The
ENCYCLOPEDIA
of
POPULAR
MUSIC

3rd EDITION

Compiled & Edited by
COLIN LARKIN

VOLUME 8
WILDE, KIM - ZZ TOP

muze

MUSIC
VIDEO
BOOKS

First edition published 1992
Reprinted 1994
Second edition published 1995
Reprinted 1997
Third edition published November 1998 by
MUZE UK Ltd
Iron Bridge House, 3 Bridge Approach
Chalk Farm, London NW1 8BD
e-mail: colin@muze.co.uk

MUZE UK Ltd is a wholly owned subsidiary of **MUZE Inc**.
304 Hudson Street, New York, NY 10013, USA
http://www.muze.com

Exclusive distribution in the UK and Rest of World except USA by
Macmillan Reference Ltd
25 Ecclestone Place, London SW1W 9NF
e-mail: macref@macmillan.co.uk

Exclusive distribution in the USA by
Grove's Dictionaries Inc.
345 Park Avenue South, New York, NY 10010, USA
e-mail: grove@grovereference.com

British Library Cataloguing-in-Publication data
A catalogue record for this book is available from the British Library
ISBN 0-333-74134-X (UK)
Library of Congress Cataloging-in-Publication Data
A catalogue record for this book is available from the Library of Congress
1-56159-237-4 (USA)

Conceived, designed, compiled and edited by Colin Larkin for
MUZE UK Ltd
to whom all editorial enquiries should be sent

Editor In Chief: Colin Larkin
Production Editor: Susan Pipe
Research Editor: Nic Oliver
Editorial Assistant: Sarah Lavelle
Executive Editor: Trev Huxley
Special thanks: Roger Kohn, Ian Jacobs, Paul Zullo, Tony Laudico
and every single Klugette

Typeset by Tin Teardrop Studio
Printed and bound in the USA by World Color

CONTENTS

ALBUM RATINGS

Outstanding

Without fault in every way. A classic and therefore strongly recommended. No comprehensive record collection should be without this album.

Excellent.

A high standard album from this artist and therefore highly recommended.

Good.

By the artist's usual standards and therefore recommended.

Disappointing.

Flawed or lacking in some way.

Poor.

An album to avoid unless you are a completist.

Wilde, Kim

b. Kim Smith, 18 November 1960, Chiswick, London, England. The daughter of 50s pop idol **Marty Wilde** and **Vernons Girls'** vocalist Joyce Smith (née Baker), Kim was signed to **Mickie Most's Rak Records** in 1980 after the producer heard a demo Kim recorded with her brother Ricky. Her first single, the exuberant 'Kids In America', composed by Ricky and co-produced by Marty, climbed to number 2 in the UK charts. A further Top 10 hit followed with 'Chequered Love', while her debut *Kim Wilde* fared extremely well in the album charts. A more adventurous sound with 'Cambodia' indicated an exciting talent. By 1982, she had already sold more records than her father had done in his entire career. While 'View From A Bridge' maintained her standing at home, 'Kids In America' became a Top 30 hit in the USA. A relatively quiet period followed, although she continued to enjoy minor hits with 'Love Blonde', 'The Second Time' and a more significant success with the **Dave Edmunds**-produced 'Rage To Love'. An energetic reworking of the **Supremes'** classic 'You Keep Me Hangin' On' took her back to UK number 2 at a time when her career seemed flagging. After appearing on the Ferry Aid charity single, 'Let It Be', Wilde was back in the Top 10 with 'Another Step (Closer To You)', a surprise duet with soul singer **Junior Giscombe**. Weary of her image as the girl-next-door, Wilde subsequently sought a sexier profile, which was used in the video to promote 'Say You Really Want Me'. Her more likely standing as an 'all-round entertainer' was underlined by the Christmas novelty hit 'Rockin' Around The Christmas Tree' in the company of comedian Mel Smith.In 1988, the dance-orientated 'You Came' reaffirmed her promise, and further Top 10 hits continued with 'Never Trust A Stranger' and 'Four Letter Word'. Her recent singles have gained only lowly positions in the charts and the subsequent *Love Is* was a pale shadow of *Close*. On *Now And Forever* Wilde abandoned pop for a slick soul groove.

● ALBUMS: *Kim Wilde* (RAK 1981)★★★, *Select* (RAK 1982)★★, *Catch As Catch Can* (RAK 1983)★★, *Teases And Dares* (MCA 1984)★★, *Another Step* (MCA 1986)★★, *Close* (MCA 1988)★★★★, *Love Moves* (MCA 1990)★★, *Love Is* (MCA 1992)★★★, *Now And Forever* (MCA 1995)★★.

● COMPILATIONS: *The Very Best Of Kim Wilde* (RAK 1985)★★★, *The Singles Collection 1981-1993* (MCA 1993)★★★, *The Gold Collection* (EMI 1996)★★★.

● VIDEOS: *Video EP: Kim Wilde* (1987), *Close* (1989), *Another Step (Closer To You)* (1990), *The Singles Collection 1981-1993* (1993).

Wilde, Marty

b. Reginald Leonard Smith, 15 April 1936, London, England. After playing briefly in a skiffle group, this UK rock 'n' roll singer secured a residency at London's Condor Club under the name Reg Patterson. He was spotted by songwriter **Lionel Bart**, who subsequently informed entrepreneur **Larry Parnes**. The starmaker was keen to sign the singer and rapidly took over his career. Reg Smith henceforth became Marty Wilde. His Christian name was coined from the sentimental film *Marty*, while the surname was meant to emphasize the wilder side of Smith's nature. Parnes next arranged a recording contract with Philips Records, but Wilde's initial singles, including a reading of **Jimmie Rodgers'** 'Honeycomb', failed to chart. Nevertheless, Wilde was promoted vigorously and appeared frequently on BBC Television's pop music programme *6.5 Special*. Extensive media coverage culminated with a hit recording of **Jody Reynolds'** alluringly morbid 'Endless Sleep' in 1957.

Soon afterwards, Parnes persuaded the influential producer **Jack Good** to make Wilde the resident star of his new television programme *Oh Boy!*. The arrangement worked well for Wilde until Good objected to his single 'Misery's Child' and vetoed the song. Worse followed when Good effectively replaced Wilde with a new singing star, **Cliff Richard**. Before long, Richard had taken Wilde's mantle as the UK's premier teen-idol and was enjoying consistent hits. Wilde, meanwhile, was gradually changing his image. After considerable success with such songs as 'Donna', 'Teenager In Love', 'Sea Of Love' and his own composition 'Bad Boy', he veered away from rock 'n' roll. His marriage to Joyce Baker of the **Vernons Girls** was considered a bad career move at the time, and partly contributed to Wilde's announcement that he would henceforth be specializing in classy, **Frank Sinatra**-style ballads. For several months he hosted a new pop show, *Boy Meets Girls*, and later starred in the West End production of *Bye Bye Birdie*. Although Parnes was intent on promoting Wilde as an actor, the star was resistant to such a move. His last major success was with a lacklustre version of **Bobby Vee's** 'Rubber Ball' in 1961. Later in the decade he recorded for several labels, including a stint as the Wilde Three with his wife Joyce, and future **Moody Blues** vocalist **Justin Hayward**. Wilde enjoyed considerable radio play and was unfortunate not to enjoy a belated hit with the catchy 'Abergavenny' in 1969. He also found some success as the writer of hits such as **Status Quo's** 'Ice In The Sun'. By the 70s, Wilde was managing his son Ricky, who was briefly promoted as Britain's answer to **Little Jimmy Osmond**. Ricky later achieved success as a songwriter for his sister, **Kim Wilde**. In 1994, Marty Wilde appeared at London's Royal Albert Hall with **Brenda Lee**, **Joe Brown**, **Eden Kane** and **John Leyton** in the nostalgic *Solid Gold Rock 'N' Roll Show*. In the following year he presented *Coffee Bar Kids*, a BBC Radio 2 documentary programme that examined the origins of rock 'n' roll in Britain.

● ALBUMS: *Wilde About Marty* (Philips 1959)★★★, *Bad Boy* (Epic 1960)★★★, *Showcase* (Philips 1960)★★★, *The Versatile Mr. Wilde* (Philips 1960)★★★, *Diversions* (Philips 1969)★★, *Rock 'N' Roll* (Philips 1970)★★, *Good Rocking - Then And Now* (Philips 1974)★★★.

● COMPILATIONS: *Wild Cat Rocker* (Jan 1981)★★★, *The Hits Of Marty Wilde* (Philips 1984)★★★.

Wilder, Alec

b. Alexander LaFayette Chew Wilder, 16 February 1907, Rochester, New York, USA, d. 23 December 1980, Gainesville, Florida, USA. A composer of popular ballads, illustrative works, jazz and classical pieces, Wilder attended Collegiate School, New York, and studied privately at the Eastman School of Music. He became an active composer in 1930 when his first popular song, 'All The King's Horses', was interpolated into the **Arthur Schwartz** and **Howard Dietz** revue *Three's A Crowd*. Thereafter, he is reputed to have written several hundred popular songs, including 'Stop That Dancin' Up There', 'It's So Peaceful In The Country', 'J.P. Dooley III' (a jazz piece recorded by **Harry James**), 'Who Can I Turn To?', 'Soft As Spring', 'Moon And Sand', 'At The Swing Shift Ball', 'While We're Young', 'I'll Be Around', 'The Long Night', 'One More Road', 'All The Cats Join In' (featured by **Benny Goodman** And His Orchestra in the 1946 **Walt Disney** cartoon *Make Mine Music*), 'Kalamazoo To Timbuktu', 'Goodbye John', 'Crazy In The Heart', 'Winter Of My Discontent', 'You're Free', 'Is It Always Like This?', 'Summer Is A-Comin' In', and 'April Age'. Artists who have recorded from his popular catalogue include **Frank Sinatra**, **Mabel Mercer**, **Bing Crosby**, **Mildred Bailey**, **Marlene Dietrich**, **Peggy Lee**, **Nat 'King' Cole**, **Jeri Southern**, and **Anita O'Day**.

UK singer **Elaine Delmar** devoted a complete album, *Elaine Sings Wilder*, to him. Among his serious works were sonatas for flute, tuba and bassoon, a concerto for saxophone and chamber orchestra, quintets and trios for various musical instruments, piano works, four operas, the *Juke Box* ballet, and several unorthodox pieces, such as 'A Debutante's Diary', 'Sea Fugue Mama', 'She'll Be Seven In May', 'Neurotic Goldfish', 'Dance Man Buys A Farm', 'Concerning Etchings', 'Walking Home In The Spring', 'Amorous Poltergeist' and 'The Children Met The Train'. For over 50 years of his life he lived in the Algonquin Hotel, Manhattan, and the Sheraton in Rochester, New York City. His memoir of the period he spent at the Algonquin was unpublished at the time of his death from lung cancer in 1980. Two of his books that did emerge are *Letter I Never Mailed* (1975), a collection of imaginary letters to real people, and *American Popular Song: The Great Innovators 1900-1950* (with James T. Maher) (1972). He hosted a weekly series based on the latter book for the National Public Radio.

● ALBUMS: *Alec Wilder And His Octet* 10-inch album (Mercury 1949)★★★, *Alec Wilder Octet* 10-inch album (Columbia 1951)★★★, *The Music Of Alec Wilder Conducted By Alec Wilder* (Columbia 1974)★★★.
● FURTHER READING: *Alec Wilder And His Friends*, Whitney Balliett.

Wilder, Joe

b. 22 February 1922, Colwyn, Pennsylvania, USA. After studying music in his home town, Wilder joined the trumpet section of the **Les Hite** band in his late teens. From Hite he graduated to the **Lionel Hampton** band and, before the 40s were over, had played with leaders such as **Dizzy Gillespie**, **Jimmie Lunceford**, **Lucky Millinder** and **Sam Donahue**. In the 50s he mostly worked in theatre bands but spent several months with **Count Basie**, and by the end of the decade had embarked upon a long stint as a staff musician in US radio and television studios. During this period, which extended into the early 70s, he found time to play with **Benny Goodman** on a tour of the Soviet Union. Later in the 70s and throughout the 80s he continued to play in studio orchestras, making occasional recordings, including a fine set with **Benny Carter**. A top-rank lead trumpeter, Wilder's technical command has ensured his successful career in the studios but that, in turn, has necessarily overshadowed his jazz playing.

● ALBUMS: with Count Basie *Dance Session* (1953)★★★★, *Wilder 'N' Wilder* (Savoy 1956)★★★★, with Benny Carter *A Gentleman And His Music* (1985)★★★, *Alone With Just My Dreams* (Evening Star 1992)★★★.

Wildhearts

Following his sacking from the **Quireboys** and a brief tenure with the **Throbs**, UK guitarist/songwriter Ginger (b. 12 December 1964, South Shields, Tyne & Wear, England) set about forming the Wildhearts around the nucleus of himself plus ex-**Tattooed Love Boys** guitarist Chris 'CJ' Jagdhar, with the duo taking on vocal duties after the departure of ex-Torbruk frontman Snake. The line-up stabilized with the recruitment of former **Dogs D'Amour** drummer Bam and bassist Danny McCormack (ex-Energetic Krusher), and the quartet signed to East West Records in late 1989. Contractual difficulties meant that the Wildhearts' debut EP, *Mondo Akimbo A-Go-Go*, was delayed until early 1992, but the poor production could not obscure the quality of the songs or the band's original style, mixing pop melodies with aggressive, heavy riffing. A Terry Date-remixed version was released as a double-pack with the *Don't Be Happy...Just Worry* EP (later reissued as a single album). This had much greater impact, and the band's following increased as they undertook a succession of support tours. Bam rejoined his old group during this period, with his predecessor Andrew 'Stidi' Stidolph filling the gap. *Earth Vs The Wildhearts* was recorded in a mere seven days, but turned out to be one of the best British rock albums for years, mixing metal, punk and pop into an adrenalized collection of songs, with their commercial appeal tempered only by the liberal use of expletives in the song-titles. Stidi was ousted shortly afterwards in favour of ex-**Radio Moscow** drummer Ritch Battersby, and following an acclaimed tour with the **Almighty**, the band broke into the UK Top 30 with 'Caffeine Bomb'. Subsequent headline dates saw the sound augmented by the keyboards of ex-**Grip** frontman Willie Dowling, while the summer of 1994 saw guitarist C.J ousted. He would later re-emerge with a new band **Honeycrack**, but was replaced by Mark Keds (ex-**Senseless Things**). Honeycrack also featured

Dowling. Later that year an exclusive 40 minute mini-album, available only through the Wildhearts' fan club, was released (still featuring CJ on guitar). *Fishing For Luckies* revealed new dimensions to the Wildhearts, stretching even to **Pogues** influences on 'Geordie In Wonderland', and the commercially available single, 'If Life Is Like A Love Bank I Want An Overdraft' brought a hit, but the band delayed their second album proper until their line-up was restored to a quartet. Auditions for a replacement were held in November, after using **Steve Vai** guitarist Devin Townsend as a stand-in. Despite the unsettling lack of a second guitarist, *P.H.U.Q.* was widely applauded as the band's strongest collection to date, with Ginger maturing as a lyricist and the group producing a much more accessible sound. Jagdhar was eventually replaced by Jef Streatfield. They countered accusations of pandering to a new audience with typically uncomplicated statements to the media such as: 'There's nothing wrong with playing a short snappy song that's got a chorus you can sing along to. What's accessible mean?' Media speculation that Senseless Things guitarist Mark Keds would be recruited permanently was confirmed in 1995, but when he joined his former band for dates in Japan and failed to return in time for the Wildhearts' appearance at the Phoenix Festival, the venture soured into acrimony on both sides. By July they were still auditioning for a new singer and guitarist, despite the release of 'Just In Lust', with Keds making his sole Wildhearts' appearance on the b-side. Confusion was rife during the Autumn of 1995: had the band broken up or not? They attempted to qualify the rumour by saying that they would break up if they failed to get a new recording contract. They were in dispute with East West records and the band decided to sell the album *Fishing For Luckies* by mail order. When East West released *Fishing For More Luckies* the band made a great deal of noise in opposing it and urged fans not to by it. The dichotomy was that it was an excellent album and one that fans would be foolish not to own. The band signed a new contract with Mushroom Records in April 1997, and released the lacklustre *Endless, Nameless* later that year amid rumours of a split. The departed bassist Danny McCormack formed the Yo-Yo's in 1998.

● ALBUMS: *Earth Versus The Wildhearts* (East West 1993)★★★, *Don't Be Happy...Just Worry* (East West 1994)★★★, *Fishing For Luckies* mini-album (East West 1994)★★, *P.H.U.Q.* (East West 1995)★★★★, *Fishing For Luckies* mini-album (1995)★★★★, *Fishing For More Luckies* (East West 1995)★★★★, *Endless, Nameless* (Mushroom 1997)★★★, *Anarchic Airwaves - The Wildhearts At The BBC* (Kuro Neko 1998)★★★.

● COMPILATIONS: *The Best Of The Wildhearts* (East West 1996)★★★.

Wildside

This Los Angeles-based glam rock quintet were formed in 1991 by vocalist Drew Hannah and guitarist Brent Wood, with Benny Rhynestone (guitar), Marc Simon (bass) and Jimmy D. (drums) completing the line-up. Contracted to **Capitol Records**, *Under The Influence* emerged in July 1992 to a lukewarm reception. Although professionally competent and technically without fault, the material proved to be both derviative and uninspired.

● ALBUMS: *Under The Influence* (Capitol 1992)★★, *Wildside* (Tony Nicole Tony 1995)★★.

Wildweeds

Formed in Windsor, Connecticut, USA, in 1966, the Wildweeds consisted of Al Anderson (guitar/vocals), Bob Dudek (drums/vocals), Al Lepak Jnr. (bass), and Martin Yakaitis (percussion). The group recorded four singles for the Cadet label, the first, Anderson's 'No Good To Cry', was a regional and a US chart success in 1967. Another three singles and an album were recorded for **Vanguard Records** but produced no hits. The group's style shifted from country-rock to R&B and psychedelia before they disbanded in 1970. A year later Anderson was drafted into **NRBQ** to replace the outgoing Steve Ferguson.

● ALBUMS: *Wildweeds* (Vanguard 1970)★★.

Wilen, Barney

b. Bernard Jean Wilen, 4 March 1937, Nice, France, d. 24 May 1996. Born of an American father and French mother, Wilen spent his first 10 years in Arizona, USA, before returning to the Côte d'Azur and serious saxophone study. Initially a follower of **Lester Young**, by the mid-50s Wilen had his own voice and was fast becoming one of the most respected European musicians. From 1955-60 he played with **Bud Powell** and **John Lewis**, joined the **Miles Davis** band and **Art Blakey**'s **Jazz Messengers**. Lewis classed Wilen as one of his four favourite saxophonists, with Lester Young, **Stan Getz** and **Eli 'Lucky' Thompson**. During the early 60s Wilen experimented with jazz rock, and from 1968-73 he lived in Africa, an experience that influenced his work during the late 70s and early 80s. Wilen returned to Nice and back to the hard bop style of playing that made him famous in the 50s.

● ALBUMS: with Miles Davis *L'ascenseur Pour L'echafaud* (1957)★★★, with Art Blakey *Les Liaisons Dangereuses* (1959)★★★★, *Paris Session* (1961)★★★, with Mal Waldron *Movie Themes From France* (1990)★★★, *New York Romance* (Columbia 1995)★★★.

Wiley And Gene

This duo are best remembered as the writers of the country standard 'When My Blue Moon Turns To Gold Again', although both had solo careers before their successful partnership started in 1939. Wiley (b. Wiley Walker, 17 November 1911, Laurel Hill, Florida, USA, d. 17 May 1966; songwriter, vocals, fiddle, dancer) learned to play fiddle and buck and wing dance as a child, and began his career as an entertainer on touring tent shows in 1925. In 1932, he began working with **Lew Childre** in New Orleans (and later Birmingham) as the Alabama Boys. In 1937, they parted and Walker played briefly with the Swift Jewel Cowboys, before moving to Shreveport. Here, while working with the **Shelton Brothers**, he met Gene Sullivan (b. 16 November 1914, Carbon Hill, Alabama, USA, d. 24 October 1984; songwriter, vocals, instrumentalist). Sullivan was a professional boxer, but in 1932, he turned to country music. After learning guitar, he worked for a time with the Tune Wranglers, before joining the Lone Star Cowboys on KWKH Shreveport. When the Shelton Brothers left the Cowboys to form their own act, Sullivan went with them and first met and worked with Walker as musicians and comedians for the Sheltons. They eventually formed a duo in 1939 and worked radio stations in Fort Worth, Lubbock, and finally ended their careers in Oklahoma City. In 1941, they recorded 'When My Blue Moon Turns To Gold Again'/'Live And Let Live' for **Columbia Records**. Their version achieved some local success but it would be the 1956 pop version by **Elvis Presley** that finally launched the song, which, in later years, has been recorded by numerous artists. In 1946, the duo registered their only chart entry, 'Make Room In Your Heart For A Friend', which became a number 2 US country hit. In the late 40s, they were regulars on Oklahoma City television but their careers ended in the early 50s. Sullivan enjoyed a solo Top 10 success in 1957 with his comedy number 'Please Pass The Biscuits'. He had originally recorded it as a demo for **Little Jimmie Dickens**, but Columbia released his version in preference.

Sullivan subsequently retired to run an Oklahoma City music store, but he made a few appearances with Walker until the early 60s. Walker died in 1966 but Sullivan, in later years, made a few solo appearances, outlasting his old partner until 1984. Some of their recordings were issued in album form after his death, by Old Homestead.

● COMPILATIONS: *Wiley Walker & Gene Sullivan Volume 1* (Old Homestead 1987)★★★.

Wiley, Lee

b. 9 October c.1910, Fort Gibson, Oklahoma, USA, d. 11 December 1975. While still in her early teens, Wiley left home to begin a career singing with the **Leo Reisman** band. Her career was interrupted when, following a fall while horse-riding, she suffered temporary blindness. She recovered her sight and at the age of 19 was back with Reisman again. She also sang with **Paul Whiteman** and later, the **Casa Loma Band**. A collaboration with composer **Victor Young** resulted in several songs for which Wiley wrote the lyrics, including 'Got The South In My Soul' and 'Anytime, Anyday, Anywhere', the latter becoming an R&B hit in the 50s. In the early 40s Wiley began a long succession of fine recording dates, singing many classic songs, usually with backing from small jazz groups, which included musicians such as **Bud Freeman**, **Max Kaminsky**, **Fats Waller**, **Billy Butterfield**, **Bobby Hackett**, **Eddie**

Condon, and **Jess Stacy**, the latter to whom she was married for a while. In 1943 she sang with Stacy's big band and subsequently continued to perform with small groups, notably with Condon-directed jazzmen, and pursued her prolific recording career.

Although she had only a small voice, she possessed a wistful and charming sound and delivered lyrics with a low-key sensuality. The warmth and intimacy she projected resulted in many of her performances becoming definitive versions of the songs. 'I've Got A Crush On You', from 1939 with Waller and Freeman in support, 'How Long Has This Been Going On?', 'Baby's Awake Now' and 'You Took Advantage Of Me', all from 1939 and 1940, and 'I've Got The World On A String', from 1945, with Condon and **Ernie Caceres**, are all excellent examples of her distinctively delicate singing style. She made fewer appearances and records in the 50s and 60s, although a 1963 television film, *Something About Lee Wiley*, which told a version of her life story, boosted interest in her work. One of her final appearances came in 1972 at the New York Jazz Festival, where she was rapturously received by audiences who were beginning to appreciate what her fellow musicians had known all along: that she was one of the best jazz singers the music had known even if, by this time, her always fragile-sounding voice was no longer at its best.

● ALBUMS: *Night In Manhattan* (1950)★★★, *Lee Wiley Sings Vincent Youmans* (1951)★★, *Lee Wiley Sings Irving Berlin* (1951)★★★★, *Lee Wiley Sings Rodgers And Hart* (1954)★★★, *Duologue* (1954)★★★, *West Of The Moon* (1957)★★★, *A Touch Of The Blues* (1957)★★★★, *One And Only Lee Wiley* (1965)★★, *Back Home Again* (Monmouth Evergreen 1971)★★, *I Got The World On A String* (1972)★★.
●COMPILATIONS: *Lee Wiley On The Air, Volume 1 (1932-36)* (Totem 1988)★★★★, *Lee Wiley On The Air, Volume 2 (1944-45)* (Totem 1989)★★★, *Rarites* (Jass 1989)★★★, *I Got A Right To Sing The Blues* (Jass 1990)★★★, *As Time Goes By* (Bluebird 1991)★★★✳, *Lee Wiley 1931-37* (Original Jazz Classics 1991)★★★★.

Wilkie, Derry, And The Pressmen

Derry Wilkie and **Freddie Starr** shared the lead vocals in **Howie Casey And The Seniors**, but the group split in 1962, leaving Wilkie to form his own band, Derry Wilkie And The Pressmen. At the Rialto Ballroom in Liverpool, they recorded 'Hallelujah I Love Her So' for the Oriole album, *This Is Merseybeat*. The recording is fairly placid but Wilkie was a wild performer, climbing up curtains and screaming like **Little Richard**. He was turned down by **Decca Records** because he would not keep still in front of the microphone. After the Pressmen folded, he formed Derry Wilkie And The Others, which was managed by Mike Jeffery who also handled - or rather, mishandled - the **Animals**. He spent some years with **Screaming Lord Sutch**'s band, being killed by Sutch every night as part of his 'Jack The Ripper' routine. When a stunt went wrong, he told Sutch, 'I can't help it, man. I'm a singer, not an actor.'

The good-natured Wilkie emigrated to Australia, no doubt continuing his quest to find the perfect group.

Wilkins, Dave

b. 25 September 1914, Barbados. Wilkins learned to play the trumpet playing in Salvation Army Bands in his native Barbados. In 1935 he moved to Trinidad to play with the well-known Blue Rhythm Orchestra which he had often heard on the radio. A couple of years later, in 1937, a small group of young West Indian musicians came to London to join **Ken 'Snake Hips' Johnson**'s West Indian Swing Band. In the 40s Wilkins played with the bands of **Ted Heath**, Harry Parry and **Joe Daniels** before retiring from music altogether.
● ALBUMS: with Harry Parry *I Can't Dance* (1942)★★★.

Wilkins, Ernie

b. 20 July 1922, St. Louis, Missouri, USA. Wilkins studied formally, learning piano and violin before taking up the saxophone. He played locally before military service and in the post-war years played in the **Jeter-Pillars Orchestra** and that led by **Earl 'Fatha' Hines**. He then freelanced as player, composer and arranger until in 1952 he joined **Count Basie**, remaining with the band until 1955, playing alto and tenor saxophones. He returned to freelancing, concentrating on writing arrangements for many bands, including those of Basie, **Tommy Dorsey**, **Dizzy Gillespie** and **Harry James**. Wilkins's charts for the James band were outstanding and helped to create one of the best bands the trumpeter led. In many respects these arrangements, loosely swinging and with tight section work, closely resembled similar work that Wilkins did for Basie and which was partly responsible for boosting the Basie band into its second period of greatness. Whether James or Basie was the first to play in this manner remains a matter of some contention. In the 60s Wilkins's career stalled due to addiction problems but he still wrote for several big bands, including that led by **Clark Terry**. In the early 70s he was A&R director for Mainstream Records and later in the decade worked again with Terry before settling in Denmark. In the 80s he formed his own Almost Big Band. As a big band arranger, Wilkins belongs firmly in the post-**Sy Oliver** tradition and has consistently adhered to the characteristics of a style which concentrates upon presenting an uncluttered ensemble sound that effectively frames the soloists.
● ALBUMS: *Ernie Wilkins /Kenny Clarke Septet* (Savoy 1956)★★★★, *The Trumpet Album* (1957)★★★, *Here Comes The Swinging Mr Wilkins* (1960)★★★, *The Big New Band Of The 60s* (1960)★★★, *A Time For The Blues* (1973)★★★, *Ernie Wilkins And The Almost Big Band* (1980)★★★, *Ernie Wilkins' Almost Big Band Live* (Matrix 1981)★★, *Montreux* (1983)★★★, *K.a.l.e.i.d.o.d.u.k.e.* (Birdology 1991)★★★.

Wilkins, Joe Willie

b. 7 January 1923, Davenport, Mississippi, USA, d. 28 March 1979, Memphis, Tennessee, USA. His reputation as a guitarist higher among his fellow musicians than it is even with those who possessed examples of his work, Wilkins has apologists who maintain that his influence reached further and deeper than is currently recognized. His father Frank bought Joe a guitar when he was 12; he was already proficient on the harmonica. He learned more from Bob Williams, Pat Rhodes and Sam Harris, members of a string band that included his father. Soon he took to the road, working in cotton-fields and playing on street corners, earning the name 'Joe Willie The Walking Seeburg'. He encountered **Sonny Boy Williamson (Rice Miller)** and **Robert Lockwood** during his travels, trading ideas with the latter. He linked up with them in 1942 in Helena, Arkansas, broadcasting on station KFFA. He was one of the King Biscuit Boys with Williamson, and promoted *Mother's Best* flour alongside Lockwood. He also met and worked with **Robert Nighthawk** and **B.B. King** in west Memphis. In Jackson, Mississippi, in 1951, he played on sessions for Williamson and **Willie Love**, and in Memphis in 1953 was on Albert Williams' session for **Sun**. He continued to work with Williamson until the latter's death in 1965. During the 70s, despite being hampered by illness, he worked the Memphis area with his own King Biscuit Boys and recorded a single and album.
● ALBUMS: *Goin' In Your Direction* (1991)★★★.

Wilkins, Robert, Rev.

b. 16 January 1896, Hernando, Mississippi, USA, d. 30 May 1987, Memphis, Tennessee, USA. Wilkins moved to Memphis during World War I, and by the 20s was playing his guitar and singing in the blues joints of Beale Street. Between 1928 and 1934, he made a series of excellent recordings, which showed a carefully crafted approach, tailoring his fingerpicked accompaniments to suit the lyrics as well as the tunes. Some of his records were issued under his middle name, Tim. There was a 30-year gap before he recorded again, following rediscovery in the days of the folk/blues boom. By this time he had renounced blues and played only religious music, having been ordained a minister in 1950. His overall style was much the same, and 'Prodigal Son' was later covered by the **Rolling Stones**.
● ALBUMS: *Memphis Gospel Singer* (1964)★★★, *Before The Reverence* (Magpie 1976)★★★, *The Original Rolling Stone* (Herwin 1980)★★★, *Remember Me* (Edsel 1994)★★★.

Wilkinson, Alan

b. 22 August 1954, Ilford, Essex, England. Wilkinson played guitar from the age of 12 and received formal education on trumpet between the ages of eight and 11. He attended a course in librarianship in Manchester for a year, then left to attend art school in Leeds. In 1978 he acquired a saxophone and played in Crow alongside alto-player Matthew Coe (aka **Xero Slingsby**), Richard Bostock (bass) and **Paul Hession** (drums). He involved himself with the British and European free improvisation scene and appeared at the Antwerp Free Music Festival in 1983 in a trio with Hession and Akemi

Kuniyoshi-Kuhn. Wilkinson played with **Derek Bailey**'s Company in Italy in 1987 and with Company Week in London in 1988. In 1988 he also recorded with the Leeds busking band Bassa Bassa. Between 1984 and 1990 he ran the Termite Club in Leeds, which presented international improvisers as well as members Wilkinson, Hession, Paul Buckton (guitar) and industrial-*bruitiste* John McMillan. Also in 1988 he led a quartet featuring pianist **Alex Maguire** and a German rhythm section. This quartet toured in 1991 and appeared at the Crawley Outside In Festival. In 1989 Wilkinson toured with pianist Maguire's big band Cat O'Nine Tails (whose concert *Live At Leeds Trades Club* was issued on cassette by *Wire* magazine). The same year he toured and recorded with Sheffield improviser Mick Beck's big band, Feetpackets. He also formed a trio with Hession and bassist/composer **Simon Fell**, which was branded as 'punkjazz' by enthusiasts. Wilkinson cites as inspirations **Ornette Coleman**, **John Coltrane** and **Albert Ayler** as well as Europeans **Peter Brötzmann**, **Mike Osborne** and **Evan Shaw Parker**. Wilkinson looks set to become a leading saxophonist of his generation, playing alto, baritone and soprano with startling weight and imagination.

● ALBUMS: with Bassa Bassa *Bassa Bassa* (1988)★★★, with Feetpackets *Listen Feetpackets* (1989)★★, with Simon Fell *Compilation II* (1991)★★★.

Will Downing - Will Downing

Highly regarded and purchased in considerable quantities by the UK soul cogniscenti, yet strangely ignored in his homeland, New York-born Downing has an exceptional voice that combines with strong songs on this, his debut and his best album. Downing was formerly a member of Arthur Baker's Wally Jump Jr And The Criminal Element and Baker produced this album. One highlight is a clever interpretation of John Coltrane's classic work 'A Love Supreme'. Sadly, Downing has not repeated this winning formula on his subsequent solo albums.

● Tracks: *In My Dreams; Do You; Free; A Love Supreme; Security; Set Me Free; Sending Out An S.O.S.; Dancin' In The Moonlight; Do You Remember Love?; So You Wanna Be My Lover.*
● First released 1988
● UK peak chart position: 20
● USA peak chart position: did not chart

Will Rogers Follies, The

This lavish production, which had music by **Cy Coleman** and a book and lyrics by Broadway veterans **Betty Comden** and **Adolph Green**, was sub-titled 'A Life In Revue'. It was summed up neatly by one critic thus: 'The time is the present, and Gregory Peck's recorded voice as impresario **Florenz Ziegfeld** instructs the theatrically resurrected Rogers, 16 showgirls, 16 other actors, and six dogs, on how to stage the life story of America's favourite humorist in the style of the *Ziegfeld Follies*.' *The Will Rogers Follies* opened at the Palace Theatre in New York on 1 May 1991, with television and film actor Keith Carradine in the central role of the folksy philosopher Rogers. He was surrounded by a production which was guaranteed to dazzle due to the presence of the master of flash and panache, director and choreographer **Tommy Tune**. Just a few of the evening's highlights featured a chorus line of girls dressed as steers, a pink powder-puff ballet, and an amazing stagewide staircase which changed colours throughout. With appearances in the real *Ziegfeld Follies*, and his celebrated newspaper columns and radio programmes, Rogers is generally accepted as being America's first multimedia superstar, but one who despite his fame stayed in touch with the people until his death in an air crash in 1935. Comden and Green attempted to sum up this facet of his character in the lyric of 'Never Met A Man I Didn't Like', the only really memorable number in a score which also included 'Let's Go Flying', 'Will-A-Mania', 'Give A Man Enough Rope', 'My Big Mistake', 'No Man Left For Me', and 'Without You'. Singer-songwriter **Mac Davies** and Larry Gatlin were two of the replacements for Carradine during the show's highly successful run of 1,420 performances. Just before it closed in September 1993, old-stager **Mickey Rooney** played the role of Rogers's father, Clem, for a time. The show won a Grammy for best original cast album, along with Drama Desk and Drama Critics Awards, and **Tony**s for best musical, score, director, choreographer, lighting, and costumes. There was some unpleasantness when Tommy Tune was accused of sexism and racism with regard to one of the show's billboards, which displayed three half-naked women, and the fact that the large cast did not contain one non-white performer.

Will The Circle Be Unbroken - Nitty Gritty Dirt Band

The Nitty Gritty Dirt Band evolved as one of the long-haired country rock bands in the late 60s, but they bridged the gap between the old music and the new with this brilliantly packaged album featuring several traditional musicians that they admired - Doc Watson, Roy Acuff, Jimmy Martin, Maybelle Carter and Earl Scruggs. There is studio chat and you hear the performances coming together, the result being six sides - yes, a triple album - of heavenly joy. In 1989 the band released a second volume featuring Emmylou Harris, Johnny Cash, Ricky Skaggs and a couple of Byrds, that was almost as good.

● Tracks: *Grand Ole Opry Song; Keep On The Sunny Side; Nashville Blues; You Are My Flower; The Precious Jewel; Dark As A Dungeon; Tennessee Stud; Black Mountain Rag; The Wreck Of The Highway; The End Of The World; I Saw The Light; Sunny Side Of The Mountain; Nine Pound Hammer; Losin' You (Might Be The Best Thing Yet); Honky Tonkin'; You Don't Know My Mind; My Walkin' Shoes; Lonesome Fiddle Blues; Cannonball Rag; Avalanche; Flint Hill Special; Togary Mountain; Earl's Breakdown; Orange Blossom Special; Wabash Cannonball; Lost Highway; Doc Watson and Merle Travis - First*

Meeting (dialogue); Way Downtown; Down Yonder; Pins And Needles (In My Heart); Honky Tonk Blues; Sailin' On To Hawaii; I'm Thinking Tonight Of My Blue Eyes; I Am A Pilgrim; Wildwood Flower; Soldier's Joy; Will The Circle Be Unbroken; Both Sides Now.
● First released 1972
● UK peak chart position: did not chart
● USA peak chart position: 68

Willard

Named after a character from James Herbert's book, *The Rats*, Willard were formed in Seattle, USA, in 1991, by Johnny Clint (vocals), Mark Spiders (guitar), Steve Wied (drums), Otis P. Otis (guitar) and Darren Peters (bass). They were picked up by Roadracer Records the same year. Subtitled *The Sound Of Fuck!*, their debut album, *Steel Mill,* released in July 1992, was a powerful and uncompromising debut, with influnces ranging from traditional metal sources like **Black Sabbath** to the more hardcore-derived output of **Nirvana** and the **Henry Rollins** Band.
● ALBUMS: *Steel Mill* (Roadracer 1992)★★★.

Willetts, Dave

b. 24 June 1952, Birmingham, West Midlands, England. A singer and actor, with a reputation as 'one of the best singing voices in town', Willetts seemed to emerge from nowhere in the 80s to take over leading roles in two blockbusting West End musicals. He had no singing, dancing or acting lessons, and before he was 20, rarely went to the theatre. However, while working during the day as a quality control supervisor for a Midlands firm of engineers, he became involved in local amateur dramatics. His sensitive performance as Charlie in the **Charles Strouse** musical *Flowers For Algernon*, came to the notice of Bob Hamlyn, artistic director of the Belgrade Theatre, Coventry. Hamlyn cast him in his first professional part, as 'the third flunky from the left', in another Strouse show, *Annie*. By now in his thirties, Willetts began his incredible rise to the top. Director **Trevor Nunn** put him into the chorus of *Les Misérables* at London's Palace Theatre, and within a year he was understudy for the lead role of Jean Valjean, which he eventually took over in 1986 after Colm Wilkinson left to join the Broadway production. In the following year, when **Michael Crawford** also departed England for the US premiere of *The Phantom Of Opera*, Willetts succeeded him at Her Majesty's in the West End's hottest ticket. He subsequently played the Phantom in Manchester, and won the *Evening News* Theatre Award. Since then, apart from his involvement as Major Lee in **Petula Clark**'s ill-fated American Civil War musical, *Someone Like You* (1990), Willetts' career has prospered. Highlights have included appearances at London's premier cabaret space, Pizza On The Park (1991), a return to the London production of *Les Misérables* (1992), and the title role of Jesus in a concert version of *Jesus Christ Superstar* at the Barbican Centre and the subsequent 1993 European tour; he also co-starred with Lorna Luft in the touring concert staging of *The Magical World Of The Musicals* (1995), and took the leading role in an acclaimed Leicester Haymarket production of *Sweeney Todd* (1996). In the same year, Willetts created the title role in a new musical by Tony Rees and Gary Young, *Jekyll*, at the Churchill Theatre, Bromley. Willetts originated leading characters in the UK premieres of *Tycoon* and *Lonely Hearts*, and has also starred in his own UK and international concerts and one-man shows. In 1997, he and Bonnie Langford headed a small cast at London's Jermyn Theatre, in *A Lot Of Living!*, an intimate revue featuring the songs of Charles Strouse. Subsequently, he portrayed Jean Valjean once again, in the 10th Anniversary production of *Les Misérables* in Sydney, Australia.
● ALBUMS: *On And Off Stage* (1990)★★★, *Stages Of Love* (1992)★★, *Timeless* (1995)★★★, and various cast and concept albums.

William Bloke - Billy Bragg

Bragg's fullest-sounding album so far does not cloud the continuing power of his songs. 'Upfield' masquerades as a 60s Motown pop song, but study the words and you will find he still has 'socialism of the heart'. 'Everybody Loves You Babe' is stripped bare so that only the lyric hits home. Heaven help the poor girl who is the subject of his wit. Bragg is at his best with guitar only; this is his real stage, from which he educates us with stinging irony in songs such as 'Northern Industrial Town'. Since *Life's A Riot*, Bragg has certainly grown but he has never sold out.
● Tracks: *From Red To Blue; Upfield; Everybody Loves You Babe; Sugardaddy; A Pict Song; Brickbat; The Space Race Is Over; Northern Industrial Town; The Fourteenth Of February; King James Version; Goalhanger.*
● First released 199616
● USA peak chart position: did not chart

Williams Brothers

This gospel group was organized by Leon Williams in 1960 when they were known as the Little Williams Brothers, a name later changed to the Sensational Williams Brothers and then simply the Williams Brothers. All the Williams Brothers were born in Smithdale, Mississippi, USA, and all came from a religious background. They have been writing and arranging and producing their music since the early 70s and recorded their first album in 1973 on the Songbird label. They have since recorded 18 albums. They have had many hits, including 'Jesus Will Never Say No,' 'He'll Understand', 'The Boat', 'Cover Me', 'A Ship Like Mine' and performed on the Winans Grammy Award song 'Ain't No Need To Worry' featuring **Anita Baker**. In 1992 the Williams Brothers formed their own record label, Blackberry Records, which was the first black owned and operated record label in Mississippi with major distribution. They have been awarded several awards, including the Stella Award for Best Performing

Group in 1991, the Best Performance by a Group in 1995 for the album *In This Place* and The Vision Award for 1991, and have performed with other gospel artists including **Mississippi Mass Choir** with **Luther Vandross** and **Phillip Bailey**.

● ALBUMS: *This Is Your Night* (Blackberry 1992)★★★, *Live/Best Of And More* (Blackberry1993)★★★, *In This Place* (Blackberry1994)★★★.

Williams, 'Uncle' Johnny

b. 15 May 1906, Alexandria, Louisiana, USA. Williams learned guitar in 1918, and divided his time between Mississippi and Chicago until 1938. He moved north permanently, and became a professional musician in 1943. He worked with many Chicago blues singers, most closely with **Theodore 'Hound Dog' Taylor**, Big Boy Spires and his cousin Johnny Young. In the late 40s, Williams played guitar behind Young on an Ora-Nelle 78, singing on one side. He and Young also recorded for **Al Benson**'s Planet/Old Swingmaster labels, and Williams shared a 1953 session with Spires for the Chance label, on which his serious, committed delivery is pehaps indicative of the Baptist minister he became in 1959.

● COMPILATIONS: *Chicago Boogie* (1974)★★, *Going Back Home* (1984)★★★.

Williams, Andre

b. 1936, Chicago, Illinois, USA. Williams made his mark in the R&B industry as both a recording artist and a producer. As a recording artist he was noted for his sly street-wise songs in which he basically talked (with a rhythmic feel) the lyrics rather than sang them. He built a parallel career as a producer of the first doo-wop vocal groups and then soul acts. Like many African-American artists, Williams began his career in the church, singing in the Cobbs Baptist Church choir in the 40s. He began singing in vocal groups in the early 50s, forming the Cavaliers. He later moved to Detroit and formed the Five Dollars, which recorded for the **Fortune** label. Williams soon disengaged himself to establish a solo career on Fortune, making his biggest impact with two jokey records, 'Jail Bait' and 'Bacon Fat' (number 9 R&B) in 1957. By the early 60s Williams was back in Chicago working as a producer for various labels. He produced **Alvin Cash** for the One-derful label complex, Joyce Kennedy for Blue Rock, and JoAnn Garrett for Checker and Duo. Meanwhile, he recorded some solo tracks for Checker, obtaining a modest chart entry with 'Cadillac Jack' (number 46 R&B) in 1968. He also recorded some singles for Avin in Detroit. In the early 70s Williams went down to Texas to produce for Duke Records, but after the label was sold to **ABC** in 1974 he returned to Chicago. Williams continued to work as an artist manager and independent producer into the early 90s.

● ALBUMS: *Fat Back And Corn Liquor* (St. George 1996)★★★.

● COMPILATIONS: *Jail Bait* (Fortune 1984)★★★.

Williams, Andy

b. Howard Andrew Williams, 3 December 1928, Wall Lake, Iowa, USA. Williams began his singing career in the local church choir with his three brothers. The quartet became popular on their own radio shows from Cincinnati, Des Moines and Chicago. They backed **Bing Crosby** on his Oscar-winning 'Swinging On A Star', from the 1944 movie *Going My Way*, and in the same year appeared in the minor musical film *Kansas City Kitty*. In the following year, Andy Williams dubbed Lauren Bacall's singing voice in her first film with Humphrey Bogart, *To Have And Have Not*. From 1947-48 the Williams Brothers worked with top pianist/singer **Kay Thompson** in nightclubs and on television. Williams went solo in 1952, and featured regularly on Steve Allen's *Tonight Show* for over two years. Signed to the Cadence label, Williams had his first success in 1956 with 'Canadian Sunset', which was followed by a string of Top 20 entries, including 'Butterfly' (number 1), 'I Like Your Kind Of Love' (a duet with **Peggy Powers**), 'Lips Of Wine', 'Are You Sincere?', 'Promise Me, Love', 'The Hawaiian Wedding Song', 'Lonely Street' and 'The Village Of St. Bernadette'. In 1961, Williams moved to **Columbia Records**, and had his first big hit for the label with the **Doc Pomus/Mort Shuman** composition, 'Can't Get Used To Losing You', which went to number 2 in the US charts in 1963. From then, until 1971 when the singles hits dried up, he was in the US Top 20 with 'Hopeless', 'A Fool Never Learns', and '(Where Do I Begin) Love Story'. Williams reached number 4 in the UK in 1973 with **Neil Sedaka**'s 'Solitaire', but it was in the album charts that he found greater success.

By the early 70s it was estimated that he had received 13 worldwide gold disc awards for chart albums such as *Moon River & Other Great Movie Themes*, *Days Of Wine And Roses* (a US number 1), *The Wonderful World Of Andy Williams*, *Dear Heart*, *Born Free*, *Love Andy* (a UK number 1), *Honey*, *Happy Heart*, *Home Loving Man* (another UK number 1) and *Love Story*. The enormous sales were no doubt assisted by his extremely successful weekly variety showcase that ran from 1962-71, and won an Emmy for 'Best Variety Show'. It also gave the **Osmond Brothers** nationwide exposure. In 1964, Williams made his film debut in *I'd Rather Be Rich*, which starred **Maurice Chevalier**, **Robert Goulet**, Sandra Dee and Hermione Gingold. It was a remake of the 1941 comedy *It Started With Eve*, and Williams sang the **Jerry Keller**/Gloria Shayne number, 'Almost There', which just failed to reach the top of the UK chart in 1965. Despite the lack of consistent television exposure in the late 70s, Williams still sold a remarkable number of albums, particularly in the UK where his *Solitaire*, *The Way We Were*, and *Reflections*, all made the Top 10. In 1984, the album *Greatest Love Classics* featured Williams singing contemporary lyrics to classical themes, accompanied by the Royal Philharmonic Orchestra. In the early 90s, Williams became the first non-country entertainer to build his own theatre along

Highway 76's music-theatre-strip in Branson, Missouri. The $8 million 2,000-seater Andy Williams Moon River Theatre is part of a complex that includes a 250-room hotel and restaurant. Williams headlines there himself, and remains one of America's most popular singers, renowned for his smooth vocal texture and relaxed approach. As a stylist, he is the equal of any popular singer from his era.

● ALBUMS: *Andy Williams Sings Steve Allen* (Cadence 1957)★★, *Andy Williams* (Cadence 1958)★★, *Andy Williams Sings Rogers And Hammerstein* (Cadence 1959)★★★, *Lonely Street* (Cadence 1959)★★★, *The Village Of St. Bernadette* (Cadence 1960)★★, *Two Time Winners* (Cadence 1960)★★★, *To You Sweetheart, Aloha* reissued as *Hawaiian Wedding Song* (Cadence 1960)★★, *Under Paris Skies* (Cadence 1961)★★★, *'Danny Boy' And Other Songs I Like To Sing* (Columbia 1962)★★★, *Moon River & Other Great Movie Themes* (Columbia 1962)★★★★, *Warm And Willing* (Columbia 1962)★★★, *Million Seller Songs* (Cadence 1963)★★★, *Days Of Wine And Roses* (Columbia 1963)★★★★, *The Andy Williams Christmas Album* (Columbia 1963)★★★, *The Wonderful World Of Andy Williams* (Columbia 1964)★★★, *The Academy Award Winning 'Call Me Irresponsible'* (Columbia 1964)★★★, *The Great Songs From 'My Fair Lady' And Other Broadway Hits* (Columbia 1964)★★★★, *Dear Heart* (Columbia 1965)★★★★, *Almost There* (Columbia 1965)★★★★, *Can't Get Used To Losing You* (Columbia 1965)★★★★, *Merry Christmas* (Columbia 1965)★★★, *The Shadow Of Your Smile* (Columbia 1966)★★★, *May Each Day* (Columbia 1966)★★★, *In The Arms Of Love* (Columbia 1967)★★★, *Born Free* (Columbia 1967)★★★★, *Love, Andy* (Columbia 1967)★★★★, *Honey* (Columbia 1968)★★★★, *Happy Heart* (Columbia 1969)★★★★, with the Osmonds *Get Together With Andy Williams* (Columbia 1969)★★, *Can't Help Falling In Love* (Columbia 1970)★★★★, *Raindrops Keep Falling On My Head* (Columbia 1970)★★★, *The Andy Williams' Show* (Columbia 1970)★★★, *Home Loving Man* (Columbia 1971)★★★★, *Love Story* (Columbia 1971)★★★, *You've Got A Friend* (Columbia 1971)★★★, *The Impossible Dream* (Columbia 1972)★★★★, *Love Theme From 'The Godfather'* (Columbia 1972)★★★, *A Song For You* (Columbia 1972)★★★, *Alone Again (Naturally)* (Columbia 1972)★★★, *The First Time Ever I Saw Your Face* (Columbia 1973)★★★, *Solitaire* (Columbia 1973)★★★, *The Way We Were* (Columbia 1974)★★★, *You Lay So Easy On My Mind* (Columbia 1974)★★★, *An Evening With Andy Williams, Live In Japan* (Columbia 1975)★★★, *The Other Side Of Me* (Columbia 1975)★★★, *Showstoppers* (Embassy 1977)★★★, *Let's Love While We Can* (Columbia 1980)★★★, *Wedding And Anniversary Album* (Columbia 1981)★★★, with the Royal Philharmonic Orchestra *Greatest Love Classics* (EMI 1984)★★★, *Close Enough For Love* (Warners 1986)★★★.

● COMPILATIONS: *Andy Williams' Best* reissued as *Canadian Sunset* (Cadence 1962)★★★, *Andy Williams' Newest Hits* (Columbia 1966)★★★, *The Andy Williams Sound Of Music* (Columbia 1969)★★★, *Andy Williams' Greatest Hits* (Columbia 1970)★★★, *Andy Williams' Greatest Hits, Volume Two* (Columbia 1973)★★★, *Reflections* (Columbia 1978)★★★, *Great Songs Of The Seventies* (Columbia 1979)★★★, *Great Songs Of The Sixties* (Columbia 1980)★★★, *Collection* (Pickwick 1980)★★★, *The Very Best Of Andy Williams* (Hallmark 1984)★★★, *Andy Williams Collection* (Castle 1987)★★★, *Portrait Of A Song Stylist* (Masterpiece 1989)★★★, *16 Most Requested Songs* (1993)★★★, *The Best Of Andy Williams* (Columbia 1996)★★★.

Williams, Bert

b. 1877, New Providence, Nassau, Bahamas, d. 5 March 1922. After moving to the USA, Williams worked in vaudeville with moderate success. In 1898 he teamed up with George Walker, and the two song and dance men became a success in New York City in the show *In Dahomey*, and also toured overseas. When Walker died in 1907, Williams continued on his own. In 1913 he met impresario **Florenz Ziegfeld**, who saw his act at the Lafayette in Harlem and was so impressed that he brought Williams into his *Ziegfeld Follies*. Williams appeared in every *Follies* until 1920, featuring such songs as 'You Ain't So Warm!' and 'Nobody', a number with which he became indelibly identified. Despite his great popularity in these shows, Williams was still subjected to severe racial discrimination; on a mundane if wounding level, he could not buy a drink in the bar of the theatre he helped to fill every night. In March 1922, Williams was onstage at the Shubert-Garrick Theatre in Detroit, in a performance of *Under The Bamboo Tree*, when he collapsed and died as a result of pneumonia.

Williams, Big Joe

b. Joe Lee Williams, 16 October 1903, Crawford, Mississippi, USA, d. 17 December 1982, Macon, Mississippi, USA. Big Joe Williams was one of the most important blues singers to have recorded and also one whose life conforms almost exactly to the stereotyped pattern of how a 'country' blues singer should live. He was of partial Red Indian stock, his father being 'Red Bone' Williams, a part-Cherokee. 'Big Joe' took his musical influences from his mother's family, the Logans. He made the obligatory 'cigar box' instruments as a child and took to the road when his stepfather threw him out around 1918. He later immortalized this antagonist in a song that he was still performing at the end of his long career. Williams' life was one of constant movement as he worked his way around the lumber camps, turpentine farms and juke-joints of the south. Around 1930 he married and settled in St. Louis, Missouri, but still took long sweeps through the country as the rambling habit never left him. This rural audience supported him through the worst of the Depression when he appeared under the name 'Poor Joe'. His known recordings began in 1935 when he recorded six tracks for Bluebird in Chicago. From then on he recorded at every opportunity. He stayed with Bluebird until 1945 before moving to **Columbia Records**. He formed a loose partnership on many sessions with **John Lee 'Sonny Boy' Williamson** that has been likened to that of **Muddy Waters** and **Little Walter**. In 1952, he worked for Trumpet in Jackson, Mississippi, then went back to Chicago for a session with Vee Jay. Other recordings made for smaller companies are still being discovered. During 1951-52, he also made recordings of other singers at his St. Louis base. Williams found a wider audience when blues came into vogue with young whites in the 60s. He continued to record and tour, adding Europe and Japan to his itinerary. He still used cheap, expendable guitars fixed up by himself with an electrical pick-up and usually festooned with extra machine heads to accommodate nine strings. With his gruff, shouting voice and ringing guitar - not to mention his sometimes uncertain temper - he became a great favourite on the club and concert circuit. He had come full circle and was living in a caravan in Crawford, Mississippi, when he died. The sheer volume of easily accessible albums recorded during his last years tended to obscure just how big a blues talent Williams really was.

● ALBUMS: *Piney Woods Blues* (1958)★★★, *Tough Times* (Fontana 1960)★★★, *Mississippi's Big Joe Williams And His Nine-String Guitar* (Folkways 1961)★★★, *Blues On Highway 49* (Delmark 1962)★★★, *Blues For 9 Strings* (Bluesville 1962)★★★, *Big Joe Williams At Folk City* (Bluesville 1963)★★★, *Studio Blues* (Bluesville 1964)★★★, *Starvin' Chain Blues* (Delmark 1966)★★★, *Classic Delta Blues* (Milestone 1966)★★★, *Back To The Country* (Bounty 1966)★★★, *Hellbound And Heaven Sent* (Folkways 1967)★★★, *Don't You Leave Me Here* (Storyville 1969)★★★, *Big Joe Williams* (Xtra 1969)★★★, *Hand Me Down My Old Walking Stick* (Liberty 1969)★★★, *Crawlin' King Snake* (RCA 1970)★★★, *Legacy Of The Blues, Volume 6* (Sonet 1972)★★★, *Guitar Blues* (Storyville 1973)★★★, *Malvina My Sweet Woman* (Old Blues 1974)★★★, *Ramblin' Wanderin' Blues* (Storyville 1974)★★★, *Tough Times* (Arhoolie 1981)★★★, *Thinking Of What They Did* (Arhoolie 1981)★★★, *Big Joe Williams 1974* (Arhoolie 1982)★★★.

● COMPILATIONS: *Field Recordings 1973-80* (L&R 1988)★★★, *Complete Recorded Works In Chronological Order Volumes 1 & 2* (Blues Document 1991)★★★, with Luther Huff, Willie Love *Delta Blues - 1951* (1991)★★★, *The Final Years* (Verve 1995)★★★.

Williams, Bill

b. 28 February 1897, Richmond, Virginia, USA, d. 6 October 1973, Greenup, Kentucky, USA. Williams claimed to have played 'Yankee Doodle Dandy' within 15 minutes of picking up a guitar in 1908, and his awesome abilities when aged over 70 with an arthritic wrist lend his claim credibility. By 1922, he had settled in Greenup to work as a trackliner after a period of wandering, and played thereafter for the local white audience. His repertoire included the 'blues, rags and ballads' of his posthumous album, songster material such as 'Chicken' and 'Railroad Bill', white fiddle pieces transposed to guitar, and pop songs such as 'Darktown Strutters' Ball' and 'Up A Lazy River'. There was even a ragtime version of 'The Star-Spangled Banner'.

Discovered in 1970, he had a brief, and professedly reluctant, career playing concerts and television shows.
● ALBUMS: *Low And Lonesome* (1971)★★★, *Blues, Rags And Ballads* (1974)★★★.

Williams, Billy

b. 28 December 1910, Waco, Texas, USA, d. 17 October 1972. Williams formed the very successful gospel group the Charioteers in the early 30s while studying theology at Wilberforce College, Ohio. The group had regular radio spots in Cincinnati and New York and worked with **Bing Crosby** on the west coast. In the 40s they had seven hits of their own and also charted with **Frank Sinatra**. In 1949 Williams left and formed the Billy Williams Quartet with Eugene Dixon (bass), Claude Riddick (baritone) and John Ball (tenor). The group were often seen on television including over 160 appearances on Sid Caesar's *Your Show Of Shows*. They recorded with little impact for **Mercury** and **MGM Records** before joining Coral in 1954 and after a few unsuccessful covers of R&B hits the group collected nine US chart entries. The biggest of these was a revival of **Fats Waller**'s 'I'm Gonna Sit Right Down And Right Myself A Letter': a US Top 3 and UK Top 30 hit in 1957. The jazzy R&B artist sadly lost his voice, due to diabetes, in the early 60s. He moved to Chicago where he became a social worker, employed on a model cities project and helping alcoholics until his death in 1972.

Williams, Blind Connie

b. c.1915, Florida, USA. Williams was recorded in 1961 in Philadelphia, having been found by a folklorist singing spirituals to his accordion accompaniment. He proved also to have a repertoire of the better-known blues, and to be an accomplished guitarist. As a result of studying at the St. Petersburg School for the Blind, he had a sophisticated grasp of harmony, and used many passing notes and altered chords. Williams' technique was also influenced by an association with **Rev. Gary Davis** in New York (though his dating of it to the late 30s is confusing, since Davis did not move to New York until 1944). Williams was also a quartet singer, though not recorded as such. He was still known to be alive in 1974, though frail and seldom performing in the streets.

● COMPILATIONS: *Philadelphia Street Singer* (1974)★★★.

Williams, Brooks

b. 10 November 1958, Statesboro, Georgia, USA. Williams began learning violin at three-years-old, moving on to guitar at the age of 10. It was not until his late teens that he started songwriting. He left his job as a teacher in 1986, and moved to Massachusetts, to take up music on a full-time basis. Beginning with appearances in colleges, bars and restaurants, he performed guest spots for such performers as **Taj Mahal**, **David Bromberg**, **Maria Muldaur** and the **Band**, especially in the north-eastern area of the USA. *North From Statesboro* produced a flood of good reviews, and national airplay, bringing Williams to a wider audience. His style combines a laid-back vocal alongside strong guitar patterns, occasionally using bottleneck. In August 1990, Williams was featured in an article on slide guitar players in *Acoustic Guitar* magazine. His follow-up, *How The Night-Time Sings*, released in 1991 and the excellent *Knife Edge* in 1995 have both consolidated his position, and he now tours more extensively, having played at the Great Woods Folk Festival alongside **Roger McGuinn** and **John Prine**.

● ALBUMS: *North From Statesboro* (Red Guitar Blue Music 1990)★★★, *How The Night-Time Sings* (Red Guitar Blue Music 1991)★★★, *Back To Mercy* (Green Linnet 1992)★★★, *Knife Edge* (Green Linnet/Redbird 1995)★★★★, *Seven Sisters* (Green Linnet 1997)★★★.

Williams, Buddy

b. Harry Taylor, 5 September 1918, Newtown suburb, Sydney, New South Wales, Australia, d. 1986. A major pioneer of Australian country music, as a child Williams never knew his parents and was placed in an orphanage, where he soon became a nuisance to the authorities by his attempts to escape. Fostered out to a farming couple in Dorrigo, he found he was treated more as an unpaid worker than as an adopted son. He heard recordings of **Jimmie Rodgers** when visiting neighbours and was immediately captivated by the music. When 15 years old, he ran away and did a series of labouring jobs. He had learned to play guitar and, while working in a quarry at Coffs Harbour, was dared to sing on the streets and was amazed at the amount of money he received. In 1936, he made a successful appearance at the Jacaranda Festival and as Buddy Williams, he continued to earn his living busking around the country, spending some time at Newcastle, before heading for Sydney. When, on 7 September 1939, singing six of his own songs, he made his first historic recordings for Regal-Zonophone (who later became **EMI**), he became the first Australian-born solo country recording artist (**Tex Morton** recorded in 1936 but he was a New Zealander). Later stating that he gained inspiration from **Goebel Reeves** and Jimmie Rodgers, he continued busking but soon gained radio exposure, where he built a reputation with his ballads and yodels. He made further recordings on 14 May 1940, including his well-known 'Australian Bushman's Yodel' and 'Happy Jackeroo'. He ran a sawmill in Walcha, supplying hardwood to the army, before enlisting for military service himself. He served as a Bren gunner and in spite of his army commitments, he recorded 30 sides during his period of war service. In 1941, he made two recordings with first wife Bernie Burnett (they were later divorced) and two more in 1943, including 'Stockmen In Uniform'. In March 1945, he recorded five songs including 'Where The Lazy Murray River Rolls Along' with Lenore Miller, who later achieved success as folk-singer Lenore Somerset in the 60s. A few weeks before the end of the war in 1945, he was seriously wounded while serving in Borneo, and

defied medical predictions by recovering.

In 1946, he recorded his noted 'The Overlander Trail' and made a film appearance. He married Grace Maidman in Brisbane on 31 January 1947, and the two formed and ran rodeo tent shows, which featured a variety of acts, including noted rodeo performers, clowns and magicians. Williams naturally sang and also did trick shooting and showed his skill with a bullwhip (sadly, in 1949, their first child Donita, then aged 21 months, tragically died in Tasmania, when she was accidentally run over by a truck driven by one of the rodeo riders in Williams' show). From the late 40s throughout the 50s, he continued to tour with his show and to record regularly. The rodeo side of the show was eventually dropped and it became a Country and Western Variety Show. His recordings were generally of Australian songs, many of his own writing, but some cover versions of American hits were made, including his very successful 1953 recording of 'Missing In Action'. Between 1958 and 1964, he recorded almost 60 sides and he was one of the last Australian artists to forsake just a solo guitar and use a backing group. In 1965, he changed labels to **RCA**. It was around this time that he was joined both on his recordings and on stage by his son Harold George (b. 23 June 1948, Rylstone, New South Wales, Australia) and daughter Kaye Elizabeth (b. 31 January 1950, Ivanoe, Victoria, Australia). Together they recorded a series of albums. In 1972, youngest daughter Karen Anne (b. 20 May 1957, Brisbane, Queensland, Australia) also became part of the Williams Family Show. In 1972, he toured in company with another pioneer, Tex Morton. In 1977 and 1978, Williams suffered heart attacks, which forced him to stop touring personally, but the Williams show continued. In 1977, he became the second artist (after Morton) to be elected to the newly created Country Music Roll Of Renown (Australia's equivalent to Nashville's Country Music Hall of Fame). In 1979, RCA presented him with a gold-plated map of Australia to celebrate his 40 years of recording country music - one of the many awards that he has received. He has written many songs and three of them, namely 'Where The White Faced Cattle Roam', 'Heading For The Warwick Rodeo' and 'Music In My Pony's Feet', are included in Australia's 50 most popular country songs. His albums include a tribute to Jimmie Rodgers and **Hank Williams**, and one also features songs written by **Shorty Ranger**, who penned Williams' hit 'The Big Banana Land'. In 1979, Williams featured in a documentary called *The Last Fair Dinkum Aussie Outback Entertainer*. There is little doubt that he has been a major inspiration for many Australian artists, and experts on the genre rate some of the recordings that he made between 1942 and 1946 among the best examples of Australian country. Harold Williams went on to record in his own right, even recording the album *Buddy Williams Jnr Sings*. He later did solo work and in 1982, with Lindsay Butler, also formed the Tamworth Country Show Band. Kaye Williams also recorded in her own right, being joined by her father for two tracks on her album *Just Between The Two Of Us*.

● ALBUMS: *Sings Jimmie Rodgers* (EMI 1962)★★★, *Buddy Williams Remembers Vol. 1* (EMI 1965)★★★★, *Buddy Williams Remembers Vol. 2* (EMI 1966)★★★, with Harold and Kaye Williams *Family Album* (EMI 1966)★★, *Country Style* (RCA 1966)★★★★, *The Williams Family* (RCA 1966)★★★, *Songs Of The Australian Outback* (Readers Digest 60s)★★★, *Buddy Sings Hank* (RCA 60s)★★★, *Family Affair* (RCA 60s)★★★, *Cowboy's Life Is Good Enough For Me* (RCA 60s)★★★★, *Sentimental Buddy* (RCA 60s)★★★, *Buddy And Shorty* (RCA 1969)★★★, *Hard Times* (RCA 1970)★★★, *Along The Outback Tracks* (RCA 1971)★★★, *Aussie On My Mind* (RCA 1972)★★★, *Bushland Of My Dreams* (EMI 1979)★★★, *Wonder Valley* (RCA 1980)★★, *An Old Hillbilly From Way Back* (RCA 1981)★★★, *Big Country Muster* (RCA 1983)★★, *Blazing The Trail* (EMI 1983)★★★, *Reflections* (RCA 1987)★★★.

Williams, Buster

b. Charles Anthony Williams, 17 April 1942, Camden, New Jersey, USA. Williams was taught to play bass by his father and later studied formally in Philadelphia. In the early 60s he played and recorded with **Jimmy Heath**, **Sonny Stitt** and others, and was also in demand for sessions with singers, notably **Betty Carter**, **Sarah Vaughan** and **Nancy Wilson**. Towards the end of the 60s he settled briefly in Los Angeles, where he played with **Miles Davis**, **Bobby Hutcherson** and others, but by the end of the decade he had moved to New York and joined **Herbie Hancock**. In the early and mid-70s he toured and recorded with Hancock and also worked with **Mary Lou Williams** and fellow bassist **Ron Carter**. In the late 70s and through the 80s Williams was in constant demand as a session musician, recording with **Kenny Barron**, **Sathima Bea Benjamin**, Sphere and the Timeless All Stars. Apart from his exemplary work as an accompanist, Williams is also an accomplished soloist.

● ALBUMS: *Crystal Reflections* (1976)★★★, *Heartbeat* (Muse 1978)★★★, *Toku Do* (Denon 1978)★★★★, *Dreams Come True* (1981)★★★, *Pinnacle* (Muse 1981)★★★, with Sphere *Four In One* (1982)★★★, with Sphere *Sphere On Tour* (1985)★★, with Sphere *Four For All* (1987)★★★, *Something More* (In And Out 1989)★★★★.

Williams, Charles

b. Isaac Cozerbreit, 8 May 1893, London, England, d. 7 September 1978, Findon Valley, Worthing, England. Williams was one of Britain's most prolific composers of light music, and he was also responsible for numerous film scores, often uncredited on screen. During his early career as a violinist he led for Sir Landon Ronald, Sir Thomas Beecham and Sir Edward Elgar. Like many of his contemporaries, he accompanied silent films, and became conductor of the New Gallery Cinema in London's Regent Street. He worked on the first British all-sound movie, Alfred Hitchcock's *Blackmail*, from which followed many commissions as composer or conductor: *The Thirty Nine Steps* (1935), *Kipps* (1941),

The Night Has Eyes (1942), *The Young Mr Pitt* (1942), *The Way To The Stars* (1945 - assisting **Nicholas Brodszky** who is reported to have written only four notes of the main theme, leaving the rest to Williams), *The Noose* (1946), *While I Live* (1947) from which came his famous 'Dream Of Olwen', *The Romantic Age* (1949), *Flesh And Blood* - from which came 'Throughout The Years' (1951) and the American film *The Apartment* (1960) which used Williams' 'Jealous Lover' (originally heard in the British film *The Romantic Age*) as the title theme, reaching number 1 in the US charts. In total Williams is reputed to have worked on at least 100 films. London publishers Chappells established their recorded music library in 1942, using Williams as composer and conductor of the Queen's Hall Light Orchestra. These 78s made exclusively for radio, television, newsreel and film use, contain many pieces that were to become familiar as themes, such as 'Devil's Galop' signature tune of *Dick Barton - Special Agent*, 'Girls In Grey' *BBC Television Newsreel*, 'High Adventure' *Friday Night Is Music Night*, 'Majestic Fanfare' *Australian Television News*. In his conducting capacity at Chappells he made the first recordings of works by several composers who were later to achieve fame in their own right, such as **Robert Farnon**, **Sidney Torch**, **Clive Richardson** and **Peter Yorke**. Williams' first recognition as a composer came in the early 30s for 'The Blue Devils' (which he had actually written in 1929 as 'The Kensington March'), followed in the 40s and 50s by 'Voice Of London', 'Rhythm On Rails', 'The Falcons', 'Heart O' London', 'Model Railway', 'The Music Lesson', 'Dream Of Olwen', 'The Old Clockmaker', 'The Starlings', 'A Quiet Stroll', 'Sleepy Marionette', 'Side Walk' and many more. For **EMI**'s **Columbia** label, with his own Concert Orchestra (as well as the Queen's Hall Light Orchestra), from 1946 onwards he conducted over 30 78s of popular light and film music.

● ALBUMS: *Charles Williams* (EMI 1993)★★★★.

Williams, Clarence

b. 8 October 1893, Plaquemine, Louisiana, USA, d. 6 November 1965. Although Williams first made his mark as a pianist, singer and dancer, it was as a composer, record producer, music publisher and entrepreneur that he made a lasting impact on jazz. Before he was in his teens he had decided upon a career in showbusiness and had run away from home to work with a travelling minstrel show. By the time he was 21 he had started composing, formed his first publishing company, and was married to blues singer **Eva Taylor**. His early associates, as performers and/or in business, included Armand Piron and **W.C. Handy**. First in New Orleans, then Chicago and finally in New York City, Williams established himself as a successful publisher, an energetic record producer and a tireless accompanist to some of the finest jazz and blues artists of the day. Among Williams' most notable recording sessions are those on which he was joined by **Louis Armstrong** and

Sidney Bechet, while his sensitive accompaniment enhanced many record dates with singers such as **Bessie Smith**, **Beulah 'Sippie' Wallace** and his wife. He was a dedicated promoter of the music of such leading pianist-composers as **James P. Johnson** and **Fats Waller**, his name often appearing as co-composer on works to which he may have contributed little that was creative but a great deal of enthusiastic effort in their promotion. By the late 30s he had decided to concentrate upon composing and, for a while, ran a business outside music. Even an accident that robbed him of his sight did not deter him and he worked steadily until his death in 1965. Williams' legacy to jazz includes many songs that bear his name as composer or co-composer and that became standards, among them 'Baby, Won't You Please Come Home', "Tain't Nobody's Biz-ness If I Do', 'Everybody Loves My Baby', 'Royal Garden Blues', 'West End Blues' and 'I Ain't Gonna Give Nobody None Of This Jelly Roll'.

● COMPILATIONS: *Clarence Williams And His Orchestra* (London 1954)★★★, *Back Room Special* (Columbia 1955)★★★, *Clarence Williams And His Orchestra Vol. 2* (London 1957)★★★, *Sidney Bechet Memorial* (Fontana 1960)★★★, *Clarence Williams Volume 1 1927-1935* (Philips 1962)★★★, *Clarence Williams Jazz Kings (1927-29)* (1979)★★★, *Clarence Williams And His Washboard Band, Volume 1 (1933-35)* (1983)★★★, *Clarence Williams And His Orchestra (1929-31)* (1986)★★★, *WNYC Jazz Festival* (1986)★★★, *Clarence Williams (1927-34)* (1988)★★★, *The Washboard Bands* (1988)★★★, *Jazz Classics In Digital Stereo* (1989)★★★, *Clarence Williams 1926-27* (Original Jazz Classics 1993)★★★, *Clarence Williams And The Blues Singers, Volumes 1 & 2* (Document 1996)★★★.

● FURTHER READING: *Clarence Williams*, Tom Lord.

Williams, Claude

b. 22 February 1908, Muskogee, Oklahoma, USA. Williams started out playing violin in local dance bands, including one led by **Oscar Pettiford**. In the late 20s he joined **Terrence Holder**'s band, staying on after Holder was replaced by **Andy Kirk**. He also spent time in the fine territory band led by **Alphonso Trent** and was briefly with the band co-led by Eddie and **Nat 'King' Cole**. In the mid-30s Williams switched to guitar to join **Count Basie**, but was replaced by **Freddie Green**. Williams continued to play guitar, working with the Four Shades Of Rhythm, Frank Martin, **Roy Milton** and other R&B bands, though he preferred to play the rarely fashionable violin. By the early 50s Williams was resident in Kansas City, but had drifted onto the sidelines. In the early 70s he returned to the spotlight, once again playing violin, and recording with **Jay McShann**, **B.B. King** and under his own name. A gutsy violinist with an energetic, swinging style, Williams has rarely attracted the attention he deserves.

● ALBUMS: with Jay McShann *The Man From Muskogee* (1971)★★★, *Call For The Fiddler* (1976)★★★, *Fiddler's Dream* (1977)★★★, *Kansas City Giants* (1982)★★.

Williams, Cootie

b. Charles Melvin Williams, 10 July 1911, Mobile, Alabama, USA, d. 15 September 1985. A self-taught trumpeter, Williams first played professionally in the mid-20s, when he was barely into his teens, appearing in the band run by the family of **Lester Young**. He later played in several New York bands, including those led by **Chick Webb** and **Fletcher Henderson**. In 1929 he replaced **Bubber Miley** in **Duke Ellington**'s orchestra, remaining there for 11 years. During this stint he made a number of records with other leaders, notably **Lionel Hampton** and **Teddy Wilson** (on some of whose sessions he accompanied **Billie Holiday**). He also led the Rug Cutters, one of the many small groups drawn from within the Ellington band. In 1940 Williams left Ellington and was briefly with **Benny Goodman** before forming his own big band. In later years, asked about his drinking habits, Williams remarked that he had not been a drinker until he had his own band. Given that his band included unpredictable musicians such as **Bud Powell** and **Charlie Parker** it is easy to understand why he turned to the bottle. For all the undoubted qualities of the band, which also featured **Eddie 'Lockjaw' Davis** and **Eddie 'Cleanhead' Vinson**, and the high standard of his own playing, by the late 40s Williams was forced to cut the band down in size.

In the early 50s he moved into the currently popular R&B field. For the next few years he continued playing R&B, leading small bands and making record dates - notably, a 1957 session, on which he was co-leader with **Rex Stewart**, by a band which boasted **Coleman Hawkins**, **Bud Freeman**, **Lawrence Brown** and **Hank Jones** within its ranks. In 1962 he rejoined Ellington, remaining in the band after the leader's death and during its brief, post-Ducal life, under **Mercer Ellington**. Although Williams was brought into the 1929 Ellington band to take over the so-called 'jungle effects' originally created by Miley, he quickly became an outstanding soloist in his own right. His full, rich tone and powerful style was showcased by Ellington on 'Concerto For Cootie' ('Do Nothing Till You Hear From Me'), recorded in 1940. Throughout his years with Ellington, and on many occasions under his own name, Williams readily displayed the command and vigour of his distinctive playing.

● ALBUMS: *The Big Challenge* (Fresh Sound 1957)★★★, *The Solid Trumpet Of Cootie Williams* (1962)★★★, *Salute To Duke Ellington* (1976)★★★.

● COMPILATIONS: *Cootie Williams And The Boys From Harlem, 1937-40* (1974)★★★, *Cootie Williams And His Rug Cutters, 1937-40* (1974)★★★, *Big Band Bounce* (1974)★★★, *Cootie Williams And Oran 'Hot Lips' Page* (1974)★★★, *New York 1944 - Sextet And Big Band* (1977)★★★, *Sextet And Orchestra* (1981)★★★, *Echoes From Harlem* (Affinity 1986)★★★, *Typhoon* (Swingtime 1986)★★★, *Memorial* (RCA 1986)★★★, *From Films, 1944-46* (Harlequin 1988)★★★.

Williams, Curley

b. Doc Williams, 1913, Southern Georgia, USA, d. 5 September 1970. He was christened Doc because family legend maintained that the seventh child would be a doctor. Little is known of Williams' early life, but in the early 40s, instead of being a doctor, he was the fiddle-playing leader of a western swing band on WALD Albany, Georgia. In December 1942, with his Sante Fe Riders, he arrived at the *Grand Ole Opry* in Nashville, where **George D. Hay** saw fit to change both his and his band's name to avoid confusion with **Doc Williams** And His Border Riders, who were then an established act on WWVA's *Wheeling Jamboree*. Williams' hair provided one simple suggestion and, being a native of Georgia (the Peach State), he became Curley Williams And His Georgia Peach Pickers. They began playing networked *Opry* shows in September 1943, and made their first recordings for **Columbia Records** in 1945 (the delay was caused by the recording ban operating at that time). Between 1945 and 1948, they relocated to play the dancehall circuits on the west coast and even appeared in a Charles Starrett B-western, *Riders Of The Lone Star*, in 1947. In the late 40s, they also starred on the *Louisiana Hayride*. Williams wrote 'Half As Much', which he recorded in 1951, at his band's last Columbia session and in 1952, **Hank Williams** took the song to number 2 in the US country charts. There has been confusion over the years, with many assuming Hank Williams, who was in fact no relation but was a friend of Curley's, to be the writer of the song (the song became a million-seller for **Rosemary Clooney**, and was also recorded successfully in the UK by **Alma Cogan** and **Lita Rosa**). During his years with Columbia, Williams also provided backing on various other artists' recordings, including on one occasion, **Fred Rose**, who at the time was recording for the label as the Rambling Rogue. In the early 50s, Williams and his band played regularly on the *Smoky Mountain Jamboree* in Georgia and for a time did sponsored shows on WSFA Montgomery, Alabama, until, in 1954, Williams tired of the showbusiness life and retired.

● COMPILATIONS: *Curley Williams - The Original Half As Much* (CowgirlBoy 1990)★★★.

Williams, Danny

b. 7 January 1942, Port Elizabeth, South Africa. Williams started singing professionally at the age of 13 and was spotted by producer Norman Newell when touring England in *The Golden City Dixies* show in 1959. The ultra-smooth ballad singer, often called 'Britain's **Johnny Mathis**', joined **HMV Records** and released his first single, 'Tall A Tree', in 1959. A regular on the television pop show *Drumbeat*, he had two minor hits with 'We Will Never Be This Young Again' and 'The Miracle Of You', before his version of the much-recorded 'Moon River' shot to number 1 in 1961. Follow-ups 'Jeannie' (co-written by **Russ Conway**) and a cover of **Andy Williams**' 'Wonderful World Of The Young', also made the UK Top 10 in

1962. In 1964 'White On White', a UK flop, gave him a US Top 10 hit. For the next decade he worked the clubs, and recordings on **Deram** and **Philips** meant little. In 1977, he briefly returned to the Top 40 with 'Dancin' Easy', a re-working of a Martini television commercial. Despite continued success in various countries, especially the Middle East, in the early 80s Williams quit show business and concentrated on his business interests. He made a comeback, touring with Eartha Kitt in 1989, and two years later starred in a concert at London's Strand Theatre. Since then, he has continued to sing at various venues throughout the UK, including the popular holiday camp circuit.

● ALBUMS: *White On White* (1964)★★★, *I'm A Song - Sing Me* (1973)★★★, *Any Time, Any Place, Anywhere* (1977)★★.

● COMPILATIONS: *Moon River And Other Great Songs* (EMI 1977)★★★★, *EMI Years* (EMI 1993)★★★★.

● FILMS: *It's All Happening* (1963).

Williams, Dar

b. *c*.1967, Mount Kisco, Massachusetts, USA. Singer-songwriter Dar Williams first gained exposure by playing tiny church halls and cramped coffee houses on the small-town Massachusetts folk circuit. Her debut album, *The Honesty Room*, was released by Grapevine Records in 1995 and attracted immediate critical acclaim. *Billboard* magazine featured Williams on its cover and ran a story concerning the 'redefinition' of the folk genre. This assertion accompanied an in-depth interview conducted by editor-in-chief Timothy White. The songs on *The Honesty Room* which inspired the media glare balanced lyrical poise with musical accessibility. The album was quickly followed by the release of *Mortal City* in 1996, a collection recorded in her own bedroom and produced by Steven Miller (a **Jane Siberry**, **Marianne Faithfull**, **Juliana Hatfield** and **Suzanne Vega** collaborator). Some critics noted that Miller's résumé also quite accurately pinpointed Williams influences, though some of the song titles, such as 'The Pointless, Yet Poignant Crisis Of A Co-Ed' and 'Southern California Wants To Be Western New York', were entirely her own. Other contributors included **John Prine** and **Eileen Ivers**. She is a departure from the stereotypical folk singer-songwriter, spending much of her time communicating via the Internet. Indeed much of her rise to prominence was attributed to word of mouth spread by 'net folkies'. Similarly she employed cutting edge ADAT recording technology for *Mortal City*, also re-packaging her debut as a special promotional double-disc available with initial quantities. Though some considered that the songs lacked the immediacy of her debut, critical reaction was once again complimentary, *Folk Roots* commenting that '. . . her energy, honesty and keen eye for observation make the end result exceptional.'

● ALBUMS: *The Honesty Room* (Grapevine 1995)★★★, *Mortal City* (Razor And Tie/Grapevine 1996)★★★, *End Of The Summer* (Razor And Tie 1997)★★★.

Williams, Deniece

b. Deniece Chandler, 3 June 1951, Gary, Indiana, USA. Williams is a gospel/soul singer whose successes span the 70s and 80s. As a child she sang in a gospel choir and made her first recordings in the late 60s for the Chicago-based Toddlin' Town label. After training as a nurse, she was hired by **Stevie Wonder** to join his Wonderlove vocal backing group. She contributed to four of his albums before leaving Wonder to pursue a solo career. Produced by Maurice White of **Earth, Wind And Fire**, her first album included the UK hits 'That's What Friends Are For' and the number 1 'Free' which was revived in 1990 by British group **BEF** for their *Music Of Quality & Distinction Vol II* album of cover versions. In 1978, Williams joined **Johnny Mathis** for the immensely popular ballad 'Too Much Too Little Too Late' This was followed by an album of duets by the couple, *That's What Friends Are For*. Returning to a solo career, Williams moved to Maurice White's own label, ARC but her next two albums made little impact. However, a revival of the 1965 song 'It's Gonna Take A Miracle', produced by **Thom Bell**, returned her to the US Top 10 in 1982. This was a prelude to the release of Williams' most well-known song, 'Let's Hear It For The Boy'. Originally made for the soundtrack of the 1984 film *Footloose*, it was issued as a single the following year and headed the US charts. Later records had no pop success although Deniece remained popular in the R&B audience and in 1988 she made her first gospel album for Sparrow. Williams is a prolific songwriter and her compositions have been recorded by **Merry Clayton**, the **Emotions**, the **Whispers**, **Frankie Valli** and others.

● ALBUMS: *This Is Niecy* (Columbia 1976)★★★★, *Songbird* (Columiba 1977)★★★, with Johnny Mathis *That's What Friends Are For* (Columbia 1978)★★★, *When Love Comes Calling* (Columbia 1979)★★★, *My Melody* (Columbia 1981)★★★★, *Niecy* (Columbia 1982)★★★★, *I'm So Proud* (Columbia 1983)★★★, *Let's Hear It For The Boy* (Columbia 1984)★★★, *Hot On The Trail* (Columbia 1986)★★★, *Water Under The Bridge* (Columbia 1987), *So Glad I Know* (Birdwing 1988)★★★, *As Good As It Gets* (Columbia 1989)★★★, *This Is My Song* (Harmony 1998)★★.

● FILMS: *Footloose* (1984).

Williams, Don

b. 27 May 1939, Floydada, Texas, USA. Williams' father was a mechanic whose job took him to other regions and much of his childhood was spent in Corpus Christi, Texas. Williams' mother played guitar and he grew up listening to country music. He and Lofton Kline formed a semi-professional folk group called the Strangers Two, and then, with the addition of Susan Taylor, they became the Pozo-Seco Singers, the phrase being a geological term to denote a dry well. Handled by **Bob Dylan**'s manager **Albert Grossman**, they had US pop hits with 'Time', 'I Can Make It With You' and 'Look What You've Done'. Following Lofton Kline's departure, they employed several replacements, result-

ing in a lack of direction, and they were as likely to record 'Green Green Grass Of Home' as 'Strawberry Fields Forever'. After Williams had failed to turn the trio towards country music, they disbanded in 1971.

He then worked for his father-in-law but also wrote for Susan Taylor's solo album via Jack Clement's music publishing company. Clement asked Williams to record albums of his company's best songs, mainly with a view to attracting other performers. In 1973 *Don Williams, Volume 1* was released on the fledgling JMI label and included such memorable songs as Bob McDill's apologia for growing old, 'Amanda', and Williams' own 'The Shelter Of Your Eyes'. Both became US country hits and JMI could hardly complain when **Tommy Cash** and then **Waylon Jennings** released 'I Recall A Gypsy Woman', thus depriving Williams of a certain winner (in the UK, Williams' version made number 13, his biggest success). Williams' work was reissued by ABC/**Dot** and *Don Williams, Volume 2* included 'Atta Way To Go' and 'We Should Be Together'. Williams then had a country number 1 with Wayland Holyfield's 'You're My Best Friend', which has become a standard and is the perennial singalong anthem at his concerts. By now, the Williams style had developed: gently paced love songs with straightforward arrangements, lyrics and sentiments. Williams was mining the same vein as **Jim Reeves** but he eschewed Reeves' smartness by dressing like a ranch-hand. Besides having a huge contingent of female fans, Williams counted **Eric Clapton** and **Pete Townshend** among his admirers. Clapton recorded his country hit 'Tulsa Time', written by Danny Flowers from Williams' Scratch Band. The Scratch Band released their own album, produced by Williams, in 1982. Williams played a band member himself in the Burt Reynolds film *W.W. And The Dixie Dancekings* and also appeared in *Smokey And The Bandit 2*. Williams' other successes include 'Till The Rivers All Run Dry', 'Some Broken Hearts Never Mend', 'Lay Down Beside Me' and his only US Top 30 pop hit, 'I Believe In You'. Unlike most established country artists, he has not sought duet partners, although he and **Emmylou Harris** found success with an easy-paced version of **Townes Van Zandt**'s 'If I Needed You'. Williams' best record is with Bob McDill's homage to his southern roots, 'Good Ol' Boys Like Me'. Moving to **Capitol Records** in the mid-80s, Williams released such singles as 'Heartbeat In the Darkness' and 'Senorita', but the material was not as impressive. He took a sabbatical in 1988 but subsequent **RCA** recordings, which include 'I've Been Loved By The Best', showed that nothing had changed. Williams' most recent album, the more sombre *Flatlands*, was released on the Carlton label. He continues to be a major concert attraction, maintaining his stress-free style. When interviewed, Williams gives the impression of being a contented man who takes life as he finds it. He is a rare being - a country star who is free of controversy.

● ALBUMS: with the Pozo-Seco Singers *Time* (Columbia

1966)★★, with the Pozo-Seco Singers *I Can Make It With You* (Columbia 1967)★★★, with the Pozo-Seco Singers *Shades Of Time* (Columbia 1968)★★★, *Don Williams, Volume 1* (JMI 1973)★★★★, *Don Williams, Volume 2* (JMI 1974)★★★, *Don Williams, Volume 3* (ABC 1974)★★★, *You're My Best Friend* (ABC 1975)★★★★, *Harmony* (ABC 1976)★★★★, *Visions* (ABC 1977)★★★★, *Country Boy* (ABC 1977)★★★, with Roy Clark, Freddy Fender, Hank Thompson *Country Comes To Carnegie Hall* (ABC/Dot 1977)★★★★, *Expressions* (ABC 1978)★★★★, *Portrait* (1979)★★★, *I Believe In You* (MCA 1980)★★★★, *Especially For You* (MCA 1981)★★★★, *Listen To The Radio* (MCA 1982)★★★★, *Yellow Moon* (MCA 1983)★★★, *Cafe Carolina* (MCA 1984)★★★★, *New Moves* (Capitol 1986)★★, *Traces* (Capitol 1987)★★, *One Good Well* (RCA 1989)★★★, *As Long As I Have You* (RCA 1989)★★★, *True Love* (RCA 1990)★★★, *Currents* (RCA 1992)★★★, *Borrowed Tales* (Carlton/American Harvest 1995)★★★, *Flatlands* (Carlton 1996)★★★.

● COMPILATIONS: *Greatest Hits, Volume 1* (MCA 1975)★★★★, *Greatest Country Hits* (Curb 1976)★★★, *Best Of Don Williams, Volume 2* (MCA 1979)★★★★, *Prime Cuts* (Capitol 1981)★★★, *Best Of Don Williams, Volume 3* (MCA 1984)★★★, *Best Of Don Williams, Volume 4* (MCA 1985)★★★, *20 Greatest Hits* (MCA 1987)★★★★, *The Very Best Of Don Williams* (Half Moon 1997)★★★★.

● VIDEOS: *Live, The Greatest Hits Collection, Volume One* (Prism 1996).

Williams, Esther

b. 8 August 1921 or 1923, Inglewood, Los Angeles, California, USA. One of MGM's top film musicals stars in the 40s and 50s, Esther Williams's mother boasted that her daughter (one of five children) swam before she walked. By the time she was 15, she had won every national swimming competition and was set to represent the USA in the Olympic Games in Finland, but they were cancelled following the outbreak of World War II. She studied for a time at the University of Southern California before joining **Billy Rose**'s Aquacade in San Francisco, in which her co-star was Johnny Weissmuller. While in the show she was spotted by MGM talent scouts, and made her film debut in 1942 as one of **Mickey Rooney**'s girlfriends in *Andy Hardy's Double Life*. She had some swimming scenes in that one, and in *Bathing Beauty* (1944). For *Zeigfeld Follies* (1946), special water ballets were created for her. Her first starring role came in *Fiesta* (1947), with Richard Montalban, and this was followed by a string of dazzling Technicolor movies in which her glamorous looks and pleasing personality were permanently on display. These included *This Time For Keeps, On An Island With You,* **Take Me Out To The Ball Game,** *Neptune's Daughter, The Duchess Of Idaho, Pagan Love Song, Texas Carnival, Skirts Ahoy!, Million Dollar Mermaid,* **Dangerous When Wet,** *Easy To Love,* and *Jupiter's Darling* (1955). With the demise of the big-budget Hollywood musicals she played several straight roles, but her appeal had diminished, and her last

picture, *The Magic Fountain*, was released in 1961. While MGM went to great lengths to show-case her superb swimming ability in some of the most lavish and spectacular aqua-sequences ever seen on the screen, and co-starred her with several attractive leading men (including cartoon characters Tom and Jerry), her acting ability was not allowed to develop, and her quite pleasant singing voice was rather neglected. However, she did sing a lovely version of 'The Sea Of The Moon' (**Harry Warren-Arthur Freed**) in *The Pagan Love Song*, and handled some of **Arthur Schwartz** and **Johnny Mercer**'s numbers extremely well in *Dangerous When Wet*. She also introduced **Frank Loesser**'s Oscar-winning 'Baby, It's Cold Outside' with Ricardo Montalban in *Neptune's Daughter*. In 1967 she married her third husband, Fernando Lamas, and continued to concentrate on her commercial swimming pool interests.

Williams, Fess

b. Stanley R. Williams, 10 April 1894, Danville, Kentucky, USA, d. 17 December 1975. As a child Williams played several instruments, receiving formal tuition from N. Clark-Smith at Tuskegee University. By his late teens he had settled on clarinet, and soon afterwards formed the first of many bands he was to lead over the coming years. In New York City in the mid-20s, he became one of the first bands to hold a residency at the Savoy Ballroom where, resplendent in top hat and diamond-studded suit, he was a great popular success. However, his music was well-laced with amiable hokum and he was soon overtaken in popularity by the more swinging bands, which were better suited to the Savoy's demanding dancers. He continued to lead a band throughout the 30s but, despite the presence of some good musicians, among them **Rex Stewart** and **Albert Nicholas**, he failed to match the successes enjoyed by other bands. Although he continued to lead bands periodically in the 40s and beyond, his later career was mostly outside music. In 1962 Williams was invited to attend a concert at New York's Town Hall, where the orchestra was directed by his nephew, **Charles Mingus**.

● COMPILATIONS: *Fess Williams And His Royale Flush Orchestra* (1978)★★★, *Fess Williams, Volume One (1929)* (1985)★★★, *Fess Williams, Volume Two (1929-30)* (1986)★★★, *Rare Masters* (1989)★★★.

Williams, Gene

b. USA. Gene Williams first entered the entertainment industry as vocalist with the **Claude Thornhill** Orchestra, before forming his own dance band in 1950 in New York City, New York, USA. The musical sidemen enrolled included Harry Wegbreit, Jack Mootz, Don Josephs, Harry Di Vito, Dick Hoch, Sam Marowitz, Charlie O'Cain, Mickey Folus, Joe Reisman, **Teddy Napoleon**, Russ Saunders and Mel Zelnick. While Gene Williams himself and Adele Castle were the featured vocalists, **Gil Evans**, Hubie Wheeler, **Chico**

O'Farrill and Joe Reisman served as the band's arrangers.

Their initial contracts came from college dates, before the membership elected to put the group on a more permanent footing. Mixing bebop instrumentals with the smooth style inherited from Williams' time with Claude Thornhill, by 1952 they had secured engagements at such venues as the Glen Island Casino. Thereafter, however, they struggled to make any headway, hamstrung by the reduced air time available to dance bands with the advent of rock 'n' roll.

Williams, George 'Bullet'
(see **Coleman, Burl C. 'Jaybird'**)

Williams, Ginger
b. 1956, Jamaica, West Indies. Williams accompanied her family in 1962 when they emigrated to the UK. After she completed her education she joined the north London group Green Mango. They played in and around the Tottenham area and although they were a popular act, she felt disenchanted with gigging and in 1972 left the group. A year later she met producer Ronnie Williams, who took her to the studio to record her debut, 'I Can't Resist Your Tenderness', which, on its eventual release in 1974, was an instant hit. The song is an early example of the burgeoning style that was later categorized as **lovers rock**. The single surfaced on Count Shelly's newly formed Paradise label. Following the birth of her third child, Williams returned to the reggae chart with 'In My Heart There Is A Place'. She was nominated in the 1974 Black Music Poll as Best Newcomer and Female Artist. In 1975 she recorded with **Dennis Harris** ('Tenderness') and the following year with Bill Campbell ('Oh Baby Come Back'). Williams continued recording with Campbell in 1977, releasing 'I'll Still Love You', 'I'm Just A Girl', and a duet with the producer, 'The Vow'. Williams was unable to repeat the success of her debut, although she has enjoyed isolated hits over the years. Notable releases included 'Love Me Tonight' and 'Strange World'. In 1996 a compilation surfaced hailing Williams as 'the first lady of lovers rock', and included 'As Long As You Love Me' and 'Tenderly'.
● ALBUMS: *B & B Super Hits* (BB 1977)★★★.
● COMPILATIONS: *Greatest Hits* (Jet Star 1996)★★.

Williams, Griff
b. La Grande, Oregon, USA, d. February 1959, Chicago, Illinois, USA. Williams studied at Stanford University and formed his first dance band on campus. His first professional employment came alongside **Anson Weeks** during his tenure at the Mark Hopkins Hotel, playing second piano. The experience encouraged him to put together his own orchestra, which was founded in San Francisco. The musical sidemen in this first incarnation of the band included Gene McDonald, Horace Perazzi, **Ray Anderson**, Albert Arnold, Jack Buck, Paul Hare, **Buddy Moreno**, Walter Kelsey, Bob

Logan and Warren Luce. Williams himself played piano, with the featured vocalist Coralee Scott, later replaced by a succession of singers including Buddy Moreno, Lois Lee and 'the Williams trio'. Their first engagement came at Edgewater Beach, where the group opened in October 1933. From the outset they styled themselves so as to appeal to hotel audiences, touring such venues almost exclusively during their active life. Included in these engagements were frequent visits to the Mark Hopkins Hotel where Williams had once played with Weeks. They also played regularly at the Stevens Hotel after the band had settled in the Chicago area during 1939. They continued to play there throughout the war years. By the end of the 30s a radically different ensemble had been recruited with Bill Clifford, Don Mulford, Walter King, Bob Kirk and Lyle Gardner among the personnel. During this time contracts with Varsity, **OKeh** and **Columbia Records** produced a number of recordings including the band's theme tune, 'Dream Music'. Williams stayed with the band until their playing opportunities began to dwindle in 1953. At that point he joined the Haywood Publishing Company, taking charge of the launch of several successful business magazines. However, he continued to appear occasionally with impromptu versions of the orchestra, before his professional commitments prevented further engagements. He became vice president of Haywood and then one of its directors, before dying of a heart attack in 1959.

Williams, Hank
b. Hiram (misspelt on birth certificate as Hiriam) Williams, 17 September 1923, Georgiana, Alabama, USA, d. 1 January 1953, on the road between Montgomery, Alabama and Oak Hill, West Virginia, USA. Misspelling notwithstanding, Williams disliked the name and took to calling himself Hank. He was born with a spine defect that troubled him throughout his life, and which was further aggravated after being thrown from a horse when he was 17 years old. Initially, his parents, Lon and Lilly, ran a general store, but Lon later entered a veterans' hospital following a delayed reaction to the horrors he had experienced during World War I. The young Williams was raised by his imposing, resourceful mother, who gave him a cheap guitar when he was seven. He learned chords from an elderly black musician, Teetot (Rufe Payne). Williams later said, 'All the musical training I ever had came from him.' It also explains the strong blues thread that runs through his work. In 1937, Lilly opened a boarding house in Montgomery, Alabama. Williams won a talent contest and formed his own band, the Drifting Cowboys. As clubs were tough, Hank hired a wrestler, Cannonball Nichols, as a bass player, more for protection than musical ability, but he could not be protected from his mother, who handled his bookings and earnings (in truth, Williams was not particularly interested in the money he made). While working for a medicine show, he met Audrey Sheppard and married her in

December 1944. Although rivals, both his wife and his mother would thump the pale, lanky singer for his lack of co-operation. Williams was a local celebrity, but on 14 September 1946, he and Audrey went to Nashville, impressing **Fred Rose** and his son Wesley at the relatively new **Acuff-Rose** publishers. On 11 December 1946 Williams made his first recordings for the small Sterling label. They included 'Callin' You' and 'When God Comes And Gathers His Jewels'. Fred Rose secured a contract with the more prestigious **MGM Records**, and he acted as his manager, record producer and, occasionally, co-writer ('Mansion On The Hill', 'Kawliga'). Williams' first MGM release, 'Move It On Over', sold several thousand copies. He then joined the prestigious radio show *Louisiana Hayride* in 1948 and was featured on its concert tours. Fred Rose opposed him reviving 'Lovesick Blues', originally recorded by Emmett Miller in 1925, and later a success for Rex Griffin in 1939; nevertheless, he recorded the song, following Miller's and Griffin's playful yodels. 'Lovesick Blues' topped the US country charts for 16 weeks and remained in the listings for almost a year. The **Grand Ole Opry**, although wary of his hard-drinking reputation, invited him to perform 'Lovesick Blues', which led to an unprecedented six encores. He and the Drifting Cowboys became regulars and the publicity enabled them to command $1,000 for concert appearances; they even upstaged comedian and film star Bob Hope. 'Wedding Bells' made number 2, as did a contender for the greatest country single ever released, the poignant 'I'm So Lonesome I Could Cry', backed with the old blues song, 'My Bucket's Got A Hole In It'; the *Opry* sponsors, disapproving of the word 'beer' in the latter song, made Williams sing 'milk' instead. In 1950, he had three country number 1 hits, 'Long Gone Lonesome Blues', 'Why Don't You Love Me?' and 'Moanin' The Blues'. The following year, he had two further chart-toppers with 'Cold, Cold Heart' and 'Hey, Good Lookin''. Another superb double-sided hit, 'Howlin' At The Moon'/'I Can't Help It (If I'm Still In Love With You)', made number 2.

In 1952, Williams went to number 1 with his praise of Cajun food in 'Jambalaya', while 'Half As Much' made number 2. Another well-balanced double-sided hit, 'Settin' The Woods On Fire'/'You Win Again', made number 2. Williams was a showman, often wearing a flashy suit embroidered with sequins and decorated with musical notes. Although MGM studios considered making films with him, nothing materialized. It is arguable that, with his thinning hair, he looked too old, or it may have been that he was just too awkward. His lifestyle was akin to the later spirit of rock 'n' roll; he drank too much, took drugs (admittedly, excessive numbers of painkillers for his back), played with guns, destroyed hotel rooms, threw money out of windows and permanently lived in conflict. His son, **Hank Williams Jnr.**, said, 'I get sick of hearing people tell me how much they loved my daddy. They hated him in Nashville.' Williams' songs articulated the lives and loves of his listeners and he went a stage further by recording melodramatic monologues as Luke The Drifter. They included 'Beyond The Sunset', 'Pictures From Life's Other Side', 'Too Many Parties And Too Many Pals' and 'Men With Broken Hearts'. Although Luke the Drifter's appeal was limited, Fred Rose saw how Williams' other songs could have wide appeal. Country songs had been recorded by pop performers before Williams, but Rose aggressively sought cover versions. Soon **Tony Bennett** ('Cold, Cold Heart'), **Jo Stafford** ('Jambalaya') and **Joni James** ('Your Cheatin' Heart') had gold records. Williams' wife, 'Miss Audrey', also made solo records, but Williams knew her talent was limited. She was frustrated by her own lack of success and many of Williams' songs stemmed from their quarrels. They were divorced on 29 May 1952 and, as Williams regarded possessions as unimportant, she was awarded their house and one half of all his future royalties. He did, however, have the sadness of losing custody of his son.

Like any professional show, the *Opry* preferred sober nondescripts to drunk superstars, and on 11 August 1952, Williams was fired and told that he could return when he was sober. However, Williams did not admit to his problem, joking about missing shows and falling off stage. He lost Fred Rose's support, the Drifting Cowboys turned to **Ray Price**, and, although the *Louisiana Hayride* tolerated his wayward lifestyle, his earnings fell and he was reduced to playing small clubs with pick-up bands. When Williams met the 19-year-old daughter of a policeman, Billie Jean Jones, he said, 'If you ain't married, ol' Hank's gonna marry you.' On 19 October 1952 he did just that - three times. First, before a Justice of the Peace in Minden, Louisiana, and then at two concerts at the New Orleans Municipal Auditorium before several thousand paying guests. The newlyweds spent Christmas with relations in Georgiana, Alabama. His biggest booking for some time was on New Year's Day 1953 with **Hawkshaw Hawkins** and **Homer And Jethro** in Canton, Ohio, but because of a blizzard, Williams' plane was cancelled. An 18-year-old taxi driver, Charles Carr, was hired to drive Williams' Cadillac. They set off, Williams having a bottle of whiskey for company. He sank into a deep sleep. A policeman who stopped the car for ignoring speed restrictions remarked, 'That guy looks dead'. Five hours later, Carr discovered that his passenger was indeed dead. Death was officially due to 'severe heart attack with haemorrhage', but alcohol and pills played their part. At the concert that night, the performers sang Williams' 'I Saw The Light' in tribute. An atmospheric stage play, *Hank Williams: The Show He Never Gave*, by Maynard Collins, filmed with Sneezy Waters in the title role, showed what might have happened had Williams arrived that night. Some commentators took Williams' then-current number 1, 'I'll Never Get Out Of This World Alive', as an indication that he knew he had little time left. **Chet Atkins**, who played 'dead string rhythm' on the record, disagreed: 'All young men of 28 or 29 feel immortal and although he wrote a lot about death, he thought it was something that would happen when he got old.' 20,000 saw Williams' body as it lay in state in an embroidered Nudie suit (designed by Miss Audrey) at the Montgomery Municipal Auditorium. His shrine in Montgomery Oakwood Cemetery is the subject of **Steve Young**'s song, 'Montgomery In The Rain'.

1953 was a remarkable year for his records. 'Kaw-Liga', inspired by a visit to South Alabama and backed by 'Your Cheatin' Heart', went to the top of the chart, and his third consecutive posthumous number 1 was with Hy Heath and Fred Rose's 'Take These Chains From My Heart'. MGM, desperate for fresh material, over-dubbed a backing onto demos for 'Weary Blues From Waitin'' and 'Roly Poly' - Hank Williams was the first deceased star to have his recordings altered. Albums of Hank Williams with strings and duets with his son followed. In 1969, Hank Jnr. completed some of his father's scribblings for an album, 'Songs My Father Left Me', the most successful being 'Cajun Baby'. In recent years, Williams and **Willie Nelson** proved a popular duo with 'I Told A Lie To My Heart', while a battered demo of 'There's A Tear In My Beer', which had been given by Williams to Big Bill Lister to perform, was magically restored with the addition of Hank Williams Jnr.'s voice and, accompanied by an even more inge-nious video, sold 250,000 copies.

Hank Williams recorded around 170 different songs between 1946 and 1952, and there are over 230 and around 130 'Tribute to Hank Williams' albums that have also been recorded, not only by country artists, but by artists including **Spike Jones**, **Del Shannon** and Hardrock Gunter. The first was 'The Death Of Hank Williams' by disc jockey Jack Cardwell. Other contem-porary ones included 'Hank, It Will Never Be The Same Without You' by **Ernest Tubb**, 'Hank Williams Will Live Forever' by **Johnnie And Jack**, 'The Life Of Hank Williams' by Hawkshaw Hawkins and 'Hank Williams Meets **Jimmie Rodgers**' by Virginia Rounders. Most tributes lack inspiration, are too morbid and too rever-ent, and are recorded by artists who would usually never enter a recording studio. The most pertinent trib-utes are **Moe Bandy**'s reflective 'Hank Williams, You Wrote My Life', **Johnny Cash**'s jaunty 'The Night Hank Williams Came To Town', **Tim Hardin**'s plaintive 'Tribute To Hank Williams', **Kris Kristofferson**'s rous-ing 'If You Don't Like Hank Williams' and **Emmylou Harris**'s isolated 'Rollin' And Ramblin''. Hank Williams *is* the Phantom of the *Opry*; his influence on Moe Bandy, **George Jones**, **Vernon Oxford** and **Boxcar Willie** is especially marked. They have all recorded albums of his songs, as have **Roy Acuff**, **Glen Campbell**, **Floyd Cramer**, **Don Gibson**, **Ronnie Hawkins**, **Roy Orbison**, **Charley Pride**, Jack Scott, **Del Shannon** and Ernest Tubb. Johnny Cash, **Jerry Lee Lewis**, **Little Richard**, **Elvis Presley**, **Linda Ronstadt** and **Richard Thompson** have also appropriated his repertoire. Major UK chart hits include 'Lovesick Blues'

by **Frank Ifield**, 'Take These Chains From My Heart' by **Ray Charles**, and 'Jambalaya' by the **Carpenters**. Before Williams was laid to rest, Lilly, Audrey and Billie Jean were squabbling for the rights to Williams' estate. Audrey's name is on his tombstone, and the inaccurate 1964 biopic *Your Cheatin' Heart*, which starred George Hamilton as Hank Williams, miming to Hank Williams Jnr.'s recordings, did not even mention Billie Jean. Both wives performed as Mrs. Hank Williams, and Billie Jean was widowed a second time when **Johnny Horton** died in 1960. A more recent development has been the claims of Jett Williams, the illegitimate daughter of Williams and country singer Bobbie Jett, who was born three days after his death. The pressures Williams suffered in his life appear to have sharpened his aware-ness and heightened his creative powers. His compact, aching songs flow seamlessly and few have improved upon his own emotional performances. Hank Williams is the greatest country singer and songwriter who ever lived. His plaque in the **Country Music Hall Of Fame** states: 'The simple beautiful melodies and straightfor-ward plaintive stories in his lyrics of life as he knew it will never die.'

● ALBUMS: *Hank Williams Sings* 10-inch album (MGM 1951)★★★★, *Moanin' The Blues* (MGM 1952/56)★★★★, *Hank Williams Memorial Album* (MGM 1953/55)★★★★, *Hank Williams as Luke The Drifter* overdubbed as *Beyond The Sunset* MGM 1963 (MGM 1953/55)★★★, *Honky Tonkin'* (MGM 1954/57)★★★, *I Saw The Light* (MGM 1954/56)★★★, *Ramblin' Man* (MGM 1954/55)★★★, *Sing Me A Blue Song* (MGM 1957)★★★, *The Immortal Hank Williams* overdubbed as *First Last And Always* MGM 1969 (MGM 1958)★★★, *The Unforgettable Hank Williams* over-dubbed MGM 1968 (MGM 1959)★★★, *Lonesome Sound Of Hank Williams* (MGM 1960)★★★, *Wait For The Light To Shine* overdubbed MGM 1968 (MGM 1960)★★★, *Let Me Sing A Blue Song* overdubbed 1968 (MGM 1961)★★★, *Wanderin' Around* overdubbed 1968 (MGM 1961)★★★, *I'm Blue Inside* overdubbed MGM 1968 (MGM 1961)★★★, *The Spirit Of Hank Williams* overdubbed MGM 1969 (MGM 1961)★★★, *On Stage-Live Volume 1* (MGM 1962)★★★, *On Stage Volume II* (MGM 1963)★★★, *Lost Highways & Other Folk Ballads* (MGM 1964)★★★, *Father And Son* overdubbed (MGM 1965)★★★, *Kawliga And Other Humerous Songs* some overdubbed (MGM 1965)★★★, *Hank Williams With Strings* overdubbed (MGM 1966)★★★, *Hank Williams, Hank Williams Jr. Again* (MGM 1966)★★★, *Movin' On - Luke The Drifter* overdubbed (MGM 1966)★★★, *Mr & Mrs Hank Williams (With Audrey)* (Metro 1966)★★★, *More Hank Williams And Strings* (MGM 1967)★★★, *I Won't Be Home No More* overdubbed (MGM 1967)★★★, *Hank Williams And Strings, Volume III* (MGM 1968)★★★, *In The Beginning* (MGM 1968)★★★, *Life To Legend Hank Williams* (MGM 1970)★★★, *The Last Picture Show Film Soundtrack* (MGM 1971)★★★, *Hank Williams/Hank Williams Jr. Legend In Story And Song* (MGM 1973)★★★, *Hank Williams/Hank Williams Jr. Insights In Story And Song* (MGM 1974)★★★, *A Home In Heaven* (MGM 1975)★★★, *Live At The Grand Ole Opry* (MGM 1976)★★★★, *Hank Williams And The Drifting*

Cowboys On Radio (Golden Country 1982)★★★, *Early Country Live Volume 1 (Hank Williams On Radio Shows Plus Others)* (ACM 1983)★★★★, *Rare Takes And Radio Cuts* (Polydor 1984)★★★, *Early Country Live Volume 2 (Hank Williams On Radio Shows)* (ACM 1984)★★★★, *Early Country Music Live Volume 3 (Hank Williams On Radio Shows* (ACM 1985)★★★★, *Just Me And My Guitar* (CMF 1985)★★★, *Hank Williams - The First Recordings* (CMF 1985)★★★★, *Hank Williams - On The Air* (Polydor 1985)★★★, *Hank Williams: I Ain't Got Nothin' But Time December 1946-August 1947* (Polydor 1985)★★★★, *Hank Williams: Lovesick Blues - August 1947-December 1948* (Polydor 1985)★★★★, *Hank Williams: Lost Highway - December 1948-March 1949* (Polydor 1986)★★★, *Hank Williams: I'm So Lonesome I Could Cry - March 1949-August 1949* (Polydor 1986)★★★★, *Hank Williams: Long Gone Lonesome Blues - August 1949-December 1950* (Polydor 1987)★★★★, *Hank Williams: Hey, Good Lookin' - December 1950-July 1951* (Polydor 1987)★★★★, *Hank Williams: Let's Turn Back The Years, July 1951-June 1952* (Polydor 1987)★★★★, *Hank Williams: I Won't Be Home No More, June 1952-September 1952* (Polydor 1987)★★★★, *There's Nothing As Sweet As My Baby* (Mount Olive 1988)★★★, *Hank Williams - Jambalaya* (Creative Sounds 1992)★★★, *Health And Happiness Shows* (Mercury 1993)★★★, *Alone And Forsaken* (Mercury 1995)★★★, *Three Hanks, Men With Broken Hearts* (Curb 1996)★★★.

● COMPILATIONS: *Greatest Hits* (Polydor 1963)★★★, *The Very Best Of Hank Williams* (Polydor 1963)★★★, *24 Of Hank Williams' Greatest Hits* (MGM 1970)★★★★, *24 Greatest Hits, Volume 2* (Polydor 1976)★★, *40 Greatest Hits* (Polydor 1978)★★★★, *The Collectors' Edition* 8-LP box set of Polydor albums listed above (Polydor 1987)★★★★★, *Rare Demos: First To Last* (CMF 1990)★★★, *The Original Singles Collection Plus* 3-CD box set (Polydor 1990)★★★★★, *Low Down Blues* (Polygram 1996)★★★.

● VIDEOS: *The Hank Williams Story* (1994).

● FURTHER READING: *Sing A Sad Song: The Life Of Hank Williams*, Roger M. Williams. *Hank Williams: From Life To Legend*, Jerry Rivers. *I Saw The Light: The Gospel Life Of Hank Williams*, Al Bock. *Hank Williams: Country Music's Tragic King*, Jay Caress. *The First Outlaw: Hank Williams*, Jim Arp. *Your Cheating Heart, A Biography Of Hank Williams*, Chet Flippo. *Hank Williams: A Bio-Bibliography*, George William Koon. *Still In Love With You: The Story Of Hank And Audrey Williams*, Lycrecia Williams and Dale Vinicur. *Ain't Nothin' As Sweet As My Baby: The Story Of Hank Williams' Lost Daughter*, Jett Williams. *Hank Williams: The Complete Lyrics*, Don Cusic. *The Life And Times Of Hank Williams*, Arnold Rogers and Bruce Gidoll. *Hank Williams: The Biography*, Colin Escott.

Williams, Hank, Jnr.

b. Randall Hank Williams Jnr., 26 May 1949, Shreveport, Louisiana, USA. The son of the most famous man in country music, **Hank Williams**, he was nicknamed Bocephus after a puppet on the *Grand Ole Opry*. Being the son of a country legend has brought financial security, but it was difficult for him to firmly establish his own individuality. His mother, Audrey, was determined that he would follow in his father's

footsteps. When only eight years old, he was touring, performing with his father's songs, and even appeared on the *Grand Ole Opry*. He also had a high school band, Rockin' Randall And The Rockets. He signed for the same label as his father, **MGM Records**, as soon as his voice broke. In the 60s, Williams had country hits with 'Long Gone Lonesome Blues', 'Cajun Baby', a revival of 'Endless Sleep', and the only version of 'Nobody's Child' ever to make the country charts. He also recorded an embarrassing narration about his relationship with his father, 'Standing In The Shadows'. Even worse was his maudlin dialogue as Luke the Drifter Jnr., 'I Was With **Red Foley** (The Night He Passed Away)'. He copied his father's style for the soundtrack of the film biography of his father, *Your Cheatin' Heart* (1964), and starred in the inferior *A Time To Sing*. He was just 15 years old and **Connie Francis** was 26 when they released a duet about adultery, 'Walk On By'.

In 1974, Williams Jnr. moved to Alabama where he recorded a hard-hitting album, *Hank Williams Jnr. And Friends*, with **Charlie Daniels** and other top-class southern country rockers. Like his father, he has had arguments with Audrey, gone through an unhappy marriage and overindulged in alcohol and drugs. 'Getting Over You' relates to his life, and in another song, he explains that it's the 'Family Tradition'. On 8 August 1975, Hank Williams Jnr. fell 500 feet down a Montana mountain face. Although close to death, he made a remarkable recovery, needing extensive medical and cosmetic surgery. Half of his face was reconstructed and he had to learn to speak (and sing) all over again. It was two years before he could perform once more. Since 1977, Williams Jnr., who is managed by his opening act **Merle Kilgore**, has been associated with the 'outlaw country music' genre. **Waylon Jennings**, for example, wrote Williams Jnr.'s country hit 'Are You Sure Hank Done It This Way?' and produced his album *The New South*. In 1983, he had eight albums on the US country charts simultaneously, yet was not chosen as Entertainer of the Year in the Country Music Awards. In 1985, Williams released his fiftieth album, *Five-O*. Williams' songs often lack distinctive melodies, while the lyrics concentrate on his macho, defiant persona. His best compositions include 'Montana Cafe', 'OD'd In Denver', the jazzy 'Women I've Never Had' and his tale of a visit to a gay disco, 'Dinosaur'. 'If The South Woulda Won' was criticized for being racist but, possibly, he was being sardonic. However, there was no mistaking of his tone towards Saddam Hussein in 'Don't Give Us A Reason'. Among his other successes are 'I Fought The Law', 'Tennessee Stud', 'Ain't Misbehavin'' and his *cri de coeur*, 'If Heaven Ain't A Lot Like Dixie'. Although Williams has shown a determination to move away from his father's shadow, he still sings about him. Many tribute songs by others - 'If You Don't Like Hank Williams' and 'Are You Sure Hank Done It This Way?' - gain an extra dimension through his interpretations. Williams himself was the subject of a tribute from **David Allan Coe**, who insisted that a man of six feet four inches and 15 stone should not be called 'Jnr'. Williams' rowdy image did not fit in well with the clean-cut 'hat acts' of the early 90s, and his record sales and air play faltered. He remains a sell-out concert draw, although a well-publicized incident during 1992 where he arrived onstage drunk, and spent most of the 20-minute performance insulting his audience, did little for his status in the Nashville community, although his father would have been proud.

● ALBUMS: *Hank Williams Jnr. Sings The Songs Of Hank Williams* (MGM 1963)★★, *Connie Francis And Hank Williams Jnr. Sing Great Country Favorites* (MGM 1964)★★, *Your Cheatin' Heart* film soundtrack (MGM 1964)★★, *Ballad Of The Hills And Plains* (MGM 1965)★★, *Father And Son - Hank Williams Sr And Hank Williams Jnr. Again* (MGM 1965)★★★, *Blue's My Name* (MGM 1966)★★★, *Country Shadows* (MGM 1966)★★, *In My Own Way* (MGM 1967)★★★, *My Songs* (MGM 1968)★★★, *A Time To Sing* film soundtrack (MGM 1968)★★, *Luke The Drifter Jnr.* (MGM 1969)★★★, *Songs My Father Left Me* (MGM 1969)★★★, *Live At Cobo Hall, Detroit* (MGM 1969)★★★★, *Luke The Drifter Jnr., Volume 2* (MGM 1969)★★★, *Sunday Morning* (MGM 1970)★★★, *Singing My Songs* (MGM 1970)★★★, *Luke The Drifter Jnr., Volume 3* (MGM 1970)★★★, with Louis Johnson *Removing The Shadow* (MGM 1970)★★, *All For The Love Of Sunshine* (MGM 1970)★★★, *I've Got A Right To Cry/They All Used To Belong To Me* (MGM 1971), *Sweet Dreams* (MGM 1971)★★★, *Eleven Roses* (MGM 1972)★★, with Johnson *Send Me Some Lovin'/Whole Lotta Lovin'* (MGM 1972)★★★, *After You/Pride's Not Hard To Swallow* (MGM 1973)★★★, *Hank Williams/Hank Williams Jr: The Legend In Story And Song* a double album in which Hank Jnr. narrates his father's life (MGM 1973)★★★, *Just Pickin' - No Singing* (MGM 1973)★★★, *The Last Love Song* (MGM 1973)★★★, *Hank Williams/Hank Williams Jr. Insights In Story And Song* (MGM 1974)★★★, *Bocephus* (MGM 1975)★★, *Hank Williams Jnr. And Friends* (MGM 1975)★★★★, *One Night Stands* (Warners/Curb 1977)★★★, *The New South* (Warners 1978)★★★★, *Family Tradition* (Elektra/Curb 1979)★★★★, *Whiskey Bent And Hell Bound* (Elektra/Curb 1979)★★★★, *Habits Old And New* (Elektra/Curb 1980)★★★, *Rowdy* (Elektra/Curb 1981)★★★★, *The Pressure Is On* (Elektra/Curb 1981)★★★★, *High Notes* (Elektra/Curb 1982)★★★, *Strong Stuff* (Elektra/Curb 1983)★★★, *Man Of Steel* (Warners/Curb 1983)★★★★, *Major Moves* (Warners/Curb 1984)★★★★, *Five-O* (Warners/Curb 1985)★★★★, *Montana Cafe* (Warners/Curb 1986)★★★★, *Hank Live* (Warners/Curb 1987)★★★, *Born To Boogie* (Warners/Curb 1987)★★★★, *Wild Streak* (Warners/Curb 1988)★★★★, *Lone Wolf* (Warners/Curb 1990)★★, *America - The Way I See It* (Warners/Curb 1990)★, *Pure Hank* (Warners/Curb 1991)★★★, *Maverick* (Curb/Capricorn 1992)★★★★, *Out Of Left Field* (Curb/Capricorn 1993)★★★, *Chronicles - Health And Happiness* (1993)★★★, *Hog Wild* (MCG/Curb 1995)★★★, *AKA Wham Bam Sam* (MCG/Curb 1996)★★, *Three Hanks, Men With Broken Hearts* (MCG/Curb 1996)★★★.

● COMPILATIONS: *The Best Of Hank Williams Jnr.* (MGM 1967)★★★, *Living Proof: The MGM Recordings 1963 - 1975* (Mercury 1974)★★★★, *14 Greatest Hits* (Polydor 1976)★★★, *Hank Williams Jnr.'s Greatest Hits* (Warners/Curb 1982)★★★, *Greatest Hits Volume Two* (Warners/Curb 1985)★★★★, *The Early Years 1976-1978* (Warners/Curb 1986)★★★, *The Magic Guitar Of Hank Williams Jnr.* (1986)★★★, *Country Store* (Country Store 1988)★★★, *Standing In The Shadows* (Polydor 1988)★★★★, *Greatest Hits Volume 3* (Warners/Curb 1989)★★★★, *The Bocephus Box: Hank Williams Jnr. Collection '79 - 92* (Capricorn 1992)★★★, *The Best Of, Volume 1: Roots And Branches* (Mercury 1992)★★★, *Hank Williams Jnr.'s Greatest Hits* (Curb 1994)★★★.

● VIDEOS: *Live In Concert* (1993).

● FURTHER READING: *Living Proof*, Hank Williams Jnr. with Michael Bane.

Williams, Iris

b. 20 April 1944, Pontypridd, South Wales. A popular singer with an attractive rich, dark voice, who came to prominence in the UK in 1979 when her recording of 'He Was Beautiful (Cavatina) (The Theme From The Deer Hunter)', entered the Top 20. While being raised by foster parents, Williams won her first talent contest at the age of seven. When aged 18 she was awarded a scholarship to the Cardiff School of Music and Drama, and later worked in a glove factory for three years. She began singing in social clubs in Wales, and soon graduated to playing club and concert dates in the UK, America, and Europe. In the early 70s, Williams had her own television series for BBC Wales, and was a regular guest on national radio and television shows. Her version of 'He Was Beautiful', on which she was backed by the BBC Midland Light Orchestra, was broadcast on Radio 2 in 1979, and generated such a favourable response that she recorded it straight away. The success of the record led to a series of television appearances and concerts at top venues, including the London Palladium. In 1981, she made her debut at London's Royal Festival Hall, supporting American singer **Vic Damone**, and was named Vocalist of the Year. A year later, she appeared with **Bob Hope** in his star-studded *Golf Classic Cabaret*. In the 80s, she spent a great deal of time in the USA, and in 1990, while listening to **Rosemary Clooney** at the Rainbow & Stars nightspot in New York, she was 'persuaded' to sing the lovely ballad, 'The Folks Who Live On The Hill'. Since then, Iris Williams has eschewed contemporary material in favour of the standard repertoire, and has performed in cabaret at venues such as the the the Cinegrill, Los Angeles, the Oak Room at the legendary Algonquin Hotel in New York, and London's Pizza On The Park.

● ALBUMS: *Many Moods Of Iris Williams* (1977)★★★, *He Was Beautiful* (1980)★★★, *Picture Me Love* (1980)★★★, *Just For You* (1981)★★, *You Belong To Me* (1982)★★, *Gentle Touch* (1984)★★★, *Beautiful* (1986)★★★, *Peace Must Come Again* (1986)★★★, *I'm Glad There Is You* (SEA-KER 1995)★★★.

Williams, J. Mayo

b. 1894, Monmouth, Illinois, USA, d. 2 January 1980, Chicago, Illinois, USA. A college graduate, Williams was nicknamed 'Ink' by musicians; he was the first, and in his time the most successful, black executive in the US record industry. In 1924, he joined Paramount, which he made perhaps the most successful of all 'race' labels in terms of both quality and quantity of output, recording **Blind Lemon Jefferson**, **Papa Charlie Jackson** and **Ma Rainey**, among others. Williams was careful to find out what black purchasers wanted; when replies to market research indicated overwhelming demand for blues, he abandoned his own preference for the likes of **Paul Robeson**. In 1927, Williams resigned to found the short-lived Black Patti label, moving on immediately to Vocalion, to whom he brought Georgia Tom, **Tampa Red** and **Jim Jackson**. In 1934, he became responsible for black A&R at **Decca**, recording **Mahalia Jackson**'s debut sides. After World War II, Williams operated a series of small labels, all of which suffered from undercapitalization and a loss of touch by Williams (as may be heard on **Muddy Waters**' first commercial recording). As an executive, his income came from a share of publishing royalties and from padding his expense accounts; he said: 'I was better than 50% honest, and in this business that's pretty good'.

Williams, Jessica

b. 17 March 1948, Baltimore, Maryland, USA. Learning to play piano as a child and studying classical music at the Peabody Conservatory of Music, Williams turned to jazz and was playing professionally at the age of 14. In Philadelphia, she was a member of the **Philly Joe Jones** Quartet and also worked with **Joe Morello** and singer Ethel Ennis. In 1977 she relocated to the west coast which remained her base into the 90s. Her reputation grew in San Francisco, Sacramento and other centres but despite playing in bands led by **Stan Getz**, **Tony Williams**, **Bobby Hutcherson**, **Charlie Rouse**, **Airto Moreira**, **John Abercrombie** and others, and some early recordings, the wider world of jazz remained largely unaware of her existence. All this began to change from the mid-80s when a succession of fine recordings began to appear. Received ecstatically by the jazz press in the USA and UK, awards followed and frequent overseas tours and appearances at international festivals helped consolidate her burgeoning reputation. By the early 90s she was widely accepted as one of the best pianists currently playing jazz and high on the list of all-time greats. In 1994 she had the distinction of seeing two albums appear in the top eight of *Jazz Journal International*'s critics poll for the best records of the year. That same year she was awarded a Guggenheim Fellowship for composition. A brilliantly incisive player, with a deft and sure touch, Williams command of her instrument is outstanding. But she is far from merely a superb technician. Her intelligent, strikingly original improvisations are built upon a sure

knowledge of the meaning of jazz and the role of the solo piano in the music's development. Her playing reveals not only her admiration for the likes of **Thelonious Monk** and **Bud Powell** but also the genius of earlier giants such as **Earl 'Fatha' Hines** and **Art Tatum**. Nevertheless, her style is distinctively her own and by the mid-90s admiration for her talent was widespread and the long years of obscurity were finally behind her.

● ALBUMS: *Jessica Williams* (1976)★★, *The Portal Of Antrim* (Adelphi 1978)★★★, *Rivers Of Memory* (Clean Cuts 1979)★★, *Portraits* (Adelphi 1981)★★, *Orgonomic Music* (Clean Cuts 1981)★★★, *Nothin' But The Truth* (Blackhawk 1986)★★★, with Charlie Rouse *Epistrophy/The Charlie Rouse Memorial Concert* (Landmark 1989)★★★, *The Golden Light* (Quanta 1989)★★★, *Heartland* (Ear-Art 1990)★★★, *And Then, There's This* (Timeless 1991)★★★★, *In The Pocket* (Hep 1993)★★★★, *Live At Maybeck Recital Hall* (Concord 1992)★★★, *The Next Step* (Hep 1992)★★★, *Arrival* (Jazz Focus 1993)★★★★, *Momentum* (Jazz Focus 1993)★★★, *Encounters* (Jazz Focus 1994)★★★, *Inspiration* (Jazz Focus 1995)★★★, *In The Pocket* (Hep 1995)★★★.

Williams, Jody

b. Joseph Leon Williams, 3 February 1935, Mobile, Alabama, USA. This legendary **Chess** studio guitarist was the leader of one of **Howlin' Wolf**'s early bands. More people are familiar with Jody Williams' guitarwork than they are with his name. Anyone with **Bo Diddley**'s 'Who Do You Love' or **Billy Boy Arnold**'s 'I Wish You Would' (Williams wrote 'I Was Fooled', the b-side of the original **Vee Jay** single) or **Billy Stewart**'s 'Billy's Blues' (the trial run for 'Love Is Strange'), has a sample of his ringing, nervy guitarwork. Though making only a handful of singles, few of them under his own name, he was an extremely busy session and house musician throughout the 50s. He arrived in Chicago in 1941, first taking up the harmonica before learning guitar with Ellas McDaniel (Bo Diddley), but to greater effect than the future star.

By 1951, they and tub bass player **Roosevelt Jackson**, had formed a band. Williams quickly became a proficient and in-demand musician, touring the USA in **Charles Brown**'s band before he was 20. That year (1955), he played on Diddley's 'Diddy Wah Diddy', Arnold's 'I Wish You Would' and soloed alongside **B.B. King** on **Otis Spann**'s 'Five Spot'. Inevitably, his own career was incidental to his other work. Singles appeared on Blue Lake, Argo and Herald as Little Papa Joe or Little Joe Lee or Sugar Boy Williams, since Joe Williams already sang with **Count Basie**'s band. In the mid-60s, he abandoned music to study electronics, and later, computer maintenance. He has made sporadic appearances since then but has not been tempted back to performing.

Williams, Joe

b. 12 December 1918, Cordele, Georgia, USA. Williams began his musical career singing in a gospel group in

Chicago and by the late 30s was performing regularly as a solo singer. He had short-lived jobs with bands led by **Jimmie Noone** and others, was encouraged by **Lionel Hampton**, who employed him briefly in the early 40s, and in 1950 was with **Count Basie** for a short spell. In 1951 he had a record success with 'Every Day I Have The Blues', but he did not make his breakthrough into the big time until he rejoined Basie in 1954. For the next few years, records by the band with Williams in powerful voice were hugely successful and, coming at a period when Basie's band was at a low commercial ebb, it is hard to say with any certainty who needed whom the most. By the time Williams moved on, in 1961, both the band and the singer had reached new heights of popularity, and they continued to make occasional concert appearances together during the following decades. In the 60s Williams worked mostly as a single, often accompanied by top-flight jazzmen, including **Harry Edison**, **Clark Terry**, **George Shearing** and **Cannonball Adderley**. He toured and recorded throughout the 70s and 80s, his stature growing as he matured and his voice seemingly growing stronger and more mellow with age. A highly sophisticated artist, whose blues singing has a burnished glow which can contrast vividly with the harsh edge of the lyrics he sings, Williams has built a substantial and devoted audience. His later appearances, with bands such as the **Capp-Pierce Juggernaut**, frequently contain popular songs which he performs with more than a tinge of blues feeling. He also favours material which allows him to display the good humour which is a characteristic of the man himself. (This artist should not be confused with the singer-pianist **Big Joe Williams**.)

● ALBUMS: with Count Basie *A Night At Count Basie's* (Vanguard 1955)★★★, with Basie *Count Basie Swings/Joe Williams Sings* (Savoy 1955)★★★★, with Basie *The Greatest! Count Basie Swings/Joe Williams Sings Standards* (Verve 1956)★★★★, with Basie *Memories Ad Lib* (Roulette 1959)★★★, with Basie *Everyday I Have The Blues* (Roulette 1959)★★★★, *Joe Williams Sings About You* (1959)★★★, *That Kind Of Woman* (1959)★★★, with Basie *Just The Blues* (Roulette 1960)★★★★, *Have A Good Time* (1961)★★★, *Together* (1961)★★★, *A Swinging Night At Birdland* (Roulette 1962)★★★, *One Is A Lonesome Number* (1962)★★★, *Me And The Blues* (1963)★★★★, *Joe Williams At Newport* (1963)★★★★, *The Song Is You* (1964)★★★, *Then And Now* (1965)★★★, *Mister Excitement* (1965)★★★, *Presenting Joe Williams And The Thad Jones-Mel Lewis Jazz Orchestra* (1966)★★★, *Something Old, New And Blue* (1968)★★, *Having The Blues Under European Skies* (1971)★★, *Joe Williams Live* (1973)★★★, with Juggernaut *Live At The Century Plaza* (1977)★★★, with Dave Pell *Prez & Joe* (1979)★★, *Nothin' But The Blues* (1983)★★★★, *Then And Now* (1983)★★★, *I Just Want To Sing* (1985)★★★, *Ballad And Blues Master* (Verve 1987)★★★, *Live At Vine Street* (Verve 1987)★★★, *Every Night* (1987)★★★, *In Good Company* (Verve 1989)★★★, *A Man Ain't Supposed To Cry* (1989)★★★, *That Holiday Feelin'* (Verve 1990)★★, with Count Basie Orchestra *Live At Orchestra Hall* (Telarc

1993)★★, *Jump For Joy* (Bluebird 1993)★★★.
● COMPILATIONS: *Joe Williams Sings Every Day* (1950-51)★★★★, *The Overwhelming Joe Williams* (Bluebird 1989)★★★★.
● FILMS: *Jamboree a.k.a. Disc Jockey Jamboree* (1957).

Williams, John (composer)

b. John Towner Williams, 8 February 1932, Flushing, Long Island, New York, USA. A composer, arranger, and conductor for film background music from the early 60s to the present. As a boy, Williams learned to play several instruments, and studied composition and arranging in Los Angeles after moving there with his family in 1948. Later, he studied piano at the Juilliard School Of Music, before composing his first score for the film *I Passed For White* in 1960. it was followed by others, such as *Because They're Young, The Secret Ways, Bachelor Flat, Diamond Head, Gidget Goes To Rome,* and *None But The Brave,* directed by, and starring **Frank Sinatra**. Williams scored Ronald Reagan's last film, *The Killers,* in 1964, and continued with *Please Come Home, How To Steal A Million, The Rare Breed* and *A Guide For Married Men.* In 1967 Williams gained the first of more than 25 Oscar nominations for his adaptation of the score to *Valley Of The Dolls,* and after writing original scores for other movies such as *Sergeant Ryker, Daddy's Gone A-Hunting,* and *The Reivers,* he won the Academy Award in 1971 for 'best adaptation' for *Fiddler On The Roof.* In the early 70s, Williams seemed to be primarily concerned with 'disaster' movies, such as *The Poseidon Adventure, The Towering Inferno, Earthquake* and *Jaws,* for which he won his second Oscar in 1975. He then proceeded to score some of the most commercially successful films in the history of the cinema, including the epic *Star Wars, Close Encounters Of The Third Kind, Superman, The Empire Strikes Back, Raiders Of The Lost Ark, E.T. The Extra Terrestrial* - still the highest-grossing film of all time more than 10 years later - and another Academy Award winner for Williams. On and on Williams marched with *The Return Of The Jedi, Indiana Jones And The Temple Of Doom, Indiana Jones And The Last Crusade, The River, The Accidental Tourist, Born On The Fourth Of July* and *Presumed Innocent* (1990). As for recordings, he had US singles hits with orchestral versions of several of his films' themes and main titles, and a number of his soundtracks entered the album charts. Real pop prestige came to Williams in 1977, when record producer Meco Monardo conceived a disco treatment of his themes for *Star Wars,* which included music played in the film by the Cantina Band. 'Star Wars/Cantina Band' by Meco, spent two weeks at number 1 in the USA. For his work in the early 90s, Williams received Oscar nominations for the highly successful *Home Alone* (the score, and 'Somewhere In My Memory', lyric by **Leslie Bricusse**), the score for Oliver Stone's highly controversial *JFK,* and 'When You're Alone' (again with Bricusse) for Steven Spielberg's *Hook.* After contributing the music to *Far*

And Away and *Home Alone 2: Lost In New York* (1992), Williams returned to Spielberg in 1993 to score the director's dinosaur drama, *Jurassic Park*, and another multi Oscar winner, *Schindler's List*. Williams himself won an Academy Award for his sensitive music for the latter picture. As well as his highly impressive feature film credits, Williams has written for television productions such as *Heidi*, *Jane Eyre* and *The Screaming Woman*.

In 1985, he was commissioned by NBC Television to construct themes for news stories, which resulted in pieces such as 'The Sound Of The News', and featured a fanfare for the main bulletin, a scherzo for the breakfast show, and several others, including 'The Pulse Of Events', and 'Fugue For Changing Times'. Williams's impressive list of blockbuster movies is unlikely to ever be beaten.

Williams, John (guitar)

b. 24 April 1941, Melbourne, Australia, This renowned exponent of the Spanish guitar took flamenco unexpectedly into the pop charts with *John Williams Plays Spanish Music*. In the later 70s, a more calculated assault on this market saw his reading of Rodrigo's Concerto de Aranjuez (with the English Chamber Orchestra conducted by Daniel Barenboim) as well as the less focussed *Travelling* and *Bridges* in the UK Top 20. With the comparative failure of *Cavatina*, Williams was faced with a choice of either a cosy career of hushed recitals for a substantial intellectual minority or transporting himself even nearer to the borders of cultured 'contemporary' pop. Adopting the latter course, he formed **Sky** with Kevin Peek (guitar), **Herbie Flowers** (bass), Francis Monkman (keyboards) and Tristan Fry (percussion). While this instrumental outfit went from strength to commercial strength, he issued solo albums and *Let The Music Take You*, an adventurous 1983 collaboration with **Cleo Laine**. Both these offerings and those of Sky were criticized in some professional quarters for an over-emphasis on technique, but many such sneers were rooted in green-eyed wonderment at Sky's million-selling records and sell-out world tours that included a concert in Williams' native Australia that was taped for release as *Sky Five Live* in 1983. The treadmill of the road was, nonetheless, among the reasons why Williams left Sky the following year. Rather than backsliding to the easy option of bringing known serious music to the masses, his output since has tended to extend his stylistic range even further - as exemplified by a prominent hand in composer Paul Hart's *Concerto For Guitar and Jazz Orchestra*, and an album with Chilean folk group, Inti-Illimani.

●ALBUMS: *John Williams Plays Spanish Music* (Columbia 1970)★★★, *The Height Below* (Cube 1975)★★★, *Concerto De Aranjuez* (1976)★★★, with Cleo Laine *Best Friends* (1978)★★★★, *Travelling* (Cube 1978)★★★, *Bridges* (Lotus 1979)★★★, *Julian Bream And John Williams* (1979)★★★, *Cavatina* (Cube 1979)★★★★, *Portrait* (Columbia 1982)★★★, *The Guitar Is The Song* (Columbia 1983)★★★, *Let The Music Take You* (Columbia 1983)★★★, *Concerto For Guitar And Jazz Orchestra* (Columbia 1987)★★★, *John Williams/Paco Pena/Inti-Illimani* (Columbia 1987)★★★, *The Seville Concert: From The Royal Alcázar Palace* (1993)★★★.

● COMPILATIONS: *Spotlight On John Williams* (Castle 1980)★★★, *Platinum Collection* (Cube 1981)★★★, *Masterpieces* (1983)★★★, *Changes* (Sierra 1985)★★★, *Images* (Knight 1989)★★★.

Williams, John (piano)

b. 28 January 1928, Windsor, Vermont, USA. He took piano lessons as a child and at the age of 12 played in a high school danceband. Four years later he joined the popular Mal Hallett band at a time when many big bands were suffering from sidemen being called into the armed forces. Later that same year, 1945, Williams returned to complete his education, then played locally until 1948 when he joined the Johnny Bothwell big band. The next year he moved to New York, mostly playing bop in nightclubs which included gigging with **Charlie Parker**. Called into the armed forces at the time of the Korean war, he returned to New York and promptly joined **Charlie Barnet** then in early 1953 began the first of two long stints with **Stan Getz**. Throughout the 50s he continued to play clubs, making records with **Cannonball Adderley**, **Phil Woods**, **Al Cohn**, **Zoot Sims** and many others. He also found time to continue his musical studies and helped pay the rent by playing second piano in the **Vincent Lopez** band at the Hotel Taft. He also played briefly with **Gerry Mulligan** then continued his round of New York club engagements until the end of the 50s when he moved to Florida where he remained, leading a trio at local clubs and also becoming involved in politics. He might have remained there in relative and contended obscurity had it not been for the joint efforts of **Spike Robinson**, who hired him to play on a Florida date, and Steve Voce, who interviewed Williams for *Jazz Journal International* in 1994. This all helped bring Williams back to the attention of the jazz world and plans were soon in hand for a resumption of his recording career. Inventive, forceful, with a commanding sense of swing and, importantly, a workmanlike view of the true role of the pianist in both mainstream and bop settings, Williams' long absence from the spotlight has been a considerable loss to jazz.

● ALBUMS: *Stan Getz At The Shrine Auditorium* (Norgran 1954)★★★, *John Williams Trio i* (Mercury 1954)★★★★, *John Williams Trio ii* (Emarcy 1955)★★★★, with Al Cohn *The Saxophone Section* (Epic 1956)★★.

Williams, Johnny (R&B)

b. 15 January 1942, Tyler, Texas, USA, d. December 1986. Williams was one of those myriad R&B singers that probably has a greater impact in the clubs than on record, because in Chicago - where he moved in 1956 - he was acclaimed for his full-bodied, deep soul style, yet his legacy on record is small. He began his career in gospel, singing with the Royal Jubilees. Williams first recorded in 1966, when he achieved a small local hit with 'My Baby's Good' for **Chess Records**. It was not a great record but two of his best, 'The Breaking Point', recorded for Twinight Records in 1967, and 'I Made A Mistake', recorded for **Carl Davis**'s Bashie label in 1969, inexplicably never found an audience. In 1972, he finally reached the national charts with 'Slow Motion (Part 1)' (number 12 R&B, number 78 pop), which was recorded in Philadelphia for **Gamble And Huff**'s **Philadelphia International Records** label. Unable to repeat this achievement, he went back to working the Chicago clubs. He had some local success with a single on the Babylon label, 'You're Something Kinda Mellow', in 1974. His death in December 1986 went unnoticed.

Williams, Joseph 'Jo Jo'

b. 1920, Coahoma, Mississippi, USA. One of a legion of musicians whose name and record follow one another with Pavlovian accuracy, Williams played in bands whose members sometimes worked with better-known artists. Raised in north-west Mississippi and on the outskirts of Memphis, his first steps in music were with baling wire strung on the wall. During the 30s he witnessed **Son House** and Willie Brown playing for country suppers. He developed his guitar-playing in Memphis in the early 40s before moving on to Chicago. In 1953 he played his first professional gig, with pianist **William 'Lazy Bill' Lucas**. Two years later, Williams formed his own group with Lucas, drummer Johnny Swanns and Lucas's niece, 'Miss Hi Fi', singing. He then teamed up with harmonica player **Mojo Buford** in a band with Dave Members and Cadillac Sam Burton. With Buford, he became a member of **Muddy Waters**' Junior Band, playing Smitty's Corner when Waters was out of town.

In 1959, he made two records, the first unnumbered, for the Atomic-H label. 'All Pretty Wimmens' epitomizes raucous, impromptu blues at its best, all the better for being obscure, as was the follow-up, 'Afro Shake Dance'. In 1962, he moved, with Lucas and Buford, to Minneapolis, playing bass in a group that recorded as Mojo & The Chi Fours, the material released on Folk Art and Vernon. Two years later, the band had two singles released on Adell. Williams recorded with Lazy Bill for Lucas's own label in 1970, and retired from music some time in the 70s.

● ALBUMS: *Lazy Bill And His Friends* (1970)★★★.

Williams, L.C.

b. 12 March 1930, Crockett, Texas, USA, d. 18 October 1960, Houston, Texas, USA. Another artist whose given names are initials, Williams grew up in Mullican, Texas, before moving to Houston around 1945. There he worked in dancehalls and bars as both singer and dancer. He also learned to play drums. Having made the acquaintance of **Lightnin' Hopkins**, he recorded for Bill Quinn's Gold Star label, nicknamed 'Lightnin' Jr.', with Hopkins backing him on guitar and piano on three singles, and pianists Leroy Carter and Elmore Nixon on one side each of a fourth, all subsequently reissued. He also recorded for Freedom, another Houston label owned by Solomon Kahal, making six records, one combining 'My Darkest Hour' and 'I Want My Baby Back' reissued on **Imperial**, mostly with Conrad Johnson's Conney's Combo. In 1951 he recorded at least four titles, including 'Baby Child' and 'Fannie Mae', for Sittin In With, owned by New Yorker **Bob Shad**. Shad probably produced Williams' final commercial session, made the same year for **Mercury** with backing by saxophonist Henry Hayes And His Rhythm Kings. Williams, addicted to cheap wine, also suffered from tuberculosis. Just prior to his death, he recorded one title with Hopkins and harmonica player Luke 'Long Gone' Miles. When asked the significance of his initials, Williams' reply was 'love crazy'. Ironic, then, that his death was from lung collapse.

● ALBUMS: *Texas Blues - The Gold Star Sessions* (1992)★★★, *The Big Three* (1992)★★★.

Williams, Larry

b. 10 May 1935, New Orleans, Louisiana, USA, d. 2 January 1980, Los Angeles, California, USA. Williams recorded a handful of raucous rock 'n' roll songs for **Specialty Records** that later influenced, among others, **John Lennon**. Williams learned to play the piano while in New Orleans, and moved to Oakland, California, with his family while in his teens. There he joined a group called the Lemon Drops. In 1954, while visiting his old home-town of New Orleans, he met and was hired as a pianist by **Lloyd Price**, who recorded for Specialty. Price introduced Williams to producer **Robert 'Bumps' Blackwell**. At that time Specialty head **Art Rupe** signed Williams. His first record was a cover version of Price's 'Just Because', which reached number 11 on the R&B chart for Williams and number 3 for Price. Backed by fellow Specialty artist **Little Richard**'s band, Williams recorded his own 'Short Fat Fannie', which reached number 1 in the R&B chart and number 5 in the pop chart during 1957.

To follow up his song about a fat girl, Williams next recorded one about a skinny girl, 'Bony Moronie', which was almost as big a hit. Williams had one final chart single for Specialty the following year, 'Dizzy, Miss Lizzy', which reached number 69 (it was later covered by the **Beatles**, with Lennon singing - they also covered 'Slow Down' and 'Bad Boy', while Lennon later recorded 'Bony Moronie' and 'Just Because', providing Williams with a steady royalties income until his death). A number of singles and an album were issued by Specialty up to 1959, none of which were hits. In that year, he was arrested for selling drugs and sent to jail, causing Specialty to drop him and his career to fade. He recorded later for **Chess Records**, **Mercury Records** and for **Island Records** and **Decca Records** in the mid-60s, by which time he was working with **Johnny 'Guitar' Watson**. In 1966 Williams became a producer for **OKeh Records** and recorded an album with Watson for that label. He was virtually inactive between 1967 and 1979, at which point he recorded a funk album for **Fantasy Records**. In January 1980, Williams was found in his Los Angeles home with a gunshot wound in the head, judged to be self-inflicted, although it was rumoured that Williams was murdered owing to his involvement with drugs and, reportedly, prostitution.

● ALBUMS: *Here's Larry Williams* (Specialty 1959)★★★, *Larry Williams* (Chess 1961)★★★, *Live* (1965)★★★, *The Larry Williams Show* (1965)★★★, with Johnny 'Guitar' Watson *Two For The Price Of One* (OKeh 1967)★★★★, *That Larry Williams* (Fantasy 1979)★★.

● COMPILATIONS: *Greatest Hits* (OKeh 1967)★★★★, *Dizzy Miss Lizzy* (Ace 1985)★★★, *Unreleased Larry Williams* (Specialty 1986)★★★, *Hocus Pocus* (Specialty 1986)★★★, *Alacazam* (Ace 1987)★★★, *Slow Down* (Specialty 1987)★★★, *The Best Of Larry Williams* (Ace 1988)★★★★, *Bad Boy* (Specialty 1989)★★★★, *Fabulous Larry Williams* (Ace 1991)★★★.

Williams, Lee 'Shot'

b. Henry Lee Williams, 21 May 1938, Tchula, Mississippi, USA. For most of his career, Williams has been a journeyman singer on the chitlin circuit, eschewing identification with the blues scene until recently. He grew up with his cousins, **Little Smokey Smothers** and **Otis 'Big Smokey' Smothers**. When his mother died in the mid-50s, he was adopted by the family of singer Arlean Brown. After spending time in Detroit, he moved to Chicago in 1958 and worked in a bakery until the pressure of gigging every night led to a full-time singing career. He made his first single, 'Hello Baby', for Foxy in 1961. Two years later, he signed to Federal and released three singles, including 'You're Welcome To The Club', later covered by **Little Milton**. Other records emerged during the 60s, on labels such as Palos, Gamma, Shama and Sussex. During much of that time, he toured the south with **Earl Hooker**'s band. In the 70s, he indulged a talent for cooking by opening Lee's Diner on Chicago's West Side. Early in the 80s, he moved to Memphis, where in 1991 he recorded *I Like Your Style* at **Otis Clay**'s studio. The following year, *Shot Of Rhythm And Blues* was recorded for the Japanese Soul Trax label. In 1993, he sang on four tracks of Little Smokey Smothers' *Bossman*, which led to a contract with Black Magic and *Cold Shot*.

● ALBUMS: *I Like Your Style* (4 Way 1991)★★★, *Shot Of Rhythm And Blues* (Soul Trax 1992)★★★, *Cold Shot* (Black Magic 1995)★★★, *Hot Shot* (Ecko 1996)★★★.

Williams, Leona

b. Leona Belle Helton, 7 January 1943, Vienna, Missouri, USA. One of the 12 children of musical parents (all played instruments), Leona worked with the family group as a child. In 1958, she had her own show on KWOS Jefferson City. She married drummer Ron Williams in 1959 and with Leona playing bass, both worked with **Loretta Lynn**. In 1968, she signed for

Hickory with whom she achieved three minor hits, including 'Once More', before moving to MCA. In 1975, she joined **Merle Haggard**'s show, initially as a backing vocalist. However, when Haggard divorced **Bonnie Owens**, she not only became the featured vocalist but on 7 October 1978, she also became the third Mrs Haggard. They combined to write several songs and recorded an album together but the marriage soon proved turbulent. In 1978, they had a number 8 US country hit with 'The Bull And The Beaver' but in 1983, when the marriage ended, they appeared in the charts with the appropriately named 'We're Strangers Again'. She later married songwriter and guitarist Dave Kirby. She also made solo recordings for **Elektra** and **Mercury** and her songs have been recorded by other stars including **Tammy Wynette**, but she has so far failed to achieve a big solo hit. Williams does hold the distinction of being the first female country singer to record a live album in a prison.

● ALBUMS: *That Williams Girl* (Hickory 1970)★★, *San Quentin's First Lady* (MCA 1976)★★★, *A Woman Walked Away* (MCA 1977)★★★, with Merle Haggard *Heart To Heart* (Mercury 1983)★★★★, *Someday When Things Are Good* (1984)★★★.

Williams, Lester

b. 24 June 1920, Groveton, Texas, USA, d. 13 November 1990, Houston, Texas, USA. Raised in Houston on the records of **Blind Lemon Jefferson** and **Lonnie Johnson**, Williams was inspired to take up the electric guitar after hearing fellow Texan **'T-Bone' Walker**. His debut recording on the small local Macy's Records - 'Wintertime Blues' - was his biggest hit. His last records were made for **Imperial Records** in 1956, although he continued to perform locally, and was rediscovered in 1986 for a tour of Europe.

● ALBUMS: *Dowling Street Hop* (Krazy Kat 1982)★★★, *Texas Troubador* (Ace 1987)★★★, *I Can't Lose With The Stuff I Use* (1993)★★★.

Williams, Lil' Ed

b. 18 April 1955, Chicago, Illinois, USA. Williams' first exposure to the blues was through the records of **Elmore James** and **Muddy Waters**, and his uncle **J.B. Hutto** taught him to play slide guitar when he was 13 years old. Williams also taught himself bass and drums. He played with Hutto, whose stinging playing is echoed in his own raunchy style, and also worked for tips in west side Chicago clubs with his half-brother James 'Pookie' Young. A three-hour session for Alligator Records in 1986 resulted in Williams' debut album and one track on the ground-breaking *New Bluesblood* compilation the following year. These recordings garnered international acclaim for Williams and his group the Blues Imperials, who have rapidly become a major attraction.

● ALBUMS: *Roughhousin'* (Alligator 1986)★★★, *Chicken, Gravy And Biscuits* (1989)★★★.

Williams, Lucinda

b. 26 January 1953, Lake Charles, Louisiana, USA. Her father, Miller Williams, is a professor of literature and a professional poet, but it was her mother, a music graduate, who influenced Lucinda the most. She played folk clubs in Texas in the mid-70s and made her first albums for **Folkways Records**. Her career failed to take off until she moved to Los Angeles some years later, but she was further stymied by an abortive development contract with **CBS Records** in the mid-80s. She describes songwriting as 'like writing a journal but I don't want it to sound self-indulgent.' Her self-titled album for **Rough Trade Records** in 1989 finally re-established her with its attendant strong press. *Sweet Old World* provided darker subject matter than most folk-country albums; the title song is about suicide and 'Pineola' similarly concerns a poet who shot himself. It included a cover version of **Nick Drake**'s 'Which Will', with musical backing by Benmont Tench, Bryce Berline and Doug Atwell. She has also performed on the tribute albums to **Merle Haggard** (*Tulare Dust*) and **Victoria Williams** (*Sweet Relief*). In the 90s **Mary-Chapin Carpenter** earned a major US country hit with her 'Passionate Kisses'. Williams is now signed to American Recordings. In 1998 Williams contributed 'Still I Long For Your Kiss' to the soundtrack of Robert Redford's adaptation of *The Horse Whisperer*.

● ALBUMS: *Ramblin' On My Mind* (Folkways 1979)★★★, *Happy Woman Blues* (Folkways 1980)★★★★, *Lucinda Williams* (Rough Trade 1988)★★★, *Sweet Old World* (Chameleon 1992)★★★, *Car Wheels On A Gravel Road* (Mercury 1998)★★★.

Williams, Mary Lou

b. Mary Elfrieda Scruggs, 8 May 1910, Atlanta, Georgia, USA, d. 28 May 1981. A child prodigy, Williams played in public at the age of six and by the time she reached her teenage years was already a seasoned professional piano player. At the age of 16 she married saxophonist John Williams, playing in his band throughout the mid-west. When her husband left to join **Terrence Holder**'s band, Mary Lou took over the leadership of the band before eventually she too joined Holder. After this band had metamorphosed into **Andy Kirk** and his Clouds Of Joy, Williams assumed additional responsibilities as the group's chief arranger. During the 30s, while still with Kirk, her arrangements were also used by **Earl 'Fatha' Hines**, **Tommy Dorsey**, **Louis Armstrong** and **Benny Goodman**, who had a hit with her composition 'Roll 'Em'. After her marriage to John Williams ended, she married **Harold 'Shorty' Baker** and co-led a band with him before he joined **Duke Ellington**. She continued to lead the band but also contributed some arrangements to Ellington. Williams was instrumental in informing **John Hammond** (senior) about the talents of **Charlie Christian**.

Throughout the 40s and early 50s she played at clubs in the USA and Europe, sometimes as a solo artist, at other times leading a small group. For a few years in the mid-50s she worked outside music, but returned to the scene in the autumn of 1957 and thereafter played clubs, concerts and festivals for the rest of her life. As an arranger, Williams's greatest contribution to jazz was her work with the Kirk band. Her charts were exemplary, providing this fine group with a distinctive voice and ably employing the individual talents of the band's members. Although her arrangements for other groups were necessarily somewhat impersonal, they were invariably first-class examples of straightforward swinging big band music. Many of her arrangements were of her own compositions and the breadth of her work in this area was such that, in the mid-40s, a classical piece, 'Zodiac Suite', was performed by the New York Philharmonic Orchestra. During this same period, she extended her writing into bop, providing charts for the **Dizzy Gillespie** big band.

Her deep religious beliefs, which had led to her leaving music for a few years in the 50s, surfaced in some of her longer compositions, which included cantatas and masses. As a pianist, her range was similarly wide, encompassing stride and boogie-woogie, swing and early bop; she even recorded a duo concert with *avant gardist* **Cecil Taylor**, though this was not an unqualified success. Throughout the later years of her career, Williams extended her repertoire still further, offering performances which, interpreted through the piano, told the story of jazz from its origins to the present day. Williams was a highly articulate and intellectually gifted individual. In interviews she displays a complex and decidedly ambivalent attitude towards life and music, perhaps fostered by the racial antagonism she encountered early in her career and dissatisfaction with the manner in which the entertainment industry demonstrated that it cared more for money than for music. Williams's importance to the fabric of jazz was recognised towards the end of her life and she was honoured by several universities.

● ALBUMS: *Mary Lou Williams In London* (1953)★★★, *On Vogue* (Vogue 1954)★★★★, *The First Lady Of The Piano* (1955)★★★★, *Black Christ Of The Andes* (1963)★★, *Mary Lou's Mass* (1977)★★★, *From The Heart* (1970)★★★, *Zoning* (Smithsonian Folkways 1974)★★★★, *The History Of Jazz* (1975)★★★, *Free Spirits* (Steeplechase 1975)★★★, *Live At The Cookery* (Chiaroscuro 1975)★★, with Cecil Taylor *Embraced* (1977)★★★, *My Mama Pinned A Rose On Me* (1977)★★★, *Solo Recital At Montreux* (1978)★★, *First Lady Of Piano* (Giants Of Jazz 1987)★★★★, with Andy Kirk *Mary's Idea* (1993)★★★, *Zodiac Suite* 1945 recordings (Smithsonian Folkways 1995)★★★.

●COMPILATIONS: *The Best Of Mary Lou Williams* (Pablo 1982).

Williams, Mason

b. 24 July 1936, Abilene, Texas, USA. This Oklahoma City University mathematics student was a self-taught guitarist who, after moonlighting in local venues, toured North America with the **Wayfarers Trio** before enlistment in the US Navy. On demobilization, he peddled topical tunes on the Los Angeles folk club circuit where he met the **Limeliters'** **Glenn Yarbrough** who introduced him to the Smothers Brothers. When this comedy duo began performing his compositions on their nationally broadcast television series, other acts - among them the Kingston Trio and **Petula Clark** - began recording his material. His most lucrative song was the 1968 novelty UK number 1 'Cinderella Rockefella', (with Nancy Ames) for **Esther And Abi Ofarim**. That year, he enjoyed a million-seller in his own right with the Grammy winning 'Classical Gas', an orchestrated instrumental (from The Mason Williams Phonograph Record song cycle). A one-hit-wonder, he, nevertheless, protracted a prolific recording career into the 70s with accompaniment by such LA session colleagues as **Hal Blaine**, Ron Tutt, Milt Holland and **Al Casey**. He also achieved success as a poet, author, cabaret entertainer and concept artist with one of his exhibitions at Pasadena Arts Museum the subject of a feature in *Life* magazine. A reissue of 'Classical Gas' in 1978 met with further success, as did his collaboration with **Mannheim Steamroller** for their album *Classical Gas* in 1987.

● ALBUMS: *Them Poems And Things* (Vee Jay 1968)★★★, *The Mason Williams Phonograph Record* (1968)★★★, *The Mason Williams Ear Show* (1968)★★★, *Music By Mason Williams* (1969)★★★, *Hand Made* (1970)★★, *Improved* (1971)★★★, with Mannheim Steamroller *Classical Gas* (American Gramophone 1987)★★★.

Williams, Maurice, And The Zodiacs

This R&B vocal group from Lancaster, South Carolina, USA, was led by Maurice Williams (pianist/songwriter). The hit record 'Stay', which went to number 3 R&B and number 1 pop in 1960, immortalized the Zodiacs as a one-hit-wonder group. (In the UK 'Stay' went to number 14 in 1961.) Williams, however, had a long history before and after the hit, forming his first group, the Gladiolas, in 1955. Besides Williams (b. 26 April 1938, Lancaster, South Carolina, USA), the group consisted of Earl Gainey (tenor), William Massey (tenor/baritone), Willie Jones (baritone), and Norman Wade (bass). Their one hit for the Nashville-based Excello label was 'Little Darlin'', which went to number 11 R&B and number 41 pop in 1957. The record was covered with greater success by the Canadian group, the Diamonds. In 1960 Williams formed the Zodiacs, consisting of Wiley Bennett (tenor), Henry Gaston (tenor), Charles Thomas (baritone), Albert Hill (double bass), and Little Willie Morrow (drums). After the unforgettable 'Stay' the group honoured themselves with many outstanding compositions, most notably 'I Remember' (number 86 pop in 1961), 'Come Along' (number 83 pop in 1961), and 'May I' (1966), but nothing close to a hit resulted. The latter song was re-recorded in 1969 by Bill Deal And The Rhondels who had a Top 40 national hit with it. The most frequently remade Williams song was 'Stay', which the **Hollies** in the UK (1963), the **Four Seasons** (1964), and **Jackson**

Browne (1978) all placed on the charts. Its timeless lyric of teenage lust and angst has been passed through the decades: 'Well your mama don't mind, well your papa don't mind', leading to the punch line, 'Oh won't you stay, just a little bit longer'. During the 70s and 80s Williams sustained a career with a new group of Zodiacs playing their classic catalogue to the Beach Music club circuit in the Carolinas.

● ALBUMS: *Stay* (Herald 1961)★★★★, *At The Beach* (early 60s)★★★ *Maurice Williams And The Zodiacs* (1988)★★★.

● COMPILATIONS: *Best Of Maurice Williams & the Zodiacs* (1989)★★★★, *Little Darlin'* (1991)★★★, *Best Of Maurice Williams & The Zodiacs* (1991)★★★★.

Williams, Midge

b. *c*.1908, California, USA, d. date unk. Despite a short period of fame, little is known about her origins, background, or even her dates of birth and death. Williams sang with a family vocal group before starting to sing professionally in the late 20s. During the early 30s she visited China and Japan, with residencies in Shanghai and Tokyo. She also recorded while in the Orient, performing popular American songs in Japanese. In 1934 she returned to the USA and for a time had her own regular radio show in Los Angeles. She then teamed up with **Fats Waller** and also sang on a radio show featuring the popular entertainer **Rudy Vallee**. She made a number of records, sometimes using leading jazz musicians of the day, including **Miff Mole** and **John Kirby**.

In 1938 she was hired as a vocalist with **Louis Armstrong**'s big band, a job she retained until 1941. After that she returned to her solo career but soon drifted from sight. Williams sang in an engaging manner with a light, finely textured voice. Her style was relatively straightforward and on her records the chief jazz interest lies in the solos heard from the musicians such as **Frankie Newton**, **Pete Brown**, **Charlie Shavers**, **Buster Bailey** and **Russell Procope**. Her records are therefore worth seeking out and she certainly does not harm the proceedings.

● COMPILATIONS: *Midge Williams And Her Jazz Jesters* (Classics 1937-38)★★★.

Williams, Otis, And The Charms

(see **Charms**)

Williams, Paul

b 19 September 1940, Omaha, Nebraska, USA. Popular composer Paul Williams entered show business as a stunt man and film actor, appearing as a child in *The Loved One* (1964) and *The Chase* (1965). He turned to songwriting, and in the 70s composed many appealing and commercially successful numbers, such as 'We've Only Just Begun', 'Rainy Days And Mondays', and 'I Won't Last A Day Without You' (written with Roger Nichols), all three of which were popular for the **Carpenters**'; 'Out In The Country' (Nicholls), 'Cried Like A Baby' (with Craig Doerge), 'Family Of Man'

(Jack S. Conrad), 'Love Boat Theme' and 'My Fair Share' (both Charles Fox), 'You And Me Against The World', 'Inspiration', and 'Loneliness' (all with Ken Ascher), 'Nice To be Around (with Johnny Williams), and 'An Old Fashioned Song', 'That's Enough For Me', and 'Waking Up Alone' (words and music by Paul Williams. Williams recorded his first solo album for Reprise in 1970 before moving to **A&M Records** the following year. None of these albums sold well, but Williams developed a highly praised night-club act in the early 70s. His first film score was for *Phantom Of The Paradise*, Brian de Palma's update of the *Phantom Of The Opera* story, in which Williams starred. This was followed by songs for *A Star Is Born* (1976), another modern version of an old movie, which starred **Kris Kristofferson** and **Barbra Streisand**, and included the Oscar-winning song 'Evergreen' (with Barbra Streisand). However, Williams's most impressive score was for the 30s pastiche *Bugsy Malone*, a gangster spoof with a cast consisting entirely of children. His later scores included *The End* (1977) and *The Muppet Movie* (1979), including 'Rainbow Connection', with Kenny Ascher).

In 1988, Williams appeared at Michael's Pub in New York. His varied programme included some numbers intended for a future Broadway musical, as well as details of his recovery from the ravages of drugs and alcohol. In 1992, he contributed music and lyrics for the songs in the feature film *The Muppet Christmas Carol*, which starred Michael Caine.

● ALBUMS: *Someday Man* (Reprise 1970)★★, *Just An Old Fashioned Love Song* (A&M 1971)★★, *Life Goes On* (A&M 1972)★★, *Here Comes Inspiration* (A&M 1974)★★, *A Little Bit Of Love* (A&M 1974)★★, *Phantom Of The Paradise* film soundtrack (A&M 1975)★★, *Ordinary Fool* (A&M 1975)★★, *Bugsy Malone* film soundtrack (A&M 1975)★★.
● COMPILATIONS: *Best Of* (A&M 1975)★★, *Classics* (A&M 1977)★★.

Williams, Pauline Braddy
(see **Braddy, Pauline**)

Williams, Robbie
b. 13 February 1974, Port Vale, England. Williams was the cheeky chappie of **Take That**; he seemed at the time to be the only one who could be badly behaved (or normal). When the band broke up the predictions were that **Mark Owen** (the nice one) and **Gary Barlow** (the voice and marketability) would succeed. Little hope was given to Williams, who immediately set about stirring up the media with anti-Gary tales. While Barlow was being groomed as the UK's new **George Michael**, Williams caused mayhem. He partied, he overindulged (drink and drugs) and he seemed to pay little attention to the music. Following a spell in a clinic for detoxification, a seemingly wiser Williams stepped out into the glare of the sunshine, blinked, and set about recording an excellent album that eclipsed Barlow's debut both musically and critically. *Life Thru A Lens* is a joy

throughout and contained the symbolic 'I Hope I'm Old Before I Die', and the huge Christmas single 'Angels'. Never before had so many pundits and critics been so wrong.
● ALBUMS: *Life Thru A Lens* (EMI 1997)★★★★.

Williams, Robert Pete
b. 14 March 1914, Zachary, Louisiana, USA, d. 31 December 1980, Rosedale, Louisiana, USA. Although he had been playing and singing blues since he was a young man, Williams first came to wider notice when he was recorded in 1958 by folklorist Harry Oster. At the time, Williams was serving a sentence for murder at the penitentiary at Angola. His sombre vocals and gentle, understated guitar accompaniments were impressive in themselves, but more significant was his unique ability to sing long, partially extemporized songs, sometimes based around a traditional formula, sometimes remarkably original and intensely personal. This exposure led to his being taken up by a younger audience, and on his release from prison he made many appearances at concerts and festivals in the USA and overseas. He also made many more records, most of which testify to his great creative imagination and artistry.
● ALBUMS: *Angola Prisoners Blues* (1958)★★★, *Blues From Bottoms* (1973)★★★, *Those Prison Blues* (Arhoolie 1981)★★★, *Live* (Wolf 1988)★★★, *With Big Joe Williams* (Storyville 1988)★★★, *Robert Pete Williams And Roosevelt Sykes* (77 Records 1988)★★★.
● COMPILATIONS: *Legacy Of The Blues Volume Nine* (Sonet 1973)★★★, *Vol. 1 - I'm Blue As A Man Can Be* (Arhoolie 1994)★★★★, *Vol. 2 - When A Man Takes The Blues* (Arhoolie 1994)★★★★.

Williams, Roosevelt Thomas
(see **Grey Ghost**)

Williams, Roy
b. 7 March 1937, Bolton, Lancashire, England. Williams first played trombone with a Manchester-based traditional jazz band. After moving to London he became a well-known figure during the trad jazz boom of the late 50s and early 60s. He played and recorded with **Monty Sunshine** and other leading lights of the era, earning praise from the many visiting American jazz stars whom he accompanied. In 1965, he joined the **Alex Welsh** band where he remained for more than a dozen years. After leaving Welsh he joined **Humphrey Lyttelton**, staying with the band until the early 80s when he began freelancing. As a member of the Pizza Express All Stars, Five-A-Slide and other mainstream bands, touring with various visitors, recording with **Spike Robinson** and others, and broadcasting, he became one of the most familiar figures on the UK jazz scene. The respect he earned travelled well and in the 80s he was invited to play at one of Dick Gibson's famous Colorado Jazz Parties and he also worked in New York. Superb technical accomplishment, allied to

impeccable phrasing, fluid swing and innate good taste, have combined to make Williams one of the best mainstream jazz trombonists in the world.

● ALBUMS: *The Melody Maker Tribute To Louis Armstrong* (1970)★★, *Something Wonderful* (Hep Jazz 1981)★★★, with Benny Waters *When You're Smiling* (Hep Jazz 1981)★★★, *Royal Trombone* (Phontastic 1983)★★, *Again! Roy Williams In Sweden* (1983)★★, with Spike Robinson *It's A Wonderful World* (1985)★★★★, *A Jazz Concert With Roy Williams* (1985)★★★.

Williams, Rudy

b. 1909, Newark, New Jersey, USA, d. September 1954. Williams played alto saxophone as a child and in the late 30s joined the **Savoy Sultans**, the very popular band led by Al Cooper at the Savoy Ballroom in Harlem. Williams was one of the Sultans' principal soloists and was a favourite of the Savoy's discerning patrons. After leaving the Sultans he played in bands led by Oran 'Hot Lips' Page, Luis Russell and others. In the mid-40s he was still active in New York, although often with lesser-known bands, and he also played with several leading bop musicians, including **Tadd Dameron** and **Oscar Pettiford**. From the end of the 40s into the early 50s he sometimes led bands of his own, playing alto, tenor and baritone saxophones as well as clarinet. Mostly, he worked on the east coast but occasionally toured farther afield, making trips to the west coast (where he played with **Gene Ammons**) and to US military bases in the Orient with Pettiford. During his career, Williams made several records with the Sultans and with leaders such as **Howard McGhee**, Dameron, **Eddie 'Lockjaw' Davis**, Ammons and **Johnny Hodges**. Although steeped in the music of the swing era and an able performer in jump band tradition, Williams made the transition to bop better than most of his contemporaries. His playing style has been likened to that of **Don Byas**, another musician who made the adjustment. Williams's career might have developed interestingly had he not drowned accidentally in 1954.

● ALBUMS: *Lifetime* (1964)★★★, *Spring* (1965)★★★, with Miles Davis *Miles In The Sky* (1968)★★★★, *Emergency* (1969)★★★, *Civilization* (1986)★★, *Angel Street* (1988)★★★, *Native Heart* (1989)★★★.

Williams, Sandy

b. Alexander Balos Williams, 24 October 1906, Summerville, South Carolina, USA. After dabbling with the tuba he began playing trombone and quickly found professional work with theatre pit bands in Washington, DC, where he was raised. At the end of the 20s he began a tour of some of the best bands of the day including **Claude Hopkins**, **Horace** and **Fletcher Henderson**, and **Chick Webb**. He joined Webb in 1933 and remained there until after the leader's death when the band continued with **Ella Fitzgerald**. In the 40s Williams was in other big bands, among them **Benny Carter**, Fletcher Henderson and **Cootie Williams**. With the decline in the fortunes and the numbers of big

bands, Williams turned to small groups, working in the mid- to late 40s with **Sidney Bechet**, **Wild Bill Davison**, **Pete Brown**, **Oran 'Hot Lips' Page**, **Roy Eldridge**, **Rex Stewart** and many others. During this period, in 1943, he spent almost a year with **Duke Ellington**. In the late 40s, Williams' lifestyle caught up with him and he was in and out of music, and hospital, for some years and by the early 50s was forced into retirement. In later years, during which he earned his living as an elevator operator, he occasionally played again. Williams drew his remarkable playing style largely from that of **Jimmy Harrison**, although it is clear that like so many musicians of his generation, regardless of instrument, he was also influenced by **Louis Armstrong**. Williams could outshine anyone when he was in the mood to do so, providing dazzling solo displays even when playing in bands led by forceful personalities such as Webb and Eldridge. Although rooted in early swing style, as the years passed William's playing took on many of the influences of later swing era music and even adopted elements of bop.

● COMPILATIONS: *The Chronological Chick Webb 1929-1934* (Classics 1929-34)★★★★, *The Chronological Chick Webb 1935-1938* (Classics 1935-38)★★★★.

Williams, Spencer

b. *c.*1889, New Orleans, Louisiana, USA, d. 14 July 1965, New York, USA. Believed to be a nephew of Lulu White, who operated Mahogany Hall, one of the most notorious brothels in New Orleans, Williams began playing piano as a child. After living in Atlanta for a while, he moved to Chicago, playing piano in an amusement park, but by 1916 was resident in New York and had embarked upon a hugely successful career as a songwriter. Among his songs, many of which became hits and have remained popular with singers and jazz instrumentalists to the present day, are 'I Ain't Got Nobody', 'Basin Street Blues', 'Tishomingo Blues', 'I Found A New Baby', 'Everybody Loves My Baby', 'Shim-me-sha-wabble', 'Mahogany Hall Stomp', 'I Ain't Gonna Give Nobody None Of My Jelly Roll' and 'Royal Garden Blues' (these last two with the unrelated **Clarence Williams**). He also composed 'Fireworks' and 'Skip The Gutter', which were recorded in 1928 by **Louis Armstrong**'s Hot Five, as was 'Squeeze Me', which Williams co-composed with **Fats Waller**. In the mid-20s he visited Paris to write special material for **Joséphine Baker**. He remained in Europe for a few years, visiting London and working with local and visiting American musicians. Around the end of the decade he was tried and acquitted on a charge of murder, and thereafter, soon moved to England, living in London until the early 50s. He then moved to Stockholm, Sweden, where he lived until 1957, finally he returned to New York, where he died.

Williams, Tex

b. Sollie Paul Williams, 23 August 1917, Ramsey, Fayette County, Illinois, USA, d. 11 October 1985,

Newhall, California, USA. His father was a keen fiddler, and by the time he was 13 years old, Williams had a local radio programme as a one-boy band. He toured with the Reno Racketeers but he soon turned to Hollywood. In 1940 he appeared alongside **Tex Ritter** in Rollin' Home To Texas and then made a long chain of westerns, many of them Saturday morning serials. He managed to overcome his limp, a legacy of childhood polio, and he became known as 'Tex', as, presumably, Illinois Williams did not have the same ring. Williams also played bass and sang with Spade Cooley's western swing band, establishing himself as a vocalist on Cooley's 1945 country hit, 'Shame On You'. In 1947, **Capitol Records** had their first million-selling record with Williams' fast-talking, deep-voiced monologue, 'Smoke! Smoke! Smoke!', which he wrote with **Merle Travis**. As his songs often praised smoking, he became known as 'The Man Who Sings Tobacco Best', but this was before the link between cigarettes and cancer was known. In 1948, Williams had success with another narration, 'Life Gits Tee-jus, Don't It?', but the composer Carson J. Robison took the main honours. Williams' other successes included 'That's What I Like About The West', 'Never Trust A Woman', 'Don't Telephone, Don't Telegraph, Tell A Woman', 'Suspicion' and 'Talking Boogie'. He and his band played dancehalls all over the USA and he promoted Nudie's stage suits, helping Nudie become the tailor to country stars. His 1963 album, *Tex Williams In Las Vegas*, was recorded at the Mint Club in 1963, featuring **Glen Campbell** and produced by one of the Crickets, Tommy Allsup. His subsequent singles included 'Too Many Tigers', 'Bottom Of The Mountain', 'The Night Miss Nancy Ann's Hotel For Single Girls Burned Down' and 'Smoke! Smoke! Smoke! '68' with Merle Travis. The smoke, smoke, smoke caught up with him and he died of lung cancer in 1985 at his home in Newhall, California.

● ALBUMS: *Dance-O-Rama-Tex Williams* (Decca 1955)★★★★, *Tex Williams Best* (Camden 1958)★★★, *Smoke! Smoke! Smoke!* (Capitol 1960)★★★, *Country Music Time* (Decca 1962)★★★ *Tex Williams In Las Vegas* (Liberty 1963)★★, *Tex Williams* (Sunset 1966)★★★, *Two Sides Of Tex Williams* (Boone 1966)★★★★, *The Voice Of Authority* (Imperial 1966)★★★, *A Man Called Tex* (1971)★★★★, *Those Lazy, Hazy Days* (1974)★★★, *Tex Williams And California Express* (1981)★★★.

● COMPILATIONS: *14 All-Time Country Hits* (1978)★★★★, *Vintage Collection Series* (Capitol 1996)★★★★.

Williams, Tony

b. 12 December 1945, Chicago, Illinois, USA, d. 23 February 1997. Williams was raised in Boston, Massachusetts, where his father, an amateur musician, encouraged him to take up drums. Williams studied with **Alan Dawson** and was sitting in at local clubs before he entered his teens. At the age of 15, he was freelancing in and around Boston and had already earned the admiration of leading drummers, including **Max Roach**. In the early 60s he went to New York, where he played with **Jackie McLean** and in 1963 joined **Miles Davis**. With Davis, Williams's rhythm section colleagues were **Herbie Hancock** and **Ron Carter** and together they made a formidable team which is still widely admired and often cited as Davis' greatest unit. During this period, both with Davis and on his many **Blue Note** recordings as leader, and sideman, Williams began reshaping modern jazz drumming, developing concepts created by some of his immediate predecessors such as **Elvin Jones**. Notably, Williams advanced the manner in which drummers could play freely yet retain a recognizable pulse. With Williams in a band, free jazz improvisers could dispense with time but were not entirely cut off from a basic rhythmic impulse. At the end of the 60s Williams left Davis to form a jazz-rock band with **John McLaughlin**. The band, named **Lifetime**, together with **Larry Young** and **Jack Bruce** set the standards to which most subsequent bands in the genre aspired but, insofar as the drumming was concerned, few achieved their aim. After McLaughlin moved on, Williams continued to lead jazz-rock bands but gradually moved back into jazz circles. In the late 70s he was with Hancock again in the V.S.O.P. quintet and also recorded with **Gil Evans** and **Wynton Marsalis**. In the late 80s Williams was leading a band with a stable personnel that included saxophonist Billy Pierce and **Mulgrew Miller**. In the mid-90s he signed to Miles Coleland's Arek 21 label and issued *Wilderness* with support from **Michael Brecker**, **Pat Metheny**, **Stanley Clarke** and Herbie Hancock.

● ALBUMS: *Lifetime* (1964)★★★, *Spring* (Blue Note 1965)★★★, *Emergency* (Polydor 1969)★★★★, *Turn It Over* (Polydor 1970)★★★, *Ego* (Polydor 1971)★★★, *Joy Of Flying* (Columbia 1979)★★★, *Foreign Intrigue* (Blue Note 1986)★★★, *Civilization* (1986)★★, *Angel Street* (Blue Note 1988)★★★, *Native Heart* (Blue Note 1989)★★★, *The Story Of Neptune* (Blue Note 1992)★★★, *New Lifetime Collection* (1993)★★★, with Wayne Shorter, Ron Carter, Wallace Roney, Herbie Hancock *A Tribute To Miles* (QWest/Reprise 1994)★★★, *Wilderness* (Ark 21 1996)★★★.

Williams, Vanessa

b. *c.*1968, Milltown, New York, USA. Williams grew up in a household surrounded by musical influences from Broadway shows, before she attended Syracuse University to major in musical theatre. A mother of three and actress as well as singer, she has come a long way since becoming embroiled in a minor scandal over her appearance in *Penthouse* magazine (after becoming the first black woman to win the Miss USA pageant). Four years later Williams began to pursue a recording contract, and found a sympathetic ear in Ed Eckstine at Wing Records (a **Mercury Records** subsidiary). Her husband, Ramon Hervey, took over her management. However, Williams' talents have nevertheless been inadequately displayed in the course of her albums. Her musical career began in 1989 with *The Right Stuff*, which provided a number 8 single in 'Dreamin'', a song recognized by ASCAP as one of the most frequently played singles of 1989 (it also contained other hits in 'He's Got The Look' and 'Darling I'). It brought her the NAACP Image Award, which she won once again for the massive-selling ballad, 'Save The Best For Last'. The album which accompanied that single, *The Comfort Zone*, achieved double platinum status. However, there was more invention and ambition displayed on a third collection, *The Sweetest Days*, delayed for three years while she gave birth to her third child, Devin, and moved back to New York from Los Angeles. This featured vocals that were pleasant rather than striking, hovering over gentle jazz, soul or Latin arrangements. The stronger material, like the warm, sensuous 'Higher Ground', was deprived of its potential stature by disappointments like 'Moonlight Over Paris' or the joyless **Sting** cover, 'Sister Moon' (with **Toots Thielemans** on harmonica).

Sting also produced, alongside other big names like **Babyface** and **Roy Ayers**. Wendy Waldman, Jon Lind, Phil Galdston and producer Keith Thomas, the team responsible for 'Save The Best For Last', wrote the title-track. The album was released while Williams was also the toast of Broadway in her role in *Kiss Of The Spiderwoman*. She has also appeared widely in film and television, including the Emmy Award winning *Motown Returns To The Apollo*, *The Boy Who Loved Christmas* and *Stompin' At The Savoy*. Earlier she had starred alongside Richard Pryor and Gene Wilder in *Another You* and Micky Rourke and Don Johnson in *Harley Davidson And The Marlboro Man*. She has also hosted her own contemporary R&B television show, *The Soul Of VH-1*. In January 1996 Williams sung the national anthem at Super Bowl XXX in Phoenix, Arizona.

● ALBUMS: *The Right Stuff* (Wing 1989)★★★, *The Comfort Zone* (Wing 1992)★★★★, *The Sweetest Days* (Wing 1995)★★, *Star Bright* (Mercury 1996)★★.

Williams, Victoria

b. 23 December 1958, Shreveport, Louisiana, USA. This talented singer-songwriter had her career disrupted by the onset of multiple sclerosis, which was diagnosed in the spring of 1992. At that time she was touring with **Neil Young** and receiving plaudits as a promising newcomer. She made her recording debut in 1987 (at that time still married to **Peter Case**), with an album produced by Anton Fier and Stephen Soles that surrounded her compositions with a varied background, including a sitar, strings and horns. The most notable accompaniment came from an award-winning Donn Pennebaker video. Williams' second set was a considerable improvement and revealed her to be a writer of depth by removing some of the extraneous instrumentation. Instead, co-producer Michael Blair (multi-instrumentalist with **Elvis Costello** and **Tom Waits**) focused on Williams' childlike, rural spirit and

inspired lyrics with simple, effective song constructions. Her rise had already been noted in the film world, and she made her acting debut in **Gus van Sant**'s lesbian epic *Even Cowgirls Get The Blues*. However, once her illness had been diagnosed, Williams' hospital bills soared, and guest musicians played a series of benefit concerts throughout 1992. This culminated in a core of friends and admirers putting together the cast for *Sweet Relief - The Songs Of Victoria Williams*, where fourteen artists contributed cover versions of her songs. **Soul Asylum**'s version of 'Summer Of Drugs' began the set, while other contributions included **Lou Reed** ('Tarbelly & Feather Foot'), **Jayhawks** ('Lights'), **Waterboys** ('Why Look At The Moon'), **Giant Sand** ('Big Fish'), **Lucinda Williams** ('Main Road'), Evan Dando of the **Lemonheads** ('Frying Pan'), **Michelle Shocked** ('Opelousas (Sweet Relief))', **Maria McKee** ('Holy Spirit'), **Pearl Jam**, **Buffalo Tom**, etc. The lyrics to 'Main Road', sung by fellow Louisianan Lucinda Williams, were perfectly apt: 'I never knew I had so many friends'. By 1994 Williams reasserted her own strength as a performer with the release of *Loose*, sustaining herself on stage with little evidence of her illness, with husband Mark Olson of the Jayhawks joining her for a duet of 'When We Sing Together' and Peter Buck and Mike Mills of **R.E.M.** on hand to support a new collection of supremely simple but deeply affecting songs. She continued her rich rein of form on 1998's *Musings Of A Creekdipper*, a typically left-field and engaging collection dominated by Williams' eerie vocals.

● ALBUMS: *Happy Come Home* (Geffen 1987)★★★, *Swing The Statue!* (Rough Trade 1990)★★★★, *Loose* (Mammoth/Atlantic 1994)★★★, *This Moment In Toronto With Victoria Williams And The Loose Band* (Mammoth/Atlantic 1996)★★★, *Musings Of A Creekdipper* (East West 1998)★★★.

● COMPILATIONS: various artists *Sweet Relief - The Songs Of Victoria Williams* (Thirsty Ear/Columbia 1993)★★★.

Williams, Willie

b. St. Ann's, Jamaica, West Indies. Williams is best known for his huge 'Armagideon Time' hit for **Coxsone Dodd** in 1979, one of the records that heralded the **dancehall** era, in which old **Studio One** rhythms were revitalized and garnished with new lyrics. In this case, the original Sound Dimension instrumental, 'Real Rock', was dusted down for Williams' lyrics. The **Clash** were sufficiently impressed to try their hand at the song. The rhythm has always been popular and there are still innumerable versions doing the rounds in the mid-90s. Williams started in the music business at the age of 14, recording 'Calling' for Dodd, and going on to run his own **sound system**, Tripletone, at the end of the decade. In the early 70s he ran his own label, Soul Sounds, producing the likes of **Delroy Wilson** and the Versatiles. He also sang alongside **Freddie McGregor** with the Generation Gap. Dodd issued a number of follow-up singles, including 'Addis Adaba' and 'Jah

Righteous Plan', though they failed to make as much of an impression. He also recorded for **Yabby You**, cutting a variation on his big hit entitled 'Armagideon Man', but further success eluded him. However, he has continued to make records, some of which, such as 'Sweet Home' for Black Victory records, were extremely good, but he is still seeking the record that will re-establish his name in the marketplace.

● ALBUMS: *Messenger Man* (Jah Muzik 1980)★★★★, *Armagideon Time* (Studio One 1982)★★★, *Unity* (Blackstar 1987)★★★, *Natty With A Cause* (Jah Shaka 1992)★★★, *See Me* (Jah Shaka 1993)★★★.

Williamson, Claude

b. 18 November 1926, Brattleboro, Texas, USA. After studying piano formally at the New England Conservatory in Boston, Massachusetts, Williamson turned to playing jazz in the late 40s. He first worked with **Charlie Barnet**, where he was featured on 'Claude Reigns', then with **Red Norvo** and also briefly led his own small group. In the early 50s he toured with **Bud Shank** before settling in Los Angeles, where he led a trio for many years. He played too with **Tal Farlow**, appeared in the second edition of the Lighthouse All-Stars with Shank, **Rolf Ericson**, **Bob Cooper** and **Max Roach**, and recorded with **Art Pepper**. Amongst Williamson's better-known compositions is 'Aquarium', recorded by the All-Stars in 1954. His trio work kept him busy but musically static for several years. However, in the late 70s and early 80s he toured Japan and the records he made there spurred his career. Although he began as mainstream player, Williamson later adapted to bop and most of his subsequent work reflects this interest. Although little known on the international scene, Japan apart, his work bears much closer attention than it has usually enjoyed.

● ALBUMS: *The Lighthouse All Stars Vol. 3* (1953)★★★, *The Lighthouse All Stars Vol. 4: Flute And Oboe* (1954)★★★, with Art Pepper *Discoveries* (1954)★★★, *Salute To Bud* (Affinity 1954)★★★★, *Keys West* (Affinity 1955)★★★★, *The Claude Williamson Trio* (1956)★★★★, *'Round Midnight* (1957)★★★★, *Claude Williamson In Italy* (1958)★★, *The Claude Williamson Quintet i* (1958)★★★, *The Claude Williamson Quintet ii* (1961)★★★, *New Departure* (1978)★★★, *Holography* (Interplay 1979)★★★, *La Fiesta* (Interplay 1979)★★★, *Tribute To Bud* (1981)★★★★, *Theatre Party* (Fresh Sounds 1988)★★★, *Mulls The Mulligan Scene* (Fresh Sounds 1988)★★★.

Williamson, James
(see **Homesick James**)

Williamson, John Lee 'Sonny Boy'

b. 30 March 1914, Jackson, Tennessee, USA, d. 1 June 1948, Chicago, Illinois, USA. Williamson learned harmonica as a child, and as a teenager in Tennessee was associated with the group of musicians around **Sleepy John Estes**. 'Sonny Boy' had been in Chicago for three years when he came to record in 1937, but his early records retained the plaintive sound, and often the songs, of Estes' circle. From the first, however, Williamson was an unmistakable musician, partly through his 'tongue-tied' singing style (probably a controlled version of his stammer), but chiefly for his harmonica playing. He worked almost invariably in 'cross-note' tuning, in which the key of the harmonica is a fourth above that of the music. This technique encourages drawn rather than blown notes, thus facilitating the vocalization, slurring and bent notes that are basic, in conjunction with intermittent hand muting and various tonguing and breath control effects, to most blues harmonica playing. In his time, Williamson was the greatest master of these techniques, and of blending voice and harmonica into a continuous melodic line; he reached a peak of technical and emotional perfection that sets the standard and defines the aesthetic for blues harmonica players to this day. Williamson recorded prolifically, as both leader and accompanist. His music developed continuously, and by the end of his life featured a powerful ensemble sound with amplified guitar. Williamson was equally adept at the expression of emotional intensity and the provision of rocking, exuberant dance music; in the musically rather bland years of the 40s, he preserved these qualities in the blues of Chicago, as if to prophesy the changes that were taking place by the time of his death. Universally liked, despite his enthusiasm for fighting when drunk, Williamson was greatly respected by his fellow musicians; he was enormously influential on more than one generation of harmonica players, from his contemporaries such as **Walter Horton** and **Drifting Slim**, to youngsters like **Junior Wells** and **Billy Boy Arnold**, and a remarkable proportion of his songs became blues standards. In Forrest City Joe, he acquired a devoted imitator, but perhaps the best indication of John Lee Williamson's importance, notwithstanding the monetary considerations that were doubtless his initial motivation, was the stubborn insistence of **Sonny Boy 'Rice Miller' Williamson**, a harmonica genius in his own right, that he was 'the original Sonny Boy Williamson'. On 1 June 1948, Williamson's life came to a tragic end following a serious assault.

● COMPILATIONS: with Big Bill Broonzy *Big Bill & Sonny Boy* (1964)★★★, *Blues Classics Volume 1* (Blues Classics 1965)★★★, *Blues Classics Volume 2* (Blues Classics 1968)★★★, *Blues Classics Volume 3* (Blues Classics 1972)★★★, *Bluebird, Number 1* (1982)★★★, *Bluebird, Number 15* (1985)★★★, *Sonny Boy Williamson* (1986)★★★, *Rare Sonny Boy* (RCA 1988)★★★, *Blues In The Mississippi Night* oral history (Rykodisc 1990)★★★★, *Sugar Mama: The Essential Recordings Of Sonny Boy Williamson* (Indigo 1995)★★★, *The Bluebird Blues* (Camden 1998)★★★.

Williamson, Robin

b. 24 November 1943, Edinburgh, Scotland. After the **Incredible String Band** split in 1974, following almost 10 years of success, multi-instrumentalist Williamson departed for Los Angeles, USA. He has released a large number of albums, many with mystical subjects. In addition to his literary projects and solo offerings, Williamson still tours, both solo and with his Merry Band. He still has a strong feel for tradition, with some material almost akin to the fantasy writer, J.R.R. Tolkien. Williamson is involved in many aspects of the business, having provided soundtracks for television series, and music for theatre productions. In addition to his many album releases, Williamson has also produced a large number of books and story cassettes. He now divides his time between the USA and Britain.

● ALBUMS: *Myrrh* (Island 1972)★★★, with the Merry Band *Journey's Edge* (1977)★★, with the Merry Band *American Stonehenge* (Criminal 1978)★★★, with the Merry Band *Glint At The Kindling* (1979)★★, *Songs Of Love And Parting* (1981)★★★, *Music From The Mabinogi* (1983)★★, *Legacy Of The Scottish Harpers* (1984)★★, *Legacy Of The Scottish Harpers Volume 2* (1986)★★, *Winter's Turning* (1986)★★★, *Ten Of Songs* (1988)★★★, with John Renbourn *Wheels Of Fortune* (Demon 1994)★★★, *Ring Dance* (Pig's Whisker 1998)★★★.

● COMPILATIONS: with the Merry Band *Songs And Music 1977* (1986)★★★.

● FURTHER READING: *English, Welsh, Scottish And Irish Fiddle Tunes*, with flexi-disc 1976. *Selected Writings 1980-83*, with cassette 1984.

Story cassettes: *The Fisherman's Son And The Gruagach Of Trick* (1981), *Prince Dougie And The Swan Maiden* (1982), *Rory Mor And The Gruagach Gair* (1982), *Music From The Mabinogi* (1983), *Five Humorous Tales Of Scotland* (1983), *Selected Writing 1980-83* (1984), *Five Humorous Tales Of Scotland And Ireland* (1984), *Five Celtic Tales Of Enlightenment* (1985), *Five Bardic Mysteries* (1985), *Five Legendary Histories Of Britain* (1985), *Five Celtic Tales Of Prodigies And Marvels* (1985), *The Dragon Has Two Tongues* (1985, film soundtrack), *Five Tales Of Enchantment* (1985), *Songs For Children Of All Ages* (1987), *Music For The Newborn* (1991).

Williamson, Sonny Boy 'Rice Miller'

b. Aleck/Alex Ford, 5 December 1899, Glendora, Mississippi, USA. d. 25 May 1965, Helena, Arkansas, USA. Being a man who would never compromise a good story by affording undue attention to veracity, and mischievous to boot, Sonny Boy's own various accounts of his life were never to be trusted and led to much confusion. Often referred to as 'Sonny Boy Williamson II' he was, in fact, older than **John Lee 'Sonny Boy' Williamson**, whose name, and associated glory, he appropriated some time in the late 30s or early 40s. Why he felt the need to do so is odd in light of the fact that he owed John Lee Williamson nothing in terms of style or ability, and alongside the latter and **Little Walter** Jacobs, was one of the most innovatory and influential exponents of the blues harmonica. He was the illegitimate child of Millie Ford, but he took to using his stepfather's name and by common association became 'Rice Miller'. He mastered his chosen instrument (he could also play guitar and drums) early in his life and seems to have taken to the road as soon as he was able, relying on his skill for a livelihood. His

wanderings throughout the south brought him into contact with many blues artists. The list includes **Robert Johnson**, **Robert Lockwood**, **Elmore James** and **Howlin' Wolf**, whose half sister, Mary, he married in the 30s. During this period Williamson used many names, working as 'Little Boy Blue', Willie Williamson, Willie Williams and Willie Miller (after his brother) and known to his friends as 'Foots' because of his habit of razoring his shoes, no matter how new they might be, to make them comfortable. He was cashing in on the popularity of John Lee Williamson (safely out of the way in Chicago) when he secured a job broadcasting over KFFA radio out of Helena on the *King Biscuit Show* in 1941. The show was heard all over the south and made Williamson famous. He continued to travel but now sought radio stations to advertise his activities. In the early 50s he recorded for Lillian McMurray's Trumpet label in Jackson, Mississippi, along with friends **Willie Love** and Elmore James. His work on this label includes many outstanding performances, with 'Mighty Long Time' being perhaps the greatest of all. On the strength of his increased popularity he extended his area of work and began to appear in the bars of Detroit, where he worked with Baby Boy Warren, and in Chicago (John Lee Williamson was dead by this time).

He began his career with **Chess Records** of Chicago in 1955 with his hit 'Don't Start Me Talkin'' and became a mainstay of the label almost until his death. In 1963, he took Europe by storm as a result of his appearances with the AFBF. His impressive appearance - tall and stooped in his famous grey/blue suit (quartered like a jester's doublet) and sporting a bowler hat and umbrella, along with his hooded eyes and goatee beard - hypnotized audiences as he weaved back and forth, snapping his fingers and clicking his tongue in a display of perfect rhythmic control. His skill on the harmonica was augmented by many tricks of showmanship such as playing two instruments at once (one with his large and plastic nose) or holding the harp end in his mouth and manoeuvring it with his tongue. If Europe took to him, Williamson seems to have enjoyed Europe: he stayed after the tour had ended and played his way around the burgeoning blues clubs, travelling as far as Poland. He recorded for the Storyville label in Denmark and with **Chris Barber** in Britain, then returned to mainland Europe, often stating his intention to take up permanent residence.

He never lived to see the days when Chess tried to convert their roster of blues singers into pop stars by uniting them with the most unlikely material and musical support, but in earlier days he had been quite happy to follow a similar route, by recording with such groups as the **Yardbirds** and the **Animals**, and a jazz band led by **Brian Auger**. Some of these efforts stand up better than others but Williamson did not care - as long as he was paid. Despite moving around extensively, he still maintained a home in the USA with his second wife Mattie Lee Gordon. He was back in Helena, appearing on the *King Biscuit Show* once more, when he died in his sleep in 1965.

Apart from his skill as a harmonica player and singer Sonny Boy Williamson was also a 'character' and anecdotes about him are legendary, both among the blues fraternity and his fans in Europe. If he was difficult, contentious, and unreliable, he was also a charming man who played upon his reputation as an evil, dangerous, hard-living blues troubadour. His music reveals that he was also capable of being both sensitive and humorous. He will always remain something of a conundrum, but as an artist his stature is recognized and his fame deserved.

● ALBUMS: *Down And Out Blues* (Checker 1959)★★★★, *Portraits In Blues Volume 4* (Storyville 1964)★★★★, *The Real Folk Blues* (Checker 1965)★★★★, *In Memoriam* (Chess 1965)★★★, *More Real Folk Blues* (Checker 1966)★★★, *Sonny Boy Williamson And The Yardbirds* (Mercury 1966)★★, with Brian Auger Trinity *Don't Send Me No Flowers* (Marmalade 1968)★★★, *Bummer Road* (Chess 1969)★★★, *One Way Out* (MCA 1976)★★★, *The Animals With Sonny Boy Williamson 1963* recording (Charly 1982)★★★, *King Biscuit Time* (Arhoolie 1989)★★★, *Goin' In Your Direction* (Trumpet 1992)★★★, *The EP Collection* (See For Miles 1994)★★★★.

Williamson, Steve

b. 1964, London, England. This tenor saxophonist has never received the media attention that near-contemporary colleague **Courtney Pine** has had and, as a very shy person, has never sought it. This may well have been to Williamson's advantage, since it meant he could develop at his own pace and on his own terms. It also meant, on the minus side, that he did not issue an album under his own name until 1990, but when the opportunity came he was in a position to make demands, such as that the album should be cut in New York - **Steve Coleman** produced the album and **Abbey Lincoln** was guest vocalist on the title track. Williamson is a mature and versatile player who convinces whether playing turbo-charged hard bop (such as at the Wembley Nelson Mandela 70th birthday concert where, accompanying dancers IDJ, he and Pine reached their biggest-ever audience), in a free jam, locking horns with the likes of **Evan Parker** in **Joe Gallivan**'s New Soldiers Of The Road, or contributing to the glorious exuberance of **Louis Moholo**'s *Viva La Black*.

He played for a week with **Art Blakey** at **Ronnie Scott**'s club, and produced some of his finest work on a 1989 four track demo disc with **Wayne Batchelor**'s Quartet which, sadly, is currently not publicly available. His first saxophone was an alto, but he switched to tenor after hearing **John Coltrane**. On occasions he also plays soprano. Of the many talented young black musicians to emerge from the London jazz scene in the late 80s, Williamson looks set to prove one of the most original and durable if he can shake off the Coltrane shadow that haunts him.

● ALBUMS: with Louis Moholo *Viva La Black* (1988)★★★★,

A Waltz For Grace (Polydor 1990)★★★★, *Rhyme Time* (Polydor 1991)★★★, *Journey To Truth* (Verve 1995)★★★.

Willing, Foy

b. Foy Willingham, 1915, Bosque County, Texas, USA, d. 24 July 1978. After first singing on local radio while still at school, he moved to New York where he appeared on radio for Crazy Water Crystals in 1933. He returned to radio work in Texas in 1935 but two years later, he moved to California, where he formed the Riders Of the Purple Sage. Initially, it comprised himself, Jimmy Dean and Al Sloey, but over the years there were many others, including Scotty Herrell, Billy Leibert, Paul Sellers and Johnny Paul. Using an instrumental line-up that included accordion, fiddle and guitar and closely resembling the **Sons Of The Pioneers**, they became very popular on several radio shows including the *Hollywood Barn Dance*. They also appeared in numerous Republic pictures with either **Roy Rogers** or Monte Hale. Their popularity saw them record for several labels and they are best remembered for their recordings of 'Ghost Riders In The Sky' (Capitol) and 'No One To Cry To' (Majestic). They formally disbanded in 1952 but later made nostalgic appearances at festivals, some further recordings and in 1959, they toured with **Gene Autry**. Foy Willing continued to appear at Western events until his death in 1978. (This group should not be confused with the **New Riders Of The Purple Sage**, a country rock band of the 70s).

● ALBUMS: *Cowboy* (1958)★★★, *New Sound Of American Folk* (1962)★★★.

Willis Brothers

Guy (b. James Willis, 5 July 1915, Alex, Arkansas, USA, d. 13 April 1981, Nashville, Tennessee, USA; guitar, vocals), Skeeter (b. Charles Willis, 20 December 1917, Coalton, Oklahoma, USA, d. March 1976; fiddle, vocals) and Vic (b. Richard Willis, 31 May 1922, Schulter, Oklahoma, USA; accordion, piano, vocals). Using clever combinations that saw any brother able to sing lead or harmony, they first appeared on KGEF Shawnee in 1932 as the Oklahoma Wranglers. In 1942, they moved to the Brush Creek Follies on KMBC Kansas City, Missouri, but their careers were interrupted by military service. In 1946, they backed **Hank Williams** when he made his first Sterling recordings in December that year. They also joined the *Grand Ole Opry* and began a long association with **Eddy Arnold**. They left the *Opry* in 1949 and during the 50s, were popular on various shows including the *Ozark Jubilee* and the *Midwestern Hayride*. They rejoined the *Opry* in 1960 and during the decade found country chart success on Starday including a Top 10 hit with 'Give Me Forty Acres'. During their career they recorded for several other labels, even worked as session musicians and toured extensively including overseas trips. They appeared in several films including *Feudin' Rhythm* and *Hoe Down*, and also hold the distinction of being the first country act to perform at the Constitution Hall in Washington. Guy retired after Skeeter died of cancer in 1976 and Vic formed the Vic Willis Trio and continued to perform.

● ALBUMS: *In Action* (Starday 1962)★★★, *Code Of The West* (Starday 1963)★★★★, *Let's Hit The Road* (Starday 1965)★★, *The Sensational Willis Brothers* (Hilltop 1965)★★★, *Give Me Forty Acres* (Starday 1965)★★★★, *Road Stop-Jukebox Hits* (Starday 1965)★★★, *The Wild Side Of Life* (Starday 1966)★★★, *The Willis Brothers Goin' To Town* (Starday 1966)★★, *Bob* (Starday 1967)★★★, *Hey, Mister Truck Driver* (Starday 1968)★★★, *Bummin' Around* (Starday 1969)★★★, *Truck Driver Hits* (Nashville 1969)★★★, *Y'All* (Nashville 1969)★★★, *For The Good Times* (Starday 1971)★★★.

● COMPILATIONS: *Country Hits* (Alshire 1969)★★★★, *The Best Of The Willis Brothers* (Starday 1970)★★★★.

Willis, Aaron 'Little Sonny'
(see **Little Sonny**)

Willis, Bruce
b. 19 March 1955, Germany. Before beginning his acting career in the mid-70s, Willis played saxophone in the R&B band, Loose Goose. His musical ambitions were overshadowed by his growing success as an actor, which culminated in his starring roles in the highly popular US television series *Moonlighting*, and the Hollywood film *Blind Date*. In 1987, Willis conceived and starred in the television special *The Return Of Bruno*, a biography (or rockumentary!) of a fictional rock star in which many real-life musicians testified to his influence on their careers. For the soundtrack, Willis revamped several classic soul songs, scoring a surprise 1987 hit with the **Staples Singers**' 'Respect Yourself', and following up with the **Drifters**' 'Under The Boardwalk', on which he was supported by the **Temptations**.

● ALBUMS: *The Return Of Bruno* (Motown 1987)★★, *If It Don't Kill You It Just Makes You Stronger* (Motown 1989)★.

Willis, Chuck
b. 31 January 1928, Atlanta, Georgia, USA, d. 10 April 1958. R&B singer Willis made his recording debut in 1951. The following year he reached number 2 in the black music charts with 'My Story', the first of several hits the artist enjoyed while signed to the renowned **OKeh** label. In 1956 Willis had his first hit for **Atlantic Records** when 'It's Too Late' reached the US R&B Top 3, and the following year he topped the same chart with the compulsive 'C.C. Rider'. In April 1958, the singer succumbed to peritonitis, in the wake of which his posthumous single, 'What Am I Living For', sold in excess of one million copies. The ironically titled b-side, 'I'm Gonna Hang Up My Rock 'N' Roll Shoes', also reached the R&B Top 10, and despite his brief life and career, Willis remained an influential stylist in the development of R&B. He composed many of his best-known recordings, and cover versions by acts as disparate as **Derek And The Dominos**, the **Animals**,

Buddy Holly, **Jerry Lee Lewis**, the **Band**, **Ted Taylor** and **Otis Redding** are a tribute to their longevity.

● ALBUMS: *Chuck Willis Wails The Blues* (Epic 1958)★★★, *The King Of The Stroll* (Atlantic 1958)★★★.

● COMPILATIONS: *Tribute To Chuck Willis* (Epic 1960)★★★, *I Remember Chuck Willis* (Atlantic 1963)★★★, *His Greatest Recordings* (Atlantic 1971)★★★, *Chuck Willis - My Story* (Official 1980)★★★, *Keep A Drivin'* (Charly 1984)★★★, *Be Good Or Be Gone* (Edsel 1986)★★★.

Willis, Kelly
b. 1 October 1968, Annandale, Virginia, USA. Willis formed her first band when aged 16, and when she moved to Austin, **Nanci Griffith** arranged an audition for her at MCA. Willis has been compared to another MCA artist, **Brenda Lee**, because her records suggest the same blend of rockabilly, rock 'n' roll and ballads, updated for the 90s. The title track of *Bang Bang*, for example, is an obscure title from rock 'n' roller Janis Martin. The songwriting credits on her albums are always interesting and 'Sincerely' was written by **Steve Earle** and **Robert Earl Keen**. **Don Was** produced her third album, which included songs she had written with John Leventhal and **Paul Kennerley**. She also duets with **Kevin Welch** on 'That'll Be Me' and took time out to add background harmonies to **Chris Wall**'s *Cowboy Nation*. She sings the Paul Kennerley song 'I Don't Want To Love You (But I Do)' on the soundtrack of *Thelma And Louise* (1991) and she appeared as Clarissa Flan in *Bob Roberts* (1992). She returned to recording with 1996's *Fading Fast EP*.

● ALBUMS: *Well Travelled Love* (MCA 1990)★★★, *Bang Bang* (MCA 1991)★★★★, *Kelly Willis* (MCA 1993)★★★.

Willis, Ralph
b. 1910, Alabama, USA, d. 1957, New York City, New York, USA. Ralph Willis moved to North Carolina in the 30s, and met **Blind Boy Fuller**, **Eugene 'Buddy' Moss** and **Brownie McGhee**; he was closely associated with McGhee in New York after he relocated there in 1944, and his recordings often have McGhee on second guitar. They range from delicate guitar duets to driving dance music, with a nice line in bawdy humour, although he could also be lazily wistful, as on his solo cover of **Luke Jordan**'s 'Church Bells'. Despite his connection with McGhee and **Sonny Terry**, Willis did not capitalize on the burgeoning folk revival. He was known as 'Bama' for his rural ways; he perhaps lacked the drive or the self-confidence to achieve mainstream success.

● ALBUMS: *Faded Picture Blues* (1970)★★★, *Carolina Blues* (1974)★★★, *East Coast Blues* (1988)★★★.

Willows
A New York doo-wop group formed in 1953 as the Five Willows, this quintet is best remembered for the up-tempo rocker 'Church Bells May Ring', a song that still enjoys airplay on US nostalgia-orientated radio stations. The group consisted of Tony Middleton,

brothers Ralph and Joe Martin, Richie Davis and John Steele. Relying on bass singer Steele's vocal acrobatics to give them an identity, they were signed to small labels Allen and Pee-Dee before recording one single for Herald, and finally, their hit for Melba. The shuffle 'Church Bells May Ring' was released in early 1956 and the chimes on the track were played by a then unknown **Neil Sedaka**. The Willows continued to record for such labels as Club, Eldorado, Gone and Heidi, and the group finally retired in 1965. They recorded no albums, but their one hit, which peaked at number 62 pop and number 11 on the R&B charts, is featured on numerous anthologies.

Wills, Billy Jack

b. 1926, on a farm near Memphis, Hall County, Texas, USA. Billy Jack was the youngest brother of **Bob Wills** and the ninth of the Wills family's children. He naturally grew up influenced by his brother Bob's music and joined the Texas Playboys in 1945. He initially played bass but, after 1949, he usually played drums and also took some vocals. He added the lyrics to the old fiddle tune called 'Faded Love' that had been written by Bob and his father John Wills. He shared the vocal when it was first recorded in 1950 and the song reached number 8 in the US country charts. It went on to become a country standard and was later a hit for **Patsy Cline** (1963), **Leon McAuliffe** (1963), **Tompall And The Glaser Brothers** (1971) and **Willie Nelson** and **Ray Price** (1980). In the mid-50s, he formed his own band and recorded for Four Star.

● COMPILATIONSS: *Billy Jack Wills & His Western Swing Band* (Western 1983)★★★, *Crazy Man Crazy* (Western 1985)★★★.

Wills, Bob

b. James Robert Wills, 6 March 1905, on a farm near Kosse, Limestone County, Texas, USA, d. 13 May 1975, Fort Worth, Texas, USA. The eldest of the ten children of John Thompkins Wills and Emmaline (Foley), Bob was a sickly child and there were fears that he would not survive his early years. His father, known locally as Uncle John, was a skilled fiddler, and later taught his son Bob to play the mandolin so that he could accompany his father's playing; however, initially Bob showed no great interest in music. In 1913, the Wills family relocated to Memphis, Texas. Bob rode his donkey behind the family wagon and the 500-mile journey took over two months. John and Bob played for farm dances along the way to raise money for food and it was at one of these dances that Bob first became interested in music played by black families, featuring trumpet and guitar. When he was 10 years old, much to his father's relief, he took up the fiddle and made his first solo public appearance. On one occasion, his father failed to appear to play at a dance, and in spite of knowing only six fiddle tunes for dancing, he kept playing alone (his father eventually arrived at 2 a.m., too drunk to play). John Wills was successful as a farmer and by 1921, he had moved to a 600-acre ranch/farm near Oxbow Crossing, which remained their home until 1931. The family continued to play for local functions; it was suggested that the Wills family, which by 1926 included nine children, produced more music than cotton. Realizing the farm could not sustain them all, in 1924, Bob moved to Amarillo where, by working on building sites and as a shoeshine boy, he made enough money to buy himself a fiddle. He then found work playing for dances on Saturday nights and made his first radio broadcasts on Amarillo's two radio stations, KGRS and WDAG. A year later, he returned home driving a Model T Ford, which enabled him to travel around playing. In 1926, he married for the first time and leased a farm, but after a crop failure in 1927, he and his wife moved to Amarillo and he gave up farming for good. He moved to Fort Worth where, sometimes in blackface, he found work in a Medicine Show. Here he met guitarist Herman Arnspiger and the two men began to appear as the Wills Family Band. They played for dances, did comedy routines and in November 1929, they recorded for **Brunswick** in Dallas, although the two songs were not released. In 1930, the duo became a quartet when Milton Brown and his brother Durwood joined as vocalist and guitarist, respectively, although Durwood was at the time still at school (Milton Brown later became famous with his own band, the Musical Brownies). They found regular work playing for dances, at times adding banjoist Frank Barnes, and played on KTAT and KFJZ where the assistant programme director of the latter station, Alton Strickland, would five years later became Wills' pianist. In 1930, Wills' band were sponsored on WBAP by the Aladdin Lamp Company (they appeared as the Aladdin Laddies), and also gained a residency at the Crystal Springs dancehall in Fort Worth. In January 1931, through the sponsorship of the Burrus Mill and Elevator Company and billed as the Light Crust Doughboys, he and the band began to advertise Light Crust Flour on KFJZ. After two weeks, in spite of their popularity with the listeners, the President of Burrus Mill, Mr. Wilbert Lee O'Daniel (later a US Senator and Governor of Texas) sacked them, because he considered their music was too hillbilly. KFJZ kept them on air without a sponsor and Wills succeeded in getting O'Daniel to resume sponsorship and pay the band as well, although for a time all members had to work a 40-hour week in the mill. Their popularity grew and soon the programme was being heard over all the south-west, even reaching as far as Oklahoma City. The band recorded for **RCA** Victor in 1932, the only recordings made by Wills with the Light Crust Doughboys. The same year, vocalist Thomas Elmer Duncan replaced Milton Brown. In 1933, after differences of opinion and occasional drinking sprees that saw him miss shows, Wills was sacked by O'Daniel. He moved to Waco, assembled a band that included his brother, **Johnnie Lee Wills**, and Duncan, and for the first time, he called his band the Playboys; he also added 'formerly the Light Crust Doughboys' (he found himself in lawsuits from O'Daniel for using the name, but eventually the courts found in his favour). He then moved to Oklahoma City, where he began to call his band the Texas Playboys, but O'Daniel stopped his programme by promising the radio station he would put on the *Burrus Mill Show* in Oklahoma if they did not broadcast Wills' band. Wills moved to KVOO Tulsa, where in February 1934, Bob Wills And The Texas Playboys finally began to broadcast and this time O'Daniel's attempts to stop them failed.

In 1935, the group made their first, historic studio recordings. The band consisted of twelve musicians, namely Bob Wills (fiddle), Tommy Duncan (vocals, piano), Johnnie Lee Wills (tenor banjo), Son Lansford (bass), Herman Arnspiger (guitar), Sleepy Johnson (guitar), Jesse Ashlock (fiddle), Art Baines (fiddle, trombone), Smokey Dacus (drums), Robert McNally (saxophone), Al Stricklin (piano) and **Leon McAuliffe** (steel guitar). Wills stayed in Tulsa and during the late 30s, he continued to shape his band; changes in personnel saw the arrival of guitarist Eldon Shamblin and saxophonist Joe Ferguson. In 1936, Leon McAuliffe first recorded his 'Steel Guitar Rag'. Wills made further recording sessions in Chicago (1936) and Dallas (1937 and 1938). When he recorded in Saginaw, Texas, in April 1940, his band numbered 18 musicians - more than the big bands of the period such as **Glenn Miller**, **Benny Goodman** and the **Dorseys** were using. It was at this session that he recorded his million-selling version of 'New San Antonio Rose', the (Tommy Duncan) vocal version of his 1935 fiddle tune, previously known as 'Spanish Two Step'. This version differed from his original fiddle one in that it featured only reeds and brass and was played in the swing style as used by the big bands of the time (over the years the song has usually been referred to as simply 'San Antonio Rose'). Wills was by this time one of the top-selling recording artists in the USA. In 1939, the demand was such that Wills decided for the first time to run a second band, which was led by his brother Johnnie Lee and also included his younger brother **Luke Wills**. Although successful with his music, Bob Wills was far from successful in marriage. He had troubles at times with excessive drinking and a fondness for the ladies. He was divorced in 1935 and married and divorced a second time in 1936. In 1938, he married again but once more was divorced within the year, and though he persuaded this wife to remarry him, they were divorced for the second time in 1939. He married again in July 1939, only to be divorced (yet again!) in June 1941.

In 1940, he appeared with **Tex Ritter** in the film *Take Me Back To Oklahoma*, even duetting with Ritter on the title track, and the following year, with his full band, he featured in the film *Go West Young Man*. In 1942, Duncan left for military service (he rejoined on discharge) but Wills maintained a band containing 15 instruments, although only four were stringed. He recorded in Hollywood and made eight B-movie westerns with Russell Hayden. He was also married that

year to Betty Anderson, a girl 18 years his junior and this time, in spite of his drinking, the marriage lasted until his death. After the filming was completed, more band members left for the US Army and Wills moved to Tulsa, finally disbanding the group in December 1942. He enlisted himself, but was discharged in July 1943. He moved to California, re-formed a band and returned to the film studios. Wills never liked Hollywood but he loved the cowboy image. He spent lavishly on horses, harnesses and dress for himself and was a popular figure on his favourite stallion, Punkin, around the California rodeo circuit. He bought a ranch in the San Joaquin Valley and stocked it with horses and a dairy herd 'just to keep my father busy'. At one stage in 1944, his band consisted of 22 instruments and 2 vocalists, but he never recorded with this unit. Duncan left in 1947 to form his own band, probably because he had tired of having to take responsibility for fronting the band when Wills failed to appear as a result of excessive drinking sprees. During 1944-45, Wills had US country and pop chart hits with 'New San Antonio Rose', 'We Might As Well Forget It' and 'You're From Texas'. He also had country number 1 hits with such war songs as 'Smoke On The Water', 'Stars And Stripes At Iwo Jima', 'Silver Dew On The Blue Grass Tonight' and 'White Cross At Okinawa'. In 1946, his 'New Spanish Two-Step' topped the country charts for 16 weeks as well as having Top 20 pop success. Wills left **Columbia Records** in 1947 to record for **MGM Records** and in 1950, he recorded his classic 'Faded Love' - a composition that he and his father wrote with some words added by brother **Billy Jack Wills**. He toured extensively and relocated to Dallas, where he invested heavily in a dancehall that he called Bob Wills' Ranch House. Due to unscrupulous advisers and accountants, he soon found himself heavily in debt. Faced with jail, he sold his Bob Wills Music Company and accidentally with it, the ownership of 'San Antonio Rose'. For two years, he struggled to raise funds; he ran two bands - one played at the Ranch House and he toured with the other. In January 1952, he finally sold the Ranch House to a Jack Ruby - a name then unknown outside Dallas, but later internationally known following the assassination of Lee Harvey Oswald (in turn, killer of President John F. Kennedy). Throughout the 50s, he recorded and toured extensively and several times moved his base of operations. Wills continued to experiment but the influence of television began to affect the dancehalls; tastes had changed and he never recaptured the earlier successes. He recorded in Nashville for the first time in 1955, and again in 1956, but most of his recordings were made in California. In 1959, he appeared at the Golden Nugget in Las Vegas but still missed a few shows through his drinking. He was reunited with Tommy Duncan, and during the period of 1960/1 they recorded over 40 sides for **Liberty Records**. In 1962, he suffered a heart attack but in 1963, he was back, even though he had sold his band to Carl Johnson. He suffered a further heart attack in 1964 and when he recovered sufficiently to work again, he always acted as a frontman for other bands. Between 1963 and 1969, he recorded almost 100 sides for either Liberty, Longhorn or Kapp Records. He was elected to the Country Music Hall Of Fame in 1968. After an appearance on 30 May 1969, he suffered a stroke and was rushed to hospital where he underwent two major operations. The stroke left him paralyzed on his right side and hospitalized for months. In 1970, he moved to Tulsa and in 1971 underwent surgery for a kidney complaint, but suffered a stroke on the left side a few hours after the operation. Months later, he recovered sufficiently to talk and to use his left arm, even telling people that he would play again. Country star **Merle Haggard** admired Wills and in 1970, he recorded his album *Tribute To The Best Damn Fiddle Player In The World (Or My Salute To Bob Wills)*, which actually featured some of the Texas Playboys. Wills was unable to attend the recordings but in 1971, he was reunited with 10 of his old Texas Playboys at Haggard's house, near Bakersfield, and watched and listened as recordings were made. In 1973, he made a few appearances, at one even holding his fiddle while Hoyle Nix used the bow. He travelled to Dallas to attend a recording session of the Texas Playboys and on 3 December even included a few of his famous yells and 'hollers' as the band recorded some of his hits. During the night, he suffered a further stroke and remained unconscious for almost 18 months until his death from pneumonia on 13 May 1975. He was buried in Memorial Park, Tulsa, a city that saw most of the glory days of Bob Wills' western swing music. It could never be said that he copied any other style - he devised his own, as the words of his song said, 'Deep within my heart lies a melody'. His long-time friend, steel guitarist Leon McAuliffe, who, though 12 years younger than Wills, had retired from the music scene, summed things up when he said, 'My desire wore out before my body, Bob never did wear out at this. His body wore out before his desire did'. There have been other bands that played the music but none that ever matched the instrumental integration or the wide variation in the styles and music of Bob Wills. His habit of uttering spasmodic high-pitched shouts during the playing of numbers, such as his famed 'Ah haaa', originated from the days when, as a young boy, he performed with his father at ranch dances in Texas. His father (and the cowboys) used similar loud cries at points when the music or the whiskey moved them to feel that something was special. As **Waylon Jennings** sang, 'When you're down in Austin, Bob Wills is still the King'.

● ALBUMS: *Bob Wills Round-Up* 10-inch album (Columbia 1949)★★★★, *Ranch House Favorites* 10-inch album (MGM 1951)★★★★, *Old Time Favorites By Bob Wills & His Texas Playboys 1* (Antone's 1953)★★★, *Old Time Favorites By Bob Wills & His Texas Playboys 2* (Antone's 1953)★★★, *Dance-O-Rama No: 2* (Decca 1955)★★★, *Ranch House Favorites ii* (MGM 1956)★★★, *Bob Wills Special* (Harmony 1957)★★★★, *Bob Wills & His Texas Playboys* (Decca 1957)★★★★, *Western Swing In Hi-Fi* (1957)★★★★, with Tommy Duncan *Together Again* (Liberty 1960)★★★, with Tommy Duncan *Bob Wills & Tommy Duncan* (Liberty 1961)★★★, *Living Legend - Bob Wills & His Texas Playboys* (Liberty 1961)★★★, *Mr Words & Mr Music* (Liberty 1961)★★★, *Bob Wills Sings And Plays* (Liberty 1963)★★★, *Best Of Bob Wills & His Texas Playboys - Original Recordings* (Harmony 1963)★★★★, *My Keepsake Album* (Longhorn 1965)★★★, *The Great Bob Wills* (Harmony 1965)★★★, *San Antonio Rose/Steel Guitar Rag* (Starday 1965)★★★, *Western Swing Band* (Vocalion 1965)★★★, with Leon Rausch *From The Heart Of Texas* (Kapp 1966)★★★, *King Of Western Swing* (Kapp 1967)★★★, *Bob Wills* (Metro 1967)★★★, *Here's That Man Again* (Kapp 1968)★★★★, *Plays The Greatest String Band Hits* (Kapp 1969)★★★, *A Country Walk* (Sunset 1969)★★★, *Time Changes Everything* (Kapp 1969)★★★, *The Living Legend* (Kapp 1969)★★★, *Bob Wills Special* (Harmony 1969)★★★, *The Bob Wills Story* (Starday 1970)★★★, *Bob Wills In Person* (Kapp 1970)★★★, *A Tribute To Bob Wills* (MGM 1971)★★★, *The History Of Bob Wills & The Texas Playboys* (MGM 1973)★★★, *The Best Of Bob Wills* (MCA 1973), *For The Last Time* (United Artists 1974)★★★★, *Bob Wills & His Texas Playboys In Concert* (Capitol 1976)★★★, *I Love People* (1976)★★★, *Lonestar Rag* (1979)★★★, *Faded Love* (1981)★★★, *31st Street Blues* (1981)★★★, *The San Antonio Rose Story* (1982)★★★, *Texas Fiddle & Milk Cow Blues* (1982)★★★, *Heaven, Hell Or Houston* (1983)★★★, *Swing Hi! Swing Lo!* (1993)★★★.

● COMPILATIONS: with Tommy Duncan *Legendary Masters - Bob Wills & Tommy Duncan* (United Artists 1971)★★★★, *The Bob Wills Anthology* (Columbia 1973)★★★★, *The Legendary Bob Wills* (Columbia 1975)★★★, *The Tiffany Transcriptions 1945-1948* (Lariat 1977)★★★, *The Tiffany Transcriptions* (Tishomingo 1978)★★★, *The Rare Presto Transcriptions Volumes 1 - 5* German releases (Outlaw 1981-1985)★★★, *Columbia Historic Edition* (Columbia 1982)★★★, *The Tiffany Transcriptions Volumes 1 - 9* (Kaleidoscope 1983-1988, reissued by Rhino in the 1990s)★★★, *The Golden Era* (Columbia 1987)★★★, *Fiddle* (CMF 1987)★★★, *Anthology 1935-1973* (Rhino 1991)★★★★, *Country Music Hall Of Fame Series* (MCA 1992)★★★★, *The Essential Bob Wills And His Texas Playboys 1935-47* (Columbia 1992)★★★★, *The Longhorn Recordings* (Bear Family 1993)★★★, *Classic Western Swing* (Rhino 1994)★★★, *Encore* 3-CD box set (Liberty 1994)★★★★, *The King Of Western Swing: 25 Hits 1935-45* (ASV 1998)★★★.

● FURTHER READING: *San Antonio Rose, The Life and Music of Bob Wills*, Charles R.Townsend. *The Life Of Bob Wills, The King Of Western Swing*, Jimmy Latham. *My Years With Bob Wills*, Al Stricklin. *Hubbin' It, The Life Of Bob Wills*, Ruth Sheldon.

Wills, Johnnie Lee

b. 2 September 1912, on a farm near Kosse, Limestone County, Texas, USA, d. 25 October 1984. Younger brother of **Bob Wills** and the fourth of the Wills family's children. He learned to play the guitar as a child but later played tenor banjo and fiddle. He made his musical debut in 1933, when he became one of brother Bob's second band, working as Johnnie Lee Wills and His Rhythmaires. He appeared with Bob in the 1940 **Tex Ritter** film *Take Me Back To Oklahoma*. In early 1941, he recorded for **Decca**, having success with 'Milk Cow Blues'. Throughout the 40s and 50s, he led western swing bands, working in conjunction with brother Bob. He played the south-west dance circuits but was mainly centred in Oklahoma City or Tulsa where, until 1964, he played a residency at *Cain's Dancing Academy*. In 1950, recording on Bullet, he achieved Top 10 US country and pop chart success with 'Rag Mop' (a number he co-wrote with Deacon Anderson that was also a pop hit for the **Ames Brothers**) and a country number 7 with 'Peter Cottontail'. He also made further recordings for Decca, **MGM** and RCA-Victor, as well as over 200 15-minute transcription discs for use on KVOO Tulsa and other stations. In 1964, he left Cain's, ran his western wear store in Tulsa and organized the Tulsa Annual Stampede rodeo. He returned to leading a band in the 70s and with some of the old Playboys, he recorded for the Flying Fish and Delta labels. In 1971, he played banjo on the Bob Wills tribute recordings made at **Merle Haggard**'s home in Bakersfield, and later made some appearances at Playboy Reunion Shows, but did not appear on the 1973 recording session in Dallas, Texas. He modestly never rated himself as a good enough solo banjo or fiddle player for people to listen to, but he was highly respected as a bandleader. He died in Tulsa in October 1984.

● ALBUMS: *Where There's A Wills There's A Way* (Sims 1962)★★★, *At The Tulsa Stampede* (Sims 1963)★★★, *Reunion* (Flying Fish 1978)★★★, *Dance All Night* (Delta 1980)★★.

● COMPILATIONS: *Best Of Johnnie Lee Wills* (Crown 1975)★★★, *Tulsa Swing* (Rounder 1978)★★★, *Rompin' Stompin' Singin' Swingin'* (Bear Family 1984)★★★★.

Wills, Luke

b. Luther J. Wills, 10 September 1920, on a farm near Memphis, Hall County, Texas, USA. Younger brother of **Bob Wills** and the seventh of the Wills family's children. He was rated so differently from the rest of the family that it became a family joke that his mother had picked up the wrong baby, after one of the many social dances held in the area. He learned to play stand-up bass as a child and made his musical debut in 1939 in the second Wills band, led by elder brother **Johnnie Lee Wills**, called the Rhythmaires. He appeared in B-movie westerns in the early 40s with Bob but in 1943, he joined the US Navy. After service, he led Bob's second band and covered the dance circuit of northern and central California, appearing first as Luke Wills And The Texas Playboys Number 2, but to avoid confusion this soon became Luke Wills' Rhythm Busters. He recorded for King and **RCA**-Victor, adopting a similar style of comments and interjections as Bob, though not in a high-pitched voice. In 1948, the Rhythm Busters were disbanded and he worked with Bob until 1950, when he

re-formed his own band and took over in Oklahoma City, when Bob returned to Texas to his new dancehall. He rejoined Bob in 1952 and played and sang with the Playboys, often fronting the band in Bob's absence, until they disbanded in 1964. He then worked outside of the music industry in Las Vegas. In 1971, he played bass on the Bob Wills tribute recordings made at **Merle Haggard**'s home in Bakersfield and later made some appearances at Playboy Reunion Shows, but did not appear on the 1973 recording session in Dallas. Although contributing in no small way to his eldest brother's legend, he was not elected to the Country Music Hall Of Fame. In the late 70s, he left the music business and retired to Las Vegas.

● COMPILATIONS: *Luke Wills' Rhythm Busters - High Voltage Gal* (1988)★★★.

Wills, Mark

b. 8 August 1973, Cleveland, Tennessee, USA. Wills is produced by the highly acclaimed **Keith Stegall.** His debut album on sold well and indicated a star in the making. Among the tracks is a country version of the **Who**'s 'Squeeze Box'. Wish You Were Here broke the artist into the country mainstream and confirmed his potential.

● ALBUMS: *Mark Wills* (Mercury 1996)★★, *Wish You Were Here* (Mercury 1998)★★★★.

Wills, Viola

b. Los Angeles, California, USA. This soul-songstress only entered the music business after having her sixth child. She was discovered by **Barry White**, who initially used her as a session vocalist, and in 1965 signed her to Bronco Records where he was A&R head. A handful of singles for the label failed to click as did a release on A Bem Soul in 1969. The next break came when she replaced Claudia Lennear on tour with **Joe Cocker**, which brought her to Europe and led to her recording in the UK for Goodear in 1974. In 1977 Wills joined **Arista Records** and in 1979 she recorded for Ariola/Hansa. It was there that she scored her biggest hit with a disco-revival of Patience And Prudence's 'Gonna Get Along Without You Now', which made the UK Top 10 in 1957. She became one of the most successful exponents of Hi-NRG music with other club successes like 'If You Could Read My Mind' and 'Up On The Roof'. She returned to the UK Top 40 in 1986 with the double a-side 'Both Sides Now'/'Dare To Dream', which she produced for the Wide Angle label. The much-recorded singer has also appeared on many labels since 1979, including **Island Records** in 1987.

● ALBUMS: *Soft Centres* (Goodear 1974)★★, *Without You* (1979)★★.

Willson, Meredith

b. Robert Meredith Reiniger, 18 May 1902, Mason City, Iowa, USA, d. 15 June 1984, Santa Monica, California, USA. An instrumentalist and musical director - then a composer-lyricist-librettist - Willson was 55-years-old when he made his Broadway debut in 1957 with the hit musical *The Music Man*. Educated at the Damrosch Institute of Musical Art in New York, Willson was a flute and piccolo soloist with **John Philip Sousa**'s concert band from 1921-23, and with the New York Philharmonic from 1924-29, playing under Arturo Toscanini. During the 30s and early 40s he worked extensively on radio as musical director on shows such as *Ship Of Joy*, *Carefree Carnival*, *Good News Of 1938*, *Maxwell House Coffee Time*, *Fanny Brice* and *John Nesbitt*. When he was in his late 30s, he composed a symphony, 'The Missions', and scored movies such as Charles Chaplin's *The Great Dictator* (1940) and Lillian Hellman's *The Little Foxes* (1941). He had composed the incidental music for Hellman's stage play of the same name, two years earlier. During World War II, Willson was a major in the Armed Forces Radio Service, and when he was released he had his own radio show from 1946 into the early 50s, and also hosted *The Big Show* with actress Tallulah Bankhead, and composed its closing theme, 'May The Good Lord Bless And Keep You'.

In December 1957, *The Music Man*, for which Willson wrote the book, music and lyrics, opened on Broadway to unanimously favourable reviews. It was set in Willson's home state of Iowa, c.1912, and starred **Robert Preston**, who was making his first appearance in a Broadway - in fact, any - musical. Preston triumphed in the role of the likeable conman, Professor Harold Hill, and **Barbara Cook** was splendid as librarian Marion Paroo. A wonderful set of songs, set in a variety of musical styles, included 'Rock Island', 'Goodnight My Someone', 'The Sadder-But-Wiser Girl', 'Marion The Librarian', 'My White Knight', 'Wells Fargo Wagon', 'Shi-poopi', 'Lida Rose', 'Will I Ever Tell You?', 'Gary, Indiana', 'Till There Was You', and the classics, 'Seventy-Six Trombones' and 'Trouble' ('Right here in River City/With a capital "T"/ That rhymes with "P"/That stands for pool!'). Willson won **Tony** and Drama Critics Circle Awards, and the show ran in New York for 1,375 performances. It was filmed in 1962 with Preston, and **Shirley Jones** who replaced Cook. Apart from the original cast and film soundtrack records, Willson and his wife Rini performed the score on an album, complete with their own individual comments.

Willson's next musical, *The Unsinkable Molly Brown* (1960), had Tammy Grimes in the title role, and ran for over a year. The appealing score included 'I Ain't Down Yet', 'Belly Up To The Bar Boys', 'Keep A-Hoppin'' and 'Are You Sure?'. **Debbie Reynolds** replaced Grimes in the 1964 film version. Willson's final Broadway score (he also wrote the book) was for *Here's Love* (1963). Adapted from George Seaton's 1947 comedy-fantasy movie about a department store's Santa Claus, it starred Janis Paige and Craig Stevens, and ran for 334 performances. The songs included 'The Big Clown Balloons', 'Arm In Arm', 'You Don't Know' and 'Pine Cones And Holly Berries'. Broadway legend **Chita**

Rivera was in the cast of Willson's stage musical swan-song, *1491*, which closed out of town in 1969.
● FURTHER READING: *And There I Stood With My Piccolo*, Meredith Willson. *But He Doesn't Know The Territory*, Meredith Willson.

Wilmer X

Comprising Nils Hellberg (guitar, vocals, songwriting), Jalle Lorenseeon (harmonica), Pelle Ossler (guitar), 'Sticky Bomb' (drums), Thomas Holst (bass) and Mats Bengtsson (keyboards), European R&B/pop band Wilmer X formed in Malmo, Sweden, in the early 90s. Immediately Hellberg focused on the southern states of the USA for his principal inspiration, as his band perfected a smooth, accessible mix of blues and R&B. Having won three domestic Grammys the group released its first English language album in 1994. The most distinctive feature of that year's self-titled release was the harmonica playing of Lorenseeon. Though Hellberg's lyrics did not translate to English as comfortably as they might have done, the group drew on the universality of R&B as a musical language with commendable tenacity.
● ALBUMS: *Mambo Fever* (MNW 1991)★★★, *Pontiac Till Himmelen* (MNW 1993)★★★, *Wilmer X* (MNW 1994)★★★.

Wilson Phillips

The daughters of **Beach Boys** leader **Brian Wilson** and his ex-wife Marilyn (formerly of the **Honeys**) and **John Phillips** and **Michelle Phillips** of the **Mamas And The Papas**, this trio proved that they were up to the task of following those famous footsteps by scoring two number 1 singles in the US charts, with 'Hold On' and 'Release Me' plus a Top 10 album at their first attempt. The girls, **Chynna Phillips** (b. Chynna Gilliam Phillips, 12 February 1968, Los Angeles, California, USA) and the Wilson sisters, Wendy (b. 16 October 1969, Los Angeles, California, USA) and Carnie (b. 29 April 1968, Los Angeles, California, USA), were all in their early twenties when they released their self-titled debut album on the newly-formed SBK Records in early 1990, although they had known each other and even sung together since early childhood. While they received moral support from their parents, the group deliberately shied away from asking for musical assistance. Their first album became one of the biggest selling debut's of all time having now sold in excess of 5 million copies. *Shadows And Light* has leapt into the US best sellers in the first week of release. This album is more introspective lyrically, and has a harder production. The band address their many childhood problems, much of their stress being caused by their respective fathers' over-indulgencies. Both **Brain Wilson** and **John Phillips** could benefit from listening to the lyrics 'Flesh And Blood' and 'Would You Fly All The Way From New York'. The unit broke up towards the end of 1992. As Carnie And Wendy Wilson, the sisters released the dreadful *Hey Santa!* late in 1993 while Phillips started a solo career. The Wilson sisters mended their estrangement from their father, and he participated with their album recorded as the Wilsons in 1997.

● ALBUMS: *Wilson Phillips* (SBK 1990)★★★★, *Shadows And Light* (1992)★★★, *Hey Santa* (SBK 1993)★, *The Wilsons* (Mercury 1997)★★★.

● VIDEOS: *So Far* (PMI 1993).

Wilson, 'Kid' Wesley

b. 1 October 1893, Jacksonville, Florida, USA, d. 10 October 1958, Cape May Court House, New Jersey, USA. With his wife, **Leola B. 'Coot' Grant**, Wilson formed a long-established and very popular black vaudeville team, who were on stage from 1912 to the mid-30s. They recorded extensively, using a number of pseudonyms, and featuring comic dialogues of marital strife in the manner of **Butterbeans And Susie**. Both also recorded solo, and Wilson duetted with Harry McDaniels (as Pigmeat Pete & Catjuice Charlie). As important as their performing was their songwriting, which produced over 400 numbers, including 'Gimme A Pigfoot', and the other three songs recorded at **Bessie Smith**'s last session. They reappeared briefly in the late 40s, recording and writing for **Mezz Mezzrow**'s King Jazz label and playing a few concerts, but had retired by the decade's end.

● ALBUMS: including *Great Blues Singers Vol. 1* (1970)★★, *Leola B. Wilson & 'Kid' Wesley Wilson* (Document 1989)★★★.

Wilson, Al

b. 19 June 1939, Meridian, Mississippi, USA. Wilson was a former member of the Jewels, and also the Rollers, a San Bernardino-based quartet who scored a hit in 1961 with 'The Continental Walk'. He was later signed as a solo act to Soul City, a short-lived label owned by singer **Johnny Rivers**. 'Do What You Gotta Do' and 'The Snake' reached the R&B chart in 1968, but it was not until the mid-70s that Al achieved a more consistent success. 'Show And Tell' (1973) was a US number 1 single while 'I've Got A Feeling (We'll Be Seeing Each Other Again)' reached number 3 in the R&B lists. Wilson's later releases were less fortunate and his last chart appearance was in 1979 with 'Count The Days'.

● ALBUMS: *Searching For The Dolphins* (1968)★★, *Weighing In* (1973)★★★, *Show And Tell* (Rocky Road 1973)★★★★, *La La Peace Song* (Rocky Road 1974)★★★, *I've Got A Feeling* (Playboy 1976)★★★, *Count The Days* (1979)★★.

Wilson, Brian

b. 20 June 1942, Hawthorne, California, USA. Brian, the spiritual leader of America's most famous group the **Beach Boys** has received as much press and publicity for his health and mental problems over the years as has his magnificent contribution as songwriter, producer, arranger and vocalist of that group. It was suggested as early as 1965 that he was a 'musical genius' and that he should go solo. He did release a solo single 'Caroline No' in 1966, but it has since been absorbed into the Beach Boys canon. For many years internal ructions

have kept Wilson and his self-appointed doctor/guru/friend Eugene Landy at loggerheads with the rest of the group. Ironically Brian was the last Wilson brother to release a solo album. *Brian Wilson* was released in 1988 to excellent reviews with Wilson bravely appearing for the major publicity that ensued. By commercial standards it was a flop, even with the high-tech production handled by Russ Titelman, **Jeff Lynne**, Lenny Waronker and Andy Paley. The suite 'Rio Grande' had strong echoes of his *Smile* period. Wilson was forced to sever his links with Landy after the rest of the Beach Boys had taken him to court. He successfully contested the ownership of his back catalogue which had been sold by his father Murray Wilson. Immediately after this Mike Love issued a writ claiming he had written 79 songs with Wilson. **Sire Records** rejected Wilson's second album *Sweet Insanity* as being 'pathetic'. In 1993 he was again working with **Van Dyke Parks** together with Andy Paley on further new songs, and, following an out of court financial settlement with Mike Love, he began writing songs with his cousin after a creative break of many many years.

The television documentary *I Just Wasn't Made For These Times* was the first in-depth interview with Wilson, and the public were at last able to make up their own mind as to his state of health. Although he was clearly enjoying singing and writing songs, there were doubts as to their quality. The accompanying **Don Was**-produced album failed to ignite, and so it was immediately on to the next project in the 'we are going to convince you that Brian Wilson is not a spent force programme'. The Van Dyke Parks project *Orange Crate Art* was more cohesive and was a co-project in the true sense. The album could best be described as interesting, there were flashes of brilliance in songs such as 'San Francisco' and the title track. Reviews were positive but any chart success proved elusive. Further good news about his health continued throughout the early 90s. Wilson had moved out of California and was living with his 2nd wife in Chicago togehter with their two adopted children. He worked long and hard on *Imagination*, and although the sales were modest, he did receive an immense amount of positive reviews and goodwill.

● ALBUMS: *Brian Wilson* (Sire 1988)★★★★, *I Just Wasn't Made For These Times* (MCA 1995)★★, with Van Dyke Parks *Orange Crate Art* (Warners 1995)★★, *Imagination* (Giant 1998)★★★.

● VIDEOS: *I Just Wasn't Made For These Times* (WEA Video 1995).

● FURTHER READING: *Wouldn't It be Nice*, Brian Wilson. *The Beach Boys And The California Myth*, David Leaf. *Heroes And Villains, The True Story Of The Beach Boys*, Steven Gaines.

Wilson, Carl

b. 21 December 1946, Hawthorne, California, USA, d. 6 February 1998. Wilson's membership of America's most famous pop group the **Beach Boys** had for over 30 years been one of their more stabilizing influences

throughout this turbulent time. His pitch-perfect, sweet voice featured lead vocal on dozens of their classic recordings, including 'Feel Flows', 'I Can Hear Music', 'Full Sail', 'Good Vibrations' and arguably his finest performance, 'God Only Knows'. During one of the Beach Boys' occasional hiatuses in 1981 (due to fragmentation), Wilson toured with his own band to promote his excellent debut solo album. Although the record sold poorly, it contained a number of melancholic ballads that highlighted his voice, notably 'Hurry Love' and 'Seems So Long Ago'. The stand-out track, however, was the beautiful 'Heaven' which became a regular number in the Beach Boys' repertoire, and was generally dedicated to the late **Dennis Wilson**. The album was co-written by Myrna Smith, who was the wife of Carl's manager Jerry Schilling. A lesser follow-up, *Youngblood*, featured more up-tempo numbers but failed to chart. Afterwards, Wilson concentrated on performances with his main band. He started litigation against his brother Brian after some comments made in the latter's autobiography. He developed brain and lung cancer in 1996 and died from complications arising from the disease in February 1998. He was survived by his second wife Gina (daughter of Dean Martin) and his two grown up children Justyn and Jonah. His greatest legacy is his pitch perfect, sweet voice on 'God Only Knows'.
● ALBUMS: *Carl Wilson* (Caribou 1981)★★★★, *Youngblood* (Caribou 1983)★★.

Wilson, Cassandra

b. 4 December 1955, Jackson, Mississippi, USA. Wilson started piano and guitar lessons at the age of nine. In 1975 she began singing professionally, primarily folk and blues, working in various R&B and Top 20 cover version bands. She emerged as a jazz singer while studying with drummer Alvin Fielder and singing with the Black Arts Music Society in her hometown. In 1981 she moved to New Orleans and studied with saxophonist Earl Turbinton. In 1982 she relocated to New York at the suggestion of trumpeter **Woody Shaw** and began working with **David Holland** and **Abbey Lincoln**. In 1985 she guested on **Steve Coleman**'s *Motherland Pulse* and was asked by the JMT label to record her own albums. Her debut was *Point Of View*, which featured Coleman and guitarist **Jean-Paul Bourelly**. New York's finest wanted to work with her. She sang with New Air, **Henry Threadgill**'s trio, and he returned the compliment by helping with arrangements on her second, more powerful album, *Days Aweigh*. Her mix of smoky, knowing vocals and expansive, lush music that travelled between psychedelia and swing was transfixing. The more conservative American audience was won over by her record of standards, *Blue Skies* (1988), which was named jazz album of the year by *Billboard* magazine. The follow-up, the innovative sci-fi epic *Jumpworld* (1990), showed that Cassandra Wilson was not to be easily categorised: it included raps and funk as well as jazz and blues. This stylistic diversity was maintained

on 1991's *She Who Weeps*. In the meantime, Wilson has continued to record on Steve Coleman's albums and has also made guest appearances with other musicians associated with Coleman's M-Base organisation, such as **Greg Osby** and Robin Eubanks. Her latest recordings on **Blue Note Records** have exposed her to a much wider market. *New Moon Daughter* (a number 1 album in the USA jazz chart) featured songs by the **Monkees**, **U2**, **Hank Williams**, **Son House** and **Neil Young**.
● ALBUMS: *Point Of View* (JMT 1986)★★★, *Days Aweigh* (JMT 1987)★★★, *Blue Skies* (JMT 1988)★★★★, *Jumpworld* (JMT 1990)★★★, *She Who Weeps* (JMT 1991)★★★, *Live* (JMT 1991), *Dance To The Drums Again* (DIW 1992)★★★, *After The Beginning Again* (JMT 1993)★★★, *Blue Light 'Til Dawn* (Blue Note 1993)★★★★, *New Moon Daughter* (Blue Note 1996)★★★★, with Jacky Terrasson *Rendezvous* (Blue Note 1997)★★★.

Wilson, Delroy

b. 1948, Kingston, Jamaica, West Indies, d. 6 March 1995, Kingston, Jamaica, West Indies. Like **Dennis Brown** and **Freddie McGregor**, Delroy Wilson was barely out of short trousers when he recorded his debut single for **Coxsone Dodd**'s **Studio One** label. His first hit, 'Joe Liges' (1963), was written by **Lee Perry**, who at the time was working as a talent-spotter, songwriter and singer for Dodd; the track was a lyrical attack on former Dodd employee and now rival, **Prince Buster** ('One hand wash the other, but you don't remember your brother, Joe Liges, Joe Liges, stop criticise'), set to a rollicking early **ska** rhythm. The record was so popular that his follow-up, 'Spirit In The Sky', another Perry-penned barb aimed at Buster, was actually credited to Joe Liges when it was released in the UK on the Bluebeat and Black Swan labels. Delroy went on to cut numerous records in the same vein for Dodd, including 'One Two Three', 'I Shall Not Remove', a duet with **Slim Smith** entitled 'Look Who Is Back Again', and the anti-Buster 'Prince Pharoah', notable for being the only occasion on which Dodd himself is heard on record, admonishing Buster in a coded, spoken outburst.
Wilson's voice broke just in time for the emergence of **rocksteady** in 1966, and his version of the **Tams**' 'Dancing Mood' of that year, one of the first rocksteady records, became a monstrous hit, alerting music fans to a new soul-styled crooner to match **Alton Ellis**. Throughout the rest of the decade, Wilson, still recording mainly for Studio One, increased his popularity with titles such as 'Riding For A Fall', another Tams cover version, 'Once Upon A Time', 'Run Run', 'Won't You Come Home', 'Never Conquer', 'True Believer', 'One One', 'I'm Not A King', 'Rain From The Skies' and 'Feel Good All Over', as well as covering the **Temptations**' 'Get Ready'. Leaving Studio One in 1969, Wilson sojourned briefly at **Bunny Lee**'s camp, which resulted in a popular reading of the **Isley Brothers**' 'This Old Heart Of Mine' (1969), before moving to **Sonia Pottinger**'s Tip Top Records, where he cut the excellent 'It Hurts' and a version of the **Elgins**' 'Put

Yourself In My Place' (both 1969). He teamed up once more with Bunny Lee and enjoyed a huge Jamaican hit with the anthemic 'Better Must Come' (1971), which was so popular that it was adopted as a theme song by Michael Manley's PNP to increase their vote among 'sufferers', during that year's election campaign. In 1972 his success continued with 'Cool Operator', again for Lee, and throughout the next few years he maintained his position as one of reggae's best-loved singers, with songs such as 'Mash Up Illiteracy' and 'Pretty Girl' for **Joe Gibbs**, 'Love' for **Gussie Clarke**, 'Rascal Man' for **Winston 'Niney' Holness**, a cover version of the **Four Tops**' 'Ask The Lonely' for **Harry J.**, 'It's A Shame' (a version of the **Detroit Spinners** song for **Joseph 'Joe Joe' Hookim**), 'Have Some Mercy' for A. Folder, and 'Keep On Running' for Prince Tony. In 1976 his career took a further step forward when he recorded a hugely popular version of **Bob Marley**'s 'I'm Still Waiting' for **Lloyd Charmers** LTD label, later followed by the well-received *Sarge*, still regarded by most aficionados as his best set. The misnomered *Greatest Hits* was also issued by Prince Tony during this period. Further recordings towards the end of the decade, including 'All In This Thing Together', 'Halfway Up The Stairs' and 'Come In Heaven' for Gussie Clarke, did well, but Wilson's career floundered somewhat during the early part of the 80s, apart from a few sporadic sides, including the popular 'Let's Get Married' for London's **Fashion Records**. The **digital** age, however, provided a revival of fortunes with the massive 'Don't Put The Blame On Me'/'Stop Acting Strange' for **King Jammy** in 1987, and 'Ease Up', a cut of the famous 'Rumours' rhythm for Bunny Lee, as well as albums such as *Looking For Love* for Phil Pratt and *Which Way Is Up*, produced by **Errol 'Flabba' Holt** for Blue Mountain, since which time he has once again drifted into semi-retirement. Despite being one of the best singers Jamaica has ever produced, Wilson was rarely able to consolidate the success that came his way; nevertheless, he remained a much-loved and respected, but sorely underused and, outside of reggae circles, underrated performer.

● ALBUMS: *I Shall Not Remove* (Studio One c.1966)★★★★, *Best Of Delroy Wilson* aka *Original 12* (c.1969)★★★, *Good All Over* (1969)★★★, *Songs For I* (1974)★★★, *Sarge* (1976)★★★★, *Looking For Love* (1986)★★★★, *Which Way Is Up* (Blue Mountain 1987)★★★★.
● COMPILATIONS: *Greatest Hits* (1976)★★★, *Collection* (Striker Lee 1985)★★★★, *Once Upon A Time - Best Of Delroy Wilson* (Trojan 1998)★★★★.

Wilson, Dennis

b. 4 December 1944, Hawthorne, California, USA, d. 28 December 1983. The former drummer with the **Beach Boys** started to develop as a notable songwriter during the late 60s when his elder brother, Brian, became less prolific. Dennis blossomed showing a hitherto unseen sensitivity which had always been clouded by his wild nature and legendary womanizing. On *Smiley Smile* he composed 'Little Bird' and the hymn-like 'Be Still' and although both songs were painfully short, the talent was unfolding. Dennis showed his class on *Sunflower* in 1970 and again in 1972 with *Carl And The Passions-So Tough*. On the former he delivered four songs but the jewel in the crown was 'Forever', one of the finest Beach Boys songs of all time. Dennis displayed lyrics as the true romantic of the group with simple yet effective lines such as 'If every word I said could make you laugh, I'd talk forever'. Wilson's 'Cuddle Up' from *So Tough* was originally criticized for its lush orchestral arrangement, but 20 years on, it stands up as a highly individual song.

Dennis continued writing similar songs although plagued by a growing drug habit. *Pacific Ocean Blue* in 1977 was a *tour de force* and must have left the other members of the band pleasantly aghast. This was a mature collection of songs, lyrically strong, melodic and expertly produced. Further rich textured orchestrations on tracks like 'Moonshine' and 'River Song' were breathtaking. The album was only a critical success and barely made the US Hot 100. Dennis, sadly became a tragic figure, his voice so badly wracked through drug and alcohol abuse ended as merely a painful croak. During a break from recording his unreleased *Bamboo* in 1983, Wilson drowned after diving from his yacht in the harbour at Marina Del Ray, California. As the only Beach Boy to have actually surfed, special dispensation was given by the USA President to the Wilson family to bury Dennis at sea.
● ALBUMS: *Pacific Ocean Blue* (Caribou 1977)★★★★.
● FURTHER READING: *Denny Remembered*, Edward Wincentsen.

Wilson, Dick

b. Richard Wilson, 11 November 1911, Mount Vernon, Illinois, USA, d. 24 November 1941. Born into a musical family, Wilson was raised in the north-western states where he was taught to play alto saxophone by **Joe Darensbourg**. He began playing professionally in 1929, having meantime switched to tenor saxophone. He played with various bands, including Darensbourg's, **Gene Coy**'s and Zack Whyte's. These engagements took him through into the mid-30s when he joined **Andy Kirk** and his **Clouds Of Joy**. Wilson quickly became the band's most impressive soloist, playing with technical assurance and advanced thinking. Although there is a strong swing era affiliation in his playing, it is also evident that he was reaching out to as yet unknown areas of music. Had Wilson not died when he did, there can be little doubt that he would have become a major influence upon a new generation of saxophonists, in the same way as his contemporary, **Lester Young**. Any one of his solos recorded with Kirk is an artistic gem, fully formed, note perfect, yet musically adventurous. Even so, there is a smooth, uncluttered aspect to his playing which makes it highly accessible to latter-day musicians.
● COMPILATIONS: *The Chronological Andy Kirk 1936-1937*,

1937-1938, 1938, 1939-1940, 1940-1942 (Classics 1936-42)★★★★.

Wilson, Edith

b. 6 September 1896, Louisville, Kentucky, USA, d. March 1981. Edith Wilson was a blues-singing stage star whose career credits include a long list of revues beginning with *Put And Take* in 1921. In the same year she made her first records in the company of Johnny Dunn And His Original Jazz Hounds. Never just a blues singer, she continued to work after the initial interest in the so-called classic blues had declined, appearing on stage and films, both as a singer and as an actress. She later appeared advertising cookies in the assumed role of 'Aunt Jemima'. She never really retired and took advantage of the increased interest in blues during the 60s to embark on a second career that saw her recording an album for the Delmark label in 1970 and performing at the **Newport Jazz Festival** in 1980. As a blues singer, what she lacked of the rawness and power associated with performers such as **Bessie Smith** and **Ma Rainey**, she made up for in urbanity and wit.

● COMPILATIONS: *Edith Wilson With Johnny Dunn's Jazz Hounds (1921-22)* (Fountain 1979)★★★, with Lena Wilson *Volume 2 1924-31* (Document 1996)★★★, with Johnny Dunn *Complete Works 1921-28, Volumes 1 & 2* (RST 1996)★★★.

Wilson, Garland

b. 13 June 1909, Martinsburg, West Virginia, USA, d. 31 May 1954. Wilson began playing piano as a child and, when he was 20, moved to New York City, where he enjoyed some success playing in Harlem clubs. His records were very well received and in 1932 he became accompanist to the popular entertainer Nina Mae McKinney, with whom he toured Europe. He stayed in Europe, playing long residencies in Paris and also appearing in London with **Jack Payne** and his band. With the outbreak of war he returned to the USA, finding work in clubs in New York and Los Angeles, but in 1951 he was back in Europe, travelling between London and Paris, where he later died in 1954.

● COMPILATIONS: *The Way I Feel (1932-51)* (Collectors Items 1986)★★★, *Piano Solos* (Neovox 1990)★★★.

Wilson, Gerald

b. 4 September 1918, Shelby, Mississippi, USA. After starting out on piano, Wilson switched to trumpet while at Manassa high school. He studied formally at Cass Tech, Detroit, before joining **Jimmie Lunceford** in 1939, where he had the unenviable job of replacing **Sy Oliver**. Like Oliver, Wilson's duties in the Lunceford band not only required him to play trumpet but also to write arrangements. He composed original material for the band, including 'Hi Spook' and 'Yard Dog Mazurka'. After leaving Lunceford in 1942 he settled in Los Angeles, served in the US Navy, where he played in the band directed by **Willie Smith** (and which included **Clark Terry**), and also played briefly in bands led by **Les Hite** and **Benny Carter**. He formed his first band in

1945, recording and touring with a measure of success. The band included trombonist-arranger **Melba Liston**, whom Wilson married. He folded the band in 1947 and resumed his studies, this time in composition. During the 50s he was active as an arranger, for **Dizzy Gillespie**, **Count Basie** and **Duke Ellington** among others, and also wrote for films and television. In 1961 he formed a new big band which recorded and played concerts and festivals, including Monterey in 1963 where the band included **Teddy Edwards**, **Joe Pass** and **Harold Land**. In 1969, he began teaching and also presented a radio series on jazz which lasted for six years. During this period he also worked extensively with singers, arranging for and accompanying **Ella Fitzgerald**, **Carmen McRae**, **Sarah Vaughan**, **Ray Charles** and others.

In 1972 he composed a classical piece, which was performed by the Los Angeles Philharmonic Orchestra under Zubin Mehta, and in later years continued to work in this field. In 1976 he directed the all-star festival band at Monterey in a programme of music that recalled the Lunceford band of the 30s and early 40s. In 1977 he continued his association with Monterey when he directed the Airmen Of Note, the US Air Force's jazz orchestra, in the premiere of his suite, 'The Happy Birthday Monterey Suite', commissioned for the festival. His orchestras have continued to present his own music, compositions and arrangements, and feature top class musicians, both veterans and newcomers, in well-rehearsed, effective performances. A sound, if little-known trumpet player in his earlier years, Wilson's contribution to jazz lies in the many fine bands he has led, in the example he has set by his undiminished enthusiasm and impeccably high standards of musicianship and, perhaps most important of all, in his distinctive writing. His son, Anthony Wilson, is an accomplished guitarist. The elder Wilson continues to record, as demonstrated by *State Street Sweet* at the age of 77.

● ALBUMS: *You Better Believe It!* (1961)★★★, *Moment Of Truth* (1962)★★, *Portraits* (1963)★★★, *On Stage* (1965)★★, *Feelin' Kinda Blue* (1965)★★★, *The Golden Sword* (Discovery 1966)★★★, *Everywhere* (1967)★★★, *Live And Swinging* (1967)★★, *California Soul* (1968)★★, *Eternal Equinox* (1969)★★★, *Lomelin* (Discovery 1981)★★★, *Groovin' High* (Hep Jazz 1981)★★★, *Jessica* (Trend 1982)★★★, *Calafia* (Trend 1984)★★, *Love You Madly* (Discovery 1988)★★★, *Jenna* (1989)★★★, *Moment Of Truth* (Pacific Jazz 1990)★★★, *Portraits* (Pacific Jazz 1992)★★★, *State Street Sweet* (MAMA Foundation 1995)★★★.

Wilson, Harding 'Hop'

b. 27 April 1921, Grapeland, Texas, USA, d. 27 August 1975, Houston, Texas, USA. Although his nickname is a corruption of 'Harp', reflecting his early prowess on the harmonica, it is as a slide guitarist that Wilson will be remembered. As well as playing conventional guitar, he played steel guitar placed horizontally on a stand, a style usually associated with C&W musicians. He played and sang with great skill and expression, encompassing a range of rhythms and moods from rocking R&B to tormented slow blues. Working in east Texas and Louisiana, he made singles for the Goldband company in 1958, and the small Ivory label (owned by drummer 'Ivory' Lee Semien) in 1960 and 1961. These, plus a handful of tracks unissued at the time but released on an album after his death, account for his entire recorded legacy; however, they are sufficient to establish Wilson as one of the most original blues artists of his time.

● ALBUMS: *Steel Guitar Flash* (Ace 1988)★★★, *Houston Ghetto Blues* (Bullseye 1995)★★★★.

Wilson, Irene
(see **Kitchings, Irene**)

Wilson, J. Frank, And The Cavaliers

This US group was formed in San Angelo, Texas by Frank Wilson (b. 11 December 1941, Lufkin, Texas, USA, d. 4 October 1991) and the Cavaliers (Phil Trunzo, Jerry Graham, Bobby Woods, and George Croyle). Their lone US chart single, 'Last Kiss' was one of the last of the particular genre known as 'death rock', in which teenagers sang about teenage lovers who meet horrifying deaths from accident, suicide, and fatal disease. (Others in this area included the **Shangri-Las**' 'Leader Of The Pack', **Mark Dinning**'s 'Teen Angel' and **Ray Peterson**'s 'Tell Laura I Love Her'.) 'Last Kiss' first charted in 1964, when it zoomed to number 2, and briefly charted again in 1973. The song was written and originally recorded without success by **Wayne Cochran** who, during the 60s had built up a career as a caucasian version of **James Brown**. Wilson got together with the Cavaliers while he was serving in the Air Force in San Angelo, Texas, and upon his discharge in 1962 the band stayed together to play in the area. The group followed 'Last Kiss' with 'Hey Little One', but it had none of the inspiration of the predecessor and charted at only number 85. Other singles followed including an album in 1971, but further success eluded the group.

● ALBUMS: *Last Kiss* (1964)★★★, *Doin' My Thing* (1971)★★.

Wilson, Jackie

b. 9 June 1934, Detroit, Michigan, USA, d. 21 January 1984, New Jersey, USA. When parental pressure thwarted his boxing ambitions, Wilson took to singing in small local clubs. He sang with the Thrillers (a predecessor group to the Royals) and recorded some solo tracks for **Dizzy Gillespie**'s Dee Gee label as Sonny Wilson, before replacing **Clyde McPhatter** in **Billy Ward And The Dominoes**. Wilson joined this notable group in 1953, but embarked on a solo career four years later with **Brunswick Records**. His first single for that label was the exuberant 'Reet Petite', a comparative failure in the USA where it crept to a lowly pop position and missed the R&B lists altogether. In the UK, however, it soared to number 6, thereby establishing

Wilson in the minds of the British pop-purchasing audience. 'Reet Petite' had been written by **Berry Gordy** and Tyran Carlo (Roquel 'Billy' Davis), who went on to compose several of Wilson's subsequent releases, including the hits 'Lonely Teardrops' (1958), 'That's Why (I Love You So)' (1959) and 'I'll Be Satisfied' (1959).

In 1960, Wilson enjoyed two R&B number 1 hits with 'Doggin' Around' and 'A Woman, A Lover, A Friend'. His musical direction then grew increasingly erratic, veering from mainstream to pseudo-opera. There were still obvious highlights such as 'Baby Workout' (1963), 'Squeeze Her Please Her' (1964), 'No Pity (In The Naked City)' (1965), but all too often his wonderfully fluid voice was wasted on cursory, quickly dated material. The artist's live appearances, however, remained both exciting and dramatic, capable of inspiring the ecstasy his sometimes facile recordings belied. Wilson's career was rejuvenated in 1966. Abandoning his New York recording base, he moved to Chicago, where he worked with producer Carl Davis. He offered a more consistent empathy and 'Whispers (Gettin' Louder)' (1966), '(Your Love Keeps Lifting Me) Higher And Higher' (1967) and the sublime 'I Get The Sweetest Feeling' (1968) stand among his finest recordings. However, it did not last; 'This Love Is Real (I Can Feel Those Vibrations)' (1970) proved to be Wilson's last Top 10 R&B entry, by which time his work was influenced by trends rather than setting them. In September 1975, while touring with the **Dick Clark** revue, Wilson suffered a near-fatal heart attack onstage at New Jersey's Latin Casino. He struck his head on falling and the resulting brain damage left him comatose. He remained hospitalized until his death on 21 January 1984.

Wilson's career remains a puzzle; he never did join Berry Gordy's **Motown** empire, despite their early collaboration and friendship. Instead, the singer's legacy was flawed - dazzling in places, disappointing in others. Immortalized in the **Van Morrison** song 'Jackie Wilson Said', which was also a UK Top 5 hit for **Dexys Midnight Runners** in 1982, his name has remained in the public's eye. Fate provided a final twist in 1987, when an imaginative video (which some claimed belittled the singer's memory), using plasticine animation, propelled 'Reet Petite' to number 1 in the UK charts. He was inducted into the **Rock And Roll Hall Of Fame** the same year.

● ALBUMS: *He's So Fine* (Brunswick 1958)★★★, *Lonely Teardrops* (Brunswick 1959)★★★★, *Doggin' Around* (Brunswick 1959)★★★, *So Much* (Brunswick 1960)★★★, *Night* (Brunswick 1960)★★★, *Jackie Wilson Sings The Blues* (Brunswick 1960)★★★★, *A Woman A Lover A Friend* (Brunswick 1961)★★★★, *Try A Little Tenderness* (Brunswick 1961)★★★, *You Ain't Heard Nothing Yet* (Brunswick 1961)★★★, *By Special Request* (Brunswick 1961)★★★, *Body And Soul* (Brunswick 1962)★★★, *Jackie Wilson At The Copa* (Brunswick 1962)★★★, *Jackie Wilson Sings The World's Greatest Melodies* (Brunswick 1962)★★★, *Baby Workout*

(Brunswick 1963)★★★, *Merry Christmas* (Brunswick 1963)★★, with Linda Hopkins *Shake A Hand* (Brunswick 1963)★★, *Somethin' Else* (Brunswick 1964)★★★, *Soul Time* (Brunswick 1965)★★★, *Spotlight On Jackie Wilson* (Brunswick 1965)★★★, *Soul Galore* (Brunswick 1966)★★★, *Whispers* (Brunswick 1967)★★★, *Higher And Higher* (Brunswick 1967)★★★, with Count Basie *Manufacturers Of Soul* (Brunswick 1968)★★★, with Basie *Too Much* (1968)★★★, *I Get The Sweetest Feeling* (Brunswick 1968)★★★★, *Do Your Thing* (Brunswick 1970)★★★, *This Love Is Real* (Brunswick 1970)★★★, *You Got Me Walking* (Brunswick 1971)★★, *Beautiful Day* (Brunswick 1973)★★, *Nowstalgia* (Brunswick 1974)★★, *Nobody But You* (Brunswick 1976)★★.

● COMPILATIONS: *My Golden Favourites* (Brunswick 1960)★★★, *My Golden Favourites - Volume 2* (Brunswick 1964)★★★, *Jackie Wilson's Greatest Hits* (Brunswick 1969)★★★, *It's All Part Of Love* (Brunswick 1969)★★★, *Jackie Wilson: S.R.O.* (1982)★★★, *Classic Jackie Wilson* (Skratch 1984)★★★, *Reet Petite* (Ace 1985)★★★★, *The Soul Years* (Kent 1985)★★★★, *The Soul Years Volume 2* (Kent 1986)★★★, *Higher And Higher* i (Kent 1986)★★★, *Through The Years* (Rhino 1987)★★★, *The Very Best Of Jackie Wilson* (Ace 1987)★★★, *Mr Excitement!* 3-CD box set (Rhino 1992)★★★★, *Higher And Higher* ii (1993)★★★, *The Dynamic Jackie Wilson* (1993)★★★★, *The Chicago Years Volume 1* (1993)★★★★, *Original Hits* (1993)★★★★, *The Jackie Wilson Hit Story Volume1* (1993)★★★★, *The Jackie Wilson Hit Story Volume 2* (1993)★★★, *The Very Best Of Jackie Wilson* (Rhino 1994)★★★★, *A Portrait Of Jackie Wilson* (Essential Gold/Pickwick 1995)★★★★, *Higher And Higher* (Rhino 1995)★★★★.

● FURTHER READING: *Lonely Teardrops: The Jackie Wilson Story*, Tony Douglas.
● FILMS: *Go Johnny Go* (1958).

Wilson, Jimmy

b. 1921, Louisiana, USA, d. 1965, Dallas, Texas, USA. Wilson was singing in California with a gospel quartet when his distinctive, bluesy lead was noticed by impresario **Bob Geddins**, who recorded Wilson as the blues singer with his band, Bob Geddins' Cavaliers, and in his own right, for his Cava Tone label, often in the company of legendary Bay Area guitarist **Lafayette Thomas**. Some of these tracks created enough of a stir for Aladdin Records to take an interest and purchase some of Wilson's masters from Geddins, and later during 1952, Wilson began recording for Aladdin and its small subsidiary 7-11. In 1953 Wilson again signed with Geddins to record for his new Big Town label, and the first release, 'Tin Pan Alley', although not a Wilson original, was a tremendous success and has since become synonymous with his name. Most of Wilson's mid-50s output was issued on Big Town, although occasional releases appeared on Irma and Elko (the latter under guitarist Jimmy Nolan's name), and four tracks were issued on the Chart label. Later recordings did not match up to the doomy Bay Area sound of his Geddins tracks, despite a couple of attempts at the 'Tin Pan Alley' sound and a good local seller, 'Please Accept My Love' on Goldband, which was covered successfully by **B.B. King**. Wilson died in 1965 of drink-related problems, virtually forgotten by the record-buying public.

● COMPILATIONS: *Trouble In My House* (Diving Duck 1985)★★, *Jimmy Wilson - San Francisco 1952-53* (1985)★★★.

Wilson, Jodie

b. Sydney, Australia. The daughter of a Scottish father and Australian mother, Wilson's family were all involved in music. Indeed her mother had her own Australian television series and had also appeared in several films. After leaving school Wilson came to the UK to further her ambitions to become a professional singer/songwriter. Her first regular employment came as the female lead opposite **Cliff Richard** in the West End musical, *Time*. She left the show, however, to concentrate on a recording career. Peter Reichhardt of **EMI Records**' publishing division was the first to spot her talent, seeing in her a similar mainstream appeal to that of **Celine Dion**. **Mercury Records** then offered her a recording contract and released her first single, 'Anything You Want', at the end of 1995. It reached number 42 in the UK charts. Written with American writer Arnie Roman, her second single was the haunting ballad 'Falling', released in March 1996. It was recorded in America with Ric Wake, previously a collaborator with Celine Dion, **Mariah Carey** and **Whitney Houston**.

Wilson, Juice

b. Robert Edward Wilson, 21 January 1904, St. Louis, Missouri, USA. Raised in Chicago, Wilson played drums in a boys' band, then took up the violin. He played in various bands in clubs in Chicago and also on pleasure boats. In the 20s he was mostly in the northeast, eventually playing in New York at the end of the decade. He visited Europe with **Noble Sissle**'s band and remained there for many years, playing with local bands and also with visiting fellow countrymen. He worked in Germany, Spain, Holland, France and North Africa, the latter region with a band led by 'Little Mike' McKendrick. He held residencies as a featured artist in Malta where he remained until the mid-50s. He continued to tour the Mediterranean region for a few more years before visiting Paris en route to the USA.

Wilson, Julie

b. Julia May Wilson, 21 October 1924, Omaha, Nebraska, USA. An actress and singer, Wilson is acknowledged as one of the greatest interpreters of standard popular songs in the world of cabaret. Her sophisticated image, with a figure-hugging gown, and a gardenia tucked into her swept-back gleaming black hair, is a reminder of a bygone era. She started young, being voted 'Miss Nebraska' when she was only 17. A year later, she joined the chorus of a touring edition of the *Earl Carroll's Vanities* which was passing through

Omaha, and ended up in New York. From there, she moved to a Miami nightclub, doing a solo act five shows a night. It was in Miami that she believes she learnt how to control an audience with the occasional aggressive 'drop-dead bitchy' remark. Next stop was Los Angeles where she won a contest on **Mickey Rooney**'s radio show. The prize was a two-week engagement at Hollywood's top nightclub, the Mocambo. Soon afterwards she was offered the part of Lois Lane in the touring version of the musical *Kiss Me, Kate,* and in 1951 recreated the role at the London Coliseum. She stayed in London for nearly four years, appearing in various shows, including *Bet Your Life* (1952), and undergoing voice training at RADA. Back in the USA, during the remainder of the 50s and throughout most of the 60s, Wilson took over roles on Broadway in *The Pajama Game* and *Kismet,* played in various regional productions, returned to London for *Bells Are Ringing,* and did some television work, including the soap opera *The Secret Storm.* In the 1969/70 Broadway season she appeared in two flop musicals, and subsequently played several cabaret engagements at New York's Brothers and Sisters club, as well as continuing to tour. In the mid-70s she went into semi-retirement in order to look after her ailing parents in Omaha. She returned to the New York cabaret scene with an evening of **Cole Porter** songs at Michael's Pub in 1984. Since then, she has attracted excellent reviews in two otherwise unsuccessful New York musicals, *Legs Diamond* (1988) and *Hannah ... 1939* (1990), recorded several superb albums, as well as, in critic Clive Barnes' words, 'putting over a torch song with the sultry heat of a flame thrower' in cabaret. There was great rejoicing at nightspots around the world, including London's Pizza On The Park, when in 1993, along with her long-time accompanist William Roy, she celebrated her 50 years in showbusiness.

● ALBUMS: *Love* (Dolphin 1956)★★★, *This Could Be The Night* film soundtrack (MGM 1957)★★, *My Old Flame* (Vik 1957)★★★, *Julie Wilson At The St. Regis* (Vik 1957)★★★, *Meet Julie Wilson* (Cameo 1960)★★★, with Kay Stevens, Connie Russell, Cara Williams *Playgirls* (Warners 1964)★★★, *Jimmy* Broadway Cast (RCA Victor 1969)★★, *Julie Wilson At Brothers And Sisters* (Arden 1974)★★★, *Bet Your Life* London Cast reissue (Blue Pear c.80s)★★★, *Sings The Kurt Weill Songbook* (DRG 1987)★★★★, *Sings The Stephen Sondheim Songbook* (DRG 1987)★★★★, *Legs Diamond* Broadway Cast (RCA Victor 1988)★★★, *Hannah...1939* off-Broadway Cast (1990)★★★, *Sings The Cole Porter Songbook* (DRG 1989)★★★★, *Sings The Harold Arlen Songbook* (DRG 1990)★★★★, *Live From The Russian Tea Room* (Cabaret Records 1993)★★★, and Ben Bagley recordings.

● FILMS: *The Strange One* (1957), *This Could Be The Night* (1957).

Wilson, Kim

b. 6 January 1951, Detroit, Michigan, USA. Kim Wilson is a member of the blues band the **Fabulous Thunderbirds**. *Tigerman*, his first solo album, predom-

inantly consisted of cover versions, performed by various combinations of ex- and current Thunderbirds, including Duke Robillard, Preston Hubbard, Fran Christina, Gene Taylor and Rusty Zinn, and also Derek O'Brien, Calvin Jones and George Rains. For much of the time, Wilson forsook his harmonica and chose to interpret songs by **Johnny 'Guitar' Watson**, **T-Bone Walker** and **Bobby Bland**. *That's Life* was a similarly disparate collection, containing tracks left over from the original sessions and newer recordings, including soul songs, 'Time Is On My Side' and 'I've Been Searchin''. During this time, the Thunderbirds remained without a recording contract, leaving a question mark over Wilson's future as a solo artist or a bandleader. Admirably equipped for either eventuality, the challenge for Wilson to reclaim old ground remained to be met.

● ALBUMS: *Tigerman* (Antone's 1993)★★★, *That's Life* (Antone's 1994)★★★.

Wilson, Mari

b. Mari MacMillan Ramsey Wilson, 29 September 1957, London, England. In the mid-80s, Mari Wilson single-handedly led a revival of the world of 50s/early 60s English kitsch. Sporting a bee-hive hairdo, wearing a pencil skirt and fake mink stole, her publicity photos depicted a world of long-lost suburban curtain and furniture styles, tupperware, garish colours (often pink) and graphic designs from the period. The songs were treated in the same way, only affectionately and with genuine feeling. The whole image was the idea of Tot Taylor who, composing under the name of Teddy Johns and gifted with the ability to write pastiche songs from almost any era of popular music, also ran the Compact Organisation label. The label's sense of hype excelled itself as they immediately released a box-set of Compact Organisation artists, all of which, with the exception of Mari, failed to attract the public's attention. (Although 'model agent' Virna Lindt was a music press favourite.) Mari was quickly adopted by press, television and radio as a curiosity, all aiding her early 1982 singles 'Beat The Beat' and 'Baby It's True' to have a minor effect on the chart. 'Just What I Always Wanted' a Top 10 hit, fully encapsulated the Wilson style. However, it was the following year's cover of the Julie London torch-song number, 'Cry Me A River' which, despite only reaching number 27, most people have come to associate with Mari. The song also generated a revival of interest in London's recordings, resulting in many long-lost (and forgotten) albums being re-released. After touring the world with her backing vocal group, the Wilsations - which included **Julia Fordham** - the return home saw a slowing-down in activity. Although for the most part Mari was out of the limelight, she provided the vocals to the soundtrack to the Ruth Ellis bio-pic *Dance With A Stranger*. In 1985, she started playing small clubs with her jazz quartet performing standards, as well as writing her own material which led to her appearance with **Stan Getz** at a

London's Royal Festival Hall. Although still affectionately remembered for her beehive, she has been able to put that period behind her and is now taken more seriously as a jazz/pop singer and is able to fill **Ronnie Scott**'s club for a season.

●ALBUMS: *Show People* (Compact 1983)★★★★, *Dance With A Stranger* film soundtrack (Compact 1987)★★, *The Rhythm Romance* (Dino 1991)★★★.

Wilson, Mary

b. 4 March 1944, Greenville, Mississippi, USA. Raised by her aunt and uncle in Detroit, Wilson began singing in her local church choir as a teenager. There she met **Florence Ballard**, with whom she formed an R&B vocal group called the **Primettes**, and subsequently the **Supremes**. Mary remained a backing vocalist with the group from their inception in 1960 until 1977, becoming the senior member after the departure of **Diana Ross** in 1969, and taking occasional lead vocals from 1974 onwards. At that time, she re-negotiated the Supremes' recording contract, so that she owned 50 per cent of the group's name, though **Motown Records** maintained a veto over its use. After the Supremes disbanded in 1977, Wilson filed a legal suit against Motown which was settled out-of-court. She then put together a fresh line-up of the group for a UK tour in 1978, before beginning a solo recording career in 1979. After the Hal Davis-produced *Mary Wilson* proved a commercial failure, Motown rejected her 1980 demos, and she was left without a recording contract. She continued to tour throughout the 80s as 'Mary Wilson of the Supremes', appearing in the 1983 film *Tiger Town* and contributing to the soundtrack album. In 1986, she published a controversial autobiography, in which she attacked both Diana Ross and Motown boss, **Berry Gordy**. In 1989 she starred in the stage production of *The Beehive* in Toronto and in 1990 published the second volume of her memoirs.

● ALBUMS: *Mary Wilson* (1979)★★.

● FURTHER READING: *Dreamgirl: My Life As A Supreme*. Mary Wilson. *Supreme Faith: Someday We'll Be Together*, Mary Wilson and Patricia Romanowski.

Wilson, Meri

b. Japan. Meri Wilson was behind the 1977 US Top 20/UK Top 10 single 'Telephone Man', released on GRT/Pye Records. She was raised in Marietta, Georgia and began singing and playing piano and flute in her childhood. After attending college in Indiana, Wilson turned professional and worked as a jingle singer in the Dallas, Texas area. The innuendo-laden song 'Telephone Man' was her own composition and the recording was produced by **Owen** 'Boomer' **Castleman** and Jim Rutledge. Although Wilson recorded two subsequent singles and an album, she never again made the charts and her future endeavours remain a mystery.

● ALBUMS: *Telephone Man* aka *First Take* (1977)★★.

Wilson, Nancy

b. 20 February 1937, Chillicothe, Ohio, USA. Wilson began singing in clubs in and around Columbus, Ohio. She attracted attention among jazz musicians, made her first records in 1956, and in the late 50s toured with a band led by Rusty Bryant. At the end of the decade she sang with **George Shearing**, with whom she recorded, and **Cannonball Adderley**. It was at Adderley's insistence that she went to New York, where she was soon signed by Capitol. During the next few years Wilson made numerous albums, toured extensively, and built a substantial following among the popular audience but always retained a connection, if sometimes tenuously so, with jazz. In the early 80s she was again working more closely with jazz musicians, including **Hank Jones**, **Art Farmer**, **Benny Golson** and **Ramsey Lewis**. Later in the decade she was active around the world, performing at major concert venues and singing in a style that revealed that the long years in the more flamboyant atmosphere of popular music had given her a taste for slightly over-dramatizing songs. Nevertheless, when backed by top-flight musicians she could still deliver a rhythmic and entertaining performance.

● ALBUMS: *Like Love* (Capitol 1959)★★★★, *Something Wonderful* (Capitol 1960)★★★★, *Nancy Wilson With Billy May's Orchestra* (1959)★★★★, *Nancy Wilson* (1960)★★★★, with George Shearing *The Swingin's Mutual* (Capitol 1961)★★★★, *Nancy Wilson With Gerald Wilson's Orchestra* (1961)★★★, *Nancy Wilson/Cannonball Adderley* (Capitol 1962)★★★, *Hello Young Lovers* (Capitol 1962)★★★★, *Broadway - My Way* (Capitol 1963)★★★★, *Hollywood - My Way* (Capitol 1963)★★★, *Nancy Wilson With Jimmy Jones's Orchestra* (1963)★★★★, *Yesterday's Love Songs, Today's Blues* (Capitol 1963)★★★★, *Today, Tomorrow, Forever* (Capitol 1964)★★★, *Nancy Wilson With Kenny Dennis's Group* (Capitol 1964)★★★, *How Glad I Am* (Capitol 1964)★★★, *The Nancy Wilson Show!* (Capitol 1965)★★★★, *Today - My Way* (Capitol 1965)★★★, *Gentle Is My Love* (Capitol 1965)★★★, *From Broadway With Love* (Capitol 1966)★★★★, *A Touch Of Today* (Capitol 1966)★★★, *Tender Loving Care* (Capitol 1966)★★★, *Nancy Wilson With Oliver Nelson's Orchestra* (Capitol 1967)★★★★, *Nancy - Naturally* (Capitol 1967)★★★, *Just For Now* (1967)★★★, *Nancy Wilson With H. B. Barnum's Orchestra* (Capitol 1967)★★★, *Lush Life* aka *The Right To Love* (Capitol 1967)★★★★, *Welcome To My Love* (Capitol 1968)★★★★, *Easy* (Capitol 1968)★★★, *The Sound Of Nancy Wilson* (Capitol 1968)★★★★, *Nancy Wilson With The Hank Jones Quartet* (Capitol 1969)★★★, *Nancy* (Capitol 1969)★★★, *Son Of A Preacher Man* (Capitol 1969)★★★, *Hurt So Bad* (Capitol 1969)★★★, *Can't Take My Eyes Off You* (Capitol 1970)★★★★, *Now I'm A Woman* (Capitol 1970)★★★, *But Beautiful* (Capitol 1971)★★★, *Kaleidoscope* (Capitol 1971)★★★, *All In Love Is Fair* (Capitol 1974)★★★, *Come Get To This* (Capitol 1975)★★★, *This Mother's Daughters* (Capitol 1976)★★★, *I've Never Been To Me* (Capitol 1977)★★★, *What's New?* (1982)★★★, *Nancy Wilson In Performance At The Playboy Jazz Festival* (1982)★★★, with Ramsey Lewis *The Two Of Us* (Capitol 1984)★★★, *Godsend* (1984)★★★, *Keep You Satisfied*

(1985)★★★, *Forbidden Love* (1987)★★★, *If I Had My Way* (Columbia 1997)★★★★.
● COMPILATIONS: *The Best Of Nancy Wilson* (Capitol 1968)★★★★, *Nancy Wilson's Greatest Hits* (Capitol 1988)★★★★, *The Capitol Years* (Capitol 1992)★★★★.

Wilson, Phil

b. Phillip Sanford Wilson, 8 September 1941, St. Louis, Missouri, USA, d. 25 March 1992, New York City, New York, USA. A strong drummer who also studied violin, Wilson was a professional from the age of 16 and worked with soul singers such as **Solomon Burke** and **Jackie Wilson** as well as with trumpeter **Lester Bowie** and saxophonists **Julius Hemphill** and **David Sanborn**. In 1965 he went to Chicago, where he worked with **Otis Rush** and played alongside Sanborn again in the **Paul Butterfield** Blues Band, a mixed-race outfit which featured often frantic versions of blues classics. During this period he became a member of the **AACM** and joined **Roscoe Mitchell**'s group. He was one of the early, transient occupants of the drum stool in the **Art Ensemble Of Chicago** (AEC), which grew out of Mitchell's quartet, and Wilson was reunited with Bowie in both of these bands. In 1972 he moved to New York and worked with **Anthony Braxton**, another AACM alumnus and his association with colleagues from the AACM continued through the 70s and 80s. In 1978 he joined a quintet led by Lester Bowie and until the early 90s (when replaced by **Don Moye**, his successor in the AEC) he was the one non-brass-playing member of Bowie's Brass Fantasy, where he provided a solid but flexible backbone for the group's rich and witty mixture of doo-wop, blues, marching band pastiches and straight ahead jazz. He also played in the gospel group, From The Root To The Scource (with **Fontella Bass** and David Peaston) and led his own groups, including a quartet with **Frank Lowe** and Olu Dara that recorded at the Moers Festival. Wilson was killed in a shooting incident in 1992.
● ALBUMS: with Paul Butterfield *The Resurrection Of Pigboy Crabshaw* (1967)★★★, *Fruits* (1977)★★, with Lester Bowie *Duet* (1978)★★★.

Wilson, Roger

b. 22 July 1961, Leicester, England. Having studied graphic design at Wolverhampton Polytechnic, Wilson, playing guitar and fiddle, became a full-time musician in 1984. He played a wide variety of folk festivals and clubs, rapidly gaining a name for himself. Coupled with British Council tours of Pakistan and Malaysia, he has played extensively in Germany and Europe. Roger has also toured Scandinavia and the British Isles, with the Lost Nation Band, which includes himself, **Sara Grey** and **Brian Peters**. Wilson's debut release, on Harbourtown, *The Palm Of Your Hand*, was highly acclaimed in the folk music media. Since the initial impact of his appearance on the folk scene, he has continued with solo performing, session work, and working with his new band, Scam.

● ALBUMS: *The Palm Of Your Hand* (Harbourtown 1988)★★★, with various artists *Urban Folk Volume 1* (1991)★★, *Stark Naked* (Whiff 1994)★★★.

Wilson, Ross

b. 18 November 1947, Australia. Along with **Joe Camilleri**, Ross Wilson is one of the father figures of the Australian music industry, being involved with innovative bands, major recording artists and eventually creative production. Wilson began playing in 1965 in Melbourne's Pink Pinks who had a hit with a cover of 'Louie Louie'. Several more R&B-influenced bands followed before the experimental outfit of Sons Of The Vegetal Mother which evolved into the highly successful **Daddy Cool**.
In 1976 Wilson moved to Mighty Kong, whose album was not a big seller. The period with the reformed Daddy Cool followed and then he subsequently found more mainstream success with Mondo Rock from 1976 onwards. While Wilson had been the main instigator and writer of his previous bands, he allowed Eric McCusker to write more of the songs for Mondo Rock. Wilson also formed his own label Oz Records for which he produced his acts leading to the successful partnership with **Skyhooks**, with whom he had total success as a producer. A solo album was always expected from Wilson, but it was not until 1989 that he found the time to record. Despite two strong songs, which charted in Australia, the album was disappointing and did not do justice to his talent.
● ALBUMS: *Dark Side Of The Man* (1989)★★★.
● COMPILATIONS: *Retrospective* (1988)★★★.

Wilson, Sandy

b. Alexander Galbraith Wilson, 19 May 1924, Sale, Cheshire, England. A composer, lyricist and author, Wilson studied at Harrow and Oxford University, where he wrote and appeared in many undergraduate productions. He began to make his mark in the West End by contributing songs to revues such as *Slings And Arrows* (1948) and *Oranges And Lemons* (1949). In 1950 he provided the lyrics for a provincial production of Michael Pertwee's musical play *Caprice*, and then was the author and composer of *See You Later* (1951) and *See You Again* (1952). His big break came in 1953 when he was asked to write the book, music and lyrics for ***The Boy Friend***, a light-hearted spoof of the musical comedies of the 20s. The delightful score included 'I Could Be Happy With You', 'A Room In Bloomsbury', 'Won't You Charleston With Me?', 'It's Never Too Late To Fall In Love', 'Fancy Forgetting', and the lively title song. After starting its life as an hour-long entertainment at the tiny Player's Theatre, in London, *The Boy Friend* moved first to the Embassy Theatre, where it was expanded, before finally transferring to Wyndhams's Theatre in the West End on 14 January 1954. It ran for over five years, and **Julie Andrews** made her New York stage debut in the Broadway production, which lasted for over a year. The show has subsequently been produced in many countries throughout the world, and enjoyed revivals in New York (1958) and London (1967 and 1993). The 1971 film version was directed by Ken Russell, and starred Twiggy, Christopher Gable, Moyra Fraser and **Tommy Tune**. As well as *The Boy Friend*, Sandy Wilson has been the composer and/or author and lyricist of some of the most civilized and enjoyable shows (British or otherwise) ever to play the West End. They included *The Buccaneer* (1955), *Valmouth* (1958), *Pieces Of Eight* (1959), *Call It Love* (1960), *Divorce Me, Darling!* (1965), *As Dorothy Parker Once Said* (1966), *Sandy Wilson Thanks The Ladies* (in which he also appeared, 1971), *His Monkey Wife* (1971), *The Clapham Wonder* (1978) and *Aladdin* (1979).

● FURTHER READING: all by Sandy Wilson *This Is Sylvia. The Boy Friend. I Could Be Happy: His Autobiography. Ivor* (a biography of Ivor Novello). *The Roaring Twenties.*

Wilson, Shadow

b. Rossiere Wilson, 25 September 1919, New York City, New York, USA, d. 11 July 1959. Early in his career, Wilson played drums with bands in the eastern states, in particular around Philadelphia. In 1939 he began an impressive swing through many of the important big bands of the period, including those led by **Lucky Millinder**, **Benny Carter**, **Lionel Hampton**, **Earl 'Fatha' Hines**, **Billy Eckstine**, **County Basie** and, in the late 40s, **Woody Herman**. In the 50s he played mostly in small groups, working comfortably with swing era stars and rising bop names: **Illinois Jacquet**, **Erroll Garner**, **Ella Fitzgerald**, **Thelonious Monk**, **Sonny Stitt**, **Lee Konitz**, **John Coltrane**. Wilson's playing style was subtle and driving, always supportive and with unfailing good taste.

●ALBUMS: with Count Basie *The Master's Touch* (Savoy 1944-49)★★★★, with Tadd Dameron *Fontainebleau* (Prestige 1956)★★★★, with Phil Woods, Gene Quill *Phil And Quill* (RCA 1956)★★★, *Thelonious Monk With John Coltrane* (Jazzland 1957)★★★.

Wilson, Smokey

b. Robert Lee Wilson, 11 July 1936, Greenville, Mississippi, USA. Wilson was eight when his father bought him his first guitar. His teenage years were spent developing his singing and playing skills. In 1961 he became a member of Junior Green And His Soul Searchers Band, which, after some years, he left to join **Roosevelt 'Booba' Barnes**, with whom he played for four years. In 1970, he moved to Los Angeles, hoping that his down-home style would be popular. He played in a number of clubs and became part-owner of the Casino Club, where he worked on a regular basis. In 1972, he sold his interest in the club and bought the Pioneer Club in south central Los Angeles. Artists such as **Percy Mayfield**, **George Smith**, **Lowell Fulson** and **Big Mama Thornton** played alongside Wilson. His first two albums featured an uncredited **Rod Piazza** on harmonica alongside a flashy rock guitarist, and inappropriate accompaniment marred the 1982 Murray

Brothers outing. He fared better four years later, when he was accompanied by harmonica player **William Clarke**'s band. *Smoke N' Fire* had guest appearances by Larry Davis and **Jimmy McCracklin**, effectively flattering Wilson's modest talent.

● ALBUMS: *Blowin' Smoke* (Big Town 1977)★★, *Smokey Wilson Sings The Blues* (Big Town 1978)★★★, *88th Street Blues* (Murray Bros 1982)★★, *Smokey Wilson & The William Clarke Band* (Black Magic 1990)★★★, *Smoke N' Fire* (Bullseye Blues 1993)★★, *88th Street Blues* (Blind Pig 1995)★★, *The Real Deal* (Bullseye Blues 1995)★★, *The Man From Mars* (Bullseye 1997)★★.

● COMPILATIONS: *Hard Times - L.A. Blues Anthology* (Black Magic 1991)★★★.

Wilson, Teddy

b. 24 November 1912, Austin, Texas, USA, d. 31 July 1986, New Britain, Connecticut, USA. Born into a middle-class family, Wilson grew up in Tuskegee where his parents moved to take up teaching posts at the university. He studied violin and piano at Tuskegee and later extended his studies at college in Alabama. In 1929, by now concentrating on piano, he became a professional musician in Detroit. He played in bands led by Speed Webb and others in the mid-west until he settled in Chicago, where he worked with Erskine Tate, Eddie Mallory, **Louis Armstrong** and **Jimmie Noone**. In the early 30s he played with **Art Tatum**, holding his own in duets, a feat of considerable distinction. In 1933 he was heard by **John Hammond**, who encouraged him to move to New York to play in **Benny Carter**'s band, and he also played with **Willie Bryant**. During this period in his career Wilson made a succession of outstanding records, with Carter in the **Chocolate Dandies**, leading small bands for which he hired the best available sidemen, and accompanying **Billie Holiday** on sessions which produced numerous masterpieces of jazz. Back in Chicago he guested with **Benny Goodman**, made records with Goodman and **Gene Krupa** and, in April 1936, became a member of the Goodman entourage, where he was featured as a member of the Benny Goodman Trio.

He remained with Goodman until 1939, usually playing as a member of the trio and later the quartet, before leaving to form his own big band. Wilson set high standards of musicianship, which militated against the band's commercial success, and it survived for barely a year. He then formed a sextet, for which he adopted similarly high standards, but fortunately this group attained a measure of success with long residencies and some excellent recordings. After a brief return visit to Goodman, Wilson worked in the studios, taught, toured and recorded over the next dozen years. By the 60s he had become a deserved elder statesman of jazz, a role which he maintained throughout the rest of his life, touring internationally as either a single or in small groups such as the Gentlemen Of Swing, in which he was joined by **Harry Edison** and Benny Carter. Although the playing style Wilson adopted early in his career owed much to the influence of **Earl 'Fatha' Hines**, by the mid-30s he was a highly distinctive performer in his own right. A naturally restrained musician, Wilson's fleet playing and the elegant poise of his solos (the latter a facet which was reflected in his personal demeanour), combined to make him an influential figure in the development of jazz piano. His influence is most directly noticeable in the work of **Nat 'King' Cole**. His accompaniments to many of Billie Holiday's classic performances were an important factor in the singer's success. The quality of the setting he provided, especially on some of the earlier sessions when Holiday's talent was still unpolished, are object lessons in their deceptive simplicity. The excellence of the arrangements, which aid the instrumental soloists as much as the singer, display his prowess, while his seemingly effortless obbligato and solo contributions add to the quality of these timeless recordings. His performances with the Goodman trio and quartet are scarcely less important, providing a brilliantly intuitive counterpoint to the leader's playing. A noted stickler for quality, Goodman never failed to praise Wilson in a manner that contrasted strikingly with his often dismissive attitude towards other important musicians. Wilson's big band was another musical landmark, although the band's failure to attain commercial success was something which still clearly rankled with its leader four decades after it had folded. The sextet of the early 40s, which included at times artists such as **Benny Morton**, **Jimmy Hamilton**, **'Big' Sid Catlett**, **Bill Coleman**, **Emmett Berry**, **Slam Stewart** and **Edmond Hall**, was yet another demonstration of his subtle and understated musicianship. Among important recording dates in later years were sessions with **Lester Young** and **Roy Eldridge** in 1956, with Carter in Japan in 1980, and several outstanding solo albums. Although a shy and retiring man, Wilson had no illusions about his musical stature. Late in his life, when an interviewer asked who was his favourite pianist, he answered, with only a hint of a disarming grin, 'I am.'

● ALBUMS: *The Didactic Mr Wilson* (1953)★★★, *Intimate Listening* (1954)★★★, *The Creative Mr Wilson* (1955)★★★★, *I Got Rhythm* (1956)★★★, *The Teddy Wilson Trio* i (1956)★★★★, with Lester Young *Pres And Teddy* (1956)★★★★, *The Impeccable Mr Wilson* (1957)★★★, *These Tunes Remind Me Of You* (1957)★★★, *The Teddy Wilson Trio At Newport* (1957)★★★, *The Touch Of Teddy Wilson* (1957)★★★, *Mr Wilson And Mr Gershwin* (1959)★★, *On Tour With Teddy Wilson* (1959)★★, *The Teddy Wilson Trio* ii (1959)★★★, *The Teddy Wilson Trio* iii (1959)★★★, *Stompin' At The Savoy* (1967)★★★, *Air Mail Special* (1968)★★★, *The Teddy Wilson Trio In Europe* (1968)★★, *The Noble Art Of Teddy Wilson* (1968)★★★★, *Swedish Jazz My Way* (1970)★★★, *Elegant Piano* (1970)★★★, *Teddy Wilson-Eiji Kitamura* i (1970)★★★, *Teddy Wilson In Tokyo* (1971)★★★, *Teddy Wilson-Eiji Kitamura* ii (1971)★★★, *With Billie In Mind* (1972)★★, *Runnin' Wild* (1973)★★★, *Teddy Wilson-Eiji Kitamura* iii (1973)★★★, *Piano Solos* (1974)★★, *Concert In Argentina* (1974)★★, *Striding After Fats* (1974)★★★,

Teddy Wilson And His All Stars (1976)★★★, *Three Little Words* (1976)★★★, *Teddy's Choice* (1976)★★★, *The Teddy Wilson Trio In Milan* (1976)★★★, *Teddy Wilson Revamps Rodgers And Hart* (1977)★★, *Cole Porter Classics* (1977)★★★★, *Lionel Hampton Presents Teddy Wilson* (1977)★★★, *Teddy Wilson Revisits The Goodman Years* (1980)★★★, with Benny Carter *Gentlemen Of Swing* (1980)★★★, *Swingin' The Forties With The Great Eight* (1983)★★★, *Traces* (1983)★★★.

● COMPILATIONS: *The Teddy Wilson Big Band (1939-40)* (1974)★★★★, one side only *I Love A Piano* 1952 recording (1979)★★, *Too Hot For Words (1935)* (1986)★★★★, with Edmond Hall *Two Of A Kind (1944)* (1987)★★★, *Teddy Wilson Collection - 20 Golden Greats* (1987)★★★, *Teddy Wilson With Billie Holiday (1935-37)* (1988)★★★★, *America Dances Broadcasts (1939)* (1988)★★★, with Benny Goodman *The Complete Small Combinations Vol. 1/2 (1935-37)* (1989)★★★★, *Fine And Dandy (30s)* (1991)★★★, *Complete All Star And V-Disc Sessions* (Victorious 1991)★★★★, *How High The Moon* (1992)★★★, *Complete Piano Solos* (1993)★★★★.

● FURTHER READING: *The Genius Of Teddy Wilson*, No author listed.

Wilson, U.P.

b. Huary Wilson, 4 September 1935, Shreveport, Louisiana, USA. Wilson learned to play on his grandmother's guitar, and after moving to Dallas, Texas, in the early 50s, he became acquainted with local bluesmen Mercy Baby, Zuzu Bollin and **Frankie Lee Sims**. Around 1954 he recorded behind Bollin, though the tracks remain unissued. In the late 50s Wilson played on a regular basis with **Robert Ealey**. During the 70s and early 80s he only occasionally played professionally, due to family commitments.

In 1988 he recorded a session for Pee Wee Records, who released one single, 'Red Lightnin''. They later released a full album, *On My Way*. *Blues And Rhythm* magazine called Wilson's music 'superb Texas blues from one of the discoveries of the 80s'. *Blueprint* magazine disagreed when it reviewed his 1996 album for JSP: '(he) affects a curiously expressionless falsetto throughout, sounding like nothing so much as *Skip James* on Mogadon'.

● ALBUMS: *On My Way* (Pee Wee 1988)★★★★, *Wild Texas Guitar* (1989)★★★, *Attack Of The Atomic Guitar* (1992)★★★, *Texas Blues Party Volume 1: The Texas Tornado Live At Schooner's* (Wolf 1995)★★★, *Boogie Boy, The Texas Guitar Tornado Returns* (JSP 1995)★★★, *This Is U.P. Wilson* (JSP 1996)★★★, *Whirlwind* (JSP 1997)★★★, *The Good The Bad And The Blues* (JSP 1998)★★★.

Wimple Winch

UK psychedelic pop band Wimple Winch comprised Lawrence Arendes (drums), Barrie Ashall (bass), Dimitrious Christopholus (vocals/guitar) and John Kelman (lead guitar). Formed in Liverpool, Merseyside, England, in the mid-60s, they were originally known as the Four Just Men. The name change resulted in a shift of musical perspective. At this time they were signed to a management deal by Mike Carr, who was in the process of turning his coffee bar into a venue, The Sinking Ship in Stockport. On the basis of their performances there as house band the group secured a recording contract with **Fontana Records** which resulted in the release of their debut single, 'What's Been Done', in 1966. Two subsequent singles, 'Save My Soul' and 'Rumble On Mersey Square South' (backed by the esoteric 'Typical British Workmanship') sold well locally but not nationally, leading to a break from Fontana. On top of this the Sinking Ship burnt down, taking all their equipment with it. They did regroup and record an unreleased debut album in the summer of 1967, but found no takers when they offered it around the major record labels. By early 1968 they had disbanded. Arendes adopted the new surname King and joined the jazz/progressive rock group Bronze, who later evolved into **Pacific Drift**. Christopholus made his name in a slightly different arena, appearing in several West End stage musicals such as *Jesus Christ Superstar*, *Hair* and *Joseph And The Amazing Technicolor Dreamcoat*. Despite their lack of success, Wimple Winch are still championed by many as purveyors of three of the finest singles of the entire psychedelic pop era, an opinion hardened by the fact that all six of their released recordings regularly crop up on compilations surveying the period.

● COMPILATIONS: *The Wimple Winch Story '63 - '68* (Bam-Caruso 1988)★★★.

Win

After the **Fire Engines** folded on New Year's Eve 1981, Davey Henderson formed Heartbeat with former Flower singer Hilary Morrison, releasing just one track, on a *New Musical Express* cassette. By mid-1984 he was working with former Dirty Reds and Fire Engines member Russel Burns (drums) once more, linking with Ian Stoddart from Everest The Hard Way to form Win in his native Edinburgh. Straight away they won Single Of The Week awards with their debut for **London Records**, 'You've Got The Power'. Live, they played advertising jingles between songs, and appropriately 'You've Got The Power' was used in a television advertising campaign by McEwans lager. With obvious irony, the band's lyrics discussed mass media communication, paranoia and conspiracy. After its release Win were augmented by keyboard player Will Perry (cousin of **Andy Stewart**), bass player Manny and guitarist/backing vocalist Simon Smeeton. As **Postcard Records** boss Alan Horne noted: 'Win are the most exciting thing I've come across since **Orange Juice** were starting out'. However, just like the Fire Engines before them, Win proved too subtle to procure a mainstream audience, splitting in 1990. The *New Musical Express* was one of many papers that mourned their passing: '(they) . . . must be both proud and guilty in the knowledge that they made some of the greatest pop never heard'. Henderson took the name **Nectarine No. 9** for an

album for Postcard, *See With Three Stars*, that included Smeeton in the line-up. Stoddart joined the ill-fated **Apples** before becoming a member of Captain Shifty. Manny joined **Jive Records** recording artists Yo Yo Honey, while Russell Burns recorded for **Creation Records** under the Pie Finger mantle. Willie Perry is believed to have moved to India via Ibiza.

● ALBUMS: *Uh! Tears Baby* (London 1987)★★★, *Freaky Trigger* (Virgin 1989)★★★.

Winans

Contemporary Christian music group the Winans are four brothers, Marvin, Carvin, Ronald and Michael Winans, from Detroit, Michigan, USA. The family has additionally produced two well-known solo/duo gospel performers, Bebe and CeCe Winans. After having sung in gospel choirs all their lives the brothers began their professional career in the 80s. Staying close to their gospel roots but always maintaining a distinctive, jazzy sound, their reputation saw them work and perform with leading artists including **Vanessa Bell Armstrong**, **Anita Baker** and **Michael McDonald**, the latter pair both appearing on their 1987 album, *Decision*. Their two QWest albums of the early 90s, *Return* and *All Out*, saw them attempt to convert their popularity into mainstream R&B success. Even this, however, was motivated by moral concerns: 'The whole purpose was to win over young people who might have been on the verge of going into a life of crime or going off track,' Ronald Winans told **Billboard** magazine in 1995. Drawn from *Return*, 'It's Time' peaked at number 5 on the US R&B charts in 1990 and was produced by **Teddy Riley**, who also rapped on the single. In consequence *Return* reached number 12 on the R&B album charts and was certified a gold record. However, *All Out* was less successful, and by 1995 and *Heart And Soul* the Winans had returned to their trademark gospel sound. As well as 11 other original songs it included a re-make of 'The Question Is', a popular stage favourite originally featured on their 1981 debut album, *Introducing The Winans*. The original version been produced by gospel legend **Andrae Crouch**, with his nephew, Keith Crouch, playing drums. The guests on *Heart And Soul* included R&B star **R. Kelly**, as well as previous collaborators Riley, McDonald and Baker.

● ALBUMS: *Introducing The Winans* (QWest 1981)★★★★, *Let My People Go* (QWest 1985)★★★, *Decision* (QWest 1987)★★, *Tomorrow* (Light 1988)★★★★, *Live At Carnegie Hall* (QWest 1989)★★, *Return* (QWest 1990)★★★, *All Out* (QWest 1993)★★★, *Heart And Soul* (QWest 1995)★★★. CeCe Winans *Alone In His Presence* (Sparrow 1995)★★★, BeBe Winans *Bebe Winans* (Atlantic 1997)★★★.

Winans, Mario

b. USA. One of the younger members of the extensively recorded **Winans** musical family, in the mid-90s, after over a decade of work in gospel music, Mario moved into contemporary R&B. He produced **R. Kelly**'s multi-platinum self-titled album of 1996, and followed this with his own effort, *Story Of My Heart*. He made his reasons clear: 'There's a gospel audience, but much more people buy R&B and pop than gospel, and for my songs to be heard, I knew it had to be done.' Apparently, the switch caused friction with his parents, Vicky and Marvin Winans, but they withdrew their objections on the condition that Winans' new R&B material did not contain anything 'offensive'. Winans began as a gospel producer at the age of 14, and has maintained his commitment to the church. As he told *Billboard* magazine in 1997, 'I know in my heart it's not bad to write a love song, because the best example of love is God.' *Story Of My Heart* was preceded by a single, 'Don't Know', which included a guest appearance from Mase, a rapper from **Sean 'Puffy' Combs'** Bad Boy Entertainment stable.

● ALBUMS: *Story Of My Heart* (Motown 1997)★★★.

Winbush, Angela

Beginning as half of the successful duo, René & Angela, Winbush has gone on to have a successful solo career in the 90s soul arena. *Angela Winbush*, recorded from November 1992 through April 1993, saw her gain full creative control with new label **Elektra Records**, and produced her best work. Premiered by the Chuck Booker-written 'Treat U Rite', this dance-orientated rhythmic track was not typical of the album's more traditional R&B concerns. A better example was her duet with husband Ronald Isley (**Isley Brothers**) on the Philly-styled 'Baby Hold On', complete with a Thom Bell string arrangement (it also included brother-in-law Ernie Isley on sitar). Winbush had already completed an album with the Isley Brothers, *Smooth Sailin'*, for **Warner Brothers** in 1987. Another track, 'Sensitive Heart', was co-written with her new family members, and Winbush also wrote material especially for the Isley Brothers, who shared her new label. However, the album's standout track was the ballad, 'I'm The Kind Of Woman'.

● ALBUMS: *Sharp* (Mercury 1987)★★★, *The Real Thing* (Mercury 1989)★★★, *Baby Hold On* (Mercury 1990)★★★, *Angela Winbush* (Elektra 1994)★★.

Winchester, Jesse

b. 17 May 1944, Shreveport, Louisiana, USA. After receiving his draft papers from the US Forces, Winchester moved to Canada where he settled. His self-titled debut album, produced by **Robbie Robertson**, was thematically reminiscent of the work of the **Band** with its evocation of life in the deep south of the USA. The moving, bittersweet memories described in 'Brand New Tennessee Waltz', plus its haunting melody line, persuaded a number of artistes to cover the song, including the **Everly Brothers**. Winchester's *Third Down, 110 To Go* was produced by **Todd Rundgren**, but in spite of its solid quality failed to sell. On *Learn To Love* (1974), he commented on the Vietnam War in 'Pharoah's Army' and was assisted by several members of the Amazing Rhythm Aces.

By 1976, Winchester was touring the USA, having received an amnesty from President Carter for his draft-dodging. He played low-key gigs abroad and continued to release albums, which veered slightly towards the burgeoning country rock market. His narrative love songs are effective and the quality of his writing is evinced by the number of important artists who have covered his songs, a list that includes **Elvis Costello**, **Tim Hardin** and **Joan Baez**. Stoney Plain Records began a CD reissue programme in 1995.

● ALBUMS: *Jesse Winchester* (Ampex 1970)★★★★, *Third Down, 110 To Go* (Bearsville 1972)★★★, *Learn To Love It* (Bearsville 1974)★★★, *Let The Rough Side Drag* (Bearsville 1976)★★★, *Nothin' But A Breeze* (Bearsville 1977)★★★, *A Touch On The Rainy Side* (Bearsville 1978)★★★, *Talk Memphis* (Bearsville 1981)★★★, *Humour Me* (Sugar Hill 1988)★★★.

● COMPILATIONS: *The Best Of Jesse Winchester* (See For Miles 1988)★★★★.

Windham Hill Records

New age record label Windham Hill Records was formed by husband and wife team Anne Robinson and **William Ackerman** in Menlo Park, California, USA, in 1976. Since that time the company has expanded to encompass one of the most important and commercially viable rosters in the new age/adult-orientated instrumental music genre. The label's best-selling artist is pianist **George Winston**, and a number of subsidiary labels have also been formed. These include Lost Lake Arts, High Street Records and Windham Hill Jazz. Among those to work with the label have been **John Gorka**, **Jim Brickman**, the **Modern Mandolin Quartet**, **Ray Obiedo**, **Ray Lynch**, the **Turtle Island String Quartet** and many others. The label also serves as distributor to George Winston's Dancing Cat label, and by the mid-90s had established satellite offices in Chicago, Atlanta, Beverly Hills and New York. Ackerman moved out of the day to day running and in 1995 Anne Robinson announced the sale of the company to BMG Entertainment North America. BMG already owned half the equity following a 50 per cent investment in May 1992, and had found the relationship to be mutually profitable. Other artists closely associated with the growth of Windham Hill have been **Mark Isham**, **Michael Hedges**, **Alex De Grassi**, **Shadowfax** and **Liz Story**.

Windhurst, Johnny

b. 5 November 1926, New York City, New York, USA, d. November 1981. After teaching himself to play trumpet, Windhurst first played in public, at Nick's in New York, while still in his early teens. Before he was out of his teenage years, he was playing professionally with **Sidney Bechet**, **Art Hodes** and **James P. Johnson**. In the late 40s he played in bands led by **Edmond Hall**, **Hilton 'Nappy' Lamare** and **Louis Armstrong**. He also led his own bands, but in these ventures chose to stay out of the main east coast centres. In the early 50s he worked with **Eddie Condon**, **Ruby Braff** and, later in the decade, with **Jack Teagarden**.

He also accompanied a number of singers who found his unassuming nature, as reflected in his discreet playing, an ideal accompaniment. During the 60s and 70s he played mostly in obscure, out-of-the-way corners of the USA, seemingly content to hide his considerable talent from the bigtime spotlight. Very much a musician's musician, highly regarded by all who heard him, Windhurst's chosen lifestyle might have robbed jazz of an important figure but, at least, he lived the life he wanted.

● ALBUMS: *The Imaginative Johnny Windhurst* (1956)★★★.

Winding, Kai

b. Kai Chresten Winding, 18 May 1922, Arhus, Denmark, d. 7 May 1983, Spain. Winding's family emigrated to the USA in 1934, and soon thereafter he began teaching himself to play trombone. In the late 30s and early 40s he was with a number of big bands including those of **Sonny Dunham** and **Alvino Rey**. After serving in the US Coast Guard during the war, he began frequenting New York clubs, including Minton's Playhouse, and eagerly assimilating bop. He played in **Benny Goodman**'s mid-40s bebop-inclined band, and then he joined **Stan Kenton** in 1946. Although he moved on the following year, his impact was substantial and he was now both a name to be reckoned with and popular with audiences. He next played with **Charlie Ventura**, **Charlie Parker** and **Miles Davis**, appearing on the *Birth Of The Cool* album. He also developed a penchant for working with other trombonists, starting with **J.J. Johnson**, with whom he formed a successful quintet in 1954. Later in the 50s he toured with his own bands, including a four-trombone and rhythm line-up, and in the 60s was musical director of the Playboy Club in New York. In the 70s he was leader, co-leader or sideman of various groups, including the Giants Of Jazz with **Dizzy Gillespie**, Giant Bones with **Curtis Fuller**, and the **Lionel Hampton** All-Star Big Band. One of the first trombone players to fully assimilate bop, Winding was an accomplished musician who could readily blend into most musical styles. His playing, in such diverse settings as Kenton's brassy powerhouse band and Davis's coolly restrained group, was always appropriate. His duets with Johnson were exquisitely formed and displayed his total command of the instrument. Towards the end of his life Winding played only when he chose to do so, spending time in semi-retirement in Spain where he died in 1983.

● ALBUMS: (NB: J.J. Johnson also indicated by 'J.J.' and 'Jay') *Jay And Kay: December 3, 1954* (1954)★★★★, *Jay And Kai At Birdland* (1954)★★★★, *Jay Jay Johnson, Kai Winding, Bennie Green* (1954)★★★, with Johnson, Frank Rosolino *Trombomania* (1955)★★★, *Jay And Kai* i (1955)★★★★, *Jay And Kai* ii (1955)★★★★, *Jay And Kai Trombone Octet* (1956)★★★, *The Kai Winding Septet* (1956)★★★, *Trombone Panorama* (1956)★★★, one side only - with the Dave Brubeck Quartet *Jay And Kai At Newport* (1956)★★★★, *Jay And Kai*

iii (1956)★★★, *The Axidentals With The Kai Winding Trombones* (1958)★★★, *The Swingin' States* (1959)★★★, *Dance To The City Beat* (1959)★★★★, *The Incredible Kai Winding Trombones* (1960)★★★, *Great Kai And J.J.* (1960)★★★, *Kai Winding And His Orchestra* i (1961)★★★, *Kai Winding And His Orchestra* ii (1962)★★★, *The Kai Winding Trombones* i (1963)★★★, with Kenny Burrell *More!!!* aka *Soul Surfin'* (1963)★★★, *January 31st And February 15th 1963* (1963)★★★, *The Kai Winding Quartet* (1963)★★★, *The Kai Winding Trombones* ii (1963)★★, *The Kai Winding Trombones* iii (1964)★★★, *The Kai Winding Trombones* iv (1964)★★★, *The Kai Winding Trombones* v (1965)★★★, *J.J. Johnson & Kai Winding* i (1968)★★★★, *J.J. Johnson & Kai Winding* ii (1968)★★★★, *Giants Of Jazz* (1971)★★★, *Kai Winding's Caravan* (1974)★★★, *Danish Blue* (1977)★★, *Showcase* (1977)★★★, *Lionel Hampton Presents Kai Winding* (1977)★★, *Duo Bones* (1978)★★★, *Giant Bones* (1979)★★★, *Trombone Summit* (1980)★★★, *Giant Bones At Nice* (1980)★★★, *Giant Bones 90* (Sonet 1980)★★★.

● COMPILATIONS: *Kai's Krazy Kats* (1945)★★★, *Kai Winding* (1989)★★★.

Windsong

This R&B vocal group, despite a 20 year plus history, remain condemned to obscurity by dint of their lack of recording opportunities. Henry Richard 'Dickie' Harmon (lead and tenor), Anthony Giusto (tenor), Jordan Montanaro (baritone) and Clinton 'Jaki' Davis (bass) formed the group as teenagers in Hackensack, New Jersey, USA. They soon found a regular source of employment at school hops and talent shows, originally operating under the title Bachelors. Although Harmon and Davis recorded with both the Connotations and Notations, the quartet itself never managed to find time to enter the studio (Harmon would also work with Strut on their solitary album for **Brunswick Records**). They changed name to Windsong in 1971 when they recruited local female singer Jackie Bland (rendering the Bachelors a suddenly inappropriate name). This formation appeared at a United in Group Harmony Association show shortly thereafter, and this finally led to a recording date in 1981 when Ronnie Italiano brought the group to Clifton Records. Their only release, an EP featuring 'Young Wings Can Fly', 'Lucky Old Sun', 'Imagination' and 'Canadian Sunset', emerged following the sessions. Windsong broke up shortly thereafter, with Harmon reappearing in the **Del-Vikings** and the **Autumns**.

Wing And A Prayer Fife And Drum Corps

This US studio ensemble was formed to capitalize on the disco craze of the late 70s. One of the aggregation's singles, a remake of the old standard 'Baby Face', reached number 14 in 1976 and became the Corps' only hit. The group of session musicians was assembled by Stephen Scheaffer and Harold Wheeler, who had launched their own Wing & Prayer record label. A crew of top vocalists (which included Linda November,

Helen Miles, Arlene Martell and Vivian Cherry) and musicians were called in to a New York studio and cut 'Baby Face' in addition to disco versions of the **Beatles'** 'Eleanor Rigby' and five other numbers for an album. Only 'Baby Face', written by Benny Davis and Harry Akst in 1926, charted, however, and after a second album the project was disbanded.
● ALBUMS: *Babyface* (1976)★★, *Babyface Strikes Back* (1977)★.

Winger
This melodic USA hard rock act was formed by experienced session musicians Kip Winger (bass/vocals) and Paul Taylor (keyboards/guitar) following their work together on **Alice Cooper**'s *Constrictor* tour. Enlisting lead guitarist Reb Beach and drummer Rod Morgenstein (ex-**Dixie Dregs**), the quartet chose the name Sahara, but were forced to change to Winger at the last moment - the original name still appeared on a corner of the debut sleeve. *Winger* proved to be an immediate success, producing US Top 30 singles in 'Seventeen', 'Madalaine' and 'Headed For A Heartbreak', while the vocalist's rugged good looks turned him into a major sex symbol. This rather worked against the band in press terms, and Winger were never really taken seriously by the UK rock press in particular, despite abilities which kept them in demand for musician-type magazines and a genuinely impressive debut. *In The Heart Of The Young* consolidated Winger's US success, producing another enormous hit in 'Miles Away', and the band were well-received on their debut European shows, but the heavy touring schedule proved too much for Taylor, who subsequently departed, later working with **Steve Perry**. The band adopted a heavier approach on the commendable *Pull* to compensate for the lack of keyboards, recruiting a second touring guitarist in John Roth, but were unable to swim against the grunge tide to emulate their earlier successes. After a lengthy US club tour, the band was put on ice while Winger pursued a solo career.
● ALBUMS: *Winger* (Atlantic 1988)★★★, *In The Heart Of The Young* (Atlantic 1990) ★★★★, *Pull* (Atlantic 1993)★★★. Solo: Kim Winger *Made By Hand* (Domo 1998)★★★.

Wingfield, Pete
b. 7 May 1948, Kiphook, Hampshire, England. Wingfield was a pianist who previously led Pete's Disciples and played sessions with Top Topham, **Graham Bond**, and **Memphis Slim**. He was also an acknowledged soul music expert who started the *Soul Beat* fanzine in the late 60s, and in the 70s would write for *Let It Rock* magazine. While at Sussex University he met fellow students Paul Butler (guitar), John Best (bass), and local teacher Chris Waters (drums) and formed the band **Jellybread**. With Wingfield doing most of the singing they made an album for their own Liphook label which they used as a demo and got themselves a deal with **Blue Horizon Records**. Although

they gained some plaudits from the media they were generally unsuccessful and Wingfield left in the summer of 1971. He next played in **Keef Hartley**'s band but that liaison ended when Hartley was invited to drum for **John Mayall**. Wingfield did further sessions for **Freddie King**, then joined **Colin Blunstone**'s band, and also backed **Van Morrison** for a spell. With Joe Jammer, he became the core of the session band the Olympic Runners, who were the brainchild of **Blue Horizon** boss **Mike Vernon**. The Runners also included DeLisle Harper (bass) and Glen LeFleur (drums) who acted as the rhythm section on Wingfield's own 1975 album *Breakfast Special* which included the hit single '18 With A Bullet'. The Olympic Runners had some success in their own right late in the 70s. Wingfield still does sessions and various studio projects, putting out the occasional single. However, he is now better known for his production credits (like **Dexys Midnight Runners'** *Searching For The Young Soul Rebels*, plus **Blue Rondo A La Turk** and the **Kane Gang**). He continues to be a regular member of the **Everly Brothers'** backing band for their UK tours.
● ALBUMS: *Breakfast Special* (Island 1975)★★★.

Wingless Angels
Wingless Angels were a group of five Nyahbingi Rastafarian drummers who were later joined by Sister Maureen. The five consisted of **Justin Hinds**, Winston 'Black Skull' Thomas, Bongo Neville, Bongo Locksey and Warren Williamson. Hinds is best remembered for the **ska** hit, 'Carry Go Bring Come', which he recorded with the Dominoes. He continued recording through to 1984, when he returned to his home-town of Steertown, Jamaica, opting for a rural lifestyle. Black Skull had previously worked with **Talking Heads** and **Bad Brains**, prior to savouring the tranquility of the Jamaican countryside. The remaining three members had only performed within the local community; Locksey was a drum-maker and fisherman, Williamson was admired for his skill in carving birds from coconut shells, while Neville was regarded as the keeper of the drums. The group played drum and chant sessions throughout the night, and this inspired local resident, **Keith Richards** of the **Rolling Stones**, to find out more about the band. Richards had acquired a villa high above Ocho Rios in 1972 when the band were recording *Goats Head Soup* in Kingston's Dynamic Recording Studio, and he befriended the group and eventually persuaded them to record in his villa. Sister Maureen had joined the band by this time, having been recruited after an impromptu performance with the group in a Steertown bar. At the beginning of the sessions, the assembly also featured the late Bongo Jackie, also known as Iron Lion. Richards' commitment to Jamaican music is widely acknowledged - he had previously recorded with **Peter Tosh** and **Max Romeo**. With the Angels, he contributed his subtle, complementary guitar licks over the African trinity of the funde, bass and kette drums. The rock 'n' roll hero known to the

band as 'bredda Keith' also recruited Frankie Gavin, a notable Irish violinist, re-emphasizing his belief in the legend of an Afro-Celtic empathy. The sessions resulted in the Angels' debut album, which featured 'Roll Jordan Roll', 'Keyman', 'Bright Soul', 'I Write My Name' and, inspired by Iron Lion's untimely demise, 'Enjoy Yourself'.

● ALBUMS: *Wingless Angels* (Island Jamaica 1997)★★★★.

Wings

Wings was **Paul McCartney**'s first post-Beatles music venture. They achieved eight Top 10 albums in both the UK and US (two and five respectively reaching number 1) and 'Mull Of Kintyre' is one of the biggest-selling singles of all time. Wings was formed during the summer of 1971, Paul and wife Linda being augmented by **Denny Laine** (b. Brian Hines, 29 October 1944; guitar/vocals, ex-**Moody Blues**), who, as Denny And The Diplomats, had supported the Beatles at the Plaza Ballroom, Dudley on 5 July 1963, and Denny Seiwell on drums. That year's *Wild Life*, intended as an 'uncomplicated' offering, was indifferently received and is regarded by McCartney himself as a disappointment. Guitarist Henry McCullough (ex-**Grease Band**) joined at the end of 1971, and the early part of 1972 was taken up by the famous 'surprise' college gigs around the UK. Notoriety was achieved at about the same time by the BBC's banning of 'Give Ireland Back To The Irish' (which none-the-less reached number 16 in the UK, and 21 in the US). Later that year 'Hi Hi Hi' (doubled with 'C-Moon') also offended the censors for its 'overt sexual references', though it penetrated the Top 10 on both sides of the Atlantic.

Early in 1973 Wings scored a double number 1 in the USA with *Red Rose Speedway* and 'My Love', taken from the album. (Both were credited to Paul McCartney and Wings.) Shortly before they were due to travel to Lagos to work on the next album, McCullough and Seiwell quit, officially over 'musical policy differences'. There is much to suggest, however, that McCartney's single-mindedness and overbearing behaviour were the real reasons, and that 'physical contact' may have taken place. Ironically, the result was Paul McCartney And Wings' most acclaimed album *Band On The Run*, with McCartney taking a multi-instrumental role. *Band On The Run* topped the album charts in the UK and USA, and kicked off 1974 by yielding two transatlantic Top 10 singles in 'Jet' and 'Band On The Run'. Towards the end of 1974, under the name the Country Hams they released 'Walking In The Park With Eloise', a song written 20 years earlier by Paul's father. At the end of the year Jimmy McCulloch (b. 4 June 1953, d. 27 September 1979, ex-**Thunderclap Newman**, **Stone The Crows**) was added on guitar and vocals, and Joe English on drums (the latter following a brief stint by ex-**East Of Eden** drummer Geoff Britton). Subsequent recordings were credited simply to Wings. The new line-up got off to a strong start with *Venus And Mars*, another number one in the UK and USA,

the single 'Listen To What The Man Said' also topping the US charts and reaching number 6 in the UK. Wings had become a major world act, and, riding on this success and 1975's *Wings At The Speed Of Sound* (UK number 2, US number 1) they embarked on a massive US tour. The resulting live triple *Wings Over America* was huge, becoming Wings' fifth consecutive US number 1 album and the biggest-selling triple of all time. Success did not bring stability, McCulloch and English both leaving during 1977. In a repeat of the *Band On The Run* phenomenon, the remaining Wings cut 'Mull Of Kintyre', which stayed at number 1 in the UK for 9 weeks. *London Town* broke Wings' run at the top of the US album charts and was poorly received. Laurence Juber and Steve Holly were added to the band, but 1979's *Back To The Egg* failed to impress anyone in particular, 'Getting Closer' not even hitting the UK singles chart. McCartney was busted for drug possession in Tokyo at the start of their tour of Japan. This was the last straw for the loyal and resilient Denny Laine, who quit in exasperation. By this time McCartney had also started recording under his own name again, and Wings were effectively no more. McCartney was knighted in January 1997.

● ALBUMS: *Wild Life* (Apple 1971)★★, as Paul McCartney And Wings *Red Rose Speedway* (Apple 1973)★★★, as Paul McCartney And Wings *Band On The Run* (Apple 1973)★★★★, *Venus And Mars* (Apple 1975)★★★★, *Wings At The Speed Of Sound* (Apple 1976)★★★, *Wings Over America* (Parlophone 1976)★★★, *London Town* (Parlophone 1978)★★★, *Back To The Egg* (Parlophone 1979)★★★.

● COMPILATIONS: *Wings' Greatest Hits* (Parlophone 1978)★★★.

● FURTHER READING: *The Facts About A Rock Group, Featuring Wings*, David Gelly.

Wink, Josh

b. *c.*1970, Philadelphia, USA. The techno artist Josh Wink combines a number of influences, from deep house to acid jazz and more experimental electronic music. His musical taste came from his family's record collection that included **Philip Glass**, **Stevie Wonder**, **Kraftwerk**, **Steely Dan** and **James Brown**. He began DJing in 1987 in underground Philadelphia clubs. In 1990 he released 'Tribal Confusion', on **Strictly Rhythm Records**, an acclaimed single produced with King Britt and credited to E-Culture that was later sampled by **Future Sound Of London**. The reaction enabled Britt and Wink to establish their own production company, WinKing Productions, in Philadelphia. Over the next five years they remixed over 20 tracks, including **Rozalla**'s 'Are You Ready To Fly?', Digital Orgasm's 'Running Out Of Time' and Book Of Love's 'Boy Pop'. In 1993 when King went on tour as the **Digable Planets**' DJ, so Wink continued as a solo artist, using a variety of names, including Wink, Winx, Winc, Winks and the Crusher. The records were released on a variety of dance labels such as Vinyl Solution, Strictly Rhythm, **Nervous**, **Limbo** and **R&S Records**. He also recorded 30-second musical compositions for television advertisements, as well as launching his own underground dance label, Ovum Recordings, in October 1994. In the mid-90s he was signed to **Virgin Records** in the USA and **Mercury Records** in Britain, releasing 'Higher State Of Consciousness' in 1995.

Winkies

This 'pub rock' attraction made its debut in the Lord Nelson in London in 1973. Touted as one of genre's most promising practitioners, it revolved around vocalist, guitarist Philip Rambow. Guy Humphries (guitar, vocals), Brian Turrington (bass, keyboards, vocals) and Michael Desmarias (drums) completed the line-up. The last-named pair were already respected session musicians. Both had appeared on **John Cale**'s *Fear*, while Turrington guested on three albums by **Brian Eno**, who in turn invited the Winkies to support him on his 1974 tour. The quartet's self-titled debut was produced by **Guy Stevens** (**Mott The Hoople**/the **Clash**), but it sadly failed to capture their in-concert fire. The Winkies disbanded in 1975 after which Rambow moved to New York. Upon his return to London he embraced punk/new wave in a solo career which engendered cult status.
● ALBUMS: *The Winkies* (Chrysalis 1975)★★.

Winley, Paul

USA-born Winley was a veteran R&B producer and songwriter, running the Paul Winley Jazzland Ballroom on Harlem's 125th Street, before setting up Winley Records in the same location. His musical interests began when his brother was a member of the Clovers in his native Washington, for whom Paul wrote songs. He went on to compose for **Ruth Brown** and **Joe Turner**. Together with **Dave 'Baby' Cortez** he formed a partnership recording doo wop groups like the Duponts, Paragons, Collegians and Jesters. His introduction to rap music came at the behest of his daughters, Tanya and Paulette, the former recorded 'Vicious Rap'. He became famed for a series of compilations entitled *Disco Brakes*, produced by DJ Jolly Roger, which won him his first admirers, combining as it did some of the most popular 'breaks' over which the park rappers would improvise routines. Popular cuts included Dennis Coffey's 'Scorpio' and New Birth's 'Gotta Get Knutt'. *Super Disco Brakes* would add standards like **James Brown**'s 'Funky Drummer' (the so-named pecussionist, Clyde Stubblefield, would later be immortalised on **Subsonic 2**'s 'Unsung Heroes Of Hip Hop') and **Incredible Bongo Band**'s 'Apache' (versions of which would appear on **Sugarhill** - the first by the **Sugarhill Gang** and the second by West Street Mob - who featured the Robinson's son, Joey Jnr.), as well as the Meters and Creative Source. Yet until the aforementioned Sugarhill started he never took the opportunity to record anything by the rappers who were buying this product. When 'Rapper's Delight' hit he finally realised its potential, releasing records by, among

others, his daughters, who rapped together on 'Rhymin' And Rappin'. Other outstanding releases included **Afrika Bambaataa**'s *Zulu Nation Throwdown Parts 1 And 2*. However, Bambaataa became hugely aggrieved at Winley's business practices, notably the release of one of his live sets as the 'Death Mix', which was of substandard quality and essentially a bootleg. Indeed, Winley would later be arrested for bootlegging activities and copyright infringement.

Winston, George

b. 1949, Michigan, USA. Following many years of listening to music, his early heroes being **Floyd Cramer**, the **Ventures** and **Booker T. And The MGs**, Winston took up the piano at the age of 18. He switched to jazz after being influenced by the 'stride' piano of **Fats Waller**. The mysterious and enigmatic Winston stopped playing in 1977 until the music of **Professor Longhair** inspired him to return. Between 1980 and 1982 he recorded a trilogy of albums which have subsequently sold millions of copies. The sparse and delicate piano music of *Autumn*, *Winter Into Spring* and *December* gave a new dimension to solo piano recording, engineered to such perfection that the instrument truly becomes part of the room the listener is in. Not one note is wasted and he plays as if each were his last. Winston was part of the original **Windham Hill Records** family of artists that pioneered the USA's west coast new-age music of the early 80s. Winston kept a low profile for almost a decade until his return with *Summer* in 1991 continuing the tradition of his best solo work. *Forest*, released in 1994 won a Grammy at the 1996 awards. His tribute to pianist **Vince Guaraldi** (composer of 'Cast Your Fate To The Wind') became a major success in 1996.
● ALBUMS: *Ballads And Blues* (Takoma 1972)★★, *Autumn* (Windham Hill 1980)★★★★, *Winter Into Spring* (Windham Hill 1982)★★★★, *December* (Windham Hill 1982)★★★★, with Meryl Streep *Velveteen Rabbit* (Windham Hill 1982)★, *Summer* (Windham Hill 1991)★★★, *Forest* (Windham Hill 1994)★★★, *Linus And Lucy: The Music Of Vince Guaraldi* (Dancing Cat/Windham Hill 1996)★★.
● COMPILATIONS: *All The Seasons Of . . .* (Windham Hill 1998)★★★.
● VIDEOS: *Seasons In Concert* (Dancing Cat Video 1997).

Winston, Jimmy

b. James Langwith, 20 April 1945, Stratford, London, England. A founder member of the **Small Faces**, organist/vocalist Winston embarked on a solo career on being fired from the band in 1965. Credited to Jimmy Winston And His Reflections, 'Sorry She's Mine' is an excellent version of a song that also appeared on the first Small Faces album. In 1967 Winston switched instruments to guitar and formed a new group, Winston's Fumbs. Tony Kaye (keyboards), Alex Paris (bass) and Ray Stock (drums) completed the line-up. Their lone single for **RCA Records** coupled the eccentric 'Real Crazy Apartment' with the psychedelic 'Snow

White'. Winston's Fumbs split up when Kaye joined **Yes**. Winston then took a role in the rock musical, *Hair*, and in 1976 released a third single, 'Sun In The Morning', for NEMS Records. He has since ceased recording.
● ALBUMS: *Mood Mosaics* (RPM 1996)★★★, *A Teenage Opera* (RPM 1996)★★★.

Winstone, Eric
b. 1 January 1915, London, England. d. 2 May 1974, Pagham, Sussex, England. A popular bandleader and composer from the 30s through to the 70s, Winston worked as a clerk at the Gas Light and Coke Company in Westminster, and played the piano in his spare time, before leaving to become a full time musician. After leading his first band at the Spanish Club in Cavendish Square, London in 1935, he learned to play the accordion, and eventually founded an accordion school. He became an accomplished arranger for the instrument, and formed his renowned Accordion Quintet and Swing Quartet. The latter outfit consisted of himself on accordion, with string bass, vibraphone, guitar and vocalist Julie Dawn.
During World War II he led the Eric Winstone Dance Orchestra and toured throughout Europe entertaining the troops. After the war his highly popular stage show played theatres and ballrooms, and was resident at Butlin's Holiday Camps in the summer for more than 20 years. Among the musicians associated with his various line-ups were Ralph Dollimore, Alan Moorhouse, Roy Marsh, Frank Deniz, Norman Payne, Bill Shakespeare, Ernie Shear, Ronnie Priest, **Jimmy Skidmore**, **Kenny Graham**, Pat Dodd, **Carl Barriteau**, Freddy Gardner, Harry Bence, and many more, along with vocalists Alan Kane, **Michael Holliday**, Elizabeth Batey and Marion Williams. For some years Winstone was the musical director for Southern Television, and he also ran an entertainment agency for a time. His best-remembered compositions include the atmospheric 'Stage Coach' (his signature tune), 'Oasis', 'Bottle Party', 'Mirage', 'Pony Express', and he also wrote several light pieces and some background music for films.
● ALBUMS: *Happy Beat For Happy Feet* (Top Rank 1961)★★★, *Eric Winstone And His Band* (President 1993)★★★.

Winstone, Norma
b. 23 September 1941, London, England. Although she studied formally as a pianist, Winstone decided to sing as a career and by her mid-teens was a professional vocalist. Although her earliest work was in the mainstream of jazz and jazz-influenced popular song, she was soon orientated towards the modern end of the jazz spectrum. In the 60s she became known for her musical associations with **Michael Garrick**, her singing developing into a frequently wordless instrumental style. In the late 60s, 70s and early 80s her reputation spread and she was a member of the trio, **Azimuth**, with **Kenny**

Wheeler and her husband **John Taylor**. She continued to work with leading contemporary musicians, including **Ralph Towner**, **Mike Westbrook** and **Eberhard Weber**.
In the late 80s and early 90s Winstone's repertoire underwent a slight shift and she was again performing many classic songs of earlier decades, often accompanied by **Tony Coe**. Although her new repertoire is rather more orthodox, Winstone brought to her material overtones of the free form work of her middle period, thus creating intriguing musical blends. In 1994 she was heard in the varied settings of London's Barbican, performing her own English lyrics to *The Songs of the Auvergne*, and as the singing voice for actress Geraldine James and in Alan Plater's BBC Television play, *Doggin' Around*. In this same year she also recorded *Well Kept Secret* with veteran pianist **Jimmy Rowles**.
In February 1995 she launched her band New Friends in a concert at **Ronnie Scott**'s. An exceptionally gifted and highly original singer, Winstone's chosen path has sometimes restricted her acceptance by the wider jazz audience, but those who have followed her work have been rewarded by the consistently high standards and indubitable integrity of her performances.
● ALBUMS: with Mike Westbrook *Love Songs* (1970)★★★★, with Michael Garrick *The Heart Is A Lotus* (1970)★★★, *Edge Of Time* (1972)★★★, *Somewhere Called Home* (ECM 1987)★★★, *In Concert* (Enodoc 1988)★★★, *Well Kept Secret* (Hot House 1994)★★★★.

Winstons
An R&B band from Washington, D.C., USA. Members were Richard Spencer (lead vocals/tenor saxophone), Ray Maritano (vocals/alto saxophone), Quincy Mattison (vocals/lead guitar), Phil Tolotta (second lead/organ), Sonny Peckrol (vocals/bass guitar), and G.C. Coleman (vocals/drums). The Winstons like many black self-contained bands during the soul years created records that sounded like a stand-up vocal group. Spencer, Mattison, and Coleman had all worked previously in **Otis Redding**'s band. The three later joined Peckrol, Tolotta, and Maritano to form a back-up band for the Chicago-based **Impressions**. They then decided to play on their own under the name Winstons. Their one hit, 'Color Him Father', written by Spencer, featured moving and heartfelt lyrics about being brought up by a wonderful father. The public was thoroughly taken by this enchanting song, making it a monster hit by buying a million copies, and going to number 1 R&B and number 7 pop in 1969. The Winstons, however, were a proverbial one-hit-wonder group. Their follow-up, 'Love Of The Common People', lacked the magic of their big hit, and only reached number 54 on the pop chart, a standing owing solely to the reflected glory of 'Color Him Father'.
● ALBUMS: *Color Him Father* (Metromedia 1969)★★★.

Winter Into Spring - George Winston

The second part of Winston's seasons series of albums opens by playing 10 piano notes in 17 seconds. This is a very spacious record that allows each track time to build. Like much of this genre's music its own lethargy allows you, in turn, to be creative. Authors with writer's block could do worse than to put on the beautiful 'January Stars' and dream. The quality of this and Winston's other 'seasons' albums is truly exceptional.

● Tracks: *January Stars; February Sea; Ocean Waves (O Mar); Reflection; Rain/Dance; Blossom Meadow; The Venice Dreamer; Introduction (Part One); Part Two.*

● First released 1984

● UK peak chart position: did not chart

● USA peak chart position: 127

Winter, Edgar

b. 28 December 1946, Beaumont, Texas, USA. Although at times overshadowed by his brother, **Johnny Winter**, Edgar has enjoyed an intermittently successful career. The siblings began performing together as teenagers, and were members of several itinerant groups performing in southern-state clubs and bars. Edgar later forsook music for college, before accepting an offer to play saxophone in a local jazz band. He rejoined his brother in 1969, but the following year Edgar released *Entrance*. He then formed an R&B revue, Edgar Winter's White Trash, whose live set *Roadwork* was an exciting testament to this talented ensemble. Winter then fronted a slimmer group - **Dan Hartman** (vocals), **Ronnie Montrose** (guitar) and Chuck Ruff (drums) - which appeared on the artist's only million-selling album, *They Only Come Out At Night*. This highly successful selection included the rousing instrumental 'Frankenstein', which became a hit single in its own right. Guitarist **Rick Derringer**, who had produced Winter's previous two albums, replaced Montrose for *Shock Treatment*, but this and subsequent releases failed to maintain the singer's commercial ascendancy. He rejoined his brother in 1976 for the *Together* album. Together with his brother Johnny, he sued DC Comics for depicting the brothers in a comic book as half-human, half-worm characters. The figures were illustrated by the creator of Jonah Hex; the Winter brothers were shown as 'Johnny And Edgar Autumn'.

● ALBUMS: *Entrance* (Epic 1970)★★, *Edgar Winter's White Trash* (Epic 1971)★★★, *Roadwork* (Epic 1972)★★★★, *They Only Come Out At Night* (Epic 1972)★★★★, *Shock Treatment* (Epic 1974)★★★, *Jasmine Nightdreams* (Blue Sky 1975)★★★, *Edgar Winter Group With Rick Derringer* (Blue Sky 1975)★★★, with Johnny Winter *Together* (Blue Sky 1976)★★★★, *Recycled* (Blue Sky 1977)★★★, *The Edgar Winter Album* (Blue Sky 1979)★★, *Standing On The Rock* (1981)★★, with Rick Derringer *Live In Japan* (Thunderbolt 1992)★★★, *Mission Earth* (1993)★★, *I'm Not A Kid Anymore* (L+R 1994)★★★.

● COMPILATIONS: *Rock Giants* (1982)★★★.

● VIDEOS: *Live In Japan* (MMG Video 1992).

Winter, Johnny

b. 23 February 1944, Leland, Mississippi, USA. Raised in Beaumont, Texas, with younger brother **Edgar Winter**, Johnny was a child prodigy prior to forging a career as a blues guitarist. He made his recording debut in 1960, fronting Johnny and the Jammers, and over the next eight years completed scores of masters, many of which remained unreleased until his success prompted their rediscovery. By 1968 the guitarist was leading Tommy Shannon (bass) and John Turner (drums) in a trio entitled Winter. The group recorded a single for the Austin-based Sonobeat label, consigning extra tracks from the same session to a demonstration disc. This was subsequently issued by United Artists as *The Progressive Blues Experiment*. An article in **Rolling Stone** magazine heaped effusive praise on the guitarist's talent and led to lucrative recording and management contracts. *Johnny Winter* ably demonstrated his exceptional dexterity, while *Second Winter*, which included rousing versions of 'Johnny B. Goode' and 'Highway 61 Revisited', suggested a new-found emphasis on rock. This direction was confirmed in 1970 when Winter was joined by the **McCoys**. Billed as Johnny Winter And - with guitarist **Rick Derringer** acting as a foil - the new line-up proclaimed itself with a self-titled studio collection and a fiery live set. These excellent releases brought Winter much-deserved commercial success. Chronic heroin addiction forced him into partial retirement and it was two years before he re-emerged with *Still Alive And Well*. Subsequent work was bedevilled by indecision until the artist returned to his roots with *Nothing But The Blues* and *White Hot And Blue*. At the same time Winter assisted **Muddy Waters** by producing and arranging a series of acclaimed albums that recaptured the spirit of the veteran blues artist's classic recordings. Winter's recent work has proved equally vibrant and three releases for Alligator, a Chicago-based independent label, included the rousing *Guitar Slinger*, which displayed all the passion apparent on those early, seminal recordings. His career may have failed to match initial, extravagant expectations, but his contribution to the blues should not be underestimated; he remains an exceptional talent. Together with his brother Edgar, he sued DC Comics for depicting the brothers in a comic book as half-human, half-worm characters. The figures were illustrated by the creator of Jonah Hex; the Winter brothers were shown as 'Johnny And Edgar Autumn'.

● ALBUMS: *Johnny Winter* (Columbia 1969)★★★★, *The Progressive Blues Experiment* (Sonobeat/Imperial 1969)★★, *Second Winter* (Columbia 1969)★★★, *Johnny Winter And* (Columbia 1970)★★★★, *Johnny Winter And Live* (Columbia 1971)★★★, *Still Alive And Well* (Columbia 1973)★★★, *Saints And Sinners* (Columbia 1974)★★★, *John Dawson Winter III* (Blue Sky 1974)★★★, *Captured Live!* (Blue Sky 1976)★★★, with Edgar Winter *Together* (Blue Sky 1976)★★★★, *Nothin' But The Blues* (Blue Sky 1977)★★★, *White Hot And Blue* (Blue Sky 1978)★★, *Raisin' Cain* (Blue Sky 1980)★★, *Raised On Rock* (Blue Sky 1981)★★, *Guitar Slinger* (Alligator 1984)★★★, *Serious Business* (Alligator

1985)★★★, *Third Degree* (Alligator 1986)★★★, *Winter Of '88* (MCA 1988)★★, *Let Me In* (Virgin/PointBlank 1991)★★★, *Jack Daniels Kind Of Day* (1992)★★★, *Hey, Where's Your Brother?* (Virgin/PointBlank 1992)★★★, with Jimmy Reed *Live At Liberty Hall, Houston* (1993)★★★, *Live In NYC '97* (PointBlank 1998)★★.
● COMPILATIONS: *The Johnny Winter Story* (GRT 1969)★★★, *First Winter* (1970)★★★, *Early Times* (1971)★★, *About Blues* (1972)★★, *Before The Storm* (Janus 1972)★★★, *Austin Texas* (United Artists 1972)★★★, *The Johnny Winter Story* (1980)★★★, *The Johnny Winter Collection* (Castle 1986)★★★★, *Birds Can't Row Boats* (1988)★★★, *Scorchin' Blues* (Epic/Legacy 1992)★★★, *A Rock N'Roll Collection* (Columbia/Legacy 1994)★★★.
● VIDEOS: *Johnny Winter Live* (Channel 5 1989).

Winter, Paul

b. 31 August 1939, Altoona, Pennsylvania, USA. While Winter was at Northwestern University, Chicago, he played the alto saxophone and the sextet he led won the Intercollegiate Jazz Festival of 1961. **John Hammond Jnr.** signed the group to **CBS Records**. The group toured Latin America in 1962 and became the first jazz group to play at the White House. The tour 'absolutely exploded our conception of what the world was' and the music Winter had heard led to the gradual change of the Sextet into the Consort. This was a band with a wholly new instrumentation - classical guitar, English horn, cello, ethnic percussion. The combination of jazz, classical and ethnic instruments has remained constant through numerous personnel changes over the following 20 years. It was difficult at the time for Winter to explain just what it was he was trying to produce and record companies found it hard to categorize. Winter now sees it as 'celebrating the convergence of both roots of American music - European and African'. He has had a series of talented musicians pass through the Consort - **Collin Walcott**, **Paul McCandless**, **David Darling** and **Ralph Towner** among them. *Icarus* was produced by **George Martin** and described by him as 'the finest album I have made'. Through the 70s Winter showed an increasing concern with conservation and became an active supporter of Greenpeace. He has recorded music accompanied by the sounds of whales off the Canadian coast and wolves in the mountains of California and Minnesota. He recorded Canyon Lullaby live in the Grand Canyon.
● ALBUMS: *Jazz Premiers: Washington* (1962)★★★, *Jazz Meets The Bossa Nova* (1962)★★★, *New Jazz On Campus* (1963)★★★★, *Something In The Wind* (1969)★★, *Icarus* (1971)★★, *Earthdance* (1977)★★★★, *Callings* (1980)★★★, *Missa Gaia/Earth Mass* (1982)★★, *Concert For The Earth* (1985)★★★, *Canyon* (1985)★★★, *Whales Alive* (1987)★★, *Earthbeat* (Living Music 1988)★★, *Canyon Lullaby* (Living Music 1997)★★★.

Winters, Tiny

b. Frederick Winters, 24 January 1909, London, England, d. 7 February 1996. A largely self-taught bass player, Winters played in many of the leading British dance bands of the 30s. He was briefly with **Roy Fox** and Bert **Ambrose** before spending five years with **Lew Stone**'s band, helping to provide the immaculate time-keeping for which this excellent orchestra was renowned. In the late 30s he was again with Ambrose and throughout the decade took time to make records, both under his own name and with **Ray Noble**, **Coleman Hawkins** and **Nat Gonella**. In the post-war years he played again for Stone and became a familiar figure in clubs and in theatrical pit bands. During the 60s he played often with **George Chisholm** and, after a short retirement in the mid-70s, was back on the scene again playing with musicians of his own age group and with those of younger generations, notably **John Barnes** and **Digby Fairweather**. Solid, dependable, in the best sense of that sometimes pejorative term, and highly regarded by his peers, he was a source of delight and information for many generations of UK musicians.
● COMPILATIONS: with Lew Stone *Coffee In The Morning (1933-34)* (1983)★★★.

Winther, Jens

b. 29 October 1960, Næstved, Denmark. Trumpeter and composer Winther was still in his teens when he enrolled in **John Tchicai**'s and Hugh Steinmetz's 'school' of free jazz and ethnic music, the Cadentia Nova Danica big band. In the 80s he joined **Erling Kroner**'s band which played a fusion of Argentinian tango and American jazz. Winther has made frequent visits to New York, USA where he has received encouragement from musicians including **Bob Brookmeyer** and has also sat in with local groups. Winther is thoroughly at home with all current styles of black American popular music and tends to eschew so-called Scandinavian 'coolness'. His lines are rhythmically exciting and avoids melodic clichés by employing unusual interval leaps. He is one among a handful of Danish jazz musicians who has recorded his own compositions with the Danish Radio Big Band. Winther's admiration for the sound of **Chet Baker** and **Miles Davis** is particularly apparent on the broodingly desolate music in parts of *The Planets*.
● ALBUMS: *Jens Winther Quintet* (Stunt 1986)★★★★, *Jens Winther And The Danish Radio Big Band* (Olufsen 1991)★★★, *Scorpio Dance* (Storyville 1991)★★★, *Nomads Of Tomorrow* (Olufsen 1993)★★★, *Looking Through* (Storyville 1993)★★, *The Planets* (Stunt 1995)★★.

Winwood, Muff

b. Mervyn Winwood, 15 June 1943, Birmingham, England. Winwood served the **Spencer Davis Group** as bass guitarist until 1967 when he joined **Island Records**' A&R department. In 1968, he supervised **Love Affair**'s version of 'Everlasting Love' before the quintet slipped through his fingers to **CBS** - and a UK number 1 with the same song. Nevertheless, having proved he had an ear for a hit, he became a freelance producer though still controller of Island's Basing Street studio. The **Sutherland Brothers (And Quiver)**, **Sparks**, **Mott The Hoople**, the **Bay City Rollers** and **Dire Straits** were among those on whom Winwood worked his magic before he joined CBS in 1978. Respected for shrewd judgement and steadiness of character, he shot up the executive ladder through his signings of **Shakin' Stevens** and **Adam And The Ants**, who both dominated the UK charts in the early 80s. Later Winwood hunches included **Bonnie Tyler**, **Altered Images**, **Paul Young**, **Bros** and **Terence Trent D'arby**.

Winwood, Steve

b. 12 May 1948, Birmingham, England. Steve and his older brother **Muff Winwood** were born into a family with parents who encouraged musical evenings at their home. Steve was playing guitar with Muff and their father in the Ron Atkinson Band at the age of eight, soon after he mastered drums and piano. The multi-talented Winwood first achieved 'star' status as a member of the pioneering 60s R&B band, the **Spencer Davis Group**. His strident voice and full sounding Hammond Organ emitted one of the mid-60's most distinctive pop sounds. The group had a successful run of major hits in the UK and USA until their musical horizons became too limited for the musically ambitious Steve. In 1965, Winwood had previously recorded the UK turntable soul hit 'Incense' under the name of the Anglos, written by Stevie Anglo. This gave fuel to rumours of his imminent departure. It was not until 1967 that he left and went on to form **Traffic**, a seminal band in the development of progressive popular music. The short-lived 'supergroup' **Blind Faith** briefly interrupted Traffic's flow. Throughout this time his talents were sought as a session musician and he became the unofficial in-house keyboard player for **Island Records**. During 1972 he was seriously ill with peritonitis and this contributed to the sporadic activity of Traffic. When Traffic slowly ground to a halt in 1974, Winwood seemed poised to start the solo career he had been threatening for so long. Instead he maintained a low profile and became a musicians' musician contributing keyboards and backing vocals to many fine albums including, **John Martyn**'s *One World*, **Sandy Denny**'s *Rendezvous*, **George Harrison**'s *Dark Horse* and **Toots And The Maytals** *Reggae Got Soul*. His session work reads like a who's who: **Jimi Hendrix, Joe Cocker, Leon Russell, Howlin' Wolf, Sutherland Brothers, Muddy Waters, Eric Clapton, Alvin Lee, Marianne Faithfull** and many others. In 1976 he performed with **Stomu Yamash'ta** and **Klaus Schulze**, resulting in *Go* and *Go 2*. He also appeared on stage with the Fania All Stars playing percussion and guitar. The eagerly anticipated self-titled solo album did not appear until 1977, and was respectfully, rather than enthusiastically, welcomed. It displayed a relaxed Winwood performing only six numbers and using first class musicians like Willy Weeks and Andy Newmark. Following its release, Winwood retreated back to his 50-acre Oxfordshire farm and shunned interviews. He became preoccupied with rural life, and took up clay pigeon shooting, dog training and horse riding. It appeared to outsiders that his musical activity had all but ceased.

During the last week of 1980 the majestic *Arc Of A Diver* was released to an unsuspecting public. With his former songwriting partner **Jim Capaldi** now living in Brazil, Winwood had been working on lyrics supplied to him by **Vivian Stanshall**, George Fleming and **Will Jennings**. The album was an unqualified and unexpected triumph, particularly in the USA where it went platinum. The stirring single 'While You See A Chance' saw him back in the charts. He followed with the hastily put together (by Winwood standards) *Talking Back To The Night*, which became another success. Winwood, however was not altogether happy with the record and seriously contemplated retiring to become a record producer. His brother, Muff, wisely dissuaded him. Winwood began to be seen more often, now looking groomed and well-preserved. Island Records were able to reap rewards by projecting him towards a younger market. His European tour in 1983 was a revelation, a super-fit Steve, looking 20 years younger, bounced on stage wearing a portable keyboard and ripped into **Junior Walker**'s 'Roadrunner'. It was as if the 17-year-old 'Stevie' from the Spencer Davis Group had returned. His entire catalogue was performed with energy and confidence. It was hard to believe this was the same man who for years had hidden shyly behind banks of amplifiers and keyboards with Traffic.

Two years later, while working in New York on his forthcoming album his life further improved when he met his future wife Eugenia, following a long and unhappy first marriage. His obvious elation overspilled into *Back In The High Life* (1986). Most of the tracks were co-written with Will Jennings and it became his most commercially successful record so far. The album spawned three hits including the superb disco/soul 'Higher Love', which reached number 1 in the USA. In 1987 his long association with **Chris Blackwell** and Island Records ended amidst press reports that his new contract with **Virgin Records** guaranteed him $13 million. The reclusive 'Midland maniac' had now become one of the hottest properties in the music business, while the world eagerly awaited the next album to see if the star was worth his transfer fee.

The single 'Roll With It' preceded the album of the same name. Both were enormous successes, being a double chart-topper in the USA. The album completed a full circle. Winwood was back singing his heart out with 60s inspired soul/pop. His co-writer once again was the talented Will Jennings, although older aficionados were delighted to see one track written with Jim Capaldi. In 1990, Winwood was involved in a music publishing dispute in which it was alleged that the melody of 'Roll With It' had been plagiarized from 'Roadrunner'. That year *Refugees Of The Heart* became his least successful album, although it contained another major US hit single with the Winwood/Capaldi composition 'One And Only Man'. Following the less than spectacular performance of that album rumours began to circulate that Traffic would be re-born and this was confirmed in early 1994. *Far From Home* sounded more like a Winwood solo album than any Traffic project, but those who love any conglomeration that has Winwood invloved were not disappointed. Later that year he participated on **Davey Spillane**'s album *A Place Among The Stones*, singing 'Forever Frozen and later that year sang the theme song 'Reach For The Light' from the animated movie *Balto*.

● ALBUMS: *Steve Winwood* (Island 1977)★★★★, *Arc Of A Diver* (Island 1980)★★★★, *Talking Back To The Night* (Island 1983)★★★, *Back In The High Life* (Island 1986)★★★★, *Roll With It* (Virgin 1988)★★★, *Refugees Of The Heart* (Virgin 1990)★★★, *Junction 7* (Virgin 1997)★★.

● COMPILATIONS: *Chronicles* (Island1987)★★★★, *The Finer Things* 4-CD box set (Island 1995)★★★★.

● FURTHER READING: *Back In The High Life: A Biography Of Steve Winwood*, Alan Clayson. *Keep On Running: The Steve Winwood Story*, Chris Welch.

Wipers

From Portland, Oregon, USA, the Wipers formed in 1977, and have been active almost continuously since. Greg Sage, formerly of 60s obscurists Beauregarde, is the only original member remaining, and the engine of all Wipers material. He had made his recording debut in the early 70s providing backing for an album by a celebrity (villain) pro-wrestler. His original partners were Dave Koupal (bass) and Sam Henry (drums). Brad Naish and Brad Visdson arrived in time for the band's best albums, *Youth Of America* and *Over The Edge*. By 1986's *Land Of The Lost*, Steve Plouf had taken over drums. Their legacy of scouring, audacious rock has recently become a subject of joy not only to hardcore archivists; a whole new generation has tuned in thanks to the public veneration of the band's achievements by **Nirvana**, all this despite an inconsistent line-up and no secure record label or pigeonhole. Sage, who has also recorded solo, is the mainstay of the band with his distinctive guitar style, a rhythmic assault with understated vocals whose dynamics were revisited by most of the late 80s/early 90s 'Seattle scene'. Sage continued to fend off offers from Nirvana for the Wipers to support them on tour, keeping a dignified distance from the vagaries of fashion.

● ALBUMS: *Is This Real?* (Park Avenue 1980)★★★, *Youth Of America* mini-album (Park Avenue 1981)★★★, *Over The Edge* (Brain Eater 1983)★★★★, *Wipers/Live 84* (Enigma 1985)★★★, *Land Of The Lost* (Enigma 1986)★★★, *Follow Blind* (Restless 1987)★★★, *The Circle* (Restless 1988)★★★, *Silver Sail* (T/K 1994)★★★, *The Herd* (T/K 1996)★★★. Solo: Greg Sage *Straight Ahead* (Enigma 1985)★★★.

● COMPILATIONS: *Best Of Wipers & Greg Sage* (Restless 1990)★★★.

Wire

This inventive UK group was formed in October 1976 by **Colin Newman** (b. 16 September 1954, Salisbury, Wiltshire, England; vocals, guitar), **Bruce Gilbert** (b. 18 May 1946, Watford, Hertfordshire, England; guitar), Graham Lewis (b. 22 February 1953, Grantham, Lincolnshire, England; bass, vocals) and Robert Gotobed (b. Mark Field, 1951, Leicester, England; drums) along with lead guitarist George Gill - the latter member had previously been a member of the Snakes, releasing a single on the Skydog label, while the rest of Wire all had art school backgrounds. Their early work was clearly influenced by punk and this incipient era was captured on a various artists live selection, *The Roxy, London, WC2*, their first recording as a four-piece following Gill's dismissal. Although not out of place among equally virulent company, the group was clearly more ambitious than many contemporaries. Wire were signed to the **Harvest Records** label in September 1977. Their impressive debut, *Pink Flag*, comprised 21 tracks, and ranged from the furious assault of 'Field Day For The Sundays' and 'Mr Suit' to the more brittle, almost melodic, interlude provided by 'Mannequin', which became the group's first single. Producer Mike Thorne, who acted as an unofficial fifth member, enhanced the set's sense of tension with a raw, stripped-to-basics sound. *Chairs Missing* offered elements found in its predecessor, but couched them in a new-found maturity. Gilbert's buzzsaw guitar became more measured, allowing space for Thorne's keyboards and synthesizers to provide an implicit anger. A spirit of adventure also marked *154* which contained several exceptional individual moments, including 'A Touching Display', a lengthy excursion into wall-of-sound feedback, and the haunting 'A Mutual Friend', scored for a delicate *cor anglais* passage and a striking contrast to the former's unfettered power. However, the album marked the end of Wire's Harvest contract and the divergent aims of the musicians became impossible to hold under one banner. The quartet was disbanded in the summer of 1980, leaving Newman free to pursue a solo career, while Gilbert and Lewis completed a myriad of projects under various identities including **Dome**, Duet Emmo and P'o, plus a number of solo works. Gotobed meanwhile concentrated on session work for Colin Newman, **Fad Gadget** and later organic farming. A posthumous release, *Document And Eyewitness*, chronicled Wire's final concert at London's Electric Ballroom in February 1980, but it was viewed as a disappointment in the wake of the preceding studio collections. It was not until 1985 that the group was resurrected and it was a further two years before they began recording again. *The Ideal Copy* revealed a continued desire to challenge, albeit in a less impulsive manner, and the set quickly topped the independent chart. *A Bell Is A Cup (Until It Is Struck)* maintained the new-found balance between art and commercial pop, including the impressive 'Kidney Bingos'. In 1990 the group abandoned the 'beat combo' concept adopted in 1985 and took on board the advantages and uses of computer and sequencer technology. The resulting *Manscape* showed that the group's sound had changed dramatically, but not with altogether satisfactory results. Following the album's release, Gotobed announced his departure. The remaining trio ironically changed their name to Wir, but not until *The Drill* had been released. It contained a collection of variations on 'Drill', a track that had appeared on the EP *Snakedrill* in 1987. The new group's first release, 'The First Letter', showed a harder edge than their more recent work, amusingly containing some reworked samples of *Pink Flag*. Wire subsequently became the subject of renewed interest in the mid-90s when indie darlings **Elastica** not only name-checked but also borrowed liberally from their back-catalogue.

● ALBUMS: *Pink Flag* (Harvest 1977)★★★★, *Chairs Missing* (Harvest 1978)★★★★, *154* (Harvest 1979)★★★★, *Document And Eyewitness* (Rough Trade 1981)★★, *The Ideal Copy* (Mute 1987)★★★★, *A Bell Is A Cup (Until It Is Struck)* (Mute 1988)★★, *It's Beginning To And Back Again* (Mute 1989)★★★, *The Peel Sessions* (Strange Fruit 1989)★★★, *Manscape* (Mute 1990)★★, *The Drill* (Mute 1991)★★. As Wir *The First Letter* (Mute 1991)★★★.

● COMPILATIONS: *And Here It Is ... Again ... Wire* (Sneaky Pete 1984)★★★, *Wire Play Pop* (Pink 1986)★★★, *On Returning* (Harvest 1989)★★★.

● FURTHER READING: *Wire ... Everybody Loves A History*, Kevin S. Eden.

Wireless

Guitar pop band Wireless were formed in the aftermath of the collapse of Manchester, Lancashire, England indie mainstays **Molly Half Head**. When that group disintegrated in 1995, songwriters Paul Bardsley and Phil Murphy elected to continue their partnership. As Bardsley confirmed to the press: 'It just got a bit stale. In the end, instead of battling away and exhausting ourselves, we decided to call it a day.' The new group was formed with the addition of Chris Picken (keyboards), Michael Darling (bass) and Basil Creese (drums). The group touted its demo recordings around various labels, with **Chrysalis Records** being the first to spot their commercial potential (they also signed a publishing contract with **Creation Records**). Their debut single, 'I Need You', premiered a more accessible sound than had been the case with Molly Half Head. Producer Bruce Lampcov replaced the heavy-going riffs, which had been such a feature of Molly Half Head, with an emphasis on sweeping string arrangements and acoustic guitars.

Wisdom, Norman

b. 4 February 1915, Paddington, London, England. A slapstick comedian, singer and straight actor, Wisdom has been a much-loved entertainer for four decades in the UK, not to mention other such unlikely places as Russia, China, and - more recently - Albania. He broke into films in 1953 with *Trouble In Store*, and during the remainder of the 50s, had a string of box-office smashes with *One Good Turn*, *Man Of The Moment*, *Up In The World*, *Just My Luck*, *The Square Peg* and *Follow A Star*. Dressed in his famous tight-fitting Gump suit, he was usually accompanied by straight man Jerry Desmonde, and, more often than not, portrayed the little man battling against the odds, eventually overcoming prejudice and snobbery, to win justice and his inevitably pretty sweetheart. He nearly always sang in his films, and his theme song, 'Don't Laugh At Me', which he co-wrote with June Tremayne, was a number 3 hit in 1954 on **EMI**/Columbia. He also made the Top 20 in 1957 with a version of the **Five Keys**' 'Wisdom Of A Fool'. In 1958, Wisdom appeared in the London production of **Where's Charley?**, a musical based on Brandon Thomas's classic farce, *Charley's Aunt*. **Frank Loesser**'s score included 'Once In Love With Amy' and 'My Darling, My Darling', and the show ran for 18 months. In 1965, he played the lead in **Leslie Bricusse** and **Anthony Newley**'s musical *The Roar Of The Greasepaint - The Smell Of The Crowd*, which toured UK provincial theatres. He was not considered sufficiently well-known in the USA to play the part on Broadway, but did make his New York debut in the following year, when he starred in *Walking Happy*, a musical version of *Hobson's Choice* with a score by **Sammy Cahn** and **Jimmy Van Heusen**. Wisdom also appeared on US television in the role of Androcles, with **Noël Coward** as Julius Caesar, in **Richard Rodgers**' musical adaptation of Bernard Shaw's *Androcles And The Lion*. His feature films during the 60s included *On the Beat*, *A Stitch In Time*, and *The Night They Raided Minsky's* with Jason Robards and Britt Ekland. Thanks to television re-runs of his films he is regarded with warm affection by many sections of the British public, and can still pack theatres, although, like many show-business veterans, he is not called on to appear much on television. In his heyday, he made two celebrated 'live' one-hour appearances on *Sunday Night At The London Palladium* in the company of Bruce Forsyth, which are considered to be classics of their kind. In 1992, with the UK rapidly running out of traditional funnymen (**Benny Hill** and Frankie Howerd both died in that year), Wisdom experienced something of a renaissance when he played the role of a gangster in the movie *Double X*, starred in a radio series, *Robbing Hood*, released the album *A World Of Wisdom*, completed a sell-out tour of the UK, and published his autobiography. In the following year he celebrated 50 years in showbusiness, and was still performing regularly. In 1995, he toured Albania as a guest of the Minister of Culture. Apparently, whereas the country's state censors banned most American and British films with their 'Marxist messages', Wisdom, in his customary role as 'the plucky proletarian', was considered politically and morally inoffensive. He was given the freedom of the capital, Tirana, met President Sali Berisha, attended several rallies in his honour, and gave a 90-minute television performance.

● ALBUMS: *I Would Like To Put On Record* (1956)★★★,

Where's Charley? stage production (1958)★★, *Walking Happy* Broadway Cast (1966)★★★, *Androcles And The Lion* (1967)★★.
● COMPILATIONS: *A World Of Wisdom* (Decca 1992)★★★, *The Wisdom Of A Fool* (See For Miles 1997)★★★.
● FURTHER READING: *Trouble In Store*, Richard Dacre. *Don't Laugh At Me*, Norman Wisdom. *'Cos I'm A Fool*, Norman Wisdom with Bernard Bale.

Wise, Chubby

b. Robert Russell Wise, 2 October 1915, Lake City, Florida, USA, d. 6 January 1996. His father was an old-time fiddler but Robert first played banjo and guitar, before changing to fiddle at the age of 12, greatly influenced by **Curly Fox** and Clayton McMichen. In 1936, Wise drove taxis in Jacksonville and played fiddle in bars in his spare time, but in 1938, he became a full-time musician. After playing for a time with the Jubilee Hillbillies, he joined **Bill Monroe** on the *Grand Ole Opry* in 1942. He remained with Monroe until 1948, in a line-up that included **Flatt And Scruggs** and played on most of the band's best-known recordings. In 1947, he co-wrote 'Shenandoah Waltz' with **Clyde Moody** and it has also been suggested that, in 1938, he may well have worked with Ervin Rouse on the writing of the fiddle classic 'Orange Blossom Special'. He returned to Monroe briefly and in the early 50s, he played with several acts including Flatt And Scruggs until 1954, when he became a member of **Hank Snow**'s Rainbow Ranch Boys. Except for a spell in 1964, he played on the *Opry*, toured extensively and recorded with Snow until March 1970. He played with Snow's band when, in 1955, they dubbed on new instrumentation to several of **Jimmie Rodgers**' classic recordings (Snow devotes almost a chapter of his autobiography to memories of the days when Wise played with him). During that time, he also recorded with **Mac Wiseman**, **Hylo Brown** and **Red Allen**. He cut a solo album for Starday in 1961 and in 1969, he began to record for Stoneway. He relocated to Livingstone, Texas, where throughout the 70s into the early 80s, he recorded a series of albums for the label, made personal appearances and also recorded as a session musician or guest with various artists and bluegrass groups, including **Charlie Moore**, Mac Wiseman, **Frank Wakefield** and the **Boys From Indiana** and cut twin fiddle albums with **Howdy Forrester**. In 1984, he moved to Florida and although he cut down his workload drastically, he still made numerous festival appearances and recorded with the Bass Mountain Boys. He continued to remain active into the 90s, recorded a twin fiddle album with **Raymond Fairchild** and late in 1995, he recorded what turned out to be his final album for Pinecastle. In December 1995, he and his wife were visiting relatives in Maryland for Christmas, when he was hospitalized with pneumonia. Soon after being released from hospital, he suffered a fatal heart seizure and died in Washington DC on 6 January 1996. Wise was one of country music's greatest fiddlers and also noted for his

humour. Once asked why he took up playing the fiddle, he replied, 'The fiddle bow fit my hand a lot better than them plough handles did'.
● ALBUMS: *Chubby Wise & The Rainbow Ranch Boys* (Starday 1961)★★★, *Chubby Wise & His Fiddle* (Stoneway 1969)★★★, *Chubby Fiddles Around* (Stoneway 1970)★★★, *Chubby Plays Uptown* (Stoneway 1970)★★★, *Chubby Plays, W.C. Averitt Sings Bluegrass* (Stoneway 1970)★★★, *Hoedown* (Stoneway 1970)★★★, *Chubby Wise Plays Bob Wills* (Stoneway 1970)★★★★, *Precious Memories* (Stoneway 1971)★★★, *Thru The Years With Chubby Wise* (Stoneway 1971)★★★, *Chubby Plays Polkas* (Stoneway 1971)★★★, *Waltzes* (Stoneway 1972)★★, *At His Best* (Stoneway 1972)★★★, *Hoedown #2* (Stoneway 1973)★★★, *Page 13* (Stoneway 1973)★★★, with Howdy Forrester *Sincerely Yours* (Stoneway 1974)★★★, with Forrester *Fiddle Favorites* (Stoneway 1975)★★★, *Grassy Fiddle* (Stoneway 1975)★★★, *The Golden Rocket* (Stoneway 1975)★★★, *The Million Dollar Fiddle* (Stoneway 1976)★★★★, *Sweet Milk And Peaches* (Stoneway 1977)★★★, *Chubby Wise Plays Hank Williams* (Stoneway 1977)★★★, *Moody Fiddle Sound* (Stoneway 1978)★★★, with Mac Wiseman *Give Me My Smokies & The Tennessee Waltz* (Gilley's 1982)★★★, *The Nashville Sound* (Guest Star 80s)★★★, with Boys From Indiana *Live At Gilley's* (Gilley's 1988)★★, with Raymond Fairchild *Cherokee Tunes & Seminole Swing* (Rebel 1990)★★★, *In Nashville* (1993)★★★, *An American Original* (Pinecastle 1993)★★★.

Wiseman, Mac

b. Malcolm B. Wiseman, 23 May 1925, Crimora, Virginia, USA. Wiseman attended the Conservatory of Music at Dayton, Virginia, and developed a great knowledge of the folk music of his native Shenandoah Valley. He first worked as a disc jockey on WSVA Harrisburg but was soon playing such shows as the *Tennessee Barn Dance* on WLOX Knoxville, where he also worked with **Molly O'Day**. During the 40s, his talent with bluegrass music saw him play and record with the bands of **Bill Monroe** and **Flatt And Scruggs**. He made his first solo recordings for **Dot** in 1951 and from 1957-61, he was the label's A&R man. After recording for **Capitol**, he returned to Dot but in the early 70s, he later recorded with **Lester Flatt** for RCA. Over the years Wiseman has worked on a variety of radio stations, played all the major US country venues and travelled extensively, including several tours to Britain, where he is always a popular artist. A prolific recording artist on various labels, his most popular recordings include such songs as 'Tis Sweet To Be Remembered'. His few actual chart hits include Top 10 successes with 'The Ballad Of Davy Crockett' and 'Jimmy Brown The Newsboy', and a minor hit with his humorous 'Johnny's Cash And Charley's Pride'. In 1979, he even charted with 'My Blue Heaven' as Mac Wiseman & Friend (the friend being Woody Herman). In 1993 he was inducted into the Bluegrass Hall Of Fame.
● ALBUMS: *I Hear You Knocking* (1955)★★★, *Songs From The Hills* (1956)★★★★, *Tis Sweet To Be Remembered* (Dot

1958)★★★, *Beside The Still Waters* (Dot 1959)★★★★, *Great Folk Ballads* (Dot 1959)★★★★, *Mac Wiseman Sings 12 Great Hits* (Dot 1960)★★★, *Keep On The Sunny Side* (Dot 1960)★★★, *Fireball Mail* (Dot 1961)★★★★, *Best Loved Gospel Hymns* (1961)★★★, *Bluegrass Favorites* (Capitol 1962)★★★, *Sincerely* (Hamilton 1964)★★★, *A Master At Work* (Dot 1966)★★★, *This Is Mac Wiseman* (Dot 1966)★★★, *Songs Of The Dear Old Days* (Hamilton 1966)★★★, *20 Old Time Country Favorites* (1966)★★★, *Mac Wiseman i* (1967)★★★, *Sings Johnny's Cash & Charley's Pride* (1970)★★★, with Lester Flatt *Lester 'N' Mac* (RCA Victor 1971)★★★, with Flatt *On The Southbound* (RCA Victor 1972)★★★, with Flatt *Over The Hills To The Poorhouse* (RCA Victor 1973)★★★, *Concert Favorites* (1973)★★★, *Country Music Memories* (CMH 1976)★★★, with Shenandoah Cut-Ups *New Traditions Volume 1* (Vetco 1976)★★★, with Shenandoah Cut-Ups *New Traditions Volume 2* (Vetco 1977)★★★, *Sings Gordon Lightfoot* (CMH 1977)★★★, *Mac Wiseman ii* (1977)★★★, with Osborne Brothers *Essential Bluegrass Album* (CMH 1979)★★★★, *Songs That Made The Jukebox Play* (CMH 1980)★★★, with Chubby Wise *Give Me My Smokies & The Tennessee Waltz* (Gilley's 1982)★★★, with Merle Travis *The Clayton McMichen Story* (CHM 1982)★★★, *Bluegrass Gold* (1982)★★★, *Live In Concert* (1982)★★, *If Teardrops Were Pennies* (1984)★★★, *Mac Wiseman iii* (1986)★★★, *Grassroots To Bluegrass* (CMH 1990)★★★★, *Teenage Hangout* (1993)★★★.

● COMPILATIONS: *Golden Hits Of Mac Wiseman* (Dot 1968)★★★, *16 Great Performances* (1974)★★★, *The Mac Wiseman Story* (CMH 1976)★★★★, *Golden Classics* (Gusto 1979), *Early Dot Recordings Volume 1* (County 1985)★★★★, *Early Dot Recordings Volume 2* (County 1985)★★★★, *Greatest Bluegrass Hits* (CMH 1989)★★★★, *Early Dot Recordings Volume 3* (County 1992)★★★, *Rare Singles And Radio Transcriptions* (Cowgirlboy 1992)★★★.

Wiseman, Val

b. 15 August 1942, West Bromwich, West Midlands, England. Wiseman began singing as a young girl and at the age of 18 joined a local jazz band. In 1963 she joined **Monty Sunshine** where she remained for three years and also sang at clubs, concerts and on radio with many other bands, including **Alex Welsh**, **Humphrey Lyttelton** and the **Al Fairweather-Sandy Brown** Allstars. In 1986 she sang with **Eggy Ley**'s Hot Shots, appearing with the band at that year's Birmingham International Jazz Festival. This performance resulted in an invitation to headline the following year's festival tribute to **Billie Holiday**. Entitled *Lady Sings The Blues*, this show subsequently toured regularly throughout the UK and Europe and featured several leading jazz instrumentalists, including **Digby Fairweather**, **Roy Williams**, **Alan Barnes** and **Len Skeat**. She has also appeared in the touring package *Drummin' Man*, singing the **Anita O'Day** songs from the **Gene Krupa** repertoire. Wiseman has also recorded extensively, appearing on albums by **King Pleasure And The Biscuit Boys**, Sunshine, and the Midland Youth Jazz Orchestra. In addition to packages and as singer with several bands, Wiseman has also toured as a solo artist and in these settings broadens her repertoire to include the great standards. Although popular in various parts of the UK, Netherlands, Belgium, Germany and Canada, Wiseman is not as well known as her skill and stylishness so clearly warrants. Her vocal sound, warm, relaxed and with effortless swing, makes her one of the best singers working in the UK jazz field in the late 90s.

● ALBUMS: *Lady Sings The Blues* (Big Bear 1990)★★★.

Wish - Cure

Undoubtedly more commercial than previous albums, *Wish* nevertheless represented the Cure doing what they do best, oblivious to prevailing musical trends. Once again, Robert Smith tore out his innards and offered them to the listener (the wrenching and chilling 'Apart'), spitting bile in 'Cut' and effectively evoking the feeling of wretched, helpless drunkenness in 'Open'. Amid the darkness, there is still time for a couple of classic pop songs, particularly the catchy 'Friday I'm In Love', and the customary obsessive love odes. Although frequently dismissed by hardcore Cure fans as too pop-orientated, *Wish* managed to strike a balance between the extremes of utter despair and intoxicating joy.

● Tracks: *Open; High; Apart; From The Edge Of The Deep Green Sea; Wendy Time; Doing The Unstuck; Friday I'm In Love; Trust; Letter To Elise; Cut; To Wish Impossible Things; End.*

● First released 1992

● UK peak position: 1

● USA peak position: 2

Wish You Were Here

In the early 50s, when Broadway audiences were enjoying such lavish musicals as **Call Me Madam**, **The King And I**, **Can-Can** and **Kismet**, *Wish You Were Here* went one better than all of them, and splashed out on a real swimming pool that was built into the stage. Perhaps the show's director, producer, choreographer, and co-librettist Joshua Logan still had fond watery memories of his association with the enormously successful **South Pacific** a few years earlier. In any event, the pool attracted a good deal of early publicity, as did a record of the title song by **Eddie Fisher** which soared to the top of the US chart just three weeks after the show opened at the Imperial Theatre on 25 June 1952. The story, which was adapted by Joshua Logan and Arthur Kober from Kober's 1937 play, *Having A Wonderful Time*, is set in Camp Karefree, a Jewish adult summer vacation resort in the Catskill Mountains. Teddy Stern (Patricia Marand) loses interest in her mature boyfriend, Herbert Fabricant (Harry Clark), when the young, suave and slinky waiter-cum-dancer Chick Miller (Jack Cassidy) sweeps her off her feet. It is all perfectly legal because, back home in New York, Chick is actually a law student. As well as the title number, which also became a hit for **Jane Froman** and **Guy Lombardo**, **Harold Rome**'s amusing and tuneful score contained another appealing ballad, 'Where Did The

Night Go', along with 'Tripping The Light Fantastic', 'Could Be', 'Ballad Of A Social Director', 'Mix And Mingle', 'Camp Kare-Free', 'Summer Afternoon', 'Shopping Around', 'Don José Of Far Rockaway' and 'Flattery'. *Wish You Were Here* was a warm and friendly show, so it was not surprising that it ran for nearly a year and a half, a total of 598 performances. The 1953 London production, with Bruce Trent, Shani Wallis, Elizabeth Larner and Dickie Henderson, stayed at the Casino Theatre (complete with swimming pool) for eight months. (The 1987 British film of the same name that starred Emily Lloyd and Tom Bell, is in no way related to this musical production.)

Wish You Were Here - Pink Floyd

Pink Floyd reaped considerable commercial acclaim with *Dark Side Of The Moon*, but it was on *Wish You Were Here* that the quartet reached an artistic maturity. The album revolves around 'Shine On You Crazy Diamond', a lengthy suite devoted to founder-member Syd Barrett, whose fragile ego snapped at the earliest whiff of success. This in mind, the group addresses music business exploitation in 'Welcome To The Machine', particularly pithy given their new-found status. A quiet determination marks this set. Roger Waters contributes some of his most openly heartfelt lyrics, while guitarist Dave Gilmour proved both economical and incisive. Free of the self-indulgence marking later work, Pink Floyd emerge as thoughtful technocrats, amalgamating and contextualizing new possibilities, rather than being swamped by them.

● Tracks: *Shine On You Crazy Diamond (Parts 1-5); Welcome To The Machine; Have A Cigar; Wish You Were Here; Shine On You Crazy Diamond (Parts 6-9)*.
● First released 1975
● UK peak chart position: 1
● USA peak chart position: 1

Wishbone Ash

In 1966 Steve Upton (b. 24 May 1946, Wrexham, Wales; drums), who had previously played with the Scimitars, joined Martin Turner (b. 1 October 1947, Torquay, Devon, England; bass/vocals) and Glen Turner (guitar) in the Torquay band, Empty Vessels. This trio then moved to London where they took the name Tanglewood. Glen Turner departed, before the similarly-titled Ted Turner (b. David Alan Turner, 2 August 1950; guitar) joined the band. He had previously played in a Birmingham band, King Biscuit. Wishbone Ash was formed when Andy Powell (b. 8 February 1950; guitar) of the Sugarband joined Upton, Turner and Turner. Heavily influenced by the music of the **Yardbirds** and the **Allman Brothers**, Wishbone Ash's hallmark was the powerful sound of twin lead guitars. Their biggest commercial success was *Argus*, released in 1973. This was a prime example of the band's preoccupation with historical themes, complex instrumentals, and folk-rock. Ted Turner departed in 1974, and was replaced by Laurie Wisefield, formerly of

Home. Wishbone Ash continued successfully, becoming tax exiles in the USA, returning to England in 1975 to play at the Reading Rock festival. In 1980 Martin Turner left. John Wetton, formerly of **Uriah Heep** and **Roxy Music**, served as his replacement, and singer **Claire Hammill** joined the band, along with Trevor Bolder. This line-up released only one album before disbanding in 1982, and it was the recruitment of Mervyn Spence to replace Bolder that seemed to give some of its former vitality back to Wishbone Ash. In 1987 the original quartet began working together again, recording *Nouveau Calls*. This project involved the renewal of their relationship with former-**Police** manager Miles Copeland, who had looked after Wishbone Ash's affairs for a brief spell in the 60s. They continue to perform to a loyal and devoted following.
● ALBUMS: *Wishbone Ash* (MCA 1970)★★★, *Pilgrimage* (MCA 1972)★★, *Argus* (MCA 1973)★★★, *Wishbone 4* (MCA 1973)★★★, *Live Dates* (MCA 1974)★★★, *There's The Rub* (MCA 1974)★★, *Locked In* (MCA 1976)★★, *New England* (MCA 1977)★★, *Frontpage News* (MCA 1977)★★, *No Smoke Without Fire* (MCA 1978)★★, *Live In Tokyo* (MCA 1978)★★, *Just Testing* (MCA 1979)★★, *Live Dates Volume II* (MCA 1979)★★, *Number The Brave* (MCA 1981)★★, *Twin Barrels Burning* (MCA 1982)★★, *Raw To The Bone* (Neat 1985)★★, *Nouveau Calls* (IRS 1987)★★, *Here To Hear* (IRS 1989)★★, *Strange Affair* (IRS 1991)★★, *BBC Radio 1 Live In Concert* (Windsong 1991)★★★, *The Ash Live In Chicago* (Permanent 1992)★★, *Illuminations* (1996)★★.
● COMPILATIONS: *Hot Ash* (MCA 1981)★★, *Classic Ash* (MCA 1981)★★★, *The Best Of Wishbone Ash* (MCA 1982)★★★, *Distillation* 4-CD box set (Repertoire 1997)★★★.
● VIDEOS: *Phoenix* (1990), *Wishbone Ash Live* (1990).

Wishplants

Indie band the Wishplants had been playing together for some time in their native Northamptonshire, England, as a trio of Ed Gilmour (guitar), James Fitzgerald (drums) and Paul Simpson (bass), before cementing the line-up with the addition of vocalist Saul in March 1992. Taking their name from an episode of science fiction television programme *Star Trek*, they played a few shows before entering a local studio to record demos with **Wonder Stuff/Neds Atomic Dustbin** producer Simon Efemey. It was he who introduced the band to their manager and set their career in motion by inviting the Wonder Stuff along to see them. The result was the support slot on that band's Scottish tour, before they had played 20 shows under their own auspices. Saul's charismatic performances soon attracted the attention of the UK indie press, prompting the *New Musical Express* to describe him as 'clearly one leg short of a full pair of trousers'. Despite record company interest the group elected to record an EP, *Circus Rain*, with Efemey, released in February 1993 on **China Records**. Afterwards they embarked on their first UK tour proper with **Power Of Dreams**, taking in both the Phoenix and Glastonbury Festivals. The *Tortoiseshell* EP followed in July to further strong reac-

tion, prefacing a well-received debut album in October.
● ALBUMS: *Coma* (China 1993)★★★, *Daddy Longlegs* (China 1996)★★★.

Witchfinder General

This Midlands-based **N.W.O.B.H.M.** group are rather better-remembered for two controversial album covers than for any of their actual music. Formed in 1979 by vocalist Zeeb and guitarist Phil Cope, with a name taken from a classic horror film, the initial line-up settled with a rhythm section of Toss McCready (bass) and Steve Kinsell (drums). Their debut single, 'Burning A Sinner' (also jokingly known as 'Burning A Singer'), revealed a primitive, **Black Sabbath**-influenced doom metal style, and was quickly followed by the *Soviet Invasion* EP, and a track on the *Heavy Metal Heroes* compilation. **Saxon** producer Peter Hinton was drafted in for *Death Penalty*, recorded in three days with a session drummer - this position remained unstable - and bassist Rod Hawkes replacing the departed Kinsell and McCready. The album showed promise, although it suffered from the rushed recording process. Most attention centred on its sleeve, which featured a mock-sacrifice scene photographed in a graveyard, with a well-known topless model and friend of the band, Joanne Latham, appearing semi-nude. The subsequent publicity reached the UK tabloids, and the band attempted to repeat the formula with *Friends Of Hell*, with the sleeve featuring several semi-naked models daubed with theatrical blood in a similar sacrifice scene, this time photographed in front of a church. This cynical effort succeeded only in losing what little support the band had garnered, and they quickly faded.
● ALBUMS: *Death Penalty* (Heavy Metal 1982)★★★, *Friends Of Hell* (Heavy Metal 1983)★★.

Witchfynde

This early UK satanist heavy metal band were formed in the late 70s, and came to prominence with the 'Give 'Em Hell' single, followed by an album of the same name. The quartet of Montalo (guitar), Steve Bridges (vocals), Andro Coulton (bass) and Gra Scoresby (drums) produced a fast and furious brand of **Judas Priest** and **Black Sabbath**-influenced metal, mixing heavy riffs with occult lyrics and imagery. *Stagefright*, a live set, followed, but the band were dissatisfied with the level of their record company's support, and took a lengthy break before finding a new label. Witchfynde resurfaced with new members Luther Beltz (vocals) and Pete Surgey (bass) on *Cloak & Dagger*. Although the album was recorded quickly with a low budget, the material again showed genuine quality, and produced the popular 'I'd Rather Go Wild'. However, the long spell of inactivity meant that the band had fallen far behind such early contemporaries as **Iron Maiden** and **Def Leppard**, and they were unable to sustain this success without major label backing. A final double set, *Lords Of Sin*, coupled with a live mini-album, *Anthems*, was released before the band disappeared.

● ALBUMS: *Give 'Em Hell* (Rondelet 1980)★★★, *Stagefright* (Rondelet 1981)★★, *Cloak & Dagger* (Expulsion 1983)★★★, *Lords Of Sin/Anthems* (Mausoleum 1985)★★★.

With A Little Help From My Friends - Joe Cocker

Joe Cocker's debut built on the promise of the title track, a hit single the previous year, which had introduced the world to the singer's astonishing blues rasp of a voice and remains to this day one of the finest Beatles cover versions committed to vinyl. The vocal pyrotechnics of that song are muted on this album, with Cocker demonstrating his fine handling of more subtle material such as Bob Dylan's 'Just Like A Woman' and 'I Shall Be Released'. Backed by his own seasoned Grease Band and stellar session players Jimmy Page and Steve Winwood, Cocker sings with a soulful intensity that shone all too briefly during his wayward career.
● Tracks: *Feeling Alright; Bye Bye Blackbird; Change In Louise; Marjorine; Just Like A Woman; Do I Still Figure In Your Life; Sandpaper Cadillac; Don't Let Me Be Misunderstood; With A Little Help From My Friends; I Shall Be Released.*
● First Released 1969
● UK peak chart position: did not chart
● USA peak chart position: 35

With A Song In My Heart

Susan Hayward gave an outstanding performance in this 1952 20th Century-Fox film which was based on the life of the popular singer **Jane Froman**. There was hardly a dry eye in the house as producer Lamar Trotti's screenplay traced Froman's brave fight back to the top following a terrible air crash during World War II that left her confined to a wheelchair. David Wayne was fine as her mentor and husband, and so was Thelma Ritter, who played her hard-bitten nurse and companion. The 22-year-old Robert Wagner had a small but effective role as a shell-shocked young airman, and also in the strong supporting cast were Rory Calhoun, Richard Allan, Una Merkel, Helen Wescott, Leif Erikson, Max Showalter and Lyle Talbot. It was Jane Froman's own voice that was heard on the soundtrack singing a marvellous selection of songs, many of which were particularly associated with her. There were especially endearing versions of 'With A Song In My Heart' (**Richard Rodgers-Lorenz Hart**), 'I'll Walk Alone' (**Jule Styne-Sammy Cahn**), 'I'm Through With Love' (**Gus Kahn**-Matty Malneck-Fud Livingstone) and 'They're Either Too Young Or Too Old' (**Frank Loesser**), along with excellent readings of 'Embraceable You' (**George** and **Ira Gershwin**), 'It's A Good Day' (**Peggy Lee**-Dave Barbour), 'Indiana' (James Hanley Ballard MacDonald), 'Blue Moon' (Rodgers-Hart), 'Deep In The Heart Of Texas' (Don Swander-June Hershey), 'Tea For Two' (**Vincent Youmans-Irving Caesar**), 'That Old Feeling' (**Lew Brown-Sammy Fain**), and several more. Musical director **Alfred Newman** won an Oscar for his scoring. Billy

Daniels staged the dance numbers and the impressive Technicolor photography was by Leon Shamroy. Walter Lang directed what was certainly one of the best films of its kind.

With The Beatles - Beatles

Released as its creators evolved from pop group to phenomenon, *With The Beatles* both affirmed promise and proclaimed genius. A slew of memorable Lennon/McCartney compositions embraced pop at its most multi-faceted; robust, melancholic, excited and wistful. Their grasp of melody and harmony startled, yet for every unusual chord sequence employed, the Beatles' vigour and sense of purpose remained true. Influences and mentors were acknowledged by a handful of cover versions, but the strength of the album lies in the group's own creations. *With The Beatles* freed artists to record their own material, and the course of pop was irrevocably changed. And Ringo's ride cymbal work is hypnotic.

● Tracks: *It Won't Be Long; All I've Got To Do; All My Loving; Don't Bother Me; Little Child; Till There Was You; Please Mister Postman; Roll Over Beethoven; Hold Me Tight; You Really Got A Hold On Me; I Wanna Be Your Man; (There's A) Devil In Her Heart; Not A Second Time; Money (That's What I Want).*
● First released 1964
● UK peak chart position: 1
● USA peak chart position: 1

Withers, Bill

b. 4 July 1938, Slab Fork, West Virginia, USA. Having moved to California in 1967 after nine years in the US Navy, Withers began hawking his original songs around several west coast companies. He was eventually signed to Sussex Records in 1971 and secured an immediate hit with his debut single, 'Ain't No Sunshine'. Produced by **Booker T. Jones**, with **Stephen Stills** amongst the guest musicians, this sparse but compulsive performance was a million-seller, a feat emulated in 1972 by two more excellent releases, 'Lean On Me' and 'Use Me'. Withers light, folksy/soul continued to score further success with 'Make Love To Your Mind' (1975), the sublime 'Lovely Day' (1977), (a single revamped by a remix in 1988) and 'Just The Two Of Us' (1981), his exhilarating duet with saxophonist **Grover Washington Jnr.**, which earned the two artists a grammy in 1982 for the Best R&B performance. 'Lovely Day' re-entered the UK pop charts in 1988 after exposure from a British television commercial, reaching the Top 5. A professional rather than charismatic performer, Withers remains a skilled songwriter.

● ALBUMS: *Just As I Am* (Sussex 1971)★★★★, *Still Bill* (Sussex 1972)★★★★, *Live At Carnegie Hall* (Sussex 1973)★★, *+'Justments* (Sussex 1974)★★★, *Making Music* (Columbia 1975)★★★, *Naked And Warm* (Columbia 1976)★★★, *Menagerie* (Columbia 1977)★★★, *'Bout Love* (Columbia 1979)★★★, *Watching You Watching Me* (Columbia 1985)★★★, *Still Bill* (1993)★★★.
● COMPILATIONS: *The Best Of Bill Withers* (Sussex 1975)★★★★, *Bill Withers' Greatest Hits* (Columbia 1981)★★★, *Lean On Me: The Best Of...* (Columbia/Legacy 1995)★★★.

Withers, Tex

b. *c.*1933. No one knows when and where Tex Withers was born, his real name or his parents. The deformed baby was abandoned in the USA, and his rise in British country music showed remarkable resilience: he was four feet tall and a hunchback with a painful history of severe spinal problems and tuberculosis. Withers wore western dress throughout the day as he longed to be an American Indian - his wife, known as White Fawn, dressed as his squaw and smoked a clay pipe. A good-natured man who laughed at his handicaps, Withers was the long-standing compere at West London's Nashville Room and won several awards as the Top UK country singer, his show-stoppers being 'These Hands' and a narration about a Red Indian's difficulties in coming to terms with society, 'The Ballad Of Ira Hayes'. *Tex Withers Sings Country Style* sold 135,000 copies, while his 1973 album, *The Grand Ole Opry's Newest Star* was recorded mainly in Nashville, Tennessee. He was championed by **Hank Snow**, but his professional career was cut short by throat illness. Withers became bankrupt and his illiteracy made work difficult. His last years were spent as a cleaner at Gatwick Airport and Haywards Heath railway station. He found his happy hunting ground on 29 December 1986, probably aged 53, and merited an obituary in *The Times*.

● ALBUMS: *Tex Withers Sings Country Style* (1970)★★★, *The Grand Ole Opry's Newest Star* (1973)★★★, *Tex Withers* (RCA 1976)★★.
● COMPILATIONS: *Blue Ribbon Country* (Homespun 1984)★★★.

Witherspoon, Jimmy

b. 8 August 1923, Gurdon, Arkansas, USA, d. 18 September 1997, Los Angeles, California, USA. Witherspoon crossed over into rock, jazz and R&B territory, but his deep and mellow voice placed him ultimately as a fine blues singer. He sang in his local Baptist church from the age of seven. From 1941-43 he was in the Merchant Marines and, during stopovers in Calcutta, he found himself singing the blues with a band led by Teddy Weatherford. In 1944, he replaced Walter Brown in the **Jay McShann** band at Vallejo, California, and toured with it for the next four years. In 1949 he had his first hit, 'Tain't Nobody's Business If I Do', which stayed on the *Billboard* chart for 34 weeks. Other recordings at the time with bands led by **Jimmy 'Maxwell Street' Davis** are fine examples of rollicking west coast R&B (collected as *Who's Been Jivin' You*). Witherspoon's popularity as an R&B singer faded during the course of the 50s, but he made a great impression on jazz listeners at the **Monterey Jazz Festival** in October 1959, performing with a group that included **Ben Webster**. Other collaborations with jazz artists included *Some Of My Best Friends Are The Blues*, with horns and strings arranged and conducted by **Benny Golson**, and a guest performance on **Jon Hendricks**' *Evolution Of The Blues Song*. He won the *Downbeat* critics' poll as a 'new star' in 1961. Frequent tours of Europe followed, beginning in 1961 with a **Buck Clayton** group and later with **Coleman Hawkins**, **Roy Eldridge**, **Earl Hines** and **Woody Herman**. He also did community work, including singing in prisons.

In the early 70s he gave up touring for a sedentary job as a blues disc jockey on the radio station KMET in Los Angeles, but resumed active music thanks to the encouragement of **Eric Burdon**. During his touring with Burdon he introduced a young **Robben Ford** as his guitarist and toured Japan and the Far East. In 1974 his 'Love Is A Five Letter Word' was a hit, though some fans regretted his neglect of the blues. A record with the **Savoy Sultans** in 1980 was a spirited attempt to recall a bygone era. *The Blues, The Whole Blues And Nothin' But The Blues* was the first album release for **Mike Vernon**'s new label Indigo. Witherspoon has been revered by generations during different eras, and his name was often cited as a major influence during the 60s beat boom; his work is destined to endure.

● ALBUMS: *New Orleans Blues* (1956)★★★, *Goin' To Kansas City Blues* (RCA Victor 1957)★★★★, with Eddie Vinson *Battle Of The Blues, Volume 3* (1959)★★★, *At The Monterey Jazz Festival* (Hifi 1959)★★★★, with Gerry Mulligan *Mulligan With Witherspoon* (1959)★★★, *Jimmy Witherspoon* (Crown 1959)★★★, *Feelin' The Spirit* (Hifi 1959)★★★★, *Jimmy Witherspoon At The Renaissance* (Hifi 1959)★★★, *Singin' The Blues* reissued as *There's Good Rockin' Tonight* (World Pacific 1959)★★★★, *Jimmy Witherspoon Sings The Blues* (Crown 1960)★★★, *Spoon* (Reprise 1961)★★★, *Hey, Mrs. Jones* (Reprise 1962)★★★, *Roots* (Reprise 1962)★★★, *Baby, Baby, Baby* (Prestige 1963)★★★, *Evenin' Blues* (Prestige 1964)★★★, *Goin' To Chicago Blues* (Prestige 1964)★★★, *Blues Around The Clock* (1964)★★★, *Blue Spoon* (Prestige 1964)★★★, *Some Of My Best Friends Are The Blues* (Prestige 1964)★★★, *Take This Hammer* (Constellation 1964)★★★, *Blues For Spoon And Groove* (Surrey 1965)★★★, *Spoon In London* (Prestige 1965)★★★, *Blues Point Of View* (Verve 1967)★★★, with Jack McDuff *The Blues Is Now* (Verve 1967)★★★, *Blues For Easy Livers* (Prestige 1967)★★★, *A Spoonful Of Soul* (Verve 1968)★★★, *The Blues Singer* (Stateside 1969)★★★, *Back Door Blues* (Polydor 1969)★★★, *Hunh!* (1970)★★★, *Handbags & Gladrags* (Probe 1970)★★★, *Blues Singer* (Stateside 1970)★★★, with Eric Burdon *Guilty!* (United Artists 1971)★★★, *Ain't Nobody's Business* (Polydor 1974)★★★, *Love Is A Five Letter Word* (Capitol 1975)★★★, *Jimmy Witherspoon And Ben Webster (That's Jazz)* (Warners 1977)★★★, with New Savoy Sultans *Sings The Blues* (Muse 1980)★★★, with Buck Clayton *Live In Paris, Big Blues* (Vogue 1981)★★★, *Midnight Lady Called The Blues* (1986)★★★, *Call My Baby* (1991)★★★, *The Blues, The Whole Blues And Nothin' But The Blues* (Indigo 1992)★★★, with Robben Ford *Live At The Notodden Blues Festival* (1993)★★★★, *Spoon's Blues* (Stony Plain 1995)★★★, with Howard Scott *American Blues* (Avenue/Rhino 1995)★★★, with Robben Ford *Ain't Nothin' New But The Blues* 1977 recording (AIM 1996)★★★★, with Robben Ford *Live At The Mint* (On The Spot 1996)★★★, *Spoonful* (ARG Jazz 1997)★★★.

● COMPILATIONS: *The Best Of Jimmy Witherspoon* (Prestige 1969)★★★★, *Never Knew This Kind Of Hurt Before: The Bluesway Sessions* 1969-71 recordings (Charly 1988)★★★, *Meets The Jazz Giants* 1959 recordings (1989)★★★, *Blowin' In From Kansas* (Ace 1991)★★★★, *Jimmy Witherspoon & Jay McShann* 40s recordings (1992)★★★.

Witnesses

This 60s showband from Northern Ireland first emerged in 1963, with a line-up comprising Harry 'Trixie' Hamilton (bass), Harry Mitchel (keyboards), Big Joe Clake (vocals), Gerry Rice (saxophone), Alex Burns (guitar), Alex Burns (guitar), George Mullen (trumpet) and David Martin (drums). An offshoot from the **Dave Glover Band**, the Witnesses' were known for their musicianship and love of jazz. With the arrival of Colm Wilkinson, in place of Mitchel, the band boasted a second vocalist, with a distinctive blues approach. Although their set was varied, the band failed to make an impact in Eire, but enjoyed successful tours of the UK before fragmenting at the end of the 60s.

Wiz, The (stage musical)

Unlike the 1903 Broadway version of *The Wizard Of Oz*, this enjoyable 1975 reworking of L. Frank Baum's novel stayed closely to the original story, and added an all-black cast and a brand new rock score. In William F. Brown's book, Dorothy (**Stephanie Mills**), is once again whisked off to the Land Of Oz on a whirlwind so that she can skip along the Yellow Brick Road with familiar characters such as the Scarecrow (Hinton Battle), the Tinman (Tiger Haynes), the Lion (Ted Ross), the extremely wicked witch (Mabel King), and wonderful Wizard (Andre De Shields). Charlie Smalls' powerful score was skilfully integrated into the plot, and contained the insinuating 'Ease On Down The Road', which became a soul-music favourite, along with 'He's The Wizard', 'Slide Some Oil On Me', 'Be A Lion', 'Don't Nobody Bring Me No Bad News', and 'If You Believe'. After surviving some predictably poor reviews (this was not a typical Broadway show), enthusiastic word-of-mouth boosted the show's appeal, and resulted in a remarkable four-year run of 1,672 performances. **Tony Awards** went to Geoffrey Holder for his brilliant costumes and direction, and *The Wiz* also won for best musical, score, supporting actress (**Dee Dee Bridgewater**), supporting actor (Ted Ross), and choreographer (George Faison). The show toured the USA, and was briefly seen again on Broadway in 1984 when Stephanie Mills recreated her original role. She portrayed Dorothy yet again in 1993, when *The Wiz* played a limited engagement at the Beacon Theatre in New York. In 1984, a London (not West End) production starred **Elaine Delmar**, Celena Duncan, and Clarke Peters. Among the cast of the 1978 film were **Diana Ross**, **Michael Jackson**, **Lena Horne**, Ted Ross, and Richard Pryor.

Wizard Of Oz, The (film musical)

It is not an easy task to conjure up a fairy tale that genuinely wins over both children and adults alike, but *The Wizard Of Oz*, released by MGM in August 1939, succeeded in every respect and became the third-highest-grossing film in the US during the 30s. To this day, this adaptation of L. Frank Baum's tale *The Wonderful Wizard Of Oz* remains a constant family favourite for new generations. Considering the many production problems that besieged the film behind the scenes, it is ironic that the film appears to have few obvious flaws and is very complete in structure. Not only did the film have three writers - Florence Ryerson, Noel Langley and Edgar Allan Woolf - but producer Mervyn LeRoy (assisted by a budding **Arthur Freed**), had numerous problems engaging an appropriate director. Having considered at least three others, Victor Fleming was assigned the prestigious job. However, even then, Fleming was not able to stay with the project until its conclusion. A few weeks before shooting was completed he was re-assigned to *Gone With The Wind*. It fell to King Vidor, Fleming's replacement, to direct the famous 'Over the Rainbow' scene, which was nearly cut at one point in the filming. Even the actors who eventually played several of the leading parts were not the director's first choice. Indeed it is only because 11 years-old Shirley Temple was unavailable that **Judy Garland**, who was six years older (and many felt, too old) won the role of Dorothy. Life for Dorothy on a farm in Kansas is miserable, and she muses 'if happy little bluebirds fly beyond the rainbow, why oh why can't I?' Suddenly a tornado strikes, and before she knows what has happened, the strength of the winds have swept her up and taken her to another land far away. Up to this point in the film, Dorothy's world has been black and white, but the moment the door is opened to Oz, everything is more colourful (Technicolor photography by Harold Rasson and Allen Darby) than she and the audience could ever have imagined. Helped by Glinda the Good Witch (Billie Burke) and over a hundred midgets playing the Munchkins, Dorothy sets off down the yellow brick road to meet the Wizard in Emerald City, and eventually to find a way back home. During her journey, she meets the Scarecrow (**Ray Bolger**) who longs for a brain, the Tin Woodman (Jack Haley) anxious for a heart, and the Cowardly Lion (Bert Lahr) who strives to be brave. Together they defeat the Wicked Witch of the West (Margaret Hamilton), only to find the giant all-powerful Oz is simply Frank Morgan shouting into a loud microphone and pulling a few levers. However, Dorothy's friends are eventually convinced that they have gained the qualities they desire, and with the help of her magical ruby slippers, Dorothy is whisked back home, or rather, she wakes up, for it has all been a dream. Faced with all her family and friends, most of whom played leading roles in her dream of Oz, Dorothy famously declares that she will never run away again and 'there's no place like home'. This ending offended many fans of Baum's books because in his writings Oz is a real place, not just a figment of the imagination. **Harold Arlen** and **E.Y. 'Yip' Harburg**'s charming score presented Garland with the immortal 'Over The Rainbow', which won an Oscar and proved to a be double-edged sword; in later years she would refuse to sing it for considerable periods of time. Other numbers included 'We're Off To See The Wizard', 'Follow The Yellow Brick Road', 'Ding-Dong! The Witch Is Dead', 'If I Were King Of The Forest', and 'The Merry Land Of Oz'. Ray Bolger gave a memorable comic performance in 'If I Only Had A Brain' (choreography was by Bobby Connolly). An extended dance sequence featuring Bolger in that number, which was removed from the final print, turned up in *That's Dancin'!*, a compilation of MGM clips which was released in 1985. Two years later, a stage version of the original film, complete with Arlen and Harburg's songs, was presented at the Barbican Theatre in London. In 1992, the Paper Mill Playhouse in New Jersey and the Muny Theatre in St. Louis, offered John Kane's adaptation of the MGM motion picture screenplay - again with the Arlen/Harburg score. The latter production starred comedienne Phillis Diller. More than 45 years after it was first released, the magic of *The Wizard Of Oz* still lingers in many forms, and this was emphasised in 1994 when a highly acclaimed documentary, *In Search Of Oz*, was screened by BBC Television.

● FURTHER READING: *The Making Of 'The Wizard Of Oz'*, Al Jean Harmetz. *Who Put The Rainbow In The Wizard Of Oz? Yip Harburg, Lyricist*, Harold Meyerson and Ernie Harburg.

Wizard Of Oz, The (stage musical)

Although it was adapted by L. Frank Baum from his own 1900 novel for children, *The Wonderful World Of Oz*, this stage show differed in several respects from the story that is so familiar to millions via the 1939 classic film which starred **Judy Garland**. It is probably true to say that it blew into the Majestic Theatre in New York on 20 January 1903, because the opening scene contains a spectacular hurricane effect which transports the young and shy Dorothy Gale (Anna Laughlin) and Imogene the Cow from their home in Kansas to the Land Of Oz. She becomes involved in some exciting adventures with most of the customary characters, including the Tin Woodman and the Scarecrow, who were played by two star comedians from vaudeville, David Montgomery and Fred Stone, and the Cowardly Lion (Arthur Hill), before eventually being confronted by the formidable Wizard (Bobby Gaylor) himself. Unlike the 1939 film of *The Wizard Of Oz*, with its wonderful score by **Harold Arlen** and **E.Y. 'Yip' Harburg**, the songs for this show were a kind of a hotch-potch cobbled together from a variety of composers and lyricists, mainly L. Frank Baum (lyrics) with Paul Tietjens and A. Baldwin Stone (music), along with others such as Theodore Morse, Vincent Bryan, Edward Hutchinson, James O'Dea, and Glen MacDonough. They included 'Hurrah For Baffins Bay',

'Sammy', 'In Michigan', 'Niccolo's Piccolo', 'Alas For A Man Without Brains', and 'When You Love Love Love'. *The Wizard Of Oz* ran for 293 performances, which meant that, in a Broadway season when 26 other musicals made their debut, it was a big hit.

Wizzard

Having already achieved success with the **Move** and the **Electric Light Orchestra**, the ever-experimental **Roy Wood** put together Wizzard in 1972 with a line up comprising Rick Price (vocals/bass), Hugh McDowell (cello), Bill Hunt (keyboards), Mike Burney (saxophone), Nick Pentelow (saxophone), Keith Smart (drums) and Charlie Grima (drums). The octet made their debut at the 1972 Wembley Rock 'n' Roll Festival and hit the charts later that year with the chaotic but intriguing 'Ball Park Incident'. Wood was at his peak as a producer during this period and his **Phil Spector**-like 'wall of sound' pop experiments produced two memorable UK number 1 hits ('See My Baby Jive', 'Angel Fingers') and a perennial festive hit, 'I Wish It Could Be Christmas Every Day'. There was even a playful stab at rivals ELO on the cheeky b-side 'Bend Over Beethoven'. Much of Wizzard's peculiar charm came from the complementary pop theatricalism of Roy Wood, who covered himself with war paint, painted stars on his forehead and sported an unruly mane of multi-coloured hair. Although less impressive on their album excursions, Wizzard's *Introducing Eddy And The Falcons* (a similar concept to **Frank Zappa**'s *Cruising With Ruben And The Jets*) was a clever and affectionate rock 'n' roll pastiche with tributes to such greats as **Del Shannon**, **Gene Vincent**, **Dion**, **Duane Eddy** and **Cliff Richard**. By 1975, the group were making in-roads into the American market where manager **Don Arden** was increasingly involved with lucrative stadia rock. Wizzard failed to persuade the management to increase their financial input, however, and swiftly folded. Wood, Rick Price and Mike Burney abbreviated the group name for the short-lived Wizzo Band, whose unusual brand of jazz funk proved too esoteric for commercial tastes. After less than a year in operation, this offshoot group self-destructed in March 1978 following which, Wood concentrated on solo outings and production.

● ALBUMS: *Wizzard Brew* (Harvest 1973)★★★, *Introducing Eddy And The Falcons* (Warners 1974)★★★, *Super Active Wizzo* (1977)★★★.
● COMPILATIONS: *See My Baby Jive* (Harvest 1974)★★★.

Wodehouse, P.G.

b. Pelham Grenville Wodehouse, 15 October 1881, Guildford, Surrey, England, d. 14 February 1975, Southampton, Long Island, New York, USA. A lyricist and librettist, and the author of a series of more than 90 humorous novels, mostly dealing with an 'hilarious, light-hearted satire on life among the British gentry, notably the inane Bertie Wooster and his impeccable valet, Jeeves'. His father was a British judge, based in Hong Kong, and Wodehouse lived in the colony with his parents until he was four, and then, for the next four years, was entrusted to a family in London, along with his three brothers. After elementary education at various boarding schools, he attended Dulwich College in the outskirts of London, and excelled at Latin and Greek. He graduated in 1900, and worked for a time at the Hong Kong & Shanghai Bank in London. A year later, he joined *The Globe* newspaper, eventually becoming the editor of the humorous column, 'By The Way'.

In 1904, he wrote the lyric for 'Put Me In My Cell', for a new show, *Sergeant Brue*, which opened in December at the Strand Theatre. Two years later, the renowned actor-manager, Seymour Hicks, offered him the job of writing song lyrics for the Aldwych shows. It was at the Aldwych Theatre that Wodehouse met the young American composer **Jerome Kern**, who was just beginning to make a name for himself. Together, they wrote the song, 'Mr. Chamberlain', a satire on the British politician, Joseph Chamberlain, for *The Beauty Of Bath*. It stopped the show each night, and became a country-wide hit. During the next few years, in between his prolific literary output which involved several trips to the USA, Wodehouse contributed sketches and lyrics to three more London shows, *The Gay Gordons*, *The Bandit's Daughter*, and *Nuts And Wine*.

In September 1914, he married an English widow, Ethel Rowley, in New York, and finally settled in the USA. Three months later, in his capacity as the drama critic of *Vanity Fair*, he attended the first night of the musical comedy **Very Good Eddie**, which had music by Jerome Kern, and a libretto by Philip Bartholomae and **Guy Bolton**. When Kern introduced Wodehouse and Bolton, it marked the beginning of collaboration during which the trio (two Englishmen and one New Yorker), contributed books, music and lyrics to a number of witty, entertaining, and highly successful Broadway musicals. Firstly though, there were two false starts: Wodehouse was called in to assist the lyricist-librettist Anne Caldwell, on *Pom-Pom* (1916), and then the new team was asked to 'Americanize' and provide a new book and some additional songs for a Viennese operetta called *Miss Springtime*. The show was a hit, and contained some charming Wodehouse lyrics in numbers such as 'Throw Me A Rose', 'My Castle In The Air', and the risqué 'A Very Good Girl On Sunday'. The trio's first original musical comedy, *Have A Heart* (1917), had music by Kern, and lyrics by Wodehouse, who also collaborated with Bolton on the book. Although critically acclaimed, the show ran for less than a 100 performances, despite an outstanding score which included 'You Said Something', 'And I Am All Alone', 'They All Look Alike', 'Honeymoon Inn', 'I See You There', and 'Napoleon'.

The young team's initial impact was made in February 1917 with *Oh, Boy!*, the first, and the more successful of their two famous **Princess Theatre Musicals**. Kern and Bolton had already worked together at the Princess in

1915, with lyricist Schuyler Greene. The tiny theatre had a capacity of only 299, and so was not able to handle the large operetta-style productions that were currently in vogue, or afford to employ established performers and writers. Kern, Wodehouse, and Bolton were interested in writing more intimate shows anyway, with songs that were integrated into plots that sometimes bordered on farce with their tales of misidentity and suchlike, but came as a welcome relief from the stodginess of the European imports. *Oh, Boy!* was a prime example of what they were aiming for, and proved to be a smash hit from the start, eventually running for over 450 performances. One of the show's stars, Anna Wheaton, helped to promote the production with her successful record of one of the hit numbers, 'Till The Clouds Roll By', and some of the other songs (nearly 20 of them) included 'Ain't It A Grand And Glorious Feeling', 'A Package Of Seeds', 'Flubby Dub', 'The Cave Man', 'Nesting Time In Flatbush', 'Words Are Not Needed', 'An Old Fashioned Waltz', and the delightfully rueful duet, 'You Never Knew About Me'. The production transferred to London two years later, where it was re-titled *Oh, Joy!*, and gave Beatrice Lillie her first role in a book musical. While *Oh, Boy!* was resident at the Princess Theatre, Wodehouse was involved with four other New York shows in 1917. Firstly, he collaborated again with Kern and Bolton for *Leave It To Jane*, a musical adaptation of George Ade's comedy, *The College Widow*. This was similar in style to *Oh, Boy!*, and included The Siren's Song', 'The Crickets Are Calling', 'Leave It To Jane', 'The Sun Shines Brighter', 'Wait Till Tomorrow', 'Cleopatterer' (an amusing piece of Egyptian hokum), and several more. The show was revived Off-Broadway more than 40 years later, in 1959, and ran for over two years. For Wodehouse, *Leave It To Jane* was followed by *Kitty Darlin'* (music by **Rudolph Friml**), *The Riviera Girl* (music by Emmerich Kalman and Kern), and *Miss 1917* (music by **Victor Herbert** and Kern). The young rehearsal pianist for *Miss 1917* was **George Gershwin**, in his first professional job in the theatre. In February 1918, Wodehouse, Bolton, and Kern completed *Oh, Lady!, Lady!!*, their final Princess Theatre show together. The all-star cast included Vivienne Segal, who sang 'Not Yet', 'Do Look At Him', 'It's A Hard, Hard World for A Man', and 'When The Ships Come Home', amongst others. It is sometimes said that disagreements over financial affairs between Kern and Wodehouse caused them to part, at least temporarily. In any event, although the three men were to work in pairs during the next few years, the brief spell when they combined to contribute to the dawn of a joyous revolution of the American musical theatre was over, except for *Sitting Pretty* (1924), which proved to be a 95 performance disappointment.
During the next two years Wodehouse contributed book and/or lyrics to productions such as *See You Later*, *The Girl Behind The Gun*, *The Canary*, *Oh, My Dear!*, *The Rose Of China*, and *The Golden Moth*, with a variety

of composer, lyricists and librettists, such as Jean Schwartz, Joseph Szulc, Ivan Caryll, George Barr, Louis Verneuill, Anne Caldwell, Louis Hirsch, and Jerome Kern, with whom he wrote 'The Church Around The Corner' and 'You Can't Keep A Good Girl Down' for *Sally* (1920). In the early 20s, he collaborated with Kern again on two successful London shows, *The Cabaret Girl* and *The Beauty Prize*. Two years later, Bolton and Wodehouse wrote the book for George and **Ira Gershwin**'s hit, *Oh, Kay!*, and they were both involved again in *The Nightingale* (1927) ('Breakfast In Bed', 'May Moon', 'Two Little Ships'), with music by Armand Vecsey. In 1927, Jerome Kern staged his masterpiece, *Show Boat*, with lyrics by **Oscar Hammerstein**. Interpolated into their score, was 'Bill', a song which was written by Kern and Wodehouse nearly 10 years previously, and cut from the original scores of *Oh, Lady! Lady!!* (1918) and *Zip Goes A Million* (1919). It was sung in *Show Boat* by **Helen Morgan**, and provided Wodehouse with the biggest song hit of his career. In the following year, he collaborated with lyricist Ira Gershwin, his brother George, and **Sigmund Romberg**, for the popular *Rosalie*, starring Marilyn Miller ('Hussars March', 'Oh Gee! Oh Joy!', 'Say So', 'West Point Song', 'Why Must We Always Be Dreaming?'). Ironically, for someone who had been at the forefront of the radical changes in American show music for the past 10 years, Wodehouse's final set of Broadway lyrics were for an operetta. With lyricist Clifford Grey and composer Rudolph Friml, he contributed numbers such as 'March Of The Musketeers' and 'Your Eyes' to **Florenz Ziegfeld**'s music adaptation of Alexander Dumas' *The Three Musketeers* (1928), which starred Vivienne Segal and Dennis King, and ran for over 300 performances. With a final flourish, Wodehouse's Broadway career ended with a smash hit, when he and Bolton provided the book for **Cole Porter**'s *Anything Goes* (1934). In that same year, Bertie Wooster and Jeeves appeared together in a novel for first time, and Wodehouse, who had been balancing several balls in the air for most of his working life, at last allowed the musical one to drop to earth. During the 30s he spent some time in Hollywood, adapting his novel, *A Damsel In Distress*, for the screen.
In July 1940, while at his villa in Le Touquet on the French Riviera, he was taken into custody by the German invading forces, charged with being an enemy alien, and interned in the local lunatic asylum at Tost in Upper Silesia. In June 1941, he was moved to Berlin, and subsequently broadcast a series of humorous talks about his experiences as a prisoner of war, which were transmitted to America. In Britain, where the population was constantly under siege from German aircraft, Wodehouse was reviled in the press and on radio, and there was talk of him being tried for treason - although most of the British population had not heard what turned out to be fairly innocuous broadcasts. Still in custody, he was transferred to Paris, and eventually

liberated in August 1944. He returned to the USA in 1947, and became an American citizen in 1955.

He continued to write constantly, and in 1971, on his 90th birthday, his 93rd volume was published. Four years later, perhaps in a belated national gesture of reconciliation, Wodehouse, was created a Knight Commander of the British Empire in the UK New Year honours list, just two months before he had a heart attack, and died in a Long Island hospital in February 1975.

● FURTHER READING: *From Wodehouse To Wittgenstein*, Anthony Quinton.

Wolf & Leopards - Dennis Brown

That the 'boy wonder', Dennis Brown, at the age of 20 was able to release an album of this calibre, gathering together only some of his hits from the previous couple of years, seems almost unbelievable. The whole set demonstrates a maturity both in content and delivery. From the spirituality of 'Emanuel God Is With Us' and 'Created By The Father' to the vengeful 'Whip Them Jah', every track oozes authority and class. Nothing Brown has done in the time subsequent to this release has lessened his impact or his appeal. He remains one of the music's most popular and influential performers.

● Tracks: *Wolves And Leopards; Emanuel God Is With Us; Here I Come; Whip Them Jah; Created By The Father; Party Time; Rolling Down; Boasting; Children Of Israel; Lately Girl.*

● First released 1978

● UK peak chart position: did not chart

● USA peak chart position: did not chart

Wolf, Kate

b. 27 January 1942, Sonoma County, San Francisco, California, USA, d. 10 December 1986. Wolf was a songwriter-singer-guitarist who worked her home area and organized the Santa Rosa folk festivals. Her first albums, *Back Roads* and *Lines On Paper*, were recorded independently and released on her own Owl label. Those albums were made with a band named after a country song, Wildwood Flower, and although country and bluegrass feature in her work, Wolf is a contemporary folk artist. In 1979 she recorded *Safe At Anchor* for the Kaleidoscope label, which many claim to be her finest set. Wolf wrote and sang beautifully, clearly and perceptively about the preciousness of life and the precariousness of relationships. She was also a fine interpreter of others' material such as the slow version of Jack Tempchin's 'Peaceful Easy Feeling'(recorded by the **Eagles**), and **John Stewart**'s 'Some Kind Of Love' on the live double-album *Give Yourself To Love*. In November 1985 she recorded a memorable television concert for *Austin City Limits*, which became *An Evening In Austin*. It was her last happy moment: she developed leukaemia and although she was not fit to record, she compiled the retrospective *Gold In California*. The title track of *The Wind Blows Wild* was recorded at her hospital bedside and she died in 1986. She had had no hits and her songs were largely

unknown, but, gradually, the quality of her work has surfaced. Her husband, Terry Fowler - the subject of 'Green Eyes' - keeps her name alive. Her songs ironically include such titles as 'Love Still Remains' and 'Unfinished Life'.

● ALBUMS: *Back Roads* (Owl 1976)★★, *Lines On Paper* (Owl 1977)★★★, *Safe At Anchor* (Kaleidoscope 1979),★★★★ *Close To You* (Kaleidoscope 1981)★★★, *Give Yourself To Love* (Kaleidoscope 1983)★★★, *Poet's Heart* (Kaleidoscope 1985),★★★ *The Wind Blows Wild* (Kaleidoscope 1988)★★, *An Evening In Austin* (Kaleidoscope 1988)★★.

● COMPILATIONS: *Gold In California* (Kaleidoscope 1986)★★★.

● VIDEOS: *An Evening In Austin*.

Wolf, Peter

b. Peter Blankfield, February 1946, Bronx, New York, USA. Formerly singer with the Boston-based **J. Geils Band**, a group he led for 15 years, Wolf went solo in 1983 following their acrimonious break-up. He only briefly emulated their commercial success with *Lights Out*, his 1984 solo debut which produced two hit singles. After the release of a follow-up collection, *Come As You Are*, his record label, **EMI** America, ceased operations. He followed executive Irving Azoff to MCA Records, for whom he recorded *Up To No Good* in 1990. However, when Azoff left the label shortly after its release, his career once more hit a hurdle. In 1996 he released his first solo effort in more than six years. *Long Line* revealed a more intimate, roots-orientated approach than had previously been the case, its reflective tone engendered by the fact that Wolf had recently turned 50. It included two songs co-written with **Aimee Mann**, 'Starving To Death' and 'Forty To One'.

● ALBUMS: *Lights Out* (EMI America 1984)★★★, *Come As You Are* (EMI America 1986)★★, *Up To No Good* (MCA 1990)★★, *Long Line* (Reprise 1996)★★.

Wolfgang Press

'None of us are very good musicians and I think that helps a lot'. Despite a reputation as **4AD Records'** longest-serving glacial post-punk outfit, such generic descriptions hardly embrace the width of the Wolfgang Press's songwriting arsenal. Comprising Andrew Gray (guitar), Mark Cox (keyboards) and Mick Allen (vocals), they took more responsibility for their packaging and image than many of their label's fellow travellers, producing an intriguing range of records, covers and videos. Their recorded fare, however, continued to be imaginative but insubstantial. Support slots on tours with the **Pixies** and **Nick Cave** had given the band a higher profile in Europe and the USA than they enjoyed domestically by the close of the 80s, where their sound collages were viewed as too eclectic to fit any particular strain of modern 'indie' music. Following several albums of edgy, fragmented pop sounds, they began the next decade with a plunge into the dance market, primarily inspired by **De La Soul**'s *Three Feet High And*

Rising. Queer won many favourable reviews, and was a successful accommodation of new musical innovations; so too 1995's *Funky Little Demons*, though this wideranging collection of songs was not the result of inflated art school egos, Allen commenting: 'You could see music as being magical but it's more like a lot of hard work, not far removed from building a house.' Whether architects of music or houses, the Wolfgang Press have grown significantly in ability as the years have passed.

● ALBUMS: *The Burden Of Mules* (4AD 1983)★★, *The Legendary Wolfgang Press And Other Tall Stories* (4AD 1985)★★★, *Standing Up Straight* (4AD 1986)★★★, *Bird Wood Cage* (4AD 1989)★★★, *Queer* (4AD 1991)★★★, *Funky Little Demons* (4AD 1995)★★★.

Wolfhounds

Formed in Essex, England, in 1985, the Wolfhounds' first recording line-up was Dave Callahan (vocals), Andrew Bolton (bass), Paul Clark (guitar), Andrew Golding (guitar) and Frank Stebbing (drums). Having spent their formative months supporting dubious pub/punk rock bands around London, the Wolfhounds became fortuitously involved in the **New Musical Express**'s C86 venture. Toying with a gritty, angular guitar framework over which Callahan's vocals wandered, the Wolfhounds were famed for having as many labels as album releases; they bounced from Pink Records to Idea and on through September and Midnight Music Records, fittingly experiencing an alarming number of personnel changes. In spite of - or perhaps because of - their stubborn outlook, the band never achieved the respect they truly warranted, and finally ground to a halt at the end of the 80s. After their demise, Dave Callahan initiated a new band called Moonshake, while Golding and Stebbing reunited in Crawl.

● ALBUMS: *Unseen Ripples From A Pebble* (Pink 1987)★★★, *Bright And Guilty* (Midnight Music 1989)★★★, *Blown Away* mini-album (Midnight Music 1989)★★★, *Attitude* (Midnight Music 1990)★★.

● COMPILATIONS: *The Essential Wolfhounds* (Midnight Music 1988)★★★, *Lost But Happy: 1986-1990* (Cherry Red 1997)★★★.

Wolfman Jack

b. Robert Weston Smith, 21 January 1938, Brooklyn, New York City, New York USA, d. 1 July 1995, Belvidere, North Carolina, USA. Wolfman Jack was one of the most influential and recognizable rock 'n' roll disc jockeys in America, and later television, during the 50s through the 70s. Infatuated with DJs **Alan Freed** and John Richbourg, Smith sought out the latter in Nashville, Tennessee, who trained him, and shortly afterwards Smith was given his own radio programme on a black station in Virginia. His croak-like voice gave him an identity, and after trying out names such as Daddy Jules, Big Smith and Roger Gordon, he settled with Wolfman Jack. The radio announcer developed an eccentric on-air personality punctuated by trademark wolf howls. His most significant radio engagement began in 1960 on station XERF, in Via Cuncio, Mexico, just nine miles south of Del Rio, Texas. Playing a mixture of R&B, rockabilly, jazz and rock 'n' roll, and shouting in black-influenced slang, Wolfman drew a huge audience. He also ran the station's business affairs and read commercials himself, selling everything from records to sex aids and becoming rather wealthy in the process. He remained something of a mystery to his audience, refusing to reveal himself, until 1963, when he began making personal appearances. In 1970, Wolfman Jack began a 16-year association with Armed Forces Radio, taping broadcasts for US servicemen. By then he had switched to a USA progressive rock station, KDAY, in Los Angeles. In 1972, the **Guess Who** paid tribute to him with a song, 'Clap For The Wolfman'. The following year he had a small role in the popular film *American Graffiti*, and during the same period he began a nine-year association as host of the live music television programme *The Midnight Special*. In 1973, Wolfman also worked briefly at New York radio station WNBC, an engagement which failed to bring in audiences. He spent the remainder of the 70s and most of the 80s making live appearances and taping commercials. In 1989 he attempted a country music radio show which failed to catch on.

Wolfsbane

This UK quartet from Tamworth, Staffordshire, UK, employed a strong biker image to augment their incendiary heavy metal anthems. Featuring Blaze Bayley (b. 1963, Birmingham, West Midlands, England; vocals), Jase Edwards (guitar), Steve 'Danger' Ellet (drums) and Jeff Hateley (bass), they incorporated elements of **Van Halen**, **Iron Maiden** and **Zodiac Mindwarp** into their own high-energy, and, at times, chaotic style. Picked up by **Rick Rubin**'s Def **American** label, they released *Live Fast, Die Fast* as an opening philosophical statement. The album failed to match the manic intensity of their live shows and was let down by weak production. Their next two releases saw some development on the songwriting front, with the addition of sci-fi and b-movie imagery, to supplement the well-worn themes of sex, booze and rock 'n' roll. After three albums their style remained loud, aggressive and, to a degree, derivative. 1993 saw them separate both from P Grant Managment and Def American, and by the following year Bayley quit to replace **Bruce Dickinson** in **Iron Maiden**. The remaining members soon abandoned their former name to become **Stretch**, releasing their debut album for Cottage Industry Records in the summer of 1995.

● ALBUMS: *Live Fast, Die Fast* (Def American 1989)★★, *All Hell's Breaking Loose Down At Little Kathy Wilson's Place* (Def American 1990)★★★, *Down Fall The Good Guys* (Def American 1991)★★★, *Massive Noise Injection* (Bronze 1993)★★★.

Wolfstone

Scottish folk-rock group formed in 1990 comprising Duncan Chisholm (b. 31 October 1968, Beauly, Scotland; fiddle), Stuart Eaglesham (b. 11 September 1965, Clydebank, Scotland; guitar/vocals), Struan Eaglesham (b. 17 January 1969, Clydebank, Scotland; keyboards), Andy Murray (b. 29 November 1963, Inverness, Scotland; guitar), and piper Allan Wilson. Ivan Drever (b. 10 June 1956, Orkney, Scotland; guitar/vocals) joined in 1991. It was this line-up, backed by session players Neil Hay (bass), and John Henderson (drums), that recorded the well received *Unleashed*. Minus Allan Wilson, who left in 1992, but additionally supported by Dougie Pincock (pipes/flute/whistle), better known for his work as a member of the **Battlefield Band**, they recorded *The Chase*. Highly acclaimed, the album brought the group to the wider attention of the music media. In July 1992, shortly after the album was recorded, Wayne MacKenzie (b. 17 November 1965; bass), and Graeme 'Mop' Youngson (b. 18 August 1960, Aberdeen, Scotland; drums), joined the band, dispensing with the need to use session players. Originally, the group had always used session pipers for live work and recordings but in 1992 Roddy McCourt (b. 1960, Edinburgh, Scotland, d. March 1993; pipes) joined them as a permanent piper, taking the place vacated by Allan Wilson. Sadly, in 1993, McCourt took his own life, and the band reverted to using guest and session pipers once more. Their recordings have won the band acclaim from many quarters, their original sound revealing a number of influences, notably that of **Horslips**.

● ALBUMS: *Unleashed* (Iona 1991)★★★, *The Chase* (1992)★★★★, *The Half Tail* (Green Linnet 1996)★★.

Wolverines

The Wolverine Orchestra was an early white jazz group, modelled loosely upon the **New Orleans Rhythm Kings**. Formed in the mid-west in 1923, the group played in clubs and restaurants in Chicago, at the Stockton Club in Hamilton, Ohio, in Cincinnati, and in Richmond, Indiana, where they recorded for the Gennett label. The recording sessions, which took place between March and November, produced 13 tracks. The personnel comprised Dick Voynow (piano), Al Gandee (trombone, appearing on two tracks only), trombonist **Georg Brunis** (trombone, appearing on two later tracks), Jimmy Hartwell (clarinet), George Johnson (tenor saxophone), and a rhythm section of Bob Gillette (banjo), Min Leibrook (tuba), Vic Moore (drums). The final member of the band, and the reason why the short-lived Wolverines warrant an important place in jazz history, was **Bix Beiderbecke**. The records were not only commercially successful, they were also influential upon jazz musicians, particularly whites, and include classic performances of 'Jazz Me Blues' and 'Riverboat Shuffle'. Subsequently, some personnel changes took place and the band recorded again with

Jimmy McPartland replacing Beiderbecke. Between 1927 and 1929 a band named the Original Wolverines led by McPartland, but with only Voynow and Moore from the original group, recorded for Vocalion. Two sides from a 1926 recording date by a small band featuring **Red Nichols** and **Miff Mole** were issued on **Brunswick** under the name of the Wolverines but were more accurately labelled on Vocalion issues as being by the **Tennessee Tooters**, a band derived from the **Original Memphis Five**. By 1930, the Wolverines had passed into history but, thanks to Beiderbecke, their records remain a constant source of interest and pleasure.

● COMPILATIONS: *The Wolverines Orchestra (1924)* (1979)★★★.

Womack And Womack

One of modern soul's most successful duos, comprising husband and wife team Cecil Womack (b. 1947, Cleveland, Ohio, USA) and Linda Cooke Womack (b. 1953). Cecil had been the youngest of the Womack Brothers, who later evolved into the **Valentinos**. With them he signed to **Sam Cooke**'s Star imprint, but Cooke's subsequent death left them homeless, and after a brief liaison with Chess Records, **Bobby Womack** left the group to go solo. Cecil later married singer **Mary Wells**, whom he managed until the couple separated. Linda, the daughter of Sam Cooke, had begun a song-writing career in 1964 at the age of 11, composing 'I Need A Woman'. She would also provide 'I'm In Love' for **Wilson Pickett** and 'A Woman's Gotta Have It' for **James Taylor**, but later forged a professional, and personal, partnership with Cecil. As she recalls: 'My father had the deepest regard for all the Womack brothers. He had talked about how talented Cecil was since I was four years old…We didn't actually meet until I was eight'. Together they worked extensively as a writing team for Philadelphia International, numbering the **O'Jays** and **Patti Labelle** among their clients. The couple achieved a notable success with 'Love TKO', a soul hit in 1980 for **Teddy Pendergrass**. This melodic ballad also provided the Womacks with their first US chart entry (and was also covered by **Blondie**), since when the duo's fortunes have prospered both in the US and UK with several excellent singles, including the club favourite, 'Love Wars' (1984) and 'Teardrops' (1988), the latter reaching the UK Top 3. They continued to write for others also, contributing 'Hurting Inside' and 'Sexy' to **Ruby Turner**. In the early 90s the couple journeyed to Nigeria, where they discovered ancestral ties to the Zekkariyas tribe. They consequently adopted the names Zeriiya (Linda) and Zekkariyas (Cecil), in a nod to the Afrocentricity movement.

● ALBUMS: *The Composers/Love Wars* (Elektra 1983)★★★, *Radio M.U.S.I.C. Man* (Elektra 1985)★★★, *Starbright* (Manhattan/EMI 1986)★★★, *Conscience* (4th & Broadway 1988)★★, *Family Spirit* (Arista 1991)★★, *Transformed Into The House Of Zekkariyas* (1993)★★.

● COMPILATIONS: *Greatest Hits* (Spectrum 1998)★★★.

Womack, Bobby

b. 4 March 1944, Cleveland, Ohio, USA. A founder member of the **Valentinos**, this accomplished musician also worked as a guitarist in **Sam Cooke**'s touring band. He scandalized the music fraternity by marrying Barbara Campbell, Cooke's widow, barely three months after the ill-fated singer's death. Womack's early solo singles, 'Nothing You Can Do' and the superb 'I Found A True Love', were all but shunned and, with the Valentinos now in disarray, he reverted to session work. Womack became a fixture at Chips Moman's American Recording Studio, but although he appeared on many recordings, this period is best recalled for his work with **Wilson Pickett**. 'I'm In Love' and 'I'm A Midnight Mover' are two of the 17 Womack songs that particular artist would record. Bobby meanwhile resurrected his solo career with singles on Keymen and **Atlantic Records**. Signing with Minit, he began a string of R&B hits, including 'It's Gonna Rain', 'How I Miss You Baby' (both 1969) and 'More Than I Can Stand (1970). His authoritative early album, *The Womack Live*, then introduced the freer, more personal direction he would undertake in the 70s. The final catalyst for change was *There's A Riot Going On*, **Sly Stone**'s 1971 collection on which Womack played guitar. Its influence was most clearly heard on 'Communication', the title track to Womack's first album for United Artists.

Part of a prolific period, the follow-up album, *Understanding*, was equally strong, and both yielded impressive singles, which achieved high positions in the R&B charts. 'That's The Way I Feel About Cha' (number 2), 'Woman's Gotta Have It' (number 1) and 'Harry Hippie' (number 8), which confirmed his new-found status. Successive albums from *Facts Of Life*, *Looking For A Love Again* and *I Don't Know What The World Is Coming To*, consolidated the accustomed mixture of original songs, slow raps and cover versions. *BW Goes C&W* (1976), a self-explanatory experiment, closed his UA contract, but subsequent work for **CBS** and **Arista** was undistinguished. In 1981 Womack signed with Beverly Glen, a small Los Angeles independent, where he recorded *The Poet*. This powerful set re-established his career while a single, 'If You Think You're Lonely Now', reached number 3 on the R&B chart. *The Poet II* (1984) featured three duets with **Patti LaBelle**, one of which, 'Love Has Finally Come At Last', was another hit single. Womack moved to MCA Records in 1985, debuting with *So Many Rivers*. A long-standing friendship with the **Rolling Stones** was emphasized that year when he sang back-up on their version of 'Harlem Shuffle'. An expressive, emotional singer, his best work stands among black music's finest moments.

● ALBUMS: *Fly Me To The Moon* (Minit 1968)★★★, *My Prescription* (Minit 1969)★★★, *The Womack Live* (United Artists 1970)★★★, *Communication* (United Artists 1971)★★★, *Understanding* (United Artists 1972)★★★, *Across 110th Street* film soundtrack (United Artists 1972)★★, *Facts Of Life* (United Artists 1973)★★★, *Looking For A Love Again* (United Artists 1974)★★, *I Don't Know What The World Is Coming To* (United Artists 1975)★★★, *Safety Zone* (United Artists 1976)★★★, *BW Goes C&W* (United Artists 1976)★★, *Home Is Where The Heart Is* (Columbia 1976)★★, *Pieces* (Columbia 1977)★★, *Roads Of Life* (Arista 1979)★★, *The Poet* (Beverly Glen 1981)★★★, *The Poet II* (Beverly Glen 1984)★★, *Someday We'll All Be Free* (Beverly Glen 1985)★★, *So Many Rivers* (MCA 1985)★★, *Womagic* (MCA 1986)★★, *The Last Soul Man* (MCA 1987)★★.

● COMPILATIONS: *Bobby Womack's Greatest Hits* (United Artists 1974)★★★★, *Somebody Special* (Liberty 1984)★★★, *Check It Out* (Stateside 1986)★★★, *Womack Winners 1968-75* (Charly 1989, 1993)★★★, *Midnight Mover: The Bobby Womack Collection* double CD (1993)★★★★, *The Poet Trilogy* 3-CD (1994)★★★, *I Feel A Groove Comin' On* (Charly 1995)★★★, *The Soul Of Bobby Womack: Stop On By* (EMI 1997)★★★.

Woman Of The Year

A vehicle for the celebrated film actress Lauren Bacall, who had enjoyed a great deal of success in the 1970 Broadway musical *Applause*. *Woman Of The Year* opened at the Palace Theatre in New York on 29 March 1981, with music and lyrics by **John Kander** and **Fred Ebb**, and a book by Peter Stone which was based on the 1942 film starring Spencer Tracy and Katharine Hepburn. Stone changed the characters of the two principals from a seen-it-all sportswriter (Tracy) who falls for a famous political commentator (Hepburn), to a satirical cartoonist, Sam Craig (Harry Guardino), who is permanently feuding with the high-powered, hard-bitten television personality, Tess Harding (Bacall). The arguments continue to rage (only more so) after they are married. According to the critics, it would have been nothing without Lauren Bacall, but the score was entertaining without being brilliant, and included 'Woman Of the Year', 'When You're Right, You're Right', 'So What Else Is New?', 'One Of The Boys', 'Sometimes A Day Goes By', and 'We're Gonna Work It Out'. The highspot of the show comes towards the end of the second act, when the super-successful Tess, and Marilyn Cooper as a downtrodden, disillusioned housewife, argue that 'The Grass Is Always Greener' (Tess: 'You can hold a husband, that's wonderful'/Cooper: 'What's so wonderful? There's more to life than husbands'/Tess: 'I could use a husband'/Cooper: 'You can have *my* husband'/Tess: 'I've already *had* your husband . . .'). During the show's run of 770 performances, two of the actresses who succeeded Lauren Bacall were also stars of the big screen - Raquel Welch and **Debbie Reynolds**. Ms. Bacall and Ms. Cooper won **Tony Awards** for their strong, amusing performances, and there were additional Tonys for the show's score and book.

Womb

This San Francisco-based group comprised Rory Butcher (vocals/percussion), Greg Young (lead guitar), Karyl Boddy (keyboards/guitar/vocals), Roluf Stuart (saxophone/flute), Christopher Johnson (bass) and Ron Brunecker (drums). Their albums revealed a penchant for improvisation and although somewhat ill-focused, offered moments of inspiration, particularly *Overdub*, which contained the extended 'Evil People'. Womb disintegrated during the early 70s with late-period member Boots Hughston (saxophone/flute) later joining the **Hoodoo Rhythm Devils**.

● ALBUMS: *Womb* (Dot 1967)★★, *Overdub* (Dot 1968)★★.

Wombles

The brainchild of producer, arranger and songwriter, **Mike Batt**, the anthropomorphic Wombles emerged from a children's television series to take the charts by storm in 1974. They enjoyed a series of hits based loosely on their Wimbledon Common lifestyle (an early attempt at ecological education for children, the Wombles recycled the rubbish found on the Common). 'The Wombling Song', 'Remember You're A Womble', 'Banana Rock' and 'Wombling Merry Christmas' were all Top 10 hits, making the group the most successful and consistent chart act of the year. By the end of 1975, however, the novelty had worn thin and Batt's solo outing 'Summertime City' was outselling his puppet counterparts.

●ALBUMS: *Wombling Songs* (Columbia 1973)★★, *Remember You're A Womble* (Columbia 1974)★★, *Christmas Package* (Columbia 1974)★★, *Superwombling* (Columbia 1975)★★, *Wombling Free* film soundtrack (Columbia 1978)★★.

● COMPILATIONS: *20 Wombling Greats* (Warwick 1977)★★★.

Wonder Man

This was the second of **Danny Kaye**'s highly original and vastly entertaining films, and the first in which he played more than one role. It was produced by Sam Goldwyn for RKO, and released in 1945. Buzzy Bellew (Danny Kaye) is a loud and audacious nightclub performer who is all set to marry his dance partner (**Vera-Ellen**) when he is killed by a bunch of hoodlums. His spirit enters the body of his twin brother, the meek and mild Edwin Dingle (Danny Kaye), and insists that he take revenge for the murder. This situation was tailor-made for Kaye to display the full range of his highly individual manic talents, which were supplemented by the ingenious Oscar-winning special effects of John Fulton and A.W. Johns. The musical highlights included two hilarious spoofs, 'Opera Number' (written by Sylvia Fine) and the mangling of the Russian folk song 'Otchi Tchorniya', along with 'Bali Boogie' (Fine) and 'So-o-o-o-o In Love' (**Leo Robin**-**David Rose**). Virginia Mayo plays Edwin's librarian girlfriend, and also in the strong supporting cast were Steve Cochran, Allen Jenkins, S.Z. Sakall, Donald Woods, Edward S. Brophy, Otto Kruger, Natalie Schafer, and, of course, the stunning Goldwyn Girls. The screenplay was written by Don Hartman, Melville Shavelson and Philip Rapp, and was based on a story by Arthur Sheekam which was adapted by Jack Jevne and Eddie Moran.

John Wray staged the dance numbers, and this popular film, which confirmed Kaye as a star of world class, was beautifully photographed in Technicolor by Victor Milner. The director who made sense out of all the confusion was Bruce Humberstone.

Wonder Stuff

Formed in Stourbridge, West Midlands, England, in April 1986, the Wonder Stuff featured Miles Hunt (vocals, guitar), Malcolm Treece (guitar), Rob Jones (b. 1964, d. 30 July 1993, New York, USA; bass, replacing original member Chris Fradgley) and former **Mighty Lemon Drops** drummer Martin Gilks. The roots of the band lay in From Eden, a short-lived local group that featured Hunt on drums, Treece on guitar and Clint Mansell and Adam Mole, later of peers **Pop Will Eat Itself**, occupying the remaining roles. After amassing a sizeable local following, the Wonder Stuff released their debut EP, *It's A Wonderful Day*, to favourable small press coverage in 1987. Along with the aforementioned PWEI and other Midlands hopefuls **Crazyhead** and **Gaye Bykers On Acid**, they were soon pigeonholed under the banner of 'grebo rock' by the national music press. Despite this ill-fitting description, the Wonder Stuff's strengths always lay in melodic pop songs braced against an urgent, power-pop backdrop. After an ill-fated dalliance with **EMI Records**' *ICA Rock Week*, a second single, 'Unbearable', proved strong enough to secure a contract with **Polydor Records** at the end of 1987. 'Give Give Give Me More More More' offered a minor hit the following year, and was succeeded by arguably the band's best early song. Built on soaring harmonies, 'A Wish Away' was the perfect precursor to the Wonder Stuff's vital debut, *The Eight Legged Groove Machine*, which followed later that year and established them in the UK charts. 'It's Yer Money I'm After Baby', also from the album, continued to mine Hunt's cynical furrow (further evident on the confrontational b-side, 'Astley In The Noose' - referring to contemporary chart star **Rick Astley**) and began a string of UK Top 40 hits. 'Who Wants To Be The Disco King?' and the more relaxed 'Don't Let Me Down Gently', both from 1989, hinted at the diversity of the group's second album, *Hup*. Aided by fiddle, banjo and keyboard player Martin Bell (ex-Hackney Five-O), the album contrasted a harder, hi-tech sound with a rootsy, folk feel on tracks such as 'Golden Green', a double a-side hit when combined with a cover version of the **Youngbloods**' 'Get Together'. The band's well-documented internal wrangles came to a head with the departure of Rob Jones at the end of the decade. He moved to New York to form his own band, the Bridge And Tunnel Crew, with his wife Jessie Ronson, but died of heart failure in 1993. 'Circlesquare' introduced new bass player Paul Clifford. A subsequent low profile was broken in April 1991 with 'Size Of A Cow'. A UK Top 10 hit, this was quickly followed by 'Caught In My Shadow' and *Never Loved Elvis*. Once again, this third album revealed the Wonder Stuff's remorseless progression. Gone were the brash, punk-inspired three-minute classics, replaced by a richer musical content, both in Hunt's songwriting and musical performances. The extent of their popularity was emphasized in late 1991 when, in conjunction with comedian **Vic Reeves**, they topped the UK charts with a revival of **Tommy Roe**'s 'Dizzy'. The group made a swift return to the Top 10 in 1992 with the *Welcome To The Cheap Seats* EP, the title track's post-punk jig (with **Kirsty MacColl** on backing vocals) typifying the direction of the following year's *Construction For The Modern Idiot*. With songs now imbued with far more optimism due to Hunt's improved romantic prospects, singles such as 'Full Of Life' and 'Hot Love Now!' replaced previous uncertainties with unforced bonhomie. Thus, it came as something as a surprise when Hunt announced the band's dissolution to the press in July 1994 long before any grapes could sour - a decision allegedly given impetus by Polydor's insistence that the band should crack the USA (a factor in striking down the label's previous great singles band, the **Jam**). They bowed out at a final gig in Stratford upon Avon, Hunt leaving the stage with a pastiche of the **Sex Pistols**' epigram 'Every Feel You've Been Treated?' ringing in fans' ears. Writer James Brown offered another tribute in his sleeve-notes to the compulsory posthumous singles compilations: 'It was pointed out that if the writer Hunter S. Thompson had been the presiding influence over the **Beatles**, they they might have looked and sounded like the Wonder Stuff'. Suitably abbreviated, it provided less accurate testimony than 'greatest hits', perhaps, but it was certainly more in keeping with the band's legacy. Former members of the band (Treece, Clifford and Gilks) regrouped in 1995 as Weknowwhereyoulive, with the addition of former **Eat** singer Ange Doolittle on vocals. Hunt also gave up his job as host of **MTV**'s *120 Minutes* to put together a new band known as Vent 414.

● ALBUMS: *The Eight Legged Groove Machine* (Polydor 1988)★★★, *Hup* (Polydor 1989)★★★, *Never Loved Elvis* (Polydor 1991)★★★, *Construction For The Modern Idiot* (Polydor 1993)★★, *Live In Manchester* (Strange Fruit 1995)★★.

● COMPILATIONS: *If The Beatles Had Read Hunter ... The Singles* (Polydor 1994)★★★★.

● VIDEOS: *Welcome To The Cheap Seats* (Polygram Music Video 1992), *Greatest Hits Finally Live* (1994).

Wonder Who

At the 1966 apogee of their chart career, Nick Massi was replaced by Joe Long in the **Four Seasons**. Included in the new line-up's year of hits was a curious joke adaptation of **Bob Dylan**'s 'Don't Think Twice It's All Right' under the *nom de turntable*, Wonder Who. The song itself mattered less than lead vocalist **Frankie Valli**'s 'baby' falsetto - supposedly his impersonation of jazz singer **Rose Murphy**. Although it reached the US Top 5, the group did intend to seriously pursue this vocational tangent beyond a couple more singles, having made the point to their record company that the

number *per se* was commercial enough without buyers knowing it was by the Four Seasons.

Wonder, Stevie

b. Steveland Judkins, 13 May 1950, Saginaw, Michigan, USA. Born Judkins, Wonder now prefers to be known as Steveland Morris after his mother's married name. Placed in an incubator immediately after his birth, baby Steveland was given too much oxygen, causing Steveland to suffer permanent blindness. Despite this handicap, Wonder began to learn the piano at the age of seven, and had also mastered drums and harmonica by the age of nine. After his family moved to Detroit in 1954, Steveland joined a church choir, the gospel influence on his music balanced by the R&B of **Ray Charles** and **Sam Cooke** being played on his transistor radio. In 1961, he was discovered by Ronnie White of the **Miracles**, who arranged an audition at **Motown Records**. **Berry Gordy** immediately signed Steveland to the label, renaming him Little Stevie Wonder (the 'Little' was dropped in 1964). Wonder was placed in the care of writer/producer Clarence Paul, who supervised his early recordings. These accentuated his prodigal talents as a multi-instrumentalist, but did not represent a clear musical direction. In 1963, however, the release of the ebullient live recording 'Fingertips (Part 2)' established his commercial success, and Motown quickly marketed him on a series of albums as 'the 12-year-old genius' in an attempt to link him with the popularity of 'the genius', Ray Charles. Attempts to repeat the success of 'Fingertips' proved abortive, and Wonder's career was placed on hold during 1964 while his voice was breaking. He re-emerged in 1965 with a sound that was much closer to the Motown mainstream, scoring a worldwide hit with the dance-orientated 'Uptight (Everything's Alright)', which he co-wrote with Henry Cosby and Sylvia Moy. This began a run of US Top 40 hits that continued unbroken (apart from seasonal Christmas releases) for over six years.

From 1965-70, Stevie Wonder was marketed like the other major Motown stars, recording material that was chosen for him by the label's executives, and issuing albums that mixed conventional soul compositions with pop standards. His strong humanitarian principles were allowed expression on his version of **Bob Dylan**'s 'Blowin' In The Wind' and Ron Miller's 'A Place In The Sun' in 1966. He co-wrote almost all of his singles from 1967 onwards, and also began to collaborate on releases by other Motown artists, most notably co-writing **Smokey Robinson** And The Miracles' hit 'The Tears Of A Clown', and writing and producing the (**Detroit**) **Spinners**' 'It's A Shame'.

His contract with Motown expired in 1971; rather than re-signing immediately, as the label expected, Wonder financed the recording of two albums of his own material, playing almost all the instruments himself, and experimenting for the first time with more ambitious musical forms. He pioneered the use of the synthesizer in black music, and also widened his lyrical concerns to take in racial problems and spiritual questions. Wonder then used these recordings as a lever to persuade Motown to offer a more open contract, which gave him total artistic control over his music, plus the opportunity to hold the rights to the music publishing in his own company, Black Bull Music. He celebrated the signing of the deal with the release of the solo recordings, *Where I'm Coming From* and *Music Of My Mind*, which despite lukewarm critical reaction quickly established him at the forefront of black music.

Talking Book in 1972 combined the artistic advances of recent albums with major commercial success, producing glorious hit singles with the poly-rhythmic funk of 'Superstition' and the crafted ballad, 'You Are The Sunshine Of My Life'. Wonder married fellow Motown artist **Syreeta** on 14 September 1970; he premiered many of his new production techniques on *Syreeta* (1972) and *Stevie Wonder Presents Syreeta* (1974), for which he also wrote most of the material. *Innervisions* (1973) consolidated his growth and success with *Talking Book*, bringing further hit singles with the socially aware 'Living For The City' and 'Higher Ground'. Later that year, Wonder was seriously injured in a car accident; his subsequent work was tinged with the awareness of mortality, fired by his spiritual beliefs. The release of *Fulfillingness' First Finale* in 1974 epitomized this more austere approach. The double album *Songs In The Key Of Life* (1976) was widely greeted as his most ambitious and satisfying work to date. It showed a mastery and variety of musical forms and instruments, offering a joyous tribute to **Duke Ellington** on 'Sir Duke', and heralding a pantheon of major black figures on 'Black Man'. This confirmed Wonder's status as one of the most admired musicians and songwriters in contemporary music.

Surprisingly, after this enormous success, no new recordings surfaced for over three years, as Wonder concentrated on perfecting the soundtrack music to the documentary film, *The Secret Life Of Plants*. This primarily instrumental double album was greeted with disappointing reviews and sales. Wonder quickly delivered the highly successful *Hotter Than July* in 1980, which included a tribute song for the late Dr. Martin Luther King, 'Happy Birthday', and a notable essay in reggae form on 'Masterblaster (Jamming)'.

The failure of his film project brought an air of caution into Wonder's work, and delays and postponements were now a consistent factor in his recording process. After compiling the retrospective double album *Stevie Wonder's Original Musiquarium I* in 1982, which included four new recordings alongside the cream of his post-1971 work, Wonder scheduled an album entitled *People Move Human Play* in 1983. This never appeared; instead, he composed the soundtrack music for the film *The Woman In Red*, which included his biggest-selling single to date, the sentimental ballad 'I Just Called To Say I Loved You'.

The album on which he had been working since 1980 eventually appeared in 1985 as *In Square Circle*. Like his next project, *Characters* in 1987, it heralded a return to the accessible, melodic music of the previous decade. The unadventurous nature of both projects, and the heavy expectations engendered by the delay in their release, led to a disappointing reception from critics and public alike.

Wonder's status as an elder statesman of black music, and a champion of black rights, was boosted by his campaign in the early 80s to have the birthday of Dr. Martin Luther King celebrated as a national holiday in the USA. This request was granted by President Reagan, and the first Martin Luther King Day was celebrated on 15 January 1986 with a concert at which Wonder topped the bill. Besides his own recordings, Wonder has been generous in offering his services as a writer, producer, singer or musician to other performers. His most public collaborations included work with **Paul McCartney**, which produced a cloying but enormous hit, 'Ebony And Ivory', **Gary Byrd**, **Michael Jackson**, and **Eurythmics**, and on the benefit records by **USA For Africa** and **Dionne Warwick** & Friends. *Conversation Peace* in 1995 was an average album with no outstanding songs, but our expectation of Wonder is different to that of most other artists. He could release ten indifferent, poor, weak or spectacular records over the next 20 years and nothing would change our fixed perception of him and of the body of outstanding music he has produced since 1963.

● ALBUMS: *Tribute To Uncle Ray* (Tamla 1962)★★★, *The Jazz Soul Of Little Stevie* (Tamla 1962)★★★, *The 12-Year-Old Genius Recorded Live* (Tamla 1963)★★★, *With A Song In My Heart* (Tamla 1963)★★, *Stevie At The Beach* (Tamla 1964)★★, *Up-Tight (Everything's Alright)* (Tamla 1966)★★★, *Down To Earth* (Tamla 1966)★★★, *I Was Made To Love Her* (Tamla 1967)★★★★, *Someday At Christmas* (Tamla 1967)★★, *For Once In My Life* (Tamla 1968)★★★★, *My Cherie Amour* (Tamla 1969)★★★★, *Stevie Wonder Live* (Tamla 1970)★★, *Stevie Wonder Live At The Talk Of The Town* (Tamla 1970)★★★, *Signed, Sealed And Delivered* (Tamla 1970)★★★★, *Where I'm Coming From* (Tamla 1971)★★★, *Music Of My Mind* (Tamla 1972)★★★, *Talking Book* (Tamla Motown 1972)★★★★★, *Innervisions* (Tamla Motown 1973)★★★★★, *Fulfillingness' First Finale* (Tamla Motown 1974)★★★, *Songs In The Key Of Life* (Motown 1976)★★★★, *Stevie Wonder's Journey Through The Secret Life Of Plants* (Motown 1979)★★, *Hotter Than July* (Motown 1980)★★★, *The Woman In Red* soundtrack (Motown 1984)★★, *In Square Circle* (Motown 1985)★★, *Characters* (Motown 1987)★★, *Conversation Peace* (Motown 1995)★★, *Natural Wonder* (Motown 1995)★★.

● COMPILATIONS: *Greatest Hits* (Tamla 1968) ★★★★, *Greatest Hits, Volume Two* (Tamla 1971)★★★★, *Anthology* aka *Looking Back* rec. 1962-71(Motown 1977)★★★★, *Stevie Wonder's Original Musiquarium I* (Motown 1982)★★★, *Song Review* (Motown 1996)★★★.

● FURTHER READING: *Stevie Wonder*, Sam Hasegawa. *The Story Of Stevie Wonder*, Jim Haskins. *Stevie Wonder*, Ray Fox-Cumming. *Stevie Wonder*, Constanze Elsner. *The Picture Life Of Stevie Wonder*, Audrey Edwards, *Stevie Wonder*, C.

Dragonwagon. *Stevie Wonder*, Beth P. Wilson. *The Stevie Wonder Scrapbook*, Jim Haskins with Kathleen Benson. *Stevie Wonder*, Rick Taylor.

● FILMS: *Bikini Beach* (1964).

Wonder, Wayne

b. Von Wayne Charles, *c*.1972, Kingston, Jamaica, West Indies. Wonder's first reggae recordings appeared in the late 80s, when he was working with producer **Lloyd Dennis**. 'You Me And She' was followed by 'Night And Day', produced by Soljie. In 1991 the beautifully crafted 'Don't Take It Personal' was also produced by Soljie. Wonder's sweet singing style was soon employed by a number of producers in Jamaica, but his most prolific output came at the Penthouse studio with **Donovan Germain** and **Dave Kelly**. In 1991 he released 'I'm Only Human' and 'Baby You And I', both of which enhanced his appeal among women. His cover version of **Delroy Wilson**'s 'I Don't Know Why' as 'Movie Star' was a classic. The song also provided **Buju Banton** with a hit when he rode the tune for 'Bonafide Love'. Another cover version found Wonder singing over a remake of a **King Jammy**'s rhythm, 'Run Down The World', for his interpretation of **En Vogue**'s 'Hold On'. A tour of the UK was arranged in 1992 featuring the Penthouse crew, including Wonder alongside **Marcia Griffiths**, **Tony Rebel** and Buju Banton. With Tony Rebel, Wonder's sweet vocals graced the enduring 'Smaddy Pickney', a toast over 'I'm Only Human' and 'Cross Over The Bridge'. Buju Banton had secured a contract with the Stateside Mercury label and Wonder provided the singing vocals on 'Searching' and 'Commitment', as well as composing the tunes with Buju. In 1994 he toured again with Buju as part of the Penthouse Showcase. By 1995 Wonder had moved on to recording with other producers and enjoyed combination hits with **Don Yute** ('Sensi Ride') and **Buccaneer** ('Trust'). He was also a featured vocalist with King Jammy's when he resurrected the Sleng Teng Rhythm, appearing on the compilation *Sleng Teng Extravaganza '95*.

● ALBUMS: with Sanchez *Penthouse Presents (Volume One & Two)* (Penthouse 1990/91)★★★, *Wayne Wonder* (VP 1991)★★★, *Don't Have To* (Penthouse 1991)★★, *One More Chance* (World 1992)★★★, *All Original Bombshell* (Penthouse 1996)★★★.

● COMPILATIONS: *The Collection* (Pickout 1997)★★★.

Wonderful Life

Cliff Richard followed-up his box-office successes *The Young Ones* and *Summer Holiday* with this 1964 offering. The **Shadows**, Melvin Hayes and Una Stubbs, each of whom also appeared in the latter film, co-starred alongside the singer and Susan Hampshire, later to find fame as Fleur in television's *The Forsyte Saga*. The plot revolved around a group of young actors who, frustrated with the outmoded ideas of a film director, attempt to complete their own version of the feature in secret. Although far from challenging, *Wonderful Life* (US title *Swinger's Paradise*) was a breezy, carefree exer-

cise, bouyed by the undoubted enthusiasm of its participants. Indeed Richard took one of its most memorable songs, 'On The Beach', to number 7 in the UK charts while the soundtrack album peaked at number 2. Nevertheless, its windkissed light-heartedness proved out-of-date when compared to the wry wit and documentary styled pop cinema pioneered by Dick Lester in the **Beatles**' *A Hard Day's Night*. However, *Wonderful Life* director Sidney Furie later reaped rewards for his work on *Lady Sings The Blues*.

Wonderful Town

Given that the score for this show was the work of the **On The Town** team of **Leonard Bernstein** (music) and **Betty Comden** and **Adolph Green** (lyrics), it does not take a great deal of imagination to realise that the wonderful, friendly, and generally too-good-to-be-true city in question is New York. This musical advertisment for the 'Big Apple' opened at the Winter Garden in New York on 25 February 1953. It had a book by Joseph Fields and Jerome Chodorov, based on their play *My Sister Eileen*, which was adapted from stories by Ruth McKinney. It concerns two young ladies, Ruth Sherwood (Rosalind Russell) and, of course, her sister, Eileen (Edie Adams), who have travelled from Ohio to the big city in an effort to find fame and fortune. Ruth is a writer who cannot seem to get a man, while Eileen the actress has difficulty holding them off. During their subsequent hilarious adventures, Eileen goes to jail for assaulting a policeman, and the editor of the classy *Manhattan* magazine, Robert Baker (George Gaynes), makes it clear that he hates Ruth's stories, but then falls in love with their writer. No big hits emerged from the effervescent, tuneful, and amusing score, which included 'Christopher Street', 'Ohio', 'One Hundred Easy Ways', 'What A Waste', 'A Little Bit In Love', 'Conga!', 'Swing!', 'It's Love', and 'Wrong Note Rag', although the lovely 'A Quiet Girl' is inclined to linger in the memory. Rosalind Russell, who had starred in the non-musical 1942 film of *My Sister Eileen*, was outstanding in this rare Broadway appearance. *Wonderful Town* ran for 559 performances in New York, and a further 207 in London with **Pat Kirkwood** and Shani Wallis. Over 30 years later, in 1986, a major West End revival starred one of Britain's favourite comedy actresses, Maureen Lipman, and in 1994 the New York City Opera offered another, with Kay McClelland and Crista Moore. The 1955 musical film, with Betty Garrett, Janet Leigh, and Jack Lemmon, reverted to the original title of the play, *My Sister Eileen*.

Wonderwall

This much-maligned film was released in 1968. Taking a highly-voyeuristic theme, it concerned the antics of an absent-minded scientist (Jack McGowran) who, having discovered a hole in a wall, peeps into another world; a flat occupied by a photographic model (Jane Birkin). He espies a peripheral world of sex and drugs and while hamstrung by the era's dalliance with triviality, *Wonderwall* does pose questions about perception. **George Harrison** contributed the atmospheric soundtrack, which became the first release on the **Beatles**' Apple label. Indian musicians provided accompaniment on the bulk of the score, but former Liverpool beat group the **Remo Four** are also featured. **Eric Clapton** contributed distinctive guitar lines, particularly on 'Microbes' and while as self-indulgent as the film inspiring it, the album does contain several notable moments. Although far from essential, *Wonderwall* is equally not as insignificant as many critics have described it.

Wonderwall - George Harrison

The first official release on the Beatles' Apple label, *Wonderwall* was the soundtrack to an elliptical film of the same name. The 'quiet' Beatle's love of Indian music was already well chronicled and here, freed from the constraints of commercial consideration, he fused raga and rock in innovatory fashion. Members of ex-Merseybeat group the Remo Four joined guitarist Eric Clapton in providing occidental perspectives, but the selections hinge on Eastern sounds and scales resulting in a serene, hypnotic selection. Harrison directs proceedings, rather than leads them, but nonetheless creates a unique and highly personal statement.
● Tracks: *Microbes; Red Lady Too; Table And Pakavaj; In The Park; Drilling A Home; Guru Vandana; Greasy Legs; Ski-ing; Gat Kirwani; Dream Scene; Party Seacombe; Love Scene; Crying; Cowboy Music; Fantasy Sequins; On The Bed; Glass Box; Wonderwall To Be Here; Singing Om.*
● First released 1969
● UK peak chart position: did not chart
● USA peak chart position: 49

Wood, Booty

b. Mitchell Wood, 27 December 1919, Dayton, Ohio, USA, d. June 1987. Wood took up the trombone in his teens, beginning his professional career towards the end of the 30s. In the early 40s he was a member of the bands of **Tiny Bradshaw** and **Lionel Hampton**. While serving in the US Navy during World War II he played in the band that included **Willie Smith** and **Clark Terry**. After the war Wood returned briefly to Hampton, then worked in bands led by **Arnett Cobb**, **Erskine Hawkins** and **Count Basie**. After a spell outside music he returned to the scene in 1959, joining **Duke Ellington** with whom he played intermittently during the next dozen years. He also appeared with **Earl 'Fatha' Hines** and in the late 70s and early 80s was with Basie again. A forceful player with a rich open tone, Wood's spell with Ellington ensured that he also became adept at using the mute, performing with colourful effect on many of the band's standards.
● ALBUMS: with Duke Ellington *Blues In Orbit* (1959)★★★★, with Ellington *Nutcracker Suite* (1960)★★★★, *The Booty Wood All Stars* (1960)★★★.

Wood, Brenton

b. Alfred Jesse Smith, 26 July 1941, Shreveport, Louisiana, USA. Smith was a veteran of several vocal groups, including the Dootones, the Quotations and Little Freddie And The Rockets, before assuming the name Brenton Wood in deference to his home district in Los Angeles. As a solo act he enjoyed fame with 'The Oogum Boogum Song' (1967), a nonsense novelty record. The follow-up, 'Gimme Little Sign' (although not a novelty), was in a similar style, but its more lasting appeal was confirmed when the single reached the UK and US Top 10. Further releases, 'Baby You Got It' (1967) and 'Some Got It, Some Don't' (1968), diluted the pattern and were less successful. Wood later recorded a duet with **Shirley Goodman**, before making a belated return to the US R&B chart in 1977 with 'Come Softly To Me'.
● ALBUMS: *Gimme Little Sign* (Liberty 1967)★★★, *The Oogum Boogum Man* (Double Shot 1967)★★★, *Baby You Got It* (1967)★★★.
● COMPILATIONS: *Brenton Wood's 18 Best* (1991)★★★.

Wood, Del

b. Adelaide Hazlewood, 22 February 1920, Nashville, Tennessee, USA, d. 3 October 1989. Wood's parents gave her a piano for her fifth birthday with the hope that she would become a classical pianist. She had different ideas and aimed for a career at the *Grand Ole Opry*. She developed a thumping ragtime style that, in 1951, saw her record her version of 'Down Yonder', a tune that had proved a million-seller for Gid Tanner and the Skillet Lickers in 1934. Wood's version on the Tennessee label reached number 5 in the US country charts and also became a million-seller. After guesting on the *Opry* in 1952 and refusing the chance of playing with **Bob Crosby**, she joined the roster in 1953. Her playing proved so popular that she toured with *Opry* shows, even to Japan. She recorded for several labels, making popular versions of such numbers as 'Johnson Rag' and 'Piano Roll Blues'. She had no more chart entries, but she won herself the nickname of 'Queen Of The Ragtime Pianists'. She remained a member of the *Opry* until her death in the Baptist Hospital, Nashville, on 3 October 1989, following a stroke on 22 September, the day she was scheduled to appear on the *Legendary Ladies Of Country Music Show*.
● ALBUMS: *Down Yonder* (RCA Victor 1955)★★★, *Hot Happy & Honky* (1957)★★★, *Mississippi Showboat* (1959)★★★, *Buggies, Bustles & Barrellhouse* (1960)★★★, *Flivvers, Flappers & Fox Trots* (1960)★★★, *Ragtime Goes International* (1961)★★★, *Ragtime Goes South Of The Border* (1962)★★★, *Honky Tonk Piano* (1962)★★★, *Piano Roll Blues* (1963)★★★, *It's Honky Tonk Time* (1964)★★★, *Roll Out The Piano* (1964)★★★, *Uptight, Lowdown & Honky Tonk* (1966)★★★, *There's A Tavern In The Town* (60s)★★, *Del Wood Favorites, Encore-Del Wood, Ragtime Favorites, Plays Berlin & Cohen Volumes, Ragtime Glory Special* (all 70s).

Wood, Haydn

b. 25 March 1882, Slaithwaite, Yorkshire, England, d. 11 March 1959, London, England. Wood's 'Roses Of Picardy' (lyrics by Fred E. Weatherly, who collaborated with **Eric Coates** and many others) has ensured his place in 20th century popular music, although he also wrote other well-remembered melodies, such as 'The Horse Guards - Whitehall', used by BBC radio since the 40s to introduce *Down Your Way*. Many of his songs (as well as 'Picardy' he composed 'A Brown Bird Singing' and 'Love's Garden Of Roses') were written for his wife, the soprano Dorothy Court, and their success has tended to overshadow the sheer volume of his musical output: 15 suites, nine rhapsodies, eight overtures, six choral compositions, three large concertante pieces as well as over 60 assorted works. A childhood spent on the Isle of Man (in the Irish sea) inspired 'Mannin Veen' (1932/3) (the title of this Manx tone poem means 'Dear Isle of Man'), and 'Mylecharane' written just after the end of World War II. His major suites included 'Moods' (1932) from which comes the concert waltz 'Joyousness', 'Paris' (distinguished by the march 'Montmartre'), 'London Landmarks' (which includes the above-mentioned 'Horse Guards - Whitehall'), 'Snapshots Of London' and 'London Cameos'. Some other notable works: 'Virginia - A Southern Rhapsody', 'Sketch Of A Dandy', 'The Seafarer - A Nautical Rhapsody', 'Soliloquy' and 'Serenade To Youth'.
● ALBUMS: *British Light Music - Haydn Wood* (Marco Polo 1992)★★★★.

Wood, Ron

b. 1 June 1947, Hillingdon, Middlesex, England. This younger brother of the **Artwoods**' leader formed the **Birds** with other students at his Middlesex art school. Although they had a minor hit with 'Leaving Here' in 1965, they are better remembered for the publicity-earning writ they served on the **Byrds** for breach of copyright. Next, Wood joined the latter-day **Creation** before entering **Jeff Beck**'s employ as second guitarist and then bass player. Ructions with Beck led to Wood's dismissal in 1969. After a brief reinstatement, he and Beck's vocalist, **Rod Stewart**, amalgamated with three former **Small Faces**. As the **Faces**, they became a major international act in the early 70s. To a lesser degree than Stewart, Wood inaugurated a parallel solo career - beginning with 1974's *I've Got My Own Album To Do*. Although mainly self-composed, a highlight was a revival of James Ray's 'If You Gotta Make A Fool Of Somebody', a Merseybeat standard recalled by **George Harrison** who, with Wood, wrote 'Far East Man' for the album, and was among the famous friends mentioned on its sleeve. The most prominent of these was **Keith Richards** who likewise served Wood on 1975's *Now Look*, and invited him to be a temporary member of the **Rolling Stones** while the group searched for a replacement for guitarist **Mick Taylor**. However, after the Faces' final tour, Wood enlisted in December 1975 as a full-time member while continuing to release

solo records such as 1979's *Gimme Some Neck* and its 'Seven Days' single. This had been penned by **Bob Dylan** who the new Stone would assist on a 1981 album. Also helping Dylan then was **Ringo Starr** whose subsequent *Stop And Smell The Roses* would include a Wood-Starr opus, 'Dead Giveaway'. Incurably addicted to jam sessions, Wood was a familiar sight in the 'impromptu' all-star performances that concluded prestigious music industry award ceremonies. He was also noticed performing during televised spectaculars, starring old idols like **Fats Domino**, **Chuck Berry** and **Jerry Lee Lewis**. Included among Wood's other extra-mural activities was an exhibition of his portrait paintings.
● ALBUMS: *I've Got My Own Album To Do* (Warners 1974)★★★, *Now Look* (Warners 1975)★★★, with Ronnie Lane *Mahoney's Last Stand* (Atlantic 1976)★★★, *Gimme Some Neck* (Columbia 1979)★★, *1, 2, 3, 4* (Columbia 1981)★★★, *Cancel Everything* (Thunderbolt 1985)★★, with Bo Diddley *Live At The Ritz* (1988)★★, *Slide On This* (Continuum 1992)★★, *Slide On Live ... Plugged In & Standing* (Continuum 1993)★★★.
● FURTHER READING: *Ron Wood: The Works*, Ron Wood with Bill German.

Wood, Roy

b. Ulysses Adrian Wood, 8 November 1946, Birmingham, England. Having been named after Homer's Greek mythological hero, Wood abandoned this eminently suitable pop star sobriquet in favour of the more prosaic Roy. As a teenager, he was a itinerant guitarist, moving steadily through a succession of minor Birmingham groups including the Falcons, the Lawmen, Gerry Levene and the Avengers and Mike Sheridan and the Nightriders. After a failed stab at art school, he pooled his talents with some of the best musicians on the Birmingham beat scene to form the **Move**. Under the guidance of **Tony Secunda**, they established themselves as one of the best pop groups of their time, with Wood emerging as their leading songwriter. By the time of 'Fire Brigade' (1967), Wood was instilled as lead singer and it was his fertile pop imagination which took the group through a plethora of musical styles, ranging from psychedelia to rock 'n' roll revivalism, classical rock and heavy metal. Never content to be bracketed to one musical area, Wood decided to supplement the Move's pop work by launching the grandly-named **Electric Light Orchestra**, whose aim was to produce more experimental albums-orientated rock with a classical influence. Wood survived as **ELO**'s frontman for only one single and album before a personality clash with fellow member **Jeff Lynne** prompted his departure in June 1972. He returned soon after with **Wizzard**, one of the most inventive and appealing pop groups of the early 70s. During this period, he also enjoyed a parallel solo career and although his two albums were uneven, they revealed his surplus creative energies as a multi-instrumentalist, engineer, producer and even sleeve designer. Back in the singles chart, Wood the soloist scored several UK hits including the majestic 'Forever', an inspired and affectionate tribute to **Neil Sedaka** and the **Beach Boys**, with the composer playing the part of an English **Phil Spector**. Wood's eccentric ingenuity continued on various singles and b-sides, not least the confusing 'Bengal Jig', which fused bagpipes and sitar!. By the late 70s, Wood was ploughing less commercial ground with the Wizzo Band, Rock Brigade and the Helicopters, while his former group ELO produced million-selling albums. The chart absence of Wood since 1975 remains one of pop's great mysteries especially in view of his previous track record as producer, songwriter and brilliant manipulator of contrasting pop genres.

● ALBUMS: *Boulders* (Harvest 1973)★★★, *Mustard* (Jet 1975)★★★, *On The Road Again* (Warners 1979)★★, *Starting Up* (Legacy 1987)★★.

● COMPILATIONS: *The Roy Wood Story* (Harvest 1976)★★, *The Singles* (Speed 1982)★★★, *The Best Of Roy Wood 1970-1974* (MFP 1985)★★★.

Woodard, Rickey

b. 5 August 1950, Nashville, Tennessee, USA. After studying saxophones under Bill Green and majoring in music at Tennessee State University, Woodard worked extensively with a wide range of performers. He worked with jazz artists such as **Jimmy Smith**, **Billy Higgins**, **Frank Capp** and **Al Grey** and also backed singers from the jazz and pop worlds including **Ella Fitzgerald**, **Ernestine Anderson**, Barbara McNair and **Prince**. He also recorded with Capp and with the big band co-led by **Jeff Clayton** and **Jeff Hamilton**. Mostly playing tenor saxophone, he established a solid if localized reputation in the USA before venturing onto the international jazz festival circuit. By the early 90s Woodard was fast becoming a popular visitor to Europe and the UK. Playing alto and soprano saxophones in addition to tenor (he also plays clarinet, flute and guitar), Woodard is a vibrant and forceful soloist, his tenor saxophone styling hinting at an affection for the work of **Wardell Grey**, **Dexter Gordon** and, especially, **Hank Mobley**. For all such stylistic mentors, however, Woodard is very much his own man and this, allied to his playing skills and an engaging personality, assures him of a continuing welcome at jazz venues at home and abroad.

● ALBUMS: *The Frank Capp Trio Presents Rickey Woodard* (Concord 1991)★★★, *California Cookin'!* (Candid 1991)★★★★, *Night Mist* (1992)★★★, *The Tokyo Express* (Candid 1993)★★★, *Yazoo* (Concord 1994)★★.

Woode, Jimmy

b. 23 September 1928, Philadelphia, Pennsylvania, USA. After extensive studies on both piano and bass, Woode settled on the latter instrument. Military service delayed the start of his professional career, but in 1946 he formed his own band which worked in the Boston area. Among his early musical associates were **Nat Pierce**, **Joe 'Flip' Phillips** and **Zoot Sims**, and he was also accompanist to **Ella Fitzgerald** and **Sarah Vaughan**. In the early 50s he was a member of the house band at **George Wein**'s Storyville Club in Boston, where he played with numerous visiting jazz stars. By 1955 his reputation was such that he was invited to join **Duke Ellington**, a job he held for five years. After leaving Ellington he settled in Europe, becoming a member of the **Clarke-Boland Big Band** throughout most of its existence. The 60s and 70s were busy years for Woode; in addition to playing with various bands on a regular basis, he gigged with visiting Americans, including **Don Byas** and **Johnny Griffin**, ran his own music publishing company, and worked in radio, television and recording studios. This pattern continued throughout the 80s, with appearances in the Paris Reunion Band, led by **Nathan Davis**, and at Ellington reunions, including Ellington '88 at Oldham, England, where he was reunited with former Ellington rhythm-section partner **Sam Woodyard**. A solid section player, Woode continues to draw the respect of his fellow musicians.

● ALBUMS: with Duke Ellington *Such Sweet Thunder* (1957)★★★★, *The Colorful Strings Of Jimmy Woode* (1957)★★★.

Woodentops

At one point, it seemed likely that the Woodentops from Northampton, England, would be commercially successful. After the offbeat 'Plenty', a one-off single for the **Food Records** label in 1984, songwriter Rolo McGinty (guitar, vocals), Simon Mawby (guitar), Alice Thompson (keyboards), Frank de Freitas (bass) and Benny Staples (drums) joined Geoff Travis's **Rough Trade Records** and issued a string of catchy singles that fared increasingly well commercially. The jolly 'Move Me' was followed by the menacing pace of 'Well Well Well' while 'It Will Come' seemed a likely hit. The band's critically acclaimed debut album, *Giant*, was an enticing mixture of frantic acoustic guitars and a warm yet offbeat clutch of songs. After 'Love Affair With Everyday Living' in 1986, McGinty decided on a change in direction, hardening up the Woodentops' sound and incorporating new technology within their live repertoire. The results were heard the following year on *Live Hypnobeat Live*, which relied on material from *Giant*, albeit performed live in a drastically revitalized way. *Wooden Foot Cops On The Highway* and the accompanying single, 'You Make Me Feel'/'Stop This Car', showed how far the Woodentops had progressed by early 1988, although it was to be their final album. Less uncompromising than their live project, the sound was more mature, with an emphasis on detail previously lacking. What the band failed to achieve in commercial terms was more than compensated for by the level of critical and public respect they earned. McGinty moved into deep house music, recording as Pluto,

● ALBUMS: *Giant* (Rough Trade 1986)★★★, *Live Hypnobeat Live* (Upside 1987)★★★, *Wooden Foot Cops On the Highway* (Rough Trade 1988)★★★★.

Woodface - Crowded House

The third and best album from the finest rock band Australia has yet produced. A good second would have been Split Enz, but they split up to become errr . . . Crowded House. The Finn brothers have been writing songs for many years and it is encouraging to see that their lyrics are as sharp, fresh and perceptive as ever. The opener 'Chocolate Cake' starts with 'not everyone in New York would pay to see Andrew Lloyd Webber, may his trousers fall down as he bows to the Queen and the crown'. Nothing lapses, no standards are dropped. No worries. This one will be around as long as the Beatles.

● Tracks: *Chocolate Cake; It's Only Natural; Fall At Your Feet; Tall Trees; Weather With You; Whispers And Moans; Four Seasons In One Day; There Goes God; Fame Is; All I Ask; As Sure As I Am; Italian Plastic; She Goes On; How Will You Go.*

● First released 1991
● UK peak chart position: 6
● USA peak chart position: 83

Woodfork, 'Poor' Bob

b. 13 March 1925, Lake Village, Arkansas, USA, d. June 1988, Chicago, Illinois, USA. Woodfork learned guitar as a youngster, but his musical career began in the US Army during World War II, when the USO spotted him in Swansea, Wales. Back in Chicago, he worked as a sideman for **Otis Rush**, and later for **Jimmy Rogers**, **Howlin' Wolf**, **George Smith** and **Little Walter**. Some mid-60s recordings under his own name were released on albums for the new European blues audience, but did not advance his career. Woodfork continued to work as a sideman and occasional leader in the Chicago clubs.

● ALBUMS: including *Blues Southside Chicago* (1966)★★★, *Have A Good Time* (1971)★★★.

Wooding, Sam

b. 17 June 1895, Philadelphia, Pennsylvania, USA, d. 1 August 1985. Largely self-taught, Wooding began playing piano professionally around 1912, before playing in clubs in New York City. After military service in World War I he formed his own band for an engagement in Atlantic City, then played other east coast venues before taking a band to Europe in 1925. He was resident in Berlin with the *Chocolate Kiddies* show, which featured some of **Duke Ellington**'s earliest music, then toured throughout central and eastern Europe, Russia, Scandinavia, and the UK. On the way back to the USA the band visited South America. After a few months in the USA, Wooding formed another band with which to tour Europe, this time returning in 1931. In the early 30s he led a band in the USA, but by the middle of the decade, and on the eve of the swing era, he abandoned performing in order to study music. In the late 30s and early 40s he taught, and also directed a gospel choir, then formed a small vocal group. In the 50s and 60s he toured as a single and in partnership with singer Rae Harrison. He continued a round of teaching and frequent appearances as a performer into old age. In 1976, as part of America's Bicentennial celebrations, he led a 10-piece band at concerts and for a recording session. Despite his widespread popularity in other lands, Wooding never gained real success in his own country. By the time he tried to establish himself in the USA, musical times were changing and the style on which he had built his overseas reputation was out of fashion. Nevertheless, Wooding was enormously important in spreading awareness of jazz and his was a significant role in helping to make jazz a truly international music. The music he played to European audiences was much closer to true jazz than was, say, the earlier music offered to Europeans by **James Reese Europe**; and Wooding's sidemen on his early visits included such leading jazzmen as **Tommy Ladnier**, **Willie Lewis** and **Gene Sedric**.

● ALBUMS: *Bicentennial* (1976)★★★.
● COMPILATIONS: *Sam Wooding And His Chocolate Kiddies Orchestra (1925-29)* (1974)★★★.

Woodman, Britt

b. 4 June 1920, Los Angeles, California, USA. Following in the footsteps of his trombone-playing father, Woodman took up the instrument in childhood to play in his father's band. In the late 30s he worked mostly on the west coast, usually in lesser-known bands, although he ended the decade with **Les Hite**. After military service in World War II he played in **Boyd Raeburn**'s musically adventurous band and was then with **Lionel Hampton**. At the end of the 40s he formalized his musical education, studying at Westlake College in Los Angeles, and then joined the **Duke Ellington** orchestra as lead trombonist. In the mid-50s he found time for record dates with **Charles Mingus**, a friend from childhood, and **Miles Davis**. His tenure with Ellington ended in 1960 and thereafter he worked in studio and theatre bands in Los Angeles and New York City. He has continued with his film and television work, but has appeared on record leading his own small band and with small groups led by **Bill Berry** and **Benny Carter**. He has also played in the big bands of Berry, **Toshiko Akiyoshi** and the **Capp-Pierce Juggernaut**. Woodman's playing style reflects his career-long immersion in big band music, but is shot through with intriguing glimpses of his interest in bop.

● ALBUMS: with Duke Ellington *Seattle Concert* (1952)★★★, with Ellington *Such Sweet Thunder* (1957)★★★, with Charles Mingus *Mingus!* (1960)★★★, with Bill Berry *For Duke* (1977)★★★, *Britt Woodman In LA* (1977)★★★.

Woodruff, Bob

b. 14 March 1961, USA. Bob Woodruff, a Nashville, Tennessee, USA-based singer-songwriter, received a generally favourable critical response on the release of his 1994 debut, *Dreams & Saturday Nights*. However, further progress was impeded by what he later described as 'philosophical differences' with his label, **Asylum Records**. He re-emerged in 1997 with *Desire*

Road, released on Imprint Records, a new Nashville label. As he told **Billboard** magazine on its release: 'The major difference with *Desire Road* is the label move from Asylum to Imprint. I was one of the first artists signed to Asylum when it opened in Nashville, and based on an artist roster including singer/songwriters like **Guy Clark** and **Emmylou Harris**, I felt like it was the perfect home for me. But towards the end of my record's promotion, I felt their philosophy changed, and after an amicable split, I and my manager, Jim Della Croce, met with Roy (Wunsch) and felt that he was starting up a label similar to Asylum, at the beginning, that would be the right place for me to make records.' Co-produced with Roy Kennedy, who occasionally adds guitar to Woodruff's live performances, this second collection added a rockier edge to many of Woodruff's compositions, and again drew praise for the artist's insightful songwriting. *Desire Road* featured nine originals, as well as cover versions of **John Fogerty**'s 'Almost Saturday Night' and two **Arthur Alexander** songs, 'Every Day I Have To Cry Some' and 'If It's Really Got To Be This Way'.

● ALBUMS: *Dreams & Saturday Nights* (Asylum 1994)★★★, *Desire Road* (Imprint 1997)★★★★.

Woods, Gay

b. Gay Corocan, Eire. Gay Woods was originally associated, alongside her husband Terry Woods (see **Woods, Gay And Terry**), with bands such as **Sweeney's Men** and **Steeleye Span** whom they left in 1970. As the Woods Band the group toured throughout Europe and recorded an adventurous self-titled debut album in 1970. Afterwards they moved back to Eire and recorded several singer/songwriter albums released on **Polydor Records**, before returning to their original home at Mulligan Records. Their musical and personal relationship sundered at the end of the 70s, at which time Gay joined Irish progressive rock band Auto Da Fe, who also included new partner Trevor Knight. They recorded several albums and singles in the mid-80s including versions of 'Something's Gotten Hold Of My Heart' and 'Magic Moments'. Much of their material, however, was never released in the UK, including several sessions produced by **Phil Lynott**. Gay then temporarily retired from performance in the late 80s to concentrate on raising her daughter. She returned to Steeleye Span in 1994 - in actual fact the first time she had played on stage with the venerable folk-rock institution despite having appeared on their debut album.

● ALBUMS: with the Woods Band *The Woods Band* (Mulligan 1970)★★★, with Auto Da Fe *Five Singles And A Smoked Cod* (Rewind 1984)★★, *Tatitum* (Rewind 1986)★★★.

Woods, Gay And Terry

Playing together in a duo during the late 60s, Gay and Terry Woods became pivotal figures in the Irish folk scene through their involvement with **Sweeney's Men**, **Steeleye Span** and **Dr. Strangely Strange**, whom they left at the end of 1970. Husband and wife, Gay and Terry, were ambitious mavericks at the adventurous end of folk rock. As the Woods Band, their debut album mixed traditional ballads and their own songs. They worked extensively in England and Europe, before disbanding and retiring to Eire. Subsequently, they signed with **Polydor**, and, with a familiar set of folk/rock musicians, recorded a series of increasingly experimental singer-songwriter albums. Gay's soft, tender vocal contrasted with Terry's lazy drawl and hypnotic Irish melodies. The finest of these is *The Time Is Right*, an appealing blend of acoustic/electric elements and intuitive compositions. *Tenderhooks* was cut for the small Mulligan label in Dublin, and was a much more upbeat piece of warm, rolling roots rock. Previously used to touring as an acoustic duo, The Woods once again assembled an electric band to promote it, and, although at the height of their creativity, decided to separate. Gay moved into prog ballad rock with Auto De Fe, and Terry temporarily revived the Woods Band before giving up music altogether. Some years later he emerged from retirement and joined the **Pogues**, where this enduring, rebellious musician continues to be influential.

● ALBUMS: *The Woods Band* (Greenwich 1970)★★★, *Backwoods* (Polydor 1975)★★★, *The Time Is Right* (Polydor 1976)★★★, *Renowned* (Polydor 1976)★★★, *Tenderhooks* (Rockburgh 1978)★★★.

Woods, Harry

b. Henry MacGregor Woods, 4 November 1896, North Chelmsford, Massachusetts, USA, d. 14 January 1970, Phoenix, Arizona, USA. A popular songwriter during the 20s and 30s, Woods sometimes wrote both music and lyrics, but collaborated mostly with lyricist **Mort Dixon**. Woods was physically handicapped, lacking three - some say all - of the fingers of his left hand, but he still managed to play the piano with the other one. He was educated at Harvard, and then served in the US Army in World War I. He started writing songs in the early 20s, and 'I'm Going' South' was interpolated into the Broadway show *Bombo*, which starred **Al Jolson**. During the late 20s Woods provided Jolson with some of his biggest hits, such as 'When The Red Red Robin Comes Bob-Bob-Bobbin' Along' and 'I'm Looking Over A Four-Leaf Clover' (with Dixon). His other 20s songs included 'Paddlin' Madelin' Home', (a hit in 1925 for **Cliff Edwards**, and still remembered over 60 years later by 'revival bands' such as the **Pasadena Roof Orchestra**), 'Me Too', 'Is It Possible?', 'Just Like A Butterfly', 'Side By Side', 'Where The Wild Flowers Grow', 'Since I Found You', 'In The Sing Song Sycamore Tree', 'She's A Great Great Girl', 'Riding To Glory' and 'Lonely Little Bluebird'.

In 1929, Woods wrote 'A Little Kiss Each Morning' and 'Heigh-Ho, Everybody, Heigh-Ho' for **Rudy Vallee** to sing in his debut movie *Vagabond Lover*. During the 30s he spent three years in England, writing songs for such movies as *Evergreen* ('When You've Got A Little

Springtime In Your Heart' and 'Over My Shoulder'), *It's Love Again* ('I Nearly Let Love Go Slipping Through My Fingers', 'Gotta Dance My Way To Heaven'), *Jack Ahoy* ('My Hat's On The Side Of My Head'), *Aunt Sally* ('We'll All Go Riding On A Rainbow'), and *Road House* ('What A Little Moonlight Can Do', a song which helped to launch **Billie Holiday**'s career). Wood also collaborated with British songwriters and music publishers **Jimmy Campbell** and **Reg Connelly** on 'Just An Echo In The Valley' and the all-time standard, 'Try A Little Tenderness'. Back in the USA in 1936, Woods wrote big hits for **Fats Waller** ('When Somebody Thinks You're Wonderful') and **Arthur Tracy** ('The Whistling Waltz'). His other songs included 'Here Comes The Sun', 'It Looks Like Love', 'River Stay 'Way From My Door', 'All Of A Sudden', 'A Little Street Where Old Friends Meet', 'Loveable', 'Pink Elephants', 'We Just Couldn't Say Goodbye', 'Oh, How She Can Love', 'You Ought To See Sally On Sunday', 'Dancing With My Shadow', 'I'll Never Say "Never" Again' and 'So Many Memories'. Among his other collaborators were **Gus Kahn**, **Arthur Freed**, **Benny Davis**, and Howard Johnson and **Kate Smith**, who worked with Woods on Smith's theme song 'When The Moon Comes Over The Mountain'. Woods retired from songwriting in the early 40s, and eventually went to live in Arizona where he died in 1970 following a car crash.

Woods, Johnny

b. 1 November 1917, Looxahoma, Mississippi, USA, d. 1 February 1990, Olive Branch, Mississippi, USA. Like his sometime partner, **Mississippi Fred McDowell**, Woods was not discovered until he was in his fifties and it was through McDowell that he had his first chance to record, although they had not seen one another for eight years at that time. A self-taught harmonica-player, he developed his technique, which relied upon rhythmic figures, by adapting the work hollers he heard in the fields in which his family worked. Because of that, Woods was at his best when performing solo on 'So Many Cold Mornings' and 'Going Up The Country', or playing a typical one-chord traditional Mississippi piece such as 'Long-Haired Doney' (also known as 'My Jack Don't Need No Water'), which he recorded with both McDowell and **R.L. Burnside**.
● ALBUMS: *Mississippi Delta Blues Vol. 1* (Arhoolie 1967/1994)★★★, *So Many Cold Mornings* rec. 1981 and 1984 (Swingmaster 1988)★★★, *The Blues Of Johnny Woods* (Swingmaster 1989)★★★.

Woods, Oscar

b. 1900, Shreveport, Louisiana, USA, d. *c*.1956, Shreveport, Louisiana, USA. Little is known about Oscar 'Buddy' Woods, who was one of the most impressive of the pre-war slide guitar blues stylists. He was closely associated with Ed Schaffer with whom he recorded as the Shreveport Home Wreckers in Memphis in 1930. In 1932, he and Schaffer took part in

what was probably one of the first integrated sessions when they lent their vocal and instrumental talents to support risqué country singer **Jimmie Davis**, later governor of Louisiana and famous for 'You Are My Sunshine'. Woods recorded some master sole tracks in 1936, in New Orleans, under the pseudonym of the Lone Wolf and later featured with Kitty Gray and others as the Wampus Cats. Finally, in 1940, he recorded five tracks for **Alan Lomax** of the Library Of Congress. He also worked with B.K. Turner, 'The Black Ace', and was last heard of working in the Shreveport area around the late 40s/early 50s.
● COMPILATIONS: *Complete Recordings: Oscar 'Buddy' Woods 1930-1938* (Document 1987)★★★.

Woods, Phil

b. 2 November 1931, Springfield, Massachusetts, USA. Woods began playing alto saxophone as a child, studied later at the Juilliard School of Music in New York and by his early 20s had already made a significant mark on jazz. Playing hard bop and acknowledging **Charlie Parker** but never slavishly so, Woods became a vital force in jazz in the late 50s. He led his own small groups, co-led a band with Gene Quill, played in bands led by artists such as **Buddy Rich**, **Cecil Payne**, **Thelonious Monk**, **Quincy Jones** and **Benny Goodman**, and worked as a studio musician and recorded extensively, including appearing on **Benny Carter**'s 1961 *Further Definitions*. During the 60s he was also active as a teacher and towards the end of the decade became resident in France, where he formed the European Rhythm Machine. Woods led this band until his return to the USA in the early 70s where, in 1973, he formed a new quartet which met with great critical and commercial acclaim. This group stayed in operation for the next few years and Woods's stature continued to grow. He also made a dynamic if somewhat anonymous impact on the pop music scene with his solo on **Billy Joel**'s hit single, 'I Love You Just The Way You Are'. In the early 80s Woods was active in the USA, touring internationally, and continuing to record albums of exceptional quality. His quartet had expanded with the addition of **Tom Harrell**. He also recorded with **Dizzy Gillespie**, **Rob McConnell** and **Budd Johnson** Although identified with the post-Parker school of alto saxophone playing, Woods has always had his own style. Early records, such as *Bird Calls*, reveal a highly sophisticated performer belying his age with the maturity of his improvisations. He plays with a rich, full sound, avoiding the harshness favoured by some of his contemporaries. By the late 80s Woods was firmly established as a major jazz musician and one of the most successful alto saxophonists the music had known. At the start of the 90s his standards of performance remained outstanding. Although this decade saw him entering his 60s the depth of his imagination was unimpaired and his playing was still filled with the enthusiasm and vitality of his youth.
● ALBUMS: *Bird's Eyes* (Philology 1947 recordings)★★★,

Wood Lore (Original Jazz Classics 1955)★★★, *The Young Bloods* (Original Jazz Classics 1956)★★★★, *Pairing Off* (Original Jazz Classics 1956)★★★, *Warm Woods* (1957)★★★, *Four Altos* (Original Jazz Classics 1957)★★★, *Phil And Quill* (Original Jazz Classics 1957)★★★★, *Bird Calls, Volume 1* (1957)★★★, *Early Quintets* (1959)★★, *Rights Of Swing* (Candid 1961)★★★, *Greek Cooking* (1967)★★, *Alive And Well In Paris* (1968)★★, *The Birth Of The European Rhythm Machine* (1968)★★★, *Stolen Moments* (JMY 1969)★★★, *Round Trip* (Vanguard 1969)★★★, *1968 Jazz* (EMI 1969)★★, *Phil Woods And His European Rhythm Machine At The Montreux Jazz Festival* (1970)★★★, *Phil Woods And His European Rhythm Machine At The Frankfurt Jazz Festival* (1970)★★, *Chromatic Banana* (1970)★★★, *Musique De Bois* (1974)★★★, *Images* (RCA 1975)v, *Live From The Showboat* (RCA 1976)★★★, *Songs For Sisyphus* (RCA 1979)★★, *I Remember...* (Telefunken 1978)★★★, *Quartet* (1979)★★★, *Crazy Horse* (1979)★★★, *European Tour, Live* (1980)★★, *The Macerata Concert* (1980)★★, *Birds Of A Feather* (1981)★★★, *Three For All* (Enja 1982)★★★, *At The Vanguard* (1982)★★★, with Rob McConnell *Rob McConnell And The Boss Brass Featuring Phil Woods* (1982)★★, *Piper At The Gates Of Dawn* (1984)★★★, *Integrity* (Red 1984)★★★, with Budd Johnson *The Old Dude And The Fundance Kid* (1984)★★★, *More Mistletoe Magic* (1985)★★, *Gratitude* (Denon 1986)★★★, *Dizzy Gillespie Meets The Phil Woods Quintet* (1986)★★, *Bouquet* (Concord 1987)★★★, *Bop Stew* (Concord 1987)★★★, *Evolution* (Concord 1988)★★★, *Here's To My Lady* (Chesky 1988)★★★, *Phil's Mood* (Philology 1988)★★, *Flash* (Concord 1989)★★★, *Phil On Etna* (Philology 1989)★★, *Embraceable You* (Philology 1989)★★★, *Real Life* (Chesky 1990)★★★, *All Bird's Children* (Concord 1990)★★★, *Flowers For Hodges* (Concord 1992)★★★, *Elsa* (Philology 1992)★★★, *Full House* (1992)★★★, *Live At The Corridonia Jazz Festival* (Philology 1992)★★, *An Affair To Remember* (Evidence 1995)★★★★, with Gordon Beck *Live At The Wigmore Hall - The Complete Concert* (JMS 1997)★★★★, with Clark Terry *Lucerne 1978* (TCOB 1997)★★★.

● VIDEOS: *The Phil Woods Quartet* (Rhapsody 1995).

Woodstock (film)

The three-day music festival in Max Yasgur's Bethil farm has passed into legend, partly through the notion of survival in adversity, but largely because of the ensuing successful documentary film and album. *Woodstock* captures the spirit of those three-days in July 1969 - the haphazard organisation, the naive ideals, the storms - but most of all it showcases many of the era's finest acts. Several would later claim that their performance at *Woodstock* was poor, but there is no denying the excitement generated by **Sly And The Family Stone** and **Santana**, the sheer power of **Joe Cocker** and the **Grease Band** and the allegorical anguish pouring out of 'The Star-Spangled Banner' when in the hands of **Jimi Hendrix**. Although several performers on the *Woodstock* bill were not featured on the film or album, enough remains in both to give the full flavour of this extraordinary event. A recent director's cut adds previously-unseen footage and a related *Woodstock Diary*

largely comprised of 'new' performances. The legend refuses to die.

Woodstock - Various

This album stands as the best live rock festival soundtrack. The story behind the festival is well known but the suggestion by Atco's marketing man, Johnny Bienstock, that 'you should put it out as a triple' was brave and bold. It worked of course, and thankfully the CD allows us to listen instead of changing sides. The best moments are here; Santana, 'Evil Ways', John Sebastian charming the crowd and the cataclysmic Joe Cocker with his stunning 'With A Little Help From My Friends'. Even the warts and all Crosby, Stills And Nash material is somehow charming, especially hearing that they were 'scared shitless'.

● Tracks: At The Hop; Coming Into Los Angeles; Dance To The Music; Drug Store Truck Drivin' Man; The Fish Cheer (medley); Freedom; Going Up The Country; I-Feel-Like-I'm-Fixin'-To-Die Rag (medley); I Had A Dream; I Want To Take You Higher; I'm Going Home; Joe Hill; Love March; Music Lover (medley); Purple Haze (medley); Rainbows All Over Your Blues; Rock And Soul Music; Sea Of Madness; Soul Sacrifice; Star Spangled Banner (medley); Suite: Judy Blue Eyes; Wooden Ships; We're Not Gonna Take It; With A Little Help From My Friends; Crowd Rain Chant; Volunteers.

● First released 1970

● UK peak chart position: 35

● USA peak chart position: 1

Woodstock Festival

The original Woodstock Art and Music Fair was forcibly moved from its planned location after protest from local townsfolk of Wallkill, New York State, USA. Their opposition to 'long-haired weirdos' was indigenous to 1969. The new location was 40 miles away at a 600-acre dairy farm in Bethel owned by Max Yasgur. If the **Monterey Pop Festival** in 1967 was the birth of the new music revolution, Woodstock was its coming of age.

A steady trail of spectators arrived up to a week before the event, which took place on 15, 16 and 17 August 1969, to make sure they had a reasonable chance to catch a glimpse of at least one of the dozens of stars scheduled to appear. The line-up was intimidating in its scale: the **Who, Jimi Hendrix, Crosby, Stills, Nash And Young, John Sebastian, Jefferson Airplane, Grateful Dead, Santana, Joe Cocker, Sly And The Family Stone, Country Joe And The Fish, Ten Years After**, the **Band, Johnny Winter, Blood, Sweat And Tears**, the **Paul Butterfield Blues Band, Sha Na Na, Janis Joplin, Ravi Shankar**, the **Keef Hartley Band**, the **Incredible String Band, Canned Heat, Melanie, Sweetwater, Tim Hardin, Joan Baez, Arlo Guthrie, Richie Havens** and **Creedence Clearwater Revival**. Estimates vary but it was generally felt that no less than 300,000 spectators were present at any one time, sharing 600 portable lavatories and inadequate water facilities. Nobody was prepared for the wave of bodies that formed, choking the highways from all directions. The world press which had previously scorned the popular hippie movement and the power of their musical message, were at last speaking favourably, as one. It was possible for vast amounts of youngsters to congregate for a musical celebration, without violence and regimented supervision. **Joni Mitchell** (who was not present) was one of the artists who eulogized the event in her song 'Woodstock': 'I'm going down to Yasgur's Farm, I'm gonna join in a rock 'n' roll band, I'm gonna camp out on the land and set my soul free'.

The subsequent film and live albums have insured Woodstock's immortality, and although there are some critics of the 'love generation' few can deny that Woodstock was a milestone in musical history. It is no exaggeration to claim that the festival totally changed the world's attitude towards popular music.

● ALBUMS: *Woodstock* (Atco 1969)★★★★, *Woodstock II* (Atco 1970)★★★, *Woodstock: Three Days Of Peace And Music - The 25th Anniversary Collection* (Atlantic 1994)★★★, *Woodstock '94* (A&M 1994)★★★.

● VIDEOS: *Woodstock 94* (Polygram 1994).

● FURTHER READING: *Woodstock: Festival Remembered*, Jean Young. *Woodstock Festival Remembered*, Michael Lang. *Woodstock Vision*, Elliott Landy. *Woodstock: An Oral History*, Joel Makowers.

Woodward, Edward

b. 1 June 1930, Croydon, Surrey, England. This UK television actor had a brief musical career as a crooner in the early 70s. He trained at the Royal Academy of Dramatic Art in London and acted in numerous stage plays before achieving national recognition in the UK television series *Emergency Ward 10* (50s/60s), as the star of the crime series *Callan* (70s) and the transatlantic *Equalizer* (80s). His recording career began in 1969 when he transferred his 'English gentleman' persona onto record in a series of albums for **DJM Records**. Woodward's repertoire ranged from ballad standards of the 30s and 40s to contemporary easy-listening hits such as 'Send In The Clowns' and 'Windmills Of Your Mind'. *Edwardian Woodward* was a selection of music hall songs. His only minor hit single was a revival of **Jerome Kern**'s 'The Way You Look Tonight' in 1971, though his second album reached the Top 20 the following year. In 1980 he released a single of the patriotic 'Soldiers Of The Queen' on the RK label.

● ALBUMS: *Grains Of Sand* (DJM 1969)★★★, *This Man Alone* (DJM 1970)★★★, *The Edward Woodward Album* (DJM 1972)★★★★, *Edwardian Woodward* (DJM 1975)★★★, *The Way You Look Tonight* (DJM 1976)★★★, *Love Is The Key* (DJM 1977)★★, *The Thought Of You* (DJM 1978)★★★, *Don't Get Around Much Anymore* (DJM 1979)★★★, *Woodward Again* (DJM 1981)★★★.

Woodyard, Sam

b. 7 January 1925, Elizabeth, New Jersey, USA, d. 20 September 1988, Paris, France. A self-taught drummer, Woodyard played in several small bands in his home state in the 40s and early 50s. In 1952 he joined **Roy Eldridge** and the following year played with **Milt Buckner**. In 1955 he joined **Duke Ellington**, a job he retained with occasional lay-offs through ill-health and personal waywardness, until the late 60s. He subsequently worked with **Ella Fitzgerald** and as an extra percussionist with Ellington and **Buddy Rich**. Occasional gigs with **Bill Berry** helped his sagging career, but by 1975 he had decided to relocate to Europe. Based in Paris, he played and recorded with local musicians such as **Guy Lafitte**, other ex-patriates including Buckner, and visitors like **Teddy Wilson**, **Buddy Tate** and **Slam Stewart**. By the 80s Woodyard's earlier years of hard drinking and wild living had begun to take their toll. The theft of his drum kit added to his decline, but in the mid-summer of 1988 he was a welcome guest at the Ellington '88 convention held at Oldham, England. Although his health was clearly at a very low ebb, he was rejuvenated by the renewal of contact with other ex-Ellingtonians, Berry, **Buster Cooper** and **Jimmy Woode**, and by the gift from the assembled delegates of a new drum kit. His playing at the convention was inevitably more tentative than of old, but he enjoyed himself and performed such crowd-pleasing favourites as 'Limbo Jazz' with his eccentric vocal. A short while later, on 20 September 1988, he died in Paris. A vigorous and skilful drummer, Woodyard's erratic temperament sometimes showed itself in his playing and he occasionally slipped into musical extravagances. At his best, however, whether in subtle accompaniments to Ellington's piano solos, or driving the big band along in thunderous performances such as the classic 1956 Newport concert, behind **Paul Gonsalves**'s legendary solo on 'Diminuedo And Crescendo In Blue', or the 1971 UK tour recording of 'La Plus Belle Africaine', he was unmatched.

● ALBUMS: *Ellington At Newport* (1956)★★★★, *Duke Ellington Plays Mary Poppins* (1964)★★★, with Ellington *Soul Call* (1966)★★★, *Duke Ellington - The Pianist* (1966)★★★, with Ellington *Togo Brava Suite* (1971)★★★, *Sam Woodyard In Paris* (1975)★★★.

Wooley, Sheb

b. Shelby F. Wooley, 10 April 1921, near Erick, Oklahoma, USA. Wooley, who is part Cherokee Indian, grew up on the family farm, learned to ride as a child and rode in rodeos as a teenager. His father traded a shotgun for Sheb's first guitar and while still at high school, he formed a country band that played at dances and on local radio. After leaving school, he found work on an oilfield as a welder, but soon tired of this work and moved to Nashville. He appeared on the WLAC and WSM radio stations and recorded for the Bullet label. In 1946, he relocated to Fort Worth, where until 1949, he became the frontman for a major show on WBAP, sponsored by Calumet Baking Powder. He then moved to Los Angeles, where he signed with **MGM Records** and with thoughts of a film career, he also attended the Jack Koslyn School of Acting. In 1949, he had his first screen role (as a heavy) in the Errol Flynn film *Rocky Mountain*. In 1952, he made a memorable appearance as Ben Miller, the killer plotting to gun down Gary Cooper in the classic western *High Noon*. During the 50s, he appeared in several other films including *Little Big Horn* (1951), *Distant Drums* (1951), *Man Without A Star* (1955), *Giant* (1956) and *Rio Bravo* (1959). He is also well remembered for his performances as Pete Nolan in the television series *Rawhide*, which ran from 1958-65 (he also wrote some scripts for the series). During his career, he appeared in over 40 films.

Other artists began to record songs he had written and in 1953, **Hank Snow** had a big hit with 'When Mexican Joe Met Jole Blon' - a parody of two hit songs. In 1958, his novelty number, 'Purple People Eater', became a million-seller and even reached number 12 in the UK pop charts. He based the song on a schoolboy joke that he had heard from Don Robertson's son and initially, MGM did not consider it to be worth releasing. Further US pop successes included 'Sweet Chile'. He first appeared in the US country charts in 1962, when another novelty number, 'That's My Pa', became a number 1. It was intended that Wooley should record 'Don't Go Near The Indians' but due to film commitments **Rex Allen's** version was released before he could record it. Wooley jokingly told MGM that he would write a sequel and came up with the comedy parody 'Don't Go Near The Eskimos'. He developed an alter-ego drunken character, whom he called Ben Colder, and in this guise, he recorded and charted it and other humorous parodies of pop/country hits, including 'Almost Persuaded No. 2', 'Harper Valley PTA (Later That Same Day)' and 'Fifteen Beers (Years) Ago'. (The name Ben Colder was the selection made by MGM from the three alternatives that Wooley offered. The other two were Ben Freezin and Klon Dyke.) He had some further minor hits with serious recordings, including 'Blue Guitar' and 'Tie A Tiger Down'. In 1969, he joined the CBS network *Hee Haw* country show, remaining with it for several years, and also wrote the theme music. Throughout the 60s and 70s, he maintained a busy touring schedule, appearing all over the USA and overseas. In 1968, Ben Colder was voted Comedian of the Year by the Country Music Association. He cut back his work during the 80s and although he has remained a popular entertainer, he has had no chart entries since 1971. Over the years, the parodies by the drunken Ben Colder have proved more popular than his serious recordings and have certainly accounted for the majority of his record sales.

● ALBUMS: as Sheb Wooley *Sheb Wooley* (MGM 1956)★★★, *Songs From The Days Of Rawhide* (MGM 1961)★★★, *That's My Pa & That's My Ma* (MGM 1962)★★★★, *Tales Of How The West Was Won* (MGM 1963)★★★★, *It's A Big Land* (MGM 1965)★★★, *Warm & Wooley* (MGM 1969)★★★. As Ben Colder *Spoofing The Big Ones* (MGM 1962)★★★, *Ben Colder* (MGM 1963)★★★, *Big Ben Strikes Again* (MGM 1966)★★★, *Wine Women & Song* (MGM 1967)★★★, *Harper Valley PTA & Other Parodies Of Top Ten Hits* (MGM 1968)★★★, *Have One On Ben Colder* (1969)★★, *Big Ben Colder Wild Again* (1970)★★, *Ben Colder* (1970)★★★, *Live & Loaded At Sam Houston Coliseum* (1971)★★★, *Wacky World Of Ben Colder* (1973)★★★.

● COMPILATIONS: as Sheb Wooley *The Very Best Of Sheb Wooley* (MGM 1965)★★★★, *Country Boogie Wild And Wooley (1948-55)* (1984)★★★, *Blue Guitar* (Bear Family 1985)★★★. As Ben Colder *The Best Of Ben Colder* (MGM 1968)★★★, *Golden Hits* (Gusto 1979)★★★.

Woolley, Shep

b. 15 October 1944, Birmingham, England. From an early age, Shep loved music, and played ukelele. His mother bought him a guitar in 1958 and he joined 15 others in a local skiffle group. In 1960, Woolley entered the Royal Navy, taking his guitar with him, and continued to play all over the world, at the same time organizing shows and groups. Woolley's first venture into a folk club came in 1969, when he was inspired by **Bob Dylan** and the songs of the American Depression. Writing his own songs, Shep found that he had a natural flair for humorous material, and jokes and monologues began to appear in his act. By 1973, he had essentially become a folk comedian, but he was also still a naval gunnery instructor, so, in 1975, Shep left the forces to concentrate on performing. In 1974, he appeared on *New Faces*, the television talent show. From 1975-85, Woolley presented the folk show on Radio Victory in Portsmouth, England. He has played all over the world and is regularly in demand for festivals. Woolley tends to play less folk clubs these days, concentrating on summer seasons and concerts. A naturally funny man, he deserves to become as widely known as others of the genre.

● ALBUMS: *Pipe Down* (Sweet Folk All 1972)★★★, *Songs Of Oars And Scrubbers And Other Dirty Habits* (Sweet Folk All 1973)★★★, *Goodbye Sailor* (Sweet Folk All 1976)★★, *First Take* (1980)★★, with various artists *Reunion* (1984)★★, *On The Button* (1986)★★, *Delivering The Goods* (1990)★★.

Woolpackers

Television soap operas have always been fertile spawning grounds for novelty spin-off records; in Britain the practice dates back as far as 1963, when Chris Sandford's 'Not Too Little, Not Too Much' was an early attempt to inject a little 'youth appeal' into *Coronation Street*. The practice was getting a little tired by 1996, however, when the single 'Hillbilly Rock, Hillbilly Roll' was recorded, supposedly by a trio of regulars from the ITV soap *Emmerdale*. This cod-country effort was released to unanimous critical derision, but still made it to the Top 10 and even spawned an album, an equally lame attempt to profit from the contemporary 'line-dancing' craze. What this had to do with the lives of a fictional West Yorkshire farming community seemed to get lost in somebody's marketing strategy.

● ALBUMS: *Emmerdance* (RCA 1996)★.

Wootton, Brenda

b. 10 February 1928, London, England, d. 11 March 1994. A singer fiercely proud of her Cornish heritage, Wootton was often said to have regretted her birth in the capital, which was accidental. She grew up in the fishing village of Newlyn, where she soon became a familiar voice in the chapel and other venues. She joined many choirs but performed as a soloist for the first time in the mid-60s, at Cornwall's first folk music club, the Count House near Batollack mine. There, only a few miles away from Land's End, she befriended **Ralph McTell**. Although she would never see the acclaim that the latter artist enjoyed, Wootton did become a major force in France, where she signed to **RCA Records**. One of her albums, *Lyonesse*, topped the French charts for several months. Among her friends in the Gallic world were President Mitterand and his family. Unfortunately the onset of ill health prevented her from accepting an invitation to sing at the 200th anniversary celebration of the French Revolution. Despite her huge continental popularity, few outside of Cornwall revered her name, a fact partially explained by her choice of the Cornish language for many of her songs. She became a Bard of the Cornish Gorsedd, and was seen widely as that culture's greatest musical ambassador.

● ALBUMS: *La Grande Cornouaillaise* (Keltia 1996)★★★.

Wootton, Miles

b. 23 March 1934, Manchester, England. Although known for his humorous material, Wootton has also written more serious songs. Having started out in revue sketches at university, he then took up the guitar and started singing at the Heritage Folk Club at Oxford. This was followed by a residency at the Court House Folk Club in Cornwall. Moving to Brighton in 1965, Miles began playing the local folk clubs, and writing songs with **Allan Taylor**. He contributed the lyrics to five tracks on Taylor's debut, *Sometimes*, in 1971. Wootton subsequently plunged into a full-time career of singing and writing, with a number of artists covering his songs. A breakthrough of sorts came when he co-wrote, with **Fred Wedlock**, 'Joggers Song', the b-side of 'The Oldest Swinger In Town'. This at least pushed his name forward to a wider audience. Miles also wrote songs weekly for Wedlock when the latter appeared regularly on the *Noel Edmonds Show* for UK television. He has also contributed songs for BBC Radio's satirical series, *Week Ending*. Miles now plays only occasionally, but his songs are much covered and imitated.

● ALBUMS: *Sunday Supplement World* (1975)★★, *The Great Fish Finger Disaster* (1980)★★.

Words And Music (film musical)

Not the 1929 college musical of that name which starred the 22-year-old John (Duke) Wayne in his fifth film, but the lavish film biography of **Richard Rodgers** and **Lorenz Hart**, one of the most celebrated songwriting teams in the history of American popular music. It has been said many times that an authentic life story of Hart - a hard drinking, homosexual depressive - would make a fascinating movie, but in 1948 Hollywood obviously was not ready for that kind of reality, and so screenwriter Fred Finklehoffe turned in the usual fudged fairy tale which was typical of most bio-pics. Hart (**Mickey Rooney**) is portrayed as a cigar-smoking nice guy, whose first working meeting with Rodgers (Tom Drake) results in the assembly of the complicated lyric to 'Manhattan', which he has seemingly jotted down in various parts of a magazine on his way over. From then on, Rodgers, who in real life could be an extremely difficult man, is portrayed as having the patience of Job, even when Hart goes off on his binges for weeks at a time - erratic behaviour which led to his death at the age of only 44. So much for the plot - it was irrelevant anyhow, given the marvellous songs and the talented performers who were on hand to sing them. In a film full of musical highlights, perhaps the most memorable were **Gene Kelly** and **Vera-Ellen**'s sizzling dance to 'Slaughter On Tenth Avenue', **Lena Horne**'s sparkling 'Where Or When' and 'The Lady Is A Tramp', Mickey Rooney and **Judy Garland** reunited on film after a break of several years with 'I Wish I Were In Love Again', Judy going to town by herself on 'Johnny One Note', June Allyson and the Blackburn Twins with the delicious 'Thou Swell', **Mel Tormé** ('Blue Moon'), **Perry Como** ('Blue Room' and 'Mountain Greenery' [with Allyn McLerie]), and not forgetting Rooney's charming version of 'Manhattan'. Also contributing were **Betty Garrett**, Ann Sothern, **Cyd Charisse**, Janet Leigh, Marshall Thompson, Dee Turnell, Jeanette Nolan, Harry Antrim, and Clinton Sundberg. Robert Alton and Gene Kelly handled the choreography, and the director who put the whole complicated affair together was Norman Taurog. *Words And Music* was photographed in Technicolor and produced by **Alan Freed**'s famous MGM unit. It grossed over $3.5 million in the USA and Canada alone, and was one of the leading musicals of the decade.

Words And Music (stage musical)

By the early 30s **Noël Coward** was at the peak of his creativity. This is clear from the material he wrote for this revue which opened at the Adelphi Theatre in London on 16 September 1932. There were normally at least one or two particularly memorable songs in any Coward show, but in *Words And Music* he really excelled himself. The score included the classic 'Mad About The Boy', 'Mad Dogs And Englishmen' (the author's most famous comedy number), and 'The Party's Over Now', which Coward subsequently used to close his cabaret act. In addition, there other, lesser-known items such as 'Let's Say Goodbye', 'Something To Do With Spring', and 'Three White Feathers'. Given the privilege and pleasure of introducing those songs were cast members John Mills, Romney Brent, Doris Hare, Norah Howard, Joyce Barbour, and Ivy St Helier.

Ironically the show failed to last for more than five months, which meant that it was the first collaboration between Coward and impresario **Charles B. Cochran** to lose money. Much of the material formed the basis of *Set To Music*, a revue which starred Beatrice Lillie, and ran for 129 performances on Broadway early in 1939.

Workers Playtime - Billy Bragg

Few singers in recent history have the honesty to sing as they sound. There is no false American twang, no hip angst vocals and no lo-fi intensity. Bragg sings like a geezer from Barking, Essex, which is exactly what he is. He is, however, blessed with a knack for writing powerful political songs of lyrical truth and romantic ballads of heart-rending openness. Long after Bragg has hung up his Burns guitar, other people with twangy American accents and plenty of angst will record songs such as 'She's Got A New Spell' and 'The Price I Pay', and they will have huge hits with them.

● Tracks: *She's Got A New Spell; Must I Paint You A Picture; Tender Comrade; The Price I Pay; Little Time Bomb; Rotting On Remand; Valentine's Day Is Over; Life With The Lions; The Only One; The Short Answer; Waiting For The Great Leap Forwards.*

● First released 1988
● UK peak chart position: 17
● USA peak chart position: 198

Working Week

The band was formed in 1983 around the nucleus of Simon Booth (guitar) and Larry Stabbins (saxophone) as an off-shoot of the soft jazz-influenced group **Weekend**. Adopting a harder jazz/Latin direction, Working Week commanded much music press attention and, in particular, 'style' magazines (*Blitz* and *The Face*), who latched on to the band's connection with the London jazz dance teams. Their radical image was strengthened by Booth and Stabbins left-wing allegiances, borne out on their 1984 debut single on Paladin/**Virgin Records**, 'Venceremos (We Will Win)'. The song, dedicated to the Chilean protest singer Victor Jara, included guest vocals from **Tracey Thorn**, **Robert Wyatt** and Claudia Figueroa. The follow-up, 'Storm Of Light' featured **Julie Tippetts** on lead vocals. In time, the group recruited a permanent lead vocalist in Juliet Roberts. After her departure in 1988, Working Week reverted back to the system of guest vocalists until the addition of a new vocalist in Yvonne Waite for 1991's *Black And Gold*. Although Working Week has centred around Booth and Stabbins for recordings and live appearances they have employed a vast array of respected UK jazz musicians who, on various occasions, have included **Harry Beckett** (trumpet), **Keith Tippett** (piano), Kim Burton (piano), **Cleveland Watkiss** (vocals), **Mike Carr** (organ), Richard Edwards and Paul Spong (brass), Dave Bitelli (reeds), **Annie Whitehead** (trombone) and Nic France (drums). Since then, the group has continued to work, turning out quality

recordings, although that initial wave of interest and impetus in the mid-80s has somewhat subsided.

● ALBUMS: *Working Nights* (Virgin 1985)★★★, *Companeros* (Virgin 1986)★★★, *Knocking On Your Door* (Virgin 1987)★★★, *Fire In The Mountain* (Ten 1989)★★★, *Black And Gold* (Ten 1991)★★★.

● COMPILATIONS: *Payday* (Venture 1988)★★★.

Workingman's Dead - Grateful Dead

Nobody who had experienced the Dead's previous albums or live performances could have believed that they could go soft. In fact, they did it in such style that people hardly noticed. This folky gem is heavily influenced by Crosby, Stills, Nash And Young, and was their first major commercial success. Robert Hunter's lyrics dominate and suit the style and themes the record conjures up. Prior to this album the Dead could only jam. After this they were respected as also being able to sing, harmonize and play. A wonderfully rootsy album that is as American as the Band's self-titled record.

● Tracks: *Uncle John's Band; High Time; Dire Wolf; New Speedway Boogie; Cumberland Blues; Black Peter; Easy Wind; Casey Jones.*

● First released 1970
● UK peak chart position: did not chart
● USA peak chart position: 80

Workman, Reggie

b. 26 June 1937, Philadelphia, Pennsylvania, USA. One of the premier bassists in post-war jazz, Workman's first involvement in music was 'singing doo-wop at a YMCA'. Piano lessons failed to interest him, but a cousin introduced him to the bass and he was hooked - though his high school's lack of an instrument meant he had to play bass lines on tuba and euphonium for a while. By the time he left school, he was working as a professional bassist playing R&B and jazz standards. At the end of the 50s he moved to New York and played with **Gigi Gryce**, **Eric Dolphy** and his mentor, **John Coltrane**, with whom he'd previously been in contact. Workman toured and recorded with Coltrane in 1961, then joined the leading hard bop group of the time, **Art Blakey**'s **Jazz Messengers**, remaining for two years and also recording with both the group's tenor saxophonist **Wayne Shorter**, on his own **Blue Note** dates such as *Night Dreamer*, *Juju* and *Adam's Apple*, and the group's trumpeter **Freddie Hubbard**. Workman next played with the radical New York Art Quartet and later worked with a variety of leaders, including **Yusef Lateef** and **Thelonious Monk**. Increasingly involved in education, in the 70s he led the Collective Black Arts organization in New York - a community self-help project that for a while published its own newspaper, *Expansions*. He also worked with **Max Roach**, **Marion Brown**, **Archie Shepp** and **Charles Tolliver**. In the 80s Workman recorded with **David Murray**, **Steve Lacy** and **Mal Waldron**, toured with **Alice Coltrane** and **Rashied Ali** in the Coltrane Legacy band, was a founder member of both the all-string Black Swan Quartet and

Trio Transition and became a regular member of pianist **Marilyn Crispell**'s groups, playing on her *Gaia*, *Circles* and *Live In Zurich*. He has also recorded a solo album, *The Works Of Workman*, and since the mid-80s led his own ensemble, whose members over the years have included Crispell, singer **Jeanne Lee**, drummers **Andrew Cyrille** or **Gerry Hemingway** and saxophonists **Joseph Jarman**, **Oliver Lake** or, most recently, **Don Byron**: their two albums are *Images* and *Synthesis*. One of the most versatile and adventurous of bass players, Workman is married to the well-known choreographer and poet Maya Milenovic.

● ALBUMS: *Conversation* (1977)★★★, *The Works Of Workman* (Denon 1979)★★★, *Synthesis* (Leo 1986)★★★★, *Black Swan Quartet* (1986)★★★, *Trio Transition* (1988)★★★, *Trio Transition With Oliver Lake* (1989)★★★, *Images* (Music And Arts 1990)★★★, *Altered Spaces* (Leo 1993)★★★★, *Cerebral Caverns* (Postcards 1995)★★★★.

World Domination Enterprises

Rock-dance fusion trio who, though passing largely unacknowledged in their own lifetime, have achieved something akin to cult status in their retirement. The band comprised Keith Dobson (guitar, vocals), Steve Jameson (bass) and Digger (drums). Dobson had formerly drummed with hippie monoliths **Here And Now**, released the album *Let's Get Professional* with his previous band 012, and set up his own cassette label, invitingly titled Fuck Off Records. World Domination Enterprises first arrived in 1985, when they played a flurry of gigs around the UK to coincide with the **Live Aid** phenomenon. This was followed by the release of their debut single, and their signature song, 'Asbestos Lead Asbestos'. Its gravelly, savage delivery neatly counterpointed Dobson's environmental concerns with a rumbling, bass-dominated resonance. Contrastingly, other material included 'Hotsy Girl', a tribute to their Morris Minor and the art of stock car racing. As the 80s developed the group played at many of the warehouse parties during the early acid house epoch, notably those organized by the Mutoid Waste Company. In the meantime they had released two LPs, but split after returning from a tour of Russia when Digger elected to pledge his faith to the Jehovah's Witness movement. There was no way back from that, and Dobson split the group and set up home in Spain, though he did return to London in 1993. Jameson joined with Steve Smith (ex-**Vapors**) in a new outfit, Cut, while Digger continues merrily on his way to this day, imparting the good news via the latest issue of *Watchtower*.

● ALBUMS: *Let's Play Domination* (Product Inc 1988)★★★, *Dub Domination* (Product Inc 1988)★★, *Love From Lead City* (Product Inc 1988)★★.

World Famous Supreme Team Show

One of **Malcolm McLaren**'s many innovative experiments in modern music, this project saw 'Talcy' pull together a team of rappers, singers and DJs from New York and Los Angeles. In their early days the group had hosted their own show on New Jersey station WHBI, alongisde the legendary Mr Magic, before the latter shifted to WBLS. The idea of their partnership with McLaren was to make a modern rap record themed on Shakespearean and Opera models, as demonstrated by the promotional single, 'Opera House'. Main vocalist Mona Lisa Young was saddled, however, by some uninspiring material, co-written between McLaren and MC Hamlet (b. Jason Van Sugars). The album includes a return to the happier times of 'Buffalo Girls'. Indeed, McLaren had formerly employed the Supreme Team on his *Duck Rock* album, where they rapped over T-Ski Valley's 'Catch The Beat'.

● ALBUMS: *The World Famous Supreme Team* (Charisma 1986)★★★, *Round The Outside! Round The Outside!* (Virgin 1992)★★.

World Machine - Level 42

Although it looks like Level 42 will never make another album, at least we have one which seems destined to endure. Mark King had already proved he could slap his bass better than almost anybody; now it was his turn to demonstrate his prowess as a classy songwriter. He succeeded in buoyant fashion with every track, very funky, very poppy and at times upliftingly wonderful, especially 'Something About You' and 'Coup D'Etat'. The winner for emotion, however, is the heartfelt 'Leaving Me Now'. Perfection, deliberately made for the age of the CD.

● Tracks: *World Machine; A Physical Presence; Something About You; Leaving Me Now; I Sleep On My Heart; It's Not The Same For Us; Good Man In A Storm; Coup D'Etat; Lying Still.*

● First released 1985

● UK peak chart position: 3

● USA peak chart position: 18

World Of Twist

Manchester, England band World Of Twist were judged late arrivals for the 'baggy' or 'Madchester' trends but in truth their sound was far more experimental and less guitar-orientated than many of their geographical peers. The group comprised Tony Ogden (vocals), Gordon King (guitar, 'gadgets'), Andy Hobson (keyboards), Julia McShells (aka MC Shells; keyboards) and Adge (visuals). In the press they claimed their former professions included those of flower arranger, Royal Marine and magician's assistant. Their breakthrough single, 'The Storm', became a minor independent chart success, bolstered by a stage show that featured women swimming in fish-tanks and extensive use of video. In November 1990 it entered the UK Top 40. By 1991 and their first session for the **John Peel** programme they had reduced to a trio of Ogden, King and percussionist Nicholas Sanderson. This broadcast included a version of the **MC5**'s 'Kick Out The Jams' in addition to their own tribute to a popular north-west holiday resort and its main attraction, 'Blackpool Tower'. However, follow-up singles such as 'She's A

Rainbow' failed to sell and the response to the group's debut album, *Quality Street*, was disappointing. The group were dropped by **Virgin Records** in 1992 after its takeover by **EMI Records**. As manager David Hardy later told the press: 'We went from being one of a handful of bands to a roster of 600 acts.' Ogden continued to work under the title World Of Twist while King started work on film soundtracks and remixes for Bob Stanley of **Saint Etienne**'s Ice Rink label.
● ALBUMS: *Quality Street* (Circa 1991)★★.

World Party

Founded on the talents of ex-**Waterboy** Karl Wallinger (b. 19 October 1957, Prestatyn, Wales), World Party have worked hard to shrug off comparisons with his former group. This is a little unjust, bearing in mind Wallinger's quite separate, but in many ways equal, songwriting abilities. Wallinger was born the son of an architect father and housewife mother. He was brought up in North Wales on a diet of 60s ephemera, from the **Supremes**, through the **Spencer Davis Group**, to Merseybeat. His first musical experience arrived in 1976 with Quasimodo, who would eventually lose their hump to become the **Alarm**. Later he moved to London to become a clerk for ATV/Northern Songs, who counted the **Beatles**' catalogue among their acquisitions. He delved back into performance in his own time, eventually going on to become musical director of *The Rocky Horror Show* in the West End of London. A short residency with funk band the Out overlapped his liaison with the Waterboys. After he split amicably from Mike Scott, Wallinger set out on a solo career that would see him sign to **Prince**'s management. He also helped **Sinead O'Connor** on her *Lion And The Cobra* set. Wallinger recorded the first two World Party albums practically single-handed, though 1993's *Bang!* saw him joined by Chris Sharrock (drums) and Dave Catlin-Birch (guitars, keyboards). The hit single 'Ship Of Fools' (from 1987) showcased Wallinger's muse, a relaxed and melancholic performance reminiscent of mid-period Beatles. This has not so much been updated as revitalized on his subsequent, sterling work, although a minor breakthrough was made with *Bang!*. Some of the reviews for *Egyptology* were unnecessarily cruel (especially the *New Musical Express*). It was by his standards another good album, which, although still locked into the Beatles' sound (this time *circa White Album* period), has some great moments, notably the gentle 'She's The One' and the meatier 'Curse Of The Mummy's Tomb'.
● ALBUMS: *Private Revolution* (Ensign 1987)★★, *Goodbye Jumbo* (Ensign 1990)★★★, *Thank You World* mini-album (Ensign 1991)★★★, *Bang!* (Ensign 1993)★★★, *Egyptology* (Chrysalis 1997)★★★★.

World Saxophone Quartet

In 1974, **Anthony Braxton** recorded a composition for a saxophone quartet on his *New York Fall 1974*. The other three players involved - **Julius Hemphill**, **Oliver**

Lake and **Hamiet Bluiett** - must have liked the format as in 1977 they and **David Murray** formed the World Saxophone Quartet. The proud name was no idle boast: these really were four pre-eminent saxophone voices. All the players are multi-instrumentalists, but in general Hemphill and Lake played alto, Murray tenor and Bluiett baritone saxophone. Wearing tuxedos as a reference to the era of big band sophistication, they became sure-fire festival favourites, starting regular European tours in 1978. They all contributed compositions, though perhaps Hemphill and Bluiett have shown most interest in the quartet's possibilities, producing thoughtful arrangements that examine ballads, bop and blues with understanding and affection. Originally located on the jazz *avant garde*, their recent albums have looked back at aspects of the black music tradition (*Plays Duke Ellington*, *Rhythm And Blues*), while the new *Metamorphosis* introduced African drums into the musical mix. In 1991, Hemphill left the group and was replaced by altoist **Arthur Blythe**, who marked his debut on *Metamorphosis*.
● ALBUMS: *Point Of No Return* (Moers 1977)★★★★, *Steppin' With* (Black Saint 1979)★★, *WSQ* (Black Saint 1981)★★★, *Revue* (Black Saint 1982)★★★★, *Live In Zurich* (Black Saint 1984)★★★, *Live At Brooklyn Academy Of Music* (1986)★★, *Plays Duke Ellington* (Elektra 1986)★★★★, *Dances And Ballads* (Elektra 1987)★★★★, *Rhythm And Blues* (Elektra 1989)★★★★, *Metamorphosis* (Elektra 1991)★★★, *Breath Of Life* (Elektra 1994)★★★, *Moving Right Along* (Black Saint 1994)★✴★★, with African Drums *Four Now* (Justin Time 1996)★★★, *Takin It 2 Level 2* (Justin Time 1997)★★★.

World War III

This short-lived American quartet came together when vocalist Mandy Lion and guitarist Tracy G were joined by the former **Dio** rhythm section of Jimmy Bain (bass) and **Vinnie Appice** (drums). Their sole, self-titled album, displayed an impressive traditional metal style, with Tracy's G's superb guitar work complemented by a thunderous backing from the Bain/Appice team, although Lion's gruff vocals and a lyrical preoccupation with his own sexual exploits and fantasies tended to detract a little from the overall effect. The album met with limited success, and the band dissolved, with Appice returning briefly to **Black Sabbath** with Ronnie James Dio before being reunited with Tracy G in a revamped Dio band. Lion later turned up in Jake E Lee's post-**Badlands** group, Wicked Alliance.
● ALBUMS: *World War III* (Hollywood 1991)★★.

World's Greatest Jazz Band

The World's Greatest Jazz Band was formed from musicians who played at Dick Gibson's Colorado Jazz Parties in the mid-to-late 60s. Led by **Yank Lawson** and **Bob Haggart** and encouraged and supported by Gibson, these players formed a semi-regular group known as the Ten Greats Of Jazz (the name changing as the numbers varied). In 1968 the band became a full-time organization and settled on the name by which they were known for the next decade. In its earliest form, the World's Greatest Jazz Band included Lawson, **Billy Butterfield**, **Lou McGarity**, **Carl Fontana**, **Bob Wilber**, **Bud Freeman**, **Ralph Sutton**, **Clancy Hayes**, Haggart and Morey Feld. Successful concerts and records kept the band busy and subsequent personnel changes maintained the high standards set by the originals. Later sidemen included **Gus Johnson**, **Eddie Hubble**, **Bobby Hackett**, **George Masso**, **Al Klink**, **Peanuts Hucko**, **Bobby Rosengarden**, **Eddie Miller**, **Nick Fatool** and **John Bunch**. Playing sophisticated dixieland and mainstream jazz, with well-rehearsed tight arrangements interspersed with vigorous solos, the band found and filled a niche in public demand for unpretentious music played by a superior selection of musicians. In 1978, with Lawson and Haggart now in their late 60s, the band broke up. However, the call remained too strong to ignore completely and thereafter the two veterans occasionally reformed a band to make special appearances and records.

● ALBUMS: *The World's Greatest Jazz Band* (World Jazz 1968)★★★, *Jazz At The Troc* (World Jazz 1969)★★, *At The Roosevelt Grill* (World Jazz 1970)★★, *What's New?* (World Jazz 1970)★★★, *Century Plaza* (World Jazz 1972)★★★, *Hark The Herald Angels Swing* (World Jazz 1972)★★★, *In Concert At Massey Hall* (World Jazz 1972)★★, *In Concert At Carnegie Hall* (World Jazz 1973)★★★, *On Tour* (World Jazz 1975)★★, *Plays Cole Porter* (World Jazz 1975)★★★, *Plays Rodgers And Hart* (World Jazz 1975)★★★, *Plays Duke Ellington* (World Jazz 1976)★★★, *Plays George Gershwin* (World Jazz 1977)★★★, *The World's Greatest Jazz Band Of Yank Lawson And Bob Haggart* (1986)★★★.

World, The

Vocalist/guitarist/songwriter **Neil Innes** and bassist Dennis Cowan formed the World in 1970 upon the break-up of their former group, the **Bonzo Dog Doo-Dah Band**. Roger McKew (guitar) and Ian Wallace (drums) joined them in this short-lived act. *Lucky Planet*, although somewhat low-key, confirmed Innes' grasp of pop melody, but the group's potential did not have time to flourish. Cowan was concurrently involved in **Viv Stanshall**'s solo recordings and in 1971 Innes opted to join **McGuinness Flint**, albeit briefly. Following this, and having completed outstanding Bonzo Dog Doo-Dah Band contractual obligations, he helped form **Grimms** before embarking on a solo career.

● ALBUMS: *Lucky Planet* (Liberty 1970)★★★.

Worth, Marion

b. Mary Ann Ward, 4 July 1930, Birmingham, Alabama, USA. She learned to play piano as a child (later adding guitar) and after initially starting nursing training, she decided to pursue a singing career. She first sang with her sister, before appearing on local radio and television in Birmingham. In 1957, she gained a number 12 US country hit with her self-penned 'Are You Willing, Willie', recorded on the tiny Cherokee label. In 1960,

another self-penned song, 'That's My Kind Of Love', recorded on Happy Wilson's Guyden label, reached number 5, which resulted in her joining **Columbia Records** (she also married Wilson). She became a regular on WSM's *Friday Night Frolics*. In 1961, her first Columbia hit, 'I Think I Know', made the Top 10, with the follow-up, 'There'll Always Be Sadness', peaking at number 21. Between 1963 and 1968, she achieved eight more *Billboard* chart entries, with 'Shake Me I Rattle' and 'Crazy Arms' both making the Top 20. She also gained Top 25 status with 'Slippin' Around', a duet with **George Morgan**. In 1967, she moved to **Decca Records** but after the self-penned 'Mama Sez', in 1968, she failed to make the charts again. Her ability to change from sultry ballads to lively barn dance-type numbers made her a popular performer on the **Grand Ole Opry**, where she was rated a singer's singer, and she was one of the first country stars to play Carnegie Hall in New York. She continued to tour in the USA and Canada and, in later years, she became a popular performer in various Las Vegas venues.

● ALBUMS: with George Morgan *Slippin' Around* (Columbia 1964)★★★★, *Marion Worth Sings Marty Robbins* (Columbia 1964)★★★, *A Woman Needs Love* (Columbia 1967)★★★.

● COMPILATIONS: *Marion Worth's Greatest Hits* (Columbia 1963)★★★.

Wrathchild

Formed in 1980 in Evesham, Worcestershire, England, as a **Black Sabbath**-influenced band, it was another two years before Wrathchild emerged at the forefront of the new glam rock scene. Original members Rocky Shads (vocals) and Marc Angel (bass) were joined by ex-Medusa personnel Lance Rocket (guitar) and Eddie Starr (drums). They subsequently released an EP on Bullet Records and toured heavily to promote it. By 1983 they had developed a melodramatic live show and perfected their **Kiss/Angel** influences, whilst retaining an 'English' quality. A year later their hard work paid off with a deal with Heavy Metal Records, but a bad choice of producer (**Robin George**) led to a slick but flat sound which was not at all representative. Soon after they entered into a long running legal battle with the company which almost killed the group off. During this time indie label Dojo released a compilation of early material which was far superior to the official album - it also contained the definitive version of live favourite and title-track, 'Trash Queen'. In 1988 they made their comeback with the aptly titled *The Bizz Suxx*. 'Nukklear Rokket', was also released and was followed with a tour that lacked the early aggression and visual drama. The follow-up album in 1989 fared badly against the more established glam rock bands like **Mötley Crüe**, and the group once again entered a legal battle, this time to stop an American thrash metal band using their moniker. They won, and their namesakes appended America to their tag. However, they disappeared from view shortly thereafter.

● ALBUMS: *Stakk Attakk* (Heavy Metal 1984)★★, *Trash*

Queens (Dojo 1985)★★★, *The Bizz Suxx* (FM Revolver 1988)★★★, *Delirium* (FM Revolver 1989)★★.
● VIDEOS: *War Machine* (1988).

Wrathchild America

This USA heavy metal quartet from Baltimore, USA seemed set for great things with the release of *Climbing The Walls*, which displayed quality **Metallica**-influenced thrash infused with melody, although the production did not quite convey the band's live guitar firepower. However, the good press accrued by Brad Divens (bass/lead vocals), Jay Abbene (guitar), Terry Carter (guitar/vocals) and Shannon Larkin (drums/vocals) went to waste as they became bogged down in litigation over the use of the Wrathchild name with the UK glam outfit of the same title. When the debut finally emerged, with America tagged on to the band's name, the pre-release publicity was long forgotten. *3D* proved the band's abilities again with a punchier sound, but stood little chance in a dwindling thrash market. The band lost their recording contract, and subsequently changed their name to Souls At Zero, pursuing a darker direction, although they later lost Larkin to **Ugly Kid Joe**.
● ALBUMS: *Climbing The Walls* (Atlantic 1989)★★★★, *3D* (Atlantic 1991)★★★, as Souls At Zero *A Taste For The Perverse* (Concrete 1995)★★★.

Wray, Link

b. 1930, Fort Bragg, North Carolina, USA. Guitarist Wray formed his first group in 1942, but his musical ambitions were thwarted by his induction into the US Army. He subsequently formed the Wraymen with Shorty Horton (bass) and Doug Wray (drums), and enjoyed a million-seller in 1958 with 'Rumble', a pioneering instrumental on which the artist's frenzied style and distorted tone invoked a gang-fight. The single incurred bans both on technical grounds and on account of its subject matter, but is now recognized as one of pop's most innovative releases, and includes the **Who**'s **Pete Townshend** as a vociferous proponent. Wray achieved another gold disc for 'Rawhide' (1959), but ensuing releases, including 'Jack The Ripper' (1960), 'The Sweeper' (1963) and 'Batman Theme' (1965), failed to match this success. He continued to record, using a home-made three-track studio built in a converted chicken shack, and a 1971 album, *Link Wray*, was the subject of critical acclaim. It drew heavily on the artist's country roots - he is part-Shawnee Indian - yet was still imbued with the primitive atmosphere of his early work. Renewed interest in Wray resulted in several archive releases, while contemporary recordings, although of interest, failed to match the promise of his initial 'rediscovery' collection.
In the late 70s the guitarist forged a fruitful partnership with new-wave rockabilly singer **Robert Gordon**, before resurrecting a solo career the following decade. Wray's primeval sound is echoed in the work of the **Cramps** and many other more contemporary groups.

He is particularly respected in the UK where his influence on 'trash' guitar groups, notably the Stingrays and **Milkshakes**, has been considerable.
In 1997 he made a new album with UK's prime R&B/Rock 'n' Roll reissue label **Ace Records**, having been previously associated with their Chiswick label. 'Rumble On The Docks' is vintage Link Wray and worth the price of the CD alone.
● ALBUMS: *Link Wray And The Raymen* (Epic 1959)★★★★, *Jack The Ripper* (Swan 1963)★★★, *Great Guitar Hits* (Vermillion 1963)★★★, *Link Wray Sings And Plays Guitar* (Vermillion 1964)★★★, *Yesterday And Today* (Record Factory 1969)★★★, *Link Wray* (Polydor 1971)★★★, *Be What You Want To Be* (Polydor 1973)★★★, *The Link Wray Rumble* (Polydor 1974)★★★, *Interstate 10* (Virgin 1975)★★★, *Stuck In Gear* (Virgin 1976)★★★, with Robert Gordon *Robert Gordon With Link Wray* (Private Stock 1977)★★★, with Gordon *Fresh Fish Special* (Private Stock 1978)★★★, *Bullshot* (Charisma 1979)★★★, *Live At The Paradiso* (Magnum Force 1980)★★★, *Live In '85* (Big Beat 1986)★★★, *Indian Child* (Creation 1993)★★★, *Shadowman* (Ace 1997)★★★.
● COMPILATIONS: *There's Good Rockin' Tonight* (Union Pacific 1971)★★★, *Beans And Fatback* (Virgin 1973)★★★, *Rockin' And Handclappin'* (Epic 1973)★★★, *Rock 'N' Roll Rumble* (Charly 1974)★★★★, *Early Recordings* reissue of *Jack The Ripper* (Chiswick 1978)★★★★, *Link Wray: Good Rocking' Tonight* (Chiswick 1983)★★★★, *Link Wray And The Wraymen* (Edsel 1985)★★★★, *Growlin' Guitar* (Ace 1987)★★★, *Mr. Guitar* (Norton 1995)★★★.
● VIDEOS: *Link Wray: The Rumble Man* (Visionary 1996).

Wray, Walter

b. 7 February 1959, Portsmouth, Hampshire, England. Melodic pop singer/songwriter Walter Wray began singing in local church choirs as a schoolboy. However, by the age of 16 he had mastered the guitar, and started writing songs with his first band, entitled Shitehot. Reading music and English literature at Sheffield University, Wray continued writing until in 1986 he, and his band, Junk, signed to local label Native Records. Junk's debut album, *Cuckooland*, and accompanying single, 'The World Doesn't Turn', were all that emerged from the deal, though the single did enter the UK indie charts. By 1988 Wray had moved on to form King Swamp. After signing to **Virgin Records** and touring extensively this outfit also petered out, despite more positive press for Wray's songs. Possibly taking the hint, he retreated instead to a more self-sufficient guitar/voice solo format, though he kept up the punishing touring schedule inaugurated by his former bands. Opening for **INXS**, **Jeff Healey**, Gary Clarke, **Julia Fordham** and **Jools Holland**, Wray went on to deliver his debut album in October 1993. Co-produced with **Sting** guitarist Dominic Miller, *Foxgloves & Steel Strings* drew fawning reviews from the critics. The first single taken from the album, 'Heaven On Our Side', was inspired by the blue and gold mask of Tutankhamun. The second excerpt, 'Can't Call It Love'/'A Hand To

Hold', conversely took its subject matter from the black US doo wop singers of the 50s and 60s.
● ALBUMS: *Foxgloves & Steel Strings* (JFD Recordings 1993)★★★★.

Wreckless Eric

b. Eric Goulden, Newhaven, Sussex, England. Launched by Stiff Records in the heyday of punk, Wreckless Eric, as his name suggested, specialized in chaotic, pub rock and roots-influenced rock. His often tuneless vocals belied some excellent musical backing, most notably by producer **Nick Lowe**. Wreckless's eccentric single, 'Whole Wide World'/'Semaphore Signals', has often been acclaimed as one of the minor classics of the punk era. During 1977/8, he was promoted via the famous Stiff live revues where he gained notoriety off-stage for his drinking. For his second album, *The Wonderful World Of Wreckless Eric*, the artist offered a more engaging work, but increasingly suffered from comparison with the other stars on his fashionable record label. Wreckless's commercial standing saw little improvement despite an attempt to produce a more commercial work, the ironically titled *Big Smash*. Effectively retiring from recording for the first half of the 80s, Wreckless returned with *A Roomful Of Monkeys*, credited to Eric Goulden, and featuring members of **Ian Dury**'s Blockheads.
He then formed the **Len Bright Combo** with ex-Milkshakes members Russ Wilkins (bass) and Bruce Brand (drums), who released two albums and found nothing more than a small cult-following on the pub/club circuit. The eventual dissolution of that group led to the formation of Le Beat Group Electrique with Catfish Truton (drums) and André Barreau (bass). Now a resident in France, and a more sober personality, Eric has found an appreciative audience.
● ALBUMS: *Wreckless Eric* (Stiff 1978)★★, *The Wonderful World Of Wreckless Eric* (Stiff 1978)★★★, *The Whole Wide World* (Stiff 1979)★★, *Big Smash!* (Stiff 1980)★★, as Eric Goulden *A Roomful Of Monkeys* (Go! Discs 1985)★★, *Le Beat Group Électrique* (New Rose 1989)★★, *At The Shop!* mini-album (New Rose 1990)★★, *The Donovan Of Trash* (Sympathy For The Record Industry 1991)★★★, as Hitsville House Band *12 O'Clock Stereo* (Casino 1994)★★★.

Wreckx-N-Effect

With their **Teddy Riley**-produced single of the same name in 1988, USA-based Wreckx-N-Effect announced the arrival of New Jack Swing. The intervening period has not been especially kind in terms of commercial fortunes, with others capitalising on their style. However, they did score a minor hit in 1992 with 'Rump Shaker' for **MCA**. The band is made up of vocalists Markell Riley (Teddy's brother) and Aquell Davidson. They were joined by a rap from **Apache Indian** on their 1994 single, 'Wreckz Shop'.
● ALBUMS: *Hard Or Smooth* (MCA 1992)★★★.

Wrencher, Big John

b. 12 February 1924, near Sunflower, Mississippi, USA, d. 15 July 1977, Clarksdale, Mississippi, USA. A self-taught harmonica player and singer, Wrencher recalled seeing many leading bluesman during his teens. He left Mississippi in 1947, though he returned frequently and on one trip was involved in a car crash that resulted in the loss of his left arm. He lived in Detroit, Michigan, and St. Louis, Missouri, before settling in Chicago during 1962, where he often worked for gratuities on Maxwell Street. He recorded for the Testament, Ja-Wes and Barrelhouse labels in the 60s and toured Europe in the early 70s, establishing a loyal following for his excellent harmonica playing and mellow vocals; he also recorded for Big Bear Records.
● ALBUMS: *Big John's Boogie* (Big Bear 1974)★★★, *Maxwell St. Alley Blues* (1978)★★★.

Wright, Betty

b. 21 December 1953, Miami, Florida, USA. A former member of her family gospel group, the Echoes Of Joy, Wright's first recordings were as a backing singer. She later embarked on a solo career and scored a minor hit with 'Girls Can't Do What The Guys Do' in 1968. 'Clean Up Woman' (1972), a US R&B number 2/pop number 6 hit, established a punchier, less passive style which later releases, 'Baby Sitter' (1972) and 'Let Me Be Your Lovemaker' (1973), consolidated. Although 'Shoorah Shoorah' and 'Where Is The Love?' reached the UK Top 30 in 1975, the singer was unable to sustain a wider success. Wright nonetheless continued recording into the 80s and has also forged a career as a US television talk show hostess.
● ALBUMS: *My First Time Around* (1968)★★★, *I Love The Way You Love* (Alston 1972)★★★, *Hard To Stop* (Atlantic 1973)★★★, *Danger: High Voltage* (Victor 1975)★★★, *Explosion* (RCA 1976)★★★, *This Time For Real* (Alston 1977)★★, *Betty Wright Live* (Alston 1978)★★★, *Betty Travellin' In The Wright Circle* (Alston 1979)★★, *Betty Wright* (Epic 1981)★★, *Wright Back At You* (Epic 1983)★★, *Sevens* (Fantasy 1987)★★, *Mother Wit* (Ms B 1988)★★, *4U2 Njoy* (Ms B 1989)★★.
● COMPILATIONS: *Golden Classics* (Collectables 1988)★★★, *Betty Wright Live* (1991)★★, *The Best Of ... The T.K. Years* (Sequel 1994)★★★★.

Wright, Billy

b. 21 May 1932, Atlanta, Georgia, USA, d. 28 October 1991, Atlanta, Georgia, USA. A promising gospel singer as a child, he would often sneak into Atlanta's famous 81 Theater to watch the secular shows and eventually turned to performing the blues. His soulful voice came to the attention of Savoy Records, who secured a US R&B Top 5 hit with his debut record 'Blues For My Baby' in 1949. Other less successful releases followed, but Wright's strength was in his live performances, earning him the nickname - Prince Of The Blues. After his Savoy tenure, Wright recorded for Peacock in 1955 and then passed on the baton to his devoted admirers

Little Richard, James Brown and Otis Redding. In the late 50s he made his final recordings for Bobby Robinson's Fire Records and tiny local labels, Carrollton and Chris, before settling down in Atlanta, where he continued to perform and introduces acts as a compere until his death in 1991.

● ALBUMS: *Stacked Deck* (1980)★★★, *Goin' Down Slow* (1984)★★★, with Little Richard *Hey Baby, Don't You Want A Man Like Me?* (1986)★★, *Goin' Down Slow* (Savoy 1995)★★.

Wright, Bobby

b. 30 March 1942, Charleston, West Virginia, USA. The son of Kitty Wells and Johnnie Wright, he appeared with his parents on the *Louisiana Hayride* at the age of eight, and three years later made his first recordings. After the family relocated to Nashville, he learned to play guitar but initially he had more interest in sports and drama. In 1962, he went to California and successfully auditioned for the role of a young guitar-playing southern boy in a proposed drama. The show did not materialize, but his performance won him the role of Willie the radio operator in a new comedy television series called *McHale's Navy*. He stayed as a regular until the series ended in 1966. He recorded for Decca (his parent's label) and in 1967, he gained his first US country chart hit with 'Lay Some Happiness On Me'. A few more minor hits followed and after further acting roles, his dislike of Hollywood saw him return to Nashville, where he began to appear with his parents. He had by this time also learned to play bass, trumpet and drums and he soon became an important part of the family show. In the early 70s, he appeared on their syndicated television series and toured extensively with them. Over the years, he has also been a popular artist on other syndicated television shows.

In 1971, he had a Top 15 country hit with 'Here I Go Again'. He recorded country cover versions of some pop hits and in 1974, he had Top 30 country success with his ABC recording of Terry Jacks' pop number 1, 'Seasons In The Sun'. He later recorded for United Artists, registering his last solo success, 'I'm Turning You Loose', on that label in 1979. He appeared in the UK with his parents at the 1974 Wembley Festival and received praise for his performance with the family at the 1988 Peterborough Festival. A talented all-round entertainer, he continues to be an important part of the family show and has not made any further attempts to pursue a solo career.

● ALBUMS: *Here I Go Again* (Decca 1971)★★★, *Seasons Of Love* (ABC 1974)★★★.

Wright, Carol Sue

b. 1945, Nashville, Tennessee, USA. The youngest of the three children of Kitty Wells and Johnnie Wright, she began to sing with her parents from an early age. In December 1955, standing on a chair to reach the microphone, Wright duetted with her mother when she recorded their well-known version of 'How Far Is Heaven?'. In the late 50s, she sang with her sister, Ruby

Wright, as the Wright Sisters, recording under the production of Chet Atkins for the Cadence label, who saw them as the female version of the label's popular Everly Brothers. She toured for a time with the family show but eventually, with no desire to pursue a singing career, she restricted her appearances and devoted her time to raising her own family. In the 80s, she and sister Ruby ran the family Museum and Tourist attraction in Nashville.

Wright, Chely

b. 1971, Wellesville, Kansas, USA. As a child the 90s country singer Chely Wright wanted to be a star and aged 11 she had her first band. When she was 18 she was working at Opryland USA in Nashville where she met songwriters and musicians. When times were tough, she would say, 'This will be great when they do the movie of my life.' She pestered producer Harold Shedd until he signed her and, with another producer Barry Beckett, she made the modern honky-tonk album *Woman In The Moon* and charted with a revival of Harlan Howard's 'He's A Good Ol' Boy'. This album brought her immediate plaudits, including the Academy Of Country Music's Best New Female Vocalist award. Despite this, the album's sales were modest. She subsequently spent a year and a half on the road, playing with Alan Jackson, Confederate Railroad, Tim McGraw and Alabama. These experiences were condensed into the performances for her second album, *Right In The Middle Of It*, on which she changed producers, employing Ed Seay. As she told *Billboard* magazine prior to its release, 'Instead of finding songs that were country and trying to make great records out of them, we tried to find great songs.' The album was accompanied by a heavily promoted attendant single, 'Listen To The Radio'. 'The Last Supper' finds a wife cooking the last meal for her cheating husband: 'He'll break the bread and drink his wine alone.' Wright disciplines herself to write in an office on Music Row and she says, 'I'm not a great singer or a great poet, but I write some good songs.'

● ALBUMS: *Woman In The Moon* (A&M 1994)★★, *Right In The Middle Of It* (A&M 1996)★★★★, *Let Me In* (MCA 1997)★★★.

Wright, Dale

b. Harlan Dale Reiffe, 4 February 1938, Middletown, Ohio, USA. As a teenager Wright was a disc jockey on WING in Dayton, Ohio. He was spotted by Harry Carlson of Fraternity Records when singing 'Walk With Me', with his group the Rock-Its, on a polio charity telethon. This song became his first single but it was his second release, the rocker 'She's Neat', that gave him his sole US Top 40 hit in early 1958. With the Rock-Its departing shortly after, Wright recorded his next single in Nashville with the Owen Bradley Quintet, subsequently forming the Wright Guys. Their first record together 'Please Don't Do It' (which also featured backing vocal duo the Dons) charted in 1958. Wright's sixth release the rocking novelty 'That's Show Biz' was his last record to create any real interest and even received airplay in the UK. In the 60s he recorded without success on the Alcar, Stardust, Boone and Revere labels, and in 1967 on Queen B on which he was backed by the label owner's son Bo Donaldson and his group the Heywoods.

Wright, Elly

b. Austria. Singing since childhood, Wright has established a considerable following in and around Vienna. She has also toured throughout Austria, sometimes working with local musicians such as pianist-composer-arranger Erwin Schmidt and guitarist Christian Havel. She has also worked with **Rolf Ericson** and **Ed Thigpen**, both of whom appeared on *A World Of My Own*. Wright's singing style is sleekly professional and she builds her repertoire from an intriguing blend of standards, jazz pieces by **Duke Ellington**, **Dave Brubeck** and others, compositions by her regular associates and a sprinkling of songs for which she herself has written either the music, the lyrics, or both.
● ALBUMS: *A World Of My Own* (RST 1994)★★★.

Wright, Frank

b. 9 July 1935, Grenada, Mississippi, USA, d. 17 June 1990, Wuppertal, Germany. Wright grew up in Memphis and, later, in Cleveland alongside **Albert Ayler**, whose influence persuaded him to switch to tenor saxophone from double bass (on which instrument he had backed visiting blues stars such as **B.B. King** and **Bobby Bland**). He developed a ferocious, vocalized saxophone style that was rooted in Ayler's innovations and, on moving to New York in 1965, associated with **John Coltrane**, Sunny Murray and **Cecil Taylor**, as well as recording two albums for the *avant garde* ESP label. In 1969 he moved to Europe with **Noah Howard**, settled in Paris with a band that included pianist Bobby Few, drummer Muhammad Ali and (later) **Alan Silva** and for many years helped to run the Center Of The World record label. Nicknamed 'the Reverend', Wright stayed in Europe for most of the 70s and 80s: though out of the jazz spotlight, he continued to play the intense, squealing, all-out free music for which he was best-known. In the early 80s he renewed his acquaintance with Cecil Taylor, touring in the pianist's Orchestra Of Two Continents and recording on his 1984 *Winged Serpent (Sliding Quadrants)*. In 1988 when he appeared at London's ICA with **Jeanne Lee** and **Lawrence 'Butch' Morris**, Wright's playing was as exciting as ever. He died of a heart attack in 1990.
● ALBUMS: *Frank Wright Trio* (ESP 1965)★★★★, *Your Prayer* (1967)★★★★, *One For John* (1970)★★★, *Center Of The World* (1972)★★★, *Last Polka In Nancy* (1973)★★, with Muhammad Ali *Adieu Little Man* (1974)★★★, with Bobby Few and Alan Silva *Solos Et Duets, Volumes 1 & 2* (1975)★★★, with Cecil Taylor *Winged Serpent (Sliding Quadrants)* (1984)★★★★.

Wright, Gary

b. 26 April 1945, New Jersey, USA. Wright attracted the attention of **Island** label owner **Chris Blackwell** when his rock group, the New York Times, supported **Traffic** on a 1967 tour of Scandinavia. An accomplished singer, composer and keyboard player, Wright was invited to join UK signing **Art**, whose career was bereft of direction. The revitalized unit, renamed **Spooky Tooth**, enjoyed considerable acclaim before Wright, who drew an increasing share of the spotlight, left for a solo career in 1970. Having contributed to sessions by **George Harrison**, **Ringo Starr** and **Badfinger**, the artist formed Wonderwheel around **Jerry Donahue** (guitar), Archie Legget (bass) and Bryson Graham (drums). Mick Jones, Legget's one-time colleague with French singer **Johnny Hallyday**, replaced Donahue prior to recording, but the ensuing releases failed to generate public interest. The group was disbanded in 1972 and while the bassist joined **Kevin Ayers**, the remaining trio became the core of a re-formed Spooky Tooth. Wright led the group for another two years before the name was finally put to rest. He resumed solo work with *The Dream Weaver*, a platinum-selling album which reached number 7 in the US chart, but this runaway success was not sustained. Despite an in-concert popularity, *Light Of Smiles* failed to reach the Top 20 while *Touch And Gone* and *Heading Home* missed the Top 100 altogether. *The Right Place* in 1981 was a much more satisfying and successful record although Wright appeared to disappear for a while. He devoted the next few years to bringing up his children as a single parent. During this time of semi-retirement he worked on a number of film music scores including *Endangered Species* but received a bigger profile when 'Dream Weaver' was used to great effect in *Wayne's World*. He continues to record and has never ruled out the possibility of a Spooky Tooth reunion.
● ALBUMS: with Wonderwheel *Extraction* (A&M 1971)★★, *Footprint* (A&M 1972)★★, *Ring Of Changes* (A&M 1972)★★; Gary Wright solo *The Dream Weaver* (Warners 1975)★★★★, *The Light Of Smiles* (Warners 1977)★★, *Touch And Gone* (Warners 1977)★★, *Headin' Home* (Warners 1979)★★★, *The Right Place* (Warners 1981)★★, *Who Am I* (Cypress 1987)★★, *First Signs Of Life* (1995)★★.
● COMPILATIONS: *That Was Only Yesterday* (A&M 1976)★★★.

Wright, Johnnie

b. John Robert Wright, 13 May 1914, on a farm near Mt. Juliet, Wilson County, Tennessee, USA. His grandfather was a champion old-time fiddler, his father a banjo player and while still at school, Wright learned to play these instruments, as well as the guitar, and began to sing locally. He relocated to Nashville in 1933, where he worked daily as a cabinetmaker and entertained at local venues. In 1936, he began to appear on radio WSIX Nashville and the following year, he met **Kitty Wells** who, as Muriel Deason, was then appearing on the station as part of the singing Deason Sisters. On 30 October 1937, they were married and with Wright's sister, Louise, the trio began to play WSIX as Johnnie Wright And The Harmony Girls. In 1939, they teamed up with their brother-in-law **Jack Anglin**, first appearing as Johnny Wright and the Happy Roving Cowboys with Jack Anglin, but by 1940, Wright and Anglin had become **Johnnie And Jack**. After Anglin's untimely death in 1963, Wright reorganized their band, the Tennessee Mountain Boys, and recorded for **Decca** as a solo artist. He made his US country chart debut in 1964 with the strangely titled 'Walkin', Talkin', Cryin', Barely Beatin' Broken Heart'. In 1965, he enjoyed a number 1 country hit with **Tom T. Hall**'s song 'Hello Vietnam'. He followed with further minor hits including 'I'm Doing This For Daddy', 'Mama's Little Jewel' and 'American Power'. During this time, he toured and worked in conjunction with Kitty Wells and in 1968, they charted with their duet 'We'll Stick Together'. After this, their careers fully merged and with their children **Ruby**, **Bobby** and **Carol Sue Wright**, they become the Kitty Wells-Johnny Wright Family Show.

● ALBUMS: *Hello Vietnam* (Decca 1965)★★★★, *Country Music Special* (Decca 1966)★★★, *Country The Wright Way* (Decca 1967)★★★, *Johnny Wright Sings Country Favorites* (Decca 1968)★★★, with Kitty Wells *We'll Stick Together* (Decca 1968)★★★, with Wells *Heartwarming Gospel Songs* (Decca 1972)★★.

Wright, Lammar

b. 20 June 1907, Texarkana, Texas, USA, d. 13 April 1973. Wright was raised in Kansas City where he took up the trumpet. In his mid-teens he played with **Bennie Moten**'s band, staying with the group until 1927 when he joined the **Missourians**. With this band he came to New York, remaining with the band through its metamorphosis into the **Cab Calloway** orchestra. In the 40s he played with **Don Redman**, **Claude Hopkins**, Calloway again, **Cootie Williams**, **Lucky Millinder** and others. Wright was also in demand for session and studio work and as a teacher. During the 50s these activities occupied much of his time although he still played jazz gigs with **Count Basie**, **Sauter-Finegan** and others, and worked briefly at the end of the decade with a band organized by **George Shearing**. Wright's technical mastery and the ease and fluency of his playing made him a valued and respected member of the jazz community. His skills were passed on to many other trumpeters through his teaching and in particular to his sons. Lammar Wright Jnr. (1927-1983) played trumpet with **Lionel Hampton**, **Dizzy Gillespie** and **Charlie Barnet**. Elmon Wright (1929-1984) also played trumpet with Gillespie, **Roy Eldridge**, **Earl Bostic**, **Buddy Rich** and **Milt Jackson**.

● ALBUMS: with George Shearing *Satin Brass* (Capitol 1959)★★★★.

● COMPILATIONS: *The Chronological Bennie Moten 1923-1927* (Classics 1923-27)★★★, *The Chronological Cab Calloway 1930-1931* (Classics 1930-31)★★★★.

Wright, Lawrence

b. 15 February 1888, Leicester, England, d. 19 May 1964, London, England. A leading pioneer in UK popular music, Wright used his real name for his music publishing business, and the nom de plume Horatio Nicholls for his songwriting activities. His father owned a music shop, and taught his son to play violin, banjo and piano. After leaving school at the age of 12, Wright worked for a printing company, before joining a concert party and learning the art of public performance. He wrote the first of his many songs, 'Down By The Stream', when he was 17, and later hired a stall in the local market to demonstrate his own compositions, and those he had bought from other songwriters. In 1910, he published 'Don't Go Down The Mine Daddy', by William Geddes and Robert Donnelly. It reputedly sold over a million sheet copies, aided, no doubt, by the Whitehaven pit disaster of the same year. He went to London in 1911 and was one of the first publishers to set up business in Denmark Street, soon to become the city's 'Tin Pan Alley'. In 1926, he founded his 'in house' journal, the *Melody Maker*, to promote his catalogue, and it still exists in the UK today. Apart from UK songs, Wright also made publishing deals with US songwriters, including **Hoagy Carmichael**, **Walter Donaldson**, **Fats Waller** and **Duke Ellington**. This policy meant that Wright introduced standards such as 'Little White Lies', 'Stardust', 'Lazybones', 'Mood Indigo', 'Ain't Misbehavin'', 'Carolina Moon', 'Basin Street Blues', and 'Memories Of You' to Britain. From 1924-56, he presented his own annual summer production, *On With The Show*, at Blackpool, to promote and try out his songs. Wright's promotional publicity stunts were legendary. For 'Me And Jane In A Plane', written by Joe Gilbert and **Edgar Leslie**, he flew the entire **Jack Hylton** Orchestra, who had made a recording of the song, around the Blackpool Tower, dropping copies of the sheet music. For 'Sahara', his own song, written with Jean Frederick, and also recorded by Hylton, he rode a camel in Piccadilly Circus.

He is said to have written over 500 songs, often in collaboration with others. His partnership with the American Edgar Leslie produced 'Shepherd Of The Hills', 'Mistakes' and, arguably his biggest hit, 'Among My Souvenirs'. The latter was performed by Hoagy Carmichael in the 1946 movie, *The Best Years Of Our Lives*, and surfaced again in 1959 as a million-seller for **Connie Francis**. Wright's best known songs with the English writer Worton David were 'That Old Fashioned Mother Of Mine', and 'Are We Downhearted? No!'. Of the 40 or so numbers he wrote with Joe Gilbert, the most famous was 'Amy, Wonderful Amy', a tribute to aviator, Amy Johnson. His other popular songs included 'When The Guards Are On Parade', 'Blue Eyes', 'Down Forget-Me-Not-Lane', 'Babette', 'The Toy Drum Major', 'Delilah', 'The Heart Of A Rose', 'Let's All Go To The Music Hall', 'London Is Saying Goodnight', 'Life Begins At Oxford Circus', 'The Festival Of Britain' and 'Adeline'. A stroke in 1943 caused him to slow down, and he was confined to a wheel-chair, but continued writing into the 50s, and retained personal control of his publishing interests. In 1962 he received an **Ivor Novello** Award for 'Outstanding Services To British Popular Music'. Two years later he died in London. After his death Lawrence Wright Music changed hands several times, and was owned for a time by US pop star **Michael Jackson**.

Wright, Mark
Wright wrote 'Paradise Tonight', a US country number 1 for **Charly McClain** and **Mickey Gilley** in 1983, but he has since established himself as a record producer. He was the co-producer with **James Stroud** of **Clint Black**'s 1989 success *Killin' Time*, and his current artists include Rhett Atkins.

Wright, Michelle
b. 1 July 1957, Chatham, Ontario, Canada. Wright grew up in a farming community in Merlin, Ontario, and her parents were both country music performers. With her distinctive low and husky voice, she became one of Canada's most popular country singers and several songs from her first album, *Do Right By Me*, were recorded for the US market by **Reba McEntire**. Wright moved to Nashville but her progress was impaired by a drink problem, which she has now overcome. Her second American album, *Now And Then*, led to 12 industry awards in one year and sales in the USA alone of over 500,000. Her powerful, husky voice was heard to good effect on 'Take It Like A Man' and she topped the Canadian charts with a touching song about adoption, 'He Would Be Sixteen'. Her more raucous performances, such as 'One Good Man', are closer to **Bonnie Tyler** than country music. Her 'good man', Joel Kane, is also her manager and bass player. She can be seen reading **Patsy Cline**'s letters on the video *Remembering Patsy* (1993). After a four-year gap in the USA, she released an album in 1996, although some momentum had been lost in her career when her record company failed to release the excellent *The Reasons Why* in 1994; the reason why, nobody really knows, but the Arista president took full responsibility for this error.
● ALBUMS: *Do Right By Me* (Savannah 1988)★★★, *Michelle Wright* (Arista 1990)★★★, *Now And Then* (Arista 1992)★★★, *The Reasons Why* (Arista 1994)★★★★, *For Me It's You* (Arista 1996)★★★.
● VIDEOS: *One Good Man* (1994).

Wright, O.V.
b. Overton Vertis Wright, 9 October 1939, Memphis, Tennessee, USA, d. 16 November 1980. One of deep soul's most impressive stylists, O.V. Wright's first recordings were in the gospel tradition and it was while a member of the Harmony Echoes that he became acquainted with Roosevelt Jamison. This aspiring songwriter penned the singer's secular debut, 'That's How Strong My Love Is', an impassioned ballad later covered by **Otis Redding** and the **Rolling Stones**. Wright's

plaintive delivery excelled on slow material, as two imploring R&B hits, 'You're Gonna Make Me Cry' (1965) and 'Eight Men, Four Women' (1967), testified. Wright's next single, 'Heartaches-Heartaches' (1967), confirmed a working relationship with producer **Willie Mitchell**, but despite excellent collaborations in 'Ace Of Spades' (1970), 'A Nickel And A Nail' (1971) and 'I'd Rather Be (Blind, Crippled And Crazy)' (1973), the singer was unable to reach a wider audience. Imprisoned for narcotics offences during the mid-70s, he re-emerged on the **Hi Records** in 1975, but intense recordings here, including 'Rhymes' (1976) and 'I Feel Love Growin'' (1978), met a similar fate. Hard living and a continuing drug problem weakened his health and in 1980, O.V. Wright died from a heart attack. For many he remains one of southern soul's most authoritative and individual artists.
● ALBUMS: *If It's Only For Tonight* (Back Beat 1965)★★★, *8 Men And 4 Women* (Back Beat 1967)★★★, *Nucleus Of Soul* (Back Beat 1968)★★★, *A Nickel And A Nail And Ace Of Spades* (Back Beat 1971)★★★, *Memphis Unlimited* (Back Beat 1973)★★, *Into Something I Can't Shake Loose* (1977)★★, *The Wright Stuff* (1977)★★★, *The Bottom Line* (Hi 1978)★★★, *Live* (1979)★★, *We're Still Together* (Hi 1979)★★★.
● COMPILATIONS: *Gone For Good* (1984)★★★, *The Wright Stuff* (1987)★★★, *Here's Another Thing* (1989)★★★, *That's How Strong Love Is* (1991)★★★, *The Soul Of O.V. Wright* (1993)★★★.

Wright, Robert
b. 25 September 1914, Daytona Beach, Florida, USA. Together with George Forrest (b. 31 July 1915, Brooklyn, New York, USA), Wright has formed one of the longest partnerships in the American musical theatre. They first met in their teens at Miami High School, where they collaborated on the show *Hail To Miami High!* After writing numerous jazzy songs together in the early 30s, the team were hired to provide some fresh material - based on non-copyright music - for the film of **Sigmund Romberg**'s stage operetta *Maytime*. So successful were they, that, during the remainder of their stay in Hollywood, the two men worked as co-lyricists for previously written stage and/or screen songs by **Rudolph Friml**, **Victor Herbert**, **Richard Rodgers**, George Posford, Edward Ward, and Herbert Stothart, amongst others. Two of their most popular film songs were 'The Donkey Serenade' (music: Friml-Stothart), which was introduced in *The Firefly* by **Allan Jones**; and the title number for one of the best of the **Nelson Eddy** and **Jeanette MacDonald** vehicles, *Sweethearts*. They also contributed to films such as *Sinner Take All*, *Maytime* ('Street Singer'), *Saratoga*, *Mannequin* ('Always And Always'), *Three Comrades*, *Balalaika* ('At The Balaika', 'The Volga Boatman', 'Ride, Cossack, Ride'), *The Women*, *Music In My Heart* ('It's A Blue World', 'Ho! Punchinello'), and *Flying With Music* ('Pennies For Peppino') (1942). In the early 40s Wright and Forrest turned to Broadway and began adapting the romantic

music of classical and operetta composers - with new lyrics - for lavish stage musicals. One of their first efforts, *Song Of Norway* (Edvard Greig, 1944), proved an enormous hit, and was followed by *Gypsy Lady* (Victor Herbert, 1946), *Magdalena* (Heitor Villa-Lobos, 1948), *The Great Waltz* (Johann Strouse (1949) and *Kismet* (Alexander Borodin, 1953). The latter contained several of their most memorable songs, including 'Stranger In Paradise', 'And This Is My Beloved', and 'Baubles, Bangles And Beads'. In 1961 Wright and Forrest wrote their first original Broadway score for *Kean* (they had written the words and music for a London production of *The Love Doctor* two years earlier), which, despite the presence of **Alfred Drake** and pleasant songs such as 'Elena' and 'Sweet Danger', folded after only three months. Four years later, *Anya*, an adaptation of **Guy Bolton** and Marcelle Maurette's play *Anastasia*, signalled a return to their previous policy - this time using the music of Sergei Rachmaninoff - but the critically acclaimed production lasted for only two weeks. *Anya* was later drastically revised and re-titled *The Anastasia Affaire*. The songwriters' latest stage musical (to date) is *Grand Hotel*, which opened on Broadway in 1989, and ran for almost three years. The score is mostly their own work, with some additional numbers by Maury Yeston. Throughout their long careers, Wright and Forrest are reputed to have contributed material to some 16 produced stage musicals, 18 stage revues, 58 motion pictures, and numerous cabaret acts. In 1994 - the year Wright celebrated his 80th birthday - they were reported to be working on three projects for the stage. In the same year they travelled from their Miami base to London, and were present at a BBC Radio 2 concert production of their best-known work, *Kismet*, which they had written over 40 years ago.

Wright, Ruby

b. 27 October 1939, Nashville, Tennessee, USA. The eldest of the three children of **Kitty Wells** and **Johnnie Wright**, she sang with her parents from an early age. At the age of 13, she was signed by **RCA Records** and under the production of **Chet Atkins**, she had single releases as Ruby Wells (there was a pop singer called Ruby Wright, but no doubt RCA believed it would help to use her mother's stage name). In the mid-50s, she was a member of a close-harmony female singing trio, Nita, Rita and Ruby (Nita was Anita Carter and Rita was Rita Robbins, the sister of **Marty Robbins'** guitarist and yodeler, Don Winters). Working with Atkins, they leaned heavily towards a pop presentation but were backed by country studio musicians, and they had minor success with numbers such as 'Rock Love' and 'Hi De Ank Tum'. They were basically only a recording act, since family touring made live appearances difficult for Nita and Ruby. Rita never conquered her stage fright; the trio broke up and she retired. Ruby began to sing with her sister, **Carol Sue Wright**, as the Wright Sisters, recording (again with Atkins) for Cadence, who

saw them as a female version of the label's popular **Everly Brothers**. In 1964, she had a Top 15 solo US country and minor pop hit with 'Dern Ya', a female answer song to **Roger Miller's** 'Dang Me'. In the late 60s, she made the country chart with her Epic label recordings of 'A New Place To Hang Your Hat' and 'A Better Deal Than This'. During the 1970s, she recorded for several small labels including Plantation and Scorpion and had some success with 'Yester-me, Yester-you, Yesterday'. She continued to appear with her parents' show but in the 1980s, along with her sister Carol Sue, took to running the family Museum and Tourist attraction in Nashville.

● ALBUMS: *Dern Ya* (Kapp 1966)★★★, as Nita, Rita & Ruby *Rock Love* (1985)★★★.

Wright, Winston

b. 1944, d. 1993. Wright's name is largely unknown outside of the committed reggae fraternity, but the sound of his organ-playing is familiar to anyone who has ever had more than a passing acquaintance with the music. Winston emerged on the Kingston music scene in the mid-60s and began playing sessions in the **rock-steady** era, initially for **Duke Reid**, but as his work became better known, he was in constant demand from many other top producers. His mastery of, and feel for, the **Hammond** organ earned him an integral role in **Tommy McCook**'s Supersonics - Duke Reid's house band. He later hit the UK charts in 1969 as one of **Harry J.**'s All Stars with 'Liquidator', and also made some of his finest recordings that same year with **Clancy Eccles'** Dynamites. Throughout the 70s he worked as part of the Dynamic Sounds nucleus of musicians, and from 1975 onwards was a member of **Toots And The Maytals'** touring band. He still continued his session work for Kingston's producers when he was at home 'resting', and his contributions to many classic 70s recordings were as uncredited and anonymous as his 60s output. More recently, he returned to Dynamic Sounds where he acted as arranger, mixer and keyboard player. His tragic and untimely death in 1993 robbed the reggae world of one of its greatest unsung talents.

● ALBUMS: with the Dynamites *Fire Corner* (Trojan/Clandisc 1969)★★★★, with the Harry J All Stars *Liquidator* (Trojan 1970)★★★★, with the Dynamites *Herbsman* (Trojan/Clandisc 1970)★★★, *Grass Roots* (Third World 1976)★★★★, *Jump The Fence* (Third World 1976)★★★★.

Wrigley, Bernard

b. 25 February 1948, Bolton, Lancashire, England. Wrigley never quite made the commercial breakthrough to the same degree as other comedian/folk artists, such as **Billy Connolly**, **Richard Digance** and **Mike Harding**. He was a self-taught guitar player who 'discovered' folk clubs as a result of the **Bob Dylan** boom during the 60s. As half of a duo called Dave And Bernard, he gave up being a Customs and Excise Officer and went professional in 1969 to provide a documentary, *The Bolton Massacre*, at the Octagon Theatre, Bolton. By 1970, the duo had split, so Wrigley joined the original Ken Campbell roadshow, during which time he wrote 'Knocking Nelly', 'Our Bill' and 'Concrete Mixer'. Actor Bob Hoskins was also a member of the roadshow at the time. In 1991, Wrigley appeared as Estragon in *Waiting For Godot* at the Octagon Theatre, alongside Mike Harding who played Vladimir. He has also done a great deal of television work, including an Alan Bennett film and a Guinness advertisement. An example of his humour can be found in the popular 'Robin Hood And The Bogey Rolling Contest'.

● ALBUMS: *The Phenomenal Bernard Wrigley* (Topic 1971)★★★, *Rough And Wrigley* (Topic 1973)★★★, *Songs Stories And Elephants* (Transatlantic 1976)★★, *Ten Ton Special* (Transatlantic 1977)★★★, *The Bolton Bull Frog* (Loofy 1981)★★★, *Rude Bits* (Loofy 1985)★★★, *Instrumental Album* (Loofy 1988)★★, *Wanted-Live!* (1991)★★, *Bugglerlugs* (1993)★★★.

● COMPILATIONS: *The Phenomenal Bernard Wrigley/Rough And Wrigley* (Loofy 1988)★★★.

Wrigley, Jennifer And Hazel

Scottish acoustic folk duo and identical twins Jennifer and Hazel Wrigley began performing immediately after leaving school in the Orkneys, near Scotland, with Hazel on guitar and keyboards and Jennifer playing the fiddle. Earlier they had enrolled in the Strathspey and Reel Society's Junior section at the age of 13. The experience of talking and playing with their peers and elders encouraged them to adopt music as their mutual career, after Jennifer had not only won the Society's Junior Fiddle Competition at the age of 15, but also took the Senior title as well. In 1991 the duo recorded their debut album for the Orkney Island's only studio, Owen Tierney's Attick Records, preceding a series of ventures into mainland Scotland and England.

● ALBUMS: *Dancing Fingers* (Attic 1991)★★★.

Writing On The Wall

Originally formed as the Jury in 1966 in Penicuik, Scotland, the nucleus of this tough, soul-based band comprised Willie Finlayson (guitar/vocals), Jimmy Hush (drums), Jake Scott (bass/vocals) and Bill Scott (keyboards). Linnie Patterson, a former member of the **Boston Dexters** and Three's A Crowd (which included the future **Rainbow** guitarist Jimmy Bain), subsequently joined as vocalist and by 1967 the Jury were a leading attraction under the managerial hand of **Tam Paton**. A new name, Writing On The Wall, was assumed when the quintet abandoned soul for a more progressive style. They then became highly popular on London's underground circuit, but their lone album on the Middle Earth label was marred by an amateurish production which negated any power the group could muster. Bound by contractual obligations, they were unable to move to another label and although a new guitarist, Robert 'Smiggy' Smith (b. 30 March 1946,

Kiel, Germany; guitar), also an ex-member of Three's A Crowd, had replaced Finlayson, the enthusiasm he brought with him rapidly disappeared. He and Patterson left the line-up, and although Finlayson returned for a final single, the group split in 1973. Most of the ex-members retained an interest in music. Finlayson worked with several bands, including Meal Ticket while Smiggy joined **Blue**. Paterson sang with a later version of the group **Beggar's Opera**, but failed to achieve due recognition. He completed a solo single, which featured several luminaries from the Edinburgh beat scene, prior to his death from asbestosis in 1990.

● ALBUMS: *The Power Of The Picts* (Middle Earth 1970)★★.

● COMPILATIONS: *Rarities From The Middle Earth* (Pie & Mash 1995)★★, *Crack In The Illusion Of Life* (Tenth Planet 1995)★★, *Burghley Road: The Basement Sessions* (Tenth Planet 1996)★★.

Wrubel, Allie

b. 15 January 1905, Middletown, Connecticut, USA, d. 13 December 1973, Twentynine Palms, California, USA. A popular songwriter from the 30s through to the 50s, who frequently wrote both music and lyrics. After studying medicine at Columbia University, Wrubel played the saxophone with several dance bands, including a one-year stint with **Paul Whiteman** in the 20s, and toured England with his own band in 1924. He spent some time working as a theatre manager before having his first song published in 1931. 'Now You're In My Arms' (written with Morton Downey), was followed by 'As You Desire Me', 'I'll Be Faithful' (**Jan Garber**) and 'Farewell To Arms' (**Paul Whiteman**). In 1934, like many of his contemporaries, Wrubel began to write songs for films, often with lyricist **Mort Dixon**. Their 'Try To See It My Way' was interpolated into the Dubin-Warren score for *Dames*. During the 30s Wrubel also contributed to *Happiness Ahead* ('Pop! Goes Your Heart'), *Flirtation Walk* ('Mr And Mrs Is The Name'), *I Live For Love* ('Mine Alone'), *In Caliente* ('The Lady In Red'), *Sweet Music* ('Fare Thee Well, Annabelle' and 'I See Two Lovers'), *The Toast Of New York* ('The First Time I Saw You'), *Life Of The Party* ('Let's Have Another Cigarette'), and *Radio City Revels* ('Goodnight Angel' and 'There's A New Moon Over The Old Mill'). The films featured some of the biggest stars of the day, such as **Dick Powell**, **Ruby Keeler**, and **Rudy Vallee**. Around that time Wrubel also collaborated with **Herb Magidson** on 'Gone With The Wind' (an all-time standard), 'The Masquerade Is Over' (popularized by Dick Robertson, **Sarah Vaughan** and **Patti Page**), and 'Music Maestro Please', one of the most popular songs of the 30s in versions by **Tommy Dorsey** and **Lew Stone**. During the 40s and 50s Wrubel continued to write songs for movies such as *Sing Your Way Home*, in which Anne Jeffreys sang Wrubel and Madgison's Oscar-nominated 'I'll Buy That Dream' ('A honeymoon in Cairo, in a brand-new autogiro/Then, home by rocket in a wink'), *Song Of The South* (the Oscar-winning 'Zip-A-Dee-Doo-Dah', written with Ray

Gilbert), *Duel In The Sun* ('Gotta Get Me Somebody To Love'), **The Fabulous Dorseys** ('To Me'), *I Walk Alone* ('Don't Call It Love'), and two full-length **Walt Disney** cartoons, *Make Mine Music* , in which the **Andrews Sisters** sang his 'Johnny Fedora And Alice Blue Bonnet', and *Melody Time*, the Andrews Sisters again, with Wrubel's story about a tiny tugboat, 'Little Toot'. During the 50s Wrubel's output declined, although he did contribute several numbers to *Never Steal Anything Small* (1959), which featured an ageing James Cagney duetting with Cara Williams on 'I'm Sorry, I Want A Ferrari'. He also wrote 'What Does A Woman Do?' for the thriller *Midnight Lace* (1960). During a career spanning nearly 30 years, his other songs included 'Gypsy Fiddler', 'The You And Me That Used To Be', 'I Can't Love You Anymore', 'I'm Home Again', 'I'm Stepping Out With A Memory Tonight' (a hit for **Glenn Miller** and **Kate Smith**), 'Where Do I Go From You?'), 'There Goes That Song Again' (revived by **Gary Miller** in the UK in 1961), 'The Lady From Twentynine Palms', '1400 Dream Street', 'Please, My Love' and 'Corabelle'. Among his collaborators were Walter Bullock, **Nat Shilkret**, **Ned Washington**, Abner Silver, and Charles Newman. Wrubel was a Charter member of the Composers Hall of Fame. He died from a heart attack in 1973 at the location mentioned in one of his popular songs - Twentynine Palms, in the state of California.

Wu Man

b. 2 January 1963, Hangzhou, near Shanghai, China. The pre-eminent female artist working in the field of Chinese classical music, Wu Man grew up in artistic surrounds. Her father is a noted painter and her mother a teacher, and both encouraged in their daughter a sense of the profound richness of Chinese culture. In turn she began to study classical music with her chosen instrument the pipa, a four-stringed, pear shaped lute. Wu Man is a member of the 'Pudong school', but this fact has often been misinterpreted in the west into meaning a place of study rather than a tradition. Pudong represents a style of performance of the classical repertoire which can be differentiated from any of the other schools, and Wu Man's actual place of study was the Central Conservatoire of Music in Beijing. There, from 1977 onwards, she was taught by 'fifth generation' Pudong master Lin Shicheng. She eventually earned a master's degree after 11 years of intense study. For a period of three years she too became a teacher, recording her debut album for the state record label in Beijing, following her victory in a national instrument competition in April 1989. She moved to the USA in 1990. Although settled in Boston, most of her performances take place in New York, where she also teaches. In September 1992 she was commissioned by the **Kronos Quartet** to appear alongside them during their appearance at the Pittsburgh New Music Ensemble, playing a composition written by Zhou Long, whose music she had recorded on her Chinese debut. Her first western album, 1993's *Chinese*

Music For The Pipa, included a piece, 'Dian (The Points)', written by Zhou Long's wife, 'Chen Yi, and saw her visit Europe for the first time.

● ALBUMS: *Overlord Removed Of His Armour* (BCD 1989)★★★, *Chinese Music For The Pipa* (Nimbus 1993)★★★.

Wu-Tang Clan

This chess-playing hip hop posse, whose ranks total eight pseudonymous rappers - Shallah Raekwon, Method Man, Rebel INS, Ol' Dirty Bastard, U-God, Ghostface Killah, The Genius (GZA) and Prince Rakeem (The RZA) - based themselves in Staten Island, New York, USA. Each of the team boasted keen martial arts prowess. Indeed their debut album was divided into two sides, Shaolin and Wu-Tang Sword, to symbolise the combat-like disciplines applied to their rapping. Both Rakeem and The Genius had also released solo records prior to their present duties, for **Cold Chillin'** and **Tommy Boy**, which sank without trace. And when the Clan as a whole signed with BMG, provision for each member to work as solo artists was enshrined in the contract. The Genius joined his third record company, **Geffen**, Method Man linked with **Def Jam** and Ol' Dirty Bastard with **Elektra Records**. Their producer/DJ, RZA, also worked alongside **Prince Paul** and Fruitkwan (ex-**Stetsasonic**) as part of the **Gravediggaz**. Affiliated group members include Shyheim The Rugged Prince, Killah Priest and Cappadonna. Wu-Tang Clan's musical armoury centres around old school rhyming and trickery, which with eight contributors offers ample opportunity for quickfire wise-cracking and playing off each other. The musical backing is one of stripped down beats, with samples culled from kung-fu movies. Such appropriation of martial culture is a theme which has occupied rap music from the days of **Grandmaster Flash** onwards. Their debut album quickly and deservedly notched gold status, setting the underground hip hop scene alight in the process. It was recorded in their own studio, its '36 Chambers' suffix alluding to the number of critical points on the body as disclosed by Shaolin theology. However, all was not well with the Clan in 1994. U-God's two-year old, Dante Hawkins, was hit in a gun battle crossfire as he played outside his babysitter's house on 13 March. The bullet destroyed one of his kidneys and damaged his hand. Just a day later a member of the band's inner circle of friends was killed in a separate incident. The Clan regrouped for 1997's **Forever**, a long sprawling record that rarely matched their debut or GZA's exceptional solo collection *Liquid Swords*. The most recent releases from the Wu-Tang stable have been Killah Priest's excellent *Heavy Mental* set, and Cappadonna's best selling *The Pillage*.

● ALBUMS: *Enter The Wu Tang (36 Chambers)* (Loud/RCA 1993)★★★★, *Wu-Tang Forever* (Loud/RCA 1997)★★★★. Solo: Cappadonna *The Pillage* (Razor Sharp/Epic 1998)★★★★. The Genius/GZA *Words From The Genius* (Cold Chillin' 1991/94)★★★, *Liquid Swords* (Geffen

1995)★★★★. Ghostface Killah *Ironman* (Razor Sharp/Epic 1996)★★★. Killah Priest *Heavy Mental* (Geffen 1998)★★★★. Method Man *Tical* (Def Jam 1994)★★★. Ol' Dirty Bastard *Return To The 36 Chambers: The Dirty Version* (Elektra 1995)★★★. Raekwon *Only Built 4 Cuban Linx* (Loud/RCA 1995)★★★.
● VIDEOS: *Da Mystery Of Kung-Fu* (MIA 1998).

Wulomei

This Ghanian group was formed in Accra by drummers Nii Ashitey and Saka Acquaye in 1973 and became the leading band in the country's acoustic highlife revival of the early to mid-70s. Forsaking electric guitars and drum kits, bands like Wulomei (whose name translates as 'Fetish Priest' in Ga) and **Dzadzeloi** featured a choir of traditional percussion instruments, acoustic guitars and melodically rich call-and-response vocals. They enjoyed a number of successful domestic hits spread over a series of early 70s albums. The band folded in 1976 shortly after an ambitious USA tour, but reformed occasionally thereafter.
● ALBUMS: *Mibi Shi Dinn* (AGL 1974)★★★, *Walatu Walasa* (AGL 1974)★★★★, *In Drum Conference* (Phonogram 1975)★★★.

Wump And His Werbles

Drummer John Cochrane (b. 24 August 1939, Wallasey, England) recalls, 'We were going to see the **Everly Brothers** at the Liverpool Empire in 1960 and on the way we were thinking of a name for our group. We wanted to send it all up by having a really stupid name and we decided on Wump And His Werbles. It worked out very well as people booked us on the strength of the name alone.' No-one would own up to being Wump but it was probably lead singer, Steve Day, the other members being Dave Georgeson (b. 8 April 1942, Wirral, England; lead guitar), Nev Humphries (rhythm guitar) and Jimmy Mellor (b. 7 November 1941, Flete Holbeton, Devon; bass). Mellor told the owner of the **Cavern** that they were back in Liverpool for a short break after an extensive tour of the Continent. The owner believed him and on 7 July 1960, they entered into Merseybeat history by playing rock 'n' roll at the club. Although the audience was none too keen, they managed to get rebooked. Although they were a popular band (holding Werble-Q's) and worked on the same bills as the **Beatles**, they broke up within two years. Steve Day fronted his own group while Cochrane played with **Freddie Starr** And The Midnighters. Cochrane and Georgeson were in the Chuckles from 1963-66. Cochrane became a librarian, writing books on car numberplates and aviation.

Wurzels

Originally Adge Cutler And The Wurzels, this English West Country group first scored a minor hit in 1967 with the comic 'Drink Up Thy Zider'. Following Cutler's tragic death in a car crash 5 May 1974, Tommy Banner, Tony Baylis and Pete Budd soldiered on as the Wurzels. Producer Bob Barrett was impressed by their country yokel parodies of well-known hits and persuaded them to provide comic lyrics to **Melanie**'s 'Brand New Key', which emerged as 'Combine Harvester', a surprise UK number 1 in the summer of 1976. The trio almost repeated that feat with their reworking of the continental hit 'Uno Paloma Blanca' retitled ' I Am A Cider Drinker'. Although they only achieved one more success with 'Farmer Bill's Cowman' (based on Whistling Jack Smith's 'I Was Kaiser Bill's Batman') they continued to appear occasionally on British television shows and maintain their popularity on the UK club circuit.
● ALBUMS: *Adge Cutler And The Wurzels* (Columbia 1967)★★, *Adge Cutler's Family Album* (Columbia 1967)★★, *Cutler Of The West* (Columbia 1968)★★, *The Wurzels Are Scrumptious* (One Up 1975)★★, *The Combine Harvester* (One Up 1976)★★, *Golden Delicious* (Note 1977)★★, *Give Me England* (Note 1977)★★, *I'll Never Get A Scrumpy Here* (Note 1978)★★, *I'm A Cider Drinker* (Encore 1979)★★.
● COMPILATIONS: *The Very Best Of Adge Cutler And The Wurzels* (EMI 1977)★★, *Greatest Hits* (Note 1979)★★, *Wurzels* (Ideal 1981)★★.

Wuthering Heights
(see **Taylor, Bernard J.**)

Wyands, Richard

b. 2 July 1928, Oakland, California, USA. In mid-teenage, he was playing piano in San Francisco jazz clubs, accompanying local musicians and visitors. In the late 50s he moved to New York where he worked with many jazz artists in both bop and mainstream. By the mid-60s he had settled into a long spell with **Kenny Burrell** with whom he toured extensively. In 1974 he left Burrell to join JPJ Trio, replacing co-founder **Dill Jones**. In the late 70s and through the 80s, he continued to play a discreet supporting role with a wide range of jazzmen. Despite such diffidence, however, Wyands is an accomplished and inventive soloist with a light touch and a subtly engaging sense of swing as can be heard on *There Here And Now*, a rare instance of Wyands as leader.
● ALBUMS: *Roamin' With Jerome Richardson* (1959)★★, with Elvin Jones *Don't Go To Strangers* (1960)★★★, with Kenny Burrell *The Tender Gender* (1966)★★★, *Then Here And Now* (Storyville 1978)★★★★, with Cecil Payne *Casbah* (1985)★★★, *The Arrival* (DIW 1992)★★★.

Wyatt, Robert

b. 28 January 1945, Bristol, Avon, England. As the drummer, vocalist and guiding spirit of the original **Soft Machine**, Robert Wyatt established a style that merged the *avant garde* with English eccentricity. His first solo album, *The End Of An Ear*, presaged his departure from the above group, although its radical content resulted in a muted reception. Wyatt's next venture, the excellent **Matching Mole**, was bedevilled by internal dissent, but a planned relaunch was forcibly abandoned following a tragic fall from a window, which left him paralyzed and confined to a wheelchair. *Rock Bottom*, the artist's next release, was composed while Wyatt lay in hospital. This heartfelt, deeply personal collection was marked by an aching vulnerability that successfully avoided any hint of self-pity. This exceptional album was succeeded by an unlikely hit single in the shape of an idiosyncratic reading of the **Monkees** hit 'I'm A Believer'. *Ruth Is Stranger Than Richard*, released in 1975, was a more open collection, and balanced original pieces with outside material, including a spirited reading of jazz bassist **Charlie Haden**'s 'Song For Che'. Although Wyatt, a committed Marxist, would make frequent guest appearances, his own career was shelved until 1980 when a single comprised of two South American songs of liberation became the first in a series of politically motivated releases undertaken for **Rough Trade Records**. These performances were subsequently compiled on *Nothing Can Stop Us*, which was then enhanced by the addition of 'Shipbuilding', a haunting anti-Falklands War composition, specifically written for Wyatt by **Elvis Costello**, which was a minor chart entry in 1983. Wyatt's fluctuating health has undermined his recording ambitions, but his commitment remains undiminished. He issued singles in aid of Namibia and the British Miners' Hardship Fund, and contributed a compassionate soundtrack to the harrowing 1982 *Animals* film. Wyatt's more recent recordings, *Old Rotten Hat* and *Dondestan*, are as compelling as the rest of his impressive work. Now relocated in Lincolnshire, after a number of years in post-Franco Spain, Wyatt returned after *A Short Break* with one of his best ever albums. *Shleep* was as brilliantly idiosyncratic as anything he has recorded. Surrounded by musicians he genuinely respected, the feeling of the album is one of mutual accord. **Brian Eno**'s production enhances Wyatt's beautifully frail vocals. Highlights include 'The Duchess', a poignant and honest song for his wife Alfie, who co-writes with him and whose gentle illustrations grace many of his album covers. Other noteworthy tracks are the wandering 'Maryan', the deeply logical 'Free Will And Testament' and the lightly mocking paean to **Bob Dylan**'s 115th Dream', 'Blues In Bob Minor'. *Shleep* is a treasure, by a man treasured by all who possess a conscience and a heart.

● ALBUMS: *The End Of An Ear* (Columbia 1970)★★★, *Rock Bottom* (Virgin 1974)★★★★, *Ruth Is Stranger Than Richard* (Virgin 1975)★★★, *Nothing Can Stop Us* (Rough Trade 1982)★★★★, *Animals* (Rough Trade 1984)★★, *Old Rotten Hat* (Rough Trade 1985)★★★, *Dondestan* (Rough Trade 1991)★★★, *A Short Break* mini-album (1992)★★★, *Shleep* (Hannibal 1997)★★★★.

● COMPILATIONS: *Going Back A Bit: A Little History Of ...* (Virgin Universal 1994)★★★★, *Flotsam Jetsam* (Rough Trade 1994)★★★.

● FURTHER READING: *Wrong Movements: A Robert Wyatt History*, Michael King.

Wyclef

b. Wyclef Jean, Haiti. Despite his parent group the **Fugees** having sold 11 million copies of their most recent album, in the process becoming the biggest rap crossover success of the 90s, lead rapper Wyclef Jean still found time to release a solo album in 1997. Long regarded as the mastermind behind the Fugees' intoxicating blend of rap, soul and Haitian music, Wyclef Jean is also active as a remixer and producer to the R&B/dance community (including the number 1 single 'No No No' by Destiny's Child). Guests on his debut solo effort included Lauryn Hill and Prakazrel Michel (his fellow Fugees), the **Neville Brothers**, the **I-Threes**, the New York Philharmonic Orchestra and Cuban superstar **Celia Cruz**. Tracks such as 'Sang Fezi' and 'Jaspora' exploited his own musical ancestry while adding modern production methods to produce an intoxicating and seamlessly rhythmic collection. The album was promoted by the release of 'We Trying To Stay Alive', a more contemporary-sounding effort that sampled the refrain from the **Bee Gees**' 'Stayin' Alive', and 'Gone Till November'.

● ALBUMS: *Wyclef Jean Presents The Carnival Featuring The Refugee Allstars* (Columbia 1997)★★★.

Wycoff, Michael

b. 1956, Torrance, California, USA. This classy and soulful singer worked as a pianist and backing vocalist for **Natalie Cole**, D.J. Rogers and **Phoebe Snow** in the 70s. He also did much session work and can be heard on **Stevie Wonder**'s chart-topping *Songs In The Key of Life*. Wycoff's first solo album was the self-composed jazz-orientated *Come To My World* in 1981. It was critically acclaimed but sold relatively few copies as did the follow-up *Love Conquers All*. He made the decision that *On The Line*, would be a less serious, lighter, more commercial and danceable album. It contained his biggest hit to date '(Do You Really Love Me) Tell Me Love' which gave him his first US R&B Top 40 single and a UK chart entry. Wycoff, who has been compared favourably with acts like Stevie Wonder, **Peabo Bryson** and **Donny Hathaway**, is possibly 'too classy' to hit. However, he could be just a one good song away from getting the break he deserves.

● ALBUMS: *Come To My World* (1981)★★★★, *Love Conquers All* (1982)★★★, *On The Line* (1983)★★★.

Wylie, Austin

b. USA. Although the Austin Wylie Orchestra essentially played at only one location, the Golden Pheasant in Cleveland, Ohio, USA, the orchestra was notable for the number of key personnel to pass through its ranks. **Claude Thornhill**, Spud Murphy, **Tony Pastor**, **Artie Shaw**, Clarence Hutchenrider, **Joe Bishop**, **Billy Butterfield**, Bill Stegmeyer, **Vaughn Monroe** and many others were among Wylie's personnel at one stage or another. Their sound, fashioned so as to make the best possible appeal to the hotel's supper dance clientele, was emblazoned with the vocals of **Helen O'Connell** and Vaughn Monroe. Their best moments were captured on labels including Beltoba and **Vocalion Records**. They were gainfully employed at the Golden Pheasant for over 10 years from the early 20s onwards, before Wylie gave up bandleading to take over management duties for Artie Shaw's group in the 40s. He briefly returned to the baton but these ventures proved unsuccessful. He eventually entered Chicago's business community instead.

Wyman, Bill

b. William Perks, 24 October 1936, London, England. Though his recruitment by the **Rolling Stones** may have saved him from a more mundane life, his frustrated artistic ambition - particularly as a composer - deserves a measure of sympathy. 1967's 'In Another Land' (b/w '2000 Light Years From Home') failed to reach the US Top 40, and only one other opus written solely by Wyman has ever been released by the group. Speculating in artist management and record production in the 60s, he was, nevertheless, able to foister some of his material onto the End, Bobbie Miller and other unsuccessful clients. By the mid-70s, his songs were heard by a much wider public when he issued his first solo record, *Monkey Grip*, on which he was accompanied mostly by Los Angeles session players. Amid hearsay that he was serving his notice with **Mick Jagger** and co., 1976's *Stone Alone* and its single - an overhaul of **Gary 'US' Bonds'** 'Quarter To Three' - employed renowned assistants like **Van Morrison** and **Sly Stone** as well as Stones associates **Nicky Hopkins**, **Ron Wood** and **Al Kooper**. Paradoxically, Wyman's resignation seemed less inevitable when 1982's witty '(Si, Si) Je Suis Un Rock Star' was the highest UK chart strike for any solo Stone. One of its follow-ups, 'A New Fashion' also sold well. Both were recorded when Wyman was labouring over the film score to *Green Ice*. His membership of the Stones guaranteed each single (and attendant album) some airplay but their chart placings testified to more intrinsic virtues in an industry where sales figures were arbiters of worth.

Among Wyman's numerous charitable works during the 80s was the shouldering of much of **Ronnie Lane**'s load in organizing fund-raising galas for Action For Muscular Sclerosis. One such London event featuring his *ad hoc* 'Willie and the Poor Boys' was immortalized on video and included an appearance by **Ringo Starr** with whom Wyman invested in 'The Brasserie', an Atlanta restaurant. Its failure did not quell his appetite for catering as shown by the opening of *Sticky Fingers*, his London eaterie. Using the Stones' mobile studio, Wyman traversed the UK on a search for deserving unknown bands via Ambition Ideas Motivation and Success (AIMS), a project that fizzled out when the Pernod drink company withdrew its sponsorship. All these ventures were, however, less interesting to the tabloid press than his courtship and consequent troubled marriage to teenager Mandy Smith whom he allegedly seduced when she was 13 years-old. Wyman

published an autobiography in 1990. Following his retirement from the Stones, Wyman has married again and now runs a successfull chain of hamburger restaurants known as Sticky Fingers.

● ALBUMS: *Monkey Grip* (Rolling Stones 1974)★★, *Stone Alone* (Rolling Stones 1976)★★, *Green Ice* film soundtrack (1981)★, *Bill Wyman* (A&M 1982)★★, with various artists *Willie And The Poor Boys* (1986)★★★.

● FURTHER READING: *Stone Alone*, Bill Wyman and Ray Coleman.

Wynder K. Frog

b. Michael Weaver, *c.*1947, Colchester, Essex, England. A pseudonym for the highly talented session organist/pianist (see **Mick Weaver**) who released three albums including the exceptional *Out Of The Frying Pan* in 1968. Dubbed the **Booker T.** of Bolton, Weaver enlisted a stellar team of musicians including **Dick Heckstall-Smith**, Chris Mercer, Alan Spenner (bass), Neil Hubbard (guitar), Bruce Rowland (drums).

● ALBUMS: *Sunshine Superfrog* (Island 1967)★★★★, *Out Of The Frying Pan* (Island 1968)★★★★, *Into The Fire* (United Artists 1970)★★.

Wyndham-Read, Martin

b. 23 August 1942, Crawley, Sussex, England. This singer and guitarist compiled a number of recordings of British and Australian songs. Martin left England in 1960 to live in Australia. In 1961, he was already playing in coffee bars in Melbourne and Sydney. He built up a large repertoire of Australian songs during this time and also recorded a number of albums for the Score label, commencing with *Moreton Bay,* the title synonymous with the imprisonment of convicts in Australia in a place now called Brisbane. Martin also recorded a live album, during the mid-60s, with **Gary Shearston**. Returning to Britain in 1967, Wyndham-Read recorded *Leviathan* for **Topic Records**, with such luminaries as Bert Lloyd, **Dave Swarbrick**, and **Martin Carthy**. *Ned Kelly And That Gang* on Trailer was Martin's first solo UK release. The album features two classics of the genre in 'The Wild Colonial Boy', and 'Moreton Bay'. On *The Valiant Sailor* and *Sea Shanties*, Martin was joined by **Alistair Anderson**, **Frankie Armstrong**, and **Roy Harris**. The later *Emu Plains* featured **Nic Jones** on fiddle, while *The Old Songs* included contributions from **John Kirkpatrick** and Sue Harris. *Maypoles To Mistletoe* features a cycle of seasonal songs and includes the much performed and recorded 'Dancing At Whitsun'. Martin regularly tours worldwide, appearing at festivals and clubs in the USA, New Zealand, Hong Kong, and India.

● ALBUMS: *Moreton Bay* (1963)★★★★, *Will You Go Lassie Go?* (1964)★★★★, *Australian Songs* (1964)★★★, *A Wench, A Whale, And A Pint Of Good Ale* (1966)★★★, *Bullockies, Bushwackers And Booze* (1967)★★★, *Leviathan* (1967)★★★★, *Ned Kelly And That Gang* (1970)★★★★, *Martin Wyndham-Read* (1971)★★★, *Great Australian Legend* (1971)★★★, *Songs And Music Of The Redcoats* (1971)★★★,

Harry The Hawker Is Dead (1973)★★★★, *The Valiant Sailor* (1973)★★★, *Sea Shanties* (1974)★★★★, *Maypoles To Mistletoe* (1975)★★★, *Ballad Singer* (1976)★★★, *English Sporting Ballads* (1976)★★★, *Andy's Gone* (1979)★★★, *Emu Plains* (1981)★★★, *A Rose From The Bush* (1984)★★★, *The Old Songs* (1984)★★★, *Across The Line* (1987)★★★, *Yuletracks* (1986)★★, *All Around Down Under* (1988)★★★, *Muscles On A Tree* (1991)★★★.

Wynette, Tammy

b. Virginia Wynette Pugh, 5 May 1942, Itawamba County, near Tupelo, Mississippi, USA, d. 6 April 1998, Nashville, Tennessee, USA. Wynette is primarily known for two songs, 'Stand By Your Man' and 'D.I.V.O.R.C.E.', but her huge catalogue includes 20 US country number 1 hits, mostly about standing by your man or getting divorced. After her father died when she was 10 months old, she was raised by her mother and grandparents and picked cotton from an early age. When aged 17, she married construction worker Euple Byrd, and trained as a hairdresser. She subsequently made an album with their third child, Tina - *George, Tammy And Tina* - in 1975. Byrd did not share her ambition of being a country singer, so she left and moved to Nashville. She impressed producer **Billy Sherrill** and had her first success in 1966 with a **Johnny Paycheck** song, 'Apartment No. 9'. She almost topped the US country charts with 'I Don't Want To Play House', in which a child shuns his friends' game because he senses his parents' unhappiness. It was the template for numerous songs, including 'Bedtime Story', in which Wynette attempts to explain divorce to a three-year-old, and 'D.I.V.O.R.C.E.' in which she does not.

Her own marriage to guitarist Don Chapel disintegrated after he traded nude photographs of her and, after witnessing an argument, country star **George Jones** eloped with her. Unaware of the turmoil in Wynette's own life, American feminists in 1968 condemned Wynette for supporting her husband, right or wrong, in 'Stand By Your Man', but she maintains, 'Sherrill and I didn't have women's lib in mind. All we wanted to do was to write a pretty love song'. The way Wynette chokes on 'After all, he's just a man' indicates pity rather than than support. Having previously recorded a country chart-topper with **David Houston** ('My Elusive Dreams'), an artistic collaboration with George Jones was inevitable. Their albums scaled new heights in over-the-top romantic duets, particularly 'The Ceremony', which narrates the marriage vows set to music. In an effort to separate Jones from alcohol, she confiscated his car-keys, only to find him riding their electric lawnmower to the nearest bar. 'The Bottle' was aimed at Jones as accurately as the real thing. 'Stand By Your Man' was used to good effect in *Five Easy Pieces* (which starred Jack Nicholson), and the record became a UK number 1 on its sixth reissue in 1975. It was followed by a UK Top 20 placing for 'D.I.V.O.R.C.E.', but it was **Billy Connolly**'s parody

about his 'D.O.G.' that went to the UK number 1 slot. Wynette also had two bestselling compilations in the UK album charts. By now her marriage to Jones was over and 'Dear Daughters' explains the position to them. Jones, in more dramatic fashion, retaliated with 'The Battle'. Even more difficult to explain to her daughters was her 44-day marriage to estate agent Michael Tomlin. After torrid affairs with Rudy Gatlin (of **Larry Gatlin And The Gatlin Brothers**) and Burt Reynolds (she saved the actor's life when he passed out in the bath), she married record producer George Richey, whose own stormy marriage had just ended. In 1978, she was kidnapped outside a Nashville car-park and was subjected to an unexplained brutal beating. She has also experienced many health problems, including several stomach operations. Throughout the traumas, she continued to record songs about married life, 'That's The Way It Could Have Been', 'Til I Can Make It On My Own', '(You Make Me Want To Be) A Mother' and 'Love Doesn't Always Come (On The Night That It's Needed)'. None of these songs have found acceptance outside the country market, but 'Stand By Your Man' has become a standard, with versions ranging from **Loretta Lynn** (who also took an opposing view in 'The Pill'), **Billie Jo Spears** and **Tina Turner**, to two male performers, **David Allan Coe** and **Lyle Lovett**. Her autobiography was made into a television movie in 1981. In 1986, Wynette entered the Betty Ford clinic for drug dependency and, true to form, followed it with a single, 'Alive And Well'. She played in a daytime soap, *Capital*, in 1987, although its drama was light relief when compared to her own life. Her stage show included a lengthy walkabout to sing 'Stand By Your Man' to individual members of the audience. Her standing in the rock world increased when she was co-opted by the **KLF** to appear on 'Justified And Ancient', which became a Top 3 UK hit in 1991. Her duet album, *Higher Ground*, was more imaginatively produced than other later albums.

Wynette's turbulent time with Jones was well documented, so much so that they were the most famous couple in the history of country music. The announcement that they were working together again came as a pleasant surprise to their many followers. Their previous reconciliation at the end of 1979 had merely been an attempt to help Jones save his washed-up career. *One*, released in 1995, was felt by many to be the best of their career; the good feeling conveyed by tracks such as 'Solid As A Rock' was the result of their having chosen to sing together for purely musical reasons. There was no longer any emotional baggage, nor any resurrection needed - perhaps for the first time in their lives, they were motivated purely by the enjoyment of making music together. One of Wynette's last appearances was as a guest singer on a cover version of **Lou Reed**'s 'Perfect Day', released in 1997 to promote BBC Radio and Television. She died from a blood clot in April 1998.

● ALBUMS: *Your Good Girl's Gonna Go Bad* (Epic

1967)★★★★, *Take Me To Your World* (Epic 1967)★★★★, *D.I.V.O.R.C.E.* (Epic 1967)★★★★, *Stand By Your Man* (Epic 1968)★★★★, *Inspiration* (Epic 1969)★★, *The Ways To Love A Man* (Epic 1969)★★★★, *Run Angel Run* (Epic 1969)★★★, *Tammy's Touch* (Epic 1970)★★★★, *The First Lady* (Epic 1970)★★★★, *Christmas With Tammy Wynette* (Epic 1970)★★, *We Sure Can Love Each Other* (Epic 1971)★★★★, with George Jones *We Go Together* (Epic 1971)★★★★, *Bedtime Story* (Epic 1972)★★★, with Jones *Me And The First Lady* (Epic 1972)★★★★, *My Man* (Epic 1972)★★★, with Jones *We Love To Sing About Jesus* (Epic 1972)★★, *Kids Say The Darndest Things* (Epic 1973)★★★★, with Jones *Let's Build A World Together* (Epic 1973)★★★, with Jones *We're Gonna Hold On* (Epic 1973)★★★★, *Another Lonely Song* (Epic 1974)★★★, *Woman To Woman* (Epic 1974)★★, *George, Tammy And Tina* (Epic 1975)★★, *I Still Believe In Fairy Tales* (Epic 1975)★★, *Til I Can Make It On My Own* (Epic 1976)★★★, with Jones *Golden Ring* (Epic 1976)★★★★, *You And Me* (Epic 1976)★★★★, *Let's Get Together* (Epic 1977)★★, *One Of A Kind* (Epic 1977)★★★, *Womanhood* (Epic 1978)★★★, *Just Tammy* (Epic 1979)★★, *Only Lonely Sometimes* (Epic 1980)★★, with Jones *Together Again* (Epic 1980)★★★, *You Brought Me Back* (Epic 1981)★★★, *Good Love And Heartbreak* (Epic 1982)★★★, *Soft Touch* (Epic 1982)★★★, *Even The Strong Get Lonely* (Epic 1983)★★★, *Sometimes When We Touch* (Epic 1985)★★★, *Higher Ground* (Epic 1987)★★★, *Next To You* (Epic 1989)★★, *Heart Over Mind* (Epic 1990)★★★, with Dolly Parton, Loretta Lynn *Honky Tonk Angels* (Columbia 1993)★★★, *Without Walls* (Epic 1994)★★★, with Jones *One* (MCA 1995)★★★.

● COMPILATIONS: *Tammy's Greatest Hits* (Epic 1969)★★★★, *The World Of Tammy Wynette* (Epic 1970)★★★, *Tammy's Greatest Hits, Volume II* (Epic 1971)★★★★, *Tammy's Greatest Hits, Volume III* (Epic 1975)★★★, with Jones *Greatest Hits* (Epic 1977)★★★★, *Tammy's Greatest Hits, Volume IV* (Epic 1978)★★★, with Jones *Encore: George Jones & Tammy Wynette* (Epic 1981)★★★★, *Classic Collection* (Epic 1982)★★★, *Biggest Hits* (Epic 1983)★★★★, with Jones *Super Hits* (Epic 1987)★★★, *Anniversary: 20 Years Of Hits* (Epic 1988)★★★★, *Tears Of Fire - The 25th Anniversary Collection* 3-CD set (Epic 1992)★★★★, *Encore* (1993)★★★, *Super Hits* (Epic 1996)★★★.

● VIDEOS: *Live In Nashville, Tammy Wynette In Concert* (Vestron Music 1987), with George Jones, *Country Stars Live* (Platinum Music 1990), *First Lady Of Country Music* (Prism Leisure 1991), *25th Anniversary Collection* (1991).

● FURTHER READING: *Stand By Your Man*, Tammy Wynette.

Wynn, 'Big' Jim

b. 21 June 1912, El Paso, Texas, USA, d. 1976, Los Angeles, California, USA. After moving to Los Angeles as a child, Wynn began his musical tuition on clarinet before switching to tenor sax and playing professionally with the band of Charlie Echols. In 1936, Wynn had his own band and began to link up with 'T-Bone' Walker; this association would last until the end of the famous blues musician's life, with the Wynn band regularly touring and recording with him. The Wynn band's own recording career lasted through R&B's golden years, when records were released on 4 Star/Gilt Edge (1945 - including his biggest hit 'Ee-Bobaliba', which was lucratively covered in various disguises by the likes of **Helen Humes** and **Lionel Hampton**), Modern (1946), **Specialty** and Supreme (1948), **Mercury** and Recorded In Hollywood (1951) and Million (1954). By the late 40s, Wynn increasingly eschewed his tenor in place of a beefy baritone saxophone, and its deep honking, coupled with his own histrionic stage act, was the role model for the next generation of west coast R&B saxophonists. A respected session musician from the late 50s into the 70s, Wynn often played with the bands of his good friends 'T-Bone' Walker and **Johnny Otis**.

● COMPILATIONS: *Blow Wynn Blow* (Whiskey 1985)★★★.

Wynn, Nan

b. c.1918, Wheeling, West Virginia, USA. A smooth, soft-voiced singer, Wynn moved to New York in her teens and joined the Hudson-DeLange Orchestra, featuring on its 1937 hit records 'Yours and Mine' and 'Popcorn Man'. She then went on to sing with Hal Kemp ('What's New?') and **Raymond Scott** ('And So Do I'). In the late 30s, she appeared on her own radio show, and with Kemp on *Time To Shine*. In the early 40s she featured in several movies, including the musicals *Pardon My Sarong*, with Abbott and Costello, and *Is Everybody Happy?*, co-starring Larry Parks. She also appeared in the comedy *Million Dollar Baby* with the future US President Ronald Reagan. Her voice, however, was heard in much more important movies than those, as she was one of the vocalists who dubbed the singing voice of **Rita Hayworth**. Because several ladies performed that function, including Anita Ellis, Martha Mears and Jo Ann Greer, there is often confusion as to who sang for Hayworth in any particular film, but it seems likely that Wynn did the honours in *You'll Never Get Rich* (1941), and *You Were Never Lovelier* and *My Gal Sal* (both 1942). In 1944 Wynn appeared on Broadway in the **Billy Rose** revue *The Seven Lively Arts*, and introduced one of **Cole Porter**'s most bitter-sweet ballads, 'Ev'ry Time We Say Goodbye'. In the late 40s she sang mostly in clubs and small theatres. Her recordings included 'You Go To My Head', 'If I Were You' and 'Laugh And Call It Love' (all with **Teddy Wilson**), 'Who'll Buy My Bublitchki?' (with Emery Deutsch), and 'Lullaby In Rhythm', 'I Said No', 'Ja-Da', 'They Didn't Believe Me' and 'Good For Nothin' But Love'.

Wynn, Steve

Guitarist/vocalist Wynn is one of the pivotal figures in the Los Angeles 'paisley underground' rock scene of the early 80s. A former member of the Suspects, which included Gavin Blair and Russ Tolman, later of True West, he briefly joined the **Long Ryders**, before founding the **Dream Syndicate** in 1981. Starved of a suitable record label, Wynn established Down There Records, which issued important early sets by **Green On Red** and **Naked Prey** in addition to his own group's debut. Dream Syndicate have since pursued an erratic career, blighted by commercial indifference. During a long hiatus in its progress, Wynn joined Gutterball and also worked with Dan Stuart from Green On Red in a ragged, bar-room-influenced collection, *The Lost Weekend*. Billed as by Danny And Dusty, the album featured support from friends and contemporaries and paradoxically outsold the musicians' more serious endeavours. *Kerosene Man* was a compelling and very personal record, which Wynn has failed to equal with subsequent releases. *Melting In The Dark* was a collaboration with indie band **Come**.

● ALBUMS: *The Lost Weekend* (Down There 1985)★★★, *Kerosene Man* (World Service 1990)★★★★, *Dazzling Display* (RNA 1992)★★★, *Fluorescent* (Mute 1994)★★★, *Take Your Flunky And Dangle* (Return To Sender/Normal 1995)★★, with Come *Melting In The Dark* (Zero Hour 1996)★★★.

Wynonna

b. Christina Ciminella, 30 May 1964, Ashland, Kentucky, USA. The mother-and-daughter duo the **Judds** was one of the most successful country acts of the 80s. After contracting chronic hepatitis, Naomi Judd decided to retire owing to ill health but, having announced this, they undertook a farewell world tour of 100 concerts. With her lead vocals and rhythm guitar, Wynonna had become the dominant part of the Judds and, indeed, their final album, *Love Can Build A Bridge*, is virtually Wynonna's solo debut. The Judds played their final concert in December 1991 and the following month Wynonna performed on her own at the American music awards in Los Angeles with, as it happens, her mother in the audience. Her solo album, *Wynonna*, led to three US country number 1s, 'She Is His Only Need', 'I Saw The Light' and 'No One Else On Earth' (which, with its synthesizer effects, was far removed from traditional country music). The album touched many musical bases and Wynonna's role model was **Bonnie Raitt**. By the mid-90s the sales had topped four million. *Tell Me Why* was an equally assured album; opening with the breezy title track, written by Karla Bonoff, there was rarely a dull moment. Songs by **Jesse Winchester**, **Sheryl Crow** and **Mary-Chapin Carpenter** enabled Wynonna to cross over into the AOR market. After contributing an excellent version of 'Freebird' for the *Skynyrd Friends* album, she came off the road when she became pregnant with her son Elijah. At that emotional time she also broke up with her manager and discovered the real identity of her father. She said that making *Revelations* kept her sane, and during the recording she married Nashville businessman Arch Kelley III (Elijah's father). This album and the following year's *The Other Side* provided a further indication of her move away from country, with strong rock and blues influences. Wynonna's position is now far removed from the cosy American family unit of the Reagan era, one that the Judds espoused.

● ALBUMS: *Wynonna* (Curb 1992)★★★, *Tell Me Why* (Curb 1994)★★★★, *Revelations* (Curb 1996)★★★★, *The Other Side* (Curb 1997)★★★.

● COMPILATIONS: *Collection* (Curb 1997)★★★★.

Wynter, Mark

b. Terence Lewis, 29 January 1943, Woking, Surrey, England. Wynter was one of several UK heart-throbs in the early 60s who took their cue from the USA. Once the extrovert champion of many a school sports day, he was serving in a general store by day, and sang with the Hank Fryer Band in Peckham Co-op Hall, London in the evening, when his well-scrubbed, good looks betrayed star potential to Ray Mackender, a Lloyds underwriter who dabbled in pop management. As 'Mark Wynter', the boy was readied for his new career with vocal exercises, tips on stage demeanour from a RADA coach, and advice about a middle-of-the-road repertoire from **Lionel Bart**. After exploratory intermission spots in metropolitan palais, he was signed to **Decca Records**, and had UK chart entries until 1964 - beginning with 'Image Of A Girl' (1960) at number 11. At the height of his fame two years later, he reached the Top 10 with covers of **Jimmy Clanton**'s 'Venus In Blue Jeans' and **Steve Lawrence**'s 'Go Away Little Girl'. From then on, he resorted to a-side revivals of such 50s chestnuts as 'It's Almost Tomorrow' and 'Only You', but was overcome, like so many others, by the burgeoning beat boom. Wynter turned his attention to the theatre, both straight and musical. He played the leading role in *Conduct Unbecoming* for more than a year at the Queen's Theatre in London, and for six months in Australia. He appeared with **Evelyn Laye** and Stanley Baxter in the musical *Phil The Fluter*, with **Julia McKenzie** in *On The Twentieth Century*, and in *Charley's Aunt*. He also starred in *Side By Side By Sondheim* in Toronto, Chichester, and on the UK tour. In the 1982 Chichester Festival season he acted in several plays including *On The Rocks* and *Henry V*, and also sang in *Valmouth*. Wynter played the male lead in Sheridan Morley's *Noël And Gertie* in London, Hong Kong, and New York. His other work in musicals during the 80s included the role of the King in a revival of *The King And I*, the title roles in *Hans Andersen* and *Barnum*, the 1986 revival of *Charlie Girl* with **Cyd Charisse** and **Paul Nicholas** in London, and the part of Robert Browning in *Robert And Elizabeth*. From 1990-92, most of Wynter's working life was spent on that famous rubbish dump in the New London Theatre which is inhabited by **Andrew Lloyd Webber**'s *Cats*. His many television appearances have included a series with Dora Bryan, *According To Dora*, *Tale Of Two Rivers* with **Petula Clark**, and his own series *Call In On Wynter*.

● ALBUMS: *The Warmth Of Wynter* (Decca 1961)★★, *Mark Wynter* (Golden Guinea 1964)★★★, *Mark Wynter* (Ace Of Clubs 1965)★★★, *Recollected* (Sequel 1991)★★★.

X

Formed in Los Angeles, California, USA, in 1977, X originally comprised Exene Cervenka (b. Christine Cervenka, 1 February 1956, Chicago, Illinois, USA; vocals), Billy Zoom (b. Tyson Kindale, Savannah, Illinois, USA; guitar), John Doe (b. John Nommensen, Decatur, Illinois, USA; bass) and Mick Basher (drums), although the last-named was quickly replaced by D.J. (Don) Bonebrake (b. North Hollywood, California, USA). The quartet made its debut with 'Adult Books'/'We're Desperate' (1978), and achieved a considerable live reputation for their imaginative blend of punk, rockabilly and blues. Major labels were initially wary of the group, but Slash, a leading independent, signed them in 1979. Former **Doors** organist **Ray Manzarek** produced *Los Angeles* and *Wild Gift*, the latter of which established X as a major talent. Both the *New York Times* and the *Los Angeles Times* voted it Album Of The Year and such acclaim inspired a recording contract with **Elektra Records**. *Under The Big Black Sun* was another fine selection, although reception for *More Fun In The New World* was more muted, with several commentators deeming it 'over-commercial'. In the meantime, X members were pursuing outside projects. *Adulterers Anonymous*, a poetry collection by Cervenka and **Lydia Lunch**, was published in 1982, while the singer joined Doe, Henry Rollins (**Black Flag**), Dave Alvin (the **Blasters**) and Jonny Ray Bartel in a part-time country outfit, the Knitters, releasing *Poor Little Critter On The Road* on the Slash label in 1985. Alvin replaced Billy Zoom following the release of *Ain't Love Grand* and X was subsequently augmented by ex-**Lone Justice** guitarist Tony Gilkyson. However, Alvin left for a solo career on the completion of *See How We Are*. Despite the release of *Live At The Whiskey A Go-Go*, X were clearly losing momentum and the group was dissolved. Doe and Cervenka have both since recorded as solo acts. They reunited in 1993 with a new recording contract for *Hey Zeus!*
● ALBUMS: *Los Angeles* (Slash 1980)★★★, *Wild Gift* (Slash 1981)★★★★, *The Decline...Of Western Civilization* film soundtrack (Slash 1981)★★★, *Under The Big Black Sun* (Elektra 1982)★★★, *More Fun In The New World* (Elektra 1983)★★, *Ain't Love Grand* (Elektra 1985)★★★, *See How We Are* (Elektra 1987)★★, *Live At The Whiskey A Go-Go On The Fabulous Sunset Strip* (Elektra 1988)★★★, *Major League* film soundtrack (Curb 1989)★★, *Hey Zeus!* (Big Life/Mercury 1993)★★, *Unclogged* (Infidelity 1995)★★.
● COMPILATIONS: *The X Anthology* (Elektra 1997)★★★★. Solo: John Doe *Meet John Doe* (DGC/Geffen 1990)★★★. Exene Cervenka with Wanda Coleman *Twin Sisters: Live At McCabe's* (Freeway 1985)★, *Old Wives' Tales* (Rhino 1989)★★, *Running Scared* (RNA 1990)★★.

X Clan

X Clan openly admitted that their recording activities were merely a front to promote the 'Blackwatch' ethos. They held a controversial Cultural Convention at London's Africa Centre in 1989 where they were heckled for their apparent endorsement of separatism and chauvinism. Blackwatch, or that part of it that the group felt able to relate to ousiders, is a movement created by black people, for black people, which invokes a larger brotherhood (specifically between different generations and strata of black society) in order to fight and defeat white oppression, through a variety of means: 'By any means necessary is one of the chief principles we have'. Membership of the rap outlet included rappers/spokesmen Professor X (b. Lumumba Carson; the son of black activist Sonny Carson and former manager of **Positive-K**), Brother J and DJ Sugar Shaft, plus associate member Lin Que/**Isis**. On record, as might be expected, they are utterly militant and uncompromising in their advocacy of their chosen lifestyle.
● ALBUMS: *To The East, Blackwards* (4th And Broadway 1990)★★★, *X Odus* (Polydor 1992)★★★.

X Press 2

Agressive UK acid house revisionists Rocky, Diesel and Daddy Ash (Ashley Beadle, of **Disco Evangelists/Black Sunshine** fame), who have run up an impressive sequence of club cuts ('Muzik Express', 'London X-Press', 'Say What', 'Rock 2 House' - remixed by **Richie Hawtin** and **Felix Da Housecat**) on Junior **Boys Own**. In addition to becoming one of that popular label's most talked-about acts, Rocky and Diesel are also well-known DJs in their own right, as is Beadle.

X Versus The World - Overlord X

At the time the most popular hardcore hip-hop album in Europe, Brit rapper Overlord X represented his clan and creed well on this debut. The lynchpin in the album's assembly is 'You Can't Do It In London', which took NWA and the gangsta rappers to task (though there was 'nuff respect for Public Enemy, who were sampled and/or paraphrased on many other cuts). Next to London Posse, this was the first evidence that UK hip-hop could hold its own against allcomers. A series of continuity links for BBC Television's *Def II* beckoned.
● Tracks: *Prologue 1990; The Predator; You Oughta Get*

Rushed; Planet Hackney; X Versus The World; Tell Yer Crew; Prelude; Definition; Suppression; The Untouchable; Powerhouse; Lyrical Turmoil; You Can't Do It In London; X Keeps Turning; O.X. Corral.

- First released 1990
- UK peak chart position: did not chart
- USA peak chart position: did not chart

X-Dream

Based in Hohenfelde, Germany, Marcus C. Maichel (b. May 1968) and Jan Mueller (b. February 1970) began writing together in 1989 and first recorded as X-Dream in 1991. Maichel was influenced by electro and reggae, and started making electronic music in 1986. Mueller trained as a sound engineer towards the end of the 80s and the pair met up to work on a session together in 1989. At first they concentrated on a techno sound and had some material released on Tunnel Records. However, after experiencing the trance scene in Hamburg during the early 90s, they switched to that style and subsequently made a number of releases under such names as C.o.p., the Delta, the Pollinator, Moondust and XME over the next few years. In October 1996 they began an association with the UK trance label **Blue Room**, releasing the single 'The Frog' and contributing the track 'No' to the compilation *Trip Through Sound*. The following year their single 'As A Child I Could Walk On The Ceiling' (as the Delta) became a favourite of many of the top trance DJs notably **Mark Allen**. In 1998 they released their debut album *Radio* as well as two new singles, 'Brain Forest/S.T.O.P.' and 'Radiohead'. At the same time as recording their own material their have remixed a number of tracks for other artists including Johann, Koxbox and the Saafi Brothers. While their music retains the simple four-on-the-floor drum patterns of the 'Goa' style and a certain dependence on riffs, X-Dream nevertheless have an unmistakable sound characterized by its solid foundations, immense aura and intense psychedelic effects and are virtually unparalleled in this kind of production.

- ALBUMS: *Radio* (Blue Room 1998)★★★★.

X-Ray Spex

One of the most inventive, original and genuinely exciting groups to appear during the punk era, X-Ray Spex were the brainchild of the colourful **Poly Styrene** (Marion Elliot), whose exotic clothes and tooth brace established her as an instant punk icon. With a line-up completed by **Lora Logic**, later replaced by Glyn Johns (saxophone), Jak Stafford (guitar), Paul Dean (bass) and B.P. Hurding (drums), the group began performing in 1977 and part of their second gig was captured for posterity on the seminal *Live At The Roxy WC2*. A series of extraordinary singles including 'Germ Free Adolescents', 'Oh Bondage Up Yours', 'The Day The World Turned Dayglo' and 'Identity' were not only riveting examples of high-energy punk, but contained provocative, thoughtful lyrics berating the urban synthetic fashions of the 70s and urging individual expression. Always ambivalent about her pop-star status, Poly dismantled the group in 1979 and joined the Krishna Consciousness Movement. X-Ray Spex's final single, 'Highly Inflammable', was coupled with the pulsating 'Warrior In Woolworths', a parting reminder of Poly's early days as a shop assistant. Although she reactivated her recording career with the 1980 album *Translucence* and a 1986 EP *Gods And Goddesses*, no further commercial success was forthcoming. In 1996 the band re-formed for the release of *Conscious Consumer*, with Elliot joined by founding members Lora Logic and Paul Dean.

- ALBUMS: *Germ Free Adolescents* (EMI 1978)★★★, *Live At The Roxy* (Receiver 1991)★★, *Conscious Consumer* (Receiver 1996)★★.

Xalam

Along with fellow Senegalese performers **Youssou N'Dour** and **Super Diamono De Dakar**, Xalam acquired a substantial international profile in the mid- and late 80s, with their interpretation and modernization of traditional mbalax music. The group was unique, however, in the extent to which it incorporated African-American jazz into the style. Founded in 1969, and working on a part-time basis in Dakar nightclubs and dancehalls, they turned professional in 1975, following a successful West African tour supporting **Hugh Masekela** and **Miriam Makeba**. Like Super Diamono, they spent 1977 and 1978 on an extended tour of Senegalese villages and market towns, supporting themselves with impromptu concerts while absorbing the traditional sounds and styles of the region. In 1979, they made their first European tour, which included an acclaimed performance at the Berlin Jazz Festival. Returning to Dakar, they were a major attraction at the annual Senegal Jazz Festival, appearing in their own right while also accompanying a wide variety of visiting soloists. In 1982, they returned to Europe to perform another widely-lauded Jazz Festival set, this time in Paris, followed, rather incongruously, by supporting **Crosby, Stills And Nash** at the Paris Hippodrome. In 1984, they contributed percussion to the **Rolling Stones**' 'Under Cover Of The Night', having met them while recording in London. During the latter half of the 80s, they toured widely throughout Europe. However, in 1989 drummer Prosper Niang died, leaving them leaderless. Singer Souleymane Faye returned to Dakar to embark on a solo career.

- ALBUMS: *Ade-Festival Horizonte Berlin* (XPS 1979)★★★, *March L'Ombre* (RCA 1979)★★★, *Goree* (Celluloid 1982)★★★★, *Apartheid* (ENC 1985)★★★, *Xarit* (1988)★★★, *Dakar-Paris-Dakar* (1989)★★.

Xanadu

Xanadu rivals *Sgt. Pepper's Lonely Hearts Club Band* as one of the greatest follies in pop/rock cinema history. Taking its cue from the Hollywood classic *The Lost Horizon*, this 1980 release attempted to weld the legend of a timeless place to a musical format. The presence of veteran dancer/choreographer **Gene Kelly** made the use of rock inappropriate, resulting in a *mélange* of anachronisms and pomposity. Singer **Olivia Newton-John**, excellent in *Grease*, is uncertain in her role, while the **Electric Light Orchestra**, their creative peak now past, play music with form but little substance. Nevertheless, the title track featuring both these acts reached the top of the UK chart when issued as a single and the soundtrack itself, a double set, peaked at number 2. This is probably a tribute to ELO and Ms Newton-John, rather than the cinematic charms of *Xanadu*.

Xavier

Eight-piece funk group featured Ernest 'Xavier' Smith (lead guitar, bass, lead vocals), Ayanna Little (lead vocals), Tim Williams (drums), Ralph Hunt Jnr (bass), Jeffrey Mitchell (guitar), Lyburn Downing (percussion), Emonie Branch and Chuck Hughes (vocals). Smith started in the mid-60s as bass player with the **Coasters**. Between 1969 and 1973 he joined **Wilson Pickett**'s backing band the Midnight Movers and later worked with **Isaac Hayes** and the **Temptations**. In the late 70s he moved to Hartford, Connecticut, where he transformed local group the Shades Of Directions into Xavier and LUV (Life's Universal Vibration). The group joined **Liberty**, shortened their name and released their first single 'Work That Sucker To Death'. This dance record with a positive message also featured Smith's old friend **Bootsy Collins**, and **George Clinton**. The record went into the R&B Top 10 and made the UK charts in 1982. Their follow-up, 'Do It To The Max', also reached the R&B chart and their album *Point Of Pleasure* narrowly missed the Top 100, yet despite this encouraging start the group were not able to chart again.
● ALBUMS: *Point Of Pleasure* (Liberty 1982)★★★.

XC-NN

This Leeds-based band of electro-industrial rockers was formed as **CNN** by ex-**All About Eve/Sisters Of Mercy** guitarist Tim Bricheno with vocalist/guitarist David Tomlinson and drummer Neill Lambert. They made their debut on 1992's *Hot Wired Monstertrux* compilation with 'Looking Forward To The Day (I Stop Breathing)', a quirkily upbeat yet lyrically nihilistic song, with a bizarrely borrowed **Buddy Holly** lyric in the pre-chorus setting out the band's humorous stall. The *Young, Stupid & White* EP followed with a publicity campaign encouraging fans to nominate celebrities whom they thought fitted that particular bill, with weekly winners featuring on that week's advertising (**Jamiroquai**'s representatives were particularly unimpressed when a caracature of their artist was used). 'Looking Forward To The Day' was re-recorded for the *Copyright* EP with a sampled intro from **2 Unlimited**'s 'No Limits', bringing legal action from producer Peter Waterman, but the legal muscle of the American news channel CNN proved rather more threatening, enforcing a name change - although the band retained a sense of identity by becoming XC-NN. They finally recruited a bassist in Nick Witherick, having previously played with sampled bass lines as a three-piece, before recording *XC-NN*. The debut's diversity and quality surprised many people who regarded XC-NN as nothing more than a frivolous gimmick band, with inventive songs ranging from the pop accessibility of '1000 Easy' to indie or industrial guitar-based blasts, while the band's live performances continued to be exhilarating.
● ALBUMS: *XC-NN* (Transglobal 1994)★★★★.

Xentrix

Originally known as Sweet Vengeance, this UK rock band was formed in Preston, Lancashire, in 1986, and originally featured Chris Astley (vocals, guitar), Kristian Havard (guitar), Paul Mackenzie (bass) and Dennis Gasser (drums). The group had done little until signing to Roadrunner Records on the strength of their *Hunger For* demo tape in 1988 (they had already recorded one track, 'Blackmail', for inclusion on the Ebony Records compilation album, *Full Force*, under the Sweet Vengeance moniker). It was their debut album, *Shattered Existence*, that brought them to the wider public's attention. Combining **Metallica**-style power riffs with Bay Area thrash pretensions, the band became popular on the UK club circuit and recorded a cover version of the **Ray Parker Jnr.** track 'Ghostbusters', a stage favourite, for their first single release. They had problems with the track, however, as they had used the *Ghostbusters* film logo for the cover without Columbia Pictures' permission. The resulting press did the band no harm and the single was released with a new cover in 1990. In the same year the band released their second album, *For Whose Advantage*. Musically similar to previous releases, it nevertheless did much to enhance their profile. With *Dilute To Taste* and *Kin* the band took a more traditional power metal approach which augured well without ever breaking them out into the mainstream. A full three-year gap preceded the release of *Scourge* in 1996, by which time vocalist/guitarist Astley had been replaced by Simon Gordon (vocals) and Andy Rudd (guitar).
● ALBUMS: *Shattered Existence* (Roadrunner 1989)★★★, *For Whose Advantage* (Roadrunner 1990)★★★, *Dilute To Taste* (Roadrunner 1991)★★★, *Kin* (Roadrunner 1992)★★★, *Scourge* (Heavy Metal 1996)★★.

XL Capris

Formed in Sydney, Australia, at the end of 1978, the XL Capris soon acquired a healthy following on the punk/alternative circuit when they formed their own Axle Records and released two singles and an album in 1980. The songs on the album were mainly written by guitarist Tim Gooding, featuring simple instrumentation, sparse production and the plaintive vocals of Johanna Pigott (bass), singing lyrics that were very Sydney-orientated. Joining Julie Anderson aka Nancy

XL Records

The brainchild of Tim Palmer, managing director of **Citybeat**, who installed Nick Halkes (b. c.1967, Portishead, Bristol, England) as A&R chief. Halkes' background spanned various labels while he DJed his way through college at Goldsmiths University in London. It was while working for Citybeat that he picked up Starlight's 'Numero Uno' as his second signing, giving the label an instant Top 10 hit. On the strength of this, he was offered his own subsidiary imprint for 'underground' dance records. XL was born, and Halkes' Midas-touch with it. XL's most notable hits included the **Prodigy**'s rich vein of form (beginning with 'Charly'), **SL2** ('On A Ragga Trip', etc.), **Liquid** ('Sweet Harmony'), **Moby** (*UHF* EP), **T99** ('Anasthasia') and **House Of Pain** ('Jump Around'). The latter was released on Ruffness, a further subsidiary founded by Halkes' friend Richard Russell. It also housed the mellow groove of Louie Rankin ('Typewriter'), licensed from the Blue Moon studios in Los Angeles. Other artists on XL included Nu-Matic (*Hard Times* EP), Cubic 22 (Peter Ramson and DJ Danny Van Wauwe - 'Night In Motion'), who also recorded under the guise of Set Up System ('Fairy Dust'). Halkes recorded alongside then-partner Russell as Kicks Like A Mule ('The Bouncer'). He defected to **EMI** in early 1993 to set up his new **Positiva** subsidiary, after being headhunted by the majors. Russell took over his A&R position.

Xmal Deutschland

This experimental and atmospheric band formed in the autumn of 1980 and were based in Hamburg, Germany. With no previous musical experience, the essential components were Anja Huwe (vocals), Manuela Rickers (guitar) and Fiona Sangster (keyboards). Original members Rita Simon and Caro May were replaced by Wolfgang Ellerbrock (bass) and Manuela Zwingmann (drums). Insisting on singing in their mother tongue and refusing to be visually promoted as a 'female' band (Ellerbrock is the 'token' male), they have continued to plough a singular, and largely lonely, furrow since their inception. They first came to England in 1982 to support the **Cocteau Twins**, joining **4AD Records** soon afterwards. The debut *Fetisch* highlighted a sound that tied them firmly to both their Germanic ancestry and the hallmark spectral musicianship of their new label. Huwe's voice in particular, was used as a fifth instrument, making the cultural barrier redundant. After the release of two well-received singles, 'Qual' and 'Incubus Succubus II', they lost drummer Zwingmann who wished to remain in England. Her replacement was Peter Bellendir who joined in time for rehearsals for the second album. After signing to **Phonogram**, the band shortened their name to X-Mal and released more mainstream material to little acclaim. They still occasionally play live from time to time.
● ALBUMS: *Fetisch* (4AD 1983)★★★, *Tocsin* (4AD 1984)★★. As X-Mal *Viva* (Phonogram 1987)★★, *Devils* (Phonogram Germany 1989)★.

Xscape

An initially rather laboured attempt at emulating the 'swingbeat' success of **SWV** and their ilk, this four-piece were brought together in Atlanta, Georgia, USA, by writer/producer Jermaine Dupri, who was previously the force behind **Kriss Kross**'s chart success. However, there was an important difference - while groups such as **TLC** (another group overseen by Dupri) had been closely identified with provocative sexuality, Xscape had roots in the gospel tradition and eschewed such salacious themes. Xscape comprise sisters Latocha 'Juicy' Scott (b. c.1973, USA), Tamika 'Meatball' Scott (b. c.1975, USA), Kandi Burruss (b. c.1976, USA) and Tameka 'Tiny' Cottle (b. c.1975, USA). The intention was to offer a 'female **Jodeci**', and they certainly achieved commercial recognition with their 'Just Kickin' It' debut single, which made number 2 on the *Billboard* Hot 100. A subsequent album, *Hummin' Comin' At Cha'*, also achieved mainstream success alongside a second single, 'Who's That Man', which was included on the soundtrack to the film *The Mask*. The group's second album, *Off The Hook*, also charted in the Top 3 of the US R&B Albums chart and went platinum. It featured more expansive song arrangements, including electric guitar and acoustic piano.
● ALBUMS: *Hummin' Comin' At Cha'* (Columbia 1994)★★★★, *Off The Hook* (Columbia 1995)★★★★, *Traces Of My Lipstick* (Columbia 1998)★★★.

XTC

Formed in Wiltshire, England, in 1972 as Star Park (Rats Krap backwards) this widely beloved UK pop unit became the Helium Kidz in 1973 with the addition of Colin Moulding (b. 17 August 1955, Swindon, Wiltshire, England), Terry Chambers (b. 16 July 1955, Swindon, Wiltshire, England) and a second guitarist Dave Cartner (b. c.1951, Swindon, Wiltshire, England), to the nucleus of. Andy Partridge (b. 11 November 1953, Swindon, Wiltshire, England; guitar, vocals). The Kidz were then heavily influenced by the **MC5** and **Alice Cooper**. In 1975 Partridge toyed with two new names for the band, the **Dukes Of Stratosphear** and **XTC**. At this time Steve Hutchins passed through the ranks and in 1976 Johnny Perkins (keyboards) joined Moulding, Partridge and Chambers. Following auditions with **Pye**, **Decca** and **CBS Records** they signed with **Virgin Records** - at which time they were joined by Barry Andrews (b. 12 September 1956, West Norwood, London, England). The band's sparkling debut, *White Music,* revealed a keener hearing for pop than the energetic new wave sound with which they were often aligned. The album reached number 38 in the UK charts and critics marked their name for further attention. Shortly after the release of *Go2,* Barry Andrews departed, eventually to resurface in **Shriekback**. Andrews and Partridge had clashed too many times in the recording studio. With Andrews replaced by another Swindon musician, Dave Gregory (b. 21 September 1952, Swindon, Wiltshire, England), both *Go2* and the following *Drums And Wires* were commercial successes. The latter album was a major step forward from the pure pop of the first two albums. The refreshingly hypnotic hit single 'Making Plans For Nigel' exposed them to a new and eager audience. Singles were regularly taken from their subsequent albums and they continued reaching the charts with high-quality pop songs, including 'Sgt Rock (Is Going To Help Me)' and the magnificently constructed 'Senses Working Overtime', which reached the UK Top 10. The main songwriter, Partridge, was able to put his sharp observations and nursery rhyme influences to paper in a way that made his compositions vital while eschewing any note of pretension. The excellent double set *English Settlement* reached number 5 on the UK album charts in 1982. Partridge subsequently fell ill through exhaustion and nervous breakdowns, and announced that XTC would continue only as recording artists, including promotional videos but avoiding the main source of his woes, the stage. Subsequent albums have found only limited success, though those of the Dukes Of Stratosphear, their *alter ego,* have reputedly sold more copies. *Mummer, The Big Express* and the highly underrated **Todd Rundgren**-produced *Skylarking* were all mature, enchanting works, but failed to set any charts alight. *Oranges And Lemons* captured the atmosphere of the late 60s perfectly, but this superb album also offered a further, perplexing commercial mystery. While it sold 500,000 copies in the USA, it barely scraped the UK Top 30. The highly commercial 'Mayor Of Simpleton' found similar fortunes, at a desultory number 46. The lyric from follow-up single 'Chalkhills And Children' states: 'Chalkhills and children anchor my feet/Chalkhills and children, bringing me back to earth eternally and ever Ermine Street.' In 1992 *Nonsuch* entered the UK album charts and two weeks later promptly disappeared. 'The Disappointed',

taken from that album, was nominated for an **Ivor Novello** songwriters award in 1993, but could just as easily have acted as a personal epitaph. In 1995 the **Crash Test Dummies** recorded 'Ballad Of Peter Pumpkinhead' for the movie *Dumb And Dumber* and in turn reminded the world of Partridge's talent. Quite what he and his colleagues in the band, and Virgin Records, feel they have to do remains uncertain. Partridge once joked that Virgin retain them only as a tax loss. It is debatable that if Partridge had not suffered from stage fright and a loathing of touring, XTC would have been one of the major bands of the 80s and would have sold millions of records. Those who are sensitive to the strengths of the band would rightly argue that this would have severely distracted Partridge and Moulding from their craft as songwriters. XTC remain one of the most original pop bands of the era and Partridge's lyrics place him alongside **Ray Davies** as one of the UK's most imaginative songwriters. After finally showing a profit the band decided to move from Virgin in 1996 and signed with Cooking Vinyl in late 1997.

● ALBUMS: *White Music* (Virgin 1978)★★★, *Go2* (Virgin 1978)★★★, *Drums And Wires* (Virgin 1979)★★★★, *Black Sea* (Virgin 1980)★★★, *English Settlement* (Virgin 1982)★★★, *Mummer* (Virgin 1983)★★★★, *The Big Express* (Virgin 1984)★★★, *Skylarking* (Virgin 1986)★★★★, *Oranges And Lemons* (Virgin 1989)★★★★, *Explode Together: The Dub Experiments 78-90* (Virgin 1990)★★★, *Rag And Bone Buffet* (Virgin 1990)★★★, *Nonsuch* (Virgin 1992)★★★★. Solo: Andy Partridge *Take Away (The Lure Of Salvage)* (Virgin 1980)★★★.

● COMPILATIONS: *Waxworks: Some Singles 1977-1982* originally released with free compilation, *Beeswax,* a collection of b-sides (Virgin 1982)★★★, *Beeswax* (Virgin 1983)★★, *The Compact XTC - The Singles 1978-1985* (Virgin 1986)★★★★, *Live In Concert 1980* (Windsong 1992)★★★, *Drums And Wireless - BBC Radio Sessions 77-89* (Nighttracks 1995)★★★, *Fossil Fuel: The Singles 1977-92* (Virgin 1996)★★★★.

● FURTHER READING: *Chalkhills And Children,* Chris Twomey.

Xymox

This atmospheric rock band was formed in Amsterdam, Netherlands, in 1981. The group's name was taken from the English word zymotic ('of fermentation') - 'It has no real significance', volunteered vocalist Ronny Moerings. The rest of the band comprised Frank Weyzig, Pieter Nooten and Anke Wolbert. After swapping a free record for entrance to a show pairing Dead Can Dance and the **Cocteau Twins**, they eventually secured a contract with parent record label **4AD**. This led to the release of 'A Day' and the album *Clan Of Xymox,* the title of which was the band's original name in their native country. Prior to this, they had released a limited edition mini-album, *Subsequent Pleasures.* Moering's romanticism moved from synthesizer-dominated landscapes to more melodic terrain as the band progressed, eventually encompassing dance rhythms. They moved from 4AD to **Polydor** for their third album, *Twist Of Shadows*, relocating to England in the process. Often dismissed as poor relations to, alternately, the **Cure** and **Depeche Mode**, Xymox's introspection has proffered diminishing rewards over recent times.

● ALBUMS: as Clan Of Xymox *Subsequent Pleasures* (1984)★★, as Clan Of Xymox *The Clan Of Xymox* (4AD 1985)★★★, *Medusa* (4AD 1987)★★★, *Twist Of Shadows* (Polydor 1990)★★, *Phoenix* (Polydor 1991)★★, *Metamorphosis* (1992)★★, *Headclouds* (1993)★★.

XYZ

This French-American Los Angeles-based hard rock act, led by vocalist Terry Ilous with Marc Richard Diglio (guitar), Patt Fontaine (bass) and Paul Monroe (drums), played initially in a blues-based style, but their sound was moulded in the studio by producer Don Dokken into an almost exact replica of **Dokken**, with Ilous in particular sounding like the producer himself. *XYZ* was not without merit, containing some high-quality songs with fiery axework from Diglio, although this inevitably led to George Lynch comparisons. However, the debut was reasonably successful as the band toured the USA with **Enuff Z'Nuff** and **Alice Cooper**, and **Capitol Records** signed XYZ for *Hungry*. With George Tutko's production the band established a more characteristic sound with a much heavier approach, also reflecting their bluesier influences with a cover of **Free**'s 'Fire And Water', but the album was a commercial failure, and the band eventually broke up.

● ALBUMS: *XYZ* (Enigma 1989)★★, *Hungry* (Capitol 1991)★★★.

Y&T

This San Francisco-based band formed in the mid-70s as Yesterday And Today, but David Meniketti (vocals, lead guitar), Joey Alves (rhythm guitar), Phil Kennemore (bass vocals) and Leonard Haze (drums) failed to make any real impact until they released *Earthshaker* as Y&T. *Earthshaker* was a classic hard rock record built on a blistering guitar barrage, Haze's thunderous rhythms and a superb collection of songs, catapulting the band into the public eye, but it also proved to be something of an albatross around the collective Y&T neck. *Black Tiger* was excellent, but subsequent records failed to maintain the standards set on *Earthshaker*. *The Open Fire* live set stopped the rot, and *Down For The Count* signalled a return to form, albeit in a more commercial direction. 'Summertime Girls' was picked up by US radio, but a disenchanted Y&T split with both their record label and drummer, feeling that Haze's image left a lot to be desired. Jimmy DeGrasso made his drumming debut on *Contagious* and Stef Burns replaced Alves for *Ten*, which were both credible hard rock albums, but the band's fortunes were waning and Y&T split in late 1990, with Burns moving on to **Alice Cooper**'s band, DeGrasso joining **White Lion** and then **Suicidal Tendencies**, and Meniketti working with **Peter Frampton**. A brief Y&T reunion came to nothing.

● ALBUMS: As Yesterday And Today: *Yesterday And Today* (London 1976)★★, *Struck Down* (London 1978)★★. As Y&T: *Earthshaker* (A&M 1982)★★, *Black Tiger* (A&M 1983)★★★, *Mean Streak* (A&M 1983)★★★, *In Rock We Trust* (A&M 1984)★★★★, *Open Fire* (A&M 1985)★★, *Down For The Count* (A&M 1985)★★★★, *Contagious* (Geffen 1987)★★★, *Ten* (Geffen 1990)★★★, *Yesterday And Today Live* (Metal Blade 1991)★★.

Ya Kid K

b. Manuella Komosi, Zaire. This pop-dance rapper was originally introduced to UK audiences through her work with **Technotronic**. She had moved to Belgium when she was 11 years old, then Chicago, Illinois, USA, where she was introduced to rap and deep house music. On her return to Belgium she teamed up with Jo Bogaert of Technotronic. Together they performed on the international hit single, 'Pump Up The Jam', though her contribution was uncredited. She then appeared alongside professional and personal partner **MC Eric** on the breakthrough hit, 'This Beat Is Technotronic', which is considered by many to be the first 'hip house' record. They teamed up again with

Technotronic for 'Get Up (Before The Night Is Over)', which was another major international hit. Afterwards Komosi appeared on Hi Tek's 'Spin That Wheel' in 1990, and contributed a song, 'Awesome', to the *Teenage Mutant Ninja Turtles II* film soundtrack. The birth of a child then interrupted her plans. Her projected solo career seems to have petered out since that time.

Yabby You

b. Vivian Jackson, 1950, Kingston, Jamaica, West Indies. Yabby acquired his nickname from the drawn-out, chanting refrain on his 1972 debut single, 'Conquering Lion': 'Be You, Yabby Yabby You'. Despite courting controversy in his repudiation of Rastafarian godhead Haile Selassie, in favour of a personalized form of Christianity, his output throughout the 70s and early 80s nonetheless rarely deviated far from the orthodox Rastafarianism typically expressed at the time. As leader of the Prophets (additional personnel at various times included Alrick Forbes, Dada Smith, Bobby Melody and the Ralph Brothers), Yabby recorded a remarkable series of roots reggae classics, including 'Jah Vengeance', 'Run Come Rally', 'Love Thy Neighbours', 'Valley Of Jehosaphat', 'Judgement On The Land', 'Fire In Kingston', 'Chant Down Babylon' and many others, mostly appearing on his own Vivian Jackson and Prophets labels in Jamaica. With the release of *Ramadam* in 1975, the UK variation of the Jamaican-issued *Conquering Lion* (several tracks were different), Yabby swiftly acquired cult status in the UK, his name becoming synonymous with reggae music of a particularly deep, spiritual nature. The subsequent **King Tubby** dub albums (*Prophecy Of Dub*, *King Tubby Meets Vivian Jackson*, *Beware Dub*) are rightly regarded as classics. Jackson also gained a reputation as a producer of other artists, including DJs **Trinity**, **Jah Stitch**, **Dillinger**, Prince Pompado, **Tapper Zukie** and **Clint Eastwood**, and singers **Wayne Wade**, **Junior Brown**, **Willie Williams**, **Patrick Andy**, **Tony Tuff** and **Michael Prophet**. In the 80s he retreated from the music business as his health deteriorated, though he made something of a comeback in the early 90s with some new productions and the reappearance of many of his classic singles and albums, re-pressed from the original stampers to cater for the large European collectors' market.

● ALBUMS: *Conquering Lion* aka *Ramadam* (Prophet 1975)★★★★, *King Tubby's Prophecy Of Dub* (Prophet 1976)★★★★, *King Tubby Meets Vivian Jackson* aka *Chant Down Babylon* and *Walls Of Jerusalem* (Prophet 1976)★★★★,

Deliver Me From My Enemies (Prophet 1977)★★★, *Beware Dub* (Grove Music 1978)★★★, *Jah Jah Way* (Island 1980)★★★, *One Love, One Heart* (Shanachie 1983)★★★, *Fleeing From The City* (Shanachie 1988)★★★.
● COMPILATIONS: *Yabby You Collection* (Greensleeves 1984)★★★, *Jesus Dread 1972 - 1977* (Blood & Fire 1997)★★★.

Yachts

Another UK new wave act to emerge from the Liverpool art school student pool of the late 70s, the Yachts started life as the seven-piece Albert And The Cod Fish Warriors. Reduced to a five-piece of Henry Priestman (vocals, keyboards), J.J. Campbell (vocals), Martin Watson (guitar), Martin Dempsey (bass) and Bob Ellis (drums), they played their debut gig at Eric's in Liverpool supporting **Elvis Costello**. This led **Stiff Records** to sign them in October 1977 and they released one Will Birch-produced single before they departed (with Costello and **Nick Lowe**) for the newly formed Radar. Campbell left at this point but with Priestman in control they released several singles including the minor new wave classic 'Love To Love You'. They recorded their debut album in New York with **Richard Gottehrer** at the helm. Dempsey left in January 1980 to join **Pink Military** and when Radar was liquidated they switched to Demon for a further single. Inevitably they disintegrated and Priestman spent some time with **It's Immaterial** before forming the **Christians**. The Yachts' popularity was fleeting but they left behind several great three-minute slices of pop, including a cover version of **R. Dean Taylor**'s 'There's A Ghost In My House'.
● ALBUMS: *The Yachts* (Radar 1979)★★★, *Yachts Without Radar* (Radar 1980)★★★.

Yaggfu Front

Despite the unfriendly acronym (Y'All Gonna Get Fucked Up [if you] Front), and their grisly personal tags: D'Ranged & Damaged, Jingle Bel and Spin 4th, this Norfolk, Virginia trio have much to offer. They came together at university, with an educative platform that has provided them with more effective ammunition than the average gun-toting gangsta rappers. There they worked as DJs on North Carolina college radio before uniting as a trio. Using live instruments, including horns and piano, they have perfected a stimulating blend of sharply observed lyrics and clever samples. Their first release was the excellent 'Looking For A Contract', which detailed the lives of starving rap aspirants. Comparisons to **A Tribe Called Quest** notwithstanding, their debut album was also a splendid, intelligent affair. There were comedic moments too, not least 'My Dick Is So Large', a thinly veiled parody of stupido ego-rappers. Nevertheless, their style was generally expressive: 'Basically the Yaggfu sound is emotional. We want to capture the way someone feels'.
● ALBUMS: *Action Packed Adventure* (Phonogram/Mercury 1994)★★★.

Yamaguchi, Momoe

b. 17 January 1959, Tokyo, Japan. Yamaguchi made her recording debut in 1973 at the age of 14 after her successful appearance in the preceding year in Star Tanjô (Birth Of A Star), a national Japanese talent show. The single, 'Toshigoro' ('Adolescence'), was promoted along with her cute, girlish image at the time when the word 'idol', in Japan, was applied to mostly female teenage stars who looked pure and innocent without any sexual suggestion or erotic overtones. However, the lyric 'I'll give you something that is most valuable to me' in 'Hitonatsuno Taiken' ('An Experience In The Summer'), was generally considered to be a reference to a girl's virginity, attracting much public attention to Momoe and her songs and making her more than an 'idol' phenomenon. She was subsequently provided with material from the songwriting team of Yôko Aki and Rhyûdouzaki, which led to a significant development in her musical career with such hits as 'Yokosuka Story' (1976) and 'Bi, Silent' ('Beauty, Silent') (1979), winning various awards in the process. Engaged to the popular film actor Tomokazu Miura, Momoe, who had experienced an unhappy childhood when young, went into retirement in late 1980 at the peak of her career to bring up her own family, in contrast to **Seiko Matsuda**, her junior by three years, who has tried to make her career compatible with married life. Momoe's popularity, however, remains so remarkable that Mrs Momoe Miura, now a wife and mother, is still regularly featured by entertainment journalists.
● ALBUMS: *Toshigoro (Adolescence)* (1973)★★★, *Aoi Kajitsu (Green Fruit)* (1973)★★★, *Momoeno Kisetsu (The Season Of Momoe)* (1974)★★★★, *Hitonatsuno Keiken (An Experience In The Summer)* (1974)★★★, *Jûgosai (Fifteen-Years-Old)* (1974)★★★, *Jûrokusaino Theme (The Theme Of Sixteen-Years-Old)* (1975)★★★, *Momoe Yamaguchi Deluxe* (1975)★★★★, *Momoe Live* (1975)★★, *Sasayakana Yokubô (Small Desire)* (1975)★★★, *Jûshichisaino Theme (The Theme Of Seventeen-Year-Olds)* (1976)★★★, *Yamaguchi Momoeno Subete (All Of Momoe Yamaguchi)* (1976)★★★, *Yokosuka Story* (1976)★★★★, *Momoe On Stage* (1976)★★, *Pearl Colourni Yurete (Swaying In Pearl Colour)* (1976)★★★, *Momoe Hakusho (A White Paper Of Momoe)* (1977)★★★, *Momoe Yamaguchi* (1977)★★★, *Golden Flight* (1977)★★★, *Momoe Monogatari (A Momoe Story)* (1977)★★★, *Momoe In Koma* (1977)★★, *Hanaza-Kari (In Full Bloom)* (1977)★★★, *Cosmos* (1978)★★★, *Playback* (1978)★★★, *Dramatic* (1978)★★★, *Momoechan Matsuri (A Momoe Festival)* (1978)★★, *Manjushage (Cluster-Amaryllis)* (1978)★★★, *A Face In A Vision* (1979)★★★, *LA Blue* (1979)★★★, *Recital* (1979)★★★, *Möbius Game* (1980)★★★, *Momoe Densetsu (Momoe Legend)* (1980)★★★★, *Fujichô Densetsu (Phoenix Legend)* (1980)★★★, *This Is My Trial* (1980)★★★, *Densetsu-Kara Shinwae (From Legend To Myth)* (1980)★★★, *Again* (1982)★★★.
● COMPILATIONS: *Densetsukara Shinwae (From A Legend To A Myth)* 5 album box-set (1981)★★★★.

Yamash'ta, Stomu

b. Tsutomu Yamashita, 15 March 1947, Kyoto, Japan. A percussionist and composer, Yamash'ta attempted to combine *avant garde* and rock music in the 70s. He studied at the Kyoto Academy of Music, making his concert debut as a soloist at the age of 16. From 1964-69 he studied and performed in the USA with both classical and jazz musicians. During the 70s, such modern composers as Hans Werne Henze and Peter Maxwell Davies created works for him which were recorded in 1972 for L'Oiseau-Lyre. From 1973, Yamash'ta created what he called 'floating music', a fusion of classical, rock and Eastern styles with his own European group, Come To The Edge. Among his shows were Red Buddha Theatre and The Man From The East, which included elements of Japanese kabuki theatre and were highly praised by British and French critics. He recorded six albums for **Island** with collaborators **Steve Winwood**, **Klaus Schulze**, Gary Boyle and **Murray Head**. *Go Too* was released by *Arista* with Dennis Mackay producing. During the 80s, Yamash'ta returned to the classical concert halls but also recorded instrumental works for new age company Celestial Harmonies.
● ALBUMS: *Contemporary* (L'Oiseau 1972)★★★, *Red Buddha* (Egg 1972)★★★, *Come To The Edge* (Island 1973)★★★, *The Man From The East* (Island 1973)★★★, *Freedom Is Frightening* (Island 1974)★★★, *One By One* (Island 1974)★★★, *Raindog* (Island 1975)★★★, *Go* (Island 1976)★★★★, *Go Live From Paris* (Island 1976)★★★, *Go Too* (Arista 1977)★★★, *Sea And Sky* (Kuckuck 1987)★★★.

Yamashita, Yosuke

b. 26 February 1942, Tokyo, Japan. Although he had played professionally at the age of 17, Yamashita went on to study at the Kunitachi College of Music (1962-67). He established himself playing in the quartets of Masahiko Togashi and **Sadao Watanabe**. The earliest influence of **Bill Evans** soon gave way to the influence of **Cecil Taylor**. When Yamashita formed his own trio with Akira Sakata (alto saxophone) and Takeo Moriyama (drums) and toured Europe (1974) the music was so wild the group was known as the Kamikaze Trio. For inspiration Yamashita looked back to 'the beginning of jazz - Europe had the system but Africa had all the feeling. All the material I use belongs to the system, but as long as I can stand on the outside and approach things from the outside, I will never be suffocated'. He kept a trio going throughout the 70s and continued to play as a sideman with the bands of Kazumi Takeda (tenor saxophone) and Seuchi Nakamura (tenor saxophone). From 1974 he made regular trips to Europe with the trio in Germany as well as playing with **Manfred Schoof** (1975), then as a soloist and in 1977 in a duo with bassist Adellard Roidinger. He disbanded the trio in 1983 when he felt that he had achieved as much as he could in that format. Yamashita formed a big band with an eclectic style and performed in many varied situations including solo performances of his own versions of classical pieces, playing with Kodo, a Japanese drum choir, and having pieces performed by the Ozaka Philharmonic Orchestra. In the early 90s he was again playing with a trio and touring Europe.
● ALBUMS: *Clay* (Enja 1974)★★★, *Distant Thunder* (1975)★★★, *Banslikana* (Enja 1976)★★★, *Ghosts By Albert Ayler* (West Wind 1977)★★★★, *A Tribute To Mal Waldron* (Enja 1980)★★★, *In Europe* (1983)★★, *It Don't Mean A Thing* (DIW 1984)★★★, *Breath With Hozan Tagoshi* (1984)★★★, *Sentimental* (1985)★★★, *Asian Games* (Verve 1988)★★★★, *Kurdish Dance* (Verve 1993)★★★★, *Dazzling Days* (Verve 1994)★★★★, *Ways Of Time* (Verve 1995)★★★★, *Spider* (Verve 1996)★★★.

Yana

b. Pamela Guard, 16 February 1932, Romford, Essex, England, d. 21 November 1989, London, England. A popular singer in the UK during the 50s and 60s, Yana became a model while still in her teens, before being 'discovered' when singing at a private party at London's Astor club. This led to engagements at several top nightspots, and a contract with **Columbia Records**. In the 50s her single releases included sultry renderings of 'Small Talk', 'Something Happened To My Heart', 'Climb Up The Wall', 'If You Don't Love Me', 'I Miss You, Mama', 'I Need You Now' and 'Mr Wonderful'. Her glamorous image made her a natural for television, and she was given her own BBC series in 1956. Later, following the advent of ITV, she appeared regularly on *Sunday Night At The London Palladium*. In 1958, Yana starred in **Richard Rodgers** and **Oscar Hammerstein II**'s *Cinderella* at the London Coliseum: her solo numbers in the show and on the Original Cast album were 'In My Own Little Corner' and 'A Lovely Night', and she duetted with **Tommy Steele** ('When You're Driving Through The Moonlight'), Betty Marsden ('Impossible') and Bruce Trent ('Do I Love You?' and 'Ten Minutes Ago'). Two years later she was back in the West End with **Norman Wisdom** in the London Palladium's longest-running pantomime, *Turn Again Whittington*. She was something of a pantomime 'specialist', and throughout the 60s and into the 70s, was one of Britain's leading principal boys. It is probably not a coincidence that the second of her three marriages was to the actor Alan Curtis, who is renowned for his performances of the 'Demon King' and other 'nasty' pantomime characters, although he is probably better known in the 90s for his PA work at important cricket matches. In her heyday Yana toured abroad, including the Middle East, and she appeared on several US variety shows hosted by **Bob Hope** and **Ed Sullivan**. She also played small roles in the British films *Zarak*, with Victor Mature and Michael Wilding, and *Cockleshell Heroes*, an early **Anthony Newley** feature. Her last performance is said to have been as the 'Good Fairy' in *The Wizard Of Oz* at an English provincial theatre in 1983. She died of throat cancer six years later.

Yancey, Jimmy

b. 20 February 1898, Chicago, Illinois, USA, d. 17 September 1951. While still a small child Yancey appeared in vaudeville as a tap dancer and singer. After touring the USA and Europe he abandoned this career and, just turned 20, settled in Chicago where he taught himself to play piano. He began to appear at rent parties and informal club sessions, gradually building a reputation. Nevertheless, in 1925, he decided that music was an uncertain way to earn a living and took a job as groundsman with the city's White Sox baseball team. He continued to play piano and was one of the prime movers in establishing the brief popularity of boogie-woogie. He made many records and played clubs and concerts, often accompanying his wife, singer Estella 'Mama' Yancey, but retained his job as grounds-man until shortly before his death in 1951. Although Yancey's playing style was elementary, he played with verve and dash, and if he fell behind such contemporaries as **Albert Ammons** and **Pete Johnson** in technique, he made up most of the deficiencies through sheer enthusiasm.

● COMPILATIONS: *Piano Solos* (1939)★★★, *The Immortal Jimmy Yancey 1940-1943* recordings (Oldie Blues 1977)★★★★, *Jimmy Yancey Vol 1 1939-40* (Oldie Blues 1988)★★★★, *In The Beginning* (Jazzology 1990)★★★, *Jimmy Yancey Vol 2 1943-50* (Document 1992)★★★★.

Yancey, Mama

b. Estella Harris, 1 January 1896, Cairo, Illinois, USA, d. 19 April 1986, Chicago, Illinois, USA. Raised in Chicago, the young Estella took an early interest in music by singing in church and learning to play the guitar. She married pianist **Jimmy Yancey** in 1919 and over the next two decades frequently sang with him at informal parties. Yancey first recorded with her husband for Session in December 1943; 'Make Me A Pallet On The Floor' became her virtual signature tune thereafter. They recorded a long session for **Atlantic Records** in July 1951, just two months before Jimmy Yancey's death. Mama Yancey more or less retired from music after that but was persuaded to make the occasional appearance and recording session. *South Side Blues* and, to a lesser extent, *Mama Yancey Sings*, were the last occasions when her bellowing church-based singing style was heard at its best. Her last album, *Maybe I'll Cry*, was recorded when she was 87 years old, three years before her death.

● ALBUMS: with Little Brother Montgomery *South Side Blues* (Riverside 1961)★★★, *Mama Yancey Sings, Art Hodes Plays Blues* (Verve-Folkways 1965)★★★, with Jimmy Yancey *Chicago Piano Vol. 1* (Atlantic 1972)★★★, *Maybe I'll Cry* (Red Beans 1983)★★★.

Yankee Doodle Dandy

James Cagney won the best actor Oscar for his magnificent portrayal of Broadway showman **George M. Cohan** in this film, which was one of the most enjoyable film biographies ever to come out of Hollywood.

Everything was right about it, especially the screenplay by Robert Bruckner and Edmund Joseph. Beginning with Cohan being called to the White House to receive the Congressional Medal of Honour from President Roosevelt for his outstanding services to the American Musical Theatre, the veteran performer then relates his spectacular rise from young vaudevillian with the family act the Four Cohans, to his position as the legendary American theatrical actor, singer, songwriter, director and much else. The supporting cast was particularly fine, too, with Walter Huston as Cohan's father, Rosemary DeCamp as his mother, and Jeanne Cagney (the actor's own sister) in the role of his sister. Richard Whorf played Sam H. Harris, who co-produced many of Cohan's hits, and Joan Leslie was George's wife Mary. Also featured were Irene Manning, George Tobias, George Barbier, **Frances Langford**, S.Z. Sakall, Eddie Foy Jnr., Walter Catlett, and Odette Myril. However, there was no doubt that it was Cagney's film. He also started out as a song-and-dance man in vaudeville, and this early training served him well. The straight-legged strut, and ebullient, cocky style suited the character perfectly. It was all a joy to see, particularly the re-enactment of scenes from one of Cohan's most successful shows, *Little Johnny Jones* (1904), which involved two immortal numbers, 'The Yankee Doodle Boy' and 'Give My Regards To Broadway'. Many of his other songs - several of them unashamed flag-wavers - were represented in the film as well, including 'Mary's A Grand Old Name', 'Harrigan', 'You're A Grand Old Flag', 'Over There', 'I Was Born In Virginia', 'The Man Who Owns Broadway', 'So Long, Mary', 'Forty-Five Minutes From Broadway', 'Oh, You Wonderful Girl', and 'Off The Record'. Musical directors Ray Heindorf and Heinz Roemheld won Oscars for their 'scoring of a musical picture', and the superb dance sequences were staged by LeRoy Prinz, Seymour Felix, and John Boyle. The excellent black and white photography was by James Wong Howe, and the film was produced by Hal B. Wallis for Warner Brothers. The director of this classic all-time great musical was Michael Curtiz.

Yankovic, 'Weird Al'

b. 1959, USA. Yankovic achieved popularity during the 80s by creating parodies of popular songs and accompanying himself with an accordion. Yankovic first found renown in 1979 with a parody of the **Knack**'s hit 'My Sharona', retitled 'My Bologna'. The song was recorded in a bathroom at a college he attended in San Luis Obispo, California, USA, and played on the syndicated Dr. Demento radio programme. It subsequently appeared on a **Rhino Records** sampler album, *Dementia Royale*, which led to further appearances on the Demento show. 'Another One Rides The Bus', Yankovic's version of **Queen**'s 'Another One Bites The Dust', became the most requested song in the 10-year history of the radio programme and was issued as a single on TK Records. In 1983 Yankovic signed to Rock 'n' Roll Records, a division of **CBS Records**, and released his self-titled debut album, produced by **Rick Derringer**. It included the Knack and Queen parodies as well as 'Ricky', a parody of the **Toni Basil** hit 'Mickey' which doubled as a salute to the *I Love Lucy* television programme. *Weird Al' Yankovic In 3-D*, also produced by Derringer (as were all of Yankovic's albums through the 80s) was released in 1984 and reached number 17 in the USA, with the single 'Eat It', a take-off of **Michael Jackson**'s 'Beat It', reaching number 12. All of his record releases were accompanied by videos that received heavy play on **MTV**, furthering Yankovic's appeal. With his Hawaiian shirts and crazed appearance, Yankovic was a natural for the video age, as a post-modern version of early 60s parodist **Allan Sherman** who was an inspiration to him. Although he included original material on his albums, all of it humorous in nature and much of it set to polka-like rhythms, Yankovic's biggest hits remained his song parodies. 'King Of Suede', a 1984 spoof of the **Police**'s 'King Of Pain', was followed by 'I Lost On Jeopardy', a parody of **Greg Kihn**'s 'Jeopardy' which changed the focus to that of the US television game show *Jeopardy*. In 1985, Yankovic took on **Madonna**, changing her 'Like A Virgin' into 'Like A Surgeon'. His final chart single of the 80s was 'Fat', which returned to Michael Jackson for inspiration, this time skewering his 'Bad'. The jacket of *Even Worse*, was itself a parody of Jackson's *Bad*. Yankovic appeared in the 1989 film *UHF*. In 1996 further parodies contained on *Bad Hair Day* included 'Amish Paradise' (parody of **Coolio** and **Stevie Wonder**'s song), and skits of **TLC**, **Soul Asylum**, **Presidents Of The United States Of America** and U2.

● ALBUMS: *'Weird Al' Yankovic* (Rock 'n' R 1983)★★, *'Weird Al' Yankovic In 3-D* (Rock 'n' R 1984)★★, *Dare To be Stupid* (Rock 'n' R 1985)★★, *Polka Party* (Rock 'n' R 1986)★★, *Even Worse* (Rock 'n' R 1988)★★, *UHF* soundtrack (Rock 'n' R 1989)★★, *Off The Deep End* (Scotti Bros 1992)★★, *Bad Hair Day* (Scotti Bros 1996)★★.

● COMPILATIONS: *Greatest Hits* (1989)★★★.

● VIDEOS: *Alapalooza: The Videos* (1994), *Bad Hair Day* (1996).

Yanni

b. Yanni Chryssomalis, *c*.1954, Kalamata, Greece. One of modern instrumental music's most distinctive and popular composers, Yanni was born and raised in Kalamata, Greece. He moved to the USA in 1972 where he attended the University of Minnesota, pursuing a degree in psychology whilst also playing with progressive rock band Chameleon. However, he is now a naturalized US citizen based in Los Angeles, California, leaving behind his academic studies to concentrate on richly orchestrated and complex keyboard compositions - he was already a self-taught musician with perfect pitch in Greece, as well as a one-time national swimming champion, though to this day he insists he cannot 'read' music. His statement of intent: 'My goal is to connect with people emotionally. I take life's experiences and translate them into music', though perhaps a

little pompous, has resulted in albums that have developed a huge following in his adopted homeland. The best example of this, and something of a career summation, was *Yanni Live At The Acropolis*. Planned over two years, this concert in front of 2,000 people in September 1993 (the first time Yanni had played live in his own country) developed an astonishing chart life when released as a double album, reaching platinum status several times over. One of the most phenomenal bestsellers of the mid-90s, it saw Yanni joined by his own band as well as the Royal Philharmonic Concert Orchestra. British Airways' use of 'Aria' as part of their advertising campaign furthered his mainstream appeal, while his relationship with actress Linda Evans brought him fame in the US tabloids. His tenth album of recordings for the Private Music label (both *Dare To Dream* and *In My Time* were Grammy nominated), *Live At The Acropolis* refreshed memories of some of the artist's most memorable compositions, including new versions of 'Keys To Imagination', 'Nostalgia', 'The Rain Must Fall' and 'Reflections Of Passion', the latter the title track to his previous platinum-selling album. The rationale behind the orchestral accompaniment ran thus: 'Symphonies can generate a tremendous amount of sound, beauty and emotion. That is part of their human feel and sweetness. Keyboards . . . give us access to millions of sounds. When I put the two together, the result is unique, and it's not only pleasing to the ear, but produces emotional responses that neither can achieve on their own.' The event was broadcast throughout the USA in March 1994, a visual *tour de force* directed by six-times Emmy-winning director, George Veras. With an international crew of more than 200 lighting, sound technicians and cameramen, it gave the whole production a visual might not seen since **Jean-Michel Jarre**'s populist Parisian spectacles. Afterwards Yanni confirmed his position as one of the few artists within the new age sphere with a rock band's appetite for touring. In 1997 he signed with **Virgin Records** who released *Tribute*, a live album recorded in India and China, the following year.

● ALBUMS: *Keys To Imagination* (Private 1986)★★★, *Out Of Silence* (Private 1987)★★★, *Chameleon Days* (Private 1988)★★★, *Nini Nana* (Private 1989)★★★, *Reflections Of Passion* (Private 1990)★★★, *In Celebration Of Life* (Private 1991)★★★, *Dare To Dream* (Private 1991)★★★, *In My Time* (Private 1992)★★★★, *Yanni: Live At The Acropolis* (Private 1993)★★, *In The Mirror* (Private 1997)★★★, *Port Of Mystery* (Windham Hill 1997)★★★, *Nightbird* (BMG 1997)★★, *Tribute* (Virgin 1998)★★★.

● COMPILATIONS: *Devotion: The Best Of Yanni* (Private Music 1997)★★★★.

● VIDEOS: *Live At The Acropolis* (Private Music 1994), *Tribute* (1997).

Yanovsky, Zalman 'Zally'

b. 19 December 1944, Toronto, Canada. A former member of the Halifax Three and the **Mugwumps**, Yanovsky founded the **Lovin' Spoonful** with songwriter

John Sebastian. Yanovsky's extrovert behaviour provided the group's visual identity while his exceptional and underrated guitar playing was a vital fixture of their overall sound. He left the band in 1967. Arrested on a drugs charge in San Francisco, he incriminated his supplier rather than face deportation. The guitarist then formed a fruitful partnership with **Jerry Yester** who, paradoxically, had replaced him in the Spoonful. The duo produced **Tim Buckley**'s *Happy Sad* as well as Yester's collaboration with **Judy Henske**, *Farewell Alderbaran* and Yanovsky's own eccentric offering, *Alive And Well In Argentina*. Its irreverent mixture of cover versions and new songs proved a commercial disaster and the artist's career withered in its wake. Although he made several unannounced guest appearances during John Sebastian concerts, Yanovsky gradually withdrew from music altogether. Sebastian reported during an interview in 1980 that Yanovsky was now a restaurateur. This has continued with his resturant Chez Piggy in Canada and his bakery Pan Chancho both flourishing.
● ALBUMS: *Zalman Yanovsky Is Alive And Well In Argentina* (Buddah 1968)★.

Yarbrough And Peoples

The duo of Calvin Yarbrough and Alisa Peoples was one of the most popular R&B pairs of the 80s, placing five singles in the R&B Top 10. The married couple had known each other since childhood, when they shared the same piano teacher in the Dallas, Texas, USA area and sang together in their church choir. They lost track of each other during their college days and Yarbrough joined the R&B group Grand Theft. He was discovered by members of the **Gap Band**, who offered him work as a backing singer, after which Yarbrough returned to his own group. Peoples soon joined him onstage and they were taken on as a duo by the Gap band's manager and producer. Yarbrough And Peoples recorded their debut album for **Mercury Records** in 1980, which yielded the number 1 R&B single 'Don't Stop The Music', which later reached the pop Top 20. Yarbrough and Peoples switched over to the Total Experience label in 1982 and continued their hit streak for four more years with the singles 'Heartbeats' (number 10 R&B in 1983), 'Don't Waste Your Time' (number 1 R&B in 1984), 'Guilty' (number 2 R&B in 1986) and 'I Wouldn't Lie' (number 6 R&B in 1986).
● ALBUMS: *The Two Of Us* (Mercury 1980)★★★, *Heartbeats* (Total Experience 1983)★★★, *Be A Winner* (Total Experience 1985)★★★.

Yarbrough, Glenn

b. 12 January 1930, Milwaukee, Wisconsin, USA. Yarbrough was best known as lead vocalist of the 60s folk group the **Limeliters**. He also recorded numerous albums and had a Top 20 single under his own name in 1965. Yarbrough sang in church as a child and became a folk-singer in the mid-50s. He was discovered in Chicago and performed on the national folk circuit,

eventually starting his own coffee-house, the Limelite, in Colorado Springs, Colorado, with Alex Hassilev. Along with Lou Gottlieb, the two formed the Limeliters, who were very successful in the early 60s, placing 10 albums on the US charts between 1961 and 1964. Yarbrough left the Limeliters in 1964 and recorded the theme song from the film *Baby The Rain Must Fall*, which reached US number 12 in 1965. Yarbrough eventually had 10 chart solo albums by the end of the 60s but only one further chart single. On *The Lonely Things*, *Each of Us* and *Glenn Yarbrough Sings The Rod McKuen Songbook*, poet Rod McKuen wrote the lyrics. Yarbrough continued to record through the 70s and 80s, without repeating his commercial success of the 60s. In the late 80s Yarbrough re-formed the Limeliters with new members.
● ALBUMS: *Time To Move On* (RCA 1964)★★★, *One More Round* (RCA 1964)★★★, *Come Share My Life* (RCA 1965)★★★, *Baby The Rain Must Fall* (RCA 1965)★★★★, *It's Gonna Be Fine* (RCA 1965)★★★★, *The Lonely Things* (RCA 1966)★★★, *Live At The Hungry i* (RCA 1966)★★, *For Emily, Wherever I May Find Her* (RCA 1967)★★★, *Honey & Wine* (RCA 1967)★★, *Best* (1967)★★★, *The Bitter And The Sweet* (1968)★★★, *Let The World Go By* (1968)★★★, *We Survived The Madness* (1968)★★, *Each Of Us Alone (The Words And Music Of Rod McKuen)* (Warners 1968)★★, *Glenn Yarbrough Sings The Rod McKuen Songbook* (RCA 1969)★★, *Somehow, Someway* (1969)★★, *Jubilee* (1969)★★, *Looking Back* (1970)★★, *My Sweet Lady* (1974)★★, *Reunion* (1974)★★, *Marilyn Child And Glenn Yarbrough* (1978)★★, *Glenn Yarbrough* (1978)★★.

Yard Tapes

Also known as 'Sound Tapes', yard tapes are simply live recordings of reggae **sound systems** in action. They first became popular around 1981, as **dancehall** began to exert a huge influence over the reggae audience. Yard tapes offered an opportunity to hear the top Jamaican sounds in action, with reggae stars performing live over **dub plates**, often showcasing material that would not be available on record for months, if ever. Although sometimes suffering from poor sound quality, their deficiencies were more than compensated for by the sense of occasion and the sheer excitement of hearing what constituted reggae in its natural habitat: the dancehall. 'Yard' means 'home' in Jamaican slang, i.e., Jamaica. Yard tapes remain a unique, perennially popular, and exclusively reggae phenomenon to this day.

Yard Trauma

Formed in Tuscon, Arizona, USA, in 1982, Yard Trauma originally comprised of Lee Joseph (bass, vocals), Joe Dodge (guitar, vocals) and Paul Sakry (drums), although the last-named was quickly replaced by Tom Larkins. Although Joseph was primarily responsible for the group's material, *Yard Trauma* revealed a debt to garage-influenced psychedelia, a feature continued on subsequent releases. Scott Fover joined the line-up when Larkins left for **Giant Sand**, a

group that later claimed Joe Dodge. Joseph still retains the Yard Trauma name, but has also recorded as a solo act. He administers the independent Dionysus label and is involved in repackaging 60s material.
● ALBUMS: *Yard Trauma* (1984)★★★, *It Must Have Been Something I Ate* (1985)★★★, *Face To Face* (1988)★★, *Take Off* (1989)★★★.
● COMPILATIONS: *No Conclusions* (1986)★★★, *Music* (1986)★★★, *Retro Spex* (1989)★★★.

Yardbirds

This pivotal UK R&B group was formed in London in 1963 when Keith Relf (b. 22 March 1943, Richmond, Surrey, England, d. 14 May 1976; vocals, harmonica) and **Paul Samwell-Smith** (b. 8 May 1943; bass), both members of semi-acoustic act the Metropolis Blues Quartet, joined forces with Chris Dreja (b. 11 November 1944, Surbiton, Surrey, England; rhythm guitar), Tony 'Top' Topham (guitar) and Jim McCarty (b. 25 July 1944, Liverpool, England; drums). Within months Topham had opted to continue academic studies and was replaced by **Eric Clapton** (b. Eric Clapp, 30 March 1945, Ripley, Surrey, England). The reconstituted line-up forged a style based on classic Chicago R&B and quickly amassed a following in the nascent blues circuit. They succeeded the **Rolling Stones** as the resident band at Richmond's popular Crawdaddy club, whose owner, **Giorgio Gomelsky**, then assumed the role of group manager. Two enthusiastic, if low-key singles, 'I Wish You Would' and 'Good Morning Little Schoolgirl', attracted critical interest, but the quintet's fortunes flourished with the release of *Five Live Yardbirds*. Recorded during their tenure at the Marquee club, the set captured an in-person excitement and was marked by an exceptional rendition of **Howlin' Wolf**'s 'Smokestack Lightning'. Clapton emerged as the unit's focal point, but a desire for musical purity led to his departure in 1965 in the wake of a magnificent third single, 'For Your Love'. Penned by **Graham Gouldman**, the song's commerciality proved unacceptable to the guitarist despite its innovative sound. Clapton later resurfaced in **John Mayall**'s **Bluesbreakers**. **Jeff Beck** (b. 24 June 1944, Surrey, England), formerly of the Tridents, joined the Yardbirds as the single rose to number 1 in the UK's *New Musical Express* chart. Gouldman provided further hits in 'Heartful Of Soul' and 'Evil Hearted You', the latter of which was a double-sided chart entry with the group-penned 'Still I'm Sad'. Based on a Gregorian chant, the song indicated a desire for experimentation prevailing in the rage-rock 'Shapes Of Things', the chaotic 'Over Under Sideways Down' and the excellent *Yardbirds*. By this point **Simon Napier-Bell** had assumed management duties, while disaffection with touring, and the unit's sometimes irreverent attitude, led to the departure of Samwell-Smith in June 1966. Respected session guitarist **Jimmy Page** (b. 9 January 1944, London, England) was brought into a line-up that, with Dreja switching to bass, now adopted a potentially devastat-

ing twin-lead guitar format. The experimental 'Happenings Ten Years Time Ago' confirmed such hopes, but within six months Beck had departed during a gruelling USA tour. The Yardbirds remained a quartet but, despite a growing reputation on the American 'underground' circuit, their appeal as a pop attraction waned. Despite late-period collaborations with the commercially minded **Mickie Most**, singles, including 'Little Games' (1967) and 'Goodnight Sweet Josephine' (1968), failed to chart. The disappointing *Little Games* was denied a UK release but found success in the USA. They followed with two bizarre successes in America: 'Ha Ha Said The Clown' and Harry **Nilsson**'s 'Ten Little Indians'. When Relf and McCarty announced a desire to pursue a folk-based direction, the group folded in June 1968. Page subsequently founded **Led Zeppelin**, Dreja became a highly successful photographer while the remaining duo forged a new career, firstly as Together, then **Renaissance**. Nonetheless, the legacy of the Yardbirds has refused to die, particularly in the wake of the fame enjoyed by its former guitarists. Relf was fatally electrocuted in 1976, but the following decade McCarty and Dreja joined Samwell-Smith - now a respected record producer - in Box Of Frogs. When this short-lived attraction folded, the former colleagues reverted to their corresponding careers, with McCarty remaining active in music as a member of the British Invasion All-Stars. The allure of his first group still flourishes and they remain acclaimed as early practitioners of technical effects and psychedelic styles. The 'blueswailing' Yardbirds have maintained enormous credibility as true pioneers of British R&B, classic experimental pop and early exponents of heavy rock.
● ALBUMS: *Five Live Yardbirds* (Columbia 1964)★★★★, *For Your Love* (Epic 1965)★★★, *Having A Rave Up With The Yardbirds* (Epic 1966)★★, *Over Under Sideways Down* (Epic 1966)★★★, *Yardbirds* aka *Roger The Engineer* (Columbia 1966)★★★, *Blow Up* film soundtrack (MGM 1967)★★, *Little Games* (Epic 1968)★★★.
● COMPILATIONS: *The Yardbirds With Sonny Boy Williamson* (Fontana 1966)★★★, *Greatest Hits* (Epic 1967)★★, *Remember The Yardbirds* (Regal 1971)★★★★, *Live Yardbirds* (Epic 1971)★★★, *Yardbirds Featuring Eric Clapton* (Charly 1977)★★★, *Yardbirds Featuring Jeff Beck* (Charly 1977)★★★, *Shapes Of Things (Collection 1964-1966)* (Charly 1978)★★★, *The First Recordings* (Charly 1982)★★★, *Shapes Of Things* box set (Charly 1984)★★★, *The Studio Sessions* (Charly 1989)★★★, *Yardbirds ... On Air* (Band Of Joy 1991)★★, *Greatest Hits* (1993)★★★, *Train Kept A Rollin': The Complete Giorgio Gomelsky Recordings* 4-CD box set (Charly 1993)★★★★, *Honey In Your Hips* recorded 1963-66 (Charly 1994)★★★, *The Best Of ...* (Rhino 1994)★★★, *Good Morning Little Schoolgirl* (Essential Gold 1995)★★★, *Where The Action Is* (New Millennium 1997)★★★, *The Complete BBC Sessions* (Get Back 1998)★★★.
● FURTHER READING: *Blues In The Night: The Yardbirds' Story*, James White. *Yardbirds*, John Platt. *Yardbirds World*, Richard Mackay and Michael Ober. *Yardbirds: The Ultimate Rave-up*, Greig Russo.

Yargo

Formed in the mid-80s, Yargo fused jazz, soul, blues and reggae forms so uniquely that the music proved too distinctive to break them commercially. However, within the annals of rock history, this Manchester quartet will reside as major innovators in black music. While vocalist Basil Clarke injected a penetrating, yearning quality into his voice, occasionally reminiscent of an urgent **Marvin Gaye**, the rhythm section of drummer Phil Kirby and enigmatic bassist Paddy Steer created a minimal but infectious backing akin to **Sly And Robbie**, alongside guitarist Tony Burnside. Primarily a live outfit at first, Yargo issued three promising singles - 'Get High' on the local Skysaw label in 1986, 'Carrying Mine' on Racket Manufacture the following February, and 'Help' on their own Bodybeat label, and attracted sizeable interest when they appeared on the UK Channel 4 television programme *The Tube*. However, it was *Bodybeat* that garnered the most praise, combining the singles with a hypnotic title track to create a sparse but mesmerizing soundtrack, set against tales of urban Manchester. In August 1989, the band's theme for Independent television's *The Other Side Of Midnight* was released, drawn from the long-awaited *Communicate*, issued in October. Smoother and fuller than *Bodybeat*, this should have established Yargo as a major commercial act, but it was sadly ignored by a nation seemingly obsessed with house music, and, as a result, it was not long before the band fragmented.
● ALBUMS: *Bodybeat* (Bodybeat 1987)★★★, *Communicate* (Bodybeat 1989)★★★.

Yazoo

This promising UK pop group was formed at the beginning of 1982 by former **Depeche Mode** keyboardist Vince Clarke (b. 3 July 1961, Basildon, Essex, England) and vocalist **Alison Moyet** (b. 18 June 1961, Billericay, Essex, England). Their debut single, 'Only You', climbed to number 2 in the UK charts in May and its appeal was endorsed by the success of the **Flying Pickets**' *a cappella* cover version, which topped the UK chart the following year. Yazoo enjoyed an almost equally successful follow-up with 'Don't Go', which climbed to number 3. A tour of the USA saw the group change their name to Yaz in order not to conflict with an American record company of the same name. Meanwhile, their album *Upstairs At Eric's* was widely acclaimed for its strong melodies and Moyet's expressive vocals. Yazoo enjoyed further hits with 'The Other Side Of Love' and 'Nobody's Diary' before completing one more album, *You And Me Both*. Despite their continuing success, the duo parted in 1983. Moyet enjoyed success as a solo singer, while Clarke maintained his high profile with the **Assembly** and particularly, **Erasure**.
● ALBUMS: *Upstairs At Eric's* (Mute 1982)★★★★, *You And Me Both* (Mute 1983)★★★.

Yazz

b. Yasmin Evans, 19 May 1963, Shepherd's Bush, London, England. Pop house singer who began her career in the music business as part of a quickly forgotten act, the Biz. After becoming a catwalk model and working as **George Michael**'s stylist, she laid plans for a return to recording work. When she did so, she found rewards immediately, joining with **Coldcut** on 'Doctorin' The House'. In its wake 'The Only Way Is Up' soared to the number 1 spot in 1988, followed shortly after by 'Stand Up For Your Love Rights'. Both of the latter were credited to Yazz And The Plastic Population. After a couple of further hits and tours she took time out to have her first baby. She returned alongside **Aswad** in 1993 for 'How Long', but this failed to break the Top 30. A new solo single, 'Have Mercy', was the first evidence of her attempts to re-establish herself via a contract with **Polydor**.
● ALBUMS: *Wanted* (Big Life 1988)★★★, *The Wanted Remixes* (Big Life 1989)★★, *One On One* (Polydor 1994)★★★.
● VIDEOS: *The Compilation* (1989)★★★, *Live At The Hammersmith Odeon* (1989)★.

Yeah Jazz

Hailing from Uttoxeter, Staffordshire, England, and formed in 1986 by Kevin Head (b. 11 April 1964, Staffordshire, England; vocals) and Chats (b. Mark Chatfield, 1 April 1962, Staffordshire, England; guitar), Yeah Jazz were completed by Stu Ballantyne (bass) and Ian Hitchens (drums). Their attempt to fuse pop and folk while chronicling the sagas of everyday life in a west Midlands rural town gained an Independent Top 30 hit in 1986 with 'This Is Not Love'. The addition of former **Higsons** saxophonist and guitarist Terry Edwards to the line-up and the transfer to the Cherry Red label strengthened the group's sound. Edwards also lent his production talents to the first Yeah Jazz album. Despite encouraging reviews and positive audience reaction, their fortunes took a downward turn. Freeing themselves from their Cherry Red contract, the band resurfaced in 1991, working on the west Midlands circuit with the promise of recording again in the near future. That promise materialized in June 1993 when they signed to Native Records and released *April*. In 1996 the group changed their name to Big Red Kite, and released *Short Stories* through German label Scout Records. In addition to Hand and Chats, the current line-up comprises Dave Blant (bass, keyboards, accordion), Freddy Hopwood (percussion) and Lee Beddow (keyboards, guitar).
● ALBUMS: *Six Lane Ends* (Cherry Red 1988)★★★, *April* (Native 1993)★★★. As Big Red Kite *Short Stories* (Scout 1996)★★★.

Yearwood, Trisha

b. 19 September 1964, Monticello, Georgia, USA. In 1985, Yearwood started working as a session singer in Nashville. She was discovered by **Garth Brooks** and sang backing vocals on his album *No Fences*. She was the opening act on his 1991 tour and became the first female singer to top the US country charts with her sparkling debut single, 'She's In Love With The Boy'. Further singles such as 'Like We Never Had A Broken Heart', 'That's What I Like About You', 'The Woman Before Me' and 'Wrong Side Of Memphis' quickly established her as a major new talent in contemporary country music. By 1994 she had accomplished major headlining tours, placed albums in the national charts and published her (ghosted) autobiography. Yearwood is at the vanguard of a wave of highly creative female country singers, including **Suzy Bogguss**, **Kathy Mattea** and **Mary-Chapin Carpenter**. Together they have breathed exciting new life into an old formula. Her mid-90s album *Thinkin' Bout You* contained irresistible light rockers such as the Berg/Randall composition 'XXX's And OOO's' (with apologies to **Richard Thompson**'s 'I Feel So Good'). Her choice of material is one of her great strengths; her use of contemporary songwriters, and her country-tinged interpretations of their songs, is inspiring. **Melissa Etheridge**'s 'You Can Sleep While I Drive' benefited greatly from the Yearwood treatment, as did **James Taylor**'s 'Bartender Blues'. Married to the **Mavericks**' bassist Robert Reynolds in 1995, she is at present riding a peak of popularity and won the CMA award in September 1997 for best female artist.

● ALBUMS: *Trisha Yearwood* (MCA 1991)★★★, *Hearts In Armor* (MCA 1992)★★★, *The Song Remembers When* (MCA 1993)★★★★, *The Sweetest Gift* (MCA 1994)★★★, *Thinkin' Bout You* (MCA 1995)★★★★, *Everybody Knows* (MCA 1996)★★★, *Where Your Road Leads* (MCA 1998)★★.

● COMPILATIONS: *Songbook: A Collection Of Hits* (MCA 1997)★★★★.

● FURTHER READING: *Get Hot Or Go Home: The Making Of A Nashville Star*, Lisa Rebecca Gubernick.

Yellen, Jack

b. 6 July 1892, Razcki, Poland, d. 17 April 1991, Springfield, New York, USA. Growing up in the USA after his family emigrated there in 1897, Yellen began writing both words and music for songs while still at school in Buffalo. Eventually he decided to concentrate on just lyrics, and, after working as a reporter on the local newspaper for a time, he moved to New York to pursue a professional songwriting career. During World War I he served in the US Army, but still had some success with 'All Aboard For Dixie Land' (1913), 'Are You From Dixie?' (both with music by George L. Cobb), and 'How's Ev'ry Little Thing In Dixie?' and 'Peaches' (both with Albert Gumble). In 1920 he wrote 'Down By The O-H-I-O' with Abe Olman. Many of his songs of this period and in the 20s were used in Broadway revues and shows such as *What's In A Name?*, *Bombo*, *Rain Or Shine*, *John Murray Anderson's Almanac*, and *George White's Scandals*. After serving in the US Army during World War I, Yellen was introduced to composer **Milton Ager**, and they began a fruitful association that initially resulted in 'A Young Man's Fancy', 'Who Cares?', 'Hard-Hearted Hannah, The Vamp Of Savannah', 'Crazy Words, Crazy Tune', and 'Ain't She Sweet?'. The latter was one of the smash hit songs that typified the 'Roaring Twenties.' In 1928, Yellen and Ager moved to Hollywood, where they collaborated on such songs as 'I'm The Last Of The Red Hot Mommas' (from the film *Honky Tonk*), 'Happy Feet', 'Glad Rag Doll' (with Dan Dougherty), 'A Bench In The Park', and 'Happy Days Are Here Again'. The latter became the theme song of the Democratic Party and President Franklin D. Roosevelt, and was synonymous with the promised emergence from the Depression and Roosevelt's 'New Deal'. Much later, it was the enduring income from **Barbra Streisand**'s highly individual, ironic and anti-political slow version of the song, which she recorded on her first album in 1963, that helped to sustain Yellen in the last bedridden days of his life. In 1925 Yellen joined with Lew Pollack on both words and music for a single song, written to record his emotions on the death of his mother. When it was sung by **Sophie Tucker**, 'My Yiddishe Momme', one of the all-time great 'sob' songs, became a huge success with audiences of all races and creeds. In the 30s, Yellen also worked with **Harold Arlen** and **Ray Henderson**, and wrote lyrics and/or screenplays for several musical films, including the early Technicolor *King Of Jazz*, *Chasing Rainbows*, *George White's Scandals*, *George White's Scandals Of 1935*, *Sing, Baby, Sing*, *King Of Burlesque*, *Happy Landing*, and two **Shirley Temple** vehicles, *Captain January* and *Rebecca Of Sunnybrook Farm*. From 1939 onwards, Yellen concentrated once more on Broadway, writing with **Sammy Fain**, Henderson and others, for shows such as *George White's Scandals*, *Boys And Girls Together*, *Son O'Fun*, and *Ziegfeld Follies Of 1943*. Among his best songs from this period were 'Are You Havin' Any Fun?' and 'Something I Dreamed Last Night' (both Fain). Over the years, Yellen was particularly associated with Sophie Tucker for whom he wrote several amusing songs, including 'Stay At Home Papa' (with Dougherty), 'No One Man Is Ever Going To Worry Me' (Ted Shapiro), 'Life Begins At Forty' (Shapiro), and 'Is He My Boy Friend?' (Ager). Yellen retired in the late 40s to concentrate on his egg farm business, and was inducted into the Songwriters Hall Of Fame in 1976. He was one of the first members of **ASCAP** in 1917, and served on its board from 1951-69.

Yello

A Swiss dance duo led by Dieter Meier, a millionaire business man, professional gambler, and member of the Switzerland national golf team. Meier provides the concepts whilst his partner Boris Blank writes the music. Previously Meier had released two solo singles and been a member of Periphery Perfume band Fresh Colour. Their first recording contract was with Ralph Records in San Francisco, a label supported by the enigmatic **Residents**. They opened their accounts there with

'Bimbo' and the album *Solid Pleasure*. In the UK they signed to the Do It label, launching their career with 'Bostisch', previously their second single for Ralph. They quickly proved popular with the Futurist and New Romantic crowds. Chart success in the UK began after a move to **Stiff Records** in 1983 where they released two singles and an EP. A brief sojourn with **Elektra** preceded a move to **Mercury Records** where they saw major success with 'The Race'. Accompanied by a stunning video - Meier saw visual entertainment as crucial to their work 'The Race' easily transgressed the pop and dance markets in the wake of the Acid House phenomenon. On *One Second*, they worked closely with **Shirley Bassey** and Billy McKenzie (**Associates**), and have recently become more and more embroiled in cinema. Soundtracks include *Nuns On The Run*, and the Polish-filmed *Snowball*, a fairytale whose creative impetus is entirely down to Yello. Meier and Blank also run Solid Pleasure, the innovative Swiss dance label. In 1995 a 'tribute' album, *Hands On Yello*, was released by Polydor, with Yello's music played by various artists including **Grid**, **Carl Craig**, **Orb** and **Moby**.
● ALBUMS: *Solid Pleasure* (Ralph 1980)★★★, *Claro Que Si* (Ralph 1981)★★★, *You Gotta Say Yes To Another Excess* (Elektra 1983)★★★★, *Stella* (Elektra 1985)★★★, *1980-1985 The New Mix In One Go* (Mercury 1986)★★★, *One Second* (Mercury 1987)★★, *Flag* (Mercury 1988)★★★, *Baby* (Mercury 1991)★★, *Zebra* (4th & Broadway 1994)★★★, *Pocket Universe* (Mercury 1997)★★★.
● COMPILATIONS: *Essential* (Smash 1992)★★, *Hands On Yello* various artists remix album (Polydor 1995)★★★.
● VIDEOS: *Video Race* (1988), *Live At The Roxy* (1991).

Yellow Balloon

Other than one fairly memorable US Top 30 hit in 1967, also titled 'Yellow Balloon', this mid-60s Los Angeles-based group is remembered mostly for its membership, which included a television comedy star, Don Grady (b. Don Agrati) of *My Three Sons* fame, and Daryl Dragon (b. 27 August, 1942, Los Angeles, California, USA), who would later go on to greater success as half of **Captain And Tennille**. Grady had recorded some solo singles before joining the group, which also included Forrest Green, Don Braught, Alex Valdez (lead singer) and Paul Canella. Guided by writer/producer Gary Zekley, the group recorded one album, for Canterbury Records, in 1967, also self-titled. They disbanded after successive recordings failed to hit. Grady briefly continued to record solo, under his real name. In 1998 the Sundazed label re-released the album with additional demos and a- and b-sides.
● ALBUMS: *Yellow Balloon* (Canterbury 1967)★★★.

Yellow Dog

This 70s act revolved around the talents of **Kenny Young** and Herbie Armstrong. American-born Young was already an established songwriter, having penned 'Under The Boardwalk' for the **Drifters** and 'Captain Of Your Ship' for **Reparta And The Delrons**. The latter proved highly popular in the UK, inspiring the composer to move his base to London where he met his future partner. Guitarist Armstrong was a former member of the Wheels, a Belfast group contemporaneous with **Them**, before founding a duo with bassist Rod Demick. The duo met up when they both joined **Fox** and enjoyed a period of UK chart success. On the break-up of Fox in 1977, Yellow Dog was formed and their self-titled album was issued in 1977. However, its brand of sweet pop clashed with the year's endemic punk explosion. **Andy Roberts** (guitar, ex-**Liverpool Scene** and **Plainsong**), Gary Taylor (bass, ex-**Herd**) and Gerry Conway (drums, ex-**Fairport Convention**) augmented the duo on this promising debut, which spawned a UK Top 10 single in 'Just One More Night'. A second album, in part completed with the assistance of Demick and keyboard player **Peter Bardens**, proved less successful and the group's name was dropped soon afterwards.
● ALBUMS: *Yellow Dog* (Virgin 1977)★★★, *Beware Of The Dog* (Virgin 1978)★★.

Yellow Magic Orchestra

Pioneers in electronic music, the influence of Yellow Magic Orchestra in this field is surpassed only by **Kraftwerk**. The band's massive commercial profile in their native country was the first example of the Orient grafting Western musical traditions into their own culture - and with Japan the birthplace of the world's technological boom in the late 70s, it was no surprise that the medium chosen was electronic. Session keyboardist **Ryûichi Sakamoto** met drummer **Yukihiro Takahashi** while recording his debut solo album. Takahashi had already released solo work, in addition to being a member of the Sadistic Mika Band (an art-rock conglomeration whose three progressive albums were released in the UK for **Harvest Records**). He had also played in a subsidiary outfit, the Sadistics. The final member of YMO was recruited when the pair met a further established musician, bass player and producer Haruomi Hosono (as well as playing he would produce the group's first six albums). Having performed with two earlier recorded Japanese outfits, his was the most advanced solo career (he was on his fourth collection when he encountered Takahashi and Sakamoto). Although the trio's debut album together was inauspicious, consisting largely of unconnected electronic pulses and flashes, *Solid State Survivor* established a sound and pattern. With English lyrics by Chris Mosdell, the tracks now had evolved structures and a sense of purpose, and were occasionally deeply affecting. *X∞ Multiplies*, however, was a strange collection, comprising comedy skits and no less than two attempts at **Archie Bell And The Drells**' 'Tighten Up'. The UK issue of the same title added excerpts from the debut album (confusingly, a US version was also available, comprising tracks from *Solid State Survivor* in the main). There were elements of both on *BGM* and *Technodelic* which predicted the beautiful synth pop produced by later solo careers, but neither were the albums cohesive or unduly attractive on their own account. More skits, again in Japanese, appeared on *Service*, masking the quality of several strong songs, leaving *Naughty Boys* to prove itself Yellow Magic Orchestra's second great album. As with its predecessor, *Naughty Boys* arrived with English lyrics now furnished by Peter Barakan (later a Takahashi solo collaborator). Accessible and less angular, the songs were no less enduring or ambitious. The band eventually sundered in the early 80s, with Ryuichi Sakamoto going on to solo and movie fame. His former collaborators would also return to their own pursuits, with Hosono enjoying success in production (Sandii And The Sunsetz, Sheena And The Rokkets, etc.) and Takahashi earning critical plaudits for his prolific and diverse solo output. News filtered through in 1993 that, on the back of interest generated by a number of techno artists name-checking or simply sampling their wares, Yellow Magic Orchestra were to re-form. The resultant *Technodon* was completed in March.

● ALBUMS: *Yellow Magic Orchestra* (Alfa 1978)★★, *Yellow Magic Orchestra* different mixes to debut (A&M 1979)★★, *Solid State Survivor* (Alfa 1979)★★★, *Public Pressure* (Alfa 1980)★★★, *X∞ Multiplies* (Alfa 1980)★★, *X∞ Multiplies* different track-listing (A&M 1980)★★, *BGM* (A&M 1981)★★★, *Technodelic* (Alfa 1981)★★★, *Service* (Alfa 1983)★★★, *After Service* (Alfa 1983), *Naughty Boys* (Alfa 1983)★★★★, *Naughty Boys Instrumental* (Pickup 1985)★★★, *Technodon* (Alfa 1993)★★★.

● COMPILATIONS: *Sealed* (Alfa 1985)★★★, *Characters - Kyoretsue Na Rhythm (Best Of)* (Restless 1992)★★★★, *Fakerholic* (Restless 1992, double CD)★★★.

Yellow Submarine

Released in 1968, and named and inspired by one of the **Beatles**' most enduring pop songs, *Yellow Submarine* was a full-length animated feature that deftly combined comic-book imagery with psychedelia. Any lingering disappointment that the Beatles did not provide the voices for their characters vanished in a sea of colour and surrealism. Creations such as the anti-music Blue Meanies and their herald, Glove, were particularly memorable and if several songs were already established Beatles favourites, the quartet did contribute some excellent new compositions, including **John Lennon**'s acerbic 'Hey Bulldog', **George Harrison**'s anthemic 'It's All Too Much' and **Paul McCartney**'s naggingly memorable 'All Together Now'. The group do briefly appear at the close singing the last-named song, but the film's strength lies in its brilliant combination of sound and visuals.

Yellowjackets

Over two decades, the Yellowjackets have achieved a formidable reputation for their live performances and critical and commercial success with their recordings of electric pop jazz. The members of the band are accomplished musicians in their own right and perhaps this

accounts for the Yellowjackets' two Grammys and six nominations. The band originally included **Robben Ford** (guitar), Russell Ferrante (keyboards), Bob Mintzer (saxophone), **Michael Franks** (vocals) and Ricky Lawson (drums). Their recording career began in 1980 with *The Inside Story*, when Ford heard Jimmy Haslip (bass) playing with veterans **Airto Moreira** and **Flora Purim** and decided to use them on his solo project. By the time of 1982's *Mirage á Trois*, Ford's presence was declining. New saxophonist, Marc Russo featured prominently on *Samurai Samba* (1983) and *Shades* in 1986 rewarded the band's steady touring with a Grammy and six-figure sales. William Kennedy was the next addition to the line-up and this prompted the band to explore some new territory. *Politics* (1988) was another Grammy winner and the band took another radical change of direction. Their next project, *The Spin* was recorded in Oslo, Norway with well-known engineer, Jan Erik Konshaug, and was a more acoustic, resolutely jazz album. *Live Wires*, the band's 1992 release successfully demonstrated the multifaceted approach the Yellowjackets like to adopt. Indeed, the simplicity of the band's sound belies the diversity of their influences: 'We spend hours experimenting, studying and listening to music from all over the world. You can't be afraid to take chances. That's what it takes to continue to grow!'. The line-up in 1997 was Mintzer, William Kennedy, Haslip and Ferrante.

● ALBUMS: *The Inside Story* (1980)★★★, *Yellowjackets* (Warners 1981)★★★, *Mirage á Trois* (Warners 1982)★★★, *Samurai Samba* (Warners 1983)★★, *Shades* (MCA 1986)★★★★, *Four Corners* (MCA 1987)★★★, *Politics* (MCA 1988)★★★★, *The Spin* (MCA 1990)★★★, *Greenhouse* (1991)★★★, *Live Wires* (GRP 1992)★★★, *Like A River* (GRP 1992)★★★, *Run For Your Life* (GRP 1994)★★★, *Dreamland* (Warners 1995)★★★, *Blue Hats* (Warners 1997)★★★.

● COMPILATIONS: *Collection* (GRP 1994)★★★★.

Yellowman

b. Winston Foster, 1959, Kingston, Jamaica, West Indies. Yellowman was the DJing sensation of the early 80s and he achieved this status with a fair amount of talent and inventive and amusing lyrics. He built his early career around the fact that he was an albino and his success has to be viewed within its initial Jamaican context. The albino or 'dundus' is virtually an outcast in Jamaican society and Foster's early years were incredibly difficult. Against all the odds, he used this background to his advantage and, like **King Stitt**, who had previously traded on his physical deformities, Foster paraded himself in the Kingston dancehalls as 'Yellowman', a DJ with endless lyrics about how sexy, attractive and appealing he was to the opposite sex. Within a matter of months, he went from social pariah to headlining act at Jamaican stage shows and his popularity rocketed; the irony of his act was not lost on his audiences. His records were both witty and relevant - 'Soldier Take Over' being a fine example - and he was the first to release a live album - not of a stage show but recorded live on a **sound system** - *Live At Aces*, which proved hugely successful and was widely imitated. It captured him at the height of his powers and in full control of his 'fans'; none of the excitement is lost in the transition from dancehall to record. Yellowman's records sold well and he toured the USA and UK to ecstatic crowds - his first sell-out London shows caused traffic jams and roadblocks around the venue. It seemed that he could do no wrong, and even his version of 'I'm Getting Married In The Morning' sold well. He was soon signed to a major contract with **CBS Records** and was 'King Yellow' to everyone in the reggae business. However, this did not last, and by the mid-80s it had become difficult to sell his records to the fickle reggae market. Nevertheless, by this time he had been adopted by 'pop' audiences all over the world as a novelty act and while he has never become a major star, he is still very popular and his records sell in vast quantities in many countries. He has released more records than a great many other reggae acts - no mean feat in a business dominated by excess. Having become both rich and successful through his DJing work, it is mainly his ability to laugh at himself and encourage others to share the joke that has endeared him to so many.

● ALBUMS: *Them A Mad Over Me* (J&L 1981)★★★, *Mr Yellowman* (Greensleeves 1982)★★★, *Bad Boy Skanking* (Greensleeves 1982)★★★, *Yellowman Has Arrived With Toyan* (Joe Gibbs 1982)★, *Live At Sunsplash* (Sunsplash 1982)★★★, with Purple Man, Sister Nancy *The Yellow, The Purple, And The Nancy* (Greensleeves 1983)★★★★, *Divorced* (Burning Sounds 1983)★★, *Zungguzungguguzungggueng* (Greensleeves 1983)★★, *King Yellowman* (Columbia 1984)★★, *Nobody Move, Nobody Get Hurt* (Greensleeves 1984)★★, with Josey Wales *Two Giants Clash* (Greensleeves 1984)★★★★, with Charlie Chaplin *Slackness Vs Pure Culture* (Arrival 1984)★★★★, *Galong Galong Galong* (Greensleeves 1985)★★, *Going To The Chapel* (Greensleeves 1986)★★, *Rambo* (Moving Target 1986)★★★, *Yellow Like Cheese* (RAS 1987)★★, *Don't Burn It Down* (Shanachie/Greensleeves 1987)★★, *Blueberry Hill* (Greensleeves/Rohit 1987)★★★, with General Trees *A Reggae Calypso Encounter* (Rohit 1987)★★, *King Of The Dancehall* (Rohit 1988)★★, with Charlie Chaplin *The Negril Chill* (ROIR 1988)★★★, *Sings The Blues* (Rohit 1988)★★, *Rides Again* (RAS 1988)★★★, *One In A Million* (Shanachie 1988)★★, *Badness* (La/Unicorn 1990)★★★, *Thief* (Mixing Lab 1990)★★, *Party* (RAS 1991)★★★, *Reggae On The Move* (RAS 1992)★★, *Live In England* (Greensleeves 1992)★★, *In Bed With Yellowman* (1993)★★, *Freedom Of Speech* (Ras 1997)★★★.

● COMPILATIONS: *20 Super Hits* (Sonic Sounds 1990)★★★★, *Operation Radication.* (Reactive 1998)★★★★.

● VIDEOS: *Raw And Rough (Live At Dollars Lawn)* (Jetstar 1989).

Yentl

With this 1984 release, which was filmed in the UK and Czechoslovakia, **Barbra Streisand** became the first woman to write, produce, direct, sing and star in a movie. Her screenplay, written in collaboration with Jack Rosenthal, was adapted from Isaac Bashevis Singer's short story, *Yentl, The Yeshiva Boy*, and set in Eastern Europe at the turn of the century. Streisand plays Yentl, the Jewish girl who disguises herself as a young man so that she can study the Torah and make her way in a male-dominated community. Complications arise when Yentl marries Hadass (Amy Irving), who just happens to be the fiancée of Avigdor (**Mandy Patinkin**), the man Yentl actually loves. Most observers noted that the scene in which Yentl, having walked away from the relationship, boards a ship bound for America, is very reminiscent of the famous 'Don't Rain On My Parade' sequence in Streisand's first picture, **Funny Girl**. The original song score, which won Academy Awards for composer **Michel Legrand** and lyricists **Alan** and **Marilyn Bergman**, was a Streisand *tour de force*, and consisted of mostly touching and emotional numbers such as 'Where Is It Written?', 'This Is One Of Those Moments', 'No Wonder', 'The Way He Makes Me Feel', 'Tomorrow Night', 'Will Someone Ever Look At Me That Way?', 'No Matter What Happens', and 'A Piece Of Sky'. An especially poignant song was 'Papa, Can You Hear Me' - the film is also a tribute from Streisand to the father she hardly knew. All in all, although far too long, *Yentl* is generally considered to be fine piece of work that certainly does not merit its sometime nickname, *Tootsie On The Roof*. Also among the cast were Steven Hill and Nehemiah Persoff, Bernard Spear, and David de Kyser. This MGM-United Artists picture was beautifully photographed in Metrocolor and Panavision by David Watkin.

Yes

During the progressive music boom of the early 70s, Yes were rivalled only by **Emerson Lake And Palmer** and **Genesis** for their brand of classical-laced rock that was initially refreshing and innovative. They evolved into a huge stadium attraction and enjoyed phenomenal success until the new wave came in 1977 and swept them aside. Yes were formed in 1968 by vocalist **Jon Anderson** (b. 25 October 1944, Accrington, Lancashire, England) and bassist **Chris Squire** (b. 4 March 1948, Wembley, London, England). Both had been experienced with 60s' beat groups, notably the Warriors and the Syn, respectively. They were completed by **Bill Bruford** (b. 17 May 1948, London, England; drums), Pete Banks (b. 7 July 1947, Barnet, Hertfordshire, England) and Tony Kaye (b. 11 January 1946, Leicester, England). One of their early gigs was opening for **Cream** at their historic farewell concert at London's Royal Albert Hall, but it was pioneering disc jockey **John Peel** who gave them nationwide exposure, performing live on his BBC radio programme *Top Gear*. Their inventive version of **Buffalo Springfield**'s 'Everydays' and the **Beatles**' 'Every Little Thing' combined with their own admirable debut 'Sweetness', made them club favourites. Banks was replaced in 1970 by guitar virtuoso **Steve Howe** (b. 8 April 1947,

London, England; ex-**Tomorrow**) who added further complexity to their highly creative instrumental passages. Neither their debut *Yes* nor *Time And A Word* made much of an impression beyond their growing following. Banks subsequently reunited with Kaye in **Flash**.

It was with *The Yes Album* that the band created major interest and sales. Kaye then departed and was replaced by the highly accomplished keyboard wizard, **Rick Wakeman** (b. 18 May 1949, London, England; ex-**Strawbs**). Wakeman's improvisational skill, like Howe's, took the band into realms of classical influence, and their solos became longer, although often they sounded self-indulgent. *Fragile* was a major success and the band found considerable support from the UK music press, especially **Melody Maker**. *Fragile* was a landmark in that it began a series of Roger Dean's Tolkien-inspired fantasy covers, integrated with his custom-calligraphed Yes colophon. The album spawned a surprise US hit single, 'Roundabout', which almost made the Top 10 in 1972. Shortly afterwards Bruford departed and was replaced by ex-**Plastic Ono Band** drummer Alan White. Later that year Yes released what now stands up as their finest work, *Close To The Edge*. Much of the four suites are instrumental, and allow the musicianship to dominate Anderson's often pretentiously abstract lyrics. Squire's bass playing was formidable on this album, and he quickly became a regular winner of musician magazine polls. Now a major band, they confidently issued a triple live album *Yessongs*, followed by a double, the overlong and indulgent *Tales From Topographic Oceans*. Both were huge successes, with the latter reaching number 1 in the UK. Artistically, the band now started to decline, Wakeman left to pursue a triumphant solo career. His replacement was ex-**Refugee** Patrick Moraz, who maintained the classical influence that Wakeman had instigated. Following *Relayer* the band fragmented to undertake solo projects, although none emulated Wakeman, who was having greater success than Yes at this time. When the band reconvened, Wakeman rejoined in place of Moraz, and continued a dual career. *Going For The One* was a less 'cosmic' album and moved the band back into the realms of rock music. Another hit single, 'Wonderous Stories', made the UK Top 10 in 1977, at the height of the punk era. Yes were the type of band that was anathema to the new wave, and while their vast following bought *Tormato*, their credibility plummeted. Internal problems were also rife, resulting in the second departure of Wakeman, immediately followed by Anderson. Astonishingly their replacements were **Trevor Horn** and Geoff Downes, who, as **Buggles** had topped the UK charts the previous year with 'Video Killed The Radio Star'. This bizarre marriage lasted a year before Yes finally said 'no' and broke up in 1981. All the members enjoyed successful solo careers and it came as a surprise in 1983 to find a re-formed Yes topping the UK singles chart with the excellent Trevor Horn-produced 'Owner Of A Lonely Heart'. The subsequent *90125* showed a rejuvenated band with short contemporary dance/rock songs that fitted with 80s fashion. No new Yes output came until four years later with *Big Generator*, and in 1989 *Anderson, Bruford, Wakeman And Howe* was released during a lengthy legal dispute. Yes could not use the name, so instead they resorted to the Affirmative; Anderson, Howe, etc. plays an 'Evening Of Yes Music' (cleverly using the famous logo). With the ownership problem solved, Yes announced a major tour in 1991, and were once again in the US Top 10 with *Union*. *Talk* was a sparkling album full of energy with two outstanding tracks 'The Calling' and 'I Am Waiting', both destined to become part of their stage shows, should they decide to perform regularly.

● ALBUMS: *Yes* (Atlantic 1969)★★★, *Time And A Word* (Atlantic 1970)★★★, *The Yes Album* (Atlantic 1971)★★★★, *Fragile* (Atlantic 1971)★★★★, *Close To The Edge* (Atlantic 1972)★★★★, *Yessongs* (Atlantic 1973)★★★, *Tales From The Topographic Oceans* (Atlantic 1973)★, *Relayer* (Atlantic 1974)★★, *Going For The One* (Atlantic 1977)★★, *Tormato* (Atlantic 1978)★★, *Drama* (Atlantic 1980)★, *Yesshows* (Atlantic 1980)★, *90125* (Atco 1983)★★★, *90125 Live-The Solos* (Atco 1986)★, *The Big Generator* (Atlantic 1987)★★, *Union* (Arista 1991)★★, *Talk* (Victory 1994)★★★, *Keys To Ascension* (BMG 1996)★★, *Open Your Eyes* (Eagle 1997)★★★.

● COMPILATIONS: *Yesterdays* (Atlantic 1975)★★★, *Classic Yes* (Atlantic 1981)★★★, *Something's Coming* recorded 1969-70 (Pilot 1998)★★★, *Friends And Relatives* (1998)★★★.

● VIDEOS: *Anderson Bruford Wakeman Howe: An Evening Of Yes Music Plus* (1995).

● FURTHER READING: *Yes: The Authorized Biography*, Dan Hedges , *Music Of Yes: Structure And Vision In Progressive Rock*, Bill Martin. *Yesstories: Yes In Their Own Words*, Tim Morse.

Yes Madam?

Bobby Howes, Bertha Belmore, and Vera Pearce, three of the stars of the original stage show that had a good run at the London Hippodrome in 1934/5, recreated their roles for this popular film version which was released by the Associated British Picture Corporation in 1938. **Binnie Hale**, who played the heroine on stage, was not present, but her part as Howes' cousin was played by the delightful Diana Churchill. In the somewhat frivolous plot, they are both obliged to work as servants for a month in order to qualify for an inheritance of more that £100,000. Obviously there will be many complications, especially when the supporting cast contains names such as Fred Emney, Wylie Watson, and Billy Milton. The score, with music by Jack Waller, Joseph Tunbridge, and Harry Weston, and lyrics by R.P. Weston, Bert Lee, and Clifford Grey, contained some jolly and engaging numbers, including 'Czechoslovakian Love Song', 'Dreaming A Dream', 'The Girl The Soldier Always Leaves Behind', 'Sitting Beside O' You', 'Too Many Outdoor Sports', 'What Are You Going To Do?', and 'Zip-Tee-Tootle-Tee-Too-

Pom-Pom'. Stalwarts Clifford Grey, Bert Lee, and William Freshman adapted their screenplay from the musical play, which itself was based on a novel by K.R.G. Browne. Norman Lee produced this popular slice of fun, and the producer was Walter C. Mycroft. An earlier, non-musical film treatment of Browne's book starred Frank Pettingell and Kay Hammond.

Yes, Mr Brown

The celebrated stage duo of **Jack Buchanan** and Elsie Randolph came to the screen in this comedy-musical which was released by British & Dominion (Woolf & Freedom) Films in 1933. Set in Vienna (as per usual) Douglas Furber's screenplay was adapted from the German play *Business With America* by Paul Frank and Ludwig Hershfield. It concerns Nicholas Baumann (Buchanan), the manager of a factory who is expecting a visit from his important American boss (Hartley Power). Just before he arrives, Nicholas's glamorous wife, Clary (Margot Grahame), walks out on him because he cannot stand the sight (or the smell) of her pet dog. Complications arise when he persuades his secretary, Ann Webber (Randolph), to stand in for her. Buchanan's deft comic touch supplemented his already established romantic image, and Randolph was her usual amusing self. Also in the cast were Vera Pearce and Clifford Heatherley. The songs included 'Leave A Little Love For Me' and 'Yes, Mr. Brown' (both Paul Abraham-Robert Gilbert-Armin Robinson-Douglas Furber). **Herbert Wilcox** was the producer, and he co-directed this diverting little film with Jack Buchanan.

Yester, Jerry

b. Joshua Tree, California, USA. A producer, songwriter and performer, Yester first gained attention as a member of the Easy Riders. From there he joined a folk ensemble, the Inn Group, which was absorbed, wholly, into the original **New Christy Minstrels**. Objecting to their commercial approach, the singer left the group to found the **Modern Folk Quartet**. Initially a traditional act, the MFQ later embraced electricity to become a fully fledged folk-rock attraction. Yester also produced material for the **Association**, a harmony group that featured his brother, Jim. Yester played guitar on **Bob Lind**'s international hit, 'Elusive Butterfly' (1966). The artist then began a solo career with two imaginative singles, before joining the **Lovin' Spoonful** in 1967, in place of guitarist **Zalman Yanovsky**. Paradoxically, the two musicians remained close friends and together produced **Tim Buckley**'s *Happy Sad* and Yanovsky's *Alive And Well In Argentina*. Yester then formed a duo with his wife, **Judy Henske**, the result of which was the atmospheric collection, *Farewell Alderbaran*. This in turn inspired their short-lived rock group, Rosebud, since when Yester has preferred production work, most notably with **Tom Waits**. However this talented individual has more recently resumed performing with a reformed MFQ. *Just Like The Big Time* was only issued in Japan.

● ALBUMS: with Judy Henske *Farewell Alderbaran* (Straight 1969)★★★★, *Just Like The Big Time* (1990)★★★.

Yesterday's News

Formed in the Bronx, New York, USA, in 1979, **a cappella** group Yesterday's News originally comprised Tony Delvecchio (lead and first tenor), Vinnie Gallo (lead and second tenor), Charlie Valentine (baritone), Vito Ferrante (second tenor) and Dennis Elber (lead and bass). Both Valentine and Ferrante were then quickly replaced by Vic Spina and Charlie Rocco, who both sang lead. With a mutual love of 50s and 60s doo-wop and harmony, they set about rehearsing a set of period standards. Like many bands of their time devoted to an earlier pantheon of vocal groups and singers, the group found a sympathetic home at United in Group Harmony Association Records in 1979. Their debut arrived in the form of 'The Mickey Mouse Chant', before shows supporting the **Skyliners**, **Chantels** and **Flamingos** at New York's Beacon Theater. They also supported seasoned doo-wop singers in the absence of their original bands - engagements that included collaborations with Earl Carroll (**Cadillacs**), Eugene Pitt (**Jive Five**), Lenny Cocco (**Chimes**) and Emil Stucchio (**Classics**).

Yetnikoff, Walter

b. 11 August 1933, New York City, New York, USA. A legend in the music industry, Walter Yetnikoff made his reputation in the 70s and 80s as the high-flying, high-spending business courtier to artists including **Billy Joel**, **Bruce Springsteen** and **Michael Jackson**. His rise began in 1961 when he moved from entertainment law to become assistant to **Clive Davis**, the **CBS Records** general attorney. By 1972 he had become head of CBS International, then president of the group in 1975. At this time he signed multi-million dollar deals with **James Taylor** and the **Beach Boys** - who promptly refused to record for four years. By 1977 Yetnikoff's bizarre behaviour was the subject of regular gossip column inches, particularly his hard-drinking approach to artist negotiations, tactics to which several artists objected. **Paul Simon**, for one, departed to rivals **Warner Brothers Records**. However, by the end of the decade Yetnikoff had secured the signatures of both **Paul McCartney** and Michael Jackson. By 1983, with Jackson's *Thriller* a multi-million seller and artists including **Culture Club** and the **Rolling Stones** on board, the executive was able to boast of soaring company profits. This allowed him to re-negotiate his own contract, with an annual salary of nearly half a million by 1984. When Sony Records acquired CBS in 1987, Yetnikoff was rumoured to have received a bonus in the region of 20 million dollars, on the condition he took over as CEO of CBS Records. However, Yetnikoff remained a controversial figure - his public disagreement with Bruce Springsteen over the artist's sponsorship of Amnesty International notwithstanding. By the end of the decade he had become head of Sony's US film and record division, with responsibility for Columbia Pictures. However, his relationships with Springsteen, former executive Tommy Mottola and Michael Jackson all conspired to bring about his downfall from Sony at the beginning of the 90s. His severance pay was reputedly 25 million dollars. The rest of the 90s were taken up with the launch of Velvel Records - an umbrella organization promoting independent labels including Razor & Tie, Hybrid and **Bottom Line Records**, and the UK's Fire Records. Evidently, the music industry has not heard the last of Walter Yetnikoff.

Yetties

The Yetties' original line-up comprised Bonny Sartin (b. Maurice John Sartin, 22 October 1943, near Sherborne, Dorset, England; percussion), Mac McCulloch (b. Malcolm McCulloch, 12 December 1945, London, England; guitar), Pete Shutler (b. Peter Cecil Shutler, 6 October 1945, Mudford, near Yeovil, Somerset, England; accordion, penny whistle, concertina, bowed psaltery) and Bob Common (b. 26 December 1940; vocals). The four eventually formed the Yetminster and Ryme Intrinseca Junior Folk Dance Display Team to play for dance evenings. Such was the problem with the name of the group, that one evening, for simplicity, they were introduced as the Yetties, and it stuck. They first performed in 1961 and shortly afterwards the group began Morris dancing with the Wessex Men, based in Yeovil, Somerset, and made their first appearance at the Sidmouth Folk Festival. The group also made subsequent regular appearances at the Yeovil Folk Dance club. They appeared on record in 1968, on an album recorded live at the Towersey Festival, along with other artists, but *Fifty Stones Of Loveliness* was their first proper release as a group. This was followed a year later by *Who's A-fear'd*. On some of the early Yetties recordings, a fiddle player, Oscar Burridge played, though he was essentially part-time. The group appeared on a **Cyril Tawney** album in 1972, *Cyril Tawney In Port*, providing background music and vocals. Another 1972 release, *Bob Arnold, Mornin' All*, featured the group providing background music and vocals for Bob Arnold. The same year, the group's version of *The Archers* theme tune, 'Barwick Green', was first used for the Sunday omnibus editions of the series on BBC radio. Bob Common left the group in 1979 and the Yetties continued as a trio. Roger Trim (fiddle), had played in various duos and trios before joining the Yetties. He joined as a full-time member of the group in 1984, but departed in 1991, leaving the group to continue once more as a trio. 1988 saw the start of the group's project, *The Musical Heritage Of Thomas Hardy*, incorporating the Hardy family manuscripts, and at one time using Hardy's own violin in the work. Originally recorded in 1985 as an album, the project continues to be performed at festivals and concerts and on radio and television, and as a result, a 1988 release materialized. Despite having

played worldwide, the Yetties have never lost the almost boyish enthusiasm which pervades their music, and still retain a loyal following.
● ALBUMS: *Fifty Stones Of Loveliness* (1969)★★★, *Who's A-Fear'd* (1970)★★★, *Keep A-Runnin'* (Argo 1970)★★★, *What The Yetties Did Next* (Argo 1971)★★★, *Our Friends* (Argo 1971)★★★, *Dorset Is Beautiful* (Argo 1972)★★★, *All At Sea* (Argo 1973)★★★, *Up In Arms* (Argo 1974)★★★, *The Yetties Of Yetminster* (Argo 1975)★★★, *The World Of The Yetties* (Argo 1975)★★★, *Let's Have A Party* (Argo 1975)★★★, *The Village Band* (Decca 1976)★★★, *Up Market* (Decca 1977)★★★, *Dorset Style* (Argo 1978)★★★, *Focus On The Yetties* (Argo 1978)★★★, *In Concert* (Decca 1979)★★★, *A Little Bit Of Dorset* (ASV 1981)★★★, *A Proper Job* (ASV 1981)★★★, *Roger Trim On The Fiddle* (1982)★★★, *Cider And Song* (1983)★★★, with John Arlott *The Sound Of Cricket* (1984)★★★, *The Banks Of Newfoundland* (1984)★★★, *Top Of The Crops* (1985)★★★, *The Yetties* (ASV 1986)★★★, *The Musical Heritage Of Thomas Hardy* (ASV 1988)★★★, *Rolling Home* (1991)★★★, *Looking For The Sunshine* (1992)★★★.
● COMPILATIONS: *Play It Again* (1989)★★★, *Singing All The Way* (ASV 1989)★★★.

Yo La Tengo

New Jersey, USA band who have crafted a formidable reputation within the US alternative rock community with their succulent, **Velvet Underground**-inspired melodicism. Comprising central duo Ira Kaplan (vocals, guitar) and Georgia Hubley (drums, vocals), plus various associates who in the 90s included James McNew (bass), the band have built a strong reputation with critics worldwide. Yo La Tengo took their name from the cry of a Spanish-speaking baseball outfielder (strictly translating as 'I Got It'), and had their debut album produced by **Mission Of Burma** bass player Clint Conley. With guest guitar from Dave Schramm, the set included a cover version of **Ray Davies'** 'Big Sky'. The oft-stated comparisons between Kaplan's vocals and those of **Lou Reed** were further endorsed by a version of the latter's 'It's Alright (The Way That You Live)' on the subsequent *New Wave Hot Dogs* collection. Two live songs from a **CBGB's** set were included on the band's most eloquent set to date, 1989's *President Yo La Tengo*. This saw the introduction of bass player Gene Holder, who also produced, on an esoteric set that included Kaplan's famed composition 'The Evil That Men Do'. Schramm returned alongside stand-up bass player Al Greller for *Fakebook*, primarily a collection of cover versions drawn from the canons of the **Kinks**, **Flying Burrito Brothers**, **John Cale** and **Cat Stevens**. Schramm would also work with Greller as Schramms the band - who recorded *Walk To Delphi* for OKra Records in 1990. *Painful* contained the usual assortment of beautiful pop moments, notably 'Nowhere Near' and 'The Whole Of The Law'. Kaplan joined Dave Grohl onstage for his post-**Nirvana** return as **Foo Fighters** in 1995, and the same year's *Electr-O-Pura*, their seventh album, saw the band picking up UK press for the first time, following a London gig performed under the title Sleeping Pill, but it was with 1997's excellent *I Can Hear The Heart Beating As One* that the band gained their best reviews to date.

● ALBUMS: *Ride The Tiger* (Coyote/Twin Tone 1986)★★★, *New Wave Hot Dogs* (Coyote/Twin Tone 1987)★★, *President Yo La Tengo* (Coyote 1989)★★★, *Fakebook* (Bar/None 1990)★★★, *Painful* (City Slang 1993)★★★, *Electr-O-Pura* (City Slang 1995)★★★, *Genius + Love = Yo La Tengo* (Matador 1996)★★★, *I Can Hear The Heart Beating As One* (Matador 1997)★★★★.

Yo Yo

b. Yolanda Whitaker, 4 August 1971, South Central Los Angeles, USA. A protégé of **Ice Cube**, Yo Yo is one of the female rappers who likes to play it as rough and dirty as her male gangsta brethren. Her long-playing debut introduced her combative attitude, with frequent interjections from Ice Cube's Lench Mob posse. However, amid the assertive, abrasive lyrics lurked a sophistication that might not have been envisaged by the casual buyer. That album's torch song was 'Sisterland', a rallying call for her fellow female MCs. Titles on her third album included 'The Girl's Got A Gun', and her duet with Ice Cube, 'The Bonnie & Clyde Theme'. Better still, she managed to invert the usual gangsta trappings by acting as a female pimp on 'Macktress'. Yo Yo had previously contributed to Ice's debut album, *AmeriKKKa's Most Wanted*, duetting on 'It's A Man's World', representing her gender in admirable style. This insight was confirmed by her leading role in the formation of the Intelligent Black Women Coalition.

● ALBUMS: *Make Way For The Motherlode* (Atlantic 1991)★★★, *Black Pearl* (East West 1992)★★★★, *You Better Ask Somebody* (East West 1993)★★★, *Total Control* (East West 1996)★★★.

Yo! Bum Rush The Show - Public Enemy

Hindsight may sometimes reduce the import of Public Enemy's debut set, particularly in the light of brilliant subsequent outings, but *Bum Rush The Show*'s impact was devastating. It introduced one of the most fearsome rhythmic talents in Terminator X and the Bomb Squad, carrying enough musical ballast to sink a battleship. 'Miuzi Weighs A Ton' is a key track here. By looping James Brown's 'Funky Drummer' break Public Enemy gave birth to the most over-used musical convention in rap. The ideology was not quite there (notably on 'Sophisticated Bitch'), though there were definite hints of greatness in 'Rightstarter (Message To A Black Man)'.

● Tracks: *You're Gonna Get Yours; Sophisticated Bitch; Miuzi Weighs A Ton; Time Bomb; Too Much Posse; Rightstarter (Message To A Black Man); Public Enemy Number 1; MPE; Yo, Bum Rush The Show; Raise The Roof; Megablast; Terminator X Speaks With His Hands.*

● First released 1987

● UK peak chart position: did not chart

● USA peak chart position: 125

Yoakam, Dwight

b. 23 October 1956, Pikeville, Kentucky, USA. Yoakam, the eldest of three children, moved with his family to Columbus, Ohio, when he was two. A singer-songwriter with an early love of the honky-tonk country music of **Buck Owens** and **Lefty Frizzell**, he has always shown a distinct antipathy towards the Nashville pop/country scene. After an abortive spell studying philosophy and history at Ohio State University, he briefly sought Nashville success in the mid-70s, but his music was rated too country even for the *Grand Ole Opry*. He relocated to Los Angeles in 1978 and worked the clubs, playing with various bands including **Los Lobos**, but for several years he worked as a truck driver. In 1984, the release of a self-financed mini-album on the Enigma label led to him signing for **Warner/Reprise Records**. Two years later, following the release of his excellent debut *Guitars Cadillacs Etc*, he registered Top 5 US country chart hits with **Johnny Horton**'s 'Honky Tonk Man' and his own 'Guitars, Cadillacs'. His driving honky-tonk music made him a popular visitor to Britain and brought him some success in the USA, but his outspoken views denied him wider fame. In 1987 he had success with his version of the old **Elvis Presley** pop hit 'Little Sister'. He followed it in 1988 with a US country number 9 hit with his idol Lefty Frizzell's classic 'Always Late (With Your Kisses)', and a number 1 with his self-penned 'I Sang Dixie'. He would also make the top of the country charts with 'The Streets Of Bakersfield', duetting with veteran 60s superstar Buck Owens. Yoakam played several concerts with Owens, after being instrumental in persuading him to come out of retirement and record again for **Capitol Records**. Like **Don Williams** and others, he retains the traditional stetson hat. There seems little doubt that Yoakam's songwriting talents and singing style will ensure further major success and much of his hip honky-tonk music has paved the way for rock audiences accepting country music of the 90s, much in the way that **Garth Brooks** has done. His straight country style is his most effective work, even though he attempted to cross over into the mainstream rock market with *La Croix D'Amour*. Although by nature shy of publicity, he earned notoriety by the bucketload when he arrived at the 1992 Academy Awards with Sharon Stone on his arm. She went public on the affair when their relationship ended, although Yoakam maintained a dignified silence. He has also recently turned his hand to acting, appearing in a Los Angeles stage production, *Southern Rapture*, directed by Peter Fonda. He came back in 1993 with the hardcore country of *This Time*. The album included the number 1 country hit 'Ain't That Lonely Yet', which won a Grammy award for Best Country Vocal Performance, while 'A Thousand Miles From Nowhere' was accompanied by an excellent video. *Dwight Live*, recorded at San Francisco's Warfield Theatre, captured the fervour of his concert performances. He wrote all the tracks on *Gone* and to quote *Rolling Stone*, 'Neither safe nor

tame, Yoakam has adopted Elvis' devastating hip swagger, **Hank Williams**' crazy-ass stare and **Merle Haggard**'s brooding solitude into one lethal package. Yoakam is a cowgirl's secret darkest dream.' After more than a decade of commercial success, Yoakam has firmly established his staying power as one of the leading country artists of the new era of country music.
● ALBUMS: *Guitars, Cadillacs, Etc., Etc.* (Reprise 1986)★★★★, *Hillbilly DeLuxe* (Reprise 1987)★★★★, *Buenas Noches From A Lonely Room* (Reprise 1988)★★★★, *If There Was A Way* (Reprise 1990)★★★★, *La Croix D'Amour* (Reprise 1992)★★★, *This Time* (Reprise 1993)★★★★, *Dwight Live* (Reprise 1995)★★, *Gone* (Reprise 1995)★★★★, *Under The Covers* (Reprise 1997)★★, *Come On Christmas* (Reprise 1997)★★, *A Long Way Home* (Reprise 1998)★★★★.
● COMPILATIONS: *Just Lookin' For A Hit* (Reprise 1989)★★★★.
● VIDEOS: *Dwight Yoakam, Just Lookin' For A Hit* (1989), *Fast As You* (1993), *Pieces Of Time* (1994), *Live On Stage* (Magnum Video 1997).

York Brothers

A popular harmony duo comprising George York (b. 17 February 1910, Louisa, Lawrence County, Kentucky, USA, d. July 1974; guitar, harmonica, vocals) and Leslie York (b. 23 August 1917, Louisa, Lawrence County, Kentucky, USA, d. 21 February 1984; guitar, vocals). George first worked in the coalmines before moving to Denver, where he played on local radio. In the late 30s, somewhat influenced by the **Delmores**, the brothers began their career in Portsmouth, Ohio, and made their first recordings for the Universal label in 1939. Their version of 'Little White Washed Chimney' (recorded as 'Going Home') sold well enough to gain them a contract with **Decca Records**. After recording for that label in 1941, and at a time when their popularity was spreading nationally, America's involvement in World War II saw both brothers drafted for service with the US Navy. After their discharge, they settled in Nashville where, until 1950, they played the *Grand Ole Opry*. They then relocated to Detroit until 1953, when they moved to Dallas, becoming regulars on the *Big D Jamboree* and the *Saturday Night Shindig*. Between 1947 and 1956, they recorded for King, and later for their own label. In the latter half of their career, their music changed from the old-time style of the usual brother harmony acts to anticipate the popular mix of nostalgia and sentimental ballads later popularized by such artists as **Red Foley**, even introducing a piano to add a honky tonk effect on some numbers. Leslie sang solo on some of their later recordings, due to the fact that George at times suffered throat problems. They eventually retired from the music but remained in Dallas where George owned a nightclub.
● ALBUMS: *The York Brothers Volume 1* (King 1958)★★★, *The York Brothers Volume 2* (King 1958)★★★, *16 Great Country Songs* (King 1963)★★★★.
● COMPILATIONS: *Early Favorites* (Old Homestead 1987)★★★.

Yorke, Peter

b. 4 December 1902, London, England, d. 2 February 1966, England. A highly respected composer, conductor and arranger, Yorke was well known in Britain through his hundreds of broadcasts, and his themes have been widely used on television and radio. In the 30s he was one of the finest dance band orchestrators in England, working with Percival Mackey, **Jack Hylton**, Louis Levy and many others. After World War II he established himself as a light music composer and conductor through BBC radio shows such as *Sweet Serenade, Our Kind Of Music* and *The Peter Yorke Melody Hours*. From the late 40s onwards he made numerous 78s for **EMI**'s **Columbia**, including some legendary titles with saxophonist Freddy Gardner (1911-50), which are regarded as models of their genre: 'I'm In The Mood For Love', 'I Only Have Eyes For You', 'Roses Of Picardy', 'These Foolish Things', 'Body And Soul' and 'Valse Vanite'. Yorke also recorded an early composition, 'Sapphires And Sables', which he used as his theme music, and his other notable pieces included 'Melody Of The Stars', 'Dawn Fantasy', 'Quiet Countryside', 'Caravan Romance', 'Carminetta', 'Faded Lilac', 'Fireflies', 'Flyaway Fidles', 'Golden Melody', 'Oriental Bazaar', 'In My Garden' - suite, 'Midnight In Mexico', 'Parade Of The Matadors', 'Royal Mile', 'Highdays And Holidays', 'Brandy Snaps', 'Miss In Mink', 'Lazy Piano', and 'Ladies Night'. From 1957-67 'Silks And Satins' was used to close the popular British television soap *Emergency Ward 10*. Most of Yorke's original works were written for various London mood music libraries especially Chappells, Francis Day & Hunter, Bosworth, Harmonic, Conroy, Paxton, Southern and Josef Weinberger. He also conducted several albums of popular songs, mainly for the American market.
● ALBUMS: *Music For Sweethearts - Romantic Compositions Of Victor Herbert* (Brunswick 1956)★★★, *Sapphires And Sables - Music In The Peter Yorke Manner* (Delyse-Envoy 1959)★★★, *Mood For Love* (EMI-World Records 1979)★★★★.

Yosefa

b. Yosefa Dahari, 13 January 1971, Eilat, Israel. Yosefa grew up hearing the music of the Arabic Middle East and North Africa from her parents (her father was originally from Yemen, her mother from Morocco), and she began singing while serving in the army. On one occasion, while stationed next to the border with Lebanon, she performed Arabic folk songs and gained a round of applause from the other side of the fence. Responses such as this encouraged her to explore her Arabic musical roots and after she had completed her national service, she became a professional singer. While many of her contemporaries have looked solely to the west for their musical inspiration, Yosefa has sought to mix western dance music styles, such as rap and soul, with the traditional vocals and rhythms of the Middle East. Her albums, *Yosefa*, released in 1994 and now deleted, and *The Desert Speaks*, released a year later, have sometimes veered too close to blandness. However, at its best, Yosefa's music represents a genuine mixture of the disparate cultural influences that make up the sound of modern Israel.

● ALBUMS: *Yosefa* (1994)★★★, *The Desert Speaks* (Hemisphere 1995)★★★.

Yothu Yindi

This, the most internationally recognizable aboriginal group, is led by spokesman and local headmaster Mandaway Yunipingu. The group is based in the remote, crocodile-infested region of Arnhem Land in the Northern Territories, Australia. Their name translating as 'mother and child', they became a force in both Australia and the rest of the world via their serene, indigenous sounds, with singing in their native Gumadj language. Their debut album was released in 1988, amid Australia's centenary jamboree, which became the focus of their cynicism. 'Treaty', from 1992, which decried Australian Prime Minister Bob Hawke's broken promise to draw up a treaty on Aboriginal rights, also crossed over to the UK dance charts. 'Our sole purpose as a band is that we're trying to develop and create an impact for our culture. And music has a universal language that can convey that.' Licensed from the Australian Mushroom label to Hollywood Records, it appeared in a remix from Melbourne DJ's Gavin Campbell and Paul Main and programmer/musician Robert Goodge. Resplendent in digeridoo, clap sticks and tribal chants, it quickly became a major club hit. However, this is only part of the group's appeal, which has also stretched to America, where *Billboard* magazine described them as the 'Flagship of Australian music.' It also saw Yunipingu recognized in his own land as Australian Band Of The Year in 1992.

● ALBUMS: *Homeland Movement* (Mushroom 1988)★★★, *Tribal Voice* (Mushroom 1991)★★★, *Freedom* (Mushroom 1994)★★★.

You Are What You Eat

This 1968 feature was directed by Barry Feinstein who co-produced it with Peter Yarrow of **Peter, Paul And Mary**. Described by its creators as an 'anti-documentary', *You Are What You Eat* featured hippies, love-ins, body painting, concerts and surfing without ever addressing the fulfilment participants felt in such counter-culture activities. Voyeuristic rather than participatory, the film is of interest for cameo appearances, rather than as a whole. Los Angeles scenemaker Vito, an ageing guru associated with the **Mothers Of Invention** and the **Byrds**, makes a rare on-screen appearance, as does San Franciscan drug supplier Super Spade, who was later murdered by less altruistic criminals. Musicians **Barry McGuire** and **David Crosby** make fleeting appearances, but the soundtrack is derived from performances by John Herald, formerly of the **Greenbriar Boys**, **Tiny Tim** (who duets memorably with Eleanor Goodman on 'I Got You Babe'), **Paul Butterfield** and the **Electric Flag**. The last-named's

contribution, 'Freak Out', sounds like an out-take from their work on the previous year's exploitation film, *The Trip*. Future **Band** producer **John Simon** was musical director and among his solo performances was 'My Name Is Jack', later a hit for **Manfred Mann**. *You Are What You Eat* is not essential viewing, but has more value than its many denigrators would claim.

You Can't Hide Your Love Forever - Orange Juice

Orange Juice were the leading attraction on Glasgow's fêted Postcard label. Critical plaudits followed the release of their first four singles and much was expected from this debut album. The insouciant charm of their windblown pop was emphasized by a clear production that focused on singer **Edwyn Collins**' sonorous croon. Songs echoing the strains of classic west coast pop deal with sorrow and rejection, a fragility matched by the group's still-untutored playing, in which their aspirations outstripped their technical abilities. The group's continued desire to broach preconceived barriers is what gives this album its implicit strength.

● Tracks: *Falling And Laughing; Untitled Melody; Wan Light; Tender Object; Dying Day; L.O.V.E.; Intuition Told Me; Upwards And Onwards; Satellite City; Three Cheers For Our Side; Consolation Prize; Felicity; In A Nutshell.*
● First released 1982
● UK peak chart position: 21
● USA peak chart position: did not chart

You Got My Mind Messed Up - James Carr

For lovers of vintage soul **James Carr** is god. Totally underrated with only a few compilation albums available, it is a mystery why this man is so overlooked. Carr, like Johnnie Taylor, was also a member of the legendary **Soul Stirrers** until he went solo for the Goldwax label. His deep and powerful 'You've Got My Mind Messed Up' was a huge R&B hit in the USA and this album followed it. There is not a bad track on the album, and one further high point is the definitive reading of Dan Penn and Spooner Oldham's 'Dark End Of The Street', the greatest ever country-meets-soul song. This album begs reissue.

● Tracks: *Pouring Water On A Drowning Man; Love Attack; Coming Back To Me Baby; I Don't Want To Be Hurt Anymore; That's What I Want To Know; These Ain't Raindrops; Dark End Of The Street; I'm Going For Myself; Lovable Girl; Forgetting You; She's Better Than You.*
● First released 1965
● UK peak chart position: did not chart
● USA peak chart position: did not chart

You Slosh

A powerful group dealing primarily in Celtic mood music. Piper Troy Donockley composed long, involved pieces for guitars and ethnic instruments (whistle, pipes, flute). The sound made by the other members of the band was big and exciting. An immensely popular college group, in late 1991 they mysteriously disbanded, just when they were starting to receive national attention. No albums were recorded.

You Were Never Lovelier

After their compatibility and box-office appeal had been established in *You'll Never Get Rich* in 1941, **Fred Astaire** and **Rita Hayworth** were brought together again a year later for this Columbia release that was set in Buenos Aires. The screenplay, by Michael Fessier, Ernest Pagano, and Delmar Daves, cast Astaire as an American nightclub dancer and gambler who goes to Argentina for the sport, but ends up working in Adolph Menjou's ritzy hotel when his money runs out. Astaire's life becomes fraught with misunderstandings, when one of Menjou's daughters, played by **Rita Hayworth**, thinks he is wooing her with expensive flowers - in fact, they are being sent by her father in an attempt to 'get her off his hands'! Naturally, Fred gets the girl in the end, with the assistance of some of **Jerome Kern**'s most endearing music and **Johnny Mercer**'s lyrics. Hayworth, whose singing was dubbed by **Nan Wynn**, 'danced her socks off' in 'Shorty George' and 'I'm Old Fashioned', and blended blissfully with Astaire for the delightfully romantic 'You Were Never Lovelier' and 'Dearly Beloved'. **Xavier Cugat** and his Orchestra provided a few genuine Latin-American rhythms in 'Chiu Chiu (Niconar Molinare)' and 'Wedding In The Spring' (both with Lina Romay), and 'Audition Dance' (with Astaire). Also in the cast was Larry Parks, just a few years before he hit the big time in *The Jolson Story*. Val Raset conceived the imaginative dance sequences, and *You Were Never Lovelier* was directed by William A. Seiter. Rita Hayworth's association with Fred Astaire had been a joy, and two years later she was marvellous all over again when she joined that other great screen dancer, **Gene Kelly**, in *Cover Girl*.

You'll Never Get Rich

Rita Hayworth fulfilled her promise as one of the screen's leading dancers, when she partnered **Fred Astaire** in this 1941 Columbia release. With America on the brink of entry into World War II, Michael Fessier and Ernest Pagano's screenplay cast Astaire as a Broadway dance director who is smitten by chorus girl Rita Hayworth. However, he is drafted into the US Army before he can consolidate his position. He turns out to be a rather perverse soldier, and spends a good deal of time in the guardhouse. While there, he performs an incredibly fast solo tap dance accompanied by a moody version of 'Since I Kissed My Baby Goodbye' by the Delta Rhythm Boys. That number was part of the superb **Cole Porter** score, which also included 'The Boogie Barcarolle', 'Dream Dancing' (a sadly underrated song), 'Shootin' The Works For Uncle Sam', and 'A-stairable Rag'. After Astaire has negotiated his release from detention in order to help to produce a musical entertainment for the troops, he serenades Hayworth (naturally, she is one of stars of the show)

onstage with the lovely 'So Near And Yet So Far' ('I just start getting you keen on clinches galore with me/When fate steps in on the scene and mops up the floor with me'), before the exuberant finalé, 'Wedding Cake Walk'. Astaire and Hayworth were perfect together, and Robert Benchley, as the amorous producer who is responsible for their romantic involvement in the first place, was excellent too. Sidney Lanfield directed, and the choreographer was Robert Alton.

You're A Big Boy Now

Released in 1967, *You're A Big Boy Now* marked the directorial debut of Francis Ford Coppola, famed for later, award-winning films, *The Godfather* and *Apocalypse Now*. This rites-of-passage feature starred Peter Kastner as a teenage stacker at the New York Public Library. He tries to leave his home for the city's downtown attractions, bewitched by the elusive Miss Thing, only to encounter an often-confusing outside world. In one memorable scene he stands in an arcade, gazing at a pornographic film, unaware his tie is caught in the machinery. An excellent comedy about sexual awakening, *You're A Big Boy Now* is a quiet masterpiece, capturing the trauma and uncertainty of late puberty. **John Sebastian** of the **Lovin' Spoonful**, who had already scored Woody Allen's **What's Up Tiger Lily**, composed the entire soundtrack, later issued on the **Kama Sutra** label. One of its tracks, the haunting 'Darling Be Home Soon', reached number 15 in the US charts when issued as a single.

You're A Good Man, Charlie Brown

Sometimes known as the 'Peanuts' musical, this show, which was based on Charles Schultz's enormously successful American comic strip of that name, opened off-Broadway at Theatre 80 St. Marks, on 7 March 1967. Music, book and lyrics were by Clark Gesner, and told of a day in the life of the strip's familiar young characters. They include the sensitive, but bemused Charlie Brown (Gary Burghoff), Lucy (Reva Rose), Patty (Karen Johnson), Schroeder (Skip Hinnant), Linus (Bob Balaban), and, of course, the lovable pooch Snoopy (Bill Hinnant), who, in his imaginary persona as a World World I pilot, is in pursuit of his opposite number, the German flying ace, the Red Baron. They all get involved in numbers such as 'My Blanket And Me', 'Little Known Facts', 'T.E.A.M.' 'Suppertime', 'You're A Good Man, Charlie Brown', 'Book Report', 'Happiness', and 'Queen Lucy'. To the surprise of many, Charlie and his friends appealed for a total of 1,597 performances in New York, while road companies carried the message throughout the USA. The concept was unfamiliar to British audiences, and the London production folded after nearly three months.

Youmans, Vincent

b. Vincent Miller (Millie) Youmans, 27 September 1898, New York, USA, d. 5 April 1946, Denver, Colorado, USA. An important composer and producer for the stage during the 20s and 30s, whose career was cut short by a long illness. He worked for a Wall Street finance company before enlisting in the US Navy during World War I, and co-producing musicals at Great Lakes Naval Training Station. On leaving the navy, he worked as a song-plugger for Harms Music, and as a rehearsal pianist for shows with music by the influential composer **Victor Herbert**. Youmans wrote his first Broadway score in 1921 for *Two Little Girls In Blue*, with lyrics by **Ira Gershwin**. One of the show's songs, 'Oh Me, Oh My, Oh You', was a hit for novelty singer **Frank Crumit**. Youmans' next show, *Wildflower* (1923), with book and lyrics by **Otto Harbach** and **Oscar Hammerstein II**, ran for a creditable 477 performances, and included 'April Blossoms', and 'Bambalina', which was recorded by **Paul Whiteman** and Ray Miller. *Mary Jane McKane* ('Toodle-oo', 'You're Never Too Old To Learn') and *Lollipop* ('Take A Little One-Step') both reached the Broadway stage in 1924, and in the following year, Youmans collaborated with lyricist **Irving Caesar** on the quintessential 20s score for *No, No, Nanette*, one of the decade's most successful musicals. It contained several hits songs, including 'Too Many Rings Around Rosie', 'You Can Dance With Any Girl At All', and the much-recorded standards, 'I Want To Be Happy' and 'Tea For Two'. It was filmed, with modifications to its score, in 1930, 1940, and in 1950 as *Tea For Two*, starring **Doris Day** and **Gordon MacRae**.

In contrast, Youmans' 1926 show, *Oh, Please*, with numbers such as 'I Know That You Know', and 'Like He Loves Me' (lyrics by Anne Caldwell), was a relative failure, despite the presence of Beatrice Lillie in the cast. A year later, Youmans composed the music for *Hit The Deck*, which ran for 352 performances, and featured 'Sometimes I'm Happy' (lyric by Clifford Grey and Irving Caesar) and 'Halleluja' (lyric by Clifford Grey and **Leo Robin**). It was filmed in 1930, and again in 1955 with an all-star cast including **Tony Martin**, **Vic Damone**, **Debbie Reynolds**, **Jane Powell**, and **Ann Miller**. The latter release contained a new Youmans song, 'Keepin' Myself For You', with a lyric by Sidney Clare. Despite containing some of his best songs, Youmans' next few shows were flops. *Rainbow* ran for only 29 performances, *Great Day*, with the title song, 'More Than You Know' and 'Without A Song' (lyrics by **Billy Rose** and Edward Eliscu), lasted for 36 performances, *Smiles*, starring Marilyn Miller, and Adele and **Fred Astaire**, and featuring 'Time On My Hands' (lyric by **Mack Gordon** and **Harold Adamson**), just 63 performances, and *Through The Years*, with the title song, 'Kinda Like You', and 'Drums In My Heart' (lyrics by Edward Heyman), a mere 20 performances. Youmans' last Broadway show, *Take A Chance*, did much better. It starred Jack Haley and **Ethel Merman**, and ran for 243 performances. Youmans contributed three songs with lyrics by **Buddy De Sylva**: 'Should I Be Sweet?', 'Oh, How I Long To Belong To You', and Miss Merman's show-stopper, 'Rise 'N' Shine', which was

also a hit for **Paul Whiteman**. Apparently disenchanted with Broadway, Youmans moved to Hollywood and wrote his only major original film score for *Flying Down To Rio* (1933). Celebrated as the film that brought **Fred Astaire** and **Ginger Rogers** together as a dance team, the musical numbers, with lyrics by **Gus Kahn** and Edward Eliscu, consisted of 'The Carioca', 'Orchids In the Moonlight', 'Music Makes Me', and the peppy title number. Youmans' previous flirtations with the big screen, *Song Of The West* and *What A Widow* (both 1930), produced nothing particularly memorable, and the film adaptation of his stage show *Take A Chance* (with Lilian Roth replacing Ethel Merman), dispensed with most of the songs. However, the aforementioned *Hit The Deck* was a box-office favourite, and *No, No, Nanette* was filmed twice - as an early talkie with Bernice Claire in 1930, and 10 years later with **Anna Neagle** in the starring role.

In the early 30s, Youmans contracted tuberculosis and spent much of the rest of his life in sanitoria. In 1934, his publishing firm collapsed, and a year later he was declared bankrupt for over half a million dollars. In 1943, he seemed well enough to return to New York to plan his most ambitious project, an extravaganza entitled *The Vincent Youmans Ballet Revue*. This was a combination of Latin-American and classical music, including Ravel's 'Daphnis And Chloe', with choreography by Leonide Massine. It was a critical and commercial disaster, losing over four million dollars. Youmans retired to New York, and then to Denver, Colorado, where he died in 1946. Despite his relatively small catalogue of songs and his penchant for rarely using the same collaborator, Youmans is rated among the élite composers of his generation, and was inducted into the Songwriters Hall of Fame. In 1971, an acclaimed revival of *No, No, Nanette* starring **Ruby Keeler**, began its run of 861 performances on Broadway.

● COMPILATIONS: *Through The Years With Vincent Youmans* (1972)★★★★, *Wildflower/Gershwin's Tiptoes'* (1979)★★★.

● FURTHER READING: *Days To Be Happy, Years To Be Sad, The Life And Music Of Vincent Youmans*, G. Bordman.

Young & Co

This funky sextet revolved around a nucleus of brothers Billy, Mike and Kenneth Young from West Virginia, USA. After moving to East Orange, New Jersey, in 1970 they formed the Young Movement with Buddy 'Hank' Hankerson, an ex-member of Aurra (bass, keyboards, guitar) and Dave Reyes (drums). The group changed their name to Flashflood in 1974 and recorded with Slave and Aurra. When vocalist and sole distaff member Jackie Thomas joined in 1979 they first recorded as Young & Co. Among the first three tracks they demoed was 'I Like What You're Doing', which helped secure a deal with **Brunswick Records**. When released, this single reputedly sold over 250,000 in the USA alone, yet never made the R&B or pop chart there. It did, however, go all the way into the UK Top 20 in 1980 when picked up by the newly formed Excalibur label. The group later recorded for Sounds Of London and **Atlantic Records** but never tasted success again.

Young Americans - David Bowie

David Bowie abandoned the glam/sci-fi personae of *Ziggy Stardust, Aladdin Sane* and *Diamond Dogs* with this radical departure. Recorded at Sigma Sound Studios, the home of Philadelphia International, it featured the label's crack house band and, as a result, confirmed the singer's growing love of soul and R&B. Pulsating dance grooves abound, in particular on the disco-influenced 'Fame', which topped the US singles chart. The song was co-written with **John Lennon**, a compliment Bowie repaid by reinventing the **Beatles'** 'Across The Universe' as a dancefloor classic. Such self-confidence abounds throughout this album which shows the singer firmly in command of yet another musical direction.

● Tracks: *Young Americans; Win; Fascination; Right; Somebody Up There Likes Me; Across The Universe; Can You Hear Me; Fame.*
● First released 1975
● UK peak chart position: 2
● USA peak chart position: 9

Young And Stupid - Josef K

This posthumous release collects material from one of Edinburgh's leading post-punk attractions. Matching Thin White Duke-period Bowie with abrasive pop, the band joined **Orange Juice** on the cult Postcard label. Several tracks culled from that period are accompanied by recordings drawn from the John Peel Show, compilations, and abandoned first drafts from sessions for the quartet's debut album. *Young And Stupid* also features one side from Josef K's first single and in so doing completes the definitive overview of a short-lived but fascinating act.

● Tracks: *Heart Of Song; Endless Soul; Citizens; Variation Of Scene; It's Kinda Funny; Sorry For Laughing; Chance Meeting; Heaven Sent; Drone; Sense Of Guilt; Revelation; Romance.*
● First released 1989
● UK peak chart position: did not chart
● USA peak chart position: did not chart

Young At Heart

Adapted by Julius J. Epstein and Lenore Coffee from Fannie Hurst's novel *Sister Act*, and the 1938 Claude Rains-John Garfield movie *The Four Daughters*, this 1954 Warner Brothers release provided a glimpse of the American suburban family viewed through the proverbial rose-coloured spectacles. The story concerns three sisters (one was dropped from the original), played by **Doris Day**, Dorothy Malone and Elizabeth Fraser, who live with their music teacher father (Robert Keith) and crusty aunt (Ethel Barrymore). Day is engaged to budding songwriter Gig Young, but one day, old chip-on-the-shoulder **Frank Sinatra** turns up on the

doorstep and ruins the whole arrangement. Day marries Sinatra, but his career prospects remain at zero (the people 'upstairs' never give him a break), and one dark, snowy night he attempts to 'take the easy way out'. His will to live is rekindled when his wife tells him they are about to become a threesome. Perhaps because of the film's sentimental character, the Sinatra-Day combination failed to work as well as might have been expected, although, individually, they had some satisfying moments. At the time, both were probably at the peak of their vocal powers, and a collection of engaging songs gave them ample chance to shine - Day with such as 'Hold Me In Your Arms' (Ray Heindorf-Charles Henderson-Don Pippin) and the more upbeat 'Ready, Willing And Able' (Floyd Huddleston-Al Rinker-Dick Gleason), and Sinatra on 'Someone To Watch Over Me' (**George** and **Ira Gershwin**), 'Just One Of Those Things' (**Cole Porter**) and 'One For My Baby' (**Harold Arlen**-**Johnny Mercer**). Sinatra sings a number of these while working in a local 'joint' for what he calls 'tips on a plate'. Other numbers included 'You, My Love' (**Mack Gordon**-**Jimmy Van Heusen**), 'There's A Rising Moon (For Every Falling Star)' (**Paul Francis Webster**-**Sammy Fain**) and 'Young At Heart' (**Carolyn Leigh**-Johnny Richards). Photographed in Warnercolor and directed by Gordon Douglas, this was the kind of film that - at the time - made audiences feel warm all over.

Young Black Teenagers

Toasted as the first to release a single on Hank Shocklee and Bill Stephney's Sound Of Urban Listeners label, YBT are in fact three white teenagers, and one Puerto Rican (ATA) from Brooklyn, New York. Their provocative moniker was chosen, they declare, to pay tribute to hip-hop's true originators, to accept that it is primarily an Afro-American format, but that outsiders too are welcome. The group, formed in 1987, comprise ATA, Kameron, Firstborn and DJ Skribble, and their debut release, 'Nobody Knows Kelli', was a tribute to cult American anti-sitcom, *Married With Children*. Although the sleeve of their debut album was a cunning take on the *Beatles For Sale* tableau, the production was haphazard, despite the presence of the Bomb Squad. They switched from SOUL to **MCA** for the single, 'Tap The Bootle', which featured a guest appearance from **Public Enemy**'s DJ **Terminator X**. Ultimately, however, they would fall out with Chuck D and Hank Shocklee, with whom Kamron had previously DJed in Roosevelt, Long Island. However, this was not before they had recorded 'To My Donna', an attack on **Madonna** for using Public Enemy's 'Security Of The First World' beat. Following the wit of their previous releases, YBT fell down heavily on political correctness. When challenged about the predominance of the word 'bitch' in their vernacular, ATA could only muster: 'When I say a girl is a bitch, I'm not saying she's a female dog. We're past that. Let's not take things at face value. Women just tend to be bitches, they tend to be moody....' Elsewhere they were more dextrous. Instead

of merely sampling on *Dead End Kidz*, they reinterpreted, to excellent comic effect and with live instruments, ancient nuggets by **Diana Ross**, the **Rolling Stones** and even **Rush**. They are currently managed and produced by **Bomb Squad** worker **Gary G-Wiz**.
● ALBUMS: *Young Black Teenagers* (SOUL 1993)★★, *Dead End Kidz Doin' Lifetime Bidz* (MCA 1994)★★★.

Young Disciples

Although their roots were in the rave scene, the 90s UK band Young Disciples' debut single, 'Get Yourself Together', combined hip-hop with jazz inflections, and featured the voice of **Carleen Anderson** and **MC Mell 'O'** on either side. The group, who comprised the duo of Mark 'O' and Femi, would win much of their notoriety through Anderson's vocal attributes. It was she who wrote and sang on many of their best recordings, including 'Apparently Nothin''. Her final release with the Young Disciples was *Dusky Sappho*, a limited edition EP, after which she concentrated on her solo career. Femi and Mark continued to use the Young Disciples banner, though the former would also undertake remix work for **Xscape** ('Just Kickin'') and others.
● ALBUMS: *Road To Freedom* (Talkin' Loud 1991)★★★.

Young Fresh Fellows

Operating out of Seattle, USA, since the early 80s, the Young Fresh Fellows have released a body of rough-hewn, understated pop gems. Their debut album was recorded in 1983 and released a year later. The band comprises Scott McCaughey (vocals), Chuck Carroll (guitar) and Tad Hutchinson (drums). *The Fabulous Sounds Of The North Pacific* picked up immediate plaudits, *Rolling Stone Record* going so far as to describe it as 'perfect'. Joined by Jim Sangster (Jimbo) (bass), they become a fully fledged offbeat new wave act, the dry humour and acute observations of their lyrics attracting a large college following. Their stylistic fraternity with the higher-profile **Replacements** was confirmed by their joint tours, both bands sharing what *Billboard* magazine described as 'a certain deliberate crudity of execution'. After the mini-album *Refreshments* they moved to Frontier Records for 1988's *Totally Lost*. Despite being dogged by a 'joke band' reputation, brought about by an aptitude for satirizing high-school traumas, the band's critical reaction was once more highly favourable. However, Carroll played his last gig for the band in winter 1989 in Washington. He was replaced by the **Fastbacks**' guitarist Kurt Bloch (who continues with both bands). Their most polished album yet, *This One's For The Ladies* highlighted McCaughey's successful adaptation of the spirit of the **Kinks**, while Bloch's guitar melodies fitted in seamlessly. Elsewhere, McCaughey released his first solo album and toured as second guitarist with **R.E.M.** in 1995.
● ALBUMS: *The Fabulous Sounds Of The Pacific Northwest* (PopLlama Products 1984)★★★, *Topsy Turvy* (PopLlama Products 1986)★★★, *The Men Who Loved Music* (PopLlama Products 1987)★★★★, *Refreshments* (PopLlama Products

1987)★★, *Totally Lost* (Frontier 1988)★★★, *Beans And Intolerance* (PopLlama Products 1989)★★, *This One's For The Ladies* (Frontier 1989)★★★, *Electric Bird Digest* (Frontier 1991)★★, *It's Low Beat Time* (Frontier 1992)★★★, *Gleich Jetzt* Japanese release (1+2 1992)★★, *Take It Like A Matador* Spanish release (Impossible 1993)★★, *Pop* Japanese release (PopLlama Products 1993)★★★.
Solo: Scott McCaughey *My Chartreuse Opinion* (PopLlama Products 1989)★★★.
● COMPILATIONS: *Includes A Helmet* UK sampler (Utility 1990)★★, *Somos Los Mejores!* Spanish release (Munster 1991)★★★.

Young Gods

This heavily experimental trio originated from Geneva, Switzerland, and specialized in hard electronic rock and rhythm. The main artistic engine was Franz Treichler (vocals), alongside original collaborators Cesare Pizzi (samples) and Frank Bagnoud (drums). Although singing mainly in French, they found an audience throughout Europe via the premier outlet for 'difficult' music, Play It Again Sam Records. Notable among their releases were 'L'Armourir', a version of **Gary Glitter**'s 'Hello Hello I'm Back Again', and *Young Gods Play Kurt Weill*, which stemmed from a commission to provide a tribute performance of the composer's works. They had already been awarded a French Government Arts grant to tour the USA in 1987, where they maintain cult popularity. Their influence is notable in Trent Reznor's hugely successful band **Nine Inch Nails**.
● ALBUMS: *The Young Gods* (Play It Again Sam 1988)★★★, *L' Eau Rouge* (Play It Again Sam 1989)★★★, *Play Kurt Weill* (Play It Again Sam 1991)★★★, *TV Sky* (Play It Again Sam 1991)★★★, *Live Sky Tour* (Play It Again Sam 1993)★★★ *Only Heaven* (Play It Again Sam 1995)★★★.

Young Hearts

An R&B vocal group from Los Angeles, California, USA. Original members were Ronald Preyer, Charles Ingersoll, Earl Carter, and James Moore. The Young Hearts were typical of the falsetto-lead stand-up vocal groups that populated the R&B scene of the late 60s and early 70s. Their impact was purely on the R&B charts, getting moderate hits with 'I've Got Love For My Baby' (number 19 R&B) in 1968 for the Minit subsidiary of **Imperial Records**, and 'Wake Up And Start Standing' (number 48 R&B) in 1974 for 20th Century. A stay at **ABC** in 1977 produced an album and several singles that did nothing, and the group faded after that.
● ALBUMS: *Sweet Soul Shakin'* (Minit 1968)★★★★, *A Taste Of The Younghearts* (20th Century 1974)★★★, *All About Love* (ABC 1977)★★.

Young Idea

This UK duo featured Tony Cox (b. 10 November 1945, London, England) and Douglas Ugo Granville Allesandro MacRae-Brown (b. 17 April 1947, Florence, Italy). MacRae-Brown, a contemporary of **Jonathan King** at Charterhouse Public School, met Cox at

university. The duo then forged a songwriting partnership and, having committed several demos to tape, hawked the finished product around London's Denmark Street-based publishers. Their talent secured a management and recording deal and the duo made their debut as the Young Idea in June 1966. They completed several singles before achieving a UK Top 10 hit the following year with a reading of the **Beatles**' song 'With A Little Help From My Friends'. The pair achieved a higher profile with non-original material, including the **Hollies**' 'A Peculiar Situation' and several poppy creations by **Les Reed** and **Barry Mason**. However, the Young Idea were unable to repeat the success of their lone chart entry.
● ALBUMS: *With A Little Help From My Friends* (MFP 1968)★★★.

Young Jessie
b. Obediah Donnell Jessie, 28 December 1936, Lincoln Manor, Dallas, Texas, USA. Young Jessie is one of the great unheralded singers of the Los Angeles R&B scene. He is best known for recording the original version of 'Mary Lou' (1955), which, although not a national hit, became a huge hit in California and Texas. The song was subsequently recorded with great success by rock 'n' roller **Ronnie Hawkins** in 1959 for Roulette and by rocker **Bob Seger** on his *Night Moves* (1976). At Los Angeles's Jefferson High, Young Jessie studied piano and saxophone alongside **Johnny 'Guitar' Watson**. His first recordings came about as a member of a doo-wop vocal group, the Hollywood Blue Jays (the other members were **Richard Berry**, Beverley Thompson, Thomas Pete Fox and Cornelius Gunther), recording for the Dolphin label a Young Jessie-penned record, 'I Had A Love'. The group then went to **Modern Records** and recorded the same song as the Flairs on the label's new Flair subsidiary. After several more singles, Young Jessie embarked on a solo career on the Modern label. His only success was with 'Mary Lou', and he left Modern in 1957. After recording with no success at **Atlantic** and then **Capitol**, Young Jessie left the music business in 1959. He returned to recording in 1961, but subsequent soul-style records on **Mercury**, Vanessa, Bit, Combo and Ro-Mark failed to find an audience.
● ALBUMS: *I'm Gone* (Ace 1995)★★★★.

Young Man With A Horn
Directed by Michael Curtiz, this film made in 1950 follows broadly upon Dorothy Baker's novel which was in its turn very loosely based on the life of **Bix Beiderbecke**. Any chance of reality went out the window with the casting of Kirk Douglas and the choice of **Harry James** to dub the character's trumpet playing. **Hoagy Carmichael** appears as a pianist but despite the fact that he actually did play piano with Bix he was ghosted by **Buddy Cole**. Amongst other musicians involved, mostly off-screen, are Babe Russin, **Nick Fatool**, **Jack Jenney**, **Willie Smith**, Stan Wrightsman and Jimmy Zito. **Doris Day** plays Douglas's long-suffering girlfriend and has a chance to sing between the melodramatics. (Alternative title: *Young Man Of Music*).

Young Marble Giants
Formed in 1978 as 'a desperate last-ditch attempt at doing something with my life' by Stuart Moxham (guitar, organ), this seminal, yet short-lived, trio from Cardiff, Wales, comprised the latter as the group's main songwriter, his brother Philip Moxham (bass) and Alison Statton (b. March 1958, Cardiff, Wales; vocals). Together they made their debut on *Is The War Over?*, a compilation of Cardiff groups, released in 1979. Their contribution reached the ears of Geoff Travis at **Rough Trade Records** who promptly invited them to record an album. Playing within minimalist musical landscapes the group utilized the superb, lyrical bass playing of Philip Moxham. The combination of Stuart's twangy/scratchy guitar and reedy organ with Statton's clear diction was evident on tracks such as 'Searching For Mr Right', 'Credit In The Straight World' and 'Wurlitzer Jukebox' from *Colossal Youth*. This highly acclaimed album was followed the next year by the impressive *Testcard* EP, which reached number 3 in the UK independent charts, by which time the group had amicably split. The brothers noted that recording separately would be the only way to maintain a healthy sibling relationship. Statton formed **Weekend** for two jazz-inspired albums, before joining Ian Devine (ex-**Ludus**) in **Devine And Statton**. *The Prince Of Wales* and *Cardiffians*. Stuart Moxham established the Gist, recording *Embrace The Herd* in 1983. This included the gorgeous 'Love At First Sight', which reached the UK Independent Top 20. Stuart's producing talents were called upon to oversee the recording of the **Marine Girls**' second album, *Lazy Ways*. Other projects in the 90s included work with **Beat Happening** and a solo album, *Signal Path*, on Feel Good All Over Records, with Statton guesting on one track. In later years his other profession, that of animation painter, gave him a credit on the film *Who Killed Roger Rabbit?*. Phil Moxham found work sessioning for both Weekend and the Gist. In 1987, the Young Marble Giants re-formed briefly to record a French release, 'It Took You'.
● ALBUMS: *Colossal Youth* (Rough Trade 1980)★★★.
● COMPILATIONS: with Weekend and the Gist *Nipped In The Bud* (Rough Trade 1984)★★★.
● VIDEOS: *Live At The Hurrah!* (Visionary 1994).

Young MC
b. Marvin Young, 10 May 1967, England, but raised in Queens, New York City. Young went to college in California, earning a degree in economics from the University Of South California, where he also wrote material for **Tone Loc** (including co-writing credits on his big hits 'Wild Thing' and 'Funky Cold Medina'). His solo work was similarly within the framework of mainstream rap, a highlight being the Top 10 hit, 'Bust A Move' - winner of the Grammy for Best Rap Record.

In its wake he started to appear on television advertising Pepsi soft drinks. He cited 'musical and ethical differences' as the reason for his move from **Delicious Vinyl** in the 90s, though he remained with 4th & Broadway/**Island** in the UK. By the time he became employed by **Capitol**, many critics pointed out that his material was becoming both overwrought and overproduced. Unlike many rappers, Young MC brought a post-AIDS conscience to his sexual boasts, as demonstrated on the second album's 'Keep It In Your Trousers'. He re-emerged in 1993 with the club hit 'Know How', a distillation of the 'Shaft' theme, produced by the **Dust Brothers** - aka his old friends from Delicious.

● ALBUMS: *Stone Cold Rhymin'* (Delicious Vinyl 1989)★★★, *Brainstorm* (Capitol 1991)★★★.

● VIDEOS: *Bustin' Moves* (1991).

Young Ones, The

Cliff Richard had already appeared in two films, *Expresso Bongo* and *Serious Charge*, prior to starring in this unashamedly teen-orientated vehicle. It combined many of the genre's sub-plots - unsympathetic adults, romance and an inevitable, jejune show that is finally performed despite adversity. Unashamedly light and frothy, *The Young Ones* (titled *Wonderful To Be Young* in the USA) also boasted a highly popular soundtrack album. The memorable title track, a number 1 single in its own right, defines the innocence of Britain's pre-**Beatles** 60s, while 'When The Girl In Your Arms Is The Girl In Your Heart' remains one of the singer's most affecting ballads. *The Young Ones* confirmed Richard's status as one of the most popular entertainers of his era. The film was released in 1962 and was directed by Sidney J. Furie. The musical interludes other than those by Cliff and the **Shadows** were composed by **Stanley Black**.

Young Rascals

This expressive act, one of America's finest pop/soul ensembles, made its debut in a New Jersey club, the Choo Choo in February 1965. **Felix Cavaliere** (b. 29 November 1943, Pelham, New York, USA; organ, vocals), Eddie Brigati (b. 22 October 1946, New York City, USA; vocals, percussion) and Dino Danelli (b. 23 July 1945, New York City, USA; drums) were each established musicians on the city's R&B circuit, serving time in several popular attractions, including **Joey Dee And The Starlighters**. It was here that the trio encountered Gene Cornish (b. 14 May 1946, Ottawa, Canada; vocals, guitar), who became the fourth member of a breakaway group, initially dubbed Felix And The Escorts, but later known as the Young Rascals. The quartet enjoyed a minor hit with 'I Ain't Gonna Eat Out My Heart Anymore' before securing a US number 1 with the energetic 'Good Lovin''. Despite a somewhat encumbering early image - knickerbockers and choir boy shirts - the group's soulful performances endeared them to critics and peers, earning them a 'group's

group' sobriquet. Now established as one of the east coast's most influential attractions, spawning a host of imitators from the **Vagrants** to **Vanilla Fudge**, the Young Rascals secured their biggest hit with 'Groovin''. This melancholic performance became an international hit, signalling a lighter, more introspective approach, and although Brigati was featured on the haunting 'How Can I Be Sure', a US Top 5 entry, Cavaliere gradually became the group's focal point. In 1968 the group dropped its 'Young' prefix and enjoyed a third US number 1 with 'People Got To Be Free'. An announcement that every Rascals live appearance must also include a black act enforced the group's commitment to civil rights, but effectively banned them from southern states. The quartet later began exploring jazz-based compositions, and although remaining respected, lost much of their commercial momentum. Brigati and Cornish left the group in 1971, and although newcomers Buzzy Feiten (guitar), Ann Sutton (vocals) and Robert Popwell (drums) contributed to final albums, *Peaceful World* and *Island Of Real*, the Rascals were clearly losing momentum and broke up the following year. **Felix Cavaliere** then enjoyed a moderate solo career while Danelli and Cornish formed Bulldog and Fotomaker. The three musicians were reunited in 1988 for an extensive US tour.

● ALBUMS: *The Young Rascals* (Atlantic 1966)★★★, *Collections* (Atlantic 1966)★★★, *Groovin'* (Atlantic 1967)★★★★, *Once Upon A Dream* (Atlantic 1968)★★★, *Freedom Suite* (Atlantic 1969)★★★, *Search And Nearness* (Atlantic 1969)★★, *See* (Atlantic 1970)★★, *Peaceful World* (Columbia 1971)★★, *The Island Of Real* (Columbia 1972)★★.

● COMPILATIONS: *Timepeace - The Rascals' Greatest Hits* (Atlantic 1968)★★★★, *Star Collection* (1973)★★★, *Searching For Ecstasy - The Rest Of The Rascals 1969-1972* (1988)★★★★.

Young Tradition

One of the leading practitioners of the English folk revival, the Young Tradition was formed in 1964 by Heather Wood (b. 1945; vocals), Royston Wood (b. 1935, d. 8 April 1990; vocals, tambourine) and **Peter Bellamy** (b. Peter Franklyn Bellamy, 8 September 1944, Bournemouth, Dorset, England, d. 24 September 1991; guitar, concertina, vocals). The trio continued the oral harmony tradition of the influential **Copper Family**, while simultaneously enjoying the patronage of the Soho circuit and the emergent 'underground' audience. Their choice of material and powerful harmonies captured what was regarded as the essence of rural folk music. The group completed three albums during their brief sojourn. Their debut included guest performances from **Dave Swarbrick** and **Dolly Collins** and their much heralded *Galleries* highlighted the divergent interests that eventually pulled them apart. Several selections featured support from David Munrow's Early Music Ensemble, a trend towards medieval perspectives that Bellamy considered unwelcome. Unable to make a commercial breakthrough, the Young Tradition broke up in 1969, although Heather and Royston Wood went on to record *No Relation*. The latter musician enjoyed a brief association with the **Albion Country Band**, before forming Swan Arcade. He died in April 1990, following a three-week coma after being run over by a car in the USA. Heather Wood teamed up with Andy Wallace to form the duo, Crossover, and now lives in America where she sings with the harmony group Poor Old Horse. Pete Bellamy, meanwhile, enjoyed a successful solo career that was abruptly cut short by his 1991 suicide.

● ALBUMS: *The Young Tradition* (Transatlantic 1966)★★★★, *So Cheerfully Round* (Transatlantic 1967)★★★★, *Galleries* (Transatlantic 1968)★★, with Shirley And Dolly Collins *The Holly Bears The Crown* 1969 recording (Fledg'ling 1995)★★★.

● COMPILATIONS: *The Young Tradition Sampler* (Transatlantic 1969)★★★★, *The Young Tradition* (1989)★★★.

Young, 'Mighty' Joe

b. 23 September 1927, Shreveport, Louisiana, USA. Blues guitarist 'Mighty' Joe Young grew up in the northern state of Wisconsin but later relocated to Louisiana before settling in Chicago in the 50s. There he briefly joined a group called Joe Little And His Heart Breakers before joining ex-**Muddy Waters** harmonica player Billy Boy Arnold in his band. He next went to guitarist **Jimmy Rogers**' blues band in 1959, meanwhile recording several unsuccessful singles on his own. Young played with guitarist **Otis Rush** from 1960-63, still recording solo with no luck. He built a reputation as a session guitarist in the 60s, recording with artists such as **Magic Sam**, **Willie Dixon** and **Tyrone Davis**. Young recorded several albums in the early 70s and became a popular blues nightclub act in Chicago. Since 1976 he has been absent from the recording scene.

● ALBUMS: *Blues With A Touch Of Soul* (Delmark 1970)★★★, *Chicken Heads* (Ovation 1974)★★, *Mighty Joe Young* (Ovation 1976)★★, *Live At The Wise Fools Pub* (1990)★★★.

● COMPILATIONS: *Legacy Of The Blues Volume Four* (Sonet 1972)★★★.

Young, Amita Tata

b. *c*.1980, Thailand. Born to American parents, Amita Tata Young symbolizes the new wave of Thai pop idols, with her urban dress and confident, irreverent attitude. She was first spotted after winning the international division of the country's premier singing contest in 1994. Since launching her professional career the following year she has helped her label to solidify its grip on the Thai pop market, selling over 1 million cassette copies of her self-titled debut album. When it reached the 1 million sales mark, Grammy reissued it with the inclusion of a new track, 'I Love You', ensuring a further million sales.

●ALBUMS: *Amita Tata Young* (Grammy 1996)★★★★.

Young, Barry

Little is known about the background of Barry Young. He was a singer specializing in impersonations of crooner **Dean Martin** when he was signed to **Dot Records** in 1966. Young recorded an old country standard, 'One Has My Name (The Other Has My Heart)', written in 1948 by Eddie Dean, Dearest Dean and Hal Blair. Young's version made it to number 13 on the US pop charts. None of Young's later singles for **Dot** or other labels ever charted, although the album containing his one hit did make a showing. Young's subsequent whereabouts is as much of a mystery as his past.

● ALBUMS: *One Has My Name* (Dot 1966)★★★.

Young, Claude

DJ and founder of Utensil Records, Claude Young is a rarity in the Detroit dance scene in that his releases do not fit neatly under the 'techno' banner. Attempting to escape the bitter urban desolation and drugs culture of the city, Young invested his time in music, but of a more soulful hue than his neighbours. Working first at radio station WHYT, he eventually ran his own two-hour show, before putting together his first musical ideas. The record to launch him was the *One Complete Revolution* EP. Proving popular in the UK, this afforded him invitations to London clubs like Rotary and Quirky, before co-opted releases on **D-Jax Up Beats** and Christian Vogel's Mosquito label. In 1994 he announced plans to set up a further, UK-based label, Frictional.

Young, Ed And Lonnie

Brothers Ed (b. *c*.1908, Como, Mississippi, USA, d. 17 July 1974, Como, Mississippi, USA) and Lonnie Young were discovered during folklore research in 1959. They were neither the first nor the finest of the Como fife and drum musicians to be recorded, but they were the first to show the increased Africanism (especially syncopation) and improvisation of the music played by the generation after **Sid Hemphill**, and the first to be brought to wider notice, playing the Newport Folk Festival and having their recordings issued on album.

● ALBUMS: *Sounds Of The South* (1960)★★★, *Roots Of The Blues* (1961)★★★, *Blues Roll On* (1961)★★.

Young, Ernie

Based in Nashville, USA, Young was a jukebox operator, record retailer and disc jockey. A move into production was therefore logical, given his access to retail outlets. Nashboro was founded in 1951 to record gospel, and Excello in 1952. Using the band led by Skippy Brooks for backing, Excello recorded many local blues artists, while Nashboro acquired a distinguished roster, including Edna Gallmon Cooke, Morgan Babb, the Consolers and the Swanee Quintet. Although there was occasional national chart success, Excello's predominant market was in the south. In 1955, Young finalized an agreement with **Jay Miller** whereby Miller recorded blues in his Crowley studio for Excello. A steady stream of classics was released, Excello's greatest chart success being **Slim Harpo**. In 1966, due to his age and ill health, Young sold the label and retired.

Young, Faron

b. 25 February 1932, Shreveport, Louisiana, USA, d. 10 December 1996, Nashville, Tennessee, USA. Young was raised on the farm his father bought just outside Shreveport and learned to play the guitar and sing country songs as a boy. Greatly influenced by **Hank Williams** (in his early days he was something of a soundalike) and while still at school, he formed a country band and began to establish a local reputation as an entertainer. In 1950, he gave up his college studies to accept an offer of a professional career and joined radio station KWKH, where he soon became a member of the prestigious *Louisiana Hayride* show and found other work in the nightclubs and honky tonks. He became friends with **Webb Pierce** and for a time toured with him as a vocalist with Pierce's band. In 1951, he made his first recordings for the Gotham label with Tillman Franks and his band, and achieved minor success with 'Have I Waited Too Long' and 'Tattle Tale Eyes' before he joined **Capitol Records**. In the summer of 1952, Faron was dating a girl called Billie Jean Jones, when she attracted the attention of Hank Williams. He persuaded Faron to arrange a double date, which resulted in Williams threatening him with a pistol and claiming Jones for himself. Young backed off and Billie Jean became the second Mrs. Hank Williams. In 1953, Young formed his own band, moved to Nashville, where he became a member of the *Grand Ole Opry* and gained his first US country chart hit with a self-penned song called 'Goin' Steady'. His career was interrupted when, because of the Korean War, he was drafted into the army. Although interrupted by this, his career certainly benefited from the exposure he received after winning an army talent competition. This led to him touring the world entertaining US forces, as well as appearing on recruiting shows that were networked to hundreds of radio stations. Young returned to Nashville in November 1954 and resumed his career, gaining his first US country number 1 the following year with 'Live Fast, Love Hard, Die Young'. This established him beyond any doubt as a major recording star, and between 1955 and 1969 he amassed a total of 63 US country chart hits, of which 46 made the Top 20. He developed the knack of picking the best material by other writers and had a number 2 hit with **Don Gibson**'s 'Sweet Dreams' and further number 1s with **Roy Drusky**'s songs 'Alone With You' and 'Country Girl'. In 1961, he recorded 'Hello Walls', thereby making the song one of the first **Willie Nelson** compositions to be recorded by a major artist. It reached number 1 in the US country charts, also became a Top 20 US pop hit and was Young's first million-seller.

In 1956, his popularity as a singer earned him a role in the film *Hidden Guns*. This led to his own nickname of The Young Sheriff and his band being called the Country Deputies (at one time **Roger Miller** was a member of the band). In later years he became the Singing Sheriff before, as he once suggested, someone queried his age and started asking 'What's he trying to prove?' After the initial success with this easily forgettable B-movie western, he made further film appearances over the years including *Daniel Boone, Stampede, Raiders Of Old California, Country Music Holiday, A Gun And A Gavel, Road To Nashville* and *That's Country*. He left Capitol for **Mercury** in 1962, immediately charting with 'The Yellow Bandanna', 'You'll Drive Me Back' and a fine duet recording with Margie Singleton of 'Keeping Up With The Joneses'. In 1965, he had a US country Top 10 hit with 'Walk Tall', a song that had been a UK pop hit for **Val Doonican** the previous year. Young quit the *Opry* in the mid-60s, finding, like several other artists, that it was not only difficult keeping up the expected number of Saturday night appearances but also that he lost many other lucrative bookings. After the success of 'Hello Walls', he perhaps unintentionally tended to look for further pop chart hits, and in consequence, his recordings, at times, became less countrified in their arrangements. He soon returned to his country roots, usually choosing his favourite twin fiddle backings. Young easily maintained his popularity throughout the 60s and 70s and toured extensively in the USA and made several visits to Europe, where he performed in the UK, France and Germany. He appeared on all the major network television shows but seemed to have little interest in having his own regular series. At times he has not endeared himself to some of his fellow performers with his imitations of their acts. In the 70s he was still a major star, with a series of Top 10 US country hits including 'Step Aside', 'Leavin' And Saying Goodbye', 'This Little Girl Of Mine' and 'Just What I Had In Mind'. 'It's Four In The Morning', another country number 1, had crossover success and also gave him a second million-seller. It also became his only UK pop chart success, peaking at number 3 during a 23-week chart run. He left Mercury Records in 1979 and briefly joined MCA. In 1988, he joined Step One Records and 'Stop And Take The Time', a minor hit, became country chart entry number 85. Over the years, he became involved in several business interests and, with the exception of heavy losses in the 60s (in respect of investments to convert an old baseball stadium into a stock-car racing track in Nashville), he was very successful. Young became involved in publishing companies, a recording studio, and a booking agency, plus co-ownership of *Music City News* newspaper. He was always noted for very plain speaking and has incurred the wrath of the establishment on several occasions for his outspoken views. A suggested association with **Patsy Cline** led to various stories of his dalliances and whether correct or not, it may well be that he revelled in the publicity they caused. In September 1972, he gained unwanted publicity by his reaction to an incident at a show. At a time when 'This Little Girl Of Mine' was a hit for him, he invited six-year-old Nora Jo Catlett to join him on stage in Clarksville, West Virginia. She refused, whereupon Young swore at the audience, stormed off stage, grabbed the child and spanked her repeatedly (the child collected autographs and had been told by her mother not to approach the stage but to wait near the front until Young finished his act). The child's father swore out a warrant for his arrest and after pleading guilty to a charge of assault, he was fined $35. The following year a civil action claiming $200,000 was filed. In his defence, Young claimed the child spat in his face. Eventually, almost two years later, the Catlett family were awarded only $3400. He has been involved in various actions, once stating, 'I am not an alcoholic, I'm a drunk', and on one occasion, he shot out the light fittings of a Nashville bar. He is reputed to have had affairs with many women while supposedly remaining happily married. In 1987, after 34 years of marriage, his wife finally obtained a divorce on the grounds of physical abuse. She claimed that he had also threatened her and their 16-year-old daughter with a gun and often shot holes in the kitchen ceiling. A fair and concise summary was offered in 1980 by Bob Allen, who parodied Young's hit song in his article entitled 'Live Fast, Love Hard And Keep On Cussin'. Faron Young is one of country music's greatest legends, while remaining relatively unknown to many. Paddy MacAloon of **Prefab Sprout** paid tribute to him when he wrote the beautiful 'Faron Young' on the group's *Steve McQueen* album. Until his death in 1996 he was semi-retired but still made concert performances as well as guest appearances on the *Opry*.

● ALBUMS: *Sweethearts Or Strangers* (Capitol 1957)★★★, *The Object Of My Affection* (Capitol 1958)★★★, *My Garden Of Prayer* (Capitol 1959)★★, *This Is Faron Young* (Capitol 1959)★★★★, *Talk About Hits* (Capitol 1959)★★★, *Sings The Best Of Faron Young* (Capitol 1960)★★★, *Hello Walls* (Capitol 1961)★★★, *The Young Approach* (Capitol 1961)★★★, *This Is Faron* (Mercury 1963)★★★★, *Faron Young Aims At The West* (Mercury 1963)★★★, *Country Dance Favorites* (Mercury 1964)★★★★, *Story Songs For Country Folks* (Mercury 1964)★★★★, *Story Songs Of Mountains And Valleys* (Mercury 1964)★★★★, *Memory Lane* (Capitol 1965)★★★, *Falling In Love* (Capitol 1965)★★★, *Pen And Paper* (Mercury 1965)★★★, *Faron Young* (Hilltop 1966)★★★, *Faron Young Sings The Best Of Jim Reeves* (Mercury 1966)★★★, *If You Ain't Lovin', You Ain't Livin'* (Capitol 1966)★★★, *It's A Great Life* (Tower 1966)★★★, *Unmitigated Gall* (Mercury 1967)★★★, *Here's Faron Young* (Mercury 1968)★★★, *I'll Be Yours* (Hilltop 1968)★★★★, *This Is Faron Young* (Merc ury 1968)★★★, *Just Out Of Reach* (Mercury 1968)★★★, *The World Of Faron Young* (Mercury 1968)★★★★, *I've Got Precious Memories* (Mercury 1969)★★★, *Wine Me Up* (Mercury 1969)★★★★, *20 Hits Over The Years* (Mercury 1969)★★★★, *Occasional Wife/If I Ever Fall In Love With A Honky Tonk Girl* (Mercury 1970)★★★, *Leavin' And Sayin' Goodbye* (Mercury 1971)★★★, *Step Aside* (Mercury 1971)★★★, *It's Four In The Morning* (Mercury 1972)★★★, *This Little Girl Of Mine* (Mercury 1972)★★★, *This Time The*

Hurtin's On Me (Mercury 1973)★★★, *Just What I Had In Mind* (Mercury 1973)★★★, *Some Kind Of Woman* (Mercury 1974)★★★, *A Man And His Music* (Mercury 1975)★★★★, *I'd Just Be Fool Enough* (Mercury 1976)★★★, *That Young Feelin'* (Mercury 1977)★★★, *Chapter Two* (1979)★★★, *Free And Easy* (MCA 1980)★★★, *The Young Sheriff (1955-1956 Radio Broadcasts)* (1981)★★★★, *The Sheriff* (Allegiance 1984)★★, with Jerry Lee Lewis, Webb Pierce, Mel Tillis *Four Legends* (1985)★★★, *Here's To You* (Step One 1988)★★★, *Country Christmas* (1990)★★, with Ray Price *Memories That Last* (1992)★★★.

● COMPILATIONS: *All-Time Great Hits* (Capitol 1963)★★★★, *Capitol Country Classics* (Capitol 1980)★★★, *Greatest Hits Volumes 1, 2 & 3* (1988)★★★★, *All Time Greatest Hits* (Curb 1990)★★★, *The Capitol Years 1952 - 1962* 5-CD box set (Bear Family 1992)★★★★, *Live Fast, Love Hard: Original Capitol Recordings, 1952-1962* (CMF 1995)★★★★, *All American Country* (Spectrum 1997)★★★★.

Young, Irma

b. *c.*1913, Thebedux, Louisiana, USA. Born into a highly musical family, she was encouraged to play the alto saxophone and joined the family band which was led by her father, W.H. Young, and which included her younger brother, **Lee Young**, on drums, and her older brother, **Lester Young**, on tenor saxophone. Her mother also played in the outfit, as did several cousins, and **Ben Webster** is reputed to have played piano with the band for a time. According to **Paul Quinchette**, himself a devoted admirer of Lester Young, Irma Young was an exceptionally fine musician and would happily jam with her brother and other jazzmen. In addition to the alto, she also played baritone and soprano saxophones. However, her preference was for none of these instruments and in the 30s she gave them all up to concentrate on dancing. Thereafter, she worked as a dancer and occasional singer until her retirement in the mid-50s. She was still living in California in the early 80s. Her daughter, Martha Young, is a professional pianist.

Young, Jesse Colin

b. Perry Miller, 11 November 1944, Manhattan, New York City, USA. One of several optimistic performers frequenting the Greenwich Village folk circuit, Young was discovered in 1963 at the renowned Gerde's Folk City club. His debut *Soul Of A City Boy*, was recorded in one four-hour session, but despite its rudimentary quality, the collection showcased the singer's haunting tenor voice and compositional skills. A second set was equally enthralling, and featured excellent assistance from **John Sebastian** (harmonica) and Pete Childs (dobro). Its title, *Young Blood*, also provided a name for the rock group Jesse subsequently founded. The **Youngbloods**' career spanned six years but ended in 1972 when the members' interests became too diverse to remain in one ensemble. Jesse had already resumed his solo career with *Together*, a selection of new material and traditional songs, but his independence was more fully asserted on 1974's *Song For Juli*. The light, intimate style of these early releases was continued on subsequent recordings. Jesse rekindled memories of his erstwhile companions by re-recording two Youngbloods favourites, 'Sugar Babe' and 'Josianne' on his 1975 album, *Songbird*, but maintained a contemporary edge with two excellent selections, *American Dreams* and *Perfect Stranger*. The latter set included 'Fight For It', a notable duet with **Carly Simon**. Angered at what he perceived as mismanagement, Young later purchased the album's master tape for re-release on an independent label, and has since avoided recording for major companies.

● ALBUMS: *The Soul Of A City Boy* (Capitol 1964)★★, *Young Blood* (Mercury 1965)★★, *Together* (Raccoon 1972)★★, *Song For Juli* (Warners 1973)★★, *Lightshine* (Warners 1974)★★, *Songbird* (Warners 1975)★★, *On The Road* (Warners 1976)★★, *Love On The Wing* (Warners 1977)★★, *American Dreams* (Elektra 1978)★★, *Perfect Stranger* (Elektra 1982)★★, *The Highway Is For Heroes* (Cypress 1988)★★.

● COMPILATIONS: *The Best Of Jesse Colin Young: The Solo Years* (Rhino 1991)★★★, *Greatest Hits* (Edsel 1998)★★★.

Young, Jimmy

b. Leslie Ronald Young, 21 September 1923, Cinderford, Gloucestershire, England. A popular ballad singer in the UK during the 50s, Young carved out a new career for himself in broadcasting when rock 'n' roll took over in the latter part of the decade. The son of a miner, he was an excellent boxer and rugby player, but turned down an offer of a professional career with top rugby league club Wigan. Always keen on music, he was taught to play the piano by his mother, and received professional voice training. He worked as a baker and an electrician before joining the Royal Air Force in 1939. After demobilization he intended to train as a teacher, but was spotted, singing at a sports club, by BBC producer George Innes. He made his first broadcast two weeks later, and subsequently toured the UK variety circuit. From 1951 he had several successful records on the small Polygon label, including 'My Love And Devotion', 'Because Of You' and 'Too Young'. In January 1953, two months after the first UK singles chart appeared in the *New Musical Express*, Young had a hit with 'Faith Can Move Mountains' for his new label, **Decca**, and followed that with 'Eternally (Terry's Theme)', from the Charles Chaplin film *Limelight*. In 1955, Young became the first UK artist to top the *NME* chart with successive releases. The first, 'Unchained Melody', made the top spot in spite of intense competition from **Al Hibbler**, **Les Baxter** and **Liberace**. The second, the title song from the movie *The Man From Laramie*, and another 1955 hit, 'Someone On My Mind', clinched Young's position as the UK's second biggest-selling artist of the year - after **Ruby Murray**. Following further 50s hits, including 'Chain Gang', 'The Wayward Wind', 'Rich Man Poor Man', 'More' and 'Round And Round', Young switched to **EMI**'s Columbia label in the early 60s, and had some success

with a recording of Charles and Henry **Tobias**'s 1929 song 'Miss You', and a re-recording of 'Unchained Melody'. In 1960, he introduced BBC Radio's popular record request programme, *Housewives' Choice*, for two weeks. It was the start of a new career that has lasted more than 30 years, initially as a conventional disc jockey and compere, and then, from 1967, as host of his own daily BBC morning radio show. This mixes records with consumer information, discussions on current affairs, and talks with figures in the public eye. He has interviewed every Chancellor and Prime Minister since 1963. For his radio work on the programme, he was awarded the OBE, and later, the CBE. In 1992, for *The Jimmy Young Story*, a silver anniversary celebration of his radio show, Young was interviewed by another distinguished broadcaster, David Frost.

● ALBUMS: *T.T.T.J.Y.S.* (Polydor 1974)★★★, *Too Young* (PRT 1981)★★★, *The Ballymena Cowboy* (1987)★★★.

● COMPILATIONS: *The World Of Jimmy Young* (Decca 1969)★★★★, *This Is Jimmy Young* (EMI 1980)★★★, *What A Wonderful World* (Flashback 1985)★★★.

● FURTHER READING: *J.Y.: The Autobiography Of Jimmy Young*, Jimmy.Young.

Young, Joe

b. 4 July 1889, New York, USA, d. 21 April 1939, New York, USA. A prolific lyricist from 1911 through to the late 30s, Young wrote many of the most memorable, singable and peppy numbers of the day, along with a number of schmaltzy ballads. Early in his career he worked as a singer, and a songplugger for music publishers, before entertaining the troops in World War I. His early songs included 'Don't Blame It All On Broadway', 'When The Angelus Was Ringing', and 'Yaaka Hula Hickey Dula'. The latter was written with Pete Wendling and Ray Goetz for **Al Jolson** to sing in *Robinson Crusoe Jnr* (1916). For the same show, Young collaborated with lyricist **Sam M. Lewis** and composer **George Meyer** on 'Where Did Robinson Crusoe Go With Friday On Saturday Night?'. The Young-Lewis lyric partnership continued for 14 years, with songs such as 'If I Knock The 'L' Out Of Kelly' (*Step This Way*), 'Arrah Go On, I'm Gonna Go Back To Oregon', 'Rock-A-Bye-Your-Baby With A Dixie Melody' (with Jean Schwartz) and 'My Mammy' (with **Walter Donaldson** for *Sinbad*), 'Just A Baby's Prayer At Twilight', 'How Ya Gonna Keep 'Em Down On The Farm?' (Donaldson), 'I'd Love To Fall Asleep, And Wake Up In My Mammy's Arms', 'Dinah' (with Harry Akst for *Kid Boots*), 'Five Foot Two, Eyes Of Blue' and 'I'm Sitting On Top Of The World' (both with **Ray Henderson**), 'In A Little Spanish Town', 'Laugh, Clown Laugh', 'King For A Day', 'I Kiss Your Hand, Madame', and 'Then You've Never Been Blue'.

In 1930, Young and Lewis combined with **Harry Warren** on one of their last projects together, the early talkie, *Spring Is Here*, which included 'Cryin' For The Carolines', 'Have A Little Faith In Me', 'Bad Baby' and

'How Shall I Tell?'. The final Young-Lewis song appears to be 'Absence Makes The Heart Grow Fonder'. In 1931, Young worked with lyricist **Mort Dixon** and Warren on 'You're My Everything', 'Ooh! That Kiss', 'Love Me Forever', and 'The Torch Song' for Ed Wynn's Broadway show, *The Laugh Parade*. From then on, during the 30s, he mostly wrote his own lyrics for songs such as 'Can't Get Mississippi Off My Mind', 'I'm Alone Because I Love You', 'In A Shanty In Old Shanty Town' (with John Siras, from the movie *The Crooner*), 'The Lady I Love', 'Lullaby Of The Leaves' (with Bernice Petkere), 'Snuggled On Your Shoulder' (with Carmen Lombardo), 'Was That The Human Thing To Do?', 'Something In The Night', 'Annie Doesn't Live Here Anymore', 'I'm Growing Fonder Of You', 'I'm Gonna Sit Right Down And Write Myself A Letter' (with **Fred Ahlert**); 'You're A Heavenly Thing', 'Sing An Old Fashioned Song', 'Dancing With You' and many more. Among his other collaborators were **Ted Fio Rito**, Ted Snyder, **Fred Ahlert**, **Victor Young**, **George W. Meyer**, **Oscar Levant**, **J. Fred Coots**, and Harry Akst.

Young, John Paul

b. 21 June 1950, Glasgow, Scotland. After fronting early 70s Sydney band, Elm Tree, former sheet metal worker Young spent the next two years in the Australian version of the stage show *Jesus Christ Superstar*. He had a hit with **Vanda And Young**'s 'Pasadena' in 1972. Two unsuccessful singles followed and then he teamed up with Vanda And Young again in 1975 for 'Yesterday's Hero' which started a run of eight Australian Top 20 singles and two Top 20 albums, mostly songs written by Vanda And Young. Some of his singles also charted in Europe and South Africa, where he performed a number of times. He formed a touring band called the All Stars, an appropriate name as members included **Kevin Borich**, Ray Goodwin (ex-**Dragon**), Johnny Dick and Warren Morgan (ex-**Aztecs**), Ian Winter (ex-**Daddy Cool**), **Phil Manning**, Tony Mitchell (ex-**Sherbet**), Ray Arnott (ex-**Dingoes**) and Vince Maloney (ex-**Bee Gees**). A happy-go-lucky artist, Young was seen to be somewhat apathetic about furthering his career. A last album, recorded on a German label IC with new writers and producers, ended his career, but Young retired gracefully and now works as a disc jockey.

● ALBUMS: *Hero* (1975)★★★, *JPY* (Midsong International 1976)★★★, *Green* (1977)★★, *Love Is In The Air* (Scotti Bros 1978)★★, *Heaven Sent* (1979)★★, *The Singer* (1981)★★, *One Foot In Front* (IC 1983)★★.
● COMPILATIONS: *All The Best* (1977)★★★, *1974-1979* (1979)★★★.

Young, Johnny (Australia)

b. John De Jong, 12 March 1945, Indonesia. In the state of Western Australia, Young became popular at Perth dances as a singer fronting his band the Kompany, which led to regular work on the local television network. Moving to east Australia, he became host of a national television pop programme which encouraged his record sales. He wrote songs for other artists such as **Russell Morris**, Ronnie Burns and Ross D. Wylie. A move to England in 1967 meant he lost his foothold in Australia, and unfortunately he did not emulate his success in England, despite recording a **Bee Gees** song. Upon his return he worked as a radio disc jockey until forming a television production company in 1970, in which he hosted a children's music show *Young Talent Time* for nearly 20 years. Unfortunately his earlier career as a writer of good pop songs was forgotten by this stage.

● ALBUMS: *Young's Golden LP* (1966)★★★, *It's A Wonderful World* (1968)★★, *Surprises* (1968)★★★, *A Young Man And His Music* (1971)★★★, *A Musical Portrait* (1973)★★★, *Mother Favourites, All My Loving* (1978)★★.

Young, Johnny (USA)

b. 1 January 1918, Vicksburg, Mississippi, USA, d. 18 April 1974, Chicago, Illinois, USA. Although he was a more than competent guitarist, Young regarded the mandolin as his main instrument. He learned both instruments, as well as harmonica, from uncle Anthony Williams, while living with him in Rolling Fork, birthplace of **Muddy Waters**. When he returned to Vicksburg, he played house parties with cousin Henry Williams, influenced by the records of **Charlie McCoy** and the **Mississippi Sheiks**. He also claimed to have worked with **Robert Nighthawk** and **Sleepy John Estes** before moving to Chicago in 1940. He joined the musicians who frequented the Maxwell Street market area, with **Floyd Jones**, **Snooky Pryor** and another cousin, **Johnny Williams**. In 1947 he made his first record, 'Money Takin' Woman', with Williams, for Ora Nelle, run by Maxwell Radio Shop owner Bernard Abrams. A year later, with Williams and Pryor, he recorded 'My Baby Walked Out' and 'Let Me Ride Your Mule' for Planet, as Man Young. Apart from two unissued songs for JOB, Young did not record again until the 60s, when he taped a number of sessions for Testament, **Arhoolie**, **Vanguard**, Milestone, Blues On Blues, Bluesway and **Blue Horizon**, in the company of artists such as **Otis Spann**, **Walter Horton**, **Little Walter** and **James Cotton**. From 1969 until his death, he was a member of the Bob Riedy Chicago Blues Band. In 1972 he toured Europe as a part of the American Folk Blues Festival.

● ALBUMS: *Johnny Young & His Chicago Blues Band* (Arhoolie 1965)★★★, *Fat Mandolin* (1969)★★★, *Chicago Boogie!* (1974)★★★, *Chicago Blues* (1993)★★★, *Johnny Young And Friends* (Testament 1994)★★★.

Young, Karen

b. 1946, Sheffield, England. After working in a record shop as a teenager, Young became interested in the local group scene and joined the Counterbeats in 1964. By the late 60s she had branched out as a soloist and following an appearance at a northern club was spotted

by the **Bachelors** who duly introduced her to their managers Dorothy and **Phil Solomon**. In 1969 she registered a Top 10 hit with the Scottish folk standard 'Nobody's Child' but failed to follow up with the **Jo Stafford/Lita Roza** hit 'Allentown Jail'. Thereafter she returned to the cabaret circuit, but before she left the pop pantheon, Karen's only hit became the subject of heated correspondence in the pop weeklies. Noting the radio/television ban on **Jane Birkin/Serge Gainsbourg**'s 'Je T' Aime . . . Moi Non Plus' (also on Solomon's Major Minor label), one reader exclaimed: 'Apparently the BBC thinks it is more beneficial for her audience to hear a hit song about a blind orphan, unfortunately sung in English, than a French song about love'.
● ALBUMS: *Nobody's Child And 13 Other Great Songs* (Major Minor 1969)★★.

Young, Kathy

b. 21 October 1945, Santa Ana, California, USA. After hearing her distinctive childlike voice, top entertainer **Wink Martindale** suggested 14-year-old Kathy should try to get a deal with Los Angeles-based Indigo Records. Her first recording was a revival of Gene Pearson And The Revileers doo-wop hit 'A Thousand Stars', and it climbed to number 3 in the US in 1960, and made the R&B Top 10. She was backed on the record by the California-based smooth harmony trio the **Innocents** and together they chalked up a further two US hits 'Happy Birthday Blues' and 'Magic Is The Night', before Kathy turned sweet 16. After a few unsuccessful singles she joined her manager Jim Lee's Monogram label in 1962, but her records both as a soloist and with **Chris Montez** failed to rekindle the public's interest. She later recorded on Starfire and married John Maus of the **Walker Brothers**.

Young, Kenny

Young first drew attention in New York's song publishing fraternity as the co-author of 'Under The Boardwalk', a 1964 hit for the **Drifters**, later popularized by the **Rolling Stones**. His next major success was 'Captain Of Your Ship', recorded in 1968 by **Reparata And The Delrons**. Although unsuccessful in the USA, the song reached number 13 in the UK. In keeping with several contemporaries, including **Carole King** and **Chip Taylor**, Young subsequently began a recording career, but his engaging singer-songwriter releases were commercially unsuccessful. He moved to London during the 70s and later formed a partnership with Herbie Armstrong. The pair formed **Fox**, who scored a Top 5 hit with 'Only You Can' (1975), and **Yellow Dog**, which reached number 8 with 'Just One More Night' (1978). However, Young's unashamedly commercial style later fell from favour and he later withdrew from performing.
● ALBUMS: *Clever Dogs Chase The Sun* (Warners 1972)★★★, *Last Stage For Silverwood* (Warners 1973)★★★.

Young, La Monte

b. 1935, USA. A composer since the mid-50s, although primarily considered within the contemporary classical sphere, Young is well known within popular music for his work with **John Cale**, who appeared in his Theatre Of Eternal Music band before joining **Velvet Underground**. He was also acknowledged by **Lou Reed** on the sleevenotes to *Metal Machine Music* as a major influence. Theatre Of Eternal Music also included other collaborators such as his wife Marian Zazeela, **Terry Riley**, jazz saxophonist **Lee Konitz**, **Andy Warhol** associate Billy Linich and **Jon Hassell**. Though his output has been sporadic, Young's experiments with 'overtones', or the range of frequencies that make up individual notes, has been acknowledged by artists as diverse as **Sonic Youth**, **Spacemen 3**, the **Orb** and the **Future Sound Of London**. Since the early 60s he has pioneered minimalist expression in his work, composing much of his work in a New York loft to the sound of a sine-wave generator to engender a 'drone' mentality. Little of his work with Theatre Of Eternal Music was ever officially released due to his well-publicized perfectionism, but he was persuaded to issue a portion of his monolithic 'life work', *The Well-Tuned Piano*, in 1987. This employed his self-customised Bosendorfer grand piano. Over five albums it expresses perfectly the linear manifesto he previously related in his 'Composition 1960 No. 10' - 'Draw a straight line and follow it'. Previous releases had included two albums recorded with his wife (with contributions from Theatre Of Eternal Music). In 1992 he founded a travelling 'rock orchestra', the Forever Bad Blues Band, whose *Just Stompin' Live At The Kitchen* is easily Young's most accessible recording.
●ALBUMS: with Marian Zazeela *The Black Record* (WG 1969)★★★★, with Zazeela *Dream House 78'17'* (Shandar 1974)★★★, *The Well-Tuned Piano* quintuple album (Gramavision 1987)★★★★, *The Melodic Version Of The Second Dream Of The High-Tension Line Stepdown Transformer From The Four Dreams Of China* (Gramavision 1991)★★★, *The Forever Bad Blues Band: Just Stompin': Live At The Kitchen* (Gramavision 1993)★★★.

Young, Larry

b. 7 October 1940, Newark, New Jersey, USA, d. 30 March 1978. His father was an organ player but at first Young played piano instead. In 1957 he joined an R&B group in Elizabeth, New Jersey and, switching to Hammond organ, recorded with tenor saxophonist **Jimmy Forrest** in 1961. In 1962 he made his vinyl debut as leader with *Groove Street*. He procured the services of top guitarist **Grant Green** and, signed to **Blue Note**, made classic records with artists such as **Joe Henderson**, **Woody Shaw**, **Donald Byrd** and **Lee Morgan**. In 1964 he visited Europe, playing piano on **Nathan Davis**'s *Happy Girl*. Affected by **John Coltrane**'s expansion of hard bop, he recorded with Coltrane and inducted drummer **Elvin Jones** into his band, recording *Unity* with him in 1965. He played electric piano on **Miles Davis**'s *Bitches Brew* in 1970, the album which launched the jazz rock genre, worked briefly with **John McLaughlin** in 1970 and then played in Lifetime, the band run by drummer **Anthony Williams**. His own *Lawrence Of Newark* featured **James 'Blood' Ulmer**, making one of his earlier appearances on record. In 1977 Young co-led a group with drummer **Joe Chambers**, recording *Double Exposure*. Young also worked under his Islamic name of Khalid Yasin. His death at the age of 38 deprived the world of an innovative and passionate player.

● ALBUMS: *Testifying* (Original Jazz Classics 1961)★★★, *Young Blues* (Original jazz Classics 1961)★★★, *Groove Street* (1962)★★★, *Into Somethin'*, (1965)★★★, *Contrasts* (1965)★★★, *Unity* (Blue Note 1966)★★★★, *Lawrence Of Newark* (1973)★★, *Spaceball* (1975)★★, with Joe Chambers *Double Exposure* (1977)★★.

●COMPILATIONS: *The Art Of Larry Young* (Blue Note 1990)★★★★.

Young, Lee

b. 7 March 1917, New Orleans, Louisiana, USA. Before settling on drums Young studied piano and various reed and brass instruments. As a child he played in the family band led by his father and which also included his brother **Lester Young**. In the early 30s he moved to Los Angeles, playing in a variety of musical settings with bands led by **Mutt Carey**, **Buck Clayton**, **Fats Waller** and others. He was one of the first black musicians to be hired on a regular basis for film studio work but continued to appear in jazz groups in the early 40s, including those led by **Lionel Hampton** and **Nat 'King' Cole**. Young also led his own small groups, one of which featured his brother, and he backed many leading artists including **Dinah Washington**. He was a regular with **Norman Granz**'s **Jazz At The Philharmonic** in the mid-40s and later in the decade he was with **Benny Goodman**. In the 50s, still working in the studios, he belatedly rejoined Cole. In the 60s he was active in record production, mostly as producer and administrator with **Vee Jay Records**, and in the late 70s was briefly with **Motown Records**. A solid player with a good sense of time, Young's career outside jazz, as both studio musician and record company executive, occupied the best of his years.

●ALBUMS: *Jazz At The Philhamonic 1944-1946* (1944-46)★★★, *Jazz At The Philharmonic 1946* (1946)★★★.

Young, Lester

b. 27 August 1909, Woodville, Mississippi, USA, d. 15 March 1959. Born into a musical family, Young was taught several instruments by his father. As a child he played drums in the family's band, but around 1928 he quit the group and switched to tenor saxophone. His first engagements on this instrument were with Art Bronson, in Phoenix, Arizona. He stayed with Bronson until 1930, with a brief side trip to play again with the family, then worked in and around Minneapolis, Minnesota, with various bands. In the spring of 1932 he joined the Original Blue Devils, under the leadership of **Walter Page**, and was one of several members of the band who joined **Bennie Moten** in Kansas City towards the end of 1933. During the next few years Young played in the bands of Moten, **George E. Lee**, **King Oliver**, **Count Basie**, **Fletcher Henderson**, **Andy Kirk** and others. In 1936 he rejoined Basie, with whom he remained for the next four years, touring, broadcasting and recording. He also recorded in small groups directed by **Teddy Wilson** and others and appeared on several classic record dates, backing **Billie Holiday**, with whom he forged a special and lasting relationship. (She nicknamed him 'Pres' or 'Prez', for president, while he bestowed on her the name 'Lady Day'.) In the early 40s he played in, and sometimes led, small groups in the Los Angeles area alongside his brother, **Lee Young**, and musicians such as **Red Callender**, **Nat 'King' Cole** and **Al Sears**. During this period he returned briefly to the Basie band, making some excellent recordings, and also worked with **Dizzy Gillespie**. Late in 1944 he was conscripted into the US Army but was discharged in mid-summer the following year, having spent part of his military service in hospital and part in an army prison. In the mid-40s he was filmed by Gjon Mili in the classic jazz short, *Jammin' The Blues*, a venture which was co-produced by **Norman Granz**. At this time he also joined Granz's **Jazz At The Philharmonic** package, remaining with the organization for a number of years. He also led small groups for club and record dates, toured the USA and visited Europe. From the mid-40s onwards Young's health was poor and in the late 50s his physical decline became swift. He continued to record and make concert and festival appearances and was featured on television's *The Sound Of Jazz* in 1957. In these final years his deteriorating health was exacerbated by a drinking problem, and some close observers suggest that towards the end he lost the will to live. He died on 15 March 1959.

One of the seminal figures in jazz history and a major influence in creating the musical atmosphere in which bop could flourish, Young's early and late career was beset by critical bewilderment. Only his middle period appears to have earned unreserved critical acclaim. In recent years, however, thanks in part to a more enlightened body of critical opinion, allied to perceptive biographies (by Dave Gelly and Lewis Porter), few observers now have anything other than praise for this remarkable artist's entire output. In the early 30s, when Young appeared on the wider jazz scene, the tenor saxophone was regarded as a forceful, barrel-toned, potentially dominating instrument. In the early years of jazz none of the saxophone family had met with favour and only the clarinet among the reed instruments maintained a front-line position. This position had been challenged, almost single-handedly, by **Coleman Hawkins**, who changed perceptions of the instrument and its role in jazz. Despite his authority, Hawkins failed to oust the trumpet from its dominating role. Nevertheless, his example spawned many imitators who attempted to replicate his rich and resonant sound. When Young appeared, favouring a light, acerbic, dry tone, he was in striking contrast to the majestic Hawkins, and many people, both musicians and audiences, disliked what they heard. Only the more perceptive listeners of the time, and especially younger musicians, heard in Young's floating melodic style a distinctive and revolutionary approach to jazz.

The solos he recorded with the Basie band included many which, for all their brevity - some no more than eight bars long - display an astonishing talent in full and magnificent flight. On his first record date, on 9 October 1936, made by a small group drawn from the Basie band under the name of Jones-Smith Inc., he plays with what appears at first hearing to be startling simplicity. Despite this impression, the performances, especially of 'Shoe Shine Swing' and 'Lady Be Good', are undisputed masterpieces seldom equalled, let alone bettered (perhaps not even by Young himself). He recorded many outstanding solos - with the full Basie band on 'Honeysuckle Rose', 'Taxi War Dance' and 'Every Tub'; with the small group, the Kansas City Seven, on 'Dickie's Dream' and 'Lester Leaps In'. On all of these recordings, Young's solos clearly indicate that, for all their emotional depths, a massive intellectual talent is at work. In 1940 he made some excellent records with a small band assembled under the nominal leadership of **Benny Goodman** which featured Basie, **Buck Clayton** and **Charlie Christian** and was clearly at ease in such illustrious company. His sessions with Billie Holiday belong to a higher level again. The empathy displayed by these two frequently-troubled people is always remarkable and at times magical. Almost any of their recordings would serve as an example, with 'Me, Myself And I', 'Mean To Me', 'When You're Smiling', 'Foolin' Myself' and 'This Year's Kisses' being particularly rewarding examples of their joint and separate artistry. Even late in their lives, after they had seen little of one another for several years (theirs was an extremely close although almost certainly platonic relationship), their appearance on the television show *The Sound Of Jazz* produced a moment of astonishing emotional impact. In a performance of 'Fine And Mellow', just after Holiday has sung, Young plays a brief solo of achingly fragile tenderness that is packed with more emotion than a million words could convey. After Young left the army his playing style was demonstrably different, a fact which led many to declare that his suffering at the hands of the military had broken his artistic will. While Young's time in the army was clearly unpleasant, and the life was something for which he was physically and psychologically unsuited, it seems unlikely that the changes in his playing were directly attributable to his army service. On numerous record dates he demonstrated that his talent was not damaged by his spell in the stockade. His playing had changed but the differences were almost certainly a result of changes in the man himself. He had matured, moved on, and his music had too. Those critics who like their

musicians to be trapped in amber were unprepared for the new Lester Young. Adding to the confusion was the fact that, apart from the faithful Hawkins-style devotees, most other tenor players in jazz were imitating the earlier Lester. His first recordings after leaving the army, which include 'DB Blues' and 'These Foolish Things', are not the work of a spent spirit but have all the elegance and style of a consummate master, comfortably at one with his world. A 1956 session with **Teddy Wilson**, on which Young is joined by **Roy Eldridge** and an old comrade from his Basie days, **Jo Jones**, is another striking example of a major figure who is still in full command of all his earlier powers; and a long-overlooked set of records made at about the same time with the Bill Potts Trio, a backing group that accompanied him during an engagement in a bar in Washington, DC, show him to be as musically alert and inventive as ever.

A withdrawn, moody figure with a dry and slightly anarchic sense of humour, Young perpetuated his own mythology during his lifetime, partly through a personal use of words which he developed into a language of his own (among other things he coined the use of 'bread' to denote money). His stoicism and a marked preference for his own company - or, at best, for a favoured few who shared his mistrustful view of life - set him apart even from the jazz musicians who admired and sometimes revered him. It is impossible to overstate Young's importance in the development of jazz. From the standpoint of the 90s, when the tenor saxophone is the dominant instrument in jazz, it is easy to imagine that this is the way it always was. That the tenor has come to hold the place it does is largely a result of Young's influence, which inspired so many young musicians to adopt the instrument or to turn those who already played it into new directions. Most of the developments in bop and post-bop owe their fundamentals to Young's concern for melody and the smooth, flowing lines with which he transposed his complex musical thoughts into beautiful, articulate sounds. Although other important tenor saxophonists have come, and in some cases gone, during the three decades since Lester Young died, few have had the impact of this unusual, introspective, sensitive and musically profound genius of jazz.

●ALBUMS: with Count Basie *Lester Young Quartet And Count Basie Seven* 10-inch album (Mercury 1950)★★★, *Lester Young* (Savoy 1951)★★★★, *The Lester Young Trio* (Mercury 1951)★★★★ *Lester Young Collates* (Mercury 1951)★★★, *Lester Young And The Piano Giants* (Verve 1950-56)★★★★, *Lester Young With The Oscar Peterson Trio* (1952)★★★, *Kansas City Style* (Commodore 1952)★★★, *Lester Young With The Oscar Peterson Quintet Vols 1 & 2* (1953)★★★★, with Illinois Jacquet *Battle Of The Saxes* (Aladdin 1953)★★★, *Lester Young Collates Vol 2* (Mercury 1953)★★★, *Lester Young - His Tenor Sax* (Aladdin 1953)★★★, *The Lester Young Trio ii* (Clef 1953)★★★★, *The President Plays* (Verve 1953)★★★★ *It Don't Mean A Thing* (1954)★★★★, *Lester Young With The Oscar Peterson Trio i* (Norgran 1954)★★★, *Lester Young With*

The Oscar Peterson Trio ii (Norgran 1954)★★★, with Paul Quinichette *Pres Meets Vice-Pres* (EmArcy 1954)★★★, *The President* (Norgran 1954)★★★★, with Harry Edison *Pres And Sweets* (Norgran 1955)★★★, *Lester Young* ii (Norgran 1955)★★★, *The President Plays With The Oscar Peterson Trio* (Norgran 1955)★★★, with Chu Berry *Tops On Tenor* (Jazztone 1956)★★★, *The Jazz Giants '56* (1956)★★★, *Lester Young And His Tenor Sax Vol 1* (Aladdin 1956)★★★★, *Lester Young And His Tenor Sax Vol 2* (Aladdin 1956)★★★★, *Lester Meets Miles, MJQ And The Jack Teagarden All Stars* (1956)★★★, *The Masters Touch* (Savoy 1956)★★★, *Pres In Europe* (1956)★★, *Lester Young In Washington DC Vols 1-4* (1956)★★★, with Teddy Wilson *Pres And Teddy* (Verve 1956)★★★★, *Pres Vols 1-4* (1956)★★★★, with others *The Sound Of Jazz* (1957)★★★, *Swingin' Lester Young* (Intro 1957)★★★, *The Greatest* (Intro 1957)★★★, *The Real Sound Of Jazz* (1957)★★★★★, *Laughin' To Keep From Cryin'* (1958)★★★★, with Roy Eldridge and Harry Edison *Going For Myself* (Verve 1959)★★★, with Roy Eldridge and Harry Edison *Laughin' To Keep From Cryin'* (Verve 1959)★★★, *Lester Young In Paris* (Verve 1959)★★, *In Memoriam* (1959)★★★★, *Lester Young Memorial Album* (Epic 1959)★★★★, *Lester Warms Up - Jazz Immortals Vol 2* (Savoy 1961)★★★, *Pres* (Charlie Parker 1961)★★★, *Pres Is Blue* (Charlie Parker 1961)★★★, *The Immortal Lester Young Vol 1* (Imperial 1962)★★★★, *The Immortal Lester Young Vol 2* (Imperial 1962)★★★, *The Influence Of Five* (Mainstream 1965)★★★, *Town Hall Concert* (Mainstream 1965)★★★, *Chairman Of The Board* (Mainstream 1965)★★★, *52nd Street* (Mainstream 1965)★★★, *Prez* (Mainstream 1965)★★★, *Pres And His Cabinet* (Verve 1966)★★★.

●COMPILATIONS: *Lester-Amadeus* (1936-38)★★★, with Count Basie, Billie Holiday *The Lester Young Story Vols 1-9* (1936-39)★★★★★, *The Alternative Lester* (1936-39)★★★, *Prized Pres!* (1936-57)★★★★, *Count Basie And His Orchestra, 1938* (1938)★★★★, with Benny Goodman *Together Again* (1940-41)★★★, *Pres At His Very Best* (1944)★★★, *Jammin' With Lester* (1944-46)★★★, *The Genius Of Lester Young* (1945-52)★★★★, *Live At The Royal Roost* (1948)★★★, *Lester Young* (1948-53)★★★, *Lester Swings* (1950)★★★, *Jammin' With Lester Vol. 2* (1950)★★★, *Lester Swings Again* (1951)★★★, *Lester Young On The Air* (1952)★★★, *Lester Young's Greatest* (Score 1958)★★★, *The Lester Young Story* (Verve 1959)★★★★, *The Essential Lester Young* (Verve 1961)★★★★, *Giants 3* (Verve 1966)★★★, *Savoy Recordings* (RCA 1986)★★★★, *Prez's Hat Vols 1-4* (Philology 1988)★★★★, *Lester Leaps In* (ASV 1995)★★★★.

●FURTHER READING: *Lester Young*, Lewis Porter. *The Tenor Saxophone And Clarinet Of Lester Young, 1936-1949*, Jan Evensmo. *You Got To Be Original Man! The Music of Lester Young*, Frank Buchmann-Moller. *You Just Fight For Your Life: The Story of Lester Young*, Frank Buchmann-Moller. *A Lester Young Reader*, Lewis Porter.

Young, Neil

b. 12 November 1945, Toronto, Canada. Having moved to Winnepeg as a child, Young began his enigmatic career as a member of several high-school bands, including the Jades and Classics. He later joined the Squires, whose indebtedness to the UK instramental combo the **Shadows** was captured on Young's composition 'Aurora'/'The Sultan'. In 1965 he embarked on a folk-based musical direction, with appearances in Toronto's bohemian Yorkville enclave. A demonstration tape from this era contains early versions of 'Sugar Mountain', a paean to lost childhood later placed on 10 different single releases, and 'Don't Pity Me', revived a decade later as 'Don't Cry No Tears'. Young then joined the Mynah Birds, a pop-soul attraction that also featured **Rick James**, but this act folded prematurely upon the latter's arrest for draft evasion. Group bassist Bruce Palmer accompanied Young on a subsequent move to California where they teamed with **Stephen Stills** and **Richie Furay** to form the **Buffalo Springfield**. Young's tenure in this seminal 'west coast' act was tempered by several 'sabbaticals', but two luxurious, atmospheric compositions, 'Broken Arrow' and 'Expecting To Fly', established the highly sculptured, orchestral-tinged sound prevalent on his debut solo record, *Neil Young*. Although originally blighted by a selfless mix that buried the artist's vocals, the album contained several excellent compositions, notably 'The Loner', 'The Old Laughing Lady', 'I've Been Waiting For You' and 'Here We Are In The Years'. The set also featured two highly effective instrumentals, Young's evocative 'Emperor Of Wyoming' and 'String Quartet From Whiskey Boot Hill', a sublime arrangement and composition by **Jack Nitzsche**. The closing track, 'The Last Trip To Tulsa', was unique in Young's canon, an overlong, surreal narrative whose performance betrayed the strong influence of **Bob Dylan**. Following his first album, Young was joined by Danny Whitten (guitar), Billy Talbot (bass) and Ralph Molina (drums) - three former members of the **Rockets** - in a new backing group dubbed **Crazy Horse**.

The now-classic *Everybody Knows This Is Nowhere* captured a performer liberated from a previous self-consciousness with the extended 'Down By The River' and 'Cowgirl In The Sand', allowing space for his stutteringly simple, yet enthralling, guitar style. While the epic guitar pieces dominated the set, there were other highlights, including the zestful 'Cinnamon Girl' and the haunting 'Running Dry', a mournful requiem featuring Bobby Notkoff on violin. The album underlined the intense relationship between Young and Crazy Horse. An attendant tour confirmed the strength of this new-found partnership, while Young also secured acclaim as a member of **Crosby, Stills, Nash And Young**. His relationship with Crazy Horse soured as Whitten grew increasingly dependent on heroin and the group was dropped following the recording of *After The Goldrush*. The set provided a commercial breakthough and included several of Young's best-known compositions, including the haunting title track, 'Only Love Can Break Your Heart', a US Top 40 hit and the fiery 'Southern Man'. The highly commercial *Harvest* confirmed this new-found ascendancy and spawned a US chart-topper in 'Heart Of Gold'; it remains his best-selling album. This commercial peak ended abruptly with *Journey Through The Past*, a highly indulgent soundtrack to a rarely screened autobiographical film. A disastrous tour with new backing group, the Stray Gators, exacerbated the gap between the artist and his potential audience, although *Time Fades Away*, a collection of new songs culled from the concerts, reclaimed the ragged feistiness of the Crazy Horse era. The set included the passionate 'Last Dance' and the superb 'Don't Be Denied', an unflinching autobiographical account of Young's early life in Canada.

The deaths of Whitten and road crew member Bruce Berry inspired the harrowing *Tonight's The Night*, on which Young's bare-nerved emotions were expounded over his bleakest songs to date. 'I'm singing this borrowed tune, I took from the **Rolling Stones**, alone in this empty room, too wasted to write my own', he intoned in world-weary fashion on 'Borrowed Tune', while in-concert Young would offer multiple versions of the grief-stricken title song. However, the final set was rejected by the record company in favour of *On The Beach*, released to coincide with a Crosby, Stills, Nash And Young reunion tour. The work was initially greeted coolly and *Rolling Stone* described it as one of the 'most despairing albums of the decade'. In common with **John Lennon**'s **Plastic Ono Band**, *On The Beach* saw Young stripping away his personality in a series of intense songs. The undoubted highlight of the set was the closing 'Ambulance Blues', arguably one of the most accomplished works of Young's career. In analyzing his place in the rock music world, Young offered a sardonic riposte to his detractors: 'So all you critics sit alone/You're no better than me for what you've shown/With your stomach pump and your hook and ladder dreams/We could get together for some scenes'. The belatedly issued *Tonight's The Night* was no longer a shock, but testified to Young's absolute conviction. The album sold poorly but was retrospectively acclaimed as one of the bravest and most moving albums of the decade.

Young next chose to team up Crazy Horse again - Talbot, Molina and new guitarist Frank Stampedro - for *Zuma*. The set's highlight was provided by a guitar-strewn 'Cortez The Killer' but, despite often ecstatic reviews, the overall performance was generally stronger than the material it supported. Another gripping recording, 'Like A Hurricane', was the pivotal feature of *American Stars 'N' Bars*, an otherwise piecemeal collection drawn from extant masters and newer, country-oriented recordings. The latter direction was maintained on *Comes A Time*, Young's most accessible set since *Harvest*, on which female vocalist **Nicolette Larson** acted as foil. The album's use of acoustic settings enhanced Young's pastoral intentions and the singer was moved to include a rare cover version: **Ian Tyson**'s folk standard, 'Four Strong Winds'. Characteristically, Young chose to follow this up by rejoining Crazy Horse for *Rust Never Sleeps*. The album rightly stands as one of Young's greatest and most consistent works. The acoustic 'My My, Hey Hey (Out Of The Blue)' and its electric counterpart 'Hey Hey, My My (Into The Black)' explained the central theme of the work - the transience of rock stardom. 'The Thrasher', one of Young's most complex and rewarding songs, reiterated the motif. 'Ride My Llama', 'Pocahontas' and 'Powderfinger' were all worthy additions to Young's classic catalogue. The album was preceded by a Young film of the same name and was followed by a double live album.

During the 80s the artist became increasingly unpredictable as each new release rejected the musical directions suggested by its predecessor. The understated and underrated *Hawks And Doves* was followed by excursions through electric R&B (*Re-Ac-Tor*), electro-techno-pop (*Trans*) and rockabilly (*Everybody's Rockin'*), before embracing ol' timey country (*Old Ways*), hard rock (*Landing On Water*) and R&B (*This Note's For You*). The last-named achieved notoriety when a video for the title song, which attacked the intertwining of rock with corporate sponsorship, was banned by **MTV**. The R&B experiment using brass (Neil And The Blue Notes) also saw Young regain some critical acclaim. Young's next project was culled from an aborted release, tentatively entitled *Times Square*. *Eldorado* invoked the raw abandonment of *Tonight's The Night*, but the five-song set was only issued in Japan and Australia. Three of its songs were latterly placed on *Freedom*, an artistic and commercial triumph which garnered positive reviews and assuaged those viewing its creator as merely eccentric. The set was generally acclaimed as Young's finest work in a decade and included some of his most intriguing lyrics, most notably the lengthy 'Crime In The City', itself an extract from an even longer piece, 'Sixty To Zero'. Young affirmed this regeneration with *Ragged Glory*, a collaboration with Crazy Horse marked by blistering guitar lines, snarled lyrics and a sense of urgency and excitement few from Neil's generation could hope to muster. Contemporary new wave band **Sonic Youth** supported the revitalized partnership on the US *Spook The Horse* tour, cementing Young's affection for pioneers.

An ensuing in-concert set, *Weld* (accompanied by an album of feedback experimentation, *Arc*), was rightly applauded as another milestone in Young's often contrary oeuvre. Following this, Young informed the media that he was making a return to a *Harvest*-type-album, and the result was, for many, another one of his best albums. *Harvest Moon* captured the essence of what is now rightly seen as a great 70s album (*Harvest*) and yet it sounded perfect for the 90s. 'From Hank To Hendrix' and the title track are but two in a collection of Young songs destined to become classics. As if this was not enough, less than a year later he produced *Unplugged*, which was a confident live set recorded for MTV. *Sleeps With Angels* mixed some of his dirtiest guitar with some frail and winsome offerings. His ability to contrast is extraordinary: 'Piece of Crap' finds Young in punkish and vitriolic form, whilst the gentle

'My Heart' would not be out of place in a school church hall. In similar mood was his ethereal 'Philadelphia', perfectly suited for the film *Philadelphia*, for which it was composed. A collaboration with **Pearl Jam** produced a good album in 1995, and once again this man thrilled, excited, baffled and amazed us; *Mirror Ball* is a gripping rock album that bought him many new (younger) fans. *Dead Man* was a challenging and rambling soundtrack of 'guitar', and neither a commercial nor listenable excursion. *Broken Arrow* received a less than positive reception from the critics, although many fans saw little difference in quality, except for the ramshackle bar-room version of 'Baby What You Want Me To Do'. *Year Of The Horse* was yet another live album, tolerated by his fans but leaving an appetite for some new material. Even with a less than perfect discography, at the time of writing his artistic standing remains at an all-time high. However, he retains the right to surprise, infuriate, and even baffle, while his reluctance to court easy popularity must be applauded. More than any other artist working in the rock field over the past 30 years, Young is the greatest chameleon. His many admirers never know what to expect, but the reaction whenever a new project or direction arrives is almost universally favourable from all quarters. He transcends generations and stays hip and in touch, with laconic ease, indifference and incredible syle. In appraising 'grunge' let it be said that it was Young who first wore check workshirts outside torn jeans, and played blistering distorted guitar (with Crazy Horse). And he did it all nearly 30 years ago.

● ALBUMS: *Neil Young* (Reprise 1969)★★★★, *Everybody Knows This Is Nowhere* (Reprise 1969)★★★★★, *After The Goldrush* (Reprise 1970)★★★★, *Harvest* (Reprise 1972)★★★, *Journey Through The Past* (Reprise 1972)★, *Time Fades Away* (Reprise 1973)★★★, *On The Beach* (Reprise 1974)★★★★★, *Tonight's The Night* (Reprise 1975)★★★★, *Zuma* (Reprise 1975)★★★★, *American Stars 'N' Bars* (Reprise 1977)★★, *Comes A Time* (Reprise 1978)★★★, *Rust Never Sleeps* (Reprise 1979)★★★★★, *Live Rust* (Reprise 1979)★★★, *Hawks And Doves* (Reprise 1980)★★★, *Re-Ac-Tor* (Reprise 1981)★★★, *Trans* (Geffen 1983)★★★, *Everybody's Rockin'* (Geffen 1983)★★, *Old Ways* (Geffen 1985)★★★, *Landing On Water* (Geffen 1986)★, *Life* (Geffen 1987)★★, *This Note's For You* (Reprise 1988)★★★★, *Eldorado* mini-album (Reprise 1989)★★★, *Freedom* (Reprise 1989)★★★★, *Ragged Glory* (Reprise 1990)★★★, *Weld* (Reprise 1991)★★★, *Arc/Weld* (Reprise 1991)★★, *Harvest Moon* (Reprise 1992)★★★, *Unplugged* (Reprise 1993)★★★, *Sleeps With Angels* (Reprise 1994)★★★★, *Mirror Ball* (Reprise 1995)★★★, *Dead Man* soundtrack (Vapor 1996)★★, *Broken Arrow* (Reprise/Vapour 1996)★★, *The Year Of The Horse* (Reprise 1997)★★★.

● COMPILATIONS: *Decade* (Reprise 1977)★★★★, *Greatest Hits* (Reprise 1985)★★, *Lucky Thirteen* (Geffen 1992)★★★.

● VIDEOS: *Neil Young & Crazy Horse: Rust Never Sleeps* (1984), *Berlin* (1988), *Freedom* (1990), *Weld* (Warners 1991), *Unplugged* (1993), *The Complex Sessions* (1994), *Human Highway* (Warners 1995).

● FURTHER READING: *Neil Young*, Carole Dufrechou. *Neil Young: The Definitive Story Of His Musical Career*, Johnny Rogan. *Neil And Me*, Scott Young. *Neil Young: Een Portret*, Herman Verbeke and Lucien van Diggelen. *Neil Young: Complete Illustrated Bootleg Discography*, Bruno Fisson and Alan Jenkins. *Aurora: The Story Of Neil Young And The Squires*, John Einarson. *Don't Be Denied: The Canadian Years*, John Einarson. *The Visual Documentary*, John Robertson. *His Life And Music*, Michael Heatley. *A Dreamer Of Pictures: Neil Young - The Man And His Music*, David Downing. *Neil Young And Broken Arrow: On A Journey Through The Past*, Alan Jenkins. *Neil Young: The Rolling Stone Files*, Holly George-Warren (ed.). *Ghosts On The Road: Neil Young In Concert*, Pete Long.
● FILMS: *Journey Through The Past* (1973), *Human Highway* (1982).

Young, Park Jin

b. Seoul, South Korea. Following graduation from Yonsei University, Park Jin Young elected to concentrate on a professional singing career. Immediately he earned a reputation for being something of a showman - shocking conservative music industry factions in Korea with his transparent vinyl trousers and outlandish dance steps. His videos and performances have helped make him his nation's most compelling and controversial artist, and it is said he enjoys 'subverting staid notions of Korean pop'. Much of his hip hop derived pop material is written in conjunction with Kim Hyoung Suk. Among his biggest hits have been 'The Proposal', a Korean number 1, and 'Elevator', which was banned from mainstream radio play for its risqué lyrics and a video that featured Korean supermodel Sora Lee.

●ALBUMS: *The Entertainer* (Orange 1994)★★★, *Best Album* (EMI Korea 1996)★★★.

Young, Paul

b. 17 January 1956, Luton, Bedfordshire, England. Prior to his major success as a solo artist Young was a former member of **Streetband**, who made the UK charts with the novelty record 'Toast'. He was then part of the much-loved **Q-Tips**, a band that did much to preserve an interest in 60s' soul and R&B. As the Q-Tips collapsed from exhaustion and lack of finance, Young signed as a solo artist with **CBS Records**. Following two flop singles, his smooth soul voice captured the public's imagination with a superb chart-topping version of **Marvin Gaye**'s 'Wherever I Lay My Hat'. The following *No Parlez* was a phenomenally triumphant debut, reaching number 1 in the UK and staying in the charts for well over two years. Now, having sold several million copies, this album remains his finest work. It was a blend of carefully chosen and brilliantly interpreted covers including 'Love Will Tear Us Apart' (**Joy Division**) and 'Love Of The Common People' (Nicky Thomas) together with excellent originals like 'Come Back And Stay'. After touring to support the album, Young experienced a recurring problem with his voice, which continues to plague his career. It was two years before he was able to record *The Secret Of Association*, but the quality of material was intact. This album also topped the UK chart and produced three top 10 singles including 'Everything Must Change' and a cover of **Daryl Hall**'s 'Every Time You Go Away'. He appeared at **Live Aid**, duetting with **Alison Moyet**, although it was obvious that his voice was once again troublesome. *Between Two Fires* was a below-par album, although his fans still made it a hit. Little was heard from Young for over a year, and while it was assumed that his voice was continuing to cause him problems, Young was merely re-assessing his life. He made an encouraging return singing **Crowded House**'s 'Don't Dream Its Over' at the Nelson Mandela Concert at Wembley in 1988, after which Young went into hibernation until 1990; this time by his own admission he was 'decorating his house'. In 1990 he returned with *Other Voices* and an accompanying tour. Once again his choice of material was tasteful and included versions of 'Don't Dream It's Over', **Free**'s 'Little Bit Of Love' and **Bobby Womack**'s 'Stop On By'. His was one of the better performances at the **Freddie Mercury** tribute concert at Wembley Stadium in May 1992. Voice permitting, Young seemed destined for continuing success, having proved that even with a sparse recorded output his sizeable following remained loyal and patient. Although his voice lacked the power and bite of old he was able to inject passion and warmth into his 90s albums. This was apparent on his excellent recording of soul classics on *Reflections*, which demonstrated the area of music where he has the closest affinity. Versions of 'Until You Come Back To Me', 'Ain't No Sunshine' and 'Reach Out I'll Be There' highlighted a man who truly has soul even though his voice is leaving him. Following the relative commercial failure of his self-titled 1997 release, Young was dropped by East West Records.

● ALBUMS: *No Parlez* (Columbia 1983)★★★★, *The Secret Of Association* (Columbia 1985)★★★, *Between Two Fires* (Columbia 1986)★★, *Other Voices* (Columbia 1990)★★★, *The Crossing* (Columbia 1993)★★, *Reflections* (Vision 1994)★★★, *Acoustic Paul Young* mini-album (Columbia 1994)★★★★, *Paul Young* (East West 1997)★★.

● COMPILATIONS: *From Time To Time* (Columbia 1991)★★★★, *Love Songs* (Columbia 1997)★★★.

Young, Snooky

b. Eugene Howard Young, 3 February 1919, Dayton, Ohio, USA. Young began playing trumpet while still a small child and by his early teens was working in **territory bands**. He was heard by **Gerald Wilson**, who was then playing in the **Jimmie Lunceford** band, and on his recommendation Young was hired. Young stayed with the Lunceford band until 1942 and in that year played with **Count Basie**, **Lionel Hampton**, **Les Hite** and **Benny Carter**. In the following year, after a brief return visit to Basie, he joined Wilson's big band in California. In the late 40s he was again with Hampton and Basie, and he was back yet again in the Basie band in the late

50s and early 60s. From the early 60s he worked in television studios in New York City, and was a member of the **Thad Jones-Mel Lewis** Jazz Orchestra from its inception. Subsequently, Young continued to play in the studios, mostly in Los Angeles, and also appeared at jazz festivals, with occasional return visits to Basie in the late 70s and early 80s. He also made a handful of records as sideman with **Ray Bryant**, and as either leader or co-leader (with **Marshal Royal**). A strong lead trumpeter, his solo gifts were frequently underused by his employers. Content to work in the studios for more than a quarter of a century, Young's infrequent jazz excursions in the past three decades have shown him to be an interesting soloist, whether on open horn or with the plunger mute.

● ALBUMS: with Count Basie *Chairman Of The Board* (1959)★★★, one side only *The Boys From Dayton* (1971)★★, with Marshal Royal *Snooky And Marshal's Album* (Concord 1978)★★★, *Horn Of Plenty* (1979)★★★.

Young, Steve

b. 12 July 1942, Noonan, Georgia, USA. Young has claimed to be the reincarnation of a cavalry officer in the American Civil War, and has written songs about reincarnation, including 'In The Ways Of The Indian'. He was raised in Alabama and his superb 'Montgomery In The Rain' is about congregating around **Hank Williams**' grave. Young played folk music in New York and various southern towns before moving to Los Angeles. In 1968 he recorded as part of the group Stone Country for **RCA**, then in 1969, he made his first album, *Rock, Salt And Nails*, for **A&M Records**, with sessionmen including **James Burton**, **Gene Clark** and **Gram Parsons**. It included a song written while he was homesick, the pastoral and mystical 'Seven Bridges Road', which has been recorded by **Rita Coolidge** and **Joan Baez** and, with commercial success, by the **Eagles**. Young's albums often repeat songs: 'I originally did "Lonesome, On'ry And Mean" as a bluesy bluegrass song in 3/4, but **Waylon Jennings** turned it into a rocker in 4/4. I got intrigued by that and so I did it that way too.' He dedicated the autobiographical 'Renegade Picker' to **Jerry Lee Lewis** because 'he refuses to play it safe'. *No Place To Fall* was delayed because RCA were busy pressing **Elvis Presley** albums following his death and Young's career lost momentum. He also had to combat drug and alcohol addiction: 'Every waking moment I was drinking and I just didn't care. I don't do drink or drugs anymore, but I am into Zen meditation, which certainly helps my creativity.' Although Young is better known as a songwriter, his only US country success is with **Willie Nelson**'s 'It's Not Supposed To Be That Way'. He has made several engaging UK appearances, often with a sense of humour that belies his grim material: 'I don't think of myself as a country singer or a folk singer. What I do comes from Southern roots, American roots, and I just let it go where it goes.' *Solo, Live*, recorded at Houston's Anderson Fair in 1990, is an effective career overview.

● ALBUMS: *Rock, Salt And Nails* (A&M 1969)★★★, *Seven Bridges Road* (Blue Canyon 1972)★★★, *Honky Tonk Man* (Rounder 1975)★★★★, *Renegade Picker* (RCA 1976)★★★★, *No Place To Fall* (RCA 1977)★★★, *To Satisfy You* (Rounder 1981)★★★, *Look Homeward Angel* (Mill 1986)★★★, *Long Time Rider* (Voodoo 1990)★★★, *Solo, Live* (Watermelon 1991)★★★★, *Switchblades Of Love* (Watermelon 1993)★★★.

Young, Tommie

A southern-soul singer about whom little biographical detail exists, Young's voice was compared to that of **Aretha Franklin** in the early 70s, although she has a rare vocal quality of her own. In the early 70s, she cut six singles and one album for Bobby Patterson's Soul Power label out of Shreveport, Louisiana, distributed by Stan Lewis' local Jewel/Paula/Ronn group. The most impressive tracks were 'Do You Still Feel The Same Way', 'She Don't Have To See You', 'You Can't Have Your Cake And Eat It Too', 'You Brought It All On Yourself', 'Everybody's Got A Little Devil In Their Soul', and a cover of **O.V. Wright**'s 'That's How Strong My Love Is'. UK Contempo issued two Young singles in 1972/3, plus two of the same sides on their 1975 album *Soul Deep Volume.1*. In 1983, a Japanese P-Vine album of Young's Soul Power output included three previously unissued sides, and UK Charly released a total of seven Young sides on their 80s compilations *Southern Soul Belles* and *Soul Jewels Volume.2*. After her Soul Power days, nothing more was heard of Young until she sang on the 1978 MCA sountrack album, *A Woman Called Moses*. The film told the story of Harriet Ross Tubman, who founded an underground railway that helped southern slaves to freedom. The score was chiefly composed by **Van McCoy**. Since then, Tommie Young seems to have faded from the soul music scene, although she resurfaced with a gospel CD in 1993, spelling her first name Tommye, and also appending West to her surname as a result of her marriage to Calvin R. West Jnr.
● ALBUMS: *Do You Still Feel The Same Way* (Soul Power 1973)★★★, *A Woman Called Moses* film soundtrack (MCA 1978)★, *Just Call Me Tommye* (Command 1993)★★★.
● COMPILATIONS: *Soul Deep Volume 1* 2 tracks only (Contempo 1975)★★, *Southern Soul Belles* 3 tracks only (Charly 1982)★★, *Do You Still Feel The Same Way/Take Time To Know Him* (P Vine 1983)★★★, *Soul Jewels Volume 2* 4 tracks only (Charly 1989)★★, *Grits & Grooves* 2 tracks only(1992)★★.

Young, Trummy

b. James Osborne Young, 12 January 1912, Savannah, Georgia, USA, d. 10 September 1984. As a child Young played trumpet and drums but by his teens was concentrating on trombone. Resident in Washington, DC, he played in local bands before relocating to Chicago and working with **Earl 'Fatha' Hines**. He remained with Hines for four years, making occasional visits to other bands. In 1937 he began a five-year stint with **Jimmie Lunceford**, becoming an important member of the band as both trombone soloist and singer. He also had a number of hit records with the band, among them 'Margie' and his own composition, 'Tain't What You Do, It's The Way That You Do It'. In the 40s he worked with bands covering a wide stylistic range, including those led by **Boyd Raeburn** and **Roy Eldridge**. He also played with **Jazz At The Philharmonic** before settling for a while in Hawaii. In 1952 he became a member of **Louis Armstrong**'s All Stars, a job he held for 12 years. After leaving Armstrong he returned to Hawaii, leading his own bands, playing with visiting musicians, and making occasional visits to the mainland for concert and festival appearances. A superbly gifted trombonist, Young's early playing style showed him to be a completely rounded soloist with an approach to his instrument that was, in many respects, very advanced for a 30s big band musician. His playing style changed after he joined Armstrong, with whom he used a deceptively simple approach. The change was highly appropriate for Armstrong's band and Young was in many ways a more suitable partner than his predecessor, the sublime **Jack Teagarden**, had been. His blistering solos and delightfully melodic ensemble lines, allied to his engagingly casual singing, helped to give the band a strength of character that it lacked after he departed.
● ALBUMS: *Louis Armstrong Plays W.C. Handy* (1954)★★★★, *Satch Plays Fats* (1955)★★★, *Trummy Young And His Fifty-Fifty Band* (1955)★★★, *A Man And His Horn* (1975)★★★, *Yours Truly: Trummy Young And Friends* (1975)★★, *Struttin' With Some Barbecue* (1979)★★★.
●COMPILATIONS: *The Complete Jimmie Lunceford 1939-40* (1939-40)★★★★.

Young, Val

Young was discovered in the late 70s by **George Clinton**, who incorporated her into the Brides Of Funkenstein, one of the many acts in his **Funkadelic** stable. After performing on the US hit 'Disco To Go', Young joined the **Gap Band**, where she was featured on the funk classic 'Oops Upside Your Head'. She recorded five albums with the group before being spotted by another black music notable, **Rick James**. Impressed as much by her striking physical appearance as by her musical talents, James promoted her as the 'black Marilyn Monroe'. He also produced her 1985 hit 'Seduction', a blatant attempt to capitalize on her erotic image. 'If You Should Ever Be Lonely' was a successful follow-up in 1986, before Young left James's stable to forge a solo career on Amherst Records.
● ALBUMS: *Seduction* (1985)★★.

Young, Victor

b. 8 August 1900, Chicago, Illinois, USA, d. 11 November 1956, Palm Springs, California, USA. A violinist, conductor, bandleader, arranger and composer, Young is said to have been responsible for over 300 film scores and themes. He studied at the Warsaw Conservatory in 1910 before joining the Warsaw Philharmonic as a violinist, and touring

Europe. He returned to the USA at the outbreak of World War I, and later, in the early 20s, toured as a concert violinist, and then became a concert master in theatre orchestras. On 'defecting' to popular music, he served for a while as violinist-arranger with the popular pianist-bandleader **Ted Fio Rito**. During the 30s, Young worked a great deal on radio, conducting for many artists including **Al Jolson**, **Don Ameche** and **Smith Ballew**. He also started recording with his own orchestra, and had a string of hits from 1931-54, including 'Gems From "The Band Wagon"', 'The Last Round-Up', 'Who's Afraid Of The Big Bad Wolf', 'The Old Spinning Wheel', 'This Little Piggie Went To Market' (featuring **Jimmy Dorsey**, **Bunny Berigan** and **Joe Venuti**), 'Flirtation Walk', 'Ev'ry Day', 'Way Back Home', 'About A Quarter To Nine' and 'She's A Latin From Manhattan' (both from the Jolson movie *Go Into Your Dance*), 'It's A Sin To Tell A Lie', 'Mona Lisa', 'The Third Man Theme', 'Ruby', 'Limelight Theme', and 'The High And The Mighty'. He also provided the orchestral accompaniments for other artists, such as **Dick Powell**, **Eddie Cantor**, **Deanna Durbin**, **Helen Forrest**, **Frances Langford**, trumpet virtuoso Rafael Mendez, **Cliff Edwards**, the **Boswell Sisters**, and western movies singer **Rex Allen**. Most notably, it was Young's orchestra that backed **Judy Garland** on her record of 'Over The Rainbow', the Oscar-winning song from the legendary 1939 film *The Wizard Of Oz*. He also backed **Bing Crosby** on two of his million-sellers: 'Too-Ra-Loo-Ra-Loo-Ral (That's An Irish Lullaby)', from *Going My Way* (the 'Best Picture' of 1944), and British doctor Arthur Colahan's somewhat unconventional song, 'Galway Bay' (1948).

Young's extremely successful and prolific career as a film composer, musical director, conductor, and arranger, began in the early 30s with Paramount. Some of his best-known film works included *Wells Fargo* (1937), *Swing High, Swing Low* (1937), *Breaking The Ice* (1938), *Golden Boy* (1939), *Man Of Conquest* (1939), *Arizona* (1940), *I Wanted Wings* (1941), *Hold Back The Dawn* (1941), *Flying Tigers* (1942), *Silver Queen* (1942), *The Glass Key* (1942), *Take A Letter, Darling* (1942), *For Whom The Bell Tolls* (1943), *The Uninvited* (1944), *Samson And Delilah* (1949), *Rio Grande* (1950), *Scaramouche* (1952), *The Greatest Show On Earth* (1952), *Shane* (1953) and *Three Coins In The Fountain* (1954). In 1956, Young was awarded a posthumous Academy Award for his score for Mike Todd's spectacular film *Around The World In Eighty Days*. His record of the title song made the US charts in 1957, and had a vocal version by Bing Crosby on the b-side. He also wrote some television themes, including 'Blue Star' for the US *Medic* series, and contributed music to two minor Broadway shows, *Pardon Our French* (1950) and *Seventh Heaven* (1955). Young's popular songs were written mostly with lyricist **Ned Washington**. These included 'Can't We Talk It Over?', 'A Hundred Years From Today' (from the revue *Blackbirds Of 1933/34*), and three beautiful and enduring ballads: 'A Ghost Of

A Chance' (co-writer, Bing Crosby), 'Stella By Starlight' and 'My Foolish Heart' (film title song). Young's other lyricists included Will J. Harris ('Sweet Sue'), Wayne King, Haven Gillespie, and Egbert Van Alstyne ('Beautiful Love'), **Sam M. Lewis** ('Street Of Dreams'), Edward Heyman ('When I Fall In Love' and 'Love Letters') and **Sammy Cahn** (the film title song, 'Written On The Wind'). Young also wrote 'Golden Earrings' with the songwriting team of **Jay Livingston** and **Ray Evans**.

● ALBUMS: *April In Paris* (c.50s)★★★, *Cinema Rhapsodies* (c.50s)★★★, *Gypsy Magic* (c.50s)★★, *Imagination* (c.50s)★★★, *Night Music* (c.50s)★★★, *Pearls On Velvet* (c.50s)★★, *Themes From 'For Whom The Bell Tolls' And 'Golden Earrings'* (c.50s)★★★, *Valentino Tangos* (c.50s)★★, *Hollywood Rhapsodies* (c.50s)★★★, *Around The World In 80 Days* film soundtrack (1957)★★★, *Forever Young* (1959)★★★, *Love Themes From Hollywood* (1959)★★★, *Wizard Of Oz/Pinocchio* (Ace Of Hearts/Decca 1966)★★, *The Quiet Man/Samson And Delilah* film soundtracks (Varese International 1979)★★★.

Young, Zora

b. 21 January 1948, Prairie, Mississippi, USA. A third cousin of **Howlin' Wolf**, Young has sufficient talent not to have to dwell on the fact. Singing in church from an early age helped her to develop both flexibility and control in her vocal technique. That continued after her family moved to Chicago in 1956, although she did not take up blues singing until 1971. During the 80s, she toured Europe on numerous occasions, while at home she played **Bessie Smith** in the stage show *The Heart Of The Blues*, alongside **Valerie Wellington**. In 1988, Young financed the recording of her first album, released on her own Black Lightning label. Three years later, she re-recorded its title track as part of *Travelin' Light*, an album of largely original material on which she was backed by members of the **Legendary Blues Band**.

● ALBUMS: *Stumbling Blocks & Stepping Stones* (Black Lightning 1988)★★★, *Travelin' Light* (Deluge 1992)★★★.
● COMPILATIONS: *Chicago Blues Ladies* (Wolf 1990)★★★.

Young-Holt Unlimited

This US group was formed in Chicago in 1965 as the Young-Holt Trio with Eldee Young (b. 7 January 1936, Chicago, Illinois, USA; bass), Isaac 'Redd' Holt (b. 16 May 1932, Rosedale, Mississippi, USA; drums) and Don Walker (piano). Young and Holt both studied at Chicago's American Conservatory Of Music. They later joined the **Ramsey Lewis** Trio and were featured on two of the group's best-known singles, 'The In Crowd' and 'Hang On Sloopy' (both 1965). The bassist and drummer then broke away to pursue their own direction - although their debut hit on **Brunswick Records**, 'Wack Wack' (1967), was as undemanding as Lewis's. In 1968 pianist Walker was replaced by Ken Chancey. Soon Chancey was out and the act was reconstituted as the Young-Holt Unlimited. Under that name, the act hit in 1968 with the million-selling 'Soulful Strut'. This instrumental was, in fact, the backing track to a **Barbara Acklin** single, 'Am I The Same Girl?', but with Floyd Morris's piano part replacing the vocal line. Ironically, neither Young, nor Holt, was on the record as the instrumental was by the Brunswick studio band. Despite that, Young-Holt Unlimited continued to make technically precise, but rather sterile records before the group's two mainstays decided to rejoin Ramsey Lewis in 1983.

● ALBUMS: *Wack Wack* (Brunswick 1967)★★★, *Young-Holt Unlimited Onstage* (Brunswick 1967)★, *The Beat Goes On* (Brunswick 1967)★★★, *Funky But!* (1968)★★, *Soulful Strut* (Brunswick 1968)★★★★, *Just A Melody* (Brunswick 1969)★★, *Young-Holt Unlimited Plays 'Superfly'* (1973)★★★.
● COMPILATIONS: *Wack Wack* (1986)★★★.

Youngbloods

Formed in 1965 in Boston, Massachusetts, the Youngbloods evolved from the city's thriving traditional music circuit. The group was formed by folk singers **Jesse Colin Young** (b. Perry Miller, 11 November 1944, New York City, New York, USA) and Jerry Corbitt (b. Tifton, Georgia, USA) who together completed a single, 'My Babe', prior to the arrival of aspiring jazz drummer Joe Bauer (b. 26 September 1941, Memphis, Tennessee, USA) and guitarist/pianist Lowell Levinger III, better known simply as Banana (b. 1946, Cambridge, Massachusetts, USA). Young began playing bass when several candidates, including **Felix Pappalardi** and Harvey Brooks, proved incompatible, and the quartet took the name 'Youngbloods' from the singer's second solo album. Having secured a residency at New York's famed Cafe Au Go Go, the group established itself as a leading folk rock-cum-goodtime attraction. Their debut, *The Youngbloods*, captures this formative era and mixes excellent original songs, including the ebullient 'Grizzly Bear', with several choice cover versions. The group's reading of **Dino Valenti**'s 'Get Together' subsequently became a hit in California where it was adopted as a counter-culture anthem. The lyric: 'Come on now people, smile on your brother, everybody get together, try and love one another right now', perfectly captured the mood of late-60s Californian rock music.

The Youngbloods then settled on the west coast. *Elephant Mountain*, their most popular album, reflected a new-found peace of mind and included several of the group's best-known songs, including 'Darkness Darkness' and 'Sunlight'. Jerry Corbitt had left the line-up during the early stages of recording allowing Bauer and Banana space to indulge in improvisational interludes. The Youngbloods gained complete artistic freedom with their own label, Racoon. However releases by Bauer, Banana and Young dissipated the strengths of the parent unit, whose final releases were marred by inconsistency. A friend from the Boston days, Michael Kane, joined the band in the spring of 1971, but they split the following year when Young resumed his solo career. Banana, Bauer and Kane continued as **Banana And The Bunch**, but this occasional venture subsequently folded. In 1984 Levinger reappeared in the Bandits, before retiring from music to run a hang-gliding shop.

● ALBUMS: *The Youngbloods* (RCA Victor 1967)★★★, *Earth Music* (RCA Victor 1967)★★★, *Elephant Mountain* (RCA 1969)★★★★, *Rock Festival* (1970)★★, *Ride The Wind* (1971)★★, *Good 'N' Dusty* (1971)★★, *High On A Ridgetop* (1972)★★.
● COMPILATIONS: one side only *Two Trips* (Mercury 1970)★★, *The Best Of The Youngbloods* (RCA 1970)★★★, *Sunlight* (1971)★★, *Get Together* (1971)★★, *This Is The Youngbloods* (RCA 1972)★★★, *Point Reyes Station* (1987)★★, *From The Gaslight To The Avalon* (1988)★★.

Younger Than Yesterday - The Byrds

With this album the **Byrds** proclaimed fully their musical genius. Distinctive three-part harmonies and chiming 12-string guitars affirmed the quartet's unique sound as a succession of superior compositions embraced folk, pop and country styles. Beguiling melodies nestled alongside experiment as the principals asserted an individuality while remaining aware of the strength of the whole. The acerbic wit of 'So You Wanna Be A Rock 'n' Roll Star' showed a group aware of commercial entrapment. On this set the Byrds rejected such advances and offered a beautiful altruism. Every individual song on this set has managed to grow in stature, especially those by Crosby and Hillman.

● Tracks: *So You Want To Be A Rock 'N' Roll Star; Have You Seen Her Face; CTA-102; Renaissance Fair; Time Between; Everybody's Been Burned; Thoughts And Words; Mind Gardens; My Back Pages; The Girl With No Name; Why.*
● First released 1967
● UK peak chart position: 37
● USA peak chart position: 24

Your Arms Too Short To Box With God
(see *Dont Bother Me I Cant Cope*)

Your Arsenal - Morrissey

Produced by the late Mick Ronson, this record has incredible tension, long before the overblown and unnecessary Morrissey/Rogan feud started. Beat group echoes, doom-laden lyrics and a full atmosphere that conjures up memories of Johnny Kidd And The Pirates, the Ventures and the Pretenders. Solo artists often mellow out and mature, but on this superlative recording, Morrissey paradoxically rocks more than ever and shows further creative maturity. 'You're Gonna Need Someone On Your Side' and 'Glamorous Glue' are only two reasons to buy this album. How many more lyrical odes does he have left?

● Tracks: *You're Gonna Need Someone On Your Side; Glamours Glue; We'll Let You Know; The National Front Disco; Certain People I Know; We Hate It When Our Friends Become Successful; You're The One For Me, Fatty; Seasick, Yet Still Docked; I Know It's Gonna Happen Someday.*

● First released 1993
● UK peak chart position: 4
● USA peak chart position: 21

Your Own Thing

By the late 60s, rock music had become the dominant force in the world of popular entertainment generally, but its first big impact on Broadway was still to come in April 1968 with *Hair*. Some three months before that, on 13 January, this modern conception of William Shakespeare's *Twelfth Night*, complete with a rock score by Hal Hester and Danny Apolinar, arrived at the off-Broadway Orpheum Theatre. Donald Driver's book takes a sly dig at men's fashionably long hair in a story that involves brother and sister Viola (Leland Palmer) and Sebastian (Rusty Thatcher), who, unbeknown to each other, are chasing the same singing job with a rock group based at a fashionable discotheque operated by Olivia (Marian Mercer). Orson (Tom Ligon), the manager of The Four Apocalypse, needs a male vocalist, so Viola adopts an effective disguise. Too effective, as it turns out, because Olivia decides that she fancies him/her, and the complications begin. After some delicate negotiations, Olivia transfers her affections to the far more suitable (and manly) Sebastian, and Viola gets the job - and Orson too. The songs, some of which had fairly predictable titles, included 'The Now Generation', 'I'm On My Way To The Top', 'The Flowers', 'I'm Me!', 'Come Away Death' (lyric-Shakespeare), and 'The Middle Years'. None of them threatened to break into the US charts, which were being headed at the time by artists such as the **Beatles**, **Aretha Franklin**, and the **Lemon Pipers**. One innovation in *Your Own Thing* was the clever use of film and slide projectors to mix traditional aspects of the piece with this contemporary treatment. The show enjoyed an impressive run of 933 performances in New York, but failed to impress in London, and was withdrawn after six weeks.

Youth Brigade

Formed in Los Angeles, California, USA, in the late 70s from the ashes of the Extremes, Youth Brigade initially comprised Shawn Stern (guitar, vocals), Adam Stern (bass, vocals), Mark Stern (drums, ex-No Crisis; Sado Nation) and Greg Louis Gutierrez (guitar). One of Los Angeles' finest hardcore bands of the period, they also formed the BYO label as a direct response to the Ellis Lodge riot of 1979 when bands including the **Go-Go's** played at a gig that was violently curtailed by riot police. BYO was housed at Skinhead Manor, an eight-bedroomed mansion in the heart of Hollywood, rented by an assortment of mavericks intent on creating an alternative media base (including fanzines, pirate radio, live shows, etc.). It was named in honour of the visiting **Sham 69**. Youth Brigade had started out as part of the Skinhead Manor collective, originally as a six-piece group with two singers. They soon crystallized into a line-up made up solely of the Stern brothers. Another band of the same name was born in Washington, DC,

at the same time (playing the same type of aggressive punk music), but luckily this group faded from view before too much confusion arose. Often compared to the **Ruts** because of their integration of reggae with punk pop, Youth Brigade's debut album was easily one of most accessible of the 'So-Cal Hardcore' scene. *Sound And Fury I* demonstrated the group's potential with a wide variety of music employed even at this early stage in their career. 'Men In Blue', for example, included a rap, and the group also tackled the doo-wop classic 'Duke Of Earl'. They embarked on a major tour playing at over one hundred venues in 1983 and 1984, covering much of the USA, Europe and Canada, but always using non-mainstream outlets to book the shows. Shawn's views were hardened by the experience: 'For me, time and time again the topic of ignorance comes up in interviews. That is the fundamental problem in the world and throughout history, and is the dominant subject of my lyrics and my whole life. Educate yourselves people!'. In 1986 they shortened their title to Brigade to accommodate 'a further progression in style'. The new line-up featured bass player Bob Gnarly, formerly of Plain Wrap (Gutierrez had long since joined Salvation Army and then the **Three O'Clock**). Their first album as the Brigade, *The Dividing Line*, featured a cameo appearance from **Jane Wiedlin** on 'The Hardest Part' (in the character of a dizzy blonde actress called Candy). Stern's lyrics were evolving and taking in matters spiritual and emotional as well as social, but Brigade never took themselves too seriously, raps and breakdancing continuing to be a feature of their live shows. However, their previous audience remained unimpressed by what they saw as Brigade's conversion to conventional hard rock. The group disbanded, with Stern subsequently forming That's It with Tony Withers, formerly of UK punk band the **Stupids**.

Ysaguirre, Bob

b. Robert Ysaguirre, 22 February 1897, Belize, British Honduras, d. 27 March 1982. As a young man he played tuba in military-style brass bands. In his early 20s he went to New Orleans where he played both tuba and string bass with various dance bands; he then moved to New York with **Armand Piron**'s orchestra. In New York during the 20s, he played with **Elmer Snowden** and Alex Jackson, then was briefly with bands led by **Fletcher** and **Horace Henderson**. He spent most of the following decade with **Don Redman**. From the 40s onwards, Ysaguirre continued to play but no longer on a full-time basis.
● COMPILATIONS: *The Chronological Don Redman 1931-1933* (Classics 1931-33)★★★★.

Yukl, Joe

b. Joseph Yukl, 5 March 1909, New York, USA, d. March 1981. After first playing violin he switched to trombone and played in college dance bands. In New York in the 20s he joined the staff of **CBS** Records but also appeared from time to time on record with jazzmen such as **Red Nichols** and **Tommy** and **Jimmy Dorsey**. In the 30s he was with **Joe Haymes** and Jimmy Dorsey, also playing dates and sometimes recording with a wide range of popular and jazz artists, including **Bing Crosby**, **Louis Armstrong**, **Frankie Trumbauer** and **Ted Fio Rito**. By this time he had relocated to the west coast where he again worked in studios. He continued these activities into the 40s and 50s, playing jazz dates with **Wingy Manone** and others. He also played on soundtracks or appeared in at least two motion pictures: *Rhythm Inn* (1951), which also featured Manone, Pete Daily and **Barrett Deems**, and *The Glenn Miller Story* (1953). In the latter film, together with **Murray McEachern**, he both coached and ghosted for James Stewart in his role as Miller. Yukl played with skill and a pleasing sound.

Yum-Yum

Chicago, Illinois, USA-based art-rock group Yum-Yum is essentially the work of one man, Chris Holmes (c.1971, Chicago, Illinois, USA). Holmes is responsible for writing all of the group's songs, and also for co-production, singing, guitar and keyboards, working alongside a constantly revolving team of sympathetic musicians and collaborators. What immediately captured critical interest about Yum-Yum's debut album, 1996's *Dan Loves Patti*, was the unusual instrumentation. Arranged by Holmes himself, the record incorporated string, horn and cello sections to animate Holmes's dense, emotive songs. An early interview in *Rolling Stone* magazine drew comparisons with both the **Beatles**' *Sgt. Pepper's Lonely Hearts Club Band* and the **Beach Boys**' *Pet Sounds*. Another comparison was drawn with the **Moody Blues** - Holmes admitting to using a Chamberlin 60s keyboard to play tapes of genuine orchestral instruments in the same manner that the Moody Blues had done two decades earlier. He also employs a mellotron, formerly used by the BBC for sound effects on the science fiction television programme *Doctor Who*. Indeed, his interest in science fiction extends to lectures on UFOs for college radio stations, and a dissertation on alien visitations at the University of Chicago. His first band, the **Hawkwind**-influenced Sabalon Glitz, were named after a *Doctor Who* character. Holmes had by now already established a reputation as an 'auteur', sharing his home with the staff of the Chicago literary journal *The Baffler*. Yum-Yum was formed in 1992 as an alternative outlet to Sabalon Glitz (he also has a third group, the ambient house project Ashtar Command). Holmes' contract with TAG/**Atlantic Records** entitles him to release music by any of the three bands (Sabalon Glitz's first album, *Ufonic*, came out in 1995). However, Holmes was forced to abandon use of the name Yum-Yum in the UK after an existing group claimed prior usage - hence *Dan Loves Patti* was released credited simply to Chris Holmes.
● ALBUMS: *Dan Loves Patti* (TAG/Atlantic 1996)★★★.

Yumuri Y Sus Hermanos

Yumuri Y Sus Hermanos, one of Cuba's most successful bands of the mid-90s, were formed by Yumuri (b. Moises Rafael Valle Moleiro, Cuba) after several years as band leader with **Orquesta Reve**. Despite that group's international and local success, Yumuri had always harboured ambitions to lead his own band, and finally established this new group with his brothers Pedro (alto saxophone), Osvaldo (tenor saxophone, flute) and Luis Alberto (trumpet) in the early 90s (Yumuri Y Sus Hermanos literally translates as Yumuri And His Brothers). They quickly became firm favourites on the Havana live circuit, with their music a mixture of Cuban styles such as son, cha-cha and salsa, as well as imported traditions such as jazz-funk. The group received numerous offers to tour internationally, Yumuri eventually accepting a commission from a consortium of Japanese owners to take a residency at a Cuban restaurant situated in the affluent Shibuya district of Tokyo. Fans of Cuban music soon flocked to that eaterie, entitled Muchaka, which also became a mecca for Japanese-based salsa musicians such as Orquesta Del Sol and **Orquesta De La Luz**. The success of this venture eventually led to a recording contract, and the release of the group's debut album, *Provocación*.
● ALBUMS: *Provocación* (JVC 1996)★★★.

Yung Wu

Yung Wu was a late 80s offshoot project of US band the **Feelies**. On the album *The Good Earth*, the Feelies' founders Glenn Mercer and Bill Million (both guitar) were joined by Brenda Sauter (bass; ex-Trypes) and percussionist Dave Weckerman. Weckerman sang lead vocals in Yung Wu, the line-up of which was completed by another former Trypes member, John Baumgartner (keyboards). *Shore Leave* had a pastoral sound, with acoustic guitars and brushed drumming. The set provided an interesting contrast to the Feelies' edgy angst, although it was slightly undermined by worthy, but unexciting, versions of songs by **Neil Young**, the **Rolling Stones** and **Brian Eno**.
● ALBUMS: *Shore Leave* (Coyote 1987)★★★.

Yuro, Timi

b. Rosemarie Yuro, 4 August 1940, Chicago, Illinois, USA. Yuro moved to Los Angeles as a child, and by the late 50s was singing in her mother's Italian restaurant. She was signed to **Liberty** by the head of the company, Al Bennett, and recorded her most famous track, 'Hurt' in 1961. Produced by Clyde Otis, who had supervised many of **Dinah Washington**'s hits, the dramatic ballad was a revival of **Roy Hamilton**'s 1954 R&B hit. Yuro's searing white soul rendering entered the Top 10 in 1961 and inspired numerous artists to cover the song, notably **Elvis Presley**, whose version was a Top 30 hit in 1976. The follow-ups 'I Apologise' and 'Smile' made less impact, but in 1962, 'What's A Matter Baby?' reached the Top 20. Yuro had minor hits with 'Make

The World Go Away' (a greater success the following year for **Eddy Arnold**) and the country song 'Gotta Travel On'. Her Liberty albums contained a mix of standard ballads such as **Mitchell Parish** and **Hoagy Carmichael**'s 'Stardust' and soul songs ('Hallelujah I Love Him So'), but mid-60s records for **Mercury** found Yuro veering towards a more mainstream cabaret repertoire. There were later records for Playboy (1975), and in 1981 a reissued 'Hurt' was a big hit in The Netherlands. This led to a new recording deal with **Polydor**. During the late 80s Yuro recorded an album of songs by **Willie Nelson**, but soon afterwards her performing career was curtailed by serious illness.

● ALBUMS: *Hurt* (Liberty 1961)★★★★, *Let Me Call You Sweetheart* (1962)★★★, *Soul* (Liberty 1962)★★★, *What's A Matter Baby?* (1963)★★★, *Make The World Go Away* (1963)★★★, *Amazing* (1964)★★★, *All Alone Am I* (1981)★★★, *Today* (1982)★★.

● COMPILATIONS: *Very Best Of Timi Yuro* (1980)★★★, *18 Greatest Hits* (1988)★★★, *The Lost Voice Of Soul* (RPM 1993)★★★.

Yvad

b. Kevin Davy. It was one of **Bob Marley**'s wishes to help young musicians to achieve their goals, and at his Tuff Gong Studios a number of performers were supported, including **Tyrone Taylor**, **Junior Tucker**, **Diana King**, **Nadine Sutherland** and one of the more recent artists, Yvad. His debut single, 'We Need Love', surfaced through the Tuff Gong label but did not make any impression on the charts. The RAS label in Washington, USA, were suitably impressed and signed the singer for the release of *Young Gifted And Dread*. He has also enjoyed media exposure on American television, including video promotion on **MTV** and Black Entertainment Television. To promote the album he was selected to support fellow RAS artists **Israel Vibration** on their US tour.

● ALBUMS: *Young Gifted And Dread* (RAS 1996)★★★.

YZ

New Jersey rapper most famous for his 'Thinkin' Of A Masterplan' cut. Bedecked in paisley shirts and dreads, YZ seemed to offer a neat distillation of **Native Tongues** philosophy with more street-orientated themes. Despite the good impression this made, it would be four years before a follow-up would be offered, by which time his DJ Tony D had been replaced by the **Trackmasterz** and God Squad, among others. As a member of the Five Per Cent Nation, a less disciplined than usual Muslim order, he produces a number of 'conscious' rhymes, but his main targets remain opposing MCs, holding **Naughty By Nature** in particular contempt.

● ALBUMS: *Sons Of The Father* (Tuff City 1989)★★★, *The Ghetto's Been Good To Me* (Livin' Large 1993)★★★.

Z

Zabriskie Point

Released in 1969 and directed by Michelangelo Antonioni, *Zabriskie Point* is a flawed, yet elegant, attempt at chronicling a malaise affecting the US counter-culture of the late 60s. In his previous feature, *Blow Up*, Antonioni had captured the spiritual ennui at the heart of 'Swinging London', but here the crux of his statement seems tantalizingly out of his grasp. The use of unknown actors, Mark Frechette and Daria Halprin, in the starring roles was ambitious, but neither acted convincingly and it was left to veteran Rod Taylor to bring cohesion to the plot. The script, in part written by Sam Shepard, carries little weight and it is for visuals and imagery that the film is best recalled. These memorable scenes include a Death Valley love-in and an apocalyptic finale, over which **Pink Floyd** contribute the eerie 'Come In Number 51, You're Time Is Up', otherwise known as 'Careful With That Axe, Eugene'. The group was initially commissioned to compose the entire score, but eventually Antonioni opted for a variety of artists, including **Kaleidoscope**, the **Youngbloods**, **John Fahey**, **Jerry Garcia** and **Patti Page**. His choices were astute and indeed the popularity of the attendant soundtrack album has outlasted that of the film generating it.

Zacharia

Billed as 'the first electric western', *Zacharia* was initially scripted by members of the **Firesign Theatre**, a radical comedy troupe blending elements of satire, 50s radio serials and counter-culture quirkiness. Their work for the film was radically altered during production, causing the group to disown the entire project. The notion of equating rock musicians with outlaws was already a cliché by the time *Zacharia* was first screened in 1971, and the final print did little to alter that notion. Coyly billed 'Ahead Of Its Time', the film boasts interesting musical cameos by the **James Gang**, **Doug Kershaw** and former **John Coltrane** drummer **Elvin Jones**, but the best moments are courtesy of **Country Joe And The Fish** who play a band of outlaws, the Crackers. This San Franciscan quintet capture the irreverence the Firesign Theatre first extolled, but the rest of the film is burdened by an aura of misplaced self-importance.

Zacharias, Helmut

b. 27 January 1920, Germany. A violinist, arranger, composer, and bandleader. At the age of three Zacharias was given a toy violin by his father, himself a professional violinist. The gift was soon replaced by the real thing, and when Zacharias was 17, he bought himself a Hammig instrument with the proceeds of a Fritz Kreisler Award. He formed his own orchestra which became popular throughout Europe. One of his biggest hits, 'When The White Lilacs Bloom Again', was also released in the USA in 1956, and almost made the Top 10. In the late 1950s Zacharias settled in Ascona, the Italian part of Switzerland, and, soon afterwards, in the early 60s, began to make an impact in the UK with several successful albums. Some of them were credited 'with Orchestra', and others 'with Magic Violins'. One of the latter was 'Love Is Like A Violin', which was enormously successful for Zacharias on the Continent, but was kept out of the UK chart by a version from singing comedian **Ken Dodd** in 1960. Four years later, Zacharias made the British Top 10, unopposed, with 'Tokyo Melody', which he wrote with Heinz Hellmer and **Lionel Bart**. It was the theme tune for the 1964 Olympic Games, the first occasion they had been held in Asia. Zacharias continued to prosper with his mixture of contemporary pops and light classics, played in a relaxed, swinging style, with the ever-present fiddle. His *Greatest Hits* contained numbers such as 'Cherry Pink And Apple Blossom White', 'Under The Linden Tree', and one of his own most attractive compositions, 'Blue Blues'.

● ALBUMS: *Rendezvous For Strings*, *Pop Goes Baroque*, *A Violin Sings*, *Super Twist*, *Crazy Party*, *Dance With My Fair Lady*, *Teatime In Tokyo*, *Romantically Yours*, *Violins Victorious*, *Happy Strings Of*, *This Is My Song*, *Plays The Hits*, *For Lovers-With Love*, *Strauss Waltzes*, *Golden Award Songs*, *On Lovers Road*, *Candlelight Serenade*, *The Best Of Everything*, *Hi-Fi Fiddle* (all 60s), *Light My Fire* (Sounds Superb 1971)★★★, *Greatest Hits* (1973)★★★.

Zacherle, John

b. 26 September 1918, Philadelphia, Pennsylvania, USA. Zacherle was a television personality on the US east coast for many years. Zacherle - who used only his surname (pronounced zack-er-ley) on the air - also found his way to the pop charts in 1958 with a novelty song, 'Dinner With Drac Part 1'. Nicknamed the 'Cool Ghoul', on Philadelphia television station WCAU, Zacherle took the role of an undertaker when hosting afternoon television programmes on which he showed popular horror films. He was switched to a late-night programme whereupon he became a vampire character. So successful was the character that Zacherle became an in-demand celebrity. **Cameo Records** approached Zacherle to record in 1958, and 'Dinner With Drac', in which Zacherle imitated Dracula, resulted. The single reached the US Top 10 that spring. He subsequently moved to a New York television station and continued to perform his role into the early 90s. Other than one album, *Monster Mash*, Zacherle never reached the charts again.

● ALBUMS: *Spook Along With Zacherle* (Cameo 1960)★★, *Monster Mash* (Cameo 1962)★★★, *Scary Tales* (Cameo 1963)★, *Zacherle's Monster Gallery* (Cameo 1963)★.

Zager And Evans

One of the biggest-selling hits of 1969 was the pessimistic look into the future, 'In The Year 2525 (Exordium & Terminus)' by Zager And Evans. The duo was Denny Zager (b. 1944, Wymore, Nebraska, USA) and Rick Evans (b. 1943, Lincoln, Nebraska, USA), who had met in 1962 and joined a band called the Eccentrics. Evans left that band in 1965 but the pair teamed up again at the end of the decade. Zager had written 'In The Year 2525' five years earlier, and they recorded it in Texas in 1968. It was released on the local Truth label and picked up the following year by **RCA Records**, climbing to number 1, where it remained for six weeks in the US charts and three weeks in the UK, ultimately selling a reported five million copies. Unable to follow this success, Zager quit in 1970; neither he nor Evans were heard of again, although RCA continued to release their recordings for some time in attempts to make lightning strike twice. 'In The Year 2525' is one of the most irritating songs ever, and yet it is still regularly played on the radio.

● ALBUMS: *2525 (Exordium & Terminus)* (RCA 1969)★★, *Zager And Evans* (RCA 1970)★, *Food For The Mind* (RCA 1971)★.

Zaiko Langa Langa

Zaire's greatest youth band, Zaiko Langa Langa, were formed in 1970, with **Papa Wemba**, N'Yoka-Longo, Manuaku Waku and Evoloko 'Joker' among the original line-up. Their style, background and musical range were considerable changes in a scene dominated, up to that point, by an older generation of rumba stars. Zaiko was made up of students, sons of the wealthy middle-class in the country's capital, Kinshasa. In the city, they were compared to the hippies, for their well-to-do backgrounds and their attitude of revolt - and specifically to the **Rolling Stones**, for introducing a hard, swaggering guitar sound into their music. While earlier Zairean bands adopted sweet melodies and neatly clipped arrangements, Zaiko blew a rude, rough-house blast of folk rhythms, hard snare drums, wild guitars and rough vocals through the whole neatly ordered system. They were not the first, but they were the wildest. The early youth sound had taken off with Jazz Baron, Bavon Marie-Marie and Thu-Zaina, from whom many of Zaiko's early line-up came, but where the earlier bands still kept their neat ambience, Zaiko took off into uncharted territory. The band immediately caught the imagination of Kinshasa youth; while

their creation of the cavacha, and later zekete zekete, put them among the key roots-rhythm bands of the early 70s. Zaiko continue today: as a band, as a legend and as the head of a family of splinter bands that followed them - collectively known as Clan Langa Langa. The first to leave the band was Shungu Wembiado, or Papa Wemba, who founded Isifi Lokole in 1970, then Yoka Lokole and Viva La Musica. Zaiko's original guitarist, Manuaka Waku, left the band in 1975 to form Grand Zaiko Wa Wa. Another prominent figure in the original line-up, Evoloko 'Joker', left in 1974 to continue his studies - his family disliked the idea of a musician in the family - and went to Europe. Here he teamed up with fellow musicians Mavuela and Bozi Boziana, now leader of Choc Stars. On his return, Evoloko joined Papa Wemba briefly, before forming Langa Langa Stars in 1981, recording a series of albums - *Requiem*, *Kalolo* and *Soleil* - which threw up new dances such as the sansaku. The 'original' Zaiko Langa Langa continue to perform and record, most recently in tandem with talented soukous vocalist, J.P. Buse

● ALBUMS: *Sarah Djenni* (FCZ 1981)★★★, *La Tout Neige* (FCZ 1983)★★★, *Bongama Kamata Position* (Disques Esperance 1987)★★★, with J.P. Buse *Zaiko Langa Langa - J.P. Buse* (Flame Tree 1993)★★★, *Avis De Recherche* (Stern's 1995)★★.

Zakary Thaks

Formed in the mid-60s in Corpus Christi, Texas, USA, Zakary Thaks was a punky blues-psychedelic-rock quintet that had no major impact in its time but is revered decades later by fans and collectors of early 'garage' band music. Consisting of singer Chris Gernoittis, lead guitarist John Lopez, rhythm guitarist Pete Stinson, bassist Rex Gregory and drummer Stan Moore, they signed to the local J-Beck label. Their first single, 'Bad Girl', was a hit in Texas and **Mercury Records** picked it up for national distribution with no success. Subsequent singles, including 'Face To Face', 'Please' and 'Mirror Of Yesterday', only fared well in their home state. J-Beck became Cee-Bee Records in the late 60s but the group's lone single for that label fared no better and they broke up in late 1968. Although they did not record an album, Zakary Thaks' singles have been collected on reissue compilations.

Zaks, Jerry

b. 7 September 1946, Stuttgart, Germany. A director and actor, mainly for the theatre, Zaks was educated at Dartmouth College and Smith College in the USA, before training for the stage with Curt Dempster. He made his first principal stage appearance in 1974, playing the role of Kenickie in the Broadway revival of *Grease*. During the next six years, as well as performing in straight theatre in New York and various other US cities, he was seen in the Broadway musicals *The 1940s' Radio Hour* (as Neil Tilden, 1978) and the critically acclaimed *Tintypes* (as Charlie, 1980). Zaks began to direct in the early 80s, but, apart from working on a major US regional tour of *Tintypes*, and the 1987 Broadway revival of **Anything Goes**, most of his efforts during that decade were concerned with non-musical productions. He also served as resident director at Lincoln Centre Theatre from 1986-90. During the 90s, Zaks' reputation as an extremely inventive 'master comedy strategist' has been affirmed with his direction of the highly successful revivals of the musicals **Guys And Dolls** (1992) and *A Funny Thing Happened On The Way To The Forum* (1996) - both starring Nathan Lane. He also helmed the **Leiber And Stoller** revue *Smokey Joe's Café* (1995), **Stephen Sondheim** and John Weidman's *Assassins* (1991, off-Broadway), and pop legend **Paul Simon**'s debut Broadway show, *The Capeman* (1998). Zaks won a **Tony Award** for *Guys And Dolls*, and three others for *The House Of Blue Leaves* (1986), *Lend Me A Tenor* (1989) and *Six Degrees Of Separation* (1991). His other honours have included Outer Circle, Obie, and Drama League awards. In addition, he was the 1994 recipient of the **George Abbott** Award for Lifetime Achievement In The Theatre. In 1996, he made his film debut directing Meryl Streep, Diane Keaton, Leonardo DiCaprio and Robert DeNiro in *Marvin's Room*.

Zamfir, Gheorghe

b. Rumania. Zamfir is the best-known exponent of the pan-pipes or nei, an ancient instrument of southern Europe consisting of reed or wooden pipes graduated in size and bound together in a row. His recording career began when he linked up with Swiss record producer Marcel Cellier, who recorded traditional folk tunes by Zamfir in the early 70s for release on his own label. Already popular in France, Zamfir found a mainstream audience in the UK in 1976 when 'Doina De Jale', a traditional funeral tune was used as the theme for a BBC Television series, *The Light Of Experience*. Released as a single by Epic, it was a Top 10 hit. The record also sold well across Europe, and Zamfir was launched on a career in middle-of-the-road music, frequently recording pan-pipe versions of western tunes, pop, classical and religious. Thus, his 1985 album *Atlantis* included film music, pieces by **Jacques Brel** and Eric Satie, plus 'Stranger On The Shore', the 1962 **Acker Bilk** hit. In 1979 Zamfir and **James Last** had a Dutch hit with the theme from 'De Verlaten Mijn', and several of his 80s albums were recorded with Dutch orchestra leader Harry van Hoof.
● ALBUMS: *Roumanian Flutes, Vol·1 and 2* (Arion 1974)★★★, *Theme Light Of Experience* (Epic 1976)★★★, *Impressions* (Epic 1978)★★★, *L'Alouette* (Philips 1978)★★★, *Picnic At Hanging Rock* (Epic 1979)★★★, *Extraordinary Pan Pipe Vol 1-3* (Columbia 1981)★★★, *In Paris* (Columbia 1981)★★★, *Roumanian Folklore Instruments* (Columbia 1981)★★, *In Paris 2* (Columbia 1981)★★★, *Rocking Chair* (Philips 1981)★★★, *Zamfir* (Columbia 1981)★★★, *Lonely Shepherd* (Philips 1982)★★★, *Music For The Millions* (Philips 1983)★★★, *Christmas Album* (Philips 1984)★★, *Romance* (Philips 1984)★★★, *Atlantis* (Philips 1985)★★★, *Zamfir In Paris Live* (Delta 1986)★★, *Classics By Candlelight* (Philips 1986)★★, *Harmony* (Philips 1987)★★★, *Beautiful Dreams* (Philips 1988)★★★, *Easyriding* (Easyriding 1988)★★, *Golden Pan Flute* (Musique International 1988)★★★, *Images* (Images 1989)★★★.
● COMPILATIONS: *Great Successes Of* (Columbia 1981)★★★, *Best Of Gheorghe Zamfir* (Philips 1985)★★★, *King Of Pan Flute* (Timeless Treasures 1986)★★★, *Greatest Hits* (Delta 1987)★★★, *The Beautiful Sound Of The Pan Pipes* (Music Club 1995)★★★.

Zanes, Dan

b. USA. Formerly lead singer with the acclaimed US alternative rock band the **Del Fuegos**, Zanes launched his solo career in 1995 with the release of *Cool Down Time*. Produced by Mitchell Froom with help from **Tom Waits** associate Tchad Blake, this collection anchored elements of blues and country as accompaniment to Zanes' dark narratives of loss, hurt and betrayal. As well as a cover version of **Mose Allison**'s 'If You Live', the artist's own writing included the affecting ballad 'Carelessly' and the tough blues of 'Rough Spot'.
● ALBUMS: *Cool Down Time* (Private Music 1995)★★★.

Zantees

This group was formed in October 1977 in New York City, USA. The Zantees (named after an episode of the science fiction television show *The Outer Limits*) drew on the raw rock 'n' roll styles of the 50s, particularly rockabilly music, emphasizing its primitive qualities rather than trying to update the sound. The original quartet consisted of Billy Miller (vocals), Billy Statile (guitar), Paul Statile (guitar) and Jimmy Devito (drums). Devito was replaced after only one performance by Miriam Linna, ex-**Cramps** drummer, who remained throughout the group's history. Although they originally had no bassist, four musicians eventually occupied that position: Chuck Forssi (whose brother Ken had been in the 60s group **Love**), Rob Norris (the last bassist of the **Velvet Underground** and later a founder-member of the **Bongos**), James Stephanik and Mike Lewis (formerly of **DMZ** and the **Lyres**). The Zantees' first record was 'Francene', a flexi-disc single released in conjunction with the US record collector magazine *Goldmine*, in 1979. Other singles followed, as did *Out For Kicks*, on the Bomp label in 1980, and *Rhythm Bound*, released on the US Midnight label in 1983. They also released a self-titled EP on Midnight in 1983. The Zantees toured the USA, as well as Scandinavian countries in the early 80s, and disbanded in December 1983. Miller, Linna and Lewis subsequently started the **A-Bones**, a band of similar qualities, in 1984. Miller and Linna also launched the popular independent record label Norton, and published their own fanzine, *Kicks*.
● ALBUMS: *Out For Kicks* (1980)★★★, *Rhythm Bound* (1983)★★★.

Zap Mama

Female vocal group Zap Mama came to international prominence in the 90s by perfecting a blend of traditional African singing and musicianship with tinges of various international pop styles. They are led, in articulate fashion, by the Belgium-based Marie Daulne (b. Zaire). After releasing their first two records on Belgium's acclaimed **Crammed Records** imprint, Zap Mama were subsequently signed to Lauka Bop by label founder **David Byrne**, who continues to take a personal interest in their development. The group's first two albums were overwhelmingly geared towards vocal music. *Adventures In Afropea 1* offered an intoxicating hybrid of African and European phrasing and rhythms. *Sabsylma* shifted the focus to Middle-Eastern and Antipodean influences, and featured new vocalist **Sally Nyolo**. These themes were continued on 1997's *7*, their first album as part of a new international deal with **Virgin Records**. However, this time the musical backing was much more forceful. As Daulne told *Billboard* magazine on its release: 'With instruments, music talks to the body; drums and bass make your body move'. The album included collaborations with **Disposable Heroes Of Hiphoprisy**'s Michael Franti on a revision of **Pheobe Snow**'s 'Poetry Man', a splendid version of **Etta James**' 'Damn Your Eyes' and a collaboration with reggae DJ **U-Roy**, 'New World'. Nyolo has also recorded solo.

● ALBUMS: *Adventures In Afropea 1* (Crammed Discs 1993)★★★, *Sabsylma* (Crammed Discs 1994)★★★, *7* (Lauka Bop/Virgin 1997)★★★.

Zap Pow

Zap Pow were formed in the early 70s. The group consisted of some of the finest musicians in Jamaica and included Max Edwards (drums, vocals), Mike Williams (bass, vocals), **Dwight Pinkney** (guitar, vocals) and **Beres Hammond** (lead vocals); the horn section featured Glen DaCosta (tenor saxophone), Joe McCormack (trombone) and David Madden (trumpet, vocals). In 1971 they recorded their debut, 'Mystic Mood', followed by the popular 'Breaking Down The Barriers', 'Nice Nice Time' and the internationally successful 'This Is Reggae Music'. These hits featured on an album released only in Jamaica, assuring their local popularity. In 1976 the group recorded 'Jungle Beat' and 'Sweet Loving Love' at **Harry J.**'s and Dynamic studios. *Zap Pow Now* featured unusual packaging, with the outer sleeve resembling a book of matches, and the album secured healthy sales within the reggae market and topped the UK chart. The success inspired **Trojan Records** to re-release their debut with the addition of 'Money', 'Crazy Woman', 'Wild Honey' and a version of **Harold Melvin And The Bluenotes**' 'If You Don't Know Me By Now'. The label released the latter as a single, which provided a minor hit. By 1980 Hammond had left the group to pursue a successful solo career. Pinkney's guitar skills were utilized in numerous sessions for artists including

Roots Radics, and at Penthouse Studios for producer **Donovan Germain**. Edwards pursued a solo career, almost crossing over into pop territory with the release of 'Rockers Arena'. Williams became known as Mikey Zap Pow, enjoying a hit with 'Sunshine People', and pursued a career in journalism, with particular emphasis on reggae. The horn section was featured on many sessions, including some for **Bob Marley** And The Wailers. They also toured individually supporting **Sly And Robbie**'s Taxi Gang and **Lloyd Parks**' We The People Band. Madden released a solo album, *David ... Going Bananas*, which featured his vocals and trumpet-playing on tracks that included 'Musical Message' and a return to 'Mystic Mood'. The album was followed by *The Reggae Trumpetaa*, while fellow horn player DaCosta released *Mind Blowing Melody*.

● ALBUMS: *Zap Pow Now* (Vulcan 1976)★★★, *Revolution* (Trojan 1976)★★★.

Zappa, Dweezil

Dweezil is the son of the legendary **Frank Zappa**. However, it was not his father's guitar playing that prompted Dweezil to form a band, but **Eddie Van Halen**. Unfortunately, this obsession led to an almost direct copy of his hero's style, right down to wielding identical guitars and dressing the same. However, Dweezil still built up a small cult following with early releases, breaking into the mainstream via the album and video, *My Guitar Wants To Kill Your Mama*, one of his father's old tunes given the Van Halen treatment. The video, which achieved mass viewing figures on **MTV** and music programmes all over the world, featured a 50s cop movie parody in black and white, and guest appearances from, among others, actor Robert Wagner. The album was completed with Bobby Blotzer (**Ratt**; drums), Steven Smith (**Journey**; drums), and vocalist Fiona. For *Shampoo Horn* the videos took on a much more surreal nature. Dweezil's brother helped out on vocals, but that Van Halen ghost still lurked.

● ALBUMS: *Having A Bad Day* (Rykodisc 1987)★★★, *My Guitar Wants To Kill Your Mama* (Chrysalis 1988)★★★, *Confessions* (Chrysalis 1991)★★, *Shampoo Horn* (Chrysalis 1993)★★★.

● VIDEOS: *My Guitar Wants To Kill Your Mama* (1988).

Zappa, Frank

b. Frank Vincent Zappa, 21 December 1940, Baltimore, Maryland, USA, d. 4 December 1993, Los Angeles, California, USA. Zappa's parents were second-generation Sicilian Greeks; his father played 'strolling crooner' guitar. At the age of 12 Frank became interested in drums, learning orchestral percussion at summer school in Monterey. By 1956 he was playing drums in a local R&B band called the Ramblers. Early exposure to a record of *Ionisation* by *avant garde* classical composer Edgard Varese instilled an interest in advanced rhythmic experimentation that never left him. The electric guitar also became a fascination, and he began collecting R&B records that featured guitar solos: **Howlin' Wolf** with **Hubert Sumlin, Muddy Waters, Johnny 'Guitar' Watson** and **Clarence 'Gatemouth' Brown** were special favourites. A schoolfriend, Don Van Vliet (later to become **Captain Beefheart**), shared his interest. In 1964 Zappa joined a local R&B outfit, the Soul Giants (Roy Collins; vocals, Roy Estrada; bass, Jimmy Carl Black; drums), and started writing songs for them. They changed their name to the **Mothers** ('Of Invention' was added at record company insistence). Produced by Tom Wilson in 1966 - the late black producer whose credits included **Cecil Taylor, John Coltrane** and **Bob Dylan** - *Freak Out!* was a stunning debut, a two-record set complete with a whole side of wild percussion, a vitriolic protest song, 'Trouble Every Day', and the kind of minute detail (sleeve-notes, in-jokes, parodies) that generate instant cult appeal. They made great play of their hair and ugliness, becoming the perfect counter-cultural icons. Unlike the east coast band the **Fugs**, the Mothers were also musically skilled, a refined instrument for Zappa's eclectic and imaginative ideas. Tours and releases followed, including *We're Only In It For The Money*, (with its brilliant parody of the *Sgt Pepper* record cover) a scathing satire on hippiedom and the reactions to it in the USA, and a notable appearance at the Royal Albert Hall in London (documented in the compulsive *Uncle Meat*). *Cruising With Ruben & The Jets* was an excellent homage to the doo-wop era. British fans were particularly impressed with *Hot Rats*, a record that ditched the sociological commentary for barnstorming jazz-rock, blistering guitar solos, the extravagant 'Peaches En Regalia' and a cameo appearance by Captain Beefheart on 'Willie The Pimp'. The original band broke up (subsequently to resurface as the Grandmothers). Both the previous two albums appeared on Zappa's own Bizarre record label and together with his other outlet Straight Records he released a number of highly regarded albums (although commercial flops), including those by the GTO's, **Larry Wild Man Fischer, Alice Cooper, Tim Buckley** and the indispensable Zappa-produced classic, *Trout Mask Replica*, by Captain Beefheart.

Eager to gain a 'heavier' image than the band that had brought them fame, the **Turtles**' singers **Flo And Eddie** joined up with Zappa for the film *200 Motels* and three further albums. *Fillmore East June '71* included some intentionally outrageous subject matter prompting inevitable criticism from conservative observers. 1971 was not a happy year: on 4 December fire destroyed the band's equipment while they were playing at Montreux (an event commemorated in **Deep Purple**'s 'Smoke On The Water') and soon afterwards Zappa was pushed off-stage at London's Rainbow theatre, crushing his larynx (lowering his voice a third), damaging his spine and keeping him wheelchair-bound for the best part of a year. He spent 1972 developing an extraordinary new species of big band fusion (*Waka/Jawaka* and *The Grand Wazoo*), working with top west coast session musicians. However, he found these excellent players

dull touring companions, and decided to dump the 'jazztette' for an electric band. 1973's *Overnite Sensation* announced fusion-chops, salacious lyrics and driving rhythms. The live band featured an extraordinary combination of jazz-based swing and a rich, sonorous rock that probably only Zappa (with his interest in modern classical music) could achieve. Percussion virtuoso Ruth Underwood, violinist **Jean-Luc Ponty**, featured in the *King Kong* project, and keyboardist **George Duke** shone in this context. *Apostrophe (')* showcased Zappa's talents as a story-teller in the **Lord Buckley** tradition, and also (in the title track) featured a jam with bassist **Jack Bruce**: it reached number 10 in the *Billboard* chart in June 1974. *Roxy & Elsewhere* caught the band live, negotiating diabolically hard musical notation - 'Echidna's Arf' and 'The Bebop Tango' - with infectious good humour. *One Size Fits All*, an under-acknowledged masterpiece, built up extraordinary multi-tracked textures. 'Andy' was a song about b-movie cowboys, while 'Florentine Pogen' and 'Inca Roads' were complex extended pieces.

In 1975 Captain Beefheart joined Zappa for a tour and despite an earlier rift, sang on *Bongo Fury*, both reuniting in disgust over the USA's bicentennial complacency. *Zoot Allures* in 1976 was principally a collaboration between Zappa and drummer Terry Bozzio, with Zappa overdubbing most of the instruments himself. He was experimenting with what he termed 'xenochronicity' (combining unrelated tracks to create a piece of non-synchronous music) and produced intriguing results on 'Friendly Little Finger'. The title track took the concept of sleaze guitar onto a new level (as did the orgasmic moaning of 'The Torture Never Stops'), while 'Black Napkins' was an incomparable vehicle for guitar. If *Zoot Allures* now reads like a response to punk, Zappa was not to forsake large-scale rock showbiz. A series of concerts in New York at Halloween in 1976 had a wildly excited crowd applauding tales of singles bars, devil encounters and stunning **Brecker Brothers** virtuosity (recorded as *Live In New York*). This album was part of the fall-out from Zappa's break-up with **Warner Brothers Records**, who put out three excellent instrumental albums with 'non-authorized covers' (adopted, strangely enough, by Zappa for his CD re-releases): *Studio Tan, Sleep Dirt* and *Orchestral Favourites*. The punk-obsessed rock press did not know what to make of music that parodied **Miklos Rosza**, crossed jazz with cartoon scores, guyed rock 'n' roll hysteria and stretched fusion into the 21st century. Undaunted by still being perceived as a hippie, which he clearly was not (*We're Only In It For The Money* had said the last word on the Summer Of Love while it was happening!), Zappa continued to tour.

His guitar-playing seemed to expand into a new dimension: 'Yo' Mama' on *Sheik Yerbouti* (1979) was a taste of the extravaganzas to come. In Ike Willis, Zappa found a vocalist who understood his required combination of emotional detachment and intimacy, and featured him extensively on *Joe's Garage*. After the mid-70s interest in philosophical concepts and band in-jokes, the music became more political. *Tinseltown Rebellion* and *You Are What You Is* commented on the growth of the fundamentalist Right.

In 1982 Zappa had a hit with 'Valley Girl', with his daughter Moon Unit satirizing the accents of young moneyed Hollywood people. That same year saw him produce and introduce a New York concert of music by Edgar Varese. *Ship Arriving Too Late To Save A Drowning Witch* had a title track which indicated that Zappa's interest in extended composition was not waning; this was confirmed by the release of a serious orchestral album in 1983. In 1984 he was quite outrageously prolific: he unearthed an 18th century composer named Francesco Zappa and recorded his work on a synclavier; he released a rock album *Them Or Us*, which widened still further the impact of his scurrilously inventive guitar; and renowned French composer Pierre Boulez conducted Zappa's work on *The Perfect Stranger*. Two releases, *Shut Up 'N Play Yer Guitar* and *Guitar*, proved that Zappa's guitar playing was unique; *Jazz From Hell* presented wordless compositions for synclavier that drew inspiration from Conlon Nancarrow; *Thing-Fish* was a 'Broadway musical' about AIDS, homophobia and racism. The next big project materialized in 1988: a 12-piece band playing covers, instrumentals and a brace of new political songs (collected respectively as *The Best Band You Never Heard In Your Life*, *Make A Jazz Noise Here* and *Broadway The Hard Way*). They rehearsed for three months and the power and precision of the band were breathtaking, but they broke up during their first tour. As well as the retrospective series *You Can't Do That On Stage Anymore*, Zappa released eight of his most popular bootlegs in a 'beat the boots' campaign. In Czechoslovakia, where he had long been a hero of the cultural underground, he was appointed their Cultural Liaison Officer with the West and in 1991 he announced he would be standing as an independent candidate in the 1992 US presidential election (almost immediately he received several death threats!). The man never ceased to astonish, both as a musician and composer: on the way, he produced a towering body of work that is probably rock music's closest equivalent to the legacy of **Duke Ellington**. In November 1991 his daughter confirmed reports that Zappa was suffering from cancer of the prostate and in May 1993 Zappa, clearly weak from intensive chemotherapy, announced that he was fast losing the battle as it had spread into his bones. He lost the fight against the disease seven months later.

In 1995 a remarkable reissue programme was undertaken by Rykodisk in conjunction with Gail Zappa. The entire catalogue of over 50 albums were remastered, repackaged and released with loving care. Ryko deserve the highest praise for this bold move. Zappa's career in perspective shows a musical perfectionist using only the highest standards of musicianship and the finest recording quality. The reissued CDs highlight the extraordinary quality of the original master tapes and Zappa's idealism. Additionally, he is now rightly seen as one of *the* great guitar players of our time. Although much of his oeuvre is easily dismissed as flippant, history will certainly recognize Zappa as a sophisticated, serious composer and a highly accomplished master of music. The use of the words 'musical genius' are carefully chosen. The additional fact that he did it all with an amazing sense of humour should be seen as a positive bonus.

● ALBUMS: *Freak Out!* (Verve 1966)★★★★, *Absolutely Free* (Verve 1967)★★★★, *We're Only In It For The Money* (Verve 1967)★★★★, *Lumpy Gravy* (Verve 1967)★★★★, *Crusing With Ruben & The Jets* (Verve 1968)★★★, *Uncle Meat* (Bizarre 1969)★★★★, *Hot Rats* (Bizarre 1969)★★★★, *Burnt Weeny Sandwich* (Bizarre 1969)★★★★, with Jean-Luc Ponty *King Kong* (1970)★★, *Weasels Ripped My Flesh* (Bizarre 1970)★★★★, *Chunga's Revenge* (Bizarre 1970)★★★★, *Live At The Fillmore East June '71* (Bizarre 1971)★★★, *200 Motels* (United Artists 1971)★★ *Just Another Band From LA* (Bizarre 1972)★★★, *Waka/Jawaka* (Bizarre 1972)★★★, *The Grand Wazoo* (Bizarre 1972)★★★, *Overnite Sensation* (DiscReet 1973)★★★, *Apostrophe (')* (DiscReet 1974)★★★★, *Roxy & Elsewhere* (DiscReet 1974)★★★, *One Size Fits All* (DiscReet 1975)★★★★, *Bongo Fury* (DiscReet 1975)★★★, *Zoot Allures* (DiscReet 1976)★★★★, *Zappa In New York* (DiscReet 1977)★★★, *Studio Tan* (DiscReet 1978)★★★, *Sleep Dirt* (DiscReet 1979)★★, *Orchestral Favourites* (DiscReet 1979)★★★, *Sheik Yerbouti* (Zappa 1979)★★★★, *Joe's Garage Act 1* (Zappa 1980)★★★★, *Joe's Garage Acts 2 & 3* (Zappa 1980)★★★★, *Tinseltown Rebellion* (Barking Pumpkin 1981)★★★, *You Are What You Is* (Barking Pumpkin 1981)★★★, *Ship Arriving Too Late To Save A Drowning Witch* (Barking Pumpkin 1982)★★★, *Baby Snakes* (Barking Pumpkin 1982)★★★, *Man From Utopia* (Barking Pumpkin 1983)★★★, *London Symphony Orchestra Volume I* (Barking Pumpkin 1983)★★★★, *Francesco Zappa* (Barking Pumpkin 1984)★★★, *Does Humor Belong In Music?* (EMI 1984)★★★, *Them Or Us* (EMI 1984)★★★, *The Perfect Stranger* (EMI 1984)★★★, *Shut Up 'N Play Yer Guitar* (Rykodisc 1984)★★★★, *Guitar* (Rykodisc 1984)★★★★, *Jazz From Hell* (Rykodisc 1984)★★★★, *Thing-Fish* (Rykodisc 1984)★★★★, *Meets The Mothers Of Prevention* (Rykodisc 1985)★★★, *London Symphony Orchestra Volume II* (Rykodisc 1987)★★★, *Broadway The Hard Way* (Rykodisc 1988)★★★, *The Best Band You Never Heard In Your Life* (Barking Pumpkin 1991)★★★★, *Make A Jazz Noise Here* (Barking Pumpkin 1991)★★★, with the Ensemble Modern *Yellow Shark* (Barking Pumpkin 1993)★★★, *Civilization Phaze III* (Barking Pumpkin 1995)★★★, *The Lost Episodes* (Ryko 1996)★★★, *Läther* (Rykodisc 1996)★★★★, *Cucamonga* pre-Mothers Of Invention (Del-Fi 1998)★★.

Beating The Bootleggers: (all released 'officially' in 1991) *'Tis The Season To Be Jelly* (Foo-Eee 1967)★★★, *The Ark* (Foo-Eee 1968)★★★, *Freaks And Motherfuckers* (Foo-Eee 1970)★★★, *Piquantique* (Foo-Eee 1973)★★★, *Unmitigated Audacity* (Foo-Eee 1974)★★★, *Saarbrucken 1978* (Foo-Eee 1978)★★★, *Any Way The Wind Blows* (Foo-Eee 1979)★★★, *As An Am Zappa* (Foo-Eee 1981)★★★.

● COMPILATIONS: *Mothermania* (Verve 1969)★★★, *Rare Meat* (Ryko 1962-63)★★★, *You Can't Do That On Stage Any More Vol 1* (Ryko 1969-88)★★★★, *You Can't Do That On Stage Any More Vol 2* (Ryko 1974)★★★★, *You Can't Do That On Stage Any More Vol 3* (Ryko 1971-88)★★★★, *You Can't Do That On Stage Any More Vol 4* (Ryko 1969-88)★★★★, *You Can't Do That On Stage Any More Vol 5* (Ryko 1992)★★★★, *You Can't Do That On Stage Any More Vol 6* (Ryko 1992)★★★★, *Strictly Commercial: The Best Of* (Ryko 1995)★★★, *Have I Offended Someone?* (Ryko 1997)★★★, *Strictly Genteel* (Ryko 1997). The entire catalogue is currently available on Ryko.
● VIDEOS: *Does Humor Belong In Music?* (1985), *200 Motels* (1988), *The True Story Of 200 Motels* (1992), *The Amazing Mr. Bickford* (1992), *Uncle Meat* (1993).
● FURTHER READING: *Frank Zappa, Plastic People Songbuch*, Carl Weissner. *Frank Zappa: Over Het Begin En Het Einde Van De Progressieve Popmuziek*, Rolf-Ulrich Kaiser. *No Commercial Potential: The Saga Of Frank Zappa: Then And Now*, David Walley. *Frank Zappa Et Les Mothers Of Invention*, Alain Dister. *The Lives & Times Of Zappa And The Mothers*, no editor listed. *Get Zapped: Zappalog The First Step To Zappology*, Norbert Obermanns. *Zappalog: The First Step Of Zappalogy (2nd Edition)*, Norbert Obermanns. *Viva Zappa*, Dominique Chevalier. *The Real Frank Zappa Book*, Frank Zappa, with Peter Occhiogrosso. *Frank Zappa: A Visual Documentary*, Miles (ed.). *Frank Zappa In His Own Words*, Miles. *Mother! The Frank Zappa Story*, Michael Gray. *Frank Zappa: The Negative Dialectics Of Poodle Play*, Ben Watson. *Electric Don Quixote: The Story Of Frank Zappa*, Neil Slaven.
● FILMS: *Head* (1968), *200 Motels* (1971), *Baby Snakes* (1979).

Zarchy, Zeke
b. Rubin Zarchy, 12 June 1915, New York City, New York, USA. Zarchy began playing trumpet as a child and was playing semi-professionally while still at high school. He first came to note as a member of the excellent dance band led by **Joe Haymes**. In 1936 he joined **Benny Goodman** and thereafter played with **Artie Shaw**, **Bob Crosby**, **Red Norvo** and **Tommy Dorsey**, before joining **Glenn Miller** in 1940. Zarchy then moved into studio work but appeared on a number of Miller recordings and during World War II played in Miller's army band. He resumed studio work in the post-war years, and also made recording dates with many leading big bands throughout the 50s and 60s. In the early 80s he began making appearances with the Great Pacific Jazz Band (comprised mostly of musicians from the Walt Disney studio orchestra) and also toured Australia and the UK with a Miller reunion band. Zarchy never risked improvising, admitting to interviewer Ralph Gulliver, 'I would have been scared witless', but he enjoyed a reputation as being one of the best and most reliable lead trumpeters of the swing era.

Zardis, Chester
b. 27 May 1900, New Orleans, Louisiana, USA, d. 1990. Zardis began playing double bass in 1916, going against the prevailing preference for brass instruments to play bass lines. In the 20s he performed with many of the leading New Orleans jazzmen, including **Chris Kelly** and **Kid Rena**. Throughout the 30s he played in his hometown and on Mississippi riverboats, also recording with **Kid Howard**. In 1942 he took part in recording dates with the rediscovered **Bunk Johnson** and the following year recorded with **George Lewis**. In the late 40s and early 50s he played in New Orleans and after a spell away from music returned to the local scene to become a member of the Preservation Hall Jazz Band. He visited Europe with this band in the mid-60s. Zardis spent the 70s in New Orleans but found time for another trip to Europe, this time with the New Orleans Joymakers in 1972. In the following decade he was still playing regularly, visiting Europe again with **Kid Thomas Valentine**. A firm player with a lovely tone, Zardis maintained a steady yet fluid beat. One of the best of the New Orleans bass players.
●ALBUMS: with Eugene Wendell *West Indies Blues* (1978)★★★.
●COMPILATIONS: with Kid Howard *Dance New Orleans Style* (1937-41)★★★.

Zaret, Hy
(see **Kramer, Alex**)

Zavaroni, Lena
b. 4 November 1963, Rothesay, Scotland. This winsome singer travelled down from the Isle of Bute in Scotland during late 1973 to sing her way to victory over a season of ITV's *Opportunity Knocks* talent showcase. She was signed to manager Dorothy Solomon, partner of 60s' impresario **Phil Solomon**. Zavaroni gained a recording contract and reached the UK Top 10 almost immediately with a revival of the **Johnny Otis** Show's 'Ma He's Making Eyes At Me' - which was tied in with a best-selling album. In 1974 too, her version of **Lloyd Price**'s 'Personality' was a lesser hit. These chart strikes were a firm foundation for the exploitation of young Zavaroni as an all-round entertainer via a world tour, extensive television guest appearances, headlining at the London Palladium, a Royal Command Performance and her own BBC 1 series. However, her career had faded to virtual semi-retirement by the 80s, blighted as it was by anorexia nervosa - and the popular media's intrusive focus on the unhappy Zavaroni's incomplete success in regaining her health.
● ALBUMS: *Ma* (Philips 1974)★★★, *If My Friends Could See Me ...* (Hallmark 1976)★★, *Presenting Lena Zavaroni* (Galaxy 1977)★★★, *Songs Are Such Good Things* (Galaxy 1978)★★, *Lena Zavaroni And Her Music* (Galaxy 1979)★★★, *Hold Tight It's Lena* (BBC 1982)★★.

Zawinul, Joe
b. Josef Erich Zawinul, 7 July 1932, Vienna, Austria. After studying music at the Vienna Conservatory Zawinul's musical ambitions soon outgrew the limited opportunities for a jazz musician in Austria shortly

after the war. But financial necessity meant that he spent the 50s almost exclusively involved in local session work. Playing piano in dance and radio orchestras, and working as the house pianist for **Polydor Records**, he played only briefly with the talented saxophonist Hans Koller in 1952. However, his fortunes improved suddenly in 1959, when he won a scholarship to **Berklee College Of Music** in Boston. Emigrating to the USA, he immediately received a huge amount of attention, and decided to spend the rest of 1959 touring with **Maynard Ferguson**. Two years with **Dinah Washington** followed this, and then in 1961 he began a musical collaboration with **Cannonball Adderley** (*Mercy, Mercy, Mercy* 1966) which was to last nine years. Although he recorded with other musicians during this period - most notably **Miles Davis** (*In A Silent Way* 1969, *Bitches Brew* 1969), it was his work with Adderley that spread his reputation as an inventive improviser and talented writer. His composition 'Mercy, Mercy, Mercy' won a Grammy Award for the group. At the end of 1970 he joined **Wayne Shorter** to form the highly influential **Weather Report**, the band with which he will always be primarily associated. When the group disbanded in 1985, after 15 years of phenomenal success, Zawinul began touring Europe and the USA again as a soloist. More recently forming Weather Update and Zawinul Syndicate, his dark and ominous chord voicings and electric piano sound will remain a distinctive part of fusion for many years to come. Recorded in Germany in 1997, *World Tour* showcased a particularly stunning performance.
● ALBUMS: *Zawinul* (Atlantic 1970)★★★, *Dialects* (Columbia 1986), *The Immigrants* (Columbia 1988)★★, *Black Water* (Columbia 1989)★★★, *The Beginning* recorded 1959 (Fresh Sounds 1990)★★, *Stories Of The Danube* (Philips 1996)★★★, *My People* (Escapade 1996)★★★, *World Tour* (Escapade 1998)★★★★.

Zed Yago

Founded in Germany by blues singer Jutta in 1985, Zed Yago were a traditional rock concern very much in keeping with the sound pioneered by fellow nationals, **Warlock**. Jutta's vocal style owed much to **Doro** from Warlock, but also saluted American singer **Ronnie James Dio**. Her band comprised Jimmy and Gunnar on guitar, Tach on bass and a larger-than-life bald powerhouse of a drummer known as Bubi. They first attracted mainstream attention in May 1989 with the release of 'Black Bone Song'. This was followed by their second album and a tour - one concert of which was broadcast live on BBC Radio 1. They vanished in 1990 having failed to make any lasting impact.
● ALBUMS: *From Over Yonder* (SPV 1988)★★★, *Pilgrimage* (BMG 1989)★★.

Zeitlin, Denny

b. 10 April 1938, Chicago, USA. Zeitlin had a classical music training before studying medicine at Johns Hopkins University and then Columbia. In 1963 he

successfully auditioned for the record producer **John Hammond Jnr.** but then moved to San Francisco where he studied psychiatry and played the piano. In 1965 he was involved in a trio with bassist **Charlie Haden**. His interest in the use of the prepared piano (in which the sound of the piano is changed by attaching nuts, bolts and screws to the strings) encouraged him to experiment with sounds available from synthesizers as these became more readily available in the late 60s. Along with his keyboard playing, he has written instrumental scores, including a film score for Philip Kaufman's *Invasion Of The Bodysnatchers* in 1978.
● ALBUMS: *Sounding* (1978)★★★, *Tidal Wave* (Palo Alto 1981)★★★, with Charlie Haden *Time Remembers One Time Once* (ECM 1983)★★★, *Homecoming* (1986)★★★★, with David Friesen *In Concert* (TM Pacific 1992)★★, *In The Moment* (Windham Hill Jazz 1992)★★, *Trio* (Windham Hill Jazz 1992)★★★, *Live At the Maybank Recital Hall Vol 27* (Concord 1993)★★★.

Zella

(see **Lehr, Zella**)

Zentner, Si

b. Simon H. Zentner, 13 June 1917, New York City, New York, USA. After learning to play the trombone as a child, Zentner played in and around New York before joining **Les Brown** in 1940. During the 40s he played in a number of bands, including those led by **Harry James** and **Jimmy Dorsey**, and at the end of the decade entered a long period of studio work. From 1957 onwards, he periodically formed a big band for studio sessions and gained a substantial following among the record-buying public. For these bands he employed studio musicians, many with strong leanings to jazz; among them were **Don Fagerquist**, Don Lodice, Joe and Ray Triscari, Alvin Stoller, **Lanny Morgan**, **Frank Capp** and Gene Goe. Perhaps the most important among the regular members of the bands Zentner formed was pianist **Bob Florence**, whose arrangements were influential in establishing Zentner's reputation among big band fans. Zentner continued his series of recordings until 1968, and thereafter continued to form big bands to accompany leading singers and also for appearances at important venues in Los Angeles and Las Vegas. Leading by example, Zentner has consistently shown that there is a substantial and enthusiastic audience for big band music, and that such music need not be repetitive or confined to recreations of old favourites.
●ALBUMS: *Introducing Si Zentner And His Dance Band/Si Zentner, His Trombone And Orchestra* i (1957)★★★★, *Si Zentner And His Orchestra* (1957)★★★, *Swing Fever/Si Zentner, His Trombone And Orchestra* ii (1957)★★★★, *Sleepy Lagoon: Si Zentner With Russell Garcia* (1957)★★, *A Thinking Man's Band* (1959)★★★, *Suddenly It's Swing* (1960)★★★★, *The Si Zentner Big Band Plays The Big Hits* (1960)★★, *Up A Lazy River* (1960-61)★★★, *The Stripper And Other Big Band Hits* (1962)★★, *Desafinado* (1962)★★★, with the Johnny

Mann Singers *Great Band With Great Voices Vols 1 & 2* (1961)★★★★, *Waltz In Jazz Time* (1962)★★★, *Rhythm And Blues* (1962)★★, *Exotica Suite* (1962)★★, *In Full Swing* (1963)★★★, *From Russia With Love* (1963)★★★, *Si Zentner Plays The Big Big-Band Hits* (1964)★★★, *It's Nice To Go Trav'ling* (1965)★★★, *Put Your Hand On My Shoulder* (1965)★★★, *Swingin' Country* (1966)★★, *Warning Shot* (1967)★★★, *Right Here* (1969)★★★.

Zephaniah, Benjamin

b. Benjamin Obadiah Iqbal Zephaniah, 1958, Handsworth, Birmingham, England. Zephaniah states that he cannot remember a time when he was not creating poetry, inspired primarily by the music and lyricists of Jamaica. His first performance was in a church in 1968, and by the age of 15 he had established a following in his home-town. In 1980 he moved to London, where his first book of poetry, *Pen Rhythm*, was published, and proved so successful that it ran to three editions. Although an eminent writer, it was his notoriety as a dub poet that brought him to prominence. The 1983 release of *Dub Ranting* led to tracks being played at rallies against sus laws, unemployment, homelessness and far-right politics. His campaign to introduce poetry to the masses was boosted by the release of *Rasta*, which prompted media interest and television appearances. The album topped the Yugoslavian pop chart and featured the **Wailers**, who had not played alongside any performer since the death of **Bob Marley**. The collaboration featured a tribute to Nelson Mandela, which led to an introductory meeting following the South African president's eventual release from prison. In 1990 he recorded *Us And Dem* and decided to promote the album outside the normal circuit, playing to audiences in Zimbabwe, India, Pakistan, Columbia and South Africa, where the oral tradition is still strong. In 1991 over a 22-day period he performed to an audience on every continent of the globe. In 1996 Zephaniah worked with children in South Africa at the behest of Nelson Mandela and hosted the president's Two Nations Concert at London's Royal Albert Hall. His musical collaborations include work with the **Ariwa Sounds** posse, **Acid Jazz**, **Bomb The Bass** and **Sinead O'Connor**.
● ALBUMS: *Dub Ranting* (Upright 1983)★★★★, *Rasta* (Upright/Helidon 1987)★★★, *Us And Dem* (Mango/Island 1990)★★★, *Back To Roots* (Acid Jazz 1995)★★, *Hazardous Dub* (Acid Jazz 1996)★★★, *Overstanding* (57 Productions 1996)★★, *Reggae Head* (57 Productions 1997)★★.

Zephyrs

This London-based quartet - John Peeby (guitar), Marc Lease (organ), John Hinde (bass) and John Carpenter (drums) - were originally known as the Clee-Shays. They made their debut in 1964 with an instrumental, 'What's That All About', before recording a version of **Bo Diddley**'s 'I Can Tell'. Although they enjoyed the services of producer **Shel Talmy**, the Zephyrs were unable to emulate the success of fellow-protégés the

Kinks and the **Who**. Their lone chart entry, 'She's Lost You', barely scraped the UK Top 50 in 1965 and the group broke up following another unsuccessful release. Pete Gage was a founder-member of the group but left prior to recording. He later formed the Ram Jam Band with **Geno Washington** and went on to join **Vinegar Joe**.
● FILMS: *Be My Guest* (1965).

Zero, Earl

b. Earl Anthony Jackson, 1952, Greenwich Town, West Kingston, Jamaica, West Indies. Zero began his recording career with **Bunny Lee**, who produced his self-penned 'None Shall Escape The Judgement'. The song was given to **Johnny Clarke**, who had previously enjoyed hits with producer **Rupie Edwards**. While Clarke's career took off, Zero had to wait until 1975 when, with singer/producer **Al Campbell**, 'Righteous Works' became a substantial hit. Guided by **Tommy Cowan** of Talent Corporation, he recorded 'Please Officer' and the legendary 'City Of The Weak Heart'. The song was covered with a slight variation to the lyrics by fellow Talent Corporation recording star **Jacob Miller**, and was included on the release of his album *Killer Miller*. By 1976 Zero had joined Bertram Brown's Freedom Sounds for the release of 'Get Happy' and was reunited with Al Campbell for 'Heart Desire'. In the following years, his output remained steady: 'Visions Of Love', 'Pure And Clean', 'Shackles And Chains', 'Jah Guide' and 'Blackbird' earned him cult status. In 1979 he recorded with the **Soul Syndicate**, featuring Carlton 'Santa' Davis, George 'Fully' Fullwood, **Tony Chin** and Earl 'Chinna' Smith, who also produced the session. In the UK, 'City Of The Weakheart' was released as 'City Of The Wicked' as a discomix through **Greensleeves Records**. The songs were featured on *Visions Of Love*, which surfaced in 1980 along with remakes of his earlier recordings, including 'None Shall Escape The Judgement', 'Shackles And Chains', 'I No Lie' and 'Please Officer'.
● ALBUMS: *Visions Of Love* (Epiphany 1980)★★★, *In The Right Way* (Student/Ital 1981)★★, *Only Jah Can Ease The Pressure* (White Label 1990)★★★.
● COMPILATIONS: with various artists *Ethiopian Kings* (RRR 1981)★★★.

Zetterlund, Monica

b. 20 September 1938, Hagfors, Sweden. During the 50s Zetterlund sang in various parts of Scandinavia, often in good jazz company such as an orchestra led by Arne Domnerus with whom she recorded. She toured elsewhere in the late 50s and early 60s, including trips to the UK and the USA. Once again, her accompanists were of the highest order and a distinguished record date with **Bill Evans** was one such example. Like her fellow countrywoman, **Alice Babs**, she also sang traditional folk songs of Sweden and also studied and sang music from the classical repertoire. Zetterlund's singing is clean and well ordered and she has a nice sense of

swing. Her interpretation of lyrics is also good and she copes comfortably with the idioms of what is to her a foreign language. In addition to singing, she has also acted, working in this capacity mostly in her homeland.
● ALBUMS: with Bill Evans *Waltz For Debby* (Philips 1964)★★★★, *Hajman* (Odeon 1975)★★★, *It Only Happens Every Time* (EMI 1977)★★★.

Zevon, Warren

b. 24 January 1947, Chicago, USA. After moving to the west coast, where he sought work as a songwriter in the mid-60s, Zevon wrote songs for the **Turtles** and **Nino Tempo And April Stevens**. He recorded several singles for the Turtles' label White Whale, including a version of **Bob Dylan**'s 'If You Gotta Go', as Lyme And Cybelle. By the late 60s, he was signed to Imperial and recorded an inauspicious debut, *Zevon: Wanted Dead Or Alive*, produced by **Kim Fowley**. One track from the album, 'She Quit Me', was featured in the movie *Midnight Cowboy*. When the album failed to sell, Zevon took a job on the road as musical director to the **Everly Brothers**. He subsequently appeared uncredited on their album *Stories We Could Tell* and also guested on Phil Everly's three solo albums. By the early 70s, Zevon was signed as a songwriter by entrepreneur **David Geffen**, and finally released his long-awaited second album in 1976. *Warren Zevon* was a highly accomplished work, which revealed its creator's songwriting power to an exceptional degree. Produced by **Jackson Browne**, the work featured the cream of LA's session musicians and included guest appearances from **Lindsey Buckingham**, **Stevie Nicks** and **Bonnie Raitt**. The material ranged from the piano-accompanied 'Frank And Jesse James' to the self-mocking singalong 'Poor Poor Pitiful Me', the bittersweet 'Carmelita' and the majestic sweep of 'Desperados Under The Eaves' with superb harmonies arranged by **Carl Wilson**. **Linda Ronstadt**'s cover of 'Hasten Down The Wind' also brought Zevon to the attention of a wider audience.
The follow-up *Excitable Boy* was released two years later and revealed another astonishing leap in Zevon's musical development. The production was confident and accomplished and the range of material even more fascinating. Zevon tackled American politics and history on 'Roland The Thompson Gunner' and 'Veracruz', wrote one of his finest and most devastating love songs in 'Accidentally Like A Martyr' and employed his satiric thrust to the heart on 'Excitable Boy' and 'Werewolves Of London'. A superb trilogy of Zevon albums was completed with *Bad Luck Streak In Dancing School* which was most notable for its inventive use of orchestration. Again, it was the sheer diversity of material and mood that impressed. The classical overtones of the title track, 'Interlude No. 2' and 'Wild Age' were complemented by Zevon's biting satire which was by now unmatched by any American artist, bar **Randy Newman**. 'Gorilla You're A Desperado' was a humorous attack on LA consumerism, while 'Play It All Night Long' was an anti-romantic portrait of rural life that

contrasted markedly with the prevailing idyllic country rock mentality. Zevon's vision was permeated with images of incest and disease: 'Daddy's doing sister Sally/Grandma's dying of cancer now/The cattle all have brucellosis/We'll get through somehow'.
Zevon's ability to attract the interest and respect of his songwriting contemporaries was once more emphasized by the presence of **Bruce Springsteen**, with whom he co-wrote 'Jeannie Needs A Shooter'. Although Zevon seemed likely to establish himself as one of the prominent singer-songwriters of the 80s, personal problems would soon undo his progress. A promising live album was followed by the much neglected *The Envoy*. This concept album sold poorly and was the last major work from Zevon for five years. During the interim, he became an alcoholic and underwent counselling and therapy. He returned in 1987 with *Sentimental Hygiene*, a welcome return to top form, which featured a new array of guest stars including **Neil Young**, Michael Stipe and Peter Buck (from **R.E.M.**), Bob Dylan, **Don Henley** (formerly of the **Eagles**), **Jennifer Warnes** and Brian Setzer (ex-**Stray Cats**). Zevon also formed a band with Peter Buck, Mike Mills and Bill Berry under the name Hindu Love Gods, and issued an album in 1990 entitled *Hindu Love Gods*. Zevon's power was not lost among the star credits and shone through on a powerful set of songs, several of which brutally detailed his fight back from alcoholism. Never self-pitying, Zevon could afford a satiric glimpse at his own situation in 'Detox Mansion': 'Well it's tough to be somebody/And it's hard to fall apart/Up here on Rehab Mountain/We gonna learn these things by heart'. Zevon promoted the album extensively and has since built upon his reputation with the finely-produced *Transverse City* and well-received *Mr Bad Example*. Those in any doubt should seek out the excellent anthology released in 1996 by **Rhino Records**.
● ALBUMS: *Zevon: Wanted Dead Or Alive* (Imperial 1969)★★, *Warren Zevon* (Asylum 1976)★★★★, *Excitable Boy* (Asylum 1978)★★★, *Bad Luck Streak In Dancing School* (Asylum 1980)★★★, *Stand In The Fire* (Asylum 1980)★★★★, *The Envoy* (Asylum 1982)★★★, *Sentimental Hygiene* (Virgin 1987)★★★★, *Transverse City* (Virgin 1989)★★★, *Mr Bad Example* (Giant 1991)★★★, *Learning To Flinch* (Giant 1993)★★★★, *Mutineer* (Giant 1995)★★★.
● COMPILATIONS: *A Quiet Normal Life - The Best Of Warren Zevon* (Asylum 1986)★★★, *I'll Sleep When I'm Dead (An Anthology)* (Rhino 1996)★★★★.

Zhané

An east coast R&B/dance duo consisting of Renee Neufville and Jean Norris, who started signing together whily studying at Philadelphia Temple University, and were discovered at a talent show by **DJ Jazzy Jeff And The Fresh Prince**. They went on to contribute backing vocals to the latter's 1991 single, 'Ring My Bell', before linking with another prominent rapper, **Queen Latifah**, as part of her Flavor Unit collective. Their debut, 'Hey Mr DJ', was first featured on the compilation album,

Roll Wit Tha Flava, before subsequent release as a single saw it reach the Top 5 in the USA. Like Latifah, they would sign on the dotted line with **Motown**, enjoying further success with follow-up single 'Groove Thang'. Both hits were produced in association with DJ Kay Gee, of **Naughty By Nature** fame, and prefaced a similarly successful debut album, the title of which offered instruction as to the pronounciation of Zhané's name. As to their musical bent: 'Our music is R&B with a jazzy attitude and hip hop flavour'.

● ALBUMS: *Zhané* (Illtown/Motown 1994)★★★, *Saturday Night* (Illtown/Motown 1997)★★★★.

Ziegfeld

Hailed as the most expensive British musical ever when it opened at the London Palladium on 26 April 1988, *Ziegfeld* had a £3.2 million budget and a 60-strong cast. This 'opulent and gaudy' show was the brainchild of veteran impresario Harold Fielding and director and choreographer Joe Layton, and purported to be a celebration of the *Ziegfeld Follies*, while also telling the life story of master showman **Florenz Ziegfeld** himself. Ned Sherrin and Alistair Beaton wrote the book in which the legendary 'girl glorifier', played by Len Cariou, is portrayed as a shifty, egotistical manipulator, and an incorrigible womanizer. One critic pointed out that it was 'dedicated to a man with no heart', and that may well have been the reason why, in spite of some great old songs, 450 costumes, 27 sets, and plenty of girls sited on revolving staircases, roulette wheels, and most other places, by August the show was in trouble. Fielding brought in his old friend **Tommy Steele** to revamp the production, and Topol, who had enjoyed a personal triumph in London with *Fiddler On The Roof* in 1967, replaced Cariou. But it was all to no avail, and *Ziegfeld* crashed in October after a run of just over five months. It recouped hardly any of its original investment, and Harold Fielding faced reported personal losses of £2.5 million. Shortly after it closed, the elaborate constumes and scenery were bought by the producers of the 'vaudeville-burlesque revue' *Ziegfeld: A Night At The Follies*, which played regional cities in the USA in the early 90s.

Ziegfeld Follies

This series of high-class, spectacular, and elaborate revues, each one containing a mixture of skits, dances, songs, variety acts, and at least 50 beautiful women, was inaugurated in 1907 by **Florenz Ziegfeld**, 'the greatest showman in theatrical history'. From 1907-10, the shows were known as the *Follies*, and presented at the Jardin de Paris in New York. One of the first of the stars to emerge from the *Follies* was Nora Bayes, who also wrote and introduced the enormously popular 'Shine On Harvest Moon' with her second husband Jack Norworth in the 1908 edition. Yet another 'moon' song, 'By The Light Of The Silvery Moon', written by Edward Madden and Gus Edwards, turned up in the *Follies* of 1909. Other artists making one or more

appearances in that first quartet of shows included Grace La Rue, Bickell And Watson, Helen Broderick, Mae Murray, **Sophie Tucker**, Lillian Lorraine, the black comedian Bert Williams, and 'funny girl' **Fanny Brice**, who appeared in nine editions of the *Follies* through until 1936. Also featured were the Anna Held Girls, named after Ziegfeld's first 'wife'. From 1911 onwards, the name up in lights became the *Ziegfeld Follies* (one of Ziegfeld's signs, 'the largest electric light sign in American history', measured 80 feet long and 45 feet high, with 32,000 square feet of glass, and weighed eight tons), and was presented annually under that title until 1927, with the exception of 1926, when, owing to contractual wrangles, it was called *No Foolin'* and then *Ziegfeld's American Revue*. During those 17 years a host of the most beautiful showgirls, along with the cream of America's vaudeville performers and popular songwriters, contributed to what was billed as 'A National Institution Glorifying The American Girl'. Unlike a book show where the score is usually written mainly by one team of songwriters (with the odd interpolation), the musical items for each edition of the *Follies* were the work of several hands, including Dave Stamper, Gene Buck, **Victor Herbert**, Raymond Hubbell, Harry Smith, Gus Edwards, **Joseph McCarthy**, and **Rudolph Friml**. Some of the many enduring numbers that first saw the light of day in the *Ziegfeld Follies* include 'Woodman, Woodman, Spare That Tree' (1911, **Irving Berlin**), 'Row, Row, Row' (1912, **Jimmy Monaco** and William Jerome), 'The Darktown Poker Club' (1914, Jean Havaz, Will Vodery and Bert Williams), 'Hold Me In Your Loving Arms' and 'Hello, Frisco!' (1915, Louis A. Hirsch and Gene Buck), 'A Pretty Girl Is Like A Melody', 'Mandy' and 'You'd Be Surprised' (1919, Irving Berlin), 'Tell Me, Little Gypsy' and 'The Girls Of My Dreams' (1920, Irving Berlin), 'Second Hand Rose' (1921, Grant Clarke and James F. Hanley), 'My Man' (1921, Channing Pollock and Maurice Yvain), 'Mr. Gallagher And Mr. Sheen' (1922, Ed Gallagher and Al Shean), and 'Shaking The Blues Away' (1927, Irving Berlin). After a break, during which Ziegfeld lost a fortune in the Wall Street Crash, the impresario mounted the last *Follies* of his lifetime in 1931, but the score consisted mainly of old numbers, such 'Half Caste Woman', 'You Made Me Love You', and the first *Ziegfeld Follies* hit, 'Shine On Harvest Moon'. After he died in July 1932, the rights to the shows' title was bought by the Shubert Brothers, who, in collaboration with Ziegfeld's widow, Billie Burke, presented further editions, notably in 1934 and 1936. Both starred the late producer's brightest star, Fanny Brice, and, somewhat ironically, introduced better songs than were in the last few 'genuine' editions, such as 'I Like The Likes Of You' and 'What Is There To Say?' (1934, **Vernon Duke** and **E.Y. 'Yip' Harburg**), and 'Island In The West Indies' and 'I Can't Get Started' (1936, Vernon Duke and **Ira Gershwin**). None of the last three *Follies*, in 1943, 1956, and 1957, were critically well received, although the 1943 show ran for 553 performances - more than any of the others in the long series. The 1957 Golden Jubilee edition was down to eight girls, but had a genuine star in Beatrice Lillie. She was the last in a glittering line of performers, most of whom owed their start to the *Ziegfeld Follies*, including Fanny Brice, Bert Williams, Ann Pennington, W.C. Fields, **Eddie Cantor**, Will Rogers, Lillian Lorraine, Leon Errol, Ray Dooley, Nora Bayes, Vivienne Segal, **Helen Morgan**, Marilyn Miller, Ed Wynn, **Ruth Etting**, and Eddie Dowling. The vast array of brilliant directors, choreographers, set and costume designers, who combined to create what are remembered as the most dazzling and extravagant shows ever seen on Broadway are too numerous to name; and the live elephants that appeared on stage in the 1914 edition were not credited individually. In the late 90s, a live recording of a complete performance of *Ziegfeld Follies 1934* was discovered, and released on CD in 1997. Eve Arden made her Broadway debut in this Follies, and star Fanny Brice is also supported by Everett Marshall, the Howard Brothers, Brice Hutchins, Judith Barron, Vivian Janis, and Buddy and Grace Ebsen. Although the transfer proved to be of fairly poor quality, it is undoubtedly a historically valuable release.

● ALBUMS: *Ziegfeld Follies 1934* (AEI 1997)★★★★.

● FURTHUR READING: *The Ziegfeld Follies*, M. Farnsworth. *Stars Of The Ziegfeld Follies*, J. Phillips.

Ziegfeld Follies (Film Musical)

William Powell, who had played the leading role in the 1936 screen biography, *The Great Ziegfeld*, portrayed the master showman again in this film which was released 10 years later. From his seat in that big theatre in the sky - heaven - **Florenz Ziegfeld** plans one final revue that will serve as his memorial. The resulting show, a collection of unconnected sketches and songs, was certainly spectacular, featuring as it did many of MGM's brightest stars of the day. Three of these, **Fred Astaire**, **Cyd Charisse** and Lucille Ball, accurately captured the Ziegfeld mood with 'Bring On The Beautiful Girls' (Earl Brent-**Roger Edens**) - followed closely by 'Bring On Those Beautiful Men', and from then on the lavish production numbers, interspersed with the laughs, followed thick and fast. The lovely **Lena Horne**, eyes ablaze, raised the temperature with 'Love' (**Ralph Blane-Hugh Martin**), **Judy Garland** sent up the much-loved Greer ('Mrs. Miniver') Garson in 'Madame Crematon', and two refugees from the world of opera, James Melton and Marion Bell, rendered 'The Drinking Song' from Verdi's *La Traviata*. However, most of the honours went to Fred Astaire who, with Lucille Bremer, provided two of the films outstanding moments, with the lovely ballad, 'This Heart Of Mine' (**Arthur Freed-Harry Warren**), and the exquisitely staged 'Limehouse Blues' (Philip Braham-Douglas Furber). Astaire also revived a number called 'The Babbitt And The Bromide' (**George Gershwin-Ira Gershwin**), which he had introduced with his sister Adele in the Broadway musical *Funny Face* (1927). In this film Astaire performed it with his main 'rival',

Gene Kelly - it was the first time they had danced on the screen together. **Kathryn Grayson**, surrounded by a substance that looked remarkably like foam, brought the curtain down on Ziegfeld's final performance, confirming the impresario's lifelong creed with 'There's Beauty Everywhere', written by Earl Brent and Arthur Freed. Freed himself produced the whole stylish and extravagant affair, which was directed by **Vincente Minnelli** and choreographed by Robert Alton.

Ziegfeld Girl

The trials and tribulations of a trio of showgirls in the most famous series of revues ever to grace Broadway - the *Ziegfeld Follies* - were discussed and dissected in this Pandro S. Berman MGM production that came to the screen in 1941. **Judy Garland**, Hedy Lamarr and Lana Turner were the three young hopefuls who were aiming for the top. Garland was the only one to make it in the end, with Lamarr and Turner swapping public acclaim for private happiness. The uneven, and sometimes maudlin screenplay was written by Marguerite Roberts and Sonia Levien. James Stewart, **Tony Martin**, Philip Dorn, and Jackie Cooper were prominent in a splendid cast that also included Ian Hunter, Edward Everett Horton, Eve Arden, **Dan Dailey**, Paul Kelly, Fay Holden, and Felix Bressart. Charles Winninger played Ed Gallagher, with Al Shean as himself, in a recreation of the question-and-answer song, 'Mr. Gallagher And Mr. Shean', which the famous vaudeville duo introduced in the *Ziegfeld Follies* of 1922. Garland was in fine form on a variety of numbers that included 'Minnie From Trinidad' (**Roger Edens**), 'You Never Looked So Beautiful' (**Harold Adamson-Walter Donaldson**), 'I'm Always Chasing Rainbows' (**Joseph McCarthy**-Harry Carroll), and, with Winninger, 'Laugh? I Thought I'd Split My Sides' (Edens), and Tony Martin gave a typically fine performance of 'You Stepped Out Of A Dream' (**Nacio Herb Brown-Gus Kahn**). **Busby Berkeley**'s staging of the dance sequences was as brilliantly imaginative as always, and the lavish sets and costumes were created by Cedric Gibbons and Adrian, respectively; the latter was coming to the end of his long and distinguished stint at MGM. The film contained several reminders of the 1936 celluloid tribute to the master showman, *The Great Ziegfeld*, including that enormous fluted spiral structure which amazed audiences again as it did the first time round. Robert Z. Leonard directed this opulent production which will be best remembered for its music and production numbers.

Ziegfeld, Florenz

b. 21 March 1867, Chicago, Illinois, USA, d. 22 July 1932, New York, USA. The most important and influential producer in the history of the Broadway musical. It is said that Ziegfeld was involved in his first real-life, but accidental, 'spectacular' at the age of four, when he and his family were forced to seek shelter under a bridge in Lake Park during the great Chicago fire of

1871. While in his teens, he was constantly running a variety of shows, and in 1893, his father, who was the founder of the Chicago Music College, sent him to Europe to find classical musicians and orchestras. Florenz returned with the Von Bulow Military Band - and Eugene Sandow, 'the world's strongest man'. The actress Anna Held, with whom Ziegfeld went through a form of marriage in 1897 (they were 'divorced' in 1913), also came from Europe, and she made her US stage debut in Ziegfeld's first Broadway production, *A Parlor Match*, in 1896. He followed that with *Papa's Wife*, *The Little Duchess*, The *Red Feather*, *Mam'selle Napoleon*, and *Higgledy Piggledy* (1904). Two years later, Held gave an appealing performance in Ziegfeld's *The Parisian Model*, and introduced two songs that are always identified with her, 'It's Delightful To Be Married' and 'I Just Can't Make My Eyes Behave'. Her success in this show, combined with her obvious star quality and potential, is said to have been one of the major factors in the impresario's decision to launch a series of lavish revues in 1907 which came to be known as the *Ziegfeld Follies*. These spectacular extravaganzas, full of beautiful women, talented performers, and the best popular songs of the time, continued annually for most of the 20s. In addition, Ziegfeld brought his talents as America's master showman to other (mostly) hit productions such as *The Soul Kiss* (1908), *Miss Innocence*, *Over The River*, *A Winsome Widow*, *The Century Girl*, *Miss 1917*, **Sally**, **Kid Boots**, *Annie Dear*, *Louie The 14th*, *Ziegfeld's American Revue* (later retitled *No Foolin'*), and *Betsy* (1926). After breaking up with Anna Held, Ziegfeld married the glamorous actress, Billie Burke. He opened his own newly built Ziegfeld Theatre in 1927 with **Rio Rita**, which ran for nearly 500 performances. The hits continued to flow with **Show Boat** (1927), **Rosalie**, *The Three Musketeers*, and **Whoopee** (1928). In 1929, with the Depression beginning to bite, he was not so fortunate with *Show Girl*, which only managed 111 performances, and to compound the failure, he suffered massive losses in the Wall Street Crash of the same year. *Bitter Sweet* (1929) was a bitter disapointment, and potential hits such as **Simple Simon**, with a score by **Richard Rodgers** and **Lorenz Hart**, *Smiles* with **Fred Astaire** and his sister Adele, the last *Follies* of his lifetime (1931), and *Hot-Cha* (1932) with Bert Lahr, simply failed to take off. It is said that he would have been forced into bankrupcy if his revival of *Show Boat*, which opened at the Casino on 12 May 1932, had not been a substantial hit. Ironically, Ziegfeld, whose health had been failing for some time, died of pleurisy in July, two months into the run. His flamboyant career, coupled with a reputation as a notorious womanizer, has been the subject of at least three films: *The Great Ziegfeld* (1936) with William Powell which won two Oscars; *Ziegfeld Follies*, William Powell again, with Fred Astaire; and a television movie, *Ziegfeld: The Man And His Women* (1978).
● FURTHER READING: *Ziegfeld, The Great Glorifier*, E. Cantor and D Freedman. *Ziegfeld*, C. Higham. *The World Of*

Flo Ziegfeld, R. Carter. *The Ziegfeld Touch*, Richard and Paulette Ziegfeld.

Ziegler, Anne, And Webster Booth

Anne Ziegler (b. Irene Frances Eastwood, 1910, Liverpool, England), and Webster Booth (b. Leslie Webster Booth, 21 January 1902, Birmingham, England, d. 22 June 1984, Llandudno, Wales). From an early age Anne Ziegler trained as a classical pianist, and later became a skilled accompanist. After studying with voice trainer John Tobin, she moved to London in 1934 and played in the chorus of the operetta *By Appointment*, and sang in restaurants and hotels. In 1936, after being chosen from 250 applicants to play the leading soprano role of Marguerita in an early colour film of *Faust*, she met the tenor, Webster Booth. He attended choir school at Lincoln Cathedral, and sang solos there at the age of seven. After his voice had broken when he was 13, he worked in accountant's office before gaining a patron for his musical education. In 1924 he joined the D'Oyly Carte Opera Company, and stayed with them for three years. Subsequently, he sang oratorios in every concert hall in Britain. He made his first recordings for **HMV** in 1928, and in the early 30s, performed at Drury Lane and Covent Garden. He married Anne Ziegler in 1938, and, two years later, they formed a double act and toured UK variety theatres. During World War II and for some years afterwards, they were extremely popular on stage, radio and records. Like so many others, their appeal faded in the mid-50s and they emigrated to South Africa, where they lived and worked until 1978. Apart from their appearances there in concerts and operettas, Booth also played the part of comedian Tommy Handley for a year in a re-creation of the famous war-time radio series ITMA. On their return to the UK they settled in North Wales, where they taught music, and continued to appear together on stage, radio and television. They sang their last duet, 'I'll See You Again', at a concert in June 1983. Booth died a year later in Llandudno.
● ALBUMS: *Sweethearts In Song* (Encore 1979)★★★, *Music For Romance* (Encore 1980)★★★, *Golden Age Of Anne Ziegler And Webster Booth* (Golden Age 1983)★★★, *Love's Old Sweet Song* (EMI 1995)★★★★, *In Opera And Song* (Memoir 1997)★★★.
● FURTHER READING: *Duet*, Anne Ziegler and Webster Booth.

Zila
(see **Pukwana, Dudu**)

Zimmer, Hans
b. 1957, Frankfurt, Germany. Apparently, from the age of six, Zimmer wanted to be a composer, although he had no formal musical education. When he was 16 he went to school in England, and, during the 70s, toured with bands throughout the UK. After spending some time at Air-Edel, writing jingles for television commercials, he collaborated with the established movie

composer **Stanley Myers**, to write the score for Nicolas Roeg's *Eureka* (1981), and several other British films during the 80s, including *Moonlighting, Success Is The Best Revenge, Insignificance*, and *The Nature Of The Beast* (1988). His solo credits around that time included movies with such themes as apartheid (*A World Apart*), a psychological thriller (*Paperhouse*), a couple of eccentric comedies (*Twister* and *Driving Miss Daisy*), a tough Michael Douglas detective yarn (*Black Rain*), and a 'stiflingly old-fashioned' version of a Stefan Zweig short story, *Burning Secret* (1988). In that year Zimmer is said to have provided the music for 14 films in the UK and abroad, including the blockbuster, *Rain Man*, starring Dustin Hoffman and Tom Cruise. *Rain Man* earned Zimmer a nomination for an Academy Award ('When they found out that I was only 30, I didn't get it!'). He continued apace in the early 90s with scores for such as *Bird On A Wire; Chicago Joe And The Showgirl* (written with Shirley Walker), *Days Of Thunder, Green Card* (starring Gerard Depardieu in his English-language debut), *Pacific Heights, Backdraft, K2* (a crashing, electro-Mahlerian score), *Regarding Henry, Thelma And Louise* ('a twanging, shimmering score'), *Radio Flyer, Toys* (with Trevor Horn), *The Power Of One, A League Of Their Own, Point Of No Return, Where Sleeping Dogs Lie* (with Mark Mancina), *The Assassin, Cool Runnings, The House Of Spirits, Renaissance Man, Drop Zone*, and *The Lion King* (Academy Award, 1995). In 1992 Zimmer composed the music for 'one of the most bizarre television re-creations to date', the 10-hour series, *Millennium*. His other work for the small screen includes the popular *First Born* (1988) and *Space Rangers* (1992). He scored *Muppet Treasure Island* in 1996 and *The Borrowers* in 1997. Zimmer is most certainly a major figure in music; his accomplishments in the film world for such a comparatively young man are already awesome.

Zion Train

UK's Zion Train formed in 1990 and have proved to be innovators in the revolutionary new wave of **dub**. While many other groups preferred a revivalist stance, the north London-based co-operative have established an enviable reputation. The cross-cultural line-up consists of Molora (vocals, percussion), Neil (DJ, beats, bass), Colin C (melodica), Dave Hake (trumpet, also part of the **Tassilli Players**) and Chris Hetter (trombone). Influenced by **Jah Shaka**, **Lee Perry** and other dub masters, the group's dub/roots dance equation was first unveiled on the sequential singles 'Power One' and 'Power Two'. As well as recording dub sounds, the collective also ran the Bass Odyssey club and their own **sound system**, produced their own magazine, *The Wobbler*, and released the first promotional dub video, *Get Ready*, and a CD-ROM to accompany *Homegrown Fantasy*, their debut release for China Records. One of their most effective and highly regarded works was the 'Follow Like Wolves' single, a fertile cross between dub and house music, with samples drawn from the

Specials' back-catalogue. In a departure from usual reggae practice, they subsequently instigated the (no copyright) Soundpool, allowing free sampling, and thus dispensing with the need for acquisitive lawyers. They have also worked with **Junior Reid**, **Maxi Priest**, **Studio One** veteran **Devon Russell** and the **Dub Syndicate**, as well as Indian tabla players and Brazilian drummers. In 1996 the group ventured into the ambient/house/acid dub territory and performed with artists including the **Shamen**, **New Model Army** and **Gary Clail**, and instigated the re-formation of **Ruts** DC for a collaboration on a live session for BBC Radio. The release of *Grow Together* featured Dave Ruffy, the Ruts' drummer, and an acid revival of the group's 1979 hit 'Babylon's Burning'. That single was followed by 'Rise', with which they achieved their first exposure on national daytime radio. Extensive touring and major festival appearances have secured the band international popularity. They later released 'Stand Up And Fight', featuring Kate Cameron on lead vocals and a 19-minute soulful reggae remix.

● ALBUMS: *Passage To Indica* (Zion 1994)★★★★, *Great Sporting Moments In Dub* (Zion 1994)★★★, *Natural Wonders Of The World* (Universal Egg 1994)★★★, *Siren* (Universal Egg 1995)★★★, *Homegrown Fantasy* (China 1995)★★★, *Grow Together* (China 1996)★★★★, *Single Minded And Alive* (China 1997)★★★.
● COMPILATIONS: *Forward Roots* cassette only (Zion 1993).

Znowhite

Standard American power metal team, with the notable exception that it boasted multiracial membership, who came together late 1983 in Chicago, Illinois, with brothers Ian and Sparks Tafoya on guitar and drums and vocalist Nicole Lee. They spent much of the following year gigging in the Bay Area of San Francisco with **Metallica**, and supported **Raven** on their US tour. Their first album was released thanks to help from influential friends Johnny Z and Doc McGhee whose better-known credits include **Anthrax** and **Mötley Crüe**. A second collection again followed the power metal mantra, but in 1988 they adopted a higher profile when they signed to **Roadrunner Records** and played gigs outside of the San Francisco scene. Musically they became much heavier and eagerly joined the thrash metal bandwagon - though with results that hardly compared to those of their new peer group. Following disappointing sales, the group sundered just after the close of the decade, with members drifting off in to a new conglomeration, Cyclone Temple.
● ALBUMS: *All Hail To Thee* (Enigma 1984)★★, *Kick 'Em While They're Down* (Enigma 1985)★★★, *Act Of God* (Roadrunner 1988)★★★.

Zodiac Mindwarp And The Love Reaction

Formed in 1985, Zodiac Mindwarp And The Love Reaction projected an image encompassing everything from sex maniacs and party animals to leather-clad

bikers. Put together by Zodiac (b. Mark Manning), a former graphic designer, their image and attitude was always more interesting than their music. With twin guitarists Cobalt Stargazer and Flash Bastard, plus Trash D. Garbage and Slam Thunderhide on bass and drums, respectively, they were the ultimate science-fiction garage band, influenced by **Alice Cooper**, **Motörhead** and the **Stooges**. After releasing the mini-album, *High Priest Of Love*, on the independent Food label, they were signed by **Mercury Records,** who funded the recording of *Tattooed Beat Messiah*. Although rigidly formularized, it spawned the hits 'Prime Mover' and 'Back Seat Education', which were accompanied by expensive and controversial videos. The creative juices soon ran dry, however. Zodiac's backing band disintegrated and Mercury dropped him from its roster in 1989. In 1991 he re-formed the band with Stargazer, Thunderhide and new bassist Suzy X, releasing the single 'Elvis Died For You'. Despite signing to European label Musidisc, little further progress was made. Manning later lived up to his reputation by collaborating with the **KLF**'s Bill Drummond in 1994 on the semi-pornographic work, *A Bible Of Dreams*.
● ALBUMS: *High Priest Of Love* (Food 1986)★★★, *Tattooed Beat Messiah* (Mercury 1988)★★★, *Hoodlum Thunder* (Musidisc 1992)★★, *The Friday Rock Show Sessions At Reading '87* (Windsong 1993)★★.
● VIDEOS: *Sleazegrinder* (1989).
● FURTHER READING: *A Bible Of Dreams*, W. Drummond and M. Manning.

Zoe

b. Zoe Pollock, Peckham, London, England. Zoe made a huge impact in 1991 with the release of her debut single, 'Sunshine On A Rainy Day', a perfect Europop cover version that went to number 4 in the UK charts. It had originally been released a year earlier when it reached the Top 60. However, subsequent efforts 'Lightning' and 'Holy Days' fared poorly. When her solo debut also flopped, she found herself in conflict with her label bosses over the extensive personal appearances she was required to perform at tawdry discos throughout Europe, and the relationship almost collapsed. Pollock had joined her first band, the soul group Cacique, after leaving stage school aged 16. She eventually regrouped in 1995 and began working on new tracks with her partner Youth (of the **Orb/Killing Joke**), whom she first met while auditioning for **Brilliant** at his Butterfly Studios in Brixton. When she presented these to her record company M&G Records, new A&R director Jack Steven was impressed, and arranged for a concurrent US release of the album by **RCA Records**. Most of the instruments on *Hammer* were played by Youth, though the duo's emotional relationship had sundered during the sessions - leaving Youth doubtlessly wondering at whom some of the more pointed lyrics were aimed. Rather than the slightly sickly pop of her debut, *Hammer* comprised a number of bittersweet lyrics and harsh vignettes, typi-

fied by 'Love Is The Beast' and the title track. Zoe's interest in the ethnic music of Ireland and India was also well represented in the Buddhist mantra 'R.A.M' and 'Down The Mountain'. 'The Lion Roars', meanwhile, was written in tandem with **Anthony Thistlewaite**, formerly of the **Waterboys**, and co-produced by revered Irish producer **Donal Lunny** in Dublin with **Davy Spillane** contributing uilleann pipes.
● ALBUMS: *Scarlet Red And Blue* (M&G 1992)★★, *Hammer* (RCA/M&G 1996)★★★.

Zoller, Attila

b. 13 June 1927, Visegard, Hungary, d. 25 January 1998, Townsend, Vermont, USA. Zoller learnt to play the violin and trumpet as a child and only turned to the guitar when he chose to make a career in music. He played in a variety of bands in Budapest after the war before political unrest at home sent him to Austria and then, in the mid-50s, to Germany. There he played with **Hans Koller** and accompanied visiting Americans like **Oscar Pettiford**. In 1959 he won a scholarship to the Lennox School of Jazz and went to the USA. He is a technically skilful guitarist who performs in a restrained style with a keen harmonic sense which sometimes reveals his east European background. He joined **Chico Hamilton**'s Quintet in 1960 and then played with **Herbie Mann** until 1965. He performed in a group specializing in modal jazz with **Dave Friedman** before playing with **Red Norvo** and then **Benny Goodman**. In 1968 he was a co-leader in a trio with **Albert Mangelsdorff** and **Lee Konitz**. In the early 80s he played with **Jimmy Raney**. In 1971 he had patented a bi-directional pick-up for the guitar and later developed a magnetic pick-up which could be used with a vibraphone.
●ALBUMS: with Albert Mangelsdorff, Lee Konitz *Z0 Ko So* (MPS 1967)★★★★, *The Horizon Beyond* (Act 1967)★★★, *Gypsy Cry* (1971)★★★★, *The K & K In New York* (L+R 1980)★★★★, *Memories Of Pannonia* (1987)★★★, *Common Cause* (1992)★★★, *Live Highlights '92* (Bhakti 1992)★★★, *When It's Time* (Enja 1995)★★★★.

Zombies

Rod Argent (b. 14 June 1945, St. Albans, Hertfordshire, England; piano), **Colin Blunstone** (b. 24 June 1945, St. Albans, Hertfordshire, England; vocals), Paul Atkinson (b. 19 March 1946, Cuffley, Hertfordshire, England; guitar), Paul Arnold (bass) and Hugh Grundy (b. 6 March 1945, Winchester, Hampshire, England; drums) formed the Zombies in 1963, although Chris White (b. 7 March 1943, Barnet, Hertfordshire) replaced Arnold within weeks of their inception. This St. Albans-based quintet won the local Herts Beat competition, the prize for which was a recording deal with **Decca Records**. The Zombies' debut single, 'She's Not There', rose to number 12 in the UK, but proved more popular still in America, where it reached number 2. Blunstone's breathy voice and Argent's imaginative keyboard arrangement provided the song's distinctive features and the group's crafted, adventurous style was then maintained over a series of excellent singles. Sadly, this diligence was not reflected in success, and although 'Tell Her No' was another US Top 10 entrant, it fared much less well at home while later releases, including 'Whenever You're Ready' and 'Is This The Dream' unaccountably missed out altogether.

The group, not unnaturally, grew frustrated and broke up in 1967 on completion of *Odessey And Oracle*. The promise of those previous releases culminated in this magnificent collection which adroitly combined innovation, melody and crafted harmonies. Its closing track, 'Time Of The Season', became a massive US hit, but despite several overtures, the original line-up steadfastly refused to reunite. Argent and Grundy were subsequently joined by ex **Mike Cotton** bassist Jim Rodford (b. 7 July 1941, St. Albans, Hertfordshire, England) and Rick Birkett (guitar) and this reshaped ensemble was responsible for the Zombies' final single, 'Imagine The Swan'. Despite the label credit, this release was ostensibly the first recording by the keyboard player's new venture, **Argent**. Colin Blunstone, meanwhile, embarked on a stop-start solo career. The band reconvened to record *New World* in 1991, which on release received respectable reviews. An ambitious and expertly produced CD box set was relased in 1997 by Ace Records, with alternate takes and unissued material. At the launch party in London the original five members played together for the first time in over 25 years. The Zombies' work is overdue for serious reappraisal, in particular the songwriting talents of Argent and White.

● ALBUMS: *Begin Here* (Decca 1965)★★, *Odessey And Oracle* (CBS 1968)★★★★, *Early Days* (London 1969),★★ *The Zombies Live On The BBC 1965-1967* (Rhino 1985)★★★, *Meet The Zombies* (Razor 1989)★★★, *Five Live Zombies* (Razor 1989)★★★, *New World* (JSE 1991)★★.

● COMPILATIONS: *The World Of The Zombies* (Decca 1970)★★★★, *Time Of The Zombies* (Epic 1973)★★★, *Rock Roots* (Decca 1976)★★★, *The Best And The Rest Of The Zombies* (Back Trac 1984)★★★, *Greatest Hits* (DCC 1990)★★★, *Best Of The Zombies* (Music Club 1991)★★★, *The EP Collection* (See For Miles 1992)★★★★, *The Zombies 1964-67* (More Music 1995)★★★, *Zombie Heaven* 4-CD box set (Ace 1997)★★★★.

Zoom Records

Camden, north London operation run by popular DJ Billy Nasty and Dave Wesson, whose clients include **Delorme** and **3:6 Philly**. The label came to prominence in 1989 with the release of two singles by Brit hip-hoppers **Red Ninja**. Later their attention turned to the dance scene, releasing a particularly harsh techno album by **Ubik** in 1992. Later Nasty's reputation as a DJ was franked by being the first to appear on the Music Unites' *Journeys By DJ* series, with a set composed of modern house standards (Havanna/**Leftfield/Gypsy**). He also recorded alongside **Morgan King** as VFN Experience. Wesson similarly colluded with Leftfield to record 'The Hunter (The Returns)' (as Herbal

Infusion). The duo have also remixed for Acorn Arts, **Saint Etienne** and Nush. Other members of the Zoom staff include the Sensory Productions team of three DJ's - Robert R. Mellow, Zaki Dee and Adam Holden, who released the double a-side 'Keep It Open'/'Jumping' for the label in 1992. Mello works behind the counter at the Zoom shop, while Dee provided a similar service at the Black Market emporium.

Zooropa - U2

If you study the wild computer graphics on the sleeve you could be expecting something frantic and electric. In fact, this is the most relaxing U2 album to date, and one on which they sound content to cruise instead of surmonizing. Brian Eno's prescence no doubt added the ambient feel that is present on most of the tracks. Bono even manages to sound like Roland Gift (Fine Young Cannibals) on 'Lemon' and a monosyllabic Lou Reed on 'Numb'. U2 took risks with this album because it broke a familiar pattern by not sounding like a U2 record. They sailed through the audition.

● Tracks: *Zooropa; Babyface; Numb; Lemon; Stay (Faraway So Close); Daddy's Gonna Pay For Your Crashed Car; Some Days Are Better Than Others; The First Time; Dirty Day; The Wanderer.*

● First released 1993
● UK peak chart position: 1
● USA peak chart position: 1

Zorba

Two years after their great success with *Cabaret*, composer **John Kander** and lyricist **Fred Ebb** reunited first for *The Happy Time*, and then for this musical, which, like *Cabaret*, had an unusual and sometimes sinister theme. *Zorba* opened at the Imperial theatre in New York on 17 November 1968, with a book by Joseph Stein that was set in Crete and based on the novel *Zorba The Greek* by Nikos Kazantzakis. It told of the earthy and larger-than-life Zorba (Herschel Bernardi) and his young friend Nikos (John Cunningham), who has inherited a disused mine on the island. In spite of financial failures, and tragedies involving the deaths of those close to him, including the French prostitute Hortense (Maria Karnilova), who was in love with him, Zorba rises above it all, secure in the passionate belief that life is for living - right to the very end. Kander and Ebbs's score caught the style and mood of the piece perfectly with songs such as 'Y'assou', 'The First Time', "Life Is', 'The Top Of The Hill', 'No Boom Boom', 'The Butterfly'. 'Only Love', 'Happy Birthday', and 'I Am Free'. Boris Aronson won a **Tony Award** for his imaginative and colourful sets, and *Zorba* ran for 305 performances. In October 1983 the show was revived on Broadway with Anthony Quinn and Lila Kedrova, both of whom had won such acclaim for their performances in the 1964 film *Zorba The Greek*. Kedrova won a Tony Award, and the production ran for longer than the original, a total of 362 performances.

Zorn, John

b. 2 September 1953, New York City, New York, USA. Zorn trained in classical composition, initial inspirations being the American composer-inventors Charles Ives, **John Cage** and Harry Partch. He developed an interest in jazz when he attended a concert given by trumpeter **Jacques Coursil**, who was teaching him French at the time. His later jazz idols have included **Anthony Braxton**, **Ornette Coleman**, **Jimmy Giuffre** and **Roscoe Mitchell**. Since 1974 he has been active on New York's Lower East Side, a leading representative of the 'downtown' *avant garde*, applying 'game theory' to structure-free improvisation, a parallel technique to **Butch Morris**'s 'conduction'. Zorn's keen study of bebop and his razor-sharp alto saxophone technique gained him respect from the jazz players: in 1977 he and guitarist **Eugene Chadbourne** were included in an 11-piece ensemble playing **Frank Lowe**'s compositions (*Lowe & Behold*). A record collector, Zorn was inspired by **Derek Bailey**'s Incus releases, and in 1983 recorded *Yankees* with him and trombonist **George Lewis**. The same year he wrote some music for Hal Willner's tribute to **Thelonious Monk**, *That's The Way I Feel Now*. In 1985 he contributed to Willner's **Kurt Weill** album *Lost In The Stars* and made a commercial breakthrough with *The Big Gundown*, which interpreted **Ennio Morricone**'s themes by deploying all kinds of unlikely musicians (including **Big John Patton** and **Toots Thielemans**). *News For Lulu* (1987), with Lewis and **Bill Frisell**, presented classic hard bop tunes from the 60s with Zorn's customary steely elegance: it was his second bebop venture, following *Voodoo* by the **Sonny Clark** Memorial Quartet (Zorn, Wayne Horvitz, Ray Drummond, Bobby Previte). Declaring that hardcore rock music had the same intensity as 60s free jazz, he championed Nottingham's **Napalm Death** and recorded hardcore versions of Ornette Coleman's tunes on the provocative *Spy Vs Spy* (1989). Naked City (Frisell - guitar, Fred Frith - bass, Joey Baron - bass) became his vehicle for skipping between sleaze-jazz, surf rock and hardcore: they made an impressive debut for Nonesuch/**Elektra Records** in 1990. In 1991 he formed Pain Killer with bassist/producer **Bill Laswell** and Mick Harris (the drummer from Napalm Death) and released *Guts Of A Virgin* on Earache, the Nottingham hardcore label. He played at Company Week 1991, proving by his commitment and enthusiasm that (relative) commercial success has not made him turn his back on free improvisation. Zorn's genre transgression seems set to become the commonsense of creative music in the 90s. He also runs his own Tzadik record label.

● ALBUMS: *School* (Parachute 1978)★★★, *Pool* (Parachute 1980)★★★, *Archery* (Parachute 1981)★★★, *The Classic Guide To Strategy Volume One* (Lumina 1983)★★★, *Locus Solus* (Eva/Wave 1983)★★★, with Derek Bailey, George Lewis *Yankees* (Celluloid 1983)★★★★, with Jim Staley *OTB* (1984)★★★, with Michihiro Sato *Ganryu Island* (Yukon 1985)★★★, *The Big Gundown* (Elektra 1985)★★★★, *The Classic Guide To Strategy Volume Two* (Lumina 1986)★★★, with the Sonny Clark Memorial Quartet *Voodoo* (Black Saint 1986)★★★, *Cobra* recorded 1985-86 (Hat Art 1987)★★★, *News For Lulu* (Hat Art 1987)★★★★, *Spillane* (Elektra 1988)★★★★, *Spy Vs Spy: The Music Of Ornette Coleman* (Elektra 1989)★★★★, with Naked City *Naked City* (Elektra/Nonesuch 1990)★★★, with Naked City *Torture Garden* (Earache 1990)★★★, with Pain Killer *Guts Of A Virgin* (Earache 1991)★★★, with Naked City *Heretic - Jeux Des Dames Cruelles* (Avant 1992)★★★, *More News For Lulu* (Hat Art 1992)★★★★, *Filmworks 1986-1990* (Elektra 1992)★★★★, with Naked City *Grand Guignol* (Avant 1993)★★★, *Masada* (DIW 1994)★★★★, *Vav* (DIW 1996)★★★, *Hei* (DIW 1996)★★★, *Bar Kokhba* (Tzadik 1996)★★★.

Zottola, Glenn

b. 28 April 1947, Port Chester, New York, USA. Zottola first played trumpet at the age of three, his early start explained by the fact that his father not only played trumpet but was also a manufacturer of trumpet mouthpieces (his brother, Bob Zottola, played with the bands of **Charlie Barnet**, **Maynard Ferguson** and **Billy May**). At the age of nine Glenn was playing in public, and within three years was performing regularly on television and had made an appearance at the Atlantic City Jazz Festival. In the early 60s he played a leading role in a documentary film, *Come Back*. In 1967 he joined the **Glenn Miller** Orchestra, then under the direction of **Buddy De Franco**. In 1970 Zottola was briefly with **Lionel Hampton** and then began a fruitful decade that saw him backing a wide range of artists including Bob Hope, **Al Martino**, **Patti Page**, **Tony Martin**, Robert Merrill and **Mel Tormé**. Towards the end of the 70s Zottola played lead trumpet in the orchestra accompanying the touring version of *Chicago*. In 1979 he joined **Tex Beneke** and that same year became a member of the **Benny Goodman** Sextet for a national tour. Zottola began the 80s in fine style, playing, singing and acting in *Swing*, a musical presented at the Kennedy Center in Washington, DC, before playing in the pit bands of several Broadway shows including *Evita*, *Annie* and *Barnum*, and also for the Stratford, Connecticut revival of *Anything Goes*, which starred **Ginger Rogers**. In the early 80s he joined **Bob Wilber**'s Bechet Legacy band, playing on record dates and international tours. Zottola has also recorded with **Butch Miles**, **George Masso**, **Keith Ingham** and **Maxine Sullivan**. In the mid-80s, in addition to his regular appearances with Wilber, Zottola led his own big band at the Rainbow Room in New York City and then joined forces with **Bobby Rosengarden** to co-lead a big band at the Hyatt Regency Hotel in Greenwich, Connecticut. He toured overseas, playing jazz festivals in Ireland, Holland and Finland, while his US festival appearances have included St. Louis, Sacramento and the Kool Jazz Festival in New York. In 1988 he was featured soloist in Wilber's recreation of Benny Goodman's 1938 Carnegie Hall concert. In 1990

Zottola was headlining at the Clearwater Jazz Festival in Florida and late in 1991 toured the UK and Europe with a band led by **Peanuts Hucko**. Unusually among brass players, Zottola is also an accomplished saxophonist, playing alto with flair. Although rooted in the mainstream of jazz and with a marked kinship for the swing era, his playing shows flashes of a deep awareness of bop and postbop developments in the music. The exceptional talent he displayed as a child has not been dissipated but has been nurtured into an impressive all-round ability.

●ALBUMS: *Live At Eddie Condon's* (1980)★★★, *Secret Love* (1981)★★★, with Bob Wilber *Ode To Bechet* (1982)★★★★, with George Masso *Pieces Of Eight* (1982)★★★, *Butch Miles Salutes Gene Krupa* (1982)★★, *Stardust* (1983)★★★, with Maxine Sullivan *The Lady's In Love With You* (1985)★★, *Christmas In Jazztime* (Dreamstreet 1986)★★.

ZTT Records

Formed in 1983 by producer Trevor Horn, a former member of the **Buggles** and **Yes**, and his wife Jill Sinclair, ZTT was one of the most innovative UK labels of the early 80s. Horn employed the sharp marketing skills of former *New Musical Express* journalist Paul Morley, whose obtuse style and interest in unearthing obscure talent was allied to a love of ephemeral pop. ZTT was an abbreviation of Zang Tumb Tuum, a phrase used by the Italian futurist Russulo to describe the sound of machine-gun fire. The artistic notions of the label were emphasized through elaborate artwork and a release policy that encouraged the use of multi-format pressings. The label was distributed by **Island Records** until 1986, after which it pursued the independent route. Among the early signings to the label were the **Art Of Noise** and **Propaganda**, both of whom enjoyed chart success and enhanced the label's *avant garde* reputation. The key act, however, was undoubtedly **Frankie Goes To Hollywood**, who conjured up a trilogy of spectacular UK number 1 hits in 1984 with 'Relax', 'Two Tribes' and 'The Power Of Love'. The release of fourteen different mixes of 'Relax' also established ZTT and Horn as pioneering forces in the remix market. Frankie's double album *Welcome To The Pleasure Dome* was quintessential ZTT, with arresting artwork, political slogans, and mock merchandising ideas included on the sleeve. The Frankie flame burned brightly until the second album, *Liverpool*, which proved expensive and time-consuming and sold far fewer copies than expected. The label continued its search for original talent, but all too often signed notably obscure acts who failed to find success in the mainstream. Among the artists who joined ZTT were Act, Anne Pigalle, Insignificance, Nasty Rox Inc. and Das Psych-Oh Rangers. **Roy Orbison** was also signed for a brief period and **Grace Jones** provided a formidable hit with 'Slave To The Rhythm'. ZTT suffered its most serious setback at the hands of former Frankie Goes To Hollywood singer **Holly Johnson**, who successfully took the label to the High Court in 1988

and won substantial damages after the group's contract was declared void, unenforceable and an unreasonable restraint of trade. The label then operated a joint venture with **Warner Brothers** for ten years, enjoying major success with **Seal** among others, before separating from the conglomerate in 1998.

Zu

Formed in London, England, in 1993, Zu combine the best traditions of dub, folk, punk and funk in an engagingly frothy and dextrous manner. Comprising Paul Godfrey (bass), Adam Woods (various instruments) and Mel Garside (vocals; ex-**Tabitha Zu**), the idea for the group originally came about when Garside met Woods in a science laboratory in Tottenham Comprehensive school. Recruiting Godfrey, the trio were the first of a series of act to sign to the small Echo Records label. Their debut EP, *Apart*, proved a typically eclectic shot at pop.

Zucchero

b. Aldelmo Fornaciari, 1956, north-west Italy. He was given the nickname Zucchero ('Sugar') as a child. He trained as a veterinary surgeon at Bologna University where a black American student taught him guitar and introduced him to soul music. Singing in a style reminiscent of **Joe Cocker**, Zucchero formed his own band in the late 70s but found initial success supplying songs for other artists. He made his first records in the mid-80s, and *Blue's* sold over a million in Italy. It also contained his best-known song, 'Senza Una Donna', which was a hit across continental Europe. Guest artists on Zucchero's 1990 album included **Jimmy Smith**, **Rufus Thomas**, **Ennio Morricone** and **Eric Clapton**, with whom he toured Europe the same year. He achieved a breakthrough in the UK when **Paul Young** duetted on a new version of 'Senza Una Donna'. The English lyrics were by Zucchero's regular collaborator Frank Musker, a British musician who had recorded in the early 80s with Bugatti & Musker. Zucchero himself translated the lyrics for Sting's Italian-language version of 'Mad About You'. Clapton played on the follow-up single, 'Wonderful World', while Zucchero dueted with **Randy Crawford** on 'Diamante' (1991).

● ALBUMS: *Rispetto* (1986)★★★, *Blue's* (1987)★★, *Ora Incenso Birra* (1989)★★★, *Zucchero Fornaciari* (1990)★★★, *Live At The Kremlin* (1991)★★, *Miserere* (1992)★★★.

Zukie, Tapper

b. David Sinclair, Jamaica, West Indies. Zukie began as a DJ in his early teens, influenced by **U-Roy** and **Dennis Alcapone**. In order to curb his youthful tendencies towards trouble, his mother sent him to England in 1973, where producer **Bunny Lee** organized some live shows and recording sessions under the aegis of the UK-based entrepreneur Larry Lawrence, for whom he cut his debut, 'Jump And Twist'. He also recorded material for Clem Bushay that later emerged as *Man A Warrior*. On his return to Jamaica he again worked for

Bunny Lee, though Zukie's ambitions to become as famous as U-Roy led him to record 'Judge I Oh Lord' for Lloydie Slim, and 'Natty Dread Don't Cry' for Lee. Zukie's frustration at Bunny Lee's indifference eventually resulted in an altercation with the producer. The police were called, but their differences were settled when Lee offered him some rhythms on which he could DJ himself. These, and others Zukie obtained from **Joseph 'Joe Joe' Hookim**, were recorded in a spare hour at **King Tubby**'s studio, and eventually issued as *MPLA* in 1976.

In 1975 he returned to the UK to find that he had gained something of a cult following owing to the belated popularity of *Man A Warrior*. An arrangement with Klik Records saw the release of 'MPLA' as a single, which met with immediate success, and Klik persuaded Zukie to let them release the whole album, which finally established his name in the higher echelons of DJs. Other recordings dating from the same period included a batch of singles for **Yabby You**, including 'Don't Get Crazy' and 'Natty Dread On The Mountain Top'. While in the UK, he appeared alongside new-wave heroine **Patti Smith**, who proved to be an admirer of *Man A Warrior*. The album was later reissued on Smith's and partner Lenny Kaye's Mer label, while Smith later contributed sleeve-notes to *Man From Bosrah*. Zukie also produced a number of artists during this period for his own Stars label, including Junior Ross and The Spear ('Babylon Fall', 'Judgement Time'), Prince Alla ('Bosrah', 'Daniel' and 'Heaven Is My Roof') and one all-time classic for **Horace Andy**, 'Natty Dread A Weh She Want'. In addition, he released two dub albums, *Escape From Hell* and *Tapper Zukie In Dub*. His protégés, **Knowledge**, were signed to **A&M Records** but subsequently dropped. His fortunes improved further with the release of *Peace In The Ghetto* and *Tapper Roots*, as well as popular singles such as 'She Want A Phensic' and his first big Jamaican hit, 'Oh Lord'. Returning to Jamaica, Zukie became active again in his local community. Largely silent during the late 80s, he has returned with a vengeance in the 90s, producing huge hits for stars such as **Dennis Brown** and **Beres Hammond**, and opening his own compact disc centre on Eastwood Park Road in Kingston in 1994.

● ALBUMS: *Man A Warrior* (Klik 1975)★★★★, *MPLA* (Klik 1976)★★, *Man From Bosrah* (Stars 1977)★★, *Escape From Hell* (Stars 1977)★★, *Tapper Zukie In Dub* (Stars 1977)★★★, *Peace In The Ghetto* (Stars 1978)★★★★, *Tapper Roots* (Stars/Front Line 1978)★★★, *People Are You Ready?* (Stars 1983)★★★, *Raggamuffin* (World Enterprise 1986)★★★.

Zuma - Neil Young

Released to universally favourable reviews, *Zuma* has lasted as a favourite Young album. On this, he pleased guitar devotees by at last attempting to sound and play like he did on stage. The tone and volume he achieves on his old Gibson throughout this record is perfection. 'Drive Back' is a shining example of the style, played over a shuffling and changing tempo. Similarly evoca-

tive are 'Danger Bird' and 'Stupid Girl', but the album's *tour de force* is 'Cortez The Killer', a lengthy song that builds, noodles and droops but is never boring. CSN make a cursory appearance at the end with 'Through My Sails'.

● Tracks: *Don't Cry No Tears; Danger Bird; Pardon My Heart; Lookin' For A Love; Barstool Blues; Stupid Girl; Drive Back; Cortez The Killer; Through My Sails*.
● First released 1975
● UK peak chart position: 25
● USA peak chart position: 44

Zumzeaux

This short-lived group, comprised Neti Vaandrager (b. 21 August 1957, Rotterdam, Netherlands; fiddle, vocals), Chris Haigh (b. 17 August 1957, Huddersfield, West Yorkshire, England; fiddle, vocals, mandolin), Bernard O'Neill (b. 4 September 1961, Dublin, Eire; double bass, vocals) and Ashley Drees (b. 25 May 1956, Paddington, London, England; cittern). Formed in 1987, the members came from a variety of musical backgrounds. Haigh had been heavily into western swing, while O'Neill had been playing jazz. Drees' earlier days of playing Irish traditional music in Dublin, had led to his teaming up with the Dutch-born Texan Vaandrager. Playing a blend of Cajun, swing, and folk music, the group impressed audiences from the start, and in 1988, they won the Ever Ready national busking competition at the BBC Radio Show. Their prize was a day in CBS Rooftop Studio which, with production help from **Andrew Cronshaw**, saw *Wolf At Your Door* emerge. Vaandrager has since joined Cajun band the Companions Of The Rosy Hours as well as Vivando, and the Poozies. O'Neill has joined the trio George Bernard Shaw. Haigh performs occasionally with Jenny Beeching; while Drees is involved in various Irish music duos and record production. The band reconvened for the quirky *Blazing Fiddles* in 1996.

● ALBUMS: *Wolf At Your Door* (1989)★★★, *Blazing Fiddles* (Black Pig 1996)★★★.

Zurke, Bob

b. 17 January 1912, Detroit, Michigan, USA, d. 17 February 1944. Learning piano as a child, Zurke displayed a remarkable talent and by his teenage years was playing semi-professionally. He worked regularly in and around Philadelphia in the late 20s and 30s, playing in numerous small bands and also as a single. In 1937 he joined the **Bob Crosby** band, achieving great success that was due in part to his ability to play convincingly sophisticated boogie-woogie during the brief craze for that style. The band's recording of 'Honky Tonk Train Blues', a feature for Zurke, was a hit. He left Crosby in 1939 to form his own band but this proved unsuccessful and he returned to solo work, playing clubs in Detroit, Chicago, Los Angeles and elsewhere. Although noted particularly for his boogie-woogie playing, Zurke had a much wider range and was an important, if erratic, factor in the Crosby band's success.

●COMPILATIONS: with Bob Crosby *South Rampart Street Parade* (MCA 1935-42)★★★, with Crosby *Big Noise From Winnetka* (MCA 1937-42)★★★★, *Bob Zurke And His Delta Rhythm Band* 1939-40 recordings (Meritt 1988)★★★.

Zwerin, Mike

b. 18 May 1930, New York, USA. Zwerin was educated at the High School of Music and Art before going to the University of Miami. During one holiday he played trombone on club dates at the Royal Roost with the **Miles Davis** nonet which later produced *Birth Of The Cool*. Zwerin moved to Paris in the early 50s but returned to New York in 1958 and worked with the big bands of **Claude Thornhill**, **Maynard Ferguson** and **Bill Russo**. Later he played with **Eric Dolphy** and **John Lewis** as well as in Orchestra USA (1962-65) and in the sextet drawn from its ranks. He toured the USSR with Earl Hines's band in 1966. During the early 60s Zwerin was president of his father's steel fabrication company and afterwards became the jazz critic for the *Village Voice* (1964-66) and was subsequently appointed its European Editor. Since then he has been music correspondent for the *International Herald Tribune*. He settled in Paris where he promotes jazz concerts for the American Centre, writes books and contributes articles to music magazines.

●ALBUMS: radio broadcast with Miles Davis *Pre-Birth Of The Cool* (1948)★★★, *Jazz Versions Of The Berlin Theatre Songs Of Kurt Weill* (1964)★★★, with Celestial Communication Orchestra *Desert Mirage* (1982)★★★, *Not Much Noise* (Spotlite 1983)★★★.

Zwingenberger, Axel

b. 7 May 1955, Hamburg, Germany. After studying classical piano for more than a decade, Zwingenberger began playing boogie-woogie in 1973. Although this was more than 30 years after the style had enjoyed its brief period of popular success, Zwingenberger's technical prowess brought him immediate public recognition in Germany. He released a successful album and was invited to tour and record in the USA, appearing with **Joe Turner**. By the end of the 70s he had established a reputation throughout Europe and was featured at concerts and festivals, sometimes as a single and also with visiting jazz luminaries such as **Lionel Hampton**. In the 80s he continued his touring and recording, working with **Sippie Wallace**, **Mama Yancey**, **Joe Newman** and others. Although rightly praised for his remarkable technique, Zwingenberger has shown himself to be a sensitive accompanist to the blues singers with whom he has performed: this, allied to his mastery of his instrument, suggests that he has even more to offer the jazz world.

●ALBUMS: *Boogie Woogie Breakdown* (Vagabond 1977)★★★, with Joe Turner *Let's Boogie All Night Long* (Vagabond 1978)★★★★, with Turner, Joe Newman *Between Hamburg And Hollywood* (1978-85)★★★, *Powerhouse Boogie* (Vagabond 1979)★★★★, *Boogie Woogie Live* (Vagabond 1979)★★★★, *Boogie Woogie Jubilee* (Vagabond 1981)★★★, *Axel Zwingenberger And The Friends Of Boogie Woogie Vols 1 & 2* (Vagabond 1982)★★★, *Lionel Hampton Introduces Axel Zwingenberger: The Boogie Woogie Album* (Vagabond 1982)★★★★, *Axel Zwingenberger With Sippie Wallace And The Friends Of Boogie Woogie* (1983)★★★, *An Evening With Sippie Wallace* (1984)★★★★, *Axel Zwingenberger And Sippie Wallace 'Live'* (Vagabond 1986)★★★★, *Axel Zwingenberger 'Live'* (1986)★★, *Axel Zwingenberger And The Blues Of Mama Yancey* (Vagabond 1988)★★★, *Axel Zwingenberger And The Friends Of Boogie Woogie: Vol 6* (Vagabond 1988)★★★, *Boogie Woogie Bros* (Vagabond 1989)★★★★, *Axel Zwingenberger And The Friends Of Boogie Woogie Volume 7 - Champion Jack Dupree Sings Blues Classics* (Vagabond 1991)★★★.

ZYX Records

Widely venerated as 'the Balearic label', ZYX is a German distributor and dance specialist that set up a UK operation in 1990, attempting to profit through 'cheaper imports and exclusive foreign product'. Their 1991 releases included De Melero featuring Monica Green's 'Night Moves' - a house standby brought up to date by Spanish brothers Cesar and Chito de Melero, DJs at Ibiza's Ku and Barcelona's The Club, respectively. 1992 brought Renee Thomas's 'I'm So In Love With You', from Fred Jorio and Sean Tucker. However, much of the label and A&R manager Alex Gold's notoriety during the 90s revolved around its public bust-ups with **Network** Records. ZYX overtures to obtain the license for Double You?'s version of **KC And The Sunshine Band**'s 'Please Don't Go' were rejected. Network got **KWS** to record a version instead, earning a five-week number 1 in the process. The same thing happened with a second KC cover, 'Rock Your Body'. Originally a number 1 hit for **Gwen McRae** in 1974, once again it jumped in front of a proposed ZYX label release - who were at that time trying to license Baby Roots' mistitled 'Rock You Baby'. When Double You?'s manager Roberton Zanetti collapsed of nervous exhaustion it could have taken few people by surprise. ZYX did at least enjoy success by licensing two contrasting Euro hits in 1992, the hard German techno of Misteria's 'Who Killed JFK?', and the clean Italian house of Jennifer Lucass' 'Take On Higher'. Other notable hits included Interactive's 'Who Killed Elvis?', LA Style's 'James Brown Is Dead' and Area 51's 'Let It Move You', a piano-rave classic. Gold went on to establish a new record label in 1994, Escapade.

ZZ Top

Formed in Houston, Texas, USA, in 1970, ZZ Top evolved out of the city's psychedelic scene and consist of Billy Gibbons (b. 16 December 1949, Houston, Texas, USA; 6-string guitar, vocals, ex-Moving Sidewalks), Dusty Hill (b. Joe Hill, 19 May 1949, Dallas, Texas, USA; bass, vocals, ex-American Blues) and Frank Beard (b. 11 June 1949, Houston, Texas, USA; drums, the last two both ex-American Blues. ZZ Top's original line-up - Gibbons, Lanier Greig (bass) and Dan

Mitchell (drums) - was also the final version of the Moving Sidewalks. This initial trio completed ZZ Top's debut single, 'Salt Lick', before Greig was fired. He was replaced by Bill Ethridge. Mitchell was then replaced by Frank Beard while Dusty Hill subsequently joined in place of Ethridge. Initially ZZ Top joined a growing swell of southern boogie bands and started a constant round of touring, building up a strong following. Their debut album, while betraying a healthy interest in blues, was firmly within this genre, but *Rio Grande Mud* indicated a greater flexibility. It included the rousing 'Francine' which, although indebted to the **Rolling Stones**, gave the trio their first hit and introduced them to a much wider audience. Their third album, *Tres Hombres*, was a powerful, exciting set that drew from delta music and high energy rock. It featured the band's first national hit with 'La Grange' and was their first platinum album. The group's natural ease was highly affecting and Gibbons' startling guitarwork was rarely bettered during these times. In 1974, the band's first annual 'Texas-Size Rompin' Stompin' Barndance And Bar-B-Q' was held at the Memorial Stadium at the University Of Texas. 85,000 people attended: the crowds were so large that the University declined to hold any rock concerts, and it was another 20 years before they resumed. However, successive album releases failed to attain the same high standard and ZZ Top took an extended vacation following their expansive 1976/7 tour. After non-stop touring for a number of years the band needed a rest. Other reasons, however, were not solely artistic, as the group now wished to secure a more beneficial recording deal. They resumed their career in 1979 with the superb *Deguello*, by which time both Gibbons and Hill had grown lengthy beards (without each other knowing!). Revitalized by their break, the trio offered a series of pulsating original songs on *Deguello* as well as inspired recreations of **Sam And Dave**'s 'I Thank You' and **Elmore James**' 'Dust My Broom'. The transitional *El Loco* followed in 1981 and although it lacked the punch of its predecessor, preferring the surreal to the celebratory, the set introduced the growing love of technology that marked the group's subsequent releases. *Eliminator* deservedly became ZZ Top's best-selling album (10 million copies in the USA by 1996). Fuelled by a series of memorable, tongue-in-cheek videos, it provided several international hit singles, including the million-selling 'Gimme All Your Lovin'. 'Sharp Dressed Man' and 'Legs' were also gloriously simple yet enormously infectious songs. The group skilfully wedded computer-age technology to their barrelhouse R&B to create a truly memorable set that established them as one of the world's leading live attractions. The follow-up, *Afterburner*, was another strong album, although it could not match the sales of the former. It did feature some excellent individual moments in 'Sleeping Bag' and 'Rough Boy', and the cleverly titled 'Velcro Fly'. ZZ Top undertook another lengthy break before returning with the impressive *Recycler*. Other notable appearances in 1990 included a cameo, playing themselves, in *Back To The Future 3*. In 1991 a greatest hits compilation was issued and a new recording contract was signed the following year, with BMG Records. *Antenna* was the first album with the new company. Over the years one of their greatest strengths has been their consistently high-standard live presentation and performance on numerous record-breaking (financially) tours in the USA. One of rock's maverick attractions, Gibbons, Hill and Beard have retained their eccentric, colourful image, dark glasses and stetson hats, complete with an almost casual musical dexterity that has won over hardened cynics and carping critics. In addition to having produced a fine (but sparse) canon of work they will also stay in the record books as having the longest beards in musical history (although one member, the inappropriately named Frank Beard, is clean-shaven). Whether it was by plan or chance, they are doomed to end every music encyclopedia.

● ALBUMS: *First Album* (London 1971)★★, *Rio Grande Mud* (London 1972)★★★, *Tres Hombres* (London 1973)★★★★, *Fandango!* (London 1975)★★, *Tejas* (London 1976)★★, *Deguello* (Warners 1979)★★★★, *El Loco* (Warners 1981)★★★, *Eliminator* (Warners 1983)★★★★, *Afterburner* (Warners 1985)★★★★, *Recycler* (Warners 1990)★★★★, *Antenna* (RCA 1994)★★★, *Rhythmeen* (RCA 1996)★★★★.

● COMPILATIONS: *The Best Of Z.Z. Top* (London 1977)★★★, *Greatest Hits* (Warners 1992)★★★★, *One Foot In The Blues* (Warners 1994)★★★.

● VIDEOS: *Greatest Hits Video Collection* (1992).

● FURTHER READING: *Elimination: The Z.Z. Top Story*, Dave Thomas.

BIBLIOGRAPHY BY ARTIST

A-Ha
Marcussen, *A-ha: The Story So Far*, Zomba Books (UK), 1986.

Abba
Borg, Christer, *ABBA By ABBA (Originally Called: The ABBA Phenomenon)*, Stafford Pemberton (UK), 1977.

Edington, Harry & Himmelstrand, Peter, *ABBA*, Magnum (UK), 1978.

Fältskog, Agnetha with Åhman, Brita, *As I Am: Abba Before And Beyond*, Virgin Books (UK), 1998.

Lindwall, Marianne, *ABBA: The Ultimate Pop Group*, Souvenir Press (UK), 1977.

No editor listed, *ABBA Annual 1982*, Stafford Pemberton (UK), 1981.

Oldham, A., Calder, T., Irwin, C., *The Name Of The Game*, Sidgwick & Jackson (UK), 1994.

Palm, Carl Magnus, *ABBA: The Complete Recording Sessions*, Century (UK), 1994.

Snaith, Paul, *Abba: The Music Still Goes On*, Castle Communications (UK), 1994.

Tobler, John, *ABBA For The Record: The Authorized Story In Words And Pictures*, Stafford Pemberton (UK), 1980.

Tobler, John, *Abba Gold: The Complete Story*, Century (UK), 1993.

Ulvaeus, Bjorn, *ABBA: A Lyrical Collection 1972-1982*, Century 21 Merchandising (UK), 1982.

York, Rosemary, *ABBA In Their Own Words*, Omnibus Press (UK), 1981.

Abbott, George
Abbott, George, *Mister Abbott*, Random House (USA), 1963.

AC/DC
Bunton, Richard, *AC/DC: Hell Ain't No Bad Place To Be*, Omnibus Press (UK), 1982.

Dome, Malcolm, *AC/DC*, Proteus Books (UK), 1982.

Dome, Malcolm (ed.), *The World's Most Electrifying Rock 'n' Roll Band*, Virgin Books (UK), 1995.

Ezra, Paul, *The AC/DC Story*, Babylon Books (UK), 1982.

Huxley, Martin, *AC/DC: The World's Heaviest Rock*, St. Martin's Press (USA), 1996.

No author listed, *HM Photo Book*, Omnibus Press (UK), 1994.

Putterford, Mark, *Shock To The System*, Omnibus Press (UK), 1994.

Putterford, Mark, *AC/DC Illustrated Biography*, Omnibus Press (UK), 1992.

Tesch, Chris, *AC/DC: An Illustrated Collectors Guide Volumes 1 & 2*, Chris Tesch (USA), 1992.

Walker, Clinton, *Highway To Hell: The Life And Times Of AC/DC Legend Bon Scott*, Sidgwick & Jackson (UK), 1995.

Acuff, Roy
Acuff, Roy, *Roy Acuff's Nashville*, Perigee Books (USA)

Dunkleberger, A.C., *King Of Country Music: The Life Story Of Roy Acuff*, Williams, 1971.

Schlappi, Elizabeth, *Roy Acuff: The Smoky Mountain Boy*, Pelican, 1978.

Adam And The Ants
Lavers, Stephen, *Adam And The Ants Kings: The Official Adam And The Ants Song Book*, Mirror Books (UK), 1981.

Maw, James, *The Official Adam Ant Story*, Futura (UK), 1981.

Rodriguez, Martha (Design), *Adam Ant Tribal Rock Special*, Kelmoss, 1981.

Vermorel, Fred & Judy, *Adam And The Ants*, Omnibus Press (UK), 1981.

Welch, Chris, *Adam And The Ants*, W.H. Allen (UK), 1981.

West, Mike, *Adam And The Ants*, Babylon Books (UK), 1981.

Adams, Bryan
Duffett, Mark, *Bryan Adams: A Fretted Biography*, Duff Press, 1995.

Gregory, Hugh, *Bryan Adams: The Inside Story*, Boxtree (UK), 1992.

Robertson, Sandy, *The Illustrated Biography*, Omnibus Press (UK), 1994.

Saidman, Sorelle, *Bryan Adams: Everything He Does*, Sidgwick & Jackson (UK), 1995.

Aerosmith
Aerosmith, *Get A Grip*, International Music Publications (UK), 1994.

Bowler, Dave & Dray, Brian, *What It Takes*, Boxtree (UK), 1997.

Foxe-Tyler, Cyrinda & Fields, Danny, *Dream On: Living On The Edge With Steven Tyler*, Dove Books (USA), 1997.

Huxley, Martin, *Toys In The Attic: The Rise, Fall And Rise Of Aerosmith*, Macmillan, 1995.

Putterford, Mark, *Live!*, Omnibus Press (UK), 1994.

Putterford, Mark, *The Fall And Rise Of Aerosmith*, Omnibus Press (UK), 1991.

Aerosmith with Davis, Stephen, *Walk This Way: The Autobiography Of Aerosmith*, Virgin Books (UK), Avon Books (USA), 1997.

Aladdin Records
Ruppli, Michael, *The Aladdin/Imperial Labels: A Discography*, Greenwood Press, 1991.

Alarm
Taylor, Rick, *The Alarm*, Omnibus Press (UK), 1986.

Alberto Y Lost Trios Paranoias
Alberto Y Lost Trios Paranoias, *Alberto's Umper Ook Of Fun*, Private Edition (UK), 1978.

Albery, Donald
Trewin, W., *All On Stage: Charles Wyndham And The Alberys*, Harrap (UK), 1980.

Alice Cooper
Alice Cooper as told to Steven Gaines, *Me, Alice: The Autobiography Of Alice Cooper*, G.P. Putnam (USA), 1976.

Bruce, Michael with James, Billy, *No More Mr Nice Guy: The Inside Story Of The Alice Cooper Group*, SAF, 1996.

Demorest, Steve, *Alice Cooper*, Popular Library (USA), 1974.
Editors of Rolling Stone, *Rolling Stone Scrapbook: Alice Cooper*, Straight Arrow Books (USA), 1975.

Allen, Fred
Allen, Fred, *Much Ado About Me*, Little, Brown (USA), 1956.

Allen, Henry 'Red'
Evensmo, Jan, *The Trumpet And Vocal Of Henry Red Allen, 1927-1942*, Evensmo.

Allen, Rex
Simpson Witt, Paula & Garrett, Snuff, *My Life-Sunrise To Sunset: The Arizona Cowboy Rex Allen*, RexGarRus Press (USA), 1989.

Allison, Mose
Jones, Patti, *One Man's Blues: The Life And Music Of Mose Allison*, Quartet (UK), 1996.

Allman Brothers Band
Freeman, Scott, *Midnight Riders: The Story Of The Allman Brothers Band*, Little, Brown (USA), 1995.
Nolan, Tom, *The Allman Brothers Band; A Biography In Words And Pictures*, Chappell Music, 1976.

Almond, Marc
Reed, Jeremy, *The Last Star: A Biography Of Marc Almond*, Creation Books (UK), 1995.

Altamont Festival
Eisen, Jonathan (ed), *Altamont*, Avon Books (USA), 1970.

Amos, Tori
Rogers, Kalen, *All These Years: The Illustrated Biography*, Omnibus Press (UK), 1994.

Anderson, Bill
Anderson, Bill, *Whisperin' Bill*, Longstreet Press (USA), 1990.
Anderson, Bill, *I Hope You're Living As High On The Hog As The Pig You Turned Out To Be*, Longstreet Press (USA), 1994.

Anderson, John Murray
Anderson, John Murray, *Out Without My Rubbers*, Library, New York (USA), 1954.

Anderson, Maxwell
Clark, B., *Maxwell Anderson: The Man And His Plays*, Samuel French (USA), 1933.
Shivers, A.S., *The Life Of Maxwell Anderson*, Stein & Day (USA), 1983.

Anderson, Stig
Oldham, A., Calder, T. & Irwin, C., *Abba, The Name Of The Game*.

Andrews, Julie
Arntz, James & Wilson, Thomas S., *Julie Andrews*, Contemporary Books (USA), 1996.

Animals
Blackford, Andy, *Wild Animals*, Sidgwick & Jackson (UK), 1986.
Burdon, Eric, *I Used To Be An Animal But I'm All Right Now*, Faber & Faber (UK), 1986.
Castello, Dionisio, *Good Times: The Ultimate Eric Burdon*, Not listed, 1991.
Kent, Jeff, *The Last Poet: The Story Of Eric Burdon*, Witan Creations, 1989.

Arlen, Harold
Jablonski, Edward, *A Life Of Harold Arlen: Happy With The Blues*, Doubleday (USA), 1961.

Armatrading, Joan
Mayes, Sean, *Joan Armatrading: A Biography*, Weidenfeld (UK), 1990.

Armstrong, Frankie
Armstrong, Frankie with Pearson, Jenny, *As Far As The Eye Can See*, The Women's Press (UK), 1992.
Henderson, Kathy & Kerr, Sandra, *My Song Is My Own*.

Armstrong, Louis
Armstrong, Louis, *Satchmo: My Life In New Orleans*, Da Capo (USA), 1986.
Bergreen, Laurence, *Louis Armstrong: An Extravagant Life*, Broadway Books (USA), 1997.
Bigard, B., *With Louis And The Duke*, London, 1985.
Boujut, Michel, *Pour Armstrong*, Filipacchi, 1976.
Collier, James Lincoln, *Louis Armstrong: An American Genius*, Oxford University Press, 1983.
Collier, James Lincoln, *Louis Armstrong: An American Success Story*, Macmillan (USA).
Giddins, Gary, *Satchmo*, Doubleday (USA), 1988.
Jones, Max & Chilton, John, *J. Louis: The Louis Armstrong Story, 1900-1971*, London, 1971.
Jones, Max, Chilton, John & Feather, Leonard, *Salute To Satchmo*, London, 1955.
Meryman, Richard, *Louis Armstrong: A Self-Portrait*, Eakins Press (USA), 1971.
Pinfold, Mike, *Louis Armstrong, His Life And Times*, Universe Books (UK).
Schiff, Ronny S., *Louis Armstrong, A Jazz Master*, MCA Music.
Tanenhaus, Sam, *Louis Armstrong*, Chelsea House.
Westerberg, Hans, *Boy From New Orleans: Louis 'Satchmo' Armstrong*, Copenhagen, 1981.

Arnaz, Desi
Arnaz, Desi, *A Book*, Warner Books (USA), 1976.

Arnold, Eddy
Arnold, Eddy, *It's A Long Way From Chester County*, Pyramid Books (USA), 1969.

Arrows
Harry, Bill, *Arrows: The Official Story*, Everest Books (UK), 1976.

Asche, Oscar
Asche, Oscar, *Oscar Asche: His Life, By Himself*, Hurst & Blackett (UK), 1929.

Ash
Bowler, Dave & Dray, Bryan, *Minds Of Fire*, Boxtree (UK), 1997.
Porter, Charley, *Ash 1977-97*, Virgin Books (UK), 1997.

Astaire, Fred
Astaire, Fred, *Steps In Time*, Harper Row (USA), 1959.
Billman, Larry, *Fred Astaire: A Bio-Bibliography*, Greenwood Press (USA), 1998.
Satchell, Tim, *Astaire. The Biography*, Hutchinson (UK), 1987.

Astley, Virginia
Brown, Robert & Rivers, Deke, *The World Of Virginia Astley*, Deke Rivers (UK), 1996.

Atkins, Chet
Atkins, Chet with Bill Neeley, *Country Gentleman*, Regnery (USA), 1974.

Atlantic Records
Gillett, Charlie, *Making Tracks: The Story Of Atlantic Records*, Souvenir Press (UK), 1988.
Guralnick, Peter, *Sweet Soul Music*, Harper & Row (USA), 1986.
Marsh, Graham & Glyn Callingham, *East Coasting: The Cover Art of NY's Prestige, Riverside & Atlantic...*, Collins & Brown, 1993.
Picardie, Justine & Wade, Dorothy, *Atlantic And The Godfathers Of Rock And Roll*, Fourth Estate (UK), 1993.

Awaya, Noriko
Awaya, Noriko, *Watashini Ii Furikoki Jinsei (My Good Furikoki Like)*, Tokyo, 1984.
Teruko Yoshitake, Bluesno Jôo (The Queen Of The Blues), *Tokyo*, 1989.

Axton, Mae Boren
Axton, Mae Boren, *Country Singers As I Know 'Em*, 1973.

Aznavour, Charles
Aznavour, Charles, *Aznavour By Aznavour: An Autobiography*, Crowell (USA), 1972.
Aznavour, Charles, *Yesterday When I Was Young*, W.H. Allen (UK), 1979.
Salgues, Y., *Charles Aznavour*, , 1964.

Babes In Toyland
Karlen, Neal, *Babes In Toyland: The Making And Selling Of A Rock And Roll Band*, Avon Books (USA), 1995.

Bachman-Turner Overdrive
Melhuish, Martin, *Bachman Turner Overdrive: Rock Is My Life, This Is My Song: The Authorized Biog*, Two Continents, 1976.

Baddeley, Hermione
Baddeley, Hermione, *The Unsinkable Hermione Baddeley*, London & New York, 1984.

Badfinger
Matovina, Dan, *Without You: The Tragic Story Of Badfinger*, Frances Glover Books (USA), Picador (UK), 1997.

Baez, Joan
Baez, Joan, *And A Voice to Sing With*, Arrow (UK), 1990.
Baez, Joan, *And Then I Wrote*.
Baez, Joan, *Daybreak: An Intimate Journey*, Dial Press (USA), 1968.
No editor listed, *The Playboy Interviews: Joan Baez*, Playboy Press (USA), 1971.
Siegmeister, Elie., *American Ballads And Folk Songs, From The Joan Baez Songbook*, Ryerson Music, 1964.
Swan, Peter, *Joan Baez, A Bio-Disco-Bibliography: Being A Selected Guide To Material In Print*, Noyce, 1977.
Swanekamp, Joan, *Diamonds And Rust: A Bibliography And Discography Of Joan Baez*, Pierian Press (USA), 1982.

Bailey, Deford
Morton, David C. & Wolfe, Charles K., *Deford Bailey: A Black Star In Early Country Music*, University Of Tennessee Press (USA), 1991.

Bailey, Pearl
Bailey, Pearl, *Talking To Myself*, New York, 1971.
Bailey, Pearl, *The Raw Pearl*, New York, 1968.

Bain, Aly
Clark, Alistair, *Aly Bain - Fiddler On The Loose*, Mainstream (UK), 1993.

Baker, Anita
Baker, Anita, *Rapture*, Columbia Pictures.

Baker, Chet
Wulff, Ingo, *Chet Baker In Concert*, Nieswand Verlag, 1992.
Wulff, Ingo (ed.), *Chet Baker In Europe 1975 - 1988*, Nieswand Verlag, 1993.

Baker, Joséphine
Hammond, Bryan & O'Connor, Patrick, *Josephine Baker*, London, 1987.
Haney, Lynn, *Naked At The Feast: The Biography Of Josephine Baker*, Robson Books (UK), 1990.
Rose, Phyllis, *Jazz Cleopatra: Josephine Baker In Her Time*, Chatto & Windus (UK), 1990.

Balanchine, George
Taper, Bernard, *Balanchine*, Harper & Row (USA), 1963.

Ball, Lucille
Gregory, J., *The Lucille Ball Story*, New American Library (USA), 1974.
Sanders, Coyne Steven & Gilbert, Tom, *Desilu: The Story Of Lucille Ball And Desi Arnaz*, William Morrow (USA), 1993.

Band
Helm, Levon with Davis, Stephen, *This Wheel's On Fire: Levon Helm And The Story Of The Band*, William Morrow (USA), 1993.
Hoskyns, Barney, *Across The Great Divide: The Band And America*, Viking (UK), Hyperion (USA), 1993.
Marcus, Greil, *Invisible Republic: Bob Dylan's Basement Tapes*, 1997.
Marcus, Greil, *Mystery Train: Images Of America In Rock And Roll Music*, 1975.

Bangs, Lester
Bangs, Lester, *Psychotic Reactions And Carburettor Dung*, Serpents Tail (UK), 1996.

Barker, Danny
Barker, Danny, *A Life In Jazz*, London, 1986.

Barker, Les
Barker, Les, *Beagles, Bangles And Beads*, 1993.

Barnet, Charlie
Barnet, Charlie with Dance, Stanley, *Those Swinging Years: The Autobiography Of Charlie Barnet*, Tulane, Louisiana (USA), 1984.

Barrett, Syd
Anderson, Pete & Rock, Mick, *Syd Barrett: The Madcap Laughs*, UFO Books (UK), 1993.
Palacios, Julian, *Lost In The Woods: Syd Barrett And The Pink Floyd*, Boxtree (UK), 1998.
Watkinson, Mike & Anderson, Pete, *Crazy Diamond: Syd Barrett And The Dawn Of Pink Floyd*, Omnibus Press (UK), 1990.

Barron Knights
Langford, Pete, *Once A Knight: History Of The Barron Knights*, International Music Publications (UK), 1993.

Barron, Kenny

Barron, Kenny, *Kenny Barron (Interviewed by Marian McPartland)*.

Basie, Count

Dance, Stanley, *The World Of Count Basie*, Charles Scribner (USA).

Horricks, Raymond, *Count Basie And His Orchestra: Its Music and Its Musicians*, Citadel Press, 1957.

Morgan, A., *Count Basie*, Tunbridge Wells (UK), 1984.

Murray, Albert, *Good Morning Blues: The Autobiography Of Count Basie*, William Heinemann (UK), 1986,

Sheridan, Chris, *Count Basie: A Biodiscography*, Greewood, Westport (USA), 1986.

Bauhaus

Shirley, Ian, *Dark Entries: Bauhaus And Beyond*, SAF (UK), 1995.

Bay City Rollers

Allen, Elkis, *Bay City Rollers*, Panther (UK).

Golumb, David, *The Bay City Rollers Scrapbook*, Queen Anne Press (UK).

Paton, Tam, *The Bay City Rollers*, Everest Books (UK), 1975.

Beach Boys

Abbott, Kingsley (ed.), *Back To The Beach - A Brian Wilson And The Beach Boys Reader*, Helter Skelter, 1997.

Anthony, Dean, *The Beach Boys*, Crescent (USA), 1985.

Barnes, Ken, *The Beach Boys: A Biography In Words & Pictures*, Sire (USA), Chappell Music (UK), 1976.

Cavanagh, Dwight, *The Smile File*, Kingsley Abbott (UK), 1995.

Elliott, Brad, *Surf's Up!: The Beach Boys On Record, 1961-1981*, Pierian Press, 1982.

Gaines, Steven, *Heroes And Villains: The True Story Of The Beach Boys*, Macmillan (UK), 1986.

Golden, Bruce, *The Beach Boys: Southern California Pastoral*, R. Reginald/Borgo Press (USA), 1976.

Hultz, Rene & Skotte, Hans Christian, *The Rainbow Files: The Beach Boys on CD*, MHRS Productions (Denmark), 1996.

Leaf, David, *The Beach Boys And The California Myth*, Grosset & Dunlap (USA), 1978.

McFarland, Stephen J, *Brian Wilson Tape 10*, PTB Publications (USA), 1992.

McFarland, Stephen J, *The Wilson Project*, PTB Productions (USA), 1991.

Millward, John, *The Beach Boys: Silver Anniversary*, Doubleday/Dolphin (USA), 1986.

Preiss, Byron, *The Beach Boys: The Authorized Illustrated Biography*, Ballantine Books (USA), 1979.

Priore, Dominic, *Look! Listen! Vibrate! SMILE*, Dominic Priore, 1989.

Tobler, John, *The Beach Boys*, Hamlyn (UK), 1978.

White, Timothy, *The Nearest Faraway Place: Brian Wilson, The Beach Boys & The Southern Californi*, Henry Holt & Co (USA), 1994.

Wilson, Brian & Gold, Todd, *Wouldn't It Be Nice: My Own Story*, Harper Collins (USA), 1991.

Wincentsen, Edward, *Denny Remembered*, Virgin Books (UK), 1991.

Wise, Nick (compiler), *In Their Own Words*, Omnibus Press (UK), 1994.

Beat (UK)

Halasha, Malu, *The Beat: Twist And Crawl*, Eel Pie (UK), 1981.

Beatles

Adams, Mike with Jones, Jeff, *Apple & Beatles Collectables*, Perry & Perry, 1991.

Adler, Bill, *Love Letters To The Beatles*, Blond & Briggs (UK), 1964.

Aldridge, Alan (ed.), *The Beatles Illustrated Lyrics*, Macdonald/Futura (UK), 1969.

Aldridge, Alan (ed.), *The Beatles Illustrated Lyrics Vol. 2*, Macdonald (UK), 1971.

Alico, Stella, *Elvis Presley - The Beatles*, Pendulum Press, 1979.

Apple Press Office, *The Beatles Press Book*, Apple (UK), 1969.

Augsburger, Jeff (etc), *Beatles Memorabilia Price Guide*, Chilton Book Co. (USA), 1994.

Bacon, David & Maslov, Norman, *Beatles' England*, Columbus Books, 1982.

Baker, Glenn A., *The Beatles Down Under: The 1964 Australia And New Zealand Tour*, Wild & Woolley, (Australia), Magnum (UK), 1982.

Barrow, Tony, *Meet The Beatles: Star Special Number 12*, World Distributors (UK), 1963.

Belmo, Jim, *The Beatles: Not For Sale*, Collector's Guide (UK), 1997.

Belmo, Mark, *The Making Of: The Beatles' Sgt Pepper*, Collectors Guide Publishing (USA), 1996.

Bennahum, David, *In Their Own Words: The Beatles After The Break-Up*, Omnibus Press (UK), 1991.

Berkenstadt, Jim & Belmo, *Black Market Beatles: Story Of The Lost Recordings*, Collectors Guide Publishing (Canada), 1995.

Best, Pete & Patrick Doncaster, *Beatle! The Pete Best Story*, Plexus (UK), 1985.

Best, Pete with Harry, Bill, *The Best Years Of The Beatles*, Headline (UK), 1997.

Bicknell, Alf & Marsh, Garry, *Baby You Can Drive My Car*, Number 9 Books (UK), 1990.

Blake, John, *All You Needed Was Love: The Beatles After The Beatles*, Hamlyn (UK), 1981.

Braun, Michael, *Love Me Do: The Beatles' Progress*, Penguin (UK), 1964.

Brown, Peter & Gaines, Steven, *The Love You Make: An Insider's Story Of The Beatles*, McGraw-Hill (USA), Macmillan (UK), 1983.

Bunt, Jan de, *The Beatles Concert-ed Effort*, Beatles Unlimited, 1978.

Burke, John, *The Beatles: A Hard Day's Night*, Pan Books (UK), 1964.

Burt, Robert & Pascall, Jeremy (eds.), *The Beatles: The Fabulous Story Of John, Paul, George And Ringo*, Octopus Books (UK), 1975.

Buskin, Richard, *The Complete Idiot's Guide To The Beatles*, Alpha (UK), 1998.

Campbell, Colin & Murphey, Allan, *Things We Said Today: The Complete Lyrics And A Concordance To The Beatles' Son*, Pierian Press (USA), 1980.

Carr, Roy, *The Beatles At The Movies*, UFO Books (UK), 1996.

Carr, Roy & Tyler, Tony, *The Beatles: An Illustrated Record*, Trewin Copplestone/New English Library (UK), 1975.

Castleman, Harry & Podrazik, Walter J., *All Together Now: The First Complete Beatles Discography 1961-1975*, Ballantine (UK), 1976.

Castleman, Harry & Podrazik, Walter J., *The Beatles Again*, Pierian Press, 1977.

Castleman, Harry & Podrazik, Walter J., *The End Of The Beatles*, Pierian Press, 1985.

Catone, Marc A., *As I Write This Letter: American Generation Remembers The Beatles*, Pierian Press (USA), 1990.

Clark, Allan, *The Beatles*, Allan Clark (USA), 1981.

Clayson, Alan, *Hamburg: The Cradle Of British Rock*, Sanctuary, 1998.

Clayson, Alan & Sutcliffe, Pauline, *Backbeat*, Pan Books (UK), 1994.

Coleman, Ray, *John Ono Lennon 1967-1980*, Sidgwick &

Jackson (UK), 1984.

Coleman, Ray, *John Winston Lennon 1940-1966*, Sidgwick & Jackson (UK), 1984.

Coleman, Ray, *Brian Epstein: The Man Who Made The Beatles*, Viking (UK), 1989.

Cott, Jonathan & Dalton, David, *The Beatles Get Back*, Apple Books (UK), 1970.

Cowan, Philip, *Behind The Beatles Songs: The Book That Sets The Record Straight*, Polytantric Press, 1978.

Cox, Perry & Lindsay, Joe, *The Beatles Price Guide For American Records-3rd Edition*, Biodisc, 1991.

Davies, Hunter, *The Beatles*, Heinemann (UK), 1968.

Davis, Edward E., *The Beatles Book*, New York (USA), 1968.

De Blasio, Edward, *All About The Beatles*, MacFadden-Bartell, 1964.

Dean, Johnny, *The Beatles Book: 1966 Christmas Extra*, Sean O'Mahoney/Beat Publications, 1966.

Di Franco, Philip J., *A Hard Day's Night With The Beatles*, Chelsea House (USA), 1970.

DiLello, Richard, *The Longest Cocktail Party*, Playboy Press (USA), Charisma Books (UK), 1972.

Dister, Alain, *Les Beatles*, Albin Michel (Paris), 1972.

Doggett, Peter, *Classic Rock Albums: Abbey Road/Let It Be*, Schirmer (UK), 1998.

Doney, Malcolm, *Lennon And McCartney*, Midas Books (UK), Hippocrene Books (USA), 1981.

Epstein, Brian, *A Cellarful Of Noise*, Souvenir Press (UK), 1964.

Evans, Mike, *Nothing To Get Hung About: A Short History Of The Beatles*, City of Liverpool Public Relations Office.

Ewing, John, *Beatles*, Orion/Carlton (UK), 1994.

Fast, Julius, *The Beatles: The Real Story*, Putnam (USA), 1968.

Fenick, Barbara, *Collecting The Beatles: An Intro And Price Guide To Fab Four Collectibles*, Pierian Press (USA), 1982.

Freeman, Robert, *Beatles Ltd*, Newnes (UK), 1964.

Freeman, Robert, *Beatles: A Private View*, Pyramid Books, 1990.

Fremon, Stephane & Hocquet, Jean -Claude, *Les Beatles: Guide de la Discographie Originale Francaise (1962-1970)*, France, 1992.

Friede, Goldie, Titone, Robin & Weiner, Sue, *The Beatles A To Z*, Methuen (UK), 1980.

Friedman, Rick, *The Beatles: Words Without Music*, Grosset & Dunlap (USA), 1968.

Fulpen, H. V., *The Beatles: An Illustrated Diary*, Plexus (UK), 1983.

Giuliano, Geoffrey, *Tomorrow Never Knows: Thirty Years Of Beatles Music & Memorabilia*, Paper Tiger (UK), 1992.

Goodgold, Edwin, *The Compleat Beatles Quiz Book*, Warner Books (USA), 1975.

Gottfridsson, Hans Olaf, *Beatles - From Cavern To Star Club*, Premium, 1998.

Greenwald, Ted, *The Fab Four In Film, Performance, Recording & Print*, Smithmark US, 1993.

Gross, Edward, *Fab Films Of The Beatles*, Pioneer, 1991.

Grove, Martin A., *Beatles Madness*, Manor Books (USA), 1978.

Guzek, Arnot, *Beatles Discography*, Beatles Unlimited, 1978.

Hamblett, Charles, *Here Come The Beatles*, New English Library (UK), 1964.

Harris, *John Lennon And The Beatles: A Special Tribute*, 1980.

Harris, *John Lennon: Beatles Memory Book*, 1981.

Harry, Bill, *The Encyclopedia Of Beatle People*, Blandford Press (UK), 1997.

Harry, Bill, *Beatlemania: An Illustrated Filmography*, Virgin Books (UK), 1984.

Harry, Bill, *Mersey Beat: The Beginnings Of The Beatles*, Omnibus Press (UK), 1977.

Harry, Bill, *Paperback Writers: An Illustrated Bibliography*, Omnibus Press (UK), 1984.

Harry, Bill, *Paperback Writers: The History Of The Beatles In Print*, Virgin Books (UK), 1984.

Harry, Bill, *The Beatles Who's Who*, Aurum Press (UK), 1982.

Harry, Bill, *Ultimate Beatles Encyclopedia*, Virgin Books (UK), 1992.

Hertsgaard, Mark, *A Day In The Life: The Music And Artistry Of The Beatles*, Macmillan (UK), 1995.

Hine, Al, *The Beatles In Help*, Mayflower Books (UK), 1965.

Hockinson, Michael J, *Nothing Is Beatleproof*, Popular Culture, 1990.

Hockinson, Michael J., *Ultimate Beatles Quiz Book*, Boxtree (UK), 1992.

Hoffman, Dezo, *With The Beatles: The Historic Photographs*, Omnibus Press (UK), 1982.

Hoffman, Dezo with Maugham, Patrick, *The Beatles*, Pyx Publications (UK), 1964.

House, Jack, *The Beatles Quiz Book*, Collins (UK), 1964.

Howard, John, *The Beatles Unseen*, Penguin (UK), 1996.

Howlett, Kevin, *The Beatles At The Beeb 62-65: The Story Of Their Radio Career*, BBC Publications (UK), 1982.

Humphery-Smith, Cecil Raymond, *Up The Beatles: Family Tree*, Achievements Ltd (UK), 1966.

Hutchins, Chris & Thompson, Peter, *Elvis Meets The Beatles*, Smith Gryphon (UK), 1994.

Janssen, Roos & Bakker, Erik M., *Dig It: The Beatles Bootleg Book*, Beatles Unlimited, 1979.

Keenan, Debra, *On Stage, The Beatles*, Creative Education (USA), 1975.

Kelly, Michael Bryan, *Beatle Myth: British Invasion Of American Popular Music*, McFarland (USA), 1991.

King, L.R.E., *Do You Want To Know A Secret*, Storyteller, 1988.

Kozinn, Allan, *The Beatles*, Phaidon Press (UK), 1995.

Larkin, Rochelle, *The Beatles: Yesterday, Today, Tomorrow*, Scholastic Book Services (USA), 1977.

Leich, Sam, *Beatles On Broadway*, World Distributors (UK), 1964.

Leigh, Spencer, *Speak Words Of Wisdom: Reflections On The Beatles*, Cavern City, 1991.

Levy, Jeffery, *Applelog IV: A Guide For The US & Canadian Apple Records Collectors*, MonHunProd Media Group, 1991.

Lewisohn, Mark, *Complete Beatles Chronicle*, Pyramid Books, 1992.

Lewisohn, Mark, *Complete Beatles Recording Sessions: The Official Story Of The Abbey Road Years*, Hamlyn (UK), 1990.

Lewisohn, Mark, *Day By Day*, Harmony (USA), 1990.

Lewisohn, Mark, *The Beatles Live*, Pavilion (UK), 1986.

Lewisohn, Mark, *The Beatles: 25 Years In The Life*, Sidgwick & Jackson (UK), 1988.

MacDonald, Ian, *Revolution In The Head: The Beatles Records And The Sixties*, Fourth Estate (UK), 1994.

Magnus, David, *All You Need Is Love*, Tracks (UK), 1997.

Martin, George, *The Summer Of Love*, Macmillan (UK), 1994.

Maugham, Patrick, *The Beatles*, Pyx Publications (UK), 1964.

McCabe, Peter & Schonfeld, Robert D., *Apple To The Core: The Unmaking Of The Beatles*, Pocket Books/Simon & Schuster (USA), 1972.

McCartney, (Peter) Michael, *Thank U Very Much: Mike McCartney's Family Album*, Weidenfeld & Nicholson (UK), 1981.

McCoy, William & McGeary, Mitchell, *Every Little Thing*, Popular Culture, 1990.

McGeary, Mitchell, *The Beatles Discography*, Ticket To Ryde, 1975.

McKeen, William, *The Beatles: A Bio-Bibliography*, Greenwood Press (UK), 1989.

Mellers, Wilfred, *Twilight Of The Gods: The Beatles In Retrospect*, Faber & Faber (UK), 1973.

Miles, *Beatles In Their Own Words*, Omnibus Press (UK), 1978.

Miles, *The Beatles: An Illustrated Discography*, Omnibus Press (UK), 1981.

Mitchell, Carolyn Lee & Munn, Michael, *All Our Loving: A Beatle Fan's Memoir*, Robson Books (UK), 1988.

Neaverson, Bob, *The Beatles Movies*, Cassell, 1997.

Neises, C.P., *Beatles Reader: A Selection Of Contemporary Views News and Reviews*, Pierian Press.

Nimmervoll, Ed & Thorburn, Evan, *1000 Beatles Facts (And A Little Bit Of Hearsay)*, J. Albert, (Australia), 1977.

No author listed, *The Beatles 1962-92: Dyskografia*, Fonopress (Poland), 1993.

No author listed, *Beatles Movies Catalog*, Japan.

No author listed, *The Complete Beatles Lyrics*, Omnibus Press (UK), 1982.

No author listed, *Ticket To Ride*, Macdonald (UK), 1989.

No author listed, *The Beatles Up To Date*, Cancer , 1964.

No editor listed, *The Beatles By Royal Command*, Daily Mirror Publications (UK), 1963.

No editor listed, *The Beatles Films*, Pop Pics, Newnes (UK), 1964.

No editor listed, *The Beatles For The Record*, Totem , 1983.

No editor listed, *The Beatles Forever*, O'Quinn Studios, 1980.

No editor listed, *The Beatles Lyrics Complete*, Futura (UK), 1974.

No editor listed, *The Beatles Memorabilia Price Guide*, My Back Pages *UK) , 1989.

No editor listed, *The Beatles On Record: A Listener's Guide*, Charles Scribner (USA) , 1982.

No editor listed, *Yellow Submarine*, New English Library (UK), 1968.

Noebel, David A, *The Beatles: A Study In Drugs, Sex And Revolution*, Christian Crusade, 1969.

Noebel, David A., *Communism, Hypnotism And The Beatles*, Christian Crusade (USA), 1965.

Norman, Philip, *Shout! The True Story Of The Beatles*, Elm Tree Books (UK), 1981.

O'Brien, *26 Days that Rocked The World*, Los Angeles, 1978.

O'Donnell, Jim, *The Day John Met Paul*, Penguin Books, 1995.

Parker, Alan, etc., *In The Lap Of The Gods And The Hands Of The Beatles*, G.C.P. , 1990.

Parkinson, Norman & Cleave, Maureen, *The Beatles Book*, Hutchinson (UK), 1964.

Patterson, Gary R., *The Walrus Was Paul: The Great Beatle Death Clues Of 1969*, Dowling Press Inc (USA), 1995.

Patterson, Gary R., *The Great Beatle Death Clues*, Robson Books (UK), 1997.

Pawlowski, Gareth L., *How They Became The Beatles: A Definitive History Of The Early Years 1960-1964*, Macdonald (UK), 1990.

Pirmanten, Patricia, *The Beatles*, Creative Education (USA), 1974.

Rayl, A.J.S., *Beatles '64: A Hard Day's Night In America*, Sidgwick & Jackson (UK), 1990.

Reinhart, Charles, *You Can't Do That: Beatles Bootlegs And Novelty Records, 1963-1980*, Pierian Press (USA), 1981.

Riley, Tim, *Tell Me Why: A Beatles Commentary*, Bodley Head (UK), 1988.

Robertson, John, *The Complete Guide To The Music Of ...*, Omnibus Press (UK), 1995.

Robertson, John, *The Essential Guide To The Music Of...*, Omnibus Press (UK), 1994.

Rosenbaum, Helen, *The Beatles Trivia Quizbook*, Signet (USA), 1978.

Russell, Ethan (photographs), *Get Back*, Apple (UK) , 1969.

Russell, Jeff, *The Beatles Album File and Complete Discography*, Blandford Press (UK), 1989.

Scaduto, Anthony, *The Beatles*, Signet (USA), 1968.

Schaffner, Nicholas, *The Beatles Forever*, Mcgraw Hill (USA), 1978.

Schaffner, Nicholas, *The Boys From Liverpool: John, Paul, George, Ringo*, Methuen (UK), 1980.

Schaumberg, Ron, *Growing Up With The Beatles: An Illustrated Tribute*, Harcourt Brace Jovanovich (USA), 1976.

Schreuders, Piet, Lewisohn, Mark & Smith, Adam, *The Beatles' London*, Hamlyn (UK), 1994.

Schultheiss, Tom, *The Beatles: A Day In The Life: The Day By Day Diary 1960-1970*, Omnibus Press (UK), 1980.

Schwartz, David, *Listening To The Beatles: Vol 1: Bootlegs And Singles*, Popular Culture, 1991.

Schwarz, Francie, *Body Count*, Straight Arrow (USA), 1972.

Shepherd, Billy, *The True Story Of The Beatles*, Beat Publications (UK), 1964.

Shipper, Mark, *Paperback Writer: The Life And Times Of The Beatles: The Spurious Chronicle*, Grosset & Dunlap (USA), Times/Mirror (UK), 1978.

Southall, Brian, *Abbey Road: The Story Of The World's Most Famous Recording Studios*, Patrick Stephens (UK), 1982.

Spence, Helen, *The Beatles Forever*, Colour Library International (UK), 1981.

Spencer, Terence, *It Was Thirty Years Ago Today*, Bloomsbury (UK), 1994.

Stannard, Neville, *The Long And Winding Road: A History Of The Beatles On Record*, Virgin Books (UK), 1982.

Stannard, Neville, *Working Class Heroes: The History Of The Beatles' Solo Recordings*, Virgin Books, 1983.

Staveacre, Tony, *The Songwriters*, BBC (UK), 1980.

Stern, Michael, *A Reference And Value Guide*, Collector Books (USA), 1993.

Stokes, Geoffrey, *The Beatles*, Omnibus Press (UK) , 1981.

Sutton, Margaret, *We Love You Beatles*, Doubleday (USA), 1971.

Swenson, John, *The Beatles: Yesterday And Today*, Zebra Books (UK).

Swenson, John, *Yesterday Seems So Far Away*, Zebra Books (UK), 1977.

Tashian, Barry, *Ticket To Ride: The Extraordinary Diary Of The Beatles's Last Tour*, Dowling Press (USA), 1996.

Taylor, Alistair, *Yesterday-My Life With The Beatles*, Pioneer, 1991.

Taylor, Alistair, *Yesterday: The Beatles Remembered*, Sidgwick & Jackson (UK), 1988.

Taylor, Derek, *As Time Goes By: Living In The Sixties*, Straight Arrow (USA), 1973.

Taylor, Derek, *It Was Twenty Years Ago*, Bantam (UK), 1987.

Todd, Michael, *Beatles For Sale:International Price Guide To LPs, EPs, 45s & CDs*, AMV Entertainment, 1993.

Turner, Steve, *A Hard Day's Write*, Little Brown (UK), 1994.

Van de Bunt, Jan & Friends, *The Beatles: Concerted Efforts*, Beatles Unlimited (Holland), 1979.

Vollmer, Jurgen, *Rock 'N' Roll Times: The Style And Spirit Of The Early Beatles*, Google Plex Books, New York, 1981.

Whitaker, Bob, *The Unseen Beatles*, Conran Octopus (UK), 1992.

Wiener, Allen J., *The Ultimate Recording Guide*, Aurum Press (UK), 1993.

Wiener, Allen J., *The Beatles: A Recording History*, Bailey Brothers & Swinfen (UK), 1987.

Wilk, Max, *The Beatles In Yellow Submarine*, New English Library (UK).

Williams, Allan, *The Man Who Gave The Beatles Away*, Elm Tree Books (UK), 1975.

Woffinden, Bob, *The Beatles Apart*, Protcus Books (UK), 1981.

Zanderbergen, George, *The Beatles*, Crestwood House (USA), 1976.

Beauty And The Beast

Frantz, Donald with Sue Heinemann, *Beauty And The Beast: A Celebration Of The Broadway Musical*, Hyperion (USA), 1996.

Bechet, Sidney
Bechet, Sidney, *Treat It Gentle*, London, 1960.
Chilton, John, *Sidney Bechet, The Wizard Of Jazz*, Macmillan (UK), 1987.
Hippenmeyer, Jean Roland, *Sidney Bechet, Ou, L'Extraordinaire Odyssee D'Un Musicien De Jazz*, Tribune Editions.

Beck, Jeff
No author listed, *Rock Fun 3: Photo Gallery*, Japan.

Bee Gees
Edwards, Henry, *Sgt. Pepper's Lonely Hearts Club Band*, Star Books (UK), 1978.
Gibb, Barry, Robin & Maurice as told to Leaf, David, *Bee Gees: The Authorized Biography*, Octopus Books (UK), 1979.
Munshower, Suzanne, *The Bee Gees*, Jove, New York, 1978.
No editor listed, *Billboard Salutes The Bee Gees*, Billboard Publications (USA), 1978.
Pryce, Larry, *The Bee Gees*, Panther/Granada (UK), 1979.
Schumacher, Craig, *Bee Gees*, Creative Education, 1980.
Stevens, Kim, *The Bee Gees: A Photo Biography*, Quick Fox (USA), 1978.
Stigwood, Robert & Anthony, Dee,*The Official Sgt. Pepper's Lonely Hearts Club Band Scrapbook*, Pocket Books (USA), 1978.
Tatham, Dick, *The Incredible Bee Gees*, Futura (UK), 1979.

Beiderbecke, Bix
Berton, R., *Remembering Bix*, New York, 1974.
James, B, *Bix Beiderbecke*, London, 1959.
Sudhalter, Richard M. & Evans, Philip R. with Dean-Myatt, *Bix, Man & Legend*, New Rochelle (USA), Arlington House (UK), 1974.

Belafonte, Harry
Shaw A.J., *Belafonte*, New York, 1961.

Belly
Brite, Poppy Z., *Courtney Love: The Real Story*, Simon & Schuster (USA), 1997.

Benatar, Pat
Magee, Doug, *Benatar*, Proteus Books (UK), 1985.

Bennett, Michael
Mandelbaum, Ken, *A Chorus Line And The Musicals Of Michael Bennett.*

Bennett, Richard Rodney
Craggs, Stewart R. (ed.), *Richard Rodney Bennett: A Bio-Bibliography*, Greenwood Press (UK), 1990.

Bennett, Tony
Bennett, Tony, *What My Heart Has Seen*, Rizzoli (USA), 1996.

Berigan, Bunny
Dupuis, Robert, *Bunny Berigan: Elusive Legend Of Jazz*, Louisiana State University Press, 1992.

Berlin, Irving
Barrett, Mary Ellen, *Irving Berlin*, Simon & Schuster (USA), 1995.
Bergreen, Laurence, *As Thousands Cheer: The Life Of Irving Berlin*, Viking (USA), 1990.
Freedland, Michael, *A Salute To Irving Berlin*, Comet (UK), 1990.
Hamm, Charles, *Songs From The Melting Pot: The Formative Years, 1907-1914*, Oxford University Press (UK), 1997.

Whitcomb, Ian, *Irving Berlin And Ragtime America*, Century (UK), 1990.

Bernhardt, Clyde
Harris, Sheldon E.B., (ed.), *I Remember Clyde Bernhardt*, Philadelphia, 1986.

Bernstein, Leonard
Bernstein, Leonard, *The Joy Of Music*, 1959.
Briggs, John, *Leonard Bernstein*, 1961.
Burton, Humphrey, *Leonard Bernstein*.
Gadenwitz, Peter, *Leonard Bernstein*, 1987.
Peyser, J., *The Private World Of Leonard Bernstein*, New York, 1968.
Peyser, Joan, *Leonard Bernstein*, New York, 1987.

Berry, Chuck
Berry, Chuck, *Chuck Berry: The Autobiography*, Simon & Schuster (USA), 1987.
De Witt, Howard A., *Chuck Berry: Rock 'N' Roll Music*, Horizon Books (USA), 1981.
Reese, Krista, *Chuck Berry: Mr Rock 'N' Roll*, Proteus Books (UK), 1982.

Berry, W.H.
Berry, W.H., *Forty Years In The Limelight*, Hutchinson (UK), 1939.

Best, Pete
Best, Pete & Doncaster, Patrick, *Beatle! The Pete Best Story*, Plexus (UK), 1995.

Big (Stage Musical)
Isenberg, Barbara, *Making It Big*, Limelight Editions (USA), 1997.

Big Bopper
Clark Alan, *Big Bopper 1930-1959: 30th Anniversary Memorial Series No 3*, West Covina, California (USA), 1989.
Knight, Tim, *Chantilly Lace: The Life & Times Of J.P. Richardson*, Port Arthur, Texas (USA), 1989.

Big Country
May, John, *Big Country: A Certain Chemistry*, Omnibus Press (UK), 1986.

Big Maceo
Oliver, Paul, *Big Maceo: The Art Of Jazz*, New York, 1959.

Bilk, Acker
Leslie, P. & Gwynn-Jones, P., *The Book Of Bilk*, London, 1961.

Bishop, Stephen
Bishop, Stephen (ed.), *Songs In The Rough*, St Martins Press (USA), 1996.

Bishop, Walter, Jnr.
Bishop, Walter, *Walter Bishop (Interviewed by Marian McPartland).*

Björk
Aston, Martin, *Björkgraphy*, Simon & Schuster (UK), 1996.
Phillips, Penny, *Post: The Official Bjork Book*, Bloomsbury (UK), 1995.

Black Crowes
Black, Martin, *The Black Crowes*, Omnibus Press (UK), 1993.

Black Grape

Middles, Mick, *Shaun Ryder: Happy Mondays, Black Grape And Other Traumas*, Independent Music Press (UK), 1997.
Verrico, Lisa, *High Life 'N' Low Down Dirty: The Thrills And Spills Of Shaun Ryder*, Ebury Press (UK), 1997.

Black Sabbath

Welch, Chris, *Black Sabbath*, Proteus Books (UK), 1982.

Black, Clint

Brown, R.D., *A Better Man*, Simon & Schuster (UK), 1993.

Blaine, Hal

Blaine, Hal with Goggin, David, *Hal Blaine And The Wrecking Crew*, Mix, 1990.

Blake, Eubie

Rose, A., *Eubie Blake*, Schirmer Books (USA).

Blasters

Alvin, Dave, *Any Rough Times Are Now Behind You*, Incommunicado, 1995.

Blondie

Bangs, Lester, *Blondie*, Fireside Books (USA), 1980.
Harry, Debbie; Stein, Chris & Bockris, Victor, *Making Tracks: The Rise Of Blondie*, Dell (USA), 1982.
Schruers, Fred, *Blondie*, Star/W.H. Allen (UK), 1980.
Sinclair, Paul, *Rip Her To Shreds: A Look At Blondie*, Cosmic Dancer, 1979.

Blood, Sweat And Tears

Alterman, Lorraine, *Blood, Sweat And Tears*, Quick Fox (USA), 1971.

Bloomfield, Mike

Ward, Ed, *Michael Bloomfield: The Rise And Fall Of An American Guitar Hero*, Port Chester, New York, 1983.

Blue Horizon Records

Fancourt, Les, *Blue Horizon Records 1965-1972*, Retrack Books, 1992.

Blue Note Records

Marsh, Graham, *The Cover Art Of Blue Note Records*, Collins Brown (UK), 1991.
Marsh, Graham, *The Cover Art Of Blue Note Records Volume 2*, Collins Brown (UK), 1997.

Blues Band

Bainton, Roy, *Talk To Me Baby: The Story Of The Blues Band*, Firebird Books, 1994.

Blur

Lester, Paul, *Blur: The Illustrated Story*, Hamlyn (UK), 1995.
Moody, Paul, *Blur: The Great Escape*, UFO Books (UK), 1996.
Postle, Paul, *Blurbook*, Harper/Collins (UK), 1995.
Roach, Martin, *Blur: The Whole Story*, Omnibus Press (UK), 1996.
St Michael, Mick, *Blur In Their Own Words*, Omnibus Press (UK), 1996.

Bogue, Merwyn

Bogue, Merwyn, *Ish Kabibble*, Louisiana State University Press (USA).

Bolan, Marc

Bolan, Marc, *The Warlock Of Love*, Lupus Music, 1969.
Bramley, John & Shan, *Marc Bolan: The Illustrated Discography*, Omnibus Press (UK), 1983.
Bramley, John & Shan, *Marc Bolan: The Legendary Years*, Gryphon (UK), 1992.
Dicks, Ted, *Marc Bolan*, Essex House (UK), 1978.
No author listed, *Marc Bolan: The Krakenmist*, T.Rex Appreciation Society (UK), 1995.
No author listed, *Marc Bolan: The Warlock Of Love*, Lupus Music, 1992.
No editor listed, *Marc Bolan Lyric Book*, Essex Music (UK), 1972.
Paytress, Mark, *Twentieth Century Boy*, Sidgwick & Jackson (UK), 1992.
Sinclair, Paul, *Electric Warrior: The Marc Bolan Story*, Omnibus Press (UK), 1982.
Tremlett, George, *The Marc Bolan Story*, Futura (UK), 1975.
Welch, Chris & Napier-Bell, Simon, *Marc Bolan: Born To Boogie*, Eel Pie (UK), 1982.
Williams, John & Thomas, Caron, *Marc Bolan: Wilderness Of The Mind*, Xanadu (UK), 1992.

Bolden, Buddy

Marquis, D, *In Search Of Buddy Bolden, First Man Of Jazz*, Baton Rouge (USA), 1978.

Bolton, Michael

Bolton, Michael, *The One Thing*, International Music Publications (UK), 1994.

Bon Jovi

Bowler, Dave & Dray, Bryan, *Bon Jovi: Runaway*, Boxtree (UK), 1995.
Dome, Malcolm, *Faith And Glory*, Castle Communications (UK), 1994.
Jeffries, Neil, *Bon Jovi*, Sidgwick & Jackson (UK), 1996.
McSquare, Eddy, *Bon Jovi: An Illustrated Biography*, Omnibus Press (UK), 1990.
Wall, Mick, *The Illustrated Biography*, Omnibus Press (UK), 1995.
Wall, Mick & Dome, Malcolm, *The Complete Guide To The Music Of ...* , Omnibus Press (UK), 1996.

Bond, Carrie Jacobs

Bond, C.J., *The Roads Of Melody*, New York, 1927.

Bond, Eddie

Komorowski, Adam, & Grint, Dact, *The Eddie Bond Story*, , 1982.

Bond, Graham

Shapiro, Harry, *Graham Bond: The Mighty Shadow*, Guinness Publishing (UK), 1992.

Boney M

Shearlaw, John, *Boney M*, Hamlyn (UK), 1979.

Bonniwell, Sean

Bonniwell, Sean, *The True Life Journey Of Sean Bonniwell*, Christian Vision Publishing (USA).

Bono, Sonny

Bono, Sonny, *And The Beat Goes On*, Pocket Books (USA), 1991.
Braun, Thomas, *Sonny And Cher*, Creative Education, 1978.

Boomtown Rats

Stone, Peter, *The Boomtown Rats: Having Their Picture Taken*, Star/W.H. Allen (UK), 1980.

Boone, Pat
Boone, Pat, *A New Song*, Lakeland (USA), 1972.
Boone, Pat, *Together: 25 Years With The Boone Family*, T. Nelson, 1979.

Bowie, David
Bowie, Angie, *Backstage Passes: Life On The Wild Side With David Bowie*, Orion (UK), 1993.
Bowie, Angie, *Free Spirit*, Mushroom, 1981.
Buckley, David, *The Complete Guide To The Music Of David Bowie*, Omnibus Press (UK), 1996.
Cann, Kevin, *David Bowie: A Chronology*, Vermilion Books (UK), 1983.
Carr, Roy & Murray, Charles Shaar, *David Bowie: An Illustrated Record*, Aaron Books (USA), Eel Pie (UK), 1981.
Charlesworth, Chris, *David Bowie: Profile*, Proteus Books (UK), 1981.
Charlesworth, Chris, *David Bowie: The Archive*, Bobcat Books (USA), 1988.
Claire, Vivian, *David Bowie! The King Of Glitter Rock*, Flash Books, 1977.
Claire, Vivian, *David Bowie: A Portrait In Words And Music*, Flash Books, 1977.
Currie, David, *David Bowie: The Starzone Interviews*, Omnibus Press (UK), 1986.
Douglas, David, *Presenting David Bowie*, Pinnacle, 1975.
Fletcher, David Jeffrey, *David Robert Jones Bowie: The Discography Of A Generalist, 1962-1979*, F. Ferguson, 1979.
Gillman, Peter & Leni, *Alias David Bowie*, Hodder (UK), 1990.
Hoggard, Stuart, *David Bowie: An Illustrated Discography*, Omnibus Press (UK), 1980.
Hopkins, Jerry, *Bowie*, Elm Tree Books (UK), 1985.
Jal de la Parra, Pimm, *David Bowie: The Concert Tapes*, Titan, 1986.
Jarman, Marshall, *Shining Star*, 1988.
Juby, Kerry, *In Other Words ... David Bowie*, Omnibus Press (UK), 1987.
Kelleher, (ed.), *David Bowie: A Biography In Words And Pictures*, Sire/Chappell Music, 1977.
Lynch, Kate, *David Bowie: A Rock 'N' Roll Odyssey*, Proteus Books (UK), 1984.
Miles, *Bowie In His Own Words*, Omnibus Press (UK), 1980.
Miles & Charlesworth, Chris, *David Bowie Black Book: The Illustrated Biography*, Omnibus Press (UK), 1980.
Muir, John, *The Life And Times Of David Bowie*, Babylon.Books (UK).
No editor listed, *David Bowie Rotterdam 87*, Sytze Annema, 1987.
Pitt, Kenneth, *David Bowie: The Pitt Report*, Design Music, 1983.
Sandford, Christopher, *Loving The Alien*, Little Brown (UK), 1996.
Sinclair, Paul, *The David Bowie Biography*, Privately printed, 1980.
Thomson, Elizabeth, and David Gutman (eds.), *The Bowie Companion*, Sidgwick & Jackson (UK), 1995.
Tremlett, George, *Living On The Brink*, Century (UK), 1996.
Tremlett, George, *The David Bowie Story*, Futura (UK), 1974.
Verlant, Gilles, *David Bowie: Portrait De L'Artiste En Rock-Star*, Albin Michel, Paris, 1981.
Zanetta, Tony, *Stardust*, McGraw-Hill (USA), 1987.

Bowlly, Al
Pallett, Ray, *Goodnight Sweetheart: The Life And Times Of Al Bowlly*, Spellmount (UK), 1986.

Boy George
Boy George, *Take It Like A Man*, Sidgwick & Jackson (UK), 1995.

Bragg, Billy
Salewicz, Chris & Bragg, Billy, *Midnights In Moscow*, Omnibus Press (UK), 1989.

Branson, Richard
Brown, Mick, *Branson: The Inside Story*, Michael Joseph (UK), 1988.
Branson, Richard, *Losing My Virginity*, Virgin Books (UK), 1998.

Braxton, Anthony
Braxton, Anthony, *Tri-axium Writings*, Synthesis Music, 1985.
Lock, Graham, *Forces In Motion: Anthony Braxton & The Meta-reality Of Creative Music*, Quartet (UK), 1989.
Radno, Ronald M., *New Musical Figurations: Anthony Braxton's Cultural Critique*, University Of Chicago Press (USA), 1993.

Brel, Jacques
Clayson, Alan, *Jacques Brel: The Biography*, Castle Books (UK), 1996.
Clouzet, J., *Jacques Brel*, Paris, 1965.

Brice, Fanny
Goldman, Herbert G., *Fanny Brice: The Original Funny Girl*, Oxford University Press (UK), 1992.
Grossman, Barbara W., *Funny Woman: The Life And Times Of Fanny Brice*, Indiana University Press (USA), 1991.
Katkov, Norman, *The Fabulous Fanny: The Story Of Fanny Brice*, Knopf (USA), 1953.

Bridges, Henry
Evensmo, Jan, *The Tenor Saxophones Of Henry Bridges, Robert Carroll, Herschal Evans*, J. Evensmo, 1976.

Brooks, Garth
Mitchell, Rick, *One Of A Kind, Workin' On A Full House*, Sidgwick And Jackson (UK), 1994.
Morris, Edward, *Garth Brooks: Platinum Cowboy*, St. Martin's Press (USA), 1993.

Broonzy, 'Big' Bill
Bruynoghe, Yannick, *Big Bill Blues: Big Bill Broonzy's Story As Told To Yannick Bruynoghe*, Cassell (UK), 1955.
Smith, Chris, *Hit The Right Lick: The Recordings Of Big Bill Broonzy*, Blues & Rhythm (UK), 1996.

Bros
Goss, Luke, *I Owe You Nothing: My Story*, Grafton (UK), 1993.

Brown, Cleo
Brown, Cleo, *Cleo Brown, Interviewed By Marion McPartland Plus Cleo Sings-Plays Piano*.

Brown, James
Brown, Geoff, *James Brown: A Biography*, Omnibus Press (UK), 1995.
Brown, James with Tucker, Bruce, *James Brown: The Godfather Of Soul*, Macmillan (USA), Sidgwick & Jackson (UK)), 1987.
Rose, Cynthia, *Living In America: The Soul Saga Of James Brown*, Serpents Tail (UK), 1990.

Brown, Milton
Ginell, Gary with Roy Lee Brown, *Milton Brown And The Founding Of Western Swing*, Urbana & Chicago, Illinois, 1994.

Brown, Ruth
Brown, Ruth with Yule, Andrew, *Miss Rhythm*, Dutton (USA), Fine Books (UK), 1995.

Brown, Sandy
Brown, Sandy, *The Jazz Manuscripts*, London, 1979.

Brozman, Bob
Brozman, Bob, *Rhythm In The Blues: The Bluesman's Bag Of Tricks And Licks*, Crossroads Music, 1996.

Brubeck, Dave
Brubeck, Dave, *Blue Rondo*, Columbia Pictures.
Brubeck, Dave, *Deluxe Piano Album*, C. Hansen II.
Brubeck, Dave, *The Genius Continues*, Columbia Pictures.
Brubeck, Dave, *The Genius Of Dave Brubeck*, Columbia Pictures.

Buchanan, Jack
Marshall, Michael, *Top Hat And Tails*, 1978.

Buffalo Springfield
Einarson, John & Furay, Richie, *For What It's Worth: The Story of Buffalo Springfield*, Quarry Music Books (USA), Rogan House (UK), 1997.

Buffett, Jimmy
Humphrey, Mark with Lewine, Harris, *The Jimmy Buffett Scrapbook*, Citadel Press (USA), 1994.

Burdon, Eric
Blackford, Andy, *Wild Animals*, Sidgwick & Jackson (UK), 1986.
Burdon, Eric, *I Used To Be An Animal But I'm All Right Now*, Faber & Faber (UK), 1986.
Castello, Dionisio, *Good Times: The Ultimate Eric Burdon*, Not listed, 1991.
Kent, Jeff, *The Last Poet: The Story Of Eric Burdon*, Witan Creations, 1989.

Burke, Solomon
Guralnick, Peter, *Sweet Soul Music*, 1994.

Burroughs, William
Bockris, Victor, *With William Burroughs*, Fourth Estate (UK), 1998.
Caveney, Graham, *'The Priest', They Called Him: The Life And Legacy Of William S.Burroughs*, Bloomsbury (UK), 1998.

Bush, Kate
Bush, Kate, *The Red Shoes*, International Music Publications (UK), 1994.
Bush, Kate, *Leaving My Tracks*, Sidgwick & Jackson (UK), 1982.
Cann, Kevin & Mayes, Sean, *Kate Bush: A Visual Documentary*, Omnibus Press (UK), 1989.
Juby, Kerry, *Kate Bush: The Whole Story*, Sidgwick & Jackson (UK), 1988.
Kerton, Paul, *Kate Bush: An Illustrated Biography*, Proteus Books (UK), 1981.
Vermorel, Fred, *The Secret Life Of Kate Bush (& The Strange Art Of Pop)*, Omnibus Press (UK), 1983.
Vermorel, Fred & Judy, *Kate Bush: Princess Of Suburbia*, Target Books.

Buzzcocks
McGartland, Tony, *Buzzcocks: The Complete History*, Independent Music Press (UK), 1995.

Bygraves, Max
Bygraves, Max, *I Wanna Tell You A Story*, London, 1976.

Byng, Douglas
Byng, Douglas, *As You Were*, London, 1970.

Byrds
Rogan, Johnny, *Timeless Flight Revisited, The Sequel*, Rogan House (UK), 1997.
Rogan, Johnny, *Timeless Flight: The Definitive Biography Of The Byrds*, Square One Books (UK), 1990.
Scoppa, Bud, *The Byrds*, Scholastic Book Services (USA), 1971.

Byrne, David
Byrne, David, *Strange Ritual: Pictures And Words*, Faber & Faber (UK), 1996.
Howell, John, *American Originals: David Byrne*, Thunder's Mouth Press (USA), 1995.

Caesar, Shirley
Caesar, Shirley, *A Miracle In Harlem*, Thomas Nelson (USA), 1997.

Cahn, Sammy
Cahn, Sammy, *I Should Care: The Sammy Cahn Story*, Arbor House (USA), W.H. Allen (UK), 1975.

Callender, Red
Callender, Red & Cohen, Elaine, *Unfinished Dream: The Musical World Of Red Callender*, London, 1985.

Calloway, Cab
Calloway, Cab, *Of Minnie The Moocher & Me*, Thomas Crowell (USA).
Calloway, Cab, *The New Cab Calloway's Catologue*.
Calloway, Cab, *The New Cab Calloway's Hepster's Dictionary*, Derby, Connecticut (USA), 1945.

Cambridge Folk Festival
Laing, Dave & Newman, Richard, *Thirty Years Of The Cambridge Folk Festival*, Music Maker Books (UK), 1994.

Campbell, Glen
Campbell, Glen, with Carter, Tom, *Rhinestone Cowboy: An Autobiography*, Villard (USA), 1994.
Kramer, Freda, *The Glen Campbell Story*, Pyramid, 1970.

Cantor, Eddie
Cantor, Eddie, *The Way I See It*, 1959.
Cantor, Eddie, *As I Remember Them*, 1963.
Cantor, Eddie, *My Life Is In Your Hands*, Harper (USA), 1928.
Cantor, Eddie & Ardmore, J.K., *Take My Life*, Doubleday (USA), 1957.
Goldman, Herbert G., *Banjo Eyes: Eddie Cantor And The Birth Of Modern Stardom*, Oxford University Press, 1998.

Captain And Tennille
Spada, James, *Captain And Tennille*, Creative Education, 1978.

Captain Beefheart
Cruickshank, Ben, *Fast And Bulbous: The Captain Beefheart Story*, Agenda (UK), 1996.
No editor listed, *The Lives And Times of Captain Beefheart*, Babylon Books (UK) 1979.
Webb, Colin David, *Captain Beefheart: The Man And His Music*, Kawabata Press, 1990.

Carmichael, Hoagy
Carmichael, Hoagy, *The Stardust Road*, Indiana University Press, 1983.
Carmichael, Hoagy with Longstreet, Stephen, *Sometimes I Wonder: The Story Of Hoagy Carmichael*, New York, 1965.

Carpenters
Coleman, Ray, *The Carpenters: The Untold Story*, Boxtree (UK), 1994.

Carr, Ian
Carr, Ian, *Music Outside-Contemporary Jazz In Britain*, Latimer New Dimensions, 1973.

Cars
Kamin, Philip, *The Cars*, Sidgwick & Jackson (UK), 1986.

Carson, Fiddlin' John
Wiggins, Eugene, *Fiddlin' Georgia Crazy: Fiddlin' John Carson, His Real World And His Songs*, University Of Illinois Press (USA), 1987.

Carter Family
Atkins, John, *The Carter Family*, Old Time Music, 1973.

Carter, Benny
Berger, M & E, *Benny Carter: A Life In American Music*, Metuchen (USA), 1982.
Evensmo, Jan, *The Alto Saxophone, Trumpet And Clarinet Of Benny Carter, 1927-1946*, J. Evensmo, 1982.

Carter, Ron
Carter, Ron, *Building A Jazz Bass Line*, R. Carter Music , 1971.
Carter, Ron, *Spielmethode Fur Jazz-Bass*, Munchen: Edition Modern, 1968.

Carter, Sydney
Carter, Sydney, *Songs Of Sydney In The Present Tense IV*, Galliard, 1971.
Carter, Sydney, *Songs Of Sydney In The Present Tense III*, Gilliard, 1970.
Carter, Sydney, *Songs Of Sydney In The Present Tense II*, Galliard, 1969.
Carter, Sydney, *Songs Of Sydney In The Present Tense I*, Galliard, 1969.
Carter, Sydney, *10 New Songs*, Clarion Photograhic Services, 1965.
Carter, Sydney, *9 Carols Or Ballads*, Clarion Photograhic Services, 1965.

Carver, Wayman
Evensmo, Jan, *The Flute Of Wayman Carver*, Jan Evensmo, 1983.

Cash, Johnny
Bowman, Kathleen, *On Stage Johnny Cash*, Creative Education, 1976.
Carpozi, George, *The Johnny Cash Story*, Pyramid, 1970.
Cash, Cindy, *The Cash Family Scrapbook*, 1997.
Cash, Johnny, *Man In Black*, Hodder and Stoughton (UK), 1977.
Cash, Johnny with Carr, Patrick, *Johnny Cash - The Autobiography*, Harper, San Fransisco (USA), 1997.
Conn, Charles Paul, *The New Johnny Cash*, Hodder and Stoughton (UK), 1973.
Govoni, Albert, *A Boy Named Cash*, Lancer Books (USA), 1970.
Smith, John L., *Johnny Cash Discography And Recording History 1954-1969*, John Edwards, 1969.
Smith, John L., *The Johnny Cash Discography 1954-1984*, Greenwood, Westport, 1985.
Smith, John L. (ed), *The Johnny Cash Record Catalogue*, Greenwood Press (USA), 1995.
Wren, Christopher S., *Johnny Cash: Winners Get Scars Too*, W.H. Allen (UK), 1973.

Cash, June Carter
Cash, June Carter, *From The Heart*, New York, 1987.

Cash, Rosanne
Cash, Rosanne, *Bodies Of Water*, Gollancz (UK), 1997.

Cassidy, David
Cassidy, David, *C'mon Get Happy. . . Fear And Loathing On The Partridge Family Bus*, Warner Books (USA), 1995.
Cassidy, David, *David In Europe: Exclusive! David's Own Story In David's Own Words*, Daily Mirror (UK), 1973.
Gregory, James, *The David Cassidy Story*, World Distributors (UK), 1973.
Hudson, James A., *Meet David Cassidy*, Scholastic Book Services, 1972.
No editor listed, *David Cassidy Annual 1974*, World Distributors (UK), 1973.

Cassidy, Shaun
Schumacher, Craig, *Shaun Cassidy*, Creative Education, 1980.

Caston, Leonard 'Baby Doo'
Todd Titon, Jeff, *From Blues To Pop: The Autobiography Of Leonard 'Baby Doo' Caston*, John Edwards Memorial Foundation, 1974.

Cave, Nick
Brokenmouth, Robert, *Nick Cave: The Birthday Party And Other Epic Adventures*, Omnibus Press (UK), 1996.
Cave, Nick, *King Ink II*, Blackspring Press (UK).
Cave, Nick, *King Ink*.
Cave, Nick, *And The Ass Saw The Angel*.
Dean, Jeremy, *Hellfire: Life According To Nick Cave*, The Dunce Directive (UK), 1995.
Johnston, Ian, *Bad Seed: The Biography Of Nick Cave*, Little Brown (UK), 1995.
Milne, Peter, *Fish In A Barrel: Nick Cave & The Bad Seeds On Tour*, Tender Prey, 1993.

Cavern, The
Leigh, Spencer & Frame, Pete, *Let's Go Down The Cavern*, Vernilion (UK), 1984.
Thompson, Phil, *The Best Of Cellars: The Story Of The World Famous Cavern Club*, Bluecoat Press (UK), 1994.

Chapin, Harry
Coan, Peter M., *Taxi: The Harry Chaplin Story*, Ashley Books (USA), 1987.

Chaplin, Saul
Chaplin, Saul, *The Golden Age of Movie Musicals And Me*, University Of Oakland Press (USA), 1994.

Chapman, Michael
Chapman, Michael, *Firewater Dreams*, Rampant Horse, 1995.

Charles, Ray
Charles, Ray & Ritz, David, *Brother Ray, Ray Charles' Own Story*, Dial Press (USA), Macdonald (UK), 1978.
Mathis, Sharon Bell, *Ray Charles*, Thomas Crowell (USA), 1973.
Olsen, David C (ed.), *Ray Charles, A Man And His Soul*, Columbia Pictures.

Chas And Dave
Hodges, Chas, *The Rock & Roll Years Of Chas Before Dave*, Lennard (UK), 1987.

Cheatham, Doc
Cheatham, Adolphus 'Doc', *I Guess I'll Get The Papers And Go Home: The LIfe Of Doc Cheatham*, Cassell (UK), 1996.

Cher
Braun, Thomas, *Sonny And Cher*, Creative Education, 1978.
Goodall, Nigel, *Cher: In Her Own Words*, Omnibus Press (UK), 1992.
Jacobs, Linda, *Cher: Simply Cher*, EMC, 1975.
Quirk, Lawrence J., *Totally Uninhibited: The Life & Times Of Cher*, Morrow (USA) and Warner Books (UK), 1991.
St. Michael, Mick, *Cher: The Visual Documentary*, Omnibus Press (UK), 1993.
Taraborrelli, J. Randy, *Cher*, St. Martins Press (USA), 1989.

Chess Records
Fancourt, L., *Chess Blues Discography*, Faversham, UK, 1983.
Fancourt, L, *Chess R&B*.
Ruppli, Michael, *The Chess Labels*, Greenwood Press, 1983.

Chevalier, Maurice
Behr, Edward, *Thank Heaven For Little Girls: The True Story Of Maurice Chevalier's Life*, Hutchinson (UK), 1992.
Chevalier, Maurice, *I Remember It Well*, 1972.
Chevalier, Maurice, *The Man In The Straw Hat*, 1949.
Chevalier, Maurice, *With Love*, 1960.
Harding, James, *Maurice Chevalier: His Life 1888-1972*, Secker & Warburg (USA), 1982.

Chicago
O'Shea, Mary J., *Chicago*, Creative Education, 1977.

Chieftains
Glatt, John, *The Chieftains: The Authorised Biography*, Century (UK), St Martins Press (USA), 1997.

Chorus Line, A
Rich, Frank (Introduction), *A Chorus Line: The Book Of The Musical, The Complete Book And Lyrics*, Applause Theatre Books (USA), 1996.
Stevens, Gary & George, Alan, *The Longest Line: Broadway's Most Singular Sensation, A Chorus Line*, Applause Theatre Books (USA), 1996.

Christian, Charlie
Broadbent, Peter, *Charlie Christian: The Story Of The Seminal Electric Guitarist*, Ashley Mark, 1997.

Chuck D.
Chuck, D. with Jah, Yusuf, *Fight The Power - Rap, Race And Reality*, Payback Press, 1997.

Chuck Wagon Gang
Terrell, Bob, *The Chuck Wagon Gang, A Legend Lives On*, Asheville, North Carolina, USA, 1990.

Cinema
Crenshaw, Andrew, *Hollywood Rock: A Guide To Rock 'N' Roll In The Movies*, Plexus (UK), 1994.
Romney, Jonathan & Wootten, Adrian, (eds.), *Celluloid Jukebox: Popular Music And The Movies Since The 50s*, BFI, 1995.

Clapton, Eric
Blake, Peter & Clapton, Eric, *Eric, 24 Nights*, Genesis, 1992.
Coleman, Ray, *Survivor: The Authorized Biography Of Eric Clapton*, Sidgwick & Jackson (UK), 1986.
Pidgeon, John, *Eric Clapton: A Biography*, Panther/Granada (UK), 1976.

Roberty, Marc, *The Complete Guide To The Music Of ...*, Omnibus Press (UK), 1995.
Roberty, Marc, *The Man, The Music, The Memorabilia*, Paper Tiger (UK), 1994.
Roberty, Marc, *Eric Clapton: The Complete Recording Sessions*, Blandford Press (UK), 1993.
Roberty, Marc, *Clapton: The Complete Chronicle*, Pyramid Books, 1991 (UK).
Roberty, Marc, *Eric Clapton: A Visual Documentary*, Omnibus Press (UK), 1985.
Roberty, Marc, *Eric Clapton: The New Visual Documentary*, Omnibus Press (UK), 1991.
Sandford, Christopher, *Edge Of Darkness*, Gollancz (UK), 1994.
Schumacher, Michael, *Crossroads: The Life And Music Of Eric Clapton*, Little Brown (UK), 1995.
Shapiro, Harry, *Eric Clapton: Lost In The Blues*, Guinness/Square One Books (UK), 1992.
Shapiro, Harry, *Slowhand: The Story Of Eric Clapton*, Proteus Books (UK), 1984.
Turner, Steve, *Conversations With Eric Clapton*, Abacus/Sphere (UK), 1976.

Clark, Dick
Clark, Dick & Robinson, Richard, *Rock, Roll & Remember*, Crowell (USA), 1976.
Clark, Dick with Bronson, Fred, *Dick Clark's American Bandstand*, Collins (USA), 1997.
Shore, Michael & Clark, Dick, *The History Of American Bandstand*, Ballantine Books (USA), 1985.

Clark, Petula
Kon, Andrea, *This Is My Song: Biography Of Petula Clark*, W.H. Allen (UK), 1983.

Clark, Roy
Clark, Roy with Eliot, Marc, *My Life: In Spite Of Myself*, Simon & Schuster (USA), 1994.

Clarke, Kenny 'Klook'
Hennessey, Mike, *Klook: The Story Of Kenny Clarke*, Quartet Books (UK), 1990.

Clash
Agent Provocateur, *The Clash Retrospective*, Retro Publishing (UK), 1997.
Gray, Marcus, *Last Gang In Town: Story Of The Clash*, Fourth Estate (UK), 1995.
Green, Johnny & Barker, Garry, *A Riot Of Our Own: Night And Day With The Clash*, Indigo (UK), 1997.
Miles & Tobler, John, *The Clash*, Omnibus Press (UK), 1981.
Smith, Pennie, *The Clash: Before & After*, Eel Pie (UK), 1980.
Wells, James, *New Visual Documentary*, Omnibus Press (UK), 1994.
Yewdall, Julian Leonard, *Joe Strummer With The 101'ers & The Clash*, Image Direct (UK), 1992.

Clayton, Buck
Clayton, Buck, *Buck Clayton's Jazz World*, Macmillan, 1986.

Cline, Patsy
Bego, Mark, *I Fall To Pieces: The Music And The Life Of Patsy Cline*. (USA).
Jones, Margaret, *Patsy: The Life And Tmes Of Patsy Cline*, Harper Collins (USA), 1994.
Nassour, Ellis, *Honky Tonk Angel: The Intimate Story Of Patsy Cline*, Virgin (UK), 1992.
Nassour, Ellis, *Patsy Cline: Sweet Dreams*, Tower Books, 1981.

Clooney, Rosemary
Clooney, Rosemary, *This For Remembrance*, New York.

Coasters
Millar, Bill, *The Coasters*, Star/W.H. Allen (UK), 1975.

Cochran, Eddie
Clark, Alan, *The Legend Continues*, West Covina, California (USA), 1994.
Clark, Alan, *Eddie Cochran: Never To Be Forgotten*, West Covina, Califronia (USA), 1991.
Clark, Alan, *The Eddie Cochran Nostalgia Book*, Alan Clark (USA), 1980.
Muir, Eddie & Scott, Tony, *Eddie Cochran*.

Cocker, Joe
Bean J.P., *Joe Cocker: With A Little Help From My Friends*, Omnibus Press (UK), 1991.

Cogan, Alma
Burn, Gordon, *Alma Cogan*, Secker & Warburg (UK), 1991.
Caron, Sandra, *Alma Cogan*, Bloomsbury (UK), 1991.

Cohan, George M.
Cohan, George M.,, *Twenty Years On Broadway*, (USA), 1925.
McCabe, John, *George M. Cohan: The Man Who Owned Broadway*, 1973.
Morehouse, Ward, *George M. Cohan: Prince Of The American Theatre*, 1943.

Cohen, Leonard
Cohen, Leonard, *Stranger Music, Selected Poems And Songs*, Jonathan Cape (UK), 1993.
Cohen, Leonard, *Beautiful Losers*, McClelland & Stewart (Canada), 1966.
Cohen, Leonard, *Death Of A Ladies Man*, Andre Deutsch (UK), 1979.
Cohen, Leonard, *Flowers For Hitler*, Jonathan Cape (UK), 1973.
Cohen, Leonard, *Poems 1956-1968*, Jonathan Cape (UK), 1969.
Cohen, Leonard, *Selected Poems 1956-1968*, Viking (USA), 1968.
Cohen, Leonard, *The Favourite Game*, Viking (USA), Cape (UK), 1970.
Cohen, Leonard, *The Spice-Box Of Earth*, Jonathan Cape (UK), 1973.
Devlin, Jim, *Leonard Cohen: In Every Style Of Passion*, Omnibus Press (UK), 1996.
Dorman, L.S. & Rawlins, C.L., *Leonard Cohen: Prophet Of The Heart*, Omnibus Press (UK), 1990.
Nadel, Ira B., *Various Positions: A Life Of Leonard Cohen*, Bloomsbury (UK), 1996.
Nadel, Ira B., *Leonard Cohen: A Life In Art*, Robson Books (UK), 1994.

Cole, Nat 'King'
Gourse, Leslie, *Unforgettable: The Life and Mystique of Nat King Cole*, New English Library (UK), 1992.
Haskins, Jim & Benson, Kathleen, *Nat King Cole: The Man And His Music*, Robson Books (UK), 1991.

Coleman, Bill
Chilton, John, *Bill Coleman On Record*, Steve Lane, 1966.
Coleman, Bill, *Trumpet Story*, Macmillan.

Coleman, Ornette
Coleman, Ornette, *A Collection Of 26 Ornette Coleman Compositions*, MJQ Music.
Litweiler, John, *Ornette Coleman: A Harmolodic Life*, William Morrow (USA), 1995.
McRae, Barry, *Ornette Coleman*, Apollo (USA), 1988.
Spellman, A. B., *Four Lives In The Bebop Business*, Pantheon (USA), 1966.

Collins, Judy
Claire, Vivian, *Judy Collins*, Flash Books (USA), 1977.
Collins, Judy, *Shameless*, Pocket Books (USA), 1995.
Collins, Judy, *Trust Your Heart: An Autobiography*, (USA(, 1975.
Collins, Judy & Haufrecht, Herbert, *The Judy Collins Songbook*, Grosset & Dunlap (USA), 1969.

Collins, Lee
Collins, Lee, *Oh, Didn't He Ramble: The Autobiography of Lee Collins*, University Of Illinois (USA), 1974.

Collins, Phil
Waller, Johnny, *Phil Collins*, Zomba Books (UK), 1986.

Coltrane, John
Cole, Bill, *John Coltrane*, Da Capo (USA), 1993.
Cole, William Shadrack, *The Style Of John Coltrane*, Middletown, Connecticut (USA), 1974.
Coltrane, John, *The Artistry Of John Coltrane*, Big 3.
Davis, Brian, *John Coltrane, Discography*, B. Davis & R. Smith.
Gelatt, Tim, (ed.), *About John Coltrane*, New York Jazz Museum (USA).
Nisenson, Eric, *Ascension: John Coltrane And His Quest*, Da Capo (USA), 1995.
Priestley, Brian, *John Coltrane*, Apollo, 1990.
Simpkins, Cuthbert Ormond, *Coltrane*, Herndon House (USA), 1975.
Thomas, J. C., *Chasin' The Trane*, Doubleday (USA), 1975.
White, Andrew Nathaniel, *Trane 'N' Me*, Andrew's Musical Enterprises.

Comden, Betty
Comden, Betty, *Off Stage*, Simon & Schuster, 1995.
Robinson, Alice M., *Betty Comden And Adolph Green: A Bio-Bibliography*, Greenwood Press, 1994.

Condon, Eddie
Condon, Eddie & Sugrue, T., *We Called It Music*, New York, 1947.
Condon, Eddie & O'Neal, Hank, *The Eddie Condon Scrapbook Of Jazz*, Galahad Books (USA), 1973.
No editor listed, *Eddie Condon's Treasury Of Jazz*, London, 1957.

Connick, Harry, Jnr.
Felix, Antonia, *Wild About Harry: The Illustrated Biography*, Taylor Publishing (USA), 1996.

Cooke, Sam
Crain, S.R., White, Clifton & Tenenbaum, G. David, *You Send Me: The Life And Times Of Sam Cooke*, William Morrow (USA), Virgin Books (UK), 1995.
McEwen, Joe, *Sam Cooke: The Man Who Invented Soul: A Biography In Words & Pictures* (USA), 1977.

Cope, Julian
Cope, Julian, *Krautrocksampler: One Head's Guide To Great Kosmische Music*, Head Heritage (UK), 1995.
Cope, Julian, *Head-On*, Magog (UK), 1994.

Copper Family
Copper Family, *The Copper Family Song Book - A Living*

Tradition, Coppersongs, 1995.
Copper, Bob, *Songs And Southern Breezes - Country Folk And Country Ways*, Coppersongs.
Copper, Bob, *Early To Rise - A Sussex Boyhood*, Coppersongs.
Copper, Bob, *A Song For Every Season-One Hundred Years In The Life Of A Sussex Farming Family*, Coppersongs.

Coppin, Johnny
Coppin, Johnny, *Between The Severn And The Wye*, Windrush Press, 1993.

Corea, Chick
Corea, Chick, *Chick Corea*, Warner Bros (USA).

Costello, Elvis
Clayton-Lea, Tony, *Elvis Costello: A Biography*, Andre Deutsch, 1998 (UK).
Gouldstone, David, *Elvis Costello: A Man Out Of Time*, Sidgwick & Jackson (UK), 1989.
Groothuizen, Richard & Kees Den Heyer, *Going Through The Motions (Elvis Costello 1982-1985)*, ECIS, 1995.
Reese, Krista, *Elvis Costello: Completely False Biography Based On Rumour, Innuendo And Lies*, Proteus Books (UK), 1981.
St. Michael, Mick, *Elvis Costello*, Omnibus Press (UK), 1986.
Thomas, Bruce, *The Big Wheel*, Viking (UK), 1990.

Cotton, Billy
Cotton, Billy, *I Did It My Way*, 1970.

County, Jayne/Wayne
County, Jayne with Smith, Rupert,*Man Enough To Be A Woman*, Serpent's Tail (UK), 1995.

Courtneidge, Cicely
Courtneidge, Cicely, *Cicely: An Autobiography*, 1953.
Hulbert, Jack, *The Little Woman's Always Right*.

Coward, Noël
Citron, Stephen, *Noel And Cole: The Sophisticates*, Sinclair-Stevenson (UK), 1992.
Cole, Lesley, *The Life Of Noel Coward*, London, 1976.
Cole, Stephen , *Noel Coward: A Bio-Bibliography*, Greenwood Press (UK), 1994.
Coward, Noel, *Autobiography*.
Fisher, Clive, *Noel Coward*, Weidenfeld (UK), 1992.
Lahr, John, *Notes On A Cowardly Lion*, Knopf (USA), 1969.
Morley, Sheridan, *Noel Coward: A Talent To Amuse*, W.H. Allen (UK), 1972.
Payne, Graham & Morley, Sheridan, *The Noel Coward Diaries*, Little Brown (USA), 1982.
Payne, Graham with Day, Barry, *My Life With Noel Coward*, Applause, 1994.

Coxhill, Lol
Nuttall, Jeff, *The Bald Soprano*, London, 1991.

Coyne, Kevin
Coyne, Kevin, *Show Business*, Serpent's Tail (UK), 1992.

Cramps
Johnston, Ian, *The Wild, Wild World Of The Cramps*, 1991.

Cranberries
Bailey, Stuart, *The Cranberries*, UFO Books (UK), 1996.

Craven, Beverly
Craven, Beverley, *Love Scenes*, International Music Publications (UK), 1994.

Crawford, Michael
Howard, Anthony, *Phantom: Michael Crawford Unmasked*, Weidenfeld & Nicholson (USA), 1991.

Cream
Mankowitz, Gered & Whitaker, Robert (Photographers), *Cream In Gear (Limited Edition)*, UFO Books (UK), 1992.
Welch, Chris, *Strange Brew*, Castle Books (UK), 1994.

Creedence Clearwater Revival
Hallowell, John, *Inside Creedence*, Bantam Books (USA), 1971.

Croce, Jim
Croce, Jim, *The Faces I've Been*, The Big 3 Music, 1975.
Jacobs, Linda, *Jim Croce: The Feeling Lives On*, EMC, 1976.

Crosby, Bing
Morgereth, Timothy A., *Bing Crosby: A Discography, Radio Programme List & Filmography*, McFarland, Jefferson, 1987.
Shepherd, Donald, *Bing Crosby: The Hollow Man*, A.W. Allen, 1981.
Thomas, Bob, *The One & Only Bing*.
Thompson, Charles, *Bing: The Authorized Biography*.
Thompson, Charles, *The Complete Crosby*, Star Books (UK), 1980.

Crosby, Bob
Chilton, John, *Stomp Off, Let's Go! The Story Of Bob Crosby's Bob Cats & Big Band*, London, 1983.

Crosby, David
Crosby, David, *Long Time Gone*, Doubleday (USA), 1990.

Crosby, Stills And Nash
Taylor, Dallas, *Prisoner Of Woodstock*, Thunder's Mouth Press (USA), 1995.
Zimmer, Dave, *Crosby, Stills & Nash: The Authorized Biography*, Omnibus Press (UK), 1984.

Crosby, Stills, Nash And Young
Rogan, Johnny, *Crosby Stills Nash & Young: The Visual Documentary*, Omnibus Press (UK), 1996.
Taylor, Dallas, *Prisoner Of Woodstock*, Thunder's Mouth Press (USA), 1995.

Crowded House
Twomey, Chris & Doole, Kerry , *Private Universe: The Illustrated Biography*, Omnibus Press (UK), 1995.

Culture Club
Dietrich, Jo, *Boy George And Culture Club*, Proteus Books (UK), 1984.
Gill, Anton, *Mad About The Boy: The Life And Times Of Boy George & Culture Club*, Holt, Rinehart & Winston (USA), 1984.
Graaf, Kasper de & Garrett, Malcolm, *Culture Club: When Cameras Go Crazy*, Virgin Books (UK), 1983.
Rimmer, Dave, *Like Punk Never Happened: Culture Club and the New Pop*, Faber & Faber (UK), 1985.

Cure
Barbarian, Lydia, Sutherland, Steve & Smith, Robert, *Ten Imaginary Years*, Zomba Books (UK), 1988.
Bowler, Dave & Dray, Bryan, *The Cure: Faith*, Sidgwick & Jackson (UK), 1995.
Butler, Daren, *The Cure On Record*, Omnibus Press (UK), 1995.
Clarke, Ross, *The Cure: Success Corruption & Lies*, Kingsfleet Publications (UK, 1992.

Hargrove, Mary Elizabeth, *The Making Of: The Cure's Disintegration*, Collectors Guide Publishing (USA), 1996.
Smith, Robert (ed.), *The Cure Songwords 1978 - 1989*, Fiction/Omnibus Press (UK), 1990.
Thompson, Dave & Greene, Jo-Anne, *The Cure: A Visual Documentary*, Omnibus Press (UK), 1988.

D'Arby, Terence Trent
Hewitt, Paolo, *Neither Fish Nor Flesh: Inspiration For An Album*, Virgin Books (UK), 1990.

Damned
Clerk, Carol, *The Damned: The Light At The End Of The Tunnel*, Omnibus Press (UK), 1988.

Dana
Dana, *Dana: An Autobiography*, Hodder & Stoughton (UK), 1985.

Daniels, Mike
Bowen, Mike, *The Mike Daniels Delta Jazz Band*, North Ferriby, 1982.

Darensbourg, Joe
Darensbourg, Joe, *Jazz Odyssey: The Autobiography Of Joe Darensbourg*, Louisiana State University Press (USA), 1987.
Darensbourg, Joe & Vacher, Peter, *Telling It Like It Is*, London, 1987.

Darin, Bobby
Darin, Dodd, *Dream Lovers*, Warner Books (USA), 1994.
Diorio, Al, *Borrowed Time: The 37 Years Of Bobby Darin*, Running Press, 1981.

Dark Ducks
Tetsu Kihaya, *Dark Ducks Tabini Utau Yamani Utau (Dark Ducks Sing When Travelling)*, Tokyo, 1990.

Davies, Dave
Davies, Dave, *Kink: An Autobiography*, Boxtree (UK), Hyperion (USA), 1996.

Davies, Ray
Davies, Ray, *X-Ray*, Viking (UK), 1994.
Davies, Ray, *Waterloo Sunset*, Viking (UK), 1997.

Davis, Clive
Davis, Clive, *Clive*, New York, 1977.

Davis, Gary, Rev.
Tilling, Robert (compiler), *Oh What A Beautiful City: A Tribute To Rev. Gary Davis 1896-1972*, Paul Mill Press, 1993.

Davis, Jimmie
Weill, Gus, *You Are My Sunshine: The Jimmie Davis Story*, Waco, Texas, 1977.

Davis, Miles
Carner, Gary (ed.), *The Miles Davis Companion*, Schirmer (USA), Omnibus Press (UK), 1998.
Carr, Ian, *Miles Davis: A Critical Biography*, Grafton (UK), 1990.
Chambers, J., *Milestones: 1. Miles Davis, 1945-60*, Toronto, 1983.
Chambers, J., *Milestones: 2. Miles Davis Since 1960*, Toronto, 1985.
Cole, Bill, *Miles Davis: The Early Years*, Da Capo Press (USA), 1995.
Davis, Miles, *Miles Davis Transcribed Solos*, J. Aebersold.

Davis, Miles, *Miles: The Autobiography*, Simon & Schuster (USA), Macmillan (UK).
Long, Daryl, *Miles Davis For Beginners*, Writers and Readers (USA), 1992.
McRae, Barry, *Miles Davis*, Apollo, 1990.
Williams, Richard, *The Man In The Green Shirt: Miles Davis*, Bloomsbury (UK), 1993.

Davis, Skeeter
Davis, Skeeter, *Bus Fare To Kentucky: The Autobiography Of Skeeter Davis*, Birch Lane Press (USA), 1993.

Dawson, Smoky
Dawson, Smoky, *Smoky Dawson, A Life*, (Australia), 1985.

Day, Doris
Braun, Eric, *Doris Day*, Weidenfeld & Nicholson (UK), 1991.
Day, Doris & Hotchner, A. E., *Doris Day: Her Own Story*, W. Morrow (USA), 1975.

De Grassi, Alex
De Grassi, Alex, *Guitar Collection*, H. Leonard Publishing (USA), 1992.

De Mille, Agnes
Easton, Carol, *No Intermissions*, Little, Brown (USA), 1996.

Dearie, Blossom
Dearie, Blossom, *Blossom Dearie (Interviewed by Marian McPartland)*.

Deep Purple
Charlesworth, Chris, *Deep Purple: The Illustrated Biography*, Omnibus Press (UK), 1984.

Def Leppard
Dickson, Dave, *Biographize: The Def Leppard Story*, Sidgwick & Jackson (UK), 1995.
Fricke, David, *Def Leppard: Animal Instinct*, Zomba Books (UK), 1988.
Rich, Jason, *Def Leppard*, Orion/Carlton (UK), 1994.

Dene, Terry
Wooding, Dan, *I Thought Terry Dene Was Dead*, Coverdale House, 1974.

Dennis, Denny
Carey, Mike, *I'll Sing You A Thousand Love Songs: The Denny Dennis Story*, Pinnacle Publishing, 1993.

Denver, John
Dachs, David, *John Denver*, Pyramid Books, 1976.
Denver, John with Tobier, Arthur, *Take Me Home: An Autobiography*, Headline Book Publishing (UK), 1994.
Fleischer, Leonore, *John Denver*, Flash Books, 1976.
Martin, James, *John Denver: Rocky Mountain Wonderboy*, Everest Books, 1977 (UK).

Depeche Mode
Corbijn, Anton, *Depeche Mode: Strangers - The Photographs*, Omnibus Press (UK), 1991.
Thomas, Dave, *Depeche Mode*, Omnibus Press (UK), 1986.
Thompson, Dave, *Depeche Mode: Some Great Reward*, Sidgwick And Jackson (UK), 1995.

Devoto, Howard
Devoto, Howard, *It Only Looks As If It Hurts: The Complete Lyrics Of Howard Devoto 1976-90*, Black Spring, 1990.

Dial, Harry
Dial, Harry, *All This Jazz About Jazz*, Storyville.

Diamond, Neil
Bovis, Jean, *Who'd Have Believed He'd Come Along*, Jade Design (UK), 1995.
O'Regan, Suzanne K., *Neil Diamond*, Creative Education, 1975.
Wiseman, Rich, *Solitary Star: Biography Of Neil Diamond*, Sidgwick & Jackson (UK), 1988.

Diddley, Bo
Kiersh, Edward, *Where Are You Now Bo Diddley?*, Doubleday (USA), 1986.
White, George, *Bo Diddley: Living Legend*, Castle Books (UK), 1995.
White, George (ed.), *The Complete Bo Diddley Sessions*, George R. White Publications (UK), 1994.

Dietrich, Marlene
Bret, David, *Marlene My Friend*, Robson Books (UK), 1993.

Dillards
Grant, Lee, *Everybody On The Truck*, Eggman Publishing (USA), 1995.

Dire Straits
Oldfield, Michael, *Dire Straits*, Sidgwick & Jackson (UK), 1984.
Palmer, Myles, *Mark Knopfler: The Unuthorised Biography*, Sidgwick & Jackson (UK), 1992.

Dixon, Willie
Dixon, Willie, *I Am The Blues*, Quartet (UK), 1989.

Dodds, Baby
Dodds, Warren 'Baby' & Gara, Larry, *The Baby Dodds Story*, Los Angeles, 1959.

Dodds, Johnny
Lambert, G.E., *Johnny Dodds*, A. S. Barnes (USA), 1961.

Dolphy, Eric
Horricks, Raymond, *The Importance Of Being Eric Dolphy*, Costello (UK), 1990.
Simosko, V. & Tepperman, B., *Eric Dolphy: A Musical Biography And Discography*, Washington, DC.

Donegan, Lonnie
McDevitt, Chas, *Skiffle: The Inside Story*, Robson Books (UK), 1998.

Doonican, Val
Doonican, Val, *The Special Years: An Autobiography*, Sphere Books (UK), 1981.

Doors
Ashcroft, Linda, *Wild Child: Life With Jim Morrison*, Hodder & Stoughton (UK), 1997.
Butler, Patricia, *The Tragic Romance Of Pamela & Jim Morrison*, Omnibus Press (UK), 1998.
Clarke, Ross, *The Doors: Dance On Fire*, Castle Communications/Penguin (UK), 1993.
Crisafulli, Chuck, *The Doors: Moonlight Drive*, Carlton Books (UK), 1995.
Densmore, John, *Light My Fire*, Delacorte (USA), 1991.
Densmore, John, *Riders On The Storm: My Life With Jim Morrison And The Doors*, Bloomsbury (UK), 1991.
Hogan, Peter K., *The Complete Guide To The Music Of...*,
Omnibus Press (UK), 1994.
Hopkins, Jerry, *The Lizard King: The Essential Jim Morrison*, Plexus (UK), 1993.
Hopkins, Jerry & Sugerman, Danny, *No One Here Gets Out Alive*, Warner Books (USA), 1980.
Jahn, Mike, *Jim Morrison And The Doors: An Unauthorized Book*, Grosset & Dunlap (USA), 1969.
Jones, Dylan, *Jim Morrison: Dark Star*, Bloomsbury (UK), 1990.
Lisciandro, Frank, *Jim Morrison: An Hour For Magic*, Eel Pie (UK), 1982.
Lisciandro, Frank, *Morrison: A Feast of Friends*, Omnibus Press (UK), 1991.
Morrison, Jim, *An American Prayer*, Private Edition: Western Lithographers (USA), 1970.
Morrison, Jim, *Jim Morrison: The Story Of The Doors In Words And Pictures*, Omnibus Press (UK), 1982.
Morrison, Jim, *The American Night Volume 2*, Viking, 1991.
Morrison, Jim, *The American Night: The Writings Of Jim Morrison*, 1991.
Morrison, Jim, *The Lords & The New Creatures*, Simon & Schuster (USA), Omnibus Press (UK), 1971.
Muller, Herve, *Jim Morrison Au Dela Des Doors*, Edition Albin Michel, Paris, 1973.
No author, *The Doors: Lyrics, 1965-71*, Omnibus Press (UK), 1992.
Riordan, James & Prochnicky, Jerry, *Break On Through: The Life and Death Of Jim Morrison*, Plexus (UK), 1992.
Seymore, Bob, *The End: The Death Of Jim Morrison*, Omnibus Press (UK), 1991.
Strete, Craig Kee, *Burn Down The Night*, Warner Books (USA), 1982.
Sugerman, Danny, *The Doors: The Illustrated History*, Vermilion (UK), 1983.
Sugerman, Danny (ed.), *The Doors Complete Illustrated Lyrics*, Macdonald (UK), 1992.
Tobler, John & Doe, Andrew, *The Doors*, Proteus Books (UK), 1984.
Wincentsen, Edward, *Images Of Jim Morrison*, Vergen, 1991.

Dorsey, Jimmy
Dorsey, Jimmy, *Beebs*, Robbins.
Dorsey, Jimmy, *Contrasts From The Solo Oodles Of Noodles*, Robbins Music.
Dorsey, Jimmy, *Dixieland Detour*, Robbins Music.
Dorsey, Jimmy, *Mood Hollywood*, Robbins Music.
Dorsey, Jimmy, *Tap Dancer's Nightmare*, Robbins Music, 1946.

Dorsey, Thomas A.
Harris, Michael, *The Rise Of Gospel Blues: The Music Of Thomas Dorsey In The Urban Church*, Oxford University Press, 1992.

Dorsey, Tommy
Haines, Connie with Stone, Robert B., *For Once In My Life*, Warner Books (USA), 1976.
Sanford, H., *Tommy And Jimmy: The Dorsey Years*, Arlington House (USA), 1972.

Dr. Feelgood
Moon, Tony, *Down By The Jetty: The Dr Feelgood Story*, Northdown (UK), 1997.

Dr. John
Rebennack, Mac with Rummel, Jack, *Dr. John: Under A Hoodoo Moon*, St Martin's Press (UK), 1994.

Drake, Nick
Housden, David, *Nick Drake*, Big Sky Studio (UK), 1994.
Humphries, Patrick, *Nick Drake: A Biography*, Bloomsbury (UK), 1997.

Drifters
Allan, Tony &Treadwell, Faye, *Save The Last Dance For Me: The Musical Legacy 1953-92*, Popular Culture Ink (USA), 1992.
Millar, Bill, *The Drifters: The Rise And Fall Of The Black Vocal Group*, Studio Vista (UK), 1971.

Drummond, Bill
Drummond, Bill & Manning, Mark, *Bad Wisdom*, Penguin Original (UK), 1996.

Dubin, Al
McGuire, P.D., *Lullaby Of Broadway: A Biography Of Al Dubin*, Sacaucus, New Jersey, 1983.

Dubliners
Hardy, Mary, *The Dubliners Scrapbook*, Wise Publications, 1978.

Duke, Vernon
Duke, Vernon, *Passport To Paris*.

Duran Duran
De Graff, Kasper & Garrett, Malcolm, *Duran Duran: Their Story*, Proteus Books (UK), 1982.

Dusty, Slim
Dusty, Slim & John Japsley, *Slim Dusty: Walk A Country Mile*, Rigby, 1979.
Phillips, Peter, *Slim Dusty Around Australia*, 1980.

Dylan, Bob
Anderson, Dennis, *The Hollow Horn*.
Auschiag, Hermann, *Small Talk*, Germany, 1982.
Bauldie, John, *The Ghost Of Electricity*, Wanted Man (UK), 1988.
Bauldie, John (ed.), *Wanted Man: In Search Of Bob Dylan*, Penguin Books (UK), 1992.
Bowden, Betsy, *Performed Literature: Words And Music By Bob Dylan*..
Cable, Paul, *Bob Dylan: His Unreleased Recordings*, Scorpion/Dark Star (UK), 1978.
Coker, Jerry, *A Concise Synopsis Of Bob Dylan's Masterpiece Renaldo & Clara Jonan Dergoth*.
Day, Aidan, *Jokerman: Reading The Lyrics Of Bob Dylan*, Basil Blackwell (UK), 1988.
Dowley, Tim & Dunnage, Barry, *Bob Dylan: From A Hard Rain To A Slow Train*, Midas Books (UK), 1982.
Dreau, Jean-Louis & Schlockoff, Robert, *Hypnotist Collectors*, My Back Pages (UK), 1989.
Dundas, Glen, *Tangled Up In Tapes*, My Back Pages (UK) , 1994.
Dylan, Bob, *Bob Dylan Drawn Blank (Folio of drawings)*, My Back Pages (UK), 1995.
Dylan, Bob, *Bob Dylan In His Own Write* (Denmark), 1974.
Dylan, Bob, *Bob Dylan: Writings And Drawings*, Alfred Knopf (USA), Jonathan Cape (UK), 1973.
Dylan, Bob, *Eleven Outlined Epitaphs & Off The Top Of My Head*, Aloes Seola.
Dylan, Bob, *Lyrics: 1962-1985*, Grafton Books (UK), 1990.
Dylan, Bob, *Poem To Joanie*, Aloes Press, 1972.
Dylan, Bob, *Tarantula*, Bootleg Editions: White Press, 1969.
Dylan, Bob, Lily, Rosemary And The Jack Of Hearts & Others, *Duophonic Print*.
Gray, Michael, *Song And Dance Man: The Art Of Bob Dylan*,
Hart-Davis (UK), 1972.
Gray, Michael & Bauldie, John (eds.), *All Across The Telegraph: A Bob Dylan Handbook*, Futura (UK), 1987.
Gross, Michael, *Bob Dylan: An Illustrated History*, Elm Tree Books (UK), 1978.
Guilbert, Jean-Claude, *Bob Dylan Et La Beat Generation*, Le Nouveau Planete, Paris, 1971.
Herdman, John, *Voice Without Restraint: A Study Of Bob Dylan's Lyrics And Their Background*, Paul Harris, 1982.
Heylin, Clinton, *The Recording Sessions 1960-1994*, Penguin (UK), 1996.
Heylin, Clinton, *A Life In Stolen Moments 1941-1995*, Omnibus Press (UK), 1996.
Heylin, Clinton, *Bob Dylan: Stolen Moments*, Wanted Man (UK), 1988.
Heylin, Clinton, *Dylan: Behind The Shades*, Viking, 1991.
Heylin, Clinton, *Rain Unravelled Tales (The Nightingale's Code Examined): A Rumourography*, Ashes and Sand, 1982.
Heylin, Clinton, *To Live Outside The Law*, Labour Of Love, 1989.
Hoggard, Stuart & Shields, Jim, *Bob Dylan: An Illustrated Discography*, Transmedia Express (UK), 1978.
Humphries, Patrick, *Complete Guide To The Music Of Bob Dylan*, Omnibus Press (UK), 1995.
Humphries, Patrick & Bauldie, John, *Absolutely Dylan*, Viking (USA), 1991.
Humphries, Patrick & Bauldie, John, *Oh No! Not Another Bob Dylan Book*, Square One Books (UK), 1991.
Karpel, Craig, *The Tarantula In Me: Behind Bob Dylan's Novel*, Klonh (USA), 1973.
Kramer, Daniel, *Bob Dylan*, Pocket Books (USA), 1968.
Kramer, Daniel, *Bob Dylan: A Portrait Of the Artist's Early Years*, Plexus (UK), 1992.
Krogsgaard, Michael, *Master Of The Tracks: The Bob Dylan Reference Book Of Recording*, Scandinavian Society For Rock Research, 1990.
Krogsgaard, Michael, *Twenty Years Of Recording: The Bob Dylan Reference Book*, Scandinavian Institute For Rock Research, 1981.
Lee, C.P., *Like The Night: Bob Dylan And The Road To The Manchester Free Trade Hall*, Helter Skelter (UK), 1998.
Liff, Dennis R., *Raging Glory*, My Back Pages (UK), 1988.
Marcus, Greil, *Invisible Republic: Bob Dylan's Basement Tapes*, Picador (UK), 1997.
McGregor, Craig, *Bob Dylan: A Retrospective*, W. Morrow (USA), 1972.
McKeen, William, *A Bio-Bibliography*, Greenwood Press, 1993.
Miles, *Bob Dylan In His Own Words*, Omnibus Press (UK), 1978.
No author listed, *Dylan: Words To His Songs*, 1972.
Pennebaker, D.A., *Don't Look Back*, Ballantine Books (USA), 1968.
Percival, Dave, *The Dust Of Rumour*, My Back Pages (UK), 1987.
Pickering, Stephen, *Bob Dylan Approximately: A Portrait Of The Jewish Poet In Search Of God; A Midra*, David Mackay (USA), 1975.
Pickering, Stephen, *Bob Dylan: A Commemoration*, No Limit (USA), 1971.
Pickering, Stephen, *Praxis One: Existence, Men & Realities*, No Limit (USA), 1971.
Pickering, Stephen, *Tour 1974*, Privately Printed, 1974.
Ribakove, Sy & Barbara, *Folk-Rock: The Bob Dylan Story*, Dell (USA), 1966.
Riley, Tim, *Hard Rain: A Dylan Commentary*, Plexus (UK), 1995.
Rinzler, Alan, *Bob Dylan: The Illustrated Record*, Harmony/Crown (USA), 1978.
Rolling Stone Editors, *Knocking On Dylan's Door*, Cassell

(UK), 1975.

Roques, Dominique, *The Great White Answers.*, Private Publication, 1980.

Scaduto, Anthony, *Bob Dylan: An Intimate Biography*, Grosset & Dunlap (USA), 1971.

Scobie, Stephen, *Alias Bob Dylan*, Red Deer College Press (USA), 1993.

Shelton, Robert, *No Direction Home: The Life And Music Of Bob Dylan*, W. Morrow (USA), Penguin (UK), 1986.

Shepard, Sam, *Rolling Thunder Logbook*, Viking (USA), 1977.

Sloman, Larry, *On The Road With Bob Dylan: Rolling With The Thunder*, Bantam (USA), 1978.

Spitz, Bob, *Dylan: A Biography*, Michael Joseph (UK), 1989.

Thompson, Toby, *Positively Main Street: An Unorthodox View Of Bob Dylan*, Coward McCann Geoghegan (USA), New English Library, 1971.

Thomson, Elizabeth M. & Gutman, David, *Dylan Companion*, Macmillan, 1990.

Thomson, Liz, *Conclusions On The Wall: New Essays On Bob Dylan*, Thin Man (UK), 1980.

Townsend, Phill, *Strangers And Prophets: CD Boots Vol II*, Next 2 Last Books (UK), 1994.

Townsend, Phill, *Strangers And Prophets: Bob Dylan CD Boots Vol1*, My Back Pages (UK), 1992.

Williams, Chris, *Bob Dylan: In His Own Words*, Omnibus Press (UK), 1993.

Williams, Paul, *Watching The River Flow (1966-1995)*, Omnibus Press (UK), 1996.

Williams, Paul, *Performing Artist: The Music Of Bob Dylan Vol. 1, 1960-1973"*, My Back Pages (UK), 1990.

Williams, Paul, *Bob Dylan: Performing Artist*, Xanadu, 1991.

Williams, Paul, *Dylan: What Happened?*, Entwhistle Books, 1980.

Wolliver, Robbie, *Bringing It All Back Home*, Pantheon Books, 1987.

Woodward, Ian, *Bob Dylan: Back Of The Tapestry*, 1992.

Wurlitzer, Rudolph, *Pat Garrett And Billy The Kid*, NAL (USA), 1973.

Wyvill, Mike & Wraith, John, *So Many Roads: Bob Dylan's 1995 Concerts*, My Back Pages (UK), 1996.

Wyvill, Mike & Wraith, John, *From Town To Town: Bob Dylan's 1994 Concerts*, My Back Pages (UK), 1996.

Wyvill, Mike & Wraith, John, *The Road Unwinds: Bob Dylan 1990 Concerts*, My Back Pages (UK), 1996.

Yenne, Bill, *One Foot On The Highway: Bob Dylan On Tour 1974*, Klonh (USA), 1974.

Eagles

Shapiro, Marc, *The Long Run: The Story Of The Eagles*, Omnibus Press (UK), 1995.

Swenson, John, *The Eagles*, Ace Books, 1981.

East 17

Jenkins, Carl, *East 17: Talk Back*, Omnibus Press (UK), 1995.

Echo And The Bunnymen

Cooper, Mark, *Liverpool Explodes: The Teardrop Explodes, Echo And The Bunnymen*, Sidgwick & Jackson (UK), 1982.

Fletcher, Tony, *Never Stop: The Echo & The Bunnymen Story*, Omnibus Press (UK), 1988.

ECM Records

No editor listed, *ECM: Sleeves Of Desire*, Lars Muller (Germany), 1996.

Edwards, David 'Honeyboy'

Edwards, David Honeyboy with Martinson, Janis & Frank, Micha, *The Life And Times Od Delta Bluesman Honeyboy Edwards*, Chicago Review Press (USA), 1997.

Electric Light Orchestra

Bevan, Bev, *The Electric Light Orchestra Story*, Mushroom, 1980.

Elektra Records

Holzman, Jac & Daws, Gavan, *Follow The Music: The Life And High Times Of Elektra Records*, First Media (USA), 1998.

Ellington, Duke

Collier, James Lincoln, *Duke Ellington: Life And Times Of A Restless Genius Of Jazz*, Michael Joseph (UK), 1987.

Dance, Stanley, *The World Of Duke Ellington*, Charles Scribner (USA), 1970.

Dodson, Leon, *Adapting Selected Compositions And Arrangements Of Duke Ellington*, 1979.

Ellington, Duke, *Autobiographie*, P. List, 1974.

Ellington, Duke, *Duke Ellington At The Piano*, Big 3.

Ellington, Duke, *Music Is My Mistress*, W.H. Allen (UK), 1974.

Ellington, Mercer, *Duke Ellington In Person*, Houghton Mifflin (USA), 1978.

Franki, Ron, *Duke Ellington*, Chelsea House.

Gammond, Peter, *Duke Ellington: His Life And Music*, Apollo, 1987.

George, Don R., *Sweet Man, The Real Duke Ellington*, Putnams (USA).

Gleason, Ralph J., *Celebrating The Duke*, Dell (USA), Little Brown (USA), 1975.

Hasse, John Edward, *Beyond Category: The Life And Genius Of Duke Ellington*, Simon & Schuster (USA), 1993.

Jackson, Quentin Leonard, *Duke Ellington (Sound Recording)*, Duke Ellington Society, 1976.

Jewell, Derek, *Duke: A Portrait Of Duke Ellington*, London, 1977.

Rattenbury, Ken, *Duke Ellington: Jazz Composer*, Yale University Press (USA), 1991.

Schaaf, Martha E., *Duke Ellington: Young Music Master*, Bobbs-Merrill (USA).

Timner, W.E., *Ellingtonia: The Recorded Music Of Duke Ellington & His Sidesman*, Scarecrow, 1988.

Travis, Dempsey J., *The Duke Ellington Primer*, Urban Research Press (USA), 1996.

Tucker, Mark, *The Duke Ellington Reader*, Oxford University Press, 1993.

Tucker, Michael, *Duke Ellington: The Early Years*, Bayou Press (USA), 1991.

Ulanov, Barry, *Duke Ellington*, New York: Creative Age, 1946.

Ellis, Don

Ellis, Don, *Notebooks On Indic Music.*

Emery, Ralph

Emery, Ralph & Carter, Tom, *The Autobiography Of Ralph Emery*, Pocket Books (USA), 1992.

Emery, Ralph with Carter, Tom *Ralph Emery: More Memories*, Putnams (USA), 1993.

Eno, Brian

Eno, Brian, *A Year With Swollen Appendices*, Faber & Faber (UK), 1996.

Tamm, Eric, *Brian Eno His Music And The Vertical Colour Of Sound*, Faber & Faber (UK), 1989.

Epstein, Brian

Coleman, Ray, *Brian Epstein: The Man Who Made The Beatles*, Viking (UK), 1989.

Epstein, Brian, *A Cellarfull Of Noise*, Souvenir Press (UK), 1964.

Erickson, Roky
Erickson, Roky, *Openers II: The Lyrics Of Roky Erickson*, 2.13.61, 1995.

Essex, David
Tremlett, George, *The David Essex Story*, Futura (UK), 1974.

Estefan, Gloria
Catalono, Grace, *Gloria Estefan*, St Martins Press (USA), 1991.

Estefan, Gloria, And Miami Sound Machine
Catalono, Grace, *Gloria Estefan*, St Martins Press (USA), 1991.

Eurythmics
Waller, Johnny, *Eurythmics: Sweet Dreams: The Definitive Biography*, Virgin Books (UK), 1985.

Evans, Dale
Stern, Jane & Michael, *Happy Trails - Our Life Story: Roy Rogers And Dale Evans*, Simon & Schuster (USA), 1995.

Evans, Gil
Horricks, Raymond, *Svengali, Or The Orchestra Called Gill Evans*, Hippocrene Books (USA), 1984.

Everett, Kenny
Lister, David, *In The Best Possible Taste: The Crazy Life Of Kenny Everett*, Bloomsbury (UK), 1997.

Everly Brothers
Aarts, Peter & Alberts, Martin, *For-Everly Yours*, Allen McPherson, Chingford (UK), 1992.
Dodge, Consuelo, *The Everly Brothers: Ladies Love Outlaws*, Cin-Dav Inc. (USA), 1992.
Hosum, John, *Everly Brothers: An Illustrated Discography*, Foreverly Music (USA).
Karpp, Phyllis, *Ike's Boys*, Pierian Press, 1988.
White, Roger, *The Everly Brothers: Walk Right Back*, Plexus (UK), 1985.

Everything But The Girl
Watt, Ben, *Patient: The History Of A Rare Illness*, Viking (UK), 1996.

Ewell, Don
Colinson, John & Kramer, Eugene, *Jazz Legacy Of Don Ewell*, Storyville, 1991.

Factory Records
Middles, Mick, *From Joy Division To New Order*, Virgin Books (UK), 1996.

Fairport Convention
Abbott, Kingsley, *Fairportfolio*, Private Press (UK), 1997.
Humphries, Patrick, *Fairport Convention: Meet On The Ledge (2nd Edition)*, Virgin Books (UK), 1997.
Humphries, Patrick, *Richard Thompson: Strange Affair*, Virgin Books (UK), 1996.
Humphries, Patrick, *Meet On The Ledge: A History Of Fairport Convention*, Eel Pie (UK), 1982.
Redwood, Fred & Woodward, Martin, *The Woodworm Era: The Story Of Today's Fairport Convention*, Jeneva Publishing (UK), 1995.

Faith No More
Chirazi, Steffan, *Faith No More: The Real Story*, Castle Books (UK), 1994.

Faith, Adam
Faith, Adam, *Acts Of Faith*, Bantam (UK), 1996.
Faith, Adam, *Adam, His Fabulous Year*, Picture Story (UK), 1960.
Faith, Adam, *Poor Me*, Souvenir Press (UK), 1961.

Faithfull, Marianne
Faithfull, Marianne & Dalton, David, *Faithfull*, Michael Joseph (UK), Little Brown (USA), 1994.
Hodkinson, Mark, *Marianne Faithfull: As Tears Go By*, Omnibus Press (UK), 1991.

Fall
Edge, Brian, *Paintwork: A History Of The Fall*, Omnibus Press (UK), 1989.

Fältskog, Agnetha
Fältskig, Agnetha with Åhman, Brita, *As I Am: Abba Before And Beyond*, Virgin Books (UK), 1998.

Farren, Mick
Farren, Mick, *The Quest Of The DNA Cowboys*, Mayflower (UK), 1976.
Farren, Mick, *The Neural Atrocity*, Mayflower (UK), 1977.
Farren, Mick, *Synaptic Manhunt*, Mayflower (UK), 1976.

Faye, Alice
Faye, Alice, *Getting Older - Looking Younger*, 1990.

Feather, Leonard
Feather, Leonard, *The Encyclopedia Of Jazz*.
Feather, Leonard, *Jazz Years: Earwitness To An Era*, Quartet (UK), 1990.

Feinstein, Michael
Feinstein, Michael, *Nice Work If You Can Get It: My Life In Rhythm And Rhyme*, Hyperion (USA), 1995.

Feldman, Victor
Schiff, Ronny S. (ed.), *Victor Feldman Fake Book*, Dick Grove.

Fender, Leo
Bacon, Tony & Day, Paul, *The Fender Book: A Complete History Of Fender Electric Guitars*, GPI Books (USA), 1992.
Smith, Richard, *Fender Custom Shop Guitar Gallery*, Hal Leonard Publications (USA), 1996.

Fields, Dorothy
Winer, Deborah Grace, *On The Sunny Side Of The Street: The Life And Lyrics Of Dorothy Fields*, Schirmer Books (USA), 1997.

Fields, Gracie
Fields, Gracie, *Sing As We Go, Her Autobiography*, London, 1960.
Hudson P., *Gracie Fields: Her Life In Pictures*, London, 1989.
Moules, Joan, *Gracie Fields*, Summersdale, 1998.

Fillmore
Kostelanetz, Richard, *The Fillmore East*, Schirmer Books (USA), 1995.

Fine Young Cannibals
Edge, Brian, *The Sweet And The Sour: The Fine Young Cannibals' Story*, Omnibus Press (UK), 1990.

Fisher, Eddie
Fisher, Eddie, *My Life, My Loves*, Harper & Row (USA), W.H. Allen (UK), 1981.

Greene, Myrna, *The Eddie Fisher Story*, P.S. Eriksson, 1978.

Fitzgerald, Ella
Colin, Sid, *Ella: The Life And Times Of Ella Fitzgerald*, Elm Tree Books (UK), 1990.
Fidelman, Mark, *First Lady Of Song*, Birch Lane Press (USA), 1995.
Haskins, Jim, *Ella Fitzgerald: A Life Through Jazz*, Hodder & Stoughton (UK), 1991.
Nicholson, Stuart, *Ella Fitzgerald*, Gollancz (UK), 1993.

Flack, Roberta
Jacobs, Linda, *Roberta Flack: Sound Of Velvet Melting*, EMC, 1975.
Morse, Charles, *Roberta Flack*, Creative Education, 1974.

Flamin' Groovies
Poncelet, Jean-Pierre, *A Flamin' Saga: The Flamin' Groovies Histoire & Discographie*, Paris, 1978.
Storey, Jon, *Bucketfull Of Groovies*, Bucketfull Of Brains (UK), 1987.

Flanders And Swann
Swann, Donald, *Swann's Way-A-Life In Song*.
Swann, Donald, *Swann's Way Out*.
Swann, Donald, *The Space Behind The Bars*.

Fleetwood Mac
Brunning, Bob, *Fleetwood Mac: Behind The Masks*, New English Library (UK), 1991.
Carr, Roy & Clarke, Steve, *Fleetwood Mac: Rumours 'N' Fax*, Harmony/Crown (USA), 1978.
Clarke, Steve, *Fleetwood Mac*, Proteus Books (UK), 1985.
Davis, Stephen, *The Crazed Story Of Fleetwood Mac*, Sidgwick & Jackson (UK), 1990.
Fleetwood, Mick & Davis, Stephen, *Fleetwood: My Life And Adventures With Fleetwood Mac*, Sidgwick & Jackson (UK), 1990.
Graham, Samuel, *Fleetwood Mac: The Authorized History*, Sire Books, 1978.

Floyd, Frank
Marcus, Greil, *Mystery Train: Images Of America In Rock And Roll Music*, , 1975.

Folkways Records
Goldsmith, Peter D., *Making People's Music - Moe Asch And Folkway's Records*, Smithsonian Institute (USA), 1998.

Formby, George
Fisher, John, *George Formby*, Futura (UK), 1975.
Randall, Alan & Seaton, Ray, *George Formby*, 1974.

Fosse, Bob
Grubb, Kevin Boyd, *Razzle Dazzle: The Life And Works Of Bob Fosse*.

Foster, George 'Pops'
Foster, G M & Stoddard, T. and Russell, R., *Pops Foster: The Autobiography of a New Orleans Jazzman*, Berkeley (USA), 1971.

Foster, Stephen
Austin William W., *The Songs Of Stephen C. Foster From His Own Time To Ours*, Macmillan (USA), 1975.
Emerson, Ken, *Doo-Dah!: Stepehn Foster And The Rise Of American Popular Culture*, Simon& Schuster (USA), 1997.

Fox, Roy
Fox, Roy, *Hollywood Mayfair And All That Jazz: The Roy Fox Story*.

Foxton, Bruce
Foxton, Bruce & Buckler, Rick with Ogg, Alex, *Our Story*, Castle Communications (UK), 1994.

Frampton, Peter
Adler, Irene, *Peter Frampton: A Photo Biography*, Quick Fox (USA), 1979.
Daly, Marsha, *Peter Frampton*, Tempo (USA), 1978.
Katz, Susan, *Frampton!: An Unauthorized Biography*, Jove, 1978.

Francis, Connie
Francis, Connie, *Who's Sorry Now*, St Martins Press (USA), 1984.

Franke, Bob
Franke, Bob, *The Folk Project Of New Jersey*, 1992.

Frankie Goes To Hollywood
Hizer, Bruno, *Give It Loads: The Story Of Frankie Goes To Hollywood*, Proteus Books (UK), 1984.
Jackson, Danny, *Frankie Say: The Rise Of Frankie Goes To Hollywood*, Virgin Books (UK), 1985.
Johnson, Holly, *A Bone In My Flute*, Boxtree (UK), 1994.

Franklin, Aretha
Bego, Mark, *Aretha Franklin*, St Martin's Press (USA), 1990.

Freberg, Stan
Freberg, Stan, *It Only Hurts When I Laugh*, Times Books (USA), 1988.

Freed, Alan
Jackson, John A., *Big Beat Heat: Alan Freed And The Early Years Of Rock 'n' Roll*, Schirmer Books (USA), 1991.

Freeman, Bud
Freeman, Bud, *Crazeology*, University Of Illinois Press (USA).

Friday, Gavin
Van Oosted De Boer, Caroline, *Gavin Friday: The Light And The Dark*, Von B Press, 1991.

Friedman, Kinky
Friedman, Kinky, *The Kinky Freidman Crime Club*, Faber & Faber (UK), 1992.
Friedman, Kinky, *God Bless John Wayne*, Simon & Shuster (USA), 1995.
Friedman, Kinky, *Elvis, Jesus And Coca Cola*, Faber & Faber (UK), 1993.
Friedman, Kinky, *Musical Chairs*, William Morrow (USA), 1991.
Friedman, Kinky, *Frequent Flyer*, William Morrow (USA), 1989.
Friedman, Kinky, *When The Cat's Away*, William Morrow (USA), 1988.
Friedman, Kinky, *A Case Of Lone Star*, William Morrow (USA), 1987.
Friedman, Kinky, *Greenwich Killing Time*, William Morrow (USA), 1986.
Friedman, Kinky, *Armadillos And Old Lace*, Simon & Schuster (USA), 1994.
Friedman, Kinky, *More Kinky Friedman*, Faber & Faber (UK), 1993.

Fripp, Robert
Tamm, Eric, *Robert Fripp: From King Crimson To Guitar Craft*, Faber & Faber (UK), 1991.

Frizzell, Lefty
Cooper, Daniel, *The Honky Tonk Life Of Country Music's Greatest Singer*, Little Brown (USA), 1995.

Fugees
Roberts, Chris, *Fugees: The Unofficial Book*, Virgin Books (UK), 1997.

Furay, Richie
Einarson, John & Furay, Richie, *For What It's Worth: The Story Of Buffalo Springfield*, Quarry Music Books (USA), 1997.

Gabriel, Peter
Bright, Spencer, *Peter Gabriel: An Authorized Biography*, Sidgwick & Jackson (UK), 1988.
St Michael, Mick, *In His Own Words*, Omnibus Press (UK), 1994.

Gainsbourg, Serge
Clayson, Allan, *Serge Gainsbourg: Viewed From The Exterior*, Sanctuary, 1998.

Galway, James
Galway, James, *James Galway*, Elm Tree Books (UK), 1978.

Garcia, Jerry
Garcia, Jerry, *Garcia: The Rolling Stone Interview*, Straight Arrow Books (USA), 1972.
Greenfield, Robert, *Dark Star: An Oral Biography Of Jerry Garcia*, Morrow (USA), Plexus (UK), 1996.
Troy, Sandy, *Captain Trips: The Life And Fast Times Of Jerry Garcia*, Thunders Mouth Press (USA), 1994.

Garland, Judy
Coleman, Emily R., *The Complete Judy Garland*, Harper Collins (USA), 1990.
Dahl, David & Kehoe, Barry, *The Young Judy*, Mason/Charter (USA), Mayflower (UK), 1975.
Deans, Mickey, *Weep No More, My Lady: An Intimate Biography Of Judy Garland*, Hawthorn (USA), W H Allen (UK), 1972.
DiOrio, Al, *Little Girl Lost: The Life And Hard Times Of Judy Garland*, Woodhill, 1975.
Edwards, Anne, *Judy Garland: A Mortgaged Life*, Simon & Schuster (USA), Constable (UK), 1975.
Finch, Christopher, *Rainbow: The Stormy Life Of Judy Garland*, Grosset & Dunlap (USA), Michael Joseph (UK), 1975.
Frank, Gerold, *Judy*, Harper & Row (USA), W H Allen (UK), 1975.
Luft, Lorna, *Me And My Shadows: Living With The Legacy Of Judy Garland*, Sidgwick & Jackson (UK), 1998.
Morella, Joe & Epstein, Edward, *Judy: The Films And Career Of Judy Garland*, Citadel Press (USA), 1969.
Sanders, Coyne Stephen, *Rainbow's End: The Judy Garland Show*, W. Morrow (USA), 1990.
Shipman, David, *Judy Garland*, 4th Estate (UK), 1992.
Shipman, David, *Judy Garland: The Secret Life Of An American Legend*, Hyperion (USA), 1995.
Smith, Lorna, *Judy With Love*, Robert Hale (UK), 1975.
Spada, James & Swenson, Karen, *Judy & Liza*, Doubleday (USA), 1983.
Tormé, Mel, *The Other Side Of The Rainbow: With Judy Garland On The Dawn Patrol*, W. Morrow (USA), 1970.
Watson, Thomas J. & Chapman, Bill, *Judy: Portrait Of An American Legend*, McGraw Hill (USA), 1986.

Garner, Erroll
Doran, James M, *Erroll Garner, The Most Happy Piano*, Rutgers University (USA), 1985.

Gaye, Marvin
Davis, Sharon, *I Heard It Throught The Grapevine: Marvin Gaye, The Biography*, Mainstream (UK), 1991.
Davis, Sharon, *Marvin Gaye*, Proteus Books (UK), 1985.
Ritz, David, *Divided Soul: The Life Of Marvin Gaye*, Michael Joseph (UK), 1985.

Geldof, Bob
Geldof, Bob, *Is That It?*, Penguin (UK), 1986.
Gray, Charlotte, *Bob Geldof*, Exley Press (UK), 1987.

Geldray, Max
Geldray, Max with John R. Vance, *Goon With The Wind*, Robson Books (UK), 1989.

Genesis
Bowler, Dave & Dray, Brian, *Genesis: A Biography*, Sidgewick & Jackson (UK), 1992.
Clarke, Steve, *Genesis: Turn It On Again*, Omnibus Press (UK), 1984.
Gallo, Armando, *Genesis: The Evolution Of A Rock Band*, Sidgwick & Jackson (UK), 1978.
Gallo, Armondo, *Genesis: I Know What I Like*, DIY Books (USA), 1980.
Poor, Kim, *Genesis Lyrics*, Sidgwick & Jackson (UK), 1979.
Welch, Chris, *Complete Guide To The Music Of Genesis*, Omnibus Press (UK), 1995.

Gerry And The Pacemakers
Marsden, Gerry with Coleman, Ray, *I'll Never Walk Alone*.

Gershwin, George
Gershwin, George, *Rhapsody In Blue*, Warner Brothers.
Jablonski, Edward, *Gershwin*, London, 1988.
Rimler, Walter, *A Gershwin Companion A Critical Inventory & Discography 1916-1984*, Pop Culture Ann Arbor (USA), 1991.
Rosenberg, Deena, *Fascinating Rhythm: The Collaborations Of George & Ira Gershwin*, E.P. Dutton (USA), 1991.

Gershwin, Ira
Furia, Philip, *The Art Of The Lyricist*, Oxford, 1996.
Gershwin, Ira, *Lyrics On Several Occasions*, London, 1977.
Kimball, Robert (ed.), *The Complete Lyrics Of Ira Gershwin*, Pavilion Books (UK), 1993.
Rosenberg, Deena, *Fascinating Rhythm: Collaboration Of George And Ira Gershwin*, Lime Tree, 1992.

Getz, Stan
Astrup, Arne, *The Stan Getz Discography*, A. Astrup, 1978.
Kirkpatrick, Ron, *Stan Getz: An Appreciation Of His Recorded Work*, Zany Publications (UK), 1992.
Maggin, Donald, *Stan Getz: A Life In Jazz*, William Morrow (USA), 1996.
Palmer, Richard, *Stan Getz*, Apollo, 1988.

Gibson, Orville H.
Carter, Walter, *Gibson Guitars: 100 Years Of An American Icon*, General Publishing, 1994.
Whitford, Eldon & Vinopal, David & Erlewine, Dan, *Gibson's Fabulous Flat-Top Guitars*, GPI Books (USA), 1994.

Gillan, Ian
Gillan, Ian with David Cohen, *Child In Time: The Life Story Of The Singer From Deep Purple*, Smith Gryphon (UK), 1993.

Gillespie, Dizzy

Evensmo, Jan, *The Trumpets Of Dizzy Gillespie, 1937-1943*, Irving Randolph, Joe Thomas, Jan Evensmo, 1982.
Frazer, Alan, *Dizzy: To Be Or Not To Bop*, Quartet (UK), 1990.
Gillespie, Dizzy, *Dizzy Gillespie Blows Kerouac*, Thornwood Music.
Horricks, Raymond, *Dizzy Gillespie And The Be-Bop Revolution*, Spellmount, 1984.
James, M, *Dizzy Gillespie*, New York, 1978.
Lees, Gene, *Waiting for Dizzy*, Oxford University Press, 1992.
McRae, Barry, *Dizzy Gillespie: His Life & Times*, Universe Books, 1988.
Tanner, Lee (ed.), *Dizzy: John Birks Gillespie In His 75th Year*, Pomegranate Artbooks, 1993.

Gin Blossoms

Gin Blossoms, *New Miserable Experience*, Warner Bros. (USA) 1994.

Glass, Philip

Kostelanetz, Richard (ed.), *Writings On Glass: Essays, Original Writings, interviews, Criticism*, Schirmer Books (USA), 1997.

Glastonbury Festival

No editor listed, *Glastonbury: The Festival*, Albedo, 1995.

Gleason, Jackie

Henry III, William A., *The Great One: The Life And Legend Of Jackie Gleason*.
Weatherby, W.J., *Jackie Gleason: An Intimate Portrait Of The Great One*.

Glitter, Gary

Glitter, Gary with Bradley, Lloyd, *Leader: The Autobiography Of Gary Glitter*, Ebury Press (UK) and Warner Books (UK), 1991.
Tremlett, George, *The Gary Glitter Story*, Futura (UK), 1974.

Go-Betweens

Nichols, David, *The Go-Betweens*, Allen & Unwin (UK), 1997.

Golson, Benny

Golson, Benny, *The Genius Of Benny Golson*, Columbia Pictures.

Gonella, Nat

Brown, Ron & Brown, Cyril, *The Nat Gonella Story*, Milestone, 1985.
Gonella, Nat, *Modern Style Of Trumpet Playing*, London, 1935.

Gong

Allen, Daevid, *Gong Dreaming*, G.A.S., 1995.

Goodman, Benny

Collier, James Lincoln, *Benny Goodman And The Swing Era*, Oxford University Press, 1990.
Connor, D. Russell, *Benny Goodman: Listen To His Legacy*, Metuchen (USA), 1988.
Connor, D. Russell & Hicks, Warren W., *BG On The Record: A Bio-Discography Of Benny Goodman*, Arlington House (UK), 1969.
Crowther, Bruce, *Benny Goodman*, Apollo, 1988.
Firestone, Ross, *Swing, Swing, Swing: The Life And Times Of Benny Goodman*, Hodder & Stoughton (UK), 1992.
Goodman, Benny, *Benny, King Of Swing*, Thames and Hudson, 1979 (UK).
Goodman, Benny & Kolodin, Irving, *The Kingdom Of Swing*, New York, 1939.

Gordon, Dexter

Britt, Stan, *Long Tall Dexter*, Quartet Books (UK), 1989.

Gordy, Berry

Gordy, Berry, *To Be Loved*, Warner Books (USA), 1994.
Gordy, Berry, *Movin' Up*, Harper & Row (USA).

Grable, Betty

Pastos, Spero, *Pin-Up: The Tragedy Of Betty Grable*, Putnams (USA), 1986.

Graham, Bill

Graham, Bill & Greenfield, Robert, *Bill Graham Presents*, Delta (USA), 1993.

Grand Ole Opry

Kingsbury, Paul, *The Grand Ole Opry History Of Country Music*, Villard Books (USA), 1995.

Grappelli, Stéphane

Horricks, Raymond, *Stephane Grappelli, Or, The Violin With Wings*, Da Capo (USA).
Smith, Geoffrey, *Stephane Grappelli: A Biography*, Pavilion (USA), 1990.

Grateful Dead

Brandelius, Jerilyn Lee, *Grateful Dead Family Album*, Warner Books (USA), 1990.
Brook, Danae, *The Book Of The Dead: The Grateful Dead England '72*, Ice Nine (USA), 1972.
Dolgushkin, Scot & Nixon, *Dead Base IX: Complete Guide To Grateful Dead Song Lists*, Dead Base (USA), 1996.
Gans, David, *Conversations With The Grateful Dead*, Citadel Underground, 1992.
Greene, Herb, *Sunshine Daydreams: Grateful Dead Journal*, Chronicle Books (USA), 1991.
Greene, Herb, *Book Of The Dead: Celebrating 25 Years With The Grateful Dead*, Delacorte (USA), 1992.
Grushkin, Paul, Grushkin, Jonas & Bassett, Cynthia, *Grateful Dead: The Official Book Of The Deadheads*, W. Morrow (USA), 1983.
Hall, Adrian, *Story Of The Grateful Dead*, Magna Books, 1993.
Harrison, Hank, *The Dead Book: A Social History Of The Grateful Dead*, Links, 1973.
Harrison, Hank, *The Grateful Dead*, Star/W.H. Allen (UK), 1975.
Hart, Mickey, *Drumming At The Edge Of Magic*, Harper (USA), 1990.
Hart, Mickey & Lieberman, Fredric, *Planet Drum*, Harper Collins, 1992 (USA).
Hart, Mickey & Stevens, Jay, *Drumming At the Edge Of Magic*, Harper Collins, 1992.
Jensen, Jamie, *Built To Last: Twenty-Five Years Of The Grateful Dead*, Penguin (USA), 1990.
Reich, Charles & Wenner, Jann, *Garcia: A Signpost To New Space*, Straight Arrow (USA).
Ruhlmann, William, *History Of The Grateful Dead*, Omnibus Press (UK), 1990.
Scott, John, Dixon, Stu & Dolguishkin, Mike, *Deadbase V*, 1992.
Scott, John, Dixon, Stu & Dolguishkin, Mike, *Deadbase '90*, 1992.
Scully, Rock with Dalton, David, *Living With The Dead*, Little Brown (USA and UK), 1996.
Troy, Sandy, *One More Saturday Night: Reflections With The Grateful Dead*, St Martin's Press (USA), 1992.
Womack, David, *Aesthetics Of The Grateful Dead*, Flying Public Press, 1992.
Wybenga, Eric F., *Dead To The Core: A Grateful Dead*

Almanack, Delta, 1998.

Green, Peter
Celmins, Martin, *Peter Green - Founder Of Fleetwood Mac*, Sanctuary (UK), 1998.
Celmins, Martin, *Peter Green: The Biography*, Castle (UK), 1995.

Grenfell, Joyce
Grenfell, Joyce, *In Pleasant Places*.
Grenfell, Joyce, *Joyce Grenfell Requests The Pleasure*.
Grenfell, Joyce, *Time Of My Life - Entertaining The Troops: Her Wartime Journals*.
Grenfell, Joyce, *Stately As A Galleon (sketches and songs)*.
Grenfell, Joyce, *George - Don't Do That . . . (sketches and songs)*.
Grenfell, Reggie & Garnett, Richard (editors), *Joyce By Herself And Her Friends*.
Roose-Evans, James (ed.), *Darling Ma: Letters To Her Mother, 1932-1944*.

Grossman, Stefan
Grossman, Stefan, *Ragtime Blues Guitarists*, Oak Publications (USA), 1970.
Grossman, Stefan & Calt, Steven, *The Country Blues Song Book*, Oak Publications (USA), 1973.

Guns N'Roses
Chin, George (ed), *The Pictures*, Omnibus Press (UK), 1994.
Elliot, Paul, *Guns N'Roses: The World's Most Outrageous Hard Rock Band*, Hamlyn (UK), 1990.
McSquare, Eddy, *Lowlife In The Fast Lane*, Omnibus Press (UK), 1994.
Putterford, Mark, *Over The Top: The True Story Of. . .*, Omnibus Press (UK), 1993.
Putterford, Mark, *In Their Own Words*, Omnibus Press (UK), 1993.
St. Michael, Mick, *Live!*, Omnibus Press (UK), 1994.
Sugerman, Danny, *Appetite For Destruction: The Days Of Guns N' Roses*, Century (UK), 1991.
Wall, Mick, *The Most Dangerous Band In The World*, Sidgwick & Jackson (UK), 1991.

Guthrie, Woody
Guthrie, Woody, *American Folksong*, M. Asch (USA), 1947.
Guthrie, Woody, *Bound For Glory*, New American Library, 1970.
Guthrie, Woody, *Pastures Of Plenty-A Self Portrait*, San Francisco, 1990.
Guthrie, Woody, *Seeds Of Man: An Experience Lived And Dreamed*, E.P. Dutton (USA), 1976.
Guthrie, Woody, *Woody Guthrie Folk Songs*, Ludlow Music.
Guthrie, Woody, ed. Robert Shelton, *Born To Win*, Collier Books, 1967 (USA).
Klein, Joe, *Woody Guthrie: A Life*, Faber & Faber (UK), Knopf (USA), 1981.
Murlin, Bill (ed.), *Woody Guthrie: Roll On Columbia*, Sing Out Corporation, 1991.
Yurchenco, Henrietta, *A Mighty Hard Road: The Woody Guthrie Story*, McGraw-Hill (USA), 1970.

Guy, Buddy
Wilcock, Donald E. & Guy, Buddy, *Damn Right I Got The Blues: Blues Roots Of Rock N Roll*, Woodford P., 1994.

Haggard, Merle
Haggard, Merle with Russell, Peggy, *Sing Me Back Home: My Life*, Timescape Books (USA), 1981.

Haircut 100
No editor listed, *Haircut 100: Not A Trace Of Brylcreem*, Medusa, 1982.
Payne, Sally, *The Haircut 100 Catalogue*, Omnibus Press (UK), 1982.

Haley, Bill, And His Comets
Von Hoelle, John & Haley, John, *Sound & Glory*, , 1991.

Hall, Henry
Hall, Henry, *Here's To The Next Time*, Odhams (UK), 1955.

Hall, Tom T.
Hall, Tom T., *How I Write The Songs, Why You Can*, Chappell Music, 1976.
Hall, Tom T., *The Songwriters Handbook*, Nashville, 1976.
Hall, Tom T., *The Storyteller's Nashville*, Doubleday, 1979.

Hamlisch, Marvin
Hamlisch, Marvin with Gardner, Gerald, *The Way I Was*.
Stevens, Gary & George, Alan, *The Longest Line*.

Hammer, M. C.
Dessau, Bruce, *M.C. Hammer: U Can't Touch This*, Boxtree (UK), 1991.

Hammerstein, Oscar, II
Citron, Stephen, *The Wordsmiths: Oscar Hammerstein & Alan Jay Lerner*, Oxford University Press (USA), 1996.
Fink, Bert (compiler), *Rodgers And Hammerstein Birthday Book*.
Green, Stanley, *The Rodgers And Hammerstein Story*.
Nolan, Frederick, *The Sound Of Their Music: The Story Of Rodgers And Hammerstein*.
Taylor, J.D., *Some Enchanted Evening: The Story Of Rodgers And Hammerstein*.
Wilk, Max, *OK! The Story Of Oklahoma!*.

Hammill, Peter
Shaw-Parker, David, *The lemming Chronicles*, Pandoras Box, 1995.

Hammond, John
Hammond, John, *Hammond On Record*.

Hampton, Lionel
Hampton, Lionel, *Hamp*, Warner Books (USA), 1989.

Hanson, John
Hanson, John, *Me And My Red Shadow: The Autobiography Of John Hanson*, W.H. Allen (UK), 1980.

Harburg, E.Y. 'Yip'
Meyerson, Harold & Ernie Harburg, *Who Put The Rainbow In The Wizard Of Oz? Yip Harburg, Lyricist*, New York.

Harris, Wynonie
Collins, Tony, *Rock Mr. Blues: The Life And Music Of Wynonie Harris*, Big Nickel Publications (USA), 1995.

Harrison, George
Clayson, Alan, *The Quiet One: A Life Of George Harrison*, Sidgwick & Jackson (UK), 1990.
Giuliano, Geoffrey, *The Illustrated George Harrison*, Sunburst, 1993.
Giuliano, Geoffrey, *Dark Horse: The Secret Life Of George Harrison*, Bloomsbury (UK), 1990.
Harrison, George, *I Me Mine*, Comet (UK), 1980.
Harrison, George, *I Me Mine: Limited Edition*, Genesis (UK),

1980.
Harrison, George & Taylor, Derek, *Fifty Years Adrift*, Genesis (UK), 1985.
Michaels, Ross, *George Harrison Yesterday And Today*, Quick Fox (USA), 1977.

Hart, Moss
Hart, Moss, *Act One*.

Hatch, Tony
Hatch, Tony, *So You Want To Be In The Music Business*.

Hawkins, Coleman
Chilton, John, *The Song Of The Hawk*, Quartet (UK), 1990.
James, Burnett, *Coleman Hawkins*, Hippocrene Books (USA), 1984.
Villetard, Jean François, *Coleman Hawkins Volume 1 (1922-44), Volume 2 (1945-57)*.

Hawkwind
Parr, Adrian, *Roadhawks Live 1969-95*, Private publication (UK), 1995.
Tate, Kris, *This Is Hawkwind, Do Not Panic*.

Hay, George D.
Hay, George D., *A Story Of The Grand Ole Opry*, , 1953.
Kingsbury, Paul, *The Grand Ole Opry History Of Country Music*, Villard Books (USA), 1995.

Heavy Metal
Arnett, Jeffrey Jensen, *Metalheads: Heavy Metal Music And Adolescent Alienation*, Westview Press (UK), 1996.
Bashe, Philip, *Heavy Metal Thunder*, Omnibus Press (UK), 1986.
Dome, Malcolm, *Thrash Metal*, Omnibus Press (UK), 1990.
Eddy, Chuck, *Stairway To Hell: The 500 Best Heavy Metal Albums In The Universe*, Harmony Books (USA), 1991.
Hale, Mark, *Headbangers: Worldwide Mega-Book Of Heavy Metal Bands*, Popular Culture Ink, 1992.
Halfin, Ross, *The Power Age*, Eel Pie (UK), 1982.
Harrigan, Brian, *The HM A-Z*, Bobcat Books (USA), 1981.
Harrigan, Brian & Dome, Michael, *Encyclopedia Metallica: The Bible Of Heavy Metal*, Bobcat (USA), 1981.
Jasper, Tony, *The International Encyclopedia Of Hard Rock & Heavy Metal*, Sidgwick & Jackson (UK), 1984.
Jeffries, Neil (ed.), *Kerrang! Directory Of Heavy Metal: The Indispensable Guide To...*, Virgin Books (UK), 1993.
Larkin Colin, *The Virgin Encyclopedia Of Heavy Rock* (Virgin Books (UK), 1999.
Larkin, Colin (ed.), *Guinness Who's Who Of Heavy Metal*, Guinness Publishing (UK), 1992.
Martyn, Lee, *Masters Of Metal*, Zomba Books (UK), 1985.
Not listed, *Giants Of Heavy Metal: Authentic Guitar - Tab Edition*, Warner Brothers (USA), 1993.
Stark, Janne, *Encyclopedia Of Swedish Hard Rock And Heavy Metal, 1970-96*, Premium Publishing (Sweden), 1996.
Stetina, Troy &Joyce, Shauna, *Secrets To Writing Killer Metal Songs*, H. Leonard Publications (USA), 1993.
Walser, Robert, *Running With The Devil: Power, Gender And Madness In Heavy Metal...*, Wesleyan University Press (USA), 1993.

Heckstall-Smith, Dick
Heckstall-Smith, Dick, *The Safest Place In The World*, Quartet Books (UK), 1989.

Hedges, Michael
Hedges, Michael, *Rhythm, Sonority, Silence*, Stropes Editions (USA), 1994.

Hell, Richard
Hell, Richard, *Artifact*, Hanuman (USA), 1990.
Hell, Richard, *The Voidoid*, Cdex (USA), 1996.
Hell, Richard, *Go Now*, Scribner (USA), Fourth Estate (UK), 1996.

Helm, Levon
Helm, Levon with Stephen Davis, *This Wheel's On Fire*, William Morrow & Co. (USA), 1993.

Helms, Bobby
Davis, Dave, *My Special Angel*.

Henderson, Chick
Wappat, Frank, *The Chick Henderson Story*, Printability Publishing, 1991.

Henderson, Fletcher
Allen, W., *Hendersonia: The Music Of Fletcher Henderson And His Musicians*, Highland Park, New Jersey (USA), 1973.

Henderson, Hamish
Henderson, Hamish, *Alias MacAlias*, Polygon, 1992.
Henderson, Hamish, *Elegies For The Dead In Cyrenaica*, John Layman, 1948.

Hendrix, Jimi
Boot, Adrian & Salewicz, Chris, *The Ultimate Experience*, Boxtree (UK), 1995.
Brown, Tony, *Hendrix: The Final Days*, Rogan House (UK), 1997.
Brown, Tony, *Jimi Hendrix: A Visual Documentary, His Life, Loves And Music*, Omnibus Press (UK), 1992.
Dannemann, Monika, *The Inner World Of Jimi Hendrix*, Bloomsbury (UK), 1995.
Dister, Alain, *Jimi Hendrix*, Editions Chiron (Paris).
Geldeart, Gary & Rodham, Steve, *From The Benjamin Franklin Studios: A Complte Guide To The Available Recordings* , Jimpress (UK), 1996.
Glebbeek, Caesar & Noble, Douglas, *The Man, The Music, The Memorabilia*, Paper Tiger (UK), 1996.
Green, Martin L. & Sienkiewicz, Bill, *Voodoo Child: The Illustrated Legend Of Jimi Hendrix*, Penguin Studio (USA), 1995.
Guiliano, Geoffrey, *The Illustrated Jimi Hendrix*, Sunburst Books (UK), 1994.
Henderson, David, *Scuze Me While I Kiss The Sky: The Life Of Jimi Hendrix*, Bantam (USA), Omnibus Press (UK), 1981.
Henderson, David, *Jimi Hendrix: Voodoo Child Of The Aquarian Age*, Doubleday (USA), 1978.
Hendrix, Jimi, *The Lost Writings Of Jimi Hendrix*, Bloomsbury (UK), 1995.
Hendrix, Jimi, *Stay Groovy Stay Free*.
Hopkins, Jerry, *Jimi Hendrix Experience*, Plexus (UK), 1996.
Hopkins, Jerry, *The Jimi Hendrix Story*, Sphere Books (UK), 1984.
Knight, Curtis, *Jimi: An Intimate Biography Of Jimi Hendrix*, Praeger (USA), W.H. Allen (UK).
Knight, Curtis, *Jimi Hendrix: Starchild*, Abelard Productions (USA), 1993.
Mankowitz, Gerad & Whitaker, Robert (photographers), *The Jimi Hendrix Experience In 1967 (Limited Edition)*, UFO Books (UK), 1992.
McDermott, John, *The Complete Studio Recording Sessions 1963-1970*, Little Brown (USA), 1995.
McDermott, John with Kramer, Eddie, *Hendrix: Setting The Record Straight*, Little, Brown (USA), 1993.
Mitchell, Mitch & Platt, John, *The Hendrix Experience*, Pyramid Books (UK), 1990.

Murray, Charles Shaar, *Crosstown Traffic: Jimi Hendrix And Post-War Pop*, Faber & Faber (UK), 1989.

Nitopi, Bill (compiler), *Cherokee Mist - The Lost Writings Of Jimi Hendrix*, Bloomsbury (UK), 1994.

Nolan, Tom, *Jimi Hendrix: A Biography In Words & Pictures*, Sire/Chappell Music (USA).

Potash, Chris (ed.), *The Jimi Hendrix Companion*, Omnibus Press (UK), 1998.

Price, Jon & Geldeart, Gary, *And The Man With The Guitar*, Jimpress (UK), 1992.

Redding, Noel & Appleby, Carole, *Are You Experienced?*, 4th Estate (UK), 1990.

Robertson, John, *Complete Guide To The Music Of*, Omnibus Press (UK), 1995.

Sampson, Victor, *Hendrix: An Illustrated Biography*, Proteus Books (UK), 1984.

Shapiro, Harry & Glebbeek, Caesar, *Jimi Hendrix: Electric Gypsy*, Heinemann (UK), 1990.

Tarshis, Steve, *Original Hendrix*, Wise (USA), 1982.

Valkhoff, Ben, *Eye Witness: The Illustrated Jimi Hendrix Concerts*, 1997.

Welch, Chris, *Hendrix: A Biography*, Omnibus Press (UK), 1982.

Willix, Mary, *Jimi Hendrix: Voices From Home*, Creative Forces (USA), 1996.

Herbert, Victor
Lee, Claire, *Victor Herbert: American Music Master*, Panther Books (UK), 1976.

Herman, Jerry
Herman, Jerry with Marilyn Stasio, *Showtune: A Memoir*, Donald I. Fine Books (USA), 1996.

Herman, Woody
Herman, Woody, *The Woodchopper's Ball*, E. P. Dutton (USA).

Herman, Woody, *Your Father's Moustache*, Mayfair Music.

Morrill, Dexter, *Woody Herman: A Guide to The Big Band Recordings, 1936-87*, Greenwood Press, 1991.

Voce, Steve, *Woody Herman*, Apollo, 1990.

Heyward, Nick
No editor listed, *Haircut 100: Not A Trace Of Brylcreem*, Medusa, 1982.

Payne, Sally, *The Haircut 100 Catalogue*, Omnibus Press (UK), 1982.

Higgins, Lizzie
Munro, Ailie, *Lizzie Higgins And The Oral Transmission Of Ten Child Ballads*, School of Scottish Studies, Edinburgh Univ., 1970.

Perrin, Stephanie, *A Study Of Lizzie Higgins As A Transitional Figure In The Development Of The Ora*, School Of Scottish Studies, Edinburgh University (UK) 1975.

Hines, Earl 'Fatha'
Courlander, Harold, *The World Of Earl Hines*, Scribners (USA).

Hinton, Milt
Hinton, Milt & Berger, David G., *Bass Line*, Temple University Press (USA), 1988.

Hip-Hop
Fernando, S.H., *The New Beats*, Payback Press (USA), 1995.

Hodes, Art
Hansen, Chadwick (ed), *Hot Man: The Life Of Art Hodes*, Bayou Press (USA), 1992.

Hodes, Art & Hansen, Chadwick (ed.), *Selections From The Gutter*, University Of California Press (USA).

Hole
Brite, Poppy Z., *Courtney Love: The Real Story*, Orion (UK), 1997.

Rossi, Melissa, *Queen Of Noise: A Most Unauthorised Biography*, Pocket Books (USA), 1996.

Wilson, Susan, *Look Through This*, UFO (UK), 1996.

Wise, Nick, *Courtney Love*, Omnibus Press (UK), 1995.

Holliday, Judy
Carey, G., *Judy Holliday*, Putnam (USA), 1982.

Holtzman, W., *Judy Holliday*, Seaview Book (USA), 1982.

Hollies
Nightingale, Anne (ed.), *How To Run A Beat Group*, Daily Mirror Press (UK), 1964.

Holloway, Stanley
Holloway, Stanley, *Wiv A Little Bit O' Luck*, London, 1967.

Holly, Buddy
Amburn, Ellis, *Buddy Holly: A Biography*, St Martin's Press (USA), 1995.

Clark, Alan, *Buddy Holly: 30th Anniversary Memorial Series No 1*, West Covina, California (USA), 1989.

Clark, Alan, *Buddy Holly And The Crickets*, Allan Clark (USA), 1979.

Dawson, Jim & Leigh, Spencer, *Memories Of Buddy Holly*, Nickel Publications (USA), 1996.

Goldrosen, John, *Buddy Holly: His Life And Music*, Bowling Green University Popular Press (USA), 1975.

Goldrosen, John, *The Buddy Holly Story*, Quick Fox (USA), 1979.

Goldrosen, John & Beecher, John, *Remembering Buddy*, Omnibus Press (UK), 1996.

Holley, Larry, *The Buddy I Knew*, Larry Holley (USA), 1979.

Laing, Dave, *Buddy Holly*, Studio Vista (UK), 1971.

Mann, Alan, *Buddy Holly, Alan Mann's A-Z*, Turnaround (UK), 1994.

Norman, Phillip, *Buddy The Biography (UK) Rave On (USA)*, Macmillan (UK), Simon & Schuster (USA), 1996.

Peer, Elizabeth & Peer, Ralph, *Buddy Holly: A Biography In Words Photographs And Music*, Peer International (USA), 1972.

Peters, Richard, *The Legend That Is Buddy Holly*, Souvenir Press (UK), 1990.

Holman, Libby
Machlin, Milt, *Libby*, Connecticut, 1980.

Perry, H.D., *Libby Holman*, Body And Soul, Boston, 1983.

Holzman, Jac
Holzman, Jac &Daws, Gavan, *Follow The Music: The Life And High Times Of Elektra Records*, First Media (USA), 1998.

Hooker, John Lee
Fancourt, Les, *Boogie Chillen: A Guide To John Lee Hooker On Disc*, Blues & Rhythm (UK), 1992.

Hopkins, Lightnin'
McCormick, M, *Lightnin' Hopkins: Blues'*, Jazz Panorama, New York, 1962.

Horn, Paul
Horn, Paul with Underwood, Lee, *Inside Paul Horn: The Spiritual Odessey of a Universal Traveller*, Harper Collins

(USA), 1991.

Horn, Shirley
Horn, Shirley, *Shirley Horn (Interviewed By Marian McPartland)*.

Horne, Lena
Haskins J. & Benson K., *Lena: A Personal And Professional Biography.*, New York.
Horne, Lena, *In Person*.
Horne, Lena with Schikel, Richard, *Lena*, New York, 1966.

Horton, Johnny
LeVine, Michael, *Johnny Horton: Your Singing Fisherman*, New York, 1982.

Housemartins
Swift, Nick, *The Housemartins, Tales From Humberside*, Music Sales, 1988.

Houston, Whitney
Bowman, Jeffery, *Diva: The Totally Unauthorised Biography Of Whitney Houston*, Headline (UK), 1995.

Howard, Jan
Howard, Jan, *Sunshine & Shadow: My Story*, Eagle, 1987.

Hughes, Spike
Hughes, Spike, *Opening Bars*, London, 1946.
Hughes, Spike, *Second Movement*, London, 1952.

Hugill, Stan
Hugill, Stan, *Sailortown*, Routledge & Kegan Paul (UK), 1967.
Hugill, Stan, *Shanties And Sailor Songs*, , 1969.
Hugill, Stan, *Shanties From The Seven Seas*, Routledge & Kegan Paul (UK), 1961.
Hugill, Stan, *Songs Of The Sea: The Tails And Tunes Of Sailors And Sailing Ships*, McGraw-Hill (USA), 1977.

Hull, Alan
Hull, Alan, *The Mocking Horse*, Spice Box Books (UK), 1973.

Human League
Nash, Peter, *The Human League: Perfect Pop*, Star/W.H. Allen (UK), 1982.
Ross, Alaska & Furmanovsky, Jill, *The Story Of A Band Called The Human League*, Proteus Books (UK), 1982.

Humperdinck, Engelbert
Short, Don, *Engelbert Humperdinck: The Authorized Biography*, New English Library (UK), 1972.

Hunt, Marsha
Hunt, Marsha, *Joy*, Century (UK), 1990.
Hunt, Marsha, *Real Life*, Headline (UK), 1987.

Hunter, Ian
Hunter, Ian, *Diary Of A Rock 'N' Roll Star*, Panther Books (UK), 1974.
Hunter, Ian, *Reflections Of A Rock Star*, Flash Books (USA), 1976.

Hunter, Robert
Hunter, Robert, *A Box Of Rain: Collected Lyrics Of Robert Hunter*, Viking (USA), 1992.
Hunter, Robert, *Night Carde*, Viking (USA), 1992.

Hunter, Tommy
Hunter, Tommy, *My Story*, 1985.

Ian, Janis
Ian, Janis, *Who Really Cares?*, Dial Press (USA), 1969.

Ice-T
Ice-T & Heidi Seigmund, *The Ice Opinion*, Pan Books (UK), 1994.

Idol, Billy
Wrenn, Mike, *Billy Idol: Visual Documentary*, Omnibus Press (UK), 1991.

Iggy Pop
Ambrosch, Connie, *Iggy Pop - Collection*, Hal Leonard Publishing (USA), 1994.
Gibbs, Alvin, *Neighbourhood Threat: On Tour With Iggy Pop*, Britannia Music Press (UK), 1996.
Nilsen, Per & Sherman, Dorothy, *Iggy Pop:The Wild One*, Omnibus Press (UK), 1988.
Pop, Iggy with Wehrer, Anne, *I Need More: The Stooges And Other Stories*, Karz-Cohl (USA), 1982.
West, Mike, *The Lives And Crimes Of Iggy Pop*, Babylon Books (UK), 1982.

Iglesias, Julio
Rovin, Jeff, *Julio!*, New York, 1986.

Imlach, Hamish
Imlach, Hamish, *Cod Liver Oil And The Orange Juice*, Mainstream Publishing (UK), 1992.

Inoue, Yosui
Inoue, Yosui, *Otono Sotogawade (Outside The Sound)*, Japan.
Takeda, Seiji, *Yosuino Kairaku (The Pleasure Of Yosui)*, Japan.

INXS
Gamblin, St John Yann (ed.), *INXS: The Official Story Of A Band On The Road*, Virgin Books (UK), 1992.

Iron Maiden
Bushell, Garry & Halfin, Ross, *Running Free: The Official Story Of Iron Maiden*, Zomba Books (UK), 1985.
Halfin, Ross, *What Are We Doing This For?*, Zomba Books (UK), 1994.
Halfin, Ross, *Iron Maiden: A Photographic History*, Zomba Books (UK), 1988.
Wall, Mick, *Run To The Hills, Iron Maiden: The Official Biography*, Sanctuary (UK), 1998.

Ives, Burl
Ives, Burl, *Wayfaring Stranger*, New York.

Iwan, Dafydd
Iwan, Dafydd, *Dafydd Iwan*, 1982.

Jackson Five
Kuliha, Ingmar, *The Record History: International Jackson Record Guide* , I. Kuliha, 1995.
Manning, Steve, *The Jacksons*, Bobbs-Merrill (USA), 1977.
Morse, Charles, *Jackson Five*, Creative Education, 1974.
Pitts, Leonard, *Pap Joe's Boys: The Jacksons' Story*, Sharon, 1983.
Taraborrelli, J. Randy, *The Magic And The Madness*, Headline (UK), 1992.

Jackson, Janet
Andrew, Bart, edited by J Randy Taraborrelli, *Out Of The Madness (The Strictly Unauthorised Biography Of...)*, Headline (UK), 1994.

Jackson, LaToya
Jackson LaToya with Ramanowski, Patricia, *LaToya Jackson*, Century (UK), 1991.

Jackson, Mahalia
Schwerin, Jules, *Got To Tell It: Mahalia Jackson Queen Of Gospel*, Oxford University Press (USA), 1992.

Jackson, Michael
Andersen, Christopher, *Michael Jackson Unauthorized*, Signet (USA), 1995.
Bego, Mark, *Michael!: The Michael Jackson Story*, Pinnacle Books, 1984.
Bego, Mark, *On The Road With Michael Jackson*, Zomba Books (UK), 1985.
Brown, Geoff, *Michael Jackson: Body And Soul: An Illustrated Biography*, Virgin Books (UK), 1984.
Brown, Geoff, *The Complete Guide To The Music Of: Michael Jackson & Jackson Family*, Omnibus Press (UK), 1992.
Campbell, Lisa D., *Michael Jackson: The King Of Pop*, Branden Books, 1993.
Dineen, Catherine, *In His Own Words*, Omnibus Press (UK), 1993.
Garland, Phyl, *Michael In Concert*, Pan Books (UK), 1984.
George, Nelson, *The Michael Jackson Story*, New English Library (UK), 1984.
Gold, Todd, *Michael Jackson : The Man In The Mirror*, Pan Books (UK), 1992.
Grant, Adrian, *The Visual Documentary*, Omnibus Press (UK), 1994.
Grant, Adrian, *Live And Dangerous*, Omnibus Press (UK), 1993.
Jackson, Michael, *Moonwalk*, Mandarin, 1990.
Jackson, Michael, *Michael Jackson: In His Own Words*, Omnibus Press (UK), 1993.
Jackson, Michael, *Moonwalk*, William Heinemann (UK), 1988.
Magee, Doug, *Michael Jackson*, Proteus Books (UK), 1984.
Michael Jackson Fact File And Official Lyric Book, Omnibus Press (UK), , 1984.
No editor listed, *The Magic Of Michael Jackson*, Omnibus Press (UK), 1984.
Pinkerton, Lee, *The Many Faces Of Michael Jackson*, Ozone, 1998.
Quill, Greg, *Michael Jackson: Electrifying*, Sidgwick & Jackson (UK), 1988.
Regan, Stewart, *Michael Jackson*, Colour Library International (UK), 1984.
Taraborrelli, J. Randy, *Michael Jackson: The Magic And The Madness*, Headline (UK), 1992.
Terry, Carol D., *Sequins & Shades: The Michael Jackson Reference Guide*, Pierian Press (USA), 1987.

Jackson, Stonewall
Henson, Billy (ed.), *From The Bottom Up: The Stonewall Jackson Story*, L.C. Parsons, 1991.

Jagger, Mick
Andersen, Christopher, *Jagger Unauthorised*, Simon & Schuster (UK), 1993.
Dowley, Tim, *Mick Jagger And The Stones*, Midas Books (UK), 1982.
Marks, J., *Mick Jagger: The Singer, Not The Song*, Abacus (UK), 1974.
Not listed, *Happy Birthday*, UFO Books (UK), 1993.
Sandford, Christopher, *Mick Jagger: Primitive Cool*, Gollancz (UK), 1993.

Jam
Agent Provocateur, *The Jam Retrospective: A Visual History*,
No publisher, 1997.
Brookes, Steve, *Keeping The Flame*, Sterling Publishing (UK), 1996.
Foxton, Bruce & Buckler, Rick with Ogg, Alex, *Our Story*, Castle Books (UK), 1994.
Hewitt, Paulo, *The Jam: A Beat Concerto, The Authorized Biography*, Omnibus Press (UK), 1983.
Honeyford, Paul, *The Jam: The Modern World By Numbers*, Eel Pie (UK), 1980.
Lowe, Richard, *The Jam*, Virgin Books (UK), 1997.
Malins, Steve, *Paul Weller: The Unauthorised Biography*, Virgin Books (UK), 1997.
Miles, *Jam*, Omnibus Press (UK), 1981.
Nicholls, Mike, *About The Young Idea: The Story Of The Jam 1972-1982*, Proteus Books (UK), 1984.
Reid, John, *Paul Weller: My Ever Changing Moods*, Omnibus Press (UK), 1996.

James, Bob
James, Bob, *Bob James And His Music*, Columbia Pictures.

James, Etta
James, Etta with David Ritz, *Rage To Survive*, Villard Books (USA), 1995.

James, Skip
Calt, Stephen, *I'd Rather Be The Devil*, Da Capo (USA), 1995.

Jan And Dean
Clark, Allan, *Jan And Dean*, Allan Clark (USA), 1981.

Japan
Pitt, Arthur A., *A Tourist's Guide To Japan*, Proteus Books (UK), 1982.

Jarre, Jean-Michel
Needham, Graham, *The Unofficial Jean-Michel Jarre Biography*, Graham Needham (UK), 1992.

Jarrett, Keith
Carr, Ian, *Keith Jarrett: The Man And His Music*, Grafton (UK), 1991.

Jefferson Airplane
Gleason, Ralph J., *The Jefferson Airplane And The San Francisco Sound*, Ballantine (USA), 1969.

Jennings, Waylon
Allen, Bob, *Waylon And Willie*, Flash Books, 1979.
Denisoff, Serge R., *Waylon: A Biography*, St Martins Press (USA), 1984.
Jennings, Waylon, *Waylon: A Man Called Hoss*, Columbia Pictures.
Jennings, Waylon, With Lenny Kaye, *Waylon: An Autobiography*, Warner Books (USA), 1997.
No author listed, *Waylon: Black On Black*, Columbia Pictures, 1982.
Smith, John L. (Ed), *The Waylon Jennings Discography*, Greenwood Press, 1995.
University Of Tennesse, *Waylon: A Biography*, Knoxville (USA), 1983.

Jesus And Mary Chain
Robertson, John, *The Jesus and Mary Chain: A Musical Biography*, Omnibus Press (UK), 1988.

Jesus Christ Superstar
Perry, George, *Jesus Christ Superstar: The Authorised Version*, Pavilion (UK), 1997.

Jobson, Richard
Jobson, Richard, *A Man For All Seasons*, Les Livres Du Crepuscule, Belgium, 1981.

Joel, Billy
Gambaccini, Peter, *Billy Joel: A Personal File*, Quick Fox (USA), 1979.

John's Children
Thompson, Dave, *John's Children*, Babylon Books (UK), 1988.

John, Elton
Bernardin, Claude & Tom Stanton, *Rocket Man: The Encyclopedia Of Elton John*, Greenwood Press, 1995.
Charlesworth, Chris, *Elton John 'Only The Piano Player', The Illustrated Elton John Story*, Omnibus Press (UK), 1984.
Clarke, Gary, *Elton, My Elton*, Smith Gryphon, 1995.
Crimp, Susan & Burstein, Patricia, *The Many Lives Of Elton John*, Birch Lane Press, 1993.
Finch, Alan, *Elton John: The Illustrated Discography*, Omnibus Press (UK), 1981.
Gambaccini, Paul, *A Conversation With Elton John And Bernie Taupin*, Flash Books, 1975.
Goodall, Nigel, *A Visual Documentary*, Omnibus Press (UK), 1993.
Jacobs, Linda, *Elton John: Reginald Dwight & Co*, EMC, 1976.
John, Elton, *The Elton John Tapes: Elton John In Conversation With Andy Peebles*, BBC (UK), 1981.
John, Elton & Taupin, Bernie, *Two Rooms: A Celebration Of Elton John & Bernie Taupin*, Boxtree (UK), 1991.
No author listed, *Candle In The Wind*, Pavilion Books (UK), 1993.
No author listed, *The Complete Lyrics Of Elton John And Bernie Taupin*, Pavilion Books (UK), 1994.
Norman, Philip, *Elton John: The Biography*, Harmony Books (USA), 1993.
Nutter, David, *Elton: It's A Little Bit Funny*, Viking (USA), 1977.
Shaw, Greg, *Elton John: A Biography In Words & Pictures*, Sire/Chappell Music, 1976.
Sobieski, Paul, *Elton John Discography*, Private Edition, 1976.
Stein, Cathi, *Elton John*, Futura (UK), 1975.
Tatham, Dick & Jasper, Tony, *Elton John*, Octopus (UK), 1976.
Taupin, Bernie, *Bernie Taupin: The One Who Writes The Words For Elton John: Complete Lyrics*, Jonathan Cape (UK).
Taylor, Paula, *Elton John*, Creative Educational Society, 1975.
Toberman, Barry, *Elton John: A Biography*, Weidenfeld & Nicolson (UK), 1988.
Tobler, John, *Elton John: 25 Years In The Charts*, Hamlyn (UK), 1995.

Johnson, Budd
Evensmo, Jan, *The Tenor Saxophones Of Budd Johnson, Cecil Scott, Elmer Williams, Dick Wilson*, Evensmo, 1977.

Johnson, Bunk
Hillman, Christopher, *Bunk Johnson: His Life & Times*, Universe Books, 1988.
Sonnier, Austin H., *Willie Geary Bunk 'Johnson'*, Crescendo.

Johnson, Holly
Johnson, Holly, *A Bone In My Flute*, Boxtree (UK), 1994.

Johnson, James P.
Brown, Scott E., *James P. Johnson*, Rutgers University (USA), 1986.
Trolle, Frank H., *James P. Johnson: Father Of The Stride Piano*, Micrography, 1981.

Johnson, Pete
Mauerer, Hans J., *The Pete Johnson Story*, Hans J. Mauerer, 1965.

Johnson, Robert
Ainslie, Scott, *Robert Johnson: At The Crossroads-The Authorative Guitar Transcriptions*, Hal Leonard (USA), 1992.
Charles, Samuel B., *Robert Johnson*, Oak Publications (USA), 1973.
Garon, P., *The Devil's Son-in-Law*, London, 1971.
Greenberg, Alan, *Love In Vain: Visions Of Robert Johnson*, Da Capo Press (USA), 1994.
Guralnick, Peter, *Searching For Robert Johnson*, E.P. Dutton (USA), 1989.

Johnson, Tommy
Evans, David, *Tommy Johnson*, Studio Vista (UK), 1971.

Jolson, Al
Freedland, Michael, *Jolie: The Story Of Al Jolson*, London, 1985.
Goldman, Herbert, *Jolson: The Legend Comes To Life*, Oxford, 1988.

Jones, George
Allen, Bob, *The Life And Times Of A HonkyTonk Legend*, Birch Lane Press (USA), 1994.
Allen, Bob, *George Jones*, Dolphin Books (USA), 1984.
Carlisle, Dolly, *Ragged But Right: The Life And Times Of George Jones*, Contemporary Books (USA), 1984.

Jones, Grace
Carlisle, Dolly, *Grace Jones: Ragged But Right*, Contemporary Books (USA), 1984.
Jungle Fever, *Goude, Jean-Paul*, Quartet Books (UK), 1982.

Jones, Grandpa
Jones, Louis M. 'Grandpa', *Everybody's Grandpa (Fifty Years Behind The Mike)*, Knoxville (USA), 1984.

Jones, Quincy
Horricks, Raymond, *Quincy Jones*, Hippocrene Books (USA), 1985.

Jones, Spike
Young, Jordan R., *Spike Jones Off The Record: The Man Who Murdered Music*, Past Times, 1994.

Jones, Tom
Hildred, Stafford & Griffen, David, *Tom Jones*, Sidgwick & Jackson (UK), 1990.
Jones, Tom, *Tom Jones: Biography Of A Great Star*, Barker, 1970.

Joplin, Janis
Amburn, Ellis, *Pearl: The Obsessions And Passions Of Janis Joplin*, Little, Brown (USA), 1993.
Caserta, Peggy as told to Knapp, Dan, *Going Down With Janis*, Dell (USA), 1973.
Dalton, David, *Janis*, Simon & Schuster (USA), 1971.
Dalton, David, *Janis Joplin: Piece Of My Heart*, Sidgwick & Jackson (UK), 1986.
Friedman, Myra, *Janis Joplin: Buried Alive*, Bantam Books (USA), 1974.
Joplin, Laura, *Love, Janis*, Bloomsbury (UK), 1992.
Landau, Deborah, *Janis Joplin: Her Life And Times*, Warner Books (USA), 1971.

Joplin, Scott
Gammond, Peter, *Scott Joplin And The Ragtime Era*, London, 1975.
Reed, A.W., *The Life And Works Of Scott Joplin*, University Of North Carolina (USA), 1973.

Jordan, Louis
Chilton, John, *Let The Good Times Roll: A Biography Of Louis Jordan*, Quartet Books (UK), 1992.

Joy Division
Curtis, Deborah, *Touching From A Distance*, Faber & Faber (UK), 1995.
Flowers, Claude, *New Order & Joy Division*, Omnibus Press (UK), 1995.
Johnson, Mark, *An Ideal For Living: An History Of Joy Division*, Proteus Books (UK), Bobcat Books (USA), 1984.

Judas Priest
Gett, Steve, *Heavy Duty*.

Judds
Judd, Naomi, *Love Can Build A Bridge*, Villard Books (USA), 1994.
Millard, Bob, *The Judds: Unauthorized Biography*, St Martins Paperbacks (USA), 1992.

Jungle
James, Martin, *State Of Bass - Jungle: The Story So Far*, Boxtree (UK), 1997.

Kahn, Si
Kahn, Si, *Si Kahn Songbook*
Kahn, Si, *Organizing: A Guide For Grassroots Leaders*.
Kahn, Si, *The Forest Service And Appalachia*.
Kahn, Si, *How People Get Power*.
Kahn, Si with Boyte, Harry, *Rural Community Organizing: History And Models*.

Kaye, Danny
Fine, Sylvia, *Fine And Danny*, 1991.
Gottfried, Martin, *Nobody's Fool-The Secret Lives Of Danny Kaye*, New York, 1994.
Singer, K., *The Danny Kaye Story*.

Keane, Ellsworth 'Shake'
Keane, Shake, *One A Week With Water*.
Keane, Shake, *The Volcano Suite*, 1979.

Keel, Howard
Leiby, Bruce R., *A Bio-Bibliography*, Greenwood Press, 1996.

Kelly, Gene
Hirschhorn, Clive, *Gene Kelly*, W. H. Allen (UK), 1974.

Kelly, Paul (Australia)
Kelly, Paul, *Paul Kelly Lyrics*, Angus & Robertson (Australia), 1993.

Kennedy, Peter
Kennedy, Peter, *The Folksongs Of Britain And Ireland*, Cassell & Schirmer, 1975.
Kennedy, Peter, *The Fiddlers Tune Book Volume 2*, Oxford University Press, 1953.
Kennedy, Peter, *Everybody Swing: Square Dances With Calls And Parts*, Chappell, 1952.
Kennedy, Peter, *The Fiddlers Tune Book Volume 1*, Oxford University Press, 1951.

Kenton, Stan
Arganian, Lillian, *Stan Kenton: The Man And His Music*, East Lansing, 1990.
Easton, Carol, *Straight Ahead: The Story of Stan Kenton*, William Morrow (USA), 1973.
Gabel, Edward F., *Stan Kenton: The Early Years*, Balboa Books (USA), 1995.
Lee, William F., *Stan Kenton*, Creative Press Of Los Angeles (USA), 1980.

Kern, Jerome
Freedland, Michael, *Jerome Kern: A Biography*, Robson Books (UK), 1990.

Kidd, Johnny, And The Pirates
Hunt, Keith, *Shaking All Over*, Magnum (UK), 1996.

Kihn, Greg
Kihn, Greg, *Horror Show*, St Martins Press (USA), 1996.

Killen, Buddy
Killen, Buddy with Carter, Tom, *By The Seat Of My Pants: My Life In Country Music*, Simon & Schuster (USA), 1993.

Kincaid, Bradley
Jones, Loyal, *Radio's Kentucky Mountain Boy: Bradley Kincaid*, Berea College (USA), 1980.

King Jammy
Lesser, Beth, *King Jammys*, Muzik Tree/Black Star, 1989.

King, B.B.
Danchin, Sebastian, *B.B. King*, Editions du Limon, Paris, 1993.
King, B.B. & Ritz, David, *Blues All Around Me, The Autobiography Of B.B. King*, Avon Books (USA), Hodder (UK), 1996.
Sawyer, Charles, *The Arrival Of B.B. King: The Authorized Biography*, Doubleday (USA), Blandford Press (UK), 1980.

King, Carole
Cohen, Mitchell S., *Carole King: A Biography In Words & Pictures*, Sire/Chappell Music, 1976.
Taylor, Paula, *Carole King*, Creative Educational Society, 1976.

Kingston Trio
Korner, Kingston, *Kingston Trio On Record*, Illinois, USA, 1987.

Kinks
Davies, Dave, *Kink: An Autobiography*, Boxtree (UK), 1996.
Davies, Ray, *Waterloo Sunset*, Viking (UK), 1997.
Davies, Ray, *X-Ray*, Viking (UK), 1994.
Hinman, Doug, *You Really Got Me: The Kinks Part One*, Privately published, 1994.
Marten, Neville & Hudson, Jeffrey, *The Kinks: Well Respected Men*, Castle Books (UK), 1996.
Rogan, Johnny, *The Kinks: The Sound And The Fury*, Elm Tree Books (UK), 1984.
Savage, Jon, *The Kinks: The Official Biography*, Faber & Faber (UK), 1985.

Kirk, Andy
Kirk, Andy, *Twenty Years On Wheels*, University Of Michigan Press (USA), 1989.

Kiss
Duncan, Robert, *Kiss*, Savoy Books, 1978.
Lendt, C K, *Kiss And Sell: The Making Of A Supergroup*, Billboard Books (USA), 1997.

Sherman, Dale, *Black Diamond: The Unauthorised Biography Of Kiss*, CGP Inc (USA), 1997.
St. Michael, Mick, *Kiss Live*, Omnibus Press (UK), 1996.
Swenson, John, *Kiss: The Greatest Rock Show On Earth*, Hamlyn (UK), 1979.
Thomas, Dave, *Still On Fire*.
Tomarkin, Peggy, *Kiss: The Real Story Authorized*, Delilah Communications (USA), 1980.

Kitt, Eartha
Kitt, Eartha, *Alone With Me: A New Biography*, H. Regenery, 1976.
Kitt, Eartha, *I'm Still Here*, New York, 1989.
Kitt, Eartha, *Thursday's Child*, Cassell (UK), 1957.

KLF
Manning, Mark & Drummond, Bill, *Bad Wisdom*, Penguin (UK), 1996.
Robinson, Pete, *Justified And Ancient: The Unfolding Story Of The KLF*, Justified & Ancient (UK), 1992.

Knight, Gladys, And The Pips
Knight, Gladys, *Between Each Line Of Pain And Glory - My Life Story*, Gollancz, 1998.

Knopfler, Mark
Palmer, Myles, *Mark Knopfler: An Unathorised Biography*, Sidgewick & Jackson, 1992.

Kool And The Gang
Kool And The Gang, *The Best Of Kool & The Gang*, Columbia Pictures.

Kooper, Al
Kooper, Al with Edmonds, Ben, *Backstage Passes: Rock 'N' Roll Life In The Sixties*, Stein and Day (USA), 1977.

Korner, Alexis
Shapiro, Harry, *Alexis Korner: The Biography*, Bloomsbury (UK), 1996.

Kostelanetz, André
Kostelanetz, André & Hammond, G., *Echoes: Memoirs Of André Kostelanetz*, New York.

Kraftwerk
Bussy, Pascal, *Kraftwerk: Man, Machine And Music*, Airlift Book Co (UK), 1993.

Kravitz, Lenny
Okun, Milton (ed.), *Best Of Lenny Kravitz*, Cherry Lane Music Co. (USA), 1994.

Kristofferson, Kris
Kalet, Beth, *Kris Kristofferson*, Quick Fox (USA), 1979.

Krupa, Gene
Crowther, Bruce, *Gene Krupa*, Omnibus Press (UK), 1988.

Kula Shaker
Cross, Nigel, *Kula Shaker*, Virgin Books (UK), 1997.

Lahr, Bert
Lahr, John, *Notes On A Cowardly Lion*, Knopf (USA), 1969.

Laine, Cleo
Collier, Graham (ed.), *Cleo And John*, Quartet Books (UK), 1976.
Laine, Cleo, *Cleo*, Simon & Schuster (UK), 1994.

Lane, Cristy
Stoller, Lee with Pete Chaney, *Cristy Lane: One Day At A Time*, St Martins Paperbacks (USA), 1993.

lang, k.d.
Bennahum, David, *An Illustated Biography*, Omnibus Press (UK), 1994.
Bennahum, David, *k.d. lang: In Her Own Words*, Omnibus Press (UK), 1993.
Robertson, William, *Carrying The Torch*, ECW Press (Canada), 1992.
Starr, Victoria, *All You Get Is Me*, St Martins Press (USA), 1994.

Lanza, Mario
Bernard, M., *Mario Lanza*, New York, 1971.
Strait, Raymond, *Lanza: His Tragic Life*.

Last Poets
Hassan, Umar Bin & Oyewole, Abiodun, *On A Mission: Selected Poems & A History Of The Last Poets*, Owl Books (USA), 1996.

Last, James
Elson, Howard, *James Last*, Proteus Books (UK), 1982.
Last, James, *James Last Story*, R. Gloss, 1975.
Willcox, Bob, *James Last*, Everest Books (UK), 1976.

Lauder, Harry
Irving G., *Great Scot: The Life Of Harry Lauder*, London, 1968.

Lead Belly
Bell, Judy, *Lead Belly*, Folkways/Big 3 Music (USA), 1976.
Garvin, Richard M. & Addeo, Edmond G., *The Midnight Special: The Legend Of Lead Belly*, Bernard Geis Associates, 1971.
Lomax, John, *Negro Folk Songs As Sung By Lead Belly*, Macmillan (USA), 1936.
Wolfe, Charles & Lornell, Kip, *The Life And Legend Of Lead Belly: A Revisionist Look*, Secker & Warburg (UK), Harper Collins (USA), 1992.

Led Zeppelin
Burston, Jeremy, *Led Zeppelin: The Book*, Proteus Books (UK), 1982.
Clarke, Ross, *Led Zeppelin: Breaking And Making Records*, Kingsfleet (UK), 1992.
Cole, Richard & Trubo, Richard, *Stairway To Heaven*, Harper Collins (USA), 1992.
Cross, Charles & Flannigan, Erik, *Led Zeppelin: Heaven & Hell*, Sidgwick & Jackson (UK), 1991.
Davis, Stephen, *Hammer Of The Gods: The Led Zeppelin Saga*, Sidgwick & Jackson (UK), 1985.
Godwin, Robert, *The Making Of: Led Zeppelin IV*, Collectors Guide Publishing (USA), 1996.
Godwin, Robert, *Illustrated Collector's Guide To Led Zeppelin*, APA Services, 1990.
Gross, Michael & Plant, Robert, *Led Zeppelin*, Popular Library/CBS, 1975.
Halfin, Ross (ed.), *The Photographer's Led Zeppelin*, 2.13.61 Publications (USA), 1996.
Kendall, Paul, *Led Zeppelin In Their Own Words*, Omnibus Press (UK), 1981.
Kendall, Paul, *Led Zeppelin: A Visual Documentary*, Omnibus Press (UK), 1982.
Lewis, Dave, *Led Zeppelin: A Celebration*, Omnibus Press (UK), 1991.
Lewis, Dave, *Led Zeppelin: The Final Acclaim*, Babylon Books (UK), 1984.

Lewis, Dave, *The Complete Guide To The Music Of...*, Omnibus Press (UK), 1994.

Lewis, Dave & Pallett, Simon, *Zeppelin: The Concert File*, Omnibus Press (UK), 1997.

Mylett, Howard, *Jimmy Page: Tangents Within A Framework*, Omnibus Press (UK), 1983.

Mylett, Howard, *Led Zeppelin*, Panther/Granada (UK), 1976.

Mylett, Howard (ed.), *On Tour With Led Zeppelin*, Mitchell Beazley (UK), 1993.

Mylett, Howard & Bunton, Richard, *Led Zeppelin: In The Light 1968-1980*, Proteus Books (UK), 1981.

Rey, Luis, *Led Zeppelin Live: An Illustrated Exploration Of Underground Tapes*, Hot Wacks Press (USA), 1995.

Welch, Chris, *Led Zeppelin - Dazed And Confused*, Carlton (UK), 1998.

Welch, Chris, *Led Zeppelin*, Orion/Carlton (UK), 1994.

Yorke, Ritchie, *The Led Zeppelin Biography*, Two Continents/Methuen (USA), 1976.

Yorke, Ritchie, *Led Zeppelin: The Definitive Biography*, Virgin Books (UK), 1993.

LeDoux, Chris

Brown, David G., *Gold Buckle:The Rodeo Life Of Chris Le Doux*, Boston, 1986.

Lee, Arthur

Brooks, Ken, *Arthur Lee: Love Story*, Agenda Books (UK), 1997.

Lee, Johnny

Lee, Johnny with Wiles, Randy, *Looking For Love*, Eakin Press, Austin (USA), 1990.

Lee, Peggy

Lee, Peggy, *Miss Peggy Lee*, Donald I. Fine (USA), 1990.

Legg, Adrian

Legg, Adrian, *The All Round Gigster* (UK), 1975.

Legg, Adrian & Colbert, Paul, *The Acoustic Guitar: A Musicians Manual* (UK), 1991.

Lehar, Franz

Czech, S., *Franz Lehár: Sein Weg Und Sein Werk*, Berlin, 1942.

Decsey, E., *Franz Lehár*, Vienna, 1924.

Grun, B., *Gold And Silver: The Life And Times Of Franz Lehár*, London, 1970.

Macqueen Pope, W. & Murray, D.L., *Fortune's Favourite: The Life And Times Of Franz Lehár*, London, 1953.

Schneiderheit, O., *Franz Lehár: Eine Biographie In Zitaten*, Innsbruck, 1984.

Leiber And Stoller

Palmer, Robert, *Baby, That Was Rock & Roll: The Legendary Leiber & Stoller*, Harcourt Brace Jovanovich (USA), 1978.

Lemonheads

St. Michael, Mick, *The Lemonheads*, Omnibus Press (UK), 1994.

True, Everett, *The Illustrated Story*, Hamlyn (UK), 1994.

Lennon, John

Baird, Julia, *John Lennon My Brother*, Grafton (UK), 1989.

Beckley, Timothy Coreen (ed.), *Lennon: Up Close*, Sunshine, 1980.

Belanger, L., Brecher, M., Kearns, J. & Lock, N., *A Tribute To John Lennon 1940-1980*, Proteus Books (UK), 1981.

Belkley, Timothy G., *Lennon: Up Close And Personal*.

Bresler, Fenton, *The Murder Of John Lennon*, Mandarin (UK), 1990.

Carpozi, George, *John Lennon: Death Of A Dream*, Manor Books, 1980.

Coleman, Ray, *John Ono Lennon 1967-1980*, Sidgwick & Jackson (UK), 1984.

Coleman, Ray, *John Winston Lennon 1940-1966*, Sidgwick & Jackson (UK), 1984.

Connolly, Ray, *John Lennon 1940-1980: A Biography*, Fontana (UK), 1981.

Diamond, Lee S., *John Lennon: All You Need Is Love*, Mar-Jam, New York.

Doncaster, Patrick, *Tribute To John Lennon: His Life, His Loves, His Work And His Death*, Mirror Books (UK), 1981.

Doncaster, Patrick, *Tribute To John Lennon: The Daily Mirror Special Issue*, Mirror Books (UK), 1980.

Du Noyer, Paul, *We All Shine On*, Carlton (UK), 1997.

Fawcett, Anthony, *John Lennon: One Day At A Time: A Personal Biography Of The Seventies*, New English Library (UK), 1977.

Garbarini, Vic & Cullman, Brian with Graustark, Barbara, *Strawberry Fields Forever: John Lennon Remembered*, Delilah/Bantam (USA), 1980.

Goldman, Albert, *The Lives Of John Lennon*, W. Morrow (USA), 1988.

Green, John, *Dakota Days: The Untold Story Of John Lennon's Final Years*, St. Martin's Press (USA), 1983.

Green, Timothy (ed.), *Lennon: What Happened!*, Sunshine, 1980.

Harry, Bill, *The Book Of Lennon*, Aurum (UK), 1984.

Heatley, Michael, *The Immortal John Lennon 1940-1980*, Longmeadow Press (UK), 1993.

Howless, Kevin & Lewisohn, Mark, *In My Life: John Lennon Remembered*, BBC (UK), 1991.

Jones, Jack, *Let Me Take You Down: Inside The Mind Of Mark Chapman*, Virgin Books (UK), 1992.

Lennon, Cynthia, *A Twist Of Lennon*, Star/W.H. Allen (UK), 1978.

Lennon, John, *AI: Japan Through John Lennon's Eyes (A Personal Sketchbook)*, Cadence Books, 1993.

Lennon, John, *A Spaniard In The Works*, Jonathan Cape (UK), 1965.

Lennon, John, *In His Own Write*, Jonathan Cape (UK), 1964.

Lennon, John, *Search For Liberation: A Conversation Between John Lennon And Swami Bhaktiredant*, Book Trust, 1981.

Lennon, John, *Skywriting By Word Of Mouth*, Harper Row (USA), Pan Books (UK), 1986.

Lennon, John, *The Penguin John Lennon*, Penguin Books (UK), 1966.

Lennon, John, *The Playboy Interviews With John Lennon And Yoko Ono*, New English Library (UK), 1982.

Lennon, John with Kennedy, Adrienne & Spinetti, Victor, *The Lennon Play*, Jonathan Cape (UK), 1968.

McCabe, Peter & Schonfeld, Robert D., *John Lennon: For The Record*, Bantam (USA), 1985.

Melody Maker Editors., *A Melody Maker Tribute*, IPC Magazines (UK), 1981.

Miles, *John Lennon In His Own Words*, Omnibus Press (UK), 1980.

Nelson, Paul, *John Lennon: A Biography In Words & Pictures*, Sire/Chappell Music.

No author listed, *John Lennon: Give Peace A Chance*, Croft (UK), 1980.

No author listed, *John Lennon: Summer Of 1980*, Chatto & Windus (UK), 1984.

No author listed, *Lennon: An Appreciation*, Choice, 1980.

No editor listed, *John Lennon: A Tribute In Words Pictures And Lyrics*, Chart Songwords, 1981.

Norman, Philip, *Days In The Life: John Lennon Remembered*, Century (UK), 1990.

Oldfield, Michael, *John Lennon: A Melody Maker Tribute*, IPC

Magazines (UK), 1980.

Pang, May, *Loving John*, Corgi Books (UK), 1983.

Pebbles, Andy, *The Lennon Tapes: Andy Peebles In Conversation With John Lennon And Yoko Ono*, BBC Publications (UK), 1981.

Robertson, John, *Lennon*, Omnibus Press (UK), 1995.

Robertson, John, *The Art & Music Of John Lennon*, Omnibus Press (UK), 1991.

Rolling Stone Editors, *The Ballad Of John And Yoko*, Rolling Stone Press (USA), 1982.

Ruhlmann, William, *John Lennon*, Smithmark (USA), 1993.

Ryan, David Stuart, *John Lennon's Secret*, Kozmik Press Centre, 1982.

Seaman, Frederic, *John Lennon: Living On Borrowed Time*, Xanadu, 1992.

Shevey, Sandra, *The Other Side Of Lennon*, Sidgwick & Jackson (UK), 1990.

Shotton, Peter & Schaffner, Nicholas, *John Lennon: In My Life*, Scarborough Books, 1983.

Smith, Ron, *John Lennon: A Tribute*, David Zentner, 1980.

Solt, Andrew & Egan, Sam, *Imagine John Lennon*, Virgin Books (UK), 1987.

Sunday Times, Editors of, *John Lennon: The Life & Legend*, The Sunday Times (UK), 1980.

Thomson, Elizabeth M. & Gutman, David, *The Lennon Companion: 25 Years Of Comment*, Macmillan (UK), 1987.

Todd, Jack, *John Lennon: 1981 (A Memorial Album)*, Friday, 1981.

Tremlett, George, *The John Lennon Story*, Futura (UK), 1976.

Tyler, Tony, *John Lennon: Working Class Hero; The Life And Death Of a Legend 1940-1980*, IPC Magazines (UK), 1980.

Wenner, Jann, *Lennon Remembers: The Rolling Stone Interviews*, Straight Arrow (USA), 1971.

Wiener, Jon, *Come Together: John Lennon In His Own Time*, Faber & Faber (UK), 1985.

Young, Paul, *The Lennon Factor*, Stein & Day (USA), 1972.

Lennox, Annie

O'Brien, Lucy, *Annie Lennox*, Sidgwick & Jackson (UK), 1991.

Lerner, Alan Jay

Citron, Stephen, *The Wordsmiths: Oscar Hammerstein & Alan Jay Lerner*, Oxford University Press (USA), 1996.

Green, Benny (ed.), *A Hymn To Him: The Lyrics Of Alan Jay Lerner*, Pavilion Books (UK), 1987.

Levant, Oscar

Kashner, Sam & Nancy Schoenberger, *A Talent For Genius; Life And Times Of Oscar Levant*, Villard (USA), 1994.

Level 42

Cowton, Michael, *Level 42: The Definitive Biography*, Sidgwick & Jackson (UK), 1989.

Lewis, George (clarinet)

Bethell, T., *George Lewis: A Jazzman From New Orleans*, Berkeley (USA), 1977.

Lewis, Jerry Lee

Cain, Robert, *Whole Lotta Shakin' Goin' On: Jerry Lee Lewis*, Dial Press (USA), 1981.

Clark, Allan, *Jerry Lee Lewis: The Ball Of Fire*, Allan Clark (USA), 1980.

De Boer, William, *Jerry Lee Lewis: Disc Special*.

Ebner, Chris, *The Works Of Jerry Lee Lewis*, Chris Ebner (Germany), 1995.

Guteman, Jimmy, *Rockin' My Life Away: Listening To Jerry Lee Lewis*, Rutledge Hill Press (USA), 1992.

Lewis, Jerry Lee & Charles White, *Killer!*, Century (UK), 1993.

Lewis, Myra with Silver, Murray, *Great Balls Of Fire: The True Story Of Jerry Lee Lewis*, Virgin Books (UK), St Martins Press (USA), 1982.

Palmer, Robert, *Jerry Lee Lewis*, Omnibus Press (UK), 1981.

Tosches, Nick, *Hellfire: The Jerry Lee Lewis Story*, Delacorte Press (USA), 1982.

Lewis, Vic

Lewis, Vic & Barrow, Tony, *Music & Maiden Overs: My Show Business Life*, Chatto & Windus (UK), 1987.

Liberace

Liberace, *Liberace*, Putnam (USA), 1973.

Thomas, B., *Liberace: The True Story*, London, 1988.

Liberty Records

Kelly, Michael 'Doc Rock', *Liberty Records*, McFarland, 1993.

Lightfoot, Gordon

Collins, Maynard, *If You Could Read My Mind*, Deneau Toronto, 1988.

Gabiou, Alfrieda, *Gordon Lightfoot*, Quick Fox (USA), 1979.

Lightfoot, Gordon, *The Pony Man*, Harper & Row (USA), 1972.

Lillie, Beatrice

Laffey, B., *Beatrice Lillie: The Funniest Woman In The World*, Wynwood Press (USA), 1989.

Lillie, Beatrice, *Every Other Inch A lady*, Doubleday (USA), 1972.

Lion King, The

Taymor, Julie, *The Lion King: Pride Rock On Broadway*, Hyperion (USA), 1998.

Lipscomb, Mance

Lipscomb, Mance with Alyn, Glen, *I Say Me For A Parable: The Oral Autobiography*, Da Capo Press (USA), 1995.

Little Richard

White, Charles, *The Life And Times Of Little Richard: The Quasar Of Rock*, Marmony Books (USA), 1984.

Lloyd Webber, Andrew

Mantle, J., *Fanfare: The Unauthorized Biography Of Andrew Lloyd Webber*.

McKnight, G., *Andrew Lloyd Webber*.

Walsh, M., *Andrew Lloyd Webber: His Life And Works*.

Lockran, Gerry

Lockran, Gerry, *Smiles And Tears*, 1983.

Lomax, Alan And John A.

Lomax, Alan, *The Land Where The Blues Began*, Methuen (UK), 1993.

Lomax, Alan, *The Penguin Book Of American Folk Songs*, Penguin Books (USA), 1964.

Porterfield, Nolan, *Cavalier: The Life And Times Of John A. Lomax 1867-1948*, University Of Illinois Press (USA), 1996.

Lombardo, Guy

Lombardo, Guy, *Auld Acquaintance: An Autobiography*, New York, 1975.

Lopez, Vincent

Lopez, V., *Lopez Speaking*, New York, 1975.

Lord, Bobby

Lord, Bobby, *Hit The Glory Road!*, Broadman Press, 1969.

Love
Brooks, Ken, *Arthur Lee: Love Story*, Agenda (UK), 1997.

Lunch, Lydia
Lunch, Lydia, *Incriminating Evidence (Last Gasp)*, Last Gasp, 1993.

Lynn, Loretta
Krishef, Robert K., *The Story Of Loretta Lynn*, Lerner, 1978.
Lynn, Loretta with Vecsey, Goerge, *Coal Miner's Daughter*, Contemporary Books (USA), 1985.
Zwisohn, Laurence J., *Loretta Lynn's World Of Music: Including An Annotated Discography*, John Edwards Memorial Foundation, 1980.

Lynn, Vera
Cross R., *We'll Meet Again*, London, 1989.
Lynn, Vera, *Vocal Refrain*, W.H. Allen (UK), 1975.

Lynott, Phil
Lynott, Phil, *Songs For While I'm Away*, Boxtree (UK), 1997.
Lynott, Philomena, *My Boy: The Philip Lynott Story*, Virgin Books (UK), 1996.
Putterford, Mark, *Philip Lynott: The Rocker*, Castle Communications (UK), 1994.

Lyttelton, Humphrey
Lyttelton, Humphrey, *Second Chorus*, London.
Lyttelton, Humphrey, *I Play As I Please*, Pan Books (UK), 1958.
Lyttelton, Humphrey, *Take It From The Top*, Robson Books (UK), 1975.
Lyttelton, Humphrey, *The Best Of Jazz, i: Basin Street To Harlem*, London, 1978.
Purser, Julian, *Humph*, Collectors Items, 1985.

Mabsant
Not listed, *Sosban Fach - CaneuonTafarn: Welsh Pub Songs*, Lolfa, 1987.
Not listed, *Caneuon Mabsant - Caneuon Gwerin: Welsh Folk Songs*, Lolfa, 1982.

MacColl, Ewan
MacColl, Ewan & Seeger, Peggy, *Traveller's Songs From England And Scotland*, Routledge & Kegan Paul (UK), 1977.

MacDonald, Jeanette
J.P. Parish, *The Jeanette Macdonald Story*.
Knowles, E., *The Films Of Jeanette MacDonald And Nelson Eddy*.

Macon, Uncle Dave
Rinzler, Ralph & Norman Cohen, *Uncle Dave Macon: A Bio Discography*, John Edwards Memorial Foundation (USA), 1970.

Maddox, Rose
Whiteside, Johnny, *The Life And Career Of Rose Maddox*, Vanderbilt University Press (USA), 1995.

Madness
Marshall, George, *Total Madness*, S T Publishing (UK), 1993.
Williams, Mark, *A Brief Case Of Madness*, Proteus Books (UK), 1982.

Madonna
Anderson, Christopher, *Madonna Unauthorized*, Michael Joseph (UK), 1992.
Cahill, Marie, *Madonna*, Omnibus Press (UK), 1991.

Lloyd, Fran, *Deconstructing Madonna*, Batsford Cultural Studies, 1994.
Madonna, *Sex*, Secker & Warburg (UK), 1992.
Matthew-Walker, Robert, *Madonna: The Biography*, Pan Books (UK), 1991.
McKenzie, Michael, *Madonna: Her Story*, Bobcat (USA), 1988.
No author listed, *Live!*, Omnibus Press (UK), 1994.
O'Brien, Glenn, *Madonna: The Girlie Show*, Prion, 1994.
Randall, Lee, *The Madonna Scrapbook*, Omnibus Press (UK), 1994.
Rosenzweig, Ilene, *The I Hate Madonna Handbook*, Virgin Books (UK), 1994.
St Michael, Mick, *Madonna: In Her Own Words*, Omnibus Press (UK), 1990.
Thompson, Douglas, *Like A Virgin: Madonna Revealed*, Sidgwick & Jackson (UK), 1992.
Turner, Kay (compiler), *I Dream Of Madonna: Women's Dreams Of The Goddess Of Pop*, Thames & Hudson (UK), 1993.
Voller, Debbi, *Madonna: The New Illustrated Biography*, Omnibus Press (UK), 1990.
Voller, Debbi, *Madonna: The Style Book*, Omnibus Press (UK), 1992.

Magny, Colette
Adureau, Sylvie, *Colette Magny, Citoyenne-Blues*.

Mairants, Ivor
Mairants, Ivor, *Great Jazz Guitarists*, Music Maker Books (UK), 1994.
Mairants, Ivor, *My Fifty Fretting Years*, 1980.

Makeba, Miriam
Makeba, Miriam with Hall, James, *Makeba: My Story*, Bloomsbury (UK), 1988.

Mamas And The Papas
Phillips, John, *Papa John*, Doubleday (USA), 1986.
Phillips, Michelle, *California Dreamin'*, Warner (USA), 1986.

Man
Leonard, Deke, *Rhinos Winos & Lunatics: The Legend Of Man*, Northdown Publishing (UK), 1996.
Mylock, Martin, *Mannerisms II*, M. Mylock (UK), 1995.
Mylock, Martin, *Mannerisms*, M. Mylock (UK), 1992.

Mancini, Henry
Mancini, Henry, *Henry Mancini (Interviewed by Marian McPartland)*.
Mancini, Henry & Lees, Gene, *Did They Mention The Music?*, Contemporary Books (USA), 1989.

Mandrell, Barbara
Conn, Charles Paul, *The Barbara Mandrell Story*, Putnam (USA).
Mandrell Barbara with Vecsey, George, *Get To The Heart: My Story*, Bantam Books (USA), 1990.

Manfred Mann
Russo, Greg, *Mannerisms: The Five Phases Of Manfred Mann*, Crossfire Publications (USA), 1996.

Manic Street Preachers
Clarke, Martin, *Manic Street Preachers, Sweet Venom*, Plexus (UK), 1998.
Shutkever, Paula, *Design For Living*, Virgin Publishing (UK), 1996.

Manilow, Barry

Clarke, Alan, *The Magic Of Barry Manilow*, Prize Books/Proteus Books (UK), 1981.

Elson, Howard, *Barry Manilow*, Proteus Books (UK), 1981.

Jasper, Tony, *Barry Manilow*, W.H. Allen (UK), 1982.

Manilow, Barry with Bego, Mark, *Barry Manilow: An Autobiography*, Grosset & Dunlap (USA), 1979.

Morse, Ann, *Barry Manilow*, Creative Education, 1978.

Peters, Richard, *The Barry Manilow Scrapbook: His Magical World In Works And Pictures*, Souvenir Press (UK), 1982.

Weir, Simon, *Barry Manilow For The Record*, Stafford Pemberton (UK), 1982.

Mansun

Middles, Mick, *Tax-Loss Lovers From Chester*, Chameleon (UK), 1998.

Manzanera, Phil

Rogan, Johnny, *Roxy Music: Style With Substance - Roxy's First Ten Years*.

Marillion

Clerk, Carol, *Marillion*, Omnibus Press (UK), 1986.

Gifford, Clive, *Marillion: The Script*, Omnibus Press (UK), 1987.

Wall, Mick, *The Authorized Story Of Marillion*, Sidgwick & Jackson (UK), 1987.

Marilyn Manson

Marilyn Manson with Strauss, Neil, *The Long Hard Road Out Of Hell*, Plexus (UK) Harper Collins (USA), 1997.

Reighley, Kurt B., *Marilyn Manson - A Biography*, Omnibus Press (UK), 1998.

Marley, Bob, And The Wailers

Booker, Cedella with Winkler, Anthony, *Bob Marley: An Intimate Portrait By His Mother*, Penguin (UK), 1997.

Boot, Adrian & Goldman, Vivien, *Bob Marley: Soul Rebel: Natural Mystic*, Eel Pie/Hutchinson (UK), 1981.

Dalrymple, Henderson, *Bob Marley: Music, Myth & The Rastas*, Carib-Arawak, 1976.

David, Stephen, *Bob Marley*, Granada Books (UK), 1984.

Davis, Stephen, *Bob Marley: The Biography*, Arthur Barker (UK), 1983.

Davis, Stephen, *Bob Marley: Conquering Lion Of Reggae*, Plexus (UK), 1993.

Lazell, Barry, *The Illustrated Legend 1945-1981*, Hamlyn (UK), 1994.

McCann, Ian, *The Complete Guide To The Music Of...*, Omnibus Press (UK), 1994.

McCann, Ian, *Bob Marley In His Own Words*, Omnibus Press (UK), 1993.

McKnight, Cathy & Tobler, John, *Bob Marley: The Roots Of Reggae*, Star/W.H. Allen (UK), 1977.

Talamon, Bruce W., *Sprit Dancer*, W.W. Norton & Co. (USA), 1994.

Taylor, Don, *So Much Things To Say: My Life As Bob Marley's Manager*, Blake (UK), 1994.

White, Timothy, *Catch A Fire: The Life Of Bob Marley*, Elm Tree Books (UK), 1983.

Whitney, Malika Lee, *Bob Marley: Reggae King Of The World*, Plexus (UK), 1984.

Marsalis, Wynton

Marsalis, Wynton & Stewart, Frank, *Sweet Swing Blues On The Road*, W. Norton (USA), 1994.

Marsden, Gerry

Marsden, Gerry with Coleman, Ray, *You'll Never Walk Alone:* *An Autobiography*, Bloomsbury (UK), 1992.

Martin, Dean

Marx, Arthur, *Everybody Loves Somebody*, 1975.

Tosches, Nick, *Dino: Living High In The Dirty Business Of Dreams*, Secker & Warburg (UK), 1992.

Martin, George

Martin, George, *Summer Of Love: The Making Of Sgt Pepper*, Macmillan (UK), 1994.

Martin, George, *All You Need Is Ears*, Macmillan (UK), 1979.

Martin, Mary

Martin, Mary, *My Heart Belongs To You*, New York, 1976.

Newman, S.P., *Mary Martin On Stage*, Philadelphia, 1969.

Martin, Tony

Martin, Tony & Charisse, Cyd, *The Two Of Us. Mason & Charter*, New York, 1976.

Maschwitz, Eric

Maschwitz, Eric, *No Chip On My Shoulder*, London, 1957.

Mathis, Johnny

Jasper, Tony, *Johnny: The Authorized Biography Of Johnny Mathis*, Comet (UK), 1984.

Matlock, Glen

Matlock, Glen with Silverton, Peter, *I Was A Teenage Sex Pistol*, Virgin Books (UK), 1996.

Matthews, Jessie

Matthews, Jessie, *Over My Shoulder: An Autobiography*, W.H. Allen (UK), 1974.

Thornton, Michael, *Jessie Matthews: A Biography*, Hart Davies (UK), 1974.

Mattoya, Yumi

Haruka Fukami, *Yuminno Toiki (Sighs Of Yumin)*, Tokyo, 1989.

Mattoya, Yumi, *Rouge-no Dengon (Message In Rouge)*, Tokyo, 1983.

May, Brian (UK)

Jackson, Laura, *Queen & I: The Brian May Story*, Smith Gryphon (UK), 1994.

Mayall, John

Newman, Richard, *John Mayall: Blues Breaker*, Castle Books (UK), 1995.

McCartney, Paul

Benson, Ross, *Paul McCartney: Behind The Myth*, Victor Gollancz (UK), 1993.

Coleman, Ray, *McCartney: Yesterday & Today*, Boxtree (UK), 1995.

Flippo, Chet, *McCartney: The Biography*, Sidgwick & Jackson (UK), 1988.

Gambaccini, Paul, *Paul McCartney In His Own Words*, Omnibus Press (UK), 1976.

Gelly, David, *The Facts About A Pop Group: Featuring Wings*, Andre Deutsch (UK), Whizzard & Harmony (USA), 1976.

Giuliano, Geoffrey, *Blackbird. The Life And Times Of Paul McCartney*, Dutton (USA), 1991.

Giuliano, Geoffrey, *Blackbird: The Unauthorized Biography of Paul McCartney*, Smith Gryphon (UK), 1992.

Grove, Martin A., *Paul McCartney: Beatle With Wings*, Manor, 1978.

Jasper, Tony, *Paul McCartney & Wings*, Octopus Books (UK),

1977.
McCartney, Linda, *Roadworks*, Little Brown (UK), 1996.
McCartney, Paul, *Paul McCartney: Composer/Artist*, Michael Joseph (UK), 1981.
Mendelsohn, John, *Paul McCartney: A Biography In Words & Pictures*, Sire/Chapell Music (USA), 1977.
Miles, Barry, *Paul McCartney: Many Years From Now* , Secker & Warburg (UK), 1997.
No author listed, *Hands Across The Water: Wings Tour USA*, Paper Tiger (UK), 1978.
Ocean, Humphrey, *The Ocean View: Paintings And Drawings Of Wings American Tour April To June 1976*, MPL Communications (UK), 1982.
Salewicz, Chris, *McCartney*, Futura (UK), 1987.
Schwartz, Francie, *Body Count*, Straight Arrow (USA), 1972.
Tremlett, George, *The Paul McCartney Story*, Futura (UK), 1975.
Welch, Chris, *Paul McCartney: The Definitive Biography*, Proteus Books (UK), 1984.

McCurdy, Ed
McCurdy, Ed, *Ed McCurdy's Song Book Of Wit And Mirth*, Hargall Music Press (USA), 1963.

McCutcheon, John
McCutcheon, John, *Water From Another Time*.

McDevitt, Chas
McDevitt, Chas, *Skiffle: The Definitive Inside Story*, Robson Books (UK), 1998.

McEntire, Reba
Cusic, Don, *Reba: Country Music's Queen*, St Martins Press (USA), 1991.
McEntire, Reba with Tom Carter, *Reba - My Story*, Bantam (USA), 1994.

McKechnie, Donna
Mandelbaum, Ken, *A Chorus Line And The Musicals Of Michael Bennett*.

McKinney's Cotton Pickers
Chilton, John, *McKinney's Music: A Bio-Discography Of McKinney's Cotton Pickers*, London, 1978.

McKuen, Rod
McKuen, Rod, *Alone*, Star Books (UK), 1976.
McKuen, Rod, *Beyond The Boardwalk*, Elm Tree Books (UK), 1980.
McKuen, Rod, *Caught In The Quiet*, W.H. Allen (UK), 1973.
McKuen, Rod, *Come To Me In Silence*, W.H. Allen (UK), 1974.
McKuen, Rod, *Coming Close To Earth*, Elm Tree Books (UK), 1977.
McKuen, Rod, *Fields Of Wonder*, W.H. Allen (UK), 1972.
McKuen, Rod, *Finding My Father: One Man's Search For Identity*, Elm Tree Books (UK), 1977.
McKuen, Rod, *In Someone's Shadow*, Michael Joseph (UK), 1971.
McKuen, Rod, *Listen To The Warm*, Michael Joseph (UK), 1968.
McKuen, Rod, *Lonesome Cities*, Michael Joseph (UK), 1971.
McKuen, Rod, *Moment To Moment*, W.H. Allen (UK), 1973.
McKuen, Rod, *Seasons In The Sun*, Star Books (UK), 1974.
McKuen, Rod, *Stanyan Street And Other Sorrows*, Michael Joseph (UK), 1968.
McKuen, Rod, *The Sea Around Me: The Hills Above*, Elm Tree Books (UK), 1976.
McKuen, Rod, *Twelve Years Of Christmas*, W.H. Allen (UK), 1972.
McKuen, Rod, *We Touch The Sky*, Elm Tree Books (UK), 1979.

McLaren, Malcolm
Bromsberg, Craig, *The Wicked, Wicked Ways of Malcolm McLaren*, Omnibus Press (UK), 1991.

McLaughlin, John
McLaughlin, John, *John McLaughlin And The Mahavishnu Orchestra*, Warner Brothers (USA), 1976.

McNeely, Big Jay
Dawson, Jim, *Nervous Man Nervous*, Big Nickel Publications, 1994.

McPartland, Marian
McPartland, Marian, *All In Good Time*, Oxford University Press, 1987.

McRae, Carmen
McRae, Carmen, *Carmen McRae (Interviewed by Marian McPartland..*

McTell, Ralph
Hockenhull, Chris, *Streets Of London: The Official Biography Of Ralph McTell*, Northdown Publishing (UK), 1998.

Meat Loaf
Meat Loaf, *Bat Out Of Hell 2 - Back Into Hell*, International Music Publications, 1994.
Robertson, Sandy, *Meatloaf: Jim Steinman And The Phenomenology Of Excess*, Omnibus Press (UK), 1981.

Meek, Joe
Repsch, John, *The Legendary Joe Meek*, Woodford House (UK), 1990.

Mega City Four
Roach, Martin, *Mega City Four: Tall Stories And Creepy Crawlies*, Independent Music Press (UK), 1994.

Mekons
No author listed, *Mekons United*, Ellipsis (USA), 1996.

Mellencamp, John
Torgoff, *American Fool: The Roots And Improbable Rise Of John Cougar Mellencamp*, St Martins Press (USA), 1986.

Melly, George
Melly, George, *Mellymobile, 1970-1981*, Robson Books (UK), 1982.
Melly, George, *Owning-Up*, Penguin, 1970.
Melly, George, *Revolt Into Style*, Oxford University Press, 1990.
Melly, George, *Rum, Bum & Concertina*, Weidenfeld & Nicholson (UK), 1977.
Melly, George, *Scouse Mouse*, Futura (UK), 1985.

Melody Maker
Hayes, Chris, *Melody Maker Memories*, Lancastian Transport Publications, 1993.
Jones, Allan (compiler), *Meoldy Maker Classic Rock Interviews*, Mandarin (UK), 1994.

Memphis Minnie
Garon, Paul & Beth, *Woman With Guitar: Memphis Minnie's Blues*, Da Capo Press (USA), 1992.

Mercer, Johnny
Bach, B., *Our Huckleberry Friend: The Life, Times And Song*

Lyrics Of Johnny Mercer, New York.

Mercury, Freddie
Clarke, Ross, *A Kind Of Magic: A Tribute To Freddie Mercury*, Kingsfleet (UK), 1992.
Hutton, Jim with Tim Wapshott, *Mercury And Me*, Bloomsbury (UK), 1994.
Jackson, Laura, *Mercury: The King Of Queen*, Smith, Gryphon (UK), 1996.
Jones, Lesley Ann, *Freddie Mercury: The Definitive Biography*, Hodder & Stoughton (UK), 1997.
Sky, Rick, *The Show Must Go On: The Life Of Freddie Mercury*, Fontana (UK), 1992.

Merman, Ethel
Merman, Ethel & Eells, G., *Merman: An Autobiography*, New York , 1978.
Merman, Ethel & Martin, P., *Who Could Ask For Anything More*, Doubleday (USA), 1955.
Thomas, B., *I Got Rhythm: The Ethel Merman Story*, New York , 1985.

Merrick, David
Kissell, Howard, *The Abominable Showman*, Applause Books (USA), 1993.

Metallica
Crocker, Chris, *Metallica: The Frayed Ends Of Metal*, Boxtree (UK), 1995.
Doughton, K.J., *Metallica Unbound*, Warner Books (USA), 1993.
Fauci, Dino, *Metallica's Lars Ulrich: An Up-Close Look At The Playing Style Of . . .*, Cheery Lane Music Co. (USA), 1993.
Halfin, Ross, *From Silver To Black*, 2.13.61 (USA), 1996.
Putterford, Mark, *In Their Own Words*, Omnibus Press (UK).
Putterford, Mark, *Metallica Live!*, Omnibus Press (UK), 1994.
Putterford, Mark, *A Visual Documantary*, Omnibus Press (UK), 1992.
Wall, Mick & Dome, Malcolm, *The Making Of: Metallica's Metallica*, Collectors Guide Publishing (USA), 1996.

Michael, George
Dessau, Bruce, *George Michael: The Making Of A Super Star*, Sidgwick & Jackson (UK), 1991.
Goodall, Nigel, *In His Own Words*, Omnibus Press (UK), 1995.
Michael, George with Parsons, Tony, *Bare*, Penguin (UK), 1992.
Rogan, Johnny, *Wham! (Confidential) The Death Of A Supergroup*, Omnibus Press (UK), 1987.

Midler, Bette
Baker, Robb, *Bette Midler*, Popular Library/CBS Coronet, 1975.
Mair, George, *Bette: An Intimate Biography Of Bette Midler*, Birch Lane Press (USA), 1995.
Midler, Bette, *A View From A Broad*, Sphere (UK), 1980.

Midnight Oil
McMillan, Andrew, *Strict Rules*.

Miller, Glenn
Butcher, Geoffrey, *Next To A Letter From Home*, Sphere (UK), 1990.
Polic, Edward F., *Sustineo Alus/I Sustain The Wings*, Scarecrow Methchen (USA), 1989.
Simon, George Thomas, *Glen Miller & His Orchestra*, Thomas Crowell (USA), 1974.

Milsap, Ronnie
Milsap, Ronnie & Carter, Tom, *Almost Like A Song*, McGraw Hill (USA), 1990.

Mingus, Charles
Coleman, Janet, *Mingus/Mingus*, Creative Arts Book, 1989.
Mingus, Charles, *Beneath The Underdog*, Payback Press (USA), 1995.
Mingus, Charles, *Revelations*, Margun Music.
Priestley, Brian, *Mingus: A Critical Biography*, Quartet Books (UK), 1982.
Weber, Horst, *Charles Mingus, Sein Leben, Seine Musik, Seine Schallplatten*, Oreos, 1984.

Minnelli, Liza
Freedland, Michael, *Liza With A Z*, W. H. Allen (UK), 1988.
Leigh, Wendy, *Liza - Born A Star*.
Luft, Lorna, *Me And My Shadows: Living With The Legacy Of Judy Garland*, Sidgwick & Jackson (UK), 1998.
Parish, James Robert, *Liza: Her Cinderella Nightmare*, W. H. Allen (UK), 1975.
Spada, James, *Judy And Liza*.

Minogue, Kylie
Stone, Sasha, *Kylie Minogue: An Illustrated Biography*, Omnibus Press (UK), 1990.
Stone, Sasha, *The Superstar Next Door*, Omnibus Press (UK), 1990.

Mission
Roach, Martin, *The Mission - Names Are For Tombstons Baby*, Independent Music Press (UK), 1993.

Mitchell, Joni
Fleischer, Leonore, *Joni Mitchell*, Flash Books (USA), 1976.
Hinton, Brian, *Both Sides Now*, Sanctuary Publishing (UK), 1996.
Mitchell, Joni, *Complete Poems And Lyrics*, Chatto & Windus (UK), 1997.
Mitchell, Joni, *A Memoir*, Chatto & Windus (USA), 1997.

Momus
No author, *Lusts Of A Moron: The Lyrics Of Momus*, Black Spring Press, 1992.

Monk, Thelonious
Bijl, L. & Canté, F., *Monk On Records: A Discography Of Thelonious Monk*.
Gourse, Leslie, *Straight, No Chaser: The Life And Genius Of Thelonious Monk*, Schirmer Books (USA), 1997.
Monk, Thelonious, *Thelonious Monk*, Consolidated Music.
Monk, Thelonious, *Works, Instrumental*, Consolidated Music.

Monkees
Adler, Bill, *Love Letters To The Monkees*, Popular Library, 1967.
Baker, Glenn A., *Monkeemania*, Plexus (UK), 1987.
Bronson, Harold (ed.), *Hey Hey We're The Monkees*, Rhino (USA), 1997.
Dolenz, Mickey & Bego, Mark, *I'm A Believer-My Life Of Monkees, Music And Madness*, Hyperion (USA), 1994.
Finn, Ed & Bone, T., *The Monkees Scrapbook*, Last Gasp, 1987.
Lefcowitz, Eric, *The Monkees Tale*, Last Gasp, 1987.
No editor listed, *Meet the Monkees*, Daily Mirror (UK), 1967.
No editor listed, *The Monkees: A 'Mirabelle' Colour Photo Souvenir*, Newnes (UK), 1967.
Reilly, Ed, McMannus, Maggie & Chadwick, Bill, *The Monkees: A Manufactured Image*, Pierian Press, 1988.

Monroe, Bill
Rooney J., *Bossmen: Bill Monroe And Muddy Waters*, Dial Press (USA), 1971.
Rosenberg, Neil V., *Bill Monroe And His Blue Grass Boys*, Country Music Foundation Press (USA), 1974.

Monroe, Marilyn
Haspiel, James, *Young Marilyn: Becoming The Legend*, Smith Gryphon (UK), 1994.
Luijters, Guus, *In Her Own Words*, Omnibus Press (UK), 1993.
Spoto, Donald, *Marilyn Monroe: The Biography*, Chatto & Windus (UK), 1993.
Summers, Anthony, *Goddess: The Secret Lives Of Marilyn Monroe*, Macmillan (USA), Gollancz (UK), 1985.

Montgomery, Little Brother
Heide, Karl Gert Zur, *Deep South Piano, The Story Of Little Brother Montgomery*, Studio Vista (UK), 1970.

Montgomery, Wes
Ingram, Adrian, *Wes Montgomery*, Ashley Mark, 1985.

Moon, Keith
Butler, Dougal, *Full Moon:The Amazing Rock & Roll Life Of Keith Moon, Late Of The Who*, Quill Books (USA), 1982.
Fletcher, Tony, *Dear Boy: The Life Of Keith Moon*, Omnibus Press (UK), Avon Books (USA), 1998.

Moore, Dudley
Donovan, Paul, *Dudley*, W H Allen (UK), 1988.
Moore, Dudley, *Off Beat: Dudley Moore's Book Of Musical Anecdotes*, Robson Books (UK), 1992.
Paskin, Barbara, *Dudley Moore: The Authorized Biography*, Sidgwick & Jackson (UK), 1997.

Moore, Scotty
Moore, Scotty & Dickerson, James, *That's Alright Elvis*, Schirmer Books (USA), 1997.

Morgan, Helen
Maxwell, Gilbert, *Helen Morgan, Her Life And Legend*.

Morissette, Alanis
Coles, Stuart, *Alanis Morissette: Death Of Cinderella*, Plexus (UK), 1998.
Grills, Barry, *Ironic - Alanis Morissette: The True Story*, Quartet Books (UK), 1998.

Morrison, Van
Collis, John, *Van Morrison: Inarticulate Speech Of The Heart*, Little Brown (UK), 1996.
DeWitt, Howard A., *Van Morrison: The Mystic's Music*, Horizon Books, 1983.
Rogan, Johnny, *Van Morrison: The Great Deception*, Proteus Books (UK), 1982.
Turner, Steve, *Van Morrison: Too Late To Stop Now*, Bloomsbury (UK), 1993.
Yorke, Ritchie, *Van Morrison: Into The Music*, Charisma/Futura (UK), 1975.

Morrissey
Bret, David, *Landscapes Of The Mind*, Robson (UK), 1994.
Reid, Pat, *Bigmouth: Morrissey 1983-1993*, Dunce Directive, 1994.
Robertson, John, *Morrissey In His Own Words*, Omnibus Press (UK), 1989.
Rogan, Johnny, *Morrissey & Marr: The Severed Alliance*, Omnibus Press (UK), 1992.
Slee, Jo, *Peepholism: Into The Art Of Morrissey*, Sidgwick & Jackson (UK), 1994.
Sterling, Linder, *Morrissey Shot*, Secker & Warburg (UK), 1992.

Morton, Jelly Roll
Balliett, Whitney, *Jelly Roll, Jabbo, And Fats*, Oxford University Press, 1983.
Charters, Samuel B., *Jelly Roll Morton's Last Night At The Jungle Inn*, Marion Boyars (UK), 1989.
Kennedy, Rick, *Jelly Roll, Bix And Hoagy: Gennett Studios And The Birth Of Recorded Jazz*, Indiana University Press (USA), 1994.
Lomax, Alan, *Mister Jelly Roll*, Berkeley: University Of California Press (USA), 1950.
Williams, M., *Jelly Roll Morton*, London, 1962.

Mothers Of Invention
Slaven, Neil, *Electric Don Quixote: The Story Of Frank Zappa*, Omnibus Press (UK), 1996.

Motley Crue
Simmons, Sylvie, & Dome, Malcolm, *Lüde, Crüde And Rüde*, Castle Communications (UK), 1994.

Motörhead
Burridge, Alan, *Motörhead: Born To Lose, Live To Win*, Babylon Books (UK), 1980.
Dadomo, Giovanni, *Motörhead*, Omnibus Press (UK), 1981.

Mott The Hoople
Cato, Phil, *All The Way To Memphis*, S.T. Publishing (UK), 1997.

MTV
Malarkey, Sarah (ed), *MTV unplugged: First Edition*, MTV Books (USA), 1995.

Muddy Waters
Hofstein, Francis, *Muddy Waters Biographie*, Actes Sud (France), 1996.
Tooze, Sandra B., *Muddy Waters: Mojo Man*, ECW Press, 1998.
Wright, Phil & Rothwell, Fred, *The Complete Muddy Waters Discography*, Blues and Rhythm (UK), 1991.

Mulligan, Gerry
Horricks, Raymond, *Gerry Mulligan's Ark*, Apollo, 1986.
Klinkowitz, Jerome, *Listen: Gerry Mulligan: An Aural Narrative In Jazz*, Schirmer Books (USA), 1991.

Musical Youth
No editor listed, *Musical Youth: Their Own Story*, Omnibus Press (UK), 1983.

Nelson, Ozzie
Nelson, Ozzie, *Ozzie*, Prentice-Hall (USA), 1973.

Nelson, Ricky
Bashe, Philip, *Ricky Nelson: Teenage Idol, Travelin' Man*, Hyperion, New York, 1992.
Selvin, Joel, *Ricky Nelson: Idol For A Generation*, Contemporary Books (USA), 1990.
Stafford, John & Young, Iain, *The Ricky Nelson Story*, Finbarr International (UK), 1988.

Nelson, Willie
Bane, Michael, *Willie*, New York, 1984.
Fowler, Lana Nelson (ed), *Willie Nelson Family Album*, H. M. Poirot & Co, Amarillo (USA), 1980.

Jackson (UK), 1994.

Nelson, Susie, *Heartworn Memories: A Daughter's Personal Biography Of Willie Nelson* (USA), 1987.
Nelson, Willie & Shrake, Bud, *Willie: An Autobiography*, Simon & Schuster (USA), 1988.
Socbey, Lola, *Willie Nelson: Country Outlaw*, New York, 1982.

New Kids On The Block
Goldsmith, Lynn, *New Kids On The Block*, Rizzoli International (USA), 1990.
McGibbon, Robin, *New Kids on The Block : The Whole Story By Their Friends*, R. McGibbon, 1990.
No author listed, *They'll Be Lovin' You Forever*, Omnibus Press (UK), 1990.

New Order
Edge, Brian, *New Order & Joy Division: Pleasures and Wayward Distractions*, Omnibus Press (UK).
Flowers, Claude, *New Order & Joy Division: Dreams Never End*, Omnibus Press (UK), 1995.

New York Dolls
Morrisey, Steven, *New York Dolls*, Babylon Books (UK), 1981.

Newton-John, Olivia
Jacobs, Linda, *Olivia Newton-John: Sunshine Supergirl*, EMC, 1975.
Ruff, Peter, *Olivia Newton-John*, Quick Fox (USA), 1979.

Nichols, Herbie
Spellman, A.B., *Four Lives In The Bebop Business*.

Nico
Witts, Richard, *The Life And Lies Of An Icon*, Virgin Books (UK), 1993.
Young, James, *Songs They Never Play On The Radio: Nico, The Last Bohemian*, Bloomsbury (UK), 1992.

Nine Inch Nails
Huxley, Martin, *Nine Inch Nails*, St. Martin's Press, 1997.

Nirvana (USA)
Arnold, Gina, *Route 666: On The Road To Nirvana*, Picador (UK), 1993.
Azerrad, Michael, *Come As You Are*, Virgin Books (UK), 1993.
Black, Suzi, *Nirvana: An Illustrated Biography*, Omnibus Press (UK), 1994.
Black, Suzi, *Nirvana: Tribute*, Omnibus Press (UK), 1994.
Crisafulli, Chuck, *Teen Spirit: The Stories Behind Every Nirvana Song*, Omnibus Press (UK), 1996.
Morrell, Brad, *Nirvana And The Sound Of Seattle*, Omnibus Press (UK), 1993.
Sandford, Christopher, *Kurt Cobain*, Carroll & Graf (USA), Penguin (UK), 1995.
Thompson, Dave, *Never Fade Away*, Pan Books (UK), 1994.
Wilson, Susan, *Nirvana: Nevermind*, UFO Books (UK), 1996.

Nix, Don
Nix, Don, *Road Stories And Recipes*, Schirmer Books (USA), 1997.

Nolans
Treasurer, Kim, *In The Mood For Stardom: The Nolans*, Midas Books (UK), 1982.

Novello, Ivor
Rose, Richard, *Perchance To Dream: The World Of Ivor Novello*, Frewin, 1974.
Wilson, Sandy, *Ivor*, Thomas Yoseff, 1974.

Nugent, Ted
Holland, Robert, *The Legendary Ted Nugent*, Omnibus Press (UK), 1982.

Numan, Gary
Coleman, Ray, *Gary Numan: The Authorized Biography*, Sidgwick & Jackson (UK), 1982.
Numan, Gary with Malins, Steve, *Praying To The Aliens*, Andre Deutsch (UK), 1998.
Vermorel, Fred & Judy, *Gary Numan By Computer*, Omnibus Press (UK), 1980.

Nyman, Michael
Nyman, Michael, *Experimental Music: Cage And Beyond*.

O'Connor, Hazel
O'Connor, Hazel, *Hazel O'Connor: Uncovered Plus*, Proteus Books (UK), 1981.

O'Connor, Sinead
Guterman, Jimmy, *Sinead: Her Life And Music*, Penguin, 1991.
Hayes, Dermott, *Sinead O'Connor: So Different*, Omnibus Press (UK), 1991.

O'Day, Anita
O'Day, Anita with Eells, George, *High Times Hard Times*, New York, 1981.

Oasis
Abbot, Tim, *Oasis Definitely*, Pavillion Books (UK), 1996.
Gallagher, Paul & Christian, Terry, *Brothers: From Childhood To Oasis: The Real Story*, Virgin Books (UK), 1996.
Gilbert, Pat, *Oasis '96*, Track (UK), 1996.
Hewitt, Paolo, *Getting High - The Adventures Of Oasis*, Boxtree (UK), 1997.
Hutton, Chris & Kurt, Richard, *Don't Look Back In Anger: Growing Up With Oasis*, Simon & Schuster (UK), 1997.
Lester, Paul, *Oasis: The Illustrated Story*, Hamlyn (UK), 1995.
Masterson, Eugene, *The World On The Street: The Unsanctioned Story Of Oasis*, Mainstream (UK), 1996.
Mathur, Paul, *Oasis: The Story*, Bloomsbury (UK), 1997.
Middles, Mick, *Oasis: Round Their Way*, Independent Music Press (UK), 1996.
Robertson, Ian, *Oasis: What's The Story*, Blake Publishing (UK), 1996.
St. Michael, Mick, *Oasis*, Sound And Media (UK), 1996.
Wheeler, Jemma, *Oasis: How Does It Feel*, Vinyl Experience (UK), 1995.

Ochs, Phil
Eliot, Marc, *Phil Ochs: Death Of A Rebel*, Anchor Press (USA), 1979.
Schumacher, Michael, *There But For Fortune: The Life Of Phil Ochs*, Hyperion (USA), 1996.

Oldfield, Mike
Moraghan, Sean, *Mike Oldfield: A Man And His Music*, Britannia Press (UK), 1994.
Newman, Richard, *True Story Of The Making Of Tubular Bells*, Music Maker Books (UK), 1993.

Oldham, Andrew Loog
Oldham, A., Calder, T. & Irwin, C., *The Name Of The Game*, 1994.

Oliver, Joe 'King'
Albertson, Chris & Rust, Brian, *King Joe Oliver*, Walter C. Allen, 1955.
Williams, M, *King Oliver And Kings Of Jazz*, London and

Newark, 19601978.
Wright, Laurie, *King Oliver*, London, 1987.

Ono, Yoko
Haskell, Barbara & Hanhardt, John G., *Yoko Ono - Arias And Objects*, Peregrine Smith Books, 1993.
Hopkins, Jerry, *Yoko Ono: A Biography*, Sidgwick & Jackson (UK), 1987.
Ono, Yoko, *Grapefruit: A Book Of Instructions*, Peter Owen (UK), 1970.

Orbison, Roy
Amburn, Ellis, *Dark Star*, Lyle Stuart (USA), 1990.
Clayson, Alan, *Only The Lonely: The Roy Orbison Story*, Sidgwick & Jackson (UK), 1989.

Orchestral Manoeuvres In The Dark
West, Mike, *Orchestral Manoeuvres In The Dark*, Omnibus Press (UK), 1982.

Orlando, Tony
Morse, Ann, *Tony Orlando*, Creative Education, 1978.

Osbourne, Ozzy
Johnson, Garry, *Ozzy Osbourne*, Proteus Books (UK), 1985.
Wall, Mick, *Diary Of A Madman: The Uncensored Memoirs Of Rock's Greatest Rogue*, Zomba Books (UK), 1986.

Osmonds
Delaney, Monica, *The Osmonds*, Creative Education, 1976.
Dunn, Paul H., *The Osmonds: The Official Story Of The Osmond Family*, Star, 1977.
Eldred, Patricia Mulrooney, *Donny And Marie*, Creative Education, 1978.
Gregory, James, *At Last ... Donny!*, World Distributors.
Gregory, James, *Donny And The Osmonds Backstage*, World Distributors, 1973.
McMillan, Constance Van Brunt, *Donny And Marie Osmond: Breaking All The Rules*, EMC, 1977.
No author listed, *Osmonds' World: The Official Year Book Of The Osmonds 1974-78*, IPC Magazines (UK).
No author listed, *The Fantastic Osmonds!*, Mirror Books (UK), 1972.
Robinson, Richard, *The Osmond Brothers And The New Pop Scene*, Pyramid, 1972.
Roeder, Lynn, *On Tour With Donny & Marie And The Osmonds*, Tempo Books, 1977.
Tremlett, George, *The Osmond Story*, Futura (UK), 1974.

Otis, Johnny
Otis, Johnny, *Upside Your Head! Rhythm And Blues On Central Avenue*, Wesleyan University Press (USA), 1995.

Otway, John
Otway, John, *Cor Baby,That's Really Me!*, Omnibus Press (UK), 1990.

Page, Jimmy
T'Vell, Adrian, *Mangled Mind Archive: Jimmy Page* A. T'Vell, (UK), 1995.

Paley, Ben
Paley, Ben, *The Swedish Fiddle Book*, 1994.

Parker, Charlie 'Bird'
Giddins, Gary, *Celebrating Bird: The Triumph Of Charlie Parker*, Hodder & Stoughton (UK), 1987.
Harrison, M., *Charlie Parker*, London, 1960.
Isacoff, Stuart, *Charlie Parker*, Amsco, 1984.

Jepsen, Jorgen Grunnet, *Discography Of Charlie Parker*, Debut Records.
Koch, Lawrence O., *Yardbird Suite*, Bowling Green State University Popular Press (USA).
Miller, Mark, *Cool Blues*, Nightwood Editions.
Parker, C. & Paudras, F., *To Bird With Love*, Poitiers, 1981.
Parker, Charles Christopher, *Charlie Parker Omnibook*, Joe Goldfeder Music.
Priestley, Brian, *Charlie Parker*, Tunbridge Wells (UK), 1984.
Reisner, R, *Bird: The Legend Of Charlie Parker*, New York, 1961.
Russell, Ross, *Bird Lives!*, Quartet Books (UK), 1976.
Russell, Ross, *Bird Lives: The High Life And Hard Times Of Charlie (Yardbird) Parker*, New York, 1973.
Watts, Charlie, *From One Charlie to Another*, UFO Jazz (UK), 1991.

Parsons, Gram
Fong-Torres, Ben, *Hickory Wind: The Life And Times Of Gram Parsons*, Pocket Books (USA), 1991.
Griffin, Sid (ed.), *Gram Parsons*, Sierra Records & Books (USA), 1990.

Parton, Dolly
Berman, Connie, *The Official Dolly Parton Scrapbook*, Grosset & Dunlap (USA), 1978.
Fleischer, Leonore, *Dolly, Here I Come Again*, Zebra Books(USA), 1988.
James, Otis, *Dolly Parton*, Quick Fox (USA), 1978.
Keely, Scott, *Dolly Parton (By Scott Keely)*, Creative Education, 1979.
Krishef, Robert K., *Dolly Parton*, Lerner, 1980.
Nash, Alanna, *Dolly*, Addison House (USA), 1979.
Parton, Dolly, *My Story*, Harper Collins (USA), 1994.
Saunders, Susan, *Dolly Parton: Country Goin' To Town*, Puffin Books.

Pastorius, Jaco
Milkowski, Bill, *Jaco: The Extraordinary And Tragic Life Of Jaco Pastorius*, Miller Freeman (USA), 1995.

Patton, Charley
Calt, Steven & Wardlow, Gayle, *King Of The Delta Blues*, Rock Chapel Press, 1988.
Fahey, John, *Charley Patton*, Studio Vista (UK), 1970.
International Symposium, *Voice Of The Delta*, Liege University (Belgium), 1987.

Paul, Les
Bacon, Tony & Day, Paul, *Gibson Les Paul Book: A Complete History Of Les Paul Guitars*, Balafon (UK), 1993.
Shaughnessy, Mary Alice, *Les Paul: An American Original*, W, Morrow (USA), 1993.

Paxton, Tom
Paxton, Tom & Rayevsky, Robert, *Belling The Cat And Other Aesop's Fables*, New York, 1990.
Paxton, Tom & Kellogg, Stephen, *Englebert The Elephant*, New York, 1990.

Payne, Jack
Payne, Jack, *Signature Tune*.
Payne, Jack, *This Is Jack Payne*.

Pearl Jam
Clarke, Martin, *Pearl Jam & Eddie Vedder: None Too Fragile*, Plexus, 1998.
Jones, Allan, *The Illustrated Story*, Hamlyn (UK), 1994.
Lorenzo, Joey (compiler), *Pearl Jam Live!*, Omnibus Press

(UK), 1994.

Morrell, Brad, *Pearl Jam: The Illustrated Biography*, Omnibus Press (UK), 1993.

Pepper, Art
Pepper, Art & Laurie, *Straight Life*, Da Capo (USA), 1979.

Perrett, Peter
Antonia, Nina, *The One And Only: Peter Perrett - Homme Fatale*, SAF, 1996.

Pet Shop Boys
Crowton, Michael, *Pet Shop Boys: Introspective*, Sidgwick & Jackson (UK), 1990.
Heath, Chris, *Pet Shop Boys, Literally*, Viking (UK), 1990.
Heath, Chris & Smith, Pennie, *Pet Shop Boys Versus America*, Viking (UK), 1993.

Peterson, Oscar
Lees, Gene, *Oscar Peterson: The Will To Swing*, Lester & Orpen Dennys, 1988.
Peterson, Oscar, *Oscar Peterson Highlights Jazz Piano*, Hansen House, 1980.

Phish
Budnick, Dean, *The Phishing Manual: A Compendium To The Music Of Phish*, Hyperion (USA), 1996.
Thompson, Dave, *Go Phish*, St. Martin's Griffin (USA), 1998.

Piaf, Edith
Berteaut, Simone, *Piaf*, Penguin, 1990.
Bret, David, *The Piaf Legend*, Robson Books (UK), 1989.
Crosland, Margaret, *Piaf*, Hodder (UK), 1990.
Lange, Monique, *Piaf*, W.H. Allen (UK), 1982.
Piaf, Edith, *The Wheel Of Fortune: The Autobiography Of Edith Piaf*, Mayflower (UK), 1968.
Piaf, Edith & Noli, Jean, *Edith Piaf: My Life*, Penguin (UK), 1992.

Piano
Lieberman, Richard K., *Steinway & Sons*, Yale University Press (USA), 1995.

Pink Floyd
Dallas, Karl, *Pink Floyd: Bricks In The Wall*, Baton Press (UK), 1984.
Hassall, Bob, *Pink Floyd Back-Stage*, Brain Damage (UK), 1992.
Jones, Cliff, *Echoes: The Stories Behind Every Pink Floyd Song*, Omnibus Press (UK), 1996.
Jones, Malcolm, *Syd Barrett: The Making Of The Madcap Laughs*, Malcolm Jones (UK), 1983.
Leduc, Jean Marie, *Pink Floyd*, A. Michel, 1977.
Mabbett, Andy, *Complete Guide To The Music Of*, Omnibus Press (UK), 1995.
MacDonald, Bruno (ed) , *Pink Floyd Through The Eyes Of ... The Band, Its Fans, Friends And Foes*, Sidgwick & Jackson (UK), 1996.
Miles, *Pink Floyd: Another Brick*, Omnibus Press (UK), 1984.
Miles, *Pink Floyd: The Illustrated Discography*, Omnibus Press (UK), 1981.
Miles & Mabbett, Andy, *Pink Floyd: A Visual Documentary*, Omnibus Press (UK), Putnam (USA), 1988.
Palacios, Julian, *Lost In The Woods: Syd Barrett And The Pink Floyd*, Boxtree (UK), 1998.
Povey, Glenn & Russell, Ian, *Pink Floyd: In The Flesh (The Complete Performance History)*, Bloomsbury (UK), 1998.
Ruhlmann, W., *Pink Floyd*, Magna Books (UK), 1993.
Sanders, Rick, *The Pink Floyd*, Futura (UK), 1976.

Schaffner, Nicholas, *Saucerful Of Secrets: The Pink Floyd Odyssey*, Sidgwick & Jackson (UK), 1991.
Thorgerson, Storm, *Mind Over Matter: The Images Of Pink Floyd*, Sanctuary (UK), 1997.
Waters, Roger, *Pink Floyd Lyric Book*, Blandford Press (UK), 1982.
Waters, Roger & Appleby, David, *The Wall*, Avon (USA), 1982.

Pirate Radio
Elliot, Chris, *The Wonderful Radio London Story*, East Anglia Productions (UK), 1997.
Skues, Keith, *Pop Went The Pirates*, Lambs' Meadow Publications (UK), 1994.

Plant, Robert
Gross, Michael, *Robert Plant*, Popular Library, 1975.
Randolph, Mike, *Led Zeppelin's Robert Plant Through The Mirror*, Tracks Publications (Lancashire UK), 1994.

Pogues
McGowan, Hewitt & Pike, *Poguetry: The Illustrated Pogues Songbook*, Faber & Faber (UK), 1990.
Scanlon, Ann, *The Pogues: The Lost Decade*, Omnibus Press (UK).

Point Of Grace
Point Of Grace, *Life, Love & Other Mysteries*, Pocket Books (USA), 1996.

Police
Goldsmith, Lynn, *The Police*, Vermilion (UK), 1983.
Miles, *The Police: A Visual Documentary*, Omnibus Press (UK), 1981.
No editor listed, *The Police Released*, Big O (UK), 1980.
Sutcliffe, Phil & Fielder, Hugh, *The Police: L'Historia Bandido*, Proteus Books (UK), 1981.
Weir, Simon, *Police Annual 1980*, Stafford Pemberton (UK), 1981.
Weir, Simon, *Police Annual 1982*, Stafford Pemberton (UK), 1981.
Welch, Chris, *Complete Guide To the Music Of: The Police And Sting*, Omnibus Press (UK), 1996.
Woolf, Rossetta, *Message In A Bottle*, Virgin Books (UK), 1981.

Ponty, Jean-Luc
Ponty, Jean-Luc, *The Musical Styles Of Jean-Luc Ponty*, Warner Brothers (USA).

Poole, Brian, And The Tremeloes
Poole, Brian, *Talkback: An Easy Guide To British Slang*, Avon Books (USA), 1996.

Poole, Charlie
Rorrer, Clifford, *Charlie Poole And The North Carolina Ramblers*, Privately published (USA), 1992.

Porno For Pyros
Thompson, Dave, *Perry Farrell: Saga Of A Hypster*, St Martins Press (USA), 1996.

Porter, Cole
Eels, George, *The Life That Late He Led: A Biography Of Cole Porter*, Putman (USA), 1967.
Gill, Brendan, *Cole*, Michael Joseph (UK), 1976.
Kimball, Robert (ed.), *Complete Lyrics Of Cole Porter*, Da Capo (USA).
No author listed, *Best Of Cole Porter*, Hal Leonard Publishing (USA), 1992.

Schwarz, Cole, *Cole Porter*, W.H. Allen (UK), 1978.

Powell, Bud
Groves, Alan with Shipton, Alyn, *The Glass Enclosure: The Life Of Bud Powell*, Bayou (USA), 1993.
Safane, Clifford Jay (ed.), *Bud Powell*, Consolidated Music.

Prefab Sprout
Birch, John, *Myths, Melodies & Metaphysics, Paddy McAloon's Prefab Sprout*, J. Birch (UK), 1994.

Presley, Elvis
Adler, Bill, *Bill Adler's Love Letters To Elvis*, Grosset & Dunlap (USA), 1978.
Adler, David, *The Life And Cuisine Of Elvis Presley*, Crown (USA), Smith Gryphon (UK), 1993.
Adler, David & Andrews, Ernest, *Elvis, My Dad*, St Martins Press (USA), 1991.
Banney, Howard F., *Return To Sender*, Pierian Press, 1988.
Barker, Kent & Pritikin, Karin, *King And I: Little Gallery of Elvis Impersonators*, Chronicle Books (USA), 1992.
Barlow, Roy, *The Elvis Presley Encyclopedia*, Albert Hand (UK), 1964.
Barry, Ron, *All American Elvis*.
Barry, Ron, *The Elvis Presley American Discography*, Maxigraphics, 1976.
Bartel, Pauline, *Everything Elvis*, Taylor Publishing Co. (USA), 1995.
Black, Jim, *Elvis On The Road To Stardom: 1955-1956*, W.H. Allen (UK), 1988.
Bowman, Kathleen, *On Stage, Elvis Presley*, Creative Education, 1976.
Bowser, James W., *Starring Elvis*, Dell (USA), 1977.
Braun, Eric, *The Elvis Encyclopedia: An Impartial Guide To The Films Of Elvis*, Batsford (UK), 1997.
Brewer-Giorgio, Gail, *The Elvis Files*, Impala Books, 1991.
Buckle, Philip, *All Elvis: An Unofficial Biography Of The 'King Of Discs'*, Daily Mirror (UK), 1962.
Bushkin, Richard, *Elvis: Memories And Memorabilia*, Salamander (UK), 1995.
Canada, Lena, *To Elvis With Love*, Scholastic Book Service, 1979.
Carr, Roy & Farren, Mick, *Elvis: The Complete Illustrated Record*, Eel Pie (UK), 1982.
Chadwick, Vernon (ed.), *In Search Of Elvis: Music, Race, Art, Religion*, Westview Press, 1997.
Cocke, Marian J., *I Called Him Babe: Elvis Presley's Nurse Remembers*, New York.
Coffey, Frank, *The Complete Idiot's Guide To Elvis*, Simon & Schuster (USA), 1997.
Cortez, Diego, *Private Elvis*, Fey Verlag (Germany), 1978.
Cotten, Lee, *All Shook Up: Elvis Day-By-Day, 1954-1977*, Pierian Press, 1985.
Cotten, Lee & DeWitt, Howard A., *Jailhouse Rock: The Bootleg Records Of Elvis Presley 1970*, Pierian Press, 1983.
Covey, Maureen, *Elvis For The Record*, Stafford Pemberton (UK), 1982.
Cranor, Rosalind, *Elvis Collectables*, Schroeder (USA), 1983.
Crumbaker, Marge with Tucker, Gabe, *Up And Down With Elvis Presley*, New English Library (UK), 1982.
Curtin, Jim E., *Candids Of The King*, Bulfinch, 1993.
DeWitt, Howard A., *Elvis: The Sun Years*, Popular Culture Ink., 1993.
Dillon-Malone, Aubrey, *The Rise And Fall And Rise Of Elvis*, Leopold Publishing (Ireland), 1997.
Dowling, Paul, *The Ultimate Album Cover Book*, Abrams (USA), 1996.
Dundy, Elaine, *Elvis And Gladys*, Pimlico (UK), 1992.
Edwards, Michael, *Priscilla, Elvis & Me*, Century (UK), 1988.

Ersson, Roger & Svedberg, Lennart, *Aren Med Elvis*, Roger Ersson (Sweden), 1992.
Escott, Colin & Hawkins, Martin, *Twenty Years Of Elvis: The Session File*, Swift Record Distributors, 1977.
Farren, Mick, *The Hitchhiker's Guide To Elvis*, Collector's Guide Publishing (USA), 1995.
Farren, Mick, *In His Own Words*, Omnibus Press (UK), 1994.
Farren, Mick & Marchbank, Pearce, *Elvis In His Own Words*, Omnibus Press (UK), 1977.
Flippo, Chet, *Graceland: The Living Legend Of Elvis Presley*, Mitchell Beazley (UK), 1993.
Friedman, Favius, *Meet Elvis Presley*, Scholastic Books, 1971.
Gelfand, Craig, Blocker-Krantz, Lynn & Noguera, Rogerio, *In Search Of The King*, Perigee Books (USA), 1992.
Goldman, Albert, *Elvis*, McGraw-Hill (USA), 1981.
Goldman, Albert, *Elvis: The Last 24 Hours*, Pan Books (UK), 1991.
Gordon, Robert, *The King Of The Road*, Hamlyn (UK), 1996.
Greenfield, Marie, *Elvis: Legend Of Love*, Morgan-Pacific, 1981.
Greenwood, Earl & Tracy, Kathleen, *The Boy Who Would Be King. An Intimate Portrait Of Elvis Presley By His Cousin*, E.P. Dutton (USA), 1991.
Gregory, Nancy & Joseph, *When Elvis Died*, Communications Press, 1980.
Gripe, Maria, *Elvis And His Friends*, Delacourte (USA), 1976.
Gripe, Maria, *Elvis And His Secret*, Delacourte (USA), 1976.
Grove, Martin A., *Elvis: The Legend Lives! One Year Later*, Manor Books (USA), 1978.
Grove, Martin A., *The King Is Dead: Elvis Presley*.
Guralnick, Peter, *Last Train To Memphis: The Rise Of Elvis Presley*, Little, Brown (USA), 1994.
Haining, Peter (ed.), *The Elvis Presley Scrapbooks 1955-1965*, Robert Hale (UK), 1991.
Hamilton, Bruce & Liben, Michael L., *Love Of Elvis*, Platinum(USA), 1979.
Hand, Albert, *A Century Of Elvis*, Albert Hand (UK), 1959.
Hand, Albert, *Elvis Special*, World Distribution (UK), 1968.
Hand, Albert, *The Elvis Presley Pocket Handbook*, Albert Hand Heanor (UK), 1961.
Hand, Albert, *The Elvis They Dig*, Albert Hand (UK), 1959.
Hanna, David, *Elvis: Lonely Star At The Top*, Leisure/Nordon, New York, 1977.
Harbinson, W. A., *The Life And Death Of Elvis Presley*, Michael Joseph (UK), 1977.
Harbinson, W.A., *Elvis Presley: An Illustrated Biography*, Michael Joseph (UK), 1975.
Harms, Valerie, *Trying To Get To You: The Story Of Elvis Presley*, Atheneum, 1979.
Harper, Betty, *Elvis: Newly Discovered Drawings Of Elvis Presley*, Bantam Books (USA), 1979.
Harrison, Ted, *Elvis People: Cult Of The KIng*, Fount Publications (UK), 1992.
Hatcher, Holly, *Elvis Is That You?*, Great American Books (USA), 1979.
Hawkins, Martin & Escott, Colin, *Elvis Presley*, Omnibus Press (UK), 1987.
Hawkins, Martin & Escott, Colin, *The Illustrated Discography*, Omnibus Press (UK), 1981.
Hill, Wanda June, *We Remember Elvis*.
Holmes, Robert, *The Three Loves Of Elvis Presley: The True Story Of The Presley Legend*, Hulton Press (UK), 1959.
Holum, Torben, Jorgensen, Ernst & Rasmussen, Erik, *Recording Sessions 1954-1974*, Elvisett, Denmark, 1975.
Holzer, Hans, *Elvis Presley Speaks*, Manor Books, 1978.
Hopkins, Jerry, *Elvis*, Abacus Books (UK), 1974.
Hopkins, Jerry, *Elvis: A Biography*, Simon & Schuster (USA), 1971.
Hopkins, Jerry, *Elvis: The Final Years*, St. Martin's Press (USA), 1980.

Hutchins, Chris, & Thompson, Peter, *Elvis Meets The Beatles: The Untold Story Of Their Entangled Lives*, Smith Gryphon (UK), 1995.

James, Antony, *Presley: Entertainer Of The Century*, Tower Books, 1976.

James, Gregory, *The Elvis Presley Story*, May Fair Books, 1961.

Jones, Peter, *Elvis*, Octopus Books (UK), 1976.

Jope, Bob, *Elvis In Wonderland*, New Guild, 1995.

Jorgensen, E., *Reconsider Baby: Definitive Elvis Sessionography*, Pierian Press (USA), 1990.

Jorgensen, Ernst, Rasmussen, Erick & Mikkelsen, Johnny, *Elvis: Recording Sessions*, Jee (Denmark), 1977.

Juanıco, June, *Elvis: In The Twilight Of Memory*, Little Brown (UK), 1997.

King, Bernd & Plehn, Heinz, *Eine Illustrierte Dokumentation*, Melze (Germany), 1978.

Lacker, Marty; Lacker, Patsy & Smith, Leslie E., *Elvis; Portrait Of A Friend*, Warner Books (USA), 1979.

Leigh, Spencer, *Presley Nation*, Raven Books (UK), 1976.

Levy, Alan, *Operation Elvis*, Andre Deutsch (UK), 1960.

Lichter, Paul, *The Boy Who Dared To Rock: The Definitive Elvis*, Dolphin/Doubleday (USA), 1978.

Lloyd, Harold, *The Graceland Gates*, Modern Age Enterprises, 1978.

Long, Reverend, *God's Work Through Elvis.*

Mann, May, *Elvis And The Colonel*, Drake (USA), 1975.

Mansfield, Rex & Elisabeth, *Elvis The Soldier*, Collectors Service, 1984.

Marchbank, Pearce, *Elvis Aron Presley: 1935-1977-The Memorial Album*, Wise (USA), 1977.

Marcus, Greil, *Dead Elvis: A Chronicle Of A Cultural Obession*, Viking, 1992.

Marsh, Dave, *Elvis*, Rolling Stone Press (USA), 1982.

Marsh, Dave, *Elvis*, Omnibus Press (UK), 1993.

Matthew-Walker, Robert, *Elvis Presley: A Study In Music*, Midas (UK), 1979.

McLafferty, Gerry, *Elvis In Hollywood*, Robert Hale (UK), 1990.

Moore, Scotty & Dickerson, James, *That's Alright, Elvis*, Schirmer Books (USA), 1997.

Moreland, Bob & Van Gestel, Jan, *Elvis, The Cool King*, Atomium Books, 1991.

Nash, Alanna, *Elvis Aaron Presley: Revelations From The Memphis Mafia*, Harper Collins (USA), 1995.

Nash, Bruce M., *The Elvis Presley Quizbook*, New English Library (UK), 1978.

No author listed, *The King Forever*, Now Dig This (UK), 1992.

No author listed, *Elvis: A Tribute To His Life*, Omnibus Press (UK), 1990.

No author listed, *Elvis: A Tribute To The King Of Rock 'N' Roll*, IPC Magazines (UK), 1977.

No author listed, *The Amazing Elvis Presley*, Amalgamated Press (UK), 1958.

No author listed, *The Official FBI File On Elvis A. Presley*, MEM, 1978.

No editor listed, *Elvis Lives!*, Galaxy (UK), 1978.

No editor listed, *Elvis Presley 1935 -1977*, Bavie.

No editor listed, *Elvis Presley Picture Parade Album*, New Musical Express (UK), 1958.

No editor listed, *Elvis Presley Poster Book*, Crown (USA), 1977.

No editor listed, *Elvis Presley: Echoes Of The Past*, Blue Suede Shoes (Netherlands), 1978.

No editor listed, *Elvis Presley: Photoplay Tribute*, Cadrant Enterprises, 1977.

No editor listed, *Elvis Special 1962*, World International (UK), 1961.

No editor listed, *Elvis The Other Side: World Spirit Message From Edie*, Golden Rainbow Press, 1980.

No editor listed, *Elvis: The Man And His Music*, World International (UK), 1981.

Not listed, *I AM Elvis: A Guide To Elvis Impersonators*, American Graphic System, 1991.

Osborne, Jerry & Hamilton, Bruce, *Presleyana*, Follet Books (USA), 1980.

Panta, Ilona, *Elvis Presley: King Of Kings*, Exposition Press (USA), 1979.

Paris, James Robert, *The Elvis Presley Scrapbook 1935-1977*, Ballantine (USA), 1975.

Parker, John, *Elvis: Murdered By The Mob*, Arrow Books (UK), 1994.

Parker, John, *Elvis: The Secret Files*, Anaya, 1993.

Pearlman, Jill, *Elvis For Beginners*, Writers & Readers, 1991.

Peters, Richard, *Elvis: The Music Lives On- The Recording Sessions 1954-1976*, Souvenir Press (UK), 1992.

Presley, Dee, Stanley, Billy, Rick & David, *Elvis: We Love You Tender*, Delacorte Press (USA), 1980.

Presley, Elvis, *His Complete Life Story In Words And Illustrated With More Than One Hundred Pict*, London Illustrated, 1956.

Presley, Vester, *A Presley Speaks*, Wimmer Brothers, 1978.

Quain, Kevin (ed), *The Elvis Reader: Texts And Sources On The King Of Rock 'n' Roll*, St Martins Press (USA), 1992.

Reggero, John, *Elvis In Concert*, Delta Special/Lorelei (USA), 1979.

Rijff, Ger J., *Long Lonely Highway: 1950's Elvis Scrapbook*, Pierian Press (USA), 1990.

Robertson, John, *The Complete Guide To The Music Of...*, Omnibus Press (UK), 1994.

Robinson, Tommy, *Elvis Bootlegs Buyer's Guide, Pts 1& 2*, Tommy Robinson (UK), 1992.

Rosenbaum, Helen, *The Elvis Presley Trivia Quiz Book*, Signet (USA), 1978.

Schroer, Andreas, *Elvis In Germany: The Missing Years*, Boxtree (UK), 1993.

Silverton, Peter, *Essential Elvis*, Chameleon, 1997.

Slaughter, Todd, *Elvis Presley*, Star/W.H.Allen (UK), 1977.

Slaughter, Todd, *Elvis Special 1982*, Albert Hand (UK), 1982.

Smith, Gene, *Elvis's Man Friday*, Light Of Day (USA), 1995.

Stanley, Bill with Erikson, George, *Elvis: My Brother*, Robert Hale (UK), 1989.

Stanley, David A. & Bego, Mark, *Raised On Rock: Growing Up At Graceland*, Mainstream (UK), 1997.

Stanley, David E., *The Elvis Encyclopaedia*, Virgin Books (UK), 1995.

Staten, Vince, *The Real Elvis: A Good Old Boy*, Media Ventures, 1978.

Stearn, Jess, *The Truth About Elvis*, Jove Books (USA), 1980.

Strausbaugh, John E., *E: Reflections On The Birth Of The Elvis Faith*, Blast Books (USA), 1995.

Tatham, Dick, *Elvis: Tribute To The King Of Rock*, Phoebus, 1977.

Taylor Jr., William J., *Elvis In The Army*, Presidio (USA), 1995.

Taylor, Paula, *Elvis Presley*, Creative Education, 1974.

Tharpe, Jac L., *Elvis: Images & Fancies*, University Press Of Mississippi (USA), 1979.

Thompson, Charles C. & Cole, James P., *The Death Of Elvis: What Really Happened*, Delacort Press (USA), 1991.

Thornton, Mary Ann, *Even Elvis*, New Leaf Press, 1979.

Torgoff, Martin, *The Complete Elvis*, Delilah Communications (USA), 1982.

Townson, John, Minto, Gordon & Richardson, George, *Elvis*, Blandford Press (UK), 1988.

Tunzi, Joseph A., *Elvis Sessions II: The Recorded Music Of Elvis Aron Presley 1953-1977*, JAT (USA), 1996.

Tunzi, Joseph A., *Elvis, Highway 51 South, Memphis, Tennessee*, JAT Publishing (USA), 1995.

Tunzi, Joseph A., *Elvis Sessions: The Recorded Music Of Elvis Aron Presley 1953-1977*, JAT Productions, 1993.

Tunzi, Joseph A., *Elvis '69, The Return*, JAT Productions

(USA), 1991.

Tunzi, Joseph & O'Neal, *Elvis, The Lost Photographs 1948-1969*, JAT Productions (USA), 1995.

Unknown, *Guts: Elvis*, Japan.

Vallenga, Dirk with Farren, Mick, *Elvis And The Colonel*, Grafton (UK), 1989.

Wallraf, Rainer & Plehn, Heinz, *Elvis Presley: An Illustrated Biography*, Omnibus Press (UK), 1979.

Wertheimer, Alfred, *Elvis '56: In The Beginning*, Cassell (UK), 1979.

West, Joan Buchanan, *Elvis: His Life And Times In Poetry And Lines*, Exposition Press, 1979.

West, Red, West, Sonny & Hebler, Dave, *Elvis: What Happened*, Ballantine (USA), 1977.

Whisler, John A., *Elvis Presley: A Reference Guide And Discography*, Scarecrow Press (USA), 1981.

Wooton, Richard, *Elvis Presley: King Of Rock 'N' Roll*, Hodder and Stoughton (UK), 1982.

Worth, Fred L. & Tamerius, Steve D., *All About Elvis*, Bantam (USA), 1981.

Worth, Fred L. & Tamerius, Steve D., *Elvis: His Life From A To Z*, Corgi (UK), Wing (USA), 1989.

Yancey, Becky & Lindecker, Cliff, *My Life With Elvis*, Mayflower/Granada (UK), 1978.

Zemke, Ken, *Elvis On Tour*, MGM/Cinema Associates, Japan, 1973.

Zmijewsky, Steven & Zmijewsky, Boris, *Elvis: The Films And Career Of Elvis Presley*, Citadel Press (USA), 1976.

Pretenders
Miles, *Pretenders*, Omnibus Press (UK), 1981.
Salewicz, Chris, *The Pretenders* , Proteus Books (UK), 1982.
Wrenn, Mike, *The Pretenders: With Hyndesight*, Omnibus Press (UK), 1989.

Pretty Things
Stax, Mike, *The Pretty Things: Their Own Story And The Downliners Sect Story*, Brisk, 1992.

Previn, André
Previn, Andre, *No Minor Chords (My Days In Hollowood)*, Doubleday (USA), 1992.

Previn, Dory
Previn, Dory, *On My Way To Where*, McCall (USA), 1971.
Previn, Dory, *Bog-Trotter: An Autobiography With Lyrics*, Weidenfeld and Nicolson (UK), 1980.
Previn, Dory, *Midnight Baby: An Autobiography*, Corgi (UK), 1978.

Price, Sammy
Price, Sammy & Richmond, Caroline (ed.), *What Do They Want? A Jazz Autobiography*, Bayou Press (USA), 1990.

Pride, Charley
Barclay, Pamela, *Charley Pride*, Mark Landkamer.
Pride, Charley with Henderson, Jim, *Pride; The Charley Pride Story*, W. Morrow (USA), 1994.

Primal Scream
Fleming, Grant, *Higher Than The Sun*, Ebury (UK), 1997.

Prince
Duffy, John W., *Prince: An Illustrated Biography*, Omnibus Press (UK), 1992.
Ewing, John, *Prince*, Orion/Carlton (UK), 1994.
Hill, Dave, *Prince: A Pop Life*, Faber & Faber (UK), 1989.
Hoskyns, Barney, *Prince: Imp Of The Perverse*, Virgin Books (UK), 1988.

Nilsen, Per, *Prince: A Documentary*, Omnibus Press (UK), 1990.
The 'Controversy' Team, *Prince By Controversy*, Virgin Books (UK), 1990.

Prodigy
Coles, Stuart, *Prodigy - An Illustrated Biography*, Omnibus Press (UK), 1998.
James, Martin, *Adventures With The Voodoo Crew*, Ebury Press (UK), 1997.
No author listed, *Prodigy: The Fat Of The Land*, Independent Music Press (UK), 1997.
Roach, Martin, *Electronic Punks: The Official Story*, Omnibus Press (UK), 1995.
Verrico, Lisa, *Prodigy: Exit The Underground*, Virgin Books (UK), 1996.

Professor Longhair
Crosby, John, *A Bio-discography*, John Crosby (UK), 1983.

Psychedelic
Perry, Charles, *I Want To Take You Higher: The Pychedelic Years 1965-69*, Chronicle Books (USA), 1997.
Strong, Martin C., *The Great Psychedelic Discography*, Canongate (UK), 1998.

Public Enemy
D., Chuck with Jah, Yusuf, *Fight The Power - Rap, Race And Reality*, Payback Press, 1997 (USA).

Public Image Limited
Heylin, Clinton, *Public Image Limited: Rise Fall*, Omnibus Press (UK), 1989.

Pulp
Aston, Martin, *Pulp*, Pan Books (UK), 1996.

Punk
Arnold, Gina, *Kiss This: Punk In The Present Tense*, Pan (UK), 1998.
Boot, Adrian & Salewicz, Chris, *Punk: The Illustrated History Of A Music Revolution*, Boxtree (UK), 1996.
Echenberg, Erica & Mark P, *And God Created Punk*, Virgin Books (UK), 1996.
Gibbs, Alvin, *Destroy: The Definitive History Of Punk*, Britannia Press (UK), 1996.
Gimarc, George, *Punk Diary 1970-1979*, St. Martins Press (USA), 1994.
Home, Stewart, *Cranked Up Really High: Genre Theory And Punk Rock*, Codex, 1997.
Lazell, Barry, *Punk: An A-Z*, Hamlyn (UK), 1995.
Manley, Frank, *Smash The State: A Discography Of Canadian Punk 1977-92*, Cargo (Canada), 1993.
Marcus, Greil, *In The Fascist Bathroom: Writings On Punk 1977-92*, Viking (USA), 1993.
Marcus, Greil, *Ranters And Crowd Pleasers: Punk In Pop Music 1977-92*, Doubleday (USA), 1993.
McNeil, Legs & McCain, Gillian, *Please Kill Me: The Uncensored Oral History Of Punk*, Grove Press (USA), Little Brown (UK), 1996.
Savage, Jon, *England's Dreaming: Sex Pistols And Punk Rock*, Faber & Faber (UK), 1991.

Quatro, Suzi
Mander, Margaret, *Suzi Quatro*, Futura (UK), 1976.

Queen
Brooks, Greg, *QueenLive: A Concert Documentary*, Omnibus Press (UK), 1996.

Clark, Stephen (ed.), *Queen Live At Wembley '86*, EMI Music Publications (UK), 1992.

Darrow, Paul, *The Novel Of Queen: The Eye*, Boxtree (UK), 1997.

Darrow, Paul, *The Art Of Queen: The Eye*, Boxtree (UK), 1997.

Darrow, Paul, *The Secrets Of Queen: The Eye*, Boxtree (UK), 1997.

Davis, Judith, *Queen: An Illustrated Biography*, Proteus Books (UK), 1981.

Dean, Ken, *Queen: A Visual Documentary*, Omnibus Press (UK), 1987.

Dean, Ken, *Queen: The New Visual Documentary*, Omnibus Press (UK), 1992.

Evans, David & Minns, David, *Freddie Mercury - More Of The Real Life*, Britannia Press (UK), 1996.

Evans, David & Minns, David, *Freddie Mercury: This Is The Real Life*, Britannia Press (UK), 1992.

Gray, Richard (ed.), *Queen: Greatest Pix 2*, Internal Music, 1991.

Gun, Jacky & Jenkins, Jim, *Queen: As It Began*, Pan Books (UK), 1993.

Hodkinson, Mark, *Queen: The Early Years*, Omnibus Press (UK), 1995.

Hogan, Peter, *The Complete Guide To The Music Of ...*, Omnibus Press (UK), 1995.

Jackson, Laura, *Mercury: The King Of Queen*, Smith Gryphon (UK), 1996.

Jackson, Laura, *Queen And I, The Brian May Story*, Smith Gryphon (UK), 1994.

Lowe, Jacques, *Queen's Greatest Pix*, Quartet (UK), 1981.

No editor listed, *Queen*, Media Overview (UK), 1982.

No editor listed, *Queen: Yesterday, Today, Tomorrow*, G C P, 1990.

Pryce, Larry, *Queen*, Star Books (UK), 1976.

Putland, Michael, *Queen Unseen*, UFO Books (UK), 1993.

Queen, *Greatest Hits - Off The Record*, International Music Publications (UK), 1994.

Tremlett, George, *The Queen Story*, Futura (UK), 1978.

West, Mike, *Queen: The First Ten Years*, Babylon Books (UK), 1981.

R.E.M.

Bowler, Dave & Dray, Bryan, *R.E.M. Documental*, Boxtree (UK), 1995.

Brown, Rodger Lyle, *Party Out Of Bounds*, Plume (USA).

Ed. Bucket Full Of Brains Staff, *A Few Chords And A Cloud Of Dust*, Total Recall (UK).

Fletcher, Tony, *Remarks: Story Of R.E.M.*, Omnibus Press (UK), 1989.

Gray, Marcus, *An R.E.M. Companion: It Crawled From The South*, Guinness Publishing/Square One Books (UK), 1992.

Greer, Jim, *R.E.M.: Behind The Mask*, Joshua Morris (USA), Sidgwick & Jackson (UK), 1992.

Hogan, Peter, *Complete Guide To The Music Of R.E.M.*, Omnibus Press (UK), 1995.

Nabors, Gary, *Remnants: The R.E.M. Collectors' Handbook*, Eclipse Publishing (USA), 1993.

No editor listed, *The Rolling Stone Files*, Sidgwick & Jackson (UK), 1995.

Rosen, Craig, *R.E.M. Inside Out*, Carlton (UK), 1997.

Storey, Jon, *R.E.M.: File Under Water, The Definitive Guide To 12 Years Of Recordings And Con*, Imaginary Books (UK), 1992.

Sullivan, Denise, *Talk About The Passion: R.E.M. An Oral History*, Pavillion Books (UK), 1995.

Race, Steve

Race, Steve, *Dear Music Lover*, Robson Books (UK), 1981.

Race, Steve, *Musician At Large*, Methuen (UK), 1979.

Radiohead

Malins, Steve, *Radiohead: Coming Up For Air*, Virgin Books (UK), 1997.

Rainbow

Makowski, Peter, *Rainbow*, Omnibus Press (UK), 1981.

Rainey, Gertrude 'Ma'

Lieb, Sandra, *Mother Of The Blues: A Study Of Ma Rainey*, University Of Massachussetts Press (USA), 1983.

Stewart-Baxter, Derrick, *Ma Rainey And The Classic Blues Singers*, Studio Vista (UK), 1970.

Wilson, August, *Ma Rainey's Black Bottom*, E. P. Dutton (USA), 1985.

Raitt, Bonnie

Bego, Mark, *Just In The Nick Of Time*, Birch Lane Press (USA), 1995.

Ramones

Bessman, Jim, *Ramones: An American Band*, St. Martin's Press (USA), 1993.

Miles, *The Ramones: An Illustrated Biography*, Omnibus Press (UK), 1981.

Ramone, Dee Dee with Kofman, Veronica, *Poison Heart: Surviving The Ramones*, Firefly (USA), 1997.

Rap

Cross, Brian with Raegan, Kelly & T-Love, *It's Not About A Salary: Rap, Race And Resistance In Los Angeles*, Verso (UK), 1994.

Fernando Jnr., S.H., *The New Beats: Exporing The Music, Culture And Attitudes Of Hip Hop*, Payback Press (USA), 1995.

Goldstein, Dan (ed), *Rappers Rappin*, Castle Books (UK), 1996.

Larkin, Colin (ed.), *Guinness Who's Who Of Rap, Techno & Dance*, Guinness Publishing (UK), 1994.

Nelson, Havelock & Gonzales, Michael A., *Bring The Noise: A Guide To Rap Music And Hip-Hop*, Harmony Books (USA), 1991.

Rose, Tricia, *Black Noise: Rap Music And Black Culture In Contemporary America*, Wesleyan/University Press Of New England (USA), 1994.

Sexton, Adam (ed.), *Rap On Rap: Straight Talk On Hip-Hop Culture*, Delta Trade Paperbacks (USA), 1994.

Stanley, Lawrence A. & Morley, Jefferson, *Rap: The Lyrics*, Penguin (UK), 1992.

Toop, David, *The Rap Attack*, Pluto Press (UK), 1984.

Raspberries

Sharp, Ken, *Overnight Sensation: The Story Of The Raspberries*, Power Pop Press (USA), 1994.

Ray, Johnnie

Sonin, Ray, *The Johnnie Ray Story*, Horace Marshall, 1955.

Razaf, Andy

Singer, Barry, *Black And Blue: The Life And Lyrics Of Andy Razaf*, Schirmer (USA), 1992.

Red Hot Chili Peppers

Lorenzo, Joey, *The Red Hot Chili Peppers*, Omnibus Press (UK), 1995.

Thompson, Dave, *True Men Don't Kill Coyotes*, Virgin Books (UK), 1993.

Redding, Otis

Schiesel, Jane, *The Otis Redding Story*, Doubleday, 1973.

Reed, Lou

Bockris, Victor, *Transformer: The Lou Reed Story*, Simon And Schuster (USA), 1994.

Clapton, Diana, *Lou Reed & The Velvet Underground*, Proteus Books (UK), Bobcat (USA), 1982.

Doggett, Peter, *Lou Reed: Growing Up In Public*, Omnibus Press (UK), 1992.

No author listed, *Rock And Roll Animal*, Babylon Books (UK), 1979.

Reed, Jeremy, *Waiting For the Man: A Biography Of Lou Reed*, Picador (UK), 1994.

Reed, Lou, *Between Thought And Expression: Selected Lyrics*, Penguin (UK), 1993.

Trevena, Nigel, *Lou Reed & The Velvets*, Bantam (USA).

Wrenn, Michael, *Between The Lines*, Plexus (UK), 1994.

Reeves, Jim

Cook, Pansy, *The Saga Of Jim Reeves: Country And Western Singer And Musician*, Crescent, 1977.

Reggae

Bader, Stascha, *Words Like Fire: Dancehall Reggae And Ragga Muffin*, M. Schwinn. (Germany), 1993.

Boot, Adrian & Thomas, Michael, *Jamaica: Babylon On A Thin Wire*, Thames & Hudson (UK), 1976.

Bradley, Lloyd, *Reggae On CD: The Essential Guide*, Kyle Cathie (UK), 1996.

Clarke, Sebastian, *Jah Music*, Heinemann Educational (UK), 1980.

Cooper, Carolyn, *Noises In The Blood*, Duke University Press (USA), 1995.

Dalke, Roger, *Record Selector: A Reference Guide To Jamaican Music Vols. 15-18*, T.S.I. Publications (UK), 1995.

Davis, Stephen, *Reggae Bloodlines: In Search Of The Music And Culture Of Jamaica*, Heineman Educational (UK), 1979.

Davis, Stephen & Simon, Peter, *Reggae International*, Alfred A. Knopf (USA), 1983.

Farmer, Paul, *Steelbands & Reggae*, Longman (UK), 1981.

Griffiths, Mark, *Boss Sounds: Classic Skinhead Reggae*, S.T. Publishing (UK), 1995.

Hausman, Gerald (ed.), *The Kebra Nagast*, St. Martin's Press (UK), 1997.

Johnson, Howard, *Reggae: Deep Roots Music*, Proteus Books (UK), 1982.

Kallyndyr, Rolston, *Reggae: A People's Music*, Carib-Arawak, 1977.

Larkin, Colin, *The Virgin Encyclopedia Of Reggae*, Virgin Books (UK), 1998.

Larkin, Colin (ed.), *Guinness Who's Who Of Reggae*, Guinness Publishing (UK), 1994.

Marshall, George, *Two-tone Story*, S.T. Publishing (UK), 1993.

Maverick Lensman, *Reggae In View*, Overheat Music Inc. (USA), 1996.

Mulvaney, Rebekah Michele, *Rastafari & Raggae: A Dictionary & Sourcebook*, Greenwood Westport (USA), 1990.

Weber, Tom, *Reggae Island: Jamaican Music In The Digital Age*, Kingston Publishers (Jamaica), 1992.

Reinhardt, Django

Abrams, M., *The Book Of Django*, Los Angeles, 1973.

Cruickshank, Ian (ed), *Django's Gypsies: The Mystique Of Django Reinhardt*, Ashley Mark Publishing (UK), 1996.

Delaunay, C., *Django Reinhardt*, London.

Rent

Larson, Jonathan, *Rent*, William Morrow & Co (USA), 1997.

Residents

Shirley, Ian, *Meet The Residents*, SAF Publishing, 1993.

Reynolds, Debbie

Reynolds, Debbie with Columbia David Patrick, *Debbie Reynolds - My Life*, Sidgwick & Jackson (UK), 1989.

Reynolds, Malvina

Reynolds, Malvina, *Cheerful Tunes For Lutes And Spoons*, Schroder Music (USA), 1970.

Reynolds, Malvina, *Little Boxes And Other Handmade Songs*, Oak Publications (USA), 1964.

Reynolds, Malvina, *Not In Ourselves Not In Our Stars Either*, Social Commentary Pamphlet (USA), 1974.

Reynolds, Malvina, *The Malvina Reynolds Songbook*, Schroder Music (USA), 1974.

Reynolds, Malvina, *The Muse Of Parker Street*, Oak Publications (USA), 1967.

Reynolds, Malvina, *There's Music In The Air*, Schroder Music (USA), 1976.

Reynolds, Malvina, *Tweedles And Foodles For Young Noodles*, Schroder Music (USA), 1961.

Rich, Charlie

Eton, Judy, *Charlie Rich*, Creative Education, 1975.

Richard(s), Keith

Bockris, Victor, *Keith Richards: The Biography*, Poseidon Press (USA), 1992.

Booth, Stanley, *Keith: Till I Roll Over Dead*, Headline (UK), 1994.

St Michael, Mick, *In His Own Words*, Omnibus Press (UK), 1994.

Richard, Cliff

Doncaster, Patrick & Jasper, Tony, *Cliff*, Sidgwick & Jackson (UK), 1981.

Ferrier, Bob, *Cliff Around The Clock*, Daily Mirror Newspapers (UK), 1964.

Ferrier, Bob, *The Wonderful World Of Cliff Richard*, Peter Davis (UK), 1964.

Harris, Jet & Ellis, Royston, *Driftin' With Cliff Richard: The Inside Story Of What Really Happens On Tour*, Hulton (UK), 1959.

Jasper, Tony, *Silver Cliff: A 25 Year Journal 1958-1983*, Sidgwick & Jackson (UK), 1983.

Jasper, Tony, *Cliff: A Biography*, Sidgwick & Jackson (UK), 1992.

Lewry, Peter & Goodall, Nigel, *The Ultimate Cliff*, Simon & Schuster (UK), 1996.

Lewry, Peter & Goodall, Nigel, *Cliff Richard: The Complete Recording Sessions, 1958-1990*, Blandford Press (UK), 1991.

No author listed, *Cliff Around The Clock*, Daily Mirror (UK), 1964.

No author listed, *Cliff Richard, Single-Minded*, Hodder & Stoughton (UK), 1989.

Read, Mike, Goodhall, Nigel & Lewry, Peter, *Cliff Richard, The Complete Chronicle*, Hamlyn (UK), 1993.

Richard, Cliff, *Happy Christmas From Cliff*, Hodder & Stoughton (UK), 1980.

Richard, Cliff, *It's Great To Be Young*, Souvenir Press (UK), 1960.

Richard, Cliff, *Me And My Shadows*, Daily Mirror Press (UK), 1961.

Richard, Cliff, *Questions: Cliff Answering Reader And Fan Queries*, Hodder & Stoughton (UK), 1970.

Richard, Cliff, *The Way I See It*, Hodder & Stoughton (UK), 1970.

Richard, Cliff, *Top Pops*, Daily Mirror Newspapers (UK), 1963.

Richard, Cliff with Bill Latham, *Which One's Cliff?*, Hodder & Stoughton (UK), 1977.

St. John, Kevin, *Cliff In His Own Words*, Omnibus Press (UK),

1981.
Sutter, Jack, *Cliff, The Baron Of Beat*, Valex, 1960.
Tobler, John, *Cliff Richard*, W.H. Allen (UK), 1983.
Tremlett, George, *The Cliff Richard Story*, Futura (UK), 1975.
Turner, Steve, *Cliff Richard: The Autobiography*, Lion (UK), 1993.
Winter, David, *New Singer, New Song: The Cliff Richard Story*, Hodder & Stoughton (UK), 1976.

Richie, Lionel
Nathan, David, *Lionel Richie: An Illustrated Biography*, Virgin Books (UK), 1985.

Rickenbacker
Bacon, Tony & Paul Day, *The Rickenbacker Book*, Balafon Books (UK), 1994.

Riddle, Almeda
Riddle, Almeda, *A Singer And Her Songs*, Louisiana University Press (USA), 1970.

Riders In The Sky
Ranger Doug, Woody Paul & Too Slim with Texas Bix Bender, *Riders In The Sky*, Layton, Utah (USA), 1992.

Riley, Jeannie C.
Riley, Jeannie C., *From Harper Valley To The Mountain Top*, Kingsway, 1981.

Rinehart, Cowboy Slim
Turner, Dallas, *Cowboy Slim Rinehart's Folio Of Country Song Hits*, Reno, (USA), 1983.

Ritchie, Jean
Ritchie, Jean, *A Garland Of Mountain Song*, Broadcast Music (USA).
Ritchie, Jean, *From Fair To Fair*, Henry Z. Walck (USA).
Ritchie, Jean, *Jean Ritchie's Dulcimer People*, Oak Publications (USA), 1975.
Ritchie, Jean, *Loves Me Loves Me Not*, Henry Z. Walck (USA).
Ritchie, Jean, *Singing Family Of The Cumberlands*, Oxford Press, 1955.
Ritchie, Jean, *The Dulcimer Book*, Oak Publications (USA), 1963.
Ritchie, Jean, *The Swapping Song Book*, Henry Z. Walck (USA).

Robbins, Marty
Pruett, Barbara J., *Marty Robbins: Fast Cars And Country Music*, Scarecrow Press (USA), 1990.

Robeson, Paul
Duberman, Martin Baumi, *Paul Robeson*, Pan (UK), 1991.
Robeson, Paul, *Here I Stand*, London, 1958.
Robeson, Paul, *Paul Robeson Speaks: Writings Speeches Interviews 1918-1974*, London, 1978.

Robinson, Smokey
Robinson, Smokey & David Ritz, *Smokey: Inside My Life*, Headline (UK), 1989.

Robison, Carson Jay
No editor listed, *Carson Jay Robison's World's Greatest Collection Of Mountain Ballads And Old Tim*, M. M. Cole.

Rodgers, Jimmie (The Singing Brakeman)
Paris, Mike & Comber, Chris, *Jimmie The Kid (The Life Of Jimmie Rodgers)*, Pocket Books (USA), 1977.
Porterfield, Nolan, *Jimmie Rodgers (The Life And Times Of America's Blue Yodeler)*, University Of Illinois Press (USA), 1979.
Rodgers, Carrie, *My Husband, Jimmie Rodgers*, Vanderbilt University Press (USA), 1995.
Rogers, Jimmie N., *Country Music Message: All About Lovin' And Leavin'*, Prentice Hall (USA), 1983.

Rodgers, Richard
Hyland, William G., *Richard Rodgers*, Yale (USA), 1998.
Nolan, Frederick, *The Sound Of Their Music (Rodgers & Hammerstein)*, Dent (UK), 1978.
Rodgers, Richard, *Musical Stages*, London, 1976.

Rogers, Kenny
Hume, Martha, *Gambler, Dreamer, Lover: The Kenny Rogers Story*, Delilah Tower, 1981.
Rogers, Kenny & Epand, Len, *Making It In Music*, New York, 1977.

Rogers, Stan
Gudgeon, Chris, *An Unfinished Conversation: The Life And Music Of Stan Rogers*, Canada, 1993.
Rogers, Stan, *Song's From Fogarty's Cove*, 1982.

Rolling Stone
Rolling Stone: The Complete Covers, 1967-1997, Abrams (UK), 1998.
Draper, Robert, *Rolling Stone Magazine: The Unsensored History*, Doubleday (USA), 1990.
Kratochvil, Laurie (ed.), *Rolling Stone: The Photographs*, Simon & Schuster (USA), 1994.
Love, Robert (ed.), *Best Of: Classic Writing From The World's Most Influential Music Mag*, Virgin Books (UK), 1994.

Rolling Stones
Aeppli, Felix, *The Rolling Stones 1962-1995; The Ultimate Guide*, Record Information Services (UK), 1996.
Aeppli, Felix, *Heart Of Stone: The Definitive Rolling Stones Discography*, Pierian Press (USA), 1985.
Aftel, Mandy, *Death Of A Rolling Stone: The Brian Jones Story*, Delilah Books (USA), 1982.
Appleford, Steve, *It's Only Rock 'N' Roll*, Carlton (UK), 1997.
Barnard, Stephen, *Rolling Stones: Street Fighting Years*, Studio Editions (UK), 1993.
Barnard, Stephen, *Street Fighting Years*, Studio Editions (UK), 1993.
Bockris, Victor, *Keith Richards: The Unauthorised Biography*, Hutchinson (UK), 1992.
Bonanno, Massimo, *The Rolling Stones Chronicle*, Plexus (UK), 1996.
Bonanno, Massimo, *The Rolling Stones Chronicle: The First Thirty Years*, Plexus (UK), 1990.
Booth, Stanley, *The True Adventures Of The Rolling Stones*, Heinemann (UK), 1985.
Carr, Roy, *The Rolling Stones: An Illustrated Record*, New English Library (UK), 1976.
Charone, Barbara, *Keith Richards*, Futura (UK), 1979.
Cohn, Nik, *The Rolling Stones: A Celebration*, Circus Enterprises (USA), 1975.
Contantin, Philippe, *Les Rolling Stones*, Editions Chiron (France), 1974.
Creem, *The Rolling Stones: Creem Special Edition*, Creem Magazine (USA), 1981.
Dalton, David, *Rolling Stones: An Unauthorized Biography In Words, Photographs And Music*, Amsco Music (USA), 1972.
Dalton, David, *The Rolling Stones*, Star/W.H. Allen (UK), 1975.
Dalton, David, *The Rolling Stones: The First Twenty Years*, Thames & Hudson (UK), Alfred A. Knopf (USA), 1981.

Dalton, David & Farren, Mick, *The Rolling Stones In Their Own Words*, Omnibus Press (UK), 1981.

Dimmick, Mary Laverne, *The Rolling Stones: An Annotated Bibliography*, University Of Pittsburgh Press (USA), 1979.

Draper, Robert, *The Rolling Stones Story* , Mainstream (UK), 1990.

Ducray, Francois, Leblanc, Jacques & Woehrle, Udo, *Le Livre Des Rolling Stones*, Albin Michel (France), 1978.

Eborn, Chris, *Not Fade Away*, Paper Tiger (UK), 1995.

Ehrlich, Cindy, *The Rolling Stones*, Straight Arrow (USA), 1975.

Elliott, Martin, *The Rolling Stones: Complete Recording Sessions 1963-1989*, Blandford Press (UK), 1990.

Elman, Richard, *Uptight With The Rolling Stones*, Scribners (USA), 1972.

Fitzgerald, Nicholas, *Brian Jones: The Inside Story Of The Original Rolling Stone*, G.P. Putnam's (USA), 1994.

Flippo, Chet, *On The Road With The Rolling Stones*, Doubleday (USA), 1985.

Fricke, David & Sandall, Robert, *Rolling Stones: Images Of The World Tour 1989-1990*, Boxtree (UK), 1991.

Giuliano, Geoffrey, *Paint It Black: The Murder Of Brian Jones*, Virgin Books (UK), 1994.

Giuliano, Geoffrey, *Not Fade Away: Rolling Stones Collection*, Paper Tiger (UK), 1992.

Goodman, Pete, *Our Own Story*, Transworrd (UK), Bantam (USA), 1964.

Greenfield, Robert, *A Journey Through America With The Rolling Stones*, E.P. Dutton (USA), Michael Joseph (UK), 1974.

Hector, James, *Complete Guide To The Music Of*, Omnibus Press (UK), 1995.

Hewat, Tim, *The Rolling Stones File*, Panther Books (UK), 1967.

Hoffman, Dezo, *The Rolling Stones*, Vermilion (UK), 1984.

Hoffmann, Dieter, *Rolling Stones: Das Weissbuch*, Germany, 1992.

Hotchner, A.E., *Blown Away: The Rolling Stones And The Death Of The Sixties*, Simon & Schuster (USA), 1990.

Hughes, William, *Performance*, Award/Universal (USA), 1970.

Jackson, Laura, *Golden Stone: The Untold Life And Mysterious Death Of Brian Jones*, Smith Gryphon (UK), 1992.

Jasper, Tony, *The Rolling Stones*, Octopus Books (UK), 1976.

Kamin, Philip & Goddard, Peter, *The Rolling Stones: Live In America*, Beaufort Books (USA), Sidgwick & Jackson (UK), 1982.

Kamin, Philip & Karnbach, James, *The Rolling Stones: The Last Tour*, Sidgwick & Jackson (UK), 1983.

Krüger, Stefan, *The Stones By Krüger*, Millbank Books (UK), 1996.

Leibowitz, Annie, *The Rolling Stones On Tour*, Dragon's Dream (UK), 1978.

Littlejohn, David, *The Man Who Killed Mick Jagger*.

Luce, Philip Carmelo, *The Stones*, Allen Wingate-Baker (UK), 1970.

MacPhail, Jessica, *Yesterday's Papers: The Rolling Stones In Print*, Pierian Press (USA), 1986.

Mankowitz, Gered, *Satisfaction: The Rolling Stones*, St. Martin's Press (USA), 1984.

Mankowitz, Gered & Whitaker, Robert (Photographers), *The Rolling Stones: Behind The Buttons (Limited Edition)*, UFO Books, 1992.

Marchbank, Pearce & Miles, *The Rolling Stones File*, Essex Music/Music Sales (UK).

Markle, Gil, *Rehearsal!: The Rolling Stones At Long View Farm*, Privately published in USA, 1981.

Marks, J., *Mick Jagger: The Singer Not The Song*, Abacus (UK), Curtis Brown (USA), 1973.

Martin, Linda, *The Rolling Stones In Concert*, Colour Library International (UK), 1982.

Miles, *A Visual Documentary*, Omnibus Press (UK), 1994.

Miles, *Mick Jagger In His Own Words*, Omnibus Press (UK), 1982.

Miles, *The Rolling Stones: An Illustrated Discography*, Omnibus Press (UK), 1980.

No author listed, *The Rolling Stones' Rock 'N' Roll Circus*, Faber & Faber (UK), 1992.

Norman, Philip, *The Life And Good Times Of The Rolling Stones*, Century (UK), 1989.

Norman, Philip, *The Stones*, Elm Tree Books (UK), 1984.

Palmer, Robert, *The Rolling Stones*, Sphere (UK), 1984.

Pascall, Jeremy, *The Rolling Stones*, Hamlyn (UK), 1977.

Quill, Greg, *The Rolling Stones 25th Anniversary Tour*, Sidgwick & Jackson (UK), 1990.

Rawlings, Terry, *Who Killed Christopher Robin*, Boxtree (UK), 1994.

Rawlings, Terry & Badman, Keith, *Good Times Bad Times: The Definitive Diary Of The Rolling Stones 1960-1969*, Complete Music (UK), 1997.

Rolling Stones, *Rolling Stones' Classics - Off The Record*, International Music Publications (UK), 1993.

Rolling Stones, *Rolling Stones In Their Own Words*, Omnibus Press (UK), 1980.

Rosenbaum, Halen, *Rolling Stones Trivia Quiz Book*, Signet (USA), 1979.

Sanchez, Tony with John Blake, *Up And Down With The Rolling Stones*, W. Morrow (USA), 1979.

Scaduto, Anthony, *Mick Jagger: Everybody's Lucifer*, W.H. Allen (UK), David McKay (USA), 1974.

Schofield, Carey, *Jagger*, Methuen (UK), 1983.

Tremlett, George, *The Rolling Stones Story* , Futura (UK), 1975.

Watts, Charlie, *Ode To A High-Flying Bird*, Beat (UK), 1964.

Weiner, Sue & Howard, Lisa, *The Rolling Stones A To Z*, Omnibus Press (UK), 1984.

Wyman, Bill & Coleman, Ray, *Stone Alone*, Viking (UK), 1990.

Zentgraf, Nico, *The Rolling Stones: The Complete Works Vol.1 1962-75*, Stoneware Publishing (Germany), 1993.

Rollini, Arthur

Rollini, Arthur, *Thirty Years With The Big Bands*, London, 1987.

Rollins, Henry

Overton, R. K., *Letters To Rollins*, Henry Rollins, 1995.

Rollins, Henry, *Get In The Van: On The Road With Black Flag*, 2.13.61.

Rollins, Henry, *Now Watch 'Em Die*.

Rollins, Henry, *Do I Come Here Often? Black Coffee Blues 2*, 2.13.61, 1997.

Rollins, Henry, *Black Coffee Blues*.

Rollins, Henry, *See A Grown Man Cry*.

Rollins, Henry, *One From None*.

Rollins, Henry, *Bang!*,

Rollins, Henry, *Art To Choke Hearts*.

Rollins, Henry, *Pissing In The Gene Pool*.

Rollins, Henry, *High Adventure In The Great Outdoors aka Bodybag*.

Rollins, Henry, *Eye Scream*, 2.13.61, 1996.

Rollins, Sonny

Baker, David N., *The Jazz Style Of Sonny Rollins*, Studio Publications/Recordings.

Blancq, Charles Clement, *Sonny Rollins: The Journey Of A Jazzman*, Twayne, 1983.

Gerard, Charley (ed.), *Sonny Rollins*, Consolidated Music.

Ronson, Mick

Gusevik, Sven, *Mick Ronson Discography*, S Gusevik (Canada), 1995.

Ronstadt, Linda
Bego, Mark, *Linda Ronstadt: It's So Easy*, Eakin Press (USA), 1990.
Berman, Connie, *Linda Ronstadt: An Illustrated Biography*, Proteus Books (UK), 1979.
Claire, Vivian, *Linda Ronstadt*, Flash Books (USA), 1978.
Kanakaris, Richard, *Linda Ronstadt: A Portrait*, L A Pop, 1977.
Moore, Mary Ellen, *The Linda Ronstadt Scrapbook*, Sunridge Press, 1978.

Rose, Billy
Conrad E., *Billy Rose: Manhatten Primitive,World*, Cleveland, 1968.
Gottlieb, Pearl Rose, *The Nine Lives Of Billy Rose*, Crown (USA), 1968.
Rose, Billy, *Wine, Woman And Words*, New York, 1948.

Rose, Fred
Rumble, John Woodruff, *Fred Rose And The Development Of The Nashville Music Industry, 1942-1954.*

Ross, Diana
Berman, Connie, *Diana Ross: Supreme Lady*, Popular Library, 1978.
Brown, Geoff, *Diana Ross: An Illustrated Biography*, Sidgwick & Jackson (UK), 1981.
Eldred, Patricia Mulrooney, *Diana Ross*, Creative Education, 1975.
Haskins, James, *I'm Gonna Make You Love Me: The Story Of Diana Ross*, Dial Press (UK), 1980.
Itzkowitz, Leonore K., *Diana Ross*, Random House (USA), 1974.
Ross, Diana, *Secrets Of The Sparrow*, Headline (UK), 1993.
Taraborrelli, J. Randy, *Call Her Miss Ross*, Birch Lane Press (USA), 1989.
Wilson, Mary, *Dreamgirl: My Life As A Supreme*, St. Martin's Press (USA), 1987.
Wilson, Mary with Patricia Romanowski , *Supreme Faith: Someday We'll Be Together*, Harper Collins (USA), 1990.

Rosselson, Leon
Rosselson, Leon, *Bringing The News From Nowhere: Songs By Leon Rosselson*, 1992.

Roth, David Lee
Roth, David Lee, *Crazy From The Heat*, Ebury Press (UK), 1997.

Roxette
Okun, Milton (ed.), *Best Of Roxette*, Cherry Lane Music Co. (USA), 1994.

Roxy Music
Balfour, Rex, *The Bryan Ferry Story*, Michael Dempsey (UK), 1976.
Lazell, Barry & Rees, Dafydd, *Bryan Ferry & Roxy Music*, Proteus Books (UK), 1982.
Rogan, Johnny, *Roxy Music: Style With Substance: Roxy's First Ten Years*, Star/W.H. Allen (UK), 1982.

Rozsa, Miklos
Palmer, C., *A Sketch Of His Life And Work* (USA), 1975.
Rozsa, Miklos, *Double Life: The Autobiography Of Miklos Rozsa* (USA), 1982.

Rubettes
Rowett, Alan, *The Rubettes Story*, AWEL, 1994.

Run DMC
Adler, B., *Run DMC*, New American Library, 1987.

Runrig
Morton, Tom, *Going Home: The Runrig Story*, Mainstream (UK) 1992.

RuPaul
RuPaul, *Lettin' It All Hang Out: An Autobiography*, Hyperion (USA), Warner Books (UK), 1995.

Rush
Banasiewicz, Bill, *Rush Visions: The Official Biography*, Omnibus Press (UK), 1988.
Harrigan, Brian, *Rush*, Omnibus Press (UK), 1982.

Russell, Pee Wee
Hilbert, Robert, *Pee Wee Russell: The Life Of A Jazzman*, Oxford University Press, 1993.
Hilbert, Robert with Niven, David, *Pee Wee Speaks: A Discography Of Pee Wee Russell*, Scarecrow Press (USA), 1993.

Russell, Tom
Russell, Tom, *And Then I Wrote*, Arsenal Pulp Press/Firebird (UK), 1996.

Sakamoto, Ryûichi
Sakamoto, Ryûichi, *Seldom-Illegal.*
Sakamoto, Ryûichi & Omori, Shôzô, *Otowo Miru, Tokiwo Kiku (Seeing Sound And Hearing Time).*

Sample, Joe
Sample, Joe, *Joe Sample*, IMP (UK).

Sandburg, Carl
D'Alessio, Gregory, *Old Troubadour: Carl Sandburg With His Guitar Friends*, Walker, 1987.

Saxophone
Lindemeyer, Paul, *Celebrating The Saxophone*, Hearst Books (USA), 1996.

Schuller, Gunther
Schuller, Gunther, *Early Jazz: Its Roots And Musical Delevopment*, New York, 1968.
Schuller, Gunther, *The Swing Era: The Development Of Jazz 1930-1945*, New York, 1989.

Scott, Ronnie
Fordham, John, *Jazz Man: The Amazing Story Of Ronnie Scott And His Club*, Kyle Cathie (UK), 1994.
Fordham, John, *Let's Join Hands And Contact The Living* , Elm Tree Books (UK), 1986.
Grime, Kitty (ed.), *Jazz At Ronnie Scott's*, Robert Hale (UK), 1979.

Scott, Tom
No author listed, *Tom Scott*, Warner Brothers (USA).

Scott-Heron, Gil
Scott-Heron, Gil, *The Vulture And The Nigger Factory*, Payback Press (USA), 1996.

Scruggs, Earl
Earl Scruggs, *Earl Scruggs And The 5-String Banjo*, Peer International (USA), 1976.

Secombe, Harry
Secombe, Sir Harry, *Arias And Raspberries*, Robson Books (UK).

Sedaka, Neil
No author listed, *Sedaka, Neil*, Breaking Up Is Hard To Do Press, 1982.

Seeger, Peggy
Seeger, Peggy, *Doomsday In The Afternoon*, Manchester University Press.
Seeger, Peggy, *Folk Songs Of Peggy Seeger*, 1964.
Seeger, Peggy & MacColl, Ewan, *Travellers Songs Of England And Scotland*, Routledge & Kegan Paul (UK).
Seeger, Peggy with Paly, Tom, *Who's Going To Shoe Your Pretty Little Foot, Who's Going To Glove Your Hand?*, 1964.

Seeger, Pete
Dunaway, David King, *How Can I Keep From Singing?*, McGraw-Hill (USA), 1981.
Reiser, Bob, *Everbody Says Freedom*, W.W. Norton (USA), 1989.
Schwartz, Jo Metcalf, *Incompleat Folksinger*, University Of Nebraska (USA), 1993.
Seeger, Pete, *Where Have All The Flowers Gone?* (USA), 1993.
Seeger, Pete, *The Foolish Frog*, Macmillan, 1973.
Seeger, Pete, *The Incompleat Folksinger*, Simon & Schuster (USA), 1976.
Seeger, Pete & Reiser, Bob, *Carry It On!: History In Song And Pictures Of The Working Men & Women Of America*, Blandford Press (UK), 1991.

Selena
Patoski, Joe Nick, *Selena: Como La Flor*, Little Brown (USA), 1996.

Sex Pistols
Agent Provocateur, *Sex Pistols Retrospective*, Retro (UK), 1997.
Bateson, Keith & Parker, Alan, *Sid's Way: The Life And Death Of Sid Vicious*, Omnibus Press (UK), 1992.
Beverley, Anne, *The Sid Vicious Family Album*, Virgin Books (UK), 1980.
Gruen, Bob, *Chaos: The Sex Pistols*, Omnibus Press (UK), 1990.
Heylin, Clinton, *Classic Rock Albums: Never Mind The Bollocks*, Schirmer (UK), 1998.
Matlock, Glen, *I Was A Teenage Sex Pistol*, Omnibus Press (UK), 1989.
Monk, Neil & Guterman, Jimmy, *12 Days On The Road: The Sex Pistols And America*, Sidgwick & Jackson (UK), 1990.
Moorcock, Michael, *The Great Rock 'N' Roll Swindle: A Novel*, Virgin Books (UK), 1980.
Morris, Dennis, *Never Mind The B*ll*cks: A Photographed Record Of The Sex Pistols*, Omnibus Press (UK), 1991.
No author listed, *Sex Pistols Retrospective*, Retro Publishing (UK), 1996.
Rotten, Johnny, *Rotten: No Irish, No Blacks, No Dogs*, St Martin's Press (USA), Hodder (UK), 1994.
Savage, Jon, *England's Dreaming: Sex Pistols And Punk Rock*, Faber & Faber (UK), 1991.
Scrivener, Tony, *Sex Pistols: Agents Of Anarchy*, Kingsfleet Publications (UK), 1992.
Stevenson, Ray, *Sex Pistols File*, Omnibus Press (UK), 1978.
Stevenson, Ray, *Sex Pistols Scrap Book*, Privately Published By Author (UK).
Vermorel, Fred & Judy, *Sex Pistols: The Inside Story*, W.H. Allen (UK), 1978.
Wood, Lee, *The Sex Pistols Diary*, Omnibus Press (UK), 1988.

Shadows
Bradford, Rob, *Funny Old World: The Life And Times Of John Henry Rostill*, Private Publication (UK), 1991.
Geddes, George Thomson, *Foot Tapping: The Shadows 1958-1978*, George Thomson Geddes, 1978.
Geddes, George Thomson, *The Shadows: A History And Discography*, G. and M. Geddes, 1981.
Shadows, *The Shadows By Themselves*, Consul Books (UK), 1961.
Shadows as told to Mike Reed, *The Story Of The Shadows: An Autobiography*, Elm Tree Books (UK), 1983.
Welch, Bruce, *Rock 'N' Roll: I Gave You The Best Years Of My Life: A Life In The Shadows*, Penguin (UK), 1990.

Shakur, Tupac
Editors of Vibe, *Tupac Shakur*, , 1997.
White, Armond, *Rebel For The Hell Of It: The Life Of Tupac Shakur*, Quartet (UK), 1997.

Shapiro, Helen
Janson, John S., *Helen Shapiro: Pop Princess*, Four Square (UK), 1963.
Shapiro, Helen, *Walking Back To Happiness*.

Shaw, Sandie
Shaw, Sandie, *The World At My Feet*, Harper Collins (UK), 1991.

Sheridan, Tony
Clayson, Alan, *Hamburg: The Cradle Of British Rock*, Sanctuary (UK), 1998.

Shore, Dinah
Cassidy, B., *Dinah!*, New York, 1979.

Short, Bobby
Short, Bobby, *Black & White Baby*, New York, 1971.
Short, Bobby with Robert Mackintosh, *The Life And Times Of A Saloon Slinger*, Clarkson Potter (USA), 1996.

Sidran, Ben
Sidran, Ben, *Black Talk*, Payback Press (USA), 1995.

Sigue Sigue Sputnik
No author listed, *Ultra*, Omnibus Press (UK), 1986.

Silvester, Victor
Silvester, Victor, *Dancing Is My Life*, London, 1958.

Simon And Garfunkel
Cohen, Michael S., *Simon & Garfunkel: A Biography In Words & Pictures*, Sire/Chappell Music.
Humphries, Patrick, *The Boy In The Bubble: A Biography Of Paul Simon*, Sidgwick & Jackson (UK), 1988.
Humphries, Patrick, *Paul Simon*, Doubleday (USA), 1990.
Humphries, Patrick, *Bookends: The Simon And Garfunkel Story*, Proteus Books (UK), 1982.
Kingston, Victoria, *Simon And Garfunkel: The Definitive Biography*, Sidgwick & Jackson (UK), 1996.
Leigh, Spencer, *Paul Simon: Now And Then*, Raven (UK), 1973.
Marsh, Dave, *Paul Simon*, Quick Fox (USA), 1978.
Matthew-Walker, Robert, *Simon And Garfunkel*, Midas Books, 1982.
Morella, Joseph & Barey, Patricia, *Simon & Garfunkel: Old Friends*, Birch Lane Press (USA), Robert Hale (UK), 1992.

Simon, Carly
Morse, Charles, *Carly Simon*, Creative Education, 1975.

Simon, Paul
Humphries, Patrick, *Paul Simon*, Doubleday (USA), 1990.
Humphries, Patrick, *The Boy In The Bubble: A Biography Of*

Paul Simon, Sidgwick & Jackson (UK), 1988.
Leigh, Spencer, *Paul Simon: Now And Then*, Raven (UK), 1973.
Marsh, Dave, *Paul Simon*, Quick Fox (USA), 1978.

Simone, Nina
Simone, Nina with Cleary, Stephen, *I Put A Spell On You: The Autobiography Of Nina Simone*, Ebury Press (UK), 1991.

Simple Minds
Bos, Alfred, *Simple Minds: Street Fighting Years*, Virgin Books (UK), 1990.
Sweeting, Adam, *Simple Minds*, Sidgwick & Jackson (UK), 1988.
Thomas, Dave, *Simple Minds: Glittering Prize*, Omnibus Press (UK), 1985.
Wrenn, Mike, *Simple Minds: A Visual Documentary*, Omnibus Press (UK), 1990.

Simply Red
Hodkinson, Mark, *The First Fully Illustrated Biography*, Omnibus Press (UK), 1994.
McGibbon, Robin & McGibbon, Rob, *Simply Mick: Mick Hucknall Of Simply Red. The Inside Story*, Weidenfeld & Nicolson (UK), 1993.

Sims, Zoot
Astrup, Arne, *The John Haley Sims (Zoot Sims) Discography*, Dansk Historisk Handbogsforlag.
Astrup, Arne, *The John Haley Sims (Zoot Sims) Discography Supplement*, Per Meistrup.

Sinatra, Frank
Ackelson, Richard W., *Frank Sinatra: A Complete Recording History*, Mcfarland & Co (USA), 1992.
Barnes, Ken, *Sinatra And The Great Song Stylists*, Ian Allan (UK), 1972.
Britt, Stan, *Frank Sinatra: A Celebration*, Hamlyn (UK), 1995.
Clarke, Donald, *All Or Nothing At All: A Life Of Frank Sinatra*, Macmillan (UK), 1997.
Coleman, Ray, *Sinatra: A Portrait Of The Artist*, Pavilion (UK), 1997.
Dellar, Fred, *Sinatra: His Life And Times*, Omnibus Press (UK), 1996.
Dellar, Fred & Peachey, Mal, *Sinatra Night And Day: The Man And His Music*, Chameleon Books (UK), 1997.
Douglas-Home, Robin, *Sinatra*, Michael Joseph (UK), 1962.
Frank, Alan, *Sinatra*, Hamlyn (UK), 1978.
Freedland, Michael, *All The Way*, Weidenfeld And Nicolson (UK), 1997.
Friedwald, Will, *Sinatra! The Song Is You: A Singer's Art*, Scribner (USA), 1995.
Gehman, Richard, *Sinatra And His Rat Pack: A Biography*, Belmont Books (USA), Mayflower (UK), 1961.
Hainsworth, Brian, *Songs By Sinatra, 1939-1970*, Hainsworth, 1973.
Hodge, Jessica, *Frank Sinatra*, Magna Books (UK), 1992.
Howlett, John, *Frank Sinatra*, Wallaby Books (USA), Plexus (UK), 1980.
Kahn, E.J., *The Voice: The Story Of An American Phenomen*, Harper And Bos (USA), 1946.
Kelley, Kitty, *His Way: The Unauthorized Biography Of Frank Sinatra*, Bantam Books (USA), 1990.
Lake, Harriet, *On Stage: Frank Sinatra*, Creative Education, 1976.
Lonstein, Albert I., *The Revised Compleat Sinatra: Discography, Filmography And Television Appearenc*, Sondra M. Lonstein (USA), 1979.
O'Brien, Ed & Sayers, Scott P., *The Recording Artistry Of Francis Albert Sinatra 1939-1992* ,1993.
Peters, Richard, *The Frank Sinatra Scrapbook: His Life And Times In Words And Pictures*, Souvenir Press (UK), 1982.
Petkov, Steven & Mustazza, Leonard (ed), *Frank Sinatra Reader: Seven Decades Of American Popular Music*, Oxford University Press (USA), 1995.
Petkove, Steven, & Mustazza, Leonard, (eds.), *The Frank Sinatra Reader*, Oxford University Press (UK), 1997.
Ridgway, John, *The Sinatra File: Part One*, John Ridgway Books, 1977.
Ridgway, John, *The Sinatra File: Part Two*, John Ridgway Books, 1978.
Ringold, Gene & Mccarthy, Clifford, *The Films Of Frank Sinatra*, Citadel Press (USA), 1971.
Rockwell, John, *Sinatra: An American Classic*, Rolling Stone Press (USA), 1984.
Scaduto, Anthony, *Frank Sinatra*, Sphere Books (UK), 1977.
Sciacca, Tony, *Sinatra*, Pinnacle Books (USA), 1976.
Shaw, Arnold, *Sinatra: A Biography*, W. H. Allen (UK), 1968.
Shaw, Arnold, *Sinatra: Retreat Of The Romantic*, Hodder (UK), 1970.
Sinatra, Frank, *Sinatra In His Own Words*, Omnibus Press (UK), 1981.
Sinatra, Nancy, *Frank Sinatra: An American Legend*, Virgin Books (UK), 1995.
Sinatra, Nancy, *Frank Sinatra: My Father*, Hodder (UK), 1990.
Taylor, Paula, *Frank Sinatra*, Creative Education, 1976.
Wilson, Earl, *Sinatra: An Unauthorized Biography*, New American Library (USA), Star Books (UK), 1976.

Siouxsie And The Banshees
Johns, Brian, *Entranced: The Siouxsie & The Banshees Story*, Omnibus Press (UK), 1989.
West, Mike, *Siouxsie And The Banshees*, Babylon Books (UK), 1982.

Sisters Of Mercy
Pinell, Andrew, *Heartland: Anthology Of Issues 1, 11 And 111*, Heartland, 1991.
Rinnell, Andrew James, *Sisters Of Mercy Discography: Heartland*, International Music Publications (UK), 1993.

Skunk Anansie
Malins, Steve, *Skunk Anansie: Skin I'm In*, Chameleon (UK), 1998.

Slade
Charlesworth, Chris, *Slade: Feel The Noize*, Omnibus Press (UK), 1984.
No author listed, *Slade*, New English Library (UK), 1972.
Pidgeon, John, *Slade In Flame*, Panther/Granada UK), 1975.
Tremlett, George, *The Slade Story*, Futura (UK), 1975.

Slick, Grace
Rowe, Barbara, *Grace Slick: The Biography*, New York, 1980.

Slik
Tremlett, George, *Slik*, Futura (UK), 1976.

Small Faces
Badman, Keith & Rawlins, Terry, *Quite Naturally*, Complete Music (UK), 1997.
Hewitt, Paolo, *The Young Mods' Forgotten Story*, Acid Jazz (UK), 1995.
Schmidt, Roland & Twelker, Uli, *Happy Boys Happy*, Sanctuary (UK), 1997.

Smashing Pumpkins
Wise, Nick, *Smashing Pumpkins*, Omnibus Press (UK), 1994.

Smith, Bessie
Albertson, Chris, *Bessie*, Stein & Day (USA), 1972.
Feinstein, Elaine, *Bessie Smith: Empress Of The Blues*, Penguin, 1990.
Moore, Carman, *Somebody's Angel Child: The Story Of Bessie Smith*, Thomas Y. Crowell (USA), 1969.
Oliver, Paul, *Bessie Smith*, A. S. Barnes, 1971.

Smith, Patti
Johnston, Nick, *Patti Smith: A Biography*, Omnibus Press (UK), 1997.
Muir, *Patti Smith: High On Rebellion*, Babylon Books (UK), 1980.
Roach, Dusty, *Patti Smith: Rock & Roll Madonna*, And Books (USA), 1979.
Smith, Patti, *Kodak*, Middle Earth (UK), 1972.
Smith, Patti, *The Coral Sea*, W. W. Norton (USA), 1996.
Smith, Patti, *Early Work: 1970-1979*, W.W. Norton And Co (USA), 1994.
Smith, Patti, *A Useless Death*..
Smith, Patti, *Babel*, Putnams (USA), 1974.
Smith, Patti, *Ha! Ha! Houdini!*, Gotham Book Mart (USA), 1977.
Smith, Patti, *Seventh Heaven*, Telegraph, Philadelphia (USA), 1972.
Smith, Patti, *The Tongue Of Love*.
Smith, Patti, *Witt*, Gotham Book Mart (USA), 1973.
Smith, Patti & Verlaine, Tom, *The Night*, Aloes Books (UK), 1976.

Smith, Stuff
Barnett, Anthony, *Desert Sands: The Recordings And Performances Of Stuff Smith*, Allardyce Barnett, 1995.

Smiths
Gallagher, Tom, Chapman, M & Gillies, M, *The Smiths: All Men Have Secrets*, Virgin Books (UK), 1995.
Middles, Mick, *The Smiths*, Omnibus Press (UK), 1986.
Rogan, Johnny, *The Smiths: The Visual Documentary*, Omnibus Press (UK), 1994.
Rogan, Johnny, *Morrissey & Marr: The Severed Alliance*, Omnibus Press (UK), 1992.
Smiths, *The Smiths: Louder Than Bombs - Off The Record*, International Music Publications (UK), 1993.

Snow, Hank
Snow, Hank with Ownby, Jack, & Burris, Bob, *The Hank Snow Story*, University Of Illinois Press (USA), 1994.

Soft Cell
Tebbutt, Simon, *Soft Cell*, Sidgwick & Jackson (UK), 1984.

Soft Machine
Allen, Daevid, *Gong Dreaming*, Gong Appreciation Society (UK), 1995.

Sondheim, Stephen
Banfield, Stephen, *Sondheim's Broadway Musicals*, University Of Michigan Press (USA), 1993.
Gordon, Joanne, *Art Isn't Easy: Theatre Of Stephen Sondheim*, Da Capo (USA), 1992.

Sonic Youth
Foege, Alec, *Confusion Is Next: The Sonic Youth Story*, Quartet (UK), 1994.

Sonny And Cher
Braun, Thomas, *Sonny And Cher*, Creative Education, 1978.

Sons Of The Pioneers
Griffis, Ken, *Hear My Song: The Story Of The Celebrated Sons Of The Pioneers* (USA), 1986.

Soul Asylum
Soul Asylum, *Grave Dancers Union*, Warner Bros (USA), 1994.

Sound Of Music, The (Film Musical)
Hirsch, Antopol, *The Sound Of Music: The Making Of America's Favorite Movie*, Contemporary Books (USA), 1996.

Soundgarden
Nickson, Chris, *Soundgarden: New Metal Crown*, St Martins Press (USA), 1996.

Sparks, Larry
Peterson, Henning, *Larry Sparks - A Discography*, , 1988.

Specials
Davies, Nick, *Specials Illustrated*, Plangent Visions Music, 1981.

Spector, Phil
Finnis, Rob, *The Phil Spector Story*, Rockon (UK), 1974.
Fitzpatrick, Jack & Fogerty, James E., *Collecting Phil Spector: The Man, The Legend, The Music*, Spectacle Press, 1991.
Ribowskys, Mark, *He's A Rebel*, Doubleday (USA), 1989.
Williams, Richard, *The Phil Spector Story: Out Of His Head*, Outerbridge & Lazard (USA), Abacus (UK), 1972.

Spector, Ronnie
Spector, Ronnie with Waldron, Vince, *Be My Baby*, Harmony Books (USA), 1990.

Spice Girls
Freeman, Dean (photographer), *Spice World: The Official Book Of The Movie*, Ebury Press (UK), 1998.
McGibbon, Rob, *Spice Power: The Inside Story*, Boxtree (UK), 1997.
Spice Girls, *Girl Power*, Chameleon Books (UK), 1997.

Spinal Tap
Occhiogrosso, Peter, *Inside Spinal Tap*, Warner Books (USA), Abacus (UK), 1992.

Spinners (UK)
Stuckey, David, *The Spinners*, Robson Books (UK), 1983.

Springfield, Dusty
O'Brien, Lucy, *Dusty*, Sidgwick & Jackson (UK), 1989.

Springsteen, Bruce
Cross, Charles R. (ed.), *Backstreets: Springsteen - The Man And His Music*, Sidgwick & Jackson (UK), 1990.
Cullen, Jim, *Born In The USA: Bruce Springsteen And The American Tradition*, Helter Skelter (UK), 1997.
Duffy, John, *Bruce Springsteen In His Own Words*, Omnibus Press (UK), 1993.
Editors of Rolling Stone, *Rolling Stone Files*, Hyperion (USA), Macmillan (UK), 1996.
Eliot, Mark, *Down Thunder Road*, Plexus (UK), 1992.
Gambaccini, Peter, *Bruce Springsteen*, Quick Fox (USA), 1979.
Heylin, Clinton & Gee, Simon, *The E. Street Shuffle*, Labour Of Love/Badlands/My Back Pages (UK), 1989.
Humphries, Patrick, *The Complete Guide To The Music Of: Bruce Springsteen*, Omnibus Press (UK), 1996.
Humphries, Patrick & Hunt, Chris, *Springsteen: Blinded By The Light*, Plexus (UK), 1985.
Lynch, Kate, *Springsteen: No Surrender*, Bobcat Books (USA), 1987.

MacInnis, Craig, *Bruce Springsteen Here & Now*, Sidgwick & Jackson (UK), 1988.
March, Dave, *Springsteen: Born To Run*, Delilah (USA), Omnibus Press (UK), 1979.
Marsh, Dave, *Glory Days*, Arrow (UK), 1990.

Squeeze
Squeeze, *Some Fantastic Place*, International Music Publications (UK), 1994.

Staines, Bill
Staines, Bill, *Moving It Down The Line*, 1987
Staines, Bill, *If I Were A Word, Then I'd Be A Song*, 1980.
Staines, Bill & Zemach, Margot, *All God's Critters Got A Place In The Choir*.

Stanley, Ralph
Wright, John, *Travellin' The HighwayHome: Ralph Stanley And The World Of Bluegrass Music*, University Of Illinois Press (USA), 1993.

Star Is Born, A
Haver, Ronald, *The Making Of The 1954 Movie And Its 1983 Reconstruction*, Knopf (USA), 1977.

Stardust, Alvin
Tremlett, George, *The Alvin Stardust Story*, Futura (UK), 1976.

Starr, Ringo
Clayson, Alan, *Ringo Starr: Straight Man Or Joker?*, Sidgwick & Jackson (UK), 1992.

Status Quo
Hibbert, Tom, *Status Quo*, Omnibus Press (UK), 1981.
Jeffries, Neil, *Status Quo: Rockin' All Over The World*, Proteus Books (UK), 1985.
Rossi, Francis, & Parfitt, Rick, *Just For The Record: The Autobioography Of Status Quo*, Bantam Press (UK), 1993.
Shearlaw, John, *25th Anniversary Edition*, Sidgwick & Jackson, 1987 (UK).
Shearlaw, John, *Status Quo: The Authorized Biography*, Sidgwick & Jackson (UK), 1979.

Stax Records
Bowman, Rob, *Soulsville USA: The Story Of Stax Records*, Books With Attitude, 1998.

Steele, Tommy
Kennedy, John, *Tommy Steele: The Facts About A Teenage Idol And An Inside:Picture Of Show Busin*, Souvenir Press (UK), 1958.
Tatham, Dick, *The Wonderful Tommy Steele: Picture-Story Album*, Record Mirror (UK), 1957.

Steely Dan
Sweet, Brian, *Steely Dan: Reelin' In The Years*, Omnibus Press (UK), 1994.

Stevens, Cat
Charlesworth, Chris, *Cat Stevens*, Proteus Books (UK), 1985.
Evans, David, *The Boy Who Looked At The Moon: Life And Times Of Cat Stevens*, Britannia Press Publishing (UK), 1995.
Stevens, Cat, *Teaser And The Firecat*, B. Jacobson (UK), 1972.

Stewart, Rex
Stewart, Rex, *Rex Stewart's 'Warm-Up' Book*, Leeds Music. (UK)
Stewart, Rex with Dance, Stanley, *Jazz Masters Of The Thirties*, New York & London, 1972.

Stewart, Rod
Burton, Peter, *Rod Stewart: A Life On The Town*, New English Library (UK), 1977.
Coleman, Ray, *Rod Stewart: The Biography*, Pavilion (UK), 1995.
Cromelin, Richard, *Rod Stewart: A Biography In Words & Pictures*, Sire/Chappell Music, 1976.
Ewbank, Tim & Hildred, Stafford, *Rod Stewart: A Biography*, Headline (UK), 1991.
Gray, John, *The Visual Documentary*, Omnibus Press (UK), 1994.
Guiliano, Geoffrey, *Rod Stewart: Vagabond Heart*, New English Library (UK), 1993.
Jasper, Tony, *Rod Stewart*, Octopus Books (UK), 1977.
Nelson, Paul & Bangs, Lester, *Rod Stewart*, Sidgewick & Jackson (UK), Delilah (USA), 1981.
Pidgeon, John, *Rod Stewart And The Faces*, Panther/Granada (UK), 1976.
Rockl, Gerd & Sahner, Paul, *Rod Stewart*, Lubbe, 1979.
Tremlett, George, *The Rod Stewart Story*, Futura (UK), 1976.

Stiff Records
Muirhead, Bert, *Stiff, The Story Of a Record Label, 1976-1982*, Sterling, 1983.

Sting
Clarkson, Wensley, *The Secret Life Of Gordon Sumner*, Blake (UK), 1996.
Sellers, Robert, *Sting: A Biography*, Omnibus Press (UK), 1989.
Welch, Chris, *Complete Guide To the Music Of: The Police And Sting*, Omnibus Press (UK), 1996.

Stone Roses
Robb, John, *The Stone Roses And The Resurrection Of British Pop*, Ebury Press (UK), 1998.

Stone Temple Pilots
Wall, Mike & Dome, Malcolm, *Stone Temple Pilots*, Omnibus Press (UK), 1995.

Stone, Lew
Trodd, K., *Lew Stone: A Career In Music*.

Stoneman Family
Tribe, Ivan M., *The Stonemans*, Urbana and Chicago, USA, 1993.

Strange Fruit Records
Garner, Ken, *In Session Tonight*, BBC (UK), 1993.

Stranglers
Black, Jet, *Much Ado About Nothing*, Stranglers' Information Service, London, 1981.
Buckley, David, *No Mercy: The Authorised And Uncensored Biography Of The Stranglers*, Hodder & Stoughton (UK), 1998.
Cornwell, Hugh, *Inside Information*, Stranglers' Information Service (UK), 1980.

Strayhorn, Billy
Hajdu, David, *Lush Life*, Farrar, Straus & Giroux (USA), Granta (UK), 1996.

Streisand, Barbra
Brady, Frank, *Barbra Streisand: An Illustrated Biography*, Grosset & Dunlap (UK), 1979.
Carrick, Peter, *Barbra Streisand: A Biography*, Robert Hale (UK), 1991.
Castell, David, *The Films Of Barbra Streisand*, BCW, 1977.
Considine, Shawn, *Barbra Streisand, The Woman, The Myth,*

The Music, London, 1986.
Eldred, Patricia Mulrooney, *Barbra Streisand*, Creative Education, 1975.
Jordan, Rene, *Streisand: Unauthorized Biography*, W.H. Allen (UK), 1976.
Keenan, Debra, *On Stage Barbra Streisand*, Creative Education, 1976.
Kimbrell, Cheri (ed), *Barbra: An Actress Who Sings Volume II*, Branden (USA), 1992.
Kimbrell, James, *Barbra: An Actress Who Sings*, Branden (USA), 1989.
Reise, Randall, *Her Name Is Barbra*, Birch Lane Press (USA), 1993.
Spada, James, *Streisand: The Intimate Biography*, Little Brown (USA), 1995.
Spada, James, *Streisand: The Woman And The Legend*, Comet Books (UK), Doubleday (USA), 1981.
Swenson, Karen, *Barbra: The Second Decade*, Citidal Press (USA), 1986.
Teti, Frank & Moline, Karen, *Streisand Through The Lens*, Sidgwick & Jackson (UK), 1982.
Waldman, Allison J., *The Barbra Streisand Scrapbook*, Citidal Press (USA), 1994.
Zec, Donald & Fowles, Anthony, *Barbra: A Biography Of Barbra Streisand*, New English Library (UK), 1982.

Stricklin, Al
Stricklin, Al, *My Years With Bob Wills*, Burnet (USA), 1976.

Style Council
Munn, Ian, *Mr Cool's Dream - The Complete History Of The Style Council*, Whole Point Productions (UK), 1996.

Styne, Jule
Taylor, Theodore, *Jule: The Story Of Composer Jule Styne.*, Random House (USA), 1979.

Suede
Membrey, York, *Suede: The Illustrated Biography*, Omnibus Press (UK), 1993.

Suicide
Vega, Alan, *Cripple Nation*, (US), 1994.

Summer, Donna
Haskins, James, *Donna Summer: An Unauthorized Biography*, Little Brown (USA), 1983.

Sun Ra
Ra, Sun, *The Immeasurable Equation,*.
Szwed, John E., *Space Is The Place: The Lives And Times Of Sun Ra*, Pantheon (USA), Payback Press (UK), 1997.

Sun Records
Escott, Colin with Martin Hawkins, *Good Rockin' Tonight: Sun Records And The Birth Of Rock 'N' Roll*, Virgin Books (UK), 1992.

Supergrass
Holorny, Linda, *Supergrass*, Omnibus Press (UK), 1996.

Supertramp
Melhuish, Martin, *The Supertramp Book*, Omnibus Press (UK), 1986.

Supremes
Bond, Johnny, *Reflections*, Los Angeles, 1976.
Turner, Tony & Aria, Barbara, *All That Glittered: My Life With The Supremes*, E.P. Dutton (USA), 1990.

Wilson, Mary, *Dreamgirl: My Life As A Supreme*, St. Martin's Press (USA), 1987.
Wilson, Mary with Romanowski, Patricia, *Supreme Faith: Someday We'll Be Together*, Harper Collins (UK), 1990.

Sutch, Screaming Lord
Sutch, David with Chippendale, Peter, *Life As Sutch: The Official Autobiography Of Monster Raving Looney*, Harper Collins (UK), 1991.

Sutcliffe, Stuart
Clayson, Alan & Sutcliffe, Pauline, *Backbeat: Stuart Sutcliffe The Lost Beatle*, Pan (UK), 1994.
Williams, Kay & Sutcliffe, Pauline, *Stuart - The Life And Art Of Stuart Sutcliffe*, Genesis Publications (UK), 1996.

Sweet
Nilsson, Christer, *The Not Even Close To Complete Sweet Encyclopedia*, Rock 'N' Records Productions (UK), 1997.

Sylvian, David
Zornes, D, Sawyer, H. & Powell H., *David Sylvian: 80 Days*, Bamboo (UK), 1990.

T. Rex
Stevenson, Ray, *Tyrannosaurus Rex*, T. Rex Appreciation Society (UK), 1991.

Take That
Morgan, Piers, *Take That: Our Story*, Boxtree (UK), 1993.
St. Michael, Mick, *The Unofficial Biography*, Bobcat Books (USA), 1994.
Take That, *Everything Changes*, International Music Publications (UK), 1994.
Taylor, Luke, *Talk Back*, Omnibus Press (UK), 1994.

Talking Heads
Davis, Jerome, *Talking Heads: A Biography*, Omnibus Press (UK), 1987.
Gans, David, *Talking Heads: The Band And Their Music*, Omnibus Press (UK), 1986.
Miles, *Talking Heads*, Omnibus Press (UK), 1981.
Reese, Krista, *The Name Of This Book Is Talking Heads*, Proteus Books (UK), 1983.

Tangerine Dream
Stump, Paul, *Digital Gothic: A Critical Discography Of Tangerine Dream*, SAF (UK), 1997.

Tatum, Art
Distler, Jed (ed.), *Art Tatum*, Music Sales.
Laubich, Arnold, *Art Tatum, A Guide To His Recorded Music*, Scarecrow (USA), 1982.
Lester, James, *Too Marvellous For Words: The Life And Genius Of*, Oxford University Press, 1994.

Taupin, Bernie
No author listed, *Elton John Bernie Taupin, The Complete Lyrics*, Pavilion Books (UK), 1994.

Taylor, Billy
Taylor, Billy, *Jazz Combo Arranging*, C. Hansen Educational Music & Books.
Taylor, Billy, *Jazz Piano*, W. C. Brown, 1983.
Taylor, Billy, *Jazz Piano: History And Development*, Dubuque, 1982.
Taylor, Billy, *Piano Solos*, C. Hansen.
Taylor, Billy, *Sketches For Jazz Trio*, Duane Music.
Taylor, Billy, *The History And Development Of Jazz Piano*,

Amherst, Massachusetts, (USA), 1975.

Taylor, Derek
Taylor, Derek, *As Time Goes By*, Abacus (UK), 1974.
Taylor, Derek, *Fifty Years Adrift (In An Open-Necked Shirt)*, Genesis (UK), 1983.
Taylor, Derek, *It Was Twenty Years Ago Today*, Bantam (UK), 1987.

Taylor, James
Taylor, James, *Live*, Waner Bros (USA), 1994.
Taylor, James, *Greatest Hits*, Warner Bros (USA), 1994.

Teagarden, Jack
Smith, Jay D. & Guttridge, Len, *Jack Teagarden: The Story Of A Jazz Maverick*, Cassell (UK), 1960.
Walters, H. Jnr., *Jack Teagarden's Music*, Stanhope, New Jersey (USA), 1960.

Tears For Fears
Greene, Ann, *Tears For Fears*, Omnibus Press (UK), 1986.
No author listed, *Tears Roll Down: Words And Music 1982-92*, EMI Music Publications (UK), 1992.

Techno
Thornton, Sarah, *Club Cultures: Music, Media And Subcultural Capital*, Wesleyan/New England (USA), 1996.

Temptations
Williams, Otis with Romanowski, Patricia, *Temptations*, Putnam (USA), 1988.

Them
Rogan, Johnny, *Van Morrison: A Portrait Of The Artist*.

Thiele, Bob
Golden, Bob, *What A Wonderful World* (USA), 1994.

Thin Lizzy
Bailie, Stuart, *The Ballad Of The Thin Man*, Boxtree (UK), 1996.
Lynott, Philip, *A Collected Works Of Philip Lynott*, Chappell, 1979.
Lynott, Philip, *Philip*, Pippen (UK), 1977.
Lynott, Philip, *Songs For While I'm Away*, Pippen (UK), 1974.
Lynott, Philomena with Jackie Hayden, *My Boy: The Philip Lynott Story*, Virgin Books (UK), 1995.
Pryce, Larry, *Thin Lizzy*, Star (UK), 1977.
Salewicz, Chris, *Thin Lizzy: The Approved Biography*, Pippin The Friendly Ranger, London, 1979.

Thompson Twins
Rouce, Rose, *The Thompson Twins: An Odd Couple*, Virgin Books (UK), 1985.

Thompson, Richard
Heylin, Clinton, *Gypsy Love Songs & Sad Refrains: The Recordings Of Richard Thompson & Sandy Denn*, Labour Of Love (UK), 1989.
Heylin, Clinton, *Richard Thompson: 21 Years Of Doom & Gloom*, Clinton Heylin (UK), 1988.
Humphries, Patrick, *Richard Thompson: Strange Affair, The Biography*, Virgin Books (UK), 1996.

Throbbing Gristle
Orridge, Genesis P., *Throbbing Gristle Scrapbook: First Annual Report*, Temple Press, 1990.

Thunders, Johnny
Antonia, Nina, *Johnny Thunders: In Cold Blood*, Jungle Books, 1987.

Tikaram, Tanita
Tikaram, Tanita, *Songs From An Invisible Woman*, International Music Publications (UK), 1994.

Tillis, Mel
Tillis, Mel with Wager, Walter, *Stutterin' Boy, The Autobiography Of Mel Tillis*, Rawson Associates (USA), 1984.

Timelords
Timelords, *The Manual*.

Tiny Tim
Stein, Harry, *Tiny Tim*, Playboy Press (USA), 1976.

Todd, Dick
O'Connell, Sheldon, *Dick Todd: King Of The Jukebox*.

Toop, David, And Max Eastley
Toop, David, *Rap Attack*.
Toop, David, *Ocean Of Sound: Aether Talk, Ambient Sound And Imaginary Worlds*, Serpent's Tail (UK), 1996.

Torme, Mel
Torme, Mel, *The Otyher Side Of The Rainbow*, W. Morrow (USA), 1970.
Torme, Mel, *Mel Torme: It Wasn't All Velvet*, Viking (USA), 1988.

Townshend, Pete
Guiliano, Geoffrey, *A Life Of Pete Townshend: Behind Blue Eyes*, Hodder & Stoughton (UK), 1996.
Townshend, Pete, *The Hores Neck*, Faber & Faber (UK), 1985.

Toyah
Evans, Gayna, *Toyah*, Proteus Books (UK), 1982.
West, Mike, *Toyah*, Omnibus Press (UK), 1982.

Travis, Randy
Cusic, Don, *Randy Travis: The King Of The New Country Traditionalists*, St Martin's Press (USA), 1990.
No editor listed, *The Randy Travis Songbook*, Hal Leonard Publications (USA).

Travolta, John
De Christoforo, Ron, *Grease*, Magnum Books, 1978.
Eisen, Arman (ed.) & Michael Sollars, *The Grease Album*, Phin, 1978.
Gilmour, H.B., *Saturday Night Fever: A Novelisation*, Bantam Books (USA), 1977.
Latham, Aaron, *Urban Cowboy: A Novel*, Corgi (UK), 1980.
Munshower, Suzanne, *The John Travolta Scrapbook: An Illustrated Biography*, Souvenir Press (UK), 1978.
No editor listed, *Grease: A Fotonovel Publications Fotonovel*, Fotonovel, 1978.
Reeves, Michael, *Travolta!: A Photo Bio*, Jove/HBJ (USA), 1978.
Schumacher, Craig, *John Travolta*, Creative Education, 1980.

Trumbauer, Frank
Trumbauer, Frank, *Tailspin*, Robbins Music.

Tubb, Ernest
Barthel, Norman, *Ernest Tubb: The Original E.T.*, Rowland (USA), 1984.
Pugh, Ronnie, *The Texas Troubadour*.

Tucker, Sophie
Tucker, Sophie, *Some Of These Days*, 1945.

Turner, Bruce
Turner, Bruce, *Hot Air, Cool Music*, London, 1984.

Turner, Tina
Turner, Tina, *Tina Turner: Easy Arrangements For Piano*, International Music Publications (UK), 1995.
Turner, Tina with Loder, Kurt, *I, Tina*, Penguin, 1987.
Welch, Chris, *The Tina Turner Experience*, Virgin Books (UK), 1994.

Twist
Dawson, Jim, *The Twist: The Story Of The Song And Dance That Changed The World*, Faber & Faber (UK), 1995.

Tyner, McCoy
Tyner, McCoy, *Fly With The Wind*, Fantasy, 1986.

Tyson, Ian And Sylvia
Tyson, Ian & Escott, Colin, *Never Sold My Saddle*, Gibbs Smith, 1994.

U2
Bowler, Dave & Dray, Brian, *U2: A Conspiracy Of Hope*, Sidgwick & Jackson (UK), 1993.
Carter, Alan, *Wide Awake In America*, Boxtree (UK), 1992.
De La Perra, Pimm Jal, *U2 Live: A Concert Documentary*, Omnibus Press (UK), 1994.
Dunphy, Eamon, *Unforgettable Fire: The Story Of U2*, Viking (UK), 1988.
Editors of Rolling Stone, *U2, The Rolling Stones File*, Sidgwick & Jackson (UK), 1994.
Fallon, B.P., *U2 Faraway So Close*, Virgin Books (UK), 1994.
Flanagan, Bill, *U2 At The End Of The World*, Bantam Press (USA), 1995.
Gardner, Elysa (ed.), *U2: The Rolling Stone Files*, Sidgwick & Jackson (UK), 1994.
Goodman, Sam, *U2: Burning Desire - The Complete Story*, Castle Books (UK), 1993.
Graham, Bill, *U2 The Early Days: Another Time, Another Place*, Mandarin (UK), 1989.
Graham, Bill, *The Complete Guide To The Music Of ...*, Omnibus Press (UK), 1995.
Hot Press editors, *The U2 File: A Hot Press U2 History*, Omnibus Press (UK).
Parkyn, Geoff, *U2: Touch The Flame. An Illustrated Documentary*, Omnibus Press (UK), 1987.
Seal, Richard, *U2: The Story So Far*, Britannia (UK), 1993.
Stokes, Niall, *Into The Heart: The Stories Behind Every U2 Song*, Omnibus Press (UK).
Stokes, Niall, *The U2 File*, Omnibus Press (UK), 1985.
Stokes, Niall, *U2: Three Chords & The Truth*, Omnibus Press (UK), 1990.
Thomas, Dave, *U2: Stories For Boys*, Bobcat (USA), 1988.
Thompson, Dave, *The Making Of: U2's Joshua Tree*, Collectors Guide Publishing (USA), 1996.
Waters, John, *Race Of Angels: The Genesis Of U2*, Fourth Estate (UK), 1994.
Williams, Peter & Turner, Steve, *U2: Rattle And Hum*, Pyramid, 1988.

UK Subs
Gibbs, Alvin, *Neighbourhood Threat*, Britannia (UK), 1995.

Ultravox
Drake & Gilbert, *The Past, Present & Future Of Ultravox*.

Valens, Ritchie
Clark, Alan, *Ritchie Valens 1941-1959: 30th Anniversary Memorial Series No 2*, West Covina, California (USA), 1989.
Mendheim, Beverly, *Ritchie Valens: The First Latino Rocker*, Bilingual Press (USA), 1987.

Van Der Graaf Generator
Shaw-Parker, David, *The Lemming Chronicles*, Pandoras Box (UK), 1995.

Van Halen
Craven, Michelle, *Van Halen*.
Dome, Malcom, *Excess All Areas*.

Vangelis
Griffin, Mark J.T., *Vangelis: The Unknown Man*, Smithy Croft, Schivas, Ythanbank, Aberdeenshire, AB1 0UA, 1994.

Vaughan, Sarah
Gourse, Leslie, *Sassy - The Life Of Sarah Vaughan*, Mainstream, 1993.

Vaughan, Stevie Ray
Patoski, Joe Nick & Crawford, Bill, *Stevie Ray Vaughan: Caught In The Crossfire*, Little Brown (USA), 1993.

Velvet Underground
Bockris, Victor & Malanga, G., *Uptight: The Velvet Underground Story*, Quill (USA), Omnibus Press (UK), 1983.
Kostek, Michael C., *Velvet Underground: A Complete Mediography*, Black Spring Press, 1992.
Kostek, Michael C., *The Velvet Underground Handbook*, Black Spring Press (UK), 1992.
No editor listed, *Velvet Underground Scrapbook*, 1991.
Shore, Stephen & Tillman, Lynne, *The Velvet Years: Warhol's Factory 1965-1967*, Pavilion (UK), 1998.
Thompson, Dave, *Beyond The Velvet Underground*, Omnibus Press (UK), 1989.

Verve
Wilding, Peter, *The Verve - Bitter Sweet*, Chameleon (UK), 1998.

Vincent, Gene
Clark, Alan, *Gene Vincent: The Screaming End*, Allan Clark (USA), 1980.
Finnis, Rob & Dunham, Bob, *Gene Vincent & The Blue Caps*, Private Edition, 1974.
Hagerty, Britt, *The Day The World Turned Blue*, Blandford Press, (UK), 1985.
Henderson, Derek, *Gene Vincent: A Discography*, Spent Brothers Productions (UK), 1992.
Muir, Eddie, *Wild Cat: A Tribute To Gene Vincent*.
Vince, Alan, *I Remember Gene Vincent*, Vintage Rock 'N' Roll Appreciation Society (UK), 1977.

Vinton, Bobby
Vinton, Bobby, *The Polish Prince*, M. Evans, 1978.

Virgin Records
Southern, Terry (ed), *A History Of Virgin Records*, Virgin (UK), 1995.

Wagoner, Porter
Eng, Steve, *A Satisfied Mind: The Country Music Life Of Porter Wagoner*, Rutledge Hill Press (USA), 1995.

Wainwright, Loudon, III
Harrison, Kevin, *So Many Fabulous Songs: Discography 1970-*

1996, BAD Press (UK), 1996.

Waits, Tom
Humphries, Patrick, *Small Change: A Life Of Tom Waits*, Omnibus Press (UK), 1989.

Wakely, Jimmy
Wakely, Linda Lee, *See Ya Up There, Baby - A Biography*, Shasta Records, 1994.

Wakeman, Rick
Wakeman, Rick, *Say Yes!*, Hodder & Stoughton (UK), 1995.
Wooding, Dan, *Rick Wakeman: The Caped Crusader*, Coverdale House, London, 1974.

Walker, Ian
Walker, Ian, *Ring Around The Moon*, 1993.

Walker, Scott
Watkinson, Mike & Anderson, Pete, *A Deep Shade Of Blue*, Virgin Books (UK), 1994.

Walker, T-Bone
Dance, Helen Oakly, *Stormy Monday*, Da Capo Press (USA), 1991.

Waller, Fats
Fox, Charles, *Fats Waller*, Barnes, 1961.
Kirkeby, Ed., *Ain't Misbehavin': The Story of Fats Waller*, Dodd Mead & Co./Da Capo (USA).
Machlin, Paul S., *Stride, The Music Of Fats Waller*, Macmillan, 1985.
Shipton, Alyn, *Fats Waller: His Life & Times*, Universe Books, 1988.
Sill, Harold D., *Misbehavin' With Fats*, Addison-Wesley.
Vance, Joel, *Fats Waller: His Life And Times*, Contemporary Books (USA), 1977.

Wallington, George
Wallington, George, *George Wallington (Interviewed by Marian McPartland)*.

Wangford, Hank
Hutt, Sam, *Hank Wangford: Volume III: The Middle Years*, Pan (UK), 1989.
Wangford, Hank, *Lost Cowboys*, Gollancz (UK), 1995.

Warner, Frank And Anne
Warner, Frank, *Frank Warner Sings American Folk Songs And Ballads*, Elektra (USA), 1952.

Warren, Harry
Thomas, Tony, *Harry Warren And The Hollywood Musical*, Citadel Press (USA), 1975.

Washington, Dinah
Haskins, James, *Dinah Washington: Queen Of The Blues*, New York, 1987.

Waters, Ethel
Waters, Ethel & Samuels C., *His Eye Is On The Sparrow*, London, 1951.

Watson, Doc
Watson, Doc, *The Songs Of Doc Watson*, Oak Publications (USA), 1971.

Weather Report
Zawinul, Josef, *The Best Of Weather Report*, Warner Brothers (USA).

Wedding Present
Hodkinson, Mark, *The Wedding Present: Thank Yer, Very Glad*, Omnibus Press (UK), 1990.

Weill, Kurt
Symonette, Lys & Kowalke, Kim, *Speak Low (When You Speak Love): The Letters Of Kurt Weill And Lotte Lenya*, Hamish Hamilton (UK), 1996.
Taylor, Ronald, *Kurt Weill: Composer In A Divided World*, Simon & Schuster (UK), 1991.

Welk, Lawrence
No author listed, *Welk, Laurence, Wunnerful, Wunnerful*, New York, 1971.
Welk, Lawrence, *Ah-One, Ah-Two: Life With My Musical Family*, New York, 1974.

Weller, Paul
Heatley, Michael, *Paul Weller: In His Own Words*, Virgin Books (UK), 1997.
Malins, Steve, *The Unauthorised Biography*, Virgin Books (UK), 1997.
Reed, John, *Paul Weller: My Ever Changing Moods*, Omnibus Press (UK), 1996.
Watson, Lawrence & Hewitt, Paolo, *Days Lose Their Names And Time Slips Away: Paul Weller 1992-95*, Boxtree (UK), 1995.

Wells, Dicky
Wells, Dicky as told to Dance, Stanley, *The Night People*, Crescendo, Boston (USA), 1971.

Wells, Kitty
Dunkleburger, A.C., *Queen Of Country Music: The Life Story Of Kitty Wells*, Nashville, 1977.
Pinson, Weize & Wolfe, *Kitty Wells: The Golden Years*, Vollersode, Germany, 1987.
Trott, Walt, *The Honky Tonk Angels: A Dual Biography*, Nova Books, 1993.

West Coast Jazz
Marsh, Graham & Callingham, Glyn, *California Cool*, Collins & Brown (UK), 1992.

Wet Wet Wet
Fowler, Simon & Jackson, Alan, *Wet Wet Wet Pictured*, Virgin Books (UK), 1995.

Wetton, John
Dancha, Kim, *My Own Time*, Northern Line, 1997.

Wexler, Jerry
Wexler, Jerry & Ritz, David, *Rhythm And The Blues: A Life In American Music*, Knopf (USA), 1993.

Wham!
Michael, George, *Bare*.
Rogan, Johnny, *Wham! (Confidential) The Death Of A Supergroup*, Omnibus Press (UK), 1988.

Wheatstraw, Peetie
Garon, Paul, *The Devil's Son-In-Law: The Story Of Peetie Wheatstraw And His Songs*, Studio Vista (UK), 1971.

Whiteman, Paul
Johnson, Carl, *A Paul Whiteman Chronology, 1890-1967*, Williams College, 1978.

Whitesnake
Hibbert, Tom, *Whitesnake*, Omnibus Press (UK), 1981.

Whitman, Slim
Gibble, Kenneth L., *Mr. Songman: The Slim Whitman Story*, Brethren Press (USA), 1981.

Who
Ashley, Brian & Monnery, Steve, *Whose Who? A Who Retrospective*, New English Library (UK), 1978.
Barnes, Richard, *Mods!*, Eel Pie (UK), 1979.
Barnes, Richard, *The Who Maximum R & B: An Illustrated Biography*, Eel Pie (UK), 1982.
Barnes, Richard & Townshend, Pete, *The Story Of Tommy*, Eel Pie (UK), 1977.
Broughton, Geoffrey, *Password 1*, Penguin (UK), 1977.
Butler, Dougal, *Full Moon:The Amazing Rock & Roll Life Of Keith Moon, Late Of The Who*, Quill Books (USA), 1982.
Butler, Dougal with Trengove, Chris & Lawrence, Peter, *Moon The Loon: The Amazing Rock And Roll Life Of Keith Moon*, Star/W.H. Allen (UK), 1981.
Charlesworth, Chris, *The Complete Guide To The Music Of ...*, Omnibus Press (UK), 1995.
Charlesworth, Chris, *The Who: The Illustrated Biography*, Omnibus Press (UK), 1982.
Clarke, Steve, *The Who In Their Own Words*, Omnibus Press (UK), 1979.
Cohn, Nik, *The Who Generation*, Circus Enterprises (USA), 1976.
Dickinson, Peter, *Hepzibah*, Eel Pie (UK), 1978.
Ehrlich, Cindy, *The Who: Ten Great Years*, Straight Arrow (USA), 1975.
Fletcher, Alan, *Quadrophenia*, Corgi/Transworld (UK) , 1979.
Fletcher, Tony, *Dear Boy: The Life Of Keith Moon*, Omnibus Press (UK), Avon Books (USA), 1998.
Fuller, John G., *Are The Kids All Right?: The Rock Generation & Its Hidden Death Wish*, Times Books/Quadrangle (USA), 1981.
Gomez, Joseph, *Ken Russell: The Adaptor As Creator*, Frederick Muller (UK), 1976.
Hanel, Ed, *The Who: An Illustrated Discography*, Omnibus Press (UK), 1981.
Herman, Gary, *The Who*, Macmillan (USA) , 1972.
Kamin, Philip & Goddard, Peter, *The Who: The Farewell Tour*, Beaufort Books (USA), 1983.
Lunden, Ollie (ed), *The Who In Sweden*, Squeeze Books (UK), 1996.
Marchbank, Pearce, *The Who File*, Wise/Fabulous Music (UK), 1979.
Marsh, Dave, *Before I Get Old: The Story Of The Who*, Plexus (UK), 1983.
Mazzone, Giacomo, *The Who* , Arcana Editore (Italy), 1980.
McKnight, Conner & Silver, Caroline, *The Who...Through The Eyes Of Pete Townshend*, Scholastic Book Services (USA), 1974.
McMichael, Joe & Lyones, Irish Jack, *The Who Concert File*, Omnibus Press (UK), 1997.
No editor listed, *Quadrophenia: Comprehensive Information*, , 1979.
Reins, Sacha, *Les Who*, Editions Chiron (France), 1974.
Sahner, Paul & Veszelits, Thomas, *The Who*, Bastei-Lubbe (Germany), 1980.
Stein, Jeff & Johnston, Chris, *The Who*, Stein & Day (USA), 1973.
Swenson, John, *The Who*, Star Books (UK), 1981.
Swenson, John, *The Who: Britain's Greatest Rock Group*, Tempo (USA), 1979.
Tremlett, George, *The Who*, Futura (UK), 1975.
Turner, Steve, *A Decade Of The Who: An Authorized History In Music, Paintings, Words And Photo*, Elm Tree Books (UK), 1977.

Von Werner, Balzert, Lore, Cortis & Lutz-W., Wolff, *The Who: Long Live Rock Songbook*, Deutscher Taschenbuch (Germany), 1980.
Waterman, Ivan, *Keith Moon: The Life And Death Of A Rock Legend*, Arrow Books (UK), 1979.

Who's Tommy, The
No author listed, *The Who's Tommy: The Musical*, Pantheon Books, 1993.

Wilber, Bob
Wilber, Bob with Webster, Derek, *Music Was Not Enough*, New York & London, 1987.

Wilder, Alec
Balliett, Whitney, *Alec Wilder And His Friends*, Houghton Mifflin (USA), 1974.

Williams, Andy
No author listed, *Andy And David On The Beach*, Mirror Books (UK), 1973.

Williams, Clarence
Lord, Tom, *Clarence Williams*, Storyville, 1976.

Williams, Hank
Arp, Jim, *The First Outlaw: Hank Williams*, King's Mountain, 1979.
Bock, Al, *I Saw The Light: The Gospel Life Of Hank Williams*.
Caress, Jay, *Hank Williams, Country Music's Tragic King*, Stein and Day (USA), 1979.
Cusic, Don (ed.), *The Complete Lyrics*, St. Martin's Press (USA), 1992.
Escott, Colin, *Hank Williams: The Biography*, Little, Brown (USA), 1994.
Flippo, Chet, *Your Cheating Heart: A Biography Of Hank Williams*, Simon & Schuster (USA), Plexus (UK), 1981.
Koon, George William, *Hank Williams: A Bio-Bibliography*, Greenwood Press, 1983.
Rivers, Jerry, *I Saw The Light: From Life To Legend*, Denver, 1967.
Rogers, Arnold & Gidoll, Bruce, *The Life And Times Of Hank Williams*, Hanley-Jones Books, 1993.
Williams, Jett & Thomas, Pamela, *Ain't Nothin' As Sweet As My Baby: The Story Of Hank Williams' Lost Daughter*, Harcourt Brace Jonanovich (USA), 1990.
Williams, Lycrecia, *Still In Love With You: The Story Of Hank And Audrey Williams*, Rutledge Hill Press (USA), 1989.
Williams, Roger M., *Sing A Sad Song: The Life Of Hank Williams*, University Of Illinois Press (USA).

Williams, Hank, Jnr.
Williams, Hank Jnr. with Bane, Michael, *Living Proof*, Putnam (USA), 1979.

Williamson, Robin
Williamson, Robin, *Home Thoughts From Abroad*, Deepdown (UK), 1972.

Wills, Bob
Latham, Jimmy, *Life Of Bob Wills: King Of Western Swing*, Texas Tech Press, Odessa, 1974.
Sheldon, Ruth, *Bob Wills: Hubbin' It*, Vanderbilt University Press (USA), 1995.
Townsend, Charles R., *San Antonio Rose: The Life And Music Of Bob Wills*, University Of Illinois Press (USA), 1976.

Wilson, Brian
White, Timothy, *The Nearest Faraway Place: Brian Wilson And*

The Southern California Experience, Henry Holt And Co. (USA), 1995.

Wilson, Dennis
Wincentsen, Edward, *Denny Remembered*, Virgin Books (UK), 1991.

Wilson, Jackie
Douglas, Tony, *Lonely Teardrops: The Jackie Wilson Story*, Sanctuary (UK), 1998.

Wilson, Teddy
No author listed, *The Genius Of Teddy Wilson*, Big 3.

Wings
Gelly, David, *The Facts About A Rock Group, Featuring Wings*, Harmony (USA), 1977.

Winwood, Steve
Clayson, Alan, *Back In The High Life: A Biography Of Steve Winwood*, Sidgwick & Jackson (UK), 1989.
Welch, Chris, *Keep On Running: The Steve Winwood Story.*, Omnibus Press (UK), 1988.
Welch, Chris, *Steve Winwood: Roll With It*, Perigee (USA), 1990.

Wire
Eden, Kevin, *Wire...Everybody Loves A History*, SAF , 1991.

Wisdom, Norman
Dacre, Richard, *Trouble In Store*.
Wisdom, Norman, *Don't Laugh At Me*.
Wisdom, Norman with Bernard Bale, *'Cos I'm A Fool*, Breedon Books (UK).

Wizard Of Oz, The (Film Musical)
Fricke, John, Scarfonr, Jay & Stillman, W., *The Official 50th Anniversary Pictorial History*, Warner Books (USA), 1989.
Harmetz, Aljean, *The Making Of The Wizard Of Oz*, Knopf (USA), 1977.

Wodehouse, P.G.
Quinton, Anthony, *From Wodehouse To Wittgenstein*, Carcanet, 1998.

Wolfman Jack
Wolfman Jack with Laursen, Byron, *Have Mercy!*, Warner Books (USA), 1995.

Wonder, Stevie
Dragonwagon, C., *Stevie Wonder*, Flash Books (USA), 1977.
Edwards, Audrey, *The Picture Life Of Stevie Wonder*, Watts (USA), 1977.
Elsner, Constanze, *Stevie Wonder*, Everest Books (UK), 1977.
Fox-Cumming, Ray, *Stevie Wonder*, Mandabrook Books, 1977.
Hasegawa, Sam, *Stevie Wonder*, Creative Education, 1975.
Haskins, Jim, *The Story Of Stevie Wonder*, Lothrop, Lee & Shepard (USA), 1976.
Haskins, Jim with Benson, Kathleen, *The Stevie Wonder Scrapbook*, Grosset & Dunlap (USA), 1978.
Taylor, Rick, *Stevie Wonder*, 1985.
Wilson, Beth P., *Stevie Wonder*, Putnams (USA), 1978.
Wonder, Stevie, *Stevie Wonder, Greatest Hits*, Columbia Pictures.

Wood, Ron
Wood, Ron with German, Bill, *Ron Wood: The Works*, Fontana (UK), 1988.

Woodstock Festival
Landy, Elliott, *Woodstock Vision*, My Back Pages (UK), 1985.
Lang, Michael, *Woodstock Festival Remembered*, Ballantine (USA), 1979.
Makower, Joel, *Woodstock: An Oral History*, Sidgwick & Jackson (UK), 1989.
Young, Jean, *Woodstock: Festival Remembered*, Ballantine (USA), 1979.

Wyatt, Robert
King, Michael, *Wrong Movements: A Robert Wyatt History*, SAF Publishing, 1994.

Wynette, Tammy
Wynette, Tammy, *Stand By Your Man*, Hutchinson (UK), 1980.

XTC
Twomey, Chris, *XTC: Chalkhills And Children*, Omnibus Press (UK), 1992.

Yamaguchi, Momoe
Masaaki, Hiraoka, *Yamaguchi Momoewa Bosatsudearu (Momoe Yamaguchi Is A Bodhisattva)*, Tokyo, 1979.
Yamaguchi, Momoe, *Aoi Toki (Adolescent Time)*, Tokyo, 1980.

Yardbirds
Mackay, Richard & Ober, Michael, *Yardbirds World*, Brisk, 1989.
Platt, John, *Yardbirds*, Sidgwick & Jackson (UK), 1983.
Russo, Greig, *Yardbirds: The Ultimate Rave-up*, Crossfire (USA), 1998.
White, James, *Blues In The Night: The Yardbirds' Story*, Privately Published (UK), 1982.

Yearwood, Trisha
Gubernick, Lisa Rebecca, *Get Hot Or Go Home: The Making Of A Nashville Star*, William Morrow (USA), 1993.

Yes
Hedges, Dan, *Yes: The Authorized Biography*, Sidgwick & Jackson (UK), 1981.
Martin, Bill, *Music Of Yes: Structure And Vision In Progressive Rock*, Open Court, 1996.
Morse, Tim, *Yesstories: Yes In Their Own Words*, St Martins Press (USA), 1996.

Youmans, Vincent
Bordman, G., *Days To Be Happy, Years To Be Sad, The Life And Music Of Vincent Youmans*.

Young, Jimmy
Young, Jimmy, *J.Y.: The Autobiography Of Jimmy Young*, Sphere Books (UK), 1975.

Young, Lester
Buchmann-Moller, Frank, *You Got To Be Original Man! The Music of Lester Young*, Greenwood Press, 1989.
Buchmann-Moller, Frank, *You Just Fight For Your Life: The Story of Lester Young*, Greenwood Press, 1989.
Evensmo, Jan, *The Tenor Saxophone And Clarinet Of Lester Young, 1936-1949*, Jan Evensmo, 1983.
Gelly, Dave, *Lester Young*, Tunbridge Wells (UK), 1984.
Luckey, Robert A., *A Study Of Lester Young And His Influence Upon His Contemporaries*.
Porter, Lewis, *A Lester Young Reader*, Smithsonian Institution Press (USA), 1992.
Porter, Lewis, *Lester Young*, Twayne.

Young, Neil

Downing, David, *A Dreamer Of Pictures: Neil Young - The Man And His Music*, Bloomsbury (UK), 1994.

Dufrechou, Carole, *Neil Young*, Quick Fox (USA), 1978.

Einarson, John, *Aurora: The Story Of Neil Young And The Squires*, Broken Arrow (UK), 1992.

Einarson, John, *Don't Be Denied: The Canadian Years*, Omnibus Press (UK), 1993.

Fisson, Bruno & Jenkins, Alan, *Neil Young: Complete Illustrated Bootleg Discography*, NYAS (UK), 1992.

George-Warren, Holly (ed.), *Neil Young: The Rolling Stone Files*, Sidgwick & Jackson (UK), 1995.

Heatley, Michael, *His Life And Music*, Mitchell Beazley (UK), 1994.

Jenkins, Alan, *Neil Young And Broken Arrow: On A Journey Through The Past*, Broken Arrow, NYAS (UK), 1994.

Long, Pete, *Ghosts On The Road: Neil Young In Concert*, The Old Homestead Press (UK), 1996.

Robertson, John, *The Visual Documentary*, Omnibus Press (UK), 1994.

Rogan, Johnny, *Neil Young: The Definitive Story Of His Musical Career*, Proteus Books (UK), 1982.

Verbeke, Herman & van Diggelen, Lucien, *Neil Young: Een Portret*, Kempen Pers (Holland), 1992.

Williams, Paul, *Love To Burn: Neil Young*, Omnibus Press (UK), 1997.

Young, Scott, *Neil And Me 2nd Edition*, Rogan House (UK), 1997.

Young, Scott, *Neil And Me*, McLelland and Stewart (Canada), 1986.

Young, Paul

Young, Paul, *The Crossing*, International Music Publications (UK), 1994.

Zappa, Frank

Chevalier, Dominique, *Viva Zappa*, Omnibus Press (UK), 1986.

Cruickshank, Ben, *Frank Zappa: A Strictly Genteel Genius Pts. 1 & 2*, Agenda (UK), 1996.

Dister, Alain, *Frank Zappa Et Les Mothers Of Invention*, Albin Michel (Paris), 1975.

Gray, Michael, *Mother! The Frank Zappa Story*, Plexus (UK), 1993.

Kaiser, Rolf-Ulrich, *Frank Zappa: Over Het Begin En Het Einde Van De Progressieve Popmuziek*, Hoon (Holland), 1971.

Miles, *Frank Zappa In His Own Words*, Omnibus Press (UK), 1993.

Miles (ed.), *Frank Zappa: A Visual Documentary*, Omnibus Press (UK), 1993.

No editor listed, *The Lives & Times Of Zappa And The Mothers*, Babylon Books (UK), 1979.

Obermanns, Norbert, *Get Zapped: Zappalog The First Step To Zappology*, Dwarf Nebula, 1981.

Obermanns, Norbert, *Zappalog: The First Step Of Zappalogy (2nd Edition)*, Rhino, Los Angeles (USA), 1982.

Slaven, Neil, *Electric Don Quixote*, Omnibus Press (UK), 1996.

Walley, David, *No Commercial Potential: The Saga Of Frank Zappa: Then And Now*, E.P. Dutton (USA), 1972.

Watson, Ben, *Frank Zappa: The Negative Dialectics Of Poodle Play*, Quartet Books (UK), 1994.

Weissner, Carl, *Frank Zappa, Plastic People Songbuch*, Zweitausendeins (Germany).

Zappa, Frank with Peter Occhiogrosso, *The Real Frank Zappa Book*, Picador (UK), Poseidon Press (USA), 1990.

Zodiac Mindwarp And The Love Reaction

Drummond, Bill & Manning, Mark, *Bad Wisdom*, Penguin Originals, 1996.

Drummond, Bill & Manning, Mark, *A Bible Of Dreams* (UK), 1994.

ZZ Top

Thomas, Dave, *Elimination: The Z.Z. Top Story*, Omnibus Press (UK), 1986.

BIBLIOGRAPHY BY SUBJECT

Black Music General

(see also Blues; R&B; Soul, Motown and Reggae).

Beckman, Jeanette & Adler, Bill, *Rap: Portraits And Lyrics Of A Generation Of Black Rockers*, Omnibus, 1991.

Behague, Gerard (ed.), *Music And Black Ethnicity: The Caribbean And South America*, Transaction Pub. US, 1993.

Bisceglia, Jacques, *Black And White Fantasy*, Corps 9 Editions.

Bisset, Andrew, *Black Roots, White Flowers*, Golden Press, 1979.

Booth, Stanley, *Rythm Oil: A Journey Through The Music Of The American South*, Pantheon, 1995.

Broughton, Viv, *Black Gospel*, Blandford Press (UK), 1985.

Carles, Philippe, *Free Jazz/Black Power*, Editions Champ Libre, 1971.

Darrell, R D, *Black Beauty*, Philadelphia, 1933.

Driggs, F, and H Lewine, *Black Beauty*, White Heat, New York, 1982.

Floyd, Samuel A., *Black Music In The Harlem Renaissance: A Collection Of Essays*, Afro-American & African Studies/Greenwood Press, 1990.

Floyd, Samuel B. Jr., *The Power Of Black Music*, Oxford University Press (USA), 1996.

Gordon, Robert, *It Came From Memphis*, Faber & Faber (UK), 1995.

Guilbaut, Joselyne, *Zouk: World Music In The West Indies*, University of Chicago Press (USA), 1993.

Hill, Donald R., *Calypso Calaloo: Early Carnival Music In Trindad*, University Press of Florida (USA), 1993.

Hill, Dr. Anthony, *Pages From The Harlem Renaissance*, Peter Lang (USA), 1996.

Kofsky, Frank, *Black Nationalism And The Revolution In Music*, Pathfinder Press (USA) 1970.

Levine, Lawrence W., *Black Culture And Black Consciousness*, Oxford University Press (USA), 1977.

Locke, Alain LeRoy, *The Negro And His Music*, The Associates In Negro Folk Education (USA), 1936.

Malone, Jackie, *Steppin' On The Blues: The Visible Rhythms Of African American Dance*, University Of Illinois Press (USA), 1996.

Morse, David, *Motown And The Arrival Of Black Music*, Studio Vista (UK), 1971.

Murray, James Briggs, *Black Visions '88: Lady Legends In Jazz*, Mayor's Office Of Minority Affairs (USA), 1988.

No author, *Black Music & Jazz Review*, Napfield, 1981.

No editor listed, *Black Music In Transition*, Holt, Rinehart and Winston (USA), 1969.

Oliver, Paul (ed.), *Black Music In Britain: Essays On The Afro-Asian Contribution To Popular Music*, Open University Press, 1990 (UK).

Peters, Erskine, *Lyrics Of The Afro-American Spiritual: A Documentary Collection*, Greenwood Press (UK), 1993.

Petrie, Gavin (ed.), *Black Music*, Hamlyn (UK), 1974.

Quarles, Benjamin, *The Negro In The Making Of America*, Collier (USA), 1969.

Reed, Tom, *The Black Music History Of Los Angeles - Its Roots*, Black Accent, 1992.

Rivelli, Pauline and Levin, Robert, *Black Giants*, New York, 1970.

Roach, Hildred, *Black American Music*, Boston: Crescendo, 1973.

Rose, Tricia, *Black Noise: Rap Music And Black Culture In Contemporary America*, Wesleyan U.P. (USA), 1994.

Rublowsky, John, *Black Music In America*, Basic Books (USA), 1971.

Savory, Chris, *UK Black Music 45s, 1950-80*, Soul Cargo Publications (UK), 1993.

Shaw, Arnold, *Black Popular Music In America*, Macmillan, 1990.

Sidran, Ben, *Black Talk*, Payback Press, 1995.

Southern, Eileen, *The Music Of Black Americans: A History*, W.W. Norton (USA), 1971.

Spellman, A. B., *Black Music: Four Lives*, Schocken Books (USA), 1970.

Stanley, Leotha, *Be A Friend: Story Of African-American Music In Song, Words And Pictures*, Zino Press Children's Books (USA), 1994.

Toll, Robert C, *Blacking Up*, Oxford University Press (USA), 1974.

Vincent, Ricky, *Funk: The Music, The People, And The Rhythm Of The One*, St. Martin's Griffin (USA), 1996.

Blues

Allen, William Francis, Ware, Charles Pickard, and Garrison, *Slave Songs Of The United States*, New York, 1951.

Arnaudon, J.C., *Dictionnaire Du Blues*, Paris, 1977.

Baker, Houston A., *Blues: Ideology And Afro-American Literature*, University Of Chicago Press (USA), 1987.

Balliett, Whitney, *Dinosaurs In The Morning*, J.B. Lippincot, 1962.

Bane, Michael, *White Boy Singin' The Blues: The Black Roots Of White Rock*, Penguin (USA), 1982.

Barlow, William, *Looking Up At Down: The Emergence Of Blues Culture*, Temple University Press (USA), 1989.

Bastin, Bruce, *Red River Blues: The Blues Tradition In The South East*, University Of Illinois Press (USA), 1986.

Bastin, Bruce, *Crying For The Carolines*, Studio Vista (UK), 1971.

Bourgeois, Anna Stong, *Blues Women*, McFarland & Co. (USA), 1996.

Bradford, Perry, *Born With The Blues*, Oak Publications (USA), 1965.

Broven, John, *Walking To New Orleans*, Blues Unlimited (UK), 1974.

Broven, John, *Rhythm And Blues In New Orleans*, Spa Books (UK), 1992.

Brunning, Bob, *Blues: The British Connection*, Blandford Press (UK), 1986.

Burley, Dan, *Dan Burley's Original Handbook Of Harlem Jive*, New York, 1944.

Campbell, James, *The Picador Book Of Blues And Jazz*, Picador (UK), 1995.

Carruth, Hayden, *Sitting In: Selected Writings On Jazz, Blues, And Related Topics*, Univ. Iowa Press (USA), 1994.

Charters, Samuel B., *The Blues Makers*, Da Capo (USA), 1991.

Charters, Samuel B., *Sweet As The Showers Of Rain: The Bluesmen Vol. 11*, Oak Publications (USA), 1977.

Charters, Samuel B., *The Bluesmen*, Oak Publications (USA), 1967.

Charters, Samuel B., *The Country Blues*, Da Capo (USA), 1977.

Charters, Samuel B., *The Legacy Of The Blues: Art And Lives Of 12 Great Bluesmen*, Da Capo (USA), 1977.

Charters, Samuel B., *The Poetry Of The Blues*, Oak Publications (USA), 1963.

Charters, Samuel B., *The Roots Of The Blues: An African Search*, Da Capo (USA), 1981.

Cohn, Lawrence (ed.), *Nothing But The Blues: The Music And Musicians*, Abbeville Press (USA), 1993.

Cone, James H, *The Spirituals And The Blues*, Seabury Press, 1972.

Cook, Bruce, *Listen To The Blues*, Da Capo (USA), 1995.

Courlander, H., *Negro Folk Music, USA*, New York and London, 1963.

Courlander, H., *Negro Songs From Alabama*, New York, 1963.

Cowley, John & Oliver, Paul (ed.), *The New Blackwell Guide To Recorded Blues*, Blackwell (UK), 1996.

Davis, Francis, *The History Of The Blues: The Roots, The Music, The People*, Hyperion (USA), 1995.

Davis, Stephen, *The History Of The Blues*, Secker (UK), 1995.

Deffaa, Chip, *Blue Rhythms: Six Lives In Rhythm And Blues*, University Of Illinois Press (USA), 1996.

Demetre, Jacques & Chauvard, Marcel, *Voyage Au Pays Du Blues 1959*, Levallois-Perret: Editions Clarb (France), 1994.

Dennison, S, *Scandalize My Name: Black Imagery In American Popular Music*, New York, 1981.

Dixon, R.M.W. & Godrich, John, *Recording The Blues*, Studio Vista (UK), 1970.

Driggs, F. and Shirley, K., *The Book Of The Blues*, New York, 1963.

Dunbar, Tony, *Delta Time: A Journey Through Mississippi*, Pantheon Books(USA).

Evans, David, *Big Road Blues: Traditions And Creativity In The Folk Blues*, Berkeley Books (USA), 1982.

Fancourt, Leslie, *British Blues On Record*, Leslie Fancourt (UK), 1989.

Fancourt, Leslie, *Blue Horizon Records 1965-1972*, Retrack Books (UK), 1992.

Feather, Leonard, *The History Of Blues*, Charles Hansen Music & Books (USA), 1972.

Ferris Jnr., William, *Blues From The Delta*, Studio Vista (UK), 1970.

Garon, Paul, *Blues And The Poetic Spirit*, Da Capo (USA), 1977.

Gart, Galen, *The History Of Rhythm And Blues: Volume 1-8*, Big Nickle, Milford (USA).

Gellert, L., *Me And My Captain*, New York, 1939.

Gellert, L., *Negro Songs Of Protest*, New York, 1936.

Godrich, John & Dixon, Robert M.W., *Blues And Gospel Records 1902-1942*, Storyville (USA), 1983.

Govenar, Alan, *Meeting The Blues: Rise Of The Texas Sound*, Da Capo (USA), 1995.

Green, Stephen, *Going To Chicago: A Year On The Chicago Blues Scene*, Woodford Publishing (USA), 1990.

Groom, Robert, *The Blues Revival*, Studio Vista (UK), 1970.

Guralnick, Peter, *Lost Highway: Journeys & Arrivals Of American Musicians*, Harper Collins (USA), 1989.

Guralnick, Peter, *Searching For Robert Johnson*, Dutton (USA), 1988.

Guralnick, Peter, *Feel Like Going Home: Portraits In Blues And Rock 'N' Roll*, Outerbridge & Dienstfrey (USA), 1971.

Guralnick, Peter, *The Listener's Guide To The Blues*, New York, 1979.

Hadley, Frank-John, *Grove Press Guide To The Blues*, Grove Press (USA), 1993.

Handy, W.C., *A Treasury Of The Blues*, New York, 1925.

Handy, W.C., *The Father Of The Blues*, Da Capo (USA), 1991.

Handy, W.C., (ed.), *Blues: An Anthology*, Da Capo (USA), 1985.

Hannusch, Jeff., *I Hear You Knockin': The Sound Of New Orleans Rhythm And Blues*, Ville Platte, Louisiana (USA), 1985.

Haralambos, Michael, *Right On: From Blues To Soul In Black America*, Da Capo (USA), 1979.

Harris, Michael W., *The Rise Of Gospel Blues*, Oxford Univ. Press (UK), 1993.

Harris, Sheldon, *Blues Who's Who: A Biographical Dictionary Of Blues Singers*, Arlington House, New York, 1979.

Harris, Sheldon, *Blues Who's Who*, Da Capo Press (USA), 1989.

Harrison, Daphne Duval, *Black Pearls: Blues Queens Of The 1920s*, Rutgers University Press (USA), 1990.

Harrison, David, *World Of Blues*, Studio Editions, 1993.

Hart, Mary L & Eagles, Brenda M., *The Blues: A Bibliographic Guide*, Garland Publications (USA), 1989.

Hatch, David & Millward, Stephen, *Blues To Rock*, Manchester University Press (UK), 1989.

Herzhaft, Gerard, *Encyclopedia Of The Blues*, University Of Arkansas Press (USA), 1992.

Herzhaft, Gerard, *Encyclopedie Du Blues*, Lyons (France), 1979.

Herzhaft, Gerard, *Long Blues In A Minor*, University of Arkansas (USA), 1991.

Hildebrand, Lee, And Michelle Vignes, *Bay Area Blues*, Pomegranate Artbooks (USA), 1993.

Hughes, Langston & Meltzer, Milton, *Black Magic: A Pictorial History Of The African-American In The Performing Art*, Da Capo (USA), 1990.

Jackson, B, *Wake Up Dead Man: Afro-American Worksongs From Texan Prisons*, Cambridge, Massachusetts (USA), 1972.

James, C.L.R., *Beyond A Boundary*, Pantheon Books (USA), 1983.

Jones, Hettie, *Big Star Fallin' Mama: Five Women In Black Music*, Viking (USA), 1974.

Jones, LeRoi, *Black Music*, William Morrow (USA), 1971.

Jones, LeRoi, *Blues People: Negro Music In White America*, Payback Press (USA), 1995.

Joseph, Pleasant & Ottenheimer, Harriet J., *Cousin Joe; Blues From New Orleans*, University Of Chicago Press (USA), 1987.

Keil, Charles, *Urban Blues*, University Of Chicago Press (USA), 1966.

Kriss, E., *Barrelhouse And Boogie Piano*, New York, 1974.

Larkin, Colin, *The Virgin Encyclopedia Of The Blues*, Virgin Books (UK), 1998.

Larkin, Colin (ed.), *Guinness Who's Who Of Blues 2nd Edition*, Guinness Publishing (UK), 1995.

Larkin, Colin (ed.), *Guinness Who's Who Of Blues*, Guinness Publishing (UK), 1993.

Leadbitter, Mike & Leslie Fancourt, *Blues Records Vol 2, 1943-1970*, Record Information Services (UK), 1995.

Leadbitter, Mike & Slaven, Neil, *Blues Records: A Complete Guide To 20 Years Of Recorded Blues: 1943-1966*, Oak Publications, 1968.

Leadbitter, Mike & Slaven, Neil, *Crowley, Louisiana Blues*, Blues Unlimited (UK), 1968.

Leadbitter, Mike & Slaven, Neil, *Nothing But The Blues: An Illustrated Documentary*, Hanover Books, 1971.

Lomax, Alan, *Land Where The Blues Began*, Methuen (UK), Pantheon (USA), 1993.

Lomax, J. A., *Adventures Of A Ballad Hunter*, New York, 1947.

Lornell, Kip, *Virginia Blues: Country And Gospel Records 1902-1943*, University Of Kentucky Press (USA), 1989.

Lornell, Kip, *Happy In The Service Of The Lord (Afro American Gospel Quartets In Memphis)*, University Of Illinois Press (USA), 1988.

Lovell, John, Jnr., *Black Song: The Forge And The Flame*, Macmillan, 1972.

Macleod, R. R., *Document Blues 1*, Pat Publications (UK), 1994.

Mann, Woody, *Bottleneck Blues Guitar*, Oak Publications (USA), 1996.

Mann, Woody, *Six Black Blues Guitarists*, Oak Publications (USA), 1973.

McKee, Margaret, And Fred Chisenhall, *Beale Black And Blue: Life And Music On America's Main Street*, Louisiana State U.P. (USA), 1993.

Mezzrow, Milton Mezz & Wolfe, Bernard, *Really The Blues*, Random House (USA), 1946.

Mitchell, George, *Blow My Blues Away*, Da Capo (1983), 1983.

Morgan, Thomas L., And William Barlow, *From Cakewalks To Concert Halls: African American Popular Music*, Elliott & Clark, 1992.

Murray, Albert, *Stomping The Blues*, McGraw-Hill (USA), 1976.

Murray, Charles Shaar, *Blues On CD: The Essential Guide*, K. Cathie (UK), 1993.

Myrus, Donald, *Ballads, Blues And The Big Beat*, Macmillan, 1966.

Napier, Simon A., *Back Woods Blues*, Blues Unlimited (UK), 1968.

Neff, Robert & Connor, Anthony, *Blues*, Godine Publications (USA), 1975.

Nicholas, A. X., *Woke Up This Mornin': Poetry Of The Blues*, Bantam (USA), 1973.

Oakley, Giles, *The Devil's Music: A History Of The Blues*, BBC (UK), Harcourt Brace (USA), 1976.

Odum, H.W. & Johnson, G.B., *The Negro And His Songs*, Chapel Hill, 1925.

Oliver, Paul, *Aspects Of The Blues Tradition*, Oak Publications (USA), 1970.

Oliver, Paul, *Blackwell Blues Guide*, Basil Blackwell (UK), 1989.

Oliver, Paul, *Blues Fell This Morning: The Meaning Of The Blues*, Cambridge University Press , 1990.

Oliver, Paul, *Blues Off The Record: Thirty Years Of Blues Commentary*, Da Capo (USA), 1984.

Oliver, Paul, *Conversation With The Blues*, Horizon Press (USA), 1983.

Oliver, Paul, *Gospel, Blues And Jazz*, Macmillan (USA), 1990.

Oliver, Paul, *Savannah Syncopators: African Retentions In The Blues*, Madison Books (USA), Studio Vista (UK), 1970.

Oliver, Paul, *Screening The Blues: Aspects Of The Blues Tradition*, Da Capo (USA), 1989.

Oliver, Paul, *Songsters And Saints: Vocal Traditions On Race Records*, Cambridge University Press, 1989.

Oliver, Paul, *The Meaning Of The Blues*, Collier Books (USA), 1963.

Oliver, Paul, *The Story Of The Blues*, Chilton Books, 1969.

Oliver, Paul (ed), *The Blackwell Guide To Blues Records*, Basil Blackwell (UK), 1991.

Oliver, Paul; Harrison, Max; Bolcom, W, *New Grove Gospel, Blues & Jazz, With Spirituals And Ragtime*, Norton (USA), 1986.

Olsson, Bengt, *Memphis Blues And Jug Bands*, Studio Vista (UK), 1970.

Oster, Harry, *Living Country Blues*, Folklore Associates, 1969.

Palmer, Robert, *Deep Blues*, Penguin Books, 1982.

Pearson, Barry Lee, *Virginia Piedmont Blues: The Lives And Art Of Two Virginia Bluesmen*, University Pennsylvania Press (USA), 1990.

Price, Sammy, *What Do They Want?*, Bayou Press (USA), 1989.

Raichelson, Richard M., *Beale Street Talks: A Walking Tour Down The Home Of The Blues*, Arcadia Press (USA), 1994.

Ramsey, F. Jnr, *Been Here And Gone*, Brunswick, New Jersey, 1960.

Roach, Hildred, *Black American Music: Past And Present*, Krieger Publishing Co (USA), 1992.

Rowe, Mike, *Chicago Blues: The City And The Music*, Da Capo (USA), 1981.

Rowe, Mike, *Chicago Breakdown*, Da Capo (USA), 1981.

Russell, Tony, *Blacks, Whites And Blues*, Studio Vista (UK), Stein And Day (USA), 1970.

Ryan, Marc, *Trumpet Records - An Illustrated History With Discography*, Big Nickel Publications (USA), 1993.

Sackheim, E, *The Blues Line: A Collection Of Blues Lyrics*, New York, 1969.

Sackheim, Eric (ed), *The Blues Line: A Collection Of Blues Lyrics From Leadbelly To Muddy Waters*, Ecco Press (USA), 1993.

Santelli, Robert, *The Best Of The Blues*, Penguin Books (USA), 1997.

Santelli, Robert, *The Big Book Of Blues*, Penguin Books, 1994 (USA).

Santoto, Gene, *Dancing In Your Head: Jazz, Blues, Rock, And Beyond*, Oxford University Press, 1994.

Scott, Frank, *The Down Home Guide To The Blues*, A Cappella Books (USA), 1991.

Seeger, M, *Anthology Of American Folk Music*, New York, 1973.

Shaw, Arnold, *Honkers And Shouters: The Golden Years Of Rhythm And Blues*, Macmillan (USA), 1978.

Sidran, Ben, *Black Talk*, Da Capo (USA), 1988.

Silverman, Jerry, *Folk Blues*, MacMillan (USA), 1967.

Smith Michael P., *A Joyful Noise: A Celebration Of New Orleans Music*, Taylor, 1990.

Sonnier, Austin Jr., *A Guide To The Blues: History, Who's Who, Research Sources*, Greenwood Press (USA), 1994.

Southern, Eileen, *The Music Of Black Americans*, W. W. Norton (USA), 1983.

Spencer, John Michael, *Blues And Evil*, University Of Tennessee Press (USA), 1993.

Springer, Robert, *Authentic Blues: Its History And Its Themes*, Edwin Mellen Press (USA), 1996.

Springer, Robert, *Authentic Blues: Its History And Its Themes*, E Mellen (Canada), 1995.

St. Pierre, Roger, *The Best Of The Blues: The Essential CD Guide*, Collins (UK), 1993.

Surge, Frank, *Singers Of The Blues*, Lerner (USA), 1969.

Sylvester, Peter, *A Left Hand Like God: A History Of Boogie Woogie Piano*, Da Capo (USA), 1989.

Taft, Michael, *Blues Lyric Poetry: An Anthology*, Garland (USA), 1983.

Titon, Jeff Todd, *Early Downhome Blues: Second Edition*, University Of North Carolina (USA), 1994.

Titon, Jeff Todd, *Downhome Blues Lyrics: An Anthology From The Post-World War 11 Era*, Boston (USA), 1981.

Titon, Jeff Todd, *Early Downhome Blues: A Musical And Cultural Analysis*, University Of Illinois Press (USA), 1977.

Tracy, Steven C., *Going To Cincinnati: A History Of Blues In The Queen City*, University Of Illinois Press (USA), 1995.

Traum, Happy, *The Blues Bag*, New York, 1968.

Trynka, Paul, and Val Wilmer, *Portrait Of The Blues: America's Blues Musicians In Their Own Words*, Hamlyn (UK), Da Capo (USA), 1996.

Walton, Ortiz M., *Music: Black, White And Blue*, William Morrow (USA), 1972.

Webb, Stan, *Will You Dance With Me*, G C P (UK), 1990.

Whitcomb, Ian, *Legends Of Rhythm And Blues Repercussions*, London, 1984.

White, N.I., *American Negro Folk-Songs*, Cambridge, Massachusetts (USA), 1928.

Wilcock, Donald E., And Buddy Guy, *Damn Right I've Got The Blues: Buddy Guy And The Blues Roots Of Rock 'N' Roll*, Woodford P., 1994.

Williams, Paul, *Blues And Outlaw*, E.P. Dutton (USA), 1969.

Wilson, Christine, *All Shook Up: Mississippi Roots Of American Popular Music*, Museum Of Mississippi (USA), 1996.

Work, John Wesley, *American Negro Songs & Spirituals*, Bonanza Books (USA), 1940.

Chess Records

Fancourt, L., *Chess Blues Discography*, Faversham, UK, 1983.

Ruppli, Michael, *The Chess Labels*, Greenwood Press, 1983.

Country

Albert, George, *The Cash Box Country Singles Charts, 1958-1982*, Scarecrow (USA), 1984.

Allan, Johnnie (ed), *Memories: A Pictorial History Of South Louisiana Music 1910-1990 (I & II)*, Jadfel (USA), 1995.

Allen, Bob (ed.), *Blackwell Guide To Recorded Country Music*, Blackwell (UK), 1994.

Ammon, W.W., *Working Lives*, Fremantle Arts Centre Press, 1984.

Ancelet, Barry Jean, *Cajun Music: Its Origin And Development*, University Of Southwestern Louisiana (USA), 1995.

Ancelet, Barry Jean and Morgan, E., *The Makers Of Cajun Music*, Austin, Texas (USA), 1984.

Artis, Bob, *Bluegrass: From The Lonesome Wail Of The Mountain Lovesong*, Hawthorn Books (USA), 1975.

Bane, Michael, *The Outlaws: Revolution In Country Music*, Doubleday (USA), 1978.

Barnard, Russell D. (ed), *The Comprehensive Country Music Encyclopedia*, Times Books (USA), 1995.

Biracee, Tom, *The Country Music Almanac*, Prentice Hall (USA) , 1993.

Boothroyd, John, L, *Bluegrass LP Issues 1957-1990*, Privately Published, Victoria (Ausralia), 1990.

Broven, John, *South To Louisiana: Music Of The Cajun Bayous*, Pelican Books (USA), 1983.

Brown, Len, *The Encyclopedia Of Country And Western Music*, Tower, 1971.

Bufwack, Mary A., and Robert K. Oermann, *Finding Her Voice: The Saga Of Women In Country Music*, Crown Publishers (USA), 1993.

Burton, Thomas, *Tennessee Traditional Singers*, University Of Tennessee Press (USA), 1981.

Byworth, Tony (ed.), *Official Music Master Country Music Catalogue Edition 2*, Waterlow Information Services (UK), 1993.

Byworth, Tony (ed.), *The Official Music Master Country Music Catalogue*, MBC Information (UK), 1991.

Cackett, Alan, *The New Illustrated Encyclopedia Of Country Music*, Salamander (UK), 1994.

Cantwell, Robert, *Bluegrass Breakdown: The Making Of The Old Southern Sound*, Da Capo (USA), 1992.

Caravan, Guy, *Voices From The Mountains*, Alfred A. Knopf (USA), 1975.

Carlin, Richard, *The Big Book Of Country Music: A Biographical Encyclopedia*, Penguin (UK), 1995.

Carr, Patrick, (ed.), *The Illustrated History Of Country Music*, Dolphin Books (USA), 1980.

Carthy, Brian, *The A-Z Of Country Irish Stars*, Gill & MacMillan (USA), 1991.

Chalker, Bryan, *Country Music*, Phoebus, 1976.

Cohen, Norman, *Long Steel Rail: The Railroad In American Folksong*, University Of Illinois Press (USA), 1981.

Conway, Jill K., *The Road From Coorain*, Alfred A. Knopf (USA), 1989.

Cooper, Lee B., & Haney, Wayne S., *Response Recordings: An Answer Song Discography 1950-1990*, Scarecrow Press (USA), 1990.

Cornfield, Robert, *Just Country: Country People, Stories, Music*, McGraw-Hill (USA), 1976.

Couch, Ernie, *Country Music Trivia And fact Book*, Rutledge Hill Press, 1994.

Country Music Catalogue, *Music Master*, Music Master (UK), 1990.

Country Music Foundation, *Country: The Music And The Musicians*, Abbeville Press (USA), 1988.

Country Music Magazine, *Complete US Country Music Encyclopedia*, Boxtree (UK), 1995.

Country Showstoppers, Columbia Pictures, c.1987.

Crump, George A, *Write It Down*, Donning.

David, Andrew, *Country Music Stars: People At The Top Of The Charts*, Domus Books, 1980.

Davis, Paul, *New Life In Country Music*, Henry Walker, 1976.

Dawidoff, Nicholas, *In The Country Of Country: People And Places In American Music*, Faber And Faber (UK), 1997.

Dellar, Fred, *The Best Of Country Music*, Octopus (UK), 1980.

Dellar, Fred & Wootton, Richard, *The Country Music Book Of Lists*, Thames & Hudson (UK), 1984.

Dellar, Fred (ed.), *The Illustrated Encyclopedia Of Country Music*, Salamander Books (UK), 1977.

Delmore, Alan, *Truth Is Stranger Than Publicity*, Vanderbilt University Press (USA), 1995.

Dew, Joan, *Singers & Sweethearts: The Women Of Country Music*, Dolphin Books, 1977.

Edwards, Don, *Classic Cowboy Songs: From The Minstrel Of The Range*, Gibbs Smith (USA), 1994.

Eichenlaub, Frank & Patricia, *The All American Guide To Country Music*, Country Roads (USA), 1992.

Ellis, William Carson, *The Sentimental Mother Song In American Country Music 1978 (USA)*, 1978.

Ellison, Curtis W., *Country Music Culture: From Hard Times To Heaven*, University Of Mississippi Press (USA), 1995.

Emery, Ralph, with Tom Carter, *Ralph Emery: More Memories*, G.P. Putnam (USA), 1993.

Endres, Clifford, *Austin City Limits*, University of Texas Press (USA), 1987.

Escallier, Pierre, *Mon Village Autrefois*, Chabottes, 1973.

Faragher, Scott, *Music City Babylon: Inside The World Of Country Music*, Carol Publishing Group (USA), 1994.

Flint, Country Joe, And Judy Nelson, *The Insider's Country Music Handbook*, Airlift (UK), 1994.

Flint, Joseph H & Nelson, Judy, *Insider's Country Music Handbook*, G M Smith (USA), 1993.

Fry, Macon, and Julie Posner, *Cajun Country Guide*, Pelican, Gretna (USA), 1993.

Gaillard, Frye, *Watermelon Wine: The Spirit Of Country Music*, St Martin's Press, 1978.

Gatlin, Larry, *My Brand Of Music*, Warner Brothers, 1982.

Gentry, Linnell, *A History And Encyclopedia Of Country, Western, And Gospel Music*, McQuiddy Press (USA), 1961.

Ginell, Cary, *The Decca Hillbilly Discography, 1927-1945*, Greenwood Press, 1989.

Gray, Andy, *Great Country Music Stars*, Hamlyn (UK), 1975.

Green, Douglas B., *Country Roots: The Origins Of Country Music*, Hawthorn Books, 1976.

Gregory, Hugh, *Who's Who In Country Music*, Weidenfeld & Nicolson (UK), 1993.

Griffiths, Grace, *The Days Of My Freedom*, World's Work, 1978.

Grissim, John, *Country Music: White Man's Blues*, Paperback Library, 1970.

Hagan, Chet, *Country Music Legends In The Hall Of Fame*, T. Nelson.

Hagan, Chet, *Grand Ole Opry: The Complete Story Of A Great American Institution And Its Stars*, H. Holt (USA), 1990.

Hall, Doug, *Country On CD*, K. Cathie (UK), 1993.

Hallowell, Christopher, *People Of The Bayou: Cajun Life In Lost America*, E.P. Dutton (USA).

Harris, Stacy, *The Best Of Country The Essential CD Guide*,

Orion Paperbacks, 1993.

Hay, George D., *A Story Of The Grand Ole Opry*, Nashville Tennessee (USA), 1953.

Heggeness, Fred, *Rarest Of The Rare Country Western Price Guide*, FH, 1991.

Hemphill, Paul, *The Nashville Sound: Bright Lights And Country Music*, Simon & Schuster (USA), 1970.

Hentoff, Nat, *Listen To The Stories; Nat Hentoff On Jazz And Country Music*, Harper-Collins (USA), 1995.

Hill, Fred, *Grass Roots: Illustrated History Of Bluegrass And Mountain Music*, Academy Books.

Hill, Thomas A., *Country Music*, Franklin Watts (USA), 1978.

Hoffmann, Frank & Albert, George, *Cash Box Country Album Charts, 1964-88*, Scarecrow (USA), 1990.

Hollaran, Carolyn, *Meet The Stars Of Country Music*, Aurora, 1977.

Hollaran, Carolyn, *Meet The Stars Of Country Music: Volume 2*, Aurora, 1978.

Horstman, Dorothy, *Sing Your Heart Out, Country Boy*, Vanderbilt University Press (USA), 1995.

Horstman, Dorothy, *Sing Your Heart Out, Country Boys*, Country Music Foundation, Nashville (USA), 1975.

Hume, Martha, *Martha Hume's Guide To The Greatest In Country Music: You're So Cold I'm Turning*, Viking Penguin (USA), 1982.

Hunter, Tommy, *My Story*, Methuen (UK), 1985.

Hurst, Jack, *Nashville's Grand 'Ole Opry*, Harry N. Abrams (USA), 1975.

Kash, Murray, *Murray Kash's Book Of Country Music*, Star (UK), 1981.

Kingsbury, Paul, *Country On Compact Disc: The Essential Guide To The Music*, Grove Press (USA), 1993.

Kingsbury, Paul, *The Grand Ole Opry: History Of Country Music*, Villard Books (USA), 1995.

Kingsbury, Paul & Axelrod, Alan, (eds.), *Country: The Music And The Musicians*, Abbeville Press (USA), 1988.

Kingsbury, Paul, Alan Axelrod & Susan Costello, *Country: The Music And The Musicians (Revised Edition)*, Abbeville Press (USA), 1994.

Kochman, Marilyn (ed), *The Big Book Of Bluegrass*, Quill (USA), 1985.

Kosser, Mike, *Hot Country Women*, Avon (USA), 1994.

Krishef, Robert K., *Western Stars Of Country Music*, Lerner, 1978.

Ladies Of Country Music, *Ladies Of Country Music*, Warner Brothers (USA), 1984.

Larkin, Colin, *The Virgin Encyclopedia Of Country Music*, Virgin Books (UK), 1998.

Larkin, Colin (ed.), *Guinness Who's Who Of Country Music*, Guinness Publishing (UK), 1993.

Levine, Arthur D., *The Nashville Number System*, Gibraltar Press, 1981.

Lewis, George H. (ed.), *All That Glitters: Country Music In America*, Bowling Green State University Press USA), 1993.

Logsdon, Guy, Mary Rogers & William Jacobson, *Saddle Serenaders*, Gibbs Smith (USA), 1995.

Lomax, John, III, *Nashville: Music City USA*, Harry Abrams (USA), 1985.

Lornell, Kip, *Virginia's Blues, Country & Gospel Records 1902-1943*, Kentucky University Press, Lexington (USA), 1989.

MacLeod, Michael, *Thomas Hennell: Countryman, Artist, And Writer*, Cambridge University Press, 1988.

Malone, Bill C., *Country Music USA: A Fifty Year History*, University Of Texas Press (USA), 1968.

Malone, Bill C., *Stars Of Country Music: Uncle Dave Macon To Johnny Rodriguez*, University Of Illinois Press (USA), 1975.

Malone, Bill C., *Singing Cowboys And Musical Mountaineers: Southern Culture/Roots Of Country*, University Of Georgia Press (USA), 1993.

Malone, Bill C., and Judith McCulloh (eds.), *Stars Of Country Music*, De Capo Press (USA), 1994.

Marshall, Rick, *New Country: Today's Brightest Stars*, Simon & Schuster (USA), 1988.

Mason, Michael, *The Country Music Book*, Scribners (USA), 1985.

McCloud, Barry (ed), *Definitive Country: The Ultimate Encyclopedia Of Country Music*, Perigree Books (USA), 1995.

McCloud, Peggy and Mike, *Bashful Brother Oswald: The Life & Times Of Roy Acuff's Right Hand Man*, B R & Eunete Kirby (USA), 1994.

Millard, Bob, *Country Music*, Harper Collins (USA), 1993.

Millard, Bob, *The Judds*, Doubleday (USA), 1988.

Morthland, John, *The Best Of Country Music A Critical & Historical Guide To The 750 Greatest Albu*, Doubleday (USA), 1984.

Nash, Alanna, *Behind Closed Doors*, A. A. Knopf (USA), 1988.

Nevell, Richard, *A Time To Dance*, St. Martin's Press (USA), 1977.

Nicholas Dawidoff, *In The Country Of Country: People And Places In American Music*, Faber & Faber, 1997.

No author, *Billboard; World Of Country Music*, Billboard (USA).

No author, *Greatest Country Classics*, Warner Brothers (USA).

No editor listed, *Country Music, A Look At The Men Who've Made It*.

No editor listed, *Who's Who In Country & Western Music.*, Black Stallion Country Press (USA).

Oermann, Robert K., *The Listener's Guide To Country Music*, Facts On File (USA), 1983.

Osborne, Jerry, *55 Years Of Recorded Country & Western Music*, C.O.L., 1976.

Peterson, Richard, *Creating Country Music*, University Of Chicago Press (USA), 1997.

Phillips, W. Robert, *Singing Cowboy Stars: The Guys, The Gals The Sidekicks*, Gibbs Smith (USA), 1994.

Porterfield, Bill, *The Greatest Honky-Tonks In Texas*, Taylor.

Price, Steven D., *Old As The Hills: The Story Of Bluegrass Music*, Viking (USA), 1975.

Price, Steven D., *Take Me Home; The Rise Of Country And Western Music*, Praeger (USA), 1974.

Randall, Paul, *Country Music: Facts, Fallacies, And Folklore*, Union & Confederacy.

Rasof, Henry, *The Folk, Country, And Bluegrass Musician's Catalogue*, St. Martin's Press (USA).

Reed, Roy, *Looking For Hogeye*, University Of Arkansas Press (USA), 1986.

Reid, Jan, *The Improbable Rise Of Redneck Rock*, Da Capo (USA), 1977.

Richards, Tad, And Melvin Shestack, *New Country Music Encyclopedia*, Simon And Schuster (USA), 1994.

Riese, Randall, *Nashville Babylon*, Congden & Weed (USA), 1988.

Rogers, Jimmie N., *The Country Music Message: All About Lovin' And Livin'*, Prentice-Hall (USA), 1983.

Roland, Tom, *Billboard Book Of Number One Country Hits*, Billboard (USA), 1991.

Rose, Michel, *Encyclopedie De La Country Et Du Rockabilly*, J. Grancher, 1985.

Rosenberg, Neil V., *Bluegrass: A History*, University Of Illinois Press (USA), 1985.

Rothel, David, *The Singing Cowboys*, A.S. Barnes Tantivy (UK).

Rovin, Jeff, *Country Music Babylon*, St Martins Press (USA), 1993.

Rubenstein, Raenne & McCabe, Peter, *Honky-Tonk Heroes: A Photo Album Of Country Music*, Harper & Row (USA), 1975.

Sakol, Jeannie, *The Wonderful World Of Country Music*, Grosset & Dunlap (USA), 1979.

Shelton, Robert, *The Country Music Story: A Picture History Of Country And Western Music*, Bobb-Merrill (USA), 1966.

Shestack, Melvin, *The Country Music Encyclopedia*, Thomas Y. Crowell (USA), Omnibus Press (UK), 19741977.

Smith, Richard D., *Bluegrass: An Informal Guide*, A Capella Books (USA), 1995.

Spears-Stewart, Reta, *Remembering The Ozark Jubilee*, Stewart, Dillbeck & White (USA), 1993.

Stambler, Irwin & Grelun Landon, *The Encyclopedia Of Folk, Country, & Western Music*, St. Martin's Press (USA), 1983.

Stambler, Irwin & Grelun, Landon, *Golden Guitars; The Story Of Country Music*, Four Winds Press (USA), 1971.

Stambler, Irwin & Landon, Grelan, *The Encyclopedia Of Folk, Country And Western*, St. Martin's Press (USA), 1969.

Taylor, Alice, *Quench The Lamp*, Brandon, 1990.

Tichi, Cecelia, *High Lonesome: The American Culture Of Country Music*, University Of Carolina Press (USA), 1993.

Tichi, Cecilia (ed), *Readin' Country Music: Steel Guitars, Opry Stars, Honky Tonk Bars*, Dale University Press (USA), 1995.

Tinsley, Jim Bob, *For A Cowboy Has To Sing*, University Press Of Florida (USA), 1991.

Tinsley, Jim Bob, *He Was Singing This Song*, University Of Central Florida (USA), 1981.

Titon, Jeff Todd, *Early Downhome Blues*, University Of North Carolina Press (USA), 1995.

Tosches, Nick, *Country: Living Legends & Dying Metaphors*, Scarborough House (USA), 1977.

Tribe, Ivan M., *The Stonemans: An Appalachian Family & The Music That Shaped Their Lives*, Univ. Illinois Press (USA), 1994.

Tribe, Ivan M., *Mountain Jamboree: Country Music In West Virginia*, Kentucky University Press (USA), 1984.

Tudor, Dean, *Grassroots Music*, Libraries Unlimited (USA), 1979.

Vaughan, Andrew, *Who's Who In New Country Music*, Omnibus Press (UK), 1989.

Vaughan, Andrew, *The World Of Country Music*, Studio Editions (UK), 1992.

Von Mattheissen, Maria, *Songs From The Hills: An Intimate Look At Country Music*, Macmillan (USA), 1993.

Wacholtz, Larry E., *Inside Country Music*, Billboard Books (USA), 1986.

Waldstein, Odo, *1899, Laugh And Tell*, Simon & Pierre (USA).

Walthall, Daddy Bob, *The History Of Country Music*, Walthall (USA), 1978.

Watson, Eric, *Country Music In Australia*, Rodeo (USA), 1976.

Whitburn, Joel, *Billboard Top Country Albums 1964-1997*, Record Research Inc. (USA), 1997.

Whitburn, Joel (ed.), *Billboard Book Of Top 40 Country Hits*, Billboard Books (USA), 1997.

Whitburn, Joel,, *Billboard Top Country Singles 1944-1988*, Record Research (USA), 1989.

White, Howard, *Every Highway Out Of Nashville*, Pickers Rest (USA), 1990.

Wigginton, Eliot (ed.), *Foxfire 3*, Doubleday (USA), 1975.

Wigginton, Eliot (ed.) & Richard M. Dorson, *Foxfire 4*, Anchor Books (USA), 1977.

Wolfe, Charles K., *Kentucky Country*, Kentucky University Press (USA), 1982.

Wolfe, Charles K., *Tennessee Strings: The Story Of Country Music In Tennessee*, University Of Tennessee Press (USA), 1977.

Wolfe, Charles K., *The Grand Ole Opry (The Early Years 1925-35)*, Old Time Music (UK), 1975.

Wooton, Richard, *The Illustrated Country Alamanac: A Day By Day History Of Country Music*, Virgin Books (UK), 1982.

Worth, Fred L., *The Country & Western Book*, Drake (USA), 1977.

Folk

Abernethy, Francis Edward (ed.), *Paisanos, A Folklore Miscellany*, Encino Press.

Abrahams, Roger & George Foss, *Anglo-American Folksong Style*, Prentice Hall (USA), 1968.

Abrahams, Roger D., *Deep Down In The Jungle*, Aldine, 1970.

Abrahams, Roger D., *Negro Folklore From South Philadelphia*, University Of Pennsylvania (USA), 1961.

Abrahams, Roger D., *Positively Black*, Prentice-Hall (USA), 1970.

Abrahams, Roger D., *Talking Black*, Newbury House.

Acuna, Rene, *El Teatro Popular En Hispanoamerica*, Universidad Nacional Autonoma De Mexico (Mexico), 1979.

Adams, Edward Clarkson Leverett, *Congaree Sketches*, Kraus (USA), 1971.

Adler, Samuel, *City By The Lake*, Schirmer (USA), 1974.

Ainsworth, Catherine Harris, *Jump Rope Verses Around The United States*, C.H. Ainsworth.

Allen, Jules Verne, *Cowboy Lore*, Naylor, 1971.

Allen, Rosa S (ed.), *Family Songs*, Newton Bicentennial Committee.

Baer, Florence E., *Sources And Analogues Of The Uncle Remus Tales*, Suomalainen Tiedeakatemia, 1980.

Baggelaar, Kristin & Milton, Donald, *The Folk Music Encyclopedia*, Thomas Y. Crowell (USA), Omnibus Press (UK) (1977), 1976.

Bagley, Julian, *Candle-Lighting Time In Bodidalee*, American Heritage Press (USA), 1971.

Baker, Ronald L., *Folklore In The Writings Of Rowland E. Robinson*, Bowling Green University Popular Press (USA).

Balmir, Guy-Claude, *Du Chant Au Poeme*, Payot, 1982.

Bayard, Samuel Preston, *Instrumental Folk Music In The North Atlantic States*.

Bayard, Samuel Preston, *Twenty Western Pennsylvania Folksongs From The Collection Of Samuel P. Bayard*, Pittsburgh Public Schools, Dept. Of Music (USA), 1946.

Bell, Michael J., *The World From Brown's Lounge*, University Of Illinois Press (USA).

Bethke, Robert D., *Adirondack Voices*, University Of Illinois Press (USA).

Blake, Susan Louise, *Modern Black Writers And The Folk Tradition 1976*

Bluegrass Handbook, W. Lafayett, N. Carlson.

Bluestein, Gene, *The Voice Of The Folk*, Univesity Of Massachusetts Press (USA), 1972.

Boette, Marie, *Singa Hipsy Doodle, And Other Folk Songs Of West Virginia*, McClain (USA).

Boggs, Ralph Steele, *On Collecting New World Folk Music.*, c1940.

Botkin, B. A. (ed.), *A Treasury Of American Folklore*, Crown (USA).

Brasch, Ila Wales and Brasch, Walter Milton, *A Comprehensive Annotated Bibliography Of American Black English*, Louisiana State University Press (USA), 1974.

Brown, Dr. Frank C., *The Frank C. Brown Collection of North Carolina Folklore*, Duke University Press (USA).

Browne, Ray B. (ed.), *The Alabama Folk Lyric*, Bowling Green University Popular Press (USA), 1979.

Buffington, Albert F., *Pennsylvania German Secular Folksongs*, Pennsylvania German Society (USA), 1974.

Burt, Olive (Woolley), *1894, American Murder Ballads And Their Stories*, Oxford University Press, 1958.

Burton, Thomas G., *Collection Of Folklore*, East Tennessee State University, 1967 (USA).

Bush, Michael E., *Folk Songs Of Central West Virginia* (USA) 1969.

Cabral, Stephen L., *Nha Distino: Cape Verdean Folk Arts*, Roger Williams Park Museum (USA).

Cadle, Peter (editor), *Nights In The Cellar: A History Of*

Bunjies, Bunjies, 1994.

Campbell, Rod, *Playing The Field*, B. Evan White Publishing, 1994.

Cannon, Hal (ed.), *Cowboy Poetry*, G. M. Smith, 1985.

Cantwell, Robert, *When We Were Good: The Folk Revival*, Harvard University Press (USA), 1996.

Cantwell, Robert S., *When We Were Good: The Folk Revival*, Harvard University Press (USA), 1996.

Carney, George O., *Sounds Of People And Places*, Rowman & Littlefield (USA), 1993.

Carroll, Gladys Hasty, *The Book That Came Alive*, G. Gannett.

Carvalho Neto, Paulo de, *Estudios De Folklore*, Editorial Universitaria.

Chesnutt, Charles Waddell, *The Conjure Woman*, Mifflin (USA), 1899.

Clark, Keith, *Folk Song And Dance*, English Folk Dance And Song Society, 1972.

Coffin, Tristram Potter, *Folklore From The Working Folk Of America*, Anchor Press, 1973.

Cohen, Anne B., *Poor Pearl, Poor Girl! The Murdered Girl Stereotype In Ballad And Newspaper*, University Of Texas Press (USA), 1973.

Cohen, John and Mike Seeger (Eds.), *Old-Time String Band Songbook*, Oak Publications (USA), 1976.

Cohen, Norm, *Long Steel Rail*, University Of Illinois Press (USA).

Cohen, Ronald D., *Wasn't That A Time: Firsthand Accounts Of The Folk Music Revival*, Scarecrow Press (USA), 1995.

Collins, Fletcher, *Alamance Play-Party Songs And Singing Games*, Norwood Editions, 1973.

Coluccio, Felix, *Diccionario De Creencias Y Supersticiones*, Ediciones Corregidor, 1983.

Coughlan, Margaret N., *Folklore From Africa To The United States*, Library Of Congress (USA), 1976.

Courlander, Harold, *Negro Folk Music USA*, Dover Publications (USA), 1993.

Crowley, Daniel J. (ed.), *African Folklore In The New World*, University Of Texas Press (USA).

Cunningham, Michael G., *American Folk Songs*, Seesaw Music, 0.

Curtis, P.J., *Notes From The Heart: A Celebration Of Traditional Music*, Torc, 1994.

Davis, Arthur Kyle, *Traditional Ballads Of Virginia*, University Press Of Virginia (USA).

De Filippi, Amedeo, *Raftsman's Dance*, c.1940.

De Turk, David A., *The American Folk Scene: Dimensions Of The Folk Song Revival*, Dell (USA), 1967.

Dorson, Richard Mercer, *America In Legend*, Pantheon Books (USA), 1973.

Dorson, Richard Mercer, *American Folklore And The Historian*, University Of Chicago Press (USA), 1971.

Dundes, Alan, *Mother Wit From The Laughing Barrel*, Prentice-Hall (USA), 1972.

Dundes, Alan, Comp. and Pagter, Carl R., *Urban Folklore From The Paperwork Empire*, American Folklore Society (USA), 1975.

Dyen, Doris Jane, *The Role Of Shape-Note Singing In The Musical Culture Of Black Communities*, 1977.

Eastham, Clark, *Two Pieces For Small Orchestra*.

Emmons, Martha, *Deep Like The Rivers*, Encino Press, 1969.

Emrich, Duncan, *American Folk Poetry*, Little Brown (USA), 1974.

Encontro Com O Folclore, *Rio de Janeiro-Guanabara*, 1964.

Fayo, Nestor A., *Musica Y Folclor*, Gaitan y Anca, 1970.

Ferris, William R., *Mississippi Black Folklore*, University And College Press Of Mississippi (USA), 1971.

Frackenpohl, Arthur Roland, *American Folk Song Suite*, Shawnee Press (USA), 1973.

Franco, Johan Henri Gustave, *When I Was Single & When I Can Read My Title Clear Composers Facsimile Edition*.

Fry, Gladys Marie, *Night Riders In Black Folk History*, University Of Tennessee Press (USA), 1967.

Fyfe, Peter, *Folk Festival Guide*.

Gainer, Patrick W., (ed.), *Folk Songs From The West Virginia Hills*, Seneca Books (USA).

Glass, Paul, *Songs Of Town And City Folk*, Grosset & Dunlap (USA), 1967.

Gordon, Robert Winslow, *Manuscript Collections Of American Folksong Texts*.

Gould, Philip, *Cajun Music And Zydeco*, Louisiana State University Press (USA), 1992.

Graetzer, Guillermo, *Antiguas Danzas Indigenas De Centro Y Sud America*, Barry.

Graham, Len (ed.), *It's Of My Rambles: Songs And Tunes From Ulster*, Harvest Home, Arts Council of Nthn. Ireland, 1993.

Green, Archie, *Only A Miner*, University Of Illinois Press (USA), 1972.

Grundman, Clare Ewing, *American Folk Rhapsody No. 3*, Boosey and Hawkes (UK).

Guion, David Wendell Fentress, *Arkansas Traveler*, Schirmer (USA).

Hagan, John Patrick, *Frederick Henry Koch And The American Folk Drama*, Bloomington, 1969.

Hamilton, James S., *Sitar Music In Calcutta*, Calgary Press, 1991.

Harris, Joel Chandler, *Nights With Uncle Remus*, Singing Tree Press.

Harris, Joel Chandler, *Uncle Remus And Brer Rabbit*, Stokes, 1907.

Harris, Joel Chandler, *Uncle Remus, His Songs And His Sayings*, D. Appleton.

Harris, Roy, *Work Song*, Belwin Mills.

Harris, Trudier, *The Tie That Binds*, (USA), 1973.

Haywood, Charles, *A Bibliography Of North American Folklore And Folksong*, Greenberg, 1951.

Helm, Everett Burton, *American Songs*, 1945.

Henry, Sam edited by Huntington, Gail, *Songs of the People*, University of Georgia Press (USA).

History Of Music Project, *A San Francisco Songster*, AMS Press, 1972.

Hoffman, Daniel, *Form And Fable In American Fiction*, Oxford University Press, 1965.

Howson, John, *Many A Good Horseman*, Veteran Tapes, Haughley, Stowmarket, Suffolk, IP14 3NX (UK), 1993.

Hudson, Arthur Palmer (ed.), *Folk Tunes From Mississippi*, Da Capo, 1977.

Hurston, Zora Neale, *Mules And Men*, J. B. Lippincott (USA), 1935.

Hurston, Zora Neale, *The Sanctified Church*, Turtle Island Foundation (USA).

Hyatt, Harry Middleton, *Hoodoo-Conjuration-Witchcraft-Rootwork*, American University Bookstore (USA).

Jackson, Bruce, *Get Your Ass In The Water And Swim Like Me*, Harvard University Press (USA), 1974.

Journal Of American Folk-Lore, *Richmond*, (USA).

Joyner, Charles W., *Folk Song In South Carolina*, University Of South Carolina Press (USA), 1971.

Kennedy, Douglas (ed.), *Community Dances Manual*, Princeton Books (USA).

Krassen, Miles, *Appalachian Fiddle*, Oak Publications (USA).

Kubik, Gail T., *Folk Song Suite, For Chamber Orchestra*, Southern Music.

Laing, Dave, Dallas, Karl, Denselow, Robin & Shelton, Robert, *The Electric Muse: The Story Of Folk Into Rock*, Methuen (UK), 1975.

Larkin, Colin, *The Virgin Encyclopedia Of World & Folk Music*, Virgin Books (UK), 1999.

Larkin, Colin (ed.), *Guinness Who's Who Of Folk Music*,

Guinness Publishing (UK), 1993.

Legg, Adrian & Colbert, Paul, *Making Music With: Acoustic Guitar*, Track Record, 1992.

Lester, Julius, *The Knee-High Man, And Other Tales*, Dial Press (USA), 1972.

Mac Aoidh, Caoimhín, *Between The Jigs And The Reels (The Donegal Fiddle Tradition)*, Drumlin Publications, 1995.

MacGall, Ewan, *Journeyman*, Sidgwick & Jackson (USA), 1991.

Mackinnon, Niall, *British Folk Scene: Musical Performance And Social Identity*, Open Uuniversity Press (UK), 1993.

Manno, Robert, *American Folk-Song Preludes*.

Martin, Claude Trimble, *Deac Martin's Book Of Musical Americana*, Prentice-Hall (USA), 1970.

McIntosh, David Seneff, *Folk Songs & Singing Games Of The Illinois Ozarks*, Southern Illinois University Press (USA), 1974.

McLean, Don, *Songs And Sketches Of The First Clearwater Crew*, North River Press (USA), 1970.

McVicar, Ewan, *One Singer One Song*, Glascow City Libraries (UK), 1991.

Michels, Barbara and Bettye White (Eds.), *Apples On A Stick*, Coward-McCann.

Minagawa, Soichi, *Amerika Foku Songu No Sekai*, Iwasaki Bijutsusha, 1973.

Modern Language Association Of America, *Report Of The Committee On Folksong Of The Popular Literature Section*, University of Florida (USA), 1953.

Morgan, Kathryn L., *Children Of Strangers*, Temple University Press, 1980.

Morgan, Kathryn L., *The Ex-Slave Narrative As A Source For Folk History*, 1970.

Museum Of American Folk Art, *American Folk Art*, Museum Of American Folk Art.

No author listed, *50 Popular Folk Songs, Pacific Coast Music.*

No author listed, *Abstracts Of Folklore Studies*, Philadelphia (USA).

No author listed, *Afro-American Folk Art And Crafts*, G.K. Hall.

No author listed, *Baking In The Sun*, University Of Southwestern Louisiana (USA).

No author listed, *The East Tennessee State University Collection Of Folklore*, Research Advisory Council Of East Tennessee State University (USA).

No author listed, *The Folk Decade*, Warner Brothers (USA).

no author listed, *Collected Reprints From 'Sing Out'*, Sing Out Corporation (USA), 1993.

No editor listed, *The Folk Directory*, English Folk Dance & Song Society (UK), 1992.

No editor listed, *Folk Visions & Voices*, University Of Georgia Press (USA).

No editor listed, *Folklore Folklife*, American Folklore Society (USA), 1984.

Not listed, *The Collected Reprints From Sing Out! Folk Song Magazine Vols. 7-12*, 1993.

O'Connor, Nuala, *Bringing It All Back Home*, BBC (UK), 1991.

Old Mother Hippletoe, *New World Records*, 1978.

Oriano, Michel, *Les Travailleurs De La Frontiere*, Payot, 1980.

Palmer, Roy, *What A Lovely War: British Soldier Songs From The Boar War to the Present Day*, Michael Joseph (UK), 1991.

Pan American Institute Of Geography and History, *Serie De Folklore Del IPGH. Coleccion Documentos*, Mexico.

Paredes, Americo and Ellen J. Stekert (eds.), *The Urban Experience And Folk Tradition*, University Of Texas Press (USA), 1971.

Peters, Harry B., (ed.), *Folk Songs Out Of Wisconsin*, State Hisorical Society Of Wisconsin (USA), 1977.

Phillips, Duncan (ed.), *Musicmaster: Folk Music Of The British Isles, Catalogue 1*, Retail Data Publishing, 1995.

Pickett, Andrew Morris, *The Use Of Black American Slave Folk Songs In The Social Studies Curiculum*, 1977.

Pooler, Marie, *Shenandoah*, C. Fischer.

Puckett, Newbell Niles, *Folk Beliefs Of The Southern Negro*, Negro Universities Press (USA).

Raim, Ethel, *Grass Roots Harmony*, Oak Publications (USA), 1968.

Randolph, Vance, *Ozark Folksongs*, University Of Missouri Press (USA), 1980.

Reuss, Richard A., *American Folklore And Left-Wing Politics*, Bloomington, 1971.

Robb, John Donald, *Hispanic Folk Music Of New Mexico And The Southwest*, University of Oklahoma Press (USA).

Roberts, Leonard W., *Sang Branch Settlers*, University Of Texas Press (USA), 1974.

Roberts, Leonard W.(ed.), *In The Pine*, Pikeville College Press, 1978.

Rose, Linda C., *Disease Beliefs In Mexican-American Communities*, R. & E Research Associates.

Scarmolin, A. Louis, *Shortnin' Bread*, Pro Art.

Schmidt, Eric Von, And Jim Rooney, *Baby Let Me Follow You Down: Illust. Story Of Cambridge Folk Years*, University Of Massachusetts Press (USA), 1994.

Schuller, Gunther (ed.), *Country Dance Music*, Margun Music.

Scott, John Anthony, *The Ballad Of America*, Grosset & Dunlap (USA), 1967.

Sharp, Cecil James, *American-English Folk-Ballads From The Southern Apalachian Mountains*, Schirmer (USA).

Shields, Hugh, *Narrative Singing In Ireland*, Irish Academic Press, 1994.

Siegmeister, Elie, *Five American Folk-Songs*, Carl Fischer.

Silverman, Jerry (ed.), *Play Old-Time Country Fiddle*, Chilton Books.

Smith, Edna (ed.), *The Griot Sings*, Medgars Evers College Press, 1978.

Solomon, Jack and Olivia, *Ghosts And Goosebumps*, University Of Alabama Press (USA).

Sper, Felix, *From Native Roots; A Panorama Of Our Regional Drama*, Caxton Printers, 1948.

Spottswood, Richard K. and Mack McCormick (eds.), *Songs Of Death & Tragedy*, Library Of Congress, Music Division (USA), 1978.

Stover, Harold, *Five Preludes On American Folk Hymns*, H. W. Gray.

Thomas, Jeannette Bell, *Devil's Ditties*, Gale Research (USA), 1975.

Thompson, Rose (ed.), *Hush, Child! Can't You Hear The Music?*, University Of Georgia Press (USA).

Townsend, Douglas, *Fantasies On American Folk Songs*, C.F. Peters.

Tracy, Steven C. (Steven Carl), *Langston Hughes & The Blues*, University of Illinois Press (USA).

Traum, Happy, *Flat-Pick Country Guitar*, Oak Publications (USA).

Trotter, Robert T., *Curanderismo, Mexican American Folk Healing*, University Of Georgia Press (USA).

Turner, Frederick W., *Badmen, Black And White Microform*, , 1965.

Turner, Martha Anne, *The Yellow Rose Of Texas*, Shoal Creek (USA).

Van der Horst, Brian, *Folk Music In America*, F. Watts, 1972.

Vassal, Jacques, *Electric Children: Roots And Branches Of Modern Folk Rock*, Taplinger, 1976.

Vassal, Jacques, *Folksong; Une Histoire de la Musique Populaire Aux Etats-Unis*, A. Michel, 1971.

Von Schmidt, Eric, *Baby, Let Me Follow You Down*, Anchor Books, 1979.

Warburton, Hilary (ed.), *Folk Directory 1994-5*, English Folk Dance & Song Society (UK), 1994.

Warner, Frank, *Folk Songs And Ballads Of The Eastern Seaboard*, Southern Press.

Wepman, Dennis, (ed.), *The Life*, University Of Pennsylvania Press (USA), 1976.

Wightman, Francis P., *Little Leather Breeches, And Other Southern Rhymes*, J.F. Taylor (USA).

Writers' Program, Georgia, *Drums And Shadows*, Anchor Books, 1972.

Yoder, Don, (ed.), *American Folklife*, University Of Texas Press (USA).

Zaninelli, Luigi, *Americana*, Shawnee Press (USA), 1975.

Zaninelli, Luigi, *Five Folk Songs*, Shawnee Press (USA).

Zenger, Dixie Robison, *Violin Techniques And Traditions Useful In Identifying And Playing North America*, 1980.

Heavy Metal

Arnett, Jeffrey Jensen, *Metalheads: Heavy Metal Music And Adolescent Alienation*, Westview Press (UK), 1996.

Bashe, Philip, *Heavy Metal Thunder*, Omnibus Press (UK), 1986.

Dome, Malcolm, *Thrash Metal*, Omnibus Press (UK), 1990.

Eddy, Chuck, *Stairway To Hell: The 500 Best Heavy Metal Albums In The Universe*, Harmony Books (USA), 1991.

Hale, Mark, *Headbangers: Worldwide Mega-Book Of Heavy Metal Bands*, Popular Culture Ink, 1992.

Halfin, Ross, *The Power Age*, Eel Pie (UK), 1982.

Harrigan, Brian, *The HM A-Z*, Bobcat Books (USA), 1981.

Harrigan, Brian & Dome, Michael, *Encyclopedia Metallica: The Bible Of Heavy Metal*, Bobcat (USA), 1981.

Jasper, Tony, *The International Encyclopedia Of Hard Rock & Heavy Metal*, Sidgwick & Jackson (UK), 1984.

Jeffries, Neil (ed.), *Kerrang! Directory Of Heavy Metal: The Indispensable Guide To...*, Virgin Books (UK), 1993.

Larkin, Colin, *The Virgin Encyclopedia Of Heavy Rock*, Virgin Books (UK), 1999.

Larkin, Colin (ed.), *Guinness Who's Who Of Heavy Metal (2nd Edition)*, Guinness Publishing (UK), 1995.

Larkin, Colin (ed.), *Guinness Who's Who Of Heavy Metal*, Guinness Publishing (UK), 1992.

Martyn, Lee, *Masters Of Metal*, Zomba, 1985.

Not listed, *Giants Of Heavy Metal: Authentic Guitar - Tab Edition*, Warner Brothers (USA), 1993.

Stark, Janne, *Encyclopedia Of Swedish Hard Rock And Heavy Metal, 1970-96*, Premium Publishing (Sweden), 1996.

Stetina, Troy, and Joyce, Shauna, *Secrets To Writing Killer Metal Songs*, Hal Leonard Publishing, (USA), 1993.

Walser, Robert, *Running With The Devil: Power, Gender And Madness In Heavy Metal...*, Wesleyan Univ. Press (USA), 1993.

Instruments

Bacon, Tony and Day, Paul, *Complete History Of Fender Electric Guitars*, Balafon: International Music Publications (UK), 1992.

Erlewine, Dan, *How To Set Up, Maintain And Repair Electrics And Acoustics*, GPI Books (USA), 1992.

Giltrap, Gordon & Neville, Martin, *History Of The Hofner Guitar And Its Players*, International Music Publications (UK), 1993.

Hoose, T. A. Van, *Gibson Super 400: Art Of The Fine Guitar*, GPI Books (USA), 1992.

Wheeler, Tom, *American Guitars: An Illustrated History*, Harper Collins, 1992.

Jazz

Abe, K., *Jazz Giants*, Billboard (USA), 1988.

Adderly, Julian, *Cannonball Adderly's Complete Jazz Fake Book*, Silhouette Music, 1976.

Aebersold, Jamey, *A New Approach To Jazz Improvisation*, Jamey Aebersold.

Agostinelli, Anthony J., *The Newport Jazz Festival, Rhode Island, 1954-1971*, Agostinelli.

Akiyoshi, Toshiko, *Transience*, Kendor Music.

Akiyoshi, Toshiko, *Notorious Tourist From The East*, Kendor Music.

Akiyoshi, Toshiko, *American Ballad*, Kendor Music.

Alkyer, Frank (ed), *Down Beat 60 Years Of Jazz*, Hal Leonard Publications (USA), 1995.

Allen, Daniel, *78-RPM Phonorecords In The Jazz Archive*, Toronto, 1972.

Allen, W.C., *Studies In Jazz Discography*, New Brunswick, 1971.

Almeida, Laurindo, *Bossa Guitarra*, Criterion.

Amstell, Billy, *Don't Fuss, Mr. Ambrose*, Spellmount, 1986.

Andriessen, Jurriaan, *Pasticcio Finale Voor Symfonicorkest*, Donemus.

Angstmann, Freddy J., *Jazz*, Silva-Verlag.

Araque, Luis, *Defensa De La Musica De Jazz*, Ediciones Alguero, 1946.

Archambault, Gilles, *Discographie De Jazz*, Service de Publicite-Radio de Radio-Canada, 1982.

Arkansas Arts Center, *Catalog Of The John D. Reid Collection Of Early American Jazz*, Arkansas Arts Center, Little Rock (USA), 1975.

Asbury, H., *The French Quarter: An Informal Histroy Of The New Orleans Underworld*, New York, 1937.

Asch, Glenn and David Reiner, *Mel Bay's Deluxe Anthology Of Jazz Violin Styles*, Mel Bay, 1982.

Assessing, Insuring, And Disposing Of Jazz Record Collection, International Association of Jazz Record Collectors.

Attali, Jacques, *Noise: The Political Economy Of Music*, Manchester University Press, 1986.

Ayoub, Nick, *Joey's Place*, Dorn.

Baats, Harry, *All Kind Of Music*, Muziekuitgeverij Van Teeseling.

Backus, R., *A Political History Of Jazz*, Chicago, 1977.

Backus, Rob, *Fire Music*, Vanguard Books (USA), 1976.

Baker, David, *Improvisational Patterns, The Bepop Era*, Charles Colin.

Baker, David N., *Contemporary Techniques For The Trombone*, C. Colin.

Baker, David N. (ed.), *New Perspectives On Jazz*, Smithsonian Institution (USA), 1991.

Balcerak, Jozef, *Magia Jazzu*, Krajowa Agenija Wydawnicza, 1981.

Balliett, Whitney, *Goodbye And Other Messages*, Oxford University Press (UK), 1992.

Balliett, Whitney, *Night Creature: Journal Of Jazz 1975-80*, Oxford University Press, 1981.

Balliett, Whitney, *New York Notes*, Houghton Mifflin (USA), 1976.

Balliett, Whitney, *Improvising: Sixteen Jazz Musicians And Their Art*, Oxford, 1990.

Balliett, Whitney, *Goodbyes And Other Messages: Journal Of Jazz 1981-1990*, Oxford University Press, 1992.

Balliett, Whitney, *Ecstasy At The Onion*, Bobbs-Merrill (USA), 1971.

Balliett, Whitney, *American Singers: Twenty-Seven Portraits In Song*, Oxford University Press, 1988.

Balliett, Whitney, *American Musicians: Fifty-Six Portraits In Jazz*, Oxford University Press, 1990.

Balliett, Whitney, *American Musicians*, Oxford University Press, 1986.

Baraka, Imamu Amiri, *The Music*, W. Morrow (USA).

Baraka, Imamu Amiri, *Blues People: Negro Music In White America*, W. Morrow (USA), 1963.

Barlow, William & Morgan, Thomas L., *From Cakewalks To Concert Halls*, Elliott And Clark Publishing (USA), 1992.

Barnet, Charles, *Those Swinging Years*, Louisiana State University Press (USA).

Barr, Walter Laning, *The Jazz Studies Curriculum*, Tempe, Arizona (USA), 1974.

Barreto, Jorge Lima, *Revolucao Do Jazz*, Editorial Inova Limitada, 1972.

Barreto, Jorge Lima, *Grande Musica Negro*, Edicoes RES, 1975.

Barreto, Jorge Lima, *Anarqueologia Do Jazz*, Regra do Jogo, 1984.

Bart, Teddy, *Inside Music City USA Nashville*, Aurora (USA), 1970.

Basie, Bill 'Count', *Good Morning Blues*, Grafton, 1990.

Batashev, Aleksei Nikolaevich, *Sovetskii Dzhaz. Ist. Ocherk. Pod Red.*, Moskva, Muzyka, 1972.

Baumgartel, Willy, *Rhythmisch-Stilistische Studien Fur Jazzposaune*, Deutscher Verlag Fur Musik.

Beckman, Monica, *Gimnasia Jazz*, Editorial Stadium.

Beeftink, Herman, *Jazz For Flute*, Muziekuiktgeverij van Teeseling.

Bellson, Louis, *Guide To Big Band Drumming*, C. Hansen.

Benham, Patrick, *Mostly Jazz*, G. Ricordi.

Berendt, Joachim E., *Jazz Book: From Ragtime To Fusion And Beyond*, L. Hill Books, (USA), 1993.

Berendt, Joachim Ernst, *The New Jazz Book, A History And Guide*, Hill and Wang, 1962.

Berendt, Joachim Ernst, *The Jazz Book*, Granada (UK).

Berendt, Joachim Ernst, *The Jazz Book*, Lawrence Hill (USA), 1975.

Berendt, Joachim Ernst, *Photo-Story Des Jazz*, Kruger.

Berendt, Joachim Ernst, *Jazz, A Photo History*, Schirmer (USA).

Berendt, Joachim Ernst, *Die Story Des Jazz*, Deutsche Verlags-Anstalt.

Berendt, Joachim Ernst, *Das Grosse Jazzbuch*, Fischer Taschenbuch (Germany), 1986.

Berger, E. (ed.), *Annual Review Of Jazz*, Scarecrow Press (USA), 1994.

Bergerot, Franck & Merlin, Arnaud, *Story of jazz, Bop And Beyond*, Thames & Hudson (UK), 1993.

Berigan, Bunny, *Modern Trumpet Studies*, Robbins Music.

Berindei, Mihai, *Dictionar De Jazz*, Editura Stiintifica Si Enciclopedica, 1976.

Berle, Arnie, *Complete Handbook For Jazz Improvisation*, Music Sales, 1972.

Berlin, Irving, *Blue Skies*, Blue Note.

Berliner, Paul F., *Thinking In Jazz: The Infinite Art Of Improvisation*, University Of Chicago Press (USA), 1993.

Berliner, Paul F., *Thinking In Jazz: The Infinite Art Of Improvisation*, University Of Chicago Press (USA), 1994.

Bernhardt, Clyde, *I Remember: Eighty Years Of Black Entertainment Big Band and Blues*, Pennsylvania University Press (USA), 1986.

Bernstein, Leonard, *Prelude, Fugue And Riffs*, Schirmer (USA).

Berry, Jason, *Up from the Cradle Of Jazz: New Orleans Music Since The War*, Da Capo (USA), 1992.

Best, William, *For Sentimental Reasons*, Capitol.

Bettonville, A., *Paranoia Du Jazz*, Brussels, 1939.

Biderbost, Marc, *Le Guide Marabout De La Musique Et Du Disque De Jazz*, Marabout.

Bird, Christiane, *The Jazz & Blues Lover's Guide To The U.S.*, Addison Wesley (UK), 1991.

Bisceglia, Jacques, *Black And White Fantasy*, Corps 9 Editions.

Bisset, Andrew, *Black Roots, White Flowers*, Golden Press, 1979.

Blackstone, O., *Index To Jazz*, Fairfax, Virginia (USA).

Blake, Ran, *A Collection Of Third Stream Compositions*, Margun Music.

Blanq, Charles Clement, *Melodic Improvisation In American Jazz*, 1977.

Blatny, Pavel, *In Mod Classico*, Editio Supraphon, 1982.

Blesh, Rudi, *Shining Trumpets*, Da Capo (USA), 1975.

Blesh, Rudi, *Eight Lives In Jazz*, Hayden (USA), 1971.

Blesh, Rudi, *Combo*, Chilton Book, 1971.

Blesh, Rudi & Harriet Janis, *They All Played Ragtime*, Alfred A. Knopf (USA), 1971.

Bohlander, Carlo, *Reclams Jazzfuhrer*, Reclam, 1970.

Bolelli, Franco, *Musica Creativa*, Squilibri, 1978.

Bolling, Claude, *Jazz Piano Course*, Hansen House, 1980.

Bolocan, David, *Jazz, Jazz, Jazz, Jazz*, Tab Books, 1985.

Bonnemere, Eddie, *Papers*, 1940.

Bonnemere, Eddie, *Help Me, Jesus*.

Bonnemere, Eddie, *Educational Cross Section*.

Boogaard, Bernard Van Den, *Panta Rhei*, Donemus.

Borneman, E., *Boogie-Woogie*, Just Jazz, London, 1957.

Bragaglia, A. G., *Jazz Band*, Milan, 1929.

Brandman, Russella, *The Evolution Of Jazz Dance From Folk Origins To Concert Stage*, 1977.

Breton, Marcela, *Hot And Cool: Jazz Short Stories*, Bloomsbury (UK), 1991.

Britt, Stan, *The Jazz Guitarist*, Sterling, 1984.

Broadbent, Alan, *Adam's Apple*.

Brooks Fox, Jules And Jo, *The Melody Lingers On*, Fifthian Press (USA), 1996.

Broonzy, William, *Big Bill Blues*, Oak Publications (USA), 1964.

Brown, Chris, *The Family Album*, Hitman, 1980.

Brown, Marion, *Recollections*, Juergen A. Schmitt.

Brown, Marion, *Faces And Places*, 1976.

Brown, Ray, *An Introduction To Jazz Improvisation*, Edward B. Marks.

Brown, Ron, *Georgia On My Mind*, Milestone.

Brown, Sandy, *The McJazz Manuscripts*, Faber & Faber (UK), 1979.

Brown, Theodore Dennis, *A History And Analysis Of Jazz Drumming To 1942*, 1976.

Brun, H., *The Story Of The Original Dixieland Jazz Band*, Baton Rouge (USA), 1960.

Bruyninckx, W., *60 Years Of Recorded Jazz: 1917-77*, Mechelen.

Bryant, Lance, *The Touch*, 1988.

Budds, M. J., *Jazz In The Sixties: the Expansion Of Musical Resources And Techniques*, Iowa City (USA), 1978.

Buerkle, J V and D Barker, *Bourbon Street Black: The New Orleans Black Jazzman*, New York: Oxford University Press, 1973.

Burns, Ralph, *Bijou*, Mayfair Music.

Burton, Jack, *The Blue Book Of Tin Pan Alley*, Century House.

Bushell, Garvin, *Jazz From The Beginning*, University Of Michigan Press (USA).

Cabanowski, Marek, *Polska Dyskografia Jazzowa*, M. Cabanowski, H. Cholinski, 1974.

Cacibauda, Joe, *No Nonsense Electric Bass*, Studio P/R.

Camarata, Salvador, *What Makes Sammy Run*, Robbins Music.

Campbell, James (ed), *The Picador Book Of Blues And Jazz*, Picador (UK), 1995.

Cane, Giampiero, *Canto Nero*, Clueb, 1982.

Caraceni, A., *Il Jazz Delle Origini Ad Oggi*, Milan.

Carey, David Arthur (ed.), *The Directory Of Recorded Jazz And Swing Music*, Delphic Press.

Carey, Joseph Kuhn, *Big Noise From Notre Dame*, University Of Notre Dame Press.

Carisi, John, *Israel*, Margun Music.

Carl Gregor, Duke Of Mecklenburg, *Die Theorie Des Blues Im Modernen Jazz*, V. Koerner, 1971.

Carles, Philippe, *Free Jazz/Black Power*, Editions Champ Libre, 1971.

Carner, Gary, *Jazz Performers: An Annotated Bibliography Of Biographical Materials*, Greenwood Press (UK), 1990.

Carr, Ian, Digby Fairweather, Brian Priestly, *Jazz: The Rough Guide*, Rough Guides (UK), 1995.

Carr, Ian; Fairweather, Digby & Priestley, Brian, *Jazz: The Essential Companion*, Grafton (UK), 1987.

Carr, Roy, *The Hip*, Faber & Faber (UK), 1986.

Carr, Roy, (ed), *Jazz On CD*, Mitchell Beazley (UK), 1995.

Carruth, Hayden, *Sitting In*, University Of Iowa Press (USA), 1986.

Carter, Willliam, *Preservation Hall*, Bayou Press (USA), 1992.

Case, Brian, *The Illustrated Encyclopedia Of Jazz*, Salamander Books (UK), 1978.

Case, Brian, *The Harmony Illustrated Encyclopedia Of Jazz*, Harmony Books (USA).

Castelli, Vittorio, *Il Jazz Su Disco*, A. Mondadori, 1983.

Castellucci, Stella, *An Approach To Jazz And Popular Music For Harp*, Miranda.

Caston, Leonard, *From Blues To Pop*, John Edwards Memorial Foundation, 1974

Cayou, Dolores Kirton, *Modern Jazz Dance*, National Press Books, 1971.

Cerri, Livio, *Mezzo Secolo Di Jazz*, Nistri-Lischi, 1981.

Chambers, Jack, *Milestones*, Beech Tree Books.

Charters, S. B. and L Kunstadt, *Jazz: A History Of The New York Scene, Garden City*, New York, 1962.

Charters, Samuel Barclay, *Jazz: New Orleans, 1885-1957*, W. C. Allen.

Charters, Samuel Barclay, *Jazz: New Orleans 1885-1963*, Oak Publications (USA), 1963.

Chaumier, J., *La Litterature Du Jazz*, Le Mans, 1963.

Chesky, David, *Contemporary Jazz Rock Rhythms*, C. Colin.

Chevigny, Paul, *After The Law: Jazz And The Cabaret Laws In New York City*, Routledge (UK), 1992.

Chilton, John, *Who's Who Of Jazz*, Macmillan, 1990.

Chilton, John, *The Song Of The Hawk*, Quartet (UK), 1990.

Chilton, John, *McKinney's Music*, Bloomsbury Book Shop, 1978.

Chilton, John, *Jazz*, Sevenoaks, 1979.

Christian, Charley, *The Art Of The Jazz Guitar*, Cherry Lane Music.

Cichero, Augusto, *Guia Del Jazz*, Editorial Huemul, 1976.

Claghorn, Charles Eugene, *Biographical Dictionary Of Jazz*, Prentice-Hall (USA).

Clark, C., *Jazz Readers' Guide*, London, 1982.

Claxton, William, *Jazz*, Twelvetrees Press.

Clayton, Peter, *Jazz A-Z*, Guinness Publishing.

Clayton, Peter & Gammond, Peter, *Guinness Jazz Companion*, Guinness Publishing (UK), 1989.

Clement, Raymond, *Jazz Im/Expressions*, RTL Editions, 1980.

Closson, David L., *One Life In Black Music*, Philadelphia (USA).

Cogno, Enrico, *Jazz Inchiesta*, Cappelli, 1971.

Cohan, Robert, *The Dance Workshop*, G. Allen & Unwin (USA), 1986.

Coker, Jerry, *The Jazz Idiom*, Englewood Cliffs (USA), 1975.

Coker, Jerry, *Patterns For Jazz*, Studio Editions.

Coker, Jerry, *Listening To Jazz*, Prentice-Hall (USA).

Coker, Jerry, *Improvising Jazz*, Simon & Schuster (USA), 1986.

Collier, Graham, *Jazz*, Cambridge University Press, 1975.

Collier, Graham, *Inside Jazz*, Quartet Books (UK), 1973.

Collier, Graham, *Compositional Devices Vol 1*, Berklee Press (USA), 0.

Collier, James Lincoln, *The Reception Of Jazz In America*, Institute For Studies In American Music.

Collier, James Lincoln, *The Making Of Jazz: A Comprehensive History*, Houghton Mifflin (USA), Macmillan (UK), 1978.

Collier, James Lincoln, *The Great Jazz Artists*, Four Winds Press (USA).

Collier, James Lincoln, *Jazz: The American Theme Song*, Oxford University Press (USA), 1994.

Collins, L., *Oh, Didn't He Ramble?*, Urbana (USA), 1974.

Complete Encyclopedia Of Rhythms And Patterns, *For All Instruments*, C. Colin.

Cook, Richard & Morton, Brian, *Penguin Guide To Jazz On CD, LP & Cassette*, Penguin (UK), 1992.

Cook, Richard & Morton, Brian, *Penguin Guide To Jazz On CD, LP & Cassette, Third Edition*, Penguin (UK), 1996.

Cooper, David Edwin, *International Bibliography Of Discographies*, Libraries Unlimited, 1975.

Coryell, Julie & Friedman, Laura, *Jazz-Rock Fusion: The People, The Music*, Marion Boyars (UK), 1978.

Courtioux, Jean, *Les Quatre Elements*, Dorn.

Coyner, Lou, *South Rampart Street Revisited*, Dorn, 1981.

Cracker, Chris, *Get Into Jazz*, Bantam (USA), 1994.

Crawford, Ralston, *Music In The Street*, Historic New Orleans Collection.

Crow, Bill, *Jazz Anecdotes*, Oxford University Press, 1990.

Crow, Bill, *From Birdland To Broadway: Scenes From A Jazz Life*, Oxford University Press, 1992.

Crowder, Henry, *As Wonderful As All That?*, Wild Trees Press.

Crowther, Bruce, And Mike Pinfold, *The Big Band Years*, David & Charles (UK), 1986.

Crowther, Bruce, And Mike Pinfold, *The Jazz Singers*, Javelin, 1988.

Crowther, Bruce, And Mike Pinfold, *Jazz Singing: The Singers And Their Styles*, Blandford (UK), Miller-Freeman (USA), 1997.

Crump, Janice D. Lapointe and Staley, Kimberly T., *Discovering Jazz Dance: America's Energy And Soul*, W C Brown (USA), 1992.

Cushman, Jerome, *Tom B. And The Joyful Noise*, Westminster Press, 1970.

Czompo, Ann I., *Recreational Jazz Dance*, AC.

D'Rozario, Rico, *North Sea Jazz Festival, 1976-1985*, 1985.

Dahl, Linda, *Stormy Weather: Music And Lives Of A Century Of Jazz Women*, Limelight Editions, 1990.

Dahl, Linda, *Stormy Weather*, Quartet (UK), 1988.

Dalaunay, Charles, *Hot Discography: Edited By Hot Jazz*, Commodore Record, 1943.

Dale, Rodney, *The World Of Jazz*, Phaidon (UK), 1980.

Dallas, Karl F., *Singers Of An Empty Day*, Kahn & Averill, 1971.

Danca, Vince, *Bunny*, Danca.

Dance Masters Of America, *Jazz Syllabus*.

Dance, Stanley, *The World Of Swing*, Scribners (USA), 1974.

Dankworth, Avril, *Jazz: An Introduction To Its Musical Basis*, Oxford University Press, 1968.

Darrell, R D., *Black Beauty*, Philadelphia, 1933.

Dauer, A.M. and Longstreet, S., *Knaur's Jazz Lexikon*, Munich, 1957.

Dauer, Alfons M., *Der Jazz, Seine Ursprunge Und Seine Entwicklung*, E. Roth-Verlag, 1958.

David, Ron, *Jazz For Beginners*, Writers And Readers, 1995.

Davis, Francis, *Outcats*, Oxford University Press, 1990.

Davis, Francis, *In The Moment*, Oxford University Press.

Davis, Francis, *Bebop And Nothingness: Jazz And Pop At The End Of The Century*, Schirmer Books (USA), 1996.

Davis, Nathan Tate, *Writings In Jazz*, Gorsuch Scarisbrick.

de Graef, Jack, *De Swingperiode (1935-1947)*, Dageraad, 1980.

de Roque, Pedro, *El Jazz*, Editorial Convergencia, 1977.

de Ruyter, Michiel, *Michiel De Ruyter, Een Leven Met Jazz*, Van Gennep, 1984.

De Stefano, Gildo, *Trecento Anni Di Jazz*, Sugar Edizioni, 1986.

De Toledano, Ralph, *Frontiers Of Jazz*, F. Ungar, 1962.

de Toledano, Ralph, *Frontiers Of Jazz*, Oliver Durrell , 1947.

Dean, Roger, *New Structures In Jazz And Improvised Music Since 1960*, Open University Press (UK), 1991.

Deffaa, Chip, *In The Mainstream: 18 Portraits In Jazz*, Scarecrow Press (USA), 1992.

Deffaa, Chip, *Voices Of The Jazz Age. Profiles Of Eight Vintage Jazzmen*, Bayou Press (USA), 1990.

Deffaa, Chip, *Swing Legacy*, Scarecrow (USA), 1989.

Delaunay, Charles, *New Hot Discography*, Criterion.

Delaunay, Charles, *Hot Discographie 1943*, Collection Du Hot Club De France, 1944.

Deutsch, Maury, *Improvisational Concepts And Jazz Patterns*,

C. Colin.

DeVeaux, Scott Knowles, *Jazz In Transition*, 1985.

Dexter Jnr., Dave, *The Jazz Story: From The '90s To The '60s*, Prentice-Hall (USA), 1964.

Dexter Jr., Dave, *Jazz Cavalcade: The Inside Story Of Jazz*, Criterion Music, 1946.

Dollase, Rainer, *Das Jazzpublikum*, Schott.

Dorigne, Michel, *Jazz 2*, New York.

Doruzka, Lubomir, *Ceskoslovensky Jazz*, Praha, 1967.

Dow, Allen, *The Official Guide To Jazz Dancing*, Chartwell Books.

Driggs, F, and H Lewine, *Black Beauty*, White Heat (USA), 1982.

Dulfer, Hans, *Jazz In China En Andere Perikels Uit De Geimproviseerde Muziek*, Bakker, 1980.

Dyer, Georff, *But Beautiful*, Jonathan Cape (UK), 1991.

Ebbesen, Niels Fink, *Dansk Jazzlitteratur: Litteratur Om Dansk Jazz*, Kobenhavns Universitet, 1980.

Edited by Barry Kernfeld, *The Blackwell Guide To Recorded Jazz*, Blackwell (UK), 1991.

Edmonds, Hank, *Great Jazz Lines*, C. Colin.

Edwards, Ernie, *Jazz Discographies Unlimited Presents Bill Harris*, Erngeobil, 1966.

Ehle, Robert C/, *Love*, Dorn.

Eldridge, Roy, *The Nifty Cat*, New World Records, 1986.

Elings, A., *Bibliografie Van De Nederlandse Jazz*, Nijmegen, 1966.

Elite Special Schallplatten, *Generalkatalog*, E. & W. Buhler, 1946.

Ellison, Mary, *Extensions Of The Blues*, Calder, 1990.

Ellison, R., *Shadow And Act*, New York, 1964.

Encyclopedia Of Jazz Duets, *For All Instruments*, C. Colin.

Englund, Bjorn, *Jazz Pa Cupol*, Svenskt Visarkiv.

Enstice, Wayne & Rubin, Paul, *Jazz Spoken Here*, Louisiana State University Press (USA), 1992.

Enstice, Wayne, And Paul Rubin, *Jazz Spoken Here*, Da Capo (USA), 1994.

Erb, Donald, *The Hawk*, Galaxy Music.

Erlich, Lillian, *What Jazz Is All About*, Julian Messner, 1962.

Escher, Wolf, *Die Trompete Im Jazz*, Universal.

European Jazz Directory, *Jazz World*.

European Jazz Federation, *List Of EJF Jazz-Clubs*, European Jazz Federation, 1976.

Evans, Lee, *The Jazz Tetrachord Approach To Keyboard Jazz Improvisation*, Belwin Mills, 1982.

Evans, Lee, *Modes And Their Use In Jazz*, E. B. Marks (USA).

Ewen, David, *The Life And Death Of Tin Pan Alley*, Funk and Wagnall (USA), 1964.

Faas, Hugo, *Der Jazz In Der Schweiz*, Pro Helvetia, 1976.

Fairbairn, Ann, *Call Him George*, Crown (USA), 1961.

Fark, Reinhard, *Die Missachtete Botschaft*, Spiess, 1971.

Fatto, Guy de, *Aux Rythmes De Dieu*, Editions du Cerf, 1978.

Fayenz, Franco, *Jazz & Jazz*, Laterza, 1981.

Fayenz, Franco, *Il Jazz Dal Mito All'Avanguardia*, Sapere, 1970.

Feather, Leonard, *The Pleasures Of Jazz*, Horizon Press (USA), 1976.

Feather, Leonard, *The Passion For Jazz*, Horizon Press (USA), 1980.

Feather, Leonard, *The New Edition Of The Encyclopedia Of Jazz*, Horizon Press (USA), 1960.

Feather, Leonard, *The Jazz Years*, Da Capo (USA), 1987.

Feather, Leonard, *The Encyclopedia Of Jazz In The Sixties*, Horizon Press (USA), 1966.

Feather, Leonard, *The Encyclopedia Of Jazz In The Seventies*, Quartet Books, 1978.

Feather, Leonard, *The Encyclopedia Of Jazz*, New York.

Feather, Leonard, *The Book Of Jazz*, Horizon Press (USA), 1965.

Feather, Leonard, *Panacea*, Mayfair Music.

Feather, Leonard, *Laughter From The Hip: The Lighter Side Of Jazz*, Da Capo (USA), 1990.

Feather, Leonard, *Inside Jazz, Inside Be-Bop*, Da Capo (USA), 1990.

Feather, Leonard, *Inside Be-Bop*, New York.

Feather, Leonard, *From Satchmo To Miles*, Da Capo (USA), 1990.

Feather, Leonard, *Encyclopedia Yearbook Of Jazz (1956)*, Da Capo (USA), 1993.

Feather, Leonard, *New Yearbook Of Jazz (1958)*, Da Capo (USA), 1993.

Feather, Leonard (intro. by), *Jazz Guitarists*, Guitar Player (USA).

Feigin, Leo, *Russian Jazz: New Identity*, Quartet Books (UK), 1985.

Ferguson, *Mainstream Jazz Reference And Price Guide, 1949-1965, Caroline House*, Ferguson.

Fernett, Gene, *Swing Out: Great Negro Dance Bands*, Da Capo Press (USA), 1993.

Finkelstein, Sidney Walter, *Jazz: A People's Music*, (USA).

Fischer-Munstermann, Uta, *Von Der Jazzgymnastik Zum Jazztanz*, Pohl.

Fischer-Munstermann, Uta, *Jazz Dance Including Aerobics*, Sterling.

Floyd, Samuel A., *Black Music In The Harlem Renaissance: A Collection Of Essays*, Afro-American & African Studies/Greenwood Press, 1990.

Fordham, John, *The Sound Of Jazz*, Hamlyn (UK), 1989.

Fordham, John, *Let's Join Hands And Contact The Living*, Elm Tree Books (UK), 1986.

Fordham, John, *Jazz On CD: The Essential Guide*, Kyle Cathie (UK), 1991.

Fordham, John, *Jazz: History, Instruments, Musicians, Recordings*, Dorling Kindersley (UK), 1993.

Fordham, John, *Shooting From The Hip: Changing Tunes In Jazz 1970-95*, Kyle Cathie (UK), 1995.

Foreman, Ronald Clifford, *Jazz And Race Records, 1920-1932* (USA), 1968.

Fortunato, Joanne Alba, *Major Influences Affecting The Development Of Jazz Dance, 1950-1971*.

Foss, Peter (ed.), *Jazz 'N' Blues*, Busker S., 1994.

Foster, Frank Benjamin, *In Defense Of Be-Bop*, F. Foster Music, 1979.

Fox, Charles, *The Jazz Scene*, Hamlyn (UK), 1972.

Fox, Charles, *Jazz In Perspective* (USA), 1969.

Fox, Roy, *Hollywood, Mayfair, And All That Jazz*, Frewin, 1975.

Francis, Andre, *Jazz*, Paris.

Frankenstein, A., *Syncopating Saxophones*, Chicago, 1925.

Fredrickson, Scott, *Scat Singing Method*.

Freeman, Bud, *Crazeology*, Bayou Press (USA), 1989.

Freeman, Lawrence, *You Don't Look Like A Musician*, Belamp.

Freeman, Lawrence, *The Eel's Nephew*, E. B. Marks Music (USA).

Freeman, Lawrence, *The Barracuda*, Robbins Music.

Freeman, Lawrence, *If You Know Of A Better Life Please Tell Me*, B. Eaves, 1976.

Freeman, Lawrence, *Dr. Peycer's Dilemma*, E. B. Marks Music (USA).

Freeman, Lawrence, *Disenchanted Trout*, E. B. Marks Music (USA).

Freeman, Lawrence, *Atomic Era*, Robbins.

Frich, Elisabeth, *The Matt Mattox Book Of Jazz Dance*, Sterling (USA).

Friedman, Carol, *A Moment's Notice*, Macmillan.

Friedwald, Will, *Jazz Singing*, Scribners (USA).

Gamble, Peter, *Focus On Jazz*, R. Hale.

Gammond, Peter, *Fourteen Miles On A Clear Night*, Greenwood Press, 1978.

Ganfield, J., *Books And Periodical Artricles On Jazz In America*

From 1926-1932, New York, 1933.

Garwood, Donald, *Masters Of Instrumental Blues Guitar*, Oak Publications (USA), 1968.

Gayford, Martin, *The Best Of Jazz: The Essential CD Guide*, Orion (UK), 1993.

Gelly, Dave & Weef, *The Giants Of Jazz*, Aurum Press (USA).

Gershwin, George, *Embraceable You*, Harms.

Giddins, G, *The Sax Section*, New York Jazz Museum (USA).

Giddins, G, *Celebrating Bird*, W. Morrow (USA).

Giddins, G., *Riding On A Blue Note: Jazz And American Pop*, New York and Oxford, 1981.

Giddins, G., *Rhythm-a-ning,* New York, 1985.

Gillenson, Lewis W., *Esquire's World Of Jazz*, Esquire (USA), 1962.

Gillespie, D, and A Fraser, *To Be, Or Not To Bop*, New York, 1976.

Gillespie, Dizzy, *Groovin' High*, MCA Music.

Gilmore, John, *Who's Who Of Jazz In Montreal*, University Of Toronto Press (Canada).

Gilmore, John, *Swinging In Paradise*, University Of Toronto Press (Canada), 1988.

Gioia, Ted, *West Coast Jazz*, Oxford University Press (UK), 1992.

Gioia, Ted, *West Coast Jazz: Modern Jazz In California 1945-60*, Oxford University Press, 1992.

Gioia, Ted, *The Imperfect Art*, Oxford University Press, 1988.

Gioia, Ted, *West Coast Jazz*, Oxford University Press, 1994.

Giordano, Gus, *Anthology Of American Jazz Dance*, Orion (UK).

Gitler, Ira, *Swing To Bop*, Oxford University Press, 1985.

Gitler, Ira, *Jazz Masters Of The Forties*, Da Capo (USA), 1990.

Gleason, Ralph J., *Jam Session: An Anthology Of Jazz*, Putnams (USA), 1958.

Gleason, Ralph J., *Celebrating The Duke, And Louis, Bessie, Billie, Bird, Carmen, Miles, Dizzy*, Little, Brown (USA), 1975.

Godbolt, Jim, *World Of Jazz: Through Printed Ephemera and Collectables*, Studio Editions (UK), 1990.

Godbolt, Jim, *All This And Many A Dog*, Quartet Books (UK), 1986.

Godbolt, Jim, *A History Of Jazz In Britain 1950-70*, Quartet Books (UK), 1989.

Godbolt, Jim, *A History Of Jazz In Britain 1919-50*, Quartet Books (UK).

Godrich, John, *Blues & Gospel Records, 1902-1942*, Storyville, 1969.

Gold, R., *A Jazz Lexicon*, New York.

Gold, Robert S., *Jazz Talk*, Bobbs-Merrill (USA).

Goldberg, Joe, *Jazz Masters Of The Fifties*, Da Capo (USA), 1990.

Goldblatt, Burt, *Newport Jazz Festival*, Dial Press (USA).

Goldstein, Gil, *Introduction To Jazz History*, Music Sales.

Golson, Benny, *Killer Joe.*, USA.

Gonda, Janos, *Jazz: Tortenet, Elmelet, Gyakorlat, Zenemukiado (Budapest)*.

Gonda, Janos (ed.), *Who's Who In Hungarian Jazz*, European Jazz Federation, 1973.

Gonzales, Babs, *I Paid My Dues*, Expubidence.

Gonzales, Babs, *Movin On Down De Line'*, Expubidence.

Gordon, Robert, *Jazz West Coast*, Quartet Books (UK), 1990.

Gottlieb, W., *The Golden Age Of Jazz*, Pomegranate (USA), 1995.

Gounelle Kline, P., *Le Theatre De Pagnol*, P. Lang.

Gourse, Leslie, *Louis' Children*, W. Morrow (USA), 1984.

Gourse, Leslie, *Every Day*, Quartet Books (UK), 1985.

Granholm, Ake, *Finnish Jazz*, Finnish Music Information Centre, 1974.

Gras, Pim, *Jazz Uit Het Historisch Archief*, Tango, 1974.

Gray, John, *Fire Music: A Bibliography of the New Jazz 1959-1990*, Greenwood Press, 1992.

Green, Benny, *The Reluctant Art: Five Studies In The Growth Of Jazz*, MacGibbon & Kee (UK), 1962.

Green, Benny, *Drums In My Ears*, Davis-Poynter (UK), 1973.

Green, John Waldo, *Murder At The Vanities. I Cover The Waterfront*, Harms.

Green, John Waldo, *Body And Soul*, Harms.

Greene, Ted, *Jazz Guitar*, Zdenek.

Gregor, Carl, *Stilformen Des Jazz. Vom Ragtime Zum Chicago-Stil*, Universal Edition.

Gregor, Carl, *International Jazz Bibliography: Jazz Books From 1919 To 1968*, P. H. Heitz Strasbourg.

Gregor, Carl, *International Jazz Bibliography (ijb) & Selective Bibli (1971/72/73 Supplement)*, Inst. for Jazz Research Universal Edition, 1975.

Gregor, Carl, *International Jazz Bibliography & International Drum & Perc. (1970 Supplement)*, Universal Edition, 1971.

Gregor, Carl, *International Bibliography Of Jazz Books*, Verlag Valentin Koerner, 1983.

Gridley, Mark C., *Jazz Styles: History & Analysis*, Prentice-Hall (USA), 1988.

Griffin, N., *To Bop Or Not To Bop?*, New York, 1948.

Griffiths, Paul, *New Sounds, New Personalites*, Faber & Faber (UK), 1986.

Grime, Kitty, *Jazz Voices*, Quartet Books (UK).

Grindley, Mark, *Concise Guide to Jazz*, Prentice-Hall (USA), 1992.

Gross, Louis D., *The Jazz Singer, A. Yokel For Lewis And Gordon.*

Grossman, S., *Ragtime Blues Guitarists*, New York, 1965.

Grundmann, Jan, *Jazz Aus Den Trummern*, Der Jazzfreund.

Gubaidulina, Sofia Asgatovna, *Kontsert Dlia Dvukh Orkestrov*, Sov. Kompozitor, 1985.

Gullickson, Gordon, *Numerical Index To Delaunay's Hot Discography*, 1941.

Gunter, John Osbon, *Good Players*, 1980.

Gunther, Helmut, *Jazz Dance*, Heinrichshofen, 1980.

Hadlock, R., *Jazz Masters Of The Twenties*, New York.

Haerle, Dan, *The Jazz Language*, Studio 224.

Hald, Jon, *10 Blues'er*, W. Hansen/Chester Music.

Hamilton, James, *Slapstick*, Robbins Music.

Hamilton, James, *Blues In My Music Room*, Robbins Music.

Hamilton, James, *Blues For Clarinet*, Robbins Music.

Hamm, C., *Music In The New World*, New York, 1983.

Hamm, C. B. Nettl and R. Byrnside, *Contemporary Music And Music Cultures*, Englewood Cliffs, 1975.

Harding, John Ralph, *A Survey Of The Evolution Of Jazz For The General Reader*, , 1981.

Harris, Howard C, *The Complete Book Of Improvistion*, DeMos Music.

Harris, Rex, *Jazz*, Penguin, 1952.

Harris, Steve, *Jazz On Compact Disc*, Harmony Books (USA).

Harris, William J., *The Poetry And Poetics Of Amiri Baraka*, University Of Missouri Press (USA), 1985.

Harrison, M., *Kings Of Jazz*, New York, 1978.

Harrison, M., *Boogie Woogie*, Jazz: New Perspectives, New York.

Harrison, M., *A Jazz Retrospect*, Newton Abbot.

Harrison, M. and others, *Modern Jazz: The Essential Records (1945-1970)*, London, 1975.

Harrison, Max, *Jazz: Retrospect*, Quartet Books (UK), 1991.

Hartmann, Walter, *Duette In Swing Und Beat*, Deutscher Verlag Fur Musik.

Haselgrove, J. R., *Readers' Guide To Books On Jazz*, Library Association (County Libraries Section), 1965.

Haskins, James, *The Cotton Club*, Random House (USA).

Hasse, J.E., *Ragtime: Its History, Composers And Music*, New York, 1985.

Hawes, H., *Raise Up Off Me*, New York, 1973.

Hayakawa, S. I., *Reflections On The History Of Jazz*, 1945.

Hayes, M, R. Scribner and P. Magee, *Encyclopedia Of Australian Jazz*, Eight Mile Plains, 1976.

Heen, Carol Louise, *Procedures For Style Analysis Of Jazz*, , 1981.

Hefele, Bernhard, *Jazz-Bibliography*, Saur, 1981.

Hellhund, Herbert, *Cool Jazz*, Schott.

Hennessey, Thomas J., *From Jazz To Swing: African American Jazz Musicians And Their M*, Wayne State University Press (USA), 1995.

Hentoff, Nat, *Jazz Is*, Random House (USA), 1976.

Hentoff, Nat, *Boston Boy*, Random House (USA), 1986.

Hentoff, Nat, *Listen To The Stories*, Harper Collins (USA), 1995.

Hentoff, Nat & McCarthy, Albert J., *Jazz: New Perspectives On The History Of Jazz*, Rinehart (USA), 1959.

Hentoff, Nat & McCarthy, Albert J., *The Jazz Life*, Dial Press (USA).

Herman, Woody, Chubby Jackson and Ralph Burns, *Northwest Passage*, Mayfair Music.

Hinton, Milt, David D. Berger, Holly Maxson, *Overtime: The Jazz Photographs Of Milt Hinton*, Pomegranate Artbooks, 1996.

Hippenmeyer, Jean Roland, *Le Jazz En Suisse, 1930-1970*, Editions de la Thiele, 1971.

Hippenmeyer, Jean Roland, *Jazz Sur Films*, Editions De La Thiele, 1973.

Hobbs, Christopher, *Three For Redlands*, Dorn.

Hobson, Wilder, *American Jazz Music*, W.W. Norton (USA), 1939.

Hodeir, Andre, *Toward Jazz*, New York.

Hodeir, Andre, *The Worlds Of Jazz*, New York, 1972.

Holcombe, Bill, *Creative Arranging At The Piano*, Musicians.

Holmes, John Clellon, *The Horn*, Penguin, 1990.

Holmes, Lowell Don, *Jazz Greats*, Holmes & Meier, 1986.

Hoskyns, Barney, *From A Whisper To A Scream*, Fontana (UK), 1991.

Houghton, Steve, *A Guide For The Modern Jazz Rhythm Section*, C. L. Barnhouse.

Howe, M., *Blue Jazz*, Bristol, 1934.

Huber, L., *New Orleans: A Pictorial History*, New York, 1971.

Hughes, Langston, *Jazz/Langston Hughes*, F. Watts, 1982.

Hughes, Langston, *Jazu, Huzu*, Showa 35 nen, 1960.

Hughes, Langston, *Das Buch Vom Jazz*, Buchheim Verlag.

Iakushenko, Igor Vasilevich, *Dzhazovyi Albom*, Muzyka, 1984.

Internationales Festival New Jazz, *Presseschau*, Stadt Moers Kulturamt.

Isadora, Rachel, *Ben's Trumpet*, Greenwillow Books.

Ita, Bassey, *Jazz In Nigeria*, Atiaya Communications.

Itoh, Kimiko, *For Lovers Only*, Columbia, 1987.

Its Evolution And Essence, *Hodeir, Andre*, Da Capo (USA).

J.J. Johnson, *Trombone*, Hansen House.

Jacquet, Illinois, *Jacquet Mood.*, Apollo, 1940.

Jalard, Michel-Claude, *Le Jazz Est-Il Encore Possible?*, Parentheses.

James, B., *Essays On Jazz*, London.

James, M., *Ten Modern Jazzmen*, London, 1960.

Jasen, D. A & Tichenor, T.J., *Rags And Ragtime: A Musical History*, New York, 1978.

Jepsen, J. Grunnet, *Jazz Records, 1942-1969: A Discography*, Holte and Copenhagen.

Johnson, Bruce, *The Oxford Companion To Australian Jazz*, Oxford University Press, 1987.

Johnson, Tom, *The Voice Of New Music: New York City 1972-1982*, Het Apollobuis, 1991.

Jones, Max, *Talking Jazz*, Macmillan (UK), 1987.

Jones, R. P., *Jazz* , Methuen (UK), 1963.

Jost, Ekkehard, *Jazzmusiker*, Ullstein, 1982.

Jost, Ekkehard, *Free Jazz*, Graz, 1974.

Jost, Ekkehard, *Free Jazz*, Da Capo (USA), 1994.

Jouvin, Georges, *Dix Etudes Speciales Pour Trompette Si b*, A.

Leduc.

Kaminsky, M. and Hughes, V.E., *My Life In Jazz*, New York, 1963.

Karpa, Gunther, *Rhythmisch-Stilistische Studien Fur Jazztrompete*, Deutscher Verlag Fur Musik.

Kater, Michael H. , *Different Drummers: Jazz In The Culture Of Nazi Germany*, Oxford University Press, 1992.

Katscher, Robert, *When Day Is Done*, Harms.

Kaufman, Fredrick, *The African Roots Of Jazz*, Alfred Knopf (USA).

Kaufman, H., *From Jehovah To Jazz*, New York, 1937.

Keepnews, Orrin, *The View From Within: Jazz Writings, 1948-1987*, Oxford University Press, 1991.

Keepnews, Orrin, *The View From Within*, Oxford University Press, 1988.

Keepnews, Orrin, and B. Grauer, *A Pictorial History of Jazz*, New York.

Kennedy, Rick, *Jelly Roll, Bix And Hoagy: Gennett Studios And The Birth Of Recorded Jazz*, Indiana University Press (USA), 1994.

Kennington, Donald, *The Literature Of Jazz: A Critical Guide*, Library Association, 1980.

Kernfeld, Barry (ed), *Blackwell Guide To Recorded Jazz*, Blackwell (UK), 1995.

Kernfeld, Barry (ed.), *The New Grove Dictionary Of Jazz*, Macmillan (UK), 1990.

Kernfeld, Barry (ed.), *Blackwell Guide To Recorded Jazz*, Blackwell (UK), 1992.

Kington, Miles, *Jazz Anthology*, Harper Collins (UK), 1992.

Kinkle, Roger D., *The Complete Encyclopedia Of Popular Music And Jazz. 1900-1950 (4 vols)*, Arlington House, 1974.

Kirk, Andy, *Twenty Years On Wheels*, Bayou Press (USA), 1989.

Kjellberg, Erik, *Svensk Jazz Historia*, Norstedt.

Klaasse, Piet, *Jam Session*, David & Charles, 1985 (UK).

Kleberg, L., *Svensk Jazzbibliografi*, Stockholm, 1964.

Koebner, F. W., *Jazz And Shimmy*, Berlin, 1921.

Konen, V., *Rozhdenie Dzhaza*, Kompozitor, 1984.

Konowitz, Bert, *The Bert Konowitz Vocal Improvisation Method*, Alfred Music.

Korall, Burt, *Drummin' Men: Heartbeat Of Jazz: The Swing Years*, Schirmer (USA), 1990.

Korte, Karl, *I Think You Would Have Understood*, Seesaw Music.

Kotek, Josef, *Kronika Ceske Synkopy*, Editio Supraphon, 1975.

Krahenbuhl, Peter, *Der Jazz Und Seine Menschen*, Francke, 1968.

Kraines, Minda Goodman, *Jump Into Jazz*, Mayfield, 1983.

Kraner, Dietrich Heinz, *Jazz In Austria*, Universal Edition, 1972.

Kreutz, Arthur, *Study In Jazz*, Mercury Music.

Kristensen, S. M., *Hvad Jazz*, Copenhagen, 1938.

Kroger, Ed, *Die Posaune Im Jazz*, Universal Edition, 1972.

Kukla, Barbara J., *Swing City: Newark Nightlife 1925-1950*, Temple University Press, (USA), 1992.

Kumpf, Hans, *Posterserielle Musik Und Free Jazz*, Musikverlag G. F. Doring.

La Porta, John, *Tonal Organization Of Improvisational Techniques*, Kendor Music.

La Porta, John, *A Guide To Jazz Phrasing And Interpretation*, Berklee Press (USA).

La Porta, John, *A Guide To Improvisation*, Berklee Press (USA).

Lacy, Steve, *Prospectus*, Margun Music .

Laing, R.D. and C Sheridan, *Jazz Records: The Specialist Labels*, Copenhagen, 1981.

Lane, Christy, *All That Jazz And More*, Leisure Press.

Lang, Iain, *Jazz In Perspective: The Background Of The Blues*, Jazz Book Club, 1957.

Lange, Horst, *Jazz In Deutshland: Die Deutsche Jazz-Chronik*,

Berlin.

Lange, Horst Heinz, *Die Deutsche 78er Discographie Der Hot-Dance Und Jazz-Musik, 1903-1958*, Colloquium Verlag, 1978.

Langridge, D, *Your Jazz Collection*, London, 1970.

Larkin, Colin, *The Virgin Encyclopedia Of Jazz*, Virgin Books (UK), 1999.

Larkin, Colin (ed.), *Guinness Who's Who Of Jazz*, Guinness Publishing (UK), 1992.

Larkin, Philip, *All What Jazz*, Faber & Faber (UK), 1985.

Lassen, Anni, *Jazzmusik Og Jazznoder*, Denmarks Biblioteksskole, 1975.

Lateef, Yusef A., *Yusef Lateef's Is Is*, Fana Music.

Lateef, Yusef A., *Transcribed Solos For Flute, Oboe & Tenor Saxophone*, Alnur Music.

Lawn, Richard & Hellmer, Jeffrey L., *Jazz Theory And Practice*, Wadsworth Publishing Co (UK), 1993.

Laycock, Ralph, *Swing-a-Ling*, T. Presser.

Lea, Barbara, *How To Sing Jazz*, T. Presser.

Leder, Jan, *Women In Jazz*, Greenwood Press.

Lee, Bill, *1002 Jumbo Jazz Album*, Silhouette Music.

Lee, Edward, *Jazz: An Introduction*, Kahn And Averill, 1972.

Lees, Gene, *Meet Me At Jim And Andy's: Jazz Musicians And Their World*, Oxford University Press, 1988.

Lees, Gene, *Waiting For Dizzy*, Oxford Univ. Press, 1994.

Leloir, Jean Pierre, *Du Jazz Plein Les Yeux*, Edica.

Lems-Dworkin, Carol, *World Music Center*, Northwestern University.

Leonard, Herman, *The Eye Of Jazz*, Viking Penguin, 1989.

Leonard, Neil, *Jazz: Myth And Religion*, Oxford University Press, 1987.

Leonard, Neil, *Jazz And The White Americans: The Acceptance Of A New Art Form*, Chicago and London, 1962.

Levey, Joseph, *The Jazz Experience*, Prentice-Hall (USA).

Levi, Ezio, *Introduzione Alla Vera Musica Di Jazz*, Edizione Magazzino Musicale, 1938.

Levitt, Rod, *Woodmen Of The World*, Associated Music.

Levy, Henry J., *The Time Revolution*, Creative World.

Lindroth, Scott, *Chasing The Trane Out Of Darmstadt*, Dorn.

Linehan, Norm, *Norm Linehan's Australian Jazz Picture Book*, Child And Henry, 1980.

Link, Harry, *These Foolish Things*, Aladdin.

Litchfield, J., *The Canadian Jazz Discography, 1916-1980*, Toronto, 1982.

Litweiler, John, *The Freedom Principle*, W. Morrow (USA), 1984.

Lock, Graham, *Chasing The Vibration*, Stride, 1994.

Locke, Alain LeRoy, *The Negro And His Music*, The Associates In Negro Folk Education, 1936.

Longstreet, Stephen, *Storyville To Harlem*, Rutgers University Press (USA).

Longstreet, Stephen, *Sportin' House: A History Of The New Orleans Sinners And The Birth Of Jazz*, Sherbourne Press, 1965.

Longstreet, Stephen, *Jazz From A to Z: A Graphic Dictionary*, Catbird Press, 1989.

Lotz, Rainer E., *The AFRS 'Jubilee' Transcription Programs*, N. Ruecker, 1985.

Lotz, Rainer E., *German Ragtime & Prehistory Of Jazz*, Storyville, 1985.

Lowe, Jacques, *Jazz: Photographs Of The Masters*, Artisan (USA), 1995.

Lowinger, Gene, *Jazz Violin*, Schirmer (USA).

Lucas, John, *Basic Jazz On Long Play*, Carleton College, 1954.

Lucas, Paul, *Jazz Chording For The Rock-Blues Guitarist*, Sole Distributorship.

Ludwig, Siegfried, *Rhythmisch-Stilistische Studien Fur Drums*, Deutscher Verlag Fur Musik.

Luigi, *The Luigi Jazz Dance Technique*, Doubleday (USA), 1981.

Lydon, Michael, *Boogie Lightning*, Dial Press (USA), 1974.

Lykiard, Alexis, *Living Jazz*, Tenormen Press, 1992.

Lyons, Len, *The Great Jazz Pianists*, Da Capo (USA), 1990.

Lyons, Leonard, *The 101 Best Jazz Albums*, W. Morrow (USA), 1980.

Lyons, Leonard, *Jazz Portraits: The Lives And Music Of The Jazz Masters*, W. Morrow (USA).

Lyttelton, Humphrey, *Why No Beethoven?*, Robson Books (UK), 1984.

Lyttelton, Humphrey, *Best Of Jazz Vol 2: Enter The Giants*, Robson (UK), 1990.

Mackenzie, Harry, *AFRS Downbeat Series*, Joyce Record Club, 1986.

Manone, W, and P Vandervoort, *Trumpet On The Wing*, New York, 1948.

Margulis, Max, *Present State Of Jazz And Swing*.

Mariano, Charlie, *Jazz Originals*, Berklee Press (USA).

Marinelli, Joseph, *Jomars LP Price Guide*, J. Marinelli, 1973.

Markewich, Reese, *The New Expanded Bibliography Of Jazz Compositions*, Markewich, 1974.

Markewich, Reese, *Jazz Publicity II*, Markewich, 1974.

Markewich, Reese, *Jazz Publicity*, Riverdale, 1973.

Marsh, Graham & Callingham, Glyn, *California Cool*, Collins And Brown (UK), 1992.

Martin, Henry, *Enjoying Jazz*, Schirmer (USA), 1986.

Martin, Henry John, *Jazz Harmony*, 1980.

Martin, Stephen Harvey, *Music In Urban East Africa*.

Martinez, Raymond J., *Portraits Of New Orleans Jazz; Its Peoples And Places*, Hope, 1971.

Matzner, Antonin, *Encyklopedie Jazzu A Moderni Popularni Hudby*, Editio Supraphon, 1983.

Mauriello, Joseph G., *The First Annual Greenwich Village Jazz Guide*, Bleecker Street (USA).

Mauro, Walter, *Jazz E Universo Negro*, Rizzoli (USA), 1972.

McCalla, James, *Jazz, A Listener's Guide*, Prentice-Hall (USA), 1995.

McCarthy, Albert, *The Dance Band Era*, Spring Books (UK), 1971.

McCarthy, Albert, *Big Band Jazz*, Putnams (USA), 1974.

McCarthy, Albert; Oliver, Paul; Harrison, Max., *Jazz On Record: A Critical Guide To The First Fifty Years: 1917-67*, London, 1968.

McGhee, Howard, *Blues Duende*, E. B. Marks Music (USA).

McKee, M and F. Chisenhall, *Beale Stret Black And Blue*, Baton Rouge (USA), 1981.

McRae, Barry, *The Jazz Handbook*, Longman (UK), 1987.

Meadows, Eddie S., *Jazz Reference And Research Materials*, Garland, 1981.

Meeker, D., *Jazz In The Movies*, London.

Megill, Donald D., *Introduction To Jazz History*, Prentice-Hall (USA).

Mehegan, John F., *The Jazz Pianist*, S. Fox.

Mehegan, John F., *Jazz Improvisation*, New York.

Mehegan, John F., *Contemporary Styles For The Jazz Pianist*, S. Fox.

Mellers, W., *Music In A New Found Land*, London, 1964.

Meltzer, David (ed.), *Reading Jazz*, Mercury House, 1995.

Mendl, R., *The Appeal Of Jazz*, London, 1927.

Merod, Jim, *Jazz As A Cultural Archive*, Duke U P (USA), 1995.

Merriam, A. P. and R. J. Benford, *A Bibliography Of Jazz*, Philadelphia.

Miller, M., *Jazz In Canada*, Toronto, 1982.

Miller, Mark, *Boogie, Pete & The Senator*, Nightwood Editions, 1987.

Miller, Norma & Jensen, Evette, *Swingin' At The Savoy: The Memoir Of A Jazz Dancer*, Temple University Press (USA), 1996.

Mingus, Charles, *Beneath The Underdog*, New York: Alfred A. Knopf (USA), 1971.

Mitchell, Jack, *Australian Jazz On Record, 1925-80*, Australian Government (Australia), 1988.

Mohr, K., *Discographie Du Jazz*, Geneva, 1945.

Moller, B., *Dansk Jazz Discography*, Copenhagen, 1945.

Montgomery, Michael R., *Studies In Jazz Style For The Double Bassist*, 1984.

Moody, Bill, *Jazz Exiles: American Musicians Abroad*, University Of Nevada Press (USA), 1993.

Morgenstern, D., *Jazz People*, New York, 1976.

Morris, Ronald L., *Wait Until Dark: Jazz And The Underworld, 1880-1940*, Bowling Green University Popular Press (USA), 1980.

Morse, Jim, *Big Band Era*, Hiawatha Publishers (USA), 1993.

Mosness, Terje, *Jazz I Molde*, Nordvest-Informasjon.

Muckenberger, Heiner, *Meet Me Where They Play The Blues*, Oreos.

Murphy, Turk, *When The Saints Go Marching In*, E. B. Marks Music (USA).

Murray, James Briggs, *Black Visions '88: Lady Legends In Jazz, February 1-March 11, 1988*, Mayor's Office Of Minority Affairs (USA), 1988.

Musica Jazz Presenta Harlem, *Musica Jazz: Rusconi Editore*, 1984.

Namyslowski, Zbigniew, *Utwory Jazzowe Na Rozny Sklad Instrumentow*, Polskie Wydawn. Muzyczne.

Nanry, C., *American Music: From Storyville To Woodstock*, E.P. Dutton (USA), 1972.

Nanry, C. & Berger, E., *The Jazz Text*, New York, 1979.

National Portrait Gallery, Washington, D.C., *A Glimmer Of Their Own Beauty*, Washington, 1971.

New York Jazz Festival, The First Annual New York Jazz Fest, *New York*, 1956.

Nicholson, Stuart, *Jazz: The Modern Resurgence*, Simon & Schuster (USA), 1990.

Nicholson, Stuart, *Jazz: The 1980s Resurgence*, Da Capo (USA), 1995.

Niemoeller, A., *Story Of Jazz*, Kansas City, 1946.

Nisenson, Eric, *Round About Midnight*, Dial Press (USA), 1982.

No author, *Rhythmisch-Stilistische Studien Fur Gitarre*, Deutscher Verlag Fur Musik, 1971.

No author listed, *Jazz On LP's*, Greenwood Press, 1978.

No author listed, *Dallas Jazz News Letter*, 1977.

No author listed, *Music Master Jazz Catalogue*, Music Master, 1990.

No author listed, *Swing And Sound*, MediaPlus, 1987.

No editor listed, *Vogue's Real Jazz Fake Book*, Golden Press.

No editor listed, *Refrains Populaires D'Amerique*, New York Mills Music.

No editor listed, *Proceedings Of NAJE Research*, NAJE.

No editor listed, *Portraits Of Jazz-Musicians*, Jazzfreund.

No editor listed, *Encyclopedia Of Jazz Standards*, Warner Brothers, 1987 (USA).

No editor listed, *Coversations With Jazz Musicians*, Gale Research, 1977.

No editor listed, *All That Jazz*, Warner Brothers (USA).

Noble, James, *Blue Flame*, Mayfair Music.

Noble, Peter, *Transatlantic Jazz, A Short History Of American Jazz*, Citizen Press (USA).

Noll, Dietrich J., *Zur Improvisation Im Deutschen Free Jazz*, Verlag Der Musikalienhandlung Wagner, 1977.

Nordisk Jazzforskning, *Rapport Fran Den Forsta Konferensen 14-16 Februari 1980 i Stockholm*, Svensk Visarkiv, 1981.

Norton, Christopher, *Microjazz: For Trumpet*, Boosey & Hawkes (UK).

Norton, Christopher, *Microjazz: For Flute*, Boosey & Hawkes (UK).

Norton, Christopher, *Microjazz For Clarinet*, Boosey & Hawkes (UK).

Norton, Christopher, *Microjazz*, Boosey & Hawkes (UK).

Ogren, Kathy J., *The Jazz Revolution*, Oxford University Press, 1989.

Ogren, Kathy J., *Jazz Revolution: Twenties America And the Meaning Of Jazz*, Oxford University Press (USA), 1992.

Oliver, J., *Jazz Classic*, London, 1962.

Oliver, Paul, *The New Grove Gospel, Blues And Jazz*, W. W. Norton (USA), 1986.

Oliver, Paul, *Savannah Syncopators*, Stein and Day (USA), 1970.

Olsen, David C., *Great Jazz Standards*, Columbia Pictures.

Ondaatje, Michael, *Coming Through Slaughter*, Penguin.

Ostransky, Leroy, *Understanding Jazz*, Englewood Cliffs: Prentice-Hall (USA), 1977.

Ostransky, Leroy, *The Anatomy Of Jazz*, Seattle, 1960.

Ostransky, Leroy, *Jazz City: The Impact Of Our Cities On the Development Of Jazz*, Englewood Cliffs (USA), 1978.

Owens, Thomas, *Bebop: The Music And The Players*, Oxford University Press (USA), 1995.

Page, Drew, *Drew's Blues*, Louisiana State University Press (USA).

Panassie, Hugues, *The Real Jazz*, Smith and Durrell (USA), 1942.

Panassie, Hugues, *Monsieur Jazz*, Stock.

Panassie, Hugues, *Guide To Jazz*, Greenwood Press, 1973.

Panassie, Hugues, *Dictionnaire Du Jazz . . . Nouvelle Edition Revue Et Augemtee*, A. Michel (Paris), 1971.

Papademetriou, Sakes, *Themata Kai Prosopa Tes Synchrones Tzaz (1950-1970)*, Ekdoseis Diagoniou, 1974.

Papademetriou, Sakes, *Eisagoge Sten Tzaz*, Ekdoseis Diagoniou, 1975.

Papo, Alfredo, *Jazz Para Cinco Instrumentos*, Distribuido Por Graf. Layetana, 1975.

Parker, Chris (ed.), *B Flat, Bebop, Scat*, Quartet Books (UK), 1986.

Pauer, Fritz, *Modale Suite*, Advance Music.

Pearson, Nathan W., *Goin' To Kansas City*, University Of Illinois Press (USA).

Pellett, Roy (ed.), *Best Of Jazz Score*, BBC (UK), 1992.

Perett, Burton W., *The Creation Of Jazz: Music, Race And Culture In Urban America*, Univeristy Of Illinois Press (USA), 1992.

Perrin, Michel, *Le Jazz A Cent Ans*, Editions France-Empire.

Perry, David, *Jazz Greats*, Phaidon (UK), 1996.

Peter Russell's Hot Record Store, *The Good Noise*, Peter Russell's Hot Record Store, 1974.

Piazza, Tom, *The Guide To Classic Recorded Jazz*, University Of Iowa Press (USA), 1995.

Placksin, Sally, *American Women In Jazz: 1900 To The Present*, Wideview Books.

Pohlert, Werner, *Praludium, Fantasie Und Suite In D*, Zimmermann.

Poindexter, Pony, *The Pony Express*, J.A.S.

Polillo, Arrigo, *Stasera Jazz*, A. Mondadori, 1978.

Polillo, Arrigo, *Jazz: La Vicenda E I Protagonisti Della Musica Afro-Americana*, A. Mondadori, 1983.

Polonsky, Bruce, *Hearing Music*, Private Books, 1981.

Poole, G., *Enciclopedia De Swing*, Buenos Aires, 1939.

Porter Ray, Keller, David (ed.), *There And Back*, Bayou Press, 1992 (USA).

Porto, Sergio, *Pequena Historia Do Jazz*, Servico de Documentacao, 1953.

Postgate, John, *A Plain Man's Guide To Jazz*, Hanover Books, 1973.

Price, Sammy, *What Do They Want?*, Bayou Press (USA), 1989.

Priestley, Brian, *Jazz On Record: A History*, Elm Tree (UK), 1988.

Raben, Erik (ed.), *Jazz Records, 1942-80 Vol 3: Bro-Cl*, Stainless/Wintermoon, 1992.

Ragland, Glenn, *Jazz Profiles In Paris*, Minerva, 1995.

Raich, S., *Criticisms Of Jazz*, Casa Provinicial de Caridad, 1958.

Ramsey, Douglas K., *Jazz Matters*, University Of Arkansas Press (USA), 1989.

Ramsey, F. Jnr, *A Guide To Longplay Jazz Records*, New York.

Ramsey, F. Jnr and Smith, C. E., *Jazz Record Book*, New York, 1942.

Ramsey, F. Jnr and Smith, C. E., *Jazzmen*, New York, 1939.

Reda, Jacques, *L'Improviste*, Gallimard.

Reda, Jacques, *Anthologie Des Musiciens De Jazz*, Stock.

Redfern, David, *David Redfern's Jazz Album*, Eel Pie (UK), 1980.

Reiff, Carole, *Nights In Birdland*, Simon & Schuster (UK).

Reisner, R., *The Literature Of Jazz*, New York.

Rimler, W., *Not Fade Away: Comparison Of Jazz Age With Rock Era Pop Song Composer*, Pierian Press (UK), 1990.

Rius, Guia, *Incompleta Del Jazz*, Grijalbo, 1987.

Rivelli, Pauline and Levin, Robert, *Black Giants*, World Books, 1970.

Roach, Hildred, *Black American Music*, Crescendo (USA), 1973.

Rockmore, Noel, *Preservation Hall Portraits*, Louisiana State University Press (USA), 1968.

Romijn Meijer, Henk, *Een Blauwe Golf Aan De Kust*, Meulenhoff.

Rose, A, & Souchon, E., *New Orleans Jazz: A Family Album*, Baton Rouge (USA), 1967.

Rose, A., *Storyville*, University of Alabama (USA), 1974.

Rose, A., *I Remember Jazz*, Louisiana State University Press (USA).

Rosenhain, Sigurd, *Fascination Jazz*, Lied Der Zeit, 1974.

Rosenthal, David H., *Hard Bop: Jazz And Black Music 1955-65*, Oxford University Press (USA), 1992.

Rosenthal, David H., *Hard Bop: Jazz And Black Music, 1955-65*, Oxford University Press (New York), 1994.

Rosenthal, George S. & Zachary, Frank, *Jazzways*, Greenberg, 1946.

Rossi, Abner, *Technica Della Chitarra Jazz*, Edizioni Musicali Farfisa.

Rossi, Nick, *Music Of Our Time*, Crescendo, 1970.

Routley, E., *Is Jazz Music Christian?*, London, 1964.

Rublowsky, John, *Black Music In America*, Basic Books (USA), 1971.

Ruppli, Michel, *The Savoy Label*, Greenwood Press, 1980.

Ruppli, Michel, *The Prestige Label*, Greenwood Press, 1980.

Ruppli, Michel, *Atlantic Records*, Greenwood Press, 1979.

Rusch, Robert D., *JazzTalk*, Lyle Stuart.

Rusch, Robert D., *Collection Of (The Periodical Literature Of Jazz) 1918-1972*, New York Public Library (USA), 1974.

Russell, Bill, *New Orleans Style*, Jazzology Press (USA), 1995.

Russell, R., *Jazz Style In Kansas City And The South West*, Berkeley (USA).

Russell, Ross, *The Sound*, E.P.Dutton (USA), 1961.

Russell, William, *Boogie Woogie Jazzmen*, New York, 1959.

Russell, William, *Technical Aspects Of Jazz*.

Russo, William, *Jazz Composition And Orchestration*, Chicago and London, 1968.

Rust, Brian, *The Dance Bands*, Arlington House, 1974.

Rust, Brian, *My Kind Of Jazz*, Hamish Hamilton, 1990.

Rust, Brian, *Jazz Records, 1897-1942*, Storyville, 1982.

Sabat, Hermenegildo, *Scat*, Instituto Salesiano de Artes Graficas.

Sacco, P. Peter, *Three Jazz Preludes*.

Saenz, Miguel, *Jazz De Hoy, De Ahora*, Siglo Veintiuno de Espana, 1971.

Sales, Grover, *Jazz: America's Classical Music*, Englewood Cliffs-Prentice Hall (USA), 1984.

Sales, Grover, *Jazz: America's Classical Music*, Da Capo (USA), 1992.

Sandole, Adolph, *The Craft Of Jazz*, A. Sandole.

Sandole, Adolph, *Reflections For Piano*, A. Sandole.

Sandole, Adolph, *Poems Of Granada*, A. Sandole.

Sandole, Adolph, *Jazz Piano Left Hand*, A. Sandole.

Sandole, Adolph, *Jazz Improvisation II*, A. Sandole.

Santisi, Ray, *Jazz Originals For Piano*, Berklee Press.

Santoro, Gene, *Dancing In Your Head: Jazz, Blues, Rock, And Beyond*, Oxford University Press, 1994.

Sargeant, Winthrop, *Jazz Hot & Hybrid*, McGraw Hill & Da Capo (USA), 1975.

Sartori, Afo, *Santi A Dispetto Del Paradiso*, Pacini.

Sbarcea, George, *Jazzul, O Poveste Cu Negri Si Mic Dictionar Al Jazzului*, Editura Muzicala A Uniunii Compozitorilor, 1974.

Schafer, W. J. and J. Riedel, *The Art Of Ragtime*, Baton Rouge (USA).

Schafer, W. J. and R. B. Allen, *Brass Bands And New Orleans Jazz*, Baton Rouge (USA), 1977.

Scheller, Elske, *Jazzdans*, Hollandia

Schenkel, Steven M., *The Tools Of Jazz*, Prentice-Hall (USA).

Schiedt, D., *The Jazz State Of Indiana*, Pittsboro (USA), 1977.

Schindler, Klaus, *Swinging*, Verlag Vogt & Fritz.

Schleman, H., *Rhythm On Record 1906 To 1936*, London, 1936.

Schmitz, Manfred, *Jazz Parnass*, Deutscher Verlag fur Musik.

Schreiner, C., *Jazz Aktuell*, Mainz, 1968.

Schuller, Gunther, *The Swing Era: The Development Of Jazz 1930-1945*, Oxford University Press, 1991.

Schuller, Gunther, *Early Jazz: Its Roots & Development*, New York, 1968.

Schulz-kohn, Dietrich, *Kleine Geschichte Des Jazz*, C. Bertelsmann, 1963.

Schwaninger, A and A. Gurwitsch, *Swing Discographie*, Geneva, 1945.

Scobey, Jan, *Jan Scobey Presents He Rambled! 'Til Cancer Cut Him Down, Pal*, 1976.

Scott, Allen, *Jazz Educated, Man*, American International, 1973.

See, Cees, *Das Schlagzeug Im Jazz*, Universal Edition.

Shapiro, Nat & Hentoff, Nat, *The Jazz Makers*, Rinehart (USA), 1957.

Shapiro, Nat & Hentoff, Nat, *Hear Me Talkin' To Ya: Story Of Jazz By the Men Who Made It*, Dover (USA), Souvenir Press (UK), 1990.

Shaw, Arnold, *The Trouble With Cinderella*, New York, 1952.

Shaw, Arnold, *The Street That Never Slept*, Coward, McCann & Geoghegan, 1971.

Shaw, Arnold, *The Jazz Age*, Oxford University Press, 1990.

Shaw, Arnold, *52nd Street: The Street Of Jazz*, Da Capo (USA), 1971.

Shearing, George Albert, *Piano Music. Selectons*, Warner Brothers (USA).

Sher, Chuck, *The Improviser's Bass Method*, Sher Music.

Sher, Chuck (ed.), *The World's Greatest Fake Book*, Sher Music.

Sidran, Ben, *Talking Jazz: An Illustrated Oral History*, Pomegranate Artbooks (USA), 1992.

Simon, George Thomas, *The Big Bands*, Macmillan (USA), 1967.

Simon, George Thomas, *Simon Says: The Sights And Sounds Of The Swing Era 1935-55*, Arlington House (USA), 1971.

Sinclair, John, *Music And Politics*, World, 1971.

Skaarup, V. and M. Goldstein, *Jazz*, Copenhagen, 1934.

Skvorecky, Josef, *Talkin' Moscow Blues*, Lester & Orpen Dennys, 1988.

Smith, Charles Edward, *Riverside History Of Classic Jazz*, Bill Grauer, 0.

Smith, Charles Edward, with Ramsey, Frederic, Jnr., *The Jazz Record Book*, Smith and Durrell (USA), 1942.

Smith, W., & Hoefer, G., *Music On My Mind*, New York, 1964.

Sol, Ydo, *Faces Of Jazz*, Nieswand Verlag, 1992.

Somma, Robert (ed.), *No One Waved Good-bye*, Outerbridge

& Dienstfrey (USA), 1971.

Southern, Eileen, *The Music Of Black Americans*, New York, 1983.

Southern, Eileen, *Readings In Black American Music*, W.W. Norton (USA), 1971.

Spagnardi, Ronald, *Great Jazz Drummers*, International Music Publishers (UK), 1992.

Spedale, Rhodes, *A Guide To Jazz In New Orleans*, Hope.

Spellman, A. B., *Four Lives In The Behop Business*, Harper & Row (USA), 1985.

Spitzer, D., *Jazzshots*, Miami, 1980.

Stagg, T. & Crump, C. , *New Orleans Revival*, Dublin, 1973.

Stanton, Kenneth, *Jazz Theory*, Taplinger, 1982.

Starr, Frederick, *Red And Hot: The Fate Of Jazz In The Soviet Union 1917-1980*, New York and Oxford, 1983.

Stearns, Marshall & Stearns, Jean, *The Story Of Jazz*, Oxford University Press, 1956.

Stearns, Marshall & Stearns, Jean, *The Jazz Dance: The Story Of American Vernacular Dance*, New York, 1968.

Stebbins, Robert Alan, *The Jazz Community*, Minneapolis, 1964.

Steen, Arild, *Molde-jazz*, Gyldendal, 1971.

Stewart, Charles, *Chuck Stewart's Jazz Files*, Little, Brown (USA).

Stewart, Milton Lee, *Structural Development In The Jazz Improvisational Technique Of Clifford Brown*, , 1973.

Stewart, Rex, *Jazz Masters Of The 30s*, New York, 1972.

Stewart, Rex with Gordon, Claire, *Boy Meets Horn*, Bayou Press (USA), 1992.

Stock, D, and Hentoff, N., *Jazz Street*, Garden City, New York, 1960.

Stoddard, Tom, *Jazz On The Barbary Coast*, Storyville.

Stoddard, Tom, *An Autobiography Of A New Orleans Jazzman*, University of California Press (USA), 1971.

Stokes, W. Royal, *Jazz Scene*, Oxford University Press, 1991.

Stokes, W. Royal, *Jazz Scene: An Informal History From New Orleans To 1990*, Oxford University Press (USA), 1993.

Stone, Gregory Prentice, *Games, Sport, And Power*, E. P. Dutton (USA), 1971.

Stramacci, Fabrizio, *New Orleans*, Alle Origini Del Jazz Lato Side.

Stratemann, Klaus, *Jazz Ball & Feather On Jazz*, Der Jazzfreund.

Strom Pa Jazzen, *I Kommission hos Attika*, 1978.

Stuart, Walter, *Encyclopedia Of Modem Jazz*, C. Colin.

Such, David Glen, *Music, Metaphor And Values Among Avant-Garde Jazz Musicians*, 1985.

Sudnow, David, *Ways Of The Hand*, Harvard University Press (USA), 1978.

Summerfield, Maurice J., *The Jazz Guitar*, Ashley Mark, 1978.

Summerfield, Maurice Joseph, *Jazz Guitar: Its Evolution, Players And Personalities Since 1900*, A. Mark Pub. Olsover Hse. Sackville Rd. Newcastle (UK), 1994.

Swenson, John, *The Rolling Stone Jazz Record Guide*, Random House (USA).

Sylvester, Peter, *A Left Hand Like God: A Study of Boogie-Woogie*, Quartet Books (UK), 1989.

Szadkowski, Dita von, *Auf Schwarzweissen Flugeln*, Focus Verlag.

Tanner, Leo, *Jazz Address Book*, Pomegranate, 1991.

Tanner, P. and M. Gerow, *A Study Of Jazz*, Dubuque, 1981.

Taylor, Art, *Notes And Tones*, Quartet Books (UK), 1988.

Taylor, Roger, *Art, An Enemy Of The People*, Harvester Press, 1978.

Tenot, F and P. Carls, *Dictionnaire Du Jazz*, Paris, 1967.

Tenot, Frank, *Le Jazz*, Larousse, 1977.

Terkel, Louis, *Giants Of Jazz, Studs Terkel With Milly Hawk Daniel*, Thomas Y. Crowell (USA), 1975.

Testoni, G. and others, *Enciclopedia Del Jazz*, Milan, 1953.

Thigpen, Ed, *The Sound Of Brushes*, E. Thigpen/Action-Reaction.

Thomas, Ianthe, *Willie Blows A Mean Horn*, Harper & Row (USA).

Thomas, Neil, *Playing Popular Piano*, Prentice-Hall (USA).

Tichenor, T. J., *Ragtime Rediscoveries*, New York, 1979.

Tiro, Frank, *Jazz: A History*, W.W. Norton (USA), 1993.

Tirro, F., *Jazz: A History*, Dent (UK), 1990.

Toll, Robert C., *Blacking Up*, Oxford University Press, 1974.

Tracy, Sheila, *Bands, Booze And Broads*, Mainstream Publishing (UK), 1995.

Traill, Sinclair, *Just Jazz (No. 4)*, Souvenir Press, (UK) 1960.

Travis, Dempsey, *An Autobiography Of Black Jazz*, Urban Research Institute, 1983.

Turner, Frederick, *Remembering Songs: Encounters With The New Orleans Jazz Tradition*, Da Capo (UK), 1994.

Turner, Frederick W., *Remembering Song*, Viking, 1982.

Ulanov, Barry, *A History Of Jazz In America*, Viking.

Ulanov, Barry, *A Handbook Of Jazz*, Viking, 1957.

Umphred, Neil, *Goldmine's Price Guide To Collectible Jazz Records*, Krause Publications (USA), 1991.

Unterbrink, Mary, *Jazz Women At The Keyboard*, McFarland, 1983.

Usinger, F., *Kleine Biographie Des Jazz*, Offenbach am Main, 1953.

Vail, Ken, *Jazz Milestones: A Pictorial Chronicle Of Jazz 1900-90*, Vail Publishing, Unit 6, French's Mill, French's Rd,..., 1993.

Vail, Ken (ed), *Jazz Milestones: A Pictorial Chronicle Of Jazz 1900-90*, Castle Communications (UK), 1995.

Valli, Raymond, *Maestro Rag*, R. Valli.

Velebny, Karel, *Jazzova Praktika*, Panton, 1983.

Velez, Ana, *En Torno Al Jazz*, Producciones Don Pedro, 1978.

Vian, Boris, *Chroniques De Jazz*, Union Generale D'Editions, 1971.

Vian, Boris, *Autres Ecrits Sur Le Jazz*, Bourgois.

Vidossich, Edoardo, *Sincretismos Na Musica Afro-Americana*, Edicoss Quiron, 1975.

Viera, Joe, *Neue Formen*, Freies Spiel.

Viera, Joe, *Grundlagen Der Jazzharmonik*, Universal Editions.

Viera, Joe, *Der Free Jazz*, Universal Editions, 1974.

Viera, Joe, *Das Saxophon Im Jazz*, Universal Editions.

Viera, Joe, *Arrangement Und Improvisation*, Universal Editions, 1971.

Vittorini, Tommaso, *Musica In Libera Uscita*, A. Mondadori, 1984.

Voigt, John, *Jazz Music In Print And Jazz Books In Print*, Hornpipe Music.

Von Physter, George, *Destiny*, Down Beat (USA).

Waite, Brian, *Modern Jazz Piano*, Spellmount, 1990.

Waldo, Terry, *This Is Ragtime*, Da Capo (USA), 1991.

Waldron, Mal, *Reflections In Modern Jazz*, S. Fox.

Walker, Leo, *Wonderful Era Of Great Dance Bands*, Da Capo (USA), 1990.

Walker, Leo, *The Big Band Almanac*, Da Capo (USA), 1978.

Wallington, George, *Virtuoso*, Denon, 1984.

Watanabe, Sadao, *Fill Up The Night*, Nichion.

Waterman, G., *The Art Of Jazz '(A Survey Of Ragtime)'*, New York, 1959.

Waterman, G., *Jazz: New Perspectives*, New York.

Wayne, Bennett, *3 Jazz Greats*, Garrard, 1973.

Weinstein, Norman C., *Night In Tunisia: Imaginations Of Africa In Jazz*, Scarecrow Press, 1992.

Welburn, Ronald G., *American Jazz Criticism, 1914-1940*.

Westerberg, Hans, *Suomalaiset Jazzlevytykset 1932-1976*, Suomen Jazzliitto, 1977.

Whannel, P., *Jazz On Film*, London, 1966.

White, Clarence Cameron, *Book Review On Henry O. Osgood's So This Is Jazz*.

White, Mark, *The Observer's Book Of Big Bands*, F. Warne (UK), 1978.

Whiteman, P. and McBride, M. M., *Jazz*, Arno Press (USA).
Wilber, Bob, *Music Was Not Enough*, Macmillan, 1987.
Wilder, Alec, *Jazz Suite*, Margun Music.
Williams, Clarence, *The Boogie Woogie Blues Folio*, Clarence Williams, 1940.
Williams, M., *The Jazz Tradition*, New York.
Williams, M., *The Jazz Heritage*, New York, 1986.
Williams, M., *Jazz Panorama*, New York and London, 1962.
Williams, M., *Jazz Masters Of New Orleans*, New York and London, 1967.
Williams, Martin, *Jazz Tradition*, Oxford University Press, 1993.
Williams, Martin T., *The Art Of Jazz: Essays On The Nature And Development Of Jazz*, Oxford University Press, 1959.
Williams, Martin T., *Jazz In Its Time*, Oxford University Press, 1989.
Williams, Martin T., *Jazz Masters In Transition, 1957-69*, Macmillan, 1970.
Williams, Martin T., *Jazz Changes*, Oxford University Press, 1992.
Williams, Richard, *Jazz: A Photographic Documentary*, Studio Editions (UK), 1995.
Williamson, Ken, *This Is Jazz*, Newnes (UK), 1960.
Williamson, Liz, *Jazz Dance & Jazz Gymnastics*, Sterling (USA)
Willioughby, Bill, *Jazz In L.A.*, Nieswand Verlag, 1992.
Wilmer, Val, *The Face Of Black Music*, Da Capo (USA), 1976.
Wilmer, Val, *Mama Said There'd Be Days Like This*, The Women's Press (UK), 1989.
Wilmer, Val, *As Serious As Your Life: Story Of The New Jazz*, Allison & Busby (UK), 1977.
Winick, S., *Rhythm: An Annotated Bibliography*, Metuchen, New Jersey, 1974.
Wolfer, Jurgen, *Handbuch Des Jazz*, Heyne, 1980.
Wood, Celia; (Steve French ed), *Jazz Musicians Guide: National UK Directory Of Jazz*, Jazz Services, 1992.
Woodward, Woody, *Jazz Americana*, Trend Books, 1956.
Wright, Rayburn, *Inside The Score*, Kendor Music, 1982.
Wylie, Floyd E. M., *An Investigation Of Some Aspects Of Creativity Of Jazz Musicians*, Detroit, 1963.
Yates, Tom, *A Boy: A Golden Trombone - And A Dream*, T. Yates.
Young, Al, *Things Ain't What They Used To Be*, Creative Arts Book, 1987.
Young, Al, *Kinds Of Blue*, Creative Arts Book, 1984.
Young, Al, *Bodies & Soul*, Creative Arts Books, 1981.
Zano, Anthony, *Mechanics Of Modern Music*, Berben.
Zinn, David, *Be-Bach*, T. Presser.
Zinsser, William Knowlton, *Willie And Dwike*, Harper & Row (USA).
Zwerin, Michael, *La Tristesse De Saint Louis*, Quartet Books (UK), 1985.
Zwerin, Michael, *Close Enough For Jazz*, Quartet Books (UK), 1983.

Liberty Records
Kelly, Michael 'Doc Rock', *Liberty Records*, McFarland, 1993.

Musicals
Banfield, Stephen, *Sondheim's Broadway Musicals*, University Of Michigan Press (USA), 1993.
Blyth, Alan (ed.), *Opera On CD: Essential Guide To The Best CD Recordings Of 100 Operas*, K. Cathie (UK), 1993.
Burton, Jack, *The Blue Book Of Broadway Musicals*, Century House, 1969.
Burton, Jack, *The Blue Book Of Hollywood Musicals*, Century House, 1953.
Gottfried, Martin, *More Broadway Musicals*, Abrams (USA), 1991.
Green, Stanley, *The Encyclopaedia Of The Musical*, Cassell (UK), 1977.
Green, Stanley, *The World Of Musical Comedy*, Thomas Yoscloff, 1960.
Hirschhorn, Clive, *The Hollywood Musical*, Pyramid Books, 1981.
Jackson, Arthur, *The Book Of Musicals: From Show Boat To Evita*, Mitchell Beazley (UK), 1979.
Raymond, Jack, *Show Music On Record: The First 100 Years From 1890-1980*, Smithsonian Institute (USA), 1992.
Rust, Brian, *London Musical Shows On Record 1897-1976*, Gramophone (UK), 1977.

Pop General
Allson, Robert Sum, *Gone Crazy And Back Again: The Rise And Fall Of The Rolling Stones Generation*, Doubleday (USA), 1981.
Alphabeat, *Who's Who In Pop*, Century 21, 1969.
Ammer, Christine, *Harper Collins Dictionary Of Music*, Harper Collins, 1991.
Anderton, Craig, *Home Recording For Musicians*, Guitar Player Books (USA), 1978.
Andrews, Bob & Summers, Jodi, *Rock Dirt: Scandals And Scoundrels of Rock 'N' Roll*, S.P.I., 1992.
Anscombe, Isabelle, *Not Another Punk Book*, Aurum Press (UK), 1978.
Arnold, Gina, *Route 666: On The Road To Nirvana*, St Martin's Press (USA), 1993.
Asbjornsen, Dag Erik, *Cosmic Dreams At Play*, Borderline Productions (UK), 1996.
Bacon, Tony, *The Ultimate Guitar Book*, Dorling Kindersley (UK), 1992.
Bacon, Tony, *Rock Hardware: The Instruments, Equipment And Technology Of Rock*, Blandford Press (UK), 1981.
Baddeley, Gavin, *Raising Hell! The Book Of Satan And Rock 'N' Roll*, Nemesis Books, 1993.
Bailey, David, *David Bailey's Rock And Roll Heroes*, Thames And Hudson (UK), 1997.
Bailey, David & Evans, Peter, *Goodbye Baby & Amen*, Corgi Books (USA).
Bailey, Derek, *Improvisation: Its Nature And Practice In Music*, The British Library National Sound Archive, 1992 (UK).
Baker, Glenn A. & Coupe, Stuart, *The New Music*, Bay Books (Australia), 1980.
Balliett, Whitney, *American Singers: Twenty-seven Portraits In Song*, Oxford University Press, 1990.
Bangs, Lester, *Psychotic Reactions & Carburetor Dung*, Vantage (USA), 1988.
Barnard, Stephen, *Rock Companion*, Paladin (UK), 1992.
Barnes, Ken, *Twenty Years Of Pop*, Kenneth Mason, 1973.
Barres, Pamela Des, *I'm With The Band: Confessions of A Groupie*, New English Library (UK), 1989.
Barrow, Tony, *On The Scene At The Cavern*, Cavern Mecca, 1984.
Bayles, Martha, *Hole In Our Soul: The Loss Of Beauty And Meaning In American Popular Music*, The Free Press (USA), 1994.
Beadle, Jeremy J., *Will Pop Eat Itself?: Pop Music In The Soundbite Era*, Faber & Faber (UK), 1993.
Beaton, Virginia, And Stephen Pedersen, *Maritime Music Greats: Fifty Years Of Hits And Heartbreak*, Nimbus Publishing, 1992.
Beckman, Jeanette & Adler, Bill, *Rap: Portraits And Lyrics Of A Generation Of Black Rockers*, Omnibus Press (UK), 1991.
Belz, Carl, *The Story Of Rock*, Oxford University Press (USA), 1969.
Bennett, T., S. Frith, L. Grossberg, J. Shepherd, G. Turner, *Rock And Popular Music: Politics, Policies, Institutions*, Routledge (UK), 1994.
Benson, Denis C., *The Rock Generation*, Abingdon (USA), 1976.
Benson, Richard (ed.), *Night Fever: Club Writing In The Face*

1980-1997, Boxtree (UK).

Bergman, Billy, *Hot Sauces*, Blandford (UK), 1985.

Best, Kenneth, *Eight Days A Week: Illustrated Record Of Rock 'n' Roll*, Pomegranate Artbooks (USA), 1992.

Betrock, Alan, *Hitsville: The 100 Greatest Rock 'N' Roll Magazine 1954-1968*, Shake Books, 1991.

Betrock, Alan, *Girl Groups: The Story Of A Sound*, Delilah Books (USA), 1982.

Bindas, Kenneth J. (ed.), *America's Musical Pulse: Popular Music In 20th Century Society*, Greenwood Press (UK), 1992.

Birch, Ian (ed.), *The Book With No Name*, Omnibus Press (UK), 1981.

Bird, Brian, *Skiffle: The Story Of Folk-Song With A Jazz Beat*, Robert Hale (UK), 1958.

Blair, Dike & Anscomb, Elizabeth, *Punk: Punk Rock Style, Stance, People, Stars*, Urizen (USA), 1978.

Blair, John, *The Illustrated Discography Of Surf Music, 1959-1965*, J. Bee, 1978.

Blair, John, *Illustrated Discography Of Surf Music, 1961-65*, Pierian Press (USA), 1990.

Blair, John and McParland, Stephen, *The Illustrated Discography Of Hot Rod Music 1961-1965*, Popular Culture, 1990.

Blake, Andrew, *The Music Business*, Batsford (UK), 1992.

Blane, Michael, *Who's Who In Rock*, Clio Press, 1981.

Bloom, Ken, *Popular Music, American Song: The Complete Broadway Musical*, Facts On File (USA), 1972.

Bloom, Ken, *Broadway: An Encyclopedic Guide*, Facts On File (USA), 1991.

Bloom, Ken, *Hollywood Song*, Facts On File (USA), 1993.

Boeckman, Charles, *And The Beat Goes On: A Survey Of Pop Music In America*, R. B. Luce, 1972.

Bogle, Donald., *Eighty Years Of America's Black Female Superstars*, Da Capo (USA), 1990.

Booth, Stanley, *Rhythm Oil*, Jonathan Cape (UK), 1992.

Booth, Stanley, *Rhythm Oil: Journey Through The Music Of The American South*, Vintage (USA), 1993.

Boston, Virginia, *Shockwave*, Plexus (UK), 1978.

Bowman, Robyn, *Book Of Rock Secrets*, Virgin Books (UK), 1982.

Bracewell, Michael, *England is Mine: Pop Life In Albion From Wilde To Goldie*, Harper Collins (UK), 1997.

Brackett, David, *Interpreting Popular Music*, Cambridge University Press, 1995.

Bradley, Dick, *Understanding Rock 'N' Roll: Popular Music In Britain 1955-64*, Open University Press (UK), 1992.

Brake, Mike, *The Sociology Of Youth Culture And Youth Subcultures*, Routledge & Paul Kegan (UK), 1980.

Breithaupt, Don And Jeff, *Precious And Few: Pop Music In The Early 70s*, St. Martin's Griffin (USA), 1996.

Bronson, Fred, *The Billboard Book Of Number One Hits*, Guinness Publishing (UK), Billboard (USA), 1992.

Bronson, Fred, *Billboard's Hottest 100 Hits*, Omnibus Press (UK), 1992.

Bronson, Fred (ed), *Billboard's Hottest Hot Hundred Hits*, Billboard Books (USA), 1995.

Broven, John, *Walking To New Orleans: The Story Of New Orleans Rhythm & Blues*, Flyright, 1977.

Brown, Len & Friedrich, Gary, *The Encyclopedia Of Rock 'N' Roll*, Tower (USA), 1970.

Brown, Len & Friedrich, Gary, *So You Think You Know Rock 'N' Roll*, Tower (USA), 1971.

Brown, Mick, *American Heartbeat: Travels From Woodstock To San Jose By Song...* , Michael Joseph (UK), 1993.

Brown, Mick, *American Heartbeat: Travels From Woodstock-San Jose By Song Title*, Penguin (UK), 1993.

Bruchac, Joseph, *The Poetry Of Pop*, Dustbooks (Canada), 1973.

Buchanan, Scott (ed.), *Rock'N'Roll: The Famous Lyrics*, Harper

Perennial (USA), 1995.

Buckle, Philip, *The Year's Top Twenty*, Mayflower/Dell (USA), 1964.

Buckley, Jonathan (ed) & Ellinghame, Mark (ed), *Rock: The Rough Guide*, Rough Guides (UK), 1996.

Bull, Andy, *Coast To Coast: A Rock Fan's US Tour*, Black Swan (UK), 1992.

Burchill, Julie & Parsons, Tony, *The Boy Looked At Johnny: The Obituary Of Rock And Roll*, Pluto Press (UK), 1978.

Burnett, Michael, *Pop Music*, Oxford University Press, 1980.

Burnett, Robert, *The Global Jukebox: The International Music Industry*, Routledge (UK), 1995.

Burt Rob & North, Patsy, *West Coast Story*, Hamlyn (UK), 1977.

Busnar, Gene, *The Superstars Of Rock: Their Lives And Their Music*, Messner, 1980.

Busnar, Gene, *It's Rock 'N' Roll*, Julian Messner, 1979.

Bussy, Patrick & Hall, Andy, *The Can Book*, SAF, 1990.

by the editors of Rolling Stone, *Rolling Stone Rock Almanac: The Chronicles Of Rock Music*, Macmillan, 1983.

Byford, Phil, *The Boys Who Rock*, Dragon's Dream (UK), 1982.

Bygrave, Mike, *Rock*, Watts (USA), 1978.

Byrne, John, *The Story Of Pop*, Heinemann Educational (UK), 1975.

Cable, Michael, *The Pop Industry: Inside Out*, W.H. Allen (UK), 1977.

Callahan, Mike, *A Guide To Oldies On Compact Disc*, Both Sides Now, 1991.

Carducci, Joe, *Rock And The Pop Narcotic*, Redoubt Press, 1992.

Cash, Dave, *All Night Long*, Minerva (UK), 1993.

Cash, Tony, *Anatomy Of Pop*, BBC (UK), 1970.

Cato, Philip, *Crash Course For The Ravers: A Glam Odyssey*, S.T. Publishing (UK), 1997.

Cavanagh, David, *The World's Greatest Rock 'N Roll Scandals*, Octopus (UK), 1990.

Cave, Nick, *And The Ass Saw The Angel*, Black Spring, 1989.

Cee, Gary, *Classic Rock*, Metro Books (USA), 1996.

Chambers, Iain, *Urban Rhythms: Pop Music And Popular Culture*, Macmillan, 1990.

Champion, Sarah, *And God Created Manchester*, Central Books, 1990 (UK).

Chapman, Robert, *Selling The Sixties: The Pirates And Pop*, Rouledge (UK), 1992.

Chapple, Steve & Garofalo, Raebee, *Rock 'N' Roll Is Here To Pay: The History & Politics Of The Music Industry Nels*, (USA), 1977.

Charlesworth, Chris, *Sex & Drugs & Rock & Roll*, Bobcat Books (USA), 1993.

Charlesworth, Chris, *A-Z Of Rock Guitarists*, Proteus (UK), 1982.

Chipman, Bruce, *Hardening Rock*, Little & Brown (USA), 1972.

Christgau, Robert, *Christgau's Record Guide : The 80s*, Pantheon (USA), 1990.

Christgau, Robert, *Christgau's Guide: Rock Albums Of The 70s*, Vermilion (USA), 1982.

Christgau, Robert, *Any Old Way You Choose It: Rock And Other Pop Music: 1967-1973*, Penguin (USA), 1973.

Clark, Al, *The Rock Yearbook 1983*, Virgin Books (UK), 1982.

Clark, Al, *The Rock Yearbook 1982*, Virgin Books (UK), 1981.

Clark, Alan, *Rock And Roll Memories Number 7*, National Rock And Roll Archives (UK), 1992.

Clark, Humphrey, *Loser: Real Seattle Music Story*, Feral House (USA), 1995.

Clarke, Donald, *The Rise And Fall Of Popular Music*, Viking, 1995.

Clarke, Donald (ed.), *Penguin Encyclopedia Of Popular Music*, Viking, 1990.

Clayson, Alan, *Death Discs*, Gollancz (UK), 1992.

Clayson, Alan, *Call Up The Groups: The Golden Age Of British Beat 1962-67*, Blandford Press (UK), 1985.

Clayson, Alan, *Beat Merchants*, Blandford Press (UK), 1995.

Clayton-Lea, Tony & Taylor, Richie, *Irish Rock: Where It Comes From etc.*, Sidgewick & Jackson (UK), 1992.

Clews, Frank, *The Golden Disc*, Brown Watson, 1963.

Clews, Frank, *Teenage Idols*, Brown Watson, 1963.

Clifford, M. (ed.), *The Harmony Illustrated Encyclopedia Of Rock, 7th Edition*, Harmony Books (USA), 1993.

Clifford, Mike (ed.), *New Illustrated Rock Handbook*, Salamander Books (UK), 1992.

Cloonan, Martin, *Banned: Censorship of Popular Music 1965-1992*, Arena (UK), 1996.

Cohen, Sam, *Pop Culture In Liverpool*, Oxford University Press, 1991.

Cohen, Stanley, *Folk Devils & Moral Panics: The Creation Of Mods & Rockers*, MacGibbon & Kee (UK), 1972.

Cohn, Nik, *Rock From The Beginning*, Pocket Books (USA), 1969.

Cohn, Nik, *Ball The Wall*, Picador (UK), 1989.

Cohn, Nik, *Awopbopaloobopawopbamboom*, Weidenfeld & Nicholson (UK), Stein & Day (USA), 1969.

Cohn, Nik And Peellaert, Guy, *Rock Dreams*, Pan Books (UK), 1974.

Coleman, Ray (ed.), *The Melody Maker File 1974*, IPC Specialist And Professional Press (UK), 1973.

Collis, John (ed.), *The Rock Primer*, Penguin (UK), 1980.

Colman, Stuart, *They Kept On Rockin': The Giants Of Rock 'N' Roll*, Blandford Press (UK), 1982.

Compiled by Perry, Neil, *Rare Singles From The Rock 'N' Roll Era*, Perry & Perry (UK), 1991.

Connelly, Will, *The Musician's Guide To Independent Record Production*, Contemporary Books, 1981.

Coon, Caroline, *The New Wave Punk Rock Explosion*, Orbach & Chambers, 1977.

Cooper, B. Lee & Haney, Wayne S., *Rockabilly: A Bibliographic Resource Guide*, Scarecrow (USA), 1991.

Cooper, B. Lee, And Wayne S. Haney, *Rock Music In American Popular Culture*, Harrington Park Press (USA), 1995.

Cooper, Mark, *Liverpool Explodes*, Sidgwick & Jackson (UK), 1982.

Coryton, Demitri & Murrells, Joseph, *Hits Of The 60s: The Million Sellers*, Batsford (UK), 1990.

Cotten, L., *Shake Rattle And Roll: Golden Age Of American Rock 'N' Roll Popular Culture*, 1990.

Coupe, Stuart & Baker, Glenn, *The New Rock 'N' Roll: The A-Z Of Rock In The '80s*, Omnibus Press (UK), 1984.

Coupland, Douglas, *Polaroids From The Dead*, Flamingo (UK), 1996.

Crenshaw, Martin, *Hollywood Rock*, Plexus (UK), 1994.

Cross, Alan, *The Alternative Music Almanac*, Collectors Guide Publishing (UK), 1996.

Cullimore, Stan, *Fighting For Fame: How To Be A Pop Star*, Piccadilly Press (UK), 1992.

Cummings, Tony, *The Sound Of Philadelphia*, Methuen (UK), 1975.

Cunningham, Mark, *Good Vibrations: A History Of Record Production*, Castle Books (UK), 1996.

Curtis, Anthony et al, *The Rolling Stone Album Guide*, Virgin Books (UK), 1993.

Dachs, David, *Inside Pop: America's Top Ten Groups*, Scholastic Book Services (USA), 1968.

Dachs, David, *Inside Pop 2: Over 25 Top Groups*, Scholastic Book Services (USA), 1970.

Dachs, David, *Encyclopedia Of Pop/Rock*, Scholastic Book Services (USA), 1972.

Dachs, David, *Anything Goes: The World Of Pop Music*, Bobbs-Merrill (USA), 1964.

Dachs, David, *American Pop*, Scolastic Book Services, 1969

(USA).

Dallas, Karl, *Singers Of An Empty Day*, Kahn And Averill (UK), 1971.

Dalley, Robert J., *Surfin' Guitars: Instrumental Surf Bands Of The Sixties*, published by author (USA), 1990.

Dalton, David & Kaye, Lenny, *Rock 100*, Grosset & Dunlap (USA), 1977.

Damsker, Matt, *Rock Voices: The Best Lyrics Of An Era*, Arthur Barker, 1980.

Dannen, Frederic, *The Hit Men*, Random House (USA), 1990.

Daufouy, Philippe & Sarton, Jean-Pierre, *Pop Music/Rock*, Editions Champ Libre, Paris, 1972.

David, Andrew, *Rock Stars: People At The Top Of The Charts*, Damus Northbrook, 1979.

Davis, Julie, *Punk*, Millington, 1977.

De Lisle, Tim (ed.), *Lives Of The Great Songs*, Pavilion (UK), 1994.

Dearling, Robert & Celia with Rust, Brian, *Guinness Book Of Music Facts & Feats*, Guinness Publishing (UK), 1976.

DeCurtis, Anthony & Warren, Holly George, *Rolling Stone Album Guide*, Virgin Books (UK), 1992.

DeCurtis, Anthony (ed), *Present Tense: Rock & Roll and Culture*, Duke U.P. (USA), 1992.

Deffaa, Chip, *Swing Legacy*, Scarecrow (USA), 1990.

Dellar, Fred & Lazell, Barry, *The Essential Guide To Rock Records*, Omnibus Press (UK), 1983.

Dellar, Fred and Lazell, Barry, *The Omnibus Rock Discography*, Omnibus Press (UK), 1982.

Dello, Phil, And Scott Woods, *I Wanna Be Sedated*, Sound And Vision, 1994.

Dempsey, Michael, *The Bible*, BIG O (UK), 1978.

Denisoff, R. Serge, *Songs Of Protest, War And Peace: A Bibliograpgy And Discography*, ABC-Clio, 1973.

Denisoff, R. Serge, *Sing A Song Of Social Significance*, Bowling Green University Press (USA), 1972.

Denisoff, R. Serge, *Great Day Coming: Folk Music And The American Left*, University Of Illinois Press (USA), 1971.

Denselow, Robin, *When The Music's Over: The Story Of Political Pop*, Faber & Faber (UK), 1989.

DeRogatis, Jim, *Kaleidoscope Eyes: Pshchedelic Rock From The 60s To The 90s*, Citadel Press, 1996.

Derogatis, Jim, *Kaleidoscope Eyes: Psychedelic Rock From The 60s To The 90s*, Citadel Underground (USA), 1996.

Des Barres, Pamela, *I'm With The Band: Confessions Of A Groupie*, Jove (USA), 1988.

Des Barres, Pamela, *Take Another Little Piece Of My Heart*, Berkley Books (USA), 1993.

Des Barres, Pamela, *Rock Bottom: Dark Moments In Music Babylon*, Little Brown, 1996.

Diamond, Wendy, *A Musical Feast*, Global Liasons, 1995.

Diamond, Wendy (ed), *A Musical Feast: Recipes From 100 Musical Artists*, Global Liasons (USA), 1996.

DiMartino, Dave, *Singer Songwriters: Performer-Composers From A To Zevron*, Billboard Publications (USA), 1994.

Dister, Alain, *Le Rock Anglais: De Tommy Steele a David Bowie*, Albin Michel, Paris, 1973.

Dister, Alain, *Story Of Rock: Smash Hits And Superstars*, New Horizons, 1993.

Dobson, Richard, *A Dictionary Of Electronic And Computer Music Technology*, Oxford University Press, 1992.

Docks, L.R., *American Premium Record Guide*, Books Americana (USA), 1991.

Dolgins, Adam, *Rock Names*, Citadel Press, 1993.

Dolgins, Adam, *Rock Names*, Pan Macmillan (UK), 1994.

Doney, Malcolm, *Summer In The City: Rock Music & Way Of Life*, Lion, 1978.

Doukas, James N., *Electric Tibet: The Chronicles And Sociology Of The San Francisco Rock Musicians*, Dominion (USA), 1969.

Downey, Pat, *The Golden Age Of Top 40 Music*, Disc Collector (USA), 1992.

Downing, David, *Future Rock*, Panther (UK), 1976.

Doyle, Michael, *History Of Marshall: The Illustrated Story Of 'The Sound Of Rock'*, Hal Leonard Publishing (USA), 1993.

Draper, Roger, *Rolling Stone Magazine: The Uncensored History*, Mainstream (UK), 1990.

Du Noyer, Paul (ed), *The Virgin Story Of Rock 'n' Roll*, Virgin Books (UK), 1995.

Duncan, Robert, *The Noise: Rock 'N Roll And The Transformation Of America*, Ticknor & Fields, 1983.

Dunson, Josh, *Freedom In The Air: Song Movements Of The 60's*, International, 1965.

Earl, Bill, *When Radio Was Boss*, Desert Rose, 1990.

Eddy, Chuck, *The Accidental Evolution Of Rock 'n' Roll*, Da Capo Press (USA), 1997.

Editor Clarke, K., *British Music Worldwide*, Rhinegold, 1991.

Editors Of Flip Magazine, *Flip's Guide To The Groups 1969-1970*, Signet (USA), 1968.

Edwards, John W., *Rock 'n' Roll Through 1969: Discographies Of All Performers Who Hit The Charts*, McFarland and Co (USA), 1992.

Edwards, Joseph, *Top 10's And Trivia Of Rock & Roll And Rhythm & Blues: 1974 Supplement*, Blueberry Hill (USA), 1974.

Eisen, Jonathan, *The Age Of Rock*, Vintage/Random House (USA), 1969.

Eisen, Jonathan (ed), *The Age Of Rock 2*, Random House (USA), 1970.

Eisen, Jonathan (ed), *Twenty Minute Fandangos And Forever Changes*, Prentice-Hall (USA), 1971.

Eliot, Marc, *Rockonomics: The Money Behind The Music*, Omnibus Press (UK), 1990.

Ellis, Robert, *The Pictorial Album Of Rock*, Salamander Books (UK), 1981.

Ellis, Royston, *The Big Beat Scene*, Four Square (UK), 1961.

Elmlark, Walli & Beckley, Timothy G., *Rock Raps Of The 70's*, Drake (USA), 1972.

Elrod, Bruce (ed.), *Your Hit Parade And American Top Ten Hits, 1935-92*, Popular Culture Ink. (USA), 1993.

Elson, Howard, *Early Rockers*, Proteus (UK), 1982.

Elson, Howard & Brunton, John, *Whatever Happened To ...? The Great Rock And Pop Nostalgia Book*, Proteus, (UK) 1981.

Emerson, Ken, *Doo-Dah!: Stephen Foster And The Rise Of American Popular Culture*, Simon & Schuster (USA), 1997.

Engel, Edward, *White & Still All Right*, Rock Culture Scarsdale, 1978.

Ennis, Philip, *Seventh Stream; Emergence Of Rock 'n' Roll In American Popular Music*, Wesleyan University Press (USA), 1993.

Erlewine, Michael (ed) and others, *All Music Guide To Rock*, Miller Freeman (USA), 1996.

Escott, Colin, *Tattooed On Their Tongues*, Schirmer Books (USA), 1996.

Evans, Liz, *Women, Sex And Rock'N'Roll*, Pandora (UK), 1994.

Evans, Liz (ed.), *Girls Will Be Boys: Women Report On Rock*, Pandora (UK), 1997.

Ewen, David, *All The Years Of American Popular Music*, Prentice-Hall (USA), 1977.

Ewen, David, *History Of Popular Music*, Constable (UK), 1961.

Ewen, David, *Great Men Of American Popular Song: The History Of The American Popular Song*, Prentice-Hall (USA), 1972.

Ewen, David, *American Popular Songs From The Revolutionary War To The Present*, Random House (USA), 1966.

Fabian, Jenny & Byne, John, *Groupie*, Mayflower-Dell (UK), 1970.

Farr, Jory, *Moguls And Madmen: The Pursuit Of Power In Popular Music*, Simon & Schuster, 1994.

Farren, Mick & Snow, George, *Rock 'N' Roll Circus*, Pierrot, 1978.

Fein, Art, *The L.A. Musical History Tour*, Faber & Faber (UK), 1991.

Feinstein, Michael, *Nice Work If You Can Get It: My Life In Rhythm And Rhyme*, Hyperion (USA), 1995.

Ferguson, Gary Lynn (compiler), *Song Finder: A Title Index To 32,000 Popular Songs 1854-1992*, Greenwood Press (USA), 1996.

Ferlingere, Robert D., *A Discography Of Rhythm & Blues And Rock 'N' Roll Vocal Groups, 1945 to 1965*, Ferlingere, 1976.

Fernando, S, H. Jr., *The New Beats: Exploring The Music Culture And Attitudes Of Hip Hop*, Payback (USA), 1995.

Fernett, Gene, *Swing Out: Great Negro Dance Bands*, Da Capo (USA), 1993.

Flanagan, Bill, *Written In My Soul*, Contemporary Books (USA), 1987.

Flattery, Paul, *The Illustrated History Of British Pop*, Wise (USA), 1973.

Fong-Torres, Ben (ed.), *What's That Sound?: The Contemporary Music Scene From The Pages of Rolling Stone*, Rolling Stone Press/Anchor Books (USA), 1976.

Fong-Torres, Ben (ed.), *The Rolling Stone Rock 'N' Roll Reader*, Bantam Books (USA), 1974.

Formento, Dan, *Rock Chronicle: A 365 Day-By-Day Journal Of Significant Events In Rock History*, Delilah (USA), 1982.

Fox, Alison, *Rock & Pop*, Boxtree (UK), 1988.

Fox, Ted, *Showtime At The Apollo*, Quartet (UK), 1988.

Frame, Pete, *The Road To Rock: A Zig Zag Book Of Interviews*, Charisma/Spice Box (UK), 1974.

Frame, Pete, *Rock Family Trees 2*, Omnibus Press (UK), 1983.

Frame, Pete, *Rock Family Trees*, Omnibus Press (UK), 1980.

Frame, Pete, *Harp Beat Rock Gazetteer Of Great Britain*, Banyan (UK), 1989.

Frame, Pete, *The Beatles And Some Other Guys*, Omnibus Press (UK), 1997.

Fredericks, Vic, *Who's Who In Rock 'N' Roll*, Fell, 1958.

Freeman, Steven & Freeman, Alan, *Crack In The Cosmic Egg: Encyclopedia Of Krautrock*, Ultima Thule (UK), 1997.

Friedlander, Paul, *Rock And Roll: A Social History*, Westview Press (USA), 1996.

Frith, Simon, *Sound And Vision: Music Video Recorder*, Routledge (UK), 1993.

Frith, Simon, *Sound Effects: Youth Leisure And The Politics Of Rock*, Constable (UK), 1983.

Frith, Simon, *Facing The Music*, Pantheon (USA), 1988.

Frith, Simon, *Performing Rites: On The Value Of Popular Music*, Oxford University Press (UK), 1997.

Frith, Simon & Goodwin, Andrew, *On Record: Rock, Pop And The Written Word*, Routledge (UK), 1990.

Fuqua, Christopher S., *Music Fell On Alabama*, Honeysuckle Imprint, 1992.

Furia, Philip, *Poets Of Tin Pan Alley: A History Of America's Great Lyricists*, Oxford UP (New York), 1994.

Furis, Philip, *The Poets Of Tin Pan Alley: A History Of America's Great Lyricists*, Oxford University Press, 1991.

Furmanovsky, Jill, *The Moment: 25 Years Of Rock Photography 1970-1995*, Paper Tiger (UK), 1995.

Gaar, Gillian A., *She's A Rebel: The History Of Women In Rock & Roll*, Blandford Press (UK), 1993.

Gabree, John, *The World Of Rock*, Fawcett Greenwich (USA), 1968.

Gambaccini, Paul, *Top 100 Albums*, GRR/Pavilion (UK), 1987.

Gambaccini, Paul, *Masters Of Rock*, BBC/Omnibus (UK), 1982.

Gambaccini, Paul, *Critics Choice Top 200 Albums*, Omnibus Press (UK), 1978.

Gambaccini, Paul and Jonathan & Tim Rice, *Guinness Hits Quiz*, Guinness (UK), 1990.

Gambaccini, Paul and Jonathan & Tim Rice, *Guinness Hits Of The 80s*, Guinness (UK), 1990.

Gambaccini, Paul and Jonathan & Tim Rice, *Guinness Book Of No 1 Hits*, Guinness (UK), 1990.

Gambaccini, Paul and Jonathan & Tim Rice, *Guinness Book Of Hits Of The 70's*, Guinness (UK), 1980.

Gambaccini, Paul and Jonathan & Tim Rice, *Guinness Book Of British Hit Singles*, Guinness (UK), 1992.

Gambaccini, Paul and Jonathan & Tim Rice, *Guinness Book of British Hit Albums*, Guinness (UK), 1992.

Gambaccini, Paul and Jonathan & Tim Rice and Read, Mike, *Guinness Hits Of The Sixties*, Guinness (UK), 1984.

Gambaccini, Paul and Jonathan & Tim Rice and Read, Mike, *Guinness Book Of 500 Number One Hits*, Guinness (UK), 1982.

Gammond, Peter, *Oxford Companion To Popular Music*, Oxford University Press, 1993.

Gammond, Peter, *A Guide To Popular Music*, Phoenix, 1960.

Garbutt, Bob, *Rockabilly Queens*, Ducktail Press, 1979.

Gardner, Graham, *Then And Now*, Graham Gardner, 1981.

Garfield, Simon, *Expensive Habits: The Dark Side Of The Music Industry*, Faber & Faber (UK), 1990.

Garner, Ken, *In Session Tonight: Complete Radio 1 Recordings*, BBC Publications (UK), 1993.

Garofalo, Reebee (ed), *Rockin The Boat: Mass Music & Mass Movements*, South End Press (UK), 1992.

Garon, Paul & Beth, *Woman With Guitar: Memphis Minnie Blues*, Da Capo (USA), 1992.

Gassen, Timothy, *The Knights Of Fuzz: Garage And Psychedelic Music Explosion 1980-1995*, Borderline Productions (UK), 1996.

George, B. and Defoe, Martha (Eds.), *International New Wave Discography: Vol 11*, Omnibus Press (UK), 1982.

George, Nelson, *Where Did Our Love Go?*, Omnibus Press (UK), 1986.

George, Nelson, *Top Of The Charts*, New Century, 1983.

George, Nelson, *The Death of Rhythm & Blues*, Pantheon (USA), 1988.

George, Nelson, *Fresh Hip Hop Don't Stop*, Random House (USA), 1985.

Giddins, Gary, *Faces In The Crowd: Players And Writers*, Oxford University Press, 1994.

Gill, John, *Hype!*, Grafton (UK), 1990.

Gillett, Charlie, *Sound Of The City*, Souvenir Press (UK), 1971.

Gillett, Charlie, *Rock File 2*, Panther/Granada, 1974.

Gillett, Charlie, *Rock File*, New English Library (UK), 1972.

Gillett, Charlie & Frith, Simon, *Rock File 5*, Panther/Granada (UK), 1978.

Gillett, Charlie & Frith, Simon, *Rock File 4 (Incorporating Rock File 1)*, Panther/Granada (UK), 1976.

Gillett, Charlie & Frith, Simon, *Rock File 3*, Panther/Granada (UK), 1975.

Gillett, Charlie and Frith, Simon, *The Beat Goes On: The Rock File Reader*, Pluto Press (UK), 1996.

Gilmore, Mikal, *Night Beat: A Shadow History Of Rock & Roll*, Doubleday (USA), 1998.

Gimarc, George & Reeder, Pat, *Hollywood Hi-Fi*, St Martins Press (USA), 1996.

Given, Dave, *The Dave Given Rock 'N' Roll Stars Handbook: Rhythm And Blues Artists And Groups*, Exposition Press, 1980.

Glassed, Timothy, *Echoes In Time: The Garage And Psychedelic Music Explosion 1980-1990*, Borderline (UK), 1992.

Godbolt, Jim, *All This And 10%*, Robert Hale (UK), 1976.

Goldman, Albert, *Freakshow: The Rocksoulbluesjazzsickjewblackhumorxpoppsych Gig And Other Scene*, Atheneum (USA), 1971.

Goldman, Albert, *Sound Bites*, Abacus (UK), 1993.

Goldman, Joe, *1991 International Steel Guitar Discography*, Self published, 1991.

Goldstein, Richard, *Goldstein's Greatest Hits: A Book Mostly About Rock 'N' Roll*, Prentice-Hall (USA), 1970.

Goldstein, Richard, *The Poetry Of Rock*, Bantam (USA), 1969.

Goldstein, Stewart and Jacobson, Alan, *Oldies But Goodies: The Rock'N'Roll Years*, Van Nostrand Reinhold (UK), 1978.

Goodgold, Edwin, *Rock 'N' Roll Trivia*, Popular Library, 1970.

Goodier, Mark, *Unbelievable: Amazing True Stories From The World Of Rock 'N' Roll*, Grafton (UK), 1993.

Goodman, Fred, *The Mansion On The Hill*, Times Books (USA), 1997.

Gordon, Robert, *It Came From Memphis*, Secker & Warburg (UK), 1995.

Gotz, Jan A., *Eurovision Collectors Guide*, Baby Baby Records (Holland), 1992.

Gratton, Virginia L., *American Women Songwriters: A Biographical Dictionary*, Greenwood Press, 1993.

Gray, Marcus, *London's Rock Landmarks*, Omnibus Press (UK), 1985.

Green, Jonathon, *Days In The Life: Voices From The English Undergound 1961-1971*, Heinemman (UK), 1988.

Gregory, Hugh, And Tony Bacon (ed.), *1000 Great Guitarists: A Guide To The World's Best Players*, Balafon (UK), 1994.

Greig, Charlotte, *Will You Still Love Me Tomorrow*, Virago Press (UK), 1989.

Gribin, Anthony J & Schiff, Matthew M., *Doo-Wop: The Forgotten Third Of Rock 'n' Roll*, Krause Publications (USA), 1992.

Griffiths, Paul, *Modern Music And After: Directions Since 1945*, Dent (UK), 1994.

Groia, Philip, *They All Sang On The Corner: New York City's Rhythm And Blues Vocal Groups*, Edmond.

Gross, Michael & Jakubowski, Maxim, *The Rock Yearbook 1981*, Virgin Books (UK), 1980.

Grove, Martin A., *Teen Idols*, Manor Books, 1979.

Guitar Playing Magazine editors, *The Guitar Players Book*, Grove Press (USA), 1979.

Gullick, Steve, *Pop Book Number One*, Independent Music Press (UK), 1995.

Gullick, Steve, *Pop Book Number 1: Photographs 1988-1995*, Independent Music Press (UK), 1995.

Guralnick, Peter, *Lost Highway: Journeys & Arrivals Of American Musicians*, David R. Godine, 1979.

Guralnick, Peter, *Feel Like Going Home: Portraits In Blues & Rock 'N' Roll*, E.P. Dutton (USA), Penguin (UK), 1971/1978.

Guterman, Jimmy, *The Best Rock 'n' Roll Records Of All Time*, Citadel (USA), 1992.

Guterman, Jimmy & O'Donnell, Owen, *Slipped Discs: Worst Rock 'N' Roll Records Of All Times*, Citadel (USA), 1991.

Halfin, Ross, *Fragile: Human Organs*, 2.13.61 (USA), 1996.

Hall, Douglas Kent & Clark, Sue C., *The Superstars: In Their Own Words*, Music Sales (UK), 1970.

Hamlyn, Nick, *Music Master Price Guide For Record Collectors*, Waterlow (UK), 1993.

Hampton's, Wayne, *Guerilla Minstrels*, University Of Tennessee, Knoxville (USA), 1987.

Hanel, Ed, *The Essential Guide To Rock Books*, Omnibus Press (UK), 1983.

Hardy, Phil & Laing, Dave, *The Encyclopedia Of Rock 1955-1975*, Aquarius, 1977.

Hardy, Phil & Laing, Dave, *The Encyclopedia Of Rock Volume 3: The Sounds Of The Seventies*, Panther/Granada (UK), 1976.

Hardy, Phil & Laing, Dave, *The Encyclopedia Of Rock Volume 2: From Liverpool To San Francisco*, Hanover/Panther (UK), 1976.

Hardy, Phil & Laing, Dave, *The Encyclopedia Of Rock Volume 1: The Age Of Rock 'N' Roll*, Panther/Granada (UK), 1976.

Hardy, Phil & Laing, Dave, *Faber Companion To 20th Century Popular Music*, Faber & Faber (UK), 1990.

Hardy, Phil & Laing, Dave, *Encyclopedia Of Rock*, Macdonald Orbis (UK), 1987.

Haring, Bruce, *Off The Charts: Ruthless Days And Reckless Nights Inside The Music Industry*, 1996.

Harker, Dave, *One For The Money*, Hutchinson (UK), 1980.

Harris, Bob, *Bob Harris' Rock Dates*, Virgin Books (UK), 1992.

Harris, Bob, *Rock And Pop Mastermind*, Orbis (UK), 1985.

Harris, Bob, *Bob Harris's Rock Dates*, Virgin Books (UK), 1992.

Hatch, David & Millward, Stephen, *From Blues To Rock: An Analytical History Of Pop Music*, Manchester University Press, 1989.

Havlice, Patricia Pate, *Popular Song Index*, Scarecrow Press (USA), 1975.

Hayes, Chris, *Melody Maker Memories: Pre-War Story Of The World Famous Music Paper*, C. Hayes, 1992.

Heatley, Michael (ed.), *The Virgin Encyclopedia Of Rock*, Virgin Books (UK), 1993.

Hedges, Dan, *British Rock Guitar*, Guitar Player Books (USA), 1977.

Helander, Brock, *The Rock Who's Who*, Schirmer Books (USA), 1982.

Henke, James (ed.) with Parke Puterbaugh, *I Want To Take You Higher: The Psychedelic Era 1965-1969*, Chronicle Books (USA), 1997.

Hennessy, Val, *In The Gutter*, Quartet Books (UK), 1978.

Herbst, Peter, *The Rolling Stone Interviews 19671980: Talking With The Legends Of Rock 'N' Roll*, Arthur Barker, 1981.

Herman, Gary, *Rock 'N' Roll Babylon*, Plexus (UK), 1989.

Heslam, David (ed), *The NME Rock 'n' Roll Years*, Hamlyn (UK), 1992.

Heylin, Clinton, *From The Velvets To The Voidoids: Pre-punk History For The Post...*, Penguin (UK), 1993.

Heylin, Clinton, *Bootleg: The Secret History Of The Other Recording Industry*, St Martin's Press (USA), 1995.

Heylin, Clinton, *The Great White Wonders*, Penguin (UK), 1994.

Heylin, Clinton (ed.), *Penguin Book Of Rock And Roll Writing*, Viking (UK), 1992.

Hibbert, Tom (ed.), *The Perfect Collection*, Proteus (UK), 1982.

Hill, Dave, *Designer Boys & Material Girls*, Blandford Press (UK), 1986.

Hinton, Brian, *Nights In White Satan: An Illustrated History Of the Isle Of Wight Pop Festival*, Cultural Services, 1991.

Hinton, Brian, *Message To Love: The Isle Of Wight Festival 1968-1970*, Castle Books (UK), 1996.

Hirshey, Gerri, *Nowhere To Run*, Times Books (USA), 1984.

Hodenfield, Chris, *Rock '70*, Pyramid Books (USA), 1970.

Hodgins, Gordon W., *The Broadway Musical: A Complete LP Discography*, Scarecrow Press (USA), 1980.

Hoffman, Abbie, *Woodstock Nation: A Talk-Rock Album*, Vintage/Random House (USA), 1969.

Hoffman, Frank, *The Literature Of Rock Vol. 2 1979-1983*, Scarecrow Press (USA), 1986.

Hoffmann, Frank, *The Literature Of Rock, 1954-1978*, Scarecrow Press (USA), 1981.

Hogg, Brian, *History Of Scottish Rock & Pop: All That Ever Mattered*, Guinness (UK), 1993.

Holegard, Roger, *The EP Book: Swedish Pressings 1954-1969*, Premium Publishing (Sweden), 1993.

Hopkins, Jerry, *The Rock Story*, Signet/New American Library (USA), 1970.

Horn, David, *The Literature Of American Music In Books And Folk Music Collections: A Fully An*, Scarecrow Press (USA), 1977.

Hoskyns, Barney, *Say It One More Time For The Broken Hearted*, Fontana (UK), 1990.

Hoskyns, Barney, *From A Whisper To A Scream*, Fontana (UK), 1991.

Hoskyns, Barney, *The Lonely Planet Boy: A Pop Romance (fiction)*, Serpents Tail (UK), 1995.

Hoskyns, Barney, *Waiting For The Sun: The Story Of The Los Angeles Music Scene*, Viking (UK), St Martins Press (USA), 1996.

Hounsome, Terry, *Single File*, Record Research (UK), 1991.

Hounsome, Terry, *Rock Record 4*, Record Research (UK), 1991.

Hounsome, Terry, *New Rock Record: A Collector's Directory Of Rock Albums And Musicians*, Blandford Press (UK), 1981.

Hounsome, Terry & Chambre, Tim, *Rockmaster*, Private Publication by Author, 1978.

Hounsome, Terry & Chambre, Tim, *Revised: New Rock Record*, Blandford Press (UK), 1981.

Humphries, John (ed.), *Music Master Tracks Catalogue*, Music Master (UK), 1991.

Humphries, John (ed.), *Music Master Singles Catalogue*, Music Master (UK), 1991.

Humphries, John (ed.), *Music Master Record Catalogue*, Music Master (UK), 1991.

Hyland, William, G., *Song Is Ended: Songwriters And American Music 1900-1950*, Oxford University Press (USA), 1995.

Jackson, John A., *Big Beat Heat: Alan Freed And The Early Years Of Rock 'N' Roll*, Schirmer (USA), 1991.

Jacobs, Arthur, *Penguin Dictionary Of Musical Performers*, Penguin, 1991.

Jacobs, David, *Pick Of The Pop Stars*, Palmer (UK), 1962.

Jacobs, Philip, *Rock 'N' Roll Heaven*, Apple Press, 1990.

Jahn, Mike, *Rock: From Elvis Presley To The Rolling Stones*, Quadrangle/Times Books (USA), 1973.

Jahn, Mike, *The Story Of Rock: From Elis Presley To The Stones*, (USA), 1973.

Jakubowski, Maxim, *The Rock Album, Volume One*, Muller (UK), 1983.

James, Sally, *Almost Legendary Pop Interviews*, Eel Pie (UK), 1981.

Jancik, Wayne, *Billboard Book Of One Hit Wonders*, Billboard Publications (USA), 1990.

Jancik, Wayne & Tad Lathrop, *Cult Rockers*, Simon & Schuster (USA), 1995.

Jasen, David A., *Tin Pan Alley*, Donald I. Fine, New York, 1988.

Jasper, Tony, *Great Rock & Pop Headlines*, Collins Willow, 1986.

Jasper, Tony, *British Record Charts 1955-1982*, Blandford Press (UK), 1982.

Jasper, Tony, *The Top Twenty Book 1955-1993*, Blandford Press (UK), 1994.

Jasper, Tony (ed.), *The Top Twenty Book*, Blandford Press (UK), 1991.

Jeffery, Tim (ed.), *Disc Jockey Directory*, Punch, 1990.

Jenkins, Alan, *How To Be A Pop Group*, Cordelia Records, 1991.

Jermy, Geoff, *Arid: Australian Rock Instrumental Discography*, Moonlight Publishing (Australia), 1995.

Jewell, Derek, *The Popular Voice: A Musical Record Of The 60s And 70s*, Andre Deustch (UK), 1980.

Johnson, Gary, *The Story Of Oi: A View From The Dead-End Of The Street*, Babylon Books, 1981.

Johnson, Paul, *Straight Outa Bristol (The Roots Of Trip-Hop)*, Hodder & Stoughton (UK), 1996.

Johnson, Phil, *Straight Outa Bristol: Massive Attack, Portishead, Tricky And The Roots Of Trip* , Hodder & Stoughton (UK), 1996.

Jones, Alan, *Chartfile 1983*, Virgin Books (UK), 1983.

Jones, Alan, *Chart File 1982*, Virgin Books (UK), 1982.

Jones, Andrew, *Plunderphonics, Pataphysics & Pop Mechanics*, Saf, 1995.

Jones, Dylan, *Easy! The Lexicon Of Lounge*, Pavillion (UK), Universe (USA), 1997.

Jones, Dylan (ed.), *Meaty Beaty Big & Bouncy: Classic Rock And Pop Writing From Elvis To Oasis*, Hodder & Stoughton

(UK), 1996.

Jones, Lesley-Ann, Eggar, Robin & Swern, Phil, *The Sony Tape Rock Review*, Rambletree Pelham, 1984 (UK).

Jones, Wayne, *Rockin', Rollin', Rappin'*, Goldmine Press.

Joyner, David L., *American Popular Music*, W. C. Brown (USA), 1993.

Joynson, Vernon, *The Acid Trip: A Complete Guide To Psychedelic Music*, Babylon (UK), 1984.

Joynson, Vernon, *Fuzz, Acid And Flowers: Comprehensive Guide To American Garage*, Borderline Productions (UK), 1994.

Joynson, Vernon, *The Tapestry Of Delights*, Borderline Productions (UK), 1995.

Juno, Andrea, *Angry Women In Rock, Vol 1*, Airlift Book Company (UK), 1996.

Kamin, Jonathan Liff, *Rhythm & Blues In White America: Rock And Roll As Acculturation And Perceptual L*, University Microfilms, 1975.

Katz, Gary J., *Rock & Roll The Untimely Deaths Of The Legends Of Rock*, Robson (UK), 1995.

Katz, Susan, *Superwomen Of Rock*, Tempo Books, 1978.

Kaufman, Paul, with Colin WHite, *Road Mangler Deluxe*, White-Boucke Publishing, 1993.

Kay, Hilary, *Rock 'n' Roll Collectables*, Pyramid Books (UK), 1992.

Kendall, Paul & Farren, Mick, *Encyclopedia Of British Beat Groups & Solo Artists Of The Sixties*, Omnibus Press (UK), 1980.

Kent, Nick, *The Dark Stuff: Selected Writings On Rock Music 1972-1993*, Penguin Books, 1994.

Keyes, Johnny, *Du-Wop*, A & R Booksearch (UK), 1992.

Keyes, Johnny, *Du-Wop*, Vesti Press, 1991.

Kinder, Bob, *The Best Of The First: The Early Days Of Rock 'N' Roll*, Adams Press, 1987.

King, Vic, Plumbley, Mike & Turner, Pete, *Isle Of Wight Rock: A Music Anthology*, Rock Archives (UK), 1995.

Kingsbury, Robert, *Rolling Stone Book Of Days*, Straight Arrow Books (USA), 1976.

Kirchherr, Astrid, And Max Scheler, *Golden Dreams*, Genesis Publishing (UK), 1997.

Kirsch, Dan R., *Rock 'N' Roll Obscurities, 2nd Edition*, Private Edition (USA), 1981.

Kirsch, Dan R., *Rock 'N' Roll Obscurities Vol 1*, Private Edition (USA), 1978.

Klanten, Robert (ed), *Localizer 1.0: The Techno House Book*, Die Gestalten Verlag (Germany), 1995.

Kureishi, Hanif & John Savage, *The Faber Book Of Pop*, Faber (UK), 1995.

Laing, Dave, *All You Need Is Love: The Story Of Popular Music*, Sheed and Ward (UK), 1969.

Laing, David, *The Sound Of Our Time*, Sheed And Ward (UK), 1969.

Lambert, Dennis, *Producing Hit Records*, Macmillan (UK), 1980.

Landau, Jon, *It's Too Late To Stop Now: A Rock And Roll Journal*, Straight Arrow Books (USA), 1972.

Lanza, Joseph, *Elevator Music - A Surreal History Of Muzak*, Quartet Books (UK), 1995.

Larkin, Colin, *The Virgin Album Guide*, Virgin Books (UK), 1999.

Larkin, Colin, *The Virgin Encyclopedia Of Country Music*, Virgin Books (UK), 1998.

Larkin, Colin, *The Virgin Encyclopedia Of Dance Music*, Virgin Books (UK), 1999.

Larkin, Colin, *The Virgin Encyclopedia Of Eighties Music*, Virgin Books (UK), 1997.

Larkin, Colin, *The Virgin Encyclopedia Of Fifties Music*, Virgin Books (UK), 1998.

Larkin, Colin, *The Virgin Encyclopedia Of Heavy Rock*, Virgin Books (UK), 1999.

Larkin, Colin, *The Virgin Encyclopedia Of Indie & New Wave*, Virgin Books (UK), 1998.

Larkin, Colin, *The Virgin Encyclopedia Of Jazz*, Virgin Books (UK), 1999.

Larkin, Colin, *The Virgin Encyclopedia Of Popular Music: Concise Edition*, Virgin Books (UK), 1997.

Larkin, Colin, *The Virgin Encyclopedia Of R&B And Soul*, Virgin Books (UK), 1998.

Larkin, Colin, *The Virgin Encyclopedia Of Reggae*, Virgin Books (UK), 1998.

Larkin, Colin, *The Virgin Encyclopedia Of Seventies Music*, Virgin Books (UK), 1997.

Larkin, Colin, *The Virgin Encyclopedia Of Sixties Music*, Virgin Books (UK), 1997.

Larkin, Colin, *The Virgin Encyclopedia Of Stage And Film Musicals*, Virgin Books (UK), 1999.

Larkin, Colin, *The Virgin Encyclopedia Of The Blues*, Virgin Books (UK), 1998.

Larkin, Colin, *The Virgin Encyclopedia Of World & Folk Music*, Virgin Books (UK), 1999.

Larkin, Colin, *All Time Top 1000 Albums*, Guinness Publishing (UK), 1994.

Larkin, Colin (ed.), *Guinness Encyclopedia Of Popular Music (2nd Edition 6 Vols)*, Guinness Publishing (UK), 1995.

Larkin, Colin (ed.), *Guinness Encyclopedia Of Popular Music (1st Edition 4 Vols)*, Guinness Publishing (UK), 1992.

Larkin, Colin (ed.), *Guinness Encyclopedia Of Popular Music Concise Edition*, Guinness Publishing (UK), 1993.

Larkin, Colin (ed.), *Guinness Who's Who Of Blues (2nd Edition)*, Guinness Publishing (UK), 1995.

Larkin, Colin (ed.), *Guinness Who's Who Of Blues*, Guinness Publishing (UK), 1993.

Larkin, Colin (ed.), *Guinness Who's Who Of Country Music*, Guinness Publishing (UK), 1993.

Larkin, Colin (ed.), *Guinness Who's Who Of Fifties Music*, Guinness Publishing (UK), 1993.

Larkin, Colin (ed.), *Guinness Who's Who Of Film Musicals & Musical Films*, Guinness Publishing (UK), 1994.

Larkin, Colin (ed.), *Guinness Who's Who Of Folk Music*, Guinness Publishing (UK), 1993.

Larkin, Colin (ed.), *Guinness Who's Who Of Heavy Metal (2nd Edition)*, Guinness Publishing (UK), 1995.

Larkin, Colin (ed.), *Guinness Who's Who Of Heavy Metal*, Guinness Publishing (UK), 1992.

Larkin, Colin (ed.), *Guinness Who's Who Of Indie And New Wave (2nd Edition)*, Guinness Publishing (UK), 1995.

Larkin, Colin (ed.), *Guinness Who's Who Of Indie And New Wave Music*, Guinness Publishing (UK), 1992.

Larkin, Colin (ed.), *Guinness Who's Who Of Jazz (2nd Edition)*, Guinness Publishing (UK), 1995.

Larkin, Colin (ed.), *Guinness Who's Who Of Jazz*, Guinness Publishing (UK), 1992.

Larkin, Colin (ed.), *Guinness Who's Who Of Rap, Dance & Techno*, Guinness Publishing (UK), 1994.

Larkin, Colin (ed.), *Guinness Who's Who Of Reggae*, Guinness Publishing (UK), 1994.

Larkin, Colin (ed.), *Guinness Who's Who Of Seventies Music*, Guinness Publishing (UK), 1993.

Larkin, Colin (ed.), *Guinness Who's Who Of Sixties Music*, Guinness Publishing (UK), 1992.

Larkin, Colin (ed.), *Guinness Who's Who Of Soul Music*, Guinness Publishing (UK), 1993.

Larkin, Colin (ed.), *Guinness Who's Who Of Stage Musicals* , Guinness Publishing (UK), 1994.

Laufenberg, Frank, *Rock And Pop Day By Day*, Blandford Press (UK), 1992.

Law, Lisa, *Flashing On The Sixties*, Chronicle Books (USA), 1988.

Law, Simon & Eric Lives, *Keep Music Legal*, Sea Dream Music, 1995.

Lax, Roger & Smith, Frederick, *The Great Song Thesaurus*, Oxford University Press, 1990.

Lazell, Barry and Rees, Dafydd, *The Illustrated Book Of Rock Records: A Book Of Lists*, Virgin Books (UK), 1982.

Lees, Gene, *Singers And The Song*, Oxford University Press, 1990.

Leichter, Albert, *A Discography Of Rhythm & Blues And Rock & Roll C. 1946-1964: A Reference Man*, Leichter, 1975.

Leigh, Spencer, *Stars In My Eyes: Personal Interviews With Top Music Stars*, Raven Books (UK), 1980.

Leigh, Spencer, *Let's Go Down The Cavern*, Vermilion Books (UK), 1984.

Leigh, Spencer & Firminger, John, *Halfway To Paradise: Britpop 1955-1962*, Finbarr International (UK), 1996.

Leo Walker, *The Wonderful Era of the Great Dance Band*, Da Capo (USA), 1991.

Lerner, Alan Jay, *The Street Where I Live*, Hodder & Stoughton (UK), 1978.

Lescroart, John, *Rock Guitarists Volume 11*, Guitar Player Books (USA), 1977.

Leslie, Peter, *Fab: The Anatomy Of A Phenomenon*, MacGibbon And Kee (UK), 1965.

Lewis, Lisa A., *The Adoring Audience: Fan Culture And Popular Music*, Routledge (UK), 1992.

Leyar, B. J. & Gossett, P, *Rock Stars/Pop Stars*, Greenwood Press (UK), 1995.

Lindsay, Joe with Bukoski, Peter & Grobman, Marc, *Picture Discs Of The World Price Guide*, BIOdisc, 1990.

Lister, Derek A.J., *Bradford's Rock 'N' Roll*, Bradford Libraries And Information Service (UK), 1992.

Logan, Nick & Woffinden, Bob, *The New Musical Express Book Of Rock*, Star Books (UK), 1975.

Logan, Nick & Woffinden, Bob, *The NME Book Of Rock 2*, Star/W.H. Allen (UK), 1977.

Logan, Nick & Woffinden, Bob, *The NME Book Of Rock*, Star/W.H. Allen (UK), 1977.

Lowe, Leslie (ed.), *Directory Of Popular Music*, Music Master (UK), 1992.

Lyall, Sutherland, *Rock Sets: Astonishing Art Of Rock Concert Design*, Thames & Hudson (UK), 1992.

Lydon, Michael, *Rock Folk: Portraits From The Rock 'N'Roll Pantheon*, Dell (USA), 1973.

Lynch, Vincent, *American Juke Box: The Classic Years*, Tiptree Book Services (UK), 1990.

Lyons, Jodie & Stevenson, Lanelle, *P.O.P.S: Principles Of Pop Singing*, Schirmer (USA), 1990.

Mabey, Richard, *The Pop Process*, Hutchinson (UK), 1969.

Macken, Bob, Fornatale, Peter & Ayres, Bill, *The Rock Music Source Book*, Anchor/Doubleday, 1980.

MacLean, Hugh & Johnson, Vernon, *An American Rock History: 4: Indiana, Iowa And Missouri*, Borderline Productions (UK), 1995.

MacLean, Hugh & Joynson, Vernon, *An American Rock History: Part Two: Texas, Arizona and New Mexico*, Borderline Productions (UK), 1991.

MacLean, Hugh & Joynson, Vernon, *An American Rock History: Part One, California The Golden State*, Borderline Productions (UK), 1989.

Maclean, Hugh & Joynson, Vernon, *American Rock History: 3. Chicago and Illinois-The Windy City And Prairie Smoke*, Borderline Productions (UK), 1992.

Marchbank, Pearce & Miles, *The Illustrated Rock Almanac*, Paddington Press (UK), 1977.

Marcus, Greil, *Rock 'N' Roll Will Stand*, Beacon Press (USA), 1969.

Marcus, Greil, *Mystery Train: Images Of America In Rock 'N' Roll Music*, E.P. Dutton (USA), 1975.

Marcus, Greil, *Lipstick Traces: A Secret History Of The Twentieth Century*, Harvard University Press (USA), 1989.

Marcus, Greil, *The Dustbin Of History*, Picador (UK), 1996.

Marcus, Greil, (ed.), *Stranded: Rock 'N' Roll For A Desert Island*, Alfred A. Knopf (USA), 1979.

Marks, J. & Eastman, Linda, *Rock And Other Four Letter Words*, Bantam (USA), 1968.

Marsh, Dave, *The Heart Of Rock And Soul*, Penguin, 1989.

Marsh, Dave, *The New Book Of Rock Lists*, Fireside (USA), Sidgwick & Jackson (UK), 1994.

Marsh, Dave, *Louie Louie*, Hyperion (USA), 1993.

Marsh, Dave (ed), *Mid-Life Confidential*, Hodder & Stoughton (UK), 1994.

Marsh, Dave with Swenson, John (eds.), *The Rolling Stone Record Guide:*, Random House (USA), 1980.

Marsh, Dave, And Kathi Kamen Goldmark, *The Great Rock 'n Roll Joke Book*, St. Martin's Griffin (USA), 1997.

Marshal, Jim; Wolman, Baron & Hopkins, Jerry, *Festival! The Book Of American Music Celebrations*, Macmillan, 1970.

Marshall, George, *Two-tone Story*, S T Publishing (UK), 1993.

Marshall, George, *The 2-Tone Story*, Zoot, 1990.

Martin, George, with Jeremy Hornsby, *All You Need Is Ears*, St. Martin's Press (USA), 1980.

Martin, Linda, And Kerry Segrave, *Anti-Rock: The Opposition To Rock 'N' Roll*, Da Capo Press(USA), 1993.

May, Chris, *Rock 'N' Roll*, Scion/Sociopack (UK) , 1974.

May, Chris & Philips, Tim, *British Beat*, Scion (UK), 1974.

McAleer, Dave, *Hit Parade Heroes: British Beat Before The Beatles*, Hamlyn (UK), 1993.

McAleer, Dave, *The Omnibus Chart Book Of The 80s*, Omnibus Press (UK), 1989.

McAleer, Dave, *Omnibus Book Of British And American Hit Singles*, Omnibus Press (UK), 1988.

McAleer, Dave, *Now That's What I Call A Decade: Rock & Pop Through The 80s*, Omnibus Press (UK), 1989.

McAleer, Dave, *Hit Parade Heroes: British Pop Before The Beatles*, Hamlyn (UK), 1993.

McAleer, Dave, *Beat Boom: Pop Goes The Sixties*, Hamlyn (UK), 1994.

McAleer, David, *Chart Beats*, Guinness (UK), 1992.

McCarthy, David, *Golden Age Of Rock And Pop*, Apple Press, 1990 (UK).

McCarthy, David & Horsham, Michael, *Wild Guide To Pop Music*, Apple Press (UK), 1991.

McColn, Bruce & Payne, Doug, *Where Have They Gone? Rock 'N' Roll Stars*, Tempo/Grosset & Dunlap (USA), 1979.

McCoy, Judy, *Rap Music In The 1980s: A Reference Guide*, Scarecrow Press (USA), 1993.

McCue, G., *Music In American Society, 1776-1976*, New Brunswick, 1977.

McCutcheon, Lynn Ellis, *Rhythm And Blues: An Experience And Adventure In Its Origin And Development*, Beatty, 1971.

McDonnell, Evelyn (ed) & Powers, Ann (ed), *Rock She Wrote: Women Write About Rock, Pop And Rap*, Delta Music (USA), Plexus (UK), 1995.

McGrath, Noel, *The Stars, The Charts, The Stories, The Legends*, Lothian (Australia), 1990.

McGrath, Tom, *MTV: The Making of A Revolution*, Running Press (USA), 1996.

McLaren, Jay, *An Encyclopedia Of Gay And Lesbian Recordings*, Jay Mclaren (Holland), 1993.

McMillan, Andrew, *Strict Rules*, Hodder & Stoughton (UK), 1989.

McNutt , Randy, *We Wanna Boogie: An Illustrated History Of The American Rockabilly Movement*, HHP Books, Fairfield (USA), 1988.

Mellers, Wilfrid, *Angels Of The Night: Popular Female Singers Of Our Time*, Basil Blackwell (UK), 1987.

Meltzer, Richard, *The Aesthetics Of Rock*, Something Else Press

(USA), 1970.

Memories Magazine (eds.), *Yearbook* , Dolphine/Doubleday (USA), 1991.

Mercer, Mick, *Gothic Rock: All You Ever Wanted To Know But Were Too Gormless To Ask*, Pegasus, 1991.

Merwe, Peter Van Der, *Origins Of The Popular Style: Antecedents Of 20th Century Popular Music*, Oxford University Press, 1992.

Middleton, R. (ed.) etc., *Popular Music Volume 12, No 1*, Cambridge University Press, 1993.

Middleton, Richard and Horn, David, *Popular Music: 2: Theory And Method*, Cambridge University Press, 1981.

Middleton, Richard and Horn, David (Eds), *Popular Music: 1: Folk Or Popular? Distinctions, Influences, Continuities*, Cambridge University Press, 1981.

Miles, *The 2-Tone Book*, Omnibus Press (UK), 1981.

Miles (ed.), *The New Wave Encyclopedia*, Omnibus Press (UK), 1981.

Miletich, Leo N., *Broadway's Prize-Winning Musicals*, Haworth Publishing (USA), 1993.

Millar, Gavin, *Pop*, Axle, 1963.

Miller, Jim, *The Rolling Stone Illustrated History Of Rock & Roll 1950-1980*, Random House (USA), 1980.

Miller, Simon (ed.), *The Last Poet: Music After Modernism*, Manchester University Press, 1993.

Miron, Charles, *Rockgold: All The Hit Charts From 1955 To 1976*, Drake, 1977.

Monnery, Steve & Herman, Gary, *Rock 'N' Roll Chronicles 1955-1963*, B. Trodd, 1991 (UK).

Morgan, Robert P., *Anthology Of Twentieth-Century Music*, W.W. Norton (USA), 1992.

Moylan, W.M., *Art Of Recording*, Van Nostrand Reinhold (UK), 1992.

Murray, Charles Shaar, *Shooting From The Hip*, Penguin (UK), 1991.

Murrells, Joseph, *The Book Of Golden Discs*, Simon & Jenkins (UK), 1978.

Murrells, Joseph, *Million Selling Records*, Arco (USA), 1984.

Musician, Player And Listener (ed.), *The Year In Rock 1981-1982 & Billboard Charts*, LSP, 1981.

Naggar, David & Brandstetter, Jeffrey D., *The Music Business (Explained In Plain English)*, DaJe Publishing (USA), 1996.

Nanry, Charles, *American Music: From Storyville To Woodstock*, Transaction Books, 1972.

Napier-Bell, Simon, *You Don't Have To Say You Love Me*, New English Library, 1982.

Natale, Frank, *Trance Dance: The Dance Of Life*, Element Books (UK), 1995.

Neal, Charles (ed), *Tape Delay*, SAF Publishing (UK), 1992.

Negus, Keith, *Popular Music In Theory*, Polity Press (UK), 1997.

Neville, Richard, *Hippie Hippie Shake*, Bloomsbury (UK), 1995.

Nicholson, Geoff, *Big Noises: Rock Guitar In The 1990's*, Quartet Books (UK), 1992.

Nick Hamlyn (ed.), *Music Master Price Guide For Record Collectors*, Music Master (UK), 1991.

Nite, Norm N., *Rock On Almanac*, Harper Collins (USA), 1993.

Nite, Norm N., *Rock On: The Illustrated Encyclopedia Of Rock 'N' Roll The Solid Gold Years*, Thomas Y. Crowell (USA), 1974.

Nite, Norm N., *Rock On Almanac: First Four Decades Of Rock 'N' Roll-A Chronology*, Harper Collins (USA), 1991.

Nite, Norm N. with Newman, Ralph M., *Rock On Vol 11: The Illustrated Encyclopedia Of Rock 'N' Roll: The Modern Years*, Thomas Y. Crowell (USA), 1978.

No author listed, *The Stars Of Rock 'N' Roll: Book 2*, Alan Keen, 1970.

No author listed, *The Stars Of Rock 'N' Roll*, Alan Keen, 1966.

No author listed, *Rhythm And Resistance*, Praeger (USA), 1990.

No author listed, *The Island Book Of Posters*, Island (UK), 1992.

No author listed, *The Moment: 25 Years Of Rock Photography*, Paper Tiger (UK), 1995.

No author listed, *What Kind Of Houseparty Is This*, MIY Publishing (UK), 1995.

No editor listed, *The Illustrated Encyclopedia Of Rock*, Hamlyn (UK).

No editor listed, *The History Of Rock*, Orbis (UK), 1982.

No editor listed, *The Bootleg Bible*, Babylon Books (UK), 1981.

No editor listed, *Soul, Pop, Rock, Stars, Superstars*, Octopus Books (UK), 1974.

No editor listed, *Rock Guitarists: From The Pages Of Guitar Player Magazine*, Guitar Player Books (USA), 1975.

No editor listed, *Rock Guitarists*, Rock Player, 1974.

No editor listed, *Rock 'N' Roll Singers Survival Handbook*, H. Leonard (USA), 1992.

No editor listed, *Music Master CD Catalogue*, MBC Information Service, 1991.

No editor listed, *It's Rock Scene*, Purnell (UK), 1964.

No editor listed, *Hot Wacks Book X1V*, Hot Wacks Press, 1990.

No editor listed, *Alphabeat: Who's Who In Pop*, Century 2, 1969.

No editor listed, *25 Years Of Rock & Roll*, Harrison House, 1979.

No editor listed, *Radio One Story Of Pop: The First Encyclopedia Of Pop*, Phoebus, 1973.

No editor listed, *Harmony Illustrated Encyclopedia Of Rock*, Harmony Books (USA).

No editor listed, *The ASCAP Biographical Dictionary (Of Composers, Authors)*, R.R. Bowker (UK), 1980.

No editor listed, *Complete NME Album Charts*, Boxtree (UK), 1995.

No editor listed, *Complete NME Singles Charts*, Boxtree (UK), 1995.

No editor listed, *Rolling Stone Images Of Rock And Roll*, Virgin Books (UK), 1995.

Norman, Philip, *The Road Goes On Forever: Portraits From A Journey In Contemporary Music*, Elm Tree Press (UK), 1982.

Norton York (ed.), *The Rock File: Making It In The Music Business*, Oxford University Press, 1991.

Nugent, Stephen and Gillett, Charlie, *Rock Almanac: Top 20 American And British Singles And Albums Of The Fifties*, Anchor Books, 1978.

O'Brien, George, *Out Of Our Minds*, Blackstaff Press (UK), 1995.

O'Brien, Karen, *Hymn To Her: Women Musician's Talk*, Virago (UK), 1995.

O'Neil, Thomas, *The Grammys For The Record*, Penguin, 1993.

Obst, Lynda Rosen, *The Sixties: The Decade Remembered Now By The People Who Lived It Then*, Rolling Stone Press/Random House (USA), 1977.

Ochs, Michael (ed), *1000 Record Covers*, Taschen (Germany), 1997.

Oliver,Vaughan, et al, *Album Cover Album 6*, Dragon's World (UK), 1993.

Olofsson, Hans, *Stora Popboken: Svensk Rock & Pop 1954-1969*, Premium Publishing (Sweden), 1996.

Olofsson, Jan, *My '60s*, Taschen (Germany), 1995.

Orloff, Katherine, *Rock 'N' Roll Woman*, Nash, 1974.

Osborne, Jerry, *The Complete Library Of American Phonograph Recordings*, Jerry Osborne, 1993.

Osbourne, Roger, Barry Lazell And Michael Gray (eds.), *Thirty Years Of NME Album Charts*, Boxtree (UK), 1994.

Palmer, Myles, *New Wave Explosion: How Punk Became New Wave Became The 80's*, Proteus (UK), 1982.

Palmer, Robert, *Rock & Roll: An Unruly History*, Harmony Books (USA), 1995.

Palmer, Robert, *Dancing In The Street: A Rock 'n' Roll History*,

BBC Books (UK), 1996.

Palmer, Tony, *Born Under A Bad Sign*, Kimber (UK), 1970.

Paraire, Philippe, *50 Years Of Pop Music*, Chambers, 1992.

Pareles, Jon, and Patricia Romanowski, *Rolling Stone Encyclopedia Of Rock & Roll*, Summit Books (USA), 1983.

Parsons, Tony, *Dispatches From The Front Line Of Popular Culture*, Virgin (UK), 1994.

Pascall, Jeremy, *The Illustrated History Of Rock Music*, Hamlyn (UK), 1978.

Pascall, Jeremy & Burt, Rob, *The Stars And Superstars Of Rock*, Octopus (UK), 1974.

Passman, Donald S., *All You Need To Know About The Music Business*, Simon & Schuster (USA).

Pavletich, Aida, *Sirens Of Song: The Popular Female Vocalist In America*, Da Capo (USA), 1982.

Pavletich, Aida, *Rock'A'Bye Baby*, Doubleday (USA), 1980.

Peace, Warren, *The Peace Record Guide*, 1988.

Pearce, Kevin, *Something Beginning With O*, Heavenly (UK), 1992.

Peck, Ira (ed), *The New Sound/Yes*, Four Winds Press (USA), 1966.

Pelletier, Paul, *The Essential 1950s British Singles Price Guide*, Record Information Services (UK), 1993.

Pelletier, Paul Maurice (Editor), *Essential British Price Guide To Collecting 45 & 78 RPM Singles*, Record Information Services (UK), 1991.

Pencil, Savage, *Rock 'n' Roll Necronomicon*, Shock Publications (UK), 1992.

Perry, Charles & Miles Barry, *I Want To Take You Higher: The Psychedelic Years 1965-69*, Chronicle Books (USA), 1997.

Perry, Neil, *Rare Singles From The Beat And Psychedelic Era*, Perry & Perry (UK), 1990.

Perry, Paul & Babbs, Ken, *On The Bus*, Plexus (UK), 1992.

Perry, Tim & Glinert, Ed, *Fodor's Rock And Roll Traveler USA*, Fodor's (USA), 1996.

Petrie, Gavin, *Rock Life*, Hamlyn (UK), 1974.

Pidgeon, John, *Classic Albums*, BBC Publications (UK), 1990.

Pleasants, Henry, *The Greatest American Popular Singers*, Victor Gollancz (UK), 1974.

Pokora, Hans, *Rare Record Cover Book*, Collect Records (UK), 1996.

Pollard, Christopher, *Good Compact Disc Guide*, Tiptree Book Services (UK), 1991.

Pollock, Bruce, *When Rock Was Young: A Nostalgic Review Of The Top 40 Era*, Holt, Rinehart & Winston (USA), 1981.

Pollock, Bruce, *In Their Own Words: Twenty Successful Songwriters Tell How They Write Their Song*, Macmillan, 1975.

Pollock, Bruce, *Hipper Than Our Kids: Rock 'N' Roll Journal Of The Baby-Boom Gener...*, Schirmer Books (USA), 1993.

Porter, Cole, *Gay Divorce/Night And Day*, Harms.

Power, Vincent, *Send 'Em Home Sweating*, , 1990.

Powers, Ann & Evelyn, McDonnell (Ed), *Rock She Wrote: Women Writing About Rock Pop And Rap*, Plexus Publishing (UK), 1995.

Prakel, David, *Rock On Compact Disc: A Critical Guide*, Salamander (UK), 1988.

Preston, Mike, *Tele-Tunes 1993*, Mike Preston Music, 1993.

Pringle, Andy, *Where Are They Now?*, Two Heads (UK), 1998.

Propes, Steve, *Those Oldies But Goodies: A Guide To 50's Record Collecting*, Macmillan, 1973.

Rachlin, Harvey, *The Songwriter's Handbook*, Funk & Wagnalls, 1977.

Rachlin, Harvey, *The Encyclopedia Of The Music Business*, Harper & Row (USA), 1981.

Ramet, Sabrina Petra (ed.), *Rocking The State: Rock Music & Politics In Eastern Europe & Russia*, Westview, 1994.

Raphael, Amy, *Never Mind the Bollocks: Women Rewrite Rock*, Virago (UK), 1995.

Raphael, Amy, *Grrrls: Viva Rock Divas*, St Martins Press (USA).

Read, Mike, *Labatt's 500: Britain's All-Time Favourite Tracks*, Mandarin (UK), 1992.

Record Collector, *Record Collector Rare Record Price Guide 1993*, Diamond Publishing (UK), 1993.

Record Collector, *Record Collector Rare Record Price Guide: 4th Edition 1997*, Diamond Publishing (UK), 1997.

Redd, Lawrence N., *Rock Is Rhythm And Blues: The Impact Of Mass Media*, Michigan State University Press (USA), 1974.

Redhead, Steve, *The End Of The Century Party: Youth And Pop Towards 2000*, Manchester University Press, 1990.

Reed, John (ed.), *Record Collector Rare Record Price Guide 1995*, Diamond Publishing (UK), 1994.

Rees, Crampton & Lazell, *Guinness Book Of Rock Stars*, Guinness Publishing (UK), 1991.

Rees, Dafydd, *Star-File Annual: Incorporating The Year's Record Information From Music Week*, Hamlyn (UK), 1978.

Rees, Dafydd & Crampton, Luke, *Q Encyclopedia Of Rock Stars*, Dorling Lindersley (UK), 1996.

Rees, Tony, *Rare Rock: A Collectors' Guide*, Blandford Press (UK), 1985.

Rees-Parnall, Hilary, *Tune In: Pop Music In Britain Today*, Harrap (UK), 1981.

Reynolds, Simon, *Blissed Out*, Serpent's Tail (UK), 1990.

Reynolds, Simon, And Joy Press, *The Sex Revolts: Gender, Rebellion And Rock & Roll*, Serpent's Tail (UK), 1995.

Rhode, H.K., *The Gold Of Rock And Roll, 1955-1967*, Arbor House (USA), 1970.

Rickard, Graham, *Famous Names In Popular Music*, Wayland, 1980.

Rimler, W., *Not Fade Away: Comparison Of Jazz Age With Rock Era Pop Song Composers*, Pierian Press (USA), 1990.

Rivelli, Pauline and Levin, Robert, *The Rock (Jazz & Pop) Giants*, World Books, 1970.

Rivelli, Pauline and Levin, Robert, *Giants Of Rock Music*, Da Capo (USA), 1981.

Roach, Martin, *The Right To Imagination And Madness*, Independent Music Press (UK), 1994.

Roach, Martin Neil, *Eight Legged Atomic Dustbin Will Eat Itself*, Independent Music Publications (UK), 1992.

Robbins, Ira (ed), *Trouser Press Guide To 90s Rock*, Fireside Books (USA), 1997.

Robbins, Ira A. (ed.), *The New Trouser Press Record Guide*, Scribners (USA), 1985.

Roberts, Chris (ed), *Idle Worship*, Harper Collins, 1994.

Robinson, Richard, *The Rock Scene*, Pyramid, 1971.

Robinson, Richard, *Rock Superstars*, Pyramid, 1973.

Robinson, Richard, *Pop, Rock And Soul*, Pyramid, 1972.

Robinson, Richard, *Electric Rock*, Pyramid, 1971.

Rockwell, John, *All American Music: Composition In The Late 20th Century*, Alfred A. Knopf (USA), 1983.

Rodnitsky, Jerome L., *Minstrels Of The Dawn: The Folk-Protest Singer As Cultural Hero*, Nelson-Hall (USA), 1976.

Rogan, Johnny, *Starmakers & Svengalis*, Macdonald/Queen Anne Press (UK), 1988.

Rogers, Dave, *Rock 'N' Roll*, Routledge & Kegan Paul (UK), 1982.

Rohde, Kandy H., *The Gold Of Rock And Roll 1955-1967*, Arbor House (USA), 1970.

Rolling Stone (ed.), *The Rolling Stone Record Review/Volume 11*, Straight Arrow/Pocket Books (USA), 1974.

Rolling Stone (ed.), *The Rolling Stone Record Review*, Straight Arrow/Pocket Books (USA), 1971.

Rolling Stone (ed.), *The Rolling Stone Interviews 1967-1980*, Rolling Stone Press/St. Martins Press (USA), 1981.

Rolling Stone (ed.), *The Rolling Stone Interviews*, Straight Arrow (USA), 1971.

Rolling Stone Editors, *What A Long Strange Trip It's Been: 20 Years Of Rolling Stones*, Ebury Press (UK), 1988.

Rolling Stone Editors, *The 100 Greatest Albums Of The 80s*, St Martin's Press (USA), 1990.

Rollinson, Anthony, *Twenty Missed Beats: The Portsmouth Music Scene 1977-1996*, Mouthy Publications (UK), 1996.

Romanowski, Patricia, And Holly George-Warren (eds.), *The New Rolling Stone Encyclopedia Of Rock And Roll*, Fireside (USA), 1996.

Ross, Michael, *Rock Beyond Woodstock*, Petersen, 1970.

Roxon, Lillian, *Lillian Roxon's Rock Encyclopedia*, Workman/Grosset & Dunlap (USA), 1969.

Runswick, Daryl, *Rock, Jazz And Pop Arranging*, Faber & Faber (UK), 1992.

Russell, Tom & Tyson, Sylvia (eds), *And Then I Wrote: The Songwriter Speaks*, Arsenal Pulp Press (USA), 1996.

Ryback, Timothy W., *Rock Around The Bloc: A History Of Rock Music In Eastern Europe & The Soviet Uni*, Oxford University Press, 1990.

Sackett, Susan, *Hollywood Sings! An Inside Look At Sixty Years Of Academy Award Nominations*, Billboard Books (USA), 1995.

Sadie, Stanley (ed.), *20th Century American Masters*, Macmillan, 1980.

Sander, Ellen, *Trips: Rock Life In The Sixties*, Scribners (USA), 1973.

Sanjek, Russell & Sanjek, David, *American Popular Music Business In The Twentieth Century*, Oxford University Press (USA), 1991.

Santelli, Robert, *Aquarius Rising: The Rock Festival Years*, Delta/Dell (USA), 1980.

Santoro, Gene, *Dancing In Your Head: Jazz, Blues, Rock And Beyond*, Oxford University Press (USA), 1994.

Saporita, Jay, *Pourin' It All Out*, Citadel Press, 1980.

Sarlin, Bob, *Turn It Up! (I Can't Hear The Words)*, Coronet (UK), 1975.

Savage, Jon, *Time Travel: From The Sex Pistols To Nirvana 1977-96*, Chatto & Windus (UK), 1996.

Savage, Jon, *Time Travel: From Sex Pistols To Nirvana*, Chatto & Windus (UK), 1997.

Savage, Jon (ed), *The Hacienda Must Be Built*, IMP (UK), 1992.

Savile, Jimmy, *Love Is An Uphill Thing*, Coronet (UK), 1976.

Savile, Jimmy, *God'll Fix It*, Mowbrays (UK), 1979.

Schafer, William J., *Rock Music: Where It's Been, What It Means, Where It's Going*, Augsburg, 1972.

Schaffner, Nicholas, *The British Invasion: From The First Wave To The New Wave*, McGraw-Hill (USA), 1982.

Scheurer, Timothy, *Born In The U.S.A.*, University Press Of Mississippi (UK), 1993.

Schinder, Scott, *Rolling Stone's Alt-Rock-A-Rama*, Delta (USA), 1996.

Schmidt, Paul William, *History Of the Ludwig Drum Company*, Centerstream Publishing (USA), 1992.

Schwartz, Daylle Deanna, *The Real Deal: How To Get Signed To A Record Label From A -Z*, Billboard Books (USA), 1997.

Scoppa, Bud, *The Rock People*, Scholastic Book Service (USA), 1973.

Scothrum, Jan, *Rock/Beat*, Politkens Forlag (Denmark), 1974.

Scott, Barry, *We Had Joy, We Had Fun*, Faber & Faber (UK), 1995.

Scott, Frank, And Al Ennis, *Roots And Rhythm Guide To Rock*, Cappella Books (USA), 1993.

Sculatti And Seay, Gene & Davin, *San Francisco Nights: The Psychedelic Music Trip 1965-1968*, Sidgwick & Jackson (UK), 1985.

Selvin, Joel, *Monterey Pop*, Plexus (UK), 1992.

Selvin, Joel, *Summer Of Love: Story Of LSD, Rock & Roll, Free Love & High Times In The Wild...*, Dutton (USA), 1994.

Selvin, Joel, *Summer Of Love: The Inside Story Of Rock 'n' Roll, LSD, Free Love, High Times*, Plume Books (USA), 1995.

Selvin, Joel, *San Francisco: The Musical History Tour*, Chronicle Books (USA), 1996.

Selvin, Joel & Marshall, Jim, *Monterey Pop*, Plexus (UK), 1992.

Shannon, Bob & Javna, John, *Behind The Hits: Inside Stories Of Classic Pop And Rock & Roll*, Warner Books (USA), 1986.

Shapiro, Harry, *A-Z Of Rock Drummers*, Proteus (UK), 1982.

Shapiro, Nat & Pollock, Bruce, *Popular Music: 1900 To The Present Day (Various Volumes)*, Gale Research (USA), 0.

Sharma, Sanjay (ed) and others, *Dis-Orientating Rhythms: The Politics Of The New Asian Dance Music*, Zed Books (UK), 1997.

Sharp, Ken & Sulpy, Doug, *Power Pop: Coversations With The Power Pop Elite*, Pop Tomes (USA), 1997.

Shaw, Arnold, *The Rockin' 50s: The Decade That Transformed The Pop Music Scene*, Hawthorn Books (USA), 1974.

Shaw, Arnold, *The Rock Revolution*, Collier (USA), 1969.

Shaw, Eddie, *Date All Those English 78s*, Private publication (UK), 1995.

Shaw, Greg, *New Wave On Record 1975-1978: Volume One England And Europe*, Greg Shaw, 1979.

Shaw, Greg, *Rolling Stone Illustrated History Of Rock & Roll*, Random House (USA), 1980.

Shevey, Sandra, *Ladies Of Pop-Rock*, Scholastic Book Service (USA), 1972.

Shirley, Ian, *Dark Entries: Bauhaus And Beyond*, SAF, 1995.

Silver, Caroline, *The Pop Makers: British Rock 'N' Roll*, Scholastic Book Services (USA), 1966.

Silver, Caroline, *The Pop Mainstream*, Scholastic Book Service (USA), 1966.

Simon, George Thomas, *The Best Of The Music Makers: From Acuff To Ellington To Presley To Sinatra To Z*, Doubleday (USA), 1979.

Simpson, Jeff (ED), *Radio 1's Classic Interviews: 25 Rock Greats In Their Own Words*, BBC Books (UK), 1992.

Sinclair, Marianne, *Those Who Died Young: Cult Heroes Of The Twentieth Century*, Plexus (UK), 1979.

Slonimsky, Nicolas, *Music Since 1900. 4th Ed.*, Scribners, 1971.

Small, Robert, Coletti, Alex and Hinckley, David, *MTV Unplugged Book*, Simon & Shuster (USA), 1995.

Smith, Geoff & Walker Smith, Nicola, *New Voices: American Composers Talk Anout Their Music*, Amadaus Press (USA), 1995.

Smith, Giles, *Lost In Music: A Pop Odyssey (fiction)*, Picador (UK), 1995.

Smith, Joe, *Off The Record: An Oral History Of Popular Music*, Warner Books (USA), 1988.

Smith, Martin & Ash, Darren, *Music Factory BPM Bible*, Music Factory, 1992.

Smith, Pete, *The Collectors Guide To U.K. Label Northern Soul*, Pete Smith (UK), 1993.

Smith, Richard, *Seduced And Abandoned: Essays On Gay Men And Popular Music*, Cassell (UK), 1995.

Smith, Steve, *Bits & Pieces: The Penguin Book Of Rock & Pop Facts & Trivia*, Penguin, 1989.

Smith, Steve, *Rock Day By Day*, Guinness Books (UK), 1987.

Smith, Timothy D'Arch, *Peepin' In A Seafood Store: Some Pleasures Of Rock Music*, Russell, 1992.

Smith, Wes, *Pied Pipers Of Rock 'N' Roll*, Longstreet Press, 1990.

Solomon, Clive, *Record Hits: The British Top 50 Charts 1952-1977*, Omnibus Press (UK), 1979.

Somma, Robert, *No One Waved Goodbye: A Casualty Report On Rock And Roll*, Fusion Magazine/Outerbridge & Dienstfrey (USA), 1971.

Southall, Brian, Vince, Peter and Rouse, Allan, *Abbey Road*, Omnibus Press (UK), 1997.

Spencer, Chris (ed.), *Who's Who Of Australian Rock*, Five Mile Press (Australia), 1994.

Spinner, Stephanie, *Rock Is Beautiful*, Dell (USA), 1970.

Spitz, Robert Stephen, *The Making Of Superstars: Artists And*

Executives Of The Rock Music World, Anchor Press/Doubleday (USA), 1978.

Spitz, Robert Stephen, *Barefoot In Babylon: The Creation Of The Woodstock Music Festival 1969*, Viking, 1979.

Stambler, Irvin (ed.), *Encyclopedia Of Pop, Rock & Soul*, Macmillan, 1993.

Stambler, Irwin (ed.), *The Encyclopaedia Of Pop, Rock & Soul*, Macmillan, 1989.

Stanley, Lawrence A., *Rap: The Lyrics*, Penguin, 1993.

Staveacre, Tony, *The Songwriters*, BBC (UK), 1980.

Stevenson, Ray, *Regeneration*, Symbiosis Books/Omnibus, 1987.

Stevenson, Ray, *Photo Past 1966-1986*, Symbiosis, 1988.

Steward, Sue & Garratt, Sheryl, *Signed, Sealed And Delivered: True Life Stories Of Women In Pop*, Serpent's Tail (UK), 1991.

Steward, Tony, *Cool Cats 25 Years Of Rock 'N' Roll Style*, Eel Pie (UK), 1981.

Stokes, Geoffrey, *Star-Making Machinery: The Odyssey Of An Album*, Bobbs-Merrill (USA), 1976.

Stone, Terri and Schwartz, David, *Music Producers*, H. Leonard Publishing (USA), 1992.

Strong, M. C., *The Great Rock Discography*, Canongate Books (UK), 1995.

Studer, Wayne, *Rock On The Wild Side: Gay Male Images In Popular Music Of The Rock Era*, Leyland/Turnaround, 1994.

Stump, Paul, *The Music's All That Matters: A History Of Progressive Rock*, Quartet Books (UK).

Sugerman, Danny, *Wonderland Avenue: Tales Of Glamour And Excess*, Penguin, 1989.

Sumrall, Harry, *Pioneers Of Rock N Roll: 100 Artists Who Changed The Face Of Rock*, Billboard Publications (USA), 1994.

Swann, Mike, *How Many Roads?*, Temple House, 1989.

Sweeney, Philip, *World Music*, Virgin Books (UK), 1990.

Swern, Phil & Greenfield, Shaun, *30 Years Of Number 1's*, BBC (UK), 1991.

Szemere, Anna, *Rockin' The Boat: Mass Music And Mass Movement*, South End Press, 1992.

Tanner, John F., *Hits Through The Years: 1956-1962 Rock 'N' Roll Era*, J.F.T., 1992.

Taylor, Paul, *Popular Music Since 1955: A Critical Guide To the Literature*, Mansell (UK), 1985.

The Songwriters Guild Of Great Britain, *Sixty Years Of British Hits*, 1968.

Thomas, Patricia and Rees, Dafydd, *Record Business: Indie Catalogue 1981-82*, Record Business (UK), 1979.

Thomson, Liz, *New Women In Rock*, Omnibus Press (UK), 1982.

Thorgerson, Storm, *Classic Album Covers Of The 60s*, Paper Tiger (UK), 1989.

Tobler, John, *Sixties: A Complete Rock 'N' Roll Chronicle*, Hamlyn (UK), 1992.

Tobler, John, *Seventies: A Complete Rock 'N' Roll Chronicle*, Hamlyn (UK), 1992.

Tobler, John, *NME's Rock and Roll Years*, Hamlyn (UK), 1992.

Tobler, John, *Guitar Heroes*, Marshall Cavendish (UK), 1978.

Tobler, John, *This Day In Rock*, Carlton (UK), 1993.

Tobler, John, *100 Great Albums Of The Sixties*, Little, Brown (UK), 1994.

Tobler, John & Frame, Peter, *25 Years Of Rock*, Hamlyn (UK), 1980.

Tobler, John & Grundy, Stuart, *The Record Producers*, BBC (UK), 1982.

Tobler, John & Grundy, Stuart, *The Guitar Greats*, BBC Publications (UK), St. Martins Press (USA), 1983.

Tobler, John & Jones, Alan, *The Rock Lists Album*, Plexus (UK), 1983.

Tobler, John (ed.), *NME Who's Who In Rock 'N' Roll*, Hamlyn (UK), 1991.

Too Fast To Live, *Too Young To Die*, Plexus (UK), 1982.

Toop, David, *Rap Attack*, South End, 1984.

Toop, David, *Ocean Of Sound: Aether Talk, Ambient Sound, Imaginary Worlds*, Serpent's Tail (UK), 1996.

Tosches, Nick, *Unsung Heroes Of Rock 'n' Roll*, Scribners (USA), 1984.

Tremlett, George, *Rock Gold: The Music Millionaires*, Unwin Hyman (UK), 1990.

Troitsky, Artemy, *Tusovka*, Omnibus Press (UK), 1990.

Troitsky, Artemy, *Back In The USSR: The True Story Of Rock In Russia*, Omnibus Press (UK), 1988.

Trow, Mike, *The Pulse Of '64: The Mersey Beat*, Vantage, 1978.

Trynka, Paul, *Rock Hardware: 40 Years Of Rock Instrumentation*, Miller Freeman (USA), 1996.

Trynka, Paul (ed.), *The Electric Guitar*, Virgin Books (UK), 1993.

Tudor, Dean and Tudor, Nancy, *Contemporary Popular Music*, Libraries Unlimited, 1979.

Turner, Steve, *Hungry For Heaven: Rock And Roll And The Search For Redemption*, Virgin Books (UK) , 1988.

Umphred, Neil, *Goldmine's Rock 'n' Roll 45rpm Record Price Guide*, Krause Publications (USA), 2147483647.

Umphred, Neil, *Goldmine's Rock 'n' Roll 45 rpm Record Price Guide*, Krause Publications (USA), 1992.

Umphred, Neil (Ed) *Goldmine's Price Guide to Collectable Record Albums 1949-89*, Krause Publications (USA), 2147483647.

Uslan, Michael & Solomon, Bruce, *Dick Clark's The First 25 Years Of Rock And Roll*, Dell (USA), 1981.

Van der Kiste, John, *Roxeventies: Popular Music In Britain 1970-79*, Kawabata Press, 1982.

Van der Merwe, Peter, *Origins Of The Popular Style: The Antecedents Of 20th-Century Popular Music*, Oxford University Press, 1991.

Vane, V., and Andrea Juno (eds.), *Incredibly Strange Music Volume 2*, Re/Search, 1994.

Various writers, *The Day The Music Died*, Plexus (UK), 1990.

Vermorel, Fred, *The Punk Encyclopedia*, Omnibus Press (UK), 1981.

Virgin, *Rock Yearbook*, Virgin Books (UK), 1993.

Vorda, Allan, *Psychedelic Psounds*, Borderline Productions (UK), 1995.

Wadhams, Wayne, *Sound Advice: Musician's Guide To the Record Industry*, Schirmer (USA), 1990.

Wagstaff, John, *International Record & CD Price Guide 1950-1990*, CD Collector, 1990.

Wale, Michael, *Voxpop: Profiles Of The Pop Process*, Harrap (UK), 1972.

Walker, Bob (ED), *Hot Wacks Book XV*, Hot Wacks Press (Canada), 1992.

Walker, Dave, *American Rock 'N' Roll Tour: Three Hundred Rock 'N' Roll Sights*, Thunder's Mouth Press (USA), 1993.

Walker, Graham (ed.), *The Chart Book 1991*, Spotlight (UK), 1992.

Wall, Mick, *Market Square Heroes*, Sidgwick & Jackson (UK), 1988.

Walters, David, *The Children Of Nuggets*, Popular Culture, 1990.

Ward, Ed; Stokes, Geoffrey; Tucker, Ken, *Rock Of Ages: The Rolling Stone History Of Rock And Roll*, Penguin (UK), Summit (USA), 1986.

Warner, Alan, *Who Sang What In Rock 'N' Roll*, Blandford Press (UK) , 1990.

Warner, Jay, *The Billboard Book Of American Singing Groups 1940-1990*, Billboard Books (USA), 1993.

Warner, Simon, *Rockspeak: Language Of Rock And Pop*, Blandford Press (UK), 1995.

Webber, Graeme, *Australian Rock Folio*, Music Industry Photos.

Wedgbury, David, and Tracy, John, *As Years Go By*, Pavilion Books (UK), 1993.

Weinberg, Max & Santelli, Robert, *Big Beat: Conversations With Rock's Great Drummers*, Billboard Publications (USA).

Weinberg, Max with Santelli, Robert, *The Big Beat*, Contemporary Books (USA), 1984.

Weisband, Eric (ed) and Craig Marks (ed), *Spin Alternative Record Guide*, Vintage (USA), 1995.

Wenner, Jann, *20 Years Of Rolling Stone*, Ebury Press (UK), 1987.

Wenner, Jann (ed.), *The Rolling Stone Interviews, Vol. 2*, Warner Books (USA), 1973.

Wheaton, Roma, *Three Steps To Heaven - Untimely Deaths In The Music World*, Warner Books (USA), 1993.

Whitburn, Joel, *Bubbling Under The Hot 100 1959-1985*, Record Research (USA), 1992.

Whitburn, Joel, *Top Rhythm & Blues Records 1972-1973*, Record Research (USA), 1974.

Whitburn, Joel, *Top Rhythm & Blues Records 1949-1971*, Record Research (USA), 1972.

Whitburn, Joel, *Top Pop Singles 1955-1990*, Record Research (USA), 1991.

Whitburn, Joel, *Top Pop Artists And Records 1952-1978*, Record Research (USA), 1979.

Whitburn, Joel, *Top LPs 1949-1972*, Record Research (USA), 1973.

Whitburn, Joel, *Top Easy Listening Records 1962-1974*, Record Research (USA), 1975.

Whitburn, Joel, *Pop Singles Annual 1955-1990*, Record Research (USA), 1991.

Whitburn, Joel, *Pop Memories 1890-1954*, Record Research (USA), 1986.

Whitburn, Joel, *Bubbling Under The Hot 100 1959-1981*, Billboard Publications (USA), 1982.

Whitburn, Joel, *Billboard Top 3000 Plus, 1955-1990*, Record Research (USA), 1991.

Whitburn, Joel, *Billboard Hot 100 Charts (The Sixties)*, Record Research (USA), 1990.

Whitburn, Joel, *Billboard Book Of Top 40 Albums*, Omnibus Press (UK), 1991.

Whitburn, Joel, *Billboard Pop Charts 1955 - 1959*, Record Research (USA), 1993.

Whitburn, Joel (ed.), *Top R&B Singles 1942-1995*, Record Research (USA), 1996.

Whitcomb, Ian, *Rock Odyssey*, Doubleday (USA), 1983.

Whitcomb, Ian, *Whole Lotta' Shakin': A Rock 'N' Roll Scrapbook*, Arrow Books (UK), 1982.

Whitcomb, Ian, *After The Ball*, Allen Lane (UK), 1973.

White, Adam, *Billboard Book Of Gold & Platinum Records*, Billboard Publications (USA).

White, Adam, And Fred Bronson, *Billboard Book Of R&B Hits*, Billboard Publications (USA), 1994.

White, Mark, *You Must Remember This... 'Popular Songwriters 1900-1980'*, Frederick Warne (UK), 1983.

White, Timothy, *Rock Lives: Profiles And Interviews*, Henry Holt (USA), Omnibus Press (UK), 1989.

White, Timothy, *Music To My Ears*, Henry Holt (USA), 1997.

Whiteley, Sheila (ed.), *Sexing The Groove: Popular Music And Gender*, Routledge (UK), 1997.

Wicke, Peter, *Rock Music: Culture, Aesthetics And Sociology*, Cambridge University Press (UK), 1990.

Wicke, Peter, *Culture Aesthetics And Sociology*, Cambridge University Press (UK), 1990.

Wilder, Alec, *American Popular Songs, The Great Innovators, 1900-1950*, Oxford University Press, 1972.

Wilkie, Jim, *Blue Suede Brogans: Secret Life Of Scottish Rock Music*, Mainstream (UK), 1990.

Wilks, Max, *They're Playing Our Song*, Atheneum Press (UK), 1973.

Williams, Paul, *Outlaw Blues: A Book Of Rock Music*, E.P. Dutton (USA), 1969.

Williams, Paul, *Rock 'n' Roll: The 100 Best Singles*, Carroll & Graf (USA), 1993.

Willis, Ellen, *Trips: Rock Life In The 60s*, Scribners (USA), 1973.

Wilson, Mary, *How To Make It In The Rock Business*, Columbus, 1988.

Wise, Herbert A., *Professional Rock 'N' Roll*, Macmillan (USA), 1967.

Wood, Graham, *An A To Z Of Rock 'N' Roll*, Studio Vista (UK), 1971.

Wooton, Richard, *Honky Tonkin': A Travel Guide To American Music*, East Woods Press, 1980.

Worth, Fred L., *Thirty Years Of Rock 'N' Roll Trivia*, Warner Books (USA), 1980.

Yamagauchi, Yoshiko, *Daremo Kakankatta Arab (Arabia No One Has Written About)*, Tokyo, 1974.

York, William, *Who's Who In Rock: An A-Z Of Groups, Performers, Producers, Session Men*, Omnibus Press (UK), 1979.

Yorke, Ritchie, *The History Of Rock 'N' Roll*, Methuen (UK), 1971.

Yorke, Ritchie, *Axes, Chops & Hot Licks: The Canadian Rock Music Scene*, M. G. Hurtig (USA), 1971.

Zalkind, Ronald, *Contemporary Music Almanac 1980/81*, Macmillan (USA), 1980.

Zollo, Paul, *Songwriters On Songwriters*, Writers Digest Book (USA), 1991.

Punk

Arnold, Gina, *Kiss This: Punk In The Present Tense*, Pan Books (UK), 1998.

Boot, Adrian and Salewicz, Chris, *Punk: The Illustrated History Of A Music Revolution*, Boxtree (UK), 1996.

Echenberg, Erica and Mark P, *And God Created Punk*, Virgin Books (UK), 1996.

Gibbs, Alvin, *Destroy: The Definitive History Of Punk*, Britannia Press (UK), 1996.

Gimarc, George, *Punk Diary 1970-1979*, St. Martins Press (USA), 1994.

Home, Stewart, *Cranked Up Really High: Genre Theory And Punk Rock*, Codex, 1997.

Lazell, Barry, *Punk: An A-Z*, Hamlyn (UK), 1995.

Manley, Frank, *Smash The State: A Discography Of Canadian Punk 1977-92*, Cargo (Canada), 1993.

Marcus, Greil, *In The Fascist Bathroom: Writings On Punk 1977-92*, Viking (USA), 1993.

Marcus, Greil, *Ranters And Crowd Pleasers: Punk In Pop Music 1977-92*, Doubleday (USA), 1993.

McNeil, Legs and McCain, Gillian, *Please Kill Me: The Uncensored Oral History Of Punk*, Grove Press (USA), Little Brown (UK), 1996.

Savage, Jon, *England's Dreaming: Sex Pistols And Punk Rock*, Faber & Faber (UK), 1991.

R&B

Berry, Jason, *Up From The Cradle Of Jazz*, University Of Georgia Press (USA).

Bryan, Bo, *Shag: The Dance Legend*, Foundation Books (USA), 1996.

Busnar, Gene, *The Rhythm And Blues Story*, J. Messner (USA).

Edwards, Joseph, *Top 10's And Trivia Of Rock & Roll And Rhythm & Blues, 1950-1980*, Blueberry Hill (USA), 1981.

Gart, Galen, *First Pressings: The History Of Rythm & Blues Vols.1: 1951 & 2: 1952*, Big Nickel Publications (USA), 1992.

George, Nelson, *The Death Of Rhythm & Blues*, Omnibus Press (UK), 1988.

Groia, Philip, *They All Sang On The Corner*, Edmund

Publishing (USA), 1974.

Guralnick, Peter, *Sweet Soul Music*, Harper & Row (USA), 1986.

Heckstall-Smith, Dick, *The Safest Place In The World: A Personal History Of British Rhythm And Blues*, Quartet Books (UK), 1989.

Hildebrand, Lee, *Stars Of Soul And Rhythm And Blues*, Billboard (USA), 1995.

Larkin, Colin, *Virgin Encyclopedia Of R&B And Soul*, Virgin Books (UK), 1998.

Merlis, Bob & Seay, Davin, *Heart & Soul: A Celebration Of Black Music Style In America 1930-1975*, Stewart Tabori & Chang (USA), 1997.

No editor listed, *Yesterday's Memories*, Freebizak (USA).

Osborne, Jerry, *Blues, Rhythm & Blues, Soul*, O'Sullivan Woodside (USA).

Pavlow, Big Al, *Big Al Pavlow's The R&B Book*, Music House (USA).

Payne, Jim , *Give The Drummer Some: The Great Drummers Of R&B, Soul And Funk*, Face The Music (USA), 1997.

Shaw, Arnold, *Honkers And Shouters: The Golden Years Of Rhythm & Blues*, Collier Books (USA), 1978.

Wexler, Jerry, And David Ritz, *Rhythm And The Blues: A Life In American Music*, Knopf (USA), 1993.

Whitburn, Joel, *Top R&B 1942-1988*, Record Research (USA), 1986.

Rap

Cross, Brian, With Raegan Kelly And T-Love, *It's Not About A Salary: Rap, Race And Resistance In Los Angeles*, Verso (UK), 1994.

Fernando Jnr., S.H., *The New Beats: Exporing The Music, Culture And Attitudes Of Hip Hop*, Payback (USA), 1995.

Goldstein, Dan (ed), *Rappers Rappin*, Castle Books (UK), 1996.

Larkin, Colin (ed.), *Guinness Who's Who Of Rap, Techno & Dance*, Guinness Publishing (UK), 1994.

Nelson, Havelock & Gonzales, Michael A., *Bring The Noise: A Guide To Rap Music And Hip-Hop*, Harmony Books (USA), 1991.

Rose, Tricia, *Black Noise: Rap Music And Black Culture In Contemporary America*, Wesleyan/University Press Of New England (USA), 1994.

Sexton, Adam (ed.), *Rap On Rap: Straight Talk On Hip-Hop Culture*, Delta Trade Paperbacks (USA), 1994.

Stanley, Lawrence A. & Morley, Jefferson, *Rap: The Lyrics*, Penguin (UK), 1992.

Toop, David, *The Rap Attack*, Pluto Press (UK), 1984.

Record Companies

Bartlette, Reginald J., *Off The Record: Motown by Master Number, 1959-89*, Popular Culture, 1990.

Benjaminson, Peter, *The Story Of Motown*, Grove Press (USA), 1979.

Bianco, David, *Heatwave: The Motown Fact Book*, Pierian Press, 1988.

Cuscuna, Michael, *The Blue Note Label: A Discography*, Greenwood Press, 1988.

Dane, Clifford Victor (ed.), *U.K. Record Industry Annual Survey*, Media Research Publishing (UK), 1993.

Davis, Sharon, *Motown: The History*, Guinness Books (UK), 1989.

Escott, Colin, *Good Rockin' Tonight*, St. Martin's Press (USA), 1991.

Escott, Colin & Hawkins, Martin, *Catalyst: The Sun Records Story*, Aquarius/Argus Books, 1975.

Escott, Colin and Hawkins, Martin, *Sun Records: The Brief History Of The Legendary Record Label*, Omnibus Press (UK), 1980.

Gillett, Charlie, *Making Tracks: The Story Of Atlantic Records*, E.P. Dutton (USA), 1974.

Kelly, Michael 'Doc Rock', *Liberty Records*, McFarland, 1993.

Knoedelseder, William, *A True Story Of MCA, The Business And The Mafia*, Harper Collins (USA), 1993.

Marsh, Graham & Callinghan, Glynn & Cromey, Felix, *The Cover Art Of Blue Note Records*, Collins & Brown (UK), 1991.

Mitchell, Elvis & Torres, Ben Fong, *The Motown Album*, Virgin Books (UK), 1991.

Morse, David, *Motown And The Arrival Of Black Music*, Studio Vista (UK), 1971.

No editor listed, *British Brunswick Singles History: 1952 to 1967*, Record Information Services (UK), 1978.

No editor listed, *British London/London Jazz E.P. Listing*, Record Information Services (UK), 1975.

No editor listed, *British Sue Complete Singles E.P.s & L.P.s Listing*, Record Information Services (UK), 1976.

No editor listed, *British Tamla Motown Complete Listing: Part One (1959 to 1970 inclusive)*, Record Information Services, 1980 (UK).

No editor listed, *British Tamla Motown Complete Listing: Part Two (1971 to August, 1975)*, Record Information Services (UK), 1977.

No editor listed, *British Top Rank - Stateside - Triumph - Palette Singles*, Record Information Services (UK), 1976.

No editor listed, *British Top Rank - Stateside Long-Play Listing*, Record Information Services (UK), 1975.

Rippli, Michel, *King Labels A Discography*, Greenwood Westport, 1985.

Ruppli, Michael, *The Savoy Label: A Discography*, Greenwood Press, 1991.

Ruppli, Michel, *The Aladdin/Imperial Labels*, Greenwood Press, 1992.

Ruppli, Michel, *Atlantic Records: A Discography*, Greenwood Press, 1979.

Ryan, Marc, *Trumpet Records: An Illustrated History With Discography*, Big Nickel Publications (USA), 1992.

Singleton, Raynoma, *Gordy, Berry, Me, And Motown*, Contemporary (USA), 1990.

Sun Records: The Discography, *Vollersode*, Germany, 1987.

Taraborrelli, J. Randy, *Motown: Hot Wax, City Cool And Solid Gold*, Plexus (UK), 1990.

Wade, Dorothy & Picardie, Justine, *Music Man: Ahmet Ertegun, Atlantic Records And The Truimph Of Rock 'N' Roll*, W.W. Norton (USA), 1991.

Westbrooks, Logan & Williams, Lance, *The Anatomy Of A Record Company*, Westbrooks (USA), 1981.

Whelan, Keith, *Directory Of Record And CD Retailers 1990-1991*, Power Communication Group, 1990.

Reggae

Bader, Stascha, *Words Like Fire: Dancehall Reggae And Ragga Muffin*, M. Schwinn. (Germany), 1993.

Boot, Adrian & Thomas, Michael, *Jamaica: Babylon On A Thin Wire*, Thames & Hudson (UK), 1976.

Bradley, Lloyd, *Reggae On CD: The Essential Guide*, Kyle Cathie (UK), 1996.

Clarke, Sebastian, *Jah Music*, Heinemann Educational (UK), 1980.

Cooper, Carolyn, *Noises In The Blood*, Duke University Press (USA), 1995.

Dalke, Roger, *Record Selector: A Reference Guide To Jamaican Music Vols. 15-18*, T.S.I. Publications (UK), 1995.

Davis, Stephen, *Reggae Bloodlines: In Search Of The Music And Culture Of Jamaica*, Heineman Educational (UK), 1979.

Davis, Stephen & Simon, Peter, *Reggae International*, Alfred A. Knopf (USA), 1983.

Farmer, Paul, *Steelbands & Reggae*, Longman (UK), 1981.

Griffiths, Mark, *Boss Sounds: Classic Skinhead Reggae*, S.T.

Publishing (UK), 1995.
Hausman, Gerald (ed.), *The Kebra Nagast*, St. Martin's Press (UK), 1997.
Johnson, Howard, *Reggae: Deep Roots Music*, Proteus (UK), 1982.
Kallyndyr, Rolston, *Reggae: A People's Music*, Carib-Arawak, 1977.
Larkin, Colin, *The Virgin Encyclopedia Of Reggae*, Virgin Books (UK), 1998.
Larkin, Colin (ed.), *Guinness Who's Who Of Reggae*, Guinness Publishing (UK), 1994.
Marshall, George, *Two-tone Story*, S.T. Publishing (UK), 1993.
Maverick Lensman, *Reggae In View*, Overheat Music Inc. (USA), 1996.
Mulvaney, Rebekah Michele, *Rastafari & Raggae: A Dictionary & Sourcebook*, Greenwood Westport (USA), 1990.
Weber, Tom, *Reggae Island: Jamaican Music In The Digital Age*, Kingston Publishers (Jamaica), 1992.

Soul

Bradley, Lloyd, *Soul On CD: The Essential Guide*, Kyle Cathie (UK), 1994.
Compiled by Perry, Neil, *Rare Soul*, Perry & Perry (UK), 1991.
Dr. Licks, *Standing In The Shadows Of Motown*, Hal Leonard Publications (USA), 1989.
Garland, Phyl, *The Sound Of Soul*, Henry Regnery, 1969.
Gill, Chris, *The Illustrated Encyclopedia Of Black Music*, Salamander Books (UK), 1982.
Gonzalez, Fernando L., *Disco-File: The Discographical Catalog Of American Rock & Roll & Rhythm And B*, Gonzalez, 1977.
Gregory Hugh, *Soul Music A -Z*, Cassell (UK), 1992.
Gregory, Hugh, *Soul Music A-Z*, Da Capo (USA), 1995.
Guralnik, Peter, *Sweet Soul Music*, Harper And Row (USA), Penguin (UK), 1986.
Hildebrand, Lee, *Stars Of Soul And Rhythm & Blues*, Billboard Books (USA), 1994.
Hoare, Ian and others (ed.), *The Soul Book*, Methuen (UK), 1975.
Hoskyns, Barney, *Say It One Time For The Broken Hearted*, Fontana (UK), 1987.
Larkin, Colin, *The Virgin Encyclopedia Of R&B And Soul*, Virgin Books (UK), 1998.
Larkin, Colin (ed.), *Guinness Who's Who Of Soul*, Guinness Publishing (UK), 1993.
Larkin, Rochelle, *Soul Music: The Sound, The Stars, The Story*, Lancer Books, 1970.
Lydon, Michael, *Boogie Lightnin'*, Dial Press (USA), 1974.
McKenna, Pete, *Nightshift*, S.T. Publishing (UK), 1996.
Osborne, Jerry, *Blues, Rhythm & Blues, Soul*, O'Sullivan Woodside, 1980.
Pascall, Jeremy, *The Stars & Superstars Of Black Music*, Phoebus, 1977.
Pruter, Robert, *Doowop: The Chicago Scene*, Big Nickel (USA), 1996.
Pruter, Robert, *Chicago Soul*, University Of Illinois Press (USA), 1991.
Pruter, Robert, *Blackwell Guide To Soul Records*, Blackwells (UK), 1993.
Pruter, Robert, *Chicago Soul*, Bayou Press (USA), 1991.
Rivelli, Pauline and Levin, Robert, *Giants Of Black Music*, De Capo (USA), 1981.
Roach, Hildred, *Black American Music: Past And Present*, Crescendo, 1973.
Roberts, John Storm, *Black Music Of Two Worlds*, Allen Lane, 1973 (UK).
Shaw, Arnold, *The World Of Soul: Black America's Contribution To The Pop Music Scene*, Thomas Crowell (USA), 1970.
Skowronski, Jo Ann, *Black Music In America: A Bibliography*, Scarecrow Press (USA), 1981.

Southern, Eileen, *Readings In Black Music*, W.W. Norton (USA), 1972.
Tee, Ralph, *Who's Who In Soul Music*, Wiedenfeld & Nicholson (UK), 1991.
Turner, Tony, *Deliver Us From Temptation*, Tony Turner, 1993.
Walton, Ortiz M., *Music, Black, White And Blue: A Sociological Survey Of The Use And Misuse Of*, W. Morrow (USA), 1972.
Winstanley, Russ & Nowell, David, *Soul Survivors: The Wigan Casino Story*, Robson Books (UK), 1997.

World Music

Akpabot, Samuel Ekpe, *Foundation Of Nigerian Traditional Music*, Spectrum Books (Nigeria), 1991.
Andersson, Muff, *Music In The Mix: The Story Of South African Popular Music*, Ravan Press (S Africa), 1981.
Barlow, Sean, And Banning Eyre, *Afropop*, Saraband Books, 1995.
Bender, Wolfgang, *Sweet Mother: Modern Africian Music*, Univerity Chicago Press (USA), 1991.
Boggs, Vernon, *Salisology: Afro-Cuban Music And The Evolution Of Salsa In New York*, Greenwood Press, 1992.
Booth, Stanley, *Rhythm Oil: Journey Through The Music Of The American South*, Vintage (USA), 1993.
Broughton, S., Ellingham, M., Muddyman, D., Trillo, R. (eds), *World Music: The Rough Guide*, Rough Guide/Penguin (UK), 1994.
Brown, Ernest Douglas, *Drums Of Life*, , 1984.
Chilvers, Garth, And Tom Jasiukowicz, *A History Of The Contemporary Music Of South Africa*, Toga Publishing, 1995.
Erlmann, Veir, *African Stars: Studies In Black South African Performance*, University Chicago Press (USA), 1991.
Ewens, Graeme, *Africa O-Ye!: A Celebration of African Music*, Guinness (UK), 1992.
Goddard, Peter & Kamin Philip (ed.), *Shakin' All Over: Rock & Roll Years In Canada*, McGraw Hill (Canada), 1989.
Graham, Ronnie, *World Of African Music*, Pluto Press (UK), 1992.
Graham, Ronnie, *The World Of African Music: Stern's Guide Vol 2*, Pluto Press (UK), 1992.
Guilbaut, Jocelyne, *Zouk: World Music In The West Indies*, University of Chicago Press (USA), 1993.
Hagensen, Rich, *Strictly Instrumental: The Canadian Scene: A Discograpy Of Canadian Instrumental*, Published By Author, 1991.
Hanly, Francis & May, Tim, *Rhythms Of The World*, BBC, 1990.
Hartigan, Royal, *West African Rhythms For Drumset*, Manhattan Music (USA), 1996.
Hill, Donald R., *Calypso Calaloo: Early Carnival Music In Trinidad*, University Press Of Florida (USA), 1993.
Jones, Stephen, *Folk Music Of China: Living Instrumental Traditions*, Oxford University Press, 1995.
Kebede, Ashenafi, *Roots Of Black Music*, Africa World Publications, 1995.
Larkin, Colin, *The Virgin Encyclopedia Of World & Folk Music*, Virgin Books (UK), 1999.
Lems-Dworkin, Carol, *World Music Center*, Program Of African Studies.
Locke, David, *African Music: Meeting In Yaounde (Cameroon) 23-27 February 1970*, La Revue Musicale.
Malone, Jacqui, *Steppin' On The Blues: The Visible Rhythms Of African American Dance*, University Of Illinois Press (USA), 1996.
Manual, Peter with Bilby, Kenneth and Jargey, Michael, *Caribbean Currents: caribbean Music From Rumba To Reggae*, Latin American Bureau, 1996.
McGowan, Chris & Pessanha, Ricardo, *Billboard Book Of Brazilian Music*, Billboard (USA), Guinness (UK), 1991.

McGrath, Noel, *Book Of Australian Rock: The Stars, The Charts, The Stories, The Legends*, Lothian, Australia, 1990.

Nketia, J. H. Kwabena, *The Music Of Africa*, W.W. Norton (USA), 1974.

Rice, Timothy, *May It Fill Your Soul: Experiencing Bulgarian Music*, University Of Chicago Press (USA), 1995.

Rudder, David & LaRose, John, *Kaiso Calypso Music*, New Beacon Books (UK), 1990.

Sharma, Sanjay (ed) and others, *Dis-Orienting Rhythms: The Politics Of The new Asian Dance Music*, Zed (UK), 1996.

Spencer, Chris, *Who's Who of Australian Rock*, Five Mile Press (Australia), 1990.

Spencer, Peter, *World Beat: A Listeners Guide To Contemporary Music On CD*, A Capella Books (USA), 1992.

Stapleton, Chris, & May, Chris, *African All-Stars*, Quartet, 1988.

Sturma, Michael, *Australian Rock 'N' Roll: The First Wave*, Kangaroo Press (Australia), 1991.

Sweeney, Philip, *Virgin Directory Of World Music*, Virgin Books (UK), 1992.

Troop, David, *Rap Attack 2: African Rap To Global Hip Hop*, Serpents Tail (UK), 1991.

Vernon, Paul, *Ethnic And Vernacular Music 1898-1960: A Resource And Guide To Recordings*, Greenwood Press, 1995.

Waterman, Christopher Alan, *Juju: Social History And Ethnography Of An African Popular Music*, University Of Chicago Press (USA), 1990.

Woodall, James, *A Simple Brazilian Song: A Journey Through The Rio Sound*, Little Brown (UK), 1997.

Woods, Peter, *The Heartbeat Of Irish Music*, Roberts Rhinhart (USA), 1997.

SELECTED FANZINES

In assembling this list we would like to thank the following for their cooperation: Alan Pearce, Aled Wilding, Arthur Davies, Axel Thomas, Ben Maynard, Charles White (Dr. Rock), Colin Miles, Cos Cimino, David Clayton, David Inquieti, Deke Rivers, Eaton 'Jah' Blake, Francois Wintein, George Matlock, James Lawrence, John Edwards, John Hellier, John Williams, Jørgen Thoresen, Kelvin Hayes, Lloyd Peasley, Nathan Lucas, Neil Rossetter, Nick Mawson, Nikki Sudden, Paul Barber, Raymond Greenoaken, Richard Rose, Scott Murphy, Tony McGartland, William Hooper. Send a sample copy to us and your fanzine will be included in subsequent editions.

Many thanks to John Williams and his invaluable Fanzine Guide, which has been running for three years and is published every two months. It is available from:

John Williams
48 Rossall Avenue
Radcliffe
Manchester M26 1JD
England

ABBA: *Abba News Service*
PO Box 21, Avonmouth, Bristol BS11 9AZ, UK

ABBA: *For All Abba Fans*
88 Whincover Drive, Old Farnley, Leeds LS12 5JT, UK

ABBA: *Report*
Alex Jones, Middle Flat 2, Old Swan House, The Croft, Neath, County Of Neath and Port Talbot SA11 1RS, Wales, UK

AC/DC: *Electric Outlaws*
N.Goff, 10 Windsor Grove, Bolton, Lancs BL1 3BR, UK

ALIEN SEX FIEND: *Fiendzine*
Blue Crumb Truck, PO Box 416, Cardiff CF1 8XU, UK

MARC ALMOND: *Obsession*
157 Brecknock Rd., London N19 5AD, UK

TORI AMOS: *Take To The Sky*
Steve Jenkins, PO Box 632 Bexleyheath, Kent DA7 5TE, UK

VIRGINIA ASTLEY: *Friends Of Virginia Astley*
Deke Rivers, Flat 2, Moon House, 1 Moon Avenue, Blackpool FY1 4HY, UK

AUTEURS: *Starstruck*
Wendy Gabriel, 88 Thorpe Road, Forest Gate, London E7 9EB, UK

KEVIN AYERS: *Why Are We Sleeping?*
Martin Wakeling, 112 Parkville Road, Withington, Manchester M20 4TZ, UK
Web Site:
http://www.users.gloalnet.co.uk/~marwak/index.html

BAND: *The Band Newsletter*
Lee Gabites, 13 Hough End Avenue, Chorlton, Manchester M21 7SF

BANGLES/SUSANNA HOFFS: *Banglemania and Hoffmania*
John Edwards, 24 Weaponness Valley Rd., Scarborough, North Yorkshire YO11 2JF, UK

BARCLAY JAMES HARVEST: *Nova Lepidoptera*
The International Barclay James Harvest Fan Club, Hamble Reach, Oslands Lane, Lower Swanwick, Southampton SO31 7EG, UK
Info Hotline: (0891) 299 736
Web Site: http://www.ftech.net/~harvest/bjh-home.htm

SYD BARRETT: *Eskimo Chain*
I. Smith, 2 White Cottages, Long Garth, Durham City, DH1 4HL

BEACH BOYS: *Beach Boys Stomp*
M. Grant, 22 Avondale Road, Wealdstone, Middlesex HA3 7RE, UK

BEATLES: *Rain*
Carol Lennie, 33 Sylam CLose, Marsh Farm, Luton, Bedfordshire LU3 3RU

BEATLES: *Beatles For Sale*
Matt, Flat A, 111 Upper Luton Road, Chatham, Kent ME5 7BJ, UK

BEAUTIFUL SOUTH: *Straight In At 37*
Catrina, 9 HopeKnowe, Earlston, Berwickshire, Scotland TD4 6HA, UK

BJORK: *Sweet Intuition*
Rachel Crookes, 25 Elmtree Road, Cosby, Leics, UK

RITCHIE BLACKMORE: *More Black Than Purple*
PO Box 155, Bedford MK40 2YX, UK

BLACK SABBATH: *Southern Cross*
Peter Scott, PO Box 177, Crewe CW2 7SZ, UK

BLONDIE/DEBORAH HARRY: *Underground Girl*
Sarah Conley or Sheryl Lee, 45 Church Lane, Lowton, Warrington WA3 2AS, UK
Web Site: www.users.globalnet.co.uk/~pmush

BLONDIE/DEBORAH HARRY: *Picture This*
Francois Wintein, 57 Church Avenue, Humberston, Grimsby, NE Lincolnshire DN36 4DJ, UK

COLIN BLUNSTONE: *Photograph*
Andy Barnes, PO Box 336, Cheltenham, Glos GL51 6YP, UK

THE BLUETONES: *In A Blue Vein*
Quarry House, 49 Bracken Park, Scarcroft, Leeds LS14 3HZ, UK

BLUR: *Blurb 7*
The Official Blur Fan Club, PO Box 525, Stoke-on-Trent ST7 2YX, UK

BLUR: *Magpie*
Suzanne Fowler, 12 Buckley Court, Stony Stratford, Milton Keynes MK11 1NH, UK

MARC BOLAN: *Electric Boogie*
Barry Smith, 11 Medoc Close, Wymans Brook, Cheltenham, Glos GL50 4SW, UK

MARC BOLAN: *Mainman*
Terry Hughes, 41 Tedder Road, Beaconside, Stafford, Staffs ST16 3QX, UK

MARC BOLAN: *Precious Star*
Alan Lauchlan, 36 Crummock St., Beith, Ayrshire KA15 2BD, UK

MARC BOLAN: *Rumblings*
Tyrannosauras Rex Appreciation Society, PO Box 297, Newhaven, East Sussex BN9 9NX, UK

MARC BOLAN: *The Never Ending Waltz*
Aled Wilding, 6 Stowe Path, Llanyrafon, Cwmbran, Gwent NP44 8SE, UK

MICHAEL BOLTON: *Bolton Bulletin*
June Allen, 9 Palm Close, Witham, Essex CM8 2PJ, UK

DAVID BOWIE: *Crankin' Out*
Steve Pafford, PO Box 3268, London NW6 4NH, UK

BOY GEORGE: *Distant Dream*
P. Bayley, 42 Winter Grove, St. Helens WA9 2JS, UK
BUDGIE: *Sabre Dance*
UK:Axel Thomas, 15 Fairfax Close, Marple, Stockport SK6 6HH
USA: c/o George Martin, 15562 Scotts Factory Rd, Smithfield, Virginia 23430
Web Site: http://www.ozemail.com.au/~sabreda/

KATE BUSH: *Homeground*
Peter, PO Box 176, Orpington, Kent. BR5 3NA, UK

THE BYRDS: *Full Circle*
Chrissie Oakes, 61 Silverbirch Close, Little Stoke, Bristol BS12 6RN, UK

CAPERCAILLIE: *Sidetaulk*
Mandy Shanks, 21 Thom Street, Hopeman Elgin, Moray IV30 2SS, UK

CARTER USM: *Blue Touch Paper*
Nathan Lucas, 20 Sear Hills Close, Balsall Common, Coventry CV7 7QL, UK

JOHNNY CASH: *The Man In Black*
Peter Lewry, 100 Boxgrove, Goring-By-Sea, Worthing, West Sussex BN12 6LX, UK

CAST: *Fine Time*
Dave Newby, 7 Brackenway, Formby, Liverpool L37 7HF, UK

THE CHARLATANS: *109*
John McGee, PO Box 94, Northwich, Cheshire CW9 5TS, UK

THE CHARLATANS: *Subterranean*
Christy, 133 Temple Street, Sidmouth, Devon EX10 9BN, UK

ERIC CLAPTON: *Where's Eric?*
Tony Edser, 3 Milverton Close, Cox Green, Maidenhead, Berks SL6 3AZ, UK
Info Hotlines: (0891) 299 762 (UK), 1 900 476 2900 (USA)

THE CLASH: *Deny*
Pete Shovlin, 5 St Andrews Terrace, Roker, Sunderland SR6 0PB, UK

JOE COCKER: *Civilized Man*
Diane Wicks, PO Box 43, Torquay TQ2 5XB, UK

JULIAN COPE: *Screaming Secrets*
146 Eglington Road, Plumstead, London SE18 3SY, UK

JULIAN COPE: *Snorer Explorer*
64 Moorland Rd., Fratton, Portsmouth PO1 5JA, UK

SHAWN COLVIN: *One In Vermillion*
M.D.Poole, 15 Lords Avenue, Bidston, Birkenhead, Merseyside. L43 7YZ, UK

ELVIS COSTELLO: *Beyond Belief*
Mark Perry, 6 Hillside Grove, Taunton, Somerset TA1 4LA, UK
Web Site: http://come.to/beyond-belief

THE CRAMPS: *The Devil's Spacecake*
Dermot Campbell, 32 Pinehill Road, Drumbo Lisburn, Co Antrim, N Ireland BT27 5TU, UK

CRANBERRIES: *The Limerick Pride*
Debrain Publications, Brian O'Donovan, Finnitterstown, Adare, Co. Limerick, Ireland

CROSBY, STILLS AND NASH: *So Far*
Andy Langran, 20 Brunswick Street, Swansea SA1 4JP, UK

CURE: *The Cure*
Cure International Information Service, PO Box 211, Hayes, Middlesex UB4 9NZ, UK

THE DAMNED: *Mystery Of The Damned*
Francois Wintein, 57 Church Avenue, Humberston, Grimsby, NE Lincolnshire DN36 4DJ, UK

DEEP PURPLE: *Darker Than Blue*
Peter Purnell, CeeDee Mail Ltd, PO Box 14, Stowmarket, Suffolk IP14 4UD, UK

DEL AMITRI: *Infidels & Popstars*
Anna Barwick, PO Box 2799, Bournemouth BH7 6ZG, UK
Web Site: http://del-amitri.linex.com

DEPECHE MODE: *Landscape*
T. Lewis, Mode Evolution, PO Box 417, Peterborough PE4 6WY, UK

DEXY'S MIDNIGHT RUNNERS: *Keep On Running*
Neil Warburton, 56 Apollo Road, Oldbury, Warley, West Midlands B68 9RS, UK

CELINE DION: *Unison*
Karl Jordinson, 28 Dunlin Drive, Ayton Washington, District 6,Tyne & Wear NE28 0EB, UK

DONOVAN: *Donovan's Friends*
Pat, PO Box 1119, London SW9 9JW, UK

DOORS: *Whiskey, Mystics And Men*
Lizard Promotions, 45 Monkton Road, Minster, Kent CT12 4ED, UK

DR ROBERT: *Keep On Digging For The Gold*
P. Duffy, 7 Wulwards Close, Farley Hill, Luton, Beds LU1 5LP, UK

DURAN DURAN: *Cherry Lipstick*
Adam Wilson, 225 Cromwell Road, Whistable, Kent CT5 1LA, UK

NICK DRAKE: *Pink Moon*
Jason Creed, 34 Kingsbridge Road, Walton on Thames, Surrey KT12 2BZ, UK

DYLAN: *Isis*
Derek Barker, PO Box 132, Coventry, West Midlands CV3 5RE, UK

EAGLES: *Natural Progressions*
D. Hirst, 15 Northcote Road, Croydon CR0 2HX, UK

ECHO AND THE BUNNYMEN: *Information Service*
1a Shepherd Road, St. Annes On Sea, Lancs FY8 3JB, UK

ECHO AND THE BUNNYMEN: *Return Of Voodoo Billy*
Dickie Straker, Willow House, Coaley, Nr. Dursley, Glos. GL11 5EG, UK

EDDIE AND THE HOT RODS: *Writing On The Wall*
Alan Heaven, 8 George Frederick Road, Streetly, Sutton Coldfield, West Midlands B73 6TB, UK

DUANE EDDY: *Twangsville*
Arthur Moir, The Duane Eddy Circle, PO Box 203, Sheffield S1 1XU, UK

ELO: *Face The Music*
FTM, PO Box 718, Sidcup, Kent DA15 7UD, UK

EMERSON, LAKE & PALMER: *Impressions*
Liv G Whetmore, PO Box 304, Walton on Thames, Surrey KT12 2YT, UK

ERASURE: *The Erasure Files*
Jonathan Grant, 36 Swanston Avenue, Inverness IV3 6QW, UK

THE EX: *The EX Newsletter*
Ex Records, Postbus 635, 1000 AP Amsterdam
Web Site: http://www.xs4all.nl/~exrcrds/

THE FALL: *The Biggest Library Yet*
Graham Coleman, 106 Fleet Road, Hampstead, London NW3 2QX, UK
Web Site: http://members.tripod.com/~GColeman/index.html

FISH: *The Company Midlands*
Adrian, 12 Colshaw Rd., Norton, Stowbridge, West Midlands D78 3AS, UK

FLEETWOOD MAC: *The Crystal*
Aine Foley, 46 St. John's Avenue, Clondalkin, Dublin 22, Ireland

FOO FIGHTERS: *Quicker Than The Human Eye*
Michael Sanderson, 2 Castle Close, Middleton, St. George, Darlington DL2 1DE, UK

FREE: *Free Appreciation Society*
David Clayton, 39 Staverton Road, Bilborough, Nottingham NG8 4ET, UK

PETER GABRIEL: *Kontakt*
Mic Smith, 23 Redshank Avenue, Winsford, Cheshire CW7 1SP, UK

GENE: *Olympian*
M. Nicholson, 21 Moffat Close, Bradford BD6 3RL, UK

GENESIS: *The Waiting Room*
Peter Morton, 97 Oldfield Rd., Stannington, Sheffield S6 6YS, UK

GENEVA: *Celeste*
Helena, 1 Lawford Close, Chorleywood, Herts WD3 5JX

ROBIN GIBB/BEE GEES: *The Rural HG Times*
Alex, Unit 21, Youngs Ind Est, Paices Hill, Aldermaston, Berks RG7 4PW, UK

THE GO-GO'S: *Beatnik Beat*
UK: PO Box 129, Southport, Merseyside PR8 6UW
USA: 4960 Almaden Expressway 186, San Jose, California 95118
Web Site: http://www.geocities.com/SunsetStrip/3981

GORDON GILTRAP: *Airwaves*
Dave Van Walwyk, 5 Vale Road, Ramsgate, Kent CT11 9LU, UK

SID GRIFFIN/COAL PORTERS: *Rebels Without Applause*
Grant Curley, 37 Dean Close, High Wycombe, Bucks HP12 3NS, UK
Web Site: http://130.159.56.1/pd/SidHome.html

PETER HAMMILL/VAN DER GRAAF GENERATOR: *Pilgrims*
Fred Tomsett, PO Box 249, Chesterfield S40 4DZ, UK

GEORGE HARRISON: *Blow Away*
Debbie Wakeford, 6 Hampden Way, Southgate, London N14 5DX, UK

JIMI HENDRIX: *Jimpress*
PO Box 218, Warrington, Cheshire WA5 2FG, UK
Web Site: http://www.u-net.com/personal/~jimpress/

JIMI HENDRIX: *UniVibes*
Caesar Glebbeek, Coppeen, Enniskeane, Co Cork, Republic of Ireland

NICK HEYWARD: *Backdated*
Sharon Curtis, Backdated, PO Box 654, High Wycombe, Bucks HP11 1LZ, UK

BUDDY HOLLY: *Chirping*
A Jenkins, 142 Burns Avenue, Feltham, Middlesex TW14 9HZ, UK

BUDDY HOLLY: *Crickets File*
412 Main Road, Sheffield S9 4QL, UK

THE INCREDIBLE STRING BAND: *Be Glad...*
Raymond Greenoaken, 11 Ratcliffe Road, Sheffield S11 8YA, UK

THE JAM: *Start*
Neil Allen, 2 Woolpack Close, Rowley Regis, Warley, West Midlands B65 8HY, UK

JAMES: *Change Of Scenery*
J. Pude, 1 Thackeray Rd., Aylesford, Kent ME20 6TH, UK

JAMIROQUAI: *Long Lost Brothers*
Unit 220, Camelot Production Studios, 222 Kensal Road, London W10, UK

ELTON JOHN: *Hercules*
UK: Hercules UK, PO Box 315, Richmond, Surrey TW9 3QX
USA: Hercules USA/Canada, c/o Sharon Kalinoski, PO Box 398, La Grange, IL 60525
Info Hotlines: (0891) 299751 (UK), 1900 2639600 (USA), 1150 5251117 (World)

WILKO JOHNSON: *Some Kind Of Hero*
Alan Grundy, 11 Darley Avenue, Farnworth, Bolton, Lancs BL4 7RU, UK

BRIAN JONES: *The Spirit*
David Reynolds, Millstone, 31 Timperley Way, Up Hatherley, Cheltenham, Glos. GL51 5RH, UK
Web Site: http://members.aol.com/jonesclub/brian/index.htm

KENICKIE: *Kenix*
Hannah, 41 The Lawns, Duston, Northampton NN5 6AF, UK

BRIAN KENNEDY: *Captured*
L. Williams, 1 Howe Grove, Knutton, Newcastle Staffs ST5 6DX, UK

KING CRIMSON: *Book Of Saturday*
PO Box 221, Leeds LS1 5LW, UK

KING CRIMSON/ROBERT FRIPP: *We'll Let You Know*
Darren Woolsey, 3 Kings Drive, Wrose, Bradford, West Yorkshire BD2 1PX, UK

KINKS: *Official Kinks Fan Club*
PO Box 30, Atherstone, Warwickshire CV9 2ZX, UK

KISS: *Goin' Blind*
Chris Hatton, 1 Matty Road, Oldbury, Warley, West Midlands B68 9RG, UK

KISS: *Kiss Renegades*
Ross Humphreys, 76 Cwmgelli Close, Treboeth, Swansea SA5 9BZ, Wales, UK

KISS: *Strike*
R. Paul, 32 Seymour Road, Lower Edmonton, London N9 0SE, UK

KRAFTWERK: *Aktivitat*
I. Calder, 108 Cummings Park Crescent, Aberdeen AB16 7AR, UK

LED ZEPPELIN: *Tight But Loose*
Dave Lewis, 14 Totnes Close, Bedford MK40 3AX, UK
Web Site: http://www.linwod.demon.co.uk/index/html

JOHN LENNON: *John Lennon International*

A. Steel, 1 Wellington Avenue, St. Ives, Cambs. PE17 6UT, UK

LEVELLERS: *On The Fiddle*
PO Box 2600, Brighton, East Sussex BN2 2DX, UK

JERRY LEE LEWIS: *Fire-Ball Mail*
Barrie Gamblin, 16 Milton Road, Wimbledon, London SW19, UK

LOVE: *The Castle*
David Peter Housden, Big Sky Studio, Stonecross House, Fitton End Road, Gorefield, Wisbech, Cambs PE13 4NQ, UK

LOVE AND ROCKETS: *Apollox*
Peter Edwards, PO Box 847, London SW18 1XA, UK

MADNESS: *Nut Inc*
Stuart Wright, 29 Hollidge Way, Dagenham, Essex RM10 9SP, UK

MADONNA: *Absolute Ciccone*
Marcus Tang, 39 Marlborough Close, Grays, Essex RM16 2SU, UK

MANIC STREET PREACHERS: *Aspire For Life*
Jason Hood, Flat 4, 121 College Road, Mosley, Birmingham B13 9LJ, UK

MANIC STREET PREACHERS: *R*e*p*e*a*t*
Richard Rose, 7 Ferry Lane, Chesterton, Cambridge CB4 1NT, UK
MANIC STREET PREACHERS: *Terrible Beauty*
Mary O'Meara, 6 Embassy Court, 76 Kenton Road, Harrow, Middlesex HA3 8BB, UK

MANIC STREET PREACHERS: *The 11th Commandment*
Katy Bennett, Blackford House, Kings School, Bruton, Somerset BA10 0EF, UK

MANSUN: *Deeside Caviar*
4 Groesfaen Terrace, Bargoed, Mid Glamorgan CF81 9GH, UK

MARILLION: *Brave Hearts Collection*
A.Williams, 19 Lilac Avenue, Humberstone, Leicester LE5 1FN, UK

BOB MARLEY: *Distant Drums*
Jeremy Collingwood, 10 The Hamlet, Chippenham, Wilts SN15 1BY, UK

STEVE MARRIOTT: *Steve Marriott International*
A. Steel, 1 Wellington Avenue, St.Ives, Cambs PE17 6UT, UK

PAUL McCARTNEY: *Club Sandwich*
PO 110, Westcliff, Essex SS0 8NW, UK

IAN McNABB: *McNabb Rag*
Paul Warry, 102 Munster Avenue, Hounslow, Middlesex TW4 5BJ, UK

JOE MEEK: *Thunderbolt*
Andrew Knott, 89 Hardy Crescent, Wimborne, Dorset BH21 2AR, UK

GUY MITCHELL: *Mitchell Music*
The Membership Secretary, The Guy Mitchell Appreciation Society, 11 Kierhill Road, Balloch, Cumbernauld, Glasgow G68 9BH, UK

MONKEES: *Band 6*
Kirk & Sue White, 19 Skipsey Avenue, East Ham, London E6 4HW, UK

MONKEES: *Head*
David Inquieti, 39 Long Mallows Rise, Ecton Brook, Northampton NN3 5AR, UK

ALANIS MORISSETTE: *The Pill*
Stephen Jones, 57 Oxford Road, Banbury, Oxfordshire OX16 9AJ, UK
Web Site: http://ds.dial.pipex.com/fivestar/alanis

VAN MORRISON: *Wavelength*
Simon Gee, PO Box 80, Winsford, Cheshire CW7 4ES, UK
Web Site: http://home.netcentral.co.uk/wavelength
MORRISSEY: *A Chance To Shine*
Bruce Duff, 12a Dyne Road, Kilburn, London NW6 7XE, UK

MUNGO JERRY: *Mun-Go For It!*
Alan Taylor, 24 Nafferton Place, Fenham, Newcastle Upon Tyne NE5 2QR, UK

NAZARETH: *Razamanewz*
Joe Geesin, Headrest, Street End Lane, Broad Oak, Heathfield, East Sussex TN21 8TU, UK

NEW ORDER: *Paradise*
David Smith, PO Box 125, Macclesfield, Cheshire SK10 5RL, UK

NINE BELOW ZERO
Sally Stokes, 62 Gresty Terrace, Crewe, Cheshire CW1 5EW, UK

OLIVIA NEWTON JOHN: *Only Olivia*
Helen Kembery, 5 Finchley Road, Ipswich IP4 2HX, UK
Web Site: http://www.netlink.co.uk/users/ermine/olivia

GARY NUMAN: *The Side Parting Is Dead*
Survival Records, 29 Townhall Street, Inverkeithing, Fife, Scotland KY11 1LX, UK

OASIS: *Lasagne*
J. Yates, 10 Oakdale Road, Binley Wds, Coventry CV3 2BL, UK

OASIS: *Listen Up!*
Micky Campbell, 72 Birkhall Road, Middlesbrough, Cleveland TS3 9LJ, UK

OASIS: *Mad For It!*
Lucy Woolard, 55 Weatheroak Close, Redditch, Worcs B97 5TF, UK

OASIS: *Must Be The Music*
Nick Mawson, 100 Arlington Street, Stockton-On-Tees TS18 3LD, UK
OASIS: *The Walrus*
Justin Smith, 4 Beech Court, Courtland Rd., Wellington, Somerset TA21 8NE, UK

OCEAN COLOUR SCENE: *On The Scene*
Berry Coffman, 48 Tower Street, Trefforest, Pontypridd, Mid Glamorgan CF37 1NR

OCEAN COLOUR SCENE: *Yesterday & Today*
Jamie Ward, 14 Gladstone Close, Hinckley, Leics LE10 1SB, UK

MIKE OLDFIELD: *Airborne*
David Porter, 17 Brogden Crescent, Leeds, Maidstone, Kent ME17 1RA

MIKE OLDFIELD: *Dark Star*
PO Box 2031, Blandford DT11 9YB, UK

ORBITAL: *Loopz*
Steve, 9 Elgin Road, Bloxwich, Walsall, UK

PEARL JAM: *Dollar Short*
Stephen Shepherd, 71 Sidmouth Road, Sale, Manchester M33 5HZ, UK

MIKE PETERS: *Spiritual*
T. Dalgarno, 13 John Street, Knutton, Newcastle Staffs ST5 6DT, UK

MIKE PETERS: *21st Century*
MPO UK, PO Box 709, Prestatyn, Denbighshire LL19 9YR, Wales, UK
Web Site: http://www.demon.co.uk/alarmpo

TOM PETTY AND THE HEARTBREAKERS: *Makin' Some Noise*
Amanda Saladine, 69 Crofthill Road, Slough SL2 1HG, UK

ANTHONY PHILLIPS: *The Pavilion*
Alan Hewitt, 174 Salisbury Road, Everton, Liverpool L5 6RQ, UK

PINK FLOYD: *Brain Damage*
Second Wave Promotions, PO Box 385, Uxbridge, Middlesex UB9 5DZ, UK

PLACEBO: *Lives, Loves And Lipstick*
Sophie Paterson, 8 Brewery Road, Horsell, Woking GU21 4LP, UK

ROBERT PLANT: *The Lemon Tree* (ISSN 1368-5619)
Liz Hames, 20 Ludford Crescent, Gainsborough, Lincs DN21 1XB, UK

ELVIS PRESLEY: *Elvis: The Man And His Music*
'Now Dig This', 19 South Hill Road, Bensham, Gateshead, Tyne & Wear NE8 2XR, UK

PRINCE: *The Interactive Experience*
PO Box 541, Sheffield S9 4YN, UK

DAVE PROWSE: *The Official International Dave Prowse Fan Club*
12 Marshlea Rd., London SE1 1HL, UK

PULP: *Pulp Friction*
Donna Nicoll, PO Box 319, Nottingham NG7 4AS

QUEEN: *Princes Of The Universe*
Neil French, 7 Chandlers Drive, Erith, Kent DA8 1LL, UK

QUEEN: *The Days Of Our Lives*
Jeanette Lea, 10 Clarence St., Leyland, Preston PR5 2WX, UK

QUEEN: *The Queen Fan Newsletter*
David Parr, 128 St. Thomas' Rd., Preston, Lancs PR1 6AY, UK

RADIOHEAD: *Radiohead World Service*
151 High Road, Trimley St. Mary, Ipswich, Suffolk IP10 0TW, UK

RAMONES: *Ramones UK Fan Club*
Veronica Kofman, 100 Albion Hill, Brighton, East Sussex BN2 2PA, UK

R.E.M: *Chronic Town*
Paul Holmes, 27 Oriel Drive, Old Roan, Liverpool L10 3JL, UK

R.E.M: *Rivers Of Suggestion*
Rob Jovanovic, 19 Cornhill Road, Carlton, Nottingham NG4 1GE, UK

R.E.M: *The Monster Mag*
R. Walton, 23 Buttermere Drive, Shropshire, Telford TF2 9RE, UK

R.E.M: *The Orange Crush*
Andrew Barber, 38 Bay View Avenue, Slyne, Lancaster LA2 6JS, UK

DARRYL READ: *Gods 'n' Angels*
Barry Smith, 11 Medoc Close, Wymans Brook, Cheltenham, Glos GL50 4SW, UK

CLIFF RICHARD: *Cliff United*
Christine Whitehead, 28 Blenheim Road, Sutton, Surrey SM1 2PX, UK

CLIFF RICHARD: *Constantly Cliff*
William Hooper, 17 Podsmead Road, Tuffley, Glos GL1 5PB, UK

ROLLING STONES: *Shattered! International*
J. Hoeksma, PO Box 3723, London SE15 1HW, UK

RUSH: *Spirit Of Rush*
M. Burnett, 23 Garden Close, Chinbrook Road, Grove Park, London SE12 9TG, UK

SAVOY BROWN: *Shades Of Savoy Brown*
Alan Pearce, PO Box 727, Cardiff CF4 1YQ, UK

SCRITTI POLITTI: *Unofficial Scritti Politti Magazine*
James Lawrence, 7 Hazely, Tring, Herts HP23 5JH, UK

JOHN SEBASTIAN: *The Red Eye Express*
John Knox, 30 Maurice Close, Dukinfield, Cheshire SK16 5JD, UK

SEX PISTOLS: *The Filth And The Fury*
Scott Murphy, 24 Muirside Street, Baillieston, Glasgow G69 7EL, Scotland, UK

SHADOWS: *Shadsfax*
Tony Hoffman, 48 Oak Tree Lane, Haxby, York YO3 3YL, UK

SHED SEVEN: *Shed Sounds*
Dave Butterfield, 116 Castleford Rd., Normanton, West Yorkshire WF6 2EJ, UK

SIMPLE MINDS: *Who's Doing The Dreaming Now?*
Simon Cornwall, 51 Cambridge Road, Girton, Cambridge CB3 0PN, UK
Web Site: http://www.simple-minds.demon.co.uk/

THE SLADE: *Feel The Noise*
Dave Jewell, c/o Cardiff Central Enterprise Centre, Roath House, 22A City Road, Cardiff CF2 3DL, S Wales, UK

SMALL FACES: *The Darlings Of Wapping Wharf Launderette E1*
John Hellier, 7 Waterdene Mews, Canvey Island, Essex SS8 9YP, UK

SMASHING PUMPKINS: *Slunk*
M. Hill, PO Box 47, Welwyn, Herts AL6 0AY, UK

SPARKS: *Looks Aren't Everything*
Tony Machin, 16 Dale Valley Road, Shirley, Southampton SO16 6QR, UK

SPEAR OF DESTINY/KIRK BRANDON: *The One-Eyed Jack*
Dave Bryant, 13 The Dingle, Uxbridge, Middlesex UB10 0DQ, UK

DUSTY SPRINGFIELD: *Dusty Springfield Bulletin*
PO Box 203, Cobham, Surrey KT11 2UG, UK

SAINT ETIENNE: *Clembuterol*
47 Brewer Street, London W1R 3FD, UK

LISA STANSFIELD: *Soul Deep*
J. Williams, 48 Rossall Avenue, Radcliffe, Manchester M26 1JD, UK

ROD STEWART: *Smiler*
John Gray, PO Box 475, Morden, Surrey SM4 6AT, UK

STIFF LITTLE FINGERS: *Get A Life*
UK: Neil Rossetter, 1d Cants Lane, Burgess Hill, West Sussex. RH15 0LQ
USA: Shirley Sexton, Montgomery Ave. #649N, Bethesda MD20814
Web Site: http://www.his.com/slf

SUEDE: *Information Service*
PO Box 3431, London N1 7LW, UK

SUEDE: *New Generation*
40 Easter, Drylaw Drive, Edinburgh, Scotland, UK

SUEDE: *Quietly Kill For You*
Clare Scothern, 24 Deer Park Road, Langtoft, Peterborough, Cambs PE6 9RB, UK

SWEET: *Cut Above The Rest*
Cos Cimino, 52 Ashbank Road, Bucknall, Stoke-on-Trent, Staffs ST2 9DR, UK

10cc: *Headline Hustler*
Phil Loftus, 45 Windsor Road, Droylsden, Manchester M43 6WB, UK

STEVE TOOK: *Shire News*
Susan Hibberd, 10 Spring Grove, Loughton, Essex IG10 4QB

ULTRAVOX: *Extreme Voice*
Cerise Reed, 19 Salisbury Street, St. George, Bristol BS5 8EE, UK

U2: *Eirinn*
Sue Fell, 28 Balmoral Court, Etterby, Carlisle, Cumbria CA3 9PW, UK

U2: *Firework*
532 Great West Road, Hounslow, Middlesex TW5, UK

U2: *Real Thing*
Jackie Harper, 6 Danebower Rd, Stoke-On-Trent ST4 8TJ, UK
or Debbi Voisey, 14 Corporation Street, Stoke-On-Trent ST4
4AU, UK
Web Site: http://www.personal.u-net.com/realthing/index.htm

U2: *Spirit*
B. Saxton, 11A Mundy Street, Heanor, Derbyshire DE75 7EB,
UK

U2: *The Zooropean U2 Magazine*
PO Box 12940, London N8 0WA, UK

URIAH HEEP: *The Official Uriah Heep Appreciation Society*
PO Box 268, Telford, Shropshire TF2 6XA, UK

VANGELIS: *Albedo*
Mark Griffin, Smithy Croft, Schivas, Ythanbank, Ellon,
Aberdeenshire AB41 7UA, UK

VENTURES: *Resurgence*
Gerald Woodage, 13 Limetree Close, Grove, Wantage, Oxon
OX12 0BJ, UK

SCOTT WALKER: *Walkerpeople*
Lynne Goodall, 71 Cheyne Court, Glengall Road, Woodford
Green, Essex IG8 0DN, UK

JIMMY WEBB: *Bruised*
Mike Howard, Oak Cottage, Furzen Lane, Ellens Green,
Rudgwick, West Sussex RH12 3AR, UK

PAUL WELLER: *Boys About Town*
David Lodge, PO Box 12318, Edinburgh EH11 1YD, Scotland,
UK
Web Site: http://www.cableinet.co.uk/bat

PAUL WELLER: *Ooh Aah Paul Weller*
Julie Kershaw, 4 Ennerdale Road, Formby, Liverpool L37 2EA,
UK

THE WHO: *Generations*
Phil Hopkins, 1 Egbert Road, Meols, Wirral, Merseyside L47
5AH, UK

THE WHO: *Naked Eye*
Matt Kent & Mark Donovan, PO Box 7331, London E18 1TE,
UK

THE WHO
Andrew Biffa, Orchard House, Layters Green Lane, Chalfont
St. Peter, Bucks SL9 8TH, UK

STEVE WINWOOD/TRAFFIC: *Coloured Rain*
Paul Minkkinen, 12 Oakfield Avenue, Slough SL1 5AE, UK

YES: *The Revealing*
Ian Hartley, 35 Field Lane, Oldswinford, Stourbridge, West
Midlands DY8 2JQ, UK

YES: *Yes Music Circle*
Progressive Society, 44 Oswald Close, Leatherhead, Surrey
KT22 9UG, UK

NEIL YOUNG: *Broken Arrow* (ISSN 1353-307X)
Alan Jenkins, 2A Llynfi Street, Bridgend, Mid Glamorgan
CF31 1SY, Wales, UK
Web Site: http://ourworld.compuserve.com/homepages/nyas

FRANK ZAPPA: *T Mershi Daween*
Fred Tomsett, PO 249, Chesterfield S40 4DZ, UK

AMERICAN/CANADIAN FANZINES

LYNN ANDERSON: *Fan Club*
Michael Dempsey, PO Box 90454, Charleston, SC 29410

ANTHRAX: *NFC*
Christine Vogel, PO Box 254, Kulpsville, PA 19443

SHIRLEY BASSEY: *The Shirley Bassey Collectors Club*
Arthur Rugg, 35 Vasa Drive, R.D. No.1, Hackettstown, NJ
07840

THE BEACH BOYS: *Fan Club*
President, PO Box 84282, Los Angeles, CA 90073

THE BEACH BOYS: *Endless Summer Quarterly*
Lee Dempsey/David Beard, PO Box 470315, Charlotte, NC
28247

THE BEATLES: *Drive My Car Fabulous Fan Club*
PO Box 159, Fairfax, VA 22030-0159

THE BEATLES: *Good Day Sunshine*
Matt Hurwitz, Phone: 310-391-0778

THE BEATLES: *Liverpool Productions*
Charles E. Rosenay, 315 Derby Ave., Orange, CT 06477

THE BEATLES: *Octopus's Garden*
Beth Shorten, 21 Montclair Avenue, Verona, NJ 07044

THE BEATLES: *Strawberry Fields Forum*
Joe Pope, 310 Franklin St., No.117, Boston, MA 02210

THE BEATLES: *Tokyo Beatles Fan Club*
Kenji Maeda, 4-9-14, Honcho, Ageo-City, Santama 362, Japan

THE BEATLES: *World Beatles Forum*
Brad Howard, 2440 Bank Street, PO Box 40081, Ottawa,
Ontario K1VOW8

THE BEE GEES: *Fan Club*
Renee Schreiber, PO Box 2429, Miami Beach, FL 33140

BIG COUNTRY: *All Of Us*
James D. Birch, 201 Gay Street, No.4, Denton, MD 21629

CLINT BLACK: *Fan Club*
Don Zullo, PO Box 299386, Houston, Texas 77299-0386

THE BLASTERS AND DAVE ALVIN: *American Music and
the Blasters Newsletter*
Billy Davis, 80-16 64th Lane, Glendale, NY 1138-6819

BLIND MELON: *Sleepy House*
Christine Vogel, PO Box 290, Kulpsville, PA 19443

TOMMY BOLIN: *Tommy Bolin Archives*
Mike Drumm, PO 11243, Denver, CO 80211

PAT BOONE: *National Fan Club*
Chris Bujnovsky, 1025 Park Road, Leesport, PA 19533

JUNIOR BROWN: *International Fan Club*
PO Box 128203, Nashville, TN 37212

SAVOY BROWN
PO Box 855, Oswego, NY 13126

ERIC BURDON: *Eric Burdon Connection Newsletter*
Phil Metzger, 448 Silver Lane, Oceanside, NY 11572

DAVID CASSIDY: *Just David International David Cassidy Fan Club*
Barbara Pazmino, 979 East 42nd Street, Brooklyn, NY 11210

THE CASSIDYS: *Friends of The Cassidys*
Cheryl Corwin, 2601 E.Ocean Blvd, No.404, Long Beach, CA 90803-2503

CHEAP TRICK: *Cheap Trick Zine*
Dana C. James, PO Box 98, Eagleville, TN 37060-0098

LOU CHRISTIE: *International Fan Club*
Harry Young, PO Box 748, Chicago, IL 60690-0748

PETULA CLARK: *The International Petula Clark Society*
Bonnie O. Miller, 50 Railroad Avenue, Madison, CT 06443

BRUCE COCKBURN: *Gavin's Woodpile*
Daniel Keebler, 7321 131st Avenue, S.E., Snohomish, WA 98290

DEBBIE COLLINS: *Fan Club*
Robin Bruce, PO Box 689, Hilliard OH 43026

THE COWSILLS: *Fan Club*
Marsha Jordan, PO Box 83, Lexington, MS 39095

THE DAMNED: *Neat Damned Noise*
PO Box 42850-123, Houston, Texas 77242-2850, USA

THE CHARLIE DANIELS BAND: *Charlie Daniels Band Volunteers*
17060 Central Pike, Lebanon, TN 37090

DION: *Official Fan Club*
119 Hutton Street, Gaithersburg, MD 20877

OSCAR D'LEON: *International Fan Club*
Betsy Quillin, 928 Myakka Ct., N.E., St. Petersburg, FL 33702-2792

THE DOORS: *The Doors Collectors Club*
Kerry Humphreys, PO Box 1441, Orem, UT 84059-1441

DURAN DURAN: Carnival: *The Duran Duran Trade Magazine*
Kimberly Blessing, 930 Sassafrass Circle, West Chester, PA 19382

DURAN DURAN: *Duck! The Duran Duran Humour Fanzine*
Janet Stroppel, 9159 Robinson Apt.2C, Overland Park, KS 66212

DURAN DURAN: *The Duranie Connection*
Kapil Mathur, e-mail:
http://www.chapman.edu/students/mather/duran.html

DURAN DURAN: *Icon Fan Club and Fanzine*
Nancy Seman or Barbara Renaud, PO Box 158, Allen Park, MI 48101-0158

DURAN DURAN: *UMF*
Tina L. Lawson, PO Box 975, Dayton, OH 45409-0975

DURAN DURAN: *ZTV*
Liz Owens, 132 St. Andrew's Court, Mt. Laurel, NJ 08054

DURAN DURAN: *Privacy: The Warren Cuccurullo Fan Club*
Cyndi Glass, PO Box 593, Vincennes, IN 47591

BOB DYLAN: *On The Tracks*
PO Box 1943, Grand Junction, CO 81 502, USA

FAMILY: *Weaver's Answer*
Patrick Little, 425 8th Street, Ann Arbor, MI 48103, USA

FISH: *The Company North America*
Eric D. Brooks, PO Box 20766, Castro Valley, CA 94546

TONY FORD: *Fan Club*
Billie Ford, 945 Windy Hill Road, 2nd Floor, Suite 5, Smyrna, GA 30080

LESLEY GORE: *International Fan Club*
Jack Natoli, PO Box 305, Pompton Plains, NJ 07444

THE GRATEFUL DEAD: *Relix*
PO Box 94, Brooklyn, NY 11229

THE GUESS WHO: *Canadian Friends of Mine*
Kevin C.Beyer, 8645 24th Ave., Southwest, Jenison, MI 49428-9543

HALL & OATES: *Rock and Soul International*
Diane Vaskas or Lori Allred, PO Box 450, Mansfield, MA 02048

BETH HART: *Fan Club*
Jerry Hill, PO Box 48214, Minneapolis, MN 55448-0214

ANNIE HASLAM: *Appreciation Society*
Joanne (Jo) Shea, PO Box 12, Folsom, PA 19033

JIMI HENDRIX: *Experience Hendrix*
Steven Roby, PO Box 4459, Seattle, WA 98014

JIMI HENDRIX: *Jimi Hendrix Information Management Institute*
Ken Voss, PO Box 20361, Indianapolis, IN 46220

ENGELBERT HUMPERDINCK: *Engelbert's 'Goils' Fan Club*
Jeanne Friedl or Dot Gillberg, 10880 Kader Drive, Cleveland, OH 44130

ENGELBERT HUMPERDINCK: *Engel's Angels in Humperdinck Heaven*
Jean Marshalek, 3024 Fourth Avenue Carney, Baltimore, MD 21234-3208

JULIO IGLESIAS: *Friends of Julio Iglesias*
Isabel Butterfield, 28 Farmington Avenue, Longmeadow, MA 01106

IRON BUTTERFLY: *Iron Butterfly Information Network*
Rick Gagnon, 9745 Sierra Avenue, Fontana, CA 92335

JONI JAMES: *International Fan Club*
Wayne Brasler, PO Box 7207, Westchester, IL 60154

JAN & DEAN: *Surfun*
Lori Brown, 328 Sumner Avenue, Summer, WA 98390

ELTON JOHN: *East End Lights*
Tom Stanton, PO Box 760, New Baltimore, MI 48047

ELTON JOHN: *Hercules International*
Sharon Kalinoski, PO Box 398, LaGrange, IL 60525

AL JOLSON: *International Al Jolson Society*
Otis R. Lowe, 2981 Westmoor Dr., Columbus, OH 43204

SHIRLEY JONES: *Fan Club*
Martina Schade, 2295 Maple Road, York, PA 17404

DOUG KERSHAW: *Fan Club*
Gail Delmonico, PO Box 24762, San Jose, CA 95154

THE KINGSTON TRIO: *Kingston Korner*
Allan Shaw, 6 South, 230 Cohasset Road, Naperville, IL 60540-3535

THE KNACK: *Fan Club*
Ethen Barborka, PO Box 1022, Provo, UT 84603

FRANKIE LAINE: *Frankie Laine Society of America*
Helen Snow, PO Box 145, Lindenhurst, NY 11757-0145
ERNIE LANCASTER: *Fan Club*
Vicki Newton, PO Box 629, Havre De Grace, MD 21078

LEAD BELLY: *Lead Belly Society*
PO Box 6679, Ithaca, NY 14851

LED ZEPPELIN: *Proximity*
Hugh Jones, PO Box 45541, Seattle, WA 98145-0541, USA

LED ZEPPELIN: *The Only One*
86 Main St., Suite 503, Dundas, Ontario, L9H 2RI, Canada

BRENDA LEE: *The Brenda Lee International Fan Club*
Bob Borum, 4720 Hickory Way, Antioch, TN 37013

THE LETTERMEN: *Fan Club*
Sharon Stewart, PO Box 570727, Tarzana, CA 91357-0727

HUEY LEWIS & THE NEWS: *Newsline 11*
Debbie Parry, PO Box 99, Payson, UT 8465¡

LIBERACE: *The Liberace Club*
Linda Claussen, 1104 Kimberly Rd. No. 603, Bettendorf, IA 52722

LITTLE JIMMY & THE BAD BOYS: *International Fan Club*
Charlie Wolf, PO Box 111604, Nashville, TN 37222

MIKE LOVE: *Fan Club*
Patricia Ferelli, 114 Gov. Winthrop Rd., Somerville, MA 02145

LOWEN & NAVARRO: *International Lowen & Navarro Fan Club*
Sue, PO Box 19285, Alexandria, VA 22320

LORETTA LYNN: *Loretta Lynn Swap Shop*
Lenny Mattison/Andy Comer, R.R.1, Box 63A, Parish, NY 13131

LYNYRD SKYNYRD: *Fan Club*
PO Box 120855, Nashville, TN 37212

MADONNA: *The Official Madonna Fan Club*
Marcia Delvecchio, 8491 Sunset Blvd., No. 485, West Hollywood, CA 90069

BARRY MANILOW: *Very Barry Kentuckiana Connection*
Ann Harris, 409 N.28th Street, Louisville, KY 40212-1905

JIM MARLBORO: *International Fan Club*
David W.Kelly, 2011 State Ave. S.W., Decatur, AL 35601

JOHNNY MATHIS: *Reflections On Mathis*
Melanie Slavin, PO Box 182, Jacksonville, NC 28541

MELANIE: *Melanie Mania*
Richard Dozier, 32 Brookfield Lane, South Setauket, NY 11720

THE MILLS BROTHERS: *The Mills Brothers Society*
Daniel R.Clemson, 604 N.Market St., Mechanicsburg, PA 17055-2727

KATY MOFFAT: *Katy Moffat World Headquarters*
PO Box 334, O'Fallon, IL 62269-0334

THE MONKEES: *Head Of The Monkees*
Teresa Jones, 262 Baltimore Avenue, Baltimore, MD 21222

THE MONKEES: *Monkeein' Around*
Janet Marie Davis, 41297 C.C. Road, Ponchatoula, LA 70454

MICHAEL MORIARTY: *Official Fan Club*
PO Box 68, Soddy Daisy, TN 37379

MOTT THE HOOPLE: *Just A Buzz*
Justin Purington, PO Box 282, Weare, NH 03281-0282, USA

ANNE MURRAY: *The Anne Murray Collectors Club*
Rita Rose, 1618 Park Ridge Way, Indianapolis, IN 46229

MICHAEL NESMITH: *Dedicated Friends*
Donna Bailey, 1807 Millstream Drive, Frederick, MD 21702

NEW COLONY SIX: *Fan Club*
Jerry Schollenberger, 24435 Notre Dame, Dearborn, MI 48124

OLIVIA NEWTON-JOHN: *Hopelessly Devoted*
Olivia Newton-John Fan Club, 465 S. Poplar Street, No.1110 Hazleton, PA 18201

ROY ORBISON: *In Dreams*
Bert Kaufman, 484 Lake Park No.80, Oakland, CA 94610

JOHN PATRICK: *Fan Club*
Laurie Ewld, 2140 W. Cass City Road, Unionville, MI 48767

PEARL JAM: *Release*
Markus Wawzyniak, 410 Gilbert Street, Apartment A, Bryan, TX 77801-3407

TOM PETTY: *Official Fanclub*
PO Box 23125, Pleasant Hill, CA 94523-0125, USA

PINK FLOYD: *Brain Damage*
Jeff Jensen or Steve Edwards, PO Box 109, Westmont, IL 60559

GENE PITNEY: *International Fan Club*
David P. McGrath, 6201 39th Avenue, Kenosha, WI 53142

ELVIS PRESLEY: *Elvis Arkansas Style Fan Club*
Beverly Rook, PO Box 898, Mabelvale, AR 72103

ELVIS PRESLEY: *Elvis's Teddy Bear Fan Club*
Mary Ann Parisi, 744 Caliente Drive, Brandon, FL 33511

ELVIS PRESLEY: *The Elvis Beat*
Troy Yeary, 2716 Terry Drive, Richmond, VA 23228

ELVIS PRESLEY: *True Fans For Elvis Fan Club of Maine*
Dot Gonyea, 62 Lowell Street, South Portland. ME 04106

ELVIS PRESLEY: *We Remember Elvis*
Priscilla A.Parker, 1215 Tennessee Ave., Pittsburgh, PA
15216-2511

LOUIS PRIMA: *Zooma-Zooma!*
Louis Prima Fans and Friends, 1209 St. Charles Ave., New
Orleans, LA 70130

PRINCE: *Uptown*
Harold Lewis, PO Box 43, Cuyahoga Falls, OH 44222

PROCOL HARUM: *Appreciation Society*
Patrick Keating, 8415 W.89th Street, Overland Park, KS 66212

EDDY RAVEN: *International Fan Club*
Sheila Futch, PO Box 2476, Hendersonville, TN 37077

LOU RAWLS: *The Lou Rawls National Fan Club*
Dottie Taylor, 904 Iverson Dr., Great Mills, MD 20634-2530

HELEN REDDY: *Helen Reddy Fan Club*
Lorraine Breault, 204 Thunder Circle, Bensalem, PA 19020

LOU REED: *Unofficial International Fan Club*
Janis, PO Box 2392, Woburn, MA 01888

MARTHA REEVES: *Martha Reeves Exclusive Newsletter*
PO Box 1987, Paramount, CA 90723

R.E.M.: *Country Feedback*
Toni Sturtevant, RR1 North Road, Jefferson, NH 03583

REO SPEEDWAGON: REO *Pals International*
Jordan Taylor, PO Box 410084, Melbourne, FA 32941-0084

REO SPEEDWAGON: *REO Speedwagon Fan Club*
Kathy Stover, 3017. .Sowers Court, Topeka, Kansas 66604

HAPPY RHODES: *Rhodeways-The International Happy
Rhodes Medium*
Sharon Nichols, PO Box 1233, Woodstock, NY 12498

CLIFF RICHARD: *Cliff Richard Fan Club of America*
Mary Posner, 8916 N.Skokie Blvd. No.3, Skokie, IL 60077

SMOKEY ROBINSON and the MIRACLES: *Fan Club*
Marie Leighton, 8 Hillside Road, Marragansett, RI 02882-2821

TOMMY ROE: *International Fan Club*
Theresa Ehler, PO Box 813, Owatonna, MN 55060-0813

THE ROLLING STONES: *Gimme Shelter*
David Conway, PO Box 163632, Austin, TX 78716

ROLLING STONES: *Sticky Fingers*
John Carr, 12190 1/2, Ventura Blvd., Box 411, Studio City, CA
91604, USA

THE ROLLING STONES: *Visual Radio*
Joe Viglione, PO Box 2392, Woburn, MA 01888

ROOT BOY SLIM: *Memorial Fan Club*
Duane Straub, 3834 Sheffield Circle, Danville, CA 94506

RUSH: *A Show Of Fans*
Steve and Mandy Streeter, 5411 E.State Street, No.309,
Rockford, IL 61108

SANTANA: *International Fan Club*
Kitsaun King, PO Box 881630, San Francisco, CA 94188-1630

PAT SHEA: *International Fan Club*
Carol MacDonald, PO Box 905, Orchard Park, NY 14127

JIM SEIBERS: *Fan Club*
PO Box 5345, Toledo, OH 43611
FRANK SINATRA: *International Sinatra Society*
Dustin Doctor, PO Box 7176, Lakeland, FL 33807

**SIR DOUGLAS QUINTET, DOUG SAHM AND AUGIE
MEYERS:** *Sir Douglas Quintet-Doug and Augie*
K.P.Kosub, PO Box 3248, Corpus Christi, TX 78463-3248

THE SMITHEREENS: *Fan Club*
PO Box 35226, Richmond, VA 23235

SPACEMEN 3: *Dreamweapon*
Matt Hunter, PO Box 2813, New Orleans, LA 70176

SPARKS: *International Official Fan Club*
Mary Martin, Box 25038, Los Angeles, CA 90025

RICK SPRINGFIELD: *Rick's Loyal Supporters*
Vivian Acinelli, 4530 E. Four Ridge Road, Imperial, MO 63052

RICK SPRINGIELD: *Rick Springfield Quarterly*
Robin Gregg, 4611 S. University Drive, Suite No.206, Davie,
FL 33328

BRUCE SPRINGSTEEN, SOUTHSIDE JOHNNY: *Backstreets*
Charles R.Cross, PO Box 51225, Seattle, WA 98115

JIM STEINMAN: *Rockman Philharmonic - The Jim
Steinman Society for the Arts*
Jacqueline Dillon, 10 Cindy Lane, Wappingers Falls, NY 12590

JOHN KAY and STEPPENWOLF: *The Howl*
The Wolfpack Fan Club, Charlie Wolf, PO Box 1435, Franklin,
TN 37065

ROD STEWART: *Smiler*
Kimberly Pingston, PO Box 766, Wayne, MI 48184

THUNDER ROAD: *Fan Club*
Barbara Gentry, 5926 Seminary Road, Smyrna, TN 37167

TRAVIS TRITT: *Travis Tritt's Country Club*
Liz Garrison, PO Box 2044, Hiram, GA 30141

TINA TURNER: *Simply The Best Tina Turner Fan Club*
Mark Lairmore, 4566 S.Park Ave., Springfield, MO 65810

U2: *U Stay 2*
Sady Azefzaf and Dana McIntosh, 5816 N.Sheridan Rd. Apt.
2B, Chicago, IL 60660

URGE OVERKILL: *Secret Society Internationale*
Christine Vogel, PO Box 354, Kulpsville, PA 19443

VELVET UNDERGROUND: *The Velvet Underground
Appreciation Society*
5721 S.E. Laguna Ave., Stuart, FL 34997

BOBBY VINTON: *Fan Club*
Julia Walker, 153 Washington Street, Mount Vernon, NY
10550-3541

VOODOO MONKEY CHILD: *V.M.C./1753*
Laurie Stansbury and Amy E. Allen, PO Box 2546, Glenview,
IL 60025-2546

JERRY JEFF WALKER: *The Tried and True Warriors*
Pam Stock, PO Box 39, Austin, TX 78767

ROGER WATERS: *Reg: The International Roger Waters Fan
Club*
Michael Simone, 214 Lake Court, Aptos, CA 95003

PAUL WELLER: *Soul Museum*
PO Box 1896, Clovis, NM 88101

HANK WILLIAMS JR: *Fan Club*
PO Box 850, Paris, TX 38242

DENNIS WILSON: *Friends of Dennis Wilson*
Chris Duffy, 1381 Maria Way, San Jose, CA 95117

WISHBONE ASH: *USASH*
Dr. John, 2428 McKinney, Boise, ID 83704

TAMMY WYNETTE: *International Fan Club*
Cynthia King, PO Box 121926, Nashville, TN 37212

DWIGHT YOAKAM: *The Dwight Yoakam Express*
Andy Comer, PO Box 3013, Zanesville, OH 43702-3013

NORMA ZIMMER: *National Fan Club*
Frances L. Young, 1604 E.Susquehanna St., Allentown, PA
18103-4398

POP & ROCK/GENERAL

Alive and Lovely (Easy Listening/Exotica)
Johnny Treble, Flat 5, 20 Simonside Terrace, Heaton,
Newcastle Upon Tyne NE6 5JX, UK

All About D And Friends (Indie)
Dee, PO Box 345, Chesham, Bucks HP5 3DT, UK

B.A.D.I.S.M. (Indie)
B.A.D. Enterprises, 18 Trinity Place, Bexleyheath, Kent DA6
7AY, UK

Ball Buster (Underground Hard Music)
Sinbad Productions, David LaDuke Publishing, PO Box 58368,
Louisville, KY 40268-0368

BangBang Buzz (Psych/Garage/Mod)
PO Box 3181, Iowa City, IA 52244-3181, USA

Bizarre (Indie)
A. Novak, PO Box 210, Northampton NN2 6AU, UK

Blueprint (Blues)
Abacabe Publishing, 10 Messaline Avenue, London W3 6JX,
UK

Blues & Rhythm (Blues)
Byron Foulger, 1 Cliffe Lane, Thornton, Bradford BD13 3DX,
UK

Bugs (Indie)
Suzanne Fowler, 12 Buckley Court, Stony Stratford, Milton
Keynes, MK11 1NH, UK

Easy (Easy Listening/Exotica)
Matthew Woodall, PO Box 11123, London SE24 OZE, UK

Easy Pieces (Indie)
Jon Jordan, c/o Stone Immaculate, Tunstall Studios, 34-44
Tunstall Road, London SW9 8DA, UK

Encyclopedia Of Cinematic Trash (Film Soundtrack)
Mason Storm, PO Box 3137, Cumbernauld, Glasgow G67
2AT, UK

ESP (General)
ESP, 17 Westvale Mews, Leeds LS13 2HD, UK

Here Be Monsters (Indie)
SAE to: Clive Roberts, 36 Folly Fields, Wheathampstead,
Hertfordshire AL4 8HL, UK

Holding Together (Jefferson Airplane/Starship/Hot Tuna/US
west coast music)
Bill Parry, 89 Glengariff Street, Clubmoor, Liverpool L13
8DW, UK

IndiePendent (Indie)
The Cottage, Nightingale Place, High Road, Cookham,
Berkshire, SL6 9HY, UK

Juke Blues Magazine (Blues)
PO Box 148, London W9 1DY, UK

Lexicon (80s Pop)
David Richards c/o Lexicon, PO Box 1734, Wheaton, MD
20915, USA

Nostalgia (Pre Rock 'n' Roll/Music Hall)
Charlie Wilson, 39 Leicester Road, New Barnet, Herts EN5
5EW, UK

Now Dig This (Rock 'n' Roll)
19 South Hill Road, Bensham, Gateshead, Tyne & Wear NE8
3XR, UK

Paintbox (Retro)
Tim Worthington, 19 Western Drive, Grassendale, Liverpool
L19 0LX, UK

Personal Vampires (Female Singer-Songwriters)
Ian Murphy, 19 Brayton Crescent, Highbury Vale,
Nottingham NG6 9DZ, UK

Progression (Progressive Rock)
PO Box 7164, Lowell, MA 01852, USA

Ptolemaic Telescope
37 Sandridge Road, Melksham, Wiltshire SN12 7BQ, UK

Real World Notes (World Music)
Fran Brooks, Real World Trading Ltd, Mill Lane, Box,
Corsham, Wiltshire SN13 8PN, UK

Rock You Sinners (Rock 'n' Roll)
Mick Hill, The British Rock 'N Roll Magazine, 117 Worlds
End Lane, Enfield, Middx EN2 7RG, UK

The Rockin' Oldies News (50-70s Rock & Roll)
531 Baltimore Pike, #106 Bel Air, MD 21014, USA

Running Down The Back Streets (Punk/Ska)
13 The Croft, Badsworth, Pontefract, West Yorks WF9 1AS, UK

Shades of Soul (Soul)
Derek Pearson, 30 Henry Street, Thornton, Bradford, West Yorks BD13 3JE, UK

Soul Renaissance (Soul)
Martyn Bradley, 26a Stafford Road, Cannock, Staffs WS12 4PD, UK

Soul Underground (Soul)
Mark Bicknell, 23 Hindley Street, Ashton-Under-Lyme, Lancashire OL7 0BX, UK

Spikey Spud (Punk)
Rob Stranger, 113 Erskine Rd., Sutton, Surrey SM1 3BJ, UK

Surfing The New Wave
Dave Richings, 9 Bantock Place, Browns Wood, Milton Keynes MK7 8DS, UK

The Modernist Review (Mod)
Paul Welsby, 14 Hawthorn Close, Addingham, Ilkley, West Yorkshire LS29 0TW, UK

The Sound Projector
Ed Pinsent, 43a Finsen Road, Camberwell, London. SE5 9AW

Totally Wired
Andy Wired, 137 Templemere, Norwich, Norfolk NR3 4EQ

Vintage Soul (Soul)
Pete Nickols, 'Acorns', 31 Strathmore Drive, Verwood, Dorset BH31 7BJ, UK

Voices From The Shadows (Soul)
Unit 2D, Hull Road, Withernsea HU19 2EG, UK

Wig Out (Indie/Lo-Fi)
Dickie Straker, Willow House, Coaley, Nr. Dursley, Glos. GL11 5EG, UK

SONG TITLE INDEX

All That She Wants, 51, 1612, 2245
All That Way For This, 1491
All That You Dream, 5367
All The Boys Love Carrie, 198
All The Cats Join In, 5830
All The Children In A Row, 4549
All The Girls Were Pretty, 5601
All The Gold In California, 2099
All The King's Horses, 1961, 5425, 5830
All The Madmen, 685
All The Man That I Need, 2611
All The Myths On Sunday, 1519
All The Quakers Are Shoulder Shakers, 3201
All The Right Moves, 5706
All The Things She Said, 4921
All The Things You Are, 639, 1734, 2366, 2976, 4779, 5435
All The Time, 2274
All The Time And Everywhere, 3636
All The Time The Lyric A Rhyme, 3018
All The Tired Horses, 1674
All The Way, 125, 884, 2861, 4325, 4928, 5607
All The Way From America, 228
All The Way From Memphis, 3815
All The Way To Heaven, 3940
All The Wishing In The World, 565
All The World Loves Lovers, 2891
All The World Will Be Jealous Of Me, 350
All The Young Dudes, 685, 1514, 1910, 3814
All This And Heaven Too, 1436, 5455, 5606
All This And More, 30
All This Love, 1450
All This Love That I'm Giving, 3558
All This Time, 5433
All Those Years Ago, 2415
All Through The Day, 1195, 5805
All Through The Night, 205, 3139, 3634, 4860, 5461
All Thru The Nite, 4297
All Time High, 714, 1224
All Together Now, 1849, 5955
All Tore Down, 2585
All Wrapped Up In You, 2216

All Writ Down, 423
All You Good Good People, 1751
All You Need Is A Quarter, 1564
All You Need Is Love, 434, 1244, 3042, 3409
All You Want To Do Is Dance, 829
All You Zombies, 2589
All Your Friends, 670
All Your Love, 1141, 3407, 4692, 5396
All Your Sins, 990
All's Fair In Love And War, 2185, 4299, 5711
All-American Redneck, 2618
Alla My Love, 2097
Allah And Justice, 711
Allah's Holiday, 2036
Alle Porte Del Sole, 3493
Alleged, 5581
Allegheny Al, 2523
Allegheny Lady, 387
Allegheny Moon, 2549, 3448, 3711, 4102
Allegro, 127
Alleluia, 1922
Allen's Got A New Hi-Fi, 3136
Allentown, 2830
Allentown Jail, 4675, 5974
Alley Cat Stomp, 138
Alley Oop, 661, 2001, 2570, 3973, 4168
Alley Special, 2575
Alley-Oop, 1386, 2019
Allez-Vous-En, 912
Alligator Man, 3929, 3983, 5598
Alligator Wine, 2436
Allison, 4256
Allison Road, 3916
Allons A Lafayette, 126
Alma Con Alma, 4742
Almaz, 1282
Almighty Father, 1080
Almighty God, 5788
Almost, 3783
Almost A Love Song, 5643
Almost Always, 2775
Almost Cut My Hair, 1307, 1465
Almost Goodbye, 1047
Almost In Your Arms, 3281
Almost Independence Day, 3795, 4720
Almost Like Being In Love, 735, 2853, 3196, 3294
Almost Paradise, 4215
Almost Paradise...Love Theme From Footloose, 2458
Almost Persuaded, 2610, 4876, 5807
Almost Persuaded No. 2, 5918
Almost Saturday Night,

1954, 5914
Almost See You (Somewhere), 1063
Almost There, 5836
Almost With You, 1082
Almost Young, 2505
Alnaaflysh, 1342
Aloha, 2037
Aloha Louie, 4224
Aloha Low Down, 1437
Alone, 782, 1102, 1884, 2025, 2867, 3293, 4328, 4869-4870
Alone (Why Must I Be Alone), 4869
Alone Again, 550, 801, 1915
Alone Again (Naturally), 1081, 4005
Alone Again In The Lap Of Luxury, 3463
Alone Again Or, 1372, 1976
Alone And Yet Alive, 2602
Alone At A Table For Two, 2528
Alone I Breathed, 4755
Alone In My Dreams, 218
Alone In The Night, 2172
Alone She Cries, 4948
Alone Together, 1520, 1950, 4776
Alone Too Long, 1886, 4776
Alone With You, 1634, 5970
Along Came Caroline, 1269
Along Comes Mary, 260, 454, 641
Along The Avenue, 4619
Along The Navajo Trail, 183, 1436, 1779
Along The Santa Fe Trail, 1639
Along With Me, 894
Alpha & Omega, 4200
Alphabetic Response, 761
Alrabaiye Take Me Up, 156, 1612
Already In Heaven, 2610
Alreet, 3998
Alright, 124, 1354, 4749
Alright Alright Alright, 3839
Alright Now, 5502
Alright With Me, 2466
Also Sprach Zarathustra, 1486-1487
Alta Songo, 87
Altar Of Love, 1017
Alternate Title, 3741
Altogether Now, 1847
Alton's Official Daughter, 1063
Alvin Stone (The Birth And Death Of A Gangster), 1844
Alvin's Harmonica, 1065
Alway-yayys Lay-yate, 2040
Always, 273, 493, 532, 617, 652, 1224, 3315, 5534, 5577
Always A Lady, 3865
Always Accused, 5328
Always Alone, 1357
Always And Always, 5669, 5929

Always And Forever, 2464
Always Coming Back To You, 5682
Always For Me, 772
Always In All Ways, 3751
Always Late, 1009
Always Late (With Your Kisses), 2039, 5960
Always On My Mind, 155, 1091, 3456, 3712, 3900, 4205, 5398
Always Something There To Remind Me, 587, 1128, 3870, 5443
Always Somewhere, 3343
Always There, 566, 2689, 5746
Always Together, 636, 3493
Always True To You In My Fashion, 3035, 3669, 4289
Always You, 3466, 5669
Always Yours, 2172
Am I Dreaming?, 5433
Am I Evil, 1507
Am I Grooving You, 4784
Am I That Easy To Forget, 2635, 3303
Am I The Same Girl, 56, 1856
Am I Wasting My Time On You, 5617
Am I Who I Think I Am?, 2205
AM:PM, 1614
Amagideon, 5668
Amanda, 677, 2051, 3589, 5843
Amanda Ruth, 4430
Amapola, 713, 897, 1598, 1697
Amateur Hour, 1990
Amazing, 156
Amazing Grace, 25, 200, 1176, 2257, 2979, 3594, 4491, 4671
Amazing Grace (Used To Be Her Favorite Song), 157
Amazons, 4229
Ambassadors Of Love, 3668
Amber, 358
Amber Mantra, 1526
Ambition, 1363, 1564, 2178, 5539
Ambrose, 5391
Ambrosia, 538
Ambulance Blues, 5978
Ambush, 3610, 4083
Ame No Blues, 292
Amelia, 3713
Amelia Earhart's Last Flight, 3565
Amen, 1711, 2683, 2733
America, 499, 664, 1509, 2261, 2797, 2949, 3936, 4557, 4916, 5771-5772
America - What Time Is Love?, 2628
America Drinks & Goes Home, 3809

Bogus Badge, 4652
Bohemia, 2904
Bohemian Rhapsody, 30, 322, 4380-4381, 4863
Bojangles, 387, 522, 569, 948, 1246, 1377, 1418, 1885, 2344, 2602, 3580, 4581, 5278, 5689
Bojangles Of Harlem, 1886, 2976
Boji, 3110
Bold Robert Emmett, 2680
Bolero, 78, 568, 727, 2237
Bolero At The Savoy, 3998
Bolero Babe, 362
Bolingo Na Ngai Na Beatrice, 2008
Boll Weevil, 931
Bolt, 5484
Boma L'Heure, 5406
Bomb, 850
Bomba, 2764
Bomba De Navidad, 4558
Bombast, 5396
Bombay Calling, 2723
Bombs Away! On Harpurhey, 3003
Bombs Over Baghdad, 5513
Bombscare, 3820
Bon Bon Vie, 5278
Bon Voyage, 913, 2287
Bona Fide, 523
Bonafide Love, 3825, 5909
Bonaparte's Retreat, 2234, 3017, 4651
Bonaventure, 1341
Bone Idol, 1631
Bone Machine, 4256
Bone Orchard Blues, 1268
Bones, 748, 988, 3657
Bongo (To The Batmobile), 5345
Bongo Bongo Bongo, 1770
Bongo Chant, 785
Bongo Gully, 3266
Bongo Massive, 5457
Bongo Natty, 3171
Bongo Nyah, 1363, 3271
Bongo Red, 2165
Bongo Rock, 1770
Bongo Stomp, 3266
Bonita, 619, 1288, 1955
Bonita Applebum, 31, 3393
Bonita Monana, 1779
Bonjour Paris, 1705, 2054
Bonnie Hielan Mary, 3137
Bonnie Jean, 2869
Bonnie Wee Jeanie McColl, 5482
Bonny Irish Boy, 3459
Bonour M. Basie, 3671
Bonsoir Jolie Madame, 5499
Bony Incus, 1696
Bony Moronie, 5853
Bonzo Goes To Bitburg, 4423
Boo-Ga-Loo, 2672
Boo-Hoo, 3300
Boogaloo Baby, 1889

Boogaloo Down Broadway, 1844
Boogaloo Party, 1926
Boogie, 673, 2967, 5743
Boogie At Midnight, 787
Boogie Chillen No. 2, 2585
Boogie Chillun, 3255
Boogie Down, 2965
Boogie Down (Bronx), 3431
Boogie In Chicago, 4328
Boogie In My Bones, 99, 573
Boogie In The Bronx, 4328
Boogie In The Park, 3325
Boogie Man, 4847
Boogie Nights, 2464
Boogie On Reggae Woman, 4520
Boogie On The Street, 3221
Boogie Oogie Oogie, 30
Boogie Rock, 99, 610
Boogie Shoes, 2949, 4752
Boogie Town, 1859
Boogie Twist, 4351, 5597
Boogie Wonderland, 1689, 1756
Boogie Woogie, 380, 1040, 3555, 3798, 4449, 4818
Boogie Woogie Amputee, 385
Boogie Woogie Bugle Boy, 183-184, 3656, 4449
Boogie Woogie Country Girl, 4277
Boogie Woogie Music, 3759
Boogie-Woogie Ball, 1918
Boogy Fool, 4351
Book Book, 681
Book Of Dreams, 5623
Book Of Life, 3838
Book Of Love, 3742, 3832
Book Of Rules, 2733, 2845, 3005, 4652
Book Report, 5963
Book Song, 1826
Books, 1396
Books On The Bonfire, 648
Boom, 728, 1605, 2700
Boom Boom, 562, 918, 976, 978, 2586-2587, 3317, 4828
Boom Boom (Out Go The Lights), 3274
Boom Boom Baby, 1272
Boom Boom Boom, 4082
Boom Boom Boomerang, 1432
Boom Bye Bye, 369, 3397
Boom Chaka Laka, 4941
Boom Sha La La Lo, 4296
Boom Shack A Lack, 206, 4494
Boom Shak Attack, 673
Boom Shaka Lacka, 3217
Boom Town, 3058
Boom Wha Dis, 370
Boom! Shake The Room, 1559, 2826, 4082
Boom-Bang-A-Bang, 2833, 3356
Boom-Boom, 3267

Boomer, 5877
Boomerang, 4980
Boop-Boop-A-Doop, 2932, 4516
Boops, 4546, 4882
Boot Heel Drag, 4499
Boot Scootin' Boogie, 753
Booted, 2217
Boothferry Bridge, 184
Boots And Shoes, 5463
Boots Of Spanish Leather, 2291
Bootzilla, 1174
Booyaka, 4503
Bop, 4798
Bop Street, 622
Bop-A-Hula, 3929
Boppin' The Blues, 570, 838, 4196, 4537
Boranda, 3354
Bordeaux Rose, 1825
Border Clash, 3956
Border Of The Blues, 2534, 5746
Border Ska, 909
Border Song, 1747, 2833
Borderline, 1881, 3539, 4888
Bordertown Woman, 387
Bored, 1494, 3033
Boredom, 198, 859, 5441
Borinquen Tiene Montuno, 3702
Boris The Spider, 1767, 1859
Born A Fighter, 4333
Born A Little Late, 5769
Born A Woman, 4292
Born Again, 1074, 1330, 5423
Born Again Black Man, 4462
Born And Raised In Compton, 1560
Born Dead, 104, 3194
Born For A Purpose, 1566, 2276
Born Free, 562, 1856, 2936, 3634, 3743, 4487, 4801
Born In A Maisonette, 3660
Born In Chicago, 2248
Born In East LA, 1041
Born In Puerto Rico, 922
Born In The Ghetto, 2054
Born In The USA, 1041
Born In Time, 1677
Born Jamaican, 4250
Born Killer, 4766
Born Lucky, 3944
Born Pressurizer, 1496
Born Slippy, 2913, 5576
Born This Way, 1222, 4082
Born To Be Blue, 4495
Born To Be Happy, 2358
Born To Be Kissed, 4818
Born To Be Loved, 2787
Born To Be Wild, 657, 1694, 2467, 3251, 4071, 4702, 4759
Born To Be With You, 923,

1069, 1535, 1707, 2311
Born To Boogie, 447
Born To Each Other, 3933
Born To Give My Love To You, 3542
Born To Live And Born To Die, 1987
Born To Lose, 1357
Born To Love You, 1172, 1569, 3542, 5487, 5522
Born To Run, 2012, 2970
Born To Wander, 4435
Born Too Late, 4278
Born Too Loose, 3094
Born Under A Bad Sign, 674, 3008, 3279, 3664
Born XY, 5527
Borrow Man, 1538
Borrowed Tune, 5978
Borstal Breakout, 4899
Bosco Stomp, 1931
Bosnia, 1276
Bosom Buddies, 246, 2505, 3428
Bosrah, 6005
Boss, 715
Boss Drum, 4576
Bossa Nova Baby, 2050, 4311
Bossanova, 3104
Bostisch, 5954
Boston Beguine, 638
Boston Blues, 5688
Boston Burglar, 3842
Boston Tea Party, 4820
Botcha-Me, 1133
Both Ends Burning, 4670
Both Sides Now, 706, 1176, 3712, 3899, 5868
Both Sides Of The Coin, 3865
Both Sides Of The Tweed, 2100
Both To Each Other (Friends And Lovers), 4396
Botheration, 2535
Bottle Of Wine, 1902, 2154
Bottle Party, 5887
Bottle Up And Go, 4925
Bottles, 4396
Bottom, 5465
Bottom Of The Mountain, 5859
Bottomless Pit, 1430
Bottoms Up, 3225
Boulder Skies, 4367
Boulder To Birmingham, 4237
Boulevard, 792
Boulevard Of Broken Dreams, 437, 480, 2801
Boum!, 5499
Bounce, 1944
Bounce In Your Buggy, 4832
Bounce Me, Brother, With A Solid Four, 4449, 4958
Bouncin' The Blues, 383
Bouncing Babies, 5324

3029, 3783, 5818
Candy Man, 3550, 3555, 3958, 4553, 4639
Candy Man Blues, 2645
Candy Skin, 1901
Candybar Express, 3335
Cannonball, 71, 4755
Canon And Gigue, 1849
Cantaloop, 5588
Cantaloupe Island, 1757
Cantante Errante, 1530
Canteloupe Island, 1358
Canter Mi Horse, 4462
Canticle, 4916
Cantina, 1404
Cantina Band, 3607
Cao Cao Mani Picao, 1320
Cap'n Crunch, 4396
Capitao Do Asfolto, 2574
Capped Teeth And Caesar Salad, 565
Caprice For Strings, 5797
Capricorn Dancer, 1096
Caps Get Peeled, 1503
Capstick Comes Home, 926
Captain Custard, 4563, 4769
Captain Dread, 1622
Captain Hook's Waltz, 4207
Captain Jack, 2830
Captain Kidd, 3799
Captain Of Love, 1788
Captain Of Your Ship, 460, 737, 3104, 4506, 5954, 5974
Captain Save A Hoe, 1681
Captain Selassie I, 2670
Captain Zlogg, 3497
Captives Of The Heart, 314
Capture Land, 1162
Car, 1191
Car Car, 2319
Car Crash, 291, 487, 2459
Car Phone, 316
Car Pound Drifter, 5685
Car Song, 1721, 2031
Cara De Payaso, 4616
Cara Mia, 2790, 3289, 3451, 5803
Caramelos, 3353, 4360
Caravan, 1735, 2726, 2955, 3479, 3736, 3762, 3795, 3984, 5451
Caravan And Skidoo, 4576
Caravan Of Lonely Men, 2954
Caravan Of Love, 25, 2175, 2608, 2720
Caravan Romance, 5961
Caravan Suite, 2904
Carceleras, 1794
Carcrash, 5564
Card Song, 941
Cards Of Love, 5432
Career Of Evil, 615
Career Opportunities, 1110
Career Time, 1080
Careful, 4802
Careful With That Axe, Eugene, 4249, 5987
Carefully Taught, 3604

Careless, 2615, 2915
Careless Hands, 2532, 3995
Careless Heart, 3865, 4607
Careless Love, 2958
Careless Memories, 1657
Careless Rhapsody, 861, 4607
Careless Whisper, 2280, 3652, 5426, 5781
Carelessly, 5989
Caresses, 3735
Carey, 1454, 3713, 5385
Caribbean, 1429, 5470
Caribbean Blue, 528
Caribbean Calypso, 540
Caribbean Love Song, 1705
Caribbean Queen, 766
Caribbean Queen (No More Love On The Run), 4012
Carino, 850, 1453
Carioca, 261
Carita, 1577
Carlo, 2731
Carlos And Yolanda, 922
Carlos Dominguez, 1256, 5457
Carlotta, 3648
Carly's Loneliness, 1763
Carmague, 647
Carmelita, 5996
Carminetta, 5961
Carnegie Hall, 1705
Carnival, 3257, 4576, 4695
Carol, 2477, 4773, 5375
Carole Ann, 1805
Carolina, 4528
Carolina (I Love You), 1380
Carolina Day, 5317
Carolina In The Morning, 1578, 1587, 2863, 2922
Carolina Moon, 282, 828, 1405, 2006, 4704, 5928
Carolina Moonshiner, 5666
Carolina On My Mind, 5313
Carolina Rua, 3774
Carolina Shout, 2846-2847, 5688
Carolina Waltz, 3760
Caroline, 348, 987, 1981, 2803
Caroline Says, 5789
Caroline, No, 5870
Carolyn, 1179
Carousel, 2756
Carousel In The Park, 4637, 5582
Carousel Waltz, 946-947, 3491
Carpet Man, 1889, 5744
Carriage Trade, 2447
Carrickfergus, 3585, 3795
Carrie, 953, 1786, 3301, 4489, 4531
Carroll Calls The Tunes, 2137
Carry Go Bring Come, 2535, 3576, 5884
Carry It On, 5530
Carry Me, 1302

Carry Me Back To Old Virginny, 738, 3532
Carry Me Back To The Lone Prairie, 4587
Carry Me Home, 2174
Carry Me Michael, 5661
Carry On, 1307, 1465, 1998, 3049, 5530
Carry That Weight, 435
Carry The Blame, 4557
Carryin' The Torch, 2034
Carrying A Torch, 3796
Carrying Mine, 5952
Cars, 1866, 3985
Cartoon Party, 3944
Carwash Hair, 3632
Casanova, 186, 310
Casanova (Your Playing Days Are Over), 186
Casanova Cricket, 942
Casbah, 3788
Cascade, 540, 1341, 2060
Casey At The Bat, 1388
Casey Jones, 2774, 4539
Casey's Last Ride, 1300
Cash For Your Trash, 5689
Cash On The Barrelhead, 3328
Cash Ready, 2222
Cashing In On Xmas, 322
Casino, 4458
Casino Royale, 147
Cassandra, 2575
Cassanova, 3209
Cassava Piece, 4096
Cassavubu, 1251, 4437
Cast A Long Shadow, 3742
Cast Iron Heart, 3250
Cast Off All My Fears, 2606
Cast Your Fate To The Wind, 106, 483, 1939, 2304, 4177, 4774, 4780, 5886
Castanets And Lace, 2533
Casting Lazy Shadows, 4367
Casting My Spell, 4254
Castle In The Sky, 671
Castle Of Dreams, 2708, 3071, 5432
Castle On The Hill, 1820
Castle Rock, 2548, 4800
Castles In Spain, 230
Castles In the Sky, 4648
Castles Made Of Sand, 5521
Casual Affair, 3605, 5462
Cat Among The Pigeons, 760
Cat Fever, 3984
Cat In The Window, 659
Cat Scratch Fever, 3984
Cat's In The Cradle, 136, 1019
Cat's Squirrel, 5397
Catalina La O, 4614
Catblack, 5277
Catch, 1335
Catch 22, 4862
Catch A Falling Star, 1195, 1326, 1495, 1977, 2468, 3678

Catch Me I'm Falling, 4455
Catch Me On The Rebop, 1421
Catch The Beat, 2138, 4251, 5921
Catch The Fire, 1631
Catch The Moon, 182
Catch The Wind, 384, 1590, 4181
Catch Us If You Can, 1099
Catcher In The Rye, 1921
Catching The Local, 3642
Cater For Woman, 79
Catfish Blues, 3861
Catfish John, 4698
Cath, 620
Cathedral, 1307
Cathedral In The Pines, 1888
Cathedral Park, 1640
Cathy Come Home, 5544
Cathy's Clown, 11, 26, 1798-1799, 2725, 5705
Catman, 212
Cats In The Cradle, 5563
Cats Squirrel, 596
Catting Around, 1067
Cattle And Cane, 2175
Cattle Call, 237, 2002, 4091, 4296, 4547, 5807
Catwalk Blues, 2156
Caught In My Shadow, 3908, 5906
Caught In The Middle, 4733
Caught In The Rapture, 337, 2170
Caught Up, 1078
Caught Up In My Heart, 4052
Caught Up In The Rapture, 337
Caught You In A Lie, 1270, 1889, 3345, 3465
Cause Cause I Love You, 1223
Cause I Need You, 3981
Caution To The Wind, 203
Cavalry Cross, 5414
Cavalry Of Cloud, 4864
Cave Bitch, 2668
Cavern Stomp, 999
Cavernism, 3839
Caviare And Chips, 1249
CB 200, 1528, 4514
Ceasefire, 2389
Ceatrix Did It, 2520
Cecilia, 2399, 2964-2965, 3324, 4916
Cecilia Ann, 676
Celebrate, 155, 169, 2134
(Celebrate) The Day After You, 607, 3529
Celebration, 1001, 2333, 3062
Celebration Generation, 5770
Celebration Of The Year, 298
Celeste Aida, 2258, 3128

Couldn't Get It Right, 1127
Couldn't Hear Nobody
Pray, 5599
Couldn't Know, 4168
Count Every Star, 588, 2447,
4561
Count Me In, 3216
Count Me Out, 4351
Count On Me, 603, 2243,
2803
Count The Days, 5870
Count Your Blessings, 494,
881, 1908, 2295, 3648
Count Your Blessings And
Smile, 3201
Count Your Blessings
Instead Of Sheep, 494, 5792
Counting Teardrops, 1468,
1970
Country And Western
Truck Drivin' Singer, 4924
Country Boy, 403, 803-804,
1513, 2473, 2897, 4172,
4947, 5356
Country Boy Blues, 2271
Country Boy's Tool Box,
5449
Country Bumpkin, 4983
Country Clown, 1616
Country Comfort, 5526
Country Cousins, 4079
Country Death Song, 5649
Country DJ, 173
Country Down To My Soul,
4143
Country Fool, 4895
Country Gardens, 4388
Country Gentleman, 2283
Country Girl, 1307, 1465,
2486, 3123, 3659, 4077,
4574, 5773, 5970
Country Girl - City Man,
1114
Country Girl Became Drugs
And Sex Punk, 4824
Country Girl-City Man,
5631
Country Girls, 4771
Country Green, 4442
Country Guitar, 417
Country Honk, 4630
Country House, 632
Country Junction, 1973
Country Life, 1966
Country Line Special, 2594
Country Living, 225, 1309,
3659
Country Man, 1913, 2897,
5631
Country Music Never Let
Me Down, 2744
Country Music Nightmare,
692
Country Music Time, 3310
Country Music's Here To
Stay, 2647
Country Of The Blind, 1829
Country Party, 3174
Country Pieces, 4388

Country Preacher, 71
Country Rock Rap, 1541
Country Sad Ballad Man,
632
Country Song, 5649
Country Sunshine, 5773
Countryfied, 4244
Countryman, 2051
County Fair, 3795
County Line, 1224
Coup D'Etat, 5921
Coupe De Ville Baby, 3608
Coupon Song, 4865
Court Of Love, 5577
Courtin' In The Rain, 5553
Courting Is A Pleasure, 4691
Cousin Kevin, 1767
Cousin Norman, 3470
Couventine, 442
Cover Girl, 3915
Cover Me, 3955, 5835
Cover Of The Rolling Stone,
4627
Covered Wagon Days, 5753
Cow Cow, 641, 1398, 3296,
3680, 4985
Cow Cow Blues, 1398-1399
Cow Cow Boogie, 1399,
1438, 2694, 2908, 3799,
4958
Cow Horn Skank, 189
Cow Thief Skak, 4200
Coward Of The County,
688, 857, 2099, 4622, 5784
Cowards Over Pearl
Harbour, 59, 1394
Cowboy, 2968, 5657
Cowboy Bill, 755, 2096
Cowboy Convention, 106
Cowboy Dreams, 3869
Cowboy Life, 3662
Cowboy Movie, 1305, 2674
Cowboy Song, 371
Cowboy's Heaven, 3497
Cowboys Ain't Supposed To
Cry, 364
Cowboys And Indians,
1308, 3379
Cowboys Don't Cry, 1432
Cowboys Stay On Longer,
5696
Cowboys To Girls, 2069,
2705
Cowgirl In The Sand, 869,
1800, 5977
Cowpuncher's Cantata, 862
Coxsone Hop, 1568
Coyote, 3713
Coz I Luv You, 4959
CPGJ's, 369
Crab In A Bag, 3802
Crab Race, 541
Crabwalking, 4335
Crack Attack, 663
Crack Killed Applejack,
2114
Crackdown, 1273
Cracker Jack, 1113
Crackin' Up, 942, 2639

Cracking Up, 2817, 3349
Cracklin Rosie, 1509
Cradle Of Love, 4317
Cradle Song, 170
Crank Face, 1528, 5504
Crank It Up (Funk Town)
Pt. 1, 784
Cranked Up Really High,
4962
Crash, 39, 1050, 1272-1273,
1867, 4330
Crash And Burn, 3476
Crash Course To Brain
Surgery, 816
Crash Crash, 200
Crash Goes Love, 2566
Crashie First Socialist, 47
Crashie Sweep Them Clean,
47
Crashing The Golden Gate,
954
Craven Choke Puppy, 740
Cravin' For Avon, 2227
Cravin' For The Avon, 3779
Crawfish, 2998, 4310, 4371
Crawfishin, 2091
Crawl, 1767, 2455
Crawl Parts 1 & 2, 804
Crawlin' Back, 4049
Crawling From The
Wreckage, 1707
Crawling King Snake, 2586
Crawling Up A Hill, 3526
Crazeology, 2405
Crazy, 651, 697, 1130, 1920,
2670, 3441, 3794, 3829,
3899, 4156, 4797, 5371-
5372, 5677
Crazy (For Me), 2740
Crazy Arms, 701, 1429,
1760, 3219, 4324, 5923
Crazy Baby, 4069
Crazy Baldhead, 172, 452
Crazy Blue Eyes, 1366
Crazy Blues, 628, 704, 4024,
4180
Crazy Boy, 2400
Crazy Chance, 1806, 2941
Crazy Country, 2637, 3465
Crazy Crazy Lovin, 955
Crazy Cuts, 2239
Crazy Daisy, 4718
Crazy Dreams, 706
Crazy Feeling, 2117, 3195
Crazy For You, 214, 2459,
2689, 3202, 3403
Crazy For Your Love, 1806
Crazy Girl, 2639
Crazy Heart, 878, 4651
Crazy Horse, 1969
Crazy Horses, 2166, 4074,
4820, 5295
Crazy In The Heart, 5830
Crazy Jane, 3974
Crazy Joe, 2763
Crazy Legs, 4476, 5495
Crazy Little Guitar Man,
1956
Crazy Little Mama, 1720, 4523

Crazy Little Thing Called
Love, 4381
Crazy Love, 1410, 2549,
2637, 3762, 4269, 4327
Crazy Mama, 890, 1720,
4523
Crazy Man, 2897
Crazy Man Crazy, 1026,
2341
Crazy Man Michael, 3236
Crazy Old Soldier, 3900
Crazy Over You, 1983, 2560
Crazy Raven, 4281
Crazy Rhythm, 35, 881,
3649
Crazy Train, 596, 4519
Crazy With Love, 2549
Crazy Woman, 5990
Crazy Words Crazy Tune,
91, 4351, 5953
Crazy World, 5643
Crazy, Crazy Nights, 3034
Crazy, He Calls Me, 4695
Crazy, Man, Crazy, 1026,
2341
Cream, 2849, 4143, 4332
Cream In My Jeans, 1256
Cream Of The Sky, 3705
Cream Puff War, 4355
Created By One, 572
Creation, 1712, 2520
Creation - The Poet And
The Fire Bird, 1648
Creation Rebel, 840
Credit In The Straight
World, 2554, 5967
Creep, 3868, 4096, 4403,
5452
Creeque Alley, 3346, 3427,
3579, 4223
Creole Blues, 2869
Creole Crooning Song, 2160
Creole Love Call, 1735, 2344
Creole Rhapsody, 1735
Crepescule With Nellie,
1090
Crescendo In Blue, 266,
2199
Crescendo In Drums, 896
Crescent City Suite, 5778
Crestfallen, 170
Crew's Gone Mad, 1222
Cricket Lovely Cricket, 3661
Cried Like A Baby, 5856
Crime Don't Pay, 4335
Crime In The City, 5978
Crime Of Passion, 3540
Crime Of The Century,
4408
Crime Story, 2315
Crimes Against Humanity,
4713
Crimes Of Passion, 4866
Criminal World, 791
Crimson And Clover, 2778,
2821
Crinoline Days, 540, 3850
Crinoline Waltz, 2488
Cripple Creek, 4359

Da Funk, 1357
Dad Gave My Dog Away, 2315, 5553
Dad Gum Your Hide, Boy, 1917
Daddy, 195-196, 2828, 3531, 3566, 4800, 5510
Daddy And Home, 4603
Daddy Cool, 656, 1395, 4450, 5360
Daddy Daddy, 1083
Daddy Dearest, 3360
Daddy Didn't Tell You, 264
Daddy Don't You Walk So Fast, 3933
Daddy Jack, 2977
Daddy Rolling Stone, 574
Daddy Sang Bass, 976, 4196
Daddy Was A Yodelling Cowboy, 2571
Daddy Was An Old Time Preacher Man, 5666
Daddy What If, 378
Daddy's Been Around The House Too Long, 378
Daddy's Come Around, 4086
Daddy's Getting Married, 518
Daddy's Girl, 5617
Daddy's Hands, 1655
Daddy's Home, 1762, 2460, 2743, 2894, 3593, 4868
Daddy's Last Letter (Private First Class John H McCormick), 4556
Daddy's Little Girl, 5617
Daddy's Little Man, 1413
Daddy's Making Records In Nashville, 3180
Daddy's Money, 4735
Daddy's Oldsmobile, 2979, 3423
Daddy, Get Your Guitar Down, 1298
Daddy, I'm Coming Home, 3156
Daddy, What's A Train?, 4221
Daddy-O, 660, 1413, 1963
Daffodil, 2336
Daisy, 2432
Daisy Age Soul, 5459
Daisy Bell, 1974
Daisy Got Me Crazy, 1124
Daisy Hill, 1872
Daisy Petal Pickin, 1902, 2154
Daisy With A Dimple On Her Chin, 1064
Daisy, Daisy, 3261
Dallas, 1728, 1930, 2154, 2736
Dallas Rag, 2868, 4209
Dalvatore Sally, 4404
Damaged, 4371
Dameron Stomp, 1368, 3195
Dameronia, 1682

Dammit, Janet, 4600
Damn Life, 3850
Damn Those Memories, 2744
Damn Your Eyes, 5990
Damn, I Wish I Was Your Lover, 2441
Damned, 5387
Damp Rag, 2214
Damp Weather, 2868
Dan's Big Log, 3384
Dana My Love, 1846
Dance, 2913, 3007, 4460, 4852, 4969, 4852, 4969, 5547
Dance A Cork, 5767
Dance A Little Closer, 1374
Dance Again, 2038
Dance All Night, 601, 4336, 4696
Dance Around In Your Bones, 1747
Dance Away, 4670
Dance Beat, 3006
Dance Can't Done, 924
Dance Class, 590, 1837
Dance Dance Dance (Yowsah, Yowsah, Yowsah), 1053
Dance Get Overload, 4468
Dance Girl, 1034, 3367
Dance Girl Dance, 2002
Dance Hall Days, 5695
Dance Hall Manic, 1008
Dance In A Greenwich Farm, 904
Dance In The Old Fashioned Way, 3493
Dance Lady Dance, 1315
Dance Man Buys A Farm, 5830
Dance Mood, 3351
Dance No More, 1681
Dance Of An Ostracised Imp, 1341
Dance Of Fury, 782, 3037, 3669
Dance Of Life, 5300
Dance Of The Eighth Veil, 3451
Dance Of The Hours, 1544, 2885, 4874
Dance Of The Marionettes, 5468
Dance Of The Snowflakes, 540
Dance Of The Spanish Onion, 4651
Dance Of The Wooden Shoes, 3409
Dance On, 292, 4835
Dance Stance, 1502
Dance Ten, Looks Three, 1070-1071, 2363
Dance The Body Music, 4072
Dance The Kung Fu, 1603
Dance The Night Away, 3523, 5605

Dance The Two Step, 127
Dance To A Dream, 922
Dance To The Locomotion, 4425
Dance To The Music, 368, 4973, 5386
Dance To The Rhythm Of Love, 5706
Dance Variations For Two Pianos And Orchestra, 2224
Dance With A Dolly (With A Hole In Her Stocking), 3047, 3786
Dance With Me, 148, 511, 784, 1627, 2704, 3318, 3461, 3733, 4063
Dance With Me Molly, 688
Dance With Me, Henry, 353, 2137
Dance With Mr Domino, 1581
Dance With The Devil, 4298
Dance With The Guitar Man, 1702, 2452
Dance With The One That Brought You, 5540
Dance With You, 3351
Dance, Dance, Dance, 4737, 5454
Dance, Everybody, Dance, 1395
Dance, Little Lady, 2340, 5397
Dance: Ten; Looks: Three, 1070-1071, 2363
Dancehall Feeling, 5338
Dancehall Style, 3144
Dancer, 556, 1459, 1962
Dancin, 1315, 1349, 5612
Dancin' Easy, 5842
Dancin' Fool, 1229
Dancin' In The Moonlight, 5390
Dancin' On A Saturday Night, 1929
Dancin' On The Sidewalk, 1837
Dancin' Shoes, 4111
Dancin' with Anson, 5753
Dancing, 1451, 2477
Dancing All The Time, 518
Dancing At Whitsun, 5935
Dancing Drums, 324
Dancing Frog, 5475
Dancing Hearts, 3864
Dancing Honeymoon, 416
Dancing In My Sleep, 1744
Dancing In Outer Space, 273
Dancing In The City, 510, 3476
Dancing In The Dark, 361, 524, 673, 1161, 1208, 1520, 2742, 4776
Dancing In The Moonlight, 3000
Dancing In The Street, 686, 1548, 2103, 3480, 4486
Dancing In Your Head, 5280

Dancing Jennie, 100
Dancing Mad, 5463
Dancing Man, 2741
Dancing Master, 1174
Dancing Mood, 3794, 5871
Dancing Nights, 1139
(Dancing) On A Saturday Night, 619
Dancing On The Ceiling, 1795, 1797, 2340, 3519, 4606, 4922
Dancing On The Floor, 5393
Dancing Queen, 37, 551, 1603, 2260, 4095
Dancing Shoes, 5667
Dancing The Devil Away, 2928, 4681
Dancing The Night Away, 3813
Dancing Tight, 1866
Dancing Time, 875, 4396
Dancing To The Music Of Love, 2774
Dancing Towards Disaster, 2643
Dancing Will Keep You Young, 3533
Dancing With A Ghost, 1428, 1744, 2822
Dancing With My Shadow, 5915
Dancing With Tears In My Eyes, 829, 1638-1639, 4818, 4880, 4818, 4880, 5571
Dancing With The Captain, 3940
Dancing With You, 5973
Dandelion, 658
Dandy, 557, 1014, 1111, 1819, 1899, 3233, 4114, 4598, 4740, 5446
Dang Me, 3679, 4976, 5930
Danger, 36, 577, 3611, 5903
Danger Ahead! (Beware), 4493
Danger Bird, 6005
Danger Of A Stranger, 4149
Danger Zone, 2426, 2763, 3297, 4465
Danger! Heartbreak Ahead, 3185, 3784
Danger, She's A Stranger, 1920
Dangerman, 90
Dangerous, 3854
Dangerous Game, 2807
Dangerous MC, 4430
Dangerous On The Dance Floor, 656, 3854
Dangerous Shoes, 3139
Daniel, 1584, 1761, 2833, 6005
Daniel Boone, 3241
Danke Schoen, 2922, 3933
Danny Boy, 448, 457, 519, 720, 1427, 3100, 3579, 3994, 4324, 4485, 4652, 4856, 5547, 5837

East Of The River Nile, 1063, 4096
East Of The Sun, 3543, 3711
East Of The Sun, West Of The Moon, 2155
East River, 722
East Side Of Heaven, 829, 3711
East Side Rendezvous, 2043
East Side Story, 4814
East Side, West Side, 463, 1361
East Texas Drag, 1691
East To The West, 203
East West, 1996
East Wind, 2348
Easter Parade, 113, 249, 493, 1516, 1692, 2555
Easter Song, 30, 4076
Easter Sunday With You, 5454
Eastern Rain, 3712
Eastwood Clint, 2166
Easy, 1193-1194, 1270, 1432, 1525, 2600, 3253, 4400, 4534, 4734
Easy Baby, 1141
Easy Come, Easy Go, 2512, 4251, 4919, 5470
Easy Easy, Baby, 1158, 1527
Easy Evil, 5695
Easy For You, 940
Easy From Now On, 966, 2408
Easy Going Fellow, 4867
Easy Living, 1858
Easy Love, 82, 205, 673, 713, 3126, 3947, 3966, 4289
Easy Lover, 333, 1177
Easy Lovin, 1936, 2271
Easy Lovin' Kind, 3297
Easy Loving, 2420, 4652
Easy Money, 2884, 3239, 4001
Easy Read, 5492
Easy Skanking, 2943
Easy Snappin, 447, 4615
Easy Street, 196
Easy Take It Easy, 1569
Easy To Believe, 1729
Easy To Live With, 216
Easy To Love, 205, 673, 713, 3126, 3947, 3966, 4289
Easy To Slip, 4719
Easy To Smile, 4821
Easy's Getting Harder, 1478
Easy, Easy Baby, 1158, 1527
Eat Drink And Be Merry, 5665
Eat It, 5949
Eat My Dust You Insensitive Fuck, 991
Eat My Goal, 1171
Eat My Shorts, 1459
Eat The Rich, 2130
Eating Competition, 4638
Ebb Tide, 1005, 1372, 2362, 4543, 5758
Ebeneezer Goode, 177, 675,

3884, 4842
Ebi Tie Ye, 85
Ebo Walker, 1527
Ebony And Ivory, 1379, 3549, 5908
Ebony Eyes, 2776, 3325, 5487, 5756
Ebony Rhapsody, 2618
Eccentric, 2348
Echate Pa' Ila, 4097
Echidna's Arf, 5991
Echo, 1698, 1756
Echo Beach, 751, 3480, 5483
Echoes, 475, 2113, 2695, 3608, 4247, 4249
Echoes Of Deaf Journalists, 225
Echoes Of Love, 3037
Eclipse, 3821
Eclipse Of The Sun, 1604, 3415
Economics, 3336
Ecstacy 0376, 2655
Ecstasy, 1339, 1816, 5468, 5589
Ecstasy - Tango, 2273
Eddie And Sheena, 1256
Eddie, My Love, 534, 1446, 1963, 3593, 5328
Edelweiss, 2531, 4607, 5377
Edge Of A Broken Heart, 5654
Edie, 81
Edina Brenya, 3444
Edith And The Kingpin, 3713
Editions Of You, 1967, 4669
Edna May's Irish Song, 989
Eds Funky Diner, 2725
Edward, The Mad Shirt Grinder, 2594, 4385
EE! But It's A Grand And Healthy Life, 1012
Ee-Bobaliba, 5937
Ee-I-Adio, 3996
Eejhanaika, 717
Eeny Meeny, 298, 4895
Efectivamente, 4387
Effervescence, 5797
Effigy, 4356
Egg, 283
Egg Shells, 4589
Ego Tripping Out, 2104
Egyptian Reggae, 3727, 4536
Egyptian Tomb, 3658
Eh Cumpari, 592
Eh Up Let's Sup, 3384
Eight Ball, 2810
8 Ball, 1561, 2668
Eight Days A Week, 437, 1151
Eight Men, Four Women, 5929
Eight Miles High, 316, 868, 870, 1100, 1186, 1890, 1940, 2646, 2683, 3069, 4145, 4353, 4501, 4670
Eight More Miles To Louisville, 2874

8 x 10, 173
Eighteen, 119, 1696
18 And Life, 4950
18 Carat Love Affair, 260
Eighteen Inches Of Rain, 118
Eighteen Is Over The Hill, 5771
18 Strings, 1360
18-39, 544
Eighteen Wheels, 2333
18 Wheels And A Crowbar, 700
18 Wheels And A Dozen Roses, 3516, 3844
18 With A Bullet, 5884
Eighteen Yellow Roses, 2142
18th Century Rock, 95
Eighth Army March, 1139
Eighth Day, 721, 3996
80's Ladies, 4073
84 Tion, 5565
80,000 Careless Ethiopians, 1081
Eileen, 178, 2501
Eileen Alanna Asthore, 606
Eine Symphonie Des Graeuns, 3742
Einmalsehen Wir Uns Wieder, 172
Einstein A Go-Go, 3121
Eire Suite, 1174
Eisenhower Blues, 3194, 4144
Eisgerwind, 3247
Eject, 4821
El Ascensor, 3365
El Barbarazo, 5615
El Bingo, 2824
El Bombón de Elena, 1240
El Buen Pastor, 3162
El Caminante, 5471-5472
El Camino, 5754
El Cantante, 3142
El Choclo, 2137
El Cid, 5750
El Conde Negro, 4614
El Condor Pasa, 734, 1871, 3805, 4916
El Coqui, 922
El Corrido De Santiago Jiminez, 2824
El Cumbanchero, 4181
El Güiro De Macorina, 4097, 4420
El Lute, 656
El Malecón, 922, 2397
El Manisero, 4121
El Metro, 5491
El Nicoya, 45
El Pantalon Blue Jean, 2824
El Paso, 2313, 3358, 3487, 4568, 5460
El Paso City, 4568
El Paso Rock, 2639
El Pio Pio, 3354
El Piro De Farra, 4614
El Pito (I'll Never Go Back To Georgia), 1323

El Pregonero, 1111
El President, 1633
El Pussy Cat, 149
El Raton, 1323
El Rey David, 4447
El Salón México, 2270
El Shaddai, 2765
El Sombrero, 1164
El Titere, 4421
El Tonto De Nadie Regresa, 4268
El Toro, 2050
El Venao, 4062
El Vino Collapso, 557
El Watusi, 393
Elbow Room, 911
Elder Greene Blues, 4159
Elderberry Wine, 1584
Eldorado, 1633
Eleanor, 3548
Eleanor Rigby, 434, 1028, 4457, 4515, 5612, 5884
Eleanor's Cake (Which Ate Her), 2903, 4354
Election Day, 217
Electric Blend, 822
Electric Blue, 2670
Electric Boogie, 2292, 4036
Electric Lady, 2121
Electric Salsa, 5617
Electricity, 1821, 1967, 2212, 4038, 4715
Electrolite, 3910
Electronic, 1727
Electronic Sonata For Souls Loved By Nature, 3079
Electronic Warfare, 5574
Elegance, 2477, 2504, 3637
Elegy For Strings, 5735
Elektronikkaa, 273
Element, 1238
Elemental Child, 5277
Elements, 2463, 5491
Elements IV:Water, 3727
Elena, 5930
Elenore, 5538
Elephant Paw, 4293
Elevation, 4453
Elevator, 77, 5979
Elevator Operator, 2113
Elevators (Me & You), 4082
11 Months And 29 Days, 4169
11 O'Clock Tick Tock, 5560
11,000 Volts, 3472
11th Hour Melody, 2516
Eli's Coming, 5422
Elite Doodz Presents Snooze, 3759
Elite Syncopations, 2891
Elitists Dance, 3648
Elixir, 4723
Elixir Of Youth, 4534
Elizabeth Montgomery's Face, 1750
Elizabeth Stride (1843-1888), 361
Elizabethan Reggae, 2086
Elk's Parade, 4878

500, 3363
500 Miles, 5774
500 Miles Away From
Home, 201, 377
500 Miles To Go, 4868
Five Knuckle Shuffle, 5427
Five Little Fingers, 173, 3541
Five Little Kisses, 1019
Five Long Years, 695
Five Man Army, 5504, 5665
Five Minutes, 3785, 4386
Five Minutes More, 884
Five O, 2700
Five O'clock Whistle, 3865
Five O'Clock World, 2979,
4516, 5655
5-7-0-5, 1090-1091
5678, 2984, 4898
Five Spot, 5850
Five String Serenade, 3170
Five Take Five, 5319
5-10-15 Hours, 787
Five To One, 1594, 5670
5 Women, 3026
Five Years, 685, 695
Five Years Old, 5670
Fix It Man, 5336
Fixin' To Die Blues, 5796
Flag Flown High, 1496
Flames, 2083, 3211, 5626
Flaming June, 808
Flamingo, 676, 2806
Flamingo Express, 4675
Flanagan, 1974
Flapperette, 4880
Flash To The Beat, 2239
Flash, Bang, Wallop!, 2342
Flash, Pop, Sizzle!, 1922
Flashback, 3821, 4151
Flashback Jack, 68
Flashdance, 524
Flashdance ... What A
Feeling, 929
Flashlight, 2061, 4141
Flat Foot Floogie, 2069
Flat Foot Sam, 5279
Flat Top, 1229
Flatliner, 4709
Flattery, 5895
Flava, 183
Flava In Ya Ear, 1190
Flawed Is Beautiful, 5387
Flea Circus, 2917
Flesh, 2130, 2328
Flesh And Blood, 5869
Flex, 3397
Flight, 25, 1127
Flight To Tennessee, 5775
Flight '76, 3845
Flight By Jet, 3788
Flight From Ashiya, 2926
Flight Of Icarus, 2711, 4237
Flight Of The Bumble Bee,
304, 2456, 3845
Flings, 3637, 3913
Flip, Flop And Fly, 5529
Flirt, 4242
Flirtation Walk, 5982
Flirtation Waltz, 276, 1005

Float On, 1940, 2685
Floatin, 5602
Floatin' In My Hoodoo
Dream, 2655
Floating, 2286, 2995, 3765
Floating In The Wind, 2625
Flood, 2788
Floodlite World, 5570
Floogie Walk, 604
Floorshow, 1327, 5608
Florence, 4124
Florentine Pogen, 5991
Florida By The Sea, 1147
Florida Feelin, 4102
Florida, The Moon And
You, 2037
Flow Joe, 1859, 4498
Flow On, 3200, 3318, 4593
Flower, 4217
Flower Lady And Her
Assistant, 4810
Flower Of Dawn, 3787
Flower Of Love, 254
Flower Of My Heart, 3753
Flower Of Scotland, 1238
Flower Of The West, 4690,
5355
Flower Power, 1385, 1590,
2153, 2564, 2625, 3829,
5681
Flower Swing, 96
Flowers For Mama, 3965
Flowers In Our Hair, 123
Flowers In The Rain, 2789,
3819, 4488
Flowers In The Sky, 4515
Flowers On The Wall, 62
Flubby Dub, 5901
FlubbyDub, The Cave Man,
4020
Fluffy, 3398
Fluffy Toy, 4709
Fluid, 4037
Fluoro Neuro Sponge, 1617
Flutes, 3935
Flutter, 3720
Fly, 807
Fly Away Home, 4096
Fly Home, Little Heart,
3007
Fly Like An Eagle, 3681,
4797
Fly Me Away, 778
Fly Me To The Moon, 4267,
4727, 4928
Fly Me To The Moon Bossa-
Nova, 2399
Fly To The Moon, 552, 3758
Fly Your Natty Dread, 3609
Fly, Robin, Fly, 4908
Flyaway Fidles, 5961
Flyin' Hawk, 3739
Flying, 1432, 3264, 5329
Flying By Foy, 2723
Flying Crow, 556
Flying Down To Rio, 1951
Flying Hero Sandwich, 4233
Flying Home, 2756, 3225,
5776

Focus On Fashion, 3788
Focus On Sanity, 1168
Fog On The Tyne, 3251
Foggy Dew, 1268, 2729
Foggy Foggy Dew, 2729
Foggy Mountain
Breakdown, 1930, 2552,
4795
Foggy Mountain Top, 4281
Foggy Road, 1106
Fold Your Wings, 2167,
3979
Folies Bergéres, 3952
Folk, 176, 831, 2889, 3519,
3561, 5569
Folk Song, 2705
Follow A Star, 1959
Follow Like Wolves, 6000
Follow Me, 892, 899, 1944,
2767, 2935, 3159, 3197,
3367, 3662, 4220, 4574
Follow Me Around, 2273
Follow Me Follow, 2673,
4872
Follow That Girl, 1960
Follow The Band, 1436
Follow The Drum, 3260
Follow The Fold, 2322
Follow The Girls, 1960
Follow The Leader, 1773,
3119
Follow The Rainbow, 5549
Follow The Swallow, 1555
Follow The Yellow Brick
Road, 2386, 5899
Follow Your Heart, 4259,
4851
Follow Your Leader, 5540
Follow Your Star, 2007
Following A Feeling, 331
Following The Feeling, 364
Following The Sun Around,
3548, 4550, 4725, 5433
Folly Ranking, 4070, 4110
Folsom Prison Blues, 867,
976
Fonso My Hot Spanish
(K)Night, 2968
Fontana Eyes, 1170
Food For Thought, 5562
Food Stamp Blues, 3124
Food, Glorious Food, 402,
4033
Fool, 2280, 3516
Fool (If You Think It's
Over), 4452
Fool For You, 4572
Fool For Your Loving, 5803
Fool From Upper Eden,
1746
Fool If You Think It's Over,
755
Fool Is A Man, 1050
Fool Killer, 278
Fool Me Once, 2346
Fool On The Hill, 3372,
4932
Fool To Cry, 552
Fool's Paradise, 3636

Fool, Fool, Fool, 785, 1136,
3266
Fooled Around And Fell In
Love, 547
Foolin' Around, 1016, 2615
Foolin' Myself, 5976
Foolin' Time, 923, 1249
Foolish Beat, 2141
Foolish Fool, 4532
Foolish Heart, 273, 4047
Foolish Little Girl, 4884
Foolish Love, 3960
Foolish Ways, 3400
Fools Fall In Love, 1627,
3326
Fools For Each Other, 180
Fools Game, 875
Fools Like Me, 1122
Fools Paradise, 2049
Fools Rush In, 604, 1622,
3630, 3896, 3937, 4927
Foot Stompin, 880
Foot Stompin' Music, 643
Foot Tapper, 4835
Football Crazy, 2352
Footlights, 1139
Footprints In The Snow,
529, 1652, 2427, 3744
Footsee, 5817
Footsteps, 956, 2205, 2909,
3684
Footsteps Of A Fool, 3370
Footstompin, 1929
For A Dancer, 3135
For A Few Dollars More,
3751-3752
For A Friend, 1194
For All Mankind, 1875
For All We Know, 409, 949,
1228, 3225
For America, 4461
For Emily, Whenever I May
Find Her, 4916
For Every Man There's A
Woman, 227, 3492
For Free, 869, 3103, 3713
For Heaven's Sake, 4944
For Her Love, 1290
For Hire And Removal,
1712
For I, 2765
For I Am An American,
2997
For Love Of Ivy, 3427, 4695
For Lovers Only, 2255
For Lovin' Me, 3241, 5556
For Loving Me, 2812
For Loving You, 174, 689,
1419, 2616
For Mama, 300, 565
For Me And My Gal, 1966,
3201, 3649
For Michael Collins, Jeffrey
And Me, 2819
For My Country, 5564
For My Lady, 4828
For No One, 376, 434, 3486,
5667
For Now And Always, 4171

5886, 5960
Funky For You, 3937
Funky Gibbon, 2207
Funky Guitar, 5577
Funky Moped, 956
Funky Music Sho' Nuff
Turns Me On, 1824
Funky Nassau - Part 1, 454
Funky Pledge, 3342
Funky Sensation, 86, 3558,
5459
Funky Street, 1205
Funky Stuff, 3062
Funky Walk, 1671
Funky Worm, 4022
Funny, 471, 781, 2540, 3153
Funny (Not Much), 1160
Funny All Over, 5634
Funny Face, 1846, 2054-
2055, 3862
Funny Familiar Forgotten
Feelings, 2887, 3926
Funny Girl, 2055, 3533,
5997
Funny How, 98
Funny How Love Can Be,
1906, 2730
Funny How Love Is, 4381
Funny How Time Slips
Away, 1408, 1733, 1873,
1879, 3767, 3899, 4233,
5677
Funny Man, 2730, 3533
Funny Neither Could I,
4891
Funny Vibe, 5654
Funny Way Of Laughin,
1143, 2729
Funny, Funny, 1583
Funny/The Duck Joke, 3860
Funtime, 693, 5365
Für Alina, 4147
Fur Den Untergang, 1719
Furry Sings The Blues, 3227,
3713
Further From Fantasy, 3476
Fusion, 5617
Futura, 3648
Futura's Promise, 3648
Futurama, 3016
Future Blues, 791
Future Daze, 4185
Future Le Funk, 1352
Future Management, 5319
Future Of Latin, 4346
Fuzz, 3500, 4568, 4911
Fuzzy, 2052, 2240, 3431,
4141
G'bye Now, 2473
G'Damn Datt DJ Made My
Day, 5340
G'Night Dearie, 1895
G.H.E.T.T.O.U.T, 1016
G.I. Blues, 5438
G.I. Jive, 2893, 3629
G.T.O., 4640
Gabbin' Blues, 527
Gaiety Glad, 2101
Gal A Di Clothes, 2038

Gal In Calico, 4776
Gal It Wouldn't Easy, 1583
Gal Wine, 381, 1008
Gal Yuh Good, 1525
Galavant, 1341
Galaxy, 875, 1273, 5697
Galaxy Of Love, 1315
Gallao Del Cielo, 1750
Gallimaufry Gallery, 3824
Gallis Pole, 3156
Gallo Del Cielo, 4700, 5556
Galloping Home, 301
Gallows Pole, 2419, 3165,
3166
Galveston, 905, 2936, 5744-
5745
Galveston Flood, 4693
Galway Bay, 3289, 4866,
5982
Galway To Graceland, 2950
Gambler's Guitar, 1621
Gambler's Love, 3400
Gambling Fury, 3904
Gambling Polka Dot Blues,
1652
Game For A Laugh, 2565
Game Seven, 768
Games, 4471
Games For May, 4247
Games People Play, 45,
2007, 2100, 5345, 5760
Games That Lovers Play,
1909
Games Up, 2477
Games Without Frontiers,
851, 2067, 4207
Gandhi's Revenge, 2051
Gang, 2619
Gang Busters, 995
Gang Starr Doundation
Sampler, 2816
Gang War, 1977
Gangsta Bitch, 3537
Gangsta Boogie, 2081
Gangsta Roll, 2584
Gangsta's Paradise, 1224,
3094
Gangstas Of The Industry,
663
Gangster Boogie, 4773
Gangster Funk, 1293
Gangster Of Love, 4720,
5731
Gangsters, 4816
Ganja Baby, 371
Ganja Man, 3425
Ganja Pipe, 808
Ganja Smuggling, 1712
Ganz Wien, 1834
Garden In The Rain, 2137
Garden Of Delights, 3293
Garden Of Eden, 2771,
3673, 3743, 5599, 5617
Garden Of Eve, 2069
Garden Of Life, 4200
Garden On The Palm, 2717
Garden Party, 1907, 3650,
3897, 4537
Garden Sequence, 4151

Garden Song, 3423
Garnett Silk Tribute, 3944
Gary Gilmore's Eyes, 82
Gary's Got A Boner, 3202
Gary, Indiana, 3852, 5869
Gas Masks Vicars And
Priests, 4053
Gaslight, 5563
Gasoline Alley Bred, 1400
Gatecrasher, 2219
Gates Of Eden, 1583, 1673
Gates Of Freedom, 5684
Gateway To The West, 1851
Gather In The Mushrooms,
2528
Gather The Rose, 2037
Gather Together, 148
Gathering Flowers For The
Master's Bouquet, 5764
Gaudete, 470
Gave You My Love, 512,
4801
Gay Paree, 5643
Gay Spirits, 4651
Gaye, 5699
Gaze Not On The Swans,
171, 1745
GBH, 1449
Gear, 3871
Gee, 1316, 2689, 2801, 3240,
4256
Gee Baby, 902
Gee Baby (I'm Sorry), 5421
Gee Baby, Ain't I Good To
You, 554
Gee Whiz, 618, 981, 2698
Gee Whiz (Look At His
Eyes), 5399
Gee, But You're Swell, 326,
2893
Gee, I Wish I Was Back In
The Army, 5792
Gee, Officer Krupke!, 499,
5771-5772
Geechy Joe, 896
Geisha Girl, 1419, 3289
Gel, 1171
Gemini Child, 5371
Gems From George White's
Scandals, 3683
Gene Vincent Sings, 1109
General Lee, 239
General Penitentiary, 562
Generals, 3853
Generate Power, 1560
Generation Belly, 1698
Genesis Hall, 5577
Genesis The Spark Of Life,
264
Genetix, 5373
Genie With The Light
Brown Lamp, 4835
Genio y Figura, 3750
Genius Of Love, 1614, 5457
Genius Rap, 1614, 4347,
5583
Geno, 1502, 5717
Gentle Gataa, 3577
Gentle Mother, 531

Gentle On My Mind, 905,
2423
Gentle To Your Senses, 3560
Gentleman Friend, 3419
Gentleman Jim, 4485
Gentleman Jimmy, 1901
Gentlemen Of The Press,
1981
Gentlemen Prefer Blondes,
2119-2120
Gently Hold Me, 4182
Genuine Way, 4675
Geordie, 2734, 2993, 4649
Geordie In Wonderland,
5831
Geordie's Down The Road,
1021
Geordie's Lost His Liggy,
2121
Geordies Gone To Jail, 5482
George Jackson, 1675
Georgette, 780, 2277, 2489
Georgette Eckins, 3440,
4095
Georgia, 1587, 1838, 2117
Georgia Bound, 592
Georgia Crawl, 200
Georgia On A Fast Train,
4264
Georgia On My Mind, 941,
1027, 2197-2198, 3900, 4180
Georgia Rag, 3601
Georgia Slop, 1608
Georgia Stomp, 419
Georgia Town Blues, 4221
Georgie Brown, 395
Georgie Porgie, 100
Georgina Bailey, 2002
Georgy Girl, 1362, 4813
Geraldine, 1720
Geraldo's Navy, 2124, 2565
Germ Free Adolescents,
5940
Germans, 3251
Geronimo, 4407, 4682, 4835
Geronimo's Cadillac, 3670
Gertcha!, 1034
Gesang, 3251
Gestapo Khazi, 599
Gesticulate, 3033
Get A Catholic Education,
5387
Get A Job, 437, 3683, 3700,
4905, 5594
Get A Life, 2205
Get A Little Dirt On Your
Hands, 174, 1149, 1474
Get Along Little Dogie, 4555
Get Away, 1837
Get Away For A Day In The
Country, 2520
Get Back, 160, 435, 3202,
4316, 4832
Get Better, 3913
Get By, 5571
Get Closer, 4798
Get Cracking, 4070
Get Dancin, 1292, 1541
Get Down, 305, 1014, 3202,

4005, 4764
Get Down Country Music, 801
Get Down Get Down (Get On The Floor), 4918
Get Down Get With It, 4959
Get Down On It, 3062, 4400
Get Down Tonight, 2949, 4896
Get Down With It, 3270, 4959
Get Down With The Genie, 5350
Get Flat, 601
Get Happy, 226, 1785, 3054, 4880, 5995
Get Here, 67
Get High, 5952
Get In My Arms Little Girlie, 4750
Get In Touch With Me, 1350, 4675
Get It, 353, 1396, 2013, 3537
Get It On, 673, 1949, 4303, 5277, 5295
Get It Right, 2013
Get It Right Next Time, 3947
Get It Together, 4826
Get It When I Want It, 2741
Get It While You Can, 2890, 4174, 4407, 4897, 5301
Get Loose, 3093
Get Lost, 2932
Get Me Home, 772
Get Me To The Church On Time, 2567, 3196, 3295, 3859
Get Me To The World On Time, 1726, 3644
Get Money, 1202, 2913
Get Off Of My Cloud, 1570, 2759, 3960, 4529, 4629
Get On Board Little Children, 1438
Get On Board, Little Chillun, 4958
Get On It, 3062, 3087, 4400
Get On My Love Train, 3095
Get On The Case, 854
Get On The Floor/Off The Wall, 4016
Get On Up, 1558, 1779
Get On Your Feet, 1781
Get Ourselves Together, 1470
Get Out And Get Under, 43
Get Out And Get Under The Moon, 2932
Get Out Baldhead, 526
Get Out Of Bed, 3515, 5317
Get Out Of Denver, 4814
Get Out Of My House, 5361
Get Out Of My Life, 2871, 5713
Get Out Of My Life Woman, 1599, 5478
Get Out Of That, 5467

Get Out Of Town, 3160, 4289, 4992
Get Out Of Your Lazy Bed, 3515
Get Out On The Dancefloor, 1352
Get Outta My Dreams, Get Into My Car, 4012
Get Over It, 3537
Get Ready, 1996, 2886, 2944, 2965, 4338, 4435, 4585, 5280, 5300, 5334, 5871
Get Ready - Rock Steady, 1741
Get Real, 3905
Get Serious, 404
Get Some, 1812
Get The Big Bass, 408
Get The Habit, 2630
Get The Message, 1727
Get The Money, 1202
Get Thee Behind Me, Satan, 1960
Get To You, 4476
Get Together, 1470, 2691, 3963, 4826, 5595, 5906, 5966, 5983
Get Up, 1558, 1779
Get Up (Before The Night Is Over), 5326, 5945
Get Up (I Feel Like Being A) Sex Machine, 775
Get Up Adinah, 53
Get Up And Boogie (That's Right), 4909
Get Up And Dance, 3623
Get Up And Get Out, 4082
Get Up And Stand Up, 189, 5474
Get Up And Use Me, 1901
Get Up Now, 1654
Get Up On It, 3087
Get Up, Stand Up, 189, 839, 1771, 4450, 5474
Get Wise, 2644
Get With It, 3270
Get With You, 886
Get Yo Body, 1457
Get Your Feet Out Of My Shoes, 670
Get Your Hands Off My Man, 5617
(Get Your Kicks On) Route 66, 1159, 5510
Get Your Lie Straight, 1148
Get Your Life Straight, 1341
Get Your Mother Off The Crack, 277
Get Your Yas Yas Out, 592
Get Yourself A Geisha, 266
Get Yourself A Redhead, 4189
Get Yourself Home, 1826
Get Yourself Together, 5966
Getaway, 571, 1234
Getcha Rocks Off, 1461
Gethsemane, 2817
Gettin' Dirty Just Shakin'

That Thing, 3897
Gettin' Ready Rag, 4408
Getting A Drag, 1438
Getting Around And About, 2968
Getting Away With It, 1727
Getting Beautiful Warm Gold Fast From Nowhere, 2161
Getting Better, 4862
Getting Closer, 5885
Getting Having And Holding, 5779
Getting In The Lifeboat, 5449
Getting Married Today, 1196
Getting Mighty Crowded, 1795
Getting Nowhere, 494, 772
Getting Nowhere Fast, 2161
Getting Out Of Hand, 367
Getting Over You, 907, 5848
Getting Sentimental Over You, 907
Getting Serious, 1109
Getting Some Fun Out Of Life, 829
Getting Tall, 3952
Getting That Joke Now, 2905
Getting The Fear, 4273
Getting To Know You, 2997, 4607, 5366
Getting Up, 4241
Getto Jam, 1580
Geurilla Warfare, 4095
Gharana, 324
Ghetto, 5685
Ghetto Bastard, 3884
Ghetto Child, 1497, 3616, 3634
Ghetto Dance, 4111, 5402
Ghetto Gospel, 4462
Ghetto Guns, 4139
Ghetto Man, 1261, 4674
Ghetto Prayer, 2296
Ghetto Youth, 924
Ghost Dance, 73, 4199, 4334
Ghost In You, 4355
Ghost Of A Chance, 896
Ghost Riders In The Sky, 4781, 5863
Ghost Town, 1047, 2050, 2352
Ghostbusters, 5941
Ghosts, 297, 2783
GI Fever, 3633
Giannina Mia, 1903, 2036, 2385
Giant, 5297, 5750
Gicicality, 5577
Giddyup Do-Nut, 689
Giddyup Go - Answer, 4175
Gideon Briggs, I Love You, 2278
Gift, 2170
Gift Of The Gods, 1242
Gifted Is, 3426

Gifts Of Love, 336
Gigantic Land Crabs In Earth Takeover Bid, 2430
Gigi, 1700, 2145
Gigi (Gaston's Soliloquy), 2144
Gigolo Aunt, 5640
Gilly, Gilly, Ossenffeffer, Katzenellen Bogen By The Sea, 862, 1992, 2549
Gimme A License, 3781
Gimme A Little Kiss, Will Ya Hugh?, 93
Gimme A Pigfoot, 5870
Gimme A Smile, 1476
Gimme All Your Lovin, 1732
Gimme Back My Foreskin, 2165
Gimme Dat Ding, 1218, 2368
Gimme Gimme, 283, 2576, 4644
Gimme Gimme Gimme (A Man After Midnight), 3159
Gimme Gimme Good Lovin, 1284
Gimme Gimme Shock Treatment, 3160, 4423
Gimme Gimme Your Love, 4489
Gimme Hope Jo'anna, 2243
Gimme Little Loving, 4251
Gimme Little Sign, 1906, 5910
Gimme Love, 3036
Gimme Me A Man, 4341
Gimme No Lip, 1379
Gimme Shelter, 1118, 1548, 2897, 3202, 4630, 5589
Gimme Some, 1301, 2188
Gimme Some Head, 139
Gimme Some Lovin, 368, 623, 1420, 2013, 2134, 5488, 5503
Gimme Some Of Your Something, 3958
Gimme Some Time, 807
Gimme Some Truth, 3192
Gimme The Heat, 1498
Gimme The Loot, 4453
Gimme Your Lovin, 273, 6007
Gimme, Gimme, Gimme, 5675
Gimmix, 1107
Gin Gan Goolie, 4763
Gin House Blues, 160, 1488, 4920
Gin'irono Michi, 1391
Gingerbread Boy, 2461
Ginny Come Lately, 2653
Gipsy Eyes, 5537
Girl, 401, 2789, 3153, 5516, 5565
Girl A Chat, 3083
Girl Crazy, 2601
Girl Don't Come, 184
Girl Don't Tell Me, 424, 2061

Goodbye Dear, I'll Be Back In A Year, 2473
Goodbye Dolly Gray, 996
Goodbye France, 421
Goodbye Freedom, Hello Mom, 4768
Goodbye Girl, 1370, 2097, 4301
Goodbye Goodbye, 1050, 3847, 4210
Goodbye Highway, 5437
Goodbye Jimmy, Goodbye, 3847
Goodbye John, 5830
Goodbye Jukebox, 3317
Goodbye King Of Rock And Roll, 1796
Goodbye Kiss, 2002
Goodbye Kisses, 1229
Goodbye Lefty, 2334
Goodbye Lonesome, Hello Baby Doll, 3306
Goodbye Lucille #1, 4308
Goodbye Mike And Goodbye Pat, 3842
Goodbye Mr. Mackenzie, 2206
Goodbye My Love, 2172, 4408, 4799, 4893, 4799, 4893
Goodbye My Lover Goodbye, 4799
Goodbye Newport Blues, 3831
Goodbye Nothing To Say, 2789
Goodbye Pork Pie Hat, 3690, 4190
Goodbye Sam, Hello Samantha, 4531
Goodbye Says It All, 571
Goodbye Stranger, 721, 4192
Goodbye Sweetheart, Hello Vietnam, 2353
Goodbye Thing, 1531
Goodbye To Love, 949, 5376
Goodbye To You, 4764-4765
Goodbye Tokyo, 3661
Goodbye Virginia, 1106
Goodbye Yellow Brick Road, 2206, 2833
Goodbye, Broadway, Hello France, 1405, 5443
Goodbye, Lenny, 2160
Goodbye, Little Darlin' Goodbye, 286
Goodbye, Love, 949, 2172, 3847, 4408, 4505, 4799, 5376
Goodbye, Mama (I'm Off To Yokohama), 3446
Goodbye, Mr. Brown, 60
Goodbye, My Lady Love, 4893
Goodbye, Old Girl, 1370
Goodfootin, 2626

Goodness Gracious Me, 3076
Goodnight, 435
Goodnight (I'm Only A Strolling Vagabond), 3994
Goodnight Angel, 3409, 3787, 5931
Goodnight Baby, 2679
Goodnight Dick, 3497
Goodnight Girl, 5779
Goodnight Is Not Goodbye, 356
Goodnight Little Angel, 3787
Goodnight Lovely Lady, 128, 5739
Goodnight Lovely Little Lady, 5739
Goodnight Midnight, 4601
Goodnight Mother, 5455
Goodnight Mrs. Flintstone, 4244
Goodnight My Love, Pleasant Dreams, 3579
Goodnight My Someone, 1219, 3852, 5370, 5869
Goodnight Sleep Tight, 1918, 4386
Goodnight Soldier, 3750
Goodnight Sweet Josephine, 5951
Goodnight Sweetheart Goodnight, 2836, 3579
Goodnight Vienna, 809, 2212
Goodnight, Girl Of My Dreams, 829
Goodnight, Irene, 926, 1427, 1956, 1958, 2107, 2810, 3156, 3323, 3677, 3836, 4476, 4820, 5410, 5518, 5743
Goodnight, Little Girl Of My Dreams, 829
Goodnight, My Love, 105, 128, 471, 534, 1863, 2216, 2583, 3727, 4511, 5453, 5795
Goodnight, My Someone, 1219, 3852, 5370, 5869
Goodnight, Sweetheart, 689, 955, 1188, 1207, 2977, 3787, 3966
Goodnight, Wherever You Are, 1658, 2549, 3786
Goodnite Sweetheart, Goodnite, 970, 5622
Goodtime Sunshine, 1046
Goodwill Games Theme, 901
Goody Goody, 1482, 1622, 2298, 2962, 3367, 3616, 3629, 4926, 5642
Goody Two Shoes, 62
Goofer Dust, 966
Goofus, 2923
Google Eye, 3324, 3879
Goon Squad, 229
Goona-Goona, 2187

Goose Never Be A Peacock, 227
Goosey Gander, 2505
Gorgeous, 211
Gorilla In Manilla, 3648
Gorilla You're A Desperado, 5996
Got A Bran' New Suit, 266, 1520, 5723
Got A Date With An Angel, 132, 1764, 2285, 2619
Got A Feeling, 5290
Got A Job, 3700
Got A Lot Of Love To Give, 1994
Got A Man On My Mind, 4413
Got A Train To Catch, 1477
Got It At The Delmar, 4821
Got It Goin' On, 2633
Got Love If You Want It, 1834, 5810
Got My Bugaloo, 3718
Got My Heart Set On You, 1205
Got My Mind Set On You, 2416
Got My Mojo Working, 530, 654, 1158, 1247, 3831, 4521, 4989, 5377
Got Myself Together, 810
Got No Shame, 760
Got No Time, 603
Got The Funk Up, 1662
Got The Jitters, 5750
Got The Moon In My Pocket, 3091
Got The South In My Soul, 5719, 5832
Got The Time, 202
Got To Be Certain, 3697
Got To Be Love, 4794
Got To Be Real, 761, 3369
Got To Be There, 2746, 2982
Got To Believe In Love, 3595
Got To Come Back, 851
Got To Find A Way, 844, 4048
Got To Get, 2920
Got To Get Enough (Of Your Sweet Love Stuff), 873
Got To Get It, 1329
Got To Get You Into My Life, 477, 1689, 4515, 4832, 5292
Got To Get You Off My Mind, 830
Got To Get Your Own, 5314
Got To Give It Up, 2104
Got To Have It, 4260, 5585
Got To Have Some, 3381
Got To Have Your Love, 2296, 3453
Got To Keep On, 1222
Got To Know You, 2636
Got To Make A Change, 3794

Got To Make It, 1742
Got What You Need, 1844
Got You On My Mind, 725-726, 2279, 4762
Gotta Be Funky, 2520
Gotta Broken Heart Again, 1540
Gotta Dance My Way To Heaven, 2726, 5915
Gotta Feelin' For You, 151
Gotta Find Me A Lover (Hours A Day), 2015
Gotta Find My Baby, 1118
Gotta Get A Date, 2675
Gotta Get It Right (One World), 1881
Gotta Get Knutt, 5886
Gotta Get Me Somebody To Love, 5932
Gotta Get Mine, 673, 2065, 3536
Gotta Get Rid Of This Band, 378
Gotta Get To Oklahoma (Cause California's Getting To Me), 2333
Gotta Get Up And Get To Work, 2644
Gotta Give A Little Love, 5406
Gotta Go Home, 656
Gotta Have Love, 68, 4746
Gotta Have Me Go With You, 227, 2130
Gotta Have Money, 4692
Gotta Have Something In The Bank Frank, 2944, 5617
Gotta Have Your Love, 4746
Gotta Keep On Moving Baby, 2077
Gotta Love For You, 2865
Gotta Love It, 2130
Gotta Pebble In My Shoe, 116
Gotta Pull Myself Together, 3969
Gotta See Baby Tonight, 536
Gotta See Jane, 5318
Gotta Serve Somebody, 1676
Gotta To Be Real, 2053
Gotta Travel On, 2234, 3745, 5986
Gotta Turn Back, 290
Govinda, 2919
Gowon Special, 3150
Grab It!, 3093
Graceland, 4919
Gracelands, 516, 2511
Graduation Day, 1991, 4666
Graffiti Bridge, 967
Grain Of Salt, 1464
Granada, 3112, 3493, 4181, 4926
Grand Canyon Suite, 264
Grand Coolie Dam, 2319
Grand Coulee Dam, 1588
Grand Hotel, 619
Grand Imperial Cirque De

Paris, 944

Grand Knowing You, 983, 4860

Grand Old Duke Of York, 4533

Grand Old Ivy, 2613, 3294

Grand Overture, 240

Grand Pianist, 3749

Grand Piano, 553, 674

Grand Vista, 1653

Grandad, 1946, 4955

Grandad's Flannelette Nightshirt, 1978, 3201

Grandma's House, 810

Grandma's Party, 3940

Grandma, We Love You, 4716

Grandmaster Flash On The Wheels Of Steel, 2239

Grandmixer Cuts It Up, 2239

Grandpa Tell Me About The Good Old Days, 2908

Grandpa's Party, 3341

Grandpa's Spells, 3800

Granny Takes A Trip, 4369

Granny's In The Cellar, 1238

Grant Avenue, 1945

Grass Won't Grow On A Busy Street, 4323

Grateful When You're Dead, 2919, 3085

Gravel, 1523

Gravel Rash, 3312

Graveyard, 354

Gravitational Arch Of 10, 2069

Gravity Grave, 5637

Gravy, 211

Gravy (For My Mashed Potatoes), 4851

Gravy Booby Jamm, 520, 2953

Graystone Chapel, 977

Grazie, Macedonia, 1787

Grazin' In The Grass, 3500

Grazing In The Grass, 2036

Grease, 2256

Grease Box, 5281

Greased Lightnin, 2256, 5497

Greasy Grit Gravy, 378

Greasy Heart, 1315

Great Balls Of Fire, 574, 1541, 2153, 2815, 3219, 4510

Great Day, 2055, 4650

Great Gosh A'Mighty, 3270

Great Place, 207

Great Southern Land, 2670

Great Things, 1699

Great Train Robbery, 4494

Great Tribulation, 3838

Great, Great Joy, 1073

Greater Reward, 4399

Greatest Living Soul, 3450

Greatest Love, 1114

Greatest Love Of All, 2611

Greatest Moment Of My Life, 400

Greed, 4108

Greed (When Will The World Be Free), 4364

Greedy Beat, 1157

Greedy Gal, 3782

Green, 2722, 3193, 3795, 4794

Green All Over, 2911

Green Among The Gold, 2950

Green Apple Quick Step, 4145

Green Bay Incident, 2761

Green Chritma, 2021

Green Door, 3610, 3788, 5617, 5742

Green Eyed American Actress, 907

Green Eyes, 897, 1598, 1697, 5548, 5902

Green Fields, 5578

Green Fields Of France, 643, 3625

Green Fingers, 5394

Green Grass, 975, 3216

Green Grass And High Tides, 4083

Green Green, 3579, 3911, 3921

Green Hills o' Somerset, 1138

Green Is The Grass, 3015

Green Jeans, 1932

Green Light, 161, 4531

Green Little Semaphore, 3989

Green Onions, 664, 810, 2266, 4376

Green Pea, 5602

Green River, 1288

Green Rocky Road, 1358

Green Shirt, 229

Green Street Green, 3921

Green Tambourine, 3189

Green's Bounce, 2268

Green, Green Grass Of Home, 2887, 3685, 4078, 4371, 4732, 5666, 5843

Green-Up Time, 3336

Greenback, 3625

Greenback Dollar, 294, 3561, 3579, 5790

Greenfields, 751, 761

Greensleeves, 1932, 3451

Greenville Strut, 1356

Greenwich Village, 4021

Greenwood, Mississippi, 3270

Greetings, 2343, 3794

Greetings (This Is Uncle Sam), 3738

Greetings Four, 26

Greetings To The New Brunette, 5288

Grey Day, 3402

Grey Farewell, 46

Grey Life, 4639

Greystone Chapel, 2838

Grief Is Very Private, 1494

Grievous Angel, 1663

Grimpon, 4874

Grits Ain't Groceries, 2835, 3268, 5535

Grits And Cornbread, 5732

Grizzly Bear, 5983

Groaning The Blues, 1141

Grocer's Devil Daughter, 954

Grocery Song, 3366

Groove Check, 4434, 5351

Groove Is In The Heart, 31, 1455

Groove Me, 2050, 3000, 3025, 3049, 3283

Groove Thang, 5997

Groovie Time, 150

Groovin, 5968

Groovin' At Small's, 1223

Groovin' In The Bus Lane, 2793

Groovin' With Mr. Bloe, 3823

Grooving, 757

Grooving Out On Life, 3217

Groovy Beat, 1352

Groovy Blues, 2614

Groovy Feeling, 1948

Groovy Kind Of Love, 772, 3100, 3688

Groovy Little Thing, 2368

Groovy Situation, 1014, 2955

Groovy Train, 1847, 1849

Ground Hog, 1060

Groupie Girl, 5801

Grow For Me, 3272

Grow Old With Me, 948

Grow Your Natty, 852

Growin' Up, 2529

Growing Pains, 1886, 5498

Growing Up, 1817, 5320, 5386, 5813

Growing Up A Catholic, 3987

Growing Up To Time, 416

Growltiger's Last Stand, 994

Guaglione, 3479, 4305

Guaguanco Triste, 4447

Guantanamera, 3428, 3576, 3817, 4737, 5736

Guardian Angel, 966, 2679

Guards Are On Parade, 1258

Guards On Parade, 1258, 2101

Guava Jelly, 1817, 2733, 3878, 4187

Gudbuy To Jane, 743

Guenevere, 899

Guess I Must Be Dreamin, 710

Guess I Was Dreaming, 1828

Guess I'll Hang My Tears Out To Dry, 884

Guess I'm Dumb, 5450

Guess It Must Be The Spring, 1745

Guess My Eyes Were Bigger Than My Heart, 179, 5548

Guess Things Happen That Way, 976, 1122

Guess Who, 25, 471

Guess Who's Back In Town, 2465

Guess Who's Coming To Dinner, 562, 4652

Guessing, 5737

Guidance, 2693, 2899

Guide Us, 559

Guiding Star, 757

Guiltiness, 1808

Guilty, 99, 103, 451, 1188, 1785, 2136, 2250, 2581, 2923, 4137, 4458, 4485, 5805, 5950

Guilty By Association, 1048, 2494

Guilty Convict, 1711

Guilty, Imagination And Turning, 5502

Guinevere, 1302, 1305

Guit-Steel Blues, 778

Guitar Boogie, 1685, 4043, 4504, 4980-4981

Guitar Boogie Shuffle, 4980, 5752

Guitar Boogie Shuffle Twist, 5652

Guitar Boy, 5590

Guitar Dance, 1476

Guitar Man, 720, 1092, 4311, 4315, 4476

Guitar On My Mind, 1184

Guitar On The Edge, 3922

Guitar Polka, 136, 1502

Guitar Rag, 2087, 2427, 5743

Guitar Shuffle, 2087, 4980, 5652, 5752

Guitar Tango, 4835

Guitars, Cadillacs, 5960

Gulf Breeze, 5617

Gully Bank, 4696

Gum Drop, 1033, 1291

Gun, 959, 1913

Gun Court, 4431

Gun From Paris, 3631

Gun Law, 2932

Gun Man, 1784, 3144, 5291

Gun Men Coming To Town, 2496

Gun Song, 259

Gun Talk, 4458, 4466

Gunchester, 1839

Gundelero, 3397

Gunfight At The O.K Corral, 5719

Gunga Din, 4145

Gunman, 4349

Gunning For Buddha, 4896

Guns Fever, 754, 4096

Guns In The Ghetto, 1062

Guns Of Brixton, 438, 2286

Guns Of Navarone, 4948

Guns Of The Magnificent Seven, 3971
Gunshot, 2930, 4431
Gunslinger, 3112
Gunsmoke, 4556
Gus, 1469, 5495
Gus, Theatre Cat, 994
Gush Forth My Tears, 3701
Guv'ment, 528
Guy Who Got A Headache And Accidentally Saved The World, 1925
Guys And Dolls, 2322, 2947, 3294
Gwan A School, 735
Gwen (Congratulations), 4086
Gypsies, Tramps And Thieves, 202, 1044, 2936
Gypsy, 1654, 1934, 3138
Gypsy Blues, 579
Gypsy Boy, 4853
Gypsy Bundle, 2463
Gypsy Eyes, 1725, 2491
Gypsy Fiddler, 5932
Gypsy Fred, 3062
Gypsy In My Soul, 645
Gypsy Jo And Me, 3368
Gypsy Joe, 5814
Gypsy Love, 1374, 2501
Gypsy Mood, 1893
Gypsy Queen, 4387
Gypsy Road, 1084
Gypsy Violin, 1358
Gypsy Wedding, 3724
Gypsy Woman, 1032, 2384, 2653, 2683, 3529, 4545, 5578, 5723
Gypsy Woman (La De Dee), 404
Ha Cha Cha, 715
Ha Ha, 121, 1939
Ha! Ha! Said The Clown, 1347, 3437, 5660, 5951
Ha-Cha-Cha, 2923
Haberna, 2182
Habit Of A Lifetime, 1021
Hacer El Amor, 4032
Hachero Pa' Un Palo, 3353
Hack The Slides Away, 1037
Had To Be, 2463
Hadashi No Kisetsu, 3514
Hail H.I.M., 99
Hail The Princess Aurora, 1483, 1545
Hail To The Chief, 259
Haile Selassie, 99
Hair, 1950, 2337, 4139, 4860
Hair Of Gold, 2666, 3360
Hair Of Gold, Eyes Of Blue, 3396
Hair Of Spun Gold, 2666
Hair Pie Bake One, 927
Haitian Fight Song, 4190
Halcyon Days, 4873, 5281
Haley's Comet, 4700
Half, 3961
Half A Heart, 1387
Half A Man, 3899

Half A Mile, 742
Half A Moment, 2801-2802
Half A Photograph, 4695
Half A Sixpence, 2342
Half As Much, 1133, 3677, 4676, 5842, 5846
Half Breed, 1044
Half Caste Woman, 5997
Half Enough, 3786
Half Man Half Boy, 2655
Half Moon, 4174
Half Past Two, 217
Half The Day's Gone And We Haven't Earned A Penny, 3369
Half The Man, 3899
Half The Way, 2106, 3844
Half Time, 3876
Half-Breed, 3325
Halfway To Paradise, 2058, 3462, 4062
Halfway To The Moon, 4754
Halfway To Where, 2031
Halfway Up The Stairs, 5872
Hall Of Shame, 3755
Hall Of The Mountain King, 3817
Halleluja, 5964
Hallelujah, 812, 910, 1569, 2228, 2543-2544, 4580
Hallelujah Chorus, 1170, 4589
Hallelujah Freedom, 907
Hallelujah I Love Her So, 352, 4336, 5832
Hallelujah Man, 3335
Hallelujah Time, 5668
Hallelujah!, 2284, 2544, 4880
Hallelujah! I'm A Bum, 3551, 4221
Hallelujah, I Love Her So, 352, 4336, 5832
Halloa, Boatman, 3688
Halloween, 3703, 3831, 4505
Halloween Parade, 3922
Halo, 5792
Ham And Eggs, 3532
Hambone, 2412, 2584, 3925, 4753
Hamburger Lady, 5427
Hamburger-I Love To Eat It, 4100
Hammacher-Schlemmer, I Love You, 3273
Hammer And A Nail, 2691
Hammer And Nails, 1986
Hammer House Of Handbag, 2866
Hammer Smashed Face, 918
Hammond Song, 4589
Hand A Handkerchief To Helen, 3521
Hand Clappin, 4352
Hand In Glove, 4857
Hand In Hand, 808, 3147, 5424

Hand In Hand With You, 1339
Hand In My Pocket, 2759
Hand Me Down Baby, 3416
Hand Me Down My Favourite Trumpet, Gabriel, 2745
Hand Me Down That Can O' Beans, 4105
Hand Of Fate, 552
Hand Of Kindness, 2375
Hand Of The Dead Body, 4766
Hand On My Heart, 4896
Hand On Your Heart, 3697
Hand Over Your Heart, 3731
Handbags And Gladrags, 1347, 1848
Handel In The Strand, 4388
Handful Of Stars, 3147
Handle With Care, 2047
Handlebars, 1494
Hands In The Air, 5517
Hands Of God, 198
Hands Of The Lord, 3129
Hands Off, 2112
Hands Off She's Mine, 2661
Hands Up (Give Me Your Heart), 4078
Handsome Gretel, 1964
Handy Man, 574, 2877, 4719, 4846, 5314
Hang It Up, 4694
Hang On In There Baby, 743, 4233
Hang On Now, 2924
Hang On Sloopy, 364, 1489, 2681, 2792, 3224, 3557, 4612, 4737, 5639, 5982
Hang On The Bell, Nellie, 1210
Hang On To A Dream, 2391, 3936
Hang On To Your Ego, 567
Hang On To Your Heart, 1806
Hang On To Your Lids, Kids, 624
Hang On To Your Love, 1591
Hang Up The Phone, 2188
Hang Up!, 1886
Hang Your Sorrows In The Sun, 4284
Hangin' Around, 5796
Hangin' Five, 1474
Hangin' On, 254, 2222, 3524
Hangin' On A String (Contemplating), 3312
Hanging Around, 3758, 4440
Hanging On The Telephone, 55, 430, 974, 3904
Hanging Tree, 1472, 3815
Hangover, 4824
Hangover Triangle, 3941

Hank And Lefty Raised My Country Soul, 1711
Hank And The Hobo, 692
Hank Williams Is Singing Again, 2377
Hank Williams Sings The Blues No More, 3298
Hank Williams' Ghost, 2377
Hank Williams' Guitar, 2420
Hank Williams, You Wrote My Life, 364, 5847
Hank, You Still Make Me Cry, 692
Hanky Panky, 2277, 2778, 4412
Hapiness Stan, 4019
Happenings Ten Years Time Ago, 4354, 5951
Happiest Days Of All, 961
Happily Ever After, 4042
Happiness, 173, 431, 1570, 1760, 2714, 2888, 3950, 3970, 4151, 4490, 4520, 4795, 4834, 5276, 5963
Happiness Comes, 2581
Happiness Forgets, 1655
Happiness In Slavery, 3953
Happiness Is, 3923
Happiness Is A Warm Gun, 723, 5381
Happiness Is Just A Thing Called Joe, 227, 876, 2386, 3110, 4866
Happiness Is Me And You, 4006
Happiness Is My Desire, 4976
Happiness Runs, 2591
Happy, 132, 268, 1807, 2383, 3720, 4305, 4529, 5522
Happy All The Time, 1930
Happy Am I, 1993
Happy And Bleeding, 1635
Happy And Free Yodel, 744
Happy And Me, 1582
Happy Anniversary, 300, 3076, 4488, 5807
Happy Are We, 1032
Happy As The Day Is Long, 3054
Happy Because I'm In Love, 4650
Happy Being Fat, 2713
Happy Birthday, 356, 2664, 5908, 6002
Happy Birthday Blues, 5974
Happy Birthday Darlin, 2614
Happy Birthday Mr. President, 3747
Happy Birthday Sweet Sixteen, 4808
Happy Birthday To Me, 173
Happy Birthday, Ginger, 308
Happy Birthday, Josh, 518
Happy Boy, 648

Happy Busman, 2010

Happy Christmas (War Is Over), 3192

Happy Country Birthday Darling, 3151

Happy Day, 4058

Happy Days, 337, 3054, 3260

Happy Days And Lonely Nights, 1963, 3847, 5617

Happy Days Are Here Again, 91, 4818, 5953

Happy Days Happy Months, 2103

Happy Ending, 4040, 4680

Happy Endings, 402

Happy Ever After, 1974

Happy Feet, 91, 3003, 5953

Happy Go Lucky Girl, 4125, 5664

Happy Go Lucky Local, 3798

Happy Go Lucky Me, 1978

Happy Guitar, 1645

Happy Guy, 3956

Happy Habit, 1886

Happy Hangovers To You, 4869

Happy Holiday, 494, 2555, 4865

Happy Hour, 2175, 2608

Happy House, 4938

Happy Is A Boy Named Me, 3588

Happy Jack, 5481

Happy Jackeroo, 5839

Happy Land, 47, 938, 3337, 5569

Happy Merry Christmas, 5402

Happy Music, 569

Happy Nation, 51

Happy New Love, 2112

Happy New Year, 1488, 2935, 3494

Happy New Year/Voice Mail No. 3, 4505

Happy Organ, 1239

Happy People, 5335

Happy Phantom, 3264

Happy Reunion, 2199

Happy Sad, 4257

Happy Side, 1149

Happy Street, 3849

Happy Talk, 928, 1371, 1578

Happy Times, 4062

Happy To Be On An Island In The Sun, 4665

Happy To Be Themselves, 538

Happy To Be Unhappy, 810

Happy To Keep His Dinner Warm, 2612

Happy To Make Your Acquaintance, 3294, 3805

Happy Together, 659, 1423, 1940, 3409, 3990, 5538

Happy Tracks, 4188, 4323

Happy Trails, 642, 3983,

4623, 5497

Happy Wanderer, 2774, 3788

Happy Yodeller, 3801

Happy Yodelling Cowgirl, 2571

Happy You, Lonely Me, 3755

Happy, Happy, Birthday Baby, 5527

Happy-Go-Lucky Local, 1978

Happy-Go-Lucky-Me, 1793

Harari, 3382

Harbour Lights, 201, 1621, 1927, 2967, 3126

Harbour Of Dreams, 4704

Harbour Of My Heart, 2544

Harbour Shark, 5669

Hard Core, 1583

Hard Day On The Planet, 5670

Hard Drugs, 735

Hard Headed Woman, 2268, 2998, 4311, 5321

Hard Hearted Hannah, 43, 91, 5331

Hard Life, 5747

Hard Livin, 2355

Hard Lovin' Woman, 1172

Hard Luck, 2897

Hard Luck Blues, 787, 2288

Hard Luck Joe, 1651

Hard Rock Bottom Of Your Heart, 5497

Hard Time, 4096

Hard Time Killin' Floor Blues, 2777

Hard Time Loving You, 4742

Hard Time Pressure, 929, 3698

Hard Times, 702, 1080, 1366, 1688, 3186, 3252, 5534

Hard Times For A Honest Man, 2608

Hard To Handle, 554

Hard To Say Goodbye, My Love, 1625

Hard To Say I'm Sorry, 1054

Hard Work, 1837

Hard-Hearted Hannah, The Vamp Of Savannah, 5953

Hardcore, 319, 1564, 1638, 2126, 3106, 3380, 3831, 3962, 4229

Hardcore U Know The Score, 2656

Hardcore Uproar, 5584

Hardee's Partee, 2389

Harden My Heart, 4378

Hardtrance Acperience, 2390, 2423, 4553

Hare Krishna, 2337

Harelip Blues, 1656

Harem Dance, 1939

Hark!, 5578

Harlem Holiday, 1280

Harlem Lady, 3603

Harlem Madness, 2805

Harlem Nocturne, 758, 858, 1297, 3362, 3394, 4077

Harlem On My Mind, 249, 493, 5723

Harlem River Shanty, 5446

Harlem Shuffle, 636, 1426, 3173, 4631, 5905

Harmonica, 1109, 2199

Harmonica Blues, 4428

Harmonica Man, 3116

Harmonique, 1184

Harmony Babies From Melody Lane, 745

Harmony Blues, 341

Harmony Hall, 3282

Harmony In My Head, 859

Harper Valley PTA, 2120, 2353, 4544, 4936

Harpsichord Concerto, 3990

Harriet, 326

Harrigan, 1152, 2121, 2285, 5948

Harry Hippie, 5905

Harry Houdini, Master Escapist, 4408

Harry The Fool, 3649

Harry The Horny Toad, 4350

Harry's House, 3713

Hart Brake Motel, 2579

Hartley Quits, 2423

Harvest For The World, 1074, 2719

Harvest In The East, 1062

Harvest Of Love, 2528

Harvest Ritual Dance, 1174

Has Anybody Here Seen Kelly?, 421, 1974, 2478

Has Anybody Seen Amy, 5818

Has Anybody Seen Our Ship?, 3146, 5462

Has I Let You Down?, 2607

Hashish, 2337

Hasten Down The Wind, 5996

Hastings Street, 592

Hat Full Of Rain, 2508

Hate Is The Thing, Rap Is The Peace, 1215

Hate The Police, 3831

Hate Yourself In The Morning, 3432

Hatikvah, 4457

Hatisitose, 514, 5331

Hats, 4079

Hats Off To Eldorado, 2665

Hats Off To Harper, 2401, 3166

Hats Off To Larry, 4846

Hattie Green, 1660

Haul And Pull Up, 4111

Haul And Pull Up Selector, 3611

Haul Away For Rosie-O, 4847

Haul The Jib, 1611

Haunted By You, 2112

Haunted Heart, 2456, 2699

Haunted House, 121, 563, 1198, 1573, 2108, 3906, 5344

Haunted Hungry Heart, 2456

Haunting Me, 1436, 3865

Haunting Memories, 2535

Hava Nagila, 4061

Havana, 2322

Have A Cigar, 2401, 4247

Have A Dream On Me, 420, 3560

Have A Drink On Me, 3317

Have A Good Forever, 1223

Have A Good Time, 803, 5414

Have A Heart, 955

Have A Little Dream On Me, 420

Have A Little Faith, 2610, 4912, 5404

Have A Little Faith In Me, 741, 3225, 5972

Have A Little Mercy, 5763

Have A Nice Day, 4668

Have A Whiff On Me, 3839

Have Blues Will Travel, 3965

Have Blues, Must Travel, 2018

Have Faith, 140

Have Guitar Will Travel, 3773

Have I Got A Girl For You?, 1196

Have I Got A New Deal For You, 3566

Have I The Right, 1441, 2582, 3611

Have I Told You Lately, 1755, 2659

Have I Told You Lately That I Love You, 3357, 3580, 3796

Have I Waited Too Long, 5970

Have Love Will Travel, 600

Have Mercy, 2908, 2970, 5872, 5952

Have Mercy Baby, 5698

Have Mercy Mr Percy, 4139-4140

Have Pity On The Boy, 4704

Have Some Mercy, 5872

Have What It Takes, 3015

Have You Come To Say Goodbye, 666

Have You Ever, 1913

Have You Ever Been Lonely (Have You Ever Been Blue?), 2528

Have You Ever Loved A Woman, 64, 654, 2131, 3014

Have You Ever Loved Somebody, 2740, 4704, 4799

Have You Ever Loved

Someone, 5716
Have You Ever Really Loved A Woman, 64
Have You Ever Seen The Rain, 1289
Have You Forgotten Who You Are, 2168
Have You Gone Crazy, 3013
Have You Got Any Castles, Baby?, 1424, 1622, 3629, 4299, 5805
Have You Heard, 1657, 2775, 4040
Have You Looked Into Your Heart?, 5593
Have You Met Miss Jones?, 2663, 4606
Have You Seen Her, 56, 1052, 2365
Have You Seen The Stars Tonite, 608, 2935
Have You Seen Your Mother Baby, Standing In The Shadow?, 2759, 4629
Have You Seen Your Saviour?, 3858
Have Your Next Affair With Me, 3218
Have Yourself A Merry Little Christmas, 586, 3488, 3611
Haven't Been Funked Enough, 3005
Haven't Got No Peace Of Mind, 4859
Haven't I Loved You Somewhere Before, 4188
Haven't You Finished With Me?, 3648
Haven't You Heard, 4694
Having A Party, 4084, 5319, 5685
Hawaiian Death Stomp, 4807
Hawaiian Honeymoon, 1280
Hawaiian Paradise, 4089
Hawaiian Sunset, 2946
Hawaiian War Chant, 2025, 2885, 3798
Hawaiian Wedding Song, 612, 3448, 4621
Hawkeye, 3112, 4717
Hawks And Eagles Fly Like Doves, 5680
Hay Fuego En El 23, 4612
Hay Ojitos, 4516
Hay Ride, 1950
Hayfever, 5492
Hayrick Song, 5339
Hazards In The Home, 1922
Haze, 3052
Hazy Shade Of Winter, 366
He, 2516, 3579
He Ain't Give You None, 4784
He Ain't Got Rhythm, 4039
He Ain't Heavy, 2564
He Ain't Heavy, He's My

Brother, 2564, 2833, 3610, 3830, 4695, 4782
He And She, 698
He Broke Your Memory Last Night, 3566
He Called Me A Fat Pig (And Walked Out On Me), 4503
He Called Me Baby, 1130, 5717
He Can Do It, 4368
He Come Down This Morning, 4414
He Doesn't Love Me, 4295
He Don't Love Me, 2097
He Don't Love You, 1423
He Fought The Law, 4860
He Got You, 3844
He Had Refinement, 669, 1886, 5498
He Hadn't Till Yesterday, 5524
He Hasn't A Thing Except Me, 2130
He Is Cola, 1156
He Loved The Weather, 658
He Loves And She Loves, 2054-2055, 2128, 3862
He Loves Me All The Way, 5309
He Loves Me All To Pieces, 1836
He Made A Woman Out Of Me, 1550, 3142
He Made The Whole World Sing, 4102
He Needs Me, 2505
He Never Looked Better In His Life, 4695
He Noticed Me, 4129
He Prayed, 840
He Sang The Songs About El Paso, 5677
He Say Yeah, 1783
He Set Me Free, 799
He Stopped Loving Her Today, 417, 702, 2872, 4372
He Talks To Me, 4495
He Taught Me How To Yodel, 136
He Thinks He'll Keep Her, 1191
He Thinks I Still Care, 3845
He Took 50 Dollars And My Yodel, When He Took My Tonsils Out, 5518
He Took Me For A Ride, 3095
He Tossed A Coin, 4662
He Touched Me, 3391
He Walks Like A Man, 3676
He Wanted To Say, 4408
He Was A Friend, 3002
He Was A Friend Of Mine, 868, 2453
He Was A Sailor, 716
He Was Beautiful, 3864, 5849
He Was Beautiful

(Cavatina) (The Theme From The Deer Hunter), 5849
He Was Her Man, 1555
He Was My Brother, 5457
He Was Really Saying Something, 2560
He Was Too Good To Me, 4606
He Was Very Kind To Me, 3137
He Wears A Pair Of Silver Wings, 307, 3091
He Went Down To The Sea, 3742
He Went To Paris, 820
He Who Feels It Knows It, 5667
He Who Has Love, 1992
He Who Loves And Runs Away, 1903
He Will Break Your Heart, 856, 2683
He Would Be Sixteen, 5929
He'd Be A Diamond, 3317
He'd Have To Get Under - Get Out And Get Under, 43, 1106, 3200
He'll Be Back, 4265
He'll Have To Go, 140, 567, 2088, 2824, 2955, 4315, 4485, 4698
He'll Have To Stay, 140, 567
He'll Never Be A Lawyer ('Cause He Can't Pass The Bar), 3618
He'll Never Love You (Like I Do), 2740
He'll Understand, 5835
He's A Bad, Bad Man But He's Good Enough For Me, 1824
He's A Cobra, 4600
He's A Good Face (But He's Down And Out), 1970
He's A Good Man To Have Around, 91
He's A Good Ol' Boy, 5926
He's A Heartache (Looking For A Place To Happen), 2032
He's A Ladies Man, 780, 2202
He's A Real Gone Guy, 3365
He's A Rebel, 720, 1322, 3339, 4255
He's A Right Guy, 3634
He's A Tramp, 1545, 3176
He's Always, 4749
He's Back!, 4873
He's Distant From Me Now, 3648
He's Frank, 3742
He's Frank (Slight Return), 3742
He's Gone, 618, 637, 1018, 3561
He's Gonna Step On You Again, 1808, 2384, 3060

He's Got No Love, 4799
He's Got The Look, 5860
He's Got The Power, 1806
He's Got The Whole World In His Hands, 3304, 5705
He's Here!, 3187
He's In Love, 3033
He's In The Jailhouse Now, 592
He's In Town, 4597, 5456
He's Mine, 3013
He's Misstra Know-It-All, 2697
He's More Than Just A Swear Word, 1257
He's My Guy, 394, 1438
He's No Good, 3239
He's Only A Working Man, 1747
He's Only Wonderful, 1824, 1923, 2386
He's Read, 4465
He's So Fine, 1057, 3677, 3855, 5456
He's So Shy, 4271
He's So Unusual, 4874
He's Solid Gone, 3561
He's Sure The Boy I Love, 1019
He's Taken, 748
He's The Greatest Dancer, 4942
He's The One, 1406
He's The Wizard, 5898
He's Too Old, 2741
He/She Danced With Me, 4969
Head, 4094, 4331, 5372
Head And Heart, 589
Head Like A Hole, 3952, 4319
Head Over Heels, 1866, 2176, 3068
Head Rag Hop, 3897
Head To Toe, 3259
Headbutts, 4078
Headed For A Heartache, 3791
Headin' Down The Wrong Highway, 1357
Heading For Self-Destruction, 2909
Heading For The Warwick Rodeo, 5839
Heading South, 4937
Headlights, 1630
Headline News, 2374
Headlines, 107
Headmaster's Ritual, 3605
Heads Down No Nonsense Mindless Boogie, 109
Heal The World, 1379
Heal Yourself, 3080
Healing, 1762, 3119
Healing Hands, 1871
Healthy Body, 79
Hear Me Calling, 2641, 3815
Hear My Call, 2636, 4190
Hear My Song, Violetta,

2456-2457, 3289, 3451, 3994

Hear My Train A-Comin, 3352

Hear No Bullshit, See No Bullshit, Say No Bullshit, 1288

Hear The Drummer (Get Wicked), 2738

Hear What The Old Man Say, 3290

Heard About My Love, 3611

Heard It In A Love Song, 3477

Hearing Is Believing, 1562

Hearsay, 4644

Heart, 79, 1233, 1370-1371, 1606, 1908, 1988, 4167, 4205

Heart (I Hear You Beating), 3933

Heart And Soul, 942, 1121, 1131, 1977, 1988, 2138, 2690, 3218, 5275, 5669

Heart Attack, 929

Heart Attack And Vine, 2436

Heart Be Still, 1746

Heart Desire, 5995

Heart Don't Leap, 3832, 5685

Heart Full Of Love, 691, 2705

Heart Healer, 5436

Heart In Hand, 1491, 3147

Heart In Pain, 4675

Heart Like A Wheel, 2949, 3570

Heart Made Of Stone, 2345, 5641

Heart O' London, 5840

Heart Of A Coon, 1732

Heart Of A Gypsy, 4880

Heart Of A Man, 4574

Heart Of A Nigger, 1732

Heart Of Darkness, 3138

Heart Of Glass, 598, 1064

Heart Of Gold, 2838, 5977

Heart Of Mine, 2015, 2037

Heart Of My Heart, 862, 1236, 1361, 2037

Heart Of Stone, 814, 1430, 2192, 2345, 3483, 4340, 4379, 5641

Heart Of The City, 3349

Heart Of The Night, 4269

Heart Of The Sunrise, 2004

Heart On My Sleeve, 2073

Heart Over Mind, 5436

Heart To Heart, 3051

Heart Trouble, 1813

Heart User, 1510

Heart Vs. Heart, 3566

Heart We Did All We Could, 4243

Heart's Bin Broken, 697

Heart's Desire, 4080

Heart-Shaped Box, 2688

Heartache, 850, 1240, 2113, 4192

Heartache Avenue, 1091, 3418

Heartache Tonight, 1683

Heartaches, 2531, 2549, 3457, 5549, 5753

Heartaches By The Number, 2615, 3711, 5438

Heartaches-Heartaches, 5929

Heartattack And Vine, 5671

Heartbeat, 458, 1763, 2083, 2569, 3847, 3944, 5448

Heartbeat - It's A Lovebeat, 1463

Heartbeat In the Darkness, 5843

Heartbeats, 5950

Heartbreak, 1099, 3068

Heartbreak Cannonball, 5603

Heartbreak Hotel, 294, 458, 704, 1249, 1274, 1748, 2021, 2036, 2599, 2754, 2859, 2895, 3679, 4310, 4451, 4699, 5353

Heartbreak Society, 4399

Heartbreak Train, 1943

Heartbreak USA, 5764

Heartbreak, Tennessee, 4169

Heartbreaker, 451, 1181, 1316, 2136, 3763, 3853

Heartbroke, 1101, 2526

Heartbroken, 4947

Heartful Of Soul, 5951

Heartical Don, 4922

Heartlight, 314, 1509

Heartline, 2122

Hearts, 348

Hearts And Flowers, 2423, 5462

Hearts Aren't Made To Break (They're Made To Love), 2278

Hearts Don't Lie, 2745

Hearts In Her Eyes, 4459

Hearts Of Fortune, 2681

Hearts Of Stone, 616, 1032, 1954, 1963, 5621

Hearts On Fire, 1714, 3613, 4146

Hearts To Cry, 2044

Heartsong, 2155

Heat It Up, 1773, 4482, 5752

Heat Of The Beat, 296

Heat Of The Moment, 257

Heat Of The Night, 63

Heat Takes A Walk, 4542

Heat Under Sufferers Feet, 4432

Heat Wave, 113, 493, 3480, 4486, 5386, 5723

Heather Honey, 4617

Heather On The Hill, 735

Heathrow Touchdown, 58

Heatwave, 249, 617, 2561, 3747, 3778, 4641, 4825

Heaute Male Ich Dein Bild,

Cindy Lou, 1499

Heave, 3723

Heave Ho, My Lads, Heave Ho, 3147

Heaven, 63, 426, 1786, 1980, 2161, 4355, 5707, 5815, 5871

Heaven Ain't High Enough, 1632

Heaven And Hell, 1767

Heaven And Paradise, 3131

Heaven Can Wait, 2253, 2687, 5606

Heaven Child, 4682

Heaven Fell Last Night, 3325

Heaven For Everyone, 1308

Heaven For Two, 1437

Heaven Gets Closer Every Day, 198

Heaven Help My Heart, 1048

Heaven In The Backseat, 3737, 4638

Heaven Is A Place On Earth, 936

Heaven Is My Roof, 6005

Heaven Is My Woman's Love, 4086

Heaven Knows, 752, 1032, 1930, 2231, 3121, 4919

Heaven Knows I'm Miserable Now, 57, 4857

Heaven Must Be Missing An Angel, 5304

Heaven Must Have Sent You, 1731, 4272

Heaven On A Freight Train, 387

Heaven On A Sunday, 3549

Heaven On Earth, 4020

Heaven On Our Side, 5924

Heaven On Their Minds, 2817

Heaven Only Knows, 1032

Heaven Sent, 2336, 2897

Heaven Tonight, 5533

Heaven's Just A Sin Away, 2965

Heaven's My Home, 666

Heaven, Hell Or Macon, 2618

Heavenly, 2466

Heavenly Angel, 665

Heavenly Father, 985

Heavenly Man, 4246

Heavy Heart, 2272

Heavy Load, 2022, 2714, 3356

Heavy Makes You Happy, 603

Heavy Manners, 5409

Heavy Metal Mania, 2575

Heavy Metal Rules, 4119

Heavy Music, 3278, 4814

Heavy Sugar, 3117

Heebie Jeebies, 234

Heed The Call, 4621

Heigh Ho, The Gang's All

Here, 69, 955, 1376, 3122

Heigh-Ho, 1543

Heigh-Ho, Everybody, Heigh-Ho, 5600, 5914

Heimatlos, 4388

Helen Is Always Willing, 2187

Helen Of Troy, 250

Helene, 1805

Hell Hath No Fury, 748

Hell In A Bucket, 2687

Hell Is Round The Corner, 3524

Hell On Earth, 801

Hell Or High Water, 789

Hell Swell, 3397

Hell Yes, I Cheated, 4087

Hell's Bells, 316

Hell's Party, 3906

Hell's Soup Kitchen, 5676

Hellhound On My Trail, 2855

Hello, 310, 911, 4535, 4606

Hello (Your World Is Next To Me), 5601

Hello Afrika, 1612

Hello Again, 2124, 2797

Hello Baby, 5854

Hello Bluebird, 2035, 2659, 3315

Hello Carol, 2165, 3593

Hello Cruel World, 1640

Hello Darlin, 1383, 5548

Hello Darling, 2276, 5448

Hello Dolly, 351, 953, 1390, 1401, 5618

Hello Fool, 1754

Hello Goodbye, 434, 3409

Hello Hag, 1179

Hello Heartache, Goodbye Love, 3458

Hello Hello, 2478, 2929

Hello Hello I'm Back Again, 5966

Hello How Are You, 1695

Hello I Love You, 1594, 2263, 4652, 5670

Hello In There, 4453

Hello Josephine, 3666, 4733

Hello Little Girl, 1999

Hello Lola, 3586, 3815

Hello Mary Lou, 848, 3214, 3431, 3896, 4255, 5763

Hello Mexico (And Adios Baby To You), 1652

Hello Mr Peters, 3459

Hello Mr. Moonlight, 1126

Hello Muddah, Hello Fadduh! (A Letter From Camp), 4874

Hello Stranger, 755, 765, 2407, 3168, 3214, 3351, 3591, 5708

Hello There, 458, 1038, 2911, 4453

Hello Tosh, 370

Hello Trouble, 879, 4494

Hello Victim, 310

Hello Vietnam, 5928

Hello Walls, 1754, 2977, 3899, 5970

Hello Y'All, 4882

Hello Young Lovers, 2367, 2997, 4607

Hello, 'Turn Your Radio On, 4838

Hello, Again, 2124, 2797

Hello, Bluebird, 2035, 2659, 3315

Hello, Dolly, 351, 953, 1390, 1401, 5618

Hello, Frisco!, 5997

Hello, Frisco, Hello, 2478

Hello, Good Morning, 4016

Hello, I Am Your Heart, 737, 3251

Hello, Little Girl, 1999

Hello, My Lover, Goodbye, 2270, 2512

Hello, New York, 540

Hello, This Is Joannie (The Telephone Answering Machine Song), 1793

Hello, Who's There, 2911

Hello, Young Lovers, 2367, 2997, 4607

Helluva Guy, 4434

Hellz A Place I Know, 4465

Help, 80, 1371, 1850, 5952

Help Me, 1258, 1397, 2098, 2254, 3713, 4023, 4069, 4987

Help Me Baby, 2043

Help Me Girl, 4084

Help Me Help Myself, 354, 4663

Help Me Make It Through The Night, 1279, 1687, 2576, 3078, 3899, 4137, 4987

Help Me Rhonda, 4551, 4560, 4737

Help Me To Help Myself, 4663

Help My Friends, 152

Help The Poor, 3278

Help The Weak, 4199

Help Yourself, 2774, 2887

Help Yourself To Happiness, 2216

Help, Get Me Some Help!, 4078

Help, I'm A Rock, 5771

Help, I'm White And I Can't Get Down, 2109

Helping Hand, 4793

Helpless, 1307, 1465, 3758, 5777

Helter Skelter, 435, 1792, 4892, 5375, 5381

Helule Helule, 5499

Hendrix, 4969

Henji Wa Iranai, 3519

Henrietta, Have You Met Her?, 716

Henry, 503, 2974

Henry Ford, 4408

Henry's Coming Home, 5456

Henry's Got Flat Feet, 353

Henry's In Love, 325

Hepcat's Boogie, 1660

Heptones Gonna Fight, 1569

Her Bathing Suit Never Got Wet, 4645

Her Beaus Are Only Rainbows, 3649

Her Eyes Are A Blue Million Miles, 1120

Her Face, 944, 3637, 4873

Her Father Didn't Like Me Anyway, 2634, 4405

Her Heart Beats, 3196

Her Jazz, 2627

Her Majesty, 1395

Her Man, 126, 944

Her Name Is..., 702

Her Royal Majesty, 1395

Herbman, 3006

Herbs Pirate, 2727

Herbsman Shuffle, 924

Herd Killing, 2060

Here, 3492

Here Am I, 179

Here Am I - Broken Hearted, 780, 4446

Here Come The Drums, 3642

Here Come The Rattlesnakes, 327

Here Come Those Tears Again, 791, 5373

Here Comes Cookie, 2216, 4511

Here Comes Heaven Again, 69

Here Comes My Baby, 5499, 5773

Here Comes Santa Claus, 286

Here Comes Summer, 2956, 5380

Here Comes That Rainy Day Feeling Again, 1981

Here Comes That Sound, 2413

Here Comes The Bandwagon, 4289

Here Comes The Dawn Again, 538, 5631

Here Comes The Hammer, 2365

Here Comes The Hot Stepper, 673

Here Comes The Judge, 263, 3309, 3466

Here Comes The Knight, 3795

Here Comes The Man, 5488

Here Comes The Morning, 3481

Here Comes The Nice, 2681, 4019, 4974

Here Comes The Night, 426, 2147, 3794, 3973, 5383

Here Comes The Rain Again, 5475

Here Comes The Rain, Baby, 3926

Here Comes The Showboat, 4650

Here Comes The Sun, 1146, 1980, 2172, 2434, 4753, 5915

Here Comes The War, 3916

Here Goes (A Fool), 3054

Here I Am, 2015, 3343, 5428

Here I Am Baby, 766, 1650

Here I Am Baby (Come And Take Me), 4514

(Here I Am) Broken Hearted, 44

Here I Am (Come And Take Me), 2266, 4139, 4514

Here I Am Drunk Again, 364

Here I Come, 2762, 3213, 4794

Here I Go Again, 460, 1254, 2414, 2563, 4897, 5567, 5803, 5926

Here I Sit, 3951

Here I Stand, 1936, 2535, 3551, 4551, 4872

Here I'll Stay, 3336

Here In Eden, 211

Here In My Arms, 1447, 4606

Here In My Heart, 1372, 3493

Here In The Real World, 704, 2736

Here In Your Bedroom, 2191

Here It Comes Again, 1981

Here Lies Love, 521, 4580

Here She Comes, 5553

Here To Go, 875

Here Today And Gone Tomorrow, 793

Here We Are, 1781, 4814

Here We Are In The Years, 5977

Here We Go, 28

Here We Go Again, 518

(Here We Go Round) The Lemon Tree, 2789

Here We Go Round The Mulberry Bush, 5488

Here Without You, 868, 1100

Here You Are, 4580

Here You Come Again, 4148

Here's A Hand, 861

Here's A Kiss, 1447

Here's A Little Girl From Jacksonville, 380

Here's A Quarter (Call Someone Who Cares), 5507

Here's A Toast, 5462

Here's Congratulations, 2043

Here's Hoping, 1228

Here's Love In Your Eye, 522, 4580

Here's Some Love, 2032, 5524

Here's That Rainy Day, 830, 4416, 4679, 4928, 5606

Here's To My Lady, 604, 3630

Here's To Romance, 3409

Here's To The Girl Of My Heart!, 5814

Here's To The Girls, 1705

Here's To The Next Time, 2347-2348

Here's To The Old Days, 5433

Here's To Your Illusions, 1824, 2386, 1923

Here's Where You Belong, 5771

Here, There And Everywhere, 434, 1769, 4515

Heritage Of A Blackman, 1460

Hermit Of Misty Mountain, 1026

Hermo Da Kope Bean, 428

Hernando's Hideaway, 79, 592, 1945, 4106, 5371

Hero, 572, 934, 1178, 1306, 3523

Hero Is He, 1251

Hero Takes A Fall, 366

Heroes, 239, 1573, 2508, 4343

Heroes And Villains, 425, 4140, 4978

Heroes Connection, 3104

Heroin, 109, 5522, 5626-5627

Heroine, 1573, 3996

Hersal Blues, 5400

Hersham Boys, 4841

Hesitation Blues, 4188, 4227

Hestia, 2953

Heureusement, Y'a Les Copains, 442

Hev Yew Gotta Loight, Boy?, 4934

Hey, 2677

Hey Babe, 2889

Hey Baby, 1017, 1539, 2398, 2438, 2662, 3552, 3684, 4233, 4524, 4867, 4976, 4982

Hey Baby, Lass Den Ander'n, 3317

Hey Bartender, 5503

Hey Bo Diddley, 237

Hey Bulldog, 435, 2180, 2223, 5955

Hey Cinderella, 488, 642

Hey Daddy, 3333, 5291

Hey Deanie, 984

Hey DJ, I Can't Dance (To The Music You're Playing), 437, 662, 663

Hey Dr. Kinsey, 2486

Hey Dude, 1184, 2919, 3085

Hey Fat Boy (Asshole), 5754

Hey Fish, 5514

Hey Frederick, 5658
Hey Girl, 14, 574, 1099, 2532, 2670, 3119, 3659, 4073, 4784, 4973, 5617, 5676
Hey Girl Don't Bother Me, 5291-5292
Hey Grandma, 1466, 2602, 5291
Hey Hey, My My (Into The Black), 4701, 5570, 5978
Hey I'm Lost, 1760
Hey Jealousy, 2157, 3916
Hey Joe (Hey Moe), 364
Hey John, 1448
Hey Jude, 210, 222, 434, 1184, 1940, 2675, 4234
Hey Judge, 3724
Hey Leroy, 986
Hey Let's Twist, 2512, 5546
Hey Little Bird, 372
Hey Little Cobra, 1211, 4551, 5327
Hey Little Girl, 14, 574, 1099, 2532, 2670, 3119, 4124
Hey Little Hen, 2103
Hey Little One, 838, 5874
Hey Little School Girl, 4124
Hey Lord, Don't Ask Me Questions, 4136
Hey Love, 3006, 3825, 5820
Hey Love You, 3818
Hey Love!, 4522
Hey Mae, 1158
Hey Mama, 5618
Hey Man Nice Shot, 1892
Hey Matthew, 1881
Hey Mister (I Need This Job), 4867
Hey Mr DJ, 3556, 5996
Hey Mr Ting-A-Ling Steel Guitar Man, 5818
Hey Mr. Deejay, 3885
Hey Mr. Rude Boy, 4462
Hey Music Lover, 4709
Hey Nineteen, 2100
Hey Pachuco!, 4671
Hey Paula, 4159, 4233, 4445, 4982
Hey Porter, 976
Hey Presto, 552
Hey Princess, 4285
Hey Ruby, 5597
Hey Schoolgirl, 4916, 4918, 4916, 4918, 5432, 5457
Hey Senorita, 80
Hey Sinorita, 4186
Hey There Little Insect, 3727
Hey There Little Miss Mary, 4979
Hey There Lonely Boy, 2572, 4680
Hey There Lonely Girl, 2572
Hey There, Good Times, 1165, 2661
Hey Venus, 5351
Hey Western Union Man, 856

(Hey Won't You Play) Another Somebody Done Somebody Wrong Song, 857, 5398
Hey Yah, Hey Yah, 808
Hey You, 1448, 2679, 3054, 3818, 4390
Hey You (Turn Up Your Radio), 1752
Hey You With The Crazy Eyes, 3204
Hey You! Get Off My Mountain, 1619
Hey! Baby, 1017, 1539, 2398, 2438, 2662, 3552, 3684, 4233, 4524, 4867, 4976, 4982
Hey! Come 'Ere, 5621
Hey! Good Lookin, 61, 1517, 2522, 3634, 3677, 4289, 4528, 4654, 5846
Hey! Schoolgirl, 4916, 4918, 5432, 5457
Hey, Babe, Hey, 673
Hey, Feller, 4893
Hey, Good Lookin, 61, 1517, 2522, 3634, 3677, 4289, 4528, 4654, 5846
Hey, Hey, 673, 2169
Hey, Joe, 803, 1457, 1820, 2299, 2356, 2400, 2490, 2937, 3111, 3161, 4653, 4724, 4836, 4984, 5617, 5764
Hey, Look At Me!, 1946
Hey, Look Me Over, 351, 1164, 3187
Hey, Miss Fannie, 1136
Hey, Mr Bluebird, 5820
Hey, Mr. Banjo, 4448
Hey, Mr. Postman, 5778
Hey, Neighbour, 1927
Hey, Pretty Legs, 2169
Hey, That's No Way To Say Goodbye, 543, 1153
Hey, There, 79, 1133, 1418, 2547, 2919, 4106, 4416, 4446, 4676, 5371
Hey, What Did The Bluebird Say?, 3054
Hey, Young Fella, 1376
Heykens Serenade/The Day Is Over, 4672
Heylom Halib, 674, 921
Hh! Cha! Cha!, 987
Hi De Ank Tum, 5930
Hi De Hi, 2181
Hi De High, 1817
Hi Fly, 5778
Hi Heel Sneakers, 1870, 2661, 4426
Hi Hi Hazel, 3482
Hi Hi Hi, 3548, 5885
Hi Ho Silver, 1508
Hi Neighbor, 5523
Hi Spook, 5873
Hi!, 2451, 5523
Hi-Desert Biker Meth Lab, 1272

Hi-Diddle-Dee-Dee (An Actor's Life For Me), 1544
Hi-Heel Sneakers, 45, 3687, 5525
Hi-Heeled Sneakers, 1490
Hi-Ho Baby, 726
Hi-Ho Silver Lining, 275, 445
Hi-Ho The Radio, 522
Hi-Jacked, 2138
Hi-Jacking, 3593
Hi-Lili, Hi-Lo, 944, 2935-2936, 3245, 4676
Hi-Tech Soul Anthem, 1531
Hi-Yo, Silver, 843, 4756, 5528
Hiawatha, 1170, 4800
Hiawatha's Wedding Feast, 1170
Hickeys On My Neck, 277
Hickory Wind, 869, 2672, 4146
Hicktown, 1973
Hidden Love, 974
Hidden Treasure, 5368
Hide And Seek, 1552, 1745, 1920, 2875, 4590, 5529
Hide The Sausage, 2730
Hide Your Heart, 2029, 3734
Hideaway, 1726, 1990, 2131, 3014
Hiding And Seeking No More, 3634
Hier Encore, 299
Higgi Higgi, 1063
High, 1453, 1867, 2585, 2655, 3242, 3534
High Adventure, 5840
High And Dry, 89, 4403, 5354
High Blood Pressure, 4210
High Brown Blues, 5523
High Coin, 4140, 5771
High Cost Of Leaving, 1806
High Energy, 146, 2364
High Enough, 1370
High Explosion, 4546
High Fidelity, 2130
High Flying Bird, 4233
High Flying Electric Bird, 4233
High Geared Daddy, 771
High Hat, 2055
High Heels, 1653
High Hopes, 884, 2548, 5607
High In High School, 3399
High In The Sky, 160, 1488
High In The Sun, 1830
High Life, 3728
High Noon, 1604, 3111, 4556, 4676, 5719
High On A Hill, 49, 3073
High On A Hilltop, 1179
High On A Windy Hill, 3073
High On Emotion, 1432
High Ridin' Heroes, 2869

High Roller, 3538, 4732
High Rollers, 2669
High Rollin, 2143
High School Dance, 3582
High School Days, 4871
High School USA, 1819
High Sign, 1510
High Society, 4235
High Society Calypso, 2522
High Stepper, 540
High Time, 2881
High Time We Went, 1949
High Times, 2860
High Up On A Hill Top, 325
High Upon High, 5793
High Water Everywhere, 4159
High Weeds And Rust, 3842
High Yellow, 2629
High, High, High, Up In The Hills, 43
High-Heeled Sneakers, 1039, 4976
Highblow, 1714
Highdays And Holidays, 5961
Higher And Higher, 1012, 1224, 2112, 4148
Higher Degree, 1012
Higher Ground, 2312, 4749, 5860, 5908
Higher Love, 2814, 2982, 5890
Higher State Of Consciousness, 5886
Higher Than A Hawk, 889
Higher Than The Sun, 2764
Highest City, 2822
Highfly, 3665
Highland, 4046
Highland Drift, 4227
Highlife Time, 1393
Highly Inflammable, 5940
Highway, 4872
Highway 61 Revisited, 4538, 4805, 5888
Highway Blues, 2401
Highway In The Wind, 2317
Highway No. 61 Blues, 2961
Highway Of Sorrow, 4374
Highway Patrolman, 978
Highway Song, 827, 4931
Highway Star, 3388
Highway To Hell, 48, 5445
Highway To Spain, 3410
Highways Are Happy Ways, 5753
Hike It Up, 1315
Hill Billie Blues, 3395
Hillbilly Boogie, 1475
Hillbilly Fever, 1513, 2600, 3487
Hillbilly Girl With The Blues, 1366
Hillbilly Heart, 388
Hillbilly Heaven, 4924
Hillbilly Hula, 939
Hillbilly Rock, Hillbilly

Roll, 5918

Hillbilly Twist, 2315

Hillbilly Valley, 4935

Hillbilly Willie's Blues, 2419

Hillbilly With A Heartache, 3149

Hillbilly With A Record Deal, 3749

Hilo March, 939

Him A Natty Dread, 541, 3945

Him Or Me, 369

Him Or Me (What's It Gonna Be), 651, 4512

Himno A La Alegria, 4550

Hindsight, 1561

Hip Coat, 1477

Hip Hip, 2645

Hip Hip Hooray, 3884

Hip Hop Be Bop (Don't Stop), 3431

Hip Hop Junkies, 3937

Hip House, 1558, 2913, 5945

Hip Housin, 2913

Hip-Hip-Hip And A Holler, 5662

Hippie Boy, 2303

Hippity Hippity Hop, 4120

Hippy Boy, 1949

Hippy Gumbo, 645

Hippy Hippy Hourrah, 1669

Hippy Hippy Shake, 999, 1468, 2123, 3274

Hiroshima, 3820

His Eye Is On The Sparrow, 1163

His Girl, 2306

His Hands, 2358

His Imperial Majesty, 5319

His Indie World, 3317

His Kiss, 2405

His Latest Flame, 3186, 4311

His Love Makes Me Beautiful, 2055

His Majesty The Baby, 5736

His Name Is Alive, 2542

His Name Is Charlie Gordon, 1946

His Spurs Are Rusty Now, 1365

His Work And Nothing More, 2807

History, 30, 2511, 2738, 3287, 5637

History Of The Beat, 1355

History Of The World, 1371

History Repeating, 410, 4349

History Sound, 3425

Hit, 2910, 3503

Hit And Miss, 400

Hit And Run, 2162, 2566

Hit Git & Split, 2816

Hit Me With Music, 1071

Hit Me With Your Morris Stick, 4072

Hit Me With Your Rhythm

Stick, 1661, 1952, 3911

Hit That Perfect Beat, 750

Hit The Deck, 4241, 5814

Hit The Ground, 1393

Hit The Road, 4449

Hit The Road Jack, 1027, 1696, 2118, 3529, 4851

Hit The Road To Dreamland, 227, 3489, 3630, 4958

Hit The Track, 5571

Hitch It To The Horse, 1844

Hitch-Hike To Mars, 4172

Hitchcock Railway, 2829

Hitchin' A Ride, 4505, 5613

Hitching To Miami, 5441

Hitchy-Koo, 43

Hitonatsuno Taiken, 5946

Hittin' The Bottle, 3054

HIV, 4794

Hiya, Sucker, 67

Ho Hum, 2512

Ho! Punchinello, 5929

Hobo, 2312

Hobo Flats, 4989

Hobo Humpin' Slobo Babe, 5781

Hobo's Lullaby, 4484

Hobo's Meditation, 695, 5505

Hockey, 4109

Hocus Pocus, 1953, 2437

Hoe Down, 308, 1705

Hoedown, 2565

Hog Inna Minty, 526, 3958

Hoity Toity, 4432

Hoketus, 2669

Hokey Cokey, 557

Hol A Fresh, 4462, 4546

Hold Back The Night, 3648, 4136, 5489

Hold Back Tomorrow, 3663

Hold Her Down, 5452

Hold It Down, 3820, 4821

Hold It Now, 416

Hold Me, 463, 1934, 2611, 3484, 4073, 4184, 4343, 4455, 4574, 5679

Hold Me Close, 945, 1780

Hold Me In Your Arms, 5965

Hold Me In Your Loving Arms, 5997

Hold Me Now, 5407

Hold Me Tight, 973, 1082, 3878, 5282

Hold Me Till The Mornin' Comes, 195

Hold Me, Hold Me, Hold Me, 105

Hold Me, Thrill Me, Kiss Me, 969, 2682, 3788, 3802

Hold My Hand, 730, 881, 1236, 1570, 2102, 2553, 2590, 3147

Hold No Hostage, 2526

Hold On, 950, 1757, 2196, 2222, 2343, 2358, 2800, 3303, 4191, 4399, 5441,

5693, 5869, 5909

Hold On (Goa Mixes), 5733

Hold On (Tighter To Love), 4364

Hold On (To This Old Fool), 52

Hold On I'm Comin, 664, 2445, 4290

Hold On Partner, 564

Hold On Tight, 2003

Hold On To My Love, 4351, 4683

Hold On To My Unchanging Love, 4351

Hold On To The Nights, 3498

Hold On To What You've Got, 5347

Hold That Sucker Down, 4079

Hold That Train, 3861

Hold That Train Conductor, 1118

Hold The Line, 5475

Hold Them, 2138, 4884

Hold Tight, 973, 1082, 2003, 2688, 3878, 5282, 5689

Hold Tight, Hold Tight, 183

Hold What You Got, 4687

Hold You Jack, 3171

Hold Your Hand Out, Naughty Boy, 1974, 4005

Hold Your Head Up, 223

Hold Your Head Up High, 5577

Holdin' A Good Hand, 1306

Holdin' On, 5726

Holding Back The Years, 1686, 4923

Holding Her And Loving You, 1206

Holding On To A Dream, 3036

Holding On To You, 1348

Holding On With Both Hands, 3496

Holding Out For A Hero, 5553

Holding The Bag, 364

Hole In My Pocket, 4596

Hole In My Shoe, 3823, 5488

Hole In The Bucket, 3056, 4015

Hole In The Ground, 3486

Hole In The Wall, 2449, 3456

Holgertron, 4503

Holiday, 450, 2603, 2808, 3402, 4244

Holiday For Flutes, 4651

Holiday For Strings, 1653, 2885, 4650

Holiday For Trombones, 4651

Holiday In Cambodia, 1441, 2030

Holiday In Disneyland, 1363

Holiday Inn, 2555

Holiday Party, 4619

Holiday Spirit, 4534

Holidays In The Sun, 4830

Holier Than Thou, 22, 3987

Holler Fe The Wok, 4155

Hollow Eyes, 4464

Hollow Horse, 2671

Holly, 1979

Holly Go Softly, 3412

Holly Holy, 1509, 1817

Hollywood Dream, 2327

Hollywood Nights, 4814

Hollywood Swingin, 521

Hollywood Swinging, 3062

Hollywood Tease, 2158

Holocaust, 5391

Holy Cow, 1035, 1598

Holy Days, 6001

Holy Fishey, 1817

Holy Ghost, 298

Holy Joe, 2449

Holy Man, 3586

Holy Manna, 2201

Holy Mount Zion, 1251

Holy Spirit, 5860

Homage, 5308

Homburg, 4344

Home, 441, 1258, 1521, 2137, 2401, 2736, 3639, 4828, 5950

Home Again, 4871, 5736

Home And Away, 4056

Home At Last, 2835

Home Coming Time In Happy Valley, 3357

Home Cookin, 3281

Home From The Forest, 2440

Home Ground, 4588

(Home In) Pasadena, 1106, 3200, 5710

Home Is Where The Hatred Is, 4222, 4790

Home Is Where The Heart Is, 1102, 1114

Home James And Don't Spare The Horses, 4181

Home Lovin' Man, 1218, 1400, 3384

Home Made Love, 726

Home Of Happy Feet, 4239

Home Of The Blues, 976

Home Of The Brave, 3444, 3677

Home Of The Whale, 3142

Home On The Range, 131, 1482, 3299

Home Sweet Heaven, 2522

Home Sweet Home In The Rockies, 4373

Home Thoughts From Abroad, 5699

Home To You, 1688

Home Tonight, 4599

Home Town, 1927, 2967

Homeboy, 190

Homecoming, 2353

Homegrown Tomatoes, 1101

Homeguard, 1621
Homeless, 2228
Homely Girl, 1052, 5562
Homenaje (Rafael Ithier), 2235
Homesick, 421
Homesick Blues, 2119, 3007
Homestead On The Farm, 960
Hometown, 380, 3893
Hometown Gossip, 5796
Homeward Bound, 253, 1270, 2229, 2581, 2944, 3291, 3576, 4386, 4916
Homeward Looking Angel, 5437
Homework, 3705, 4692, 5655
Homing Pigeon, 2815
Homing Waltz, 3372
Hominy Grits, 3173
Hommage A Baba Cissoko, 3070
Homophobia, 1081
Homophobic Asshole, 4821
Honaloochie Boogie, 3814
Hondo's Song, 2042
Honest And Truly, 4651
Honest I Do, 2001, 2698, 4477, 5312, 5375, 5408
Honestly Sincere, 862
Honesty, 339, 4139-4140, 4281
Honey, 857, 1540, 2194, 2582, 2812, 2857, 3754, 4877, 5600, 5805
Honey (Oh How I Need You), 87
Honey At The Core, 2036
Honey Babe, 5750
Honey Be Good, 516, 2511
Honey Bop, 294, 2753
Honey Boy, 843, 3976, 5659
Honey Bunny Baby, 3106
Honey Child, 4671
Honey Chile, 3206, 3480, 4838
Honey Come Back, 905
Honey Don't, 4196, 4522, 4594
Honey Gal, 758
Honey Honey, 3367, 4235
Honey Hush, 838, 1074, 1625
Honey I Need, 4319
Honey I Still Love You, 873
Honey In The Honeycomb, 876-877
Honey Love, 1413, 1627, 1873, 1993
Honey On The Moon, 2311
Honey Pie, 5521
Honey Thief, 2541
Honey White, 3789
Honey-Babe, 3763
Honeybun, 3490
Honeycomb, 4602, 5829
Honeymoon By The Sea, 4137

Honeymoon Hotel, 1638, 1965
Honeymoon Inn, 2432, 5900
Honeymoon Isle, 441
Honeymoon On A Rocket Ship, 3508
Honeysuckle And The Bee, 2664
Honeysuckle Dreamin, 4102
Honeysuckle Rose, 95, 4450, 5419, 5443, 5688-5689, 5976
Hong Kong, 2436
Hong Kong Blues, 942
Hong Kong Flu, 1784
Hong Kong Garden, 3247, 4938
Honky Tonk, 789, 1502, 1573, 2290
Honky Tonk Blues, 771, 1502, 1753, 3223, 3320, 3721, 6005
Honky Tonk Cinderella, 2783
Honky Tonk Girl, 5410
Honky Tonk Hardwood Floor, 2599
Honky Tonk Man, 1298, 2311, 2599, 4569, 5960
Honky Tonk Mona Lisa, 2635
Honky Tonk Moon, 5496
Honky Tonk Saturday Night, 2546
Honky Tonk Season, 5678
Honky Tonk Song, 4240, 5603
Honky Tonk Teachers, 3618
Honky Tonk Town, 5432
Honky Tonk Train Blues, 1753, 3223, 3320, 6005
Honky Tonk Wine, 2964
Honky Tonk Woman, 494, 1217, 2727
Honky Tonk Women Love Red Neck Men, 2791
Honky Tonkin' Again, 883
Honky Tonkitis, 268, 855
Honolulu, 1273
Honour And Love, 3748
Honour Your Father And Mother, 1466
Hoochie Coochie Man, 2400, 3830-3831, 4620, 4847, 5377
Hoochie Coochie Woman, 531
Hoodoo Blues, 3242
Hoodoo Man, 5763
Hoodoo Party, 5406
Hook And Sling, 635
Hooked, 988
Hooked On A Feeling, 618, 4242, 5398
Hooked On You, 2424
Hooker Street, 3610
Hooligan, 1569
Hoop De Dingle, 1495
Hoop-Dee-Doo, 1963

Hoops, 361
Hooray Festival, 1817
Hooray For Captain Spaulding, 192, 2928, 4680-4681
Hooray For Hazel, 4617
Hooray For Hollywood, 1411, 1622, 3629, 5805
Hooray Hooray It's A Holi-Holiday, 656
Hoot Mon, 4563
Hoot Nanny Hoot, 5473
Hootchy Kootchy Henry (from Hawaii), 5470
Hootie Blues, 790
Hoots Mon, 651, 3316
Hoots Mon, 651, 3316
Hooverville (They Promised Us The World), 1074
Hop Along Rock, 2086
Hop La Tu As Vu, 1378
Hop Scotch Polka, 3763
Hop, Skip And Jump, 3687
Hope, 3515, 5667
Hope Fell Down, 1522
Hope Slumbers Eternal, 1823
Hope You Find Your Way, 681
Hopeful Village, 2727
Hopefully Yours, 3131
Hopeless, 5836
Hopelessly Devoted To You, 2256
Hopelessly In Love, 205, 5408
Hopes And Dreams, 2242
Hoping That You're Hoping, 3328
Hoppy, Gene And Me, 4623
Hopscotch, 2318
Horizontal Heroin, 1079
Hornet's Heart, 5391
Hornpipe Boogie, 1470
Horny, 1971
Horror Business, 3703
Hors D'Oeuvres, 158
Horse Feathers, 2272
Horse Fever, 3967
Horse Out In The Rain, 3724
Horse With No Name, 2389
Horseplay, 1701
Horses, 2599
Horsey, Horsey, 4574
Hot And Bothered, 1735
Hot And Cold, 4200, 4096
Hot As Sun, 4104
Hot Blooded, 2145
Hot Child In The City, 1064, 2146-2147
Hot Chocolate Crazy, 2932
Hot Day In The South, 986
Hot Diggity, 2549, 2563, 3448, 4704
Hot Diggity (Dog Ziggitty Boom), 1195
Hot Dog, 5468
Hot Dog Joe, 116

Hot Dog That Made Him Mad, 2753, 4598
Hot For Love, 1805, 3462, 5277
Hot For Teacher, 3954
Hot Fun, 740, 3462
Hot Girls In Love, 3344
Hot Hot Hot, 242, 2831
Hot House, 2150, 4637
Hot In The City, 1064, 2146-2147, 2673, 3346
Hot Like Fire, 1277
Hot Like The Sun, 3237
Hot Line, 381
Hot Lips, 321, 332, 496, 826, 853, 885, 992, 1269, 1721, 1792, 1887, 2321, 2473, 2850, 2874, 2893, 2933, 3212, 3351, 3516, 3654, 3765, 3773, 3806, 3940, 4101, 4103, 4171, 4300, 4790, 4855, 4932, 4936, 4984, 5300, 5342, 5723, 5774, 5802, 5841, 5858
Hot Lips And Seven Kisses, 700
Hot Love, 673, 1805, 1949, 3462, 5277
Hot Love Cold World, 5756
Hot Love Now!, 5907
Hot Lunch Jam, 1837
Hot Metal, 82
Hot Milk, 1569
Hot Music, 4107
Hot Pants, 5769
Hot Pastrami, 1395
Hot Patootie (Bless My Soul), 4600
Hot Pistol, 3299
Hot Potato, 2022, 2029
Hot Pretzels, 2166
Hot Rock, 955
Hot Rockin, 2907
Hot Rod Lincoln, 655, 1193
Hot Rod Poppa, 2638
Hot Shot, 619
Hot Smoke And Sasafrass, 808, 2701
Hot Spot, 3766
Hot Stepper, 370, 1810
Hot Stuff, 552, 1602
Hot This Year, 1538
Hot Time In The Old Town Tonight, 960
Hot Toddy, 1927, 2462
Hot Wire My Heart, 1293
Hot, Hot, Hot, 242, 2831
Hotel California, 205, 524, 2032, 5733
Hotsy Girl, 5921
Hottentot Potentate, 266, 5723
Hotter This Year, 808
Hound Dog, 139, 462, 739, 1644, 1671, 2438, 2895, 2995, 3179, 3186, 4077, 4310, 4451, 5319, 5405, 5417, 5836
Hound Dog Man, 1816, 4277

How You Gonna See Me Now, 5304

How You Keep A Dance, 5767

How You Say It, 3190

How You So Hot, 1944

How'd Ja Like To Love Me?, 1424

How'd You Like To Spoon With Me?, 2975, 5435

How'dja Like To Make Love To Me?, 3293

How're You Getting On?, 4748

How's About It?, 2412

How's Chances?, 249

How's Ev'ry Little Thing In Dixie?, 5953

How's Your Bird, 311

How?, 3123, 3171, 3176

Howard Beach, 541

Howard Blaikley, 2613

Howdy Friends And Neighbours, 1438

Howdy Judge, 2443

Howlin' At The Moon, 5846

Howling At The Moon, 1242

Howzat, 4872

Hu Ba Lua, 1437

Huckleberry Duck, 3147

Huffety Puff, 2989

Huge Ever-Growing..., 4054

Hugette Waltz, 5592

Huggin' And Chalkin, 3091

Hula Drums, 3562

Hula Love, 1541, 3052

Hullo, My Darlings!, 1618

Hully Gully, 5316

Hully Gully Again, 3263

Hully Gully Baby, 1606

Hully Gully Guitars, 4476

Hully Gully Slip And Slide, 4663

Human, 2633, 2639

Human Again, 441

Human Behaviour, 551, 1752

Human Disease (S.K.U.M.M.), 4953

Human Features, 551

Human Fly, 1275

Human Nature, 1092, 1415, 5426

Human Racing, 2977

Human Work Of Art, 4327

Humanity, 1761

Humanoid, 2060

Humble Lion, 4940

Humblebee, 1883

Hummer, 4898

Humming, 944, 2489, 3215

Humoresque, 756, 1638

Humphrey The Camel, 584

Humpty Dumpty, 4385

Humpty Dumpty Heart, 4181

110th Street And 5th Avenue, 3776

130 Steps, 324

100% Chance Of Rain, 3791

100 lbs Of Clay, 4251

100 Pounds Of Clay, 4674

Hundreds Of Girls, 3389

Hung Up, 5761

Hungarian Rhapsody No. 2, 756

Hungry, 1884, 3616, 4512

Hungry Eyes, 941

Hungry For Love, 2986, 3684

Hungry For You, 2986, 3475, 3684

Hungry For Your Lovin, 1526

Hungry Freaks, Daddy, 3809

Hungry Like A Wolf, 1657

Hungry Like The Wolf, 3828

Hunt Ya Down, 281

Hunted, 4152

Hunting After Dark, 1012

Hunting High And Low, 33

Hurdy Gurdy Man, 81, 859, 1590

Hurrah For Baffins Bay, 5899

Hurrah For Today, 3761

Hurray! It's Lovely Up Here, 4039

Hurricane, 1675, 1796, 2584, 4341, 4710

Hurricane Fighter Plane, 121

Hurricane Hattie, 511, 1124

Hurry Blues, 951, 2879

Hurry Don't Linger, 762

Hurry Down Sunshine, 951

Hurry Home, 3244, 3649

Hurry Hurry Baby, 3416

Hurry Love, 3649, 5871

Hurry On Down, 806, 3365

Hurry Over, 665

Hurry Sundown, 355, 3270

Hurry Up, 2899

Hurry Up Harry, 4841

Hurry Up Sundown, 355

Hurry! It's Lovely Up Here!, 3122

Hurry, Mr Peters, 5520

Hurt, 2362, 3933, 3953, 5985-5986

Hurt Her Once For Me, 4698, 5820

Hurt In Your Heart, 2228

Hurt Me If You Will, 3465

Hurt On Hold, 2060

Hurt So Bad, 3262

Hurt So Good, 2407, 4200

Hurt The Heart, 304

Hurt The One You Love, 4683

Hurting Inside, 3659, 5904

Hurting Me, 5290

Hurts Me To My Heart, 65

Hurts So Bad, 4425

Hurts So Good, 679, 880,

2748, 3617, 4639

Husband Hunting, 180

Hush, 618, 670, 1457, 3085, 3145, 4458, 5465

Hush Hush, 3077

Hush Hush Hush, 1161

Hush Ma Mouth, 2185

Hush Up, 3478

Hush, Here Comes A Whizzbang, 4021

Hush-A-Bye Island, 69

Hush-A-Meca, 982

Hush-Hush, 4723

Hushabye, 3866, 4277

Hushabye Island, 3580

Hushabye Mountain, 1066

Hushpuckiny, 2443

Hussars March, 5901

Hustling, 4780, 5559

Hybrid, 1681, 1696

Hydrolic Pump, 1131

Hydroplane, 5580

Hymn, 376, 2093, 3722-3723

Hymn For Sylvia, 720

Hymn Number 5, 2070

Hymn Of Love, 3046

Hymn To A Sunday Evening, 862

Hymn To Her, 4318

Hymn To The Snark, 2643

Hymne A L'Amour, 108, 4229

Hyperactive, 1576

Hyperballad, 551

Hyperphoria Parts One And Two, 2902

Hyperreal, 4552

Hyperspaced, 2693

Hypnosis, 3829

Hypnotic Love, 3195, 3215

Hypnotise Me, 5695

Hypnotised, 875, 3030

Hypnotize The Moon, 5679

Hypnotized, 2879

Hypnotizing Eyes, 2955

Hypocrite, 3934

Hypocrites, 2019, 4940

I (Who Have Nothing), 2125, 3010, 3186

I A Tell, 4050

I Admire You, 3478-3479

I Adore Mi Amore, 1181

I Adore You, 1309, 5785

I Ain't A-Studyin' You, Baby, 2141

I Ain't Blue, 3055

I Ain't Down Yet, 5581, 5869

I Ain't Goin' Hungry Anymore, 2420

I Ain't Gonna Eat Out My Heart Anymore, 189, 5968

I Ain't Gonna Give Nobody None Of My Jelly Roll, 5841, 5858

I Ain't Got Nobody, 4660, 4973, 5523, 5858

I Ain't Got Noth'n But The

Blues, 4359

I Ain't Living Long Like This, 1314, 2813

I Ain't Mad At You, Pretty Baby, 3765

I Ain't Never, 701, 5436

I Ain't No Beatle (But I Want To Hold Your Hand), 3836

I Ain't No Joke, 1773

I Ain't No Miracle Worker, 748

I Ain't Sharin' Sharon, 1966

I Ain't Superstitious, 2620

I Ain't The One, 4348

I Almost Felt Like Crying, 3589

I Almost Lost My Mind, 1432, 1601, 2641, 4138

I Alone, 2031, 2237, 3173, 3852, 4568

I Always Get A Souvenir, 1179

I Always Knew, 196

I Always Was Your Girl, 2673

I Am, 1810, 1952, 2342

I Am ... I Said, 1509

I Am A Cathedral, 4748

I Am A Child, 3133, 4753

I Am A Clown, 983

I Am A Girl Of Constant Sorrow, 2737

I Am A Horse, 281

I Am A Man Of Constant Sorrow, 247

I Am A Pilgrim, 3567

I Am A Rabbit, 3190

I Am A Rock, 4916, 4918, 4916, 4918, 5372

I Am A Witness, 2639

I Am A Woman, 4571

I Am All Alone, 2432

I Am Changing, 1625

I Am Damo Suzuki, 5396

I Am Easily Assimilated, 913

I Am For Ever Dated, 919

I Am Free, 6002

I Am Going To Like It Here, 1945

I Am In Love, 912

I Am Just A Rebel, 1203

I Am Loved, 4289

I Am Not Willing, 3723

I Am One, 4977

I Am Only Human After All, 1647, 2095

I Am Right, 2602

I Am So Eager, 3852

I Am So Ordinary, 1161

I Am So Proud, 765, 3055

I Am That Type Of Badmarsh, 324

I Am That Type Of Badmarsh II, 324

I Am The Blues, 1556, 3991

I Am The Conqueror, 2575

I Am The Don, 4976

I Am The Fly, 1007

1095, 1490, 3824, 4206, 4315
I Want To Know (Quiero Saber), 3904
I Want To Know (What You Do When You Go Round There), 1636
I Want To Know Her Again, 5701
I Want To Know What Love Is, 1975
I Want To Know Who You Are Before We Make Love, 2546
I Want To Love And Be Loved, 407
I Want To Make Magic, 1837
I Want To Marry A Lighthouse Keeper, 26
I Want to Marry A Male Quartet, 2036
I Want To Marry You, 777, 1235, 1469
I Want To Meet Him, 4674
I Want To Play House With You, 3399
I Want To Ring Bells, 1228
I Want To See Me In Your Eyes, 4182
I Want To See The People Happy, 520, 1745
I Want To Sing In Opera, 247
(I Want To) Squeeze You Hold You, 5280
I Want To Stay Here, 2221, 3148, 3663
I Want To Take You Higher, 2727, 4973, 5386
I Want To Tell You, 2415, 4515
I Want To Wake Up With You, 2086, 2318
I Want To Walk In The Rain, 5333
I Want To Walk Through This World With You, 5717
I Want To Whisper Something, 595
I Want Tomorrow, 1768
I Want What I Want When I Want It, 606, 3720
I Want Yer, Ma Honey, 620
I Want You, 599, 875, 2380, 2724, 3719, 4112, 4152, 4754
I Want You (All Tonight), 2337
I Want You (Forever), 1268
I Want You Back, 1510, 1861, 2735, 2746, 3077
I Want You Now, 2983
I Want You Right Now, 2983
I Want You To Be My Baby, 1406, 5815
I Want You To Be My Boy, 1806

I Want You To Be My Girl, 3367, 5815
I Want You To Love Me, 106, 4987
I Want You To Want Me, 106, 1038, 3277, 4987, 5416
I Want You With Me, 4987
I Want You, I Need You, I Love You, 4310
I Want Your Body, 222
I Want Your Love, 1053, 1756, 5492
I Want Your Lovin (Just a Little Bit), 2338
I Want Your Sex, 1829, 3652, 3902
(I Want) A Butter And Egg Man, 234
I Want'a Do Something Freaky To You, 2450
I Wanta Make Up With You, 4613
I Was A Boy When You Needed A Man, 5690
I Was A Fool, 2057
I Was A Fool To Care, 3155
I Was A Kamikaze Pilot, 2584
I Was Anything But Sentimental, 1258, 2630, 5285
I Was Born In Virginia, 5948
I Was Born On Christmas Day, 4721
I Was Born To Be Loved, 2787
I Was Born To Be Me, 3509
I Was Born To Love You, 3632
I Was Born With A Broken Heart, 4372
I Was Country When Country Wasn't Cool, 3436
I Was Dancing In The Lesbian Bar, 4536
I Was Doing All Right, 2129
I Was Fooled, 5850
I Was Kaiser Bill's Batman, 4979, 5933
I Was Lucky, 1957
I Was Made For Dancing, 2094
I Was Made For Lovin' You, 3034
I Was Made For Loving You, 1057
I Was Made For You, 1057, 2015, 3034
I Was Made To Love Her, 2944
I Was Much Better Off In The Army, 2103
I Was Never Kissed Before, 589, 1745, 2308, 5745
I Was Only 19, 4471
I Was So Young (You Were So Beautiful), 694
I Was Taken By Storm, 151

I Was The One, 1748
I Was With Red Foley (The Night He Passed Away), 1956, 5848
I Washed My Face In Muddy Water, 2751
I Wasn't Born To Follow, 1694, 3011
I Wasn't The One (Who Said Goodbye), 1004
I Watch The Love Parade, 987
I Went Off And Cried, 179
I Went To Your Wedding, 1918, 2885, 4102, 4583, 4676
I Whistle A Happy Tune, 2997
(I) Who Have Nothin, 409, 3050
I Will, 1374
I Will Always Care, 5648
I Will Always Love You, 2148, 2351, 2612, 4148, 5357
I Will Always Think About You, 3912
I Will Be Free, 3782
I Will Be In Love With You, 5317
I Will Be Master, 416
I Will Be There, 2182, 4720, 4798, 4720, 4798
I Will Be With You, 5275, 5317
I Will Cry, 179
I Will Dance With You, 757
I Will Drink The Wine, 4704
I Will Follow, 5560
I Will Follow Him, 3458, 3521
I Will Follow You, 3593
I Will Get Along, 3619, 4493
I Will Hold You, 5613
I Will I Won't, 801
I Will Love You, 1939, 5317
I Will Love You (Every Time When We Are Gone), 2057
I Will Love You All My Life, 1383, 3121
I Will Miss You, 5601
I Will Remember You, 5403
I Will Survive, 242, 888, 2107, 2247
I Will Wait, 1990
I Will Wait For You, 3183
I Will Whisper Your Name, 2853
I Wish, 3683
I Wish I Could Forget You, 4151
I Wish I Could Shimmy Like My Sister Kate, 4254, 4500
I Wish I Could Tell You, 604
I Wish I Didn't Have To

Miss You, 2274, 4813
I Wish I Didn't Love You, 1990
I Wish I Didn't Love You So, 2447, 3125, 3293, 4889
I Wish I Had A Girl, 2922
I Wish I Had A Nickel, 5672
I Wish I Had Never Met Sunshine, 5538
I Wish I Knew, 539, 2217, 2447, 4786, 5711
I Wish I Never Saw The Sunshine, 4640
I Wish I Was Here, 1573
I Wish I Was In Love Again, 30
I Wish I Was Queer So I Could Get Chicks, 602
I Wish I Were In Love Again, 308, 4606, 5919
I Wish I Were Twins, 3649
I Wish It Could Be Christmas Every Day, 5900
I Wish It Could Be Otherwise, 3230
I Wish It So, 596
I Wish It Would Rain, 3263, 4545, 4683, 5325, 5334, 5804
I Wish John Stetson Made A Heart, 5686
I Wish That We Were Married, 4640
I Wish Things Were Simple Again, 1179, 2334
I Wish You A Waltz, 356
I Wish You Belonged to Me, 4444
I Wish You Love, 3373, 5499
I Wish You Peace, 4047
I Wish You Well, 1144
I Wish You Were Dead, 4768
I Wish You Would, 237, 359, 5850, 5951
I Wished On The Moon, 522, 2556
I Woke Up, 3327
I Won't Be Going South, 4110
I Won't Be The Fool Anymore, 2459
I Won't Conga, 5573
I Won't Dance, 1552, 1885, 2366, 2976, 3580, 4503, 4570
I Won't Forget The Dawn, 1438
I Won't Forget You, 2615, 4485
I Won't Go Huntin' With You Jake But I'll Go Chasin' Women, 2358
I Won't Go Huntin' With You, Jake, 1446
I Won't Grow Up, 3187, 4207
I Won't Hold You Back, 5475

I'm A Brass Band, 1165, 1886
I'm A City Girl, 3704
I'm A Convict With Old Glory In My Heart, 3566
I'm A Country Song, 4619
I'm A Cult Hero, 1334
I'm A Ding Dong Daddy From Dumas, 420
I'm A Dreamer Aren't We All, 780, 2489
I'm A Fool, 1533, 2452, 4174
I'm A Fool To Care, 400, 1357
I'm A Good Man, 2663
I'm A Happy Man, 2825
I'm A Hog For You, 3858
I'm A Hog For You Baby, 1660
I'm A Honky Tonk Girl, 3370
I'm A Jonah Now, 2685
I'm A King Bee, 4247, 4967
I'm A Levi, 3211
I'm A Little Aeroplane, 3727
I'm A Little Bit Fonder Of You, 881, 3206
I'm A Little Blackbird Looking For A Bluebird, 93, 1106, 3649
I'm A Little On The Lonely Side, 4575
I'm A Lonesome Fugitive, 179, 2333, 4024
I'm A Long Gone Daddy, 5664
I'm A Lover, 2805, 4472, 5600
I'm A Lover (Not A Fighter), 1419, 3154
I'm A Man, 1039, 1055, 1152, 1420, 1517, 2663, 2825, 3203, 3676, 3731, 4024, 4277, 4897, 5381
I'm A Man Not A Boy, 2435
I'm A Man You Don't Meet Every Day, 4685
I'm A Married Man, 3731
I'm A Medicine Man For The Blues, 103
I'm A Midnight Mover, 5905
I'm A Millionaire, 5463
I'm A Monarchist, 597
I'm A Moody Guy, 1876
I'm A One Woman Man, 2599
I'm A One-Man Girl, 2339, 2619, 3824
I'm A Pig, 192
I'm a Popular Man, 1152
I'm A Ram, 530
I'm A Rastawoman, 2242
I'm A Secretary, 273
I'm A Star, 780
I'm A Stranger Here Myself, 4047
I'm A Sucker For Your

Love, 3462
I'm A Telling You, 856
I'm A Tiger, 3356
I'm A Train, 2368, 4265
I'm A Truck, 4924
I'm A Winner, Not A Loser, 2693
I'm A Woman, 3040, 3122, 3186, 3834
I'm A Wonderful Thing, Baby, 2984
I'm A'Tingle, I'm Aglow, 2120
(I'm A) Stand By My Woman Man, 2032
I'm Afraid Of Me, 1330
(I'm Afraid) The Masquerade Is Over, 3409, 5669
I'm Alive, 618, 2564, 3953, 4533
I'm Alone, 953, 3852
I'm Alone Because I Love You, 5973
I'm Already Blue, 2965
I'm Already Taken, 5703
I'm Alright, 1441, 3297
I'm Always Chasing Rainbows, 1195, 1578, 2447, 2708, 3548, 5998
(I'm Always Touched By Your) Presence Dear, 598
I'm An Indian, Too, 153, 197
I'm An Old Cowhand, 3629
I'm An Old Rock 'n' Roller, 5767
I'm An Ordinary Man, 2417, 3295, 3859
I'm Available, 4448
I'm Away, 161, 1195, 1960, 2333
I'm Awfully Glad I Met You, 3649
I'm Awfully Strong For You, 1152
I'm Back, 468, 4460
I'm Back For More, 3356
I'm Back In Circulation, 1886, 4471
I'm Back To Collect, 1148
I'm Bad, 3283, 4472
I'm Banking Everything On You, 2664
I'm Beginning To See The Light, 1734, 1736, 2694, 4265, 4528
I'm Biting My Fingernails And Thinkin' Of You, 183, 5518
I'm Blowin' Away, 161
I'm Blue (The Gong Gong Song), 230, 2677
I'm Brandin' My Darlin' With My Heart, 2318
I'm Bringing A Red Red Rose, 2922, 5814
I'm Calm, 2056
I'm Casting My Lasso

Towards The Sky, 5807
I'm Chillin, 608
I'm Comin' Hardcore, 5577
I'm Comin' Home, 2778, 1887, 4526, 5355
I'm Coming Out, 4657
I'm Coming Virginia, 1302, 5322, 5723
I'm Completely Satisfied With You, 3783, 3785
I'm Confessin, 3374, 3956
I'm Considering A Move To Memphis, 1182
I'm Cool, 4481
I'm Counting On You, 1551
I'm Cracking Up I Need A Pill, 312
I'm Cramped, 1275
I'm Crying, 193, 4843
I'm Dangerous, 1450
I'm Doin' Fine Now, 3923
I'm Doin' Time In A Maximum Security Twilight Home, 121
I'm Doin' What I'm Doin' for Love, 91
I'm Doing Fine Now, 3923, 4150
I'm Doing This For Daddy, 5928
I'm Doris The Goddess Of Wind, 864
I'm Dynamite, 4182
I'm Easy, 952, 1830, 3122
I'm Every Woman, 1350, 2612, 2982, 5452
I'm Falling, 620
I'm Falling In Love, 4520
I'm Falling In Love Tonight, 4710
I'm Falling In Love With Someone, 3885
I'm Feathering A Nest (For A Little Bluebird), 91
I'm Feelin' Like A Million, 746
I'm Feeling Fine, 821
I'm Flying, 3187, 4207
I'm Forever Blowing Bubbles, 843, 1146, 2810, 3383, 4818
I'm Free, 858, 1366, 4494
I'm Gettin' Tired Of Babyin' You, 4182
I'm Getting Married In The Morning, 2567, 5956
I'm Getting Myself Ready For You, 3924
I'm Getting Nowhere Fast With You, 2535
I'm Getting Sentimental Over You, 1482, 5719
I'm Getting Tired So I Can Sleep, 5395-5396
I'm Glad, 2777, 5526
I'm Glad I Waited, 2284, 4265
I'm Glad I'm Not Young Anymore, 1051, 2144,

3197, 3295
I'm Goin' Back (To The Bonjour Tristesse Brassiere Company), 2562
I'm Going Crazy, 1363
I'm Going Home, 1654, 3562, 4600
I'm Going Out, 5281
I'm Going Shopping With You, 2185
I'm Going To Find A Girl, 3160
I'm Going To Get Lit Up, 3032
I'm Going To See You Today, 2282
I'm Going' South, 5914
I'm Gone, 4884
I'm Gonna Be, 4344
I'm Gonna Be A Wheel Someday, 3709
I'm Gonna Be Strong, 3444, 4255, 4653
I'm Gonna Cross That River, 4541
I'm Gonna File My Claim, 3747
I'm Gonna Find My Baby, 5684
I'm Gonna Get Married, 4323, 4445, 5535
I'm Gonna Get Me A Gun, 1488
I'm Gonna Get My Baby, 4477
I'm Gonna Get You, 236, 447, 551, 3250, 4442, 5345
I'm Gonna Hang My Hat, 1960
I'm Gonna Hang Up My Rock 'N' Roll Shoes, 5864
I'm Gonna Hate Myself In The Morning, 69
I'm Gonna Hire A Wino To Decorate Our Home, 2039
I'm Gonna Knock On Your Door, 507, 1272, 2548, 4073
I'm Gonna Laugh You Right Out Of My Life, 1164
I'm Gonna Leave Off Wearin' My Shoes, 2607
I'm Gonna Leave You, 4297
I'm Gonna Live Till I Die, 2549, 2971
I'm Gonna Love Her On The Radio, 4326
I'm Gonna Love That Gal, 1195
I'm Gonna Love That Guy, 2462
I'm Gonna Love You Anyway, 3122
I'm Gonna Love You Forever, 1315
I'm Gonna Love You Just A Little More Baby, 5795
I'm Gonna Love You Too, 2631
I'm Gonna Make You Eat

2976, 3630, 5963
I'm On A See-Saw, 158, 1744, 2823
I'm On Fire, 84, 2303, 5544
I'm On My Way, 218, 663, 3196, 4105
I'm On My Way Home Again, 5797
I'm On My Way To A Better Place, 1007
I'm On My Way To Mandalay, 843
I'm On My Way To The Top, 5984
I'm On The Crest Of A Wave, 780, 4535
I'm On The Outside (Looking In), 3262, 4425
I'm On The Road To Memphis, 106
I'm On The Water Wagon Now, 716
I'm One, 1349, 4682, 5871
I'm Only Dreaming, 2037, 2385
I'm Only Human, 2403, 5909
I'm Only In It For The Love, 753, 1205
I'm Only Sleeping, 434, 4515
I'm Only Thinking Of Him, 3431
I'm Only Walking, 5785
I'm Outta Here, 2205
I'm Over You, 940
I'm Partial To Your Abracadabra, 3911
I'm Past My Prime, 3230
I'm Popeye The Sailor Man, 3197
I'm Praying Humble, 675
I'm Praying To St. Christopher, 4866, 5659
I'm Proud, 2683, 3055, 3059, 3416, 4688
I'm Pulling Through, 3039
I'm Putting All My Eggs In One Basket, 493, 1960
I'm Qualified, 2731, 5686
I'm Ready, 3830
I'm Ready For Love, 3480
I'm Real, 775
I'm Riffin, 3536
I'm Ruined, 2662
I'm Rushin, 68, 824, 2202
I'm Sending A Letter To Santa, 1210
I'm Sending You Red Roses, 2000, 5672
I'm Shadowing You, 1448
I'm Shooting High, 3054, 3580
I'm Shy Mary Ellen I'm Shy, 5690
I'm Simply Mad About The Boys, 2037
I'm Sitting On Top Of The World, 2489, 2862, 3225,

4934, 5972
(I'm So) Afraid Of Losing You Again, 2019
I'm So Attractive, 4229
I'm So Bored With The USA, 1110
I'm So Crazy For Love, 921
I'm So Excited, 3170
I'm So Glad, 1459, 2777, 5526
I'm So Glad I Met You, 2310
I'm So Glad I'm Standing Here Today, 1145, 1318
I'm So Glad You're Mine, 1317
I'm So Green, 1714
I'm So Happy, 1640, 3367
I'm So High, 1807
I'm So In Love With You, 5820, 6006
I'm So Into You, 807
I'm So Jealous, 1052
I'm So Lonesome I Could Cry, 705, 866, 1266, 3607, 3721, 4209, 5398, 5846
I'm So Proud, 2683, 3416, 4688
(I'm So) Sad, 3407
I'm So Sorry, 5661
I'm So Thankful, 2678
I'm So Very Glad, 1459
I'm So Young, 5454
I'm Sorry, 421, 725, 1124, 1471, 1485, 3170, 3976, 5395, 5408, 5659, 5661, 5700
I'm Sorry Fr You, My Friend, 364
I'm Sorry I Didn't Say I'm Sorry When I Made You Cry Last Night, 1133
I'm Sorry I Made You Cry, 843
I'm Sorry, I Want A Ferrari, 5932
I'm Standing, 33, 2834, 4293
I'm Starting All Over Again, 5524
I'm Stepping Out With A Memory Tonight, 3409, 5932
I'm Stickin' With You, 3052
I'm Sticking With You, 683
I'm Still, 3209
I'm Still Here, 837, 1959, 2252, 3039, 3976
I'm Still In Love, 3013
I'm Still In Love With You, 1569, 1741, 2266, 3055, 3276, 5845
I'm Still Standing, 33, 2834
I'm Still Waiting, 3648, 4445, 4696, 5408, 5872
I'm Stone In Love With You, 464, 3513
I'm Straight, 4356
I'm Stranded, 4721
I'm Strong, 3825

I'm Sure Of Everything But You, 3649
I'm Sure We Won't Fall Out Over This, 817
I'm Talking Through My Heart, 522
I'm Tellin' The Birds And Bees (How I Love You), 1708
I'm Telling The Birds, I'm Telling The Bees, 2035
I'm Telling You, 856, 3941
I'm Telling You Now, 923, 2021-2022
I'm The Boss, 2615, 2920
I'm The Echo, 1886
I'm The Face, 1962, 5810
I'm The Girl In The U.S.A, 4952
I'm The Greatest, 1698
I'm The Greatest Star, 2055-2056
I'm The Kind Of Woman, 5882
I'm The Last Of The Red Hot Mamas, 91, 5523, 5953
I'm The Leader Of The Gang (I Am), 2162, 2172, 3158
I'm The Lonesomest Gal In Town, 779
I'm The Man, 202, 2816, 3197
I'm The Medicine Man For The Blues, 103, 1106
I'm The One, 1349, 4424, 4682
I'm The One Who Loves You, 29, 368
I'm The One You Need, 2561, 3700, 5727
I'm The Only Hell (Mama Ever Raised), 4169
I'm The Toughest, 4599, 5473
I'm The Urban Spaceman, 662, 2697
I'm Thinking Of You Thinking Of Him, 3218
I'm Thinking Tonight Of My Blue Eyes, 59, 267, 960, 5764
I'm Through With Love, 2923, 3747, 5896
I'm Through With You, 946
I'm Throwing A Ball Tonight, 3634, 4118
I'm Tired, 5436
I'm Tired Of Being Pushed Around, 1894
I'm To Be Married Today, 4021
I'm Too Sexy, 4543
I'm Too Sexy For You, 1339
(I'm) Tore Down, 3014
I'm Tore Up, 5531
I'm Trembling On The Brink Of Love, 4414
I'm Trusting In You, 4651

I'm Trying, 1008
I'm Turning The Town Upside Down, 5285
I'm Turning You Loose, 5926
I'm Under The Influence Of Love, 5313
I'm Unlucky At Gambling, 1891
I'm Up Early, 2023
I'm Using My Bible For A Road Map, 4503
I'm Waiting For The Man, 5626-5627
I'm Waiting Just For You, 2439, 3187
I'm Walkin, 403, 1463, 3896
I'm Walking, 4879, 5785
I'm Walking Backwards For Christmas, 2213
I'm Walking Behind You, 1908, 4493
I'm Wanting You, I'm Needing You, 2739
I'm Wastin' My Tears On You, 4555
I'm Way Ahead, 1886
I'm Weak But Willing, 5647
I'm Wise, 635
I'm Wishing, 1543
I'm With You, 476, 683, 946, 1207, 3052
I'm Writing You This Little Melody, 5753
I'm You, You Are Me, 3509
I'm Your Baby Tonight, 2611
I'm Your Boogie Man, 2949
I'm Your Girl, 459, 3604
I'm Your Hoochie Coochie Man, 1556
I'm Your Man, 1654-1655, 2949
I'm Your Part Time Love, 1173
I'm Your Puppet, 459, 2514, 3303, 4031, 4368
I'm Your Toy, 1244
I'm Your Woman, 4351
I'm Yours, 1236, 1908, 2270, 4593
I'se A Muggin, 5389
I've A Shooting Box In Scotland, 4288
I've Alrcady Cheated On You, 1149
I've Always Been Crazy, 2813
I've Always Got Time To Talk To You, 694
I've Been A Bad, Bad Boy, 2881, 4342
I've Been A Fool, 3374, 4786
I've Been Around Enough To Know, 4771
I've Been Carrying A Torch For You For So Long That It's Burned A Great Big Hole In My Heart, 5333

In The Dark, 67
In The Days Of Ford Cortina, 1236
In The Dim Dim Dawning, 68
In The Evening By The Moonlight, 5660
In The Eye Of The Storm, 696
In The Future, 3605
In The Garden, 1870
In The Garden Of My Heart, 350, 843, 1702
In The Ghetto, 438, 880, 997, 1413, 2895, 4312, 5510
In The Gold Fields Of Nevada, 3200
In The Groove Again, 4080
In The Hall Of The Mountain King, 3903
In The Heat Of The Moment, 87
In The Hills, 3068
In The Jailhouse Now, 4240-4241, 4603, 5591
In The Land Of Beginning Again, 1106, 3649
In The Land Of La la La, 4594
In The Land Of Let's Pretend, 103, 1106
In The Light, 4229, 4265
In The Long Run, 1766
In The Middle Of A Heartache, 2753
In The Middle Of An Island, 480, 1973, 2998, 3012
In The Middle Of Nowhere, 69, 3580
In The Middle Of The House, 1621
In The Middle Of Two Hearts, 4188
In The Midnight Hour, 333, 664, 1301, 1308, 2356, 2678, 4234, 4670, 5361, 5456, 5503
In The Mission Of St. Augustine, 808, 4061
In The Mix, 301, 2636
In The Mood, 474, 1422, 1659, 1887, 2088, 2444, 2586, 3015, 3320, 3670, 3674, 4450, 5696
In The Moonlight, 345, 2985
In The Morning, 3496
In The Mystic Land Of Egypt, 2980
In The Name Of Love, 5407
In The Navy, 5644
In The Neighbourhood, 5671
In The Night, 4391
In The Past, 5739
In The Queue, 4964
In The Rain, 1619, 2624, 2912
In The Raw, 5791

In The Realm Of The Senses, 409, 2305
In The Rhythm Of My Heart, 3461
In The Right Way, 5319
In The Same Old Way, 3550, 3661, 4541
In The Shade Of The New Apple Tree, 227, 2589
In The Shade Of The Old Apple Tree, 782, 843, 2589, 2930
In The Shelter, 820
In The Sing Song Sycamore Tree, 1555, 5914
In The Springtime, 4327
In The Still Of The Night, 1535, 1703, 1919-1920, 2522, 3947, 3994, 4289, 4482, 5549
In The Summertime, 1676, 3823, 3839, 4372, 4450
(In The Summertime) You Don't Want Love, 3679
In The Sweet Bye And Bye, 961
In The Temple Of Radjah Krishnu, 2261
In The Thick Of It, 4682
In The Twilight Zone, 264
In The Valley (Where The Evening Sun Goes Down), 2426
In The Valley Of The Moon, 829
In The Ways Of The Indian, 5980
In The World Of Marnie Dreaming, 1184
In The Year 2525, 685, 5652, 5988
In The Year 2525 (Exordium & Terminus), 5988
In This Life, 4449, 4495
In Thoughts Of You, 2059
In Time, 1827, 4297, 4940
In Times Like These, 3560
In Too Deep, 3981
In Tune, 1886, 4482
In Twilight, 1090
In Walked Bud, 3739
In Walked Love, 3325
In Whatever Time We Have, 1058
In Your Arms, 3263
In Your Blood, 311, 647
In Your Bones, 2913
In Your Car, 1223
In Your Care, 219
In Your Eyes, 1350, 2942
In Your Heart, 723
In Your Own Little Way, 1228
In Your Own Quiet Way, 227, 2386
In Your Own Sweet Way, 794
In Your Room, 366

In Your System, 542
In-Between, 1705
Inbetween Days, 4056
Inbetweener, 4964
Inca Roads, 5991
Incendiary Device, 2839
Incense, 3676, 5890
Incense And Peppermints, 81
Inch Allah, 63
Inchworm, 2946, 3294
Incompatibility, 227, 2768
Inconvenience, 277
Increase Your Knowledge, 1007
Incredible, 2167, 2912, 4059, 4171, 4503
Incredible Miss Brown, 2183
Incubus Succubus II, 5942
Incurably Romantic, 3204, 3747, 5618
Indelible Shuffle, 3848
Independence, 762
Independence Cha Cha, 1511, 2928
Independence Day, 1199, 1607, 3542, 3668
Independence Ska, 754
Independent, 1769, 1839, 3850, 3913, 4965
Independent Deterrent, 145
Independent Jamaica, 2717, 3316
Independent Love Song, 4766
Independent Woman, 4668
Indestructible, 1997
India, 1186, 2683, 2860, 3267
India Kinda, 5440
Indian Chief, 4723
Indian In-Laws, 2907
Indian Lady, 1741
Indian Lake, 1267
Indian Love Call, 1703, 2028, 2037, 2366, 2385, 2682, 3326, 4153, 4648, 4880, 4967, 5807
Indian Outlaw, 2907, 3575
Indian Pacific, 1663
Indian Rag, 540
Indian Reservation, 1845, 3254, 3325, 4512
Indian Rope, 1024
Indian Summer, 1639, 2099, 2501
Indiana, 1918, 4570, 5896
Indiana Moon, 1405
Indiana Style, 2524
Indiana Wants Me, 5318
Indianapolis, 679
Indians, 201
Indigo, 3045
Indiscretion, 5778
Indispensable Thomas Hensible, 82
Indo Smoke, 2065
Indulge, 3906

Industry, 1117
Inequality, 2002
Infamy, 1759
Infatuation, 4038
Infidelity, 4923
Infinite Depth, 1242
Infinity, 1453, 1768, 2316
Inflation, 4546
Influenza (Relapse), 2113
Info Freako, 1519, 2818
Information Blues, 4579
Informer, 1944, 3104, 3425
Informer Fe Dead, 673
Ing' Song, 4589
Inglan' (England) Is A Bitch, 2850
Inherit The Wind, 4396
Inhlonipho, 421
Inhuman Condition, 3503
Iniquity Worker, 648
Injected With A Poison, 4305
Inka Dinka Doo, 1658
Inkis' Butt Crack, 4433
Inna Jah Children, 2138
Innamorata, 3484, 5593
Inner Cities, 5338
Inner City Blues, 2104, 4790, 5782
Inner City Boundary, 2697
Inner City Life, 2191
Inner Mind, 1768
Innocence, 586
Innocent, 4004
Inoculated City, 519
Inolvidable, 4616
Ins And Outs, 4946
Insane, 3523
Insane In The Brain, 1343
Insanity, 1441
Insatiable, 5661
Insect Love, 3480
Insensitive, 221
Inside, 1756, 3844, 4495, 4661
Inside Looking Out, 193
Inside Of Your Heart, 3890
Inside Out, 193, 2312, 4015, 4404
Insomnia, 1832
Insomniac's Dream, 3450
Inspiration, 1692, 3939, 5857
Instant Death, 4458
Instant Karma, 3191
Instant Knockout, 242
Instant Love, 5470
Instant Party, 3198, 5381
Instant Pussy, 3511
Instead-Of-Song, 5426
Instinct De Mort, 5515
Institute, 4390
Institution, 840
Instructions Of Life, 1350, 2800
Insult To Injury, 4205
Intense Energy, 92
Intense Song For Madonna

It's No Sin, 1992
It's Not Easy, 3172
It's Not For Me To Say, 1993, 3513
It's Not Love, 5483
It's Not Love (But It's Not Bad), 1143
It's Not Me, 2685
It's Not Supposed To Be That Way, 2966, 3899, 5735, 5980
It's Not Surprising, 648
It's Not The End Of The World, 1755
It's Not The World - It's The People, 5391
It's Not Unusual, 2887, 3684, 4478
It's Not What You Say, 4110
It's Not Where You Start (It's Where You Finish), 1165, 1886, 5527
It's Not Wrong, 2346
It's Not You, 1744, 4233
It's Not You, It's Not Me, 2949
It's Now Or Never, 3303, 4311, 4771
It's Obvious, 277
It's On, 1945, 3300
It's On You, 4455
It's Only A Game, 395
It's Only A Paper Moon, 227, 1159, 1708, 2386, 3764, 3951, 4650
It's Only A Phonograph Record, 3746
It's Only Love, 63, 569, 3648, 4923
It's Only Make Believe, 905, 1057, 1144, 1551, 2059, 2217, 3565, 3651, 5547-5548
It's Only Rock 'n' Roll, 2813, 4630, 4898
It's Our Turn, 1757
It's Our Turn To Sing With Ol' Willie, 3900
It's Over, 2053, 2753, 3010, 3207, 3293, 4049, 4055, 4572, 4941, 5426, 5496
It's Over Now, 404, 936, 1217, 1221, 4628, 5373, 5568, 5599
It's People Like You, 1437
It's Power House Brooklyn Style, 3981
It's Raining, 1247, 1396, 1417, 5401, 5676
It's Raining Men, 5551, 5740
It's Raining On Prom Night, 2256
It's Raining Sunbeams, 4045
It's Sad To Belong, 1760
It's Shocking What They Call Me, 2077
It's So Easy, 2569
It's So Hard, 4174
It's So Hard Being A

Loser, 1215
It's So Nice, 2077
It's So Nice To Come Home, 3189
It's So Peaceful In The Country, 5830
It's So Simple, 336
It's Somebody Else's Moon, 1933
It's Sort Of Romantic, 3419
It's Still Cloudy In Saudi Arabia, 3355
It's Still Nowhere, 95
It's Still Rock 'N' Roll To Me, 2830
It's Such A Small World, 1315
It's Summertime, 70
It's Super Nice, 2723
It's Superman, 2723
It's That Time Of Night, 777
It's The Animal In Me, 522
It's The Dreamer In Me, 5606
It's The Drum, 694
It's The End Of The World As We Know It, 1568, 4394
It's The Girl, 326
It's The Going Home Together, 2187
It's The Irish In Me, 3847
It's The Little Things (That Piss Me Off), 2952
It's The Natural Thing To Do, 2473
It's The Only Way To Travel, 4563
It's The Rhythm In Me, 4328
It's The Same Old Dream, 884, 2723
It's The Same Old Song, 1997, 2561, 4242
It's The Talk Of The Town, 2253
It's Tight Like That, 1599, 2552, 5291, 5655
It's Time, 518, 884, 1627, 1784, 2120, 2723, 3190, 3299, 3325, 5773, 5881
It's Time for A Love Song, 3122
It's Time For Love, 1052
It's Time For Your Dreams To Come True, 4132
It's Time To Pay The Fiddler, 4983
It's Time To Say Goodnight, 2035, 3649
It's Today, 2505, 3428, 4021
It's Too Late, 954, 1063, 1222, 2194, 2291, 3011, 3815, 4234, 5297, 5352, 5864
It's Too Late Now, 3047
It's Too Soon To Know, 4055, 4061
It's True, 511, 4520
It's True I'm Gonna Miss

You, 2015
It's Tulip Time In Holland, 5805
It's Twelve and A Tanner A Bottle, 1747
It's Up To Me, 2723
It's Up To You, 3896
It's Up To You, Petula, 1706
It's Whatcha Do With Whatcha Got, 1438, 4449
It's When It's Wrong It's Right, 1351
It's Wonderful, 4683
It's Wonderful To Be In Love, 2741, 4084
It's Written All Over Your Face, 753
It's Yer Money I'm After Baby, 5906
It's You, 227, 564, 733, 893, 1369, 1551, 1744, 2130, 2894, 3531, 3896, 4233, 4455, 4467, 4563, 4843, 5422, 5483, 5606
It's You I Love, 3271, 5325
It's You Only You (Mein Schmerz), 3346
It's You Or No One, 4636
It's You That I Need, 1758
It's You That's On My Mind, 5299
It's Your Love, 2529, 3575
It's Your Thing, 2719, 2727, 4726
It's Your Time, 3299
It's Yours, 1432, 1460, 1886, 2800, 4679, 5276
It's Yourself, 3406
Ital Feast, 2764
Italian Lullaby, 1960
Italian Street Song, 2501, 3885
Italian Sunset, 95
Itchycoo Park, 2681, 3379, 4019, 4974
Its A Mystery, 5483
Its A Shame, 3424
Its All Over Now, 3545
Its All Right, 3218
Its All Up To You, 921
Its Alright, 4293
Its Goodbye, 2170
Its Got To Be Mellow, 4639
Its Grim Up North, 3043
Its Just Another Groove, 1220
Its My Life, 193
Its My Turn, 2636
Its Not You, 1022
Its The Darndest Thing, 3580
Its Too Late Baby, 2705
Itsari, 4823
Itsy Bitsy Teenie Weenie, Honolulu Strand Bikini, 5595
Itsy Bitsy Teeny Weeny Yellow Polka Dot Bikini, 651, 1326, 1495, 2653, 2936

Ivory Tower, 949, 1033, 2943
Ivy, 942, 5371
Ivy Ivy, 3179
Izinyembezi, 421
J'ai Fait Mon Edée, 3127
J'Aime Les Filles, 1669
J'arrive, 2263
J'Attendrai, 2009
J'en Ai Morre, 36
J'Y Pense Et Puis J'Oublie, 2009
J.P. Dooley III, 5830
Ja Da, 4979
JA People, 3634
Ja-Da, 308, 2837, 5937
Jack & Jill Shuffle, 447
Jack And Diane, 3617
Jack And Jill, 4138
Jack And Jill Boogie, 4428
Jack And Neal/California Here I Come, 5671
Jack Daniels If You Please, 1149
Jack Horner's Holiday, 3304
Jack In The Box, 3734, 4601
Jack Named The Planets, 251
Jack Of Diamonds, 1358
Jack Of My Trade, 2138, 4939
Jack Tar On Shore, 2354
Jack The Bear, 1736, 5355
Jack The Groove, 4451
Jack The Lad, 3494
Jack The Ripper, 3283, 5832, 5924
Jack To The Sound Of The Underground, 2545
Jack Your Body, 2606, 2644
Jack! Jack! Jack!, 4989
Jack-Ass, 4013
Jacket Hangs, 610
Jackie, 2017, 3381, 4782, 5682
Jackie Blue, 4093
Jackie Wilson Said, 1503, 3795, 4720, 5465, 5874
Jackie's Racing, 5802
Jackie's Still Sad, 1519
Jackpot, 2138
Jackpot Jack, 4642
Jackson, 977, 979, 2452, 2838, 4931, 5784
Jackson Ain't A Very Big Town, 1651
Jacob's Ladder, 3218, 3742
Jacqueline, 2480
Jacques Chirac, 2761
Jacques Derrida, 4794
Jaded Figurine, 3742
Jag Maste Ga Nu, 5329
Jag Var Sa Kar, 37, 1837
Jagged Edge Of A Broken Heart, 1403
Jaguar, 1380
Jah Army, 5546
Jah Bring I Joy, 5409
Jah Calling All Over The

World, 2670
Jah Children Cry, 2762
Jah Find Babylon Guilty, 778
Jah Fire Will Be Burning, 3838
Jah Glory, 2727
Jah Guide, 5473, 5995
Jah Heavy Load, 3211
Jah Holds The Key, 4696
Jah I, 2822
Jah Is Calling, 5319
Jah Is Here, 4468
Jah Is My Light, 2822
Jah Jah Children, 3487, 4675
Jah Jah Fire, 767
Jah Jah Forgive You, 2763
Jah Jah Go Before Us, 2165
Jah Jah Jehovah, 1417
Jah Jah Loving, 648
Jah Jah Me, 4468
Jah Judgement, 3576
Jah Kingdom Come, 5546
Jah Light, Jah Love, 5640
Jah Lion, 2761
Jah Live, 4200
Jah Made Them All, 648
Jah Man A Come, 5716
Jah Mek Us Fe A Purpose, 4942
Jah Rulez, 2133
Jah Says The Time Has Come, 3838
Jah Screw, 311
Jah See Dem A Come, 2889
Jah Shaky, 1569
Jah Stay, 1472
Jah Vengeance, 5945
Jah Wonderful, 5716
Jahoviah, 1373, 2242, 3210
Jail Bait, 5836
Jailbirds Can't Fly, 981
Jailbreak, 4640
Jailhouse, 4494
Jailhouse Affair, 5767
Jailhouse Nuh Nice, 4766
Jailhouse Rock, 517, 1858, 3186, 5503
Jake On The Make, 2075
Jake Walk Blues, 127
Jalouse, 2921
Jalousie, 3111
Jam, 522, 995, 2466, 2824, 3135, 3603
Jam It Jam, 4860
Jam J, 2769
Jam Rock Style, 4791
Jam Song, 2740
Jam Tonight, 2740
Jam Up, 4541
Jam Up Jelly Tight, 4617
Jam With Sam, 341
Jamaica Farewell, 457, 897
Jamaica Salute, 3647
Jamaica Say You Will, 791
Jamaican Child, 3649
Jamaican Collie, 1029
Jamaican In New York, 370, 4882

Jambalaya, 116, 616, 725, 1581, 1993, 2670, 3170, 3677, 3836, 4393, 4651, 4654, 5846-5847
Jambalaya (On The Bayou), 1954
James, 4017, 5314
James (Hold The Ladder Steady), 3325, 5414
James Alley Blues, 786
James Bond Theme, 400
James Brown, 875, 3030
James Brown (Part 1), 1651
James Brown Is Dead, 6006
James Dean, 791
Jamestown Ferry, 5524
Jamie, 2559
Jamie D, 1939
Jamming, 1808, 3891, 5652
Janaam - The Message, 2051
Jane, 2803-2804
Jane, Stop This Crazy Thing!, 3538
Jango, 4447
Janie Baker's Love Slave, 4867
Janie Took My Place, 3122
January, 4244
January February, 1515
January Man, 2225
January/After Midnight Polkas, 2276
Japanese Boy, 189
Jarabi, 4713
Jarrow Song, 4322
Jasmine, 1761
Jason, 2789, 5342
Jason And The Arguments, 382
Jaspora, 5934
Jassamine, 2846
Java, 773, 1062, 4096, 5478
Java Jive, 2694
Jawbreaker, 1906
Jay Moon Walk, 2733
Jazz Baby, 5417
Jazz Carnival, 302
Jazz Is The Teacher, 1868, 3979
Jazz Ma Ass, 1353
Jazz Marimba, 5432
Jazz Me Blues, 5904
Jazz Pizzicato, 179
Jazz Praises, 2095
Jazz Sonatas For Solo Guitar, 3418
Jazz Thing, 2081, 2799-2800
Jazz Up Your Lingerie, 2284
Jazzboat, 2488
Jazzman, 3011
Jazzy, 1180
Jazzy Notions, 3426
Jazzy Sensation, 86, 337, 2800, 4214, 5459
JB Dick + Tin Turner (sic) Pussy Badsmell, 672
Je M'en Fous, 1378
Je Ne Regrette Rein, 4229
Je Suis Bien, 2263

Je Suis Un Rock Star, 4631
Je T' Aime . . . Moi Non Plus, 544, 2071, 2733, 5974
Je T'ai Dans La Peau, 442
Je T'Aime, 2908, 2915, 4849
Je T'Appartiens, 442
Je Tire Ma Révérence, 4711-4712
Je Vous Aime, 4695
Jealous, 3536, 3809
Jealous Again, 554
Jealous Eyes, 2533
Jealous Guy, 2680, 3192, 4103, 4670
Jealous Heart, 958, 1708, 1963, 2085, 4494, 4573
Jealous Hearted Me, 5764
Jealous Kind Of Fellow, 2269
Jealous Lies, 4324
Jealous Lover, 767, 5840
Jealousy, 170, 572, 1453, 2059, 2411, 5501, 5591
Jealousy Fe Done, 3697
Jealousy, Heartache And Pain, 4070
Jean, 758, 3068, 3588
Jean And Dinah, 3661
Jean Genie, 105
Jeanie Girl, 1032
Jeanie Loved The Roses, 2783
Jeanie With The Light Brown Hair, 1986
Jeannie, 5842
(Jeannie Marie) You Were A Lady, 4086
Jeannie Needs A Shooter, 5996
Jeannie, I Dream Of Lilac Time, 282, 4880
Jeanny, 1834
Jeans On, 1653
Jeep's Blues, 1735, 2548
Jeepers Creepers, 1622, 2962, 3629, 4299, 4928, 5711
Jeepster, 673, 1696, 1949, 4273, 5277
Jeeves Is Past His Peak, 2801
Jeffrey Goes To Leicester Square, 2819
Jehovah's Witness At The Door, 382
Jekyll And Hyde Variations, 2224
Jekyll's Plea, 2807
Jelly Babies, 1768
Jelly Roll, 2469, 4469
Jelly, Jelly, 1700
Jellybread, 664
Jellyhead, 1319
Jennie Lee, 2779-2780
Jennifer (Fly My Little Baby), 1184
Jennifer Johnson And Me, 3057
Jennifer Juniper, 1590
Jennifer's Rabbit, 4168

Jenny, 307, 2130, 2915, 3146, 4259
Jenny Artichoke, 2926
Jenny Jenny, 3270
Jenny Pluck Pears, 5458
Jenny Take A Ride, 4705
Jeopardy, 505, 2988, 5949
Jericho, 3593, 4345
Jerk It, 2323
Jerome, Jerome, I'm A Hell Of A Guy, 1968
Jerri O, 292
Jerry, 2687, 3531, 5807
Jersey Bounce, 3674, 4263
Jersey Girl, 5671
Jersey Thursday, 1828
Jeru, 545, 3836
Jerusalem, 709
Jesamine, 872, 987
Jesse James, 99
Jessie, 2921
Jester, 363
Jestering, 3593
Jesu, Joy Of Man's Desiring, 209
Jesus, 2065
Jesus And Mama, 1203
Jesus Built My Hotrod, 3692
Jesus Es Mi Senor, 922
Jesus Hold My Hand, 799
Jesus I Love To Call His Name, 1114
Jesus In A Leather Jacket, 4098
Jesus Is Just Alright, 1431
Jesus Is Way Cool, 3002
Jesus Loves Amerika, 4842
Jesus Loves You, 3052
Jesus Met The Woman At The Well, 4243
Jesus Saves, 4755
Jesus Skrew Superstar, 4955
Jesus To A Child, 4029
Jesus Was A Crossmaker, 4907
Jesus, I Need To Talk To You, 1971
Jet, 361, 475, 2410, 3548, 4511, 5885
Jet Airliner, 3680
Jet Boy, Jet Girl, 928, 3805-3806
Jet Set Junta, 3742
Jet Song, 499
Jet Star, 1350
Jeun Ko'ku, 3088
Jewel, 4348
Jewel In The Crown, 3519
Jewelry, 336
Jezebel, 299, 1339, 3111, 3677, 4520, 4692, 5337
Je'Ne Sais`Pas Pour Qui, 3697
Jibaro Soy, 3162
Jidai, 3870
Jig A Jig, 1690
Jig Hope, 1894
Jig Jigaloo, 103, 1106
Jig Time, 5753

Judy Says (Knock You In The Head), 5640
Judy Staring At The Sun, 991
Judy Teen, 1146
Judy's Turn To Cry, 2219, 4639
Judy, Judy, Judy, 5438
Jug Band Music, 1429
Jug Of Punch, 1093
Jugband Blues, 392, 4247, 4354
Juggling, 4111
Juice Head Baby, 5647
Juicebox, 28, 3538
Juicy Crocodile, 1002
Juke, 820, 1039, 3274, 5354
Juke Box Baby, 1195
Juke Box Fury, 2884
Juke Box Jive, 4678
Juke Box Saturday Night, 3956
Juke Joint, 2995
Jukebox, 822, 2315, 4491, 4505
Jukebox Help Me Find My Baby, 2315
Jukebox In My Mind, 2143
Jukebox Junkie, 3618
Jukebox Saturday Night, 1132, 2962, 3729
Julia, 435, 2235, 3838, 4167, 4452
Julia Says, 5779
Julianne, 4710
Juliano The Bull, 2789
Julida Polka, 2550
Julie, 1107, 1220
Julie Ann, 2970, 3483
Julie Do Ya Love Me?, 5792
Julie Is Her Name, 4903
Julie Ocean, 5575
Julie-O, 5537
Juliet, 1994, 2017
July 13th 1985, 2391
Jumbo, 450, 1129
Jump, 524, 2737, 3077, 3954, 4946, 5530, 5605
Jump (For My Love), 4271
Jump And Prance, 4107
Jump And Spread Out, 1944
Jump And Twist, 6004
Jump Around, 1557, 2608, 5942
Jump Back, 5405
Jump Children, 2174
Jump For Joy, 2205, 5750
Jump In My Car, 3838
Jump Jim Crow, 3533
Jump Little Children, Jump, 1365
Jump Mk2, 4228
Jump On The Wagon, 1210
Jump Out Of The Frying Pan, 2535
Jump Start, 1161
Jump To It, 2013
Jump Up, 79
Jump Up In The Air, 3671

Jump, Little Chillun!, 1923
Jump, Red, Jump, 4352
Jump, Shout, Boogie, 1229
Jumpin' At The Jubilee, 407
Jumpin' At The Woodside, 405
Jumpin' Blues, 2405, 4133
Jumpin' Jack, 2927
Jumpin' Jack Flash, 2611, 4529, 4630, 5744
Jumpin' Jive, 2040
Jumpin' Punkins, 1738
Jumping, 937, 6002
Jumping Bean, 1851
Jumping Jack, 603
Jumping Jehosaphat, 3798
Jumping Someone Else's Train, 1334
Junco Partner, 5737
June Bride, 1438, 4825
June Brought The Roses, 4880
June In January, 2003, 4413, 4580
June Is Bustin' Out All Over, 946-947, 4607
June Love, 2037, 4580
June Night, 325, 2035, 3373
Junge Komm Bald Wieder, 4389
Jungle, 3642, 3667, 3708, 3873, 4080, 4931, 4979
Jungle Beat, 5990
Jungle Boogie, 3062
Jungle Bungle, 371
Jungle Fever, 1008
Jungle Green, 4471
Jungle High, 615
Jungle Kisses, 4969
Jungle Lion, 4200
Jungle Rock, 3719, 4594
Jungle-Ist, 1479
Junglistic Bad Boy, 4503
Junior, 214, 589, 1326, 1635, 1969, 2684, 3829, 5290, 5459, 5595
Junior And Julie, 1483
Junior Wants To Play, 653
Junior's Farm, 3548
Junk Food Junkie, 2294
Junker's Blues, 624
Junkhead, 120, 1538
Jupiter Forbid, 861
Jury Of Love (Men, Women), 1148
Just A Baby's Prayer At Twilight, 5972
Just A Baby's Prayer At Twilight (For Her Daddy Over There), 843
Just A Breath Away, 2517
Just A Catchy Little Tune, 4932
Just A City, 5656
Just A Closer Walk, 610
Just A Closer Walk With Thee, 956, 1129, 1956
Just A Cottage Small By A Waterfall, 1439

Just A Coupl'a Sisters, 3987
Just A Dream, 1094, 3758, 4223, 5290, 5621
Just A Dream Away, 3196
Just A Feeling, 5319
Just A Friend, 550, 4948
Just A Friendly Game Of Baseball, 3417
Just A Gigolo, 881
Just A Girl, 3961
Just A Groove, 3970
Just A Kiss, 4832
Just A Kiss Apart, 2120
Just A Little, 288, 438, 5395
Just A Little Bit, 2217, 5408, 5575
Just A Little Bit More, 1886
Just A Little Bit Of Loving, 1120
Just A Little Bit Too Late, 1963
Just A Little Closer, 3649
Just A Little Fond Affection, 2103
Just A Little Love, 3566, 4956
Just A Little Lovin' Will Go A Long Way, 237
Just A Little Misunderstanding, 1215
Just A Little Ring, 606
Just A Little Talk With Jesus, 766
Just A Little Too Much, 838, 3896
Just A Little Touch Of Your Love, 5450
Just A Little War, 3282
Just A Minute, 4949
Just A Patsy, 4899
Just A Smile, 4244
Just A Song Before I Go, 3877
Just A Step From Heaven, 1782
Just A Tear, 4233
Just A Touch, 3239
Just A Wave, Not The Water, 2154
Just A-Settin' And A-Rockin, 5355
Just A-Wearyin' For You, 653
Just About Now, 2529
Just Ain't No Love, 56
Just An Echo In The Valley, 1207, 5600, 5915
Just An Hour Of Love, 672
Just An Illusion, 2679
Just Another Cowboy Song, 2570
Just Another Day, 3825, 4803
Just Another Day In Paradise, 2518
Just Another Dream, 1481
Just Another Fool Along The Way, 3755
Just Another Girl, 1569

Just Another Illusion, 2645
Just Another Kiss, 4880
Just Another Lonely Day, 3825
Just Another Night, 2760
Just Another Onionhead, 31
Just Another Pretty Boy, 82
Just Another Rhumba, 2129
Just Another Woman In Love, 3845
Just Anuddah Day, 3106
Just Around The Corner, 1144, 5660
Just Around The Eyes, 2529
Just Arrived, 1229
Just As Long As I've Got You, 656
Just As Long As You Need Me, 2690
Just As Soon As The Feeling's Over, 1460
Just As Though You Were Here, 1436, 4238
Just As You Are, 1870
Just Be Good To Me, 438, 4710
Just Be My Lady, 2232
Just Be True, 1014
Just Because, 4323, 4445, 4865, 5853
Just Because You're You, 4207
Just Before Dawn, 3802
Just Before Daybreak, 2847
Just Between The Two Of Us, 179
Just Between You And Me, 1069, 1122, 2233, 4326
Just Blew In From The Windy City, 889
Just Call Me Lonesome, 1986, 2289
Just Came Back, 2770
Just Can't Cry No More, 3306
Just Can't Win, 863
Just Cool Melba, 3505
Just Crusin, 1559
Just Crying In The Rain, 3677
Just Dance And Leave The Music To Me, 3258
Just Doin' Our Job, 2018
Just Don't, 3974
Just Don't Wanna Be Lonely, 3576
Just Driftin, 4355
Just Dropped In (To See What Condition My Condition Was In), 3142, 3926, 4621
Just En Reve, 4530
Just Enough Rope, 5502
Just Enough To Keep Me Hanging On, 2714
Just Enough To Start Me Dreaming, 4813
Just Fades Away, 5527
Just Fascination, 875

Just For A Second, 4062
Just For A Thrill, 232, 5363
Just For Kicks, 1649
Just For Old Times Sake, 2289, 3579
Just For Once, 1886
Just For The Money, 2389
Just For Tonight, 5388
Just For What I Am, 4986
Just For You, 653, 1918, 2021, 2172, 2647, 2923, 3380, 4322, 4372, 4648
Just For Your Love, 1834, 3623
Just Friends, 881, 1532, 1907, 2074, 3225
Just Get Up And Close The Door, 2395, 4613
Just Girls, 1223
Just Give Me What You Think Is Fair, 2222, 2812
Just Go Away, 4125
Just Go The The Movies, 27
Just Good Friends, 1907, 2074
Just Good Ol' Boys, 364
Just Got Lucky, 2828
Just Got Paid, 4434
Just Got To Know, 3007, 3557
Just Heaven, 1129, 1335, 1533, 2212, 3036
Just Hold My Hand, 3802
Just Imagine, 780, 2202
Just In Case, 1976, 3729
Just In Case You Change Your Mind, 765
Just In Lust, 5831
Just In Time, 468, 480, 1191, 2562
Just Jammin' Fresh And Def, 2826
Just Keep It Up, 574, 1099
Just Keep Right On, 1233
Just Kickin, 5966
Just Kickin' It, 5942
Just Leave Everything To Me, 2477
Just Let It Come, 122
Just Let Me Look At You, 1886, 2976
Just Like A Butterfly, 1555, 5914
Just Like A Dream, 3758
Just Like A Fool, 3063
Just Like A Gypsy, 421
Just Like A Man, 3173
Just Like A Melody Out Of The Sky, 282
Just Like A River, 1162, 2138
Just Like A Song, 2714
Just Like A Story Book, 3548
Just Like A Widow, 2859
Just Like A Woman, 2893, 3015, 3437, 4726, 5461, 5896
Just Like Daddy's Gun, 1632
Just Like Eddie, 1142,

2473, 3611
Just Like Gold, 4295
Just Like Heaven, 1335, 1533, 3036
Just Like Honey, 2817
Just Like Me, 3621, 3712, 4512
Just Like Romeo And Juliet, 4487, 4751
Just Like That, 4490
Just Like The Bluebird, 2117
Just Like Tom Thumb Blues, 3540
Just Like You, 2950, 3548, 4633
Just Look At Us, 4150
Just Look At You Fool, 5799
Just Love, 266, 713, 1193, 1569, 3196, 3931, 4255, 4431, 4928
Just Loving You, 2404, 4986
Just Lust, 5831
Just Me, 1459, 1532, 3621, 3712, 3755, 4512
Just Moved In, 2672
Just My Imagination, 134, 1889, 2965, 3303, 5334, 5576
Just My Salvation, 134
Just My Soul Responding, 4585
Just Now, 2529
Just Once, 1886, 2693, 3842
Just Once In My Life, 2181, 4543
Just Once More, 5601
Just One Fix, 846, 1156
Just One Kiss, 3864, 4680
Just One Look, 1829, 2563, 3426, 5512
Just One More Night, 5954, 5974
Just One More Time, 2454, 3196
Just One Of Those Things, 266, 713, 912, 2522, 2596, 2906, 3947, 4289, 4928, 5965
Just One Smile, 3931, 4255
Just One Time, 2141, 2393, 2454, 3196, 4986, 5745
Just One Way To Say I Love You, 3705
Just Out Of My Reach, 1459
Just Out Of Reach, 830, 1459
Just Playin' Possum, 1583
Just Remember I Love You, 1902
Just Rock, 1866
Just Say No, 2099, 2525, 3283, 4025, 5455
Just Say Who, 1569
Just Someone I Used To Know, 5666
Just Suck, 1350
Just The Lonely Talking Again, 3168
Just The Two Of Us, 179,

3083, 5897
Just The Way It Is Baby, 4499
Just The Way You Are, 2830, 5378, 5795
Just The Way You Like It, 4710
Just This One Time, 5745
Just Thought I'd Let You Know, 3218
Just To Be Close To You, 1193
Just To Be Near You, 1438
Just To Be With You, 4152
Just To Satisfy You, 689
Just To See Her, 4585
Just To See You, 4121
Just To See You Smile, 2031
Just Wait Until I Get You Home, 1460
Just Walkin' In The Rain, 4340, 4446
Just Watch Me, 1459
Just What I Always Wanted, 5876
Just What I Had In Mind, 5970
Just What I Needed, 957, 5358
Just What You Want, Just What You Get, 2833
Just When I Needed You, 1513
Just When I Needed You Most, 5613
Just When We're Falling In Love, 4695
Just When You Thought It Was Safe, 5484
Just You, 1069, 1918, 2021, 2103, 2172, 2404, 2647, 2923, 2950, 3380, 3548, 3859, 3896, 4322, 4372, 4633, 4648, 4986
Just You And Me, 1069, 1122, 2233, 4326
Just You Wait, 3859
Just You Watch My Step, 3160
Justice, 4408
Justice (Just Us), 4703
Justice In Freedom, 2655
Justice Love And Harmony, 3505
Justified And Ancient, 3043, 5936
Justify, 3380
Justify My Love, 3075, 3403, 4731
Justify Your Love, 4056
Juvenile Delinquent, 559
K Sera Sera, 3043
K-K-K-Katie, 5443
K.C. Boogie, 1604
K.C. Lovin, 3186, 3275
Ka Ding Dong, 1510, 2063
Ka-Lu-A, 875
Kachusha, 1391
Kaguya Hime, 2914

Kaigoon, 4563
Kakuda, 236
Kalamazoo To Timbuktu, 5830
Kaleidoscoptic, 4885
Kanashiki Kuchibue, 3704
Kanawha March, 2979
Kandy Pop, 546
Kanga Roo, 812
Kangewah, 4621
Kansas City, 416, 437, 1816, 2418, 3186, 3275, 3390, 3894, 4025, 4582, 5361
Kansas City Blues, 2736, 4159
Kansas City Kitty, 3200
Kansas City Lights, 5703
Kao-tic Harmony, 3526
Kara Lee, 3986
Karabitz!, 2723
Karen, 2175
Karma (A Study Of Divination's), 4970
Karma Chameleon, 364, 693, 1330, 4719
Karma Coma, 5504
Kashama Nkoi, 3228
Kashmir, 1263, 3165, 4229
Kate (Have I Come Too Early Too Late), 1361
Kate Warren Breakdown, 5710
Kathleen Mine, 2512
Kathy's Song, 4918
Kathy's Waltz, 5440
Kathy-O, 1510
Katie Went To Haiti, 1635, 3634
Katie's Kisses, 1551
Katinka, 2036, 5454
Katisha's Warning, 2602
Katmandu, 3278
Katrina, 1438
Katsumi Love Theme, 5734
Katy Cruel, 1397
Kaw-Liga, 692, 4651, 5846-5847
Kawasaki, Hotter Than Chapati, 1236
Kay Sarah, 1446
Kaya, 85, 2763, 2943
Kayleigh, 1907, 3463, 3704
Kaze Wa Akiiro, 3514
KC, 2949, 4539
KC Railroad Blues, 419
Keem-O-Sabe, 1724
Keen, 5351
Keep A Dollar In Your Pocket, 4202
Keep A Hold Of What You've Got, 4892
Keep A Knockin, 571, 2070, 3270, 4083
Keep A Light At The Window, 3681
Keep A Twinkle In Your Eye, 604
Keep A-Hoppin, 5869

King Without A Throne, 4919
King's Call, 3374
King's Dilemma, 5643
King's Lead Hat, 1765
Kingdom, 5569
Kings Of Kings, 4459, 5665
Kingston Tuffy, 541, 2576, 4644
Kingston 11, 4336
Kingston Hot, 3144
Kingston Town, 1817, 3316, 5291, 5562
Kingston Tuffy, 541, 2576, 4644
Kingston Twelve Tuffy, 4644
Kinky Afro, 4244
Kinky Love, 4109
Kisap Mata, 4557
Kiss, 89, 245, 2887, 4123, 4332
Kiss An Angel Good Morning, 4137, 4326
Kiss And Make Up, 1916, 4721
Kiss And Ride, 715
Kiss And Say Goodbye, 3441
Kiss Crazy Baby, 2836
Kiss From A Rose, 4797
Kiss From Your Lips, 1915
Kiss In The Dark, 2501
Kiss Me, 1644, 5782
Kiss Me Another, 2137
Kiss Me Baby, 4311
Kiss Me Deadly, 1971
Kiss Me Goodbye, 1406
Kiss Me Goodnight, 5486
Kiss Me Honey Honey, Kiss Me, 409
Kiss Me Kate, 3035
Kiss Me No Kisses, 5782
Kiss Me Now, 4385, 4500
Kiss Me Quick, 691, 4277, 4311, 4672, 4897
Kiss Me Where It Smells Funny, 602
Kiss My Ass, 3984, 5612
Kiss Of Death, 4749
Kiss Of Fire, 2137, 3492
Kiss Off, 5649
Kiss Somebody, 4514
Kiss The Baby Goodnight, 247
Kiss The Boys Goodbye, 4769, 5669
Kiss The Children, 2262
Kiss The Girl, 255, 3268
Kiss The Hurt Away, 1606
Kiss The Road Of Rarotonga, 1897
Kiss Them For Me, 4938
Kiss This Thing Goodbye, 1467
Kiss Tomorrow Goodbye, 1925
Kiss Waltz, 829
Kiss What I Miss, 742
Kiss You All Over, 1064,

1806, 4652
Kiss-a-me Baby, 1873
Kissed By The Rain, Warmed By The Sun, 375
Kisses, 658
Kisses Don't Lie, 1640
Kisses On The Wind, 1047
Kisses Sweeter Than Wine, 4602, 5617, 5743
Kissin In The Back Row Of The Movies, 3384
Kissin, 2672
Kissin' And Twistin, 1816
Kissin' Cousins, 2718
Kissin' Cousins (Number Two), 3037
Kissin' In The Back Row Of The Movies, 1628, 3303
Kissin' Time, 4705
Kissing Bug, 3119
Kissing Time, 2160
Kissing Under Anaesthetic, 3021
Kissing You, 3419
Kita Kita, 3143
Kitchen Blues, 1413
Kitchen Man, 625
Kites, 1657
Kitten On The Keys, 1203
Kitty, 4309
KJZ, 4228
KKK (Koffee Koloured Kids), 2584
KKK Bitch, 640
Klact-oveeseds-tene, 4134
Klactoveesedstein, 616
Klunk, 2265
Knee Deep In The Blues, 1759, 3677, 3711, 4568
Knievel, 4795
Knife Edge, 4236
Knight In Rusty Armour, 3407, 4206
Knight In Shining Armour, 2167
Knightsbridge March, 1139
Knit One - Purl Two, 2965
Knock Knock, 778, 1942
Knock Knock Knock, 778
Knock Knock Who's There, 3805
Knock Me A Kiss, 2893
Knock Me Down, 4463
Knock Me Out, 4201
Knock On My Door, 3817
Knock On Wood, 1301, 1947, 2184, 3050, 5399
Knock Three Times, 1272, 1423, 4062, 5433
Knock Wood, 1301, 1947, 2184, 3050, 5399, 5523
Knock! Knock! Who's There?, 2591, 5753
Knocked It Off, 4574
Knocked Out, 584
Knockin' Lost John, 359
Knockin' On Heaven's Door, 1384, 1675, 2261, 2314, 3107, 4154, 4501

Knocking Nelly, 5931
Knocking The Boots, 2167
Knockout Artist, 2418
Know By Now, 4112
Know Far I, 4644
Know How, 1473, 5968
Know How Fi Chat, 4882
Know Myself, 3838, 4494
Know Tomorrow, 5542
Know When To Leave The Party, 3426
Know Yourself Blackman, 2761
Knowing Me Knowing You, 37, 2260
Knowing When To Leave, 4348
Knowledge Me, 4060
Knowledge...Put Your Brain in Gear, 3057
Knoxville Station, 281
Ko Ko Mo (I Love You So), 1033, 1195, 1291, 3641, 4144
Ko Ko Mo Indiana, 4957
Kodachrome, 447, 4918
Kodak Ghosts, 1021
KoKo, 406, 4134, 5359
Kokofe Hene Mbabut, 5516
Kokomo, 239, 426, 4223, 5784
Kokomo Blues, 4415
Kokomo, Indiana, 3808, 3865
Kollage, 4306
Kommisar, 1834
Kon Tiki, 4835
Kon-Tiki, 2968
Koochie Ryder, 2020, 2574
Kookie Little Paradise, 5617
Kookie, Kookie, Lend Me Your Comb, 871, 5705
Kookoo Macka, 4338
Kooks, 685
Kool Roc Bass, 3287
Kose Kose, 1453
Kosmos, 5760
Koteja, 3188
Kow Kow, 717
Krakpot, 2443
Kray Twins, 4503
Kreepin' Through Your Hood, 663
KRS-One Attacks, 3080, 4509
Kryll, 1696
Kuff, 5429
Kuff N Dem, 3662
Kumbaya, 4737
Kumbayah, 2303
Kundiluni Express, 3335
Kung Fu, 251
Kung Fu Ballet, 2763
Kung Fu Fighting, 1603, 5412
Kunte Kinte, 4096
Kuos, 358
Kylie Said To Jason, 3043
Kyrie, 3826

L'Amerique (La Petite), 2073
L'Amour Est Bleu, 3159, 3521
L'apres-Midi D'une Faune, 1242
L'Ecole Est Fini, 4863
L'Elite, 5515
L'Enfant Au Tambour, 3817
L'Inventoire '66, 1476
L-O-V-E, 2267, 2922
L-O-V-E-U, 715
L.A. Angels, 4171
L.A. Lujah, 2110
La Ambulancia, 4121
La Ballenta Della Tromba, 4659
La Bamba, 730, 1468, 2162, 4675, 5578, 5594
La Bilirrubina, 2306
La Bomba, 522, 5456
La Cage, 2784
La Cage Aux Folles, 3095
La Cathedrale Engloutie, 3870
La Chanson De Prevert, 2071
La Cinquantaine, 2505
La Comparsa, 3164
La Cucaracha, 68, 2600
La Cuesta De La Fama, 4646
La Culebra, 362
La Cuna Blanca, 3162
La Dee Dah, 537, 1482
La Defence, 2784
La Do-Dada, 2438
La Dolce Vita, 1109
La Dolly Vita, 4977
La Donna E Mobile, 2258
La Donna Riccia, 3729
La Duboney, 1833, 4097, 4113, 4743
La Engañada, 3881
La Esencia Del Guaguanco, 4614
La Femme Fetal, 1523
La Firenze, 5767
LA Freeway, 1101
La Golondrina, 2473, 5595
La Grange, 6007
La Gringa, 5596
La Hija De Lola, 4114
La Isla Bonita, 648, 3403
La Javanaise, 2071
La, La, 1950, 3303
La La La Hey Hey, 4082
La La La La La, 1583, 4160
La La Land, 4879
La La Lu, 1545
La La Means I Love You, 464, 1471, 5433
La Leçon De Twist, 2125
La Loteria, 2397
La Maja De Goya, 2273
La Mamma, 2073
La Mer, 3147, 5499
La Mer (Beyond The Sea), 1390
La Negra Tomasa, 885

Les Gestes, 3818

Les Hommes Qui Passent, 2921

Les Neiges Du Kilimandjaro, 1378

Les Orgues De Barbarie, 3818

Les Sucettes, 2073

Les Trois Cloches, 793, 1196, 4181

Les Vendanges De L'Amour, 2125, 3108

Lesley, 50

Less Than Senseless, 3612

Less Than Zero, 1244

Lessons In Loneliness, 5344

Lessons In Love, 142, 3207

Lest We Forget, 4478

Lester Leaps In, 5976

Lester, Bill And Me, 3482

Let 'Em In, 3548

Let A Smile Be Your Umbrella, 1824

Let A Woman Be A Woman - Let A Man Be A Man, 1671

Let Bygones Be Bygones, 658

Let George Do It, 4615

Let Go, 493, 1172, 1491, 1960, 3759

Let Go Of The Stone, 388

Let Her Go, 1172

Let Her In, 5497

Let Her Love Me, 3161

Let Him Have It, 827

Let It All Blow, 1431

Let It All Hang Out, 757, 1061, 3015, 4242

Let It Be, 262, 435, 3614, 4267, 4761, 5829

Let It Be Me, 442, 1555, 1742, 1795, 1878, 2120, 3900, 4733

Let It Be You, 5757

Let It Bleed, 4631

Let It Blurt, 367

Let It Flow, 1095, 4807

Let It Grow, 1996

Let It Happen, 950

Let It Move You, 6006

Let It Out (Let It All Hang Out), 2578

Let It Please Be You, 946, 1492, 3718

Let It Rain, Let It Pour, 282, 1587, 2035

Let It Rock, 500

Let It Roll, 127, 1101, 3154, 3950

Let It Shine, 2395

Let It Slide, 4985

Let It Snow! Let It Snow! Let It Snow!, 884, 3748

Let It Whip, 1431

Let Jah Be Praised, 2765

Let Love Abide, 5319

Let Love Come Between Us, 4368

Let Love Go, 1491

Let Love In, 4306

Let Love Shine, 4293

Let Me Awake, 606

Let Me Be, 4970, 5538

Let Me Be Good To You, 4444, 5399

Let Me Be Right, 950

Let Me Be The One, 589, 1920, 3289, 4835, 5511, 5677

Let Me Be There, 3934, 4444, 1869

Let Me Be Your Angel, 3136

Let Me Be Your Fanstasy, 4346

Let Me Be Your Fantasy, 310

Let Me Be Your Lovemaker, 5925

Let Me Be Your Lover, 5559

Let Me Be Your No. 1, 3949

Let Me Be Your Salty Dog, 3790

(Let Me Be Your) Teddy Bear, 4310

Let Me Be Your Tupperwear, 2472

Let Me Call You Sweetheart, 843, 1202, 5522

Let Me Cover You, 3593

Let Me Dance For You, 1070

Let Me Die A Young Man's Death, 3279

Let Me Down Easy, 3122, 3142

Let Me Down Gently, 1167

Let Me Drive, 1537

Let Me Entertain You, 2324

Let Me Go, 3759

Let Me Go Free, 2254

Let Me Go Girl, 5578

Let Me Go, Devil, 5748

Let Me Go, Lover, 725, 729, 958, 3027, 3677, 3847, 4102, 5748

Let Me Good To You, 4444, 5399

Let Me Have My Dream, 103, 1106

Let Me In, 398, 1963, 2447, 4074, 4820

Let Me Live, 2765

Let Me Live And Die In Dixie, 606

Let Me Look At You, 227

Let Me Love You, 938, 3676

Let Me Love You Now, 3356, 4733

Let Me Love You Once Before You Go, 1824

Let Me Love You Tonight, 4367

Let Me Move You, 2897

Let Me Off At The Corner, 5773

Let Me Off Uptown, 1722, 3998

Let Me Party With You, 4902

Let Me Ride Your Mule, 5973

Let Me Roll It, 361

Let Me Shake Your Tree, 3030

Let Me Show You, 2919

Let Me Sing And I'm Happy, 493, 2862, 2864

Let Me Start Tonite, 1611

Let Me Take You Dancing, 63

Let Me Take You There, 663

Let Me Tell Ya, 198

Let Me Tell You About Love, 2908

Let Me Tell You Boy, 3832

Let Me Tickle Your Fancy, 2743

Let Me Try Again, 2006, 4928

Let Me Turn You On, 550

Let My Days Be Long, 47

Let My Love Open The Door, 5481

Let No Man Put Asunder, 1905

Let No Man Steal Your Thyme, 4190

Let Old Mother Nature Have Her Way, 4984

Let Sleeping Dogs Lie, 4696

Let The Battle Begin, 1906

Let The Big Wheel Roll, 2303

Let The Blood Run Red, 5416

Let The Curtain Come Down, 4865

Let The Day Begin, 893

Let The Drummer Have Some, 1903

Let The Four Winds Blow, 403, 1581, 2682, 4505, 5282

Let The Good Times Roll, 105, 352, 2269, 2893, 3277, 3641, 4581, 4884

Let The Good Times Roll & Feel So Good, 4902

Let The Grass Grow, 2023

Let The Great Big World Keep Turning, 295, 540, 2284

Let The Heartache Ride, 4509

Let The Heartaches Begin, 347, 3383, 5540

Let The Horns Blow, 437

Let The Jukebox Keep On Playing, 4196

Let The Kids Dance, 1808

Let The Little Bird Fly, 1601

Let The Little Girl Dance, 585

Let The Man Who Makes The Gun, 3466

Let The Music (Lift You Up), 1693, 3215

Let The Music Move U, 4451

Let The Music Play, 4845

Let The Music Use You, 4958

Let The Mystery Be, 1478

Let The People Sing, 2102, 3152

Let The Pony Run, 5437

Let The Power Fall, 4638

Let The Power Fall On I, 3958

Let The Red Wine Flow, 4520

Let The Rest Of The World Go By, 350, 2447

Let The Rhythm Pump, 3154

Let The River Run, 4917

Let The Sunshine In, 2337, 4179

Let The Whole World Sing It With Me, 707

Let The Words Flow, 1060

Let Them Free, 203

Let There Be, 1058

Let There Be Country, 4240

Let There Be Drums, 1197, 2682, 3203, 3897

Let There Be House, 5770

Let There Be Love, 1160

Let There Be Music, 2386, 5419

Let There Be Rock, 2388, 4050

Let Us Go Down The River, 520, 1745

Let Us Go Down To The River, 1745

Let Your Backbone Slide, 1624

Let Your Body Go Downtown, 1971

Let Your Fingers Do The Walking, 2298

Let Your Hair Down, 5335

Let Your Heart Not Be Troubled, 902

Let Your Yeah Be Yeah, 4251

Let Yourself Go, 493, 1960

Let's All Get Down, 3937

Let's All Go Down The River, 3677

Let's All Go Down The Strand, 4307

Let's All Go Down To The River, 4169

Let's All Go To The Music Hall, 5928

Let's All Help The Cowboys Sing The Blues, 2813, 2970

(Let's All) Turn On, 2584

Let's All Unite, 3838

Let's Be Buddies, 3634, 4118

Let's Be Common, 3338

Let's Be Friends, 3878

Let's Be Sentimental, 1744

Let's Begin, 4570

Let's Build A World Together, 5309

Linger A Little Longer In The Twilight, 1207
Linger Awhile, 4654, 5802
Lining Your Pockets, 3803
Lion Hunts The Tiger, 1922
Lion In A Cage, 2949
Lion In Your Heart, 1241
Lion Of Judah, 4435
Lion Tamer, 3408
Lion's Den, 1230
Lionheart, 3257
Lions And Tigers And Bears, 3109
Lions In My Own Garden, 4307
Lip And Tongue, 5641
Lip Service, 5779
Lipgloss, 4363
Lips Can't Go, 121
Lips Like Red Wine, 1186
Lips Of Wine, 2765, 5836
Lipsing Jam Ring, 5276
Lipstick, 81
Lipstick On Your Collar, 2006, 3651, 4937
Lipstick Promises, 1640
Lipstick Traces, 3258, 4002
Lipstick Traces (On A Cigarette), 3693
Lipstick, Powder And Paint, 1222, 4838
Liquid, 1969, 2469, 3979
Liquid Bass, 2839
Liquid Cool, 1456
Liquid Poetry, 2693
Liquor, 2763
Lisa, 2335
Lisa Knew, 4105
Lisa Marie, 438
Lisbon Antigua, 3678, 4539
Listen, 3782, 5585
Listen Little Girl, 2961
Listen People, 3260
Listen To Me, 3648
Listen To The Bass Tone, 1341
Listen To The Beat, 1211, 3171
Listen To The Lion, 3795, 4720, 5354
Listen To The Mocking Bird, 2002, 2340
Listen To The Music, 1591, 5425
Listen To The Radio, 5926
Listen To The Rhythm Flow, 2302, 4453
Listen To What The Man Said, 3548, 5885
Listen To Your Father, 3402
Listen To Your Heart, 4849
Listen, Dear, 2036
Listen, It's Convenient, 4613
Listen, The Snow Is Falling, 2072, 4049
Listening, 3769
Litany, 727
Little Altar Boy, 1374

Little America, 4459
Little Angel, 1654
Little Arrows, 1551, 2368, 3175
Little Baby, 62, 1819, 5601
Little Baby Nothing, 3318
Little Baby Swastikkka, 4955
Little Band Of Gold, 2777
Little Bird, 2036, 2531, 3107, 5872
Little Bird, Little Bird, 3431
Little Biscuit, 2768
Little Bit O' Soul, 3850
Little Bit Of Love, 2022, 5980
Little Bitty Pretty One, 100, 105, 1426, 2414, 3119, 3598
Little Black Book, 2142
Little Black Dress, 2033
Little Black Train, 2020
Little Blue Bird, 2531
Little Blue Wren, 4592
Little Blue-Eyed Blonde Goodbye, 4373
Little Bluebird, 1888
Little Boat, 1745
Little Bottom Drawer, 4932
Little Boxes, 4518, 4812
Little Boy, 511, 727, 1251, 1374, 3018, 4672
Little Boy And Girl, 3053
Little Boy Blew His Top, 4328
Little Boy Blue, 585, 2961, 3171, 5862
Little Boy Blues, 1744
Little Boy Lost, 2563, 5681
Little Boy Sad, 838, 1625, 4181, 4221
Little Boy's Prayer, 4086
Little Boys, 490, 4470
Little Boys And Little Girls, 4682
Little Britain, 1622
Little Brown Hand, 1685
Little Brown Jug, 571, 717, 1318, 2170, 3674, 4533
Little By Little, 2726, 4268, 5763
Little Canole, 4226
Little Child, 2398, 3951
Little Children, 2682, 3074, 4897
Little Children No Cry, 915, 2670
Little Darlin, 1510
Little Darlin''s Not My Name, 1897
Little Darling, 2561
Little Darling Pal Of Mine, 960-961
Little Debbie, 1653
Little Demon, 2436
Little Devil, 4808
Little Dianne, 1468
Little Did I Dream, 69
Little Did You Know, 5325
Little Dipper, 3670
Little Does She Know, 3087

Little Donkey, 511, 1887, 3951
Little Drop Of Gin, 1012
Little Drops Of My Heart, 2099
Little Drops Of Rain, 227, 2386
Little Drops Of Silver, 3747
Little Drummer Boy, 511, 727, 1251, 4672
Little Dutch Mill, 395, 2025
Little Egypt, 3456, 4665
Little Fish In A Big Pond, 3705
Little Fluffy Clouds, 4054
Little Fox Run, 176
Little Games, 5951
Little Girl, 227, 369, 459, 1253, 1324, 1339, 2043, 2073, 2551, 3085, 4459, 4615, 4808, 5594
Little Girl (With Blue Eyes), 4363
Little Girl Baby, 5601
Little Girl Blue, 539, 2890, 2911, 4606, 4650
Little Girl Don't Cry, 2738
Little Girl Gone, 1846
Little Girl Of Mine, 1121, 1510
Little Girl, Little Girl, 779
Little Girls, 195-196
Little Green, 3272
Little Green Apples, 3679, 4976
Little Green Bag, 340
Little Green Snake, 3637
Little Green Valley, 4587
Little Hans, 4767
Little Heaven Of The Seven Seas, 2473
Little Hitler, 2818, 3349
Little Honda, 1333, 2162, 2581
Little Jazz Bird, 3107
Little Jimmy's Goodbye To Jimmie Rodgers, 4945
Little Joe, 877
Little Joe The Wrangler, 131, 2184, 4484
Little Johnny Chickadee, 1133, 1228
Little Johnny Jewel, 2676
Little Known Facts, 5963
Little Lady, 67, 189, 942, 4894, 5486
Little Latin Lupe Lu, 3022, 4543
Little Lies, 1413, 1587, 1934, 2025, 2447, 4636, 5294, 5928
Little Life, 196
Little Lonely One, 2916
Little Love Letters, 3137
Little Maggie, 3167
Little Man, 2620, 4021
Little Man With A Candy Cigar, 1482
Little Man, You've Had A

Busy Day, 132, 1482, 2348, 2549, 5736
Little Marian Parker, 2809
Little Me, 894, 1221, 3268, 5963
Little Miracles, 1291
Little Miss Belong To No One, 684
Little Miss Can't Be Wrong, 4268
Little Miss Go-As-You-Please, 1745
Little Miss Lonely, 4848
Little Miss Melody, 694
Little Miss Wooden Shoes, 3705
Little Mohee, 2948
Little Musgrave, 2881
Little Nell, 1325
Little Niles, 5778
Little Nut Tree, 3619
Little Old Country Home Town, 1046
Little Old Lady, 67, 942, 4894, 5486
Little Old Log Cabin In The Lane, 4180, 4359
Little Old New York, 638
Little Ole Wine Drinker, Me, 3484
Little One, 1769, 2522, 2916
Little Orphan Annie, 1225, 1779
Little Pal, 282, 780
Little Palaces, 3002
Little Pictures, 62
Little Pine Log Cabin, 799
Little Pink Stars, 4403
Little Princess, 3316
Little Queen Bee, 4967
Little Queenie, 501, 2174
Little Ramona (Gone Hillbilly Nuts), 701
Little Ray Of Sunshine, 293
Little Red Corvette, 4332
Little Red Monkey, 1005
Little Red Rooster, 1221, 1429, 2288, 2620, 4371, 4628
Little Rock, 1536, 4449
Little Rock Getaway, 2869
Little Rock Rag, 713
Little Rosa, 707
Little Sad Eyes, 985
Little School Girl, 2551
Little Serenade, 2899, 5458
Little Sheila, 99, 573
Little Ship With A Red Sail, 892
Little Ships Come Sailing Home, 4021
Little Shop Of Horrors, 3272
Little Side Car, 3131, 5298
Little Sir Echo, 1248, 2473, 3473, 5455
Little Sister, 1217, 4277, 4311, 4897, 5960
Little Star, 1728

Mama, Keep Your Big Mouth Shut, 2518
Mama, Mama, 3805
Mama, Teach Me To Dance, 2221, 2549, 3449
Mama, Tell 'Em What We're Fightin' For, 2353
Mama, That Moon Is Here Again, 522
Mamas Don't Let Your Cowboys Grow Up To Be Babies, 5801
Mambo, 3313
Mambo Caliente, 3428
Mambo Italiano, 1133, 3636, 4304
Mambo Jambo, 4181, 4304
Mambo Jazz, 4447
Mambo Mado, 4057
Mambo Of The Pines, 1323
Mambo Of The Times, 1323
Mambo Rock, 2341
Mambo Sha-Mambo, 1033
Mambo Show, 4114
Mamie Is Mimi, 2120
Mamma Goes Where Papa Goes, 43
Mamma Mia, 37
Mammas, Don't Let Your Babies Grow Up To Be Cowboys, 796, 2143, 2813, 3900, 5735, 5801
Mammy Blue, 1084
Mammy Oh, 2520
Mammy's Little Coal Black Rose, 5805
Mammy, I'll Sing About You, 2174
Mampie, 4837
Mamselle, 1427, 2217, 2447, 4238
Man, 241, 1133, 4838
Man A Me Yard, 4837
Man Ah Rush Me, 5429
Man And Wife, 1922
Man And Woman, 5429
Man At C&A, 1375
Man Beware, 4966
Man From Madrid, 4070
Man From Russia, 607
Man From Warieka, 3211
Man In A Cage, 4766
Man In A Hurry, 540
Man In Black, 977, 4954, 5807
Man In Me, 3520
Man In The Box, 120
Man In The Hills, 840
Man In The Meadow, 3582
Man In The Mirror, 319, 3787
Man In The Moon, 4395, 4792, 5450, 5644
Man Makes Machines, 2712
Man Me Love, 4155
Man Next Door, 4970
Man Of Constant Sorrow, 98
Man Of Gallilee, 959

Man Of My Heart, 216, 3979
Man Of Mystery, 2968
Man Of Straw, 4714
Man Of The World, 1933, 2681
Man On Fire, 5319, 5617
Man On The Flying Trapeze, 1012
Man On The Moon, 285
Man On The Silver Mountain, 2542, 4909
Man Or Mouse, 4131
Man Out Of Time, 1244
Man Overboard, 1564
Man Shortage, 1817
Man Sized Job, 3131
Man To Man Talk, 4042
Man Walks Among Us, 3969
Man Wanted, 1229
Man With Money, 1813
Man With The Agony, 5483
Man With The Golden Arm, 3798
Man With The Horn, 4533
Man With The Light Bulb Head, 2544
Man's Temptation, 1014
Man, Not A Mouse, 2227
Managua, Nicaragua, 3091, 3300
Mañana, 3176
Manchester, 349, 2474
Manchester Et Liverpool, 3108
Manchild, 651, 1047
Mandalay, 3366
Mandela Day, 4922
Mandella Story, 4458
Mandinka, 3996
Mandjou, 2954
Mandolin Twist, 849
Mandolin Wind, 1800
Mandolins In The Moonlight, 2273
Mandy, 224, 493, 896, 2985, 3104, 3443, 5792, 5997
Mandy Make Up Your Mind, 93, 1106, 3649
Maneater, 2344
Mangoes, 1429
Mangos, 1133, 4704
Manha De Carnaval, 3626
Manhattan, 2095, 3674, 3860, 4606, 4818, 5997
Manhattan Downbeat, 383
Manhattan Masquerade, 151
Manhattan Moonlight, 151
Manhattan Playboy, 1851
Manhattan Serenade, 151
Manhattan Skyline, 4752
Manhattan Spiritual, 4087
Manhattan Square Dance, 4651
Manhattan Tower, 2810
Manhunt, 922, 1817, 3670
Maniac, 4773

Manic Monday, 209, 366, 4332
Manic-Depressive Pictures presents . . ., 5581
Manifest, 2081, 2816, 5823
Mankind, 924, 5749
Mannequin, 4246, 5891
Mannin Veen, 5911
Mannish Boy, 3133, 3830
Manny Oh, 610
Mansion On The Hill, 866, 5846
Mansions, 3427
Manteca, 2048, 3940, 4133
Mantra For A State Of Mind, 4709
Manuel Goodbye, 3458
Manuela, 2677
Many A Mile, 4956
Many A New Day, 4025
Many Are Called, 3470
Many Are Called But Few Get Up, 3430
Many Clouds Of Smoke, 5474
Many Moons Ago, 4042
Many Rivers To Cross, 1125, 2296, 5364, 5562
Many Tears Ago, 2006
Many Ways, 4444
Manzanar, 1016
Map Of The City, 4673
Maple Leaf Rag, 2891, 2930
Maple On The Hill, 1444, 3417
Marble Breaks Iron Bends, 1499
Marbles, 5443
March, 982
March Eccentrique, 1499
March From The River Kwai And Colonel Bogey, 3678
March Glorious, 2899
March Of The Bowmen, 1341
March Of The Boyds, 1893
March Of The Flower Children, 4810
March Of The Grenadiers, 1703, 2284, 3338
March Of The Mods, 4805
March Of The Musketeers, 2037, 2284, 5901
March Of The Siamese Children, 350, 2997
March Of The Spacemen, 4596
March Of The Toys, 309
March Of The United Nations, 1499
March Winds And April Showers, 4302
March With Me, 1031, 3246
March, March, 2724
Marche Tout Troit, 2009
Marcheta, 1486, 4769
Marching Along Together, 1555

Marching Down Through Rochester, 1150
Marching Song, 2212
Marching Strings, 2725, 3491
Marcus Garvey, 840
Marcus Say, 2764
Mardi Gras, 2295, 3364, 4346
Mardi Gras In New Orleans, 4346
Mardi Gras Mambo, 1282, 3908-3909
Mardi Gras Waltz, 2830
Margaret, 3832, 5685
Margaret's Dream, 3832, 5685
Margaritaville, 820
Margie, 920, 1405, 1792, 2488, 2962, 5981
Margie's At The Lincoln Park Inn, 377, 2353
Margo, 1499
Margot, 1491
Marguerita, 4328
Maria, 499, 4343, 5771-5772
Maria Cervantes, 3776
Maria Cristina, 4613
Maria Elena, 3319, 4181, 4255, 4695
Maria La O, 3164
Maria Magdalena, 1763
Maria's Curse, 5788
Marian The Librarian, 3852
Marianne, 762, 2534
Marie, 493, 1599, 1998, 2203, 4880, 5600
Marie Colere Marie Douceur, 3108
Marie Laveau, 378
Marie Marie, 154, 1158
Marie's Law, 1901
(Marie's The Name) His Latest Flame, 4277
Marieke, 2756
Marigold, 3528
Marijuana In My Brain, 1528
Marijuana In My Soul, 5412
Marilyn Dreams, 304
Marilyn Monroe, 599
Marimba, 178
Marimba Jive, 4463
Mario, 5596
Marion The Librarian, 3852, 5869
Marionette, 236, 5748
Marjie, 1568
Marjorine, 1144
Mark, 4862
Mark Chapman, 5684
Mark My Word, 1742
Mark My Words, 3129
Mark Of Cain, 3965
Mark Of The Beast, 3575
Marked With Death, 2463
Market Square Heroes, 1907, 3462
Marlene, 1200

Messiah, 5294

Messin' Around, 3624

Messin' With The Kid, 2726, 5763

Metal Anarchy, 5702

Metal Guru, 5277

Metastasis, 3871

Metro, 3647

Metropolis, 2060, 3648

Mewsette, 227, 2386

Mexcal Road, 3573

Mexican Divorce, 1071

Mexican Funeral In Paris, 3387

Mexican Hat Rock, 211

Mexican Joe, 4485, 5470

Mexican Jumping Beat, 1437

Mexican Whistler, 5809

Mexico, 88, 347, 3766, 4596

Mexico Big Sky, 2282

Mi Amor, 95

Mi Debilidad, 4389

Mi Desengaño, 4618

Mi God Mi King, 665, 3018, 4120, 5565

Mi Lover Mi Lover, 5434

Mi Madre, 2397

Mi Rule, 3487

Mi Vecina, 4117

Mi Vida Loca, 5437

Miami, 1083, 3273

Miami Bass, 2685, 3538, 5550

Miami, My Amy, 5806

Michael, 2009, 2526, 3568

Michael (The Lover), 1149

Michael Caine, 3402

Michael From Mountains, 3712

Michael Murphy's Boy, 1049

(Michael) Parkinson's Theme, 2565

Michael Row The Boat, 3663

Michael Stipe, 4095

Michele's Meditation, 2861

Michelle, 1218, 1220, 1400, 4085, 5621

Michoacan, 4718

Mickey, 671, 1064, 3654, 5753, 5949

Mickey Way, 25

Mickey's Monkey, 2561, 3700-3701

Microbes, 5910

Microgravity, 4393

Microphone Fiend, 1961

Mid The Green Fields Of Virginia, 961

Middle Aged Blues Boogie, 4715

Middle Aged Whore, 81

Middle Mass, 4545

Middle Of The Road, 567, 4318

Middle Of The Road Man, 5564

Middle Road, 2098

Middleman, 5342

Midlander, 486

Midnight, 280

Midnight At The Masquerade, 3861

Midnight At The Oasis, 711, 3834

Midnight At The Onx, 1436

Midnight Blue, 829, 844, 2233, 3201, 3432, 3657, 3795, 4716

Midnight Blues, 951, 4527

Midnight Confession, 2245, 3129, 4522

Midnight Cowboy, 1877

Midnight Feast, 5724

Midnight Fire, 3170, 5703

Midnight Hauler, 333

Midnight Hour Blues, 951

Midnight In A Perfect World, 1561

Midnight In Manhattan, 1387

Midnight In Mexico, 5961

Midnight In Montgomery, 1584, 2736

Midnight In Moscow, 350

Midnight In Paris, 3409

Midnight Lady, 3814

Midnight Magic, 810

Midnight Mary, 4304

Midnight Moonlight, 1660, 1905

Midnight Moses, 2426

Midnight On The Trail, 645

Midnight Plane To Houston, 5742

Midnight Rambler, 4630

Midnight Rider, 143, 1145

Midnight Riding, 1946

Midnight Rock, 5401

Midnight Rodeo, 1797

Midnight Sleigh Ride, 4754

Midnight Special, 1958, 4559

Midnight Sun, 1327, 3170, 3630

Midnight To Moonlight, 1660, 1905, 3409

Midnight To Six Man, 4319

Midnight Train To Georgia, 3048, 5742

Midsummer New York, 2679

Might Be Stars, 5696

Might Just Take Your Life, 832

Mighty Cloud Of Joy, 3658

Mighty Joe, 4886

Mighty Long Time, 5862

Mighty Love Part 1, 1497

Mighty Mighty, 1390

Mighty Mighty Spade And Whitey, 2683

Mighty Quinn, 1347, 3438

Mighty Redeemer, 99

Mighty Ruler, 4874

Mighty Wings, 1038

Migration, 820

Mihon, 273

Mil Noches, 4516

Miles Apart, 3612

Milestones, 5694

Militant Dread, 2763

Militant Man, 2763

Militant Style, 4430

Military Life (The Jerk Song), 894

Military Man, 4281

Milk, 2084, 5846

Milk And Alcohol, 1613

Milk And Honey, 1422, 2637

Milk Cow Blues, 239, 1059, 1782, 2273, 5367, 5868

Milkcow Blues Boogie, 4309

Milkman's Son, 5563

Milkman, Keep Those Bottles Quiet, 1438, 3004, 3799, 4449

Mill Hill Self Hate Club, 349

Millennium, 2994

Miller's Blues, 3723

Miller's Cave, 377, 1122

Millie Girl, 2254

Million And More, 1944

Million Dollar Bash, 1674, 3015

Million Dollar Hero, 4400

Million Dollar Secret, 2634

Millions Like Us, 4369

Milord, 3818, 4230, 5617

Milquetoast, 2480

Milton's Boogie, 3687

Milwaukee Here I Come, 3222

Mimi, 1051, 1703, 3337, 4606, 5479

Mimi On The Beach, 4899

Mimi's Song, 1794

Minator, 4228

Mind, 1273, 3522

Mind Adventures, 1489

Mind Blowing Decisions, 2464

Mind Body And Soul, 1924

Mind Excursion, 5487

Mind Filter, 5451

Mind Gardens, 868

Mind If I Make Love To You?, 2522

Mind Of A Razor, 2315

Mind Of A Toy, 5652

Mind Over Matter, 1506, 1980

Mind Playing Tricks On Me, 2131

Mind The Gap, 4241

Mind Train, 2679

Mind Your Motion, 562

Mind Your Own Business, 447, 1083, 1476

Mind, Body And Soul, 1924

Mindboggler, 2693

Mindflux, 3867

Mindgames, 3288

Mine, 4041, 4518

Mine 'Til Monday, 5498

Mine Alone, 1555, 5931

Mine And Mine Alone, 3148

Mine Till Monday, 1886

Miner's Lifeguard, 800

Miner's Prayer, 2311

Ming's Incredible Disco Machine, 762, 3288

Mini Mini Mini, 1669

Mini Skirt Vision, 4638

Mini-Bus Driver, 4494

Miniature Suite, 1138

Minimalism, 2423

Ministry, 2573

Minka, 4704

Minnie, 4412

Minnie From Trinidad, 1705, 5998

Minnie The Moocher, 521, 623, 896, 1246, 2945, 5503

Minnie The Moocher's Wedding Day, 3054

Minnie's In The Money, 2081

Minor Threat, 3697

Minuet By Candlelight, 3528

Minuet In Boogie, 2523

Minute By Minute, 807, 938

Mira, 944

Mira Mira, 4460

Miracle, 495, 4031

Miracle Of Life, 1882, 4482

Miracle Of Miracles, 1882

Miracles, 348, 2803

Mirage, 1139, 2778, 5887

Miriam, 2583

Mirriam, 1184

Mirror And A Blade, 1342

Mirror In The Bathroom, 430, 1375, 2661

Mirror Man, 2633

Mirror Mirror, 1508, 1577, 2996, 4250, 4735

Mirror Of Yesterday, 5988

Mirror Of Your Mind, 5739

Mirrors, 4030

Mis'ry River, 2139

Misalliance, 1928

Miserable Woman, 1586

Misere, 5515

Miserlou, 1236

Misery, 4848

Misery (Someone Is Winning), 4792

Misery Loves Company, 4476, 5666

Misery's Child, 5829

Misfit, 1335-1336, 4594

Misirlou, 279, 1362

Miss Alice Martin, 1871

Miss America, 525, 2664

Miss America, You're Beautiful, 4075

Miss Annabelle Lee, 4535

Miss Azami's Lullaby, 3870

Miss Brown, 1939, 2610

Miss Brown To You, 522, 2556, 5805

Miss Chatelaine, 2693
Miss Dandys, 362
Miss DJ (Rap It Up!), 4859
Miss Goody Goody, 5342
Miss Hit And Run, 619
Miss Ida, 1698
Miss In Mink, 5961
Miss Jamaica, 511, 3060
Miss Lindy Lou, 3054
Miss Marmelstein, 2659, 3140
Miss Melanie, 540
Miss Molly Colly, 1913
Miss My Schooldays, 4801
Miss Otis Regrets, 864, 1520, 3947, 4289
Miss Pauline, 1172
Miss Playgirl, 1761
Miss Ska-Culation, 149
Miss The Girl, 1288
Miss The Mark, 2061
Miss The Mississippi And You, 805, 2106, 4604, 4728
Miss Trudy, 2220
Miss Turnstiles, 4040
Miss Universe, 3788
Miss White And Wonderful, Miss Black And Beautiful, 4445
Miss Williams' Guitar, 2792
Miss Wire Waist, 1062, 1071, 3422
Miss You, 4631, 5453, 5972
Miss You Blind, 1330
Miss You Much, 2742, 2781
Miss You Nights, 4531
Miss You So, 4017
Miss You So Badly, 1016
Missing, 1801, 5345
Missing In Action, 1685, 5519, 5839
Missing The Moon, 1883
Missing Words, 1375, 4816
Missing You, 1432, 2982, 3048, 3265, 4213, 4657, 5670
Missing You Baby, 2351
Mission, 1212, 5454
Mission Bell, 755
Mission From Hank, 5448
Mission Impossible, 4522, 4770, 5641
Mission Motherland, 2479
Mission To Moscow, 4301
Missionary Man, 1787, 4512
Missions Impossible, 4546
Mississippi, 1824, 4371
Mississippi Boweavil Blues, 4159
Mississippi Cotton Picking Delta Town, 1597, 4326
Mississippi Delta, 2120
Mississippi Delta Blues, 4604
Mississippi Dream Boat, 780
Mississippi Mud, 395, 1302, 3003
Mississippi Queen, 5775
Mississippi Steamboat, 4582

Mississippi Town, 2306
Mississippi Valley Blues, 982
Mississippi, You're On My Mind, 1711
Missouri, 5495
Mistakes, 3201, 4182, 5928
Mister And Mississippi, 1427, 4102
Mister And Missus Fitch, 2100
Mister And Mrs Mississippi, 1427
Mister Five By Five, 1438
Mister Jelly Lord, 3800
Mister Love, 1427, 5453, 5820
Mister Moonlight, 4231
Mister Porter, 3805
Mister Sandman, 1988
Mister Skol, 1174
Mister Snow, 947
Mister Tango, 3624
Mister Won't You Please Help My Pony, 5754
Mistreated, 832, 2299
Mistreatin' Heart, 4742
Mistress Of Deception, 1922
Mistrustin' Blues, 4222
Misty, 830, 943, 2091, 3513, 4324, 5639
Misty Blue, 828, 3421, 3754, 3767
Misty Islands Of The Highlands, 2967
Misty Roses, 631, 2391
Misunderstanding, 1350, 1645, 2645
Mittageisen (Metal Postcard), 4938
Mix And Mingle, 5895
Mix It Up, 4476
Mix Me Down, 5526
Mix Up, 3001, 4476
Mixed Emotions, 1655, 4631
Mixed Up Confusion, 1672
Mixed Up Shook Up, 3694
Mmm...Skyscraper, I Love You, 5575
MMMBop, 1662, 2382
Mmmm Mmmm Mmmm, 1277, 2178
Mo' Onions, 664
Moanin', 127, 158, 227, 1363, 1710, 2572, 2589, 2857, 3273, 3721, 4413, 5299, 5365, 5376, 5846
Moanin' At Midnight, 2857, 3721
Moanin' For You, 158
Moanin' Low, 2572, 3273, 4413, 5299
Moanin' The Blues, 127, 1363, 5846
Moaning For My Baby, 3721
Mobile, 842
Moby Dick, 3165-3166
Mock Turtles, 3788

Mockin' Bird Hill, 4102
Mocking Bird, 1992, 2340, 4980
Mocking Bird Hill, 2600
Mocking Bird Yodel, 5415
Mockingbird, 376, 2004, 4917, 5313
Mockingbird Hill, 3661, 4181
Mockingbird Yodel, 4772
Model Girl, 1291, 3404
Model Railway, 5840
Model With Me, 4549
Modelling Crowd, 4749
Modelling Girl, 2871
Modelling Queen, 1712
Modern Day Delilah, 571
Modern Day Romance, 753, 3959
Modern Day Slavery, 4095
Modern Don Juan, 3487, 3892
Modern Girl, 686, 1323, 1647, 1693, 1880
Modern Love, 686, 3203
Modern Pleasures, 1632
Moderne Man, 3379
Modus Vivendi, 3885
Mohair Sam, 2019, 4527, 4976
Moira Jane's Cafe, 1462
Mojo Boogie, 104
Mojo Navigator, 3732
Mojo Rocksteady, 1569
Molina, 1289
Molly Darling, 3226
Molly O'Halloran, 989
Molly O'Reilly, 3191
Molly On The Shore, 4388
Molly The Marchioness, 1253
Molly's Lips, 1891, 5616
Molten Gold, 3067
Mom-e-le, 1686
Moment Of Weakness, 1297
Moments In Love, 1642, 3006
Moments In The Moonlight, 2535
Moments In The Woods, 2704
Moments Like These, 4233
Moments Like This, 3293
Moments Of Happiness, 994
Moments To Remember, 1992
Momma's Gotta Die Tonight, 640
Momma, Momma, 2659
Momma, Where's My Daddy, 2950
Mommy For A Day, 2615-2616, 5765
Mommy, Can I Still Call Him Daddy, 5773
Mon Belle Amour, 804
Mon Coeur Balance, 1387
Mon Credo, 3512

Mon Dieu, 4229
Mona, 1517, 3589
Mona Lisa, 419, 1160, 1217, 1427, 2339, 3281, 3360, 3445, 3836, 5547, 5982
Mona Lisa's Lost Her Smile, 1149, 3368
Monday Monday, 15, 3427, 4223
Monday Morning 5:19, 4523
Mondo Cane, 1633
Money, 317, 744, 1404, 1739, 1951, 2543, 3981, 4476, 4952, 5360, 5479, 5551, 5990
Money Blues, 2614
Money Burns A Hole In My Pocket, 3281
Money Can't Buy It, 1548
Money Changes Everything, 1879
Money Don't Matter 2 Night, 4332
Money First, 370
Money For Nothing, 762, 1537, 3828
Money Friend, 311
Money Honey, 1627, 1748, 1775, 5780
Money In My Pocket, 770, 2138, 3056, 3605, 4336, 4379, 5409
Money In The Bank, 177, 4735
Money Is A Problem, 748
Money Is Everything, 1580
Money Is The Root Of All Evil, 3073
Money Isn't Everything, 127
Money Man Skank, 2343
Money Money, 874, 2636, 2931, 3974
Money Move, 3213
Money Palaver, 5567
Money Takin' Woman, 5973
Money Talks, 890, 2738, 4678
Money To Burn, 2342
Money Tree, 1496
Money Won't Change You, 775
Money Worries, 3593
Money's Too Tight To Mention, 4923
Money, Marbles And Chalk, 267
Money, Money, 874, 2636, 2931, 3974
Money, Money, Money, 3974
Mongolian Hip Hop Show, 3718
Monie In The Middle, 3341
Monk's Mood, 1090, 2118
Monkberry Moon Delight, 4418
Monkey, 850, 3653

Monkey Business, 4652
Monkey Fashion, 4675
Monkey Gone To Heaven, 1593, 4256
Monkey Man, 512, 3060, 3532, 4251
Monkey On My Back, 2367
Monkey Say, Monkey Do, 5770
Monkey Spanner, 381, 1397, 4140, 4546
Monkey Suit, 4261
Monkey Time, 4156
Monkey Wrench, 1964
Monkey's On Juice, 4465
Monotonous, 837, 3039
Monsieur Dupont, 4857
Monster, 4260, 5758
Monster Mania, 264
Monster Mash, 2570, 4168, 4234, 4954
Monster Pussy, 5616
Monster's Holiday, 4234
Montana Cafe, 5848
Montana Song, 56
Montego Bay, 157, 603, 2286, 2679
Monterey, 193, 3573
Monterey I, 991
Montgomery In The Rain, 5847, 5980
Montmartre, 5911
Mony Mony, 1284, 2673, 2778
Mood, 1735, 3447, 4125
Mood Indigo, 283, 533, 1734-1736, 1991, 2596, 4215, 4265, 4345, 5928
Moods, 5911
Moody River, 668
Moody's Mood For Love, 2805
Moog Eruption, 1441
Mooking, 4467
Moon, 3490, 3836, 5997
Moon And Sand, 5830
Moon Country, 942, 3629
Moon Dog, 4308
Moon Glow, 2197
Moon Hop, 4374
Moon In June, 5392
Moon In My Window, 1563
Moon Love, 441, 1401, 2962, 3068
Moon Mist, 3873
Moon Of Manakoora, 3293, 3928
Moon Over America, 3366
Moon Over Memphis, 360
Moon Over Miami, 3200
Moon Over Naples, 3493
Moon River, 721, 2286, 3433, 3630, 5842
Moon Song, 4021
Moon Taj, 935
Moonage Daydream, 685
Moonbeam, 1555
Moonbeams, 606, 2501, 4465

Moonburn, 205, 942, 2512
Moonchild, 1885
Moondance, 844, 1838, 3569, 3657, 5648
Moondreams, 2569, 3198, 5357
Moondust, 3764
Moonfall, 3865
Moonglow, 569, 1436, 1654, 4177
Moonglow And Theme From Picnic, 990, 3579
Mooning, 2256
Moonlight And Roses, 2289
Moonlight And Shadows, 1888
Moonlight And Skies, 4604
Moonlight Bay, 2386, 3122, 5443
Moonlight Becomes You, 1303, 3539, 3898, 4563, 5606
Moonlight Cocktail, 4561
Moonlight Cocktails, 3728
Moonlight Drive, 1594
Moonlight Gambler, 2533
Moonlight In Heaven, 151
Moonlight In Vermont, 2117, 4990, 5805
Moonlight Lover, 3168
Moonlight Madness, 1228
Moonlight Masquerade, 3147, 5528
Moonlight Mile, 4630
Moonlight Mood, 3898
Moonlight On The Alster, 4725
Moonlight On The Ganges, 355
Moonlight On The Highway, 829
Moonlight Over Paris, 5860
Moonlight Serenade, 4561
Moonlight Shadow, 4030
Moonlight Sonata, 2364, 3188
Moonlighting, 4761
Moonraker, 409
Moonrise Blues, 665
Moonshadow, 5325
Moonshake, 2059
Moonshine, 345, 5872
Moonshine Lullaby, 197
Moonstruck, 4079
Moose The Mooch, 5537
Moose Turd Pie, 4221
Mooving (sic) Version, 4200
Mope-Itty Mope, 401
Moppety Mo, 171, 1745
More, 1195, 1374, 2169, 3787, 4481, 4942, 5972
More & More Hits, 3937
More And More, 911, 2386, 2911, 2976, 2990, 4240
More Bits And Pieces, 1158, 2511
More Dogs To The Bone, 1810
More Good Old Rock 'N'

Roll, 1099
More Human Than Human, 5793
More I Cannot Wish You, 2322, 3294
More Love, 118, 1880, 2547, 2714, 4752
More Love Than Your Love, 1886
More Music, 773
More Nights, 748
More Of The Same, 356
More Pretty Girls Than One, 4980
More Questions Than Answers, 1158
More Scorcher, 3511
More Slavery, 2520
More Than A Dream, 1850
More Than A Feeling, 677
More Than A Whisper, 2291
More Than A Woman, 450, 4752, 5304
More Than Ever, 2547
More Than Ever (Come Prima), 1686, 5618
More Than Everything, 101
More Than I Can Say, 1292, 1339, 3325, 4761, 5622
More Than Just A Chance, 1560
More Than Likely, 4267
More Than One Way Home, 2950
More Than Satisfied, 4824
More Than The Sun, 552
More Than This, 288
More Than Words, 1811
More Than Words Can Say, 118
More Than Yesterday, 879
More Than You Know, 639, 1785, 2055, 2543, 3770, 4650, 5549, 5964
More Walnuts, 46
More Whisky, 99
More, More, More, 127, 940
Moreau, 5394
Moreno Soy, 3354
Morento, 3454
Moreton Bay, 5935
Morgen, 2922
Morgus The Magnificent, 1970
Moriat, 5426
Moritat, 279
Mornin' Ride, 2279
Morning, 777, 1593
Morning After, 3888
Morning Child, 1223
Morning Comes Too Early, 777
Morning Desire, 4622
Morning Dew, 1769, 2299, 4653
Morning Girl, 984, 3902
Morning Glory, 812, 1623, 2205, 2644, 2779, 4008

Morning Has Broken, 478
Morning Morning, 2046, 3086
Morning Rain, 2059
Morning Side Of The Mountain, 2345, 4073-4074
Morning Train, 1693
Morningtown Ride, 4518, 4813
Morphic Resonance, 1242
Morphine Tango, 3036
Morris Dance, 2126
Morris Minor, 3790
Morse Avenue, 3971
Mortamer, 4747
Moschino, 2166
Moscow Idaho, 982
Moses, 1717
Moses Brown, 1632
Moses Supposes, 1705, 2959, 4933
Mosese, 1840
Moskow Diskow, 5330
Mosquito, 2766
Mosquito One, 111
Mosquitoes, 4780
Most Emphatically, Yes!, 5528
Most Exclusive Residence For Sale, 1819
Most Gentlemen Don't Like Love, 266, 2522, 3160, 4289
Most Likely You Go Your Way, 2387
Most Of All, 1236, 3764, 4523
Most Of The Time, 1677, 4019
Motel Blues, 5669
Motel Time Again, 4169
Moten Swing, 1659
Mother, 723, 1386, 3191, 3386, 4262, 4983
Mother Africa, 3781
Mother And Child Reunion, 892, 1125, 2286, 4652, 4918
Mother Country Music, 2032
Mother Earth, 3624
Mother In Law, 1029
Mother Knows Best, 4686
Mother Left Me Her Bible, 2377
Mother Machree, 350
Mother Matty, 4966
Mother May I, 180
Mother Maybelle, 3985
Mother Moon, 246
Mother Mother, 658
Mother Nature And Father Time, 842
Mother Of Mine, 4495
Mother Of Mine, I Still Have You, 2796
Mother Of Pearl, 4670
Mother Of Shame, 2566
Mother Of The Dead Man, 590
Mother Popcorn, 775

Mrs Edgar Linton, 2463
Mrs Rita, 3916
Mrs Simpson, 269
Mrs Winder, 1759
Mrs. A., 4549
Mrs. Krauses's Blue-Eyed
Baby Boy, 1951
Mrs. Lennon, 2679
Mrs. Robinson, 664, 2229,
2727, 2988, 3190, 4916
Ms Grace, 4639, 5554
Mt. Healthy Blues, 3390
MTV Makes Me Want To
Smoke Crack, 444
Much More, 1845
Much Smarter, 3609
Much Too Young (To Feel
This Damn Old), 3167
Muchacha, 3670
Mucho Corazón, 3779
Muck It Out, 1850
Mucking About In The
Garden, 4748
Muddy Water, 528, 4535,
4816
Muff Diving Size Queen,
3701
Muhômatsu No Isshô, 3840
Mulder And Scully, 988
Mule, 704, 2562
Mule Skinner Blues, 3760
Mule Train, 1973, 2675,
2774, 2908, 3111, 3396,
3671, 3677, 4424
Mule Train Parts One And
Two, 3670
Mulema Mwam, Elimba
Dikalo, 3324
Muleskinner Blues, 1621,
1875, 4728
Mull Of Kintyre, 3111,
3548, 5885
Multiplication, 1390
Mum And Dad, 3465
Mumbles, 2600, 5343
Mummy You're A Wreck,
5639
Mums And Dads, 595
Munching The Candy, 48
Munich City, 520
Murder By Guitar, 1293
Murder Dem, 3956
Murder In My Heart For
The Judge, 3723
Murder Man, 4078
Murder Mystery, 1498
Murder Of Liddle Towers,
190
Murder Of The Planet
Earth, 2722
Murder She Wrote, 1008,
4972
Murder We Wrote, 1007
Murder Weapon, 3697,
3956
Murder, He Says, 4889
Murder, Murder, 2807
Murderah Man, 3398
Murderer, 369, 4117

Murders, 5463
Muriel, 1568, 1740, 2774,
3671
Muriella, 3491
Murphy And The Bricks,
3843
Murphy's Law, 1045, 2638
Mursheen Durkin, 3567
Muscle Bustle, 3849
Muscle Shoals Blues, 5400,
5688
Musclehead, 2637, 3017,
3944
Muscles, 3622, 4657
Musetta's Song, 1794
Mushroom Festival In Hell,
5754
Mushroom Hill, 5649
Music, 591, 647, 1483, 2202,
2732, 2805, 3350, 3665,
4037
Music (Takes Control), 301
Music And Lights, 2679
Music And Politics, 1546,
2656
Music And The Mirror,
2363
Music Box Dancer, 3684
Music Field, 3171, 4884
Music For Electric Violin
And Low Budget Orchestra,
3892
Music For Gong Gong, 4072
Music For Money, 2818
Music For The World, 2665
Music Fraternity, 4458
Music Goes Round And
Round, 2108
Music Got Soul, 3217
Music Hath Charms, 3003
Music In My Heart, 151,
1885
Music In My Pony's Feet,
5839
Music In The Moonlight,
2287, 5964
Music Is Better Than
Words, 2252, 2724
Music Is Life, 5749
Music Is Love, 1305
Music Is Shit, 3913
Music Is So Wonderful,
4969
Music Is The Answer, 2606
Music Is The Key, 2606,
2644
Music Like Dirt, 53, 1466
Music Madness, 3452
Music Makers, 4449
Music Makes Me, 1951,
5964
Music Man, 1596
Music Market, 189
Music Melody, 5577
Music Music Music, 728,
4820
Music Must Change, 3761
Music On The Wind, 1853
Music Smooth As Glass, 2168

Music Stop, 4410
Music Takes Me Up, 4090
Music Takes You, 3820
Music To Watch Girls By,
1292, 2526
Music! Music! Music!, 997,
4182
Music, Harmony And
Rhythm, 752
Music, Maestro Please,
1428, 1927, 3091, 3409,
5931
Music, Part 1, 1350
Musica De Amor, 29
Musical Alphabet, 111
Musical Chariot, 4791
Musical Freedom (Moving
On Up), 75
Musical Message, 5990
Musical Pleasure, 3832
Musical Terrorist, 3002
Musical Workshop, 754
Musically Red, 3832
Musik, 1560
Muskrat, 5495
Muskrat Love, 926
Muskrat Ramble, 2930,
3579, 4066
Muss I Den, 2135
Must Be Love Coming
Down, 3119
Must Be Madison, 3320
Must Be Santa, 4488
Must Be The Magic, 2657
Must Get Paid, 745
Must You Throw Dirt In
My Face?, 3328
Mustang Sally, 1834, 4234
Mustang Wine, 1687
Mustapha, 5601
Mutant Jazz, 5276
Mutant Rock, 3644
Mutate Me, 2703
Mutations, 4056
Muthaphukkin' Gs, 1612
Mutual Attraction, 1015
Muzik Express, 5939
My Sharona, 1064, 1494,
3045, 5948
My Adidas, 4687
My Adobe Hacienda, 1532,
2615, 3504
My Adorable One, 4917
My Adventure, 2185
My Aim Is To Please You,
1806
My Alabama Home, 286
My Angel, 189, 1657, 2480,
4592, 5618, 5655, 5802
My Angel (Angela Mia),
3315
My Angel Baby, 5454
My Anthem, 4462
My Arabian Baby, 5470
My Attorney Bernie, 1448
My Autumn Love, 1377
My Babe, 809, 1039, 3274,
4254, 5354, 5983
My Baby, 227, 282, 466, 545,

689, 1055, 2289, 2890, 3608,
3688, 4547, 5334, 5454,
5470
My Baby Dearest Darling,
1032
My Baby Don't Dance To
Nothing But Ernest Tubb,
778
(My Baby Don't Love Me)
No More, 1465
My Baby Just Cares For Me,
920, 1587, 2922-2923, 4920,
5338, 5753, 5814
My Baby Left Me, 502, 621,
1317, 3124, 4171
My Baby Looks But He
Doesn't Touch, 1211
My Baby Loves Me The
Way That I Am, 3542
My Baby Loves Western
Guys, 725
My Baby Specialises, 1114
My Baby Sucks, 3465
My Baby Thinks He's A
Train, 980
My Baby Walked Out, 5973
My Baby Walks All Over
Me, 3719, 4796
My Baby's Arms, 5432
My Baby's Been Watching
TV, 4847
My Baby's Coming Back,
4462
My Baby's Gone, 3328,
4758, 4852, 4758, 4852,
5686
My Baby's Gone Away, 2097
My Baby's Gone, On, On,
2837
My Baby's Good, 5853
My Baby's Love, 982
My Back Pages, 199, 868,
1673
My Beautiful Lady, 4249
My Best Friend, 1055, 5290
My Best Friend's Girl, 957,
3400, 5358
My Best Friend's Man, 225,
1309
My Best Girl, 957, 3352,
3400, 3428, 5358
(My Best Pal's In Nashville)
Never Mind, 2291
My Big Best Shoes, 5601
My Big Mistake, 5834
My Big Moment, 589
My Bill, 1125
My Bird of Paradise, 843,
2037
My Black Girl, 3213
My Blackbirds Are
Bluebirds Now, 881, 2035
My Blanket And Me, 5963
My Blue Heaven, 132, 282,
1581, 1587, 3337, 5802,
5893
My Blue Ridge Mountain
Home, 4587
My Body, 1166, 3239

3993, 5782

My Home's Across The Blue Ridge Mountains, 239, 254, 945

My Home's In Alabama, 103

My Hometown With The Red Sunset, 3661

My Honey Said Yes Yes, 2035

My Honey's Lovin' Arms, 3649

My House, 4207, 5342

My Husband Makes Movies, 3952

My Husband The Pig, 3270

My Ideal, 4580, 5805

My Immediate Pleasure, 1813

My Jamaican Girl, 1817

My Joe, 941, 2810

My Juanita, 1297

My Kid's Singing Swing Songs, 1436

My Kind Of Carryin' On, 3773

My Kind Of Girl, 732, 3712, 3743

My Kind Of Man, 51, 2284

My Kind Of Town, 885, 5607

My Kinda Love, 151

My Lady, 602, 1376, 1503, 1885, 4249, 5499, 5837

My Last Band, 4233

My Last Dance With You, 3528

My Last Date, 1419

My Last Dollar, 3551

My Last Goodbye, 2615

My Last Love, 4139-4140

My Last Night With You, 242

My Life, 679, 2830, 4085

My Life Belongs To You, 3979

My Life In The Bush, 2507

My Life Is Love, 3415

My Life's A Jigsaw, 4369

My Little Baby's Shoes, 1293

My Little Book Of Poetry, 3850

My Little Corner Of The World, 2533

My Little Georgia Rose, 2592, 3745

My Little Girl, 1292, 3225, 3886

My Little Grass Shack, 4469

My Little Gray Haired Mother In The West, 971

My Little Home In Tennessee, 961

My Little Javanese, 2277

My Little Lady, 602, 5499

My Little Red Book, 3334

My Little Town, 447, 4916, 4918, 4916, 4918

My Little World Is All Blue, 660

My Lord And Master, 2997

My Love, 151, 483, 615, 913, 982, 1102, 1309, 1377, 1390, 1647, 1794, 2037, 2402, 2512, 2533, 2677, 2898, 3548, 3849, 4139-4140, 4337, 4545, 4652, 4784, 5422, 5578, 5669-5670, 5719, 5803, 5885

My Love And Devotion, 5972

My Love And Little Me, 684

My Love For You, 1428, 3513

My Love Forgive Me (Amore, Scusami), 2225

My Love Is A Flower (Just Beginning To Bloom), 4536

My Love Is Alive, 2660

My Love Is Coming Down, 967

My Love Is For Real, 40

My Love Is Getting Stronger, 3967

My Love Is On Fire, 4400

My Love Is On the Way, 2187

My Love Loves Me, 3281

My Love Parade, 1703, 2284, 3338

My Love Will Never Die, 618, 1017, 1141

My Love, My Love, 2775

My Lovely Elizabeth, 4625

My Lucky Star, 780, 1439, 1961, 4043

My Mama Never Heard Me Sing, 1272

My Mammy, 517, 1587, 2383, 2796, 2862, 2864, 3225, 4934, 5802, 5972

My Man, 43, 527, 731, 881, 937, 2055, 2260, 2271, 2355, 3385, 3423, 3911, 4536, 4648, 5309, 5710, 5997

My Man - He's A Loving Man, 3142

My Man A Sweet Man, 2748

My Man I A Lover, 4017

My Man O'War, 937

My Man's Gone Now, 4286

My Margarita, 2473

My Maria, 753

My Marionette, 2277

My Mary, 843, 2358

My Melancholy Baby, 282, 545, 689

My Melanie Makes Me Smile, 846

My Mellow Man, 2271

My Melody Of Love, 5648

My Memories Of You, 2402

My Mind, 3838, 5647

My Mind Has A Heart Of Its Own, 666, 2006

My Mind Is Going, 679

My Mind's Eye, 3471, 4973

My Mind's Gone To Memphis, 2098

My Mistake, 4903, 5834

My Momma Said, 3885

My Moonlight Madonna, 5750

My Most Requested Song, 4171

My Mother (Yes I Love Her), 2800

My Mother Was A Friend Of The Enemy Of The People, 633

My Mother Would Love You, 4118

My Mother's Eyes, 325, 4493

My Mother-In-Law, 5686

My Motter, 217

My Mummy's Dead, 4262

My Music, 3297, 4398

My Music - My Songs, 4398

My My Darling, 1019, 3294, 3396, 5788, 5892

My My My, 2147

My My, Hey Hey (Out Of The Blue), 5978

My Name Is Jack, 3438, 4918, 5962

My Name Is Mud, 4001, 4331

My Name Is Prince, 4332

My Name's Candide, 1884

My Next Ex-Wife, 3263

My Oh My, 213, 4713, 4959, 4713, 4959

My Old Faded Rose, 4796

My Old Flame, 3176

My Old Friend The Blues, 1687, 2033, 4103

My Old Hampshire Home, 5660

My Old Kentucky Home, 1986

My Old Man, 2355, 3385, 3423, 3911

My Old Man's A Dustman, 1588

My Old Man's A Fatso, 192

My Old Man's A Fireman On The Elder-Dempster Line, 1588

My Old Pal, 4603

My Old Pal Of Yesterday, 286

My Old School, 1252

My One Ambition Is You, 5433

My One And Only, 2055

My One And Only Highland Fling, 383, 2130, 5711

My One And Only Love, 4928

My One Great Love, 1766

My Only Chance, 4652

My Only Defence, 922

My Only Love, 4652

My Own, 69, 218, 1424, 2615, 3580

My Own Best Friend, 1055

My Own Brass Bed, 5581

My Own Home, 1545

My Own Kind Of Hat, 2334

My Own Native Land, 4568

My Own Peculiar Way, 1576

My Own Planet, 1924

My Own True Love, 1094, 1401, 1657, 2175

My Own Way, 1576

My Paradise, 2385

My Perfect Cousin, 5575

My Picture In The Papers, 2187

My Pink Half Of The Drainpipe, 662

My Pledge Of Love, 177, 2805, 5695

My Poor Brain, 1964

My Prayer, 69, 1873, 2189, 2485, 2694, 2967, 3747, 4263, 4445, 5522, 5676

My Prerogative, 523, 767, 4733

My Pretty Baby, 3608

My Problem Is You, 2664

My Queen, 1654, 3338

My Rainbow, 989

My Real Gone Rocket, 726

My Resistance Is Low, 69, 338, 942, 5523

My Reverie, 1131, 3131, 5669

My Rival, 5654

My River, 4719, 5802

My Rockin' Days, 1292

My Romance, 483, 539, 1789, 2876, 2911, 4606, 4650, 5521

My Rose Of Old Kentucky, 3745

My Rules, 2205

My Second Home, 3149

My September Love, 1794, 5803

My Sharona, 1064, 1494, 3045, 5948

My Shawl, 68

My Shining Hour, 227, 1622, 2253, 3630

My Ship, 2130, 3105, 3146, 5755

My Ship Is Coming In, 2017, 5677

My Shoes Keep Walking Back To You, 4324

My Silent Love, 2512

My Silent Mood, 68

My Simple Heart, 1647, 5422

My Sin, 43, 780, 1439, 3218

My Singing Bird, 989, 2634

My Sister And I, 3073, 5669

My Sister Rose, 2685

My Smile Is Just A Frown, 1279

My Son, 2616

My Son John, 5803

My Son, My Son, 1686, 3372

My Song, 52, 66, 69, 164, 606, 780, 941, 965, 1662, 2489, 2597, 3289, 3634, 5797
My Song Goes Round The World, 2967
My Song Of The Nile, 3649
My Soul's Got A Hole In It, 5301
My Souvenir Things, 1968
My Spanish Rose From Mexico, 5767
My Special Angel, 1657, 2480, 5618, 5655
My Special Friend, 5708
My Special Prayer, 5676
My Spine Is the Bassline, 4896
My Springtime Thou Art, 606
My Story, 2825, 3988, 5864
My Summer Love, 2533
My Summer's Gone, 1990
My Sunbeam From The South, 716
My Sweet Darling, 3745
My Sweet Dream, 3988
My Sweet Hunk O' Trash, 2557
My Sweet Lady, 1503
My Sweet Lord, 125, 1057, 1200, 2415
My Sweetest Song Of All, 606
My Sweetheart, 4183
My Sweetheart 'Tis Of Thee, 2512
My Sweetheart's The Man In The Moon, 5416
My Sweetie, 5395
My Talking Day, 5601
My Thang, 775
My Thanks To You, 2103
My Thing Is Your Thing, 4157
My Three Sons, 3766
My Time, 3213
My Time After Awhile, 2108, 2461
My Time Ain't Long, 4604
My Time Of Day, 2322, 3294
My Toot Toot, 3049, 3132, 3607
My Town, 447, 1210, 2197, 3993, 4289, 4916, 4918, 5782, 5802
My True Heart, 596
My True Love, 1094, 1401, 1657, 2175, 4784
My True Story, 2825
My Truly, Truly Fair, 1372, 3636, 3711
My Tune, 1223
My Two Timin' Woman, 2568
My Unfinished Symphony, 5803
My Valuable Hunting

Knife, 2308
My Very Good Friend The Milkman, 829, 5689
My Waltz For You, 5468
My Way, 195, 326, 1228, 1444, 2009, 2032, 2147, 2258, 3263, 4830, 4900, 4928, 5309, 5642
My Way Or The Highway, 3239
My Weakness, 925
My Weakness (Is None Of Your Business), 1751
My White Bicycle, 2618, 3886, 5459
My White Knight, 3852, 5869
My Whole World Ended, 4683
My Whole World Is Falling Down, 173, 1569
My Wife, 1767, 2660
My Wife And My Dead Wife, 2544
My Wife Thinks You're Dead, 778
My Wife, My Dog, My Cat, 3501
My Wild Irish Rose, 1079, 3033
My Wild Love, 5670
My Wild Mountain Rose, 1383
My Winter Coat, 4589
My Wishing Doll, 1401
My Woman, 2197
My Woman My Woman My Wife, 4568
My Woman's Love, 4545, 5578
My Woman, My Woman, My Wife, 4568
My Wonderful Dream, 4769
My Wonderful One, 1705
(My) Wonderful One, 2295
My World, 450, 1333, 4650
My World Fell Down, 2730, 3921, 4717
My World Is Empty Without You, 2654
My Yiddishe Momma, 658, 4866
My Yorkshire Lassie, 4079
My Zelda, 4874
My, How The Time Goes By, 69
Mylecharane, 5911
Myrah, 3179
Myself When I Am Real, 3691
Mysteries, 3094
Mysteries Of Love, 3094
Mysterious Girl, 183
Mysterious Lady, 4207
Mysterious Ways, 53, 3505
Mystery Dance, 3857
Mystery Girl, 1212
Mystery Of Love, 1558, 3824
Mystery Train, 1748, 4131,

4310, 5547
Mystery Voice, 1651, 5540
Mystery Wind, 4686
Mystic Eyes, 5383
Mystic Mood, 5990
Mystic Stepper, 3820
Myth Of The Rainy Night, 3512
N'Ecoute Pas Les Idoles, 2073
N'Sel Fik, 1822
N-N-Nervous, 5791
N-R-G, 68
N17, 4758
Na Buy Apartheid, 3051
Na Fry No Fat, 3487
Na Lef Jamaica, 5676
Na Na Hey Hey Kiss Him Goodbye, 357, 3990
Na Na Na It'll Be Alright, 3303
Naci Moreno, 3354, 5595
Nadia's Theme, 399, 1939
Nadine, 501, 1238
Nag Nag Nag, 702, 875
Nagasaki, 1555, 5710
Nagasaki No On'na, 2939
Nah Fight Over Woman, 4549
Nah Get Nutten, 4462
Nah Get Rich And Switch, 4494
Nah Go A Funeral, 4333
Nah Watch Nah Clock, 4923
Nah Wear Nuh Versace, 371
Naija Must Sweet Again, 3108
Nail It To The Wall, 3136
Naima, 1184, 2084
Naive, 2994
Najwieksza Milosc, Najciezszy Grzech, 4610
Naked, 3325, 4481
Naked And Crying, 935
(Naked) But Still Stripping, 1351
Naked In The Rain, 615, 3884
Naked Under Leather, 1042
Name And Number, 1336
Name Brand, 1583, 3425, 4466, 5693
Name Dropping, 1953
Name Of The Game, 551
Namely You, 1047, 1438, 3230, 3630
Names, 1300, 1897, 3393
Nana, 4251, 4966
Nana's Medley, 3593
Nanci, 5453
Nancy (Let Your Hair Down For Me), 4308
Nancy (With The Laughing Face), 5607
Nancy Boy, 4259
Nancy Jane, 782
Nanita, 586
Nanny Goat, 526, 1569,

3478, 4489
Nanny Skank, 1817
Nanny Version, 526
Nantucket Sleighride, 4378
Napoleon, 2386, 2432, 2768, 3677, 5900
Napoli, 940
Narayan, 5362
Narcissus, 2282
Nargin, 2860
Narra Mine, 2912
Narragansett Bay, 1234
Narrator, 2536
Nashville Cats, 2929
Nashville West, 3879
Nastee, 673, 3089
Nasty Girl, 5613
Nasty Rhythm, 762
Natchez Burning, 1530
Nation Of Girls, 2166
National Avenue, 4463
National Working Women's Holiday, 2978
Nationale Seven, 3626
Native New Yorker, 4015
Natty Bal' Head, 2764
Natty Chase The Barber, 2765
Natty Don't Make War, 4431
Natty Dread, 3236
Natty Dread A Weh She Want, 6005
Natty Dread Don't Cry, 6005
Natty Dread In A Greenwich Farm, 904
Natty Dread Is Not The Prodigal Son, 4939
Natty Dread On The Mountain Top, 6005
Natty Dread She Want, 6005
Natty Dread Time, 1742
Natty Dread Upon A Mountain Top, 790
Natty Kung Fu, 1528
Natty Loving, 4096
Natty Step It Inna Greenwich Farm, 790
Natty The Collie Smoker, 4431
Natural Born Bugie, 2633
Natural Born Killers, 5276
Natural Collie, 3575
Natural Day, 50
Natural Fact, 904
Natural High, 602, 1761, 1962, 2664, 5634
Natural Man, 5610
Natural One, 4802
Natural Reaction, 559
Natural Sinner, 1827-1828
Natural Thing, 2698
Natural Woman, 3107
Naturally, 1462, 2861
Nature Boy, 484, 775, 1004, 1159
Nature Boy (Uptown), 193

No War Into This Dance, 4139
No Way, 1220, 4047
No Way No Better Than Yard, 79
No Way Out, 1068, 5565
No Way Out Of This Town, 3509
No Way, No How, 561
No Woman No Cry, 172, 452, 2046, 2351, 3105, 3279, 3468, 3883, 3902, 5375
No Wonder, 5956
No Words, 492
No Words For Dory, 4321
No You Don't, 715
No, No Nora, 920
No, No, A Thousand Times No!, 4874
No, No, Nanette, 2385
No, No, No, 1019, 3586, 3944, 5934
No, No, No (World A Respect), 681, 4187
No, Not Much, 1993
No-One Driving, 2004
No-One Else Will Do, 4528
Nobody, 308, 1705, 5837
Nobody Answered Me, 799
Nobody But Me, 1532, 2632, 2775, 4893-4894
Nobody But My Baby, 4233
Nobody But You, 1099, 4233, 4527
Nobody Cares, 5716
Nobody Cares If I'm Blue, 103
Nobody Does It Better, 2364, 4716, 4917, 4716, 4917
Nobody Does It Like Me, 409, 1165, 1886
Nobody Else But Me, 1532, 4893-4894, 4893-4894
Nobody Has A Better Dream Than Me, 4848
Nobody Home, 5380
Nobody I Know, 4206
Nobody In His Right Mind Would've Left Her, 1529
Nobody Knows, 4529, 4852
Nobody Knows If, 4262
Nobody Knows Kelli, 5965
Nobody Knows What A Red Headed Mama Can Do, 1639, 1824
Nobody Loves A (Fat) Fairy When She's Forty, 4005
Nobody Loves Me, 2049
Nobody Loves Me Like You, 1926
Nobody Loves Me Like You Do, 3845
Nobody Loves You When You're Down And Out, 625
Nobody Makes A Pass At Me, 4251
Nobody Move, 4281
Nobody Needs Your Love,

3931, 4255
Nobody Said It Was Easy (Lookin' For The Lights), 3154
Nobody Thought Of It, 932
Nobody Told Me, 3964
Nobody Wants To Cha Cha With Me, 2741
Nobody Wants To Shine, 3828
Nobody Wins, 1986, 3170, 4534
Nobody's Changing Places With Me, 1994
Nobody's Chasing Me, 2278, 4289
Nobody's Child, 5787, 5848, 5974
Nobody's Darling But Mine, 1410, 2675, 4555, 4796
Nobody's Diary, 5952
Nobody's Fool, 1084, 3297
Nobody's Heart, 861, 4607
Nobody's Perfect, 2660, 3747
Nobody's Scared, 2178
Nobody's Sweetheart, 4772
Nobody's Sweetheart Now, 2923
Nobody's Using It Now, 2284, 3338
Nocturne, 495, 4806, 5279
Nodding Roses, 5638
Noises From The Darkness, 2693
Nola, 236, 3315, 4166, 4587, 5753
Non Aligned Movement, 4456
Non Ho L'Eta Per Amarti, 1088
Non Lateral Hypothesis, 1562
Non Stop, 370
Non, Je Ne Regrette Rien, 4230
Non-stop Dancing Craze, 441
None But The Lonely Heart, 4046
None Of My Business, 935
None Shall Escape The Judgement, 1107, 3171, 5995
Nonny, Nonny, No, 1744, 2822
Nora Creina, 3842
Nora Malone, 5659
Norma, 1012
Norma Jean Riley, 1508
Norma Jean Wants To Be A Movie Star, 3747
Norman, 1455, 3068, 3325, 5414
Norman Bates, 3121
Normandy, 4042
North Country Boy, 5330
North To Alaska, 126
North Wind, 2823, 3333, 5763

Northeast Arkansas Mississippi County Bootlegger, 796, 4323
Northern Industrial Town, 5835
Northern Lights, 1021, 4501
Northern Sky, 807, 1830
Northern Soul, 386, 2143, 4840
Northwest Passage, 914, 2505, 4625
Norwegian Wood, 433, 1089, 1237, 2415, 4677, 4845
Nose Out Of Joint, 1050
Nosey Joe, 2738
Nostalgia, 1272, 4185, 5949
Nostradamus, 1300
Not A Day Goes By, 3638
Not A Little Girl Any More, 1962
Not A Soul Around, 3084
Not Anymore, 458, 4414
Not Anyone, 553
Not Counting You, 755
Not Cricket To Picket, 4251
Not Dead Yet, 1263
Not Enough Hours In The Night, 87
Not Enough Magic, 4549
Not Every Day Of The Week, 1942
Not Fade Away, 526, 2532, 2568, 4628, 4691, 5352
Not For All The Rice In China, 249, 493, 617
Not Forgotten, 784, 3179, 4081, 4938
Not Human, 1526, 5542
Not In Front Of Baby, 1012
Not In Love (Hit By A Truck), 5569
Not John, 4248, 5363, 5670
Not Just A Flower In Your Hair, 88
Not Just Another Girl, 3909
(Not Just) Knee Deep, 2052
Not Me, 1784, 3731, 3942
Not Mine, 1933
Not My Kind Of People, 3218
Not Now But Later, 2036
Not Now John, 4248, 5363
Not On The Bottom, 692
Not On The Outside, 3734
Not On Your Love, 957
Not One Minute More, 4482
Not Over Yet, 808, 4194
Not Ready For My Loving, 4466
Not Since Ninevah, 3033
Not So Manic Now, 1640
Not That Sort Of Person, 4079
Not The Little Girl She Knew, 1253
Not Time, 5802
Not Too Little, Not Too

Much, 5918
Not Too Much To Ask, 1191
Not Too Young To Get Married, 636
Not With Me, 3731
Not Yet, 808, 1263, 2975, 4021, 4194, 5901
Nothin' But The Blues, 151
Nothin' But You, 3177
Nothin' To Do, 2563
Nothing, 1070, 1689, 1948, 2018, 2363, 4734
Nothing Better To Do, 2207
Nothing But A Child, 1687
Nothing But A Heartache, 1940, 2323
Nothing But Hard Rocks, 4762
Nothing But Love, 2318, 4052
Nothing But Sea And Sky, 2023
Nothing But The Radio On, 3071
Nothing But The Truth, 4344
Nothing Can Divide Us Now, 1591
Nothing Can Last Forever, 51
Nothing Can Stop Me, 1014
Nothing Can Stop Me Now, 733, 4565
Nothing Can Stop My Loving You, 4963
Nothing Can Stop Us, 4721
Nothing Compares 2 U, 3997, 4332
Nothing Else Matters, 3644
Nothing Ever Happens, 1467
Nothing Ever Happens To Me, 1744
Nothing Ever Hurts Me, 702
Nothing Ever Was, Anyway, 4173
Nothing From Nothing, 4316
Nothing Good, 940
Nothing I Can Do It About It Now, 3946
Nothing In Common, 2590
Nothing In The World Can Hurt Me (Except You), 52
Nothing Is For Nothing, 1810
Nothing Is Forever, 4372
Nothing Lasts Forever, 4260
Nothing Like The City, 4408
Nothing Like You've Ever Known, 565
Nothing Means Nothing, 2681
Nothing More, 1484, 1986
Nothing Personal, 1662
Nothing Really Matters, 3648
Nothing Rhymed, 4005

4179, 4762, 5305
Part Time Punks, 5329
Part Two, 3981
Parthenogenesis, 916
Parting (Is Such Sweet
Sorrow), 2349
Parting Shot, 2292
Partly Bill, 3255
Partners, 1526
Party, 655, 2450, 2774, 2981,
3313
Party - Part 1, 3387
Party All Night, 2004
Party Doll, 683, 3052, 3148,
4215
Party Down, 3263
Party Fears Two, 260
Party Hearty, 1004, 4720
Party Lights, 1098, 4256
Party Man, 1649
Party Mix, 242
Party Night, 2004, 3698,
5526
Party Now, 5615
Party Of A Lifetime, 1030
Party Pack, 2701
Party Pops, 1216
Party Time, 3659, 4082
Party Train, 2083
Party Vibe, 4450
Pasadena, 5331, 5973
Paseo And Corrida, 3509
Pass It On, 3551, 5668
Pass It On Down, 103
Pass Me By, 1165, 2349,
3187, 4613
Pass That Peace Pipe, 1705,
2202, 3488
Pass The Beer And Pretzels,
2284
Pass The Booze, 5519
Pass The Dutchie, 3090,
3659, 3853, 5325
Pass The Kouchie, 3659,
3853
Pass The Toilet Paper, 4082
Pass The Tushenpeng, 3144
Passage To Windward, 1653
Passe, 3649
Passepied, 5458
Passin' Thru, 1251
Passing By, 4219
Passing Me By, 4219
Passing Of Salome, 2904
Passing Strangers, 1700,
5570
Passion, 1752, 1854, 1952,
2866, 5443
Passionate Friend, 5324
Passionate Kisses, 947, 5855
Past Meets Present, 5753
Past My Prime, 3230
Past Present And Future,
4843
Past The Point Of Rescue,
2378, 2979
Pastel Blue, 4853
Pastime Paradise, 1224,
3094

Pastoral Symphony, 1544
Pastures Of Plenty, 681,
2319
Pat Ha Fe Cook, 1248
Pata Pata, 1511
Pata Pata Rock Steady, 4437
Patanio, The Pride Of The
Plains, 529
Patch It Up, 4396
Patches, 967, 1007, 1122,
2286, 3005, 3172
Patchwork, 5443
Path Through A Forest,
1820
Patha Patha, 3420
Pathetique, 3936
Pathway To The Moon,
3720
Patience, 2314
Patience of Angels, 2511,
4453
Patiently Smiling, 3185
Patio, 2220
Patio Set, 1750
Pato And Roger A Go Talk,
370
Patricia, 1195, 3340, 4181,
4304
Patsy, 4455
Patterns, 4973
Paul McCartney, 3137
Paula (An Improvised Love
Song), 2205
Paula C, 4421
Pause, 4687
Pavan For My Lady, 244
Pavane, 2224
Pavanne, 5411
Pavlova, 2945
Pay For Me, 5781
Pay To Cum, 319, 2659,
4365
Pay To The Piper, 1007
Payaso, 3162
Payback's A Mother, 3006
Paying For That Back Street
Affair, 4240, 5764
Pea Vine Special, 2586
Peace, 762, 1452, 2165,
2733, 5783
Peace And Harmony, 762
Peace And Love, 590, 767,
1261, 2535, 4572
Peace Conference In A
Western Kingston, 5504
Peace In The Valley, 1956
Peace In The Valley Of
Love, 4204
Peace Lovin' Man, 606
Peace Must Come, 3648
Peace Of Mind, 3411, 5660
Peace On Earth, 1545
Peace On You, 4527
Peace Pipe, 1321
Peace Throughout The
World, 4327
Peace To My Lonely Heart,
606
Peace To The World, 4327

Peace Train, 5337
Peace Truce, 4780
Peaceful Easy Feeling, 1684,
5902
Peach On the Beach, 3964
Peach Picking Time In
Georgia, 4604
Peaches, 4173, 4309, 5953
Peaches 'N' Cream, 2678
Peaches En Regalia, 5991
Peacock Alley, 713
Peacock Suit, 2468
Peanie Peanie, 4432
Peanie Wallie, 1569
Peanut, 4877
Peanut Butter, 2792, 3456,
5639
Peanut Butter Conspiracy,
820
Peanut Polka, 1851
Peanut Punch Mek Man
Shit Up Gal Bed, 3106
Peanut Vendor, 754, 2795,
3388
Peanuts, 3266, 5546, 5963
Peanuts And Diamonds,
702
Pearl, 1022, 2533, 4773
Pearl Harbour Blues, 1118
Pearl's A Singer, 755, 3186
Pearly Queen, 5489
Peasant Army, 4474
Peck Up A Pagan, 2787
Pecos Bill, 4556
Peculiar Number, 47
Pedro the Fisherman, 1887,
2273, 3260
Peek-A-Boo, 880, 3921
Peel Me A Grape, 1448
Peel Me A Nanner, 1634
Peep Game, 2734
Peg, 100, 3176
Peg Leg Stomp, 200
Peg O' My Heart, 1427,
1909, 3360, 5753
Peg O'My Heart, 843
Peggy Blue Skylight, 2844
Peggy Day, 816
Peggy Sue, 201, 816, 838,
1233, 1551, 2568, 3192
Peggy Sue Got Married,
1292, 5357
Penelope Tree, 1872
Pennies For Peppino, 5929
Pennies From Heaven, 829,
1303, 4958
Pennsylvania 6-5000, 2253,
3674
Pennsylvania Turnpike,
5455
Penny Arcade, 3122, 4055
Penny For Your Song, 1071,
2581, 4791
Penny Lane, 434, 2635,
3409, 3517, 3521, 4629
Penny Reel, 754, 1162, 4335
Penny Royal Tea, 3957
Penny Serenade, 1248, 2473,
3300

Pentagram Ring, 1037
Pentecost Hotel, 3956
People, 2055-2056, 3637,
5554
People All Around The
World, 954
People Are Fighting, 3781
People Are Still Having Sex,
3136
People Are Strange, 1594,
1698
People Bawling, 2765
People Can Fly, 264
People Dancing, 84
People Everyday, 242
People Funny Boy, 1698,
2138, 4200, 4489
People Get Ready, 446,
1010, 2683, 3107, 3529,
3848, 4301, 5612
People Got To Be Free, 5968
People Hold On, 1157
People Like Frank, 5454
People Like Us, 4969
People Like You And Me,
2172, 2216, 4058
People Like You And People
Like Me, 2172
People Livin' Today, 2060
People Magazine, 1166,
3239
People Make The World Go
Round, 1071
People Rock Steady, 5578
People Say, 1549, 2175,
4413, 4461
People Who Died, 955
People Will Say We're In
Love, 2367, 2876, 4025-
4026, 4607
People You Were Going To,
5602
Pepe, 5595
Pepper, 959
Pepper Pot, 3511
Pepper Rock, 4335
Pepper-Hot Baby, 3784
Peppermint Twist, 1040,
1454, 2512, 5546
Percolator, 537
Percussion Piece, 5467
Percy's Song, 1826, 5577
Perdido, 2926, 4613, 5451
Perdoname, 4739
Perennial Cross Swords,
1462
Perfect, 763, 1825, 4453,
5966
Perfect Circle, 3841
Perfect Day, 1078, 1242,
3777, 4479, 5936
Perfect Fit, 4036
Perfect Kiss, 3918
Perfect Lady, 2637
Perfect Motion, 1847
Perfect Skin, 1159
Perfect Strangers, 3865
Perfect Turkey Blues, 1820
Perfect Woman, 1990

Plastic Girl, 3560
Plastic Jesus, 4395, 4588
Plastic People, 3809
Plastic Smile, 3640
Plastic Surgery, 4261
Plateau, 3607
Platinum Blonde, 4308
Platt Skank, 4306
Play, 2195, 5733
Play A Simple Melody, 493, 2412, 5386, 5720
Play At Your Own Risk, 1727
Play De Music, 4877, 4987, 4877, 4987
Play Dead, 551
Play Gypsies - Dance Gypsies, 1252
Play Hank's Song Once Again, 698
Play It Again, 565
Play It All Night Long, 5996
Play It Loud, 1507, 3825
Play Me An Old Fashioned Melody, 539
Play Me Like You Play Your Guitar, 1702, 3384
Play Me No Hearts And Flowers, 1493
Play More Music, 1212
Play My Funk, 4921
Play Orchestra Play, 3146, 5462
Play Play, 3146, 3470, 5462
Play That Funky Music, 5612, 5822
Play The Music For Me, 2807
Play The Saddest Song On The Jukebox, 5309
Play The World, 2996
Play To Me Gypsy, 2348, 2967, 5486
Play With Me, 1811
Play, Fiddle, Play, 3146
Playboy, 2113, 3014, 3495, 4445, 5312
Playboy Of Paris, 1555
Playboy Short, 1681
Playboy Theme, 3187
Playboy's Theme, 1164
Playboys, 1669
Player's Anthem, 2913, 3244
Playground, 2404
Playground In My Mind, 2573
Playground Twist, 4938
Playing Croquet, 3267
Playing Golf, 1839
Playing The Dozens, 4219
Playing To Win, 4435
Playing With Fire, 5539
Playing With Knives, 551, 615
Playmates, 3091
Plaything, 5455
Pleasant Valley Sunday, 2181, 3011, 3741
Please, 521, 4413, 4580, 5988

Please Accept My Love, 5875
Please Be Kind, 884, 1020
Please Be Love, 2253
Please Be Mine, 982, 1999
Please Be The One, 661
Please Believe In Me, 946
Please Believe Me, 768, 946
Please Come Back, 4459, 4615
Please Come Home For Christmas, 1683
Please Come To Boston, 1091, 3900
Please Do Not Go, 5649
Please Don't Ask, 1645
Please Don't Ask About Barbara, 5622
Please Don't Cry, 4796
Please Don't Do It, 5926
Please Don't Ever Change, 1292
Please Don't Fight, 317
Please Don't Flirt With Me, 5463
Please Don't Go, 1602, 2047, 2949, 3090, 3906, 4182, 4478, 6006
Please Don't Go Girl, 3915
Please Don't Leave Me, 1581, 4591
Please Don't Let Me Love You, 3783
Please Don't Make Me Cry, 2296
Please Don't Monkey With Broadway, 746, 4289
Please Don't Stop Loving Me, 4148, 5666
Please Don't Talk About Me When I'm Gone, 282, 4325
Please Don't Tease, 4530, 4834
Please Don't Tell Me, 4965
Please Don't Tell Me How The Story Ends, 378
Please Don't Think I'm Nosey, 5708
Please Don't Touch, 2162, 2454, 2986, 3644, 3812
Please Don't Treat Me Like A Child, 4774
Please Forget Her, 2915
Please Forgive Me, 52
Please Go 'Way And Let Me Sleep, 5660
Please Hello, 4099
Please Help Me I'm Falling, 751, 1419, 2032, 3289
Please Let Me Go, 2254
Please Let Me In, 386
Please Let Me Love You, 867, 2816, 3783
Please Let Me Wonder, 5454
Please Listen To My Demo, 1769
Please Love Me Forever, 2801
Please Make The Love Go

Away, 5783
Please Mark 2, 2486
Please Mr. Disc Jockey, 4820
Please Mr. Please, 5757
Please Mr. Postman, 949, 2559, 2561, 3495, 3813, 4061, 4751, 4872, 4751, 4872
Please Mr. Sun, 1712, 4446
Please Mrs Henry, 1674, 3438
Please Officer, 5995
Please Pass The Biscuits, 1446, 5832
Please Phil Spector, 275
Please Please Me, 433, 983, 999, 2675
Please Read Me, 450
Please Release Me, 1947
Please Say You Want Me, 1121, 4773
Please Send Her Back To Me, 1990
Please Send Me Someone To Love, 1936, 3529, 3764, 4223, 4690
Please Sing A Song For Us, 2634
Please Sing Satin Sheets For Me, 4351
Please Stay, 2019, 2384, 3478
Please Stop Your Lying, 1654
Please Surrender, 2039, 5775
Please Take Me Back, 588
Please Talk To Me, 4919
Please Talk To My Heart, 3512
Please Tell Him That I Said Hello, 1374
Please Think Of Me, 3787
Please Warm My Weiner, 966
Please, Mr Johnson, 2842, 2844
Please, Mrs Henry, 1674, 3438
Please, My Love, 5875, 5932
Please, Please, Please, 409, 775, 5381
Pleasure, 265
Pleasure And Pain, 1549, 5332, 5725
Pleasure And Privilege, 4662
Pleasure Seekers, 3168
Pleasures Of The Harbour, 5579
Pledge Of Love, 1230-1231
Pledge To The Sun, 5320
Pledging My Love, 52, 729, 3575, 5438
Plenty, 5912
Plenty Of Pennsylvania, 4259
Plenty To Be Thankful For, 2555
Plink, Plank, Plunk, 179

Pluckin' The Bass, 896
Plug Me In (To The Central Love Line), 4767
Plutonic, 551
Po' Folks, 173
Po-Jama People, 4047
Pocahontas, 899-900, 5978
Pocket Calculator, 1199
Pocket Full Of Gold, 2147
Pocket Of Peace, 3536
Pocketful Of Sunshine, 5350
Poco Man Jam, 4749
Pocomania Jump, 4749
Poems, 4099
Poetry In Motion, 5438-5439
Poetry Man, 5990
Pogo Dancing, 5640
Poinciana (Song Of The Tree), 4650
Poinconneur Des Lilacs, 2071
Point Blank, 4806
Point Me At The Sky, 4247
Point Of No Return, 3560
Point Of View, 5566
Pointed Toe Shoes, 4196
Poison, 119, 459, 1275, 2630, 4460
Poison Arrow, 39, 5368
Poison Arrows Shot At Heroes, 4960
Poison Ivy, 1138, 3117, 3203, 3381, 4126, 5418
Poison Love, 271, 1403, 2836
Poison Red Berries, 375, 3926
Poisoning Pigeons In The Park, 3186
Polaris, 5470
Poles Apart, 5360
Police And Thieves, 693, 2761, 3848, 5358
Police Beat, 3660
Police In Helicopter, 2576, 3144
Police Officer, 1856, 4978, 5565
Police On My Back, 4736
Police Patrol, 5614
Police Story, 1367
Political, 166, 3853, 4904
Political Confusion, 2822
Political Science, 4719
Political Song For Michael Jackson To Sing, 5732
Politician, 79, 414, 767, 796, 1356, 4546
Politics And Poker, 1901
Politics Of Ecstasy, 5294
Polk Salad Annie, 4312, 5801
Polka, 1012
Polka Dot, 5402
Polka Dots, 1895
Polka Dots And Moonbeams, 1789, 4927, 5606, 5731

Pressure Drop, 3532, 5364

Pressure In A Babylon, 3487

Pretend, 1160, 1417, 3445, 3479

Pretend Best Friend, 5342

Pretend We're Dead, 3094

Pretending, 4695, 4874

Pretty, 650, 783, 1241, 2999, 4366, 5388

Pretty Africa, 53

Pretty Baby, 1202, 2752, 2922, 4648

Pretty Ballerina, 3179

Pretty Brown Babies (Pro Seed), 2130

Pretty Brown Eyes, 1576

Pretty Colours, 1456

Pretty Flamingo, 2881, 3437

Pretty Girl, 1212, 2138, 2700, 5409, 5872

Pretty Girl, Pretty Clothes, Pretty Sad, 4323

Pretty Girls Everywhere, 1083, 5356, 5677, 5681

Pretty In Pink, 4355

Pretty Jenny, 1212

Pretty Lady, 4099

Pretty Little Angel Eyes, 532, 3155, 3172

Pretty Little Black-Eyed Susie, 3711

Pretty Little Cemetery, 4831

Pretty Little Martha, 5670

Pretty Little Picture, 2056

Pretty Looks, 1569, 2496

Pretty Me, 189

Pretty Mess, 5613

Pretty Miss Kitty, 1966

Pretty Paper, 3899

Pretty Polly, 642, 4924

Pretty Pretty, 2889

Pretty Saro, 3559

Pretty Shitty Days, 300

Pretty Song, 4352

Pretty Suicide, 3989

Pretty Suzanne, 3742

Pretty Thing, 237, 1039, 1399, 1517

Pretty To Walk With, 2768

Pretty Vacant, 3514, 3908, 4830, 5399

Pretty Woman, 2516, 4431, 5550

Price Of Cotton Blues, 127

Price You Pay, 4384

Pride, 785, 873

Pride (In The Name Of Love), 5380, 5561

Pride And Ambition, 4976

Pride And Joy, 589, 1263, 2903

Priestess, 2400

Priests, 1153

Primary, 1334

Primary Rhyming, 3539

Prime Mover, 3159, 6001

Prime Time TV, 405

Primero Fui Yo, 4032

Primitive, 3723

Primitive Painters, 1872

Primrose, 1376, 3979

Primrose Hill, 3494, 4593

Primrose Lane, 4327

Prince Ali, 104

Prince Charming, 62, 989

Prince Edward Island Is Heaven To Me, 3305

Prince In The Pack, 4199

Prince Of Peace, 3914

Prince Of Punks, 882, 4586

Prince Of Techno, 419, 5574

Prince Of The Punks, 882, 4586

Prince Of Wails, 4772

Prince Pharoah, 5871

Princess, 1971

Princess Black, 1913

Princess In Rags, 4255

Princess Zenobia, 4042

Princess, Princess, 5438

Principles, 2043

Printemps A Rio, 5499

Printhead, 1616

Prison Blues Come Down On Me, 3666

Prison Oval Rock, 3144, 3213

Prison Song, 3877

Prisoner Of Ignorance, 2985

Prisoner Of Love, 775, 1188, 1195, 1700, 2694, 3068, 3168, 4580

Prisoner's Farewell, 1475

Prisoners, 5614

Prisoners In Niggertown, 2337

Private Cecil Gant, 2082

Private Dancer, 1537

Private Eye, 3358, 4037

Private Eye Suite, 3241

Private Investigations, 1537

Private Life, 2873, 4318

Private Number, 464, 1114, 1420

Private Property, 2186, 5426

Private Psychedelic Reel, 1523

Private World, 2087

Privileged, 623

Prize Of Gold, 4488

Probably A Robbery, 4503

Problem Everywhere, 4906

Problematic, 1920

Problems, 804, 1466, 1686, 1798

Problems Get You Down, 767

Problems Of The World Today, 1866

Prodigal Son, 453, 5833

Production Plan, 2138

Professional Widow, 168, 698, 5606

Professor Black, 3321

Profound Gas, 4734

Progen, 4552

Progress, 3336, 5693

Progress Is The Root Of All

Evil, 3230

Prohibition Blues, 421

Project 'Ho, 3538

Prologue, 1965

Prologue Jellicle Songs For Jellicle Cats, 994

Promenade, 179

Promise, 3720, 4714

Promise Me A Rose, 3637, 5284

Promise Me, Love, 5836

Promised Land, 126, 501, 1558, 2093, 4674, 4948, 5292, 5319

Promised You A Miracle, 4921

Promises, 859, 1095, 1570, 3477, 4546, 5285, 5496

Prop Me Up (Beside The Jukebox), 1522

Proper Education, 1622

Property Of Jesus, 1676

Prophecy, 47, 99, 1270, 3272, 3576, 4546

Prophecy Call, 2822

Prophets Of Rage, 4357

Prospect Street, 525

Protect And Serve, 5817

Protect And Serve/Bad Things, 3255

Protection, 3955

Protocoligorically Correct, 4969

Proud Mary, 801, 1040, 1288, 2534, 2727, 2965, 4312, 5532, 5535

Proud Of Mandella, 3055

Prove Your Love, 1430

Prove Yourself, 4403

Proverb, 3802

Proverbs, 541

Provócame, 3162

Prowler, 2710-2711

Prowlin' Nighthawk, 3948

Psalm, 29

Psalm 121, 2764, 4306

PSK, 974, 4773

Psyche, 2993

Psychedelic Rock, 1569

Psychedelic Shack, 4354

Psychiatric Explorations Of The Fetus With Needles, 1925

Psycho, 556, 3318, 4171

Psycho Killer, 1952, 5287-5288

Psycho Kong, 1563

Psycho Street, 4686

Psychonaut, 1885

Psychosis, 850

Psychotic Reaction, 1251, 3985, 4885

Psychoticbumpschool, 1174

Pscyle Sluts, 1107

Psykick Dancehall, 1616

Psyko Funk, 663

Pu-leeze, Mr. Hemingway, 2971

Public Enemy Number 1, 4357

Public Execution, 2485

Public Image, 4358

Public Melody Number One, 227, 3054

Publicity, 1436

Pucker, 97

Pucker Up Buttercup, 2184

Puckwudgie, 1618

Puddin N' Tain (Ask Me Again, I'll Tell You The Same), 137-138

Pueblo Latino, 4614

Puff The Magic Dragon, 2684, 4208

Puffin' Billy, 5797

Puffin' On Down The Track, 3500

Pull Down The Blind, 729

Pull My Daisy, 3890

Pull Out The Pin, 5361

Pull Up, 5292

Pull Up To The Bumper, 2873

Pulling Mussels (From The Shell), 224

Pulling Weeds, 1857

Pulp Fiction, 4105, 4474

Pulse, 1523

Puls(t)ar, 3236

Pulsar Glich, 616

Pulstar, 5611

Pum-Pa-Lum, 3148

Pump Action Sunshine, 5342

Pump It Up, 5397

Pump That Bass, 4060

Pump The Move, 3044

Pump Up Chicago, 3825, 5497

Pump Up England, 3825

Pump Up The Jam, 4455, 5326, 5945

Pump Up The Volume, 214, 850, 1157, 1183, 1773, 1989, 3393, 3472

Pump Your Fist, 1288

Pumping To Playboy, 2165

Pumpkin Belly, 5338

Pumps And Pride, 5504

Punany, 79, 4941

Punch And Judy, 3462

Punchinello, 1341

Punchlines, 2565

Punish Me With Kisses, 2173

Punishment Kiss, 5385

Punk Is Dead, 1867

Punk Rock Dream Come True, 716

Punk Rock Girl, 1442

Punk Rock Rap, 1157

Punk's Not Dead, 4366

Punka, 2966

Punks Give Me Respect, 4408

Punky Brewster, 808

Punky Reggae Party, 4200

Punky's Dilemma, 664

Puny Puny, 3477

Puppet Life, 4365
Puppet Man, 3309, 4809
Puppet On A String, 1249, 3483, 3521, 4857
Puppetmaster, 1760
Puppy Love, 194-195, 1146, 3956, 4073, 4148
Pure, 151, 763, 959, 2302, 3243, 3411
Pure And Clean, 5995
Pure Gal, 4766
Pure Love, 3687, 4396, 5995
Pure Love - Pure Energy, 1350
Pure Pleasure, 4081
Pure Power, 4640
Pure, Impure, 4810
Purify Your Heart, 4546
Purlie, 4368
Purple Haze, 1535, 2490, 4411, 4885
Purple Hazy Melancholy, 720
Purple Heather, 3795
Purple Pas de Deux, 1179
Purple People Eater, 5918
Purple Rain, 4332
Purple Robe, 4014
Pursuance, 29
Pursuit, 336
Push, 3511
Push Button Cocktail, 3257
Push Come To Shove, 3576
Push Daughter Push, 4549
Push De Button, 2386, 2768
Push It, 3093, 4725-4726
Push It In, 863
Push Lady Push, 4548
Push Me In The Corner, 3832
Push Out The Boat, 2526
Push Push, 889, 4061, 4490, 4548-4549, 5735
Push The Beat, 921, 1237
Push The Button, 227
Push The Feeling On, 3948
Push Up Your Lighter, 5466
Pushed But Not Forgotten, 2523
Pushin, 2625, 4443, 4810
Pushin' Against The Flow, 4443
Pushin' Too Hard, 2625, 4810
Pushover, 1109, 2772
Puss In Boots, 62
Pussy Cat, 164
Pussy Control, 4333
Pussy Foot, 2192
Pussy Price, 99
Pussy Summit Meeting, 139
Pussy Whipped, 385
Pussy Wiggle Stomp, 1741
Put A Light At The Window, 1993
Put A Little Love Away, 1979
Put A Little Love In Your Heart, 1492, 1788, 2267,

2558, 2682
Put A Ring On Her Finger, 3610
Put A Tax On Love, 4635
Put Another Chair At The Table, 3683
Put Another Nickel In (Music! Music! Music!), 164
Put Down Your Guns, 767
Put It In A Magazine, 1040
Put It In The Book, 4565
Put It Off Until Tomorrow, 2965, 4221
Put It On, 1309, 4250
Put It On Me, 3436
Put It There, Pal, 4563
Put It Where You Want It, 1318
Put Me Down, 1275
Put Me In My Cell, 5900
Put Me In The Picture, 3640
Put Me In Your Pocket, 782, 3997
Put Me To The Test, 1263, 1373, 2130
Put On A Happy Face, 862
Put On An Old Pair Of Shoes, 2528
Put On Your Old Gray Bonnet, 4359
Put On Your Sunday Clothes, 2477-2478, 2504
Put Out The Light, 1145
Put Some Drive Into Your Country, 5507
Put That Down In Writing, 2185
Put The Blame On Mame, 1909, 2450
Put The Needle On The Record, 337
Put You Arms Around Me Honey, 3399
Put You Back In Your Place, 1459
Put You In The Picture, 4967
Put Your Arms Around Me, 5792
Put Your Arms Around Me Honey, 1202, 2385, 2447, 5659
Put Your Dreams Away, 3187
Put Your Hand In The Hand, 2929, 4011
Put Your Hands Together, 1350, 4002, 5345
Put Your Handz Up, 5814
Put Your Head On My Shoulder, 194, 2094
Put Your Love In Me, 2601
Put Yourself In My Place, 1731, 1768, 2561, 5871
Put Yourself In My Place, Baby, 942
Putsch, 4662
Puttin' In Overtime At Home, 4527

Puttin' On The Ritz, 617, 1376
Puttin' On The Style, 1247
Putting On The Dog, 1437
Putting On The Style, 1588
Putting The Damage On, 5490
Putting Up Resistance, 2368, 2638
Pyjamarama, 4669
Pyramid Of The Night (Past, Present And Future), 3391
Qmart, 1717
Qu'Elle Est Belle, 3512
Qu'est-Ce Que Tu Deviens, 2009
Quadlibet For Tenderfeet, 2246
Quadrophenia, 84
Quahogs, Anyone?, 2364
Quaker City Jazz, 4756
Qual, 5942
Quality, 922
Quality Time, 2963
Quand Fera-T-Il Jour Comrade, 3512
Quand On N'A Que L'Amour, 724
Quand Tu Danses, 442
Quando M'Innamoro (A Man Without Love), 4737
Quando, Quando, Quando, 5595
Quarter Gram Pam, 4294
Quarter To Three, 655, 5935
Quarter To Twelve, 4466, 4923
Quartette, 88
Quasimodo's Dream, 4482
Quat, 4749
Que Hablen, 3881
Que Humanidad, 3233
Que Maravilla Fue Sentirte, 4745
Que Pena Me Da, 4616
Que Que Sera, 4667
Que Reste-Il De Nos Amours?, 5499
Que Sera Sera, 680, 1159, 1446, 3043, 3678, 4675
Quedate, 3835
Queen For A Day, 3436
Queen Jane Approximately, 1358
Queen Lucy, 5963
Queen Majesty, 1762, 2961, 4137, 4493, 5325
Queen Of Clubs, 2949
Queen Of Hearts, 1707, 3933, 4382
Queen Of My Heart, 2037
Queen Of My House, 2930
Queen Of The Beach, 3011
Queen Of The Hop, 1390
Queen Of The House, 2930, 3676
Queen Of The Jungle, 2260
Queen Of The Minstrels,

904, 1569
Queen Of The Night, 3393
Queen Of The Rapping Scene, 3728
Queen Of The Reich, 4383
Queen Of The Road, 2211, 3676
Queen Of The Senior Prom, 3683
Queen Of The Silver Dollar, 1397, 2570
Queen Wahine's Papaya, 4123
Queenie, 715
Queenie's Ballyhoo, 4893
Question, 401, 1907, 4324
Questions, 3133, 5549
Quick Joey Small, 816, 2937
Quick, Fast, In A Hurry, 3923
Quicksand, 1729, 2561, 3480
Quicksilver, 136, 744
Quicksilver Girl, 3680
Quiéreme, 885
Quiereme Mucho, 3428, 4889
Quiet, 2416, 4898, 5910
Quiet Countryside, 5961
Quiet Joys Of Brotherhood, 1484
Quiet Life, 2783
Quiet Night, 4042
Quiet Nights On Quiet Stars, 3178
Quiet Please, 1032
Quiet Village, 419, 1484
Quill Blues, 2631
Quiniela, 1779
Quinn The Eskimo, 1674
Quino - phec, 207
Quite Extraordinary, 2665
Quittin' Time, 947, 2636
Quiz, 3788
Quoth, 207
R Subway Train That Came To Life, 5392
R To The A, 3215
R&B Swinger, 1861
R.A.M., 6001
R.I.P., 121
R.M. Blues, 3687, 4690
R.O.C.K. In The USA, 3617
R2D2 I Wish You A Merry Christmas, 652
Rabbit, 317, 786, 825, 917, 1034, 2022, 2548, 3067
Rabbit Blues, 665
Rabbit Stew, 4443
Rabbits, 2336
Race With The Devil, 2162, 2312, 5645
Racemixer, 4095
Rachel, 3493
Rachel's Comin' Home, 2041
Rachel's Dream, 48
Racing With The Clock, 4106

Right At The Start Of It, 5425

Right Back To You, 2805

Right Back Where We Started From, 3949, 4937

Right Ball, 2211

Right Behind You Baby, 5320

Right Beside You, 2441

Right Between The Eyes, 5734

Right By Your Side, 1787, 5475

Right Down The Line, 1091

Right From The Start, 1206

Right Here, 5568

Right Here Waiting, 3498

Right Here, Right Now, 2818

Right In The Middle, 4553

Right In The Middle (Of Falling in Love), 3142

Right In The Palm Of Your Hand, 3560

Right Now, 603, 947, 1288

Right On, 372, 4150

Right On Jody, 4157

Right On The Tip Of My Tongue, 725, 3557

Right On Time, 1586, 3659

Right On, Right On, 1215

Right Or Left At Oak Street, 452

Right Or Wrong, 879, 1606, 2650, 2753, 4494

Right Place, Wrong Time, 1615, 4157

Right Said Fred, 3486, 5495

Right Side Of A Good Thing, 1938

Right String Baby But The Wrong Yo Yo, 4231

Right Time, 1586, 2588, 3659, 4514

Right Time Of The Night, 3546, 4445, 5706

Right To Work, 1042

Right Track, 854

Righteous Man, 1363, 3271, 3866

Righteous Works, 5995

Righthand Heart, 3735

Ring 'Em, 2365

Ring Around Rosie, 2515

Ring Around The Rosy, 2706, 5429

Ring Finger, 4319

Ring My Bell, 3047, 5698, 5996

Ring Of Fire, 977, 1122, 1172, 2311, 2618, 2990, 5460

Ring Of Gold, 798

Ring Of Ice, 4692

Ring On Her Finger, Time On Her Hands, 2966

Ring Out The Blues, 954

Ring Ring, 37

Ring Ring Ring (Ha Ha

Hey), 1435

Ring The Alarm, 4546, 5338, 5636

Ring, Ring, Ring, 3393

Ring-A-Ding Girl, 956

Ringo I Love You, 1044

Ringo Rock, 149

Ringo-Mura Kara, 3661

Rings, 1343, 4499, 5460

Rings Of Gold, 5773

Rinky Dink, 1239

Rio, 2145, 3828, 3905

Rio Bravo, 5750

Rio Grande, 5870

Rio Junction, 3241

Rio Rita, 3548, 4550, 4880, 5433

Riot, 2623, 3500

Riot Grrrl, 2627, 4792, 4900, 5517

Riot In Cell Block No. 9, 503, 2414, 4580

Riot Inna Juvenile Prison, 1472

Riot On 103rd Street, 3807

Riotousness And Postrophe, 2542

Rip In Heaven, 3476

Rip It Up, 575, 1583, 2341, 3203, 3270, 4593

Rip Off, 3175

Rip Van Winkle, 1501

Ripe Cherry, 111

Ripper, 5580

Ripple, 160

Ripple Wine Dream, 5621

Rippling Stream, 1387

Rise, 147, 340, 1071, 1073, 3382, 3400, 4358, 6000

Rise 'N' Shine, 3634, 5283, 5964

Rise Above, 1367

Rise And Fall, 99, 4653

Rise And Shine, 981, 1606, 3064, 3634, 5668

Rise From Your Grave, 1417, 1560

Rise Sally Rise, 3161

Rise To The Occasion, 1128

Rising From The Dread, 5564

Rising Star, 3519, 3975

Rising Sun, 2717, 3609

Rising Tide, 1288

Rising To The Top, 4851

Risingson, 3505

Risky, 2004

Rita Valentine, 967

Ritual, 1610, 4476

Riturnella, 3456

River, 3713

River Boy, 3899

River Deep Mountain High, 400, 1457, 2277, 2299, 2944, 5532

River Edge Rock, 2389

River In The Rain, 528

River John Mountain, 790

River Jordan, 1568, 1698

River Of Smack, 2053

River Of Tears, 855

River Road, 5557

River Song, 3648, 5872

River To Another Day, 3338

River To The Bank, 754, 1247

River's Invitation, 3529

River, Stay 'Way From My Door, 1555, 4991, 5915

Riverboat Jamboree, 1438

Riverboat Shuffle, 941, 5904

Rivers Of Babylon, 656, 3060, 3619

Rivers Of Girls, 3631

Rivers Of Justice, 1468

Rivers Of Salt, 1879

Riverside Blues, 2884

Riviera Paradise, 2686

Rizla, 852

Rizla Bass, 663

Rizla Skank, 852

Roach In The Corner, 4780

Road, 829, 3118, 3577, 3928, 4498, 4563, 4769, 4849, 4914, 5487

Road Block, 1204, 4216

Road By The River, 3459

Road Mi Waan Come, 311

Road Of Truth, 1321

Road Runner, 1039, 2988, 5681

Road Scholar, 4143

Road To Madness, 4383

Road To Morocco, 4563, 5606

Road To Nowhere, 5288, 5459, 5492

Road To Rio, 4534

Road To The Precinct, 2393

Roadblock, 673, 2689

Roadhouse Blues, 1594, 3793, 4175

Roadrunner, 3727, 4536, 5890

Roads, 3118

Roam Jerusalem, 1698

Roane County Prison, 920

Roast, 590

Roast Fish And Cornbread, 5685

Rob's Theme, 5330

Robber Man, 3213

Robbers' Chorus, 250

Robbins Nest, 4695

Robbins' Nest, 5408

Robe Of Cavalry, 2042

Robert De Niro's Waiting, 357

Robertson County, 5705

Robin Hood, 1759, 2771, 3673, 4328

Robin Hood And The Bogey

Rolling Contest, 5931

Robins And Roses, 829, 3201

Robinson Crusoe, 1325

Robot, 5470

Robot Criminal, 1929

Rocco, 1449

Rochdale Cowboy, 2392

Rock & Roll Lullaby, 3005, 3303, 5398

Rock & Roll Music, 426, 500

Rock & Roll Part 1, 2920

Rock & Roll Revival, 1916

Rock & Roll Show, 1083

Rock 'n Roll, 2781

Rock 'N' Me, 1949, 3680

Rock 'n' Roll Ain't Noise Pollution, 48

Rock 'N' Roll All Nite, 3034

Rock 'N' Roll Baby, 918, 976

Rock 'N' Roll Friend, 1980

Rock 'n' Roll Heaven, 3997, 4543

Rock 'N' Roll Is Here To Stay, 1384-1385

Rock 'N' Roll Lifestyle, 888

Rock 'N' Roll Opera, 3148

Rock 'N' Roll Ruby, 955, 976

Rock 'n' Roll Star, 376

Rock 'N' Roll Suicide, 685

Rock 2 House, 2913, 5939

Rock A Beatin' Boogie, 4591

Rock A Hula Baby, 612

Rock A Man Soul, 2165

Rock All My Babies To Sleep, 4359

Rock And A Hard Place, 4631

Rock And Groove, 5668

Rock And Roll, 3158, 3165, 3288, 4932

Rock And Roll Ain't Noise Pollution, 48, 317

Rock And Roll Blues, 5694

Rock And Roll Doctor, 1867

Rock And Roll Fever, 904

Rock And Roll Is Back Again, 2396

Rock And Roll Is Dead (And We Don't Care), 4679

Rock And Roll Lullaby, 3303, 5398

Rock And Roll Music, 426, 500

Rock And Roll Pussy, 31

Rock And Roll Queen, 3815

Rock And Roll Rhapsody, 1989

Rock And Roll Shoes, 5398

Rock And Roll The Place, 3737

Rock And Roll To The Rescue, 426

Rock And Roll Woman, 819

Rock Around Mother Goose, 2214

Rock Around The Clock, 1085, 1452, 2341, 2939, 3203, 3465, 3623, 3951, 4591, 4593, 5330, 5767

Rock Around The Rock Pile, 2159

Rock Around The Symbol, 2826

Rock Around With Ollie Vee, 1339
Rock Awhile, 967
Rock Back, 3104
Rock Bitch, 2265
Rock Boll Weevil, 5784
Rock Boppin' Baby, 796
Rock Bottom, 1438, 3808, 4223, 4769, 5562
Rock Box, 4687, 4915
Rock Dis Funky Joint, 4281
Rock Everybody Rock, 3715
Rock H-Bomb Rock, 1876
Rock Hard, 4679
Rock Hearts, 3488
Rock House Boogie, 2586
Rock Island, 3852, 5869
Rock Island Line, 806, 1390, 1588, 1958, 2021, 3156
Rock It, 2871, 3649
Rock Little Baby, 2083
Rock Lobster, 303, 5353
Rock Love, 1963, 4100, 5930
Rock Me, 1949, 2147, 2581, 3680, 3951
Rock Me (In The Cradle Of Love), 129
Rock Me All Night Long, 4443
Rock Me Amadeus, 1834
Rock Me Baby, 983, 1107, 1834
Rock Me On The Water, 791
Rock Me Tonight (For Old Times Sake), 2740
Rock Me, Baby, 983, 1107, 1834
Rock Music, 742, 4256
Rock My Baby, 4867
Rock My World (Little Country Girl), 753
Rock Of Ages, 2241
Rock On, 1780, 4923
Rock Savoy Rock, 5431
Rock Star's Lament, 3057
Rock Steady, 2030, 4493, 5791
Rock The Beat, 111, 305, 4482, 5706
Rock The Casbah, 1110
Rock The Joint, 21, 2341, 4593
Rock The Nation, 3757
Rock The Night, 1786
Rock This Party Right, 5555
Rock To The Beat, 111, 4482
Rock With Me Baby, 1107
Rock With The Cavemen, 402
Rock With You, 2746, 4016
Rock You Baby, 6006
Rock You Like A Hurricane, 3335
Rock Your Baby, 3090, 3558, 3906
Rock Your Little Baby To Sleep, 3052

Rock'n'Roll Mercenaries, 3606
Rock, Rock, Rock, 249
Rock-A-Beatin' Boogie, 2341, 4591
Rock-A-Billy, 3711
Rock-A-Billy Baby, 1652
Rock-A-Bye The Boogie, 4449, 4958
Rock-A-Bye Your Baby With A Dixie Melody, 2862, 3225, 5972
Rock-A-Doodle-Doo, 3221
Rock-Bye-Boogie, 4958
Rockabilly Can Rock, 3546
Rockabilly Guy, 4273
Rockabilly Rebel, 3510
Rockabye Baby, 3850
Rockabye Your Baby With A Dixie Melody, 2863
Rockafeller Skank, 1220
Rockall, 3650
Rocker, 64, 545, 1281
Rockers, 778, 3659, 4543, 4594
Rockers Arena, 5990
Rockers Don't Move You, 2579
Rockers Medley, 572
Rockers No Crackers, 2138
Rockers Time Now, 3217, 4070
Rockers To Rockers, 4060
Rocket, 2657
Rocket Charms, 349
Rocket Man, 2833, 4176
Rocket To The Moon, 732
Rocket USA, 3311
Rockfort Rock, 2637
Rockhouse, 5547
Rockin' All Over The World, 1954, 3170
Rockin' And Rollin' With Granmaw, 4587
Rockin' Around The Christmas Tree, 3170, 3614, 5829
Rockin' At Cosimo's, 132
Rockin' At The Cannon Ball, 2227
Rockin' At The Phil, 4781
Rockin' Chair, 332, 941, 1722, 2197, 3558, 3683, 4180, 4949
Rockin' Daddy, 653
Rockin' Dolly, 1147
Rockin' In America, 5767
Rockin' In The Coconut Top, 4818
Rockin' In The Congo, 5410
Rockin' In The Free World, 524
Rockin' It, 1866
Rockin' Little Angel, 1873
Rockin' On The Dancefloor, 4640
Rockin' Over The Beat, 5326
Rockin' Pneumonia And

The Boogie Woogie Flu, 2402, 4559, 4988
Rockin' Robin, 636, 1426, 2746, 4503
Rockin' Soul, 2626
Rockin' The Boogie, 756
Rockin' With Red, 4231
Rockin' Years, 2872, 4866
Rocking Chair, 3412, 4383
Rocking Chair Daddy, 1947
Rocking Dolly, 3144
Rocking Goose, 2837
Rocking Pneumonia And The Boogie Woogie Flu, 3458
Rocking The 5000, 4431
Rocking Time, 2955, 3758, 4337
Rocking' In Rhythm, 1735
Rockingham Twist, 3316
Rockit, 2239, 2373, 3132
Rocks In My Bed, 4265
Rocks Off, 5802
Rocky, 839, 1846, 3172
Rocky Mountain Music, 4396
Rocky Mountain Way, 5691
Rocky Road, 4003
Rocky Top, 803-804, 4067
Rod Hull Is Alive - Why?, 2343
Rod Of Correction, 1698
Rodeo Cowboys, 77
Rodeo Eyes, 3185
Rodeo Romeo, 364
Rodney K, 1351
Roger The Ugly, 5540
Roi, 723
Rok Da House, 437, 1222, 4522
Rok The Nation, 2920
Rolaids, Doan's Pills And Preparation H, 1643
Roland The Thompson Gunner, 5996
Rolene, 3490, 3694
Roll 'Em, 3525
Roll Along Covered Wagon, 2967
Roll Along Kentucky Moon, 695
Roll Along Prairie Moon, 5659
Roll And Tumble Blues, 3925
Roll Away The Stone, 3815
Roll It On Robbie, 4471
Roll Jordan Roll, 99, 5885
Roll Muddy River, 5820
Roll On Babe, 3123
Roll On Columbia, 681, 2319
Roll Out The Barrel, 183
Roll Over Beethoven, 500-501, 998, 1725, 2847, 3222, 3279
Roll The Dice, 667, 1249, 2468, 5485
Roll Truck Roll, 4924

Roll Um Easy, 1549
Roll Up the Ribbons, 2660
Roll Wit Tha Flava, 4382
Roll With It, 2814, 4008, 5783, 5890
Roll With Me, Henry, 353, 2771
Roll With The Punches, 70, 3688
Roll Yer Socks Up, 3913
Roll Your Own, 3560
Roller Skate Rag, 2055
Rollercoaster, 3974
Rollerskates, 2636
Rollin, 68, 916, 1541, 1780, 1963, 1985, 2984, 3687, 3830, 4341, 4527, 5693, 5847
Rollin' Down the River, 68
Rollin' Home, 5693
Rollin' In My Sweet Baby's Arms, 3687
Rollin' Stone, 1780, 1963, 3830, 4341
Rollin' With Kid 'N Play, 2984
Rollin' With Rai, 1541
Rollin' With The Flow, 4527
Rolling Down To Bowling Green, 3808
Rolling Down To Old Maui, 4847
Rolling Home, 673
Rolling Stone, 371, 4468
Roly Poly, 4652, 5847
Roman Candle, 1936
Romance, 310, 1491, 2273, 2501, 4814
Romance Dance, 5367
Romance For Mouth-Organ, Piano And Strings, 78
Romance In Durango, 1675
Romance In The Dark, 2271
Romance On The North Sea, 2433
Romancing To The Folk Song, 562
Romantic Rhapsody, 4534
Romantica, 3784
Romany Life, 2501
Rome, 3832
Romeo, 1102, 2468, 2681, 2967, 3823, 5625
Romeo And Juliet, 613, 1537, 1831, 2691, 3513
Romeo Had Juliette, 3922
Romeo's Tune, 1967
Romeo's Twin, 2942
Rompe Saragüey, 3142
Roobarb & Custard, 1881, 5484
Roobarb And Custard, 5484
Roof Space, 336
Room 504, 2137
Room At The Top, 62
Room Enuff For Us, 3230
Room Five Hundred And Four, 3499

Room Full Of Roses, 1338, 2153, 2447, 3783, 5736
Room In Your Heart, 3280
Room Of Shadows, 263
Room Service, 1626
Room To Move, 3527, 5536
Roomin' House Boogie, 105, 3663, 4583
Rooms, 3427
Rooms For The Memory, 2706
Roosevelt In Trinidad, 269
Rooster, 120, 1538
Rooster Blues, 3242
Roots And Culture, 681, 4794
Roots Girl, 681, 735
Roots Man Skanking, 4431
Roots Natty, 2165
Roots Natty Roots Natty Congo, 2763
Roots Pon Mi Corner, 648
Roots Reality And Culture, 681
Roots With Quality, 5393
Rootsman Revival, 1621
Rooty Toot, 2756
Rope In, 4780
Rope The Moon, 3754
Rosa, 1601
Rosa Rosetta, 421
Rosabella, 3294, 3805
Rosalee, 2626
Rosalie, 2473, 4153, 4289, 4704
Rosalie's Good Eats Cafe, 3356
Rosalie/Cowgirl's Song, 3276
Rosalita, 1502
Rosalita (Come Out Tonight), 5381
Rosalyn, 4319, 4454
Rosanna, 5475
Rosco's Rhythm, 2217
Rose Coloured Glasses, 1205
Rose Garden, 180, 4673
Rose Garden Waltz, 1685
Rose Marie, 1280, 1703, 2385, 4648, 4967
Rose O'Day, 3004
Rose Of Bel-Air, 4651
Rose Of England, 3979
Rose Of My Heart, 3729
Rose Of The Rio Grande, 3200, 5710
Rose Of The World, 2502
Rose Of Washington Square, 4648
Rose Petals Fall From Her Face, 5702
Rose Room, 533, 1073, 2516
Rose Rose, I Love You, 3111, 3677
Rose Tint My World, 4600
Rose's Turn, 2324, 3635
Rose, Rose, I Love You, 3111, 3677
Rose-Marie, 2037, 2366

Rosecrans Blvd, 5744
Rosemary, 778, 1543, 2613, 4591, 4782
Rosemary's Baby, 2342
Rosencrans Boulevard, 5690
Roses, 5707
Roses And Revolvers, 4449
Roses Are In Bloom, 653
Roses Are Red, 213, 956, 2420, 3384, 5648
Roses Are Red (My Love), 1793
Roses At The Station, 2237
Roses For Mama, 3543
Roses In December, 667, 2003, 3409
Roses In The Hospital, 3442
Roses of Picardy, 1280, 2531, 5911, 5961
Roses Red And White, 1064
Roses Remind Me Of You, 1405
Rosetta, 1999, 4322
Rosie, 862, 4149, 4282, 4656
Rosie (Make It Rosy for Me), 1106
Rosme, 4388
Rote Lichter, 4108
Rothschild And Sons, 4662
Rotterdam, 440
Rough And Tough, 1162
Rough Boy, 6007
Rough Boys, 5481
Rough Justice, 357
Rough Kids, 2989
Rough Rider, 2661
Rough Spot, 5989
Rough This Year, 1008
Rougher Yet, 1569, 3305
Roughneck Fashion, 5338
Roughside, 5815
Roulette, 1216
Round, 944, 3841
Round And Round, 909, 1195, 1845, 2231, 5391, 5760, 5972
Round Midnight, 2118, 5279
Round Round Round, 2965
Round Table Talk, 3104, 4120
Round The Corner, 4725, 5463
Round The Gum Tree, 1901
Round The Marble Arch, 2102
Round The World, 5665
Roundabout, 1647, 2004, 5957
Route 66, 501, 1135, 4044
Route 90, 2091
Roving Cowboy, 2948
Roving Gambler, 2403
Row Mr. Fisherman, 790
Row, Row, Row, 935, 3735, 5997
Rowdy Blues, 332
Roxanne, 4082, 4274, 4456
Roxanne Roxanne, 4456,

4668, 5560
Roxanne's Revenge, 4668
Roxie, 1055
Roxy Roller, 2147
Roy, 194, 454, 1610
Royal Blue Waltz, 3451
Royal Garden Blues, 5841, 5858
Royal Mile, 5961
RU 486, 4105
RU Single, 3341
Rub & Squeeze, 1569
Rub A Dub Session, 4110
Rub A Dub Soldier, 601
Rub A Dub Style, 3654
Rub It Down, 4801
Rub It In, 1272
Rub Me Out, 1278, 5638
Rub Sister Rub It, 4431
Rub Up Push Up, 2535, 4139-4140
Rub You The Right Way, 2147
Rub-A-Dub, 4458
Rub-A-Dub-Dub, 5410
Rubb It In, 4453
Rubber Ball, 292, 4255, 5622, 5829
Rubber Biscuit, 1065
Rubber Duck, 1650
Rubber Glove Blues, 5769
Rubber Neck Blues, 3746
Rubbers, 2080, 2958
Rubbish, 962
Ruby, 419, 2447, 4946, 5982
Ruby Ann, 4568
Ruby Baby, 1272, 1469, 1627, 1822, 5370
Ruby My Dear, 2118, 3739, 5537
Ruby Tuesday, 201, 962, 2100, 3616, 4629
Ruby, Are You Mad At Your Man, 1260
Ruby, Don't Take Your Love To Town, 1394, 2109, 4181, 4621, 5436
Rude Boy Gone A Jail, 1569, 4490
Rude Boy Life, 852
Rude Boy Skank, 4070
Rude Boy Step, 4780
Rude Boy Train, 1466
Rude Boys, 601
Rude Girl Sandra, 3611
Rude Mood, 5348
Rudi Got Married, 99
Rudi's In Love, 2336, 3292
Rudie, 1569
Rudie Bam Bam, 1097
Rudie Gone A Jail, 1097
Rudie Got Soul, 1466
Rudolph, The Red-Nosed Reindeer, 287, 880, 1375, 2885
Rudy, 4729, 5600
Rudy's Rock, 2341, 4590
Ruff An' Tuff, 2222
Ruff Disco, 5457

Ruff Neck Soldier, 2765
Ruff Ruff, 2022
Ruffneck, 3537
Rufus Is A Tit Man, 5670
Rule The Nation, 5559
Ruler Of My Heart, 5401
Rules And Regulations, 5739
Rules Of Love, 4063
Rum, 1012
Rum And Rodeo, 3864
Rum Bumper, 2576
Rum-Bar Stylee, 2995
Rumba Rhapsody, 3776
Rumble, 5771, 5924
Rumble On Mersey Square South, 5881
Rumbón Mélon, 3702
Rumor Has It, 5679
Rumors, 1281
Rumors Are Flying, 936, 959
Rumours, 1107, 1354, 1356, 1757, 2276, 3027, 4406, 4466, 5872
Rumours Are Flying, 183, 475, 3492
Rump Shaker, 5925
Rumplestiltskin, 3407
Run, 3153
Run Around Girl, 681
Run Around Woman, 4110
Run Babylon, 3533
Run Back, 1603
Run Baldhead Run, 2727
Run Boy Run, 2452, 2916
Run Come, 4137, 4545
Run Come Call Me, 5338
Run Come Celebrate, 5325
Run Come Rally, 5945
Run Down The Man, 5426
Run Down The World, 3958, 5909
Run Fatty, 4966
Run For Home, 3251
Run Girl, 526, 681, 1721, 4713
Run Home Girl, 4713
Run Joe, 754, 1032, 1162, 2893
Run Like Hell, 4206
Run Little Girl, 1721
Run Me Down, 2526
Run Mr Nigel Run, 5404
Run Rudolph Run, 4529
Run Run, 1311, 1927, 2102, 2452, 2623, 2727, 2916, 3925, 4529, 5319, 5525, 5871
Run Through The Jungle, 1955
Run To Him, 2094, 5622
Run To Me, 450, 1602, 3758
Run To The Door, 1969
Run To The Hills, 2710
Run To You, 63, 3172, 4364, 4459
Run, Baby, Run, 1311, 3925, 5525
Run, Catch, And Kill, 675

Sending Up My Timber, 1163

Senor (Tales Of Yankee Power), 1675

Senorita, 3037, 5843

Sensation, 4228

Sensation For Strings, 2273

Sense Of Doubt, 2508

Sense Sickness, 1467

Senses, 4813

Senses Working Overtime, 5943

Sensi, 3425

Sensi Come From, 370

Sensi Crisis, 2899

Sensi Ride, 808, 1583, 5909

Sensimella, 3090

Sensimilia Babe, 765, 4466

Sensitive Heart, 5882

Sensitivity, 4042, 5502

Sensitize, 5351

Sensityzed, 1714

Sensoria, 875

Sensual Enjoyments, 5617

Sensuality, 2719

Sensurround, 5388

Sentiment, 3301

Sentimental, 1268

Sentimental Agitation, 5285

Sentimental Feelings, 2019

Sentimental Journey, 779, 1427, 3639

Sentimental Lady, 5756

Sentimental Me, 164, 2095, 4606

Sentimental Ol' You, 1537

Sentimental Reason, 4532

Sentimental Reasons, 4639

Sentimental Souvenirs, 3930

Sentimental Street, 3948

Sentinel Beast, 4822

Senza Una Donna, 6004

Separate Lives, 547, 1178

Separate Ways, 2900, 4499

Sepian Bounce, 4133

September, 1689

September Gurls, 529, 4401

September In The Rain, 2652, 3300, 4861, 5711, 5716

September Song, 180, 1103, 1658, 2591, 2884, 3045-3046, 3231, 4443, 5755

September's Sweet Child, 2598

Serenade, 336, 606, 884, 1457, 3129, 3185, 4637, 4833, 5807

Serenade For Small Orchestra, 2899

Serenade In Blue, 4058, 5711

Serenade In The Night, 2967, 3451

Serenade To A Lost Love, 2447

Serenade To The Stars, 69, 3397

Serenade To Youth, 5911

Serenata, 179, 604

Serenata d'Amore, 3451

Serenata Nortena, 2613

Serenata Ritmica, 3776

Sergeant Black, 2763

Sergeant Fury, 4820

Series Of Dreams, 1677

Serious, 17, 21, 129, 800, 1801, 1940, 2687, 2899, 3036, 5295, 5486

Serious Drugs, 635, 2145

Serious Man, 767

Serious Thing, 2165

Serious Time, 1525

Seriously, 762, 1810

Serrana, 2235

Serve Me Long, 5767

Sesame Street, 4791

Sesame's Treet, 470, 5484

Session Man, 1819, 2594

Set Adrift On Memory Bliss, 4016, 4267, 4833

Set Fire To Me, 1181

Set Him Free, 1419

Set It Off, 3417

Set Me Apart, 3324

Set Me Free, 2231, 3023, 3950, 4371, 4527

Set My Heart On Fire, 4400

Set The Controls For The Heart Of The Pelvis, 69

Set The Controls For The Heart Of The Sun, 409, 4247, 4249

Set The Stage Alight, 5740

Set Up Yourself, 5504

Set You Free, 3970

Set You Free This Time, 868, 1100, 5528

Set Your Face At Ease, 3832

Set Yourself Free, 3781

Settin' By The Fire, 4469

Settin' The Woods On Fire, 1625, 4651, 5846

Setting Sun, 1042, 1523

Settle Down Girl, 4110

Settle Down In A One-Horse Town, 5720

Settle For Me, 2871

Seul Sur Son Etoile, 442

Seven & Seven Is, 1353

Seven And A Half Cents, 4488

7 And 7 Is, 3334

Seven Ate Sweet, 2926

Seven Beers With The Wrong Woman, 2937

Seven Bridges Road, 5980

Seven Daffodils, 1045

Seven Day Weekend, 4277, 4897

Seven Days, 660, 725, 857, 1316, 2137, 3598, 4866, 5911

Seven Days And One Week, 4293

Seven Days Of Crying Makes One Weak, 2389

Seven Drunken Nights, 1639

750, 4431

747 (Strangers In The Night), 4759

720 In The Books, 69, 4756

Seven Into The Sea, 2687

Seven Letters, 3010

Seven Little Girls, 3684

Seven Little Girls Sitting In The Back Seat, 292, 651, 1793, 2533

Seven Lonely Days, 660, 725, 857, 1316, 2137

Seven Nights To Rock, 476, 3836

Seven Old Ladies Locked In A Lavatory, 712

7 Reasons, 4512

Seven Seas Of Rhye, 4380-4381

7 Seconds, 3867

777 Expansion, 1617

7-6-5-4-3-2-1 (Blow Your Whistle), 1218

Seven Spanish Angels, 3900, 4799, 4906, 4799, 4906

Seven Steps To Heaven, 1869, 5537

728 Texas, 3543

7 Ways To Love, 1156

Seven Years With The Wrong Man, 3365

Seventeen, 476, 1621, 1963, 3202, 5617, 5884

17, 2776

Seventeen Tons, 5495

Seventeeth Summer, 1060

Seventh Son, 3381, 4559

75 Years In Indiana, 3296

74-75, 1207

77 Sunset Strip, 3670

Seventy-Six Trombones, 2185, 2998, 30123852, 4317, 5869

Severance, 5376

Sex Daze, 656

Sex 4 Daze, 656

Sex And Drugs And Rock And Roll, 721, 1661, 3453

Sex Beat, 4239

Sex Bomb Baby, 1940

Sex Crazy Baby, 76

Sex Drive, 1750

Sex Machine, 671, 2030, 4973

Sex Maniac, 4431

Sex Pot, 5682

Sex Shooter, 209

Sex Sux (Amen), 5616

Sex Without Stress, 277

Sexappeal, 2123

Sexdrive, 4863

Sexercise Pts 1 & 2, 2748

Sexorcist, 5685

Sextet, 1323, 2258, 5420

Sexthinkone, 4896

Sexual, 5564

Sexual Healing, 1788, 2104-2105, 2254, 3477, 3524, 3657, 4545, 4696

Sexual Prime, 3504

Sexuality, 419, 708, 1584

Sexually Free, 1165, 2661

Sexy, 3508, 5583, 5904

Sexy Cream, 1859, 5762

Sexy Eiffel Towers, 683

Sexy Eyes, 200, 1655

Sexy Gal, 3302

Sexy Gale, 2082

Sexy Lover, 3631, 4383

Sexy Mama, 3734

Sexy MF, 4332

Sexy Ways, 353

Sgt Rock (Is Going To Help Me), 5943

Sgt. Early's Dream, 696

Sh-boom, 954, 1070, 1291, 1396, 1510, 2021, 2980, 3503

Sha La La, 3437

Sha La La La Lee, 3369, 3806, 4261

Sha-La-La-La-Lee, 3471, 4897, 4973, 4897, 4973

Shabby Old Cabby, 2473

Shack Up, 25

Shackin Up, 3501

Shackles And Chains, 4067, 5995

Shaddai Children, 5641

Shaddap You Face, 1576, 5570

Shades Of A Blue Orphanage, 5790

Shades Of Blue, 3914, 4254

Shades Of Hudson, 111, 2623

Shades Of Orange, 1758

Shadow Captain, 1307

Shadow Dancing, 1137, 2136

Shadow Is Light, 2666

Shadow Of The Wasp, 4673

Shadow Waltz, 1982, 2185, 4299, 4534

Shadow-Line, 1938

Shadowed, 1895

Shadows, 1920

Shadows And Reflections, 58

Shadows Of My Mind, 1797

Shadows On the Moon, 2923

Shadows On The Sand, 68

Shady Grove, 5774

Shady Grove Blues, 1985

Shady Lady, 4255

Shaft, 5968

Shagging In The Streets, 3450

Shake, 1221, 2083, 2404, 2949, 4076, 4836, 6057

Shake 'N' Stomp, 1362

Shake A Hand, 65, 1083, 1993, 3792

Shake A Leg, 3782

Shake A Tail Feather, 1878, 1916, 4048, 4368

Shake And Fingerpop, 5681

Shake Baby Shake, 4428
Shake Down The Stars, 1436, 5606
Shake Hands, 1499
Shake Holler & Run, 2586
Shake It, 3518, 3538
Shake It And Break It, 2805, 4159
Shake It Easy Baby, 4156
Shake It Off With Rhythm, 227, 780
Shake It Up Tonight, 3355, 3369, 3576
Shake It Well, 1619
Shake Me, 571, 1084, 2218
Shake Me I Rattle, 5923
Shake My Tree, 1263
Shake Rattle And Roll, 22, 105, 2341, 4591, 5357, 5529
Shake Sherry, 1215, 1852, 2218
Shake That Rump, 3310
Shake That Tambourine, 2394-2395
Shake The Sugar Tree, 5437
Shake With Me, 571
Shake You Down, 39
Shake Your Body, 4275
Shake Your Body (Down To The Ground), 2754
Shake Your Groove Thing, 4173
Shake Your Head, 4071
Shake Your Head From Side To Side, 884
Shake Your Hips, 4967
Shake Your Love, 2141
Shake Your Mini, 4895
Shake Your Money, 2725
Shake Your Moneymaker, 2771
Shake Your Rump, 4160
Shake Your Rump To The Funk, 372
Shake Your Tambourine, 3458
Shake Your Thang, 4725
Shake, Rattle And Roll, 22, 105, 2341, 4591, 5357, 5529
Shakedown, 2636, 4815
Shakermaker, 3964, 4008
Shakin' All Over, 995, 1480, 2041, 2306, 2986, 3317, 4667, 5377
Shakin' Street, 3539
Shakin' The Blues Away, 493, 1785
Shaking Story, 2058
Shaking The Blues, 4169
Shaking The Blues Away, 153, 1692, 3337, 3669, 5997
Shakiyla (JHR), 4281
Shakti (The Meaning Of Within), 3749
Shall I Carry The Budgie Woman?, 656
Shall I Take My Heart And Go?, 2192
Shall We Dance?, 807, 2367,

2997, 4607, 5366
Shall We Take A Trip, 3975
Shallow, 2465
Shalom, 3668
Sham, 4758
Shame, 1717, 3014, 4709, 4754
Shame (Whole Heart Howl), 2113
Shame And Scandal, 5473
Shame On Me, 377, 1363
Shame On The Moon, 4815
Shame On You, 1223, 1393, 4625, 5859
Shame Shame, 3407
Shame Shame Shame (On You Miss Roxy), 1085
Shame, Shame On Me, 1363
Shame, Shame, Shame, 1172, 3221, 3225, 5357
Shameless, 755, 4645
Shamrocks And Shenanigans, 2608
Shang A Doo Lang, 4295
Shang I, 1062
Shang-A-Lang, 420, 1250, 3483
Shanghai, 1237
Shanghai Lil, 1369, 1638, 1965, 5710
Shanghai Rooster, 1058
Shanghai Surprise, 720
Shanghai-Di-Ho, 205
Shangri-La, 1374, 1990
Shannon, 981, 4832
Shanti, 2860
Shape Of My Heart, 5336
Shape Of Things To Come, 1333, 3523
Shapes Of Things, 3621, 5951
Share My Love, 1756
Share The Land, 2307
Share Your Love, 359, 2166, 2637, 2701, 2899
Sharing You, 1173, 5622
Shark Out Deh, 2576
Sharp Dressed Man, 1732, 6007
Sharpen Up Your Knives, 4367
Sharpen Your Wits, 2108
Shashamane City, 3210
Shatter, 4864
Shattered, 4631
Shattered Dreams, 2838
Shaunty O'Shea, 4989
Shauri Yako, 4058
Shavin' My Neck, 2113
Shaving Cream, 460, 1817
Shaw Nuff, 4134
Shazam, 443, 1702, 2452, 4755
She, 300, 1192, 1693, 3076, 4434
She Ain't Gonna Do Right, 4031
She Aint Nothing But The Real Thing, 4919

She Bangs The Drums, 5378
She Believes In Me, 857, 4622
She Belongs To Me, 3507, 3897, 3936
She Blinded Me With Science, 1576
She Bop, 3139, 4860
She Called Me Baby, 2153, 2615, 4527
She Came From Fort Worth, 118, 3057
She Came In Through The Bathroom Window, 435
She Can Put Her Shoes Under My Bed (Anytime), 1652
She Can See The Angels Coming, 2421
She Cheats On Me, 375
She Comes In Colours, 1353
She Could Shake The Maracas, 5464
She Could Toodle-Oo, 3925
She Cracked, 3727
She Didn't Know (She Kept On Talking), 5713
She Didn't Say Yes, 5435
She Doesn't Cry Anymore, 4867
She Don't Have To See You, 4157, 5981
She Don't Know I'm Alive, 1181
She Don't Know She's Beautiful, 2978
She Don't Let Nobody, 1008
She Don't Use Jelly, 1925
She Don't Wanna, 5523
She Done Give Her Heart To Me, 2777
She Dreams, 1047
She Drives Me Crazy, 1894
She Even Woke Me Up To Say Goodbye, 3926
She Finally Spoke Spanish To Me, 1750
She Gave Her Heart To Jethro, 2353
She Goes Down, 1613
She Goes Walking Through My Mind, 5677
She Gonna Marry Me, 1472
She Got The Goldmine (I Got The Shaft), 4476
She Has A Girlfriend Now, 4481
She Is His Only Need, 5938
She Is My Daisy, 3137
She Is Not Thinking Of Me, 3197
She Just A Draw Card, 4976
She Just Satisfies, 1962, 4100
She Just Started Liking Cheating Songs, 177
She Left Love All Over Me, 333
She Left Me On A Friday, 4862

She Lied To Me, 4034
She Likes Basketball, 4348
She Likes To Dance, 4372
She Lives With Me, 3196
She Loves Me, 638, 4860
She Loves Me Just The Same, 1225
She Loves Me Now, 2368
She Loves Me, She Loves Me Not, 3974
She Loves My Cock, 2754
She Loves The Jerk, 1191
She Loves The Rub A Dub, 2765
She Loves You, 433, 2724, 4282
She Loves You - Yes Siree, 1977
She Makes My Day, 4112
She Means Nothing To Me, 1798
She Moved Through The Fair, 1826, 3141, 3585, 3795, 4922
She Must Be A Witch, 3299
She Needs Love, 1963
She Never Lets It Go To her Heart, 3575
She Never Spoke Spanish To Me, 1750, 2373, 2829, 4718, 5348
She Picked It Up In Mexico, 128
She Put The Hurt On Me, 4336
She Quit Me, 5996
She Reminds Me Of You, 2216, 4511, 5739
She Said, 76, 3310
She Said She Said, 434, 4353
She Said Yeah, 661
She Said Yes, 101
She Say Oom Dooby Doom, 1510
She Sells Sanctuary, 1328
She Shot A Hole In My Soul, 1337, 2021
She Smiled Wild, 3703
She Talks To Angels, 554
She Taught Me Everything There Is To Know About Poultry, 1090
She Taught Me How To Yodel, 651, 4572
She Taught Me To Yodel, 136
She Thinks I Still Care, 2872, 3172, 4315
She Thinks That She'll Marry, 4609
She Told Me Lies, 3496
She Too Young, 4794
She Twists The Knife Again, 5413
She Understands Me, 5438
She Used To Call Me, 1392
She Want A Phensic, 6005
She Wanted A Little Bit More, 4188

Sitting In La La, 5434
Sitting In The Park, 1742, 1837
Sitting On A Log, 1203
Sitting On Top Of The World, 2620
Sitting Tenant, 5387
Sitting There Standing, 4551
Sitting There That Night, 1938
Situation-Wise, 2724
Siva, 2163
Six, 1769, 5455
Six & Seven Books Of Moses, 1569
6am Jullandar Shere, 1237
Six Celan Songs, 3990
Six Day Rock, 401
Six Days On The Road, 416, 1336, 1643
Six Flats Unfurnished, 3425
Six Guns, 203
Six Hours On The Cross, 2788
Six Lessons From Madame La Zonga, 3736
Six Million Ways To Die, 2053
Six Months Out Of Every Year, 1370
Six More Miles, 3998
Six Nights A Week, 1291
Six Nights And Seven Days, 4396
6 O'Clock, 5555-5556
Six Or Seven Times, 896
Six Sixth Street, 852, 3345, 3465
Six String Poet, 483, 4500
634-5789, 1947, 3050
Six Times A Day, 1336
Six White Horses, 981, 3760
Sixpence, 4638
Sixteen, 3012, 3853
Sixteen (Into The Night), 5522
16 Candles, 752, 1291, 3404
16 Dreams, 3311
Sixteen Tacos, 5495
Sixteen Tons, 878, 1493, 1973, 1977, 2547, 2563, 3112, 4736, 5495
Sixteen Years, 2793
16th Avenue, 1366, 4710
Sixty Days & Sixty Nights, 99
68 Guns, 106
65 Love Affair, 1417
Sixty Minute Man, 1636, 2315, 5698
Sixty Minute Teaser, 1148
60 Minutes Of Your Love, 368
69, 1343, 1860
69 Année Erotique, 544
61 Storm, 929
Sixty Seconds Together, 3683
Sixty To Zero, 5978

Size Of A Cow, 5906
Size Seven Round (Made Of Gold), 5309
Ska Rock, 328
Ska-ba, 3068
Ska-Core The Devil And More, 3660
Ska-ing West, 4939
Skank Bloc Bologna, 4794
Skank In Bed, 478, 1071, 2733, 2845
Skankin' Queen, 640
Skanking Easy, 4096
Skanking On The Banking, 1063
Skanless, 3006
Skate Now, 1259
Skateboard, 4468
Skateboard Romance, 518
Skeleton, 2474, 2721
Sketch Of A Dandy, 5911
Skettel Concerto, 808
Ski Surfin' Sanctuary, 3169
Skid Row, 3272
Skid Row Joe, 2420
Skin, 1695, 4955
Skin Deep, 468, 1554, 2462, 5635
Skin Her Alive, 1543
Skin It A Go Peel, 1183
Skin On Skin, 4194
Skin Tight, 5290
Skin To Skin, 2403
Skinhead Moon Stomp, 4374
Skinhead Train, 99
Skinned, 594
Skinnin' A Cat, 4368
Skinny Dip (Got It Goin' On), 1701
Skinny Legs And All, 5347
Skinny Lizzie, 190
Skinny Minnie, 1339
Skins, 1784
Skip A Rope, 935
Skip Away, 2424
Skip The Gutter, 5858
Skipping Along, 2447
Skirt Lifter, 818
Skoda Lasky, 2166
Skokiaan, 3479, 4304
Skokiian, 1992
Skopul, 1784
Skweeze Me Pleeze Me, 4959
Sky Blue And Black, 792
Sky Gone Grey, 640
Sky High, 2822
Sky Juice, 2138
Sky Rocket, 2708
Skylark, 942, 1700, 2563, 3630, 4889
Skylarking, 188, 1569, 4335, 4957
Skylight, 3788
Skyline, 4241
Skyline Pigeon, 1220, 2833
Skyliner, 389, 3766
Skyride, 1499

Skyscraper Fantasy, 4222
Skyway, 4507
Slack, 304, 550, 2114, 2222, 4334
Slackness Style, 4431
Slam, 453, 1817, 2958
Slam Country, 2959
Slam Dance, 1313, 3825
Slam Fashion, 1817
Slam Of The Century, 1817
Slap That Bass, 4841
Slaphead, 3536
Slaughtahouse, 3505
Slaughter In The Vatican, 1941
Slaughter On Tenth Avenue, 346, 646, 2959, 4042, 4467, 4606, 5632, 5919
Slave, 4333
Slave Annie, 68
Slave Ship, 2685
Slave Ships, 740
Slave To Love, 1879
Slave To The Rhythm, 2873, 5276, 6004
Slavery Days, 840
Slaves (Don't You Know My Name?), 4783
Slaves No More, 607
Slaving, 773, 4139-4140
Sledgehammer, 2067, 4964
Sleep, 676, 3464
Sleep Baby Sleep, 2346, 4180, 4603, 4605
Sleep Freak, 2469
Sleep Of The Just, 3002
Sleep Walk, 1158, 1933, 4746
Sleep Well Tonight, 2112
Sleep With Me, 5502
Sleep's Dark And Silent Gate, 792
Sleep, Baby, Sleep, 2346, 4180, 4603, 4605
Sleeper, 278, 4068, 4148
Sleepin' Single In A Double Bed, 3436
Sleepin' With The Radio On, 3550
Sleeping Bag, 4168, 6007
Sleeping Beauty, 2937
Sleeping Gas, 5324
Sleeping Satellite, 218-219
Sleepwalk, 5570
Sleepy Eyed John, 268
Sleepy Head, 3683
Sleepy Maggie, 3389
Sleepy Marionette, 5840
Sleepy Time, 4469
Sleepy Time Gal, 282, 843, 5805
Sleepy Town, 614
Sleigh Bell Ride, 3113
Sleigh Ride, 179, 1895, 2192, 3113
Sleng Teng Finish Already, 5448
Slick, 2949, 5544

Slid, 1948
Slide, 3358
Slide Some Oil On Me, 5898
Slide's Derangement, 2372
Slight Return, 630
Slim Thing, 5504
Slip Away, 966, 4006, 4204, 4918
Slip In Mules, 1490
Slip Of The Tongue, 1857
Slip Slide, 640
Slip Sliding Away, 4204
Slip-In Mules, 1039
Slipped Her The Big One, 1379
Slipped Tripped And Fell In Love, 4179
Slippery When Wet, 1193
Slippin' And Slidin, 4327
Slippin' Around, 3783, 4186, 5438, 5518, 5672, 5805, 5923
Slipping Away, 2636, 3638, 4869
Sliver, 3957
Slogan On The Wall, 5641
Sloop Dance, 5639
Slop Time, 4877
Sloppy Heart, 2018
Slot Machine, 1586
Sloth, 1827
Slow And Easy, 384
Slow And Sexy, 2147
Slow Boat To China, 307, 1970, 2161, 3091
Slow Burning Fire, 2139
Slow But Sure, 93
Slow Country Dancing, 331
Slow Dancin' Don't Turn Me On, 73
Slow Dancing, 331, 1652
Slow Daze, 4726
Slow Death, 1924
Slow Down, 1690, 3665, 5853
Slow Down And Cool It, 4231
Slow Fizz, 4746
Slow Freight, 805
Slow Hand, 4271
Slow It Down, 1690
Slow Jam, 5588
Slow Jerk, 3169
Slow Love, 4746
Slow Mood, 3672
Slow Motion (Part 1), 5853
Slow Poison, 2836
Slow Poke, 1927, 2439, 4651
Slow Tongue (Working Your Way Down), 2748
Slow Train To Dawn, 1047
Slow Twistin, 1583
Slow Walk, 283, 1574
Slower, 216
Slowly, 1446, 2714, 4240, 4417
Slowly The Day, 3407
Slowpoke, 3017
Sluefoot, 1355, 3630

So You Want To Be A Rock 'N' Roll Star, 868
So You Win Again, 355, 2601
So You're The One, 579
So Young, 2379
So-o-o-o-o In Love, 5906
So. Central Rain, 4394, 4459
Sobbin' Women, 1438, 3630, 4825
Sobredosis, 399
Soca Rhumba, 4618
Societally Provoked Genocidal Contemplation, 1807
Society's Child, 2666, 3800
Socio-Genetic Experiment, 1546
Sock It To Me, Baby, 1292
Soda Fountain Rag, 1735
Sodom In Jamaica, 4431
Sodomy, 2337
Soft, 3336, 4285, 4352
Soft And Warm, 3865
Soft And Wet, 4331
Soft As Spring, 5830
Soft Lights And Sweet Music, 493, 1818
Soft Shoe, 3836
Soft Summer Breeze, 1510, 1670, 2513
Softly As I Leave You, 3743, 5460
Softly As In A Morning Sunrise, 1457, 1703, 2366, 3916, 4637, 5372
Softly Awakes My Heart, 3148
Softly In The Night, 5421
Softly Whispering I Love You, 1204, 1218, 4132
Softly, As I Leave You, 3743, 5460
Softly, As In a Morning Sunrise, 1457, 1703, 2366, 3916, 4637, 5372
Softly, Softly, 3847, 4574
Soho, 5791
Soko Soko, 3150, 4346
Solace, 4796
Solace I, 2891
Solace II, 2891
Solar System, 4806
Sold, 3754
Sold American, 2034
Sold Out, 422, 2086
Soldier And Police War, 2761
Soldier Baby, 915
Soldier Boy, 1846, 1990, 4450, 4768
Soldier Of Love, 114, 4073
Soldier Round The Corner, 2761
Soldier Take Over, 5767, 5955
Soldier's Blues, 2530
Soldier's Joy, 3395
Soldier's Last Letter, 5518

Soldier's Prayer in Viet Nam, 3482
Soldier's Return, 3120
Soldiers Joy, 4924
Soldiers Of Peace, 1308
Soldiers Of The Queen, 996, 5917
Soldiers Who Want To Be Heros, 3588
Soldiers' Gossip, 4151
Soley Soley, 3655
Solid Air, 3494-3495
Solid As A Rock, 4875, 5936
Solid Glass Spine, 281
Solid Gold Easy Action, 1487, 5277
Solid Potato Salad, 1438, 4449
Solid Rock, 2177, 3420
Solidarity, 3622, 5608
Soliloquy, 604, 946-947, 4416, 4607, 5911
Solitaire, 714, 5709, 5836
Solitary Ashtray, 2697
Solitary Confinement, 3622
Solitary Lovers, 1882
Solitary Man, 1508, 4139-4140, 4871
Solitary Party Groover, 1633
Solitary Stranger, 1960
Solitude, 1436, 2199, 2344, 4265
Solitude Book, 4783
Solo, 555, 731, 1385, 1484, 1506, 2272, 2803, 2936, 3089, 3163, 3872, 4254, 4380, 4640, 4688-4689, 4828, 5798
Solo Flight, 3839
Solo Na Mutsai, 1499
Solomon, 2403, 3848, 3990, 4289, 5757
Solomon Grundy, 4235
Solomon Song, 5426
Solomon's Day, 740
Som'thin' From Nuthin, 740
Sombrero, 989
Some Bartenders Have The Gift Of Pardon, 1719
Some Bright Morning, 1946
Some Broken Hearts Never Mend, 5843
Some Candy Talking, 2817
Someday, 934, 1687, 1898, 2310, 2736, 2805, 3748, 3948, 3956, 4186, 4192, 4619
Some Day, 2037, 2725, 2752, 5592
Some Day My Prince Will Come, 1543
Some Day We're Gonna Love Again, 4799
Some Days Are Diamonds, 857
Some Days Everything Goes Wrong, 5782
Some Do, Some Don't, 2142

Some Enchanted Evening, 726, 1195, 2367, 2790, 4607
Some Find Love, 2524
Some Fools Never Learn, 5703
Some Girls, 4398, 5568
Some Girls Are Bigger Than Others, 418
Some Got It, Some Don't, 5910
Some Guys Have All The Luck, 4038, 4112, 4204, 4327, 5522
Some Have, Some Have Not, 2237
Some Justice, 1898, 4619
Some Kind Of Love, 5902
Some Kind Of Trouble, 5525
Some Kinda Fun, 3753
Some Kinda Woman, 5488
Some Like It Dread, 1622
Some Like It Hot, 4303
Some Little Girl, 4021
Some Memories Just Won't Die, 4568
Some Might Say, 4008
Some Misunderstanding, 4849
Some Of Shelly's Blues, 3959
Some Of These Days, 125, 746, 758, 4159, 4648, 5523
Some Of Us Belong To The Stars, 538, 565
Some Old California Memory, 935
Some Other Guy, 530, 998
Some Other Spring, 3038
Some Other Time, 1191, 4041
Some People, 1455, 2324, 3635, 4450
Some Sing Some Dance, 4103
Some Sort Of Somebody, 5638
Some Sunday Morning, 2447
Some Sweet Day, 2725, 2752
Some Sweet Someone, 2928, 4680
Some Things Just Stick In The Mind, 5616
Some Things You Never Get Used To, 2770
Some Velvet Morning, 2452, 3359, 4931, 5391
Some Women Do, 5647
Somebody, 63, 924, 2488, 4459
Somebody (Somewhere) Needs You, 368
Somebody Always Paints The Wall, 3297
Somebody Bad Stole De Wedding Bell, 3039, 3788
Somebody Changed The Lock On My Door, 5758

Somebody Did All Right For Herself, 356
Somebody Done Hoodooed The Hoodoo Man, 2893
Somebody Done Stole My Cherry Red, 5647
Somebody Else Is Taking My Place, 3787
Somebody Else's Guy, 5590
Somebody Else's Sweetheart, 5695
Somebody Help Me, 1420, 1710, 5545
Somebody Is Lying, 1551
Somebody Knew, 101
Somebody Lied, 4866
Somebody Loan Me A Dime, 4582
Somebody Loves Me, 1439, 2128, 4519, 5802
Somebody Loves You, 2289, 4516
Somebody Paints The Wall, 3149, 3297
Somebody Please Help Me, 5545
Somebody Put Something In My Drink, 3644
Somebody Should Leave, 2615, 3566
Somebody Somewhere, 3805
Somebody Stole My Gal, 1247, 2283, 2488, 4446, 5753
Somebody Stole My Synthesiser, 2137
Somebody To Love, 26, 90, 288, 2259, 2687, 2802, 3117, 3409, 4381, 4966, 5737
Somebody Touched Me, 3052
Somebody's Baby, 792
Somebody's Been Sleeping, 3432, 4045
Somebody's Changing My Sweet Baby's Mind, 4762
Somebody's Gonna Do It Tonight, 369
Somebody's Gonna Love You, 2278
Somebody's Gotta Win, Somebody's Gotta Lose, 1215
Somebody's Love, 2979
Somebody's Lying, 588
Somebody's Thinking Of You Tonight, 3446
Somebody's Watching Me, 4600
Someday, 934, 1687, 1898, 2310, 2736, 2805, 3748, 3948, 3956, 4186, 4192, 4619
Someday (You'll Want Me To Want You, 744
Someday Baby, 3861, 5367
Someday I Suppose, 3660
Someday I'll Be Saturday

South African Man, 643
South America, Take It Away, 894, 1495, 2093, 4637, 4645
South American Joe, 2035
South American Way, 1607, 1639, 2962, 3580, 3701
South By South West, 3671
South California Purples, 1055
South Carolina Rag, 5684
South Of The Border, 158, 1356, 1888, 2967, 3492
South Rampart Street Parade, 417, 2335
South Street, 211, 900, 4063
South To A Warmer Place, 3573
South To Louisiana, 126
South Wind Of Summer, 1930
Southbound Special, 2171
Southend, 5574
Southend On Sea, 1719
Southern California, 688
Southern California Wants To Be Western New York, 5842
Southern Comfort, 1608
Southern Freeze, 2026
Southern Grace, 3274
Southern Holiday, 2348
Southern Home, 540
Southern Humoresque, 4880
Southern Loving, 777, 4086
Southern Man, 88, 1998, 3374, 5977
Southern Nights, 905
Southern Rag, 592
Southern Rains, 5436
Souvenir, 3549
Souvenir De Granada, 2078
Souvenir Of Love, 4719
Soweto, 4969
Soweto Trembles, 2941
Sowing The Seeds Of Love, 5324
Space (He Called From The Kitchen), 2725
Space And Time, 3866
Space Bass, 1859, 5762
Space Funk, 1637, 4422, 4576
Space Guitar, 5730
Space Hopper, 5542
Space Is The Place, 3719, 4553
Space Oddity, 685-686, 1642, 4748, 5653
Space Plucks, 3020
Space Race, 4316
Space Station No. 5, 3757
Space Time, 3866
Spaceball Ricochet, 5376
Spaceman, 312, 1994, 4201
Spacer, 1053
Spain, 2875
Spanglish, 1886

Spanish Blues, 1813
Spanish Castle Magic, 294
Spanish Dance Suite, 1174
Spanish Eyes, 3493
Spanish Eyes (Moon Over Naples), 2922
Spanish Flea, 147
Spanish Harlem, 2916, 3010, 3186, 4746
Spanish Heart, 1717
Spanish Lace, 1995, 4277, 4897
Spanish Omega, 111
Spanish Stroll, 3694
Spanish Two Step, 5866
Spare Chaynge, 87
Sparkle, 1795, 4268, 5543
Sparklin' Look Of Love, 2105
Sparkling Blue Eyes, 3417
Sparky's Dream, 2237, 5329
Sparrow, 1783
Sparrow In The Tree Top, 183, 3636, 3711, 3913
Spasticus Autisticus, 1661
Spastik, 2443
Speak Low, 4047, 5755
Speak No Evil, 5578
Speak Now Or Forever Hold Your Peace, 4495
Speak Softly Love, 3493, 4660
Speak The Truth, 3838, 4494
Speak To Me Pretty, 3170
Speak Your Mind, 189
Speaking Of Happiness, 3373
Speaking Of The Weather, 2185, 2386
Spear Burning, 840
Special, 824, 920, 2870, 3711
Special Brew, 321
Special Care, 3133
Special Delivery Stomp, 4854
Special Guest, 924
Special Kind Of Love, 954
Special Lady, 1910, 4445
Special Occasion, 1460
Special Request To The Manhattans, 2019
Special Train To Pankow, 3251
Specialization, 3204, 3747
Spectre Versus Rector, 1616
Speed Freak, 3722
Speed King, 1458, 1636
Speed Of The Sound Of Loneliness, 943, 2291, 4339
Speed Your Love To Me, 4921
Speedo Is Back, 880
Speedoo, 880, 1284
Speedy Gonzales, 668, 2125
Speeed King, 5387
Spencer The Wild Rover, 3026
Spend My Money, 2841

Spend One Night In A Babylon, 3005
Spend Some Time, 5726
Spend The Night, 1223
Sperm, 310
Sperm Rod, 4923
Spice, 1768
Spicks And Specks, 449
Spiders And Snakes, 464
Spike Heeled Shoes, 852
Spike Milligan's Tape Recorder, 3622
Spikee, 2913
Spill The Wine, 826, 5697
Spilled Perfume, 5437
Spin, 1922
Spin That Wheel, 5326, 5945
Spin The Black Circle, 4175
Spin The Wheel, 4621
Spinal Meningitis, 5754
Spinning, 3311
Spinning Around, 556
Spinning Around (I Must Be Falling In Love), 3416
Spinning Rock Boogie, 838
Spinning Wheel, 600-601, 1119
Spiral Dance, 469
Spirit Body And Soul, 3969
Spirit In The Dark, 2013
Spirit In The Sky, 1566-1567, 2273, 2756, 5871
Spirit Of America, 2846
Spirit Of Love, 189
Spirit Of Radio, 4691
Spirit Of Summer, 1486
Spirit Of The Falklands, 3916
Spirits In The Material World, 371, 4274
Spiritual High, 3016, 3758
Spiritual Thang, 474
Spirituals For Orchestra, 2224
Spiritus, 2317
Spiritwalker, 1328
Spit In The Rain, 1467
Spit In The Sky, 1569, 4199
Spitfire Prelude And Fugue, 5694
Splanky, 274, 2472
Spliff Tail, 4110
Splish Splash, 1032, 1390, 1618, 1775
Spo-Dee-O-Dee, 838, 4138
Spoil The Child, 1810
Spoilt By Your Love, 3168
Spoin Kop, 4593
Sponono, 4227
Spontaneous Apple Creation, 767
Spooks, 3663
Spooky, 271, 1111, 2682, 5679
Spooky Ookum, 606
Spoon, 1714
Spoonful, 1556, 4924
Sposalizio, 3805

Spot The Lights, 395
Spray, 2059
Spread A Little Happiness, 1588, 1744-1745, 2285, 3824
Spread Love, 200, 2030
Spreadin Honey, 5732
Spring, 357, 543
Spring Fever, 604
Spring Is Here, 2661, 4606, 4814
Spring Will Be A Little Late This Year, 3293
Spring, Spring, Spring, 1438, 3630, 4825
Springtime For The World, 607
Springtime Suite, 1139
Sprinkle Me, 1681
Spy In The House Of Love, 5714
Spy vs Spy, 4390
Spybreak, 4349
Square Bash, 3670
Square Biz, 3462
Square Room, 5384
Squaws Along The Yukon, 3226, 4226, 5410
Squeeze Box Boogie, 1043
Squeeze Her Please Her, 5874
Squeeze Me, 4639, 5688, 5858
St Jago De La Vega, 4966
St Lawrence Suite, 2224
St Louis Blues Mambo, 3425
St Louis Shuffle, 2437
St. Andrew Fall, 594
St. Columbia's Hymn, 3585
St. Elmo's Fire (Man In Motion), 4144
St. George And The Dragonet, 2021
St. James Infirmary, 1208, 1233, 2198, 4101
St. John's Shop, 5739
St. Louis, 1695, 5703
St. Louis Blues, 545, 782, 894, 2377, 3141, 3674, 3683, 4595, 4750, 5359, 5723
St. Louis Cyclone Blues, 894
St. Olav's Gate, 2291, 2952
St. Paul's Walking Through Heaven With You, 1098
St. Pierre, 2384
St. Stephen, 206
St. Swithin's Day, 1640
St. Therese Of The Roses, 5618, 5698
St. Thomas, 4761
St. Tropez, 1561
Stab Up De Meat, 3106
Stack Is Back, 1568
Stack O'Lee Blues, 4781
Stack-O-Lee, 220, 4323
Stadium House, 2916
Stage Coach, 5887
Stagefright, 594
Stagger Lee, 2775, 5535
Stainsby Girls, 4452

Stairway, 1499
Stairway Of Love, 2563, 4568
Stairway To Heaven, 668, 1621, 2388, 2413, 3165-3166, 4348, 4393, 4808
Stairway To The Stars, 307, 2962, 3091, 4130, 4903
Stalactite, 3198
Stalag, 2114, 2930, 5338
Stalag 17, 4546
Stamina, 1880
Stamina Man, 2584
Stamp, 4293
Stamp Out Loneliness, 2751
Stan' Up And Fight, 941
Stand, 2263, 4394, 5386
Stand And Deliver, 62
Stand Back, 3686, 3943, 5661
Stand Beside Me, 1446
Stand By Me, 306, 423, 1087, 2007, 2153, 3010, 3186, 3192, 4009, 4948, 5509
Stand By Your Man, 772, 3345, 3370, 4876, 5747, 5936
Stand Down Margaret, 430
Stand In For Love, 4002
Stand On My Own Two Knees, 688
Stand Tall, 1331
Stand Up, 360, 2839, 4364, 4723
Stand Up And Fight, 4886, 6000
Stand Up For Your Love Rights, 437, 5952
Stand Up Strong, 3758
Stand!, 3186
Standin' At The Big Hotel, 2373
Standing Around Crying, 530
Standing By The River, 216
Standing In The Rain, 4080, 4821
Standing In The Road, 571
Standing In The Shadows, 5848
Standing In The Shadows Of Love, 2561
Standing On Guard, 1835
Standing On The Corner, 1993, 2296, 2998, 3012, 3294, 3484, 3805
Standing On The Top, 5335
Standing Ovation, 2066
Standing Proud, 3138
Standing Room Only, 314, 3436
Standing Tall, 857, 3786
Standing Up, 1170
Stanislavsky, 2945
Star, 349, 605, 759, 1454, 1867, 2550, 4978, 5890
Star 69, 3749
Star Dust, 4130

Star Eyes, 1438, 3820
Star Love, 4268
Star Over Parvati, 1592
Star Quality, 2227
Star Spangled Banner, 2491, 4411
Star Tar, 1369
Star Wars Theme, 3607
Star Wars/Cantina Band, 5851
Star-Studded Sham, 2477
Starburst, 1893
Stardust, 941-942, 1160, 1279, 1780, 2444-2445, 2516, 2810, 2875, 3131, 3336, 4237, 5333, 5698, 5928, 5986
Starfish And Coffee, 4902
Staring At The Embers, 1898
Staring At The Rude Boys, 4703
Starlight, Starbright, 1437
Starman, 685
Starrclub, 5802
Starry Crown Blues, 4890
Starry Eyed, 2563
Starry Eyes, 4459
Stars, 188, 904, 923, 1063, 1569, 1640, 2219, 2456, 4139-4140, 4958, 5291
Stars And Stripes At Iwo Jima, 5866
Stars And Stripes Forever, 536
Stars And Stripes Of Corruption, 1442
Stars Are The Windows Of Heaven, 164
Stars Fell On Alabama, 820, 3300, 4130, 4957, 5322
Stars N' Stripes, 2241
Stars Over Bahia, 713
Stars Shine In Your Eyes, 2535
Stars, Stars, Stars, 518
Starship, 2803
Starship Trooper, 5382
Starsign, 5328
Starsky And Hutch, 790, 1761, 5314
Start, 1717, 2767
Start Afresh, 559
Start Me Up, 4631
Start Moving (In My Direction), 3689
Start Off Each Day With A Song, 1658
Start Talkin' Love, 3412
Start Today, 5642
Starting Again, 1910
Starting All Over Again, 2403, 3615
Starting On A Journey Feels Like A Freesia, 3514
Starvation, 2188
Starve The City (To Feed The Poor), 1727
Starving To Death, 5902

State Occasion, 1851
State Of Grace, 5488
State Of Independence, 178
State Of Self-Decline, 2064
State Of Shock, 673, 2754
State Of The Art, 2036, 2301, 3486
Stately As A Galleon, 2282
Statement, 4272
Statesboro Blues, 3601, 4553, 5642
Stateside, 5436
Static Airplane Jive, 2308
Static Friendly, 1273
Stating A Fact, 3950
Station HOBO Calling, 4484
Statue Of A Fool, 2274
Statue Of Snow, 4428
Statues, 2646
Statues & Liberties, 2631
Statues Without Hearts, 2099
Stavin' Chain, 647
Stay, 792, 854, 1497, 1563, 1782, 3252, 4023, 4128, 4838, 4944, 5574, 5856
Stay (Don't Walk Away), 750
Stay (I Missed You), 3293
Stay A Little Bit Longer, 1761
Stay A Yard And Praise God, 1247
Stay Another Day, 1690
Stay As Sweet As You Are, 2216, 4511
Stay At Home Papa, 5953
Stay Away From Cali, 2081
Stay Away From Me, 3119
Stay Away From My Baby, 5319
Stay Away From The Apple Tree, 688
Stay Awhile, 467, 720
Stay Beautiful, 3442
Stay Free, 2164
Stay In My Corner, 1474, 1936
Stay Loose Mama, 1784
Stay On The Right Side Of The Road, 603
Stay On The Right Side Sister, 3054
Stay Out Of Automobiles, 3543
Stay People Child, 211
Stay Pon Guard, 4923
Stay Well, 3322
Stay With Me, 613, 1091, 1718, 1746, 1819, 3187, 3706
Stay With Me (Death On The Dole), 1692
Stay With Me Baby, 3757, 4407, 4495, 4652, 5534, 5677
Stay With Me Till Dawn, 5557
Stay With The Happy

People, 2532
Stayin' Alive, 450, 1114, 5934
Stayin' In, 3325
Staying Alive, 3318, 4752
Staying Out For The Summer, 1572
Staying Together, 2141
Staying Young, 5284
Steady As She Goes, 2446
Steady Date, 5421
Steady Eddie Steady, 1856
Steady F. King, 3537
Steal Away, 1956, 2628, 2731, 3522
Steal Your Fire, 2312
Stealin' Apples, 2623
Steam, 1690
Steam Heat, 4102, 4106
Steamboat, 1627
Steamboat Bill, 4602
Steamboat Row, 4405
Steaming Train, 5290
Steamy Windows, 5801
Steel Claw, 706
Steel Guitar Rag, 2427, 2480, 3541, 5743, 5866
Steel Guitar Stomp, 4189
Steel Guitar Tango, 904
Steel Guitar Wiggle, 904
Steel Man, 5809
Steel Orchards, 3323
Steel Rail Blues, 2360
Steel Rails, 3075
Steel Strings, 974
Steeling The Blues, 866
Steeling The Chimes, 866
Steevo, 4826
Stella, 2767, 4393
Stella By Starlight, 3674, 5719, 5982
Step Aside, 2287, 5970
Step Aside Shallow Waters, 3929
Step By Step, 752, 1291, 3190, 3404, 4396, 4918
Step Down, 1106
Step In The Right Direction, 5516
Step In Time, 3499
Step Inside Love, 564
Step Into A Dream, 5793
Step Into Lite, 5276
Step Into My Life, 1756
Step Into My Shoes, 4486
Step Into My World, 2645
Step Into The Projects, 3887
Step It Brother Clem, 852, 3465
Step It Down A Shepherds Bush, 4431
Step It In A Freedom Street, 790
Step It Up Youthman, 767
Step Off, 3617
Step On, 2384, 3060, 4244
Step On The Gas, 3018
Step Out, 3086
Step Out Of Your Mind, 161

Strange Cargo, 4958
Strange Dream, 4465
Strange Enchantment, 3293
Strange Fruit, 167, 2067, 2557, 3932
Strange Girl In Clothes, 290
Strange Kind Of Love, 3335
Strange Kind Of Woman, 1458, 3401
Strange Land, 2049
Strange Little Girl, 4713
Strange Love, 1285, 2030, 4475
Strange Love Affair, 1596
Strange Museum, 5761
Strange Things, 1569, 4475
Strange Walking Man, 3436
Strange Way, 1902
Strange Young Girls, 3427
Stranger, 1651, 2032
Stranger At The Door, 1162
Stranger In A Strange Land, 569, 2711, 5528
Stranger In Love, 1107, 2700, 4514
Stranger In Moscow, 2543
Stranger In My Home Town, 4514
Stranger In My House, 4495
Stranger In Paradise, 480, 1236, 1988, 2990, 3033, 3492, 4956, 5930
Stranger In The House, 2872
Stranger In Town, 5439
Stranger On Home Ground, 1829
Stranger On The Shore, 536, 1071, 2266, 2714, 5989
Stranger Than Fiction, 4400, 5752
Stranger Things Have Happened, 3687
Strangers Again, 1655
Strangers In The Night, 2922, 4928
Stranglehold, 5566
Strato Cruiser, 3364
Straw Hat In The Rain, 103
Strawberries Are Growing In My Garden, 1485
Strawberry Fair, 2672, 3926
Strawberry Fields Forever, 434, 915, 2635, 3409, 3619, 4353, 4629, 4689, 5843
Strawberry Roan, 529
Strawberry Samba, 4022
Strawberry Shortcake, 2791
Strawberry Tea, 2177
Strawberry Wine, 488, 3858
Stray, 1633
Stray Cat Blues, 3676
Streamline Cannonball, 692
Streamline Train, 5650, 5815
Streamlined Yodel Song, 3254
Streams Of Whiskey, 4270
Street Corner Serenade,

3623, 5779
Street Fighting Man, 3676, 4630-4631
Street Hassle, 4921
Street Justice, 4416
Street Life, 1282, 1318, 2814, 4669, 4730
Street Lover, 541
Street Of Dreams, 3004, 3225, 5533, 5982
Street Player, 810
Street Player - Mechanik, 1856
Street Scenes From My Heart, 5794
Street Singer, 61, 3971, 5929
Street Songs, 1942
Street Spirit (Fade Out), 5354
Street Talk, 1292, 3516
Street Tuff, 4458
Street Walkin' Daddy, 2288
Street Waves, 4193
Street-Walkin' Daddy, 1429
Streets And Alleys, 2697
Streets Of Baltimore, 377, 2615, 5460
Streets Of Derry, 5498
Streets Of Greenspoint, 1880
Streets Of Hell, 3626
Streets Of London, 202, 2034, 3602
Streets Of New York, 3063, 5696
Streets Of Paradise, 4297
Streets Of Your Town, 2176
Stress, 2930, 4059
Stretch, 3524
Strictly USA, 1705, 5284
Strike Up The Band, 2117
Strike While The Iron Is Hot, 1994
String Along, 164, 3896
String Around My Heart, 1121
String Of Diamonds, 3546
String Of Pearls, 474, 2253, 2329
String Quartet From Whiskey Boot Hill, 5977
String Quartet In D Major, 1401
Stringmusic, 2224
Strings Of Life, 3526, 5326, 5491
Strings Of Love, 732
Strip City, 3204
Strip Me Down, 281
Strip Polka, 183, 3004, 3091, 3629, 4958
Stripped Me Naked, 3823
Stripped To The Bone, 404
Stripper Vicar, 3450
Strive, 4882
Strobelite Honey, 3775
Stroke It, 2603
Stroke You Up, 1016
Strokin, 2450

Stroll On, 607
Strollin' On, 4327
Strolling In The Park, 1012
Strong Enough, 1311
Strong Enough To Be Gentle, 558
Strong Enough To Bend, 3946, 5524
Strong Love, 2888, 4282
Strong Survive, 4494
Strong Woman, 4878
Strong Woman Number, 2664
Stronger Than Before, 2660, 4716
Struggle In Babylon, 648
Struggling In A Babylon, 1605
Strut, 1596
Strutter, 5580
Stubborn Kind Of Fellow, 2103, 3480, 4061
Stuck In The '90s, 3822
Stuck In The Middle With You, 265, 1714
Stuck On You, 4257
Stuck With You, 3218
Stuff Like That There, 3656
Stuff That Works, 1101
Stumblin' Blocks, Steppin' Stones, 230
Stumblin' In, 4379
Stumbling, 1204, 5802
Stumpy, 2437
Stupid Cupid, 2006, 4808
Stupid Girl, 2084, 4629, 6005
Stupid Thing, 5783
Stupidity, 909, 5316, 5575
Stutter, 1452
Stutter Rap, 3790
Style, 541, 940, 1107, 3408, 4250, 4341, 4401, 4644, 5607, 5920
Style Wars, 2526
Stylee, 1913
Styrofoam, 3312, 5552
Su Su Pon Rasta, 2138
Su-i-side, 1149
Suavecito, 3233, 3424
Sub Rosa Subway, 3040
Subculture, 3918
Subhuman, 2084
Sublime, 3248
Substitute, 3117, 5811
Substitute Lover, 1525, 2343
Subterranean Homesick Blues, 741, 1583, 1673, 2578, 3951, 4396
Suburban Girl, 2112
Suburbia, 4205
Subway Song, 3419
Success, 908, 3370, 4408
Success Is The Word, 663, 3452
Such A Good Feeling, 762, 1541
Such A Merry Party, 3267
Such A Night, 1615, 1627,

1748, 1775, 2396, 4446
Such A Small Love, 4782, 5682
Such A Sweet Thing, 5765
Such Is Life, 3316
Such Sweet Thunder, 1736
Suck'n'Swallow, 2388
Sucker MCs, 987, 2678, 4347, 4687
Sucu Sucu, 2849, 3320, 3951
Suddenly, 173, 2042, 4919
Suddenly He's Gone, 765
Suddenly It Happens, 4969
Suddenly It's Spring, 830, 5607
Suddenly Last Summer, 3806
Suddenly Seymour, 3272
Suddenly There's A Valley, 1102, 2243, 3147
Suddenly You Love Me, 5499
Suds And Soda, 1498
Sue Me, 578, 1567, 2322, 3294
Sue's Gotta Be Mine, 4846
Suedehead, 3797, 5654
Sueno, 5516
Sueño Latino, 3526
Suffer The Children, 3873
Sufferation, 5319
Sufferer Of The Ghetto, 1261, 4675
Suffering On The Land, 1783
Suffocated Love, 3524
Suffragette City, 5374
Sufriendo Penas, 4516
Sugar And Spice, 1321, 2429, 4799
Sugar Babe, 768, 1224, 5972
Sugar Baby Love, 1354, 4678
Sugar Baby Parts 1 & 2, 4301
Sugar Bee, 917, 4938
Sugar Blues, 3556
Sugar Bridge, 620
Sugar Candy Kisses, 3037
Sugar Cane, 1106
Sugar Cane County, 793
Sugar Coated Love, 3154
Sugar Daddy, 2574, 4751, 4807, 4751, 4807
Sugar Foot Stomp, 2437, 2930
Sugar Frost (Azucare), 4097
Sugar Hill, 299
Sugar Honey Ice Tea, 2207
Sugar Love, 1354, 2888, 3154, 4678
Sugar Mama, 5300
Sugar Me, 1438
Sugar Mountain, 3712, 5977
Sugar On Sunday, 1132
Sugar Pantie, 4137
Sugar Pie Guy, 2889
Sugar Plum, 5350, 5669
Sugar Plum Plum, 5669
Sugar Rappin, 3617

Take Me Home, Country Roads, 1485, 2687, 3934, 4490
Take Me I'm Yours, 1077, 3593
Take Me In The Lifeboat, 3417
Take Me In Your Arms, 2561, 5777
Take Me In Your Arms And Hold Me, 129, 5679
Take Me On The Merry-Go-Round, 989
Take Me Or Leave Me, 4505
Take Me Out To The Ball Game, 1359, 3976, 5284, 5659
Take Me To Alabam, 5453
Take Me To That Midnight Cakewalk Ball, 43
Take Me To The Hotel Johanna (And Let's Trash The Joint), 916
Take Me To The Mardi Gras, 1277, 4918
Take Me To The Next Phase, 2720
Take Me To The River, 2856, 3194, 4952, 5287
Take Me To Your Heart Again, 2531
Take Me Up, 3016, 4037
Take Me With U, 209
Take Me, Take Me, 980
Take My Breath Away, 492, 525, 1087
Take My Hand, 2687, 4872, 5436
Take My Heart, 713, 3493
Take My Love, 2935
Take My Ring Off Your Finger, 3218
Take Off, 3585
Take Off Some Time, 5421
Take On Higher, 6006
Take On Me, 33, 4481
Take On The World, 2907
Take That, 1537, 4848
Take That Look Off Your Face, 565, 3284, 5746
Take That Situation, 2512
Take The 'A' Train, 1477, 3873
Take The High Ground, 5719
Take The High Road, 4908
Take The Long Way Home, 721
Take The Moment, 1563
Take The Money And Run, 68, 1949, 3947
Take The Skinheads Bowling, 909
Take These Chains From My Heart, 3728, 4419, 4651, 5847
Take This Job And Shove It, 1149, 4169
Take This Time, 3413

Take Time To Know Her, 4963, 5787
Take To The Mountains, 4386
Take You To The Dance, 3425
Take Your Chance, 2050
Take Your Girl, 3007, 3979
Take Your Hand Out Of Your Pocket, 3795
Take Your Hands Off My Heart, 4243
Take Your Memory With You, 2147
Take Your Partner By The Hand, 4577
Take Your Partners For The Waltz, 1745
Take Your Shoes Off Moses, 2788
Take Your Time, 2296, 3724, 4851
Take Your Time (Do It Right) Part 1, 4710
Take Your Time And Take Your Pick, 4259
Take Your Time, Yeah!, 3137
Taken For A Ride, 1960
Taken My Love, 3507
Takes Two To Tango, 332, 2549, 3448
Takin' Care Of Business, 316
Takin' Miss Mary To The Ball, 4989
Takin' Retards To The Zoo, 1442
Taking A Chance On Love, 625, 876-877, 1647, 4928
Taking Off, 782, 1023
Taking The Heart Out Of Love, 1473
Taking The Sun From My Eyes, 298
Tales From The Crack Side, 2920
Tales Of Brave Aphrodite, 431
Tales Of Brave Ulysses, 1546, 5667
Tales Of The Three Blind Mice, 540
Talk, 4235
Talk About Love, 2962, 4137, 4306
Talk About Love/First The Girl, 4306
Talk Back Trembling Lips, 256, 2546, 3325, 5438
Talk Dirty To Me, 3310, 4272
Talk In Toytown, 4276
Talk Of The Town, 3798, 4318, 4431, 5432
Talk Talk, 243, 3852, 5286
Talk Talk Talk, 3104
Talk To An Angel, 5693
Talk To Her, 518

Talk To Me, 1451, 1476, 2153, 2657, 3310, 4272, 4944, 5823
(Talk To Me Of) Mendocino, 2939
Talk To Me Lonesome Heart, 4001
Talk To Me, Baby, 3630
Talk To Me, Talk To Me, 2153, 2835
Talk To The Animals, 733, 1418, 1567, 3927
Talk To Your Daughter, 3194
Talk To Your Heart, 4324
Talkative Toes, 5425
Talkin' 'Bout A Revolution, 1022
Talkin' About The Love I Have For You, 2741
Talkin' All That Jazz, 2685
Talkin' Baseball, 981
Talkin' Silver Cloud Blues, 2440
Talkin' To My Heart, 579
Talkin' To Myself, 3409, 5753
Talkin' To The Wrong Man, 3841
Talkin' Vietnam Pot Luck Blues, 4168
Talking About The Good Times, 4319
Talking About The Man, 2851
Talking Back To The Night, 2814
Talking Boogie, 5859
Talking Facts, 1341
Talking In Your Sleep, 1218, 1221, 2106, 3567, 3844, 4636
Talking John Birch Paranoid Blues, 1332
Talking John Birch Society Blues, 1672
Talking Like a Man, 5411
Talking Off The Wall, 653
Talking Parrot, 4120
Talking The Teenage Language, 3322
Talking To Hank, 1047
Talking To The People, 70
Talking To The Walls, 3390
Talking With Myself, 1723
Tall 'n' Handsome, 4126
Tall A Tree, 5842
Tall Cool One, 4260, 5668
Tall Dark Stranger, 725
Tall Oak Tree, 838
Tall Paul, 195
Tall Ships, 4894
Tall Tale, 3163
Tall Tall Grass, 2423
Tall Trees, 2736
Tallahassee Lassie, 918, 1292
Tally Ho!, 1119
Tallyman, 445, 2225
Talon, 5394

Talula, 5490
Tam Lin, 1826
Tam Tam Pour Ethiopie, 5720
Tamalpais High, 2674
Tambo, 4614
Tame The Lion, 4520
Tammy, 164, 2183, 3281, 4516
Tampico, 923, 1076, 1909, 3122, 4626
Tan Ta Ra, 3722
Tanga, Rumba-Afro-Cubana, 3428
Tangerine, 897, 1598, 1697, 1867, 1933, 3165, 3630, 4100, 4769, 4866
Tangled Mind, 2708
Tangled Up In Blue, 1675-1676
Tango In D, 3147
Tango In The Night, 3451
Tango Maureen, 4505
Tango Of The Bells, 3491
Tango-Ballad, 5426
Tank Park Salute, 2560
Tansy, 5766
Tantalise (Wo Wo Ee Yeh Yeh), 2825
Tantra, 5326
Tantric Trance (Animus), 5661
Tantric Wipeout, 5684
Tap Dance Concerto, 2224
Tap The Bottle, 5574
Tap Turns On The Water, 1001, 3066
Tap Your Troubles Away, 3389
Tape Loop, 3777
Tapestry, 456
Tappin' Off, 896
Tar, 5652
Tar And Cement, 1576
Tara, 1825
Tara's Theme, 1094, 1401, 1657
Tarbelly & Feather Foot, 5860
Tarzan Boy, 3728
Taste Of India, 3953
Taste Of Rain, 4410
Taste Of You, 3733
Taste Your Love, 774
Tasty Fish, 4076
Tasty Love, 2740
Tattle Tale Eyes, 5970
Tattva, 2919, 3085
Tatty Seaside Town, 3622
Taxi, 1019-1020
Taxi Blues, 3270
Taxi War Dance, 5976
Taxman, 434, 2415
TB Blues, 1255
TCB, 1099, 4490
Tchaikovsky, 2945
Tchaikowsky, 2130
Te Compro Tu Novia, 4062
Te Estoy Estudiando, 4032

1888, 2345, 3176, 3384, 5896
That Old Gang Of Mine, 1555, 2489, 4650
That Old Piano Roll Blues, 5617
That Old Soft Shoe, 646
That Old Sweet Roll (Hi De Ho), 3011
That Old Sweet Song, 4003
That Ole Devil Called Love, 1909, 2280, 3822
That Once A Year Feeling, 932
That Piano Track, 2913
That Reminiscent Melody, 178
That Rhythm Man, 2197
That Ring On Your Finger, 1495
That Road Not Taken, 1522
That Rock Won't Roll, 1537, 4509
That Same Old Feeling, 3384
That See Me Later Look, 4372
That Set The West Free, 4083
That Shirt, 3605
That Silver Haired Daddy Of Mine, 286, 982
That Sounds Good, 2825
That Summer, 118
That Terrific Rainbow, 4107
That Thing You Do!, 1988
That Was A River, 4449
That Was Nearly Us, 2802
That Was Yesterday, 1846, 3668
That Wild And Wicked Look In Your Eye, 3941
That Woman's Got Me Drinking, 3387
That Wonderful Sound, 1565
That'll Be Me, 5864
That'll Be The Day, 816, 1292, 1310, 2568, 4100, 4215, 4377, 4641, 5352
That'll Be The Last Thing, 2608
That'll Show Him, 2056
That's A Crime, 2709
That's A Lie, 5464
That's A No No, 180
That's A Plenty, 2930
That's All, 982, 1973
That's All I Want From You, 3784
That's All Right, 563, 621, 1317, 2695, 4062, 4568, 4620
That's All Right (Mama), 4309
That's All There Is To That, 1992
That's Alright, 1748, 4301
That's Amore, 3484, 5711

That's Enough, 4584
That's Enough For Me, 5857
That's Entertainment, 361, 1520, 2298, 4776
That's For Me, 578, 2447, 3736, 5857
That's Him, 4047
That's How A Love Song Was Born, 842
That's How Heartaches Are Made, 5716
That's How I Feel, 62, 3428
That's How I Got My Start, 3037
That's How I Love The Blues, 506
That's How I Need You, 3547
That's How It Goes, 720
That's How It Is, 4048
That's How It Is (When You're In Love), 1114
That's How Love Is, 3543
That's How Much I Love You, 2001, 3556, 5818
That's How Strong My Love Is, 2194, 2684, 4470, 4936, 5929, 5981
That's How You Know When Love's Right, 5703
That's How Young I Feel, 3428
That's Just The Way It Is, 3536
That's Just The Way It Is To Me, 1829
(That's Just My Way Of) Forgetting You, 2695
That's Just Too Much, 26
That's Life, 2857, 4296
That's Love, 1350, 4606
That's Me, 540, 578, 2447, 3137, 3484, 3542, 3736
That's Me Without You, 2777
That's My Baby, 1992
That's My Biography, 2227, 3779
That's My Desire, 1017, 3111, 4820
That's My Doll, 3106, 5617
That's My Girl, 1406
That's My Home, 536, 2197
That's My Kind Of Love, 5923
That's My Little Suzie, 5594
That's My Pa, 5918
That's My Story, 4449, 5457
That's My Weakness Now, 2932
That's Nice, 1074
That's Not Cricket, 266
That's Right, 563, 621, 1317, 1458, 2695, 4062, 4568, 4620
That's Rock And Roll, 984
That's Show Biz, 5927
That's That, 2853
That's The Chance I'll Have

To Take, 2812
That's The End, 872
That's The Joint, 2053
That's The Kind Of Woman, 196
That's The Reason Noo I Wear A Kilt, 3137
That's The Rhythm Of The Day, 1376
That's The Stuff You Gotta Watch, 2844
That's The Thing About Love, 3187
That's The Time She Go Love You, 1817
That's The Way, 2582, 3165
That's The Way (I Like It), 2949
That's The Way All My Money Goes, 1299
That's The Way God Planned It, 210, 1200, 4316
That's The Way I Feel About Cha, 5905
That's The Way I Like It, 1443
That's The Way I Love, 955
That's The Way I've Always Heard It Should Be, 4917
That's The Way It Could Have Been, 5936
That's The Way It Is, 1681, 3536, 3614, 5443
That's The Way Love Goes, 1512, 2040, 4613
That's The Way Love Is, 2805, 3614, 3869, 5336
That's The Way Of The World, 1350, 1481
That's The Way The Money Goes, 1299, 5501
That's The Way The Money Grows, 932
That's What Friends Are For, 314, 1545, 2943, 3122, 4716, 4876, 5441, 5713, 5843
That's What Girls Are Made For, 1496
That's What Her Memory Is For, 338
That's What I Call Love, 540
That's What I Get For Loving You, 5420
That's What I Like, 2825, 3281
That's What I Like About The South, 1863, 2412, 4181
That's What I Like About The West, 5859
That's What I Like About You, 5953
That's What I Tell My Heart, 2075
That's What I Told Him Last Night, 1886
That's What I Want, 3456
That's What I Want for Christmas, 3466, 4235, 5333

That's What I Want For Janie, 1164
That's What I Want To Be, 4495
That's What It's Like To Be Lonesome, 173
That's What It's Like To Be Young, 4565
That's What Life Is All About, 4478
That's What Love Is, 2617
That's What Love Is All About, 650
That's What Love Will Do, 777, 3268
That's What Made Me Love You, 3319
That's What Makes Paris Paree, 885
That's What Makes The Juke Box Play, 364
That's What The Blues Is All About, 3008
(That's) What The Nitty Gritty Is, 1743
That's What You Always Say, 3358
(That's What You Do) When You're In Love, 1975
That's What You're Doing To Me, 5698
That's What Your Love Does To Me, 1655
That's When I Cried, 2877
That's When She Started To Stop Loving You, 2964
That's When The Crying Begins, 179
That's When The Music Takes Me, 4809
That's When Your Heartaches Begin, 4309
That's Where My Baby Used To Be, 980
That's Where The South Begins, 1959
That's Why (I Love You So), 1404, 5874
That's Why Darkies Are Born, 780
That's Why I Love You, 251
That's Why I Love You Like I Do, 2777
That's Why I'm Crying, 2730
That's Why The Poor Man's Dead, 4220
That's Worth Waiting For, 326
That's Your Mistake, 1033
Thats All, 2116
(The) Girl Don't Care, 1014
The Girl I Left Behind Me, 3201
The Look Of Love, 39, 314, 1080, 3626, 5368
The Moon Was Yellow, 93, 3201
The Most High, 1080

About Goodbye, 331
There's A Lovely Lake In London, 1794
There's A Lull In My Life, 2216, 4511
There's A Man Who Comes To Our House Every Single Day (Poppa Comes Home And The Man Goes Away), 958, 4305
There's A Moon Out Tonight, 925
There's A Mother Waiting For You At Home, Sweet Home, 5417
There's A New Face In The Old Town, 1994
There's A New Moon Over My Shoulder, 1410, 4555
There's A New Moon Over The Old Mill, 5931
There's A New World, 2967
There's A Quaker Down In Quaker Town, 843
There's A Rainbow 'Round My Shoulder, 4650, 4934
There's A Reward, 2520
There's A Rising Moon (For Every Falling Star), 1824, 5965
There's A Small Hotel, 554, 646, 4042, 4107, 4606
There's A Star Spangled Banner Waving Somewhere, 744
There's A Sucker Born Ev'ry Minute, 390, 1165
There's A Tear In My Beer, 5847
There's A Telephone Ringing, 753
There's A Time And A Place For Everything, 993
There's A World, 2967
There's Always A Happy Ending, 713, 2549
There's Always Me, 3652, 4593
There's Always Room At Our House, 3711
There's Always Something Fishy About The French, 1216
There's Always Something There To Remind Me, 314, 1401, 2261, 2851, 4857
There's Always Tomorrow, 809, 1022, 1744, 3888, 4426
There's Beauty Everywhere, 5998
There's Danger In A Dance, 1202
There's Danger In The Waltz, 2967
There's Danger In Your Eyes, Cherie, 4535
There's Gonna Be One Hell Of A Storm, 305
There's Got To Be A Better

Way, 3866
There's Got To Be A Word, 2929
There's Gotta Be Something Better Than This, 1165, 1886, 5633
There's Honey On The Moon Tonight, 1228, 3315
There's Life In The Old Girl Yet, 1031
There's More To Life Than This, 1451
There's More To Love, 1194
There's More To The Kiss Than XXX, 694
There's Never Been Anything Like Us, 1374
There's No Business Like Show Business, 197, 210, 361, 494, 2447, 3634
There's No Deeper Love, 4553
There's No Fool Like An Old Fool, 3649
There's No Getting Away From You, 249
There's No One With Endurance Like The Man Who Sells Insurance, 1318
There's No Other (Like My Baby), 1322
There's No Other Way, 632, 1965
There's No Place Like Your Arms, 645
There's No Reason In The World, 3668
(There's) No Room To Rhumba In A Sports Car, 2050, 3449
There's No Tomorrow, 2549, 3492
There's No-One Quite Like Grandma, 730
There's Not One Thing, 1992
There's Nothing Else To Do In Ma-La-Ka-Mo-Ka-Lu But Love, 2035
There's Nothing I Won't Do, 2917
There's Nothing Like A Song, 3808, 3865
There's Nothing Like This, 5287
There's Nothing Too Good For My Baby, 920
There's Nothing Wrong With A Kiss, 3206
There's Nowhere To Go But Up, 1703, 3046
There's Only One Of You, 1993
There's Only One Union, 3406
There's Poison In Your Heart, 1123
There's Room In My Heart For Them All, 3054

There's So Much I'm Wanting To Tell You, 2383
There's Something About A Lady, 1651
There's Something About A Soldier, 1258, 2102
There's Something About A Uniform, 1152
There's Something About An Empty Chair, 1370
(There's Something About An) Old Fashioned Girl, 780
There's Something About You, 4235
There's Something At The Bottom Of The Well, 3764
There's Something In That, 3649
There's Something In The Air, 69, 1888, 3580
There's Something Spanish In Your Eyes, 2035
There's Something Wrong With You, 2436
There's Yes! Yes! In Your Eyes, 997, 2035
There, I've Said It Again, 2334, 2962, 3748, 5648
There, There My Dear, 1502
Therese, 640
Thermodynamically Yours, 2233
These Are My Children, 1837
These Are Not My People, 5760
These Are The Days, 1242, 4623
These Are The Good Old Days, 4623
These Are The Laws, 5557
These Arms Of Mine, 4470
These Boots Are Made For Walking, 489, 5822
These Charming People, 5446
These Crazy Thoughts, 3390
These Days, 791, 2673, 3239, 4394, 5387
These Dreams, 2458, 4101
These Early Days, 2673
These Eyes, 2307, 2622
These Foolish Things, 713, 1516, 2137, 3499, 5698, 5961, 5976
These Golden Rings, 2825
These Hands, 3663, 3965, 5897
These Lonely Hands Of Mine, 5436
These Old Heavy Burdens, 1554
These Things Are Worth Fighting For, 4576
These Thousand Hills, 5719
They Ain't Makin' Jews Like Jesus Anymore, 2034
They All Fall In Love, 4289
They All Laughed, 2129-

2130, 4841
They All Look Alike, 2432, 5900
They All Start Whistling At Mary, 1246
They All Went To Mexico, 3900
They Always Follow Me Around, 5720
They Always Pick On Me, 5660
They Call Him A Bum, 2992
They Call Him Boxcar Willie, 1971
They Call It Dancing, 493, 3850
They Call It Democracy, 1144
They Call It Making Love, 702
(They Call Me) A Wrong Man, 1109
They Call Me Guitar Shorty, 2310
They Call The Wind Maria, 384, 3196, 3294, 3464, 4105
They Came In Peace, 1807
They Can't Fool Me, 2726
They Can't Take That Away From Me, 383, 659, 1732, 2129-2130, 4841, 4928, 5521
They Didn't Believe Me, 730, 2975, 3128, 3266, 4021, 5435, 5463, 5937
They Die, 170, 1766
They Died With Their Boots Laced, 1438
They Don't Care About Us, 2543
They Don't Know, 1706, 3385
They Don't Make Them Like That Any More, 3152, 4219
They Don't Make Them Like They Used To, 314
They Don't Need Another Fuehrer, 3251
They Fell, 299
They Go Wild, Simply Wild, Over Me, 3548
They Hold Us Down, 4644
They Like Ike, 494, 893
They Long To Be Close To You, 4295
They Met In Rio, 5350
They Only Come Out At Night, 4888
They Reminisce Over You (T.R.O.Y.), 4593
They Saved Hitler's Cock, 192
They Say, 4704
They Say It's Wonderful, 197, 494, 1195, 3634, 4695
They Shoot Horses Don't They, 4399
They Suffocate At Night, 4363

True Believer, 2765, 5871
True Blue, 3403
True Blue Gil, 2410
True Blue Lou, 4580
True Born African, 2763, 2787
True Companion, 1155
True Confessions, 1567, 5799
True Experience, 4336
True Faith, 3918
True Friends, 3794
True Grit, 565
True Groove Thing, 525
True Life Country Music, 333
True Love, 118, 1062, 1130, 1454, 2522, 3180, 3347, 4289, 4300
True Love (You Took My Heart), 1795
True Love And Apple Pie, 1220
True Love Goes On And On, 2729
True Love Is A Treasure, 5635
True Love Tends To Forget, 1675
True Love Ways, 816, 1780, 2153, 2569, 4206, 5357
True Religion, 827
True To Me, 1766
True To The Game, 1449, 3538
True True True, 4137
Truly, 1569, 2588, 3528, 4535
Truly Scrumptious, 1066
Trumpet No End, 341
Trumpet Sorrento, 289
Trumpet Tarantella, 289
Trust, 808, 3890, 5909
Trust In Me, 91, 469, 1532, 1545, 2772, 5357
Trust Me, 91, 469, 1532, 1545, 2637, 2740, 2772, 2890, 4119, 5357, 5643
Trust The Book, 863
Trust Your Mechanic, 1442
Trusting My Luck, 4719
Truth & Rights, 1063
Truth Is Marching On, 134
Truth Must Reveal, 2727
Truth Of Self Evidence, 3044
Truthfully, 1458
Try, 772, 2890
Try A Little Sunshine, 1820
Try A Little Tenderness, 1207, 1785, 3821, 3937, 4077, 5915
Try Again, 1012, 1605, 5665
Try Again Tomorrow, 4606
Try Again, Johnny, 1253
Try And Love Again, 2604
Try For The Sun, 1828
Try Hard, 677
Try It, 4021

Try It Baby, 2218
Try Jah Love, 5393
Try Just A Little Bit Harder, 1746
Try Love Again, 1605, 2604
Try Me, 526, 775, 3359, 3522, 4860
Try Rock And Roll, 3709
Try The Impossible, 186
Try To Forget, 987, 2385
Try To Learn To Love, 5397
Try To Remember, 164, 1388, 1845, 4054, 4770
Try To See It My Way, 1369, 1555, 5931
Try To Understand, 848
Tryin, 464, 955, 1259, 2269, 2662, 3122, 3443
Tryin' To Find My Woman, 1259
Tryin' To Forget About You, 3122
Tryin' To Get Over You, 2662
Tryin' to Get The Feeling Again, 3443
Tryin' To Get To You, 955, 2662
Tryin' To Hold On, 2269
Trying, 1601, 2534, 5621
Trying To Beat The Morning Home, 4871
Trying To Hold Onto My Woman, 1611
Trying To Live My Life Without You, 1114, 2741
Trying To Love Two Women, 4006
Trying To Make A Fool Out Of Me, 1471
Trying To Make You Love Me, 5717
Trying To Rope The Wind, 1083
Trying To Satisfy You, 1601
Tschaikowsky, 3105
TSOP, 2839, 3651, 5422
Tu Le Regretteras, 442
Tu Loco Loco, Y Yo Tranquilo, 4617
Tú Solo Tú, 4817
Tu-Li Tulip Time, 1248, 2473
Tu-Sheng-Peng, 790
Tubby, 665, 3428
Tubby The Tuba, 2945
Tubby's In Full Swing, 3006
Tube Disasters, 1948
Tubthumping, 1081
Tubukula Beach Resort, 5454
Tubular Bells, 717, 4346
Tuck Me To Sleep In My Old 'Tucky Home, 3649
Tuesday Sunshine, 4384
Tuesday's Dead, 5325
Tuesday's Gone, 4348
Tufaan, 2265
Tuff, 918, 2514, 4685

Tuff Scout, 3611
Tulane, 501, 2137
Tulips And Heather, 725
Tulips From Amsterdam, 862
Tulsa Telephone Book, 2353
Tulsa Time, 1345, 2051, 5843
Tumba La Caña, 3180
Tumbleweed, 4210
Tumbling Tumbleweeds, 958, 1338, 3607, 3969, 4541, 4750, 5807
Tune In Light Up, 3981
Tune In, Turn On, Drop Out, 1860
Tune Up/Voice Mail No. 1, 4505
Tunnel Of Love, 2050, 3420, 5527
Tuntuneco, 1240
Tupelo County Jail, 5436
Tupelo Honey, 5354
Turbo Charge, 648
Turkey Buzzard Blues, 200
Turkey In The Straw, 356, 2979, 4575, 4587
Turkey Lurkey Time, 3583
Turkish Bath, 1741
Turn And Stab, 1944
Turn Around, 4196
Turn Around And Take A Look, 3189
Turn Around, Look At Me, 5655
Turn Back, 3678
Turn Back The Clock, 2838
Turn Back The Hands Of Time, 1114, 1422, 1908, 3222
Turn Back Time, 213
Turn Back The Years, 2550
Turn Blue, 3364
Turn Down Day, 1345
Turn It Loose, 2908
Turn It On Again, 1645
Turn It Up, 183, 1557, 5326
Turn Me Loose, 1816, 2605, 3344, 4277
Turn Me Loose And Let Me Swing, 4188
Turn Me On, Turn Me Off, 2581
Turn Me Out, 1342, 2002
Turn Me To Love, 5806
Turn Me Up, 399
Turn Of The Century, 2182
Turn Off The Lights, 4184
Turn Off Your Light, Mr. Moon-Man, 421, 3976
Turn On A Friend, 4174
Turn On The Heat, 780
Turn On The Love-light, 2553
Turn On the Moon, 69
Turn On The Music, 2102
Turn On The Night, 3034
Turn On The Old Music Box, 1544

Turn On The Red Heat (Burn The Blues Away), 151
Turn On Your Lovelight, 585, 1869, 2641, 3278
Turn On, Tune In, Cop Out, 3288
Turn Out The Lights, 2705, 5283
Turn Out The Stars, 1789
Turn The Aerials Away From England, 1500
Turn The Pencil Over, 5666
Turn The Tables, 4307
Turn Those Wheels Around, 967
Turn To Me, 4683
Turn To Stone, 5691
Turn To The Sky, 3458
Turn Up The Bass, 1558, 5555
Turn Up The Radio, 284
Turn Your Love Around, 1962
Turn Your Radio On, 101, 799, 4838
Turn! Turn! Turn!, 868
Turn Up The Beat, 222
Turnaround, 1501
Turning Japanese, 2145, 5614
Turning My Love On, 4171
Turnip Greens, 1036
Turquoise, 1590
Turquoise Tandem Cycle, 2789
Turtle Dove, 2729
Turtle Tail, 2328
Turtle-Dovey, 1374
Turvy, 1163
Tutoring, 1248
Tutti Frutti, 575, 1583, 1816, 3270, 5361
Tuxedo Junction, 397, 404, 1396, 1779, 2439, 3441, 3674, 4756
TV, 81, 4679, 5785
Twangy, 1702, 2432, 4594
Tweedle Dee, 343, 729, 2137, 4073, 5617
Tweedle Dee, Tweedle Dum, 3655
Tweedledee, 2137
Tweetie Pie, 1239
Twelfth Street Rag, 690, 2638-2639, 3580, 4181, 5468
Twelfth Street Rag Mambo, 1736
Twelve Days To Christmas, 4860
Twelve O'Clock And All's Well, 1960
12 Reasons, 3861
Twelve Thirty, 3427
12,600 Lettres A Franco, 2009
20th Century Fox, 3806
Twentieth Century Blues, 996
20th Century Boy, 5277

Twentieth Century Express, 1653
20th Century Schizoid Man, 5580
Twentieth-Century Blues, 1265
Twenty Below, 1417
Twenty Feet Of Muddy Water, 4982
21st Century Schizoid Man, 1968, 2999
25 Lovers, 4692
25 Minutes To Go, 4911
Twenty Flight Rock, 1142, 2159, 4934
24 Hour Bullshit, 3869
24 Hours, 695, 1041, 5503
24 Hours A Day, 3970
Twenty Four Hours From Tulsa, 314, 384, 1401, 4255, 5693
Twenty Four Hours Of Sunshine, 3763
Twenty Miles, 1970
20 Miles, 785
20 Million Things To Do, 3265
Twenty One Years, 3383
20-75, 3717
26 Miles (Santa Catalina), 1995
Twenty Tens, 5651
20,000 Hardcore Members, 3641
23 Minutes In Brussels, 3358
Twenty Tiny Fingers, 64
20-20 Vision, 3488
Twenty-First Century Boy, 4904
Twenty-Five Minutes To Go, 2838
Twenty-Four Hours, 2902
Twice My Age, 4432
Twiggy, 4965
Twiggy Twiggy, 4257
Twiggy Vs James Bond, 4257
Twilight, 3825
Twilight On The Prairie, 971
Twilight On The Trail, 151
Twilight Time, 3445, 4263, 5373, 5418
Twilight Zone, 2189
Twin Cadillac Valentine, 4793
Twin Engines, 593
Twin Guitar Special, 4841
Twine Time, 976, 4048
Twingy Baby, 3794
Twinkie Lee, 5679
Twinkle, 5789
Twinkle, Twinkle Little Star, 1728, 3409
Twinset And Pearls, 4341
Twist, 237, 537
Twist & Crawl, 1375, 2661
Twist & Shout, 497, 1008,

1027, 1040, 2719, 2727, 3169, 3252, 4265, 4280, 4282, 4401, 4612, 4725, 4768, 5546, 5695
Twist A San Tropez, 5330
Twist Baby, 3316
Twist In My Sobriety, 5434
Twist Of Cain, 1463
Twist Polka, 5546
Twist Twist, 655, 1008
Twist Twist Senora, 655, 5546
Twist With The Morningstars, 4625
Twist-Her, 3204
Twisted, 2254, 3713, 4656, 5365
Twistin England, 1385
Twistin' All Night Long, 5546
Twistin' Bells, 5546
Twistin' Matilda, 5546
Twistin' Postman, 3495, 5546
Twistin' The Night Away, 1221
Twistin' U.S.A., 1385, 5546
Twisting, 2512
Twisting By The Pool, 5546
Twisting The Night Away, 1040, 2070, 5546
Twitterpated, 1544
2 A.M., 4184
Two Bad Boys (Just Out Makin' Noise), 354
2 Be Reel, 1360
2,665,866,746,664 Little Devils, 5788
2014, 123
Two Bits Worth Of Nothing, 4853
Two Blue Singin' Stars, 1143
Two Bouquets, 2967
Two Broken Hearts, 1469
Two Brothers With Checks, 5569
Two Can Dream As Cheaply As One, 4528
Two Can Play, 285
Two Car Garage, 5398
2 Chairs, 237
Two Cigarettes In The Dark, 5750
Two Clouds In The Sky, 4480
Two Days, 1238, 1371
Two Different Worlds, 1657, 2535, 3784, 5758
Two Divided By Love, 2965
Two Dollar Novels, 2355, 4986
Two Dollars In The Jukebox (Five In A Bottle), 4396
Two Doors Down, 3185
Two Dozen Roses, 3540
Two Dreams Met, 1607
Two Faced Woman, 5737
Two Faces Have I, 1075
Two Fatt Guitars, 1681

Two Finger Boogie, 1327
Two Fingers Pointing At You, 4352
Two Folk Songs, 3645
2 Foot Walk, 1007
2468 Motorway, 4587
Two Friends, 3046
Two Girls From Little Rock, 2119, 3747
Two Girls In Love, 49
2 Good 2 B Bad, 2205
Two Guitars, 345, 1681
Two Gunslingers, 3917
Two Guys At Harvard, 1922
Two Headed Dog, 290
Two Hearts, 667, 1033, 1469, 3686
Two Heavens, 4480
200 Bars, 3153
Two Is Better Than Too Many, 3236
Two Ladies, 874, 2285
Two Ladies In De Shade Of De Banana Tree, 227, 2607
Two Laughing Irish Eyes, 606
Two Lesbians, 4548
Two Little Boys, 1621, 2412, 3470, 4869, 5503
Two Little Girls From Little Rock, 2119, 3747
Two Little Orphans, 3663
Two Little Rosebuds, 1552
Two Little Ships, 5901
Two Lost Souls, 1370-1371, 3784, 5632
Two Lovers, 2211, 4585, 5765
Two Make A Home, 4284
Two Mexican Pictures, 2273
Two Minute Man, 929
Two Minutes To Midnight, 2711
Two More Bottles Of Wine, 3542, 3552, 4378
Two Mules Pull This Wagon, 4698
295, 2974
Two Of A Kind, 755, 1576, 3754, 3934
Two Of Us, 435
214, 4557
Two Out Of Three Ain't Bad, 410
Two People, 307, 490, 522, 565, 942, 3091, 3293, 5689
Two People In Love, 3785
Two Princes, 4268
Two Purple Shadows, 5593
Two Sevens Clash, 1329, 5409
Two Sides To Every Story, 1109
Two Sisters, 1404
Two Six Packs Away, 1643
Two Sleepy People, 307, 522, 942, 3091, 3293, 5689
Two Spoos In An Igloo, 1893

Two Step, 2492
Two Steppin' Mind, 3575
Two Steps Forward And Three Steps Back, 127
2,000, 4677
2000 Light Years, 4956
2000 Light Years From Home, 5935
2000 Miles, 4318
2000 Years, 2019, 4956, 5441
2300 Skiddoo, 3941
Two Tickets To Georgia, 1228
Two Tickets To Paradise, 3737
Two Times I Love You, 4425
Two Timing Lover, 1856, 3168, 3195
Two Trains Running, 2841
Two Tribes, 2012, 5702, 6004
2 Wedden Skank, 773, 4335
Two Weeks Past, 4795
Two Wrongs, 4051
Two Years In The Making, 2192
Two's Company, 3460
Two-Faced Man, 1083
Two-Faced Woman, 1950
Tying The Leaves, 3357
Tyler, 1380
Type Of Loving, 3487
Typic, 5406
Typical, 2018
Typical British Workmanship, 5881
Typically English, 733, 809
Tyree's Got A Brand New House, 1558
Tyrone, 325, 4124
Tyrone's Rap, 1837
Tzena, Tzena, 1372, 2810, 3677, 4130
U Can't Touch This, 2365
U Da Man, 4978
U Don't Have To Say U Love Me, 4453
U Don't Have To Say You Love Me, 3671
U Got 2 Know, 922
U Got 2 Let The Music, 922
U Got Me Up, 886
U Got The Look, 1693, 4902
U Make Me Feel So Good, 1633
U Will Know, 1347
U.S. Male, 4315, 4476
Uamh An Oir, 3392
Uciekali, 3647
Ueo Muite Aruko, 4722
UFOrb, 363
Ugly, 3955, 4440
Ugly Child, 4142
Ugly Girl, 2688
Ugly Women And Pick-Up Trucks, 4171, 5460
Uglyman, 1363

Vivienne, 916
Vivir Sin Ella, 4739
Vivre, 2017
Vo-Do-Do-De-O Blues, 91
Você Já Foi à Bahia, 1000
Vodka, 345
Vogue, 3403
Voice In The Wilderness, 1809
Voice Mail No. 2, 4505
Voice Mail No. 4, 4505
Voice Mail No. 5, 4505
Voice Of Africa, 1541
Voice Of Liberty, 2527
Voice Of London, 5840
Voice Of The People, 559
Voice Of The Poor, 1270, 3291
Voice Of The Trade Winds, 4089
Voice Your Choice, 3522, 4399
Voices Carry, 5435
Voices In The Sky, 2686
Voices Of Old People, 664
Void, 3671, 4292
Voila An American Dream, 4264
Volare, 1618, 3484, 3493, 3729, 4130, 4705
Voodoo Chile, 1249, 1725, 2491, 4411, 4870, 5469, 5667
Voodoo Doll, 4956
Voodoo Fire, 1807
Voodoo Idol, 1548
Voodoo Ray, 28
Voodoo Woman, 1739, 2194
Voodte, 2437
Vote Elvis, 4284
Vote For Love, 962
Vote With A Bullet, 1239
Vote, Baby, Vote, 1455
Vous Qui Passez Sans Me Noir, 4711
Vow, 2084
Voyage, 3851
Voyager, 2078
Vuela La Paloma, 4616
VX Gas Attack, 4953
W-O-L-D, 1019
W. Tex. Teardrops, 4027
W.P.A. Polka, 2166
Wa Do Dem, 3144
Wabash Cannonball, 59-60, 350, 692, 960-961, 1260, 1336, 1407, 2352
Wack Wack, 5982
Wacky Dust, 68
Wade In The Water, 654, 1023, 3224, 4856, 5308, 5377
Wages Of Love, 2173
Wagon Wheels, 2528
Wah Wah, 305
Wah Wah Lament, 3556
Wah Watusi, 211
Wah-Hoo, 2035

Wah-wah, 3556, 5667
Wahre Arbeit, Wahrer Lohn, 1518
Wahzinak's First Letter, 922
Wahzinak's Letter, 922
Wait, 607, 5792
Wait A Little Longer Son, 2679
Wait A Minute, 3322
Wait And See, 2426
Wait For Me, 933, 1151, 3198, 4488, 5618
Wait For Me Mary, 2447, 5453
Wait For Me, Lili, 172
Wait For You, 658
Wait One Minute More, 1092
Wait Til' My Bobby Gets Home, 3339
Wait Till The Sun Shines Nellie, 4359, 5660
Wait Till Tomorrow, 2975, 3160, 5901
Wait Till We're Sixty-Five, 4039
Wait Till You See Her, 861, 4607
Wait Till You See Paris, 3865
Wait Until Dark, 3281
Wait Until Tonight, 2015
Wait'll You See My Brand New Home, 2383
Waiter's Gavotte, 2477
Waitin' At The End Of Your Run, 373
Waitin' For My Dearie, 735, 3196
Waitin' In School, 838, 4537
Waitin' In Your Welfare Line, 4088
Waiting, 2385, 3647
Waiting And Drinking, 700
Waiting At The Gate For Katy, 2923
Waiting For A Girl Like You, 1975
Waiting For A Star To Fall, 694
Waiting For An Alibi, 5390
Waiting For Billy, 1960
Waiting For Love, 118
Waiting For Magic, 51
Waiting for Our Daughter, 1960
Waiting For The Light To Shine, 528
Waiting For The Lights, 1807
Waiting For The Man, 2400, 4123
Waiting For The Night, 1807
Waiting For The Rain, 1547
Waiting For The Robert E. Lee, 308
Waiting For The Sun, 2792
Waiting Hopefully, 1349

Waiting In Sweetheart Valley, 4528
Waiting In The Lobby Of Your Heart, 2251, 5410
Waiting In The Wings, 94, 422, 1766
Waiting In Vain, 1808
Waiting On My Angel, 2606, 4338
Waiting On You, 1263, 4941
Waiting Phase One, 4285
Waiting Phase Two, 4285
Waiting Round The Corner, 4021
Wakare No Blues, 292
Wakare No Ippon Sugi, 2939
Wakare Uta, 3870
Wake Me Into Love, 611, 828
Wake Me Up Before You Go Go, 5781
Wake The Town, 4493, 5559
Wake Up, 1385, 2093, 2765, 3609
Wake Up (It's 1984), 4023
Wake Up And Live, 1436
Wake Up And Make Love To Me, 1661, 3910
Wake Up And Sing, 2035
Wake Up And Start Standing, 5966
Wake Up Everybody, 3568
Wake Up Jacob, 1437
Wake Up Jamaica, 111
Wake Up Little Susie, 804, 1798, 2998
Wake Up My Mind, 5564
Wake Up, Wake Up!, 5449
Wakey News, 2038
Waking Or Sleeping, 216, 3979
Waking Up, 1721
Waking Up Alone, 5857
Waldo P. Emerson Jones, 4235
Waldorf Suite, 3860
Walk, 1779, 2179, 5662
Walk An' Wine, 2222
Walk And Skank, 4958
Walk Away, 565, 2770, 2915, 3187, 3317, 3743, 4179, 4846, 5667
Walk Away From Love, 200, 4683
Walk Away Renee, 1997, 3179, 3749, 4976, 5516
Walk Don't Run, 5629
Walk Hand In Hand, 956, 3492
Walk Him Up The Stairs, 4368
Walk Into The Sun, 4059
Walk Like A Duck, 3086
Walk Like A Man, 1292, 1995
Walk Like An Egyptian, 366
Walk Me Home From The Party, 1098

Walk Me To The Door, 5548
Walk Of Faith, 4495
Walk Of Life, 762, 1537, 2122
Walk On, 488, 1292, 4093, 5424
Walk On By, 291, 314-315, 954, 1610, 3210, 4400, 4768, 4979, 5604, 5713, 5800, 5848
Walk On Gilded Splinters, 1615, 2638, 5761
Walk On Stalks Of Shattered Glass, 2630
Walk On The Ocean, 5452
Walk On The Water, 1324
Walk On The Wild Side, 248, 622, 654, 685, 1644, 1946, 1971, 3467, 4479, 4989, 5491, 5638
Walk On Water, 1324
Walk Out The Door If You Wanna, 1824
Walk Out To Winter, 300
Walk Right Back, 1339, 1798, 3325
Walk Right In, 919, 1394, 4642
Walk Right Now, 2742
Walk So Lonely, 3885
Walk Softly On My Heart, 3120
Walk Softly On The Bridges, 3151
Walk Softly On This Heart Of Mine, 2974, 3120
Walk Tall, 1593, 5970
Walk The Dinosaur, 5714
Walk The Way The Wind Blows, 3993, 4516
Walk This Way, 83, 4415, 4679, 4687
Walk Through This World With Me, 1359
Walk Upon The Water, 1288, 2475
Walk With Me, 4813, 5926
Walk With Me My Angel, 1026
Walk With Your Chin Up, 4722
Walkabout Rock 'n' Roll, 3254
Walked All Night, 665
Walkin' A Broken Heart, 3250
Walkin' After Midnight, 4217
Walkin' Away A Winner, 4848
Walkin' Back To Happiness, 4848
Walkin' Blues, 1691, 3770, 4300
Walkin' By Myself, 4620
Walkin' By The River, 579
Walkin' Down The Line, 2953

Walkin' In The Park, 654, 1182, 5667

Walkin' In The Rain With The One I Love, 3339, 5795

Walkin' My Baby Back Home, 93, 1160, 3484, 4446, 5753

Walkin' My Cat Named Dog, 5293

Walkin' On New Grass, 4323

Walkin' On The Sun, 1976

Walkin' Shoes, 3836

Walkin' Tall, 5617

Walkin' The Dog, 664, 758, 1359

Walkin' To Missouri, 726, 3636, 4676

Walkin' To New Orleans, 1026

Walkin' To School, 2927

Walkin' With Mr. Lee, 132

Walkin, Talkin, Cryin, Barely Beatin' Broken Heart, 5928

Walking After Midnight, 1129-1130, 1266

Walking Along, 1510, 1810

Walking Along With Billy, 1202

(Walking) Among My Yesterdays, 2384

Walking Away Whistling, 2278, 3294

Walking Back To Happiness, 4774

Walking Blues, 791, 1656, 3830

Walking Down Madison, 3386

Walking Down Their Outlook, 2522

Walking Dr Bill, 3861

Walking Home In The Spring, 5830

Walking In Different Circles, 2191

Walking In Memphis, 1044, 1155, 1388

Walking In Rhythm, 569

Walking In Space, 2337

Walking In The Park With Eloise, 5885

Walking In The Rain, 344, 636, 923, 1249, 3444, 3728, 4640, 5677

Walking In The Sunshine, 321

Walking In Your Footsteps, 4455

Walking Into Sunshine, 1004

Walking My Baby Back Home, 4535

Walking My Lord Up Calvary's Hill, 1228

Walking On Air, 2018

Walking On Broken Glass, 1548

Walking On Ice, 4050, 4557, 5740

Walking On New Grass, 4188

Walking On Sunshine, 2940, 3082

Walking On The Chinese Wall, 333

Walking On The Moon, 4274, 4491, 4700

Walking On The Water, 2195

Walking On Thin Ice, 4050, 5740

Walking The Blues, 791, 1656

Walking The Dog, 1483, 2385, 4841, 5375, 5405

Walking The Floor Over You, 5518-5519

Walking The Streets In The Rain, 923, 1249

Walking The Tou Tou, 1285

(Walking Through The) Sleepy City, 3658

Walking To New Orleans, 403, 1581

Walking Up A One Way Street, 5328

Walks Like A Woman, 413

Wall Around Your Heart, 3994

Wall Of Death, 4888

Wall Of Sound, 1322, 4542, 5900

Wall To Wall Love, 2075

Walla Walla, 4489

Wallflower, 534, 3727, 3742, 4549

Walls Come Tumbling Down, 893

Walter T., 158

Walter, Walter, 1887

Waltz Across Texas, 3900, 5519

Waltz At Maxim's, 2144, 3197

Waltz For A Lonely Heart, 3528

Waltz For Debby, 1789, 5694

Waltz In Swing Time, 1886

Waltz Me No Waltzes, 4886

Waltz Of My Heart, 1376, 3979

Waltz Of The Bubbles, 4651

Waltz Of The Flowers, 2185

Waltz Of The Gypsies, 2967

Waltz Of The Wind, 59, 622

Waltzing Bugle Boy, 3491

Waltzing In The Clouds, 2923

Waltzing Is Better Than Sitting Down, 4886

Waltzing Matilda, 2426

Wan Light, 4295

Wand'rin' Star, 3196, 3294, 4105

Wander Where You

Wander, 5470

Wanderin' Eyes, 2229, 3564, 4001, 5617

Wandering, 1071

Wandering Child, 4218

Wandering Heart, 660

Wang Dang Doodle, 1039, 1556, 4271, 5316

Wang Wang Blues, 164, 853, 5802

Wanna Be Dancin' (Buck Whylin'), 494?

Wanna Be Down, 2015

Wanna Be Loved, 4137

Wanna Be Starting Something, 1511

Wanna Make Love, 3794

Wanna Take You Home, 2514

Want Ad Reader, 2165

Want Ads, 2582, 4137

Want You To Rock Me, 726

Wanted, 1195, 1593, 2736, 3493

Wanted Dead Or Alive, 652, 4970

Wanted Man, 977, 2838

Wanting Things, 4348

Wanting You, 3916

War, 2763, 2787, 2816, 3487, 4124, 4566, 5804

War And Crime, 4458

War Baby, 4587

War Bytes, 4465

War Fever, 5539

War Is War, 1447

War Of The Worlds, 3130

War Pigs, 2020, 4126

War Rationin' Papa, 671

War Start, 4766

Wardance, 2993

Warder, 311

Waremouse, 3820

Warhead, 3503, 5628

Warm, 1839

Warm All Over, 3805

Warm And Tender Love, 1248, 5787

Warm and Willing, 3581

Warm Aspirations, 5424

Warm It Up, 3077

Warm Leatherette, 3855

Warm Love, 2115

Warm Up To Me Baby, 683

Warm Valley, 2548

Warn Them, 4468

Warning, 75, 1650

Warning Of Eve, 3090

Warning Sign, 2513, 4851

Warpaint, 751

Warpath, 5277

Warricka Hill, 2138

Warrior, 778, 1472

Warrior Charge, 265, 1080, 5566

Warrior Groove, 1350

Warrior In Woolworths, 2126, 5940

Warrior Woman, 2974

Warrior's Drum, 3001

Warsaw Concerto, 4534

Wartime Letters, 3150

Warum, 5431

Warum Nur Warum, 565, 2915

Was It Rain?, 3126, 5486

Was It Worth It?, 762

Was She Prettier Than I?, 2522

Was That A Smile, 3239

Was That The Human Thing To Do?, 5973

Was There Life Before This Love?, 2712

Wash His Back, 3868

Wash Wash, 1817

Wash Your Face In My Sink, 171, 1624

Wash Your Necks With A Cake Of Beck's, 4281

Washboard Blues, 941

Washing Machine, 3824-3825, 4090, 5497

Washing The Dishes, 3899

Washington Bullets, 4736

Washington Square, 4883

Wasn't Born To Follow, 868

Wasn't It Beautiful While It Lasted?, 1951

Wasn't It Nice?, 2037

Wasn't It Wonderful?, 1438

Wasn't That A Handsome Punch-Up, 5781

Waspman, 3761

Wasted, 909, 2594, 3923

Wasted Days And Wasted Nights, 1873-1874, 4718

Wasted On The Way, 1307

Wasted Union Blues, 2723

Wasted Years, 2711

Wastin' My Time, 97

Watashi Konogoro Youtsuyo, 292

Watashiwa Machino Ko, 3704

Watch Dog, 5330

Watch Me, 3785, 4848, 4902

Watch Me Rock, I'm Over 30, 5670

Watch That Girl Destroy Me, 4294

Watch The Birdie, 1437

Watch The Gun, 681

Watch This Sound, 1032, 2019, 4545, 5578

Watch What Happens, 3183

Watch Your Step, 2856, 4133, 4317, 4434, 4521, 5515

Watcha Gonna Do, 4382

Watching Mary Go Round, 4975

Watching My Dreams Go By, 829

Watching Scotty Grow, 1413, 2194

Watching The Clock, 3649, 4695

Watching The Clouds Roll By, 2928
Watching The Detectives, 1244
Watching The Wheels, 1754
Watching You, 1706, 2929
Watching You Watching Me, 2242
Water, 1635
Water Come A Mi Eye, 5676
Water From The Moon, 1536
Water Jelly, 3647
Water Of Love, 2908
Water Pumpee, 3647, 5526
Water Pumping, 4070
Water Under The Bridge, 1647
Water Water, 402
Water With The Wine, 2826
Water Woman, 4099
Waterfall, 1125, 1693, 5378, 5768
Waterfalls, 1284
Waterfront, 4921
Waterline, 25, 1573
Waterloo, 37, 182, 350, 358, 1088, 1566, 2481, 2751, 3324, 5443
Waterloo Road, 2789
Waterloo Sunset, 2392, 3023, 5289
Watermelon Crawl, 867
Watermelon Man, 783, 858, 2373, 3097, 3373, 4740
Watermelon Party, 421
Watermelon Weather, 1908
Watersports, 1450
Watford Gap, 2401
Watteau, 250
Wau Wau Wau, 3351
Wave, 2827
Wave Bye Bye To The Man, 3255
Wave Of Mutilation, 4256
Wave To Me My Lady, 744
Waves, 1119
Waving Not Drowning, 1526
Wax Dolls, 1907
Way Back Home, 527, 1251, 5982
Way Back In The 1960s, 2689
Way Down, 4312
Way Down Deep, 388
Way Down Home, 282
Way Down In Arkansas, 3925
Way Down In North Carolina, 5700
Way Down Now, 2205
Way Down South In Greenwich Village, 3086
Way Down Upon The Swanee River, 2174
Way Down Yonder In New Orleans, 918, 3153, 4328
Way In My Brain, 4958

Way Of Life, 1261, 2368, 4675
Way Of The World, 3622
Way Out, 281, 297, 2926, 3099, 3739, 4114, 4647
Way Out There, 3566, 3969
Way Over There, 3700, 4585
Way To Reason, 5716
Way You Dog Me Around, 1506, 1980
Wayfaring Stranger, 2327
Waylon And Willie, 2813
Ways To Be Wicked, 3304
Wayz Of The Wize, 549
We A Blood, 1472
(We Ain't Got) Nothin' Yet, 625
We All Feel Better In The Dark, 762
We All Gotta Go Sometime, 3325
We Almost Got It Together, 5434
We Are All One, 3487
We Are Family, 309, 1053, 4942
We Are Free, 840
We Are Glass, 3985
We Are Hardcore, 4346
We Are In Love, 184, 864, 4520, 4663
We Are Indelible, 3848
We Are Neighbours Whether We Want To Be Or Not, 2714
We Are Ninja, 2010
We Are One, 291, 3487
We Are Rolling, 1162
We Are The Champions, 4381
We Are The Gentlemen Of Japan, 2602
We Are The Lucky Ones, 1953
We Are The Moles, 1657
We Are The One, 291
(We Are) The Road Crew, 52
We Are The World, 457, 943, 1028, 1081, 1676, 2747, 2883, 3900, 4535, 4622, 4919, 5475, 5535, 5588
We Believe In Happy Endings, 1206, 2218
We Belong Together, 127, 1483, 3852, 4570
We Built Fires, 4281
We Built This City, 1087, 2804, 4101, 4966, 5304
We Call It Acieed, 1350
We Can Be, 1267, 5759
We Can Be Brave Again, 230
We Can Be Together, 5658
We Can Do It (Wake Up), 1756
We Can Do This, 1157
We Can Fly, 1267
We Can Help You, 3956

We Can Make It, 4549, 4682
We Can Make It Pretty Baby, 4061
We Can Work It Out, 433, 1542, 2637, 2937
We Can't Go On This Way, 3194
We Can't Live Like This, 767
We Care A Lot, 1829
We Close Our Eyes, 2175
We Come Alive, 5332
We Could Be Together, 2141, 4906
We Could Find Happiness, 5695
We Could Send Letters, 300
We Danced Anyway, 488
We Did It, 2856
We Did It Before And We Can Do It Again, 2035, 5454
We Didn't Ask To Be Brought Here, 1390
We Do It, 5487
We Do What We Can, 1311-1312
We Don't All Wear D'Same Size Boots, 3406
We Don't Care, 4702
We Don't Go Together, 2505
We Don't Matter At All, 2723
We Don't Need Another Hero, 5535
We Don't Need Nobody Else, 5789
(We Don't Need This) Fascist Groove Thang, 2464
We Don't Talk Anymore, 4531
We Don't Work For Free, 3617
We Drink Bitter, 916
We Gettin' Down, 2713
We Girls, 511, 704
We Go A Long Way Back, 602
We Go Together, 2256, 2505, 3496, 3764
We Gonna Funk, 1560
We Got A Love Thang, 762, 2644, 4186
We Got Love, 900
We Got More Soul, 1671
We Got The Beat, 2176
We Got The Funk, 4293
We Got The Neutron Bomb, 5755
We Got To Get You A Woman, 4688
We Gotta Get Out Of This Place, 193, 508, 3444
We Gotta Go, 3239
We Had A Dream, 3239
We Had It All, 4798
We Hate To Leave, 170
We Have A Dream, 4575
We Have All The Time In

The World, 5444
We Have Been Around, 1578
We Just Couldn't Say Goodbye, 3300, 5915
We Just Disagree, 3502
We Kinda Music, 3876
We Kiss In A Shadow, 2997, 4607, 4634, 5669
We Let The Stars Go, 2891
We Live In Two Different Worlds, 3222, 4651
We Love Each Other, 369
We Love You, 2594, 3349, 4629, 5462
We Loved It Away, 5309
We Loves Ya, Jimmy, 4471
We Made Memories, 692, 1464
We Make A Beautiful Pair, 4868
We May Never Love Like This Again, 3574
We Might As Well Forget It, 5866
We Miss Him When The Evening Shadows Fall, 4605
We Musn't Say Goodbye, 3736
We Must Be Vigilant, 829
We Must Have Been Out Of Our Minds, 1359, 2872
We Nah Go Suffer, 572
We Need A Little Christmas, 2505, 3428
We Need Love, 5986
We Need Some Money (Bout Money), 768
We Need Somebody, 2996, 4138
We Need To Be Locked Away, 1710
We Never Talk Much, 748
We No Lotion Man, 924
We Open In Venice, 3035, 3669
We Parted On the Shore, 3137
We Propose, 3470
We Rap Mellow, 2239, 3617
We Rap More Mellow, 3617
We Refuse The Right To Refuse Service To You, 2034
We Rule, 4794
We Said We Wouldn't Look Back, 4723, 4960, 4723, 4960
We Saw The Sea, 1960
We Shall Overcome, 99, 326, 2451, 3130, 4812
We Should Be In Angola, 3803
We Should Be Together, 4516, 5333, 5843
We Stand Alone, 4899
We Stand Around, 2665
We Still Love Songs In Missouri, 1235
We Still Survive, 4489

White Light, 4590
White Lightning, 521, 2871, 4566
White Line Fever, 1949
White Lines, 1658, 5280
White Lines (Don't Do It), 2239, 3617
White Love, 2392, 4966
(White Man) In Hammersmith Palais, 1110
White Man's Got A God Complex, 3133
White Mice, 3721
White On White, 5842
White Orchids, 2273
White Punks On Hope, 1278
White Rabbit, 484, 1371, 2259, 2802, 4353, 4966
White Room, 422, 783, 796
White Russians, 4714
White Sands, 311, 563, 2086, 2514
White Silver Sands, 563, 2086, 2514
White Trash Blues, 2298
White Wedding, 2673, 5732, 5797
Whiter Shade Of Pale, 1125, 2261, 2332, 3194
Whitlam Square, 1519
Whizzin' Away Along De Track, 941
Who, 809, 2339, 2385, 4036
Who Am I Kidding, 1229
Who Am I?, 453, 3199, 4207
Who Are They To Say, 1432
Who Are We, 2535, 3372
Who Are We To Say, 2923
Who Are You?, 1228, 1884, 3196
Who Bit the Wart Off Grandma's Nose, 957
Who Blew Out The Flame?, 1424, 5669
Who But You, 1555
Who Can Be True, 1915
Who Can I Turn To?, 733, 3926, 4565, 5830
Who Can It Be Now?, 3625
Who Can Make You Feel Good, 410
Who Cares, 2129
Who Could Be Bluer?, 3317
Who Could Be Loving You, 4658
Who Couldn't Dance With You?, 2237
Who Dares Believe In Me, 1417
Who Dem Fi Rate, 1080
Who Did You Fool, After All?, 421
Who Do I Know In Dallas?, 1143
Who Do Think You Are, 914, 4881
Who Do You Know In California?, 4442

Who Do You Love, 1517, 2440, 2909, 3133, 4385, 4576, 4746, 5636, 5850
Who Do You Think You Are, 914, 4881
Who Do You Think You Are Kidding Mr. Hitler, 1927
Who Got The Props, 3904
Who Have Eyes To See, 757, 2576, 4644
Who Hit Me?, 3191
Who Is It?, 762
Who Is Silvia?, 5549
Who Killed Bambi, 2258, 5339
Who Killed Elvis?, 6006
Who Killed JFK?, 6006
Who Killed Marilyn?, 3704
Who Knows, 2659
Who Knows What Tomorrow Might Bring?, 5488
Who Knows Where The Time Goes, 1826
Who Knows?, 1438, 4449
Who Loves Who, 2390
Who Loves You As I Do?, 3649
Who Loves You?, 1228, 1996
Who Needs Roses?, 3389
Who Needs The Peace Corps, 3809
Who Needs To Dream?, 1229
Who Needs You, 1804, 1993
Who Needs You Baby, 5679
Who Protects Us From You?, 2133
Who Put the Benzedrine In Mrs Murphy's Ovaltine?, 2142
Who Put The Bomp?, 3444, 5653
Who Put The Lights Out, 1374
Who Put The Turtle In Myrtle's Girdle, 3018
Who Said I Would, 3962
Who Say, 3825
Who Say Jah Jah, 4468
Who Say Jah No Dread, 3676
Who Says There Ain't No Santa Claus?, 1923
Who Says You Can't Have It All, 2736
Who She Love, 4432
Who Shot Sam?, 1755, 2534, 2872
Who Slapped John?, 622
Who Takes Care Of The Caretaker's Daughter, 3630
Who Taught Her Everything, 2056
Who Taught You All Those Things You Taught Me?, 540

Who The Am Dam Do You Think I Am?, 697
Who The Cap Fits, 4882
Who The Hell Are You?, 3196
Who The X Is Alice?, 2196
Who Threw The Whiskey In The Well?, 2414
Who Told You So, 3605
Who Walks In (When I Walk Out?), 2025, 2549
Who Wants to Be A Millionaire?, 2522
Who Wants To Be The Disco King?, 5906
Who Wants To Live Forever, 29
Who Was That Guy, 2741
Who Were You Thinkin' Of, 5348
Who Will Answer?, 164
Who Will Buy, 402, 3322
Who Will Buy The Wine, 3719
Who Will Follow Norma Jean ?, 4321
Who Will Save Your Soul, 2821
Who Will The Next Fool Be?, 4527
Who Would Have Dreamed?, 4118
Who Would've Thought?, 2205
Who Wouldn't Be Blue?, 829, 1405
Who Wouldn't Love You, 307, 3091
Who Ya Know, 3077
Who'd She Coo?, 4022
Who'll Buy My Bublitchki, 1746
Who'll Join Me On This Escapade?, 2643
Who's Afraid Of Love?, 4046
Who's Afraid Of The Big Bad Wolf, 5982
Who's Afraid Of Virginia Woolf, 4989
Who's At The Bottom Of Your Swimming Pool, 5482
Who's Been Listening To My Heart?, 192, 2928, 4680
Who's Been Mowing The Lawn (While I Was Gone), 4188
Who's Been Polishing The Sun, 2102
Who's Been Talking?, 2858, 3708
Who's Calling You Sweetheart Tonight?, 3746
Who's Cheating Who?, 3268, 3550
Who's Complaining?, 1263
Who's Crying Now, 2900
Who's Gonna Bring Me Laughter, 3443

Who's Gonna Fill Their Shoes, 388
Who's Gonna Love Me, 395, 3262
Who's Gonna Play This Old Piano, 2287
Who's Gonna Ride Your Wild Horses, 53
Who's Gonna Sing The Last Country Song, 4132
Who's Gonna Walk The Dog And Put The Cat Out, 4188
Who's Got The Pain, 5632
Who's Holding Donna Now?, 1450
Who's In The House, 437
Who's In The Strawberry Patch With Sally, 1423
Who's It Gonna Be, 3299
Who's Johnny?, 1451
Who's Lonely Now, 753, 2525
Who's Lovin' You, 725, 5522
Who's Making Love, 368, 2525, 5316, 5696
Who's Making Love To Your Old Lady While You're Out Making Love?, 5503
Who's Number 1, 1123
Who's Sorry Now, 125, 1434, 2006, 2928, 4074, 4681, 4937
Who's Taking You Home Tonight?, 1210
Who's That Girl, 210, 1219, 1787, 1952, 3403, 5475
Who's That In Your Love Life?, 1438, 4449
Who's That Lady?, 2719
Who's That Man, 2956, 5942
Who's That Woman?, 1219, 1959
Who's The Fool Now, 1620
Who's The Lady With My Man?, 3462
Who's The Lady?, 520, 1745
Who's The Man, 5574
Who's This Geezer Hitler?, 595
Who's Yehoodi?, 1483, 3091
Who's Your Sweetheart?, 251
Who-Dun-It?, 2520
Whoa, 1983
Whoa Back Buck, 3156
Whoa Sailor, 5410
Whodunit, 5304
Whoever You Are, 4348
Whoever's In New England, 3566
Whole, 4371
Whole Lot Of Sugar, 773
Whole Lot Of Women, 2441
Whole Lotta Love, 1001, 3066, 3165-3166, 4100,

4132, 4260, 4416, 4519, 5467
Whole Lotta Love On The Line, 5448
Whole Lotta Loving, 403
Whole Lotta Rosie, 48, 2674, 4039
Whole Lotta Shakin' Goin' On, 527, 998, 1122, 1816, 2352, 3219, 5361
Whole Lotta Woman, 4414
Whole New Thing, 369
Whole Wide World, 5925
Whoop-De-Oodle-Do, 875
Whoopee Blues, 3005
Whoot, There It Is, 86, 3955
Whose Baby Are You?, 2723
Whose Been Sitting In My Chair?, 2192
Whose Girl Are You, 398
Whose Heart Are You Breaking Tonight?, 1406
Whose Honey Are You?, 1228
Whose Law (Is It Anyway?), 2316
Whose Little Angry Man, 4414
Whose Little Girl Are You?, 5540
Whose Problem, 3806
Why, 14, 289, 371, 868, 1305, 1326, 1350, 1481, 1890, 2672, 3390, 3724, 3926, 4073, 4917, 5425, 5809
Why (Is There A Rainbow In The Sky), 1228, 1406
Why Am I A Hit With The Ladies?, 1147
Why Am I Always The Bridesmaid, 1747, 4005
Why Am I Me, 4868
Why Am I So Gone About That Gal?, 3199
Why Am I So Lonely?, 2141
Why Am I So Romantic?, 192
Why Are You Leaving, 2059
Why Baby Why, 670, 2871, 4116, 4238, 4240
Why Be Afraid To Dance?, 1844
Why Begin Again?, 4449
Why Can't I Be Two People?, 4969
Why Can't I Be You?, 1335
Why Can't I Have You, 1424
Why Can't I Wait Till Morning, 2000
Why Can't I Wake Up With You, 5285
Why Can't I?, 416, 539, 1335, 4606
Why Can't The English?, 2417, 3196, 3295, 3859
Why Can't This Be Love, 5605

Why Can't We Be Friends?, 4976, 5697
Why Can't We Be Lovers, 1611, 4682
Why Can't We Live Together, 1507, 1562, 3524
Why Can't You, 2493
Why Can't You (Birdies Sing In Cages Too), 780
Why Can't You Leave Dreadlocks Alone, 5433
Why Daddy Don't Live Here Anymore, 4087
Why Did I Have To Meet You?, 4382
Why Did I Kiss That Girl, 780
Why Did Nellie Leave Home?, 1152
Why Did She Fall For The Leader Of The Band?, 2967
Why Did She Go, 3412
Why Did The Chicken Cross The Road?, 1428
Why Did Ya Do It, 749
Why Did You Call Me Lily?, 1745
Why Did You Do It, 2083, 3575, 5626
Why Did You Say I Do To Me (When You Still Meant To Do It With Him)?, 1339
Why Do All Girls Think They're Fat, 4481
Why Do Everything Happen To Me, 2440
Why Do Fools Fall In Love?, 1151, 1187, 1363, 1510, 3195, 3215, 3367, 4657, 5815
Why Do Girls, 673
Why Do I Cry, 4498
Why Do I Love You?, 1439, 2366, 2975, 4880, 4892-4893
Why Do I?, 2160
Why Do Lovers Break Each Other's Heart?, 636
Why Do The Heathen Rage?, 2303
Why Do They Always Pick On Me?, 2478
Why Do Ya Roll Those Eyes?, 1022
Why Does It Have To Be (Wrong Or Right), 4509
Why Does Love (Have To Go Wrong)?, 422
Why Does Love Get In The Way?, 51
Why Does The Rain?, 1287, 3295
Why Don't The Telephone Ring, 867
Why Don't They Dance The Polka?, 2160
Why Don't They Leave Us Alone, 1166, 3239
Why Don't They Understand?, 2360, 2488

Why Don't We Do This More Often?, 3091
Why Don't We Get Drunk And Screw?, 820
Why Don't We Go Somewhere And Love, 3999
Why Don't You Believe Me, 1915, 2775, 4102, 4676
Why Don't You Do Right, 2271, 3176
Why Don't You Eat Where You Slept Last Night, 647
Why Don't You Fall In Love With Me?, 5736
Why Don't You Go To Dallas, 4182
Why Don't You Haul Off And Get Religion, 666
Why Don't You Haul Off And Love Me, 4428
Why Don't You Love Me, 575, 4428
Why Don't You Smile Now, 1609
Why Don't You Spend The Night, 4445
Why Don't You Try Me, 3522
Why Don't You Write Me, 879
Why Don't You?, 725, 3176, 3548, 4419, 5846
Why Dream?, 522
Why God, Why?, 3706
Why Have You Left The One You Left Me For?, 2106
Why I Sing The Blues, 1098
Why I'm Walking, 1759, 2751
Why Is Everybody Going Home, 4761
Why Is It Always The Woman Who Pays?, 88
Why Is There Ever Goodbye?, 933, 3979
Why Is Tomorrow Like Today, 3575
Why Lady Why?, 3791
Why Look At The Moon, 5860
Why Lovers Turn To Strangers, 2420
Why Me, 929, 2908, 3050, 3078, 3791, 4102, 4257, 4710
Why Me Lord, 3487
Why Me Ralph, 1128
Why Must We Always Be Dreaming?, 5901
Why Not Confess, 4954
Why Not For Me, 4341
Why Not Katie?, 4259
Why Not Me, 2908, 3050, 4341, 4710
Why Not Now/Can This Be Love, 3743
Why Not Tonight?, 2628
Why Not Your Baby, 5362
Why Oh Why, 1309, 2543

Why Paddy's Not At Work Today, 3843
Why Play Games, 5308
Why Should I Be Lonely?, 726
Why Should I Cry Over You?, 3729
Why Should I Suffer With The Blues, 804
Why Should We Stop Now, 3884
Why Shouldn't I?, 2906, 4289
Why The Stars Come Out Tonight, 3966
Why There's A Tear In My Eye, 960, 4604
Why Try To Change Me Now?, 1164
Why Was I Born?, 2976, 3784, 5435
Why Why, 670, 1309, 2543, 2871, 4116, 4238, 4240, 5487
Why Why Why, 1267
Why Won't You Love Me?, 3481
Why Worry, 421, 2722
Why You Do That, 4639
Why You Treat Me So Bad, 1137
Why You Wanna Treat Me So Bad?, 4331
Why'd You Come In Here Looking Like That, 936
Why's Everybody Always Pickin' On Me, 602
Why, I'm Walking, 1759, 2751
Why, Oh Why, 1309, 2543
Why?, 421, 522, 750, 842, 901, 1548, 3078, 3160, 4880
Wichita Lineman, 905, 1433, 3871, 5744
Wicked Can't Run, 2761
Wicked Funk, 1952
Wicked Game, 2716
Wicked In Bed, 4432
Wicked Inna Bed, 1525
Wicked Intention, 5319
Wicked Man, 371, 452
Wicked Mathematics, 3945
Wickedest Sound, 5338
Wickedest Thing In Life, 929, 2222
Wicker Vine, 3817
Widdicombe Fair, 2184
Wide Awake In A Dream, 534
Wide Eyed And Legless, 1828
Wide Open Road, 5504
Widow Maker, 3488
Wife And Sweetheart, 4780
Wife Of A Gangsta, 1212
Wigged Criminal, 2585
Wiggle It, 1342
Wiggle Wobble, 1034
Wiggle, Wiggle, 4824

You Don't Have To Be A Baby To Cry, 930, 3123, 3636, 4976
You Don't Have To Be A Star, 1890, 3554
You Don't Have To Be In The Army To Fight In The War, 3839
You Don't Have To Be So Nice, 2168
You Don't Have To Go, 1052, 3416, 3708, 4477, 5312
You Don't Have To Know The Language, 4563, 5606
You Don't Have To Say You Love Me, 1748, 2017, 3874
You Don't Hear, 981
You Don't Know, 188, 2277, 2787, 4848, 5869
You Don't Know Like I Know, 4301, 4727
You Don't Know Me, 2153, 3728, 4188, 5593, 5678-5679, 5758
You Don't Know Paree, 1891, 4289
You Don't Know What Love Is, 1437, 4761
You Don't Know What You're Missing (Till It's Gone), 1806
You Don't Know What You've Got (Until You Lose It), 1590
You Don't Love (No No No), 681, 2638
You Don't Love Me, 27, 1140, 3144, 3463, 4187, 5679
(You Don't Love Me) True, 2107
You Don't Love Me When I Cry, 3991
You Don't Mess Around With Jim, 2508
You Don't Miss Your Water, 464, 869, 3892
You Don't Need A Licence For That, 1977
You Don't Need Me, 3619, 4493
You Don't Need Someone New, 3324
You Don't Own Me, 607, 1385, 2219
You Don't Pull No Punches But You Don't Push The River, 3795
You Don't Tell Me, 3964
You Don't Treat Me Right, 2310
You Don't Wanna See Me, 1131
You Don't Want Me, 5665
You Doo Right, 910
You Dream Too Much, 4686
You Dropped A Bomb On

Me, 2083
You Facety Whitey, 2685
You Fascinate Me So, 1164
You Finally Said Something When You Said Goodbye, 3333
You Forgot Your Gloves, 2003
You Found Me And I Found You, 4021
You Fucked Up, 5754
You Fucked Up My Life, 922
You Gave Me A Mountain, 850, 4568
You Gave Me Love, 1315
You Gave Me Something, 1844
You Get To Me, 4396
You Give A Little Love, 821
You Give Good Love, 2611
You Give Love A Bad Name, 652, 1057, 4970
You Give Me You, 4524
You Give Me Your Love, 2186
You Go To My Head, 1228, 1885, 3912, 5937
You Go Your Way (And I'll Go Crazy), 4511
You Gonna Make Me Love Somebody Else, 2866
You Gonna Miss Me, 2844
You Got It, 3865, 3904, 4055, 4415
You Got It (The Right Stuff), 3915
You Got Me Running, 5460
You Got Me So I Don't Know, 4235
You Got Me This Way, 3091
You Got Soul, 3878
You Got The Love, 4453, 4684
You Got The Papers (But I Got The Man), 3049
You Got The Power, 5697
You Got To Be Faithful, 2844
You Got To Be Happy, 541
You Got To Be Holy, 3802
You Got What It Takes, 2852, 4133
You Gotta Be, 1489-1490
You Gotta Be A Football Hero, 4874
You Gotta Believe, 3342, 4453
You Gotta Die Sometime, 3458
You Gotta Eat Your Spinach, Baby, 4281
You Gotta Give The People Hoke, 205
You Gotta Have A Gimmick, 2324, 4567
You Gotta Have A License, 1179
You Gotta Love That, 3556

You Gotta Move, 4630
You Gotta Pull Strings, 69, 2260
You Gotta Pull The Strings, 2260
You Gotta Stop, 4311
You Gotta Work, 4090
You Have Cast Your Shadow On The Sea, 698, 4607
You Have Placed A Chill In My Heart, 1788
You Have Taken My Heart, 2810
You Have The Right To Remain Silent, 4194
You Have The Ring, 1766
You Hit The Spot, 2216
You Hung The Moon (Didn't You, Waylon)?, 1184
You Hurt My Soul, 5704
You I Love, 748, 4828, 5747
You In The Night, 1856
You Just Can't Win, 5383
You Just Get Better All The Time, 2608
You Just Might See Me Cry, 4078
You Keep Coming Back Like A Song, 494, 617, 4889
You Keep Me Hangin' On, 5829
You Keep Me Hanging On, 1775, 2561, 3800, 4179, 5612, 5623
You Keep The The Love, 1717
You Know, 188, 2277, 2787, 3787, 4848, 5869
You Know All I Want, 1760
You Know How To Love Me, 2654
(You Know How To Make Me) Feel So Good, 880
You Know It Ain't Right, 2540
You Know Me Better Than That, 1060
You Know What I Mean, 659, 1177, 1819, 5538, 5634
(You Know) You Can Do It, 1003
You Know You Wanna Be Loved, 399
You Know, I Know, 218, 4301, 4727
You Lay A Lotta Love On Me, 4449
You Lay So Easy On My Mind, 4524
You Learn, 5703
You Leave Me Breathless, 2025
You Leave Me Like This, 1804
You Left The Water Running, 3369, 3522, 4399
You Lied To Your Daddy, 5291

(You Lift Me) Up To Heaven, 3566
You Light Up My Life, 667-668
You Like It, 4219
You Like Me Don't You, 2743
You Little Thief, 4849
You Little Trustmaker, 5554
You Look So Good In Love, 682, 4609
You Love Us, 2466, 3442
You Lucky People You, 4563
You Made A Believer (Out Of Me), 186, 762
You Made Me Love You, 352, 746, 1705, 2088, 2708, 2773, 2862-2863, 3337, 3446, 3547, 3735, 4535, 5997
You Made Me So Very Happy, 2286
You Made This Love A Teardrop, 2291
You Make It Happen, 4717
You Make It Move, 1398
You Make Loving Fun, 4686
You Make Me Feel, 5912
You Make Me Feel (Mighty Real), 1195
You Make Me Feel Like Dancing, 4761
(You Make Me Feel Like) A Natural Woman, 2013
You Make Me Feel So Good, 264
You Make Me Feel So Young, 2217, 3865, 4928
You Make Me Real, 1594
You Make Me Wanna, 5588
(You Make Me Want To Be) A Mother, 5936
You Make Me Want To Love You, 679
You Make Me Want To Make You Mine, 3933
You Make My Life Complete, 2572
You Me And She, 5909
You Mean The World To Me, 719, 2610, 4529
You Meet The Nicest People On A Honda, 1333
You Messed Up My Mind, 2368
You Might Need Somebody, 156, 1282
You Might Want To Use Me Again, 4613
You Move Me, 1605, 1807, 4798
You Musn't Be Discouraged, 837
You Musn't Kick It Around, 4107
You Must Be Fool, 2222
You Must Be True, 1720
You Must Believe Me, 829,

GENERAL INDEX

A

A Band Of Angels, 25, 1347, 1542, 3437
A Cappella, 25 and *passim*
A Certain Ratio, 25-26, 2843, 4566, 4588, 5564
A Class Crew, 2701, 2899
A Day And Her Knights, 1428
A Flock Of Seagulls, 27, 3828, 3894, 3920
A Foot In Cold water, 27-28
A Guy Called Gerald, 28, 886, 1717, 3538, 4343, 4379, 5584
A Homeboy, A Hippie And A Funki Dredd, 28
A House, 28 and *passim*
A II Z, 29
A Noh Radio, 5806
A Man Called Adam, 29-30
A Taste Of Honey, 30
A Tribe Called Quest, 31-32, 171, 561, 853, 1353, 1435, 1455, 2466, 2713, 2826, 2912, 3044, 3232, 3299, 3393, 3417, 3657, 3876, 3883, 4004, 4059, 4071, 4191, 4219, 4303, 4687, 5368, 5946
A Tribo, 2903
A Witness, 31 and *passim*
A&M Records, 32 and *passim*
A's, 32
A+, 32
A-Bones, 32-33, 5989
A-Ha, 33, 4452, 6029
A.B. Skhy, 33, 2001
A.C., 33 and *passim*
A.D., 34 and *passim*
A.G. And Kate, 4014, 4106, 4460
A13 Productions, 34
A=440, 34, 243, 1520
Aaarrg Records, 2577
AACM, 34, 44, 96, 176, 182, 244, 382, 553, 634, 717, 821, 1168, 1287, 1465, 1784, 1803, 1862, 2028, 2200, 2406, 2592, 2783, 2810, 3114, 3217, 3347, 3544, 3581, 3716, 3762, 3862, 4514, 4656, 4982, 5297, 5420, 5878
Aaliyah, 34, 908, 1740, 2158, 2963
Aaltonen, Juhani, 34
Aardvark, 15, 35, 246, 5419
Aaron, Danny, 1379
Aaron, Lee, 35, 113, 275, 2380, 2684, 4742, 4805, 5471, 5704
Aarons, Alex A., 35, 2025, 2054, 2159
Aarons, Alfred E., 35
Aaronson, Irving, 36, 1049,

2040, 2258, 3128, 5750
Aaronson, Kenny, 1489, 2332, 2621, 3748, 5420
Aaronsrod, 36
Aatabou, Najat, 36
AB/CD, 36
Abaddon, 5628
Abangithandayo, Baningi, 3581
Abarbanell, Lina, 3399
Abarca, Jerry, 2482
Abatiello, Sal, 3342
Abato, Jimmy, 4658
Abattoir, 36-37, 3551
Abba, 37-38, 50, 182, 236, 551, 566, 680, 889, 1004, 1048, 1239, 1773, 1837, 2033, 2260, 2916, 3043, 3167, 3616, 3964, 4031, 4297, 4468, 4524, 4575, 4669, 4715, 5376, 6029-6030, 6047, 6122
Abba, Eden, 50
Abbey, John, 1573, 2670
Abbey, Leon, 1163, 2088, 4984
Abbey, Rufford, 3137
Abbittibbi Blues Print, 1492
Abbot, Gary, 3022
Abbot, Jacqui, 440
Abbot, Tim, 3763, 4009, 6066
Abbott And Costello, 183, 351, 419, 1437-1438, 1764, 2255, 3433, 3638, 3648, 4449, 4695, 5433, 5937
Abbott Records, 39, 4485
Abbott, Bud, 2255
Abbott, Chris, 362, 2693
Abbott, Darrell, 4119
Abbott, Drew, 4814
Abbott, George, 38, 498, 506, 1370, 1900-1901, 1941, 1983, 2056, 2931, 3637, 4042, 4106, 4337, 5498, 5787, 5989, 6029
Abbott, Gregory, 38
Abbott, John, 5564
Abbott, Kris, 4370
Abbott, L.B., 1567
Abbott, Larry, 5817
Abbott, Russ, 95, 1165, 3268, 4034
Abbott, Vince, 4119
ABC, 39 and *passim*
ABC Records, 39 and *passim*
Abdelhak, Cheb, 4409
Abdelkrim, 3667
Abdelli, 39-40
Abdul, Mussa, 1813
Abdul, Paula, 40, 404, 2644, 3093, 5715
Abdul-Malik, Ahmed, 40
Abdullah, Ahmed, 40-41, 701, 2200, 2591
Abdulsamad, Bilal Dinari, 697

Abdulsamad, Hakeem Saheed, 697
Abdulsamad, Hakim, 4297
Abdulsamad, Hasan Khiry, 697
Abdulsamad, Ustadi Tajh, 697
Abel, Robert, 1748, 3203
Abel, Walter, 2035
Abeloos, Oliver, 5279
Abeni, Queen Salawah, 3058
Abercoed, Frank, 1942
Abercrombie, John, 41, 492, 722, 1465, 1586, 1701, 1775, 2084, 2098, 2365, 2559, 3826, 3988, 4214, 4441, 4779, 5480, 5674, 5850
Abernathy, Mack, 5438
Abiam, Nana Danso, 4117
Abineri, Daniel, 319
Abiodun, Dele, 42, 74-75, 1359
Abnak Records, 2866
Abner, Ewart, 42
Abney, Don, 3771
Abong, Fred, 469, 5428
Abou-Khalil, Rabi, 1751
Above All, 42 and *passim*
Above The Law, 42-43 and *passim*
Abraham, Alex, 1329
Abraham-Robert, Paul, 5958
Abrahams, Brian, 43, 4174
Abrahams, Doris, 43
Abrahams, Maurice, 43, 337, 1106, 2217, 3201
Abrahams, Mick, 12, 44, 596, 1074, 2819, 4747, 5397, 5399
Abrahams, Paul, 4481
Abramo, Pete, 4518
Abrams, Bernard, 5511, 5973
Abrams, Bryan, 1181
Abrams, Dan, 5511
Abrams, Ja-Vanti, 1497
Abrams, Lawrence, 1914-1915
Abrams, Max, 44, 5435, 5635
Abrams, Muhal Richard, 34, 44, 96, 382, 561, 681, 717-718, 780, 953, 1287, 1344, 1784, 1803, 1862, 2028-2029, 2592-2593, 2796, 2810-2811, 3087, 3217, 3544, 3716-3717, 3862-3863, 4156, 4363, 5297, 5420, 5691
Abrams, Philip, 898
Abramson, Herb, 44, 268, 272, 1775, 3327, 5535, 5780
Abromavage, Mark, 3020
Abruscato, Sal, 3238
Absalom, Mick, 45
Abshire, Nathan, 45-46, 347-348, 887, 1931, 3676
Absolute Beginners, 46, 381, 686-687, 1088, 1404, 1414,

1718, 2027, 3729, 4144, 4150, 4714, 4782, 4978, 4714, 4782, 4978, 5339
Absolute Grey, 46
Absu, 46
Abubaka, Jazzboe, 4436
Abueta, Oscar Alberto, 3938, 4117
Abyssinians, 47, 938, 1300, 1329, 1363, 2638, 2822, 4438, 4489, 4675, 4751, 5279
AC/DC, 29, 36, 47-48, 285, 293, 310, 316, 362, 410, 475, 743, 823, 1000, 1069, 1089, 1461, 1539, 1589, 1695, 1845, 1905-1906, 1921, 1967, 1991, 2121, 2388, 2429, 2467-2468, 2525, 2674, 2754, 2819, 2838, 2907, 3040, 3079, 3211, 3271, 4053, 4672, 4679, 5429, 5482, 5515, 5586, 5808, 6029, 6122
Acacia, 48, 2455, 5370
Academy, 48-49 and *passim*
Acadia, 887
Accelerators, 49
Accent (UK), 49
Accents, 49 and *passim*
Accept, 49-50 and *passim*
Accolade, 50 and *passim*
Accra Rhythmic Orchestra, 2133, 3627, 5710
Accrington, Stanley, 50
Accuser, 50, 479
Ace, 45-46 and *passim*
Ace Lane, 51, 2096
Ace Of Base, 51, 70, 947, 1729, 2920, 4455
Ace Of Clubs, 51 and *passim*
Ace Records, 52 and *passim*
Ace, Buddy, 52, 4563
Ace, Charlie, 381, 4200
Ace, Georgina, 1949
Ace, Johnny, 52-53, 585, 635, 918, 1409, 2217, 2519, 3013, 4579
Ace, Martin, 1949, 3429, 3813
Ace, Richard, 486, 1979, 2519
Aces, 53 and *passim*
Aces (reggae), 53
Aceto, Eric, 4924
Acher, Markus, 3978
Acher, Michael, 3978
Acheron, 53
Achilles, Peter, 124
Achimota, 2133, 5710
Achor, James, 4671
Acid, 53-54 and *passim*
Acid Bath, 54, 121, 1137, 1941
Acid House, 28, 54, 264, 267, 311, 518, 694, 875, 1042, 1155, 1157, 1268, 1350, 1450, 1456,

Armstrong, Bob, 982, 2796
Armstrong, Brock, 929
Armstrong, Dee, 2989
Armstrong, Floyd, 230
Armstrong, Frankie, 231, 609, 736, 3285, 3594-3595, 4658, 4811, 5935, 5985, 6030
Armstrong, Herbie, 2002, 5786, 5954, 5974
Armstrong, Howard, 3483
Armstrong, Jim, 5383
Armstrong, Julie, 2862
Armstrong, Kevin, 1576, 4152, 4348
Armstrong, Lillian, 232, 2391, 2750, 2790, 2825, 2852, 2878, 3281, 3710, 4156, 4604, 5609
Armstrong, Louis, 7-8, 19, 22-23, 40, 72, 122, 130, 148-149, 154, 232-235, 240-241, 286, 342, 350, 372, 420, 428, 443-444, 455, 468, 475, 486, 491, 505, 507, 542, 545, 548, 568, 578, 608, 678, 704, 707, 786, 800, 803, 814, 852, 858, 876-877, 884-885, 890, 895, 941, 976, 1038, 1061, 1066, 1102, 1115, 1122, 1132, 1160, 1163, 1167, 1177, 1201, 1265, 1302-1303, 1365, 1372, 1378, 1383, 1408, 1436-1437, 1452, 1455, 1506, 1513, 1571, 1647, 1655, 1669, 1706, 1722, 1732, 1774, 1793, 1828, 1862, 1866, 1912, 1918, 1976, 1985, 2070, 2073, 2094, 2111, 2120, 2135, 2151, 2159, 2170-2171, 2189, 2197, 2209, 2215, 2241, 2268, 2304-2305, 2329, 2335, 2347-2348, 2354, 2360, 2362, 2370-2372, 2377, 2428, 2437, 2439, 2477, 2487, 2518, 2522, 2528-2529, 2536-2538, 2545, 2573, 2617, 2623, 2625, 2639, 2654, 2722, 2750, 2773, 2794, 2796, 2798, 2810, 2843, 2848, 2851, 2869, 2879-2880, 2884, 2892, 2895, 2928, 2946, 2971, 3009, 3019, 3030, 3056, 3090, 3108, 3110, 3126, 3129, 3150, 3200, 3226, 3376, 3401, 3448-3449, 3466, 3499, 3503, 3517, 3554, 3557, 3584, 3600, 3655, 3658, 3672, 3683, 3690, 3710, 3736, 3752, 3765, 3773, 3781, 3786-3787, 3804, 3875, 3919, 3930, 3932, 3937, 3939, 4024, 4035, 4040, 4059, 4066, 4089, 4128, 4180, 4211-4213, 4255, 4291, 4300, 4323, 4328, 4370, 4427, 4450, 4472, 4500, 4513, 4526, 4584, 4604, 4608, 4662, 4694, 4699, 4736, 4750, 4753, 4815, 4855, 4877, 4915, 4936, 4981, 4985, 4988, 5278, 5301, 5322, 5359, 5365, 5368, 5400, 5426, 5507, 5533, 5598, 5606, 5611, 5688, 5711, 5718, 5724, 5732, 5741, 5756, 5815, 5817, 5840, 5855, 5858, 5879, 5882, 5981, 5985, 6030
Armstrong, Mo, 1356
Armstrong, Nancy, 1682
Armstrong, Roger, 52, 1066
Armstrong, Rollo, 4079

Armstrong, Sam, 4820, 6030
Armstrong, Stretch, 2053
Armstrong, Tommy, 443, 1862, 2375
Armstrong, Vanessa Bell, 1631, 2829, 5881
Army Of Lovers, 236
Arnaud, Delmar, 5349
Arnaud, Michele, 2071
Arnaz, Alberto, IV, 1532
Arnaz, Desi, 236, 351, 1532, 3428, 5464, 6030-6031
Arnaz, Desi, Jnr., 351, 3428
Arnaz, Lucie, 236, 351, 2363, 2797, 5388
Arndt, Felix, 236
Arne, Peter, 1066
Arnesen, Peter, 2640
Arnett, Wiley, 4713
Arnez, Alberto, 236
Arnez, Lucie, 3389
Arnheim, Gus, 236, 308, 2025, 2287, 3366, 4695, 5453
Arno, Fritz, 2167
Arno, Lou, 4391
Arnold, 237 and *passim*
Arnold, Albert, 5845
Arnold, Arnita, 981
Arnold, Billy Boy, 237, 1399, 1517, 1671, 2253, 2856, 2879-2880, 5333, 5680, 5861, 5969
Arnold, Bob, 274, 3455, 5959
Arnold, Bruce, 4064, 6085
Arnold, David, 4349
Arnold, Dek, 4378
Arnold, Eddy, 173, 237-238, 704, 803, 828, 864, 944, 958, 1143, 1229, 1256, 1419, 1421, 1526, 1956, 2001, 2010, 2102, 2143, 2289, 2311, 2395, 2444, 2481, 2880, 3017, 3030, 3290, 3308, 3310, 3325, 3783-3784, 3862, 3926, 4062, 4091, 4310, 4315, 4373, 4547, 4887, 5678-5679, 5729, 5774, 5818, 5863, 5986, 6030
Arnold, Edward, 197, 237, 3281, 4635, 5284
Arnold, Franz, 611
Arnold, Harry, 238-239, 4001, 4204
Arnold, Harvey, 4083
Arnold, Horace, 1981
Arnold, James 'Kokomo', 239
Arnold, Jerome, 1691, 1879
Arnold, Jerry, 563
Arnold, Jimmy, 239-240
Arnold, Joe, 3455
Arnold, Lee, 1123
Arnold, Malcolm, 78, 240
Arnold, P.P., 228, 240, 437, 1125, 1402, 1462, 2678, 2932, 3471, 3936, 4012, 4458, 4974, 5543
Arnold, Patricia, 240
Arnold, Paul, 4085, 6001
Arnold, Richard Edward, 237, 5284
Arnold, Tim, 2828
Arnold, Tom, 240-241, 1758
Arnold, Vance, 1144
Arnondrin, Sidney, 241
Arnone, Mike, 1657
Arnott, Dave, 726

Arnott, Ray, 5973
Arnoux, Jean Pierre, 3422
Arnspiger, Herman, 781, 3240, 5865-5866
Arnstein, Nicky, 731, 1493, 2055-2056
Arntz, James, 186, 6030
Aroche, Elizardo, 3313
Arodin, Sidney, 241, 941, 4328
Aronoff, Kenny, 639, 3477
Aronson, Billy, 4505
Aronson, Boris, 874, 876, 1196, 4099, 6002
Arpeggio Records, 810
Arquette, Rosanna, 4217
Arran, Rod, 1013
Arrested Development, 241-242, 1224, 1546, 1854, 2312, 3133, 4007, 4836, 5369, 5585
Arrington, Barbara, 3412
Arrington, Charlie, 5705
Arrington, Harvey, 942
Arrington, Jabbo, 3487
Arrington, Joseph, Jnr., 5347
Arrington, Robert, 1777
Arrival, 242 and *passim*
Arrogant Worm, 929
Arrow, 242 and *passim*
Arrows, 242-243 and *passim*
Arrows (Canada), 243
Arroyo, Joe, 243, 398, 3939
Arroyo, Pedro, 2235, 3835, 4618
Ars Nova, 243-244, 1230
Art, 244 and *passim*
Art Bears, 588, 2493, 5394
Art Ensemble Of Chicago, 34, 96, 244, 408, 688, 1226, 1341, 1463, 1616, 1701, 1784, 1862, 2783, 3042, 3716, 3762, 3822, 4363, 5311, 5362, 5878
Art In America, 245
Art Of Noise, 102, 245, 349, 1237, 1642, 1702, 2286, 2887, 3006, 3229, 4123, 4709, 6004
Artch, 245
Artery, 246, 3768, 5618
Arthey, John, 4150
Arthur, Art, 582, 1405, 1733, 3360, 3908-3909, 4750
Arthur, Beatrice, 246, 1882, 3428, 5426
Arthur, Bob, 2591, 3807
Arthur, Charline, 246
Arthur, Davey, 2057-2058, 4894
Arthur, Emry, 247
Arthur, J., 1102, 2128, 5659-5660
Arthur, Jack, 246, 1217, 2785, 5691
Arthur, Jean, 498, 2562, 4207
Arthur, Neil, 260, 585
Arthur, Robert, 125, 899, 976, 3808, 4706
Arthur, Robert Alan, 125
Arthur, Wayne, 478
Arthurs, Andy, 81
Arthurs, Debra, 3237
Arthurs, George, 247
Articles Of Faith, 247
Artificial Records, 1378
Artillery, 248, 1823, 1926, 2347, 3258, 4147, 4177, 4533
Artis, Bob, 3489, 6091
Artisan, 248, 2272, 4537, 6102

Artistics, 248, 1407
Artwoods, 50, 248, 1457, 1573, 2423, 5633
Arundel, Alex, 5712
Arusha Jazz, 4913
Arvan, Chris, 4398
Arvee Records, 457
Arvis Records, 2994
Arwin Records, 2779
As The Girls Go, 69, 249
As Thousands Cheer, 249, 493-494, 748, 1516, 2422, 2602, 3326, 5723, 6035
As You Were, 249, 672, 789, 864, 1141, 1326, 1436, 3603, 4238, 6038
Asafo-Agyei, Herman, 2514
Asakawa, Tommy, 5712
Asante, Okyerema, 2471
ASAP, 250
Asare, Kwame, 3628
ASCAP, 14, 68, 93, 250, 604, 1033, 1166, 1214, 1218, 1401-1402, 1596, 1766, 1783, 1824, 2224, 2270, 2364, 2597, 2785, 2967, 3285, 3629, 3844, 4181, 4502, 4509, 4654, 4664, 4677, 4736, 4777, 5709, 5719, 5750, 5860, 5953, 6114
Asch, Moses, 4904, 5344
Asche, Oscar, 250-251, 1078, 6030
Ascher, Kenny, 5857
Ascher, Robert, 4658
Ash, 251 and *passim*
Ash Ra Temple, 4303
Ash, Daniel, 251, 418, 1989, 3335, 3843, 5461
Ash, Darren, 3612, 6116
Ash, Debbie, 2601
Ash, Jerome, 3003
Ash, Leslie, 4376, 5520
Ash, Mike, 280
Ash, Paul, 251, 1455, 2932
Ash, Vic, 2082
Ashall, Barrie, 1992, 5880
Ashbourn, Peter, 1081
Ashburn, Bernie, 1193
Ashburn, Peter, Affair, 1979
Ashby Players, 252
Ashby, Dorothy, 251-252, 2339, 5769
Ashby, Hal, 680
Ashby, Harold, 252, 3348
Ashby, Irving, 252, 2370
Ashby, John, 252, 4510
Ashley, Leon, 254
Ashcroft, Peggy, 4577
Ashcroft, Ray, 544
Ashdown, Doug, 252
Asher, Bea, 356
Asher, John, 422, 796, 1285
Asher, John Symon, 422, 796, 1285
Asher, Peter, 252, 1509, 2686, 4206, 5313, 5337
Ashes, 253 and *passim*
Asheton, Ron, 1494, 2676, 4401
Ashfield, Tony, 2576
Ashford And Simpson, 230, 253, 722, 1459, 1678, 2104, 3048, 3686, 4571, 4910, 4925
Ashford, Geoff, 2204
Ashford, R.T., 2171

Barksdale, Chuck, 150, 994, 1033, 1473
Barksdale, Everett, 383, 4786
Barlam, Alan, 230, 2476
Barlow, Andrew, 3115
Barlow, Barriemore, 2819, 3423
Barlow, Bill, 383
Barlow, Bruce, 1193
Barlow, Colin, 3242
Barlow, Dale, 383, 2108
Barlow, Dave, 1403
Barlow, Dean, 4944
Barlow, Gary, 383, 4087, 5285, 5857
Barlow, Jack, 384
Barlow, Jonathan, 5420
Barlow, Lou, 1533, 1957, 2853, 4802, 4944
Barlow, Louise, 4463
Barlow, Phil, 1921
Barlow, Randy, 384
Barman, Tom, 1498
Barnabus, 189, 4514
Barnaby Records, 820, 2570
Barnacle, Gary, 4703
Barnacle, Pete, 2148, 2158
Barnacles, Gary, 3379
Barnard, Bob, 5648
Barnard, Eric, 5545
Barnard, Glenn, 5824
Barnard, Ivor, 4725
Barner, Micah, 3990
Barnes And Barnes, 384-385 and *passim*
Barnes Howel, Joshua, 2619
Barnes, Adam, 2630
Barnes, Al, 3450, 5628
Barnes, Alan, 385, 1035, 1151, 2884, 3932, 4760, 5894
Barnes, Artie, 384
Barnes, Benny, 385
Barnes, Binnie, 746, 996
Barnes, Chris, 917, 4010, 4943
Barnes, Christopher Daniel, 3268
Barnes, Clive, 2285
Barnes, Danny, 321
Barnes, Dee, 1612
Barnes, Eddie, 1326
Barnes, Emile, 638, 1189
Barnes, Fae, 2880
Barnes, Frank, 4719, 5865
Barnes, Fred, 707, 1242
Barnes, George, 385-386, 707, 1965, 3076, 4257, 4305, 4786, 5631
Barnes, J.J., 386, 3432
Barnes, James Jay, 386
Barnes, Jeffrey, 717
Barnes, Jim, 415, 3348
Barnes, Jimmy, 386, 1057, 1156, 3850
Barnes, John, 385-386, 3376, 3658, 4760, 5766, 5889
Barnes, Kathy, 2323
Barnes, Ken, 15, 427, 2007, 4930, 6032, 6078, 6106
Barnes, Lloyd, 387, 742, 1487, 3271, 4201
Barnes, Mae, 387
Barnes, Max, 387, 1322, 2147, 4798, 5496
Barnes, Mike, 4592
Barnes, Neil, 3179

Barnes, Paul, 388, 3179, 5445
Barnes, Paul 'Polo', 388
Barnes, Peggy-Ann, 4182
Barnes, Phil, 204
Barnes, Raymond, 746, 3131
Barnes, Richard, 4386, 5812, 6085
Barnes, Ricky, 2426, 4156
Barnes, Roosevelt 'Booba', 388
Barnes, Sid, 2741, 4660
Barnes, Skipper, 4719
Barnes, Stephen, 5419
Barnes, Sylvia, 415-416, 3348
Barnes, Walter, 388, 2750, 3765
Barnes, William, 3151
Barnes, Winifred, 511
Barnet, Beres, 3758
Barnet, Charlie, 107, 375, 388-389, 421, 504, 507, 779, 897, 914, 925, 1433, 1437, 1455, 1774, 1817, 1877, 1885, 1927, 2085, 2100, 2150, 2199, 2406, 2472, 2560, 2596, 2738, 2924, 2993, 3045, 3127, 3142, 3178, 3516, 3525, 3544, 3599, 3766, 3785, 3875, 3932, 3967, 3978, 4075, 4151, 4215, 4342, 4626, 4686, 4716, 4844, 5343, 5852, 5861, 5928, 6003, 6031
Barnet, Jim, 431
Barnet, Miguel, 3779
Barnet, Mike, 513
Barnett, Andy, 250
Barnett, Angela, 685
Barnett, Anthony, 6079
Barnett, Bobby, 389
Barnett, Derrick, 4717
Barnett, Gene, 1539, 3246
Barnett, Grace, 2258, 2802-2803
Barnett, Horace, 2456
Barnett, Irving, 3635
Barnett, James, 226
Barnett, Jan, 4662
Barnett, Jerry, 4885
Barnett, Rikki, 4717
Barnett, Tommy, 844
Barney, Steve, 824
Barnfield, John, 4184
Barnhart, Ralph, 4701
Barnova, Vera, 4042
Barnum, 389-390 and *passim*
Barnum, H.B., 1595, 1614, 3973, 4580
Barnum, P.T., 1165, 1281
Barnwell, Carl, 3516
Barnwell, Duncan, 4921
Barnwell, Timothy, 241
Baró, Armando, 85
Barohn, Josh, 285
Baron Demus, 1906
Baron Rojo, 390, 3936
Baron, Bob, 3492
Baron, Calvin, 3789
Baron, Don, 2800
Baron, Joey, 496, 2038, 3870, 4571, 6003
Baron, Lynda, 1959, 3268
Baron, Peter, 5290
Baron, Steve, 4819
Baron, Tommy T., 1237
Barone, Richard, 432, 3255
Barovero, Fabio, 3520
Barovier, Carl, 5393
Barr, George, 729, 1978, 5901

Barr, John, 1064
Barr, Ralph, 3958
Barra, David, 4851
Barraclough, Mike, 4373
Barraclough, Roy, 4873, 4969
Barracudas, 390, 4354
Barragan, Larry, 2482
Barratt, John, 4372
Barratt, Steve, 2504
Barratt, Willy, 2624
Barre, Martin, 2819, 5505
Barreau, André, 5925
Barrelhouse Buck, 390, 5621
Barrelhouse Records, 711, 2561
Barrell, Ernie, 3562
Barren Cross, 390, 3902
Barrere, Paul, 391, 3265
Barresi, Joe, 2975
Barret, Charlie, 1922
Barret, Sweet Emma, 2635
Barreto, Don Marino, 1939
Barreto, Justi, 137
Barrett Brothers, 65, 839, 3468
Barrett Sisters, 391
Barrett, Betty, 2785
Barrett, Bob, 840, 5933
Barrett, Brent, 1296
Barrett, Carlton, 4050, 4401, 5583
Barrett, Clive, 1905
Barrett, Curt, 512
Barrett, Dan, 112, 391, 3505, 4191, 4736
Barrett, Dave, 4260
Barrett, Dicky, 3660, 4425
Barrett, Fanita, 606
Barrett, Geoff, 5351
Barrett, Howard, 1565, 4124, 4962, 5301
Barrett, James, 606, 4821, 4867
Barrett, Jeff, 2466, 4066
Barrett, Jonathan, 3410
Barrett, KK, 558
Barrett, Malcolm, 728, 6068
Barrett, Marcia, 656
Barrett, Nick, 4184
Barrett, Norman, 2250
Barrett, Patrick, 4458
Barrett, Richard, 5421, 5598
Barrett, Richie, 1018
Barrett, Rob, 918
Barrett, Roger, 392, 4247
Barrett, Roger Keith, 392
Barrett, Ronald, 1595, 3131
Barrett, Russell, 1022
Barrett, Sweet Emma, 391-392, 2636, 4762
Barrett, Syd, 325, 392-393, 1229, 1456, 1715, 1774, 2145, 2250, 2425, 2541, 2544, 2858, 3334, 4007, 4248-4249, 4354, 4885, 5330, 5396, 5545, 5895, 6031, 6068, 6122
Barrett, Wild Willie, 393, 4078
Barretto, Marino, 993, 4645
Barretto, Ray, 301, 393-394, 507, 576, 872, 1320-1321, 1530, 1833, 1841, 1855, 2398, 3163, 3233, 3354, 3657, 3702, 3938, 4098, 4114-4115, 4361, 4421, 4611, 4742, 5446
Barri, Steve, 79, 394, 795, 1211, 1531, 1844, 2245, 3579, 4522, 4970, 5398

Barrie, Amanda, 2665
Barrie, Barbara, 1196
Barrie, Dick, 3147
Barrie, George, 885, 1196
Barrie, Grace, 3366
Barrie, Gracie, 394, 3147, 5798
Barrie, J.J., 395, 2615, 3755, 4126, 4344
Barrie, James, 735
Barrie, Linda, 3019
Barrie, Mona, 4046
Barrie, Wendy, 522
Barrier, 395 and *passim*
Barrier Brothers, 395
Barrier, Eric, 1773, 4104
Barrier, Henry Ray, 395
Barrier, Herman, 395
Barrigo, Don, 2197, 3323
Barringer, Ambrose, 3583
Barrington, Chris, 3920
Barrington, Johnny, 715
Barrington, Roy, 4374
Barrington, Rutland, 1253
Barrio, Querido, 1323, 4611
Barris, Chuck, 918
Barris, George, 760
Barris, Harry, 251, 332, 395, 1302, 1885, 2555, 3002, 4522, 4932, 5453
Barrish, Jesse, 396
Barrison, Mabel, 309
Barrister, 396, 1976, 2046, 2643, 3058, 4528
Barrister, Wasiu, 396, 2046
Barriteau, Carl, 397, 1733, 2848, 5635, 5810, 5887
Barrois, Raymond, 830
Barron Knights, 397, 3325, 5385, 5481, 6031
Barron, Bill, 397-398, 1338
Barron, Blue, 397-398, 939, 1927, 4111
Barron, Chris, 626
Barron, Curly, 1358
Barron, Douglas, 1246
Barron, James, 3196
Barron, Kenny, 115, 130, 182, 383, 397-398, 404, 614, 738, 1338, 1928, 2016, 2038, 2133, 2331, 2445, 2448, 2621, 3321, 3716, 3946, 4584, 4786, 5386, 5770, 5840, 6032
Barron, Muriel, 4192
Barron, Tony, 398
Barron, Wally, 2535
Barros, Adolfo, 399
Barros, Alberto 'El Conejo', 398-399
Barros, José, 398
Barroso, Abelardo, 1899, 3181, 4121
Barroso, Ary, 4695
Barrow, Ernest, 2755
Barrow, Geoff, 1047, 1649, 4291
Barrow, George, 168, 622
Barrow, Keith, 399
Barrow, Ricky, 147
Barrow, Willie T., 399
Barrowman, John, 1922, 3509
Barrows, April, 635
Barry And The Tamerlanes, 399
Barry Sisters, 3019
Barry, Anna, 2342

Bennett, Mark, 4619
**Bennett, Michael, 356, 478,
1049, 1070-1071, 1625, 1959,
2363, 3583, 5527, 6035, 6063**
Bennett, Mick, 1139, 4110
Bennett, Mikey, 1944, 3405,
4120, 4468
Bennett, Mikie, 2186
Bennett, Nigel, 3622, 5640
Bennett, Patricia, 1057
Bennett, Pinto, 478, 5685
Bennett, R., 1813
Bennett, Ray, 1929, 4208
Bennett, Rex, 4819
Bennett, Richard, 479, 719,
1029, 1640, 2409, 2546, 3018,
3755, 5785, 6035
**Bennett, Richard Rodney, 479,
719, 3018, 3755, 5785, 6035**
**Bennett, Robert Russell, 479-
480, 1499, 2101, 2159, 4025**
Bennett, Ronnie, 857, 2534
Bennett, Roy, 2214, 5654
Bennett, Roy C., 5654
Bennett, Russell, 479-480, 1499,
2101, 2159, 4025
Bennett, Stan, 4268
Bennett, Sylvia, 2372
**Bennett, Tony, 23, 79, 406-407,
480-481, 803-804, 1164, 1185,
1243, 1483, 1504, 1534, 1788-
1789, 1793, 1831, 1851, 1883,
1928, 2329, 2399, 2524, 2595,
2768, 2900, 3099, 3105, 3187,
3261, 3268, 3322, 3348, 3473,
3553, 3630, 3664, 3677, 3709,
3789, 3857, 4075, 4208, 4374,
4565, 4616, 4654, 4782, 4801,
4850, 4928, 5846, 6035**
Bennett, Trevor, 1946, 2096
Bennett, Val, 4429
Bennett, Ventura, 476
Bennett, Vernie, 1782
Bennett, Veronica, 4639
Bennett, Wayne, 481, 6105
Bennett, Wilda, 3850
Bennett, Wiley, 5856
Bennett, Willie P., 1865
Bennett, Winston, 3634
Benney, David, 3323
**Bennink, Han, 151, 182, 330-
331, 481, 591, 727-728, 763,
3070, 3102, 3388, 3627, 4135,
4773, 5310, 5607**
**Benno, Marc, 265, 403, 482,
1095, 4698**
Benns, Jon, 226
**Benny Goodman Story, The,
136, 482, 1085, 1419, 2209-
2210, 2226, 2773, 3042, 3082,
3433, 5439**
Benny Profane, 482, 4642
Benny, Buck, 175, 332, 1427,
2412, 2749, 4694
Benny, Jack, 78, 130, 451, 522,
746, 955, 1418, 1426-1427, 2020,
2287, 2412, 2948, 3638, 4580,
5439, 5773
**Benoit, David, 483, 2300-2301,
2304, 4231, 4552**
Benoit, Tab, 483
Benorick, Steve, 4619
Bensman, Ben, 2938
Benson Orchestra, 483, 828, 3081

Benson, Al, 484, 4144
Benson, Bobby, 2524, 3150
Benson, Bruce, 372, 558, 2370
Benson, Edgar, 483, 2193
Benson, Edgar A., 483
Benson, F.R., 250
Benson, Fred, 1332, 2938
**Benson, George, 150, 283, 296,
465, 484-485, 724, 759, 877,
889, 969, 1280, 1282, 1431,
1785, 1853, 1883, 1981, 2068,
2338, 2370, 2464, 2517, 2689,
2795, 2882, 2983, 3044, 3177,
3233, 3258-3259, 3502-3503,
3565, 3833, 4279, 4699, 4832,
4848, 4850, 4990, 5450, 5583,
5750**
Benson, Howard, 3003
Benson, Ivy, 485, 3279
Benson, Jo Jo, 4787, 4790, 4936
Benson, Jodi, 1284, 3268
Benson, John, 350, 1794, 3259,
4695
Benson, Julie, 2862
Benson, Kathleen, 1161, 5909,
6041, 6086
Benson, Leo, 2501
Benson, Lorraine, 2501, 3868
Benson, Marie, 4125
Benson, Nathaniel, 150
Benson, Peter, 2941
Benson, Ray, 257, 4986
Benson, Renaldo, 1997
Benson, Robby, 440, 2120
Benson, Sally, 3611, 5654
Benson, Sharon, 2602
Bensusan, Pierre, 2309
Bent, Phillip, 486, 2797
Benti, Phil, 5421
Bentine, Michael, 2111, 2213,
4397, 4804
**Bentley Rhythm Ace, 486, 1488,
2317, 4954**
Bentley, Ed, 1306
Bentley, Fatso, 486
Bentley, Gladys Alberta, 486
Bentley, Irene, 466
Bentley, Jay, 322
Bentley, John, 1319, 3159
Bentley, Mary Denise, 1968
Benton, Arley, 487
**Benton, Brook, 254, 486-487,
1011, 2610, 2882, 2976, 3632,
4075, 4326, 4847, 4936, 4975,
5496, 5620, 5716-5717**
Benton, Buster, 487, 1167
Benton, Carl, 2258
Benton, Christopher, 447
Benton, Jim, 4017
Benton, Robert, 2723
Benton, Sonny, 1424
Bentyne, Cheryl, 3441
Beny, Puente Homenaje A,
1321, 4361, 4614
Benz, 487
Benz Records, 487, 3538
**Benz, Spragga, 487, 2015, 2038,
2959, 3425**
Benzell, Mimi, 3668
Benzini Brothers, 2604
Beraldi, Frank, 2625
Berber, Ignaz, 738
Berdy, Vickie, 2396
Berea Three, 5784

Berecz, András, 4803
Bereman, Bobby, 4471
Berendt, Joachim, 2408, 3655,
6097
Berens, Harold, 2456
Berenyi, Miki, 3363, 3775
Beres, Jeff, 4941
Beresford, Steve, 482, 1150,
1269, 1951
Berg, Billy, 2142
Berg, Bob, 487, 2625
Berg, Cia, 5780
Berg, George, 2625
Berg, Icee, 488
Berg, Matraca, 488, 642
Berg, Mole, 4370
Berg, Ron, 596, 2910
Berg, Steve, 2678
Berg, Thilo, 3793
Berg, Tony, 1016, 5340
Bergcrantz, Anders, 3141
Bergen, Edgar, 3967, 5600
Berger, David, 2540, 6053, 6101
Berger, Ernest, 2464
**Berger, Karl, 488, 2732, 3102,
4682, 5698**
Berger, Michel, 488
Berger, Morroe, 964
Bergerac, Jacques, 3199, 4620
Bergere, Roy, 282
Bergeron, Alphee, 488
Bergeron, Shirley, 488, 3127
Berggren, Wes, 5506
Bergh, Totti, 489, 1154, 1365
Berghofer, Chuck, 489, 543, 925
Bergin, David, 4623
Bergin, Mary, 490
Berghofer, Chuck, 489, 543, 925
Bergland, Bob, 2672
Berglund, Henrik, 274
**Bergman, Alan And Marilyn,
356, 490, 1824, 1942, 2363-
2364, 2784, 2876, 3183, 3574,
5956**
Bergman, Eddie, 3015
Bergman, Ingrid, 2183, 2644,
4181
Bergman, Peter, 1904
Bergman, Stefan, 1480
Bergonzi, Jerry, 490
Bergreen, L., 235, 494
Bergren, Jenny, 51
Bergren, Jonas, 51
Bergren, Malin, 51
Bergström, Henry, 70
Bergus, Clay, 1455
Berigan, Buddy, 1599
**Berigan, Bunny, 279, 332, 355,
491, 537, 550, 677, 823, 1208,
1599, 1731, 1776, 2208, 2535,
3586, 3736, 3815, 4075, 4342,
4525, 4528, 4818, 4877, 4880,
5476, 5713, 5780, 5802, 5982,
6035, 6097**
Bering, Ted, 4441
Berio, Luciano, 187, 4491
Berk Brothers, 2838, 4318
Berk, Dave, 325, 1371, 2839
**Berkeley, Busby, 308, 491, 539,
920, 1084, 1368, 1965-1966,
1982, 2081, 2185, 2571, 2951-
2952, 2985, 3492, 4054, 4299,
4535, 4636, 4648, 5284, 5710,
5814**

Berkeley, Tyrone, 5576
Berkeley, William, 491
Berkey, Bob, 4176
Berkhout, Fred, 1778
**Berklee College Of Music, 41,
101, 172, 187, 490, 492, 571,
597, 658, 738, 742, 745, 759,
786, 844, 847, 872, 885, 925,
951, 1035, 1162, 1172, 1186,
1220, 1424, 1531, 1554, 1565,
1586, 1624, 1682, 1776, 1783,
1785, 1890, 2038, 2075, 2082,
2095, 2139, 2226, 2305, 2332,
2395, 2415, 2441, 2483, 2540,
2562, 2786, 2882, 2898, 2988,
3072, 3079, 3099, 3113, 3130,
3178, 3253, 3280, 3316-3317,
3333, 3366, 3451, 3459-3461,
3473-3474, 3502, 3512, 3553,
3568, 3645, 3772, 3826, 3967,
4093, 4111, 4245, 4277, 4288,
4302, 4473, 4499, 4542, 4608,
4640, 4731, 4747, 4751, 4779,
4852, 4913, 5292, 5295, 5478,
5569, 5585, 5592, 5653, 5691,
5720, 5725, 5757, 5994**
Berkley, Winston, 4706
Berkowitz, Mike, 859
Berle, Milton, 112, 955, 1274,
2252, 2591, 2895, 3204, 3466,
5439, 5454
Berlin, 492 and *passim*
**Berlin, Irving, 21, 43, 113, 196-
197, 249, 261, 295, 354, 492-
494, 617, 668, 678, 829, 837,
893, 1005, 1133, 1147, 1498,
1516, 1647, 1700, 1868, 1886,
1909, 1912, 1959-1960, 2028,
2107, 2221, 2260, 2273, 2422,
2448, 2488, 2544, 2555, 2616,
2654, 2729, 2862, 2922, 2985,
3148, 3200, 3212, 3337, 3362,
3452, 3481, 3555, 3580, 3634,
3705, 3710, 3747, 3788, 3850,
3984, 4212, 4827, 4850, 4855,
5396, 5466, 5619, 5757, 5791,
5832, 5997, 6035, 6097**
Berlin, Jeff, 798
Berlin, Steve, 587, 1090, 1937,
2539, 3320, 5517
Berline, Byron, 334, 494, 1252,
1277, 1527-1528, 1950, 3745
Berliner, Emile, 17, 2545, 4276
Berliner, Ernie, 4451
Berlinger, Warren, 2285, 2613
Berlmon, Joni, 3344
Berman, Al, 1469
Berman, Bess, 1919
Berman, Brigitte, 455, 550
Berman, David, 4909
Berman, Harry, 1358
Berman, Pandro S., 5998
Berman, Saul, 495
Berman, Shelley, 2742
**Berman, Sonny, 495, 2506,
4404, 5379**
Bermann, Frank, 157
Bernabel, Memo, 495, 4176
Bernadette, 495
Bernard, Al, 3076
Bernard, Barrie, 2822, 4250
Bernard, Chuck, 762
Bernard, Clem, 1246
Bernard, Dudley, 2841

Blackburn, Bryan, 2017
Blackburn, Clifton, 1784
Blackburn, Jeff, 396, 569
Blackburn, Kenneth, 569
Blackburn, Tom, 4135
Blackburn, Tony, 569, 2410, 4252
Blackbyrds, 569-570, 865
Blackeyed Susan, 570, 743, 1540
Blackfeather, 570, 4583
Blackfoot, 293, 368, 402, 570-571, 1566, 2436, 3808, 5697
Blackfoot Sue, 570-571, 1563, 4083
Blackford, Andy, 194, 827, 1014, 4323, 6030, 6038
Blackford, Richard, 2996
Blackhawk, 417, 546, 571, 795, 1225, 1411, 1415, 1792, 1822, 1869, 1984, 2028, 2196, 2379, 2403, 2572, 2618, 2667, 2768, 2785, 2895, 2943, 2964, 3085, 3091, 3181, 3250, 3446-3447, 3722, 3740, 4538, 4740, 5451, 5484, 5850
Blackhurst, Keith, 1453
Blackjacks, 3195, 5746
Blackledge, Spencer, 2910
Blackley, David, 2970
Blackman, Arthur, 4596
Blackman, Bernard, 5732
Blackman, Cindy, 571, 2487, 3540
Blackman, Donald, 5425
Blackman, Honor, 3152
Blackmer, Sidney, 2522
Blackmon, Karen, 4373
Blackmon, Larry, 767, 2318
Blackmore, Amos, 5763
Blackmore, Jon, 2148, 3388, 5824
Blackmore, Ritchie, 503, 571-572, 647, 668, 1074, 1175, 1269, 1457, 1534, 1730, 2148, 2174, 2264, 2269, 2473, 2686, 3145, 3388, 3401, 3423, 3496, 4083, 4183, 4411, 4751, 5533, 6122
Blackout, 572, 1575, 1804, 2372, 2508, 3342, 4273, 4774, 4781, 5355
Blacksteel, 2857
Blackston, Harvey, 2399
Blackstones, 572, 1605
BLACKstreet, 523, 572-573, 772, 793, 4243, 4545
Blackthorne, 573, 659, 3385
Blackton, Jay, 1499, 4025
Blackwards, 5939
Blackwatch, 3249, 5939
Blackwater, 150, 2378, 2782, 2978
Blackwell, Arthur, 942
Blackwell, Chris, 99, 303, 573, 824, 1125, 1234, 1420, 1710, 1781, 1783, 2214, 2254, 2717, 2814, 2873, 3211, 3407, 3468, 3494-3495, 3531-3532, 3681, 3956, 4260, 4490, 5489, 5509, 5565, 5646, 5651, 5890, 5927
Blackwell, Chuck, 890, 4881
Blackwell, Dwayne, 755, 1935
Blackwell, Ed, 40, 412, 488, 567, 574, 603, 701, 1026, 1046, 1167, 1405, 2023, 2331, 3474, 3731,

4028, 4321, 4472, 5698, 5778, 6090-6091, 6101
Blackwell, Elizabeth, 574
Blackwell, Francis Hillman 'Scrapper', 574
Blackwell, Gino, 1353
Blackwell, Middleton Joseph, 573
Blackwell, Otis, 150, 574, 1995, 2835, 3219, 4310
Blackwell, Robert 'Bumps', 575
Blackwell, Rory, 3316, 4142
Blackwell, Willie '61', 575
Blackwells, 575, 1878, 6120
Blackwood Brothers, 575-576, 2880, 5666
Blackwood, Roy, 575
Blackwood, Cecil Stamps, 575
Blackwood, Doyle, 575
Blackwood, Hugh, 5441
Blackwood, James Webre, 575
Blackwood, Lloyd, 1269
Blackwood, R.W., 575
Blackwood, Sarah, 1640
Blackwood, Terry, 187
Blackwood, Tim, 3154
Blackwoods, 2071
Blackwych, 576
Blade, 576 and *passim*
Blade Records, 230, 749, 1860, 2474, 2503, 2909, 3879, 4119, 4294, 4337, 4773, 4822
Blade Runner, 576, 4903, 5555
Blade, Jay C., 4092
Blades, Jack, 1370, 3893, 3947-3948, 3984, 4854, 4858
Blades, Rubén, 301, 393, 576-577, 922, 1180-1181, 1842, 1900, 2235, 2397, 3142, 3233-3234, 3779, 4098, 4361, 4421, 4447, 4559, 4612, 4614, 4618
Blades, Steve, 1805
Blaeholder, Henry, 512
Blaggers ITA, 577, 1608, 4023
Blaha, Axel, 4124
Blahzay Blahzay, 577
Blaikley, Alan, 1398, 2502, 2582, 2613, 2616
Blaikley, Howard, 1398, 2502, 2582, 2613, 2616, 3517
Blaine, Hal, 578, 4559, 4665, 4737, 5589, 5856, 6036
Blaine, Jerry, 45, 1019
Blaine, Terry, 578
Blaine, Vivian, 578, 2016, 2322, 2942, 3294, 4075, 4107
Blair, Anthony, 304
Blair, Betsy, 124
Blair, Billy, 2785
Blair, Bobby, 4441
Blair, Doug, 5663
Blair, Gavin, 5514, 5937
Blair, Gordon, 4081
Blair, Gordy, 2240
Blair, Harry, 903
Blair, Janet, 579
Blair, John, 2866, 6107
Blair, Joyce, 371
Blair, Judith, 1259
Blair, Lionel, 3107
Blair, Michael, 2033, 5860
Blair, Nicky, 5654
Blair, Ron, 4215
Blair, Timothy, 1573

Blair, Warren, 621
Blair, William, 1185
Blaisdell, Geoffrey, 2807
Blake Babies, 579, 708, 2430, 3190, 3448
Blake, Amanda, 3245
Blake, Andy, 3430
Blake, Arthur, 592
Blake, Barbara, 372, 2583
Blake, Blind, 592, 628, 919, 2243, 2552, 2744, 3174, 3754, 3804, 4750, 5402, 5405
Blake, Charlie, 1267, 2355
Blake, Cicero, 3063
Blake, Cyril, 993
Blake, David, 1560, 4152
Blake, Eubie, 72, 149, 341, 579-580, 1068, 1267, 2007, 2345, 2596, 2639, 3939, 4450, 4897, 4940, 4990, 6036
Blake, Fitzroy, 2636
Blake, Gary, 4039
Blake, Ginger, 163, 1211, 2583
Blake, Howard, 738, 861
Blake, Ian, 4373
Blake, Jacqui, 4842
Blake, James, 579, 4450
Blake, Jamie, 580
Blake, Jim, 2535
Blake, John, 436, 580, 4632, 5776, 6032, 6075
Blake, Josephine, 4549
Blake, Keith, 2138, 4333
Blake, Lesley, 2077
Blake, Mary, 4732
Blake, Norman, 580-581, 634, 4152, 4460, 4664, 5328
Blake, Paul, 601, 4165
Blake, Paul Emerson, 601
Blake, Ran, 561, 581, 591, 861, 1682, 1972, 2192, 3056, 3102, 3173-3174, 3316, 3762, 4204, 5292, 6097
Blake, Richard, 1943
Blake, Ron, 4989
Blake, Sam, 3871
Blake, Tchad, 1610, 1897, 5989
Blake, Tim, 2198, 2442
Blake, Tom, 5675
Blake, Westbrook, 5776
Blake, William, 580, 774, 1594, 2046, 2155, 2764, 2916, 3086, 3585, 5776
Blakely, Alan, 1075, 5498
Blakely, John, 3869
Blakely, Mike, 1075
Blakely, Paul, 927, 1332
Blakely, William, 1469
Blakemore, Michael, 1091, 3239
Blakemore, Rick, 1841, 5533
Blakeney, Andy, 581, 2087
Blakeslee, Susanne, 1968
Blakewell, William, 2185
Blakey, Art, 40, 43, 65, 128, 165, 203, 244, 393, 582-583, 591, 614, 722, 769, 865, 877, 913, 1026, 1035, 1140, 1223, 1433, 1523, 1586-1587, 1615, 1700, 2150-2151, 2155, 2195, 2268, 2400, 2415, 2508, 2622, 2684, 2786, 2795, 2819, 2870, 2942, 3344, 3439-3440, 3460, 3474-3475, 3479, 3500, 3592, 3678, 3722, 3739-3740, 3752, 3785,

3929, 3941, 4027, 4215, 4245, 4363, 4420, 4634, 4640, 4696, 4858, 4879, 4910, 4989, 5278, 5412, 5442, 5543, 5568, 5693, 5702, 5770, 5778, 5831, 5863
Blakey, Arthur, 582
Blakk, Pete, 3000
Blakley, Alan, 1925
Blakley, Ronee, 1675
Blakley, Ronnee, 583
Blakwell, Chuck, 5282
Blam Blam Blam, 762, 1750, 3856
Blameless, 583
Blamey, Chris, 588
Blamire, Robert, 3847, 4184
Blanc, Jean-Claude, 5505
Blanc, Jean-Marc, 3198
Blanc, Mel, 2020, 3903
Blanch Family, 583
Blanch, Arthur, 583
Blanchard, Edgar, 583, 3757
Blanchard, Jack, And Misty Morgan, 584
Blanchard, Lowell, 2579
Blanchard, Red, 584, 3904
Blanchard, Steve, 2602
Blanchard, Terence, 128, 582, 584, 2415, 3474
Blanchflower, Olly, 2418
Blancmange, 260, 585, 1881, 2101, 3302, 3920
Blanco Y Negro, 28-29, 357, 363, 516, 988, 1045, 1274, 1287, 1533, 1623, 1670, 1772, 1801, 2511, 2816-2817, 3017, 3742, 4062, 4453, 4663, 5569-5570
Bland, Billy, 585, 5756
Bland, Bobby, 33, 52, 394, 481, 503, 585-586, 787, 1098, 1409, 1412, 1422, 1784, 2071, 2217, 2289, 2520, 2532, 2566, 2610, 2741, 2774, 2844, 2858, 2878, 3010, 3244, 3268, 3558, 3661, 3717, 3795, 3843, 3902, 3908, 4015, 4131, 4186, 4211, 4225, 4521, 4527, 4579, 4886, 5405, 5532, 5655, 5684, 5799, 5803, 5876, 5927
Bland, Ian, 1623
Bland, Jackie, 787, 5883
Bland, James, 2858, 3532
Bland, Joyce, 2212
Bland, Leroy, 40
Bland, Michael, 4332
Bland, Milton, 2520, 4048, 4582
Bland, Robert Calvin, 585
Blane, Ralph, 506, 586, 2589, 2637, 3326, 3487, 3574, 3611, 3694, 3865
Blandick, Clara, 911
Blando, Deborah, 586
Blandon, Richard, 1639
Blane Sisters, 5443
Blane, Marcie, 586
Blane, Ralph, 506, 586, 2589, 2637, 3326, 3487, 3574, 3611, 3694, 3865
Blank Generation, The, 586-587, 2475, 3195
Blank, Boris, 5953
Blank, Dorothy Ann, 1543
Blank, Roger, 701
Blanke, Toto, 5639

Blankfield, Peter, 5902

Blanks, Jonothan, 2585

Blant, Dave, 4394, 5952

Blanthorn, Tim, 5721

Blanton, Jimmy, 587, 716, 1306, 1736, 2279, 2321, 2819, 3096, 3479, 3653, 4407, 5355, 5509

Blanton, Joe, 4671

Blaquiere, Roland, 2915

Blasko, Chuck, 5655

Blasquiz, Klaus, 3410

Blast First Records, 1693, 3359-3360

Blasters, 132, 149, 154, 431, 447, 587, 610, 1137, 1174, 1180, 1548, 1568, 2571, 2705, 3368, 3557, 3970, 4108, 4429, 4461, 5355, 5528, 5939, 6036, 6128

Blatt, Edgar, 295

Blatt, Melanie, 124

Blau, Eric, 2756, 4897

Blauvelt, Howie, 4418

Blavat, Jerry, 4561

Blaxhill, Ric, 5467

Blaze, Steve, 3245

Blazer, Judy, 2159, 5449

Blazing Apostles, 587

Blazyca, Rita, 1517

Bleach, 587-588 and *passim*

Bleach, Annabel, 916

Bleach, Sarah, 1192

Bleasdale, Alan, 1244

Bledsoe, Fern, 1855

Bledsoe, Jim, 1253

Bledsoe, Jules, 282, 4893

Bleed, 588 and *passim*

Blend-Aires, 4537

Blender, Everton, 304, 784, 2728, 4379, 4590

Blenders, 442, 588-589, 1915, 2844, 4137

Blenders (Chicago), 588

Blene, Gerard, 5603

Blennerhassett, James, 566

Blesh, Rudi, 2797, 4513, 6097

Bless The Bride, 171, 589, 1141, 1745, 2308, 5745

Bless, Roland, 4366

Blessed Death, 589

Blessed, Brian, 993, 3647

Blessid Union Of Souls, 589-590

Blessing, 590 and *passim*

Blessing, Michael, 3904

Blevins, Ken, 5721-5722

Blevins, Leo, 462

Blevins, Rubye, 3749-3750

Blevins, Gaines, 4787

Bley, Carla, 224, 381, 590-591, 763, 800, 847, 1344, 1445, 1776, 2038, 2068, 2330, 2381, 2793, 3073, 3102, 3451, 3503, 3980, 4173, 4472, 4636, 4696, 4735, 4871, 5318, 5321, 5698

Bley, Johann, 615, 2914

Bley, Paul, 133, 154, 171, 298, 590-591, 701, 847, 1295, 1341, 1553, 1700, 1789, 2038, 2155, 2164, 2196, 2249, 2330, 2732, 2793, 2856, 3056, 3451, 3501, 3810, 4173, 4231, 4243, 4584, 4982, 5568

Bleyer, Archie, 592, 1069, 5438

Bleyer, Janet, 1069

Blige, Mary J., 155, 523, 592, 774, 853, 974, 1190, 1538, 1791, 1858, 2011, 2238, 3588, 3977, 4545-4546, 4801, 5584, 5783

Blind Andy, 2809

Blind Blake, 592, 628, 919, 2243, 2552, 2744, 3174, 3754, 3804, 4750, 5402, 5405

Blind Boy Fuller, 592-593, 945, 1004, 1250, 1708, 2315, 2408, 2493, 2612, 2744, 2881, 3274, 3571, 4379, 4521, 4750, 5300, 5344, 5444, 5503, 5655, 5715, 5864

Blind Date, 593 and *passim*

Blind Faith, 593 and *passim*

Blind Fury, 4750

Blind Illusion, 4331

Blind Melon, 593-594, 736, 6128

Blind Vision, 3813

Blinkhorn, Smilin' Billy, 594

Blinky, 466, 594, 1310

Bliss Band, 594

Bliss Blood, 1807, 4105

Bliss, John, 4481

Bliss, Lucille, 1544

Bliss, Paul, 594, 1573

Blissed, 594 and *passim*

Blithe Spirit, 72, 1258, 1265, 2101, 2522, 3246

Blitz!, 595 and *passim*

Blitz, Johnny, 1440

Blitz, May, 345, 402, 692, 3525, 5636

Blitzkrieg, 559, 595, 611, 4423, 4442, 4662, 4749

Blitzstein, Marc, 354, 595-596, 669, 1273, 2095

Blizzard Of Ozz, 4519-4520

Bloch, Alan, 1201

Bloch, Kurt, 5966

Bloch, Ray, 1361

Bloch, René, 637

Block, Geoffrey, 4894

Block, Jesse, 2985

Block, Ken, 4941

Block, Rory, 596

Blockheads, 459, 1661, 1952, 2170, 2261, 2857, 2990, 3520, 3851, 3910-3911, 4174, 4955, 5925

Blodwyn Pig, 44, 596-597, 1127, 2819, 4099, 5397

Bloedow, Oren, 1573

Blomfield, Derek, 2725

Blon, Tommy, 5281

Blonde On Blonde, 597, 1673-1675, 1677, 2425, 3064, 3993, 5348, 5792

Blonde Redhead, 597, 3253

Blondel, 156, 597-598, 3940, 4524

Blondell, Joan, 94, 1368-1369, 1965, 2185, 4299

Blondheim, Philip, 3586

Blondie, 362, 367, 395, 406, 425, 430, 579, 598, 1000, 1044, 1064, 1078, 1393, 1440, 1658, 1721, 1746, 1930, 2176, 2223, 2313, 2418-2419, 2450, 2559, 2567, 2796, 3045, 3195, 3458, 3667, 3904, 3913, 3922, 4087, 4125, 4239, 4330, 4427, 4564, 4592,

4730, 4911, 4730, 4911, 5444, 5453, 5492, 5577, 5637, 5656, 5790, 5904, 6036, 6122

Blondy, Alpha, 463, 598-599, 1855, 2972, 3433, 3729

Blood, 599 and *passim*

Blood Brothers, 599 and *passim*

Blood Of Abraham, 599, 1697, 4498, 4703

Blood On The Saddle, 366-367, 600, 3307, 4556

Blood Sausage, 600

Blood, Dave, 1442

Blood, Sweat And Tears, 161, 380, 426, 600-601, 626, 722, 749, 819, 977-978, 1001, 1054-1055, 1119, 1188, 1334, 1407, 1723, 1793-1794, 2181, 2305, 2423, 2487, 2565, 2672, 3011, 3064, 3553, 3823, 3924, 3931, 3951, 3991, 4153, 4672, 4899, 5916, 6036

Bloodfire Posse, 601, 3018, 4468

Bloodgood, 601, 3902

Bloodgood, Mike, 601

Bloodhound Gang, 601

Bloodhunter, 2476

Bloodrock, 602, 3050, 3959-3960

Bloods And Crips, 602

Bloodstone, 291, 602, 612, 3792, 4793, 5634

Bloodvessel, Buster, 321, 3408, 4816

Bloom, Benny, 3076

Bloom, Bobby, 603, 2679, 2929

Bloom, Eric, 346, 615

Bloom, Howie, 2678

Bloom, Jane Ira, 603, 4327

Bloom, Jeff, 5330

Bloom, Ken, 14, 3214, 6107

Bloom, Luka, 603, 2728

Bloom, Marty, 4649

Bloom, Mickey, 2841

Bloom, Molly, 3039

Bloom, Rube, 569, 603, 1622, 3054, 3629-3630, 3679, 4681

Bloom, Walter, 4176

Bloomer Girl, 227, 479-480, 604, 1436, 2386

Bloomery, Laurel, 2255, 4347

Bloomfield, Brett, 2149

Bloomfield, Jo, 5647

Bloomfield, Mike, 20, 442, 604-605, 629, 728, 756, 858, 1055, 1347, 1615, 1691, 1724, 1782, 1879, 1972, 2187, 2248, 2262, 2369, 2890, 2923, 2980, 3009, 3020, 3064-3065, 3242, 3255, 3664, 3753, 3807, 3830, 3853, 4208, 4692, 4753, 5301, 5413, 5506, 6036

Bloomfield, Steve, 3510

Bloomquist, Elmer, 4226

Bloor, Rich, 5446

Blore, Eric, 540, 708, 1957, 2100, 4636, 4841, 5466

Blore, Louis, 1635

Blosl, Sean, 4733

Blossom Time (stage musical), 605, 3245

Blossom Time (film musical), 605

Blossom Toes, 606, 1263, 1629, 1852, 2178, 2196, 3123, 4282

Blossom White, 1361

Blossom, David, 1890

Blossom, Henry, 606, 2502, 3719

Blossom, Henry, Jnr., 606

Blossoms, 606-607 and *passim*

Blount, John, 1476

Blow, 607 and *passim*

Blow Monkeys, 607, 1539, 3529, 5761

Blow Up, 607 and *passim*

Blow, Kurtis, 607-608, 1400, 1460, 1858, 1866, 2238, 3342, 4915, 4992, 5813

Blow, Sydney, 708

Blow, Will, 2983, 2999

Blowers, Johnny, 608

Blowzabella, 170, 231, 608-609, 1612, 1943, 3526

Bloxsom, Ian, 1310

Blubbery Hellbellies, 670, 1239

Bludd, Joe, 3852

Bludgeon Riffola Records, 1461

Blue, 609 and *passim*

Blue Aeroplanes, 502, 609, 1050, 5502

Blue Angels, 191, 2298, 3817

Blue Barron, 397-398, 939, 1927, 4111

Blue Beat Records, 610, 3593

Blue Blazers, 496

Blue Blood Group, 49

Blue Bludd, 610, 5502

Blue Blue World, 141, 191, 2090, 2304, 4930, 5416, 5469, 5645, 6083

Blue Bonnett Girls, 1266

Blue Boys, 611 and *passim*

Blue Cheer, 364, 611, 1043, 2299, 2925, 3407, 3699, 3976, 4076, 4909, 5420

Blue Emotions, 1756

Blue Eyed English, 1118

Blue For A Boy, 611

Blue Goose Records, 664

Blue Grass Cut-Ups, 4868

Blue Gum Band, 1245

Blue Hawaii, 475, 612, 1191, 1303, 2118, 2896, 3127, 4123, 4311-4312, 4315, 5621

Blue Horizon Records, 612 and *passim*

Blue Lu, 380

Blue Magic, 272, 612-613, 1859, 2895, 2898, 3505, 4220

Blue Mink, 395, 463, 613, 1071, 1218, 1220, 1400, 1946, 1971, 2273, 4131-4132

Blue Murder, 210, 240, 324, 613, 696, 1905, 2162, 3001

Blue Nile, 31, 613, 2116, 2430, 2454, 2884, 3194, 4690

Blue Note Records, 613-614 and *passim*

Blue Orchids, 614, 5455

Blue Oyster Cult, 91

Blue Paradise, The, 615, 4637, 4814

Blue Pearl, 526, 551, 615, 1206

Blue Planet Corporation, 1952

Blue Ridge Mountain Folk, 894

Blue Ridge Playboys, 1356,

3836, 5438

Blue Ridge Rangers, 615-616, 1954-1955

Blue River Boys, 1876

Blue Rodeo, 616, 1865

Blue Rondo A La Turk, 405, 616, 5440, 5884

Blue Skies, 617 and *passim*

Blue Sky Boys, 230, 329, 617, 1799, 2289, 2811, 2823, 2937, 3247, 3328, 3383, 3489, 4106, 4238

Blue Sky Records, 2831

Blue Stars, 617-618, 1447, 1658, 3635, 3722, 5398

Blue Swede, 618

Blue Thumb Records, 618, 752, 859, 3259, 3502

Blue Tick Hounds, 3842

Blue Velvets, 619, 1288, 1955, 2195

Blue Zoo, 526, 619, 2584, 4384

Blue, 'Little' Joe, 2888, 5365

Blue, Amanda, 4843

Blue, Andrew, 2528, 3608

Blue, Barry, 460, 619, 1441, 3157

Blue, Ben, 1966, 2523

Blue, Billy, 1830

Blue, David, 266, 619-620, 2831, 3252, 3409, 4501

Blue, Desmond, 1493

Blue, Dion, 3868

Blue, Jimmy, 499, 4809, 4990, 5717

Blue, Joe, 619, 2488, 2888, 3009

Blue, Ruby, 4680

Blue, Vicki, 4688

Bluebeats Showband, 462

Bluebell In Fairyland, 620

Bluebell, Bobby, 620

Bluebells, 620, 1244, 3287, 3302, 4043, 4295

Bluebird Cajun Band, 1931

Bluebird Records, 620 and *passim*

Blueblood, 3594, 4907

Bluegrass Album Band, 621, 1314, 3150

Bluegrass Alliance, 621, 1277, 2147

Bluegrass Cardinals, 621-622, 1490, 5652

Bluegrass Kinsmen, 337-338

Bluejacks, 3465

Bluerunners, 1266

Blues, The, 626-630 and *passim*

Blues Ambassadors, 5400

Blues Band, 622 and *passim*

Blues Boy Kingdom, 5597

Blues Brothers, 622-623 and *passim*

Blues Brothers, The, 283, 544, 547, 623, 626, 664, 775-776, 896, 1028, 1065, 1087, 1246, 1301, 2013-2015, 2321, 2587, 3408, 3437, 3552, 3843, 3888, 4277, 5448, 5503

Blues Busters, 623

Blues Company, 2461, 4322-4323

Blues Council, 624, 4156

Blues Force, 2870, 5777

Blues Image, 624, 4246

Blues In The Night, 227, 586, 624-625, 1264, 2224, 2547, 2772, 3130, 3269, 3322, 3630, 4667, 4815, 4863, 4936, 5647, 5697, 5861, 5951, 6086

Blues Keepers, 376

Blues Machine, 842, 3013, 3770, 5316

Blues Magoos, 161, 625, 1958, 2678, 2702, 4353

Blues Mob, 2530

Blues Project, 625-626 and *passim*

Blues Serenaders, 283, 2640

Blues Traveler, 626, 4496

Blues, Bill, 153, 760, 1621, 2369, 3861, 6037, 6097

Blues, Saraceno, 4272

Bluesbreakers, 28, 146, 477, 630, 760, 796, 1094, 1285, 1402, 1573, 1650, 1933, 2022, 2180, 2272, 2423, 3526-3527, 3603, 3733, 4260, 4645, 4667, 4692, 4891, 5318

Bluesland, 2530

Bluetones, 630, 1572, 6123

Bluestone, 4188

Bluett, Bay, 3019

Bluiett, Hamiet, 40, 630, 2592-2593, 3846, 5922

Blulight, 4703

Blum, Edwin, 2257

Blum, Joel, 4893

Blum, Richard, 1516

Blumenfeld, Roy, 626, 4801

Blumfeld, 631, 3978

Blunder, B.B., 606, 2178

Blunstone, Colin, 98, 223, 631, 1313, 2391, 2766, 3383, 3517, 3882, 4144, 6001-6002, 6122

Blunt Records, 2905

Blunt, Martin, 1024

Blunt, Nigel, 889, 2296

Blunt, Robbie, 750, 4260, 4911

Blur, 631-632 and *passim*

Blurt, 632-633, 4229, 4968

Blush, Edwina, 2905

Bly, Robert, 3208

Blyden, Larry, 210, 1945, 2056

Blyth Power, 13, 276, 633, 1278

Blyth, Ann, 633, 3033-3034, 3784, 4648

Blyth, Tom, 2201

Blyth, Vernon, 985

Blythe Spirit, 634

Blythe, Arthur, 634, 773, 844, 1230, 1311, 1405, 1417, 1465, 2841, 3243, 3286, 3544, 3740, 3833, 3846, 5297, 5362, 5568, 5922

Blythe, Jimmy, 634, 2552, 4112

Blythe, Lance, 5547

BMG Records, 1276, 1486, 1746, 2117, 2350, 3594, 3797, 4664, 6007

BMX Bandits, 634-635, 926, 1785, 3559, 5328

BNA Records, 840, 1047, 3307, 4817

Bo Street Runners, 635, 1052, 2829

Bo, Eddie, 358, 635

Boals, Mark, 3423, 5281

Boardman, Harry, 4654

Boardman, Phil, 5419

Boardwalk Records, 1888, 2821, 3925

Boast, Tony, 3806

Boatman, Mark, 2453

Boatner, Joseph, 2695

Boatwright, Dave, 558

Boatwright, Ginger, 635, 1527

Boatwright, Grant, 635

Bob And Earl, 636, 1426, 2571, 3173, 4037

Bob And Marcia, 188, 636, 2292, 4489, 5509

Bob B. Soxx And The Blue Jeans, 606, 636, 3339, 4219

Bob Delyn, 636

Bobbettes, 637

Bobbin Records, 4232

Bobby And The Consoles, 2836

Bobby And The Midnights, 637

Bobby Sue, 4473

Bobby, Senator, 4819

Bobin, John, 3181

Bobo, Eric, 1344

Bobo, Jim, 3719

Bobo, William, 1551

Bobo, Willie, 637, 1234, 1833, 2626, 3181, 4361, 4739-4740, 4858, 5447, 5451

Bobrow, Norm, 4903

Bobs, 638

Bocage, Peter, 638, 3895, 4560

Bocage, Spider, Orchestra, 635

Bock, Charlie, 169

Bock, Jerry, 211, 336, 475, 638, 1023, 1418, 1882, 1901, 2399, 3674, 4661, 4859, 4874

Bock, Steve, 3980

Bockholt, Albert, 1579

Bockner, Rick, 3398

Bockris, Victor, 598, 846, 4479, 4529, 4632, 5627, 6036, 6038, 6073-6074, 6083

Bodacious D.F., 348, 639, 2295

Boddy, Karyl, 5905

BoDeans, 525, 639

Bodimead, Jacqui, 916, 2162

Bodimead, Tony, 916

Bodine, 639

Bodines, 639-640, 3570

Bodnar, Andrew, 4136

Body Count, 560, 640, 931, 2669, 3549, 4018, 4406, 6034, 6063

Bodysnatchers, 466, 1375, 4520, 5994

Boe, Peter, 1283

Boean, Alan, 1593

Boehm, Carl, 1127

Boehm, David, 2185

Boel, Hanne, 4956

Boenzye Creque, 640, 4352

Boers, Robin, 3639, 5563

Boerstler, John, 4373

Boettcher, Curt, 260, 454, 640, 3668, 4717, 5589

Bofill, Angela, 641, 1212, 3513

Bofill, Sergio, 3163, 3738, 4121, 4421, 4611, 5471

Bogaert, Jo, 5945

Bogan, Henry, 1691

Bogan, Lee, 1522

Bogan, Lucille, 641, 1813, 3556, 4626

Bogan, Nazareth, 641

Bogan, Ted, 3483

Bogan, Tony, 3652

Bogardus, Stephen, 2522, 3457

Bogart, Humphrey, 756, 2518, 2644, 3296, 3448, 5836

Bogart, Neil, 815, 3529

Bogdan, Henry, 2479

Bogdanovich, Peter, 266

Bogen, Harry, 2659

Bogen, Joel, 2765

Bogert, Tim, 102, 210, 445, 637, 641, 692, 878, 5611

Boggs, Dock, 247, 254, 642, 4810

Boggs, Moran Lee, 642

Boggs, Noel, 642, 805, 4132

Boggs, Vernon W., 1842

Bogguss, Suzy, 216, 270, 488, 642, 947, 1206, 1444, 2143, 4509, 5785, 5953

Bogie, Douglas, 4394

Bogle, Bob, 5629

Bogle, Eric, 643, 903, 4471

Bogtrotters, 1653, 5700

Bogue, Merwyn, 643, 3091, 6036

Bogus Records, 2738

Bogus, Blind, 1264

Bohannon, Hamilton, 643, 1146

Bohannon, Jim, 4176

Bohlken, Eike, 631

Bohm, Carl, 5688

Bohman, Adam, 1213

Bohmler, Craig, 1766

Bohn, George, 2625

Bohn, Tom, 293

Boiarsky, Andres, 3177, 4623

Boiled In Lead, 643

Boine, Marie, 644

Boines, Houston, 665

Bois, Curt, 1263, 3861, 5350

Boisot, Louise, 1234

Boissy, Gerard, 731

Boivenue, Ron, 4064

Bok, Gordon, 644, 2225, 2992, 3348

Bokelo, Jean, 657

Boladian, Armen, 5775

Bolan, Marc, 607, 644-645, 1045, 1325, 1473, 1727, 1940, 1949, 2219, 2812, 2833, 3401, 3537, 3874, 4142, 4180, 4239, 4264, 4808, 5277, 5376, 5482, 5555, 6036, 6123

Bolan, Rachel, 4950

Bolan, Tommy, 5704

Boland, Clay, 645

Boland, Francy, 645-646, 1108, 1110, 1498, 3519, 3600

Boland, Greg, 5556

Boland, Jacqueline, 3056

Boland, Mary, 1818, 2906

Bolas, Niko, 4724, 4787

Bolcato, Jean, 4779

Bolden, Andrea, 4737

Bolden, Buddy, 646, 2087, 2752, 2842, 2975, 3377, 3801, 3939, 5356, 6036

Bolden, Charles Joseph, 646

Bolder, Trevor, 5587, 5895

Bolero, Conjunto, 229

Bowman, Rob, 2602, 6080
Bowman, Ronnie, 621, 3321
Bowman, Simon, 222, 3705
Bown, Alan, 690, 750, 1354,
2275, 3956, 4112, 4601, 5646
Bown, Andy, 2502, 2906, 5281
Bown, Patti, 690-691
Bowne, Dougie, 1159
Bowron, Robert, 4649
Bowser, Erbie, 464, 691, 2639
Bowties, 4592
Bowyer, Brendan, 518, 691,
2957, 4593, 4672
Bowyer, Geoff, 4369
Box Of Frogs, 691, 3550, 3609,
3621, 4732, 5951
Box Of Laughs, 1271
Box Tops, 216, 461, 691-692,
1061, 2041, 2121, 2539, 4186,
4262
Box, Clive, 563
Box, Elton, 2834, 2968, 4574
Box, Mick, 5586-5587
Boxcar, 883, 1525, 2333, 3552,
4399
Boxcar Willie, 60, 692, 1181,
1206, 1464, 1971, 3325, 4440-
4441, 4654, 4698, 5847
Boxem, Jan, 572
Boxer, 692 and *passim*
Boy Friend, The, 692-693 and
passim
Boy George, 86, 364, 523, 670,
683, 693, 1329-1330, 1443,
3338, 3405, 3463, 3537, 3590,
3654, 4267, 4543, 4829, 5382,
5534, 5568, 6037, 6042, 6123
Boy Howdy, 693-694
Boy Meets Girl, 694 and *passim*
Boy's Own Records, 694
Boy, Andy, 694
Boy, Jimmy, 4377
Boy, The, 694 and *passim*
Boyce And Hart, 694-695, 3033,
3740-3741, 5369
Boyce, Dave, 4564
Boyce, Denny, Band, 1382
Boyce, Keith, 2468, 5320
Boyce, Mark, 4122
Boyce, Tommy, 694-695, 2679,
3740, 5369
Boycott, Bus, 5715
Boyd, Adam, 4968
Boyd, Bill, 695, 764, 771, 2708,
3931
Boyd, Bill And Jim, 695
Boyd, Bruce, 2298
Boyd, Craig, 1486, 2585, 3161
Boyd, Don, 1718
Boyd, Eddie, 612, 629, 695, 775,
1049, 1324-1325, 1496, 2737,
3291, 3719, 4014
Boyd, Eva Narcissus, 3264
Boyd, Jenny, 1590
Boyd, Jim, 695, 2517, 3931
Boyd, Jimmy, 1210, 1877, 2163,
3112
Boyd, Joe, 695, 1324, 1370,
1616, 1618, 1826, 2939, 3517,
3570, 3712, 4247, 4706, 5337,
5505, 5617, 5725
Boyd, Kit, 3533
Boyd, Patti, 2415
Boyd, Reggie, 4582

Boyd, Rocky, 3847
Boyd, Roger, 2453
Boyd, Stephen, 539, 2911
Boyd, Whitney, 2501
Boyd, William, 695, 3180
Boyd, Willie, 2410
Boyd-Jones, Ernest, 1942
Boyelle, Jimmy, 3787
Boyer, Charles, 1844, 2345, 3688
Boyes, Jim, 696
Boyes, Nick, 306
Boyes, Terry, 2077
Boykin, Gary, 1688
Boykins, Ronnie, 701
Boyko, Mike, 4768
Boylan, Jeffrey, 2327
Boylan, John, 5317
Boylan, Pat, 1906
Boylan, Terry, 212, 696
Boyle, Billy, 919
Boyle, Dee, 3309
Boyle, Denny, 3027
Boyle, Gary, 1783, 2721, 5947
Boyle, John, 4831, 5556, 5948
Boyle, Maggie, 696, 4502, 5439
Boyle, Paddy, 696
Boyle, Ray, 1785
Boymerang, 697
Boyne, Jeff, 2366
Boyo, Billy, 370, 1183, 3144,
3505, 4431-4432, 5685
Boys (punk) 697 and *passim*
Boys (soul) 697 and *passim*
Boys Don't Cry, 697
Boys From Indiana, 698, 5893
Boys From Syracuse, The, 38,
108, 346, 698, 745, 2728, 2867,
3487, 4607
Boys Of The Lough, 334, 699,
2068, 2100, 2232, 3561
Boysie, Count, 1124, 4429
Boyte, Harry, 2924, 6057
Boyte, Randy, 5739
Boyter, George, 2454
Boyz II Men, 312, 459, 699, 853,
934, 1190, 1632, 2218, 2296,
3077, 3814, 4529, 4801, 5707
Boyzone, 699-700, 1367, 2941,
3413, 4276
Boyzz, 303, 700
Boze, Calvin, 700
Boziana, Bozi, 5988
Bozulich, Carla, 2124
Bozzio, Dale, 3706
Bozzio, Terry, 446, 2717, 2937,
3706, 5469, 5991
Bozzo, Rick, 4712
BPeople, 700
BR5-49, 700
BPM Records, 2860
Brabbs, Mark, 599, 1649, 5295
Braben, John, 5647-5648
Bracco, Ralph, 3956
Bracebridge, Chris, 5654
Braceful, Fred, 1397
Bracewell, Angela, 2947
Bracey, Ishmon, 701, 5743
Bracey, Marty, 3435
Brack, John, 701
Brackeen, Charles, 40, 701,
2200, 3810
Brackeen, Joanne, 582, 701,
1853, 2131, 2196, 2538, 2770,
3541, 3752

Bracken, C., 970, 5621
Bracken, Eddie, 1933, 5464
Bracken, James, 42, 970, 5622
Bracken, Sam, 1917, 5385
Brackenridge, Joe, 4265
Bracket, 326, 702, 824, 1490,
1657, 2043, 2662, 2776, 2927,
2985, 3561, 3654, 3763, 4380
Brackett, Al, 253, 4173
Brackman, Jacob, 4917
Brad, 702 and *passim*
Bradbury, Bob, 2477
Bradbury, Brad, 2103
Bradbury, John, 4816
Bradbury, Matt, 4819
Bradbury, Ray, 4176
Braddock, Bessie, 1019
Braddock, Bobby, 488, 702,
2615, 4372
Braddock, Eddie, 3222
Braddy, Pauline, 703, 2703,
4444, 5857
Braden, Bernard, 1483, 2404
Braden, Larry, 117
Braden, Tommy, 1989, 2404
Bradfield, James, 3442, 3974
Bradford, Alex, 3350
Bradford, Bobby, 703, 968,
1167, 1311, 1626, 1670, 2195,
3791, 3846, 5733, 5770
Bradford, Brett, 4791
Bradford, Eddie, 2731
Bradford, Elaine, 2726
Bradford, Geoff, 703
Bradford, Jimmy, 3350, 3869
Bradford, Perry 'Mule', 704
Bradley, Addie, 704
Bradley, Alton, 2189
Bradley, Betty, 704, 1049
Bradley, Billy, 2847
Bradley, Buddy, 1154, 1797,
2726, 4719
Bradley, Carrie, 723
Bradley, Dave, 5654
Bradley, Don, 5639
Bradley, Hank, 1119
Bradley, Harold, 704-705, 864
Bradley, Jan, 704
Bradley, Kenny, 3952
Bradley, Liam, 2949
Bradley, Mark, 2657
Bradley, Michael, 441, 5575
Bradley, Mike, 4564
Bradley, Oscar, 4328
Bradley, Owen, 704, 828, 1129,
1154, 1256, 2568, 3125, 3128,
3170, 3370, 4156, 5371, 5548,
5764-5765, 5926
Bradley, Patrick, 2899
Bradley, Rolland, 1032
Bradley, Susan, 2426
Bradley, Vic, 1216
Bradley, Will, 705, 914, 985,
2535, 2623, 2895, 3587, 3966,
4449, 4624, 4958
Bradshaw, Brett, 1857
Bradshaw, Carl, 1375, 2390,
3866
Bradshaw, Kim, 325, 3362
Bradshaw, Kym, 4721
Bradshaw, Myron, 705
Bradshaw, Simon, 5276
Bradshaw, Steve, 1987
Bradshaw, Terry, 705

Bradshaw, Tiny, 705-706, 890,
1010, 1178, 2001, 2271, 2393,
2867, 2885, 3090, 3517, 3592,
3880, 3940, 4197, 4263, 4345,
4853, 5536, 5910
Bradt, Grace, 108
Bradt, Hollis, 2903
Brady, Alice, 2101, 2185, 4045
Brady, Chris, 2860, 4278
Brady, Eunan, 2570
Brady, Heather, 696
Brady, James, 1471
Brady, Jim, 351, 4737
Brady, Joseph, 170, 2185
Brady, Ken, 2077
Brady, Pat, 706, 1910, 2860
Brady, Paul, 706, 1479, 2165,
2388, 2712-2713, 2814, 2860,
2949, 3051, 3540, 3943, 3994,
4001, 4261, 4415
Brady, Phil, 706-707, 2534, 5793
Brady, Phil, And The Ranchers,
706-707, 2534
Braeden, Mari Anne, 2263
Braff, Reuben, 707
Braff, Ruby, 112, 130, 386, 480,
707, 781, 1178, 1399, 1504,
1513, 1534, 1572, 1632, 1871,
1943, 2209, 2654, 2956, 3043,
3130, 3200, 3348, 3351, 3799-
3800, 3875, 4183, 4301, 4535,
4948, 5301, 5409, 5592, 5611,
5883
Brage, Tommy, 293
Bragg, Billy, 437, 707-708, 729,
1441, 1546, 1584, 2163, 2175,
2179, 2281, 2290, 2319, 2812,
3057, 3080, 3280, 3547, 3699,
3767, 4658, 4709, 4886, 5288,
5725, 5821, 5835, 5920, 6037
Bragg, Johnny, 4340
Braggs, Al, 2289, 2629, 2844,
5597
Braham, Philip, 416, 540, 708,
3301, 4042
Braham-Douglas, Philip, 5998
Braheny, Kevin, 4562
Brahms, Caryl, 2233
Brain, Brian, 4358
Brain, Guy, 5603
Brain Ticket, 4303
Brainiac, 709
Braithwaite, Daryl, 709, 4872
Braithwaite, Frederick, 1815
Braithwaite, J.B., 4047
Braithwaite, Jeff, 1023
Braithwaite, Junior, 3467, 5667
Braithwaite, Shorn, 3536
Braithwaite, Stuart, 3730
Bralower, Jim, 4119
Bramage, Dane, 593
Bramah, Martin, 614, 1835
Bramall, Peter, 5320
Braman, Winston, 2061
Bramante, Anthony, 3982
Brambell, Wilfred, 919, 2387
Bramble, Derek, 2231, 2242,
4037, 4985
Bramble, Mark, 709, 1982
Bramlett, Bonnie, 482, 710,
1470, 2678, 4881
Bramlett, Delaney, 710, 989,
1470, 3788, 4881
Bramley, Clyde, 2584

2559, 5777
Brian, Lewis, 2183, 4627
Briar, 730 and *passim*
Briard, John, 3037
Briarhoppers, 730-731, 975
Brice, Fanny, 341, 354, 493, 731, 829, 1106, 1909, 2055-2056, 2136, 2260, 3850, 3939, 4648-4650, 5869, 5997-5998, 6037
Brice, Richard, 5597
Brice, Trevor, 5613
Bricheno, Tim, 123, 4942, 5941
Brick Layer Cake, 731
Brickell, Edie, 731, 2109, 3312, 4919
Brickell, Edie, And The New Bohemians, 731, 2109, 3312
Bricker, Gene, 3457
Brickley, Audrey, 4063
Brickley, Shirley, 4063
Bricklin, 732
Bricklin, Brian, 732
Bricklin, Scott, 732
Brickman, Jim, 732, 5882
Brickman, Marshall, 2901, 4223
Bricusse, Leslie, 95, 309, 336, 732, 1418, 1567, 2806, 3049, 3246, 3373, 3433, 3926-3927, 4063, 4235, 4565, 4795, 4804, 4873, 5643, 5745, 5851, 5892
Brides Of Funkenstein, 2052, 5981
Bridge, 733-734 and *passim*
Bridge, Danny, 2938
Bridgeman, Dan, 1825, 2926
Bridgeman, Noel, 3768, 4023, 4950
Bridges, Alicia, 734
Bridges, Fred, 186, 762
Bridges, Gil, 4435
Bridges, Hank, 1368
Bridges, Henry, 734, 2934, 3195, 6037
Bridges, Steve, 5896
Bridgewater, Dee Dee, 734, 3098, 5898
Bridgewater, Ron, 734
Bridgewood, Jonny, 3988
Brierly, Ben, 5640
Brigadier Jerry, 734, 3103, 4432, 4717, 4881, 4922, 4941
Brigadoon, 735, 1024, 1436, 2025, 2547, 2619, 2960, 3196, 3294, 3336, 3696, 5500
Brigandage, 735-736
Brigati, Dave, 5592
Brigati, Eddie, 1454, 5968
Briggs, Anne, 231, 736, 3285, 5725
Briggs, Bill, 4498
Briggs, David, 222, 736, 890, 3271, 3849, 4186, 4672
Briggs, Gideon, 2278
Briggs, Jack, 4620
Briggs, Jimmy, 2287
Briggs, Matt, 1202
Briggs, Raymond, 5598, 5724
Briggs, Vic, 194, 278, 660
Brigham, Kenneth, 1290
Bright, Ann, 1443
Bright, Bette, 736, 1443, 3402
Bright, Clive, 737, 5338
Bright, Garfield, 4837

Bright, Gerald, 2124
Bright, Kevin, 4499
Bright, Len, Combo, 737, 5925
Bright, Nicola, 2732
Bright, Ronnie, 1343, 5598
Bright, Sid, 132
Bright, Tom, 1212
Brighter Side Of Darkness, 737
Brightman, Sarah, 258, 352, 566, 737, 993, 1146, 1219, 1281, 1580, 2601, 3284-3285, 4218, 4531, 5372
Brightman, Stanley, 416
Brighton Rock, 323, 738, 4863
Brighty, Luke, 590
Brignardello, Mike, 2135
Brignola, Mike, 738, 2506
Brignola, Nick, 738, 1324, 2506, 4987
Brigode, Ace, 738
Briley, Alexander, 5644
Briley, Martin, 738
Brill Building, 17, 364, 517, 739, 1322, 1386, 1495, 1509, 2223, 2639, 2939, 3160, 3444, 3924, 3930, 3991, 4031, 4808, 5486, 5543, 5622, 5628, 5689, 5748
Brill, Jeremy, 1477
Brill, Marty, 2335
Brill, Rob, 492
Brill, Wally, 1881, 3115
Brilleaux, Lee, 1613, 3221
Brilliant, 739 and *passim*
Brilliant Corners, 739, 2572, 3739-3740, 5687
Brim, Grace, 739, 4477
Brim, John, 739, 3460, 4144, 4895
Brimfield, Billy, 176
Brimfield, Len, 4781
Brimmer, Annie, 4833
Brimstone, 740 and *passim*
Brimstone, Derek, 740, 926
Brindle, Nian, 3686
Bring In 'Da Noise, Bring In 'Da Funk, 740
Bringas, Ernie, 4551
Brinkley, Grace, 1951, 4016
Brinsford, Martin, 715, 4029
Brinsley Schwarz, 453, 741, 1060, 1087, 1641, 1706, 1716, 1719, 2196, 2818, 3027, 3232, 3349, 3673, 4136, 4597, 4686, 4777, 5578
Brintley, Andre, 3626
Brio, Con, 490-491, 3013, 3141, 3254, 5537
Briody, Mark, 2758
Brion, Jon, 1835
Briquette, Pete, 98, 665
Brisco, Erald, 1762
Brise-Glace, 741
Brisker, Gordon, 492, 742, 2626-2627, 3309
Brisset, Annette, 742, 2857
Brisson, Carl, 250, 742-743, 1031
Brisson, Frederick, 743, 4337
Bristol, Johnny, 743, 2057, 4074, 4683, 4763
Bristow, Dave, 4735, 4805
Bristow, John, 57
Britain, John, 2178

British Electric Foundation, 453, 743
British Lions, 743, 1910, 3609, 3621, 3814
Britny Fox, 743-744, 1084, 5737
Brito, Felo, 2396
Brito, Phil, 1584
Britt, Elton, 136, 512, 744, 3447, 3542, 3783, 4572-4573, 4605, 4771
Britt, Mai, 1418
Britt, Michael, 3307
Britt, Stan, 2215, 2799, 6050, 6078, 6097
Brittan, Barbara, 1933
Brittan, Robert, 4414
Britten, Benjamin, 1288, 3286, 4112
Britten, Buddy, 744, 897, 4920
Britten, Charlie, 2776
Britten, Ray, 4088
Britten, Terry, 395, 2073, 2494, 4531, 5544
Brittnam, Marion, 804
Britton, 744 and *passim*
Britton, Chris, 5336, 5508
Britton, Geoff, 1012, 1690, 3438, 4662, 5885
Britton, Marsha, 745
Britton, Pamela, 170
Britton, Tony, 3965, 5618
Broad, Charlie, 3045
Broad, James, 4909
Broad, William, 2115
Broadbent, Alan, 492, 745, 4428, 6097
Broadcasters, 132, 622, 1024, 1459, 1621, 1796, 2452, 2785, 3024, 3172, 3413, 3667, 3786, 4291, 5477
Broadrick, Justin, 2179, 3873, 4780
Broadway, 745 and *passim*
Broadway Angel Records, 745
Broadway Dance Band, 5404, 5564
Broadway Dance Orchestra, 5564
Broadway Grand, 66, 94, 3187
Broadway Melody, The, 745, 782, 2025
Broadway Wrangler, 4484
Broadway, Orquesta, 746-747, 1435, 1833, 1899, 3737, 4121, 4744, 5471-5472
Broc, K.B., 526
Brocas Helm, 747
Brocco, Joe, 1916
Broccoli, Albert R., 1066
Brock, 'Big' George, 519
Brock, Dave, 747, 897, 1649, 2441-2442, 3407
Brock, Hal, 4250
Brock, Paul, 3820
Brock, Terry, 5289
Brock, Tony, 313, 5670
Brockenborough, Dennis, 3660
Brockman, Jake, 1699
Brockman, Polk, 957, 2809
Brockway, Chris, 2380
Broderick, Dean, 4734
Broderick, Helen, 249, 361, 747, 955, 1891, 5466, 5997
Broderick, Matthew, 2613, 3256

Brodie, Nicky, 1192
Brodsky Quartet, 1244-1245
Brodsky, Irving, 945
Brodszky, Nicholas, 748, 884, 3128, 3147, 3337, 4533, 5632, 5840
Brodt, Dottsy, 1601
Brody, Bruce, 3304, 3584
Brody, Francine, 2680
Brody, Lane, 748, 3174
Broekema, Klaas, 4906
Brogan, Sonny, 2068
Brogna, Guy, 4768
Brogues, 748
Brohez, Fred, 738
Brohn, William David, 4408
Brokaw, Chris, 1148, 1191, 4217
Broken Arrow, 89, 586, 5979, 6087, 6128
Broken Bones, 748-749 and *passim*
Broken English, 749 and *passim*
Broken Hope, 749
Brokop, Lisa, 1537, 1804, 4848
Brom, Gustav, 2347
Broman, Tom, 4819
Bromberg, Bruce, 2441, 3666, 5682
Bromberg, Craig, 3590
Bromberg, David, 596, 749-750, 1122, 1508, 2211, 2806, 5838
Bromiley, Dorothy, 2725
Bromley, Gary, 1520
Bron, Eleanor, 932, 2771, 5501
Bron, Gerry, 5586
Bronco, 750 and *passim*
Bronco Records, 3162, 3835, 4647, 5595-5596, 5868
Bronhill, June, 3639, 4569
Bronski Beat, 146, 750, 1194-1195, 3039
Bronski, Steve, 750
Bronson, Art, 5975
Bronson, Betty, 4934
Bronson, Charles, 4264
Bronson, Harold, 4519, 6064
Bronson, Ichabod, 466
Brontë Brothers, 750
Bronz, 750, 2303, 3950
Bronze Records, 750, 985, 2122, 3714, 3812, 4072, 5332, 5586-5587
Bronze, David, 5512
Brood, Herman, 751, 1325
Brook Brothers, 751, 2429, 5692
Brook, Clive, 996
Brook, Geoffrey, 751
Brook, Michael, 751, 1765, 2981-2983, 3844, 5560
Brook, Paul, 51, 5789
Brook, Richie, 3229
Brook, Ricky, 751
Brooke, Hugh, 2167
Brooke, Jonatha, 751-752
Brooke, Mike, 1378
Brooke-Taylor, Tim, 2207
Brooker, Gary, 547, 752, 851, 1095, 1588, 2914, 4126, 4144, 4344
Brookes, Bruno, 2733, 2825
Brookes, Chris, 749
Brookes, Jon, 1024

Buck, Alan, 1994, 4087
Buck, Chris, 4680
Buck, Gary, 810
Buck, Gene, 2502, 5997
Buck, Mike, 1684, 1818, 3197, 5860, 5996
Buck, Peter, 708, 1719, 1868, 1938, 2535, 2691, 3296, 4224, 4394, 5508, 5517, 5572, 5676, 5860, 5996
Buck, Steve, 2229
Buckeroos, 106, 670, 2471, 2570, 2757, 4587, 5518
Bucketheads, 810
Buckett, Billy, 5533
Buckingham, Bonnie, 2311
Buckingham, Jamie, 4545
Buckingham, Lindsey, 810, 838, 1934, 3603, 3943, 5996
Buckingham, Steve, 4495, 4866, 5502
Buckinghams, 811, 1054, 2305
Buckler, Ethan, 4969
Buckler, Paul Richard, 2766
Buckler, Rick, 2003, 2766-2767, 6048, 6055
Buckley, Betty, 336, 811, 953, 994, 2664, 3269, 3865, 4104, 4348
Buckley, David, 390, 6037, 6080
Buckley, Dennis, 1640
Buckley, Jeff, 510, 811-812, 1632, 1830, 2228, 2796
Buckley, Lord, 109, 812, 1904, 2142, 2486, 4914, 5991
Buckley, Richard, 812
Buckley, Tim, 811-813, 1006, 1147, 1230, 1623, 1729, 2116, 2205, 2347, 2384, 2578, 2853, 3651, 3892, 3942, 3971, 4028, 4140, 5317, 5379, 5760, 5991
Buckley, Vernon, 3533
Buckman, Sid, 2003, 2197
Buckmaster, Paul, 4897, 5337, 5392, 5650
Buckner And Garcia, 813
Buckner, Jan, 328
Buckner, Jerry, 813
Buckner, Milt, 813, 1011, 1140, 2370, 3205, 3576, 4203, 4932, 5530, 5726, 5917
Buckner, Richard, 813
Buckner, Sherman, 921
Buckner, Teddy, 444, 814, 1390, 2486, 4077, 4206, 4369, 4702, 5536, 5747, 5823
Buckner, Tom, 3716-3717
Bucknor, Sid, 2588, 2733, 2845, 3593, 5545
Bucks, 814 and passim
Bucks Fizz, 814-815, 1577, 1593, 2064, 5602
Buckton, Paul, 1871, 2510, 5834
Buckwell, Ollie, 1596
Buckwheat Zydeco, 815, 4664
Buda, Max, 2926
Budbill, Dave, 4733
Budd, Arthur, 1469
Budd, Eric, 1902
Budd, George, 3583, 4019
Budd, Harold, 751, 815, 1148, 1158, 1765
Budd, Pete, 5933
Budd, Roy, 815, 2345, 5595

Buddah Records, 815 and passim
Buddle, Errol, 126
Buddy, 816 and passim
Buddy Boy, 1250, 2414, 5715
Buddy Holly Story, The, 816, 1087, 2569-2570, 4449, 5357, 6053
Budgie, 816-817 and passim
Budgie (stage musical), 817
Budimir, Dennis, 2359
Budwig, Monty, 817, 2506, 3349, 3446
Budzak, David, 2396
Buena Vista Social Club, 87, 817-818, 1218, 2201
Buerk, Michael, 3276
Buerkle, Jack V., 380
Buerstate, Phil, 3132
Buettner, Peter, 1295
Buffalo, 818 and passim
Buffalo Club, 818
Buffalo Gals, 818
Buffalo Springfield, 15, 22, 89, 268, 277, 517, 616, 630, 818-819, 848, 988, 1306, 1308, 1358, 1528, 1775, 2057, 2283, 2769, 2775, 2901, 3133, 3297, 3308, 3639, 3642, 3753, 3809, 3887, 3942, 3960, 4180, 4268, 4418, 5311, 5578, 5977, 6038, 6049
Buffalo Tom, 819, 1157, 2688, 3057, 4044, 4658, 5860
Buffalo, Norton, 2398, 3274, 4623
Buffett, Jimmy, 39, 819-820, 1016, 1122, 1634, 1710, 1953, 2814, 3368, 3540, 3665, 3902, 6038
Buford, 'Mojo' George, 820-821
Buford, Ross, 1034
Bugatti, Dominic, 1647
Bugger All Stars, 821
Buggles, 821, 2309, 2760, 5957, 6004
Bugnel, Jim, 1924
Bugsy Malone, 821, 1837, 5857
Buick MacKane, 1778, 5376
Built To Spill, 822
Buirski, Felicity, 822
Bukowski, Charles, 2734
Bula Sangoma, 2947
Bulen, Lance, 413
Bulimia Banquet, 822
Bull, Geoff, 2376
Bull, Graham, 5495
Bull, John, 1572, 3025, 4523
Bull, Peter, 1567
Bull, Prince David, 3150, 4346
Bull, Richie, 3087
Bull, Sandy, 822, 5611
Bull, Tim, 1943
Bulldozer, 520, 822-823, 1245
Bullen, Charles, 1839, 5394
Bullen, Nick, 3873, 4780
Bullen, Roger, 1377
Bullet Lavolta, 1037, 3190, 3821
Bullet Records, 559, 1558, 3008, 3154, 5923
Bullet, Jim, 269
Bulletboys, 823
Bullet, 823 and passim
Bullitt, Nick, 4118

Bulloch, Martin, 3730
Bullock, Chick, 823, 2210, 3736, 4511, 4654
Bullock, Gerald, 1120
Bullock, John, 4969
Bullock, Tim, 4251
Bullock, Tommy, 1888-1889
Bullock, Walter, 2081, 5932
Bullocks, Lester, 1528
Bullseye, 823 and passim
Bullseye Blues, 768, 855, 1114-1115, 1120, 1412, 1656, 1686, 1974, 2049, 2851, 2888, 3016, 3083, 3369, 3557, 3763, 4179, 4475-4476, 4643, 4664, 4983, 5874, 5879
Bully Wee Band, 823
Bullyrag, 824
Bulmer, Bill, 5790
Buloff, Joseph, 4905
Bulsara, Frederick, 3632, 4380
Bultitude, Paul, 4805
Bumble Bee Slim, 824, 2216, 2779, 5798
Bumbry, Grace, 4287
Bump, 824 and passim
Bumpass, Thomas, 4093
Bumpus, Cornelius, 1592, 4457
Bumrush, 824
Bunbury, Fergal, 28
Bunch Of Fives, 825, 1917, 2913
Bunch, Boyd, 2035
Bunch, Carl, 2569
Bunch, Gacy, 3399
Bunch, John, 130, 825, 2007, 5923
Bunch, William, 5784
Bundles Of Piss, 5280
Bundrick, John 'Rabbit', 825
Bunetta, Al, 2211
Bunker, Clive, 597, 2819, 3540, 3673, 5511
Bunker, Larry, 489, 825
Bunn, Alan, 1089
Bunn, Alden, 105, 3131, 5297
Bunn, Roger, 4232, 4669
Bunn, Teddy, 72, 825-826, 2851, 3771, 4347
Bunnage, Avis, 538, 4021
Bunnage, Michael, 1456
Bunnell, Dewey, 160
Bunny Lie-Lie, 4432
Bunny Rugs, 785, 1913, 5393
Bunting, David Michael, 1337
Bunuel, Louis, 4501
Bunyan, Vashti, 5616-5617
Buono, Nick, 2773
Bupp, Dave, 3411
Burbank, Albert, 826, 5445
Burbela, Kate, 4592
Burce, Suzanne, 4300
Burch Trio, 1403
Burch, Curtis, 621
Burch, Johnny, 1285
Burch, Shelley, 3952
Burchardt, Mathias, 2079
Burchell, Chas, 826
Burchill, Charlie, 4042, 4921-4922
Burchill, Julie, 3917, 6107
Burchill, Simon, 5634
Burden, Ernest, 3672
Burden, Ian, 2633
Burden, Lynell, 1996

Burden, Martin, 1486
Burden, Sev, 2265
Burdett, Christopher, 169
Burdette, Wayne, 5349
Burdon, Eric, 15, 193-194, 449, 825-827, 1028, 1334, 1385, 2491, 3651, 3682, 3737, 3753, 3931, 4084, 4274, 4322, 4353, 4591, 5697, 5898, 6030, 6038, 6129
Bureau, 827 and passim
Burford, Roger, 605, 1374, 2660
Burg, China, 3472
Burgan, Jerry, 5738
Burge, John, 3039
Burge, Ross, 3856
Burger, Bruce, 4457
Burger, Gary, 3741
Burgess, Bernie, 3847
Burgess, Bob, 2431, 3753
Burgess, Chris, 2112
Burgess, Colin, 47
Burgess, Dale, 1926
Burgess, Dave, 1013, 4448, 5339
Burgess, James, 3121
Burgess, John, 3486, 4900
Burgess, Leroy, 556
Burgess, Mark, 1011, 5782
Burgess, Marlina, 4856
Burgess, Paul, 898, 2671, 3410
Burgess, Randy, 680
Burgess, Ricci, 2603
Burgess, Sally, 1406, 4893
Burgess, Sonny, 154, 827-828
Burgess, Tim, 1024, 1042, 4721, 5275
Burgess, Wilma, 611, 828, 2287, 2349, 3753
Burghdoff, Randy, 4435
Burghoff, Gary, 5963
Burgi, Chuck, 346, 712, 3606, 4411
Burgos, Bob, 3510
Burgoyne, Mick, 2031
Burk, Mike, 5668
Burke, Alex, 4895
Burke, Betsy, 1447
Burke, Billie, 383, 5899, 5997, 5999
Burke, Billy, 2260
Burke, Byron, 5336
Burke, Ceele, 4059
Burke, Clem, 81, 1043, 4087
Burke, Clement, 598
Burke, Fiddlin' Frenchie, 828
Burke, Gregg, 1070
Burke, Hazel, 669
Burke, James, 4014
Burke, Jim, 1171
Burke, Joe, 828, 830, 1405, 1414, 1638-1639, 3201, 3936, 5453
Burke, Johnny, 40, 829, 1207, 2091, 2182, 3303, 3736, 4416, 4563, 4769, 4932, 5606-5607
Burke, Joseph Francis, 830
Burke, Keni, 1920
Burke, Kevin, 679, 2276, 2713, 3950, 4155
Burke, Laddie, 4895
Burke, Leslie, 1586
Burke, Marcella, 3397
Burke, Marie, 4893
Burke, Matt, 3913

Cannata, Jeff, 216, 916
Cannavino, Rob, 4085
Canned Heat, 20, 181, 431, 728, 916-917, 1025, 1823, 1843, 2585, 2587, 2668, 3232, 3241, 3434, 3753, 3809, 4099, 4366, 4466, 4950, 5364, 5511, 5916
Cannibal And The Headhunters, 917, 2969
Cannibal Corpse, 917, 4943, 4964
Canning, Cerne, 5704
Cannon's Jug Stompers, 918
Cannon, Ace, 563, 918, 2018, 2267, 2514
Cannon, Buddy, 5540
Cannon, Freddy, 918, 1809, 2063, 3057
Cannon, Gus, 918-919, 2743, 3224, 4642
Cannon, Henry, 4175
Cannon, Johnny, 918, 2915
Cannon, Maureen, 506, 5582
Cannonball, Wabash, 3290, 5834
Canova, Judy, 3147
Cansfield, Ford, 1332
Cansino, Margarita Carmen, 2450
Canslar, Bob, 4198
Canterbury Records, 5954
Canterbury Tales, 323, 919, 930, 3031, 5527
Cantor, E., 5999
Cantor, Eddie, 103, 350-351, 491, 493, 881, 919-920, 1405, 1587, 1659, 2278, 2285, 2602, 2863-2864, 2922, 2952, 2985, 3466, 3491, 3635, 3649, 4635, 5453, 5582, 5711, 5814, 5982, 5998, 6038
Cantrall, Bobby, 2837
Cantrell, Jerry, 120, 4242
Cantrelli, Tjay, 2127
Cantwell, Dennis, 2175, 4552
Cantwell, Michael, 3638
Canty, Brendan, 1477, 2045
Canty, James, 3419
Canyon Records, 3870, 4132
Canzano, Dominic, 1624
Cap-Tans, 921, 1316, 3501
Cap, Andy And Flip, 920, 5786
Capaldi And Frog, 3503, 5488, 5742
Capaldi, Jim, 803, 825, 921, 1095, 1456, 2001, 2262, 2466, 3502-3503, 5368, 5487-5489, 5890
Capella, 921-922, 2701, 4372, 6093, 6121
Capeman, The, 922, 4919, 5989
Capercaillie, 922, 2265, 2707, 3138, 3261, 3361, 4888, 6123
Capers, Virginia, 4414-4415
Capetta, Donnie, 758
Capitol, 923 and *passim*
Capitol Records, 923 and *passim*
Capitols, 924, 3131, 3591
Capizzi, Leonard, 4234
Capleton, 924, 929, 2114, 2242, 2275, 3956, 4117, 4458, 4766, 4922
Caplin, Paul, 2449

Caplinger, Warren, 920
Capo Records, 1566
Capó, Bobby, 229, 4114, 4361, 4744
Capone, Al, 812, 1529, 3875, 4417, 5688
Capone, Tom, 4385
Capote, Truman, 227, 2606-2607
Capozzi, Dave, 5792
Capozzi, Ernie, 2535
Capp, Al, 3191, 5912
Capp, Andy, 924, 4322
Capp, Frank, 925, 1942, 4239, 5912, 5994
Capp-Pierce Juggernaut, 175, 184, 925, 1713, 2854, 4674, 5851, 5913
Cappadona, John, 91
Capps, Jimmy, 4226
Capra, Frank, 3668
Capricorn Records, 547, 558, 624, 710, 1047, 1550, 2653, 3161, 3477, 5695, 5779
Capris (50s), 925
Capris (60s), 925
Capstick, Tony, 926, 2100, 2470
Captain America, 635, 926, 1785, 1891, 4152, 5616
Captain And Tennille, 32, 578, 926, 2858, 2904, 4809, 5954, 6038
Captain Animal, 2296
Captain Beefheart, 15, 31, 367, 379, 618, 764, 816, 842, 926-927, 997, 1112, 1120, 1215, 1217, 1237, 1456, 1498, 1716, 1723, 1843, 2018, 2097, 2388, 2474, 2493, 2603, 2620, 2754, 2929, 3234, 3392, 3422, 3448, 3636, 3809-3810, 3828, 3857, 3942, 4028, 4180, 4193, 4202, 4258, 4263, 4372, 4508, 4678, 4715, 4823, 4888, 4914, 5333, 5511, 5514, 5542, 5651, 5671, 5754, 5991, 6038
Captain Beyond, 927
Captain Boycott, 155
Captain Rapp, 928
Captain Sanjar, 210
Captain Sensible, 325, 437, 682, 928, 1278, 1342, 1371, 1578, 2544, 2641, 2697, 2838-2839, 3806, 3918, 4543, 5355
Captain Shifty, 211, 5881
Captain Sinbad, 225, 798, 929, 1856, 2222, 3266, 3647, 4120
Captain Tractor, 929
Capurro, Alfredo, 1617
Caputo Keith, 3238
Caputo, Chris, 2387
Car Park, 999, 2597, 2974, 5773
Cara, Irene, 524, 929, 2988
Caravan, 929-930 and *passim*
Caravan Singers, 881
Caravans, 132, 882, 1305, 1646, 2508, 2566, 4575
Caravanserai, 930, 4740-4741, 4740-4741
Caravelles, 930, 1921, 3123, 3636, 4976
Carawan, 64, 931, 2968, 3299, 6091

Carawan, Candie, 931
Carawan, Guy, 64, 931, 2968, 3299, 6091
Caraway, Mimi, 4039
Carbon, Lisa, 273
Carbone, Anthony, 4523
Carbone, Joey, 125
Carbone, John, 1916
Carbonnaro, Joe, 2355
Carcass, 931 and *passim*
Carcrashh Records, 2112
Card, Jon, 1565
Card, The, 931-932 and *passim*
Cardall, Ralph, 4440
Carden, Cornelius, 1764
Carden, Joan, 3793
Cárdenas, Henry, 1900
Cardew, Cornelius, 165, 1764
Cardiac Arrest, 353, 900, 932, 949, 1858, 3402, 4569, 5402
Cardiacs, 932, 4900
Cardigans, 932-933 and *passim*
Cardinal, 933 and *passim*
Cardinali, Pete, 4917, 5642
Cardinals, 621-622, 933, 1490, 2749, 3598, 5652
Cardona, Charlie, 3938
Cardwell, Jack, 5847
Cardwell, Tiffanie, 4833
Career Records, 897, 2232, 4442, 5855
Carefree, 933 and *passim*
Careless Rapture, 933, 1516, 3979
Carelli, Gerard, 934
Caretaker Race, 636, 934, 1050, 1930, 3296
Carey, Alfonso, 125
Carey, Bob, 3492, 5299
Carey, Danny, 5465
Carey, Dave, 2799
Carey, David, 6097
Carey, Denis, 4960
Carey, Jake, 1926
Carey, John, 3410
Carey, Lynn, 3639
Carey, Macdonald, 3105
Carey, Mariah, 155, 312, 699, 934, 1190, 1424, 3782, 5875
Carey, Mutt, 219, 581, 934-935, 1571, 3672, 4066, 5401, 5975
Carey, Pat, 1608
Carey, Phil, 889
Carey, Scott, 4128
Carey, Thomas, 934, 4893
Carey, Tony, 935, 4411
Carey, Zeke, 1926
Carfax, Bruce, 4893
Cargill, Henson, 935
Cargman, Jerry, 1844
Cargo Cult, 521
Cargo Records, 504, 3386, 5352
Caribs, 601, 1817
Carillo, 935, 2188, 2678
Carillo, Frank, 935, 2188, 2678
Cariou, Len, 210, 1374, 3269, 5997
Carisi, John, 6097
Carisi, Johnny, 935, 5309
Carl, Barry, 4594
Carl, Max, 935
Carl, Rudiger, 3732
Carle, Frankie, 475, 659, 690, 936, 1176, 1402, 2253, 2355,

2473, 3146, 3231, 4586
Carle, Richard, 684, 4732
Carlens, Steff kamil, 1498
Carless, Dorothy, 2124, 4063, 5500
Carless, Mick, 2387
Carless, Ray, 1306, 2689, 3869
Carleton, Billie, 694
Carleton, Bob, 308
Carlier, Ramona, 3721
Carlill, Neil, 1472
Carlin, Bill, 2355
Carlin, Ioanna, 2418, 3883
Carlino, Mike, 1495
Carlisle, Belinda, 63, 936, 1078, 2126, 2176, 3190, 4056, 4638, 4956, 5709
Carlisle, Bill, 269, 666, 937, 5500
Carlisle, Billy, 1639
Carlisle, Bob, 138, 936
Carlisle, Cliff, 937, 2249, 4750
Carlisle, Dicky, 1209
Carlisle, Elsie, 158, 936, 4181
Carlisle, Una Mae, 286, 937, 2885
Carlisles, 376, 937-938
Carlone, Francisco, 936
Carlone, Freddie, 1195
Carlos, Bun E., 1038, 2059
Carlos, Don, 173, 562, 648, 1029, 1270, 3144, 4675
Carlos, Ray, 702
Carlos, Wendy (Walter), 938, 1133
Carlotti, Rose, 2459
Carlsen, Dave, 3817
Carlsen, Les, 601
Carlson, Angie, 3203
Carlson, Brad, 1038, 2059
Carlson, Butch, 2758
Carlson, Chas, 1249
Carlson, Ed, 1944
Carlson, Frank, 2505
Carlson, Howard, 2347
Carlson, Jack, 2801
Carlson, Paulette, 938, 2524-2525
Carlson, Reynold, 5281
Carlson, Sannie Charlotte, 5788
Carlson, Scott, 990
Carlsson, Maurits, 1716
Carlton And His Shoes, 47, 938, 1569, 1856, 2822, 2955, 3337
Carlton Records, 49, 5533
Carlton, Bob, 4510
Carlton, Clipper, 1132, 1551
Carlton, Harry, 3994
Carlton, Jim, 1246
Carlton, Larry, 161, 163, 483, 938-939, 1318, 1414, 1972, 4294, 4554, 5364
Carlton, Peter, 2726
Carlton, Simon, 3410
Carlyle, Louise, 939
Carlyle, Russ, 939
Carman, 939-940, 1012, 1018, 1728, 2381, 3159, 4981, 5403, 6079
Carman, Brian, 1018
Carman, Paul, 3159
Carmassi, Denny, 2078, 2332, 2458, 3757, 5803
Carmel, 678, 940, 954, 1200, 1427, 2161, 3351, 4730, 5730

Carson, Lori, 958, 2190
Carson, Lumumba, 5939
Carson, Martha, 959, 1225, 3099-3100, 3482, 3508, 4571-4572
Carson, Martha Lou, 959, 3099-3100, 4571-4572
Carson, Mindy, 959, 1927, 3636, 3642, 3711
Carson, Nelson, 1228
Carson, Norma, 843
Carson, Ron, 3884
Carson, Rose Lee, 957
Carson, Salli, 587
Carson, Sonny, 5939
Carson, Sunset, 4787
Carson, Terry, 1483
Carste, Hans, 5453
Cartellone, Michael, 1370, 3948, 3984, 4854, 4858, 5289
Carter And Lewis, 959, 1291, 1905, 1946, 3456, 3587, 3850, 4100
Carter Family, 59, 270, 422, 959-963, 966, 968-969, 971, 977-980, 1079, 1126, 1931, 2020, 2289, 2334, 2827, 2994-2995, 4006, 4072, 4180, 4475, 4539, 4604, 4664, 4984, 5378, 5410, 5728, 6039
Carter USM, 576, 636, 962, 1452, 2754, 3431, 3612, 4282, 4772, 6123
Carter, A.P., 959, 961-963, 1256, 2995, 4539
Carter, Alice, 1206
Carter, Alison, 2862
Carter, Anita, 666, 960, 963, 5930
Carter, Arlie, 2456
Carter, Benny, 71, 112, 154, 216, 219, 375, 378, 380, 383, 391, 415, 468, 477, 500, 502, 516, 568, 691, 716, 806, 814, 845, 861, 937, 963-965, 992, 1038, 1065, 1068, 1083, 1100, 1102, 1156, 1162-1163, 1171, 1176, 1178, 1414, 1437-1438, 1475, 1513, 1527, 1602, 1700, 1720, 1722, 1803, 1849, 1866, 1885, 1912, 2120, 2122, 2150, 2171, 2230, 2244, 2254, 2268, 2283, 2348, 2406, 2409, 2427, 2437, 2457, 2487, 2513, 2518, 2529, 2548, 2626, 2629, 2684, 2773, 2792, 2794, 2805, 2843, 2845, 2848, 2854, 2868, 2878, 2895, 3038, 3109, 3175, 3227, 3249, 3423, 3447, 3554, 3587-3588, 3597, 3599, 3602, 3752, 3757, 3765, 3837, 3863, 3975-3976, 4191, 4275, 4290-4291, 4301, 4323, 4345, 4369, 4380, 4388, 4417, 4427, 4497, 4528, 4561, 4656, 4664, 4696, 4760, 4876, 4915, 4984, 5303, 5402, 5419, 5449, 5464, 5515, 5529, 5533, 5537, 5634, 5718, 5744, 5749, 5762, 5817, 5830, 5858, 5873, 5879-5880, 5913, 5980, 6039
Carter, Betty, 806, 965, 1028, 1465, 2268, 2275, 2371, 2750, 3176, 3568, 3678, 3752, 4339,

4685, 4705, 4915, 5353, 5461, 5840
Carter, Big Lucky, 965
Carter, Bill, 1256, 3227, 4095, 4793
Carter, Bo, 620, 966, 1036, 3707, 4300
Carter, Bob, 3256, 4339
Carter, Brian, 4747
Carter, Calvin, 970, 4265, 5622
Carter, Carlene, 963, 966, 978-979, 1566, 2408, 3137, 3349, 3550, 4064, 4508, 4984, 5757
Carter, Carmet, 2029
Carter, Carroll, 242
Carter, Chris, 1071-1072, 5427
Carter, Clarence, 143, 966-967, 1007, 2351, 2888, 4031, 4186, 5686, 5695
Carter, Clive, 2463, 5307
Carter, Colin, 1929
Carter, David, 412, 1079, 1791, 2362
Carter, Deana, 488, 967
Carter, Delaney, 959
Carter, Derrick, 967
Carter, Desmond, 1022, 1374, 1744, 2102, 2128-2129, 2259, 2822, 3107
Carter, Doug, 4921
Carter, Drew, 5813
Carter, Earl, 5834, 5966
Carter, Edward, 3823
Carter, Elliott, 3493, 3895
Carter, Ezra J., 960
Carter, Fred, 935, 967
Carter, Fred F., Jnr., 935, 967
Carter, Goree, 967
Carter, Hal, 4935
Carter, Hank, 5417
Carter, Helen, 968, 979, 2862
Carter, Ian, 3829, 4565
Carter, J.T., 1291
Carter, Jack, 5654
Carter, James, 42, 968, 3752, 4217, 4496, 4921, 5621, 5770, 5966
Carter, Jamie, 3731
Carter, Jerry, 14, 4978
Carter, Jimmy, 535, 575, 1914, 3607, 3691, 3791, 3901, 4790, 5744
Carter, Joe, 53, 961, 968, 4291
Carter, John, 14, 412, 502, 703, 846, 959, 962, 968, 977, 980, 1344, 1414, 1557, 1626, 1905, 2195, 2362, 2483, 2667, 2730, 3567, 3806, 3846, 3850, 3921, 4496, 4717, 5770, 6039
Carter, John Wallace, 968
Carter, Johnny, 150, 979, 1474, 1926, 3063, 4388
Carter, Jonathan, 4254
Carter, Judy, 1839
Carter, June, 42, 580, 960, 962-963, 966, 968, 977-980, 1342, 1513, 2579, 2838, 2990, 4984, 5784, 6039
Carter, Kent, 3102
Carter, Leon, 1293
Carter, Leroy, 5853
Carter, Leslie, 962
Carter, Linval, 4335
Carter, Lonnie, 1033

Carter, Lorraine, 965
Carter, Lou, 1742
Carter, Lynda, 5703
Carter, Maybelle, 270, 960-963, 966, 968-969, 979, 1256, 3985, 4566, 5834
Carter, Mel, 969, 2311, 3802
Carter, Mother Maybelle, 960, 963, 968, 979, 1256
Carter, Neil, 4971, 5563, 5823
Carter, Nell, 95, 196
Carter, Obadiah, 1919
Carter, Paul, 437, 4007
Carter, Penny, 3158
Carter, Peter, 1970, 4847
Carter, R., 5999, 6039
Carter, Ralph, 4415, 6046, 6091
Carter, Ray, 806, 965, 1028, 1929, 2703
Carter, Ron, 27, 31, 296, 398, 543, 969, 1414, 1579, 1757, 1778, 1791, 2016, 2094, 2310-2311, 2349, 2359, 2373-2374, 2488, 2622, 3114, 3285, 3415, 3475, 3637, 3664, 3756, 3861, 4080, 4155, 4560, 4634, 4663, 4786, 4891, 5359, 5619, 5840, 5859, 6039
Carter, Roy, 1004, 1080, 3687
Carter, Russel, 1857
Carter, Sara, 959-962, 969, 1256, 4604
Carter, Sheila, 2802
Carter, Stephen, 1777
Carter, Sydney, 969-970, 4897, 5315, 6039
Carter, Tom, 906, 1754, 2992, 3567, 3687, 6038, 6046, 6057, 6063-6064, 6091
Carter, Virgil, 777
Carter, Vivian, 42, 970, 5621-5622
Carter, Vivian, And James Bracken, 42, 970, 5621
Carter, Wilf, 970-971, 1105, 1662, 2598, 3180, 3254, 3305, 3443, 3749, 4145, 4429, 4605, 5807
Carteret, John, 2382
Cartey, Rick, 2777
Carthage Records, 4706
Carthy, Eliza, 736, 971-972, 5724-5725
Carthy, Eliza, And Nancy Kerr, 971-972
Carthy, Martin, 110, 184, 333, 382, 465, 715, 970-972, 1234, 1447, 1672, 1966, 1984, 2374, 2422, 2513, 3031, 3285, 3348, 3594, 4185, 4658, 4804, 5279, 5724-5725, 5935
Carthy, Ron, 2200
Cartledge, Glenn, 5801
Cartoone, 972
Cartwright, Alan, 1800, 4344
Cartwright, Christine, 4873
Cartwright, Deidre, 2307
Cartwright, Erik, 1955
Cartwright, George, 3134
Cartwright, Lionel, 972
Cartwright, Peggy, 2212
Cartwright, Root, 4338
Caruso, Carmine, 4441
Caruso, Enrico, 678, 968, 1195,

2545, 4451
Carver, Johnny, 973
Carver, Lynne, 746, 3532
Carver, Siegfried, 4167
Carver, Warner, 1259
Carver, Wayman, 65, 973, 2431, 2513, 5744, 6039
Carvettes, 2289
Carvey, George, 4377
Carvey, Tom, 1799
Cary And His Dixieland Doodlers, 973
Cary, Clara, 428
Cary, Dick, 973
Caryl, Ronnie, 1925
Caryll, Ivan, 1064, 4079, 4249, 5901
Casa Loma Orchestra, 455, 790, 897, 973-974, 1009, 1131, 1274, 1654, 1742, 2143-2144, 2226, 2252-2253, 2329, 2638, 2648, 2879, 2895, 3142, 3146, 3565, 3842, 4747
Casablanca Records, 816, 1997, 2029, 2147, 2450, 2950, 3034, 4738, 5644
Casady, Jack, 348, 827, 1315, 1725, 2491, 2603, 2674, 2802, 2935, 2941, 2949
Casagrande, Steve, 1297
Casal, Luz, 3365
Casale, Bob, 1501
Casale, Gerald, 1501
Casals, Pablo, 4660
Casanova, Héctor, 4098, 4421
Casas, Jorge, 1263, 4803
Cascades, 302, 399, 622, 857, 974, 1591, 1939, 2534, 2848, 4640, 5746
Cascales, John, 4532
Cascone, Kim, 4905
Case, 974 and *passim*
Case, Brian, 2799, 5656, 6098
Case, Paul, 2680
Case, Peter, 430-431, 974, 3904, 4266, 5860
Case, Rodney, 698
Case, Russ, 2535, 3446, 5323
Casebolt, Arika, 1089
Caselotti, Andriana, 1543
Casey, Al, 974, 1104, 1188, 1779, 3601, 4819, 5435, 5604, 5689, 5856
Casey, Ben, 4417
Casey, Bobby, 1853
Casey, Claude, 730, 975
Casey, Harry, 4752
Casey, Harvey, 5464
Casey, Howie, And The Seniors, 112, 975, 4220, 5832
Casey, Jayne, 526, 763, 4249
Casey, John, 459, 4281
Casey, Martyn, 5504
Casey, Nollaig, 566, 1853, 4303
Casey, Patrick, 3406
Casey, Sean, 301
Casey, Warren, 2256
Casey, Wayne, 2949, 3558
Cash Crew, 975, 1392, 1557, 2054, 3981
Cash Money And Marvellous, 975, 4965
Cash, Al, 304
Cash, Alvin, 976, 4048, 5836

Cash, Bernie, 976, 2690
Cash, Eddie, 1634
Cash, Fred, 2683
Cash, Jack, 976
Cash, John R., 979
Cash, Johnny, 77, 263, 286, 321, 429, 431, 448, 580, 688, 705, 757, 801, 918, 961, 966, 976-981, 1001, 1101, 1109, 1122, 1187, 1206, 1256, 1326, 1341, 1381, 1478, 1521, 1674, 1740, 1759, 1799, 1872, 1987, 2098, 2255, 2333-2334, 2481, 2494, 2525, 2615-2616, 2702, 2788, 2812-2814, 2827, 2838, 2871, 2896, 2908, 2963, 2970, 2977, 2990, 3068, 3078, 3081, 3108, 3135, 3220, 3241, 3325-3326, 3358, 3445, 3523, 3719, 3745, 3879, 3889, 3893, 3900-3901, 3959, 4006, 4024, 4056, 4169, 4171, 4196-4197, 4225, 4240, 4476, 4526, 4559, 4594, 4679, 4736-4737, 4795, 4853, 4876, 4881, 4911, 4947, 4980, 5348, 5428, 5460, 5737, 5745, 5784, 5834, 5847, 6039, 6123
Cash, June Carter, 979-980, 5784, 6039
Cash, Nick, 1821, 2989, 3953
Cash, Philip, 211
Cash, Rosanne, 756, 947, 976, 978, 980, 1101, 1314-1315, 1339, 2147, 3013, 3130, 3301, 4197, 6039
Cash, Steve, 1184, 2813, 4093
Cash, Tommy, 980-981, 2033, 5843
Cashan, James, 3003
Cashman And West, 981, 1425, 2161
Cashman, Terry, 981, 1425
Cashmeres, 981
Casiano, Dino Guy, 4618
Casino Steel, 697, 2570, 3302
Casino, Conjunto, 3354, 4614
Casinos, 981-982 and passim
Caskie, Douglas, 2116
Casman, Nellie, 1020
Casnoff, Philip, 4928
Cason, James E., 3665
Cason, Yvette, 4265
Casonovas, 982
Casper, Adam, 4879
Casper, Jackie, 70
Caspers, 2688
Cass And The Cassanovas, 530, 2119, 2867
Cass County Boys, 286, 982
Cassandra Complex, 982, 5589
Cassavetes, John, 189, 498, 3925, 4417, 5464
Casser, Brian, 2867
Cassidy, Al, 2841
Cassidy, David, 460, 599, 839, 982-984, 1267, 1343, 2700, 2858, 2885, 3147, 3157, 3616, 3856, 3951, 4149, 4524, 5440, 6039, 6129
Cassidy, Ed, 892, 1217, 2060, 4466, 4553, 5282, 5541
Cassidy, Eileen, 1951
Cassidy, George, 3507
Cassidy, Jack, 982-984, 2699,

2723, 2885, 4149, 4860, 5894
Cassidy, John, 983, 5296
Cassidy, Larry, 4807
Cassidy, Patrick, 983-984, 3481
Cassidy, Shaun, 983-984, 6039
Cassidy, Spike, 54, 1352
Cassino, Peter, 2192
Cassisi, John, 821
Casson, Jim, 1608
Casson, Reginald, 1747
Cast, 984 and passim
Castaldo, Aniello, 985
Castaneda, Ricky, 3936
Castaways, 155, 984, 1051-1052, 1311, 2244, 2399, 3879, 4145, 4491, 4874-4875
Castel, Vic, 214
Castellano, Vince, 4445
Castelles, 984-985, 4407
Castells, 985, 5289
Castelluccio, Frank, 5601
Castelnuovo-Tedesco, Mario, 4539
Castillo, Cesar, 3428
Castillo, Efrain Rivera, 4558
Castillo, Orlando, 4613
Castillo, Randy, 4071
Castle Communications, 985, 1131, 1580, 1865, 2058, 3024, 3124, 4823, 4974, 5645, 6029, 6036, 6044, 6048, 6061, 6065, 6105
Castle, Adele, 5844
Castle, Bill, 2399
Castle, Geoff, 4172
Castle, Irene, 261-262, 275, 383, 493, 985-986, 1786, 2928, 4118, 4620, 4681, 5720
Castle, Jimmy, 1984
Castle, Lee, 985, 3177, 3875, 4172
Castle, Nick, 205, 1607, 3939, 4046, 4058, 4673
Castle, Roy, 538, 3373, 3788, 4235, 4748, 4804, 4933
Castle, Vernon And Irene, 261-262, 275, 383, 493, 985-986, 1786, 2928, 4118, 4620, 4681, 5720
Castleman, Owen, 986, 3214, 5877
Castling, Harry, 2967
Caston, Leonard 'Baby Doo', 986
Castor, Jimmy, 986-987
Castro Sisters, 1432-1433, 1438
Castro, Adolfo, 885
Castro, George, 747, 4115
Castro, Joe, 1712
Castro, Julio, 1111, 3835, 3946-3947, 4065, 4612
Castro, Peppy, 113, 346, 625
Castro, Ray, 1111, 3947
Castro, Raymond, 1111, 3946, 5447
Castronari, Mario, 4564
Casual, 987 and passim
Casual Gods, 2416
Casuals, 872, 987, 2878, 3169, 4982
Caswell, Dave, 256, 2423
Cat And The Fiddle, The, 987, 1141, 1285, 1703, 2385, 2976, 4814

Cat Iron, 987
Cat Mother And The All Night Newsboys, 987-988
Catalano, Bill, 1821
Catalina, Santa, 1995
Cataline, Glen, 2181
Catamount Records, 3718
Catania, Tony, 4767
Catatonia, 988
Catch, 988 and passim
Catch My Soul, 240, 988-989, 1470, 2097, 2149, 2204, 2434, 3219, 4343, 5801
Catch Of The Season, The, 989
Catch Us If You Can, 7, 989, 1086, 1099, 2134
Catchpole, Tony, 690
Cate Brothers, 989
Cate, Earl, 989
Cates, George, 989, 1654
Cates, Phoebe, 4836
Cates, Ronnie, 4213
Catfish Keith, 990
Cathcart, Dick, 990, 4206
Cathcart, Patti, 5521
Cathedral, 990 and passim
Cathedral, Grace, 442, 2304, 5451
Catherine Wheel, 870-871, 991, 1078, 3465, 3914, 5287
Catherine, Philip, 991, 1241, 3461, 5609
Cathey, Rory, 1157
Cathey, Tully, 3727
Catholic Discipline, 327, 991, 4229
Catilin, Pauline, 765, 1605
Catingub, Matt, 991-992, 4560
Catlett, 'Big' Sid, 233, 481, 2703, 2779, 4111
Catlett, Nora Jo, 5971
Catlett, Walter, 1544, 2284, 3861, 4039, 4724, 5581, 5948
Catley, Bob, 3412
Catlin-Birch, Dave, 5922
Catling, Victor, 5786
Cato's Vagabonds, 992
Cato, Bob, 3723
Cato, Pauline, 992, 3553-3554
Caton, Juliette, 3481
Caton, Lauderic, 993
Caton, Tommy, 2604
Catron, Johnny, 993
Cats, 993-994 and passim
Cats 'N' Jammers, 994
Cats And The Fiddle, 994-995, 1989
Cats In Boots, 995
Cats Jazz Band, 4819
Cats, Bob, 417, 1305, 3672, 6042
Cattini, Clem, 209, 214, 995, 2970, 2986, 5470
Cattle Records, 405, 1421, 1444, 3226, 3305, 4001, 4237
Catto, Jamie, 1832
Catto, Malcolm, 4194
Cattouse, Nadia, 970
Cauchi, Les, 752
Caudle, Rick, 4617
Caufield, Joan, 617
Caughlin, Jim, 4367
Caughron, J.C., 828
Caught On The Hop, 995
Cauld Blast Orchestra, 996, 3138

Cauld Blast Orchestra, 996, 3138
Cauley, Ben, 371-372
Caulfield, Bryce, 137-138
Caupin, Bobby, 2679
Causi, Jerry, 372, 558
Causley, Charles, 275
Cauty, Jimmy, 739, 2481, 2916, 3042, 4053, 5441
Cavalcade, 996 and passim
Cavalera, Max, 2045, 3869, 4822-4823
Cavaliere, Felix, 996, 1454, 5968
Cavallari, Tony, 2327
Cavallaro, Carmen, 128, 996-997, 1361, 1641, 2942, 3366
Cavalli, Freddy, 751
Cavallo, Rob, 2264
Cavanagh, Dean, 2166
Cavanagh, Don, 4518
Cavanagh, Paul, 4642
Cavanaugh, Hobart, 4648
Cavanaugh, James, 395
Cavanna, Joe, 1756
Cavannagh, Frank, 1892
Cavazo, Carlos, 1379, 2645, 4386
Cavazo, Tony, 1379, 2645
Cave, Alan, 3551
Cave, Lloyd, 2857
Cave, Nick, And The Bad Seeds, 322, 998, 1293, 4258
Caveman, 998, 1557, 2019, 2178, 3128, 3594, 4945
Caven, Mark, 2166
Cavendish, Charles, 261, 361, 4673
Cavern, The, 998-1000 and passim
Cavestany, Rob, 1449, 4059
Caviezel, Romy, 4823
Cavill, Chris, 2042
Caws, Matthew, 3868
Cawthorn, Joseph, 2160, 2185, 2260, 3885
Cawthorne, Stewart, 273
Cawthra, Mark, 932
Caxon, Gordon, 1199
Caymmi, Dori, 1000
Cayou, Billy, 3132
Cazares, Dino, 798, 1138, 1864, 3869
Cazazza, Monte, 2692
CBGB's, 1000 and passim
CBS Records, 1000 and passim
CCS, 1001, 1947, 3066, 3805, 4132, 4416, 4909
Cease, Jeff, 554-555
Ceballos, Larry, 2185, 4934
Ceballos, Wayne, 280, 1784
Ceberano, Kate, 1001
Ceccon, Andrea, 3520
Cecil, Malcolm, 5463
Cecilia Records, 1297
Cedar, Tim, 4190
Cederblom, Henrik, 1480
Cee, Rodney, 2053-2054
Cee-Bee Records, 5988
Cekalovich, Greg, 1495
Celebration, 1002 and passim
Celestin, Oscar 'Papa', 1002
Celibate Rifles, 95, 1002, 3831
Cellamare, Rosalino, 4638
Cellier, Frank, 5284, 5573

Chris Mosdell, 5954
Chrisman, Tony, 4747
Christ, John, 1386, 4729
Christ, Tommy, 4768
Christchurch Symphony, 3052
Christensen, Alex, 4767, 5561
Christensen, Don, 5798
Christensen, Kelly, 1796
Christensen, Jon, 469, 1072, 2084, 2786, 2890, 3286, 5653, 5748
Christensen, Marty, 990
Christensen, Tim, 1557
Christgau, Robert, 148, 4792, 4963, 6107
Christi, Ellen, 3791, 4139
Christian Death, 80, 1072, 5630
Christian Stars, 4878
Christian, Charlie, 417, 500, 629, 734, 825, 844-845, 864, 974, 1072-1073, 1108, 1175, 1269, 1283, 1742, 1848, 1943, 2099, 2152, 2208, 2210, 2269, 2321, 2346, 2370, 2395, 2819, 2851, 2853, 2971, 2993, 3008, 3018, 3076, 3223, 3756, 3772, 4069, 4133, 4429, 4497, 4727, 5342, 5413, 5500, 5683, 5855, 5976, 6040
Christian, Chris, 1073, 1904
Christian, David, 1192
Christian, Earl, 2783
Christian, Fletcher, 3856
Christian, Garrison, 1073-1074
Christian, Garry, 1073-1074
Christian, James, 2164, 2607
Christian, Jodie, 34
Christian, Little Johnny, 1074, 1423
Christian, Mark, 525
Christian, Neil, 44, 220, 1074
Christian, Rick, 13-14, 1074
Christian, Roger, 427, 1074, 1211, 4541, 4551, 5589
Christian, Terry, 1839, 4009, 6066
Christian, Timothy, 5464
Christians, 1074 and *passim*
Christiansen, Rob, 1715, 2282
Christie, 1075 and *passim*
Christie, Anna, 3637, 3913, 5284, 5632
Christie, Audrey, 946, 2661
Christie, Ian, 1863, 3838
Christie, Julie, 1802, 2624, 2647, 3023, 4216, 5462
Christie, Keith, 124, 1075
Christie, Lou, 1075, 1228, 5544, 6129
Christie, Lyn, 331
Christie, Martin, 2705
Christie, Mike, 3184
Christie, Stevie, 678
Christie, Tony, 508, 1075, 1802, 3260, 4809
Christina, Fran, 4579, 5876
Christine, Christina, 4715
Christiné, Henri, 2284
Christlieb, Pete, 543, 1004, 1075-1076, 1942, 4681
Christmann, Günter, 1076
Christmas, David, 1369
Christmas, Keith, 13, 1076, 3407

Christo, Johnnie, 1777
Christopher, Gavin, 2242
Christopher, Homer, 730
Christopher, Johnny, 3900, 6039
Christopher, Nick, 2240
Christopher-Jones, John, 2205
Christopherson, Peter, 1155, 2250, 2541, 4355, 5427
Christopholos, Dee, 1992
Christy Minstrels, 226, 277, 348, 943, 1100, 1331, 1485, 1986, 3579, 3651, 3904, 3911, 4621, 4823, 5958
Christy, Don, 661
Christy, Ed, 1986
Christy, June, 1076-1077, 1210, 1225, 1438, 1682, 2120, 2972-2973, 4493, 4626, 5635
Christy, Sonny, 661
Chrome, 1077 and *passim*
Chrome Dog, 517
Chrome Molly, 311, 1077, 2108
Chron Gen, 1077-1078, 1541, 4366
Chrysalis Records,1078 and *passim*
Chu Chin Chow, 250, 540, 1078, 3415
Chubb Rock, 1078, 3106, 3351, 3467, 4496
Chuck D., 650, 1079, 1865, 1932, 2063, 3064, 3080, 3467, 3825, 4085, 4346, 4356-4357, 4731, 4860, 4942, 5340, 5497, 5965, 6040, 6071
Chuck Wagon Gang, 799, 1079-1080, 6040
Chuckleberry, 487, 3425
Chuckles, 2589, 4425, 4592, 5421, 5933
Chudd, Lew, 358, 1080, 1581, 2682, 3641
Chudnick, Robert, 4609
Chuk, Papa, 4120
Chukki Star, 1080
Chumbawamba, 448, 1080-1081, 1288, 1556, 4046, 4236
Chumchal, Dave, 415
Chung, Geoffrey, 6, 47, 1081-1082, 1979, 2496, 3980, 5393
Chung, Marc, 1719
Chung, Mikey, 1081-1082, 3980, 4514
Chung, Wang, 2861, 5695
Chunk Records, 4795
Church, 1082-1083 and *passim*
Church Door Records, 4191
Church, Allen, 2347
Church, Bill, 2332, 3757
Church, Cindy, 1083, 5557
Church, Eugene, 1083
Church, Sandra, 2324
Churchill, Chick, 5337
Churchill, Danny, 308, 2159
Churchill, Diana, 5957
Churchill, Frank, 1543-1544, 3147, 5750
Churchill, Gary, 3198
Churchill, Sarah, 4673
Churchill, Savannah, 716, 937, 1083, 1998
Churchill, Trevor, 52, 1066
Churchill-Dries, Dennis, 5302
Churney, Russell, 2913

Chute, Tony, 4377
Chylinski, Mike, 1632
Ciacci, Antonio, 3274
Ciafone, John, 3758
Ciambotti, Johnny, 1135
Cianide, 1083
Ciccone Youth, 1083-1084
Ciccone, Melanie, 2494
Ciccone, Tony, 3635
Ciconne, Don, 1297
Cidre, Cynthia, 3428
Cieka, Robert, 662
Cimarons, 1084, 2286, 3520, 5566
Cimarosti, Rob, 1723
Cimarosti, Robert, 2295
Cimarron, 1130, 1343, 3541, 4269, 4651, 5438
Cimarron Records, 3541
Cimarrón, Orquesta, 3946
Cincinnati Pops Orchestra, 3112, 4801
Cinderella, 1084 and *passim*
Cinderella (film musical), 1084
Cinderella (stage musical), 1084
Cinderellas, 5450
Cindi, Abe, 3424
Cinema, 1084-1088 and *passim*
Ciner, Al, 161, 4684
Cini, Alfred, 3493
Cinnamon Records, 1793
Cinnamons, 5522
Cinquetti, Gigliola, 1088
Cintarea, 4283
Cintron, 1088, 2704, 3835
Cintron, David, 2704
Cintron, Eliut, 3835
Cintron, George, 1088
Ciola, Al, 2501
Cipollina, John, 1088, 1232, 1285, 1534, 1843, 2249, 2385, 3563, 4385, 5343
Cipollina, Mario, 2941, 3217
Cipriani, John, 1999
Circa Records, 174, 1948, 3775
Circle, 1088-1089 and *passim*
Circle Game, 906, 3103, 3712, 4693, 5358
Circle Jerks, 192, 322, 555, 1089, 1386, 1564, 4469, 4826, 5731, 5793-5794
Circle Records, 1571
Circle Star Cowboys, 3226
Circuit Records, 817, 1233, 1290, 1927, 2200, 3059, 4738, 4746, 4758, 4902, 5477, 5581
Circus, 1089 and *passim*
Circus Lupus, 1089
Circus Of Power, 1089-1090
Cirith Ungol, 1090
Cirklen, Gyllene, 2355
Cisneros, Freddie, 1684
Cissokho, Issi, 4057
Cistone, Toni, 4278
Citizen Fish, 1090, 3352
Citizen Kane, 935, 1090, 1273, 1473, 2509, 2932
Citizen's Utilities, 1090
Citorello, Paola, 780
Citrin, Lenny, 5653
Citroen, Soesja, 1090
City, 1090 and *passim*
City Boy, 1090-1091, 2359,

3418, 5971-5972
City Of Angels, 178, 1091, 1165, 2205, 2686, 3700-3701
City Records, 447, 1098, 1123, 1506, 1546, 1578, 2162, 2464, 2510, 2996, 4451, 5476, 5611, 5640, 5744
City, Charles, 4829
Citybeat, 656, 2026, 3855, 5942
Ciurciu, Alexandru, 5297
CIV, 1091-1092
CJ Records, 4983
CJSS, 1035, 1092
Claassen, Fee, 727, 1092
Claes, Johnny, 2206, 4788, 5810
Claesson, Gert, 3159
Claff, Harry, 4488
Clague, Dave, 662, 4939
Clail, Gary, 1092, 4042, 4194, 4576, 4875, 4877, 5280, 5326, 6000
Clail, Gary, And The On U Sound System, 1092, 4042
Clair, Mark, 1991
Clair, René, 1051
Clairborne, Lillian, 921
Claire, Anna-Juliana, 2203
Claire, Bernice, 3965, 5964
Claire, Bob, 5770
Claire, Dorothy, 870, 1092
Claire, Ina, 2160, 4377
Clambake, 1092, 1600, 1815, 2204, 4311-4312, 4315
Clambotti, Gina, 757
Clan Alba, 996, 1092, 2100, 4904
Clan McPeake, 1093, 5467
Clan Of Xymox, 5943-5944
Clancy, 1093 and *passim*
Clancy Brothers, 898, 1093, 1639, 2057, 2510, 2992, 5487, 5611
Clancy Brothers And Tommy Makem, 1093, 1639, 5487
Clancy, Tom, 1093
Clancy, Willie, 490, 2068
Clandinning, Linda, 1170
Clane, George, 1262
Clannad, 1094, 1201, 1768, 2068, 2707, 3097, 3361, 5722
Clanton, Jimmy, 1094, 2174, 2569, 3013, 3510, 4809
Clapp, Jack, 1094
Clapton, Eric, 8, 125, 143, 146, 312, 340, 359, 435, 445-446, 517, 547, 593, 629-630, 650, 695, 706, 710, 722, 796, 839, 841, 851, 890, 898, 1056, 1094-1096, 1169, 1177-1178, 1224, 1241, 1249, 1283, 1285, 1299, 1312, 1369, 1402, 1410, 1470, 1489, 1497, 1546, 1606, 1615, 1636, 1690, 1734, 1776, 1828, 1874, 1919, 1972, 1996, 2048, 2272, 2387, 2415-2416, 2455, 2461, 2490-2491, 2530, 2620, 2814, 2839, 2868, 2896, 2929, 2953, 3009, 3014, 3051, 3066, 3083, 3133, 3161, 3169, 3171, 3191, 3276, 3300, 3434, 3468, 3495, 3526-3527, 3558, 3603, 4038, 4126, 4197, 4207, 4262, 4283, 4291, 4404, 4632, 4692, 4698, 4838, 5318, 5354, 5356,

Claw Hammer, 1112, 5511
Clawfinger, 1112, 3703, 4422
Clawfist Records, 1939
Clawson, Cynthia, 1112, 1259
Claxton, Rozelle, 1113
Claxton, William, 2799, 6098
Clay Allison, 1113, 1343, 4051
Clay Records, 1114, 1541, 1707, 1805
Clay, Al, 1467, 4945
Clay, Andrew Dice, 5715
Clay, Clinton, 1939
Clay, Henry, 2212, 3326
Clay, James, 703, 2400, 2519, 2750, 4280
Clay, Jesse, 3176
Clay, Joe, 1113
Clay, Judy, 464, 1113-1114, 2916, 5311, 5631-5632
Clay, Otis, 804, 1114-1115, 2741, 2856, 3543, 3552, 3717, 4762
Clay, Roger, 1631
Clay, Shirley, 415, 1115, 3423, 3711
Clay, Sonny, 176, 814
Clay, Tom, 1115
Clay, W.C., 1115
Clayden, Jonathan, 4254
Clayden, Mark, 4254
Clayderman, Richard, 1115-1116, 3134, 4231
Claypool, Les, 4331, 5642
Claypool, Philip, 1116
Clayson, Alan, 13, 437, 724, 921, 1421, 2416, 3502, 4056, 4873, 5488, 5601, 5891, 6032, 6037, 6051, 6067, 6077, 6080-6081, 6086, 6107-6108
Clayton Brothers, 1117, 4719
Clayton Squares, 1116, 4522, 5344
Clayton, Adam, 908, 1765, 2151, 3361, 3891, 4784, 4847, 5560
Clayton, Bessie, 466
Clayton, Buck, 112, 332, 368, 391, 405, 475, 482, 537, 548, 674, 707, 814, 861, 895, 1007, 1010, 1116, 1178, 1190, 1267, 1396, 1399, 1412, 1706, 1792, 1885, 1932, 2273, 2323, 2378, 2557, 2634, 2749, 2792, 2796, 2844, 2854, 2934, 3093, 3105, 3108, 3178, 3348, 3376, 3505, 3773, 3799-3800, 3863, 4203, 4239, 4420, 4582, 4694, 4736, 4743, 4809, 5300, 5332, 5371, 5408, 5611, 5709, 5741, 5762, 5898, 5975-5976, 6040
Clayton, Dick, 2642
Clayton, Freddie, 2124
Clayton, J., 1118, 3008, 3291, 4608
Clayton, Jan, 4893-4894
Clayton, Jay, 947, 1643, 3174
Clayton, Jeff, 856, 1116-1117, 2362, 5912
Clayton, Jenny Mae, 4833
Clayton, John, 674, 1090, 1117, 2361, 3072, 4404, 4681
Clayton, Keith, 1867
Clayton, Kenny, 391, 1483
Clayton, Lee, 1117-1118, 1643
Clayton, Lou, 1658, 3924

Clayton, Mary, 1118
Clayton, Merry, 1118, 1539, 3339, 4195, 4404, 5843
Clayton, Michael, 5552
Clayton, Mike, 3662
Clayton, Patty, 939
Clayton, Paul, 1127, 1958
Clayton, Peter, 1118, 1404, 6098
Clayton, Peter J. 'Doctor', 1118
Clayton, Robin, 250
Clayton, Sam, 391, 3265
Clayton, Sam, 391, 3265
Clayton, Steve, 438, 5485, 5735
Clayton, Terry, 4102
Clayton, Vikki, 1118, 4406
Clayton, William, 1867, 3093
Clayton, Willie, 1118, 1301, 3553
Clayton-Thomas, David, 600, 1119, 2887
Clea And McLeod, 708, 1119
Clean, 1119 and passim
Clean, Dean, 1442
Cleanliness And Godliness
Skiffle Band, 569, 1119
Clear Blue Sky, 1119-1120
Clear Vision, 452
Clearlight, 1120
Clearwater Jazz Festival, 6004
Clearwater, Eddy, 1120, 1167, 1916, 2737
Cleary, Jon, 3763, 5282
Cleary, Michael, 3409, 5719
Cleaver, Chuck, 259
Cleaver, Paul, 4910
Cleaves, Jessica, 1689, 2036
Clee, Michael Kevin, 1865
Cleese, John, 2103, 2207, 3406
Clefs, 1120, 3210, 3224, 5502
Cleftones, 1121, 1510
Clegg, Johnny, 1121, 2590, 2910, 3060, 3534, 3581, 4758
Cleghorn, Ronald, 956
Clemens, Bill, 5675
Clemens, Brian, 2849
Clement Irie, 369, 1880, 1944, 3611
Clement, Dick, 538
Clement, Frank A., 1942
Clement, Jack, 377, 795, 976, 1121-1122, 2051, 2142, 3172, 3836, 4326, 4516
Clement, Jack Henderson, 1121
Clement, Rene, 3108
Clement, Ron, 105
Clements, John, 4569
Clements, Otis, 2708
Clements, Rod, 2734, 3251-3252
Clements, Stanley, 1122, 2182
Clements, Terry, 2890
Clements, Vassar, 580, 749, 1122, 1314, 2244-2245, 2249, 2955, 3745, 4027, 5317, 5650
Clements, Zeke, 1122, 2002, 2254, 2617
Cleminson, Zal, 3886, 4820, 5323
Clemmens, Jeffrey, 2063
Clemmons, Clarence, 4761
Clemmons, Larry, 1545
Clemonson, Merle, 3821
Clempson, Dave, 345, 797, 871, 1012, 1123, 1182, 2275, 2633, 4662

Clench, Jim, 213, 316
Clenndining, Linda, 1170
Clere, Slim, 5553
Cless, Rod, 1123
Cleuver, Hans, 1953
Cleveland Cavaliers, 467
Cleveland City Records, 1123
Cleveland Gospel Chimes
Singers, 1554
Cleveland, George, 3808
Cleveland, James, Rev., 1123, 1173, 1551, 1554, 1603, 3421, 3773, 4768
Cleveland, Jimmy, 499, 1124, 2310, 2371, 3350, 4634, 5717
Cleversley, Keith, 2631
Cleyndert, Andy, 1124, 3932
Cliburn, Rick, 4978
Cliff, Jimmy, 280, 422, 452, 511, 573, 1087, 1124-1125, 1466, 1920, 2140, 2214, 2286-2287, 2351, 2390, 2638, 3059, 3380, 3468, 3878, 4327, 4418, 4489, 4644, 5364, 5473, 5669, 5676, 5688
Cliff, Laddie, 540, 1552, 2383
Cliff, Les, 4652, 4854
Cliff, Marcus, 3978
Cliff, Tony, 452, 4439, 4532, 6073
Clifford, Bill, 1125, 5845
Clifford, Bob, 937
Clifford, Buzz, 1126
Clifford, Camille, 466, 989
Clifford, Doug, 619, 1288, 2195, 4718
Clifford, Gordon, 2405
Clifford, Greg, 5398
Clifford, James, 3415
Clifford, John, 1203, 2538, 5442, 5754
Clifford, Julia, 1853
Clifford, Linda, 1126, 1340, 3529
Clifford, Mark, 1148, 4810
Clifford, Max, 770, 4301, 4634
Clifford, Mike, 1126, 6108
Clifford, Paul, 5906
Clifford, Reese Francis, III, 1126
Clifford, Sandy, 1784
Clifford, Stephen, 2671
Clifford, Winston, 411, 2109, 4278
Clift, Anne, 1821
Clift, Montgomery, 2573, 2906, 3042
Clifton Records, 3718, 5883
Clifton, Bill, 329, 1126-1127, 4238, 4460, 5774
Clifton, Verlen, 902, 2785
Climax, 1127 and passim
Climax Blues Band, 1127, 2223, 2309, 2838, 4939, 5399
Climie Fisher, 1127-1128, 2229, 3326, 3870
Climie, Simon, 1127-1128, 3326, 3870
Cline, Alex, 496, 2195, 2200
Cline, Charlie, 1128, 3306
Cline, Curly Ray, 1128, 3306
Cline, Ezra, 1128, 3306
Cline, Gerald, 1129
Cline, Lee, 1128, 3306
Cline, Ned, 3306

Cline, Nels, 2124, 2195
Cline, Patsy, 8, 192, 294, 578, 692, 705, 1087, 1128-1130, 1206, 1229, 1255-1256, 1274, 1644, 2001-2002, 2102, 2141, 2439, 2836, 2963, 3125, 3222, 3370, 3459, 3523, 3589, 3864, 4049, 4156, 4217, 4418, 4485-4486, 4547, 4869, 5371-5372, 5428, 5460, 5677, 5773, 5865, 5970, 6040
Cline, Tammy, 1130-1131, 3864
Cline, Tammy And Dave, 1130
Clink, Mike, 2314, 3643, 4796, 5803
Clinkscales, J.T., 1915
Clint Eastwood And General
Saint, 1131, 2276, 3139, 4245
Clint, Johnny, 5835
Clinton Special, 70
Clinton, Bill, 4288, 4942
Clinton, George, 70, 86, 386, 608, 711, 1131, 1468, 1612, 1910, 2052, 2125, 2663, 2668, 2775, 3107, 3299, 3536, 3847, 4021, 4078, 4141, 4329, 4354, 4463, 4591, 4707, 4723, 4731, 4953, 4973, 5612, 5714, 5775, 5941, 5981
Clinton, Larry, 116, 1131-1132, 3147, 3446, 3736, 5455, 5669
Clipper Carlton, 1132, 1551
Clique, 234, 327, 559, 1108, 1132, 1455, 1977, 2585, 2920, 3955, 4373, 5770, 5811
Clivilles And Cole, 3758
Clivillés, Robert, 873
Clock DVA, 1132, 2691, 4938
Clock Records, 1239
Clockwork Orange, A, 26, 76, 430, 1133, 1183
Clooney, Betty, 4153
Clooney, Dave, 1239
Clooney, Rosemary, 79, 287, 516, 667, 742, 1117, 1133-1134, 1175, 1208, 1227, 1303, 1457, 1868, 1943, 2358, 2515, 2946, 3057, 3147, 3187, 3492, 3597, 3636, 3677, 3711, 3804, 4106, 4153, 4191, 4220, 4304, 4539, 4676, 4828, 4980, 5333, 5632, 5752, 5777, 5791, 5804, 5842, 5849, 6041
Close Lobsters, 1134
Close, Bob, 4247
Close, Glenn, 200, 390, 811, 1134, 1165, 3284
Close, Julian, 1424, 4461
Cloud 9, 1182, 1339, 3734
Cloud Nine, 1134-1135, 1179, 1778, 2416, 2917, 3373, 3971, 4259, 5335
Clouds, 1135 and passim
Clouds Of Joy, 19, 1135, 2553, 3028-3029, 3147, 3658-3659, 5305, 5319, 5389, 5722, 5855, 5872
Clough, Adam, 5276
Clough, Brian, 395
Clougherty, Kevin, 823
Clouter, Bobby, 5512
Cloven Hoof, 1135, 1649
Clover, 1135-1136 and passim
Clovers, 1136 and passim

Colao, Jim, 3871
Colbeck, Rik, 4069
Colbert, Charles, 161, 1430, 3528, 4684
Colbert, Claudette, 1051, 4874
Colbert, Laurence, 4540
Colbert, Paul, 3183, 6059, 6095
Colbourn, Chris, 466, 819
Colbourn, Richard, 466
Colby, Fred, 2340
Cold Blood, 1156, 1654, 2882-2883, 3422, 3718, 4271, 5430, 6082
Cold Chillin' Records, 1156
Cold Chisel, 386, 1156-1157, 4471
Cold Crush Brothers, 303, 1157, 3157, 5340
Cold Hard Facts, 2069, 5666
Cold Sweat, 1157 and *passim*
Cold Water Flat, 1157, 3057, 4515
Coldcut, 271, 526, 1157-1158, 1450, 1462, 1558, 1773, 3955, 4494, 5726, 5752, 5952
Colder, Ben, 2647, 5918
Coldrick, Matt, 2265
Cole, Andy, 1809
Cole, Ann, 1158
Cole, B.J., 12, 670, 1141, 1158, 1738, 4653
Cole, Bill, 1186, 1416, 2441, 4242, 6041, 6043
Cole, Bob, 670
Cole, Buddy, 2447, 3448, 4681, 4853, 5967
Cole, Charlie, 3820
Cole, Cindy, 2801
Cole, Courtney, 83, 784, 3015, 4906
Cole, Cozy, 415, 806, 896, 1163, 1659, 2457, 3524, 5322, 5402
Cole, D. Cane, 804
Cole, Dale, 4787
Cole, David, 873, 4290
Cole, Fred, 3299
Cole, Gardner, 4385
Cole, Gary, 748
Cole, George, 480, 1160-1161, 1337, 4861, 5722, 6068
Cole, Holly, 1158
Cole, Jack, 153, 2119, 2862, 3033, 3199, 3204, 3761, 4040, 5387, 5632
Cole, Joe, 4633
Cole, Johnny, 2519, 2903, 4502
Cole, Larry, 2143
Cole, Lloyd, 1159, 2176, 4706
Cole, Lloyd, 1159
Cole, Mike, 3839, 4944
Cole, Nat 'King', 18, 1160-1161, 1326, 2105, 2512, 2947, 3073, 3772, 5594, 6041
Cole, Natalie, 807, 856, 923, 1160-1161, 2064, 2690, 2963, 3258-3259, 3280, 3435, 3513, 4571, 4928, 5934
Cole, Paddy, 518, 923
Cole, Paula, 1161, 3245
Cole, Ralph, 3242
Cole, Richie, 1162, 2805, 2884, 3522, 4681, 5701
Cole, Roy, 3635
Cole, Stranger, 512, 670, 754,

1162, 2138, 2763, 3060, 3659, 4437, 4493, 5325
Cole, William 'Cozy', 1162
Coleman Brothers, 1158, 1163, 1476, 2107, 4160
Coleman, Bernice, 2427
Coleman, Bill, 113, 203, 823, 1066, 1163-1164, 1190, 2223, 2428, 2529, 2531, 2739, 3108, 3227, 4203, 4662, 4783, 4936, 5530, 5748-5749, 5762, 5880, 6041, 6075
Coleman, Bobby, 1476
Coleman, Burl C. 'Jaybird', 1164
Coleman, Cy, 390, 480, 1091, 1164-1166, 1418, 1495, 1885-1886, 2479, 2661, 3072, 3187, 3239, 3268, 3843, 4041, 5633, 5834
Coleman, Cynthia, 1158
Coleman, G.C., 5887
Coleman, Gary 'BB', 1166
Coleman, George, 115, 128, 224, 603, 1124, 1166, 1220, 2870, 2963-2964, 3415, 3572, 3833, 3861, 4562, 5384, 5693, 5727
Coleman, Jaybird, 2398, 3556
Coleman, Jaz, 245, 1642, 2993, 4879
Coleman, Jesse 'Monkey Joe', 1166
Coleman, Johnny, 332, 3528
Coleman, Kevin, 4976
Coleman, Lander, 1163
Coleman, Lisa, 4331, 5768
Coleman, Margi, 1167
Coleman, Michael, 390, 730, 1167, 3364, 4816, 5729
Coleman, Ornette, 20, 71, 176, 297, 381, 412, 496, 567, 574, 591, 614, 701, 703, 718, 780, 786, 792, 822, 927, 968, 1006, 1016, 1046, 1076, 1149, 1167-1169, 1184, 1214, 1296, 1466, 1579, 1596, 1880, 2023, 2095-2096, 2168, 2330-2331, 2376, 2398, 2404, 2519, 2667, 2732, 2750, 2856, 3080, 3096, 3275, 3347, 3410, 3420, 3473-3474, 3506, 3569, 3582, 3590, 3592, 3645-3646, 3716, 3730, 3752, 3848, 3870, 3973, 4028, 4069, 4138, 4329, 4472, 4634, 4636, 4760, 4775, 4844, 4940, 5309, 5339, 5376, 5507, 5511, 5553, 5568, 5626, 5770, 5834, 6003, 6041
Coleman, Pat, 1466, 2519, 3248
Coleman, Ray, 436-437, 949, 1096, 1169, 1771, 2128, 3193, 3549, 3620, 3986, 4632, 5889, 5935, 6032-6033, 6039-6040, 6046, 6049, 6059, 6062, 6066, 6075, 6078, 6080, 6108
Coleman, Richard, 946
Coleman, Rob, 5574
Coleman, Shepard, 2478
Coleman, Silvia, 5441
Coleman, Steve, 130, 681, 1169, 2559, 3323, 3870, 3887, 4071, 5675, 5863
Coleman, Stuart, 1158, 5574

Coleman, T. Michael, 4816, 5729
Coleman, Warren, 4286
Colenso Parade, 1170
Coleridge-Taylor, Samuel, 1170
Coles, Brian, 260
Coles, Johnny, 1170, 1282, 1791
Coles, Richard, 1194
Coley, Daryl, 2016
Coley, John Ford, 1651, 1759-1760, 2309, 4798
Coley, Keith, 4912
Coliauta, Vinny, 168
Colicos, Nicolas, 2802
Colin, Paul, 341, 6098, 6112
Colin, Sid, 1913, 6048
Colina, Javier, 1506
Colla, Johnny, 3217
Collage, 26, 168, 365, 425, 459, 1011, 1272, 1554, 1626, 1719, 1862, 1871, 1987, 2109, 2691, 2919, 3254, 3723, 3733, 3858, 4023, 4039, 4147, 4295, 4439, 4512-4513, 4775, 4862, 5712, 5754, 5794
Collapsed Lung, 1170-1171, 1453, 1697, 1765, 3900
Collard, Dave, 2178, 2828
Collazo, Fernando, 3313
Collazo, Julito, 1833, 4739
Collective Soul, 1171, 3125
Collectors, 1171 and *passim*
College Boyz, 1171
Collegians, 404, 429, 706, 2439, 2494, 4144, 4266, 4773, 5499, 5886
Collen, Phil, 1461, 2158
Colleran, William D., 3489
Collette, Buddy, 410, 1171-1172, 2359, 2545, 3445, 5297, 5412
Colley, Dana, 1209, 3789
Collianni, John, 2900
Collie, Bif, 1172
Collie, Mark, 1172, 3523
Collie, Max, 1172, 1189, 3141, 4275, 4819
Collie, Shirley, 1143, 3899
Collier, Graham, 307, 353, 447, 1172, 2139, 3111, 3177, 3478, 4174, 4538, 4982, 5315, 5384, 5785, 6058, 6098
Collier, Ian, 1395
Collier, James Lincoln, 235, 1738, 2209-2210, 2798, 6030, 6046, 6050, 6098
Collier, Ken, 2275
Collier, Kevin, 3154, 4626
Collier, Lucille Ann, 3668
Collier, Mike, 3027, 3407, 4538
Collier, Mitty, 1173
Collier, Pat, 1285, 5639-5640
Colliur, Ron, 516
Collier, Scott, 760, 5785
Collier, William, 3850
Collimore, Stan, 2608
Collinge, Craig, 3438, 4888
Collings, David, 4795
Collingwood, Chris, 1988, 2730
Collins Kids, 1173
Collins, Aaron, 879, 1929, 5328
Collins, Albert, 114, 139, 618, 630, 1173-1174, 1230, 1283, 1402, 2110, 2455, 2587, 2639,

2668, 2670, 3558, 3769, 3823-3824, 4322, 4475, 4784, 4895, 5417, 5819
Collins, Allen, 1174, 3374, 4659
Collins, Allen, Band, 1174
Collins, Ansell, 381, 773, 1397, 2764, 4140, 4200, 4489, 4514, 4546, 4780, 5325, 5401, 5509, 5559
Collins, Anthony, 1174
Collins, Art, 616, 1971
Collins, Arthur, 758, 843, 5659
Collins, Barnabas, 3305
Collins, Bernard, 47, 92, 938, 4751
Collins, Berice, 583
Collins, Bill, 1544, 3719, 4541, 5658
Collins, Bob, 515, 2931
Collins, Bootsy, 77, 86, 775, 1131, 1174, 1455, 2190, 2416, 3093, 3133, 4141, 4642, 4706, 4724, 5769, 5941
Collins, Cal, 1175, 5658
Collins, Calvin, 1175
Collins, Charlie, 60, 1132, 2751, 3028
Collins, Clarence, 3262
Collins, Dalon, 2369
Collins, Dave, 2984, 3809
Collins, Dennis, 3709
Collins, Dixie, 1810
Collins, Dolly, 1178, 1395, 5968-5969
Collins, Dorothy, 1959
Collins, Edwyn, 29, 854, 1175, 1980, 2010, 4053, 4295, 4588, 4599
Collins, Frances, 1322
Collins, Frank, 242, 3057, 3269
Collins, Gail, 4122
Collins, Glenda, 1175, 4083
Collins, Grenville, 3023, 4100
Collins, Henrietta, 4633
Collins, Herb, 2279
Collins, Ida, 583
Collins, Jack, 3407
Collins, Joan, 822, 2140, 3118, 3926-3927, 4563, 4639, 5462
Collins, Joe, 1206
Collins, John, 848, 1089, 1175, 1283, 3823, 4725
Collins, José, 3415
Collins, Josie, 1078
Collins, Joyce, 1176
Collins, Judy, 172, 515, 681, 712, 819, 848, 947, 970, 1153, 1176-1177, 1302, 1728, 1756, 1879, 2140, 2257, 2319, 2510, 2578, 2689, 2827, 2890, 2955, 3057, 3269, 3577, 3712, 3931, 4003, 4140, 4168, 4518, 4542, 4547, 4871, 4883, 5530-5531, 5556, 5784, 5812, 6041
Collins, Keith, 290, 4755
Collins, Larry, 1173, 3023
Collins, Lawrencine, 1173
Collins, Lee, 241, 380, 505, 1177, 2346, 2375, 2868, 3650, 3781, 6041
Collins, Lester R., 1178
Collins, Lewis, 3623, 3733
Collins, Lorrie, 1173
Collins, Louis, 3824

4957, 4989, 5299, 5322, 5438, 5453, 5469, 5486, 5518, 5600, 5606, 5631-5632, 5672, 5678, 5703, 5711, 5739, 5791, 5802, 5830, 5836, 5838, 5982, 5985, 6042

Crosby, Bob, 417, 507, 550, 675, 779, 829, 858, 884, 936, 990, 1061, 1302, 1304-1305, 1347, 1407, 1427, 1438, 1493, 1516, 1862, 2120, 2335, 2433, 2962, 2996, 3115, 3118, 3150, 3569, 3577, 3629, 3672, 3688, 3798, 3993, 4075, 4238, 4275, 4351, 4511, 4539, 4563, 4608, 4769, 4876, 5322, 5419, 5753, 5910, 5993, 6005-6006, 6042

Crosby, David, 6, 89, 150, 419, 608, 791, 818-819, 867-868, 1100, 1301-1302, 1305-1307, 1465, 1775, 1965, 2074, 2086, 2590, 2674, 2691, 2802-2803, 2839, 2887, 2935, 3103, 3131, 3200, 3577-3578, 3712, 3823, 3911, 4353, 4574, 5370, 5528, 5745, 5962, 6042

Crosby, Gary, 1306, 2795, 3459, 4083

Crosby, Israel, 1306, 2346, 2487, 2768, 3223, 4861

Crosby, Justin, 14, 1632

Crosby, Kim, 2704

Crosby, Rob, 840, 1306

Crosby, Robbin, 3245, 4439

Crosby, Stills And Nash, 18, 25, 88, 150, 160-161, 266, 272, 624, 819, 868-869, 1120, 1301-1302, 1305-1308, 1465, 1634, 1775, 1820, 1889, 1898, 1998, 2042, 2086, 2110, 2230, 2246, 2564, 2887, 2901, 3025, 3075, 3103, 3276, 3432, 3713, 3877, 3963, 4021, 4802, 4822, 5747, 5916, 5920, 5940, 5977-5978, 6042, 6123

Crosby, Stills, Nash And Young, 150, 161, 266, 272, 624, 819, 869, 1120, 1301, 1307, 1465, 1889, 1998, 2086, 2230, 2901, 3103, 3713, 3877, 4021, 4822, 5747, 5916, 5920, 5977-5978, 6042

Crosland, Alan, 2796

Cross, 1308 and passim

Cross Country, 1308 and passim

Cross, Al, 529, 1257, 5738

Cross, Ben, 2664

Cross, Beverley, 465, 2342, 2381

Cross, Brian, 5733, 6072, 6119

Cross, Bridget, 97, 5580

Cross, Chris, 5570

Cross, Christopher, 134, 314, 1309, 4038, 4716, 5570, 5800

Cross, Dan, 4194

Cross, David, 2999

Cross, Hector, 2857

Cross, Hugh, 1309, 1331, 1910, 5786

Cross, Ian, 732

Cross, Joe, 460

Cross, Rosie, 4373

Cross, Sandra, 99, 225, 1309, 2857, 3345, 4941

Cross, Tim, 5539

Cross, Victor, 225

Crossa, Lou, 1360

Crossan, George, 1952

Crossan, Keith, 2949

Crossfield, Lorrance, 3708

Crossfire, 1310 and passim

Crossfires, 1310, 5538

Crossley, Alfred, 4250

Crossley, Nigel, 2343

Crossley, Syd, 4382

Crossman, Bud, 4441

Crossman, Joe, 158

Crossmen, 1743

Crosstown Blues Band, 4577

Croston, Jill, 1366

Croswell, John, 1090

Crothers, Connie, 1310

Crothers, Rachel, 5463

Crotty, Eddie, 1921

Crouch, Andrae, 219, 939, 1310-1311, 1330, 1384, 2441, 5881

Crouch, Dick, 3177, 4172

Crouch, Keith, 699, 713, 1268, 4157, 5881

Crouch, Le Roy, 1892

Crouch, Nicky, 1852, 3733

Crouch, Reverend Samuel, 1620

Crouch, Stanley, 634, 703, 1311, 1626, 3845

Croucier, Juan, 1575, 4439

Crousare, Terry, 3411

Crouse, Russell, 205, 893

Crouse, Timothy, 205

Crover, Dale, 3622

Crow, 1311 and passim

Crow, Jim, 297, 1708

Crow, Joe, 3286, 3949, 5815

Crow, Phil, 3365

Crow, Sheryl, 1311-1312

Crow, Terry, 3879

Crowbar, 1312-1313, 1607, 1812, 5527

Crowd (UK), 1313 and passim

Crowd (USA), 1313 and passim

Crowded House, 469, 1313, 1355, 1897-1898, 2030, 2994, 3135, 3361, 4142, 4236, 5913, 6042

Crowder, Paul, 81

Crowder, Bob, 1313-1314

Crowdy, Andy, 3641

Crowe, Cameron, 2458, 4175

Crowe, Dave, 4358

Crowe, J.D., 135, 621, 1314, 1508, 1604, 2526, 3149-3150, 3488, 4664, 4947, 5806

Crowe, Simon, 665, 3832

Crowe, Wallace, 1825

Crowell, Rodney, 756, 789, 792, 848, 966, 978, 980, 1101, 1314-1315, 2408-2409, 2525, 2615, 3137, 3301, 4339, 4378, 4815, 4947

Crowism, Jim, 2997

Crowl, Charles, 2791

Crowley, Gary, 850, 4766

Crowley, Tony, 4832

Crowley, Vincent, 53

Crown Heights Affair, 1315

Crown Of Thorns, 730, 1315-1316, 4791

Crown Records, 1080, 3728

Crows, 1316 and passim

Crowsdell, 1316

Crowther, Bruce, 12-15, 2210, 3082, 6050, 6058, 6098

Crowther, Caroline, 3374, 5390

Crowther, Leslie, 2404, 3374, 3710, 5390

Crowther, Pete, 3823

Croxton, Frank, 843

Croydon, Nicky, 2664

Croyle, George, 5874

Crozier, Larry, 561

Crozier, Trevor, 1316

Crozza, Chi Chi, 2501

Crudup, Arthur 'Big Boy', 1316-1317

Cruickshank, John, 2298

Cruickshank, Pete, 2298, 2501

Cruise, Julee, 1317

Cruise, Tom, 426, 3583, 6000

Cruiser, 910, 1317, 1487, 1921

Cruman, Lester, 5498

Crumb, Ann, 258, 566, 2205, 3952

Crumbley, Elmer, 1317

Crumbo, Minisa, 2357

Crumbsuckers, 944, 1317, 4343

Crume, Ray, 2525

Crumit, Frank, 1317, 2277, 4880, 5659, 5964

Crummey, Christopher, 4799

Crump, Albert, 2459, 4868

Crump, Bruce, 3734

Crump, Jesse, 1268, 1318

Crump, Simon, 2630

Crump, William, 1459

Crunt, 309, 1318

Crunz, Ponzi, 2938

Crusader Records, 3501

Crusaders, 1318-1319 and passim

Crush, 1319 and passim

Crush, Bobby, 1319, 2488, 4231

Crustene Roundup Gang, 4538

Crutcher, Bettye, 368

Crutchfield, James, 1319

Crutchfield, Jerry, 1116

Crutchley, Lee John, 4260

Cruz Records, 123

Cruz, Anthony, 2235, 4065

Cruz, Antonio Maria, 3313

Cruz, Bobby, 576, 1841, 4421, 4446-4448

Cruz, Celia, 109, 393-394, 508, 1180-1181, 1319-1321, 1349, 1816, 1841, 1855, 2397, 3097, 3354, 4064, 4098, 4114, 4361, 4421, 4558, 4611, 4614, 4742, 4744, 4742, 4744, 5596, 5934

Cruz, Don, 362

Cruz, Kenny, 3835

Cruz, Miguel, 2234

Cruz, Ray, 3233, 4446-4448

Cruz, Roberto, 4446

Cruz, Simón, 1319

Cruz, Tito, 508, 1320, 1349, 2235, 4098, 4114, 4361, 4421, 4618, 4744

Cruz, Vera, 2034, 5594

Cruzados, 1321, 1676, 2192-2193

Cry Of Love, 1321, 2491, 5789

Cryan' Shames, 1321, 2309

Crybabys, 1321-1322

Cryer, Bruce, 1845

Cryer, David, 1845, 3389

Cryer, Gretchen, 2664

Cryptic Slaughter, 1322

Crypto Records, 2079

Crystal Ball Records, 1810, 2383

Crystal, Angela, 989

Crystal, Conrad, 1810

Crystal, Lee, 2821

Crystals, 1322 and passim

Csapo, George, 508

Csoóri, Sándor, 3857

CTI Records, 1486, 3149

Cua, Rick, 1322

Cub Records, 2879

Cuba, Joe, 1323, 3163, 4114, 4387, 4420-4421, 4610-4611, 4711, 4742, 4711, 4742

Cuba, Joe, 1323, 3163, 4114, 4387, 4420-4421, 4610-4611, 4711, 4742, 4711, 4742

Cuban Heels, 1323

Cubanate, 1324

Cubanismo, 1324, 4611, 4902

Cubanos, Ritmos, 468

Cube Records, 228

Cuber, Ronnie, 1324, 4115

Cubert, Joe, 4705

Cubitt, Robert, 3883

Cuby And The Blizzards, 873, 1324-1325

Cuca Records, 543

Cuccioli, Robert, 2806

Cuckoo Patrol, 1086, 1325, 2022

Cud, 1325, 3658

Cuda, Barry, 1313

Cuddly Toys, 1325, 2958

Cuddy, Jim, 616

Cuddy, Shawn, 1325

Cuden, Steve, 2806

Cuervo, Alma, 5449

Cues, 449, 588, 1326, 2078, 2384, 3459

Cuevas, Manual, 3984

Cuevas, Tony, 3936

Cuff Links, 1326, 1386, 2574

Cuff, Bob, 3866, 4824

Cuffe, Laurie, 1323

Cuffe, Tony, 4075

Cuffee, Ed, 1326

Cuffey, Ronald, 1920

Cuffley, John, 1970

Cugat, Xavier, 68, 820, 894, 1080, 1326-1327, 3776, 3903, 4097, 4113, 4420, 4615, 4695, 5963

Cugini, Christopher, 169

Cujo, 1327, 5454

Cuka, Frances, 4795

Cukor, George, 3198, 3204, 3859, 4044

Culbertson, Rod, 544

Culhane, T.H., 808

Cullen, Angus, 1290

Cullen, Boyce, 3121

Cullen, Gerry, 4672, 5656

Cullen, Keith, 28

Cullen, Wayne, 1642, 5664

Cullerier, Lyn, 1045

Culley, Frank 'Floorshow', 1327

Culley, John, 563, 1291

Culley, Wendell, 1327

Culleyvoe Band, 2643
Culliman, A. Darius, 5350
Cullinan, Tom, 4386
Cullum, Jim, 1327, 2622, 3844, 5592
Cullum, John, 4039, 4041, 4867
Cullum, Ross, 675
Culprit, 1328, 1845, 5577
Cult, 1328-1329 and *passim*
Culture, 1330 and *passim*
Culture Beat, 1329
Culture Club, 62, 98, 307, 416, 683, 686, 693, 714, 763, 1329-1330, 1457, 1706, 2069, 2420, 2471, 2518, 2924, 2996, 3276, 3301, 3326, 3463, 3590, 3819, 3920, 4267, 4719, 5534, 5649, 5651, 5958, 6042
Culture Shock, 868, 1330, 1558, 1966, 3352
Culture, Louie, 2728, 4946
Culture, Peter, 225, 6118
Culverwell, Andrew, 1330
Cumberbache, Williams, 2380, 5526
Cumberland Rangers, 3482
Cumberland Ridge Runners, 1309, 1330, 1956, 2592, 2937, 3112, 3881
Cumberland Three, 1331, 3022
Cumberland Valley Boys, 2752
Cumberland, Enid, 2955
Cummingham, Mark, 2464
Cummings, Burton, 1331, 2306
Cummings, Dave, 2526
Cummings, David, 1467
Cummings, Donnie, 1602
Cummings, Irving, 1578, 1607, 3861, 4281, 5350
Cummings, Jack, 746, 3903, 5654
Cummings, Jim, 3256
Cummings, John, 3730, 4423
Cummings, Krysten, 1922, 5661
Cummings, Robert, 427, 1659, 2227, 3761
Cummings, Sean, 3076
Cummings, Steve, 1331
Cummins, Bernie, 1331
Cummins, Michael, 1890
Cun, Medo, 3854
Cunha, Rick, 1332, 2460
Cunico, Gino, 1806
Cunliffe, Whit, 247
Cunnah, Peter, 1352
Cunniff, Albert, 2814
Cunniff, Jill, 3363
Cunningham, Abe, 1463
Cunningham, Agnes 'Sis', 1332
Cunningham, Alicia, 1333
Cunningham, Bill, 1061, 2578
Cunningham, Billy, 691
Cunningham, Carl, 371
Cunningham, David, 1910, 1951
Cunningham, Father Kit, 319
Cunningham, Jeremy, 3207
Cunningham, John, 1196, 4907, 5449, 6002
Cunningham, Johnny, 1332, 3950, 4497
Cunningham, Kevin, 4906
Cunningham, Larry, 1940, 3459-3460, 3658
Cunningham, Mark, 3472, 6108

Cunningham, Neil, 2036
Cunningham, Paul, 273, 326, 1940
Cunningham, Phil, 334, 382, 2949, 3464, 4907
Cunningham, Phil And Johnny, 1332, 4497
Cunningham, Sis, 144
Cunningham, Steve, 4461
Cunningham, Tom, 5779
Cunninghams, 1117, 1332-1333
Cunnington, Graham, 5346
Cuomo, Jim, 1093, 2172
Cuomo, Rivers, 5754
Cuomo, Sal, 4489
Cup Of Tea Records, 1715
Cupid, 1361, 2006, 2254, 2589, 2721, 3618, 4795, 5369
Cupid's Inspiration, 1333
Cupido, Josefina, 2307
Cuppini, Gil, 1333, 4662
Curb Records, 464, 666, 840, 957, 1116, 1333-1334, 1491, 1762, 2489, 2546, 2979, 3575, 4194, 4871, 5695, 5728
Curb, Mike, 129, 840, 1333-1334, 3651, 4074, 4547, 4551, 4755, 5429, 5822
Curbelo, José, 393, 4360, 4615-4616
Curbishley, Bill, 3117
Curcetti, Georgio, 3982
Curcio, E.L., 4904
Curcio, Paul, 3733
Curd, John, 57, 2466, 3658
Cure, 1334-1335 and *passim*
Cure, Martin, 1052
Curiosity Killed The Cat, 1335, 1435
Curless, Dick, 1336-1337, 3305, 5786
Curley, John, 84, 259
Curly And The Country Boys, 3305
Curly Dan And Wilma Ann, 3874
Curnon, Ian, 98
Curran, Alvin, 4135, 4666
Curran, Andy, 1202
Curran, Ciarán, 150
Curran, Dave, 5581
Curran, Eamonn, 2949
Currence, Loren, 2294
Current, 1337 and *passim*
Currie, Alannah, 307, 2419, 3318, 5407
Currie, Billy, 2619, 5570-5571, 5652
Currie, Cherie, 1337, 4688
Currie, Clive, 2212
Currie, John Boy, 1069
Currie, Kevin, 2809, 5824
Currie, Nicholas, 3735
Currie, Steve, 5277
Currier, Ben, 97
Currier, Jane, 3784
Curry, Ben, 1264
Curry, Butch, 186
Curry, Clifford, 1337, 2070, 3976
Curry, David R., 3707
Curry, Debian, 1182
Curry, Doris, 1645
Curry, Florence, 1266

Curry, John, 4046
Curry, Laurie, 1911
Curry, Mickey, 63, 1328, 4224
Curry, Tim, 1337, 3860, 4600, 5426, 5686, 5724
Curson, Ted, 397, 738, 1124, 1338, 3206, 3253, 3803, 3847
Curtain, Richard, 4820
Curtin, Dan, 1338
Curtis, Adrian, 2312, 2316
Curtis, Alan, 1520, 5947
Curtis, Andy, 1678, 4435
Curtis, Betty, 4195
Curtis, Bill, 1860, 4077
Curtis, Chris, 1457, 4799
Curtis, Connie, 1283
Curtis, Dave, 1457, 1521, 1931
Curtis, Eddie, 1006
Curtis, Herman, 5655
Curtis, Ian, 1295, 2283, 2902, 3347, 3918, 5444, 5579
Curtis, James 'Peck', 1338
Curtis, Jeff, 2112
Curtis, Jimmy, 1050, 1538, 1920, 2073, 2861
Curtis, John, 1046, 1657, 3803
Curtis, Jon, 1022
Curtis, Justina, 2191
Curtis, Keene, 4662
Curtis, Keith, 31, 3623
Curtis, Ken, 944, 1338, 1910, 4132, 5708
Curtis, Lee, 532, 999, 1852, 3155, 3172, 4213
Curtis, Lee, And The All-Stars, 507, 1339, 4667
Curtis, Mac, 4142
Curtis, Mann, 103, 442, 2549, 2971
Curtis, Nathaniel, 2426
Curtis, Paul, 169, 2312
Curtis, Peck, 1338
Curtis, Phil, 1454, 1932
Curtis, Randy, 3105
Curtis, Robert, 3004, 4832
Curtis, Sam, 2312, 2316, 4761
Curtis, Sonny, 814, 1292, 1339, 1531, 1596, 2568-2569, 3052, 5806
Curtis, Stan, 3407
Curtis, Tony, 3747, 4439
Curtis, Winston, 2581, 2774, 4652
Curtiss, Dave, 2618
Curtiz, Michael, 507, 3947, 4636, 5395, 5792, 5948, 5967
Curtola, Bobby, 1339
Curtom Records, 1149, 1339, 3976
Curve, 1340 and *passim*
Curved Air, 1231, 1340, 1716, 3077, 3462, 4546, 4669, 4747
Curvin, Jamaica Papa, 173
Curzon, Frederic, 1340-1341
Curzon, Gary, 3732
Cusack, Peter, 4734
Cuscuna, Michael, 614, 718, 1341, 6119
Cush, Frank, 3349
Cushing, Steve, 5784
Cushman, Robert, 2386
Cusic, Don, 3567, 5497, 5848, 6063, 6082, 6085
Cusimano, Larry, 1756

Cusseaux, Zulema, 1829, 4090
Cussick, Ian, 3113
Custy, Mary, 4847
Cusumano, John, 2535
Cut Le Roc, 4954
Cut To Kill, 1341, 4345
Cutest Rush, 5285
Cutfather, 4985
Cuthbert, Pete, 4523
Cutlass, Frankie, 2053, 3904
Cutler, Adge, 1316, 5933
Cutler, Chris, 1226, 2493, 4193, 5400
Cutler, Eric, 285
Cutler, Ian, 98, 823-824
Cutler, Kate, 1942
Cutler, Paul, 98, 700
Cutliffe, John, 5478
Cutrer, T. Tommy, 1341, 3929
Cutshall, Cutty, 1342
Cutshall, Robert Dewees, 1342
Cutting Crew, 1342
Cutting Records, 1342 and *passim*
Cutting, Andy, 609, 5724
Cuttone, Joe, 2605
Cuvillier, Charles, 2284
Cybertrax, 495
Cyborg, John L., 1077
Cyclone, 1342-1343 and *passim*
Cyclone Rangers, 2900
Cyclone Temple, 6000
Cymande, 3253, 4774
Cymarron, 1343, 4499
Cymbal, Johnny, 1343, 2936
Cymone, Andre, 4331
Cynan, Geraint, 2776
Cynic, 1343 and *passim*
Cynics, 1343 and *passim*
Cypher, Jon, 518
Cypress Hill, 1343-1344 and *passim*
Cyriis, John, 36, 91, 1802
Cyrille, Andrew, 96, 130, 763, 1295, 1344, 1514, 2024, 2080, 2200, 2249-2250, 2811, 3174, 3375, 3732, 4623, 4777, 5309, 5921
Cyrkle, 1344-1345, 2956, 4813, 4918
Cyrus, Billy Ray, 1345, 3618, 4483, 5507
Czech Philharmonic Orchestra, 4819
Czolgosz, Leon, 259
Czukay, Holger, 909-910, 1345, 2032, 2764, 4056, 5617

D

D Records, 804, 1810, 1958, 4230
D'Abo, Michael, 1347
D'Amico, Hank, 1347
D'Andrea, Franco, 1347
D'Angelo, 1347
D'Arby, Terence Trent, 1348
D'León, Oscar, 1348
D'Molls, 1349
D*Note, 1349, 1596, 4083
D, Cliff, 3991, 5499
D, Davey, 371, 1222, 1400, 4992
D, Donald, 1350, 6102

D, Hank, 4836, 5965
D., Howie, 318
D, Mikey, 3417
D, Willie, 1351, 2131
D-Code, 663
D-Influence, 155-156, 475, 1349, 3135, 5568
D-Jax Records, 4961
D-Mob, 54, 1222, 1349-1350, 1392, 1481, 1881, 4129, 5752
D-Nice, 860, 1350, 4382, 4675
D-Train, 1350, 1727
D-Zone Records, 1350, 2800
D., Donald, 1350, 6102
D., Petey, 160, 4595
D.A.D., 1351 and *passim*
D.A.F., 348, 749, 1351, 3096
D.C. Star, 1351
D.R.I., 1322, 1352
D.O.C., 410, 1351-1352, 1612, 3536, 3653, 3988, 4703, 5463, 5495
D.O.P., 1352, 2305, 2801, 3840, 4056
D07, 4882
D:ream, 873, 1352-1353, 2657, 2733, 3338, 4523, 5819
Da Bulldogs, 1701
Da Bush Babees, 1353
Da Costa, Howard, 5736
da Costa, Paulinho, 2474
Da Gradi, Donald, 1545, 3498
Da Happy Headz, 1353
Da Lench Mob, 437, 1353, 1468, 2305, 2663, 2668, 4376
Da Luniz, 1353
Da Mango, Linda, 2307
Da Silva, Ana, 4412
Da Silva, Felix, 680
Da Silva, Howard, 1273, 4025, 4827
Da Silva, Jose, 1803
Da Twinz, 2065
Da Vinci, Paul, 1354, 3196, 4678
Da Yeene, 1354
Da Youngstas, 32, 437, 1560
Daamen, Stefan, 1343
Dab Hand, 1354, 2357, 3553-3554
Dabney, Ford, 780
DaCosta, Glen, 4250, 5990
DaCosta, Morton, 3852
Dacre, Harry, 2664
Dacre, Richard, 5893, 6086
Dacres, Desmond, 1466
Dacus, Donnie, 1013, 1054
Dacus, Smokey, 5866
Dada (70s), 1354
Dada (90s), 1354
Daddy Ash, 5939
Daddy Colonel, 200, 4430, 5447, 5565
Daddy Cool, 1355, 4681, 5360, 5878
Daddy Dewdrop, 1355
Daddy Freddie, 1355, 1462
Daddy G, 373, 3504
Daddy Kool, 572, 4335
Daddy Lilly, 3611
Daddy Lizard, 1944, 2015
Daddy Long Legs, 201, 262, 946, 1355, 3630, 3973
Daddy Longlegs, 1356, 5896

Daddy Noddy, 3944
Daddy Rich, 4329
Daddy Rings, 1356, 1496
Daddy Screw, 1525, 5483
Daddy Stovepipe, 1356
Daddy-O, 1356 and *passim*
Dadmun-Bixby, Danny, 2258
Daemon Records, 2350
Daenen, Helen, 1067
DAF, 1351, 2717, 3855, 3959
Daffan, Ted, 1356, 2413, 2708
Daffern, Willy, 927
Daffodil Records, 1143, 1448, 3040
Dafis, Dafydd, 2776
Daft Punk, 1357
Daggett, Larry, 4408
Dagle, Gabe, 448
DaGrease, Dewey, 2295
Dahari, Yosefa, 5961
Dahl, Arlene, 210
Dahl, Glen, 1981
Dahlgren, Eva, 1357
Dahlheimer, Patrick, 3275
Dahlander, Bert, 1357
Dahlor, Norman, 3671
Dahlstrom, Johan, 4909
Dahlström, Petter, 274
Daigrepont, Bruce, 887
Dailey, Albert, 3333, 4610
Dailey, Bernard, 2841
Dailey, Cliff, 1358
Dailey, Dan, 308, 506, 894, 1024, 1357, 1555, 2107, 2203, 2227, 2252, 2434, 2724, 2960, 2987, 3492, 3635, 3808, 4651, 5386, 5998
Dailey, Frank, 1358
Dailey, Pete, 3557
Dailey, William, 671
Daily Flash, 1358
Daily, Janet, 4266
Daily, Pappy, 1358, 2871, 4238
Daily, Pete, 785, 1359, 3580, 5323, 5985
Daintees, 1359
Dainton, Marie, 1064
Dainty, Billy, 4488
Dairo, I.K., 74, 1359, 2910, 4009
Daisley, Bob, 1056, 4071, 4411, 5587, 5816
Daisy Chainsaw, 1276, 1360, 4046
Dakar Records, 3119
Daker, Rhoda, 4520
Dakeyne, Paul, 1360
Daking, Geoff, 625
Dakota, 1360 and *passim*
Dakotas, 1360 and *passim*
Dalbello, 5642
Dalby, Andy, 3020
Dale And Grace, 764, 1360, 2407, 3802, 4718
Dale, Alan, 1236, 1361, 1583, 1823
Dale, Allan, 1987
Dale, Betty, 3320
Dale, Bill, 3057
Dale, Bob, 2124, 4396
Dale, Carlotta, 4756
Dale, Chris, 273, 1514
Dale, Colin, 1361, 2984
Dale, Dick, 129, 373, 427, 1085,

1211, 1236, 1361-1362, 2866, 3849, 5542, 5589, 5639
Dale, Dick, And The Deltones, 2866
Dale, Flora, 2489
Dale, Glen, 1981
Dale, Jim, 390, 932, 1165, 1362, 2429, 3012, 4034, 4142, 4813, 4943, 5501, 5544, 5746
Dale, Jimmy, 5708, 5710
Dale, Kenny, 1363
Dale, Larry, 624, 1363, 2068
Dale, Paul, 3475
Dale, Roger, 688, 5518
Dale, Stanley, 3566, 4808
Dale, Ted, 3366
Dalek I Love You, 1363, 4038, 5324
Daley, Arthur, 5722
Daley, Cass, 1933
Daley, Earl, 1686
Daley, Jack, 5569
Daley, Jared, 583
Daley, Joe, 770, 4697
Daley, Lloyd, 47, 526, 770, 1251, 1363, 1741, 1784, 2165, 3271, 4674, 5578, 5669
Daley, Paul, 29, 3179, 4734
Daley, Richard, 1008, 2696, 5392
Daley, Winston, 214
Dalglish, Malcolm, 1413
Dalhart, Vernon, 1256, 1364, 2354, 2809, 3365, 4020, 4359, 4587, 4880, 5810
Dalhover, Scott, 1379
Dali, 32, 78, 917, 3159, 5293, 5649
Dali's Car, 1364
Dalida, 1364
Dalienst, 2008, 3440
Dalio, Marcel, 4040
Dall, Bobby, 4272
Dall, Cindy, 1364
Dall, Evelyn, 158, 1960, 3705
Dallas, Karl, 4248, 5534, 6068, 6094, 6098, 6108
Dallas, Ken, And The Silhouettes, 4210
Dallas, Leroy, 1364, 1710
Dallas, Lorna, 4893
Dallas, Lucio, 4638
Dallas, Rex, 1365
Dallas, Yodelin' Slim, 1365
Dallaway, Robin, 1278, 5638
Dallin, Sarah, 357
Dalling, Richard, 825
Dalling, Tim, 4029
Dallion, Susan, 4937
Dallwitz, Dave, 462, 1365
Dalquist, Michael, 4907
Dalrymple, Dick, 1411
Dalseth, Laila, 489, 1154, 1365-1366
Dalto, Jorge, 4361
Dalton, Billy, 2975, 4672
Dalton, David, 1832, 2247, 2891, 4632, 5642, 6033, 6047, 6050, 6056, 6074-6075, 6108
Dalton, John, 1286, 3023-3024, 3465, 5444
Dalton, Kathy, 1366
Dalton, Lacy J., 702, 1366, 3058, 3345, 3729, 3900, 4876, 5309

Dalton, Larry, 1366
Dalton, Nic, 3190
Dalton, Timothy, 4573
Daltrey, Peter, 1825, 2926
Daltrey, Roger, 414, 1088, 1095, 1366, 1830, 2435, 2643, 3261, 3476, 5381, 5458, 5481, 5589, 5810, 5813
Dalwood, Dexter, 1240
Daly Wilson Big Band, 516, 1367, 2538
Daly, Chris, 4056
Daly, Gary, 1063
Daly, Jackie, 1433, 2713, 4155-4156
Daly, Mick, 1993
Daly, Mike, 2143
Daly, Steven, 4053
Daly, Tyne, 2324, 3140
Daly, Warren, 1367
Daly, William, 2385
Dalziel, Denis, 2582
Damage, 1367 and *passim*
Damaged Goods Records, 2594, 2994
Damba, Fanta, 1368
Dambala, 3253
Dambuster Records, 1524
Dameron, Tadd, 332, 614, 769, 1368, 1683, 1700, 1893, 2195, 2199, 2301, 2405, 2882, 3195, 3885-3886, 4170, 4203, 4634, 4664, 4696, 4879, 4915, 5536, 5858, 5879
Damery, Norman, 5300
Dames, 1368-1369 and *passim*
Dames At Sea, 1369, 4209
Damian, 1220, 1369, 2542, 2641, 2669, 4315, 4434, 4954, 5351, 5575
Damien Thorne, 1369
Damita Jo And The Red Caps, 4583
Damita, Lili, 729, 5397
Damjuma, Ras, 3634
Dammers, Jerry, 430, 1078
Damn The Machine, 1369-1370
Damn Yankees, 1370 and *passim*
Damn Yankees (film musical), 1370
Damn Yankees (stage musical), 1370
Damned, 1371-1372 and *passim*
Damon, Cathryn, 1942
Damon, Stuart, 1030
Damond, Tony, 2077
Damone, Vic, 151, 313, 748, 954, 1372-1373, 1457, 1831, 2543, 2589, 3033-3034, 3322, 3425, 3533, 3930, 4075, 4290, 4833, 5849, 5964
Damrell, Dave, 2299
Damrell, Joseph, 2925
Damron, Dick, 810
Damsel In Distress, A, 262, 933, 1373, 2129-2130, 3966, 4118, 5901
Dan Reed Network, 1723, 4476
Dan, Michael, 1373, 2252, 3258
Dana, 1373-1374 and *passim*
Dana, Vic, 1374, 1935, 3931
Danby, Chris, 5303

Dance A Little Closer, 1374, 2801, 3197
Dance Band, 1374 and *passim*
Dance Craze, 1374-1375 and *passim*
Dance Mania Records, 1847
Dance On Arrival, 663
Dance, Charles, 1692, 4218
Dance, George, 1064
Dance, Helen Oakley, 1039, 2208, 3039
Dance, Stanley, 389, 1738, 2054, 2536, 2634, 2934, 5762, 6031-6032, 6046, 6080, 6084, 6098
Dancehall, 1375 and *passim*
Dancer, Prancer And Nervous, 1375
Dancey, Mark, 523
Dancho, Dante, 2791
Dancin', 1375
Dancing Cat Records, 428
Dancing Did, 1087, 1376
Dancing Lady, 1376 and *passim*
Dancing Years, The, 1376 and *passim*
Dandelion Records, 438, 1377, 4564, 4939, 5485, 5735
Danderliers, 1377
Dando Shaft, 650, 1377, 2470, 2613, 2811, 5789
Dando, Evan, 579, 1192, 1768, 2430, 2672, 2727, 3189, 3968, 5731, 5860
Dandridge, Dorothy, 940-941, 4286-4287
Dandridge, Putney, 1115, 1377, 4421
Dandurand, Tommy, 3881
Dandy And Audrey, 1378, 2345
Dandy, Jim, 558, 1378
Dandys, 1378
Dane Stephens And The Deepbeats, 1826
Dane, Barbara, 716, 1010, 1378, 4904
Dane, Dana, 1378
Dane, Faith, 2324
Dane, Patrick, 4386
Dane, Warrel, 4733
Danel, Pascal, 1378
Daneman, Paul, 899
Dangel, Richard, 5668
Danger, Danger, 1378-1379 and *passim*
Dangerface, 1379
Dangerfield, Matt, 697, 3302
Dangerhouse Records, 138, 327, 1785, 5755
Dangerous Birds, 544, 1191
Dangerous Toys, 1379, 1857
Dangerous When Wet, 1379, 2278, 3630, 5692, 5806, 5844
Dangers, Jack, 3605
Daniel Band, 1379, 3367
Daniel Fred, 1492
Daniel, Casey, 4826
Daniel, Charlie, 3418
Daniel, Dale, 1380
Daniel, Davis, 1380
Daniel, Eliot, 1388, 3930
Daniel, John, Quartet, 2000
Daniel, Jonathan, 1723
Daniel, Ken, 2970
Daniel, Kenny, 2970

Daniel, Ted, 634, 1344
Daniel, Willie C., 4204
Daniele, Graciela, 2205, 4549
Daniele, Pino, 1380
Daniell, Henry, 1903, 3199
Daniels, Bebe, 1982, 3366, 4118, 4550, 5433, 5710
Daniels, Billy, 66, 803, 1380, 1418, 1474, 2188, 2221, 2478, 2962, 5597
Daniels, Charlie, 1203, 1380-1381, 1634, 2618, 2929, 3167, 3174, 3333, 3375, 5519, 5848, 6129
Daniels, Danny, 508
Daniels, David, 1551, 4259
Daniels, Eddie, 100, 1381, 2188, 2300, 2898
Daniels, Errol, And The Garments, 3634
Daniels, Henry, 1551, 3611
Daniels, Henry H., Jnr., 3611
Daniels, Howard, 1023, 4948
Daniels, Jack, 2354, 2524, 5889
Daniels, Jeffrey, 3686, 4840
Daniels, Jerry, 2694
Daniels, Joe, 1382, 1738, 2101, 2565, 3364, 4671, 5833
Daniels, Joey, 1720
Daniels, Julius, 1382
Daniels, Koran, 272
Daniels, Lee, 951, 3174
Daniels, Leon, 1720
Daniels, Luke, 1382
Daniels, Maxine, 1382, 3368, 5601
Daniels, Mike, 1061, 1383, 2638, 3141, 6043
Daniels, Paul, 2943
Daniels, Phil, 721, 1383, 4376-4377, 5482
Daniels, Phil, And The Cross, 1383
Daniels, Ritchie, 1471
Daniels, Roly, 1383, 3121
Daniels, Tom, 843, 3375
Daniels, William, 272, 539, 4827
Danielson, Kurt, 5280
Danielson, Palle, 1775, 3286, 5315
Danish Brew, 3766
Danish Radio Big Band, 1112, 2886, 3079, 5768, 5889
Dankers, Harold, 2785
Danko, Rick, 172, 359-360, 1095, 1383, 1634, 1673, 2440, 4576
Dankworth, Alec, 1384, 2898
Dankworth, Jacqueline, 3638
Dankworth, Jacqui, 1383
Dankworth, John, 124, 223, 381, 447, 998, 1097, 1289, 1383-1384, 1498, 1733, 1869, 2139, 2435, 2595, 3017, 3026, 3155, 3350, 3599, 3638, 3755, 3768, 3804, 4255, 4374, 4658, 4986, 5315, 5407, 5785
Danleers, 1384
Danlierop, Nikki, 4305
Danneman, Monika, 2491
Dannen, Frederick, 2110
Danniebelle, 1384
Danny And Dusty, 1384, 2265, 5938

Danny And The Juniors, 39, 975, 1384-1385, 2859, 3203, 4256, 5546
Danny Dread, 1183, 3944, 3958, 4468
Danny Wilson, 525, 1385, 3466, 4930
Danoff, Bill, 1858
Danoff, Taffy, 1858
Danova, Cesare, 5654
Dansak, 2286
Danse Society, 526, 619, 1385
Dantalians, 4274
Dantalion's Chariot, 1385
Dante And The Evergreens, 1386, 2019
Dante, Frankie, 2397-2398, 4114, 4744
Dante, Nicholas, 1070
Dante, Ron, 220, 1326, 1386, 1495, 3033
Dantzer, Scott, 4356
Danus, Vicens, 3319
Danvers, Lindsey, 3648
Danville Mountain Boys, 3874
Danyls, Bob, 1841
Danzenie, Billy, 3380
Danzig, 542, 554, 909, 990, 1089, 1138, 1239, 1345, 1386-1387, 1564, 1572, 2467, 3065, 3092, 3704, 4463, 5555
Danzig, Evelyn, 1387
Danzig, Glenn, 1386, 3020, 3703, 4729
Daou, Peter, 3981
Daouda, Tou Kone, 1387
Daphne's Flight, 1387
Dara Records, 3298
Dara, Olu, 496, 681, 5878
Darbone, Luderin, 2328
Darby And Tarlton, 1387
Darby, 'Blind' Teddy, 1388
Darby, Allen, 5899
Darby, Gerry, 940
Darby, Ken, 899, 1388, 2997, 3927, 4286
Darby, Teddy, 1388
Darby, Tom, 1387
Darbyshire, Keith, 1295
Darbyshire, Richard, 1388, 3280
Darcel, Denise, 1379
Darch, Frank, 3777
Dardanelle, 722, 1388-1389, 1848, 2331, 3573, 4001, 4230
Dare, 1389 and *passim*
Dare, Ada, 466
Dare, Danny, 2555, 5582
Dare, Eric, 2906
Dare, John, 2456
Dare, Phyllis, 217, 466, 620
Dare, Tracey, 3395
Dare, Zena, 989, 3007
Darensbourg, Joe, 233, 1389-1390, 3115, 3782, 5872, 6043
Dareweski, Herman, 3994
Darewski, Max, 247, 708
Darford, David, 5805
Darin, Bobby, 45, 268, 272, 517, 659, 1100, 1326, 1390-1391, 1618, 1775, 1966, 2183, 2257, 2391, 2568, 2755, 2956, 3032, 3041, 3147, 3230, 3577, 3630, 3670, 4136, 4180-4181, 4698,

4782, 4897, 5426, 5464, 5499, 5628, 5659, 6043
Darion, Joe, 3187, 3430
Dark Angel, 1391, 4700, 4713, 4845
Dark Ducks, 1391, 6043
Dark Heart, 1159, 1391, 2453, 5783
Dark Lord, 1391-1392
Dark Room, 191, 5616
Dark Star, 14, 1392, 1595, 2642, 3278, 3846, 4056, 6044-6045, 6049, 6067, 6126
Dark Throne, 3530
Dark Wizard, 1392
Dark, Tommy, 2672
Dark, Tony, 4038, 4393-4394
Darkboy, 487
Darkman, 908, 1392, 1560, 1977
Darko, George, 1290, 1393, 2153, 2524, 3060, 5404-5405
Darling Buds, 1393, 1756, 2868, 3363
Darling, David, 1393, 1863, 1977, 3545, 4731, 5889
Darling, Denver, 1393
Darling, Erik, 822, 1394, 3492, 3559, 4642, 5299, 5743
Darling, Jill, 1428, 1744, 2822-2823
Darling, Michael, 5892
Darling, Tom, 5545
Darlings Of Rhythm, 803
Darlington, Jay, 3085
Darlington, Sandy, 422
Darnell, August, 2984
Darnell, Bill, 2942
Darnell, Larry, 716, 1394, 2108, 3889
Darnell, Linda, 2642
Darnell, Stoney, 2984
Darrell And The Oxfords, 5456
Darrell, Johnny, 963, 1394, 3754, 4371, 5436
Darren, James, 443, 1394-1395
Darriau, Matt, 3042
Darrieux, Danielle, 748
Darrington, Steve, 728
Darroch, Paul, 1002
Darron, Benny, 265, 482
Darrow, Chris, 1241, 1395, 1714, 2275, 2926-2927, 3958
Darryl-Ann, 1395
Darshan, 1952
Dartells, 1395
Darts, 1395-1396 and *passim*
Darvill, Benjamin, 1277
Darway, Chris, 1297
Darwell, Jane, 4046, 4281
Daryl And The Chaperones, 5793
Darxon, 1396
Das Combo, 4413
Das-EFX, 1396, 1479
Dash, Julian, 1396
Dash, Leslie, 2470
Dash, Sarah, 3100
Dashboard Saviours, 3296
DaSilva, John, 3365
Dassin, Joe, 1396
Dassin, Jules, 1396
Datchler, Clark, 2838
Datchler, Fred, 2838

2923, 3232, 3258, 3490, 3931, 3960, 4126, 4140
Desi And Billy, 1532, 2452
DeSilva, Leon, 1723
Desire, 1492 and *passim*
Desjardins, Richard, 1492
Deslandes, Michael, 1071
Desmarais, Mike, 5552
Desmarias, Michael, 5886
Desmond And His Cherry Pies, 53
Desmond, Florence, 212, 250, 1031, 3372, 4725, 5397
Desmond, Johnny, 578, 1233, 1236, 1361, 1492-1493, 3579, 4107
Desmond, Norma, 811, 1102, 1134, 3284, 3362, 4104
Desmond, Paul, 516, 718, 784, 794-795, 1493, 1582, 1892, 2349, 2943, 3387, 3569, 3780, 3836-3837, 4760
Desmond, Ritchie, 4711
Desmonde, Jerry, 465, 3303, 5892
Desni, Tamara, 1939
Desolation Angels, 320
Desperate Bicycles, 1493-1494
Dessau, Paul, 721
Destiny, 1494 and *passim*
Destri, James, 598, 3667
Destroy All Monsters, 1494, 2676, 3539
Destruction, 1494 and *passim*
Destructors, 1494-1495
Destry Rides Again, 1495, 1519, 2252, 2379, 2987, 3293, 3636, 4416, 4637
Desvarieux, Jacob, 3200, 3867
Desvigne, Sidney, 391, 1248, 2019, 2348, 3895, 4762
Detective, 1495 and *passim*
Detectives, 2166, 2280, 2333
Detente, 722, 1495
Detergents, 1386, 1495-1496
Determine, 1496, 2537, 3356, 3904, 5741
Deth, Lawnmower, 55, 3145
Detmers, Maruschka, 3428
Detours, 80, 1245, 1274, 4410, 5481, 5810
Detrick, Ritchie, 3987
Detroit Emeralds, 1496, 1978, 5775
Detroit Junior, 1496, 3013
Detroit Spinners, 272, 464, 743, 1008, 1098, 1471, 1496-1497, 2057, 4137, 4220, 5713, 5872
Detroit's Most Wanted, 1497
Detroit, Marcella, 1095, 1497, 4838
Detroit, Nathan, 578, 2322, 3208
Dette, John, 4963, 5346
Deuce, 1497 and *passim*
Deuces Wild, 104, 528, 2053, 3010, 3112
Deuchar, Jimmy, 645, 1383, 1498, 1704, 2634
Deupree, Jerome, 3789
dEUS, 1498, 3238, 5616
Deutsch, Adolph, 197, 1020, 1498, 1705, 2054, 4025, 4825
Deutsch, Emery, 3146, 5937
Deutsch, Helen, 944, 2935, 3245

Deutsch, Josh, 1026
Deutsch, Stephanie, 946
Deutsch, Stu, 4261
Deutschendorf, Henry John, Jnr., 1485
Deutscher, Drafi, 1499
Devas, 3817
DeVaughn, William, 1499
Devera Ngwena, 1499-1500
Deveraux, Matthew, 4109
DeVere, Margie, 5708-5709
Devereaux, Wesley, 2414
Deverill, Jon, 4203, 5737
Devey, Willie, 879
Devi, Annapurna, 2981
Devi, Kalpana, 558
Deviants, 1500 and *passim*
Devillard, Remy, 1009
DeVille, Willy, 1500, 3051, 3694, 4277, 5280
Devine And Statton, 1500, 3355, 5753, 5967
Devine, Ian, 1500, 3355, 5967
Devine, John, 420
Devine, Loretta, 2562
Devine, Rachel, 5331
DeVito, Hank, 980, 1315, 1993, 2408
Devito, Jimmy, 5989
DeVito, Nick, 1993, 1995
DeVito, Ralph, 2383
DeVito, Tommy, 1993, 1995
Devlin, Adam, 630
Devlin, Barry, 2599
Devlin, Johnny, 1500
Devlin, Shaun King, 2474
Devo, 651, 1112, 1237, 1501, 1765, 2691, 2743, 4085, 4402, 4590, 4679, 4701, 4939
Devoe, Biv, 459, 699, 2063, 3129, 3535, 3912, 5502
DeVoe, Ronnie, 459, 3912
DeVol, Frank, 1402, 2473, 3244, 5805
DeVol, John, 1328
Devonport, Mick, 3988, 4405
Devotion, Sheila B., 1053
Devotions, 618, 1501
Devoto, Howard, 859, 1501-1502, 3355, 3405, 5396, 5441, 6043
Devoux, Paul, 663
Devoux, Ted, 663
Devril, Chris, 4287
Dew, Tom, 1884
Dewar, Jim, 3356, 3673, 5511
Dewayon, Paul Ebongo, 2008
Dewbury, Russ, 895
DeWese, Mohandas, 3063
Dewey, Greg, 639, 1254, 1716, 2295, 3398
Dewey, Nick, 4515
Dewey, Notcho, 1716, 2295
Dewhirst, Ian, 3507
Dewhurst, William, 4719
Dewing, Thomas, 1148
DeWitt, Alan, 4756
Dexter, Al, 765, 1143, 1502, 3709, 4750
Dexter, Alan, 4105
Dexter, C.K., 2522
Dexter, Jeff, 160
Dexter, Julie, 2795
Dexter, Roscoe, 4933

Dexter, Sally, 2495, 4034
Dexys Midnight Runners, 274, 612, 788, 1487, 1502, 2994, 3640, 3795, 4667, 4805, 5465, 5717, 5874
Dey, Georgia, 2970
Dey, Rick, 3621
Dey, Tony, 1358, 3621
DeYoung, Cliff, 1503
DeYoung, Dennis, 1503
DFC, 1198, 1503, 3535-3536, 4202
Dharma Bums, 1504
Dharma Records, 3594
Dharma, Ritchie, 44
Dharmas, 1504
DHM Records, 1507
Dhomhnaill, Michael O, 4497
Di Bart, Tony, 5451
Di Benedetto, Joe, 1999
Di Gillio, Victor Williams, 358
Di Maio, Dick, 4518
Di Mario, Matt, 1756
Di Mercado, Geoffrey, 2642
Di Novi, Gene, 1504
Di Rose, Diana, 4647
Di Rossi, Renato, 1563
Di Salvo, Jim, 4807
Di Vito, Harry, 5844
Di'Anno's, Paul, Battlezone, 1504
Diabate, Keletigui, 1506, 3070
Diabate, Lamine Youl, 3435
Diabate, Mama, 1505
Diabate, Sidiki, 4713
Diabate, Sekouba 'Bambino', 357
Diabate, Sona, 1505
Diabate, Toumani, 1505, 3069, 5409, 5477
Diablos, 1506, 1585, 1980, 2816
Diadem Records, 1532
Diagram Brothers, 1543, 4109
Diagram, Andy, 1542-1543, 2769, 4109
Dial, Harry, 1506, 4486, 5689, 6044
Diallo, Medoune, 85, 3416
Diamant, Shanty, 3642
Diamond D, 1506-1507, 1701, 2678, 2800, 4836, 4895
Diamond Head, 549, 1507, 1716-1717, 2036, 3453, 3643, 3922, 3977, 4124, 4759, 5421, 5851
Diamond Horseshoe, 178, 367, 539, 997, 1507, 2217, 2227, 2447-2448, 2959, 4118, 4650, 5711
Diamond Rio, 789, 1508, 4143, 4538, 4735, 5420
Diamond, Anne, 5482
Diamond, Brent, 4063
Diamond, Charlie, 3776
Diamond, David, 492, 4132
Diamond, I.A.L., 4636
Diamond, Jack, 296, 3015
Diamond, Jim, 351, 362, 1313, 1508, 3824, 4219, 5734
Diamond, Lance, 2201
Diamond, Lee, 6059
Diamond, Leo, 1508, 2447
Diamond, Max, 1618
Diamond, Michael, 3035, 3184

Diamond, Neil, 314, 365, 400, 479, 578, 777, 923, 1457, 1508-1509, 1854, 2099, 2616, 2790, 2797, 3183, 3670, 3741, 3778, 4763, 4782, 4763, 4782, 5562, 5715, 6044
Diamonde, Dick, 1695
Diamonds (Canada), 1509
Diamonds (USA), 1510
Dianno, 1504, 1510, 2182
Diarra, Zoumana, 476, 2924, 2930
Diatta, Pascal, 1510
Díaz, Felipe, 4420
Diaz, Herman, 1779
Díaz, Juana, 3353
Diaz, Mirelle, 873
Díaz, Tato, 4744
Dibala, Diblo, 1511
Dibango, Manu, 14, 535, 1511, 1651, 1841, 2239, 2924, 2935, 2987, 3134, 3228, 3324, 3416, 4026, 4704, 5406, 5720
Dibari, Vince, 2287
Dibble, Martin, 5416
DiBiase, Joe, 1860
DiBuono, Toni, 1968
diCaprio, Leonardo, 5989
Dice, Tito, 4616
Dicey, Bill, 1511
Dick And Dee Dee, 1512
Dick, Charlie, 1129-1130
Dick, Derek William, 1907, 3462
Dick, Guy, 3045
Dick, Johnny, 2903, 5973
Dick, Michael, 867, 1902, 1949, 6040
Dick, Nigel, 1774, 2296
Dick, Robert, 1626, 2483, 3157
Dick, Paul, 889, 2463, 4348, 5439
Dicken, Bernard, 2902, 3918
Dicken, Jeff, 3823
Dickens, Charles, 255, 1512, 4033
Dickens, H., 884
Dickens, Hazel, 931, 1512, 2127, 4810
Dickens, James Cecil, 1513
Dickens, Jerry, 2585
Dickens, Little Jimmy, 328, 714, 828, 1429, 1513, 1755, 2600, 2615, 2714, 3487, 4296, 4374, 4567, 4750
Dickens, Rob, 2156
Dickenson, James Luther, 1834
Dickenson, Vic, 406, 707, 1178, 1412, 1513, 2329, 2378, 2513, 2592, 2749, 2847, 2895, 3093, 4183, 4239, 4533, 5747
Dickerson, Carroll, 233, 963, 1115, 1513, 1793, 2354, 2536, 2614, 2750, 3710, 4581, 4936, 4988
Dickerson, Dez, 4331
Dickerson, Herbert, 1023
Dickerson, Lance, 1193
Dickerson, Nathaniel, 3464
Dickerson, R.Q., 3708
Dickerson, Walt, 1417, 1514
Dickerson, Walter Roland, 1514
Dickeson, Andrew, 2108
Dickey, Gwen, 4649
Dickey, Robert Lee, 4368

Donahue, Al, 201, 1584, 2962
Donahue, Jack, 309, 1933, 2723, 3903
Donahue, Jerry, 318, 1585, 1986, 2418, 4269, 5927
Donahue, Jonathan, 3632
Donahue, Patty, 2567, 5671
Donahue, Sam, 107, 504, 830, 1585, 5830
Donahue, Tom, 288, 438, 1585, 1953, 2438, 3608
Donald And The Delighters, 1585-1586
Donald, Barbara, 1586, 4915
Donald, Chris, 4832
Donald, Duck, 271, 1459, 1543, 1897
Donald, Howard Paul, 5285
Donald, Keith, 2680, 3820
Donald, Leo Edward, 1394
Donald, Peter, 1586
Donald, Timmy, 609
Donald, Tony, 4921
Donaldson, Alasdair, 4907
Donaldson, Bo, 4122, 5927
Donaldson, Dustin, 5418
Donaldson, Eric, 1586
Donaldson, Jim, 2707
Donaldson, John, 2517
Donaldson, Lou, 393, 614, 1223, 1586-1587, 2393, 3833, 4141, 4158, 4611, 4989, 5537
Donaldson, Pat, 1385, 1986, 2860, 4269
Donaldson, Walter, 70, 1587, 2028, 2035, 2304, 2596, 2861, 2922, 3201, 3225, 3337, 5814, 5928, 5972
Donaldson, Will, 2128
Donaldson, William, 4518
Donat, Robert, 2841, 4676
Donath, Ludwig, 2258, 2862-2863
Donath, Peter, 3317
Donato, Chris, 1290
Doncaster, Patrick, 436, 507, 4532, 6032, 6035, 6059, 6073
Done Lying Down, 1587
Donegal, Arthur, 730, 1942
Donegan, Anthony, 1588
Donegan, Dorothy, 1587-1588, 2614, 2749, 4855
Donegan, Lawrence, 620, 1159
Donegan, Lonnie, 20, 350, 374, 806, 998, 1588-1589, 1629, 1652, 1830, 2074, 2203, 2526, 3156, 3357, 3663, 4372, 4649, 4781, 4943, 5544, 5650, 6044
Donegan, Norman, 61
Donegan, Patrick, 2167, 4490
Donelly, Tanya, 170, 469, 722-723, 991, 1589, 2509, 4194, 5396, 5428
Donen, David, 935
Donen, Stanley, 498, 1370, 1457, 1589, 2054, 2724, 2960, 4106, 4467, 4673, 4825, 4933, 5284
Dones, Tito, 1865
Donga Tribe, 4379
Donida, Carlo, 4195
Donight, Will, 4445
Donihue, Jack, 1279
Donin, Rob, 525

Donington Festival, 48, 250, 321, 554, 1263, 1589, 3778, 4299, 4550
Donlevy, Brian, 545, 3238
Donlinger, Jim, 206
Donlinger, Tom, 206
Donmell, Obie, 2816
Donna Darlene, 2751
Donna, Jim, 984
Donne, David, 2659
Donnell, Blind Joe, 5281
Donnellan, Declan, 3481
Donnellan, Jay, 3334, 3788
Donnelly, Ben, 2695
Donnelly, Declan, 4257
Donnelly, Dorothy, 605, 1457, 4637
Donnelly, John, 4758
Donnelly, Maeve, 3820
Donnelly, Phillip, 2290, 3594
Donnelly, Ruth, 1965, 3147
Donnelly, Ted, 1135
Donnelly, Thomas, 1134
Donnely, Dan, 3536
Donner, Ral, 106, 1590, 4461
Donnolly, Philip, 1117
Donockley, Troy, 2707, 5962
Donohue, Al, 645
Donohue, Jack, 153, 889
Donovan, 1590-1591 and passim
Donovan, Dan, 519, 1622
Donovan, Jason, 173, 1591, 1664, 1940, 2653, 2897-2898, 3589, 3697, 3849, 4525, 4601, 4772
Donavan, Jeff, 4108
Donovan, Mick, 3476
Donovan, Terence, 519, 607
Dont Bother Me I Cant Cope, 5983
Dontinos, 264
Doo Doo Ettes, 700
Doobie Brothers, 538, 910, 1029, 1135, 1591-1592, 2719, 2859, 3064, 3131, 3265, 3297, 3563, 3724, 3886, 3948, 3963, 4457, 4915, 5317, 5333, 5358, 5568, 5631, 5705-5706, 5738
Doodletown Pipers, 908
Doof, 1592 and passim
Dooley, Eric, 4573
Dooley, John, 1592
Dooley, Mike, 1759, 5288, 5482
Dooley, Ray, 5998
Dooley, Simmie, 181
Dooleys, 1592-1593
Doolittle, Alfred P., 883, 2567, 3859
Doolittle, Clarence, 170
Doolittle, Jesse, 3881
Doolittle, Spud, 1960
Doonan Family Band, 1593
Doonan, Kevin, 1593
Doonan, Mick, 1593, 2470
Doonican, Val, 1339, 1387, 1593-1594, 1635, 3884, 3917, 4397, 4729, 5970, 6044
Doonican, Wilmott, 3884
Door Knob Records, 4182
Doors, 1594-1595 and passim
Doorsen, Wendy, 2213
DooTone Records, 2519, 3608, 4186

Dootones, 1595-1596, 3608, 5910
Dor, Gil, 3965
Dora, Steven, 2116
Dorado Records, 177, 1050, 1349, 1596, 4083
Dorados, El, 667, 970, 1290, 1720, 1810, 3063, 5622
Doran, James M., 2092, 6049
Doran, Joanna, 5329
Doran, Johnny, 2309
Doran, Mary, 745
Dorane, Michael, 1373
Dorane, Mike, 3634, 4639
Dore Records, 32, 1792, 5327, 5791
Dore, Charlie, 1536, 1596
Dorff, Stephen, 317
Dørge, Pierre, 1596, 5321
Dorham, Kenny, 1296, 1596-1597, 1646, 1700, 1774, 2487, 2527, 2795, 2885, 2892, 3084, 3233, 3753, 3803, 4065, 5693, 5726, 5778
Dorman, Harold, 1597, 4326
Dorman, L.S., 1154, 6041
Dorman, Lee, 927, 2709
Dormer, Martyn, 1376
Dorn, Joel, 2211, 4321, 4786
Dorn, Philip, 5998
Dornacker, Jane, 1893, 4174
Dornberger, Charley, 1342
Dorney, Tim, 1945, 4508
Doro, 1597, 5703-5704, 5816, 5994
Doroschuk, Colin, 3626
Dorough, Bob, 942, 1597, 2796
Dorough, Robert L., 1597
Dorrell, Dave, 850, 3393, 3472
Dorrian, Lee, 990, 3873
Dorrington, Paul, 5751
Dorris, Kiven, 1093
Dors, Diana, 2226, 3175, 3491, 3779, 4237, 4574
Dorset, Ray, 2272, 3462, 3839
Dorsett, Chris, 1213
Dorsey Brothers, 19, 355, 870, 985, 1131, 1551, 1598-1600, 2028, 2503-2504, 3399, 3587, 3786
Dorsey, Bob, 550, 2971, 4539, 4876, 5479
Dorsey, Glenn, 1909, 2391, 2889, 3147
Dorsey, Irving Lee, 1598
Dorsey, Jimmy, 68, 151, 201, 417, 421, 497, 603-604, 677, 779, 785, 823, 830, 870, 897, 941, 985, 1009, 1172, 1598-1600, 1697, 1708, 1742, 1877, 1894, 1909, 1918, 1933, 2085, 2120, 2131, 2163, 2169, 2193, 2226, 2288, 2447, 2895, 2948, 2957, 2971, 3031, 3073, 3126, 3147, 3226, 3434, 3466, 3505, 3516, 3525, 3672, 3674, 3798-3799, 3942, 3993, 4181, 4472, 4480, 4536, 4609, 4695, 4700, 4760, 4876, 4958, 5299, 5322, 5408, 5439, 5464, 5476, 5606, 5631, 5982, 5985, 5994, 6044
Dorsey, Lee, 358, 415, 460, 567, 1598-1599, 2406, 3013, 3645, 4582, 5478, 5719

Dorsey, Thomas A., 547, 894, 1123, 1599, 2123, 2745, 2790, 2852, 5291, 6044
Dorsey, Tommy, 128, 151, 308, 326, 385, 389, 417, 468, 491, 495, 550, 603, 645, 675, 677, 823, 852, 870, 877, 884, 892, 914, 985, 1009, 1047, 1058, 1117, 1131, 1243, 1302, 1304, 1338, 1390, 1433, 1436, 1482, 1585, 1598-1600, 1682, 1746, 1816, 1862, 1895, 2027, 2113, 2137, 2139, 2273, 2295, 2304, 2336, 2361, 2382, 2386, 2391, 2447-2448, 2503, 2542, 2773, 2882, 2929-2930, 2996, 3042-3043, 3082, 3147, 3150, 3178, 3195, 3200, 3226, 3250, 3359, 3446, 3448, 3471, 3474, 3489, 3509, 3539, 3544, 3565, 3672, 3688, 3733, 3765, 3842, 3854, 3895, 4035-4036, 4191, 4237-4238, 4284-4285, 4302, 4342, 4370, 4451, 4525, 4528, 4535, 4539, 4561, 4668, 4700, 4818, 4853, 4876-4878, 4889, 4927, 4930-4931, 4989, 5322, 5476, 5510, 5606, 5634, 5719, 5723, 5756, 5802, 5833, 5855, 5931, 5993, 6044
Dos, 108, 638, 802, 818, 1349, 1530, 1600, 2163, 2355, 3080, 3097, 3181, 3314, 3424, 3820, 3877, 4098, 4283, 4389, 4558, 4614, 4691, 5447, 5502
Doss, Alan, 2072
Doss, Buster, 2849
Doss, Tommy, 1600-1601, 1853, 5708
Dostal, Frank, 313
Dot Records, 1601 and passim
Dothan Sextet, 3550, 3660, 4368
Dotson, Big Bill, 1601
Dotson, Dotty, 1259, 1984
Dotson, Jimmy, 1601, 1984, 2550
Dotson, Ward, 4239
Dott, Gerald, 2689
Dottsy, 1601
Doty, Don, 1391
Double M Records, 3844
Double Six, 2152, 3327
Double Trouble, 1602 and passim
Double You?, 1602 and passim
Doubleday, Marcus, 1724, 2890
DoublePlusGood, 3758
Doucet, David, 439
Doucet, Michael, 439, 887, 1964
Doucette, 1602
Doucette, Jerry, 1602
Doug E. Fresh, 650, 1602, 3398, 3720, 4150, 4965, 5497
Doug-e-tee, 4293
Dougall, Bernard, 4570
Dougan, Rob, 4079
Dougans, Brian, 2060
Dougherty, Dan, 91, 5953
Dougherty, Eddie, 1602
Dougherty, Joseph, 1337
Doughterty, Steve, 840
Doughton, Shannon, 723
Doughty, Andy, 2910
Douglas, Alan, 1341, 2491

1661, 1821, 3797, 3847, 4031, 5654

Dury, Ian, 1661, 1952, 2152, 2170, 2389, 2414, 2461, 2631, 2989-2990, 3453, 3520, 3851, 3910, 3922, 3953, 4072, 4402, 4972, 5351, 5790

Duryea, Andre, 1270

Duryrea, Larry, 5290

Duskeys, 2963

Duskin, 'Big' Joe, 1661

Dust Brothers, 430, 1025, 1042, 1473, 1662, 1713, 2382, 2913, 3179, 3257, 3619, 3893, 5733, 5968

Dust Junkies, 3539, 4909

Dust Junkys, 1662

Dusted Records, 1489

Dusterloh, Jurgen, 1832

Dusty, Slim, 385, 1245, 1365, 1425, 1662-1664, 2976, 3031, 3596, 4145, 4429, 6045

Dutch Swing College Band, 1382, 1669, 3503, 5648

Dutfield, Dave, 3782

Dutrey, Honore, 1571, 1669, 4035

Dutronc, Jacques, 1669

Dutt, Anjali, 4008, 4627

Dutt, Hank, 3080

Dutton, Dave, 2476, 5308

Dutton, Garrett, 2063

Dutton, Mark, 841

DuValle, Reginald, 941

Duvivier, George, 1389, 1669, 3941, 4875

Duyn, Willem, 3818

DVC, 1669

Dvoracek, J., 2967

Dvorak, Ann, 5349-5350

Dvorak, Anton, 1638

Dvorak, Jim, 3115

Dvorkin, Judith, 1670

DWA Records, 1237

Dwain Records, 1916

Dweeb, 1670, 5587

Dweeb, Chris, 1670

Dwyer, Ada, 5706

Dwyer, Bernie, 2021

Dwyer, Carl, 929

Dwyer, Del, 395

Dwyer, Eugene, 2403

Dwyer, Gary, 5323

Dwyer, Lloyd, 4474

Dyall, Valentine, 4969

Dyani, Johnny Mbizo, 1670, 1880, 2559, 5331

Dyatt, Walter, 2288

Dyble, Judy, 1826, 3540, 5486

Dyche, Mick, 5824

Dycke, Michael, 5494

Dye, Bill, 3265

Dye, Graham, 12, 4144, 4767

Dye, Steven, 4767

Dyeas, Frank, 1529

Dyer, Ada, 1670

Dyer, Bob, 1671

Dyer, Des, 2822

Dyer, Johnny, 1671

Dyer, Liz, 2225

Dyer, Wilbur, 2288

Dyke And The Blazers, 1671, 2449

Dyke, Roy, 256, 4500, 5494

Dykes, Gene, 395

Dykes, Omar, 1671

Dykes, Van, 5604

Dykstra, Jorrit, 224

Dylan, Bob, 11, 20, 27, 43, 199, 266, 326, 337, 359, 382, 414, 433, 435, 452, 504, 515, 543, 597, 600, 605, 608, 620, 637, 650, 685, 696, 706, 732, 739, 741, 749, 804, 867, 869, 906, 926, 967, 972, 977, 1001, 1059, 1087-1088, 1095, 1107, 1119, 1125, 1187, 1200, 1244, 1312, 1332, 1398, 1409, 1413, 1492, 1535, 1619, 1631, 1634, 1651, 1671-1678, 1694, 1702, 1740, 1746, 1787, 1826, 1828, 1847, 1900, 1908, 1958, 2026, 2048, 2110, 2115, 2140, 2154, 2157, 2175, 2183, 2187, 2211, 2230-2231, 2247, 2291-2292, 2297, 2319, 2369, 2373, 2387-2388, 2398-2399, 2408, 2415, 2425, 2434, 2440, 2460, 2464, 2479, 2491, 2510, 2515, 2525, 2567, 2615, 2636, 2641, 2684, 2687, 2718-2719, 2731, 2824, 2827, 2832, 2838, 2906, 2953, 2977, 3055, 3064, 3078, 3104, 3108, 3113, 3133, 3151, 3182, 3235, 3241, 3276, 3304, 3373, 3438, 3494, 3507, 3516, 3520, 3555, 3578, 3589, 3592, 3598, 3623, 3632, 3634, 3713, 3765, 3767, 3778, 3801, 3814, 3817, 3822, 3838, 3851, 3872, 3878, 3893, 3901, 3943, 3991, 3993, 3997, 4019, 4049, 4055, 4084, 4109, 4112, 4154, 4166, 4168, 4195, 4208, 4216, 4258, 4261, 4270, 4307, 4422, 4439, 4501, 4518, 4529, 4543, 4566, 4576, 4585, 4591, 4641, 4698, 4718, 4741, 4748, 4756, 4795, 4804, 4831, 4904, 4906, 4967, 4970, 4972, 4986, 5293, 5319, 5353, 5363, 5367, 5379, 5383, 5398, 5423, 5456, 5487, 5493, 5512-5513, 5516, 5538, 5588, 5591, 5607-5608, 5620, 5633, 5680, 5690, 5713-5715, 5764, 5780, 5806, 5911, 5918, 5930, 5977, 5991, 5996, 6045-6046, 6129

Dylan, Jakob, 5690

Dylans, 1678

Dymond, John, 1397, 3125

Dymonds, 5495

Dynametrix, 1678

Dynamic Superiors, 1678-1679

Dynamic Superiors, 1678-1679

Dynamites, 1679 and *passim*

Dynes, Alison, 1097

Dyre, Arthur, 3809

Dysart And Dundonald, 3261

Dysarz, Edward, 36

Dyson, Bobby, 611

Dyson, Ronnie, 273, 1679, 5749

Dzadzeloi, 1679, 5933

Dziony, Wolfgang, 4780

E

E Street Band, 655, 1967, 3295, 3606, 3889, 4591, 5608

E-40, 1681, 2734

E-Culture, 5885

E-Lustrious, 1681, 1693, 3365

E-Mello, 408

E-Zee Posse, 2449, 3537

E., Sheila, 301, 1681, 1778, 4010, 4332, 4361-4362, 5513

Eacrett, Chris, 4079

Eade, Dominique, 1682

Eade, Winston, 4341

Eadie, Irene, 1682, 3038

Eadie, James, 2703

Eager, Allen, 1682, 3069, 3581

Eager, Johnny, 2935

Eager, Jimmy, 1014

Eager, Vince, 1683, 3610, 4142

Eagles, 23, 205, 212, 266, 524, 620, 696, 791, 818, 848, 910, 921, 1086, 1312, 1358, 1455, 1493, 1527, 1683-1684, 1760, 1767, 1902, 1949, 1953-1954, 2032, 2057, 2098, 2213, 2261, 2485, 2492, 2559, 2604, 2675, 2736, 2770, 2839, 3067, 3157, 3264, 3290, 3309, 3518, 3613, 3781, 3943, 3959, 4046-4047, 4083, 4147, 4195, 4213, 4237, 4268-4269, 4280, 4448, 4509, 4574, 4641, 4687, 4860, 5507, 5524, 5671, 5680, 5691, 5747, 5902, 5980, 5996, 6046, 6089, 6124

Eagles, Steve, 2291, 4229

Eaglesham, Bobby, 1917

Eaglesham, Struan, 5904

Eaglesham, Stuart, 5904

Eaglin, Snooks, 403, 1282, 1684, 1958, 2049, 2051, 4347, 4541

Ealey, Robert, 403, 1684, 5880

Eanes, Homer Robert, Jnr., 1684

Eanes, Jim, 269, 376, 1684-1685, 1752, 3745, 3766, 4238, 4868, 4978, 4980-4981, 5302, 5786

Earache Records, 267, 801, 1137, 1541, 1638, 1811, 2045, 2179, 3703, 3777, 4254, 5570

Eardley, Jon, 4374

Earforce, 1685

Earl Brutus, 1685

Earl Carroll's Vanities, 1686

Earl Of Wharncliffe, 998

Earl Sixteen, 1261, 1270, 1621, 1686, 2138, 3144, 3179, 4338, 4675

Earl, Colin, 3839

Earl, Edison, 2537

Earl, James, 1014, 3149, 3256, 4230, 4710, 5609, 5681

Earl, Jimmy, 1380, 2842, 5301, 5762

Earl, Richard, 1543

Earl, Robert, 147, 1686, 2016, 2291, 2952, 3345, 5396, 5864

Earl, Roger, 1955, 4757

Earl, Ronnie, 907, 1409, 1686, 2016, 3214, 3291, 3651, 4291, 4399, 4642, 5758

Earl, Scott, 1328

Earl, Vince, 1686-1687

Earl, Vince, And The Talismen, 1687

Earl, Vince, And The Zeros, 1687

Earl, Vince, Attraction, 1687

Earl-Jean, 1222, 1687, 2181

Earland, Charles, 1211, 3576, 3833, 5280

Earle, Josephine, 4414

Earle, Kenny, 5618

Earle, Steve, 84, 338, 1101, 1232, 1687, 2291, 2310, 2409, 2589, 2608, 2813, 2969, 3671, 3900, 4414, 5460, 5591, 5609, 5758, 5864

Earlie, Dave, 3774

Earls, 1687-1688, 1925, 2075, 5382

Earls Of Suave, 1925, 2075

Early, Dellareese, 3609

Early, Margaret, 308

Earnshaw, Spencer, 5664

Earth Band, 2594, 3438-3439, 4563, 4666

Earth Messengers, 1688

Earth Mother And The Final Solution, 1893

Earth Nation, 1688, 5491

Earth Opera, 676, 1688, 1728, 2275, 2294, 2808, 4666, 4801

Earth Quake, 1688-1689, 2988

Earth, Wind And Fire, 31, 273, 333, 553, 671, 943, 1087, 1682, 1689, 1756, 1936, 2145, 2170, 2517, 2657, 2659, 3136, 3149, 3224, 3435, 3603, 3659, 3924, 4832, 4878, 5843

Earthling, 687, 1689, 3032

Earthquake, 168, 505, 1232, 1556, 1688, 1703, 1726, 1994, 2428, 2444, 2610, 2715, 2724, 3230, 3844, 4139-4140, 4679, 4709, 4732, 4709, 4732, 5851

Earthshaker, 1690, 1982, 5316, 5945

Earthworks, 42, 94, 137, 353, 412, 798, 1290, 1900, 2919, 2938, 3382, 3414, 3454, 3692, 3867, 4058, 5405

Earwig Records, 847

East 17, 1288, 1497, 1541, 1690, 1730, 1812, 2067, 2657, 2702, 2733, 4276, 4728, 5589, 5802, 6046

East Of Eden, 438, 929, 1127, 1690-1691, 2286, 2728-2729, 3418, 3438, 4655, 5418, 5555-5556, 5650

East Orange, 1113, 1162, 1428, 1691, 3396, 3763, 3884, 4158, 4382, 4395, 5713, 5964

East Texas Serenaders, 1691

East West Records, 147, 168, 310, 367, 940, 1349, 1921, 2153, 2480, 2848, 3028, 4007, 4523, 5342, 5574, 5662-5663, 5830-5831, 5980

East, Brian, 4755

East, Chris, 3181

East, Ernest, 902

East, John, 2709, 6130

East, Nathan, 337, 2000, 4554

Easter Brothers, 1691-1692

Easter Parade, 1692 and *passim*

Easter Russell, 1691

Evans, Lynn, 1069
Evans, M.S., 4773
Evans, Mal, 259, 1792
Evans, Marion, 4774
Evans, Marjorie Ann 'Margie', 1792-1793
Evans, Mark, 47, 1893, 2465, 4551, 5712
Evans, Matt, 4969
Evans, Maureen, 1793, 3449, 4061
Evans, Maurice, 4414
Evans, Mick, 5414
Evans, Mike, 57, 1116, 1443, 2327, 3279, 3658, 6033
Evans, Nick, 4734, 5448
Evans, Paul, 778, 1790, 1793, 2349, 2533, 2927, 2996, 4231, 4594, 5648
Evans, Paul A., 1793
Evans, Paul Wesley, 1790
Evans, Pete, 539, 2607, 3988
Evans, Peter, 4409, 6106
Evans, Philip, 455, 6035
Evans, Ray, 1793, 2590, 3281, 5982
Evans, Rex, 2119
Evans, Richard, 455, 4856, 6035
Evans, Rick, 5988
Evans, Robert, 1246, 1763, 4978
Evans, Rod, 927, 1457
Evans, Roland, 1776, 4173, 4203
Evans, Sandy, 331
Evans, Shane, 1171
Evans, Skeets, 1796
Evans, Slim, 4430
Evans, Stuart, 2116
Evans, Stump, 1793
Evans, Sue, 1793
Evans, Tania, 1329
Evans, Terry, 1793, 2607, 2885, 3566, 3823
Evans, Tolchard, 1794, 3711
Evans, Tom, 323-324, 2729
Evans, Tommy, 946, 6056
Evans, Tornado, 1074
Evans, Tyrone, 5325
Evans, Warwick, 5503
Evans, Wayne, 557
Evans, Wilbur, 3648, 5582
Evans, William, 3135
Evans, Winston, 915, 2670
Evans, Yasmin, 5952
Eve Records, 2407
Eve, Hallows, 2355
Eve, Mick, 2200
Eve, Trevor, 2522
Evelyn, Alison, 4082
Evelyn, Clara, 295, 540
Even Dozen Jug Band, 1688, 1794, 2294, 2297, 3834, 4542, 5513
Even, Sieges, 4901
Evenson, Casper, 542
Evensong, 156, 1794, 3152
Event Records, 981, 2791
Ever Green, 1031, 1141, 1794, 1797, 2340, 3519, 4606, 4922
Everall, Rob, 4287
Everclear, 163, 702, 1795
Everett, Betty, 42, 856, 1044, 1118, 1795, 3221, 5713
Everett, Clifford, Jnr., 4844
Everett, Edward, 250, 2081,

2101, 4841, 5466, 5523, 5998
Everett, Kenny, 1086, 1795-1796, 1825, 2601, 2643, 2926, 3021, 4252, 5467, 6047
Everett, Mark, 1713
Everett, Matt, 3628
Everett, Rupert, 1676, 1900, 2460
Everett, Steve, 1695, 4094
Everett, Tanya, 1882
Everett, Timmy, 3852
Everette, Jack, 1796
Everette, Leon, 1796-1797
Evergreen, 1797 and *passim*
Evergreen Blueshoes, 414, 1797
Everlast, 1797 and *passim*
Everly Brothers, 26, 61, 118, 141, 329, 439, 442, 489, 592, 617, 734, 751, 753, 781, 803-804, 838, 978, 995, 1109, 1117, 1132, 1476, 1606, 1797-1799, 1949, 2120, 2143, 2291, 2438, 2725, 2814, 2937, 3031, 3086, 3168-3169, 3301-3302, 3325, 3328, 3589, 3654, 3730, 3886, 4055, 4296, 4430, 4628, 4654, 4710, 4881, 4916, 5327, 5362, 5457, 5495, 5665, 5670, 5705, 5747, 5882, 5926, 5930, 5933, 5996, 6047
Everly, Bob, 3589
Everly, Don, 118, 1101, 1797-1799, 2141, 2314, 3328, 4654
Everly, Phil, 848, 995, 1180, 1799, 2291, 2548, 2569, 3265, 4531
Everman, Jason, 3689, 3957
Everpresent Fullness, 1799
Evers, Barbara, 4873
Eversand, Richard, 2724
Everson, Lottie, 428
Evertson, Dave, 4414
Every Mother's Nightmare, 1799
Every Mother's Son, 1800
Every Which Way, 1402, 1798, 1800, 3625, 3936, 4396, 4527, 5436
Everybody's Cheering, 1800
Everyday's A Holiday, 1800
Everything But The Girl, 932, 1045, 1284, 1705, 1801, 2131, 2146, 2673, 3259, 3464, 4663, 4766, 5409, 5416, 5731, 6047
Evetts, Steve, 160
Evil Dead, 37, 1802
Evil Superstars, 1802
Evita, 27, 565, 993, 1048, 1075, 1264, 1780, 1802, 1968, 2801-2802, 2862, 2882, 3284-3285, 3362, 3403, 4104, 4154, 4337, 4524-4525, 5746, 6003, 6106
Evo, Paul, 5702
Evora, Cesaria, 1803
Ewans, Kai, 1803
Ewart, Douglas, 176, 1803, 2200, 3217, 3435
Ewbank, Tim, 6080
Ewell, Don, 1790, 1803-1804, 2348, 2614, 3178, 5435, 6047
Ewell, Lois, 1981
Ewell, Tom, 201, 983, 2159
Ewen, David, 494, 2129, 2976, 3860, 4290, 4608, 6099, 6109

Ewens, Kai, 257
Ewing, Skip, 1804, 5795
Ex, 1804 and *passim*
Ex-tras, 3005
Excalibur, 1804-1805, 1955, 4166, 5620, 5965
Excellents, 1805
Excello Legends, 2070
Excello Records, 177, 2310, 2550, 3136, 3153, 3242
Exciter, 1805-1806, 5580
Exciter (The Netherlands), 1805
Exciters, 399, 1021, 1806, 1916, 2277, 2783, 4412
Exclusive Records, 407, 4502
Excuse 17, 4963
Executives, 1806 and *passim*
Exhorder, 1941
Exile, 1806-1807 and *passim*
Exile Records, 32, 1806, 4066
Exist Dance, 1807
Exit Records, 1906
Exit-13, 801, 1807
Exkano, Paul, 1914
Exner, Billy, 2625
Exodus, 1807-1808 and *passim*
Expanding Headband, 2532, 3323, 5463
Experimental, 1808 and *passim*
Exploding White Mice, 1808
Exploited, 1808 and *passim*
Explorer, 1809 and *passim*
Export, 1809 and *passim*
Express, 1809 and *passim*
Expressive Records, 1809
Expresso Bongo (film musical), 1809
Expresso Bongo (stage musical), 1809
Exquisites, 1810
Extended Family Band, 2795
Exterminator, 1810-1811 and *passim*
Extreme, 1811 and *passim*
Extreme Noise Terror, 672, 1811, 2467, 2628, 3043
EYC, 1812
Eye Q Records, 1688, 4460
Eyehategod, 1812
Eyeless In Gaza, 412, 1269, 1812
Eyemark Records, 395
Eyen, Tom, 1625
Eyes, 1812-1813 and *passim*
Eyes Of Blue, 1488, 1813, 2118, 4930
Eynsford-Hill, Freddy, 3859
Eyre, Ian, 1340
Eyre, Mickey, 1876
Eyre, Richard, 2522, 3987
Eyre, Tommy, 1144, 1650, 2149, 3113, 4820
Eysler, Edmund, 615
Eythe, William, 3191
Eyton, Frank, 2102, 2270, 2512, 5425
Eyuphuro, 1813
Ezba, Danny, 3650
Ezell, Ralph, 4867
Ezell, Will, 641, 1813
Ezio, 1813, 1843, 3418, 3490, 6102
Ezo, 1814
Ezrin, Bob, 658, 3034, 4066, 5427

F

F-Beat Records, 1479
F.I.S.T, 1214
F.O.S., 1040, 4976
F9s, 1815, 3057
Fab 5 Freddy, 1815, 5707
Fabares, Michelle, 1815
Fabares, Shelley, 1092, 1815, 2160, 2553, 4540
Faber, Shane, 408
Fabian, 99, 289, 443, 1100, 1809, 1815-1816, 2605, 2642, 2923, 3139, 4540, 4705, 4737, 5429, 6109
Fabiani, Joe, 2664
Fabray, Nanette, 361, 809, 884, 1815, 2520, 3204, 3336, 3488
Fabre, Candido, 1816
Fabricant, Herbert, 5894
Fabulon Records, 1198
Fabulous, 1816
Fabulous Dorseys, The, 579, 1085, 1598, 1600, 1697, 1816, 2462, 5932
Fabulous Five Inc., 1817, 3347
Fabulous Flames, 1698, 1817
Fabulous Phineas, 3925
Fabulous Rhinestones, 1817-1818, 2678
Fabulous Stars, 472
Fabulous Thunderbirds, 403, 757, 1707, 1818, 2051, 2489, 2941, 3390, 3909, 4579, 4621, 5618, 5620, 5876
Face The Music, 1818
Face To Face, 1818
Facedancer, 1819
Facenda, Tommy, 1819
Faces, 1819-1820 and *passim*
Factory (UK 60s), 1820
Factory (UK 70s), 1820
Factory Records, 1820 and *passim*
Fad Gadget, 1719, 1821, 3855, 5478, 5891
Fadden, Jimmie, 3958-3959
Faddis, Jon, 543, 1287, 1821-1822, 2151, 3475
Fadela, Chaba, 1822, 4409
Fadela, Chaba, 1822, 4409
Fafara, Dez, 1138
Fagan, Bevin, 3520
Fagan, Glaister, 3520
Fagen, Donald, 100, 696, 845, 1324, 1489, 1822, 2790, 2900, 4320, 5370, 5624, 5706
Fagenson, Don, 5714
Fagerquist, Don, 1534, 1822, 3082, 4626, 5994
Fagerstedt, Hakan, 5738
Fagg, Billy, 1828
Fagin, Joe, 1823
Fagin, Sandra, 3738
Fahey, Brian, 1823
Fahey, John, 55, 1395, 1434, 1823, 2777, 2961, 3069, 4159, 5490, 5611, 5987, 6067
Fahey, Siobhan, 357, 620, 1497, 1787, 4838, 4880
Fahlgren, Peter, 5397
Faiella, Benny, 2760
Fain, Sammy, 170, 569, 780,

Farnum, Dorothy, 1794
Faron And The Tempest
Tornadoes, 4316
Farr, Gary, 1852, 5275
Farr, Hugh, 1256, 1852
Farr, Karl, 231, 1852-1853
Farr, Lucy, 1853
Farr, Steve, 4375
Farragher, Noel, 588
Farragher, Rita, 588
Farran, Fred, 216
Farran, Maggie, 4235
Farrar, David, 3260
Farrar, Jay, 5572, 5821
Farrar, Jimmy, 3734
Farrar, John, 2256, 2463, 3497, 3934, 4525, 4531, 5498
Farrell And Farrell, 196, 246, 484, 1853, 1924, 2781, 3573, 4510, 4858
Farrell, Bob, 1853
Farrell, Bobby, 656
Farrell, Brian, 2312, 4078
Farrell, Charles, 246, 3019
Farrell, Eileen, 1851-1852, 3573, 5804
Farrell, Glenda, 2185
Farrell, James, 1924
Farrell, Joe, 484, 1853, 2445, 2870, 4176, 4509-4510, 4858
Farrell, Louie, 2312
Farrell, Perry, 2780, 3299, 4287, 6068
Farrell, Stephen, 3838
Farrell, Wes, 216, 1854, 4149
Farren, Charlie, 4199
Farren, Chris, 693, 4852
Farren, David, 321, 6075
Farren, Mick, 1500, 1854, 4131, 4314, 4632, 5545, 6047, 6069, 6071, 6075, 6109, 6112
Farrent, Robert, 3764
Farrington, Mollie, 4020
Farris, Dionne, 1854
Farris, Steve, 168, 3826
Farriss, Andrew, 2706
Farrow, Ernie, 1184
Farrow, Mia, 733, 3694, 3927
Farry, Eithne, 5290
Faryar, Cyrus, 1854, 2140, 3650, 5790
Fascinations, 618, 1855, 4486
Fashek, Majek, 1855, 3068
Fashion, 1856 and passim
Fashion Records, 1856 and passim
Faso, Tony, 263
Fasoli, Claudio, 2632
Fassbinder, Rainer Werner, 172
Fassert, Charles, 4489
Fast Forward, 1856-1857
Fastball, 15, 1857
Faster Pussycat, 1857, 3442
Fastest Bat, 1857
Fastest Guitar Alive, The, 1857, 4055-4056, 4728
Fastway, 1106, 1857-1858, 1952, 5737
Fat Boys, 426, 1858, 3283, 4953, 5434, 5589, 5813
Fat Cat Records, 3519
Fat City, 622, 842, 1189, 1858-1859, 2364
Fat Fantango, 1859

Fat Joe Da Gangsta, 745, 1859, 4433
Fat Larry's Band, 1859
Fat Lilly, 4231
Fat Mattress, 1859, 1946, 2491, 2718, 4563
Fat, Colin, 924, 4922
Fataar, Rikki, 4703
Fatback Band, 792, 1859
Fatboy Slim, 438, 1220, 1860, 4954
Fate, 1860
Fates Warning, 1860, 5816
Fathead, 3139, 3647, 3654, 3929
Father, 1860-1861
Father Abraham And The Smurfs, 1861
Father Shark, 4266
Fatima Mansions, 616, 1861, 3654, 4284, 4769
Fatman And Sons, 3876
Fatool, Nick, 973, 1861, 4206, 4515, 4854, 5923, 5967
Faubert, Peter, 2431
Faubert, Pierre, 2431
Fauerso, Paul, 3288
Faulkner, Dave, 2584
Faulkner, Eric, 420
Faulkner, Jack, 1987
Faulkner, John, 2949
Faulkner, Roy, 1910
Faulkner, Tony, 2594
Faulkner, Vic, 2477
Faulkner, William, 1550, 3930
Fauntleroy, Tom, 5577
Faust, 1862
Faust, Luke, 2699
Fautheree, Jimmy Lee, 3512
Faux, George, 1150, 5534
Fauz-Pas, Voco, 4715
Favale, Joe, 1756
Favaretto, Alex, 1392
Favata, Mike, 5416
Faver, Colin, 1361
Favio, Tony, 1496
Favors, Malachi, 244, 1784, 1862, 2200, 2527, 2783, 3716, 5362
Favre, Pierre, 1862-1863, 4777, 5383, 5733
Fawcett, Tom, 3883
Fawkes, Wally, 1061, 1863, 2547, 4513, 5744
Fay, Bob, 4802
Fay, Colin, 3648
Fay, Johnny, 4484, 5489
Fay, Martin, 1056
Fay, Susan, 4752
Fayad, Frank, 3169, 3334
Faye, Adama, 4804
Faye, Alice, 113, 159, 493, 1863-1864, 1885, 2081, 2203, 2216, 2257, 2412, 2434, 2478, 3491-3492, 3580, 3635, 4039, 4118, 4281, 4648, 5350, 5443, 5600, 5711, 5797-5798, 6047
Faye, Frances, 4449
Faye, Habib, 4706
Faye, Joey, 2479, 2520
Fayne, Greta, 4042
Fazan, Adrienne, 2144
Fazio, Enrico, 447
Fazola, Irving, 236, 537, 1304, 1743, 1864

Fazzio, Joe, 1812
FBI, 262, 640, 849, 983, 3455, 3988, 4357, 4472, 4578, 5723, 5732, 6070
Fean, Johnny, 2601
Fear, 1864 and passim
Fear Factory, 798, 801, 1137-1138, 1617, 1864, 2325, 3238, 3914, 4964
Fearing, Stephen, 1865, 2281
Fearless Four, 608, 1541, 1865-1866, 4915
Fearless, Richard, 1449
Fearman, Eric, 1430-1431
Fearn, Ray, 3964
Fearnley, James, 4270
Fearon, Clinton, 2165, 5404
Fearon, Phil, 1866, 2931, 4346
Feaster, Carl, 1527, 2980
Feaster, Claude, 1070, 2980
Feather, Leonard, 235, 925, 950, 964, 1866, 3135, 3739, 3896, 4134, 4634, 5476, 5716, 6030, 6047, 6089, 6099
Featherbed Records, 2290
Featherby, Marcus, 1385
Feathers, Charlie, 534, 1866-1867, 2995
Featherstonehaugh, Buddy, 3292
Febland, Nicholas, 3120
Febles, José, 301, 1111, 3142, 3353, 4614, 4647
Federal Records, 47, 1565, 3119, 3275, 3341, 5282
Federici, Tony, 4619
Federow, Gabriel, 3410
Fedlkamp, Elmer, 3349
Fee-Fi-Fo-Fum, 3141
Feeder, 1867
Feehan, Pat, 3757
Feehan, Tim, 34, 243
Feelies, 1854, 1867-1868, 2730, 3358, 4663, 5662, 5985
Feely, Fergus, 823
Feemster, Herbert, 4172
Feeney, Seamus, 4284
Feeny, Harry, 4598
Fehlmann, Thomas, 1868
Feiffer, Jules, 4019
Feigin, Leo, 13, 2080, 3194, 6099
Feinberg, Samuel, 1823
Feingold, Michael, 5426
Feinstein, Barry, 5962
Feinstein, David, 1534, 4617
Feinstein, Michael, 1868, 3122, 3488, 5804, 6047, 6109
Feist, Leo, 3164
Feiten, Buzzy, 3826, 5968
Felber, Dean, 2590
Feld, Mark, 644, 5277
Feld, Morey, 1869, 5923
Felder's Orioles, 1869
Felder, Don, 1683
Felder, Jerome, 4277
Felder, Wilton, 1318, 4730
Feldham, Andreas, 1034
Feldman, Bob, 2223
Feldman, Bobby, 1508
Feldman, Dennis, 346
Feldman, Eric, 566, 4193, 4258
Feldman, Eric Drew, 566, 4193
Feldman, Jack, 255, 1229
Feldman, Joel, 1805

Feldman, Mark, 1626, 4571
Feldman, Morton, 2471, 4441, 5664
Feldman, Nick, 5695
Feldman, Richard, 4838
Feldman, Victor, 169, 841, 1299, 1869, 4155, 4475, 4586, 4850, 6047
Feldmann, John, 1725, 2190
Feldon, Barbara, 3583
Feldon, Roy, 356
Feldthouse, Solomon, 2926
Feldttahn, Eberhard, 1034
Felice, John, 4455
Feliciano, Cheo, 576, 1323, 1841, 2397, 3702, 4113, 4115, 4361, 4387, 4421, 4618, 5596
Feliciano, Frankie, 3904
Feliciano, José, 1323, 1869-1870, 3567
Feliciano, Nelson, 2234, 4612
Feline, 994, 1296, 1577, 1870, 1939, 3176, 3284
Felipe, Don, 2273
Felix, 1870
Felix Da Housecat, 55, 850, 1417, 1870, 3945, 5939
Felix, Hugo, 3399
Felix, John, 2735, 5948
Felix, Julie, 970, 1870-1871, 3805, 4416
Felix, Julie (90s), 1871
Felix, Lennie, 1836, 1871
Felix, Mike, 3661
Felix, Seymour, 1262, 2260, 2985, 3808, 4039, 5948
Felix, Steve, 849
Fell, Simon, 1871, 2011, 2510, 5834
Fell, Terry, 1871, 2350
Fell, Terry, 1871, 2350
Fellensby, Fred, 4492
Feller, Dick, 1872, 5460
Feller, Sid, 39
Fellini, Federico, 3943, 4304, 4659
Fellows, Stephen, 1199
Fellside Records, 1872 and passim
Felt, 1872-1873
Feltham, Mark, 2074, 2399, 3952
Felton, Leslie, 4895
Felton, Verna, 1544-1545
Felts, Narvel, 56, 1873
Fem 2 Fem, 5661
Femme Fatale, 1873
Fenda, Jaymes, And The Vulcans, 5626
Fender, B., 1873-1874
Fender, Freddy, 1104, 1873-1874, 3479, 3512, 3650, 4718, 5348, 5411, 5844
Fender, Griff, 1395
Fender, Leo, 1361, 1874-1875, 2143, 5495, 6047
Fendermen, 1875
Fenelley, Colin, 2975
Fenholt, Jeff, 228, 2899
Fenimore, Howard, 3366
Fenn, Al, 254, 1451, 3410
Fenn, Alastair, 254, 1451, 3410
Fenn, Eddie, 4545
Fenn, Rick, 3503, 5336, 5540

Fureys, 2057-2058, 2074
Furgason, Gary, 1016
Furia, Philip, 2130, 6049, 6109
Furious Four, 3398, 5497
Furious, Danny, 291
Furlong, Michael, 2058
Furlong, T.C., 2911
Furness, Joe, 1918
Furness, Slim, 5528
Furnier, Vince, 538
Furniss, Paul, 5648
Furniture, 2058 and *passim*
Furrell, Frank, 4761
Furry Freaks, 2514
Fursdon, Phil, 4398
Furth, George, 1196
Fury Records, 1598, 3047
Fury, Billy, 907, 1087, 1876,
2058-2059, 2203, 2432, 2665,
2916, 3931, 4062, 4125, 4143,
4264, 4304, 4667, 5351-5352,
5377, 5470, 5547, 5752
Fury, Don, 5574
Fury, Rocco, 160
Fury, Stone, 3020, 4903
Fusco, Giovanni, 1470
Fuse, 2059
Futter, Brian, 991
Future Generation, 303, 2727,
3553
Future Sound Of London, 1440,
2060, 4933, 5741, 5885, 5974
Fuzzbox, 1006, 1780, 2060,
3949, 5425, 5739-5740
Fuzztones, 548, 2060, 2436,
5290
Fuzzy, 2061
Fuzzy Duck, 187, 2061, 4375
Fyffe, Will, 1747, 2383

G

G Love And Special Sauce,
2063, 4024
G-Clefs, 918, 1510, 1998, 2063,
5691
G-Force, 1718, 2063, 3768, 4345
G-Man, 2384, 3720, 4635, 5807
G-Note, 1681
G-Wiz, Gary, 650, 2063, 5966
G., Bobby, 2064, 2964, 4524
G., Gilly, 2064
G., Gina, 2064
G., Johnny, 454, 1571, 1809,
6044
G., Kenny, 2063-2065, 3070,
3339, 4047, 4552, 4761, 4807,
4928
G., Warren, 1503, 2065, 2678,
3536
G.B.H., 202, 813, 2065, 2302
G.G.F.H., 2066, 3674, 3858
G.Q., 2066
Gabbard, Harley, 698, 2788
Gabbidon, Basil, 1568
Gabel, Moriarty, 335
Gabinelli, Gerald, 2066
Gabis, Claudio, 3461
Gable, Christopher, 4969, 5879
Gable, Clark, 1376, 1703, 1705,
2088, 4732, 5696
Gable, Guitar, 496, 2310
Gable, June, 2756

Gable, Mark, 1069
Gabler, Milt, 2066, 2922
Gables, Coral, 4616
Gabor, Zsa Zsa, 452, 3204, 3245,
4517, 4881
Gabrels, Reeves, 686, 5442
Gabriel, Debby, 818
Gabriel, Gilbert, 1623
Gabriel, Guitar, 1003, 1902,
2310, 2881, 3410
Gabriel, Gunter, 692
Gabriel, Peter, 78, 179, 335,
851, 1022, 1177, 1638, 1902,
1907, 2063, 2067, 2115, 2139,
2350, 2367, 2373, 2968, 3126,
3141, 3216, 3462, 3848, 3867,
4018, 4066, 4207, 4457, 4498,
4576, 4587, 4754, 4845, 4885,
4899, 5640, 5775, 6049, 6124
Gabrielle, 12, 118, 361, 520,
1557, 1729, 2067, 2175, 2265,
2765, 2801, 3260, 3363, 4079,
4635
Gadd, Paul, 2172
Gadd, Renee, 2383
Gadd, Steve, 731, 1029, 1838,
2067, 2073, 2295, 2301, 3417,
4178, 4751
Gaddis, Ron, 3785
Gaddy, Bob, 1363, 2068
Gadenwitz, Peter, 499, 6035
Gadler, Frank, 3980
Gadson, James, 5732
Gadye, Donna, 4444
Gael Linn, 490, 1094, 2068
Gaer, Murray, 3366
Gaetan, Oscar, 3840
Gaff, Billy, 2068, 2502, 3617
Gaffney, Burke, 4063
Gaffney, Chris, 154, 2069, 4063
Gaffney, Eric, 4802
Gage, Josephus, 2119
Gage, Mark, 2069
Gage, Pete, 228, 755, 1354, 5717,
5995
Gage, Yvonne, 2069
Gagel, Wally, 1589, 4027
Gagliardi, Edward, 1975
Gagnon, Erika, 2420
Gagnon, Wayne, 5665
Gahagan, John, 415
Gaham, Bill, 2535
Gaillard, Slim, 1124, 1624,
2069-2070, 2142, 2212, 2293,
2359, 4668, 5464, 5731
Gails, Irving Lee, 880
Gaina, Velerie, 4837
Gainer, George, 4746
Gaines, Charlie, 2070
Gaines, Earl, 2070
Gaines, Grady, 1684, 2070-
2071, 2629
Gaines, Jim, 5349
Gaines, Julius, 5328
Gaines, Lee, 1477
Gaines, Reg E., 740, 2070
Gaines, Richard, 3337
Gaines, Ron, 1690
Gaines, Rosie, 4076, 4332
Gaines, Roy, 2071
Gaines, Steve, 37, 3375, 4373
Gaines, Steven, 120, 427, 436,
5870, 6029, 6032
Gianes, Tata, 1324

Gaines, Walter, 4061, 5656
Gainey, Earl, 5856
Gains, Bill, 2116-2117
Gainsbourg, Serge, 544, 2071,
2073, 4123, 4849, 6049
Gaisberg, Fred, 1754
Gaither Vocal Band, 2411, 5403
Gaither, Bill, 576, 939, 2071-
2072
Gaither, Bill (country), 2071
Gaither, Danny, 2072
Gaither, Tommy, 4061
Gaitsch, Bruce, 4385, 4956
Gakkel, Seva, 2261
Galactic Cowboys, 2072
Galahad, Kid, 1959, 2985, 4311,
4315
Galante, Marie, 3784
Galas, Diamanda, 69, 1626,
2072, 2878, 3132, 3855
Galati, Frank, 3322, 4408
Galaxie, 2072, 2370, 3073, 3358,
4584, 4881, 4944
Galaxie 500, 2072, 3073, 3358,
4881, 4944
Galaxy Records, 4753
Galbraith, Barry, 88, 3771, 4292
Galbraith, Erle, 2864
Galbreath, Frank, 2073
Galby, Pete, 5492
Galdez, Claudio, 310
Galdo, Joe, 2987
Gale, Al, 3081
Gale, David, 1842, 3976
Galé, Diego, 3938, 4117
Gale, Dorothy, 5899
Gale, Eric, 212, 1280, 1842,
2068, 2073, 2520, 2770, 3133,
4048, 4428, 5327
Gale, Everod, 4717
Galé, Grupo, 399, 1530, 3938,
4117
Gale, Juliette, 4247
Gale, Ken, 2073
Gale, Len, 2073
Gale, Moe, 1039
Gale, Trevor, 1400, 4992
Galeforce, 2073
Galeon, Andy, 1449, 4059
Gales, Larry, 2268, 3739
Galfas, Stephan, 1063, 4050
Galfo, George, 3866
Galga, Eddie, 570
Galhardo, Jose, 2967
Galindo, Danny, 5393
Galione, Albie, 4152
Galisha, Joe, 2434
Gall, France, 488, 2073, 2947
Gall, Robert, 2073, 2323
Gallacher, Doug, 295
Gallagher And Lyle, 2073-2074,
3123-3124, 3578
Gallagher, Audrey, 4768
Gallagher, Benny, 2073, 3123,
3438, 3578
Gallagher, Ed, 5997-5998
Gallagher, Garvan, 2953
Gallagher, George, 4269
Gallagher, Helen, 2520, 3965,
4108
Gallagher, Jimmy, 691, 4152
Gallagher, Mary, 4434
Gallagher, Mickey, 459, 1661,
2005, 2170, 2631, 4954

Gallagher, Nicky, 4174
Gallagher, Noel, 315, 445, 1042,
1523, 1947, 2481, 3964, 4012,
4975, 5637, 5761
Gallagher, Peter, 1884, 2322
Gallagher, Regina, 4506
Gallagher, Rob, 2074
Gallagher, Rory, 12, 691, 1588,
1874, 2069, 2074, 2174, 3113,
3219, 4276, 4820, 5300
Gallagher, S.T., 4695
Gallant, Charles, 3642
Gallanti, Roberto, 1774
Gallardo, Maestro, 470
Gallaway, Peter, 4021
Galleon Jazz Band, 1294
Galletta, Joey, 4892
Galley, David, 362
Galley, Mel, 2393, 2628, 4219,
5492, 5803
Galley, Tom, 4219
Galliano, 54, 408, 711, 1573,
2074, 3133, 4078, 4315, 5287,
5579, 5585, 5741
Gallico, Al, 5309, 5535
Gallico, Paul, 898, 944, 3245,
3637
Galliland, Henry, 4575
Gallimore Sisters, 4440
Gallimore, Rosanne, 4440
Gallimore, Stan, 2292
Gallinger, Karen, 2075
Gallion, Bob, 2075
Gallo Records, 456, 3534
Gallo, Vinnie, 5958
Gallon Drunk, 1925, 2075,
2526, 5444
Gallop, Sammy, 604
Galloway, Jim, 1039, 2075, 2547
Galloway, Peter, 1889
Gallucci, Don, 1582, 3021-3022
Gallup, Cliff, 622, 5644
Gallup, Simon, 1334
Galper, Hal, 722, 2075, 2539
Galper, Harold, 492
Galpin, Sam, 3423
Galvin, John, 770, 3734
Galvin, Larry, 618
Galvin, Ritchie, 4316
Galway, James, 1057, 1250,
1485, 2076, 3111, 3433, 5686,
6049
Gamans, Erik, 1157, 5737
Gambaccini, Paul, 2835, 3248,
3549, 4525, 6056, 6062, 6109-
6110
Gambale, Frank, 2076
Gambale, Johnny, 1111
Gamble And Huff, 317, 460,
517, 1697, 2076-2077, 2705,
2753-2754, 2760, 2866, 3621,
3651, 3658, 3991, 4002, 4220,
4234, 4444, 4917, 5393, 5421,
5652
Gamble, Daisy, 4039
Gamble, Kenny, 464, 943, 2076,
2344, 2866, 3991, 4002, 4160,
4851, 5421
Gamble, R.C., 304
Gamble, Roger, 3022
Gamblers, 2077
Gamboa, 3419
Game, 2077 ad *passim*
Game Theory, 2077-2078, 5545

Gamet, Cliff, 738
Gamley, Douglas, 2078
Gamma, 2078-2079
Gamma Ray, 1937, 2079, 2479, 3092
Gammond, Peter, 1738, 2891, 6046, 6057, 6098-6099, 6110
Gamon, Mitt, 2399
Gamson, David, 1681, 4794
Ganafoul, 2079
Gancher, Tina, 2517
Gandee, Al, 5904
Gandelman, Leo, 2474, 3461
Ganden, Tami, 1044
Gander, Andrew, 2716, 2888
Gandhi, Mahatma, 249
Gandy, Fred, 1826, 2588
Gane, Mark, 3479-3480
Gane, Tim, 3479-3480, 3547, 3775
Ganelin Trio, 1042, 2079, 3058, 3194
Ganelin, Vyacheslav, 1042, 2079-2080
Gang Green, 1322, 2080
Gang Of Four, 1825, 2080, 2597, 2738, 3029, 3363, 3707, 4356, 4453, 4679, 4907, 5337, 5564
Gang Starr, 711, 865, 1047, 1222, 1224, 1523, 1538, 1560, 1571, 1906, 2080-2081, 2799, 2816, 3393, 3538, 3876, 3887, 4071, 4433, 4945, 5368, 5571
Gang War, 3074, 5430, 5772
Gang's All Here, The, 2081
Gangale, Eddie, 1892
Gangelin, Paul, 729
Gangie, Rudy, 877
Gangsta Pat, 2081, 2670
Ganja Kru, 2082
Ganley, Allan, 124, 1733, 2082, 3478, 4658
Ganley, Len, 2343
Gannel, Paul, 292
Gannon, Craig, 81, 556, 614, 620, 1839, 2352, 3137, 3287, 3797
Gannon, Jim, 563, 2002
Gannon, Kim, 2971, 3865, 5736
Gano, Gordon, 4944, 5649
Ganryu, Michihiro Sato, 6003
Ganser, Margie, 4843
Gant, Cecil, 951, 2082-2083
Gant, Don, 3902
Gant, Frances, 1441
Gantry, Elmer, 1388, 2083, 2885, 4102, 5626
Ganxsta Rid And The Otha Side, 2083
Ganyou, George, 4530
Ganz, Bobby, 1200
Ganz, Bruno, 1701
Ganzie, Terry, 1944, 4462
Gap Band, 145, 2083, 3603, 3618, 3632, 4004, 4528, 4985, 5950, 5981
Gara, Larry, 1571, 6044
Garace, Fred, 3266
Garage, 2083
Garbage, 2084 and *passim*
Garbarek, Jan, 23, 469, 1186, 1211, 1465, 1701, 2038, 2084, 2163, 2316, 2331, 2786, 2983,

3078-3079, 3286, 3663, 4696-4697, 4706, 5315, 5616, 5639, 5653, 5785
Garber, Jan, 103, 398, 495, 509, 829, 1020, 1047, 1489, 1984, 2085, 2169, 2948, 3281, 3842, 4176, 5931
Garber, Matthew, 3498
Garber, Victor, 259, 1047, 1371, 3268
Garbo, Greta, 78, 2237, 3429, 4905-4906
Garborit, John, 1300
Garbutt, Vin, 2085, 4900
Garcia, Adam, 4752
García, Andriano, 3738, 4121, 4611, 5471
Garcia, Antonio, 4837
Garcia, Arcelio, 3424
Garcia, Dean, 1340
Garcia, Gary, 813
García, Henry, 5602
Garcia, Jake, 3366
Garcia, Jerry, 23-24, 33, 52, 160, 728, 1122, 1285, 1307, 1534, 1955, 2086, 2246, 2275, 2294, 2387, 2421, 2521, 2598, 2641, 2674, 2803, 2923, 2935, 3085, 3200, 3731, 3877, 3919, 4027, 4666, 4753, 5672, 5725, 5987, 6049
Garcia, Juan, 36, 91, 1779, 1802
García, Louis, 4618
Garcia, Nestor, 5526
Garcia, Oscar, 5342
Garcia, Roy, 2657
Garcia, Ruben, 815
Garcia, Russ, 4212
Garcia, Ted, 1870
Garcia, Vincent, 1631
Garde, Betty, 4025
Gardella, Tess, 4893
Garden, Charlie, 3817
Garden, Graeme, 2207
Gardener, Hirsh, 3913
Gardenia, Vincent, 356, 3272
Gardiner, Boris, 1686, 2007, 2086, 2318, 2733, 3252, 4801, 5583
Gardiner, Mark, 1811
Gardiner, Reginald, 266, 1202, 1373, 1578
Gardiner, Ricky, 454
Gardner, Ava, 2448, 3509, 4643, 4892
Gardner, Bunk, 2127, 3809
Gardner, Carl, 1138, 4580
Gardner, Charles, 1595
Gardner, Dave, 2086
Gardner, Dick, 4036
Gardner, Don, 3142, 5716
Gardner, Edward, 669
Gardner, Egga, 2787
Gardner, Freddy, 3258, 3966, 5887, 5961
Gardner, Gerald, 2364, 6051
Gardner, J.E., 1068
Gardner, Jack, 3399
Gardner, James, 3167
Gardner, Jenny, 382
Gardner, Joanna, 3312
Gardner, Kim, 256, 544, 1286, 3300, 4500
Gardner, Lyle, 5845

Gardner, Mark, 1296, 1504, 3984
Gardner, Mike, 2121, 3984
Gardner, Morris, 1625
Gardner, Rita, 1845
Gardner, Robert Alexander, 3382
Gardner, Suzi, 3094
Gardner, Ted, 3299
Gardner, Thomas, 1639
Gardner, Tracy, 3942
Gardner, Vernon, 1458
Gardner, Willi, 4967
Gardner, William, 3533
Gardoni, Fredo, 2308
Gare, Leslie, 165, 2086, 4321
Gare, Lou, 165, 2086
Garelts, Monica, 2172
Garf, Gene, 3896
Garfat, Jance, 1614
Garfield, Henry, 4633
Garfield, John, 5754
Garforth, Jim, 1248
Garforth, Richard, 1981
Garfunkel, Art, 18, 414, 547, 1971, 2073, 2087, 2186, 2261, 2368, 2643, 2966, 3086, 3945, 4072, 4408, 4710, 4860, 4916, 4918, 5372, 5386, 5457, 5745
Garibaldi, David, 5479
Garidel, Lucien, 4249
Garland, Beverly, 2861
Garland, Dave, 637
Garland, Ed 'Montudie', 2087
Garland, Frank, 1992
Garland, Hank, 847, 864, 1142, 1229, 2087-2088, 2618
Garland, Joe, 2088, 2090, 2444, 3667, 3683, 4450
Garland, Judy, 134, 196, 227, 261, 307-308, 383, 402, 494, 586, 710, 746, 782, 876, 881, 1152, 1296, 1299, 1302, 1478, 1589, 1659, 1692, 1703, 1705, 2025, 2035, 2088-2090, 2130, 2159, 2216-2217, 2386, 2422, 2426, 2447, 2488, 2515, 2538, 2549, 2565, 2900, 2909, 2959, 3109, 3122, 3226, 3340, 3399, 3406, 3488, 3491-3492, 3547-3548, 3573, 3611, 3629, 3669, 3674, 3694-3696, 3747, 3864, 4253, 4285, 4488, 4539, 4643, 4650-4651, 4729, 4732, 5419, 5435, 5469, 5523, 5692, 5711, 5777, 5899, 5919, 5982, 5998, 6049, 6064
Garland, Lily, 3586, 4041
Garland, Marjory, 3639
Garland, Red, 71, 393, 1170, 1186, 1222, 1338, 1414, 1788, 2048, 2090, 2437, 3667, 4327
Garland, Terry, 630, 2090
Garland, William M., 2090
Garlow, Clarence, 2091
Garments, 604, 3253, 3634, 4886
Gårnas, Agnes Buen, 2084-2085
Garner, Bob, 1286, 3640
Garner, Erroll, 279, 507, 830, 895, 913, 1176, 1200, 2091-2092, 2096, 2142, 2171, 2345, 2507, 2847, 3350-3351, 3466, 3768, 4134, 4230, 4697, 4915, 5309, 5774, 6049

Garner, Henry, 4648
Garner, James, 796, 2813, 2922, 5604, 5642
Garner, Kate, 2449
Garner, Larry, 630, 2092
Garner, Laurent, 3722
Garner, Paul, 2449, 3407
Garnes, Sherman, 3367
Garnett, David, 258
Garnett, Gale, 2092-2093
Garnett, Richard, 2283, 6051
Garni, Kelly, 4386
Garnier, Laurent, 54, 1268, 1357, 2093, 3906
Garon, Jesse, 2093, 4309
Garon, Jesse, And The Desperadoes, 2093
Garon, Paul, 5784, 6063, 6084, 6089, 6110
Garone, Ralph, 3046
Garrahan, Kyle, 3321
Garrett, Amos, 3833-3834, 4718
Garrett, Betty, 893, 2093, 3669, 3903, 4040-4041, 5284, 5909, 5919
Garrett, Denise, 734
Garrett, JoAnn, 5836
Garrett, John, 1060
Garrett, Kenny, 2093-2094, 3678
Garrett, Leif, 2094
Garrett, Lesley, 2463, 5307, 5720
Garrett, Matt, 2577
Garrett, Mike, 3244
Garrett, Nicky, 4829
Garrett, Pat, 135, 558, 1529, 1675, 1678, 1937, 3078, 3151, 3272, 4154, 6046
Garrett, Peter, 1519, 3657
Garrett, Rafael, 3348
Garrett, Robert 'Bud', 2094
Garrett, Scott, 2577
Garrett, Siedah, 711, 1709
Garrett, Snuff, 135, 2094, 3052, 3232, 3315, 6030
Garrett, Tommy, 2094, 5622
Garrick Gaieties, The, 1447, 1647, 2095, 2386, 2572, 3629, 4606
Garrick, David, 871, 2095, 2729
Garrick, Michael, 2095, 2206, 2268, 2404, 2950, 2983, 3177, 3350, 3478, 3914, 4502, 5384, 5458, 5887
Garrier, Tony, 2953
Garris, Gerdy, 2043
Garrison, David, 5449
Garrison, Jim, 1241
Garrison, Jimmy, 29, 1046, 1168, 1184-1185, 2095, 2551, 2683, 2795, 3504, 3610, 4634, 4844
Garrison, Sean, 3020
Garrity, Eddie, 4962
Garrity, Freddie, 1325, 2021
Garros, Christian, 3328
Garry, Len, 4377
Garryish, Sonny, 2539
Garside, Katie Jane, 1360
Garside, Mel, 6004
Garson, Mike, 4747
Garson, Mort, 2533
Garthwaite, David, 2903
Garthwaite, Terry, 2903

General, Mikey, 1270, 3210, 3662, 4945
General, Ricky, 370
Generation X, 57, 82, 2115, 2178, 2640, 2673, 3303, 4184, 4194, 4829, 4903, 5277
Genesis, 82, 268, 278, 307, 459, 614, 712, 845, 1023, 1155, 1169-1170, 1177-1178, 1295, 1452, 1484, 1624, 1644-1645, 1719, 1819, 1834, 1841, 1897, 1902, 1907, 1925, 1985, 2067, 2109, 2115-2116, 2180, 2250, 2303, 2329-2330, 2691, 2870, 2933, 2968, 3079, 3081, 3113, 3159, 3462, 3614, 3661, 3704, 4147, 4207, 4284, 4306, 4355-4356, 4548, 4576, 4702, 4745, 4758, 4817, 4845, 4891, 5311, 5427, 5485, 5501, 5561, 5577, 5956, 6040, 6049, 6051-6052, 6081-6083, 6112, 6124
Genetic, 598, 627, 1617, 2126, 2768, 2838, 4864
Geneva, 2116
Genevieve, 2116
Genies, 873, 1582, 2116
Genis, Ed, 3641
Genitorturers, 2117, 3463, 3777
Genius, 2117
Genius Jerry, 2835
Gennaro, Peter, 4106
Gennaro, Sandy, 650, 5494
Gennett Records, 937, 3121, 3583
Genockey, Liam, 3732
Genocky, Leon, 2148
Genovese, Stu, 3791
Genrich, Ax, 2316
Gensler, Lewis E., 1439, 2284
Gent, Chris, 4459, 4805
Gentle Faith, 1883
Gentle Giant, 1657, 1813, 2118, 3135, 4334, 4619, 5653, 5824
Gentle Soul, 2118-2119, 2743, 3942, 4917, 5311, 5860
Gentle, Johnny, 432, 995, 2119, 4143, 5653
Gentlemen Marry Brunettes, 1851, 2119-2120, 3577, 5600
Gentlemen Of Swing, 462, 965, 3446-3447, 4984, 5879-5880
Gentlemen Prefer Blondes, 69, 95, 942, 1018, 1436, 2119-2120, 2225, 2520, 3487, 3747-3748, 3930, 3965, 4580, 5387
Gentlemen Prefer Blondes (film musical), 2119
Gentry, Art, 713
Gentry, Bobbie, 905, 1322, 2120, 2351, 3142, 4468
Gentry, Charles T., 2120
Gentry, Chris, 3628
Gentry, Chuck, 2120, 4854
Gentry, Ian, 4781
Gentry, Ruby, 2120, 2447
Gentry, Teddy, 103
Gentrys, 857, 2120-2121, 2678
Geoghan, John, 4245
Geoghegan, Mick, 3660
Geordie, 2121 and *passim*
George Lane, 2853, 3197
George M!, 2121 and *passim*
George Records, 1065, 1542,

2792, 3933
George White's Scandals, 2121
George, Alan, 1071, 1978, 2077, 2129, 2364, 2416, 3559, 4039, 6040, 6051
George, Barbara, 415, 1196, 1208, 1959, 2121, 4336
George, Derek, 5795, 6003, 6052
George, Fatty, 1294, 2121, 2371
George, Holgar, 293
George, Izzy, 3583
George, Jon, 4080
George, Karl, 2122
George, Langston, 3047
George, Lowell, 15, 136, 391, 891, 1549, 1820, 2018, 2122, 2246, 2303, 2884, 3264-3265, 3352, 3809, 4112, 4415, 4719, 4803, 5450, 5478, 5879
George, Nelson, 209, 2218, 2748, 4061, 6055, 6110, 6118
George, Robin, 1507, 2122, 3977, 5923
George, Ron, 89, 1791
George, Samuel, 924
George, Sergio, 229, 399, 3938, 4064
George, Siwsann, 3382
George, Sophia, 2122, 3252
George, Steve, 1849, 3169, 3826, 4698
George, Suzanne, 3382
George, Terry, 350, 3583, 4361, 5851
George, Wayne, 216
Georgeiva, Eva, 3154
Georges, Bernard, 5428
Georges, Trevor Michael, 2712
Georgeson, Dave, 5933
Georgia Cotton Pickers, 373, 3804, 5742
Georgia Crackers, 2122-2123, 3672, 4979
Georgia Peach Pickers, 2480, 5842
Georgia Peanut Band, 4787
Georgia Satellites, 318, 334, 1322, 1991, 2123, 2293, 3589, 4592, 5513
Georgia Slim, 894, 1979
Georgia Tom, 1599, 2123, 2552, 3921, 5850
Georgia Wildcats, 804-805, 4951, 5495
Georgia, Cordele, 768, 2787, 5850
Georgiades, Michael, 3157
Georgie Porgie Boys, 764
Georgieva, Eva, 5505
Georgio, 70, 882, 1041, 2123-2124, 3982
Georgio, Tony, 882
Geppert, Christopher, 1309
Geraci, Sonny, 1127, 4084
Geraghty, Billy, 816
Geraghty, Tony, 3652
Gerald, Francis, 5516
Gerald, Michael, 2991
Geraldine Fibbers, 2124
Geraldine, Vinita, 5820
Geraldo, 2124 and *passim*
Geraldo, Neil, 472, 1468
Gerard, Danyel, 2125, 3108
Gerard, Gabrielle, 361, 3260

Gerard, Teddie, 708
Gerardo, 2125, 2707
Geray, Steve, 1374
Gerber, Scott, 2135
Gerdes, George, 5669
Gere, Richard, 1246, 2256, 3134, 3481, 4866
Geremia, Paul, 2125
Gerhard, Ake, 4574
Gerhardt, Mark, 3984
Germain, Donovan, 79, 1583, 2017, 2125, 2186, 2345, 2350, 2765, 2958, 3397, 3593, 4190, 4250, 4337, 4468, 5338, 5426, 5909, 5990
German, Edward, 2126
Germann, Greg, 259
Germano, Lisa, 2126, 2135, 4201
Germano, Margaret, 3446
Germino, Mark, 2281
Germs, 2126-2127 and *passim*
Gerhard, Phil, 3288, 4671
Gernoittis, Chris, 5988
Gero, Mark, 3695
Geronimo Black, 2127, 3809
Geronimo, Mic, 299
Geronomi, Clyde, 1544-1545
Gerrard, Alice, 1512, 1897, 2127, 2785, 4810
Gerrard, Denny, 2127
Gerrard, Denver, 2127, 5704-5705
Gerrard, Lisa, 1440-1441
Gerrard, Rod, 2504
Gerrie, Malcolm, 4454, 5520-5521
Gerritsen, Rinus, 2188-2189
Gerry And The Pacemakers, 14, 999, 1169, 1187, 1234, 1313, 1483, 1770, 1878, 2012, 2127-2128, 2362, 2825, 3475, 3486, 3917, 4385, 4522, 4675, 4749, 4784, 4799, 4749, 4784, 4799, 5547, 6049
Gerry, Alex, 3245
Gerry, Vance, 1545
Gers, Janick, 2148, 2182, 2711, 5793
Gersch, Gary, 709
Gersch, Vernon, 5388
Gerschwitz, Martin, 5511
Gersh, Gary, 1795, 1964
Gershe, Leonard, 1495, 2054, 4905
Gershman, Don, 2938
Gershwin, George, 77-78, 107, 112, 236, 261, 283, 480, 569, 581, 672, 694, 728, 853, 858, 877, 881, 1202-1203, 1218, 1243, 1434, 1439, 1498, 1647, 1831, 1868, 1894, 2128-2129, 2284, 2295, 2366, 2385, 2537, 3068, 3107, 3122, 3148, 3231, 3487, 3727, 3788-3789, 3845, 3984, 4212, 4286, 4509, 4518, 4646, 4784, 4850, 4894, 5534, 5619-5620, 5798, 5815, 5901, 5923, 5998, 6049, 6100
Gershwin, Ira, 35, 78, 162, 227, 308, 837, 1022, 1133, 1284, 1373, 1439, 1647, 1868, 1912, 2095, 2107, 2128-2130, 2159, 2221, 2385-2386, 2495, 2923,

2945, 2976, 3105, 3107, 3122, 3146, 3237, 3408, 3862, 4016, 4020, 4286, 4519, 4646, 4650, 4841, 4875, 4886, 5363, 5711, 5755, 5896, 5901, 5964-5965, 5997, 6049
Gershwin, Jackie, 4958
Gershwin, Marc, 138
Gershwin, Ronnie, 138
Gerst, Bill, 1784
Gertz, Irving, 1654
Gerughty, Larry, 1760
Gerun, Tom, 2615
Gesner, Clark, 5963
Gessle, Per, 2033, 4669
Geston, Paul, 1453
Get Low Records, 2734
Get Set VOP, 2130
Geter, Gus, 4864
Getman, Ron, 5485
Geto Boys, 853, 1351, 1460, 2131, 4433, 4766, 5392, 5550
Getting My Act Together And Taking It On The Road, 811, 2664
Getz, Dave, 1254
Getz, Stan, 107, 116, 141, 145, 171, 187, 398, 410, 479, 482, 489, 519, 638, 641, 669, 753, 825, 842, 847, 865, 1072, 1140, 1185, 1417, 1465, 1556, 1682, 1714, 1801, 1849, 1853, 2076, 2082, 2131-2133, 2146, 2208, 2336, 2355, 2371, 2419, 2448, 2506, 2721-2722, 2768, 2789, 2792, 2796, 2827, 2846, 2892, 2924, 2943, 2971, 3018, 3069, 3084-3085, 3113, 3183, 3213, 3250, 3258, 3327, 3460, 3522, 3568, 3584, 3653, 3690, 3760, 3766, 3780, 3826, 3836-3837, 3987, 4195, 4211, 4296, 4368, 4374, 4420, 4427, 4626, 4636, 4668, 4754, 4760, 4788, 4909, 4925, 4990, 5379, 5405, 5440, 5646, 5800, 5831, 5850, 5852, 5876, 6049
Geva, Tamara, 346, 1950, 4042, 4058
Geyer, Dennis, 33
Geyer, Renee, 673, 2108, 2133
Geyer, Stephen, 4765
Geza X Gideon, 327
Ghanaba, Kofi, 2133, 5710
Ghetto Mafia, 2133
Gholar, Kenneth, 5660
Ghomeshi, Jean, 3822
Ghost, 2134 and *passim*
Ghost Dance, 248, 2134, 2689, 4949, 5715
Ghost Goes Gear, The, 1086, 1420, 2134, 2142
Ghostwriters, 2134
GI Blues, 1925, 2135, 2162, 4311
Giacalone, Paul, 1903
Giaimo, Chuck, 1571
Giamblavo, Lenny, 459
Giammalvo, Chris, 3400
Giammanco, Anthony, 652
Giant, 2135 and *passim*
Giant Records, 525, 532, 955, 1486, 1857, 2264, 3205, 3561, 4935, 5679, 5699

Grunge, 2300 and *passim*
Gruning, Thomas, 290
Gruntruck, 2300, 4273
Gruntz, George, 159, 445, 781, 2195, 2300-2301, 3663, 3803, 3987, 4327, 4727, 4773, 4950, 5321, 5687
Grushinskaya, Elizaveta, 2237
Grusin, Dave, 283, 483, 490, 669, 2299, 2301, 4231, 4554, 4586
Grusin, Don, 2301, 4554
Gruska, Jay, 5422
Gryce, Gigi, 706, 1424, 1849, 2301-2302, 2371, 2882, 3461, 3572, 3581, 4129, 4626, 5920
Gryphon, 753, 2302, 6033, 6036, 6049, 6056, 6062, 6064-6065, 6069-6070, 6072, 6075
Gschoesser, Harry, 4398
Gschwend, Achim, 318
GTO, 460, 1374, 1593, 1778, 2002, 2034, 2172, 2302, 3157, 3917-3918, 4012-4013, 4276, 4453, 4640, 5359, 5677
GTOs, 2302-2303
GTR, 751, 2303, 2329, 2619
Guadalcanal Diary, 2303
Guana Batz, 2303-2304, 3644
Guaragna, Salvatore, 5710
Guaraldi, Vince, 2304, 5886
Guaranteed Records, 1793, 5890
Guard, Dave, 1331, 2503, 3022, 3650, 5790
Guard, Pamela, 5947
Guard, Philip, 1960
Guardian Records, 1391, 3866
Guardino, Harry, 204, 5905
Guare, John, 5549
Guarente, Frank, 2304
Guariento, Al, 1391
Guarnieri, Johnny, 88, 705, 2304, 2347, 2847, 3118, 4854, 5756
Guay, Tom, 5793
Guayacán, Orquesta, 3938
Gubara, Mohamed, 4724
Gubby, Robert, 814, 2064
Gubenko, Julius, 2139
Gudgeon, Chris, 4625, 6074
Gudinski, Michael, 3849
Gueist, Gus, 2599
Guercio, James William, 426, 2304-2305
Guercio, Jim, 811, 1054, 2304
Guerilla Records, 2305
Guerin, John, 163, 543
Guerin, Paul, 4462
Guérin, Roger, 2305, 3327
Guernsey, Otis L., Jnr., 2817
Guerra, Carlos, Jnr., 1530
Guerra, Joey, 5433
Guerra, Juan Luis, 2305
Guerra, Marcelino, 2397, 3233, 3776
Guerrero, Corazón, 1181
Guesnon, Creole George, 2306
Guess Who, 315-316, 668, 717, 1331, 2306-2307, 3010, 5808, 5903, 6129
Guess, Don, 2568
Guest Stars, 2307 and *passim*
Guest, Annette, 1905
Guest, Edgar A., 881, 2295

Guest, Elenor, 3047
Guest, Reg, 4782, 5677, 5682
Guest, Roy, 2047, 2968
Guest, Val, 1809, 2664, 3705
Guest, William, 3047
Guest, Willie, 1916, 3997
Guétary, Georges, 162, 589, 1745, 2307-2308, 5745
Guffin, Lum, 2778
Guida, Frank, 655, 1819
Guida, Jerry, 2299
Guided By Voices, 168, 1037, 2308, 3510, 4802
Guidotti, G.G., 2465
Guidry, Doc, 797
Guidry, Greg, 2308
Guidry, Robert Charles, 1026
Guilbeau, Gib, 1950, 3879, 4116, 4145
Guilbeau, Ronnie, 4116
Guild, 2309
Guilfoyle, Frank, 2355
Guilino, Sam, 1699
Guillemain, Gaston, 2309
Guillemand, Marcel, 4249
Guillén, Nicolás, 1205
Guillory, Isaac, 1321, 2309, 4502
Guillot, John Allan, 126
Guinaldo, Clay, 2657
Güines, Tata, 1832, 5447
Guinn, Ed, 1212
Guinn, Janis Lee, 1355
Guinness, Alec, 931, 1102, 4795
Guitar Gable, 496, 2310
Guitar Gabriel, 1003, 1902, 2310, 2881, 3410
Guitar Nubbit, 2310
Guitar Shorty, 2310, 2493
Guitar Slim, 575, 635, 1027, 1394, 1409, 1663, 2295, 2310, 2321, 2449, 2870, 3013, 3117, 4690, 4718, 4829, 5528, 5799
Guitar, Bonnie, 1567, 2311, 2992, 3678, 5699
Guiteau, Charles, 259
Guitierrez, Louis, 1354
Guitierriez, Juan, 1506
Guizar, Tito, 522
Gulda, Friedrich, 1235, 1381, 2195, 2311
Gulewar, 2768
Gull Records, 1840
Gullaghan, Steve, 1812
Gulland, Brian, 2302, 3422
Gullane, Roy, 5296
Gulliksen, Eric, 4064
Gullin, Lars, 1357, 1582, 2311-2312, 3854, 4655, 5816
Gulliver, Ralph, 5993
Gulotta, James, 274
Gumball, 84, 306, 317, 1533, 2342, 2475, 2554
Gumble, Albert, 5953
Gumbleton, Ethel, 3151
Gumbo, 2312
Gumede, Sipho, 3731
Gumina, Tommy, 1433-1434
Gumm, Albert, 5659
Gumm, Ethel, 2088
Gummoe, John, 974
Gun (60s), 2312
Gun (90s), 2312
Gun Club, 327, 1275, 1548,

2313, 4239, 4356, 4942-4943
Gundry-White, Patrick, 3039
Gunn, Andy, 2911
Gunn, Ben, 4942
Gunn, Debbie, 4822
Gunn, Peter, 201, 623, 1779, 2111, 2695, 3433, 3447
Gunn, Tommy, 163, 699, 3617
Gunn, Tony, 1906
Gunnar, 327, 1494, 1682, 3620, 3893, 3902, 5994
Gunnarsson, Eythor, 3650
Gunne, Jo Jo, 266, 1649, 1876, 2826, 2911
Gunnell, Rik, 1848, 4004
Gunner, Jim, 2173
Gunnerfeldt, Pelle, 1904
Gunning, Sarah Ogan, 1512, 2737
Guns N'Roses, 2313-2314 and *passim*
Guns, Tracii, 2313, 3093
Gunshot, 2314-2315
Gunter, Arthur, 2315, 5378
Gunther, Cornelius, 5967
Gunther, Cornell, 1138
Gunter, Hardrock, 2315, 5847
Gunther, John, 2144
Gunther, Ulrich, 3317
Gunton, Bob, 528
Guppy, David, 4472
Guppy, Shusha, 4897
Guralnick, Peter, 272, 1205, 2351, 2855, 3100, 4314, 4528, 6031, 6038, 6056, 6069, 6089, 6110, 6119
Guran, Tom, 3491
Gurevitz, Brett, 1112, 3074
Gurl, Steve, 204, 307, 5824
Gurley, James, 522, 1037
Gurley, Michael, 1354
Gurov, Andre, 1562
Gurtu, Trilok, 1751, 2316, 3591, 4059
Guru Guru, 2316 and *passim*
Guru Josh, 2316, 3379
Gurvitz, Adrian, 335, 2312, 2316, 3759
Gurvitz, Paul, 2312
Gusevs, Rob, 243
Guss, Randy, 5452
Gussow, Adam, 4750
Gust, Neil, 2463
Gustafson, Bobby, 4085
Gustafson, John, 2148, 2388, 2394, 2868, 4378, 4669
Gustafsson, Rune, 1582
Gustavson, Kjell, 4909
Guster, Keith, 3198
Gusto Records, 3880
Gut Records, 1272
Guthrie, Andy, 133, 358, 1696, 2317, 4046, 4293, 4306, 5506
Guthrie, Arlo, 120, 681, 1515, 1740, 1756, 2211, 2317, 2319, 2601, 3423, 3560, 3810, 3889, 4140, 4155, 4242, 4501, 4812, 5706, 5916
Guthrie, Gwen, 1651, 2318, 2831, 5610
Guthrie, Jack, 1749, 2318-2319
Guthrie, Robin, 214, 1147-1148, 1175, 1521, 1872, 2313, 3363, 3608, 4239, 5396, 5624

Guthrie, Woody, 20, 64, 108, 121, 144, 444, 680-681, 931, 947, 1332, 1672, 1674, 1740, 1749, 1828, 1958, 2058, 2074, 2317-2320, 2378, 2426, 2431, 2503, 2609, 2712, 2827, 3156, 3182, 3299, 3361, 3562, 3571, 3767, 3893, 4013, 4484, 4693, 4811-4812, 4829, 5344, 5363, 5531, 5743, 5821, 6051
Gutierrez, Greg Louis, 5984
Gutiérrez, Hernán, 3314, 4117
Gutiérrez, Julio, 3314, 4610, 4616
Gutsy, Suzi, 4970
Guttenberg, Steve, 911
Gutteridge, Peter, 1119
Guttierez, Louis, 5424
Guy, 2320
Guy Called Gerald, A, 28, 886, 1717, 3538, 4343, 4379, 5584
Guy, Athol, 4813
Guy, Barry, 13, 2320, 3070, 3302, 3394, 4135, 4544, 4702, 4777, 5664, 5733
Guy, Billy, 1138, 4580
Guy, Buddy, 18, 481, 483, 627, 629-630, 695, 750, 898, 1049, 1264, 1341, 1369, 1402, 1608, 1636, 1743, 1933, 2131, 2142, 2320-2321, 2419, 2461, 2530, 2546, 2726, 3009, 3026, 3125, 3135, 3364, 3432, 3831, 3889, 3948, 4210, 4303, 4475, 4620, 4692-4693, 4870, 5316, 5400, 5473, 5531, 5611, 5726, 5763-5764, 6051, 6090
Guy, Freddie, 2279, 2321, 3682, 4692
Guy, George, 2320, 2528
Guy, Joe, 2150, 2321, 2557, 2792, 3682
Guy, Michael, 2607, 3364, 4849
Guy, Phil, 1423, 2321, 3364, 3564, 4702
Guy, Terry, 2134
Guy, Vernon, 357, 4852
Guyana, Berbice, 228
Guys And Dolls, 112, 578-579, 846, 997, 1577, 1968, 1993, 2237, 2322, 2427, 2547, 2612-2613, 2807, 2867, 2876, 2940, 2947, 2987, 3208, 3294, 3356, 3574, 3586, 3805, 3999, 4054, 4154, 4557, 4927, 4930, 4932, 5602, 5664, 5736, 5745, 5989
Guys And Dolls (film musical), 2322
Guzmán, Andy, 3750, 3835
Guzman, Ben, 4481
Guzman, Edward, 4435
Guzmán, Paquito, 2925, 4031-4032, 4065, 4387, 4745
Guzman, Randy, 3724
Guzzo, Francis, 1970
Gwaltney, Tommy, 2322-2323, 2329, 2895
Gwangwa, Jonas, 1875, 2323, 3419, 3441, 3499, 4362
GWAR, 2323
Gwendal, 2323
Gwerin, Caneuon, 2731, 4266, 6061
Gwilym, Tich, 2776

Gwylym, Danny, 1064
Gwynne, Fred, 1246
Gwyther, Geoffrey, 874
Gyasi, Dr. K., And His Noble Kings, 3060
Gyasi, K., 3060
Gyenis, Katalin, 5661
Gymslips, 2323, 3723, 4503, 4592
Gynt, Greta, 3303
Gypsies, 360, 459, 1010, 1044, 1252, 1376, 1940, 2001, 2323, 2381, 2491, 2865, 3138, 3540, 3664, 3913, 4364, 4497, 4676, 4759, 5430, 5468, 5486, 5646, 6073
Gypsy (60s), 2324
Gypsy (90s), 2324
Gypsy (film musical), 2324
Gypsy (stage musical), 2324
Gypsy Kings, 326, 1842
Gypsy Queen, 45, 2324-2325, 4387
Gyrlz, 2325, 5342, 5583
Gysi, Wädi, 4492
Gysin, Brion, 3102
GZA, 2117, 5932
GZR, 560, 2325

H

H, Mike, 1300, 4160, 5628
H.P. Lovecraft, 206, 728, 2327, 3890, 3931, 4836
H.P. Zinker, 3510
H2O, 2327, 2344
Haaby, Elizabeth Jane, 179
Haade, William, 4932
Haakon, Paul, 2589, 3648
Haarmann, Fritz, 3383
Haas, Andy, 3479
Haase, Gary, 4288
Habberly, P.J., 892
Haberfield, Edwin, 1662, 4429
Habibiyya, 2327, 3658
Habicht, Jutta, 3467
Haçienda, 2283, 2328
Hackberry Ramblers, 887, 2328
Hackeman, Vicki, 1397
Hackett, Albert, 1692, 1903, 3885, 4648, 4825
Hackett, Andy, 4598
Hackett, Bobby, 480, 608, 675, 781, 877-878, 915, 1009, 1123, 1513, 1632, 2152, 2170, 2226, 2323, 2328-2329, 2348, 2473, 2806, 3178, 3226, 3473, 3505, 3733, 3800, 4075, 4699, 4774, 4805, 5301, 5435, 5592, 5819, 5832, 5923
Hackett, Buddy, 3147, 3268, 3852
Hackett, Peter, 1992
Hackett, Steve, 254, 2115, 2303, 2329, 2619, 3525, 4767
Hackl, Cornelius, 1281, 2477
Hackman, Paul, 2475
Hackwith, Scott, 1523
Hadary, Jonathan, 259
Haddaway, 2330
Hadden, Martin, 4907
Hadden, Roger, 2522
Haddock, Durwood, 2330

Haddock, Kenny, 337
Haddock, Rubby, 3354, 4065
Haddock, Simon, 2905
Haddon, Peter, 5573
Haddow, Steven, 1717
Haden, Charlie, 130, 341, 398, 574, 590-591, 603, 701, 745, 856, 1016, 1046, 1167-1168, 1776, 2023, 2038, 2085, 2163, 2330, 2448, 2519, 2732, 2786, 2875, 3061, 3212, 3333, 3590, 3645-3646, 3810, 4028, 4155, 4472-4473, 4727, 4779, 4727, 4779, 5994
Haden, Petra, 4505
Haden, Sara, 4281
Hadfield, Mark, 3906
Hadfield, Pete, 1453
Hadi, Shafi, 2331, 3690
Hadjidakis, Manos, 3817
Hadley, Brian, 1389
Hadley, Dardanelle, 2331
Hadley, Jerry, 1406, 4893
Hadley, Mike, 906
Hadley, Skip, 1389
Hadley, Tony, 423, 2726, 2817
Hadley, Walter, 1389
Hadlock, Richard, 2798
Hadwin, Julie, 529
Haenning, Gitte, 2163
Haese, Kelly, 2464
Haffkine, Ron, 1380
Hafner, Robert, 2527
Hag Records, 3207
Hag, Rowland, 293
Hagan, Cass, 3212
Hagans, Buddy, 3040
Hagans, Tim, 2331, 3333, 4339, 4801, 5658
Hagar, Fred, 4024
Hagar, Regan, 702, 2266, 3312
Hagar, Sammy, 1461, 2079, 2332, 2458, 2621, 3757, 4208, 4713, 5605-5606
Hage, Martin, 88
Hageman, Brian, 5391
Hageman, Richard, 2258
Hagen, Earle, 2119
Hagen, Jean, 4933
Hagen, John, 3345
Hagen, Mary, 1210
Hagen, Nina, 1864, 2332-2333
Hagens, Tim, 3334
Hager, John, 2333
Hagers, 2333, 4700
Haggard, Lee, 3825
Haggard, Merle, 125, 154, 179, 257, 564, 653, 688, 820, 848, 923, 957, 1143, 1179, 1256, 1290, 1488, 1508, 1521, 1804, 2019, 2033, 2039-2040, 2094, 2157, 2333-2335, 2702, 2736, 2873, 2956, 2979, 3123, 3301, 3400-3401, 3541, 3545, 3618, 3672, 3687, 3719, 3864, 3900-3901, 3905, 4024, 4067, 4087-4088, 4102, 4169, 4469, 4538, 4566, 4605, 4700, 4728, 4842, 4924, 5438, 5496, 5507, 5519, 5609, 5679, 5699, 5715, 5854-5855, 5867, 6051
Haggard, Piers, 5788
Haggart, Bob, 417, 830, 832, 858, 1304, 2335, 2622, 3043,

3150-3151, 3178, 3569, 3672, 3688, 3815, 4655, 5922-5923
Haggerty, John, 3871
Haggerty, Neil, 4371
Haggerty, Sara, 2463
Hagler, Sherry, 545
Haglof, Karen, 360
Hagman, Larry, 3490
Hagstrom, Helen, 944
Hague, Albert, 1885, 2335, 4259, 4471
Hague, Ian, 1402, 1848
Hague, Mel, 2335-2336
Hague, Stephen, 58, 1194, 1714, 3918, 4205, 4508, 5768
Hahm, Alfred, 2383
Hahn, Jerry, 1898, 2376
Hahn, Tom, 1343
Haig, Al, 107, 1534, 1682, 2082, 2131, 2150, 2336, 3210, 5384
Haig, Alan, 1060
Haig, Paul, 2336, 2896
Haigh, Anna, 4712
Haigh, Chris, 452, 6005
Haigh, Kersten, 4821
Hailey, Jo Jo, 3937
Haimsohn, George, 1369
Hain, Kit, 14, 3476
Haines, Connie, 1361, 1482, 1599, 2336, 6044
Haines, Gibby, 4095
Haines, Herbert E., 989
Haines, Norman, 2336, 3292
Haines, Paul, 1776, 2381, 4348
Haines, Will, 1210, 2968
Hair, 2336-2337 and *passim*
Hairspray, 661, 2337, 2419, 3458, 3544, 4817
Hairston, Curtis, 2337-2338
Haisman, Gary, 1350
Haissem Records, 3642
Haji-Mike, 305
Hajischacalli, Sugar, 3893
Hajnallik, Nem Arról, 3857
Hajnallot, Amerröl, 3857
Hajos, Militza, 2167
Hake, Alan, 1717
Hake, Dave, 5299, 6000
Hakim, Omar, 114, 2338, 2441, 2895, 3083, 5584, 5741
Hakim, Sadik, 2338, 2806
Hakmoun, Hassan, 2338
Hakusho, Momoe, 5946
Hakzanchi, Deepak, 103
Halcomb, Robin, 3791
Halcox, Pat, 374, 2338
Halcrow, Caroline, 609, 5502
Haldane, Stan, 690
Hale, Alan, 2523, 3947, 5395
Hale, Andrew, 4714
Hale, Barbara, 2523, 2863
Hale, Binnie, 295, 748, 1031, 1141, 1744, 2285, 2339-2340, 2619, 3824, 3965, 5957
Hale, Bob, 4468
Hale, Camilla, 2919
Hale, Chester, 4648
Hale, Corky, 2339, 4457
Hale, Fred, 925
Hale, Jack, 3623
Hale, Monte, 2339, 5863
Hale, Robert, 2339-2340, 6049, 6069-6070, 6076-6077, 6080, 6107, 6110

Hale, Sonnie, 1428, 1552, 1794-1795, 1797, 2102, 2339-2340, 2726, 3152, 3303, 4043, 4719, 5397, 5643
Hale, Theron, And His Daughters, 2340
Hale, William, 3262
Haley Sisters, 507, 2340
Haley, Bill, 21, 476, 1009, 1026, 1326, 1916, 2024, 2083, 2893, 3017, 3523, 3882, 4312, 4700, 4838, 5529, 5544, 5767
Haley, Bill, And His Comets, 829, 1085, 1583, 2340-2341, 2568, 3203, 3302, 4084, 4590-4591, 4593, 4639, 6051
Haley, Jack, 113, 1961, 2523, 2699, 3109, 3694-3695, 3761, 4281, 5283, 5806, 5899, 5964
Haley, Jimmy, 3150
Half A Sixpence, 246, 1030, 1810, 2285, 2342, 2417, 2665, 3373, 4219, 5459, 5745
Half A Sixpence (film musical), 2342
Half Japanese, 2342-2343, 3073, 4880, 5522, 5625
Half Life, 182, 1626, 2483
Half Man Half Biscuit, 2343
Half Moon Six, 4781
Half Pint, 2343
Halfan, Buzz, 2002
Halford, Paul, 2838
Halford, Rob, 560, 1535, 1891, 2906, 3422, 4793
Halifax Three, 1575, 2343-2344, 3833, 5949
Halkes, Nick, 5942
Hall And Oates, 291, 583, 934, 1787, 2344, 2346, 2678, 2966, 3477, 4030, 4342, 4379, 4451, 4683, 4689, 4764, 5588
Hall, Aaron, 4726
Hall, Adelaide, 569, 1066, 1100, 1735, 1885, 2016, 2344-2345, 3320, 3580, 5303, 5533, 5724
Hall, Adrian, 1066, 2247, 6050
Hall, Al, 2345, 4422
Hall, Alexander, 3269
Hall, Audrey, 1378, 2345, 2350
Hall, Avery Fisher, 3314, 4154
Hall, Barbara, 1460
Hall, Bettina, 205, 987
Hall, Bob, 1649, 1788, 2247, 2298, 2345, 2958, 4172, 4198, 4757, 5489
Hall, Bruce, 4506
Hall, Carol, 506, 2664
Hall, Charles, 1384
Hall, Charlie, 1269, 6132
Hall, Chris, 4393-4394
Hall, Christopher, 2192
Hall, Clifton, 1981
Hall, Connie, 2346
Hall, Daryl, 1787, 1881, 2344, 2346, 5588
Hall, Dave, 449, 1649, 2704, 2865, 4506, 4593, 4713, 4905
Hall, Donna, 5779
Hall, Ed, 1263, 3672
Hall, Edmond, 133, 233, 475, 614, 707, 1010, 1269, 1280, 1647, 2075, 2346-2347, 2592, 2815, 2847, 2867, 3216, 3932,

4407, 4427, 4750, 4819, 5880, 5882
Hall, Francis, 4537, 4988
Hall, Frederick, 1477
Hall, Gary, 2347
Hall, George, 969, 981, 1296, 1977, 2346-2347, 4566
Hall, Gerry, 4988
Hall, Greg, 4713
Hall, Henry, 132, 716, 964, 1005, 1866, 1976, 2347-2348, 3323, 4180, 4574, 6051
Hall, Herb, 2348
Hall, Hillman, 2348
Hall, Jack, 2349
Hall, James, 614, 1124, 1280, 2349, 2847, 3420, 3673, 6061
Hall, Jan, 4393
Hall, Jay Hugh, 2352, 3167, 3417, 3760
Hall, Jerry, 1879, 4262, 4291
Hall, Jim, 519, 753, 847, 969, 1493, 1788-1789, 2038, 2076, 2082, 2163, 2192, 2196, 2349, 2375, 2435, 3637, 3716, 4197, 4634, 4861, 5292
Hall, Jimmy, 510, 753, 1290, 2349, 2968, 5292, 5779
Hall, Joe, 569, 3764
Hall, Joey, 3266
Hall, John, 1772, 2071, 2985, 3002, 3073, 3963, 4062, 4393, 4451, 4880, 4885, 5703
Hall, John S., 2071, 3002, 3073, 4880
Hall, Juanita, 1387, 1944-1945, 2607
Hall, Judson, 590, 2617
Hall, Kelvin, 3024, 4689, 5296
Hall, Khristen, 2350
Hall, Lani, 3626
Hall, Larry, 2350, 2938, 4868
Hall, Leo, 861
Hall, Leon, 4865
Hall, Lorenzo, 2705
Hall, Marcel, 550
Hall, Martin, 988, 1783
Hall, Minor, 2350, 2354
Hall, Natalie, 3851
Hall, Nathaniel, 2912
Hall, Pam, 1817, 2345, 2350, 3005
Hall, Patrick, 2081, 6107
Hall, Peter, 946, 2302, 3017, 4154
Hall, Phil, 2807
Hall, Randall, 1174
Hall, Reg, 1398, 5347
Hall, Reginald, 2878
Hall, Richard, 773, 3722
Hall, Rick, 143, 2013, 2351, 2628, 2730-2731, 3849, 4476, 4867, 4876
Hall, Robert, 2246, 2347
Hall, Robin, 2351-2352, 2968
Hall, Robin, And Jimmie MacGregor, 2351
Hall, Roy, 2352, 3167
Hall, Ruth, 2985
Hall, Simon, 4379
Hall, Steve, 3417
Hall, Steven, 694, 2913
Hall, Stuart Warren, 2511
Hall, Terry, 357, 763, 1183,

1699, 2050, 2176, 2352, 2481, 2913, 4078, 5504
Hall, Tom T., 587, 981, 1643, 2348, 2353-2354, 3632, 4073, 4566, 4613, 4795, 4853, 6051
Hall, Tommy, 5393
Hall, Tony, 242, 1227, 2354, 3494
Hall, Tubby, 2350, 2354, 3081
Hall, Vera, 2354
Hall, Wendell, 2354, 4587
Hall, Willie, 664, 1656, 2081, 2349
Hall, Willis, 538, 817, 931, 3012
Hallam, Jesse, 978
Hallberg, Bengt, 1582, 2355, 3079, 3250, 4204
Hallett, Mal, 936, 1822, 2226, 2228, 2355, 2812, 3081, 3842, 3844, 5852
Halley, David, 2355
Halliday, Hidegarde, 2095
Halliday, Hugh, 5578
Halliday, Lin, 115
Halliday, Neil, 1717
Halliday, Pete, 2504
Halliday, Richard, 3489
Halliday, Robert, 1491, 3916, 4814
Halliday, Toni, 1340, 3180
Halligan, Dee Dee, 2330
Halligan, Dick, 600
Hallin, Gunnar, 3902
Hallinhan, Tim, 4266
Halliwell, Andy J., 5509
Hallman, Art, 2970
Hallman, Bill, 2188
Hallom, Gerry, 2355, 2881
Hallor, Edith, 3160
Halloran, Jack, 954
Hallowell, John, 1289, 6042
Hallows Eve, 2355
Halls, Nick, 1574
Hallucinogen, 133, 1592, 1617, 2692, 4293, 4969, 5446
Hallvarosdottir, Hardis, 2718
Hallyday, Johnny, 2356, 2947, 4863, 5320, 5927
Hallyday, Lee, 2356
Halo Of Flies, 2356
Halop, Bill, 624
Halperin, Jerry, 49, 808
Halpin, Kieran, 2357, 2949, 3553
Halprin, Daria, 5987
Halsall, Ollie, 692, 4703, 4763, 5332
Halsey, Bill, 1242
Halsey, Jim, 1103, 2357
Halsey, John, 1869, 4158, 4703
Halstead, Henry, 2357, 3446
Halstead, Neil, 3732, 4971
Ham And Scram, 849
Ham, Bill, 564, 4271
Ham, Greg, 3625
Ham, Jacquie, 5589
Ham, John Lee, 3174
Ham, Pete, 323-324, 2729
Ham, Warren, 61
Hamada, Cheikh, 4409
Hamada, Mari, 2358
Hamady, Ousmane, 4803
Hamalainen, Eero, 4092
Hamar, Dániel, 3857

Hambel, Bobby, 541
Hamblen, Stuart, 512, 2358, 5538, 5709
Hamblin, Lee, 177
Hambly, Mark, 5640
Hambra, Al, 3016
Hamburger, Michel, 488
Hamefarers, 2642-2643
Hamelaers, Thijs, 4809
Hamely, Chris, 1089
Hamer, Harry, 1081
Hamer, Stu, 2514
Hames, Mike, 821
Hamill, Buck, 2905
Hamill, Chris, 2924
Hamill, Claire, 2358, 3841
Hamilton, Andrew, 1850
Hamilton, Andy, 13, 1891, 3303, 5451
Hamilton, Anthony, 5733
Hamilton, Arthur, 2765
Hamilton, Bill, 2287
Hamilton, Chico, 41, 145, 296, 446, 634, 681, 1171, 1579, 2359, 2796, 2884, 3285, 4673, 4985, 5720
Hamilton, Cosmo, 466, 989
Hamilton, David, 914, 968, 3260, 4167, 4264
Hamilton, Don, 2362, 5275
Hamilton, Ferdy, 2175
Hamilton, Frank, 931, 2362, 2602, 4812, 5275, 5743
Hamilton, Fred, 442
Hamilton, George, 329, 1206, 1336, 1398, 1419-1420, 1872, 2204, 2287, 2359-2361, 2422, 2488, 2534, 2615, 2848, 2963, 3121, 3305, 3324-3325, 3729, 4980, 5787, 5847
Hamilton, George, IV, 329, 1206, 1336, 1419-1420, 1872, 2204, 2287, 2359-2361, 2488, 2534, 2615, 2848, 2963, 3121, 3305, 3324-3325, 3729, 4980
Hamilton, Gerald, 1316
Hamilton, Gil, 5429
Hamilton, Gloria, 3191
Hamilton, Graeme, 1894
Hamilton, Graham, 277, 2801
Hamilton, James, 1349, 2361, 6094, 6100
Hamilton, Jeff, 144, 1117, 2361, 3072, 3785, 5912
Hamilton, Jimmy, 412, 968, 1734, 2362, 4040, 4673, 5880
Hamilton, Joe, 2362, 4958, 5275
Hamilton, Joe Frank And Reynolds, 2362, 5275
Hamilton, John, 442, 1739, 2362, 5451
Hamilton, John 'Bugs', 2362
Hamilton, Kenny, 2881
Hamilton, Lawrence, 625, 2602, 4265
Hamilton, Margaret, 5899
Hamilton, Mark, 13, 251, 4801
Hamilton, Mike, 4271
Hamilton, Page, 360, 2479, 2494
Hamilton, Peter, 3260
Hamilton, Prilly, 929
Hamilton, Richard, 1879
Hamilton, Roy, 486, 1001, 1187, 2362-2363, 4160, 4644, 4762

Hamilton, Russ, 2280, 2363
Hamilton, Rusty, 5416
Hamilton, Scott, 344, 391, 516, 707, 825, 865, 1154, 1175, 1943, 2409-2410, 2884, 3505, 3585, 3664, 3837, 4191, 4801, 4915, 4987, 5300, 5332, 5451, 5460, 5591-5592, 5631, 5820
Hamilton, Tim, 1739
Hamilton, Tom, 82
Hamlett, Ian, 1213
Hamlisch, Marvin, 255, 490, 566, 842, 1070, 2363-2364, 3187, 4209, 4525, 4542, 4716, 4917, 6051
Hamlyn, Bob, 5835
Hamm, Stuart, 2364, 3069
Hammell, Dick, 2903
Hammen, Cloet, 1691
Hammer, Alvin, 2562
Hammer, Jan, 316, 446, 544, 647, 846, 1843, 2364-2365, 2549, 3355, 3413, 3502, 3590, 3761, 3984, 4772
Hammer, Ken, 4319
Hammer MC, 1559, 1689, 1755, 2365-2366, 2702, 4433
Hammerbox, 2211, 4168
Hammerdoll, 3400
Hammered, 68, 206, 1087, 1350, 1593, 1648, 1983, 5296, 5680
Hammerhead, 2356, 2366
Hammersmith, 2366 and *passim*
Hammersmith Gorillas, 1066, 2219
Hammerstein, Arthur, 2366
Hammerstein, Oscar, II, 21, 127, 197, 947, 1210, 1219, 1491, 1520, 1578, 1944, 2036, 2252, 2278, 2366, 2385, 2523, 2596, 2661, 2928, 2975, 2997, 3140, 3784, 3916, 4025, 4039, 4607, 4637, 4650, 4681, 4814, 4880, 4892, 5378, 5964, 6051
Hammerstein, William, 2366
Hammertones, 2688
Hammett, Bill, 4441
Hammett, Kirk, 1807, 3643, 4751
Hammill, John, 4371
Hammill, Peter, 1907, 2367, 5602, 6051, 6124
Hammock, Cleveland, Jnr., 1625
Hammody, Joey, 80
Hammon, Ronnie, 355
Hammond, Albert, 1400-1401, 1536, 1576, 1839, 2367-2368, 2564, 3407, 3788, 4251, 4716
Hammond, Andy, 674, 1213
Hammond, Beres, 304, 369, 1810-1811, 2368, 2638, 3462, 3825, 4250, 4514, 4794, 5291, 5676, 5990, 6005
Hammond, Bryan, 342, 6031
Hammond, Clay, 2368, 5305
Hammond, Dave, 1132
Hammond, Dill, 1477
Hammond, Fred, 2369, 5680
Hammond, Gene, 1358
Hammond, John, 359, 405, 530, 580, 605, 674, 948, 1268, 1306, 1615, 1672-1673, 1741, 2013, 2066, 2090, 2208, 2268, 2297,

4369, 5509
Heywood, Heather, 2277, 2513
Heywood, Leroy, 2700, 3405
Heywood, Pete, 1889, 2513
Heywood, Terri, 1360
Hexworth, John, 1291
Hex, 1158, 1835-1836, 2078, 2511, 2988-2989, 3955, 4272, 4356, 4909, 5888
Hi Records, 2514 and passim
Hi-Bias Records, 2514
Hi-C, 2514
Hi-Five, 2829, 2963, 4675
Hi-Life International, 2514, 4419
Hi-Lites, 1052, 4640
Hi-Lo's, 2515 and passim
Hiatt, John, 740, 1218, 1312, 1314, 1515, 1631, 2489, 2515, 2590, 3121, 3274, 3349, 3866, 3943, 4415
Hibari, Misora, 3704
Hibbard, Bruce, 2515
Hibbert, Jimmy, 109
Hibbert, Lennie, 5685
Hibbert, Oscar, 1471
Hibbert, Ossie, 1008, 3002, 5319, 5426
Hibbert, Toots, 1265, 2054, 2351, 2516
Hibbler, Al, 1737, 2516, 3074, 3973, 4407, 5972
Hibler, Son, 842
Hibler, Winston, 1544
Hibtone Records, 4394
Hichin, Pat, 2363
Hickey, Chris, 2516
Hickey, Jack, 5528
Hickey, Kenny, 5555
Hickey, Mike, 990
Hickinbotham, Gary, 4414
Hickland, Tom, 1917
Hickman, Art, 846, 2003, 2516
Hickman, Darryl, 4519
Hickman, Dwayne, 2612, 4949
Hickman, John, 494, 1277
Hickman, Johnny, 1271
Hickman, Sylvester, 994
Hickory Records, 60, 256, 2814, 3925, 4001, 4189
Hickory Wind, 2287, 2516, 3368, 4147, 6067
Hickox, Charlie, 639
Hickox, Richard, 2320
Hicks, Aaron, 2279
Hicks, Bert, 2344
Hicks, Bobby, 343, 621, 1314, 1967, 3150, 3745, 4868
Hicks, Charley, 3250, 5742
Hicks, Colin, 995, 1810, 1987, 3779, 5470
Hicks, Dan, 396, 569, 618, 1025, 2516-2517, 2723, 3258-3259
Hicks, David, 4512
Hicks, Edna, 2517
Hicks, Hiriam, 1632
Hicks, Jacqui, 2517
Hicks, Joe, 1888, 2629
Hicks, John, 631, 2483, 3772, 4473
Hicks, Johnny, 2517
Hicks, Les, 597
Hicks, Nathan, 5705
Hicks, Otis, 3242

Hicks, Robert, 344, 373, 5742
Hicks, Seymour, 250, 620, 989, 5900
Hicks, Thomas, 1809
Hicks, Tom, 985
Hicks, Tommy, 995, 4143, 5459
Hicks, Tony, 316, 2549, 2563, 3877, 5435
Hicks, Ulysses K., 1917
Hickson, Joan, 932
Hicksville, 816, 1533, 1617, 2517, 2830, 3029
Hidalgo, David, 815, 974, 3320
Hidalgo, Giovanni, 3984
Hideaways, 999, 2517-2518
Hierlehy, Alison, 2601
Higginbotham, J.C., 130, 1163, 1269, 1932, 2279, 2518, 3644, 3683, 4370, 5402
Higginbottom, Robert, 5525
Higginbottom, Geoff, 2518
Higgins, Bertie, 2518
Higgins, Billy, 476, 591, 701, 822, 856, 1016, 1046, 1167, 1712, 1802, 2023, 2519, 2885, 2892, 3646, 3722, 3731, 4473, 4634, 4663, 5376, 5435, 5619, 5912
Higgins, Chuck, 2082, 2519, 3969, 5730
Higgins, Cub, 2938
Higgins, Donald, 2519
Higgins, Henry, 1010, 1771, 2417, 3859
Higgins, Joel, 1884
Higgins, Lizzie, 2513, 2519-2520, 6053
Higgins, Monk, 2520, 2950, 4048, 4582, 4762
Higginsen, Vy, 3426
Higgs, D.M., 2961
Higgs, Dave, 1701, 3221
Higgs, Joe, 610, 840, 1125, 1568, 1698, 1711, 2520, 3060, 3211, 3467, 5667, 5669
Higgs, Paul, 3882
High, 2520
High Broom, 2789
High Button Shoes, 38, 659, 884, 1151, 1564, 2520-2521, 3204, 3487, 4567
High Country, 78, 343, 1508, 1954, 2521
High Inergy, 2521
High Llamas, 427, 2036, 2521, 3654
High Note Records, 2521
High On Love, 372, 4635
High Roller, 5740
High Society, 2521-2522 and passim
High Spirits, 2522 and passim
High Stepper, 3297
High Street Records, 257, 1610, 2350, 3130, 5882
High Tide, 525, 2127, 2522-2523, 3407, 4632, 5427, 5636
High Times Band, 2140, 5411
High Tones, 975
High, Wide And Handsome, 2523, 2976, 3118, 3429
Higham, C., 5999
Higher And Higher, 2523 and passim

Higher Intelligence Agency, 513, 542, 2523
Higher State Records, 2523
Highhatters, 3365
Highland, Ken, 2165
Highlife, 2524 and passim
Highlights, 2524
Hightone Records, 265, 1362, 3306, 4462, 5728
Hightower, Rosetta, 463, 2262, 2524, 4063
Hightower, Willie, 1570
Highway 101, 938, 1537, 2524-2525, 2615, 5799
Highway QC's, 2525
Highway Robbery, 2525
Highway, John, 4249
Highwaymen, 978, 1331, 2526, 2813, 3078, 3900, 5348
Highwood, Steven, 138
Higson, Charlie, 2526
Higsons, 858, 1850, 2113, 2526, 5952
Higuchi, Masayuki, 4122
Hijack, 166-167, 305, 608, 908, 1033, 2413, 2526, 2935, 2939, 4350, 4677
Hijas Del Sol, 2527, 4899
Hijazi, Tanya, 2776
Hijbert, Fritz, 3072
Hijuelos, Oscar, 4616
Hila Y, 672
Hilaire, Andrew, 505, 1219
Hilbert, Robert, 4700, 6076
Hilberts, Edy, 4371
Hild, Daved, 3073, 5442
Hilda, Bernard, 3784
Hildebrand, Diane, 2211
Hildebrand, Ray, 4159
Hildebrandt, Herbert, 4439
Hildegarde, 159, 2527, 4890, 4906, 5426
Hildenbeutel, Ralf, 1688, 4460
Hilder, Tony, 2527
Hildred, Stafford, 2887, 6056, 6080
Hildyard, David, 1882
Hill, Adrian, 2534
Hill, Aimée, 929
Hill, Albert, 5856
Hill, Alexander, 5689
Hill, Alfred Hawthorne, 2528
Hill, Andrew, 561, 614, 844, 1010, 1338, 1341, 1506, 1514, 1579, 1862, 2155, 2487, 2527-2528, 2648, 3521, 4908, 5297
Hill, Andy, 814, 4345
Hill, Arthur, 5899
Hill, Beau, 97, 1540, 1786, 1856, 1900, 3040, 4843
Hill, Benny, 1066, 1100, 2243, 2528, 2842, 3418, 4426, 5571, 5633, 5892
Hill, Bertha 'Chippie', 2528
Hill, Billie, 1780
Hill, Billy, 1537, 2528
Hill, Bob, 2181, 2938
Hill, Brendan, 626
Hill, Byron, 494
Hill, Chris, 2942
Hill, Chuck, 4518
Hill, Dan, 2529, 5456
Hill, Daniel, Jnr., 2529
Hill, Dave, 1478-1479, 2688,

4333, 4958, 6071, 6111
Hill, David, 574, 5633
Hill, Don, 429, 2993, 5499
Hill, Dule, 740
Hill, Dusty, 161, 6006-6007
Hill, Eddie, 602, 660, 864, 1876, 2714, 2836
Hill, Erin, 5449
Hill, Ernest, 2529
Hill, Faith, 1537, 2489, 2529, 3575, 4735
Hill, George Roy, 5418
Hill, Goldie, 2529-2530, 3563, 4240, 4984, 5520
Hill, Harold, 108, 2660, 3852-3853, 4317, 5869
Hill, Harry, 1911
Hill, Ian, 1839, 2906, 5394
Hill, James, 2450, 3554, 5368
Hill, Jason, 3693
Hill, Jeff, 2605
Hill, Jessie, 358, 2121, 2530
Hill, Joe, 1039, 1178, 2600, 2878, 2961, 3004, 3325, 5647, 5669, 5916, 6006
Hill, Joel Scott, 3653
Hill, Joseph, 1329
Hill, Ken, 4218
Hill, Lauryn, 2046, 5934
Hill, Lester, 3325
Hill, Marion, 1341, 4860
Hill, Michael, 1434, 2530
Hill, Olive, 2348, 2353
Hill, Richard, 919, 3266
Hill, Rob, 290
Hill, Robert, 4300
Hill, Rosa Lee, 2483-2484, 2530
Hill, Rose, 465, 1897, 2533, 5312
Hill, Scott, 2044, 3653
Hill, Scotti, 4950
Hill, Sharon Lee, 336, 597, 1946
Hill, Steve, 602
Hill, Steven, 5956
Hill, Teddy, 429, 1108, 1163, 1178, 1437, 1527, 1721, 2150, 2321, 2362, 2531, 2993, 4345, 4582, 5713, 5762
Hill, Theodore, 2531
Hill, Thomas Lee, 4204
Hill, Tiny, 958, 2531
Hill, Tom, 2121
Hill, Tony, 2522-2523, 3708
Hill, Vince, 2531-2532
Hill, Walter, 2669
Hill, Wareika, 4437, 4614
Hill, Z.Z., 161, 534, 1098, 1422, 2289, 2532, 2731, 2741, 2888
Hillage, Steve, 1024, 1144, 1633, 1715, 2198, 2532, 2574, 2697, 2981, 3235, 3503, 4921, 5463
Hille, Rodger, 2299
Hiller, Holger, 4108
Hiller, Tony, 761
Hillery, Dave, 5534
Hillhouse, Christa, 1994
Hilliard, Bob, 313, 1824, 2532
Hilliard, Brenda, 1829
Hilliard, George, 5554
Hilliard, Harriet, 1960, 3896
Hilliard, Lee, 1995
Hilliard, Vera, 4382
Hillier, Steve, 1640
Hillin, Jim, 440
Hillis, Craig, 3322

Hoffman, Ingfried, 1577
Hoffman, Jean, 572
Hoffman, Mathias, 5819
Hoffman, R.S., 3066
Hoffman, Randy, 934
Hoffmaster, Pat, 575
Hoffnung, Gerald, 240
Hoffs, Susanna, 366-367, 2550, 3245, 3534, 6122
Hofner, Adolph, 2517, 2550
Hofner, Dolph, 2550
Hofrenning, Barbara, 5551
Hofseth, Bendik, 4825
Hogan, Anne, 1954
Hogan, Annie, 3456
Hogan, Arval, 730
Hogan, Carl, 500, 5598
Hogan, Don, 1625
Hogan, Jimmy, 923
Hogan, John, 2550
Hogan, Louanne, 4518
Hogan, Noel, 1275
Hogan, Silas, 1601, 2550, 2958, 3676, 5399, 5406
Hogan, Tweet, 5523
Hogarth, Nicky, 1105, 3047
Hogarth, Steve, 1907, 3463
Hogberg, Sven Ake, 838
Hogg, Dave, 191, 2707
Hogg, John, 2551
Hogg, Smokey, 473-474, 1080, 2551, 2586, 4377, 4833
Hogg, Willie 'Smokey', 2551
Hoggard, Jay, 1626, 2483, 2551
Hoggs, Billy, 1215
Hogman, Pete, 3621
Hogwood String Band, 422
Hoh, Eddie, 3651
Hohki, Kazuko, 2010
Hohl, Daryl Franklin, 2344
Hoile, Jed, 2875
Hoist, Allen, 4611
Höjberg, Örjan, 1937
Hokanson, Alan, 2322
Hokenson, Ed, 752
Hokey Pokey, 1179, 2551-2552, 2578, 5411, 5413-5414
Hokkanen, Erik, 1109, 4210
Hokum Boys, 786, 1599, 2552, 4581
Holcombe, Wendy, 2552
Hold Everything!, 35, 780, 829, 1439, 1516, 1951, 1961, 2552, 3109
Hold My Hand, 2102, 2340, 2553, 3123, 3519, 3802
Hold On!, 2553
Hold, Lucien, 4594
Holdbrook, Ian, 4598
Holdclaw, Andrea, 404
Holden, Adam, 4076, 6002
Holden, Bob, 1582
Holden, Brendan, 1050
Holden, Fay, 5998
Holden, Guy, 2100-2101
Holden, Jim, 5564
Holden, Mark, 680
Holden, Randy, 611, 4076
Holden, Rob, 2252
Holden, Ron, 1468, 2553, 2858
Holden, Steve, 3734
Holden, William, 1933, 1988
Holder, Frank, 4544
Holder, Gene, 1431, 5959

Holder, Geoffrey, 1567, 5898
Holder, Irma, 3252
Holder, Nicky, 2514
Holder, Noddy, 2162, 2688, 3707, 4958
Holder, Roy, 1443
Holder, Terrence, 861, 1792, 2553, 2842, 2933, 4984, 5300, 5341
Holderby, Scott, 3777
Holdridge, Lee, 1509, 3110
Holdsworth, Allan, 445, 798, 2198, 2364, 2553, 2646, 2675, 3189, 4678, 5332, 5435
Holdsworth, Dave, 2320, 4092
Hole, 2554 and *passim*
Hole, Dave, 2554
Holgate, Ronald, 2056, 4827
Holidai, Peter, 4400
Holiday Inn, 261-262, 396, 494, 617, 1303-1304, 1394, 1774, 2555, 2712, 4169, 4225, 5791
Holiday Records, 671, 3554
Holiday, Billie, 8-9, 19, 105, 279, 339, 380, 382, 428, 480-481, 537, 548, 578, 585, 608, 755, 852, 940, 974, 1000, 1039, 1061, 1085, 1115, 1140, 1158, 1175, 1180, 1187, 1221-1222, 1249, 1267, 1365, 1412, 1433, 1602, 1792, 1803, 1912-1913, 2067, 2132, 2253, 2271, 2321, 2391, 2419, 2485, 2513, 2555-2558, 2566, 2596-2597, 2617, 2634, 2772, 2835, 2971, 2978, 2987, 3038, 3043, 3081, 3086, 3105-3106, 3132, 3142, 3176, 3216, 3249, 3261, 3348, 3375, 3414, 3466, 3504, 3554, 3593, 3599-3600, 3629, 3644, 3691, 3736, 3752, 3771, 3791, 3799, 3814, 3919, 3998, 4211, 4216, 4422, 4584, 4657, 4668, 4695, 4697, 4789-4790, 4816, 4870, 4877, 4915, 4985, 5509, 5530, 5620, 5675, 5724, 5730, 5774, 5841, 5879-5880, 5894, 5975-5977
Holiday, Bob, 2723
Holiday, Clarence, 2555
Holiday, Doc, 935
Holiday, Harold, 554, 1710, 2596
Holiday, Jimmy, 2558, 3693
Holiday, Johnny, 942, 5734
Holiday, Valerie, 5422
Holland, 2558-2559
Holland, Annie, 1720
Holland, Bernie, 12, 1878, 2829
Holland, Brian, 1611, 2559, 2561, 3495, 4448, 5318, 5682, 5777
Holland, Chris, 2463
Holland, Dave, 41, 154, 159, 331, 488, 718, 738, 815, 1089, 1122, 1170, 1203, 1227, 1234, 1287, 1415, 1465, 1682, 1701, 1714, 1785, 2031, 2098, 2122, 2194, 2559, 2628, 2684, 2716, 2907, 3217, 3439, 3590, 3646, 4155, 4221, 4250, 4327, 4560, 5492, 5674, 5687, 5785-5786
Holland, David, 1203, 2463, 5871

Holland, Deborah, 193, 1231
Holland, Doug, 1298, 4017
Holland, Eddie, 1611, 2218, 2559-2561, 3813, 5804
Holland, Fred, 5444
Holland, Gary, 744, 2259
Holland, Greg, 1537
Holland, Herbert Lee, 2560
Holland, Jools, 224, 788, 1237, 1349, 1691, 2560, 2910, 3135, 4231, 4738, 5520, 5924
Holland, Julian, 2560
Holland, Maggie, 176, 1150, 1761, 2560
Holland, Malcolm, 2953
Holland, Milt, 5856
Holland, Nick, 4340
Holland, Nicola, 262
Holland, Peanuts, 389, 2305, 2560, 2934, 5342, 5500
Holland, Steve, 3734
Holland, Tom, 303
Holland, Willie, 4204
Holland/Dozier/Holland, 253, 763, 1611, 1717, 1731, 1924, 1977, 1997-1998, 2559-2561, 2719, 2965, 3175, 3432, 3480, 3700, 3813, 4170, 4923, 5314, 5318, 5681, 5777, 5804
Hollander Boys, 2111
Hollander, Frederick, 205, 1207, 3197, 3293, 3467, 4580
Hollaway, Ann, 5549
Holleman, Regina, 3496
Holler, Dick, 1535
Holler, Jerry, 4703
Holles, Antony, 729, 2167, 5397
Holley, 'Lyin" Joe, 2561
Holley, Joe, 231, 2561
Holley, Major, 489, 2562, 3657, 4444
Holley, Willie, 3496
Holliday, Jennifer, 1608, 1625, 2016, 2562, 3239
Holliday, John, 1263, 1777
Holliday, Judy, 467-468, 1033, 1190, 2562-2563, 3484, 3837, 4608, 6053
Holliday, Michael, 313, 1187, 2563, 3448, 3673, 4125, 4568, 4729, 5887
Holliday, Mike, 2563, 4512
Holliday, Rick, 304
Hollies, 14, 18, 223, 433, 514, 999, 1144, 1306, 1308, 1400, 1777, 1798, 2142, 2225, 2260, 2330, 2368, 2563-2564, 2567, 2682, 2724, 2729, 2734, 2771, 2833, 2916, 3384, 3486, 3725, 3830, 3877, 4142, 4292, 4436, 4454, 4499, 4533, 4679, 4696, 4704, 4782, 4784, 4897, 5311, 5335, 5374, 5512, 5567, 5618, 5679, 5856, 6053
Holliman, Shirlie, 4192, 5781
Hollingsworth, John, 479, 2078
Hollins, Tony, 1411
Hollis, George, 1929
Hollis, Mark, 2726, 5286
Hollis, Peter, 1052
Hollis, Richard, 1545
Hollis, Tommy, 4408
Hollister, David, 573, 4546
Holloway, Brenda, 56, 2565,

4683, 5744
Holloway, James W., 2566
Holloway, Jean, 5436
Holloway, Ken, 2565
Holloway, Laurie, 2565, 3755
Holloway, Loleatta, 553, 921, 1460, 2566, 4215, 4902
Holloway, Nicky, 347
Holloway, Red, 2566, 3493
Holloway, Stanley, 565, 1011, 1552, 1894, 2544, 2566-2567, 3826, 3859-3860, 4932, 5782, 6053
Hollowell, Alton, 1835
Holly And The Italians, 2223, 2567
Holly, Buddy, 6, 22, 127, 162, 194, 209, 385, 433, 503, 521, 705-706, 744, 781, 804, 816, 948, 1087, 1109, 1154, 1233, 1246, 1290, 1339, 1412, 1419-1420, 1452, 1468, 1551, 1593, 1749, 1874, 1902, 1930, 2219-2220, 2360, 2435, 2564, 2567-2570, 2755, 2812, 2999, 3052, 3315, 3592, 3623, 3678, 3753-3754, 3886, 3892, 3995, 4027, 4058, 4100, 4181, 4215, 4257, 4280, 4312, 4317, 4449, 4641, 4693, 5352, 5357, 5388, 5457, 5594, 5622, 5662, 5864, 5941, 6053, 6124
Holly, Doyle, 2570, 4088
Holly, Maria, 2568-2569
Holly, Steve, 3548, 5885
Hollyday, Christopher, 2192, 3613
Hollywood Argyles, 414, 1386, 2001, 2019, 2570, 4168, 4954, 5327
Hollywood Beyond, 2570
Hollywood Blue Jays, 503, 5967
Hollywood Brats, 697, 2570-2571, 3302
Hollywood Fats, 587, 2571, 4461
Hollywood Flames, 636, 1426, 2571
Hollywood Hillbillies, 1910
Hollywood Hotel, 420, 492, 1411, 1584, 1658, 1899, 2304, 2571, 2890, 3126, 3629, 4119, 4299, 5805
Hollywood Records, 850, 1582, 1792, 1857, 2117, 2329, 2519, 2699, 3239, 4792, 5276, 5962
Hollywood, Jimmy, 5588, 6044
Holm, Celeste, 604, 2522, 3761, 4025
Holm, Dallas, 734
Holm, Eleanor, 2785, 4649
Holm, June, 2571-2572
Holm, Michael, 2572
Holman, Bill, 143, 389, 1713, 2111, 2572, 2626, 2973, 3210, 3223, 3227, 4195, 5789
Holman, Eddie, 2572, 4680
Holman, Fred, 43, 3924
Holman, Libby, 130, 2095, 2270, 2512, 2572-2573, 3273, 3924, 4413, 5425, 6053
Holman, Spencer, 191
Holmes Brothers, 2573
Holmes, Charlie, 944, 2573, 3683

Hopkins, Keith, 3189, 5774

Hopkins, Lightnin', 2593 and *passim*

Hopkins, Linda, 788, 5766, 5817, 5875

Hopkins, Lymon, 1050

Hopkins, Mark, 2470, 2942, 2964, 3015, 5294, 5609, 5753, 5845

Hopkins, Mike, 2673, 3189, 4378

Hopkins, Miriam, 3850

Hopkins, Nicky, 214, 365, 445, 728, 1402, 1588, 1758, 2593-2594, 3680, 4100, 4231, 4269, 4385, 5343, 5456, 5935

Hopkins, Richard, 597

Hopkins, Rick, 2770

Hopkins, Robert, 1916, 4732

Hopkins, Sam, 2593

Hopkins, Sarah, 4562

Hopkins, Steve, 3847

Hopkins, Sylvester, 1919-1920

Hopkins, Trevor, 4393

Hopkins-Harrison, James, 3113

Hoppe, Kelly, 529

Hoppen, Lance, 4062

Hoppen, Larry, 4062

Hopper, 2594

Hopper, Dennis, 1415, 1694, 3877, 5505

Hopper, Hal, 4237

Hopper, Hugh, 392, 929, 2721

Hopper, Otis, 4724

Hopper, Sean, 1135, 3217

Hopping, Bill, 5397

Hoppoh Records, 3086

Hopscotch, 1623, 2170

Hopwood, Aubrey, 620

Hopwood, Avery, 2185

Hopwood, Keith, 2504

Horak, Brian Michael, 3238

Horan, Jimmy, 5441

Horbury, Terry, 1540, 5614

Hord, Eric, 3579

Hordern, Michael, 4969

Hordichuk, Kenny, 2915

Horenstein, Stephen, 1553

Horgan, Patrick, 336

Horizon 222, 2594

Horizon Records, 49, 294, 612, 1933, 4939, 5884, 6036, 6089

Horler, Dave, 2595, 3627

Horler, John, 347, 1289, 2594

Horler, Ronnie, 2594

Horn, Jim, 1702

Horn, M.F., 1877

Horn, Paul, 169, 1176, 1853, 2359, 2595, 4173, 4845, 6053

Horn, Shirley, 2419, 2595, 4231, 6054

Horn, Trevor, 226, 272, 821, 1577, 2767, 2782, 2873, 2887, 3699, 4030, 4797, 5957, 6000, 6004

Hornaday, Jeffrey, 1070

Hornblow, Arthur, Jnr., 4025

Hornby, Alan, 5419

Hornby, Paul, 1574, 4249

Horne, Alan, 1902, 2175, 3889, 4295, 5881

Horne, Bob, 27

Horne, Cora Calhoun, 2596

Horne, Lena, 177, 227, 381, 389,

457, 569, 586, 604, 713, 876-877, 969, 1033, 1117, 1246, 1299, 1504, 1669, 1705, 1851, 1881, 1913, 2344-2345, 2359, 2386, 2406, 2449, 2595-2597, 2767, 2844, 2884, 3054, 3190, 3488, 3709, 4104, 4177, 4207, 4581, 4928, 4930, 5292, 5301, 5419, 5435, 5620, 5724, 5817, 5898, 5998, 6054

Horne, Marilyn, 941, 1973

Horne, Trader, 459, 3540, 4281, 5486

Horner, Ashley, 4109

Horner, Daren, 4648

Horner, Harry, 5823

Horner, James, 2597, 2814

Horner, Penelope, 2342

Horning, William A., 2144

Hornsby, Bruce, 847, 1790, 2247, 2598, 3218, 3561, 4415, 5411

Hornsby, Bruce, And The Range, 2598

Hornsby, Clive, 1483

Hornsby, Jim, 4308

Hornsby, Paul, 2606

Horovitz, Richard, 2338

Horowitz, Cecil, 4492

Horowitz, Jimmy, 1652

Horowitz, Sam, 2347

Horowitz, Ted, 4283

Horoya Band, 1505

Horrocks, James, 4453, 4522

Horsburgh, Wayne, 2598

Horse, 2598

Horse, Mark, 656

Horslips, 882, 2599, 3426, 4689, 5904

Hortis, Throm, 2147

Horton, Bill, 4905

Horton, Edward Everett, 2081, 2101, 4841, 5466, 5523, 5998

Horton, Everett, 251, 2081, 2101, 4841, 5466, 5523, 5998

Horton, Gladys, 3495-3496

Horton, Holly, 3931

Horton, Johnny, 230, 268, 653, 753, 1298, 1446, 1629, 2287, 2456, 2599-2600, 2990, 3011-3012, 3214, 3298, 3326, 3358, 3512, 4882, 5847, 6054

Horton, Monte, 2495

Horton, Ron, 1035

Horton, Roy, 1255-1256

Horton, Sampson, 5660

Horton, Shorty, 5924

Horton, Vaughan, 1394, 2600

Horton, Walter 'Shakey', 2600

Horton-Jennings, Colin, 2261

Horvath, John, 2605

Horváth, Károly, 3421

Horvath, Kornel, 4803

Horvath, Ronald, 1686, 4642

Horvitz, Bill, 3791

Horvitz, Wayne, 1105, 3791, 3870, 4139, 4896, 5354, 6003

Horwitt, Arnold B., 893, 2335, 2699, 3419

Horwitz, Murray, 94, 4883

Hoschna, Karl, 545, 1202, 2385, 3399

Hosert, Rick, 1615

Hosie, Alan, 3138

Hosking, Mark, 1925

Hoskins, Bob, 1237, 1246, 2315, 2389, 5931

Hoskins, Tom, 2645

Hosler, Mark, 3891

Hosono, Haruomi, 4722, 5954

Hossack, Michael, 1591-1592

Host, 2601

Hoste, Michael, 2669

Hostnik, Tomaz, 3110

Hot And Blue, 35, 977-978, 1047, 1658, 2590, 2651, 2676, 2854, 3327, 3634-3635, 4289-4290, 4468, 5501, 5888

Hot Butter, 1496, 2601

Hot Chocolate, 355, 566, 1325, 2230, 2242, 2592, 2601, 3145, 3235, 3805, 4083, 4416

Hot Gossip, 737, 993, 2601, 5440

Hot Knives, 2602

Hot Mikado, 1477, 2602-2603, 4341, 4581

Hot Rize, 3993

Hot Rod Gang, 2603, 5645

Hot Shot Records, 4024

Hot Streak, 2603

Hot Tuna, 259, 592, 827, 1285, 1315, 1534, 1859, 1892, 2603-2604, 2803, 2941, 6132

Hot Wax Records, 1611

Hot, Roland, 3302

Hotchner, A.E., 1165, 4632, 6043, 6075

Hotel, 2604

Hothouse Flowers, 563, 1275, 1898, 2604, 2691, 2703, 2728, 4886

Hotlegs, 2180, 2225, 2604, 3260, 3689, 5335

Hott Records, 3906

Houchens, Kenneth, 4305

Houghton Weavers, 2605

Houghton, Chris, 1376

Hould-Ward, Ann, 441

Hound Dog, 222, 1388, 1701, 1816, 2256, 2579, 3186, 4197, 4221, 5353, 5417

Hound-Dog Man, 2605

Hounds, 851, 1106, 1408, 1545, 2020, 2314, 2437, 2605, 2635, 2854, 3842, 5295, 5873

Hounsham, Toby, 4523

Houpt, Debbie, 2602

Houpt, Mike, 2602

Hour Glass, 142-143, 1427, 2605-2606

House, 2606 and *passim*

House Band, 2606

House Of Flowers, 227, 332, 2606-2607

House Of Lords, 50, 189, 657, 1389, 1889, 2019, 2164, 2607, 2682

House Of Love, 1170, 1287, 1409, 1693, 1962, 2241, 2607-2608, 3212, 3570, 4138, 4540, 4797, 5774

House Of Pain, 542, 549, 1344, 1557, 1560, 1797, 2052, 2480, 2608, 3065, 3318, 3954, 4292, 4593, 5459, 5574, 5814, 5942

House, James, 2608, 3671

House, Kenwyn, 4480

House, Simon, 2442, 2522, 3407

Househunters, 1891

Houseman, John, 2562

Housemartins, 25, 379, 438, 440, 1220, 1860, 2175, 2608-2609, 2720, 4394, 4456, 4766, 4824, 6054

Houser, Brad, 731

Houserockers, 139, 1363, 1671, 1866, 2068, 2851, 3265, 4090, 4137, 5319, 5686-5687

Houses And Gardens, 3282

Housman, John, 595, 1273

Houston, Bee, 2610

Houston, Bob, 3308

Houston, Cisco, 64, 144, 680, 1332, 1958, 2319, 2426, 2609, 3108

Houston, Cissy, 1113, 2609, 2739, 3742, 5512, 5713, 5742

Houston, Dale, 764, 1360

Houston, David, 2609-2610, 3436, 4371, 5936

Houston, Edward 'Bee', 2610

Houston, Gilbert Vandine, 2609

Houston, Joe, 694, 2238, 2374, 2610, 5529

Houston, K., 5513

Houston, Norman, 745

Houston, Sam, 2609, 5437, 5918

Houston, Thelma, 857, 2610-2611

Houston, Whitney, 87, 225, 719, 767, 934, 1088, 1181, 1268, 1424, 1536, 1812, 2013, 2064, 2139, 2609, 2611-2612, 2743, 2788, 2814, 3392-3393, 3435, 3529, 3975, 4148, 4184, 4186, 4383, 4455, 4571, 4851, 5357, 5403, 5610, 5680, 5808, 5875, 6054

Hovey, David, 2476

Hovey, Tim, 3397

Hovington, Frank, 2612

Hovington, Steve, 304

Hovorka, Bob, 1501

Hovorka, John, 5528

How To Stuff A Wild Bikini, 195, 289, 1086, 2612, 3022, 4643

How To Succeed In Business Without Really Trying, 846, 1376, 1983, 2278, 2612, 3294, 3568, 3583, 4540, 5600

Howard And Blaikley, 1398, 2502, 2582, 2613, 2616, 3517

Howard And David, 465, 4349

Howard Pickup, 81

Howard The Duck, 400-401, 2990

Howard, Adina, 1739, 2613

Howard, Alan, 1398, 1925, 2502, 2582, 2613, 5499

Howard, Ann, 1358, 3034, 3036, 4648, 5798

Howard, Avery, 2617

Howard, Barry, 53, 3443, 6062

Howard, Bob, 826, 2613-2614

Howard, Bruce, 607, 3096, 6057

Howard, Camille, 1564, 2614, 3687, 4690

Howard, Chuck, 957, 2614, 6035

Howard, Clint, 254, 5728

Howard, Clinton, 1477

Howard, Darnell, 963, 992, 1730, 2536, 2614, 5301
Howard, Dean, 4623, 4734, 5275
Howard, Don, 2614, 3508, 4118
Howard, Donnee, 2626
Howard, Eddy, 43, 1106, 2615, 2914, 3293, 5453
Howard, Eugene, 2159, 5798, 5980
Howard, Gene, 1049
Howard, Harlan, 118, 377, 1129, 1143, 1256, 2525, 2615-2616, 3755, 3802, 4088, 4372, 5436, 5460, 5717
Howard, Harry, 1293, 1477, 2951
Howard, Henry, 3715, 3885
Howard, Jack, 2643
Howard, James, 490, 1757, 2616, 3134, 4717, 6058
Howard, James Newton, 490, 2616, 4717
Howard, Jan, 174, 2395, 2615-2616, 4504, 6054
Howard, Jane, 1361
Howard, Jean, 4290
Howard, John, 1875, 2347, 2875, 3230, 4544, 6033, 6109
Howard, Johnny, 826, 2616
Howard, Joseph E., 4956
Howard, Ken, 1398, 1925, 2502, 2582, 2613, 2616, 4827, 4944
Howard, Ken, And Alan Blaikley, 1398, 2502, 2582, 2613, 2616
Howard, Kid, 826, 2019, 2375, 2617, 2958, 4583, 5993
Howard, Leslie, 2055, 4181, 4894
Howard, Linda, 2521
Howard, Lou, 4463
Howard, Marcia, 2177
Howard, Michael, 6042
Howard, Miki, 2617, 3209
Howard, Myron, 5398
Howard, Noah, 2617, 5927
Howard, Norah, 1744, 5919
Howard, Paul, 404, 778, 2087, 2137, 2370, 2408, 2617, 2752, 3778, 4694, 5285, 5778
Howard, Pete, 1110, 1695, 5628
Howard, Randy (fiddle), 2618
Howard, Randy (singer-song-writer), 2618
Howard, Robert, 607, 746, 5761
Howard, Ron, 2290, 3577, 3778
Howard, Rosetta, 2396, 2618, 3776, 5718
Howard, Rowland S., 390, 1293, 1719, 1989, 3360
Howard, Shane, 2177
Howard, Sidney, 3294
Howard, Simon, 5314
Howard, Sydney, 708, 1939, 2055
Howard, Tim, 4102
Howard, Willy, 2159
Howarth, David, 2203
Howarth, Peter, 5540
Howarth, Tod, 2029, 4826
Howbs, Neil, 89
Howe II, 2618
Howe, Brian, 320, 5793
Howe, Carey, 3159

Howe, Darcus, 723
Howe, Greg, 2618
Howe, James Wong, 5948
Howe, Mark, 3644
Howe, Mike, 2503, 3642
Howe, Steve, 46, 174, 256, 2004, 2303, 2329, 2359, 2618-2619, 2684, 3799, 4479, 5382, 5459, 5544, 5956
Howel, Alton, 854
Howell, Alphonso, 4820
Howell, Brad, 1846, 3681
Howell, Dan, 4449
Howell, Hammy, 1395
Howell, Jerry, 3817
Howell, John, 871, 4386, 6038
Howell, Kurt, 839
Howell, Leonard P., 4438
Howell, Myles, 3021
Howell, Notch, 673, 2011
Howell, Owen, 1170
Howell, Paul, 1316
Howell, Peg Leg, 200, 2619
Howell, Peter, 92
Howell, Porter, 3273
Howell, Rob, 1922
Howell, William, 244
Howells, Derek, 2239
Howells, Johnny, 2688
Howells, Pete, 832
Howells, Phil, 1881
Howerd, Frankie, 2056, 3289, 3847, 5892
Howes, Andrew, 4122
Howes, Basil, 3824
Howes, Bobby, 649, 1552, 1744-1745, 2285, 2339, 2619, 3204, 3824, 4105, 5957
Howes, Dave, 5534
Howes, Sally Ann, 79, 112, 1066, 2619, 4105, 5782
Howie B., 305, 318, 1478, 2790, 3381, 3721, 4577
Howie Casey And The Seniors, 112, 975, 4220, 5832
Howie, Mitch, 1135
Howland, Beth, 1196
Howland, Stet, 570, 5663
Howlett, Liam, 3867, 4345, 5484
Howlett, Mike, 204, 228, 2198, 4185
Howlett, Steve, 1829
Howlin' Wilf, 2619-2620
Howlin' Wolf, 2620-2621 and passim
Howlin, Olin, 911
Howling At The Moon, 4029
Howson, Pat, 1978
Howton, Lou, 4900
Hoy, Jayni, 1319
Hoy, Steve, 2962
Hoy, Tom, 3410, 3883
Hoyland, Dave, 2598
Hoyland, Mal, 1992
Hoyland, Martin, 4370
Hoyle, Ian, 50
Hoyle, Linda, 84, 2621
HR, 1003, 2327, 4436
Hradistan, 992
HSAS, 2332, 2621, 5420
HSE Records, 508
HTD Records, 556, 4501, 5824
Hu Xi, 5738
Hubba Hubba Records, 2621

Hubbard, Bruce, 4893, 5935
Hubbard, Freddie, 115, 128, 393, 398, 571, 614, 622, 742, 758, 770, 856, 877, 969, 1010, 1059, 1220, 1381, 1465, 1506, 1627, 1757, 1788-1789, 1862, 2016, 2023, 2082, 2094, 2108, 2187, 2268, 2275, 2311, 2373, 2395, 2405, 2445, 2448, 2487, 2538, 2621-2622, 2684, 2795, 2841, 2879, 2963, 3098, 3415, 3504, 3541, 3752, 3772, 3895, 4051, 4081, 4129, 4203, 4483, 4562, 4685, 4858, 4896, 5653, 5778, 5800, 5920
Hubbard, Gregg, 4758
Hubbard, Jerry, 4476
Hubbard, Johnny Ray, 827
Hubbard, Neil, 2257, 2524, 2909, 3057, 3169, 3290, 4686, 5742, 5935
Hubbard, Preston, 1743, 1818, 4579, 5876
Hubbard, Ray Wylie, 2355, 2622, 3322
Hubbell, Raymond, 606, 5997
Hubble, Eddie, 2622, 5923
Hubler, Richard, 4290
Hubley, Georgia, 203, 4944, 5959
Huckle, Roger, 548
Hucklebee, Dorothy, 2112
Hucko, Peanuts, 502, 1049, 1869, 1918, 2623, 4736, 5322, 5923, 6004
Hudd, Roy, 1927, 4748
Huddlestone, Trevor, 3435, 3499
Hudgins, Johnny, 569
Hudson Brothers, 2623, 2858
Hudson, Al, 1453, 2170
Hudson, Barbara, 5568
Hudson, Bob, 553
Hudson, Brian, 3969
Hudson, Curtis, 2603
Hudson, D., 4003
Hudson, David, 983, 4562
Hudson, Doug, 5526-5527
Hudson, Earl, 319, 2327
Hudson, Eric, 358
Hudson, Garth, 358, 1673, 4576
Hudson, George, 630
Hudson, Harry, 3615
Hudson, Ian, 2113, 2625
Hudson, Joe, 2755
Hudson, Johnny, 4281
Hudson, Keith, 111, 533, 670, 1062, 1937, 2623, 4096, 5559
Hudson, Lee, 5577
Hudson, Lord Tim, 2624-2625, 3299
Hudson, Mark, 2623
Hudson, Mick, 5808
Hudson, Paul, 319, 2327
Hudson, Reid, 3525
Hudson, Richard, 2083, 2440, 2625, 5626
Hudson, Rochelle, 4284, 4859
Hudson, Saul, 2313, 4961
Hudson, Will, 550, 569, 1436, 2625
Hudson-Ford, 2625, 5626
Hue And Cry, 281, 2625, 3911
Huerta, Baldemar G., 1873

Hues Corporation, 1978, 2626
Huff, Bob, 1280
Huff, Dann, 2135
Huff, Henry, 1784, 3581
Huff, Leon, 464, 2076, 3967, 3991, 3997, 4002, 5421
Huff, Luther, 2626, 5838
Huffman, Joe, 2072
Hufstetter, Steve, 908, 1906, 1942, 2626
Hug, Armand, 2627
Hugenberger, Mark, 4892
Hugg, Mike, 1046, 1086, 1657, 2627, 3437-3438, 5582
Huggins, Ben, 2072
Huggins, Harley, 104
Huggy Bear, 535, 600, 2627, 5443
Hugham, Bill, 2869
Hughart, Jim, 1076
Hughes, Alex, 2908, 4334
Hughes, Andy, 2336
Hughes, Bill, 3635
Hughes, Billy, 975, 1872
Hughes, Brian, 975, 3585
Hughes, Bruce, 1271
Hughes, Bryan, 439
Hughes, Chris, 62, 675, 1363
Hughes, Chuck, 5941
Hughes, Dave, 1363, 4038
Hughes, David, 832, 2348, 2627-2628, 2645
Hughes, Don, 4701
Hughes, Dusty, 3647
Hughes, Frances, 1792
Hughes, Glenn, 285, 560, 832, 1458, 2174, 2628-2629, 3975, 4219, 5644
Hughes, Harry, 1135
Hughes, Howard, 2626, 3843, 3952
Hughes, J.D., 2250
Hughes, Jimmy, 637, 1393, 2628, 2730
Hughes, Joe 'Guitar', 2629
Hughes, Langston, 2331, 3669, 3691, 3888, 5778, 6089, 6095, 6101
Hughes, Leon, 1138, 3119, 4580
Hughes, Lynn, 5462, 5598
Hughes, Lynne, 1025, 5461
Hughes, Lysbeth, 1248
Hughes, Marjorie, 936
Hughes, Martin, 204
Hughes, Mary Beth, 2257, 4058
Hughes, Maureen, 495
Hughes, Mike, 13, 3259
Hughes, Nick, 4203
Hughes, Patrick C., 2629
Hughes, Randy, 1130, 1229
Hughes, Red, 3253
Hughes, Rita, 2801
Hughes, Sean, 1548, 1861
Hughes, Spike, 131, 500, 964, 973, 2629, 3620, 6054
Hughes, Steve, 3256
Hughes, Ted, 231, 4897
Hughes, Tom, 558, 3156
Hughes, Tony, 4375
Hughes/Thrall, 285, 2628-2629
Hughey, Dan, 2995
Hughey, John, 653, 2629, 2995, 5547
Hughston, Boots, 2585, 5906

Hutch, Willie, 3700
Hutchence, Michael, 2111, 2648, 2706, 3697
Hutchenrider, Clarence, 973, 2648, 5934
Hutcherson, Bobby, 1506, 2076, 2527, 2648-2649, 2672, 2749, 3541, 3772, 4081, 4560, 4663, 4730, 5554, 5840, 5850
Hutcherson, Burt, 411, 5705
Hutcheson, David, 5397
Hutchings, Ashley, 110, 415, 650, 1179, 1618, 1620, 1826-1827, 2422, 2649, 3031-3032, 3519, 3782, 3825, 5583, 5724
Hutchins, Jalil, 5813
Hutchins, Marshall, 4518
Hutchins, Sam, 5312
Hutchins, Steve, 5943
Hutchinson, Charles, 89
Hutchinson, Dolly, 2649, 2869
Hutchinson, Frank, 1708
Hutchinson, Graeme, 2558
Hutchinson, Gregory, 43
Hutchinson, Johnny, 530, 2868
Hutchinson, Leslie 'Hutch', 2649
Hutchinson, Leslie 'Jiver', 2649-2650
Hutchinson, Mick, 1105, 5602
Hutchinson, Nigel, 635
Hutchinson, Sheila, 2171
Hutchinson, Tad, 5966
Hutchinson, Trevor, 4847
Huth, Harold, 5284
Huth, Todd, 4331
Hutson, Leroy, 1340, 2650, 2683, 3884
Hutson, Roy, 2650
Hutt, Allen, 5696
Hutt, Sam, 5696, 6084
Hutter, Lenny, 1916
Hutter, Ralf, 3071
Hutto, J.B., 627, 629, 1014, 1475, 1671, 2571, 2650, 2771, 3244, 3533, 3581, 3594, 3853, 5611, 5854
Hutton, Barbara, 249, 479
Hutton, Betty, 196-197, 261, 509, 1933, 2412, 2651, 3204, 3547, 3649, 4118, 4695
Hutton, Danny, 3740, 5422
Hutton, Ina Ray, 758, 1631, 2625, 2651-2652, 2702
Hutton, Jack, 1169, 3620
Hutton, Joe, 2652, 5431
Hutton, June, 2652, 4238
Hutton, Marion, 2652, 2962, 3315, 3674, 4058
Hutton, Mick, 5315
Hutton, Tim, 3633
Hutton, Will, 2625
Huwe, Anja, 5942
Huws, Owen, 2776
Huxley, Rick, 1098
Huxter, Chris, 273, 3912
Hwang, Jason, 4139
Hyacinthe, Jimmy, 1387
Hyams, Leila, 521
Hyams, Margie, 1848, 2505, 2652, 4861
Hyams, Mark, 2625
Hyatt, John, 5423
Hyatt, Karl, 5545

Hyatt, Susan, 4243
Hyd, Lybuk, 1004
Hyde, Karl, 2032, 5575
Hyde-White, Wilfred, 3859
Hyde-Whyte, Alex, 4218
Hyder, Ken, 2652
Hydra, 2653, 3416, 5475
Hyland, Brian, 1027, 1326, 1806, 2183, 2653
Hylton, Jack, 1027, 1452, 1482, 1961, 2437, 2462, 2653, 2694, 2742, 3201, 4170, 4227, 4748, 5340, 5928, 5961
Hylton, Jeniffer, 772
Hylton, Sheila, 2653-2654, 2733
Hyman, Bernard, 4732
Hyman, Dick, 391, 707, 1243, 1776, 2654, 2956, 3132, 3525, 3923, 3941, 4194, 4655, 4875, 4984, 5389, 5426, 5727, 5766
Hyman, Jeffrey, 4423
Hyman, Jerry, 601
Hyman, Phyllis, 1211-1212, 2654
Hyman, Rob, 2589, 4068
Hyman, Ron, 3139
Hymas, Tony, 446, 4219
Hymer, Warren, 2985
Hynd, Richard, 5348
Hynde, Chrissie, 478, 1071, 1854, 2583, 2706, 2839, 3024, 3758, 4318, 4591, 4641, 4921, 4928, 5562
Hynde, Sheila, 4518
Hynes, Danny, 5740
Hynes, Dave, 778
Hyoung Suk, Kim, 5979
Hype-A-Delics, 2655
Hyper Disc Records, 3872
Hyper Go-Go, 1453, 2655, 3979, 4293
Hyperhead, 2103, 2655, 5570
Hypnotics, (Thee), 1768, 2655
Hypnotist, The, 28, 2265, 2656, 4552-4553
Hypnotone, 2656
Hypocrisy, 2656
Hyskos, 2656-2657
Hyslop, Kenny, 4921, 4967
Hyson, Carl, 1515-1516
Hyson, Dorothy, 1516, 2383, 4932
Hysterix, 2655, 2657
Hytner, Nicholas, 947
Hyts, 2657

I

I Can Get It For You Wholesale, 1358, 2659, 3140, 3636, 4637
I Could Go On Singing, 2035, 2089-2090, 2386, 2659
I Do! I Do!, 2660
I Give My Heart, 225, 929, 1374, 2660, 4488
I Love My Wife, 246, 1165, 2661
I Luv Wight, 1825
I Married An Angel, 346, 1703, 2661-2662, 2728, 4606, 4814
I Mother Earth, 2662, 5642
I Roy, 370, 773, 1183, 1637, 1711, 2317, 2575, 2665-2666,

3006, 3171, 3282, 3648, 3832, 3875, 4139-4140, 4306, 4335-4336, 4489, 4675, 5685
I Want To Get Off, 732-733, 1419, 1869, 2225, 2285, 3452, 3636, 3926-3927, 4154, 4235, 4264, 4565, 5745
I'd Rather Be Right, 2663
I'll Be Your Sweetheart, 2663-2664
I'll Get By, 2664
I'm Getting My Act Together And Taking It On The Road, 2664
I've Gotta Horse, 2665
I, Ludicrous, 2665
I-Rails, 4330
I-Threes, 742, 2292, 2351, 2638, 2665, 2981, 3468, 3470, 3821, 3883, 5934
Iadevaio, John, 5816
Iadevaio, Michael, 5816
Iam, 2666
Ian And Sylvia, 1718, 2666, 2955, 3241, 4122, 4700, 5556-5557, 5611, 6083
Ian And The Zodiacs, 2666
Ian, Janis, 511, 1958, 2666-2667, 3034, 3800, 5293, 5485, 5638, 5785, 6054
Ian, Scott, 201, 3646, 5400
Ibbotson, Jim, 2211, 3959
Ibert, Jacques, 2706
Ibrahim, Abdullah, 475, 630, 712, 1046, 1151, 1670, 2406, 2667, 2938, 3441, 3474, 3499, 3541, 3663, 3731, 4441, 4562, 4871, 5698-5699
Ice, 2667
Ice Records, 2242
Ice, Richard, 878
Ice-T, 163, 524, 560, 640, 1288, 1350, 1462, 1766, 1797, 2064, 2526, 2608, 2668-2669, 2928, 3259, 3299, 3617, 4018, 4128, 4340, 4433, 4939, 4963, 5424, 5585, 5612, 5771, 6054
Iceberg Records, 4767
Icebreaker, 187, 2669
Icehouse, 989, 1017, 2580, 2589, 2669-2670
Ichiban, 179, 186, 296, 487, 622, 783, 967, 1053, 1118, 1166, 1351, 1422-1423, 1454, 1497, 1567, 1620, 2081, 2609, 2670, 2851-2852, 2898, 2994, 3089, 3182, 3369, 3529, 3536, 3538, 3543, 3626, 3889, 4160, 4211, 4475, 4521, 4674, 4787, 5305, 5405, 5512, 5766, 5795
Ichiban Records, 1166, 1454, 3538, 4211
Icho Candy, 915, 2670, 2762, 4096
Icicle Works, 454, 2671, 3243, 3595
Icon, 2671 and passim
ID Records, 2240, 2303
Ideals, 2671-2672
Ides Of March, 2672, 5383
Idha, 349, 2672, 4540
Idle Cure, 2672
Idle On Parade, 2488, 2672, 3926-3927

Idle Race, 606, 2137, 2673, 3189, 3373, 3803, 3819, 4872, 5321
Idle, Eric, 2697, 4703
Idol, Billy, 464, 2115, 2601, 2673-2674, 3303, 6054
Idren, 1417
If, 2674
If You Feel Like Singing, 2089, 2674
If?, 2674
Ifang Bondi, 2675
Ifield, Frank, 1187, 1410, 2035, 2675, 4125, 5847
Iggy Pop, 147, 163, 345, 686, 1159, 1440, 1518, 1563, 1783, 1816, 2050, 2126, 2283, 2451, 2515, 2675-2676, 3134, 3159, 3309, 3364, 4017, 4443, 4591, 4722, 4891, 5365, 5462, 5520, 5642, 5653, 5714-5715, 6054
Iglauer, Bruce, 139, 1173, 2530, 2668, 3026, 3263, 3888, 4715
Iglesias, Enrique, 2676-2677
Iglesias, Julio, 108, 195, 1401, 2676-2677, 3071, 3081, 3179, 3900, 6054, 6129
Ignorance, 2677 and passim
Ignorant, Steve, 1203, 1278
Igoe, Kim, 58
Igoe, Sonny, 1793
Iguana Foundation, 1987
Iguana Records, 3909
Iidesuka, Ikiteitemo, 3870
Iijima, Yoshiaki, 4122
Ikeda, Thomas, 3860
Ikettes, 230, 240, 710, 2581, 2677-2678, 3563
Ilda, Lewis, 2968
Iliffe, Steve, 4251
Ill (Featuring Al Skratch), 2678
Illegal, 2678
Illegal Substance, 2678
Illegitimate Jug Band, 3567, 3958
Illinois Speed Press, 2305, 2678, 4268
Illkid Records, 2816
Illman, Margaret, 4467
Illsley, John, 1537
Illusion, 2678
Illusion Of Safety, 741
Ilson, Carol, 4337
IM Records, 3702
Imaginary Records, 56, 4481
Imagination, 2678-2679 and passim
Imaginations, 561, 2023, 2217, 2679, 6105
Imagine, 2679-2680 and passim
Imagine (stage musical), 2679
Imagine Records, 1378, 4008
Imago Records, 1161, 1746, 3338
Imbimbo, Tony, 3956
Imbres, Victor, 111
Imbrie, Liz, 2522
Imi, Toni, 4969
Imlach, Hamish, 736, 2680, 3494, 6054
Immaculate Fools, 2681

Immature, 2681
Immediate Records, 364, 889, 1933, 2681, 3198, 4100, 5704
Immerwahr, Steve, 1148
Impact Records, 2072, 2527, 4744
Impalas, 2681, 2822
Impelliteri, Chris, 111, 2681
Imperial Bodyguard Band, 94
Imperial Drag, 2808
Imperial Records, 2682 and *passim*
Imperial Seven, 2878
Imperial Teen, 1830, 2682, 3898, 5638
Imposter, 1244, 2130, 3481, 5445
Impressions, 2683 and *passim*
Imps, 2684, 3517, 3714
Impulse! Records, 2684 and *passim*
In Brackets, 3071
In Crowd, 2684
In Crowd (reggae), 2684
In Dahomey, 2685, 5837
In Tua Nua, 2687, 5721
In-Be-Tweens, 2688
Inabnett, Marvin, 1994
Inbreds, 2688
Inca Records, 4031, 4646
Incantation, 167, 2688-2689
Incognito, 419, 1536, 1573, 2689, 2906, 3089, 3240, 5585
Incorvaia, Richie, 122
Incredible Bongo Band, 1770
Incredible String Band, 423, 695, 1125, 1139, 1337, 1616, 1729, 1732, 1840, 1975, 2220, 2508, 2680, 2689, 3561, 4110, 4354, 4362, 4725, 5352, 5364, 5861, 5916, 6125
Incredibles, 2690
Incubus Succubus, 2690
Incus Records, 4092, 4135
Ind, Peter, 826, 976, 1306, 2541, 2690, 3802, 5317, 5507
Independents, 2690 and *passim*
Indigo Girls, 750, 1857, 2350, 2604, 2690-2691, 3205, 3245
Indigo Records, 3544, 4577, 5974
Indochina Records, 1715
Indolent Records, 1644, 4944, 4964
Indus Creed, 4896
Industrial Music, 2691 and *passim*
Inez, Mike, 4961
Infante, Frank, 598
Infante, Pedro, 471
Infascelli, Silvia, 2692-2693
Infectious Grooves, 2692
Infinite Wheel, 2692
Infiniti, 271
Infinity Project, The, 1592, 1617, 2692-2693, 5446
Infonet Records, 362, 2693
Ingalls, Sam, 1888
Ingam, Michael, 2807
Ingber, Elliot, 2018
Ingels, Marty, 2885
Ingemansson, Hans, 1289
Ingersoll, Charles, 5966
Ingeveld, Victor, 1008

Ingham, Barrie, 2807
Ingham, Beryl, 1977
Ingham, Keith, 128, 2693, 3200, 3840, 4988, 6003
Ingle, Red, 2693, 2885, 5753
Ingle, Steve, 1288
Ingleson, Kevin, 4452
Inglez, Roberto, 1217
Inglis, Doug, 2179
Ingmann, Jorgen, 3317
Ingo, Gus, 3598
Ingoldsby, Dennis, 1782, 2107
Ingraham, Roy, 5453
Ingram, Aaron, 4747
Ingram, Adrian, 3756, 6065
Ingram, Ashley, 2678
Ingram, B.J., 3542
Ingram, Bobby, 3734
Ingram, James, 283, 943, 3209, 3563, 4545, 4622, 4641, 4717, 5403, 5588
Ingram, John, 1064, 2679
Ingram, Luther, 368, 2694, 5733
Ingram, Neville, 5641
Ingram, Philip, 4171
Ingram, Raphael, 1917
Ingram, Rex, 876-877
Ingram, Ripley, 1917
Ingram, Wally, 5440
Ingrams, Ashley, 1490
Ingrams, Bobby, 770
Injeti, Chin, 408, 3389
Ink Spots, 72, 340, 475, 765, 921, 933, 1023, 1293, 1326, 1573, 1909, 1912, 1915, 1998, 2189, 2257, 2694-2695, 2825, 2960, 3039, 3147, 3441, 3560, 3593, 4061, 4090, 4263, 4949
Inky Blacknuss, 2695, 4712
Inman, Autry, 2695
Inmates, 204, 225, 601, 1180, 2695, 2721, 3174, 3277, 4152, 4341, 4343, 4468, 4770, 5640
Inmon, John, 3322
Inner Circle, 534, 1081, 1264, 1565, 2372, 2460, 2696, 2718, 2765, 3676, 4595, 4987, 5393, 5749, 5932
Inner City, 2696
Inner City Posse, 2080, 2699
Inner City Unit, 2697
Inner Sanctum, 1340, 2697, 4957, 5555
Innerzone Orchestra, 3721
Innes, Andrew, 4329, 4515
Innes, Brian, 5331
Innes, Dick, Jnr., 318
Innes, George, 3710, 5972
Innes, Neil, 661, 2293, 2697-2698, 2911, 3578, 4522, 4703, 4881, 5923
Innis, Dave, 4509
Innis, Louis, 2752, 3173
Innocence, 2698
Innocence (techno), 2698
Innocents, 281, 1051, 1773, 2001, 2085, 2698, 4122, 5805, 5974
Inoue, Tetsuo, 2698
Inoue, Yosui, 6054
Inoura, Hideo, 5571
Insane Clown Posse, 2699
Insect Trust, 2699, 3762

Inside U.S.A., 2699-2700
Inspiral Carpets, 614, 2700, 3237, 3257, 3844, 3855, 4008, 4341, 4481, 4576, 5354
Inspirational Choir, 68, 2280
Inspirations, 71, 109, 403, 1113-1114, 1662, 2071, 2407, 2609, 2714, 2845, 3087, 3133, 3303, 4251, 4482, 4705, 4977, 5280, 5834, 6003
Instant Action Jug Band, 1119, 1253, 3562, 3621
Instant Funk, 2700
Instant Records, 358, 2980
Instigators, 2700-2701 and *passim*
Instinct Records, 3722
Instone, Anthony, 3383
Inta Warriors, 2296
Intangible Records, 4138
Intellect, 663, 832, 1518, 1836, 2065, 2325, 2554, 4281, 4332, 4347, 4578
Intelligent Hoodlum, 2701, 3876
Inter 1 Records, 4306
Intermezzo, 3461, 3727, 4181, 4462
Internal Records, 2701, 4056
International Artists Records, 1101, 2701
International Foot Language, 2702
International Rude Boys, 1562
International Stussy Tribe Force, 4640
International Submarine Band, 1491, 2452, 2702, 4146, 5506
International Sweethearts Of Rhythm, 703, 843, 1072, 1408, 1416, 1659, 2652, 2702-2703, 4444
International Youth Band, 781, 1333, 2196, 2300, 4655
Interscope Records, 251, 573, 850, 1112, 1994, 4294, 5349, 5453, 5690
Into Another, 2703 and *passim*
Into Paradise, 2009, 2703
Into The Woods, 893, 2704, 3586, 4151, 4209
Intrigue, 2704
Intrinsic, 2704
Intruders, 2705 and *passim*
Intveld, James, 2705
Investigators, 2705 and *passim*
Invincibles, 2705, 4140
Invisibl Skratch Piklz, 1615
Invisible Girls, 1107, 2706, 3847, 4185, 4864
Invisible Man's Band, 2706
Invitation To The Dance, 1024, 1525, 2706, 2960
INXS, 169, 310, 1157, 2111, 2648, 2706, 3271, 3632, 3697, 3725, 3792, 4439, 4735, 4969, 5924, 6054
Ioan, Gareth, 2776
Iommi, Jimmy, 4550
Iommi, Tony, 559, 1507, 2628, 2707, 2819, 4126, 4378
Iona, 2707
Iona And Andy, 2707
Iovine, Jimmy, 1450, 1613,

2707, 3304, 3344, 4042, 4703, 4815, 4921
Iovino, Frank, 1915, 3046
IPG Records, 5625
IQ, 1946, 2707-2708, 3536, 4259
IQ Procedure, 2708, 3536
Irakere, 1324, 1842, 2380, 3935, 4610
Irby, Jerry, 2708
Ireland, Sam, 1517
Irene, 2708-2709
Irewolede Denge, 2910
Irie, Clement, 369, 1880, 1944, 3611
Irie, Henkel, 1880
Irie, Penny, 1525
Irie, Welton, 3305, 4431, 4548-4549, 4749, 5319, 5767
Iris, Donnie, 2709, 2760
Iris, Donnie, And The Cruisers, 2709
Irma La Douce, 110, 1917, 2227, 2709, 2893, 3636, 3779, 5527
Irmler, Joachim, 1862
Iron Butterfly, 268, 272, 517, 624, 657, 927, 1775, 2530, 2688, 2702, 2709-2710, 3533, 3902, 4246, 4435, 6129
Iron Curtain, 405, 930, 2711, 3527, 3944
Iron Eagle, 80, 3001
Iron Fist, 2478, 2710, 3812, 5295
Iron Lion, 5884
Iron Maiden, 29, 36, 145, 250, 288, 322, 390, 475, 601, 652, 726, 747, 991, 1141, 1294, 1328, 1369, 1391, 1504, 1514, 1589, 1732, 1782, 1809, 1860, 2456, 2467, 2710-2711, 2991-2993, 3257, 3282, 3476, 3778, 3879, 3922, 4076, 4237, 4306, 4689, 4731, 4755, 4759, 4828, 4937, 5370, 5430, 5468, 5494, 5515, 5737, 5793, 5896, 5903, 6054
Iron Man, The, 2712, 4858, 5379, 5812
Ironhorse, 316, 2712
Ironing Board Sam, 2712
Irons, Jack, 4175, 4463
Irons, Jeremy, 946, 2181, 3256, 3864, 5746
Irvin, James, 2058, 2342
Irvin, Jeremy, 4511
Irvin, Smitty, 2402
Irvine, Andy, 706, 1616, 2100, 2232, 2378, 2712-2713, 3394, 4001, 4155-4156, 4261, 4653
Irvine, Bruce, 5552
Irvine, Doug, 3462
Irvine, Stephen, 1159
Irvine, Weldon, 792, 2713
Irving Davies, Belita, 2706
Irving, Amy, 5956
Irving, Bill, 1969-1970
Irving, Brian, 553
Irving, Clifford, 3952
Irving, David, 494, 4713
Irving, Don, 439, 3635
Irving, Ethel, 1253
Irving, G., 3137, 6058
Irving, George S, 2119
Irving, Henry, 295, 2126
Irving, Kevin, 1137

Jones, Nasir, 3876
Jones, Neal, 2880
Jones, Neil, 159, 1827
Jones, Nic, 465, 831, 1150, 1984, 2354-2355, 2649, 2881, 4185, 4653-4654, 5279, 5534, 5935
Jones, Nick, 973, 2469, 3442
Jones, Nigel Maslyn, 2880
Jones, Norman, 2115
Jones, Norris, 118, 4940
Jones, Nyles, 2310, 2881
Jones, O.P., 2793
Jones, Oliver, 1662, 2487, 2875, 2881, 3212, 4231, 4673, 5343
Jones, Ollie, 588, 1326, 4442
Jones, Palmer, 2266
Jones, Paul, 25, 29, 240, 252, 401, 622, 695, 797, 966, 988, 1095-1096, 1347, 1456, 1474, 1695, 1802, 2072, 2160, 2410, 2458, 2828, 2878, 2881-2882, 2897, 3020, 3036, 3065, 3164-3165, 3284, 3437, 3548, 3610, 3625, 3667, 3706, 4100, 4252, 4290, 4342, 4454, 5430, 5534, 5701, 5746, 5802
Jones, Pearl, 855, 2167, 2884, 4175-4176
Jones, Peggy, 671, 4948
Jones, Percy, 712, 3279
Jones, Peter, 2238, 3342, 3538, 4314, 6070
Jones, Phalin, 371
Jones, Phil, 84, 1271, 1363, 1811, 3519
Jones, Philly Joe, 71, 398, 481, 489, 619, 1170, 1222, 1344, 1368, 1414, 1670, 1789, 1862, 2090, 2095, 2250, 2288, 2486, 2882, 3373, 3478, 3504, 3519, 3667, 3792, 3848, 4128, 4374, 4475, 4634, 5530, 5769, 5786, 5850
Jones, Pim, 2541
Jones, Puma, 562
Jones, Quincy, 239, 283, 329, 380, 406, 490, 565, 575, 622, 690, 909, 1124, 1416, 1624, 1647, 1700, 1813, 1850, 1883, 2078, 2219, 2302, 2355, 2371, 2487, 2621, 2693-2694, 2746-2747, 2750, 2770, 2842, 2882-2883, 3078, 3118, 3149, 3177, 3212, 3261, 3270, 3373, 3461, 3502, 3525, 3637, 3690, 3895, 3910, 3978, 4016, 4156, 4204, 4239, 4376, 4420, 4423, 4534, 4537, 4656, 4673-4674, 4695, 4770, 4782, 4818, 4879, 4926-4927, 4930, 5283, 5301, 5588, 5610, 5717, 5915, 6056
Jones, Ramona, 766, 2874, 5470
Jones, Randy, 794, 3131, 3528, 5644
Jones, Ray, 1360, 2655, 2776, 2978, 3074, 3543, 4865
Jones, Rena, 1012
Jones, Reunald, 2883, 5747
Jones, Richard, 534, 547, 1127, 1437, 1620, 2704, 2750, 2883-2884, 3817, 4035, 4577, 5450
Jones, Richard M., 534, 547, 1437, 1620, 2750, 2883-2884, 4035, 4577

Jones, Richie, 1463
Jones, Rick, 4767
Jones, Rickie Lee, 751-752, 757, 1057, 1311, 1615, 2884, 3215, 3263, 3323, 3720, 3991, 4038, 4054, 5450, 5648
Jones, Rob, 3438, 5667, 5906
Jones, Robert, 684, 827, 1196, 2310, 2862, 2878, 2881, 6037
Jones, Robert Elliott, 2878
Jones, Robert L., 2310, 2881
Jones, Robin, 873, 4593
Jones, Rocky, 1558, 3053
Jones, Rodney, 2884
Jones, Ron, 1404, 1925, 3637, 3756
Jones, Russell, 3644, 4239
Jones, Rusty, 5565
Jones, Ruth, 5431, 5716
Jones, Salena, 2622, 2884
Jones, Sam, 71, 740, 778, 813, 2539, 2884, 2892, 3699, 4051, 5359
Jones, Sandie, 1551
Jones, Sandra, 562
Jones, Shay, 1457
Jones, Sheila, 2943
Jones, Shirley, 946-947, 983-984, 1014, 1034, 1219, 1604, 2700, 2866, 2885, 3394, 3396, 3852-3853, 4025-4026, 4149, 5869, 6130
Jones, Shiva, 4389
Jones, Sianed, 3972
Jones, Simeon, 2889
Jones, Simon, 13, 2905, 5637
Jones, Slick, 2885
Jones, Sonia, 2463
Jones, Sonny, 2622
Jones, Sophie, 1631
Jones, Spike, 727, 2885, 4695, 4769, 4859, 5495, 5847, 6056
Jones, Spud, 5462
Jones, Stacy, 3205, 5637
Jones, Stephen, 311, 881, 4284, 5897, 6120, 6126
Jones, Steve, 29, 291, 598, 695, 1043-1044, 1095, 1662, 1951, 2263, 2314, 2508, 2676, 2886, 3548, 3612, 4076, 4303, 4346, 4829, 5339, 5430, 5641
Jones, Taree, 241
Jones, Teren Delvon, 1468
Jones, Terry, 4271, 4674
Jones, Thad, 126, 203, 630, 992, 1117, 1243, 1572, 2301, 2331-2332, 2869-2870, 2874, 2886, 3018, 3223, 3637, 3691, 3709, 3785, 3940, 3978, 4635, 5390, 5770
Jones, Thymme, 741
Jones, Tim, 3769
Jones, Tom (vocalist), 2886-2887 and *passim*
Jones, Tom (lyricist), 2888
Jones, Tomas Squip, 452
Jones, Tommy Lee, 3371, 3567
Jones, Trefor, 520, 2167
Jones, Treolo, 5639
Jones, Trevor, 1008, 2763, 3512
Jones, Tutu, 2888
Jones, Valerie, 2866
Jones, Vince, 383, 1786, 2888, 3048, 3539

Jones, Virginia, 2227
Jones, Vivian, 12, 2762, 2888
Jones, Willie, 114, 5856
Jones, Willy, 4450
Jones, Wizz, 65, 2889, 3290, 3562
Jones-Smith Inc., 4984, 5976
Joneses, 2872, 2889
Jonsson, Tommy, 1693
Jonutz, Jerry, 1156
Jonutz, Larry, 1156
Jonzun, Michael, 5459
Jook, 641, 2833, 2855, 2883, 2889, 4626
Joolz, 1107, 4511
Joos, Herbert, 2890
Joplin, Janis, 18, 20, 449, 463, 497, 522, 543, 722, 1001, 1037, 1087, 1153, 1188, 1254, 1268, 1407, 1446, 1746, 2015, 2249, 2297, 2781, 2890-2891, 2911, 2953, 3078, 3583, 3656, 3753, 4166, 4174, 4216, 4291, 4407, 4409, 4653, 4833, 4938, 5301, 5454, 5916, 6056
Joplin, Scott, 17, 96, 2654, 2891, 4136, 4230, 4542, 6057
Jordan, Al, 3743
Jordan, Brad, 2131, 4766
Jordan, Charley, 2891, 5758
Jordan, Clay, 1297
Jordan, Clifford, 614, 1105, 1220, 2155, 2405, 2528, 2891-2892, 3243, 3253, 4156, 4626, 5295, 5442, 5693, 5702
Jordan, Cyril, 1924
Jordan, Danny, 1386, 1495
Jordan, Dave, 3387
Jordan, David, 3964
Jordan, Duke, 1030, 2892, 2894, 3722, 4170, 4475
Jordan, Fred, 2892
Jordan, Greg, 4649
Jordan, Jack, 506, 1005, 1843, 4400
Jordan, Jack, Jnr., 506
Jordan, James, 2895, 3243, 4049
Jordan, Jimmy, 4675
Jordan, John, 854, 1517, 1636, 1998, 2894
Jordan, Jojo, 5464
Jordan, Julie, 946-947
Jordan, Kent, 3474
Jordan, Kidd, 2200
Jordan, Louis, 19, 105, 127, 209, 374, 622, 700, 768-769, 826, 1246, 1422, 1517, 1573, 1712, 1916, 2174, 2414, 2457, 2744, 2850, 2854, 2892-2894, 3004, 3073, 3339, 3641, 3781, 3787, 3895, 4362, 4388, 4583, 4586, 4761, 4925, 5744, 6057
Jordan, Luke, 2894
Jordan, Marabeth, 1762
Jordan, Michael, 1059
Jordan, Montell, 183, 2894
Jordan, Neil, 1249
Jordan, Randy, 2042
Jordan, Ronny, 1063, 1571, 2894
Jordan, Sheila, 2405, 2892, 2894, 3085, 3321, 3803, 3843, 4292, 4696, 5418, 5461, 5687
Jordan, Stanley, 614, 2895, 4492

Jordan, Steve, 1571, 1949, 2895, 2983, 5318
Jordan, Taft, 806, 1602, 2895, 5609, 5744
Jordan, Tommy, 1495, 2110
Jordan, William, 981
Jordanaires, 60, 174, 587, 774, 1298, 1300, 1652, 1973, 2334, 2358, 2616, 2895-2896, 2908, 2963, 3125, 3290, 3370, 3565, 3755, 4156, 4310, 5371, 5547, 5754
Jordon, Christian, 2054
Jordu, Roach, 770
Jorge, Ben, 472, 2145
Jorge, Reinaldo, 3233, 4032
Jorgenson, John, 1491, 5728
Jorio, Fred, 1716, 6006
Jormin, Christian, 1480
Jormin, Rikard, 1693
Jorrín, Enrique, 1833, 3313, 4121
Jory, Sarah, 1206, 2896
Jory, Victor, 2167
Josch, Friedemann, 1546
José José, 2896 and *passim*
José, Alvaro, 243
Josef K, 1750, 1901, 2336, 2896-2897, 4295, 5492, 5965
Josefus, 2897
Joseph And The Amazing Technicolor Dreamcoat, 983, 993, 1212, 1591, 2801, 2897-2898, 3284-3285, 3638, 4073, 4524-4525, 4772, 5690, 5881
Joseph, Chuck, 1565
Joseph, Delroy, 3090
Joseph, Donovan, 2898, 4772, 5441
Joseph, Edmund, 5948
Joseph, Felix, 558
Joseph, George, 740, 2035, 3015, 4316
Joseph, Hugh, 2185, 2708
Joseph, John, 1298
Joseph, Julian, 2898
Joseph, Lee, 2010, 5950
Joseph, Marc, 1884
Joseph, Margie, 1460, 2898
Joseph, Martyn, 2898-2899
Joseph, Nerious, 929, 1856, 2166, 2637, 2701, 2899, 3195, 5338
Joseph, Patrick, 1049
Joseph, Richard, 1214
Josephs, Don, 5844
Josephs, Wilfred, 2899
Josephson, Barney, 2557
Josephson, Nancy, 818
Joshi, Pandit Bhimsen, 3886
Joshua, 2899 and *passim*
Josi, Christian, 130, 2899, 5458
Josie Records, 880, 981, 1019, 1065, 3046
Joslyn, Allyn, 4886
Jost, Ekkehard, 5310, 6101
Jostyn, Mindy, 2589, 2900
Jouannest, Gérard, 2263
Joubert, Andre, 3260
Jouer, Gioca, 557
Jourard, Jeff, 3806
Jourgenson, Al, 3692, 3697, 4513
Journey, 2900-2901 and *passim*
Journey Through The Past,

2901, 4701, 5978-5979, 6087
Journey Within, 1026, 3286
Journeymen, 1546, 1575, 1727, 1747, 2344, 2468, 2901-2902, 3427, 3586, 4146, 4223-4224, 4653, 5775
Jovanotti, 1380
Jovet, Roger, 4261
Joy, 2902
Joy And Jane, 3542, 4091
Joy Division, 284, 448, 700, 1134, 1295, 1491, 1820-1821, 2026, 2283, 2379, 2384, 2902, 2993, 3101, 3347, 3725, 3913, 3918-3919, 4180, 4291, 4343, 4403, 4512, 5332, 5337, 5392, 5444, 5579, 5627, 5712, 5979, 6047, 6057, 6066
Joy Of Cooking, 2903
Joy Records, 372, 2902-2903, 3562, 4640
Joy, Eddie, 5748
Joy, Gale, 506
Joy, Jimmy, 1411, 2903, 4101
Joy, Marjorie, 1253
Joy, Ruth, 2903, 3082
Joyce Records, 1291
Joyce, 2903-2904
Joyce, Archibald, 2904
Joyce, Chris, 1660, 4128, 4249, 4923, 5667
Joyce, Don, 3891
Joyce, Ed, 4036
Joyce, Heather, 2281
Joyce, Jackie, 3818
Joyce, James, 1201, 2283
Joyce, John, 5626
Joyce, Leroy, 1916
Joyce, Mike, 81, 860, 3605, 3797, 4358
Joyce, Miranda, 466
Joyce, Teddy, 485, 1065
Joyce, Yootha, 1895
Joye, Col, 2904
Joyner, Frank, 5695
Joyous Noise, 2904
Joyrider, 2905
Joystrings, 2905, 4488
Jozefowicz, Janusz, 3647
JPJ Quartet, 2749, 2842, 2869, 4183
JSD Band, 1917, 2905
JSP Records, 821, 4100, 4932
Ju Ju Hounds, 2314
Ju Ju Space Jazz, 2905, 3515
Juan Trip, 2905
Juan, Don, 64, 1582, 1875, 2103, 2117, 2929, 3728
Juan, Olga San, 617, 4105
Juanita, Donna, 357
Jubilee, 2906
Jubilee Hillbillies, 5893
Jubilee Kings, 982
Jubilee Records, 1920, 1990, 2399, 2405, 4412
Judas Jump, 160, 2906
Judas Priest, 50, 197, 560, 1369, 1805, 1891, 2122, 2173-2174, 2456, 2467, 2476, 2710-2711, 2832, 2906-2907, 2991, 3257, 3276, 3345, 3412, 3422, 3450, 3476, 3879, 3948, 4011, 4076, 4092, 4319, 4398, 4755, 4792-4793, 4909, 4937, 5286, 5580,

5610, 5712, 5781, 5896, 6057
Judd, Cledus 'T', (No Relation), 2907
Judd, Naomi, 2907-2908, 5938, 6057
Judd, Nick, 277, 2017
Judd, Phil, 1759
Judds, 2615, 2907-2908, 2970, 3999, 4002, 4073, 4086, 4495, 4710, 5938, 6057, 6092
Judels, Charles, 1544
Judge Dread, 2908-2909, 4334, 5509
Judge Jules, 1123, 2909
Judge, Alan, 1739
Judge, Buddy, 1835
Judge, Dick, 3446
Judge-Smith, Chris, 5602
Judkins, Mike, 70
Judson, Edward C., 2450
Judy And Johnny Band, 3255
Judy Jack And The Beanstalks, 680
Jug Stompers, 918-919, 1958, 3224, 3921, 5607
Juggernaut, 2909 and passim
Juggs, 5583
Juhos, Fred, 2077
Juiceful Records, 2655
Juicy Groove, 657
Juicy Lucy, 692, 1517, 1539, 2200, 2909-2910, 3708, 3780, 4727, 5332, 5636
Juille, Don, 738
Juju, 2910 and passim
Juke Box Jury, 400, 2077, 2560, 2910, 3453, 4198, 4245
Juke Boy, 659, 2910
Jukebox Records, 2937, 4690
Jules And The Polar Bears, 3518, 4860
Jules, John, 5574
Julia, Raul, 3187, 3431, 3952, 5549
Julian, Don, 3131
Julian, Ivan, 2475
Julian, Jo, 492
Juluka, 1121, 2910
July, 2910-2911
Jumbo, 38, 178, 480, 491-492, 539, 1427-1428, 1658, 1691, 1705, 2205, 2309, 2911, 4253, 4260, 4606, 4650, 4828, 5692, 5802, 5922, 6102
Jumbo (film musical), 2911
Jumonville, Jerry, 4399
Jump 'N The Saddle Band, 2911
Jump Street Records, 5568
Jump, Joe Joe, 3365, 5631
Jump, Wally, Jnr., 1608-1609
Jumpin' The Gunn, 2911
Jumpleads, 2911
June Brides, 2912, 5624
June, Ray, 1258, 2054, 2260
Jungle, 2912 and passim
Jungle Book, The, 469, 1545, 1547, 2412, 2512, 2912, 4328-1329, 4676, 4876
Jungle Brothers, 31, 438, 561, 1052, 1123, 1908, 2054, 2108, 2636, 2685, 2912, 3134, 3341, 3511, 3721, 3883, 4303, 4349, 5591
Jungle Milk, 517
Jungr And Parker, 708, 2281,

2912-2913
Jungr, Barb, 2281
Junior, 2913 and passim
Junior Boy's Own Records, 2913
Junior Cat, 3945
Junior Demus, 1375, 3945, 4494
Junior MAFIA, 1367, 2913, 3244
Junior Melody, 852
Junior Olympia Brass Band, 3910
Junior's Eyes, 2913-2914
Junior, Bobby, 1098, 1502, 2566, 5799
Junior, Byles, 863, 2138, 2407, 2575, 2588, 4200, 4438, 4489, 4514, 4595
Junior, Detroit, 1496, 3013
Junior, Guitar, 757, 2351, 3470, 4038
Junior, Marvin, 1473-1474, 1808
Junkhouse, 1865
Junkyard, 521, 545, 554, 1843, 2265, 2417, 2914, 3697, 4367, 5793
Junkyard Angels, 2417
Juno Reactor, 616, 2914, 3318, 3979
Jupiter, Donnie, 5545
Jupp Band, 1395
Jupp, Mickey, 2908, 2914, 3181, 3255, 3346
Jupp, Mike, 84
Jupp, Pete, 1580, 4731
Jurgens, Curt, 5426
Jurgens, Dick, 2615, 2914-2915, 3781, 4480, 5736
Jürgens, Udo, 2915
Juris, Vic, 2332, 3109, 3573
Jurmann, Walter, 2935
Jury, 2915
Juskiewicz, Krzysztof Henryk, 4952
Just A Gigolo, 686-687, 1520, 2915, 4329, 5365
Just Four Men, 1358, 1992, 5880
Just For Fun, 648, 1234, 1336, 1572, 2875, 2915, 3958, 5438, 5622, 5648
Just Ice, 2916, 4376, 5591
Just Records, 46, 198, 608, 714, 1396, 1762, 1977, 2069, 2511, 2520, 2766, 2950, 3034, 3334, 3423, 3494, 3634, 3768, 3988, 4730, 4821, 5543, 5578, 5734
Just Us, 2916
Justice Records, 483, 2114, 2813
Justice, Dick, 2894
Justice, Jimmy, 720, 2916, 3325
Justified Ancients Of Mu Mu, 1633, 2916, 3042, 3319, 5441, 5483
Justin Time Records, 777
Justin, Sidney, 4841
Justis, Bill, 1515, 1581, 2917, 4370, 4526, 5621
Jústiz, Pedro 'Peruchín', 3779
Justman, Seth, 2110
Justo, Rodney, 271
Justus, Vern, 4187
Jutta, 726, 2541, 3467, 5994
JX, 2585, 2917

K

K Klass, 1453, 1693, 1847, 2843, 2919, 4442, 5276
K Sridhar And K Shivakumar, 2919
K-9 Posse, 2919
K-Doe, Ernie, 358, 2919, 3693, 4138, 5478
K-Klass, 4037, 4138
K-Passa, 2920
K-Solo, 1560, 1770, 2920, 4472, 4593
K-Tel Records, 1561, 2550, 2920, 2963, 3356
K., Leila, 947, 1354, 1357, 2920, 5349
K., Paul, 2834, 2920-2921
K7, 2921, 3605, 4366, 5459
Ka-Spel, Edward, 3182, 4954
Kaa, James, 1313
Kaapana, Ledward, 2546
Kaas, Patricia, 2921, 4423
Kaasinen, Sari, 5615
Kabak, Milton, 4328
Kabaka International Guitar Band, 4060
Kabaka, Godwin, 4060
Kabaka, Remi, 98, 306
Kaballero, Karlos, 1514
Kabaret Noir Records, 281
Kabasele, Joseph, 1511, 2927
Kabes, Jiri, 4262
Kabibble, Ish, 3091, 6036
Kabuki, 281, 2587, 2939, 4099, 5947
Kabulie, Moses, 2921
Kadison, Joshua, 2921
Kador, Ernest, Jnr., 2919
Kadovitz, Jerry, 1892
Kaeding, Rudi, 1845
Kaempfert, Bert, 2329, 2542, 2921-2922, 3493, 3513, 3933, 4873
Kaffinette, Dave, 4435
Kagan, Harvey, 4718, 4938
Kagan, Peter, 644
Kagan, Shel, 4315
Kagel, Mauricio, 3892
Kahal, Irving, 1824, 4649
Kahal, Lief, 4767
Kahal, Solomon, 5853
Kahala, Tomomi, 3059
Kahane, Rob, 850
Kahleel, Kurtis, 3452
Kahn, Gus, 103, 782, 1587, 1951, 2035, 2270, 2596, 2922, 2935, 3054, 3885, 4046, 4769, 5350, 5805, 5814, 5915, 5964
Kahn, John, 2086, 2724, 2923, 3835, 4027, 4753
Kahn, Lewis, 4559
Kahn, Madeline, 266, 4041
Kahn, Norman, 2924
Kahn, Peter, 2724
Kahn, Roger Wolfe, 35, 505, 843, 881, 2544, 2923, 3019, 3124, 3250, 4775, 5631
Kahn, Si, 1897, 2923-2924, 2949, 3559, 6057
Kahn, Steve, 1018, 1241
Kahn, Tiny, 1534, 2924, 3145
Kahne, David, 1908
Kai, Takayuki, 1690

Kerr, Gordon, 678
Kerr, Janet, 4943
Kerr, Jean, 2192
Kerr, Jeremy, 25
Kerr, Jim, 1718, 4042, 4318, 4921-4922
Kerr, Nancy, 971-972
Kerr, Patrick, 4454
Kerr, Richard, 2814, 4259
Kerr, Sandra, 231, 333, 971, 3595, 4811, 4943, 5746, 6030
Kerr, Stuart, 2036, 3335, 5347
Kerr, Tim, 521, 1823, 2144, 2543, 3055, 4412, 4445
Kerr, Walter, 4045
Kerridge, Roland Vaughan, 4452, 4487
Kerrison, John, 1769
Kerryson, Paul, 4099, 4549
Kersh, David, 2977
Kerschenbaum, Howard, 2790
Kersey, Jim, 513, 2219
Kersey, Kenny, 2792
Kersey, Paul, 2637
Kersey, Ron, 4752, 5489
Kershaw, Andy, 4018, 4028, 4054, 4225, 4625, 5803
Kershaw, Doug, 710, 1634, 2977-2978, 3609, 3676, 5784, 5987, 6130
Kershaw, Emma, 4341
Kershaw, Liz, 2825, 3304
Kershaw, Nik, 2435, 2455, 2977, 5553
Kershaw, Pee Wee, 611
Kershaw, Sammy, 2099, 2978, 4116
Kershenbaum, David, 1022
Kerslake, Lee, 2180, 4071, 5455, 5586
Kert, Larry, 4416, 5772
Kesey, Ken, 4353
Kessel, Barney, 347, 805, 817, 865, 925, 1682, 2076, 2245, 2258, 2427, 2507, 2716, 2779, 2794, 2978-2979, 3303, 3327, 3356, 3471, 3998, 4500, 4554, 4854, 5317, 5620, 5684
Kesselman, Wendy, 4608
Kessinger Brothers, 2979
Kessinger, Clark, 2979
Kessler, Kent, 4697
Kessler, Woody, 3508
Kestenbaum, Denis, 1805
Kesteven, Ben, 98
Kesteven, Sam, 98
Kestrels, 846, 1218, 1400, 4251
Ketchum, Cavalliere, 5289
Ketchum, Dave, 1202
Ketchum, Hal, 118, 2378, 2635, 2979, 3423, 3994, 5799
Ketchum, Michael, 2979
Ketelbey, Albert William, 2979
Ketteridge, George, 2522
Kettering, Frank, 2589
Kettle, John, 5296
Kettley, Steve, 996
Ketzer, Willi, 1685
Kewley, Ian, 2980, 4375
Key, cEVIN, 4953
Key, Phil, 3096
Key, Tara, 203
Key, Ted, 2608
Keyes, Bobby, 277, 2356, 4630

Keyes, Daniel, 336, 1946
Keyes, Evelyn, 2862
Keyes, Horace, 3366
Keyes, Jimmy, 1070, 2980
Keyes, Johnny, 3412, 6112
Keyes, Steve, 4594
Keynotes, 951, 1070, 3459
Keys, Cherry, 1262
Keys, Nelson, 1961
Keyser, Alex, 1699
Keyser, Diane, 3605
Keyser, Doug, 5720
Keystone, Blakey, 3475
Kezdy, Pierre, 3871
KGB, 605, 2262, 2980
Khac Chi Ensemble, 2980-2981
Khaled, 1275, 1822, 2981, 4409, 4968, 5302
Khaled, Cheb, 1822, 2981, 4409
Khalsa, Giti, 4826
Khambatta, Jim, 4545
Khan, 2981
Khan, Ali Akbar, 2376, 2981-2982, 5721
Khan, Allauddin, 2981, 4845
Khan, Chaka, 366, 422, 453, 547, 1087, 1217, 1350, 1497, 1651, 1757, 1854, 2000, 2296, 2424, 2611, 2660, 2689, 2982, 3048, 3053, 3136, 3427, 3909, 4202, 4384, 4684, 4838, 4985, 5450, 5576, 5610, 5701
Khan, George, 414, 1978, 2689, 2989
Khan, Imrat, 3394, 5721
Khan, Morgan, 892
Khan, Nusrat Fateh Ali, 751, 2982, 3886, 4457, 4717
Khan, Praga, 4305
Khan, Rashid, 3886
Khan, Salamat Ali, 5721
Khan, Shakeel, 5487
Khan, Shere, 1545
Khan, Shujaat, 3886
Khan, Steve, 2983, 5741
Khan, Ustad Amjad Ali, 3886
Khan, Ustad Bilayat, 3886
Khan, Ustad Bismillah, 3886
Khan, Ustad Vilayat, 3886
Khanyile, Jabu, 421
Kharito, Nicholas, 1436
Khaury, Herbert, 5444
Khomo, Thapelo, 422
Khorn, Peter, 1845
Khouri, Ken, 99, 3980
Khoury, George, 45, 4224
Khoza, Rufus, 3440
Kiamichi Mountain Boys, 461
Kiani, Mary, 2983, 5517
Kiara, Dorothy, 1968
Kibbee, Guy, 1368, 1965, 1982, 2185
Kibbee, Martin, 1820, 2018
Kibbey, Sue, 2983
Kibble, Mark, 5283
Kibby, Walter, 1908
Kick, Johnny, 3400
Kick, Richard, 736
Kickin' Records, 2984
Kid 'N Play, 976, 2984
Kid Chrysler And The Cruisers, 2381
Kid Creole And The Coconuts, 2984

Kid From Spain, The, 103, 491-492, 881, 920, 2227, 2928, 2984, 4681
Kid Frost, 2043, 2052, 2985, 3136, 3605
Kid Galahad, 1959, 2985, 4311, 4315
Kid Koala, 1562, 3955
Kid Livi, 99
Kid Millions, 351, 920, 1587, 2923, 2985, 3635
Kid Sensation, 2670, 2985
Kid Sheik Cola, 2376, 5435
Kidd Glove, 4713
Kidd, Carol, 2082, 2975, 2985-2986, 3376, 3932
Kidd, Jerry, 4463
Kidd, Johnny, 114, 995, 1263, 1272, 1438, 1457, 2306, 2454, 2986, 3684, 4254, 4667, 4808, 4920, 5653, 5702, 5983, 6057
Kidd, Johnny, And The Pirates, 995, 1263, 1457, 2454, 2986, 4667, 4808, 4920, 5653, 5702, 5983, 6057
Kidd, Kenneth, 2986
Kidd, Michael, 361, 912, 1438, 1495, 2205, 2252, 2322, 2477, 2724, 2960, 2986, 3230, 4825
Kiddus I, 280, 4595
Kidjo, Angelique, 2987, 3135, 4457
Kidron, Adam, 4794
Kids Are Alright, The, 1767, 2987-2988, 5381, 5811-5812
Kids From Fame, 112, 1837, 2988
Kiedis, Anthony, 4463
Kiefer, Tommy, 3079
Kiek, James Llewelyn, 3456
Kiek, Mara, 3456
Kiely, Andy, 872
Kiergerl, Stephen, 1272
Kiernan, Thomas, 3842
Kiger, Al, 5658
Kihayà, Tetsu, 1391
Kihn, Greg, 505, 1689, 2988, 4751, 6057
Kik Tracee, 2988
Kikoski, Dave, 3772
Kikuchi, Masabumi, 2539, 2988-2989
Kikuchi, Takashi, 1616
Kila, 2989
Kilanoski, Eddie, 5498
Kilbey, Reginald, 2758
Kilbey, Steve, 2176
Kilbride, Pat, 415
Kilburn And The High Roads, 1661, 2152, 2989-2990, 3953
Kilburn, Duncan, 4355
Kilcher, Jewel, 2821
Kilduf, Vinnie, 2687
Kilduff, Frank, 1482
Kilduff, Vinnie, 490
Kiles, Marlin, 3583
Kiley, Richard, 2990, 3034, 3430-3431, 3583, 3964, 4471, 5632
Kiley, Tony, 607
Kilfeather, Eddie, 4036
Kilgallon, Eddie, 4537
Kilgore, Merle, 977, 2990, 3011, 5848
Kilgore, Rebecca, 2991

Kilgour, David, 1061, 1119
Kilgour, Hamish, 1119
Kilkenny, Sean, 1572
Kill City Records, 1578, 2464
Kill For Thrills, 2991
Kill Rock Stars Records, 1477, 3317, 4960
Killbilly, 321
Killbridge, Sean, 2449
Killdozer, 1518, 2991, 4791
Killen, Buddy, 857, 2311, 2991-2992, 3264, 3543, 5347, 6057
Killen, Ked, 2992
Killen, Kevin, 3216, 4899
Killen, Louis, 1093, 1398, 1984, 2375, 2992
Killen, Sally, 2992
Killer Of Heavenly Kings, 1036
Killers, 2992-2993
Killerwatt Records, 1450
Killgo, Keith, 569
Killian, Al, 406, 2993
Killian, Sean, 5649
Killing Joke, 615, 739, 908, 2103, 2479, 2655, 2993-2994, 3584, 3643, 4053, 4078, 4348, 4514, 4879, 5317, 5783, 6001
Killinger, Chris, 2841
Killjoys, 1502, 2162, 2994, 4366
Kilmer, Doug, 5598
Kilminster, Ian, 4598
Kilo, 2670, 2693, 2994, 3058, 5446
Kilpatrick, Dean, 3375
Kilpatrick, Walter D., 1483
Kilzer, Jobie, 5777
Kim, Andy, 220, 400, 1999, 3033
Kimball, Bobby, 5474
Kimball, James, 1481
Kimball, Jennifer, 752
Kimball, Jim, 3834
Kimball, Richard, 4290
Kimball, Stuart, 1818
Kimball, Terry, 3816
Kimball, Walt, 1904
Kimberley, Colin, 1507
Kimble, Paul, 2240
Kimble, Perry, 30
Kimbrough, Charles, 1196
Kimbrough, James, 2994
Kimbrough, Junior, 2994
Kimbrough, Lottie, 428, 2574-2575
Kimbrough, Sylvester, 428
Kimmel, Bob, 4641
Kimmel, Jack, 2535
Kimmett, Ralph, 2889
Kimmins, Anthony, 2726, 4382
Kimono, Ras, 2995, 3068
Kimsey, Kim, 1890
Kin, Joe, 614
Kinard, Gig, 864
Kincaid, Bradley, 405, 774, 2592, 2936, 2995, 3357, 3881, 4605, 6057
Kincaid, Jan, 711
Kincaid, Jesse Lee, 4553
Kincaid, Mark, 1726
Kincaide, Deane, 298, 2995
Kinch, Steve, 1820
Kinchen, Mark, 2996, 3044, 4138, 5577
Kinchen, Ricky, 3698
Kinchla, Chan, 626

Kitson, Vikki, 2911
Kitsyke Will, 3039
Kitt, Eartha, 382, 1163, 2006, 2251, 2695, 3039, 3187, 5695, 5817, 5842, 6058
Kitt, Niki, 2463
Kittrell, Christine, 2614, 3040
Kittringham, Eric, 5300
Kix, 753, 3040, 3541
Kizys, Algis, 711
Kjelberg, Anna, 1617
Kjellemyr, Bjorn, 4706
Kjellman, Carin, 1957-1958
Kjoo, 4376
KK, 558, 1500, 2053-2054, 3422, 3464-3465, 4356, 4780, 4805
Klaatu, 3040
Klages, Raymond, 151
Klark Kent, 1231, 3040-3041, 3616, 4274
Klass, Charlie, 497
Klaudt Indian Family, 3041
Klaudt, Ronald, 3041
Klaus And Gibson, 1023, 1777, 3475, 3548, 4099-4100, 5653, 5660
Klaus, Ron, 1750
Klauser, Art, 4101
Klavatt, Dean, 3514
Klaven, Jeff, 1141
Klearview Harmonix, 2857
Kleban, Edward, 1070, 2363-2364
Klebe, Gary, 4886
Kleeb, Bill, 3019
Kleemeyer, Ray, 2940
Kleenex, 3041, 3247
Kleign, Jeroen, 1395
Klein, Alan, 3921, 5637
Klein, Allen, 435, 900, 1792, 3041, 4629
Klein, Carol, 4808
Klein, Danny, 2110
Klein, Emmanuel, 3041
Klein, Joe, 2320, 6051
Klein, Jon, 4938
Klein, Larry, 1159, 1189, 3714
Klein, Manny, 482, 603, 3041-3042, 4528
Klein, Marlon, 1547
Klein, Oscar, 1669
Klein, Peter, 4287
Klein, Robert, 210, 351, 2363, 5388
Klein, Warren, 1820, 2018
Kleinbard, Annette, 4551, 5327
Kleingers, Dan, 259
Kleinhans, Werner, 295
Kleinman, Jon, 3749
Kleinow, Pete, 1420, 1949-1950, 3713, 4146, 4195, 5364
Kleist, Ken, 1797
Kleive, Audun, 4706
Kleive, Iver, 3236
Klemann, Suzanne, 3298
Klemmer, John, 745, 3042, 3212
Klepacz, Julian, 5569
Klett, Peter, 913
Klezmatics, 3042
Klezmer Conservatory Band, 872
KLF, 526, 763, 962, 1571, 1633, 1811, 1992, 2026, 2481, 2628, 2636, 2916, 3042-3043, 3319,

3759, 4054, 5441, 5483, 5590, 5936, 6058
Klimek, Jamie, 1724, 3703
Kline, Augie, 4305
Kline, Kevin, 3362, 4041, 4641
Kline, Lofton, 5843
Kline, Merrill, 3349
Kline, Olive, 615
Klinger, Frank, 2347
Klingman, Moogy, 4688
Klink, Al, 474, 2562, 3043, 5923
Klinke, Markus, 1272
Klopfenstein, Scott, 4481
Kloss, Eric, 3803
Klot, Lillie, 772
Klotz, Florence, 3269, 4099
Kluger, Irv, 263
Kluger, Irving, 2376, 3043
Klugh, Earl, 484, 2300, 3044, 3149, 3259, 4510
Klugman, Jack, 2324, 2659
Klyngeld, Adolf, 2473
KMD, 3044
KMS Records, 3044
Knack, 3044-3045 and passim
Knapp, George, 2347, 3966
Knapp, John, 2324
Knapp, Orville, 3045, 3966, 4036
Knapp, Roy C., 3081, 5780
Knapp, Terry, 3050
Knauss, Richard, 3457
Knechel, Larry, 3137
Knechtel, Larry, 720, 1702, 2839, 4559
Knee, Bernie, 356
Knellar, Richard, 4327
Knepper, Jimmy, 67, 2956, 3045, 3691, 4626, 5332
Knetchel, Larry, 1004
Knibbs, Lloyd, 4948
Knibbs, Ted, 2230
Knickerbocker Holiday, 180, 1703, 2990, 3045-3046, 3322, 5755
Knickerbocker, Bob, 1893
Knickerbockers, 2337, 3046, 4543, 5968
Knight Brothers, 3046, 4233, 4727
Knight, Alex, 2695, 4712
Knight, Bob, Four, 1019, 3046
Knight, Clifton, 2705
Knight, Curtis, 1105, 2490, 2492, 3047, 6052
Knight, Dave, 1426
Knight, Esmond, 4467
Knight, Evelyn, 1956, 3047
Knight, Frederick, 1215, 1459, 3025, 3047, 5698, 5733
Knight, Gladys, 87, 155, 253, 314, 467, 490, 557, 848, 1117, 2147, 2275, 2963, 2982, 3513, 4077, 4795, 4895, 4928, 5708, 5713
Knight, Gladys, And The Pips, 353, 816, 1262, 2041, 2104, 3047-3048, 3081, 3358, 3557, 3813, 4204, 4582, 4895, 5308, 5742, 5799, 5804, 6058
Knight, Grace, 1786, 2888, 3048-3049, 4859
Knight, Graham, 1970, 3470
Knight, Holly, 4764

Knight, Ivor, 3788, 4781
Knight, Jean, 3025, 3049
Knight, Jerry, 4036, 4137
Knight, Jim, 2664
Knight, Jonathan, 3915
Knight, Jordan, 3915
Knight, June, 746, 5283
Knight, Kelvin, 1476
Knight, Kevin, 4341
Knight, Larry, 2941
Knight, Marie, 5350
Knight, Oliver, 5724-5725
Knight, Pedro, 1320
Knight, Peter, 14, 1430, 2016, 2097, 2422, 2452, 2664, 3032, 3049, 3759, 3788, 4782, 5650, 5682
Knight, Phil, 4879
Knight, Phillip, 3182
Knight, Richard, 186, 762
Knight, Robert, 762, 3049, 3688, 4937
Knight, Sonny, 3050
Knight, Stanley, 557
Knight, Steve, 1426, 3816
Knight, Terry, 602, 2043, 2236, 3050, 5822
Knight, Tony, 4952
Knight, Trevor, 5914
Knightley, Steve, 226, 4894
Knights Of The Occasional Table, 3050
Knights, Barron, 397, 3325, 5385, 5481, 6031
Knightsbridge, John, 2627
Knitting Factory Works, 1561, 3253
Knoblich, Michael, 4765
Knobloch, Fred, 3050, 3786, 4710
Knoblock, Edward, 1794, 3033
Knock, Darryl, 2463
Knockshot, Jackie, 1183
Knooks, George, 4336
Knopf, Edwin H., 3245
Knopfler, David, 1537, 3051, 3420
Knopfler, Mark, 177, 228, 270, 565, 706, 728, 890, 1299, 1369, 1500, 1537-1538, 1676, 1874, 2147, 2321, 2455, 2812-2813, 2908, 3051, 3361, 3977, 4001, 4225, 5497, 5535, 5757, 6044, 6058
Knorr, Al, 1796
Knott, James, 4135
Knott, Ray, 307
Knotts, Don, 2290
Knotts, Phyllis, 854
Knowledge, 3051
Knowledge, Michael, 3051
Knowles, Bert, 4484
Knowles, Bill, 549
Knowles, Chris, 5738
Knowles, E., 1704, 6061
Knowles, Keith, 3475-3476
Knowles, Pamela, 3052
Knowling, Ransom, 2396, 3052, 5356
Knox, Buddy, 683, 1541, 3041, 3052, 3754, 4621
Knox, Chris, 1119, 1759, 3052, 5288, 5482
Knox, Jimmy, 3052, 4728

Knox, Nick, 1275, 1724
Knuckles, Frankie, 1847, 1881, 2083, 2606, 3052-3053, 3249, 3775, 4090, 4338
Knudsen, Keith, 1592
Knudsen, Kenneth, 3053
Knust, Michael, 1880
Kobart, Ruth, 2056
Kobel, Allan, 2306
Kobelk, Oscar, 3019
Kober, Arthur, 5894
Koblin, Ken, 819
Kobluk, Mike, 3709
Kobrin, Barry, 4498
Koch Records, 3078, 4236, 6067
Koch, Ingmar, 96
Koch, Lydia, 3359
Kocjan, Krysia, 3883
Koda, Cub, 793, 3053
Kodaks, 2735, 3053-3054, 4773
Kodaly, Zoltan, 4803
Kodjo, Charles, 4419
Kodo, 1521, 3054, 5947
Koebler, Ronnie, 1317
Koehler, Esther, 894
Koehler, Ted, 226, 603, 881, 2489, 3054, 3122, 3581, 3736
Koehler, Trevor, 2699
Koehler, Violet, 1224
Koelewijn, Peter, 2196
Koenig, Lester, 1214, 2435
Koerner, 'Spider' John, 3055
Koerner, John, 3055, 4445
Koerner, Ray And Glover, 1728, 3055, 4445, 4661
Koester, Bob, 1475
Kofi, 99, 765, 866, 2133, 2514, 2795, 3055, 3060, 3444, 5710
Kofi, Tony, 2795
Koffman, Moe, 4154
Koga, Masao, 3840
Kogan, George, 2659
Kogel, Mike, 3319
Koger, George, 2967
Koglmann, Franz, 591, 1150, 3056, 4173
Kohler, George, 4518
Kohler, Mark, 3079
Köhler, Sven, 4937
Kohlmar, Fred, 862, 4107
Kohn, Margaret, 3845
Kohn, Tony, 3561
Kohner, Frederick, 3397
Koite, Sourokata, 3056
Koivusaari, Tomi, 167
Koja, Misako, 3902
Kojak And Liza, 2138, 3056, 4780
Koji, Enibasun, 41
Kojima, Sachihio, 5571
Kokane, 3056, 4498, 4703
Koko Records, 368, 2694
Koko, Pia, 5654
Kokomo, 239, 242, 1093, 2550, 3057, 3275, 3835, 4370, 5784
Kokomo (UK), 3057, 3835
Kokomo (USA), 3057, 4370
Kokov, Anatoly, 2652
Kólan, Li, 3229-3230
Kolbe, Bernie, 1579, 1769
Kolber, Larry, 3172, 3444
Kold Sweat, 1678, 1815, 2939, 3057, 3077, 5571
Kolderie And Slade, 580, 658,

Le Freak, Kermit, 4702
Le Gall, Robert, 2323
Le Gardes, 3180
Le Gassick, Damian, 2669
Le Gop, 3154
Le Grand Orchestra Parisien, 3154
Le Grande Kalle, 2927
Le Griffe, 3154
Le Jeune, Eddie, 888
Le Laverne, Johnny, 2966
Le Laverne, Lauren, 2966
Le Mar, Bryan, 2325
Le Mercier, Paddy, 335
Le Mesurier, John, 1325, 3406
Le Mystère Des Voix Bulgares, 3154, 5505
Le Noble, Martyn, 2781, 4287
Le Port, Gary, 3764
Le Roux, 3154-3155
Le Roy, Chester, 4492
Le Sage, Bill, 1001, 3155
Le Strange, Bebe, 2458
Le Super Tentemba, 3729
Lea, Barbara, 942, 3155, 3573, 6102
Lea, Clive, 4597
Lea, Jim, 2162, 2688, 3707
Lea, Jimmy, 4959
Lea, Larry, 3307
Lea, Tim, 46
Leach, Alan, 4862
Leach, Ben, 1849
Leach, Billie, 2938
Leach, Clare, 4893
Leach, Craig, 2357
Leach, Curtis, 173
Leach, Jimmy, 1210, 2968
Leach, Lillian, And The Mellows, 3155
Leach, Roger, 1884
Leach, Scott, 4819
Leach, Wilford, 3865
Leach, Winston, 1332
Lead Belly, 144, 422, 444, 1015, 1198, 1217, 1260, 1588, 1958, 2189, 2231, 2319, 2419, 2804, 3155-3156, 3299-3300, 3571-3572, 3828, 4445, 5487, 6058, 6130
Leadabrand, Mike, 3392
Leadbury, Peter, 2643
Leader, Bill, 1620-1621, 4576, 4653, 4924
Leader, Harry, 2485, 5989
Leaders Of The New School, 32, 650, 853, 2713, 3028, 3157, 4778
Leaders Trio, 3243
Leadhen, John, 2453
Leadon, Bernie, 1241, 1332, 1526-1527, 1683, 1949, 2032, 2291, 2460, 3157, 3613, 3959, 4641, 4687, 4791, 5362
Leady, Don, 3197
Leaf, David, 427, 451, 5870, 6032, 6035
Leahy, Dick, 420, 460, 2605, 2926, 3157, 5781
Leahy, Ronnie, 5323, 5492
Leak, Maysa, 2689, 5585
Leake, Danny, 2849
Leake, Lafayette, 3158
Leaky Radiators, 1948
Lean, Cecil, 615, 3965

Lean, David, 1265
Leander, Mike, 2172, 2477, 2665, 2878, 3158, 4342, 5544, 5549
Léandre, Joëlle, 1226, 3158, 3217, 3946, 4777
Leandros, Vicky, 3159
Leanear, Kevin, 3660
Leaner, Ernie, 4048
Leaner, George, 4048
Leaner, Tony, 4048
Leapy Lee, 2368, 3175
Lear, Amanda, 3159
Lear, Graham, 4740
Learmouth, Peter, 5526-5527
Learned, Rod, 492
Leary, Paul, 321, 859, 2859
Leary, Timothy, 349, 3506, 4173, 4353, 4356, 4953
Leary, Wilma Lee, 1227
Lease, Marc, 5995
Leather Nun, 3159
Leather Records, 5483, 5652
Leatherman, Ronnie, 5393
Leatherwolf, 3159-3160
Leatherwood, Stu, 3062
Leave It To Jane, 649, 2975, 3160, 4020, 4338, 5901
Leave It To Me!, 35, 153, 2959, 3160-3161, 3489, 3947, 4016, 4047, 4289, 5524
Leavell, Chuck, 142, 510, 554, 626, 2349, 2770, 3161, 4719
Leaves, 3161 and *passim*
Leavey, Tom, 2127
Leavill, Otis, 854, 3119, 3161
Leavitt, Phil, 1354, 1509-1510
Leavitt, Raphy, 3161-3162, 4745, 5624
Leavitt, Sam, 941
Leavy, Calvin, 3162
Lebaigue, Jim, 821
LeBail, Christine, 2125
Lebedeff, Ivan, 3532
LeBlanc And Carr, 3162, 4719
LeBlanc, Fred, 1266
LeBlanc, Keith, 3162, 4319, 4875, 4877, 5280, 5459
LeBlanc, Lenny, 3162
LeBoeuf, Alan, 334
LeBoy, Grace, 2922-2923
Lebrón Brothers, 3163-3164
Lebrón, Angel, 3163
Lebrón, José, 3163
LeCausi, Richard, 2679
Lech, Emil, 2899
Lechesseur, John, 2684
Leckenby, Lek, 2504
Leckie, John, 984, 1783, 3245, 4087, 4292, 4403, 4677, 5381, 5492, 5768
Leckie, Mandy, 4968
LeClaire, Alan, 5320
Lecuona, Ernestina, 3164
Lecuona, Ernesto, 901, 3164, 3313, 5594
Lecuona, Marguerita, 4695
Led Zeppelin, 8, 23, 83, 191, 240, 272, 318, 324, 401, 429, 528, 530, 561, 658, 682, 972, 1003, 1169, 1197, 1263, 1328, 1507, 1514, 1538, 1556, 1621, 1696, 1723, 1776, 1814, 1839, 1858, 1911, 1962, 1971, 1982,

2169, 2243, 2259, 2297, 2401, 2413, 2425, 2467, 2583, 2609, 2722, 2734, 2759, 2839, 2878, 2994, 3020, 3043, 3164-3167, 3184, 3259, 3293, 3458, 3523, 3610, 3706, 3799, 3811, 3912, 3924, 4028, 4094, 4100, 4182, 4229, 4260, 4283, 4343, 4495, 4548, 4672, 4692, 4726, 4746, 4792, 4911, 4952, 4977, 5275, 5321-5322, 5951, 6058-6059, 6125, 6130
Leddy, Eugene, 1659
Ledeé, Alberto Antonio, 3354
Ledeé, Toñito, 3354
Lederer, Charles, 912, 3033
Lederer, Otto, 2796
Ledford String Band, 3167
Ledford, Lily Mae, 1224-1225
Ledford, Rosie, 1224-1225
Ledford, Steve, 2352, 3167, 3417, 3760
Ledford, Steve, 2352, 3167, 3417, 3760
Ledigo, Hugh, 350
Ledin, Tomas, 3167
LeDoux, Chris, 3167-3168, 6059
Lee Curtis And The All-Stars, 507, 1339, 4667
Lee Highway Boys, 1752
Lee, 'Little' Frankie, 3168
Lee, Adam, 1064
Lee, Adrian, 1019, 3661, 4702
Lee, Albert, 792, 805, 966, 1074, 1292, 1588, 1707, 1756, 1798, 1848, 1943, 2088, 2137, 2218, 2262, 2291, 2408, 2454-2455, 2571, 2970, 3169, 3601, 3799, 4947, 5505, 5747, 6001
Lee, Alex, 4453
Lee, Alvin, 187, 446, 1021, 1052, 3169, 5337, 5890
Lee, Amy, 1599, 3029
Lee, Anna, 2036
Lee, Annabelle, 4396
Lee, Arthur, 1468, 1976, 2958, 3169-3170, 3174, 3334, 3527, 4076, 4833, 4978, 6059, 6061
Lee, Aubrey, 698, 4979
Lee, Baayork, 1071
Lee, Babbacombe, 1827
Lee, Barbara, 214, 1057
Lee, Barry, 1174, 3722, 6090
Lee, Benny, 2016
Lee, Bernard, 2626, 3201
Lee, Bernie, 1333
Lee, Bert, 247, 1593, 2553, 5957-5958
Lee, Bertha, 4159
Lee, Beverly, 4883
Lee, Bill, 2510, 5786, 6102
Lee, Billy, And The Rivieras, 4705
Lee, Bob, 225, 1112, 2822, 3469, 6062
Lee, Brenda, 125, 173, 704-705, 725, 838, 856, 959, 1256, 1452, 1491, 1973, 2105, 2481, 2615, 2976, 3078, 3125, 3170-3172, 3665, 3766, 3899, 3901, 4125, 4148, 4476, 4547, 4598, 4798, 4863, 4866, 5395, 5829, 5864, 6130

Lee, Brian, 2183, 2862, 4464
Lee, Bunny, 65, 92, 99, 111, 149, 188, 369, 452-453, 534, 670, 767, 790, 904, 1062, 1107, 1417, 1446, 1636, 1711, 1742, 2138, 2575-2576, 2665, 2961-2962, 3001-3002, 3006, 3171, 3405, 3554, 3718, 4096, 4116, 4120, 4137, 4335, 4545, 4594, 4639, 4884, 4976, 5282, 5325, 5412, 5505, 5545, 5559, 5578, 5635, 5872, 5995, 6004-6005
Lee, Byron, 610, 624, 924, 1008, 1124, 1742, 1817, 2291, 2637, 2774, 3153, 3171, 3217, 3505, 3532, 3878, 4137, 4142, 4465, 4966, 5282, 5290, 5325
Lee, Byron, And The Dragonaires, 610, 1124, 1817, 2774, 3153, 3171, 3217, 3505, 3878, 4142, 4465
Lee, C.P., 109, 1678, 6045
Lee, Carol, 1227-1228, 1959, 2119
Lee, Caroline, 767
Lee, Charles, 623, 1223, 3004, 5804, 6060
Lee, Chin Y., 1944-1945
Lee, Chris, 581, 1610, 2137, 5418, 6060
Lee, Coco, 3172
Lee, Craig, 327, 991, 4367
Lee, Curtis, 507, 532, 999, 1339, 1852, 3155, 3172, 4213, 4667
Lee, D.C., 2799, 5760-5761
Lee, Danny, 1044
Lee, Dave, 505, 526, 878, 1848, 2031, 2332, 2618, 2641, 3076, 3172, 3543, 4252, 4461, 5567, 5592, 5707, 5792
Lee, Davey, 4934
Lee, David, 34, 111, 446, 823, 1857, 2300-2301, 2831, 3003, 3842, 3954, 4028, 4508, 4650, 4660-4661, 4831, 4982, 5286, 5604-5606, 5705, 6076, 6128
Lee, Dickie, 4499
Lee, Dixie, 3305, 3998, 5823
Lee, Donna, 518, 718
Lee, Ed, 1213, 2152, 6050
Lee, Eddie, 1137, 1376, 2949, 3029, 5544
Lee, Ellie, 3174
Lee, Erick Erick, 1275
Lee, Ernie, 3172-3173
Lee, Eugene, 4408
Lee, Frances, 3885, 5634
Lee, Frankie, 1173, 1674, 1684, 2832, 2841, 2906, 3168, 4377, 4925, 5597, 5645, 5880
Lee, Gaby, 3249
Lee, Garrett, 1198
Lee, Geddy, 3585, 4691, 5642
Lee, George, 336, 1219, 1317, 1424, 2842, 2848, 2933, 3028, 3173, 3175, 3195, 3269, 4041, 4133, 4680, 4695, 5463, 5528, 5975
Lee, George E., 1317, 2842, 2848, 2933, 3028, 3173, 3175, 3195, 4133, 5528, 5975
Lee, Graham, 15, 1300, 3175, 5504
Lee, Hamilton, 2058, 5491

Linnell, John, 5387
Linnell, Mike, 3658
Linnenberg, Bettina, 736
Linns, Ivan, 5616
Linscott, Joan, 3057
Linsley, Brian, 955
Linsley, Steve, 955
Linton, Charles, 1912
Linton, Jack, 2347
Linton, Slim, 1309
Linus, 3256, 5886, 5963
Linville, Albert, 1370
Linx, 2242, 3256, 4707, 5933
Linzer, Sandy, 3249, 5278
Lion, 3256
Lion King, The, 105, 1041, 1545, 2834, 3256-3257, 3268, 4525, 6000, 6060
Lion, Alfred, 613-614, 758, 2488, 4380
Lion, Mandy, 5922
Lion, Walt, 553
Lionel Records, 4765
Lionel, Edwin, 189
Lioness, 3257
Lionheart, 851, 1269, 3257
Lionrock, 1453, 3257, 4576
Lionsheart, 2292, 3257-3258
Lip Service, 257, 5397
Lipere, Thebe, 331, 3732
Lipford, Cindy, 1904
Lipman, David, 3860
Lipman, Harry, 4670
Lipman, Maureen, 72, 499, 2282-2283, 3012, 5582, 5909
Lipman, William R., 3269
Lippman, Sidney, 3047
Lipps, Burkhard, 1685
Lipscomb, Dennis, 5577
Lipscomb, Mance, 1043, 2778, 2840, 3258, 6060
Lipscombe, Richard, 3172
Lipsius, Fred, 600
Lipson, Robert, 2229
Lipson, Stephen, 2788
Lipson, Steve, 2441, 3194
Lipton, Rusty, 3510
Lipton, Sydney, 132, 689, 1686, 2462, 3049, 3258, 3839
LiPuma, Tommy, 618, 752, 3258, 4737
Liquid, 3259
Liquid Jesus, 3259
Liquid Records, 5789
Liquor Cabinet, 3296
Liroy, 454, 3259
Lisa Lisa And Cult Jam, 873, 3259
Lisberg, Harvey, 1075, 2180, 2502, 2504, 3260
Lisbon Story, The (film musical), 3260
Lisbon Story, The, (stage musical), 3260
Lisbona, Eddie, 1210
Lisher, Greg, 909
Lishrout, Jay, 322
Lisi, Rick, 4537
Lismor Records, 3260
List, Garrett, 3119
Lister, Alfred, 217
Lister, Eve, 611
Lister, Jean, 4382
Lister, Lance, 4042, 5397

Lister, Mick, 5516
Lister, Perry, 2601
Lister, Sim, 954, 4287
Liston, Melba, 1554, 1572, 3253, 3261, 4673, 5295, 5778, 5873
Liszt, George, 2860
Lisztomania, 1366, 3261, 3940, 5673
Litherland, Harry, 3261
Litherland, James, 1123, 1182, 5667, 5780
Lithgow, John, 125
Lithman, Phil, 1060, 3658
Litt, Scott, 432, 1043, 2691
Litter, 1497, 1546, 2317, 3262
Little Angels, 145, 306, 355, 1805, 2767, 2815, 3098, 3262, 3871, 4251, 4952, 5360
Little Anthony And The Imperials, 694, 995, 1065, 1333, 1784, 2193, 3262, 4002, 4425, 4674, 5421
Little Beaver, 3262-3263
Little Bennie And The Masters, 3887
Little Big Band, 914, 1823, 2423-2424, 2462, 2770, 3263, 5446
Little Buddy, 1290, 4181, 5787
Little Buro, 370
Little Caesar, 612, 618, 1367, 1468, 3263, 3956
Little Caesar And The Romans, 1468, 3263, 3956
Little Charlie And The Nightcats, 3263
Little Culture, 2717
Little Dippers, 2977, 3264, 3543
Little Egypt, 3264
Little Eva, 53, 900, 1222, 1531, 2181, 2713, 3011, 3032, 3264, 4153
Little Feat, 136, 161, 391, 891, 1217, 1366, 1549, 1740, 1820, 1867, 2018, 2122, 2303, 2884, 3131, 3264-3265, 3809, 4112, 4140, 4174, 4348, 4367, 4400, 4415, 4592, 4719, 4803, 5333, 5367, 5706, 5730, 5745
Little Foxes, 511, 595, 5635, 5869
Little Harry, 1183, 3144, 4125, 4431
Little Hatch, 3265
Little Hero, 3631
Little Hudson, 4895
Little Joe And The Thrillers, 3265-3266, 4773, 5546
Little Joe Blue, 2888, 5365
Little Joey And The Flips, 3266
Little John, 370, 767, 776, 929, 1933, 2070, 2610, 2835, 3042, 3144, 3266, 3274, 3647, 3863, 3880, 4165, 4213, 4431-4432, 4700, 5356, 5535
Little Johnny Jones, 730, 1152, 2879, 3266, 3409, 4073, 5948
Little Kirk, 2038
Little Louie Vega, 3267, 3758, 4194
Little Mack, 2737, 4783
Little Mary Sunshine, 745, 3267
Little Me, 3267-3268

Little Melvin And The Downbeats, 1264
Little Mermaid, The, 104, 255, 440, 1545, 3257, 3268, 4913
Little Milton, 408, 629, 687, 902, 953, 1039, 1098, 1404, 1454, 1470, 1490, 2094, 2112, 2558, 2888, 3268-3269, 3339, 3342, 3421, 3552, 3581, 3661, 3862, 4090, 4211, 4658, 4720, 5454, 5535, 5733, 5742, 5777, 5854
Little Miss Marker, 186, 3269, 4413, 4580, 5333
Little Night Music, A, 811, 1115, 2435, 2622, 3152, 3235, 3269-3270, 4337
Little Richard, 11, 22, 132, 140, 402, 444, 575, 667, 767, 787, 975, 1085, 1143, 1180, 1262, 1583, 1601, 1809, 1816, 1908, 1951, 1958, 2052, 2070, 2159, 2210, 2407, 2490, 2503, 2519, 2834, 2866, 2893, 2953, 3040, 3085, 3117, 3203, 3270-3271, 3280, 3302, 3365, 3510, 3708, 3757, 3796, 4111, 4181, 4230-4231, 4316, 4451, 4470, 4537, 4591, 4628, 4690, 4705, 4718, 4800, 5361, 5403, 5695, 5731, 5803, 5832, 5847, 5926, 6060
Little River Band, 1850, 3271, 5544
Little Roy, 237, 502, 660, 1063, 1083, 1229, 1363, 2481, 3222-3223, 3271-3272, 4801, 5818
Little Shop Of Horrors (film musical), 3272
Little Shop Of Horrors (stage musical), 3272
Little Show, The, 69, 130, 1520, 1894, 1950, 2022, 2129, 2572, 2644, 2940, 3246, 3272-3273, 4776, 5425
Little Son Joe, 3273, 3624
Little Sonny, 1049, 3014, 3273, 3533, 3550, 3824, 3880, 5864
Little Steven And The Disciples Of Soul, 3273, 5608
Little Texas, 693, 1048, 2004, 3264, 3273-3274, 3844, 3960
Little Tony, 3274
Little Village, 1218, 1271, 2515, 3274, 3349
Little Walter, 18, 297, 460, 621, 627, 629, 739, 753, 786, 858, 1039, 1049, 1140, 1671, 1985, 2346, 2398, 2407, 2619, 2641, 2726, 2755, 2867, 3151, 3265, 3274, 3291, 3327, 3533, 3551, 3555, 3717, 3830, 3853, 3888, 3942, 3961, 4303, 4498, 4582, 4620, 4987, 5354, 5680, 5763, 5784-5785, 5838, 5862, 5913, 5973
Little Whisper And The Rumors, 802
Little Whitt And Big Bo, 3274
Little, Ayanna, 5941
Little, Booker, 1029, 1579, 3275, 4339, 5675
Little, Carlo, 1946, 2466, 4628
Little, Cleavon, 4368
Little, David, 573, 3367

Little, Jack, 298, 489, 522, 1228, 3425, 5454, 6042
Little, Joe, 175, 876, 2070, 2762, 2888, 3083, 3209, 3265-3266, 3273, 3624, 4431, 4470, 4773, 4877, 5365, 5546, 5850, 5969
Little, Levi, 573, 4546
Little, Little Jack, 298, 489, 522, 1228, 3425, 5454, 6042
Little, Marie, 5308
Littlefield, 'Little' Willie, 532, 2217, 3275, 3960, 4230
Littlefield, Lucien, 2257
Littlejohn, Darrell, 3738
Littlejohn, Johnny, 519, 847, 3275
Littlejohns, Allan, 2594
Littler, David, 2605
Littler, Denis, 2605
Littleton, Kelly, 3244
Littlewood, Joan, 1895, 3384, 5540
Littman, Julian, 1596
Littman, Tony, 1840
Litton, Martin, 4819
Littrell, Brian, 318
Litweiler, John, 2797, 5309, 5311, 6041, 6102
Live, 3275-3276
Live Aid, 29, 62-63, 220, 360, 666, 686, 957, 1086, 1096, 1178, 1200, 1244, 1537, 1576, 1676, 1751, 1787, 1858, 1892, 1979, 2111, 2155, 2230, 2391, 2760, 2834, 2966, 3251, 3276, 3403, 3425, 3434, 3822, 3962, 4216, 4248, 4318, 4381, 4529, 4683, 4788, 5365, 5417, 5535, 5557, 5561, 5670, 5724, 5811, 5921, 5980
Live Skull, 1037, 1191
Live, David, 686-687, 1947, 2245, 2344
Liver Birds, 3279, 5433
Liverpool Express, 3279, 3640
Liverpool Scene, 999, 1116, 1633, 2293, 2422, 2916, 3279-3280, 3574, 4061, 4564, 4571, 4763
Livesey, Jack, 3260
Livesey, Sam, 4414
Livestock, 712, 1817, 3585, 5339
Livgren, Kerry, 61, 159, 2933, 3280
Livin' Joy, 3280
Living Colour, 202, 320, 513, 1575, 1723, 1908, 2248, 2407, 3270, 3280, 3299, 3871, 4331, 4476, 4496, 5479, 5551, 5654
Living In A Box, 1388, 3121, 3280-3281
Living It Up, 1845, 2922, 3206, 3281, 3484
Living, Bernie, 3438
Livingston, Bob, 3322
Livingston, Fud, 1732, 2923, 3281
Livingston, Jay, 1793, 2590, 3281, 5982
Livingston, Jerry, 1401, 1544, 2549, 3187, 5750
Livingston, Joe, 4746
Livingston, John, 1006, 2525
Livingston, Paul, 5492

Lynch, Willie, 2518, 3682
Lynde, Paul, 862
Lyndell, Liz, 4483
Lyndon, Barry, 1056, 4655
Lynn, Bambi, 4025
Lynn, Barbara, 757, 815, 1166, 2345, 2888, 3369, 3540, 4718
Lynn, Bonnie, 710, 1470, 4881
Lynn, Cheryl, 761, 2053, 2242, 3369-3370, 5610
Lynn, Chris, 1694, 2423
Lynn, Gail, 5432
Lynn, Judy, 1877, 3370, 4296
Lynn, Loretta, 387, 705, 838, 1256, 1478, 1824, 1971, 1995, 2002, 2105-2106, 2629, 2783, 3125, 3170, 3343, 3370-3371, 3785, 4086, 4149, 4182, 4566, 4765, 4798, 4911, 5453, 5496, 5505, 5519, 5548, 5820-5821, 5854, 5936-5937, 6061, 6130
Lynn, Mara, 3204
Lynn, Marc, 1063
Lynn, Oliver Vanetta, 3370
Lynn, Robbie, 2871
Lynn, Robert, 1081-1082, 3371, 3980
Lynn, Sandy, 3046
Lynn, Tami, 3371
Lynn, Van, 5603
Lynn, Vera, 95, 158, 212, 595, 1027, 1088, 1210, 1438, 1604, 2251, 2348, 2938, 2971, 3201, 3320, 3372, 3584, 4531, 6061
Lynn, Carol, 520, 2823, 5745
Lynne, Gillian, 993, 2342, 3372, 4565
Lynne, Gloria, 520, 3373
Lynne, Jeff, 436, 1677, 1702, 1725, 2047, 2415, 2455, 2673, 2703, 2887, 3194, 3373-3374, 3486, 3641, 3819, 3865, 3931, 4055, 4080, 4216, 4846, 4872, 5493, 5870, 5911
Lynne, Shelby, 2529, 2618, 3374, 4495
Lynon, George, 2250
Lynott, Phil, 462, 1313, 2263, 2389, 2765, 3051, 3374, 3768, 4024, 4950, 5390, 5430, 5736, 5914, 6061
Lynton, Everett, 4573
Lynton, Peter, 2101
Lynton, Rod, 3198
Lynyrd Skynyrd, 255, 539, 570, 700, 1174, 1203, 1271, 1321, 2293, 2429, 2754, 2914, 2974, 3064, 3374-3375, 3754, 3799, 4028, 4348, 4373, 4592, 4659, 5507, 6130
Lyon, Andy, 190
Lyon, Greg, 1310
Lyon, Iain, 2905
Lyons, Barry, 1917, 3825, 5498
Lyons, Colette, 1578, 4893
Lyons, Gary, 5779
Lyons, Gill, 5448
Lyons, James L., 3375
Lyons, Jamie, 1723, 3850
Lyons, Jeff, 1968
Lyons, Jimmy, 1344, 2427, 3174, 3286, 3375, 3752, 3762, 3847-3848, 5309-5310, 5699
Lyons, John, 3002, 4539

Lyons, John Henry, 4539
Lyons, Leo, 5337, 5737
Lyons, Richard, 3891
Lyons, Roger, 3257, 4576
Lyons, Rory, 3002
Lyons, Stuart, 4969
Lyons, Tigger, 2648
Lyons, Toby, 1183
Lyons, William, 5298
Lyons, Willie James, 902, 905, 2971, 3376
Lyra Records, 4756
Lyric, Dora, 1926
Lyrichord Records, 1511
Lytell, Bert, 3105
Lytell, Jimmy, 2648, 3376, 4060
Lytle, Donald Eugene, 4169
Lyttelton, Humphrey, 385-386, 536, 674, 682, 806, 1116, 1153, 1188, 1382, 1384, 1836, 1863, 2231, 2268, 2281, 2354, 2725, 2798, 2869, 2944, 3376-3377, 3388, 3486, 3804, 4069, 4137, 4233, 4374, 4513, 4694, 4848, 4951, 5332, 5530, 5725, 5744, 5767, 5857, 5894, 6061, 6102
Lyttle, Jim, 4626
Lytton, Paul, 2320, 3344, 3675, 4135

M

M, 3379 and *passim*
M People, 1125, 1453, 2328, 3379, 4007, 4079, 4130, 4635
M&O Band, 1626, 3380
M&S Productions, 3380
M-BASE, 130, 1169, 2484, 4071, 5871
M.A.F.I.A., 3977
M.A.R.S., 147, 214, 1183, 3380, 3383
M.O.P., 323, 3380
MA1 MA2, 1562
Maal, Baaba, 3135, 3287, 3380, 3848, 4185, 4293, 4803
Maas, Frederica, 4886
Maas, Peter, 2026
Mabele, Aurlus, 1548
Maben, Luther, 1288
Maberly, Kate, 4806
Mabern, Harold, 115, 1166, 3756
Mabey, Richard, 2910, 4454, 6113
Mabiala, Youlou, 1840
Mabie, Milton, 3504
Mabley, Moms 'Jackie', 3381
Mabon, Willie, 53, 484, 757, 3291, 3381
Mabsant, 3382, 4720, 6061
Mabuse, Sipho, 3382, 3425, 3534
Maby, Graham, 2744
Mac And Bob, 3382-3383
Mac And Little Addie, 4014
Mac And Slim, 4014
Mac, Andy, 2077
Mac, Steve, 1935, 3970, 5601, 6048
Mac-O-Chee Valley Folks, 2279
Macabre, 3383
Macainish, Greg, 4957
MacAlise, Thomas, 1970

Macalpine, Tony, 3380, 3383, 4183, 5281
MacArthur, Neil, 631, 3383
Macaskill, Doug, 243
MacAuland, Paul, 2449
Macauley, Richard, 2478
Macauley, Tony, 347, 1180, 1347, 1400, 1628, 1702, 1706, 1951, 1987, 3383, 4235
MacBaine, Robert, 1960
Macbeth, David, 3384
Macbeth, Peter, 1987
MacBride, Donald, 2202
Macc Lads, 3384
MacCallum, Catherine, 1987
Maccara, Nigel, 5290
MacCaw, Craig, 4284
MacColl, Ewan, 231, 465, 736, 831, 970-971, 2100, 2225, 2351, 2355, 2992, 3285, 3299, 3384-3385, 3594, 3767, 4453, 4811, 5467, 6061, 6077
MacColl, Kirsty, 98, 708, 1706, 2252, 2839, 3023, 3248, 3384-3385, 4270, 4453, 5398, 5907
MacColl, Neil, 4453
MacCormick, Bill, 1716, 3453
MacDaniel, Rudy, 5280
MacDermot, Galt, 2336-2337, 3386, 5549
MacDonald Salisbury, Barbara, 3663
MacDonald, Alsy, 5504
MacDonald, Andy, 2481, 5420
MacDonald, Ballard, 1439, 2128, 4570, 4650
MacDonald, Brian, 2277
MacDonald, Calum, 4689
MacDonald, Catriona, 3236
MacDonald, Christie, 466
MacDonald, Eddie, 106
MacDonald, Francis, 634-635, 5328
MacDonald, Hank, 3386
MacDonald, Iain, 416, 4075
MacDonald, Ian, 436-437, 1826, 2277, 3917, 6033
MacDonald, Ian Matthews, 1826
MacDonald, Jeanette, 550, 809, 987, 1051, 1702-1704, 1903, 2185, 2212, 2284, 2662, 2923, 3123, 3184, 3337-3338, 3386, 3429, 3532, 3639, 3751, 3885, 3916, 4044, 4648, 4732, 4880, 5446, 5592, 5929, 6061
MacDonald, Jeanette, And Nelson Eddy, 550, 1702-1704, 2662, 3386, 3885, 3916, 4648, 5929, 6061
MacDonald, Laurel, 3386
MacDonald, Neville, 4952
MacDonald, Pat, 5440
MacDonald, Ralph, 3386
MacDonald, Richie, 773
MacDonald, Robert, 4689, 4732
MacDonald, Rory, 4689
Macdonald, Tesfa, 915
Macdonell, Jimmy, 3327
MacDonough, Glen, 309, 2502, 5899
Macdonough, Harry, 615, 716, 1942
Mace, Ralph, 685

Maceo And The King's Men, 3387
Macero, Attilio Joseph, 3387
Macero, Teo, 2372, 3387, 4496
Macey, Tommy, 3366
MacFadyen, John, 4245
MacFarland And Gardner, 3383
MacFarland, Barrelhouse Buck, 5621
MacFarland, Lester, 3382
MacFarlane, Danny, 4250
MacFarlane, Earl, 3051
MacGill, Alan, 4333
MacGill, Moyna, 3127
MacGillivray, John, 1856
MacGowan, Geraldine, 4023
MacGowan, Kenneth, 5443
MacGowan, Shane, And The Popes, 3387
MacGowan, Shay, 4023
MacGregor, Freddie, 4139
MacGregor, Jimmie, 473, 2351-2352
MacGuire, Daniel, 2134
MacGuire, Mike, 2914
Machado, Celso, 4384
Machin, Alex, 27
Machin, Denry, 931
Machinations, 259, 695, 932, 1533, 1741, 1922, 2108, 2612, 2682, 3514, 3890-3891, 4130, 4331, 4399, 5379, 5663
Machine Head, 1138, 1458, 1941, 2297, 2453, 3388, 3401, 4713, 5278, 5649
Machito, 216, 418, 641, 1323, 2150, 2152, 2868, 3233, 3353, 3388, 3445, 3776, 4000, 4114, 4170, 4304, 4360, 4420, 4447, 4615-4616, 4743, 5447, 5530
Machlin, Milt, 2573, 6053
MacInnes, Iain, 5296
MacInnes, Maggie, 4075
Macino, John, 4333
Macintosh, Adrian, 3376, 3388
MacIntyre, Marguerite, 196
MacIsaac, Ashley, 3389
MacIsaac, Dave, 2728, 3395
Mack And Mabel, 1013, 1369, 2505, 2862, 3389, 3636, 4209, 4317
Mack Nicholson, Mary Rachel, 508
Mack Smith, Retha, 508
Mack 10, 5779
Mack The Knife, 1391, 1912, 2846, 4321, 5368, 5426
Mack, Bill, 3019, 4547
Mack, Bob, 2778
Mack, Bobby, 1985, 3390
Mack, Cecil, 780, 5659
Mack, Craig, 1859
Mack, Jimmie, 4966
Mack, Jimmy, 4177
Mack, Johnny, 3017, 3563, 4555
Mack, Leroy, 2973
Mack, Lonnie, 77, 139, 647, 1634, 3390, 3960, 4798, 5620
Mack, Lorraine P., 508
Mack, Marlene, 4172
Mack, Paul, 3019
Mack, Steve, 1043, 1518, 5351
Mack, Ted, 667, 3121
Mack, Warner, 1872, 2481,

Magnets, 1761, 3890, 5492, 5614
Magnificent Men, 1258, 1469, 2213, 3411-3412
Magnificents, 3412
Magnum, 3412 and *passim*
Magnum, Jeff, 1440
Magnus, Kerry, 3022
Magnuson, Ann, 657, 3073, 4880-4881
Magnusson, Bob, 3531
Magny, Colette, 3412-3413, 6061
Magog, Dominic, 4847
Magoo, Phil, 322
Magoogan, Wesley, 430
Maguire, Alex, 3413, 3967, 4231, 5834
Maguire, Barry, 3631
Maguire, Les, 2127
Maguire, Ricky, 3625
Maguire, Sean, 2642, 3413
Mahaffey, John, 4093
Maharaj, Pandit Birju, 3886
Maharaj, Pandit Kishan, 3886
Maharis, George, 4075
Mahavishnu Orchestra, 514, 544, 637, 797, 1140, 1790, 1941, 2364, 3413, 3590-3591, 4279, 4839, 5674, 6063
Maher, Brent, 2258, 2615, 2908
Maher, Fred, 1159, 2475, 2953, 3511, 4794
Maher, George, 1849
Maher, James T., 5830
Maher, John, 859, 1727, 1913, 3847, 5667
Maher, Johnny, 3796
Maher, Liam, 1945
Maher, Siobhan, 4556
Mahlan, John, 80
Mahlathini, Simon Nkabinde, 3414
Mahler, Bruno, 3851
Mahler, Gustav, 1475, 5664
Mahogany, 1087, 3414-3415, 3464, 3637, 4657, 5858
Mahogany Rush, 3414, 3464
Mahogany, Kevin, 3415
Mahon, John, 4824
Mahon, Teddy, 3658
Mahon, Tom, 1671
Mahone, Wardell, 2919
Mahoney, Damien, 2645
Mahoney, Dave, 1988, 3857
Mahoney, Desmond, 561
Mahoney, Frank, 1990
Mahoney, Janet, 3415
Mahoney, Paul, 4050
Mahoney, Timothy J., 5424
Mahoney, William, 955
Mahony-Bennett, Kathleen, 2602
Mahotella Queens, 3188, 3414-3415, 3420, 3534, 5516
Mahramas, Michael, 1990
Maichel, Marcus C., 5940
Maid Of The Mountains, The, 250, 540, 2382, 3415, 4426
Maida, Raine, 4079
Maida, Sal, 3667, 4669
Maiden Voyage, 1850, 2347, 2374, 2547, 3224, 3415, 4157, 4751, 5283, 5449
Maiden, Sidney, 1604, 3415

Maiden, Tony, 4684, 6060
Maidman, Grace, 5839
Maids Of Gravity, 3608, 4399
Maiga, Boncana, 85, 1505, 1605, 3416
Maiken, Gilda, 4957
Maile, Vic, 2162, 2454, 2991, 4671
Mailhouse, Rob, 1574
Maimone, Tony, 3138, 3815, 4193, 5388
Maimro, Jean-Claude, 3200
Main, 3416
Main Attraction, 1912, 2269, 2284, 2485, 2767, 2794, 3169, 3219, 3395, 3546, 3919, 3971, 4379, 4908, 5432, 5921
Main Ingredient, 3416 and *passim*
Main Source, 3416 and *passim*
Main Squeeze, 462, 2890, 3650
Main Street Crew, 2213, 4465-4466, 4765
Main, Graham, 1901
Main, Marjorie, 2426, 3611, 4648
Main, Paul, 5962
Maine, Simon, 133
Mainegra, Richard, 1343, 4499
Mairants, Ivor, 2124, 2186, 3177, 3417-3418, 3715, 6061
Mainer, J.E., 3167, 3417, 3760, 3790, 4133, 4978
Mainer, Wade, 1552, 3167, 3417, 3760, 3790
Maines, Lloyd, 1749, 3322, 3573
Maini, Joe, 1944
Mainieri, Mike, 2196, 2295, 3417
Mainstream Records, 52, 1880, 1893, 2634, 2848, 5833
Mair, Alan, 198, 438, 4049
Mair, Alexander, 275
Mairants, Ivor, 2124, 2186, 3177, 3417-3418, 3715, 6061
Mais, Don, 4349, 4431
Maisonet, Luisito, 3162
Maisonettes, 1091, 3418
Maita, Joe, 1892
Maitland, Chris, 4285
Maitland, Duncan, 4236
Maitland, Graham, 2170
Maitland, Joan, 595
Maitland, Lena, 5573
Majewski, Andy, 3392
Majewski, Hank, 1993, 1995
Majidi, Arman, 4899
Majola, Ronnie, 3440
Major Mackerel, 3130, 4155, 4922
Major Minor Records, 2910
Major Surgery, 69, 1114, 1230, 1463, 1979, 2813, 3358, 3418, 4569, 4605, 4978, 5760
Major, Harold, 1316
Major, Ray, 743, 1910, 3814, 4147, 4243
Majors, 3418
Makarova, Natalia, 4042
Makassi, Neng, 5406
Makassy, Mzee, 4057
Make Me An Offer, 110, 842, 3418-3419
Make Mine Manhattan, 3109, 3419

Make You Whistle, 649, 809, 2549, 2653, 4426, 5397, 5821
Make-Up, 3419
Makeba, Miriam, 457, 675, 1505, 2250, 2987, 3057, 3341, 3419-3420, 3441, 3499-3500, 3535, 3669, 5940, 6061
Makeda, Lisa, 3059
Makeham, Elliot, 5285
Makem, Tommy, 1093-1094, 1414, 1639, 2992, 5487
Makonde, 4018
Makower, Joel, 6086
Makowicz, Adam, 3420
Mákvirág, 3421
Malaco Records, 3421 and *passim*
Malara, Bob, 1624
Malarky, John, 1323
Malavasi, Mauro, 1015
Malcolm, Calum, 2454
Malcolm, Christopher, 4600
Malcolm, Horace, 2396
Malcolm, Victor, 2121, 3665
Malcom, Carl, 3421-3422 and *passim*
Maldem, Pete, 2275
Malden, Karl, 2324
Maldonado, Jorge, 229, 4421, 5471
Maldonado, Ray, 4447
Maldonado, Ricardo, 4446
Maldonado-Palmieri, Isabel, 4113
Maldoon, Clive, 2618
Male, Andrew, 4012
Male, Johnny, 4508
Male, Kerilee, 1700, 2486, 3353
Malekani, Jerry, 4704
Malevolent Creation, 3422
Malfatti, Radu, 3675
Malheiros, Alex, 302
Malherba, Didier, 4706
Malice, 3422
Malicorne, 3154, 3422, 5739
Malignac, Alain-Philippe, 3159
Malik, Raphé, 5310
Malika B, 305, 1559, 2939
Malina, Luba, 3648
Malino, Louis, 1144
Malis, Jody, 2801
Malkmus, Steve, 631, 1316, 4167
Mallard, 825, 927, 1101, 3422-3423
Mallet Playboys, 4577
Mallet, Alain, 752
Mallet, Sam, 1893
Mallett, Dave, 3282, 3423
Mallett, Saundra, 1731
Mallett, Timmy, 651
Mallinder, Stephen, 875-876
Mallon, Josh, 4563
Mallory, Eddie, 2171, 3423, 3554, 5879
Mallory, Lee, 3668
Malloy, David, 714, 980, 3558
Malloy, Donald, 368
Mallozzi, Charlie, 4434
Malm, Eddy, 2467
Malmsteen, Yngwie, 111, 1391, 1624, 2456, 2618, 2951, 3380, 3423, 4183, 4660, 5286, 5533, 5592
Malnati, Rob, 1805

Malneck, Matty, 2215, 2923, 3293, 3629, 4130
Malo, 1180-1181, 1841, 2212, 3143, 3424, 3523, 3671, 3938-3939, 4083, 4746
Malo, Gina, 2212
Malo, Raul, 3523, 3671
Malombo Jazz, 328, 3424
Malone, Bill C., 1223, 1254, 2249, 2589, 4730, 4951, 5765, 6092
Malone, Bugsy, 821, 1837, 5857
Malone, Cindy, 848
Malone, Dave, 4400
Malone, Debbie, 4364
Malone, Dorothy, 2034, 3947, 5965
Malone, Geneva, 3424
Malone, George, 3742
Malone, J.J., 2980, 3424, 5794
Malone, Kenny, 2106
Malone, Linda, 2307
Malone, Marcus, 4740
Malone, Michelle, 2407
Malone, Molly, 5799
Malone, Pat, 1538
Malone, Russell, 3072
Malone, Steve, 1799
Malone, Terry, 2881
Malone, Today, 4514
Maloney, Bunny, 3271, 3832, 4177
Maloney, Hattie, 4118
Maloney, Vince, 301, 5973
Malopoets, 280, 3425, 3534
Malsch, Dan, 5816
Maltby, David, 1572
Maltby, H.F., 5285, 5573
Maltby, Richard, 94, 310, 518, 3425, 3705, 3942, 4608, 4883
Maltby, Richard, Jnr., 94, 310, 518, 3425, 3705, 3942, 4608, 4883
Maltese, Tony, 1756
Malvo, Anthony, 765, 785, 1944, 3425, 4466, 4922-4923
MAM Records, 1438, 2061
Mama Records, 3426
Mama's Boys, 3426
Mama, I Want To Sing, 3426-3427, 5512
Maman, Alan, 5814
Mamas And The Papas, 18, 79, 366, 578, 982, 1575, 1610, 1739, 1919, 2344, 2901, 3085-3086, 3346, 3427-3428, 3431, 3579, 3586, 3753, 3833, 4109, 4122, 4173, 4222-4224, 4557, 5311, 5371, 5738, 5869, 6061
Mamas Boys, 98, 1610, 5311
Mambo Kings, The, 351, 1320, 3428, 4616
Mame, 246, 351, 581, 1190, 2221, 2504-2505, 2935, 3095, 3127, 3235, 3246, 3389, 3428, 3586, 3669, 4317, 4620
Mamedov, Gussan, 253
Mameli, Patrick, 4205
Mamet, David, 3403, 4680
Mammoth, 3428
Mamonas Assassinas, 3429
Mamoulian, Rouben, 1051, 1703, 2523, 3337-3338, 3429, 4285-4286, 4906

Messiah Force, 3641
Messina, Jim, 818-819, 3133, 3297, 3642, 4268
Messina, Rich, 1019
Messingham, Andrew, 2732
Messini, Jimmy, 689
Messner, Johnny, 3642
Metal Blade Records, 230, 749, 1860, 2474, 2503, 2909, 3879, 4119, 4294, 4337, 4773, 4822
Metal Church, 2503, 3642, 4939, 5816
Metalheadz, 2191, 2296, 3642-3643, 4474
Metallica, 37, 50, 120, 145, 151, 204, 208, 640, 1298, 1317, 1369, 1507, 1518, 1541, 1807, 1891-1892, 1944, 1988, 2072, 2184, 2297, 2467, 2575, 2697, 2958, 2991, 2993, 3020, 3092, 3465, 3506, 3612-3613, 3642-3644, 3660, 3777, 3866, 3879, 4050, 4085, 4124, 4127, 4540, 4597, 4751, 4937, 4962, 5286, 5352, 5628, 5636, 5657, 5712, 5720, 6000, 6052, 6064, 6096
Metamoros, Miguel, 1205
Metaxa, George, 550
Metcalf, Byron, 5773
Metcalf, Ken, 1784
Metcalf, Louis, 1267, 3644
Metcalfe, Andy, 2544
Metcalfe, Clive, 4247
Metcalfe, Hugh, 821
Metcalfe, Keith, 4464
Metcalfe, Martin, 2206
Metcheer, Kevin, 5452
Metchick, Don, 3733
Meteor Records, 553, 5797
Meteors, 879, 2303, 3396, 3638, 3644-3645
Meters, 3645 and passim
Meth, Max, 4108
Metheny, Pat, 15, 161, 492, 591, 686, 722, 847, 1168, 1380, 1466, 1701, 2038, 2139, 2316, 2331, 2448, 2491, 2519, 3276, 3461, 3531, 3645-3646, 3714, 3803, 3965, 4017, 4153, 4473, 4492, 4779, 4836, 5494, 5616, 5859
Method Man, 32, 1042, 1766, 2053, 2117, 4027, 5932-5933
Method Of Destruction, 3646
Metis, Frank, 2718
Metro, 3646-3647
Metro, Peter, 370, 3104, 3144, 3505, 3647, 3697
Metronome All Stars, 878, 3736
Metroplex, 271, 2002, 3647, 4482, 5326
Metropolis, 3647-3648
Metsers, Paul, 3648, 5534
Mettome, Doug, 2208
Metty, Russell, 5418
Metz, Bennie, 3635
Metz, Janet, 3389, 3457
Metz, Steve, 3249
Metzner, Doug, 1254
Mew, Dave, 934
Mewes, Ken, 618
Mexican Hayride, 1886, 3648, 4289
Mexicano, 3648-3649, 4445
Meyer, Ben, 3879, 4127

Meyer, Edgar, 1604
Meyer, Eric, 1391
Meyer, George, 91, 93, 569, 1106, 3201, 3225, 3649, 5972-5973
Meyer, George W., 91, 93, 569, 1106, 3201, 3225, 3649, 5973
Meyer, Joe, 877
Meyer, John, 843, 4649
Meyer, Joseph, 35, 881, 1022, 1439, 2035, 3649, 4650
Meyer, Mandy, 1141, 3079
Meyer, Mark, 3820
Meyer, Russ, 2258
Meyer, Sig, 3580
Meyer, Skip, 1604
Meyers, Augie, 440, 1874, 2824, 3649, 4718, 4938, 5348, 6131
Meyers, Billy, 2923
Meyers, Larry, 1843
Meyerson, Harold, 2387, 5899, 6051
Mezcal, 3366
Mezias, Jay, 4011
Mezzoforte, 316, 3650
Mezzrow, Mezz, 72, 154, 826, 1116, 1177, 1437, 1571, 1651, 1885, 2212, 2243, 2547, 2852, 3031, 3081, 3108, 3650, 3768, 4380, 4533, 4809, 4936, 6090
MFG, 5491
MFQ, 1855, 3650-3651, 5958
MFSB, 613, 1499, 1626, 1724, 1905, 3651, 3967, 4752, 5422
MGM Band, 2006, 4867, 5460
MGM Records, 3651 and passim
Mia, Cara, 5804
Miall, Terry Lee, 62
Miami Showband, 3652, 4593, 4737
Miami Sound Machine, 1781-1782, 1900, 3652, 4803, 6047
Miaow, 440, 954, 1239, 3652
Mice, 3652 and passim
Michael, Eddie, 1444
Michael, George, 56, 776, 850, 983, 1001, 1152, 1188, 1829, 1990, 2013, 2110, 2347, 2748, 2834, 2882, 3045, 3157, 3276, 3434, 3652-3653, 3740, 3808, 3874, 4029, 4192, 4349, 4381, 4435, 5426, 5570, 5719, 5781, 5815, 5857, 6064, 6084
Michael, Jean-Francois, 488
Michael, Jorg, 290, 4183
Michael, Morris, 4342, 4795
Michael, Peter, 436, 847, 1681, 3417, 3570, 3805, 4416, 6033
Michael, Ryan, 544
Michael-Phillips, David, 3001
Michaeli, Michael, 1786
Michaelis, Robert, 3184
Michaels, Andy, 4917
Michaels, Arjen, 268
Michaels, Bert, 336
Michaels, Bret, 4272
Michaels, David, 2327
Michaels, Frank, 3428
Michaels, Hilly, 2424
Michaels, Jesse, 4052, 4424
Michaels, Jill, 4771
Michaels, Lee, 1839, 3653, 4822
Michaels, Nick, 508

Michaels, Rollie, 4518
Michaels, Russ, 3015
Michaels, Shaun, 318
Michaels, Shirley, 2389
Michaelson, Nick, 4821
Michall, Ernest, 701
Michals, Mark, 1857
Michalski, John, 1251
Michalski, Mike, 1343
Michalski, Richard, 295
Micheaux, Oscar, 2806, 2869, 4577
Michel'le, 3154, 3422, 3653, 6103
Michel, Jean, 850, 2469, 2784, 4054, 4422
Michele, Lea, 4408
Michell, Chris, 5797
Michell, Keith, 124, 171, 811, 2709, 3431, 4569
Michelle, Yvette, 2053
Michelot, Pierre, 3328, 3653, 4079, 4664
Michels, Stephanie, 3239
Michener, Dean, 2187
Michigan And Smiley, 1569, 1609, 1713, 3139, 3144, 3654, 4717, 5767
Mickell, Lt. Eugene, Snr., 963
Mickey And Sylvia, 344, 1539, 2469, 3654, 5509
Mickey And The Milkshakes, 3668
Micki And Maude, 3768
Mickle, Elmon, 1629
Microdisney, 170, 1861, 2521, 3654
Micus, Stephan, 3654
Middel, Willy, 1324
Middle Earth Records, 218
Middle Of The Road, 3655 and passim
Middlemass, Frank, 1578
Middleton, Charles, 2761
Middleton, George, 649, 6124
Middleton, Guy, 1012
Middleton, Herb, 5708
Middleton, Malcolm, 215
Middleton, Mark, 573, 4406
Middleton, Max, 445, 3495, 4298, 4452
Middleton, Ray, 197, 3046, 3336, 4570, 5798
Middleton, Robert, 1258
Middleton, Tom, 4210
Middleton, Tony, 4498, 5864
Middleton, Velma, 234, 3655, 4750
Midfield General, 4954
Midgely, Vernon, 2456, 3289
Midgett, Tim, 4907
Midgley, Bobby, 5467
Midland Youth Jazz Orchestra, 224, 5894
Midler, Bette, 393, 1312, 1486, 1489, 2226, 2291, 2295, 2324, 3432, 3441, 3443, 3655-3656, 3712, 4449, 4571, 4653, 4716, 5454, 5671, 5709, 6064
Midnight And Peanut, 4787
Midnight Court, 2446, 2950, 5556
Midnight Oil, 1519, 2134, 2672, 3436, 3657, 4534, 5513, 6064

Midnight Runners, 274, 612, 788, 827, 1487, 1502, 1584, 2526, 2994, 3486, 3640, 3795, 4142, 4667, 4800, 4805, 5351, 5465, 5717, 5874, 6123
Midnight Serenaders, 3775
Midnight Star, 1487, 3093, 5813
Midnight Well, 3547, 3773-3774
Midnite Follies Orchestra, 385-386, 1153, 1188, 1747, 1828, 3657, 3941
Midsong Records, 5497
Midway Still, 3658
Midwest Playboys, 2378
Mielle, Gary, 5303
Mielziner, Joe, 127
Miessner, Brian, 82
Miettinen, Miri, 2293
Miezitis, Chris, 1524
Migdol, Brian, 555
Migenes, Julia, 1882
Mighell, Norman, 4058
Might Dub Katz, 1860
Mighty Avengers, 2822, 2878, 3658, 4031
Mighty Avons, 3658
Mighty Baby, 51, 58, 1060, 1076, 1852, 2327, 3018, 3658, 4354, 5414, 5634, 5704
Mighty Clouds, 2764, 3658-3659, 5305, 5319
Mighty Clouds Of Joy, 3658-3659, 5305, 5319
Mighty Diamonds, 1062, 1107, 1309, 1356, 1650, 2588, 2727, 2761, 2763, 3533, 3593, 3609, 3659, 3958, 4431, 4514, 4543, 4595, 4675, 4941, 5290-5291, 5505, 5651
Mighty Fatman, 790, 2700, 2762
Mighty Frontline, 1605
Mighty Glad, 3686
Mighty Houserockers, 2068
Mighty Irokos, 137
Mighty Jah Shaka, 778, 4741
Mighty Lemon Drops, 3659-3660, 5822, 5906
Mighty Maytones, 3533, 4595
Mighty Mighty, 3660
Mighty Mighty Bosstones, 3660, 4425, 4481
Mighty Sam, 3550, 3660-3661, 4368
Mighty Sparrow, 3171, 3661, 4717
Mighty Two, 468, 2138, 3082, 5409-5410
Mighty, Ray, 4979
Mightymo Destructimo, 3145
Migil Five, 2600, 3661
Migilacio, Gerson, 1844
Miglans, John, 1183
Migliacci, Franco, 3729
Mignon, Philly, 2882
Migone, Scott, 2325
Mihas, Eddie, 4492
Mihashi, Michiya, 3661
Mihm, Danny, 1924, 2299, 2602, 3307
Mike And The Mechanics, 51, 952, 1388, 2116, 2379, 3661-3662, 4391, 4702
Mike And The Thunderbirds, 871

Mike And The Utopians, 49
Mike Stuart Span, 3211, 3662
Miketta, Bob, 4328
Mikey General, 1270, 3210, 3662, 4945
Miki And Griff, 3663
Mikkelborg, 2502, 3053, 3663, 4065, 4542, 4696, 4706
Mikkelborg, Palle, 2502, 3053, 3663, 4065, 4542, 4696, 4706
Miklaszewska, Maryna, 3647
Miklis, Peter, 3086
Miksa, Florian Pilkington, 1340
Mikus, Heinz, 1831
Milani, Roberto, 3666
Milano, Billy, 3646
Milano, Freddie, 469, 1535
Milburn, Amos, 77, 105, 132, 532, 768, 1007, 1496, 1568, 2217, 2414, 3275, 3641, 3663-3664, 4089, 4223, 4583, 4946, 5730
Milder, Joakim, 1565, 2084
Milem, Percy, 5818
Milenovic, Maya, 5921
Miles, Ant, 1987
Miles, Barry, 1416, 3549, 6043, 6063, 6115
Miles, Bernard, 381, 2849, 3017, 3288
Miles, Buddy, 360, 1724, 2381, 2491, 2526, 3133, 3664, 4705, 4724, 4740-4741, 4724, 4740-4741
Miles, Butch, 3664-3665, 6003-6004
Miles, Colin, 4809, 6122
Miles, Dick, 2233, 2532, 3665
Miles, Garry, 3665, 3684
Miles, Gaynor, 4569
Miles, George, 3258, 3664, 4725, 6003
Miles, Henry, 268, 4010
Miles, Herbie, 995
Miles, John, 297, 549, 794, 1110, 1415, 3665, 4677, 6040, 6059
Miles, Kevin, 2112
Miles, Lizzie, 2517, 3665, 4579
Miles, Luke, 3666
Miles, Lynn, 3666
Miles, Phyllis, 3508
Miles, Reid, 614, 844
Miles, Richard, 1416
Miles, Robert, 1453, 3280, 3666, 4569
Miles, Sue, 3665
Miles, Trevor, 4078
Miles-Kingston, June, 3721
Miles-Kingston, Paul, 737
Milestone Records, 1287, 1629, 4352
Milestone, Lewis, 205
Miley, Bubber, 72, 475, 963, 1735, 2713, 3667, 3873, 4497, 5841
Miley, James Wesley, 3667
Milhaud, Darius, 78, 794, 4491, 4684
Milheim, Keith, 2589
Milhûn, 1004, 3667, 4408
Militiades, George, 3615
Milito, Helicio, 3717
Milk And Cookies, 3667

Milk And Honey, 2504, 3192, 3667-3668
Milkboilers, 1475
Milkshakes, 1475, 1485, 1750, 3668, 4341-4342, 5382-5383, 5924
Milkwood, 801, 2211
Millán, William, 1899-1900, 4744
Milland, Ray, 522, 2709, 3106, 3548, 5432
Millar, Gertie, 295, 1031, 3184, 4079, 4377
Millar, Larry, 5572
Millar, Mary, 441
Millar, Robin, 552
Millar, Ronald, 4569
Millar, Stuart, 2659
Millar, Will, 276
Millars, Jean-Pierre, 3949
Millas, Larry, 2672
Millenium, 1060, 1853, 2181, 2631, 2833, 3252, 3592, 3852, 4330, 4574, 4717, 5307, 5351, 5542
Millennium Records, 752, 2011
Miller, Andy, 1572, 3679, 4343, 4570
Miller, Ann, 1020, 1692, 2543, 3035-3037, 3428, 3488, 3668-3669, 4040-4041, 4118, 4511, 4570, 4643, 5798, 5964
Miller, Barry, 1837, 3639, 4752
Miller, Ben, 1494, 3680, 5918
Miller, Bernie, 2347
Miller, Besti, 4349
Miller, Big, 1942, 3669
Miller, Bill, 3669, 5322, 5790
Miller, Billy, 32, 76, 5989
Miller, Blue, 1823, 2143
Miller, Bob, 675, 744, 958, 1790, 1942, 3670, 4305
Miller, Bobbie, 5935
Miller, Bobby, 1213, 1474, 3035, 3748
Miller, Bobsy, 1183
Miller, Brian, 928, 2225, 2721, 4593
Miller, Cedric, 5569
Miller, Charles, 5697
Miller, Chris, 14, 928, 1035, 1146, 1371, 3302
Miller, Chuck, 3670
Miller, Cleo, 1731
Miller, Count Prince, 1980, 2581, 2774, 2908, 3670
Miller, Craig, 2928
Miller, Daniel, 1487, 1821, 2145, 2630
Miller, Dave, 2143, 4583
Miller, David, 1896, 3356, 5298, 5343
Miller, Dean, 3671
Miller, Diane Disney, 1545
Miller, Dominic, 5924
Miller, Don, 1013, 5655
Miller, Donald, 671, 2267
Miller, Donnie, 3671
Miller, Drew, 643
Miller, Duncan, 3671
Miller, Dwain, 2951
Miller, Ed, 3671, 5998, 6114
Miller, Edd, 318
Miller, Eddie, 1129, 1304, 2330,

2627, 3115, 3580, 3671, 3705, 4206, 4275, 4328, 5819, 5923
Miller, Elva, 3678
Miller, Emmett, 2289, 3672, 4469, 5846
Miller, Ernest 'Punch', 3672
Miller, Flournoy, 569, 579, 4896
Miller, Frankie, 825, 2017, 2906, 3559, 3673, 3813, 4268, 4344, 5306, 5399, 5511
Miller, Fred, 2493
Miller, Gary, 215, 313, 350, 3673, 3743, 4860, 5790, 5932
Miller, Gertie, 4079
Miller, Glenn, 19, 144, 184, 201, 235, 355, 375, 398, 421, 474, 507, 543, 675, 705, 726, 877, 936, 941, 985, 1049, 1060, 1085, 1162, 1171, 1288, 1401, 1433, 1436, 1492, 1584, 1659, 1697, 1741, 1776, 1864, 1887, 1895, 1909, 1927, 2007, 2088, 2120, 2128, 2159, 2170, 2216, 2253, 2300, 2329, 2391, 2462, 2533, 2549, 2623, 2652, 2708, 2812, 2944, 2962, 2971, 2996, 3043, 3068, 3081, 3126, 3146-3148, 3292, 3315, 3320, 3348, 3433, 3492, 3499, 3525, 3563-3564, 3581, 3587, 3615, 3630, 3638, 3674-3675, 3705, 3728, 3748, 3763, 3815, 3820, 3865, 3898, 3966, 4057, 4130, 4181, 4237, 4275, 4370, 4451, 4561, 4700, 4760, 4822, 4866, 5322, 5606, 5711, 5789-5790, 5866, 5932, 5985, 5993, 6003, 6064
Miller, Gregg, 1574
Miller, Hank, 2516
Miller, Harold, 4450
Miller, Harry, 763, 3675, 3732, 4069, 4362, 5448
Miller, Helen, 4391
Miller, Henry, 874, 876, 2017, 3158, 3669, 3678
Miller, Herb, 3675
Miller, Hilda, 1219, 4259
Miller, Horace, 1895, 3705
Miller, Husky, 940-941
Miller, Irwin C., 1027
Miller, J.D., 3153, 3676
Miller, J.D. 'Jay', 3676
Miller, Jack, 985, 1374, 2347, 3045, 3815, 4275, 5894
Miller, Jacob, 1082, 1264, 2696, 3676, 4050, 4096, 4595, 5995
Miller, Jay, 46, 177, 2091, 2310, 2550, 2755, 2977, 3154, 3307, 3889, 4967, 5406, 5969
Miller, Jerry, 1013, 1068, 1280, 3723-3724
Miller, Jimmie, 3384, 3672
Miller, Jimmy, 201, 453, 485, 1864, 3676, 3956, 4012, 4630, 4793
Miller, Jo, 1256, 3341, 3677
Miller, Jody, 3676-3677, 4169
Miller, John, 15, 1953, 2103, 2961, 3672
Miller, Johnny, 241, 1236, 1909
Miller, Jonathan, 499, 513-514, 2103
Miller, Kincaid, 4746
Miller, Larry, 1494

Miller, Les, 1035
Miller, Leza, 3626
Miller, Marcus, 792, 1790, 2165, 3677, 4155, 5539, 5800
Miller, Marilyn, 249, 2216, 2284-2285, 4207, 4478, 4637, 4646, 4724-4725, 5901, 5964, 5998
Miller, Mark, 4135, 4343, 4758, 5286, 6067, 6102
Miller, Max, 212, 485, 862, 1516, 3372, 4005
Miller, Maxine, 387
Miller, Mitch, 480, 1000, 1133, 1187, 1208, 1998, 2021, 2024, 2563, 3111, 3231, 3632, 3673, 3677, 3711, 4554, 5593, 5748
Miller, Mrs, 1256, 3678
Miller, Mulgrew, 383, 2094, 2267, 3678, 3772, 5859
Miller, Ned, 3678-3679, 5284
Miller, Oscar, 2903, 4746
Miller, Pat, 4807
Miller, Paul, 579, 1332, 1561, 2216
Miller, Perry, 4782, 5971, 5983
Miller, Peter, 2791, 4106
Miller, Phil, 1297, 1473, 1584, 2429, 3511, 3882
Miller, Ray, 579, 603, 1697, 2623, 2971, 3679, 4328, 4593, 4874, 5798, 5964
Miller, Rhett, 4027
Miller, Robert, 1025, 1731, 2178, 5833
Miller, Robin, 1369
Miller, Roger, 173, 528, 531, 702, 838, 1198, 1256, 1755, 2674, 2736, 2906, 2966, 2992, 3078, 3671, 3679-3680, 3707, 3901, 3926, 4324, 4344, 4418, 4559, 4866, 4960, 4976, 5591, 5970
Miller, Ronnie, 1262
Miller, Rufus, 5479
Miller, Sammy, 5762
Miller, Scott, 90, 2077, 5591
Miller, Shirley, 2441
Miller, Slim, 1331, 3112
Miller, Sonny, 1027, 1039, 1374, 2285, 2771, 4351
Miller, Stan, 1688, 2657
Miller, Steve, 15, 33, 501, 717, 923, 930, 1269, 1410, 1473, 1769, 1898, 1949, 1953, 2044, 2187, 2291, 2309, 2586, 2594, 2839, 3502, 3548-3549, 3639, 3680-3681, 3753, 4231, 4257, 4268, 4354, 4477, 4514, 4720, 4763, 4896, 4900, 5343, 5369, 5578, 5650, 5731
Miller, Steve, Band, 33, 501, 717, 923, 1949, 2044, 2594, 2839, 3502, 3680-3681, 3753, 4268, 4354, 4514, 4720, 4763, 4720, 4763, 5343, 5578
Miller, Steven, 5842
Miller, Thomas, 3675, 4762, 5633, 6064
Miller, Tom, 3727, 5399
Miller, Tommy, 877, 1929, 2657, 4451
Miller, Trevor, 28
Miller, Vern, 4498

Moore, Johnny, 768, 1627-1628, 2440, 3275, 3641, 3770, 4912, 4948
Moore, Johnny B., 3770
Moore, Jon, 176, 2560, 2911
Moore, Jonathan, 1157, 1558, 2511, 3955
Moore, Keith, 239, 379, 3715
Moore, Kevin, 1624, 1860, 2950
Moore, Lee, 710, 1804, 3770-3771, 5302, 5731
Moore, Marilyn, 3771
Moore, Mark, 1275, 2181, 2978, 4522, 4709
Moore, Melanie, 5554
Moore, Melba, 924, 2337, 2740, 3039, 3322, 3771, 4368, 4506
Moore, Michael, 2222, 4648, 5301
Moore, Mick, 290, 595
Moore, Milton Aubrey, 3766
Moore, Monette, 1950, 2556, 3771, 4421
Moore, Nicky, 3428, 4731
Moore, Ollie, 4241, 4467
Moore, Oscar, 768, 1159, 1176, 3770, 3772, 4197
Moore, Owen, 4859
Moore, Patrick, 4510
Moore, Paul Joseph, 613
Moore, Pete, 2007
Moore, Phil, 2345, 4483
Moore, R. Stevie, 3772
Moore, Ralph, 1393, 2268, 3772, 4213
Moore, Ray, 524, 3772
Moore, Rev. James, 3421, 3707, 3773
Moore, Rev. James, And The Mississippi Mass Choir, 3772-3773
Moore, Robert, 4975
Moore, Robin, 4714
Moore, Roger, 258, 1214, 2873, 3574, 3771
Moore, Roger Lee, 3771
Moore, Rosie, 5582
Moore, Russell 'Big Chief', 3773
Moore, Ruth, 644
Moore, Sam, 1601, 2553, 4591, 4727
Moore, Sammie, 2712
Moore, Sandy, Jnr., 508
Moore, Sara Jane, 259
Moore, Scotty, 563, 955, 1748, 2438, 2896, 3290, 3773, 4197, 4225, 4309, 4311, 4314, 4876, 5377, 5737, 6065, 6070
Moore, Sean, 3442
Moore, Shirley, 995, 3421
Moore, Simon, 4902, 5307, 5582
Moore, Stan, 578, 5988
Moore, Terry, 1060, 1355, 2526
Moore, Thom, 3773
Moore, Thurston, 84, 317, 672, 710, 1083, 1530, 1804, 2475, 3968, 5625, 5698, 5731
Moore, Tim, 2344, 2978
Moore, Tiny, 2580, 3774
Moore, Tom, 3821
Moore, Vic, 603, 5904
Moore, Victor, 205, 259, 672, 1981, 2055, 2185, 2552, 2602,

3160, 3326, 3850, 4016, 4020, 4468
Moore, Vinnie, 3774, 5641
Moore, Wayne, 3879
Moore, William, 791, 1919, 2586, 3765, 4468
Moore, Willie C., 3774
Moorehead, Agnes, 1122
Moorer, Alvis, 1779
Moorer, Betty, 1779
Moorer, Gilbert, 1779
Moorer, Lana, 3537
Moorhouse, Alan, 5887
Mooridian, Jeff, 2366
Moors Murderers, 1231, 2839, 3040, 4318
Moorshead, Jem, 1695
Moose, 1022, 1030, 1129, 1733, 2738, 3050, 3316, 3612, 3774-3775, 4207, 4475, 5598
Mootz, Jack, 2287, 5844
Mopro Records, 14, 1175, 5658
Mora, Pepe, 3314
Moraes, Angel, 3775
Morais, Trevor, 2875, 4179, 4686
Morales, David, 551, 2083, 2689, 3053, 3083, 3249, 3775, 4090, 4186, 4222, 4619, 5276, 5338, 5727
Moráles, Edwin, 3834
Morales, Efrain, 4421
Morales, Frankie, 3163, 3233, 3249, 4032, 4613
Morales, Hermanos, Orchestra, 3776
Morales, Matthew, 942
Morales, Michael, 3632
Morales, Noro, 86, 2396, 2925, 3232, 3314, 3775-3776, 4360, 4420, 4615-4616, 4646
Morales, Obdulio, 3353
Morali, Jacques, 5644
Moran, Eddie, 5906
Moran, Gayle, 3414
Moran, Jackie, 3397
Moran, Jerry, 163
Moran, Kenny, 2514
Moran, Lois, 4016
Moran, Mae, 428
Moran, Mike, 1308, 1438, 2148, 3060, 4104
Moran, Robert, 346
Morand, Eric, 2093
Morand, Herb, 826, 2396, 2517, 3776
Morandi, Gianni, 3790
Moranis, Rick, 3272, 3585
Morath, Kate, 5423
Moraz, Patrick, 1024, 1402, 2736, 3759, 4487, 5957
Morbid Angel, 649, 913, 1767, 3777, 3873, 3968, 5342
Morcheeba, 871, 3777
Mordred, 899, 1591, 3777
More, 3777-3778
More American Graffiti, 3778
More, Anthony, 3778, 5394
Moré, Beny, 86, 508, 1321, 1349, 1899, 2200, 2397, 3143, 3702, 3779, 4361-4362, 4389, 4610, 4614, 4742, 5472
More, Julian, 442, 1809-1810,

2226-2227, 2709, 3779
More, Kenneth, 4795, 4969
More, Robin S., 1354
Morehand, Marc, 4542
Morehouse, Chauncey, 3779
Morehouse, Ward, 1153, 6041
Moreira, Airto, 156, 1714, 2000, 2131, 2163, 2421, 3085, 3590, 3780, 3877, 4368, 4483, 4509-4510, 4636, 5721, 5741, 5850, 5955
Moreira, Diana, 2000
Moreira, Gil, 2145
Moreland, Bruce, 5685
Moreland, Prentice, 1636
Morell, André, 4969
Morello, Joe, 794, 2088, 3780, 4178, 5850
Morello, Tom, 4406
Morells, 3780-3781
Moreno, Bobby, 3781
Moreno, Buddy, 3781, 5845
Moreno, Chino, 1463
Moreno, Lydia, 5598
Moreno, Rita, 1018, 2997, 5771-5772
Morer, Jack, 5289
Moreshead, John, 1263, 2466
Moret, Neil, 2923, 5453, 5805
Moreton, Ivor, 2946
Moreu, G., 4574
Morey, Larry, 1543-1544
Morgan Heritage, 3781
Morgan, Adrian, 1249
Morgan, Al, 958, 2293, 3781
Morgan, Alun, 2798, 3756
Morgan, Barry, 613, 1001, 3722, 4269, 4350, 4785
Morgan, Brian, 2731, 4720
Morgan, Carey, 178
Morgan, Chad, 1664
Morgan, Charles, 1251
Morgan, Charlie, 4132, 4626
Morgan, Cindy, 3782
Morgan, Clifford, 250
Morgan, Dave, 356, 3295, 3412, 4598, 5564
Morgan, Dennis, 421, 1491, 2186, 2259, 3125, 3436
Morgan, Derek, 3782
Morgan, Derrick, 512, 573, 610, 1568, 2908, 3006, 3060, 3171, 3782, 4376
Morgan, Diana, 4806
Morgan, Dick, 1429
Morgan, Dorinda, 3050
Morgan, Earl, 1686, 2496
Morgan, Eddie, 415
Morgan, Elaine, 3782
Morgan, Eula, 2257
Morgan, Fay, 1206
Morgan, Frank, 746, 2260, 2508, 3782-3783, 3885, 4183, 4646, 5419, 5899, 5994
Morgan, Freddy, 4515
Morgan, George, 238, 866, 1706, 2481, 2695, 3783, 3785, 4171, 4596, 5438, 5679, 5806, 5818, 5923
Morgan, Harry, 4058
Morgan, Helen, 151, 633-634, 1022, 2174, 2243, 2512, 3429, 3783-3784, 4021, 4183, 4535, 4892-4893, 5600, 5901, 5998, 6065

Morgan, Ian, 746, 2825, 3612, 5973
Morgan, Jane, 442, 3428, 3784
Morgan, Jaye P., 354, 3784
Morgan, John, 908, 3292, 4821
Morgan, Jonathan, 5298
Morgan, Lanny, 908, 3309, 3785, 5994
Morgan, Laurie, 5762
Morgan, Lee, 398, 403, 614, 618, 770, 803, 1166, 1276, 2293, 2302, 2395, 2400, 2486-2487, 2519, 2538, 2879, 3564, 3722, 3785, 4203, 4626, 4989, 5376, 5442, 5693, 5726, 5974
Morgan, Lloyd, 2763
Morgan, Lorrie, 1380, 1804, 3731, 3785, 4495, 4848, 5806
Morgan, Mark, 532, 1726
Morgan, Mary Margaret, 3784
Morgan, Melissa, 3507, 4675
Morgan, Merlin, 511
Morgan, Michele, 2523
Morgan, Mike, 1684, 3786, 4408
Morgan, Miles, 301
Morgan, Pamela, 1891
Morgan, Paul, 2026, 2919
Morgan, Ray, 3306
Morgan, Richard, 505, 2370, 4981
Morgan, Rick, 2859
Morgan, Ron, 1726
Morgan, Royce, 611
Morgan, Russ, 829, 884, 1401, 1984, 2919, 3786-3787, 4176, 4181, 4480, 4515, 4958
Morgan, Sally, 5814
Morgan, Sam, 1002, 3781, 3787, 4583
Morgan, Stanley, 2695
Morgan, Sunny, 2249
Morgan, Theodis, 4255
Morgan, Tom, 1253, 3190
Morgan, Tommy, 2625
Morgan, Warren, 301, 5973
Morgan, Wendy, 4283
Morganfield, McKinley, 3026, 3830
Morgenstein, Rod, 1550, 5884
Morgenstern, Dan, 2798
Mori, Romi, 2313, 4239
Moriarty, Cathy, 3428
Morias, Trevor, 1852
Morillo, Erick 'More', 3787
Morin, Frank, 4718, 4938
Morini, Luca, 3520
Morisse, Lucien, 1364, 2125
Morissette, Alanis, 211, 658, 757, 2455, 2680, 2759, 3666, 3765, 3787-3788, 3838, 4069, 6065, 6126
Moritt, Fred G., 4569
Moritz, Edward, 4782
Moriyama, Takeo, 5947
Morks, Jan, 1669
Morlay, Gaby, 2144
Morley, Angela, 3788
Morley, Bob, 573
Morley, Carol, 4819
Morley, Ed, 2287
Morley, Luke, 5340, 5429
Morley, Malcolm, 453, 2482, 4728
Morley, Paul, 245, 2012, 3623,

Mosley, Bernard, 3552
Mosley, Bob, 3723-3724
Mosley, Ian, 3462
Mosley, Lawrence L., 3804
Mosley, Ronald, 4680
Mosley, Snub, 1651, 2047, 2073, 2640, 3602, 3804, 4369, 5342, 5500
Mosley, Wenzon, 5604
Moss, Anne Marie, 4129
Moss, Brian, 1632
Moss, Buddy, 373, 593, 1512, 1655, 2408, 2493, 2744, 3595, 3804, 4521, 5444, 5715
Moss, Clayton, 1308
Moss, Danny, 204, 1001, 1383, 3116, 3189, 3804, 4736
Moss, Dave, 1561
Moss, Geoff, 2791, 3804
Moss, Ian, 1156
Moss, Jeff, 467
Moss, Jerome, 354
Moss, Jerry, 32, 147, 801, 2455, 3626, 3804, 4978, 5757
Moss, Joe, 1961, 3464
Moss, Jon, 98, 693, 763, 1329, 1371, 1706, 3301
Moss, Kathi, 3952
Moss, Larry, 4978
Moss, Russell, 3642
Moss, Tom, 2111
Moss, Wayne, 222, 379
Most Happy Fella, The, 1968, 1993, 2998, 3294, 3360, 3804-3805, 4209, 4656
Most Wanted, 163-164, 650, 681, 1198, 1497, 1503, 2454, 2668, 2670, 3419, 4294, 4340, 5960
Most, Arthur, 3366, 4776
Most, Mickie, 193, 220, 1001, 1045, 1064, 1146, 1187, 1871, 2504, 2770, 2838, 2878, 2970, 3260, 3356, 3651, 3805, 3879, 4378, 4416, 4495, 5800, 5951
Mostel, Josh, 3860
Mostel, Zero, 638, 1882, 2056
Mostert, Alan, 4389
Motello, Elton, 3805, 4261
Motels, 3806 and *passim*
Moten, Bennie, 378, 405-406, 861, 1113, 1659, 2790, 3175, 3195, 3524, 3765, 3806, 4102, 4694, 4983, 5278, 5341, 5528, 5718, 5748, 5928, 5975
Moth Macabre, 3806-3807
Mother Earth, 54, 185, 596, 926, 1212, 1652, 1893, 2133, 2662, 2890, 3050, 3625, 3807, 3898, 4514, 4517, 4834, 4957, 5407, 5642, 5761
Mother Earth (60s), 3807
Mother Earth (90s), 3807
Mother Goose, 413, 3703, 3762, 3807
Mother Love Bone, 2266, 2609, 3312, 3808, 4174-4175, 5332, 5335
Mother Maybelle, 960-963, 968, 979, 1256, 4604
Mother Maybelle And The Carter Sisters, 961, 963, 968, 979
Mother Records, 1101, 1759, 3309, 3477, 4769, 5479, 5561

Mother Superia, 3808
Mother Wore Tights, 1358, 2227, 3399, 3808, 3865, 3927
Mother's Finest, 3808
Motherlode, 776, 3419, 3808-3809, 5960
Mothers Of Invention, 166, 311, 414, 767, 819, 916, 926, 1397, 1456, 1646, 1650, 1784, 1820, 1907, 1940, 2001, 2020, 2127, 2303, 2530, 2603, 2944, 3161, 3264, 3388, 3410, 3651, 3731, 3809-3810, 3907, 4047, 4263, 4508, 4706, 5538, 5549, 5572, 5638, 5650, 5739-5740, 5962, 5993, 6065, 6087
Mothersbaugh, Bob, 1501
Mothersbaugh, Mark, 1501
Moti Special, 1763
Moti, Majik, 4689
Motian, Paul, 130, 496, 591, 701, 1295, 1788, 2038, 2192, 2331, 2786-2787, 3096, 3102, 3333-3334, 3740, 3810, 4173, 4473, 4584, 4790
Motion, Tim, 2799
Mötley Crüe, 63, 293, 552, 743, 995, 1589, 1613, 1857, 2220, 2380, 2456, 2468, 2758, 2838, 3040, 3053, 3342, 3810-3811, 3879, 3893, 4407, 4439, 4597, 4677, 4792, 4892, 4950, 4962, 5434, 5550, 5555, 5563, 5737, 5923, 6000
Motley, Frank, 3811, 5502
Motlow, Johnny, 2289
Motola, George, 4878
Motor Town Revue, 3811
Motorcycle Boy, 3812, 4889
Motörhead, 51-52, 54, 145, 321-322, 548, 1066, 1089, 1105-1106, 1135, 1298, 1389, 1449, 1494, 1518, 1813, 1857-1858, 1921, 2162, 2214, 2394, 2442, 2454, 2467, 2598, 2710, 2991, 3047, 3134, 3238, 3777, 3812-3813, 3817, 3866, 3871, 3922, 3963, 4015, 4092, 4203, 4235, 4598, 4726, 4728, 4808, 4964, 5295, 5303, 5342, 5430, 5570, 5702, 5740, 5823, 6001, 6065
Motors, 32, 353, 1291, 1641, 1895, 3813, 3892, 5320
Motown Records, 3813 and *passim*
Mott, 1125, 1514, 3814-3815, 4719
Mott The Hoople, 685, 743, 750, 1321, 1487, 1910, 2223, 2298, 2640, 3025, 3334, 3391, 3609, 3621, 3814-3815, 4390, 4418, 4641, 5513, 5816, 5886, 5890, 6065, 6130
Motte, Frank, 2215
Motter, Paul, 1631
Mottola, Tommy, 934, 1001, 1188, 2344, 5959
Mould, Bob, 247, 1231, 2190, 2240, 2420, 2646, 2836, 3411, 3815, 3979, 4706, 5388, 5651
Moulding, Colin, 4224, 5942
Moule, Ken, 2944
Moules, Peter, 5578
Mound City Blue Blowers,

3124, 3586, 3815
Mounka, Pamelo, 3198, 3815
Mounsey, Paul, 3816
Mount Rushmore, 3816
Mount, Dave, 3829
Mount, Peggy, 1893
Mountain, 3816 and *passim*
Mountain Ash Band, 3816
Mountain Melody Boys, 3770
Mountain Music Clan, 3874
Mountain, Valerie, 1086, 1455
Mountbatten, Philip, 4673
Mounteer, Jules, 929
Mountjoy, Monte, 2531
Mouquet, Eric, 1456
Mourneblade, 3816
Mourning Reign, 3085, 3817
Mousa, Murad, 3464
Mouse And The Traps, 2485, 3817
Mouse Records, 39, 3817
Mouse, John, 4462
Mouse, Stanley, 2246
Mouskouri, Nana, 457, 1218, 1387, 1962, 2280, 2939, 3159, 3513, 3817-3818, 5306
Moustaki, Georges, 3818
Mouth And McNeal, 3818
Mouth Music, 3392, 3818, 4538, 4888
Mouzon, Alphonze, 172, 2187, 3819, 5609
Move, 3819 and *passim*
Movement Ex, 3819
Movement 98, 5408
Mover, Bob, 2268, 2508, 4608
Mover, Jonathan, 3462, 4751
Movin' Melodies, 3819
Moving Cloud, 3820
Moving Hearts, 2378, 2446, 2599, 2680, 2776, 3298, 3361, 3767, 3820, 4261, 5474
Moving Pictures, 1332, 1345, 3820, 3907, 4691
Moving Shadow Records, 3820
Moving Sidewalks, 3821, 6007
Moving Targets, 3821
Mowat, Will, 2987
Mowatt, Judy, 1914, 2292, 2665, 3056, 3468, 3470, 3781, 3821, 3866, 4458, 4941
Mowbray, Alan, 153, 2997, 4039, 4635, 4648
Mowforth, Chris, 4911
Mowrey, Dude, 3822
Moxham, Philip, 5400, 5967
Moxham, Stuart, 3448, 5967
Moxley, Gina, 2456
Moxon, Simon, 5491
Moxy, 35, 3344, 3822
Moxy Früvous, 3822
Moy, Sylvia, 5907
Moyake, Nick, 3575, 4362
Moye, Famoudou Don, 244, 3822
Moyer, Mike, 1809
Moyes, Jim, 3406
Moyet, Alison, 118, 1487, 1821, 1825, 2707, 3201, 3243, 3344, 3822, 4012, 5952, 5980
Moynihan, Johnny, 736, 2712, 4261
Moyse, David, 97
Mozart, Leopold, 3475

MPS Records, 4932
Mr. Blobby, 2898, 5285
Mr Bo, 3824
Mr Brown, 790, 809, 4426, 5821, 5958
Mr. Easy, 471, 2959, 4225
Mr Fabulous, 1581
Mr Fingers, 1558, 3824-3825, 4090, 5556
Mr Flymo, 3145
Mr Lee, 132, 637, 1353, 3171, 3825, 5497, 5865
Mr Million, 2708
Mr Modo Records, 5733
Mr Piano, 2488, 3836
Mr Resister, 4390
Mr Scruff, 3115, 4566
Mr T Experience, 2202
Mr Thankyou Very Much, 2905
Mr. Big, 320, 1723, 1760, 1901, 2648, 2682, 3049, 3271, 3395, 3823, 4054, 4324, 4398, 5286, 5427, 5734
Mr. Big (70s), 3823
Mr. Big (80s), 3823
Mr. Bloe, 3823
Mr. Bo, 3823
Mr. Bungle, 1830, 2298, 3824
Mr. Cinders, 1744-1745, 2285, 2339, 2619, 3824
Mr. Fox, 1917, 3825
Mr. Gerbik, 1615
Mr. Mister, 1090, 1144, 1273, 3826
Mr. Tram And Company, 4875
Mraz, George, 1862, 2245, 3421, 3596, 3756, 3826, 4383, 4668
Mraz, Jirí, 3826
Mrs Brown You've Got A Lovely Daughter, 3826
Mrs Miller, 1256, 3678
Ms Melodie, 3826
Mseleku, Bheki, 2898, 3826
MSG, 98, 573, 659, 3113, 3257, 3827, 4299, 4769, 4820, 4849, 5563
MSL Records, 3589
Mthimkhulu, Joseph, 3415
MTMT Records, 3819
Mtoto, Pepo, 4327
Mtukudzi, Oliver, 1499, 3827
MTV, 3827-3828 and *passim*
Mu, 574, 1046, 1633, 1843, 2916, 3042-3043, 3059, 3319, 3636, 3828, 4592, 5441, 5483
Muana, Tshala, 3828
Much Ado, 130, 3829, 5307, 6030, 6080
Muckram Wakes, 1150, 3829
Mucky Pup, 50, 3829
Mud, 3829-3830 and *passim*
Mudboy And The Neutrons, 1515
Mudd, Fred, 3832
Mudd, Jeff, 3832
Muddy Waters, 8, 18, 21, 140, 359, 374, 409, 460, 500, 519, 621, 627, 629, 681, 695, 739, 747, 771, 775, 820, 842, 858, 902, 905, 965, 1039, 1049, 1079, 1158, 1166, 1247, 1260, 1517, 1608, 1686, 1743, 1985, 2074, 2142, 2230, 2262, 2314, 2320, 2346, 2349, 2394, 2410, 2424,

2427, 2554, 2566, 2571, 2593, 2600, 2620, 2778, 2847, 2851, 2855-2856, 2878-2879, 2889, 2958, 2980, 3013, 3026, 3133, 3144, 3151, 3175, 3182, 3242, 3274, 3291, 3299, 3326, 3381, 3460, 3533, 3551, 3715, 3721, 3746, 3830-3831, 3948, 4014, 4028, 4156, 4172, 4197, 4231, 4283, 4291, 4327, 4329-4330, 4372, 4393, 4413, 4445, 4465, 4472, 4543, 4564, 4606, 4608, 4620, 4627, 4809-4810, 4856, 4987, 5318, 5354, 5356, 5367-5368, 5375, 5417, 5522, 5583, 5618, 5743, 5763, 5784, 5806, 5838, 5854, 5888, 5890, 5973, 5991, 6065, 6090

Mudhoney, 120, 2126, 2266, 2300, 2554, 3622, 3831-3832, 3957, 4174, 4292

Mudie, Don, 293, 879

Mudie, Harry, 526, 1247, 1251, 2496, 2576, 3007, 3832, 4437, 5685

Mudlarks, 292, 3832, 4125, 4639

Mudriczki, Jamie, 4367

Mueller, Andrew, 163, 2116

Mueller, Anna, 1457

Mueller, Ernest, 3751

Mueller, Jan, 5940

Mueller, Jens, 3536

Mueller, Michael, 5582

Mueller, Teddy, 293

Mueller-Westernhagen, Marius, 3832

Muen, T.B., 4092

Muermans, Richard, 288

Mugwumps, 1575, 1739, 2344, 3346, 3833, 4122, 4551, 5949

Muhammad, Idris, 1416, 3833, 4779

Muhammed, Elijah, 2701, 3890

Muhammed, Shaheed, 31, 4071, 4191

Muir, Ian, 1952, 5737

Muir, Jamie, 331, 2999

Muir, Lewis, 43, 1106

Muir, Lewis F., 43

Muir, Mike, 2692

Muir, Nick, 3626

Mukwesha, Virginia, 3833

Mulcahy, Russell, 2670

Muldaur, Geoff, 3089, 3833-3834, 4316

Muldaur, Maria, 43, 695, 1794, 2923, 2955, 3089, 3569, 3833-3834, 4031, 4148, 5797, 5838

Muldoon, Clive, 1500

Muldowney, Dominic, 3834

Muldrow, Cornell, 5582

Muldrow, Michelle, 3806

Mule, 3834 and *passim*

Mulenze, 3750, 3834-3835, 4739, 4745, 4739, 4745

Mulford, Don, 5845

Mulhern, Johnny, 5556

Mulholland, Keith, 3988, 4405

Mulholland, Rosie, 1447

Mulkerik, John, 1463

Mull, George, 1796

Mullaney, Jan, 935

Mullard, Arthur, 1325

Mullen, Andrea, 1921

Mullen, George, 5898

Mullen, Jim, 278, 381, 2674, 2974, 3057, 3798, 3835, 4172, 4232, 4494, 5646

Mullen, Keith, 1849

Mullen, Larry, 1765, 3891, 5560

Mullen, Laurence, 5560

Müller, Heiner, 1701

Muller, Henry, 1358

Muller, Randy, 715, 3923

Müller, Torsten, 1076

Mullican, Aubrey, 3835

Mullican, Moon, 476, 799, 1129-1130, 1356, 3835-3836, 4566, 5438

Mulligan Records, 5914

Mulligan, Declan, 438

Mulligan, Gerry, 20, 107, 141, 374, 380, 410, 442, 468, 489, 753, 794-795, 825, 1097, 1124, 1414, 1493, 1774, 1791, 1845, 1849, 2128, 2132, 2196, 2293, 2300-2301, 2562-2563, 2572, 2632, 2721, 2739, 2796, 2972, 3061, 3071, 3082, 3145, 3223, 3375, 3443, 3502, 3525, 3531, 3568, 3664, 3716, 3739-3740, 3752, 3836-3837, 3932, 4090, 4147, 4212, 4239, 4439, 4534, 4640, 4655-4656, 4664, 4673, 4727, 4731, 4760, 4779, 4925, 5416, 5468, 5770, 5852, 5898, 6065

Mulligan, Jerry, 162

Mulligan, John, 1856, 3568

Mulligan, Mick, 1294, 2562, 3227, 3838, 4137, 4818

Mulligan, Oliver, 696

Mullins, Danny, 1844

Mullins, Darrin, 1630

Mullins, Michael J., 3728

Mullins, Paul, 698

Müllrich, Uve, 1546

Mulraine, Gordon, 2763

Mulreany, Paul, 610, 2793, 4329

Mulry, Ted, 3838, 5610

Mulvany, Maeve, 923

Mulvey, Andi, 4270, 5323

Mulvey, Linda, 3355

Mulvihill, Jane, 4379

Mulvihill, Pete, 4379

Mumford, Gene, 5698

Mummers, Tzotzil, 5310, 5699

Munbar, Hal, 2501

Munde, Alan, 580, 1252, 3488

Mundell, Ed, 3749

Mundell, Hugh, 2276, 3838, 4096, 4494, 5688

Munden, Dave, 5499

Mundi, Billy, 414, 3809, 4519

Mundi, Coati, 2984

Mundy, 1927, 2359, 2362, 2536, 3457, 3838-3839, 5747, 6128

Mundy, Jimmy, 2359, 2362, 2536, 3839, 5747

Mungo Jerry, 2272, 2508, 3462, 3510, 3839, 4372, 6126

Munier, Gregg, 4747

Munkacsi, Kurt, 2168

Munn, Billy, 2028, 3258, 3839, 4912

Munnerlyn, John, 1691

Munoz, Eddie, 4266

Muñoz, Ernesto, 3313

Munoz, Hector, 5513

Muñoz, Rafael, 3775, 4113

Munro, Ailie, 2520, 6053

Munro, Jane, 277

Munro, Kevin, 3834

Munro, Nigel, 4052

Munroe, Dave, 2240

Munroe, Mike, 2173

Munroe, Pete, 1500

Munroe, Tony, 544

Munshin, Jules, 893, 1692, 2959, 3669, 4040-4041, 4905, 5284

Munslow, Bryan, 1378

Munson, Otis, 4189

Munting, Eppie, 4809

Munzing, Michael, 3297, 5617

Mura, Corinna, 3648

Murad, Jerry, 2447

Muranyi, Joe, 3840

Murata, Hideo, 3840

Murch, Russell, 290

Murcia, Billy, 3923, 5430

Murder Inc., 3840, 4348

Murder Junkies, 140

Murdoch, Bruce, 619

Murdoch, Richard, 2653, 3032, 3372, 3491

Murdoch, Stuart, 465

Murdock, Glen, 3808

Murfin, Jane, 4570

Muriel, Frankie, 3003

Murk, 2621, 3840

Murmaids, 3840

Murmur Records, 5614

Murnau, F.W., 5307

Murph, Randolph, 737

Murphey, Michael Martin, 642, 986, 2042, 2635, 3174, 3841, 4086, 4671, 4710

Murphy's Law, 3841

Murphy, Ann, 2661

Murphy, Audie, 3144

Murphy, Bernard, 725

Murphy, Brian, 1993, 4021

Murphy, C.W., 421

Murphy, Chris, 1504, 4970

Murphy, Clive, 1417

Murphy, Colm, 1433

Murphy, David Lee, 3842

Murphy, Delia, 2232, 3842

Murphy, Derrick, 711, 4714

Murphy, Donal, 1993

Murphy, Donna, 1968, 2998, 4151

Murphy, Dudley, 552

Murphy, Dwayne, 2365

Murphy, Eddie, 159, 974, 2611, 2776, 4841, 4843

Murphy, Edward, 4831

Murphy, Floyd, 544, 3843

Murphy, George, 746, 1777, 1966, 2985, 3580, 4570, 5395-5396

Murphy, Gerry, 5534

Murphy, Greg, 1591

Murphy, James, 912, 1448, 4010, 5346

Murphy, Jeff, 3511, 4886

Murphy, Jessie, 1919

Murphy, John, 2113, 4886

Murphy, Keith, 1611

Murphy, Kevin, 161, 2179, 4684

Murphy, Lyle 'Spud', 3842

Murphy, Marion, 1777

Murphy, Mark, 908, 1164, 1734, 1977, 2016, 2895, 3018, 3443, 3531, 3573, 3842-3843, 4681, 4801, 5374, 5701

Murphy, Martin, 169, 3628

Murphy, Marty, 4436

Murphy, Matt, 3625, 3843, 5758

Murphy, Melvin, 3844

Murphy, Michael, 1485, 3741, 4506

Murphy, Mick, 1551

Murphy, Noel, 3843

Murphy, Pete, 304, 2937, 3843, 5323

Murphy, Peter, 418, 1364, 2821

Murphy, Phil, 3733, 5892

Murphy, Ralph, 3844

Murphy, Roscoe, 3211

Murphy, Rose, 769, 803, 2742, 3844, 4181, 4230, 5907, 6122

Murphy, Shaun, 3265

Murphy, Spud, 1743, 5934

Murphy, Stanley, 295

Murphy, Turk, 1378, 1790, 2087, 2355, 3844, 4513, 4779, 5323, 5732, 6103

Murphy, Walter, 3844-3845, 4752

Murrah, Roger, 3187

Murray Brothers, 1283, 1671, 4839, 4987, 5879

Murray The K, 1019, 1469, 4461, 4478, 4537

Murray, Alfred, 1942

Murray, Andy, 5904

Murray, Anne, 679, 905, 923, 1655, 1718, 2408, 2440, 3172, 3187, 3596, 3845, 4012, 4622, 6130

Murray, Arthur, 201, 419, 1122, 3847

Murray, Bill, 3272

Murray, Billy, 43, 843, 1555, 2385, 4465, 4649, 4680, 5659

Murray, Bobby, 560, 1873, 2381

Murray, Charles Shaar, 687, 2492, 3917, 6037, 6053, 6090, 6114

Murray, Chrissie, 2799

Murray, Clive, 553

Murray, D.L., 3185, 6059

Murray, Dave, 1198, 2710

Murray, David, 182, 298, 371, 412, 561, 688, 703, 844, 872, 953, 968, 1311, 1405, 1465-1466, 1626, 1670, 1784, 2362, 2381, 2508, 2592-2593, 3114, 3544, 3689, 3791, 3845-3846, 3848, 4210, 4760, 5297, 5467, 5568, 5778, 5920, 5922

Murray, Dee, 1421, 4764

Murray, Deidre, 5420

Murray, Denis, 3652

Murray, Don, 1310, 5538

Murray, Elizabeth, 3399

Murray, Evan, 291

Murray, George, 1794, 4987

Murray, Graeme, 4110

Murray, Gwendolyn, 4448

Murray, Ian, 796

Murray, J. Harold, 1818, 3548, 4550, 5433

Murray, Jeff, 698

Murray, Jerry, 2672

Murray, Jim, 1088, 4385

Murray, Keith, 2053, 3846

Murray, Ken, 3817

Murray, Larry, 2460, 4791

Murray, Lee, 3202

Murray, Lindley, 2885

Murray, Mae, 5997

Murray, Martin, 560, 2582, 3703, 3724, 4049

Murray, Martin Glyn, 3724, 4049

Murray, Mike, 1692

Murray, Mitch, 1075, 4122

Murray, Neil, 560, 682, 1182, 2182, 2272, 2440, 3475, 3882, 4219, 4693, 4850, 5803

Murray, Patrick, 370

Murray, Paul, 1961

Murray, Pauline, 2706, 3821, 3847, 4049, 4184

Murray, Pauline, And The Invisible Girls, 2706, 3847

Murray, Peg, 874, 876

Murray, Pete, 4401, 4943, 5467

Murray, Phil, 1593, 2470, 2734

Murray, Robert, 1447

Murray, Ron, 840

Murray, Roy, 3424, 6037

Murray, Ruby, 958, 1187, 2488, 2725, 3847, 4125, 4574, 5972

Murray, Sonny, 574

Murray, Stephen, 2547, 4626

Murray, Steve, 4194, 5920

Murray, Sunny, 290, 297, 1257, 1862, 2024, 2370, 2405, 2593, 2617, 2652, 2795, 3846-3848, 4288, 4584, 4697, 4852, 4908, 5309, 5553, 5659, 5698, 5927

Murray, Ted, 1406, 3525

Murray, Tom, 512, 3262

Murray, Tony, 4262, 5508

Murray, Wayne, 988

Murray, William, 156, 5284

Murray, Wynn, 308, 698

Murrell, Keith, 98, 3257, 3426

Murrough, Mac, 2068

Murrow, Ed, 4750

Mursal, Maryam, 3848

Murtceps, 3848, 4681

Murumets, Susan, 4370

Murvin, Junior, 172, 557, 2138, 3848, 4200, 4595, 4644

Murzyn, Alex, 4010

Musa, Jali, 2153, 2790

Muscat, Brent, 1857

Muscle Beach Party, 195, 289, 419, 1086, 1362, 3849

Muscle Shoals, 403, 447, 476, 570, 583, 650, 710, 890, 966, 1114, 1173, 1551, 1675, 1852, 1898, 2013, 2157, 2351, 2376, 2417, 2461, 2539, 2606, 2730, 2741, 2748, 2772, 2965, 3162, 3175, 3421, 3445, 3522, 3550, 3849, 3899, 4224, 4234, 4368, 4399, 4719, 4763, 4790, 4831, 4867, 4888, 5305, 5330, 5400-5401, 5686, 5695, 5717, 5795, 5819

Musclehead, 2899

Muse, 3849

Muse Records, 2811

Muse, Clarence, 4286

Muse, David, 1902

Musel, Bob, 1047, 1207

Musenbilcher, Robby, 2860

Muses Rapt, 1617

Musgrave, Sharon, 409

Musgrove, George, 3268

Mushroom Records, 3849 and *passim*

Music Box Revue, 178, 493, 731, 1141, 2940, 3850

Music Explosion, 3850 and *passim*

Music From China, 931, 3431

Music In The Air, 3851 and *passim*

Music Machine, 3852 and *passim*

Music Man Records, 264, 5489

Music Man, The, 108, 195, 499, 673, 745, 802, 862, 913, 983, 1096, 1219, 1363, 2163-2164, 2185, 2492, 2548, 2660, 2885, 3268, 3352, 3852, 4063, 4116, 4149, 4259, 4317, 4569, 5370, 5581, 5869, 5977, 6040, 6052, 6086

Music Man, The (film musical), 3852

Music, Frank, 79, 102, 813, 1005, 1234, 1543, 1646, 2896, 3358, 3804, 3811, 5301, 5805, 6096

Musical Brownies, 764, 771, 782, 787, 799, 1410, 3240, 5865

Musical Millers, 3482, 4296

Musical Journey Band, 4475

Musical Youth, 969, 2055, 3659, 3853, 5320, 5325, 6065

Musicor Records, 1533, 2925, 4616, 4744, 5471, 5786

Musicraft Records, 3853

Muskee, Harry, 1324-1325

Musker, Dave, 5330

Musker, Frank, 1647, 6004

Musker, Joe, 1443, 5667

Musker, John, 105, 3268

Muskett, Hunter, 2639

Musselwhite, Charlie, 224, 318, 630, 1127, 2187, 2248, 2398, 3274, 3434, 3639, 3824, 3853-3854, 3898, 4172, 4413, 5634

Musser, Tharon, 1071, 1625

Musso, Vido, 817, 1104, 2571, 2972, 3854, 4686

Mussolini, Romano, 3854, 4662

Mussorgsky, M., 1042, 4752

Mussulli, Boots, 1009, 5629

Must Bust, 4923

Mustafa, Tim, 2175

Mustafov, Ferus, 3854

Mustaine, Dave, 1507, 3612, 4733

Mustang Records, 1468

Mustangs, 3506, 4157

Mustard, 38, 106, 1787, 1962, 2661, 2766, 3151, 5323, 5912

Mustard Seed Faith, 1962

Musto And Bones, 3854-3855

Musto, Tommy, 656, 1808, 3854-3855, 4920, 5521

Mutabaruka, 83-84, 1637, 1913, 2242, 3855, 4110, 4945

Mute Records, 3855 and *passim*

Mutiny!, 1780, 2935, 2988,

3524, 3855-3856, 4229, 4540, 5430

Mutler, Stuart, 3775

Mutrix, Floyd, 162

Mutsaers, Wilbert, 5474

Mutton Birds, 3856

Mutukudzi, Oliver, 3856

Muud, Jal, 3311

Muzingo, Patrick, 2914

µ-Ziq, 3856

Muzsikás, 3857

Mwenda, Jean, 675

MX-80 Sound, 3857

My Bloody Valentine, 1276, 1287, 1985, 2075, 2178, 2604, 2721, 3343, 3570, 3608, 3632, 3775, 3857-3858, 4515, 4792, 4810, 4964, 5569, 5789

My Dad Is Dead, 2112, 5490

My Dear Watson, 2905, 3858

My Dying Bride, 267, 3858, 4715

My Fair Lady, 185, 217, 480, 535, 707, 883, 899, 913, 1001, 1010, 1068, 1133, 1161, 1187, 1208, 1553, 1567, 1831, 1851, 1878, 1968, 2023, 2186, 2417, 2422, 2447, 2533, 2567, 2619, 3049, 3196-3197, 3235, 3294-3295, 3373, 3393, 3446-3447, 3498, 3706, 3804, 3859-3860, 3888, 4063, 4080, 4118, 4126, 4212, 4320-4321, 4361, 4724, 4773, 4724, 4773, 5308, 5646, 5987

My Fair Lady (film musical), 3859

My Favorite Year, 518, 1337, 2205, 3860

My Gal Sal, 2450, 3861, 4118, 4413, 4580, 5937

My Heart Goes Crazy, 3303, 3861

My Life Story, 278, 2563, 3048, 3386, 3861, 4569, 5401, 6058

My One And Only, 102, 1347, 2055, 3618, 3862, 3896, 3952, 5363, 5527, 5603

Myatt, John, 3825

Mycroft, Walter, 605, 1747, 5958

Myddle Class, 3019, 3862, 5459

Mydland, Brent, 2246, 2598, 2687, 5755

Myer, Jeff, 4755, 5343

Myers Brothers, 530, 5362

Myers, Alan, 1501

Myers, Alice, 70

Myers, Allan, 2123

Myers, Amina Claudine, 44, 3194, 3862, 5420

Myers, Billy, 4124

Myers, Brett, 1518

Myers, Bumps, 3863

Myers, Colvin, 932

Myers, Craig, 2059

Myers, Dave, 53, 2527, 3863

Myers, Dave, And The Surftones, 2527

Myers, David, 3274, 5763

Myers, Dwight, 2466

Myers, John, 3863

Myers, Louis, 53, 1196, 3182, 3274, 3853, 3863, 4291, 4582,

5473, 5763

Myers, Pamela, 1196

Myers, Paul, 2178, 4346

Myers, Randy, 2558

Myers, Richard, 1744, 2095, 2475, 2512, 3147, 3824, 4580

Myers, Sammy, 519, 2051, 3863, 4255, 5645

Myers, Stanley, 565, 2302, 3863, 6000

Myers, Steve, 2240

Myers, Ted, 3321

Myhill, Jill, 5600

Myhill, Richard, 3864

Myhr, Ken, 4899

Myles, Alannah, 413, 1718, 3177, 3477, 3864

Myles, Billy, 3014, 3618

Myles, Dave, 3523

Myles, Donnie, 1424

Myles, Frank, 1144, 2257

Myles, Geoff, 1042

Myles, Heather, 3864

Myles, John, 4269

Myles, Tony, 4269

Myles, Willie, 3342

Mylett, John, 3988, 4405

Myman, Bob, 1844

Mynah Birds, 818, 2775, 5977

Myofist, 1911, 3864

Myrick, Gary, 2432

Myrick, Weldon, 222

Myrie, Mark, 369

Myril, Odette, 5948

Myrow, Joseph, 2217, 3865

Myrrh Records, 198, 1073, 1853, 1905, 2223, 2271

Mysels, Sammy, 2533

Mysterious, William, 198, 4518

Mystery Duo, 3480, 3931

Mystery Of Edwin Drood, The, 811, 3865

Mystery Trend, 1660, 3732, 3865-3866, 3869, 4780

Mystery Trio, 3638

Mystic Records, 92, 3962

Mystic Revealers, 304, 3866

Mystica, 4194

Mystics, 601, 1193, 1538, 2508, 2783, 2790, 3496, 3866, 4152, 5545, 6124

Mythra, 3866

Myton, Cedric, 1204, 2459, 4336, 4696

Myung, John, 1624

N

N/X, 4703

N'Dour, Youssou, 3867 and *passim*

N-Joi, 1453, 3867

N-Tense, 3868

N-Troop, 3868

N.R.T., 3868

N.W.O.B.H.M., 29, 311, 369, 2096, 2467, 2476, 2504, 2558, 2575, 2648, 2697, 3643, 3777-3778, 3868, 3988, 4203, 4307, 4405, 4452, 4747, 5434, 5509, 5896

N2-Deep, 3868

Na Fili, 3868

Na Má, Ahí, 301-302, 1240
Naa-Koshie, Terri, 2944
Nabbie, Jimmie, 765, 2694
Nacao Zumbi, 4777-4778, 4777-4778
Nacardo, Vinny, 925
Nacci, Alberto, 2084
Nada Surf, 3868
Nadel, Warren, 2718
Nader, Richard, 3203
Naftalin, Mark, 858, 1691, 3807
Nagel, Freddy, 3868
Nagle, Ron, 1585, 1660, 3866, 3869
Nagy, John, 1688
Naideau, Jeff, 3980
Naiff, Lynton, 84, 2667
Nail, Jimmy, 3869, 4308, 4659
Nailbomb, 2045, 3869, 4823
Naish, Brad, 5891
Naish, J. Carroll, 1607
Naismith, Laurence, 899, 4795
Naismith, Monty, 4374
Najee, 3070
Najma, 3869
Nakajima, Miyuki, 3870
Nakajima, Yuki, 2468
Nakamura, Seuchi, 5947
Nakatani, Michie, 4887
Naked City, 2038, 2399, 2768, 3525, 3870, 4676, 5874, 6003
Naked Eyes, 1127, 3870, 3918
Naked Prey, 2135, 3871, 4413, 5938
Naked Raygun, 3871
Naked Skinnies, 163
Naked Truth, 568, 816, 2189, 3621, 3871
Nakonechny, Keith, 5694
Nalesso, Gable, 1391
Namchilak, Sainkho, 2652
Namlook, Peter, 542, 1361, 3719, 3871, 4553
Namyslowski, Zbigniew, 96, 3058, 3421, 3872, 5585, 6103
Nanaco, 3872
Nance, Delores, 4517
Nance, Jack, 827, 5547
Nance, Ray, 937, 1159, 1734, 1736, 2199, 3873, 4128, 4407, 5530
Nance, Willis, 3873
Nanini, Joe, 327, 558, 1937, 5685
Nanjô, Fumiwaka, 3688
Nanton, Joe 'Tricky Sam', 3873
Napalm Death, 412, 474, 649, 798, 801, 990, 1767, 1811, 2179, 3870, 3873, 4123, 5342, 6003
Napier, Alan, 1258
Napier, Alex, 5586
Napier, Bill, 200, 3766-3767, 3874
Napier, John, 993, 3199
Napier-Bell, Simon, 645, 2243, 2783, 2832, 3874, 5781, 5951, 6036, 6114
Napoleon XIV, 2001, 3875
Napoleon, Jo, 263
Napoleon, Marty, 263, 1163, 2739, 3875, 5629
Napoleon, Marty, 263, 1163, 2739, 3875, 5629
Napoleon, Phil, 1399, 3733,

3875, 4060, 4903
Napoleon, Phil, And His Memphis Five, 3875, 4060
Napoleon, Teddy, 3875, 5844
Napolitano, Johnette, 1201, 2567
Napper, Kenny, 124
Napper, Tom, 1354, 2357, 3553
Naptali, Raymond, 2700, 3875-3876
Naranjo, Valerie, 3731
Narcizo, David, 723, 5428
Nardini, Peter, 3559
Nardo Ranks, 2351
Narell, Andy, 3876
Naro, Phil, 1006, 5286
Nas, 31, 101, 299, 1560, 1773, 3232, 3417, 3876-3877, 4417, 4433, 4593, 4682
Nascence, Harrison, 584
Nascimento, Milton, 2904, 3877, 4571, 5616
Nasco Records, 1819
Nash, Art, 3501
Nash, Brian, 2012
Nash, David, 1302, 1306, 3131, 5655
Nash, George, Jnr., 474
Nash, Graham, 608, 792, 1301-1302, 1305-1307, 1347, 1465, 1634, 1775, 1777, 2563-2564, 2803, 2935, 3103, 3131, 3502, 3570, 3574, 3713, 3877, 4907, 5337, 5679
Nash, Jim, 5734
Nash, Jimmy, 422, 3508
Nash, Joey, 2535
Nash, Johnny, 422, 1158, 2107, 2200, 2360, 2535, 2733, 3067, 3468, 3877-3878, 4187, 4987, 5282
Nash, Len, And His Country Boys, 1852
Nash, Mary, 5436
Nash, N. Richard, 4286
Nash, Ogden, 1033, 1647, 4047, 5755
Nash, Peter, 2633, 4329, 5392, 6054
Nash, Robin, 5467
Nash, Ted, 3525
Nash, Vernon, 1144, 2257
Nashboro Records, 1603, 4017
Nashua, Joe, 2767
Nashville Bluegrass Band, 1252, 3878
Nashville Superpickers, 417, 1755, 4566-4567
Nashville Teens, 193, 220, 424, 783, 1086, 1609, 2199, 3220, 3324, 3805, 3879, 3931, 4667
Nashville West, 3879, 4145, 5796, 5897
Naskov, Nikolai, 2220
Nason, Steven, 276, 1244
Nasralla, Ronnie, 2714, 3171
Nassour, Ellis, 452, 1130, 6040
Nastanovich, Bob, 4167
Nastasi, Dan, 1572, 3829
Nasty Idols, 3879
Nasty Savage, 3879-3880
Nasty, Billy, 1633, 6002
Natal, Nanette, 3880
Naté, Ultra, 5568

Natel, Jean-Marc, 3076, 3199
Nathan, Morty, 3508
Nathan, Sid, 766, 3836, 4939
Nathan, Stephen, 2180-2181
Nathan, Sydney, 3880, 4188
Nathanson, Roy, 2796
Nathonson, Eric, 945
Nati, 393, 1530, 3354, 3880-3881, 3938, 4421
Natinal, Jamel, 3199
Nation Of Ulysees, 3419, 5517
Nation Records, 3881 and passim
National Barn Dance, The, 135, 226, 286, 584, 804, 843, 1122, 1309, 1330-1331, 1444, 1532, 1645, 1956, 2161, 2354, 2443, 2579, 2589, 2592, 2937, 3030, 3112, 3357, 3489, 3504, 3744, 3881-3882, 4305, 4448, 4484, 4652
National Champion Hillbillies, 4448
National Health, 930, 1406, 1473, 1715, 2430, 3882
National Jazz Ensemble, 2403, 2722, 3212, 3525, 3882, 4636
National Youth Jazz Orchestra, 224, 255, 381, 546, 788, 1124, 1403, 1738, 2517, 2974, 3018, 3882, 4327, 4538, 5455, 5725
Native Hipsters, 13, 3882-3883, 5693, 5801
Native Records, 875, 1393, 1756, 4977, 5924, 5952
Native Tongues Posse, 31, 561, 1052, 1435, 3341, 3883, 4191
Natoli, Nat, 2841
Natschinski, Gerd, 336, 4874
Natt, Eddie, 200
Natty Dread, 172, 533, 1622, 2733, 3468-3469, 3883, 4438, 5668
Natural Acoustic Band, 3410, 3883
Natural Four, 1340, 3883-3884
Natural Milk Hotel, 211
Natural Mystics, 601
Natural, Ras, 4468
Naturals, 3884, 5481, 5686
Naturists, 3884
Natwick, Mildred, 266, 1258, 3037, 4828
Naughtie, Andrew, 1156
Naughton And Gold, 1927
Naughton, Bucky, 872
Naughton, David, 3884
Naughton, Francis, 3856
Naughton, James, 1091, 2661
Naughton, Jay, 5667
Naughton, Tony, 4639
Naughty By Nature, 437, 526, 1344, 1350, 1571, 2022, 3094, 3799, 3884-3885, 3955, 3961, 4376, 4687, 5986, 5997
Naughty Marietta (film musi-cal), 3885
Naughty Marietta (stage musi-cal), 3885
Naumann, Paul, 15, 27, 5487
Naura, Michael, 3885
Nauseef, Mark, 1730, 2063, 2148
Navarre, Ludovic, 3885
Navarro, Dave, 2781, 4463, 5793

Navarro, Fats, 165, 614, 769, 878, 1368, 1682, 1700, 2090, 2150, 2208, 2371, 2395, 2846, 3127, 3348, 3350, 3572, 3885-3886, 4137, 4296, 4339, 4634, 4664
Navarro, Ramon, 93
Navarro, Theodore, 3885
Navetta, Frank, 1490
Navidad, Feliz, 1874, 3143, 4558
Navras Records, 3886
Navy, Judy, 1055
Nawaz, Aki, 2051, 3881
Naylor, Jerry, 3886
Naylor, Liz, 953
Naylor, Maria, 4076
Naylor, Randy, 4280
Naylor, Shel, 4100
Naysmith, Graeme, 4109
Nazareth, 641, 803, 2174, 2314, 2618, 2785, 3483, 3542, 3886-3887, 4820, 5459, 6126
Nazarian, Bruce, 285, 793, 1718
Nazario, Ednita, 922
Nazaroff, Nicolai, 3532
Nazz, 119, 1038, 3887, 4688
Nazzaro, Fred, 5528
Ndegé Ocello, Me'Shell, 3887 and passim
Ndjock, Yves, 1505
Ndonfeng, Samuel Thomas, 5405
Neabore, David, 1572, 3829
Neagle, Anna, 550, 809, 1022, 1030, 1141, 2212, 2709, 3007, 3106, 3152, 3492, 3548, 3887-3888, 3965, 4488, 5432, 5486, 5618, 5821, 5964
Neal Brothers Blues Band, 3888
Neal, Bob, 3773, 4310
Neal, Dave, 4378
Neal, Jack, 5644
Neal, Kenny, 139, 630, 2332, 3364, 3888-3889
Neal, Mark, 3515
Neal, Pat, 2120
Neal, Raful, 2321, 2846, 3888
Neal, Rochester, 4084
Neal, Thurman, 3931
Neale, Zora, 772, 2950, 3888, 6094
Nealey, Ken, 2943
Neame, Ronald, 2659, 4795
Near, Holly, 3559, 3889, 5537
Nearly Band, 324, 2509, 3003, 3831, 4114
Neason, Terry, 4341
Neat Records, 274, 595, 1135, 1453, 1911, 2468, 2476, 2761, 4203, 4442, 5702, 5793
Nebbish, Ocher, 1151
Necros, 523, 3889
Nectarine No.9, 1902, 3889-3890, 5881
Ned B, 1349, 3678, 5719
Ned's Atomic Dustbin, 3890 and passim
Nedderman, Ross, 5457
Neddo, Joe, 640
Nedich, Marty, 1444
Nedwell, Robin, 735
Needham, Margie, 1069
Needham, Waxy Max, 5822
Neesam, John, 5684

Novis, Donald, 521, 2287, 2911, 4044

Novos, Tony, 4360

Novoselic, Krist, 1964, 3957, 5731

Now Generation, 1062, 1081-1082, 1979, 2086, 2496, 3980, 4991

Nowack, Georg, 4859

Nowels, Rick, 4222

Nowherefast, 3980

Nowlan, George, 1407

Nowlen, Jeff, 4076

Nowlin, Bill, 1951, 4664

Noy, Derek, 2780

Nozedar, Adele, 4522

NRBQ, 1419-1420, 3980, 4197, 4803, 5831

NRG, 310, 2100, 4697, 5553

NSO Force, 3980-3981

Ntimih, Billy, 1557

Nu Colours, 908, 3053, 3135, 3351, 3379, 3981, 5403

Nu Groove Records, 656, 3981

Nu Roy, 370, 1417

Nu, Pete, 4734

Nua, Onipa, 3982

Nuba, Jimmy Lyons, 1344, 3174

Nubbit, Guitar, 2310

Nubian, Brand, 711, 1052, 1507, 2237, 2393, 3508, 4043, 4462, 4593, 4714, 4965, 5585

Nubiles, 1921, 1939, 3963, 3982

Nuclear Assault, 55, 201, 801, 3982

Nuclear Valdez, 3982

Nucleus, 3982-3983

Nudds, Dick, 3026

Nude Records, 2116

Nudeswirl, 3983

Nudie, 855, 1255, 3370, 3983-3984, 4146, 4323, 5410, 5665, 5847, 5859

Nuese, John, 2702, 4146

Nueva Manteca, 3984

Nueva, Grupo, 3880

Nuevo, Todo, 3750-3751

Nugent, Elliot, 5582

Nugent, Geoff, 5575

Nugent, Moyra, 996

Nugent, Ted, 83, 158, 320, 1370, 2456, 2637, 3184, 3449, 3606, 3734, 3948, 3984-3985, 4617, 4833, 4858, 5326, 6066

Nugget Records, 967

Null, Cecil, 3985

Null, Jeffrey, 5657

Null, Lisa, 1890

Numan, Gary, 88, 454, 686, 1169, 1443, 1814, 2004, 3071, 3347, 3985-3986, 4112, 4838, 5326, 5521, 5570, 5754, 5806, 6066, 6126

Number One Cup, 3986

Nunes, Tommy, 4822

Nunez, Alcide 'Yellow', 3986

Nuñez, Arturo, 3779

Nunlee, Darrel, 1215

Nunley, Chris, 4671

Nunley, Louis D., 2976

Nunn, Bobby, 1138, 4580

Nunn, Gary P., 756, 3322, 3986

Nunn, Larry, 308

Nunn, Terri, 492

Nunn, Trevor, 258, 336, 993-994, 1048, 3199, 3284, 3986, 5835

Nunnally, Keith, 2644, 4364

Nunnen, Jimmy, 914

Nuns, 3987

Nunsense, 354, 3987

Nuridin, Jalal, 371, 3133

Nurm, Gary, 3841

Nurse With Wound, 1337, 1954, 3182

Nurse, Robert, 5661

Nuss, Otto, 4561

Nussbaum, Adam, 42, 3235, 3987

Nut, 3988

Nutmegs, 25, 1756, 3988

Nutt, Garry, 5294

Nutt, Joe, 89

Nuttal, Tim, 736

Nuttall, Jeff, 1269, 6042

Nutter, Alice, 1081

Nutz, 751, 3988, 4405

Nuyens, Frank, 4376

NWA, 164, 429, 1271, 1344, 1352, 1450, 1459, 1561, 1612, 1697, 2668-2669, 2678, 3653, 3988-3989, 4060, 4340, 4357, 4433, 4703, 5771, 5939

Nwanne, Obi, 4060

Nwapa, Alban, 1612

Ny Antsaly, 4417

NY Loose, 3989

Nyame, E.K., 2524, 3989

Nyboma, 1757, 1840, 3199-3200, 3440

Nye, Peter, 5762

Nye, Steve, 2303, 4185

Nyholt, Jim, 206

Nyll, Nat, 5603

Nylons, 25, 95, 3989-3990

Nyman, Michael, 346, 1548, 2032, 2320, 2669, 3990, 4135, 4347, 6066

Nymph Errant, 1141, 1428, 1436, 3146, 3990, 4289-4290, 5757

Nymphs, 932, 1544, 3465, 3991

Nype, Russell, 893, 2192

Nyro, Laura, 266, 996, 1001, 1188, 1407, 1889, 2110, 2884, 3100, 3651, 3753, 3924, 3991, 4208, 5422, 5638

Nyson, Liam, 984

Nystrom, Jeff, 3864

Nystrom, Lene, 213

O

O Lucky Man, 3993, 4322-4323

O'Brien, Floyd, 3993

O'Brien, Tim, 3993

O'Connell, Helen, 3993

O'Connell, Maura, 3993-3994 and *passim*

O'Connor, Cavan, 3994-3995 and *passim*

O'Connor, Des, 3995 and *passim*

O'Connor, Donald, 3995 and *passim*

O'Connor, Hazel, 3995-3996 and *passim*

O'Connor, Mark, 3996

O'Connor, Sinead, 3996-3997 and *passim*

O'Daniel, Wilbert Lee, 3997

O'Day, Alan, 3997

O'Day, Anita, 3997-3998 and *passim*

O'Day, Molly, 3998-3999

O'Dell, Kenny, 3999 and *passim*

O'Dhomhnaill, 4497

O'Donnell, Daniel, 3999-4000 and *passim*

O'Farrill, Arturo 'Chico', 4000

O'Flynn, Bridget, 4000

O'Flynn, Liam, 4000-4001

O'Gwynn, James, 4001

O'Hara, Jamie, 4001

O'Hare, Husk, 4001

O'Jays, 4002 and *passim*

O'Kanes, 4002-4003

O'Keefe, Danny, 4003

O'Keefe, Johnny, 4003

O'Neal, Alexander, 4003-4004 and *passim*

O'Neal, Shaquille, 4004

O'Neill, Sharon, 4004 and *passim*

O'Rahilly, Ronan, 4004

O'Shea, Tessie, 4005

O'Sullivan, Gilbert, 4005-4006 and *passim*

O, Rodney, 4609

Oaishimashô, Sakuban, 3520

Oak Records, 558, 1820, 2077, 3662

Oak Ridge Boys, 216, 1345, 1386, 1537, 1995, 2019, 2253, 2357, 3745, 4006-4007, 4442, 4538

Oakenfold, Paul, 264, 305, 347, 892, 1440, 1617, 2018, 3693, 3898, 4007, 4194

Oakes, Betty, 983

Oakes, Bill, 1734

Oakes, Trevor, 4894

Oakey, Phil, 2632, 5701

Oakie, Jack, 236, 521, 2257, 2278, 2478, 2544, 5443

Oakland, Ben, 3197, 3409

Oakley Dance, Helen, 1039, 2208, 3039

Oakley, Annie, 196-197, 287, 1403, 1886, 3634

Oakley, Berry, 142, 510, 3276

Oakley, Glenroy, 2286

Oakley, Helen, 1039, 2208, 3039

Oakley, Vic, 872, 3195

Oakman, Pete, 778

Oaks, Sherman, 1259, 1280, 1388

Oaktown's 3-5-7, 4007

Oasis, 8, 16, 251, 315, 389, 423, 445, 466, 516, 518, 531, 618, 632, 662, 850, 1287, 1462, 1474, 1515, 1572, 1717-1718, 1751, 1923, 1947, 2112, 2169, 2212, 2169, 2481, 2592, 2968, 3024, 3038, 3570, 3763, 3964, 3974, 4008-4009, 4012, 4345, 4364, 4456, 4627, 4730, 4789, 4830, 4944, 4949, 4975, 5331, 5392, 5421, 5494, 5637, 5783, 5802, 6066, 6111, 6126

Oates, Ian, 1820

Oates, Warren, 5550

Oattes, 3249

Oaxaca, 614

Oban, George, 265, 2581

Ober, Dillion, 738

Öberg, Sebastian, 1937, 3355

Oberlé, David, 2302

Oberlin, Brent, 5418

Oberstein, Arnold, 4226

Obey, Ebenezer, 42, 74-75, 1359, 2835, 2910, 4009

Obiedo, Ray, 4010, 5882

Obispo, Luis, 1726, 4822, 5948

Obituary, 4010 and *passim*

Objects Of Desire, 2016, 2503, 5623

Oblivians, 4011

Obsessed, 4011 and *passim*

Obsession, 4011

Obuadade, 73

Obus, 4011

Ocasek, Ric, 320, 957, 2337, 4011, 5358, 5754

Ocean, 4011-4012

Ocean Colour Scene, 240, 3803, 4012, 5761, 6126

Ocean Records, 2655

Ocean, Billy, 272, 1608, 2171, 4012-4013, 5534

Ochs, Larry, 4665-4666

Ochs, Phil, 326, 619, 712, 1015, 1070, 1398, 1728, 1740, 1958, 2157, 2290, 2333, 2578, 3182, 4013, 4028, 4168, 4661, 5379, 5450, 5531, 5607, 6066

Ockrent, Mike, 518, 1284, 2159

October, Gene, 1042

Octopus, 4013 and *passim*

Oddie, Bill, 2207

Odell, George, 1358

Odell, Larraine, 1213

Odell, Mac, 4013

Odell, Roger, 1213, 4838

Oden, Henry, 4014, 5681

Oden, James Burke, 4014

Odenstrand, Anders, 3628

Odeon Records, 2827

Odet, Clifford, 1033, 5823

Odetta, 64, 457, 515, 681, 712, 1093, 1671, 1958, 2297, 2510, 2890, 4014-4015, 4468, 5607, 5611

Odgers, Brian, 209, 4350

Odmark, Matt, 2788

Odom, Andrew, 4015

Odoni, Eleni, 581

Odum, Bernard, 3387

Odum, Dab, 2453

Odum, Lynford, 740

Oduro, Kwabena, 2514

Odyssey, 4015 and *passim*

Oermann, Robert, 1053, 6091-6092

Oeters, Don, 1931

Of Perception, 4015 and *passim*

Of Thee I Sing, 479, 649, 745, 2129-2130, 2940, 4016, 4468, 5363

Ofarim, Esther And Abi, 4016, 5856

Offbeets, 5739

Offen, Arthur, 97

Offenbach, 2967, 4017, 4218, 6105

Pepper, Art, 339, 352, 489, 855, 1011, 1214, 1822, 1944, 2028, 2108, 2301, 2330, 2435, 2519, 2572, 2798, 2861, 2870, 2931, 2972, 3045, 3210, 3212, 3446, 3476, 3716, 3783, 4103-4104, 4191-4192, 4195, 4197, 4534, 4624, 4687, 4760, 4844, 4863, 5646, 5675, 5770, 5861, 6068
Pepper, Dave, 5704
Pepper, Jack, 4620
Pepper, Jay, 5434
Pepper, Jim, 1241, 4197, 5675
Pepper, Will, 1768, 2645, 2655
Pepperell, Rob, 2511
Pepperd, Garry, 2760
Peppiatt, Frank, 2471
Peppie, Harold, 2357
Pepsi And Shirlie, 4192
Pepys, Samuel, 171, 1745, 2496
Perano, Greg, 2643
Perata, Lloyd, 5770
Peraza, Armando, 3984, 4740, 5404
Perazzi, Horace, 5845
Perber, Dave, 3020
Perch, Floyd, 3056
Perchance To Dream, 241, 442, 3979-3980, 4192, 6066
Percival, Eric, 3950
Percival, Lance, 2724
Percival, Walter, 3719
Percy, 4192-4193
Percy, Dave, 4564
Percy, Esme, 3260
Percy, Mike, 1443
Pere Ubu, 31, 1112, 1467, 2112, 2190, 2201, 3138, 3234, 3632, 3815, 4193, 4461, 4596, 4663, 5369, 5399-5400
Perelman, S.J., 4047
Peres, Trevor, 4010
Peretti, Hugo, 475, 4602, 5456
Peretz, Jesse, 3189
Pérez, Bernie, 4647
Pérez, Dave, 4115, 5446-5447
Perez, David Charles, 2400
Pérez, Delfin, 3354
Pérez, Eddie, 1240, 2234-2235
Perez, Enrique, 4086
Pérez, Héctor, 2234, 3142, 3354, 4032
Perez, John, 4577, 4938
Perez, Julian, 1558
Perez, Larry, 4308
Pérez, Lou, 229, 746, 1833, 3314, 4742, 5472
Pérez, Luis, 3142
Perez, Manuel, 1580, 1730, 3939, 4193, 4577, 4579, 5445
Perez, Marc, 2598
Pérez, Mike, 1833, 1899-1900
Perez, Paul, 605, 2660
Pérez, Pichy, 3354, 4033
Pérez, Ray, 1348, 2397
Pérez, Rubby, 5615
Pérez, Simón, 4032
Pérez, Victor, 2234-2235
Perfect Disaster, 469, 723, 4193-4194
Perfect Jazz Repertory Quintet, 2654
Perfect Stranger, 3805, 4194, 4871, 5972, 5992

Perfect, Christine, 1055, 1933, 3602-3603, 4194
Perfect, Pete, 1631
Perfecto Fluoro, 4194
Perfecto Records, 807, 4007, 4194, 5490
Perfume, 486, 829, 1457, 1873, 1942, 1976, 2238, 3201, 3357, 4123, 4195, 5782, 5953
Peri, Bill, 3675
Perialas, Alex, 589, 3605, 4343
Pericoli, Emilio, 4195
Perignon, Don, 3354, 3750, 3835, 4065, 4558, 4739, 5596
Period, Sean J., 1353
Perkins, Al, 907, 1478, 1950, 2409, 3137, 3431-3432, 4195
Perkins, Anthony, 1196, 2278, 3294, 5287
Perkins, Bill, 1906, 1942, 2435, 2506, 2930-2931, 3716, 4195
Perkins, Brian, 1474
Perkins, Carl, 433, 517, 700, 795, 838, 918, 966, 976-979, 981, 1250, 1541, 1707, 2415, 2908, 3220, 3298, 3367, 3445, 3773, 3980, 4056, 4196-4197, 4225, 4310, 4313, 4418, 4566, 4594, 5646, 5694
Perkins, Carl (jazz), 4197
Perkins, Eddy, 1740
Perkins, Frank, 1250, 4130
Perkins, James, 4195
Perkins, Jay, 4196
Perkins, Jerry, 1478, 2355, 3220, 4197, 4313
Perkins, Joe Willie, 4197
Perkins, John, 1291
Perkins, Johnny, 918, 4225, 5943
Perkins, Judy, 3173
Perkins, Lascelles, 1568
Perkins, Luther, 976, 5737
Perkins, Millie, 5823
Perkins, O.C., 4872
Perkins, Osgood, 2185
Perkins, Percell, 1914
Perkins, Pinetop, 3026, 3182, 3460, 4197, 4291, 5531
Perkins, Polly, 48, 854, 4198
Perkins, Ray, 1291
Perkins, Red, 4198, 5341
Perkins, Stephen, 2692, 2781, 4195, 4287
Perkins, Terence, 1603
Perkins, Wayne, 650, 5737
Perko, Lynn, 2683
Perkowski, Jacek, 4364
Perks, Jeff, 4659
Perks, Vickie, 5739-5740
Perks, William, 4628, 5935
Perla, Gene, 2298
Perlberg, William, 4886
Perlman, Ben, 4743
Perlman, Itzhak, 2349, 3042, 4321, 5664
Perlman, Marc, 2792
Perlmutter, Lior, 264
Perloff, John, 3515
Pernice, Joe, 4795
Pernice, Sal, 336
Pero, A.J., 5547
Peron, Jean Herve, 1862
Peron, Juan, 1802
Perowsky, Ben, 3323

Perras, Anita, 679
Perrault, Charles, 1545
Perrett, Peter, 1760, 2567, 4048-4049, 4198, 5430, 6068
Perrin, Glyn, 3430
Perrin, Joe, 4492
Perrin, Johnny, 3635
Perrin, Nat, 2985, 4635
Perrin, Roland, 5526
Perrin, Tony, 1751
Perrin-Brown, Steve, 1547
Perrodin, Gabriel, 2310
Perrone, Marc, 3032
Perrson, Bent, 4199
Perrson, Hans, 1937
Perry Brothers, 1692, 3383
Perry, Antoinette, 5463
Perry, Bill, 4199
Perry, Brendan, 1440
Perry, Chris, 1105, 3047
Perry, Dale, 621
Perry, Darthard, 5732
Perry, Dave, 6068
Perry, Elizabeth, 4185
Perry, Fred, 1163
Perry, George, 4218, 6055
Perry, Ivor, 1692
Perry, J.B., 2978
Perry, Jeffrey, 4341
Perry, Jimmy, 83, 1927, 2730
Perry, Joe, 82-83, 1636, 2130, 2214, 2575, 4199, 4687, 6033
Perry, Joe, Project, 83, 4199
Perry, John, 930, 2244, 3407, 4049
Perry, Kathryn, 569
Perry, Lee, 65, 85, 99, 111, 225, 257, 280, 381, 863, 880, 1204, 1397, 1471-1472, 1524, 1566, 1569, 1586, 1621, 1636-1637, 1650, 1686, 1698, 1784, 2138, 2214, 2296, 2407, 2458, 2496, 2575, 2624, 2665, 2714, 2738, 2761, 2787, 2955, 3006, 3171, 3468, 3609, 3620, 4078, 4096, 4116, 4199-4201, 4335, 4429, 4436, 4638, 4696, 4939, 4972, 5304, 5326, 5409, 5412, 5441, 5545, 5559, 5583, 5635, 5668, 5688, 5871, 6000
Perry, Lincoln, 5817
Perry, Linda, 1994, 4201
Perry, Lynnette, 4048, 4408
Perry, Mark, 152, 325, 4201, 4365-4366, 6123
Perry, Matthew, 4099
Perry, Mitch, 5286
Perry, Neil, 3707, 6108, 6115, 6120
Perry, Oliver 'King', 4202
Perry, Phil, 1267, 3751
Perry, Rainford Hugh, 4199
Perry, Richard, 1843, 2177, 2677, 2887, 3270, 3432, 4202, 4486, 4716, 4761, 4917, 5496
Perry, Ron, 1064
Perry, Steve, 385, 1936, 2900, 4202, 5289, 5421, 5588, 5884
Perry, Steven, 2465
Perry, Stu, 3673
Perry, Will, 5881
Perryman, Lloyd, 512, 958, 1256, 1338, 4202, 5708
Perryman, Rufus 'Speckled

Red', 4203
Perryman, William, 4203, 4231
Persen, Mari Boine, 4203
Pershey, Bernard, 5511
Persian Risk, 1064, 4203
Persiany, André, 4203
Persip, Charlie, 1556, 2310, 3987, 4203-4204, 5727
Perskin, Spencer, 4885
Persoff, Nehemiah, 5823, 5956
Persoff, Sam, 2535
Person, Houston, 581, 2854, 2871, 4204
Personality Boys, 3638
Perspective Records, 2824, 3698
Persson, Aake, 645
Persson, Nina, 932
Persson, Thomas, 4462
Persuader, 871, 1283, 4317
Persuaders, 312, 401, 4204
Persuasions, 25, 2281, 3042, 4158, 4204, 4594
Pert, Maurice, 712
Pertwee, Jon, 2056, 3012
Pertwee, Michael, 1994
Peruse, Julian, 2606
Pesce, Joey, 5435
Peshay, 2202, 3643, 4228, 4496
Pestilence, 285, 649, 1343, 1456, 4205, 4822
Pet Lamb, 4205
Pet Shop Boys, 58, 760-762, 883, 962, 1727, 1772, 1827, 1897, 2286, 2677, 2702, 2725, 3053, 3695, 3722, 3918, 4079, 4118, 4142, 4205-4206, 4455, 5768, 5772, 6068
Petal, 810, 1902, 2154
Pete Kelly's Blues, 4206
Pete Tong, 1832, 1881, 2800, 2926
Pete, Robert, 2125, 5857
Peter And Gordon, 252, 433, 1005, 1223, 1542, 2059, 2689, 3521, 3548, 4206, 5313, 5327, 5690
Peter And The Test Tube Babies, 4206-4207
Peter Pan, 241, 440, 498, 733, 1190, 1516, 1544-1545, 1824, 2405, 2660, 2946, 3147, 3187, 3258, 3268, 3490, 3927, 3986, 4207-4208, 4259, 4567
Peter, Paul And Mary, 1015, 1413, 1485, 1672, 1879, 2105, 2140, 2164, 2297, 2684, 2853, 3064, 3241, 3423, 3516, 4208, 4256, 4422, 4862, 5705, 5962
Peterbank, Wesley, Jnr., 1678
Peterik, Jim, 4208
Peterkin, Keith, 4336
Peterman, Barbara, 3344
Peters And Lee, 2017, 4208-4209
Peters Sisters, 3766
Peters, Ben, 3786
Peters, Bernadette, 565, 1369, 2121, 2205, 2364, 2704, 3389, 4041, 4209
Peters, Bethan, 1476
Peters, Brian, 2285, 4209, 5878
Peters, Brock, 941, 3322, 4286-4287
Peters, Clarke, 625, 1916, 2893,

2996, 3939, 5898
Peters, Dale, 2769
Peters, Dan, 2266, 3831, 3957
Peters, Darren, 5835
Peters, Dave, 117, 778
Peters, David, 3154
**Peters, Debra, And The Love
Saints, 4209-4210**
Peters, Frank, 707, 4930
Peters, Jeff, 778
Peters, Joey, 2240
Peters, Lennie, 4208-4209
Peters, Linda, 5411, 5413-5414
Peters, Michael, 1625, 3428
Peters, Mark, And The
Cyclones, 4210
Peters, Mark, And The Method,
4210
**Peters, Mark, And The
Silhouettes, 4210**
Peters, Mike, 106, 5526, 6126
Peters, Nick, 4518
Peters, Richard, 2570, 3443,
4314, 4930, 6053, 6062, 6070,
6078
Peters, Rob, 2196, 2511
Peters, Scott, 929
Peters, Sir Shina, 75, 4210
Petersburski, J., 2967
Petersen, Detlef, 3113
Petersen, Dick, 3022
Petersen, Herb, 2521
Petersen, John, 438
Petersen, Patricia, 4455
Petersen, Paul, 1815
Peterson, Albert, 862
Peterson, Anders, 1693
Peterson, Bernice, 941
Peterson, Cole, 4212
Peterson, Colin, 449-450
Peterson, Colleen, 1083, 5557
Peterson, Debbi, 366-367
Peterson, Dickie, 611, 2299,
5420
Peterson, Ella, 467-468, 1913,
2562, 2782
Peterson, Garry, 2306
Peterson, Gary, 1978
Peterson, Gilles, 54, 895, 2689,
4037, 4758, 5578, 5585
Peterson, Henning, 6079
Peterson, James, 4210-4211
**Peterson, Lucky, 3026, 4210-
4211, 4878**
Peterson, Marvin 'Hannibal', 4211
Peterson, Oscar, 101, 115, 235,
261, 344, 346, 468, 516, 786,
815, 844, 901, 965, 1434, 1556,
1627, 1722, 1732, 1735, 1742,
1785, 1821-1822, 1909, 1913,
2132, 2192, 2244, 2371, 2433,
2437, 2445, 2457, 2484, 2515,
2562, 2749, 2782, 2792, 2881,
2885, 2978, 3116, 3613, 3632,
3739, 3768, 3826, 4065, 4093,
4151, 4211-4213, 4231, 4526,
4626, 4932, 5294, 5301, 5389,
5619-5620, 5638, 5659, 5748-
5749, 5976-5977, 6068
Peterson, Ralph, Jnr., 872, 4656
**Peterson, Ray, 134, 399, 4213,
4626**
Peterson, Sylvia, 1057
Peterson, Tom, 1038

Peterson, Vicki, 366-367
Peterson, Walter, 2398
Petersson, Tom, 1038, 2059,
3887
**Petit, Buddy, 233, 443, 826,
1389, 2346, 3216, 3754, 3939,
3971, 4213, 5479**
Petit, Christopher, 4402
Petit, Margaret, 946
Petit, Roland, 205, 1355, 2381
Petkere, Bernice, 5973
Petra, 4213
Petri, Tony, 5547
Petrie, Hay, 2660, 4467
Petrillo, James Caesar, 4213
Petrovic, Gedomir, 2214
Petrucci, John, 1624
Petrucci, Roxy, 1873, 3399, 5654
**Petrucciani, Michel, 1789,
2245, 2349, 3286, 3327, 3553,
4094, 4214**
Petrus, Jacques Fred, 1015
Petters, John, 1065
Pettersson, Jonas, 3628
**Pettibone, Shep, 58, 337, 1481,
2636, 3403, 3855, 4214, 4455,
5459, 5617**
Petticoato, Toto, 410
**Pettiford, Oscar, 70, 168, 548,
1104, 1231, 1294, 1682, 2302,
2845, 3210, 3653, 3739, 3771,
3810, 3925, 4215, 4298, 4407,
4534, 4664, 4985, 5412, 5509,
5726, 5841, 5858, 6001**
Pettigrew, Charles, 1025
Pettigrew, Craig, 5701
Pettigrew, Jason, 2112
Pettingell, Frank, 4719, 4932,
5285, 5958
Pettis, 'Alabama' Junior, 4215
Pettis, Coleman, Jnr., 4215
Pettis, Fred, 248
Pettis, Jack, 3919
Pettit, Jimmy, 1750
Pettitt, Tony, 1884
Pettus, Kenny, 1430
**Petty, Norman, 683, 744, 1233,
1292, 1651, 2510, 2568-2569,
3315, 4055, 4215, 4280, 5388**
**Petty, Tom, 334, 447, 869, 980,
1234, 1271, 1370, 1467, 1519,
1631, 1676-1677, 1787, 1953,
2047, 2416, 2703, 2707, 3304,
3373, 3511, 3865, 3943, 3958,
4055, 4215-4216, 4430, 4846,
4865, 5493, 6126, 6130**
Petulia, 401, 4216
Petway, Robert, 3551
Petz, Manfred, 4388
Peverell, J., 3947
Peverett, Dave, 1955, 4757
Pew, Tracy, 545
Peyronel, Danny, 2468, 5563
Peyroux, Madeleine, 4216
Peyser, Joan, 499, 2129, 6035
Peyton, Dave, 505, 2750, 3584,
4936
Peyton, Lawrence, 1997
Pez Band, 4217
Pezzati, Marco, 3871
Pfanmuller, Harmut, 1718
Pfeiffer, Darrin, 2190
Pflayer, Jim, 4021
PFM, 2202

**Phair, Liz, 658, 1806-1807,
2766, 3245, 3510, 3765, 4217,
5637**
Phajja, 4217
Phang, George, 735, 1810, 2343,
3266, 3794, 3958, 5676
Phantom Blue, 4217-4218, 4805
**Phantom Of The Opera, The,
73, 258, 352, 538, 566, 737, 815,
1146, 1281, 1703-1704, 1968,
2704, 2711, 2806, 3284, 3373,
3393, 3493, 4218, 4337, 4565,
5307, 5372, 5835, 5857**
**Pharcyde, 189, 198, 408, 711,
1473, 1507, 2468, 4219, 4731**
Pharoah, Jaarone, 2810
Pharr, Coburn, 197, 4039
Pharr, Kelsey, 1477
Phay, Danny, 1068
**Phd, 362, 396, 488, 1277, 1508,
2193, 2391, 2428, 2732, 2860,
4219, 4518, 5306, 5584**
Phelan, Eileen, 4900
Phelan, Margaret, 1164
Phelan, Martin, 3652, 4737
Pheloung, Barrington, 4749
Phelps, Doug, 761, 2974
Phelps, George, 3708
Phelps, Joel, 4907
Phelps, Ricky Lee, 761, 2973-
2974
Phenomena, 4219
Phield, Paddy, 1325
Phil the Albino Priest, 3287
**Phil The Fluter, 956, 3152,
4219, 5938**
**Philadelphia International
Records, 4220 and** *passim*
Philbin, Greg, 4506
Philips Records, 4220 and
passim
Philips, Dave, 3296
Philips, Stu, 3547
Philips, Van, 1207
Philips, Woolf, 2452
Philles Records, 1640
Phillinganes, Greg, 337, 5283
Phillip, Rob, 3862
Phillipet, Gary, 1088, 1232
Phillipps, Martin, 1060, 1119
Phillips, Aaron, 3296
Phillips, Andrew, 2901
Phillips, Anthony, 930, 2329,
6126
Phillips, Arlene, 196, 2601, 4752,
5440
**Phillips, Barre, 331, 591, 1863,
2559, 3070, 3158, 3439, 4220,
5505**
Phillips, Bill, 3875, 4221
Phillips, Bobby, 880
Phillips, Brewer, 4221
**Phillips, Bruce 'Utah', 4221-
4222 and** *passim*
Phillips, Bunny, 4903
**Phillips, Chynna, 4222, 4224,
5869**
Phillips, Danny, 202
Phillips, Dave, 906
Phillips, Don, 3475, 4222
Phillips, Doug, 1395
Phillips, Eddie, 1286, 3465
Phillips, Esther, 409, 446, 1608,

3264, 3275, 3350, 4153, 4222-
4223, 4790, 5766
Phillips, Ethan, 3860
Phillips, Eugene Floyd, 4223
Phillips, Flip, 391, 417, 2622,
2792, 3875, 4223, 4526, 5379
Phillips, Gary, 1689, 2988, 5690
Phillips, Gene, 4223
Phillips, Glen, 5452
Phillips, Grant Lee, 2240, 5428
Phillips, Gregory, 2659, 4500,
4737
Phillips, Gretchen, 5551
Phillips, Gus, 740
Phillips, Harry, 4225, 4227
Phillips, Hugh, 4932
Phillips, J., 5998
Phillips, Jamal, 2678
Phillips, Jim, 3428, 3964, 4224
Phillips, Joe 'Flip', 4223
**Phillips, John, 848, 1575, 1756,
2344, 2901, 3427-3428, 3431,
3586, 3753, 3879, 4222-4224,
4653, 4932, 5371, 5869, 6061**
Phillips, Jon, 5740
Phillips, Joseph, 272
Phillips, Julian, 3464
Phillips, Kevin, 4949
Phillips, Leslie, 3199, 4224
Phillips, Linn, 1929
Phillips, Marc, 2604
Phillips, Mark, 2994, 4225
Phillips, Marvin, 471, 3496
Phillips, Mary Bracken, 3647
Phillips, McKenzie, 3427, 4223
**Phillips, Michelle, 1575, 1660,
2901, 3427-3428, 4222-4224,
5869, 6061**
Phillips, Paul, 1630, 3860
Phillips, Phil, 496, 4224
Phillips, Ray, 816, 3879
Phillips, Reuben, 2854, 5762
Phillips, Ricky, 313, 320, 1263,
5670
Phillips, Robert, 3398, 6092
Phillips, Robin, 258, 2807
Phillips, Roy, 1606, 4179, 4227
Phillips, Russ, 2531
**Phillips, Sam, 21, 653, 665, 726,
827-828, 838, 976, 1122, 1550,
1616, 1947, 2044, 2315, 2394,
2620, 2730, 2815, 2840, 3325,
3444, 3960, 3974, 4055, 4131,
4196, 4224-4225, 4309-4310,
4526, 5403, 5547, 5690**
Phillips, Sam (singer), 4225
Phillips, Shawn, 1971, 2010,
5304
Phillips, Shelley, 4271
Phillips, Shola, 5733
**Phillips, Sid, 44, 158, 477, 1097,
1482, 3292, 4225, 4227**
Phillips, Simon, 1716, 3453,
3475, 3827, 5475, 5811
Phillips, Stacy, 5506
**Phillips, Steve, 15, 1299, 3051,
3641, 3977, 4225**
Phillips, Stu, 3439, 4226
Phillips, Teddy, 4226
Phillips, Terry, 255, 4271
Phillips, Todd, 621, 1314, 2294
Phillips, Tom, 2165, 4474
Phillips, Utah, 1522-1523, 4222
Phillips, Washington, 4227

Phillips, Woolf, 4227
Phillipus, Frans, 4809
Philo Records, 105, 1478, 3641, 4221
Philpotts, Tex, 2261
Phipps Family, 961, 3746
Phipps, Chris, 5520
Phipps, Jim, 1799
Phipps, Joyce, 2282
Phipps, Nicholas, 3106
Phipps, Pete, 1480, 2171
Phipps, William, 1544
Phiri, Ray Chipika, 2934, 3534, 4227
Phish, 626, 3720, 4227-4228, 6068
Phisst Records, 3335
Phoebus, Chad, 3335
Phoenix, 4228
Phoenix, Rain, 5387
Phoenix, River, 430, 5728
Phonogram Records, 123, 146, 312, 1015, 1090, 1479, 2074, 2293, 2392, 2707, 2925, 3961, 4012, 4781, 5324, 5379, 5779
Phonokol Records, 264
Photek, 2296, 3643, 3721, 4228, 4474
Photoglo, Jim, 4687
Photos, 4228-4229
Phranc, 991, 4229
Phuture Records, 1560
Physter, George, 3635, 6105
Piaf, Edith, 299, 442, 793, 1102, 1159, 1803, 2033, 2709, 3218, 3467, 3512, 3818, 4104, 4181, 4217, 4229-4230, 4700, 5557, 6068
Piano C. Red, 4231
Piano Red, 71, 527, 1222, 2090, 4203, 4231-4232
Piano Slim, 2880, 4232
Piano, Mike, 522, 3125, 4737, 5776
Piantadosi, Al, 1106, 3548
Piazza, Joe, 4973
Piazza, Rod, 318, 630, 1538, 1671, 2571, 4232, 4621, 5879
Piazza, Sammy, 2603
Piazzolla, Astor, 3080, 3233, 3727, 3837, 4110, 4232
Piblokto!, 307, 414, 784, 2118, 4232-4233
Pic And Bill, 4233
Picard, John, 4233
Picard, Simon, 4623
Picardo, Tommy, 1297
Picariello, Freddy, 918
Piccadilly Records, 25, 1869, 4301
Piccioni, Dave, 301
Picciotto, Guy, 2045
Piccoli, Michel, 2263
Piccolo, Greg, 4642
Piccolo, John, 4885
Pichon, Walter 'Fats', 4233-4234
Picken, Chris, 5892
Pickens, Buster, 2283, 4234
Pickens, Charles, 4233
Pickens, Earl, 1344
Pickens, J.P., 4824
Pickens, Lee, 602
Pickens, Slim, 135

Pickerell, Mark, 4794
Pickering, Andy, 3733
Pickering, Ben, 3776
Pickering, Mike, 1453, 2328, 3379, 4130
Pickert, Rolly, 308
Pickett, Bobby 'Boris', 4234
Pickett, Dan, 355, 4234
Pickett, Kenny, 1286, 3465
Pickett, Lenny, 5479
Pickett, Phil, 4719
Pickett, Wilson, 142-143, 272, 664, 670, 917, 1262, 1301, 1834, 1920, 2077, 2240, 2351, 2539, 2609, 2628, 2678, 2969, 3010, 3050, 3455, 3664, 3849, 3960, 4021, 4234-4235, 4454, 4762, 5316, 5361, 5377, 5395, 5456, 5695, 5700, 5904-5905
Pickettes, 4027
Pickettywitch, 4235
Pickford Hopkins, Gary, 1813, 5824
Pickford, Mary, 261, 4619, 5578
Pickles, Andy, 2825, 3612
Picklesimer, Juanita, 3770
Pickney, Fayette, 5421-5422
Picks, Glen, 1973
Pickwick, 4235
Picon, Molly, 1882, 3668
Picone, Vito, 1728
Picôt, Carl Eugene, 2755
Picou, Alphonse, 884, 1389, 4235, 4368
Picture, 4235-4236
Pictures At An Exhibition, 1753, 4236
Picture House, 4236
Pidgeon, Rebecca, 4680
Pidgeon, Walter, 1457, 1659, 2055, 2543, 4814, 5284
Pie Plant Pete, 405, 4236-4237
Piech, Jennifer, 5449
Pied Piper, The, 1242, 1590, 2028, 4063, 4237, 4700, 5372
Pied Pipers, 212, 1482, 1927, 2007, 2623, 2652, 3454, 4237-4238, 4695, 6116
Piek, Fred, 2051
Pierce Brothers, 799, 2249, 4603
Pierce, Andy, 3879
Pierce, Billie, 4238
Pierce, Charlie, 3366
Pierce, Dave, 3522
Pierce, De De, 2636, 4238, 4583
Pierce, Don, 389, 1358, 3673, 4238
Pierce, Jack, 4603, 5338
Pierce, Jason, 3153, 4194
Pierce, Jeffrey Lee, 2313, 4239
Pierce, Jennifer, 2766
Pierce, John, 97, 2712, 4095
Pierce, Les, 4157
Pierce, Lonnie, 1277
Pierce, Nat, 389, 877, 925, 2472, 2506, 3461, 3522, 3544, 4239, 4388, 4560, 5912
Pierce, Paula, 4119
Pierce, Ralph, 4701
Pierce, Rick, 4375
Pierce, Tim, 3477
Pierce, Tony, 1034
Pierce, Webb, 329, 799, 864, 1009, 1179, 1429, 1483, 1706,

1759, 2097, 2328, 2481, 2533, 2990, 3220, 3326, 3358, 3487, 3901, 3929, 3983, 4240-4241, 4296, 4568, 4984, 5436-5437, 5665, 5678, 5746, 5764, 5820, 5970-5971
Piercy, Andy, 88, 5516
Pierre, Amedee, 4923
Pierrepoint, Hughie, 4079
Pierson, Clark, 2890, 3255
Pierson, Jon, 243
Pierson, Kate, 303, 2676, 4395
Piesmack, Stefan, 2380
Pietklewicz, Krystof, 873
Pietsch, Walter, 295
Pigalle, Anne, 6004
Pigbag, 2648, 2692, 3139, 3311, 3524, 4241, 4282, 4968
Pigeon Pie Records, 4241
Pigeonhed, 4241-4242
Pigg, Gary, 1904
Piggot, Charlie, 1433
Piggott, Johanne, 1617
Piggott, Mike, 4190
Piglets, 4242
Pigmeat Pete, 2241, 5870
Pignagnoli, Larry, 5788
Pigott, Johanna, 5941
Pigsty Hill Light Orchestra, 3928, 4242
Pihl, Gary, 2332
Piirpauke, 4242
Pike, Andy, 3476
Pike, Cisco, 3078, 4718
Pike, Dave, 3077, 3476, 4243, 5747
Pike, Jim, 1995, 3205
Pike, Pete, 849
Pike, Simon, 2026
PiL, 98, 2190, 2781, 2910, 3179, 3212, 3642, 4243, 4357-4358, 5564, 5640
Pilate, Felton, 1199-1200
Pilatus, Rob, 1846, 3681
Pilcher, Barry Edgar, 1213
Pilf, Philip, 932
Pilgrim Records, 4412
Pilgrim Travelers, 4243
Pilgrim, Jerry, 306
Pilgrim, Jimmy, 5544
Pilgrim, John, 5815
Pili-Pili, 2987
Pilkington, Rosemary, 2612
Pillars, Hayes, 2819, 5500
Pillbox, 4243
Piller, Eddie, 54, 5287
Pilloud, Rod, 1300
Pillow, Ray, 1172, 4243-4244, 4869
Pills, Jacques, 442
Pilnick, Paul, 1443
Pilot (UK), 4244
Pilot (USA), 4244
Pilot, Mike, 4104
Pilots Of The Impossible, 4767
Pilson, Jeff, 1575
Piltch, David, 1158
Piltch, Rob, 3386
Piltdown Men, 1995, 4244, 4518
Pilz, Michel, 2172, 3070
Pina, Eugene, 4307
Pinado, Bob, 4244
Pinchers, 1007-1008, 1525,

1810-1811, 2738, 2764, 3144, 3662, 4165, 4245, 4733, 4794, 4733, 4794, 5669
Pinchley, Amos, 3267
Pincock, Dougie, 415, 2513, 4245, 5904
Pincombe, Ian, 1500, 3355
Pindell, Reginald, 3322
Pinder, Mike, 3759
Pine Grove Boys, 45
Pine Ridge String Band, 920
Pine State Playboys, 975
Pine Valley Boys, 2521
Pine, Courtney, 447, 582, 844, 1107, 1991, 2760, 2795, 2797, 2799, 3188, 3474, 3826, 4129, 4245, 4458, 5408, 5726, 5863
Pineapple, Samuel, 1064
Pineda, Leopoldo, 5447
Pinedo, Nelson, 1240, 4032, 4616
Pinera, Mike, 14, 119, 624, 878, 2709, 4246, 4435
Pinero, Frank, 4328
Pingatore, Mike, 3763
Pini, Eugene, 4492
Pini, Gil, 700
Pink Fairies, 392, 1060, 1233, 1500, 1813, 1826, 1854, 2303, 2442, 2631, 2914, 3407, 3806, 3812, 4246, 5545
Pink Floyd, 166, 194, 274, 319, 349, 358, 392-393, 410, 615, 695, 923, 928, 1187, 1623, 1652, 1747, 1755, 2109, 2155, 2305, 2425, 2469, 2474, 2618, 2812, 2994, 3098, 3503, 3608, 3619, 3632, 3720, 3856, 3889, 4054, 4066, 4147, 4180, 4216, 4246-4249, 4285, 4338, 4353, 4391, 4752, 4964, 5293, 5360, 5363, 5372, 5380, 5462, 5482, 5510, 5570, 5686, 5707, 5724, 5895, 5987, 6031, 6068, 6126, 6130
Pink Floyd At Pompeii, 4249
Pink Industry, 526, 763, 1717, 4249
Pink Lady, The, 4249
Pink Military, 526, 763, 1444, 1717, 4249, 5946
Pink Records, 962, 1873, 4249, 5903
Pink, Celinda, 4188, 4250
Pinkard, Maceo, 93, 4650
Pinker, Jeff, 859
Pinkerton's Assorted Colours, 4250
Pinkham, Stuart, 4196
Pinkins, Tonya, 2807, 4264
Pinkney, Bill, 1627
Pinkney, Dwight, 4250, 4644, 5990
Pinky, Bill, And The Turks, 2917
Pinlar, Les, 4278
Pinne, Peter, 4341
Pinnick, Chris, 1054
Pinnock, Delroy, 4034
Pinocchio, 639, 1174, 1535, 1543-1544, 1708, 2946, 4250, 5719, 5982
Pins And Needles, 2479, 4250-4251, 4338, 4637, 4800, 5835
Pinski Zoo, 298, 1168, 4251

Prince Rakeem, 1766, 2117, 4707, 4898, 5932

Prince Allah, 2019, 2738, 4333, 5318

Prince, Bill, 1545, 3295, 4599

Prince, Faith, 1901, 2322, 3942, 4074

Prince, Hal, 38, 499, 3638, 4099, 4337, 4893

Prince, Harold, 874, 876, 1196, 2056, 2976, 3269, 3393, 4337, 4859, 6131

Prince Heron, 1247, 3832

Prince, Hughie, 4449

Prince Huntley, 3487

Prince, Joe, 111, 3467, 4654

Prince, Mark, 5627

Prince, Michael, 1316, 1349, 2030, 3184, 4953

Prince, Norman, 2605

Prince, Rod, 808, 2019

Prince, Tony, 1621, 2494, 2666, 4140, 4336, 5559, 5872

Prince, Viv, 1105, 2913, 4319, 5602

Prince, Wesley, 1159

Princess Pang, 4337

Princess Sharifa, 99, 4337

Princess Theatre Musicals, 649, 2975, 4338, 5900

Principal Edwards, 1127, 4338

Principle, Jamie, 3053, 4338

Prine, James, 1439

Prine, John, 898, 1221, 1750, 2211, 2291, 2832, 3058, 4339, 5572, 5839, 5842

Pringle, Bryan, 538

Prins, Patrick, 3819

Printemps, Yvonne, 1216

Printup, Marcus, 4339

Prinz, Eddie, 1376

Prinz, LeRoy, 2523, 3947, 4519, 4563, 4892, 5395, 5948

Prior, Les, 109

Prior, Maddy, 470, 736, 1300, 2354, 2393, 2422, 2881, 4265, 4339, 4904, 4907, 5279, 5533

Prior, Nick, 4766

Prior, Richard, 577, 5733

Priority Records, 1167, 4340, 4703

Priory Records, 3528

Priske, Rich, 517

Prism, 4340 and *passim*

Prisonaires, 3325, 4340-4341, 4446

Prisoner Cell Block H - The Musical, 4341, 5760

Prisoners, 4341-4342

Prisonshake, 4342

Pritchard, Barry, 1981

Pritchard, Bill, 3508

Pritchard, Charlie, 1212

Pritchard, Chris, 4907

Pritchard, Dave, 2673, 4872

Pritchard, John, 4886

Pritchard, Mark, 4498

Pritchard, Mel, 376

Pritchett, James Arthur, 666, 1685, 4980

Pritikin, Arnold, 3635

Private Lives, 1031, 1141, 1147, 1265, 3035, 3066, 3146, 3261, 4342, 4949

Private Stock Records, 2573, 3149, 3845

Privilege, 4342

Privin, Bernie, 2622, 4342

Pro-Ject X, 4342-4343

Pro-Pain, 67, 1317, 4343

Probe Records, 647, 2443, 5634

Probert, George, 1904

Proby, P.J., 401, 959, 988, 995, 1380, 1700, 1839, 1953, 1970, 2001, 2204, 3730, 3931, 3960, 4049, 4343-4344, 4468, 4478, 4533, 4720, 4784, 4892, 5679, 5772

Process Records, 405, 4237

Proclaimers, 379, 3822, 4344, 4405

Procol Harum, 30, 423, 448, 520, 752, 1141, 1234, 1452, 1609, 1800, 1949, 2026, 2359, 2414, 2861, 3164, 3619, 4126, 4262, 4264, 4344-4345, 4488, 4865, 5399, 5511, 6131

Procope, Russell, 330, 374, 706, 937, 963, 2487, 3027, 4345, 5856

Procter, John, 2665

Proctor, Harold, 963

Proctor, Judd, 4533

Proctor, Philip, 1904

Proctor, Rob, 3879

Proctor, Steve, 509

Proctor, Wayne, 5739

Prodigy, 4345-4346 and *passim*

Production House, 4346 and *passim*

Profane, Benny, 482, 4642

Professional Seagulls, 3150, 4346

Professionals, 495, 1068, 1184, 1650, 1693, 1724, 2138, 2263, 2597, 2784, 2849, 2886, 3554, 3605, 3733, 3742, 4006, 4139-4140, 4346, 4401, 5463, 5780

Professor Frisky, 784

Professor Griff, 908, 1079, 1815, 1865, 3890, 4346, 4357, 4860

Professor Longhair, 139, 352, 567, 856, 1581, 1684, 2530, 3013, 3364, 3763, 4138, 4346-4347, 5718, 5886, 6071

Professor X, 3249, 5939

Proffit, Mason, 3501

Proffitt, Frank, 4347, 5705

Proffitt, Wiley, 4347

Profile Records, 4347 and *passim*

Profit, Clarence, 4347

Profitt, Louie, 5312

Profus, Chuck, 91

Prohourn, Chris, 1565

Project Soul, 1199

Prokop, Skip, 3242, 4166

Prokopczuk, Stef, 51, 2096

Promises, Promises, 4348

Prong, 4348 and *passim*

Pronk, Rob, 548

Prongo, Jark, 2030

Proops, Jim, 1840, 4920

Propaganda, 4348-4349

Propatier, Joseph, 4765

Propellerheads, 410, 1488, 4349

Proper-Sheppard, Robyn, 2177

Propes, Duane, 3273

Prophet, Billy, 2825

Prophet, Chuck, 2265, 4349, 5514

Prophet, Michael, 2019, 2343, 3144, 4349, 4432, 4546, 5665, 5945

Prophet, Orvel, 4350

Prophet, Ronnie, 4350

Prophets Of The City, 4350

Prosen, Sid, 5457

Prosper Mérimeé, 940

Prosser, Alan, 5526

Protheroe, Brian, 4350

Prototype Records, 2296

Protrudi, Rudi, 2060

Prout, Brian, 1508

Prouty, Jed, 745

Province, Clara, 4360, 5471

Provine, Dorothy, 427, 4350

Provisor, Danny, 2585

Provost, Joe, 3534

Prowler, 2044, 2525, 2711, 3436, 4024

Prowse, Jane, 5582

Prowse, Juliet, 354, 912, 1055, 1165, 2135, 2660, 4118

Pruden, Hal, 1984, 4351

Prudence, Ron, 2261

Prudence, Steve, 2760

Pruett, Jack, 4351

Pruett, Jeanne, 3985, 4351

Pruett, Sammy, 1628, 2480

Pruette, William, 1068

Pruitt, Joseph, 1844

Prunes, 349, 1562, 1694, 1726, 2033, 3862, 4885, 5639, 5651

Pryce, Debbie, 1222

Pryce, Jonathan, 402, 1596, 1802, 3393, 3705-3706, 3952, 4034

Pryde, David, 1778

Pryor, Arthur, 1787, 2128, 4880

Pryor, Laurie, 985

Pryor, Richard, 729, 3523, 4680, 5860, 5898

Pryor, Snooky, 1399, 1641, 1985, 2346, 2580, 2871, 2880, 4351, 4882, 5973

Prysock, Arthur, 407, 796, 3544, 4153, 4351-4352, 5756

Prysock, Wilbert 'Red', 4352

Prytcherch, Harry, 4500

Psilias, Paul, 823

Psychaos, 616, 5491

Psyche-Out, 4352, 5429

Psyched Up Janis, 4352

Psychedelic, 4353-4355 and *passim*

Psychedelic Furs, 545, 2349, 2379, 3248, 3338, 4355, 4697, 4942, 5398, 5782

Psychic Deli, 133, 1526

Psychic TV, 152, 1087, 1155, 1719, 2286, 2692, 2697, 3614, 3718, 4355-4356, 5427

Psychick Warriors Ov Gaia, 615, 1633, 4356

Psychodots, 458

Psychonauts, 2765

Psychopod, 5446

Psychotic Records, 4609

Psychotics, 4821

Psycka, Rodney, 721

Psyclone Rangers, 4356

Ptacek, Rainer, 2135, 4413

Puba, Grand, 592, 711, 745, 1880, 2237, 2387, 2468, 3398, 3508, 3537, 4043, 4294, 4837, 4965

Public Enemy, 202, 205, 208, 429, 487, 558, 640, 663, 776, 883, 975, 1079, 1344, 1459-1460, 1546, 1865, 1932, 2063, 2387, 2393, 2413, 2608, 2668-2669, 2701, 2723, 2738, 2972, 3064, 3080, 3341, 3508, 3535, 3825, 3887, 3890, 4085, 4128, 4191, 4295, 4346, 4356-4357, 4433, 4593, 4679, 4731, 4915, 4939, 4942, 4965, 5340, 5369, 5497, 5513, 5543, 5612, 5939, 5960, 6071

Public Image Limited, 356, 360, 1275, 2103, 2367, 2764, 3134, 3392, 4044, 4243, 4357-4358, 5324, 5407, 5520, 6071

Puck, Eva, 2160, 2277, 4893

Puckett, Gary, 1111, 2388, 2944, 4171, 4358-4359, 5460

Puckett, Gary, And The Union Gap, 2388, 4171, 4358-4359, 5460

Puckett, Holland, 4359

Puckett, Riley, 744, 804, 1309, 2808, 4359-4360, 4951, 5699, 5728

Puckett, Si, 4359

Puders, Peter, 4172

Pudgee The Phat Bastard, 4360, 4384

Pudim, Alafia, 3133

Puente, Ernesto Antonio, Jnr., 4360

Puente, Rafy, 1899

Puente, Tito, 137, 230, 301, 577, 637, 1240, 1320, 1323, 1327, 1841, 1855, 2048, 2925, 3090, 3097, 3181, 3232, 3314, 3354, 3428, 3702, 3752, 3776, 4064, 4097-4098, 4113-4114, 4360-4362, 4420-4421, 4447, 4558, 4613-4616, 4646-4647, 4731, 4739-4740, 4743-4744, 5447

Puente, Valdez, 4361, 4740

Puente, Vaya, 4361

Puerling, Eugene Thomas, 2515

Puerta, Joe, 159, 2598

Puerto Rican Power, 508, 4065, 4647

Puerto Rican Supremes, 641

Puerto, Al, 3938

Puff Daddy, 1190, 4362

Pugh, Bryan, 2730

Pugh, Joe Bennie, 1975, 4362

Pugh, John, 2040

Pugh, Martin, 227

Pugh, Mick, 932

Pugh, Mike, 3709

Pugh, Steve, 129, 1799

Pugliano, Jim, 2760

Pukulski, Jan Marek, 1938

Pukwana, Dudu, 43, 224, 260, 447, 482, 1227, 1880, 3500, 3575, 3627, 3675, 4135, 4174, 4362, 5999

Pullen, Don, 65, 614, 630, 1341, 2028, 2249-2250, 3822, 3833, 3848, 4363, 4536, 5691, 5794

Pullum, Joe, 694, 2216

5714-5715, 5806, 5938, 5996, 6072
Raitt, John, 947, 2806, 4025, 4075, 4106, 4339, 4415-4416, 5371
Rajas, Miguel Martinez, 4086
Rak Records, 1064, 2468, 2838, 2970, 3649, 4416, 5829
Rake, 4416-4417 and *passim*
Rakestraw, Fred, 3412
Rakha, Ustad Alla, 2647
Rakim, 1773, 1897, 1960-1961, 2451, 3077, 3808, 3981, 4104, 4129, 4417, 4898, 5497, 5727
Rakotozafy, 4417
Raksin, David, 3630, 3789, 4417
Raleigh, Ben, 4304
Raleigh, Sir Walter, 4418
Raley, Dennis, 3424
Raley, Leo, 799
Ralfini, Jan, 2485
Rall, Tommy, 2055, 2706, 3035, 3668, 4825
Ralph And Elmer, 3497
Ralph Records, 321, 1049, 1173, 4508, 5539, 5953
Ralph, Jessie, 4046, 4732
Ralphs, Mick, 156, 320, 750, 3814, 4418
Ralske, Kurt, 5569
Ralston, Aonghus, 4236
Ralston, Teri, 1196
Ralton, Bert, 2516
Ram Jam, 216, 1354, 1848, 2200, 3189, 3236, 3593, 4418, 5552, 5646, 5717, 5995
Ram, Buck, 39, 1186, 2971, 4263, 5373
Ram, Raja, 2692, 4389, 5446
Ramacon, Phil, 4418
Ramazzotti, Eros, 674, 4419
Rambeau, Eddie, 1999, 4419
Ramblers International Dance Band, 4419
Rambling Mountaineers, 271, 282, 660, 666, 4460
Rambling Rogue, 5842
Rambow, Philip, 3309, 5780, 5886
Ramdani, Abdellah, 3667
Ramey, Ben, 3624, 4833
Ramey, Gene, 674, 3600, 4420, 5342
Ramey, Samuel, 1219
Ramírez, Carlitos, 3162
Ramirez, Carlos, 3947
Ramírez, Chamaco, 229, 4031-4032
Ramirez, Gabby, 4945
Ramírez, Humberto, 3750, 4618, 4647, 5623
Ramirez, Joe, 558, 1937
Ramirez, Louie, 4420-4421 and *passim*
Ramirez, Ram, 1377, 4421
Ramirez, Rick, 802
Ramirez, Tomas, 3322
Ramistella, John, 4559
Rammelzee, 4422
Rammstein, 4422
Ramon, Paul, 3680
Ramone, Dee Dee, 413, 2460, 3094, 4423, 6072
Ramone, Joey, 1000, 1478, 2567,

3923, 4423
Ramone, Johnny, 3923, 4423
Ramone, Marky, 4423
Ramone, Phil, 2853, 3193, 4422, 5715
Ramone, Tommy, 4423
Ramones, 52, 123, 145, 192, 251, 334, 367, 413, 454, 587, 701-702, 860, 1000, 1078, 1357, 1440, 1472, 1478, 1514, 1516, 1523, 1758, 1891, 1930, 2065, 2134, 2225, 2460, 2475, 2584, 2676, 2839, 3002, 3091, 3159-3160, 3195, 3362, 3801, 3913, 3935, 4152, 4180, 4201, 4330, 4365-4366, 4423, 4439, 4455, 4561, 4590, 4592, 4596, 4821, 4891, 4939, 5290, 5303, 5336, 5342, 5351, 5388, 5542, 6072, 6127
Ramos, Jackie, 366
Ramos, Jerome, 5625
Ramos, Juan, 2516
Ramos, Kid, 1818
Ramos, Larry, 3911
Ramos, Ray, 1899
Rampage, Randy, 197, 1564
Rampal, Jean-Pierre, 3149
Rampart Records, 917
Rampling, Charlotte, 2784
Rampling, Danny, 264, 347, 349, 1453, 1617, 2265, 2656, 3570, 4007, 4424
Ramrod Records, 1909
Ramrods, 1542, 2417, 4424
Ramsahoye, Nadia, 1030
Ramsden, Mike, 4906
Ramsden, Nico, 697
Ramsey, Alan, 3216
Ramsey, Dorothy, 208
Ramsey, Frederic, 2798, 2843, 4513, 6104
Ramsey, Kevin, 3238
Ramsey, Mary, 1522, 5337
Ramsey, Steve, 4127, 4749, 4957
Ramsey, Tom, 2188
Ramson, Peter, 5942
Ran-Dells, 4424
Ranaldo, Lee, 710, 1084, 1533, 1804, 1963, 5731
Rance Allen Group, 134, 4424
Ranch Boys, 343, 958, 1634, 2274, 3308, 4044, 4203, 5893
Ranch Hands, 385, 3029, 3805, 4499
Ranch Romance, 3341
Rancho Records, 839
Rancid, 4424-4425 and *passim*
Rand, Ayn, 4178, 4691
Rand, Odell, 2396
Rand, Randy, 284
Randall, Aaron, 197
Randall, Alan, 1978, 6048
Randall, Alex, 806, 1694, 4818
Randall, Bobby, 2912, 4758
Randall, Carl, 3850, 4020
Randall, Dick, 4719
Randall, Freddy, 350, 806, 1294, 1871, 2101, 3189, 4425, 4513, 4818, 4870, 5409, 5530
Randall, Jess, 3045
Randall, Jimmy, 2826
Randall, Jon, 4425
Randall, Ronnie, 3642

Randall, Tony, 3204
Randazzo, Teddy, 2512, 4425, 4674, 5421
Randell, Buddy, 3046
Randholph, Homer Louis, III, 4425
Randle, Bill, 1291
Randle, Vicki, 5537
Randolph, Bill, 4271
Randolph, Boots, 270, 725, 1162, 1274, 1748, 2249, 3052, 4426, 4566, 4761
Randolph, Elsie, 649, 809, 1022, 1031, 1744, 1961, 2549, 4426, 5397, 5958
Randolph, Irving, 4427, 6050
Randolph, Lester, 4441
Randolph, Mouse, 4427
Randolph, Patsy, 4963
Randolph, Trevor, 5569
Randolph, Zilner, 2750, 4427
Random Records, 1462
Random, Eric, 875
Randrianantoandro, Clémont, 5599
Rands, Bernard, 4544
Randy And The Rainbows, 4427
Raney, Doug, 339, 4428
Raney, Jerry, 431
Raney, Jimmy, 753, 2131, 2789, 3243, 3780, 4427-4428, 5405, 6001
Raney, Sue, 745, 1942, 4428
Raney, Wayne, 766, 1475, 1758, 2173, 3298, 4428, 5480
Rang, Bunny, 2501
Range Ramblers, 5806
Range Riders, 1394
Rangell, Nelson, 4428-4429, 4761
Ranger Doug, 4541, 6074
Ranger, Shorty, 1662-1663, 3254, 3596, 4429, 5839
Ranglin, Ernest, 116, 149, 1137, 1306, 1980, 2254, 2795, 4429, 4493, 4912, 5565, 5669
Rank And File, 431, 1491, 1529, 1778, 3873, 3987, 4430, 4908, 5513
Rank, Bill, 2193, 4430, 5322
Ranken, Andrew, 4270
Rankin Family, 4430
Rankin R.S., 4430
Rankin, Billy, 741, 1641, 3027, 3886, 4820
Rankin, Brian, 3496, 4834
Rankine, Alan, 260
Rankine, Lesley, 4680, 4911
Ranking Ann, 225, 4430-4431, 4941
Ranking Barnabus, 189
Ranking Dread, 4431, 5412, 5688
Ranking Ivan, 2857
Ranking Joe, 767, 1686, 2138, 2762, 4110, 4431, 5526, 5559
Ranking Roger, 370, 430, 2114-2115, 4283
Ranking Toyan, 370, 767, 3144, 3945, 4110, 4431
Ranking Trevor, 370, 2588, 3422, 3945, 4548, 5505, 5665, 5767

Ranking, Peter, 3647
Ranking, Roy, 2700, 3876
Ranking, Squiddly, 3647, 4549, 5767
Ranking, Tony, 4458
Ranks, Bucky, 3944
Ranks, Cutty, 304, 924, 1147, 2368, 2579, 2762, 3405, 4406, 4432, 4458, 4546, 5429
Ranks, Shabba, 249, 265, 369, 453, 487, 1008, 1107, 1147, 1496, 1525, 1817, 2015, 2114, 2147, 2167, 2186, 2276, 2579, 2584, 2764, 3059, 3080, 3134-3135, 3324, 3397-3398, 3462, 3511, 3956, 4155, 4382, 4406, 4432, 4462, 4593, 4795, 4801, 4837, 5429, 5676
Ranks, Shawnie, 3618
Ranno, Richie, 2476
Ransley, Tony, 1657
Ransom, Benny, 1449
Ransome, Mick, 4306-4307, 5303
Rantzen, Esther, 2103
Ranwood Records, 373
Rap, 4433 and *passim*
Rap-A-Lot Records, 4433
Rapallo, Calo, 4937
Rapeman, 110, 521, 723, 2818, 3957, 4258, 4433, 4792, 4864, 4907, 5280, 5589
Rapetti, Guilio, 4195
Rapfogel, Ben, 2347
Raphael, Don, 618
Raphael, Gordon, 4956
Raphael, Jeff, 3987
Raphaelson, Samson, 2796
Rapid, Stephen, 4400
Rapination, 3297, 4434
Rapino Brothers, 4434
Rapone, Al, 4382
Raposo, Joe, 639
Rapp, Anthony, 4505
Rapp, Barney, 4176, 4434
Rapp, Barry, 4165
Rapp, Danny, 1384
Rapp, Philip, 5906
Rapp, Tom, 4176
Rappaport, John, 4424
Rappin' Is Fundamental, 4434
Rapson, John, 2195
Rare, 4434-4435
Rare Bird, 256, 1023, 1062, 1111, 4124, 4435, 4492, 5780
Rare Earth, 3500, 3596, 3814, 4435, 4563, 5318
Rare Silk, 2821
Rarebell, Herman, 4781
Ras Elroy, 562
Ras Tafari, 4338, 4438, 4940
Ras, Michael, And The Sons Of Negus, 562, 1081-1082, 1204, 1251, 4435, 4437
Rasa, Tabula, 1719, 1932, 4147
Rasboro, Jonathan, 4905
Rascel, Renato, 3129
Rasch, Albertina, 361, 746, 1903, 1950, 2182
Rascher, Sigurd, 1139
Rasec, Julio, 3429
Raset, Val, 1262, 2478, 3861, 5963
Rasey, Uan, 5464

Reckless Records, 512
Reco, Ezz, And The Launchers,
4459, 4615
Record Station Records, 182
Record, Eugene, 56, 372, 1052-
1053, 1377, 3161
Recordiau, 4720
Records, 4459 and *passim*
Recorte Records, 3956
Rector, Bobby, 2188
Rector, John, 5810
Rector, Red, 580, 766, 1126-
1127, 2580, 3746, 4460
Recycle Or Die, 2423, 4460,
5617
Red Bandit, 4460
Red Beans, 348, 766, 1264, 3121,
4547, 5948
Red Beans And Rice, 348, 3121
Red Bird Records, 2193, 4413,
4460
Red Bone, 2936
Red Box, 4461
Red Cadillac And A Black
Moustache, 3358
Red Clay Ramblers, 2127
Red Crayola, 1780, 2701, 3315,
4193, 4461
Red Devils, 3353, 4461, 4895
Red Dogs, 4462
Red Dragon, 369, 785, 1525,
1810, 1944, 2186, 2764, 3405,
3425, 3697, 4462, 4466, 4546
Red Flame Records, 246, 1521
Red Fox, 1752, 2020, 4462, 4815
Red Fun, 4462
Red Guitars, 4463
Red Hot Chili Peppers, 273,
602, 671, 1442, 1864, 1892,
1908, 2781, 3259, 3299, 3622,
3689, 3787, 3829, 4175, 4463-
4464, 4679, 4791, 4827, 4921,
5387, 5424, 5731, 5793-5794,
6072
Red House Painters, 4464
Red Jasper, 4464
Red Knuckles And The
Trailblazers, 3993
Red Letter Day, 819, 4464
Red Light, 1208, 1284, 2514,
2796, 3954, 5697
Red Lightnin Records, 2071
Red Lights, 4239
Red Lorry Yellow Lorry, 2134,
4464-4465, 5601
Red Menace, The, 38, 506, 1941-
1942, 2931, 3694-3695, 4337
Red Mill, The, 606, 2501, 3396,
4465
Red Nelson, 4465
Red Ninja, 4465, 6002
Red Rat, 2213, 4465-4466
Red Rhino Records, 4948
Red Rider, 1143, 4956
Red River Dave, 3565-3566,
4068, 4466
Red River Rangers, 1105, 4572,
4979
Red River Rustlers, 2097
Red River Valley Boys, 655
Red Robin Records, 1636, 4412,
4582
Red Rockers, 1266, 4461
Red Roosters, 4466

Red Rose, Anthony, 765, 785,
929, 1944, 3001-3002, 3006,
3631, 3958, 4458, 4466, 5466
Red Shoes, The, 518, 851, 1589,
3583, 3637, 4466-4467, 4879,
6038
Red Shoes, The (film musical),
4466
Red Shoes, The (stage musical),
4467
Red Sky Covern, 4511
Red Snapper, 147, 2272, 4066,
4467, 4609, 5707
Red Tops, 1793
Red Zone Entertainment, 4726
Red, Buryl, 1259
Red, Danny, 4468
Red, Hot And Blue!, 35, 1047,
1658, 2590, 2651, 2676, 3327,
3634-3635, 4289-4290, 4468
Red, Ida, 1475
Red, White And Blue(grass),
635
Red-Tahney, Loretto, 1611
Redbone, 4468-4469, 4566
Redbone, Leon, 4469
Redburn, Julia, 2601
Redd Kross, 2703, 4469
Redd, Ernie, 4198
Redd, Freddie, 758, 2376
Redd, Gene, 676
Redd, Jeff, 1880
Redd, Johnny, 4198
Redd, Ramona, 5470
Redd, Vi, 4469, 4673
Redding, David, 1859
Redding, Noel, 222, 462, 892,
1014, 1859, 2381, 2490, 2492,
3817, 4563, 6053
Redding, Otis, 268, 272, 453,
464, 789, 830, 1041, 1114, 1143,
1197, 1205, 1221, 1301, 1539,
1606, 1661, 1721, 2049, 2054,
2194, 2491, 2539, 2628, 2662,
2890, 2996, 3010, 3204, 3302,
3380, 3454-3455, 3552, 3568,
3598, 3752-3753, 3960, 4076,
4350, 4470, 4585, 4725, 4847,
4881, 4936, 5316, 5360, 5369,
5377, 5395, 5399, 5733, 5768,
5794, 5799, 5864, 5926, 5929,
6072
Reddy, Helen, 134, 599, 1403,
1806, 2390, 2546, 2817, 3537,
3997, 4470-4471, 4914, 6131
Rede, Emma, 3173
Redeye, 91, 4471
Redfern, David, 2799, 6104
Redfield, Irene, 803
Redknapp, Jamie, 3326
Redford, Robert, 577, 1874,
3140, 3218, 3900, 5524
Redgrave, Lynn, 2479, 4977
Redgrave, Vanessa, 607, 721,
899, 5462
Redgum, 3353, 4471
Redhead, 4471-4472 and
passim
Redhead Kingpin And FBI,
4471-4472
Redhead, Jimmy, 3510
Redman, 4472
Redman, Brian, 2534, 5746
Redman, Dewey, 128, 130, 574,

1046, 1168, 2331, 2786, 2795,
3540, 3569, 3645, 3810, 4028,
4472-4473, 5778
Redman, Don, 233, 332, 341,
378, 418, 429, 704, 861, 870,
937, 992, 1010, 1068, 1437,
2171, 2268, 2431, 2486-2487,
2513, 2560, 2625, 2750, 2805,
2825, 2842, 2852, 2868, 2883,
2885, 2960-2961, 2993, 3031,
3473, 3580, 3588, 3799, 4028,
4290, 4301, 4427, 4472-4473,
4511, 4581, 5406, 5412, 5713,
5718, 5928, 5984
Redman, Joshua, 115, 795,
3613, 4473, 4483
Redman, Roy, 4483, 5475
Redmix Records, 4986
Redmon, Jesse, 148
Redmond, Colin, 5667
Redmoon, August, 278
Rednex, 4473
Redpath, Jean, 4473
Redshaw, Wayne, 4754
Redskins, 379, 1781, 4474
Redunzo, Tony, 3769
Redwing, 2165, 4474
Reece, Alex, 3350, 3721, 4474
Reece, Alphonso, 4475
Reece, Brian, 589, 2628
Reece, Colin, 823-824
Reece, Damon, 1699
Reece, David, 50, 366
Reece, Dizzy, 1416, 2082, 2155,
2795, 3722, 4475
Reed Brothers Records, 4475
Reed, A.C., 1173, 4415, 4475,
5784
Reed, Alan, 1545, 4110
Reed, Alyson, 1070
Reed, Andy, 4749
Reed, Ashley, 110
Reed, B. Mitch, 2625
Reed, Bill, 1509-1510, 2916
Reed, Blind Alfred, 4475
Reed, Bob, 4591, 5492
Reed, Bobby, 5597
Reed, Brett, 4424
Reed, Bud, 4480
Reed, Buddy, 318
Reed, Carol, 4033
Reed, Chris, 4464, 4814
Reed, Dalton, 4475
Reed, Dan, Network, 1723,
4476
Reed, David, 350, 922, 1922
Reed, Dizzy, 2314
Reed, Dock, 2354
Reed, Earl, 3339
Reed, Ernie, 2357
Reed, Francine, 3345
Reed, Henry, 3339
Reed, Herb, 4263
Reed, Ishmael, 2381
Reed, Jerry, 270, 977, 1073,
1872, 3301, 3487, 3594, 4086,
4226, 4311, 4315, 4326, 4476-
4477
Reed, Jimmy, 18, 77, 177, 193,
481, 629, 647, 739, 747, 757,
970, 1032, 1166, 1298, 1671,
2090, 2315, 2398, 2407, 2550,
2855-2856, 2916, 2934, 2986,
3136, 3281, 3552, 3680, 4210,

4477, 4498, 4967, 5312, 5357,
5375, 5583, 5622, 5889
Reed, John, 13, 352, 970, 1609,
2290, 3943, 4210, 4342, 4823,
5622, 5761, 5794, 6084, 6115
Reed, John X., 352, 4210
Reed, Johnny, 4061
Reed, Larry, 1619
Reed, Les, 62, 863, 1099, 1488,
2078, 2887, 3995, 4182, 4478,
4573, 5967
Reed, Lou, 31, 117, 179, 218,
367, 492, 672, 685, 891, 922,
1266, 1299, 1609, 1623, 1650,
2043, 2207, 2475, 2619, 2664,
2793, 2953, 3138, 3295, 3309,
3457, 3642, 3922, 3943, 3979,
3991, 4048-4049, 4217, 4441,
4478-4479, 4590-4591, 4678,
4727, 4845, 5457, 5491, 5522,
5608, 5626-5627, 5792, 5860,
5959, 5974, 6002, 6073, 6131
Reed, Lucy, 4480
Reed, Lulu, 4478, 5414
Reed, Lydia, 2522
Reed, Nancy Binns, 2614
Reed, Napoleon, 941
Reed, Ola Belle, 4480
Reed, Oscar, 2903
Reed, Rex, 4875
Reed, Robert, 3138, 4478
Reed, Tommy, 2378, 4480, 5484
Reed, Willie, 114
Reeder, Eskew, 358
Reeder, Leon, 1012
Reeder, Randy, 117
Reeder, Russ, 5729
Reedus, Tony, 1790, 2094
Reedy, Winston, 3005, 4177,
4639
Reef, 4480 and *passim*
Reegs, 1011, 4481
Reekie, Anna, 1883
Reel Big Fish, 2190, 4481
Reel Houze, 4076
Reel 2 Real, 2909, 3787, 4293,
4481
Reels, 4481-4482
Rees, John, 3625
Rees, Roger, 4467
Rees, Stephen, 215
Rees, Tony, 2807, 5835, 6115
Rees, Wyndham, 1813
Rees-Jones, John, 4819
Rees-Mogg, William, 4629
Reese Project, 824, 2296, 2696,
2831, 4482
Reese, Della, 4075, 4482
Reese, Ingrid, 635
Reese, James, 1786, 1936, 4444,
4940, 5913
Reese, Jim, 2048
Reese, Lloyd, 2545, 3690
Reeve, Ada, 1942
Reeve, Jimmie, 2055
Reeves, Barry, 606
Reeves, David, 608, 1400, 3902
Reeves, David, Jnr., 608
Reeves, Del, 688, 1464, 2194,
2278, 3754, 4372, 4482-4483
Reeves, Dianne, 964, 4483, 5283
Reeves, Eddie, 1343
Reeves, Garth, 2211
Reeves, Glen, 294

Rice, Jim, 801
Rice, Larry, 870, 2533
Rice, Mack, 1834, 2694
Rice, Martin, 2830
Rice, Oscar, 4671
Rice, Robert Gene, 4524
Rice, Ronnie, 3912
Rice, Sylvester, 1408, 1930
Rice, Tim, 37, 97, 104, 205, 240, 255, 414, 441, 983, 993, 1048, 1591, 1733, 1802, 1968, 2453, 2463, 2643, 2801, 2817, 2834, 2882, 2897, 3260, 3283, 3856, 4104, 4218, 4524-4525, 4531, 5673, 6109-6110
Rice, Tony, 70, 269, 580-581, 621, 947, 1277, 1314, 2294, 2533, 2955, 3150, 4947
Rich Kids, 3514, 4525, 4967, 5390, 5570, 5585, 5652
Rich Kids On LSD, 2202
Rich, Allan, 4527
Rich, Bernard, 4525
Rich, Buddy, 95, 203, 279, 352, 418, 476, 825, 1162, 1599, 1626, 1706, 1732, 1893, 1981, 2139, 2163, 2371, 2447, 2572, 2622, 2690, 2739, 2773, 2792, 2842, 2845, 3069, 3082, 3099, 3113, 3226, 3388, 3417, 3434, 3459, 3473, 3522, 3553, 3629, 3632, 3664, 3699, 3753, 3958, 4178, 4285, 4302, 4370, 4525-4526, 4636, 4664, 4853-4854, 4878, 4985, 5332, 5468-5469, 5629, 5713, 5750, 5785, 5915, 5917, 5928
Rich, Charlie, 682, 838, 977, 1001, 1122, 1188, 2019, 2032, 2420, 2615, 2636, 2917, 2966, 3473, 3632, 3999, 4371, 4526-4528, 4876, 4936, 4976, 5320, 5676, 6073
Rich, Don, 106, 2757, 4088
Rich, Frank, 1071, 1917, 6040
Rich, Fred, 491, 1252
Rich, Freddy, 417, 2812, 4127, 4528, 4775
Rich, Herbie, 1724, 3553
Rich, Irene, 249
Rich, John, 1713, 2835, 3307
Rich, Larry, 183
Rich, Max, 2216-2217, 4526
Rich, Paul, 4307, 4528
Rich, S., 1704
Rich, Tommy, 163, 491
Richey, Buck, 2318
Richey, George, 389, 2471, 5309, 5936
Richard, Belton, 4529
Richard, Cleby, 4529
Richard, Cliff, 8, 18, 23, 125, 173, 289, 352, 354, 392, 402, 414, 477, 517, 568, 720, 737, 751, 842, 975, 983, 995, 1085, 1099, 1124, 1180, 1187, 1387, 1535, 1687, 1712, 1755, 1798, 1809-1810, 1830, 1876, 1893, 1971, 2027, 2041, 2156, 2203-2204, 2291, 2356, 2463, 2643, 2777, 2927, 3274, 3284, 3317, 3483, 3497, 3509, 3604, 3658, 3670, 3754, 3779, 3796, 3917, 3934, 4125-4126, 4218, 4327,

4408, 4450, 4488, 4525, 4530-4532, 4729, 4774, 4809, 4834-4835, 5284, 5307, 5409, 5440, 5544, 5549, 5653, 5699, 5747, 5752, 5829, 5875, 5900, 5909, 5968, 6073-6074, 6127, 6131
Richard, Gary, 348, 2795, 5549
Richard, Judine, 3238
Richard, Paul, 80, 1971, 2766, 4606, 5637
Richard, Robert, 2809, 3717, 4204, 4875
Richard, Roy, 681, 719, 995, 2601, 4580
Richard, Rudi, 2846
Richard, Stephen, 4519
Richard, Willie, 1180, 3255
Richard, Zachary, 3121
Richards, Abraham S., 4535
Richards, Angela, 1766, 2522
Richards, Ben, 2603
Richards, Billy, 1517, 3679, 4302
Richards, Carol, 4905
Richards, Carole, 735, 893
Richards, Cully, 4253
Richards, Cynthia, 1062, 1679, 1698, 1980, 3671, 4532
Richards, Dave, 3518, 4259
Richards, Digby, 1949
Richards, Donald, 1896
Richards, Drew, 1870
Richards, Earl, 1062, 1081, 3754
Richards, Eddie, 54, 1905, 3288
Richards, Emil, 4834
Richards, J.R., 1542
Richards, Jeff, 4825
Richards, Jim, 4505
Richards, Johnny, 2152, 2972, 3187, 4302, 4532, 4695
Richards, Judy, 2970
Richards, Keith, 440, 501, 1517, 1676, 2312, 2759, 3589, 3823, 4410, 4529, 4627, 4631-4632, 4638, 4831, 5637, 5884, 5911, 6073-6074
Richards, Keni, 284, 1540
Richards, Mark, 1785
Richards, Martin, 825
Richards, Milo, 162
Richards, Nick, 697
Richards, Paula, 13, 2323, 4503
Richards, Ralph, 2531, 4518
Richards, Red, 4533
Richards, Rick, 2123, 4873
Richards, Rod, 4435, 4563
Richards, Ron, 3486, 3589, 4533, 4831
Richards, Sally, 4518
Richards, Tom, 4671
Richards, Tony, 5663
Richards, Trevor, 785
Richardson, Allen, 3883
Richardson, Barry, 453
Richardson, Bill, 2388, 5278
Richardson, Charles, 748, 2525, 2700, 4533
Richardson, Chuck, 5683
Richardson, Claytoven, 4010
Richardson, Clive, 748, 4533, 5840
Richardson, Colin, 649, 1448, 1864, 4767
Richardson, Dan, 1317, 4343
Richardson, Dave, 699

Richardson, Dawn, 1994
Richardson, Derek, 4394
Richardson, Garth, 2975, 3622
Richardson, Geoff, 930, 5650
Richardson, Jack, 2307
Richardson, Jape, 4317
Richardson, Jerome, 788, 4534, 5933
Richardson, Jim, 528, 2674
Richardson, Joe, 1239, 2460
Richardson, John, 3639, 3883, 4678
Richardson, Kevin, 318
Richardson, Larry, 3306
Richardson, Lee, 2525, 2799
Richardson, Mark, 306, 3262, 4955
Richardson, Natasha, 874, 876, 2522
Richardson, Peter, 321, 2166, 5840
Richardson, Ralph, 1928, 3993, 4414
Richardson, Ron, 528, 4368
Richardson, Rudy, 3304
Richardson, Scott, 318, 2460
Richardson, Steve, 4735
Richardson, Sylvan, 4923
Richardson, Tich, 699
Richardson, Tony, 3414
Richardson, Van Earl, 612
Richardson, Wendel, 2022, 4072
Richbourg, John, 4831, 4917, 5903
Richey, George, 389, 2471, 5309, 5936
Richey, Kim, 4534
Richie, Lionel, 103, 911, 1193, 1200, 2218, 3497, 3814, 4534-4535, 4657, 5588, 6074
Richling, Greg, 5690
Richman, Alex, 859
Richman, Boomie, 4535
Richman, Harry, 1885, 2035, 3146, 3580, 4511, 4535-4536, 5524, 5798
Richman, Jonathan, 431, 505, 634, 1807, 2072, 2342, 2416, 2793, 3135, 3726-3727, 4536, 4598, 4663, 5433
Richman, Milton, 4979
Richmond, Dannie, 65, 182, 1972, 3690-3691, 3941, 4363, 4536, 5687, 5691
Richmond, Dave, 3437
Richmond, Fritz, 2955, 3089, 4803
Richmond, June, 3799, 4536-4537
Richmond, Kim, 1942
Rici, Paul, 2535
Rick And The Ravens, 1594
Rick, Slick, 1602, 2894, 3937, 4593, 4965-4966
Rickard, Stephen, 5394
Rickem Jazz, 1840
Rickenbacker, 316, 867, 869-870, 1874, 2283, 2309, 2734, 2767, 2969, 3578, 3823, 3840, 4216, 4410, 4537, 4799, 6074
Rickenbacker, Adolph, 1874, 4537
Rickers, Manuela, 5942
Rickett, Nooney, 1531

Ricketts, David, 757, 1059
Ricketts, Lloyd, 1417, 2714, 2727
Rickfors, Mickael, 2564
Rickles, Don, 535
Rickman, Jonathon, 1715
Ricks, Glen, 929, 1525, 1817
Ricks, Jimmy, 4442
Ricks, Tommy, 1625
Ricky And The Hallmarks, 4537
Rico And Ronnie, 1585
Rico Records, 1855, 4065, 4447
Rico, Layne, 4078
Ricochet, 515, 687, 1565, 3203, 3958-3959, 4537-4538, 4735, 4913, 5293, 5376
Ricordi Records, 4195
Ricotti, Frank, 255, 3140, 3476, 4538
Ricros, André, 4779
Ridarelli, Robert, 4705
Riddell, Kirk, 1089
Riddell, Richard, 528
Riddick, Claude, 2189, 5838
Riddim Kings Band, 3487
Riddington, Barry, 5824
Riddle, Almeda, 4538, 6074
Riddle, Jimmy, 4538
Riddle, Leslie, 960, 4539
Riddle, Nelson, 30, 409, 439, 958, 1159, 1191, 1706, 1731, 1912, 2687, 3799, 3936, 4105, 4212, 4428, 4539-4540, 4548, 4641, 4927, 4931, 4936, 4991
Riddle, Paul, 3477
Riddles, Kevin, 191, 3523
Ride, 4540 and *passim*
Ride The Wild Surf, 1086, 1816, 1844, 2642, 2780, 4540
Ridel, Stefanie, 5823
Rideout, Mark, 2707
Riderick, David, 4542
Riders In The Sky, 2598, 3510, 4541, 4968, 5808, 6074
Ridge Records, 4689
Ridge Runners, 1309, 1330-1331, 1956, 2592, 2937, 3112, 3247, 3881, 4480, 5302
Ridge, Glen, 897
Ridgeley, Andrew, 5781
Ridgley, Tommy, 3510, 4541, 5401
Ridguard, Nicky, 562
Ridgway, Stan, 168, 1231, 1937, 4541, 5685
Riding, Joanna, 947, 3107, 3269
Ridley, Greg, 244, 2633, 5650
Ridley, Neil, 5630
Ridley, Wally, 1151, 2534, 5618
Ridon Records, 3921
Riebling, Scott, 3205
Riedel, Georg, 239, 1582
Riedel, Oliver, 4422
Riedy, Bob, 5973
Rieflin, William, 4513
Riehn, Rainer, 883
Riel, Axel, 4542
Riera, Pedro, 2325
Riff Brothers, 1983
Riff Raff, 707, 1707, 2200, 2674, 4542, 4600
Riffburglers, 1021
Rifkin, Joshua, 1794, 2891, 3834, 4542

1262, 1489, 1843, 2231, 2236, 2297, 2344, 2424, 2532, 3606, 3887, 3913, 4355, 4370, 4587, 4688-4689, 5442, 5475, 5521, 5553, 5882
Rundless, Ernestine, 3609
Running Wild, 4689 and *passim*
Runrig, 922, 1603, 2776, 3261, 3911, 4236, 4689-4690, 5355, 5360, 6076
Runswick, Daryl, 4593, 6116
Runyman, Jerry, 2181
Runyon, Damon, 983, 2322, 3269, 3294
Ruoff, Charles, 2347
RuPaul, 4690, 5276, 6076
Rupe, Art, 575, 629, 1221, 2571, 4690, 5853
Rupe, Bob, 638, 4908
Rupe, Lee, 2571
Rupert, Michael, 2807, 3457, 4154
Rupert, Mike, 2384
Rupkina, Yanka, 5505
Rupp, Glen, 2605
Rusay, Bob, 917
Rusby, Kate, 736, 1464, 1772, 3559, 4281, 4572, 4690-4691, 4857
Rusby, Kate, And Kathryn Roberts, 1464, 4572, 4690, 4857
Rush, 4691 and *passim*
Rush, Bobby, 3376, 4691-4692
Rush, Jennifer, 1580, 4692, 4956, 5426
Rush, Joe, 3839
Rush, Merrilee, And The Turnabouts, 4692
Rush, Neil, 4122, 4692
Rush, Otis, 143, 237, 530, 612, 627, 629-630, 754, 844, 902, 905, 1049, 1074, 1141, 1402, 1475, 2110, 2131, 2238, 2847, 2923, 3008, 3014, 3135, 3158, 3364, 3754, 4172, 4303, 4399, 4692, 5396, 5413, 5473, 5522, 5531, 5611, 5620, 5633, 5655, 5878, 5913, 5969
Rush, Richard, 4122, 4352, 4755
Rush, Tom, 15, 695, 756, 791, 1101, 1261, 1517, 1729, 1740, 1782, 3064, 3712, 4122, 4316, 4661, 4693, 5358, 5585, 5677
Rushakoff, Harry, 1201
Rushen, Neil, 3899
Rushen, Patrice, 1348, 4679, 4693-4694
Rushent, Martin, 152, 2196, 4864, 5652
Rushing, Jimmy, 18, 353, 355, 406, 496, 499, 502, 645, 825, 951, 1116, 1438, 1572, 1656, 1763, 2378, 2566, 2842, 2844, 2854, 3178, 3474, 3669, 3792, 3806, 3873, 4077, 4103, 4138, 4302, 4694, 5300, 5342, 5371, 5408, 5611, 5709, 5762
Rushlow, Tim, 3273
Rushton, Alan, 4593
Rushton, Geoff, 4355
Rushton, Joe, 4694
Rushton, Neil, 2696, 3905-3906
Rushton, Nicky, 170

Rushton, Robbie, 1321
Rusk, Corey, 3889
Russaw, Lester, 1238
Russell, Al, 1564
Russell, Alistair, 415
Russell, Andy, 4694
Russell, Arthur, 4965
Russell, Bert, 1806
Russell, Bill, 561, 1728, 4888, 6104
Russell, Billy, 368, 1200, 3027
Russell, Bob, 151, 898, 1483, 2335, 2935, 4695, 4782, 5778
Russell, Bobby, 2194, 3149, 3226
Russell, Brenda, 67, 1490, 4985
Russell, Brian, 1171, 1766
Russell, Connie, 4181, 5876
Russell, Curley, 2150, 4696
Russell, Dave, And The Renegades, 1812
Russell, David, 3779, 6116
Russell, Devon, 4696, 6000
Russell, Erik, 5539
Russell, George, 171, 329, 339, 412, 488, 546, 561, 590, 691, 693, 1029, 1046, 1579, 1788-1789, 1849, 1853, 1972, 2084, 2139, 2332, 2722, 2793, 2894-2895, 3323, 3553, 3663, 3691, 4173, 4655, 4696-4697, 4871, 5292, 5383
Russell, Graham, 97, 1578
Russell, Guy, 2535
Russell, Hal, 1701, 4697, 5553
Russell, Henry, 1436
Russell, Ivo Watts, 2126
Russell, Jack, 941, 2259, 4697
Russell, Jane, 578, 2119-2120, 3747, 4304, 4623
Russell, Janet, 4697-4698, 4985, 5746
Russell, Jim, 2695
Russell, John Bright, 4698
Russell, Johnny, 688, 799, 4698
Russell, Judy, 3981
Russell, Ken, 693, 3261, 4112, 5458, 5811, 5813, 5879, 6085
Russell, Kurt, 1748
Russell, Leon, 32, 147, 265, 458, 482, 710, 890, 1096, 1200, 1224, 1234, 1410, 1470, 2041, 2090, 2094, 2097, 2401, 2415, 2485, 2829, 3009, 3014, 3161, 3216, 3250, 3456, 3487, 3502, 3747, 3900-3901, 3914, 3960, 3974, 4219, 4404, 4566, 4698-4699, 4865, 4881, 5485, 5890
Russell, Lillian, 159, 1863-1864, 2923, 2935, 3927
Russell, Luis, 122, 219, 233, 372, 496, 533, 706, 823, 1163, 1177, 1513, 1985, 2271, 2448, 2518, 2531, 2573, 2750, 2810, 3401, 3644, 3904, 3939-3940, 4233, 4300, 4427, 4444, 4699, 4913, 5278, 5406, 5858
Russell, Marc, 5816
Russell, Nigel, 4625
Russell, Paul, 2172
Russell, Pee Wee, 367-368, 707, 781, 941, 1201-1202, 2248, 2378, 2437, 2793, 2929, 2957, 3178, 3226, 3773, 3896, 3942, 4206, 4239, 4328, 4584, 4699-

4700, 5301, 5780, 6076
Russell, Peggy, 2335, 6051
Russell, Ray, 14, 295, 4444, 4593
Russell, Richard, 4304, 4360, 5942
Russell, Robert, 479-480, 734, 1499, 1941, 2101, 2159, 3637, 4025, 4700, 5284, 5893
Russell, Rosalind, 499, 743, 1018, 2095, 2324, 3428, 3488, 5909
Russell, Roscoe, 488, 902
Russell, Ross, 1985, 2797-2798, 2934, 4134-4135, 5342, 6067, 6104
Russell, S.K., 4695
Russell, Terry, 4781
Russell, Tom, 154, 2291, 3730, 4700, 5556-5557, 5803, 6076, 6116
Russell, Tony, 2929, 4360, 6090
Russell, William, 231, 3216, 4513, 6104
Russell, Willy, 599
Russin, Babe, 298, 2170, 2208, 4700, 5967
Russo, Andy, 2355
Russo, Bill, 221, 1097, 2527, 2973, 3912, 4195, 4701, 5507, 5785, 6006
Russo, Dan, 1898, 2923
Russo, Danny, 4701
Russo, Frank, 4523
Russo, Marc, 4010, 5955
Russo, William, 4901, 6104
Rust Never Sleeps, 736, 1501, 2300, 4701, 5978-5979
Rust Records, 1200, 2383
Rust, Brian, 2381, 6066, 6104, 6106, 6108
Rust, Vernon, 3541
Rutan, Wally, 3045
Ruth Ruth, 4701
Ruth-Ann, 4031
Rutherford, Ann, 3674, 4058
Rutherford, Daryl, 1212
Rutherford, Jack, 5814
Rutherford, John, 5814
Rutherford, Margaret, 2212, 2282
Rutherford, Mike, 2115, 3661, 3914, 4702
Rutherford, Paul, 763, 1076, 2012, 2031, 2172, 2320, 3578, 3627, 3914, 4623, 4702, 5776
Rutherford, Rudy, 4702
Ruthless Blues, 3550
Ruthless Rap Assassins, 556, 1788, 4702
Ruthless Records, 4703 and *passim*
Rutland, Georgia Slim, 894
Rutland, John, 692 693
Rutledge, Jim, 602, 5877
Rutledge, Lenny, 4733
Rutles, 725, 1087, 2698, 4158, 4522, 4703, 4881
Rutlin, Ajule, 553
Ruts, 4703-4704 and *passim*
Rutsey, John, 4691
Ruttenberg, Joseph, 2144, 2706, 3033
Ruttenberg, Rich, 34
Rutter, Steven, 306

Ruvell, Norman, 2938
Ruzz, Kim, 716, 3633
Ry-co Jazz, 4704
Ryan, Barry, 2724, 4478, 4704
Ryan, Buck, 2402
Ryan, David, 2061, 2406-2407, 3190, 6060
Ryan, Dennis, 5284
Ryan, Don, 1297, 4511
Ryan, Eamonn, 4511
Ryan, Eddie, 923, 4434
Ryan, Frank, 911
Ryan, Gary, 2821
Ryan, Gordy, 2440
Ryan, Irene, 4252
Ryan, Jack, 1799
Ryan, Jim, 1297
Ryan, Jimmy, 1722
Ryan, John, 4000
Ryan, Kelley, 265
Ryan, Marion, 1990, 2724, 3509, 4704
Ryan, Mark, 639
Ryan, Mick, 1098
Ryan, Mike, 252, 639
Ryan, Nicky, 1768
Ryan, Paul, 639, 1799, 2802, 4704
Ryan, Paul And Barry, 2724, 4478, 4704
Ryan, Phil, 784, 1813, 3430, 4233
Ryan, Roma, 1768
Ryan, Ron, 4551
Ryan, Ross, 252
Ryan, Sean, 490
Ryan, Sheila, 2081
Ryan, Stephen, 4511
Ryan, Sue, 4850
Ryan, Tommy, 398, 4704
Ryanes, Warren, 3742
Ryce, Daryle, 3573, 4705
Rydell, Bobby, 443, 751, 862, 900, 1040, 1100, 1625, 1809, 1999, 2414, 3729, 4181, 4705
Ryder, Buck, 1724
Ryder, Carl, 5513
Ryder, Jean, 720
Ryder, John, 1818
Ryder, Mark, 2831, 4523
Ryder, Mitch, 1916, 2167, 2187, 3255, 3309, 3664, 4700, 4705-4706, 5374
Ryder, Mitch, And The Detroit Wheels, 4705
Ryder, Paul, 2384
Ryder, Steve, 3838
Ryder, Wynona, 4217
Rydcr-Prangley, David, 4398
Ryderson, Frank, 2355
Rye, Mark, 4809
Rye, Steve, 2299, 2958
Ryerson, Art, 5674
Ryerson, Florence, 5899
Ryestraw, 1704
Rykiel, Jean-Phillippe, 4706
Rykodisc Records, 2190, 3994, 4706, 5487
Rylance, Alex, 4307
Ryley, Dave, 2045
Rymdimperiet, 3949
Rymer, Gene, 3312
Rynhart, Philip, 3540
Ryota, Sugiyama, 3435

Samuel Prody, 2789
Samuel, Leroy, 5305
Samuels, Arthur, 4284
Samuels, Bill, 994
Samuels, Calvin, 3431
Samuels, Clarence, 787
Samuels, David, 128, 1977, 3545, 4731
Samuels, Everton, 1080
Samuels, Frank, 5597
Samuels, Fuzzy, 3169, 3432
Samuels, James, 53
Samuels, Jerry, 3875
Samuels, Lesser, 2278, 2726, 4719
Samuels, Michael, 1977, 3051
Samuels, Milt, 2938
Samuels, Peter, 3481
Samuels, William, 1919
Samuelson, Gars, 3612
Samwell, Ian, 4530, 4973
Samwell-Smith, Paul, 691, 1279, 2359, 3725, 4500, 4732, 4917, 5456, 5951
San Francisco, 4732 and *passim*
San Fransciso Jazz Band
San Miguel, Valentine, 1629
Sanabria, Bobby, 3984
Sanborn, David, 115, 183, 650, 858, 1283, 1714, 1791, 1842, 2338, 2640, 2770, 2806, 2929, 3071, 3177, 3387, 3677, 4116, 4368, 4428, 4732, 4761, 5450, 5878
Sanches, Fernando, 4011
Sanchez, 4732-4733 and *passim*
Sánchez, Armando, 229, 3180, 4611
Sanchez, David, 3613, 4733
Sánchez, Ernesto, 2234, 4065
Sanchez, Gil, 1784
Sanchez, Julienne Oviedo, 87
Sánchez, Lionel, 5447
Sanchez, Mel, 36-37
Sanchez, Michel, 1456
Sanchez, Mike, 532
Sánchez, Nestor, 2397, 4612, 4647
Sánchez, Papo, 4618
Sanchez, Paul, 1266
Sanchez, Phil, 1805
Sanchez, Poncho, 2626
Sánchez, Ralph, 3775
Sanchez, Ray, 1501
Sanchez, Raymond
Sanchez, Roger, 3904, 4047, 4733
Sanchez, Tony, 2760, 4632, 6075
Sancious, David, 722, 797, 1775
Sanctuary, 4733 and *passim*
Sand, Paul, 4080
Sandall, Simon, 2201
Sandall, Stuart, 2201
Sandals, 4734 and *passim*
Sandberg, Peter, 121
Sandburg, Carl, 4734, 6076
Sandell, Robert, 1538
Sandeman, Mary, 189
Sanden, Doug, 5810
Sanders, Bev, 3348
Sanders, Coyne Steven, 236, 351, 6031
Sanders, David
Sanders, Ed, 2046, 3086, 4734

Sanders, Fat, 975
Sanders, Felicia, 281
Sanders, George, 893, 1216, 1545, 3634, 3928, 4876
Sanders, Jeff, 2704
Sanders, Joe, 1225, 4734, 5800
Sanders, Larry, 2845, 3094
Sanders, Leroy, 3263
Sanders, Mark, 1213, 1445, 4135, 4623, 4734-4735
Sanders, Paul, 2366, 4135
Sanders, Pharoah, 128, 406, 590, 1006, 1108-1109, 1168, 1185, 1981, 2405, 2684, 2716, 2788, 2845, 3521, 3541, 3610, 3822, 3827, 3833, 4211, 4735, 4852, 5404, 5778, 5800
Sanders, Ric, 1300, 1827, 2156, 4735, 4805
Sanders, Rick, 4248, 6068
Sanders, Sonny, 4448, 4751
Sanders, Steve, 2405, 4006
Sanders, Tim, 2018
Sanders, William, 4448
Sanders, Willie Roy, 1888
Sanderson, Alan, 2077
Sanderson, Duncan, 1500, 4246
Sanderson, Julia, 730, 1318, 2160, 4880
Sanderson, Nicholas, 5921
Sanderson, Nick, 1132, 2313
Sanderson, Tommy, 2142
Sanderson, Vic, 5647
Sandford, Amos, 4232
Sandford, Chris
Sandford, Christopher, 1096, 2760, 3958, 6037, 6040, 6055, 6066
Sandford, Trevor, 5721
Sandii And The Sunsets, 4735-4736, 5571, 5955
Sandke, Randy, 4736
Sandland, Colin
Sandler, Harry, 4064
Sandlin, Johnny, 2606
Sandman, 3515, 3644, 3715, 3789, 3951, 4309
Sandman, Mark, 4309
Sandolar, Andy, 3679
Sandole, Dennis, 786
Sandon, Erik, 3962
Sandon, Johnny, 4500, 4736-4737, 4799
Sandoval, Arturo, 3428
Sandoval, Pete, 3777, 5342
Sandoval, Phil E., 230
Sandow, Alan, 4872
Sandow, Eugene, 5999
Sandow, Ted, 3366
Sandpebbles, 873, 4737
Sandpipers, 3258, 4737, 5736
Sandrich, Mark, 933, 1960, 2101, 2555, 4841, 5466
Sands, 4737 and *passim*
Sands, Bobby, 3498
Sands, Evie, 2916
Sands, Jeremy, 1766
Sands, Rena, 3605
Sands, Tommy, 309, 578, 694, 3459, 4088, 4737, 4931
Sandstrom, Bobby, 5823
Sandstrom, Brian, 4697
Sandstrom, Renee, 5823
Sandy And Jeannie, 422

Sandy And Johnny, 1484
Sane, Dan, 2961, 4738
Sanford, Dick, 2533
Sanford, Herb, 1598, 1600
Sanford, Rick, 3184
Sangaré, Oumou, 4738
Sangster, Jim, 5966
Sangster, John, 126, 331, 462, 1365, 4738, 5648
Sanguinetti, James, 3777
Sanko, Anton, 5623
Sanlin, Johnny, 1459
Sanlin, Kevin, 3751
Sanna, Piero, 5339
Sano, Kenji, 682
Sansom, Frank, 4364
Sanson, Veronique, 488
Santa Esmeralda, 475, 4738
Santa Rosa, Gilberto, 154, 3750, 4031-4032, 4065, 4647, 4739, 5623
Santaella, Antonio, 3354
Santamaria, 925, 2770, 5453
Santamaría, Mongo, 229, 393, 508, 637, 1234, 1833, 1841, 1981, 2073, 2373, 2925, 3097, 3181, 3233, 3314, 4098, 4114, 4360-4361, 4421, 4611, 4739-4740, 4744
Santamaría, Ramón, 4739
Santamaria, Ray, 5453
Santana, 15, 45, 291, 301, 355, 398-399, 626, 706, 1156, 1185, 1271, 1285, 1407, 1676, 1681, 1863, 1892, 1933, 2097, 2230, 2364, 2587, 2655, 2841, 2934, 2954, 3064, 3104, 3235, 3276, 3435, 3461, 3533, 3591, 3664, 3733, 3823, 3900, 3938, 3948, 4027, 4095, 4187, 4361, 4562, 4694, 4740-4741, 4777, 4896, 5364, 5404, 5513, 5674, 5916, 6131
Santana, Jorge, 1841, 3424, 4746
Santana, Miguel, 2172
Santana, Steve, 99, 4741
Santanna, Carlo, 4122
Santarelli, Vince, 1936
Santen, Kathy, 2205
Santers, 35, 4742, 5508
Santers, Rick, 4742, 5508
Santi, Ralphy, 137, 4421
Santiago, Adalberto, 137, 393-394, 1321, 1855, 2397-2398, 2925, 3738, 4121, 4361, 4421, 4611, 4618, 4646, 4742, 5446
Santiago, Al, 1180, 1320, 1899, 2925, 3097, 3314, 4097, 4114, 4121, 4361, 4420, 4558-4559, 4612, 4646-4647, 4742-4744, 5447, 5471
Santiago, Burnell, 220
Santiago, Eddie, 3835, 4065, 4614, 4745
Santiago, Elena, 2568
Santiago, Herman, 3367, 4121
Santiago, Isaac, 3981
Santiago, Joe, 3702
Santiago, Joey, 567, 4256
Santiago, Marvin, 4031, 4745, 5595-5596
Santiago, Pupy, 3835, 4065
Santiago, Ray, 1899-1900
Santiago, Renaly, 922

Santic, 4177, 4520
Santiel, Terrai, 4648
Santiglia, Peggy, 191
Santilli, Ivana, 408
Santisiero, Drew, 580
Santley, Joseph, 3850
Santly, Lester, 91, 325, 1405
Santo And Johnny, 938, 1158, 1933, 2236, 4746, 5546
Santollo, Joe, 1657
Santonio, Reese, 4482
Santora, Joseph, 3718
Santoro, Tony, 570
Santoro, Vince, 1315
Santos, Cuqui, 2235
Santos, Daniel, 1111, 1240, 3143, 4098, 4421, 4611
Santos, Héctor, 2234
Santos, Patti, 2723
Santos, Ray, 2234, 3776, 4616-4617
Santos, Rui, 558
Santos, Todos, 3791
Santuione, Franco, 2172
Saoco, Wilson, 399, 1435
Sapherson, Barry, 4704
Sapo, 3424, 4746
Sapp, Hosea, 3687
Sapp, Jane, 2924
Sapper, Howard, 4457
Sapphire, 334, 544, 1903, 1941, 2097, 2273, 3495, 4112, 4736
Sapphires, 1220, 4746, 5961
Sappho, Dusky, 174, 5966
Saquito, Nico, 4746
SAR Records, 1222, 1899, 4121, 4243, 4611, 5471
Sara, Cathy, 2802
Saracen, 4747
Saraceno, Joe, 4665, 5275
Saraf, Amir, 3095
Sarah Records, 13, 1883, 2465, 4062, 4747, 4796, 5290, 5624
Saratoga, Leonardson, 2190
Saraya, 1379, 4747
Saraya, Sandi, 4747
Sardi, Sam, 2303
Sardo, Frankie, 2569
Sardou, Michel, 1115
Sargeant, Bob, 2337, 4747
Sargeant, Gary, 3585
Sargent, John, 1688
Sargent, Kenny, 973, 1274, 2253, 4747
Sargent, Kit, 5782
Sargent, Laurie, 1818
Sargent, Stefanie, 4827
Sargon, Pierre, 3260
Sarig, Tom, 4678
Sarita, Al, 2462
Sarko, Rick, 2031
Sarkoma, 4747
Sarmanto, Heikki, 4747
Sarne, Mike, 959, 1406, 1800, 4142
Sarnoff, Dorothy, 2997
Sarony, Leslie, 4748
Sarpilä, Antti, 4191, 4748, 5591
Sarstedt, Peter, 2309, 2932, 4748-4749
Sarstedt, Richard, 2932, 4749
Sarstedt, Robin, 538, 942, 2932, 4748-4749
Sartin, Bonny, 5959

3348, 3681, 4855
Shaw, Charles 'Bobo', 4855-4856
Shaw, Chris, 1363, 4126, 5754
Shaw, Ciggy, 4598
Shaw, Clarence, 767, 5934
Shaw, Dale, 600
Shaw, Daoud, 3731
Shaw, David, 701, 1577, 4471
Shaw, Dinah, 4889
Shaw, Donald, 922, 2761, 3659, 5974
Shaw, Dorothy, 2119
Shaw, Eddie, 831, 3408, 3741, 4856, 6116
Shaw, Eddie 'Vaan', 4856
Shaw, Elliott, 4880
Shaw, Floyd, 2938
Shaw, George Bernard, 1068, 2945, 3012, 3196, 6005
Shaw, Greg, 651, 2835, 3732, 4119, 4887, 6056, 6116
Shaw, Howard, 3292
Shaw, Ian, 4278, 4856
Shaw, Jim, 1276
Shaw, Joe, 1416, 1577, 5579
Shaw, Marion, 4492
Shaw, Martin, 222, 5725
Shaw, Mark, 319, 5384
Shaw, Marlena, 4856
Shaw, Martin, 222, 5725
Shaw, Milt, 1641
Shaw, Oscar, 1951, 3850, 4020, 5638
Shaw, Pat, 1464, 3519, 4691, 4856
Shaw, Pat, And Julie Matthews, 4691
Shaw, Randy, 1132
Shaw, Reta, 3498, 4106
Shaw, Richard, 853, 2131
Shaw, Rick, 2533
Shaw, Robert, 691, 694, 1660, 1986, 2283, 4767, 4857
Shaw, Robin, 1905, 1946, 5792
Shaw, Ron, 996
Shaw, Ronny, 3436
Shaw, Sandie, 184, 314, 453, 564, 587, 1400, 1476, 2399, 3475, 3483, 4126, 4857, 5701, 6077
Shaw, Sebastian, 729
Shaw, Snowy, 3000, 3633
Shaw, Thomas, 2805, 4858
Shaw, Timmy, 2769
Shaw, Todd, 5465
Shaw, Tommy, 389, 847, 1370, 2304, 3671, 3893, 3948, 3984, 4525, 4854, 4858, 5756
Shaw, Victoria, 1537, 4858
Shaw, Winifred, 5710
Shaw, Woody, 614, 701, 844, 1416, 1853, 2094, 2305, 2445, 2622, 3243, 3678, 4858-4859, 4910, 5579, 5699, 5800, 5871, 5974
Shaweez, Chapaka, 1282
Shay, Dorothy, 3636, 4859
Shayka, Richard, 89
Shayler, Pat, 1064
Shayne, Gloria, 5836
Shayne, Tamara, 2723, 2862-2863
Shayon, Robert, 4880

Shazamme, Ace, 1678
She, 4859 and *passim*
She Done Him Wrong, 4859
She Loves Me, 4859-4860 and *passim*
She Rockers, 305, 1222, 2413, 4860
She Trinity, 2243, 3475, 4860
Shea, Gary, 111, 3913
Shea, Jere, 4151
Shea, Robert, 3042
Shea, Tom, 4795
Sheaff, Lawrence, 165, 2086
Sheahan, John, 3387
Shean, Al, 3851-3852, 4732, 5997-5998
Shear, Ernie, 5887
Shear, Jules, 316, 1714, 1801, 3086, 3139, 3444, 3518, 4589, 4860, 5435, 5783
Sheard, John, 2495
Shearer, Brian, 1056
Shearer, Don, 1132
Shearer, Douglas, 2258
Shearer, Marc, 4013
Shearing, George, 158, 175, 445, 516, 520, 637, 795, 813, 841, 1160-1161, 1175, 1306, 1836, 1851-1852, 2206, 2244-2245, 2349, 2448, 2652, 2718, 2796, 2874-2875, 2956, 3019, 3176-3177, 3210, 3226, 3446, 3502, 3573, 3597, 3600, 4191, 4211, 4225, 4231, 4361-4362, 4695, 4801, 4861-4862, 4951, 5389, 5451, 5469, 5851, 5877, 5928, 6104
Shearlaw, John, 657, 6036, 6080
Shears, Billy, 2005, 4832
Shears, Steve, 5570
Shearsby, Ed, 2841
Shearston, Gary, 1084, 4808, 4862, 5935
Sheater, Mark, 1119
Shechtman, George, 2940
Shed Seven, 310, 1378, 1572, 4862, 6127
Shedhouse Trio, 2183
Sheehan, Billy, 3383, 3823, 4660, 5286, 5420
Sheehan, Bobby, 626
Sheehan, Eddie, 5474
Sheehan, Fran, 676
Sheehan, Gladys, 2456
Sheekman, Arthur, 2985, 4635, 5425
Sheeley, Evan, 4375
Sheeley, Sharon, 1045, 1142, 1491
Sheen, Bobby, 636
Sheena And The Rokkets, 5955
Sheenan, John, 1551
Sheenan, Paul, 4407
Sheep On Drugs, 1276, 4523, 4862-4863
Sheeran, Kevin, 3367
Sheets, Toby H., 4945
Sheffler, Ted, 1300
Shehan, John, 1639
Sheik, Duncan, 4863
Sheiks, 114, 966, 1036, 1166, 1565, 2857, 3707, 3718, 4738, 5282, 5647, 5778, 5973
Sheila, 4863 and *passim*

Sheils, Brian, 5419
Shekoni, Kayode, 2947
Shelby, Jeff, 2034
Shelby, Jewford, 2034
Shelby, Thomas Oliver, 3114
Sheldon, Chris, 145, 5574
Sheldon, Doug, 1533
Sheldon, Ernie, 2098, 3248
Sheldon, Gene, 1578
Sheldon, Jack, 339, 489, 1214, 1250, 3083, 3973, 4197, 4863, 5461, 5646
Sheldon, Sydney, 4471
Shell, Ed, 3923
Shell, John, 2495, 2517-2518
Shell, Mark Jude, 336
Shellac, 110, 521, 621, 629, 731, 1255, 4864, 5280, 5655
Shellenbach, Kate, 429
Sheller, Marty, 4740
Shelley, Carole, 2725, 4893
Shelley, Count, 1565, 2581, 3171, 4639, 5685, 5716
Shelley, Joshua, 3419
Shelley, Pat, 1374
Shelley, Pete, 27, 198, 859, 3847, 4864
Shelley, Steve, 2475, 4412, 4729
Shelleyan Orphan, 4864, 5396
Shells, 866, 873, 1640, 2176, 2688, 2729, 3026, 3070, 3177, 3366, 4737, 4864-4865, 5621, 5884, 5921
Shelly, Peter, 1263
Shelly, Steve, 1530
Shelnut, Andrew, 1550
Shelnut, Dale, 1550
Shelnut, Randy, 1550
Shelor, Sammy, 5652
Shelski, Steve, 1202
Shelter Records, 32, 265, 4698, 4865
Shelton Brothers, 2002, 2156, 4865, 5832
Shelton, Aaron, 1154
Shelton, Anne, 158, 172, 1210, 2016, 3298, 3705, 3788, 4220, 4222, 4290, 4574, 4865-4866, 5659
Shelton, Bob, 4865
Shelton, Curly, 4865
Shelton, Don, 4932
Shelton, Earl, 1860
Shelton, Jack, 4187
Shelton, Ricky Van, 388, 2964, 3540, 4866-4867, 5436, 5497
Shelton, Robert, 1672, 1678, 2320, 6046, 6051, 6093-6094
Shelton, Roscoe, 2070, 4867
Shelton, Seb, 1502, 4805
Shelton, Yvonne, 4260
Shenandoah, 1598-1599, 1685, 1752, 2330, 2340, 3075, 3540, 3744, 4064, 4133, 4368, 4867, 6095
Shenandoah (stage musical), 4867
Shenandoah Cut-Ups, 4868, 5302, 5894
Shendar, Jacob E., 544
Shenkman, Eric, 626
Shep And The Limelites, 671, 2459, 4868
Shepard, Franklin, 3638

Shepard, Jean, 1181, 1971, 2439, 2647, 3370, 4093, 4243-4244, 4869
Shepard, Sam, 1266, 1676, 1678, 2577, 4019, 5987, 6046
Shepard, Thomas Z., 639, 1219
Shepard, Wally, 4316
Sheperd, Brad, 2584
Shephard, Gerry, 2171
Shephard, Tommy, 4226
Shepherd Brothers, 2874, 5495
Shepherd Sisters, 4869
Shepherd, Andy, 5574
Shepherd, Cybill, 266, 4289
Shepherd, Dave, 516, 608, 1221, 1382, 1828, 3189, 3804, 4425, 4870
Shepherd, Dick, 3017, 5447
Shepherd, Ella, 1911
Shepherd, Gerry, 1480
Shepherd, John, 650
Shepherd, Judy, 4869
Shepherd, Keith, 1992
Shepherd, Kenny Wayne, 4870
Shepherd, Tony, 516, 2511
Shepherd, Vicki, 5421
Shepp, Archie, 224, 688, 727, 780, 800, 844, 1026, 1046, 1184-1186, 1405, 1553, 1643, 1670, 1789, 2249, 2293, 2405, 2617, 2648, 2684, 2732, 2793, 2845, 3079, 3098, 3174, 3206, 3504, 3576, 3736, 3803, 3848, 3892, 3941, 4065, 4138, 4141, 4165, 4203, 4211, 4220, 4278, 4542, 4562, 4584, 4685, 4870-4871, 4908, 4982, 5309, 5321, 5388, 5609, 5920
Sheppard, Andy, 546, 591, 1186, 1481, 2898, 4697, 4760, 4871, 4950, 5448, 5616
Sheppard, Audrey, 5845
Sheppard, Chris, 456
Sheppard, James, 1120, 2459, 4868
Sheppard, Nick, 1240
Sheppard, P., 1782
Sheppard, T.G., 174, 488, 757, 1143, 4871
Sheppard, Terrence, 2919
Sheppard, Tim, 187
Sheppard, Vonda, 2529
Sheppards, 4872
Shepperd, Paul, 2594
Sher, Rick, 1609
Sherba, John, 3080
Sherbet, 563, 709, 1950, 3735, 4872
Sheridan, Ann, 421, 3976
Sheridan, Art, 42, 1014, 1213
Sheridan, Chris, 407, 1514, 6032
Sheridan, Karen, 4395, 4588
Sheridan, Lee, 761, 2770
Sheridan, Mike, 2673, 3373, 4872-4873, 5911
Sheridan, Mike, And The Nightriders, 4872-4873, 5911
Sheridan, Paul, 5285
Sheridan, Tony, 432, 436, 477, 1286, 2922, 4156, 4276, 4439, 4873, 5320, 6077
Sheridan-Price, 4872-4873
Sheriff, Dave, 507, 2340
Sherik, 5517

Slaughter And The Dogs, 743, 2283, 3796, 4256, 4962

Slaughter, Alfred, 921

Slaughter, John, 374

Slaughter, Mark, 4962, 5646

Slaughter, Walter, 620

Slaughterhouse, 304, 4767, 4962, 4767, 4962

Slave Raider, 4962

Slaven, Mick, 4658

Slaven, Neil, 12-13, 181, 3810, 5633, 5993, 6065, 6087, 6089

Slavin, Sandy, 62, 4550

Slawson, Bob, 1055

Slay, Frank, 537, 918

Slay, Frank C., Jnr., 537

Slayer, 4962 and *passim*

Sleak, Norman, 109

Sleater-Kinney, 4963

Sledd, Patsy, 4963

Sledge, Percy, 272, 464, 1459, 2255, 2539, 2730-2731, 4031, 4186, 4963-4964, 5395, 5695, 5787, 5789

Sledge, Robert, 472

Sledgehammer, 1723, 2265, 2575, 3551, 3661, 4964

Sleep, 4964 and *passim*

Sleep, Wayne, 874, 876, 993, 1297

Sleeper, 378, 763, 1311, 1452, 2293, 3243, 3271, 4013, 4054, 4545, 4944, 4964, 5381

Sleeping Bag Records, 2416, 4965

Sleeping Beauty, 959, 1041, 1483, 1545, 3147, 3268, 4965

Sleepy People, 5570

Sleet, Gary, 51

Slezak, Walter, 893, 1843-1844, 2661, 3851-3852, 4253, 4814

Slice Of Saturday Night, A, 4965, 5722

Slick, 4965 and *passim*

Slick Rick, 1602, 2894, 3937, 4593, 4965-4966

Slick, Aaron, 3281, 4889-4890

Slick, Earl, 147, 319, 1540, 3263, 4966, 5670

Slick, Earl, Band, 4966

Slick, Grace, 288, 819, 827, 2258-2259, 2674, 2802-2804, 2934-2935, 3200, 3731, 4174, 4201, 4271, 4966, 5709, 6078

Slick, John, 4213

Slickers, 739, 2138, 2390, 2885, 3960, 4251, 4695, 4966, 5364

Slide Records, 3700, 4969

Slider, Albie, 4841

Sligh, J.F., 3551

Slijngaard, Mario, 2213

Slik, 1087, 2760, 3157, 3483, 4525, 4921, 4967, 5390, 5570, 5585, 5652, 6078

Slim And Jack, 344, 804

Slim Chance, 1275, 2295, 3123-3124, 4967

Slim Harpo, 77, 612, 1918, 2320-2321, 2755, 2846, 3136, 3543, 3676, 3770, 3888, 4967, 5399, 5970

Slimani, Abdel Ali, 4968

Slimmon, Tannis, 543

Slingbacks, 4968

Slinger, Cees, 727

Slingsby, Xero, 4968, 5833

Slinky Wizard, 1617, 1952, 4968-4969

Slint, 723, 3730, 4108, 4969

Slip 'N' Slide Records, 4969

Slipper And The Rose, The, 3788, 4876, 4969

Slits, 4970 and *passim*

Sloan, 4006, 4970

Sloan, Allen, 1550

Sloan, Elliot, 589

Sloan, Frank, 3640

Sloan, P.F., 79, 105, 394, 795, 848, 1844, 2245, 2553, 3579, 4126, 4522, 4592, 4970, 5398, 5538, 5771

Sloan, Philip, 4971

Sloane, A. Baldwin, 178, 2277

Sloane, Carol, 1572, 4801, 4971

Sloane, Nicola, 1766

Sloane, Tod, 3266

Sloane, Tommy, 2736

Slocum, Tom, 2408

Sloey, Al, 5863

Sloman, John, 518, 3305, 5587

Sloman, Larry, 1678, 6046

Slone, Bobby, 2973

Slovak, Hillel, 4463

Slow Drag, 866

Slowdive, 854, 1022, 3732, 3858, 4971-4972

SLR Records, 3003

Slumberland Records, 5624

Sly And Robbie, 172, 228, 452, 528, 562, 665, 785, 790, 1008, 1062, 1082, 1108, 1335, 1375, 1472, 1511, 1524-1525, 1650-1651, 1661, 1771, 1797, 1810, 2007, 2017, 2138, 2186, 2578, 2654, 2715, 2761, 2873, 2930, 3080, 3134, 3210, 3324, 3405, 3465, 3511, 3631, 3671, 3781, 4034, 4052, 4401, 4432, 4468, 4490, 4545, 4615, 4732, 4906, 4972, 5291, 5305, 5325, 5427, 5441, 5641, 5767, 5952

Sly And The Family Stone, 241, 368, 1407, 1920, 2230, 2232, 2454, 2719, 3533, 4316, 4354, 4792, 4972-4973, 5334, 5386, 5916

Slye, Leonard, 1852, 3969, 4623

Smale, Pete, 4180

Small Faces, 220, 275, 318, 632, 1086, 1141, 1819, 1859, 2112, 2123, 2681, 3085, 3123, 3471, 3589, 3887, 4019, 4031, 4436, 4667, 4897, 4954, 4973-4974, 5430, 5462, 5481, 5760, 5811, 5886, 5911, 6078, 6127

Small Wonder Records, 1278, 1334, 1913, 3229, 4272

Small, Bobby, 4278

Small, Danny, 4864

Small, Drink, 4974

Small, Florrie, 4725

Small, Heather, 3379

Small, Henry, 4340

Small, Jon, 2830

Small, Leroy, 1562, 1977

Small, Michael, 2299, 2912

Small, Millie, 573, 1710, 2345

Small, Patrick, 4242, 6084

Small, Phil, 1156

Small, Steve, 1156, 1391, 5760

Small, Winston, 5585

Smallcombe, Derek, 2789

Smalle, Ed, 1555

Smaller, 4974-4975

Smalley, Dave, 123, 1069, 1490, 1607, 4436

Smallman, Gary, 4184

Smalls, Cliff, 4975

Smalltown Parade, 4975

Smart, Bob, 90

Smart, Bobby, 925

Smart, Keith, 356, 3189, 5564, 5900

Smart, Leroy, 311, 370, 851, 1106, 1525, 2575, 2588, 2822, 3171, 3697-3698, 4050, 4111, 4595, 4749, 4975

Smart, Nicker, 4110

Smart, Philip, 3171

Smart, Terry, 4530

Smash Mouth, 4976

Smash Records, 4976 and *passim*

Smash, Chas, 3401

Smashing Orange, 4976-4977

Smashing Pumpkins, 1048, 1395, 1514, 1892, 1988, 2084, 2163, 2730, 2829, 2975, 3083, 3299, 3608, 3618, 4443, 4627, 4709, 4898, 4977, 5506, 5637, 6078, 6127

Smashing Time, 72, 3299, 4977, 5459

Smear, Pat, 1964, 2126, 3958, 5731

Smeck, Roy, 164, 4977

Smeda, Nat, 1019

Smedley, Major Oliver, 897, 4253

Smedley, Martin, 304

Smeenk, Paul, 1325

Smeeton, Simon, 5881

Smells Like Records, 597, 4729

Smet, Jean-Philippe, 2356

Smethurst, Allan, 4934

Smif N Wessun, 4977

Smile, Sara, 386

Smiley Culture, 1414, 1856, 3018, 4327, 4337, 4494, 4978, 5447, 5565-5566, 5801

Smiley, Arthur Lee, 4978

Smiley, Red, 328, 1314, 1685, 2402, 3400, 3598, 3766, 4460, 4503-4504, 4868, 4978, 5302, 5786

Smiling Mountain Boys, 376, 2173, 3247

Smillie, Johnny, 5428

Smillie, Phil, 5296

Smirnov, Andrei, 5340

Smith, 4978-4979 and *passim*

Smith And Mighty, 4979, 5424, 5735

Smith Brothers, 4895, 4979, 5278

Smith Hurt, John, 2645

Smith, 'Whistling' Jack, 4979

Smith, Adrian, 250, 2710-2711

Smith, Al, 2663, 3189, 4477

Smith, Alex, 1340, 3820

Smith, Alexis, 1959, 3895, 3947, 4518

Smith, Alfred Jesse, 5910

Smith, Andrew, 3496, 3628, 5762

Smith, Andy, 906, 5762

Smith, Anthony, 1295, 2816, 4518, 5461

Smith, Arlene, 1018

Smith, Art, 82, 4518, 5529

Smith, Arthur, 271, 666, 730, 1128, 1475, 1685, 1979, 2360, 2752, 3366, 3571, 3751, 4196, 4504, 4979-4981, 5711

Smith, Arthur 'Fiddlin'', 4980-4981

Smith, Arthur Q., 666, 1685, 4980-4981

Smith, Arvid, 5473

Smith, Baron, 2708

Smith, Barry, 5652, 6123, 6127

Smith, Bennie, 519

Smith, Bernadine Boswell, 1855

Smith, Bessie, 17, 100, 209, 233, 294, 344, 382, 527, 552, 628, 641, 678, 729, 766, 806, 852, 1015, 1513, 1792, 1813, 2268, 2369-2370, 2513, 2635, 2639, 2745, 2787, 2798, 2880, 2890, 2892, 3080, 3413, 3466, 3863, 3898, 4015, 4024, 4101, 4217, 4238, 4413, 4981, 4985, 4990, 5278, 5353, 5359, 5688, 5717, 5723, 5815, 5841, 5873, 5982, 6079

Smith, Betty, 3189, 4981, 5498

Smith, Big Robert, 2070

Smith, Bilge, 1960, 2544

Smith, Bill, 274, 794, 1238, 4159, 4233, 4377, 4594, 4764, 4982, 4986, 5278

Smith, Bill 'Major', 4159, 4233, 4982

Smith, Billy, 1424, 2231, 2418, 3057, 4093, 5912

Smith, Blake, 1891

Smith, Bobby, 403, 2249, 3573, 5945

Smith, Bobby Earl, 3573

Smith, Brian, 415, 1233, 1925, 2725, 4172, 4982, 6075

Smith, Brix, 2968, 5382, 5396

Smith, Broderick, 1531, 4471, 4982

Smith, Bruce, 198, 2369, 4282, 4358, 4551, 4970

Smith, Buster, 703, 1656, 2934, 3133, 3806, 4133, 4983

Smith, Byron, 1162, 1446, 4674

Smith, Byther, 2321, 3175, 4983

Smith, Cal, 177, 2481, 2978, 4132, 4188, 4983, 5519

Smith, Carl, 653-654, 803, 855, 966, 977, 979, 1009, 1483, 1526, 2040, 2530, 2553, 3218, 3386, 3926, 4093, 4171, 4240, 4425, 4568, 4750, 4983-4984, 5436, 5694

Smith, Carl 'Tatti', 4984

Smith, Carlton, 1062, 4979

Smith, Carrie, 788, 1039, 3573, 4984

Smith, Carson, 4984-4985

Smith, Chad, 4463, 5387, 5794

Smith, Charlene, 4985

Smith, Charles, 1040, 2544,

Stowell, Damon, 3935
Strachen, Keith, 2679
Strachey, Jack, 212, 1552, 1747, 3499, 5182
Strachwitz, Chris, 13, 224, 1604, 2745, 3416, 3764
Stradlin, Izzy, 2313-2314
Stradlin, Izzy, And The Ju Ju Hounds, 5182
Stradling, Danny, 4029
Stradling, Harry, 2055, 2381, 4254, 5436
Stradling, Rod, 176, 1761, 2560, 4029
Stradling, Rod And Danny, 4029
Straeter, Ted, 5669
Straight Records, 119, 5991
Straight, Charley, 5183
Strain, Sammy, 1065, 3262, 4002
Strain, Tony, 1893
Strait, George, 682, 789, 857, 867, 878, 1059, 1322, 1529, 2040, 2753, 3137, 3559, 4012, 4487, 4698, 4735, 4771, 4871, 5183-5184, 5410, 5496, 5679, 5730
Straker, Nick, 682, 3520
Straker, Peter, 625, 4218
Straker, Rob, 5793
Strand, Darron, 4434
Strandberg, Per, 1987
Strange Creek Singers, 1512, 2127, 3915, 4810, 5184
Strange Folk, 1722, 5184, 5584
Strange Fruit Records, 31, 1811, 2161, 5185, 6080
Strange, Alex, 4408
Strange, Billy, 2944
Strange, Dobie, 3263
Strange, Pete, 3658, 5185
Strange, Richard, 6, 1568, 1827, 5413, 6047, 6082
Strange, Steve, 3728, 4229, 5585, 5652
Strange, Todd, 1312, 1607
Strangelove, 135, 1133, 2849, 3851, 4142, 4909, 5185
Strangeloves, 364, 497, 683, 1508, 2223, 2681, 5186
Stranger, 5186 and *passim*
Strangers, 5186-5187 and *passim*
Strangeways, 4343, 4820, 4851, 5187
Stranglers, 448, 553, 832, 1218, 1237, 1612, 2191, 2909, 3276, 3315, 3963, 4150, 4349, 4367, 4384, 4440, 5187-5189, 5373, 5578, 5639-5640, 5653, 6080
Strapping Fieldhands, 5189
Strapping Young Lad, 5189
Strapps, 4378, 5189
Straropoli, Chris, 5350
Strasberg, Lee, 504, 1497, 2095, 4054
Strasberg, Susan, 4352
Strasen, Robert, 2515
Strassen, Michael, 2495
Stratas, Teresa, 4893
Stratton, Dennis, 2710, 3257, 4307
Stratton, Gil, Jnr., 506
Stratton, Harley, 2995
Stratton, Maria, 5189

Stratton, Nick, 3778
Stratton, Rob, 3245-3246
Stratton-Smith, Tony, 1023, 1800, 2115, 3465, 4435, 5189-5190, 5653
Stratus, 1140, 2237, 3257, 4307, 5190
Straughan, Dick, 668
Strauks, Freddie, 853, 4957
Strauss, Johann, Jnr., 2259
Strauss, Johann, Snr., 2259
Strauss, Justin, 3667
Strauss, Oscar, 1068
Strauss, Richard, 444
Straw, Syd, 588, 1431, 1468, 1868, 2190, 2355, 5190
Strawberry Alarm Clock, 81, 89, 3374, 4352, 5190
Strawberry Statement, The, 5190-5191
Strawberry Switchblade, 5191
Strawbridge, David, 3151
Strawbs, 160, 727, 1260-1261, 1484, 1642, 1826-1827, 1901, 2083, 2248, 2393, 2574, 2625, 5191, 5626, 5653, 5673
Strawhead, 5192
Stray, 5192 and *passim*
Stray Cats, 1707, 3589, 3638, 4197, 4594, 4832, 5192, 5356
Stray Dog, 2355, 5192-5193
Strayhorn, Billy, 102, 581, 690, 1737-1738, 2427, 2548, 2596, 2837, 3597, 3629, 3791, 4040, 4668, 4903, 5193, 5355, 5694, 6080
Strazza, Peter, 1724
Strazzeri, Frank, 489, 4195
Stream, Harold, III, 180
Streamliners, 4291
Streep, Meryl, 721, 3362, 5886, 5989
Street Beat, 810, 1087, 3866, 4340, 4884, 5285
Street Rhythm Band, 5732
Street Sense, 3380
Street, Charles, 4416
Street, Mel, 1206, 2978, 3151, 3296
Street, Patricia, 1394
Street, Patrick, 1993, 2265, 2276, 2713, 4099, 4155-4156
Street, Richard, 3738, 5335
Street, Stephen, 1275, 1426, 3464, 4964, 5654, 6074
Streetband, 2980, 4375, 5193, 5979
Streeter, Roberta Lee, 2120
Streetman, Chick, 2950
Streets, 5193 and *passim*
Streetwalkers, 293, 1020-1021, 1838, 2262, 2710, 5193-5194
Streetwise Records, 337, 1460
Strehli, Angela, 352, 403, 5194
Streisand, Barbra, 227, 354, 451, 490, 524, 547, 566, 578, 731, 777, 943, 1018, 1034, 1164, 1181, 1243, 1281, 1296, 1299, 1489, 1509, 1555, 1604, 1660, 1968, 2055-2056, 2136, 2226, 2301, 2477-2478, 2495, 2574, 2607, 2616, 2659, 2931, 2960, 3078, 3140, 3143, 3187, 3258-3259, 3284, 3574, 3637, 3857, 3892, 3924, 3991, 4039, 4078,

4202, 4422, 4508, 4517, 4571, 4637, 4648, 4763, 4851, 4883, 4928, 5194-5196, 5610, 5709, 5857, 5956, 6080-6081
Stress Records, 5196
Stressball, 1812, 5196
Stretch, 5196
Strick, John, 3863
Strickland, Andy, 934, 1050, 3295
Strickland, Charlie, 93
Strickland, Don, 499
Strickland, Keith, 303
Strickland, Larry, 2908
Strickland, Milt, 921
Strickland, Napoleon, 5196
Strickland, Perry, 5649
Strickland, Robert, 2202
Stricklin, Al, 5196-5197, 5866-5867, 6081
Strictly Ballroom, 5197
Strictly Rhythm, 824, 1417, 1560, 1562, 1714, 1716, 1870, 2202, 3380, 3775, 3787, 3904, 3910, 4481, 4733, 4807, 5198, 5345, 5350, 5885
Strictly Roots, 745, 5198
Strictly Underground, 5198
Stride, Pete, 697, 3362
Strife, 5198 and *passim*
Strike Under, 3871
Strike Up The Band, 308, 407, 480, 491-492, 1705, 2025, 2090, 2117, 2128-2129, 2224, 2329, 2462, 2861, 2940, 3107, 3696, 4016, 4643, 4764, 5199, 5363, 5802
Strike, Johnny, 1293
Striker, 5199 and *passim*
Striknine, Aldine, 4273
String Trio Of New York, 365, 4855, 5199
String-a-Longs, 5199
String-Driven Thing, 5199-5200
Stringbean, 1058, 2471, 3482, 3744, 4787, 5200, 5531
Stringbean And Peanut, 4787
Stringer, Becky, 482, 4642
Stringer, Gary, 4480
Stringfellow, Ken, 4292, 4956
Strip, The, 169, 235, 321, 446, 588, 871, 983, 1162-1163, 1372-1373, 1907, 2094, 2166, 2688, 2809, 3411, 3812, 4352, 4594, 4671, 4681, 4822, 4861, 5200, 5345
Striplin, Steve, 3884
Stritch, Elaine, 159, 179, 578, 1196, 1219, 1959, 2192, 2532, 4042, 4108, 4893, 5200-5201
Strob, Neil, 5542
Strohm, John, 579, 3190
Strollers Dance Band, 1290
Strolling Yodeler, 541
Stroman, Guy, 1976
Stroman, Susan, 1284, 4893
Stromberg, Hunt, 1903, 2259, 3532, 3885
Strong, Al, 4342
Strong, Barrett, 248, 1404, 2559, 5201, 5334, 5576, 5804
Strong, Benny, 3636, 5201
Strong, Bob, 3814, 5455

Strong, Nolan, 1506, 1980
Strong, Philip, 3386
Strong, Ronnie, 1585
Strong, Willie, 2668
Strongman, Phillip, 1849
Stroud, Charlie, 925
Stroud, Claude, 3337
Stroud, James, 4491, 5201, 5929
Stroud, Jimmy, 3976
Strouse, Charles, 66, 195-196, 210, 862, 1033, 1374, 1418, 1946, 2188, 2477, 2723, 3942, 4581, 4777, 5201-5202, 5835
Strouse, Johann, 5930
Strozier, Frank, 1166, 3275
Structure Records, 5202
Strum, Dana, 1495, 4962, 5646
Strummer, Joe, 519, 1066, 1089, 1110, 3303, 4044, 4270, 4365, 4703, 4709, 6040
Strunk, Gilbert, 5530
Strunk, Jud, 5202
Struthers, Dave, 188
Strutt, Nick, 2184, 2336, 3825, 5202-5203
Stryker, Paul, 3637, 4467
Strykert, Ron, 3625
Stryper, 139, 3902, 4119, 5203
Strzelecki, Henri, 417, 611, 4226, 4566
Strzempka, Greg, 4406
Stuart, Alice, 3809, 5203
Stuart, Babe, 2785
Stuart, Barry, 100
Stuart, Dan, 1384, 2265, 3871, 5938
Stuart, Fred, 3583
Stuart, Glen, 3410
Stuart, Gloria, 2185, 4281, 4635
Stuart, Hamish, 291, 1623, 3549
Stuart, Jay Alison, 3217
Stuart, Leslie, 61-62, 466, 606, 1942
Stuart, Margie, 4492
Stuart, Marty, 338, 855, 3984, 5203-5204, 5507, 5799
Stuart, Michael, 3211
Stuart, Mike, 3211, 3662
Stuart, Peter, 1573
Stuart, Roluf, 5905
Stuart, William, 4340
Stubblefield, Clyde, 775, 5886
Stubblefield, John, 3690, 4288
Stubbles, Joe, 1834
Stubbs, Eddie, 2839
Stubbs, Joe, 1215, 1834, 4045, 4061
Stubbs, Ken, 412
Stubbs, Levi, 1007, 1834, 1997, 3272, 5288
Stubbs, Una, 5909
Stucchio, Emil, 1111, 5958
Stuckey, David, 6079
Stuckey, Henry, 4089, 5204
Stuckey, Nat, 4986, 5204
Stud, 606, 1883, 2784, 2990, 4639, 5205, 5834
Stud Brothers, 1883
Student Bodies, 2517
Student Prince In Heidelberg, The, 5205
Student Prince, The, 633-634, 748, 2382, 3128-3129, 4054, 4118, 4637, 5205, 5500

Studer, Fredy, 800, 5205-5206
Studholme, Joe, 1030
Studio One, 47, 62, 111, 149, 170, 188, 200, 305, 447, 526, 534, 670, 681, 704-705, 735, 742, 754, 766-767, 770-771, 840-841, 877, 902, 904, 915, 927, 929, 938, 1007, 1032, 1097, 1137, 1261, 1329, 1417, 1528, 1566, 1569-1570, 1586, 1634, 1636, 1686, 1711, 1740-1742, 1753, 1784, 2007-2008, 2023, 2105, 2148, 2165-2166, 2291-2292, 2496, 2575-2576, 2581, 2588, 2623, 2705, 2727, 2733, 2787, 2845, 2955, 2999, 3005-3006, 3129-3130, 3271, 3305, 3316, 3337, 3423, 3468-3470, 3477-3479, 3531-3533, 3575-3576, 3582, 3593, 3654, 3659, 3662, 3698, 3718, 3958, 4041, 4070, 4096, 4124, 4137, 4139-4140, 4165, 4185, 4187, 4250, 4334-4336, 4431, 4436-4437, 4445, 4494, 4514, 4532, 4599, 4644, 4696, 4751, 4778, 4801, 4814, 4882, 4912, 4946, 4948, 4957, 4972, 5206, 5290, 5299, 5325, 5338, 5380, 5427, 5526, 5578, 5641, 5669, 5688, 5735, 5747-5748, 5767, 5860-5861, 5871-5872, 6000
Studio Tone, 1681
Study, Sidney, 3015
Stull, Michael, 859, 5664
Stump, 1793, 2127, 5206, 5294, 6081, 6117
Stupids, 2388, 5206, 5984
Stupp, Mick, 2697
Sturgess, Ian, 1426
Sturgis, Michael, 5541
Sturmer, Andy, 2808
Sturr, Jimmy, 5206
Sturr, Harold, 2841
Stutzer, Morten, 248
Stuyvesant, Peter, 2301, 3046
Style Council, 271, 383, 873, 1487, 2074, 2146, 2767, 3276, 3640, 4384, 5207, 5485, 5760-5761, 6081
Styler, Marshall James, 1645
Styler, Trudie, 1728
Stylistics, 146, 464, 602, 1440, 1471, 1580, 1626, 2654, 3068, 3262, 3557, 4220, 5207-5208
Styne, Jule, 170, 371, 467-468, 565, 721, 731, 884, 942, 1190, 1564, 1589, 1824, 1868, 2055-2056, 2119-2120, 2324, 2520, 2532, 2562, 2596, 2722, 2785, 2959, 3140, 3187, 3281, 3293, 3409, 3634, 3637, 3747, 4207, 4290, 4467, 4580, 4636, 5208-5209, 5607, 6081
Styrenes, 1724, 3138, 3703, 5209
Styx, 80, 90, 97, 121, 138, 205, 439, 847, 916, 1263, 1289, 1360, 1370, 1503, 1566, 1760, 1841, 1891, 2460, 3184, 3913, 3950, 3978, 4506, 4564, 4858, 4876, 4892, 4955, 5209-5210
Suarez, Gil, 747
Suarez, Zeke, 1810

Sub Pop Records, 5210 and *passim*
Sub Sub, 5210
Subcircus, 5210
Subdudes, 5210
Subete, Momoeno, 5946
Subhumans, 3352, 4046
Subhumans (Canada), 5211
Subhumans (UK), 5211
Sublime, 5211
Submission Records, 5815
Subramaniam, E.M., 5560
Subramaniam, Dr. L., 644, 5211-5212
Subsonic 2, 1560, 5212
Subterfuge, 2693, 4063, 5212
Subterraneans, The, 1371, 1479, 3303, 3837, 5212
Subtle Oppression, 452
Suburban Base, 3536, 3763, 4496, 5212-5213, 5484
Subway Organisation Records, 1050
Success!, 5213, 5307
Sucedo, Jose, 5817
Suck Me Plasma, 1562, 4969
Sudano, Bruce, 122, 752
Suddeeth, William, III, 272
Sudden, Nikki, 390, 1287, 1768, 2755, 3570, 5213, 6122
Suddenly, Tammy!, 5213
Sudhalter, Dick, 892, 942, 2298, 2693, 5213, 5802
Sudy, Joe, 4492
Sudy, Joseph, 3015, 4492
Sudy, Sidney, 3015
Sue And Sunny, 5213-5214
Sue Records, 1602, 2121, 5214, 5512, 5531, 5716
Suede, 5214-5215 and *passim*
Suedo, Julie, 4382
Sueref, George, 3325
Suesse, Dana, 2512, 4649, 5215
Sufit, Alisha, 3406, 5215-5216
Sugama, Shinki, 2468
Sugar, 5216 and *passim*
Sugar (stage musical), 5216
Sugar And Dandy, 2345, 3282, 4919
Sugar Babies, 3281, 3488, 3669, 4643, 5216
Sugar Blue, 1231, 1710, 1897, 4816, 5609
Sugar Cane, 793, 5408, 5773
Sugar Hill Records (Country), 5217
Sugar J, 90
Sugar Merchants, 278
Sugar Ray, 1102, 4643, 5217
Sugarcreek, 1289, 5217
Sugarcubes, 551, 1451, 2118, 3238, 3257, 3650, 4046, 4576, 4709, 5217-5218, 5492
Sugarhill Gang, 608, 651, 892, 1609, 3617, 3898, 4433, 4730, 5218, 5280, 5465, 5886
Sugarhill Records, 5218-5219 and *passim*
Sugden, Chris, 3026
Sugerman, Danny, 1595, 2314, 6044, 6051, 6117
Sugg, Patrick, 2577
Suggs, 1337, 1443, 3324, 3401-3402, 5219
Suhler, Jim, 1684, 3786

Suicidal Tendencies, 521, 1322, 2692, 3463, 3961, 4406, 5219-5220, 5346, 5945
Suicide, 5220 and *passim*
Sukaesih, Elvi, 4736
Sulack, Cy, 125
Suleyman, Sunay, 3312
Sulieman, Idrees, 2893, 5220-5221
Sulley, Susanne, 2632
Sullivan Family, 2618
Sullivan, Barry, 1006, 3449, 3588
Sullivan, Big Jim, 1034, 2309, 3145, 3588, 5221
Sullivan, Chris, 616
Sullivan, Ed, 242, 433, 511, 862, 1006, 1099, 1113, 1145, 1196, 1362, 1672, 1749, 1976, 2225, 2282, 2568, 2745, 3098, 3466, 3512, 3545, 4167, 4211, 4628, 4934, 5524, 5598, 5695, 5947
Sullivan, Eddie, 4672
Sullivan, Floyd, 2785
Sullivan, Francis L., 1428
Sullivan, Frankie, 4208
Sullivan, Gene, 4865, 5832
Sullivan, Gordon, 2026
Sullivan, Ira, 1714, 5221
Sullivan, Jacqui, 357, 4880
Sullivan, Jeff, 554, 1630
Sullivan, Jeri, 2785
Sullivan, Jim, 156, 1034, 2309, 3145, 3588
Sullivan, Jo, 3294, 3804, 5426, 5788
Sullivan, Joe, 154, 1790, 2346, 2868, 4291, 5221, 5529
Sullivan, John, 129, 3310
Sullivan, Matt, 5298
Sullivan, Maxine, 391, 1436, 1943, 2323, 2329, 2537, 2693, 2740, 3027, 3132, 3376, 3573, 4199, 4801, 4853, 5221-5222, 5416, 5582, 5606, 5711, 5819, 6003-6004
Sullivan, Niki, 1292, 2568
Sullivan, Peter, 2886
Sullivan, Rollin, 3310
Sullivan, Sir Arthur, 2126
Sully, Eve, 2985
Sultans, 1225, 1231, 1538, 2007, 2024, 2892, 2960, 3736, 4183, 4523, 4533, 4588, 4757, 5222, 5536-5537, 5858, 5898
Sultans Of Ping FC, 5222-5223
Sulton, Kasim, 4688
Sulzmann, Stan, 3519, 3882, 5223, 5315
Sumac, Yma, 1923, 4251, 5223
Sumlin, Hubert, 612, 2620, 3550, 3863, 4856, 5223-5224, 5991
Summer Holiday (1948), 586, 1894, 1947, 2134, 2196, 3429, 4643, 5224, 5284. 5555, 5692, 5791, 5909
Summer Holiday (1962), 568, 1085, 3497, 4531-4532, 5224
Summer Records, 1122, 1384
Summer Stock, 112, 837, 1020, 1434, 1966, 2089-2090, 2217, 2674, 2959-2960, 3148, 5224-5225, 5453, 5692, 5711
Summer, Donna, 122, 146, 266,

400, 752, 888, 2109, 2301, 3034, 3157, 3695, 3853, 4038, 4914, 5225, 5568, 5610, 5623, 5644, 6081
Summer, Mark, 5537
Summer, Mike, 5484
Summerfield, Eleanor, 2725
Summerfield, Peter, 4103
Summerfield, Saffron, 3540, 5226
Summers, Andy, 194, 228, 1270, 1385, 1783, 2037, 3737, 3870, 4274, 4653, 5226
Summers, Don, 3821
Summers, Eddie, 602
Summers, Elijah, 899
Summers, Graham, 1456
Summers, Hilary, 3990
Summers, Jazz, 526, 619, 1367, 1617, 5781
Summers, Jeff, 5740
Summers, Jerry, 1606
Summers, Walter, 4414
Summey, Clell, 59, 1260, 3017
Summitt, Scott, 2190
Sumner, Bernard, 1717, 1727, 3918
Sumner, Gordon, 4274, 6080
Sumner, Marion, 2824
Sun Birds, 5543
Sun City Girls, 5226
Sun Dial, 5227
Sun Ra, 13, 133, 290, 365, 591, 618, 780, 1035, 1185, 1257, 1417, 1514, 1553, 2028-2029, 2155, 2286, 2474, 2487, 2788, 2793, 2795-2796, 3194, 3348, 3435, 3789, 3980, 4156, 4231, 4327, 4358, 4595, 4735, 4908, 4933, 4940, 5227-5229, 6081
Sun Records, 5229-5230 and *passim*
Sun Valley Serenade, 2216, 2962, 3674, 3939, 4058, 4370, 5230, 5711
Sun J, 257
Sun, Joe, 3729, 5230
Sunbeam Records, 1465, 2235
Sunbonnet Girl, 1331
Suncatcher, 5230
Sunday In The Park With George, 2505, 4151, 4154, 4209, 5230-5231
Sundays, 269, 1830, 2118, 2712-2713, 2990, 3047, 3333, 4142, 4246, 4663, 5231
Sundazed Records, 5231
Sundberg, Clinton, 383, 1692, 2202, 3037, 4040, 5919
Sunderberg, Joe, 2059
Sundgaard, Arnold, 4063
Sundholm, Norm, 3022
Sundial, 331, 5231-5232
Sundin, Per, 1716
Sundowners, 77, 4013, 4499, 5232, 5445, 5621
Sundquist, Jim, 1875
Sundqvist, Dan, 2947
Sundrud, Jack, 2258
Sune, 4352
Sunflower Records, 1355, 3684
Sunny, 5232 and *passim*
Sunny Alade Records, 74
Sunny And The Sunglows, 5232

Thomson, Barry, 649
Thomson, Chris, 1089, 2036
Thomson, Craig, 5415-5416
Thomson, Fred, 649
Thomson, Henrik, 1583
Thomson, Kristin, 5517
Thomson, Liz, 1678, 6046, 6117
Thor, 1450, 4662, 5416
Thor, Matt, 4662
Thorkelson, Peter Halsten, 3740
Thorn, Stan, 4867
Thorn, Thomas, 1724
**Thorn, Tracey, 1045, 1705,
1801, 3463, 3505, 5416, 5920**
Thornalley, Phil, 29, 2068, 2680,
2838
Thornbar, Kraig, 4510
Thornbury, James, 917
Thorne, Damien, 1369
Thorne, John, 4747
Thorne, Kathryn, 5749
Thorne, Mike, 3928, 5379, 5435,
5891
Thorne, Raymond, 196
Thorngren, Brett, 3849
**Thornhill, Claude, 36, 116, 187,
476, 758, 935, 1210, 1453, 1764,
1791, 1864, 1943, 1993, 2226,
3045, 3060, 3836, 3865, 3966,
4275, 4328, 4609, 4696, 5416,
5844-5845, 5934, 6006**
Thornhill, Rebecca, 441
Thornton, Barry, 1663
Thornton, Big Mama, 527, 530,
1806, 2071, 2410, 2610, 3186,
4579, 4987, 5417, 5611, 5879
Thornton, Blair, 316
Thornton, Charles, 3664
Thornton, Clifford, 2551, 2793,
3233, 3599, 4156
Thornton, Frank, 3604
Thornton, James, 5416-5417
Thornton, John, 993
Thornton, Johnny, 5777
Thornton, Keith, 1615, 5569
Thornton, Kevin, 1181
Thornton, Michael, 3005,
3519, 6062
Thornton, Thomas, 4316, 5521
**Thornton, Willie Mae 'Big
Mama', 5417**
**Thorogood, George, 275, 4664,
5417**
**Thoroughly Modern Millie,
185-186, 498, 885, 1018, 1204,
3246-3247, 5417-5418, 5607**
Thorp, William, 5721
Thorpe, Billy, 5418
Thorpe, Lionel, 1070
Thorpe, Melvin P., 506
Thorpe, Peter, 4663
Thorpe, Richard, 2258, 2723
Thorpe, Suzanne, 3632
Thorpe, Tony, 4678
Thorson, Lisa, 5418
Thorstensen, Gary, 5280
Thorty, J.Y., 1290
Thorup, Peter, 1001, 3066
Thorvald, John, 3931
**Those Were The Happy Times,
3146, 5418**
Thought Industry, 5418-5419
Thoughts, 5419
Thoughts Of Mary, 448, 1918

**Thoumire, Simon, 3559, 4029,
5419**
Thousand Yard Stare, 5419
**Thousands Cheer, 144, 249,
351, 493-494, 586, 646, 748,
1434, 1516, 1705, 2025, 2089-
2090, 2255, 2386, 2422, 2596-
2597, 2602, 2959-2960, 3326,
3488, 4300, 4643, 5419-5420,
5723, 5736, 6035**
Thrall, Pat, 257, 285, 2628-2629,
5494
Thrasher, 1627, 4701, 5420
Thrasher, Andrew, 1627
Thrasher, Neil, 5420
Thrasher Shiver, 5420
Thrashler, Walter, 1449
**Threadgill, Henry, 96, 561, 681,
1341, 1784, 1803, 2592-2593,
2797, 3431, 3511, 3544, 3689,
3716, 3862, 5420**
Three Beat Records, 5420-5421
**Three Bells, 793, 1196, 1941,
5421**
Three Blazers, 105, 534, 768,
1554, 3727, 3770, 3772, 4502,
4690
Three Cheers For Tokyo, 1572
**Three Chuckles, 4425, 4592,
5421**
3 Colours Red, 3514, 5421
**Three Degrees, 146, 1001, 1187,
1647, 4902, 5421-5422**
**Three Dog Night, 39, 223, 294,
354, 394, 624, 1403, 2515, 3673,
3740, 3891, 3897, 3931, 3951,
4761, 5422**
Three Johns, 5423
3 lb. Thrill, 5423
Three Hats Record, 5416
Three Little Maids, 958
Three Maids, 958, 3489
Three Man Posse, 5424
Three Men When Stood Side By
Side Have A Wingspan Of Over
12 Feet, 1988
**3 Mustaphas 3, 643, 1067, 3061,
3972, 4358, 5298, 5424**
Three O'Clock, 5424
311, 3065, 3196, 5424
3Phase, 3979, 5424-5425
3T, 5425
Three Tree Posse, 5425
Three Vocal Trio, 5450
Three Way Records, 785
Three Weary Willies, 3728
Three's A Crowd, 5425
**Threepenny Opera, The, 246,
323, 595, 721, 1296, 1337, 1390,
1419, 2447, 2488, 3574, 4054,
5425-5426, 5754**
Threesome, 108, 116, 2724,
2875, 3038, 3788, 5965
**Threshold Records, 2775, 3759,
5426, 5492**
**Thriller U, 80, 1810, 1944, 3129,
3611, 4590, 5426-5427**
**Throbbing Gristle, 1071, 1077,
1132, 1473, 1484, 1992, 2469,
2691-2692, 3159, 3608, 3855,
4355, 4953, 5425, 5427, 5741,
6082**
Throbs, 2459, 4046, 5427, 5830
Throckmorton, Sonny, 702, 2615

Throndson, Sjor, 526
Throup, Andy, 4807
Thrower, Stephen, 1155
**Throwing Muses, 170, 469, 722,
1589, 1632, 1636, 1780, 1989,
2509-2510, 3057, 3312, 4194,
4278, 4792, 5396, 5428**
Thrown Ups, 3831
Thrum, 5428
Thunder, 5429 and *passim*
Thunder Alley, 195, 5429
Thunder, Johnny, 221, 5429
Thunder, Leslie, 1055
Thunder, Shelly, 3080, 5429
Thunder, Theodore, 362
Thunderbeats, 3062
Thunderbolts, 726-727, 3214,
4596, 5343
**Thunderclap Newman, 2952,
3117, 3406, 5399, 5429-5430,
5481**
Thunderhead, 5430
**Thunders, Johnny, 413, 1046,
1106, 1328, 2283, 2460, 2475,
3094, 3748, 3923, 4198, 4938,
5430, 5642, 6082**
Thunders, Johnny, And The
Heartbreakers, 1046, 2283, 4938
**Thunderstick, 4731, 5430-5431,
5468**
Thunes, Scott, 5722
Thurgood, Deborah Lynn, 129
Thurlow, Jon, 1078
Thurman, Ed, 4340
Thurman, John, 2639, 5393
Thursaflokkurim, 5431
Thursby, Robert, 5627
Thurston, Colin, 272, 2782,
4049
Thurston, Peter, 2055
Thurston, Scott, 1783, 2676
Thwaite, Jeff, 4365
Thyne, Robin, 3410, 3883
Ti Jaz, 3154
Tiara Records, 2274
Tibbenham, Mark, 3418
Tibbett, Lawrence, 2284, 3916
Tibbetts, Steve, 1701
Tibbs, Andrew, 5431
Tibbs, Casey, 3864
Tibbs, Gary, 62, 1854, 4669,
5640
Tiberi, Frank, 2506, 5431
Tibet, David, 1337
Tic Tac Toe, 5431
Tice, Dave, 818, 1251
Tichy, John, 1193
**Tickell, Kathryn, 1382, 2652,
4029, 5431-5432**
**Tickle Me, 2366, 2385, 2743,
4311, 4315, 5432**
Tickle, David, 1994
Tickler, Nigel, 4839
Tickner, Eddie, 2408-2409
Tickner, George, 2044, 2900
Tickner, Myrtle, 4273
Tico All-Stars, 229, 3314, 4097,
4113, 4361
**Tico And The Triumphs, 4918,
5432, 5457**
Tico Records, 1320, 1323, 1832,
1841, 3097, 3181, 4115, 4360,
4615, 4744
Tidmarsh, Christopher, 1074

Tielli, Martin, 5694
Tieman, Tommy, 4823
Tieres, Wharton, 5581
Tiernan, Paul, 2953
Tierney, Bobby, 576
Tierney, Gene, 4040
**Tierney, Harry, 1405, 1703,
2708, 3547, 4550, 5432**
Tierney, Louis, 104
Tierney, Mancel, 104
Tierney, Mike, 2633
Tierney, Tony, 3356
Tierra, 5433 and *passim*
Tierrazo Records, 1240, 4613
Tietjens, Paul, 5899
Tiffany, 5433 and *passim*
Tiffany's Thoughts, 5433
Tiffen, Harry, 1262
Tiger, 5433 and *passim*
Tiger (Reggae), 5433-5434
Tiger Moth, 176, 1150, 1760,
2560
Tiger Records, 3501, 4460, 4581
Tigertailz, 4805, 5434
Tighe, Michael, 812
Tighe, Rachael, 2703
Tigrane, Armik, 4839
Tihai Trio, 4758
Tijuana Brass, 32, 147, 358, 1004
**Tikaram, Tanita, 223, 423, 750,
1299, 2291, 2717, 5434-5435,
5502, 6082**
Tikis, 288, 439, 2401, 4973, 5333
Tikk Takk, 158
**Til The Butcher Cuts Him
Down, 5435**
Til Tuesday, 687, 3476, 5435
Tilbrook, Adrian, 316, 5435
Tilbrook, Glenn, 1522, 5095-
5096
Tilbury, John, 165
**Till The Clouds Roll By, 144,
153, 1024, 2089-2090, 2160,
2255, 2449, 2596-2597, 2976,
3127, 3160, 3492, 3696, 4889-
4890, 4930, 5435-5436**
Till, Gus, 4969
Till, John, 2890
Tiller, Mary, 198
Tillery, Donald, 768
Tillery, Linda, 3288
Tilley, Sandra, 3480, 5625
Tilley, Vesta, 465, 2405, 3032
Tilling, Robert, 1409, 6043
**Tillis, Mel, 688, 1104, 1872,
2287, 2992, 3220, 3555, 3598,
3754, 3822, 4086, 4221, 4241,
4931, 5436-5437, 5971, 6082**
**Tillis, Pam, 388, 488, 1537,
2896, 4817, 5436-5437**
Tillison, Roger, 890
Tillman, Floyd, 1356, 5438
Tillman, Georgeanna Marie,
3495
Tillman, Jesse, 854
Tillman, Keith, 1650
**Tillotson, Johnny, 256, 1407,
2546, 2915, 3170, 3325, 3369,
3755, 4186, 5438-5439**
Tilo, Amadou, 5476
Tilsley, Harry, 4573
Tilson, Martha, 25
Tilston, Steve, 696, 4502, 5439
Tilton, Mark, 3622, 4545

Vance, Dick, 379, 3093, 5609
Vance, Frank, 984
Vance, Johnny, 5320
Vance, Kenny, 162, 2790, 4202
Vance, Paul, 1326, 1495, 2573
Vance, Tommy, 1459, 4252, 5628
Vance, Vivian, 351, 2589
Vancouver Playboys, 3974
Vancouver Symphony Orchestra, 2547
Vanda And Young, 1695, 2244, 3858, 5610, 5973
Vanda, Emil, 3019
Vanda, Harry, 47, 1694, 2244, 3858, 5610
Vandebroek, Bert, 1802
Vandekauter, Marnix, 4076
Vandekerckhove, Hans, 4076
Vanden, Peter, 1692
Vandenberg, 3961, 5610, 5803
Vander, Christian, 3409
Vander Ark, Brad, 5638
Vander Ark, Brian, 5638
Vandergelder, Horace, 2477
Vandergelder, Peter, 2258
Vandergucht, Mark, 2074
Vanderhoof, Kurt, 3642
Vanderloo, Herbie, 268
Vanderpapeliere, Renaat, 4393
Vanderpool, Sylvia, 344, 3654
Vandross, Luther, 1063, 2013, 2165, 2295, 2466, 2694, 2806, 3237, 3283, 3370, 3393, 4383, 4571, 5610, 5713, 5836
Vandyke, Les, 1830
Vanessi, Lilli, 3035
Vangelis, 178, 207, 648, 2359, 2866, 4525, 4825, 5611, 6083, 6128
Vangu, Dianzenza, 657
Vanguard Records, 5611 and *passim*
Vanhamel, Tim, 1802
Vanian, Dave, 928, 1371-1372, 1910, 4976
Vanilla Fudge, 210, 268, 272, 446, 641, 878, 1457, 1775, 2456, 2678, 3164, 3508, 3731, 3800, 5611-5612, 5968
Vanilla Ice, 305, 1344, 1450, 1559, 2365, 3537, 4433, 5392, 5612, 5822
Vanilla, Cherry, 1046, 5612
Vanishing Point, 4329, 5612
Vanity, 5612-5613 and *passim*
Vanity 6, 209, 4332, 5612-5613
Vanity Fare, 741, 1056, 3027, 5613
Vanleer, Jimmy, 372
Vann, Joey, 1657
Vann, Teddy, 5429
Vann, Tony, 4737
Vannata, Larry, 214
Vanwarmer, Randy, 1206, 1245, 4006, 5613
Vapirov, Anatoly, 3087, 3194, 5613
Vapnick, Isaac, 2770
Vapors, 138, 3220, 5613-5614
Varda, James, 5614
Varden, Norma, 1567, 2119
Vardis, 1540, 5598, 5614
Vardy, Ian, 4308

Varela, Jairo, 398, 3937
Vargas, Sergio, 109
Vargas, Wilfrido, 5614-5615
Variety Records, 429, 5774
Varley, Bill, 5650
Varley, Paul, 242
Varnaline, 5615
Varnel, Marcel, 1374, 2660, 3201
Varney, Mike, 1489, 1889, 2671, 3069, 3380, 3423, 3774, 3987, 4217, 5281, 5641
Varro, Johnny, 5591
Varsity Records, 5683
Vartan, Sylvie, 1763, 2356
Värttinä, 5615
Vasco, Dave, 1093
Vasconcelos, Monica, 5616
Vasconcelos, Nana, 172, 1046, 1149, 1731, 2084, 2163, 2316, 2428, 2903, 4584, 4871, 5480, 5494, 5560, 5616, 5674, 5699
Vaselines, 926, 1785, 1891, 3828, 5616
Väsen, 5616
Vashti, 5462, 5616-5617
Vasquez, Angel, 2206
Vásquez, Frankie, 3233
Vasquez, Junior, 1146, 2083, 2839, 3618, 4383, 5338, 5617, 5823
Vass, Tim, 4451
Vassell, Elaine, 1462
Vaszary, John, 2661
Vath, Sven, 273, 1688, 2423, 3234, 4293, 5617
Vaughan Williams, Ralph, 2225, 3285
Vaughan, Clarence, 1697
Vaughan, Cooney, 3754
Vaughan, Denny, 2124
Vaughan, Frankie, 95, 476, 1151, 1604, 1935, 1982, 2016, 2724, 2944, 3204, 3340, 3394, 3560, 3673, 3743, 3747, 3788, 3818, 3888, 4039, 4488, 4574, 4602, 5617-5618, 5659, 5742
Vaughan, Henry, 2650
Vaughan, Ivan, 4377
Vaughan, Jerry, 3019
Vaughan, Jimmie, 1517, 4579, 5618
Vaughan, Jimmy, 1818, 4488
Vaughan, Malcolm, 326, 1686, 2480, 4621, 5618
Vaughan, Maurice John, 139, 5618
Vaughan, Michael, 4122
Vaughan, Norman, 2456
Vaughan, Ray, 147, 403, 630, 927, 1249, 1362, 1807, 1818, 2455, 2686, 2770, 2888, 3008, 3203, 3390, 5348-5349, 5376, 5618, 5620-5621, 5667, 5687, 5873, 6083
Vaughan, Sarah, 19, 43, 79, 107, 175, 407, 604, 646, 691, 1159, 1365, 1417, 1700, 1712, 1851, 1866, 1883, 1909, 1913, 2192, 2301, 2364, 2379, 2536, 2597, 2770, 2869, 2877, 2960, 2987, 3081, 3110, 3176, 3178, 3200, 3213, 3425, 3443, 3531, 3574, 3636, 3736, 3752, 3804, 3853,

4104, 4111, 4285, 4668, 4684, 4697, 4782, 4789-4790, 4833, 5294, 5301, 5461, 5619-5620, 5638, 5717, 5749, 5777, 5840, 5873, 5912, 5931, 6083
Vaughan, Steve, 2142, 2765
Vaughan, Stevie Ray, 147, 403, 630, 1249, 1362, 1818, 2455, 2686, 2770, 2888, 3008, 3203, 3390, 5348-5349, 5376, 5618, 5620-5621, 5667, 5687, 6083
Vaughn, Billy, 1601, 1963, 2169, 2534, 2917, 2922, 5426, 5621
Vaughn, Danny, 5289, 5552, 5737
Vaughn, Jimmy, 3339, 5621
Vaughn, Kenny, 3541
Vaughn, Richard, 5621
Vaughn, Yvonne, 1846
Vaughton, Brian, 3506
Vault Records, 3241
Vaya Records, 2397, 3181, 4098, 4389, 4447
Vázquez, Javier, 1833, 3181, 3233, 3938, 4031, 4098, 4389, 4558, 4742
Veal, Dave, 3464
Veal, Reginald, 2898, 3474
Vearncombe, Colin, 551
Vecsey, Armand, 5901
Vecsey, George, 3371, 3436, 6061
Vecsey, Roz, 4341
Vedder, Eddie, 880, 4174-4175, 5335, 5502, 5731, 6067
Vedette Jazz, 2768
Vee, Bobby, 1136, 1292, 1339, 1495, 1625, 1687, 1809, 1970, 2094, 2181, 2569, 2915, 3011, 3032, 3216, 3232, 3999, 4140, 4255, 4264, 5440, 5622, 5630
Vee, Jerry, 3817
Vee Jay Records, 5622 and *passim*
Vega, Alan, 1061, 4679, 5623, 6081
Vega, David, 2230
Vega, Little Louie, 3267, 3758, 4194
Vega, Louie, 719, 3267, 3507, 3758, 4194, 5521, 5623
Vega, Nikki D., 5623
Vega, Sergio, 4385
Vega, Suzanne, 1610, 1793, 2516, 2717, 2759, 3190, 3245, 4237, 4886, 4899, 5537, 5623, 5842
Vega, Tania, 4782
Vega, Tata, 5623
Vega, Tony, 1320, 1349, 3162, 3750, 4065, 4116, 4361, 4421, 4558, 4647, 5623
Veidt, Conrad, 1743
Veilloa, Leroy, 1964
Veitch, Tim, 1728
Veitch, Trevor, 4693
Vejtables, 288, 3085, 3733, 5624
Vejvoda, Jaromir, 780, 2166
Vela, Rosie, 5624
Velarde, Benny, 3181
Velasco, Chris, 492
Velázquez, Victor, 747, 4113, 4420

Veldt, 5624
Vélez, Chuíto, 4742
Velez, Jerry, 2491
Vélez, Kito, 1240, 2234
Velez, Loraine, 1837
Velez, Martha, 477, 2223, 4939
Velgas, Magnus, 3949
Velichkov, Stoyan, 5505
Velker, J.J., 3639
Velocette, Gene, 4968
Velocity Girl, 5517, 5624
Velocity Records, 3849, 5624
Velours, 1065, 5625
Velvelettes, 357, 2560, 2852, 5625, 5804
Velvet Crush, 1644, 2145, 5625
Velvet Monkeys, 305-306, 1533, 2343, 5625
Velvet Opera, 727, 2083, 5626
Velvet Underground, 47, 117, 161, 189, 454, 583, 685, 860, 891, 910, 955, 1119, 1456, 1498, 1609, 1765, 1868, 1930, 1987, 2072, 2175, 2308, 2384, 2599, 2636, 2781, 2896, 3277, 3287, 3321, 3400, 3642, 3651, 3726-3727, 3808, 3922, 3943, 4175, 4180, 4355, 4376, 4478-4479, 4536, 4590, 4729, 5290, 5369, 5375, 5491, 5522-5523, 5626-5627, 5638, 5789, 5792, 5974, 5989, 6073, 6083, 6131
Velvet, Jeffrey, 539
Velvetones, 2306, 2753, 2761, 4526
Velvets, 306, 619, 891, 1288, 1955, 2195, 3766, 4479, 4582, 5626-5627, 6073, 6111
Velvett Fogg, 5627-5628
Venable, Evelyn, 1544
Venable, Kim, 1111
Venables, Mark, 1510
Vencier, Ray, 2206
Vendetta, 2316, 2789, 3290, 4829, 5355
Vendors, 149, 1569, 1741, 2688, 3718, 4187, 4436, 4899, 5688
Venegas, Kenny, 4660
Venegas, Victor, 3180, 4739
Venesa, Amy, 729
Venet, Nik, 424, 4321, 5628
Venezolana, Alma, 3097
Vengerova, Isabella, 498
Venner, Cliff, 3918
Venneri, Joseph, 5456
Venom, 5628 and *passim*
Venom P. Stinger, 1540
Venosa, Arthur, 1728
Vent 414, 5628-5629, 5907
Ventura, Charlie, 373, 476, 1908, 2244, 2267, 2406, 2739, 3072, 3082, 3544, 3584, 3716, 3771, 3875, 4526, 5600, 5629, 5768, 5883
Ventura, Chico, 1813
Ventura, Johnny, 3702
Ventura, Ray, 2111
Ventura, Rick, 4550
Ventures, 5629-5630 and *passim*
Venus And The Razorblades, 2001, 3667
Venus Fly Trap, 4130, 5630
Venuti, Joe, 107, 116, 355, 386,

417, 823, 941, 1009, 1302, 1455,
1669, 1746, 2111, 2193, 2226,
2244-2245, 2449, 2580, 2929,
3002, 3124-3125, 3142, 3178,
3200, 3585, 3597, 3875, 3942,
4069, 4206, 4469, 4480, 4528,
4842, 4903, 4925, 5460, 5630-
5631, 5650, 5664, 5766, 5802,
5982
Vera, Billy, 432, 538-539, 1114,
1262, 2916, 5311, 5631-5632
Vera, Joey, 202, 230
Vera-Ellen, 261, 466, 893, 1047,
2946, 2959, 3492, 3634, 3669,
4040-4042, 4118, 5632, 5711,
5791, 5906
Veras, George, 5949
Verbeek, Tjeerd, 5489
Verbraak, Stan, 2478
Vercambe, Laurent, 3422
Verckys, 1757, 5632
Vercruysse, Rudy, 4076
Verdon, Gwen, 125, 912, 1020,
1054-1055, 1370, 1886, 1983,
2642, 2990, 3583, 3913, 4040,
4054, 4471, 4557, 5632-5633
Verdun, Kitty, 5787
Verdusco, Darrell, 2949
Verebes, Ernest, 1552
Vereen, Ben, 125, 2055, 2807,
4252
Veres, Mariska, 4886
Verghese, Kevin, 1137
Verity Records, 2369, 2951
Verity, John, 223, 1029, 4228
Verlaine, Tom, 812, 2475, 3138,
3286, 3471, 4354, 4642, 4679,
5514, 5633, 6079
Verlaines, 1060, 5633
Vermouth, Apollo C., 662
Vernal, Ewan, 1439, 3138
Verner, David, 1692
Verneuill, Louis, 5901
Verney, Lowell, 3306
Vernie, D.D., 4085
Vernieri, Larry, 1454
Vernin, Ron, 4888
Verno, Jerry, 4467
Vernon Girls, 2203
Vernon, Billy, And The
Celestials, 5749
Vernon, Charles, 5460
Vernon, H.M., 357
Vernon, Kenny, 3255
Vernon, Mike, 49, 477, 554,
602, 612, 629, 1056, 1642, 1953,
2298, 2546, 3558, 4090, 4577,
5633, 5884
Vernon, Ralph, 3789
Vernon, Richard, 4199
Vernon, Virginia, 465
Vernon, Wentworth, 4139-4140
Vernons, 612, 720, 1236, 3279,
5634, 5829
Vernons Girls, 720, 1236, 3279,
5634, 5829
VerPlanck, Billy, 3573, 4302,
5634
VerPlanck, Marlene, 1243,
3573, 3630, 5634-5635
Verrell, Ronnie, 5635, 5810
Verrett, Harrison, 1581
Versalettes, 1586, 5635
Versatiles, 863, 1889, 2138,

2407, 3418, 3554, 5860
Versatility Birds, 544
VerScharen, Joe, 4958
Version, 5635-5636 and passim
Versye, Bernie, 91
Verta-Ray, Matt, 3400
Vertex, 217, 4439
Vertigo Records, 5636 and
passim
Veruca Salt, 1891, 2766, 3205,
5637
Verve, 5637 and passim
Verve Pipe, 5462, 5637
Verve Records, 5637-5638 and
passim
Very Good Eddie, 649, 1031,
2975, 3636, 4338, 5638, 5900
Very Things, 5638 and passim
Vesala, Edward, 35, 171, 3194,
5639
Vesala, Martti, 5639
Vescara, Mike, 4011
Vessel, Jerry, 4464
Vestal, Scott, 622
Vester, Gil, 1259
Vestine, Henry, 916, 1823, 2777,
3809
Vestoff, Virginia, 2664
Vetta, Patti, 3573
Vez, Otra, 1181, 1240, 2234,
3354, 3835, 4117, 4558, 4613,
4618, 4647, 5602
Vezner, Jon, 3516
Viáfara, Andrés, 3938
Viagas, Robert, 1071, 1845, 4771
Vian, Boris, 1955, 6105
Vibert, Rose, 258
Vibes Corner Collective, 2636
Vibrasonic, 5639
Vibrations, 5639 and passim
Vibrato, Prof Vic, 5639
Vibrators, 14, 1854, 2380, 3813,
4294, 4366-4367, 5639-5640
Vibronics, 2761, 5640
Vibronics, Stevie, 5640
Vice Squad, 812, 1077, 1546,
4261, 5640
Viceroys, 1363, 2703, 4546,
5412, 5641, 5735
Vicious Rumors, 5641
Vicious, Sid, 1110, 2258, 3514,
3590, 4185, 4365, 4829-4831,
4899-4900, 4937, 5430, 5641-
5642, 6077
Vick, Harold, 3803
Vick, William, 1896
Vickers, Bernie, 5725
Vickers, Eric, 5307
Vickers, Howie, 1171
Vickers, John, 226
Vickers, Mike, 3437, 5642
Vickers, Robert, 2176
Vickers, Walter, 1780
Vickery, Graham, 4839
Victor, 5642
Victor Records, 5642 and
passim
Victor, Frank, 2535
Victor, Kid Augustin, 2348
Victor, Tommy, 123, 4348
Victor, Tony, 1111
Victor/Victoria, 185-186, 733,
1968, 3433, 4318, 5642-5643
Vidacovich, John, 3763

Vidal, Maria, 1057, 3344
Vidalin, Maurice, 442
Vidican, John, 2926
Vidor, Charles, 2381, 2861, 3337
Vieco, Al, 618
Vienna, Louise, 1125
Vieu, Jane, 247
Vig, Butch, 1518, 1754, 2084,
2480, 2859, 3908, 4724, 4977,
5586
Vigil, Selene, 4827
Vigilante, Lavoe, 1181
Vigliatura, Jack, 1966
Vik Records, 1720, 5421
Vikernes, Varg, 848, 3530
Vikings, 520, 1469, 2054, 4367,
4532, 5643, 5824
Vikstrom, Kenny, 4285
Vikström, Sven-Erik, 5643
Vikström, Thomas, 5643
Vilato, Orestes, 3984, 4097, 4740
Vile Bodies Swing Orchestra,
2971
Villa, Joe, 4672
Villa-Lobos, Heitor, 3727, 5930
Village, 5644
Village Boys, 3542
Village Of Sangoona, 3978
Village People, 911, 1087, 3807,
5537, 5644
Village Stompers, 4883
Villaneuva, Adrian, 4685
Villanueva, Tom, 1488
Villard, Jean, 1196, 4181
Villareal, 187
Villari, Guy, 4489
Villariny, Tommy, 3750
Villasenor, Rico, 3442
Villeneuve, Craig, 2778
Villiers, Doreen, 2124
Villiers, James, 2342
Villon, Francois, 5592
Villot, Julito, 4114
Vinall, Phil, 2112
Viñas, Mike, 577
Vince Melamed, 4687
Vince, Harry, 5655
Vincent Rocks And The
Bluecaps Roll, 622, 5645
Vincent, Bob, 5484, 6083
Vincent, Crawford, 2328
Vincent, David, 3777, 5342
Vincent, Gene, 18, 350, 414,
446, 458, 622, 705, 837-838,
923, 955-956, 1000, 1085, 1142,
1377, 1396, 1437, 1502, 1819,
1981, 2001, 2159, 2203, 2217,
2360, 2432, 2603, 2727, 2868,
3148, 3911, 4088, 4476, 4628,
5495, 5644-5645, 5822, 5900,
6083
Vincent, John, 5645
Vincent, Johnny, 519, 3124,
5645
Vincent, Joyce, 1423
Vincent, June, 911
Vincent, Kim, 1611
Vincent, Larry, 5454
Vincent, Lee, 543, 4424
Vincent, Leo, 2816
Vincent, Monroe, 5645
Vincent, Nick, 566
Vincent, Robby, 4005
Vincent, Roland, 1476

Vincent, Vinnie, 3034, 3884,
5646
Vinchon, Betty, 3379
Vinci, John, 2678
Vincson, Walter, 1166, 3707
Vinding, Mads, 1112
Vine, Emma, 1756
Vinegar Joe, 690, 755, 1127,
1354, 4112, 5646, 5717, 5995
Vinestock, Simon, 4907
Ving, Lee, 1864
Vinnegar, Leroy, 489, 1712,
2128, 2794, 3446, 3666, 5646
Vinson, Eddie 'Cleanhead',
4643
Vinson, Mose, 1432, 2600,
3141, 5647
Vinson, Walter, 5647
Vintage Jazz And Blues Band,
5647-5648
Vinton, Bobby, 186, 1793, 1990,
3041, 3083, 4371, 5648, 6083,
6132
Vinx, 5648
Vinyl Records, 82, 1939, 2388,
3208, 3912, 4342, 4456, 4511,
4587, 4599, 4625, 5539
Vinyl Solution Records, 1939,
2388
Viola, Joe, 492, 1776
Violence, 5649
Violent Femmes, 532, 1498,
2240, 2509, 3979, 4294, 4909,
4944, 5649
Violent J., 2699
Violin, 5650 and passim
Violinski, 5650
Vipers Skiffle Group, 5650,
5756
Vipond, Dougie, 1439, 3138
VIPs, 244, 2417, 5650
Virgin Mary, 319, 495, 1861,
2434, 3139, 3623, 3997
Virgin Prunes, 349, 2033, 5651
Virgin Records, 5651 and
passim
Virgin Steele, 5652
Virginia Cut-ups, 239
Virginia Squires, 5652
Virginia String Band, 2403
Virgo, Jimmy, 3465
Virtue, Frank, 1724, 5652
Virtue, Mickey, 5561
Virtues, 5652 and passim
Visca, Christian, 5617
Visconti, Tony, 84, 106, 152,
272, 529, 685, 721, 1260, 1502,
1522, 1723, 1949, 2118, 2515,
2592, 2729, 2914, 3883, 4229,
4273, 4488, 4797, 5277, 5652
Viscounts, 858, 1297, 2119,
2429, 2635, 2886, 3073, 3684,
5653
Visdson, Brad, 5891
Visser, Erik, 1249
Visser, Jan, 340
Visser, Peter, 510
Vita Records, 1186
Vital Escape, 5653
Vital Information, 2076, 2901
Vitale, Bruce, 4011
Vitale, Joe, 5691
Vitale, Steve, 291
Vitaliano, Genaro Louis, 5593

Watkins, Mack, 2965
Watkins, Mitch, 3765
Watkins, Peter, 4342
Watkins, Sammy, 3484
Watkins, Tom, 760, 1497, 1690, 2657
Watkinson, Nick, 2760
Watkinson, Terry, 3523
Watkiss, Cleveland, 1306, 2191, 2795, 2797, 3643, 3826, 4083, 4458, 5726, 5920
Watkiss, Trevor, 5726
Watley, Jody, 4840, 5727
Watling, Jack, 729
Watmough, Ralph, Jazz Band, 998
Watrous, Bill, 543, 738, 3083, 4428, 4636, 5727
Watson, Alan, 3661
Watson, Arthel, 5728
Watson, Ben, 13, 1295, 5993, 6087
Watson, Betty Jane, 249, 4025
Watson, Bob, 5648
Watson, Bobbie, 1199
Watson, Bobby, 52, 1124, 1481, 2182, 2277, 2708, 3603, 4684, 5543, 5727
Watson, Bruce, 523
Watson, Chris, 382, 559, 875, 1035, 1387
Watson, Dale, 5728
Watson, David, 5651
Watson, Derek, 1074, 4873
Watson, Doc, 254, 270, 580, 1122, 1413, 1931, 1951, 1958, 2650, 3745-3746, 3959, 3996, 4359, 4549, 4816, 4886, 5495, 5728-5729, 5731, 5834, 6084
Watson, Dusty, 3184
Watson, Eric, 3103, 3159, 4145, 6093
Watson, Fraser, 4270, 5492
Watson, Gene, 810, 1143, 2019, 3058, 4698, 5729-5730
Watson, Harry, Jnr., 5446
Watson, Harvey, 4359
Watson, Helen, 940, 1150, 1387, 2839, 2913, 3829, 3922, 4857, 5730, 5997
Watson, Jeff, 3948
Watson, Joe, 765, 1914
Watson, Johnnie, 1001
Watson, Johnny, 52, 69, 575, 1356, 1517, 1523, 1646, 2082, 2519, 2816, 3728, 3858, 4878, 5730-5731, 5853-5854, 5876, 5967, 5991
Watson, Johnny 'Guitar', 1646, 5730-5731
Watson, Junior, 917
Watson, Leo, 825, 955, 5731
Watson, Lloyd, 1716, 3453
Watson, Mamie, 1516
Watson, Martin, 5946
Watson, Mike, 57, 1379
Watson, Milton, 251
Watson, Neil, 4711
Watson, Nigel, 2272, 4299
Watson, Paul, 5611
Watson, Peter, 336
Watson, Reg, 4341
Watson, Roger, 1150, 3829
Watson, Scott, 587

Watson, Stan, 464, 1471
Watson, Stuart, 4911
Watson, Susan, 862
Watson, Valerie, 1137
Watson, Winston A., 4723
Watt, Ben, 1045, 1705, 1801, 3017, 3464, 5731, 6047
Watt, Hamilton Wesley, 1786
Watt, John, 1170
Watt, Mike, 1084, 1600, 1903, 3699, 4302, 5731
Watt, Norman, 61
Watt-Roy, Garth, 1690, 2061, 2261, 2980, 4375
Watters, Cyril, 5732
Watters, Lu, 2444, 2843, 3844, 4513, 4779, 5732
Watters, Lucious, 5732
Watters, Sam, 1181
Wattis, Richard, 1066
Watts 103rd Street Rhythm Band, 5732
Watts Prophets, 5732-5733
Watts, Andy, 4797
Watts, Arthur, 4785
Watts, Barry, 4375
Watts, Bertha, 2112
Watts, Charlie, 1153, 1758, 2346, 2620, 2759, 3065-3066, 4135, 4595, 4628, 4631, 4698, 4950-4951, 5368, 5801, 6067, 6075
Watts, Clem, 3636
Watts, David, 124
Watts, George, 906
Watts, Howard, 1628, 1930
Watts, James, 2277
Watts, Jeff, 5478
Watts, John, 1907, 2382
Watts, Louise Mary, 1081
Watts, Mario, 1577
Watts, Martin, 1426
Watts, Peter, 3814
Watts, Ron, 728
Watts, Skidillion, 2342-2343
Watts, Steve, 728, 1479
Watts, Tony, 1193
Watts, Trevor, 2320, 3286, 3732, 3914, 4702, 5448, 5733
Watts-Russell, Ivo, 1147, 1989, 5396
Wattstax, 3268, 3615, 5733
Watusi, Orlando, 4421
Watwood, Tommy, 1943
WAU! Mr Modo Records, 5733
Wauquaire, Phil, 1821
Wax, 5734
Wax Trax Records, 1896, 2692, 5734
Waxman, Franz, 2034, 3281, 5734-5735
Waxman, Lou, 3723
Way We Live, 438, 2116, 5485, 5735
Way Out West, 903, 1417, 3037, 3447, 4401, 4634, 5696, 5735
Way, Darryl, 1340
Way, Pete, 1106, 1146, 1857, 2829, 5562-5563, 5737
Waybill, Fee, 118, 5521
Waye, Michael, 467
Wayfarers, 660, 5855
Waylon, Nelson, 263, 1149, 2813, 3333, 4499, 4891, 5680, 5745

Waymon, Eunice, 4920
Wayne And Charlie, 2443, 5735
Wayne, Artie, 4304
Wayne, Bob, 524, 1963
Wayne, Bobby, 1718, 2447
Wayne, Carl, 3145, 3819, 5746
Wayne, Chris, 2713, 2878, 3819, 5641, 5735
Wayne, Chuck, 1504, 1534
Wayne, David, 108, 578, 1896, 2384, 2704, 3642, 4107, 4893, 5896
Wayne, Don, 4983
Wayne, Harry, 2949, 3558
Wayne, James, 3167, 3327
Wayne, Jeff, 1780, 1947, 3759, 5736
Wayne, Jerry, 713, 2289, 2322, 2547, 5736
Wayne, John, 54, 370, 905, 1211, 1339, 2034, 2358, 2412, 2430, 2599, 3002, 3253, 3399, 3752, 3896, 4091, 4517, 4623, 5919, 6048
Wayne, Mabel, 325, 1374, 2549, 3225, 4650, 5736
Wayne, Mick, 825, 2631, 2913-2914, 4246
Wayne, Patrick, 5496
Wayne, Paula, 2188
Wayne, Richard, 3270, 3532
Wayne, Sid, 1195
Wayne, Thomas, 1935, 5737
Wayne, Wee Willie, 5737
Waynes, Art, 2938
Wayouts, 3871
Waysted, 1106, 1858, 1952, 3257, 5552, 5563, 5737
Wayward Souls, 5737-5738
Waywha, 5738
WDR Big Band, 3626
We Are Going To Eat You, 5738
We Five, 5556, 5595, 5738, 5770
We Free Kings, 3030, 4204, 5738-5739
We Saw The Wolf, 1233, 5739
We The People, 2017, 2275, 3605, 4139-4140, 4432, 4717, 4773, 4717, 4773, 5690, 5739, 5990
We The Raggamuffin, 3662, 3944
We're Not Dressing, 5739
We've Got A Fuzzbox And We're Gonna Use It, 5739-5740
WEA Records, 5740 and *passim*
Weakley, Michael, 1726
Weapon, 5740
Weapon Of Choice, 3312
Wearen, Shane, 4109
Weather Girls, 873, 5551, 5740
Weather Report, 119, 671, 712, 800, 1775, 1842, 2164, 2338, 2441, 2469, 2841, 3053, 3350, 3780, 3819, 4153, 4457, 4636-4637, 4890, 5653, 5740-5741, 5994, 6084
Weatherall, Andy, 349, 1238, 1273, 1779, 1847, 2379, 2389, 2574, 2681, 2764, 3179, 3257, 3858, 4043, 4066, 4329, 4712, 4725, 4793, 4712, 4725, 4793, 5326, 5574, 5741, 5770
Weatherall, Kevin, 2681

Weatherall, Paul, 2681
Weatherford, Teddy, 368, 5741, 5897
Weatherhead, 3697
Weatherly, Fred E., 1138, 5911
Weatherly, Jim, 5741-5742
Weathers, Barbara, 273
Weathers, John, 1813, 2118, 2257, 3430, 4233, 5824
Weathersby, Carl, 5742
Weathersby, Alan, 986
Weaver, Curley James, 344, 5742
Weaver, Denis, 1339
Weaver, Elviry, 4175
Weaver, Ernie, 3583
Weaver, Fritz, 335
Weaver, Jesse B., 4773
Weaver, Ken, 2046, 4734
Weaver, Louie, 4213
Weaver, Marco, 4332
Weaver, Mick, 1826, 2257, 2423, 3503, 3673, 4693, 5282, 5488, 5742, 5935
Weaver, Sylvester, 2778, 3491, 5742
Weavers, 144, 422, 441, 681, 1076, 1215, 1394, 1624, 2098, 2156, 2234, 2503, 2605, 2810, 2955, 3156, 3394, 3889, 4642, 4811, 5295-5296, 5299, 5456, 5527, 5611, 5743, 5780
Weavers, Houghton, 2605
Webb Family, 4182
Webb, 'Boogie' Bill, 5743
Webb, Artie, 4611
Webb, Bernard, 3548, 4206
Webb, Bill, 5743
Webb, Brenda Gail, 2105
Webb, Chick, 65, 68, 116, 216, 233, 418, 481-482, 629, 852, 963, 973, 1038, 1178, 1280, 1437, 1553, 1912, 1932, 2047, 2268, 2362, 2394, 2417, 2431, 2457, 2518, 2529, 2548, 2573, 2805, 2868, 2883, 2892, 2895, 3027, 3031, 3082, 3388, 3478, 3600, 3664-3665, 3765, 3786, 3799, 3932, 3939, 4345, 4422, 4427, 4731, 4800, 5299, 5309, 5514, 5609, 5743, 5762, 5774, 5841, 5858
Webb, Clara, 2105, 3370
Webb, Clifton, 130, 249-250, 1950, 3273, 4497, 5425
Webb, Danny, 1384
Webb, David, 927, 6038
Webb, Gary, 2570
Webb, Gavin, 3506
Webb, George, 806, 1863, 3326, 4513, 4547, 5744
Webb, Harry Roger, 4530
Webb, Jack, 990, 4206
Webb, Jay Lee, 3343, 3370, 4182
Webb, Jimmy, 118, 629, 752, 905, 1889, 1917, 2146, 2412, 2611, 2876, 3253, 3398, 3486, 4765, 5744-5745, 6128
Webb, June, 3303, 5745
Webb, Keith, 1263, 4495, 4547
Webb, Kenneth, 2100
Webb, Laura, 637
Webb, Lizabeth, 2628
Webb, Marti, 565-566, 932,

Westside Connection, 5779
Westville, Gene Estes, 1176
Westwood, John, 92
Westwood, Liz, 3763
Westwood, Richard, 5498
Westwood, Tim, 3341
Westwood, Vivienne, 3589
Westworld, 807, 3763, 5382
Wet Wet Wet, 5779 and *passim*
Wet Willie, 510, 2349, 3477, 5779
Wettling, George, 2793, 2929, 3993, 4699, 5780
Wetton, John, 256, 1838, 2554, 2619, 2999, 3113, 4219, 4669, 5587, 5650, 5780, 5895, 6084
Wetzel, Ray, 2505
Wetzels, Theo, 4371
Wexler, Dan, 2671
Wexler, Haskell, 680
Wexler, Jerry, 14, 272, 364, 403, 463, 517, 1114, 1515, 1537, 1615, 1662, 1675, 1775, 1870, 2013, 2351, 2731, 3356, 3849, 4718, 4727, 4790, 4891, 5361, 5363, 5512, 5620, 5780, 6084, 6119
Weyel, Eberhard, 50
Weygandt, Gene, 518
Weymouth, Martina, 5287, 5457
Weymouth, Nigel, 244, 2385
Weymouth, Tina, 2384, 3327, 3470, 4498, 5287, 5457
Weyzig, Frank, 5943
Whale, 5780-5781
Whale, Andy, 649
Whale, James, 4892
Whale, Pete, 741, 3027
Whalen, Michael, 4281
Whaley, Ken, 1641-1642, 2482, 5552
Whaley, Paul, 611, 2925
Whalley, Jay, 2030
Whalley, Steve, 2257
Whalley, Wade, 935
Wham!, 33, 62, 526, 797, 1212, 1642, 1739, 1829, 1910, 2018, 2204, 2825, 2834, 3157, 3390, 3652-3653, 3874, 4029, 4192, 4974, 5330, 5343, 5376, 5781, 5849, 6064, 6084
Wharton, Alex, 3805
Wharton, Darren, 1389
Wharton, Gib, 2573
Wharton, Mark Ramsey, 55, 990
What A Crazy World, 778, 5781
What Are Records?, 4730
What Lola Wants, 1370, 5782
What Makes Sammy Run?, 112, 846, 2619, 3148, 4863, 5782, 6097
What's Up Tiger Lily, 5783
Whatnauts, 3734, 5783
Wheat, Brian, 5345
Wheatley, Glen, 3271, 3507
Wheatley, Phyllis, 174
Wheatley, Tim, 2229
Wheaton, Ann, 4020, 5432
Wheatstraw, Nick, 3299
Wheatstraw, Peetie, 239, 826, 1388, 1656, 2551, 2852, 2891, 4446, 5784, 6084
Wheeler, Audrey, 2740
Wheeler, Bert, 5433

Wheeler, Big, 1124, 5784-5785
Wheeler, Billy Edd, 688, 5784
Wheeler, Caron, 765, 1605, 1962, 3083, 3345, 3887, 4037, 5566, 5784
Wheeler, Cheryl, 5785
Wheeler, Edd, 688, 5784
Wheeler, Golden, 5784-5785
Wheeler, Harold, 5883
Wheeler, Hubie, 5844
Wheeler, Hugh, 874, 913, 2708
Wheeler, Ian, 374, 1189, 2890, 3503, 5579
Wheeler, John, 1465, 1564, 2032, 2431, 4856
Wheeler, Karen, 4188
Wheeler, Kenny, 67, 172, 224, 299, 603, 718, 770, 788, 800, 1001, 1076, 1124, 1150, 1172, 1287, 1383, 1465, 1701, 1863, 2031-2032, 2172, 2431, 2559, 2595, 2632, 2882, 2890, 3140, 3350, 3407, 3478, 3519, 4135, 4374, 4697, 4856, 5315, 5579, 5659, 5711, 5785, 5810, 5887
Wheeler, Onie, 5786
Wheeler, Paul, 301, 1076, 5784
Wheeler, Steve, 770, 1863, 3887
Wheeler, Tim, 251
Wheeling Jamboree, The, 134, 373, 580, 972, 1198, 1227, 1419, 1685, 2075, 2097, 2173, 2184, 2249, 2315, 2377, 2439, 2695, 2751, 3305, 3514, 3771, 4067, 4503-4504, 4573, 4619, 4787, 4978-4979, 5786
Wheels, 5786-5787
Wheels, Dave, 2523, 4836
Whelan, Albert, 1374
Whelan, Andy, 4102
Whelan, Bernie, 3113
Whelan, Dave, 4459
Whelan, Gary, 2384
Whelan, Gavan, 2769
Whelan, Thomas, 4109
Whelan, Tim, 2058, 2523
Wheland, Gerard, 169
Whelans, Mike, 699
When People Were Shorter And Lived Near The Water, 4880
Where The Boys Are, 1086, 1960, 2006-2007, 5787
Where's Charley?, 5787-5788
Wherry, Jake, 2501
Whetherall, Winston, 5275
Whetsol, Artie, 552, 1734, 5788
Whetstine, John, 1776
Whetstone, Dave, 3032
Whetstone, Richard, 1726
Which Witch, 1616, 4229, 5788
Whigby, Mandy, 3257, 4576
Whigfield, 4276, 5788
Whigham, Haydn, 5789
Whigham, Jiggs, 1704, 5789
While, Chris, 784, 928, 1171, 1387, 1905, 3519, 4236, 4574, 4857, 5525
Whiley, Jo, 4588, 5467, 5704
Whimple, Essie, 4471
Whiplash, 2673, 2769, 2912, 2991, 3398, 3812, 3985, 5509
Whipped Cream, 147, 821, 5789
Whippersnapper, 254, 1377,

2588, 2811, 5439, 5789
Whipping Boy, 4909, 5789
Whipple, Armide, 2287
Whirlwind, 5790 and *passim*
Whiskey, Nancy, 1246, 2188, 3561-3562, 5459, 5790
Whiskeyhill Singers, 1854, 3022, 3650, 5790
Whiskeytown, 4027
Whisky Priests, 633, 1097, 5790
Whispers, 5791 and *passim*
Whistler, Kevin, 601
Whitaker, David, 1385
Whitaker, Forest, 543, 3209
Whitaker, Hugh, 2608-2609, 4824
Whitaker, Jessie, 4243
Whitaker, Ruby, 1050
Whitaker, Steve, 390
Whitbread, Paul, 4358
Whitburn, Joel, 537, 4325, 6093, 6118-6119
Whitby, Francis, 4198
Whitby, John, 513, 2219
Whitby, Susan, 3315
Whitcomb, Dale, 635
Whitcomb, Ian, 5791, 6035, 6090, 6118
White Buffaloes, 2240
White Christmas, 153, 494, 668, 1133, 1161, 1303-1304, 2267, 2946, 3176, 4219, 4771, 5632, 5703, 5791-5792
White Hots, 2778
White Lion, 119, 189, 1271, 1378, 2019-2020, 3003, 5502, 5541, 5552, 5792, 5945
White Plains, 846, 959, 1218, 1706, 1905, 1946, 2730, 4252, 5792-5793
White Sisters, 5625
White Spirit, 2148, 2711, 5793
White Town, 2197, 5793
White Whale Records, 1799, 3020
White Witch, 2181
White Zombie, 560, 2126, 3002, 5346, 5793
White's, George, Scandals, 5794
White, 'Schoolboy' Cleve, 5794
White, Alan, 146, 356, 459, 2000, 2619, 2672, 3191, 4008, 4262, 5957
White, Andrew, 1186, 1689, 5794, 6041
White, Andy, 1236, 1898, 2604, 5794
White, Anthony, 1157, 2619
White, Artie 'Blues Boy', 5795
White, Barry, 524, 731, 911, 913, 1078, 1375, 1626, 2601, 2694, 2830, 2932, 3081, 3136, 3204, 3209, 3283, 3338-3339, 3419, 4137, 5313, 5378, 5617, 5795, 5868
White, Bill, 158, 1966, 2275, 3700
White, Bob, 70, 1197, 2354, 3469
White, Brett, 2281
White, Bruce, 4682
White, Buck, 4753, 5796, 5802
White, Buddy, 3961

White, Bukka, 2090, 2778, 3008-3009, 3594, 3833, 4159, 4693, 4721, 5642, 5655, 5796
White, Calvin, 4737
White, Carl, 194, 3119, 4561
White, Carol, 3401, 4281
White, Charles, 1136, 3220, 3271, 6060, 6122
White, Charlie, 5698
White, Chris, 3807, 6001
White, Christine, 110
White, Clarence, 869, 1109, 2222, 2275, 2829, 2955, 2973, 3616, 3835, 3879, 4145, 5541, 5796, 6105
White, Clifford, 3120, 5797
White, Daniel, 405, 616, 3515
White, Danny, 1977, 3777, 4256
White, Dave, 1384-1385, 3579
White, David, 3204, 3806, 4256, 4807
White, Don, 730, 5760
White, Edward, 5797, 6109
White, Effie, 1625
White, Eric, 2973, 5308
White, Ernie, 291
White, Forrest, 1874
White, Franklyn, 5325, 5577
White, George, 435, 1059, 1517, 1911, 2121, 2159, 2651, 2841, 3044, 4519, 5794, 5797, 6044
White, George L., 1911
White, Georgia, 4580, 5798
White, Gladys, 2489
White, Glodean, 5795
White, Gonzel, 405
White, Grace, 3771
White, H.C., 5796
White, Harold, 3635
White, J.D., 3123
White, James, 1215, 2090, 3777, 5798, 5951, 6086
White, Jane, 4042, 4513, 4590
White, Jeff, 3075
White, Jim, 1540
White, Joe, 989, 2622, 3209, 3832, 4159, 4296, 4884, 5695, 5800-5801
White, John, 1156, 1186, 3833, 4859, 5798, 5951
White, John I., 5798
White, Josh, 64, 759-760, 1015, 1093, 1294, 1836, 2351, 2573, 2728, 3074, 3156, 3302, 3571, 3804, 5281, 5495, 5607, 5684, 5799
White, Joy, 781, 1172, 1203, 1537, 2489, 3071, 5290, 5757, 5799
White, Joy Lynn, 781, 1172, 1203, 1537, 2489, 5757, 5799
White, Karyn, 3093
White, Ken, 1119
White, Kenny, 4111
White, Kitty, 2339
White, L.E., 329
White, Lari, 1219, 5420
White, Lavelle, 2844, 5799
White, Lenny, 2297, 4483, 4510, 5799-5800
White, Lillias, 3238-3239
White, Lulu, 5858
White, Lynn, 781, 1172, 1203, 1537, 2489, 5757, 5799-5800

White, Mac, 4150

White, Mark, 39, 1732, 2303, 3614, 6105, 6118

White, Martin, 1161, 1354, 2724

White, Maurice, 273, 1509, 1651, 1689, 1756, 3224, 5843

White, Michael, 2376, 2495, 3541, 4372, 5661, 5792, 5800, 6088

White, Mick, 3644

White, Norma, 5408

White, Onna, 862, 3852, 4033

White, Pete, 4464

White, Peter, 168

White, Priscilla, 564, 999

White, Ralph, 321, 1545

White, Ray, 981, 1394, 4093

White, Reuben, 925, 1050

White, Richard, 441, 2407, 2955, 6060

White, Rick, 1773

White, Robert, 1492, 3212, 5298

White, Roger, 1799, 3879, 6047

White, Roland, 1252, 3745, 3878

White, Ronnie, 3700, 4585, 5907

White, Sam, 2889

White, Sammy, 2160, 2277, 3281, 4893

White, Sheila, 3268

White, Simon, 109, 3628

White, Snowy, 4653, 5390

White, Sonny, 2348, 3119

White, Stan, 3650

White, Steve, 337, 1184, 2813, 4893, 5314, 5760

White, Sylvan, 5319

White, Tam, 677, 5800

White, Ted, 2013, 3106

White, Teddy, 5797

White, Tim, 82, 2000, 2604

White, Timothy, 163, 427, 3469, 4534, 5472, 5842, 6032, 6062, 6085, 6118

White, Tony, 70, 989, 1392, 2622, 3764, 4682, 5695, 5800-5801

White, Tony Joe, 989, 2622, 5695, 5800-5801

White, Trevor, 2818, 2889, 4402

White, Walter, 2778, 5800

White, Willard, 4287

White, William, 4093

White, Williard, 1406

White-Irving, J.H., 1012

Whitehead, Alan, 3470

Whitehead, Annie, 3883, 4135, 5801, 5920

Whitehead, Don, 1689

Whitehead, John, 3568

Whitehead, Martin, 1930

Whitehead, Neville, 4244

Whitehead, Paul, 975

Whitehead, Peter, 5462, 5644

Whitehead, Steve, 412, 3382

Whitehead, Tim, 412, 3312, 5801

Whitehorn, Geoff, 317, 4344

Whitehouse, Dick, 1491

Whitehouse, Jay, 1263

Whiteley, Ken, 543

Whiteman, Ian, 58, 2327, 3658, 5414

Whiteman, Paul, 19, 77, 91, 178, 205, 218, 289, 308, 332,

395, 420, 455, 483, 491, 505, 579, 823, 829, 897, 1009, 1022, 1302, 1304, 1403, 1482, 1598-1599, 1961, 1976, 2027, 2042, 2095, 2128, 2186, 2193, 2284, 2295, 2449, 2486, 2528, 2911, 2957, 3002, 3019, 3028-3029, 3125, 3142, 3250, 3281, 3359, 3417, 3425, 3565, 3629, 3733, 3941, 3975, 4075, 4111, 4214, 4263, 4380, 4413, 4430, 4457, 4519, 4522, 4650-4651, 4903, 5299, 5322, 5416, 5425, 5439, 5515, 5631, 5678, 5736, 5780, 5801-5802, 5814, 5832, 5931, 5964, 6084

Whiteman, Steve, 3040

Whiteman, Wilberforce, 3028-3029, 3359

Whiteout, 5802

Whiteread, Rachel, 3043

Whites, 5802

Whiteside, David, 4435

Whitesnake, 88, 98, 107, 275, 307, 311, 601, 610, 613, 639, 652, 744, 832, 1141, 1182, 1263, 1271, 1458, 1461, 1589, 2109, 2234, 2393, 2454, 2645, 3036, 3380, 3475, 3879, 3936, 4100, 4219, 4299, 4834, 4849, 4943, 4946, 4952, 5489, 5511, 5552, 5562, 5592, 5610, 5802-5803, 5824, 6085

Whitfield, Alice, 2756

Whitfield, Anne, 5792

Whitfield, Barrence, 4700, 5803

Whitfield, Cyrus, 654

Whitfield, David, 95, 241, 505, 4493, 4574, 4676, 5803-5804

Whitfield, Joe, 3238

Whitfield, Johnny, 654

Whitfield, June, 51

Whitfield, Mark, 4990

Whitfield, Norman, 1135, 1824, 2083, 2560, 2965, 3048, 4354, 4435, 5334, 5576, 5625, 5804

Whitfield, Thomas, 68

Whitfield, Weslia, 3573, 5804

Whitford, Brad, 82-83, 4199

Whiting, Barbara, 1379

Whiting, George, 282, 350, 493, 1587

Whiting, Jack, 2589, 4606, 4719, 5283

Whiting, Margaret, 354, 666, 782, 849, 1379, 1482, 1622, 2775, 3073, 3573, 4493, 4958, 5438, 5469, 5582, 5672-5673, 5777, 5804-5806

Whiting, Richard, 103, 522, 782, 1379, 1622, 2923, 3197, 3629, 3751, 4044, 4338, 4493, 4580, 5283, 5805

Whiting, Steve, 3708, 4719

Whitley, Chris, 1083, 5806

Whitley, Keith, 239, 338, 1206, 1314, 1339, 1508, 2051, 2355, 2736, 3075, 3618, 3785, 4086, 4710, 4946-4947, 5806

Whitley, Ray, 268, 894, 3365, 4499, 5291, 5806

Whitlock, Bobby, 1470, 1489, 2455

Whitman, Byron, 5808

Whitman, Paul, 4967, 5350

Whitman, Slim, 704, 707, 971, 1080, 1206, 1280, 1339, 2456, 2598, 2682, 3302, 3326, 4499, 4967, 5807-5808, 6085

Whitmore, Andy, 4985

Whitmore, George, 2026

Whitmore, James, 3035, 4025-4026

Whitnall, Tim, 2203

Whitney, Chapman, 362, 1020-1021, 1838, 4030

Whitney, Charlie, 293, 1838, 1847, 1865

Whitney, Delmos, 3884

Whitney, Eleanore, 522

Whitney, Joan, 1402, 3073, 4070

Whitney, Joe, 1925

Whitney, John, 2139, 2262

Whitney, Leonard, 4958

Whitney, Lou, 3780-3781

Whitney, Malika Lee, 3469, 6062

Whitney, Marva, 1634

Whitney, Steve, 4823, 5808

Whitney, Steve, Band, 4823, 5808

Whitsell, George, 4596

Whitsell, Leon, 4596

Whitsett, Carson, 664

Whitstein Brothers, 3333, 5808

Whitstein, Charles, 3333, 5808-5809

Whitstein, R.C., 5808

Whitstein, Robert, 3333, 5808

Whitt Brothers, 5809

Whittaker, Natalie, 5810

Whittaker, Roger, 4215, 5809-5810

Whittaker, Tim, 1443-1444

Whitten, Chris, 3549, 5721

Whitten, Danny, 1284, 4596, 5977

Whitten, Jessie, 2464

Whitter, Henry, 1364, 2255, 2403, 5810

Whittier, Jim, 1492

Whittingham, Jack, 3260

Whittingham, Richard, 889, 4060

Whittinghill, Whit, 4237

Whittington, Bill, 748, 1839

Whittle, Tommy, 385, 1075, 2411, 2595, 2791, 4225, 4374, 4948, 5332, 5340, 5409, 5635, 5810

Whitwam, Barry, 2504

Whitworth, Gene, 2039

Who, 5810-5812 and passim

Who's Tommy, The, 5813 and passim

Whodini, 908, 1460, 1567, 1727, 2826, 3283, 3342, 4992, 5560, 5727, 5813-5814

Whodunit Band, 2950

Wholey, Dennis, 4819

Whooliganz, 4376, 5814

Whoopee!, 491-492, 920, 1587-1588, 1785, 2035, 2227, 2596, 2922, 2952, 2958, 3182, 3281, 3619, 3921, 4036, 4926, 5582, 5749, 5814, 5999

Whoopee! (stage musical), 5814

Whorf, Richard, 624, 5436, 5948

Why, Johnny, 3770

Whycliffe, 5815

Whycliffe, Donovan, 5815

Whyke, Roy, 51

Whylie, Majorie, 2795

Whyte Boots, 848

Whyte, Duncan, 2186

Whyte, Ronny, 719, 5815

Whyte, Tom, 3769

Whyte, Zack, 378, 948, 1010, 1368, 1513, 3904, 4035, 4582, 4800

Whyton, Wally, 5650, 5815

Wibberley, Frank, 975

Wicked Maraya, 67, 5816

Wickens, Barry, 2681

Wickens, Holger, 1034

Wickersham, Johnny, 880

Wickes, Mary, 2523, 3852, 5792

Wickett, Andy, 1657

Wickham, Alan, 1382

Wickham, Brad, 1773

Wickham, Chrissie, 2601

Wickham, Steve, 2687, 5721

Wickham, Vicki, 3100, 4454

Wickman, Dick, 5816

Wickman, Putte, 1582, 3221, 3716, 5816

Wicks, John, 4459

Wicks, Johnny, 542

Wicks, Tommy, 4820

Wicksten, Par, 5696

Wiczling, Dogdan, 1895

Wide And Handsome, 2523, 2976, 3118, 3429

Widelitz, Stacy, 1539

Widemann, Benoit, 3410

Widerberg, Noel, 1474

Widger, Paul, 1132

Widlake, Terry, 4085

Widmark, Richard, 2596

Widmoser, Christopher, 1481

Widowmaker (UK), 5816

Widowmaker (USA), 5816

Wied, Steve, 5835

Wiedemeier, Chrigi, 4823, 5808

Wiederhorn, Jon, 4765

Wiedlin, Jane, 936, 2176, 3138, 5817, 5984

Wiedoeft, Rudy, 843, 2841, 4760

Wiedoft, Herb, 5817

Wiendoeft, Rudy, 4036

Wiener, Stu, 1200

Wienevski, Matt, 1349

Wietz, George, 5797

Wig Records, 128

Wigan's Chosen Few, 5817

Wiggan, Audley, 2704

Wigges, James, 239

Wiggins, Dwayne, 4921

Wiggins, Gene, 957

Wiggins, Gerry, 895, 5817-5818

Wiggins, Herb, 4198

Wiggins, John, 146, 1504, 1510, 3279, 5818, 6039

Wiggins, John And Audrey, 5818

Wiggins, Keith, 2238

Wiggins, Little Roy, 237, 660, 1229, 2481, 5818

Wiggins, Phil, 1004, 5818

Wiggins, Raphael, 31, 5464

Wiggins, Roland, 1981

Wiggins, Roy, 237, 660, 1229, 2481, 5818

Williams, Taff, 4233
Williams, Teddy, 1990, 3351, 4230, 5655
Williams, Terence, 1480
Williams, Terry, 725, 1537, 1707, 3338, 3429-3430, 3813, 3911, 4279, 4599, 4621, 4873, 4897
Williams, Tex, 805, 923, 1223, 3057, 3541, 3983, 4188, 4625, 5415, 5480, 5495, 5858-5859
Williams, Tig, 4330
Williams, Tim, 5941
Williams, Tom, 275, 5841, 6085
Williams, Tony, 23, 571, 969, 1341, 1414, 1424, 1757, 1778, 1977, 2053, 2076, 2374, 2538, 2684, 2876, 3239, 3285, 3291, 3415, 3590, 3664, 3678, 3861, 4081, 4263, 4358, 4483, 4560, 4562, 4640, 4645, 4664, 4891, 4957, 5359, 5850, 5859
Williams, Travis, 2432, 5480
Williams, Trevor, 277, 2906
Williams, Troy, 2466
Williams, Trudy, 4943
Williams, Tyrone, 1156, 4668
Williams, Vanessa, 1268, 2956, 3632, 5403, 5859
Williams, Vaughan, 2225, 2399, 3285, 5717
Williams, Vern, 1796, 3400
Williams, Victoria, 2792, 3245, 5855, 5860
Williams, Walter, 3146, 3180, 4002
Williams, Wendell, 337
Williams, Wendi, 4455
Williams, Wendy O., 2117, 4261
Williams, Willie, 767, 1569, 5644, 5847, 5860, 5862, 5945
Williams, Winnie, 3089
Williamson, Claude, 4844, 5861
Williamson, Cliff, 1696
Williamson, Heather, 2513
Williamson, James, 2580, 2676, 3863, 4492, 5861
Williamson, John, 1306, 3547, 5861-5862
Williamson, John Lee 'Sonny Boy', 621, 3415, 4362, 5708, 5861
Williamson, Kitty, 3997
Williamson, Lisa, 4942
Williamson, Robin, 1179, 2276, 2508, 2680, 2689, 2992, 3782, 3883, 4110, 4502, 5352, 5861, 6085
Williamson, Roy, 1238
Williamson, Skeets, 328, 376, 3999
Williamson, Sonny Boy 'Rice Miller', 1039, 1049, 1338, 2626, 2771, 3144, 3551, 4351, 5708, 5777, 5833, 5862-5863
Williamson, Steve, 411, 582, 1306, 1571, 2191, 2702, 3826, 4083, 4458, 5477, 5588, 5720, 5863
Williamson, Wade, 715
Williamson, Warren, 5884
Willie And The Poor Boys, 348, 1288-1289, 5935
Willie D, 1351, 2131

Willie, Joe, 3342, 4197, 4421, 4477, 5595, 5647, 5708, 5833
Willie, Washboard, 2018, 3824, 5708, 5715
Willing, Foy, 2339, 3357, 5863
Willingham, Doris, 1646
Willingham, Jimmy, 4153
Willington, Cecil, 3944
Willis Brothers, 655, 5818, 5863-5864
Willis, Aaron 'Little Sonny', 3273
Willis, Alan, 1483, 4642
Willis, Bobby, 564
Willis, Brian, 4378
Willis, Bruce, 500, 711, 1686, 3567, 5864
Willis, Carolyn, 607, 2581
Willis, Carroll, 1280
Willis, Chick, 1166
Willis, Chuck, 1033, 1222, 2068, 2071, 4024, 4521, 4787, 4800, 5864
Willis, David, 3718, 3891
Willis, Ian, 4598
Willis, Jez, 5589
Willis, Kelly, 2970, 3137, 5864
Willis, Larry, 380, 4858
Willis, Milton, 3960
Willis, Pete, 1461, 2182, 4564
Willis, Ralph, 593, 2618, 5715, 5864
Willis, Rollie, 1033
Willis, Roy, 1032
Willis, Ted, 1280, 2725
Willis, Vic, 5864
Willis, Victor, 5644
Willison, Mike, 1891
Willman, Tyler, 2263
Willmer, Eric, 1739
Willner, A.M., 3185
Willner, Hal, 845, 2033, 2796
Willock, Dave, 2081
Willoughby, Mike, 5584
Willow Spring, 664, 1301, 3455
Willows, 1510, 2181, 2391, 2396, 2418, 3012, 4353, 5372, 5864-5865
Willows, Glen, 2396
Wills Fiddle Band, 781
Wills, Alan, 3324, 3450
Wills, Billy Jack, 3774, 5865-5866
Wills, Bob, 19, 257, 642, 700, 765, 769, 781, 945, 1123, 1223, 1256, 1357, 1652-1653, 1756, 2156-2157, 2254, 2334, 2456, 2517, 2617, 2708, 2872-2873, 2956, 3240, 3542, 3566, 3672, 3719, 3774, 3899, 3931, 3997, 4091, 4143, 4171, 4187-4188, 4325, 4441, 4499, 4575, 4726, 4728, 4750, 4841, 5378, 5436, 5460, 5673, 5678, 5865-5868, 5893, 6081, 6085
Wills, John, 3311, 4824, 5865
Wills, Johnnie Lee, 104, 4440, 4842, 5865-5868
Wills, Luke, 5866, 5868
Wills, Luther J, 5868
Wills, Mark, 3450, 5868
Wills, Martin, 563
Wills, Nat, 3200
Wills, Oscar, 5279

Wills, Rick, 1141, 1975, 2005, 4669, 4974
Wills, Robin, 390
Wills, Viola, 5795, 5868
Willsher, Pete, 5762-5763
Willson, Meredith, 3852, 5868-5869
Willson, Rick, 1519
Willson-Piper, Marty, 123, 1082-1083, 3652
Willsteed, John, 2176
Willy Wonka And The Chocolate Factory, 733, 1418, 3927
Wilmer X, 5869
Wilmer, Valerie, 674, 2795, 2798, 3575
Wilmot, Al, 3242
Wilmot, Gary, 1228-1229, 2205, 3443
Wilmott, Anthony, 3866
Wilner, A.M., 605
Wilner, Hal, 958, 3740
Wilsey, Frankie, 217, 4796
Wilsh, Mike, 1994
Wilsher, Mark, 1830
Wilsher, Mick, 3921
Wilson Phillips, 163, 1755, 2391, 4222, 4224, 4763, 5869-5870
Wilson, 'Kid' Wesley, 5870
Wilson, Al, 1611, 2082, 3068, 4340, 4484, 5870
Wilson, Alan, 916, 2585
Wilson, Allan, 3406, 5904
Wilson, Andy, 2173, 2575, 3006
Wilson, Ann, 1922, 2458
Wilson, Anthony, 1660, 5873
Wilson, B.J., 1144, 2914, 3164, 4126, 4344
Wilson, Barrie, 635
Wilson, Barry, 13, 2829
Wilson, Ben, 663, 5341
Wilson, Bernard, 3621
Wilson, Bert, 3348
Wilson, Bob, 2137, 2585, 2673, 5321
Wilson, Bobby, 870, 2755, 4852
Wilson, Brad, 702
Wilson, Brent, 5701
Wilson, Brian, 146, 163, 195, 336, 424-427, 504, 905, 936, 1333, 1404, 1758, 1958, 2036, 2285, 2521, 2581, 2583, 2612, 2780, 2808, 2858, 3334, 3373, 3753, 3849, 4140-4141, 4206, 4222, 4354-4355, 4541, 4551, 4560, 4722, 4978, 5450, 5454, 5589, 5649, 5715, 5869-5870, 6032, 6085
Wilson, Bryce, 299, 1016, 2296, 5543
Wilson, Carl, 424-425, 427, 3000, 4692, 5870-5871, 5996
Wilson, Cassandra, 96, 681, 1159, 1169, 3245, 4071, 5871
Wilson, Cec, And The Panhandlers, 3490
Wilson, Charlie, 606, 3618, 6132
Wilson, Chris, 390, 1924, 3312, 3338, 6132
Wilson, Cindy, 303
Wilson, Clive, 785, 4398
Wilson, Clyde, 3432, 4045

Wilson, Danny, 525, 1385, 3466, 4930
Wilson, Delroy, 111, 512, 562, 610, 758, 877, 1557, 1569, 2138, 2254, 2575, 2581, 2623, 2700, 3006, 3018, 3282, 3461, 3670, 3802, 4199, 4545, 4801, 4946, 5409, 5487, 5860, 5871-5872
Wilson, Dennis, 424-426, 2036, 2226, 5313, 5550, 5871-5872, 6086, 6132
Wilson, Dick, 1135, 1270, 2842, 2934, 3028, 5341, 5872, 6056
Wilson, Don, 5629
Wilson, Dooley, 604, 877, 2523, 2644
Wilson, Earl, 1357, 3068, 4214, 4930, 6078
Wilson, Ed, 1367, 2602
Wilson, Edith, 5873
Wilson, Eileen, 506, 3635, 4070
Wilson, Eric, 703
Wilson, Ernest, 1063, 1097, 1569, 2138, 3018, 3575, 4546
Wilson, Errol, 2351, 4674
Wilson, Frank, 1143, 1997, 2565, 3659, 4982, 5703, 5874
Wilson, Garland, 5704, 5873
Wilson, Gary, 246
Wilson, Gerald, 169, 703, 814, 1004, 1124, 1171, 1221, 1296, 1579, 2516, 2574, 2648, 2750, 2842, 2845, 2867, 3212, 3545, 4090, 4191, 4786, 5297, 5530, 5770, 5873, 5877, 5980
Wilson, Gordon, 3335
Wilson, Grace, 226, 3881
Wilson, Gus, 5500, 5747
Wilson, Hank, 704, 4699
Wilson, Happy, 2315, 2615
Wilson, Harding 'Hop', 5873-5874
Wilson, Harold, 22, 999, 1056, 3819, 4808
Wilson, Harry, 2173, 2642, 3019
Wilson, Huary, 5880
Wilson, Ian, 2257, 4180, 4713
Wilson, Irene, 2501, 5874
Wilson, J., 1143-1144, 2914, 3164, 4126, 4344, 4982, 5874, 6032
Wilson, J. Frank, 1143, 4982, 5874
Wilson, J. Frank, And The Cavaliers, 1143, 4982, 5874
Wilson, Jackie, 56, 162, 343, 787, 800, 1194, 1215, 1224, 1396, 1404, 1407, 1497, 1595, 2073, 2112, 2217, 2559, 2755, 2769, 2844, 2852, 3215, 3557, 4077, 4585, 4656, 4720, 4836, 5354, 5374, 5388, 5465, 5698, 5765, 5874-5875, 5878, 6086
Wilson, Jake, 1109, 3834
Wilson, Jeremy, 1504
Wilson, Jim, 606, 2099
Wilson, Jimmy, 1249, 2461, 3969, 5403, 5875, 5877
Wilson, Jodie, 5875
Wilson, Joe, 1111, 1262
Wilson, John, 122, 442, 3018, 3637, 4390, 4452, 5300, 5383, 5869
Wilson, Johnny, 814, 3155, 5873

Woodmansey, Mick, 685
Woodroffe, Patrick, 2276
Woodroffe, Pete, 1670
Woodrow, Craig, 1146
Woodruff, Bob, 5913
Woodruff, Barbara, 3964
Woodruff, John, 4652, 4754, 6076
Woodruffe, Jezz, 4260
Woods, Adam, 1922, 6004
Woods, Arthur, 2383
Woods, Aubrey, 1946
Woods, Belita, 5576
Woods, Bernie, 2938
Woods, Bob, 5525
Woods, Bobby, 5874
Woods, Brian, 5495
Woods, Carol, 625, 2205, 3322, 4209
Woods, Danny, 1006-1007
Woods, Donald, 3608, 3947, 5690, 5906
Woods, Erika, 4680
Woods, Gay, 5914
Woods, Gay And Terry, 2422, 5914
Woods, Geoff, 4236
Woods, Georgie, 1905
Woods, Harry, 603, 1207, 1555, 1797, 2726, 2863, 5914
Woods, Holly, 5471
Woods, Ilene, 1544
Woods, Jimmy, 3718
Woods, John, 2938, 5646
Woods, Johnny, 3564, 5915
Woods, Lesley, 277
Woods, Mark, 3114
Woods, Melanie, 4900
Woods, Oscar, 552, 1410, 5915
Woods, Paul, 2932
Woods, Phil, 159, 403, 410, 445, 738, 865, 913, 1137, 1162, 1424, 1850, 1928, 2076, 2152, 2300, 2311, 2403, 2508, 2632, 2795, 3183, 3553, 3780, 4069, 4157, 4361-4362, 4761, 4971, 5344, 5690, 5852, 5879, 5915-5916
Woods, Sheryl, 4893
Woods, Sonny, 353, 865, 913
Woods, Terrell, 306
Woods, Terry, 814, 2422, 2942, 4270, 5914
Woods, Wayne, 955
Woods-Wright, Tomica, 4703
Woodson, Craig, 5579
Woodson, Mary, 2267
Woodstock, 5916 and *passim*
Woodstock Festival, 150, 1145, 1307, 1674, 1697, 1720, 1776, 2046, 2423, 2434, 2491, 2802, 2829, 3615, 3816, 4405, 4740, 4802, 4832, 4845, 4915, 4973, 5337, 5599, 5683, 5916-5917, 6086, 6117
Woodward, Alun, 1472
Woodward, Ben, 4180
Woodward, Dave, 3013
Woodward, Davey, 739
Woodward, Edward, 1563, 2522, 4784, 5736, 5917
Woodward, Kaye, 413
Woodward, Keren, 357
Woodward, Mark, 2887
Woodward, Pat, 2705

Woodward, Robert, 1919, 3236
Woody Paul, 1853, 4541, 6074
Woody, Dan, 2460, 4836
Woodyard, Sam, 813, 4128, 5912, 5917
Woolam, Steve, 1725
Wooldridge, Gaby, 3249
Wooler, Bob, 999, 1852, 2518
Wooler, John, 2911
Wooley, Bruce, 1576
Wooley, Sheb, 1122, 2647, 5917-5918
Woolf, Julia, 1744
Woolf, Simon, 1403
Woolf, Walter, 1252
Woolfe Records, 1507
Woolfe, Tom, 3379
Woolfenden, Guy, 5549
Woolfolk, Andrew, 1689
Woolfson, Eric, 4144
Woolfson, Richard, 5479
Woollard, Ken, 898
Woollcott, Alexander, 2940
Woolley, Monty, 350, 2906, 3033, 3947, 4042
Woolley, Shep, 5918
Woolley, Stan, 3783, 4608
Woolnough, Peter, 133
Woolpackers, 5918
Woolsey, Phil, 2905
Woolsey, Robert, 4284, 5433
Woolverton, Linda, 3256
Wooly Mammoth, Are You My Mother?, 1988
Woon, Basil, 1939
Woonton, Andrew, 2631
Woosey, Dominic, 4460
Wooster, Bertie, 2801, 3921, 5900-5901
Wooten, Roy, 1932
Wooten, Victor, 1932
Wooton, Roger, 1199
Wootton, Bob, 963
Wootton, Brenda, 4910, 5919
Wootton, Miles, 5919
Wootwell, Tom, 509
Wopat, Tom, 818
Worchell, August, 2838
Word Records, 198, 422, 1943, 2264, 2340, 2369, 3659, 3782, 4271, 5403
Word Sound And Power, 172, 1062, 1082, 2318, 4514, 5473
Words And Music (film musical), 5919
Words And Music (stage musical), 5919-5920
Words And Pictures, 38, 142, 871, 1595, 4930, 6029-6030, 6037-6038, 6044, 6059, 6078, 6088
Wordsworth, Linda, 3922
Wordsworth, Richard, 3288
Working Week, 1511, 1825, 2053, 3379, 3857, 4572, 5395, 5753, 5801, 5920
Workman, Brandon, 4955
Workman, Geoff, 1575, 2332
Workman, Reggie, 872, 1185, 1295, 1344, 2683, 2783, 3114, 3174, 3576, 5920
World Circuit Records, 817, 1290, 2200, 3059, 4738, 4746, 4758, 4902, 5477

World Domination Enterprises, 5921
World Domination Records, 4356, 5921
World Famous Supreme Team Show, 3590, 5921
World In Pain, 4348
World Music Records, 3341
World Of Trombones, 2372, 4583
World Of Twist, 1685, 1948, 5921-5922
World Party, 1059, 1486, 2205, 2671, 5721, 5922
World Saxophone Quartet, 561, 634, 2483, 3114, 3846, 5922
World War III, 1091, 1374, 1622, 5363, 5922
World's Greatest Jazz Band, 5922-5923
Worley, Jo Anne, 441
Worley, Paul, 3542
Worloou, Lambros, 2307
Woronzow Records, 512-513
Worrall, Bruce, 4872
Worrall, Simon, 4128
Worrell, Bernie, 1061, 1131, 1174, 2416, 4404
Worrell, Lewis, 5321
Worsley, Tony, 3449
Worster, Howett, 3916, 4748, 4893
Worth, Billy, 256
Worth, Bobby, 3486
Worth, Johnny, 1830, 2531, 2916
Worth, Marion, 3783, 5438, 5923
Worthington, Harold, 5577
Worthy, David, 214, 2952
Worthy, James, 946
Wortley, Gary, 3189
Wortmann, Kurt, 4548
Worwood, Mark, 5686
Wow Records, 2868, 3671, 4023, 5507
Wozencroft, Keith, 3924
Wozitsky, Jan, 853
Wrafter, Tony, 3524
Wrangler, Jack, 1622
Wrap Records, 2670, 3538
Wrathchild, 1459, 2122, 5923-5924
Wrathchild America, 5924
Wratten, Robert, 1883
Wray Brothers, 4449
Wray, Doug, 5924
Wray, Fay, 1023, 5397
Wray, John, 1688, 5906
Wray, Link, 1066, 2217, 2485, 3255, 5382, 5767, 5924
Wray, Stephen, 2037
Wray, Walter, 5924
Wreck Records, 2053
Wreckless Eric, 325, 737, 3668, 4402, 5383, 5925
Wrecks, 4270
Wreckx-N-Effect, 4545, 5925
Wreede, Katrina, 5537
Wren, Christopher S., 979, 6039
Wren, Jenny, 2233
Wren, Steve, 2429, 5384
Wrencher, Big John, 5925
Wright Special, 2508

Wright, Adrian, 1547, 2632
Wright, Aggi, 4152
Wright, Albert, 4090
Wright, Andy, 1073
Wright, Ben, 2704
Wright, Bernard, 1602, 4198
Wright, Bette, 3673
Wright, Betty, 106, 784, 1041, 1098, 3005, 3026, 3263, 5925
Wright, Billy, 511, 4800, 5925
Wright, Bob, 59, 4185
Wright, Bobby, 2836, 4372, 4908, 5764, 5926
Wright, Carol Sue, 5764, 5926, 5928, 5930
Wright, Charles, 5732
Wright, Cherly, 5926
Wright, Chris, 1078, 1746
Wright, Chuck, 573, 2164, 2607, 2682, 4800
Wright, Clifton, 1017
Wright, Clive, 1144
Wright, Dale, 5926
Wright, Darlene, 606, 1322, 3339
Wright, Dave, 1469, 3313, 5336, 5508
Wright, David, 1924
Wright, Delroy, 4494
Wright, Denny, 473, 1542, 1652, 1828, 2244
Wright, Edna, 607, 1310, 2581-2582
Wright, Edythe, 645, 1599
Wright, Elly, 5927
Wright, Elmon, 5928
Wright, Eric, 1697, 3988
Wright, Ernest, Jnr., 3262
Wright, Frank, 734, 1257, 2024, 2264, 2617, 3070, 3679, 4855, 4908, 5927
Wright, Gary, 244, 2356, 2613, 2660, 3761, 4653, 5927
Wright, Gavyn, 4185
Wright, Gene, 794
Wright, George, 1978, 2236, 2259, 2734, 3033, 3492, 3532
Wright, Gil, 2976
Wright, Gilbert, 3039
Wright, Ginny, 1342
Wright, Heath, 4537
Wright, Helena-Joyce, 2602
Wright, Hugh, 295, 693
Wright, Hugh E., 295
Wright, Ian, 1717, 4635
Wright, Jeff, 5717
Wright, Jeffrey, 740
Wright, Jimmy, 1914, 2971
Wright, John, 427, 1478, 2836, 3962, 5717, 5927, 6080
Wright, John Lincoln, 427
Wright, Johnnie, 192, 2836, 5712, 5764-5765, 5926-5928, 5930
Wright, Johnny, 318, 2353, 5764, 5928
Wright, Judi, 1931
Wright, Lammar, 5928
Wright, Larry, 2778, 5658
Wright, Laurie, 4035, 6067
Wright, Lawrence, 1207, 3201, 3620, 3940, 3966, 4222, 4227, 5928-5929
Wright, Lonzine, 4737

QUICK REFERENCE GUIDE

A Band Of Angels
A Cappella
A Certain Ratio
A Flock Of Seagulls
A Guy Called
    Gerald
A Homeboy, A
    Hippie And A
    Funki Dredd
A House
A II Z
A Tribe Called
    Quest
A Witness
A&M Records
A's
A+
A-Bones
A-Ha
A.C.
A.D.
A13 Productions
A=440
AACM
Aaliyah
Aaltonen, Juhani
Aardvark
Aaron, Lee
Aarons, Alex A.
Aaronson, Irving
Aaronsrod
Aatabou, Najat
AB/CD
Abattoir
Abba
Abbott, George
Abbott, Gregory
ABC
ABC Records
Abdelli
Abdul, Paula
Abdul-Malik,
    Ahmed
Abdullah, Ahmed
Abeni, Queen
    Salawah
Abercrombie,
    John
Abiodun, Dele
Abner, Ewert
Above All
Above The Law
Abrahams, Brian
Abrahams, Doris
Abrahams,
    Maurice

Abrahams, Mick
Abrams, Max
Abrams, Muhal
    Richard
Abramson, Herb
Absalom, Mick
Abshire, Nathan
Absolute
    Beginners
Absolute Grey
Absu
Abyssinians
AC/DC
Acacia
Academy
Accelerators
Accent (UK)
Accents
Accept
Accolade
Accrington,
    Stanley
Accuser
Ace
Ace Lane
Ace Of Base
Ace Of Clubs
Ace Records
Ace, Buddy
Ace, Johnny
Aces
Aces (reggae)
Acheron
Acid
Acid Bath
Acid House
Acid Jazz
Acid Jesus
Acid Reign
Ackah, Jewel
Ackerman,
    William
Ackles, David
Ackles, Stephen
Acklin, Barbara
Acoustic
    Alchemy
Acquaye, Saka
Acrophet
Act
Actifed
Action
Action Pact
Acuff, Roy
Acuff, Roy, Jnr.
Acuff-Rose Music

AD (80s)
AD (90s)
Ad Libs
Adair, Tom
Adam And The
    Ants
Adam Ant
Adam Bomb
Adam, Mike And
    Tim
Adamo
Adams, Bryan
Adams, Cliff
Adams, Derroll
Adams, Faye
Adams, George
    Rufus
Adams, Glen
Adams, J.T.
Adams, Jody
Adams, Johnny
Adams, Lee
Adams, Marie
Adams, Oleta
Adams, Pepper
Adams, S.A.
Adams, Stanley
Adams,
    Woodrow
Adams, Yolanda
Adamski
Adamson, Barry
Adamson, Harold
Adastra
ADC Band
Adcock, Eddie
Adderley,
    Cannonball
Adderley, Nat
Addinsell,
    Richard
Addison, Bernard
Addison, John
Addrisi Brothers
Addy, Mustapha
    Tettey
Addy, Obo
Ade, King Sunny
Adeboye, Kengbe
Adepoju,
    Lanrewaju
Adeva
Adewale, Segun
Adicts
Adkins, Hasil
Adkins, Trace

Adkins, Wendel
Adler, Danny
Adler, Larry
Adler, Lou
Adler, Richard
Admiral Bailey
Admiral Tibet
Admirations
Adolescents
Adrenalin
Adrenalin OD
Adult Net
Adventures
Adventures Of
    Stevie V.
Advertising
Adverts
Aerial
Aerosmith
Afari, Yusus
Affinity
Afghan Whigs
Afraid Of Mice
African Brothers
Africando
Afrika
    Bambaataa
Afro-Celt Sound
    System
Afro-Cuban All
    Stars
Afro-Planes
Afros
After 7
After Hours
After Hours (film
    musical)
After Tea
After The Ball
After The Fire
Afterglow
Aftermath
Age Of Chance
Agee, Ray
Agent
Agent Orange
Agent
    Provocateur
Agent Steel
Agentz
Ager, Milton
Aggression
Aggrovators
Agincourt
Agnes Strange
Agnew, Charlie

Agnostic Front
Ahlert, Fred E.
Ahmad
Ahmed,
    Mahmoud
Ahola, Sylvester
Ain't Broadway
    Grand
Ain't Misbehavin'
Ainsworth, Alyn
Air
Air (jazz)
Air Condition
Air Liquide
Air Miami
Air Raid
Air Supply
Airborne
Aire, Jane, And
    The Belvederes
Airey, Don
Airforce
Airhead
Airrace
Aisha
Aitken, Laurel
Akendengue,
    Pierre
Akens, Jewel
Akers, Doris
Akers, Garfield
Akinyele
Akiyoshi, Toshiko
Akkerman, Jan
Akst, Harry
Alaap
Alabama
Alabama Boys
Aladdin
Aladdin Records
Alaimo, Steve
Alan Brown
Alarm
Alaska
Albam, Manny
Albany, Joe
Albert, Christine
Albert, Don
Albert, Eddie
Albert, Morris
Alberto Y Lost
    Trios Paranoias
Alberto, José 'El
    Canario'
Albery, Donald
Albini, Steve

Albion Country Band
Alcapone, Dennis
Alcatraz
Alcatrazz
Alcorn, Alvin
Alda, Robert
Alden, Howard
Aldo, Steve, And The Challengers
Aldrich, Ronnie
Alessi
Alexa
Alexander's Ragtime Band
Alexander, Alger 'Texas'
Alexander, Arthur
Alexander, Daniele
Alexander, Dave
Alexander, Eric
Alexander, Monty
Alexander, Peter
Alexander, Ray
Alexander, Van
Alexander, Willie
Alexandria, Lorez
Alexis
Alger, Pat
Ali Dee
Ali, Rashied
Alias
Alice Cooper
Alice In Chains
Alice's Restaurant
Alien (Sweden)
Alien (USA)
Alien Sex Fiend
Alienoid
Alisha's Attic
Alive And Kicking
Alix, May
Alkaholics, Tha
Alkatrazz
All
All About Eve
All Night Long
All Saints
All Sports Band
All That Jazz
Allan, Gary
Allan, Jack
Allan, Jan
Allan, Johnnie
Allanson, Susie
Allegro
Allen Brothers
Allen, Annisteen
Allen, Bob
Allen, Carl
Allen, Davie, And The Arrows
Allen, Deborah

Allen, Donna
Allen, Fred
Allen, Geri
Allen, Harry
Allen, Henry 'Red'
Allen, Jackie
Allen, Jules Verne
Allen, Lee
Allen, Leonard
Allen, Les
Allen, Lillian
Allen, Mark
Allen, Marshall
Allen, Pete
Allen, Peter
Allen, Red
Allen, Rex
Allen, Rex, Jnr.
Allen, Ricky
Allen, Rosalie
Allen, Steve
Allen, Terry
Allen, Tito
Allen, Tony
Alley Cats (50s)
Alley Cats (80s)
Alley, Shelly Lee
Alliance
Allied Forces
Allies
Alligator Records
Allin, G.G.
Allison, Gene
Allison, Joe
Allison, Luther
Allison, Mose
Allisons
Allman Brothers Band
Allman, Duane
Allman, Gregg
Allyn, David
Allyson, June
Allyson, Karrin
Almanac Singers
Almeida, Laurindo
Almighty
Almond, Johnny
Almond, Marc
Almost Summer
Alomar, Carlos
Aloof
Alpert, Herb
Alpert, Herman 'Trigger'
Alpha And Omega
Alpha Band
Alpha Centauri
Alphaville
Alphonso, Roland
Alston, Ovie
ALT
Altairs
Altamont Festival

Altan
Altar Of The King
Altena, Maarten
Alter, Louis
Altered Images
Altern 8
Alternative TV
Althea And Donna
Altheimer, Joshua
Alton, Robert
Altschul, Barry
Alvarez, Adalberto
Alvin, Danny
Alvin, Dave
Alvis, Hayes
Alwyn, William
Ama, Shola
Amadin
Amampondo
Amazing Blondel
Amazing Catsfield Steamers
Amazing Mr. Smith
Amazing Rhythm Aces
Amazulu
Amber
Ambersunshower
Amboy Dukes
Ambrose
Ambrosetti, Franco
Ambrosia
Ameche, Don
Amen Corner
America
Americade
American Angel
American Blues
American Breed
American Flyer
American Graffiti
American Hot Wax
American In Paris, An
American Music Club
American Noise
American Spring
American Tears
Ames Brothers
Ames, Ed
AMG
AMM
Ammons, Albert
Ammons, Gene 'Jug'
Amon Düül
Amon Düül II
Amorphis
Amory Kane
Amos, Tori

Ampex
Amps
Amran, David Werner, III
Amy, Curtis
An Emotional Fish
Anastasia Screamed
Anathema
Anchors Aweigh
Ancient Beatbox
And All Because The Lady Loves
And So To Bed
Anders And Poncia
Andersen, Arild
Andersen, Eric
Andersen, Lale
Anderson, Al
Anderson, Alistair
Anderson, Angry
Anderson, Bill
Anderson, Carleen
Anderson, Cat
Anderson, Eddie
Anderson, Ernestine
Anderson, Fred
Anderson, Ian A.
Anderson, Ivie
Anderson, Jhelisa
Anderson, Jimmy
Anderson, John
Anderson, John Murray
Anderson, Jon
Anderson, Kip
Anderson, Laurie
Anderson, Leroy
Anderson, Liz
Anderson, Lynn
Anderson, Maxwell
Anderson, Miller
Anderson, Moira
Anderson, Pinkney 'Pink'
Anderson, Ray
Anderson, Stig
Andersson, Stefan
Andrade, Leny
Andre, Peter
Andrews Sisters
Andrews, Andy
Andrews, Chris
Andrews, Ernie
Andrews, Harvey
Andrews, Julie
Andrews, Lee, And The Hearts
Andrews, Ruby

Andrews, Tim
Andriessen, Louis
Andromeda
Andrus, Blackwood & Co.
Andrus, Chuck
Andrus, Pete
Andwella's Dream
Andy, Bob
Andy, Horace
Andy, Patrick
Aneka
Angel
Angel (dance)
Angel Corpus Christi
Angel, Dave
Angelic Upstarts
Angelica
Angelo, Bobby, And The Tuxedos
Angels (Australia)
Angels (USA)
Angels With Dirty Faces
Angelwitch
Anglin Brothers
Anglin, Jack
Angry Samoans
Animal Crackers
Animal Logic
Animal Nightlife
Animals
Animals That Swim
Anka, Paul
Annette
Annie
Annie (film musical)
Annie Get Your Gun
Annihilator
Annointed Pace Singers
Anointed
Anotha Level
Another Pretty Face
Ant And Dec
Anthem
Anthony, Chubby
Anthony, Eddie
Anthony, Julie
Anthony, Mike
Anthony, Ray
Anthony, Richard
Anthrax
Anti
Anti-Nowhere League
Anti-Pasti
Antietam

Antoinette
Antolini, Charly
Anvil
Any Trouble
Anyone Can
  Whistle
Anything Goes
  (film musical)
AOR
Aorta
Apache Indian
APB
Apes, Pigs &
  Spacemen
Aphex Twin
Aphrodite's Child
Apocalypse
Apocalyptica
Apocrypha
Apollas
Apollo
Apollo 440
Apollo100
Apollonia 6
Appice, Carmine
Applause
Apple
Apple Tree, The
Apple, Fiona
Applejacks (UK)
Applejacks (USA)
Apples
Apples In Stereo
Applesauce!
Appletree
  Theatre
Appleyard, Peter
April Wine
Aqua
Aquarian Age
Aquarian Dream
Aquatones
Ar Bras, Dan
AR Kane
Ar Log
Arab Strap
Arabian Prince
Arata, Tony
Arbello,
  Fernando
Arbors
ARC
Arc Angel
Arc De Triomphe
ARC Records
Arcade
Arcadia
Arcadians, The
Arcadium
Arcangel
Arceneaux,
  Fernest
Archer, Harry
Archer, Martin
Archer, Tasmin
Archers
Archers Of Loaf

Archey, Jimmy
Archibald
Archies
Arden, Don
Arden, Jann
Ardley, Neil
Ardoin, Amadie
Are You
  Lonesome
  Tonight?
Area Code 615
Arena, Tina
Argent
Argent, Rod
Argüelles, Julian
Argüelles, Steve
Arhoolie Records
Arista Records
Ariwa Sounds
Arizona Smoke
  Revue
Arkarna
Arkie The
  Arkansas
  Woodchopper
Arlen, Harold
Armageddon
Armatrading,
  Joan
Armenra, Dolly
Armenteros,
  Alfredo
  'Chocolate'
Armored Saint
Armoury Show
Armstead,
  'Joshie' Jo
Armstrong Twins
Armstrong, Billy
Armstrong,
  Frankie
Armstrong,
  Lillian
Armstrong, Louis
Army Of Lovers
Arnaz, Desi
Arndt, Felix
Arnheim, Gus
Arnold
Arnold, Billy Boy
Arnold, Eddy
Arnold, Harry
Arnold, James
  'Kokomo'
Arnold, Jimmy
Arnold, Malcolm
Arnold, P.P.
Arnold, Tom
Arodin, Sidney
Arrested
  Development
Arrival
Arrow
Arrows
Arrows (Canada)
Arroyo, Joe
Ars Nova

Art
Art Ensemble Of
  Chicago
Art In America
Art Of Noise
Artch
Artery
Arthur, Beatrice
Arthur, Charline
Arthur, Emry
Arthurs, George
Articles Of Faith
Artillery
Artisan
Artistics
Artwoods
As The Girls Go
As Thousands
  Cheer
As You Were
ASAP
ASCAP
Asche, Oscar
Ash
Ash, Daniel
Ash, Paul
Ashby, Dorothy
Ashby, Harold
Ashby, Irving
Ashby, John
Ashley, Leon
Ashdown, Doug
Asher, Peter
Ashes
Ashford And
  Simpson
Asian Dub
  Foundation
Ashkhabad
Ashley, Clarence
  Tom
Ashley, Steve
Ashman, Howard
Ashphalt Ballet
Ashton
Ashton, Bill
Ashton, Gardner
  And Dyke
Ashton, Mark
Ashton, Tony
Ashworth, Ernie
Asia
Asleep At The
  Wheel
Asmussen, Svend
Aspects Of Love
Aspey, Gary And
  Vera
Asphalt Ribbons
Aspinall, Neil
Ass Ponys
Assassins
Assegai
Assembly
Associates
Association
Astaire, Fred

Astley, Rick
Astley, Virginia
Aston, John
Astor, Bob
Astor, Tom
Astors
Astral Projection
Astralasia
astroPuppees
Aswad
Asylum Choir
Asylum Records
At Home Abroad
At Long Last
  Love
At The Drop Of
  A Hat
At The Gates
Atari Teenage
  Riot
Atcher, Bob
Atchison, Tex
Atco Records
Atheist
Atilla
  (Netherlands)
Atilla (USA)
Atilla The Hun
Atkin, Pete
Atkins, Bobby
Atkins, Chet
Atkins, Juan
Atkins, Ray
Atkins, Rhett
Atlanta Rhythm
  Section
Atlantic
Atlantic Records
Atlantic Starr
Atlas, Natasha
Atmosfear
Atom Heart
Atom Seed
Atomic Rooster
Atomic Swing
Atomkraft
Atrophy
Attack
Atteridge, Harold
Attic Records
Attila The
  Stockbroker
Attractions
Atwell, Winifred
Au Go-Go
  Singers
Au Pairs
Audience
Audio Active
Audio Two
Audioweb
Auger, Brian
August Redmoon
August, Jan
August, Joe 'Mr.
  Google Eyes'
Auldridge, Mike

Aum
Aungier, Cliff
Aura
Aural Assault
Auric, Georges
Ausgang
Austin, Bobby
Austin, Cuba
Austin, Gene
Austin, Harold
Austin, Jesse
  'Wild Bill'
Austin, Lovie
Austin, Patti
Austin, Sil
Australia
Autechre
Auteurs
Autograph
Autoharp
Automatic
Automatic Man
Automatix
Autopsy
Autosalvage
Autrey, Herman
Autry, Gene
Autumn Records
Autumns
Avalon
Avalon (USA)
Avalon, Frankie
Avant garde
Avant Gardeners
Avatar
Avenger
  (Germany)
Avenger (UK)
Avengers
Average White
  Band
Aviary
Aviator
Avion
Avons
Awaya, Noriko
AWBH
Aweke, Aster
Axe
Axe Victims
Axewitch
Axiom
Axis
Axis Point
Axton, Hoyt
Axton, Mae
  Boren
Axxis
Ayala, Bob
Ayer, Nat D.
Ayers Rock
Ayers, Kevin
Ayers, Roy
Ayler, Albert
Ayler, Donald
Ayres, Mitchell
Ayshea

Ayuba, Adewale
AZ
Az Yet
Azimuth
Aznavour,
　Charles
Aztec Camera
Aztec Two-Step
Azteca
Aztecs
Azuli
Azuquita, Camilo
Azymuth
B'zz
B-52's
B-Boy Records
B-Movie
B. Bumble And
　The Stingers
B., Anthony
B., Derek
B., Lisa
B., Stevie
B.A.L.L.
B.B. Blunder
b.l.o.w.
B.Q.E.
B.T. Express
B12
Baah, Kwaku
　'Reebop'
Babbington, Roy
Babbitt, Harry
Babble
Babe Ruth
Babes In Arms
Babes In Toyland
Babes In Toyland
　(stage musical)
Babes On
　Broadway (film
　musical)
Babs, Alice
Baby
Baby Animals
Baby Chaos
Baby D
Baby Ford
Baby Ray And
　The Ferns
Baby Tuckoo
Baby Wayne
Babyface
Babylon AD
Babylon Zoo
Babys
Baca, Susana
Baccara
Bacharach, Burt
Bachelors
Bachman-Turner
　Overdrive
Back Door
Back Street
　Crawler
Back To The
　Planet

Backbeat
Backbone Slide
Backroom Boys
Backstreet Boys
Backwater
Bacon Fat
Bacsik, Elek
Bad Boy
Bad Boy Johnny
　And The
　Prophets Of
　Doom
Bad Brains
Bad Company
Bad English
Bad Livers
Bad Manners
Bad News
Bad Religion
Bad Seeds
Bad Steve
Badarou, Wally
Baddeley,
　Hermione
Badfinger
Badini, Gerard
Badlands
Badmarsh
Badowski, Henry
Badu, Erykah
Baer, Abel
Baez, Joan
Bagneris, Vernel
Bags
Bagwell, Wendy,
　And The
　Sunliters
Bahmadia
Bahula, Julian
Bailes Brothers
Bailey Brothers
Bailey, Benny
Bailey, Buster
Bailey, Deford
Bailey, Derek
Bailey, Judy
Bailey, Kid
Bailey, Mildred
Bailey, Pearl
Bailey, Philip
Bailey, Razzy
Bailey, Roy
Baillie And The
　Boys
Bain, Aly
Bainbridge,
　Merril
Baird, Dan
Bajourou
Baka Beyond
Baker Gurvitz
　Army
Baker Street
Baker's Wife,
　The
Baker, Adrian
Baker, Anita

Baker, Arthur
Baker, Belle
Baker, Billy
Baker, Bonnie
Baker, Butch
Baker, Carroll
Baker, Chet
Baker, David
　Nathaniel, Jnr.
Baker, Duck
Baker, Etta
Baker, George,
　Selection
Baker, Ginger
Baker, Harold
　'Shorty'
Baker, Joséphine
Baker, Kenny
Baker, Kidd
Baker, LaVern
Baker, Mickey
Baker, Tom
Baker, Willie
Bakerloo
Balaam And The
　Angel
Balalaika
Balance
Balanchine,
　George
Balanescu
　Quartet
Baldock, Ken
Baldry, Long John
Balearic
Balfa Brothers
Balham Alligators
Balin, Marty
Ball Of Fire
Ball, Dave
Ball, David
Ball, Ed
Ball, Ernest R.
Ball, Kenny
Ball, Lucille
Ball, Marcia
Ball, Michael
Ball, Ronnie
Ballad In Blue
Ballamy, Iain
Ballard, Florence
Ballard, Hank,
　And The
　Midnighters
Ballard, Kaye
Ballard, Russ
Ballen, Ivin
Ballew, Smith
Ballin' Jack
Balloon Farm
Ballroom
Baltzell, John
Bambi
Bambi Slam
Bambino,
　Sekouba
Bamboula, The

Banana And The
　Bunch
Banana Splits
Bananarama
Banashak, Joe
Banchee
Banco De Gaia
Band
Band Aid/Live Aid
Band Of Blacky
　Ranchette
Band Of Gypsies
Band Of Susans
Band Wagon,
　The (stage
　musial)
Banda El Recodo
Bandit
Bandit Queen
Bandulu
Bandy, Moe
Bang
Bang Records
Bang Tango
Bang The Party
Bang, Billy
Bangalore Choir
Bangles
Bangor Flying
　Circus
Bangs
Bangs, Lester
Banished
Banks, Billy
Banks, Darrell
Banks, Homer
Banks, Jeff,
　Bishop
Banks, Rose
Banned
Bannon, R.C.
Banshee
Banton, Buju
Banton, Buro
Banton, Mega
Banton, Pato
Banton, Starkey
Bantu
Bar Mitzvah Boy
Bar-Kays
Barbara And the
　Uniques
Barbarians
Barbarin, Louis
Barbarin, Paul
Barbecue Bob
Barbee, John
　Henry
Barber, Ava
Barber, Bill
Barber, Chris
Barber, Glenn
Barber, Patricia
Barbieri, Gato
Barbour, Dave
Barbour, Fiddling
　Burk

Barclay James
　Harvest
Bardens, Peter
Bare, Bobby
Barefield, Eddie
Barefoot Jerry
Barely Works
Barenaked Ladies
Barfield, Johnny
Bargeron, Dave
Barker, Danny
Barker, Dave
Barker, Guy
Barker, Les
Barker, Louis
　'Blue Lu'
Barker, Sally
Barker, Thurman
Barkleys Of
　Broadway, The
Barksdale,
　Everett
Barlow, Dale
Barlow, Gary
Barlow, Jack
Barlow, Randy
Barnes And
　Barnes
Barnes, Alan
Barnes, Benny
Barnes, George
Barnes, J.J.
Barnes, Jimmy
Barnes, John
Barnes, Lloyd
Barnes, Mae
Barnes, Max
Barnes, Paul
　'Polo'
Barnes, Roosevelt
　'Booba'
Barnes, Walter
Barnet, Charlie
Barnett, Bobby
Barnum
Baron Rojo
Barracudas
Barrelhouse Buck
Barren Cross
Barrere, Paul
Barrett Sisters
Barrett, Dan
Barrett, Sweet
　Emma
Barrett, Syd
Barrett, Wild
　Willie
Barretto, Ray
Barri, Steve
Barrie, Gracie
Barrie, J.J.
Barrier
Barrier Brothers
Barris, Harry
Barrish, Jesse
Barrister
Barrister, Wasiu

Barriteau, Carl
Barron Knights
Barron, Bill
Barron, Blue
Barron, Kenny
Barron, Tony
Barros, Alberto 'El Conejo'
Barrow, Keith
Barry And The Tamerlanes
Barry, Jeff
Barry, Joe
Barry, John
Barry, Len
Barry, Sandra
Bart, Lionel
Barth, Bobby
Bartholomew, Dave
Bartley, Chris
Barton, Lou Ann
Bartz, Gary
Bascomb, Dud
Bascomb, Paul
Basehead
Basement Boys
Bashful Brother Oswald
Bashful Harmonica Joe
Basia
Basie, Count
Basil, Toni
Basin Street Boys
Bass Bumpers
Bass Is Base
Bass, Fontella
Bass, Ralph
Bass-O-Matic
Bassey, Shirley
Bassheads
Basso, Gianni
Bastard
Batchelor, Wayne
Bate, Dr. Humphrey, (And The Possum Hunters)
Bates, Django
Bates, Martyn
Bathory
Batiste, Alvin
Baton Rouge
Bators, Stiv
Bats
Batt, Mike
Battered Ornaments
Battin, Skip
Battiste, Harold
Battle, Edgar 'Puddenhead'
Battleaxe
Battlecry

Battlefield Band
Battling Butler
Batts, Will
Batu
Bauduc, Ray
Bauer, Billy
Baugh, Phil
Bauhaus
Bauza, Mario
Bawl
Baxter, Andrew And Jim
Baxter, Blake
Baxter, Les
Baxter, Phil
Bay Bops
Bay City Rollers
Bay, Francis
Bayes, Nora
Bayete
Baylor, Helen
Bayou Seco
Be Glad For The Song Has No Ending
Be Sharp
Be-Bop Deluxe
Beach Ball USA
Beach Boys
Beach Party
Beacon Street Union
Beal, Charlie
Beaman, Lottie
Beamer, Keola
Bear Family Records
Beason, Bill
Beastie Boys
Beat (UK)
Beat (USA)
Beat Club
Beat Farmers
Beat Happening
Beat Publique
Beat Rodeo
Beaters
Beatles
Beatmasters
Beatnuts
Beats International
Beatstalkers
Beau
Beau Brummels
Beau Geste
Beau Nasty
Beau, Heinie
BeauSoleil
Beautiful South
Beauty And The Beast
Beauty Prize, The
Beaver And Krause
Beaver, Pappy Gube

Beavers
Becaud, Gilbert
Because They're Young
Bechet, Sidney
Bechstein
Beck
Beck, Bogert And Appice
Beck, Gordon
Beck, Jeff
Beck, Joe
Becker, Jason
Becker, Margaret
Becker, Walter
Beckett, Barry
Beckett, Harry
Beckford, Theophilus
Becky Sharp
Bedford, David
Bedhead
Bedlam
Bedlam Rovers
Bedouin Ascent
Bedrocks
Bee Gees
Bee, Molly
Beeching, Jenny
Beefeater
Beenie Man
Bees Make Honey
BEF
Beggars Banquet Records
Beggars Hill
Beggars Opera
Beginning Of The End
Begley, Philomena
Beiderbecke, Bix
Bekker, Hennie
Bel Biv DeVoe
Bel Canto
Bel, M'bilia
Bel-Airs
Belafonte, Harry
Belew, Adrian
Belew, Carl
Belfast Gypsies
Belfegore
Bell And Arc
Bell Biv Devoe
Bell Notes
Bell Records
Bell, Archie, And The Drells
Bell, Benny
Bell, Carey
Bell, Chris
Bell, Delia, And Bill Grant
Bell, Edward 'Ed'
Bell, Eric
Bell, Freddie, And The Bellboys

Bell, Graeme
Bell, Jimmie
Bell, Jimmy
Bell, Lurrie
Bell, Madeline
Bell, Maggie
Bell, Nyanka
Bell, T.D.
Bell, Thom
Bell, William
Bellamy Brothers
Bellamy, Peter
Belle
Belle And Sebastian
Belle Of Mayfair, The
Belle Of New York, The
Belle Stars
Belle, Regina
Bells
Bells Are Ringing (stage musical)
Bellson, Louie
Bellus, Tony
Belly
Belmonts
Beloved
Beltram, Joey
Beltran, Lola
Belvin, Jesse
Bembeya Jazz
Ben Folds Five
Ben, Jorge
Ben, Mohammed Malcolm
Benatar, Pat
Benbow, Steve
Bender, D C
Bendix, Ralf
Benediction
Beneke, Tex
Benét, Eric
Benford, Tommy
Bengal Tigers
Benitez, Jellybean
Benjamin, Bennie
Benjamin, Sathima Bea
Benkadi International
Bennett, Betty
Bennett, Boyd
Bennett, Brian
Bennett, Cliff
Bennett, Cuban
Bennett, Duster
Bennett, Joe, And The Sparkletones
Bennett, Lorna
Bennett, Michael
Bennett, Pinto
Bennett, Richard Rodney
Bennett, Robert Russell

Bennett, Tony
Bennett, Wayne
Bennink, Han
Benno, Marc
Benny Goodman Story, The
Benny Profane
Benoit, David
Benoit, Tab
Benson Orchestra
Benson, Al
Benson, George
Benson, Ivy
Bensusan, Pierre
Bent, Phillip
Bentley Rhythm Ace
Bentley, Gladys Alberta
Benton, Brook
Benton, Buster
Benz
Benz, Spragga
Berg, Bob
Berg, Matraca
Berger, Karl
Berger, Michel
Bergeron, Shirley
Bergh, Totti
Bergin, Mary
Berghofer, Chuck
Bergman, Alan And Marilyn
Bergonzi, Jerry
Berigan, Bunny
Berkeley, Busby
Berklee College Of Music
Berlin
Berlin, Irving
Berman, Sonny
Bernabei, Memo
Bernadette
Bernard, James
Bernard, Rod
Berne, Tim
Bernhardt, Clyde
Bernie, Ben
Berns, Bert
Bernstein, Artie
Bernstein, Elmer
Bernstein, Leonard
Berry, Bill
Berry, Chu
Berry, Chuck
Berry, Dave
Berry, Emmett
Berry, Heidi
Berry, John
Berry, Mike
Berry, Nick
Berry, Richard
Berry, W.H.
Berryhill, Cindy Lee

Bert, Eddie
Bertelmann, Fred
Berton, Vic
Bertrand, Jimmy
Beserkley
    Records
Best Foot
    Forward (stage
    musical)
Best Little
    Whorehouse In
    Texas, The
Best Things In
    Life Are Free,
    The
Best, Denzil De
    Costa
Best, Johnny
Best, Pete
Best, Tony
Betancourt, Justo
Betesh, Danny
Bethlehem
Bethlehem
    Gospel Singers
Bethnal
Betsy
Bettencourt,
    Frank
Bettencourt,
    Nuno
Better 'Ole, The
Better Days
Better Than Ezra
Bettie Serveert
Betts, Richard
    'Dickie'
Betty
Beverley Sisters
Beverley's
Beverly Hillbillies
Bevis Frond
Beyond
Beyond Records
Beyond Religion
Beyond The
    Fringe
BG The Prince Of
    Rap
BGO Records
Bhundu Boys
Biafra, Jello
Bibb, Eric
Bible
Bickert, Ed
Biddell, Kerrie
Bienstock, Freddy
Bienstock, Johnny
Bif Naked
Biff Bang Pow!
Big
Big 8
Big Audio
    Dynamite
Big Bad Smitty
Big Beat, The
Big Ben

Big Ben Banjo
    Band
Big Bertha
Big Black
Big Bopper
Big Boys
Big Broadcast,
    The
Big Brother And
    The Holding
    Company
Big Bub
Big Chief
Big Country
Big Daddy
Big Daddy Kane
Big Dish
Big F
Big Flame
Big Fun
Big Head Todd
    And The
    Monsters
Big House
Big In Japan
Big Joe
Big Life Records
Big Maceo
Big Maybelle
Big Mountain
Big Pig
Big River
Big Slim, The
    Lone Cowboy
Big Sound
    Authority
Big Star
Big Sugar
Big Three
Big Three Trio
Big Timber
    Bluegrass
Big Time Sarah
Big TNT Show
Big Tom And The
    Mainliners
Big Top Records
Big Town
    Playboys
Big Twist And
    The Mellow
    Fellow
Big Wheel
Big Youth
Bigard, Barney
Bigeou, Esther
Biggs, Barry
Bihari Brothers
Bikel, Theodore
Bikini Beach
Bikini Kill
Bile, Moni
Bilk, Acker
Billboard
Billie And Lillie
Billie Joe And The
    Checkmates

Billings, Vic
Billion Dollar
    Babies
Billy
Billy And The
    Beaters
Billy Rain
Billy Rose's
    Diamond
    Horseshoe
Billy Rose's
    Jumbo
Billy Satellite
Billy The Kid
Bing Boys Are
    Here, The
Binge, Ronald
Bingi Bunny
Binkley Brothers
Biohazard
Biondi, Ray
Biosphere
Bird
Bird On A Wire
Bird Sisters
Birdland
Birdlegs And
    Pauline
Birds
Birkin, Jane
Birth Of The
    Beatles
Birth Of The
    Blues
Birtha
Birthday Party
Bis
Biscoe, Chris
Bishop, Billy
Bishop, Elvin
Bishop, Joe
Bishop, Stephen
Bishop, Wallace
Bishop, Walter,
    Jnr.
Bisiker And
    Romanov
Bitch
    (Switzerland)
Bitch (USA)
Bitch Magnet
Bitches Sin
Bite It! Records
Biting Tongues
Bitter Sweet
Bivona, Gus
Bivouac
Biz Markie
Bizarre Inc.
Björk
Bjorn Again
Black
Black 'N' Blue
Black Ace
Black Alice
Black And Tan
Black Angels

Black Artists
    Group
Black Bob
Black Box
Black Boy Shine
Black Cat Bones
Black Crowes
Black Dog
    Productions
Black Flag
Black Grape
Black Ivory
Black Ivory King
Black Joy
Black Lace
Black Lace (USA)
Black Moon
Black Oak
    Arkansas
Black Pearl
Black Radical Mk
    II
Black Randy And
    The Metro
    Squad
Black Rebels
Black Roots
Black Rose (UK)
Black Rose (USA)
Black Sabbath
Black Saint And
    Soul Note
    Records
Black Sheep
Black Sheep (rap)
Black Slate
Black Train Jack
Black Uhuru
Black Velvet
    Band
Black Widow
Black, Bill
Black, Cilla
Black, Clint
Black, Don
Black, Frances
Black, Frank
Black, James
Black, Jeanne
Black, Mary
Black, Roy
Black, Stanley
Blackbirds Of
    1928
Blackburn And
    Snow
Blackburn, Tony
Blackbyrds
Blackeyed Susan
Blackfeather
Blackfoot
Blackfoot Sue
Blackhawk
Blackman, Cindy
Blackmore,
    Ritchie
Blackout

Blackstones
Blackstreet
Blackthorne
Blackwell, Chris
Blackwell, Ed
Blackwell, Francis
    Hillman
    'Scrapper'
Blackwell, Otis
Blackwell, Robert
    'Bumps'
Blackwell, Willie
    '61'
Blackwells
Blackwood
    Brothers
Blackwych
Blade
Blade Runner
Blades, Rubén
Blaggers ITA
Blahzay Blahzay
Blaine, Hal
Blaine, Terry
Blaine, Vivian
Blair, Janet
Blake Babies
Blake, Eubie
Blake, Jamie
Blake, John
Blake, Norman
Blake, Ran
Blakeney, Andy
Blakey, Art
Blakley, Ronee
Blakley, Ronnie
Blameless
Blanch, Arthur
Blanchard, Edgar
Blanchard, Jack,
    And Misty
    Morgan
Blanchard, Red
Blanchard,
    Terence
Blancmange
Bland, Billy
Bland, Bobby
Blane, Ralph
Blando, Deborah
Blane, Marcie
Blane, Ralph
Blank
    Generation,
    The
Blanton, Jimmy
Blasters
Blazing Apostles
Bleach
Bleed
Blegvad, Peter
Blenders
Blenders (Chicago)
Bless The Bride
Blessed Death
Blessid Union Of
    Souls

Blessing
Bley, Carla
Bley, Paul
Bleyer, Archie
Blige, Mary J.
Blind Blake
Blind Boy Fuller
Blind Date
Blind Faith
Blind Melon
Blinkhorn, Smilin'
   Billy
Blinky
Bliss Band
Blissed
Blitz!
Blitzkrieg
Blitzstein, Marc
Block, Rory
Blodwyn Pig
Blonde On
   Blonde
Blonde Redhead
Blondel
Blondie
Blondy, Alpha
Blood
Blood Brothers
Blood Of
   Abraham
Blood On The
   Saddle
Blood Sausage
Blood, Sweat And
   Tears
Bloodfire Posse
Bloodgood
Bloodhound Gang
Bloodrock
Bloods And Crips
Bloodstone
Bloom, Bobby
Bloom, Jane Ira
Bloom, Luka
Bloom, Rube
Bloomer Girl
Bloomfield, Mike
Blossom Time
   (stage musical)
Blossom Time
   (film musical)
Blossom Toes
Blossom, Henry,
   Jnr.
Blossoms
Blow
Blow Monkeys
Blow Up
Blow, Kurtis
Blowers, Johnny
Blowzabella
Blue
Blue Aeroplanes
Blue Beat
   Records
Blue Bludd
Blue Boys

Blue Cheer
Blue For A Boy
Blue Hawaii
Blue Horizon
   Records
Blue Jays
Blue Magic
Blue Mink
Blue Murder
Blue Nile
Blue Note
   Records
Blue Orchids
Blue Oyster Cult
Blue Paradise,
   The
Blue Pearl
Blue Ridge
   Rangers
Blue Rodeo
Blue Rondo A La
   Turk
Blue Skies
Blue Sky Boys
Blue Stars
Blue Swede
Blue Thumb
   Records
Blue Velvets
Blue Zoo
Blue, 'Little' Joe
Blue, Barry
Blue, David
Bluebell In
   Fairyland
Bluebells
Bluebird Records
Bluegrass Album
   Band
Bluegrass Alliance
Bluegrass
   Cardinals
Blues
Blues Band
Blues Brothers
Blues Brothers,
   The
Blues Busters
Blues Council
Blues Image
Blues In The
   Night
Blues Magoos
Blues Project
Blues Traveler
Bluetones
Bluiett, Hamiet
Blumfeld
Blunstone, Colin
Blur
Blurt
Blyth Power
Blyth, Ann
Blythe, Arthur
Blythe, Jimmy
BMX Bandits
Bo Street Runners

Bo, Eddie
Boatwright,
   Ginger
Bob And Earl
Bob And Marcia
Bob B. Soxx And
   The Blue Jeans
Bob Delyn
Bobbettes
Bobby And The
   Midnights
Bobo, Willie
Bobs
Bocage, Peter
Bock, Jerry
Bodacious D.F.
BoDeans
Bodine
Bodines
Body Count
Boenzye Creque
Boettcher, Curt
Bofill, Angela
Bogan, Lucille
Bogert, Tim
Boggs, Dock
Boggs, Noel
Bogguss, Suzy
Bogle, Eric
Bogue, Merwyn
Bohannon,
   Hamilton
Boiled In Lead
Boine, Marie
Bok, Gordon
Bolan, Marc
Boland, Clay
Boland, Francy
Bolden, Buddy
Boles, John
Bolger, Ray
Bolin, Tommy
Bolland, C.J.
Bollin, A.D.
   'Zuzu'
Bolling, Claude
Bollock Brothers
Bolo, Yammie
Bolshoi
Bolt Thrower
Bolton, Guy
Bolton, Michael
Bolton, Polly
Bomb Squad
Bomb The Bass
Bombalurina
Bombers
Bomp Records
Bon Jovi
Bon Rock And
   The Rhythem
   Rebellion
Bonamy, James
Bonano, Sharkey
Bond, Carrie
   Jacobs
Bond, Eddie

Bond, Graham
Bond, Johnny
Bond, Peter
Bonds, Gary
   'U.S.'
Bonds, Son
Bone Orchard
Bone Thugs-N-
   Harmony
Bones, Frankie
Boney M
Bonfire
Bonfire, Mars
Bongo Man,
   Kanda
Bongwater
Bonham
Bonham, Tracy
Bonn, Issy
Bonner And
   Gordon
Bonner, Weldon
   'Juke Boy'
Bonnet, Graham
Bonney, Betty
Bonney, Graham
Bonnie Lou
Bonnie Lou And
   Buster
Bonnie Sisters
Bonniwell, Sean
Bono, Sonny
Bonoff, Karla
Bonzo Dog Doo-
   Dah Band
Boo Radleys
Boo, Betty
Boo-Yaa
   T.R.I.B.E.
Boogie Beat
   Records
Boogie Down
   Productions
Bookbinder, Roy
Booker T. And
   The MGs
Booker, Charley
Booker, James
Boom, Barry
Boomtown Rats
Boone, Claude
Boone, Debby
Boone, Larry
Boone, Pat
Boones
Booth And The
   Bad Angel
Booth, Paul Eric
Booth, Shirley
Booth, Tim, And
   Angelo
   Badalamenti
Booth, Tony
Booth, Webster
Boothe, Ken
Boothill Foot-
   Tappers

Bootsauce
Booze, Beatrice
   'Bea'
Bop Brothers
Bop Chords
Borbetomagus
Bordoni, Irene
Boredoms
Borich, Kevin
Born Jamericans
Born To Boogie
Born To Dance
Born To Swing
Borsato, Marco
Bortolotti,
   Gianfranco
Borum, Willie
Bosco, Jean
   Mwenda
Bose, Miguel
Bose, Sterling
Boss
Bosstown Sound
Bostic, Earl
Boston
Boston Dexters
Boswell Sisters
Boswell, Connee
Boswell, Eve
Botany 5
Bothy Band
Bottle Rockets
Bottom Line
   Records
Bottrell, Marie
Boublil, Alain
Boucher, Judy
Boulevard
Bouncer, Peter
Bound For Glory
Bounty Killer
Bourelly, Jean-
   Paul
Bourke, Rory
   Michael
Boutté, Lillian
Bovell, Dennis
Bow Wow
Bow Wow Wow
Bowen, Jimmy,
   And The
   Rhythm
   Orchids
Bowers, Bryan
Bowers, Robert
   Hood
Bowes, Margie
Bowie, David
Bowie, Joe
Bowie, Lester
Bowling, Roger
Bowlly, Al
Bowman, Dave
Bowman, Don
Bowman, Euday
   L.
Bown, Alan

Bown, Patti
Bowser, Erbie
Bowyer, Brendan
Box Of Frogs
Box Tops
Boxcar Willie
Boxer
Boy Friend, The
Boy George
Boy Howdy
Boy Meets Girl
Boy's Own
Boy, Andy
Boy, The
Boyce And Hart
Boyd, Bill And
   Jim
Boyd, Eddie
Boyd, Joe
Boyes, Jim
Boylan, Terry
Boyle, Maggie
Boymerang
Boys
Boys Don't Cry
Boys From
   Indiana
Boys From
   Syracuse, The
Boys Of The
   Lough
Boyz II Men
Boyzone
Boyzz
Boze, Calvin
BPeople
Bracey, Ishmon
Brack, John
Brackeen,
   Charles
Brackeen, Joanne
Bracket
Brackman, Jim
Brad
Braddock, Bobby
Braddy, Pauline
Bradford, Bobby
Bradford, Geoff
Bradford, Perry
   'Mule'
Bradley, Betty
Bradley, Harold
Bradley, Jan
Bradley, Owen
Bradley, Will
Bradshaw, Terry
Bradshaw, Tiny
Brady, Pat
Brady, Paul
Brady, Phil, And
   The Ranchers
Braff, Ruby
Bragg, Billy
Braham, Philip
Brainiac
Braithwaite,
   Daryl

Bramble, Mark
Bramlett, Bonnie
Bramlett,
   Delaney
Bramstormer
Branca, Glenn
Branch, Billy
Brand New
   Heavies
Brand Nubian
Brand X
Brand, Oscar
Brandt, Paul
Brandwynne, Nat
Brandy
Branigan, Laura
Brannen, John
Branson, Richard
Brasfield, Rod
Brass
   Construction
Brass Monkey
Brassy
Bratmobile
Brats
Bratton, John W.
Braud, Wellman
Braun Brothers
Brave Belt
Brave Combo
Braxton, Anthony
Braxton, Toni
Braxtons
Breach, Joyce
Bread
Bread Love And
   Dreams
Breakaways
Breaking Glass
Breathless
Breau, Harold
   John
Brecht, Bertolt
Breckenridge,
   Dardanelle
Brecker Brothers
Brecker, Michael
Brecker, Randy
Breeders
Breen, Ann
Breese, Lou
Breeze, Jean
   'Binta'
Brel, Jacques
Bremner, Billy
Brenda And The
   Tabulations
Brennan, Rose
Brennan, Walter
Brenston, Jackie
Brent, Tony
Bresh, Thom
Breslau
Brett Marvin And
   The
   Thunderbolts
Brett, Paul

Breuer, Carolyn
Breuker, Willem
Brewer And
   Shipley
Brewer's Droop
Brewer, 'Blind'
   James
Brewer, Teresa
Brewster's
   Millions
Brian And
   Michael
Brian, Donald
Briar
Briarhoppers
Brice, Fanny
Brick Layer Cake
Brickell, Edie
Brickell, Edie,
   And The New
   Bohemians
Bricklin
Brickman, Jim
Bricusse, Leslie
Bridge
Bridges, Alicia
Bridges, Henry
Bridgewater, Dee
   Dee
Brigadier Jerry
Brigadoon
Brigandage
Briggs, Anne
Briggs, David
Bright, Bette
Bright, Len,
   Combo
Brighter Side Of
   Darkness
Brightman, Sarah
Brighton Rock
Brignola, Nick
Brigode, Ace
Briley, Martin
Brill Building
Brilliant
Brilliant Corners
Brim, Grace
Brim, John
Brimstone
Brimstone, Derek
Bring In 'Da
   Noise, Bring In
   'Da Funk
Brinsley Schwarz
Brise-Glace
Brisker, Gordon
Brisset, Annette
Brissette,
   Annette
Brisson, Carl
Brisson,
   Frederick
Bristol, Johnny
British Electric
   Foundation
British Lions

Britny Fox
Britt, Elton
Britten, Buddy
Britton
Britton, Marsha
Broadbent, Alan
Broadway
Broadway Angel
   Records
Broadway
   Melody, The
Broadway,
   Orquesta
Brocas Helm
Brock, 'Big'
   George
Brock, Dave
Broderick, Helen
Brodszky,
   Nicholas
Brody, Lane
Broggs, Peter
Brogues
Broken Bones
Broken English
Broken Hope
Bromberg, David
Bronco
Bronski Beat
Bronte Brothers
Bronz
Brood, Herman
Brook Brothers
Brook, Michael
Brooke, Jonatha
Brooker, Gary
Brooklyn Bridge
Brooklyn Dreams
Brookmeyer, Bob
Brooks And Dunn
Brooks, 'Big'
   Leon
Brooks, Baba
Brooks, Cedric 'Im'
Brooks, Donnie
Brooks, Elkie
Brooks, Garth
Brooks, Hadda
Brooks, Harvey
Brooks, Karen
Brooks, Lonnie
Brooks, Meredith
Brooks, Mike
Brooks, Randy
Brooks, Shelton
Brooks, Terry
Brooks, Tina
Broom, Bobby
Broonzy, 'Big' Bill
Bros
Brosnan, Mike
Brother Cane
Brother D
Brother Phelps
Brotherhood
Brotherhood Of
   Man

Brothers Four
Brothers In
   Rhythm
Brothers Johnson
Brothers Of Soul
Brötzmann,
   Peter
Broudie, Ian
Broughton,
   Edgar, Band
Broussard, Van
Brower, Cecil
Brown Dots
Brown Sugar
Brown's Ferry
   Four
Brown, Al
Brown, Andrew
Brown, Angela
Brown, Arthur
Brown, Barry
Brown, Bessie
Brown, Bobby
Brown, Buster
Brown, Charles
Brown, Chuck,
   And The Soul
   Searchers
Brown, Clarence
   'Gatemouth'
Brown, Cleo
Brown, Clifford
Brown, Danny
   Joe, Band
Brown, Dennis
Brown, Derwood
Brown, Dusty
Brown, Foxy
Brown, Friday
Brown, Gabriel
Brown, Georgia
Brown, Gerry
Brown, Glen
Brown, Greg
Brown, Henry
Brown, Horace
Brown, Hylo
Brown, J.T.
Brown, James
Brown, Jeri
Brown, Jim Ed
Brown, Joe
Brown, Junior
Brown, Junior
   (reggae)
Brown, Lawrence
Brown, Lee
Brown, Les
Brown, Lew
Brown, Lillyn
Brown, Marion
Brown, Marshall
   Richard
Brown, Marty
Brown, Maxine
Brown, Milton
Brown, Nacio Herb

Brown, Nappy
Brown, Olive
Brown, Oscar, Jnr.
Brown, Pete (UK)
Brown, Pete (USA)
Brown, Peter
Brown, Prezident
Brown, Pud
Brown, Randy
Brown, Ray (Australia)
Brown, Ray (USA)
Brown, Richard 'Rabbit'
Brown, Rob
Brown, Robert
Brown, Roy James
Brown, Roy Lee
Brown, Ruth
Brown, Sam
Brown, Sandy
Brown, Shirley
Brown, T. Graham
Brown, Tom
Brown, Tommy
Brown, Tony
Brown, U.
Brown, Vernon
Brown, Walter
Brown, Willie
Browne, Duncan
Browne, Jackson
Browne, Jann
Browne, Tom
Brownmark
Browns
Brownstone
Brownsville Station
Brozman, Bob
BRS-49
Brubeck, Dave
Bruce And Terry
Bruce, Ed
Bruce, Ian
Bruce, Jack
Bruce, King
Bruce, Tommy
Bruce, Vin
Bruford, Bill
Bruhl, Heidi
Brujeria
Brumley, Al
Brumley, Albert
Bruner, Cliff
Bruninghaus, Rainer
Brunis, Georg
Brunner, John
Brunswick Records
Bruntnell, Peter

Brush Arbor
Brutal Truth
Brutality
Bruton, Stephen
Bruzer
Bryan, Mike
Bryant, Anita
Bryant, Beulah
Bryant, Boudleaux
Bryant, Clora
Bryant, Don
Bryant, Felice
Bryant, Jimmy
Bryant, Ray
Bryant, Slim
Bryant, Willie
Bryden, Beryl
Bryndle
Brynner, Yul
Bryson, Peabo
BT
Bubble Puppy
Buccaneer
Buccaneers
Buchanan And Goodman
Buchanan, Colin
Buchanan, Ian
Buchanan, Jack
Buchanan, Roy
Buck, Gary
Bucketheads
Buckingham, Lindsey
Buckinghams
Buckley, Betty
Buckley, Jeff
Buckley, Lord
Buckley, Tim
Buckner And Garcia
Buckner, Milt
Buckner, Richard
Buckner, Teddy
Bucks
Bucks Fizz
Buckwheat Zydeco
Budd, Harold
Budd, Roy
Buddah Records
Buddy
Buddy Holly Story, The
Budgie
Budgie (stage musical)
Budwig, Monty
Buena Vista Social Club
Buffalo
Buffalo Club
Buffalo Gals
Buffalo Springfield
Buffalo Tom

Buffett, Jimmy
Buford, 'Mojo' George
Bugger All Stars
Buggles
Bugsy Malone
Built To Spill
Buirski, Felicity
Bulimia Banquet
Bull, Sandy
Bulldozer
Bulletboys
Bullett
Bullock, Chick
Bullseye
Bully Wee Band
Bullyrag
Bulter, Joe
Bumble Bee Slim
Bump
Bumrush
Bunch Of Fives
Bunch, John
Bundrick, John 'Rabbit'
Bunker, Larry
Bunn, Teddy
Burbank, Albert
Burchell, Chas
Burdon, Eric
Bureau
Burgess, Sonny
Burgess, Wilma
Burke, Fiddlin' Frenchie
Burke, Joe
Burke, Johnny
Burke, Ray
Burke, Solomon
Burke, Sonny
Burkes, Conish 'Pinetop'
Burks, Eddie
Burland, Dave
Burleson, Hattie
Burn
Burnap, Campbell
Burnel, Jean Jacques
Burnett, Carol
Burnett, Chester
Burnett, T-Bone
Burnette, Billy
Burnette, Dorsey
Burnette, Johnny
Burnette, Legendary Hank C.
Burnette, Rocky
Burnette, Smiley
Burnin' Daylight
Burning Rome
Burning Spear
Burning Tree
Burns, Eddie
Burns, Norman

Burns, Ralph
Burns, Ray
Burns, Tito
Burnside, R.L.
Burnside, Vi
Burr, Henry
Burrage, Harold
Burrage, Ronnie
Burrell, Dave
Burrell, Kenny
Burrell, Philip 'Fatis'
Burris, J.C.
Burroughs, Alvin
Burroughs, William
Burrows, Abe
Burrows, Tony
Burse, Charlie
Burtnick, Glen
Burton, Aron
Burton, Gary
Burton, James
Burton, Lori
Burton, Wendell
Burzum
Bus Boys
Busby, Buzz
Busch, Lou
Bush
Bush Records
Bush, Johnny
Bush, Kate
Bush, Stan
Bushay, Clement
Bushell, Garvin
Bushkin, Joe
Bushman
Bushwackers
Busse, Henry
Busta Rhymes
Butler, Bernard
Butler, Billy
Butler, Billy, And The (En)Chanters
Butler, Carl And Pearl
Butler, Frank
Butler, George 'Wild Child'
Butler, Henry
Butler, Jerry
Butler, Larry
Butler, Rosemary
Butterbeans And Susie
Butterfield 8
Butterfield, Billy
Butterfield, Paul
Butthole Surfers
Butts Band
Buzzcocks
Buzzov.en
Bwchadanas
By Jeeves
By Jupiter

Byard, Jaki
Byas, Don
Bye Bye Birdie
Bygraves, Max
Byles, Keith 'Chubby' Junior
Byng, Douglas
Byrd, Billy
Byrd, Bobby
Byrd, Charlie
Byrd, Donald
Byrd, Gary
Byrd, Jerry
Byrd, Joseph
Byrd, Robert
Byrd, Tracy
Byrds
Byrne, Bobby
Byrne, David
Byrne, Mike
Byrnes, Edd
Byron, David
Byron, Jon
Bystander
Bystanders
C & The Shells
C+B
C+C Music Factory
C, Roy
C.I.V.
Cabana
Cabaret
Cabaret (film musical)
Cabaret Girl, The
Cabaret Voltaire
Cabin In The Sky
Cabin In The Sky (stage musical)
Cables
Cables, George
Cabot, Chuck
Caceres, Ernie
Cacophony
Cactus
Cactus Brothers
Cadd, Brian
Caddick, Bill
Cadets
Cadets/Jacks
Cadillac Tramps
Cadillacs
Cadogan, Susan
Caesar, Irving
Caesar, Shirley
Cafe Orchestra
Café Society
Cafferty, John, And The Beaver Brown Band
Cage, James 'Butch'
Cage, John
Cagle, Buddy
Cagney, James

Cagnolatti, Ernie
Cahn, Sammy
Caiazza, Nick
Caicedo, José
  Harbey 'Kike'
Caifanes
Cain, Benny And
  Vallie
Cain, Jackie
Caiola, Al
Cajmere
Cajun And
  Zydeco
Cajun Moon
Cake
Cake Like
Cake Records
Calamity Jane
Calder, Tony
Caldwell, Bobby
Caldwell, Happy
Cale, J.J.
Cale, John
Calennig
Calibre Cuts
California
  Ramblers
California, Randy
Californians
Calikes, David
Call
Call Me Madam
Call Me Mister
Call, Bob
Callahan
  Brothers
Callender, Red
Callicott, Joe
Callier, Terry
Callies
Calloway, Cab
Calvert, Eddie
Calvert, Reg
Calvert, Robert
Camarata, Tutti
Cambridge Folk
  Festival
Camel
Camelot
Camelots
Cameo
Cameo Records
Cameo-Parkway
  Records
Camero De
  Guerra,
  Candido
Cameron, G.C.
Camilleri, Joe
Camilo, Michel
Camp Creek
  Boys
Camp Lo
Camp, Steve
Campbell, 'Little'
  Milton
Campbell, Al

Campbell, Alex
Campbell, Archie
Campbell, C. Eddie
Campbell, Cecil
Campbell,
  Choker
Campbell,
  Cornell
Campbell, Don
Campbell, Glen
Campbell, Ian,
  Folk Group
Campbell, Jimmy
Campbell, John
Campbell, Junior
Campbell, Kate
Campbell, LInslee
Campbell, Luther
Campbell, Mike
Campbell, Naomi
Campbell, Sarah
  Elizabeth
Campbell, Tevin
Camper Van
  Beethoven
Can
Can't Help
  Singing
Can't Stop The
  Music
Can-Can
Canales, Angel
Cancer
Candide
Candido
Candlebox
Candlemass
Candlewick
  Green
Candoli, Conte
Candoli, Pete
Candy And The
  Kisses
Candy Flip
Candy, Icho
Candyland
Candyman
Canis Major
Cannanes
Cannata
Canned Heat
Cannibal And
  The
  Headhunters
Cannibal Corpse
Cannon's Jug
  Stompers
Cannon, Ace
Cannon, Freddy
Cannon, Gus
Canterbury Tales
Cantor, Eddie
Cap-Tans
Cap, Andy And
  Flip
Capaldi, Jim
Capella

Capeman, The
Capercaillie
Capitol
Capitol Records
Capitols
Capleton
Capp, Andy
Capp, Frank
Capp-Pierce
  Juggernaut
Capris (50s)
Capris (60s)
Capstick, Tony
Captain America
Captain And
  Tennille
Captain
  Beefheart
Captain Beyond
Captain Rapp
Captain Sensible
Captain Sinbad
Captain Tractor
Cara, Irene
Caravan
Caravanserai
Caravelles
Carawan, Guy
Carcass
Card, The
Cardiacs
Cardigans
Cardinal
Cardinals
Carefree
Careless Rapture
Carelli, Gerard
Caretaker Race
Carey, Mariah
Carey, Mutt
Carey, Tony
Cargill, Henson
Carillo
Carisi, Johnny
Carl, Max
Carle, Frankie
Carlisle, Belinda
Carlisle, Bob
Carlisle, Elsie
Carlisle, Una Mae
Carlisles
Carlos, Wendy
  (Walter)
Carlson, Paulette
Carlton And His
  Shoes
Carlton, Larry
Carlyle, Russ
Carman
Carmel
Carmen Jones
Carmen, Eric
Carmen, Jenks
  'Tex'
Carmichael,
  Hoagy
Carnations

Carne, Jean
Carnes, Kim
Carney, Harry
Carnival
Carnivore
Carolina Cotton
Carolina Slim
Carolina Tar
  Heels
Carollons
Carolons
Carols
Caron, Leslie
Carousel
Carousel (film
  musical)
Carpenter, Mary-
  Chapin
Carpenter,
  Thelma
Carpenter,
  Wingie
Carpenters
Carr, Cathy
Carr, Ian
Carr, James
Carr, Leroy
Carr, Michael
Carr, Mike
Carr, Pearl, And
  Teddy Johnson
Carr, Valerie
Carr, Vikki
Carrack, Paul
Carradine, Keith
Carrie
Carroll, Baikida
Carroll, Barbara
Carroll, Cath
Carroll, David,
  And His
  Orchestra
Carroll, Dina
Carroll, Earl
Carroll, Jim
Carroll, Joe
Carroll, Johnny
Carroll, Ronnie
Carrott, Jasper
Carry, Scoops
Cars
Carson, Fiddlin'
  John
Carson, Jeff
Carson, Jenny
  Lou
Carson, Ken
Carson, Lori
Carson, Martha
  Lou
Carson, Mindy
Carter And Lewis
Carter Family
Carter USM
Carter, Anita
Carter, Benny
Carter, Betty

Carter, Big Lucky
Carter, Bo
Carter, Carlene
Carter, Clarence
Carter, Deana
Carter, Derrick
Carter, Fred F.,
  Jnr.
Carter, Goree
Carter, Helen
Carter, James
Carter, Joe
Carter, John
  Wallace
Carter, Maybelle
Carter, Mel
Carter, Ron
Carter, Sara
Carter, Sydney
Carter, Vivian,
  And James
  Bracken
Carter, Wilf
Carthy, Eliza
Carthy, Eliza,
  And Nancy
  Kerr
Carthy, Martin
Cartoone
Cartwright,
  Lionel
Carver, Johnny
Carver, Wayman
Cary, Dick
Casa Loma
  Orchestra
Cascades
Case
Case, Peter
Casey, Al
Casey, Claude
Casey, Howie,
  And The
  Seniors
Cash Crew
Cash Crew (UK)
Cash Crew (USA)
Cash Money And
  Marvellous
Cash, Alvin
Cash, Bernie
Cash, Johnny
Cash, June Carter
Cash, Rosanne
Cash, Tommy
Cashman And
  West
Cashmeres
Casinos
Casonovas
Cass County Boys
Cassandra
  Complex
Cassidy, David
Cassidy, Jack
Cassidy, Patrick
Cassidy, Shaun

Cast
Castaways
Castelles
Castells
Castle Communications
Castle, Lee
Castle, Vernon And Irene
Castleman, Owen
Caston, Leonard 'Baby Doo'
Castor, Jimmy
Casual
Casuals
Cat And The Fiddle, The
Cat Iron
Cat Mother And The All Night Newsboys
Catatonia
Catch
Catch My Soul
Catch Of The Season, The
Catch Us If You Can
Cate Brothers
Cates, George
Catfish Keith
Cathcart, Dick
Cathedral
Catherine Wheel
Catherine, Philip
Catholic Discipline
Catingub, Matt
Catlett, 'Big' Sid
Cato's Vagabonds
Cato, Pauline
Caton, Lauderic
Catron, Johnny
Cats
Cats 'N' Jammers
Cats And The Fiddle
Cats In Boots
Cattini, Clem
Caught On The Hop
Cauld Blast Orchestra
Cavalcade
Cavaliere, Felix
Cavallaro, Carmen
Cave, Nick, And The Bad Seeds
Caveman
Cavern, The
Caymmi, Dori
CBGB's
CBS Records
CCS
Ceberano, Kate

Celebration
Celestin, Oscar 'Papa'
Celibate Rifles
Cellos
Celtic Frost
Cement
Cemetary
Centaurus
Central Line
Cephas, John
Ceroli, Nick
Cetera, Peter
Ceyleib People
Chaabi
Chacksfield, Frank
Chad And Jeremy
Chadbourne, Eugene
Chain
Chain Reaction
Chairmen Of The Board
Chaix, Henri
Chaka Demus And Pliers
Chakachas
Chalice
Chalker, Curly
Challenger
Challis, Bill
Chaloff, Serge
Chaloner, Sue
Chamberlain, Richard
Chambers Brothers
Chambers, Henderson
Chambers, Joe
Chambers, Paul
Chamblee, Eddie
Chameleons
Champagne Charlie
Champaign
Champion
Champion Records
Champion, Gower
Champlin, Bill
Champs
Chance Element
Chance Records
Chance, James
Chandler, Chas
Chandler, Gene
Chandler, Len
Chandra, Sheila
Change
Change Of Seasons
Changing Faces
Channel
Channel 3

Channel Light Vessel
Channel One
Channel One Records
Channel, Bruce
Channels
Channing, Carol
Chantays
Chantels
Chanters
Chants
Chaperones
Chapin, Harry
Chaplin, Saul
Chapman Whitney
Chapman, Marshall
Chapman, Michael
Chapman, Mike
Chapman, Roger
Chapman, Tracy
Chapterhouse
Chaquito Orchestra
Charig, Phil
Chariot
Charioteers
Charisma Records
Charisse, Cyd
Charlatans (UK)
Charlatans (USA)
Charlene
Charles And Eddie
Charles Lloyd - Journey Within
Charles, Bobby
Charles, Dennis
Charles, Don
Charles, Hugh
Charles, Jimmy
Charles, Ray
Charles, Sonny, And The Checkmates Ltd
Charles, Teddy
Charlie
Charlie Chaplin
Charlie Girl
Charlie's Angels
Charlot, André
Charly Records
Charmers, Lloyd
Charms
Charney, Suzanne
Charnin, Martin
Charon
Charro
Chartists
Charts
Chas And Dave

Chase, Allan
Chase, Bill
Chase, Tommy
Chastain, David T.
Chateaux
Chatmon, Sam
Chau, Emil
Chavez
Chavis, Wilson 'Boozoo'
Cheap 'N' Nasty
Cheap Trick
Cheatham, Doc
Cheatham, Jeannie
Checker Records
Checker, Chubby
Checkmates, Ltd.
Cheech And Chong
Cheeks, Judy
Cheeky Records
Cheetah
Chefs
Chekasin, Vladimir
Chelsea
Chemical Brothers
Chenier, C.J.
Chenier, Clifton
Chequered Past
Cher
Cheré, Tami
Cheri
Cherokees
Cherrelle
Cherry Red Records
Cherry Smash
Cherry Vanilla
Cherry, Don (trumpeter)
Cherry, Don (vocalist)
Cherry, Neneh
Chesney, Kenny
Chesnut, Mark
Chesnutt, Vic
Chess
Chess Records
Chessmen
Chester, Bob
Chester, Johnny
Chesterfields
Chestnuts
Cheung, Jacky
Chevalier, Maurice
Chevy
Cheynes
Chi-Ali
Chi-Lites
Chiavola, Kathy
Chic
Chicago

Chicago (stage musical)
Chicago Loop
Chicken Chest
Chicken Shack
Chicory Tip
Chieftains
Chiffons
Child
Child, Desmond, And Rouge
Child, Jane
Childers, Buddy
Childre, Lew
Children Of Eden
Children Of The Day
Childs, Andy
Childs, Billy
Childs, Toni
Chill EB
Chill, Rob G.
Chilli Willi And The Red Hot Peppers
Chilliwack
Chills
Chilton, Alex
Chilton, John
Chimes (UK)
Chimes (USA)
Chin, Clive
Chin, Tony
Chin-Loy, Herman
China Black
China Crisis
China Drum
China Sky
Chinatown
Chinese Honeymoon, A
Chinn And Chapman
Chipmunks
Chips
Chisholm, George
Chiswick Records
Chittison, Herman
Chitty Chitty Bang Bang
Chiweshe, Stella
Chixdiggit
Choates, Harry
Chocolate Dandies
Chocolate Soldier, The
Chocolate Starfish
Chocolate Watch Band
Chocolate Weasel
Choir

Choir Invisible
Choirboys
Chordettes
Chords
Chorus Line, A
Chorus Line, A
  (film musical)
Chosen Few
Chris And Cosey
Christensen, Jon
Christian Death
Christian, Charlie
Christian, Chris
Christian, Garry
Christian, Little
  Johnny
Christian, Neil
Christian, Rick
Christians
Christie
Christie, Keith
Christie, Lou
Christie, Tony
Christlieb, Pete
Christmann,
  Günter
Christmas, Keith
Christy, June
Chrome
Chrome Molly
Chron Gen
Chrysalis Records
Chu Chin Chow
Chubb Rock
Chuck D.
Chuck Wagon
  Gang
Chudd, Lew
Chukki Star
Chumbawamba
Chung, Geoffrey
Chung, Mikey
Church
Church, Cindy
Church, Eugene
Churchill,
  Savannah
Cianide
Ciccone Youth
Cimarons
Cinderella
Cinderella (film)
Cinderella (stage
  musical)
Cinema
Cinquetti,
  Gigliola
Cintron
Cipollina, John
Circle
Circle Jerks
Circus
Circus Lupus
Circus Of Power
Cirith Ungol
Citizen Fish
Citizen Kane

Citizen's Utilities
Citroen, Soesja
City
City Boy
City Of Angels
CJSS
Claassen, Fee
Clail, Gary, And
  The On U
  Sound System
Claire, Dorothy
Clambake
Clan Alba
Clan McPeake
Clancy
Clancy Brothers
  And Tommy
  Makem
Clannad
Clanton, Jimmy
Clapton, Eric
Clapton, Richard
Clare, Alan
Clare, Kenny
Clarendonians
Clarion
Clark, Buddy
Clark, Chris
Clark, Claudine
Clark, Dave
Clark, Dave, Five
Clark, Dee
Clark, Dick
Clark, Garnet
Clark, Gene
Clark, Guy
Clark, June
Clark, Petula
Clark, Roy
Clark, Sanford
Clark, Sonny
Clark, Terri
Clark, Yodelling
  Slim
Clark-Hutchinson
Clarke, 'Fast'
  Eddie
Clarke, Eric
Clarke, Grant
Clarke, Gussie
Clarke, John
  Cooper
Clarke, Johnny
Clarke, Kenny
  'Klook'
Clarke, Loni
Clarke, Stanley
Clarke, Terry
Clarke, Tony
Clarke, Vince
Clarke, William
Clash
Clásico, Conjunto
Classics
Classics IV
Classix Nouveaux
Clausen, Thomas

Claw Hammer
Clawfinger
Clawson, Cynthia
Claxton, Rozelle
Clay Allison
Clay, Joe
Clay, Judy
Clay, Otis
Clay, Shirley
Clay, Tom
Clay, W.C.
Clayderman,
  Richard
Claypool, Philip
Clayton Squares
Clayton, Buck
Clayton, Jeff
Clayton, John
Clayton, Lee
Clayton, Merry
Clayton, Peter J.
  'Doctor'
Clayton, Vikki
Clayton, Willie
Clayton-Thomas,
  David
Clea And McLeod
Clean
Cleanliness And
  Godliness
  Skiffle Band
Clear Blue Sky
Clearlight
Clearwater, Eddy
Clefs
Cleftones
Clegg, Johnny
Clement, Jack
Clements, Vassar
Clements, Zeke
Clempson, Dave
Cless, Rod
Cleveland City
  Records
Cleveland, James,
  Rev.
Cleveland, Jimmy
Cleyndert, Andy
Cliff, Jimmy
Clifford, Bill
Clifford, Buzz
Clifford, Linda
Clifford, Mike
Clifton, Bill
Climax
Climax Blues
  Band
Climie Fisher
Cline, Charlie
Cline, Curly Ray
Cline, Patsy
Cline, Tammy
Clint Eastwood
  And General
  Saint
Clinton, George
Clinton, Larry

Clipper Carlton
Clique
Clock DVA
Clockwork
  Orange, A
Clooney,
  Rosemary
Close Lobsters
Close, Glenn
Clouds
Clouds Of Joy
Cloven Hoof
Clover
Clovers
Clower, Jerry
Club Ecstasy
Club Nouveau
Clue J And His
  Blues Blasters
Cluster Of Nuts
  Band
Clutch
Clyne, Jeff
Coal Chamber
Coasters
Coates, Eric
COB
Cobb, Arnett
Cobb, Jimmy
Cobb, Julius
Cobbs, Willie
Cobham, Billy
Cobra (reggae)
Cobra (rock)
Cobra Records
Cochise
Cochran, Charles
  B.
Cochran, Eddie
Cochran, Hank
Cochran, Wayne
Cochrane, Tom
Cock Robin
Cockburn, Bruce
Cocker, Joe
Cockney Rebel
Cockney Rejects
Coco Steel And
  Lovebomb
Cocoa Tea
Cocoanuts, The
Cocteau Twins
Coday, Bill
Codeine
Codona
CODs
Cody, Betty
Coe, David Allan
Coe, Pete
Coe, Tony
Coetzee, Basil
  'Manenberg'
Coffee
Cogan, Alma
Cohan, George
  M.
Cohen, Alan

Cohen, Leonard
Cohen, Paul
Cohn, Al
Cohn, Marc
Cohn, Zinky
Coil
Coker, Henry
Cola Boy
Cold Blood
Cold Chillin'
Cold Chisel
Cold Crush
  Brothers
Cold Sweat
Cold Water Flat
Coldcut
Cole, Ann
Cole, B.J.
Cole, Holly
Cole, Lloyd, (And
  The
  Commotions)
Cole, Nat 'King'
Cole, Natalie
Cole, Paula
Cole, Richie
Cole, Stranger
Cole, William
  'Cozy'
Coleman
  Brothers
Coleman, Bill
Coleman, Burl C.
  'Jaybird'
Coleman, Cy
Coleman, Gary
  'BB'
Coleman, George
Coleman, Jesse
  'Monkey Joe'
Coleman, Margi
Coleman, Michael
Coleman,
  Ornette
Coleman, Ray
Coleman, Steve
Colenso Parade
Coleridge-Taylor,
  Samuel
Coles, Johnny
Collapsed Lung
Collective Soul
Collectors
College Boys
Collette, Buddy
Collie, Bif
Collie, Mark
Collie, Max
Collier, Graham
Collier, Mitty
Collins Kids
Collins, Albert
Collins, Allen
Collins, Anthony
Collins, Bootsy
Collins, Cal
Collins, Edwyn

Collins, Glenda
Collins, John
Collins, Joyce
Collins, Judy
Collins, Lee
Collins, Phil
Collins, Sam
Collins, Shad
Collins, Shirley
   And Dolly
Collins, Tommy
Collinson, Lee
Collister,
   Christine
Colman, Stuart
Colón, Willie
Color Me Badd
Colorado
Colorblind James
   Experience
Colosseum
Colour Box
Colour Field
Coloured Balls
Colourman
Colours
Colston, Mary
Colter, Jessi
Colton's, Tony,
   Big Boss Band
Coltrane, Alice
Coltrane, John
Colts
Columbia
   Records
Columbia
   Records (UK)
Columbo, Russ
Colville,
   Randolph
Colvin, Shawn
Colyer, Ken
Combelle, Alix
Combs, Sean
   'Puffy'
Comden, Betty
Come
Comet Gain
Coming Up Roses
Commander
   Cody And His
   Lost Planet
   Airmen
Commodores
Common
Communards
Como, Perry
Compagnons De
   La Chanson
Company
Company (stage
   musical)
Company Caine
Company Of
   Wolves
Compton
   Brothers

Compton's Most
   Wanted
Compulsion
Comsat Angels
Comus
Con Funk Shun
Concert For
   Bangla Desh,
   The
Concords
Concrete Blonde
Condell, Sonny
Condition Red
Condon, Eddie
Coney Hatch
Coney Island
Confederate
   Railroad
Conflict
Confrey, Zez
Congo Ashanti
   Roy
Congos
Congregation
Conjunto
   Céspedes
Conlee, John
Conley, Arthur
Conley, Earl
   Thomas
Conlon, Bill
Conn, Mervyn
Connecticut
   Yankee, A
Connells
Connelly, Reg
Connick, Harry,
   Jnr.
Conniff, Ray
Connolly, Billy
Connolly, Kevin
Connor, Chris
Connor, Tommie
Connors, Bill
Connors, Carol
Connors, Chuck
Connors, Gene
   'Mighty Flea'
Connors,
   Norman
Conqueroo
Conrad, Jess
Conscious
   Daughters
Consolidated
Constellation
   Records
Conte, Paulo
Contemporary
   Music Unit
Contemporary
   Records
Conti, Bill
Continental
   Singers And
   Orchestra
Contortions

Contours
Contraband
Controllers
Conversation Piece
Convict
Conway, Russ
Conway, Steve
Cooder, Ry
Cook And
   Greenaway
Cook, Barbara
Cook, Doc
Cook, Don
Cook, Junior
Cook, Norman
Cook, Roger
Cook, Willie
Cooke, Micky
Cooke, Sam
Cookie Crew
Cookies
Cool Notes
Cooley, Spade
Coolidge, Rita
Coolio
Cooltempo
Coon Creek Girls
Coon, Carleton
Coon-Sanders
   Nighthawks
Cooper, Al
Cooper, Bob
Cooper, Buster
Cooper, Jerome
Cooper, Lindsay
Cooper, Mike
Cooper, Pete
Cooper, Stoney,
   And Wilma
   Lee
Cooper, Trenton
Coots, J. Fred
Copacabana
Copas, Cowboy
Cope, Julian
Copeland, Greg
Copeland, Johnny
Copeland, Ken
Copeland, Martha
Copeland, Ray
Copeland, Stewart
Copley, Jeff
Copper Family
Copperhead
Coppin, Johnny
Cops 'N' Robbers
Coral Records
Corason Records
Cordelia's Dad
Cordell, Denny
Cordet, Louise
Corea, Chick
Corkscrew
Corley, Dewey
Cornelius
   Brothers and
   Sister Rose

Cornelius, Helen
Cornell, Don
Cornell, Lynn
Cornells
Cornershop
Cornick, Glenn
Cornwell, Hugh
Corona
Coroner
Coronets
Corridor
Corries
Corrigan, Briana
Corrosion Of
   Conformity
Corsairs
Cortez, Dave 'Baby'
Cortijo, Rafael
Cortinas
Corvettes
Coryell, Larry
Cosmic Baby
Cosmic Force
Cosmosis
Cosmotheka
Costa, Don
Costa, Johnny
Costanzo, Sonny
Costello, Elvis
Coster, Stan
Cote, Nathalie
Cotten, Elizabeth
   'Libba'
Cotton Club, The
Cotton Club, The
   (stage musical)
Cotton, Billy
Cotton, James
Cotton, Joseph
Cotton, Larry
Cotton, Mike
Cotton, Sylvester
Cottrell, Louis,
   Jnr.
Couchois
Cougar, John
Cougars
Coughlan, Mary
Coulter, Phil
Counce, Curtis
Council, Floyd
Count Bishops
Count Five
Count Ossie
Countess Maritza
Counting Crows
Country Gazette
Country
   Gentlemen
Country Girl, A
Country Jim
Country Joe And
   The Fish
Country Music
   Association
Country Music
   Foundation

Country Music
   Hall Of Fame
   And Museum
Countrymen
County,
   Jayne/Wayne
Courage Of
   Lassie
Couriers
Coursil, Jacques
Court Jester, The
Courtneidge,
   Cicely
Courtney, Del
Courtney, Lou
Courtney, Ragan
Cousin Emmy
Cousin Jody
Cousin Joe
Cousins, Dave
Cousins, Roy
Couza, Jim
Covay, Don
Cover Girl
Coverdale Page
Coverdale, David
Covert, Robert
Covey, Julian,
   And Machine
Covington, Blind
   Bogus Ben
Covington, Julie
Covington,
   Robert
Cowan, Tommy
Coward, Noël
Cowboy Junkies
Cowboy Loye
Cowboy Mouth
Cowboy Records
Cowboy, Copas
Cowens, Herbert
Cowsills
Cox, Carl
Cox, Deborah
Cox, Harry
Cox, Ida
Cox, Jess
Cox, Michael
Coxhill, Lol
Coxsone, Lloyd
Coy, Gene
Coyne, Kevin
CPO
Craaft
Crabby Appleton
Crack The Sky
Cracker
Crackjaw
Cracknell, Sarah
Craddock, Billy
   'Crash'
Cradle Of Filth
Cradle Will Rock,
   The
Craig, Carl
Craig, Francis

Cramer, Floyd
Crammed
    Records
Cramps
Cranberries
Cranes
Cranium HF
Cranshaw, Bob
Crary, Dan
Crash 'n' Burn
    (Film)
Crash 'N' Burn
    (heavy metal)
Crash Test
    Dummies
Crass
Cravats
Craven, Beverly
Cravin' Melon
Crawdaddys
Crawford,
    Carolyn
Crawford, Hank
Crawford, Jack
Crawford, Jesse
Crawford, Jimmy
Crawford, Johnny
Crawford,
    Michael
Crawford, Randy
Crawford, Ray
Crawford,
    Sugarboy
Crawler
Crawley
Cray, Robert
Crayton, Pee
    Wee
Crazy Elephant
Crazy For You
Crazy Horse
Crazyhead
Creach, 'Papa'
    John
Cream
Creamer, Henry
Creaming Jesus
Creath, Charlie
Creation
Creation Records
Creatures
Credit To The
    Nation
Creed
Creedence
    Clearwater
    Revival
Creek
Creeps
Creese, Malcolm
Crenshaw,
    Marshall
Crentsil, A.B.,
    And The
    Ahenfo Band
Crescendos
Cressida

Crests
Crew-Cuts
Crewe, Bob
Crickets
Crickets (R&B)
Crime
Crime And The
    City Solution
Crimmins, Roy
Crimson Canary,
    The
Crimson Glory
Crispell, Marilyn
Crispy
    Ambulance
Criss, Peter
Criss, Sonny
Criswell, Kim
Critchenson, John
Criterions
Critters
Cro-Mags
Croce, Jim
Crockett, G.L.
Crockett,
    Howard
Croisille, Nicole
Croker, Brendan
Crombie, Tony
Crome Cyrcus
Cronos
Cronshaw,
    Andrew
Crook Brothers
Crook, General
Crook, Lewis
Cropper, Steve
Crosby And Nash
Crosby, Bing
Crosby, Bob
Crosby, David
Crosby, Gary
Crosby, Israel
Crosby, Rob
Crosby, Stills And
    Nash
Crosby, Stills, Nash
    And Young
Cross
Cross Country
Cross,
    Christopher
Cross, Hugh
Cross, Sandra
Crossfire
Crossfires
Crothers, Connie
Crouch, Andrae
Crouch, Stanley
Crow
Crowbar
Crowd (USA)
Crowd, The
Crowded House
Crowder, Rob
Crowe, J.D.
Crowell, Rodney

Crown Heights
    Affair
Crown Of Thorns
Crows
Crowsdell
Crozier, Trevor
Crudup, Arthur
    'Big Boy'
Cruise, Julie
Cruiser
Crumbley, Elmer
Crumbsuckers
Crumit, Frank
Crump, Jesse
Crunt
Crusaders
Crush
Crush, Bobby
Crutchfield,
    James
Cruz, Celia
Cruzados
Cry Of Love
Cryan' Shames
Crybabys
Cryptic Slaughter
Crystals
Cua, Rick
Cuba, Joe
Cuban Heels
Cubanate
Cubanismo
Cuber, Ronnie
Cuby And The
    Blizzards
Cuckoo Patrol
Cud
Cuddly Toys
Cuddy, Shawn
Cues
Cuff Links
Cuffee, Ed
Cugat, Xavier
Cujo
Culley, Frank
    'Floorshow'
Culley, Wendell
Cullum, Jim
Culprit
Cult
Culture
Culture Beat
Culture Club
Culture Shock
Culverwell,
    Andrew
Cumberland
    Ridge Runners
Cumberland
    Three
Cummings,
    Burton
Cummings, Steve
Cummins, Bernie
Cunha, Rick
Cunningham,
    Agnes 'Sis'

Cunningham, Phil
    And Johnny
Cunninghams
Cupid's Inspiration
Cuppini, Gil
Curb, Mike
Cure
Curiosity Killed
    The Cat
Curless, Dick
Current 93
Currie, Cherie
Curry, Clifford
Curry, Tim
Curson, Ted
Curtin, Dan
Curtis, James
    'Peck'
Curtis, Ken
Curtis, Lee, And
    The All-Stars
Curtis, Sonny
Curtola, Bobby
Curtom Records
Curve
Curved Air
Curzon, Frederic
Cuscuna, Michael
Cut To Kill
Cutrer, T.
    Tommy
Cutshall, Cutty
Cutting
Cutting Crew
Cyclone
Cymarron
Cymbal, Johnny
Cynic
Cynics
Cypress Hill
Cyrille, Andrew
Cyrkle
Cyrus, Billy Ray
Czukay, Holger
D'Abo, Michael
D'Amico, Hank
D'Andrea, Franco
D'Angelo
D'Arby, Terence
    Trent
D'León, Oscar
D'Molls
D*Note
D-Influence
D-Mob
D-Nice
D-Train
D-Zone Records
D., Donald
D.A.D.
D.A.F.
D.C. Star
D.C. Talk
D.R.I.
D.O.C.
D.O.P.
D:ream

Da Bush Babees
Da Happy Headz
Da Lench Mob
Da Luniz
Da Vinci, Paul
Da Yeene
Da Youngstas
Dab Hand
Dada (70s)
Dada (90s)
Daddy Cool
Daddy Dewdrop
Daddy Freddie
Daddy Long Legs
Daddy Longlegs
Daddy Rings
Daddy Stovepipe
Daddy-O
DAF
Daffan, Ted
Daft Punk
Dahlgren, Eva
Dahlander, Bert
Dailey, Dan
Dailey, Frank
Dailey, Pete
Daily Flash
Daily, Pappy
Daily, Pete
Daintees
Dairo, I.K.
Daisy Chainsaw
Dakeyne, Paul
Dakota
Dakotas
Dale And Grace
Dale, Alan
Dale, Colin
Dale, Jim
Dale, Kenny
Dale, Larry
Dalek I Love You
Daley, Lloyd
Dalhart, Vernon
Dali's Car
Dalida
Dalienst
Dall, Cindy
Dallas, Leroy
Dallas, Rex
Dallas, Yodelin'
    Slim
Dallwitz, Dave
Dalriada
Dalseth, Laila
Dalton, Kathy
Dalton, Lacy J.
Dalton, Larry
Daltrey, Roger
Daly Wilson Big
    Band
Damage
Damba, Fanta
Dameron, Tadd
Dames
Dames At Sea
Damian

Damien Thorne
Damn The
  Machine
Damn Yankees
Damn Yankees
  (film musical)
Damn Yankees
  (stage musical)
Damned
Damone, Vic
Damsel In
  Distress, A
Dan, Michael
Dana
Dana, Vic
Dance A Little
  Closer
Dance Band
Dance Craze
Dancehall
Dancehall Queen
Dancer, Prancer
  And Nervous
Dancin'
Dancing Did
Dancing Lady
Dancing Years,
  The
Dandelion
  Records
Danderliers
Dando Shaft
Dandridge,
  Putney
Dandy, Jim
Dandys
Dane, Barbara
Dane, Dana
Danel, Pascal
Danger, Danger
Dangerface
Dangerous Toys
Dangerous When
  Wet
Daniel Band
Daniel, Dale
Daniel, Davis
Daniele, Pino
Daniels, Billy
Daniels, Charlie
Daniels, Eddie
Daniels, Joe
Daniels, Julius
Daniels, Luke
Daniels, Maxine
Daniels, Mike
Daniels, Phil, And
  The Cross
Daniels, Roly
Danko, Rick
Dankworth, Jacqui
Dankworth, John
Danleers
Danniebelle
Danny And Dusty
Danny And The
  Juniors

Danny Wilson
Danse Society
Dantalion's Chariot
Dante And The
  Evergreens
Dante, Ron
Danzig
Danzig, Evelyn
Daouda, Tou
  Kone
Daphne's Flight
Darby And
  Tarlton
Darby, 'Blind'
  Teddy
Darby, Ken
Darbyshire,
  Richard
Dardanelle
Dare
Darensbourg, Joe
Darin, Bobby
Dark Angel
Dark Ducks
Dark Heart
Dark Lord
Dark Star
Dark Wizard
Darkman
Darko, George
Darling Buds
Darling, David
Darling, Denver
Darling, Erik
Darnell, Larry
Darrell, Johnny
Darren, James
Darrow, Chris
Darryl-Ann
Dartells
Darts
Darxon
Daryll Ann
Das-EFX
Dash, Julian
Dassin, Joe
Dauner, Wolfgang
Dave And Ansell
  Collins
Dave And Sugar
Dave Dee, Dozy,
  Beaky, Mick
  And Tich
Davenport, Bob
Davenport,
  Charles
  Edward 'Cow
  Cow'
Davenport, Jed
Davenport,
  Lester
Davern, Kenny
Davey D
David And Jonathan
David Devant
  And His Spirit
  Wife

David, Hal
David, Mack
Davidson, Brian
  'Blinky'
Davies, Cyril
Davies, Dave
Davies, Debbie
Davies, Gail
Davies, Iva
Davies, John R.T.
Davies, Litsa
Davies, Ray
Davis, 'Billy'
  Roquel
Davis, 'Blind' John
Davis, Anthony
Davis, Art
Davis, Benny
Davis, Billie
Davis, Carl
Davis, Carl (R&B)
Davis, Carlene
Davis, CeDell 'Big
  G'
Davis, Clive
Davis, Danny,
  And The
  Nashville Brass
Davis, Eddie
  'Lockjaw'
Davis, Ernestine
  'Tiny'
Davis, Gary, Rev.
Davis, Geater
Davis, James
  'Thunderbird'
Davis, Jesse
Davis, Jesse 'Ed'
Davis, Jimmie
Davis, Jimmy
  'Maxwell
  Street'
Davis, Johnny
  'Scat'
Davis, Larry
Davis, Lem
Davis, Linda
Davis, Mac
Davis, Martha
Davis, Meg
Davis, Miles
Davis, Nathan
Davis, Paul
Davis, Richard
Davis, Ronnie
Davis, Roy, Jnr.
Davis, Sammy,
  Jnr.
Davis, Skeeter
Davis, Spencer
Davis, Spencer,
  Group
Davis, Stu
Davis, Tyrone
Davis, Walter
Davis, Wild Bill
Davison, Wild Bill

Dawkins, Jimmy
Dawn
Dawn, Billy,
  Quartette
Dawn, Dolly
Dawson, Alan
Dawson, Dana
Dawson, Jim
Dawson, Smoky
Dax, Danielle
Day In
  Hollywood, A
Day, Bobby
Day, Curtis
Day, Dennis
Day, Doris
Day, Francis
Day, Jill
Day, Jimmy
Day, Margie
Day, Steve, And
  The Drifters
Daylighters
Dayne, Taylor
Dazz Band
dB's
dc Talk
De Berry, Jimmy
De Burgh, Chris
De Castro Sisters
De Castro, Leo
De Coque, Oliver
De Dannan
De Franco, Buddy
De Grassi, Alex
De Haven, Gloria
De La Fé, Alfredo
De La Luz,
  Orquesta
De La Soul
De Lange, Eddie
De Mille, Agnes
De Paris, Sidney
De Paris, Wilbur
De Paul, Gene
De Paul, Lynsey
De Sylva, Brown
  And Henderson
De Sylva, Buddy
Deacon Blue
Dead Boys
Dead Can Dance
Dead Dead Good
Dead End Kids
Dead Famous
  People
Dead Kennedys
Dead Milkmen
Dead Or Alive
Dead Ringer
Deaf Dealer
Deaf School
Deal, Kelley
Dean, Billy
Dean, Bob And
  Cindy
Dean, Eddie

Dean, Elton
Dean, Jimmy
Dean, Joanna
Dean, Nora
Dean, Paul
Déanta
Dearest Enemy
Dearie, Blossom
Dearly Beheaded
Death
Death Angel
Death In Vegas
Death Mask
Death Of Vinyl
Death Row
DeBarge
DeBarge, Bunny
DeBarge, Chico
DeBarge, El
Decameron
Decca Records
Deceptive
  Records
DeConstruction
Dede, Amakye,
  And The
  Apollo Kings
  International
  Band
Dederick, Rusty
Dee, David
Dee, Joey, And
  The Starliters
Dee, Kiki
Dee, Lenny
Deems, Barrett
Deene, Carol
Deep Blue
  Something
Deep Feeling
Deep Forest
Deep Freeze
  Mice
Deep Freeze
  Productions
Deep Fried
Deep In My Heart
Deep Purple
Deep River Boys
Deep Switch
Deére, Darron
Dees, Rick, And
  His Cast Of
  Idiots
Dees, Sam
Def FX
Def Jam Records
Def Jef
Def Leppard
Def Wish Cast
DeFaut, Volly
Defiance
Definition Of
  Sound
DeFranco Family
Defries, David
Deftones

Defunkt
Degrees Of
    Motion
DeHaven, Penny
Deicide
Deighton Family
Deiseal
Déjà Vu
Dejan, Harold
DeJohn Sisters
DeJohnette, Jack
Dekker,
    Desmond
Del Amitri
Del Fuegos
Del Lords
Del Tha Funky
    Homosapien
Del-Fi Records
Del-Satins
Del-Vikings
Delafose, John
Delaney And
    Bonnie
Delaney, Eric
Delerue, Georges
Delfonics
Delgado, Junior
Delgados
Delicatessen
Delicious Vinyl
Delivery
Dell-Vikings
Dello, Pete
Dells
Delltones
Delmar, Elaine
Delmark Records
Delmonas
Delmore
    Brothers
Delpech, Michel
Delroys
Delta 5
Delta Rhythm
    Boys
Delta 72
Deltones
Demensions
Dement, Iris
Demolition 23
Demon
Demon Boyz
Demon Records
Den
Den Fule
Dene, Terry
Denim
Denison/Kimball
    Trio
Deniz, Joe
Dennerlein,
    Barbara
Dennis, Cathy
Dennis, Denny
Dennis, Jackie
Dennis, Matt

Dennisons
Denny, Jim
Denny, Martin
Denny, Sandy
Dentists
Denton, Richard,
    And Martin
    Cook
Denver, John
Denver, Karl
Denzil
Deodato
Department S
Depeche Mode
Depth Charge
Derailers
Deram Records
Derek And The
    Dominos
Derek B
Derringer, Rick
Derwin, Hal
Des Barres,
    Michael
Des'ree
DeSanto, Sugar
    Pie
Descendents
Desert Rose Band
Desert Song, The
DeShannon,
    Jackie
Desire
Desires
Desjardins,
    Richard
Desmond, Johnny
Desmond, Paul
Desperate
    Bicycles
Desperate Danz
    Band
Destiny
Destroy All
    Monsters
Destruction
Destructors
Destry Rides
    Again
Detective
Detente
Detergents
Determine
Detroit Emeralds
Detroit Junior
Detroit Spinners
Detroit's Most
    Wanted
Detroit, Marcella
Deuce
Deuchar, Jimmy
dEUS
Deutsch, Adolph
Deutscher, Drafi
DeVaughn,
    William
Devera Ngwena

Deviants
DeVille, Willy
Devine And
    Statton
Devlin, Johnny
Devo
Devotions
Devoto, Howard
Dexter, Al
Dexys Midnight
    Runners
DeYoung, Cliff
DeYoung, Dennis
DFC
Dharma Bums
Dharmas
Di Novi, Gene
Di'Anno's, Paul,
    Battlezone
Diabate, Mama
Diabate, Sekouba
    'Bambino'
Diabate, Sona
Diabate,
    Toumani
Diablos
Dial, Harry
Diamond D
Diamond Head
Diamond
    Horseshoe
Diamond Rio
Diamond, Jim
Diamond, Leo
Diamond, Neil
Diamonds
    (Canada)
Diamonds (USA)
Dianno
Diatta, Pascal
Dibala, Diblo
Dibango, Manu
Dicey, Bill
Dick And Dee
    Dee
Dickens, Charles
Dickens, Hazel
Dickens, Little
    Jimmy
Dickenson, Vic
Dickerson,
    Carroll
Dickerson, Walt
Dickies
Dickinson, Bruce
Dickinson, Kim
Dickson, Barbara
Dickson, Dorothy
Dictators
Diddley, Bo
Die Cheerleader
Die Kreuzen
Die Krupps
Die Monster Die
Died Pretty
Diesel
Diesel Park West

Dietrich, Marlene
Dietz, Howard
Dif Juz
Different Drums
    Of Ireland
Diffie, Joe
Difford And
    Tilbrook
DiFranco, Ani
Dig
Dig Records
Digable Planets
Digance, Richard
Diggers
Digi Dub
Digital
Digital B
Digital
    Underground
Digital, Bobby
Digitalis
Dill, Danny
Dillard And Clark
Dillard, Bill
Dillard, Doug
    And Rodney
Dillard, Moses
Dillard, Varetta
Dillards
Dillinger
Dillon, Dean
Dillon, Phylis
Dils
Dim Stars
Dimensión Latina
Dimension
    Records
DiMeola, Al
Dimitri
DiMucci, Dion
Dingle Spike
Dingoes
Dinning Sisters
Dinning, Mark
Dino
Dino, Desi And Billy
Dino, Kenny
Dinosaur Jr
Dinosaurs
DiNovi, Gene
Dio, Ronnie
    James
Dion And The
    Belmonts
Dion, Celine
DiPiero, Bob
Dire Straits
Dirt Nation
Dirtsman
Dirty Blues Band
Dirty Dancing
Dirty Dozen
    Brass Band
Dirty Looks
Dirty Three
Dirty Tricks
Dirty White Boy

Disc Jockey
    Jamboree
Discharge
Disco Evangelists
Disco Four
Disco Magic
    Records
Disco Tex And
    The Sex-O-
    Lettes
Dishwalla
Disk-O-Tek
    Holiday
Disley, Diz
Dislocation
    Dance
Dismember
Disney, Walt
Disorder
Disposable
    Heroes Of
    Hiphoprisy
Dissidenten
Distel, Sacha
Distractions
Dittman, Kyat-
    Hend
Divine Comedy
Divine Horsemen
Diving For Pearls
Divinyls
Dixie Cups
Dixie Dregs
Dixie Echoes
Dixie Flyers
Dixie
    Hummingbirds
Dixie Melody
    Boys
Dixies
Dixon Brothers
Dixon, Adele
Dixon, Bill
Dixon, Charlie
Dixon, Don
Dixon, Floyd
Dixon, Fostina
Dixon, Jesse
Dixon, Mary
Dixon, Mort
Dixon, Reginald
Dixon, Willie
DIY
Dizzy Miss Lizzy
DJ Biznizz
DJ Dag
DJ Duke
DJ Flowers
DJ Food
DJ Gusto
DJ Hollywood
DJ Hurricane
DJ International
DJ Jazzy Jeff And
    The Fresh
    Prince
DJ Krush

DJ Magic Mike
DJ Mark The 45 King
DJ Pete Jones
DJ Pierre
DJ Pogo
DJ Premier
DJ Quik
DJ S The Karminsky Experience
DJ Shadow
DJ Spooky
DJ SS
DJ Talla 2XLC
DJ Vadim
Djaimin
Django Reinhardt
Djavan
Djax Up Beats
DJM Records
DMZ
DNA
Do I Hear A Waltz?
Do Ray Me Trio
Do Ré Mi
Do Re Mi (stage musical)
DOA
Dobrogosz, Steve
Dobson, Dobbie
Dobson, Dobby
Dobson, Richard
Doc Holliday
Doctor Alimantado
Doctor And The Medics
Doctor Butcher
Doctor Dolittle
Doctor Ice
Doctor West's Medicine Show And Jug Band
Doctors Of Madness
Dodd, Coxsone
Dodd, Deryl
Dodd, Ken
Dodds, Baby
Dodds, Johnny
Dodge City Productions
Dodgion, Dottie
Dodgy
Dog Eat Dog
Dog Soldier
Dog's Eye View
Dog, Tim
Doggett, Bill
Dogs D'Amour
Dogstar
Dogwood
Doherty, Denny
Dokken
Dolan, Joe
Dolby, Ray, Dr.

Dolby, Thomas
Dolce, Joe
Doldinger, Klaus
Doll
Doll By Doll
Dollar
Dollar, Johnny
Dollface
Dolly Mixture
Dolly Sisters, The
Dolphy, Eric
Domain
Domingo, Placido
Dominique, Lisa
Dominique, Natty
Domino
Domino, Fats
Dominoes
Domnérus, Arne
Don And Juan
Don And The Goodtimes
Don Patrol
Don Yute
Don't Knock The Rock
Don't Knock The Twist
Don't Look Back
Donahue, Al
Donahue, Jerry
Donahue, Sam
Donahue, Tom
Donald And The Delighters
Donald, Barbara
Donald, Peter
Donaldson, Eric
Donaldson, Lou
Donaldson, Walter
Done Lying Down
Donegan, Dorothy
Donegan, Lonnie
Donelly, Tanya
Donen, Stanley
Donington Festival
Donner, Ral
Donovan
Donovan, Jason
Dont Bother Me I Cant Cope
Doobie Brothers
Doof
Dooleys
Doonan Family Band
Doonican, Val
Doors
Dootones
Dorado Records
Dore, Charlie
Dørge, Pierre
Dorham, Kenny
Dorman, Harold

Doro
Dorough, Bob
Dorsey, Jimmy
Dorsey, Lee
Dorsey, Thomas A.
Dorsey, Tommy
Dos
Doss, Tommy
Dot Records
Dotson, Big Bill
Dotson, Jimmy
Dottsy
Double Trouble
Double You?
Doucette
Doug E. Fresh
Dougherty, Eddie
Douglas, Blair
Douglas, Carl
Douglas, Carol
Douglas, Craig
Douglas, Isaac, Rev.
Douglas, Jerry
Douglas, Johnny
Douglas, K.C.
Douglas, Keith
Douglas, Mike
Douglas, Tommy
Doumbia, Nahaw
Dove, Ronnie
Dovells
Dowd, Tom
Dowell, Joe
Dowlands
Down
Down Argentine Way
Down By Law
Down River Nation
Down South
Downchild Blues Band
Downing, Big Al
Downing, Will
Downliners Sect
Downs, Johnny
Downy Mildew
Doyle, Charlie
Doyle, Teresa
Dozier, Lamont
Dr. Alban
Dr. Cosgill
Dr. Dre
Dr. Feelgood
Dr. Hook
Dr. Jeckyll And Mr Hyde
Dr. John
Dr. Mastermind
Dr. Nico
Dr. Octagon
Dr. Phibes And The House Of Wax Equations
Dr. Strangely Strange

Dr. Umezu
Dragon
Dragonfly Records
Drain
Drake, Alfred
Drake, Charlie
Drake, Nick
Drake, Pete
Dramatics
Dranes, Arizona Juanita
Dransfield, Barry
Dransfield, Robin And Barry
Dransfields
Draper, Rusty
Dread Zeppelin
Dread Zone
Dread, Mikey
Dream
Dream Academy
Dream Frequency
Dream Police
Dream Syndicate
Dream Theatre
Dream Warriors
Dream Weavers
Dreamers
Dreamgirls
Dreamlovers
Drennon, Eddie
Dresser, Mark
Drew, Kenny
Drew, Martin
Drew, Patti
Drifters
Drifting Cowboys
Drifting Slim
Driftwood, Jimmy
Driscoll, Julie
Drive
Drive, She Said
Driven
Driver
Driver 67
Drivin' N' Cryin'
Drizabone
Droge, Pete
Drones
Droogs
Drootin, Buzzy
Drop Nineteens
DRS
Dru Hill
Drug Free America
Drugstore
Drum Club
Drum Theatre
Drummond, Bill
Drummond, Don
Drummond, Tim
Drusky, Roy
Du Barry Was A Lady
Du-Droppers

Duarte, Chris, Group
Dub
Dub Federation
Dub Plate
Dub Poetry
Dub Syndicate
Dub War
DuBarry Was A Lady
Dube, Lucky
Dubin, Al
Dubliners
Dubs
Dubstar
Ducanes
DuCann, John
DuChaine, Kent
Duchin, Eddy
Duchin, Peter
Ducks Deluxe
Dudek, Gerd
Dudes
Dudgeon, Gus
Dudley, Anne
Dudley, Dave
Dudziak, Urszula
Dufay, Rick
Duff, Jeff
Duff, Mary
Duffy
Duffy's Nucleus
Dugites
Duke Bootee
Duke Jupiter
Duke Of Paducah
Duke Wore Jeans, The
Duke, Doris
Duke, George
Duke, Patty
Duke, Vernon
Dukes
Dukes Of Dixieland
Dukes Of Stratosphear
Dukes, 'Little' Laura
Dulcimer
Dulcimer, Appalachian and Hammered
Dulfer, Candy
Dummer, John, Blues Band
Dumpy's Rusty Nuts
Dunbar, Aynsley
Dunbar, Aynsley, Retaliation
Dunbar, Scott
Dunbar, Sly
Duncan, Darryl
Duncan, Hank
Duncan, Johnny
Duncan, Johnny, And The Blue Grass Boys

Duncan, Lesley
Duncan, Tommy
Duncan, Trevor
Dundas, David
Dunford, Uncle
    Eck
Dunham, Sonny
Dunhill Records
Duning, George
Dunkley, Errol
Dunn, Holly
Dunn, Johnny
Dunn, Ronnie
Dunn, Roy
Dunwich Records
Dupree, Big Al
Dupree,
    Champion Jack
Dupree, Simon,
    And The Big
    Sound
Duprees
Duran Duran
Durante, Jimmy
Durbin, Deanna
Durham, Eddie
Durham, Judith
Durkin, Kathy
Durocs
Durst, Lavada
    'Dr. Hepcat'
Durutti Column
Dury, Ian
Duskin, 'Big' Joe
Dust
Dust Brothers
Dust Junkys
Dusty, Slim
Dutch Swing
    College Band
Dutrey, Honore
Dutronc, Jacques
Duvivier, George
DVC
Dvorkin, Judith
Dweeb
Dyani, Johnny
    Mbizo
Dyer, Ada
Dyer, Bob
Dyer, Johnny
Dyke And The
    Blazers
Dykes, Omar
Dylan, Bob
Dylans
Dynametrix
Dynamic
    Superiors
Dynamites
Dyson, Ronnie
Dzadzeloi
E-40
E-Lustrious
E., Sheila
E.V.C.
Eade, Dominique

Eadie, Irene
Eager, Allen
Eager, Vince
Eagles
Eaglin, Snooks
Ealey, Robert
Eanes, Jim
Earforce
Earl Brutus
Earl Carroll's
    Vanities
Earl Sixteen
Earl, Robert
Earl, Ronnie
Earl, Vince
Earl-Jean
Earle, Steve
Earls
Earth Messengers
Earth Nation
Earth Opera
Earth Quake
Earth, Wind And
    Fire
Earthling
Earthshaker
East 17
East Of Eden
East Orange
East Texas
    Serenaders
Easter Brothers
Easter Parade
Easterhouse
Eastern Bloc
Eastman, Madeline
Easton, Elliot
Easton, Sheena
Easy
Easy Action
Easy Baby
Easy Come, Easy Go
Easy Mo
Easy Rider
Easybeats
Eat
Eater
Eaton, Connie
Eavesdropper
Eavis, Michael
Eazy E
Ebb, Fred
Eberle, Ray
Eberly, Bob
Ebonys
Eccles, Clancy
Echo And The
    Bunnymen
Echobelly
Echoes
Eckstine, Billy
Eclection
ECM Records
Ed.Og And Da
    Bulldogs
Eddie And The
    Hot Rods

Eddy And The
    Soul Band
Eddy, Duane
Eddy, Nelson
Eddy, Nelson,
    And Jeanette
    MacDonald
Edelhagen, Kurt
Edelman, Judith
Edelman, Randy
Edens, Roger
Edenton, Ray
Edge
Edison
    Lighthouse
Edison, Harry
    'Sweets'
Edmunds, Dave
Edsels
Edwards, Alton
Edwards, Archie
Edwards, Bobby
Edwards,
    Clarence
Edwards, Cliff
Edwards, David
    'Honeyboy'
Edwards, Dennis
Edwards, Don
Edwards, Eddie
Edwards, Frank
Edwards, Jackie
Edwards,
    Jonathan
Edwards,
    Jonathan And
    Darlene
Edwards, Moanin'
    Bernice
Edwards, Rupie
Edwards, Scott
Edwards, Stoney
Edwards, Teddy
Edwards, Tommy
Eek A Mouse
eels
Ef Band
Efford, Bob
EFX And Digit
Egan, Joe
Egan, Mark
Egan, Walter
Ege Bam Yasi
Egg
Egg (dance)
Eggs
Eggs Over Easy
Eggstone
8 Ball Records
8 Eyed Spy
808 State
801
Eight Records
18 Wheeler
8th Day
Eighth Wonder
Eikhard, Shirley

Einstein
Einsturzende
    Neubaten
Eire Apparent
Eitzel, Mark
Ekyan, André
El Din, Hamza
El Dorados
El Venos
Elastica
Elbert, Donnie
Elders, Betty
Eldridge, Joe
Eldridge, Roy
Elecampane
Electrafixion
Electribe 101
Electric Angels
Electric Boys
Electric Ceilidh
    Band
Electric Eels
Electric Flag
Electric Hellfire
    Club
Electric Indian
Electric Light
    Orchestra
Electric Love
    Hogs
Electric Prunes
Electric Sun
Electro
Electro Hippies
Electronic
Electropathics
Elegants
Elegies For
    Angels, Punks
    And Raving
    Queens
Eleison, Victoria
Elektra Records
Elements
Elend
Elevate
11:59
Eleventh Dream
    Day
Elf
Elgar, Charlie
Elgart, Larry
Elgart, Les And
    Larry
Elgins
Elias, Eliane
Elio E Le Storia
    Tese
Elixir
Elizalde, Fred
Elledge, Jimmy
Ellefson, Art
Elliman, Yvonne
Elling, Kurt
Ellington, Duke
Ellington, Marc
Ellington, Mercer

Ellington, Ray
Elliot, 'Mama' Cass
Elliott, Bern, And
    The Fenmen
Elliott, Mike
Elliott, Missy
Elliott, Ramblin'
    Jack
Elliott, Ron
Ellis, Alton
Ellis, Don
Ellis, Herb
Ellis, Hortense
Ellis, Mary
Ellis, Red
Ellis, Seger
Ellis, Shirley
Ellis, Terry
Ellis, Tinsley
Ellis, Vivian
Ellis, Wilbert 'Big
    Chief'
Ellison, Andy
Ellison, Lorraine
Elman, Ziggy
Eloy
Elsdon, Alan
Elstree Calling
Elvis On Tour
Elvis That's The
    Way It Is
Elvis The Movie
Ely, Brother Claude
Ely, Joe
Embarrassment
Embrace
Embry, 'Queen'
    Sylvia
Embryo
Emergency
Emerson, Bill
Emerson, Billy
    'The Kid'
Emerson, Darren
Emerson, Keith
Emerson, Lake
    And Palmer
Emery, Ralph
EMF
EMI Records
Emilio
Emmons, Buddy
Emotionals
Emotions
Emotions (male)
Emotive Records
Emperor
Empire Bakuba
En Vogue
Enchantment
End
Enemy
Energy Orchard
Engine Alley
England Dan And
    John Ford
    Coley

England's Glory
England, Ty
Engle, Butch, And
  The Styx
English Country
  Blues Band
English, John
English, Junior
English, Logan
English, Michael
Englishman
Enid
Enigma
Enjoy Records
Ennis, Ethel
Ennis, Seamus
Ennis, Skinnay
Eno, Brian
Enter The
  Guardsman
Entombed
Entwistle, John
Enuff Z'Nuff
Envy
Enya
Eon
Epic Soundtracks
Episode Six
Epitaph
Epitaph Records
Epps, Preston
Epstein, Brian
Equals
Equation
Erasure
Eric B And Rakim
Eric Steel Band
Eric's Trip
Erickson, Roky
Ericson, Rolf
Ether
Eros
Erskine, Peter
Ertegun, Ahmet
Ervin, Booker
Erwin, George
  'Pee Wee'
Escape Club
Escorts (UK)
Escorts (USA)
Escovedo
Escudero, Ralph
Eskimos And
  Egypt
ESP
Espiritu
Esquires
Esquivel
Essential Logic
Essex
Essex, David
Estefan, Gloria
Estefan, Gloria,
  And Miami
  Sound Machine
Estes, Sleepy John
Eternal

Eternals
Ethel The Frog
Etheridge, John
Etheridge,
  Melissa
Ethiopians
Ethix
Ethnic Heritage
  Ensemble
Ethos
Etting, Ruth
Eubanks, Kevin
Eugenius
Euphoria
Eurogliders
Europe
Europe, James
  Reese
Eurovision
Eurythmics
Eusebe
Evans, Bill
  (pianist)
Evans, Bill (saxo-
  phonist)
Evans, Dale
Evans, Doc
Evans, Gil
Evans, Herschel
Evans, Jay
Evans, Joe, And
  Arthur McLain
Evans, Lucky
Evans, Mal
Evans, Marjorie
  Ann 'Margie'
Evans, Maureen
Evans, Paul
Evans, Ray
Evans, Stump
Evans, Sue
Evans, Terry
Evans, Tolchard
Even Dozen Jug
  Band
Evensong
Ever Green
Everclear
Everett, Betty
Everett, Kenny
Everette, Jack
Everette, Leon
Evergreen
Evergreen
  Blueshoes
Everlast
Everly Brothers
Everpresent
  Fullness
Every Mother's
  Nightmare
Every Mother's
  Son
Every Which
  Way
Everybody's
  Cheering

Everyday's A
  Holiday
Everything But
  The Girl
Evil Dead
Evil Superstars
Evita
Evora, Cesaria
Ewans, Kai
Ewart, Douglas
Ewell, Don
Ewing, Skip
Ex
Excalibur
Excellents
Exciter
Exciter (The
  Netherlands)
Exciters
Executives
Exile
Exist Dance
Exit-13
Exodus
Experimental
Exploding White
  Mice
Exploited
Explorer
Export
Express
Expresso Bongo
  (film musical)
Expresso Bongo
  (stage musical)
Exquisites
Exterminator
Extreme
Extreme Noise
  Terror
EYC
Eyehategod
Eyeless In Gaza
Eyes
Eyes Of Blue
Eyuphuro
Ezell, Will
Ezio
Ezo
F.M.
F9s
Fab 5 Freddy
Fabares, Shelley
Fabian
Fabre, Candido
Fabric, Bent
Fabulous
Fabulous
  Dorseys, The
Fabulous Five Inc.
Fabulous Flames
Fabulous
  Rhinestones
Fabulous
  Thunderbirds
Face The Music
Face To Face

Facedancer
Facenda, Tommy
Faces
Factory (UK 60s)
Factory (UK 70s)
Factory Records
Fad Gadget
Faddis, Jon
Fadela, Chaba
Fagen, Donald
Fagerquist, Don
Fagin, Joe
Fahey, Brian
Fahey, John
Fain, Sammy
Fair, Yvonne
Fairchild, Barbara
Fairchild,
  Raymond
Fairfield Parlour
Fairground
  Attraction
Fairies
Fairport
  Convention
Fairweather
Fairweather,
  Digby
Fairweather-Low,
  Andy
Fairytale
Faith
Faith Brothers
Faith Hope And
  Charity
Faith No More
Faith Over
  Reason
Faith, Adam
Faith, Percy
Faithful Breath
Faithfull,
  Marianne
Faithless
Fajardo, José
Falco
Falco's, Tev,
  Panther Burns
Falcons
Falkner, Jason
Fall
Fallon, Jack
Falls, Ruby
False Prophets
Falsettoland
Fältskog,
  Agnetha
Fame
Fame, Georgie
Family
Family Cat
Family Dogg
Family Fodder
Family
  Foundation
Family Tree
Famous Jug Band

Famous Potatoes
Fan Fan, Mose
Fan Fan, Mosese
Fandango
Fandango (UK)
Fania All Stars
Fankhauser,
  Merrell
Fankhauser,
  Merrell, And
  HMS Bounty
Fanny
Fanny (stage
  musical)
Fantacy Hill
Fantasia
Fantastic Baggys
Fantastic Four
Fantastic Johnny
  C
Fantasticks, The
Fantasy Records
Fardon, Don
Farewell
  Performance
Fargo
Fargo, Donna
Farian, Frank
Farina, Mimi
Farina, Richard
Farinas
Farka, Ali Toure
Farley And Heller
Farley And Riley
Farley Jackmaster
  Funk
Farley, Eddie
Farlow, Tal
Farlowe, Chris
Farm
Farmer, Addison
Farmer, Art
Farmers Boys
Farnham, John
Farnon, Robert
Faron's
  Flamingos
Farr, Gary
Farr, Hugh
Farr, Karl
Farrell And
  Farrell
Farrell, Joe
Farrell, Wes
Farren, Mick
Farris, Dionne
Faryar, Cyrus
Fascinacion,
  Grupo
Fascinations
Fashek, Majek
Fashion\
Fashion Records
Fast Forward
Fastball
Faster Pussycat
Fastest Bat

Fastest Guitar
  Alive, The
Fastway
Fat Boys
Fat City
Fat Fantango
Fat Joe Da
  Gangsta
Fat Larry's Band
Fat Mattress
Fatback Band
Fatboy Slim
Fate
Fates Warning
Father
Father Abraham
  And The
  Smurfs
Fatima Mansions
Fatool, Nick
Faust
Favors, Malachi
Favre, Pierre
Fawkes, Wally
Faye, Alice
Fazola, Irving
Fear
Fear Factory
Fearing, Stephen
Fearless Four
Fearon, Phil
Feather, Leonard
Feathers, Charlie
Feeder
Feelies
Fehlmann,
  Thomas
Feinstein, Michael
Feld, Morey
Felder's Orioles
Feldman, Victor
Feliciano, José
Feline
Felix
Felix Da
  Housecat
Felix, Julie
Felix, Julie (90s)
Felix, Lennie
Fell, Simon
Fell, Terry
Feller, Dick
Fellside Records
Felt
Felts, Narvel
Femme Fatale
Fender, Freddy
Fender, Leo
Fendermen
Fennelly, Michael
Fenton, George
Fenton, Shane
Fentones
Ferguson, Ernest
Ferguson, H-
  Bomb
Ferguson, Jay

Ferguson, Johnny
Ferguson,
  Maynard
Ferrante And
  Teicher
Ferrari, Frederick
Ferrell, Rachelle
Ferris Wheel
Ferron
Ferry Across The
  Mersey
Ferry, Bryan
Festival
Fesu
Fever Tree
Feza, Mongezi
Ffrench, Robert
ffrr Records
Fiel Garvie
Field, Frank
Fields Brothers
Fields Of
  Ambrosia, The
Fields, Herbie
Fierce Heart
15-16-17
Fifth Angel
Fifth Avenue
  Band
Fifth Dimension
Fifth Estate
Fifty Foot Hose
Fifty Million
  Frenchmen
53rd & 3rd
Fig Dish
Figgy Duff
Fight
Fillmore
Filter
Fina, Jack
Final Four
Final Solution
Finch
Finckel, Eddie
Findask
Finders Keepers
Fine And Dandy
Fine Young
  Cannibals
Finegan, Bill
Fingerprintz
Fings Ain't Wot
  They Used
  T'Be
Finian's Rainbow
Finian's Rainbow
  (film musical)
Finitribe
Fink, Cathy
Finn
Finn, Mickey
Finn, Tim
Finnegan, Larry
Finnegan, Mike
Fio Rito, Ted
Fiol, Henry

Fiona
Fiorello!
Fire
Fire Engines
Fire Merchants
Fireballs
Firefall
Fireflies
Firefly, The
Firefly, The (film
  musical)
Firehose
Firehouse Five
  Plus 2
Fireside
Firesign Theatre
Fireworks
Firm
First Choice
First Choice
  Records
First Class
First Down
First Strike
Fischer Z
Fischer, Clare
Fischer, John
Fischer, Larry
  'Wild Man'
Fish
Fishbone
Fisher, Cilla, And
  Artie Trezise
Fisher, Doris
Fisher, Eddie
Fisher, Fred
Fisher, Mark
Fisher, Martin
Fisher, Miss Toni
Fisher, Morgan
Fisher, Shug
Fisk Jubilee
  Singers
Fisk, Charlie
Fist (Canada)
Fist (UK)
Fitzgerald, Ella
Fitzgerald, Mark
Fitzgerald,
  Patrick
Fitzroy, Edi
5 Royales
5X
Five Americans
Five Blind Boys
  Of Alabama
Five Blind Boys
  Of Mississippi
Five Boroughs
Five Breezes
Five Chances
Five Crowns
Five Discs
Five Dutones
Five Guys Named
  Moe
Five Hand Reel

Five Keys
Five Pennies, The
Five Red Caps
Five Satins
Five Sharps
Five Stairsteps
Five Star
Five Thirty
Fivepenny Piece
Fix, The
Fixx
Fjellaard, Gary
Flack, Roberta
Flahooley
Flame
Flamin' Groovies
Flaming Ember
Flaming Lips
Flaming Star
Flaming Stars
Flaming Youth
Flamingoes
Flamingos
Flanagan And
  Allen
Flanagan, Ralph
Flanagan,
  Tommy
Flanders And
  Swann
Flares
Flash
Flash Cadillac
  And The
  Continental
  Kids
Flash Faction
Flatmates
Flatt And Scruggs
Flatt, Lester
Flatville Aces
Flavin, Mick
Flavor Flav
Fleagle, Brick
Fleck, Bela
Flee-Rekkers
Fleet's In, The
Fleetwood Mac
Fleetwoods
Fleischman,
  Robert
Fleming, Mike
Flemming, Herb
Flemons, Wade
Flesh For Lulu
Flesh Quartet
Flesheaters
Fleshtones
Fletcher, Darrow
Fletcher, Liz
Fletcher, Tex
Flight From Folly
Flinch
Flint
Flint, Shelby
Flintlock
Flipper

Flirtations
Flo And Eddie
Floaters
Floating Bridge
Flock
Flood, Dick
Floodgate
Floorjam
Flora, The Red
  Menace
Floradora
Florence, Bob
Flores, Rosie
Florida
Florida Boys
Flory, Chris
Flory, Med
Flotsam And
  Jetsam
Flourgon
Flower Drum
  Song
Flower Drum
  Song (stage
  musical)
Flowered Up
Flowerpot Men
Flowers And
  Frolics
Flowers For
  Algernon
Flowers, Herbie
Flowers, Mike,
  Pops
Floyd, Eddie
Floyd, Frank
Fluffy
Fluke
Flux Of Pink
  Indians
Fly Records
Flying Aces
Flying Burrito
  Brothers
Flying Circus
Flying Colors
Flying Down To
  Rio
Flying High
Flying Lizards
Flying Machine
Flying Pickets
Flying Records
Flying Rhino
Flying Squad
Flys
FM
Focus
Foetus
Fogelberg, Dan
Fogerty, John
Fogerty, Tom
Foghat
Fol, Raymond
Foley, Betty
Foley, Red
Foley, Sue

Folies Bergère De Paris
Folk Implosion
Folk Och Rackare
Folk Stringers
Folks Brothers
Folkways Records
Follies
Follow A Star
Follow That Dream
Follow That Girl
Follow The Boys
Follow The Fleet
Follow The Girls
Follow Thru
Folly To Be Wise
Folque
Fomeen, Basil
Foncett, Frankie
Fong, Oden
Fontaine, Claudia
Fontana Records
Fontana, Carl
Fontana, Wayne
Fontane Sisters
Fontenot, Allen
Fontenot, Canray
Foo Fighters
Food Records
Foot In Coldwater, A
Footlight Parade
For Love Not Lisa
For Me And My Gal
For Squirrels
Foran, Dick
Forbert, Steve
Forbidden
Forbidden Broadway
Force Inc
Force MD's
Ford, Benjamin Francis 'Whitey'
Ford, Clinton
Ford, David
Ford, Dean, And The Gaylords
Ford, Emile, And The Checkmates
Ford, Frankie
Ford, Gerry
Ford, Joy
Ford, Lita
Ford, Martyn
Ford, Mary
Ford, Ricky
Ford, Robben
Ford, Tennessee Ernie
Forde, Florrie
Fordham, Julia
Forehand, Edward 'Little Buster'

Foreigner
Forest
Forest City Joe
Forester Sisters
Foresythe, Reginald
Forever Plaid
Forehand, Edward 'Little Buster'
Formanek, Michael
Formation Records
Formations
Formby, George
Formerly Fat Harry
Forrest
Forrest, George
Forrest, Helen
Forrest, Jimmy
Forrester, Howdy
Forrester, Sharon
Forster, Robert
Fortnox
Fortress
Fortune Records
Fortune, Lance
Fortune, Sonny
Fortunes
Forty-Five Minutes From Broadway
44 Magnum
44xes
42nd Street
Fosse, Bob
Foster And Lloyd
Foster, Al
Foster, Chris
Foster, Chuck
Foster, Frank
Foster, George 'Pops'
Foster, Joe
Foster, Leroy 'Baby Face'
Foster, Little Willie
Foster, Radney
Foster, Stephen
Fotheringay
Foul Play
Found Free
Foundation
Foundations
Fountain, Pete
Fountains Of Wayne
Four Aces
4AD Records
Four Blazes
Four Bucketeers
Four Buddies
Four Coins
Four Esquires

Four Fellows
Four Freshmen
4 Hero
Four Horsemen
400 Blows
Four Just Men
Four Knights
Four Lads
Four Lovers
Four Men And A Dog
Four Musketeers, The
4 Non Blondes
Four Pennies
Four Preps
4 Runner
Four Seasons
4 Skins
430 West Records
Four Tops
Four Tunes
Four Vagabonds
Four Voices
4 Yn Y Bar
Four-Evers
Fourmost
Fourplay
14 Iced Bears
Fourth World
Fowler, Wally
Fowley, Kim
Fowlkes, Charlie
Fowlkes, Eddie
Fox
Fox, Curly, And Texas Ruby
Fox, Norm, And The Rob-Roys
Fox, Roy
Fox, Samantha
Foxton, Bruce
Foxworthy, Jeff
Foxx, Inez And Charlie
Foxx, John
FPI Project
Frampton, Peter
Francis, Cleve
Francis, Connie
Francis, David
Francis, Joe
Francis, Winston
Francisco, Don
Franco
Francois, Claude
Frank And Walters
Frank Chickens
Frank, J.L.
Frank, Jackson C.
Franke And The Knockouts
Franke, Bob
Frankie
Frankie And Johnny

Frankie Goes To Hollywood
Franklin, Aretha
Franklin, C.L., Rev.
Franklin, Carolyn
Franklin, Chevelle
Franklin, Erma
Franklin, Guitar Pete
Franklin, Kirk, And The Family
Franklin, Rodney
Franks, Michael
Franz, Johnny
Fraser, Andy
Fraser, Dean
Fraternity Of Man
Frazier Chorus
Frazier, Calvin
Frazier, Dallas
Frazier, Josiah
Frazier, Philip
Freak Of Nature
Freakwater
Freaky Realistic
Freberg, Stan
Fred, John, And His Playboy Band
Freda'
Freddie And The Dreamers
Freddie Foxxx
Free
Free As Air
Free I
Free Kitten
Free Movement
Free Music Production
Freed, Alan
Freed, Arthur
Freed, Ralph
Freedley, Vinton
Freedom
Freedom Of Speech
Freeez
Freeform
Freeman, Alan
Freeman, Bobby
Freeman, Bud
Freeman, Chico
Freeman, Ernie
Freeman, Louis
Freeman, Russ
Freeman, Von
Freestyle Fellowship
Frehley's Comet
Frehley, Ace
Frenté
Frenzal Rhomb

Fresh Fruit Records
Fresh Gordon
Fresh Maggots
Freshies
Freshmen
Fresu, Paulo
Freur
Frey, Glenn
Fricke, Janie
Frida
Friday, Gavin
Friedhofer, Hugo Wilhelm
Friedman, Dean
Friedman, Kinky
Friedman, Marty
Friend And Lover
Friend, Cliff
Friends Again
Friends Of Distinction
Frijid Pink
Friml, Rudolph
Fripp, Robert
Frisco Kid
Frisell, Bill
Frishberg, Dave
Frith, Fred
Frizzell, David
Frizzell, Lefty
Froeba, Frank
Froggatt, Raymond
Frogmorton
From A Jack To A King
Froman, Jane
Fromholz, Steven
Front (1)
Front (2)
Front 242
Frost
Frost, Frank
Frumious Bandersnatch
Fruup
Fu Manchu
Fu-Schnickens
Fudge Tunnel
Fugain, Michel
Fugazi
Fugees
Fugs
Fuji
Fulford, Tommy
Full Force
Fuller, Bobby
Fuller, Curtis
Fuller, Gil
Fuller, Jesse 'Lone Cat'
Fuller, Johnny
Fulson, Lowell
Fun Boy Three
Fun Factory
Fun In Acapulco

Fun Lovin'
   Criminals
Fun-Da-Mental
Funderburgh,
   Anson
Fundis, Garth
Fungus
Funicello,
   Annette
Funkadelic
Funkdoobiest
Funkees
Funki Porcini
Funkmaster Flex
Funkmasters
Funky Four (Plus
   One More)
Funky Poets
Funny Face
Funny Face (film
   musical)
Funny Girl
Funny Girl (film
   musical)
Funny Lady
Funny Thing
   Happened On
   The Way To
   The Forum, A
Fuqua, Harvey
Furay, Richie
Fureys
Furlong, Michael
Furniture
Fury, Billy
Fuse
Future Sound Of
   London
Fuzzbox
Fuzztones
Fuzzy
Fuzzy Duck
G Love And
   Special Sauce
G, Shawnie
G-Clefs
G-Force
G-Wiz, Gary
G., Bobby
G., Gilly
G., Gina
G., Kenny
G., Warren
G.B.H.
G.G.F.H.
G.Q.
Gabinelli, Gerald
Gabler, Milt
Gabriel, Peter
Gabrielle
Gadd, Steve
Gaddy, Bob
Gael Linn
Gaff, Billy
Gaffney, Chris
Gage, Mark
Gage, Yvonne

Gaillard, Slim
Gaines, Charlie
Gaines, Earl
Gaines, Grady
Gaines, Reg E.
Gaines, Roy
Gainsbourg,
   Serge
Gaither, Bill
Gaither, Bill
   (country)
Gaither, Danny
Galactic Cowboys
Galas, Diamanda
Galaxie 500
Galbreath, Frank
Gale, Eric
Galeforce
Gall, France
Gallagher And
   Lyle
Gallagher, Rory
Galliano
Gallinger, Karen
Gallion, Bob
Gallon Drunk
Galloway, Jim
Galper, Hal
Galway, James
Gambale, Frank
Gamble And Huff
Gamblers
Game
Game Theory
Gamley, Douglas
Gamma
Gamma Ray
Ganafoul
Ganelin Trio
Gang Green
Gang Of Four
Gang Starr
Gang's All Here,
   The
Gangsta Pat
Ganja Kru
Ganley, Allan
Gant, Cecil
Gantry, Elmer
Ganxsta Rid And
   The Otha Side
Gap Band
Garage
Garbage
Garbarek, Jan
Garber, Jan
Garbutt, Vin
Garcia, Jerry
Gardiner, Boris
Gardner, Dave
Gare, Lou
Garfunkel, Art
Garland, Ed
   'Montudie'
Garland, Hank
Garland, Joe
Garland, Judy

Garland, Red
Garland, Terry
Garlow, Clarence
Garner, Erroll
Garner, Larry
Garnett, Gale
Garnier, Laurent
Garon, Jesse, And
   The
   Desperadoes
Garrett, Betty
Garrett, Kenny
Garrett, Leif
Garrett, Robert
   'Bud'
Garrett, Snuff
Garrick Gaieties,
   The
Garrick, David
Garrick, Michael
Garrison, Jimmy
Gas Mark 5
Gaskin
Gaskin, Barbara
Gaskin, Leonard
Gaslini, Giorgio
Gass
Gateley, Jimmy
Gates, David
Gateway Singers
Gathering Field
Gatlin, Larry,
   And The Gatlin
   Brothers Band
Gattis, Keith
Gatton, Danny
Gaughan, Dick
Gay Divorce
Gay Divorcee,
   The
Gay's The Word
Gay, Al
Gay, Connie B.
Gay, Noel
Gaye Bykers On
   Acid
Gaye, Marvin
Gayfeet Records
Gaylads
Gayle, Crystal
Gayle, Michelle
Gaynor, Gloria
Gaynor, Mitzi
Gayten, Paul
Gebert, Bobby
Geddes Axe
Geddins, Bob
Gee Street
   Records
Gee, Jonathan
Geesin, Ron
Geezinslaw
   Brothers
Geffen Records
Geffen, David
Geggy Tah
Geils, J., Band

Geldof, Bob
Geldray, Max
Geller, Herb
Gem
Gems
Gene
Gene And Debbe
Gene Krupa
   Story, The
Gene Loves
   Jezebel
General Echo
General Kane
General Levy
General Public
General Trees
Generation X
Genesis
Geneva
Genevieve
Genies
Genitorturers
Genius
Gentle Giant
Gentle Soul
Gentle, Johnny
Gentlemen Marry
   Brunettes
Gentlemen
   Prefer Blondes
Gentlemen
   Prefer Blondes
   (film musical)
Gentry, Bobbie
Gentry, Chuck
Gentrys
Geordie
George M!
George White's
   Scandals
George, Barbara
George, Fatty
George, Karl
George, Lowell
George, Robin
George, Sophia
Georgia Crackers
Georgia Satellites
Georgia Tom
Georgio
Geraldine Fibbers
Geraldo
Gerard, Danyel
Gerardo
Geremia, Paul
Germain,
   Donovan
German, Edward
Germano, Lisa
Germs
Geronimo Black
Gerrard, Alice
Gerrard, Denny
Gerry And The
   Pacemakers
Gershwin,
   George

Gershwin, Ira
Get Set VOP
Geto Boys
Getz, Stan
Geyer, Renee
Ghanaba, Kofi
Ghetto Mafia
Ghost
Ghost Dance
Ghost Goes Gear,
   The
Ghostwriters
GI Blues
Giant
Giant Sand
Gibb, Andy
Gibb, Barry
Gibb, Robin
Gibbons, Carroll
Gibbons, Steve
Gibbs, Georgia
Gibbs, Joe
Gibbs, Mike
Gibbs, Terri
Gibbs, Terry
Gibby
Gibson, Bob
Gibson, Clifford
Gibson, Debbie
Gibson, Don
Gibson, Harry
   'The Hipster'
Gibson, Lacy
Gibson, Lorne
Gibson, Orville H.
Gibson, Wayne,
   And The
   Dynamic
   Sounds
Gibson/Miller
   Band
Gidea Park
Gifford, Gene
Gift
Gifted
Gigi
Gigolo Aunts
Gil, Gilberto
Gilbert, Bruce
Gilbert, Jim
Gilberto, Astrud
Gilberto, João
Gilder, Nick
Gilgames J
Gill, Johnny
Gill, Vince
Gillan, Ian
Gillespie, Dana
Gillespie, Dizzy
Gillett, Charlie
Gilley, Mickey
Gillum, William
   McKinley 'Jazz'
Gilmer, Jimmy,
   And The
   Fireballs
Gilmore, Boyd

Gilmore, Jimmie
Dale
Gilmore, John
Gilmour, David
Giltrap, Gordon
Giltrap, Joe
Gimble, Johnny
Gimmie Shelter
Gin Blossoms
Ginsberg, Allen
Ginuwine
Gipsy Kings
Girard, Adele
Girard, Chuck
Girl
Girl Crazy
Girl Crazy (film
musical)
Girl Friend, The
Girl From Utah,
The
Girl Happy
Girls Against
Boys
Girls At Our Best
Girls Next Door
Girls Of The
Golden West
Girls On The
Beach, The
Girls! Girls! Girls!
Girlschool
Giscombe, Junior
Gismonti,
Egberto
Gist
Gitte
Giuffre, Jimmy
Giuffria
Gizmos
Glad
Gladiators
Glahe, Will
Glam Metal
Detectives
Glamma Kid
Glamorous
Hooligan
Glamorous Night
(film musical)
Glamorous Night
(stage musical)
Glaser, Don
Glaser, Tompall
Glasgow,
Deborahe
Glass House
Glass Menagerie
Glass, Philip
Glastonbury
Festival
Glazer, Tom,
And The Do-
Re-Mi Gleason,
Jackie
Glenn, Lloyd
Glencoe
Glenn And Chris

Glenn Miller
Story, The
Glenn, Garry
Glenn, Tyree
Glinn, Lillian
Glitter Band
Glitter, Gary
Global Village
Trucking
Company
Globe Unity
Orchestra
Glory Bell's Band
Glosson, Lonnie
Glove
Glover, Dave,
Band
Glover, Roger
Gloworm
Go Into Your
Dance
Go Johnny Go
Go West
Go! Discs
Go-Betweens
Go-Go's
Goanna
Goats
God Machine
Goddard, Vic,
And The
Subway Sect
Godding, Brian
Goddo
Godfathers
Godflesh
Godley And
Creme
Gods
Gods Little
Monkeys
Godspell
Godz
Goedert, Ron
Goffin, Gerry
Goffin/King
Gogmagog
Goins Brothers
Going Hollywood
Going My Way
Going Steady
Goins, Herbie
Golbey, Brian
Gold Diggers Of
Broadway
Gold, Andrew
Gold, Brian And
Tony
Gold, Harry
Goldberg, Barry
Goldberg, Stu
Golden Apple,
The
Golden Boy
Golden Carillo
Golden Dawn
Golden Disc, The
Golden Earring

Golden Gate
Quartet
Golden
Palominos
Golden Smog
Goldfinger
Goldie
Goldie And The
Gingerbreads
Goldilocks
Goldings, Larry
Goldkette, Jean
Goldman, Albert
Goldner, George
Goldsboro, Bobby
Goldsmith, Jerry
Goldwax Records
Golia, Vinny
Golliwogs
Golowin, Albert
Golson, Benny
Gomelsky,
Giorgio
Gomez, Eddie
Gomez, Roy
Gomm, Ian
Gompie
Gone To Earth
Gonella, Nat
Gong
Gonks Go Beat
Gonsalves, Paul
Gonzales, Babs
Gonzalez
Gonzalez, Celina
Gonzalez, Dennis
Gonzalez, Ruben
Goo Goo Dolls
Goober Patrol
Good Boy
Records
Good Looking
Records
Good News (film
musical)
Good News
Records
Good News!
(stage musical)
Good Rats
Good Rockin'
Charles
Good Rockin'
Tonite
Good Times
Good, Jack
Goodacre, Tony
Goodbye Girl,
The
Goodbye Mr.
Mackenzie
Goode, Coleridge
Goodfellaz
Goodhand-Tait,
Philip
Goodies
Gooding, Cuba
Goodman, Benny

Goodman, Dickie
Goodman, Steve
Goodness
Goodnight Vienna
Goodwin, Henry
Goodwin, Myles
Goodwin, Ron
Goofy
Goombay Dance
Band
Goons
Gopthal, Lee
Gordi
Gordon, Alan
Gordon, Archie
Gordon, Barry
Gordon, Claude
Gordon, Dexter
Gordon, Jimmie
Gordon, John
Gordon, Mack
Gordon, Robert
Gordon, Rosco(e)
Gordy, Berry
Gordy, Emory,
Jnr.
Gore, Charlie
Gore, Lesley
Gorefest
Gorilla
Gorillas
Gorka, John
Gorky Park
Gorky's Zygotic
Mynci
Gorme, Eydie
Gosdin, Vern
Gospel Fish
Gospel Seed
Gota And The
Low Dog
Gottehrer, Richard
Goudie, Frank
'Big Boy'
Goudreau, Barry
Gould, Morton
Goulder, Dave
Gouldman,
Graham
Goulet, Robert
Gowans, Brad
Goykovich, Dusko
Gozzo, Conrad
Grab Me A
Gondola
Grable, Betty
Grace, Teddy
Gracie, Charlie
Gracious
Graduate
Graduate, The
Graettinger, Bob
Graham Central
Station
Graham, Bill
Graham, Chick,
And The
Coasters

Graham, Davey
Graham, Jaki
Graham, Kenny
Graham, Larry
Graham, Len
Graham, Tammy
Grainer, Ron
Grainger, Richard
Gramm, Lou
Grammer, Billy
Gran Combo, El
Granahan, Gerry
Granata, Rocco
Grand Funk
Railroad
Grand Hotel
Grand Ole Opry
Grand Prix
Grand Puba
Grand, Otis
Grandaddy IU
Granderson, John
Lee
Grandmaster
Flash
Grandmaster
Slice
Grandmixer DST
Graney, Dave,
And The Coral
Snakes
Granmax
Grant Lee Buffalo
Grant, Amy
Grant, Coot, And
Sox Wilson
Grant, David
Grant, Della
Grant, Earl
Grant, Eddy
Grant, Gogi
Grant, Julie
Grant, Leola B.
'Coot'
Grant, Peter
Granz, Norman
Grapefruit
Grappelli,
Stéphane
Grass Roots
Grass-Show
Grateful Dead
Grauso, Joe
Grave Digger
Gravediggaz
Gravenites, Nick
Graves, Josh
Graves, Milford
Gravity Kills
Gravy Train
Gray, Arvella
Gray, Barry
Gray, Billy
Gray, Claude
Gray, David
Gray, Dobie
Gray, Dolores
Gray, Glen

Gray, Henry
Gray, Jerry
Gray, Mark
Gray, Otto, And
    His Oklahoma
    Cowboys
Gray, Owen
Gray, Wardell
Grayson, G.B.
Grayson, Hal
Grayson, Jack
Grayson, Kathryn
Grease
Grease (stage
    musical)
Grease Band
Greasy Bear
Great American
    Broadcast, The
Great Awakening
Great Caruso,
    The
Great Guitars
Great Hussar,
    The
Great Plains
Great Rock'n'Roll
    Swindle, The
Great Society
Great Waltz, The
Great White
Great Ziegfeld,
    The
Greatest Show
    On Earth
Greaves, R.B.
Grebenshikov,
    Boris
Grech, Ric
Greco, Buddy
Gréco, Juliette
Greedies
Green Apple
    Quick Step
Green Bullfrog
Green Day
Green Jelly
Green Linnet
    Records
Green Nuns Of
    The Revolution
Green On Red
Green River
Green, Adolph
Green, Al
Green, Bennie
Green, Benny
Green, Charlie
Green, Clarence
Green, Dave
Green, Freddie
Green, Garland
Green, Grant
Green, Jack
Green, Johnny
Green, Keith
Green, L.C.

Green, Leothus
    'Pork Chops'
Green, Lil
Green, Lilly
Green, Lloyd
Green, Peter
Green, Philip
Green, Urbie
Greenaway,
    Roger
Greenbaum,
    Norman
Greenberg,
    Florence
Greenbriar Boys
Greene, Jack
Greene, Richard
Greene, Tony
Greenslade
Greenslade, Dave
Greensleeves
    Records
Greenthal,
    Stanley
Greentrax
    Records
Greenway, Brian
Greenwich
    Village Follies
Greenwich, Ellie
Greenwillow
Greenwood,
    Charlotte
Greenwood, Lee
Greer, 'Big' John
Greer, Jim
Greer, Sonny
Greger, Max
Gregg, Ricky
    Lynn
Gregory, John
Gregory, Steve
Gregson And
    Collister
Greig, Stan
Gren
Grenadine
Grenfell, Joyce
Gretsch
Gretton, Rob
Grey Ghost
Grey, Al
Grey, Clifford
Grey, Joel
Grey, Sara
Greyhound
Gribbin, Tom
Grid
Grier, Jimmie
Griff, Ray
Griffin
Griffin Brothers
Griffin, Chris
Griffin, Johnny
Griffin, Ken
Griffin, R.L.
Griffin, Rex

Griffin, Sid
Griffith, Andy
Griffith, Nanci
Griffith, Shirley
Griffiths, Marcia
Grifters
Grim Reaper
Grimes, Carol
Grimes, Henry
Grimes, Tiny
Grimms
Grine, Janny
Gringos Locos
Grisman, David
Groce, Larry
Groenemeyer,
    Herbert
Grofé, Ferde
Grogan, Clare
Grolnick, Don
Grootna
Groove
    Corporation
Groove Theory
Grooverider
Groovy, Winston
Grope
Grossman, Albert
Grossman, Stefan
Grossman, Steve
Grosz, Marty
Grotus
Groundhogs
Group 'B'
Group Therapy
Growl
GRP Records
Grunge
Gruntruck
Gruntz, George
Grusin, Dave
Grusin, Don
Gryce, Gigi
Gryphon
GTO
GTOs
GTR
Guadalcanal
    Diary
Guana Batz
Guaraldi, Vince
Guarente, Frank
Guarnieri, Johnny
Guercio, Jim
Guerilla
Guérin, Roger
Guerra, Juan Luis
Guesnon, Creole
    George
Guess Who
Guest Stars
Guétary, Georges
Guided By Voices
Guidry, Greg
Guild
Guillory, Isaac
Guitar Gable

Guitar Gabriel
Guitar Nubbit
Guitar Shorty
Guitar, Bonnie
Gulda, Friedrich
Gullin, Lars
Gumbo
Gun (60s)
Gun (90s)
Gun Club
Guns N'Roses
Gunshot
Gunter, Arthur
Gunter, Hardrock
Gurtu, Trilok
Guru Guru
Guru Josh
Gurvitz, Adrian
Guthrie, Andy
Guthrie, Arlo
Guthrie, Gwen
Guthrie, Jack
Guthrie, Woody
Guy
Guy, Barry
Guy, Buddy
Guy, Freddie
Guy, Joe
Guy, Phil
Guys And Dolls
Guys And Dolls
    (film musical)
Gwaltney, Tommy
Gwangwa, Jonas
GWAR
Gwendal
Gymslips
Gypsies
Gypsy
Gypsy (film musi-
    cal)
Gypsy (stage
    musical)
Gypsy Queen
Gyrlz
GZR
H.P. Lovecraft
H2O
Habibiyya
Haçienda
Hackberry
    Ramblers
Hackett, Bobby
Hackett, Steve
Haddaway
Haddock,
    Durwood
Haden, Charlie
Hadi, Shafi
Hadley,
    Dardanelle
Hagans, Tim
Hagar, Sammy
Hagen, Nina
Hagers
Haggard, Merle
Haggart, Bob

Hague, Albert
Hague, Mel
Haig, Al
Haig, Paul
Haines, Connie
Haines, Norman
Hair
Haircut 100
Hairspray
Hairston, Curtis
Hakim, Omar
Hakim, Sadik
Hakmoun,
    Hassan
Halcox, Pat
Hale, Binnie
Hale, Corky
Hale, Monte
Hale, Robert
Hale, Sonnie
Hale, Theron,
    And His
    Daughters
Haley Sisters
Haley, Bill, And
    His Comets
Half A Sixpence
Half A Sixpence
    (film musical)
Half Japanese
Half Man Half
    Biscuit
Half Pint
Halifax Three
Hall And Oates
Hall, Adelaide
Hall, Al
Hall, Audrey
Hall, Bob
Hall, Connie
Hall, Daryl
Hall, Edmond
Hall, Gary
Hall, George
Hall, Henry
Hall, Herb
Hall, Hillman
Hall, James
Hall, Jim
Hall, Jimmy
Hall, Khristen
Hall, Larry
Hall, Minor
Hall, Pam
Hall, Rick
Hall, Robin, And
    Jimmie
    MacGregor
Hall, Roy
Hall, Terry
Hall, Tom T.
Hall, Tony
Hall, Tubby
Hall, Vera
Hall, Wendell
Hallberg, Bengt
Hallett, Mal

Halley, David
Hallom, Gerry
Hallows Eve
Hallyday, Johnny
Halo Of Flies
Halpin, Kieran
Halsey, Jim
Halstead, Henry
Hamada, Mari
Hamblen, Stuart
Hamill, Claire
Hamilton, Chico
Hamilton, George, IV
Hamilton, James
Hamilton, Jeff
Hamilton, Jimmy
Hamilton, Joe Frank And Reynolds
Hamilton, John 'Bugs'
Hamilton, Roy
Hamilton, Russ
Hamilton, Scott
Hamlisch, Marvin
Hamm, Stuart
Hammer
Hammer, Jan
Hammerhead
Hammersmith
Hammerstein, Oscar, II
Hammill, Peter
Hammond, Albert
Hammond, Beres
Hammond, Clay
Hammond, Fred
Hammond, John, III
Hammond, John, Jnr.
Hampel, Gunter
Hampton, Lionel
Hampton, Slide
Hamsters
Hancock, Butch
Hancock, Herbie
Hancock, Hunter
Hancock, Keith
Hand Of Glory
Handle, Johnny
Handsome Beasts
Handy, 'Captain' John
Handy, George
Handy, John, II
Handy, W.C.
Hank The Drifter
Hankins, Esco
Hanlon, Jerry
Hanly, Mick
Hanna, Jake
Hanna, Roland, Sir
Hannant, Beaumont

Hannett, Martin
Hannover Fist
Hanny
Hanoi Rocks
Hanrahan, Kip
Hans Christian Andersen
Hansen, Randy
Hanshaw, Annette
Hanson, John
Happenings
Happy
Happy Goodman Family
Happy Mondays
Happy Time, The
Hapshash And The Coloured Coat
Harbach, Otto
Harburg, E.Y. 'Yip'
Hard 2 Obtain
Hard Day's Night, A
Hard Meat
Hard Response
Hard Rock Café
Hard Stuff
Hard Times
Hard-Ons
Hardbag
Hardcastle, Paul
Hardee, John
Harden Trio
Harden, Arlene
Harder They Come, The
Hardfloor
Hardin And York
Hardin, Lil
Hardin, Tim
Harding, Buster
Harding, Mike
Hardkiss
Hardknocks
Hardline
Hardman, Bill, Jnr.
Hardman, Rosie
Hardstuff
Hardwicke, Otto 'Toby'
Hardy, Emmett
Hardy, Françoise
Hare, Auburn 'Pat'
Harem Holiday
Harem Scarum
Hargrove, Linda
Hargrove, Roy
Harle, John
Harlem Hamfats
Harlequin
Harley Quinne
Harley, Steve

Harlow, Larry
Harman, James
Harmolodics
Harmonica
Harmonica Fats
Harmony Grass
Harnell, Joe
Harnick, Sheldon
Harper, Ben
Harper, Billy
Harper, Charlie
Harper, Roy
Harpers Bizarre
Harpsichord
Harptones
Harrell, Bill
Harrell, Kelly
Harrell, Tom
Harriott, Derrick
Harriott, Joe
Harris, Alfred
Harris, Anita
Harris, Barry
Harris, Beaver
Harris, Benny
Harris, Betty
Harris, Bill
Harris, Craig
Harris, Corey
Harris, David Ryan
Harris, Dennis
Harris, Don 'Sugarcane'
Harris, Eddie
Harris, Edward P.
Harris, Emmylou
Harris, Gene
Harris, Gil
Harris, Hi Tide
Harris, Jet, And Tony Meehan
Harris, Johnny
Harris, Larnelle
Harris, Major
Harris, Marilyn
Harris, Max
Harris, Peppermint
Harris, Phil
Harris, Richard
Harris, Rolf
Harris, Roy
Harris, Simon
Harris, Ted
Harris, Thurston
Harris, Wee Willie
Harris, William
Harris, Wynonie
Harrison, Bobby
Harrison, Donald 'Duck'
Harrison, George
Harrison, Jerry
Harrison, Jimmy
Harrison, Mike

Harrison, Noel
Harrison, Rex
Harrison, Vernon 'Boogie Woogie Red'
Harrison, Wilbert
Harrold, Melanie, And Olly
Harry Crews
Harry, Deborah
Hart, Alvin Youngblood
Hart, Billy
Hart, Clyde
Hart, Corey
Hart, Freddie
Hart, Grant
Hart, Hattie
Hart, Lorenz
Hart, Mickey
Hart, Mike
Hart, Moss
Hart, Tim, And Maddy Prior
Hartford, John
Harthouse Records
Hartley, Keef, Band
Hartley, Trevor
Hartman, Dan
Hartman, Johnny
Harvest Ministers
Harvest Records
Harvey
Harvey Girls, The
Harvey, Alex
Harvey, PJ
Harvey, Richard
Harvey, Roy
Hashim, Michael
Hasselgård, 'Stan' Ake
Hassell, Jon
Hastings, Lennie
Hatch, Tony
Hatcher, George, Band
Hatfield And The North
Hatfield, Juliana
Hathaway, Donny
Haughton, Chauncey
Haunted
Haurand, Ali
Havalinas
Havana 3A.M.
Havana Black
Have A Heart
Haven, Alan
Havens, Bob
Havens, Richie
Haver, June
Havohej
Hawaii
Hawdon, Dickie

Hawes, Hampton
Hawkes, Chesney
Hawkins, 'Screamin' Jay'
Hawkins, Coleman
Hawkins, Dale
Hawkins, Edwin, Singers
Hawkins, Erskine
Hawkins, Hawkshaw
Hawkins, Ronnie
Hawkins, Roy
Hawkins, Sophie B.
Hawkins, Ted
Hawkins, Walter
Hawkins, Walter 'Buddy Boy'
Hawkwind
Hawthorne, Vaughan
Hawtin, Richie
Hay, George D.
Hayes, Bill
Hayes, Clancy
Hayes, Edgar
Hayes, Isaac
Hayes, Louis
Hayes, Martin
Hayes, Tubby
Hayes, Wade
Hayman, Richard
Haymer, Herbie
Haymes, Dick
Haymes, Joe
Haynes, Roy
Haysi Fantayzee
Hayton, Lennie
Hayward, Justin
Haywire
Haywire Mac
Haywood, Leon
Hayworth, Rita
Haza, Faisal
Haza, Ofra
Haze
Hazel, Monk
Hazlehurst, Ronnie
Hazlewood, Lee
Head
Head East
Head Machine
Head, Murray
Head, Roy
Headboys
Headgirl
Headpins
Heads, Hands And Feet
Headswim
Healey, Jeff
Heap, Imogen
Heap, Jimmy, And The Melody Masters

Hear 'N' Aid
Hear My Song
Heard, J.C.
Heard, John
Hearn, George
Heart
Heart Throbs
Heartbeats
Heartbreakers
Heartland Reggae
Hearts And
  Flowers
Hearts Of Fire
Heartsman,
  Johnny
Heartwood, Kiya
Heath Brothers
Heath, Al
  'Tootie'
Heath, Jimmy
Heath, Percy
Heath, Ted
Heathcliff
Heatmiser
Heatwave
Heaven
Heaven 17
Heaven And
  Earth
Heaven's Edge
Heavenly
Heavenly Records
Heavy D And The
  Boyz
Heavy Jelly
Heavy Load
Heavy Metal
Heavy Metal Army
Heavy Metal Kids
Heavy Pettin
Heavy Stereo
Hebb, Bobby
Heberer, Thomas
Heckmann,
  Thomas
Hecksher, Ernie
Heckstall-Smith,
  Dick
Hedgehog Pie
Hedgehoppers
  Anonymous
Hedges, Michael
Hedningara
Hedzolleh
  Soundz
Hee Haw
Hefti, Neal
Hegamin, Lucille
Heidi Of
  Switzerland
Heidt, Horace
Heintje
Heinz
Heir Apparent
Heitor
Helen And The
  Horns

Helium
Helix
Hell, Richard
Hellanbach
Hellcats
Hellfield
Hellhammer
Hellion
Hello
Hello, Dolly! (film
  musical)
Hello, Dolly!
  (stage musical)
Hello, Frisco,
  Hello
Helloise
Helloween
Hellzapoppin
Helm, Levon
Helmet
Helms, Bobby
Helms, Don
Helms, Jimmy
Help
Help Yourself
Help!
Helstar
Hemingway,
  Gerry
Hemphill, Jessie
  Mae
Hemphill, Julius
Hemphill, Sid
Hemphills
Henderson, Bill
Henderson,
  Bobby
Henderson, Bugs
Henderson, Chick
Henderson,
  Dorris
Henderson, Duke
Henderson, Eddie
Henderson,
  Fletcher
Henderson,
  Hamish
Henderson,
  Horace
Henderson, Joe
Henderson, Joe
  'Mr Piano'
Henderson,
  Kelvin
Henderson, Lyle
  'Skitch'
Henderson,
  Michael
Henderson, Mike
Henderson, Ray
Henderson, Rosa
Henderson, Scott
Hendricks, Jon
Hendricks, Scott
Hendrix, Jimi
Hendryx, Nona
Heneker, David

Henley, Don
Henley, John Lee
Hennessys
Henry Cow
Henry, Big Boy
Henry, Clarence
  'Frogman'
Henry, Ernie
Henry, Haywood
Henry, Joe
Henry, Marcia
Henry, Pauline
Henry, Stuart
Henry, Thomas
Henrys
Henshall, Ruthie
Henske, Judy
Hensley, Ken
Henson, Leslie
Heptones
Herbal Mixture
Herbaliser
Herbert, Victor
Herbolzheimer,
  Peter
Herd
Here We Go
  Round The
  Mulberry Bush
Heretic
Herfurt, Skeets
Heritage
Herman's
  Hermits
Herman, Jerry
Herman, Lenny
Herman, Woody
Hermeljin, Dylan
Herndon, James
Herndon, Ty
Heron
Heron, Mike
Herring, Vincent
Herrmann,
  Bernard
Hersh, Kristin
Hession, Paul
Hester, Carolyn
Hewerdine, Boo
Hey Boy! Hey
  Girl!
Hey Let's Twist
Heyman, Edward
Heyward, Nick
Heywood, Eddie
Heywood,
  Heather
Hex
Hi Records
Hi-Bias Records
Hi-C
Hi-Life
  International
Hi-Lo's
Hiatt, John
Hibbard, Bruce
Hibbler, Al

Hickey, Chris
Hickman, Art
Hickory Wind
Hicks, Dan
Hicks, Edna
Hicks, Jacqui
Hicks, Johnny
Hideaways
Higginbotham,
  J.C.
Higginbottom,
  Geoff
Higgins, Bertie
Higgins, Billy
Higgins, Chuck
Higgins, Lizzie
Higgins, Monk
Higgs, Joe
High
High Button
  Shoes
High Country
High Inergy
High Llamas
High Note
  Records
High Society
High Spirits
High Tide
High, Wide And
  Handsome
Higher And
  Higher
Higher
  Intelligence
  Agency
Higher State
  Records
Highlife
Highlights
Hightower,
  Rosetta
Highway 101
Highway QC's
Highway Robbery
Highwaymen
Higsons
Hijack
Hijas Del Sol
Hildegarde
Hilder, Tony
Hill, Andrew
Hill, Benny
Hill, Bertha
  'Chippie'
Hill, Billy
Hill, Dan
Hill, Ernest
Hill, Faith
Hill, Goldie
Hill, Jessie
Hill, Michael
Hill, Rosa Lee
Hill, Teddy
Hill, Tiny
Hill, Vince
Hillage, Steve

Hilliard, Bob
Hillman, Chris
Hillside
Hillside Singers
Hillsiders
Hilltoppers
Hilton, Ronnie
Himber, Richard
Hinds, Justin
Hindu Love Gods
Hines, Deni
Hines, Earl
  'Fatha'
Hines, Marcia
Hines, Simone
Hinnen, Peter
Hino, Motohiko
Hino, Terumasa
Hinojosa, Tish
Hinsons
Hinton, Eddie
Hinton, Joe
Hinton, Milt
Hinze, Chris
Hip-Hop
Hipgnosis
Hipp, Jutta
Hipsway
Hirax
Hired Man, The
Hirt, Al
His Name Is Alive
Hiseman, Jon
Hissanol
Hit The Deck
  (film musical)
Hit The Deck
  (stage musical)
Hitchcock, Nicola
Hitchcock, Robyn
Hite, Les
Hithouse
Hittman
HMV Records
Ho'op'i'i Brothers
Hoax
Hobbs, Becky
Hockridge,
  Edmund
Hodeir, André
Hodes, Art
Hodges, Eddie
Hodges, Johnny
Hodgkinson,
  Colin
Hoez With
  Attitude
Hoffman, Al
Hoffs, Susanna
Hofner, Adolph
Hogan, John
Hogan, Silas
Hogg, John
Hogg, Smokey
Hogg, Willie
  'Smokey'
Hoggard, Jay

Hokum Boys
Holcombe,
Wendy
Hold Everything!
Hold My Hand
Hold On!
Holden, Ron
Holder, Terrence
Holdsworth,
Allan
Hole
Hole, Dave
Holiday Inn
Holiday, Billie
Holiday, Jimmy
Holland
Holland, Brian
Holland, Dave
Holland, Eddie
Holland, Jools
Holland, Maggie
Holland, Peanuts
Holland/Dozier/H
olland
Holley, 'Lyin" Joe
Holley, Major
Holliday, Jennifer
Holliday, Judy
Holliday, Michael
Hollies
Holloway, Brenda
Holloway, Ken
Holloway, Laurie
Holloway,
Loleatta
Holloway, Red
Holloway, Stanley
Holly And The
Italians
Holly, Buddy
Holly, Doyle
Hollywood
Argyles
Hollywood
Beyond
Hollywood Brats
Hollywood Fats
Hollywood
Flames
Hollywood Hotel
Holm, June
Holm, Michael
Holman, Bill
Holman, Eddie
Holman, Libby
Holmes Brothers
Holmes, Charlie
Holmes, Chris
Holmes, Clint
Holmes, David
Holmes, Richard
'Groove'
Holmes, Rupert
Holmes,
Winston, And
Charlie Turner
Holmes, Wright

Holness, Winston
'Niney'
Holocaust
Holt, Errol
Holt, John
Holts, Roosevelt
Holy Barbarians
Holy Ghost Inc
Holy Modal
Rounders
Holy Moses
Holzman, Jac
Hombres
Home Service
Home T
Homer And
Jethro
Homesick James
Homo Liber
Hondells
Honey Bane
Honey Boy
Honey Cone
Honeybus
Honeycombs
Honeycrack
Honeydogs
Honeydrippers
Honeyman-Scott,
James
Honeymoon Suite
Honeys
Honeysmugglers
Honky
Honourable
Apache
Hoodoo Gurus
Hoodoo Rhythm
Devils
Hooj Toons
Hook
Hooker, Earl
Hooker, John Lee
Hookey Band
Hookfoot
Hookim, Joseph
'Joe Joe'
Hooper, Les
Hooray For
What!
Hoosier Hot
Shots
Hooters
Hootie And The
Blowfish
Hope, Bob
Hope, Elmo
Hope, Lynn
Hopkin, Mary
Hopkins, Claude
Hopkins, Doc
Hopkins, Fred
Hopkins, Joel
Hopkins,
Lightnin'
Hopkins, Nicky
Hopper

Horizon 222
Horler, John
Horn, Paul
Horn, Shirley
Horne, Lena
Horner, James
Hornsby, Bruce,
And The Range
Horsburgh,
Wayne
Horse
Horslips
Horton, Johnny
Horton, Vaughan
Horton, Walter
'Shakey'
Host
Hot Butter
Hot Chocolate
Hot Gossip
Hot Knives
Hot Mikado
Hot Rod Gang
Hot Streak
Hot Tuna
Hotel
Hothouse
Flowers
Hotlegs
Houghton
Weavers
Hound-Dog Man
Hounds
Hour Glass
House
House Band
House Of Flowers
House Of Lords
House Of Love
House Of Pain
House, James
Housemartins
Houston, Cisco
Houston, Cissy
Houston, David
Houston, Edward
'Bee'
Houston, Joe
Houston, Thelma
Houston,
Whitney
Hovington, Frank
How To Stuff A
Wild Bikini
How To Succeed
In Business
Without Really
Trying
Howard And
Blaikley
Howard, Adina
Howard, Bob
Howard, Camille
Howard, Chuck
Howard, Darnell
Howard, Don
Howard, Eddy

Howard, Harlan
Howard, James
Newton
Howard, Jan
Howard, Johnny
Howard, Ken,
And Alan
Blaikley
Howard, Kid
Howard, Miki
Howard, Noah
Howard, Paul
Howard, Randy (1)
Howard, Randy (2)
Howard, Rosetta
Howe II
Howe, Steve
Howell, Peg Leg
Howes, Bobby
Howie B.
Howlin' Wilf
Howlin' Wolf
Hoyle, Linda
HR
HSAS
Hubba Hubba
Records
Hubbard, Freddie
Hubbard, Ray
Wylie
Hubble, Eddie
Hucko, Peanuts
Hudson Brothers
Hudson, Keith
Hudson, Lord
Tim
Hudson, Will
Hudson-Ford
Hue And Cry
Hues
Corporation
Huff, Luther
Hufstetter, Steve
Hug, Armand
Hugg, Mike
Huggy Bear
Hughes, David
Hughes, Glenn
Hughes, Jimmy
Hughes, Joe
'Guitar'
Hughes, Spike
Hughes/Thrall
Hughey, John
Hugill, Stan
Hula
Hulbert, Jack
Hull, Alan
Hull, Papa
Harvey, And
Long Cleve
Reed
Hullaballoos
Hum
Humair, Daniel
Human Beast
Human Beinz

Human League
Human Nature
Humble Pie
Humble, Derek
Humblebums
Humes, Helen
Hummon, Marcus
Humperdinck,
Engelbert
Humphrey, Percy
Humphrey, Willie
Humphries, Tony
100 Proof Aged
In Soul
Hunley, Con
Hunningale,
Peter
Hunsecker, Ralph
Blane
Hunt
Hunt, Clive
Hunt, Fred
Hunt, Geraldine
Hunt, Marsha
Hunt, Pee Wee
Hunt, Tommy
Hunter Muskett
Hunter, 'Long
John'
Hunter, Alberta
Hunter, Alfonzo
Hunter, Chris
Hunter, Ian
Hunter, Ivory Joe
Hunter, James
Hunter, Robert
Hunter, Tab
Hunter, Tommy
Hunter, Willie
Hunters And
Collectors
Hunting Of The
Snark, The
Hupfeld, Herman
Hurley, Michael
Hurley, Steve
'Silk'
Hurrah!
Hurricane
Hurricane #1
Hurt, Mississippi
John
Husband, Gary
Husik, Lida
Hüsker Dü
Husky, Ferlin
Hussain, Zakir
Hustler
Hustlers
Convention
Hustlers HC
Hutchenrider,
Clarence
Hutcherson,
Bobby
Hutchings, Ashley
Hutchinson, Dolly

Hutchinson, Leslie 'Hutch'
Hutchinson, Leslie 'Jiver'
Hutson, Leroy
Hutto, J.B.
Hutton, Betty
Hutton, Ina Ray
Hutton, Joe
Hutton, June
Hutton, Marion
Hyams, Margie
Hyder, Ken
Hydra
Hyland, Brian
Hylton, Jack
Hylton, Sheila
Hyman, Dick
Hyman, Phyllis
Hype-A-Delics
Hyper Go-Go
Hyperhead
Hypnotics, (Thee)
Hypnotist, The
Hypnotone
Hypocrisy
Hyskos
Hysterix
Hyts
I Can Get It For You Wholesale
I Could Go On Singing
I Do! I Do!
I Give My Heart
I Love My Wife
I Married An Angel
I Mother Earth
I Roy
I'd Rather Be Right
I'll Be Your Sweetheart
I'll Get By
I'm Getting My Act Together And Taking It On The Road
I've Got Horse
I, Ludicrous
I-Threes
Iam
Ian And Sylvia
Ian And The Zodiacs
Ian, Janis
Ibrahim, Abdullah
Ice
Ice Cube
Ice-T
Icebreaker
Icehouse
Ichiban
Icho Candy
Icicle Works
Icon

Ideals
Ides Of March
Idha
Idle Cure
Idle On Parade
Idle Race
Idol, Billy
If
If You Feel Like Singing
If?
Ifang Bondi
Ifield, Frank
Iggy Pop
Iglesias, Enrique
Iglesias, Julio
Ignorance
Ikettes
III (Featuring Al Skratch)
Illegal
Illegal Substance
Illinois Speed Press
Illusion
Imagination
Imaginations
Imagine
Imagine (stage musical)
Imlach, Hamish
Immaculate Fools
Immature
Immediate Records
Impalas
Impelliteri, Chris
Imperial Records
Imperial Teen
Imposter
Impressions
Imps
Impulse! Records
In Crowd
In Crowd (reggae)
In Dahomey
In Tua Nua
In-Be-Tweens
Inbreds
Incantation
Incognito
Incredible String Band
Incredibles
Incubus Succubus
Ind, Peter
Independents
Indigo Girls
Industrial
Infascelli, Silvia
Infectious Grooves
Infinite Wheel
Infinity Project, The
Infonet Records

Ingham, Keith
Ingle, Red
Ingram, James
Ingram, Luther
Ink Spots
Inky Blacknuss
Inman, Autry
Inmates
Inner Circle
Inner City
Inner City Unit
Inner Sanctum
Innes, Neil
Innocence
Innocence (techno)
Innocents
Inoue, Tetsuo
Inoue, Yosui
Insane Clown Posse
Insect Trust
Inside U.S.A.
Inspiral Carpets
Instant Funk
Instigators
Intelligent Hoodlum
Internal Records
International Artists Records
International Foot Language
International Submarine Band
International Sweethearts Of Rhythm
Into Another
Into Paradise
Into The Woods
Intrigue
Intrinsic
Intro
Intruders
Intveld, James
Investigators
Invincibles
Invisible Girls
Invisible Man's Band
Invitation To The Dance
INXS
Iommi, Tony
Iona
Iona And Andy
Iovine, Jimmy
IQ
IQ Procedure
Irby, Jerry
Irene
Iris, Donnie, And The Cruisers
Irma La Douce
Iron Butterfly

Iron Maiden
Iron Man, The
Ironhorse
Ironing Board Sam
Irvine, Andy
Irvine, Weldon
Irvis, Charlie
Irwin, Big Dee
Isaacs, Barry
Isaacs, Bud
Isaacs, David
Isaacs, Gregory
Isaacs, Ike
Isaacs, Mark
Isaak, Chris
Isham, Mark
Ishii, Ken
Ishola, Haruna
Islam, Yusuf
Island Records
Islanders
Islandica
Isle Of Wight Festivals
Isley Brothers
Isley, Jasper, Isley
Ismailov, Enver
Isola, Frank
Isotonik
Isotope
Israel Vibration
Israels, Chuck
It Bites
It Happened At The World's Fair
It Happened In Brooklyn
It's A Beautiful Day
It's A Bird, It's A Plane, It's Superman
It's Alive
It's All Happening
It's All Over Town
It's Always Fair Weather
It's Great To Be Young
It's Immaterial
It's In The Air
It's Love Again
It's Magic
It's Trad Dad
It's Your Thing
Itals
Its Alive
Ivansay
Ivers, Eileen
Ives, Burl
Ivey, Don
Iveys
Ivor Biggun
Ivy

Ivy League
Ivy, Quin
Iwan, Dafydd
Izenzon, David
Izit
J-Blast And The 100% Proof
J., Harry
J., Ollie
J.T. The Bigga Figga
Jack
Jack Frost
Jack The Lad
Jackie And Roy
Jackie And The Starlites
Jacks
Jacks, Terry
Jackson Five
Jackson Heights
Jackson, 'New Orleans' Willie
Jackson, Alan
Jackson, Armand 'Jump'
Jackson, Aunt Molly
Jackson, Bo Weavil
Jackson, Bullmoose
Jackson, Carl
Jackson, Chad
Jackson, Chubby
Jackson, Chuck
Jackson, Cliff
Jackson, Dee D.
Jackson, Deon
Jackson, Dewey
Jackson, Freddie
Jackson, George
Jackson, J.J.
Jackson, Jack
Jackson, Jackie
Jackson, Janet
Jackson, Jermaine
Jackson, Jim
Jackson, Joe
Jackson, John
Jackson, Larry
Jackson, LaToya
Jackson, Lee
Jackson, Li'l Son
Jackson, Mahalia
Jackson, Michael
Jackson, Millie
Jackson, Milt 'Bags'
Jackson, Oliver
Jackson, Papa Charlie
Jackson, Peg Leg Sam
Jackson, Preston
Jackson, Quentin
Jackson, Ronald Shannon

Jackson, Shot
Jackson, Stonewall
Jackson, Tommy
Jackson, Tony
Jackson, Walter
Jackson, Wanda
Jacksons
Jackyl
Jacob's Mouse
Jacobites
Jacobs, 'Boogie Jake'
Jacobs, Dick
Jacobsen, Erik
Jacques Brel Is Alive And Well And Living In Paris
Jacquet, Illinois
Jade
Jade Warrior
Jae, Jana
Jaffa, Max
Jag Panzer
Jag Wire
Jagged Edge
Jagger, Chris
Jagger, Mick
Jaggerz
Jags
Jaguar
Jaguars
Jah Free
Jah Lion
Jah Screw
Jah Shaka
Jah Stitch
Jah Stone
Jah Warriors
Jah Wobble
Jah Woosh
Jahmali
Jahson, David
Jai
Jailhouse Rock
Jakszyk, Jakko
Jale
Jam
Jamaica
Jamal-Ski
Jamaneh, Bubacar
Jamboree
James
James Gang
James, Bob
James, Calvin
James, Colin
James, Dick
James, Elmore
James, Etta
James, Frank 'Springback'
James, George
James, Harry
James, Jesse

James, Jimmy
James, Jimmy, And The Vagabonds
James, John
James, Joni
James, Nicky
James, Rick
James, Siân
James, Skip
James, Sonny
James, Steve
James, Tommy
James, Tommy, And The Shondells
James, Wendy
James, Willie Bee
Jameson, James
Jamiroquai
Jammin' The Blues
Jan And Arnie
Jan And Dean
Jan And Kjeld
Jan Dukes De Grey
Jane's Addiction
Janis
Jankowski, Horst
Jansch, Bert
Jap, Philip
Japan
Jaramillo, Jerry
Jarman, Joseph
Jarmels
Jarre, Jean-Michel
Jarre, Maurice
Jarreau, Al
Jarrell, Tommy
Jarrett, Art
Jarrett, Keith
Jarrett, Pigmeat
Jarrett, Winston
Jars Of Clay
Jarvis, Clifford
Jarvis, J.D.
Jason And The Scorchers
Jason Crest
Jaspar, Bobby
Javells
Jawara, Jali Musa
Jaxon, Frankie
Jay And The Americans
Jay And The Techniques
Jay, Barbara
Jay, Peter, And The Jaywalkers
Jaydee
Jaye, Jerry
Jayhawks
Jayhawks (R&B)
Jaynetts
Jazz At The Philharmonic

Jazz Butcher
Jazz Composer's Orchestra Association
Jazz Dance
Jazz Festivals
Jazz In Exile
Jazz Is Our Religion
Jazz Jamaica
Jazz Messengers
Jazz On A Summer's Day
Jazz Passengers
Jazz Singer, The
Jazz Warriors
Jazz writing
Jazzamatazz
Jazzie B.
Jazzy Jason
Jazzy Jay
Jazzy Jeff
Jazzy M.
JC001
Jean, Cathy, And The Roomates
Jeannie And The Big Guys
Jeeves
Jefferson
Jefferson Airplane
Jefferson Starship
Jefferson, Blind Lemon
Jefferson, Eddie
Jefferson, Hilton
Jefferson, Marshall
Jefferson, Thomas
Jeffery, Robert
Jeffrey, Joe, Group
Jeffrey, Paul H.
Jeffreys, Garland
Jeffries, Herb
Jekyll & Hyde
Jelly Beans
Jelly's Last Jam
Jellybean
Jellybread
Jellyfish
Jemini The Gifted One
Jenkins, Andrew
Jenkins, Billy
Jenkins, Bobo
Jenkins, Freddie
Jenkins, Gordon
Jenkins, Gus
Jenkins, Leroy
Jenkins, Martin
Jenkins, Snuffy, And Pappy Sherrill
Jenner, Peter
Jenney, Jack

Jennings, Tommy
Jennings, Waylon
Jennings, Will
Jensen, Kris
Jensen, Papa Bue
Jepson, Tony, And The Whole Truth
Jerome, Henry
Jerome, Jerry
Jeru The Damaja
Jerusalem Slim
Jessie, Obie Donmell 'Young'
Jesters
Jesus And Mary Chain
Jesus Christ Superstar
Jesus Jones
Jesus Lizard
Jet
Jet Star
Jetboy
Jeter-Pillars Orchestra
Jethro Tull
Jets
Jett, Joan, And The Blackhearts
Jeunemann, Margeurite
Jewel
Jewels
Jewels (reggae)
Jigsaw
Jill Darling
Jilted John
Jim And Jesse
Jiminez, Flaco
Jiminez, Santiago, Jnr.
Jimmy Jam And Terry Lewis
Jimmy The Hoover
Jive Bombers
Jive Bunny And The Mastermixers
Jive Five
Jive Records
Jivin' In Bebop
JJ Fad
Jo Jo Gunne
Jo Jo Zep And The Falcons
Jobim, Antonio
JoBoxers
Jobriath
Jobson, Richard
Jocasta
Jodeci
Jody Grind
Joe

Joe Popp
Joel, Billy
Joey Negro
Johansen, David
Johansson, Jan
John's Children
John, Elton
John, Little Willie
John, Mable
John, Monday
John, Robert
Johnboy
Johnnie And Jack
Johnnie And Joe
Johnny And The Hurricanes
Johnny Crash
Johnny Hates Jazz
Johnny Moped
Johnny Vicious
Johns, Glyn
Johns, Sammy
Johnson Mountain Boys
Johnson, 'Big' Jack
Johnson, 'Blind' Willie
Johnson, Alfred 'Snuff'
Johnson, Alphonzo
Johnson, Arnold
Johnson, Bessie
Johnson, Bill
Johnson, Bryan
Johnson, Budd
Johnson, Buddy
Johnson, Bunk
Johnson, Charlie
Johnson, Denise
Johnson, Edith
Johnson, Ella
Johnson, Ellen
Johnson, Ernie
Johnson, Ginger
Johnson, Gus
Johnson, Harry 'J'
Johnson, Henry
Johnson, Holly
Johnson, Howard
Johnson, J.J.
Johnson, James 'Stump'
Johnson, James P.
Johnson, James
Johnson, Jimmy
Johnson, Johnnie
Johnson, Johnny, And The Bandwagon
Johnson, Keg
Johnson, Ken 'Snakehips'
Johnson, Kenny
Johnson, Kevin
Johnson, L.J.

Johnson, Larry C.
Johnson, Laurie
Johnson, Lem
Johnson, Linton
Kwesi
Johnson, Lonnie
Johnson, Lou
Johnson, Luther
'Georgia Snake
Boy'
Johnson, Luther
'Guitar Junior'
Johnson, Luther
'Houserocker'
Johnson, Manzie
Johnson, Marv
Johnson, Mary
Johnson, Matt
Johnson, Merline
Johnson, Michael
Johnson, Mike
Johnson, Money
Johnson, Oliver
Johnson, Pete
Johnson, Plas
Johnson, Robb
Johnson, Robert
Johnson, Ruby
Johnson, Sy
Johnson, Syl
Johnson, Teddy
Johnson, Tex
Johnson, Tommy
Johnson, Wilko
Johnson, Willie
Johnston, Bruce
Johnston, Daniel
Johnston, Freedy
Johnston, Jan
Johnston, Tom
Johnstone,
Clarence
Nathaniel
Johnstons
Joi
Jojo
Joker Is Wild,
The
Joli, France
Jolley, Steve
Jolly, Pete
Jolson - The Musical
Jolson Sings
Again
Jolson Story, The
Jolson, Al
Jomanda
Jon And Robin
And The In-
Crowd
Jon And The
Nightriders
Jon And Vangelis
Jon Pleased
Wimmin
Jonathan
Fire*eater

Jones Girls
Jones, Albennie
Jones, Allan
Jones, Bessie
Jones,
Birmingham
Jones, Booker T.
Jones, Carmell
Jones, Casey,
And The
Engineers
Jones, Catherine
Zeta
Jones, Claude
Jones, Coley
Jones, Curtis
Jones, Davey
Jones, David Lynn
Jones, Dill
Jones, Dolly
Jones, Dyer
Jones, Eddie
Jones, Eddie
'Guitar Slim'
Jones, Elvin
Jones, Etta
Jones, Floyd
Jones, Frankie
Jones, George
Jones, Grace
Jones, Grandpa
Jones, Hank
Jones, Howard
Jones, Isham
Jones, Jack
Jones, Janie
Jones, Jimmy
Jones, Jimmy
(R&B)
Jones, Jo
Jones, Joe
Jones, John Paul
Jones, Jonah
Jones, Leroy
Jones, Linda
Jones, Little Hat
Jones, Little
Johnny
Jones, Maggie
Jones, Mazlyn
Jones, Mick
Jones, Moody
Jones, Neal
Jones, Nic
Jones, Nyles
Jones, Oliver
Jones, Paul
Jones, Philly Joe
Jones, Quincy
Jones, Reunald
Jones, Richard M.
Jones, Rickie Lee
Jones, Rodney
Jones, Salena
Jones, Sam
Jones, Shirley
Jones, Slick

Jones, Spike
Jones, Steve
Jones, Thad
Jones, Tom
(vocalist)
Jones, Tom (lyri-
cist)
Jones, Tutu
Jones, Vince
Jones, Vivian
Jones, Wizz
Joneses
Jook
Joos, Herbert
Joplin, Janis
Joplin, Scott
Jordan, Charley
Jordan, Clifford
Jordan, Duke
Jordan, Fred
Jordan, Louis
Jordan, Luke
Jordan, Montell
Jordan, Ronny
Jordan, Sheila
Jordan, Stanley
Jordan, Steve
Jordan, Taft
Jordanaires
Jory, Sarah
José José
Josef K
Josefus
Joseph And The
Amazing
Technicolor
Joseph, Julian
Joseph, Margie
Jospeh, Martyn
Joseph, Nerious
Josephs, Wilfred
Joshua
Josi, Christian
Jostyn, Mindy
Journey
Journey Through
The Past
Journeymen
Joy
Joy Division
Joy Of Cooking
Joy, Jimmy
Joy, Ruth
Joyce
Joyce, Archibald
Joye, Col
Joyous Noise
Joyrider
Joystrings
JSD Band
Ju Ju Space Jazz
Juan Trip
Jubilee
Judas Jump
Judas Priest
Judd, Cledus 'T',
(No Relation)

Judds
Judge Dread
Judge Jules
Juggernaut
Juicy Lucy
Juju
Juke Box Jury
Juluka
July
Jumbo
Jumbo (film musi-
cal)
Jump 'N The
Saddle Band
Jumpin' The
Gunn
Jumpleads
June Brides
Jungle
Jungle Book, The
Jungle Brothers
Jungr And Parker
Junior
Junior Boy's Own
Records
Junior MAFIA
Junior's Eyes
Junkyard
Juno Reactor
Jupp, Mickey
Jurgens, Dick
Jürgens, Udo
Jury
Just A Gigolo
Just For Fun
Just Ice
Just Us
Justice, Jimmy
Justified Ancients
Of Mu Mu
Justis, Bill
JX
K Klass
K Sridhar And K
Shivakumar
K-9 Posse
K-Doe, Ernie
K-Passa
K-Solo
K-Tel Records
K., Leila
K., Paul
K7
Kaas, Patricia
Kabulie, Moses
Kadison, Joshua
Kaempfert, Bert
Kahn, Gus
Kahn, John
Kahn, Roger
Wolfe
Kahn, Si
Kahn, Tiny
Kaira Ben
Kaiser, Henry
Kajagoogoo
Kak

Kako
Kaleef
Kaleidoscope
Kaleidoscope
(UK)
Kalin Twins
Kaliphz
Kalle, Joseph
Kalle, Le Grande
Kallen, Kitty
Kalmar, Bert
Kam
Kama Sutra
Records
Kamen, Michael
Kaminsky, Max
Kamissoko,
Aminata
Kamoze, Ini
Kamuca, Richie
Kander, John
Kandidate
Kane Gang
Kane, Amory
Kane, Big Daddy
Kane, Eden
Kane, Helen
Kane, Kieran
Kansas
Kansas City Jazz
Kansas City Red
Kante, Mory
Kantner, Paul
Kanza, Lokua
Kaper, Bronislaw
(Bronislau)
Kaplan, Bruce
Kaplansky, Lucy
Kapp Records
Karas, Anton
Karklins, Ingrid
Karl And Harty
Karn, Mick
Kasenetz-Katz
Singing
Orchestral
Circus
Kash, Murray
Kashmir
Kaspersen, Jan
Kassell, Art
Kasseya, Souzy
Kassner, Eddie
Kasuga, Hachirô
Kat
Katch 22
Katon, Michael
Katrina And The
Waves
Katz, Al
Katz, Jeff
Kaufman, George
S.
Kaukonen, Jorma
Kaukonen, Peter
Kavana
Kavana, Ron

Kavanagh, Niamh
Kavelin, Al
Kawaguchi,
   George
Kay, Connie
Kay, Herbie
Kay, Janet
Kay, Karen
Kaye Sisters
Kaye, Cab
Kaye, Carol
Kaye, Danny
Kaye, Sammy
Kaye, Stubby
Kayirebwa, Cecile
Kayo
Kayser, Joe
Kazebier, Nate
Kazee, Buell
KC And The
   Sunshine Band
Keane, Dolores
Keane, Ellsworth
   'Shake'
Keane, Sean
Keb' Mo'
Kebnekaise
Kee, Rev. John P.,
   And The New
   Life Keel
Keel, Howard
Keeler, Ruby
Keen, Robert Earl
Keen, Speedy
Keene, Nelson
Keene, Steven
Keep On Rockin'
Kefford, Ace,
   Stand
Keineg, Katell
Keisker, Marion
Keita, Salif
Keith
Keith And Enid
Keith And
   Rooney
Keith And Tex
Keith, Bill
Keith, Toby
Kellaway, Roger
Keller, Jerry
Kelley, Eileen
Kelley, Peck
Kellin, Orange
Kelly Brothers
Kelly Family
Kelly, Arthur Lee
   'Guitar'
Kelly, Chris
Kelly, Dave
Kelly, Dave 'Rude
   Boy'
Kelly, Gene
Kelly, George
Kelly, Jack
Kelly, Jo Ann
Kelly, Keith

Kelly, Pat
Kelly, Paul
Kelly, Paula
Kelly, R.
Kelly, Sandy
Kelly, Vance
Kelly, Wynton
Kemp, Hal
Kemp, Wayne
Kemper, Ronnie
Kendalls
Kendricks, Eddie
Kenickie
Kennedy Rose
Kennedy, Brian
Kennedy, Jerry
Kennedy, Jesse
   'Tiny'
Kennedy, Jimmy
Kennedy, Nigel
Kennedy, Peter
Kennedy, Ray
Kennedys
Kenner, Chris
Kennerley, Paul
Kenney, Mart
Kenny
Kenny And The
   Kasuals
Kensit, Patsy
Kent, Stacey
Kent, Walter
Kent, Willie
Kente
Kenton, Stan
Kentucky
   Colonels
Kentucky
   Headhunters
Kenyon, Carol
Kepone
Keppard, Freddie
Kerbdog
Kern, Jerome
Kernaghan, Lee
Kerr, Anita
Kersh, David
Kershaw, Doug
Kershaw, Nik
Kershaw, Sammy
Kessel, Barney
Kessinger
   Brothers
Ketchum, Hal
Ketelbey, Albert
   William
Kewley, Ian
Keyes, Jimmy
KGB
Khac Chi
   Ensemble
Khaled
Khan
Khan, Ali Akbar
Khan, Chaka
Khan, Nusrat
   Fateh Ali

Khan, Steve
Kiani, Mary
Kibbey, Sue
Kickin' Records
Kid 'N Play
Kid Creole And
   The Coconuts
Kid From Spain,
   The
Kid Frost
Kid Galahad
Kid Millions
Kid Sensation
Kidd, Carol
Kidd, Johnny, And
   The Pirates
Kidd, Kenneth
Kidd, Michael
Kidjo, Angelique
Kids Are Alright,
   The
Kids From Fame
Kihn, Greg
Kik Tracee
Kikuchi,
   Masabumi
Kila
Kilbey, Steve
Kilburn And The
   High Roads
Kiley, Richard
Kilgore, Merle
Kilgore, Rebecca
Kill For Thrills
Killdozer
Killen, Buddy
Killen, Ked
Killen, Louis
Killers
Killian, Al
Killing Joke
Killjoys
Kilo
Kimbrough,
   James
Kimbrough,
   Junior
Kimono, Ras
Kincaid, Bradley
Kincaide, Deane
Kinchen, Mark
King
King (stage musi-
   cal)
King And I, The
King And I, The
   (film musical)
King Brothers
King Creole
King Crimson
King Curtis
King Diamond
King Floyd
King Harvest
King Jammy
King Just
King Kobra

King Kong
King Kurt
King Missile
King Of Jazz
King Of The Hill
King Of The
   Slums
King Pins
King Pleasure
   And The
   Biscuit Boys
King Sisters
King Solomon
   Hill
King Sounds
King Sporty
King Stitt
King Sun
King Tee
King Tubby
King's Rhapsody
King, Al
King, Albert
King, B.B.
King, Ben E.
King, Carole
King, Claude
King, Dave
King, Denis
King, Diana
King, Don
King, Earl
King, Eddie
King, Evelyn
   'Champagne'
King, Freddie
King, Henry
King, Jigsy
King, Jonathan
King, Little
   Jimmy
King, Morgan
King, Morgana
King, Norah Lee
King, Pee Wee
King, Peter
King, Peter
   (reggae)
King, Reg
King, Sandra
King, Saunders
King, Sid
King, Solomon
King, Stan
King, Teddi
King, Wayne
King, Yvonne
Kingbees
Kingdom Come
Kingdom Come
   (70s)
Kingdom Come
   (80s)
Kingfish
Kinghorse
Kingmaker
Kings X

Kingsmen
Kingston Trio
Kinks
Kinky Machine
Kinnaird, Alison,
   And Christine
Kinney, Fern
Kinsey Report
Kinsey, Big Daddy
Kinsey, Tony
Kipper Family
Kippington Lodge
Kirby, John
Kirby, Kathy
Kirby, Pete
Kirk
Kirk, Andy
Kirk, Eddie
Kirk, Mary
Kirk, Rahsaan
   Roland
Kirk, Red
Kirk, Roland H.
Kirkland, Kenny
Kirkland, Leroy
Kirkpatrick, Anne
Kirkpatrick, Don
Kirkpatrick, John
Kirkwood, Pat
Kirshner, Don
Kirwan, Dominic
Kismet
Kismet (film
   musical)
Kiss
Kiss Me Kate
   (film musical)
Kiss Of Life
Kiss Of The
   Gypsy
Kiss Of The
   Spider Woman
Kiss The Boys
   Goodbye
Kissin' Cousins
Kissing Bandit,
   The
Kissoon, Mac And
   Katie
Kitamura, Eiji
Kitarô
Kitchens Of
   Distinction
Kitchings, Irene
Kitsyke Will
Kitt, Eartha
Kittrell, Christine
Kix
Klaatu
Klark Kent
Klaudt Indian
   Family
Kleenex
Klein, Allen
Klein, Manny
Klemmer, John
Klezmatics

KLF
Klink, Al
Kluger, Irving
Klugh, Earl
KMD
KMS Records
Knack
Knapp, Orville
Knepper, Jimmy
Knickerbocker
   Holiday
Knickerbockers
Knight Brothers
Knight, Bob, Four
Knight, Curtis
Knight, Evelyn
Knight, Frederick
Knight, Gladys,
   And The Pips
Knight, Grace
Knight, Jean
Knight, Peter
Knight, Robert
Knight, Sonny
Knight, Terry
Knights Of The
   Occasional
   Table
Knobloch, Fred
Knopfler, David
Knopfler, Mark
Knowledge
Knowles, Pamela
Knowling,
   Ransom
Knox, Buddy
Knox, Chris
Knuckles, Frankie
Knudsen,
   Kenneth
Koda, Cub
Kodaks
Kodo
Koehler, Ted
Koerner, 'Spider'
   John
Koerner, Ray And
   Glover
Kofi
Koglmann, Franz
Koite, Sourokata
Kojak And Liza
Kokane
Kokomo (UK)
Kokomo (USA)
Kold Sweat
Kolderie And
   Slade
Koller, Fred
Koller, Hans
Kollington
Komeda,
   Krzysztof
Komuro, Tetsuya
Konadu, Alex
Konders, Bobby
Köner, Thomas

Kong, Leslie
Kongos, John
Konimo
Konitz, Lee
Konte, Dembo
Konte, Lamine
Koobas
Kool And The
   Gang
Kool G Rap And
   DJ Polo
Kool Gents
Kool Herc
Kool Moe Dee
Kool Rock Jay
Kooper, Al
Korgis
Kormoran
Korn
Korner, Alexis
Korngold, Erich
   Wolfgang
Kortchmar,
   Danny
Kossoff, Kirke,
   Tetsu And
   Rabbit
Kossoff, Paul
Kostelanetz,
   André
Kota, Tera
Kotch
Kotick, Teddy
Kottke, Leo
Kotzen, Richie
Kouyaté, Kandia
Kouyate,
   Ousmane
Kouyaté, Tata
   Bambo
Kowald, Peter
Koz, Dave
Kpiaye, John
Kraftwerk
Kral, Irene
Kral, Roy
Krall, Diana
Kramer
Kramer, Alex
Kramer, Billy J.
   And The
   Dakotas
Kramer, Wayne
Krause, Dagmar
Krauss, Alison
Kravitz, Lenny
Kreator
Kress, Carl
Kretzmer, Herbert
Kreuger, Bernie
Kreuz
Kriegel, Volker
Krispy 3
Kriss Kross
Kristina, Sonja
Kristofferson,
   Kris

Krivda, Ernie
Krog, Karin
Krokus
Kroner, Erling
Kronos Quartet
KRS-1
Kruger, Jeffrey
Krupa, Gene
Krush
Kuban, Bob, And
   The In-Men
Kubek, Smokin'
   Joe
Kubis, Tom
Kubota, Toshi
Kuepper, Ed
Kuhn, Joachim
Kühn, Rolf
Kuhn, Steve
Kula Shaker
Kulka, Leo de
   Gar
Kunkel, Leah
Kunz, Charlie
Kunze, Heinz
   Rudolf
Kupferberg, Tuli
Kurious
Kursaal Flyers
Kuryokhin, Sergey
Kut Klose
Kuti, Fela
Kwamé
Kweskin, Jim, Jug
   Band
KWS
Ky-mani
Kyle, Billy
Kyoung, Park Mi
Kyper
Kyser, Kay
Kyuss
(Les) Fleur De
   Lys
L'Aventure Du
   Jazz
L'Trimm
L.A. And Babyface
L.A. Guns
L.A. Mix
L.V.
L7
La Beef, Sleepy
La Bouche
La Cage Aux
   Folles
La Costa
La Cucina
La De Das
La Dusseldorf
La Faro, Scott
La Lugh
La Lupe
La Momposina,
   Toto
La Roca, Pete
La Vallee

La Velle
La's
LaBarbera, Joe
LaBarbera, Pat
Labeef, Sleepy
LaBelle
LaBelle, Patti
Labradford
Lace, Bobbi
Lacey, Rubin,
   Rev.
Lacy, Steve
Ladies And
   Gentlemen...Th
   e Rolling
   Stones
Ladnier, Tommy
Lady And The
   Tramp
Lady Anne
Lady B
Lady G
Lady In The Dark
Lady Is A Square,
   The
Lady Of Rage
Lady Saw
Lady Sings The
   Blues
Lady, Be Good!
Ladysmith Black
   Mambazo
LaFarge, Pete
Lafitte, Guy
LaForet, Marie
Lagbaja
Lagrene, Bireli
Lahr, Bert
Lai, Francis
Laibach
Laine, Cleo
Laine, Denny
Laine, Frankie
Laine, Papa Jack
Lair, John
Laird, Rick
Lake
Lake County
   Revellers
Lake, Greg
Lake, Oliver
Lakeman
   Brothers
Lakeside
Lalor, Trudi
Lamare, Hilton
   'Nappy'
Lamb
Lamb, Annabel
Lamb, Paul
Lambchop
Lambe, Jeannie
Lambert, Dave
Lambert, Donald
Lambert,
   Hendricks And
   Ross

Lambert, Kit
Lambert, Lloyd
Lambrettas
Lamond, Don
Lamour, Dorothy
Lamplighters
Lancaster, Byard
Lancastrians
Lance, Major
Land, Harold
Land, Jon
Landers, Jake
Landreth, Sonny
Landry, Art
Landsborough,
   Charlie
Landscape
Lane, Burton
Lane, Christy
Lane, Lois
Lane, Lupino
Lane, Red
Lane, Ronnie
Lang, Don
Lang, Eddie
Lang, Eddie
   (blues)
Lang, Eddie (jazz)
Lang, Jonny
lang, k.d.
Lang, Kid Johnny
Langa Langa
   Stars
Langford, Frances
Lanier, Jaron
Lanin, Sam
Lanois, Daniel
Lanor Records
Lanphere, Don
Lansbury, Angela
Lanson, Snooky
Lanza, Mario
Laquan
Lara, Jennifer
Larkin, Kenny
Larkin, Patty
Larkins, Ellis
Larks
Larks (Apollo)
Larson, Nicolette
LaSalle, Denise
Lashley, Barbara
Last Crack
Last Exit
Last Of The Blue
   Devils, The
Last Poets
Last Waltz, The
Last, James
Laswell, Bill
Lateef, Yusef
Later With Jools
   Holland
Latimore
Latin Alliance
Latour
Lattimore, Kenny

Lattislaw, Stacy
Lauder, Harry
Lauderdale, Jim
Laugh
Laughing Buddah
Laughing Clowns
Laughner, Peter
Laula, Carol
Lauper, Cyndi
Laurel And Hardy
Lauren, Rod
Laurence Olivier
 Awards
Laurence, Chris
Laurents, Arthur
Laurie, Annie
Laurie, Cy
Laurin, Anna-
 Lena
Laury, Booker T.
Laury, Lawrence
 'Booker T'
Lavelle, Caroline
LaVere, Charles
LaVert
Lavette, Betty
Lavoe, Héctor
Lavoy, Fernando
Lawal, Gasper
Lawes, Henry
 'Junjo'
Lawhorn, Sammy
Lawnmower Deth
Lawrence, Denise
Lawrence, Derek
Lawrence, Elliot
Lawrence,
 Gertrude
Lawrence, Jack
Lawrence, Lee
Lawrence, Steve
Lawrence, Syd
Lawrence, Tracy
Lawrence, Vicki
Laws, Hubert
Laws, Ronnie
Lawson, Doyle
Lawson, Rex
Lawson, Tim
Lawson, Yank
Lawton, Jimmy
Lay, Rodney
Lay, Sam
Laycock, Tim
Laye, Evelyn
Layne, Joy
Layton And
 Johnstone
Layton, Linda
Layton, Turner
Lazarus, Ken
Lazy Lester
Lazy, Doug
Le Gop
Le Griffe
Le Mystère Des
 Voix Bulgares

Le Roux
Le Sage, Bill
Lea, Barbara
Leach, Lillian,
 And The
 Mellows
Lead Belly
Leaders Of The
 New School
Leadon, Bernie
Leahy, Dick
Leake, Lafayette
Leander, Mike
Léandre, Joëlle
Leandros, Vicky
Lear, Amanda
Leather Nun
Leatherwolf
Leave It To Jane
Leave It To Me!
Leaves
Leavill, Otis
Leavitt, Raphy
Leavy, Calvin
LeBlanc And
 Carr
LeBlanc, Keith
Lebrón Brothers
Lecuona, Ernesto
Led Zeppelin
Ledford, Steve
Ledin, Tomas
LeDoux, Chris
Lee, 'Little'
 Frankie
Lee, Albert
Lee, Alvin
Lee, Arthur
Lee, Brenda
Lee, Bunny
Lee, Byron, And
 The Dragonaires
Lee, Coco
Lee, Curtis
Lee, Dave
Lee, Dickie
Lee, Ernie
Lee, George E.
Lee, Jackie
Lee, Jackie (USA)
Lee, Jeanne
Lee, Joe, And
 Jimmy Strothers
Lee, John
Lee, Johnny
Lee, Julia
Lee, Laura
Lee, Peggy
Lee, Phil
Lee, Ranee
Lee, Robin
Lee, Will
Lee Davis, Janet
Leecan, Bobby,
 And Robert
 Cooksey
Leeman, Cliff

Leeman, Mark,
 Five
Lees, Gene
Lefevre,
 Raymond
Left Banke
Left Hand Frank
Leftfield
Lefty Dizz
LeGarde Twins
Legarreta, Félix
 'Pupi'
Legend
Legendary Blues
 Band
Legendary Pink
 Dots
Legg, Adrian
Legrand, Michel
Legs Diamond
Lehár, Franz
Lehr, Zella
Lehrer, Tom
Leiber And
 Stoller
Leigh, Carolyn
Leigh, Mitch
Leigh, Richard
Leiner, Robert
Lema, Ray
LeMarc, Peter
Lemer, Pepi
Lemon Pipers
Lemon Popsicle
Lemon Tree
Lemon, Brian
Lemonheads
Lend An Ear
Lennon Sisters
Lennon, John
Lennon, Julian
Lennox, Annie
Lenoir, J.B.
Leo Records
Leo, Philip
Leon, Craig
Leonard, Deke
Leonard, Harlan
Leonard, Jack
Leonardo
Lerner, Alan Jay
Lerner, Sammy
LeRoi Brothers
Lerole, Elias, And
 His Zig Zag Jive
 Flutes
Les Aiglons
Les Amazones
Les Bantous De
 La Capitale
Les Girls
Les Misérables
Les Quatre
 Étoiles
Lesberg, Jack
Lesh, Phil
LeShaun

Leslie, Edgar
Lesurf, Cathy
Let George Do It
Let It Be
Let Loose
Let The Good
 Times Roll
Let's Active
Let's Face It!
Let's Make Love
Letman, Johnny
Lettermen
Letters To Cleo
Levallet, Didier
Levant, Oscar
Level 42
Levellers
Leven, Jackie
Levene, Sam
LeVert, Gerald
Levert, Gerald,
 And Eddie
 Levert
Levey, Stan
Levi Roots
Levi Smiths Clefs
Levi, Ijahman
Leviathan
Leviathan (UK)
Leviathan (USA)
Leviev, Milcho
Levine, Henry
 'Hot Lips'
Levitation
Levitt, Rod
Levy, Barrington
Levy, Hank
Levy, Lou
Levy, Ron
Lewie, Jona
Lewis And Clarke
 Expedition
Lewis, Barbara
Lewis, Bobby
Lewis, Bobby
 (country)
Lewis, Bobby
 (rock 'n' roll)
Lewis, C.J.
Lewis, Darlene
Lewis, Donna
Lewis, Ed
Lewis, Gary, And
 The Playboys
Lewis, George
Lewis, George
 (clarinet)
Lewis, George
 (trombone)
Lewis, Hopeton
Lewis, Huey, And
 The News
Lewis, Hugh X
Lewis, Jeannine
Lewis, Jerry Lee
Lewis, John
Lewis, Lew

Lewis, Linda
Lewis, Linda Gail
Lewis, Little Roy
Lewis, Meade
 'Lux'
Lewis, Mel
Lewis, Noah
Lewis, Ramsey
Lewis, Sabby
Lewis, Sam M.
Lewis, Smiley
Lewis, Ted
Lewis, Texas Jim
Lewis, Vic
Lewis, Walter
 'Furry'
Lewis, Willie
Ley, Eggy
Ley, Tabu
Leyton Buzzards
Leyton, John
LFO
Li Kolan
Li'l Abner
Li'l Abner (film
 musical)
Liberace
Liberty Cage
Liberty Grooves
Liberty Records
Libre, Conjunto
Lick The Tins
Lieb, Oliver
Lieberson,
 Goddard
Liebert, Ottmar
Liebman, Dave
Liebrand, Ben
Lien, Annbjørg
Lieutenant
 Pigeon
Lieutenant
 Stitchie
Life And Times
Life Begins At
 8:40
Life Of Agony
Life, Sex And
 Death
Life, The
Lifers Group
Lifetime
Ligabue
Liggins, Jimmy
Liggins, Joe
Light Crust
 Doughboys
Light Of The
 World
Light, Enoch
Lightfoot,
 Alexander
 'Papa George'
Lightfoot,
 Gordon
Lightfoot, Terry
Lighthouse Family

Lighthouse
Lightnin' Slim
Lightning Seeds
Lightsey, Kirk
Lijadu Sisters
Lil' Ed And The
   Blues Imperials
Lil' Louis
Lil' Kim
Lilac Time
Lilac Time (stage
   musical)
Lili
Lilith Fair
Lillian Axe
Lillie, Beatrice
Lilliput
Lilly Brothers
Lillywhite, Steve
Limahl
Limbo
Limelight
Limerick, Alison
Limit
Limmie And The
   Family Cooking
Lin Que
Lincoln, Abbey
Lincoln, Abe
Lincoln, Charley
Lind, Bob
Lind, Ove
Linde, Dennis
Lindenberg, Udo
Lindisfarne
Lindley, David
Lindner, Patrick
Lindo, Kashief
Lindsay, Arto
Lindsay, Erica
Lindsay, Jimmy
Lindsay, Mark
Lindsay, Reg
Lindsey, Judy
Lindsey, LaWanda
Line Records
Linkchain, Hip
Linn County
Linus
Linx
Lion
Lion King, The
Lioness
Lionheart
Lionrock
Lionsheart
Lipscomb, Mance
Lipton, Sydney
LiPuma, Tommy
Liquid
Liquid Jesus
Liroy
Lisa Lisa And
   Cult Jam
Lisberg, Harvey
Lisbon Story, The
   (film musical)

Lisbon Story,
   The, (stage
   musical)
Lismor Records
Liston, Melba
Lisztomania
Litherland, Harry
Litter
Little Angels
Little Anthony
   And The
   Imperials
Little Beaver
Little Big Band
Little Caesar
Little Caesar And
   The Romans
Little Charlie
   And The
   Nightcats
Little Dippers
Little Egypt
Little Eva
Little Feat
Little Hatch
Little Joe And
   The Thrillers
Little Joey And
   The Flips
Little John
Little Johnny
   Jones
Little Louie Vega
Little Mary
   Sunshine
Little Me
Little Mermaid,
   The
Little Milton
Little Miss
   Marker
Little Night
   Music, A
Little Richard
Little River Band
Little Roy
Little Shop Of
   Horrors (film
   musical)
Little Shop Of
   Horrors (stage
   musical)
Little Show, The
Little Son Joe
Little Sonny
Little Steven And
   The Disciples
   Of Soul
Little Texas
Little Tony
Little Village
Little Walter
Little Whitt And
   Big Bo
Little, Booker
Littlefield, 'Little'
   Willie

Littlejohn, Johnny
Live
Live Aid
Liver Birds
Liverpool Express
Liverpool Scene
Livgren, Kerry
Livin' Joy
Living Colour
Living In A Box
Living It Up
Livingston, Fud
Livingston, Jay
Livingston,
   Ulysses
Livingstone,
   Dandy
Livingstone, John
   Graeme
Lizzie
Lizzy
Lizzy Borden
LL Cool J
Lloyd Webber,
   Andrew
Lloyd, A.L.
Lloyd, Charles
Lloyd, Jon
Lloyd, Richard
Lloyd, Robert
Lo-Fidelity
   Allstars
Lo, Cheikh
Lo, Ismaël
Loaded Records
Loading Zone
Lobo
Lock Up Your
   Daughters
Locke, Josef
Locklin, Hank
Lockran, Gerry
Locks, Fred
Lockwood, Didier
Lockwood,
   Robert
Lockyer, Malcolm
Locomotive
Locust
Lodestar
Lodge, J.C.
Loeb, Lisa
Loesser, Frank
Loewe, Frederick
Lofgren, Nils
Loft
Lofton, Cripple
   Clarence
Logan, Ella
Logan, Jack
Logan, Josh
Loggins And
   Messina
Loggins, Kenny
Logic Records
Logsdon, Jimmy
Lohan, Sinéad

Loïs Lane
Lolita
Lollapalooza
Lollipop Shoppe
Lomax, Alan And
   John A.
Lomax, Jackie
Lombardo, Guy
Londin, Larrie
London (UK)
London Calling!
London Jazz
   Composers
   Orchestra
London Posse
London Records
London SS
London Town
London, Jimmy
London, Julie
London, Laurie
Londonbeat
Lone Justice
Lone Pine, Hal,
   And Betty
   Cody
Lone Ranger
Lone Star
Lonesome Pine
   Fiddlers
Lonesome
   Strangers
Lonesome
   Sundown
Lonestar
Loney, Roy (And
   The Phantom
   Movers)
Long And The
   Short
Long Ryders
Long, George
Long, Hubert
Long, Johnny
Long, Shorty
Longbranch
   Pennywhistle
Longdancer
Longo, Pat
Longpigs
Lonzo And Oscar
Look Twice
Looking Glass
Looking Through
   A Glass Onion
Loop
Loose Ends
Loose Gravel
Loose Tubes
Loosegroove
   Records
Loot
Lopez, Trini
Lopez, Vincent
Lora Logic
Lorber, Jeff
Lord Creator

Lord
   Rockingham's
   XI
Lord, Bobby
Lord, Mary Lou
Lordan, Jerry
Lords
Lords Of
   Brooklyn
Lords Of The
   New Church
Lords Of The
   Underground
Lords, Traci
Lore And The
   Legends
Lori And The
   Chameleons
Los Bravos
Los Del Rio
Los Indios
   Tabajaras
Los Lobos
Loss, Joe
Lost
Lost And Found
Lost Generation
Lost Gonzo Band
Lost In The Stars
Lost Jockey
Lost Tribe
Lota, Tera
Lothar And The
   Hand People
Lotion
Lotis, Dennis
Lottin, Eboa
Lotus Eaters
Louchie Lou And
   Michie One
Loudermilk, John
   D.
Louis, Big Joe
Louis, Joe Hill
Louise
Louisiana
   Hayride, The
Louisiana
   Purchase
Louisiana Red
Louiss, Eddy
Lounge Lizards
Loup Garou
Loussier, Jacques
Louvin Brothers
Louvin, Charlie
Lovano, Joe
Love
Love Affair
Love And Money
Love And
   Rockets
Love Canal
Love City Groove
Love In Las Vegas
Love Life
Love Me

Love Me Or
  Leave Me
Love Me Tender
Love Me Tonight
Love Parade, The
Love Sculpture
Love Spit Love
Love To Infinity
Love Unlimited
Love Unlimited
  Orchestra
Love, Clayton
Love, Darlene
Love, Geoff
Love, Laura
Love, M'Pongo
Love, Monie
Love, Preston
Love, Willie
Love/Hate
Lovebug Starski
Loved Ones
Loveless, Patty
Lovelites
Lovens, Paul
Lover Speaks,
  The
Loverboy
Lovers Rock
Lovett, Lyle
Lovich, Lene
Lovin' Spoonful
Low
Lowe, Frank
Lowe, Jez
Lowe, Mundell
Lowe, Nick
Lown, Bert
Lowrell
Lowther, Henry
LTJ Bukem
Lubinsky,
  Herman
Lubitsch, Ernst
Lucas
Lucas, Al
Lucas, Carrie
Lucas, Clyde
Lucas, Dick
Lucas, Nick
Lucas, Robert
Lucas, Trevor
Lucas, William
  'Lazy Bill'
Lucca, Papo (and
  Sonora
  Ponceña)
Luciano
Lucky People
  Center
Ludus
Lukather, Steve
Luke, Robin
Lukie D
Lulu
Lulu Belle And
  Scotty

Luman, Bob
Luna
Lunachicks
Lunceford,
  Jimmie
Lunch, Lydia
Lund, Art
Lundberg, Victor
Lundy, Ted
Lunn, Robert
Lunny, Donal
Lupino, Stanley
Lupone, Patti
Lurie, Evan
Lurkers
Luscious Jackson
Lush
Lusher, Don
Lusk, Professor
  Eddie
Lutcher, Joe
Lutcher, Nellie
Luther, Frank
Luvdup Twins
Luz
Lyle, Kami
Lyman, Abe
Lyman, Arthur,
  Group
Lyme And
  Cybelle
Lymon, Frankie,
  And The
  Teenagers
Lymon, Louis,
  And The Teen-
  Chords
Lynam, Ray
Lynch Mob
Lynch, Brendan
Lynch, Claire
Lynch, Kenny
Lynch, Ray
Lynn, Barbara
Lynn, Cheryl
Lynn, Gloria
Lynn, Judy
Lynn, Loretta
Lynn, Tami
Lynn, Vera
Lynne, Gillian
Lynne, Gloria
Lynne, Jeff
Lynne, Shelby
Lynott, Phil
Lynyrd Skynyrd
Lyons, James L.
Lyons, Jimmy
Lyons, Willie
  James
Lytell, Jimmy
Lyttelton,
  Humphrey
M
M People
M&O Band
M&S Productions

M.A.R.S.
M.O.P.
Maal, Baaba
Mabley, Moms
  'Jackie'
Mabon, Willie
Mabsant
Mabuse, Sipho
Mac And Bob
Macabre
Macalpine, Tony
MacArthur, Neil
Macauley, Tony
Macbeth, David
Macc Lads
MacColl, Ewan
MacDaniel, Rudy
MacDermot, Galt
MacDonald, Hank
MacDonald,
  Jeanette
MacDonald,
  Jeanette, And
  Nelson Eddy
MacDonald,
  Laurel
MacDonald,
  Ralph
Maceo And The
  King's Men
Macero, Teo
MacGowan,
  Shane, And
  The Popes
Machine Head
Machito
Macintosh,
  Adrian
MacIsaac, Ashley
Mack And Mabel
Mack, Bobby
Mack, Lonnie
Mack, Warner
Macka B
Mackay, Andy
Mackel, Billy
Mackenzie
  Theory
MacKenzie,
  Talitha
Mackenzies
MacKillop, Gavin
Mackintosh, C.J.
Mackintosh,
  Cameron
Mackintosh, Ken
Mackness,
  Vanessa
MacLean, Dougie
MacMaster,
  Natalie
Macon, John
  Wesley
  'Shortstuff'
Macon, Uncle
  Dave
Macrae, Dave

MacRae, Gordon
Macumba
Mad About Music
Mad Cobra
Mad Lads
Mad Lion
Mad Professor
Mad River
Mad Season
Madam X
Madame Sherry
Madball
Madder Rose
Maddox, Rose
Made
Madison, Bingie
Madison, Kid
  Shots
Madness
Madonna
Madriguera, Enric
Maestro Fresh
  Wes
Maestro, Johnny
Maffay, Peter
Mafia And Fluxy
Magazine
Magellan
Maggie May
Magic Carpet
Magic Christian,
  The
Magic Lanterns
Magic Mixture
Magic Muscle
Magic Sam
Magic Show, The
Magic Slim
Magical Mystery
  Tour
Magicians
Magidson, Herb
Magma
Magna Carta
Magnapop
Magnetic Fields
Magnetic North
Magnificent Men
Magnificents
Magnum
Magny, Colette
Maguire, Alex
Maguire, Sean
Mahavishnu
  Orchestra
Mahlathini,
  Simon
  Nkabinde
Mahogany
Mahogany Rush
Mahogany, Kevin
Mahotella
  Queens
Maid Of The
  Mountains, The
Maiden, Sidney
Maiga, Boncana

Main
Main Ingredient
Main Source
Mairants, Ivor
Mainer, J.E.
Mainer, Wade
Mainieri, Mike
Maisonettes
Major Surgery
Majors
Make Me An
  Offer
Make Mine
  Manhattan
Make-Up
Makeba, Miriam
Makowicz, Adam
Mákvirág
Malaco Records
Malcom, Carl
Malevolent
  Creation
Malice
Malicorne
Mallard
Mallett, Dave
Mallory, Eddie
Malmsteen,
  Yngwie
Malo
Malombo Jazz
Malone, Geneva
Malone, J.J.
Malopoets
Maltby, Richard
Maltby, Richard,
  Jnr.
Malvo, Anthony
Mama Records
Mama's Boys
Mama, I Want To
  Sing
Mamas And The
  Papas
Mambo Kings,
  The
Mame
Mammoth
Mamonas
  Assassinas
Mamoulian,
  Rouben
Man
Man Called
  Adam, A
Man Jumping
Man Of La
  Mancha
Man Parrish
Man Who Fell To
  Earth, The
Man, Wu
Manassas
Mance, Junior
Mancha, Steve
Manchester,
  Melissa

Mancini, Henry
Mandators
Mandel, Harvey
Mandel, Johnny
Mandela Day
Mandingo Griot
  Society
Mandinka
Mandrake
  Memorial
Mandrake
  Paddlesteamer
Mandrell, Barbara
Mandrell, Louise
Manfila, Kante
Manfred Mann
Manfred Mann
  Chapter Three
Manfred Mann's
  Earth Band
Manga, Bebe
Mangelsdorff,
  Albert
Mangione, Chuck
Mangwana, Sam
Manhattan
  Brothers
Manhattan
  Transfer
Manhattans
Manhole
Manic Street
  Preachers
Manifold, Keith
Manilow, Barry
Manly, Gill
Mann, Aimee
Mann, Barry
Mann, C.K.
Mann, Carl
Mann, Herbie
Mann, Johnny,
  Singers
Mann, Peggy
Manne, Shelly
Manners, Zeke
Mannheim
  Steamroller
Manning, Bob
Manning, Dick
Manning, Phil
Manning, Phil,
  Band
Manone, Joseph
  'Wingy'
Manowar
Mansun
Mantaray
Mantas
Mantler, Michael
Mantovani
Mantra, Michael
Mantronix
Manuel And His
  Music Of The
  Manzanera,
  Phil

Mapfumo, Thomas
Maphis, Joe, And
  Rose Lee
Maple Oak
Mar-Keys
Mara
Marathons
Marauders
Marbles
Marc And The
  Mambas
Marcellino,
  Muzzy
Marcels
March Of The
  Falsettos
March Violets
March, Little
  Peggy
Marchan, Bobby
Marcus, Steve
Mardi Gras
Mares, Paul
Maresca, Ernie
Margo
Margolin, Bob
Margolis, Kitty
Mariano, Charlie
Mariano,
  Torcuato
Marie, Donna
Marie, Kelly
Marie, Teena
Marillion
Marilyn
Marilyn Manson
Marine Girls
Mariners
Marino, Frank
Marion
Marionette
Marionettes
Mark Four
Mark IV
Mark, Louisa
Marketts
Markham,
  Pigmeat
Marks, Gerald
Marky Mark And
  The Funky
  Bunch
Marlene, Das
  Musical
Marley Marl
Marley, Bob
Marley, Cedella
  Booker
Marley, Rita
Marley, Ziggy,
  And The
  Melody Makers
Marmalade
Marmarosa,
  Dodo
Marquee Club
Marr, Johnny

Marrero,
  Lawrence
Marriott, Steve
MARRS
Mars
Mars, Chris
Mars, Johnny
Marsala, Joe
Marsala, Marty
Marsalis,
  Branford
Marsalis,
  Delfeayo
Marsalis, Ellis
Marsalis, Wynton
Marsden, Bernie
Marsden, Beryl
Marsden, Gerry
Marseille
Marsh, Tina
Marsh, Warne
Marshall Hain
Marshall Law
Marshall Tucker
  Band
Marshall,
  Amanda
Marshall, Carla
Marshall, Jim
Marshall, John
Marshall, Kaiser
Marshall, Keith
Marshall, Larry
Marshall,
  Wendell
Martell, Lena
Martell, Linda
Marterie, Ralph
Martha And The
  Muffins
Martha And The
  Vandellas
Martika
Martin Guerre
Martin, Asa
Martin, Benny
Martin, Bill
Martin, C.F.
Martin, Carl
Martin, Claire
Martin, Dean
Martin, Eric
Martin, Fiddlin'
  Joe
Martin, Freddy
Martin, George
Martin, Grady
Martin, Horace
Martin, Hugh
Martin, Jimmy
Martin, Judy
Martin, Mac, And
  The Dixie
  Travelers
Martin, Mary
Martin, Ray
Martin, Sara

Martin, Tony
Martin, Vince
Martindale, Wink
Martino, Al
Martino, Pat
Martyn, Barry
Martyn, Beverly
Martyn, John
Marvelettes
Marvellos
Marvelows
Marvels
Marvin And
  Johnny
Marvin, Hank B.
Marvin, Johnny
  And Frankie
Marx, Richard
Marxman
Mary Poppins
Maschwitz, Eric
Masekela, Hugh
Maskman And
  The Agents
Maslak, Keshavan
Mason Dixon
Mason Proffit
Mason, Barbara
Mason, Dave
Mason, Harvey
Mason, Nick
Mason, Rod
Mason, Wood,
  Capaldi And
  Frog
Masqueraders
Mass Order
Massacre
Massey, Cal
Massey, Louise,
  And The
  Westerners
Massiah, Zeitia
Massive Attack
Massive Dread
Masso, George
Master Ace
Master's
  Apprentices
Master Musicians
  Of Jajouka
Mastercuts Series
Masterminds
Masters At Work
Masters Family
Masters Of
  Ceremony
Masters Of
  Reality
Masters, Frank
Masters, Valerie
Mastren, Carmen
Matador
Matador Records
Matassa, Cosimo
Matchbox
Matchbox 20

Matching Mole
Matchuki, Count
Material
Material Issue
Matheny, Dmitri
Mathieu, Mireille
Mathis, Country
  Johnny
Mathis, Johnny
Matlock, Glen
Matsu, Tokyo
Matsuda, Seiko
Matsui, Keiko
Matsuri
  Productions
Matt Bianco
Mattea, Kathy
Matthews
  Southern
  Comfort
Matthews, Al
Matthews, Dave
Matthews, Dave,
  Band
Matthews,
  George
Matthews, Iain
Matthews, Jessie
Matthews, Julie
Matthewson, Ron
Mattôya, Yumi
Matumbi
Mau Mau
Maughan, Susan
Maupin, Bennie
Mauriat, Paul
Maurice And Mac
Maurizio
Mauro, Turk
Mavericks
Max And The
  Broadway
  Metal Choir
Max Frost And
  The Troopers
Max Webster
Max-A-Million
Maxey, Leroy
Maximum Joy
Maxwell
Maxwell, Jimmy
May Blitz
May, Billy
May, Brian
May, Derrick
May, Tina
May, Wuta
Mayall, John
Maye, Arthur Lee
Mayer, Nathaniel
Mayerl, Billy
Mayes, Pete
Mayfield, Curtis
Mayfield, Percy
Mayhem
Maynard, Ken
Mayor, Simon

Mays, Bill
Mays, Curley
Mays, Lyle
Maytals
Maytime
Maytime (film
musical)
Maytones
Mayweather,
Earring George
Maze (60s)
Maze (featuring
Frankie
Beverly)
Mazzy Star
Mbaqanga
Mbarga, Nico,
Prince
Mbulu, Letta
MC 900ft Jesus
MC Brains
MC Breed
MC Buzz B
MC Duke
MC Eric
MC J
MC Kinky
MC Lyte
MC Mell 'O'
MC Pooh
MC Ren
MC Serch
MC Shan
MC Shy D
MC Solaar
MC Trouble
MC Tunes
MC5
McAfee, Johnny
McAll, Barney
McAlmont
McAlmont And
Butler
McAnally, Mac
McAuley, Jackie
McAuliffe, Leon
McBee, Cecil
McBride And The
Ride
McBride, Frankie
McBride, Janet
McBride, Laura
Lee
McBride, Martina
McCafferty, Dan
McCain, Jerry
McCall, C.W.
McCall, Cash
McCall, Mary Ann
McCall, Steve
McCall, Toussaint
McCalmans
McCandless, Paul
McCann, Eamon
McCann, Les
McCann, Lila
McCann, Peter

McCann, Susan
McCarters
McCarthy
McCarthy, Joseph
McCartney, Paul
McCarty's, Jim,
Meltdown
McCarty, Jim
McClain, Charly
McClain, Mighty
Sam
McClean, Bitty
McClennan,
Tommy
McClintock,
Harry
McClinton,
Delbert
McClinton, O.B.
McClure, Bobby
McClure, Ron
McConnell, Rob
McConville, Tom
McCoo, Marilyn
McCook, Tommy
McCord, Castor
McCorkle,
Susannah
McCormack,
Count John
McCoy, Charlie
McCoy, Clyde
McCoy, Joe
McCoy, Neal
McCoy, Robert
McCoy, Van
McCoys
McCracken, Bob
McCracklin,
Jimmy
McCrae, George
McCrae, Gwen
McCray, Larry
McCulloch, Ian
McCullough,
Henry
McCurdy, Ed
McCusker, John
McCutcheon,
John
McDaniel, Floyd
McDaniel, Mel
McDaniels, Gene
McDermott's
Two Hours
McDermott, John
McDermott,
Michael
McDevitt, Chas
McDonald And
Giles
McDonald, Billy
McDonald, Brian,
Group
McDonald,
Country Joe
McDonald, Kathi

McDonald,
Michael
McDonald,
Shelagh
McDonald, Skeets
McDonough, Dick
McDowell,
Mississippi Fred
McDowell,
Ronnie
McDuff, Brother
Jack
McEachern,
Murray
McEnery, Peter
McEnery, Red
River Dave
McEntire, Pake
McEntire, Reba
McEuen, John
McEvoy, Johnny
McFadden And
Whitehead
McFarland Twins
McFarland, Gary
McFerrin, Bobby
McGann, Bernie
McGarity, Lou
McGarrigle, Kate
And Anna
McGear, Mike
McGee, Alan
McGee, Sam And
Kirk
McGhee, Brownie
McGhee,
Granville
'Sticks'
McGhee, Howard
McGhee, Wes
McGlohon,
Loonis
McGough And
McGear
McGovern,
Maureen
McGraw, Tim
McGregor, Chris
McGregor,
Freddie
McGriff, Jimmy
McGuffie, Bill
McGuinn, Clark
And Hillman
McGuinn, Roger
McGuinness Flint
McGuire Sisters
McGuire, Barry
McHargue, Rosy
McHugh, Jimmy
Mchunu, Moses
McIntyre,
'Kalaparush'
Maurice
McIntyre, Hal
McIntyre, Ken
McKagan, Duff

McKay, Freddie
McKay, Kris
McKay, Marion
McKechnie,
Donna
McKee, Maria
McKellar,
Kenneth
McKendrick, 'Big
Mike'
McKendrick,
'Little Mike'
McKenna, Dave
McKenna, Mae
McKennitt,
Loreena
McKenzie, Bob
And Doug
McKenzie, Julia
McKenzie, Red
McKenzie, Scott
McKibbon, Al
McKinlay, Bob
McKinley, L.C.
McKinley, Ray
McKinleys
McKinney's
Cotton Pickers
McKinney, Bill
McKinnie, La
Velle
McKnight, Brian
McKuen, Rod
McLachlan, Craig
McLachlan, Sarah
McLagan, Ian
McLain, Tommy
McLaren,
Malcolm
McLaughlin, John
McLaughlin, Ollie
McLawler, Sarah
McLean, Don
McLean, Jackie
McLean, Nana
McLin, Jimmy
MCM
McMahon,
Andrew
'Blueblood'
McMillan, Terry
McMorland,
Alison
McMullen, Fred
McNabb, Ian
McNamara,
Robin
McNamara, Tim
McNeely, Big Jay
McNeil, Rita
McNulty, Chris
McPartland,
Jimmy
McPartland,
Marian
McPeak Brothers
McPhatter, Clyde

McPhee, Joe
McPherson,
Charles
McQuater,
Tommy
McRae, Carmen
McRae, Teddy
McShann, Jay
'Hootie'
McShee, Jacqui
McTell, 'Blind'
Willie
McTell, Ralph
McVea, Jack
McVie, Christine
McVie, John
McWilliams,
Brigitte
McWilliams,
David
McWilliams,
Paulette
Me And Juliet
Me And My Girl
Me And You
Mean Machine
Meanstreak
Meat Beat
Manifesto
Meat Loaf
Meat Puppets
Meaux, Huey P.
Meco
Medallions
Media Records
Medicine
Medicine Ball
Caravan
Medicine Head
Meditation
Singers
Meditations
Medley, Bill
Meehan, Tony
Meek, Joe
Meeks, Carl
Meet Me In St.
Louis
Mega Banton
Mega City Four
Megabass
Megadeth
Mehldau, Brad
Meirelles, Helena
Meisner, Randy
Mekon
Mekons
Mel And Kim
Mel And Tim
Melachrino,
George
Melanie,
Melcher, Terry
Meldrum, Molly
Melendes, Lisa
Melle Mel And
The Furious 5

Mellencamp, John
Mello K
Mello-Kings
Mellons, Ken
Mellotron
Mellow Man Ace
Mellowmoods
Mellows
Melly, George
Melodians
Melodic MC
Melody Maker
Melony
Meltdown
Melton, Barry
Melvin, Harold, And The Blue Notes
Melvins
Members
Membranes
Memory
Memphis Horns
Memphis Jug Band
Memphis Minnie
Memphis Slim
Men At Work
Men Of Vizion
Men They Couldn't Hang, The
Men Without Hats
Menace To Society
Mendes, Sergio
Mendoza, Vince
Mengelberg, Misha
Menken, Alan
Mensah, E.T.
Mensah, Kwaa
Menswear
Mental As Anything
Mental Hippie Blood
Menza, Don
Mercedes Ladies
Mercer, Johnny
Mercer, Mabel
Merchant, Natalie
Merciless
Mercury Records
Mercury Rev
Mercury, Freddie
Mercy
Mercy Dee
Mercyful Fate
Merger
Merlin
Merman, Ethel
Meroff, Benn
Merrell And The Exiles
Merrick, David

Merrill, Bob
Merrill, Helen
Merrily We Roll Along
Merritt, Max, And The Meteors
Merry Macs
Merry Widow, The
Merry-Go-Round
Merryweather, Neil
Merseybeats
Merseys
Merton Parkas
Mertz, Paul
Mesner Brothers
Messer, Mike
Messiah
Messiah Force
Messina, Jim
Messner, Johnny
Metal Church
Metalheadz
Metallica
Metcalf, Louis
Meteors
Meters
Metheny, Pat
Method Of Destruction
Metro
Metro, Peter
Metroplex
Metropolis
Metsers, Paul
Mexican Hayride
Mexicano
Meyer, George W.
Meyer, Joseph
Meyers, Augie
Mezzoforte
Mezzrow, Mezz
MFQ
MFSB
MGM Records
Miami Showband
Miami Sound Machine
Mice
Michael, George
Michaels, Lee
Michel'le
Michelot, Pierre
Michigan And Smiley
Mickey And Sylvia
Microdisney
Micus, Stephan
Middle Of The Road
Middleton, Velma
Midler, Bette
Midnight Oil
Midnite Follies Orchestra

Midway Still
Mighty Avengers
Mighty Avons
Mighty Baby
Mighty Clouds Of Joy
Mighty Diamonds
Mighty Lemon Drops
Mighty Mighty
Mighty Mighty Bosstones
Mighty Sam
Mighty Sparrow
Migil Five
Mihashi, Michiya
Mike And The Mechanics
Mike Stuart Span
Mikey General
Miki And Griff
Mikkelborg, Palle
Milburn, Amos
Miles, Buddy
Miles, Butch
Miles, Dick
Miles, Garry
Miles, John
Miles, Lizzie
Miles, Luke
Miles, Lynn
Miles, Robert
Miley, Bubber
Milhûn
Milk And Cookies
Milk And Honey
Milkshakes
Millenium
Miller, Ann
Miller, Big
Miller, Bill
Miller, Bob
Miller, Chuck
Miller, Clarence 'Big'
Miller, Count Prince
Miller, Dean
Miller, Donnie
Miller, Duncan
Miller, Ed
Miller, Eddie
Miller, Emmett
Miller, Ernest 'Punch'
Miller, Frankie
Miller, Gary
Miller, Glenn
Miller, Harry
Miller, Herb
Miller, J.D. 'Jay'
Miller, Jacob
Miller, Jimmy
Miller, Jody
Miller, Marcus
Miller, Mitch
Miller, Mrs

Miller, Mulgrew
Miller, Ned
Miller, Ray
Miller, Roger
Miller, Steve
Milli Vanilli
Millian, Baker
Millican And Nesbitt
Millie
Millinder, Lucky
Millns, Paul
Mills Blue Rhythm Band
Mills Brothers
Mills Sisters
Mills, Frank
Mills, Garry
Mills, Gordon
Mills, Irving
Mills, Jeff
Mills, Mrs.
Mills, Stephanie
Milltown Brothers
Milsap, Ronnie
Milton, Roy
Mimms, Garnet, And The Enchanters
Minami, Haruo
Mince, Johnny
Mindbenders
Mindfunk
Mindset
Mindstorm
Mineo, Sal
Mingus
Mingus, Charles
Mini Allstars
Ministry
Ministry Of Sound
Minit Records
Mink DeVille
Minnelli, Liza
Minnelli, Vincente
Minogue, Dannii
Minogue, Kylie
Minor Threat
Minott, Echo
Minott, Sugar
Mint Condition
Mint Juleps
Mint Tattoo
Minter, Iverson
Mintzer, Bob
Minutemen
Miracles
Miranda Sex Garden
Miranda, Carmen
Miranda, Ismael
Miro
Mirrors
Misery Loves Co.
Misex

Misfits
Misiani, Daniel
Misora, Hibari
Miss Hook Of Holland
Miss Liberty
Miss London Ltd.
Miss Saigon
Missing Persons
Mission
Mission Of Burma
Mississippi Mass Choir
Mississippi Sheiks
Missourians
Mister Rock And Roll
Misty In Roots
Misunderstood
Mitchell, Billy
Mitchell, Blue
Mitchell, Bobby
Mitchell, Chad, Trio
Mitchell, George
Mitchell, George (jazz)
Mitchell, Guy
Mitchell, Joni
Mitchell, Kim
Mitchell, Louis
Mitchell, Malcolm
Mitchell, McKinley
Mitchell, Red
Mitchell, Roscoe
Mitchell, Walter
Mitchell, Willie
Mitchell-Ruff Duo
Mittoo, Jackie
Mix Tapes
Mixed Company
Mixmaster Morris
Mize, Billy
Mizell, Hank
Mlle. Modiste
MLO
MMW
MN8
Mo' Wax Records
Mo-Dettes
Mobb Deep
Mobley, Hank
Moby
Moby Dick
Moby Grape
Mock Turtles
Mockingbirds
Models
Modern English
Modern Jazz Quartet
Modern Lovers
Modern Mandolin Quartet
Modern Records
Modernaires

Modibo, Askia
Modugno,
   Domenico
Moffatt, Hugh
Moffatt, Katy
Moffett, Charles
Mogg, Ambrose
Mogwai
Mohamed, Pops
Mohawk, Essra
Moholo, Louis
Moire Music
   Drum
   Orchestra
Moist
Mojave 3
Mojo Mavigator
Mojo Men
Mojos
Mole, Miff
Molly Half Head
Molly Hatchet
Moloko
Molton, Flora
Moments
Momus
Monaco
Monaco, James V.
Moncur, Grachan,
   III
Mondello, Toots
Money Mark
Money, Eddie
Money, Zoot
Monguito 'El
   Unico'
Monitors
Monk, Meredith
Monk, T.S.
Monk, Thelonious
Monkees
Monks
Monochrome Set
Monotones
Monro, Matt
Monroe, Bill
Monroe, Birch
Monroe, Charlie
Monroe, Gerry
Monroe, James
Monroe, Marilyn
Monroe, Melissa
Monroe, Michael
Monroe, Vaughn
Monsieur
   Beaucaire
Monsoon
Monster Magnet
Montage
Montana Rose
Montana Slim
Montana, Patsy
Montanez, Andy
Montclairs
Monte Carlo
Montenegro,
   Hugo

Monterey Jazz
   Festival
Monterey Pop
   Festival
Monterose, J.R.
Montez, Chris
Montgomery,
   Bob
Montgomery,
   John Michael
Montgomery,
   Little Brother
Montgomery,
   Marian
Montgomery,
   Melba
Montgomery,
   Monk
Montgomery,
   Wes
Montoliu, Tete
Montrell, Roy
Montreux
   International
   Jazz Festival
Montrose
Montrose, Ronnie
Monyaka
Mood II Swing
Mood Six
Moodswings
Moody Blues
Moody Boyz
Moody, Clyde
Moody, James
Moog, Robert A.
Moon
Moon Martin
Moon Over
   Miami
Moon, Keith
Moondoc, Jemeel
Moondog
Moondogg
Mooney, Art
Mooney, John
Moonglows
Moontrekkers
Moore, 'Whistlin'
   Alex
Moore, Abra
Moore, Alton
Moore, Arnold
   Dwight
   'Gatemouth'
Moore, Billy
Moore, Bob
Moore, Brew
Moore, Butch
Moore, Charlie
Moore, Christy
Moore, Dorothy
Moore, Dudley
Moore, Freddie
Moore, Gary
Moore, Glen
Moore, Grace

Moore, GT, And
   The Reggae
   Guitars
Moore, Jackie
Moore, James
Moore, Johnny
Moore, Johnny B.
Moore, Lee
Moore, Marilyn
Moore, Melba
Moore, Monette
Moore, Oscar
Moore, R. Stevie
Moore, Ralph
Moore, Ray
Moore, Rev.
   James, And
   The Mississippi
   Mass Choir
Moore, Russell
   'Big Chief'
Moore, Scotty
Moore, Thom
Moore, Tiny
Moore, Vinnie
Moore, Willie C.
Moose
Moraes, Angel
Morales, David
Morales, Noro
Morand, Herb
Morbid Angel
Morcheeba
Mordred
More
More American
   Graffiti
More, Anthony
Moré, Beny
More, Julian
Morehouse,
   Chauncey
Moreira, Airto
Morello, Joe
Morells
Moreno, Bobby
Morgan Heritage
Morgan, Al
Morgan, Cindy
Morgan, Derrick
Morgan, Elaine
Morgan, Frank
Morgan, George
Morgan, Helen
Morgan, Jane
Morgan, Jaye P.
Morgan, Lanny
Morgan, Lee
Morgan, Lorrie
Morgan, Mike
Morgan, Russ
Morgan, Sam
Morillo, Erick
   'More'
Morissette, Alanis
Morley, Angela
Morning

Moroccos
Moross, Jerome
Morphine
Morricone, Ennio
Morris Brothers
Morris Minor And
   The Majors
Morris, Audrey
Morris, Gary
Morris, Jenny
Morris, Joe
Morris, Lawrence
   'Butch'
Morris, Marlowe
Morris, Russell
Morris, Sarah
   Jane
Morrison,
   Barbara
Morrison, James
Morrison, Mark
Morrison, Neville
Morrison, Van
Morrissey
Morrissey, Dick
Morrissey, Louise
Morrissey-Mullen
Morrow, Buddy
Morse, Ella Mae
Morse, Steve,
   Band
Morta Skuld
Morton, 'Jelly
   Roll'
Morton, Benny
Morton, George
   'Shadow'
Morton, Pete
Morton, Tex
Morwells
Mosby, Johnny
   And Jonie
Mosca, Sal
Moses, Bob
Moses, J.C.
Moses, Pablo
Mosley, Snub
Moss, Buddy
Moss, Danny
Most Happy Fella,
   The
Most, Mickie
Motello, Elton
Motels
Moten, Bennie
Moth Macabre
Mother Earth
Mother Earth
   (60s)
Mother Earth
   (90s)
Mother Goose
Mother Love
   Bone
Mother Superia
Mother Wore
   Tights

Mother's Finest
Motherlode
Mothers Of
   Invention
Motian, Paul
Mötley Crüe
Motley, Frank
Motor Town
   Revue
Motorcycle Boy
Motörhead
Motors
Motown Records
Mott
Mott The Hoople
Mould, Bob
Mound City Blue
   Blowers
Mounka, Pamelo
Mounsey, Paul
Mount Rushmore
Mountain
Mountain Ash
   Band
Mourneblade
Mourning Reign
Mouse And The
   Traps
Mouse Records
Mouskouri, Nana
Moustaki, Georges
Mouth And McNeal
Mouth Music
Mouzon, Alphonze
Move
Movement Ex
Movin' Melodies
Moving Cloud
Moving Hearts
Moving Pictures
Moving Shadow
   Records
Moving Sidewalks
Moving Tragets
Mowatt, Judy
Mowrey, Dude
Moxy Frivous
Moye, Famoudou
   Don
Moyet, Alison
Mr Bo
Mr Fingers
Mr Lee
Mr. Big
Mr. Big (70s)
Mr. Big (80s)
Mr. Bloe
Mr. Bo
Mr. Bungle
Mr. Cinders
Mr. Fox
Mr. Mister
Mraz, George
Mrs Brown
   You've Got A
   Lovely
   Daughter

Ms Melodie
Mseleku, Bheki
MSG
Mtukudzi, Oliver
MTV
Mu
Muana, Tshala
Much Ado
Muckram Wakes
Mucky Pup
Mud
Muddy Waters
Mudhoney
Mudie, Harry
Mudlarks
Mueller-
  Westernhagen,
  Marius
Mugwumps
Muhammad, Idris
Mukwesha,
  Virginia
Muldaur, Geoff
Muldaur, Maria
Muldowney,
  Dominic
Mule
Mulenze
Mullen, Jim
Mullican, Moon
Mulligan, Gerry
Mulligan, Mick
Mulry, Ted
Mundell, Hugh
Mundy
Mundy, Jimmy
Mungo Jerry
Munn, Billy
Muranyi, Joe
Murata, Hideo
Murder Inc.
Murk
Murmaids
Murphey, Michael
  Martin
Murphy's Law
Murphy, David
  Lee
Murphy, Delia
Murphy, Lyle
  'Spud'
Murphy, Mark
Murphy, Matt
Murphy, Noel
Murphy, Peter
Murphy, Ralph
Murphy, Rose
Murphy, Turk
Murphy, Walter
Murray, Anne
Murray, David
Murray, Pauline,
  And The
  Invisible Girls
Murray, Ruby
Murray, Sunny
Mursal, Maryam

Murtceps
Murvin, Junior
Muscle Beach
  Party
Muscle Shoals
Muse
Mushroom
Mushroom
  Records
Music Box Revue
Music Explosion
Music From
  China
Music In The Air
Music Machine
Music Man, The
Music Man, The
  (film musical)
Musical Youth
Musicraft Records
Musselwhite,
  Charlie
Musso, Vido
Mussolini,
  Romano
Mustafov, Ferus
Musto And Bones
Musto, Tommy
Mutabaruka
Mute Records
Mutiny!
Mutton Birds
Mutukudzi, Oliver
μ-Ziq
Muzsikás
MX-80 Sound
My Bloody
  Valentine
My Dear Watson
My Dying Bride
My Fair Lady
My Fair Lady
  (film musical)
My Favorite Year
My Gal Sal
My Heart Goes
  Crazy
My Life Story
My One And Only
Myddle Class
Myers, Amina
  Claudine
Myers, Bumps
Myers, Dave
Myers, Louis
Myers, Sammy
Myers, Stanley
Myles, Alannah
Myles, Heather
Myofist
Myrow, Joseph
Mystery Of Edwin
  Drood, The
Mystery Trend
Mystic Revealers
Mystics
Mythra

N'Dour, Youssou
N-Joi
N-Tense
N-Troop
N.R.T.
N.W.O.B.H.M.
N2-Deep
Na Fili
Nada Surf
Nagel, Freddy
Nagle, Ron
Nail, Jimmy
Nailbomb
Najee
Najma
Nakajima, Miyuki
Naked City
Naked Eyes
Naked Prey
Naked Raygun
Naked Truth
Namlook, Peter
Namyslowski,
  Zbigniew
Nanaco
Nance, Ray
Nanton, Joe
  'Tricky Sam'
Napalm Death
Napier, Bill
Napier-Bell,
  Simon
Napoleon XIV
Napoleon, Marty
Napoleon, Phil
Napoleon, Teddy
Naptali, Raymond
Narell, Andy
Nas
Nascimento,
  Milton
Nash, Graham
Nash, Johnny
Nashville
  Bluegrass Band
Nashville Teens
Nashville West
Nasty Idols
Nasty Savage
Natal, Nanette
Nathan, Sydney
Nati
Nation Records
National Barn
  Dance, The
National Health
National Jazz
  Ensemble
National Youth
  Jazz Orchestra
Native Hipsters
Native Tongues
  Posse
Natural Acoustic
  Band
Natural Four
Naturals

Naturists
Naughton, David
Naughty By Nature
Naughty Marietta
  (film musical)
Naughty Marietta
  (stage musical)
Naura, Michael
Navarre, Ludovic
Navarro, Fats
Navras Records
Naylor, Jerry
Nazareth
Nazz
Ndegé Ocello,
  Me'Shell
Neagle, Anna
Neal, Kenny
Neal, Raful
Near, Holly
Necros
Nectarine No.9
Ned's Atomic
  Dustbin
Nefertiti
Nefilim
Negativland
Negrocan
Neidlinger, Buell
Neighbors, Paul
Neil, Fred
Neil, Vince, Band
Nelson
Nelson Brothers
Nelson, 'Big Eye'
  Louis
Nelson, Bill
Nelson, Gene
Nelson, Jimmy
  'T-99'
Nelson, Louis
Nelson, Oliver
Nelson, Ozzie
Nelson, Ricky
Nelson, Romeo
Nelson, Sandy
Nelson, Shara
Nelson, Skip
Nelson, Tracy
Nelson, Willie
Nemesis
Nenes
Neon Cross
Neon
  Philharmonic
Neon Rose
Neptune's
  Daughter
Nero And The
  Gladiators
Nero, Peter
Nerves
Nervous Norvus
Nervous Records
Nesbitt, John
Nesmith, Michael
Nestico, Sam

Network
Network Records
Neu
Neuro Project
Neuropolitique
Neurosis
Nevada Slim
Neville Brothers
Neville, Aaron
Neville, Art
Neville, Ivan
Nevins, Jason
New Birth Brass
  Band
New Bomb Turks
New Celeste
New Christy
  Minstrels
New Colony Six
New Cranes
New Edition
New England
  (UK)
New England
  (USA)
New Fast
  Automatic
  Daffodils
New Frontier
New Girl In Town
New Grass
  Revival
New Idol Son
New Jazz
  Orchestra
New Kids On The
  Block
New Kingdom
New Lost City
  Ramblers
New Model Army
New Moon, The
New Musical
  Express
New Musik
New Order
New Orleans
New Orleans
  Rhythm Kings
New Riders Of
  The Purple
  Sage
New
  Romanticism
New Seekers
New Strangers
New Tweedy
  Brothers
New Vaudeville
  Band
New Victory
  Band
New Wave
New Wave Of
  British Heavy
  Metal
New World

New York City
New York Dolls
New York Jazz
  Repertory
  Orchestra
New York Skyy
New York, New
  York
New Yorkers,
  The
New, Howard
Newbeats
Newbern,
  'Hambone'
  Willie
Newberry,
  Booker, III
Newborn,
  Phineas, Jnr.
Newbury, Mickey
Newley, Anthony
Newman, Alfred
Newman, Chris
Newman, Colin
Newman, David
Newman, David
  'Fathead'
Newman, Jimmy
  C.
Newman, Joe
Newman, Lionel
Newman, Randy
Newman, Roy
Newport Jazz
  Festival
Newton, David
Newton, Frankie
Newton, James
Newton, Juice
Newton, Wayne
Newton-John,
  Olivia
Newtown
  Neurotics
Next Step Up
Nexus 21
NG La Banda
Ngonda, Wally
Ní Chathasaigh,
  Máire
Niagara
Nice
Nice And Smooth
Nice And Nasty
  Three
Nice Jazz Festival
Niche, Grupo
Nicholas
  Brothers
Nicholas,
  'Wooden' Joe
Nicholas, Albert
Nicholas, Big
  Nick
Nicholas, Paul
Nicholls, Horatio
Nicholls, Sue

Nichols, Cowboy
  Sam
Nichols, Herbie
Nichols, Keith
Nichols, Penny
Nichols, Red
Nicholson, J.D.
Nick And Nora
Nicks, Stevie
Nico
Nico Junior
Nicodemus
Nicol, Simon
Nicolette
Nicols, Maggie
Niehaus, Lennie
Nielsen-
  Chapman, Beth
Niemack, Judy
Nieves, Tito
Night And Day
Night Ranger
Nightcrawlers
Nighthawk,
  Robert
Nightingale,
  Annie
Nightingale,
  Maxine
Nightingales
Nightman
Nightmares On
  Wax
Nightnoise
Nightwing
Nilsson, Harry
Nina And
  Frederick
Nine
Nine Below Zero
Nine Inch Nails
9 Lazy 9
999
1994
1910 Fruitgum
  Company
95 South
Ninja Tune
  Records
Ninjaman
Nino And The
  Ebb Tides
Nirvana (UK)
Nirvana (USA)
Nistico, Sal
Nitty Gritty
Nitty Gritty Dirt
  Band
Nitzer Ebb
Nitzinger, John
Nitzsche, Jack
Nix, Don
Nix, Willie
Nixon, Elmore
Nixon, Hammie
Nixons
NME

No Doubt
No Exqze
No Face
NoFX
No Means No
No Nukes
No Strings
No Sweat
No Way Sis
No, No, Nanette
Noa
Noack, Eddie
Noakes, Rab
Noble, Leighton
Noble, Patsy Ann
Noble, Ray
Noble, Steve
Nobles, Cliff (And
  Co.)
Nock, Mike
Nocturnus
Noel And Gertie
Noiseworks
Nokemono
Nolan, Bob
Nolans
Nolen, Jimmy
Nomad
Nomi, Klaus
Nomos
Nookie
Noonan, Steve
Noone, Jimmie
Noone, Peter
Noor Shimaal
Nordenstam,
  Stina
Norma Jean
Norman, Jimmy
Norris, Walter
North, Alex
North, Freddie
Northcott, Tom
Northern Uproar
Northside
Norum, John
Norum, Tone
Norvo, Red
Norworth, Jack
Notations
Notes From The
  Underground
Noto, Sam
Notorious
Notorious B.I.G.
Notting Hillbillies
Nottingham,
  Jimmy
Notwist
Nova Mob
Nova, Aldo
Nova, Heather
Novamute
  Records
Novello, Ivor
Now Generation
Nowherefast

NRBQ
NSO Force
Nu Colours
Nu Groove Records
Nua, Onipa
Nubiles
Nuclear Assault
Nuclear Valdez
Nucleus
Nudeswirl
Nudie
Nueva Manteca
Nugent, Ted
Null, Cecil
Numan, Gary
Number One
  Cup
Nunez, Alcide
  'Yellow'
Nunn, Bobby
Nunn, Gary P.
Nunn, Trevor
Nuns
Nunsense
Nussbaum, Adam
Nut
Nutmegs
Nutz
NWA
NY Loose
Nyame, E.K.
Nylons
Nyman, Michael
Nymph Errant
Nymphs
Nyro, Laura
O Lucky Man
O'Brien, Floyd
O'Brien, Tim
O'Connell, Helen
O'Connell, Maura
O'Connor, Cavan
O'Connor, Des
O'Connor,
  Donald
O'Connor, Hazel
O'Connor, Mark
O'Connor, Sinead
O'Daniel, Wilbert
  Lee
O'Day, Alan
O'Day, Anita
O'Day, Molly
O'Dell, Kenny
O'Donnell, Daniel
O'Farrill, Arturo
  'Chico'
O'Flynn, Bridget
O'Flynn, Liam
O'Gwynn, James
O'Hara, Jamie
O'Hare, Husk
O'Jays
O'Kanes
O'Keefe, Danny
O'Keefe, Johnny
O'Neal, Alexander

O'Neal, Shaquille
O'Neill, Sharon
O'Rahilly, Ronan
O'Shea, Tessie
O'Sullivan,
  Gilbert
Oak Ridge Boys
Oakenfold, Paul
Oaktown's 3-5-7
Oasis
Obey, Ebenezer
Obiedo, Ray
Obituary
Oblivians
Obsessed
Obsession
Obus
Ocean
Ocean Colour
  Scene
Ocean, Billy
Ochs, Phil
Octopus
Odell, Mac
Oden, James
  Burke
Odetta
Odom, Andrew
Odyssey
Of Perception
Of Thee I Sing
Ofarim, Esther
  And Abi
Offenbach
Offitt, Lillian
Offspring
Ogada, Ayub
Ogholi, Evi-Edna
Oh! Calcutta!
Oh, Boy!
Oh, Joy!
Oh, Kay!
Oh, Lady! Lady!!
Oh, What A
  Lovely War!
Ohio Express
Ohio Knox
Ohio Players
Ohman, Phil
Ohrlin, Glenn
Oi Polloi
Oingo Boingo
Oisin
OK Jazz
OK Jive
Okasili, Martin
OKeh Records
Okey Dokey
  Stompers
Oklahoma! (film
  musical)
Oklahoma! (stage
  musical)
Okoshi, Tiger
Okosun, Sonny
Ol' Dirty Bastard
Olaiya, Victor

Olatunji, Babatunde
Olatunji, Babtunji
Old And In The Way
Old And New Dreams
Old Grey Whistle Test, The
Old 97's
Old Rope String Band
Old Swan Band
Oldfield, Mike
Oldfield, Sally
Oldham, Andrew Loog
Oldham, Spooner
Olive
Olivencia, Tommy
Oliver!
Oliver! (film musical)
Oliver, Frankie
Oliver, Joe 'King'
Oliver, Sy
Olivier, Laurence, Awards
Ollie And Jerry
Olsen, George
Olympic Records
Olympics
Om Records
Omar
Omartian, Michael
OMD
Omen
On A Clear Day You Can See Forever
On The Avenue
On The Riviera
On The Road With Duke Ellington
On The Town (film musical)
On The Town (stage musical)
On The Twentieth Century
On U Sound System
On Your Toes
Once Upon A Mattress
One Dam Thing After Another
One Dove
One Hit Wonder
One Hour With You
110 In The Shade
One Hundred Men And A Girl

100th Monkey
One In A Million
One Little Indian Records
One Love Records
One More Time
One Night Of Love
101 Ranch Boys
101ers
One Records
1,000 Violins
One Touch Of Venus
One Trick Pony
One, The
One-derful Records
Ongala, Remmy
Only Child
Only Ones
Only The Lonely
Ono, Yoko
Onslaught
Onuora, Oku
Onyeka
Onyx
Opal
Open Road
Operation Ivy
Ophichus
Optimystic
Opus III
Oral
Orange
Orange Juice
Orb
Orbach, Jerry
Orbison, Roy
Orbit, William
Orbital
Orchestra Baobob
Orchestra Makassy
Orchestra Wives
Orchestral Manoeuvres In The Dark
Orchestre Jazira
Orchestre Super Mazembe
Oregon
Orendorff, George
Organization
Organized Konfusion
Oriental Brothers Band
Original Concept
Original Dixieland Jazz Band
Original Memphis Five

Original Rockers
Originals
Oriole Records
Orioles
Orion
Orlando
Orlando, Ramón
Orlando, Tony
Orleans
Orlons
Ornadel, Cyril
Orphan
Orpheus
Orquesta Reve
Orrall, Robert Ellis
Ørsted Pedersen, Niels-Henning
Ortiz, Mario
Orton, Beth
Ory, Edward 'Kid'
Oryema, Geoffrey
Osadebe, Osita
Osborne Brothers
Osborne, Jeffrey
Osborne, Jimmie
Osborne, Joan
Osborne, Mary
Osborne, Mike
Osborne, Tony, Sound
Osborne, Will
Osbourne, Johnny
Osbourne, Ozzy
Osby, Greg
Oscar The Frog
Osibisa
Oslin, K.T.
Osmond, Donny
Osmond, Little Jimmy
Osmond, Marie
Osmonds
Osser, Glenn
Ossian
Ostrogoth
Other Half
Other Records
Other Two
Otis, Johnny
Ottawan
Otway, John
Ougenweide
Oui 3
Our Daughters Wedding
Our Kid
Our Lady Peace
Our Miss Gibbs
Our Tribe
Out Cold Cops
Out Of My Hair
Out Of The Blue
Outcaste Records
Outcasts

Outer Rhythm Records
Outfield
Outhere Brothers
Outkast
Outlaw Posse
Outlaws
Outlaws (UK)
Outside
Outside Edge
Outsiders
Ovans, Tom
Ovations
Overbea, Danny
Overdose
Overflash
Overkill
Overlanders
Overlord X
Overstreet, Paul
Overstreet, Tommy
Oviedo, Papi
Owen, Jim
Owen, Mark
Owen, Reg
Owens, Bonnie
Owens, Buck
Owens, Calvin
Owens, Harry
Owens, Jack
Owens, Jay
Owens, Jimmy
Owens, Robert
Owens, Tex
Owoh, Orlando
Oxford, Vernon
Oxley, Tony
Oysterband
Oz
Ozark Jubilee, The
Ozark Mountain Daredevils
Ozone
Ozone, Makoto
Ozric Tentacles
Ozz
P
P.O.W.E.R.
Pablo
Pablo Cruise
Pablo Gad
Pablo, Augustus
Pacheco, Johnny
Pacheco, Tom
Pacific Drift
Pacific Gas And Electric
Pacific Overtures
Paddy, Klaus And Gibson
Page, Cleo
Page, Jimmy
Page, Larry
Page, Martin
Page, Oran 'Hot Lips'

Page, Patti
Page, Stu
Page, Walter
Pagliaro
Pahinui Brothers
Pahinui, Gabby
Paich, Marty
Paige, Elaine
Pain Teens
Paint Your Wagon
Paisley, Bob
Pajama Game, The
Pajama Game, The (film musical)
Pajama Game, The (stage musical)
Pal Joey
Pal Joey (film musical)
Pal Joey (stage musical)
Palace Brothers
Palace Guard
Palais Schaumburg
Pale
Pale Fountains
Pale Saints
Paley, Ben
Paladins
Palladinos
Pallas
Palma, Triston
Palmer, Carl
Palmer, Clive
Palmer, Earl
Palmer, Holly
Palmer, Jimmy
Palmer, Michael
Palmer, Robert
Palmer, Roy
Palmer, Tony
Palmieri, Charlie
Palmieri, Eddie
Palomino Road
Pama Records
Pampini, Gabino
Pan African Orchestra
Pan Head
Pan, Hermes
Panama Hattie
Panasonic
Pandemonium
Pandora
Pandora's Box
Pandoras
Pannell, Bill
Pantera
Papa Bue
Papa Chuk
Papa Levi, Phillip
Papa San

Papadimitriou, Sakis
Papaíto
Papas Fritas
Papasov, Ivo
Paper Lace
Pappalardi, Felix
Parade
Paradis, Vanessa
Paradise Lost
Paradise - Hawaiian Style
Paradons
Paradox
Paragons (R&B)
Paragons (reggae)
Paramor, Norrie
Paramounts
Paras, Fabio
Pardon, Walter
Parenti, Tony
Parham, Tiny
Pariah (UK)
Pariah (USA)
Paris
Paris Angels
Paris Blues
Paris Sisters
Paris, Barbara
Paris, Jackie
Paris, Jeff
Paris, Mica
Parish, Mitchell
Park, Graeme
Park, Simon
Parker, 'Little' Junior
Parker, Alan
Parker, Andy, And The Plainsmen
Parker, Billy
Parker, Bobby
Parker, Byron
Parker, Charlie
Parker, Evan
Parker, Fess
Parker, Graham
Parker, John 'Knocky'
Parker, Johnny
Parker, Ken
Parker, Leo
Parker, Maceo
Parker, Ray, Jnr.
Parker, Robert
Parker, Sonny
Parker, Terrence
Parker, Tom, 'Colonel'
Parker, William
Parkes, Lloyd
Parkinson, Doug
Parks, Lloyd
Parks, Van Dyke
Parkway Records

Parlan, Horace
Parliament
Parlophone Records
Parnell, Jack
Parnell, Lee Roy
Parnes, Larry
Parr, John
Parrish, Andy
Parrot Records
Parsons, Alan
Parsons, Bill
Parsons, Gene
Parsons, Gordon
Parsons, Gram
Pärt, Arvo
Partch, Harry
Partners In Crime
Parton, David
Parton, Dolly
Parton, Stella
Partridge Family
Partridge, Andy
Partridge, Don
Party Party
Party Posse
Pasadena Roof Orchestra
Pasadenas
Pasquall, Don
Pass, Joe
Passion
Passions (UK)
Passions (USA)
Pastels
Pastels (UK)
Pastels (US)
Pastor, Tony
Pastorius, Jaco
Pat Garrett And Billy The Kid
Pate, Johnny
Patinkin, Mandy
Patitucci, John
Paton, Tam
Patra
Patrick Street
Patrick's, Bobby, Big Six
Patrick, Pat
Patt, Frank 'Honeyboy'
Patterson, Ann
Patterson, Bobby
Patterson, Ottilie
Patterson, Rahsaan
Patterson, Ray And Ina
Patto
Patton, 'Big' John
Patton, Charley
Paul And Paula
Paul, Billy
Paul, Clarence
Paul, Emmanuel

Paul, Frankie
Paul, Henry, Band
Paul, Les
Paupers
Pavageau, Alcide 'Slow Drag'
Pavement
Pavlov's Dog
Pavone, Rita
Paw
Paxton, Gary S.
Paxton, Tom
Paycheck, Johnny
Payne, Cecil
Payne, Freda
Payne, Jack
Payne, Jimmy
Payne, Leon
Payne, Scherrie
Payne, Sonny
Payton, Earlee
Paz
Peace, Love And Pibulls
Peaches And Herb
Peacock, Annette
Peacock, Gary
Peanut Butter Conspiracy
Pearce, Dick
Pearl Harbor And The Explosions
Pearl Jam
Pearl, Minnie
Pearl, Ray
Pearls Before Swine
Pearson, Duke
Pearson, Johnny
Peart, Jeff
Peart, Neil
Peavey, Doris
Pebbles
Pecora, Santo
Peddlers
Peebles, Ann
Peel, John
Peeping Tom
Peer, Ralph
Peers, Donald
Pegg, Dave
Peggy-Ann
Peggy Sue
Peiffer, Bernard
Pell, Axel Rudi
Pemberton, Bill
Pendarvis, Paul
Pendergrass, Teddy
Pendragon
Penetration
Penguin Cafe Orchestra
Penguins
Peniston, Ce Ce
Penn, Dan

Penn, Dawn
Penn, Michael
Penn, William, And His Pals
Pennington, Ray
Penny, Hank
Pentagons
Pentagram
Pentangle
Penthouse
Peoples, Dottie
Peplowski, Ken
Pepper, Art
Pepsi And Shirlie
Perchance To Dream
Percy
Pere Ubu
Perez, Manuel
Perfect Disaster
Perfect Jazz Repertory Quintet
Perfect Stranger
Perfect, Christine
Perfecto Records
Perfume
Pericoli, Emilio
Perkins, Al
Perkins, Bill
Perkins, Carl
Perkins, Carl (jazz)
Perkins, Carl (rock 'n' roll)
Perkins, Pinetop
Perkins, Polly
Perkins, Red
Perrett, Peter
Perrson, Bent
Perry, Bill
Perry, Joe, Project
Perry, Lee
Perry, Linda
Perry, Mark
Perry, Oliver 'King'
Perry, Ray
Perry, Richard
Perry, Steve
Perryman, Lloyd
Perryman, Rufus 'Speckled Red'
Perryman, William
Persen, Mari Boine
Persian Risk
Persiany, André
Persip, Charlie
Person, Houston
Persson, Aake
Persuaders
Persuasions
Pestilence
Pet Lamb

Pet Shop Boys
Pete Kelly's Blues
Peter And Gordon
Peter And The Test Tube Babies
Peter Pan
Peter, Paul And Mary
Peterik, Jim
Peters And Lee
Peters, Bernadette
Peters, Brian
Peters, Debra, And The Love Saints
Peters, Mark, And The Silhouettes
Peters, Sir Shina
Peterson, James
Peterson, Lucky
Peterson, Marvin 'Hannibal'
Peterson, Oscar
Peterson, Ray
Petit, Buddy
Petra
Petrillo, James Caesar
Petrucciani, Michel
Pettibone, Shep
Pettiford, Oscar
Pettis, 'Alabama' Junior
Petty, Norman
Petty, Tom
Petulia
Peyroux, Madeleine
Pez Band
Phair, Liz
Phajja
Phantom Blue
Phantom Of The Opera, The
Pharcyde
Phd
Phenomena
Phil The Fluter
Philadelphia International Records
Philips Records
Phillips, Barre
Phillips, Bill
Phillips, Brewer
Phillips, Bruce 'Utah'
Phillips, Chynna
Phillips, Don
Phillips, Esther
Phillips, Gene
Phillips, Joe 'Flip'

Phillips, John
Phillips, Michelle
Phillips, Phil
Phillips, Sam
Phillips, Sam
   (singer)
Phillips, Sid
Phillips, Steve
Phillips, Stu
Phillips, Teddy
Phillips, Utah
Phillips,
   Washington
Phillips, Woolf
Phiri, Ray Chipika
Phish
Phoenix
Photek
Photos
Phranc
Piaf, Edith
Piano C. Red
Piano Red
Piano Slim
Piazza, Rod
Piazzolla, Astor
Piblokto!
Pic And Bill
Picard, John
Pichon, Walter
   'Fats'
Pickens, Buster
Pickett, Bobby
   'Boris'
Pickett, Dan
Pickett, Wilson
Pickettywitch
Pickwick
Picou, Alphonse
Picture
Pictures At An
   Exhibition
Picture House
Pie Plant Pete
Pied Piper, The
Pied Pipers
Pierce, Billie
Pierce, De De
Pierce, Don
Pierce, Jeffrey
   Lee
Pierce, Nat
Pierce, Webb
Pigbag
Pigeon Pie
   Records
Pigeonhed
Piglets
Pigsty Hill Light
   Orchestra
Piirpauke
Pike, Dave
PiL
Pilgrim Travelers
Pillbox
Pillow, Ray
Pilot

Pilot (US)
Piltdown Men
Pinado, Bob
Pinchers
Pincock, Dougie
Pine, Courtney
Pinera, Mike
Pink Fairies
Pink Floyd
Pink Floyd At
   Pompeii
Pink Lady, The
Pink Military
Pink, Celinda
Pinkerton's
   Assorted
   Colours
Pinkney, Dwight
Pinocchio
Pins And Needles
Pinski Zoo
Pioneers
Pipkins
Pippin
Pirate Radio
Pirate, The
Pirates
Piron, Armand
Pisces
Pitch Shifter
Pitchford, Lonnie
Pitney, Gene
Pitt, Kenneth
Pittman, Barbara
Pixies
Pixies Three
Pizzarelli, Bucky
Pizzicato Five
PJ And Duncan
PJ Harvey
Placebo
Plain And Fancy
Plainsong
Planet 4
Planet Dog
   Records
Planet Jazz
Plant, Robert
Planxty
Plasmatics
Plastic Bertrand
Plastic Fantastic
Plastic Ono Band
Plastic Penny
Plastic People Of
   The Universe
Plater, Bobby
Platt, Eddie
Platters
Platz, David
Plava Trava
   Zaborava
Play It Cool
Play On!
Playmates
Pleasure Bombs
Pleasure Elite

Pleasure Fair
Pletcher, Stew
Plethyn
Plimsouls
Plus 8
PM Dawn
Poacher
Poco
Poe
Poet And The
   One Man Band
Poets
Pogues
Point Blank
Point Of Grace
Pointer Sisters
Pointer, Bonnie
Poison
Poison Girls
Poison Idea
Pokrovsky,
   Dmitri
Polcer, Ed
Polecats
Police
Pollack, Ben
Pollock, Marilyn
   Middleton
Polo, Danny
Polo, Jimmy
Poly Styrene
Polydor Records
Polygon Window
PolyGram
   Records
Pomeroy, Herb
Pomus, Doc
Ponce, Daniel
Pond
Poni-Tails
Ponomarec,
   Valery
Ponsford, Jan
Pontrelli, Pete
Ponty, Jean-Luc
Pooh Sticks
Poole, Brian, And
   The Tremeloes
Poole, Charlie
Poor
Poor Cow
Poor Little Rich
   Girl
Poor Righteous
   Teachers
Poor Souls
Poormouth
Poozies
Pop Art
Pop Down
Pop Gear
Pop Group
Pop Will Eat
   Itself
Popa Chubby
Popeluc
Popguns

Popinjays
Poppy
Poppy Family
Popsicle
Porcino, Al
Porcupine Tree
Porgy And Bess
Porky's
   Productions
Porno For Pyros
Portal, Michel
Porteous,
   Wyckham
Porter, Art
Porter, Billy
Porter, Cole
Porter, David
Porter, Gene
Porter, Mark
Porter, N.F.
Porter, Yank
Portishead
Portnoy, Jerry
Posey, Sandy
Posies
Positiva
Positive Black
   Soul
Positive Force
Positive-K
Possessed
Possum Dixon
Post, Mike
Posta, Adrienne
Postcard Records
Poster Children
Potter, Dale
Potter, Tommy
Pottinger, Philip
   'Leo'
Pottinger, Sonia
Poulsen, Hans
Pourcel, Franck
POV
Powell, Bobby
Powell, Bud
Powell, Cozy
Powell, Dick
Powell, Eleanor
Powell, Eugene
Powell, Jane
Powell, Jesse
Powell, Jimmy
Powell, Keith
Powell, Mel
Powell, Richie
Powell, Rudy
Powell, Seldon
Powell, Teddy
Power
Power Station
Power Steppers
Power, Bob
Power, Brendan
Power, Duffy
Powers, Joey
Powers, Ollie

Pozo, Chano
Prado, Perez
Praga Khan
Prairie Ramblers
Prana
Pratt, Phil
Praying Mantis
Preager, Lou
Precious Metal
Prefab Sprout
Prelude
Premiers
Presidents Of
   The United
   States Of
Presley, Elvis
Pressgang
Pressure Drop
Pressure Of
   Speech
Prestige/Folklore
   Records
Preston, Billy
Preston, Earl,
   And The TTs
Preston, Johnny
Preston, Mike
Preston, Robert
Pretenders
Pretty Maids
Pretty Things
Previn, André
Previn, Dory
Prevost, Eddie
Price
Price, 'Big'
   Walter
Price, Alan
Price, Jesse
Price, Kenny
Price, Lloyd
Price, Ray
Price, Ronnie
Price, Sammy
Pride And
   Prejudice
Pride, Charley
Pride, Dickie
Priest, Maxi
Priester, Julian
Priestley, Brian
Prima, Louis
Primal Scream
Prime Minister
   Pete Nice A nd
   Daddy Rich
Prime Time
Primer, John
Primes
Primettes
Primitive Radio
   Gods
Primitives
Primus
Prince
Prince Allah
Prince Bakaradi

Prince Buster
Prince Far I
Prince Hammer
Prince Jazzbo
Prince La La
Prince Lincoln
Prince
  Mohammed
Prince Paul
Prince, Harold
Princess Pang
Princess Sharifa
Princess Theatre
  Musicals
Principal Edwards
Principle, Jamie
Prine, John
Printup, Marcus
Prior, Maddy
Priority Records
Prism
Prisonaires
Prisoner Cell
  Block H - The
  Musical
Prisoners
Prisonshake
Private Lives
Privilege
Privin, Bernie
Pro-Ject X
Pro-Pain
Proby, P.J.
Proclaimers
Procol Harum
Procope, Russell
Prodigy
Production
  House
Professor Griff
Professor
  Longhair
Proffitt, Frank
Profile Records
Profit, Clarence
Promises,
  Promises
Prong
Propaganda
Propellerheads
Prophet, Chuck
Prophet, Michael
Prophet, Ronnie
Prophets Of The
  City
Protheroe, Brian
Provine, Dorothy
Pruden, Hal
Pruett, Jeanne
Pryor, Snooky
Prysock, Arthur
Prysock, Wilbert
  'Red'
Psyche-Out
Psyched Up Janis
Psychedelic
Psychedelic Furs

Psychic TV
Psychick
  Warriors Ov
  Gaia
Psyclone Rangers
Pubin, Joel
Public Enemy
Public Image
  Limited
Puckett, Gary,
  And The Union
  Gap
Puckett, Holland
Puckett, Riley
Pudgee The Phat
  Bastard
Puente, Tito
Pugh, Joe Bennie
Pukwana, Dudu
Pullen, Don
Pulp
Pulse 8 Records
Pungent Stench
Punishment Of
  Luxury
Punk
Punk In London
Pur
Purdie, Bernard
  'Pretty'
Pure Food And
  Drug Act
Pure Mania
Pure Prairie
  League
Puressence
Purify, James And
  Bobby
Purim, Flora
Purlie
Purnell, Alton
Purnell, Keg
Purple Gang
Purple Hearts
Pursell, Bill
Pursuit Of
  Happiness, The
Purtill, Moe
Purvis, Jack
Pusherman
Pussy Galore
Pussycat
Putman, Curly
PWL
Pye Records
Pyewackett
Pyle, Artimus,
  Band
Pyle, Pete
Pyne, Chris
Pyne, Mike
Pyramids
? And The
  Mysterians
Q Magazine
Q-Tips
Q5

Q65
QDIII
Quadrophenia
Quaker Girl, The
Qualls, Henry
Quarrymen
Quarterflash
Quartz
Quatermass
Quatro, Suzi
Quattlebaum,
  Doug
Quaye, Finley
Que Bono
Quealey, Chelsea
Quebec, Ike
Queen
Queen Ida
Queen Latifah
Queen Of Hearts
Queen Yemisi
Queensrÿche
Quest
Quest, J.
Questions
Qui Xia He
Quick
Quickly, Tommy
Quicksand
Quicksilver
  Messenger
  Service
Quickspace
Quiet Five
Quiet Riot
Quijano, Joe
Quill, Greg
Quillian, Rufus
  And Ben
Quilter, Roger
Quin-Tones
Quinichette, Paul
Quinn, Freddy
Quintana, Ismael
  'Pat'
Quintessence
Quintette Du Hot
  Club Du France
Quireboys
Quirk
Quiver
Quotations
R. Cajun And The
  Zydeco
  Brothers
R.A.F.
R.E.M.
Rabbitt, Eddie
Rabin, Oscar
Rabin, Trevor
Rabinowitz,
  Harry
Race, Steve
Racer X
Racey
Rachel Stamp
Rachell, Yank

Racic, Robert
Racing Cars
Radar Brothers
Radcliff, Bobby
Radiants
Radiator
Radiators
Radiators (UK)
Radiators (USA)
Radiators From
  Space
Radical Dance
  Faction
Radics Sowell
Radics, Jack
Radio Birdman
Radio
  Luxembourg
Radio On
Radio Tarifa
Radiohead
Radish
Radle, Carl
Rae, Jesse
Raeburn, Boyd
Raelettes
Rafferty, Gerry
Raga
Rage (UK)
Rage Against The
  Machine
Rage
Ragga
Raging Slab
Raglin, Junior
Ragovoy, Jerry
Ragtime
Rah Band
Raheem
Rai
Railroad Gin
Railway Children
Rain
Rain Parade
Rainbow
Rainbow Bridge
Rainbows
Raincoats
Raindance
Raindrops
Rainer
Rainey, Ma
Rainger, Ralph
Rainravens
Rainwater,
  Marvin
Raise The Roof
Raisin
Raitt, Bonnie
Raitt, John
Rak Records
Rake
Rakim
Rakotozafy
Raksin, David
Raleigh, Sir
  Walter

Ralphs, Mick
Ram Jam
Ramacon, Phil
Ramazzotti, Eros
Rambeau, Eddie
Ramblers
  International
  Dance Band
Ramey, Gene
Ramirez, Louie
Ramirez, Ram
Rammelzee
Rammstein
Ramone, Phil
Ramones
Rampling, Danny
Ramrods
Ran-Dells
Rance Allen
  Group
Rancid
Randall, Freddy
Randall, Jon
Randazzo, Teddy
Randolph, Boots
Randolph, Elsie
Randolph, Mouse
Randolph, Zilner
Randy And The
  Rainbows
Raney, Jimmy
Raney, Sue
Raney, Wayne
Rangell, Nelson
Ranger, Shorty
Ranglin, Ernest
Rank And File
Rank, Bill
Rankin Family
Rankin R.S.
Ranking Ann
Ranking Dread
Ranking Joe
Ranking Toyan
Ranks, Cutty
Ranks, Shabba
Rap
Rap-A-Lot
  Records
Rapeman
Rapino Brothers
Rapp, Barney
Rappin' Is
  Fundamental
Rare
Rare Bird
Rare Earth
Ras, Michael, And
  The Sons Of
  Negus
Rasha
Raspberries
Raspberry,
  Raymond
Rasta Music
Rastafarianism
Rat Race, The

Ratcat
Ratt
Rattle 'N' Reel
Rattles
Rattlesnake
 Annie
Rattlesnake Kiss
Rausch, Leon
Rava, Enrico
Ravan, Genya
Ravazza, Carl
Rave
Raven
Raven, Eddy
Ravens
Ravikiran
Raw Breed
Raw Fusion
Raw Stylus
Rawls, Lou
Ray, Carline
Ray, Danny
Ray, Dave
Ray, Goodman
 And Brown
Ray, Harmon
Ray, Johnnie
Ray, Ricardo
 'Richie', And
 Bobby Cruz
Ray, Wade
Rayber Voices
Rayburn, Margie
Raydio
Raye, Collin
Raye, Don
Raye, Susan
Rays
Rayvon
Razaf, Andy
Raze
Razorblade Smile
Razorcuts
RCA Records
Re-Animator
Re-Flex
Rea, Chris
React Records
Reader, Eddi
Ready, Steady,
 Go!
Reagon, Bernice
 Johnson
Reagon, Toshi
Real Breaks
Real Kids
Real Life
Real McCoy
Real People
Real Roxanne
Real Sounds
Real Thing
Real World
 Records
Realm
Reardon, Caspar
RebbeSoul
Rebel MC

Rebel, Tony
Rebello, Jason
Rebennack, Mac
Reckless
Reco, Ezz, And
 The Launchers
Records
Rector, Red
Recycle Or Die
Red Bandit
Red Bird Records
Red Box
Red Crayola
Red Devils
Red Dogs
Red Dragon
Red Fox
Red Fun
Red Guitars
Red Hot Chili
 Peppers
Red House
 Painters
Red Jasper
Red Letter Day
Red Lorry Yellow
 Lorry
Red Mill, The
Red Nelson
Red Ninja
Red Rat
Red River Dave
Red Roosters
Red Rose,
 Anthony
Red Shoes, The
Red Shoes, The
 (film musical)
Red Shoes, The
 (stage musical)
Red Snapper
Red, Danny
Red, Hot And
 Blue!
Redbone
Redd Kross
Redd, Vi
Redding, Otis
Reddy, Helen
Redeye
Redgum
Redhead
Redhead Kingpin
 And FBI
Redman
Redman, Dewey
Redman, Don
Redman, Joshua
Rednex
Redpath, Jean
Redskins
Redwing
Reece, Alex
Reece, Dizzy
Reed, A.C.
Reed, Blind
 Alfred
Reed, Dalton

Reed, Dan,
 Network
Reed, Jerry
Reed, Jimmy
Reed, Les
Reed, Lou
Reed, Lucy
Reed, Ola Belle
Reed, Tommy
Reef
Reegs
Reel Big Fish
Reel 2 Real
Reels
Reese Project
Reese, Della
Reeves, Del
Reeves, Dianne
Reeves, Goebel
Reeves, Jim
Reeves, Martha
Reeves, Reuben
Reeves, Ronna
Reeves, Vic
Reflections
Reflex
Refreshments
Refugee
Regal Zonophone
Regan, Joan
Regan, Russ
Regents
Reggae
Reggae George
Reggae
 Philharmonic
 Orchestra
Reggae Regular
Reggae Sunsplash
Regina Regina
Regurgitator
Reich, Steve
Reichel, Hans
Reichman, Joe
Reid, Billy
Reid, Duke
Reid, Eileen
Reid, Irene
Reid, Junior
Reid, Mike
Reid, Neil
Reid, Rufus
Reid, Terry
Reid, Vernon
Reign
Reinforced
 Records
Reinhardt,
 Django
Reisman, Leo
Relativity
Relativity
 Records
Reload
Remains
Rembrandts
Remington, Herb
Remingtons

Remler, Emily
Remo Four
Rena, Kid
Renaissance
Renaldo And
 Clara
Renaud, Henri
Renbourn, John
Rendell, Don
Rene Brothers
Renees
Renegade
 Soundwave
Renk Records
Reno And Smiley
Reno, Don
Reno, Jack
Rent
Rentals
Renton, Charlie
REO Speedwagon
Reparata And
 The Delrons
Rephlex Records
Replacements
Reprazent
Represent
 Records
Reprise Records
Republic Records
Republica
Residents
Restless Heart
Return To
 Forever
Return To The
 Forbidden
 Planet
Reunion
Rev, Martin
Rev. Hammer
Reveille With
 Beverly
Revel, Harry
Revenants
Revenge
Revere, Paul, And
 The Raiders
Revillos
Revival
 Movement
Revolting Cocks
Revolution
Revolutionaries
Revolutionary
 Ensemble
Revolver
Revolving Paint
 Dream
Rey, Alvino
Reyna, Cornelio
Reynolds, Allen
Reynolds, Blind
 Joe
Reynolds, Debbie
Reynolds, Donn
Reynolds, Jody
Reynolds, Malvina

Reynolds,
 Tommy
Rezillos
Rhapsody In Blue
Rhino Records
Rhinoceros
Rhoads, Randy
Rhoda With The
 Special AKA
Rhoden, Donna
Rhoden, Pat
Rhodes, Emitt
Rhodes, Eugene
Rhodes, Sonny
Rhodes, Todd
 Washington
Rhodes, Walter
Rhythm albums
Rhythm And
 Blues Inc
Rhythm Boys
Rhythm Heritage
Rhythm Invention
Rhythm King
Rhythm Saints
Rhythmatic
Rialto
Ribitones
Rice, Bobby G.
Rice, Tim
Rich Kids
Rich, Buddy
Rich, Charlie
Rich, Freddy
Rich, Paul
Richard, Belton
Richard, Cliff
Richards, Cynthia
Richards, Johnny
Richards, Keith
Richards, Red
Richardson, Clive
Richardson,
 Jerome
Richey, Kim
Richie, Lionel
Richman, Boomie
Richman, Harry
Richman,
 Jonathan
Richmond,
 Dannie
Richmond, June
Rickenbacker
Ricky And The
 Halmarks
Ricochet
Ricotti, Frank
Riddle, Almeda
Riddle, Jimmy
Riddle, Leslie
Riddle, Nelson
Ride
Ride The Wild
 Surf
Riders In The Sky
Ridgley, Tommy
Ridgway, Stan

Riel, Axel
Riff Raff
Rifkin, Joshua
Riggins, J., Jnr.
Riggs
Right Said Fred
Righteous Brothers
Rikki And The
  Red Streaks
Riley, Howard
Riley, Jeannie C.
Riley, Jimmy
Riley, Marc
Riley, Mike
Riley, Teddy
Riley, Terry
Riley, Winston
Rimes, LeAnn
Rimington,
  Sammy
Rinehart, Andy
Rinehart, Cowboy
  Slim
Ringo, Johnny
Rink, The
Rinzler, Ralph
Rio Rita
Rios, Miguel
Riot
Riot On Sunset
  Strip
Riot Squad
Rip Chords
Rip Rig And Panic
Riperton, Minnie
Rippingtons
Riptides
Rising High
  Collective
Rising High
  Records
Rising Sons
Ritchie, Jean
Ritenour, Lee
Ritter, Tex
River City People
River Maya
Rivera, Chita
Rivera, Ismael
Rivera, Mon
Rivers, Johnny
Rivers, Mavis
Rivers, Sam
Riverside Records
Rivingtons
RME
Roach, Max
Roach, Steve
Roachford
Road
Road To
  Singapore
Roadhouse
Roadie
Roadnight,
  Margret
Roadrunners

Roadside Picnic
Roane County
  Revellers
Roar Of The
  Greasepaint-
  The Smell Of
  The Crowd,
  The
Roaring Jelly
Rob Base And DJ
  E-Z Rock
Robbins, Hargus
  'Pig'
Robbins, Jerome
Robbins, Marty
Robert And
  Elizabeth
Robert And
  Johnny
Robert, Yves
Roberta (film
  musical)
Roberta (stage
  musical)
Roberts, Andy
Roberts, Bruce
Roberts, Hank
Roberts, James
Roberts, Joe
Roberts, Juliet
Roberts, Kane
Roberts, Kenny
Roberts, Luckey
Roberts, Malcolm
Roberts, Marcus
Roberts, Paddy
Roberts, Rick
Robertson, B.A.
Robertson, Dick
Robertson, Eck
Robertson,
  Jeannie
Robertson, Justin
Robertson,
  Robbie
Robertson,
  Sherman
Robertson, Zue
Robeson, Paul
Robey, Don
Robichaux, John
Robichaux,
  Joseph
Robillard, Duke
Robin, Leo
Robins
Robinson,
  'Lonesome'
  Jimmy Lee
Robinson, Alvin
Robinson, Banjo
  Ikey
Robinson, Bill
  'Bojangles'
Robinson, Bobby
Robinson, Eli
Robinson, Fenton

Robinson,
  Freddie
Robinson, Janice
Robinson, Jessie
  Mae
Robinson, Jim
Robinson, John
Robinson, L.C.
  'Good Rockin''
Robinson, Perry
Robinson, Prince
Robinson, Roscoe
Robinson,
  Smokey
Robinson, Spike
Robinson, Sugar
  Chile
Robinson, Tom
Robison, Carson
  Jay
Robs' Records
Robson And
  Jerome
Roby, Charlie
ROC
Roché, Betty
Roche, Suzzy
Rochell And The
  Candles
Roches
Rochester,
  Anthony
Rock 'n' Roll High
  School
Rock 'n' Roll
  Revue
Rock And Roll
  Hall Of Fame
  And Museum
Rock Around The
  Clock
Rock City Angels
Rock Goddess
Rock
  Marketplace,
  The
Rock Rock Rock
Rock Workshop
Rock, Dickie
Rock, Pete
Rock, Salt And
  Nails
Rock-A-Bye Baby
Rock-A-Teens
Rockabilly
Rockapella
Rockers
Rockers (film)
Rocket
Rocket From The
  Crypt
Rocket From The
  Tombs
Rocketones
Rockets
Rockfield Studio
Rockhead

Rockin' Berries
Rockin' Dopsie
Rockin' Sidney
Rockin' Vickers
Rockingbirds
Rockpile
Rocksteady
Rocksteady Crew
Rockwell
Rocky Horror
  Picture Show,
  The
Rocky Horror
  Show, The
Roden, Jess
Rodford, Jim
Rodgers, Andy
Rodgers, Clodagh
Rodgers, Jesse
Rodgers, Jimmie
  (country)
Rodgers, Jimmie
  (pop)
Rodgers, Mary
Rodgers, Paul
Rodgers, Richard
Rodgers, Sonny
Rodin, Gil
Rodito, Claudio
Rodman, Judy
Rodney O And
  Joe Cooley
Rodney, Red
Rodowiz, Maryla
Rodríguez,
  Alfredo
Rodríguez,
  Arsenio
Rodríguez, Bobby
Rodríguez,
  Johnny
Rodriguez, Lalo
Rodríguez, Pete
  'El Conde'
Rodriguez, Rico
Rodríguez, Tito
Rods
Roe, Tommy
Roena, Roberto
Roger, Roger
Rogers, Buddy
Rogers, Ce Ce
Rogers, David
Rogers, Ginger
Rogers, Jimmy
Rogers, Julie
Rogers, Kenny
Rogers, Paul
Rogers, Roy
  (blues)
Rogers, Roy
  (Country)
Rogers, S.E.
Rogers, Shorty
Rogers, Smokey
Rogers, Stan
Rogie, S.E.

Rogue Male
Roker, Mickey
Roland, Gene
Roland, Walter
Rollerskate
  Skinny
Rolling Stone
Rolling Stones
Rolling Stones
  Rock And Roll
  Circus, The
Rollini, Adrian
Rollini, Arthur
Rollins, Henry
Rollins, Sonny
Rollo
Roman Scandals
Roman, Murray
Romance On The
  High Seas
Romano, Aldo
Romano, Joe
Romantics
Romao, Dom Um
Romberg,
  Sigmund
Rome, Harold
Romeo's
  Daughter
Romeo, Max
Ron
Ron C
Ronald And Ruby
Ronco Records
Rondo, Gene
Ronettes
Roney, Wallace
Ronin Records
Ronnie And The
  Hi-Lites
Ronny And The
  Daytonas
Ronson, Mick
Ronstadt, Linda
Rooftop Singers
Roogalator
Room
Roomful Of Blues
Rooney, Mickey
Roots (Rap)
Roots Radics
Roots, Rock And
  Reggae
Rope Ladder To
  The Moon
Roppolo, Leon
Ros, Edmundo
Rosalie
Rosario, Willie
Rose Garden
Rose Marie
Rose Of
  Avalanche
Rose Of
  Washington
  Square
Rose Royce

Rose Tattoo
Rose, Biff
Rose, Billy
Rose, David
Rose, Doudou
  N'Diaye
Rose, Fred
Rose, Judy
Rose, Michael
Rose, Samantha
Rose, Tim
Rose, Tony
Rose, Vincent
Rose, Wesley
Rosengarden,
  Bobby
Rosengren, Bernt
Rosenman,
  Leonard
Rosewoman,
  Michele
Rosie And The
  Originals
Rosolino, Frank
Ross, Annie
Ross, Diana
Ross, Doctor
Ross, Jackie
Ross, Jerry
Ross, Ricky
Ross, Ronnie
Ross, Spencer
Rosselson, Leon
Rossi, Francis
Rossington
  Collins
Rosso, Nini
Rostaing, Hubert
Rota, Nino
Rotary
  Connection
Rotenberg, June
Roth, Dave Lee
Roth, Lillian
Rothberg, Patti
Rothchild, Paul A.
Rothschilds, The
Rotondo, Nunzio
Rough Cutt
Rough Diamond
Rough House
Rough Silk
Rough Trade
  Records
Roulettes
Round Midnight
Rounder Records
Rouse, Charlie
Roussos, Demis
Roustabout
Routers
ROVA
  Saxophone
  Quartet
Rover Boys
Rowan Brothers
Rowan, Peter

Rowe, Dick
Rowe, Normie
Rowlands, Dennis
Rowles, Jimmy
Rox
Roxanne Shanté
Roxette
Roxy
Roxy Music
Roy, Harry
Royal Crown
  Revue
Royal Court Of
  China
Royal Guardsmen
Royal Rasses
Royal Scots
  Dragoon
  Guards
Royal Showband
Royal Teens
Royal Trux
Royal Wedding
Royal, Billy Joe
Royal, Ernie
Royal, Marshal
Royalettes
Royals
Royaltones
Royce, Earl, And
  The Olympics
Roz
Roza, Lita
Rozalla
Rozsa, Miklos
RPLA
RPM
Rub Ultra
Rubella Ballet
Ruben, Spooky
Rubettes
Rubin, Rick
Rubin, Vanessa
Rubinoos
Ruby
Ruby And The
  Romantics
Ruby Blue
Ruby, Harry
Rucker, Ellyn
Rudd, Mike
Rudd, Roswell
Ruegg, Matthias
Ruffhouse
Ruffin, Bruce
Ruffin, David
Ruffin, Jimmy
Rufus
Rugburns
Ruggiero,
  Antonella
Rugolo, Pete
Ruiz, Hilton
Rumble
Rumillajta
Rumour
Rumpf, Inga

Rumsey, Howard
Run C&W
Run DMC
Runaways
Rundgren, Todd
Running Wild
Runrig
RuPaul
Rupe, Art
Rusby, Kate, And
  Kathryn
  Roberts
Rush
Rush, Bobby
Rush, Jennifer
Rush, Merrilee,
  And The
  Turnabouts
Rush, Otis
Rush, Tom
Rushen, Patrice
Rushing, Jimmy
Rushton, Joe
Russell, Andy
Russell, Bob
Russell, Curley
Russell, Devon
Russell, George
Russell, Hal
Russell, Jack
Russell, Janet
Russell, Johnny
Russell, Leon
Russell, Luis
Russell, Pee Wee
Russell, Tom
Russin, Babe
Russo, Bill
Russo, Danny
Rust Never
  Sleeps
Ruth Ruth
Rutherford, Mike
Rutherford, Paul
Rutherford, Rudy
Ruthless Rap
  Assassins
Ruthless Records
Rutles
Ruts
Ry-co Jazz
Ryan, Marion
Ryan, Paul And
  Barry
Ryan, Tommy
Ryce, Daryle
Rydell, Bobby
Ryder, Mitch
Ryder, Mitch,
  And The
  Detroit Wheels
Rykiel, Jean-
  Phillipe
Rykodisc Records
Rypdal, Terje
RZA
S'Express

S*M*A*S*H
S-1000
S-K-O
S.A.D.O.
S.O.B. Band
S.O.S.
S.O.S. Band
Sabater, Jimmy
Sabbat
Sablon, Jean
Sabres Of Paradise
Sabrettes
Sabri Brothers
Sabrina
Sabu
Sacko, Fanta
Sacred Reich
Sad Cafe
Sad Lovers And
  Giants
Sadat X
Sade
Sadler, Barry,
  Staff Sgt.
Sadness
Safaris
Saffire - The
  Uppity Blues
  Women
Safka
Safranski, Eddie
Saga
Sager, Carole
  Bayer
Sagittarius
Sagittarius Band
Sagoo, Billy
Sahko Recordings
Sahm, Doug
Sailcat
Sailing Along
Sailor
Sain (Recordiau)
  Cyf
Sain, Oliver
Saint Etienne
Sainte-Marie,
  Buffy
Saints
Sakamoto, Kyu
Sakamoto,
  Ryuichi
Salad
Salad Days
Salas, Stevie,
  Colorcode
Salem, Kevin
Salim, Abdel
  Gadir
Sally
Sally In Our Alley
Sallyangie
Salt-N-Pepa
Salt Tank
Salter, Sam
Salty Dog
Saluzzi, Dino

Salvador, Sal
Salvation
Sam And Bill
Sam And Dave
Sam Apple Pie
Sam Gopal
Sam Gopal's
  Dream
Sam The Sham
  And The
  Pharaohs
Sam, Ambrose
Samhain
Sammes, Mike
Sammy
Sample, Joe
Samples
Samples, Junior
Sampling
Sampson, Edgar
Samson
Samuels, David
Samwell-Smith,
  Paul
San Francisco
Sanborn, David
Sanchez
Sanchez, David
Sanchez, Roger
Sanctuary
Sandals
Sandburg, Carl
Sanders, Ed
Sanders, Joe
Sanders, Mark
Sanders, Pharoah
Sanders, Ric
Sandii And The
  Sunsetz
Sandke, Randy
Sandon, Johnny
Sandpebbles
Sandpipers
Sands
Sands, Tommy
Sane, Dan
Sangaré, Oumou
Sangster, John
Santa Esmeralda
Santa Rosa,
  Gilberto
Santamaría,
  Mongo
Santana
Santana, Steve
Santers
Santiago,
  Adalberto
Santiago, Al
Santiago, Eddie
Santo And Johnny
Sapo
Sapphires
Saquito, Nico
Saracen
Sarah Records
Saraya

Sargeant, Bob
Sargent, Kenny
Sarkoma
Sarmanto, Heikki
Sarony, Leslie
Sarpilä, Antti
Sarstedt, Peter
Sasha
Sassafras
Sassafras (The
Promoter)
Satan
Satan And Adam
Satchmo The
Great
Satherley, Art
Satintones
Sato, Masahiko
Satriani, Joe
Saturday Night
Fever
Satyricon
Saunders, Jane
Saunders, Merl
Saunders, Red
Sauter, Eddie
Sauter-Finegan
Orchestra
Savage
Savage Garden
Savage Grace
Savage
Resurrection
Savage Seven,
The
Savalas, Telly
Savatage
Savitt, Jan
Savopoulos,
Dionysis
Savoy Brown
Savoy Sultans
Saw Doctors
Sawhney, Nitin
Sawyer Brown
Saxon
Saxon, Sky
Saxophone
Sayer, Leo
Sayles, Charlie
Sayles,
Emmanuel
Sayles, Johnny
Sbarbaro, Tony
SBK Records
Scafell Pike
Scaffold
Scaggs, Boz
Scala, Primo
Scales, Harvey,
And The Seven
Sounds
Scandal (featur-
ing Patty
Smyth)
Scanner
Scanner (dance)

Scarbury, Joey
Scarce
Scare Dem Crew
Scarface
Scarfo
Scarlet
Scarlet Fantastic
Scarlet Party
Scars
Scat Opera
Scatman John
Scatterbrain
Scenic
Scepter Records
Schenker,
Michael
Schertzer, Hymie
Schertzinger,
Victor
Schickele, Peter
Schifrin, Lalo
Schmidt, Harvey
Schmidt, Irmin
Schneider, John
Schneider, Mary
Schoebel, Elmer
Schofield, Phillip
Schon And
Hammer
Schonberg,
Claude-Michel
Schoof, Manfred
School Of
Violence
Schoolboys
Schoolly D
Schroeder, Gene
Schroeder, John
Schubert
Schuller, Gunther
Schulze, Klaus
Schutt, Arthur
Schutze, Paul
Schuur, Diane
Schwartz, Arthur
Schwartz,
Stephen
Schwarz, Brinsley
Schweizer, Irène
Science, Chico
Scientist
Scientists Of
Sound
Sclavis, Louis
Scobey, Bob
Scofield, John
Scorcher, Errol
Scorn
Scorpio Records
Scorpions
Scorpions (UK)
Scott, Bobby
Scott, Buddy
Scott, Casey
Scott, Cecil
Scott, Freddie
Scott, Hazel

Scott, Isaac
Scott, Jack
Scott, John
Scott, Linda
Scott, Little
Jimmy
Scott, Marylin
Scott, Mike
Scott, Peggy, And
Jo Jo Benson
Scott, Ramblin'
Tommy
Scott, Raymond
Scott, Robin
Scott, Roger
Scott, Ronnie
Scott, Shirley
Scott, Tom
Scott, Tommy
Scott, Tony
Scott-Adams,
Peggy
Scott-Heron, Gil
Scottsville
Squirrel
Barkers
Scotty
Scrap Iron
Scientists
Scratch Acid
Scrawl
Scream
Screaming Blue
Messiahs
Screaming Jets
Screaming Trees
Screwdriver
Scritti Politti
Scrooge
Scruggs, Earl
Scud Mountian
Boys
Sea Hags
Sea Urchins
Sea, Johnny
Seahorses
Seal
Seals And Crofts
Seals, Dan
Seals, Son
Seals, Troy
Seamen, Phil
Searchers
Sears, Al
Sears, Zenas
'Daddy'
Seaton, B.B.
Seaton, Lynn
Seatrain
Sebadoh
Sebastian, John
Sebestyén, Márta
Secada, Jon
Seck, Mansour
Seck, Thione
Secombe, Harry
Second Chorus

2nd Heat
2nd II None
Second Vision
Secret Affair
Secret Cinema
Secret Garden
Secret Garden,
The
Secret
Knowledge
Secret Life
Secrets
Section 25
Secunda, Tony
Sedaka, Neil
Sedric, Gene
Seducer
See For Miles
Seeds
Seefeel
Seeger, Mike
Seeger, Peggy
Seeger, Pete
Seekers
Seely, Jeannie
Segal, Vivienne
Seger, Bob
Segure, Roger
Seifert, Zbigniew
Seldom Scene
Selecter
Selena
Sellers, Brother
John
Sellers, Jason
Selvin, Ben
Semenya,
Caiphus
Semien, 'Ivory'
Lee
Semple, Archie
Senator Bobby
Send No Flowers
Sensational Alex
Harvey Band
Sensations
Senseless Things
Senser
Senter, Boyd
Sentinals
Sentinel Beast
Sepultura
Sequel Records
Serendipity
Singers
Sergeant
Serious Drinking
Serpent Power
Servants
Sessions, Ronnie
Sevåg, Øystein
7 Year Bitch
Seven Brides For
Seven Brothers
Seven Mary Three
707
702

7 Seconds
7669
1776
70, Girls, 70
Severinson, Doc
Seville, David
Seward, Alec
Sex Gang
Children
Sex Pistols
Sex, Love And
Money
Sexsmith, Ron
Sexton, Ann
Sexton, Charlie
Seyton, Denny,
And The
Sabres
Sgt. Pepper's
Lonely Hearts
Club Band
Sha Na Na
Shabazz, Lakim
Shack
Shad, Bob
Shade, Will
Shades
Shades Of Blue
Shades Of Joy
Shadow King
Shadowfax
Shadows
Shadows Of
Knight
Shadz Of Lingo
Shag
Shaggs
Shaggy
Shah
Shai
Shakatak
Shake, Rattle And
Roll
Shakespears
Sister
Shakey Jake
Shakey Vick
Shakin' Stevens
Shakin' Street
Shako Lee
Shakta
Shakti
Shakur, Tupac
Shalamar
Shall We Dance
Sham 69
Shamblin, Eldon
Shamen
Shampoo
Shanghai
Shangri-Las
Shanice
Shank, Bud
Shankar,
Lakshminaraya
na
Shankar, Ravi

Shannon
Shannon, Del
Shannon, Mem
Shannon, Preston
Shannon, Sharon
Shanty Crew
Shapiro, Artie
Shapiro, Helen
Shapiro, Tom
Shara, Yuni
Sharam, Max
Shark Island
Sharkboy
Sharkey, Feargal
Sharman, Dave
Sharon, Ralph
Sharp Nine
Sharp, Cecil
Sharp, Dee
Sharp, Dee Dee
Sharp, Jonah
Sharp, Kevin
Sharpees
Sharrock, Sonny
Shaver, Billy Joe
Shavers, Charlie
Shaw Blades
Shaw, Allen
Shaw, Artie
Shaw, Arvell
Shaw, Charles 'Bobo'
Shaw, Eddie
Shaw, Eddie 'Vaan'
Shaw, Ian
Shaw, Marlina
Shaw, Pat, And Julie Matthews
Shaw, Robert
Shaw, Sandie
Shaw, Thomas
Shaw, Tommy
Shaw, Victoria
Shaw, Woody
Shay, Dorothy
She
She Done Him Wrong
She Loves Me
She Rockers
She Trinity
Shear, Jules
Shearing, George
Shearston, Gary
Shed Seven
Sheep On Drugs
Sheik, Duncan
Sheila
Sheldon, Jack
Shellac
Shelley, Pete
Shelleyan Orphan
Shells
Shelter Records
Shelton Brothers
Shelton, Anne

Shelton, Ricky Van
Shelton, Roscoe
Shenandoah
Shenandoah (stage musical)
Shenandoah Cut-Ups
Shep And The Limelites
Shepard, Jean
Shepherd Sisters
Shepherd, Dave
Shepherd, Kenny Wayne
Shepp, Archie
Sheppard, Andy
Sheppard, T.G.
Sheppards
Sherbet
Sheridan, Mike, And The Nightriders
Sheridan, Tony
Sheridan-Price
Sherlock Holmes - The Musical
Sherman, Al
Sherman, Allan
Sherman, Bim
Sherman, Daryl
Sherman, Richard M., And Robert B.
Sherock, Shorty
Sherriff
Sherrill, Billy
Sherrys
Shertzer, Hymie
Shervington, Pluto
Sherwood, Adrian
Sherwood, Bobby
Shew, Bobby
Shields
Shields, Lonnie
Shihab, Sahib
Shihad
Shilkret, Jack
Shilkret, Nat
Shillelagh Sisters
Shimmy-Disc
Shindell, Richard
Shindig
Shindigs
Shinehead
Shines, Johnny
Shirati Jazz
Shire
Shire, David
Shirelles
Shirley And Lee
Shirley, Roy
Shirts
Shiva
Shiva's Headband

Shockabilly
Shocked, Michelle
Shocking Blue
Shocking Miss Pilgrim, The
Shoes
Shok Paris
Sholes, Steve
Shondell, Troy
Shonen Knife
Shooglenifty
Shoot
Shooters
Shooting Star
Shop Assistants
Shore, Dinah
Short, Bobby
Short, J.D.
Shorter, Wayne
Shortino, Paul
Shotgun Express
Shotgun Messiah
Shots
Shout
Show Boat
Show Is On, The
Showaddywaddy
Showbiz And AG
Showers, 'Little' Hudson
Showmen
Showstoppers
Shri
Shriekback
Shrieve, Michael
Shuffle Along
Shuman, Mort
Shusha
Shut Up And Dance
Shy
Shyheim
Sibèba
Siberry, Jane
Sick Of It All
Sidi Bou Said
Sidmouth Folk Festival
Sidran, Ben
Siebel, Paul
Siegal-Schwall Blues Band
Sieges Even
Sierra Maestra
Siffre, Labi
Sigler, Bunny
Signal
Signatures
Signorelli, Frank
Sigue Sigue Sputnik
Silber, Irwin
Sileás
Silent Majority
Silent Rage
Silent Records
Silhouettes

Silk
Silk Stockings
Silk, Garnett
Silkie
Silkscreen
Silkworm
Sill, Judee
Silly Sisters
Silly Wizard
Silos
Silva, Alan
Silver Convention
Silver Dream Racer
Silver Jews
Silver Metre
Silver Mountain
Silver, Horace
Silver, Mike
Silverchair
Silverfish
Silverhead
Silverstein, Shel
Silvertones
Silvester, Victor
Silvestri, Alan
Simba Wanyika
Simeon, Omer
Simeone, Harry, Chorale
Simmons, 'Little' Mack
Simmons, Gene
Simmons, Jeff
Simmons, John
Simmons, Norman
Simmons, Patrick
Simmons, Russell
Simmons, Sonny
Simms, Ginny
Simon And Garfunkel
Simon Chase
Simon, Carly
Simon, Joe
Simon, John
Simon, Paul
Simon, Tito
Simone, Nina
Simonelli, Victor
Simper, Nick
Simple Aggression
Simplé E
Simple Minds
Simple Simon
Simpleton
Simplice, Sery
Simply Red
Simpson, Martin
Simpson, Red
Simpson, Valerie
Sims, Clarence 'Guitar'
Sims, Frankie Lee
Sims, Zoot

Sinatra, Frank
Sinatra, Frank, Jnr.
Sinatra, Nancy
Sindecut
Sing As We Go
Sing You Sinners
Singer, Harold 'Hal'
Singers Unlimited
Singh, Talvin
Singin' In The Rain
Singing Fool, The
Singing Nun
Singing Postman
Singing Stockmen
Singletary, Daryle
Singleton, Margie Creath
Singleton, Shelby
Singleton, Zutty
Sinitta
Sinner
Sinners
Siouxsie And The Banshees
Sir Douglas Quintet
Sir Lord Comic
Sir Mix-A-Lot
Sire Records
Siren
Sirone
Sissle, Noble
Sista Rebeka
Sister Allison
Sister Carol
Sister Hazel
Sister Love
Sister Nancy
Sister Sledge
Sister Souljah
Sisters Of Mercy
Sisters Unlimited
Six Feet Under
6.5 Special
Six Teens
16 Horsepower
1600 Pennsylvania Avenue
6ths
60 Foot Dolls
Sixty Six
Size, Roni
Sizemore, Asher, And Little Jimmy
Sizzla
Ska
Skagarack
Skaggs, Ricky
Skatalites
SKB
Skeat, Len
Skeletal Family

Skellern, Peter
Ski Party
Skibberean
Skid Row (Eire)
Skid Row (USA)
Skidmore, Alan
Skidmore, Jimmy
Skids
Skillet Lickers
Skin
Skin Alley
Skin The Peeler
Skinner, Jimmie
Skinny Boys
Skinny Puppy
Skint Records
Skip And Flip
Skip Bifferty
SKO
Skrew
Skull
Skunk Anansie
Sky
Sky Cries Mary
Sky, Amy
Sky, Patrick
Skyclad
Skyhooks
Skylarks
Skyliners
SL
Slack, Freddie
Slade
Slade, Julian
Slam
Slant 6
Slapp Happy
Slash's Snakepit
Slater, Luke
Slaughter
Slaughter And
   The Dogs
Slave Raider
Slayer
Sleater-Kinney
Sledd, Patsy
Sledge, Percy
Sledgehammer
Sleep
Sleeper
Sleeping Bag
   Records
Sleeping Beauty
Slice Of Saturday
   Night, A
Slick
Slick Rick
Slick, Earl, Band
Slick, Grace
Slickers
Slik
Slim Chance
Slim Harpo
Slimani, Abdel Ali
Slingbacks
Slingsby, Xero
Slinky Wizard

Slint
Slip 'N' Slide
   Records
Slipper And The
   Rose, The
Slits
Sloan
Sloan, P.F.
Sloane, Carol
Slowdive
Sly And Robbie
Sly And The
   Family Stone
Small Faces
Small, Drink
Smaller
Smalls, Cliff
Smalltown
   Parade
Smart, Leroy
Smash Mouth
Smash Records
Smashing Orange
Smashing
   Pumpkins
Smashing Time
Smeck, Roy
Smif N Wessun
Smiley Culture
Smiley, Red
Smith
Smith And
   Mighty
Smith Brothers
Smith, 'Whistling'
   Jack
Smith, Arthur
   'Fiddlin''
Smith, Arthur
   'Guitar Boogie'
Smith, Bessie
Smith, Betty
Smith, Bill
Smith, Bill 'Major'
Smith, Brian
Smith, Broderick
Smith, Buster
Smith, Byther
Smith, Cal
Smith, Carl
Smith, Carl
   'Tatti'
Smith, Carlene
Smith, Carrie
Smith, Carson
Smith, Clara
Smith, Clarence
   'Pine Top'
Smith, Connie
Smith, Darden
Smith, Derek
Smith, Ernie
Smith, George
Smith, Gulliver
Smith, Huey
   'Piano'
Smith, J.B.

Smith, J.T. 'Funny
   Papa'
Smith, Jabbo
Smith, Jack
Smith, Jimmy
Smith, Joe
Smith, Johnny
Smith, Kate
Smith, Keely
Smith, Keith
Smith, Larry
Smith, Leo
Smith, Lonnie
   Liston
Smith, Mamie
Smith, Margo
Smith, Moses
   'Whispering'
Smith, O.C.
Smith, Patti
Smith, Rex
Smith, Robert
   Curtis
Smith, Russell
Smith, Sammi
Smith, Slim
Smith, Stuff
Smith, Tab
Smith, Tommy
Smith, Trixie
Smith, Wayne
Smith, Will
Smith, Willie
Smith, Willie
   'The Lion'
Smith, Willie Mae
   Ford
Smither, Chris
Smithereens
Smiths
Smog
Smoke
Smokey Babe
Smokey Joe's
   Cafe: The
   Songs Of
   Leiber And
   Stoller
Smokie
Smooth, Joe
Smoothe The
   Hustler
Smothers, Little
   Smokey
Smothers, Otis
   'Big Smokey'
Smythe, Pat
Snafu
Snake Thing
Snakefinger
Snakepit Rebels
Snakes Of Shake
Snap!
Snapper
Sneaker Pimps
Sneetches
SNFU

Sniff 'N' The
   Tears
Sniper
Snobs
Snoman
Snoop Doggy
   Dogg
Snow
Snow White And
   The Seven
   Dwarfs
Snow, Hank
Snow, Phoebe
Snow, Valaida
Snowblind
Snowden, Elmer
Snowpony
Snuff
Sobule, Jill
Soca Stéreo
Social Distortion
Soda, Frank
Sodom
Soft Boys
Soft Cell
Soft Machine
Softley, Mick
Soho
Sojourn
Solal, Martial
Soldiers Of The
   King
Solitaires
Solitude
Solitude
   Aeturnus
Soloff, Lew
Solomon, King
Solomon, Lenny
Solomon, Phil
Solution AD
Soma Records
Somaton
Some Bizzare
   Records
Some Like It Hot
Some People
Someone Like
   You
Somerville,
   Jimmy
Sommers, Joanie
Son House
Son Of Bazerk
Son Of Noise
Son Volt
Sondheim,
   Stephen
Sonet Records
Song And Dance
Song Is Born, A
Song Of Norway
Song Remains
   The Same, The
Songhai
Sonia
Sonic Boom

Sonic Unyon
   Records
Sonic Youth
Sonics
Sonnier, Jo-El
Sonny And Cher
Sonora
   Matancera, La
Sons Of Adam
Sons Of Blues
Sons Of
   Champlin
Sons Of Jah
Sons Of The
   Pioneers
Sons Of The San
   Joaquin
Sony Broadway
Sophisticated
   Ladies
Soprano Summit
Sopwith Camel
Sorrels, Rosalie
Sorrows
Sortilege
Soul Agents
Soul Asylum
Soul Brothers
Soul Children
Soul Coughing
Soul For Real
Soul Sonic Force
Soul Stirrers
Soul Survivors
Soul Syndicate
Soul II Soul
Soul, David
Soul, Jimmy
Souled American
Souls Of Mischief
Soulsonics
Sound
Sound Barrier
Sound Factory
Sound Of Jazz,
   The
Sound Of Miles
   Davis, The
Sound Of Music,
   The
Sound System
Soundgarden
Sounds Nice
Sounds Of
   Blackness
Sounds
   Orchestral
Soup Dragons
Source
Sousa, John Philip
South Central
   Cartel
South Pacific
South Shore
   Commission
South Side
   Movement

South, Eddie
South, Joe
Souther Hillman
   Furary Band
Souther, J.D.
Southern Pacific
Southern, Jeri
Southernaires
Southlanders
Southside Johnny
   And The
   Asbury Jukes
Southwind
Sovine, Red
Space
Space Streakings
Spacehog
Spacek, Sissy
Spacemen 3
Spagna, Ivana
Spand, Charlie
Spandau Ballet
Spaniels
Spanier, Muggsy
Spanky And Our
   Gang
Spann, Lucille
Spann, Otis
Spanner Banner
Spanos, Danny
Spargo, Tony
Sparklehorse
Sparks
Sparks Brothers
Sparks, Terry
Sparrow
Sparrows
   Quartette
Spartan Warrior
Spaulding, James
Spear
Spear Of Destiny
Spear, Roger
   Ruskin
Spears, Billie Jo
Specht, Paul
Special Ed
Special EFX
Specials
Specialty Records
Spector, Phil
Spector, Ronnie
Spectres
Spectrum
Spedding, Chris
Speech
Speedball Baby
Speedway
Speedway
   Boulevard
Speedy J
Spell
Spellbinders
Spellbound
Spellman, Benny
Spence,
   Barrington

Spence, Skip
Spencer's, John,
   Blues Explosion
Spencer, J.
Spencer, John B.
Spencer, Tim
Spice Girls
Spice I
Spice Trade
Spice, Mikey
Spider (UK)
Spider (USA)
Spiders
Spielman, Fred
Spikes Brothers
Spillane, Davy
Spin
Spin Doctors
Spinal Tap
Spinanes
SpinART Records
Spinners (UK)
Spinners (USA)
Spinout
Spiral Starecase
Spiral Tribe
Spirea X
Spires, Arthur
   'Big Boy'
Spirit
Spirit Level
Spirit Of The
   West
Spirits
Spirits Of
   Rhythm
Spitfire
Spivak, Charlie
Spivey, Addie
   'Sweet Peas'
Spivey, Victoria
SPK
Splinter
Split Beaver
Split Enz
Splodgenessabou
   nds
Spoelstra, Mark
Sponge
Spontaneous
   Combustion
Spontaneous
   Music
   Ensemble
Spooky
Spooky Tooth
Spoonie Gee
Sports
Spotnicks
Sprague, Carl T.
Spread Eagle
Spriguns
Spring Parade
Spring, Bryan
Springfield, Dusty
Springfield, Rick
Springfields

Springsteen,
   Bruce
Spud
Spy
Spyro Gyra
Spys
Squadron
Squadronaires
Squarepusher
Squeeze
Squier, Billy
Squire, Chris
Squires, Dorothy
Squires,
   Rosemary
Squirrel Bait
Squirrel Nut
   Zippers
SRC
Srinivas, U.
St Louis Blues
St. Clair, Isla
St. John, Barry
St. John, Bridget
St. John, Jeff
St. Louis Union
St. Louis Woman
St. Paradise
St. Peters,
   Crispian
Stabbins, Larry
Stabile, Dick
Stackhouse,
   Houston
Stackridge
Stackwaddy
Stacy, Jess
Stafford, Jim
Stafford, Jo
Stafford, Terry
Stage Dolls
Stage Door
   Canteen
Stained Glass
Staines, Bill
Stakka Bo
Stalk Forrest
   Group
Stalling, Carl
Stallings, Mary
Stallone, Frank
Stamey, Chris
Stamm, Marvin
Stampede
Stampfel, Peter
Stamping Ground
Stampley, Joe
Stand Up And
   Sing
Standells
Stanford Prison
   Experiment
Stanko, Tomasz
Stanley Brothers
Stanley, James
   Lee
Stansfield, Lisa

Stanshall, Vivian
Staple Singers
Staples, Mavis
Staples, Pops
Stapleton, Cyril
Stapp, Jack
Star Is Born, A
Star Spangled
   Rhythm
Starcastle
Starcher, Buddy
Starchild
Stardust
Stardust, Alvin
Starfighters
Stargard
Stargazers
Starjets
Stark, Bobby
Starland Vocal
   Band
Starlets
Starlight Express
Starlites
Starr, Edwin
Starr, Freddie
Starr, Jack
Starr, Kay
Starr, Kenny
Starr, Maurice
Starr, Ray
Starr, Ringo
Starry Eyed And
   Laughing
Stars On 45
Starship
Starsound
Start
Starvation
Starz
State Fair
State Fair (stage
   musical)
Statetrooper
Statler Brothers
Staton, Candi
Staton, Dakota
Status Quo
Stax Records
Stay Away Joe
Steady B
Steagall, Red
Stealers Wheel
Stealin' Horses
Steam
Steam Packet
Steamhammer
Stearns, June
Steel Forest
Steel Pier
Steel Pole
   Bathtub
Steel Pulse
Steele, Blue
Steele, Chrissy
Steele, Tommy
Steeler

Steeler
   (Germany)
Steeler (USA)
Steeleyard Blues
Steeleye Span
Steelwind
Steely And Clevie
Steely Dan
Steelyard Blues
Steeplechase
Stegall, Keith
Stegmeyer, Bill
Steig, Jeremy
Stein, Lou
Steiner, Max
Steinman, Jim
Stelin, Tena
Stephan, Tom
Stephens, Leigh
Stephens, Richie
Stephens, Tanya
Stephenson,
   Martin, And
   The Daintees
Steppenwolf
Stepper, Reggie
Steppin' Out
Steps Ahead
Stept, Sam
Stereo MC's
Stereolab
Stereophonics
Stereos
Sterling Cooke
   Force
Sterling, Keith
Stern's Records
Stern, Joseph W.
Stern, Mike
Stetsasonic
Stevens', Steve,
   Atomic
   Playboys
Stevens, Cat
Stevens, Connie
Stevens, Dodie
Stevens, Garry
Stevens, Guy
Stevens, John
Stevens, Jon
Stevens, Ray
Stevens, Shakin'
Stevens, Stu
Stevenson, B.W.
Stevenson,
   Mickey
Stevo
Steward, Herbie
Stewart, Al
Stewart, Andy
Stewart, Andy M.
Stewart, Bill
Stewart, Billy
Stewart, Bob
Stewart, Dave,
   And Barbara
   Gaskin

Stewart, David A.
Stewart, Delano
Stewart, Gary
Stewart, John
Stewart, Louis
Stewart, Mark,
    And The Maffia
Stewart, Redd
Stewart, Rex
Stewart, Rod
Stewart, Slam
Stewart, Tinga
Stewart, Wynn
Stidham, Arbee
Stiff Little Fingers
Stiff Records
Stigers, Curtis
Stigwood, Robert
Stiles, Danny
Stilgoe, Richard
Stillborn
Stills, Stephen
Stills-Young Band
Stiltskin
Sting
Stingray
Stitt, Sonny
Stiv Bators
Stivell, Alan
Stobart, Kathy
Stock, Aitken
    And Waterman
Stockard, Ocie
Stockhausen,
    Markus
Stockton's Wing
Stockwood, Kim
Stokes, Frank
Stokes, Simon
Stoller, Alvin
Stoller, Mike
Stone City Band
Stone Fury
Stone Poneys
Stone Roses
Stone Temple
    Pilots
Stone The Crows
Stone, Cliffie
Stone, Doug
Stone, Henry
Stone, Jesse
Stone, Kirby,
    Four
Stone, Lew
Stone, Sly
Stoneground
Stoneman Family
Stooges
Stop The
    Violence
    Movement
Stop The World I
    Want To Get
    Off
Stordahl, Axel
Stories

Storm
Storm, Gale
Storm, Rory
Stormbringer
Stormtroopers
    Of Death
Stormwitch
Stormy Weather
Story Of Vernon
    And Irene
    Castle, The
Story, Carl
Story, Liz
Storyteller
Storyville
Stothart, Herbert
Stott, Wally
Stovall, Don
Stovall, Jewell
    'Babe'
Stovepipe No.I
Stowaway
Strachey, Jack
Stradlin, Izzy,
    And The Ju Ju
    Hounds
Straight, Charley
Strait, George
Strange Creek
    Singers
Strange Folk
Strange Fruit
    Records
Strange, Pete
Strangelove
Strangeloves
Stranger
Strangers
Strangeways
Stranglers
Strapping Young
    Lad
Strapps
Stratton, Maria
Stratton-Smith,
    Tony
Stratus
Straw, Syd
Strawberry
    Alarm Clock
Strawberry
    Statement, The
Strawberry
    Switchblade
Strawbs
Strawhead
Stray
Stray Cats
Stray Dog
Strayhorn, Billy
Street, Mel
Streetband
Streets
Streetwalkers
Strehli, Angela
Streisand, Barbra
Stress Records

Stressball
Stretch
Strickland,
    Napoleon
Stricklin, Al
Strictly Ballroom
Strictly Rhythm
Strictly Roots
Strictly
    Underground
Strife
Strike Up The
    Band
Strike Up The
    Band (film
    musical)
Striker
String Trio Of
    New York
String-a-Longs
String-Driven
    Thing
Stringbean
Strip, The
Stritch, Elaine
Strong, Barrett
Strong, Benny
Stroud, James
Strouse, Charles
Structure
Strunk, Jud
Strutt, Nick
Stryper
Stuart, Alice
Stuart, Marty
Stuckey, Henry
Stuckey, Nat
Stud
Student Prince In
    Heidelberg,
    The
Student Prince,
    The
Studer, Fredy
Studio One
Stump
Stupids
Sturr, Jimmy
Style Council
Stylistics
Styne, Jule
Styrenes
Styx
Sub Pop Records
Sub Sub
Subcircus
Subdudes
Subhumans
    (Canada)
Subhumans (UK)
Sublime
Subramaniam,
    Dr. L.
Subsonic 2
Subterfuge
Subterraneans,
    The

Suburban Base
Success!
Sudden, Nikki
Suddenly,
    Tammy!
Sudhalter, Dick
Sue And Sunny
Sue Records
Suede
Suesse, Dana
Sufit, Alisha
Sugar
Sugar (stage
    musical)
Sugar Babies
Sugar Hill
    Records
    (Country)
Sugar Ray
Sugarcreek
Sugarcubes
Sugarhill Gang
Sugarhill Records
Suggs
Suicidal
    Tendencies
Suicide
Sulieman, Idrees
Sullivan, Big Jim
Sullivan, Ed
Sullivan, Ira
Sullivan, Joe
Sullivan, Maxine
Sultans
Sultans Of Ping
    FC
Sulzmann, Stan
Sumac, Yma
Sumlin, Hubert
Summer Holiday
    (1948)
Summer Holiday
    (1962)
Summer Stock
Summer, Donna
Summerfield,
    Saffron
Summerhill
Summers, Andy
Sun
Sun City Girls
Sun Dial
Sun Ra
Sun Records
Sun Valley
    Serenade
Sun J
Sun, Joe
Suncatcher
Sunchilde
Sunday In The
    Park With
    George
Sundays
Sundazed
    Records
Sundial

Sundowners
Sunny
Sunny And The
    Sunglows
Sunny Day Real
    Estate
Sunnyboys
Sunnyland Slim
Sunnysiders
Sunrays
Suns Of Arqa
Sunscreem
Sunset Boulevard
Sunshine
    Company
Sunshine, Monty
Super Deluxe
Super Diamono
    De Dakar
Super Etoile De
    Dakar
Super Furry
    Animals
Super Junky
    Monkey
Super Stocks
Superbs
Supercat
Supercharger
Superchunk
Superdrag
Supereal
Superfly
Supergrass
Supergroove
Supermodel
Supernaturals
Supernaw, Doug
Supersax
Supersister
Supersuckers
Supertramp
Supremes
Sure Is Pure
Sure!, Al B.
Surf Party
Surface
Surfaris
Surgin
Surman, John
Surrender
Survivor
Suso, Foday Musa
Suso, Jali Nyama
Sutcliffe, Stuart
Sutherland
    Brothers
Sutherland,
    Nadine
Sutton, Ralph
Suzuki, Kenji
Suzuki, Tsuyoshi
Sven Gali
Sven Klang's
    Kvintett
SVT
SWA

Swain, Tony
Swallow, Steve
Swallows
Swamp Dogg
Swampwater
Swan Arcade
Swan Silvertones
Swan, Billy
Swann, Bettye
Swann, Donald
Swans
SWAPO Singers
Swarbrick, Dave
Sweat, Keith
Sweathog
Sweatman, Wilbur
Sweaty Nipples
Sweeney Todd
Sweeney's Men
Sweet
Sweet Adeline
Sweet And Low-Down
Sweet Beat
Sweet Charity
Sweet Charity (film musical)
Sweet Exorcist
Sweet Honey In The Rock
Sweet Inspirations
Sweet Love, Bitter
Sweet Pain
Sweet Ride, The
Sweet Savage
Sweet 75
Sweet Sister
Sweet Talks
Sweet Tee
Sweet Water
Sweet, Matthew
Sweet, Rachel
Sweetback
Sweethearts (film musical)
Sweethearts (stage musical)
Sweethearts Of The Rodeo
Sweetie Irie
Swell Maps
Swemix Records
Swervedriver
Swift, Duncan
Swift, Kay
Swing Out Sister
Swing Shift Band
Swing Time
Swingbeat
Swingin' Medallions
Swinging Blue Jeans
Swinging UK

Swingle Singers
Swingmen In Europe
Switch
Sword
SWV
Sye
Sykes, Bobby
Sykes, Roosevelt
Sylla, Ibrahima
Sylvain Sylvain
Sylvers
Sylvester
Sylvia
Sylvian, David
Symarip
Symbols
Symphony In Black
Symposium
Syms, Sylvia
Syn
Syncopation
Syndicate Of Sound
Syndicats
System 7
Syzygy
Szabo, Frank J.
Szabo, Gabor
Szymczyk, Bill
T. La Rock
T Power
T'Pau
T-Bones (UK)
T-Bones (USA)
T-Empo
T-Power
T-Ride
T. Rex
T.A.S.S.
T.I.M.E.
T.O.B.A.
T.S. Monk
T.V. Slim
T99
Tabackin, Lew
Tabor, June
Tackhead
Tacuma, Jamaaladeen
Tad
Taffola, Joey
Tages
Taggart, Blind Joe
Tairrie B
Tait, Lynn
Taj Mahal
Takahashi, Tatsuya
Take 6
Take A Chance
Take Me Along
Take Me High
Take Me Out To The Ball Game
Take My Tip

Take That
Talas
Talion
Talisman
Talk Show
Talk Talk
Talkin' Loud
Talking Heads
Tall Dwarfs
Tall Stories
Talley, Bob
Talley, James
Talmy, Shel
Talulah Gosh
Tamam Shud
Tamla-Motown Records
Tamlins
Tampa Red
Tams
Tan Tan
Tana, Akira
Tananas
Tanega, Norma
Tangerine Dream
Tangier
Tangled Feet
Tania Maria
Tank
Tankard
Tanksley, Francesca
Tannahill Weavers
Tannen, Holly
Tanner, Gid
Tansads
Tapscott, Horace
Tarafel Soporul De Cimpie
Tarheel Slim
Tarika Sammy
Tarleton's Jig
Tarleton, Jimmie
Tarnation
Tarriers
Tarto, Joe
Tarver, Quindon
Tassilli Players
Taste
Taste Of Honey, A
Tate, Baby
Tate, Buddy
Tate, Erskine
Tate, Frank
Tate, Grady
Tate, Howard
Tate, Tater
Tati, Cheb
Tattoo Rodeo
Tattooed Love Boys
Tatum, Art
Taupin, Bernie
Tavares
Tawney, Cyril

Taylor, 'Little' Johnny
Taylor, 'Sam The Man'
Taylor, Allan
Taylor, Art
Taylor, Bernard J.
Taylor, Billy
Taylor, Bobby, And The Vancouvers
Taylor, Bram
Taylor, Carmol
Taylor, Cecil
Taylor, Chip
Taylor, Derek
Taylor, Earl
Taylor, Eddie
Taylor, Eric
Taylor, Eva
Taylor, Felice
Taylor, James
Taylor, James, Quartet
Taylor, Jeremy
Taylor, John
Taylor, Johnnie
Taylor, Kingsize, And The Dominoes
Taylor, Koko
Taylor, Lewis
Taylor, Livingston
Taylor, Martin
Taylor, Melvin
Taylor, Mick
Taylor, Montana
Taylor, R. Dean
Taylor, Rod
Taylor, Roger
Taylor, Ted
Taylor, Theodore 'Hound Dog'
Taylor, Tyrone
Taylor, Vince
Tchaikovsky, Bram
Tchicai, John Martin
Tea And Symphony
Tea Party
Teagarden, Charlie
Teagarden, Cub
Teagarden, Jack
Teagarden, Norma
Teague, Thurman
Tear Gas
Teardrop Explodes
Teardrops
Tears For Fears
Techniques
Techno
Technotronic
Technova

Teddy Bears
Teddybears
STHLM
Tee Set
Tee, Richard
Tee, Willie
Teen Queens
Teenage Fanclub
Teenage Jesus And The Jerks
Tekla
Telescopes
Television Personalities
Telex
Telstar Ponies
Tembo, Biggie
Temiz, Okay
Temperance 7
Temperley, Joe
Tempest
Temple Of The Dog
Temple, Johnny
Temple, Shirley
Templeman, Ted
Tempo, Nino, and April Stevens
Temptations
10cc
Ten City
Ten Feet Five
10,000 Maniacs
Ten Years After
Tenaglia, Danny
Tenneva Ramblers
Tennors, Clive
Tenor Fly
Tenor Saw
Tenores Di Bitti
Tenpole Tudor
Terem Quartet
Terminator X
Ternent, Billy
Terraplane
Terrell, Pha
Terrell, Tammi
Territory Bands
Terror Fabulous
Terrorizer
Terrorvision
Terry And Monica
Terry And The Pirates
Terry Dactyl And The Dinosaurs
Terry, Clark
Terry, Karl, And The Cruisers
Terry, Helen
Terry, Sonny
Terry, Todd
Teschemacher, Frank

Tesla
Test Department
Testament
Tester, Scan
Tetsuhiro, Daiku
Tex, Joe
Texas
Texas Tornados
Tha Brigade
Tha Dogg Pound
Thackray, Jake
Thackery, Jimmy
Thanks A Million
Tharpe, Sister
  Rosetta
That Kid Chris
That Night In Rio
That Petrol
  Emotion
That Summer
That'll Be The Day
That's A Good
  Girl
The Age Of
  Electric
The Girl Can't
  Help It
The Point
The Story
The The
Theatre Of Hate
Theatre Owners
  Booking
  Association
Thee Headcoats
Thee Mighty
  Caesars
Thelin, Eje
Them
Themen, Art
Then Jerico
Theodorakis,
  Mikis
Therapy (Folk)
Therapy?
There's No
  Business Like
  Show Business
Thermadore
These Animal
  Men
They Might Be
  Giants
They're Playing
  Our Song
Thiele, Bob
Thielemans,
  Toots
Thigpen, Ben
Thigpen, Ed
Thilo, Jesper
Thin Lizzy
Thin White Rope
Think
Thinking Fellers
  Union Local
  282

3rd Bass
Third Ear Band
Third Eye Blind
Third Rail
Third World
Thirlwell, Jim
Thirteenth Floor
  Elevators
38 Special
Thirty Ought Six
This Heat
This Is The Army
This Is The Army
  (film musical)
This Mortal Coil
This Perfect Day
This Year Of
  Grace!
This'll Make You
  Whistle
Thistlethwaite,
  Anthony
Thomas Group
Thomas, B.J.
Thomas, Carla
Thomas, Charles
Thomas, Chris
  (UK)
Thomas, Chris
  (USA)
Thomas, David
Thomas, David,
  And The
  Pedestrians
Thomas, Earl
Thomas, George
Thomas, Hersal
Thomas, Hociel
Thomas, Ian,
  Band
Thomas, Irma
Thomas, Jah
Thomas, James
  'Son'
Thomas, Jesse
  'Babyface'
Thomas, Joe
  (saxophone)
Thomas, Joe
  (trumpet)
Thomas, Joe
  Lewis
Thomas, Keith
Thomas, Kenny
Thomas, Kid
Thomas,
  Lafayette Jerl
Thomas, Leone
Thomas, Nicky
Thomas, Pat
Thomas,
  Ramblin'
Thomas, Rene
Thomas, Rufus
Thomas, Sam
  Fan
Thomas, Tabby

Thomas, Timmy
Thomas, Walter
  'Foots'
Thomas, Willie B.
Thompson Twins
Thompson,
  'Lucky'
Thompson,
  Barbara
Thompson, Butch
Thompson,
  Carroll
Thompson,
  Charles, Sir
Thompson,
  Danny
Thompson, Eddie
Thompson, Errol
Thompson, Gina
Thompson, Hank
Thompson, Joe
  And Odell
Thompson, Linda
Thompson, Linval
Thompson, Odell
Thompson,
  Richard
Thompson,
  Richard And
  Linda
Thompson,
  Sonny
Thompson, Sue
Thompson, Uncle
  Jimmie
Thoms, Shirley
Thomson, Craig
Thor
Thorn, Tracey
Thornhill, Claude
Thornton, James
Thornton, Willie
  Mae 'Big
  Mama'
Thorogood,
  George
Thoroughly
  Modern Millie
Thorpe, Billy
Thorson, Lisa
Those Were The
  Happy Times
Thought Industry
Thoughts
Thoumire, Simon
Thousand Yard
  Stare
Thousands Cheer
Thrasher
Thrasher Shiver
Threadgill, Henry
3Phase
Three Beat
  Records
Three Bells
Three Chuckles
3 Colours Red

Three Degrees
Three Dog Night
311
Three Johns
Three Man Posse
3 Mustaphas 3
Three O'Clock
3 lb. Thrill
3T
Three Tree Posse
Three's A Crowd
Threepenny
  Opera, The
Threshold
  Records
Thriller U
Throbbing Gristle
Throbs
Throwing Muses
Thrum
Thunder
Thunder Alley
Thunder, Johnny
Thunder, Shelley
Thunderclap
  Newman
Thunderhead
Thunders, Johnny
Thunderstick
Thursaflokkurim
Tibbs, Andrew
Tiberi, Frank
Tic Tac Toc
Tickell, Kathryn
Tickle Me
Tico And The
  Triumphs
Tierney, Harry
Tierra
Tiffany
Tiffany's
  Thoughts
Tiger
Tiger (Reggae)
Tigertailz
Tikaram, Tanita
Til The Butcher
  Cuts Him
  Down
Til Tuesday
Tilbrook, Adrian
Till The Clouds
  Roll By
Tillis, Mel
Tillis, Pam
Tillman, Floyd
Tillotson, Johnny
Tilston, Steve
Tilton, Martha
Timbuk 3
Time
Time Records
Time Unlimited
Timelords
Times
Timmons, Bobby
Tin Huey

Tin Machine
Tin Pan Alley
Tin Tin Out
Tina
Tindersticks
Tinsley, John
Tintern Abbey
Tiny Monroe
Tiny Tim
Tio, Lorenzo
Tiomkin, Dimitri
TIP Records
Tip-Toes
Típica 73
Tippa Irie
Tippett, Keith
Tippetts, Julie
Tippin, Aaron
Tir nA nOg
Tissendier,
  Claude
Titanic
Titelman, Russ
Titus Groan
Tityo
Tizol, Juan
TJ Rhemi
Tjader, Cal
TLC
To Hell With
  Burgundy
Toad The Wet
  Sprocket
Toadies
Tobias Brothers
Tobias, Charles
Tobin, Amon
Tobin, Christine
Toby Beau
Toby, Glenn
  'Sweet G'
Todd, Art And
  Dotty
Todd, Dick
Todd, Nick
Todd, Phil
Toddy Tee
Toe Fat
Together
Tokens
Tom And Jerry
Tom Tom Club
Tomato Records
Tomkins, Trevor
Tomlinson,
  Ernest
Tommy
Tommy (film
  musical)
Tommy Boy
Tommy Steele
  Story, The
Tomorrow
Tomorrow
  Records
Tompall And The
  Glaser Brothers

Tompkins, Ross
Tone Loc
Toneff, Radka
Tones On Tail
Toney, Oscar, Jnr.
Tongue And Groove
Tongueman
Tonic
Tonight At 8.30
Tonight At Noon
Tonight Let's All Make Love In London
Tonight's The Night
Tonolo, Pietro
Tonto's Expanding Headband
Tony Awards
Tony! Toni! Tone!
Too Late Blues
Too Many Girls
Too Much Joy
Too Short
Tool
Toop, David, And Max Eastley
Top Cat
Top Hat
Top Of The Pops
Topic Records
Torch, Sidney
Torme, Bernie
Tormé, Mel
Torn, David
Tornados
Törnqvist, Rebecka
Torok, Mitchell
Toronto
Torres, Roberto
Tortoise
Tory Voodoo
Toscano, Eli
Tosh, Andrew
Tosh, Peter
Toss The Feathers
Total Devastation
Total Touch
Toto
Touch
Touchables, The
Tough, Dave
Touré Kunda
Touré, Ali Farka
Tourists
Tournesol
Toussaint, Allen
Toussaint, Jean
Tovey, Frank
Tower Of Power
Tower Struck Down

Towering Inferno
Towles, Nat
Town Hall Party
Towner, Ralph
Towns, Colin
Townsend, Ed
Townsend, Henry
Townshend, Pete
Toxic Ephex
Toy Dolls
Toy Love
Toyah
Toyin
Toys
Toytown Techno
Trace, Al
Tracey, Clark
Tracey, Stan
Tracie
Tractor
Tractors
Tracy, Arthur
Trader Horne
Tradewinds
Tradition
Tradition Records
Traffic
Tragically Hip
Tramline
Trammps
Tramp
Trance Induction
Trance Syndicate Records
Trans-Global Underground
Transcendental Love Machine
Transcription Carriers
Transeau
Transient Records
Transmat Records
Transvision Vamp
Trapeze
Trash
Trash Can Sinatras
Trashmen
Trask, Diana
Traum, Happy
Traveling Wilburys
Travellers 3
Travers, Pat, Band
Travis
Travis And Bob
Travis, Geoff
Travis, Gus, And The Midnighters
Travis, Merle
Travis, Randy

Travolta, John
Trax Records
Treacherous
Tree Grows In Brooklyn, A
Trees
Tremaine, Paul
Tremblers
Tremeloes
Trenet, Charles
Trenier Twins
Trent, Alphonso
Trent, Bruce
Trent, Buck
Trent, Jackie
Trespass
Tresvant, Ralph
Trettine, Caroline
Trevino, Rick
Tribble, Thomas E., 'TNT'
Tribe After Tribe
Tribute To Nothing
Tribute To The Blues Brothers, A
Trice, Richard
Trice, Willie
Tricky
Triffids
Trinity
Trio
Trio Bulgarka
Trio Cornemuse
Trip, The
Tripping Daisy
Trischka, Tony
Tristan
Tristano, Lennie
Tritt, Travis
Triumph
Troggs
Trojan Records
Trotman, Lloyd Nelson
Trouble
Trouble Funk
Trouble With Girls, The
Troup, Bobby
Trout, Walter, Band
Trower, Robin
Troy, Doris
Trudell, John
True Believers
True Endeavor Jug Band
True Life Mathematics
True West
Trueheart, John
Truly
Truman's Water
Trumbauer, Frank

Trunkles
Truss And Bucket Band
Trust
Truth (pop)
Truth (R&B)
Tshole, Makgona, Band
Tsiboe, Nana
TSOL
Tsunami
TTF
Tuatara
Tubb, Ernest
Tubb, Justin
Tube, The
Tubes
Tubeway Army
Tuck And Patti
Tucker, Barbara
Tucker, Cy, And The Friars
Tucker, Junior
Tucker, Luther
Tucker, Maureen
Tucker, Orrin
Tucker, Sophie
Tucker, Tanya
Tucker, Tommy
Tucky Buzzard
Tuff
Tuff, Tony
Tumbaito
Tundra
Tune Weavers
Tune, Tommy
Tungsten
Tunnell, Bon Bon
Tura Satana
Turasakis, Mark
Turbans
Turbines
Turner, 'Big' Joe
Turner, Bruce
Turner, Dallas
Turner, Danny
Turner, Gil
Turner, Grant
Turner, Ike
Turner, Ike And Tina
Turner, Jay
Turner, Jesse Lee
Turner, Joe
Turner, Joe Lynn
Turner, Other
Turner, Ruby
Turner, Sammy
Turner, Steve
Turner, Tina
Turner, Titus
Turney, Norris
Turnham, Edythe
Turrentine, Stanley
Turrentine, Tommy

Turtle Island String Quartet
Turtles
Tuttle, Wesley
Tuxedomoon
TV Smith
TV Smith's Explorers
TV 21
Twain, Shania
Twang!!
Twardzik, Dick
28th Day
25th Of May
24-7 Spyz
29th Street Saxophone Quartet
21 Guns
21-3 Productions
20/20
22 Brides
22 Pistepirkko
Twice
Twice As Much
Twilights
Twilley, Dwight
Twin Hype
Twink
Twinkeyz
Twinkle
Twinkle Brothers
Twist
Twist Around The Clock
Twisted Sister
Twister Alley
Twitty, Conway
Two A Penny
Two Gentlemen Of Verona
200 Motels
Two Lane Blacktop
2 Live Crew
2 Live Jews
Two Nice Girls
Two Tons O' Fun
2 Too Many
2 Tribes
2 Unlimited
Tygers Of Pan Tang
Tyketto
Tyla, Sean
Tyler, Bonnie
Tyler, Charles
Tyler, T. Texas
Tymes
Tyner, McCoy
Type O Negative
Typically Tropical
Tyrannosaurus Rex
Tyree
Tyrrel Corporation

Tyrrell, Sean
Tyson, Ian
Tyson, Ian And
  Sylvia
Tyson, Sylvia
Tzelniker, Meir
Tzuke, Judie
U-Krew
U-Roy
U., Srinivas
U.T.F.O.
U2
U96
UB40
Ubik
UFO
Ugly Ducklings
Ugly Kid Joe
Uglys
Uhurus
Ui
UK Decay
UK MCs
UK Players
UK Reggae
UK Subs
UK Swings Again
Ukrainians
Ukwu, Celestine
Ullman, Tracey
Ulloa, Francisco
Ulmer, James
  'Blood'
Ultimate Kaos
Ultimate Spinach
Ultra Naté
Ultra Vivid Scene
Ultramagnetic
  MC's
Ultramarine
Ultrasound
Ultraviolence
Ultravox
Umbruglia,
  Natalie
UMC's
Uminosachi
Ummm
Unanimous
  Decision
Uncanny Alliance
Uncle Cyp And
  Aunt Sap
Uncle Sam
Uncle Tupelo
Under Your Hat
Under Your Hat
  (film musical)
Undercover
Underdog
Underground
  Resistance
Understand
Undertakers
Undertones
Underworld
Unifics

Union City
Union City
  Recordings
Unique 3
Uniques
Unit Four Plus
  Two
United Artists
United Future
  Organization
United Jazz And
  Rock Ensemble
United States Of
  America
United States Of
  Sound
Unrest
Unsane
Unsinkable Molly
  Brown, The
Up In Arms
Up In Central
  Park
Up On The Roof
Up The Junction
Upchurch, Phil
Upper Crust
Upsetters
Upton, Eddie
Uptown Records
Urban Cookie
  Collective
Urban Dance
  Squad
Urban Folk
Urban South
Urban Species
Urbaniak, Michal
Ure, Midge
Urge Overkill
Uriah Heep
Urusei Yatsura
Us3
USA For Africa
Usher
Usher, Gary
Ut
Utah Saints
Uwaifo, Victor
V-Roys
V., Stevie
Vaché, Allan
Vaché, Warren,
  Jnr.
Vagabond King,
  The
Vagabonds
Vagrants
Vai, Steve
Vain
Valance, Ricky
Valdambrini,
  Oscar
Vale, Jerry
Valens, Ritchie
Valente, Caterina
Valenti, Dino

Valentin, Bobby
Valentin, Charlie
Valentine, Cal
Valentine, Dickie
Valentine, Kid
  Thomas
Valentines
Valentino, Sal
Valentinos
Vali, Justin, Trio
Valino, Joe
Vallee, Rudy
Valley Of The
  Dolls
Valli, Frankie
Valmouth
Valoy, Cuco
Vamp
Van Day, David
Van Der Graaf
  Generator
Van Helden,
  Armand
Van Hove, Fred
Van Der Linden,
  Dolf
Van Dyke, Earl
Van Dyke, Leroy
Van Dykes
Van Eps, George
Van Halen
Van Halen, Eddie
Van Heusen,
  Jimmy
Van Ronk, Dave
Van Straten,
  Alfred
Van Walls, Harry
Van Zandt,
  Steven
Van Zandt,
  Townes
Van't Hof, Jasper
Van, Garwood
Vance, Dick
Vanda And
  Young
Vandenberg
Vandross, Luther
Vangelis
Vanguard
  Records
Vanilla Fudge
Vanilla Ice
Vanilla, Cherry
Vanishing Point
Vanity
Vanity 6
Vanity Fare
Vanwarmer,
  Randy
Vapirov, Anatoly
Vapors
Varda, James
Vardis
Vargas, Wilfrido
Varnaline

Värttinä
Vasconcelos,
  Monica
Vasconcelos,
  Nana
Vaselines
Väsen
Vashti
Vasquez, Junior
Vath, Sven
Vaughan, Frankie
Vaughan, Jimmie
Vaughan,
  Malcolm
Vaughan, Maurice
  John
Vaughan, Sarah
Vaughan, Stevie
  Ray
Vaughn, Billy
Vaughn, Jimmy
Vee, Bobby
Vee Jay Records
Vega, Alan
Vega, Suzanne
Vega, Tata
Vega, Tony
Vejtables
Vela, Rosie
Veldt
Velocity Girl
Velours
Velvelettes
Velvet Crush
Velvet Monkeys
Velvet Opera
Velvet
  Underground
Velvets
Velvett Fogg
Venet, Nik
Venom
Vent 414
Ventura, Charlie
Ventures
Venus Fly Trap
Venuti, Joe
Vera, Billy
Vera-Ellen
Verckys
Verdon, Gwen
Verlaine, Tom
Verlaines
Vernon, Mike
Vernons
Vernons Girls
VerPlanck,
  Marlene
Verrell, Ronnie
Versalettes
Version
Vertigo Records
Veruca Salt
Verve
Verve Pipe
Verve Records
Vervette, Irving

Very Good Eddie
Very Things
Vesala, Edward
Vibrasonic
Vibrations
Vibrators
Vibronics
Vice Squad
Viceroys
Vicious Rumors
Vicious, Sid
Vickers, Mike
Victor
Victor Records
Victor/Victoria
Vikings
Vikström,
  Thomas
Village
Village People
Vincent, Gene
Vincent, Johnny
Vincent, Monroe
Vincent, Vinnie
Vinegar Joe
Vinnegar, Leroy
Vinson, Eddie
  'Cleanhead'
Vinson, Mose
Vinson, Walter
Vintage Jazz And
  Blues Band
Vinton, Bobby
Vinx
Violence
Violent Femmes
Violin
Violinski
Vipers Skiffle Group
VIPs
Virgin Prunes
Virgin Records
Virgin Steele
Virginia Squires
Virtues
Visconti, Tony
Viscounts
Vital Escape
Vito And The
  Salutations
Vitous, Miroslav
Viva Las Vegas
Vivid
Vixen (USA)
Vocaleers
Vocalion Records
Vogues
Voice
Voice Masters
Voice Of The
  Beehive
Voice Squad
Voisine, Roch
Voivod
Vokes, Howard
Vollenweider,
  Andreas

Volume 10
Volumes
Von Battle, Joe
Von Ohlen, John
Von Schlippenbach, Alex
Von Tilzer, Albert
Von Tilzer, Harry
Vontastics
Voorman, Klaus
Voxpoppers
Voyeurz
Vujicsics
Vulcan's Hammer
Vulgar Boatmen
W., Kristine
W.A.S.P.
Wabash Avenue
Wachsmann, Phil
Wackers
Wade, Adam
Wade, Norman
Wade, Wayne
Wadsworth Mansion
Wagon Christ
Wagoner, Porter
Wah!
Wah-Wah
Wailer, Bunny
Wailers
Wailers (USA)
Wailing Souls
Wain, Bea
Wainwright, Loudon, III
Waite, John
Waitresses
Waits, Tom
Wakefield, Frank
Wakely, Jimmy
Wakeman, Rick
Walcott, Collin
Wald, Jerry
Walden, Narada Michael
Waldman, Herman
Waldron, Mal
Wales, Josey
Walkabouts
Walker Brothers
Walker, Billy
Walker, Charles
Walker, Charlie
Walker, Clay
Walker, Eddie
Walker, Gary
Walker, Hezekiah
Walker, Ian
Walker, Jerry Jeff
Walker, Jimmy
Walker, Joe Louis
Walker, John

Walker, Johnny 'Big Moose'
Walker, Junior, And The All Stars
Walker, Philip
Walker, Scott
Walker, T-Bone
Walker, Willie (blues)
Walking Seeds
Walks, Dennis
Wall
Wall Of Voodoo
Wall, Chris
Wall, The
Wallace Brothers
Wallace, Bennie
Wallace, Beulah 'Sippie'
Wallace, Herman 'Ace'
Wallace, Jerry
Wallace, Leroy 'Horsemouth'
Wallace, Wesley
Waller, Fats
Waller, Gordon
Wallflowers
Wallington, George
Wallis, Bob
Walrath, Jack
Walsh, Joe
Walsh, Peter
Walter, Mitchell
Walters, Charles
Walters, Hank
Walters, Jamie
Walters, John
Walton, Cedar
Walton, Wade
Walton, William, Sir
Waltons
Wammack, Travis
Wand Records
Wanderers
Wang Chung
Wangford, Hank
Wannadies
War
Ward, Alex
Ward, Anita
Ward, Billy, And The Dominoes
Ward, Carlos
Ward, Chris
Ward, Clara
Ward, Clifford T.
Ward, Fields
Ward, Helen
Ward, Robert
Ward, Robin
Wardell, Anita
Warden, Monte

Ware, Leon
Ware, Martyn
Ware, Wilbur
Warfare
Warfield, Justin
Warhorse
Wariner, Steve
Waring, Fred
Warlock
Warlop, Michel
Warm Dust
Warm Jets
Warm Sounds
Warmack, Paul, And The Gully Jumpers
Warner Brothers Records
Warner, Frank And Anne
Warnes, Jennifer
Waronker, Lenny
Warp
Warp 9
Warrant
Warren, Alister
Warren, Baby Boy
Warren, Dale
Warren, Diane
Warren, Earle
Warren, Fiddlin' Kate
Warren, Guy
Warren, Harry
Warren, John
Warren, Paul
Warrior
Warrior Soul
Warriors
Warwick, Carl 'Bama'
Warwick, Dee Dee
Warwick, Dionne
Was (Not Was)
Was, Don
Washboard Doc
Washboard Slim
Washboard Willie
Washington, Baby
Washington, Delroy
Washington, Dinah
Washington, Ella
Washington, Geno (And The Ram Jam Band)
Washington, George
Washington, Grover, Jnr.
Washington, Isidore 'Tuts'
Washington, Jack
Washington, Jeanette

Washington, Jerome
Washington, Justine
Washington, Kenny
Washington, Lamont
Washington, Larry
Washington, Maurice
Washington, Melodie
Washington, Ned
Washington, Oddball
Washington, Renee
Washington, Steve
Washington, Tony
Washington, Walter 'Wolfman'
Waso
Wassy, Brice
Watam
Watanabe, Sadao
Watch Your Step
Watchtower
Water Into Wine Band
Water Lily Records
Waterboys
Waterford, Charles 'Crown Prince'
Waterlillies
Waterman, Dennis
Waters, Benny
Waters, Crystal
Waters, Ethel
Waters, Roger
Waterson, Lal, And Oliver Knight
Waterson, Norma
Watersons
Wates, Matt
Watford, Michael
Watkins, Doug
Watkins, John 'Mad Dog'
Watkins, Julius
Watkiss, Cleveland
Watley, Jody
Watrous, Bill
Watson, Bobby
Watson, Dale
Watson, Doc
Watson, Gene
Watson, Helen
Watson, Johnny 'Guitar'
Watson, Leo
Watt, Ben

Watt, Mike
Watters, Cyril
Watters, Lu
Watts 103rd Street Rhythm Band
Watts Prophets
Watts, Trevor
Wattstax
WAU! Mr Modo Records
Wax
Wax Trax Records
Waxman, Franz
Way We Live
Way Out West
Wayne And Charlie
Wayne, Chris
Wayne, Jeff
Wayne, Jerry
Wayne, Mabel
Wayne, Thomas
Wayne, Wee Willie
Waysted
Wayward Souls
Waywha
We Are Going To Eat You
We Five
We Free Kings
We Saw The Wolf
We The People
We're Not Dressing
We've Got A Fuzzbox And We're Gonna Use It
WEA Records
Weapon
Weather Girls
Weather Report
Weatherall, Andy
Weatherford, Teddy
Weatherly, Jim
Weathersby, Carl
Weaver, Curley James
Weaver, Mick
Weaver, Sylvester
Weavers
Webb, 'Boogie' Bill
Webb, Chick
Webb, George
Webb, Jimmy
Webb, Lizabeth
Webb, Marti
Webb, Peta
Webb, Sonny, And The Cascades

Webb, Speed
Webb, Stan
Webber, Aj
Webber, Merlene
Weber, Eberhard
Weber, Joan
Webster, Ben
Webster, Et
Webster, Freddie
Webster, Katie
Webster, Paul
Francis
Weckl, Dave
Wedding Bells
Wedding Present
Weddings,
Parties,
Anything
Wedlock, Fred
Wee Papa Girl
Rappers
Weedon, Bert
Weekend
Weeks, Anson
Weems, Ted
Ween
Weezer
Weil, Cynthia
Weill, Kurt
Wein, George
Weir, Bob
Weirdos
Weiss Brothers
Weiss, George
Weiss, Sammy
Weiss, Sid
Welch, Bob
Welch, Bruce
Welch, Elisabeth
Welch, Kevin
Welch, Lenny
Welch, Mike
Weldon, Casey
Bill
Weldon, Liam
Welk, Lawrence
Well Hung
Parliament
Well Oiled
Sisters
Weller, Don
Weller, Freddy
Weller, Paul
Wellington,
Sheena
Wellington,
Valerie
Wellins, Bobby
Wells, Brandi
Wells, Dicky
Wells, Houston,
And The
Marksmen
Wells, Jean
Wells, Junior
Wells, Kitty
Wells, Mary

Wells, Viola 'Miss
Rhapsody'
Wellstood, Dick
Welsh, Alex
Welton Irie
Welz, Joey
Wemba, Papa
Wendy And Lisa
Wentzel, Magni
Werner, Susan
Werth, Howard
Wesley, Fred
Wess, Frank
West
West Bam
West Coast Jazz
West Coast Pop
Art
Experimental
Band
West Coast Rap
All-Stars
West Side Story
West Side Story
(film musical)
West Street Mob
West, Bruce And
Laing
West, Dodie
West, Dottie
West, Harold
'Doc'
West, Hedy
White, Bryan
West, Keith
West, Leslie
West, Shelly
Westbound
Records
Westbrook, Kate
Westbrook, Mike
Westerberg, Paul
Weston, John 'So
Blue'
Weston, Kim
Weston, Paul
Weston, Randy
Westside
Connection
Wet Wet Wet
Wet Willie
Wettling, George
Wetton, John
Wexler, Jerry
Whale
Wham!
What A Crazy
World
What Lola Wants
What Makes
Sammy Run?
What's Up Tiger
Lily
Whatnauts
Wheatstraw,
Peetie
Wheeler, Big

Wheeler, Billy
Edd
Wheeler, Caron
Wheeler, Cheryl
Wheeler, Golden
Wheeler, Kenny
Wheeler, Onie
Wheeling
Jamboree, The
Wheels
Where The Boys
Are
Where's Charley?
Whetsol, Artie
Which Witch
Whigfield
Whigham, Jiggs
Whipped Cream
Whippersnapper
Whipping Boy
Whirlwind
Whiskey, Nancy
Whiskeyhill
Singers
Whisky Priests
Whispers
Whitcomb, Ian
White Christmas
White Lion
White Plains
White Spirit
White Town
White Zombie
White's, George,
Scandals
White,
'Schoolboy'
Cleve
White, Andrew
White, Andy
White, Artie
'Blues Boy'
White, Barry
White, Buck
White, Bukka
White, Clarence
White, Clifford
White, Edward
White, George
White, Georgia
White, James
White, John I.
White, Josh
White, Joy Lynn
White, Lavelle
White, Lenny
White, Lynn
White, Michael
White, Tam
White, Tony Joe
Whitehead,
Annie
Whitehead, Tim
Whiteman, Paul
Whiteout
Whites
Whitesnake

Whitfield,
Barrence
Whitfield, David
Whitfield,
Norman
Whitfield, Weslia
Whiting,
Margaret
Whiting, Richard
Whitley, Chris
Whitley, Keith
Whitley, Ray
Whitman, Slim
Whitney, Steve,
Band
Whitstein
Brothers
Whittaker, Roger
Whitter, Henry
Whittle, Tommy
Who
Who's Tommy,
The
Whodini
Whooliganz
Whoopee!
Whoopee! (stage
musical)
Whycliffe
Whyte, Ronny
Whyton, Wally
Wicked Maraya
Wickman, Dick
Wickman, Putte
Widowmaker
(UK)
Widowmaker
(USA)
Wiedlin, Jane
Wiedoft, Herb
Wigan's Chosen
Few
Wiggins, Gerry
Wiggins, John
And Audrey
Wiggins, Little
Roy
Wiggins, Phil
Wiggins, Spencer
Wiggs, Johnny
Wikman, Eric
Wikström, Rolf
Wilber, Bob
Wilburn Brothers
Wilco
Wilcox, Herbert
Wilcox, Toyah
Wild Angels
Wild Angels, The
Wild Cherry
Wild Flowers
Wild Horses
Wild In The
Country
Wild Orchid
Wild Party, The
Wild Pitch

Wild Rose
Wild Swans
Wild Turkey
Wildchild
Wilde, Kim
Wilde, Marty
Wilder, Alec
Wilder, Joe
Wildhearts
Wildside
Wildweeds
Wilen, Barney
Wiley And Gene
Wiley, Lee
Wilkie, Derry,
And The
Pressmen
Wilkins, Dave
Wilkins, Ernie
Wilkins, Joe
Willie
Wilkins, Robert,
Rev.
Wilkinson, Alan
Will Rogers
Follies, The
Willard
Willetts, Dave
Williams
Brothers
Williams, Andre
Williams, Andy
Williams, Bert
Williams, Big Joe
Williams, Bill
Williams, Billy
Williams, Blind
Connie
Williams, Brooks
Williams, Buddy
Williams, Buster
Williams, Charles
Williams,
Clarence
Williams, Claude
Williams, Cootie
Williams, Curley
Williams, Danny
Williams, Dar
Williams,
Deniece
Williams, Doc
Williams, Don
Williams, Esther
Williams, Fess
Williams, Gene
Williams, George
'Bullet'
Williams, Ginger
Williams, Griff
Williams, Hank
Williams, Hank,
Jnr.
Williams, Iris
Williams, J. Mayo
Williams, Jessica
Williams, Jody

Williams, Joe
Williams, John (composer)
Williams, John (guitar)
Williams, John (jazz)
Williams, Johnny
Williams, Johnny (R&B)
Williams, Joseph 'Jo Jo'
Williams, L.C.
Williams, Larry
Williams, Lee 'Shot'
Williams, Leona
Williams, Lester
Williams, Lil' Ed
Williams, Lucinda
Williams, Mary Lou
Williams, Mason
Williams, Maurice, And The Zodiacs
Williams, Midge
Williams, Otis, And The Charms
Williams, Paul
Williams, Pauline
Williams, Robert Pete
Williams, Roosevelt Thomas
Williams, Roy
Williams, Rudy
Williams, Sandy
Williams, Spencer
Williams, Tex
Williams, Tony
Williams, Vanessa
Williams, Victoria
Williams, Willie
Williamson, Claude
Williamson, James
Williamson, John Lee 'Sonny Boy'
Williamson, Robin
Williamson, Sonny Boy 'Rice Miller'
Williamson, Steve
Willie D
Willing, Foy
Willis Brothers
Willis, Aaron 'Little Sonny'
Willis, Bruce
Willis, Chick
Willis, Chuck
Willis, Kelly
Willis, Ralph
Willows
Wills, Billy Jack
Wills, Bob
Wills, Johnnie Lee

Wills, Luke
Wills, Mark
Wills, Viola
Willson, Meredith
Wilmer X
Wilson Phillips
Wilson, 'Kid' Wesley
Wilson, Al
Wilson, Brian
Wilson, Carl
Wilson, Cassandra
Wilson, Delroy
Wilson, Dennis
Wilson, Dick
Wilson, Edith Goodall
Wilson, Garland
Wilson, Gerald
Wilson, Harding 'Hop'
Wilson, Irene
Wilson, J. Frank, And The Cavaliers
Wilson, Jackie
Wilson, Jimmy
Wilson, Jodie
Wilson, Juice
Wilson, Julie
Wilson, Kim
Wilson, Mari
Wilson, Mary
Wilson, Meri
Wilson, Nancy
Wilson, Phil
Wilson, Roger
Wilson, Ross
Wilson, Sandy
Wilson, Shadow
Wilson, Smokey
Wilson, Teddy
Wilson, Up
Wimple Winch
Win
Winans
Winans, BeBe And CeCe
Winans, Mario
Winbush, Angela
Winchester, Jesse
Windham Hill Records
Windhurst, Johnny
Winding, Kai
Windsong
Wing And A Prayer Fife And Drum Corps
Winger
Wingfield, Pete
Wings
Wink, Josh
Winkies
Winley, Paul

Winston, George
Winston, Jimmy
Winstone, Eric
Winstone, Norma
Winstons
Winter, Edgar
Winter, Johnny
Winter, Paul
Winters, Tiny
Winther, Jens
Winwood, Muff
Winwood, Steve
Wipers
Wire
Wireless
Wisdom, Norman
Wise, Chubby
Wiseman, Val
Wiseman, Mac
Wish You Were Here
Wishbone Ash
Wishplants
Witchfinder General
Witchfynde
With A Song In My Heart
Withers, Bill
Withers, Tex
Witherspoon, Jimmy
Witnesses
Wiz, The
Wizard Of Oz, The
Wizard Of Oz, The (film musical)
Wizzard
Wodehouse, P.G.
Wolf, Kate
Wolf, Peter
Wolfgang Press
Wolfhounds
Wolfman Jack
Wolfsbane
Wolfstone
Wolverines
Womack And Womack
Womack, Bobby
Woman Of The Year
Womb
Wombles
Wonder Man
Wonder Stuff
Wonder Who
Wonder, Stevie
Wonder, Wayne
Wonderful Life
Wonderful Town
Wonderwall
Wood, Booty

Wood, Brenton
Wood, Del
Wood, Haydn
Wood, Ron
Wood, Roy
Woodard, Rickey
Woode, Jimmy
Woodentops
Woodfork, 'Poor' Bob
Wooding, Sam
Woodman, Britt
Woodruff, Bob
Woods, Gay
Woods, Gay And Terry
Woods, Harry
Woods, Johnny
Woods, Oscar
Woods, Phil
Woodstock
Woodstock Festival
Woodward, Edward
Woodyard, Sam
Wooley, Sheb
Woolley, Shep
Woolpackers
Wootton, Brenda
Wootton, Miles
Words And Music
Words And Music (film musical)
Working Week
Workman, Reggie
World
World Domination Enterprises
World Famous Supreme Team Show
World Of Twist
World Party
World Saxophone Quartet
World War III
World's Greatest Jazz Band
Worth, Marion
Wrathchild
Wrathchild America
Wray, Link
Wray, Walter
Wreckless Eric
Wreckx-N-Effect
Wrencher, Big John
Wright, Betty
Wright, Billy
Wright, Bobby
Wright, Carol Sue

Wright, Cheryl
Wright, Dale
Wright, Elly
Wright, Frank
Wright, Gary
Wright, Johnnie
Wright, Lammar
Wright, Lawrence
Wright, Mark
Wright, Michelle
Wright, O.V.
Wright, Robert
Wright, Ruby
Wright, Winston
Wrigley, Bernard
Wrigley, Jennifer And Hazel
Writing On The Wall
Wrubel, Allie
Wu Man
Wu-Tang Clan
Wulomei
Wump And His Werbles
Wurzels
Wuthering Heights
Wyands, Richard
Wyatt, Robert
Wyclef
Wycoff, Michael
Wylie, Austin
Wyman, Bill
Wynder K. Frog
Wyndham-Read, Martin
Wynette, Tammy
Wynn, 'Big' Jim
Wynn, Chris
Wynn, Nan
Wynn, Steve
Wynonna
Wynter, Mark
X
X Clan
X Press 2
X-Dream
X-Ray Spex
Xalam
Xanadu
Xavier
XC-NN
Xentrix
XL Capris
XL Records
Xmal Deutschland
Xscape
XTC
Xymox
XYZ
Y&T
Ya Kid K
Yabby You
Yachts

Yaggfu Front
Yamaguchi,
  Momoe
Yamash'ta,
  Stomu
Yamashita,
  Yosuke
Yana
Yancey, Jimmy
Yancey, Mama
Yankee Doodle
  Dandy
Yankovic, 'Weird
  Al'
Yanni
Yanovsky,
  Zalman 'Zally'
Yarbrough And
  Peoples
Yarbrough, Glenn
Yard Tapes
Yard Trauma
Yardbirds
Yargo
Yazoo
Yazz
Yeah Jazz
Yearwood, Trisha
Yellen, Jack
Yello
Yellow Balloon
Yellow Dog
Yellow Magic
  Orchestra
Yellow
  Submarine
Yellowjackets
Yellowman
Yentl
Yes
Yes Madam?
Yester, Jerry

Yesterday's News
Yetnikoff, Walter
Yetties
Yo La Tengo
Yo Yo
Yoakam, Dwight
York Brothers
Yorke, Peter
Yosefa
Yothu Yindi
You Are What
  You Eat
You Slosh
You Were Never
  Lovelier
You'll Never Get
  Rich
You're A Big Boy
  Now
You're A Good
  Man, Charlie
  Brown
Youmans,
  Vincent
Young & Co
Young At Heart
Young Black
  Teenagers
Young Disciples
Young Fresh
  Fellows
Young Gods
Young Hearts
Young Idea
Young Jessie
Young Man With
  A Horn
Young Marble
  Giants
Young MC
Young Ones, The
Young Rascals

Young Snakes
Young Tradition
Young, 'Mighty'
  Joe
Young, Amita
  Tata
Young, Barry
Young, Claude
Young, Ed And
  Lonnie
Young, Ernie
Young, Faron
Young, Irma
Young, Jesse
  Colin
Young, Jimmy
Young, Joe
Young, John Paul
Young, Johnny
  (Australia)
Young, Johnny
  (USA)
Young, Karen
Young, Kathy
Young, Kenny
Young, La Monte
Young, Larry
Young, Lee
Young, Lester
Young, Neil
Young, Park Jin
Young, Paul
Young, Snooky
Young, Steve
Young, Tommie
Young, Trummy
Young, Val
Young, Victor
Young, Zora
Young-Holt
  Unlimited
Youngbloods

Your Arms Too
  Short To Box
  With God
Your Own Thing
Youth Brigade
Ysaguirre, Bob
Yukl, Joe
Yum-Yum
Yumuri Y Sus
  Hermanos
Yung Wu
Yuro, Timi
Yvad
YZ
Zabriskie Point
Zacharia
Zacharias,
  Helmut
Zacherle, John
Zager And Evans
Zaiko Langa
  Langa
Zakary Thaks
Zaks, Jerry
Zamfir, Gheorghe
Zanes, Dan
Zantees
Zap Mama
Zap Pow
Zappa, Dweezil
Zappa, Frank
Zarchy, Zeke
Zardis, Chester
Zaret, Hy
Zavaroni, Lena
Zawinul, Joe
Zed Yago
Zeitlin, Denny
Zella
Zentner, Si
Zephaniah,
  Benjamin

Zephyrs
Zero, Earl
Zetterlund, Monica
Zevon, Warren
Zhané
Ziegfeld
Ziegfeld Follies
Ziegfeld Follies
  (film musical)
Ziegfeld Girl
Ziegfeld, Florenz
Ziegler, Anne,
  And Webster
  Booth
Zila
Zimmer, Hans
Zion Train
Znowhite
Zodiac Mindwarp
  And The Love
  Reaction
Zoe
Zoller, Attila
Zombies
Zoom Records
Zorba
Zorn, John
Zottola, Glenn
ZTT Records
Zu
Zucchero
Zukie, Tapper
Zumzeaux
Zurke, Bob
Zwerin, Mike
Zwingenberger,
  Axel
ZYX Records
ZZ Top